TALL, DARK

ALPHA

Reapers Series

_____

Donna Grant

St. Martin's Griffin

"Dark Alpha's Claim" Copyright © 2015 by Donna Grant.

"Dark Alpha's Embrace" Copyright ? 2016 by Donna Grant.

"Dark Alpha's Demand" Copyright ? 2016 by Donna Grant.

www.stmartins.com

Jacket photographs: Jacket photographs: couple © kiuikson/Shutterstock.com; smoke © Stieber/Shutterstock.com

Author photo © Kim Rocha

eISBN 9781250155542 (ebook)

ISBN 9781250158055 (tradepaperback)

First eBook Edition: July 2017

DARK ALPHA'S CLAIM

Chapter One

Edinburgh. Baylon surveyed the city from the shadows of an alley. For hundreds of years it had been a mecca in Scotland, bringing in tourists from all over the world.

But the city was no longer just ancient architecture and legends. An evil had taken up residence—Dark Fae. The city burned while the Dark killed hundreds of humans in a single night.

All the while, the mortals were ignorant of what was going on. They were helplessly drawn to the Dark Fae, completely unaware there was a supernatural war going on in Edinburgh and every major city in the UK between the Dark and the Dragon Kings. It was a war where the Reapers weren't involved, but that didn't mean Baylon wasn't rooting for the Kings.

Baylon had only been in Edinburgh a few hours, but during that time he happily exacted his justice on any Dark Fae he ran across.

And there were many.

The Fae were a race of magical beings that had a fondness for the humans who lived upon Earth. The mortals are what brought the Fae. The Light, for the most part, kept their dalliances with the humans to a single time.

The Dark, however, were addicted to the mortals. For every time they had sex with a human, the Dark fed off their souls. The Dark didn't stop until nothing was left of the individuals but a dead shell.

Being the first to arrive at the announced destination, Baylon studied the pub before he walked inside.

He didn't use any glamour to hide his features even though every human in the pub looked his way. Baylon was a Light Fae, but more than that, he was a Reaper—and damn proud of it.

Death recruited him two thousand years earlier after a betrayal that took his life. Even now, Baylon could feel that cold knot of treachery. He'd trusted implicitly, and what had it gained him? Weeks in the Dark palace where he was tortured by his best friends between them taking human females as they willingly turned Dark.

He was his friends' first Fae kill. But Death held onto his soul, allowing him to live—and gave him the opportunity to become a Reaper. His first order from Death had been to execute his friends.

Baylon hadn't hesitated. The surprise and fear in their red eyes did little to ease his soul. But if Baylon thought he'd never trust again, he was never more wrong once he met the other Reapers.

There were seven of them. Though the Reapers weren't created for the humans. No, the Reapers were a group specifically formed to be judge, jury, and executioner to the Fae—Dark and Light.

For the past several centuries, they'd been on the Fae realm trying to straighten out the mess left by their race. It was so bad the queen of the Light, Usaeil, abandoned the Realm, preferring to live exclusively in Ireland.

The king of the Dark, Taraeth, however, found the Fae realm just to his liking. The Dark numbers continued to grow, as did Taraeth's power.

Which worried Baylon.

The two Fae factions were always at war with each other in some form or another. The few times it had become an all-out civil war, the Reapers had stayed out of it. Though they watched from the sidelines.

Baylon took a seat toward the back of the pub and ordered a pint from a pretty young waitress. As she walked away, he leaned back in his chair and let his eyes slowly wander from table to table picking up on conversations. What was it with their leader, Cael, always wanting to meet in a pub?

There was a reason, though Baylon had yet to discern what it was. Perhaps he'd ask today. It would be better if they gathered in secret, but Cael continually chose somewhere very public. At least for the start of their meetings. Cael said it was to get everyone relaxed and remind them this wasn't the Fae realm.

As if Baylon could forget. He was surrounded by mortals. They were oblivious to the fact the Fae were on their realm. Oddly enough, they were also clueless that the Dragon Kings called Earth home.

"Here you go," the waitress said as she set down his ale.

Baylon shot her a smile of thanks. Most of the time the Reapers gathered after one or more of them had to exact justice. So having a drink or two with the group did help get everyone focused before Cael gave them a new assignment.

Baylon sighed. Another assignment so quickly after their last. It's not that he minded removing evil from a realm. It's just that he felt there was a heaviness to his soul from all the people he had killed.

"Always first, aye, Baylon," said a voice with a thick Irish accent.

Baylon looked up to find Kyran. He nodded to the Dark Fae. Kyran's black and silver hair fell to his shoulders while he used glamour to hide his red eyes.

The Reapers were made up of both Dark and Light Fae. Baylon didn't know how any of them were chosen to be Reapers, since none of them spoke of the time before they were Reapers.

Nor did he know what it was the two Dark of their group had done to be asked by Death to join the Reapers, but he trusted Fintan and Kyran with his life.

"I was thirsty," Baylon said and took a drink of ale.

Kyran pulled out the chair across the table from Baylon. He waved away the waitress when she walked over. Baylon had yet to get the reason why Kyran never drank. Perhaps one day.

Kyran leaned his forearms on the table. "The Dark wreaked havoc on this city."

"All over England and Scotland. The Dragon Kings are putting things back in order quickly, though."

"What was the Darks' purpose?"

"I know," Cael said as he approached with Fintan, Talin, and Eoghan.

Baylon looked up at the four of them. They each took a seat and placed their drink order while Cael held out a mobile phone to Baylon.

He took it from Cael and watched the video with a mixture of shock and disgust at seeing the Dragon Kings fighting the Dark on Dreagan—in dragon form. "Talaeth's plan?"

Cael shook his head and waited until the waitress set their drinks down. She openly flirted with them, but they paid her no heed.

It was a curse—or a blessing, depending on what Fae you talked to—that humans were attracted to them. It wasn't a minor attraction, but one so vast and irresistible that the mortals couldn't ignore it.

"Taraeth might've used his men to shoot the video of the Dragon Kings, but we think its Ulrik behind it all," Cael said.

Kyran's lips twisted ruefully. "Not good news for the Dragon Kings."

"The Kings will have their hands full going forward. By the way, Daire won't be joining us," Cael said as his silver eyes looked around the table.

Talin frowned and turned his gaze to their leader. "Surely he's not still following Rhi."

"He is," Cael said with a nod of his head, his long black hair pulled back in a queue. "He'll be with her for as long as it takes."

Baylon, like the rest of the Reapers, was curious as to why Death was so interested in a Light Fae. Granted, Rhi was one of the best warriors the Light ever had. She was even the lone female Queen's Guard.

Rhi's skills with a sword could've caught Death's attention, but Baylon had a feeling it could have something to do with Rhi once having a Dragon King lover.

Fintan set down his glass of whisky and raised his silver eyes rimmed in red to Cael. "We just got the assignment to bring the Dark to a halt here, yet you're talking as if we have another."

"We do." Cael released a breath.

Baylon noticed that Cael wasn't pleased with whatever he was about to impart. In fact, if Baylon had to guess, Cael was debating on whether to pass on the assignment.

A first for sure. Cael always did whatever Death wanted—they all did. It was one of the rules. Death was the judge. The Reapers were the executioners. Death was the one who decided who the Reapers would visit and exact their justice.

The Reapers answered to just one entity—Death.

Baylon glanced at Eoghan who had yet to speak. Then again, Eoghan never said anything. Eoghan's brow was furrowed as deeply, his gaze on the table.

"Isn't this the time we leave?" Talin asked. "We're drawing enough attention as Faes, not to mention our Irish accents."

Cael tossed back his whisky. As he did, he used his magic so that the others in the pub wouldn't be able to make out what they were saying.

Baylon sat up straighter. What was so important that Cael wouldn't take them out of the pub to discuss their assignment at length as he always did?

"In case none of you noticed, the city was overrun with Dark just a few hours ago. They've begun another war with the Dragon Kings," Cael said. "I saw many of the Dark using glamour to hide themselves."

Baylon nodded, turning the pint glass in a circle with his fingers. "You worried the Dark will see us?"

"Of course not," Cael said with a flat look. "We're to keep with our first orders of removing any Dark in the city."

"Are we to help the Kings as well?" Kyran asked.

Cael gave a quick shake of his head. "We'll be staying out of their way. The Kings don't need our help."

"After the video you just showed us?" Talin asked skeptically.

"We have our directives." Cael set the empty whisky glass on the table with finality. "Although as a race the Fae are supposed to stay away from humans, we all know that isn't possible. The Dark take their victims, but the Light give in to desire and have a night with mortals."

Baylon had a sick feeling in his gut at where this was going.

"Many times the Light leaves having no idea they've left their lover behind with a child growing in the womb."

Eoghan's silver eyes turned hard as he glared at Cael. "No."

No one had a chance to even register that Eoghan spoke because Cael continued talking. "We're to find the humans with Fae blood and remove them from this realm."

Talin face scrunched up as he looked at Cael in disgust. "You mean kill the humans?"

"Yes."

Fintan shook his head. "They're human."

"They're part Fae," Cael stated.

"And human," Kyran argued. "We've never touched a human before. Only Fae. That's what we do."

Baylon pushed away his pint glass. "Our job is to go after Fae. I'm not going to kill a mortal."

"Look, I'm not thrilled with this either." Cael ran a hand down his face. "We don't get to choose what orders we accept or decline. We all knew when we accepted our roles what it entailed."

"We understand that," Baylon said. "But this is so . . . sudden. Why is Death wanting to target the humans now?"

Cael shrugged, his gaze dropping to the table. "I don't know."

"We don't always know why Death sends us after anyone," Fintan said. "I've always followed orders without question."

"Thank you," Cael said.

Fintan raised a white brow. "But this time I'm questioning them."

Cael blew out a breath and looked at each of them.

"If you disobey Death's order, you'll be permanently removed from existence."

Eoghan rose and walked out of the pub.

Cael watched him, then sighed as he turned back to the group. "We're to begin hunting these half-Fae mortals immediately. If you encounter more Dark roaming the streets, kill them. Understood?"

None of them said a word as they looked at Cael. Baylon remained seated as Cael got to his feet and followed Eoghan outside. Humans? Death didn't even care if a human knew they were Reapers. Why all of a sudden would she target a half-Fae?

"I can't do it," Talin said.

Fintan pushed back his chair and stood. He held his hand over the table as money appeared in a pile to pay for their drinks. "We've orders."

Baylon turned his gaze at Kyran who looked as if he were about to be sick.

Kyran raised his eyes to Baylon's before sliding them to Talin. "In all the time humans have been on this realm, we've never hunted half-Fae. The number of mortals with Fae blood could number in the millions by this time."

"I can't do it," Talin said again.

Baylon laid his hands flat on the table and pushed up as he got to his feet. "Something is going on. I, for one, am going to find out what it is."

"How?" Fintan asked. "Are you going to try and contact Death yourself?"

"If that's what it takes."

It was true only Cael spoke to Death as leader of the Reapers. The Reapers only saw Death once, when they were offered the position. None of them ever had need to speak to Death before or after.

But if that's what he had to do, then Baylon would see it done. Executioner or assassin, when Death sent them after a Fae, it was with good reason. Never had Baylon killed an innocent—that he knew of.

He walked from the pub and turned to the left. Baylon veiled himself and wandered the streets of the city as night began to fall.

There was no way he could kill a half-Fae. If he did, it would tear his soul in two, he was sure of it.

Once, long ago, he'd found a pretty female on a Greek isle. He'd intended to walk away, but the longer he admired her beauty, the more he wanted her.

Baylon experienced an incredible night in her arms. By the time the sun broke the horizon, he was gone. He didn't forget her after. Years later, Baylon checked in on her. To his shock, she had a young daughter. Thankfully, Baylon discovered the child wasn't his.

Though it left him . . . empty somehow. He'd been terrified he might have impregnated the mortal. Then there came an instant of relief to know the child wasn't his.

Right on the heels of that emotion came the sorrow that he didn't have a child.

And as a Reaper, he never would.

Baylon gave up all thoughts of a wife and family when he accepted his role as a Reaper. They were solitary with no ties of any kind. It was just what they needed to be.

It had been centuries since Baylon thought of that female in Greece. Except for a chance of fate, that child could have been his. Then he would be hunting his own blood.

Baylon paused when he caught sight of the Dragon King Darius standing in the shadows outside a hospital. There was much the Reapers didn't know of the Kings, but Baylon didn't have to know Darius's story to know the King carried guilt around with him. It weighed Darius down as nothing else could.

He was curious as to what would keep the Dragon King waiting around a hospital. Then a tall redhead came out of the hospital, and Baylon had his answer.

Darius couldn't take his eyes from her. For a moment, he thought Darius would let her walk past without a word. But the female stopped and turned.

Baylon felt like an interloper watching the two stare at each other, the attraction and desire so blatant and palpable that it made him take a step back.

In two strides, Darius was in front of the woman. They didn't speak, but there was no need to. He brought her to him and kissed her.

In moments, Darius had her against a building with her skirts up. Baylon turned away when they began to make love. He'd already intruded on something private.

Baylon walked away feeling at odds with everything. Their new order made no sense. The humans with Fae blood didn't even know about their ancestry. They might have some special ability, but that's as far as it went.

There was no need to wipe them from the realm as if they were some dirty secret being swept under the rug.

And what if the Dragon Kings discovered what was being done?

That brought Baylon up short. The Kings protected the humans to such lengths that they had sent their own dragons away. There was nothing the Dragon Kings wouldn't do to protect the mortals.

Then again, with all the Kings had going on, their attention would be focused elsewhere. At least that's what Baylon hoped, because he really didn't want to get into a war with the Kings.

He rather liked them. It had raised all kinds of eyebrows within the Fae when Rhi had taken a King as her lover.

Baylon had seen them once. The Dragon King and

the Light Fae. They made a striking pair. He didn't know what went wrong between the two, but the affair had ended suddenly.

That wasn't something Baylon ever needed to worry about. He was well and truly single from now until the end of time.

It was a price he willingly paid to be a Reaper.

It was one he would pay again in a heartbeat.

Chapter Two

Jordyn Patterson stepped to the side to dodge a man hurrying down the narrow aisle with a cup of coffee. She rolled her eyes and made her way to her desk.

She'd barely sat down and rolled her chair into place when her boss, Detective Inspector Dougal MacDonald walked from his office to stand by her desk.

"It's been a few days since the American, Lexi Crawford, has been in. Did she make her way home?" he asked.

Jordyn gave a nod. "I made sure I'd get notified by the airline when she checked in. She's back in South Carolina now, sir."

"Good. Good," he said again with a nod. "Too much craziness has been going on in this town. At least the killings have stopped. That's a relief."

Jordyn merely smiled as he walked away. She never told MacDonald her thoughts, because they went against everything he was. From the first time Lexi Crawford came into the station and repeated her story to MacDonald in her southern accent, Jordyn had been enthralled.

Red eyes! She hadn't believed Lexi either at first. Mac-Donald dismissed Lexi's story as nonsense, but Jordyn felt the need to look deeper into the case. Especially when more and more people were being killed every night.

There had been a day—only a few hours really—when everyone whispered about red eyes.

Jordyn went home and frantically searched through the mountain of books she accumulated on the Fae. She read in one that some of the Fae had red eyes.

She stayed up all night looking for that passage. An hour before dawn, she finally found it. Jordyn had sat on the floor with the open book in hand and stared numbly.

For as long as she could remember, the Fae were talked about in her family. Sometimes when someone did something unique and amazing, her family would say it was because of the Fae within them.

Other times when someone did something horrible, the Fae were mentioned with words laced in fear.

Jordyn's curiosity about the Fae grew as she did, until it consumed her. She began researching them when she was thirteen. Now, twenty years later, she was still gathering information about them, only she was doing it in Edinburgh hours away from her family. There was really only so much a person could do in a small village. Jordyn had needed a city.

She knew the Fae were real. There couldn't be that many stories—folktales or otherwise—without the beings being real. However, she had yet to meet one.

Over the last five years, she'd begun to try and discover how to find the Fae. She thought she would have to do all sorts of tricks to see one, but it seemed that all she had to do was go out on the streets of Edinburgh.

The very next day she had, and she'd been shaken to her very core. Every book she read described the Fae differently, from tiny winged creatures to giants. She didn't know what to expect, but the sheer number of Fae walking around with red eyes gave her pause.

Then she saw them killing. And it wasn't with a knife or gun. They killed with sex.

Jordyn shuddered in her chair. She'd been hunting the Fae for most of her life. What she found made her wish she didn't know of them.

But they were the dark side of the Fae. Dark Fae to be exact. Their use of glamour aside, they had red eyes and their black hair had silver in it.

Some of the Dark had more silver than others, and that gave her pause. She wanted to think it meant they were older, but she suspected it meant something else entirely.

Their laughter as they killed human after human made her ill. She ran away that night and ducked behind an alley to empty her stomach.

After that, she desperately wanted Lexi to come into the station again and tell MacDonald more of what she had seen, but Lexi didn't return.

For a while, Jordyn began to suspect that Lexi was dead with dozens of other humans. Then the notice from the airline came, and Jordyn breathed a sigh of relief.

Halloween was the worst. Even now, a few days later, it still appeared as if the Fae had a hold on the city. Most of them were gone, but she could tell where a Dark was just by where the men and women gathered, fawning over them as they tried to get close.

Jordyn didn't know why she wasn't drawn to the Dark like everyone else, but she was glad she wasn't. Perhaps it was all she'd read about the Fae. Despite not knowing what was true and what was fiction, she did know they were real.

A glance at the clock confirmed she had a few hours before she could take her lunch. Jordyn came across mention of a book that might shed more light on the Fae.

She tried to purchase it, but no one had it. It was fortunate that she called the library and they actually had a copy.

The new librarian, however, was a bit of a prude and refused to hold the book for her until after work. If Jordyn wanted it, she was going to have to race over there during her lunch.

She kept busy until noon, then Jordyn grabbed her purse and hurried from the office. She flagged a taxi and gave the address. There wasn't much time to get to the library and return to work before lunch ended.

Normally she would walk, but it was too far away. She'd never make it back in time. Jordyn drummed her fingers on the door of the taxi as it drew to a halt at a stoplight. Every second spent sitting still was a second wasted.

Her stomach rumbled in hunger. If she were lucky, she would be able to grab some chips and stuff a few in her mouth before she was back at her desk.

By the time the taxi pulled up to the library, Jordyn was anxious to get out. She threw a few bills at the driver as she opened the door and said, "Keep the rest."

She ran up the steps as a gust of wind barreled down the street. Jordyn pulled her arms tight against her, wishing she hadn't forgotten her coat.

The man exiting the library saw her but didn't hold the door open. She shook her head. Where were the men who held doors and were still gentlemen? Apparently, they went the way of the dodo bird.

"Jerk," she mumbled beneath her breath as she entered the library.

As soon as she stepped inside, Jordyn smiled. There

was a special smell to a library. It was leather, wood, and the pages of books.

She'd always had a love of books. The feel of the weight of it in her hand, the smell of the pages, the words written that could give her facts or take her off on a visual story.

Now wasn't the time to wander the aisles though. Jordyn walked up to the counter. "Excuse me. I have a book being held."

"Your name?" the woman asked without turning around.

Jordyn frowned at the back of her. It was like the woman studied what a librarian should be and copied it from the tight bun, the glasses, and the frumpy, plain clothes. "Jordyn Patterson."

The woman looked at her watch. "With just a few minutes to spare." She bent and pulled out the book from the beneath the counter and turned, setting it down beside her.

Jordyn was taken aback at the woman. She was pretty with her dark hair and pale blue eyes. Not at all what she expected with such a bitchy voice from the phone, or the image she got from the back of her in her prim button-down, cardigan, and long, plaid skirt.

"Here," she said, handing the card over to Jordyn to sign out the book.

Once she filled it out, Jordyn pulled the book into her

arms. "Thanks for holding it."

"You have two weeks. The book will need to be returned then," the librarian said as she met Jorydn's gaze.

"Yep." Jordyn turned her back on the woman and rolled her eyes.

Had she been able to find the book online, she wouldn't have had to deal with the librarian from Hell. If the book held as much information as Jordyn hoped it did, she was going to have to widen her search for it, because a book like it belonged in her own library, not the city's, where no one would check it out.

Jordyn fought the urge to open the book as she walked down the steps of the building. By the time she reached the bottom, her will crumpled. She had it open and was flipping through pages in a heartbeat.

Her eyes scanned page after page as her brain soaked up everything. Jordyn couldn't wait to get home and begin making notes.

With her stomach rumbling again, Jordyn turned to find some food when she ran into someone. Her shoulder was jarred so that she nearly lost her hold on the book. "Sorry," she said and looked up into the most amazing silver eyes.

"Must be an interesting book," he said.

She nodded, unable to find words for a moment. The man was the most gorgeous person she'd ever seen. Her reaction to him was instantaneous, earth-shattering.

He was mouth-wateringly gorgeous, heart-stoppingly magnificent. His short coal black hair was wavy and full. Her fingers itched to run through the locks and see if they felt as shiny as they looked.

His beautiful face was lean and hard, with his chiseled jaw and chin. Not to mention his wide, thin lips. His gaze was direct, intense. Relentless.

While he sized her up, she let her gaze fall to his chest. An olive green long-sleeved tee showed off broad shoulders and arms that rippled with muscles. She imagined when he took off that shirt that he would be toned and supple, with just the right amount of hard sinew. Black jeans were slung low on his narrow hips with black boots completing his look.

"It is," she finally answered when she looked back up into his face.

"Fae, huh?" He glanced down at the page before his silver eyes returned to hers.

His gaze was molten, holding her still and making her blood heat. The desire, the yearning to have his lips on hers made her heart skip a beat and her stomach flutter.

Jordyn had never felt such attraction before. Another gust of wind hit her, but she didn't feel the chill. Her body was too heated.

That's when she registered the Irish accent. "Research."

"Good luck with your research," he said and bowed his head.

Jordyn had the urge to stay and talk to him, but her stomach growled, reminding her she had little time to get food and make it back to the office. She reluctantly walked away from the handsome Irishman to the pub down the street.

It was the first time in a long time that she actually wanted to interact with a man, because the Irishman knocked her off her feet with just a few words and an intense look from his silver eyes.

In no time, she had an order of chips to go. With food in hand, she hailed another taxi and gobbled the grease-soaked potatoes and flipped through the book. Though she found herself looking out her window for another glimpse of the Irishman.

It was the worst sort of punishment to have to put the book away and get back to work. The day crawled as she constantly looked at the clock, waiting for her workday to end so she could get to her research.

~

Baylon was sitting on the steps outside the library watching the mortals when he saw her. She stood out amongst the humans like a star in the midnight sky.

Her beauty was undeniable, catching the attention of everyone around her-though she didn't seem to notice. He liked the way her dark blond hair was cut short and trendy with it swept to the side in the front. A pixie cut, he thought he heard a human call it.

The mortal was tall and thin, with every curve just the right size. Her turquoise eyes were large, and there was a hint of innocence about them that drew him again and again.

She wore large earrings that brought more attention to her beautiful oval face. Her brows were thin and arched delicately over her eyes. When she smiled, she dazzled. Her lips were just wide and full enough to be alluring.

He'd laughed when he heard her mumble "jerk" to the man who hadn't held the door for her.

He knew immediately that she had Fae blood. It wasn't just her beauty. There was an air about her that was as distinctive as a beacon. And he was happy he found her before the others.

Baylon waited outside the library for another glimpse of her. She walked out a short time later carrying a large book. She was entranced by it. Several people had to walk around her because she wasn't looking where she was going—she was too intent on reading.

He wanted to see what kind of book was so interesting.

When he put himself in her path, he never expected to look down at a tome all about the Fae.

His shock was quickly replaced with a blinding and penetrating desire when they bumped into each other. Then she looked up at him.

He was completely taken by her, tumbling into incredible turquoise eyes.

If he didn't speak, he was liable to do something stupid—like kiss her. His gaze lowered to her lips, an ache gripping him, begging him to take her. To taste her.

"Sorry," she said.

Her Scots accent was soft and lilting. Beautiful, just as she was. What was it about this half-Fae that held him enthralled so? "Must be an interesting book."

Her gaze slowly raked over him, heating his blood to such a degree that he fisted his hands to keep from touching her. Didn't she realize she was playing with fire?

If her gaze wasn't so guileless, Baylon would have suspected she was proficient in teasing a man to such a degree. But it was the need in her own eyes that made his cock instantly hard.

"It is."

He glanced down at the page she was reading. "Fae, huh?"

"Research," she said breathlessly.

Warning bells went off in Baylon's head. Research?

Did she know she had Fae blood? It was time he found out more about her. Besides, he was going to make sure none of the other Reapers found her.

"Good luck with your research." He bowed his head and walked around her.

He then stopped and turned to watch her, wondering if she would look back at him. To his exasperation, she didn't.

Baylon veiled himself and followed her all the way to the police station. From there, he watched her. She was friendly and always had a smile. Everyone liked her.

She didn't give anyone a second look, preferring to concentrate on her work. She was quick and accurate in everything she did.

Baylon wondered if she knew how the others looked at her, watched her. She was graceful and striking without being flamboyant. She had her own kind of elegance that screamed Fae.

But mortals wouldn't know that.

To another Fae, it was like a beacon.

He'd stumbled onto a half-Fae without even trying. Fate couldn't be that cruel to him, surely. There was something about the order from Death that was just wrong. Humans, even those with Fae blood, had never been targeted by the Reapers.

Perhaps Baylon needed to have a talk with Cael. Disobeying Death's orders wasn't an option, but that's exactly what Baylon was going to do for the time being. It felt wrong to target half-Fae.

He was about to leave to find Cael, but then the mortal smiled. She was safe. The others weren't in the area, so they wouldn't be looking for her.

Why then wasn't Baylon leaving?

Because he couldn't. A feeling in his gut kept him right where he was, continuing to watch her. He found it humorous as just about every man in the station tried to get her attention while all the women made a point of talking to her.

The humans couldn't help it. It was the Fae blood within the mortal that drew them.

Just as she captivated him.

Chapter Three

Jordyn sighed in happiness when the day was finally over. It was one of the longest days of her life, made even longer with the book next to her, waiting to be read.

She looked at it often, the cover teasing her about what she knew was within the pages. More information on the Fae. How much of it would be true, though?

Now that she knew there were Dark Fae with red eyes and black and silver hair, there had to be Light Fae. If only she knew what they looked like.

If she could talk to one, she might be able to find all the answers she was looking for. But that was a huge if.

As many years as she looked for Fae, she hadn't been successful. Then again, she'd been looking for tiny winged creatures at one point.

Remembering her first expedition at fourteen made her smile. She'd searched everywhere for the small winged creatures she thought were Fae.

Her obsession made it difficult to keep friends. They didn't understand the need that pushed her to learn all she could of the Fae. It didn't help that she couldn't explain what pressed her to find answers.

More often than not, Jordyn was alone. She found comfort in her books when her friends disappeared one by one, making fun of her when she did see them at school.

She developed a thick shell—or at least she told herself she did. Their words, to this day, still hurt when she thought about them.

Once she actually attempted to put aside her obsession. It lasted all of a day. Of course, her grandmother supplied her with all kinds of stories of the Fae that spurred her interest.

Her grandmother was the only one who truly understood her fascination with the Fae. Probably because it had been her grandmother's as well.

Losing her when Jordyn was sixteen had been a hard blow for her. She lost the one advocate she had.

Jordyn looked up as she walked from the police station as thunder rumbled overhead. Rain was on the way, and with the temperatures dropping so rapidly, she wouldn't be surprised if there might be snow flurries.

Her steps were quick and light as she hurried down the streets. She was impatient to fully dive into the book that weighted down her arms.

She stopped at a crosswalk and tapped her toes as the light stayed green, keeping her from crossing the street.

Unable to help herself, she opened the book for a quick peek inside.

It was people rushing past her that alerted Jordyn it was time to move. She put her finger in the book to keep her page for the next crosswalk and tucked it against her body.

She managed to read three pages by the time she reached the last crosswalk before her flat. She was moving to the next page when something prickled on the back of her neck. She closed the book and tucked it underneath her arm again as her gaze slowly moved around her.

That's when she saw him. A Dark Fae.

Her heart missed a beat as fear rushed through her. Panic tried to set in, but Jordyn managed to keep her head. Luckily, he was across the street talking to a young couple who couldn't keep their hands off him.

Jordyn turned her gaze forward pretending she didn't see the Dark, but the feeling didn't go away. She crossed the intersection and suppressed a shiver that had nothing to do with the icy wind.

Her blood turned to ice when she spotted the two Dark standing along the sidewalk right where she had to pass to reach her flat.

The panic she managed to suppress a moment ago returned with a vengeance. Her steps slowed as she debated what to do. She didn't want to draw their attention, so suddenly stopping and turning around wasn't an option. Her only choice was to walk past them and hope they ignored her.

There had to be a way to kill a Fae, and it was something she was going to begin searching for immediately. Walking the streets of Edinburgh alone was becoming a hazard.

~

Baylon stifled a growl when he saw the three Dark Fae. Staying veiled, he crossed the street and grabbed the Dark talking to the couple and teleported him away. Baylon plunged his sword in the Dark's gut, killing him instantly.

Within seconds he returned to the female. The two Dark would be nothing to kill, but he wasn't yet ready to show his true self to the human.

He stayed close to her. She was alert, her body nearly vibrating with tension—and trepidation. At least she understood the Dark were dangerous. That was a plus. Sort of. If she didn't calm down, the two Dark would notice her.

Baylon eyed the two. Their cockiness and laughter at killing humans as if they were no more than cattle grated on his nerves. Not because he particularly cared about the mortals, but because of the unadulterated evil within the Dark.

The Dark cared about nothing and no one but themselves.

Baylon grimaced when the female walked as far from the Dark as she could. Her stiff back and the fact she kept her gaze straight ahead was like a light flashing over her. It did exactly what Baylon had been afraid of—it drew the Darks' attention.

"Well, hello there," said one of the Dark.

The woman ignored them and kept walking.

The second dark laughed as he hurried to catch up with her. "That's not very nice. We're just a couple of Irishmen saying hello."

"It's cold, and I'm in a hurry," she murmured.

Baylon tightened his grip on his sword. The Dark were beginning to notice that she wasn't interested in them. One of them touched her, which should've been enough to stop her in her tracks and turn her full attention on them.

But not the half-Fae. She shrugged off his hand and walked faster.

"Shit," Baylon mumbled to himself.

The two Dark quickly moved to block her path. "We're not done with you," said the first.

"It's not natural that you ignore us," said the second.

The woman didn't back up. She stood her ground, but the Dark took it as an invitation. To be fair, anything she did would've been taken as an offer to assault her.

Baylon moved to stand behind the Dark and unveiled himself. "You just don't know when to quit, do you?" he asked them.

They spun around gapping at him in surprise—and a bit of fear. Baylon shoved his sword in the second Dark while the first attempted to throw a ball of magic at him.

Baylon easily blocked it, pivoting as he lopped off the Dark's head. With a few words, the two Dark bodies began to turn to dust and fly away in the breeze.

It was the quiet behind him that altered Baylon. There was no hysterics, no demands of who he was and what was going on.

He put away his sword, making it disappear until he needed it again. Then he slowly turned to face the woman. Her large eyes were open wide. Her chest heaved from fear—and he suspected excitement.

"Thank you," she said. She swallowed and licked her lips. "My God. You're Fae."

Baylon studied her, wondering why he wanted to give her an answer instead of lying.

"How did you kill them?" she asked, glancing at the ground where the dust of the bodies had been.

Jordyn watched the Fae's head cock to the side and his beautiful silver eyes observe her with a bit of wariness and a dash of interest.

He was the same man who ran into her at the library. She had the same visceral reaction to him now as she did then. All the questions in her head evaporated with him being so near.

She couldn't seem to pull in a coherent thought as she imagined his body pressed against hers.

Jordyn gave a shake of her head to try and clear it. He stood with his feet apart, his weight on both of them as if he were waiting to whip out his sword again.

His sword! How could Jordyn have forgotten it? She had stood like an idiot with her mouth gaping as he swung the weapon quickly and effortlessly. There was a ruthless edge about him that made her heart flutter—and the desire grow.

Jordyn lifted her gaze to his face to find one of his brows lifted. She shrugged and tried to make light of being caught gawking. "I'm not one to let such a striking man pass without looking my fill."

'Again' was left unsaid, but it hung in the air between them.

A slow smile pulled up one side of his lips. He didn't say a word as his gaze slowly lowered to her mouth and then her chest.

Jordyn found it difficult to breathe at his deliberate perusal of her body. Her knees grew weak and her palms began to sweat. The desire rushing and swelling through her was flagrant and commanding, shameless and controlling.

By the time his gaze returned to her face, she was panting with need. His silver eyes darkened with unabashed passion. Jordyn grasped the building next to her to keep on her feet.

The stone rasped her palm, but all she felt was her heart pounding in her chest and need clawing through her.

In two steps, he was next to her. He gently cupped both sides of her face and gazed into her eyes. His head gradually lowered.

Jordyn's lids slid closed, her breath locked in her lungs as she waited to feel his mouth on hers. The first touch was a brush of his lips against hers. It left her both eager and aching for more.

Then with a groan, he slanted his mouth over hers and kissed her.

She sighed, dropping her book and purse to slide her arms around him. He kissed her slowly, thoroughly, sapping her of strength and filling her with a passion that burned hotter with every second.

It was as if the world was suddenly righted around her.

Everything that felt wrong and at odds was put right. She clung to him, wanting, needing more of what he was giving her.

When he suddenly broke off the kiss, it took her a moment to get her bearings and open her eyes. She had to blink to focus and push past the longing for more.

There was regret in his gaze when he caressed a cheek. "You've no idea what you are, do you?"

She drank in more of his Irish accent. Belatedly, she realized he'd asked her a question. Jordyn shook her head. If he wanted her to find words, he was going to have to put some distance between them.

"I didn't think so." He sighed heavily. "You're not safe."

Jordyn was still trying to figure out his words when he released her and bent to pick up her purse and book. She was frowning when he stood.

He glanced around him. "There are things you need to know, female."

"Jordyn," she said, her voice a mere whisper.

Now it was his turn to frown. "What?"

"My name. It's Jordyn Patterson."

The Fae shot her another crooked smile. "We need to talk, Jordyn Patterson."

She didn't know how she found the strength to push away from the wall and take her items from him. Jordyn motioned him to follow as she walked on wobbly legs to the door of her building.

They didn't say a word in the lift up to her flat or while she unlocked her door. Once inside, Jordyn sat her purse on the dining table and laid the book beside it. It was the first time since she got the book that she wasn't interested in opening it.

Jordyn then faced the Fae. Her lips still throbbed from his kiss. His taste still upon her tongue. And she wanted more.

"You have a lot of books," he said as he looked around her flat.

She cleared her throat and glanced at the kitchen. "Do you want a drink?"

"I'm not interested in a drink." His gaze was heated, his words obvious as he looked her way.

Jordyn shrugged out of her coat as her blood heated even more. She had to grab a hold of the chair when her knees threatened to buckle at the hungry look he raked over her body.

He finally pulled his gaze away and walked along the bookshelves lining every wall. "It appears your interest is in one subject."

"Yes," she finally managed after two tries.

He turned to face her. "Why do you have an interest in us?"

Jordyn was happy he wasn't trying to tell her he wasn't

a Fae. By that question, he confirmed what she blurted out on the street.

She shrugged helplessly. "My family used to say we were part Fae. That along with stories my grandmother used to tell me. It was said as a joke, but it got me interested."

"Apparently," he said and looked at all the books again.

Jordyn couldn't imagine how neurotic she looked in his eyes. She was a bit embarrassed. "Will you tell me your name?"

He cut his gaze to her, a small smile about his seductive lips. Lord, the man could kiss!

"Baylon."

"Baylon," she repeated, letting it roll around her tongue.

He briefly closed his eyes before he turned his back to her. Jordyn wasn't sure if she had done something wrong. She tracked him for several quiet moments as he looked over more of her bookshelves.

"What have you learned from all these books?" he asked.

"That few have met a Fae, and even fewer know anything about you."

He turned around to face her. "Yet you knew the Dark. And me."

Chapter Four

Baylon kept his distance from Jordyn. He was still reeling from their kiss and how deeply it touched him. He kept far away from humans, especially those that he was attracted to.

But there was something fascinating and engaging about Jordyn. She was gorgeous to be sure, but there was a quality about her he couldn't pinpoint that kept him completely and utterly charmed and enticed.

He hungered for another kiss, craved to hold her against him. He longed to take her as his lover.

That thought alone was like being dunked in ice.

He was a Reaper. There were no entanglements.

Ever.

Death saw that they had females when the need arose, which with a Fae was often. But a human? Even a half-Fae? He could never cross the line and take her to his bed. It would be disastrous for them both.

Why then did he want her so desperately?

Baylon loved the way Jordyn's forehead puckered in the middle when asked something she wasn't sure how to answer. She was never hasty with a response. She thought over her words carefully.

"It was the red eyes," she answered. "I was working at the police station when an American came in trying to explain that it was a red-eyed man who killed her friend."

Was it coincidence that Jordyn worked at the very place Lexi Crawford had gone for help before the Dragon Kings entered her life? If there was one thing Baylon learned in his thousands of years of existence, it was that there was no such thing as coincidence.

"And," he prompted when Jordyn fell silent.

She motioned to the bookshelves. "I remembered reading something about red eyes. I was running into men and women with red eyes everywhere, and the evil coming off them was gagging. I realized that the book had it right. The red-eyed people I'd been seeing were Dark Fae."

"How did you know I was Fae?" Was it vanity that prompted him to ask? Or did he truly want to know how much knowledge she had of the Fae?

Jordyn pivoted and walked into the kitchen. She took down a wine glass from the cupboard and set it on the counter. She then grabbed the bottle of wine next to the toaster and uncorked it before pouring it in her glass.

She lifted the bottle and glanced at him, silently asking if he wanted some. Baylon shook his head as he watched her lift the glass to her lips and take a drink of the red wine.

"I think I was hoping you were Fae." Jordyn leaned against the counter, her gaze colliding with his. "I never believed the Fae were tiny winged creatures as some of the books claim. I always pictured someone like you when I thought of the Fae."

He fought the invisible strings that kept tugging him closer to her.

"The way you move, the way you talk. The way you fight," she continued. "And your eyes. No one could ever mistake you for a human. Everything about you shouts unique, special, and . . . captivating."

Damn. She really needed to stop talking. If she didn't, he would kiss her again. And if he kissed her again, he wouldn't be able to stop. He hungered for her that much.

Her gaze dropped as if she became embarrassed by her confession. Baylon found the action endearing and delightful.

He was so screwed.

"Why are the Dark here?" she asked, once more looking his way.

A safe topic. Just what he needed. Baylon remained across the flat as he said, "Because they've begun a war."

"With you?"

He scrunched up his face, wishing he hadn't told her

the truth. "With other beings."

"Others?" she asked worriedly. "What others?"

Baylon could kick himself for not lying to her again. What was wrong with him? He was a proficient liar. Except with her, for some reason. "You're not going to let this go are you?"

She gave him a flat look. "You've seen my books. Do you think I'll let it go if you don't tell me?"

He ran a hand down his face. "The Dragon Kings."

Jordyn's face went slack. "*Dragon* Kings?"

"Aye. They've been around since the beginning of time. They sent their dragons away, but they can shift between human and dragon form."

"Oh. Well if you make it sound as if it's nothing, then it must be," she said sarcastically.

The more she talked, the more Baylon liked her. "You don't need to worry about them. They vowed to protect humans, and they've won many wars against others who wanted this realm and humans."

"Wow," she mumbled before taking a long drink. "I think I'm going to need another bottle of wine. Wait. You killed the Dark tonight."

"Because it's what I do."

"What's that supposed to mean?"

He waved away her question. "That's not a concern."

"Then what is?"

"You."

She held the wine glass at her cheek and furrowed her brow. "That's right. You said I didn't know what I was. What am I?"

It wasn't that Baylon was afraid she couldn't handle the news. He hesitated because once he told her, everything would change.

He should walk away from now, disappear and forget her. Baylon snorted inwardly. Forget Jordyn? That wasn't possible. He would never be able to stay far from her, worried that one of the other Reapers would find her and kill her.

"Baylon?" she urged.

"You've read all these books about the Fae, but you don't know us."

She motioned to him with her wine glass. "I've got thousands of questions. If you want to tell me, then tell me."

"You saw the way humans react to the Dark."

Her head gave a slight nod.

"Humans are drawn to us against their will. They don't understand it, nor can they resist the temptation to be with us. The Dark will lure or kidnap mortals from this realm and take them away."

"Where?" Jordyn asked.

"Sometimes to the Fae realm. Sometimes to Ireland

where the Fae have taken over."

She swallowed and inhaled. "What do they do with them?"

"They have sex with them. Each time drains the mortal of their soul, leaving nothing but a dead husk behind."

She sat there for a moment before tilting back the glass and draining it. Jordyn then turned and poured more wine. "Do you do that?"

"The Light for the most part keep their distance from humans. When we do give in to the need, we sleep with the mortals only once."

"I wasn't attracted to the Dark," she said with her back to him.

Baylon didn't want to discuss the need tearing through him. He didn't want to think about the passion piercing him. And he couldn't allow himself to consider what it might be like to sink between Jordyn's thighs.

He fisted his hands at his sides. "The Fae don't feel the same overwhelming draw that humans do."

Jordyn spun around, her lips parted. She stared at him in silence for several moments. Then she asked, "Perhaps there are some Fae more appealing than others."

"You saw the Dark tonight. Can you tell me they weren't handsome?"

Her lips flattened briefly. "They were. I've also seen how they casually and happily kill humans. That's why I don't find them remotely attractive."

"Liar."

She rolled her eyes. "I'm not lying."

He liked how her brogue deepened when she became annoyed. "You might not want to have ripped off your clothes for them, but they were gorgeous."

"Yes," she said grudgingly. "I didn't want them because they're evil."

"That could be one explanation."

"One?" she asked with brows raised.

Baylon thought she was ready to hear the truth. All of her research and knowledge of Fae pointed to that fact. Now he wasn't so sure. But he'd already come this far. It was better to just tell her instead of beating around the bush.

"The Fae aren't drawn to each other like humans are drawn to us."

She shrugged. "That makes sense I guess. What does that have to do with me not finding the Dark appealing?"

"You're half-Fae, Jordyn."

She laughed and gave a little shake of her head before taking a drink. Her gaze returned to him, and her smile slowly died. "My God. You're not joking."

"No, I'm not."

"I don't understand. How?"

It was Baylon's turn to smile. "It happens in the usual

way."

She waved his words away. "I know *that*. I mean, how?"

"Somewhere in your family line one of your ancestors had an affair with a Fae. The *who* may have gotten lost over time, but they never forgot there was Fae blood in your family."

"That would explain all the mentions of Fae throughout the years," Jordyn said, shock lining her voice. Then her face cleared as if everything was beginning to make sense to her. She slid her gaze to him. "What does this mean for me?"

Baylon glanced at the floor. "It used to mean nothing. There were added benefits to mortals that had Fae blood. Beauty, talent, and sometimes unexplained abilities could occur."

"Used to," she repeated in a strangled voice. "Why do I get the feeling that I'm not going to like your next explanation?"

"Because it isn't good."

She sat her wine glass down. "That isn't comforting me."

"Any humans with Fae blood are being hunted."

"What?" she said with a choked gasp. "Why? What did we do?"

Baylon lifted one shoulder in a shrug. "I wish I knew."

"Is there a way for me to stay hidden?"

"Perhaps for a time, but not forever."

She walked to the table and pulled out a seat, visibly shaken. Jordyn sank into the chair before propping her elbow on the table and dropping her head in her hands. "This can't be happening." Her head lifted and she speared him with her turquoise eyes. "How do you know we're being hunted?"

Baylon had never been in a position where he told someone he was a Reaper. They weren't forbidden from telling humans, because there had never been an instance to interact with a human.

The Fae, on the other hand, they were barred from telling. Part of the fear and dread surrounding the Reapers was that no one knew who they were.

He'd never had an encounter with a half-Fae before, so he wasn't sure what side of the fence Death might consider her. So Baylon decided to think of her as human, because it was easier for him. She hadn't been a part of the Fae world before, so she wouldn't know anyone.

"Your silence is frightening," Jordyn said.

Baylon walked to his right slowly. "I'm part of an elite group of Fae who are judge, jury, and executioner for our people who have done wrong."

"So you were sent to kill me?" she asked, her voice rising. She got to her feet. "You should've just done it instead of kissing me! That was plain wrong."

"I didn't mean to kiss you!" he yelled in exasperation.

"Stop talking. I can't sit around waiting to be killed. If you're going to do it, just do it!"

Baylon stared at her standing tall and proud, her beautiful eyes filled with anger. "My orders are to kill any half-Fae I came across. But I never intended to carry through with them."

Chapter Five

Jordyn could only stare at Baylon. She wasn't sure whether to believe him or not. Why would he kill the Dark and tell her everything only to then take her life himself? Then again, it could all be a ploy.

As if her silence hurt him, Baylon said, "You must believe me."

"This has all been some kind of horrible mistake. I'm not Fae. Sure, my family is wacky enough to say it as a jest, but I've no special qualities or abilities. I'm as plain as the next woman on the street."

Baylon raised a black brow and snorted. "You're far from plain, and you're certainly not anything like any other woman. You're not just amazingly beautiful, Jordyn, but everyone likes you."

"I'm nice to people," she said with a shrug.

"Others are nice, too, and yet everyone has enemies. Except a Fae among humans. Even one drop of Fae blood can change a mortal."

"Oh." Could he be right? It's not like she looked around for enemies, but not everyone liked everyone.

That was just a fact of life. Yet Baylon made it sound as if she were something special.

Could she be? What if all the stories she heard from her grandmother were true? What if she really was half-Fae?

Her knees threatened to give out. What if she really did have Fae blood? Could that be why she was so intent on finding the Fae? Did she somehow know? Was it some instinct to find those like herself?

Jordyn drew in a deep breath. A part of her was excited to not only have found Baylon, a real Fae, but to also learn she was half-Fae. That thrill was quickly joined by dread and terror at the thought of being hunted.

By Baylon and others like him.

"Do you have a list with names on it?" she asked.

"No. A Fae knows another Fae."

Jordyn couldn't handle any more. To be told she was Fae, and that because of it she was being hunted, pushed her over the proverbial edge.

She pointed to the door. "You need to leave. Now."

Baylon frowned and took a step toward her. "Jordyn, you're not safe."

"It appears it's you I should be worried about, since you're the one with orders to kill me."

"There are others in my group. If they find you, they'll kill you."

She swallowed, her thoughts going back to the mind-blowing kiss they shared. Jordyn hated being this confused. She didn't know what to do. "What are you proposing? That you'll protect me?"

"Yes."

Jordyn blinked, surprised at his instant response. "Why?"

"Because it's not your fault you have Fae blood. We've never harmed one of you before. I'm not going to start now."

"What happens if your friends discover you've not followed orders?"

He turned his head away, which was answer enough.

"You just met me," she said. "Why would you risk so much to keep me alive?"

His gaze swiveled to hers, burning with a silver light that mesmerized her. "Do you really need to ask?"

"Yes."

Suddenly he was standing before her, his arms tight as he held her securely. From shoulder to hip their bodies were pressed together. She felt the heat and hard muscles of him through her clothes as her hands came up automatically to grasp his arms.

His face loomed above her. Desire smoldered, passion burned. Her lips parted of their own accord as she waited for him to kiss her once more.

She couldn't draw enough air into her lungs. Her body was on fire, aching for him. A rush of air passed through her lips when his gaze dropped to her mouth.

Baylon was wreaking havoc on her senses so that she was left adrift and drowning with yearning. Every fiber of her pulsed in expectation, burned in need.

His head lowered so that his cheek softly brushed against hers. With his mouth near her ear, he whispered, "I can't keep my hands from you."

If Jordyn thought to hold back, those seven words would've shattered any reservations.

To her surprise, he pulled her against him in an embrace. She rested her head on his shoulder and closed her eyes. It felt good to be in his arms.

It felt even better to have him holding her so securely.

Which seemed wrong knowing he was sent to kill her, but she couldn't change how she felt.

"I intended to stay away from any half-Fae," Baylon said. "Then I saw you on the library steps. You were so engrossed in the book that I had to know what you were reading."

Jordyn smiled. "I'm glad you did."

"I knew as soon as I saw you that you were half-Fae. I followed you the rest of the day."

As disturbing as that was, Jordyn didn't pull away. "How did I not see you?"

"I can veil myself so that no one can see me."

She was impressed at his ability. "You went to the station?"

"I did. I saw you with your co-workers and how they look at you. You've no idea how much they want you, do you?"

"No."

There was a beat of silence before he said, "You are one special half-Fae, Jordyn Patterson."

She sighed against him. She hadn't realized just how much she needed to be held in such a way until then. Not quite ready to give it up, she remained where she was.

Jordyn leaned back to look at him, but didn't step away. "How long can you remain veiled?"

"As long as I needed. I had to know how much you knew of the Fae," he continued. "I hadn't intended to make myself known to you tonight. Then the Dark approached." Baylon lightly touched her face. "I should've veiled myself after."

"Why didn't you?" she asked breathlessly.

"The way you looked at me."

So he felt it to, whatever it was between them. Jordyn had felt desire and lust before, but whatever the emotion was now was a hundred times more forceful.

"The way you're looking at me now," he said in a husky voice pitched low.

"I thought you said I wouldn't feel your appeal."

There was a slight smile to his lips as he said, "You aren't."

"Then what's happening?"

Baylon's head lowered once more. "I wish I knew."

Jordyn lifted her face as his lips pressed against hers. She moaned as his tongue slipped into her mouth.

This kiss wasn't slow and sensual as it had been below. This one sizzled in its intensity, blazed with its potency.

Singed with its fervor.

She never stood a chance at resisting Baylon, not that the thought ever crossed her mind. Jordyn slid her arms up his neck and held tight.

The world, the Fae, and everything else simply disappeared as they gave into their passion that refused to be denied.

~

Cael stood with Eoghan on the walls of Edinburgh Castle. They remained in the shadows staring over the city. Cael had followed Eoghan from the pub, waiting for the time when he might be able to talk.

Eoghan's past was one he refused to speak of, but it was one that drastically shaped the Fae into who he was now.

As leader, Cael knew the pasts of his men. He never mentioned them—none of them did. Death felt that he should know to better understand his men and gain their trust.

That was the only reason he had such information.

"I don't make the orders," Cael said.

Eoghan continued to stare straight ahead.

Cael drew in a deep breath and released it. "We don't have a choice. You know that. We all knew that when we became Reapers. I'm not any happier about this than you."

"Then you should've told Death that."

It took Cael a moment to process what he said since Eoghan so rarely spoke. "I didn't see Death this time. A message arrived."

Death normally liked to meet with Cael and give the orders, but on rare occasions Death sent a message. Though with something as big as this assignment, Cael expected a face-to-face meeting.

"You don't think the others will follow the order, do you?" Cael asked.

Eoghan cut his eyes to him and simply glowered.

"I didn't think so." Cael grasped his hands behind his back. The truth was, he didn't want to kill any half-Fae either.

But it wasn't as if they had a choice.

"You know what happens if we don't follow Death's orders," Cael said.

Eoghan turned his head forward. "I'm prepared."

Cael jerked his head to Eoghan in shock and disbelief. He wasn't sure what to say to his friend. Eoghan was prickly at the best of times. He carried the weight of the world on his shoulders, which was slowly crushing him.

Cael couldn't remember the last time he saw Eoghan smile. He was part of the group, but he kept himself separate at all times. Despite that, Eoghan never let the group down. He was always there when needed.

"*Cael!*"

He gritted his teeth when he heard Kyran's voice in his head. Cael wasn't ready to leave Eoghan after his admission, but he had to get to Kyran and find out what he needed.

"We'll finish this talk later," Cael said.

He waited for Eoghan to acknowledge his words, but the Light Fae merely stood as silent as a statue. Cael gave a shake of his head and teleported to Kyran.

He found the Dark Fae with Talin in the same warehouse the Dragon Kings Thorn and Darius had used to burn the bodies of the Dark they killed.

Kyran was pacing, his red eyes filled with uncertainty. Talin sat on a table and looked as if he were preparing to face Death.

Cael worried his men would have this reaction. Hell, he'd had the same reaction. But they were Reapers. They didn't get to choose how they felt about their orders. Nor did they get to choose who they killed.

The problem was, none of them had ever felt this way before. There was something inherently wrong with killing the half-Fae.

"I can't," Kyran said as he glanced at Cael. "I can't do this. I realize by disobeying Death's orders that I forfeit my life. These are mortals, Cael. We've never gone after them before."

Talin lifted his silver eyes to Cael. "I tried to do as ordered. I found a half-Fae in Norway, but I couldn't kill him."

That was three of the six on this mission. With Daire watching Rhi, perhaps it was time Cael checked in on Baylon and Fintan. He suspected the only one who would follow Death's command was Fintan.

Not because the Dark Fae liked to kill, but because Fintan was able to close off any and all emotions to carry out his duty. It made him a cold bastard, but that's what a Reaper was.

"Why is Death after the half-Fae?" Kyran asked. He raked a hand through his black and silver hair. "It doesn't make sense."

"I didn't get to talk to Death."

That brought Kyran up short. He stopped and gawked at Cael. "Death didn't summon you?"

"Not this time," Cael admitted.

Talin slid off the table, his brow furrowed. "I think we should request a meeting."

Cael held up his hand to stop Talin from speaking further. "I've already decided to see Death. Eoghan is at the castle. I'm going to find Baylon and Fintan. There will be no killing of the half-Fae until I get some answers."

"You know Death may strike you down for issuing such a command," Talin said.

Cael shot them a smile. "Then one of you could be in charge next."

Chapter Six

Baylon couldn't stop kissing Jordyn. Her taste was incredible, but with the wine on her tongue, it left him heady.

And wanting more.

He lifted her to sit on the table. Her hands roamed his back as he stood between her legs. His cock twitched and swelled even more.

His chest heaved as he deepened the kiss and she responded with a moan. She was driven mad with longing. He wanted to remove her clothes, to have her bared so he could see every wonderful inch of her.

Baylon laid her back on the table. Her legs came around him and she locked her ankles behind him. Unable to help himself, he rocked against her. Jordyn groaned and tightened her legs.

He wanted her, needed her with a desperation that shook him. Each kiss only inflamed the desire spreading through him like wildfire. Every fiber demanded that he take her. He didn't understand the hurry that clawed at him, or why there was a part of him that craved to make sure that everyone knew she was his.

"*Baylon.*"

He wanted to ignore Cael's call, but if he didn't respond, Cael would find him. The last thing Baylon wanted was for Cael to know he was hiding a half-Fae.

Baylon ended the kiss and looked down at Jordyn. Her eyes were glazed, her lips swollen. She was so beautiful it hurt to look at her.

"What's wrong?" she murmured huskily.

"I have to go." Baylon straightened and pulled her up with him. "I'll be back soon."

She tilted her head to the side, her eyes questioning. "You're leaving?"

"Cael is calling for me. If I don't go, he'll come here."

That seemed to snap Jordyn out of her daze. "What if another Fae comes?"

"They shouldn't. They haven't seen you. Just don't leave the flat until I return."

"All right."

Baylon touched her face and teleported to Cael. All he had to do was follow the sound of Cael's voice that brought him to the underground city beneath Edinburgh.

He saw Cael leaning against a section of an entrance that arched overhead. It was a segment that had yet to be unearthed by the mortals, so there was no electricity.

Cael had an orb of magic over him shedding a pale blue light.

As soon as Baylon appeared, Cael pushed away from the wall. "Where have you been?"

"Around the city."

"Hm," Cael said. "I've already spoken to the others. I'm going to talk to Death. Until I return, don't kill any mortals with Fae blood."

Baylon was happy to hear Cael's words, but he knew what Cael proposed wasn't without retribution. "I gather you didn't talk to Death when you got the order."

"No, and I'm going to rectify that now. The order never sat well with me, but after listening to all of you, I have to see Death."

"I know you," Baylon said. "You have a suspicion."

Cael looked away for a moment. "The humans have never done anything to the Fae. Why would Death suddenly decide to wipe out all of them who have any Fae blood? Death never has cared about them before."

"So why now?" Baylon asked.

Cael nodded firmly. "Exactly. Something isn't right. I thought it was just me, but the rest of you felt the same way."

"Are you sure about this, Cael? If Death does want us to kill the half-Fae, we're disobeying orders. You know what that means for you."

"Keep killing the Dark about the city. I'll be back as soon as I can," Cael stated and vanished.

Baylon immediately returned to Jordyn.

~

Each Reaper knew of the Fae doorway that only a Reaper could see. Cael looked through the doorway. The meeting could go one of two ways.

He'd never worried about his own neck, which was what led him to become a Reaper in the first place. He'd never expected to lead them, but here he was. It was a position he accepted with pride, because he knew what it meant for Death to choose him.

Cael stepped through the door and paused. No matter how many times he visited Death's realm, he was never prepared.

It wasn't Hell. There was no fire or damnation. It wasn't desolate either.

There was green everywhere. Lush plants, vibrant flowers.

Life.

It surrounded him, besieged him.

Cael walked through the immaculate garden to the large white stone tower. No one visited Death. Only animals occupied the realm. Death was feared by every

Fae—and human.

Out of the corner of his eye he saw something through the tall vines running along a stone wall. Cael walked around the wall, but there was no one there. Only a leaf swinging told him someone brushed past.

"Never have you come to me on your own. Not in all the centuries I've known you," came a voice behind him.

For a millisecond Cael couldn't move. Then he turned and looked Death in the face. It wasn't a skeleton or a hideous beast he gazed upon, but a woman more beautiful than all the Fae put together.

"Erith," he said and bowed his head.

Her blue-black hair hung to her hips in soft waves. She turned her back to him and began walking. Her black dress flowed about her like gossamer, hugging her trim frame and showing off her ample curves before dropping to the ground. Wide black lace edged her sleeves that stopped just below her elbow and at her neckline. That same lace bordered her long skirts that trailed behind her by several feet.

Erith looked over her shoulder at Cael, pinning him with her lavender eyes. "Why are you here? Was my order difficult to understand?"

Her voice was smooth and lyrical. There wasn't anything about Erith that wasn't stunning and exquisite. But he wasn't fooled by her soft words. Erith was ferocious and fierce.

A combination Cael found infinitely pleasing.

"Cael?" she prodded, her voice edged with irritation.

He followed her through the maze of flowers, watching her hand trail across the blooms. "Have I ever questioned you about an order

"No. I'd suggest you not begin now." She paused and leaned down to smell a yellow flower.

Cael knew he had to tread carefully and phrase his responses just right. "We've had no problem taking out the Dark who remain in Edinburgh."

"Good. Most of the Dark have pulled back from all the cities in Scotland and England, but a few remain. Concentrate on Edinburgh first since that's where Taraeth began. The Dark who descended upon the helpless mortals have been judged." She cut her lavender eyes to Cael. "You're their executioner."

"It's a position I enjoy."

"And yet you're here." She narrowed her gaze at him before she faced him fully.

Cael was always taken aback when he saw Erith. Her ethereal beauty could make him forget his words.

Before he'd known her true mantel, he had sought to win her. How he had longed to run his hand down her face and trace her high cheekbones.

How he still longed for that.

He burned to get close enough and see if it was a deep purple or black that ringed her amazing eyes. He ached to know if her plump mouth was as kissable as it looked.

But those thoughts ended as quickly as falling off a cliff. Even after several millennia, his breath was always snatched away when he beheld her and realized something so magnificent was real.

And completely out of his reach.

Erith walked to Cael, stopping a foot from him. "You don't mind killing the Dark. Why then are you here? Does it have to do with your men?"

"No," Cael told her.

"Then say whatever it is you came to say." Her gaze hardened a fraction. "Now."

Cael towered over her by a foot, but she had a way of looking at him that made him feel he was no taller than a bug. "Was killing the Dark your last order to me?"

"Yes."

Cael squeezed the bridge of his nose with his thumb and forefinger. He and his men had nearly killed innocents not condemned by Death. That alone would have been a death sentence for each of them.

"I think it's time you told me all of it."

Cael opened his eyes, but Erith was gone. He looked around and found her walking toward the tower in what he could only call a glide. He wondered if her feet even touched the ground. Cael lengthened his strides to catch up with her.

Erith's nostrils flared in anger as she stared straight ahead. "Why do you think I would send you another mission?"

"It came to me via the robin as you've sent messages before."

"Only three times. In ten thousand years," she corrected. "What was the new order?"

The door to the tower opened on its own. Cael waited until they were inside before he said, "For us to hunt all half-Fae and kill them."

Erith had lifted her skirts and already started up the stairs. She whirled around, her eyes wide and her face pale with shock. "What?" she yelled in disbelief.

Her chest rose and feel rapidly. After a few tense moments, she turned back around and ascended the stairs that wound around the perimeter of the tower.

"No one knows I get the robin from you," Cael explained. "Not even my men."

"Did any of you kill a half-Fae," she asked tightly.

Cael got ahead of her on the stairs and stopped as he faced her. "No. We all had misgivings. Which is why I'm here."

Erith raised a black brow, questioning his statement.

Cael blew out a breath. "You know Fintan doesn't feel

anything. You formed the Reapers to keep the Fae in check. There is no one you've sent us after that didn't deserve the justice we served them."

"And yet you took that order and told your men."

Cael stepped to the side and bowed his head. "I did."

"Defeat doesn't become you, Cael," she said as she came even with him. "You did exactly as you were supposed to."

"Had I forced my men, you would've had to kill all of us."

She faced forward, a frown wrinkling her brow. "Yes. Leaving me with no one to keep the Fae in check."

Cael waited until the last of her skirts passed him before he continued after her. "Do you know who it might be?"

"There are a few candidates. No one knows I'm Death, but obviously you've been watched."

"We've been on the Fae realm, not Earth. It could be Taraeth."

She turned off the stairs when she reached a landing and walked into a spacious room. In the middle there was a large white rug with a black swirling pattern. Atop it was a simple wooden desk with a feminine feel and a chair.

Around the walls were shelves containing immaculately kept of records of every Fae—including the Reapers.

Erith walked to one of the windows. "There could be someone after the Reapers."

"True," he acknowledged. "Whispers of us are everywhere among the Fae. After we're done with Edinburgh, they'll know we're back. Or someone could be after you."

Erith's lavender gaze swung to him causing her long black locks to swirl around her. "I should be able to see this evil that has interfered with us, but I can't. Had you not come to me, I wouldn't have even known."

"Not until you had to kill us," he added.

Her gaze lowered to the ground. "I need to know who is doing this."

"Then let me find them."

He waited anxiously as she contemplated his request. She was silent so long that he added, "They used the robin, Erith. They put in a false order in your name. They're either out to remove all Reapers. Or they're after you."

"Let them come at me, then," she said as she met his gaze.

Cael had seen in her battle once—before he knew she was Death. He pitied anyone who dared to take her on.

Finally, she gave a single nod.

Chapter Seven

Jordyn thought taking a shower might help cool her body, but there was no halting the desire that raged like a volcano within her.

She tied her robe and ran her fingers through her short hair as she looked in the mirror. A Fae. Could she really have Fae blood?

All the times her family mentioned the Fae now took on a new meaning. Baylon was certain she was Fae. His conviction then swayed her.

Eyes a bright blue green mixture stared back at her. Very few people in her family had her color eyes. They only happened once a generation on her father's side. Her grandmother had called them Fae eyes.

But Jordyn knew what Fae eyes looked like. Silver ringed by a band of dark silver. Those were Fae eyes. Beautiful eyes that could make her body heat with just a look.

She closed her eyes and lowered her head as she put her hands on the sink to steady herself. It had been a long time since she accepted a date from anyone.

The men always became attached to her so quickly before any kind of feelings could form within her. There was no casual dating for her. The men wanted a commitment sometimes before the first date. Jordyn had learned to keep to herself.

Was she now feeling for Baylon what others had felt for her? Her stomach rolled at the thought.

She took a deep breath and opened her eyes. Then she pushed away from the sink. She opened the door and walked from the bathroom, only to stop dead in her tracks when she saw Baylon standing in the middle of her flat.

He had actually returned. Part of her never expected to see him again. "You're back."

"I said I would be."

Jordyn's mouth went dry as she met his gaze. She had been trying to convince herself that Baylon wasn't nearly as handsome as she thought he was. But seeing him again confirmed what she had already known.

The Fae was seriously hot.

"You have a reprieve. None of us are hunting half-Fae," he said.

"That's good."

It wasn't good. It was great, but all she seemed to be able to think about was Baylon. His kisses and his touch.

His eyes held hers, refusing to let her look away. "Do

you want me to leave?"

"No," she said in a rush, anxious to make sure that he never left.

Baylon smiled then. That half smile where only one side of his mouth lifted always seemed to make her stomach do a fluttery thing. "That pleases me."

And his words certainly pleased her.

He closed the distance between them, halting before her. She gazed into his silvery eyes and became lost, floating on a sea of silver that promised indescribable pleasure.

Baylon grabbed the ties to her robe with his hands and tugged. The bow came loose so that the silk robe fell open a fraction, getting caught on her breasts.

The room swam when his eyes lowered and a muscle in his jaw jumped as he caressed a finger along the edge of the robe along the swell of her breast.

Jordyn was a puddle of need. The only way she remained standing was by locking her knees.

His finger didn't stop until he reached her waist. With deliberate slowness, he opened each side of the robe until the garment hung on the outsides of her breasts.

"So beautiful," he mumbled.

He then set both hands at her neck where the robe was. Leisurely, he pushed the silk over her shoulders until it fell down her arms to sink into a puddle of white silk at her feet.

"I feel like I've waited eternity to see you," he said.

Baylon wasn't lying. All he had been thinking about was getting her out of the clothes so he could have an unblocked view of her amazing body.

And was it ever incredible. She was tall with all the seductive curvature of the Fae. His fingers grazed the indent of her waist to rest on the flare of her hip.

Baylon couldn't tear his eyes away from her perfect breasts. They were just a handful, pert and round, with nipples a deep pink.

As he stared, her nipple hardened, making his balls tighten in response. He was so hard for her he ached.

There wasn't a blemish on her supple skin. When his gaze lowered to her sex and saw the dark blond curls trimmed into a narrow strip of hair, his breath locked in his chest.

Unable to keep his hands off her anymore, he wound a hand around her waist and dragged her against him. Her hands rested on his chest as she looked up at him with a little smile of excitement.

"No one will bother us now."

She touched his lips with her finger. "I think I'll scream if they do."

"Oh, you'll be screaming. That I promise you."

Her turquoise eyes widened a fraction. "Let me see

you."

With a mere thought, his clothes vanished.

Jordyn spread her fingers and let her hands run over his wide shoulders before caressing down his washboard stomach to his trim waist.

There wasn't a scrap of hair on his upper body, and she found she liked that. He stayed still and let her look—and feel—at her pleasure.

She couldn't stop touching his warm skin and feeling his hard muscles beneath her hands. When she spotted his thick arousal jutting between them, she sighed in expectation.

But she wanted to explore him first, because once she kissed him, she would become lost.

Jordyn trailed her hand across his chest as she walked around to his back. Just as in the front, every muscle was defined and shaped into firm sinew.

She loved feeling his muscles move beneath her palms. After exploring his back and arms, she lowered her eyes to his behind. He had a spectacular ass.

Suddenly, Baylon spun around and yanked her against him before his mouth descended on hers. The kiss seized, it captured.

And ensnared.

Jordyn was sinking into oblivion. She tightened her arms around Baylon's neck to make sure he came with her. As she responded to his kiss, he ground his arousal against her.

The next thing she knew, they were lying in her bed, sinking into the thick down comforter. Their limbs tangled as they rolled with wild abandon.

She had to get closer to him. It irritated her that their skin separated them. Something strong and unyielding drove her onward, urging her to have their bodies become one.

Baylon had never been so wild for a female before. He craved her, hungered for her as if she were the very essence of his life force.

Somewhere in the dark recesses of his mind, he knew if he made love to Jordyn that disaster would come his way in great waves of pain. He knew it with as much certainty as he did that being with Jordyn would be like finding a lost piece of himself—a piece he hadn't known was missing.

A piece that centuries of being a Reaper had chipped away from his soul. Something he hadn't even realized until that moment.

With her in his arms.

He had to have her. There was no other choice, no other option.

She tore her lips from his and moaned when he cupped her breast and rolled a nipple between his fingers. Jordyn was panting, her hips rocking against him.

Baylon trailed kisses down her neck and over a perfect breast to a turgid peak. He wrapped his lips around it and suckled.

"I'm on fire," she said hoarsely, her back arching.

He smiled. Yes, that's exactly how he wanted her. Burning from the inside out with the same desire he felt.

"But I want to feel you," he said kissing the valley between her breasts.

He held her arms above her head with one of his hands. Baylon raised his head to look at her. Jordyn's lips were puffy and wet with his kisses. Her chest heaved from her rapid breaths.

His gaze glanced down to her lovely breasts and her nipples that responded so quickly to his touch. And lips.

He slowly ran his free hand down her stomach to her sex. She sucked in a breath, watching him with her mouth parted. He stopped just short of touching her.

"I want to feel all of you." As soon as he said the last word, he slid a finger inside her.

Her eyes rolled in her head and her back arched. She moaned, her chest deflating as she released her breath. Baylon couldn't resist. He claimed her lips as he delved his finger deep into her tight sheath.

He added a second finger. Inwardly he smiled when her legs parted wider to allow him more access. He made use of the opportunity by teasing her clit with his thumb.

Her entire body began to shake. Baylon didn't make her wait for the orgasm. He gave her the release she sought. And when her eyes flew open, her lips parted on a silent scream as her walls clamped around his finger, he watched it all with amazement.

Jordyn had never experienced a climax so shattering that she felt as if she were soaring. Even as the last vestiges of the orgasm wracked her body, Baylon's fingers were moving in and out of her.

His thumb flicked over her sensitive clit, sending her on another mini-climax.

And all it did was make her want him even more.

Jordyn shoved at his shoulder and rolled him onto his back. She rose up on her knees over him. His silver eyes watched her, daring her to do whatever it was she wanted.

Oh, the things she wished to do to Baylon. She feared she could spend eternity in bed with him, and it wouldn't be nearly long enough.

She reached between them and grasped his engorged cock. He sucked in a breath when she ran her hands up and down his length.

Holding his gaze, she brought him to her entrance. As soon as she felt the blunt head of his arousal, Jordyn lowered herself upon him.

She dropped her head back, her eyes sliding closed at

the feel of him stretching her, filling her. It felt . . . right.

Once she was fully seated, she lifted her head and looked down at him. A fine sheen of sweat covered his skin. His hands were braced on her hips, and the fire of desire in his eyes made her heart skip a beat.

Jordyn began to rock back and forth slowly. The tighter his fingers dug into her hips, the faster she moved. She had to brace her hands on his chest at one point.

But their gazes never broke.

She could feel the tightening of her body as passion and pleasure reigned. Their breathing was harsh, their bodies sliding against the other sensually.

A moan slipped past her lips as her body wound tighter. The climax hit her quickly, sending her spiraling into oblivion.

Baylon ground his teeth together, intent on holding firm control over himself as pleasure erupted over Jordyn's face as her body jerked around his cock.

He lasted until he could wait no longer. Then Baylon flipped her onto her back and rose up on his knees. He drove within her hard and deep.

If he thought she couldn't take anymore, he was surprised when her legs rose up and locked around his waist, her ankles urging him to go faster and deeper.

He looked down into a face that was branded in his mind. She opened herself and her body to him without any reservations. She touched him—deeply. Deeper than anyone ever had.

Baylon gave a final jerk of his hips as he buried himself so deep he touched her womb. He whispered her name as the climax took him.

Chapter Eight

For the first time Baylon knew what paradise was because he lying next to her. Jordyn's arms and legs were wrapped about him as if cocooning him.

It was a place he never wanted to leave.

But even as he rejoiced in the tranquility, he knew it wouldn't last.

She kissed his head and ran her hands through his hair. Baylon closed his eyes, and for the first time since becoming a Reaper, he wished he hadn't accepted Death's offer.

"Where have you been all my life?" Jordyn asked in a voice deepened by pleasure.

His cock jumped at the seductive sound. He was in big trouble if the sound of her voice could stir him so. He rose up and looked down at her. "If I'd known you were out there, I would've begun searching for you thousands of years ago."

Her smile was soft and glorious. "That was the perfect response."

"It's the truth."

Her smile vanished as a frown took its place. "What is it? What's wrong? Is it that a Fae isn't supposed to have sex with a human? Because technically, I've got some Fae in me."

How he wanted to pull her against him and shield her from every horrible thing out there. But he couldn't. She was going to have to face it all.

"It has nothing to do with you being human," he finally answered. Baylon ran the back of his hand down her side. "It's about who I am and what I do."

"And that is?" she prompted when he paused.

Baylon didn't want to tell her. He wanted to go on pretending that he was a normal Fae and there was nothing out there that could destroy the treasure he'd found.

She took his face between her hands and gazed fixedly at him. "Tell me. I can handle it."

"You weren't raised as a Fae, so you wouldn't have heard of the Reapers."

She smiled then as her hands fell away. "I know exactly what a Reaper is. They're said to collect the souls of the dead."

"In the human world that's what it means." He watched her as his words sank in.

"What does Reaper mean in your world?"

"Reapers are Fae who come for a Fae who has crimes they must answer for."

Jordyn's frowned deepened. "So your Reapers don't take dead souls? They kill?"

By the way she said the last part, she thought it abhorrent.

"They do."

"Well. That's just weird, but whatever. The Fae have magic, so I guess I understand that things would be different." She finished off her words with a shrug and a smile. "I bet there are stories regarding the Reapers to scare the Fae."

He chuckled softly. "There are. I heard them all as a child."

"What do the Reapers have to do with you though?"

Baylon inhaled a deep breath. "We're not hindered from telling humans what we do, but we're forbidden from telling other Fae."

"And I'm a bit of each," Jordyn said with a firm nod. "So you're not sure what to tell me. What will happen if they consider me a Fae and you tell me?"

"I'll be killed. As will you."

Her eyes grew big as she gaped at him. "You're serious."

"I am. It's not to be taken lightly, Jordyn." Baylon rolled off her and fell onto his back to stare at the ceiling.

Jordyn moved to her side and propped herself up on her elbow. "Then don't tell me what you do. I don't have to know."

"There are rules I have to follow," he said in a tone roughened by regret.

Her chest constricted. "What rules?"

"There aren't a lot." His Irish brogue had deepened. "We have very little dealings with humans, which is why it doesn't matter if they know who we are. The Fae, on the other hand, must never discover our names or faces."

The more he talked, the more her mind began to wonder if he was a Reaper. "Why?"

"Fae are magical and live an extremely long time. In human terms, we're immortal, since no human weapon can kill us. So the Fae have to have something to fear."

Jordyn felt her chest tighten even more. "And the other rules?"

"No relationships. Of any kind."

The fact he wouldn't look at her was like a kick in the stomach. Jordyn tried to swallow past the lump of emotion in her throat. "So this has to be just a one-time thing?"

"Yes," he replied in a strangled voice.

"I see."

His head turned to her as his eyes blazed with some unnamed emotion. "That's just it, you don't. I knew I should've never returned to you. I told myself it was to let you know that for now you're not being hunted. Then I saw you standing there in that silk robe." He rose up on his elbow to face her. "When it comes to you, I have no control."

Jordyn smiled, relief easing away the pain in her chest.

"But none of that matters," he finished.

Her smile died instantly. "I can feel what's between us is special."

"I took vows." His gaze lowered to the bed. "I've forsaken ever having a lover or wife or family. There can be nothing that would take me from my duties."

There was something about the way he said duties that confirmed he was a Reaper. She should be appalled that he went out and killed Fae as he had the Dark outside her building, but those kinds of Fae were evil.

So many questions rattled around in her head, but she knew she could never ask him. No one could know that she had figured out he was a Reaper. Jordyn would never want to put his life in danger because of her curiosity.

She wasn't sure what brought Baylon into her life that day, but she didn't regret it. Now she understood why she hadn't felt anything deep for any of the men she tried to date. She'd been waiting for Baylon.

It seemed wrong to have a small taste of him, only to be told it was the only time she had with him. It made her sad and angry at the same time.

But she wouldn't fight or argue. Not when she didn't

know how much longer she had with him.

Jordyn buried the scream of frustration and put on a smile when he looked at her. "How much time do we have?"

"Not nearly long enough."

She leaned forward and kissed him. His arms came around her as he fell back and brought her with him. He was already hard, and she ached to feel him inside her once more.

"We shouldn't," he murmured between kisses.

"I know." But she couldn't stop touching him.

She ran her hands over his chest and shoulders. Before she knew it, she was face down on the bed with him behind her.

He lifted her hips and slid into her. Jordyn closed her eyes in ecstasy as she rose up on her hands. He leaned over her, his hands on her breasts, kneading them as he placed kisses along her back.

The feel of him moving in and out of her was glorious. She moved back against him, bringing him deeper. He groaned and pinched her nipple.

Jordyn turned her head to the side and suddenly his lips were on hers, kissing her in time with his thrusts. It was erotic and sensual and unbelievable.

She wished she had the power to stop time so they could have as long as they wanted. But in truth, one night would never be enough for her. Each time she thought of Baylon leaving, it felt as if someone were squeezing her heart. So she stopped thinking about it and concentrated on what he was doing to her body.

"I can't get enough of you," he rasped.

She rotated her hips, smiling when he groaned again. "Don't stop. Don't ever stop touching me."

"I fear I'll never be able to."

Those words gave her hope, but for what she wasn't sure. She became lost in the pleasure, the bliss that was Baylon's hands and mouth on her body.

His swirled a finger around her clit, making her shudder in response.

"Yes," he whispered. "I want to hear you cry out in pleasure again."

"All you have to do is touch me."

His chest rumbled in a growl. Then he began to plunge deeper, harder while teasing her swollen clit.

She was so close to peaking. As if he knew, he paused for a few seconds before he repeated the process all over again.

It wasn't long until she was panting, her body on fire for release. She felt his lips on her neck. "Please," she begged.

"Not yet," he whispered.

She whimpered as he pounded her body and aroused

her even more. It wasn't until her body was shaking, her sex swollen and primed for orgasm when he said, "Now. Come for me now."

As if on cue, her body exploded.

Jordyn screamed her release, the pleasure so forceful that she felt like she was having an out-of-body experience.

Then she felt Baylon fill her one more time before he climaxed. The feel of him releasing his seed within her caused her peak on top of the orgasm she was already experiencing.

Long moments later, her body finally stopped pulsing. Baylon's arms wrapped around her and brought her against him as he lay on his side.

He kissed her check, holding her tight.

~

Cael couldn't remember the last time he was so furious. He returned to Edinburgh and the castle to find the others waiting for him. All except Baylon.

Fintan shrugged when Cael looked his way. "We've not seen Baylon since the pub earlier."

"I've tried calling to him," Talin said. "He's not responding. Eoghan went looking for him."

Cael turned to Eoghan, but the Light Fae stared over

the city. "Should I assume by your silence that Baylon isn't in danger?"

Eoghan gave a single nod.

Cael was going to have to prod deeper when the others weren't around. With Eoghan, he never knew if the Fae was being his usual silent self, or if it was because he didn't want to share what he knew.

"What did you discover?" Kyran asked.

"A lot." Cael let out a sigh. "Death didn't issue the order."

For the first time in the thousands of years that he had known the Reapers, none of them had anything to say. They stared at him with various degrees of alarm and shock.

"I suspect that was my reaction when I spoke with Death. The fact that someone not only knows who I am, but how Death contacts me is . . . troubling."

"Troubling?" Fintan repeated with a snort. "I'd say it's a sight more than that."

Cael looked around at the men. "We're going to find who did this. What's unclear is if they're targeting us or Death. Regardless, we're going to find them and end it before they can do anything else."

"Now this order I can eagerly jump onto," Kyran stated.

Fintan smirked. "Whoever this fucker is has no idea

what's coming for him."

"He—or they—will find out soon enough," Talin said.

Cael was glad his men were on board. Though he would feel better if Baylon were there. They could also use Daire, but he needed to stay with Rhi. "Before any of you get too excited, we have no clue as to who the culprit might be."

"No Fae is supposed to know who we are," Kyran said.

Cael faced Talin. What the others didn't know was that Talin had been working undercover in the court of the Light, trying to get close to Queen Usaeil.

Talin thought he had kept his affair with another Fae private, but Cael had seen Talin with the female. Talin hadn't touched her, but it was the way Talin looked at her that gave him away.

"Why are you looking at Talin?" Fintan demanded.

Talin drew in a deep breath. "Those times I've left the group? Well, it was to go undercover at Usaeil's court."

"Now that's an assignment I'd have liked," Kyran said with a cocky grin.

Talin looked to Cael. "No one knows. I swear."

That's all Cael needed to hear. He trusted his men implicitly. "We all know how treacherous court can be. Is there anyone there that gave you concern?"

"Several," Talin said. "Usaeil spends a lot of time away from the castle as she pretends to be an American. She quite likes being a movie star. It's a rare thing if she's at court."

"And when she is?" Fintan pressed.

"She spends a lot of time in her rooms. There's rumor she's taken a lover. I can confirm that fact."

Eoghan looked at Cael and raised a brow in question.

Cael was equally curious. "Who is the lover?"

"That is the question," Talin said with a twist of his lips. "Some have suggested it's a Dragon King."

Cael didn't like that news at all. "Does Rhi know?"

"Daire would know that better than I," Talin answered.

Kyran crossed his arms over his chest. "How can we go after someone if we don't know who it is? We don't even have any suspects."

"Could it be a human?" Fintan asked.

Eoghan grunted and gave a shake of his head.

"I agree with Eoghan," Cael said. "The mortals think of Reapers in an entirely other light. They have no reason to fear us. Besides, it would take someone with magic to send the message from Death."

"It's not like we can ask past Reapers," Kyran said.

Eoghan turned to Cael, his face lined with dread.

"They're dead. Death saw to that when they tried to side with the Dark during the Fae Wars," Cael said to him. To the others he explained, "Eoghan and I are the only ones left of that group. Besides. The only way we stop being Reapers is when we die."

But Eoghan didn't look convinced. Which made Cael begin to think back to the time of the last group of Reapers.

Chapter Nine

Jordyn woke to Baylon lying between her legs, his mouth on her sex. She moaned and grabbed his head. His tongue was doing amazing, erotic things to her.

She opened her eyes to see it was still dark outside. Jordyn had fought to stay awake, fearing that she would fall asleep and wake to find Baylon gone.

But he was still with her. Why couldn't she have some magic that gave her the ability to prolong time to keep them secluded?

She sighed as her mind went empty as pleasure swarmed her. It wasn't fair that he had such power over her body as he did. The orgasm was growing closer. She tried to keep it at bay, but Baylon wouldn't let her. She screamed his name as she climaxed.

Her sex still throbbed with her orgasm when he thrust inside her. She reached for him, loving the feel of his weight atop her.

~

Cael sent Talin, Fintan, and Kyran away to see what they could find about anyone having a grudge against the Reapers.

"What aren't you telling me?" he asked Eoghan when they were alone.

"Leave it."

Cael shook his head. "You know I can't. Why isn't Baylon here."

"He will."

"But he wasn't here where I told him to be." Cael sighed. "Baylon doesn't disregard orders. If he's not in danger, then my only other conclusion is that it's a female."

When Eoghan didn't answer, Cael clenched his teeth together. He understood why Erith made them all vow never to have any sort of relationships, even friendships. The only ones they could depend on were other Reapers.

Those were the rules that protected them. If others knew who the Reapers where, they could try and take advantage or turn them. Their jobs were difficult enough without that added burden.

"Give him the night," Eoghan said.

Cael looked at his old friend. It was uncommon for Eoghan to speak, and even rarer when he asked for something.

"Do I need to be worried?"

Eoghan's gaze lowered to the ground before he swung around and looked back over the city.

That was all the answer Cael was going to get, but it was all he needed. Whatever Eoghan saw must've been serious.

It was the last thing the Reapers needed right now. It wasn't the first time Cael had seen a Reaper try to forsake his vow.

Bran, one of the first Reapers, had fallen in love. Cael and the others discovered the relationship and demanded Bran end it. Instead, Bran turned against them. The result had been catastrophic—for everyone.

Cael prayed Baylon was smart enough to walk away from the female before it was too late. Cael didn't want to lose another Reaper.

Without a word, Cael veiled himself and thought of Baylon. He was immediately taken to a flat in Edinburgh. Cael looked at all the books in wonder as he turned around.

Then he saw the bedroom. Upon the bed was Baylon making love to a half-Fae female, her cries of ecstasy filling the flat.

Cael immediately teleported to Daire. He was surprised to find himself at Dreagan, though it took everything he had to remain veiled.

The room they were in was large, and upon the bed lay

the Light Fae, Rhi. She was unharmed, though he saw the burn in her shirt that indicated Dark magic was used on her.

Daire unveiled and let out a sigh. "The Dragon Kings' magic is powerful. It's damn hard to remain here veiled."

Cael unveiled himself and nodded. "The Kings wouldn't be happy to know we've been here. They know of us, but they've not had reason to interact. Perhaps we should keep it that way. I don't want them as enemies."

"Absolutely," Daire said. He then looked at Rhi. "There was a battle involving Ulrik. I didn't see him send the magic at her, but it could only have been him. Also, most of the Kings have come to see Rhi. Rhys is here often. And when he comes, he stays for awhile."

"Curious."

"Con healed her below. I'm not sure why she still sleeps."

Cael shrugged absently. "Only time will tell."

"There's something else." Daire glanced at the bed and the sleeping Fae. "Rhi had another visitor today."

Cael raised a brow. "Who?"

"A Warrior named Phelan."

"So the Warriors are still around. And ones who control their god instead of the god controlling them. Impressive."

"There are several Warriors at MacLeod Castle," Daire

said.

That was news to Cael. Perhaps he needed to look into the Warriors and see what was going on. "So why did one visit Rhi?"

Daire ran a hand down his face. "He's half-Fae."

Cael eyed the decanter of whisky he saw on the table. After the day he'd had, he could use a drink or two. "I came to let you know that we got a new order to kill every half-Fae we find."

"What?" Daire demanded, shock making his face go slack. "Since when do we kill humans?"

Cael held up a hand to quiet him. "The order came from a messenger. I questioned the orders, and the others refused to carry out the order. So I spoke to Death. The new command didn't come from Death."

"If not Death, then who?" Daire asked.

"That's the question. As hard as it is, remain veiled here and see if you can find out anything about who would want to attack us or Death."

Daire gave a nod. "Certainly. And if Rhi wakes?"

"Stay with her. No matter what."

"You really think she's that important?"

"Death does, and that means I do as well."

～

Jordyn came awake slowly. For a moment she didn't move, afraid she would find herself alone. Then she heard Baylon's breathing.

A second later she realized she was on her side facing him while he lay on his back. Her leg lay across him while his hand rested on her bare ass.

Her eyes opened to find sunlight streaming through the windows. Baylon slept, giving her the opportunity to study him.

His black hair was mussed in a way that made her smile. She had begun to think there wasn't a part of the Fae that was ever out of place. And the way he made her feel.

Lord, he was dangerous to her soul.

Her smile faded as she thought of their night. She lost track of how many times they made love. Jordyn hadn't realized she was such a wanton. But in his arms, she became someone else. As if he brought out the Fae in her.

Jordyn was confused at the myriad emotions she felt for Baylon. The thought of him leaving left her reeling so much so that she didn't think she would ever right her world again.

Then there was Baylon himself. She couldn't be near him and keep her hands off him. Jordyn had heard of couples who were so insanely attracted to the other that nothing else mattered. Well, she experienced it firsthand.

It was glorious.

And frightening.

To hunger for someone in such a way. It linked them on a level she hadn't known existed before. Then there was the fact he couldn't have any sort of relationship.

They had one night together. That one night ruined her for anyone else. Not because Baylon was Fae, but because he stirred something within her that had been waiting to be found.

No other male—human or Fae—would ever be able to touch her as deeply as Baylon.

Jordyn slowly removed his hand and climbed out of bed. She walked from the bedroom and found her robe. After she had it on, she made her way to the kitchen and started the coffee brewing.

A glance at the clock told her she had a couple of hours before she had to get to work. Jordyn yawned as she got down a mug from the cupboards. It took forever for the coffee to finish.

She poured the steaming liquid into her mug and added milk and sugar until the coffee was a light tan color. Jordyn took a sip and looked into her bedroom where Baylon still slept.

A soft knock jarred her. She walked to the door and peered through the peephole to see it was from a delivery service. It must be the books she ordered last week.

Jordyn unlocked the door and opened it. "Morning."

The man smiled, showing dimples in his handsome face. "Morning, Miss Patterson. I've got a delivery for you."

"Great. You can bring it up now."

He hesitated and glanced down the stairs. "The thing is, a couple of boxes busted. I'm not sure what all belongs to you. Could you come down and take a look?"

"Mine are the books."

"There were three boxes of books," he said. "I want to make sure everyone gets what they ordered. It was my screw up, and I really don't want to get fired."

Jordyn sighed. "Let me get some clothes on."

She was turning away when the Irish accent hit her. She had gotten so used to listening to Baylon all night that she almost hadn't recognized it.

Her gaze returned to the deliveryman to see that he was insanely good looking. His hair was blond and his eyes green. She hadn't bothered to ask Baylon if Light Fae had different color hair and eyes. Then again, he could be using glamour.

"Something wrong?" he asked.

Jordyn smiled and shook her head. "It's a little early for deliveries, isn't it?"

He shrugged and looked at his clipboard. "I've got a lot of stops, so I thought I'd start early."

"Look," Jordyn began, but her words ended when four Dark stepped out behind the driver.

One of them threw a large iridescent bubble at the driver, killing him instantly. The four Dark stepped over his body and started toward her.

For a moment, Jordyn couldn't move. Her mind wasn't able to process the fact that the Dark were there and coming right at her.

She spun around and tried to run, but a Dark wrapped his arm around her neck, jerking her back. Jordyn shrieked as her coffee spilled on her arm and shoulder, burning her through the silk.

"Time to die," the Dark said in her ear.

The other three Dark stood around her with their magic at the ready and smirks on their faces. They were going to enjoy killing her.

There was a loud bellow. Jordyn looked toward the bedroom in time to see Baylon launch himself from the bed with his sword over his head.

He crossed the flat in a blink before he killed one of the other Dark, but the one holding her dragged her out of her flat into the hallway. Jordyn tried to grab hold of the doorjamb, but her fingers couldn't get a good hold. She stared at Baylon watching him go from one Dark to another, killing them.

Then she was out in the hall, the Dark's grip became

lethal as he continued to drag her. Suddenly there was another man standing in front of her. His silver eyes blazed with fury directed at the Dark. His black hair hung long and straight to his shoulders.

The Light Fae held up his hand and said one word that Jordyn didn't understand. The Dark holding her gurgled as if he were choking. His hold loosened, and Jordyn tried to get away.

But the Dark held fast even as he struggled to breathe.

"Jordyn!" Baylon bellowed from inside the flat where he killed the last two Dark.

Chapter Ten

Jordyn reached for Baylon as the Dark holding her began to fall backward. There was nothing but stairs there, and she doubted she could survive the fall.

The Light who had killed her attacker grabbed her hand and pulled her away from the Dark. Jordyn turned and watched the Dark fall down a flight of steps, only to disintegrate a second later.

"Jordyn."

She turned her head to Baylon and started to go to him, when she noticed his tight expression. Jordyn halted, wounded that he would treat her in such a fashion.

"You're hurt," the Fae said.

Jordyn blinked and looked at him. Hurt? Yes, her heart hurt. That's when she realized he was holding her injured arm where the coffee had burned her.

Her robe was ruined, but that's not why she wanted to cry. It was because her time with Baylon was over. It hurt far worse than she thought it would.

"Perhaps we should take this matter inside," the Fae

said to Baylon.

Baylon nodded woodenly and strode past them. Jordyn watched him, her chest feeling as if her heart had been ripped from her with a spoon.

She let the Fae guide her inside her flat. He didn't release her as he closed the door behind them. The Dark who attacked her was gone, as was the deliveryman. She wasn't sure what happened to him, and she was fairly certain she didn't want to know.

"I'm Cael," the Fae said as he ushered her to the sofa. He gave her a tender shove to sit and followed her.

Jordyn winced when he gently pulled the silk away from her burns. The material was beginning to latch onto her skin, and it was painful to have it drawn away.

"Your skin is blistered."

She didn't bother answering him. Nor did she look at her arm. She just wanted both of them to just go away so she could begin to try to pick up the pieces of her life.

Her gaze was on the floor staring at the pattern of her rug when she saw a pair of boots step in front of her. Baylon. Her body reacted instantly to his nearness.

Cael then put her hand atop her leg and patted it.

"It's not as bad as I feared. I don't think you'll even scar," he said and stood.

Out of the corner of her eye, Jordyn saw him go to the window. She glanced at her arm to find her robe no longer ruined. The pain of her arm was lessening by the moment. Had Cael healed her? "Thank you."

"What the hell happened?" Baylon demanded of Cael. "Why did they attack her?"

His questions had Jordyn curious. She lifted her head and looked at Cael. His fingers gripped the windowsill as if he would rather break the glass than look out of it.

"I didn't see you last night," Cael said in response.

Baylon briefly closed his eyes, wondering yet again why he hadn't left Jordyn in the middle of the night. But then he knew the answer. He hadn't been able to.

Cael turned his head to Baylon before he then looked to Jordyn. She rose to her feet and tried to walk away. "Please stay," Cael said. "This involves you now."

Baylon didn't like the sound of that.

Cael shifted so that he leaned back against the windowsill, his hands resting on either side of him. "Someone wants half-Fae dead."

"I don't understand," Baylon said. "Why?"

"We're trying to find out." Cael's gaze slid to Jordyn. "How long have you known you were half-Fae?"

She lifted her chin and replied, "Since last night."

Cael raised a brow and motioned around the flat with his hand. "Yet, you've been studying the Fae."

"They've always interested me."

"Cael," Baylon said, fast losing his patience.

The leader of the Reapers turned his eyes to Baylon. "Someone has made it their mission to find half-Fae humans and kill them, if this morning is any indication."

There was something Cael wasn't saying. Baylon didn't press him since he knew Cael would reveal nothing in front of Jordyn.

"If I'm going to face more Fae, then I'd like to do it with my clothes on," Jordyn said as she got to her feet. "I'm sure you lads can entertain yourselves as I shower."

Baylon wished Cael wasn't there so he could join Jordyn in the shower. His cock hardened as he imagined pressing her against the wall with the water running over them, soap allowing their bodies to glide against the other.

It was everything Baylon could do not to follow Jordyn to the bathroom. He stared for long moments at the closed door as the water turned on. His few hours with Jordyn had changed something within him. He couldn't pinpoint what it was, but he knew he would fight to his last breath for it.

Baylon waited for Cael to ream him for missing the meeting. Instead, Cael remained silent. Baylon finally looked at him.

Cael regarded him with a curious look. "Death didn't send us the order to kill the half-Fae."

"I'm relieved. Who did then?"

"That's what we need to find out. It's unclear whether they are targeting Death or us."

Baylon crossed his arms over his chest. "Or both."

"Or both," Cael replied with a nod. "I'm keeping Daire with Rhi. She's at Dreagan for the moment, and he could find out something there."

"You really want to drag the Dragon Kings into this?"

Cael shot him a perturbed look. "Absolutely not. Hopefully, they'll never know Daire was there. I've sent the others out looking for anything that might help us find whoever knows about us."

"Why did they attack Jordyn?" Baylon ran a hand down his face and dropped his arms. He glanced at the door, remembering how his heart had lurched in his chest when he woke to find Dark surrounding her.

"You stopped them from taking her away. Smart thinking putting that spell on her."

Baylon gave a little shake of his head. "I did it while she slept last night. I had a feeling something might happen. I knew that she stood a chance if one of us was near to help her, but if the Dark took her, I'd never find her."

"What is she to you?"

He wasn't yet ready to tell Cael, mainly because he wasn't sure he could admit to what he was feeling. It was all too new, too raw.

Too visceral.

"We can have sex with Fae," Baylon said.

Cael raised a black brow. "Death would rather we stayed away from humans. I suppose you figured since Jordyn was half-Fae you were in the clear?"

"What I knew was that I couldn't keep my hands off her," Baylon said in a harsh whisper. He looked at the bathroom and turned his back on it. "I was going to leave her this morning."

"Are you sure about that?"

"I was. She knew it as well."

"Then you woke to the Dark," Cael said.

Baylon briefly looked sideways at him. "In all the years you've been alive, even before you were a Reaper, was there ever something you wanted so desperately that you were willing to do anything for it?"

There was a long pause. Then Cael responded in a voice pitched in a whisper, "Yes."

Now this was something Baylon had never expected Cael to answer, let alone admit. He looked at him in a new light. Was that why Cael had yet to tell him that he had to leave Jordyn behind forever?

Cael rubbed a hand along his jaw. "I came to get you this morning. It was a surprise to arrive and find Dark attacking Jordyn. They've targeted her. And not to take her back to their realm for sex. They want her dead."

"I know." It tore Baylon to pieces that she had been so

close to being killed. "I should've warded the flat so Dark couldn't get in."

"She'll have to leave the flat eventually," Cael pointed out.

Baylon turned to meet his gaze. "She'll be safe if she's with us."

"That's not possible. She can't know of us. She's Fae."

"She's also human," Baylon argued. "Death doesn't care if we tell humans."

Cael pushed away from the window and shook his head. "She's either human or Fae, Baylon. You can't keep changing who she is to suit your purpose."

"Then I stay with her."

"You can't," Cael said, his forehead furrowed deeply. "Your place is with us."

Baylon walked to stand in front of Cael. "I'll not let her die."

"If you remain with her, Death will see it as abandoning your duties." Cael's face was a mask of confusion. "You'll die. Who will protect her then?"

Baylon heard the shower cut off. "For whatever reason, she was brought into my life and I into hers. It doesn't matter why, really. All I know is that I have to protect her."

Cael simply looked at him, no emotion on his face.

So Baylon tried again. "She's lived her entire life as a

human. She'll continue to be human. It's not her fault she has Fae blood."

"That can be said about any mortal with Fae blood."

"Exactly," Baylon said earnestly. "We can't allow the Dark to kill them."

Cael looked away and sighed. "Even if we wanted to help, it's not our mission."

"No. Our mission was to kill the Dark that remained in Edinburgh. I'd say that's one and the same."

Cael laughed and swiveled his head to Baylon. "Nice thinking. It'll work for those in Edinburgh and through-out the UK, but the others around the world won't be so lucky."

"We can do this, Cael."

"You're risking a lot for her."

Baylon was willing to risk everything. "Yes."

A moment later Jordyn walked out of the bathroom in her robe once more. She didn't look at them as she en-tered her bedroom and closed the door behind her.

Baylon wanted to go to her, to pull her in his arms and kiss her until she melted against him. He didn't like see-ing her put up walls around herself as if she were trying to keep him out.

He saw her clearly last night, and he refused to have anything less. They laid each other's souls bare. Baylon had tried to pull away, but it was impossible with Jordyn.

She had a way of making him want to tell her everything. He wanted no secrets between them. She tried to hide her disappointment when he hadn't told her he was a Reaper, but he had seen it through her smile.

"She's going to have to leave her life behind," Cael said.

Baylon shook his head. "No, she doesn't. We need to find out who is after us. The best way is to get some answers out of those trying to kill her."

"Do you think she'll agree to your plan to use her as bait?"

"I won't know until I ask." Baylon stood straighter when the bedroom door opened a moment later.

Jordyn emerged wearing a pale pink button-down, opened enough to reveal a white shirt beneath and a pair of jeans. Her short dark blond hair was still damp, and there wasn't a stitch of makeup on her face.

"So what's the verdict?" she asked as she put her hands in her back pockets.

Cael smiled at her. "How do you feel about helping us catch whoever is after you?"

Chapter Eleven

Jordyn stared at Cael for a moment before her gaze swung to Baylon. It wasn't as if she had any choice really. The Dark were coming for her, and if there was even a shred of hope that she might escape them, then she had to help Baylon and Cael.

"I believe it's the right thing," she replied.

Baylon's head lowered as his gaze dropped to the ground. A part of her had hoped—okay, really all of her—that he'd see she could be brave, that she could do her part.

Surely he didn't think her mortal half made her weak and a coward.

"Baylon," Cael said.

Baylon lifted his head and looked directly at Jordyn. "I'd have preferred to keep you out of this, but in order to find the truth, we need you."

Jordyn relaxed as she realized he didn't think her weak. He just hadn't wanted her involved. He was protecting her.

"Don't be too hasty," Baylon cautioned. "It'll mean

walking away from all of this," he said, motioning to her flat.

She looked at her bookshelves and all the books on the Fae. For decades she'd been soaking up any and all information about them. Now there were two standing in front of her. Whether she learned everything or only a little, it was much more than she had before last night.

Then there were the Dark. Without Baylon, she didn't stand a chance against them. She might have Fae in her blood, but she had no magic, or anything that might be used to fight the Dark.

But it wasn't just the place she lived that she'd be walking away from. It was her friends. Her family.

Cael stode to her. "It's a lot that we ask of you."

"But my other option is death," she finished for him. "I get it. I'm just thinking of my family."

"The less they know, the better," Baylon said.

Jordyn looked from him to Cael. "If the Dark know I have Fae blood, can they find my family?"

When Cael gave a single, curt nod, the room began to spin. She had to warn them, to let them know they were in danger.

Jordyn hurried to her purse and rummaged in it looking for her mobile. Her hands shook as she searched for her parents' number. Right as she was about to press dial, a hand covered the phone.

"Where are they?" Baylon asked.

She gazed into his silver eyes. "Stonehaven."

In a blink he was gone. Jordyn lowered her hand and looked to Cael who stood with a frown marring his face. He wasn't happy, but she didn't care. This was her family.

Cael's eyes hardened a fraction. "How much has Baylon told you?"

"He told me of the Fae, of who I am. He also mentioned there was a war started by the Dark. If you're wondering if he told me who he is, let me set your mind at ease. I know whatever he's doing is important. I know that he's not supposed to have any relationships, and I know he'll disappear out of my life soon."

For long moments, Cael watched her. "You've had one night with him, and yet you look at him as if you've known him for centuries."

"Because that's what it feels like." She pulled out a chair at the table and sat as she drew in a shaky breath. Worry settled like lead in her stomach. "I expected to find him gone when I woke this morning. I'm thankful that he was here, but I know the longer I'm near him, the harder it's going to be to let him go."

Cael moved to the opposite side of the table and rested his hands on the back of the chair. "You're going to have to let him go. If he stays with you, he'll be executed."

"I won't let that happen," she said and lifted her chin.

She was putting on a valiant face that she didn't feel. It was a mask she was going to have to wear from now on. For herself.

For Baylon.

"He told you something else," Cael said suddenly.

Jordyn looked away. She couldn't stand to have Cael's silver eyes, so similar to Baylon's, watching her. "He told me about the Fae."

"What, specifically?"

She rubbed her temple as her leg began to bounce. Her mind was on her family, not on the conversation the night before. "He told me some differences in my world and his."

"Like?" Cael pressed.

Jordyn slammed her hand on the table and swung her head to him. "He didn't tell me!"

"But you figured it out." Cael snorted and shook his head. "What did he say that had you piecing it together?"

"Does it matter? The only thing you need to know is that he didn't tell me. And I didn't tell him that I pieced it together."

Cael clenched his teeth, a muscle jumping in his jaw. "There's a reason we never share our secret with other Fae, Jordyn. It's to keep ourselves safe. Now you've put Baylon and yourself in danger."

"I'm already in danger," she said and leaned back in the

chair.

"The Dark don't stand a chance against Death, because that's who we answer to."

Jordyn slumped in the chair. She should've kept her mouth shut. "None of this is Baylon's fault. It's mine. He was very careful about not divulging anything. I wanted to know differences in our cultures. He told me about Reapers. I began to suspect last night that he might be one."

"What confirmed it?"

She gave a half-hearted shrug. "Nothing specific. Just the way he acted, the things he knew. I would never have come out and asked him. If Death wants to punish anyone, let it be me. Baylon is innocent."

"He's hardly innocent," Cael said and ran a hand down his face as he turned away. "He knew not to stay the night with you."

"So none of you can . . . be . . . with another?"

Silence dragged on, making Jordyn wonder if Cael was going to answer her.

Then he said, "We can, but some of us choose not to. The risks are too great."

"You mean like if one of you developed feelings for someone."

"Exactly. That's why we get one time with a female."

Not a night? But a single time? Interesting. "Has it

happened before?"

Cael turned back to her. "Yes. And the end result was horrific. Should I be concerned about you and Baylon?"

Jordyn thought about Baylon, about how she needed his touch, how she longed to have him near. Were there feelings? Oh, yes. Would she tell Cael? Hell no.

"The sex was good, but that's all it was," Jordyn lied.

Cael started to say something when Baylon appeared next to him. Jordyn met Baylon's gaze, waiting for him to tell her that her family was all right.

But his expression of regret said it all.

Baylon was at Jordyn's side in an instant as she began to hyperventilate. He kneeled in front of her and took her face in his hands. "Jordyn, look at me. Look at me. That's it. Focus on me."

He used just enough magic to help her get her bearings. Though he was tempted, Baylon didn't take away her pain. She needed to cope with what life had given her. That was true of all beings—mortal or immortal.

"How?" she asked as tears gathered and spilled down her cheeks.

Baylon would never tell her the hideous way the Dark killed her family. He might not be able to save her from the pain of losing them, but he could spare her the details.

"Baylon?"

He looked into her turquoise eyes filled with agony and remorse. Baylon used his thumb to wipe away a trail of tears that did nothing to stop her crying. "It was the Dark."

"Did they suffer?" she asked.

Cael blew out a harsh breath. "It was the Dark, Jordyn. They don't do anything gently."

When her face dropped into her hands as she cried silent tears with her shoulders shaking, Baylon released her and stood.

He looked at Cael and shook his head to let Cael know it had been a vicious scene. That was the Dark's answer for their stopping the attack this morning.

"We need to get her away and form a plan with the others," Cael said as he glanced around. "We've got this one shot at discovering who is after us. We need to do it right."

Baylon heard his name being said in his mind. "Kyran is calling for me."

"Don't tell him to come here," Cael said hastily. He hurried to Jordyn and grabbed her arm to pull her to her feet. "We go to Edinburgh Castle."

Baylon met Jordyn's gaze and gave her a smile he hoped comforted her. As soon as she and Cael disappeared, Baylon heard movement outside her door. Dark Fae.

How he wanted to stand and fight them. But it wasn't the time. Baylon teleported to the castle as the door was blasted off the hinges.

~

Bran stared into the flat, his gaze roaming the area. The half-Fae female had been there. Of that he was sure. She had no magic, which meant one of the Reapers helped her get away.

"Keep running, Cael. I'll catch you soon enough," he whispered.

Bran motioned to the Dark behind him. They filed into the flat as they began searching for anything about her. Bran strode slowly to the bookshelves. A smile formed and grew when he saw that all of the half-Fae's books were on the Fae.

Which one of the Reapers had found her? It wasn't Cael. The bastard didn't have a shred of feeling within him. It's what made him a perfect Reaper.

Bran hoped that Erith enjoyed having Cael as leader of the Reapers, because when he was finished with Cael, there would be nothing left.

"Here, Bran," one of his men called.

Bran pivoted and walked into the bedroom that smelled of sex. How . . . interesting. A Reaper had taken the half-Fae. Bran suspected that Cael was anything but happy about that. What a predicament that was for Cael and all the Reapers.

Did they tell the female who they were since she was human? Or did they keep it a secret because of her Fae blood? That would tie Cael up in knots for a while.

"Look," the Dark said and pointed to the bed.

Bran leaned close and saw that part of the iron scrollwork of the headboard was bent. "The sex must have been very good."

"Magic lingers there."

He shrugged and turned on his heel. "We'll never figure out which of the Reapers was in bed with the half-Fae. Not from that, at least."

"I thought she'd be here," another Dark said angrily.

Bran halted and leisurely turned to look at the Dark in question. He smiled. "You wiped out her entire family a moment ago. As for the female, we'll find her soon enough."

"But you said she'd be here," the Dark argued.

He wouldn't have anyone question him ever again. Bran lifted his hand and sent a blast of magic that evaporated the Dark were he stood.

Bran looked around at the other Dark. "Anyone else want to bitch about the female not being here?"

Chapter Twelve

One minute Jordyn was in her apartment, and the next she was in a castle—Edinburgh Castle if she heard Cael correctly.

She sniffed through her tears and turned around the room looking for a window so she could see out, but there was no window. Jordyn wrapped her arms around herself as the coldness of reality sank into her bones.

There would come a time for her to mourn her family properly, but now wasn't the time. Now she had to concentrate on the task at hand and remain alive with the only people-or Fae-that could help her.

With great amount of effort, she forced her attention away from the ancient stones of the castle to the room. It was a good-sized room with an arched ceiling.

Rugs that looked as ancient as the room itself lined the floor in haphazard fashion that she found appealing. At odds with the chamber itself were the two leather Chesterfield sofas and three chairs, all of which looked worn and completely comfortable.

She noticed that the light came from dozens upon

dozens of candles of all sizes. Some were lined up along the walls. Others were atop shelves and on the mantle of the massive fireplace. But it was the ones that hung seemingly midair that made her do a double take.

That's when she had to remind herself that she was with Fae.

"Um . . . Cael?" said a male voice behind her.

Jordyn whirled around and found four men behind her. As soon as she saw the one with black and silver hair and red eyes, she took a step back. Right into Baylon's arms.

"It's all right," he reassured her in a warm, soft tone. "That's Kyran. He's Dark, but he's a friend."

"Uh, huh. Sure," she mumbled. Then her gaze took in the man with long white hair staring at her. His eyes were silver, but rimmed in red. It was beyond eerie.

Cael motioned to her. "This is Jordyn. As I'm sure you've deduced, she has Fae blood. The Dark are after her, which is why she's here. She's going to act as bait to help us determine who we're up against."

"Death isn't going to be happy about this," said a main with shoulder-length black hair and light silver eyes.

Cael's nostrils flared. He then turned his head to her. "These are the men that are going to help protect you. There's Kyran, who Baylon already pointed out. Next to him is Talin who doesn't know when to keep his mouth shut."

Jordyn pressed her lips together to keep from laughing when Talin looked at Cael as if had lost his mind. Behind her, Baylon chuckled.

"Going down the line we have Fintan. If you haven't guessed by his red-rimmed eyes, he's Dark as well."

Fintan turned his unusual eyes on her. "We all have our pasts."

Cael ignored him and pointed to the last man who stood slightly apart. "The silent one is Eoghan. Don't get upset if he doesn't talk, because he doesn't talk to any of us."

Eoghan watched her curiously. She shot him a smile, and to her shock, his lips lifted in what must be his idea of a grin.

"The only one missing is Daire," Baylon said as he came around her. "He's on another assignment."

Jordyn found it more than a little uncomfortable to have six pairs of eyes focused entirely on her. She cleared her throat and rocked back on her heels. "So. What do I do?"

"Nothing." Cael sank into one of the Chesterfield chairs, and rested his arms on the rounded arms.

Baylon motioned her to follow him to a sofa. Jordyn tentatively tracked him, his path taking her between Talin and Fintan.

Baylon sat on the edge of the sofa, his arms lying on his knees. "Dark arrived as we were leaving."

"I know," Cael said. "I also thought about putting our plan into action right then, but we weren't ready. We need all six of us on this, not just you and me, if there's even a small chance of Jordyn coming out of this with her life."

She raised her brows at Cael's choice of words. It wasn't as if she hadn't known the danger, but he said it as if it were an everyday occurrence. And perhaps for them it was.

Jordyn sat next to Baylon. A moment later, Eoghan sank onto the other side of her. She glanced at the silent Reaper to find him looking at her.

Fintan reclined on the other sofa while Talin and Kyran sat in the remaining chairs. They all seemed as disturbed by her appearance as she was to be there.

"They came for Jordyn this morning," Baylon explained. "Cael and I were able to dispatch them."

Fintan eyed her as he cocked his head to the side. "Why didn't they teleport her away?"

"I made sure they couldn't."

Baylon's words made the others look at him with mixtures of disbelief and alarm. All except for Talin, whose gaze was on the floor.

Kyran crossed his ankle over his knee. "How much

does she know?"

"Nothing," Baylon replied.

It was Cael who then said, "That's not true."

Jordyn shifted when Baylon's gaze slid to her. She glanced at him and shrugged. "I pieced it together."

Baylon's face fell. He rose to his feet and ran both hands through his hair. "Shite."

"I'm not going to tell anyone," she assured him as she stood. "I wasn't even going to let you know that I figured it out. I swear."

Fintan laughed then. "I'll be damned. Now we know why Baylon missed out on our meeting last night."

"The fact is," Cael's voice rang out through the chamber, "we have an enemy. We need to know who it is and what they're after exactly. The Fae blood within Jordyn makes her a priority since the Dark have singled her out."

Talin pointed to Jordyn and said, "Is she Fae or human? Because a Fae can't know of us."

Jordyn plopped down on the couch and blew out a breath. She was a part of both worlds, but which one dictated her life? If she was Fae, the Reapers could protect her. But if she was Fae, she couldn't know of them.

"No one told her," Cael said. "She guessed. Because she's human, I confirmed her suspicion."

Baylon's eyes were troubled. "And when this is over? Say we win and discover who is after us and take them out. We've saved Jordyn. What then? She's left behind her world, Cael. She can't just show up."

"That will be dealt with later."

Jordyn didn't like Cael's answer. She cut her eyes to him, letting him see her displeasure. "If that reply means that you'll kill me later, I'd rather you do it now."

Cael's eyes went cold. "Are you telling me you wouldn't remain and help possibly save Baylon's life?"

"Cael," Baylon said in a dangerous voice.

Neither she nor Cael paid attention to anyone else in the room. She knew what Cael was asking, and she hated him for it. Because there was only one answer.

The thought that she might spend days, weeks, or even months with the group while putting herself out as bait and being that close to Baylon was exciting and scary. But mostly exhilarating because she would be with Baylon.

Yet it wasn't fair to be able to get to know Baylon on such a level, only to realize that she might be killed for discovering all their secrets.

The room was utterly silent. She couldn't hear anyone breathing as she and Cael stared at each other. Beside her, Jordyn could feel Baylon's eyes on her.

She wanted to throw her arms around Baylon and have him hold her. Tears threatened again as she recalled that she was now totally alone. All of her family was dead, slaughtered by the Dark.

"You know I will," she answered Cael.

All the tension in the room immediately eased as Cael relaxed once more. "There is no Fae who know what I'm about to tell you. We keep it from all Fae because no one can know our names or our faces. We're a tale told to frighten."

Jordyn felt the sofa next to her sink as Baylon took his seat. He hadn't stopped staring at her yet, and she was afraid to look at him. Afraid that she would tell him that she couldn't face the next day without him by her side.

"We're Reapers," Cael continued. "We don't collect the souls of humans. We're sent by Death to hunt down and kill Fae for their crimes."

She grew confused at that. "Then wouldn't you take out all Dark Fae?"

Cael motioned to Kyran and Fintan. "Death chose each of us—both Dark and Light—for a reason. There can't be Light without Dark or Dark without Light. Death's responsibility is keeping the balance."

"But the Dark are evil."

"And there are Light Fae who do bad things. Does that mean we should kill them?" Cael asked.

To Jordyn, things were black and white. She couldn't wrap her head around the fact that Dark Fae were allowed to live.

"Just as we'll never go after Taraeth, the King of the

Dark," Cael said. "He's the one who orchestrated the attack on your city recently."

She gaped, now truly confused. "He's done evil."

"He's dark," Fintan said. "Of course he's done evil."

Jordyn shook her head in bewilderment. "Don't you go after the bad Fae?"

Cael bowed his head in acknowledgment. "That means we go after as many Light Fae as we do Dark. It's also why it's so imperative that our identities remain hidden. The same for Death."

"Death has a name?" she asked in surprise.

"Of course," Talin replied as if everyone knew that fact.

Kyran picked up where Cael left off. "We only take orders from Death."

"We've never hunted humans in any capacity," Fintan said. "Until yesterday."

Jordyn's gaze swung to Baylon. "Why did that change?"

"Someone wants to hurt us or Death," he clarified. "Cael spoke to Death and learned the new order came from somewhere else."

She looked around the room at the Reapers. "Do you think a human is involved?"

"Not possible," Cael said.

Baylon then explained further. "There was magic involved. It was a Fae."

"But the Fae don't know of you, right?"

Talin said, "We've gone to great lengths to ensure that. Any Fae who we think might have a clue to one of us is killed instantly."

She winced at the thought. It was callous to take a life so, but the men had no choice. What was it Baylon told her last night? There were rules.

"It's harsh to some," Cael said. "We do it because we can't be compromised. Neither can Death. There are rules we must follow."

Jordyn lowered her head and glanced at Baylon. Rules. Their night together broke one rule already, and now they were telling her their secrets.

Baylon's eyes met hers, and she knew in that instant that it was all worth it for him.

Chapter Thirteen

Baylon wished to hell he were alone with Jordyn. He yearned to have her beneath him, on top of him, or however she wanted as long as he was inside her.

He hadn't been able to take a steady breath since she admitted to Cael that she was staying to help. As if her life didn't matter.

Didn't she understand she was the important one? He wasn't one of the first Reapers, and he knew there would be more after him.

To sit so close to Jordyn that their legs touched and their arms brushed against the other, but to not be able to pull her into his arms was pure torment.

Her eyes were still red from the tears she shed at her flat. The fact she was able to push the pain aside for the moment boggled his mind. He knew she was still agonizing over losing her family.

The others knew he'd taken her to his bed. And he was glad of it. That was one thing he would no longer have to hide.

Baylon wasn't sure he could conceal his craving for

her, the need that clawed and ripped through him to declare Jordyn as his. It would be a death sentence, but to live without her . . . that was also a death sentence.

He rubbed his pinkie against hers and saw a faint smile. Jordyn had no idea what that simple reaction did to him. It eased his worry a fraction, but it also made him proud.

"Now that Jordyn knows our secret, can we get to planning how we're going to find these fuckers?" Kyran asked.

Cael caught Baylon's gaze. "They went looking for Jordyn at her flat. They'll go to places she frequents now."

"Won't they figure out I'm with you?" she asked.

That gave Baylon pause. "If they know of us, then it's safe to say they know we'd keep her protected."

"That's a good point," Fintan said.

Talin nodded. "We need to assume they'll know our every move."

"They don't know of this place," Cael said.

Baylon saw Eoghan's frown. "What is it?" he asked Eoghan.

The Fae shook his head once, though he and Cael exchanged a silent look.

Cael pressed his lips together in irritation as he looked away. "There is one meeting place that I didn't change after the last Reapers were killed."

"Where?" Kyran asked.

"It's right here in Edinburgh. Below the library."

Baylon now understood why Eoghan was worried. If their enemy knew of that meeting place, than all they had to do was look for other such places in the city.

"Wait," Jordyn said. "There were other Reapers? And they were killed? Why?"

There was a beat of silence as each Reaper thought about the ones before them. It was a story only told once—but that's all that was needed.

"I was the seventh Reaper of the last group," Cael said. "I was brought on last. Youngest of the group. There were three Dark and four Light. The same rules we have now were enforced then." Cael paused for a moment. "For thousands of years we did Death's bidding."

"While we were being betrayed by one of our own," Eoghan said.

Jordyn's head jerked to him. Even Baylon was surprised to hear Eoghan voice anything to do with that time.

Cael's eyes turned distant. "Aye. One of them deceived us. He told a few powerful Fae who he was. They gave him things in return for favors like not killing them or taking out a rival."

Baylon knew how important it was that the seven of them trust each other. How difficult it must have been for

Eoghan and Cael to feel such betrayal when they learned the truth.

"As awful as that was," Cael continued. "Another of us fell in love. Our leader at the time tried to put a stop to it. For a while, we took his word that the affair was over, but it was all a lie. He chose her, telling her who he was because he believed he could have her and be a Reaper."

This was Cael's way of reminding Baylon of what could never be. As if Baylon needed that reminder. He knew all too well what the future held.

Jordyn turned to Baylon when Cael stopped talking. "And?" she asked expectantly.

Baylon glanced at Cael who was looking at the floor, lost in the past. Even Eoghan's thoughts had turned inward. Baylon was going to have to finish the story.

"These seven were the first Reapers. Death gave those Reapers time to fix their mistakes," Baylon said.

Jordyn's eyes went wide. "You mean kill those who knew."

"Aye. When they didn't, Death killed every Fae who'd been told."

Fintan then added, "The Reaper who kept his lover secret went crazy when he learned of her death. He and the other Reaper who deceived the group joined forces and turned other Reapers to their side."

"It was three against four," Kyran said. "Cael and

Eoghan should've won, but their leader tried a peaceful approach instead of battle. The others killed him first."

Baylon looked at Eoghan to find his head turned away, his hand in a fist.

"Then it was three against three," Talin said. "Friends against friends."

Baylon took Jordyn's hand as her gaze moved to him. "Eoghan and Cael were both wounded. The Reaper who stood with them was killed. Before either Cael or Eoghan could end the battle, Death arrived and took the betrayers."

"And killed them?" Jordyn asked.

Baylon nodded.

Jordyn's gaze swung to Eoghan and Cael. "They got what they deserved."

Baylon was surprised when she put a comforting hand on Eoghan's arm. Eoghan didn't look at her, but he didn't pull away either. When Baylon eyed his friends, he saw they were as surprised as he.

Cael took a deep breath and crossed his arms over his chest. "Let's see how well our enemy knows us. We visit none of the usual places. We don't go anywhere alone."

"How do you propose to trick them?" Kyran asked.

Cael shot him a look. "This new enemy thinks they know us. We're going to prove they don't."

"Not at first," Baylon said. "We let them think they

have us cornered."

Fintan sat forward on the couch and cocked his head to the side. "I like it. But you realize that'll put Jordyn in danger."

"I'm already there," she said with a smile as she dropped her hand from Eoghan and turned to Fintan. "I trust all of you."

"That's either very brave, or very foolish," Talin said.

Baylon met Jordyn's gaze and saw her nod of acceptance. He then looked to Cael. "We go to one of the places they're expecting us and set the trap."

Cael's smile was cold, cruel. "Shall we get down to planning then?"

For the next few hours they planned every detail. Eoghan used his magic and made a model-sized scale of the city. A table appeared to set it on with all six of them standing around it.

"There will be more than one Dark after Jordyn," Fintan said.

Cael's lips flattened as he looked at the model of the city. "They'll try to kill her, but they may well go after us as well."

"What about the other half-Fae?" Kyran suddenly asked.

Baylon had been so intent on Jordyn, he hadn't even thought about the others. By Cael's look, neither had he.

None of them had.

Cael gave a nod. "If you know where a part-Fae is, visit them now, get them to safety, and then return immediately."

Fintan, Kyran, Talin, and Eoghan teleported away in a blink. Baylon glanced at Jordyn to find her asleep on the sofa behind him.

"I need you to find a Warrior named Phelan," Cael said.

Baylon whipped his head around. "A Warrior?"

"Daire found him at Dreagan. He knows Rhi."

"He has Fae blood?"

Cael nodded. "Don't let him see you, but check on him. He has a cottage hidden away."

Baylon veiled himself and teleported away. It took him longer than he would've liked to find the cottage by the loch. Small flakes of snow began to fall.

He walked to the cottage and felt magic surrounding it. Druid magic. The door of the cottage banged open and a tall man with long dark hair and blue gray eyes stood imposingly on the porch.

"Who's out there?" he demanded.

A heartbeat later a woman with fawn-colored eyes and long wavy black hair joined him. "Something has touched the barrier."

Baylon watched the couple for a moment before he

came to a conclusion. If Phelan was half-Fae, then of course he'd sense Baylon. The longer Baylon remained silent, the angrier Phelan would get. So, Baylon stayed veiled and said, "I'm a friend."

"Then show yourself," Phelan said tightly. He released his god, his skin turning gold and dark gold claws sprouting from his fingers. Phelan peeled back his lips to show fangs and growled while searching the area.

Baylon smiled, liking Phelan immediately. "I can't."

"Irish accent," the woman said. "A Fae."

"Who can remain veiled a verra long time," Phelan stated.

There was something different about the Druid. Baylon couldn't quite put his finger on it, but the magic within her was stronger than what a Druid should have. "I am a Fae. I come because you're in danger. There is a threat out there who is searching out any human with Fae blood and killing them."

"That has nothing to do with me."

Baylon sighed loudly. It was going to take more than mere words to convince the Warrior. "I was protecting a human with Fae blood. A group of Dark came after her earlier, and not to take her away. They attempted to kill her."

"Who are you?" the Druid asked.

Baylon knew by keeping his identity secret he was

making it more difficult for the couple, but he didn't have a choice. "I can't say. I was only supposed to check to make sure Phelan was still alive, not warn you of what was coming."

"I can take care of myself," Phelan said and walked down the few steps off the porch. "Your words could be false."

"But they're not."

Phelan's gold Warrior eyes narrowed. "How do you know me?"

"Quite by accident. We have a mutual acquaintance. Rhi."

Phelan snorted, his lips curling in a sneer. "Rhi would never have told you anything."

"You're right. She didn't. I gather she's been protecting your heritage carefully, but she's not the only one who knows, is she?"

Phelan looked over his shoulder to the woman. She frowned and moved to the edge of the porch. "Aisley?" Phelan asked.

Baylon filed the Druid's name away. He wanted to know more about her and why her magic was different, but that would come later. There were more pressing matters at hand. "The female I protected had her entire family slaughtered when they couldn't get to her. You should prepare."

"Let them try," Phelan said as he turned back around. "We won't go down easily."

"No, you won't." And Baylon was glad of it.

Just as he was about to teleport away, Aisley said, "Thank you."

"Be ready," Baylon warned and teleported back to Edinburgh.

Chapter Fourteen

Bran stood in the room beneath Edinburgh's library. It seemed eons ago that it had been one of his favorite places to meet up with the other Reapers.

He raised the ball of light higher so he could see more of the room. By the cobwebs and dust, Cael had switched locations.

It wasn't surprising. Nor was he shocked to learn Cael had taken over as leader. Eoghan was too . . . broken to lead. But Cael thrived on it.

Bran had hoped to catch the Reapers here. Cael and the others had no idea who was after them, so they wouldn't have had time to switch locations.

Cael would keep a place in Edinburgh. It's just the type of Fae he was. He would retain the roots of the Reapers—just change it up.

Bran shook his head as he laughed. Cael was so predictable. He thought himself smart and strong. Cael turned his back on him when Bran needed him most, and for that Cael would pay.

Anger burned within Bran. It took him far longer to

claw his way out of the Netherworld. But he was back.

And he was going to unleash hell.

~

Baylon returned to the chamber in time to see Eoghan cover Jordyn with a blanket.

"Curious, I know," Cael said as he came to stand beside Baylon. They both watched Eoghan gently tuck the blanket around her.

Eoghan then straightened and walked away as if he hadn't done anything out of the ordinary.

"That's the first I've seen him interact with anyone other than us," Baylon said.

Cael lifted one shoulder in a shrug. "I'm as confused as you. I'd never have expected Jordan's arrival to provoke such a reaction from him."

"Perhaps it's not Jordyn. What if it's the fact she's part Fae?"

"Have you seen him around Fae?" Cael asked with a shudder. "It has nothing to do with that and everything to do with her. Since you appear calm, I gather Phelan is fine."

Baylon couldn't look away from Jordyn. Her arm was tucked under her head as a pillow. "He is."

"Good. You spoke to him, didn't you?"

Baylon glanced at Cael and nodded. "He needed to be warned. There's a Druid with him. I think it's his wife."

"I trust you remained veiled."

"Of course."

"A Druid," Cael said. "I suppose it was inevitable that a Warrior and Druid would come together. It was Druids, after all, who made the Warriors. I think when this little problem is dealt with that we look in on the Warriors. Daire said they're at MacLeod Castle."

Baylon watched Eoghan walk through arches several feet behind the sofa into more rooms. "Is Eoghan the only other one back?"

"He is." Cael's sigh was full of frustration and fury. "Eoghan knew of a human with Fae blood within the city. That human, as well as his family, have been killed."

Baylon shook his head at the pointlessness of it all. "Damn."

Cael opened his mouth to speak when Talin appeared. Their attention was riveted on the Fae as his nostrils flared.

"The Dark killed him," Talin stated.

In quick succession Fintan and Kyran arrived. Fintan was holding his side that bled from what was obviously a shot of magic.

"The two I checked on are dead," Kyran stated furiously.

Fintan leaned against one of the pillars of the arch. "I arrived as the Dark were killing. I tried to save the human, but the Dark had done too much damage."

Cael motioned to his wound with his head. "Is that how you got wounded."

"No." Fintan's eyes lowered to the floor, rage rolling off him in thick waves. "I took a blast meant for the mortal's infant."

Finally, some good news. Baylon smiled. "At least you saved the baby. Where did you take it?"

"He didn't save it," Cael said into the silence.

Baylon turned to Fintan.

The Dark Fae lifted his gaze and shook his head. "There were so many of them. I didn't see the ones coming from the back of the house."

"You tried. That's what counts," Cael said.

Whoever led these Dark were intent on wiping out every half-Fae. They were Dark, so nothing bothered them. Not even the slaying of an infant.

The Dark had to be stopped, because if they weren't, millions of humans could be wiped out within the next week. Baylon looked at Jordyn again. A surge of relief swept through him knowing she was safe.

Or as safe as she could be since she was being used as bait.

She had no idea how lucky she was to be with them.

Or rather, he was the lucky one. If he hadn't found her, if he hadn't followed her, she would be dead. And he would never know the sweet taste of her kisses.

"How the fuck are the Dark finding them?" Talin demanded angrily.

Talin's words pulled Baylon back to the problem at hand.

Kyran stood with his hands clenched at his sides. "We don't even know all the mortals with Fae blood, but these Dark somehow do."

"I don't have any answers," Cael said. This his eyes went hard. "But that's going to change."

$\sim$

Jordyn wasn't sure what woke her. She opened her eyes to find the chamber eerily quiet. The edge of the blanket tickled her nose. She sat up, wondering who gave her a blanket.

A popping drew her attention. She looked to the right to find a fire roaring in the fireplace and Cael standing before it, his hands clasped behind his back as he gazed into the flames.

"Has something happened?" she asked tentatively.

Cael's head lifted at the sound of her voice. "The Dark have begun killing mortals with Fae blood."

"Dear God."

"Yes, I do believe that's an appropriate statement." Cael kept his back to her as he said, "Those humans died needlessly. We need to discover who is doing this, and time is of the essence."

"I'm ready to help."

"Let's hope so."

Then Cael vanished. Jordyn swung her legs off the couch and stood. She hated that the Reapers could pop in and out at will. Now *that* would've been something cool to have with the Fae blood within her.

She looked around the chamber for a sign of Baylon. It wasn't until she caught a glimpse of light coming from behind the sofa that she followed it.

Jordyn was amazed to find a small hallway after walking beneath the arch, and then more rooms. Her steps slowed then halted when she saw Baylon.

He stood in the middle of the room with his gaze locked on a map that had to be at least fifteen feet wide and ten feet tall.

Whatever the map was, it had nothing to do with Earth, as far as Jordyn could tell. But she was less interested in the map than she was in Baylon.

The object of her attention turned his head as if he had heard her. Then he faced her and smiled.

Jordyn returned his smile and walked to him. It was

the first time they had been alone since the night before. It seemed as if it happened years ago, and not hours, since so much had happened.

She stopped beside him and motioned to the map with her thumb. "Is that important?"

"It's a map of the Fae realm."

Jordyn nodded, trying not to look at his mouth. "Do you miss it?"

"I miss what it once was. We were there for a long time cleaning up some of the mess from our last civil war. We just returned to your realm."

"Why are you here?"

"Because the Fae are." He turned so that he faced her. "We left so you could get some sleep. I don't remember you doing much of that last night."

The mention of the previous night made her stomach flutter at the many hours of pleasure spent in his arms. She had to try twice to swallow. "I think it was the quiet that woke me. Where are the others?"

"Getting our plan into action."

Being alone with him was a mistake. She wanted him too desperately to stand this close and not touch him. Jordyn took a couple of steps back, but he followed.

She continued until she bumped into a wall. Baylon pressed her against it, his mouth mere breaths from hers. His hands were on either side of her, and his breathing was harsh.

"One night," he said in a raw, primal voice. "That's all we can have."

Jordyn didn't remember grabbing him, but somehow her fingers gripped his shirt. Her breathing was ragged, the desire heating her blood. "I know."

"I can't," Baylon whispered as his head lowered.

Her lids fell closed as his lips were about to touch hers. When he stopped, Jordyn wanted to scream in exasperation.

She knew for them to give into the need, they could both be killed. But how could either of them ignore something so irresistible, so vast?

Baylon let out a groan a second before his lips covered hers. The kiss was as savage and untamed as their desire.

Jordyn held him tightly. Her body melted against him, aching to feel his skin against hers.

One night. That's all Baylon was allowed, but it wasn't enough. Forever would never be enough. Jordyn sank into him as their kiss consumed them.

She no longer knew where she ended and he began. They were one-endless and unbroken. She knew in the very depths of her soul that she was meant to be with Baylon. However long she had.

"If we continue, we die," Baylon said.

Jordyn touched his face. "If I don't have you inside me,

I die."

With a groan, he took her mouth again. One moment their clothes were in the way, and the next, there was nothing but skin to skin.

She moaned and slid her fingers in his thick black hair. His large hands moved down her back and over her bottom. He grasped her, lifting and spreading her legs as he did.

Jordyn wrapped her legs around his waist as he held her above his engorged cock. She ended the kiss and looked at him, consumed with such deep emotions that they took her breath and her thoughts.

All her life she never felt the need to break any rules, but it was different with Baylon. She couldn't stop herself—even when her very life was on the line.

But it wasn't just her life. It was Baylon's. If they made love again, Death would kill him. How could she put him in that position?

"I have to have you," he said, his chest rising and falling rapidly. "I can't have you this close and not be touching you."

Jordyn felt her eyes sting with tears. Was it truly possible to feel so intensely about someone that you would gladly give up your own life?

Love.

That's what it was called.

But it couldn't be love. She'd only known Baylon a short time, and yet there was no denying what she did feel was genuine and acute.

"I'm yours," she whispered.

A strange light came into his silver eyes. Then he lowered her onto his arousal. Jordyn's eyes rolled back in her head at the pleasure. He held her securely as he began to rock his hips, sliding in and out of her.

Anyone could come upon them. But they didn't care. They were too lost in their desire, in the ecstasy that enveloped them.

The threat of Death coming for Baylon, along with the Dark after her ramped up their need to such a degree. Sweat glistened their bodies, their harsh breaths filling the alcove.

"Can't hold back," Baylon bit out.

Jordyn couldn't speak as the climax tore through her, snatching her breath as it did. She clung to Baylon as he buried himself deep and put his face in her neck.

"Jordyn," he said with a strangled voice as he orgasmed.

After a few seconds, Baylon lifted his head. He looked at her with his large eyes, and there was a hint of regret there. With a smile, he pulled out of her. In the next moment, their clothes were back in place.

Baylon took a couple of steps back from her. "You

heard what happened to the other Reaper who took a lover."

She nodded, her throat closing as she realized what Baylon was doing.

"You're already being hunted by the Dark. Let's leave Death out of it."

It was probably already too late for that, but Jordyn didn't bother to say the words. She waited until he walked away before she slid down the wall and brought her knees up to her chest. She rested her forehead on her knees and didn't try to stop the tears.

She wasn't sure if she cried for her family or for the fact that she had lost Baylon. The pain of both was devastating. She was crushed beneath the weight of each.

How stupid to think she could let Baylon walk out of her life. She talked big, but it was all a lie. She couldn't even be alone in the same room with him.

This last time made everything even harder. Because she hadn't been strong enough to walk away, she might very well have sealed his fate. She wondered if she could talk to Death and try to explain.

The tears came faster then. There was an emptiness inside her, a void that began the moment she opened her eyes that morning. The longer she remained near Baylon, the wider that abyss became.

She was surrounded by Fae, but Jordyn had never felt

more alone in her life. There was no one she could talk to, no one she could confide in.

No longer did she have a family, and she walked away from her friends. How utterly alone she was now.

Something was placed in her fingers. She grabbed the item and realized it was a handkerchief. Jordyn lifted her head enough to see who had given it to her.

While she had been crying, Eoghan came to sit so close beside her they were nearly touching. He said nothing, but his mere presence gave her much needed comfort.

Jordyn sniffed and tucked the handkerchief against her. Eoghan gave her a nod. She laid her head back on her knees as a fresh wave of tears came.

～

Baylon stood at the corner and watched Jordyn, fighting not to go to her. It killed him that Eoghan could sit beside her, but he couldn't. Baylon didn't dare. He was ready to tell Death to kiss off just so he could be with Jordyn for as long as he wanted.

But that wasn't how it worked being a Reaper.

Each tear that fell from Jordyn's eyes was like a blade plunging in his heart. He pressed his face against the cool stones, but it did nothing to ease the storm within him.

A storm that raged more fiercely with each heartbeat he was away from Jordyn.

Chapter Fifteen

The time had come. Jordyn rubbed her hands together in an effort to keep them warm as she looked around at the beautiful loch, though not even the fires of Hell could warm her at this point.

The weather was frigid, and she was petrified at being the bait against an unknown enemy in a valley with tall hills and thick forest around her. But that's not why she was so cold. It was knowing Baylon was lost to her forever that froze her from the inside out.

Was it just an hour earlier that she woke, after crying herself to sleep, to find an array of clothes for her? At least with the Fae, she'd never have to worry about having something to wear.

Fintan walked up beside her. "Ready?"

She glanced at the Dark Fae, watching his breath billow around him. "It's now or never, right?"

"That's right," he replied with a smile.

She wasn't surprised that Baylon decided not to stay with her. After their lovemaking and his words, it was better for them both to remain as far apart as they could.

In fact, she hadn't laid eyes on him since their last words. Jordyn had no idea where he was, but she knew he was near. She could feel his eyes on her.

"The others have surrounded the area."

She glanced at Fintan before looking back at the secluded area an hour outside of Edinburgh filled with numerous trees, hills, and a loch. The sun was bright when it wasn't hiding behind the clouds, making her squint when it peeked out. "I know."

"I can tell you his location so you don't have to keep looking."

Jordyn seriously wanted to hurt Fintan. She took a few steps away to give herself some breathing room. "I'm looking for whoever is after us, you imbecile."

Fintan came up behind her and leaned down to whisper, "I'm not Cael or Death. There's no need to lie."

"What happened between Baylon and I was one night. Everyone is making a big deal out of nothing."

Fintan snorted as he moved to stand in front of her. "And last night?"

Jordyn gaped at him. As far as she had known, no one else had been around.

"I was walking from the other room," Fintan explained.

"How much did you see?"

Fintan gave her a pitying look. "All of it."

"Oh." What could she say to that? She could only hope she hadn't looked as pathetic as she felt. And still felt. "Do none of you develop feelings for others?"

"Some put themselves in situations that could lead to that."

"But not you?" she asked with a raised brow.

Fintan made a sound at the back of his throat. "Do I really look like the kind of male capable of tenderness or love?"

Now that he mentioned it, that would be a big, fat no.

"Exactly," he said with a dry laugh.

Jordyn listened to the sound of the loch lapping softly against the shore. It was too bad they couldn't have found a more open spot, but as Cael had informed her, it was a place they used before to meet up.

She caught up with Fintan when he began to walk slowly around the loch. "All of you are thousands of years old. Surely there has to be someone in the group who fell for another, despite what happened with the first Reaper group."

"Sure there was."

That made Jordyn feel a little better.

"They're dead now. Death killed them before history could repeat itself."

What little bit of relief she experienced went up in a blast of flames. This wasn't good news. She wracked her

Donna Grant

brain for some way to help Baylon. Then it came to her. "All right. I get that. But what about feeling strongly, but not acting on it."

Fintan's pale silver eyes ringed in red slid to her. He raised a white brow. "What gets us in such a pickle is acting on it. If we don't, then I suppose we're safe."

"Then Baylon is safe. He walked away."

"Wars have been won or lost with the same feelings between the two of you," he said before turning his head forward. "And stop using names. We don't know who might be listening."

Jordyn halted, feeling more deflated than before. "He won't betray any of you. No matter what. He wouldn't do that."

Fintan stopped walking. He stood there for a moment before he turned on his heel to face her. "You think you know him that well?"

"He's proven it several times already. To me. To you. To Death. What else must he do?"

"That's not for me to say," Fintan stated.

"I'm trying to make sure he lives."

"Then perhaps you should never have taken him to your bed."

Jordyn blinked, completely taken aback by his words. He didn't state it harshly, but neither was it done in a kind voice. "I could no sooner deny him than I could stop

164

breathing."

"That's lust."

"Does it matter what it is? It was there and palpable. Both of us acted on it."

Fintan gave a shake of his head and looked away with a disapproving look. "Baylon knew. He should've stayed away from you."

"Are you telling me you never felt lust before?"

"Of course I have," he said with a curt look.

She walked to him, angry that he made light of what she felt for Baylon. Jordyn stopped inches from him and glared up into his red-rimmed eyes. "Either you're a liar or you've never felt what I did."

Fintan's gaze went hard as ice. He became as still as stone. "I'm not a liar."

The words were clipped and violent.

What stood before her was more beast than man. Fintan hide his viciousness, but he was showing it to her now. And it frightened her to such a degree that she took a step back.

"One day," she said, her voice shaking from her fear. "One day you'll find a woman that will make you want to do anything just to be with her."

He smiled wryly, the beast back in his cage. "That's never going to happen."

Jordyn waited until he had walked far enough away before she whispered, "Don't ever say never."

~

Baylon watched Jordyn from his station atop the hill. He was veiled, but even if hadn't been, the trees would've hidden him. How he wished he knew what Jordyn was talking to Fintan about. She was in turns shocked and angry. It irritated Baylon that he wasn't down there with her.

It shocked Baylon when Fintan stated he would guard Jordyn. Baylon knew he couldn't have that duty and allow Jordyn to do as she must in order for them to catch the Dark. But it still vexed him.

Baylon stood guard in the chamber below Edinburgh Castle all night as Jordyn slept. It was as close as he would allow himself to her, and as far as he could get without feeling as if he would shatter if he didn't see her.

After leaving Jordyn in such a fashion, Baylon wondered if she would talk to him. Their lovemaking had slayed him. Proving that he needed her as much then as he had that first night—more, actually.

Walking away and ending whatever was developing quickly between them was the hardest thing he had ever done.

It wouldn't compare to walking out of her life forever

though.

Baylon pushed such thoughts from his mind. He needed to concentrate on the threat at hand. The rest . . . well, he would deal with it later.

Twenty minutes passed with nothing. Baylon was beginning to wonder if their new enemy would show himself. His attention sharpened when Talin appeared next to Jordyn and Fintan just as planned.

Baylon counted to a hundred and Kyran teleported to the others right on schedule. Another count of a hundred, and Cael was with them.

As soon as Cael emerged, all hell broke loose.

Eight Dark materialized around them. It was exactly what Cael had expected—and planed for. Baylon watched his friends battle the Dark and protect Jordyn.

They closed in around Jordyn. Fintan shoved her to the ground while they stood with their backs to her and blocked the Dark's magic aimed at her.

Eoghan unveiled himself behind three of the Dark and killed them with one swipe of his sword. It startled the attackers enough that Fintan and Talin were able to kill the remaining five.

The quiet of the valley was unnatural. It seemed that every living thing around the area had simply vanished. Baylon remained veiled, impatiently waiting for the next part of the plan.

So far everything they did had been exactly what the previous group of Reapers had performed. The next portion was something new.

To make everything appear genuine, all Jordyn knew of the plan was that she was bait and the others would protect her. It was imperative that their enemy believe the attack was a shock to all of them.

"Keep her down!" Cael bellowed.

Kyran raised his sword. "No more humans with Fae blood are going to die."

Baylon looked around the loch as he felt more Fae. There were more Dark in the trees. By now the other Reapers would've felt their presence as well. It was going to be a concentrated assault. But the Dark Fae had no idea that they weren't just fighting any Fae. They were fighting Reapers.

Bubbles of magic came hurtling out of the trees. Cael shoved most of them into the loch with his magic, but a few got past Kyran, Fintan, and Talin.

Eoghan vanished and emerged a moment later in the thick of the Dark, his sword swinging savagely. None of it deterred the Dark from their mission. They didn't break ranks or flee as expected.

Instead, they began to walk toward Jordyn and the Reapers. Baylon saw a Dark come up behind Eoghan. Without hesitation, Baylon teleported to them. He unveiled himself and plunged his sword in the Dark just as Eoghan spun around.

Baylon glanced down at the tip of Eoghan's sword that had stopped at his throat. "You're welcome."

Eoghan gave a nod and turned back to the Dark. The Dark had now seen Baylon. There was no returning to his hiding position and looking for the one controlling the Dark.

With precision and lethal speed, Baylon cut his way through the Dark, one Fae at a time. They were so intent on killing Jordyn that they didn't even attempt to defend themselves.

Only twice was Baylon struck with magic. Both times had left him gasping for breath. Whoever these Dark were, their magic was stronger than any others.

With a flick of his wrist, Baylon sent his sword cutting through the air, taking off a Dark's head. Before the body hit the ground, Baylon spun around with his sword pointed at the Fae he felt sneaking up on him.

The Fae smiled, though it didn't reach his red eyes. He glanced down at the point of the sword that was leveled at his heart. "What are you waiting on?"

"Who are you?" Baylon demanded.

The Fae chuckled and knocked the blade away. Baylon immediately brought it back into place, pushing it against the Fae's chest.

"Either kill me or put that away," the Dark said, the smile gone.

"I asked you a question."

"And you can go fuck yourself."

Baylon studied the Fae as the tip of his sword entered through flesh. "You first."

Chapter Sixteen

Jordyn looked anxiously around. Dark Fae were coming at them from every direction. Magic was literally flying through the air.

She wasn't sure how the Reapers were able to deflect most of the magic, but they did. Jordyn could tell that it wasn't normal for them to stay so close to each other in battle. They wanted to spread out and not be bottled together. But they were protecting her.

Which made them easy targets.

A bubble of magic the size of a bowling ball landed on the other side of Fintan. Jordyn watched as the ground sizzled like grease in a hot skillet as the bubble sank into the dirt.

If that's what it did to the earth, what would it do to her? Jordyn didn't want to find out. Matter of fact, she was certain she didn't want to be there anymore.

Helpless and vulnerable, that's what she was. A freaking sitting duck. The only thing standing between her and death were the Reapers. And how much more could they take?

She glanced up to see that each of the Reapers had been hit more than once with magic. With every blast that came into contact with them, they merely flinched as if stung by a bee.

Yet she saw what it did to their clothes and skin. The pain must be terrible. How did they continue fighting and ignore the pain?

Her gaze sought out Baylon. She managed to get a glimpse of him through the Reapers' legs as he stood talking to someone in the trees.

Then he was no longer talking. He was fighting. She could only stare in mute fear as his sword moved like lightning to block and repel the blasts of magic coming from the Dark Fae.

Jordyn was suddenly knocked forward into a pair of legs. She heard a curse and hastily looked up to see she had fallen into Kyran.

"Sorry!" she yelled and pushed herself back into her squatting position.

But she couldn't manage to right herself correctly. She kept falling over. Pinpricks of black began to fill her vision. She tried to rub her eyes, but her right arm wouldn't work.

Jordyn looked down wondering where all the smoke was coming from. She couldn't get her eyes to focus. Nor did she understand why she couldn't move her arm.

"Oh, shit. Cael!" someone shouted.

She blinked, struggling to keep her eyes open. Why were the Dark beginning to back away? Had the Reapers won? Did they have their enemy?

"Jordyn? Jordan, can you hear me?"

Was that Cael? She opened her eyes, wondering when she had shut them. Someone touched her arm and the pain made her begin to black out again.

She really wished whoever was screaming would shut up. It was distracting. She kept trying to tell the Reapers to go help the person, but the words got stuck in her throat.

Then she just stopped trying.

~

The fact the Dark Baylon fought moved nearly as fast as he did confirmed what he suspected. The Dark they were fighting had been given a boost to their magic by someone. And the Reapers really needed to find that someone.

Baylon gripped the hilt of his sword tighter and used it to punch the Dark in the nose. Blood spurted everywhere.

He used the momentum to drive the Fae against a tree. Baylon pressed the blade of his sword against the Fae's neck. "Now," he said. "Who the hell are you?"

The Dark began to laugh as he looked over Baylon's shoulder. "We did what we were sent to do."

Baylon's hearing picked up the voices of the other Reaper's behind him as well as screaming. Then the Dark in his grasp vanished.

He dropped his arms, glaring at the tree. The Dark shouldn't have been able to get away. Not when he was held by a Reaper.

Baylon pivoted and started walking toward the others when he realized all the Dark were gone. He turned his attention back to the others. The screaming registered then. It was a woman's scream.

Baylon's heart stopped, falling to his feet like lead when he realized it was Jordyn who lay on the ground unmoving with Cael leaning over her. He teleported to them, not even wasting the few seconds to run.

"Jordyn," he said and shoved Talin and Kyran out of the way.

Baylon stared down at her helplessly. He fell to his knees, grimacing when he saw her arm, bloody and burnt from the Dark magic.

"I don't know how it got past Kyran and me," Fintan said.

Eoghan knelt on the other side of Jordyn and put his hand at her throat. His gaze lifted to Baylon as he gave a small smile.

"She's still alive?" Baylon asked, hope surging.

Eoghan nodded.

"Let's get her out of here," Cael said.

Baylon carefully lifted her in his arms and teleported back to the castle. As soon as he was in the chamber, he walked through the arch and down the corridor.

Fintan was a few steps ahead of him. Baylon walked to the last room to the left and found Eoghan and Cael were already there along with a bed.

Baylon laid her down just as Kyran snapped his fingers and a fire roared to life in the hearth. Baylon ran his fingers along her brow to smooth away her hair.

"What can we do?" Fintan asked from beside Baylon.

Eoghan put his hand on Jordyn's forehead and closed his eyes.

"Nothing," Cael said.

Baylon jerked his gaze to Cael. "Nothing? What do you mean nothing?"

"You know we don't have the ability to heal others," Cael said.

Kyran and Talin stood at the foot of the bed. Kyran look askance at Cael. "Surely there has to be someone we can ask."

"The Dragon Kings perhaps?" Cael asked in a mocking tone. "We're Reapers. This is why we aren't allowed to have relationships. We put ourselves and Death in a bind by caring and owing others."

Baylon pointed to Jordyn, fury spiking dangerously inside him. "She put her life on the line to help us. And you expect us to sit idly by and watch her die!"

Cael's face went hard, his eyes narrowing in anger. "Do not mistake my actions to mean that I don't care. We have rules, Baylon. Need I remind you of them?"

Baylon felt magic well up in his hand. Before he could throw it, Fintan put a hand on his chest and shoved him back.

Fintan then stood between Baylon and the bed. "Don't do this. Not here. Not over her bed."

All the fight went out of Baylon. He looked back at Jordyn. Fintan was right. Now wasn't the time. Baylon focused on Jordyn. He couldn't heal, but he could hope. And pray.

Eoghan finally opened his eyes and removed his hand from her brow. Without a word, he walked to the back of the room and leaned against the wall.

Baylon made a chair appear so he could sit. He scooted it close to Jordyn's bed and took her hand.

"If I could, I'd heal her," Cael said.

Baylon shrugged. "I put her in danger so she could help us."

"You didn't do anything. It was her choice. Jordyn wanted to help."

"Because I dragged her into this. I should never have told her what she was."

Cael blew out a breath. "You saved her. Had you not found her and stayed the night with her, she would be dead. And we wouldn't be any closer to finding out who is behind any of this."

Baylon swallowed and sat back in the chair. "We didn't come away completely empty handed. The Dark attacking your group had a single-minded purpose."

"Aye," Talin said. "Jordyn."

"They didn't even try and defend themselves against me and Eoghan," Baylon said. He looked up and around the bed at his fellow Reapers. "But a Dark came up behind me. He didn't seem to care about Jordyn."

Fintan's brow furrowed. "What did he want?"

"I've no idea." Baylon shook his head in confusion. "We fought. He was fast. Nearly as fast as me."

Kyran made a sound as an appalled expression came over his face. "Impossible."

"Trust me. It wasn't. He was incredibly fast, and just as lethal. But the worst part was when I had my hand on him and my sword at his throat."

Cael looked at him warily. "Did you kill him?"

"That's the thing," Baylon said as he rubbed his thumb along the back of Jordyn's hand. "He teleported away."

No one gasped aloud, but their expressions said it all.

Baylon nodded in understanding. "Exactly."

"Has Death set another group upon us?" Talin asked.

Cael cut him a sharp look. "No. That doesn't benefit Death or us. This is something else. Whoever it is, they don't mind losing Fae to battle us."

"The ones attacking us didn't move as fast," Fintan said. "But their magic seemed stronger than a normal Fae's should."

Baylon squeezed the bridge of his nose with his thumb and forefinger. "Perhaps who I spoke with is running things."

"Doubtful," Cael said. "He's not a lackey like the rest of the Dark we fought, however."

Kyran leaned his hands upon the footboard. "At least we let them believe we were taken by surprise."

"That's the only thing that worked," Talin mumbled.

Baylon looked at Jordyn wondering if he would ever get to gaze into her turquoise eyes again. One by one the others left, until only he remained.

Not even Death could make him leave Jordyn's side. She wouldn't be alone when she breathed her last.

~

Bran stood in the Louvre staring at the sarcophagus box of Ramses III when he felt the approach of Searlas behind him. "Well?" he asked without turning around.

"The half-Fae the Reapers made off with is dead."

Bran leaned close to see the engravings of the seventh and eighth chapters of the "Book of Amduat". "Are you sure she's dead?"

"She was hit with magic and screaming. Cael was leaning over her, but she became quiet fast."

Bran straightened and turned to Searlas. "One more down then."

"Is it time to strike directly at Cael?"

Bran walked to the next exhibit with Searlas beside him. "Oh, yes."

"I fought a Reaper. You should've seen his face when I vanished while he held me."

Bran laughed and clapped Searlas on the shoulder as they stopped. "I bet it was priceless. Who did you fight?"

"Baylon."

"And who was protecting the mortal?"

Searlas gave a little shrug. "All of them except for Daire, Eoghan, and Baylon."

"If you were fighting Baylon, where was Eoghan and Daire?"

"Daire wasn't there at all," Searlas said. "Unless he was veiled and I didn't see him."

Bran rubbed his hand along his jaw. "If Daire was there, he would've joined in. That means he's somewhere else. And Eoghan?"

"Was fighting our Dark."

"It's too bad. I would've liked to know who had taken an interest in the mortal."

Searlas smiled widely. "You struck at them quick and true today."

"But I didn't hurt them nearly as much as I could have. The Reapers better watch themselves. I'm waiting for the day one of them falls in love. Because I'll be there to tear their world apart like Cael and Eoghan did mine. And it'll happen. It's just a matter of time."

Chapter Seventeen

Baylon had the entire room alight with candles. He didn't want darkness creeping in from anywhere. Not for Jordyn. Not if he had any say in it.

He ran a hand down his face and wearily got to his feet. Though he was loath to not touch her, if he didn't move, didn't burn off some of the anger festering within him, he was going to burst.

Baylon rolled his neck as he walked around the room. Since he could do nothing for Jordyn, his mind turned to the Dark he had fought.

"What is it?" Fintan asked as he leaned a shoulder against the archway.

Baylon shook his head and paced before the bed. "A Fae doesn't just get more magic. That's not how it works."

"Right. It was Death who gave us the extra boost."

"Death," Baylon repeated and glanced at Fintan. "Who else has such abilities?"

Both of Fintan's brows lifted as he snorted. "Death is the only one I know, and I didn't know Death was even real until I stood before her."

"Aye. For me as well. Damn. There has to be someone else."

"You don't think the Fae we fought just had more magic?"

Baylon halted and turned to look at Fintan. "Do you?"

"Not for an instant. But I wanted to know your thoughts."

"Whoever is killing mortals with Fae blood is targeting us. They wanted us to carry out the false order they sent."

Fintan nodded, picking up Baylon's words. "And when we didn't, they went after the mortals themselves, knowing we'd protect them."

"But we've never really cared about the mortals. Why would they think we would save them now?"

Fintan's gaze moved to the bed. "Because they have Fae blood."

Fae blood that was doing nothing for Jordyn. Baylon closed his eyes and lowered his chin to his chest. Ever since he became a Reaper, nothing had stood in his way. His strength, his magic, his speed all increased the day he accepted Death's offer.

Now none of it did any good.

"Baylon," Fintan said.

But Baylon couldn't look at Jordyn. It was wrong to see her lying so still upon the bed, her life draining from her gradually as the Dark magic ate away at her.

"Baylon," Fintan said more urgently.

Baylon whirled around angrily. "What?" he demanded.

Fintan now stood by Jordyn's bed. He didn't move his gaze from her as he pointed.

Baylon focused on her chest, waiting to see if she had stopped breathing. Relief surged through him when he saw the steady breathing. If Fintan wasn't pointing out that Jordyn was dead, then what did he want?

With his irritation clearly showing, Baylon walked back to his chair where Fintan stood. That's when he spotted Jordyn's arm and how the wound was healing.

Baylon turned to Fintan, unable to find words.

Fintan's smile started slowly. He slapped Baylon on the back and pivoted as he began to yell for the others.

Baylon sank back into the chair and watched the healing process. It was much slower than a full-blooded Fae, but the fact she was healing was the best news Baylon had heard in a long time.

He once more took Jordyn's hand, as the grip on his chest began to ease. Baylon looked up to find the others surrounding the bed.

"I'll be damned," Cael said with a smile.

Kyran shook his head, though he was grinning. "Now this I wasn't expecting."

"Let's hope it doesn't take her long to wake." Talin elbowed Kyran. "We're anxious to get our retribution for what they've done to Jordyn."

As usual, Eoghan simply looked for long moments at Jordyn before he walked away. Baylon had long since given up hoping to one day carry on a conversation with Eoghan. Eoghan's choice to refrain from speech wasn't because of some vow of silence.

No, Eoghan didn't talk because he was broken in ways none of them would ever be able to discern. Baylon wasn't sure if Cael even knew all the particulars.

And none of it mattered. Eoghan was a Reaper. They were a family of sorts. A rag-tag, lethal family, but still a family.

All they had was each other. That forced them to bond on a level few beings ever experienced.

"What now?" Fintan asked. "We can't remain here. I agree with Talin and Kyran. I want to find these fuckers and lay waste to them."

Baylon nodded and shifted his gaze to Cael. "I agree. We must retaliate."

"And we will," Cael assured them. "We're going to make sure we hurt them as they've tried to hurt us."

Fintan's red-rimmed gaze was filled with reckoning. "I've got an idea."

～

Jordyn smiled as she felt the caress on the back of her hand. She didn't need to open her eyes to know it was Baylon. He'd done that same stroke the times they cuddled between making love.

At least he was touching her again. That was a vast improvement from before. Though she wasn't quite sure why he was with her while she slept.

She opened her eyes to find him sitting by her bed smiling at her. He really had no idea of how gorgeous he was. And his smile. It always made her feel as if her stomach was filled with butterflies.

"Hello," he said.

His smile, his eyes, and that Irish brogue? She was a total goner. "Hello."

"How do you feel?"

Now this was getting odd. "I feel great. How about you?"

His smile slipped. "You don't remember, do you?"

"Remember what?"

"A ball of Dark magic hit you."

Jordyn sat up and spread her arms. "I'm fine."

"But you weren't." He motioned to her arm with his head.

She looked down, and her heart stopped. The sleeve of

her sweater was completely gone, the edges burned at the shoulder and along her side. "I don't remember any pain."

"That's probably a blessing."

Her head snapped up to look into his dark silver eyes. "What happened?"

"You were dying. We brought you back here, but then you began to heal."

"I saw what Dark magic did to the ground. There's no way I could heal from that."

Baylon winked at her. "I did tell you that you have Fae blood."

Could she really have gotten that lucky? Her gaze lowered and she saw the burned hole in Baylon's shirt. She looked back at him pointedly. "Did Cael heal my coffee burn at my flat?"

"We can't heal others."

"But the stain on my robe was removed."

Baylon's grin grew. "That we can do."

Well. She didn't think she could be surprised any more, but obviously she was wrong. "And your wounds? I saw you had a few."

He laughed and showed her he was healed. "The pitfalls of fighting Dark."

"Can a Fae not be killed with magic?"

The laughter died in Baylon's eyes. "They can. Imagine magic is like swordplay. You must attack your opponent while deflecting and halting his blade from reaching your body. In a Fae battle, that's what we must do."

"And sometimes magic gets through," she said and reached over to touch his side.

"Sometimes."

Jordyn refused to look back into his eyes. She knew she would see desire and longing there. If she was going to make sure Death didn't kill him, Jordyn needed to be sure and not put herself in a position where she gave into him.

But how she wanted to feel his arms around her, to rest her head on his shoulder.

"Look at me," he urged her in a soft voice.

Jordyn shook her head. Her heart missed a beat when his hands cupped her face and he tilted her head back so their eyes locked.

"I almost lost you. Do you have any idea what I went through?"

She saw the torment in his eyes, the pain he allowed her to see. "Don't do this."

"I have to."

"No," she said and put her hands on his wrists. She tried to pull his arms away, but he didn't budge. "Death will kill you."

"Then I'll die happy. Because I'll have you."

"Baylon," she implored. She wanted nothing more

than to throw her arms around him, but she was also trying to save him. Didn't he know that?

But he was looking at her as if he had waited an eternity to hold her. How could any women stand against that?

His kiss was slow, heady. Erotic. There was no need for words when his kiss told her exactly how much he had feared her death, how he yearned to make love to her.

How he ached.

For her.

Her arms wrapped around his neck as he laid her back on the bed. His body covered hers as the kiss deepened. Baylon groaned when she wound one leg around him.

He ended the kiss and looked down at her, breathing rapidly. "I know being with you means my death, but after the night I spent thinking you were dying, I don't care. I need you. Do you understand that? I *need* you."

"I understand perfectly," she whispered. "Because I need you as well."

"I've never felt this before. I . . . I'm not even sure what it is."

Jordyn knew. She'd known for awhile now, but had been too frightened of it to admit it. Fintan had called it lust, but it went much deeper than that. The emotion that filled her now was much more potent. "I thought I'd always be alone. I was searching for someone and didn't even know it. That someone was you."

His lips softened. He placed a brief kiss on her lips. "If only I'd known you were out there. I wouldn't have become a Reaper, and we could be together."

"You found me because you're a Reaper."

"I want forever with you, Jordyn. Not hours or days."

"I'll take whatever I can get." She smoothed her hands along his cheek and then slid her fingers into his thick hair. "Despite the danger and near-death, it feels right that I'm with you."

She put a finger over his lips when he began to speak. Jordyn smiled and looked down at his mouth. She traced his lips, recalling the decadent things he could do to her with that mouth.

"Fate put me in your path," she said, pulling her eyes back up to his. "I don't know why, and it doesn't matter. I belong here. With you."

"Then we stand together."

"Together," she repeated with a grin, feeling as if things might really work in their favor somehow. "No matter what the consequences or the outcome."

He nodded and ran his fingers along the back of her cheek. "We'll figure out a way to be together."

"I like the sound of that."

Baylon's smile froze in place. His head slowly turned to the side. Jordyn followed his eyes and found Eoghan watching them.

Eoghan had been kind to her, but by the look in the Reaper's eyes now, all that was going to change.

"The others are waiting," Baylon said as he climbed off her to stand by the bed. He held out his hand to help her down. "You'll find everything you need to shower and change in the next room."

As soon as Jordyn's feet were on the ground, Baylon yanked her against him.

"Nothing will keep me from you," he whispered before he turned and walked away.

She watched him leave, her smile growing by the moment. Surely she'd be able to talk to Death and explain their love.

Chapter Eighteen

Baylon was practically walking on air when he met the others in the main room. Eoghan was staring at him with a closed expression. Baylon wasn't sure what his friend was thinking, and he really didn't care.

Jordyn was alive. Alive and healed.

And he wanted her.

It would mean the end of his life, but he couldn't deny what was between them. The more he tried to keep his distance, the more he needed her.

It was a desperation, a driving necessity to be near her. He was prepared to lie, cheat, steal, and even kill if it meant he could be with Jordyn.

Baylon also realized what that meant for his fellow Reapers.

Death's words to him so long ago about how important it was that the Reapers only had each other hit home. Now he understood Death's rules.

But it didn't change anything.

"How is she?" Cael asked.

Baylon shrugged, unable to hide his grin. "She feels

great. She doesn't remember any of the pain."

"That's a blessing," Talin said.

Kyran nodded slowly. "That's for sure. How is that even possible?"

"It must be her Fae blood," Baylon said. It was the only explanation.

Cael crossed his arms over his chest. "It must be."

Baylon held Cael's gaze. He didn't even try to pretend he didn't know why the room was charged with tension. Baylon took a deep breath, a calm settling over him. "Say whatever it is that needs to be said."

"There's nothing." Every head in the room turned to Eoghan. His gaze was on Baylon, but he didn't say anything more.

Baylon gave a nod to Eoghan and turned his attention to the others. "Our problem isn't going to go away. We need to find out who these Dark are and how they got their magic increased to such a degree."

"Agreed," Cael said. "We used the one card we had, and Jordyn nearly died in the process. That doesn't leave us much."

Kyran crossed his arms over his chest. "Let's back up a moment. They wanted us to kill the humans with Fae blood at first."

"Because that would've made us seem to go against Death, and then Death would've had to kill us," Talin

said.

Baylon shook his head as anger settled around him. "Which would've left Death with no Reapers."

"But that didn't happen," Fintan pointed out. "We didn't kill the humans."

A muscle flexed at Cael's jaw. "No, that plan was brought to a halt when I went to Death."

"That puts us where?" Talin asked.

Kyran lifted his shoulders in a shrug. "The Dark didn't wait around on us. They began to kill any human with Fae blood. Why?"

"There has to be a connection there," Baylon said.

He felt Jordyn's presence before he saw her. Baylon turned to find her in the shadows. He waited for her to step forward. As soon as the light from the candles landed on her, Baylon found himself smiling.

She was so beautiful. And she was his. It made him want to shout to the world how happy he was.

But Jordyn wasn't smiling. A deep frown marked her brow. "Baylon said that humans with Fae blood had abilities."

"Some do," Cael admitted.

Baylon waited until Jordyn was even with him before he asked, "Why? What are you thinking?"

Her turquoise eyes shifted to him. "I just think it odd that we're being annihilated. Why would they do that? If the focus is not on any of you now, and we don't have the magic that a full-blooded Fae does, then why kill us? What do they stand to gain?"

The room was quiet as they considered Jordyn's words. Baylon couldn't think of a single reason why the Dark were doing what they were to the half-Fae.

"Fuck!" Cael said and turned to punch the wall. Stone crumbled beneath his fist to fall at his feet. "I should've seen it from the beginning."

Kyran dropped his arms. "Seen what?"

Cael whirled around, his silver eyes alight with an unnatural shine that showed just how angry he was. "This is about Death. If we weren't here, Death would have to do the work we're sent for."

"And if we can't control the Dark, Death will come to help," Baylon finished.

Fintan ran a hand through his long white hair. "This is fucked up. It has to be someone who knows about Death and us. Who spilled our secrets?"

Each of them looked at the other. Baylon was the first to say, "It wasn't me."

"I'd never share our secrets," Kyran said.

Talin threw up his hands. "It wasn't me."

"Please," Fintan said with a roll of his eyes.

Eoghan gave them a droll look.

Cael blew out a long breath. "It wasn't me either. Daire

has been following Rhi, but I know he hasn't said anything."

"If it wasn't any of us, then who?" Baylon asked.

Eoghan's silver eyes stared hard at Cael as some unspoken communication passed between them. Baylon watched the two carefully before he exchanged a worried glance with the others.

"No," Cael said aloud. "It's not possible."

Talin raised a brow. "What isn't possible?"

Cael lowered his gaze to the floor where he stared at it for a long time. Baylon felt Jordyn move closer to him, and on instinct laced his fingers with hers.

Eoghan turned his head away, a resigned and furious expression on his face.

"Cael," Fintan stated, his voice pitched low.

Finally Cael drew in a deep breath, but he didn't look at them. "It's not possible, Eoghan, because they're dead. There's no way any of the others survived Death's fury. They're gone."

Now Baylon understood. "Both of you saw their deaths?"

Eoghan shook his head.

"Death's action was swift and lethal. They're dead," Cael repeated.

Kyran asked, "Are you sure of that? Because it sounds like you're trying to convince yourself."

Cael's head snapped up, his gaze pinning Kyran. "Death wouldn't have let them survive."

"Why not ask Death?" Jordyn asked.

Cael gave her a cursory glance. "There's no need. If Death thought for a moment they survived, we would know of it."

"Fine," Talin said. "So the Reapers who betrayed you and Eoghan are dead. That leaves us exactly zero suspects."

Baylon knew they were going to get nowhere at this rate. He looked at Jordyn and felt his heart catch. She was in danger. They all were, and if they didn't figure out a way to stop the Dark Fae, she would end up dead.

He'd already been down that road. He didn't want to go down it ever again.

Her face softened as she gazed up at him. In her turquoise depths, he saw how much she cared. The warmth spreading through him told him his feelings went deep. Deep enough that he knew without having to even think about it that he loved her.

They way they had met, the circumstances that put her in his arms all pointed to the fact that they were supposed to be together.

"Consider it," Baylon told Cael. He shifted his attention their leader. "Let's just for a moment think about the possibility that one or more of the traitors managed to live."

Cael gave a half-hearted shrug. "All right. Say they did."

"They'd be pissed," Talin.

Fintan snorted. "I know I would be, and I'd be gunning for revenge in the worst way."

Cael ran a hand down his face. "Yes. All of that and more, but Death would never have left them alive."

"Perhaps she didn't know they were," Kyran said.

Baylon tightened his grip on Jordyn's hand. "These Dark know things, Cael. They know too much to have just been told."

"If it is one of them, then we've got a serious problem," Cael said. He swiveled his head to Eoghan. "If it is them, they're coming for the both of us and Death."

Fury passed over Eoghan's face before his eyes went stony. There was no need for words. Everything was written plainly on Eoghan's face. He was ready and waiting for the Fae he'd once considered friends.

"Yeah. Me, too," Cael said.

Talin rocked back on his heels. "We're going to need to know everything about the three who turned against you. Not just the story, but who these Fae were and why they became Reapers."

"Right," Baylon said. "We need to make sure they no longer have the element of surprise."

Cael nodded woodenly. "We need to find another

place. If it is them, it won't be long before they find us. Locate somewhere else for us to meet. This place is no longer safe."

"Where are you going?" Fintan asked.

Cael looked around the room. "I'm going to see Death."

After Cael vanished, they stood around for a moment. It was Eoghan who looked at them, and with a nod, disappeared.

"Well, shit," Talin mumbled.

Fintan turned to Baylon and Jordyn. "If these assholes find out Jordyn is still alive, they'll not stop until she's dead."

"Especially if it's Bran," Kyran said. "Death took away his woman. He won't like knowing you have one."

Jordyn lifted her chin as she looked from Kyran to Baylon. "I'm not going to hide meekly anymore. I may not have any magic, but you have weapons that can be used. I want one. I'll not be caught unawares again."

"Agreed," Baylon said. He'd already thought of that himself.

It was Fintan who pulled two daggers from the waist of his jeans and walked to Jordyn. He handed them to her hilt first with a smile. "These blades were forged in the Fires of Erwar. They were specifically made to kill Fae. They've served me well. Let them serve you."

Baylon gave a nod of thanks to Fintan once Jordyn had wrapped her hands around the pommels and held the long knives in her hands.

With Jordyn occupied handling the blades, Baylon took the sheaths from Fintan. The weapons weren't enough, but it was a start.

"Some of our best warriors are females," Talin said with a grin. "One of the best is named Rhi."

Baylon stood to the side and watched Jordyn rotate her wrists as she twirled the knives. "You're going to need to be trained. Starting immediately."

"We can each take turns," Kyran said. "We'll all have a lot to do in preparation."

Jordyn lowered her arms to her sides. "So. This is war?"

Baylon nodded. "This is war."

$\sim$

Bran walked around the room between the Reapers and the half-Fae Baylon had taken as a lover. Bran couldn't have gotten any luckier had he tried.

If his lover was taken, then Bran would be the one to take Jordyn. It was fair after all.

He smiled as he passed Cael. The mighty Cael, leader of the Reapers, didn't have a clue that Bran was there. Cael hadn't put any magic up on the secret room, but still none of the Reapers realized Bran was veiled and among them.

Reapers, by Death's command, were the most lethal, strong, and powerful of the Fae. Bran nearly laughed aloud. It was all going to be so very easy.

It didn't matter that Eoghan and Cael suspected him, or that Death would search for him in the Netherworld. Soon, Death and the Reapers–minus Daire–would be after him.

But that's not what made Bran pause. He wanted to know where Daire was. Death kept the Reapers together unless it was for something special. Perhaps Bran needed to find Daire and see what Death had him doing.

Bran walked from the room with a smile. Let them find a new place. He would run them to ground quick enough. Especially now that he had Jordyn's scent.

Chapter Nineteen

Cael walked through the Fae doorway and was instantly surrounded by vivid shades of green and every color flower imaginable.

Seeing Erith twice in such a short period was unusual. And both times he'd sought her out.

She hadn't been happy to see him the first time. He didn't imagine things would change this time around.

A butterfly glided past him, its black and blue markings spectacular on its large wings. Cael followed the flight of the butterfly over and behind him. He turned, his gaze caught by the graceful beauty of the insect that reminded him of Erith.

The way she seemed to glide instead of walk. The way she had to touch the leaves of the plants she passed, as if they alone were the reason she breathed. The way she never stayed still for long.

As soon as the butterfly landed on a pink rose with white tips, he saw her. Death.

Her large lavender eyes were trained on him. There was no welcoming smile, but when was there ever? Her blue-black hair fell over her left shoulder in waves of inky blackness. And a small pink flower was tucked behind her right ear.

She wore another black dress that dipped low to show ample cleavage and a hint of bright pink lining. Slim straps kept the dress atop her shoulders while the bodice molded to her narrow waist before flaring out in layers of elaborate lace.

Erith said not a word as she turned and started toward the white tower. Cael followed, noting how the train of her dress seemed to float just above the ground, the black fading to pink before it returned to black and started the process all over again.

No words were spoken until they reached the room that Cael had dubbed the library. It was the only place he'd seen in the entire white tower, the only place she ever allowed him to enter. All the others doors were kept closed at all times.

Erith walked to the middle of the room and faced him with one blue-black brow raised.

He'd hoped she would demand why he was there, but then again, Erith never did anything expected. After thousands of years working with her, Cael should know that.

Cael stood just inside the door, his gaze holding Death's. She was the only female in all the realms who had the ability to make him feel as insignificant as an ant, and then on the other hand as mighty as the universe.

It was a battle of wills that kept them both silent. Cael needed her to ask why he was there. Death wasn't all-knowing, though some thought she was.

"Two visits in a matter of days. When I didn't summon you," Erith said and raised her chin. "You know I don't like to be disturbed."

Cael drew in a breath and slowly released it. "When have I ever come simply to visit? I'm here for a reason."

"Did you find who is killing the half-Fae then?"

"I've a suspicion."

Her lavender gaze narrowed slightly. "Surely you're not here to get my permission to kill these Fae."

"How did you know it was Fae?"

She looked askance at him. "And who else would it be?"

True. Cael took a step to the right, but remained near the door. "It's not one Fae, Erith. It's an army."

There was a beat of silence before she asked, "How many?"

"We can't be sure. I set a trap for them."

"And?" she urged when he paused.

"There was a half-Fae Baylon found. She agreed to act as bait to draw them out after they wiped out her family. There were over two dozen Dark who attacked us. The half-Fae was hit."

Erith moved to sit on a padded bench beneath a window whose shudders had been pushed open. "Is she dead?"

"It took awhile, but her body healed."

"Did you see the leader of this army?"

Cael shook his head. "These Dark knew us. They knew where to find us, how we'd fight, and they knew our ways. Baylon had one in his grasp, with his sword at the Dark's throat, and the Dark was able to teleport away."

"Impossible," she stated, offended that he would even suggest such a thing.

Cael shrugged on shoulder. "It happened. They don't move as fast as us, but it's close. Their magic is more powerful than a Dark's should be."

Erith leveled a glare at him. "Are you suggesting that I sent another group after you?"

"No. If you wanted us dead, we'd be dead."

"But someone gave these Dark added powers."

"Whoever the leader is has focused his attention on the Reapers—and you."

Erith studied him a moment. "You know who it is."

"I think so, but it couldn't be possible."

"Who?"

"Bran." Cael didn't know what he expected Erith to do, but to sit there without so much as a bat of her eyes was like a punch to his stomach.

Erith turned her head to look out the window. "Bran is no more."

"Did you kill him?"

Her gaze snapped around to glower at him. "You dare to question me?"

"Yes, when it's your life in danger. Not to mention ours and every half-Fae on Earth."

Erith moved a loose curl that had fallen over her eyes to the side. "Bran is somewhere he can never escape."

Cael closed his eyes, the knot of dread forming. He'd prayed Eoghan was wrong, but it looked like his old friend had known what Cael refused to admit. Bran wasn't dead.

"Where is Bran?"

Erith leaned an arm on the sill of the window and held out her hand. A moment later a dragonfly with wings that were clear except for a two thick bands of dark green on each of the four wings landed on her finger. "Far, far away."

"Have you checked on him?"

"No need."

Cael could no longer control the anger that spiked within him. "Why the hell didn't you just kill him?"

His shout echoed around the tower. Erith didn't immediately respond. She waited until the dragonfly had flown away before she turned back to him.

Lavender eyes pinned him as she rose to her feet. "After what Bran did, you ask me that? He killed Theo and was about to kill you and Eoghan."

"Then you should've ended him."

She smiled, but there was no humor there. "He broke my rules, Cael. He took a lover and told her who he was. He told her about each of you. Then he turned on you. Dying was too easy."

Listening to her talk of Bran's lover reminded Cael that Baylon was walking the same path as Bran. The only difference was that Cael willingly allowed Jordyn into the group in order to stop whoever was killing half-Fae.

But what if Cael had sealed Baylon and Jordyn's fate?

Then he realized that what was between the two of them couldn't be stopped. Whether Jordyn had the protection of the Reapers or not, Baylon would still have given his heart to the half-Fae.

"Check to see if Bran is still where you put him," Cael urged.

Erith stared at Cael for a long time. She didn't like being told what to do—in any capacity. She was Death, after all. She made the decisions.

Yet, there was something in Cael's words that alerted her. Cael wasn't prone to fanciful thoughts. If he asked about Bran it was because Cael had enough information to believe it was him.

With a wave of her hand, the door closed to the room. Despite the extra power and magic she gave Cael, he wouldn't be able to leave that room without her permission.

The last thing she wanted was him wandering the tower-or her realm. It was her sanctuary, and there were things she didn't want him to see.

And she shouldn't like the thought of him in her tower.

"I'll return shortly," she said and teleported out.

Erith stood in the Netherworld, unmoved by the malicious winds that blew constantly. The sky was a murky orange that never changed across the desolate landscape.

The entire realm was made up of nothing but sand and the howling wind. It was a Hell for Fae that weren't killed–a prison world that kept them trapped for eternity.

Those who were imprisoned in the Netherworld learned to survive by digging holes in the earth, otherwise the small shards of rock carried in the wind would slowly slice off pieces of skin day after day.

Erith thought of Bran, expecting to be taken to him instantly. But nothing happened.

She looked around. No one had ever escaped the Netherworld. No one.

Yet there was no denying Bran wasn't there.

With no other choice, Erith returned to her tower. She found Cael standing at one of the windows looking out as a pair of butterflies danced near the purple wisteria that climbed the tower on one side.

"He's gone, isn't he?" Cael asked without turning around.

Erith was sick to her stomach at the thought that Bran had somehow escaped and she hadn't known. Was she so confident in herself that she didn't see when something was going wrong?

No. That couldn't be right. She knew her limits all too well.

"Yes," she admitted.

Cael turned to face her. "Where did you put him?"

"The Netherworld."

Cael's silver eyes widened. "And he escaped? How the bloody hell did that happen?"

"It's what we need to find out." She walked to stand next to Cael, something she rarely did. He always made her feel flustered, rattled when he got too near. "Bran is the one causing this havoc. He needs to be stopped."

"This time I'm going to kill him."

The statement, made by a man who never failed her, was why she chose him as a Reaper. Well, it was one reason. Then there was the fact he was the type of man that others followed. His instincts were usually right on the money as well.

There was another reason, but that she kept locked away.

Erith smiled. "If you don't, I will."

"Will you join this fight?"

"Eventually. I need to see if Bran had help getting out of the Netherworld."

Cael crossed his arms over his chest. "We're stretched thin with Daire gone. We could use him."

"No," she stated. "Daire stays with Rhi."

Cael bowed his head. "As you say."

"Bran knows I killed his lover. He's going to want to strike at the Reapers in such a way." She left the rest unsaid to see what reaction she would get from Cael. There was the tiniest flash in his silver eyes, but it was all she needed to see.

"Bran won't be able to hurt us in such a way."

Erith looked up at Cael with his long black hair loose about his shoulders, and his silver eyes set in a determined glint. "This half-Fae female who allowed herself to be used as bait, do I need to be concerned?"

"No."

Said much too quickly. Erith felt a piece of her wither inside. She never wanted to be put in this situation again, and yet her she was.

She turned to the window, allowing her fingers to

graze Cael lightly. In an instant an image of the half-Fae filled her mind. Jordyn Patterson.

"How many humans with Fae blood have we lost?" she asked, to change the subject.

They way Cael's shoulders relaxed was a telling sign. There was something going on between one of the Reapers and Jordyn. Was it Cael?

She cut him a look out of the corner of her eye. No, not Cael and not Eoghan. Those two saw firsthand what it had done to the group before.

Nor was it Fintan. The Dark would never allow himself to become involved with another. Daire was with Rhi. That left Kyran, Talin, and Baylon.

And Baylon was the one who found her.

Death had high hopes for Baylon. She didn't want to kill him or Jordyn, but neither of them were giving her a choice.

"We've not tallied it up yet," Cael replied. "My guess is in the hundreds. We don't have names or locations of the humans with Fae blood, so it will take us time to find them."

"Time we don't have," she said. "I'll do what I can."

Cael nodded and turned on his heel. Erith opened the door with her mind before he reached it. She remained in the tower watching as Cael walked to the doorway that would take him back to the realm of Earth.

His strides were long, purposeful. He was a Fae who didn't let anything stand in his way. Cael was the perfect Reaper–and the very one she'd modeled the group after.

Chapter Twenty

The weight of the daggers sat heavily in Jordyn's hands before she slid them into their sheaths at her waist. She practiced with them as much as she could, but an hour was nothing. Jordyn needed years.

It helped knowing she wasn't completely weaponless. She might not know how to use the daggers properly, but let one of the Dark get close enough and she'd be happy to sink a blade into their bodies.

If they didn't strike her down with magic first.

Jordyn felt like she was about to get sick. She might have Fae blood, but she was still a human. The shred of magic she had took hours to heal her from the blast of Dark magic. She had nothing but her daggers, her wits–and Baylon–to protect her from the Dark.

Baylon. She turned her gaze to him as they walked along the streets of Edinburgh looking for a place the Reapers could plan their next assault.

Baylon gave her a brief nod. His attention was on the people along the streets. Though it seemed odd not to run across any Dark in the half hour they'd been walking.

"What about my flat?" Jordyn suggested.

Baylon glanced at her. "They know of it."

"Yep, but that also means they'll assume we won't go back."

Baylon paused at a corner and looked behind him before he looked to each side. "That could work."

Jordyn chuckled. "Since your group normally hides under ancient structures, I'd say that's a yes."

"I'll let the others know," Baylon said with a wink.

Jordyn's steps were lighter than they had been in hours. Her life had gone to hell in a matter of seconds, and she no longer had any family. But there was Baylon. She had him and the knowledge of who she was.

She was confident the Reapers would stop this enemy, and then Jordyn could mourn her family. Right after she begged Death to allow Baylon to live.

Neither of them spoke about the future since their last conversation. His fingers slid against hers, intertwining. There wasn't a need for more words. They said all that needed to be said.

Jordyn smiled when she saw her building. By the time they reached her flat, Kyran and Talin were already inside. They were looking through her numerous Fae books and comparing them.

"They're like bairns. They have to touch everything," Fintan said behind them.

Jordyn turned to find him leaning against her kitchen counters and drinking her wine. He lifted the glass and shot them a half smile.

Baylon chuckled. "At least those two had an adult to watch over them."

"As if," Talin shot over his shoulder. "Fintan was the first one here and showed us the books."

When Jordyn looked back at Fintan, he merely smiled and shrugged before he took a long drink of wine. She stood looking at the four Fae–two Dark and two Light–in her home.

Just a few days earlier she'd wondered if she would ever encounter a Fae, preferably one who wasn't Dark. How odd that she no longer feared Fintan and Kyran. She trusted them as much as she trusted Baylon and the rest of the Reapers.

The door to the flat opened and Eoghan strode in followed by Cael. Neither looked happy.

At once, Kyran and Talin set aside the books and came toward the kitchen table. Fintan moved closer, though he didn't relinquish his wine glass.

"By your face, I'm guessing it's Bran we're after," Fintan stated.

Cael gave a nod. "Death put him in the Netherworld."

"How the hell did he get out?" Talin asked in a mixture of shock and anger.

Cael put his hands on the back of a chair and slowly released a breath. "Death is attempting to sort that bit out."

"Why didn't she just kill him to begin with?" Kyran asked with a frown.

Cael and Eoghan exchanged a look. It was Cael who said, "Because he killed Theo and nearly killed me and Eoghan. Death wanted Bran to pay by living in the Netherworld for eternity."

Jordyn didn't know what this Netherworld was, but it obviously wasn't a place that people escaped from. The fact Bran did meant he wasn't just intelligent but was cunning as well.

Baylon leaned down and whispered, "The Netherworld is like Hell for Fae."

That's what she assumed. It must be bad for Death to put Bran there instead of killing him. But that meant Bran was royally pissed, and now he was after them.

"This was a good place to meet," Cael told her.

Jordyn grinned, pleased at the praise.

"We need to draw Bran out," Fintan said.

Each man nodded their heads in agreement. Jordyn was used to working at the police station where men acted like they always had the answers and knew what to do.

This was completely different. These Fae knew exactly what had to be done, and they had most of the answers.

There was no acting with these men. Each and every one of them was bossy, assertive, and overbearing in their own ways.

And she found she liked it. Not just because they protected her, but because they protected each other and the humans.

They were the elite of the Fae, and though none of them spoke of it, she could tell their duties took a toll on them. They were assassins. No one-not even a Reaper-could kill that many people and not have it stain their soul somehow.

Cael looked to Eoghan. "Eoghan and I are going to scout the city. We know what Bran looks like."

"I think we'd be better setting a trap for him now instead of waiting," Kyran said.

Cael nodded. "That's coming. First I want to find him."

Jordyn screamed as the door to her flat was busted in and a tall man with pitch black hair that fell to his jaw stood in the doorway smiling as his silver eyes looked at each of them.

Behind him were several Dark who were all but salivating to get inside and start killing.

Jordyn felt Baylon's nudge and she gradually slid behind him. There was something about Bran that made her feel as if someone walked over her grave.

His eyes were that of a Light Fae, but there was something decidedly evil about him.

"You don't need to look, Cael. I'm right here," Bran said, his smile growing. "I actually thought I was going to have more of a fight with you, but this is entirely too easy."

While Jordyn's hands shook as she parted her coat and put her hands on the hilts of the daggers, the six men around her stood as tall as oaks and as daunting as giants.

Bran rubbed his hand along his jaw as he smirked at Cael and Eoghan. "I walked among you before you went to see Death and ask if I was dead. How did that conversation go, Cael?"

"Swimmingly," Cael said, as if they were talking about what to order for dinner.

"It didn't take a great amount of effort to locate where the Reapers would meet up. There are always hidden rooms in ancient buildings. Edinburgh Castle was an obvious choice. And you didn't even put any magic around the rooms."

Cael shrugged indifferently. "There wasn't a point."

Bran laughed and took two steps into the flat. "The great Cael didn't have a clue I was veiled and listening to your conversation. I discovered quite a bit. And something very interesting," he said as his gaze landed on Jordyn.

Her heart seized. Bran knew of her and Baylon's affair.

The malic she glimpsed in his gaze was enough to make her realize he was coming for her.

Suddenly Baylon's large form blocked Bran from her view. Which only made Bran chuckle.

"If I don't kill her, Death will," Bran said to Baylon.

Baylon's sword materialized in his hand. "Try."

Jordyn found herself squeezed between Kyran and Talin as Fintan moved to stand just behind Baylon. The tension in the flat was running high.

When she suggested her place, she never thought there might be a battle. There were innocent people all around. One of them could die.

Jordyn looked around and saw Eoghan watching her. There was anger in his gaze, but it was for Bran. Eoghan stood calm and collected. Then he gave her a split-second smile.

Was that supposed to help her? She didn't know him well enough to know what that was supposed to mean. All she knew was that there was about to be a war, and once more, everything was aimed at her.

"Who did you come for, Bran?" Cael asked. "Me or Jordyn?"

Bran's smile widened. "All of you."

There was a moment where no one moved. They didn't even breathe. Their gazes were locked, the intensity so thick she could've cut it with a knife.

For the first time in her life, Jordyn knew what real fear felt like. Before with the Dark on the streets, she had been scared. She'd been frightened at the loch when she was used as bait.

Both times she'd thought she was scared out of her skin.

But that was before this.

She stood on a precipice of life and death. Now she fully grasped what terror, true debilitating horror and distress, felt like.

It gripped her body, making it impossible for her to move. She couldn't draw a breath into her lungs or even think past the idea that this could be her end.

She wanted to touch Baylon, to feel his strength against her once more. If she could get to him she might be able to gather some courage and fight.

Jordyn reached out her hand, sliding past Fintan's body. Just as she was about to wrap her fingers around Baylon's arm, the first volley of magic was thrown by Bran.

Chapter Twenty-one

In all his years as a Reaper, Baylon had been the one sent to assassinate. He was the one who took lives without hesitation, because it was his duty, his promise to Death.

For the third time in as many days, he was protecting. It felt right. Perhaps it was because the one he was defending was Jordyn, but it didn't matter. All he knew was that by doing so, the pit in his stomach that had been worrying him for centuries began to dissipate.

He lifted his sword, the blade stopping a ball of magic aimed for his head. Baylon spun in a circle, bending down to one knee as one of the Dark approached. He swung his blade, slicing the Dark's legs in half.

The Dark fell with a cry of agony. Baylon stood and plunged his sword in the Dark's gut. He wanted to look for Jordyn, but there wasn't time. He had to accept that the others were shielding her.

Baylon leaned to the side to miss a ball of magic, only to be hit in quick succession by two blasts. One in his thigh, the other in his gut.

He shook off the pain and found himself standing next

to Cael. Eoghan was on Cael's other side as they fought shoulder to shoulder in Jordyn's small flat.

Her books were being destroyed, the bookshelves disintegrating upon impact of the magic. Glass shattered, furniture splintered, dishes clattered to the floor and broke.

Baylon couldn't properly move his sword to defend or attack. He allowed it to disappear and focused on his magic instead.

The others soon did the same, and the Reapers were able to keep the Dark bottlenecked at the door. But that only lasted for a short time before they demolished the door and the wall on either side.

Eoghan took a nasty hit to his chest from Bran that sent him flying backwards. Baylon felt someone on his other side and glanced over to see Fintan. That meant that Kyran and Talin were with Jordyn.

Baylon knew what it meant to lose. He'd felt the helplessness, the futility as his friends betrayed and killed him. Only a few hours ago, he'd experienced much the same thing when he thought Jordyn was dying.

But it had been a very long while since he'd lost. In all his battles as a Reaper, he'd always won. And he was going to make sure he did today as well.

The smile Bran had so confidently worn was slowly fading as more and more of his Dark were being cut down by the magic of the Reapers.

Baylon felt assured they were going to win. He advanced on Bran, even as he heard Cael call him back. But Baylon wanted this ended with Bran right then.

As if anticipating such a move, Bran eagerly went one-on-one with Baylon. Bran's punches were like having rocks slammed into him. But Baylon was a Reaper. He dodged and weaved, landing his own blows, adding magic to them when he did.

He thought of Jordyn, and what Bran and the Dark would do to her, which gave Baylon the strength to continue even as he bled from his wounds.

Hit after hit, he slammed his fists into Bran with enough force to kill a lesser Fae. Baylon didn't stop until Bran was on his knees.

Bran then looked up at him and grinned. "So cocky. You're going to know how it feels to lose the woman you love."

The words barely had time to register before the flat was filled with Dark. Baylon tried to turn and rush to Jordyn, but he was grabbed from behind and had blast after blast of magic pounded into him until it was all he could do to keep his eyes open.

He heard Bran laugh even as there was a loud battle cry that sounded like it came from Eoghan. Baylon's body struggled to heal the damage that had been done while the Dark tramped on him as they rushed into the flat.

Kyran shouted Jordyn's name. Then Baylon heard her scream. He gritted his teeth and rolled onto his side. That's when he got a look at the carnage.

Bodies of the Dark littered the floor. Cael and Eoghan were cut off from the others by a large group of Dark. Kyran and Talin stood in front of Jordyn as they battled the Dark. Fintan had been singled out by Bran, but Baylon couldn't make out what Bran was saying.

Whatever Fintan said in response angered Bran by his mottled face. Baylon dragged himself toward Jordyn, Talin, and Kyran. He would be there to help protect her.

Baylon called up his sword and rolled onto his back, jerking the blade up into the spine of a Dark. Then he moved out of the way before the Dark fell on him.

It seemed to take forever for Baylon to get anywhere. There were so many Dark, but the Reapers were holding their own, even as wounded as each of them were.

Baylon was nearly to Jordyn. He caught her gaze and shot her a smile. She returned it, her face softening. Out of the corner of his eye, Baylon saw Bran turn toward Jordyn. Fintan shouted her name while he swung his sword at Bran.

And all Baylon could do was watch in horror as the bubble of magic hit Jordyn in the chest. She fell back, unmoving.

"I told you I'd take everything," Bran whispered in Baylon's ear.

Baylon forgot his pain. He forgot that his body was riddled with holes of Dark magic as he jumped to his feet and plunged his sword toward Bran, but the Fae teleported away.

While the others continued to fight any Dark that remained, Baylon limped his way to Jordyn. He fell to his knees and gently pulled Jordyn into his arms.

She was no longer breathing. All life was gone from her body. Baylon had never known such emptiness before. He thought what his friends had done to him was the worst that could happen. How very wrong he'd been.

Now he understood the true meaning of pain—pain of the mind, of the heart.

Of the soul.

It took him a moment to realize that there were no more sounds of fighting. His friends stood around him, their silence conveying their sorrow.

Baylon touched Jordyn's cheek, recalling what a vibrant force she'd been. Nothing had stopped her once she set her mind to something.

"Baylon," Cael said and touched his shoulder.

He looked up to find ashes of the dead Dark disappearing out the window. Then he spotted Death. She wore a black dress with long, fitted sleeves and a high neckline. The train of her gown trailed behind her with a hint of white at the edges that faded to gray and then to black.

Baylon no longer feared what she would do to him. He'd lost the one thing that was precious to him, the one person who righted his soul.

Death walked to him without a word. She stood looking down at him with a closed expression in her lavender eyes. Baylon held Jordyn tighter while he gazed at the vision of Death.

She was so beautiful that it hurt to look at her. Baylon recalled the first time she'd come to him. She'd held his soul, telling him he was a formidable warrior who'd had the misfortune of being betrayed. Then she asked if he wanted to join the Reapers. She told him of the extra powers he would get, as well as the added strength to become her executioner.

After what had just happened to him, Baylon couldn't refuse. He gladly accepted her offer and hadn't looked back.

Death knelt at Jordyn's side and touched her forehead before her gaze slid back to Baylon. "She's gone."

He'd already known it, but to hear it said was too much. Baylon felt the emotion well within him, but he didn't stop it. Nor did he care that tears fell down his face.

"You loved her," Erith said.

Baylon simply nodded, unable to speak the words.

"Even though you knew my rules."

He blinked and looked at Death. This was where she would take his life. "Yes. It's my fault alone. I talked Cael into using Jordyn as bait to catch our enemy. None of the others were happy with the situation. I take full responsibility."

She raised a blue-black brow.

"I know by taking her to my bed more than once I've broken your rule and forfeited my life. The Reapers are going to need someone to fill my place to fight Bran. I hope you have someone in mind."

"I do," she responded.

Cael said, "Erith."

She held up a hand, her gaze still locked on Baylon. "Do you know why I have those rules in place?"

"I do," Baylon answered. "We carry out your orders. No one can know of us so they can't bribe us as what was done before. Thereby, we're also forbidden from forming any emotional attachment in case it jeopardizes our decisions in battle."

Death looked at each Reaper. "All of you agreed to my rules when you accepted my offer to be a Reaper."

This was what Baylon feared. He was the only one who should be punished for his decision, not any of the others. But before he could speak, Death halted him with a look.

She took a breath and released it. "I've watched you and Jordyn, Baylon. She was courageous, even though she knew she was going to die. She stood by the Reapers, willingly helping you ferret out your enemy.

"I also saw something else," Death continued. "I saw the Reapers knowingly accept Jordyn into the group."

"Because she was using herself as bait."

Erith shook her head. "Cael knew you were in love with her. He could've forbidden it and used another half-Fae. He didn't. Nor did any of the others balk at having Jordyn among you."

"What are you saying?" Cael asked.

Death got to her feet. "Forbidding my Reapers from finding love is like demanding you not breathe. What happened with Bran will repeat over and over again unless something changes."

Baylon wasn't sure he heard her correctly. Surely Death didn't just say the rules were being altered.

"Baylon, if Jordyn agrees to be yours, she will be a part of the Reapers. There are things she can do to help the group."

Fintan crossed his arms over his chest and rocked back on his heels. "You're making Jordyn a Reaper?"

"No," Baylon said. "I don't want her killing anyone."

Erith's gaze narrowed on him. "It may come to a point sometime where she needs to take a life, but no, I don't plan on sending her as I do the seven of you. I've other plans for Jordyn."

"What if the rest of us find someone?" Talin asked.

"Just as all of you were chosen to be Reapers, if you fall in love, the women must prove themselves as Jordyn has." Erith paused. "I'm not issuing a blanket acceptance for anyone. The Reapers still need to remain a secret. Jordyn will have to remain as anonymous as the rest of you or this endeavor will fail."

Cael stepped forward. "It won't. I won't allow it."

"Baylon, take Jordyn from this place," Death said.

He climbed to his feet with Jordyn in his arms. "When will you talk to her?"

There was a small smile upon Erith's lips. "I already have. She'll wake soon."

"What about Bran?" Kyran asked.

Fury contorted Death's face. "He believes he killed Jordyn. Let him. But be warned, any of you who show feelings toward another, Bran will be there."

"Unless we stop him," Fintan said.

Eoghan nodded, his jaw clenched tight.

Death turned her head to Cael. "He had help escaping from the Netherworld. I've got a name."

"Let me have a talk with them," Cael bade.

When Cael and Death moved away to talk in low tones, Baylon couldn't stop staring at Jordyn. Not only was he not going to be killed, but Death saved Jordyn while allowing her into the Reapers.

"I'm happy for you," Kyran said as he slapped Baylon on the back.

Talin nodded with a grin. "It's certainly going to be different."

"We need to find another place to hide," Fintan said.

Eoghan snapped his fingers to get their attention. He pointed out the window, far in the distance, toward the sea.

"Lead the way," Kyran told Eoghan.

Baylon gave a nod of thanks to Death before he teleported away.

Chapter Twenty-two

Jordyn came awake and found herself cradled in arms she knew all too well. The pain from the blast of magic that killed her might never fade from her memory, but it was the knowledge that she was alive once more and with Baylon that made it acceptable.

"How do you feel?" Baylon asked.

She shifted her head to look up at him with a smile. "I'm with you. I feel amazing."

He gave her a quick kiss. "I know from experience that you'll never forget how you were killed."

"I'm still reeling over the fact that Death is a woman, a beautiful woman. And she gave me a place with the Reapers."

"What did Death say to you?"

Jordyn thought back to the moments after she was killed. Her mind had been full of regrets for everything she hadn't been able to do with Baylon. And then suddenly, all the misery and pain were gone. Standing before her was a woman in all black wearing a kind smile.

Death hadn't been at all what Jordyn expected. Erith

was nothing like the Grim Reaper, but then again, perhaps that story came about because of the Reapers.

That's when Death told her she had been watching her and Baylon and saw everything Jordyn did to help them. Somehow, Jordyn impressed her. Though Death made it known that her rules wouldn't be broken twice.

Then to Jordyn's shock, Death had offered her a deal.

"Jordyn?" Baylon nudged.

She turned and looked around at the room, noticing it for the first time. They were in a plush bed with a large fireplace before them, keeping her warm.

"Death told me there was a place for me among the Reapers. I wouldn't be sent out killing as all of you do, but that there are other things she has need of me for. I wasn't prepared to leave you yet, and I want to catch Bran. So I agreed." She looked back at him. "I no longer have any family, Baylon. You and the Reapers are all I have now. You are my family."

He said nothing as he brought her against him and held her. They stayed that way for long moments, with the only sound coming from the wood that popped in the fire.

"Bran had help escaping the Netherworld," Baylon finally said. "Cael is questioning the man now."

"I'm surprised you aren't with him."

Baylon's lips twisted as he loosened his hold. "All of us

want to be, but Cael is doing this alone."

"Where are we?"

"In some caves along the coast. It'll do for now."

She snuggled against him. "Will we go after Bran again?"

"Definitely. He must be stopped. He'll not quit coming after us or Death until he's dead."

Jordyn recalled Death saying something similar to her. "When do we start?"

"As soon as you're up to it."

She sat up. "Tell me."

Baylon smiled as he rose from the bed. Jordyn was quick to follow him out of the cavern that was their room down a tunnel lit by candles hanging along the walls in midair.

They didn't stop until they reached a large space. Jordyn gaped when she saw her bookshelves and all her books, as well as hundreds of others.

"This is your place," Baylon said. "You've made a life doing research, so we've given you a place to do it."

She walked to the books and touched them. "Bran destroyed these."

"Magic," Baylon said with a wink.

Jordyn laughed and shook her head. "I don't think I'll need books on the Fae anymore."

"You'd be surprised. Every book has some kernel of

truth in it. It might just be one sentence, but it's important."

"Wow," she said walking along the books, allowing her fingers to touch the spines. "I'm amazed."

Baylon came up behind her. "Whatever you need, you only have to ask. We'll get it for you."

She turned in his arms. "All I need right now is you."

"I was hoping you'd say that," he murmured as he lowered his head. Right before their lips touched he said, "I love you, Jordyn Patterson."

She thought her heart would burst from her chest, she was so happy. Not only did she have the answers to her ancestry, she had been brought back from the dead, was working with Death and the Reapers, and to top it off, she had the man of her dreams.

"I love you, too."

"This is the start of our life," Baylon said.

Jordyn rose up on her toes and kissed him. "If you don't take me to bed and make love to me, we won't be starting our new life until tomorrow."

With a laugh, Baylon grabbed her hand and tugged her after him as they ran back to their room.

Tomorrow and locating Bran would come soon enough. Today was theirs.

Epilogue

Eoghan watched Baylon and Jordyn run to their room. Their happiness was palpable. He should be happy for them, and he was. But it brought back so many memories he'd thought he buried deep.

Apparently not deep enough.

"It's only ever been us males," Kyran said as he walked up. "This might take some getting used to."

Eoghan shrugged. It never took long to get used to a female.

"I wish Cael would get back so we could hunt Bran."

Eoghan nodded, because it's all he could think about. Bran had killed Reapers before. He could do it again. But Eoghan was prepared to do whatever it took to stop him this time. History wouldn't repeat itself.

Of that he would make sure.

~

Bran was walking the halls of Edinburgh Castle. He'd driven the Reapers out easily enough. It wouldn't take long to remove them from Edinburgh. He'd already made the first step in killing Jordyn.

Searlas appeared at the juncture ahead, his expression tight.

"What is it?" Bran asked.

"They have Seamus."

Bran shrugged. "So? The idiot is the one who helped us. If he was too stupid to get caught, then he'll pay for it with his life."

"What if he tells the Reapers something?" Searlas asked.

Bran laughed as he continued walking. "He doesn't know anything."

One by one the Reapers would fall. Then there would only be Death. Bran wasn't so cocky that he didn't realize battling Death would be difficult.

But he was preparing for that as well.

DARK ALPHA'S
EMBRACE

Chapter One

EDINBURGH, SCOTLAND
NEW YEAR'S EVE

Kyran stared curiously at the large gray structure of Edinburgh's Central Library. What was it about such places that called to some mortals? Even the half-Fae Jordyn found it one of the most amazing places in the city.

He didn't get it.

"Just a building full of books," Kyran mumbled.

Talin smacked him in the arm as he came to stand beside Kyran. "Don't knock it. Many of the books on Jordyn's list are in that place. The more she has, the more information we get."

"I know." That didn't mean he liked it.

Talin turned his silver eyes to him. "What's the problem?"

Kyran shot him a look. "We're Fae, Talin. Reapers. We kill those Death chooses. We don't break into libraries and take books. Our skills are being wasted."

"It's a change, that's for sure." Talin chuckled softly and

rubbed his hands together. "I attempted to check out one of the books on Jordyn's list, but the librarian is fierce. She told me I was asking about a book in the ancient section, as if I was supposed to know what that meant."

Kyran rubbed his eyes with his thumb and forefinger. He'd already heard this story four times, and each time the librarian became more and more ferocious. "Aye."

"When I asked what that was, she looked at me as if I'd grown another head. Then she said, in that uptight tone of hers, 'You're Irish.' As if that makes a difference."

"I told you to get a human to ask for them."

With a snort, Talin ran his hands through his long black hair. "We're getting the books tonight. What difference does it make?"

"Why can't we just use magic and find them someplace else?"

Talin rolled his eyes. "Did you not listen to Jordyn when she briefed us on this? These books are extremely rare. There is only one edition for each."

"And some just happen to be in this library?" No, Kyran wasn't buying it. "Why this place?"

Talin looked around, his hands held out. "We're in Edinburgh. It's one of the oldest cities. Where else would these books be?"

"Private owners."

"Let it go," Talin said with a shake of his head.

But Kyran didn't want to let it go. Why did he have to get stuck with the library instead of going to some of the private collectors? He'd much rather do that than sneak around a building.

There was no adventure in it. They'd be in and gone without anything happening.

"The library closed at eight," Talin said. "It's after midnight now. We'll have the books in hand and return to Jordyn in a blink."

"That's the problem. There's no danger."

"Ah. I see." Talin walked backward into the middle of the narrow street that was empty of people and cars. "You want danger? We'll get it as soon as we get the books. Then we can locate Bran."

The anger within Kyran sizzled at the mention of the ex-Reaper. Bran betrayed his group and was sent to the Netherworld by Death.

Except Bran managed to escape the inescapable prison and was now after them. Bran had already killed Jordyn in his bid to take the Reapers out.

But Death stepped in and made Jordyn one of them. Though she was a Reaper—the first female Reaper—Jordyn didn't assassinate as they did.

Her job was coordinating everything, as well as research. Jordyn's first order of business was discovering all she could about the Netherworld.

Kyran couldn't wait to find Bran. Con and Eoghan might be the only ones who survived from the first group of Reapers, but Kyran would be the one to help take Bran down for good.

"Let's get going then," Kyran said.

With a wink, Talin veiled himself. Kyran watched the Light Fae and tried not to laugh. They'd become friends immediately, which still shocked Kyran since he was a Dark Fae.

Then again, each Reaper suffered some kind of betrayal in one form or another. That's what drew them all together, what bonded them. The seven of them only had each other. Well, they were eight now.

Kyran veiled himself so no human—or Fae—could see him. All Fae had the ability to veil themselves, but most could only hold it for a minute or so. Only the Reapers could remain that way indefinitely. It was one of the gifts of accepting Death's offer.

He walked across the street and up the steps to the main entrance to the library. It was locked and barred, which kept out the majority of the humans.

Kyran lifted his head to the cameras placed around the building. Some were in plain sight while others were hidden. The security system managed to keep out most of the criminals, but the mortals were resourceful when they really wanted something.

If the mortals knew of the books in the ancient section of the library and how much they were worth, no security system on the realm would keep the humans out.

But Kyran wasn't mortal. He teleported inside the library without a single hindrance. A long sigh fell from his lips. He was itching for a good fight ever since Bran got away a few weeks ago.

Death had been oddly quiet. There had been no assignments, and they were all growing restless. Except for Daire. The bastard was trailing a Light Fae Death wanted information on—Rhi. Kyran had no idea where Daire was. He only hoped Daire was having more fun than he was.

They'd also not seen a glimpse of Cael since Death told him who helped Bran escape the Netherworld. Each of the Reapers wanted a piece of the Fae responsible for that, but Cael departed before anyone could go with him.

Kyran looked at the help desk standing in front of him where Talin had tried—unsuccessfully—to get one of the books from the library.

He unveiled himself, his magic keeping him hidden from the cameras as he strode to the stairs and descended to the next level. Talin decided to come in from the roof and take the top three floors while Kyran searched the bottom.

Talin bet him before they arrived that the books were

stored in the top hidden floor of the library. Frankly, Kyran didn't care where they were as long as they found the books and left.

His hands itched to hold his sword. More than anything Kyran wanted to find Bran and sever his head from his body. It would go a long way in helping him feel better about being tracked by Bran and his Dark Fae army—and for what happened to Jordyn.

She and Baylon might be in love, but Kyran thought of her like a sister. As soon as that thought went through his mind, he inwardly cringed.

Even now, so many thousands of years later, the thought of his sister could make him feel as if he were being crushed on all sides. He hadn't been the only one betrayed that rainy night in Dublin.

There was never a good time for those memories to be brought into the light, but on the anniversary of the day he became a Reaper, Kyran allowed a few of those memories loose.

They never did him any good. They only served as a reminder, but it was one he needed. Because time had a way of making someone forget important facts. It was the mind's way of allowing a person to move on.

But Kyran didn't want to move on.

He reached the next floor and quickly went about searching rooms, hoping that behind every door would be the place he sought.

Kyran explored the next two floors but came up empty. Frustration soured his mood. He turned around and nearly ran into Talin who was standing behind him.

"You look vexed," Talin said. "Are you vexed, Kyran?"

For some odd reason, Talin was fixated on that word. He used it as often as he could, annoying everyone in the process. Kyran glared at him. "If I wasn't, I am now."

Talin's smile was wide. "Everyone should be vexed once in a while."

"Find another word," Kyran growled as he pushed past Talin.

Talin leaned a shoulder against the wall. "I didn't find a damn thing on my floors. I even double-checked the main level. Nothing. I know it's here."

"Aye, it's here. We just have to find it."

Pushing away from the wall, Talin stood and slowly turned in a circle. "We're missing it."

"It's hidden somehow."

"Not with magic."

Kyran eyed the books around him. "But maybe magic will help show it."

"And you thought this wouldn't be adventurous."

Kyran snorted. "If you think this is exciting, then we need to have a talk." Suddenly Talin moved to block him from walking away. Kyran lifted a brow. "Something on your mind?"

"Are you all right?"

"You mean besides wanting to find Bran? Aye."

Talin waved away his words. "We all want Bran. This is something else."

Kyran put his hand out and shoved at Talin's shoulder as he walked past. "Look on the left side of the room. I'll take the right."

"You haven't been the same since Baylon brought Jordyn into the group."

That stopped Kyran in his tracks. He turned and gawked at Talin. "What are you going on about?"

"Death changed the rules. Baylon wasn't killed for loving Jordyn, and now she's one of us."

"So?"

Talin ran a hand down his face. "Are you lonely?"

"What the hell kind of question is that?"

"One that, as your friend, I'm asking you to answer."

Kyran stared at him a long time before he let out a deep breath. "When Death asked me to join the Reapers, I knew what the rules were. We tell no Fae who we are, or they die. We develop no attachments to humans or Fae so no one can be used against us. We leave all family and friends behind, letting them believe we're dead."

"You still haven't answered the question. That vexes me."

"I have the six of you. I have our assignments, doling out justice."

Talin folded his arms over his chest. "So you are lonely."

Each time that emotion threatened Kyran, he hastily shoved it away. "We're Reapers, gifted by Death with more power and magic than any other Fae. We don't have time to be lonely."

"Of course." Talin dropped his arms and turned away.

"You're lonely, aren't you?"

Talin halted. Without turning around he said, "Maybe."

"Just because Death allowed Jordyn to be a Reaper doesn't mean any of us will get that same privilege. Jordyn proved herself worthy."

"I know."

Kyran watched his friend walk away without another word. He'd known when Cael sent Talin undercover to the Light Fae court that something was going to happen.

Talin ended up wooing the daughter of an influential advisor to the queen, Usaeil. Kyran had warned Talin to remember that while at court, everything was a lie, but it seems his friend forgot his advice.

Now with Baylon and Jordyn's romance condoned by Death, Talin had hope. Which was the worst thing for any of them. Hope was viciously and ruthlessly snatched from them when they were betrayed. Death gave them a purpose.

But even Kyran could admit to being a tad jealous of Baylon for having the one thing all of them thought would never happen—love.

Kyran pivoted and walked to the far wall. He was about to use his magic when he saw a door half hidden by a large bookshelf. He walked around the bookshelf and spotted the opening that was just large enough for the door.

He let out a whistle to Talin while staring at the keypad that unlocked the door.

"This is it," Talin said as he ran up and saw it.

Kyran put his hand over the keypad and loosed a pulse of magic.

Chapter Two

River White stood looking at the dozen books she spent the last fourteen years accumulating. While everyone else celebrated a new year with parties, alcohol, and kisses, she was with the only thing that mattered—her books.

Each one was special, though she hid her reasons from the board of directors who approved her requests and sanctioned the use of funds to purchase them.

As Ancient Acquisitions Manager, she took tremendous pride in her work and everything it involved. She put on the white gloves in the humidity-controlled room. The lights—specialized bulbs—were dimmed and turned away from each of the books so as not to deteriorate them any more than they already were.

Each of the dozen books was in a glass case for protection from dust and pollutants. The library had spent a considerable sum between the precautions to keep the books in good condition and the room itself that was triple-coded to prevent anyone from stealing them.

The public assumed all the money given to the library

was used in its renovation. However, part of the reason for the renovation was for the ancient books to have a place to be stored.

Luckily, Edinburgh had wealthy patrons who loved to give money during charity events. A large sum of those monies went to buying the books she now stood with.

There were more, however. The next one she was after was being sold on the black market, but River didn't have enough money for it. Nor did she think the Board would give her access to more so soon after her last purchase.

But it was imperative the books stay out of the hands of certain individuals who could use the knowledge within the pages to harm others.

River walked to the tome in front of her. The leather binding was worn around the edges, and the gold clasp locking it was worn smooth by use.

She punched in her fifteen-digit code to unlock the case. As the glass panel slid open, River carefully grasped the book and lifted it.

The last time she'd touched it was more than a year ago when she placed it inside its case. She didn't know what prompted her to go to this book tonight, but she didn't question it.

River walked slowly with the book to the podium and gently set it down. She took a deep breath and slowly released it. Unable to help herself, she ran her gloved finger down the spine of the book. The gold letters were faded now. Only portions of each were visible.

The words were written in an obscure language that she told her boss she was searching for ways to transcribe. But River already knew what it said.

"*The Hidden,*" she whispered, her finger running over the gold letters on the front of the book. Just as with the spine, there wasn't much left of the title.

She flipped the gold clasp and opened the book. The creak of leather was loud in the silence. With the barest of touches, she turned each page, skimming them.

River already knew what the book said because she'd sat in front of her great-aunt's hearth and read it when she was only five. She hadn't understood what it meant then, not really.

If only she'd had the same knowledge then that she had now. So much would be different. She wouldn't be facing a world of monsters on her own.

"*I'm not strong enough,*" she'd told Aunt Maureen.

But Maureen had simply held River's face in her gnarled hands and smiled down at her with the same blue eyes River saw in the mirror. "*Oh, aye, my girl. You're more than strong enough.*"

If only Aunt Maureen could see her now. Everything she did was because of the heritage she learned on her visits to Ireland.

Her final trip came at the age of thirteen when she found her aunt dead.

River closed her eyes, shutting out those agonizing memories. But she couldn't think about her aunt without thinking of that day. Maureen changed her life, but it was Maureen's death that set River on a course that would define her life.

She read a few more pages of the book before she gently closed and latched it. Taking it from its case was hazardous, but she'd wanted to touch something that once belonged to her aunt.

With the book in hand, she was turning to replace it when she heard voices. Male voices. River quickly returned the book to the case. She yanked off the gloves and hid in the shadows.

"I told you," said a man in a thick Irish accent. He was smiling as he held out his arms and turned in a circle. His hair was long and black, and his silver eyes darted from one book to the next.

She recognized him immediately. He'd come into the library the day before, asking for one of the ancient books. River should've known the Fae would return.

It was the man behind him that made her stomach fall to her feet though. His shoulder-length black hair was laced with silver. Eyes the color of blood surveyed the room slowly, as if he knew she was there.

"See if they have the ones we need," he stated.

River didn't wonder how they got into the library and her vault, because she knew what they were—Fae. But how peculiar for a Light and a Dark to be working together. They were usually at odds with one another.

Ever since the Dark openly descended upon Edinburgh in October, River made sure to have her blade with her at all times. She bent and pulled the long, curved knife from the hidden scabbard attached to her leg beneath her skirt.

The Dark walked to the book she'd just been reading. "Some of the titles are gone."

"I know. The ones I can read are on the list."

"I think they're all on the list. We'll take all of them. What we don't need, you'll return."

The Light cut him a flat look. "Are you trying to vex me?"

"Is it working? I'm not returning for another go at this," the Dark said with a harsh look.

River heard enough. She stepped into the light. "You'll not be taking anything."

The Light Fae looked at her with confusion while the Dark's red gaze honed in on her. She glowered at each of them. Neither said a word as they continued to stare at her.

"I didn't stutter," River said. "Turn around and leave

now."

It was the Dark who said, "We can. But we'll be back."

"And I'll be waiting for you."

The Light frowned at her after he glanced at the Dark Fae. "You're supposed to be at home."

"Doesn't look like I am."

The Light held up his hands. "We need these books. It's important."

"And it's important to me that they remain right where they are," she told him.

When the Light Fae went to use his magic on the code to open the glass box, she swung her arm up, the blade in hand.

The Dark was suddenly there, his hand on her wrist. River twisted out of his grip and pointed the knife at his neck. "These are my books."

"I thought they belonged to the library," the Dark said calmly, as if they hadn't briefly clashed.

River wasn't going to split hairs. Let the library think the books belonged to them, but in fact each and every one of them were hers.

"Leave," she ordered.

The Dark moved closer, the point of her weapon nicking his skin so that a bead of blood formed. "Do you know what you are?"

"I have a Fae blade in my hand. Of course I know what

I am."

"Where did you get the dagger?" the Light asked.

River didn't budge even as more blood welled from the prick on the Dark's neck. "Wouldn't you like to know?"

"Talin," the Dark cautioned when the Light began to move toward her.

"Yes, Talin," River said. "I think you'd better stay right where you are."

Talin dropped his arms and heaved a sigh. "Kyran, do something."

River's gaze was locked with Kyran. She'd seen many Fae over the years, but there was something fascinating and absorbing about this Dark that made her heart race—from something other than fear. If only she could lay her finger on what it was.

She knew what the Dark Fae did to humans, how they had sex with them, giving the humans ultimate pleasure. And all the while the Dark drained them of their souls. It was a horrendous way to die.

But Kyran seemed different. She didn't get a vibe of evil from him despite his hair and eyes. All Dark had red eyes and silver in their black hair. Despite what he was, she couldn't deny his attraction. Perhaps it was the way he held her gaze, looking at her as if he couldn't get enough.

Her stomach quivered, and she moved a half step closer, even as her mind warned her to keep her distance. But she couldn't. She had to get nearer.

He didn't look away. With a simple look, he invited her to get closer. It was a temptation she wasn't sure she could refuse.

He was enigmatically gorgeous, despite being Dark. Kyran's eyes were a deep red, outlined with black. His face was harshly beautiful with hallowed cheeks and cheekbones no man should have. She had the irresistible urge to run her hands along his jaw and chin before pressing her mouth against his lips.

At the thought, she nearly moaned. It had been so long since she felt any sort of attraction, and her body reacted rapidly.

And wantonly.

Lustful thoughts ran through her mind about all she wanted to do to the Dark—and what she wanted him to do to her.

Unable to help herself, River's gaze lowered to his wide chest. The black shirt stretched over defined muscles that begged to be caressed. That impressive chest tapered to a narrow waist and hips where his jeans rode low.

It was the visible outline of his arousal that made her breath catch in her throat.

His large hand wrapped around her wrist again, this time more gently. Her gaze snapped to his face and she jerked as something electric passed between them.

It was so unexpected that for a second, she couldn't react. She saw his eyes widen for just a fraction of a moment, telling her he experienced it as well.

The room suddenly felt small, as if there wasn't enough air for all of them. She wanted to lower her weapon and toss it aside so she had both hands to rub over his body.

In all the Fae she'd run into, none of them made her feel like this. It was as if she was just now waking, as if she had been waiting for him.

But if she gave in now, everything she worked for would be for nothing. She couldn't allow that to happen. Somehow, she pushed aside the desire flooding her body and recalled why she had a blade to his throat.

"Leave," she said.

Kyran didn't back away. "Give me your name."

"River."

"You're afraid of me, River."

She lifted her chin. "I'm not."

"I feel your pulse. It races. If not in fear, they why?" he asked with a knowing look.

If a simple touch from him could cause such a reaction, she could only imagine what might happen if he kissed her. The thought of a kiss from Kyran made her knees week.

Talin moved to the right so he could see her clearly. "River, we need the books to battle someone."

"I've spent half my life gathering these books. You're not taking them." To prove her point, she pressed the dagger against Kyran's throat, reminding them all she had a weapon.

A drop of blood rolled down his neck and disappeared into his shirt.

"If you have a Fae blade, then you saw the destruction on Halloween," Kyran said.

River gave a nod. "I did."

"It's only the beginning."

That she knew as well. It'd been foretold by one of her ancestors. "If you want these books, you're going to have to kill me. That's the only way they're leaving this room."

She was ready to defend what was hers at all cost. Then everything suddenly changed as four Dark appeared around them.

"Shite," Talin said as a sword appeared in his hand.

River ducked as one of the Dark took a swing at her. Kyran shoved her behind him as he battled two of the Dark. Out of the corner of her eye, River saw one of the Dark eyeing her with a grin.

She smiled and motioned him to her as she tossed

away her glasses. Let him think she'd be an easy kill. Let him think he could overpower her.

Let him think she was a mere mortal.

River slashed and spun, her blade cutting across his chest. The Dark snarled and reached for her. She wasn't quick enough though. His meaty paw yanked her back against him, but she didn't panic.

She threw back her head, slamming it into his nose. He growled in anger and tightened his grip on her neck. His other hand grasped her right hand and squeezed.

Her fingers grew numb, but River wasn't going to lose her grip. She tossed her knife from her right to her left hand and stabbed him in the belly, yanking the blade upward.

Almost immediately Kyran and Talin were there, plunging their blades into him.

River pulled her weapon out and watched the Dark fall and then disintegrate into ash before floating away as the others had. She checked each of the books to make sure none was damaged. Only then did she breathe easily.

"I think we need to talk," Kyran said as he came to stand beside her.

River faced him. "And I think you need to leave."

Chapter Three

Kyran wasn't going anywhere. There was a half-Fae before him who not only managed to get her hands on a Fae weapon, but knew how to use it. She also knew a lot about the Fae.

He heard Talin moving behind him, but Kyran was too engrossed with the librarian. River. The name evoked fluidity, refinement, and strength.

When he'd first seen her standing there with her dark hair pulled back in a bun so severe it looked painful, her black glasses, and the frumpy clothes, he nearly laughed.

Then Kyran saw her fight. She moved as if she'd been born to the weapon. With her glasses gone, he saw how pale her blue eyes were. They were a beacon in her face, drawing everyone's gaze to their odd color.

The battle had shaken her tight bun so that long dark brown hair hung straight and glossy down the middle of her back. Kyran wanted to sink his fingers into the length and grab hold of it, to keep her steady as he kissed her.

She watched him with one thin chocolate brow arched. With her hair down, she didn't look so stern.

She had impossibly high cheekbones and lips so full they made him long to have them on his skin.

Kyran lowered his gaze from her beautiful face and unusual eyes. The battle had done its damage to her clothes as well. The top two buttons of her shirt had come undone, giving him a glimpse of the swells of her breasts.

And bright pink lace.

He ached for

He looked at her plain blue plaid skirt and navy shirt. They were clothes an elderly human would wear. Not a woman like River.

But how he ached. For her.

To have her, to hold her.

To make love to her.

Kyran wanted-no, he yearned—to have her near again so he could inhale her fresh scent and femininity. They way she stood up to him turned him on as nothing else could.

Her pale blue eyes glittered with anger as she held the dagger to his neck. Never had he seen anything so stunning—or wanted anything more.

River.

If they were alone, he'd already have her in his arms, kissing her, touching her. He wanted to feel her melt against him, to feel her give into the attraction that had both of them in its grip.

Her lips parted as their gazes held. Kyran barely held himself back from reaching for her.

"We need to tell Cael about this," Talin said as he came up beside Kyran.

"Then go tell him."

River cocked her head to the side. "Both of you go tell him. I want you gone. Now."

"Not going to happen," Kyran said.

She raised her dagger in front of her. "If I have to make you, I'll do it."

"How do you know of us?" Kyran asked.

She glanced away. "The how doesn't matter. I do."

Talin made a sound. "Actually, it does matter."

"Why?" She shot him a look, her pale blue eyes pinning him. "Your kind comes here, sleeps with a mortal, and leaves without a second thought. You don't care how you left the mortal or the consequences of such a union. All you care about is your pleasure."

Talin shifted feet uncomfortably. "Those are a lot of generalities."

"Tell me it isn't true," River demanded. "Tell me the Light don't do that."

"I can't."

"Now tell me about the Light who return and see if they have any offspring? Or better yet, tell me about the females who keep the babies in the Fae world."

Kyran was amazed at how much River knew of their world. She was roasting Talin. And he wasn't keen on her turning that ire on him.

Talin shrugged helplessly. "The half-Fae offspring don't always have magic. They could never survive in our world."

"Then why mix with us?" she asked, her voice rising.

Though Kyran loved the sound of her Scottish brogue, he wanted her calm. Until she was in his arms. Then he wanted all that fiery passion unleashed. The mere thought made his balls tighten.

He took a step toward her, and just as he wanted, her attention swung to him. "Is it my turn now?"

"Leave. And never return."

"That's not going to happen. We need these books."

She smiled tightly. "Then I'll have to kill you, because these books aren't leaving this room."

Talin blew out a breath. "She knows of us, Kyran. Why not just tell her?"

"Have you lost your mind?" Kyran asked, looking at him sideways.

"Perhaps."

River motioned to the door with her blade. "I don't want to know anything. I just want you gone."

Kyran let just enough magic leave his hand to knock the dagger from hers. In the next instant, he had her up against the wall, their bodies pressed together.

For a heartbeat, he couldn't move. It felt so good to have her against him, to feel the heat of her. Then he made the mistake of looking down.

She watched him with wide eyes, her lips parted and the pulse at her throat beating double. Kyran meant to frighten her enough to help them, but all he'd managed to do was fill his body with lust.

"We're trying to be nice," he murmured.

Her mouth was so close to his. And her eyes. By the stars but they were even more amazing up close. He saw lines of silver in their depths as well as a thick ring of silver around the iris.

Their first look at her brought to mind anything but a Fae. Now that she was exposed, it was so blatantly clear he couldn't believe her disguise worked.

Thick black lashes fell as she blinked and composed herself. "I've gone to great lengths to keep the Fae out of my life. They're just books."

"We need them," he attempted to explain.

Kyran didn't want to steal them, not now, not after talking with River, but she was leaving them no choice.

She turned her head to the side, refusing to look at him. Kyran frowned. Her words disturbed him, especially when he put them together with her earlier declaration that she'd worked most of her life to gather these books.

"We need to go," Talin said.

Kyran glanced at him over his shoulder. "Don't touch a single book."

River's head snapped back to him. "What?" she asked in confusion.

"I get the feeling there's something important you aren't telling us." Kyran released her and took a few steps back. "The fact is, River, you're going to have Fae here."

Talin nodded. "And not just us."

"The other Dark," she said.

Kyran bent and retrieved her weapon. He held it by the blade and handed it back to her. "Aye, the other Dark. They were hunting half-Fae."

River's forehead crinkled as she pieced it together. "And killing us."

"Viciously," Kyran said. "Your concealment was good enough to even mask you from us, but the others know of you now. You're not safe."

"Great," she mumbled sarcastically.

Talin walked from one case to the next. "We could use magic to keep the Dark out."

"That might work," Kyran said. Then he looked at River. "If she remains in this room."

"And this is why I dress like this," she said with a roll of her eyes. "Almost two decades I've hidden. In one night both of you ruined that."

Kyran held up his hands. "We had no idea."

"No, all you cared about was getting what you wanted," she rebuked him.

Kyran exchanged a look with Talin before he said, "You're right. We wanted them to help us stop the Dark from killing any more half-Fae."

"Sure you did," River said as she went to examine one of the cases to make sure it wasn't damaged.

"Why don't you believe us?" Talin asked.

"You're Irish."

Now that intrigued Kyran. "We're Fae."

"Who have Irish accents," she said as she went to the next case.

Talin raised both brows high in his forehead and turned away with his hands up, leaving Kyran to sort through River's statements.

"It's how all Fae speak."

River didn't respond.

He watched her walk from case to case, growing more fascinated as the minutes passed. "My accent is why you won't talk to me or help us?"

"My reasons are my own." She straightened from looking at one of the keypads. "If you're going to take the books, make it look like a robbery. I don't want to be accused."

Talin produced a bubble of magic. "That's reasonable."

Kyran walked to him and shoved down his hand. Then he turned back to River. "We'll leave. But be warned, River, more of those Dark will be here looking for their companions and whatever else it is they want, which I suspect is the books. They'll eventually find out who you are."

"That's my problem."

"You know what the Dark do," Talin said. "Let us help you."

"Will you leave the books?"

Kyran shook his head. "We can't. I told you why we need them."

"And I need them to."

"Why?" Talin asked.

Kyran could see how upset she was, and he hated it. "You know you won't win against us no matter how hard you fight. We're fighting against evil."

She drew in a long breath and released it. Then she retrieved her broken glasses and put them in a pocket of her skirt. With the dagger tucked along her arm, she turned on her heel and walked from the room.

The door sealed behind her with a soft click. Kyran stared at it for a long minute.

"I know that look. What are you thinking?" Talin asked.

Kyran crossed his arms over his chest. "I'm thinking River White has something to hide, and she wants to make sure it stays that way."

"Aye. I get that same feeling. She knew too much about the Fae."

"But not about us."

Talin twisted his lips. "That's a good thing. More of Bran's men will come. They'll see the books and take them simply because we were here."

"I know." Kyran wanted to leave them behind. There was something about the way River spoke of the books that struck a chord deep within him. "We can't allow Bran to get ahold of them."

Talin briefly looked at the door. "She fought so hard to protect them. It feels wrong to take the books."

It did at that. "We're trying to keep her safe. If the books are gone, then Bran has no reason to focus on River."

"You hope," Talin mumbled.

Kyran dropped his arms to his side and walked to the case nearest him. The glass protecting the books was thick, blocking out the elements. "We take the books, but for anyone who comes to check, make it appear as if they're still here."

"I like that," Talin said.

Kyran knew that was enough for the humans to leave

River alone, but it wasn't going to keep her safe from others. If Kyran had his way, he'd take River with them. But he was certain Cael wouldn't be thrilled with him kidnapping anyone.

Nor would River for that matter.

Somehow Kyran was going to have to keep an eye on her. It wasn't just out of obligation, but because he couldn't deny the need to protect her.

Within minutes they collected the books and used magic to return everything to how it was. Then they teleported back to the caves.

Kyran led the way into the section where Jordyn's library was. She was bent over a table reading a book. She looked up at them and smiled.

"You found them." Jordyn rushed to take the ones from Kyran, but he held them away from her. She looked at him askance. "Kyran?"

He glanced at Talin, who nodded in agreement. Kyran then swung his gaze back to Jordyn. "Look through these as quickly as possible. We need to return them."

"Return them?" Jordyn asked in shock. "That's not what was discussed. We need them here."

Talin gently set his stack of books on the table. "We return them, Jordyn."

"It might take me months to go through each of these."

Kyran shook his head. "Then work faster. These are ancient texts that were being stored in pristine conditions. They need to be returned exactly as they are."

Jordyn threw out her hands to her sides, before letting them slap against her thighs. "I don't have that kind of facility."

"Then we'll see to it," Talin said.

Kyran handed his books to Talin to protect with magic. He turned away and found Cael blocking his path.

"Something you want to tell me?" their leader asked.

Behind Kyran Talin said, "We found a half-Fae."

"What?" Jordyn asked in disbelief.

Kyran blew out a breath. "It's the librarian."

"No way," Jordyn said in awe.

Talin laughed. "Yes way. You should've seen her fight."

Kyran could've kicked him.

"Fight?" Cael asked with a frown.

"Some of Bran's men arrived. They must've tracked us," Kyran explained.

Jordyn shrugged. "Or found out about the books as well."

That was something Kyran hoped to hell wasn't a possibility, because if it was, then Bran would eventually look for River.

Talin grinned. "You should've seen her, Cael. The Fae dagger is gorgeous. I don't know who taught her how to use it, but she's good."

"Really?" Cael looked between the two of them. "I think I'd like to meet this half-Fae Kyran is so adamant about returning the books to."

"Well, someone needs to talk to her," Jordyn said.

Kyran and Talin turned to look at her. "Why?" Kyran asked.

Jordyn held up the first book, opened to the middle. "Because it's in a language I don't understand."

Chapter Four

River closed the door and leaned against it. Her dagger fell to the floor as her fingers, numb from fear, lost their grip.

She looked down at her hands to find that they were shaking. A moment later, her knees buckled. She slid down the door to the floor and buried her face in her hands as the tears came.

Never had she felt so stupid and foolish. All those years of thinking she could handle herself if a Fae approached her. All those years of practicing. None of it did any good.

Aunt Maureen warned her that knowledge was power, but when it came to the Fae, it was all about the magic. River never really believed her. She put all her effort into the books, believing that was all she needed.

River learned her lesson tonight.

Not even the warding marks she learned from her books and inscribed with her own blood around the vault door prevented the Fae from entering.

She looked down at her clothes and squeezed her eyes

shut. Maureen cautioned her to dress ugly, to be ugly to keep the Fae away. For years that worked. What changed tonight?

River glared at the dagger. If she hadn't pulled the weapon there was a chance the Fae would never have discovered what she was.

That wasn't true. Kyran would have. There was nothing that went on around him that he didn't take note of and catalogue. He must have been laughing at her. The poor, pitiful half-Fae trying to stand up to them.

She slid her dagger into the sheath at her leg and yanked her skirt down. Then she got to her feet and wiped her face. Tears never did anyone any good. It was an emotional release because she couldn't scream her fury.

River squared her shoulders. Whatever came, she was prepared. Her family had suffered for generations because of the Fae. It'd been silly to think she would escape the curse.

She made her way to the back of the library and the entrance she used. After gathering her purse and putting on her coat, she walked outside.

Snow was piled along the edges of the sidewalk. Her sensible shoes had good rubber grips that kept her from sliding on the icy patches.

Since she lived less than a three-minute walk from the

library, she was home in no time. River unlocked her door and stepped inside.

"Great," she mumbled when she was met with cold air.

The heater was out again. It was the third time in less than a month. River was too tired to call the landlord or try to fix the problem herself.

She went to her stash of wood and started a fire in the hearth. When the fire blazed high, she dragged her chair closer and sat.

With her legs curled up and two quilts atop her, she stared into the fire. Her thoughts kept returning to one thing—Kyran. She hadn't expected him to be so nice. He could've easily killed her, but neither he nor Talin harmed her.

All they did was take her books. River couldn't even think about that. As soon as the board learned they were gone, she would be out of a job.

The work and time she put into finding her family's library was for naught. She'd lost what books she worked hard to acquire. Even then, they hadn't been hers. They belonged to the library, and thereby the city of Edinburgh.

River closed her eyes and moaned. She was going to make herself ill if she continued to think along this vein. Perhaps she'd call in sick tomorrow. It would be her first time, but she was going to have to start a new life anyway.

The wood popped in the fire, sizzling into the silence of the room. Just as she'd sizzled when Kyran was close to her.

He'd moved so quickly. She blinked and he was there, pressing her against the wall with his hard body. His touch had been firm, but gentle. A complete contradiction to what her aunt warned her.

River snuggled deeper into the quilts. She didn't fight the sleep when it claimed her.

~

Kyran stared at the books. Every one of them was in a different language.

"It's Fae," Cael said.

Fintan snorted, his red-rimmed white eyes passing over each book. "Ancient Fae. These languages have been dead for eons."

"Shouldn't you be able to use magic to read it?" Jordyn asked.

Baylon smiled at his woman. "If only it were that easy."

"There are some things our magic can't do," Cael explained. "With the humans, if you don't learn the language, it dies. That's what happened with our race as well."

Kyran motioned to the books. "We got cocky, is what

happened. The Fae believed these languages would never die."

"They didn't just die," Fintan said. "They were obliterated from record."

Jordyn pointed to the books. "There are twelve different languages here. How many were there?"

"At one time, over thirty," Cael said.

Her turquoise eyes widened. "How many are there now?"

"One," Talin answered.

Anticipating her next question, Baylon said, "The thirty languages represent the thirty most powerful families—both Dark and Light. The families warred. When one of them would win, they eradicated that language."

"So who won in the end?" Jordyn asked.

They were all silent. Kyran didn't like to think of the past, because his family played a major role in it. Only Cael knew the particulars, and that was how Kyran wanted it.

"We speak the common tongue now," Cael responded. "Every Fae knew the language. At the end, when there was hardly anyone left of the thirty families, the majority of the Fae rose up against them. It was the one time the Light and Dark were united."

Jordyn softly closed the book in front of her. "Then you can take these back to River. If I can't read them, they do me no good."

"But they were on your list," Baylon pointed out.

Kyran caught Jordyn's gaze. "Where did you find that list, by the way?"

"I did a search for all books containing any information on the Fae, fairies, Death, hell, and the Netherworld. I already had most of the books, and none of them offered anything that could help. So then I went to a black site and did the same search. A list of thirty books came up related to the Fae."

Cael's shock was evident on his face. "Thirty. I'll be damned."

"How did the books get into mortal hands?" Fintan asked.

Baylon nodded. "I'd like to know that as well."

"Kyran, didn't River say she'd been collecting these? She may know that list as well."

He could've happily punched Talin into the next millennia. Kyran didn't want River involved any more than she already was, but by the look in Cael's eyes, that hope went flying right out the door.

"Let's go pay River a visit," Cael said.

Kyran shook his head. "It's late."

"Which means she'll be alone," Fintan added.

Cael looked at Kyran with his silver eyes. "She's half-Fae, and you were attacked by Bran's men. If we don't get to her first, they will."

"She won't talk to us," Talin said.

Kyran nodded when Cael returned his gaze to him. "She buttoned up pretty quick."

"Then unbutton her," Fintan stated.

Baylon rubbed his hand over his chin. "I agree with Fintan and Cael. Whether she tells us anything or not, keeping another half-Fae alive and out of Bran's grasp is a good thing."

Each of them turned to the corner where Eoghan stood. He watched them with hooded silver eyes. After a moment, he gave a nod to Cael. It was all they would get from him. Eoghan didn't speak.

"Let's go," Cael said.

Baylon hurried around the table. "You've not told us if you caught the person responsible for helping Bran escape the Netherworld."

"We'll get to that soon enough," Cael said.

Kyran knew that meant whatever Cael had to say wouldn't be good. None of them could force him to talk now. Cael would tell them when he was good and ready.

"Do you know where she lives?" Cael asked Kyran.

Talin answered for him. "No. I'm sure she's left the library by now."

All Kyran had to do was think about River and a picture of her formed in his head. "I found her," he said and teleported out, not waiting on the others.

When he arrived at the flat, Kyran saw her sitting before a dying fire. He didn't have time to stoke the fire before Cael, Talin, and Jordyn arrived.

He didn't bother asking why Jordyn was there. Cael had his own reasons that he rarely shared with any of them. That was the responsibility of being leader to the Reapers.

"It's freezing," Jordyn said in a whisper.

With only a thought Kyran had the fire roaring. It would last until River left.

"There are too many," Kyran said. "She'll see all of you and freak out."

Cael shrugged, then motioned to River. "Wake her."

"She looks exhausted," Jordyn said. She took a closer look at River and blew out a harsh breath. "And different. She's stunning. I couldn't tell with the way she dressed and held herself."

Talin walked around the flat. "She did it on purpose to hide from the Fae."

"That means she knows quite a bit about us," Cael said, his forehead creased as he stared at River. "She knew a Fae would recognize her and went to great lengths to hide herself. I want to know why."

Kyran moved closer to River and squatted down. He'd already scared her once. He didn't want to do it again.

"She's not going to be pleased to see us again. She has something against the Fae and anything Irish."

"Wake her," Cael ordered.

Kyran put his hand on her leg. Her eyes flew open immediately, the pale blue orbs focusing on him. He held up both hands before him. "We're not here to hurt you."

"We?" she asked as she shook off her sleep. River sat up and looked around, taking in each of them. She paused at Jordyn and narrowed her eyes. "You never returned the book you checked out."

Jordyn made an apologetic face. "I don't intend to. I need it. It's in the library I'm creating."

"So you're the Jordyn who sent them after my books?" River asked, disdain dripping from her voice.

"Those aren't your books. They belong to the library."

River threw off the blankets and stood. "Same thing, sweetheart. I worked decades to locate those books. I dealt with the scum of the earth in black market deals just to acquire them."

Kyran was more impressed the longer River talked. She had backbone and a wealth of courage that helped her overcome a lot. He hoped it was enough to get her through what was coming.

River turned to face the fire, putting her back to all of them. "I don't care why you came, but you're not welcome. Leave. All of you."

Kyran looked at Talin who gave him a shrug. Both knew this was how it would go. Jordyn's appearance hadn't helped anything.

Cael walked quietly to stand next to River. He clasped his hands behind his back and stared at the fire with her. "My men tell me you disguised yourself to hide the Fae within you."

"It worked for years until tonight," she said without any heat.

"Who taught you that?"

River remained silent.

Cael turned his head to her. "You saw for yourself the Dark we're fighting. I'm sure you observed the Dark Fae who razed the city at Halloween and before. The Dark who attacked tonight are stronger and more powerful. They hunt those like you."

"We've been hunted from the beginning."

Kyran frowned and started to move toward her, but Cael held up a hand, halting him. If River had been hounded, it explained her reaction to them.

"No one is supposed to hunt any half-Fae," Cael said.

River snorted and cut her pale blue eyes to him. "Tell that to those who've killed my family."

Chapter Five

River should've known the Fae would find her. The fact they hadn't killed her yet was a plus. But there was little hope she'd last until morning. They wanted information from her, and until they got it, she would remain alive.

The Fae beside her was tall and striking—as all Fae was. His silver gaze was direct, his tone frank. As imposing as he was, though, she had to stop herself from looking at Kyran.

She didn't know what it was about the Dark that drew her attention, but she hated it. It was bad enough she associated with Fae, but to have a Dark turn her on? Maureen was probably rolling over in her grave.

"The Dark we fought tonight are killing half-Fae all over the world. They wiped out Jordyn's entire family," Talin said. "We want to protect other half-Fae."

She slid her gaze to him. "If you want my help, the least you could do is give me the truth."

Kyran held up a hand to stop anyone from talking. He moved toward River as Cael sidestepped to make room for him. "It's true we need something. The truth is, those

Dark want our group dead. They began by killing half-Fae to get our attention. Jordyn's family was wiped out. We saved her, and we'd like to save more half-Fae."

"Don't waste your time with me." She turned to him and met his gaze. "Let me guess. You can't read the books."

"Each one contains a dialect that died out thousands of years ago."

River inhaled deeply and blinked.

That's when Kyran nearly smiled. She could read them. He didn't know how, but that didn't matter at the moment. The important thing was that she could help.

They just had to convince her.

Kyran gave Cael a subtle look. The next second, only Kyran and River remained.

She looked around, brows raised. "Are they veiled?"

"They're gone. It's just us."

"So you can convince me to give up my secrets."

"So I can persuade you how much we need your help."

She sat in her chair and turned to the fire, resting the side of her face against the chair. "No."

Kyran didn't expect her to agree immediately, but the way she said the word, as if a gavel fell at the same time. The finality disturbed him.

"You will condemn other half-Fae to die?"

"Everyone dies." She glanced at him. "Even the half-

Fae."

He did a quick look behind him to see the kitchen without a single dish out of place. "That's true. The Dark are making them suffer."

"You're Dark."

"I am, but not in the same way."

She snorted, letting him know what she thought of that statement.

Kyran knew there was only one way to get River's cooperation. And that was to tell her the whole truth. "You act as if you know the history of the Fae. Do you?"

"Maybe."

He wished she would look at him, but her eyes didn't waver from the flames. Kyran walked to get one of the two chairs at the kitchen table and brought it to the fire. He sat and leaned his forearms on his thighs.

River looked sideways at him, then returned to studying the fire.

"If you do know our history, then you must've read about the existence of Reapers."

River lifted one shoulder in a careless shrug. "Maybe."

"That's what I am, River. A Reaper."

There was a beat of silence before she slowly turned her head to him. "The Reapers are nothing more than a Fae folktale."

"We're very real. There are seven of us who do Death's

bidding. We're a mix of both Light and Dark Fae. It's why I'm not like other Dark you've seen. Becoming a Reaper shifts a Fae's focus. We bind ourselves to Death and the group."

Her interest was evident in the way her pale blue eyes glittered in the firelight. "How does Death choose you? Or do you volunteer?"

"Each of us suffered a betrayal of some sort that resulted in our deaths. Before our soul left us, Death was there to offer us an opportunity to keep the balance of good and evil."

River looked down at her hands. "I'm sorry you were betrayed."

"I am too. However, it brought me to the Reapers. Those men—and now Jordyn—are my family."

Her gaze returned to him as her head leaned to the side. "How is Jordyn a part of this?"

"The Dark who attacked us tonight are led by a Fae named Bran. He was part of the first group of Reapers. Death had rules. A Reaper was never to tell a Fae who they were. If a Fae discovered it, that Fae must be killed immediately."

"Wow," River murmured.

"A Reaper could never have any relationship with any species."

River fiddled with the edge of one of the quilts.

"Meaning you could never have a family."

"Right. Our focus needs to be entirely on the Reapers and what Death asks of us. But Bran fell in love. When Death ordered him to kill the woman, he refused and turned half of the Reapers to his side. He then killed the original leader, Theo, and attempted to kill Cael and Eoghan. They survived."

River gave him a baleful look. "You can't stop there. I know there's more."

"Death took Bran. Cael and Eoghan thought Bran was killed, but Death instead took him to the Netherworld."

"A place he should still be in," River said.

Kyran nodded. "Aye. He should. He had help escaping."

"Now he seeks vengeance on the Reapers, right?"

"And Death."

River rolled her eyes. "He sounds idiotic to be going after Death."

Kyran couldn't help but grin. "That he is." The smile died though. "He attempted to trick us into killing the half-Fae by making Cael believe the order came from Death. When we didn't carry out the plan, he and his men began their annihilation of all half-Fae on this realm."

"How does Jordyn fit into this?"

"Baylon found her when the Dark attacked. He saved

her. We ended up telling her everything, and in exchange, she offered to use herself as bait."

River flattened her lips. "That's never a good idea."

"It was the only one we had at the time."

"Did it work?"

Kyran gave a single shake of his head. "It led us to figure out it was Bran, but in the end he cornered us and killed Jordyn."

"She looked very much alive a few minutes ago."

"Death offered her a position with the Reapers. She doesn't execute as we do."

River's exasperated look told him exactly what she thought of Jordyn. "So she's a Reaper now?"

"In a manner."

"She and Baylon fell in love, didn't they?"

Kyran sat back, surprised at her assessment. "How did you know?"

"A good guess. So Death changed the rules."

"Aye. Death realized if the rules didn't shift then history would repeat itself."

River folded her hands in the quilt. "Too bad Death didn't figure that out to begin with."

"Everyone makes mistakes. Even Death."

River returned her look to the fire. "Now you must find a way to rid yourself of Bran."

"When we become Reapers, Death gives us more

magic and power. Somehow Bran has passed that on to other Dark and increased his own in the process."

She shook her head and swung her gaze to him. "No. Bran wouldn't be able to do such a thing. It has to be either a person or item that is giving him that extra boost of power and allowing other Dark to have it as well."

"How do you know this? We don't know this."

"I read a lot," was her response.

Kyran rubbed his hands together. "You've obviously had some bad encounters with the Fae, and I'm sorry for that. We need your help, River. I know you can read the books."

She smiled then, though it held a wealth of irritation. "Yes, I can."

"How?"

"One member of my family every few generations has the gift. Those who couldn't read the books were told the stories to pass them down through the family until the next one of us who could read them came along."

Kyran blew out a breath. The answer to their problems sat right in front of him. "Will you read them to us? Will you help us?"

"Where were you or Death when my family was being summarily slaughtered? Every generation. I'm the last of my line. As soon as I have a child and it's old enough to know our secrets, I'll be killed."

Kyran frowned, thoroughly confused. "I don't understand. Are you sure it's the Fae doing this to your family?"

"Oh yes. I saw them tear my aunt apart."

"Your parents?"

"They were killed while I was away. That's how they found Maureen. They tracked me to her. They hadn't known of her until then. The Dark wanted to be sure there was no one left but me."

Kyran couldn't imagine such suffering. No wonder she had problems with the Fae, especially the Dark. "You said you've been tracking the books. Were they at your aunt's?"

"Yes. The Dark took great enjoyment out of stealing everything from me."

"None of this makes sense. It had to be a Light Fae who gave your family the Fae blood."

River remained silent, her gaze lowering.

Kyran closed his eyes and sighed. A Dark. When had there ever been a Dark who left a human alive? He lifted his lids and stared at River, seeing her with new eyes.

"I don't want your pity," she stated and once more looked at the fire.

"I'm not giving it."

"Good."

Kyran stretched his legs out and crossed them at the ankles. "You're needed, River. It's not by accident that you know what you do about the Fae and were put in our path. You're destined to aid us in this."

When she didn't respond, he tried again. "Think of all the innocents, like your family and Jordyn's, who were killed. You have a chance to help us put an end to such things for everyone. The half-Fae will no longer need to fear for their lives. And I promise you I'll figure out who has hunted your family and end it."

Her resigned look cut through him. "You can't do that. You work for Death. I doubt you'll be given leave to help me."

"Let me deal with that. Whether you help me or not, I'm going to find out why the Dark are hunting your family. And then I'm going to make sure it never happens again."

River swung her gaze to him. She tucked a long length of hair behind her ear. "Do I have your word you'll stop whoever is after me?"

"Aye." Kyran held out his hand.

River stared at it a moment before she leaned up and took it. They shook, her small hand in his. "Then I'll help you."

"Good. You need to get somewhere warm."

He didn't give her any time to change her mind. Kyran kept hold of her hand and teleported them to the caves.

She weaved on her feet. Instantly, his arms were

around her. "A little warning would've been nice," she said.

It took Kyran a minute to respond. Being close to her again was playing havoc with his body. She felt good in his arms, her softness against him. "Sorry," he mumbled.

Her eyes opened and clashed with his. Kyran had the insane urge to lean down and kiss her. Twice in a matter of hours. If he were smart, he'd put some distance between them.

Then again, only a fool would walk away from someone like her.

And Kyran wasn't a fool.

Chapter Six

"He did it!" shouted a male voice close to River.

She jerked, suddenly realizing she was standing in Kyran's arms and looking into his red eyes. River stepped away from him and took a look around.

The cave might be rough looking, but it was warmer than her flat. Fae magic was visible from the barrier that kept the harsh winter weather out to the hundreds of candles that hung midair casting everything in a warm glow.

Talin came up to her with a smile. "We're glad you're helping."

Jordyn walked up with a Light Fae beside her, who River deduced was Baylon. Behind them stood two men, one with long white hair and red-rimmed white eyes. He bowed his head at her, but didn't come closer.

The Fae who obviously led the Reapers strode to her from a connecting room, a smile in place. "We're glad to have you, River. I'm Cael."

"I'll do what I can."

"Of course." Cael looked around the room and motioned to Jordyn and her man. "That's Baylon. The white one in the back is Fintan. And next to him is Eoghan."

Eoghan didn't even acknowledge her.

"He doesn't talk," Kyran whispered in her ear from behind.

Cael spread his arms wide. "It's not much, but it's our base for now. We'll be here until Bran ferrets us out."

"Or we find him first," Fintan stated.

There was a half-smile on Cael's lips as he said, "Aye."

River smothered a yawn. She was sure she got only a half-hour of sleep before Kyran and the others arrived at her flat. They were in a hurry for information, but she was dead on her feet.

"Let's get started," Jordyn said and marched to the right.

River leaned to the side and saw a short tunnel that diverted to several openings.

"She's very excited," Baylon said. He ran a hand through his short black hair and smiled after her. "Jordyn hates that she can't read the books."

Fintan pivoted and went back the same way he'd come. Talin clapped his hands together and winked at her before he followed Jordyn, with Baylon on his heels.

"If you're not up to this—" Kyran began.

But River interrupted him. "I'm fine. Let's begin."

She felt Eoghan's gaze on her as she trailed after the

others. River looked into each entrance as she walked past. One looked like an office, another looked like a social room with sofas and chairs.

It was the third opening she came to that she found Jordyn standing in front of a large table with River's books. River walked inside, and even she was impressed with the number of books lining the shelves that took up all the wall space in the cavern.

As River moved further into the room, she looked at the books. Every one of them was about the Fae in some fashion.

"They're my collection," Jordyn said proudly.

River turned to her. "How many are stolen from libraries?"

Jordyn's smile slipped. "Only about four."

"Do you have any idea the funding libraries have to go through to get books? Most times books that don't get returned aren't purchased again. That means you've taken away someone else's privilege to read it."

Jordyn put her hands on the table and scowled. "Tell me, how many times was my book checked out in the last year?"

"That's not the point. You wanted it. There could be someone else who does as well."

"If that's the case, then we need to be worried," Jordyn said.

River nodded, the full impact of what she was involved in hitting her. "You're right."

"Now that that's taken care of," Baylon said. "Where do we start?" He reached for one of the books.

River reacted on instinct from years of handling ancient texts. "Don't!" she yelled, her hands outstretched to snatch the book from him.

"It's all right," Kyran said as he walked up beside her. "I protected them with magic. I saw what you did for them at the library. They'll not be harmed."

Baylon smiled as he opened the book and flipped through the pages. "It's like each page has its own protection spell. It can't be ripped, burned, or soaked."

"That's good," she said and dropped her arms to her sides.

Kyran walked to the table, his long black and silver hair shoved away from his face. "The books are important to us as well."

"Which one do we start with?" Jordyn asked excitedly.

River looked for the book that began it all. "It's not here."

"Looks like we've got eighteen books to find, lads," Talin said.

Kyran tapped the book nearest him. "Do they go in order?"

"In a manner. That's how I read them, but with our

timing, I don't have to start there."

Talin turned and walked from the cavern as he said, "I'll tell Cael we need to find those other books immediately."

"I'll go help them," Kyran said.

River nodded, unsure of why he was telling her. After a few whispered words, Baylon left as well. Leaving her alone with Jordyn.

It wasn't that River hated people, she just liked being alone. Others always disappointed her. Besides, she'd spent her life hiding from the Dark. Making friends wasn't part of the package.

"I'm really glad you're here," Jordyn said.

River looked to find Jordyn's turquoise eyes trained on her. Jordyn's blond locks were cut short, the pixie cut showcasing her narrow face and high cheekbones.

"Yeah." She removed her coat and walked around the table until she came to *The Hidden*. She took it and moved to one of the Chesterfield chairs where she curled up.

Jordyn had a laptop in hand when she took the chair next to her. "Were these really your books?"

"My family's, yes." River ran her hand over the cover. "I used to read them in front of my aunt's hearth. I knew they were old, but I had no idea I shouldn't have held them or read while eating."

"They've aged well."

"Aunt Maureen always cleaned them after I handled each book." Holding it again as she had so many years ago brought back a torrent of emotions.

River opened the book and the antiquated Fae dialect was as easy to read as English.

"What are the books about?"

She shrugged and glanced at Jordyn. "The Fae. It's the accounting of each family. Some knew more than others, but they all had knowledge, that when combined is important."

"How did your family come to have the books?"

River felt eyes on her and looked up to find Eoghan leaning a shoulder against the entrance, watching them.

"He's not being rude," Jordyn said. "He doesn't talk."

River kept eye contact with him as she told Jordyn, "I never thought he was being rude."

She recognized another soul who preferred solitude to the company of others. That wasn't the reason Eoghan didn't speak. If River had to guess, it had something to do with Bran's betrayal, or even something farther back.

His lips softened just a fraction as he nodded at her and walked away.

"You never said how your family came to have all thirty books," Jordyn prompted.

River shrugged and went back to looking at the pages.

"I don't know. They were always there. I never thought to ask how we had them until it was too late, and I couldn't get answers."

～

Kyran returned with three of the books. He was surprised to find he was the first one back. When he walked into the library, as Jordyn had dubbed the cavern, he found River asleep, a book opened on her lap.

Jordyn smiled at him. "I didn't want to wake her."

"It's fine, lass," Kyran told her as he set the books on the table.

While he walked to River, Jordyn was busy crossing off the books on her list. Kyran took the book from River's hands and closed it to set it with the others. Then he lifted her in his arms and strode from the library.

He took her to a room Cael had set up for her. The chamber wasn't large, but the bed was soft and warm. Kyran laid her down and removed her boots before covering her.

River immediately rolled onto her side and sighed. He touched her face before letting a long strand of her dark brown hair slide through his fingers.

What was it about her that pulled at him? It couldn't be her strength, because Jordyn had that as well. It wasn't just her beauty, though River was striking.

Perhaps it was the sadness she tried so desperately to hide. There was a wealth of hurt and anger there as well. Kyran still couldn't believe she agreed to help them.

"Do you trust her?" Fintan asked from the doorway.

Kyran looked over his shoulder at his friend. He glanced down at River before he walked to the door. "Aye," he told Fintan before he moved around him.

Fintan followed him down the corridor to the library. "No one else can read those words but her. How do you know she won't lie to us?"

"What would she gain?" Talin asked as he set his books down and faced them.

Jordyn nodded. "Exactly. Why lie?"

"She didn't want to help. Listening to Kyran and Talin, she was ready to kill them at the library to keep them from taking the books."

Kyran folded his arms over his chest as Cael and Baylon appeared in the room with the last of the books. "What are you getting at?"

"I'm saying she agreed too easily," Fintan said.

Cael leaned his hands on the table. "She doesn't trust Fae."

"It could be a ruse." Fintan lifted a shoulder.

Kyran shifted his feet wider. "I get your point, brother, but I don't think that's our problem."

"You've already considered that?" Cael asked.

Kyran rubbed his jaw as he tried to put his thoughts into words. "Not until Fintan said something. Talin and I spent the most time with her. There is a lot of rage there. It's in her eyes, in her voice, in her very breath. She's not a decoy of Bran's."

"You're assuming a lot from talking to her only a little," Fintan stated.

"Kyran's right," Talin said. "All she thought about tonight was protecting those books. She wanted us gone."

Cael jutted his chin toward Kyran. "There's something that concerns you. What is it?"

"If anything, River won't tell us everything. As Fintan pointed out, she's the only one who can read the books."

Baylon blew out a breath. "We need to earn her trust."

"That's not going to happen overnight," Jordyn added.

Fintan motioned to the thirty books on the table. "We've no choice but to take her word for it."

"She's here of her own free will," Kyran pointed out. "I promised I'd find out who is hunting her family. I need to discover who it is, and stop them."

"That'll go a long way in the trust department," Cael said. "What did she tell you about them?"

Kyran dropped his arms, unease running through him. Ever since he'd learned it was a Dark family, he'd had a bad feeling that churned in his gut.

"It's obviously the Dark killing off her family," Fintan said.

Cael's forehead puckered. "Kyran?"

"Aye, it's the Dark," he said.

Baylon said, "Then our next step would be to find which of the Light fathered the first of her line and their connection to the Dark hunting her."

"That's where we'll hit a snag." When every eye was on him, Kyran said, "It was a Dark who gave her family the Fae blood."

Chapter Seven

"A Dark?" Fintan asked in shock.

Kyran ran a hand through his hair. "I'm fairly certain I wore that exact same expression when she told me."

Talin shook his head in confusion. "Since when does a Dark leave a human after one coupling?"

"Never," Fintan and Kyran answered in unison.

A muscle in Cael's temple jumped. "We need to find the answer. I agree with Kyran, there's something going on here."

"How does River know it's a Dark?" Jordyn asked.

Kyran lifted a shoulder. "I didn't ask specifics."

"Let's find who is targeting her first," Cael said.

Baylon asked, "Can't we get that information from Death?"

Kyran shifted his gaze to Cael. As leader, it was Cael who ventured into Death's domain on occasion. Each time he went, Kyran noticed he was different when he returned. Cael was wound as tight as a bowstring and on edge. He hid it well—but not nearly well enough.

"We're Reapers. We'll take care of this," Cael stated.

Baylon gave a nod of acceptance. "Fair enough."

"I want to help," Jordyn said. She looked around at her books helplessly. "It doesn't state in any of my books about a mortal family being hunted by Fae."

Fintan's face twisted with anger. "The Dark do much worse for less. Can you trace her family, Jordyn?"

"Sure. River White, yes?" Jordyn asked as she punched in the name on her laptop.

As they waited for the results, Kyran thought over everything River told him. How she'd hidden in plain sight, how her great-aunt had taken extreme precautions.

"The list is pulling up," Jordyn told them.

Kyran grinned as he realized what River had done. "Don't bother looking. You won't find River on that list."

"She changed her surname," Talin said, coming to the same conclusion.

Cael said, "That would be the smart move if the Dark are looking for a certain name."

"Nay." Kyran frowned as he recalled her story. "She was at her great-aunt's in Ireland."

Talin's eyes widened. "Ireland?"

Kyran nodded to him and continued. "That's who taught her all she knows. Maureen had the books. From what River said, Maureen lived in secret for most of her life. Yet the Dark tracked River there and killed Maureen in front of her."

"Where in Ireland?" Jordyn asked as she began to punch keys on her laptop.

"Dublin. River would've been a child."

While Jordyn did her search, Cael looked at each of them. "We need to know what it is about River's family that has them being hunted."

"And why haven't they killed her?" Fintan asked.

Kyran swallowed. "River said the Dark allow one of her family to live. She said once she has a child and that child is old enough to know about its heritage, the Dark will come and kill her."

"Shite," Talin murmured.

Cael pointed to Kyran and Fintan. "Go to the Dark. See what you can find. Talin—" he began.

"I know," Talin interrupted. "I'll go to the Light court and see if anyone knows anything."

Behind them Eoghan clapped his hands and pointed to Talin. Kyran had forgotten he was even in the room. Eoghan was always there, watching and listening. It made Kyran wonder just what the silent Reaper saw that they didn't.

"All right," Cael said. "Eoghan will go with Talin. Baylon, stay with the women."

Baylon winked at Jordyn. "Fine with me."

"And you?" Fintan asked Cael.

Cael hesitated for a moment. "I've got a visit to make."

"Is this when you tell us about catching the one responsible for letting Bran out?" Kyran asked.

Cael shook his head and pivoted. As he walked away he said, "Not now."

"When?" Talin asked as he frowned after their leader.

Fintan slapped Talin on the back. "He'll tell us when he wants to."

"Which isn't right," Baylon said. "Not after what we went through."

Kyran had to agree. He walked into the corridor and looked down the tunnel to River's chamber. While she slept, he was going to find answers.

"Ready?" Fintan asked.

Kyran was anything but ready to return to the world of the Dark. "Aye."

Both used glamour to alter their appearance, Fintan so he wouldn't stand out with his white hair and eyes. Kyran did it because of his family. Even though it had been over six thousand years since he was betrayed, he wasn't going to take a chance of anyone recognizing him.

With a nod, he and Fintan teleported to the Fae doorway on the edge of the cliffs in the city of Portpatrick. Across the Irish Sea, Kyran could see Northern Ireland.

Fintan didn't falter before he walked through the doorway, which would lead them to the Dark world. Kyran took a deep breath and followed him.

As soon as Kyran entered the Fae doorway, he was surrounded by Dark. At one time, this had been everything to him. He'd put aside his own wants and needs for those of his family. The ever dutiful son.

And look where that had gotten him.

"You good?" Fintan asked.

Kyran was in the heart of the Dark—Taraeth's palace. He was far from good. It was a place he hated almost as much as his family home. "Nay."

"Me either. Let's get this done and return to the others."

"Agreed."

They proceeded along the extensive hallway, passing dozens of Dark. Kyran spotted Balladyn talking to the Dark king, Taraeth, and halted. Balladyn was a legend among the Fae. He'd once been the Light queen's most trusted and lethal warrior in her Queen's Guard—until the Dark captured him and turned him.

What made him of even more interest to the Reapers had to do with Rhi, the Light Fae Daire was following. Balladyn had been in love with her for ages. And he was endeavoring to win her love.

But it was Balladyn who had ambushed and killed Kyran.

Fintan blew out a breath as he too saw Balladyn. "I wonder how long it's going to take the Dragon Kings to discover Balladyn is in pursuit of Rhi?"

"Who says they don't already know?" Kyran glanced at Fintan. "Daire would know, but we've not seen him for weeks."

"And likely won't until Death has all that's needed of Rhi."

Kyran stared at Balladyn and Taraeth. "Do you think either of them are involved with Bran?"

"If Taraeth knew how strong Bran was, the king would have killed him already. Taraeth knows nothing."

"And Balladyn?"

Fintan crossed his arms over his chest. "He could go either way in this. Balladyn could've helped Bran, but to what end?"

Kyran cut a dry look to Fintan. "You know as well as I it's only a matter of time before Balladyn takes over. I'm surprised Taraeth hasn't killed him yet."

"Aye. Then again, Balladyn is the kind of Fae who does things himself. He wouldn't rely on others to help him steal the throne."

Kyran nodded slowly. "Balladyn wouldn't want to be indebted to anyone."

"Then there's no reason for Balladyn to help Bran."

"How long until Bran focuses his intent right here?"

Fintan released a long breath. "I'd rather like to believe we'll kill his stupid arse before then."

"Aye."

They continued walking, neither speaking. Being back at the Dark Palace was like opening doorways to his past that Kyran would rather have kept boarded and locked forever.

It never entered his mind to tell Cael another Reaper should be sent. He and Fintan were the only two Dark Fae. They knew how the Dark acted, how they thought. None of the other Reapers could learn to interpret the nuances of their behavior as he and Fintan could.

In all the years Kyran had been away, he found it humorous that nothing had changed. There were still the immense areas where humans were caged, moaning and begging the Dark to take them.

Even more mortals were on the floor, writhing in pleasure as Dark after Dark took them—killing them slowly. It disgusted Kyran.

"Don't look," Fintan said.

As if Kyran could ignore it. It had been part of his life once. Not looking at it wouldn't change any of that.

When Fintan stopped at the second of such areas, Kyran knew he was going in.

"This is where the information flows," Fintan said in a low voice.

Kyran nodded. "Right."

Fintan went in first, walking among the Dark and the

mortals as if he was still very much a part of the world. Kyran remained at the doorway. He leaned his shoulder against it and merely watched Fintan.

A female Dark rose from her stack of pillows on the floor and approached him, a goblet in hand. Kyran took in every detail about her from her average height, her straight black hair that just touched the tops of her shoulders.

The silver streaking her hair was abundant, the strips thick and wide. She wore a silver bracelet on her left wrist with a chain that connected to the ring on her middle finger.

Her red silk dress stopped mid-thigh and was of the highest quality. She showed just enough cleavage to bring a man's attention to her breasts, but she didn't bare herself like some of the lower-class Dark had a habit of doing.

She stopped before him and smiled seductively. "See something that catches your eye?" she asked in a husky voice.

Kyran looked down into her large red eyes. "Maybe."

Her smile widened at his words. For long minutes she stared at him as she drank from her goblet.

"Finish your inspection?" he asked after her gazed raked him from head to toe twice.

"Maybe."

He chuckled and glanced to where Fintan was talking with a group of Dark. "What does your family think of you being here alone?"

Her smile dropped instantly. "Excuse me?"

Kyran nodded to her bracelet. "No one here must know you're part of the Nighttail family or else they wouldn't talk to you. They aren't exactly a family who'd allow a female to venture to the palace unescorted."

"I don't need anyone following me or telling me what to do," she said tightly. "Is that why you're here? To take me back?"

"I don't care what you do. I'm here for information."

As soon as she realized Kyran wouldn't return her home, she relaxed. "Information I have loads of. I'll get you anything you want to know as long as you don't tell anyone I'm here."

"Sounds fair. Though you should hide that bracelet."

She rolled her eyes. "Already did that. My father made sure that it isn't just permanently on my wrist, it's now unable to be touched by magic."

That meant her father was mostly likely the head of the Nighttail family.

"What do you want to know?" she asked.

"I hear there is a group of Dark who hunts a mortal family. They leave one in each generation to continue the line, but then hunt and kill them."

"Why do you want to know this?" she asked, skeptically.

Kyran smiled. "So I can join them, of course."

Chapter Eight

"That doesn't sound like your speed."

Kyran pushed away from the doorway and smiled down at the female. "I'm in need of fun."

She hesitated. "This crowd I'm talking about doesn't allow just anyone in. And once in, they'll never let you out."

"Thanks for the warning." Kyran watched as she nervously glanced around. "What are you afraid of?"

Her red gaze jerked to him, becoming hard. "You're a male. You wouldn't understand."

He understood perfectly because he'd had a sister. Kyran remembered how she suffered, how she'd borne the weight of her obligations in silence and sadness.

"This is a bad idea," the female said and began to turn away.

Kyran reached out and snagged the wrist bound with the bracelet and chain, stopping her. When she didn't jerk out of his grip, he asked, "If you had a choice, if you were free, what would you do?"

"I don't know."

He smiled sadly. "You're lying. You've thought of it a hundred times or more and planned every detail."

She cocked her head to the side. "Who are you?"

"No one."

"Now who's lying?" she asked with a raised black brow. Her red eyes narrowed as her head straightened. "My father sent you, didn't he?"

Kyran released her hand. "No. I recognize the bracelet."

"And only those close to my family know what it means."

"Those in the nobility know it."

Her eyes widened as her lips parted. "So one of the other families have decided to help my father curb my . . . activities."

"Nay," Kyran said and shook his head. "At least not that I know of."

She swallowed and turned her face away, looking into the room. "I'd go somewhere no one knew me. I'd remove this bracelet and any connection to my family. I'd make my own decisions. I'd be the one to decide who I married."

"Removing the bracelet will give you freedom, but if you ever need your family, that link will be severed."

"I know." Her chest expanded as she took a deep breath. "I also comprehend I'll have no one to protect me."

Kyran spotted Fintan ending his conversation. "And if I could help you with that?"

"Why would you do that?"

"An exchange," Kyran told her. "I get you free, and you tell me who is hunting the mortal family."

The female closed her eyes.

Kyran gave a small shake of his head to Fintan as he approached. Without missing a beat, Fintan changed course and walked to a group of females.

"I'm Maiti." Her eyes opened, and she met Kyran's gaze squarely. "Don't make me regret trusting you."

He bowed his head. "Kyran."

"How soon can you get me out of here?"

Kyran nodded his head toward Fintan. "I've come with a friend. He'll help. First, we need to remove the bracelet. If not, your family will only track you."

Maiti rolled her eyes. "Did you not hear me? My father made sure no magic can touch this."

"Trust me," Kyran told her. He motioned Fintan over.

Fintan studied Maiti before he looked at Kyran. "I guess this means you found what you were looking for?"

"This is Maiti," Kyran said. "Maiti, this is Fintan."

Fintan took one look at her bracelet and said, "Night-tail."

"She knows the group hunting the mortals," Kyran

said.

Fintan's gaze slid from the bracelet to Kyran. "And I suppose we're to help her somehow."

"To escape my family," Maiti said.

Fintan let out a string of curses beneath his breath. He then put his hands on his hips and stared in a mixture of shock and anger at Kyran. "Have you lost your damn mind?"

"I'm helping her," Kyran stated.

"This isn't wise."

Maiti moved closer to them. "The family hunting the mortals is the Lightslayers. Does that ease your mind? Now, will you please help me?"

The room began to swim around Kyran. He couldn't catch his breath. Sound rushed like a waterfall in his ears. Suddenly, Fintan's face appeared in Kyran's line of vision. Fintan's lips were moving, but Kyran couldn't hear anything.

This couldn't be happening. The name couldn't be right.

But he knew it was.

As awful as the truth was, Kyran couldn't deny it.

"Kyran," Fintan called.

He blinked and was able to focus his gaze on his friend's concerned face.

Fintan's frown was deep. "You all right?"

"Aye." How could he be? Kyran was going to have to tell River that it was his family killing hers.

"We need to get moving," Maiti said.

Kyran followed her, his mind still reeling.

"How do you know it's the Lightslayers?" Fintan demanded.

Maiti shrugged and glanced over her shoulder at them. "I overheard my father and the head of the Lightslayer clan once. Another time when I was sneaking back into my house, I saw a group of Lightslayer men arrive, rejoicing at another kill. Rarely do Dark have blood on them when they take a mortal soul."

After she led them to a small corner in the palace, Kyran braced his hand on the stone wall and hung his head. Of course it would be his family. His father always had to prove to everyone they were the most evil, the most bloodthirsty.

Kyran blew out a breath. He'd deal with this later. Right now he had to remove Maiti's bracelet. He straightened and dropped his arm to his side.

"You weren't expecting that name, were you?" she asked him.

He shrugged. "I should've known."

"Do you know why they hunt the mortals?" Fintan asked.

Maiti chuckled wryly. "You're not getting anything

else from me until I'm far from my family."

Fintan looked pointedly at the bracelet. "That's got to come off first."

"Good luck with that," she stated sarcastically.

Kyran explained, "She's tried to remove it before. Her father spelled it so no magic could touch it."

"Wonderful," Fintan murmured. He flattened his lips as he shook his head at Kyran. "Do you search out the most difficult tasks? It must be your gift."

Kyran didn't bother to answer Fintan. Instead, he held out his hand, waiting for Maiti to lay her wrist in his palm. Once she did, he wrapped his hands around the silver.

Magic pulsed into his fingers. Strong magic. Old magic. But still not nearly as powerful as a Reaper's. Kyran pushed his magic against the bracelet. The magic in the bracelet fought back.

"We don't have time for this," Fintan murmured. He put his hand atop Kyran's and added his magic to the mix.

With both of them forcing their Reaper magic against the bracelet, the old Dark power didn't stand a chance. The binding charm faded away without much of a fight.

Kyran and Fintan dropped their hands. Maiti's gaze was on her wrist. She waved her other hand over the bracelet, and with a click, the cuff unlocked.

She removed it and the ring. Maiti held it for a moment, silently staring at the thing that chained her to her family for thousands of years.

"I'm free," she whispered in happiness.

Her smile began slowly but soon took up her entire face. With a few words, the cuff vanished. Maiti then looked at them. "How did you do that?"

"Magic," Fintan replied.

She rolled her eyes, her smile fading. "Smart-ass."

Kyran stepped in before Fintan could say more. "You're free to go wherever you want."

"There's a Fae doorway on the west side of the palace. Help me get there, and I'll tell you the family who set the Lightslayers on the mortals."

Kyran motioned with his hand for her to start walking. "Agreed."

Fintan remained ten steps behind them to make sure no one stopped them. Neither Kyran nor Maiti spoke in the ten minutes it took them to reach the west side of the palace.

They walked through dozens of rooms where numerous people saw them, and a few even tried to get Maiti's attention. She never stopped. Their pace was sedate, as if they didn't have a destination in mind.

By the time they maneuvered the corridors, dozens of guards, and hundreds of Dark, Maiti was frazzled. They stopped just inside the palace and stared out over a courtyard where a Fae doorway stood unguarded.

"There it is," she said.

Kyran glanced at Fintan to see if he knew where the doorway led. Fintan shrugged and looked down the hallway. "We got you here."

Maiti turned and smiled at him. "So you did. Who are you, Kyran?"

"I already told you. I'm no one."

"Perhaps. But I saw your reaction when I mentioned the Lightslayers. You know that family as well."

Kyran shrugged.

She shot him a quick smile. "You kept your word. I'm surprised."

"I had something to gain."

"You did," she replied with a nod. "I also get the feeling your word means a lot to you."

Fintan turned and whispered urgently, "Hurry up."

"You could've tricked me. I was desperate," Maiti said.

Kyran chose not to respond. "The other name, please."

"Who else but my own family?"

He bowed his head. "Thank you."

"I owe you, Kyran."

Now this shocked him. "We made a deal. I helped you in exchange for information."

"This information was nothing to what you and Fintan did for me." She stepped out into the courtyard and looked back at Kyran. "If you ever need anything, I'll be there."

Kyran watched her walk to the doorway and step through. He didn't know how long Fintan stood beside him.

"We could've gotten that information without helping her. She's a Dark, Kyran."

"Maiti reminded me of my sister."

There was a beat of silence before Fintan said, "I didn't know you had a sister."

"She hated the life of the Dark." Kyran turned from the courtyard. "Hated it so much she decided to do something a Dark never does—she was going to the Light."

"Oh, fuck," Fintan murmured.

Kyran took a deep breath and pulled himself from his memories. "Aye, we had to help Maiti."

"So your sister is a Light Fae now?"

Kyran shook his head. "She's dead. She never made it to the Light. She was betrayed by her family."

Chapter Nine

River woke, confused as she looked around. Where was she? It took her a full minute to remember everything that happened and why she wasn't in her flat.

She sat up and swung her legs over the side of the bed, her hands on either side of her. The last thing she remembered was reading one of the books. She must have fallen asleep. That meant that someone carried her to bed.

Was it Kyran? She hoped it was Kyran.

That drew her up short. No, she didn't want it to be Kyran. He was far too dangerous for her mind and body.

River stood and looked around the chamber. The bed was a simple iron bed. At its base was a bench with three sets of clothes folded neatly. The only other furniture was a table and chair off to the side where a large bowl sat atop the table.

She walked to it, amazed to find the bowl filled with water. River dipped her finger in it to find out how cold it was, only to discover it was warm. She had to smile, because what else would the water be with Fae around?

It wasn't until she began to take off her clothes that

she realized she wasn't the least bit cold. In fact, she was downright cozy.

River washed herself as best she could. Then she turned to the bench and the clothes. One was a set very similar to what she'd worn most of her life. It was her normal, her safety net.

The second set was a pair of jeans and a sweater. The third set was a black pair of pants and a shirt that dipped low in the front.

She shook her head, wondering who picked out the clothes. River wasn't surprised at all to find the sweater and jeans fit to perfection. She zipped the boots and stood, running her fingers through her hair before putting it in a loose plait.

Her stomach was growling viciously when she started toward the door. She was steps from reaching it when there was a soft knock.

"River?" Jordyn's voice said through the wood.

River opened the door. Jordyn smiled, then let her gaze wander down. The smile was gone and her face registered surprise when she once more met River's gaze.

"Wow."

River swallowed past her nervousness. "Did you pick out the clothes?"

"Yeah. I wanted to give you some choices in case you might want something different."

"Thanks." It had been so long since River had someone do something for her that the gratitude felt weird.

Jordyn waved away her words. "How about some food?"

"That sounds great."

She followed Jordyn through the tunnel. "How long have you been here?"

"This place is new," Jordyn said over her shoulder. "We were set up below Edinburgh Castle, but Bran found us."

That didn't give River confidence in the Reapers. She put a lot of faith in them to keep her safe. As long as she didn't have a child, she was relatively safe, but how long would that last? When would they get tired of waiting and just kill her?

If she never had a child, her line would die with her. Perhaps that was for the best.

Then she thought of the books, of how only she could read them. If she didn't carry on her line, no one would ever be able to read those words again. As much as that saddened her, it was better than knowing her family would continue to be killed over and over in the future.

River turned with Jordyn and entered another cavern that was set up with a table and an assortment of food. She looked over croissants, sausage, bacon, toast, eggs, cereal, pancakes, different pastries, and fruit.

"I'm guessing it's dawn?" River asked.

Jordyn grinned. "It does become difficult to keep track of time in these caves. I keep a watch so I know. The guys don't understand. I suppose it's my human side that likes to know what time it is."

"I think I'd be the same way." River grabbed a croissant and an apple.

"Coffee?"

River wrinkled her nose. "I hate the smell of it."

"I don't think I've ever heard that before," Jordyn said with a laugh. "Just tell Baylon what you'd like."

River carried the apple as she ate the croissant on the way to the library. They had a lot to do and only a little time to do it.

She settled back in the chair from the night before and looked at the books spread out on the table. Thirty books with different stories, each in a long-forgotten Fae language, and each with something in the pages that could help them.

"Do you remember reading anything about the Netherworld?" Baylon asked.

River looked up to find him at the doorway. "Yes. It's mentioned at least once in each of the books. Some just speak of it in passing. Something like the way humans would talk about Hell. The way it's worded, sometimes it seems as if they expected whoever was reading the books to know a lot."

"And in others?" Jordyn asked.

River pointed to the book in dark green leather. "In that one, there's an entire chapter devoted to it. It speaks about the horrors of the Netherworld. About how all Fae are terrified of that place."

Baylon moved into the cavern and picked up the book she spoke of. "Did any make mention of escaping?"

"No."

Jordyn sank into her chair with a sigh. "If you can get into a place, then you can get out."

"That was my thought," River said.

But Baylon was shaking his head. "The Netherworld is a prison."

"People break out of prisons all the time," River stated.

Jordyn made a face. "This is getting us nowhere fast. Who made the Netherworld?"

"No one made it. It just came into being like the rest of the universe," Baylon explained.

River finished her croissant and dusted off her hands. "Who decided to make it into a prison?"

At this, Baylon shrugged. "I don't know."

"Death probably," Jordyn said.

River leaned up, grabbed the green leather book, and flipped the pages to look for the chapter on the Netherworld.

"Do you really remember all that you read?" Baylon

asked.

She glanced up at him. "You're Fae, and you actually sound surprised at the idea of that."

"I am," he admitted.

"You shouldn't be. I don't recall all of it word for word. Some pieces stuck with me while others didn't. The Netherworld intrigued me, because you could read the fear each family had of it in the written words."

Jordyn tucked one leg under her. "You must remember a lot, because you know what's in each book."

"I couldn't recite the books front to back, no. You must understand that before I could read, I heard the stories. Once I learned to read, I devoured the books as often as I could."

Baylon leaned a hip against the table. "How often was that?"

"Up until I was thirteen, it was once, maybe twice a year. I used to beg to see Aunt Maureen more. She loved having me there, and my parents adored her. It wasn't that far to see her, so I never understood why we didn't visit more. Until she was killed, and I learned the truth. Every time I visited, I put her at risk."

Jordyn's smile was sad as she caught River's eye. "Apparently your aunt felt the risk was great enough."

"It killed her."

Baylon stood, his silver gaze direct and unflinching.

"The risks she took to teach you would've killed her eventually. She lived far longer than any of your other family."

"Yes." That was true. And River would probably live longer than Aunt Maureen.

Jordyn cleared her throat. "Do you have any kids?"

"No. And before you ask, I don't plan to. This ends with me." River looked from Jordyn to Baylon. "No one else will have to suffer."

"You can't be the only one who wanted this," Baylon said.

River looked away. Out of the corner of her eye she saw Kyran and Fintan appear. "My aunt and her two sisters vowed to end it."

"But your line continued." Jordyn frowned. "How?"

River picked up the apple and turned it in her hand. "Maureen's youngest sister, Mary, was gang-raped. They took her one night and kept her for a week. By the time Maureen and the family found her, Mary had lost her mind. She had to be committed."

"Damn," Fintan murmured.

"After my mother was born, Mary somehow got ahold of a razor and slit her wrists. She died before the Dark could kill her."

Kyran ran a hand down his face.

River knew exactly how he felt. It was her family, and yet there were times she could barely take it all in. "My mother was raised by my great-grandmother and Michelle, the middle sister."

"Not Maureen?" Jordyn asked.

River smiled as she thought of her great-aunt. "She was the one to initially take my mother to raise. I don't know how it was decided or why, but Maureen left the family here in Scotland and moved to Ireland."

"Smack in the middle of the Fae," Baylon said.

Jordyn made a face. "Not something I'd have done."

"But a perfect place to hide. They didn't look for her there. Between that and hiding her beauty, Maureen was able to watch my mother grow and learn her heritage from her family."

Kyran caught her gaze. "When were Michelle and your great-grandmother killed?"

"The day after my mother's thirteenth birthday." River didn't know what the significance of thirteen was other than puberty. They were too young to survive on their own.

"Did your mother know the family history?" Jordyn asked.

River nodded. "Of course."

"But she had a child," Fintan said. "Why would she continue the line?"

She wistfully thought of her parents. So carefree, so naïve. "My father convinced Mum that if they didn't speak of it to me, then the Fae would leave us alone. If I wasn't taught, then how could it be passed on?"

"But you went to Maureen's," Baylon argued.

"Yes." River set aside the apple, no longer able to think about eating. "That was Mum's doing. In her heart, she knew I had to learn. If she couldn't teach me, then she would make sure Maureen could. She kept it from Dad. He thought Maureen was from my grandfather's side."

Fintan's white eyes focused on her. "Whatever woman decided not to have children must have been per-suaded—or forced—in some way. The same could hap-pen to you."

"Why do you think I've taken such precautions to stay hidden?" River asked. She stood, the book in hand. "You laughed at my clothes before, but believe it or not, they helped."

She watched as Fintan's gaze slowly ran down her body from the sweater that gently hugged her to the jeans that conformed becomingly against her legs. When he looked back into her eyes, she saw desire in his gaze.

"It's not just the clothes," Jordyn said. "It's the hair, the glasses, and the attitude. You were still pretty though few noticed. Dressed are you are now, everyone would be looking."

"Aye," Kyran said.

River's gaze slid to him. She wondered what he

thought of her change in clothes. If he desired her, he hid it well—unlike Fintan.

While Fintan said and did whatever he wanted, not caring how it affected others, Kyran was like a caged beast. Waiting for the time he could escape and decimate everything around him.

Why then was it Kyran she found herself attracted to? Why was it him she wanted to look at her as if he could devour her with one kiss? Why was it him that she yearned to have claim her?

She looked for him when he wasn't in the room. She sought him out when he was. How? Why? She managed to stay away from guys after she graduated school in nearly every capacity. Why was this happening now?

"Oh crap," Jordyn said. "I left my laptop in our chamber. I need to get it."

River didn't move as both Jordyn and Baylon left. A moment later, Fintan turned on his heel and walked away. Leaving her alone with Kyran.

He moved around the table and came to stand in front of her. "You've suffered a great deal."

"My family has suffered."

"Aye. Now everything is on your shoulders. It's a heavy burden, but you carry it well."

River turned her head to the side and crossed her arms over her chest. "I don't want it. Nor will I put this on another's shoulders. It will end with me."

"Aye," he whispered.

She looked to find him within inches of her. His red gaze was hooded and focused on her mouth. Her heart skipped a beat when his finger caressed her jaw with the softest of touches.

"It will end," he vowed, his red eyes meeting hers. His head lowered slowly, almost as if he wasn't sure if he should.

River lifted her face, both eager for the kiss and frightened of where it might lead. Then she looked into his eyes. That's when she saw it, there in his gaze.

"You know who's been killing my family."

A mask fell over his face as he took a step back. "I do."

"Who is it? Is it the same one who began this whole mess?"

He gave a firm shake of his head. "Nay, but after I have a talk with them, their attacks on you and your family will end."

Chapter Ten

Cael strode through the jungle of flowers. He didn't carefully pick his way through as he usually did. This time he didn't care if he pissed off Death—because he was too furious.

The white tower rose toward the clouds, the sunlight nearly blinding. Bees buzzed, birds chirped, the breeze rustled the leaves.

But he heard none of it.

He reached the tower and tried the metal handle. It didn't budge. If Cael thought he could break through the oak door, he'd do it in a heartbeat. But it was fortified by Death's magic. Nothing was getting through that Death didn't want.

Cael took a few steps back and looked up. He saw the shutters open high above him. "You can't keep me out forever."

"Of course I can," came the soft reply behind him.

He whirled around and came face-to-face with Death. One of the fiercest creatures in the universe only reached as high as his shoulders. Death wasn't a skeleton or even a man.

Death was a woman.

She blinked at him with eyes a soft shade of lavender. Long, thick black lashes framed the unusual hue. Wide lips, full and alluring, didn't tilt up in a smile—though that wasn't out of the norm.

Hair as black as pitch fell past a slim waist to narrow hips. An onyx silk gown encased a figure that made his hands ache to touch. The skirt was full, as typical, with crimson edging the trim. It faded to black, mixing with the black.

He held Death's gaze, waiting. It wouldn't do any good to argue. Because Death never lost.

"Let me inside," he said between clenched teeth.

Erith sighed. She turned her head to the side when a dragonfly circled her face, the sunlight glinting off its iridescent wings.

She held out her hand, and the dragonfly alit upon her palm. To his shock, Cael saw her lips tilt up in a smile. In all the thousands of years he'd known her, not once had he seen such.

As if she realized she wasn't alone, the grin disappeared. A moment later, the dragonfly flew away. Erith slid her gaze to him. "I don't want to beat the information out of Seamus, Cael. I want to flip him to our side."

"He ventured into the Netherworld for Bran. Seamus

isn't going to switch sides so easily."

Death's head cocked to the side. "I can be very . . . persuasive . . . when needed."

Without a doubt he knew that to be true. It only took one look for males of all species to want her. It was one of the reasons Erith kept to her own realm where no one dared to venture.

All across the universe, Death was feared. And she used it to her advantage.

"I need to see him." The bastard needed to be gutted several times over for releasing Bran back into the world.

Death closed the distance between them and laid her palm on his chest. "Calm your anger."

Cael stared down at her in shock. The only other time she touched him was when he became a Reaper. Erith always kept her distance from anyone and anything. Yet she was touching him now.

He could feel the warmth of her hand through his shirt, sinking into his skin. Though he couldn't discern any magic being used, his anger began to fade.

She was so close he could see the dark purple encircling her irises. He could smell the scent of the flowers she loved so much clinging to her, as if they needed her almost as much as . . .

Cael didn't finish the thought. He couldn't.

Erith lowered her gaze to the ground before she

dropped her arm. She then stepped around him. The door of the tower opened as she approached.

He turned, watching her. He drank in every moment with her, because it might be a millennia before he saw her again. Seeing her, talking to her always affected him deeply. She had no idea how acutely he coveted every morsel of time with her.

Nor would she.

Cael's gaze followed the flow of her hair down her back, itching to touch a lock. He kept his hands to himself and observed how the train of her gown floated upon the air, inches from the ground.

Cael took a deep breath and slowly released it. Erith then paused as she began to ascend the stairs. She looked over her shoulder at him and gave a nod.

He strode inside the tower, taking the stairs three at a time to catch her. Halfway up, the sound of the tower door closing reached him.

"Don't say a word," Erith ordered Cael when she reached the fourth landing.

Cael flashed her a smile. "I always behave myself."

Her gaze cut him a baleful look before she touched the door with her palm. It swung open without a sound. Erith's chin lifted as she proceeded into the chamber.

Cael peered inside, not at all sure what he might find. He'd seen Death's mercy. He'd witnessed her anger. And he'd beheld her vengeance. The one thing he wasn't ever sure of was Death's mood.

He walked into the chamber to see it looked like a guest room one would find at a mortal's home. Cael remained by the door as Erith moved to the window where Seamus sat with his back to Cael, staring out over the beautiful sea of flowers below.

There was more silver in the Dark's hair than black, which told Cael how much evil Seamus had done in his lifetime. Seamus wasn't tied to the chair or otherwise bound. He held a mug of tea in one hand, sipping at his leisure.

Just what was Death about?

"I've learned more about you, Seamus." Erith stood beside the window, her gaze directed outside as well.

Cael raised a brow. Death already knew all there was about Seamus. It was her ability anytime someone came on her radar. With a mere word, she could have Seamus cowering upon the floor, begging for his life.

Erith must have a good reason for taking this approach. And Cael was curious to discover what it was.

Seamus shrugged. "Find anything interesting?"

"Actually, I did. As I told you before, I already know how you've made a name for yourself in the Dark world as a Fae who can procure anything. That takes a fair amount of skill."

Though Cael hated to admit it, he was impressed. If Seamus managed such a feat, then he was someone who could help the Reapers. No wonder Erith was going to such extremes.

Which meant, the Dark had no idea he was speaking to Death. Because Erith was taking such precautions, she intended to let Seamus live—if he could serve them in some capacity.

Erith leaned a shoulder next to the window. A brush of wind blew back strands of her hair. Cael stood entranced as sunlight fell upon the contours of her face. She looked wistful and frail in that instant. So much so, for that brief space in time, Cael forgot who she was and the power she commanded.

He had to stop himself from going to her and taking her in his arms. Cael needed to remember that Erith was acting for Seamus's benefit and nothing more. If there was one thing Death was not, it was vulnerable.

Seamus turned his head to Erith and watched her for a long moment. "I was pulled out of my home, which, I might add, should never have happened. There are dozens of spells not even Taraeth could break through to reach me."

"Only a man who has something to fear locks himself inside his home," Erith said, her gaze remaining out the window.

Seamus snorted. "Or a man who values his life. There are those who would gladly kill me."

"As I said, fear."

Cael was listening to the exchange with interest. He crossed his arms over his chest and leaned back against the wall.

"You call it fear, I call it taking action," Seamus said. "A man in my position must take precautions. By helping one Fae, I alienate others."

"What a lonely life."

Death's words caused a pang within Cael's chest. Lonely. The word hung in his brain, tolling through his mind like a bell.

He'd never thought himself lonely until Baylon found Jordyn. Seeing how happy the two of them were brought it all home. The fact Erith changed the rules for the Reapers so the two could be together was huge. Only he and Eoghan knew just how much.

"It's how I prefer it," Seamus said.

Erith finally turned her head to look at him. Her lavender gaze was focused solely on the Dark. "I don't believe you."

Seamus merely shrugged in answer.

Death walked to the other side of the window. "You have questions. As do I. How about we make a trade? I'll answer one of yours for one of mine."

"All right," the Dark said. He took a drink from the mug, his eyes never leaving Erith's face. "Who took me from my home?"

"I did."

Cael was surprised she gave Seamus the truth. The Dark's next question could very well be to ask who Erith really was.

Seamus nodded. "Your turn."

"Who contacted you about helping Bran from the Netherworld?"

At that question, Seamus's entire attitude changed. He stilled instantly. "How do you know of that?"

"We had a deal. Answer the question," Erith commanded.

Cael dropped his arms to his sides. Tension filled the room, all of it coming from Seamus.

"You can't know of that," the Dark said, fear filling his voice. "No one was supposed to know."

Erith lifted a single black brow. "We're Fae. We eventually discover the truth."

Seamus set down the mug beside him on the floor, then ran a hand down his face. "I received a message."

"From who?" Erith urged.

The Dark shrugged, shaking his head. "It wasn't signed. It simply stated that if I wanted to never have to fear for my life again that I should find the doorway to the

Netherworld."

Erith's gaze met Cael's before she returned her attention to Seamus. "When did you receive the message?"

"I've already answered two in a row. It's your turn to answer a question. How do you know of Bran and my helping him?"

Erith waved her hand and a chair materialized behind her. She gracefully lowered herself down. "Bran was never to leave the Netherworld. It came to my attention he somehow escaped, and it didn't take me long to discover who helped him. Now, when did you receive the message?"

"Thousands of years ago. It's taken me this long to find a way into the Netherworld. I thought the message was a joke at first, but I was curious. The more I looked into the superstition of the Netherworld, the more I discovered was fact."

Cael saw the tightening of Erith's hands that rested in her lap. The news disturbed her, but she was doing her best to hide it. Though there wasn't much about Death that escaped him.

"Who are you?" Seamus asked.

Erith released a deep breath. "Right now, Seamus, you're of value to me. If I tell you the truth, I'll have to kill you. I'd rather not."

"I'd rather you didn't either," he said.

"Good. Now, how did you find a way in?"

He glanced down at his hands. Seamus slowly fisted them before stretching them wide. Only then did he meet Erith's gaze. "By accident. There's a doorway in Dublin on the grounds of an old castle's ruins. I'd tried every Fae doorway I could find over my lifetime. I heard whispers of this one."

"And?" Death prodded when he paused.

"It's different. I almost didn't walk through it. It felt . . . wrong."

Cael frowned. Fae doorways were constructed by Fae themselves. So for one to be there, a Fae had to have erected it. Then Cael's eyes slid to Erith.

Or Death.

Seamus cleared his throat. "I'm Dark. Evil is part of my life, but there was something about this doorway that made me want to go the opposite direction."

"But you walked through it anyway," Erith stated.

Cael looked at Seamus. Had the Dark been paying attention, he would've heard the anger and censor in Erith's voice. Seamus would've seen the power she kept under wraps around him.

But the Dark was too occupied thinking of that doorway.

"Not at first," Seamus admitted. "I returned to it four times before I was able to step through it."

Death didn't utter a sound as her gaze narrowed on the Dark.

Seamus continued, unaware. "I found myself standing in what can only can be described as a large bubble. All around me was chaos, fire, and wind. None of it touched me, but I could still feel it. I knew then that somehow I was looking at the Netherworld."

Chapter Eleven

Kyran stood at the entrance to the caves. His promise to River reverberated through him. Even if it hadn't been her family targeted, he still would've made that promise—just to himself.

The roar of the sea below as well as the wind buffeting the cliffs was deafening, but he still knew River was behind him. He didn't turn around. Not because he didn't want to see her, but because he very much wanted her near.

Twice now he'd nearly kissed her. He couldn't put himself in that position a third time. He only had so much control. And those new clothes she wore that showed every wonderful curve made his mouth water.

"Would you rather be alone?"

She spoke softly, her Scottish brogue making him want to groan in need. Without thinking about it, Kyran shook his head. The next thing he knew, River stood beside him, shoulder to shoulder.

"Wow," she murmured.

He turned his head toward her and saw her rapt attention as she looked over the dark blue sea. Her eyes were wide, her lips slightly parted in wonder.

Had his face ever held such an expression? Had there ever been a time when he looked at something so beautiful and wanted to keep the memory forever?

No matter how Kyran sorted through his wretched memories, he found nothing. River had no idea how being half-human gave her the ability to find joy and splendor in such simple pleasures. A Dark didn't have that ability.

"No wonder you're here," River said, a small smile about her lips. She pulled her gaze away from the opening and looked at him.

Kyran struggled to breathe. He couldn't look away from her pale blue gaze no matter how hard he tried. River looked at him as if he were special. It was as if she didn't see his red eyes or the silver in his hair.

She made him feel as if his past had never been, as if he'd always been the man he was with the Reapers.

And she couldn't possibly grasp how much that affected him.

Their fingers brushed. A shock of something vibrant and brilliant, of something compelling and penetrating crackled through him.

River also experienced it by the way her eyes widened a fraction. There was no need for words, no need to try and question what was there. It hung between them like a dominant, evocative force that wouldn't be denied.

Kyran wound his fingers with hers. As one they turned toward each other. He stared into her eyes, losing himself in the pure blue depths.

With his other hand, he caressed up her arm to her shoulder and then her neck, her dark locks sliding silkily against the back of his fingers. His mind cautioned him to back away, but his entire body demanded he kiss River.

Slowly, he slid his hands into the thick tresses of her hair. Her face tilted upward as desire filled her eyes. Kyran lowered his head while his heart pounded in his chest. Her lids slid closed right before their lips met.

The first contact of their mouths was like the calm before a storm. It was a faint brush of lips, hesitant and teasing. Kyran pulled back a little to look down at her in shock and wonder at the urgent need swirling through him to make her his—in the most primal way possible.

River's hands came up to his shoulders and pulled him down. Kyran splayed his hands on her back and kissed her as he'd been yearning to do.

It started slowly, but quickly turned wild, the desire raging like a tempest between them. He couldn't get enough of her taste, of her smell. Kyran's cock ached to be buried inside her.

Her hands were everywhere, touching every part of

him. He groaned when her nails scoured his back through his shirt. In answer, she pressed her body tighter against him.

The feel of her full breasts to his chest made his balls tighten. Kyran held her tight, hating the clothes that stood between them being flesh to flesh.

He wound his hands in her hair and pulled her head back. She gasped and opened her eyes. Their breaths drowned out the sounds outside the cave.

The craving was so fervent that if Kyran didn't get them somewhere private, he was likely to take her right there.

As he stared down at River's lips, swollen from his kisses, there was no question she would be his. The fire within her matched his.

He teleported them to the cavern he claimed as his own. There was no bed, only a pile of pillows and blankets scattered on the floor.

River's hands were beneath his shirt against his bare skin in a second. Kyran's need was too great for him to take the few moments to discard their clothes. Instead, he used magic.

When she saw their clothes gone, River smiled and pulled his head back down for another kiss. Kyran released his hold on her hair.

Skin to skin, breath to breath. Each touch, each kiss

sent him spiraling into an abyss that felt like home. He didn't question the rightness of having River in his arms or the perfection of how they matched each other.

All Kyran knew was that he had to have her, he had to mark her as his. The need, the longing was driving every move and decision he made since he first laid eyes upon her.

Whatever fleeting thoughts he had about ignoring the feelings within him were banished the moment his lips met River's. Regardless of the consequences, he wasn't going to deny himself or her.

With a slight tug on her hand, he knelt. She followed, never breaking the kiss. Kyran kept one arm around her and used his other to brace them as he laid River down.

He groaned when River wrapped one long leg around him. Kyran loved the feel of her smooth skin and how it warmed beneath his palm.

Like a blind man, he learned her through touch. He felt the firm muscles from repeated use of her weapons. He learned the slender column of her neck and her slim shoulders. He counted each vertebra down her back before he leisurely caressed around her slim waist and over flared hips.

But it was her long legs that he couldn't get enough of. Powerful muscles were evidence of the many hours of training. The slender limbs made his mouth water. He stroked first one leg then the other, learning she had a spot just behind her knees that was ticklish.

Kyran saved his two favorite places for last. He deepened the kiss, settling between her legs. With great effort, he ended the kiss and rose up on his elbows to look down at River.

She'd been beautiful with her glasses and bun.

She'd been enthralling while she fought the Dark with her hair down and fire in her eyes.

But now . . . she was enchanting. With her lips swollen, her chest heaving, and her eyes heavy-lidded, Kyran had never seen anything more precious or stunning in his long life.

He softly caressed his fingers along her cheek. It boggled his mind that she was with him, that she wanted him. No Light Fae would look twice at him because he was Dark, and he had no interest in any Dark female after he became a Reaper.

It had been many centuries since he last had a woman, and he didn't want to do anything wrong. He wanted everything to be perfect.

His eyes closed when River's hand lay alongside his jaw. The emotions swirling chaotically within left him laid bare—and he hated it. After his family's betrayal, he swore he'd never open himself up in such a way again.

"What is it?" River whispered.

Kyran opened his eyes and looked down at her. "Are you sure this is what you want?"

In response, she took his hand and brought it between their bodies. She then pushed one of his fingers inside her. "Do you feel that? Yes, Kyran, I want you. *You*," she repeated.

He pushed his finger in further, feeling her heat, her wetness. Kyran pulled his finger out and circled her clitoris. A smile pulled at his lips when her eyes rolled back in her head and she moaned loudly.

Alternating between pushing his finger inside her and stroking her swollen clit, he teased her mercilessly. Her legs fell open, allowing him to see her dark curls and her glorious sex.

Her back arched when he added a second finger to the first. Kyran's gaze was drawn to her breasts. They were large and full. Her hardened nipples were a dark pink and begging to be sucked.

Kyran leaned down and wrapped his mouth around one stiff peak.

River gasped at the pleasure that spiked through her. Every inch of her had been touched by Kyran. His skilled hands brought her unimaginable rapture.

She couldn't catch her breath, the ecstasy was so overwhelming. River wanted to learn his body as he'd learned hers, but he hadn't given her a chance. Her body was an instrument, and he the master.

"Louder," he said.

Louder? What was he talking about? She wasn't making any noise. River forgot his words as his lips found her other nipple and began to suck.

Her hands clung to him, trying to hold on as she fell through a void of bliss that had her spinning out of control. The only thing keeping her grounded was Kyran.

The orgasm came upon her unexpectedly. It slammed into her with the force of a tidal wave. Her breath locked in her lungs as the climax swept over her, lifting her up and carrying her to untold heights.

It seemed like an eternity later before she felt herself back in her own body. She opened her eyes to find Kyran above her.

His red eyes were dark with desire. "I need you."

Her chest clenched. How long had she dreamed of someone saying those exact words to her? River reached between them and grasped his cock.

He was incredibly hard. If only she had time to explore his body. But that would come next time. For now, she was content to hold him for a moment before she guided his arousal to her entrance.

She watched in amazement as his eyes closed and pleasure filled his face as the head of his cock entered her. Then he pushed inside her.

The feel of him slowly stretching her, filling her made her heart skip a beat. When he buried deep, he opened his eyes. Their gazes met, and something profound passed between them.

River couldn't name it, nor did she try. She was living in the moment—something she'd never done before.

Kyran was a Dark Fae, but that's not what she saw when she looked at him. She saw a man who was devoted to his friends and his cause. She saw a man who was haunted by his past.

She saw a man who made her think of the future.

Their gazes held as he began to thrust his hips in a slow, steady rhythm. His thrusts were long and deep. Sweat soon glistened their skin so their bodies slid sensuously against each other.

The tempo soon increased so that she once more clung to him. Their harsh breaths filled the air with their moans. River was drowning in a sea of red, but she wasn't afraid. She was in Kyran's arms, and she knew he would protect her.

She gasped when one of his hands took a handful of her hair and tugged. He was straining as he attempted to hold back. But she was having none of it.

"If you want me, take me," she dared him.

As if the leash had come off, he growled and began to pound her body with his. He tugged her hair harder, but still she held his gaze.

"Together," Kyran bit out.

River smiled in response. As if it had been waiting for just such a command, her body stiffened as the orgasm exploded.

Kyran buried himself deep inside her, their gazes holding as the climax swept through both of them.

Chapter Twelve

River was afraid to move, afraid to even breathe. Because it might very well disrupt the perfect rapture she'd found in Kyran's arms.

As she rested on his chest with his arms wrapped securely around her, River almost pinched herself to make sure it was all real. But as she listened to his heartbeat, there was no denying the man—the Fae—who lay beneath her.

Had Aunt Maureen told her she would have sex with a Dark Fae and want it, River would've laughed at her. All those Dark she trained to kill to protect herself. She'd nearly killed Kyran that first night.

Well, that was a lie. She knew what she needed to do, but she'd been unable to do it. Even then, before she knew who Kyran was, she recognized something different about him. As if somewhere deep inside her she acknowledged he would help.

River drew in a deep breath. After all the generations of her family hunted and killed by the Dark, Kyran was going to stop it. He hadn't just learned who was killing her family, but he was willing to end it.

Why? No one, not even Fae, did things for others without wanting something in return. Was Kyran different? There were the occasional people out there who did things for others out of the goodness of their hearts, but she wasn't sure Kyran was one of them.

She thought back to their conversation about the Dark family who hunted hers. There had been something in his voice when he spoke of them. Almost as if he had a grudge against them himself.

Was that why he offered to help her? Because it would benefit him as well? What if it did? Why should she care? As long as she stopped being hunted, that was all that mattered.

"Does your mind ever stop?"

She couldn't help but grin. "When I sleep."

"I somehow doubt that."

River was suddenly rolled onto her back with Kyran leaning over her. His red gaze searched hers. She smoothed his long black and silver hair back from his face. "There's a fire between us."

"Aye. I felt it from the beginning."

Her hands lowered down his muscular arms then back up again to roam over his thick shoulders and hard sinew of his chest. "I'd ask something of you."

"Name it."

No hesitation, no reluctance. Was Kyran truly real or a figment of her imagination?

A slight frown marred his forehead. "River?"

"Tell me the truth. Always. No matter how much it might hurt me, I have to have honesty."

He gave a nod. "I give you my vow. And expect the same from you."

"I promise." She licked her lips. "I . . . I've steered clear of relationships for years, and I've never had one with a Fae. How does this work?"

Kyran rolled onto his back, his gaze on the ceiling of the cavern. "I don't know."

River remained where she was. She glanced around the chamber to see a few candles in various places hanging in midair. The dim lights created a sensual atmosphere.

And it also allowed her to feel hidden.

Because at that moment she felt more exposed than ever before.

"Let's not think too hard on what this is right now," Kyran said as he turned his head to her. "We have Bran to find and the Dark to stop from hunting you. After all of that is settled, perhaps we'll have an answer for this."

River nodded in agreement. "I like that."

"We should probably go find the others."

"Yeah. I need to continue translating the books."

Kyran rose to his feet and faced her. River drank in the sight of all his glory. He stood tall and proud and gorgeous. Every muscle was defined and sculpted from his shoulders that tapered to his narrow waist and hips to his legs. His long hair was mussed, but there was a small smile pulling at his lips.

He held out his hand for her. River accepted it, and by the time she stood beside him, her clothes were in place. She looked down at his chest, saddened to see his superb body once more hidden behind the clothes.

"You can't know how you've touched me," he whispered. The intensity of his gaze told her how much those words cost him.

River brought his hand up to her mouth and kissed it. "I think I do."

"No Fae knows I'm a Reaper. All they see when I'm around is a Dark Fae. And I can't stand to be around the Dark."

She covered his hand with her other one. "Because they're evil?"

"Yes. And because I was once like them."

"There's more to this story, isn't there?"

He glanced away. "All I wanted to do was please my father. He had high expectations for me, and he made them clear from a young age. I did everything he asked without question. I climbed the social ranks of the Dark quickly, and was sought after by many Dark families as a husband to their daughters."

River saw the strain on Kyran's face as he spoke. He didn't like to talk of his family or his past, that much was clear.

"I had no time for my sister or the rest of the family. I was too busy doing everything my father planned. He gave me assignments almost daily, and expected them carried out immediately. I got such a task one night. I was to find and kill the Dark blackmailing my family."

He paused, and she moved closer to him. Kyran now stared at a spot on the ground, a muscle ticking in his jaw. "It's all right. You don't need to finish."

Kyran squeezed her hand tighter and slid his gaze to hers. "I found the Dark easily enough despite the hooded cape he wore. I snuck up on him. I was furious that anyone would dare to blackmail my family. I didn't even bother to confront him. I simply plunged the dagger in the Dark's back. He collapsed to the ground, and the hood fell away to reveal my sister."

River could only stare in mute silence at Kyran. Pain filled his eyes and regret rolled off him in thick waves.

"Before she died, she told me she was going to the Light. She hated being Dark. I held her until her life drained away, her eyes saying all that her lips never could. Then I carried her home. My family refused to allow her inside the house."

"That's horrible," River murmured.

As if he didn't hear her, Kyran continued. "I burned her body alone. As I watched the flames devour her, I thought of all the times she asked to speak with me, and I didn't make time for her. I thought of how I readily did whatever my father wanted without asking questions. I thought about all the Fae I'd killed and began to wonder what they really did to deserve it."

Kyran pulled his hand away and turned his back to her. His shoulders sagged and his head dropped to his chest. "I killed my sister. The weight of that will never lessen. Her death made me reevaluate my existence.

"Nothing I'd done had been what I wanted. Not only was I uninterested in continuing my father's plan for me to climb the social hierarchy of the Dark, but I didn't like who I was. I couldn't look at myself in the mirror. And the hate for my family consumed me. I vowed then that I'd bring down Dark Fae like my father."

River fisted her hands to keep from touching Kyran. He obviously wanted distance since he turned away from her. But she wanted to be near him, to help him bear some of the weight he carried with him.

Kyran blew out a breath. "I began with those closest to my father. I looked into their dealings and associates. It didn't take me long to discover their treachery against their own kin. And I killed them. One by one. I should've been more observant, however. My aunt had been watching me. She alerted my father, who then went to Taraeth."

The king of the Dark. River shivered at the thought of him.

"Taraeth sent his best weapon—Balladyn. I didn't know I was being trailed until I walked into the ambush and felt the blade in my back. Balladyn didn't confront me. He simply killed me. As I'd done my sister."

River could no longer stand it. She closed the distance between them and wrapped her arms around Kyran from behind as she lay her head on his back. "I'm so sorry you endured all of that."

He covered one of her hands with his. "Dark Fae are evil. They do evil things to each other, but there is an unspoken rule that you never harm family."

She held him tighter, wishing she could take away his pain with a hug. "Families hurt each other all the time."

"They don't kill their daughters because they don't like their choices."

"Unfortunately, some do. I hate that you had to suffer such things, but look at the man you are now. You wouldn't be here doing the things for the Reapers without it."

He turned and wound his arms around her. "You really feel that way?"

"We said honesty, and that's what I'm giving you."

"Do you still want me?"

River rose up on her toes and placed her lips on his for a hard kiss. "Now more than ever. You were faced with difficult choices and made the right ones."

"It doesn't absolve me for my sins."

"You must learn to forgive yourself."

He kissed her deeply, fiercely. It was a lengthy, carnal kiss that made her wish they had more time alone, because she wasn't ready for any of this to end.

When he tried to end the kiss, River refused to let him. He spun her, pushing her back against a wall of granite. His thick arousal pressed into her stomach.

"I burn for you," he rasped between fiery kisses.

She moaned in response. His words sent chills racing over her skin.

There was a soft gasp behind them before Jordyn said, "Oh. Sorry."

Kyran ended the kisses and rested his forehead against hers as Jordyn's footsteps hurried away. They looked at each other and began to smile, which soon turned into laughter.

River couldn't remember the last time she had laughed in such a fashion. There hadn't been anything in her life to cause such a reaction. It certainly wasn't something she expected being with the Reapers or Kyran since he was such a somber Fae. And now she knew why.

His smile faded. "My eyes will always be red. My hair will always have silver."

Not to be outdone, River lifted her chin. "My eyes will always be blue. My hair will always be brown. Neither of us look like a Light Fae. And I'm okay with that."

He stepped aside, his smile back in place. They walked from his chamber together. River glanced at him often. To her surprise, his smile didn't waiver. It was one of those half-smiles, the kind that people didn't even know they wore.

And she loved it.

She'd given him that. River was proud of herself. Kyran deserved to smile. They all did.

When they walked into the library, River looked at each of the Reapers, wondering about their stories. Her gaze landed on Fintan, and she imagined his story was even worse than Kyran's—if that were possible.

But no one was looking at her. They all stared at Kyran. River moved to her chair and sat. She went to the first book in the thirty and drew it into her lap while covertly observing Kyran.

He had an easygoing attitude now. One that hadn't been there before, and by the way the others were acting, one they'd never seen.

Kyran looked up and met her gaze. "Ready?"

"Ready," she said and settled back in her chair.

River was ready—for whatever came her way, regardless if it was Dark Fae, Bran, or anything else. She had strength she hadn't had before.

Because of Kyran.

Chapter Thirteen

Bran was impatient. He should've killed Cael already. But it was enough that he slayed Baylon's woman. Bran smiled, thinking about how Baylon's bellow echoed around the flat that day.

How shaken Talin, Kyran, and Fintan had looked. The murderous expression on Eoghan's face. The best part had been Cael. He'd been shocked and enraged.

Those images were what kept Bran focused. Thousands of half-Fae had already been killed—and he was just getting started.

Searlas strode toward him, his boot heels resonating throughout the empty room. It hadn't taken much for Bran to convince the occupants of the manor to leave—and never return.

He stared out the window toward the North Sea and watched a storm rolling inland. By the way Searlas strode with heavy footfalls, Bran's good mood would soon disappear.

As his lieutenant approached, Bran turned to face him. The occupants hadn't just left the house, they also took all the furniture.

With a snap of his fingers, the study was filled with furniture, down to pictures on the walls and a roaring fire in the hearth.

Bran walked to the sofa before the fire and sat. A moment later, Searlas halted next to the hearth. "Spit it out," Bran demanded.

"The men we sent out for the books never returned."

What were the odds that the Reapers had been at the library? Next to none. Bran leaned back and spread his arms along the back of the sofa. "And the books?"

"It's magic making them appear to be there, but they've been taken."

Bran raised a brow as he turned his head to Searlas. "All of them?"

"The ones that you asked for, aye."

His men dead and the books gone. Coincidence? Not likely. "Bring me the librarian. She'll know something."

"I looked for her. She's missing."

"Cael," Bran said through clenched teeth.

How had the Reapers learned of the books? If they had them, then that put things in a new perspective. "Find Seamus. If anyone can locate these books, it's him."

"He's not returned to his home. I told you he disappeared."

"You told me he couldn't be found."

Searlas shrugged. "I went looking for him again."

It took every effort Bran had to keep his calm. The element of surprise he had was now gone. The Reapers—and Death—knew he was after them.

But he still had something they didn't—the need for vengeance.

Death obliterated the woman he loved. Bran was going to make Erith pay for such a transgression. Cael and Eoghan would experience their own special kind of torture Bran had thought of while he was in the Netherworld.

As for the rest of the Reapers, he would allow his army of Dark to kill them—while Death, Cael, and Eoghan watched.

Bran imagined how Baylon felt losing his woman. He would be nothing but trouble for Cael as Baylon struggled with the loss, anger, and helplessness.

"You're smiling?" Searlas asked in confusion.

Bran nodded. "I killed Baylon's woman. I know what he's going through right now, and that pain trumps anything the Reapers might gain."

"What's the plan then?"

"No one else could've gotten those books or killed my men. Check on the other books on that list. There are thirty of them, but I can guess they're all missing."

"Which means the Reapers have them," Searlas

interjected.

"Precisely."

Searlas crossed his arms over his chest. "How does the librarian factor into this? They wouldn't need her."

"You spoke with her?"

"No. She was helping someone else. It was another mortal I dealt with."

Bran leaned forward and rested his forearms on his knees. "Is there any chance she's half-Fae?"

"You know as well as I that half-Fae are beautiful. This woman was . . . plain. I'd have known if she had Fae in her."

"Then where is she?" Bran asked. "Where would she go? She has no reason to vanish."

Searlas lifted one shoulder in a shrug.

"We need to find her. Now."

Bran listened to his instincts that were shouting for him to locate the librarian posthaste. He didn't know why, but she was important.

The question was, did the Reapers know that as well?

～

Erith felt Cael's eyes on her as she took her seat before Seamus. Warmth spread over her where his gaze touched. She refused to look his way, refused to acknowledge that she felt anything.

After Seamus's confession about finding the Netherworld, she'd needed time alone. She left Cael in the tower and walked among her flowers—or so she told him.

That doorway Seamus found was created by her. It should've never been discovered by anyone. Erith went to Ireland to see the doorway for herself, and to her shock, something had changed.

It was now visible. Her magic wasn't losing potency, so what would alter it? She didn't have time to find the answer. Erith created another doorway to the Netherworld on her realm, then returned to Ireland and demolished the one Seamus used.

She didn't like the idea of the doorway to the Netherworld attached to her realm, but she no longer had a choice. No one else could escape from the prison.

Erith added a shield around the doorway so that anyone who might attempt an escape would be trapped and she would be alerted. It was a quick fix until she could understand what happened to turn her doorway visible to any Fae.

"You look troubled," Seamus told her.

She folded her hands neatly in her lap. "Your words trouble me. The Netherworld is a prison. Fae are sent there. No one wants to go."

"But everyone wants to leave," Seamus stated with a

small smile. "No matter how secure, every prison can be broken out of. You just have to find the way."

Unwittingly, Erith glanced at Cael to see his focus on Seamus. "And you found the way."

Seamus twisted his lips. "I've always loved solving puzzles. The more difficult it is, the more I dig in."

"That's how you saw finding a way into the Nether-world?"

"Aye. That's how I look at everything people ask me to locate for them. It's a puzzle. I excel at them."

"So I see." She took a breath. "How did you find Bran?"

"I didn't. He found me. I was in that place for only a few minutes, and I was turning to leave when someone shouted my name. I barely heard him over the roar of the wind. When he reached me, the wind and heat had burned off much of his skin and all of his hair."

She didn't flinch at the description. Erith knew exactly what the Netherworld could do to a person. "Was there anyone else with him?"

"No. I asked how he knew where the doorway was, and he told me he'd been looking for it."

"So he saw it?" At Seamus's nod, Erith felt as if she'd been ripped open by magic. This couldn't be happening. In all her thousands of years, her magic had never failed her. Never.

Why had it now? All of this was her doing. She led

Cael and Eoghan to believe she killed Bran. She hadn't wanted to explain at the time why she put him in the Netherworld. Neither of the men would've cared that Bran would suffer untold tortures there. All they'd wanted was his death.

But Erith wanted to punish Bran in the most heinous way possible. All would've remained as it was had the doorway not been visible to the Fae. If it had remained hidden as it was supposed to have been, Seamus would've never found it, and he would've never helped Bran escape.

"My words have troubled you even more," Seamus said.

Erith jerked her gaze to him. "Do you know who Bran is?"

"No. I searched for record of him in both the Dark and Light Fae, but found nothing. He told me I was lucky to have him as an ally and not as an enemy."

She didn't need to look at Cael to see his anger. It radiated off him in surges. "You're also a liability to Bran."

"Because I released him," Seamus said with a nod. "I've already thought of that."

"He'll likely kill you."

Seamus raised his brows and looked around the room. "I suspect that would be difficult here."

"Why do you say that?"

"I like puzzles, remember? Anyone with a brain would soon realize you're much more than a beautiful face. As nice as this chamber is, we're not on the Fae realm."

Erith didn't want to like him, but Seamus had a way about him that drew people in. No wonder he'd done so well for himself. "And for a Dark Fae, you've not been able to take your eyes off my flowers."

"I'm a complicated Fae," he replied with a smile. "Has it come time for you to tell me who the Fae is standing behind me? At first, I thought he might be here to guard you, but now I've come to the conclusion that he's here because of me."

She gave a nod to Cael who wasted no time in walking toward them. Erith would never admit it, but she loved watching him. Cael moved with lethal grace in everything he did. Even before she approached him to be a Reaper, she'd watched him, utterly enthralled.

Cael was a warrior, through and through. Deadly accuracy, alarming skill, and terrifying brutality. He was also fair and honest. A perfect combination.

He halted a few feet from her, but even that made Erith uncomfortable. Anytime they got close, she chanced forgetting the boundaries set. He made her forget everything—but him.

"Bran is my enemy," Cael said. "He killed my friends, and now that he's loose, he's coming after my group again."

Seamus rested his hands on his knees as he regarded Cael. "I know that look about you. Bran has it as well. Neither of you will be satisfied until one of you is dead."

"All I need is him dead," Cael said. "Bran wants me and my men lifeless. He's set about killing any half-Fae he can find."

Erith affirmed Cael's statement by saying, "Thousands of half-Fae have been killed in a matter of days. Bran has wiped out entire families."

"Because of Fae blood?" Seamus asked in alarm.

Cael snorted. "You've no idea what you let out of the Netherworld. Did it never occur to you that those Fae are put there for a reason?"

"What's your name?"

"Cael."

Seamus scratched his temple. "Well, Cael, you and I both know innocents get put in prisons all the time. How was I to know Bran wasn't one of those?"

"How dare—"

"Enough," Erith said over Cael. "What's done is done. It can't be reversed or changed. All we can do is stop any more damage."

Seamus looked between the two of them before he focused on Erith. "Is this where you have him kill me?"

"If I wanted you dead, I'd kill you myself. I don't need

Cael for that."

"But you do need him."

Erith chose to ignore Seamus's statement. "I'm going to offer you a place among us. This offer comes only once."

Seamus's red eyes were filled with intelligence as he looked at Cael. "How am I supposed to respond when I don't even know who any of you are?"

Erith stood. "I'm Death. And Cael is leader of the Reapers."

Chapter Fourteen

Kyran listened as River read aloud from the first book. He, Talin, and Baylon jotted notes. Normally Kyran liked to be out doing something instead of being cooped up, but this was different.

This was listening to River's amazing Scot's brogue as she read from a Fae book. Every so often, she'd look up and smile at him.

He knew the others saw, and he didn't care. River was helping them, just as Jordyn had. If Death had an issue with that, then Kyran had a ready argument.

It took hours for River to get through the first book. Her voice was hoarse, but she didn't complain. She rolled her neck from side to side before she rose and walked to Jordyn who was on her computer.

"Jordyn recorded her," Baylon said. "Next Jordyn is going to scan in the pages of the book."

Kyran frowned. "Are you sure that's a good idea? One copy of these is enough. What if the file gets out?"

"What if the books are taken from us?" Talin asked.

They had a point, but Kyran still wasn't sure about

having the books on the computer either. They needed to keep them out of Bran's reach—or everyone's, really. Having more than one copy could come back to bite them in the arse.

"Kyran."

He turned to find Fintan behind him. Kyran rose from the stool and followed Fintan out of the library and down the tunnel. "What is it?" he asked when Fintan finally halted.

"Is there something going on between you and River?"

"Aye. Is that what you called me out here for?"

Fintan's white eyes stared at him for a long moment. "Does River know it's your family hunting hers?"

Kyran glanced away with a sigh. He put his hands on his hips and shook his head. "I tried to tell her last night, but I couldn't get the words out. I'm embarrassed to tell her it's my family."

"Embarrassed? Or worried that she'll hate you once she learns the truth?"

There was that as well. Kyran regarded Fintan. As the only two Dark Fae in the Reapers, they had bonded quickly. Fintan kept everyone at a distance, but out of all of them, Kyran was the closest to him.

"You weren't a fan of Jordyn at first, either."

Fintan's face remained impassive. "I like River fine. I don't think there is a place for women in our group."

"It's just been by happenstance that the Reapers have always been men. I think if Death found the right female, that would change."

"Be that as it may, having attachments changes the dynamic."

Kyran dropped his arms to his sides. "I know."

"I watched the Nighttails today," Fintan said, changing the subject. "That family rivals yours for being messed up. It's a good thing you helped Maiti. Her father and brothers have let it be known that she's to be killed on sight for her embarrassing behavior."

Kyran couldn't believe his ears. "Does no one value family anymore?"

"Few ever did. You're an exception."

Kyran didn't want to believe that. Surely there were others out there who believed family should be cherished, loved, and forgiven. "Did you happen to learn who it was who dallied with River's family?"

"I'd need to get closer to them, and they don't trust easily. Only family members are used as guards around the property. Outsiders aren't allowed into the main house either."

"We need that information. Stopping my family from hunting River's can be done, but the Nighttails will find someone else to do the hunting unless they're stopped."

Fintan ran a hand through his long white hair. "Perhaps we first need to learn why River and her family have been hunted. Not the stories River's been told, but the truth."

"From the source," Kyran finished with a nod. "That means paying a visit to the Nighttails."

"The sooner it's done, the better."

"I'll be going in Kyran's stead," Cael said.

Kyran and Fintan turned to find him standing in the tunnel.

"Why?" Fintan asked. "We're the two Dark. We should be going together."

Cael walked toward them. "That's true. However, Death has requested Kyran remain close to River."

Not for an instant did Kyran believe that Death had given approval for him and River. In fact, he felt just the opposite.

"I'm gathering by your expression that something has developed between you and the half-Fae?" Cael asked.

Kyran wasn't going to hide any of it. Baylon tried that, and it hadn't done any good. "It has."

"That's what I suspected when she gave me this order. Don't read anything into it."

"I won't."

Cael gave a nod. "Good. Now bring me up to date on what's been going on."

"River has translated one book with Jordyn recording

it," Kyran explained. "Also, Baylon, Talin, and I took notes."

"She's working fast, but not fast enough. We're going to have to use magic and time to our advantage. There's something else," Cael prodded.

Kyran gave a half shrug. "Baylon mentioned that Jordyn was going to scan the books into the computer. They all think it's a good decision in case the books are stolen."

"Why do you have reservations?" Fintan asked him.

Kyran shifted his feet wider. "It's more of a feeling than anything. These books are important. Yes, there's a chance they could be stolen, just as we took them. If we have those scans, will we pay as much attention to the books themselves?"

"Probably not," Cael answered. "You have a valid argument."

Fintan snorted loudly. "River won't ever let those books out of her sight again. Those are her family legacy."

"And yet they don't truly belong to her," Cael stated.

Kyran looked from one to the other. "If we can stop her family from being hunted, she wouldn't need the books."

"She might want to keep them because of the past," Fintan said.

Kyran looked to Cael. "I know where we can put the books."

"With Death," Cael said as he nodded. "That's a good idea. No one will ever be able to get to them."

Fintan made a face. "Not to put a damper on things, but Bran knows how to get to Death's realm."

"Not anymore," Cael said.

Kyran waited for Cael to explain, but there was only silence. He and Fintan exchanged looks.

"Fintan, what about you?" Cael asked.

In quick order Fintan and Kyran filled Cael in on what Maiti Nighttail told them and Fintan's observation of the Nighttails.

"You did good helping her," Cael told Kyran. "Stay with River and guard her. I don't suspect it'll take Bran long to realize we have her. From there, he'll begin to wonder why, and then he'll set out to take her."

Kyran clenched his hands. "That's not going to happen."

"Exactly. We need River to translate all thirty books, and quickly. The rest of you will remain here guarding the women and the books while Fintan and I pay the Nighttail family a visit," Cael ordered.

Kyran watched the two of them walk away. He hadn't wanted to leave River, not after he'd watched Bran kill Jordyn. If not for Death, Baylon would be drowning in misery. Kyran never wanted to experience River taken from him in any form.

He turned and retraced his steps to the library. River looked up from reading when she heard him. Her eyes crinkled in the corners in greeting, but she didn't stop.

She read fast and spoke clearly. Even with that, it was going to take her days to get through all thirty books. But it was better than her translating them by hand.

Kyran tapped Talin to get his attention. They made the rounds of the tunnels and caves, adding magic to keep anyone other than Reapers, River, and Death out. Bran had snuck up on them once and heard their plans. Kyran didn't want that happening ever again.

He wanted River safe in the caves. He wanted all of them safe. They might have to move soon, but until then, this was a place that would offer them all a bit of peace.

They also took Cael's advice and used magic to lengthen time for a twenty-four-hour period to give River more time to read the books.

"River could go to the Fae realm," Talin said.

Kyran shook his head, his steps slowing as they returned to the library. "There's no place there that would offer her safety."

"Neither does this realm."

Kyran's attention was jerked to River as he heard something that reminded him of the Reapers. There was nothing spoken directly about them, and if he hadn't been a Reaper, he might not even associate it, but he made the connection.

He grabbed the pad of paper he'd been making notes on and saw where he'd scribbled a similar set of words. He began to wonder if the Reapers, like the Netherworld, were mentioned in all the books as well.

Perhaps he should pay better attention to what was being said. It wasn't just family history and accounts being written about, but important information sprinkled throughout. Too bad the families didn't make it easy by having a chapter on just such information instead of throughout the massive tome.

"Did you hear that reference to Death's crew?" Talin whispered.

Baylon walked to them and nodded. "I did. And it isn't the first time."

"Aye," Kyran said and held up the paper. "I heard it both times."

"Why not just state Reapers?" Talin asked.

Kyran shrugged. "Perhaps they thought it wise not to mention us directly."

"Each family goes into great detail about everything else," Baylon said with a frown.

"That's true. They talk of Fae doorways, where they're located, where they go to, and which ones that particular family erected," Kyran said.

Talin raised his brows. "So why not mention the

Reapers?"

"Maybe we didn't have a name?"

Kyran's frown grew. "These books are ancient. Death was around, but the Reapers hadn't been formed yet. The families couldn't mention us because we didn't have a name."

"Not true," River said as she stopped reading.

Kyran's head swung to her. "What do you mean?"

"Aunt Maureen told me tales of the Reapers."

Talin's face twisted. "So did my family."

River's smile was patient. "Every story Maureen told me came from these books. Remember when I said not everyone could read them? They learned to memorize the stories and pass them down until another one of us could read them."

"And the Reapers were mentioned by name?" Baylon asked.

"Yes."

Kyran shook his head as he tried to line up everything he knew. "That's not right. It's not what we've been told. There was only one group before us, and they were gathered together well after these families ceased to exist."

"I'm just telling you what I remember. It'll be in one of these books, and all of you will know the truth. Death is cited several times already. Whatever the Reapers were, they were greatly feared. Just as the Netherworld was,"

River said.

A bad feeling churned in Kyran's gut. Could this revelation about the Reapers be why Bran wanted the books? He had no need of learning about the Netherworld since he escaped. And though Kyran fully expected each of the thirty books to hold some vital facts or evidence on different things, none of that mattered at the moment.

River returned to her reading while Kyran listened aptly, trying to take it all in—the important and the nonsense. Because what was nonsense now might become important later. The families must've known the books would be needed later. Why else would all thirty write them down, each touching on the same subjects multiple times within the volumes?

Kyran first thought the idea of finding the tomes was silly, but once they had them everything would be fine. He now suspected they just opened a huge can of worms.

Chapter Fifteen

River lost track of time as she read one book after another. Her throat began to hurt, and just when she thought she might have to stop and take a break, Kyran was there. He handed her a mug and told her to drink.

She should've known it would contain some type of magic. Within a few sips, her throat no longer ached. She continued reading and sipping on the brew. Kyran never let her mug empty. Again and again he refilled it.

When her eyes became itchy and her voice harsh, they took a ten-minute break where River did nothing but sit there with her eyes closed, listening to the others go over all she'd read aloud.

With each word read, the stories came flooding back as Aunt Maureen had told them. There was very little changed from the telling to the book. It was human nature to embellish a story, but her family had done the opposite. Somehow, they kept the original stories through the generations from the last one who could read the books.

"How do you feel?"

River turned her head to the sound of Kyran's voice. She nodded but kept her eyes shut.

"Good. Keep drinking. It'll help your voice as well."

He sounded calm, but River knew it was a front. There were thirty huge books to be read, and only four of them had been translated. If she managed five a day, it would take her nearly a week to complete.

They didn't have that kind of time. Every day that passed was another day that more and more half-Fae were killed by Bran and his men.

River hated the human part of her that needed rest. She could work well past a mortal, but she couldn't keep up with a Fae. If only the Fae part of her was stronger, then she wouldn't need to rest.

"You're doing great," Kyran said, as if sensing her thoughts.

She appreciated his words, but that didn't stop the worry that surrounded her. River opened her eyes and leaned forward to grab the next book. She opened the cover and took a deep breath before she began reading.

It wasn't until she finished the fifth book that River realized something was amiss. She was still tired, but there was something different in the air that she couldn't explain.

River finished the last of the hot drink. When Kyran went to mix more, she found Talin staring at her from his spot near the wall. He sat on a stool and leaned back against the stone wall while he propped his feet on the table holding the books.

"Can you get through all of these?" he asked.

River stood and walked around to get the blood flowing in her body. "Of course."

"Tonight?"

"I read fast, but not that fast."

He gave her a flat look. "We're Fae, River. We've used magic to pause time."

"Excuse me?" Was that even possible?

Baylon mumbled Talin's name. "What he means is that here, in the caves, time is paused so we can get this done."

River frowned, her mind jumbling at the thought. "If time has stopped for us, won't it keep going for everyone else?"

"Yes," Jordyn said. "Pausing is the wrong word. Think of it as stretching. We've taken this day and stretched it. When dawn comes on the following day, we'll be back in alignment with everyone else."

No wonder River always hated science. It didn't make sense to her, but the rest of them accepted it as truth. Who was she to argue the point when she didn't even understand it?

She spotted Eoghan pass by the library entrance without looking inside. It was like he didn't care what they were doing, then again it was hard to read the Reaper since he didn't speak.

River piled the books in the order she'd read them, then she went to the next. The sequence had been ingrained in her mind from the very beginning. She hadn't understood why it was so important, and even now she wondered why Maureen had cautioned her to read them in succession.

Already there was much she hadn't remembered from the stories she read. How much more had she forgotten? Maureen told her it was all important, that she must retain it all, but River hadn't.

Because she'd been able to read the books, she hadn't retained the stories as her ancestors had. There could be a critical piece of knowledge that could help Kyran if she'd done as Maureen instructed.

She refused to think about it, because it wouldn't help any of them now. All she could do was get through each of the books as fast as she could.

River picked up the next book and returned to her chair. She gave Jordyn a nod to start recording, then River began to read. She hadn't gotten through the first page when Kyran returned with another mug of his special brew. She didn't know what was in it, and it didn't matter. It made her feel good so she could finish what she'd begun.

The idea of being able to help the Reapers gave her a purpose—something she needed. She hadn't realized she wanted it until it was there, but there was no denying it now.

At one time River thought gathering the books stolen from Maureen—or merely keeping away from the Fae—was her purpose. But the truth stood before her.

She had a chance to help the Reapers make a difference in her world as well as theirs. She wasn't going to let it pass by.

~

By the time the sun rose the following day, Kyran was antsy for River to finish the last of the thirty books. It was only the use of magic—and lots of it—that allowed her to get through all of them in one day.

And it had taken its toll on her.

A Fae wouldn't have needed magic. A mortal wouldn't have been able to handle the dose of magic used. A half-Fae could only take so much before the mortal part of it shut down completely.

"She'll be fine," Talin whispered.

Both Talin and Baylon had been saying that for hours, but no one believed it. Even Eoghan looked upon River with worry on one of his many passes.

When River read the last sentence of the thirtieth book, Kyran grabbed it from her and closed it, setting the book on the table with the others. He turned and found River already standing with a smile on her face.

Then her lids fell shut and she crumpled. Kyran easily caught her up in his arms before she hit the floor and strode from the library to her cavern.

Once there, he used magic to pull back the covers and remove her boots before he laid her upon the bed. Kyran pulled the covers up, then he leaned down and kissed her forehead.

When he turned, Eoghan stood in the doorway. Kyran glanced at River's sleeping form. "I'm worried."

Eoghan gave a small shake of his head before he walked to River's side and rested the back of his hand upon her forehead. After a moment, he looked at Kyran and gave a thumbs-up. As if that was supposed to make everything all right.

Kyran followed him out, asking, "What's that mean?"

Eoghan held up his thumb again and added a nod.

Kyran moved in front of him to block Eoghan. "Are you telling me she'll be all right?"

In answer, Eoghan gave a single nod.

Kyran let out a breath. "I gave her a lot of magic, but she's strong."

Eoghan merely stared at him.

"I know, I know. It's absurd to fret so. She's half-Fae. Each holds a different Fae aspect. I've seen her fight. She moves like a Fae. But we've never given so much magic to a half-Fae before."

There was no response from Eoghan. He merely slapped Kyran on the shoulder and walked around him.

To take his mind off River, Kyran went looking for Cael and Fintan in the hopes they'd returned, but they weren't in the caves.

"What is it?" Talin asked when he caught up with him.

Kyran didn't want to tell Talin what he was going to do, but someone had to know in case things went bad. "I'm going to see my family."

"What?" Talin shouted in shock. His hand landed on Kyran's arm, jerking him to a stop. "What the fuck do you mean, you're going to see your kin?"

"They're the ones who've been hunting River's family. I'm going to make sure they stop."

Talin stared at him for a long moment with a mixture of alarm and concern. Then he ran a hand down his face. "You know you can't see them. It's one of the rules Death gave us. No contact."

"I have to do this."

"Death will kill you. Or throw you in the Nether-world." Talin blew out a breath. "I know why you want to do this."

Kyran highly doubted that. "Do you?"

"Aye," Talin said, his gaze narrowed slightly. "You care for River, probably more than you should. You want to fix things for her, especially since it's your kin causing her so much pain. But you can't."

He looked at Talin more closely. Had the time his friend spent at the Light court wooing a certain Fae affected him?

"Why are you looking at me like that?" Talin said. "It vexes me."

Kyran ground his teeth together at that word. "Did you fall for the Light Fae Cael wanted you to seduce?"

"How the hell did this come back to me? We're talking about you."

"Now we're talking about you."

Talin snorted loudly. "I don't think so. You want to get out of talking about what you shouldn't be doing by turning this on something you think I'm doing or not doing."

"I'm not."

"You're vexed."

Kyran wanted to strangle Talin. "I am now. Stop using that word."

"If you go, I'm going with you."

Kyran closed his eyes in an effort to remain calm. He knew Talin was looking out for him, but what Kyran had to say to his family wasn't for anyone else to hear.

When he looked up at Talin, he was in control once more. "Nay."

"You won't be able to stop me. Besides, Cael told you to stay here and protect River. What will she think when she wakes and finds you gone?"

"I intend to be back long before then."

Talin scrunched up his face. "Why? So River can see Death kill you for disobeying one of her rules. She spared Baylon. Do you really want to test her again so soon?"

Damn Talin for making a good point. Kyran didn't want to die, but he couldn't stand there and not do something about his family.

"We go using glamour," Talin said. "You get to confront your family without letting them know it's you, and I'll be just another Dark watching your back."

It wasn't how Kyran had wanted to do this, but it was the right way to do it. "All right. Be warned though. Don't trust anything you see or hear from my family."

"The way your face darkens each time you speak of them already vexes me."

Kyran let out a growl of frustration. "Say it one more time and I'll hit you."

Talin merely laughed in response.

Chapter Sixteen

Cael arrived back at the caves in a foul mood. The Nighttails were as atrocious as he'd expected. And just as Fintan said, they couldn't get close enough to learn anything.

Until Cael used glamour to get inside.

Within the confines of the Nighttail house, Cael couldn't wait to get out. Evil fairly bled from the walls. How anyone living with such maliciousness every day could manage not to be as vindictive as the monarch of that family boggled his mind.

Yet the youngest Nighttail daughter had done just that.

Cael stood in the large cavern quietly going over everything in his mind from gaining entrance into the house, to speaking to Nolan, the head of the Nighttail family, to learning the darkest secret of the family.

"How'd you do it?" Fintan asked.

Cael had forgotten he was there. He faced Fintan and smiled. "I told Nolan exactly what he wanted to hear. I led him to believe he was the greatest Dark who ever lived, and that he ran his family exactly as a Dark should."

"You fed his ego," Fintan said with a grin.

"Nolan isn't as tough as he lets everyone believe. Men like him are all the same. They want their egos stroked."

Fintan flattened his lips. "That's all it took to get him to divulge family secrets?"

"It took a little more finesse," Cael said with a grin. "Let's find the others, and I'll fill everyone in."

He turned and Erith was suddenly standing before him. This time her black dress faded to gold from her knees down. It plunged deep at the front, giving him a glimpse of the swells of her breasts—and made his balls tighten in response.

"You need to find Kyran and Talin immediately," she stated.

Cael frowned at her words. "They're here."

"No," she said. "They went to Kyran's family."

Fintan growled, then said, "Fuck. I knew he'd do it."

Cael pointed to Fintan and said, "Remain here. Don't leave until I return."

In a blink, Cael put his Dark glamour back in place and teleported to the Dark side of the Fae realm and the Lightslayer clan. Despite both Kyran and Talin using glamour to disguise themselves, Cael was able to pick them out.

He appeared in front of them as they approached the large mansion that used to be Kyran's home.

"Fuck," Kyran mumbled.

Talin jumped back before running into Cael. "I do believe he's vexed, Kyran."

"No shit," Kyran replied.

Cael looked from one to the other. "You know you can't be here."

"I have to do this," Kyran said. "I disguised myself."

"It doesn't matter."

Kyran moved closer until they stood nose to nose. "It does. And you know why. All of that, and then to learn it's my fucked-up family who has been hunting and killing River's? I have to do this."

Cael swallowed and looked away. He understood why Kyran felt such a need. Cael would as well in his place, but that still didn't change anything.

"None of them will know it's him," Talin said. "The whole point of Death wanting us to stay away from our families was so they didn't know it was us."

"I know exactly what my rules mean," Erith said from behind them.

Cael wondered how long she'd been there. She wouldn't look at him, however. Her gaze was locked on Kyran as she walked around him to stand next to Cael.

"May I plead my case?" Kyran asked.

Death inclined her head.

Kyran looked at the house and grimaced. "I never

wanted to see this place again. I never want to see anyone in my family again. After what they did to me, I chose not to be a part of them even before I was killed."

"Then why come now?" Erith asked.

Cael couldn't take his gaze off Death. Anyone looking her way would see just another Dark female. But Cael was used to seeing her long, wavy black hair and lavender eyes.

It was disturbing to see her disguised, with the thick stripes of silver in her hair and the red eyes that were focused on Kyran, as if Cael didn't exist at all.

Why had she sent him if she planned to come herself? Or was this some test? Neither pleased him.

Kyran took a deep breath and met Death's gaze. "My family has done enough damage. They need to be stopped. I know them. I know when they issue false promises."

"Now isn't the time," Erith said. "Return to the caves. Now."

With that, she disappeared.

Cael put a hand on Kyran's arm when he tried to walk around him. "You heard Death."

"I'm right here," Kyran argued. "It won't take me long."

"Now isn't the time," Cael repeated Erith's words.

Talin grimaced. "Cael, let him do this."

Cael looked at each of them. "I learned a long time ago

to read into Death's words. *Now* isn't the time. She didn't say you couldn't, Kyran, only not now."

"All right," Kyran said, and teleported away.

Talin blew out a breath. "We need to watch him. He'll confront them."

"I know," Cael said.

But Kyran wouldn't be alone. Cael would be with him.

∿

River woke and simply lay upon the bed unmoving. All thirty books were translated. The Reapers had no more use of her. There was no reason to remain in the caves.

And that made her feel so wretched that tears stung her eyes.

She didn't want to leave. For once in her life she wasn't worried about a Dark hunting and killing her. She knew with the Reapers she was safe.

The burden of hiding and pretending had fallen away. She hadn't realized what a heavy load it was until it was gone. How could she go back to her life before? She couldn't. She wouldn't.

Even if Kyran did manage to stop the Dark family from hunting her, she'd never really believe she was free. The moment she let her guard down is when they would strike. Kyran might stop one Dark family, but he couldn't stop them all.

The only way for River to make sure this ended was to remain as detached as ever. She was never having children, so she didn't have to worry about the curse falling upon another's shoulders.

River rolled onto her back. Out of the corner of her eye she saw movement and gasped when she turned her head and spotted a woman so breathtakingly beautiful, there were no words to describe her.

"Hello, River," she said with a softening of her lips at the corners.

"Hello."

River gazed into lavender eyes and knew this woman was much more than a Fae. The fact she was in the caves must mean the Reapers allowed her inside.

The woman walked around the foot of the bed and stopped. River spotted an ebony lace and silk gown draped along the woman's petite form. Her jet black hair matched the gown so perfectly, they blended together.

"Do you know who I am?" she asked.

River shook her head as she sat up to lean against the iron headboard. "No."

"My name is Erith, though many know me by my other name—Death."

River's mouth parted in shock. *This* was Death? This magnificent, tiny individual ruled the Reapers? Then

River looked past the beauty and saw the spine of steel, the determination in Erith's gaze. Yes, this woman was certainly Death, because who else would dare to take on such a role?

"I wasn't expecting a visit," River said.

Erith stood elegantly. "I thought it'd be better if you and I spoke alone before the lads knew."

"All the books are translated."

She held up a hand to stop River. "I never had a doubt you would translate them. That's not why I'm here."

"Oh." River wondered if this was when Death would send her away. Would she be able to say good-bye to Kyran? She really hoped so.

"Tell me, River, what do you see in your future?"

Future? Was Death joking? River looked for a smile, a hint that Erith wasn't serious, but there was nothing. "More of what I've had."

"Really? That's all you see?" Death said with a hint of surprise.

River shrugged. "I'm the last of my family. I'm going to be the one to ensure that the Dark can't hunt us anymore."

"That's an admirable plan, but it's going to be a little difficult."

"I've made sure of it."

"Until Kyran."

For the second time in minutes, River was astonished into silence.

Death walked around the bed and placed her hand on River's stomach. "Yes, my dear, you're carrying Kyran's child."

River wasn't sure how to feel. There was excitement at the prospect of having a life growing inside her that was a part of Kyran.

Then she remembered what it was to be born into her family.

"Do you trust Kyran?" Erith asked, removing her hand.

River put her hands protectively over her stomach. "Yes."

"Then have faith that he'll take care of the Dark hunting your family."

"Then I'll be safe?"

A black brow rose. "I didn't say that. There's still Bran, and he's intelligent enough to figure out what part you play in all of this. He'll be coming for you."

"Then I'll be ready."

"*We'll* be ready," she corrected.

River swallowed. "Are you angry about Kyran and me?"

Death resumed her spot at the foot of the bed. "You know why I put those rules in place, don't you?"

"Yes. They made sense."

"At one time, they did. Until I realized that history was doomed to repeat itself. No one is meant to be alone. All of you—human and Fae—were born for someone."

River noticed that Death didn't include herself, but she didn't question it. There were some things better left unsaid.

"Even my Reapers," Erith said. "Jordyn is a benefit to the group. Will she become a liability one day? Possibly. But she's strong and determined. Just as you are."

"Are you telling me I'm a part of this group now?"

One corner of Death's mouth lifted in a smile. "That will be up to you and Kyran. You're carrying his child. No matter how hard you try to keep that secret, Bran will find out."

"Unless we stop him."

Erith's smile grew. "Exactly. I hear you're an excellent fighter. Be ready, River. You'll be called upon."

River blinked and Death was gone. She looked down at her stomach. Pregnant. She was pregnant? After all the precautions she took, it had been the last thing she'd been thinking when she was with Kyran.

All she wanted was him, to get as close to him as she could. The fire, the passion between them ran hot and fierce. No wonder she hadn't been thinking about protecting herself from getting with child.

Though it was going to be tough, she didn't regret the child growing within her. Now more than ever she needed to stop Bran. She was tired of hiding, tired of worrying about someone coming after her.

If it was the last thing she did, she was going to make sure her child never had the same fears. Her child would know only love and happiness and peace in their childhood.

River threw off the covers and stood. When she looked up, Kyran was walking into her chamber.

Without a word, he strode to her and pulled her against him. She held him tight, giving him the comfort he needed.

"Is everything all right?"

"It is now," he said.

Chapter Seventeen

Bran watched the rain as it trickled down the window. In order for him to find the Reapers, he needed to think like Cael. Cael might be a worthy opponent, but he was also predictable.

Since the Reapers' regular places where they used to gather were now compromised, that meant Cael would take them somewhere completely different.

There were a number of places Cael might have gone, but Bran knew the Reapers were still in Scotland—and not far from Edinburgh.

Too much was happening in Edinburgh for the Reapers to leave. With the librarian and the books Bran sought now gone, it affirmed what he already suspected.

And it infuriated him that Cael managed to beat him. Bran hoped Cael was enjoying his victory, because it wasn't going to last long.

Searlas entered the study and softly closed the door behind him. "We only have a few more historical sites to look through. The Reapers will be at one of them."

"No, they won't," Bran said as he faced Searlas. "Cael

has taken them out of the city."

"To where?"

"It'll be someplace away from mortals. Cael wouldn't bring attention to themselves that way."

Searlas nodded as he listened. "They need somewhere to gather that will be private and difficult for others to get to them."

"As well as shelter for the librarian."

"You really think they have her."

Bran turned and looked at his reflection in the window. His black hair was thick. He knew the face staring back at him, but he wasn't the same Fae. Death had seen to that. Magic might have restored his looks that the Netherworld had eaten away day after day, but magic did nothing to repair his shredded soul.

"I do," Bran replied and swiveled his head back to Searlas. "If she's not shown up to work or returned to her flat, there's no other explanation. Did you check her family?"

"She doesn't have any."

Now that was curious. "And you're sure you didn't detect any Fae blood within her?"

"I'll stake my life on it," Searlas declared.

"It might very well come to that."

Searlas's face darkened with anger, his red eyes narrowing. "Why?"

"I've gone over everything, and the only reason the

Reapers would take the librarian is if her life was in danger or she was of some use to them."

"She's not a Fae, so we wouldn't have targeted her. So that rules out that scenario."

Bran shrugged. "Why would they need her if she's simply a human?"

"They wouldn't," Searlas said with a snort. "They're Reapers. They wouldn't trouble themselves with a mortal."

Bran waited for his lieutenant to realize the conclusion he'd spoken aloud.

Searlas ran a hand down his face. "Shite. If they took her, she's half-Fae."

"And you missed it."

"She didn't look anything like a Fae," Searlas stated in his defense. "She wasn't even remotely appealing."

Bran appreciated Searlas's cleverness with magic and freely used his skills in battle, but something like this slipping through could wreck all of Bran's plans.

He watched lightning fork across the sky before he looked at Searlas. "Nearly all half-Fae have no idea what they are. They either use their beauty, or don't care about it. Have you ever heard of someone who would go out of their way to hide it?"

"No."

"Me either. Do you know what that means?"

Searlas barely kept his anger in check. "Of course. She knows she has Fae blood."

"If she knows, then she was making sure to disguise herself from Fae. I need to know why. Immediately."

Searlas turned and motioned for two men at the door to begin the investigation. "You'll have the information soon."

"Within an hour." Bran listened to the rain patter harder against the window as the wind began to howl. "Now, that brings me back to the Reapers. They might've helped her because she has Fae blood, just as they did Baylon's woman."

"But you don't think that's the reason."

Bran shook his head. "My suspicion is that she's somehow tied to the books."

"These books have been missing from the Fae realm for eons."

"Isn't it curious that this half-Fae who knows of her heritage would be working at the very place that has the books?"

A muscle jumped in Searlas's jaw. "No Fae would just give those books to a human."

"Someone did. No mortal found their way onto our realm and took them. Half-Fae or not."

"I'll find out."

Bran took a deep breath when Searlas teleported away.

Once Bran got the information he needed about the librarian and her connection to the books, he'd understand why the Reapers had taken her.

Even if Searlas and the rest of the Dark failed him, there was only one ending for the librarian—death.

The longer Bran thought about a half-Fae escaping his grasp and Cael having the books, the more furious he became. He hadn't spent thousands of years trapped in the Netherworld suffering indescribable pain not to get his revenge.

Bran walked from the study to the lower part of the manor. The owners tried to hide the fact the house had once had a dungeon, but he'd found it anyway.

He entered the small dungeon and the smell of rot and dampness assaulted him. Bran didn't pay the two Dark guards any mind. He stopped in front of the prisoner with her arms chained above her head and latched to the ceiling.

Blood ran from a cut at the corner of her mouth. Dirt and blood stained her face, hair, and clothes, but she still glared at him with anger in her silver eyes.

"Get on with it if you're going to kill me," she said vehemently, her Scot's accent so thick the words were hard to discern.

Bran's smile was slow as he cocked his head to the side and regarded her. "Oh, I'm not going to kill you."

"You're a sick Irish fuck."

"You don't know the half of it." Bran took a step closer to her. He had to give her credit for not flinching as he neared, but her pulse let him know she was scared. "I've got something special in store for you. Soon you'll learn what you are. Soon you'll learn what I can do for you."

She rolled her eyes. "Go to hell. I'll be happy to show you the way."

Bran grabbed the collar of her sweater and tore it down the middle. Then with a snap of his fingers her bra ripped at the juncture of her breasts and fell open, exposing her.

"That's better."

She lifted her chin. "You can beat me. You can rape me. You can abuse me any way you want, but you'll never touch my soul."

Bran cupped her breast and lightly ran his thumb over her nipple. It peaked instantly. He smiled. "You want me. You want this. I can see it in your eyes, hear it in the way your breathing has changed. I can feel it."

To prove his point, he tweaked her nipple. At her quick intake of breath, Bran lowered his head until his lips were nearly touching hers. "You're mine, Thea. I own your body, your mind, and even your soul." He threaded his fingers in her brown locks and held her head steady. "Accept what I offer."

"No."

Bran released her because she was already breaking. Four days ago, her response had been shouted. This time was but a whisper.

"Bran."

He glanced to the side to find Searlas. Bran kissed her cheek and whispered in her ear, "You have a reprieve."

With a nod to Searlas, he returned to the main floor of the house. Bran might have an army of Dark he recruited, but that didn't mean he trusted them.

Not until they were back in the study that Bran had spelled against eavesdropping did he turn to Searlas. "That was quick."

"We're not the only ones asking questions."

Cael. Again. Bran was really going to have to do something about him. "Tell me."

"The Nighttails have put out a bounty on their youngest daughter, Maiti. Apparently she was spotted with two Dark at Taraeth's palace before disappearing."

Bran shrugged. "So? What do I care about some female?"

"Maiti tried to leave before. She wore a slave bracelet that couldn't be removed with any magic."

Bran chuckled as he poured himself some Irish whiskey. "How puny the Dark are compared to the power within a Reaper. It must've been Kyran and Fintan that helped her."

"That's my guess as well. None of the descriptions I got matched, so they used glamour."

"Any smart Fae would."

Searlas paused for a moment. "Maiti was in deep conversation with the Reapers."

"But you don't know about what?"

"Give me some credit," he said tightly. "I went to the source."

That made Bran grin. "The Nighttail family. And?"

"Nolan had a visitor a few hours before. A Dark who he had never seen before somehow made it into the house and had an audience with him."

"It was Cael. What did he want of Nolan Nighttail?"

"He asked about a family of humans."

Bran's attention was now riveted. "And?"

"Nolan didn't want to talk, but I convinced him. It seems that his brother fell in love with a mortal."

Bran downed his whiskey. "A Dark Fae and a human. That certainly couldn't work."

"It didn't. Nat was ordered to kill her, but he didn't. He had sex with her once. The two faked her death. He got away with it for a little while until the woman gave birth—to twins."

Bran's brows shot up in his forehead. "Not exactly a surprise. A Fae can get a mortal pregnant easy enough."

"Except Nat wanted her as his wife. He tried to talk his father into allowing it, which of course they didn't. Nat then tried to run away with the mortal. The Nighttails caught up with the couple easily enough."

"I suppose that somehow this mortal woman who birthed the twins is an ancestor of the librarian?"

"I do believe so. The Nighttails wanted her and the children slain."

"Let me guess," Bran said. "Nolan's father didn't want their blood on his hands."

One side of Searlas's mouth curved in a grin. "The Nighttails are close to the Lightslayers. The Lightslayers stepped in and killed Nat, but they left the female and her whelps alive."

"Why?"

"To have something else to hunt in a few years."

Bran clapped his hands together. "Brilliant! The Lightslayers wait until the half-Fae are a certain age, most likely with a child or two of their own to carry on the line."

"Precisely. The Lightslayers get to have fun through generations, and the Nighttails are rid of a problem."

"Except they aren't." Bran blew out a breath. "The librarian knows what she is and hid it because she knows she's going to be hunted soon. But would that be enough to send her to the Reapers? It could be. Cael always did like to play the hero."

"This explains how the librarian could hide her Fae blood from me."

"It doesn't explain the books and her connection," Bran stated.

There was a knock at the door before it opened and two Dark filled the doorway. "We found them," one of the Dark said.

This made all the troubles vanish as if they didn't exist. Bran had another chance to kill Cael and the Reapers before he took on Death.

"Where?" Bran demanded.

The second Dark smiled and said, "They're at some cliffs outside of Edinburgh."

"Let's go get them," Searlas said.

Bran looked out the window to the night and the storm that raged. "They'll be expecting something right now."

"The storm will keep our approach quiet," one of the soldiers said.

Bran made one mistake already because he'd been too confident. If he would've only taken a moment and thought things over, he could've ended it all the first time. He wouldn't make the same misstep again.

"Get the men ready," Bran told the two Dark. When they were gone, he turned to Searlas. "This is exactly when I would attack, and Cael knows that. We're going to attack when they least expect it. In a way they won't be anticipating."

"When and how?"

Bran laughed. "Get ready, Searlas. The Reapers are about to come to an end."

Chapter Eighteen

River was more than a little anxious when Cael gathered all of them together. She sat nervously next to Jordyn, who reminded River of that particular student in class who made the others groan at her excitement and happiness.

It was all River could do to keep the small amount of breakfast from coming up. She felt out of place among the Reapers, and her new secret weighed heavily upon her.

"Cael wouldn't have called us unless he has some information," Jordyn leaned over to whisper.

River caught Baylon's grin. She cut her eyes to Jordyn. "You do know that whispering is pointless in a roomful of Fae, right?"

Jordyn's smile was infectious. "I keep forgetting those small things."

Small things. River's hand immediately lay protectively over her stomach. A life was growing inside her. Hers and Kyran's. Would it be a boy? Or a girl? Who would the bairn look like?

River didn't have the first clue what to do with a baby. She'd never held one before. Panic began to set in as she thought about raising an infant and everything she didn't know about them.

Kyran walked into the room, drawing her gaze. Instantly, she felt calmer. She would tell him of the bairn, because if she didn't, Death would. But River had no illusions. There wasn't a place for her with the Reapers.

The only thing River could do, Jordyn was already doing. All River would be was someone who got in the way, and someone for them to worry about.

She refused to be that person.

Kyran smiled at her, though his red eyes still held a hint of sadness. He hadn't told her what was wrong earlier. They'd remained locked in their embrace for a long time before he gave her a kiss on the forehead and walked away.

She wanted to know what was wrong so she might help, but she couldn't if he wouldn't talk to her. He'd come to her for comfort, though. For a man who was used to dealing with everything himself, that was a huge step.

And for a woman who wasn't used to sharing anything with anyone, she found it all too easy to fall into being needed and wanted.

Kyran frowned at her, a question in his eyes.

Her own eyes stung with unshed tears. He knew something troubled her from across the room. Her heart missed a beat, because she knew then that she wasn't just carrying Kyran's child, she was also in love with him.

He pushed away from the wall, intending to go to her. River gave a discreet shake of her head, but his frown remained in place. With no other choice, she forced a smile.

Kyran's shoulders lifted and fell back into place as he took a deep breath then released it. One black brow lifted, telling her he wasn't fooled.

Cael strode into the cavern, stern and focused. He stood in front of them, looking at each of them before he began. "Thanks to River, we have all thirty books translated. Eoghan, Baylon, Jordyn, and I have been poring over them searching for anything to do with the Netherworld."

"And finding quite a lot," Jordyn added.

Cael gave her a nod. "That we have. Death found Seamus after Bran attacked Jordyn. I also got a chance to question him." Cael held up his hand for silence when Talin started to speak. "It was Kyran and Fintan going back to the Dark that gave us the name of the family responsible for the Fae within River's family. They're the Nighttails."

River glanced around and noted that the tension

ratcheted within the room. It was also apparent that everyone knew something she didn't.

"River," Cael said to get her attention. "We now know that Nat Nighttail is the one who got your ancestor with child. They aren't the ones who have been hunting your family. Those are the Lightslayers."

She felt every eye on her, as if everyone was watching her reaction. "Why another family?"

"The Nighttails didn't want to bloody their hands with the death of family," Kyran explained.

She supposed that made sense. That didn't dispel the knot of apprehension growing in the pit of her stomach. "So it's two families that have to be convinced to stop hunting mine."

River swallowed, her hand clutching her stomach. She'd sworn not to bring a child into the world to be hunted by the Dark. It was the one thing she'd wanted to do.

For a brief time, River actually believed the Reapers would be able to carry through with the promise to stop the Dark. How foolish of her to believe they could do it. This was the Dark she was talking about.

Kyran's red eyes caught and held her gaze. "I gave you a promise, River. I intend to keep it. No matter how long it takes, no matter what I have to do, the Nighttails and Lightslayers will cease."

"We all will," Cael said. "We owe you, River. This is the least we can do for you."

River lowered her gaze and out of the corner of her eye saw the way Jordyn was staring. River made her hand relax from gripping her stomach. No one could know about the child yet. River wasn't ready to share it with anyone, and when she did, it would be Kyran first.

When she looked up, Kyran was still staring at her. She gave him a nod, to let him know she believed his words. And she did. She knew he would keep his word—if Bran didn't get to Kyran first.

Talin sat forward on the couch. "You know I'll help with River's issue, but I'd like to get back to Seamus and Bran."

"It seems that Seamus knew Bran needed help because Bran sent him a message," Cael said.

You could've heard a pin drop the cavern grew so quiet. River shivered with a feeling that Maureen used to say was akin to someone walking over your grave.

River never liked it before, but now she detested the feeling.

"What the hell?" Fintan asked.

Cael shook his head. "Neither Death, Seamus, nor I know how Bran did it. There's no way Bran could've known what Death would do to him."

"Perhaps he did it as a precaution," Baylon said.

Eoghan let out a loud snort.

"I agree," Cael said as he glanced at Eoghan. "Bran might've known Death would step in when he and the others attacked me, Eoghan, and Theo, but why would he send a note like that on the off chance Death might send him to the Netherworld instead of killing him?"

Kyran said, "It's the only theory we have."

"Point made." Cael then said, "Seamus is a puzzle-solver. When he got Bran's note, he immediately set out trying to find the entrance into the Netherworld. He searched for thousands of years and found nothing. Every Fae doorway was checked, but nothing led to the Netherworld. Just as he was about to give up, he heard of a doorway seen in a remote part of Ireland in the ruins of a castle. He visited and found what he was looking for."

"That easily?" Talin said in shock.

River looked over at Eoghan to see him glaring at the floor, a vein throbbing in his temple.

"Apparently so," Cael answered. "It took Seamus a few tries before he was brave enough to venture through the doorway. He said it felt wrong. When he did, he found himself in the Netherworld where Bran was waiting."

Fintan's face was lined with agitation. "Wait. You're telling me that he just happened to find the very door that would lead him to the Netherworld, and despite it feeling wrong, he walked through it? And then, Bran was waiting. There's something wrong here, Cael."

"Aye," Cael admitted.

Everyone was so wrapped up in the story and talking among themselves that none of them noticed how Cael was careful not to say anything about Erith. River knew Fae made the doorways, and she suspected it was Death who created the one Seamus found.

When Cael met her gaze, he didn't hide the burden he carried quickly enough. Cael knew the truth and was protecting Death. It was sweet, especially since Erith didn't need anyone to protect her. She was the ultimate badass.

"Look," Cael said to quiet the room. "Seamus didn't know how Bran knew where to go. All Bran told him was that he'd begun looking for the doorway as soon as he was put in the Netherworld. Then he waited for Seamus to find him."

Baylon gave a nod. "All right. Let's assume Seamus is telling the truth."

"He was. Death made sure of it."

"How was there even a doorway visible to the Netherworld? Wouldn't Death have located any and concealed them?"

River winced, because it didn't matter how much Cael wanted to protect Erith, the truth was about to come out.

Eoghan slapped his hand against the wall. He and Cael stared silently at each other for a long time before Cael nodded. Eoghan relaxed slightly.

"Though nothing was confirmed, I believe Death created that doorway," Cael stated.

Kyran said, "It would've been concealed."

"I know. Something has happened." Cael blew out a breath. "Whatever occurred to show Seamus that doorway allowed Bran to find the one in the Netherworld. It could also be what has given him extra power as well as the ability to share that power with his army of Dark Fae."

Fintan stood. "We need to find it then, because if it weakens Death's magic, it makes it easier for Bran to kill her."

River's stomach fell to her feet. Death couldn't die. "Has any of your magic diminished at all?"

The Reapers looked at each other, shaking their heads. It was Kyran who said, "Not that we've noticed."

"Then you might be Death's only hope."

Cael's eyes went hard, anger practically glowing from him. "Bran won't get near her."

Eoghan shook his head, his arms crossed over his chest as he agreed with Cael.

"We won't let anything happen to her," Kyran said.

Cael pointed to Talin and Baylon. "We need to find a new place as a few Dark have been spotted near here. We've been here too long already."

Instantly, the two disappeared. Cael walked past River

and Jordyn and crossed the hallway to the library. River turned in her seat and watched Cael gather some of the thirty books she'd translated into his arms before he teleported out.

"What's he doing?" River asked.

Kyran came to stand beside her. "He's taking them to the one place Bran will never go—Death's realm."

Which meant River couldn't touch or read them again. It wouldn't have been a big deal if she wasn't pregnant, but she wanted to pass on the tradition of her family to her child.

"It's going to be all right," Kyran said. He put his finger beneath her chin and turned her face to him. "You do believe me, don't you?"

How could she not with his devastating looks and amazing Irish accent? "Yes."

"I won't let you down, River."

"I know you won't. We'll worry about my problem after Bran is dealt with. You and the others need to concentrate on him."

Kyran glanced away, his lips flattening. "That may be a moot point. Bran wants the books, which means he'll know everything about them."

"Meaning, he'll know about me," River said, realization dawning. "Do you think he knows I'm half-Fae?"

"I can guarantee it. Bran will want allies. If he discovers your family's past, then he'll try to use it to his advantage."

River closed her eyes. "This can't be happening."

"It is," Kyran said and drew her up to her feet and into his arms. "But we'll deal with all of it. One thing at a time. Cael is getting the books out of Bran's reach. He might get the translations, but we'll still have the books themselves."

She nodded, leaning her head back so she could look at him. "That's all well and good, but he'll still have the information."

"Not after Jordyn changes out the translations with various audiobooks. We're not about to let him get anything so easily. The next thing is getting somewhere safe. Cael is right, we've been here too long."

One thing at a time. As long as River focused on that, then her anxiety was kept to a minimum. It would be so easy to get overwhelmed with everything and make a mistake.

That's most likely exactly what Bran was hoping for. But he wouldn't be getting it.

River smiled up at Kyran. "I'm so glad I met you."

In answer, Kyran lowered his head and kissed her slowly, passionately . . . seductively.

Chapter Nineteen

Erith stood hidden behind a wall of rose bushes as she watched Cael bring the books to her realm. She should be there, directing him where to place them, but she couldn't be near him anymore.

She spent entirely too much time with him already. Any more could be detrimental to her well-being. Then there was the fact something was going on with her magic. She didn't want Cael to know until she discovered the root of the problem and fixed it.

The sun shown on Cael's long black hair, seemingly being sucked into the midnight locks. Once she'd dared to run her fingers through the thick strands as he lay dead.

Waiting for him to die an agonizingly slow death had nearly done her in. After three hours she hadn't been able to listen to his garbled breathing another moment. Cael was the only Reaper whose natural death she intervened with. It took only one touch from her for his last breath to leave his body.

Erith had revived him instantly. She hadn't been able

to see him without life inside him. That's when she'd known he was her weakness—one she should've removed immediately.

But she hadn't been able to. Cael was born to be a Reaper. Just as he'd been born to lead. He listened and observed, taking everything in before he made a decision. He wasn't quick in his actions like Baylon. Nor was he reckless as Talin was.

But Cael didn't shut off his feelings as Fintan did, or withdraw into himself as Eoghan had. Unlike Kyran who focused on one thing at a time, Cael could juggle numerous issues with ease. The only one who came close to replicating Cael was Daire, though Daire second-guessed himself at times.

To Erith, Cael was perfection in body, mind, and spirit. In all her never-ending eons of life, he was the only one who made her wish she could have someone. But it wasn't meant to be. Ever.

Her gaze followed Cael as he walked from the tower. He stopped, his head swiveling slowly as he searched for her. She gripped the rose branches, the thorns cutting into her palm, to keep herself still.

"Erith," Cael called. "I know you're here."

There was no way he could. Or was that part of her magic also failing?

"I don't think you should leave Seamus alone. I don't

care if he's agreed to help us or not. Trust needs to be earned from him," Cael said.

She smiled. Of course Cael would think along those lines. He would know that she spelled the tower so that Seamus couldn't venture into some places, but Cael was the type of male who needed to state his concerns.

He blew out a breath and lowered his chin to his chest. After a moment, he raked a hand through his coal black hair. His face was set, worry bracketing his sensuous mouth. "I know something is going on with your magic. You made the doorway in Ireland to the Netherworld. I know you. You would've hidden it. The fact it became visible means there's a problem."

Erith felt blood run down between her fingers before it dropped to the ground.

"I'm going to help whether you wish it or not. This . . . hiccup . . . in your magic could be all Bran needs to attack you. And win. I won't let that happen."

She released the branch and turned her back to Cael. His words affected her too deeply. If she didn't get away now, she might answer him.

Erith stilled. Someone was behind her, close enough she could feel the heat from his body. She knew his scent of cedar and rain. Her eyes closed as she imagined allowing herself to lean back against his hard chest, to have his arms come around her and hold her tight.

"You can't run from me," Cael said.

Her gaze snapped open. Run? She wasn't running—not yet anyway. Erith turned to face him, shocked to discover how close he was. She had to tilt her head up to look into his face. "I'm dealing with this."

A small frown formed briefly. "Is it so hard to admit you might need help?"

"I've always been alone, Cael. I've done everything myself. Why would that change now?"

"Because I'm offering. You don't have to do it all alone."

She most certainly did, especially since she wanted nothing more than his help because she was terrified of what was happening to her.

He took a step back, his silver eyes going cold. "If you change your mind, you know where to find me."

The moment he was gone she wanted to call him back. She began to turn when a figure caught her eye. She found Seamus leaning a shoulder against the open doorway of the tower, his hands in his pants pockets.

"Ignoring it won't make it go away," he said.

Erith shot him a look. "What are you going on about?"

"Your feelings for Cael." Seamus then straightened and turned on his heel to disappear inside the tower.

She was going to have to find some other place to put him, because she missed her solitude.

∼

Kyran remained as near to River as he could. Leaving the caves was the right thing to do, but he couldn't dispel the feeling that something was about to happen. And by something, he meant someone—Bran.

The hunting lodge Talin and Baylon located wasn't as roomy as anything they had before, but it was their only choice.

"Something isn't right," Kyran said.

Fintan stood by one of the windows looking out. "Aye."

"Cael wants to stay close to Edinburgh. We found this," Baylon stated.

Talin grunted and jerked his chin to Baylon. "Only because every time we thought we found a place, we'd see a Dark."

Kyran's gut clenched. "We need to leave. Now."

"And go where?" Jordyn asked. "We're protected here."

"Nay." Kyran strode to the front of the house and looked out one of the windows. "We need to leave."

River looked nervously around. "Why? What's going on?"

"I've a bad feeling about this place," he explained.

Fintan turned from the window and crossed his arms over his chest. "The longer I'm here, the more I feel I need to leave."

"There's one other place," Talin said as he looked at Baylon.

But Baylon was shaking his head. "Bran will know to look for us there."

"How do you know he didn't lead us here?" Fintan asked. "You say the places you checked you saw Dark. This was all that was left open for us that was secluded and near the city."

Eoghan strode into the room and pointed to Fintan and Talin before motioning to the doors. Kyran took River's arm and pulled her with him as he moved her to a wall.

"Are we under attack?" she asked.

Kyran shrugged. "Possibly."

"I need my dagger."

He turned his head to her, ready to tell her that she needed to stay put. Bran would hit them on all sides, and Kyran couldn't be everywhere at once. River had trained for years with her weapon. She knew how to use it, as she'd already proven.

Kyran held out his hand and her blade appeared. Her eyes widened as she took it from him.

"I wondered where it went."

He gave her a wink. "I found it on the bed and put it away until you needed it."

"Did you?" she asked with a sly look. "What do you mean by 'put away'?"

"With magic. It's where all our weapons go when we aren't using them."

River gave a small shake of her head. "Of course that's what happens."

Kyran then thought of his sister's sword. He called for it, then handed it to River. "It's bigger than your dagger, but the weight will feel the same."

"It's beautiful," she said in amazement as she turned the sword one way, then the other to look at the blade. "Thank you."

Kyran watched as she strapped the dagger's sheath along her outer thigh and tucked the blade in place. She then began to walk around the room thrusting, turning, and lunging with the sword.

She was a natural warrior. Had she been born a Fae, no doubt she'd be in the Fae army. Her skills were that good. Even with only a small portion of Fae blood within her, she moved as if she were full-bloodied Fae.

Kyran reached out and snagged her arm when she turned, tugging her against him. Her pale blue eyes were alight with pleasure. He smoothed his hand over her dark locks, amazed that he had such a connection.

"What is it?" she asked.

"I don't know what's going to happen, but stay near

me. Bran will try and separate you from the rest of us. So be vigilant."

She nodded. "Okay."

"We'll be outnumbered, and these Dark have as much strength as we do."

"Great," she mumbled.

Kyran grinned. "I've seen you fight, remember? I know how lethal you are. We need you."

"We?"

"I," he corrected. "I need you."

Her gaze softened. He bent and pressed his mouth to hers, intending only to give her a quick kiss. Then he felt the softness of her lips. Her tongue licked at his mouth.

With a groan, he tightened his arms around her and kissed her passionately, fervently. His senses came alive at her taste, and his body craved to be inside her once more.

It was Fintan's cursing that broke through Kyran's haze of desire. He ended the kiss and lifted his head.

"Get the women," Talin shouted as he teleported out.

A moment later, Eoghan and Fintan were gone as well. Kyran held out his hand for River as Baylon and Jordyn vanished. Kyran gave River a nod and teleported.

Except they didn't leave. He looked at River and tried again, but nothing happened. It felt as if he were tied down, unable to get away.

River released him. "Try now."

"I'm not leaving you." It didn't matter if he could teleport without her or not, he wasn't going to.

"Get away. Fight another day," she urged.

Kyran shook his head. "We stand together."

"Just try it."

He sighed, but did as she asked. Sure enough, he was able to get away and return to her.

"I knew it," she said.

Kyran blew out a harsh breath. "Bran's done something to keep you locked in one place."

"Perhaps it isn't me exactly, but this house."

Kyran ran a hand down his face. Of course it was the house. They had been tricked into going there, but because Bran wanted River.

She took his hand and swallowed hard. "I have to tell you something."

"All right." By the way she gripped his hand and the apprehension in her gaze, he wasn't so sure he wanted to know.

"I was going to tell you. You have to know that. I just didn't want to do it during all of this. Once Bran was taken care of, I'd have told you."

"Told me what," he urged.

River fretfully licked her lips. "Death visited me."

Kyran felt as if he'd been kicked in the stomach.

"She was beautiful and nice," River said.

Donna Grant

"What did she say?"

River shrugged. "She asked what I saw in the future."

When River didn't continue, Kyran held on to his patience. "And?"

"I'm carrying your child."

Kyran blinked, unsure if he'd heard her correctly. Then it penetrated his mind. His child was growing within River. His child.

Their baby.

He smiled and gathered River in his arms. "Are you sure?"

"Death certainly was."

Kyran released River, his smile fading. There would be time to celebrate later. Right now he needed to prepare for Bran. He looked at River. "Ready for this?"

"With you by my side I could face anything," she said as she lifted her chin and adjusted her grip on the sword.

Kyran had never been more proud of anyone in his life than he was of River. She was his woman, his lover . . . his.

Nothing was going to come between them.

Chapter Twenty

River wished her hand would stop shaking. She wished her entire body would stop trembling, but the thought of Bran and his Dark army closing in on her shot that right to hell.

The weight of the sword in her hand gave her a smidgen of comfort. She wasn't used to fighting with a longer blade, but Kyran was right, it weighed the same as the dagger—and that she knew very well.

If something happened and she lost the sword, her dagger was waiting. River wouldn't go down without a fight. It wasn't just herself she was protecting, it was her unborn babe.

No one—not human or Fae—was going to harm her child.

"Do you trust me?"

She turned her head to Kyran. "Yes."

His smile melted her heart. "I love you."

The words barely penetrated her mind before he vanished. River knew he'd only veiled himself, but still. He hadn't given her time to respond to his declaration. A part of her wanted to tell him right then of her feelings.

But her heart urged her to wait. She wanted to look into his red eyes and see the love shining there before she said the words.

"You're going to pay for that later," she told the room.

She had no idea where Kyran was, but she knew he hadn't left her. He wasn't that kind of man.

The door to the hunting lodge opened slowly to reveal a tall Fae. His silver eyes were trained on her, and the wind ruffled the black locks that fell to his jaw.

He was gorgeous with his wide lips, cheekbones that could cut marble, and fine body. All Fae were stunning, but he had confidence and anger that gave him an edge.

Bran.

Behind him stood two Dark with red eyes glittering with a need to kill.

River lifted her chin, waiting for him to make the first move. She should've known Bran was the kind who liked to make an entrance. He stood staring at her a long time before he took two steps inside.

"They actually left you," he said with a smile.

River didn't bother to reply. The others had left, but only because they didn't know she was trapped. Kyran, however, was there. River couldn't wait until Kyran made himself known. All this with Bran could end that night.

Bran chuckled and shook his head as he walked

around her. River remained facing the door, her gaze on the numerous Dark Fae waiting to be allowed entrance into the lodge to kill her.

"I'm shocked," Bran said as he came to stand right behind her. He leaned over her shoulder. "This is unlike Cael."

River had to bite her tongue not to respond. Let Bran come to his own conclusions. She'd learn more that way than by lashing out and telling him to go bugger himself.

"Tell me, River, are they planning an attack?"

She glanced at him. It bothered her that he knew her name.

"Oh, I've learned a great deal about you besides your name," he said as he came to stand in front of her. His hands were clasped behind his back. "I know it was a Dark who got your ancestor's belly full with a child. I know that Dark fell in love with her."

Now that was something River hadn't known.

"It's too bad there wasn't a happy ending to the story." Bran's gaze searched her face. "The Dark was killed, thereby starting the continual hunting of your family. The fact it is another Dark family entirely who hunts and kills your line is fascinating."

He was so close River could drive the sword into his gut. If only it were that easy. Bran probably expected her to do exactly that. So she'd wait, biding her time.

"I know you're the last of your line," Bran continued. "I'm guessing by how you've lived your life you intend to end things so your line can't carry on."

Anyone who knew her story could figure that out. She returned his stare, giving her face just enough of a bored expression to make him narrow his gaze.

"We'll get back to that in a moment." Bran briefly looked at the floor, his lips turning up in a smile. "I also know of the books. Give them to me."

She held out her empty hand and looked around the lodge.

The smile dropped as he stepped closer. "I know they're not here. Tell me where they are."

"Death has them," she readily told him. Then it was her turn to smile as his cheeks blotched red with his anger.

"It hasn't taken me much to learn all there is to know of you and your family, River. I also did a bit of digging on the books. Do you know most Fae believe the books are nothing more than a myth? Much like the Reapers."

Could she kill him now? She didn't want to hear anything else he had to say.

"There are a few who have stories about the Thirty. That's how the books are referred to. The Thirty. Not very original, I agree, but then again, does it really matter?"

The fact he smiled at his own stupid joke made her want to gag.

Bran refused to let her look away. "It seems each of the books was written in a different language created by each of the thirty families. All of which are no longer spoken."

Dammit. He'd figured out why she was with the Reapers. It was one thing she'd wanted to keep from him, but she should've known he'd discover it, just as Kyran and the others had.

"I'd stake my life on the fact you can read all of them," Bran said with a pleased smile.

The response on her tongue was to tell him to fuck off, which would only anger him. Not what she wanted quite yet.

"You've nothing to say?" he asked.

River blinked and sighed sarcastically.

Bran looked down and noticed her weapons. "Are those yours?"

"I have them, don't I?" Damn. She really needed to keep her mouth shut.

He glanced behind him at the door. "I hope you know how to use those weapons, River, because you may well need them. Unless," he paused, letting the silence lengthen until she wanted to scream. "Unless you join me."

Was he serious? He couldn't be serious. She looked into his silver eyes, which were clear and focused. Shit. He was serious. "I'll pass."

"You don't even know what I offer."

"It doesn't matter."

He raised a brow. "You aided the Reapers."

"So?"

"That was your first mistake. Let's not make another. You do want to live, don't you? I can make sure the Dark who've been hunting you stop. I can also make sure no other Fae—Dark or Light—bother your family ever again. In other words, River, I'm offering you a normal future like every other mortal has. Go out and find a man, get married, have children, and whatever it is that happens next."

She understood then what Maureen had always known—River wasn't meant for normal. She needed the atypical, the unusual. The magical.

She needed Kyran and the crazy life of a Reaper.

"As I said, I'll pass," River repeated.

Bran shrugged one shoulder. "Then let me put it in simpler terms. Help me first get the books and then translate them, or die."

"There is nothing on this realm or another that could convince me to help you."

"That's too bad." He stepped to the side, turning so that he half-faced the front door. "I'm sure this is where you expect the Reapers to come and help you, but I've ensured they can't get through my field around the house."

River swallowed, attempting to dispel the terror that began to grip her. There were too many Dark for her and Kyran to take down by themselves.

It wouldn't do any good to tell Kyran to remain veiled or even to leave, because he wouldn't. He would stand beside her no matter what.

She felt a presence beside her. Kyran. It gave her the courage to take a deep breath and widen her stance. There was no room for fear in battle. She needed a clear mind, focused entirely on her opponents.

And it was time to get the show on the road.

"Are you done talking?" River asked. "Because I can't take another word out of your mouth."

Bran simply smiled. In a blink, two Dark at the doorway rushed her. River lifted her sword, holding it with both hands as she stopped one of their blades above her head.

She then spun, using her weapon to block a blast of magic. While the two Dark were surprised at her ability, she used that time to slice open the neck of one and pierce the heart of the other.

They fell to the floor before disintegrating and floating away in the wind.

"You certainly move like a Fae," Bran said. He jerked his chin to a Dark who pushed through the group at the door. "Is this who you saw at the library, Searlas?"

Searlas looked her up and down. "I'd say no, but it's the tilt of her chin I recognize."

"I never imagined a different hairstyle, dowdy clothes, and glasses could change an appearance so much," Bran said. He bowed his head to her. "You did a good job. It's really too bad you have to die."

River felt anything but confident, yet she had to make Bran think she was. "If I do, who will read the books?"

"I've no doubt Cael already had you translate them. I'll simply find the translations."

"And if I told him something wrong perhaps?" she asked innocently. "I mean, they're Reapers. What if I wanted to ensure they had to continue to protect me?"

Bran burst out laughing. "Well, you keep surprising me. It's too bad I have a toy of my own right now, or I'd take you with me. Besides, I think you're buying yourself time."

"I'm not. I really did tell them three things that were wrong. I did it to make sure they keep protecting me from the Fae hunting me."

Bran strode to her and gripped her chin roughly in his fingers. He stared into her eyes for a long time before he murmured, "I'll be damned."

She let out a shaky breath when he released her. River was shocked he'd actually believed her lie. Then again, she was growing desperate. Battling two Dark that she surprised with her skills was one thing, but if she had to fight more, she wasn't sure she'd win.

Her left hand fisted at her side to keep from covering her stomach protectively. She had a child to fight for.

A large hand covered her fisted one. Kyran was still veiled, but he was letting her know he was there. A small squeeze of his hand told her it was time to finish the battle.

She stood straighter as she glared at Bran. It was time to mess with him a bit before he was killed. After all he'd done to the Reapers, he deserved no less.

"Tell me what the three things are," Bran demanded.

River gave him a flat look. "Do I appear that dim-witted? I not only read each of those thirty languages, I know which parts I erroneously told the Reapers. You can kill me and attempt to steal the translations, which I might add isn't going to happen. But even if by some stroke of luck you manage it, you'll never know which three parts are wrong. They could be the very things you need."

"You tell me this as if you're proposing to help me. I've already made that offer."

"It does appear that way, doesn't it?" she said with a small nod. "I just wanted to get your hopes up for minute. I'm not going to help you in any way."

Bran's lips peeled back in a sneer as he bellowed and released three blasts of magic in quick succession. River pivoted away in time to see Kyran unveil himself and block each of the bubbles of magic.

The Dark outside the lodge began to yell and pour into the house. River readied her sword and faced those coming at her.

Chapter Twenty-one

Kyran wanted to remain focused on Bran, but with the sheer number of Dark descending upon them, he couldn't. He'd done his best to alert the others to what was going on, but he had no idea if his call reached them.

If Bran had locked River to this location, then shielded it so no one else could get in, it was a damn good thing Kyran hadn't left to get the others. He might not have gotten back in to help River.

He stood back-to-back with his woman as they fought the onslaught of Dark. He heard her wince and looked over to find her limping from a wound of magic on her leg.

Just like the scourge that he was, Bran moved away to watch the battle instead of engaging Kyran as they'd begun.

"Coward!" Kyran yelled at Bran.

Bran merely chuckled. "Who'll be alive when this is all over? It won't be you."

"Want to bet on that?" asked Cael as he suddenly appeared next to Bran.

Bran's face contorted with fury as he launched himself at Cael. Kyran wanted to watch the two of them go at it, but he turned his attention to River.

They stood side by side and fought as Fintan and Eoghan made their way to them. Kyran caught a glimpse of Baylon and Jordyn, as well as Talin.

There was a violent bellow that drew everyone's attention. Kyran saw that Bran's gaze was riveted on Jordyn. When she noticed, she gave him a wink and a smile.

That's all it took to get the fighting started again. Kyran could see that River had more than one wound. He wasn't sure of her healing abilities yet, and the thought of her in any kind of pain left him breathless.

Then there was the child growing inside her.

"Kyran," Fintan said.

Kyran wrapped his arms around River and spun her away as Fintan took out a Dark and Eoghan killed two more who were intent on killing River.

"Get her out of here," Fintan said angrily.

River pushed out of his arms and looked into Kyran's face. "I can help. You need me."

Before he could answer, she lunged and sunk her sword into a Dark coming up behind Kyran. He shot her a quick smile as they went back to fighting.

This time it was the Reapers who'd gotten an upper hand with the Dark. Bran hadn't brought as many because he thought he planned well enough to only need a few, and it was going to cost him heavily.

When Kyran next looked up, there were only six Dark left alive while Cael and Bran continued to battle it out. River stood beside Kyran, breathing heavily as the others took care of the remaining Dark.

"Cael will win, right?" River asked.

Kyran snorted. "Of course."

In a matter of moments, Cael had Bran on the floor, pounding his face with punches. He was getting ready to end it with a surge of power to Bran's face when Kyran heard River's intake of breath.

He looked over in time to see a Dark rush through the door toward Cael. Kyran could only watch in amazement as River threw her dagger, embedding it deep in the Dark's spine. With a gargled sound, he crumbled to ash.

Kyran slid his gaze to Cael to find him looking at River with surprise. Unfortunately, Kyran's shout of warning to Cael was too late as Bran used Cael's momentary lapse of attention to his advantage.

There was a loud boom as smoke billowed everywhere and the house vibrated to the very foundation. As one, the Reapers quickly approached Cael, clearing the smoke with magic.

They found Cael unconscious and Bran leaning over him with a dagger, getting ready to plunge it in Cael's heart. Eoghan growled and lunged for Bran. But by the time Eoghan reached him, Bran had teleported away.

"He can't be gone," River said as she looked around. "Tell me Bran didn't get away."

Talin kicked at a chair that was knocked on its side. "He's clever."

"And a coward," Kyran added.

Fintan grunted. "Most definitely that."

Cael sat up, shaking his head to clear it. He propped one foot on the floor and draped an arm over his knee. "Bastard got away again, didn't he?"

"Aye," Jordyn mumbled. "We were so close."

"And he was close last time," Baylon said.

Kyran wrapped an arm around River. "Had my message not reached you, he would've killed both of us."

"What message?" Talin asked.

Kyran frowned. "If you didn't get my call, how did you know?"

"When you and River didn't follow us, we knew something was wrong," Baylon said.

Fintan crossed his arms over his chest. "We arrived back here to find Dark and a spell blocking us from entering."

"So how did you get in?" River asked.

Cael smiled as he climbed to his feet. "We're Reapers. Bran may be able to cast some impressive spells, but you get all of us together, and we can usually break through any type of magic."

"We heard him talking for a bit," Talin said. "River, you've got a healthy dose of courage."

Eoghan walked to River and stopped when he stood before her. He took her hand in his and gave her a nod before he walked out of the lodge.

River looked to Kyran who said, "That's his way of letting you know he thanks you for what you did, and also appreciates your courage."

"Wow," she said and smiled.

Cael looked around as if searching for Bran. "We need to get out of here."

"And go where?" Jordyn asked.

Fintan dropped his arms. "Anywhere but here."

"We'll meet up soon," Cael said.

Kyran didn't have to be told twice. He slid his hand into River's and teleported away.

Cael waited until everyone was gone before he walked out of the hunting lodge to find Eoghan standing in the moonlight next to a stone wall that surrounded the property.

"Was it luck or skill that got us out of this tonight?" Cael asked him.

Eoghan glanced at him, but didn't answer.

"Aye. A little of both. Had there been more Dark Fae,

we wouldn't have won."

"Who says we did?"

Cael looked at Eoghan when he spoke. "Everyone is alive. Bran didn't get to any of us."

This time Eoghan remained as silent as he usually was.

Cael blew out a harsh breath and raked his hand through his hair. "I nearly had him. I took my concentration off him for just a second. That's all he needed to get away. How many more chances will I have to do that again?"

Eoghan shook his head slowly.

"I didn't think so either. So I lost my chance. Now he knows Jordyn is alive, that we have the books, and that River can translate them. Just once I'd like to keep a secret from him."

Eoghan leaned forward and rested his hands on the stones. He looked out over the rolling landscape covered in shadows chased away only by the meager light of the moon.

"I think Kyran is in love with River."

Eoghan looked at him over his shoulder and smiled as he nodded.

"She saved my life."

Eoghan issued a small grunt.

"Kyran and Talin were right. She has great skill with a weapon."

Without a sound, Eoghan turned back to the scenery.

Cael clapped him on the back. "We need to find a new place for everyone. Somewhere Bran won't think of. Somewhere we can remain for as long as needed."

Eoghan straightened and put his hand on Cael. In a blink they were standing on an island. Cael looked around at the large concrete structures surrounding him. Upon inspection, the isle couldn't be more than about one hundred meters by two hundred meters.

Across the dark waters he could see the lights of the mainland. "Edinburgh," he said when he recognized the silhouette of some buildings.

Eoghan walked down a path deeper into the buildings. But Cael had already seen all he needed. This was a perfect location, near to the city but away from the humans. It also afforded them a way to protect it so no Dark could easily stumble upon them.

Cael followed the trail Eoghan had taken and found him within one of the buildings. "This is perfect. I'll begin calling the others here. Start setting up the magic to keep the Dark out."

Eoghan gave a nod and walked away. Cael watched his friend. He missed the man Eoghan used to be. But circumstances changed people, and it had left a permanent scar upon Eoghan that was never going to heal.

The other Reapers might find love, but Cael knew he

and Eoghan would remain alone. Eoghan because no one would replace what had been lost.

And him because he couldn't have the one he wanted.

Cael turned and stopped in his tracks when he found Erith standing in the doorway. He couldn't see her face because of the shadows, but he knew every curve.

"He got away," Cael told her.

Erith nodded and took two steps that put her in the moonlight that poured through a window. "I'm sorry."

"No, I'm sorry. I had him, Erith. I was about to kill him."

"And what happened?" she asked.

Cael shook his head as he shrugged. "A Dark came out of nowhere, coming right for me. I had my hands on Bran. I saw the others about to react, but River was quicker. She threw her dagger and killed the Dark."

"Bran used your break of focus to get away."

"He did." Cael wasn't going to tell her how close Bran came to killing him. It wasn't sitting well with him, and he didn't want anyone to discuss it.

Erith looked around. "I like this place."

"Eoghan found it."

"It's been one of his spots he comes to in order to be alone."

Cael's gaze jerked to her. "I didn't know."

"Eoghan wouldn't want you to know. Keep it safe for

him."

He bowed his head in a silent promise.

She then drew in a long breath and released it. "None of the Reapers or River died tonight."

"I claim it as a win, but it feels like a loss."

"What do you think of River?"

Since when did she want his thoughts on the Reapers' lovers? Cael shifted uncomfortably. "She's more than capable as a warrior. She was an asset tonight."

"She saved your life."

"I know. She was the only one who could read those books, and she helped us when we asked."

Erith lifted her brows. "I know her qualities, Cael. I want to know what you think of her personally."

"I've not been around her much." He swallowed and thought about the times he'd watched Kyran and River. "I believe Kyran is in love with her, and I think she is falling for him, if she hasn't already. She's . . . calmed him. And he's shown her her purpose."

"They're a good match."

"They are. Why are you telling me this?"

Erith's head tilted slightly to the side. "Because in a few days or weeks they're going to announce some grand news. River is pregnant."

Cael was so shocked he could only stare at Erith. He heard her laughter as if from far away. When he finally blinked, he found himself alone.

Things were definitely changing.

Chapter Twenty-two

For two glorious days River had been in Kyran's arms. They had talked about a great many things except for love and the baby.

River walked along the beach of their new home. It was a small island off the east coast of Scotland. She could see Edinburgh from where she stood.

If the concrete buildings were any indication, they were on the island of Inchmickery. It was used as a gun emplacement during both World Wars.

The noise of different gulls rivaled that of the waves. So far River had seen nesting pairs of common eider and Sandwich terns.

"What do you think?" Kyran asked as he appeared beside her and fell in step.

She lifted her face to the breeze and smiled. "I like it."

He put his hand on her to halt her. River turned and looked at him. Kyran swallowed and dropped his hand, as if he didn't know what to do with it.

"Whatever it is, just tell me. Remember, we promised honesty."

"I remember." He looked over her shoulder for a moment before he met her gaze. "There's something I should've told you as soon as I found out, but I was embarrassed and furious. Then the longer I held off, the harder it became to say."

"It's best to just say it." Her stomach turned into a ball of twisting worry and anxiety. Was he going to tell her it was over?

Kyran's shoulders lifted as he took a deep breath. "The Lightslayers were the ones who hunted your family."

"I know." She folded her arms across her chest. It must be really bad for him to take so long to tell her.

"I'm so sorry, River, but the Lightslayers are my family."

She waited for more, and when there was nothing, she realized he'd been worried about telling her it was his family. River put her hands on either side of his face and made him look at her.

"I'll say this as much as it needs to be heard. Those people might be your blood, but they're not your family. They turned their backs on you and betrayed you. Family doesn't do that. The Reapers are your family."

"And you?" he asked softly. "Are you my family?"

She glanced at his mouth that had done wonderfully wicked things to her body. She felt his hands on her, hands that had caressed her to the point of exhaustion, then held her tenderly.

"Yes, Kyran, I'm your family." She brought his head down and kissed his lips.

"I wanted to give you time to take everything in," Kyran said. "I didn't bring up the bairn because of it."

She grinned as he smoothed the hair back that had blown across her face from the breeze. "What you said at the lodge. Did you mean it?"

"With every ounce of my being."

"And you're sure?"

His red eyes crinkled at the corners. "You and my feelings for you are the one thing I am sure of, River."

"I love you, Kyran. I love you deeper than I thought possible. You hold my heart in your hands."

"And you hold mine, my love," he whispered right before he kissed her.

River melted against him, winding her arms around his neck and basking in the love that surrounded them.

Someone cleared their throat next to them. They looked to the side to find Cael.

"I do hate to interrupt, but since this mission includes the both of you, I thought you might want to be involved," Cael said.

Kyran's body grew still. "Now?"

"Now," Cael confirmed.

River dropped her arms and stepped back from Kyran.

"Would someone like to fill me in?"

Suddenly Erith appeared next to Cael. "We're going to pay the Lightslayers a visit," Death said. She looked at River. "A promise is owed."

River was still digesting the thought of meeting Kyran's family when she found herself not only wearing black pants and a red shirt that showed nearly all of her breasts, but she was no longer on the beach.

"You're on the Fae realm," Kyran whispered as they began walking.

She looked at him to see his eyes, but a different face. River turned her head to find Cael and Erith had also changed their looks. It made her curious to see what she looked like, then she thought better of it.

"Whatever happens," Erith told her. "Stay quiet."

They began walking down a driveway toward an imposing house in the distance. No one said a word as they approached the massive gates.

Death stood before the black iron and waited. Kyran positioned River to stand behind and to the side of Erith while he and Cael flanked them.

They didn't have to wait long for the gates to open. Erith strode forward as if she'd been there before. The closer River got to the house, the more she wanted to turn and run away.

She didn't want to see the people who had hurt Kyran.

His hand brushed hers, as if he knew what she was thinking. She inwardly berated herself. Here she was worried about how she was going to act when it was *his* family, *his* house. *His* feelings.

By the time they reached the front door, two tall Dark Fae stood blocking their entrance.

"Move," Death said. When they didn't budge, she lifted a brow. "They opened the gates for us, so what does that tell you?"

The two Dark looked at each other, and then stepped to the side. Death walked forward, opening the door as she did. River suppressed a shiver as she stepped inside the house of evil.

Kyran frowned as he watched Death walk through his house as though she knew it as well as he. Her strides were long and purposeful as she made her way to his father's study at the back of the house.

They passed the parlor where his mother was taking tea with his aunts. His mother rushed to the doorway and started to talk, but Erith simply lifted her hand, halting his mother's ability to speak.

Kyran had to bite the inside of his mouth to keep from laughing at the surprised look on his mother's face. That was almost worth being back in the house.

In minutes they were standing inside his father's study. It was the first time he'd ever seen Alor intimidated by anyone, but that's exactly the expression his father wore as he looked at Death.

Erith simply stared silently at Alor, causing him to fidget in his chair. Finally, he got to his feet and took a step back.

"Do you remember me?" Death asked.

Alor nodded. "I'll never forget your face."

"Good, because you know how serious I am."

"Aye," Alor said, not taking his eyes from her. "I'll do whatever you want."

Death walked to the front of the desk and rested her hands upon the wood. "Your family has been hunting and killing a mortal family for hundreds of years. It stops now."

"Some other Dark family will take over. The Nighttails will see to that," Alor said.

"No, they won't." Death lifted her chin. "Your hunting ceases now. If I have to return, I'll annihilate your entire lineage."

"They're just mortals," he argued.

Erith narrowed her eyes to glare at him. "You know as well as I that they were half-Fae."

Alor swallowed. "It stops immediately."

With that, Death turned on her heel and marched out. No sooner had they departed the house than they were all teleported back to the beach, the glamour to alter their appearance gone.

Erith turned to River. "Your family line will never have to worry again."

"Who did my father think you were?" Kyran asked.

Death smiled. "The first time I met him I led him to believe I was one of Taraeth's assassins."

Kyran began to laugh as he looked down at River. "It's over, love."

"It's about to be," Erith said. "I'm going to pay a visit to the Nighttails to ensure it is."

Cael faced her. "I'll come with you."

Kyran watched them as Death stared at Cael for a long, silent moment before she inclined her head. Then they were both gone.

"Is it really over?" River asked.

Kyran put his hands around her waist and lifted her over his head. "Aye. There's just one more thing I need to ask you."

"Ask," she urged when her feet were back on the sand.

"Will you be mine? I want you by my side and in my bed forever. I want you as my wife."

Her eyes glistened as she threw her arms around his neck as she shouted, "Yes!"

Kyran spun around, more happy than he thought possible. Nothing was going to dim the light that surrounded them.

Epilogue

Bran rose from the sofa and walked to Alor Lightslayer. "I never thought I'd see you back down."

"You don't want to know who that was."

But he did know. It was Death, and it appeared as if she were giving her blessing to the Reapers finding love. Which only increased his fury tenfold.

"I know who she is," Bran said. "I also know the group working with her. If she's not around, she can't dictate what you can and can't do."

Alor smiled slowly. "I like the sound of that."

"I know just how to get to them."

"Do you now?" Alor asked, intrigued. "Tell me."

Bran laughed and walked to the door. "Don't worry, Alor. You'll know everything soon enough. I'll be in touch."

Bran waited until he was away from the Fae realm before he removed the glamour. Then he teleported to Ireland. He looked up at the palace of the Light queen. It was time he paid Usaeil a visit.

Donna Grant

DARK ALPHA'S DEMAND

CHAPTER ONE

Talin pushed open the thirty—foot double doors and entered . . . Hell. The court of Queen Usaeil was a gorgeous one. All around him, Light Fae with their midnight hair and silver eyes—their beauty a trait of being a Fae—danced, laughed, and plotted.

He paused steps into the massive room and surveyed the huge chamber. Everything glittered—per Usaeil's demand. The decorations were white and gold, with splashes of vivid, breathtaking flowers in various colors everywhere.

There wasn't an inch of the Queen's castle that didn't bespeak wealth and beauty. Add in the Light Fae, and the brilliance made it difficult to gaze upon.

Even for a Fae.

But then again, Talin wasn't just any Light Fae. He was a Reaper—chosen by Death to be an executioner for all Fae. Except no one knew his true identity.

If he wanted to ensure that everyone lived, then they could never know.

Talin walked through the crowd gathered, in the hopes that Usaeil might make an appearance. The Fae, as a general rule, were a race of beings that cared only about themselves.

There were a few exceptions—Rhi, for instance. But the Light Fae who'd once had a well—documented affair with a Dragon King was another matter entirely.

The Fae around him now had no idea their queen pretended to be a very well-known American movie star. So they wouldn't know she was on location shooting her next film and wouldn't be in attendance that night.

Then again, the Fae didn't care. Their thoughts were on something else entirely.

Talin paused when the whispers reached him. *Reapers.* They whispered the word as if speaking it would bring them to life. Their voices were filled with fear, panic.

Dread.

And they should feel such emotions. Every Fae was subject to Death's judgment, be they Light or Dark.

The Dark Fae preferred to use their magic for evil,

which changed them physically by adding silver to their black hair and turning their eyes red. They fed off humans by having sex with them, stealing their souls in the process.

Light Fae were those who grasped the magic they were given and only dallied with a human every now and again, though never killing them.

That didn't mean the Light weren't judged. In some cases, Death was harder on the Light than the Dark. Balance. There always had to be balance.

As Talin listened to the scheming and constant conspiring, he could understand why. Those among the court were devious, calculating, conniving, and treacherous. It wasn't always done to get in favor with the queen. In fact, a lot of it was done for marriages, business dealings, and even position among the Light.

Talin didn't understand the need to have a social standing. The humans had all but gotten rid of theirs, but the Fae made up for it by structuring their entire race around such things. Though it had always been so.

Since his arrival at court, Talin had been begged, bribed, and even threatened by families to marry their daughters. All of which, turned his stomach.

The machinations to get a man to notice a certain woman made Talin wary. He'd seen the same trickery directed at him on several occasions.

He quickly moved to the side of the room and up the four steps to one of a dozen white granite pillars. From this vantage point, he could see in almost every direction.

Talin leaned a shoulder against the column and crossed his arms over his chest. He wasn't sure why Death had chosen him to spy upon the Light court, but a Reaper didn't question orders.

Well, that wasn't entirely true. It had happened only once, and it was a good thing the orders were questioned, because it turned out Death hadn't sent the directive for them to kill all half—Fae among the humans.

Turns out, that order had somehow come from an old enemy out to end the Reapers—and Death. The fact this new nemesis was none other than a former Reaper Death had sent to the Netherworld for his crimes only made things more difficult.

Talin had no idea what Death hoped he might find spying upon the Light court. All he'd discovered so far was that the Light somehow knew the Reapers were on Earth.

No one knew who the Reapers were, or if, in fact, they were real. The Reapers were a story told to the young to scare them as well as deter them from turning Dark. The Dark, well, he wasn't sure what they were told.

The fact was, there wasn't a Fae alive—Light or Dark—who wasn't frightened of the Reapers. Just the mention of them put the Fae on high alert.

If no one knew whether the Reapers were even real, why would the Fae somehow know they'd returned to Earth? It was a question Talin asked himself over and over again with no answer in sight.

While he attempted to figure it out, he watched those at court. There were the ones who had prestige and position within Fae society.

Those few individuals walked around with a cocky smile in place, their heads held high as if they were above reproach. In their wake were others, whispering and plotting as jealousy threatened to swallow them whole. That was the next tier of Light—those who wanted the top positions.

These Fae never stopped scheming or conspiring. Their goal was to be on top, and they were going to get there one way or another. This group was by far the largest, with its own social hierarchy that made Talin's head hurt each time he thought about it.

The last group was those who managed to make their way to the castle by the queen's invitation, some trade or bargain, or another such endeavor. These Fae were rendered bright—eyed by the opulence and allure, and most didn't realize they needed to guard themselves against it all.

With the right connections, these lowest of the Fae

could manage to get into the second level easily enough. However, working their way through that hierarchy was trickier than maneuvering through a battlefield.

"Hello, lover," whispered a sexy feminine voice in his ear as hands wound around him from behind.

Talin smiled, unable to help himself. He looked over his shoulder at Neve. She raised a black brow, her silver eyes searching his.

Desire struck him quickly, making him instantly hard. Neve managed to bring such a reaction from him every time he heard her voice, felt her touch, or looked at her.

In other words, simply her existence filled him with lust. It knotted tightly within him, demanding that he claim her body. He drew in a shaky breath as he ached to taste her, to hold her luscious body against his.

"You walked right past me." She lifted her chin, her dark pink lips tightening subtly. "I should be offended."

Talin took her hand and pulled her around to face him. His skin prickled at the feel of her soft curves against him. His heart quickened when he breathed in her scent.

How he craved this woman.

"But you won't."

He took in her heart—shaped face and high cheek-bones with skin that seemed to glow. Her ebony locks were pulled away from her face in several rows of braids before being clasped at the back of her head, leaving the rest of her locks to fall about her shoulders.

Black brows arched over large, almond—shaped eyes that tilted up at the corners. Her lashes were thick, her lips full.

The long, slim column of her throat tempted him to lean down and nip at the delicate skin while running his hands over her delicious curves.

She shot him an icy look before she let her eyes run up and down him. "Why's that?"

"You'll forget all about it when I take you down the corridor and into one of the many hidden alcoves." He looked down at the bright pink gown that accentuated her breasts and small waist. Talin ran his finger along the swell of one breast. "I'll tear off that dress and have you screaming in pleasure."

"You're confident."

He met her gaze as he slid his finger between the plump swells of her breasts. "I should be. I've done it with you often enough."

Neve smiled and wrapped her arms around him and said, "Hmm. I like your thinking." Then she gave a little pout. "You've been gone a long time."

"I'm here now." He squeezed her breast before wrapping both arms around her. So far, Talin had been able to dodge any questions she posed regarding his whereabouts, but Neve was getting more pointed in her questioning.

"Yes, you are. None too soon, either."

That made Talin cautious. There was always something going on at court. Hopefully, this didn't pertain to him or Neve. "What? Besides the usual."

"You haven't seen it?" she asked with a frown.

"Apparently, not."

Neve took his hand and dragged him behind her as she meandered through the people until they came to a crowd of onlookers gawking at something.

Talin maneuvered around her and shouldered his way to the front. Hanging on the wall was the front of a human magazine with a picture of Usaeil and a man taken through the window of a hotel room.

The man was out of focus, but Talin knew who it was—Constantine. He was King of the Dragon Kings, and he wasn't going to be happy about this.

Talin wondered if Con and the other Dragon Kings had learned of this. More importantly, had Rhi? Talin looked around to see if he could catch a glimpse of Rhi. This was definitely something she would post in the middle of court.

"Who are you looking for?" Neve asked.

Talin kept his hold on Neve's hand and moved them away from the crowd. "Have you seen Rhi?"

"She always hated being at court, but no one has seen

her in a long while. There was a rumor that she quit the Queen's Guard."

He ran a hand through his hair. There was one person who would know if Rhi was responsible for this. Daire was veiled and following Rhi wherever she went, per Death's orders. Death had a peculiar interest in Rhi that none of them understood.

"Why are you asking about Rhi?" Neve questioned.

Talin shrugged and dropped his hand to his side. "Rhi's pissed at Usaeil."

"So you think she posted the magazine cover?" Neve asked with brows raised.

He glanced back at the crowd and halted before he faced Neve. "Yes."

Neve licked her lips and took a step closer to him, her voice lowering. "Right now, everyone is shocked about Usaeil's escapades as an actor."

"She didn't purposefully hide it. Did she?"

Neve lifted one shoulder in a shrug. "It explains why our queen has been gone so much. The fact is, that's what everyone is talking about. Now. Soon, it'll turn to the man she was photographed with."

"And?" Talin wanted to know if the Light thought it was a human or a Dragon King.

"Some speculate it's a human. That doesn't bode well for our queen."

Talin may not have known Neve for long, but in the time he'd spent with her, he'd come to recognize that she formulated her own opinions, thoughts, and answers without concern as to what the rest of the court thought or did.

"And you?"

Neve looked him in the eye and said, "I have other thoughts."

"Like?" he pressed.

"I believe it's a Dragon King."

Several seconds passed before he reacted. "Why do you think that?"

"I've never met Usaeil, but I've seen her often enough. She's a queen, Talin. She's not going to give herself to just any man, especially not a human."

"Even a queen has needs."

That brought a small smile to Neve's lips. "She's taken lovers within the court every few hundred years, but none know their identity."

"Then how do you know she's taken a lover?"

Neve gave him a flat look. "How do you know anyone has taken a lover?"

"Point taken." Talin started walking. He waited until they were outside the castle walls and strolling through the cold night air with dark, heavy clouds threatening rain before he asked, "Do you really think Usaeil would take a Dragon King as her lover?"

"You mean because of what happened with Rhi?"

He nodded. "Do you know the story?"

"Every Fae knows that story. Or at least what we were told."

"Which is?"

"I know Rhi was in love. I know the queen didn't like the fact that a Light in the Queen's Guard was seeing a Dragon King. There are some Light who believe Usaeil was the one who caused the end of the affair."

"Do you?"

Neve moved her hand in the mist that had begun to form. The cold didn't bother the Fae as it did the humans. "No other Fae has been with a Dragon King before or since. It's one of those unspoken rules."

"Is it?" he asked with a frown. "I didn't know."

"How could you not? It's because of Rhi. Usaeil might not have responded before or after the affair, but the fact she remained mute about it said more than if she'd made a speech."

"True. How does everyone feel about Rhi quitting the Queen's Guard?"

"So it's true?"

"Yes."

"Just the rumors have shocked the court. She's been gone so long, many have assumed the rumor is true.

They're not necessarily afraid without her. More uneasy. People trusted her. When Rhi gave her word, she carried through with it."

Talin put all this to memory to share with the other Reapers later.

"You know," Neve said. "I almost feel sorry for Usaeil."

"Why?" he asked as he turned to her.

She gave a shake of her head. "If Usaeil has taken a King as a lover, it's inevitable that Rhi finds out. The vibrant, impulsive Rhi will go after her."

That was exactly Talin's thought, as well.

Chapter Two

Neve watched Talin carefully. He was always secretive, though he used his charm to make others forget they wanted to know anything about him.

But she didn't forget.

She hated secrecy, mostly because Neve had lived with it her entire life. The Everwoods had been members of the Light court for more generations than they could count.

Neve grew up learning the ins and outs of the court, as well as how to work others to get what she wanted. If one wished to survive at court, then you did what you had to do.

Since Neve didn't have the option of refusing the mantle placed upon her by her family, she worked the system effortlessly. It should bother her how easily she was able to manipulate people, but when she stepped back and saw them for who they truly were, Neve couldn't bring herself to feel much of anything.

The Light Fae. As a race, they were supposed to be all about good and decency, but there wasn't a shred of either emotion within the walls of Usaeil's castle.

Neve observed Talin examining everything around him—from the castle, the Fae walking outside, the trees, and even the sky. His pale silver eyes missed nothing. She wondered what he saw, and how he catalogued things.

His long, black hair had the barest hint of a wave to it as it hung to the shoulders of his pale blue shirt. He shoved one side behind an ear and tilted his head as if listening.

She didn't think he realized she was still beside him, not that she minded. It gave her a chance to fill her gaze with his sharply chiseled features.

The hard planes of his jaw and chin were in direct contrast to his wide lips and thick eyelashes. It was difficult to look at Talin and notice anything but those beautiful eyes.

Except when she did look down, she saw a body that made her hands itch to touch him. His shirt barely contained wide shoulders that tapered to narrow hips where navy pants encased his legs. Every muscle was honed and defined.

As eye—catching as Talin's personal package was, it didn't hold a candle to what drew her interest—his bearing. The way he stood, walked, talked.

In a castle full of Light who believed themselves above others, the only one who had the attitude and demeanor to carry it off was Talin.

He didn't care about furthering his standing. In fact, Neve didn't know his ranking in society, and she didn't care. She had no idea how he'd gotten to court. The fact that he acted as though he belonged there ensured no one questioned him.

Talin spoke to everyone from the lowest ranked to the highest. None knew his goals, and with the easy way he talked to everyone, no one seemed to mind—which was rare in court.

Neve looked down at their joined hands and the way his long fingers held her hand securely. She wasn't the only female to want his attention. She still wasn't sure why he'd chosen her.

The first time he'd arrived at court, she'd seen him walk through the doors. He'd taken a deep breath and strode straight into the crowd.

In a matter of moments, those around him forgot they didn't know him and were introducing him to others. Neve had been awed by his interaction.

She'd stayed on the outskirts of the main floor and followed his progression through the melee of Light. Men shook his hands. Women flirted outrageously, touching him and rubbing themselves against him.

He was never unkind. In fact, he went out of his way to be fair and generous to all. In a castle full of cads, he was . . . nice.

The entire day, Neve was never far from him. She noticed how he made sure not to reveal anything about himself. All the while, she thought she was being careful while she stalked him.

He let her know how wrong she was when he came up behind her and asked her to dance in that deep, spine—tingling seductive voice of his.

In his arms, Neve felt like they were the only two in the entire castle. She forgot everyone and everything. They didn't speak, merely looked into each other's eyes. From that moment on, he was hers.

And she was his.

Suddenly, he turned his head to her. She knew that look. He was leaving again. Neve smiled, pushing aside the disappointment.

"Nice try," he said as he faced her. He brought her into his arms and caressed her cheek with the back of his fingers. "But I know I've upset you."

There was no sense in denying it. Neve gave him a quick kiss. "Go do what you need."

But he didn't move. Talin remained with his arms locked around her. "Only once have you asked where I go."

"Is there a question in there somewhere?" she asked with a quirk of a brow.

Talin chuckled, but the smile quickly faded as he searched her gaze. "There's something wrong."

"Nothing I can't handle." Neve stepped back, missing his touch instantly. "Do whatever it is you do."

He kissed her cheek. "I'll return shortly."

She wrapped her arms around herself as he disappeared. He always said the same thing. Most times, he did return quickly. But there were other times, like this last trip, where he was gone much longer.

Neve wanted to bolt back to the castle but she made herself remain still. Even though she felt someone watching her. She thought of the black roses that had been placed on her bed and barely held back a shiver.

"Neve."

She turned at the sound of her brother's voice. Atris strode through the mist, a frown in place. She walked toward him, thankful to no longer be alone.

When she reached him, Atris held out his arm for her. She looped her arm through his as they started back to the castle. The feeling of being watched didn't diminish.

"Did you tell him?"

She shook her head. "Talin had to leave."

"Dammit, Neve."

She knew Atris wanted to stop and speak his mind, but he continued on, his muscles tightening beneath her hand. "When he gets back I will."

"You wouldn't have told me had I not found the roses."

"I think it's a prank."

"That's shite," he mumbled.

She thought so too, but Neve didn't want anyone worried. The fact was, she'd begun to suspect that someone wanted to scare her. Yet she couldn't prove it. That was the only reason she had waited so long to speak to Talin about it.

"I don't want you alone," Atris said.

Neve nodded as they entered the castle. "Whoever it is, is here."

Atris let out a string of curses that would've made their mother blush. "It could be anyone. Da has a fair amount of enemies."

"Everyone at court does," she reminded him.

"I still don't know why they'd target you. Why not me?"

Neve shrugged, wishing Talin were with her. He always made everything better.

"Could it be about a suitor?"

She cut her brother a dark look. "You know I've not led anyone on. The ones who were interested, I'm friends with."

"After turning them down," Atris pointed out. "All except Talin."

Shock reverberated through Neve. Until she recalled

how well liked Talin was. "No. It can't be about Talin."

"Perhaps a woman who wanted him, wants you to pay?"

Now that she could see. "Let's see what we can find."

"I think we should tell Mum and Da."

Neve held him in place, forcing him to look at her. "No. I'll not involve them until there's a need."

"All right." Atris blew out a frustrated breath. "But I want it on record that I argued for telling them."

She smiled up at her brother. "Consider it done."

"Good. Now let's go find this bitch."

$\sim$

Talin arrived on the small isle of Inchmickery that the Reapers had claimed as their own. It was close enough to the east coast of Scotland that they could see Edinburgh.

He strode through the main corridors of the concrete building. Though the Reapers hadn't touched the outside of the buildings once used for battle, the insides were another matter entirely. Magic transformed the cold look of the concrete to one of charm and warmth.

Talin found Eoghan first. Eoghan and the Reaper's leader, Cael, were the only two left of the first group of Reapers. Eoghan stood in one of the corridors alone.

He was always alone. Eoghan chose not to speak. Talin

wasn't sure what had happened in Eoghan's past to make it so he didn't talk, but Eoghan communicated in other ways.

Eoghan raised a brow when he saw Talin.

"Everything good here?" Talin asked.

Eoghan gave a slow nod.

"Cael return yet?"

Eoghan blew out a loud breath.

"Damn." Talin ran a hand through his hair.

There was the sound of soft footsteps before Kyran appeared. "What's going on?"

"A lot." Talin met Kyran's red eyes and quickly filled the two of them in on what he'd learned at court.

"Shit," Kyran murmured. He then glanced over his shoulder into the library where his woman, River, sat amid a pile of books.

Eoghan crossed his arms over his chest, his lips twisted. It was Eoghan's version of "shit."

"Do you think it was Rhi?" Kyran asked.

Talin shook his head. "If Rhi knows Usaeil is seeing a Dragon King, she'll do a lot more than simply put up a copy of the picture."

Eoghan snorted as he nodded.

"Perhaps it's time we talk to the Dragon Kings," Kyran suggested.

Talin was beginning to think it might be. "That's ultimately Cael's decision, but I'm in agreement. I've got to return to court."

"You mean Neve."

Talin paused and slowly turned his head to Kyran. He knew Kyran was worried about his growing feelings for Neve, as if Kyran had any right since he'd recently fallen in love. At least both Kyran and Baylon were allowed to have their women with them.

He would never have that option. River and Jordyn were both half—Fae. It was their human half that had prevented them from being killed the moment they discovered who the Reapers were.

That wouldn't be the same for Neve. If any Fae learned who a Reaper was, they were to be killed immediately. It didn't matter how Talin felt about Neve because he could never have her.

Eoghan touched his shoulder. Talin swung his head to Eoghan, who gave him a reassuring nod. Thinking it better to not respond to Kyran, Talin teleported back to Ireland.

"He's in love with her," Kyran stated when Talin was gone.

Eoghan slowly released a breath and faced Kyran. Then he shrugged before pointing to River in the library.

Kyran's jaw clenched. "That's different."

Eoghan just stared at Kyran. No words were needed.

Finally, Kyran blew out a harsh breath and hung his head. "Neve is a Light Fae. You know what Death will make Talin do to her."

Eoghan nodded.

Kyran ran a hand through his black and silver hair. The Reapers were made up of both Light and Dark Fae, and though it went against a Light Fae's instincts, Eoghan trusted both Kyran and Fintan with his life—despite both being Dark.

"Talin can't kill her," Kyran stated. "I won't let my friend go through that."

Eoghan hadn't planned to allow that to happen. If Neve had to die, then he would be the one to do the deed. Talin wouldn't carry the weight of that.

He exchanged a look with Kyran, a silent promise made between the two of them.

Chapter Three

Talin returned to court, his gaze immediately searching for Neve. He began to get worried when he couldn't find her.

That's when he noticed something was definitely off within the castle. There was an undercurrent of widespread alarm. The fear was palpable, the terror tangible.

Talin kept to the fringes of the massive chamber, picking through pieces of conversations. And they all said the same thing—a Reaper was at court.

Who the hell knew he was there? No one but the other Reapers and Death. No one could know it was him. No one.

But it wasn't just coincidence that a rumor had been put in circulation about a Reaper. That could only mean that somehow Bran was at court.

Talin nearly sent up a call to Cael and the other Reapers, but he stopped. It would be just what Bran wanted. Since Bran managed to escape the Netherworld, his goal had been to kill the Reapers and Death.

He'd failed twice. Talin never thought Bran would actually show himself at the Light court, but then again, Bran wasn't exactly sane.

In all the times Talin had been at court, not once had he spotted Bran. He knew what that son of a bitch looked like. There was no forgetting that face. Ever.

Then again, Bran seemed to hold on to the same powerful magic given to Reapers. Which meant he could remain veiled as long as he wanted.

But Talin should be able to see him, even veiled. At the very least, sense him. All Reapers could. Something definitely wasn't right.

And Talin began to fear that it was all going to blow up at court.

The longer Talin went without finding Neve, the more he worried that Bran had already gotten to her. Talin then began to search for Atris and the few females Neve normally spoke with.

Talin found one of the females and hurried to her. "Have you seen Neve?" he asked.

She blinked up at him. "Have you heard? There's a Reaper at court. So that must mean they're real. What do they want, do you think?"

"Where's Neve?"

"Reapers," she repeated and put a hand to her throat, her eyes wide with shock.

Talin drew in a deep breath for patience and calm.

"Neve. Have you seen her?"

"Not in a while. Who do you think the Reaper is?"

Talin didn't respond as he turned on his heel and began to search the parts of the castle he and Neve had been to together. His heart was thumping wildly in his chest. The last time he'd felt such distress was the night he was killed.

He refused to think about it, preferring to concentrate on Neve. She was strong and sharp. There wasn't a situation the woman couldn't talk her way out of, but she had a rebellious streak that was the bane of her family's existence.

The sound of footsteps behind him caught Talin's attention. Someone was following him. He turned the corner and flattened his back against the wall. A bubble of magic formed in his hand as he waited.

He drew his arm back, prepared to throw the magic as the footsteps drew closer. Then the person turned the corner. Talin recognized Neve's face and managed to toss the magic aside.

Her silver eyes were wide as she met his gaze. "Talin?"

Without a word, he drew her against him and simply held her. "Are you all right?"

"Yes. What was that about?"

"I thought someone was following me."

"Me," she said and held him tighter.

Talin felt her shaking. "I'm sorry. I didn't mean to scare you."

"There's something wrong here."

He leaned back to look her in the face. "The rumor about the Reaper?"

"If the Reapers are real, it wouldn't surprise me to find one among us."

Now that shocked him. She'd said it calmly, the exact opposite reaction of everyone else at court. A thread of worry wound through him that she'd figured out his secret somehow. "Why do you say that?"

"No one knows for sure if the Reapers are real or what they do."

"But you have a theory?"

She shot him a quick smile. "Since we were children, we're taught to fear the Reapers. I'm not so sure that's how we should see them."

"Interesting. But that's not what's bothering you. Tell me."

The confident woman suddenly became cautious and wary. She lowered her gaze, hesitating too long for Talin's comfort.

"Has someone bothered you?" he asked. "Did someone threaten you in some way?"

Her gaze jerked to Talin. "What?"

"Tell me, Neve. Now. Tell me everything."

She pulled out of his arms. "How did you know something is wrong?"

He shook his head, unable to fathom why she was upset. "It was just a guess."

"Stop," she stated, her eyes blazing with anger. "Stop the lies right now."

Talin drew up short. Not once had she questioned him about any of his responses. Had she known all along? If so, then why not call him on it before? "Why the sudden change?"

"Don't you dare deflect."

He was at a loss because he couldn't tell Neve the truth, but he couldn't lie to her anymore either. "I'm not deflecting. I'm wondering why you're questioning me. I'm trying to help you."

"Is it you?"

"What do you think is me?"

Her face crumpled. "If it's you, just make it stop. I won't say anything."

He'd had enough. "Neve, what the hell are you talking about?"

"You. Trying to scare me."

Talin felt as if he'd had the rug pulled from underneath him. He stared at Neve. How long had this been going on? Why hadn't she come to him before? Did she honestly think he was doing this to her?

"It's not me," he said around the emotion choking him.

She threw herself into his arms. "I didn't think so until I saw the magic. I thought you were trying to kill me."

"Never," he murmured, burying his face in her neck.

"But you thought someone was following you. You were worried enough to protect yourself."

Talin squeezed his eyes closed. He was tired of the lies so he gave her the closest thing to the truth he could. "It's court. We all have enemies."

"What aren't you telling me, Talin?"

"If I could tell you, I would. Please believe that."

Her hands delved into his hair. Then she turned her head and whispered in his ear, "I do."

Talin clutched her tighter before he let her go. "I think it's time you tell me what's been happening."

He held out his hand, waiting for her to slide her palm against his. With their fingers entwined, they slowly walked back toward the ballroom.

"It's just little pranks."

Talin could tell she was trying to make light of the situation, but she was scared enough to consider even him. No way was he going to let her get away with saying it was nothing.

"What kind of pranks?"

She looked straight ahead. "Things left in my room and such."

Talin halted and faced her. He took Neve by the shoulders. "You're scared."

"I'm not anymore. Not with you here."

He searched her gaze until he was satisfied that she told the truth. "If anything else happens, will you let me know immediately?"

"I promise."

"I'm going to hold you to that."

She laughed then. "I overreacted. It's easy to do with the scheming that goes on in court. This kind of thing happens all the time to others. It's just the first for me. I'm sure it's nothing."

"Have you told your family?"

"Atris knows. I feel like such an idiot now."

Talin pulled her after him and into one of the many rooms. He closed the door. "Are you sure about it being a joke?"

"It's probably meant to get my father's attention. I'll be sure to tell him tonight."

He was glad she planned to inform her parents. Prank or not, it needed to stop. The fear was gone from her eyes, which eased the band around his chest.

Talin slid his hand around to the back of her neck and drug her against him for a kiss. Her hands rested on his waist before caressing up his chest.

He moaned at the sensual taste of her that set his

blood on fire. The attraction he felt for Neve went beyond anything he could comprehend. He'd noticed her the moment he entered court the first time.

When she'd followed him, listening and watching, he'd grown more intrigued. There had been no question of him having her. The fact that she felt the same attraction only heated his blood more.

Neve's passion spurred his own. The hunger, the yearning to be inside her drove out all thoughts but that. He walked her backward until they reached the plush chair.

Talin spun her around so her back was pressed against his front. He clasped one hand around her throat while the other fondled her breast.

Her lips were parted, her breathing ragged as she turned her head to the side and closed her eyes. Talin didn't worry about undressing her. With a snap of his fingers, her gown was gone.

He cupped a breast and rolled a nipple between his fingers. She groaned and reached behind her to find his arousal. Her hand ran up and down his length beneath his pants.

Talin turned her around before pushing her into the chair. She was smiling as she reclined in the large seat. He knelt before her, placing a leg over each arm of the chair and exposing her sex to him.

Having her bared made him smile. She was unabashed in her passion. Most Fae were, but with Neve, it was different. *She* was different. He couldn't put a finger on what exactly made her so, only that she stood out radiantly in a crowd.

He ran his hands up from her ankles to her thighs, stopping just short of touching her swollen sex. Her eyes glittered with desire and need, causing his balls to tighten.

Talin held her gaze as he leaned forward and tasted her. Her fingers dug into the arms of the chair. His tongue licked and laved over her sensitive clit until she was panting with need.

Only then did he delve a finger inside her. She moaned as he thrust in time with his tongue. Her cries grew louder. He added a second finger and pumped faster.

Her body tensed a heartbeat before the climax claimed her. With her lips parted, her scream was silent as her body convulsed with the force of the orgasm.

Talin felt her body contracting around his fingers. The need to be inside her was too great. With a thought, his clothes were gone.

Neve's eyes opened when he pulled his fingers from her. He stood, and her gaze lowered to his cock. Her smile was slow as she sat up and wrapped her fingers around him.

He watched as her lips slid over his length. Her warm mouth and tongue sent him spiraling much too quickly. He fought the passion, fought the need to give in—because he wanted to hear her scream again.

Talin pulled away from her and yanked her up. She laughed huskily—a wanton, inviting sound that made his balls tighten. With Neve, he was always smiling. She brought that out in him.

He sat in the chair. She began to climb on top of him when he held up a finger to stop her. "Turn around," he bade.

Without question, she turned her back to him. She looked over her shoulder and bent her knees as she shoved her fine ass toward him.

Talin sucked in a breath when she ran her hands over the globes of her butt. Her knowing smile at what she was doing to him only made him want her all the more.

His breath locked in his chest when she bent at the waist. Talin had to clench his hands not to grab her, stand, and thrust into her glorious body.

She slowly stood, her hands running up her legs while her gaze never left his. His cock jumped, eager to be inside her. Neve saw it, and her tongue peeked out to lick her lips.

He groaned, recalling how those lips had been around his arousal just moments before as her hot mouth sucked him. It didn't matter how many ways, or how many times Talin had been with Neve, it was never enough.

It would *never* be enough.

That thought should send him running, but all he could think about was giving her pleasure. The same indescribable pleasure she gave him.

Just when Talin was about to lose the hold on his control, Neve stepped back so that her legs were on either side of his and sat. He grasped her waist and lifted her until she hovered over his straining, hungry cock.

"Please, Talin," she whispered wantonly.

The need he heard in her voice made his rod jump again. Neve was going to be the death of him. But until then, he was going to revel in the ecstasy he found in her arms.

Gradually, he lowered her onto his arousal. As soon as the head of him entered her, she sucked in a breath. Her head fell back and the ends of her hair teased his chest as he filled her inch by inch until she'd taken all of him. He leaned up and nipped at her shoulder before reaching around to tease her nipples.

"Talin."

"Aye, love?"

"I need you."

He didn't have to be told twice.

Chapter Four

Neve sucked in her breath when Talin grasped her hips and began to rock them back and forth. She closed her eyes as pleasure filled her until her entire body hummed with it.

He placed her hands on the arms of the chair as her breasts bounced with each movement. Neve then held herself up before lowering herself once more.

Talin groaned her name, causing her stomach to clench in need. He began to pump his hips, sliding in and out of her. All Fae were sexual creatures, but Talin touched her on a level she hadn't dreamed could happen.

Hadn't known existed.

He required her to hold nothing back, and in turn, he gave her all of himself.

Every wild, wicked, wonderful part of him.

"Beautiful," he said huskily. "And all mine."

Sweat beaded upon her skin as he began to thrust deeper, harder. Just as she liked it. Just as she needed it.

He swept her hair aside and nipped the lobe of her ear with his teeth. His warm breath fanned over her face. She wanted to touch him, to run her hands over his fine body, but Talin ensured that this time would be all his.

His hands moved from her neck to her breasts to mercilessly tease her nipples before dipping lower to fondle her swollen clit. Desire tightened low in her belly.

Time ceased as they gave in to the pleasures of the flesh. Every breath, every sigh tightened the growing bond between them. His skilled hands wrung cry after carnal cry from her.

Their bodies were slickened with sweat by the time he moved them to the floor. Neve was on her hands and knees as he kneeled behind her. His large hands held her hips steady as he began to pound into her.

In no time, the climax consumed her, sweeping into a maelstrom of ecstasy and rapture. She understood the true meaning of bliss because she experienced it each time she was in Talin's arms.

His fingers dug into her hips as he said her name and thrust deep before spilling his seed within her. For several minutes, neither moved as the sound of their breathing filled the room.

"You're going to be the death of me," Talin said.

Neve laughed as they fell to the side, limbs entangled. Her back was still against his chest, his arms wound around her. She grinned, amazed at how lucky she was to have him in her life.

"What are you smiling about?"

She grunted. "You can't see me. You've no idea if I'm smiling."

"I can tell," he said and lifted his head. "Yep. Smiling. I'm that good, aye?"

"Anyone ever tell you that you're conceited?"

He barked in laughter. "Kyran does all the time."

She wanted to ask who Kyran was, but she somehow knew he wouldn't tell her. It was the first time Talin had let something of his life slip out, and she was going to accept the little that he offered without questioning it.

"Now tell me why you're really smiling," he urged. Then he kissed the side of her head.

"I'm happy. Truly, delightfully happy."

"You sound surprised."

It was on the tip of Neve's tongue to tell him how she'd dreamed of having the kind of love Rhi and her Dragon King had. Not that Neve wanted the same ending as Rhi. But the story of Rhi and her Dragon King lover's affair had been told to thousands of young girls.

It was retold as a cautionary tale, but that's not how Neve heard it. All she knew was that the kind of love she'd always hoped for existed. The kind of love where the person was the other half of another.

The kind of love where nothing could tear two people apart.

The kind of love that defied time.

True love.

Her greatest fear was having the type of marriage her parents had. They were pleasant to each other, but there was no love—never had been. It was a marriage that gave both families advantages.

Neve refused to be a pawn, but her father was getting tired of her not picking a husband and settling down. How much longer did she have on her own?

Surprised that she was happy? Yes, that was true. Neve turned over to face Talin. "How long do I have with you?"

"I'm not leaving anytime soon," he said with a wink.

Neve stared at him until she saw the realization cross his face. There had been a small kernel of hope buried deep that he would never leave. But she had her answer.

"How did you know?" he asked, all traces of a smile gone.

"You speak often and about many things, but never yourself. You keep everything completely private. You're gone for long periods, and you're secretive. Anyone who has a brain can put two and two together."

"Not just anyone," he said softly. His pale silver eyes held hers. "Only someone who knows me as you know me."

"Why me?"

His hand touched her cheek. "Because I had to have

you."

"Will you ever tell me who you really are?"

"That I can't do. Ever."

She swallowed, hurt more deeply than she could handle. Neve took several steadying breaths until she had a handle on her emotions. "Why?"

"It's for your protection. And mine."

It was on the tip of Neve's tongue to argue and tell him that she'd never disclose anything he told her, but it would be pointless.

"I didn't want to upset you," he said.

Neve lowered her eyes to his chest. "I think it's better if I know the truth of things instead of hoping for something I'll never have." She returned her gaze to his. "You."

"Neve," he whispered. He held her tenderly, firmly.

Her heart constricted painfully. Until that moment, she hadn't realized just how hard she'd fallen for Talin. She was in love with a man who could never be hers.

Was this what Rhi felt like? Neve had idolized the Light Fae her entire life. Although Neve wanted a love like Rhi's, what she'd gotten instead was comprehension of the pain of loss.

"If I could remain, I would."

"Don't," Neve said and shoved away from him. She sat up, needing some distance. "Don't you dare say things you don't mean."

There was a brief pause before Talin put his hand on her back. "I'm speaking the truth."

Tears prickled her eyes, but she refused to cry. She was an Everwood. She would wait until she was alone in her chamber before she gave in to the need to cry.

Neve climbed to her feet, summoning her clothes as she did. When she faced Talin, she was once more dressed without the threat of tears.

"Neve?"

Was that worry in his voice? Trepidation? Perhaps even a little fear? That made her feel a little better, but only slightly. "My family expects me to choose my husband soon. I've put it off long enough."

Talin's frown was deep. He jumped to his feet as his eyes narrowed with concern.

She waited for him to say he was her man, that she didn't need to look anywhere else. Yet Talin remained silent. All the while she'd been falling in love with him, and he felt nothing. Had he used her?

Neve couldn't even fathom the thought. It was better for all concerned if she didn't proceed with questions of that sort because she feared just what the answer might be.

There was so much she wanted to say to Talin, so much she wanted him to understand about her. Neve wasn't known for holding her tongue. She spoke her mind. But the words wouldn't come this time.

She walked from the room with her head high—even as her heart broke. How would she ever manage to find someone to marry after having a man like Talin?

Neve turned the corner and nearly collided with someone. She looked up to find Atris.

"Where have you been?" he asked in a low voice as he cautiously looked around.

"With Talin."

Atris rolled his eyes. "Just as I expected."

Neve wasn't in the mood for his jests. "I'm not feeling well. I'm going home."

"Sorry, sis. Not happening." He turned and clasped her arm as he began walking, tugging her beside him. "Father is searching for you."

Damn. "For how long?"

"Long enough to notice that you've been gone entirely too long."

"You didn't cover for me?"

He shot her a droll look. "Of course, I did. For as long as I could. The only thing saving your ass is the fact that no one saw you leave with Talin."

"Because I didn't." Neve jerked her arm from his hold before they returned to the main ballroom. "I'm a grown woman."

"In the eyes of humans, yes."

"In the eyes of the Fae, as well," she argued.

Atris sighed and put his hands on his hips as he shook his head. "It took weeks for both of us to convince our parents to let you move out on your own. Take what you can."

"No."

Concern and worry clouded her brother's silver gaze. He raked a hand through his short, black hair. "What are you thinking of doing now?"

"I know the rules of the court and society, but I just don't care anymore. I'm tired of it all."

"This has to do with Talin," Atris guessed. "What did he do?"

It was more what he hadn't done, but Neve kept that to herself. "Talin was a fling."

"Right," Atris said with a loud snort.

"He was. Now, since I'm tired, I'm going home. Tell Father you found me as I was leaving. I'll talk to him to-morrow."

Neve walked to the outside of the castle where the spells preventing just anyone from teleporting in and out stopped. Then she used her magic to transport her to her flat in Castlebar.

As soon as she was alone, the tears came. Neve stood in the middle of her flat and buried her face in her hands as she cried for the hope that withered and died horribly, for the love that would never grow.

She didn't know how long she stood there. When she lifted her head, her eyes hurt and her nose was clogged. She wiped at the trail of tears and walked to her bedroom.

There were times she missed living in her parents' large estate. There were always people about, working at the house. As well as visitors. But on days like today, Neve enjoyed her solitude more than ever.

The silence of her flat was resounding. Thoughts of Talin and their conversation were on constant replay in her head. Neve grabbed the remote to the radio and clicked it on as she walked past.

She removed her gown and hung it in her closet before she grabbed a pair of jeans, a white tee shirt, and a green cardigan.

Neve turned and came to a halt when she saw one of the drawers of her bureau open. She looked inside to see her panties shoved this way and that as if someone had been digging through the drawer.

She whirled around, testing the magic of her flat. No one was supposed to be able to get past her spells, but someone had. This wasn't the first time she'd come home to notice something amiss.

This time—like the black roses upon her bed—was something she couldn't shake off as imagined or forgetful. Someone definitely wanted her attention.

In order to get this to stop, Neve was going to have to find out why.

Chapter Five

Cael remained veiled in the corner of the hallway, listening to Neve and her brother. Usaeil and the Queen's Guard took great precautions to ensure that no one could be veiled or teleport within the castle, except with special permission.

Then again, Cael was a Reaper and had special abilities.

Leading the Reapers gave him insight into each of the men that the others didn't know. It's why he was at the Light court. He had no doubt Talin could complete his orders, but that's not what worried Cael. It was the fact that Talin might have feelings for Neve.

Cael waited until Neve and Atris were gone before he unveiled himself in the deserted corridor and walked into the room where Talin remained.

From his position on the chair, Talin's head jerked at the sound of the door, but the hope that spread across his face died as soon as he saw Cael. "What are you doing here?"

"This isn't exactly a pleasant place to be. Then there's

the tidbit of information you shared with Kyran and Eoghan," Cael stated.

Talin merely nodded, his thoughts seemingly elsewhere.

Cael had been right to come. "I was told you believe the Dragon Kings need to know what's going on here."

"I do." Talin's gaze was on the floor, his arms resting casually along the arms of the chair.

But Cael wasn't fooled. Talin was good at concealing his emotions, burying them deep, but he wasn't an expert like Fintan. Yet. Fintan repressed everything to a dangerous extreme. Cael didn't want Talin going down that road.

"You've a valid point," Cael stated. "I'm going to see Con soon, and I'd like you there to add what you've experienced and seen personally."

"All right."

Cael released a deep breath. "Neve isn't like Jordyn or River."

"I'm well aware," Talin bit out.

The show of anger relieved Cael. It meant Talin wasn't pushing aside all his emotions. Not yet, anyway. "I'm sorry. I know you have feelings for her."

"Like you said, Neve isn't half—Fae. She's Light." Talin pushed himself to his feet. "Odd, isn't it? How Baylon and Kyran manipulated the situation to their benefits, pushing the women's human side ahead of the Fae. But it's the Fae part that allows them to be Reapers."

Cael had known this would eventually come to a head. He'd discussed it with Death, but Death assured him that it would be taken care of.

"Even Death seemed to forget Jordyn and River's Fae part. Hell, River knew she was a Fae. At least with Jordyn, she didn't have a clue!" Talin shouted.

There was nothing Cael could say that would make the situation better. And apologizing again would be useless, other than to rile Talin more.

A tingling along his spine was all the warning Cael received before he heard a sultry voice behind him say, "I didn't forget anything."

Cael turned and sucked in a breath as he took in Death. Her lustrous ebony locks were piled behind her with curls falling about her face and shoulders in a way that tantalized him.

Lavender eyes glanced his direction before she once more concentrated on Talin. Erith wore another of her favorite gowns. The full, trailing skirt was the same lavender shade as her eyes with black tulle covering it.

The black bodice fit snuggly against her, emphasizing her tiny waist and full breasts. The entire dress hung on her shoulders by thin, black straps and dipped so low in the front that Cael had an eyeful of cleavage.

Talin stared at Death with a mixture of anger and reverence.

She looked around the room and raised a brow at all the gold. With a roll of her eyes, Erith shook her head. "I've often wondered what Usaeil was thinking when she decorated."

Death rarely interacted with the Reapers. Cael was the one who spoke to her, and even that was irregular. Or it had been. Bran's escape from the Netherworld changed many things—including how much time Cael spent with Erith.

He could wholly admit she was the most beautiful thing he'd ever gazed upon. The fact she barely reached his shoulders, but had more magic and power than all the Light at court combined, always made him smile.

It's because he knew her that he understood why she was speaking of Usaeil's choice in decorations instead of continuing the conversation with Talin. She was giving Talin time to calm down.

"It's been a long time since I stepped foot in this castle. I was here when she first claimed it as a Light stronghold all those thousands of years ago." Erith turned to Cael, but there was no smile in greeting. "You and the rest of the men need to know this place inside and out."

That got Cael's attention. Death only gave that order if she suspected there was a need to defend—or attack—in the future. "I'll see it done."

"Veiled," she ordered.

Talin replied, "Someone knows I'm here already. The rumor is spreading throughout the court faster than lightning."

Erith moved to stand closer to Cael as she faced Talin. "Is it Bran?"

"I've not seen him," Talin said. "And I've been looking."

Cael added, "The rumor could've been started by anyone. Bran or one of his cronies."

"True." Erith slowly nodded. "Has anyone said it was you, Talin?"

Talin's lips twisted. "Not yet. Everyone is watching everyone else, though."

"That could work to our benefit," Death said, a slow smile pulling at her lips.

Cael couldn't look away from her mouth. She had no idea how enticing she was—and she never would. Because he'd never let it pass his lips.

"How?" Talin asked.

Erith held out both of her arms. "Look where we are. The Queen of the Light's castle. Where is Usaeil?"

"Gone. Again," Cael answered.

Erith dropped her arms and turned her head to him. "Exactly. As she has been of late. A Reaper at court isn't the only rumor swirling, is it?"

"No." Talin laughed. "Everyone is also whispering about the photo of Usaeil with a man. The speculation is it's a Dragon King."

Erith nodded, smiling. "Usaeil isn't here to squash any rumors or get her court under control. The Queen's Guard has been in disarray since Rhi left. This leaves the court very vulnerable."

Cael frowned as he faced her. "Are you telling me you believe someone might take over?"

"No," Death replied.

One word and no explanation as to what she meant. This was how most of the conversations with Erith went. Cael should be used to it after all these thousands of years, but sometimes, it irritated him.

"So, what do you mean?" Talin asked.

Erith was silent for a moment. "Tensions are going to begin to run high. First, about the Dragon King. It might've been ages since Rhi's fling with her King, but the Light don't forget easily."

"No Fae does," Cael murmured.

Death cut her gaze to him for a moment. "As fast as that rumor will continue to circulate, it's the fear of a Reaper at court that will keep that one going. You've been accepted here, Talin. Use it to your advantage. Continue to make your rounds and listen. I think you'll be surprised at what you hear."

"I could do more veiled," he said.

Before Cael could respond, Death said a cool, "No."

Talin bowed his head. "I'll get on it immediately."

Cael watched Talin leave the room. He'd seen first-hand what could happen to a Reaper who fell in love with a Fae. Bran had destroyed the Reapers from the inside out because of it.

"You're worried about him," Erith said, breaking into his thoughts.

Cael turned his head to her at her statement. "I worry about all my men."

"They're not Bran."

"I didn't think Bran was capable of killing us, but I was wrong."

Erith arched a black brow. "So you question your judgment?"

"You choose the Fae to be Reapers."

Erith's eyes widened before she looked at him with something akin to admiration. "So you question *my* judgment."

Cael squeezed his eyes shut a moment. It hadn't been a question. "You chose each of us because we were betrayed in some way that brought about our deaths. We're all fighters."

"But?"

"There is no but. It's a simple fact. We fight for justice, for you, and for the continuation of things as they should be."

She tilted her head to the side and regarded him, her black locks moving with her. "You've always had a higher sense of right and wrong than most. You aren't hasty in your decisions, and you weigh all your options. It's why you're a leader. You should've been leader of the first group."

"I was the newest. Theo did a good job."

"He wasn't you."

Cael had never heard such praise from Death before.

She drew in a deep breath. "You knew what Bran was going to do."

He lowered his gaze, not wanting to think about that time. Theo had had his hands full with the Reapers splitting apart.

"You told Eoghan," Erith continued as she moved closer to him. "You tried to tell Theo."

"I was too late."

"It was your observations that saved both you and Eoghan."

Cael slid his eyes back to her. "That's not true. Bran and the others were winning. They would've killed Eoghan and me had you not arrived."

"I think your memories of that night are clouded with

yet another betrayal, as well as the magic Bran aimed at your head. When I arrived, all that was left was Bran. I had to pull you off him."

Cael shook his head. "That's not how I remember it."

"Eoghan had been knocked out with a blast of magic. The same one that Bran aimed at your head. It bounced off you and hit Eoghan so you weren't unconscious as Bran wanted when he attacked."

Cael searched his memories, but just as Erith said, they were clouded.

"As good as every Reaper now is, I chose the right one to lead."

He rubbed his chin. "Then hear me when I say we could have a problem with Talin."

"Because he's in love with Neve?"

"You know?" Cael asked with a frown.

Erith lifted one shoulder in a shrug. "It was fairly easy to deduce after his blowup earlier."

"You changed the rules for Baylon and Kyran."

Death hastily looked away. "I did it because neither of those half—Fae had connections to the Fae. River knew of her heritage, but she'd never interacted with a Fae."

Cael hung his head, furious and sad for Talin at the same time. It was going to devastate Talin, who'd watched his best friend fall in love and get the girl.

"Talin chose one of the most connected families to get

involved with," Erith continued. "Neve is an Everwood. That family has always been a part of court. They're respected. There's no way Neve could know who he is and not let it slip eventually."

"I know." Cael's heart broke for Talin.

"I've watched Neve."

Cael's head jerked up. "You've watched her?"

"I wanted to see who Talin managed to connect with. I was thrilled to discover it was the Everwoods, and that it happened by accident."

"Talin is charming and likable."

Erith bowed her head. "It's why I chose him for this assignment. His interaction with Neve hinted at something deeper, something more profound. I never expected him to fall in love."

"But he has."

She met his gaze. "If he tells Neve–"

"He won't," Cael spoke over her before she could finish the sentence.

Chapter Six

For two days, Talin walked the castle, listening to the inane talk of those at court. The longer he went without seeing Neve, the harder it was for him to keep a smile in place.

He missed her terribly. He wanted to search her out, but for his own sanity, he kept away.

Just as Death had expected, talk of Usaeil and the Dragon King was overshadowed by the idea of a Reaper at court. Then it shifted away from the Reapers, briefly, when anger began to build as the males became irate with the idea of Usaeil choosing a Dragon King over one of them.

The reasons and excuses as to why Usaeil should take one of the Light as her husband were varied, but all focused on one thing—children.

The Light may have sided with the Dragon Kings against the Dark eons ago, but that didn't mean they wanted any involvement with them.

The exception to the rule seemed to be Rhi. The outrageous, wild, and sometimes reckless Light Fae was beloved by the majority of Light.

Talin was shocked by this. He thought it might have something to do with her affair with the Dragon King and the way it had so abruptly ended. Not to mention the love everyone knew she still carried for her King.

Then he heard a story about how Rhi had been so brokenhearted, she'd walked into the Dark side of the Fae realm where few come back. There was a small group who claimed that it was Usaeil who saved her. However, the masses said they knew it was her King.

No one knew why the affair ended, or why the King continued to keep his distance from Rhi—though there was also speculation that Usaeil had a hand in ending the relationship. One thing was for certain, everyone trusted Rhi.

Talin wondered if Daire knew all of this since he was trailing after Rhi. He couldn't wait to ask Daire and compare notes.

The anger throughout the court might have begun with the thought of Usaeil with a Dragon King, but it didn't take long for things to turn back to the Reapers. And that's when everything got interesting.

All Talin had to do was sit back as one after another, the Fae began to claim others were the Reaper. Fights broke out. After one was broken up, another started. Magic was thrown until everyone quickly subdued both attackers.

After the fights came the explanations of why those accused weren't Reapers. Talin learned countless things about the families at court, and he suspected there were many secrets spilled, as well.

By the third day, the accusations and fights continued. He kept out of the way, never condemning or taking sides. He merely observed.

During a fight, he saw some new rumor making the rounds as people began to talk. It didn't take long for it to reach him.

"Did you hear?" the person next to him asked. "They say Neve Everwood has been hurt. It's why she hasn't been at court."

"Hurt how?" Talin demanded.

The woman shrugged. "I don't know."

His orders to stay away from Neve be damned. He had to know what was going on. Talin stalked out of the ballroom, searching for anyone from her family.

It was Atris who found him.

"Talin," Atris called.

He turned his head to find Neve's brother running down the corridor to his right. "What's going on with Neve?"

"Thank the Light I found you," Atris said when he reached him. "You need to come with me."

Talin didn't budge. "Not until you tell me what's going on."

Atris halted, his brow furrowing. "Didn't Neve tell you?"

"Tell me what?"

Atris's shoulders sagged. "Someone has been stalking her."

Dammit. He knew he should've pressed her further the other day. Talin's need to get to her right then was overwhelming. "Is she all right?"

"She was poisoned. I found her."

Poisoned? The room spun around Talin at the thought. "Where is she?"

Atris moved to stand in front of him. "First, you have to calm down. My parents don't know yet."

"They should."

"They will soon. I need you with Neve first. You're the only one I trust right now."

Talin nodded. "Where is she?"

"At her flat. Listen, Talin, someone has been going through her things and moving items around in the house."

Talin's first thought was Bran. If he were at court, it would make sense that he would've seen Neve with Talin and gone after Neve as he had with Jordyn and attempted with River.

"What else?"

Atris hesitated for a second. "There were black roses left on her bed."

In the world of the Fae, black meant Dark. None of the Reapers knew how Bran passed on the powers given to him by Death—or how he managed to retain them.

When Talin saw Bran, he hadn't been Dark. Then again, Bran could've used glamour to hide that fact.

"I'll go to Neve. You find your parents," Talin said.

Atris nodded and turned on his heel before hurrying away. Talin made his way outside the castle and teleported to Neve's flat.

His stomach was in knots. His chest was so heavy it felt as if every Dark pummeled him with magic. Talin was veiled as he walked around her building, looking for signs of Bran or anyone else.

There was nothing, which only frustrated him more. Talin unveiled himself in an alley and hurried up to her flat. He felt the magic around her door before he reached it.

As a Reaper, there wasn't much magic that could keep him out. He sensed Atris's magic added to Neve's. That meant someone had passed through Neve's strong magic.

A Dragon King could do that, but they had no reason to target Neve. That left Bran or one of his many Dark underlings. Talin didn't know how long he had before Atris showed up with Neve's parents.

He passed through the magic shields and spells to open the door. As soon as he entered the flat, he smelled the distinct aroma of poison infused with Dark magic. He paused long enough to put his own spell in place to keep anyone out that wasn't a friend to Neve or himself.

Talin rushed into the bedroom where Neve lay upon the bed, unmoving. His heart stopped until he saw her chest move.

Humans believed the Fae were immortal. That wasn't true at all. A Fae could be killed using a blade forged in the fires of Erwar—or by magic.

He slowly made his way to the bed. Talin sat and gathered one of Neve's hands in his own. Her eyes fluttered open. It took her a moment to focus on him.

"Talin," she murmured.

"It's me. I'm going to watch over you until Atris returns with your parents."

She swallowed, a shadow of pain crossing her face.

He rubbed his thumb in circles on the back of her hand. "Why didn't you tell me someone was bothering you?"

"I thought it was my imagination at first." She had difficulty swallowing again.

Talin looked around and saw the glass of wine knocked over, the red liquid staining the carpet. The poison must've been in the wine. If he took it to Cael, they might be able to figure out what kind of poison—and magic—was used.

"And the flowers?" he urged.

She shrugged and looked away. "Perhaps a prank."

"I wish you would've told me. I could've protected you."

Neve's gaze returned to him. "On one of the few occasions you're here?"

He bowed his head. "Point taken. But had I known, measures could've been taken."

"I took them," she said angrily. Then she paused as she put a hand to her throat. "Whoever this is, got through the layers of magic I used."

"Do you know who it is?"

She shook her head. "Atris and I looked into it a few days ago, but we found nothing."

"You need to be somewhere more secure. I'm fairly certain your parents will feel the same when they arrive." Talin glanced over his shoulder. Where was Atris?

"I can still feel the poison within me."

That shocked him. He'd just assumed Atris was able to remove it all. Talin put his hand over her throat and mumbled a spell that would pull the poison from her.

Except it didn't work. Not properly, at least. Talin felt some of the poison fade away, but not enough to heal her as she needed.

"You need to fight the poison and magic," he told her.

She gave him a wry look. "I have been."

"For how long?"

"Hours. Days," she said with a shrug.

Talin didn't like feeling helpless, and he was getting to that very quickly. "I think we should leave."

"I'm not strong enough to teleport," she said and closed her eyes. "I tried multiple times."

If he took her with him, Neve would know one of his secrets. But if he didn't get her out, there was a chance her attacker could return.

Though Talin wanted a look at him.

What he didn't want was Neve caught in the middle of a battle, because that was exactly what would happen.

"*Eoghan. Kyran,*" he called mentally.

He knew his friends would come immediately. Talin ran a hand over Neve's forehead, using magic to make her sleep. He then stood and gathered the wine glass and the little bit of wine that was left within.

Talin walked into the kitchen as the door opened and Eoghan and Kyran entered the flat. He glanced into the bedroom to make sure Neve still slept as he greeted his fellow Reapers.

"What's going on?" Kyran asked.

Talin held up the wine glass. "Neve's been poisoned.

There's magic added to it."

Eoghan frowned and jerked his chin toward the bedroom.

"She's fighting the effects. Her brother found her. I thought Atris removed the poison, but I don't think he could. I tried, but I was only able to eradicate a tiny bit."

Kyran's forehead furrowed deeply. "Do you know who did this?"

"No. It's someone who has been harassing her, though. Atris told me her drawers have been gone through, things moved around the flat, and black flowers placed on her bed."

"Now this." Kyran crossed his arms over his chest.

Eoghan raised a brow and pointedly looked at Talin.

Talin sighed as he nodded. "I know it could be because of me. I've not seen Bran or any of his companions. A Dark, even one using glamour, would stick out at court."

"Could this be because of her family?" Kyran asked.

Talin lifted one shoulder in a shrug. "It's what she believes."

"But you don't."

"No."

Kyran grunted loudly. "I don't either. It's no coincidence Neve was targeted after mention of a Reaper at court made the rounds."

"We still need to check out her family. I want to rule

out every possibility."

Eoghan walked past them and began to look around the flat. Talin didn't stop him. After all, no one knew Bran better than Eoghan and Cael.

"We need to get her out of here," Kyran said.

Talin ran a hand down his face. "I know. I'm waiting for Atris to return with their parents. The two of you will need to hide when they arrive."

"Of course. When do you expect him?"

"I've been expecting him. He found me first to watch over Neve while he found his parents. Atris said he didn't trust anyone."

"Eoghan and I'll stay with Neve. Perhaps you should go look for Atris."

Talin looked to the bedroom. "I left Neve alone once and she was nearly taken from me. I'll not leave her again."

Chapter Seven

An hour later, Talin had changed his mind. He, Eoghan, and Kyran had searched the entire flat. There were obvious instances where things had been shoved around in drawers instead of neatly placed as others were, but there was no hint of who poisoned Neve.

"It's been over an hour," Kyran said.

Talin clenched his teeth together. He knew exactly how long it had been. With every minute that passed where Atris hadn't returned with his and Neve's parents, Talin knew something had happened.

"When I leave, you must take Neve somewhere," Talin told Kyran as he turned to face him.

The look on Kyran's face said he wasn't thrilled with that request. When he opened his mouth to respond, it was Eoghan who walked to them and gave Talin a nod.

"Thank you," Talin told Eoghan.

He knew why Kyran faltered. Neve was a Fae, and Kyran was worried that Talin was in love with her. The problem was that Talin had begun to wonder himself if he had such feelings for Neve.

"Should you return to court alone?" Kyran asked.

Talin knew it was a risk he had to take. "I've no choice. I've always been alone."

"I don't think that's wise this time."

Talin shifted his gaze to Eoghan and shot him a questioning look. Eoghan looked to Kyran and nodded.

"All right," Talin said. "Kyran will come with me. Where are you taking Neve?"

Eoghan shrugged and strode into the bedroom. He gathered Neve in his arms before returning to the living area. Eoghan pointedly looked at the wine glass.

Talin placed it on its side on Neve's chest, the liquid still pooled within. Then Eoghan was gone. Talin didn't like not knowing where he was taking Neve, but he trusted Eoghan to keep her safe.

"Ready?" Kyran asked.

He looked into his friend's red eyes. "You're going to need glamour to hide your hair and eyes."

With a snap of his fingers, the silver in Kyran's hair was gone, and his red eyes were replaced with silver. He smiled at Talin. "Satisfied?"

"Yeah. Let's go."

They arrived outside of the castle with the snow falling heavily. Talin looked at everyone around them. The Light were grouped in small numbers and talking quietly amongst themselves.

"The Dark court is loud," Kyran leaned over and whispered.

"So is the Light normally."

Talin made his way to the doors and entered the castle. There was an unusual and odd hush over the entire castle that prickled his skin with warning.

"Talin," Kyran said.

He nodded as they proceeded further. "I know."

They both walked cautiously through the main corridor. There were few Fae about. The ones they did see were gathered together, whispering.

Neither Reaper said a word. Talin couldn't shake the feeling that somehow this involved Neve or her family.

Their boots didn't make a sound as they strode into the main chamber. Of all the times Talin had been at court, he'd never heard the ballroom quiet. It was disconcerting.

He motioned for Kyran to follow him as he moved to the fringes. Talin didn't trust anyone at court, so he wasn't going to just walk up to anyone.

But it was easy to overhear things.

Just as Talin expected, it didn't take long for him to discover what was going on. He came to a group of females huddled tightly together.

"The Reapers are real," one said.

He and Kyran halted immediately. Kyran backed behind a pillar so he couldn't be seen while Talin leaned against the wall.

"Does anyone know who it is?"

"No."

"You'd think Usaeil would return after this."

"Where is she anyway?"

"You mean with who?"

"Reapers. I just can't believe it."

"The Everwoods were taken so violently. Why do the Reapers want them?"

"Can't be for good."

"Perhaps we should leave court?"

"You can't be serious? Where else would we get first-hand knowledge like this?"

"I don't want any part of the Reapers."

"Honey, if the legends are true, the Reapers will find you wherever you are."

"Does anyone know if Neve was taken, as well?"

"Surely she was."

"I haven't seen her for a few days."

"What if the Reapers took her first?"

"By all that's magical, that must be what happened!"

Talin didn't need to hear more. He pivoted and walked out of the ballroom. Neve's brother and parents had been taken. He knew the Reapers hadn't been part of it, but someone sure wanted the rest of the Light to think otherwise.

Bran.

"We don't know where they were taken," Kyran said as he caught up with Talin.

"It doesn't matter."

"It does. And you know it."

Talin halted and faced Kyran. He lowered his voice and said, "It's somewhere in this damn castle. How else would everyone know?"

"We'll learn a lot if we find the place."

He knew Kyran was right, but Talin needed to get back to Neve. She had no idea about her family, and he wasn't sure how much longer she could fight the affects of the poison.

As soon as Talin was outside, he thought of Neve and teleported away. Imagine his shock when he found himself in the middle of a forest with snow falling so thick he could only see a few feet in front of him.

"Where the hell are we?" Kyran asked from beside him.

Talin should've known Kyran would follow. He shrugged and walked through the piling snow. After a hundred yards or so, he stopped short when he saw the cottage.

It looked as if it had been plucked right out of the days of the Celts. It was large and round, with smoke coming out of the chimney.

"What is this place?" Kyran asked.

Talin felt the magic around it—Reaper magic. "I think it's Eoghan's. It must be where he goes off to sometimes."

"I'll be damned. Scotland? Why not Ireland?"

Talin walked to the door, Kyran a step behind him. When he reached the door, he thought Eoghan might be there to welcome them. But as he opened it, he discovered why he wasn't.

Eoghan was sitting on a stump he used as a stool near the bed where Neve lay. He held his hands over her with his eyes closed. There was magic coming from him, but it wasn't going into Neve. Instead, Eoghan was using his magic to pull the poison into himself.

After a few minutes, Eoghan tried to rise, but fell to his knee and dry heaved as the poison entered his body.

Talin rushed to him, grabbing Eoghan by the shoulders. Kyran helped Eoghan back onto the stool. Eoghan's face was pale, and thick beads of sweat dotted his brow and ran down his face.

"What are you doing?" Talin demanded.

Eoghan had trouble holding up his head. He nodded toward Neve and then pointed at himself.

"This could kill you," Kyran stated.

At this, Eoghan merely smiled sardonically. His eyes slid shut a second before he fell to the side.

Talin and Kyran were there to grab him, but then an extra pair of hands appeared. Talin looked up to find Fintan.

The Dark cut his white eyes to Talin. "Cael will be here shortly."

"That's good," Kyran said through clenched teeth. "He's damn heavy."

Talin used his magic to call up another bed, and the three moved Eoghan to it. Only then did Talin turn back to Neve. She was so pale.

"How did Cael know where we were?" Kyran asked Fintan.

Fintan snorted as he crossed his arms over his chest. "Cael is almost as all—seeing as Death."

"Eoghan must've told him," Talin said.

Fintan shoved him in the back. "I had Kyran going. You should've kept quiet."

Kyran rolled his eyes. "I didn't believe you."

"Uh, huh. Whatever you say."

Talin rubbed the back of his neck. "Where's the wine glass?"

"Cael," Fintan said.

That gave him a measure of peace. If anyone could discover what had been used, it was Cael. Not that it would do Neve any good in her present condition.

A shadow filled the doorway. They turned to find Cael,

who walked inside to stand next to Neve. Talin had a dozen questions, but he held himself quiet until Cael looked at him.

"Eoghan has been pulling the poison from her since he brought her here," Cael explained. "She was nearly dead, Talin."

Talin's knees almost gave out. "He saved her."

"For now." Cael released a breath. "The poison is a common one among humans called hemlock. It's the added magic that's causing the problem."

"Because it's dark magic," Talin guessed.

Cael nodded. "Death is seeing if the specific spell can be determined. It was a good call getting the wine and the glass."

Talin wasn't sure it would be enough. He looked at Eoghan. "Will he be all right?"

"Yes. His body needs rest is all."

At least there was that. Talin sank onto the tree stump. "Neve's parents and brother were taken at the castle."

"Taken?" Fintan repeated, surprise lacing his voice.

Kyran said, "I didn't want Talin going alone. I heard the same thing he did. Everyone at the castle believes it was a Reaper who took the Everwoods."

"The more I hear, the more I think Neve's poisoning has to do with you, Talin," Cael said.

Talin clasped his hands together and rested his forearms on his knees. "I've already come to that conclusion. I searched that castle. I looked at everyone. I never found Bran or anyone who I believed worked with him."

"That just means they're good at hiding," Kyran said.

Fintan nodded his head of solid white hair. "Most likely, they were following you so they knew exactly when to stay out of the way."

"I should've known." Talin squeezed his hands into fists as the fury wound around him.

Kyran laid a hand upon his shoulders. "This isn't your fault."

"He's right," Cael said. "If it's Bran or one of his men, he would know exactly what you'd do. What any Reaper would do."

"Then we need to start thinking like Bran," Fintan said.

Cael's brows drew together. "I wouldn't recommend that. It means you'd travel down the same dark path as he has. And you'd no longer be Reapers."

"Then how do we fight him?" Talin demanded.

There was a long stretch of silence before Kyran said, "At court."

Talin turned his head to look at his friend. "Have you lost your mind? We don't want anyone to know we're Reapers."

"I never said we'd tell them."

Fintan chuckled and dropped his hands to his sides. "I

actually like this plan. Does this involve telling Neve who we are?"

"No," Talin said the same time as Cael.

It was Cael who spoke then. "Neve will need to know about her family. She'll do what any of us would in her place."

Talin nodded as he looked at Neve. "She'll want to return to where they were taken."

"That's where we'll be waiting," Cael said. "Veiled."

Chapter Eight

Bran stared at the three Light Fae held before him with magic. They were seated—not that they would get anywhere with the Dark army surrounding them.

He first looked at the father. Carsir Everwood held Bran's gaze, but there was fear reflected in the silver depths. The mother had yet to stop crying, nor would she look at him.

The son, well, Atris was another matter entirely. He stared at Bran with open hostility.

"You want to hurt me?" Bran asked.

Atris looked him up and down with complete contempt.

That made Bran smile. "I've felt that way before. It's what turned me into who I am now."

"What do you want with us?" Carsir asked.

Bran ignored him, preferring to focus on Atris. There was a possibility they could turn Atris to his side. And wouldn't that just be the cherry on top of the cake?

He stood in front of Atris with his hands clasped behind his back. Silver eyes blazed with resentment and hatred. None of it bothered Bran. Not after spending what felt like an eternity in the Netherworld.

"Have you figured it out yet?" he asked Atris.

Atris's lips peeled back in a sneer. "You're the one who's been watching my sister."

"What?" the mother exclaimed.

Bran laughed softly. "So you do have a brain."

"Why poison her?" Atris demanded.

"If I tell you that, it'll spoil the surprise." The mother began to cry harder. Bran rolled his eyes and leaned down so he was level with her face. "Neve isn't dead. Yet."

Bran straightened, watching as Carsir tried to comfort his wife with soft words, encouraging her to keep faith. His attention soon returned to Atris.

"You ran off, like a good lad, and found Talin. Just as I wanted."

Atris's brow furrowed, uncertainty tingeing his visage.

This was the part Bran loved. When someone began to suspect the Reapers weren't who they said they were. Soon, Bran would tell Atris who Talin really was. That would most likely be the tide that turned Atris.

Bran inhaled and slowly released the breath. It was so great being him. Never mind the stumbles he'd made recently. This plan would be all he needed to get Cael—and Death.

And they would never see him coming.

It was all so close to coming together that he could barely contain himself. It no longer mattered that Death managed to find Seamus. He wasn't useful anymore.

Bran wasn't worried about anything Seamus could tell Death because he'd made sure Seamus knew nothing that could incriminate him.

He walked around the family until he stood behind Atris. Bran looked across the room to the man who was his right hand, Searlas.

Searlas waited patiently for Bran's instructions, just as every Dark Fae who joined him did. The thrill of total and utter control was a high Bran suspected only Death truly understood.

"I used to be terrified of the Reapers," Bran said. "The stories my family told me scared me terribly. The tales did their job. I didn't turn to the Dark."

Atris snorted.

Bran moved around to the front of the trio. "You think I lie?"

Atris jerked his chin to the Dark. "Have you looked around?"

"They're mine. I gifted them with more power and magic than you can comprehend. They are under my command to do as I instruct."

Atris looked bored. "Why? Because someone hurt your feelings?"

"Let me tell you the real story of the Reapers." With a "come here" motion, Bran called a chair to him. It slid across the marbled floor directly behind him. He sat, placing his hands on his knees. "We're not created to keep the Fae from turning Dark."

"We're?" Atris asked with a laugh. "You're telling me you're a Reaper."

Bran's smile was slow and wide. "Oh, yes. I was one of the first. You see, Death is judge and jury to all Fae. But the Reapers, we're the executioners."

"You're lying."

"Am I?" Bran twisted his lips. "Death watches the Fae. She finds those who are warriors at heart. Those Fae who die because of a betrayal are sometimes selected to be a Reaper. There are seven of us at any given time. Well," he said as he thought about the current Reapers. "Sometimes there are more.

"But Death has rules. No one can know of us. If any Fae learns who we are, they are immediately killed."

Atris's nostrils flared. "Then why tell us?"

Bran shrugged indifferently. "I like to do things my way."

"Because you're no longer a Reaper."

The fact Atris guessed the truth did nothing to dampen Bran's good mood. "For all intents and purposes, I'm still very much a Reaper."

"What did you do to get kicked out?" Atris asked.

"I fell in love and told her who I was." Bran thought of his love as an image of her filled his mind. "Death killed her."

Atris rolled his eyes. "You want me to feel sorry for you because you couldn't follow the rules?"

"No." Bran rubbed his hands on his thighs a few times. "As Reapers, all we do is kill. Most times, we don't even know why. Death sends us a name, and we deliver justice."

"So why is there still Dark?"

"That's a question you should ask Death yourself. To Death, the Dark will always be evil. It's who they are. Death judges them on those terms. The Light are weighed on a different scale."

Atris shook his head. "That's not very fair."

"Life isn't fair. It's why I decided to make my own rules."

"And kill whoever you want?"

Bran leaned forward. "You don't have to die."

Atris looked to his parents before his gaze slid back to Bran. "You tried to kill my sister. You terrorized her for weeks. You've taken us hostage. Why would I listen to you?"

"Then don't. The choice is yours. As for your sister, she was a means to an end."

"Talin," Atris guessed.

Bran smiled as he looked at each of the Everwoods. "How does it make you feel to know your daughter was taking a Reaper to her bed? Talin is one of the current seven. My guess is he's at court to spy for Death."

"Talin is a good man," Atris said.

Bran wrinkled his nose. "That depends on who you talk to. I'm fairly certain those he's killed in the name of Death wouldn't agree."

"Why do you hate him?"

The more Atris conversed with him, the more Bran realized how much more of a spine he had than either of his parents. It was too bad Atris was so against joining him. He would be a brilliant addition.

"Talin is part of a larger problem," Bran explained. "Talin stands in my way of getting to those who are to blame."

"Because you broke the rules?"

"I followed my heart."

Atris barked in laughter. "You can't even admit you did wrong, can you? In your eyes, everyone else is to blame. Not yourself. Did you ever think you're the reason the Fae you loved is dead?"

In a flash, Bran was out of his chair with his hand around Atris's throat. He squeezed, leaning the chair on its back two legs as he glared. "You insolent bastard."

Atris merely grinned in triumph.

Bran released him, letting the chair fall back on all four legs again. He turned and stalked away, taking a deep breath to gain control of his anger.

"Shall I kill him now?" Searlas asked when Bran approached.

Bran gave a small shake of his head. "No. I need him for the parents and Neve. When the time comes to kill them, they're all yours, my friend."

Searlas smiled in response.

Bran turned back to the threesome. "I know how nervous everyone at court was to hear there was a Reaper among them. Did none of you think of Talin?" When the family didn't answer, Bran shrugged. "I don't know why not. Talin was new to court. He never spoke of his family or said anything about himself, and none of you thought that odd?"

He sighed loudly. "Had you been more observant of others, instead of furthering your own standing, you might've seen Talin for what he is. Do you wonder why he chose Neve?"

"He cares for her," Atris said when his mother cried harder.

Bran rolled his eyes, tsking. "You can't possibly believe that. Talin wants something from Neve. Otherwise, he would've chosen another female."

"You can say whatever you think, but I saw them together."

"We Reapers are great at pretending to fit in anywhere. We have ten times more power and magic than any of you. We can remain veiled for hours at a time. Talin was a spy."

"That doesn't mean he doesn't have feelings for Neve," Atris argued.

Bran scrunched up his face. "I admit, Neve has fallen for him. That much is obvious. But did she tell you why she hasn't seen him in a few days?"

Atris remained silent, his face closing off.

"So she didn't," Bran said with a grin. "I'm betting it's because she wanted more, and Talin refused. Because to give her more, he must tell her who he is. And we both know how that ends. Your sister was being used. As was your family."

Atris suddenly smiled. "You're good. I'll admit that. You almost made me believe your lies."

"Lies?" Bran raised his brows, surprised. "Why do you think it was lies?"

"Because you want Talin. In order to get to him, you kidnapped us and hurt my sister. If he felt nothing for Neve or my family as you suggest, you would never have taken us."

It was Atris's victorious smile that made Bran fume.

Damn the man for being so smart. Usually, Bran could talk his way into—or out of—anything he wanted. What made Atris so different?

"You took us because you knew Talin would feel obligated to find us," Atris said.

Bran nodded in agreement. "That's true."

"And you plan to kill him? Are you Reapers that easy to kill?"

"What I do with Talin is my own business. As for how easy we are to kill, a normal Fae would never succeed. Your magic would be like the bite of a gnat. Even if you managed to use a sword from Erwar, you'd never get close enough."

"There have to be other ways to kill you."

"Keep thinking on that," Bran said with a smile.

Atris lifted his chin. "I will. Because I'll be the one to end you."

Bran liked his courage and his intelligence. It was really too bad he couldn't turn him. But he had plenty of men in his army, with more added every day.

"I honestly would like to see you try," Bran admitted.

Atris looked down at the chair. "Release me."

"Oh, that wouldn't be a fair fight," he said with a laugh. "Besides, I can't wait to hear what Talin has to say to you. As soon as your sister finally succumbs to the effects of the poison—with my magic added, of course—Talin will be on the warpath. He'll come looking for me no matter what the other Reapers tell him."

"And you'll be waiting."

"Well," Bran said as he thought of his plan. "In a manner."

Atris looked at him with ridicule. "So you don't even have the balls to meet him yourself."

"He's a fine catch, Atris, but Talin isn't who I'm really after. Talin will be a fun kill that will outrage Cael. Just as I intend."

Chapter Nine

Talin paced the area in front of Neve's bed. It had only been an hour since they arrived at Everwood Manor. The servants simply thought Neve was sleeping. So far, none of them knew the rest of the Everwoods were missing.

Cael's plan was simple. Almost too simple. Yet it hinged Talin her parts while omitting so much more to Neve. That wasn't what had Talin tied in knots. It was the fact that Cael wanted to send her back to court.

It was thanks to Eoghan, who managed to drain all of the magic infused poison from Neve's body that they were even contemplating the plan. But Talin had been part of such a plan before.

He recalled all too well how Jordyn had been struck by Dark magic. As a half—Fae, none of them knew what power she might have possessed. It was by sheer fortune that the Fae part of her had allowed her body to slowly heal. None of them had realized that, however, so Baylon had sat by her side, waiting for her to pass.

The torture that had put Baylon through was extreme. It didn't matter that Neve was Fae. In fact, it made things worse. Because Bran would stop at nothing to kill her—along with Talin and the other Reapers.

Talin ran a hand down his face as he halted. They had to stop Bran. That wasn't up for debate. Talin wished there was another way to get to him instead of using Neve, but no matter how he racked his brain, he couldn't come up with anything.

Bran hadn't just kept his Reaper powers. They seemed to be stronger. The Reapers had yet to find him, and they looked continuously.

Talin wasn't sure about Death. Erith could find anyone at anytime, so why hadn't she done something about Bran. Unless he was able to shield himself from her, as well.

That put a whole new spin on things. That could be why Cael was so adamant about his latest plan. Talin had died once already, and though he didn't want to do it again, he didn't fear it.

For Death's life to be extinguished . . . now that was something to truly dread.

Talin knew Neve had more of an advantage than any half—Fae. Neve was a powerful Light. She was strong and confident. She was determined and well—versed in the intricacies of deception.

Neve wouldn't back down from Bran. She would focus everything on getting her family back. Talin could only hope there was a way that could happen. Knowing Bran, they were likely already dead.

Any moment, Cael would return from visiting Daire and filling him in. Eoghan was already veiled at the Light court to see what he could learn.

Fintan and Kyran were even now taking a stroll through Taraeth's court. With Bran's link to the Dark, it made sense that information would pass through there, as well. And if it did, Fintan and Kyran would find it.

Baylon remained at Inchmickery with his woman Jordyn and River to guard their sanctuary. Bran had already discovered many of their hideouts. This one had to be defended at all times.

Cael didn't want Talin at court in any fashion. His fear—justifiably so—was that Talin would see Bran and attack. But Talin wasn't going to allow Neve to go into that next of vipers and not have her back.

Five of the seven Reapers would be at court. If Bran or any of his men showed up, the Reapers would be ready.

Talin looked over his shoulder and saw Cael standing at the doorway. How long had he been there? Talin pivoted and walked from Neve's room. Cael turned to the side to allow him to pass before following him down the hallway.

"Everything is set," Cael said. "We're just waiting for Neve to wake."

"And for me to deliver the news."

Cael studied him silently for a moment. "She knows you, Talin. It has to be you. Otherwise, I'd do it."

He knew that, but that didn't mean he had to like it. Talin looked to the side. "Bran's people are most likely already at court and veiled as Eoghan is."

"Eoghan isn't alone."

Talin's gaze slid back to Cael. "Does that mean Kyran and Fintan didn't learn anything?"

"Whispers of Reapers, just as you reported at the Light court. Nothing more than that. Taraeth is attempting to squash those rumors, but Fintan did see something interesting."

"What's that?"

"Balladyn wasn't helping Taraeth."

Balladyn was once a highly regarded Light Fae and a close friend of Rhi's. He'd been turned and was now the Dark King's right—hand lieutenant.

Everyone knew Balladyn would eventually take over the Dark throne. If he wasn't stopping the rumors of the Reapers, it was either because he knew they were real, or he didn't care. Either option could be catastrophic.

"We need to watch them," Talin said.

Cael nodded. "I agree. But that's later. Right now, this is about Bran, Neve, and her family."

"Yes. One power—hungry megalomaniac at a time."

Cael smiled as he turned away. "I'm going to remain here until Neve goes to court."

Talin watched Cael take two steps away before he said, "You mean you're going to stay to make sure I don't follow her."

"Not true." Cael's feet halted. Slowly he turned to face Talin. "Even though I've told you why you shouldn't be there, I know you'll go. Because we need you. And because you need her."

With that, Cael vanished.

Talin took a deep breath. Time and again, Cael had proven why he was leader of the Reapers. He didn't just see what others missed, he knew their hearts and minds, as well. And he had a knack for using that information to his advantage.

And knowing when it was pointless to fight something.

Talin forgot all about Cael when he heard movement within Neve's chamber.

～

Neve arched her back as she stretched. She felt lethargic, as if magic had been used to make her sleep. As she looked around the room, she slowly realized that she was at her parent's house, not her flat.

And then it all came rushing back.

Neve sat up, her head swinging toward the door as Talin walked in. There was a smile on his face, but the regret in his eyes alerted her to the fact that something was wrong.

"Where's Atris?" she asked.

Talin came to stand at the foot of her bed. "How do you feel?"

"Tired. Other than that, I'm fine. Where's Atris?"

"That's good," he said with a nod.

Neve's heart began to pound as she realized he wasn't going to tell her where her brother was. So she asked something else. "I fought to get the poison out, but I couldn't. Who removed it?"

"A friend."

"My friend?" she asked, brows raised.

Talin gave a shake of his head. "My friend."

"I'd like to thank them."

"He's gone."

With each passing second, Neve became increasingly more concerned. And frightened. She tried to remain calm, telling herself she was just jumpy because someone had tried to kill her.

But it didn't help.

She'd observed Talin long enough to know that there was something he needed to say. Whatever it was, it bothered him enough that he was putting off the unavoidable.

Neve threw off the covers and rose from the bed. She walked to Talin and stared deeply into his pale silver eyes. "Tell me what you so desperately don't want to."

He briefly looked away. "Atris was taken."

"Taken?" she repeated, shock rolling through her, turning her blood to ice. "By who? Are my parents looking for me?"

Talin visibly grimaced. "Your parents were with him."

Neve took a step back as she fought to draw breath into her lungs. "They were taken as well?"

He gave a single nod.

It must have been shock that kept her upright and silent. Because in her mind, she was screaming.

"Who?" she demanded when she was able to speak past the lump of grief and panic in her throat. "Who took them?"

"Those at court say the Reapers."

There was something about the way he said it, as if it took everything Talin had to get the words out. Neve narrowed her gaze on him. "You don't believe that?"

"I wasn't there. I was with you."

She had no way of knowing since she'd been out of her mind from the poison. Then something occurred to her. How had Talin gotten into her flat? Both she and Atris had put spells in place so that no one could get into her place without one of them present.

But Atris hadn't come with Talin to her flat. Talin had told her Atris went to find their parents. So how had Talin gotten in?

Talin couldn't hold her gaze. He turned to the window and stared out across the rain—drenched landscape of western Ireland. "I'm sorry, Neve. I did as much for you as I could until Eoghan arrived. Then I went looking for your family."

"Look at me," she demanded.

Talin swiveled his head and met her gaze. She looked deep into his eyes. Neve had seen the way Talin could easily slip over the truth or not speak of it at all in order to keep his secrets.

What she saw in his gaze was nothing but honesty. It surprised her as much as the news of her family. Every time she and Talin had been together, he'd always kept a wall up between them, as if he were afraid to get too close.

There were two names he'd let slip now—whether on purpose or not. Kyran and Eoghan. Men from his life she'd never heard of before.

Neve decided to test Talin to see if what she suspected was right. "Where you alone when you went to court for my family?"

"No. Kyran was with me."

The truth lay bare before her. Neve dropped her chin to her chest and covered her face with her hands. "Why is this happening to my family?"

"Because of me."

Her head jerked up. She thought back to all she knew of Talin. For a while, she'd begun to deduce that Talin was spying on the Light court. What she hadn't figured out was why or for who?

Neve squared her shoulders. "Can I get my family back?"

"I don't know."

At least, she had the truth, but that wasn't going to stop her. "Whether this involves you or not, they're my family. I want to see where they were taken from."

"It happened at court."

"And I want to know everything you know about the Reapers."

He hesitated before he blew out a breath. "I know what you know."

There it was, that easy way he manipulated words or phrases in order to lie. Neve wanted to pound his chest and get him to admit all that he knew, but she didn't.

She needed to save her energy for dealing with whoever took her family. It didn't matter why they were kidnapped. All that mattered was getting them back.

Neve was used to doing things her own way so she didn't ask Talin for his advice as she walked to her wardrobe and threw open the doors.

If she were going to court, she was going to have to dress the part. Everyone would expect it. The Light, the queen . . . the Reapers.

And even her family's kidnapper.

She waved her hands down her body, using magic to change her clothes, add jewelry, and fix her hair. Only after, did she face Talin.

"Thank you for saving me."

He held her gaze, disappointment tightening his face. "Don't believe everything you see or hear. Trust your heart." Talin closed the distance between them and cupped her face as he kissed her slowly, sensuously. When he pulled back, he whispered, "Be careful."

Neve didn't ask how he knew she planned to go to court alone. Instead of responding, she teleported to the castle.

Chapter Ten

Talin veiled himself and followed Neve to the Light court. She looked spectacular in a gown of white that dipped into a V at the neckline. The dress was Grecian in style and flowed down her body, showcasing her glorious curves.

Thin, gold straps held the gown on her shoulders. The only other embellishment was the wide, gold belt of tiny beads that encircled her waist.

Her mane of black hair was left unadorned to fall straight down her back. With her head held high and her back rigid, Neve Everwood strode through the castle doors.

Despite the threat of Reapers, the majority of Light hadn't left the castle. When they caught sight of her, their talking ceased as they stared wide—eyed at Neve's arrival.

He smiled as he watched her. Talin didn't know of another woman who would have faced this alone. Just his Neve.

His.

That brought him up short. Until he realized he'd thought of her as his from the moment their gazes had first locked. She knew he kept secrets, and though she wanted to know what they were, she didn't pressure him.

It was that same fortitude, that same resolve that had her walking through the castle alone.

As Talin followed behind her, he heard some Light whisper that she wasn't afraid. That wasn't true. Talin could see the apprehension in the way she held her head and how her walk wasn't as carefree as normal.

Other Light wondered why the Reapers hadn't taken her. One such Fae asked that question loud enough for Neve to hear. Talin thought Neve might respond, but she simply looked at the female in question as she walked past.

With the white skirts of her gown billowing around her, Neve continued to explore corridor after corridor. She didn't stop to talk, not even if someone called her name. She had a single—minded purpose—to locate the place where her family had been kidnapped.

Not that it would do any good, but Talin understood her need for some kind of connection to her loved ones. He wondered if they would even be able to know where that place was.

Then they turned down another hall. It was long, narrower than most with a fifty—foot section of nothing but windows overlooking the sea. He heard his name whispered in his head. It was a warning from Kyran that they were close.

Neve's steps faltered, then slowed before halting altogether. Talin walked around her and felt anger sizzle along his skin.

On the opposite wall from the windows, written in blood, was the mark of the Reapers. A triskelion inside a circle inside a triangle pointed downward. If there had been any doubt Bran was responsible for the Everwoods kidnapping, there wasn't any longer.

Neve stared at the symbol for a long time, as if committing it to memory. Then she turned in a full circle, looking around her.

Talin got close enough to touch her. He could sense her pain, the anger that was close to consuming her. There were no words he could give to comfort her because to do so would mean her death.

But how he wanted to draw her into his arms, to hold her as he gave her his vow to kill Bran and return her parents. Her brother. He might not be able to say the words aloud, but they were shouted. In his heart.

Neve inhaled deeply and slowly released the breath. Then she walked to the Reaper sign and put her hand next to it. "Who are you?" she demanded of Bran. "What do you want with my family?"

A chuckle behind them had Neve spinning around. Talin watched as the veil dropped and a Dark appeared, leaning against one of the windows with his arms crossed.

Neve gasped and took a step back. "No Dark is allowed in this place."

"Your queen isn't here to stop me," came the smug reply.

Talin hated to admit it, but the Dark was right. Usaeil set the rules, and without her in residence, there was no one to uphold them besides the Queen's Guard. But they weren't there either.

He recognized the Dark from their battles with Bran. The Dark was always near the former Reaper. Capturing him would be a boon for sure.

"Then I'll stop you," Neve replied.

The Dark raised a brow. "Do you really believe you can? Alone?"

"Yes."

Talin wanted to cheer her courage, even though it put her in danger.

Neve took a step toward him. "I want the name of the Dark who kidnapped my family."

"Searlas is my name," he stated.

"Why do you want my family?"

He shrugged and crossed one ankle over the other. His

short black hair was liberally laced with silver while his red eyes watched her with interest. "I'm not the one you should be asking that question."

"So you're not the one in charge." Neve briefly looked upward and sighed loudly. "Why should I bother with you then?"

"Because I'll be the one giving you information on your family."

"What are you waiting for?"

"Say please."

Talin fisted his hands in an effort to keep himself still. They had to know where Bran was. As much as he wanted to go after Searlas now, it wouldn't be wise.

So he had to stand there and listen to the Dark taunt his woman. It was one of the hardest things Talin had ever done. The urge, the *need* to protect her warred with his orders from Cael.

Several seconds passed before Neve looked Searlas in the eye and said, "Please."

"That's better." The Dark laughed and dropped his arms as he pushed away from the windows. "All three are alive for now."

"What happens next? I need to know what to do to get my family released."

Searlas smiled slowly. "Why are you here alone?"

"Because this is my family."

567

"You don't happen to have anyone walking around veiled?"

Neve's brow furrowed as she shrugged. "No. You'd know anyway since no Fae can remain veiled that long."

Searlas just chuckled in response.

That only angered Neve. "I'm here because this is my battle. I don't need anyone to help. You took my family, and I want them back. What do you want in exchange?"

"We'll get to that eventually."

"What's that supposed to mean?" she snapped.

Searlas looked behind Neve, right to where Talin stood. There was no way the Dark could know he was there, but Talin didn't like it regardless.

"Perhaps you should return with someone to help you . . . negotiate," Searlas said.

Neve took another step toward him. "No."

"That isn't a request," Searlas said before he vanished.

Neve whirled around and slammed her hand against the wall. She put her forehead against the stone and closed her eyes.

Talin looked behind him. Since Reapers could remain veiled indefinitely—and used the ability often—Death made sure they could see each other, even when invisible to others.

Cael and Eoghan were stationed directly behind him. Coming down the opposite direction were Fintan and

Kyran. Cael motioned for Talin to follow him as the other Reapers set up a perimeter around Neve.

Talin trailed Cael into a room where he promptly closed the door and ensured that no one would be able to come in or hear them. While Cael did that, Talin made sure there were no unwanted visitors within the room.

Cael dropped the veil and waited for Talin to do the same. Only then did he say, "They're going to ask for you."

"I know." Talin rubbed a hand along his jaw. "Bran is going to force the issue where I either have to tell Neve who I am—or she guesses."

"Either way means her death."

Talin didn't want to think about that. "Is there another way?"

"We have to let this play out."

"I doubt we'll have a chance to get Bran. He'll stay away. We could take Searlas."

Cael's grin was wide. "I was thinking the same thing."

"Bran takes something close to one of us. We'll take something close to him."

"It won't gain the release of the Everwoods."

Talin wanted to punch something. "I know." It was Cael studying him that made Talin frown. "What?"

"How do you do it? I've not figured it out."

Talin shrugged, unsure of what Cael meant. "Do

what?"

"We're assassins, Talin. We kill. It's our job, it's everything we do."

"Not everything. We've been fighting Bran of late."

Cael cut his hand through the air. "All those Baylon killed came close to destroying his soul, but then he found Jordyn. Kyran loves the danger of what we do. It's because he was Dark, and though he may never admit it to anyone, I know that killing gets to him sometimes."

Talin looked away, because he now knew what Cael was getting at.

"Eoghan feels everything deeply. In order to deal with the killings, he goes off by himself. Daire feels as if he must make up for his past, so each death against those doing wrong or evil balances him. Fintan," Cael said and then paused. "Fintan buried his emotions so deeply he's forgotten what they are. He feels nothing."

"And you?" Talin asked.

Cael ignored the question. "I see you attempting to push aside your feelings. Don't. I wouldn't want you to follow Fintan's path."

Talin thought of all those he'd slain in the name of Death's judgment. He saw their faces constantly, but they didn't haunt him as they did others.

"I knew what Death asked of me. I understood I'd be killing for eternity." Talin looked at Cael. "I trust Death's judgment. If she says someone needs to die, then my sword is at the ready."

Cael sighed as he nodded. "That same calmness you exhibit daily is why Death sent you here. It's what you're going to need to help Neve get through this. Because we both know Bran is going to kill her family. It's your nature to protect, but you must do it veiled this time."

"You're asking the impossible."

"No, wanting Death to not kill Baylon and Jordyn because they fell in love was asking for the impossible. Look how that turned out. Bran has been ahead of us for the last time. Death is waiting for us to bring Searlas."

That made Talin smile. "I'd like to be the one to capture him."

"Of course. Let's get back out there."

He turned to the door when Talin said, "I love her, Cael."

Cael halted and looked over his shoulder at him. "I've known for some time."

"How? I just figured it out."

"It doesn't matter how. Have you told her?"

Talin shook his head. "I don't know if I should."

"You'll be leaving her after this is over. Perhaps it'd be wise not to say anything."

"Probably." But that's not what Talin wanted to do. The sudden, crushing need to tell Neve his feelings consumed him.

Death had changed the rules to allow the Reapers to find love, but had she meant with half—Fae only? Surely if Death intended to exclude the Fae she would've said something. Talin saw Cael staring at him with a frown.

Talin veiled himself and walked from the room, returning to his post beside Neve.

Chapter Eleven

Neve was terrified. It was the first time in her life that she'd ever experienced such an emotion. And she hated it.

Reapers she was prepared to deal with—only because she didn't know specifics about them. But a Dark? A Dark, who brazenly appeared within the halls of the Light Queen?

There was much Neve knew how to handle, but with this, she was out of her depth. She wished Talin were with her. He always seemed to know what to do in any situation.

He handled the court as if it were mere child's play. Neve didn't think anyone could outdo her father in such a way, but Talin did it without even trying.

She stood with her back to the windows, staring at the giant symbol on the wall. It meant something. Though she'd never seen it before, there was a connection, and she guessed that somehow it would lead back to the Reapers.

Everything led back to them.

Neve turned and strode away. She needed to know about the Reapers, and if Talin wouldn't tell her, then she would go to the next best source—the Queen's library.

After having been watched for so long, Neve knew the feeling well. Someone else was following her. She was tired of being spied on.

The thought of spying drew her up short, right as she reached the doors to the library. From the moment she'd first seen Talin, she'd thought him a spy. Though she'd never asked because she really didn't want to know.

Now, she wanted to know everything.

Neve pushed the door open and walked into the library. A three—story room stretched endlessly before her. In the center of it all, high above them, was a dome of windows, allowing light to stream in. There were comfy chairs, sofas, and even tables one could go to.

Though she'd rather do her research in private, that wasn't possible since she was being watched. The millions of books before her gave her pause, but just for a second.

"Reapers. Origin and facts," she said aloud.

All around the library, small, hovering lights appeared next to the books that mentioned Reapers. Neve walked to the closest book and opened it.

Since she was being observed, Neve wasn't going to be able to write down the things she found. It would all have to stay in her head.

She went to each and every book regarding the Reapers. Neve was shocked at just how many there were in the library, but most merely mentioned them as a legend.

Just as she was about to give up, Neve saw something within a small book titled The Truth of Legends. Within the pages, she learned that the Reapers were real.

The volume went on to tell her that Reapers weren't around to ensure a Fae didn't turn Dark. Though it never told her exactly what a Reaper did, the author was explicitly clear that they should be avoided at all costs because they were highly dangerous.

Neve closed the book and moved on. Twenty books later, she ran across another obscure text that mentioned the Reapers as being harbingers of Death. This author surmised the Reapers were not to be feared, but accepted as part of Fae culture.

She looked at the book and how pristine the pages were. It was at least a million years old, but no one had read it.

Neve spent another hour finishing off the rest of the books containing anything about Reapers. The last book held the most information, however. On the back cover, in the lower left—hand corner was the same symbol painted on the wall.

She opened the book, flipping through pages and searching for information on Reapers. Then the light coming from the dome above struck a page. And she saw the faint watermark of the symbol once more. It was on the upper inner corner and was so small it would be missed unless someone knew what they were looking for.

If only she'd read this one first, she could've saved herself a lot of time.

On the same page as the watermark, she found a poem.

> The seven there are, warriors all.
> Do not do wrong or their blade will fall.
> Their appearances shrouded.
> Their approach, clouded.
> Against evil they fight.
> Power and magic are their might.
> They serve only one.
> If you expose their identity—run.
> Secrecy is their defense.
> If the truth escapes, Death will commence.

Neve read the poem thrice more. Each time, her gaze stopped on Death. It was no happenstance that the word was capitalized. The poet spoke of a person, not an event. It made sense that the Reapers worked for Death.

Seven. Could this mean there were seven Reapers? It didn't seem like much of an army. Neve always assumed the Reapers numbered in the hundreds of thousands. But if the poem were right, with secrecy and magic, much could be accomplished. Especially with Death leading the charge.

Neve closed the book as she repeated the verse in her head. There was nothing more in the library for her. She needed to think over all she'd read.

She slowly made her way back to where her family had been taken. Her thoughts kept returning to the symbol. She'd suspected it had something to do with the Reapers. Now she was sure of it.

Her heels clicked loudly on the marble floor. Whoever watched her was close. It was the tingling along her skin that made her heart skip a beat.

There was only one who could do that to her with just a look.

Talin.

Neve's steps didn't slow as she began to list everything in her mind.

Talin had gotten into her flat without Atris. That would take a considerable amount of magic to break through hers and Atris's spells.

He was most likely a spy. She'd never outright called him that, but she knew he had secrets, and then there were the many times he'd disappear.

He'd said her family's abduction was because of him.

Talin refused to speak of the Reapers. It was obvious he knew something, but it was as if talking about it would be a crime.

Then she recalled a part of the poem.

> Secrecy is their defense.
> If the truth comes out, Death will commence.

The halls of the castle were all but deserted, especially where she was. Whoever watched her did so veiled. And she recognized Talin's gaze on her.

When she added all of that up, it pointed to one thing—Talin was a Reaper.

As soon as she came to that conclusion, everything made sense. Chills raced over her skin as she realized she'd taken a Reaper as a lover.

If their identities were to be kept secret, someone had to know who he was to spread the rumor of a Reaper at court. Neve halted before the symbol painted in blood.

Talin hadn't been lying. This was about him, about the Reapers. Whoever took her family and tried to kill her did it to get to the Reapers.

And if she knew Talin at all, she knew he wouldn't leave her on her own. For all his secrets and mystery, he was, without a doubt, a defender of anyone who needed it.

If he were a Reaper as she assumed, then that was why he'd told her he wouldn't be remaining at court long. It was also why he'd divulged nothing of himself. No one knew a Reaper or what they did because they didn't speak of it.

And those that did learn, didn't say anything . . . because they couldn't.

Death would commence.

Neve wasn't sure if Death would be lenient on her because she'd pieced it together on her own, but it was a chance she would gladly take. Because it was her family. They were all she had. If she lost them . . .

She couldn't even finish the thought. It didn't matter that she'd fallen in love with Talin. They could never be. It was easy to accept now that she knew the truth about who he was. *What* he was.

All she could hope for—pray for—was that she was given time to free her family before Death came for her. Neve had never been brave before. There hadn't been a need, not in court.

She smiled when she was supposed to, kept her mouth shut when she had to, and proved she was an Everwood when needed. She learned how to flirt, how to charm, how to lure, and even how to seduce.

But to be brave? That was saved for Atris. The only thing she'd ever needed courage for was when she entered court. And that really didn't count because she wore armor. It was invisible, and really only in her mind, but in order to survive at court, a Fae learned to ignore everything that might hurt them.

That invisible, mental armor did nothing for her now. She was a crumbling mess of emotions. At any moment, she expected her knees to give out.

The ones responsible for abducting her family weren't anyone she could charm, entice, or seduce. How silly she must look to Talin for thinking she could take on this foe.

But she knew there was really only one who could.

Neve turned to where she knew Talin stood behind her. "Show yourself, Talin."

A heartbeat later, the veil dropped, and she found herself staring into familiar pale silver eyes.

Chapter Twelve

Talin was filled with both joy and distress that Neve had figured it out. But then again, he knew she might after her search in the library.

"Who took my family?" she asked.

Talin held her gaze. "His name is Bran."

"What are the chances my family will live? The truth," she added, tight—lipped.

"Slim."

Talin wanted to rush to her when he saw her breath leave her in a rush, but she remained standing tall despite the news. It took everything he had to allow her to stand on her own instead of bearing the burden for her.

She turned her head to the symbol. "That stands for Reapers, doesn't it?"

He didn't want to answer her. It might already be too late in Death's eyes. Neve's intelligence in putting it all together might be all it took to seal her fate, but Talin didn't want to give Death another excuse.

When he didn't answer, Neve swiveled her head back to him. "I know you're a Reaper. I also know that by admitting what I know—aloud—my life is in jeopardy." Then her gaze narrowed. "You're not alone, are you?"

Shite. There wasn't much that got past Neve. Any other moment, Talin would've beamed with pride at his woman. Now, all he wanted to do was shield her from what he knew was coming.

Talin decided to try and change the subject. "Atris said you were being watched before. That was most likely Searlas or Bran. Neither of which can remain veiled here now."

"Why is Bran after you?"

"Because he fell in love," Talin said. "Bran told the Fae who he was. It's one of the cardinal rules that can't be broken without reprisal."

Neve's pulse beat wildly in her throat. "What happened?"

"She was killed. Bran didn't take it well."

She turned her head away, her eyes closing. "I knew it. He's a Reaper."

"Was," Talin corrected.

Neve opened her eyes as she looked at him. "Does it really matter? He's here, and he has my family."

"Neve," he began.

She held up a hand to stop his words. "Right now, Bran doesn't know I know of him or that you're a Reaper. Let's use that to our advantage."

"We're going to take Searlas."

"Not until I know where my family is," she stated angrily. "I don't care how remote of a chance it is, I'm going to try and get them back."

"And I'm going to help you."

She looked taken aback, as if that were the last thing she'd expected him to say. "I'm going to need it."

Talin didn't care that the others were there watching. He walked to Neve and claimed her lips in a savage kiss born of desire and desperation.

When she ended the kiss, she put her lips next to his ear as she held him and whispered, "I'm so glad you're with me."

He closed his eyes, his chest feeling as if an iron band were wrapped about him, cutting off his air. Talin didn't know how long he had with Neve, but he was going to make the most out of every second.

Resentment unfurled within him. It wasn't fair that Baylon and Kyran were able to bring their women into the Reapers' sanctuary, with the half—Fae essentially becoming Reapers themselves.

Why couldn't he have the same? Neve was just as deserving. She had the heart of a warrior. And he loved her.

"It was my decision," she whispered. "I knew what would happen if I called you out. I carry the weight of this."

"Why did you do it? I would've been beside you. I wouldn't have let anything happen to you."

"I know." She briefly tucked her face into his neck. "This way, I can talk to you and know what it is the Reapers plan instead of trying to figure it out on my own. It's the best way for my family."

But not for her. Talin wanted to roar his anger, howl his outrage. Instead, he held on to the woman who had stolen his heart so effortlessly he hadn't realized it happened.

Neve stepped out of his arms. "Can I see the others?"

"It's better if you don't."

Cael dropped his veil and pushed away from the wall. "Actually, I disagree."

Talin eyed Cael, ready to fight him if he attempted to slay Neve. Cael met his gaze and gave a subtle shake of his head, letting Talin know it wouldn't happen now.

Neve faced him. "Have all of you been here veiled?"

"Just today. I'm Cael," he introduced himself. "I lead the Reapers."

Neve nodded in greeting. "I have no right, but I would ask something of you."

Talin looked between the two of them, suddenly wary of what Neve might be thinking.

"All right," Cael consented.

"When my time comes, will you let me know?"

Talin immediately said, "No."

"Yes," Cael replied calmly, a heartbeat later.

Neve graced him with a small smile. "Thank you."

Talin looked at the ceiling and prayed for patience. This couldn't be happening. There had been a remote chance Death might let Neve live, but now that Cael had showed himself and talked to her, it sealed Neve's fate.

"Would you like to see the others?" Cael offered.

"Very much so."

Talin could only stare at her, his chest tightening.

"The Reapers are made up of Light and Dark," Cael explained. "Each of us proves our worth before Death chooses us."

Kyran unveiled himself and came to stand beside Talin. He held out a hand to Neve, bowing his black and silver head. "I'm Kyran. I'm usually the one who keeps him in line," he said as he motioned to Talin.

That made Neve's smile widen. "You need to keep a better eye on him."

"I know," Kyran replied wryly.

Next was Fintan. His white hair and eyes startled Neve for a moment, but she recovered quickly and greeted him with a smile.

"I usually shock the Light," he said.

Without missing a beat, Neve said, "It'll take more than your hair and eyes to shock me."

"I'm Fintan," he said with a crooked grin.

Eoghan came up to stand beside Cael. Neve turned to him and waited for him to speak.

Cael said, "This is Eoghan. He and I are two of the original Reapers. He chooses not to speak."

Neve grasped his hand and held it between her own as she looked into his silver eyes. "Thank you for saving me."

Eoghan placed his other hand atop hers and smiled before he touched his chest above his heart and bowed his head.

Her gaze moved to Talin where her look softened. Despite the circumstances, he recognized she was happy to get a peek into his life. He hadn't appreciated how much it would mean to her.

Or to him.

"Where are the other two?" she asked.

Talin took her hand in his after Eoghan had stepped away. "Daire is on another assignment. Baylon is safeguarding our base."

He left out Jordyn and River. Since he didn't think it fair that two half—Fae were allowed in, he was certain Neve wouldn't either. Besides, it was easier to omit their existence. Thankfully, none of the other Reapers said anything.

Neve's fingers entwined with his. "So, Bran wants Talin."

"He wants me and Eoghan," Cael said. "And any Reaper he can hurt until he gets to us."

Neve glanced at Talin. "Because Bran fell in love with a Fae. Did one of you kill her?"

"Death did," Fintan replied.

Talin looked at the symbol on the wall. Until that moment, he'd been proud to be a Reaper. The fact that Neve was taking everything in stride, including her upcoming death, left him with a bitter taste in his mouth.

"I see," Neve said.

Cael said, "Bran divided us, turning Reaper against Reaper until only four were left standing. He murdered our leader and came after us. Before I could kill him, Death intervened and took him away."

"Why didn't she kill him?" Neve asked.

Kyran rolled his eyes. "A question each of us has asked."

"She wanted him to suffer. So she put him in the Netherworld," Cael explained.

Neve's brows shot up as her eyes widened. "So that place is real?"

"Very much so," Talin said.

Neve's brow puckered as she looked at Talin. "Who let him out?"

"He escaped," Kyran said. "He's been after us ever since."

"You're Reapers. You can't stop him?"

Talin shot her a wry look. "If only it were that easy. He's got an army of Dark that he's somehow managed to give the same powers we have as Reapers."

"Oh," she murmured.

Cael brought everyone's attention to him when he called Neve's name. "We're going to attempt to rescue your family. Searlas is going to want to take you to them. Go."

"What?" she exclaimed.

Talin squeezed her hand. "I'm going to be with you. He told you to get someone to help. That's me."

"What if they have magic to stop you all?" she asked.

Fintan smiled, but there was no humor in it. "The magic will be down enough for Searlas to teleport you both in."

Neve bit her bottom lip as she nodded, listening. "All right. Then what?"

"Talin will let us know where he's at," Kyran said.

Fintan rubbed his hands together. "Then we attack."

"What of the Dark army?" Neve pointed out.

Cael looked at Talin and said, "We have two objectives after we find where the Everwoods are being held. We get them and Neve out. And we capture Bran. If Bran isn't there for some reason, we take Searlas."

"I'll stay with Talin," Kyran said.

Eoghan pointed to himself and put his fist into his hand.

Cael nodded. "I know. We'll each have a go at Searlas or Bran. Bran wants a Reaper, but he's focused on Eoghan and me. Eoghan and I will then capture Bran."

"While I'm kicking some Dark ass," Fintan said with a wink.

It was a good plan, and the smiles they wore helped convince Neve that it would work. But she hadn't been in battle. Nor had she been up against Bran. She had no idea how things could turn from going their way to going against them.

And she had been right to mention the Dark army. They had no idea how many were now with Bran, and the more they had to fight, the longer it gave Bran to get away.

Then there were the Everwoods and Neve. That was another concern. There was no use planning anything because it would all depend on where they were being held, how many were there, if the Everwoods were injured, and what magic Bran had put in place.

All of that would have to be acknowledged and dealt with while fighting the Dark and keeping an eye on Neve. It was a catastrophe waiting to happen.

"I don't like this," Talin said. He could no longer keep silent because he knew the odds of Neve and her family coming out alive were diminishing by the second.

Neve turned to him and touched his cheek. "I know you don't. I'm also sure your friends have thought of another way to do this, but even I can see this is it. Bran and Searlas expect me. You'll have the element of surprise. Have you had that before?"

"We thought we did once. It didn't turn out well."

"But this will," she said determinedly. "Use this, Talin."

When he began to argue, she rose up on her tiptoes and placed her lips on his, quickly ending whatever he'd thought to say.

Chapter Thirteen

Neve reluctantly ended the kiss, but she wasn't done with Talin. Not even close. She ignored the presence of the other four Reapers as she said, "I want to be alone."

In the next blink, she found herself teleported to a room inside the castle. Talin pressed her against the wall and savagely took her lips.

It was a kiss meant to set her ablaze. And as always, it worked. She was engulfed by desire, her blood heating as her heart raced with excitement—and yearning.

As if Talin knew she needed to feel, there were no words spoken. None were needed. Everything could be seen and felt in the deepest, most profound and genuine way.

With a mere thought, she removed his clothes so her hands could run over his sculpted body. The Fae often took beauty for granted since it was what made them who they were.

But there was nothing about Talin that could be taken for granted. Not his soft silver eyes, not his luxurious mane of long, black hair. Not his body that made her mouth water.

And especially not his heart.

It was on the tip of Neve's tongue to tell him of her love, but she forgot about words as her gown vanished and his lips wrapped around a nipple. Her eyes closed as she clung to him while he licked and laved and mercilessly teased the turgid peaks.

Then it was nothing but hands, lips, and tongues as they caressed, stroked, and embraced each other. Sighs of pleasure echoed in the room, matched only by the moans of desire.

Her breasts swelled, her skin sizzled with longing—and a hunger only Talin could quench.

She slid her fingers into his thick strands of hair and held his head as he kissed her senseless. There was a thread of desperation in his kiss—because they each knew this could be the last time they were together.

His hands skimmed along her ribs before he grasped her hips and lifted her. Neve immediately wrapped her legs around his waist. He broke the kiss and looked into her eyes as he held her.

With one hard thrust, he buried himself inside her. The breath lodged in Neve's lungs from the exquisite feel of him filling her. Where she ended, he began.

They were as close as two people could get, and it felt right. As if this moment had been planned for them. That second, that very instant in time, seemed to have been set aside just for her.

A hint of a smile played about Talin's lips as a triumphant look came into his eyes. He palmed her butt and began to rock his hips.

The fear of what was to come, the anxiety of her impending death, and even the excitement of learning that Talin was a Reaper all ramped up her emotions until she crackled with them.

The tempo of his thrusts grew. Neve could feel herself falling into the abyss of pleasure. Her orgasm got closer each time he drove inside her.

"Together," he whispered.

Neve nodded, unable to form words for the pleasure flooding her. She could feel her own heartbeat, could hear the ragged breaths that passed her lips.

The carnal way their bodies slid against each other, the decadence of how he felt moving inside her made her blood race and her heart swell with love.

Because he was hers.

And she was his.

The words might never be spoken aloud, but her heart repeated them often. And would for eternity.

The orgasm approached quickly. She tightened her legs. Talin plunged hard and fast, sending her over the edge. She screamed his name as her body was racked with pleasure. Fingers dug into her hips when he buried himself deep and whispered her name.

They stared into each other's eyes as they climaxed together. In that special moment, time stood still for them. Everything she had ever been, everything she was, and everything she would be was given to Talin.

Freely. Willingly.

And for the first time, she saw the way he looked at her. As if she were the most precious thing he'd ever held, as if she were all that he wanted.

As if he would die if he let her go.

Neve put her hand over his heart. No longer could she hold back her feelings. "This is the wrong time, but we might not have another chance. I love you, Talin. I think I have from the first day you arrived at court. No matter what happens, I wouldn't want anyone else beside me."

His throat worked as he tried to swallow. To her surprise, his beautiful eyes filled with emotion—and tears.

"Don't say anything," she hurried to say as she put a finger on his lips. "This is the best moment of my life."

She rested her head on his chest with him still inside her. Neve felt the tears burn her eyes, but she refused to shed them. Life, even for a Fae, wasn't always fair.

Magic couldn't fix everything, and rank and power rarely healed. That was all Neve had. Except for Talin. She had him for a brief time, and in that interval, she was going to fix a wrong for both of them.

All the while, her heart shattered and she wanted to scream her frustration and devastation. The only way she could face what was to come was because of Talin.

"Each Reaper is betrayed, which brings about our death," Talin murmured into the silence. "I was employed by a very powerful family in Belfast to watch over their children. I'd done it with my own siblings, so it seemed a natural fit. And so it was for several years. There were two boys with the youngest being a girl."

Neve leaned back to look at him, unsurprised that he'd always been a protector. She was grateful he was sharing part of his history, and she wanted to see his face as he did.

"They grew up, as kids do," he continued. "The girl believed she'd fallen in love with me. I did nothing to encourage her. In fact, I informed her parents as soon as I found out."

"And?" Neve asked.

"They laughed and said she'd get over it. I went about my job as always. There was another employed by the family that caught my eye. Corla was in charge of teaching the children spells. We began to see each other privately."

Neve didn't like the sudden flare of jealousy that reared its head.

"The boys made her life difficult. And the girl, she came to me crying, saying I had deceived her. I tried to tell her that there was nothing between her and I, but she wouldn't listen. The next day, the boys told their parents that Corla used magic to punish them."

Talin paused as he pulled out of her and released her legs so she was standing. He took a step back, but he held on to Neve's hand. "Corla feared she would be let go, but the parents simply reprimanded her after hearing she hadn't done anything to the kids. The children were outraged. For several days, they refused to allow Corla near them. And then, she was found in her room with a knife through her heart."

Neve covered her mouth with her free hand in shock. Her hand dropped to her side as she realized who was at fault. "It was the kids, wasn't it?"

"Yes, though I couldn't prove it. The parents didn't believe their children could do any wrong. The girl's affections grew bolder, and I knew I was going to have to leave. I told the parents, but asked that they not tell anyone else until I'd departed."

"The kids found out, didn't they?"

"The girl came into my room while I slept. When I refused to have sex with her, she ran out crying. I thought that was the last of it, but I was wrong. It was my last day at the estate when one of the boys told me his sister had walked through a Fae doorway. I immediately ran to find her. Only there was no doorway."

Neve held his hand tighter, waiting helplessly for the rest of the story.

"It was a trick to get me in place. The girl lay upon the ground, and I was shoved from behind. I landed on her. I tried to roll away, but the boys used magic to keep me in place. I was so shocked that I stilled for a moment. It was during that time the parents walked out. The girl began screaming that I'd raped her. I threw off the magic and got to my feet. That's when both brothers stabbed me, one from behind and one from the front."

"Betrayed by those you were supposed to protect." Neve swallowed, anger for what had happened consuming her. "I'm so sorry, Talin."

"It's been difficult keeping things from you. I wanted to tell you everything about me."

"But you were protecting me."

"I wish—"

"I know," she said over him with a smile. "I wish it, too."

His gaze slid away. "I suppose we should get back."

Neve was ashamed of herself for taking time for her and Talin when she should be fighting for her family. With her dress back in place, she turned to Talin. He stood tall and formidable in his jeans and T-shirt.

"Ready?" he asked as he held out his hand

She put on a smile, took his hand, and lied through her teeth. "Yes."

In the next second, they were once more standing in the corridor. Talin gave her a nod.

Neve looked around to find the other Reapers veiled as planned. For the next thirty minutes, she paced, stared out the window, and paced some more. She and Talin didn't speak as each thought over what was to come.

Then her patience ran out. "Searlas! I want to see my parents!"

"Perhaps he didn't hear you," Talin said.

She looked at him and frowned. "I can't wait any longer."

"You'll wait as long as we want you to," Searlas said from behind her.

Neve spun around to see the Dark smirking at her. How she'd love to wipe that sneer off his face. "You told me to find someone to help me negotiate. I've done that."

"Why him?" Searlas asked without looking at Talin.

She raised a brow. "Because he's the only one willing to come here with me. The other Light are too frightened of the Reapers."

Searlas laughed loudly. "What if I told you Talin is a Reaper?"

"I'd call you a liar," she replied easily.

"You think you know him so well, aye?"

She stared into the red eyes of the Dark and said without hesitation, "Yes."

"He'll do," Searlas said angrily.

"Good. Let's start negotiating. What do you want?"

But Searlas no longer looked at her. His attention was over her right shoulder where Talin stood. "Where are they?"

Talin shrugged as he came to stand beside Neve. "Who?"

"Don't play dumb, Reaper. Where are the others?" Searlas demanded.

Neve kept her gaze on Searlas, whose bitterness showed in every facet of his face from his pinched lips to his narrowed eyes and frown.

"It's just me," Talin said. "I knew you'd want them, so I made sure they wouldn't know what happened here."

Searlas barked with laughter. "You think to protect them?"

"It's what I do."

Neve's heart swelled with pride at the man beside her. All he wanted to do was protect those he cared about, and in the end, it had cost him his life. Yet he was protecting once more—her.

"Once Bran has you, Cael will come," Searlas stated confidently.

Talin lifted one shoulder. "Not if he thinks it's a trap."

"We both know that's a lie. Cael would never leave one of his men behind."

Neve shifted her feet. "I don't know who this Cael is or why he matters. I just want my family. I've done as you asked and brought Talin. Let me see my parents and brother."

Searlas's red gaze moved to her as he grinned. "The rest of the negotiations will conclude with Bran." He held out his hand. "Come, Light. It's time to see your family."

"She's not going anywhere without me," Talin declared.

"I was hoping you'd say that."

Neve suppressed a shudder as she and Talin walked to Searlas and took his hands.

Chapter Fourteen

Death stood before a window in her tower, looking out over the many shades of flowers surrounding the area but she didn't see them. Her thoughts were on Talin's mission.

There was a sound behind her. She waited for Seamus to speak. Though he was still her prisoner, she allowed him to wander a few places throughout the tower.

"You look troubled," Seamus said as he walked to stand beside her.

"Cael is going after Bran with his men."

"There's something else."

She sighed and turned her head to look at him. "I like my privacy. Perhaps it was a mistake to allow you to roam."

Seamus threw up his hands and took a step back. "I thought you might want to talk. My mistake."

When he turned and began to leave, Erith discovered she didn't want to be alone. How odd, since she'd always been alone. And liked it that way. "I should be with them."

"No, you shouldn't," Seamus said as he faced her. "I still agree with Cael, you should remain here."

"I don't hide."

"No one said you were."

Erith held out her arms. "That's exactly what I'm doing. I don't fear Bran."

Seamus lifted a brow, silently questioning her outburst.

Fine. Maybe she did fear him. A little. But she was Death! She'd never feared anything before.

"We need to know how Bran is getting his power and passing it on to his army," Seamus said into the silence.

Erith wearily shook her head. "I've tried."

"While doing a million other things. Let me," Seamus urged. "It's what I do, Erith. I solve puzzles."

He'd solved how to free Bran from the Netherworld. If anyone could figure this out, it was Seamus. It was too bad he couldn't determine why her magic seemed to be fading.

"Yes. My library is yours to search," she told him.

But Seamus didn't leave. "I shouldn't have been able to find the doorway leading to the Netherworld."

"That's right." Her magic had hidden it for millions of years.

"If the doorway became visible that means—"

"Something is happening to my magic," she interrupted him, her tone terse. He was putting it together anyway. The Puzzle Solver.

Erith sighed and turned her head away. Her magic had never failed her. Never. Why now? Why, when she needed it the most?

The only thing she could be thankful for was that Bran had been the only one to escape the Netherworld. She'd since moved the doorway from Ireland to her own realm, but that didn't alleviate her worry.

"If I may be so bold," Seamus said. "How long have you noticed?"

"I didn't. Not until we discovered that Bran escaped, and I learned how you helped him." That had been a vicious blow. If she'd known the particulars, she never would've allowed Cael to be in the room as she questioned Seamus.

As it was, Cael also knew something was off with her magic. It's why he didn't want her involved with catching Bran. It didn't feel right to have anyone—especially Cael—trying to shield her.

Erith had never needed anyone.

It stung that she did now. Seamus was right, she couldn't focus all her energy on finding out how Bran was growing his magic because she had other duties.

"There might be a connection," Seamus said, tapping his chin with his forefinger.

Erith watched him with his brow furrowed and his face deep in thought. His silver—laced black hair became unruly as he raked his hands through it again and again. A habit when he was deep in thought. She could practically see him turning everything over in his mind.

"Yes. A connection," he murmured to himself, his wide—set eyes looking about the room but seeing what was in his mind instead of what was actually there.

Without another word, he walked from the chamber. She watched him before turning back to the window and the sun sinking into the horizon.

The sky was a vivid pink and orange. It was a stunning sight she enjoyed immensely. Each sunrise and sunset was different. She never knew what colors would appear until it happened.

It was one of the few surprises that she actually enjoyed.

When the sun sank below the skyline, she turned away from the window and thought about Talin. And how he'd fallen in love with a Fae.

She wasn't sure why she hadn't killed Neve yet. Maybe it was because Neve's family had been taken by Bran. Perhaps it was because Neve had pieced Talin's identity together on her own without Talin letting anything slip.

It might even be because Neve knew what she'd risked by alerting Talin and the others to her knowledge of them being Reapers.

Erith also knew that Talin was furious with the entire situation. It wasn't like she took pleasure in killing those who learned of the Reapers.

None would ever know how it took a piece of her soul each time she had to do it. But rules were rules. If only Neve were half—Fae and knew nothing of the Fae like Jordyn and River, then things would be different.

But Neve was from a large family with ties to the Light court and society. One small slip and everything could be ruined for the Reapers.

It wasn't a chance Erith was willing to take. Above all else, the Reapers' identities must be protected and kept secret.

~

Daire watched as Balladyn kissed Rhi. He wanted to gag. The Dark shouldn't be anywhere near Rhi, but it wasn't as if he'd say anything.

His mission to watch and follow Rhi while remaining veiled—and silent—had shown him a lot about the infamous Light Fae. Rhi had a thing for driving her Lamborghini around Austin, Texas.

She shopped endlessly for anything, but mostly shoes. It was like she couldn't get enough. And the more unusual or beautiful, the more she had to have them.

Rhi loved to surprise the Dragon Kings—especially Con. She went out of her way to rile the King of Kings. And did it effortlessly. With style.

She had an obsession with nail polish, but not just any polish. It had to be OPI. Her collection rivaled that of her shoes and contained every color. When OPI came out with a new set of colors, Rhi was the first in line to get them.

And she didn't just look at the polish. She used them. Rhi had her nails done constantly. A favorite nail tech named Jesse was the only one who ever touched her nails and painted the special designs.

What he learned most, however, was that she loved her people. Rhi looked out for the Light continuously. They had no idea how many times she'd put her life on the line for them.

Then there were the Dragon Kings. There were a few of the Kings she considered friends. She'd helped save their arses more times than he could count, and she had no intention of stopping.

Rhi was loyal beyond measure, exceedingly focused, and decidedly motivated. Right now, all of that was geared toward reminding the queen, Usaeil, that their people were more important than some movie.

At least, he wished she were focused on that instead of

wrapping her arms around Balladyn's neck.

Rhi was a gem of the Light, and Balladyn—regardless of the hero he'd been while he was a Light—was going to be king of the Darks one day.

Despite Balladyn capturing Rhi and attempting to turn her Dark, she'd forgiven him and taken him as a lover.

On one hand, Daire could understand. Rhi had been alone for so very long. She had no idea why the affair with her Dragon King ended or why her love went unanswered. She needed someone, and Balladyn had been relentless as he pursued her.

On the other hand, if Rhi still loved her Dragon King, she shouldn't be with anyone. Much less the Dark who'd tortured her and tried to turn her.

Sometimes it was difficult for Daire to remain silent as he watched Rhi make decisions he could see were impacting her future. Yet they were her decisions to make.

"What is it?" Balladyn asked her.

Rhi pulled out of his arms and looked at the tropical isle she'd claimed as her own. "Did you find out any more on the Reapers?"

"Isn't what we learned enough?" he asked, his face scrunched.

Rhi shrugged and kicked at the sand. "Are the Dark still talking about them?"

Balladyn's lips compressed briefly. "More so now than ever. Stop looking, Rhi. You keep looking, and you're bound to gain their attention."

It's what she wanted. Daire knew that, but Balladyn didn't. She kept things from Balladyn, like her desire to talk to a Reaper—and the magazine that showed Usaeil with a blonde man.

Daire knew it all. Mostly because he followed her, but Rhi knew he was there. She spoke to him, not that he could answer. She let him see her sadness, her pain, and her heartache as no one else had witnessed.

It's why Daire knew Balladyn wasn't for her. Many times, he'd been tempted to answer when she spoke. There had even been one occasion recently where he'd almost told her he was a Reaper.

But he knew the rules.

Though none of the Reapers knew Death's interest in Rhi, the fact was there was one. If he told Rhi who he was, she would have to die.

Daire agreed with Death—Rhi was important to the future of all the races on Earth—human, Fae, and Dragon King.

To what capacity, though?

Balladyn sighed loudly. "I must return. Taraeth is calling for me."

After a quick kiss, he teleported away. Daire remained

next to the palm tree, waiting to see what Rhi would do next. She spent a lot of time at the isle. When she wasn't there she also liked to know what was going on with the Dragon Kings and their fight with one of their own—Ulrik.

"Your disapproval is like a cloud," Rhi said as she turned to face Daire.

She couldn't see him. She wasn't even supposed to know he was there, but from the very first, she'd sensed him.

He crossed his arms over his chest. Damn right, he disapproved.

"I deserve some happiness," she stated.

Everyone did. But most especially her. Rhi had hurt for so very long.

She faced the ocean. The wind blew the long, black strands of her hair about her. "I've seen Balladyn's eyes turn silver."

Now that truly shocked Daire. He moved to stand beside her, coming as close as he dared.

She bent and picked up a seashell. "He loves me, and I think there might be a chance to change him back to Light."

The chance was slim, but Daire couldn't argue that there was a possibility. It had been done before. Most recently with a female Dark who'd fallen in love with a

Dragon King. But Shara had wanted to become Light.

Balladyn wanted to be king of the Darks. He couldn't do that as a Light.

"He's what the Light needs," Rhi murmured, turning the seashell in her fingers.

Now that, he'd argue with. What the Light needed was their queen to remember her role, but that was unlikely to happen anytime soon. In the meantime, what the Light needed was Rhi.

Daire felt a disturbance he'd never felt before, like a shockwave went around the world. He waited to hear one of the Reaper's voices, but there was only silence.

Unease shifted through him. His gaze jerked to Rhi.

A frown suddenly creased her forehead. She lifted her beautiful face to the sun. "Something has happened at court."

In a blink, she was gone. Daire had no trouble following her. He appeared beside her in the hallowed halls of Usaeil's castle.

It had been so long since he'd stepped foot in the castle, that he had the sudden urge to leave. But Rhi—and whatever had drawn her—held him there.

The quiet sent a chill of foreboding down his spine. There wasn't a Fae in sight. It was as if everyone had vanished. Or fled.

As a Reaper, he wasn't surprised to register that some-

610

thing had happened with the Fae. It wasn't the first time, nor would it be the last. But Rhi? He was curious as to how she'd found out that something was wrong.

Always more questions where the Light Fae was concerned. And he suspected he'd never learn the answers to any of them.

Daire was surprised when Rhi veiled herself as if she too sensed the lingering danger. Where were the Reapers? Daire held off calling to them until he learned what was going on.

He glanced over at Rhi. His Reaper magic allowed him to continue to see her, even veiled, but the same didn't apply to her.

Her ability to remain veiled far longer than other Fae was something that confounded him. It was another reason he suspected Death was curious about the Fae.

Rhi took a deep breath and lifted her chin. The warrior rising to the surface in a rush. Her silver eyes stared straight ahead as if attempting to see through walls.

She cast a glance in his direction and gave a nod. Daire flexed his fingers as she called to her sword. It appeared in her hand as she took the first step.

They walked through the hallways and tall corridors, each on edge, waiting to find the source of what drew them.

They turned a corner, and Daire saw the other

Reapers. That's when he knew—this was about Bran.

Chapter Fifteen

The moment Talin and Neve arrived at the manor with Searlas, he was prepared for anything. Beside him, Neve held her head high, ready to face whatever came.

She was strong, but was she resilient enough for whatever Bran had in store for them? Because Talin could only imagine what the ex—Reaper planned.

There was laughter behind them. Talin whirled around to find Bran standing next to an enormous granite hearth with intricately carved details of cherubs and flowers.

Bran's silver eyes crinkled at the corners as he looked at them. "I knew you'd come," he told Talin.

The urge to move closer to Neve was great, but Talin held himself in check. The more he showed his feelings for her, the worse Bran would do to her and her family. "You requested someone to help negotiate."

"Enough," Bran stated harshly. Gone was all trace of mirth as he now glared. "We both know you came with the beautiful Neve because you've been wooing her."

"So I have." There was no need for Talin to deny it. Bran already knew. But just how much did Bran really *know*? That's what Talin would have to determine while talking to a psychopath who sought everyone's destruction.

Bran's gaze moved to Neve. He took two steps toward her, appreciation filling his expression. "I've watched you for some time now. You're amazing."

"I'd thank you for such a compliment, if you hadn't kidnapped my family," she replied coolly.

Bran's smile grew. "Ah, I do love that pluck. I'd caution you, however, because it could get your family killed."

She held his gaze for a long minute. "What do you want from me?"

"It's simple, really," Bran said. He turned and clasped his hands behind his back as he stared at the fire, his head bent forward. "You have a choice to make."

"What choice?"

"We'll get to that in a moment."

Talin had a sick feeling in his gut. Whatever Bran planned was far from good. The air was heavy with Dark magic, and he had no idea where the rest of Bran's army was.

He could take out Searlas, but that would be too . . . easy. In the times Talin had battled Bran, he'd discovered that Bran liked to come at the Reapers with a move they weren't expecting.

Talin had to make a quick decision. Go for Searlas,

leaving Neve to defend against Bran. Or wait.

As difficult as it was, Talin waited. He clenched his hands at his sides, the need to go after Bran overwhelming as it mixed with his fury.

Bran's head turned, his gaze locking with Talin's. A small smile lifted one side of Bran's lips as if he knew exactly the struggle within Talin.

"I want to see my family," Neve said into the silence.

Talin glanced at her, silently urging her to remain quiet. But it was her family at stake. How could he expect her to stand there, waiting for the maniac to make a move?

Ignoring Talin, Neve said, "I've done what you asked of me."

"Not all." Bran's gaze returned to the fire as if he were bored with them.

Talin looked behind him. The capacious room was filled with furniture from the human world, the opulence dripping from every piece staggering. In the far corner, dozens of steps away, was Searlas, wordlessly watching the entire scene.

As Talin turned back to Bran, he let his gaze wander the room, but he saw no sign of any Reapers, veiled or not. The situation was going from bad to worse.

They'd all assumed Kyran would be able to follow them to wherever Searlas had taken them, but what if he hadn't. Talin would have to assume he'd fight Bran alone.

He wasn't afraid to face Bran, but it wasn't just Bran. It was Searlas and an entire Dark army as well. Talin was good, but not nearly good enough to defeat all of them and keep Neve safe.

His other option was to attempt to leave with Neve. She'd never forgive him for abandoning her family, but at least she'd be safe.

For how long, though? Bran would continue coming after her. Talin wanted to bellow his frustration.

"How much do you love your family, Neve?" Bran asked.

She briefly met Talin's gaze. "Deeply."

"I was so hoping you'd say that."

~

Rhi looked around the corridor that stood as empty as every other room in Usaeil's castle. Yet she knew she wasn't alone.

It wasn't just her watcher either. There were others there. Veiled. Watching.

Waiting.

The fact that they could see her when she veiled—same as her watcher—was like a kick in the pants. Had she been right all along in thinking her watcher was a Reaper? Were those surrounding her also Reapers?

Rhi wanted to demand an answer, but she held back the words before they passed her lips. If her watcher had told her nothing, what made her think these others would?

She looked to where her watcher stood on her right. For all these many weeks he'd followed her, veiled. Not once had he spoken or shown himself.

He had touched her—briefly.

Though she didn't know her watcher, she felt safe with him. Perhaps she was going mad. And perhaps she didn't care anymore.

She lowered her sword and looked first one way down the hall and then the other. When no other Fae appeared, she dropped her veil and glanced out the windows as thick raindrops began to hit the glass.

Then she turned and saw the symbol painted with blood on the wall. For several seconds, she couldn't move as she imagined all sorts of things that had happened at the castle.

"I don't know who you are," she said aloud to those watching her. "I don't care. But if you had anything to do with what happened to my people, I will hunt you down and kill you myself."

She faced her watcher. Then, deliberately, she turned

to where she sensed each of the other three. Seconds stretched to minutes. Rhi wasn't the most patient of individuals, and she was about to make a demand when a deep, rich voice filled the space.

"It wasn't us."

She turned to her right where she detected the owner of the voice stood next to the window. "You expect me to believe that when you won't show yourselves? I was born in the morning, but not this morning, sugar."

Was that a snort of laughter she heard behind her? Rhi didn't turn to find out. She waited for her watcher to say something, anything. But he remained silent, as usual.

"The Light are safe," the voice said. "They ran."

Well, that was good news. "And Usaeil? Was she here?"

Silence.

As if she expected a different answer. Rhi rolled her eyes. She drew in a deep breath and glanced at the symbol in blood. "What does that mean?"

"Nothing."

It was her turn to snort—loudly. And loaded with sarcasm. "I'm going to find answers. I'm going to get the truth. It doesn't matter how long it takes. I won't stop looking."

"A family was kidnapped," the voice replied, choosing to ignore her threats.

Rhi didn't like being ignored. Obviously this individual had no idea who she was.

Worse, maybe he did. And didn't care.

Now that was a new feeling for her. Her reputation gave her enough respect, admiration, and even fear that others didn't bother her.

This group could give a rat's ass.

She grimaced when an image of Con flashed in her mind. Ugh. She did *not* want to be thinking of that jackass right now.

"What family?" Rhi asked.

"The Everwoods."

"Well, hell," she mumbled. She liked the Everwoods. "All four?"

"All but Neve."

Rhi turned her back to the windows and leaned against the glass. Why would they leave Neve? Unless she hadn't been around when the rest were taken. She needed to find Neve immediately.

Just as Rhi was about to leave, she drew up short and turned to glare at the spot where the disembodied voice had been coming from. "Neve already knows, doesn't she?"

"Yes."

"Yes," she mimicked in a mocking voice. "You might've told me."

"I wanted to see how quickly you'd figure it out."

"I'm really not liking you," Rhi said with a shake of her head. "Where is Neve?"

"Why?"

She threw up her hands in exasperation. "So I can sing her a song. Why do you think?"

This time, she was sure she heard a bark of laughter that was quickly covered up.

She couldn't stop her own smile as she raised a brow at the voice. "How are you liking my quick wit, sweetcheeks?"

"I'm not," he said tightly.

"It takes a certain kind to get me," she said with a shrug.

There was a loud sigh. "If I tell you where Neve is, what will you do?"

"Help her if she needs it." Rhi pushed away from the window, her mind racing. "You know who kidnapped the family?"

"I do."

"Why aren't you going after them?"

"We were about to."

It had been a while since she'd been in a good battle. "Can I join you? I'm wicked good with a blade," she said, swinging her sword around her in a dancing arc.

The silence was deafening. Though she couldn't see them, Rhi could imagine they were debating whether to include her or not. She lowered her sword, waiting.

"Not this time."

And then they were gone. All but her watcher.

Rhi couldn't believe they'd left her behind. But she wasn't going to give up that easily. If Usaeil wasn't there to protect the Light, then Rhi would do it.

She strode to the symbol. If the man she'd just spoken with hadn't made the mark, then the one who took the Everwoods had.

And that meant Rhi could find them.

Her fingertips tingled with magic as she raised her hand. Her watcher rushed to her side as if to halt her, but he stopped just short of touching her. Again.

Just once, she wanted him to put his hand against her, to feel her. He never allowed himself to get that close, and it was really beginning to frustrate her.

Rhi put her hand in the blood and pushed her magic into it. She'd never had to use her magic like this before, but she knew it could be done.

Gossamer visions of Fae passed around—and through—her, moving quickly as if on rewind. She saw Neve, but couldn't clearly make out the man beside her. Or those around her. There was an awesome amount of magic being used to prevent her from seeing faces.

Rhi used more magic in an attempt to get a better view, but her focus changed when a Dark arrived. She gasped at the intrusion, but the Dark teleported Neve and the man with her.

The black trail of the Dark's magic was faint. Rhi turned to see it floating through the air, leaving a winding path and telling her exactly where she needed to go.

She dropped her hands and looked at her watcher. "Don't you dare try to stop me," she said before following the black trail.

Chapter Sixteen

Neve stood her ground. She didn't have another choice. The man standing before the fire was clearly deranged. But the fact that he was also clearly brilliant was what scared the hell out of her.

Every time she asked about her family, they seemed further and further out of reach. The idea that she might never see them again made tears sting her eyes.

Bran ran a hand through his jaw—length black hair before he turned to her. Silver eyes bored into hers. It was all she could do not to take a step back. While the outside of him was as beautiful as any Fae, she could see the anger and evil twisting him on the inside.

It showed in his words and his eyes.

"You don't like me," he stated.

Neve kept control of the many vile things she wanted to spew at him. Instead, she said, "What do you expect? You took my parents."

"Because of Talin."

At his name, Talin took a step toward Bran. "Your fight is with me."

Bran dragged his eyes from her and looked at Talin. "Do you love her?"

"I'm not going to stand by while you continue to kill innocents, whether they're half—Fae or someone I happen to look at."

"Oh, you've done more than look," Bran said with a knowing smile. "I'd say you . . . explored . . . Neve, inside and out, thoroughly. Many times."

Neve nearly gagged at the thought of Bran watching them make love. Beside her, Talin didn't so much as bat an eye.

"I was spying on the castle," Talin said. "I took what information I could get. Anywhere I could get it."

If Neve hadn't spoken to Talin earlier, she might actually think he'd exploited her. Then she realized she could use his words to her advantage.

She gasped and moved away from him. "You . . . used me?" she asked, affronted.

Talin didn't even look her way when he said, "I had my orders."

"Bravo," Bran said as he clapped loudly. Then he threw back his head and laughed. "Nice try, you two."

"I don't know what you're talking about," Neve said. "I trusted Talin. Look where that's gotten me. You think I mean something to him, so you take my family? Obviously, we were both wrong."

Bran never quit smiling. His eyes swung to Talin, his brows raised expectantly.

Talin merely released a long breath.

Bran chuckled as he grinned at Talin. "How did you miss that I was there?"

A muscle ticked in Talin's jaw, but he said nothing. Neve wanted to take his hand to offer him—and her—comfort.

"I saw you watching her," Bran continued as he walked around Talin slowly. "The hunger that burned in your gaze each time you saw Neve. And the obsessive way you kept her all to yourself."

Neve tried to swallow, but her mouth was too dry. Had Talin really looked at her like that?

Bran stopped between them. "You glanced at no other women. Because you wanted only one. Her," Bran said and pointed at Neve.

She lowered her gaze to the floor, unsure of what Bran's intentions were. Neve was ill—prepared for any of this, and she didn't want to do or say anything that would impede Talin's attack.

"And you," Bran said as he faced her. "Your father pushed male after male before you. You ignored all of them until Talin. You took one look at him and were his."

Her head jerked up. "How long have you been at court?"

Bran merely smiled. "You wanted him, and you went after him. How far were you prepared to go to get him, dear Neve?"

"As far as I needed. So I feel for him? What of it?"

"You admit your love?"

Somehow, Neve realized too late that she'd mis-stepped. Royally. There was no way she could backtrack or attempt to say something else. Her feelings were out there for any and all to see.

Out of the corner of her eye, she saw Talin staring at her. There was no turning back now.

"I do," she answered, her voice coming out hoarse and wispy.

Bran's smile was wide. "This makes up for discovering that Jordyn didn't die, or that I couldn't get my hands on River."

Neve had no idea who those women were. She glanced at Talin, but he was scowling intently at Bran. Neve returned her gaze to Bran to watch as he spun around and looked at each of them.

"You're going to know how I felt," he said.

His eyes were too bright for Neve's liking. He'd just stepped onto the crazy train, and she was about to get pulled onto it, as well.

Bran raised a brow at Talin. "What? No cutting re-mark?"

"There's nothing to say," Talin replied.

Neve wanted to get things back on track. "Please. My family."

"Family," Bran murmured as if recalling a memory. His eyes went soft for a moment before anger once more filled his gaze. He glared at Talin. "That's what Cael and the others were to me."

"You made your choices," Talin said. "You knew the rules."

"Rules Death is now changing. Why now?"

Neve covertly looked around the expansive room but she didn't see the grand decor, antique tables, or the fine furniture. She was looking for any hint of her family or the rest of the Reapers.

But there was nothing.

Panic began to set in. This wasn't the plan.

She tried to pull her magic to her to use it against Bran, but it took massive amounts of effort to call even a thimbleful.

Bran must've done something. The bastard.

Neve understood what hate was. He was the cause of all of this. And she was nearly fed up, playing along with whatever psycho scenario Bran had in mind.

"You didn't give Death a choice," Talin said, pulling Neve's mind back to the conversation.

A large bubble of magic the size of a bowling ball appeared in Bran's hand. Iridescent streams of power swirled within. He looked down at the orb before slowly lifting silver eyes filled with hatred to Talin. "Not true. I was in love. Why should we have to choose?"

Choose? What was this? Neve's throat felt like it was closing up as she searched Talin's face for a hint that Bran was out of his mind.

Bran barked out a dry laugh. "Ah, Neve. There is so much you don't know about Talin. For instance, he's a Reaper."

Neve shook her head, unable to voice the words that would keep Bran thinking she didn't know the truth.

"Oh, yes. He's the very thing everyone fears. He's not allowed to tell you, because if he does, he'll have to kill you."

Neve turned her head away. Not because Bran was saying things she already knew, but because Talin refused to look at her. It was almost as if he were preparing himself for some secret about to be exposed. But she knew everything.

Didn't she?

"We're not permitted to have relationships. Or we weren't," Bran continued.

Neve's heart nearly burst with hope. But then shattered into a million pieces a second later.

"Well, some of the Reapers are allowed. Death saved

Jordyn's life so she could be with Baylon. Is Jordyn living with the Reapers now, Talin?"

Neve glanced at him, a muscle working in Talin's jaw. This. This was what he hadn't wanted Bran to tell her, but she still wasn't sure why.

"That's what I thought. That brings me to River," Bran said. "Kyran must be ecstatic to know that she's able to look past him being Dark and love him. All the while, Death once more giving approval for a Reaper to keep his woman with him."

Bran paused as he walked to Talin and held the orb of magic between them so that it brushed against Talin's shirt, singing it.

Neve wanted to push Bran away, but she remained where she was. Because, above all else, she knew Talin could handle himself in any situation. He was a Reaper, after all.

"Neve, my sweet," Bran said with a smile, his gaze still clashing with Talin's. "Do you know the difference between you and those women?"

A long stretch of silence filled the room. She realized Bran waited for her response. "No," she replied.

"They're half—Fae. They have no concept of being Fae in any form." Bran then looked at her, a look of pure delight filling his face as comprehension dawned within her.

She was Light. And for whatever reason, Death didn't look favorably on such a union with a Reaper. Neve had known she was going to lose Talin, but she hadn't realized it was because of this 'rule.'

And Talin had known all along. He had used her, but she'd accepted that. It was his assignment. But what of the feelings between them, the passion and desire? Those, she thought, were more than his mission.

Now she wasn't so sure. And that infuriated Neve.

Because she was totally, completely in love with Talin.

Bran let out a long whistle before he smiled and looked back at Talin. "I almost feel sorry for you. Neve loves you. Will it be you who kills her now that she knows? Or will Death do the honors?"

"My family," Neve stated, no longer asking.

Bran ignored her, continuing his story. "Death killed my woman. My beautiful, honorable Light Fae lover."

"You knew the rules," Talin bit out.

"So did Baylon!" The ball of magic in Bran's hand grew, burning through Talin's shirt to touch the skin on his chest. "Baylon knew what would happen."

"And he was prepared to die for Jordyn. You changed the rules for us."

Shocked, Bran took a step back, as if he couldn't absorb what Talin had just stated. Neve looked at the wound on Talin's chest and watched as it began to heal.

She might have her magic bound, but at least Bran hadn't stopped their healing ability. That she knew of.

Talin's smile was callous, vicious, and unforgiving. "It's all you, Bran. You tried to trick us, and when that didn't work, you began killing the half—Fae. We had to do something. You succeeded in killing Jordyn, but Death realized Baylon could turn into you. She decided to allow Jordyn to become a Reaper. None of this would've happened had you not come to hunt us and Death," he said with a harsh laugh.

Furious, Bran threw the ball of magic at Talin, who didn't so much as flinch. Neve sucked in her breath as it skimmed by Talin's head, burning the ends of his hair.

The orb landed behind them on an accent table that held a Ming vase. All of which exploded with the impact.

Neve whirled back around to see what Bran would do next. Talin's words seemed to send him right over the edge, and she wasn't sure that's where they needed Bran to be. Because a crazy Bran meant he was unpredictable.

His gaze swung to her. Bran's smirk was ruthless as he said, "You've been asking for your family. Perhaps now is the time to show you."

Dread filled her, causing chills of apprehension to rush over her. She shook her head. But it was already too late.

Bran snapped his fingers. Beside him, two Dark appeared, holding Atris between them. Neve's heart sank as she saw that he'd been tortured. Blood coated the side of his face from a cut at his hairline that had already healed. There was blood on his clothes, as well.

But it was the vacant look in his eyes that turned her blood cold. The brother she knew, the one who made her laugh and always looked out for her was gone.

"I thought he'd hold out longer. Being an Everwood and all," Bran said matter—of—factly. He then shrugged. "I guess bloodlines don't count as much as they used to. Though I was going to get what I wanted in the end. No matter what."

Neve swallowed and took a step toward her brother. "Atris. Look at me."

"You can try to reach him all you want, but he's mine." Bran held her gaze and said, "Just as you will be."

Chapter Seventeen

Daire was seconds behind Rhi when she arrived at the manor. He wasted no time wrapping his arms around her to stop her from doing anything stupid. Like charging Bran when she spotted him.

"I'll just drop my veil," she whispered, seemingly undisturbed that he had his arms around her.

Daire smiled at her bravery. She had no way of knowing that he hadn't used just his arms to stop her. With her being up against him, his veil automatically wrapped around her as well. It didn't matter what she did.

He looked over Rhi's black head to find Cael watching him. The magic surrounding the manor was thick, but Kyran had been able to piggyback on Talin. As soon as they arrived, Kyran had begun working to systematically destroy Bran's spells. It meant that Kyran had to venture out of the room with Talin and Neve.

Now that six of the seven Reapers were at the manor, no amount of magic could stand in their way. Yet, Cael and the others didn't blast away Bran's magic.

That would alert him to their presence. And that time

hadn't arrived yet.

"You son of a bitch," Rhi murmured through clenched teeth.

Ah. So she'd dropped her veil. Daire drew in a breath, inhaling her intoxicating scent of the sea, sun, and lavender. And might.

By the heavens, he craved her.

Her hands grasped the outside of his thighs. She stood as still as a statue as they listened to Bran talk about Neve's brother.

The sight of Atris made Daire want to kill something. He wasn't part of the mission to destroy Bran. His assignment was Rhi. Who happened to be there. If she fought, then so could he.

Neve's tears flowed freely as she tried, repeatedly, to get her brother's attention. But Bran was right. Atris was gone. Neve didn't seem to understand that Bran had an identical plan for her.

The same couldn't be said for Talin. He was losing what little control he had over his anger. Any moment now, Talin was going to attack.

The Reapers were fanning out, surrounding Bran. He was too confident in his magic to believe that the Reapers could get into the manor without him knowing.

Rhi's nails dug into Daire's leg when two more Dark appeared. Each held one of Neve's parents before them.

Neve's eyes widened when she saw them.

"It's time for your choice, Neve," Bran said and motioned to her parents. "Come willingly with me, and I'll let them live."

Neve's father was fiercely shaking his head no at his daughter. The entire room appeared to hold its breath, waiting for Neve's decision.

Bran walked to the mother and touched her cheek that was soaked with tears. He looked into her silver eyes and asked, "Do you want your daughter to die? Or would you rather her be alive?"

"I'd rather kill you myself," the matriarch said, raising her chin.

Daire could see Rhi's smile of approval as he glanced down. He had to admit, he was impressed by any Fae who stood against Bran. No one knew who he was, but everyone seemed to understand that he wasn't someone to be trifled with.

"I escaped the Netherworld," Bran told her with a grin. "Do you really believe your meager little Light Fae magic could hurt me?"

His confession about the Netherworld seemed to throw a switch within Neve. Her tears stopped. She dashed them from her cheeks and squared her shoulders. Then she did as her mother had and lifted her chin.

"I've made my decision," she called to Bran.

He turned to her, a smile in place. "Let me be clear. If you refuse me, I'll kill your parents slowly while you watch. Then I'll kill you. Do you understand?"

"Perfectly," came her succinct reply.

Rhi turned in Daire's arms. He sucked in a breath when her hands roamed up his chest and then around his neck. She rose up on her tiptoes and leaned in close to his ear. "Let me fight. I can help."

Even as he told himself not to, his hands came to rest on her narrow waist. His cheek brushed hers, and his eyes slid closed. How he'd wanted to hold her just like this.

But now wasn't the time.

"No," he whispered.

Her hands cupped his face as she searched to try and see him. She could feel him, which was more than he'd allowed before. Out of the corner of his eye, he saw Fintan watching them with interest.

~

Every eye in the room watched Neve. Talin held his breath, hoping she made the right decision. Atris was Dark. All he had to do to complete the turn was kill.

And Talin knew who Bran was going to have Atris murder.

Talin didn't think he could get more disgusted with Bran, but he was wrong. So very wrong. He was tearing a family apart simply because Talin had been courting Neve.

The Light palace was the one place Talin had thought he'd be safe from Bran's interference. Why would Bran go to the Light? There was nothing for him there. His goal was to wipe out the half—Fae and destroy the Reapers and Death.

But once more, they'd underestimated him.

Talin wanted to rip him apart for watching him with Neve. He didn't share. Anything. But especially his women—in any way. Knowing that Bran spied on them made Talin insane with jealousy and fury.

It warred with the part of him that rejoiced to know that Neve had fallen in love with him. Yet not even that lasted long because he knew what awaited Neve when this was all over.

So did she.

Talin's gut clenched. Neve knew she was going to die. Why would she refuse Bran and fight her way free only to be killed once they returned to the castle?

"Neve," Talin said.

Her head turned to him. Her beautiful silver eyes were clear. Black lashes spiked with tears dipped against her cheek when she blinked. She was calm.

Too damn calm for Talin's liking.

Kyran moved to his side, but Talin was more concerned with Neve's decision. She wasn't going to simply choose Bran. Because then Talin would have to kill her.

That's what made him want to bellow with frustration and resentment. It didn't matter what decision Neve made. She was going to die either way.

She was going to attempt to save her parents. Except Talin knew it was only a ruse. There was only one chance to stop her.

"Do you know what happens when a Light turns Dark?" he asked.

Bran rolled his eyes. "Admit defeat, Talin. I've won."

Neve shook her head.

Talin took a half—step toward her. "A Light is repeatedly tortured until their light is gone. They accept the dark." He pointed to Atris. "Just as your brother has."

"He could've held out longer," Bran stated.

Talin glanced at Daire to see Rhi now faced Daire with her hands on his face. But her gaze was directed at Bran, and there was hate shooting from her eyes.

"That's the ones who are forced to become Dark. The others who eagerly accept it bypass the torture," Talin told Neve. "But accepting the dark into you doesn't seal the deal of a Fae becoming Dark."

Bran walked to Neve with all the confidence of someone who thought he'd won. "She's a smart one, Talin. I'm sure she knows."

"Tell me," she urged Talin, ignoring Bran.

"Look at your brother," Talin urged her. "His eyes are still silver. And they'll remain that way until he makes his first kill. Whether he drains the soul of a human or murders someone, it matters not."

Neve's head swung to Atris, who now stared at her as if he'd never seen her before. "I see."

"Still ready to make your decision?" Bran asked her.

She drew in a deep breath and slowly released it. Then she answered, "Yes."

Talin wasn't going to stand there and watch as Neve turned Dark. It would destroy him completely. More so than the betrayal that had Death seeking him out to become a Reaper.

Kyran moved in front of him. No words were spoken since Bran would be able to hear. Kyran's face said it all. His red eyes were narrowed, his face stern.

It was Kyran's way of telling him it still wasn't time to attack. But Talin was tired of waiting. How much more were the Everwoods going to have to suffer before the Reapers made their presence known?

No one should have to witness a sibling turning Dark. It was asking too much of Neve. She was strong, but everyone had their limits.

Neve walked around Bran to her parents. She hugged both of them while everyone looked on with interest. Her parents told her they loved her, and she responded in kind.

While her parents shed tears aplenty, Neve's eyes were dry. That alarmed Talin. The cocky smile Bran threw his way said that Bran also noticed that little detail.

It was only Kyran's hand on Talin's arm that held him back from stalking to Neve and hauling her against him. But what could he promise? A life sheltered by the Reapers?

That wasn't possible, as wrong as it was.

Talin had to think about what would be the easiest death for her. He inwardly snorted. There was no easy death. Both scenarios sucked royally.

He looked at Neve's parents. They'd seen one child turn Dark against his will. How much more painful would it be to see the other willingly go to the Dark?

Talin couldn't imagine. He didn't *want* to imagine. But he had no choice. It was laid out before him like a buffet, and Bran was gorging himself.

The Everwoods stood tall, knowing they were going to die. They didn't beg for their lives. The strength of the Everwood line lay in the parents for all to see.

Talin gave Neve's father a nod. He responded in kind, acceptance of his fate reflected in his eyes. Neve's mother silently begged Talin with her eyes to protect her daughter.

It was all Talin wanted to do.

And he was going to do it. All of this was Bran's fault. The Everwoods didn't have to be dragged into this messy affair, and they wouldn't have been, had Talin not dallied with Neve.

There was no changing the past now. It was done. All that could be dealt with was what was in front of him. And Talin was going to make sure the right decisions were made.

"I'm sorry," he whispered, the message meant for Death. Talin was going against her and the Reapers by attacking Bran on his own.

Kyran's forehead dipped into a frown. He gave a shake of his head, but not even his friend was going to stop Talin. As if sensing his decision, Kyran dropped his hand with a sad smile.

"This vexes me," Kyran mumbled.

That nearly made Talin smile. Kyran hated the word vexed, so Talin made sure to use it often whenever he was around Kyran just to annoy him.

And it was Kyran's way of saying good—bye.

Bran's gaze narrowed on Talin. For a second, Talin thought Bran might've heard Kyran. Then Bran's head turned back to Neve as she moved to Atris.

She hugged her brother while his arms remained by his sides. Neve kissed his cheek and whispered something Talin couldn't hear.

Then she turned to Bran. "My answer is—"

"No!" bellowed another female voice.

At the same moment, Rhi pushed away from Daire, out of his veil. She whirled toward Bran, her sword held high.

Chapter Eighteen

Neve stared speechlessly at Rhi. She wasn't sure who was more shocked, she or Bran at the sight of the Light Fae.

"I don't know who you are," Rhi said as she stalked slowly toward Bran. "But you're going back to whatever Hell you slithered from."

"How did you get here?" Bran demanded.

Rhi smiled and spread her feet with her sword held out at her side. "I think you're shit outta luck there, crazy pants. That tidbit, I'm keeping to myself."

"We'll see about that," he stated.

In a blink, the two Dark guarding Atris attacked. Neve watched in awe as Rhi quickly dispatched both Fae with two swings of her sword.

It was no wonder everyone was always in awe of the Light Fae. Neve had constantly wanted to be Rhi. It wasn't just the way Rhi dressed (a sexy badass look few could pull off) or the way she talked with such sass.

It was the way she held herself when confronting adversaries. There was no doubt in her gaze that she was going to win. That confidence was in her bearing, in the way she moved.

And most knew enough to respect her for it.

Not so with Bran. Neve couldn't wait for Rhi to take him down.

Neve glanced at Talin. He was looking off to his left at an empty spot. The Reapers must be there. But why weren't they helping Rhi?

"Is that all you got?" Rhi asked with a raised black brow.

Bran's face filled with fury. "You're going to regret this."

"I highly doubt it." Rhi flicked her sword, removing the blood of the Dark from her blade.

This time, four Dark appeared. They didn't advance on Rhi, but used magic instead. She twisted and turned to dodge the orbs. The few that hit her, she didn't even acknowledge.

Neve met Talin's gaze and gave him a pointed look. The barely discernable shake of his head told her that for now, the Reapers were letting Rhi shake things up with Bran.

And that wasn't right. Neve knew it was likely because Rhi didn't realize who the Reapers were, nor did they want her to know because then she'd have to die.

Neve tested her magic and found that it came to her easily. She created two orbs—one in each hand—and threw them at the Dark attacking Rhi.

Rhi winked at Neve right as she slit the throat of one Dark. Neve didn't stop. She managed to throw three more balls of magic before Bran turned to her with a growl.

In the next instant, Neve found herself held against the wall, several feet off the floor. Bran's magic was slowly squeezing her throat, cutting off her air.

Talin let loose a bellow of fury. She could only watch while a sword with a long blade appeared in his hand. Talin took a step, lunging and swinging his weapon.

He managed to get close enough to Bran to cut his arm. Neve smiled at the sight of Bran's blood. But the smile was soon gone as Bran whipped his head to Atris and barked his name.

The room stilled once more. Without a second's hesitation, her brother casually walked to their mother. A dagger appeared in his hand a heartbeat before he sunk it into her heart.

Neve screamed as her mother's silver eyes widened in surprise. She crumpled to the ground, lifeless. Neve watched in horror as Atris sidestepped to their father.

Her father glanced at Neve and gave her a reassuring smile before he touched Atris's face. A second later, her brother slit his throat.

Although Neve's mouth was open on a scream, there was no sound. The shock was debilitating, devastating.

Unbearable.

The trauma of what she'd just witnessed left her shuddering with disbelief. She was numb, her heart shriveling at the blow Bran had just served her.

Neve couldn't look away from her parents, who lay unmoving on the floor. Their match had been one to solidify and strengthen the family. They hadn't shared a great love, but in death, their fingers were touching, as if despite it all, they'd needed each other in the end.

It was Bran's laughter that pulled her gaze from her parents. Neve found herself staring into her brother's face, but gone were his familiar silver eyes. Now, a blood—red gaze glared back at her.

"Can I kill her next?" Atris asked Bran.

"Over my fucking dead body," Talin ground out.

Rhi whistled to get Atris's attention. "How about we have a go at it if you're looking for someone else to kill?"

Neve fought to get out of the grip of Bran's magic, but his hold was unbreakable. He wasn't even paying attention to her. Bran's gaze was riveted on Talin as if he were waiting for Talin to make another move.

The violence in Talin's beautiful, silver gaze blazed. His chest heaved as he pinned Bran with a look. Neve guessed the other Reapers were holding him back.

What were they waiting on?!

Without looking at Atris, Bran gave him a nod. In the

next heartbeat, Atris was lobbing orbs of magic at Rhi. She was as graceful as a swan, as agile as a feline.

And extremely lethal.

Her blade rarely missed its mark. Neve could only watch as Rhi cut her brother time after time. It was almost as if she were playing with Atris, because there were plenty of times where she could have delivered the killing blow. But she never did.

Neve couldn't understand why. She knew how accurate Rhi was, how deadly her blade was. It was then that it dawned on Neve. Rhi was weakening Atris so it would be one less Fae to fight.

Neve's throat clogged with emotion. Her brother was lost, but Rhi was preventing her from having to see him killed after just watching her parents' murders.

She looked over at Talin to find him and Bran facing off with each other. They were slowly circling one another, their gazes locked.

Anger burned in Neve. Why weren't the Reapers attacking? They had a perfect opportunity to take Bran out. She was held against her will, helpless to do anything but watch the proceedings.

Suddenly, Bran smiled as Searlas came up behind Talin. Now Talin had to turn to the side to keep both men in view.

Just as she was about to shout for the Reapers, Searlas

fell to his knees, his eyes wide as blood blossomed over his chest. Kyran dropped his veil and yanked his sword from Searlas's chest.

Bran's face erupted with rage. He let out a bellow, and the room was suddenly filled with Dark.

His army.

At that moment, the rest of the Reapers dropped their veils. Cael immediately went after Bran. Their swords clanged, magic swirling around each of them.

Talin was working his way through the Dark to get to her. Kyran, Eoghan, and Fintan were all battling several Dark at the same time.

There was another Reaper, one Neve hadn't seen before. The Light Fae had long, black hair, and his silver gaze glanced at Rhi often. He was never far from her.

Neve found Atris, who worked his way over to the nearest wall. Blood ran down his chest, arms, neck, and legs. Rhi's sword had been made in the Fires of Erwar, preventing a Fae's body from healing as it normally would.

He fell to his knees, his chin dropping to his chest. Neve didn't want her brother dead, but it was better than knowing he was Dark.

$\sim$

Talin gritted his teeth against the blasts of magic he sustained during his attempts to reach Neve. At least, she was out of the fray of battle.

That was the only good thing in the whole fucked up setting.

No matter how many Dark he killed, more took their place. The many cuts from their weapons mixed with the blasts of magic were slowing him. It didn't help that this army had the same kind of strength and added power to their magic as he did as a Reaper.

If they were normal Dark Fae, the Reapers would've made quick work of them. Talin ducked a blade coming at his head. They really needed to find out how Bran was passing on the magic. None of the other Reapers were able to do that. So what made Bran so special?

Talin caught a glimpse of Daire near Rhi. Even in the heat of battle, the infamous Light Fae had noticed each of the Reapers. He hoped Cael had a way of dealing with Rhi's new knowledge, because Talin was fairly certain Death didn't want Rhi killed.

But if Rhi were able to live after knowing of the Reapers, then Talin was going to fight with everything he had to make sure the same was true for Neve.

Even if he couldn't have her.

He hissed as an orb of magic hit where he'd already been burned with Dark magic earlier. His skin sizzled as the magic scorched him, going through muscle all the way to the bone.

Talin pushed aside the pain. He'd deal with it later. Right now, he had to be strong and fierce for Neve. She needed him. No longer were his sights set on killing Bran. Talin merely wanted to reach Neve and keep her safe.

Then he could focus on killing the evil bastard.

Talin pivoted, his gaze catching a glimpse of Cael and Bran fighting. For the first time since Bran had begun this war, the Reapers had surprised him.

It made Talin inwardly grin. They were Reapers. They could—and would—stop Bran this night. No longer would Bran wreak havoc among the Reapers and threaten Death. No longer would the Reapers have to worry about protecting the few half—Fae left among the humans.

Talin plunged his sword into the gut of the Dark nearest him while he threw up magic to block a blast from another. He withdrew his sword as the Dark disintegrated before he rammed his shoulder into another Fae.

His path to Neve was slow. Too damn slow for his peace of mind. It didn't seem to matter how many Dark the Reapers killed—and it was a significant number—there were always more.

Talin frowned as he came face to face with a Dark he'd just killed with his sword. What the hell was going on?

He killed the Dark again, with the same thrust of his blade through the Dark's stomach. For the second time, Talin watched him turn to dust.

It was Bran's bark of laughter that made apprehension grip Talin. There was more at work here than any of the Reapers knew. They assumed they knew Bran's mind, which was difficult.

But they'd made a fatal mistake in thinking whatever was giving him power was nothing to be concerned with. They were wrong.

Talin soon found himself standing next to Kyran in the battle. By the look of trepidation on his friend's face, Kyran had come to the same conclusion.

With great effort, Talin and Kyran cleared a path to Neve. She clawed at her throat, at the invisible bonds that choked her.

"Kill him!" Talin yelled at Cael.

It was the only way they would be able to free Neve from his magic. Because Bran wasn't going to do it willingly. Bran wanted to inflict pain, wanted to kill anything the Reapers cared about.

Cael wasn't just fighting Bran. There were several Dark attacking him, as well. The Reapers were outnumbered, and if something wasn't done soon, they were going to lose the chance to kill Bran that they'd been given.

Bran plunged his sword into Cael's thigh.

Everyone stilled mid—fight as Cael's lips peeled back in a grimace. Talin held his breath as Cael looked down at the blade sticking out of his thigh before gradually raising his head.

His breaths were labored, the blood flowing down his leg in thick rivulets.

"No!" Eoghan shouted.

The shock of Eoghan speaking quickly dissipated at the feel of malevolence. Bran held out his hands, magic filling the room and expanding rapidly. Talin fought against the weight of it, but in the end, he fell to his knees as Bran's magic swelled in an attempt to swallow each of them.

Talin's gaze met Kyran's as each were held by Bran's magic, unable to move. Talin gritted his teeth in pain as it felt as if his skin were pulling away from his body.

Suddenly, something off to his left began to glow. The manor started to tremble as if the very ground fought against Bran's hold.

Talin managed to turn his head enough to see that it was Rhi who glowed. Light emanated from every pore of her body. The brighter she glowed, the more the house shook.

Cracks appeared in the walls. The ceiling groaned and shifted, splintering into several veins. Rhi, however, seemed unfazed.

Her magic clashed with Bran's, pushing his back with a vengeful roar.

But there were consequences to such power. The mixture of two such powerful magics created a maelstrom. A vicious swirl of magic that whirled about them like a tornado. Rhi didn't seem to notice. Anger twisted her face, consuming her.

Bran took advantage of the storm and focused it on one person—Cael.

It was pulling him into the vortex. Wounded, Cael fought valiantly against the magic dragging him. He strained until his feet were yanked out from beneath him. Even then, Cael clawed at the floor.

Every Reaper attempted to reach Cael, but the magic—and the magical storm—made it nearly impossible.

Talin sucked in a breath when Rhi's magic pressed against him, making his body shake with the force of it. It would soon devour Bran's—and everything else.

"Rhi!" Daire shouted. He was the one nearest her, and he crawled to her even as blood dripped from his ears.

Cael was about to be swallowed by the magical storm. Talin yelled his fury when he saw something move out of the corner of his eye.

In a rush, Eoghan got to his feet and shoved Cael out of the way—only to be sucked into the tempest himself.

With Eoghan's disappearance, Bran shut down his magic and teleported away, his laughter echoing off the walls of the manor.

Daire managed to take Rhi's hand as he said her name again. Rhi blinked. Then, with a shuddering breath, the glowing diminished until it faded completely. Everyone was silent for a moment as they looked around to find the Dark gone. Except for one—Atris.

Chapter Nineteen

Neve drew in a deep breath of air. The fall had been farther than she'd thought, with her knees giving out upon impact. She fell forward, catching herself with her hands. She touched her throat, thankful to no longer feel Bran's magic.

She looked at Talin, but his gaze was locked on the spot Eoghan had vanished. Neve couldn't imagine how the Reapers were feeling. Just as she wasn't able to wrap her head around what she'd witnessed Rhi do.

The Light Fae had actually *glowed*!

There was always talk around court regarding Rhi's powerful magic, but Neve hadn't known those murmurings were based on truth. She guessed few had observed it in the flesh.

A moan from her right drew Neve's attention. She gasped when she saw Atris. Without thinking of the consequences, Neve half—crawled, half—stumbled her way to him.

"Atris," she murmured as she reached him.

He began to crumple to the side. Instinctively, she cradled his head, wrapping her arms around him. She situated herself with her back against the wall.

"I've got you," she said, soothing him.

His eyes were closed, and she was thankful for that small reprieve. She wasn't yet ready to see the red eyes that made him Dark.

Nor could she look at her parents' bodies. It was just too painful. So she didn't turn their way or think about Atris killing them.

"I'm . . . sorry," Rhi said into the quiet and stillness of the room.

The fire in the hearth crackled and popped. Blood—Dark Fae blood—dripped from Rhi's sword. The sound of that single drop hitting the floor seemed to slam into Rhi. In the next moment, the sword vanished.

A shaky breath left her. Then she walked to Cael and withdrew the sword from his thigh without a warning. His face twisted in agony. He looked up at her as he rolled to his back.

Neve was spellbound, watching as Rhi went down on one knee and examined the wound. No one moved. No one uttered a single syllable.

"It's not going to heal," Rhi finally said.

Cael shrugged. The look on his face said he already knew the verdict. "It doesn't matter."

Neve rocked her brother, a frown forming at Cael's

words. What did he mean 'it doesn't matter?'

"If you want to kill Bran and find your friend it does," Rhi said matter—of—factly. She met Cael's gaze and held her hand over his wound, then her hand began to glow.

Neve could actually see the magic moving from Rhi's hand into Cael's wound, healing him. If Neve had been shocked at Rhi's power before, now she was dumbstruck. Fae with Rhi's kind of ability were myth and legends—not true beings.

Then again, so were the Reapers.

Neve's skin warmed as she felt Talin's gaze on her. She turned her head to the side and looked his way. No matter how hard she tried, she couldn't read his closed—off expression.

He stood and made his way to her. There he knelt beside her and smoothed a lock of her hair behind her ear. It felt so good to have his touch again that Neve closed her eyes and leaned her cheek against his palm.

"We didn't get him," Talin said.

Neve opened her eyes and gave him a reassuring smile. "Next time."

"How many more will we get?" Kyran asked the room. "We should've had Bran."

Fintan shook his head of white hair. "Where is he getting his fucking power?"

Rhi's head snapped to him, and for the longest time, she simply stared at Fintan. She then looked at each of the Reapers until she came to the one Neve hadn't met. Daire.

Daire looked away from Rhi and said to Cael, "We need to know how Bran is getting his power if we're to beat him."

"Agreed," Talin said.

Cael stood, testing his leg that was now fully healed. He gave a nod to Rhi. "Thank you. As for Bran, I also agree. We'll have two missions. Find Eoghan, and discover Bran's secret."

"Which could stem from how he escaped from the Netherworld," Kyran said.

"Well stick a fork in me," Rhi suddenly said, a smile on her face. "You're Reapers."

Neve waited for one of them to admit it, but the only one who would meet the Light Fae's gaze was Cael. Neve knew exactly how Rhi felt. The Reapers were closed—mouthed about themselves, but she knew why. Rhi had yet to figure that out.

"You're wrong about them," Neve told Rhi. "There's no such thing as a Reaper."

Rhi turned to look in her direction. Behind her, Cael gave Neve a nod she assumed was in thanks for her attempt. Unfortunately, it was a failed attempt, because Rhi obviously didn't believe her.

"We'll have to agree to disagree on that, baby girl," Rhi said. She then walked to Neve and sat down before her, staring at Atris.

Neve swallowed. "Will he wake?"

"Undoubtedly." Rhi's silver eyes met hers. "Are you sure you want him to?"

"Because if he's Dark I might have to kill him?"

"There's not a 'might' about it," Talin told her.

Neve shook her head. "My family has been dealt enough. I'll not kill my own blood."

"We'll do it for you," Cael said as he walked up with the other Reapers behind him.

That didn't make Neve feel any better. She hugged Atris tighter. He'd been a good soul, a kind soul. Perhaps he wasn't as strong as past Everwoods mentally, but that didn't make him a bad person.

Rhi laid her hand atop hers and gave a little squeeze. "You saw what Bran was."

"Yes," Neve said, swallowing.

"He controls Atris. We can't allow that to continue."

Neve knew that, but the thought of her brother dead left her eyes stinging with unshed tears.

Talin wrapped an arm around her, giving her his strength and his shoulder. She'd never needed it more. It felt like at any moment, she was about to fall apart.

She sniffed and blinked to clear her vision. Then she looked at Cael. "Can it be done together?"

"What?" Rhi asked. She looked between Neve and Cael several times before she shot Neve a hard look. "Why do you want to die?"

"I don't." It was the truth, and Neve wasn't sorry for saying it. She looked at Talin and saw the pain in his eyes. He was prepared to fight for her, but she wouldn't allow that.

Look where it had gotten Bran.

"Then fight," Rhi said, affronted.

Neve cupped Talin's face. "You know the rules. You know what has to be done."

"Nay. I don't," Talin said.

"You do," she insisted. Neve gave a firm shake of her head when Talin was about to continue arguing. "No. I won't have you end up like Bran."

"Whoa, there," Rhi said holding up hands. "Let's put the brakes on for a sec while someone catches me up on what the feck you're talking about."

Neve smiled through her watery eyes as she stared at Talin, wanting to remember every detail of his face. Then she said without looking at Rhi, "Leave it."

"The hell I will." The Light Fae craned her head up and around to Cael. "You're not going to lay a hand on Neve. She's under my protection."

"Which means nothing," Cael said without any heat.

Rhi shot him the finger and took hold of Neve. In the next instant, Neve found herself in a lavish room with Atris still in her arms.

She looked around at the white and gold comforter on the bed with half a dozen pillows of gold in various shapes and sizes. There was a gigantic white and gold shag rug beneath the bed.

Two beautiful tables sat on either side of the king—sized bed, painted white with glamorous twirls and swirls of gold. A dainty chair with gold arms and legs and a white back and seat sat near a window next to a small, round, white table with a massive bouquet of white flowers.

A large white vanity with gold knobs on the drawers and gold trim along the edges was accompanied by a white stool. There was a white sofa with white and gold pillows, as well.

Rhi stood in the middle of the room next to Neve, putting a spell in place. When she finished, she looked down at Neve before she walked to the sofa.

Neve hadn't thought much about Rhi's black pants, black spiked heels, and black and bright pink pinstriped shirt. Until now.

She didn't need to ask where they were. Neve might never have been in this room, but she knew the feel of Usaeil's castle.

"This is my room," Rhi said as she curled a foot beneath her and sat. "We'll be safe here."

"It's pointless. You shouldn't have interfered."

"Tell me why? You obviously love Talin. And he feels the same."

That didn't make Neve feel any better. Yes, she wanted nothing more than for Talin to love her, but she didn't want him to turn into Bran.

"Neve?" Rhi pressed.

She looked down at her brother. "There are rules."

"Rules are made to be broken." Rhi snorted. "Trust me. I've broken enough to know."

Neve smoothed back Atris's hair from his brow. "This rule can't be broken."

"This goes back to that Bran character, right?" Rhi bit her lip as she stretched an arm out along the back of the sofa and tapped her foot on the floor. "He broke this rule."

"Yes."

"And Talin has as well?"

Neve nodded. She looked up at Rhi. "Talin is needed. He can't turn into Bran."

"So how do the Reapers work?"

She almost fell into Rhi's trap, but Neve caught herself in time before she spoke about the group. "I don't know what you're talking about."

"I'll find out one way or another. Might as well tell me."

"I've got a favor to ask instead."

The curiosity shone brightly in Rhi's silver eyes. She shoved back her length of black hair over her shoulder. "Fire away."

"I don't want Talin or any of the Reapers to take my life. I request the greatest of the Light Fae to do it. You."

Rhi's mouth went slack. Her brows drew together as she stared, unblinking. "Don't ask this of me."

"But I am."

"Neve?"

She looked down when she heard Atris's voice. "I'm here."

His eyes opened flashing between red and silver. In a heartbeat, Rhi was beside them.

"Listen to me, Atris," Rhi said hurriedly. "You have a choice to make. Pick either the light or the dark. You can't have both."

"I . . ." he squeezed his eyes closed. "What happened . . . to me?"

Neve smoothed her hand along his cheek. "We'll discuss that later. Look to the light, Atris. Come home to me."

His body was racked with pain, bowing in her arms.

Neve held him tightly, repeating his name again and again, hoping he would hear her calling him home.

Finally, he grew still. His body was soaked in sweat. His eyes fluttered open to reveal . . . silver.

Rhi let out a loud sigh and fell back on her butt. "That was close."

"Too close," Cael said from behind Rhi.

Neve looked up into Talin's eyes and knew the time had come.

Atris was unsteady as he climbed to his feet. He frowned at Talin. "What's going on? How did I get here?"

"Easy there, tiger," Rhi said as she came to stand in front of him and Neve.

Neve stood and tried to walk around Rhi, but the Light Fae wouldn't let her. Neve met Cael's gaze. "I'm not running. Let's leave. Now."

"I agree." Cael gave a nod to Kyran. But it was Talin who approached her.

Atris shouted Neve's name as he pulled her against him. "Talin, tell me why I get the feeling you're about to hurt my sister? I thought you cared for her."

"I do," Talin said in a voice that broke with emotion.

Neve turned to face Atris. She had to make her brother understand. "It's fine. Talin and I have details to work out. Besides, you need to rest."

"Details?" he asked, confused.

She nodded and smiled up at him. If only her parents could know that Bran's hold hadn't been as strong as they'd thought. Atris, the pride of the Everwood family, was once more a Light Fae. His brief stint as a Dark—and the things he'd done—would never be spoken of.

"He's not going to hurt you?" Atris asked.

Neve smiled, knowing she wasn't actually lying when she said, "Talin would never hurt me. You know that."

"Because he loves you. And you love him."

"Yes." Neve was thrilled that she was about to be able to leave Atris without him knowing the true reason.

Before the Reapers took her life, she was going to make sure Talin led Atris to believe that they were living somewhere far away. If she had her way, Atris would never know how she died.

Or why.

"You love him," Atris repeated.

It was Neve's turn to frown. There was something different in his voice. His fingers dug into her arms as a cruel smile formed on his face.

The same time his eyes went red.

Neve barely registered the pain as the blade sank into her heart.

Chapter Twenty

Talin rushed to Neve, catching her before she could hit the ground. He lowered them to the floor. Already, she was gasping for breath. Though he wanted to kill Atris, Talin let the others attempt to catch him while he held on to the love of his life.

"Neve," he whispered and caressed her face. Time was running out, quickly. He swallowed past the lump of emotion in his throat. "I love you. I should've told you before."

She smiled, but any words she might've said were gone as the life faded from her eyes.

Talin couldn't move. He held Neve close, unable to believe that Atris had fooled them all and killed his sister. Had it been Bran's plan all along?

It had been Talin's secret hope that Rhi would be able to take Neve somewhere they could never reach her. But he'd known how futile that was. Death could find anyone at any time. There was no hiding from her.

None of that mattered now. Neve was gone, regardless.

She hadn't deserved this. None of her family had. The

blame lay with Bran, and Talin was going to make him pay. He wasn't going to kill Bran quickly. He wanted the son of a bitch to suffer for eternity.

Kyran put a hand on his shoulder. "I'm sorry, Talin. Atris got away."

Rhi squatted beside him. "Talin, I know someone who can help. They can bring someone back from the dead. I'll ask him."

There was a shimmer in the air and Death appeared before them. Her midnight locks were loose, hanging to her waist. Her sleeveless gown was solid black with a high neck and a long train.

"How the hell are all of you getting through my spells?" Rhi demanded, affronted.

Death turned to Rhi. "It's not time for us to meet yet."

"That's too fecking bad," she retorted.

Rhi was too busy being indignant to realize that Daire had moved behind her. With a wave of Death's hand, Rhi was unconscious. Daire caught her, lifting her in his arms.

"She won't remember anything to do with Reapers when she wakes," Erith said.

"Is that wise?" Cael asked. "She's going to be pissed when she eventually figures it out."

"It's not time," was Death's reply. "Daire, take Rhi back to her island."

And with that, Daire was gone.

Talin didn't bother to hide his anger when he raised his gaze to Death as she squatted before him. "You got what you wanted. Neve is dead."

"You're mistaken if you think I wanted this."

He looked into her lavender eyes and snorted. "They're your rules. You were going to make sure Neve died one way or another."

"I didn't send her brother to betray her, Talin." Erith held his gaze. "You know that."

So he did. He needed an outlet, and that's exactly what Death was. Someone had to feel the wrath of his pain. Who better, than the one person who could take it?

Death put her hand atop one of his. "Reapers are chosen when they've been betrayed. Neve was betrayed by her brother and Bran."

Talin blinked. Was Erith saying what he thought she was saying? It was too much hope for him to deal with if he was wrong.

"I can bring her back," Death said.

Talin squeezed his eyes closed and hugged Neve's body. "As a Reaper?"

"It's the only way you can be with her now."

Eternity alone.

Or an eternity with Neve.

But to have her as a Reaper taking lives . . . Talin and the others had lived some of that life before Death offered them roles. Neve hadn't.

Would she be able to handle it? She was strong mentally, but that didn't mean she would be up to the challenge of taking lives. It would change her, harden her.

His sweet, beautiful Neve.

But to never look into her eyes again. To never hold her hand or feel her body against his. To never hear her laughter—or her cries of pleasure.

How stupid Talin felt for thinking he could give himself to one such as Neve and walk away when his mission was finished. His heart had known he wouldn't be able to leave her.

His brain was just now catching up.

Yet Bran had taken that choice from him. Bran had taken choices from all of them, but mostly Neve. Talin's throat tightened as emotion choked him.

"I leave it in your hands whether I offer the role to Neve. Even if you say yes, she might not," Erith cautioned.

"Yes," Talin said in a rush. "My answer is yes."

He knew as soon as the words were out that there hadn't been another answer for him. It wasn't because he wanted Neve beside him—although that played a huge role in his decision.

No, it was because it was time that Neve had her own choice. Whatever that would be, Talin would live with it.

No matter how hard it would be.

Death gave a single nod and lightly squeezed his hand. "Now the choice is in Neve's hands."

Talin remained with Neve in his arms, waiting for Erith to talk to Neve's soul as she'd done with Jordyn. But Death had other ideas.

"When I came to each of you, you were alone. It'll be the same with Neve," Erith said softly.

Kyran came up beside him. "Talin."

He loosened his hold on Neve. Quick as a flash, Death was gone with Neve. Talin ran a hand through his hair. When he looked down, he saw Neve's blood all over his shirt, mixing with his own and that of the Dark.

Blood. So much blood.

His life was bloody and hard. He saw death and fought evil daily. It wore away at his soul, chipping away one millimeter at a time.

How much longer until he turned out like Fintan?

Neve had shone a light upon his world that he'd forgotten existed. Reapers lived whatever life they wanted when they weren't hunting for Death, but it was the hunting, the killing that had dimmed the light within him.

With Neve, she reminded him of who he'd been, of the Fae who had been proud and hopeful. Talin had been Death's executioner for so many thousands of years, he'd forgotten who he was.

"Neve loves you," Kyran said. "She'll choose to be a Reaper."

Fintan nodded as he walked around the room. "There's no denying Neve's feelings."

"They're right," Cael said as he came up on Talin's other side.

Talin drew in a deep breath. "Being a Reaper will destroy Neve. I can't bear that."

"Jordyn doesn't kill," Kyran reminded them. "Perhaps Neve won't either."

Cael tensed but didn't reply.

Talin turned his head to look at Kyran. River wasn't a Reaper. She carried Kyran's child, and Death had given her a place with the Reapers so she could become Kyran's.

Would the same chance have been given to Neve had Talin gotten her with child? Would Death do the same with Neve as she had with Jordyn and not make her kill?

Talin knew the answer—no.

It all came down to the others being half—Fae, and Neve being a Light. There must be a reason for the difference, but he had yet to figure it out.

And it pissed him off. His anger grew, expanded.

"Why?" he asked the room. "Why is Death treating Neve differently than the others? Why are the half—Fae given more consideration than Fae? Neve lost her family.

She had to watch her parents be killed by her own brother. Only to have Atris then kill her. She's suffered."

"So have you," Fintan pointed out.

Talin shook off Kyran's hand on his shoulder. He rose and stalked around the room, his hands balled into fists at his side. "We're Fae! More concessions shouldn't go to the half—Fae than one of our own."

"The half—Fae are our own," Kyran said.

Talin halted, facing his friend. "Really? Why then do the Fae never return for the children that result from a union with a human? Why do the female Fae leave the spawn of a human in the forest, forgetting her indiscretion? Why do the Fae not bring the half—Fae into our world?"

"Because they have human blood," Fintan stated.

"Exactly." Talin snorted, his fury building. "Neve was going to be killed because she figured out who we were. She figured it out because her family was taken and Bran made sure she was pointed in the direction of the Reapers."

Cael nodded, his voice reassuring as he said, "I know."

"Rhi knows. She's *seen*. But Death doesn't kill her. Why? Because there are plans for Rhi? Why aren't there plans for Neve?"

He was shouting by the end of it, but Talin couldn't help it. It wasn't fair that everything had been stacked against Neve. She'd more than proven her worth as Jordyn had. But Jordyn was half—Fae, so apparently, that gave her something more than Neve.

His gorgeous, wonderful Neve.

The room was silent. Talin needed some time alone. He was too angry to be around anyone else. He teleported out of Usaeil's castle, out of Ireland altogether.

He found himself on a mountain in the middle of the Highlands. Snow fell in thick sheets. It was piled along the rocky slopes.

It wasn't until he turned around and saw the man behind him that he realized where he had inadvertently taken himself—Dreagan.

Chapter Twenty—one

Neve.

She opened her eyes and blinked. Neve found herself looking up at brilliant blue skies and towering trees with birds of all shapes and colors flying around.

Neve sat up, confused when she found herself on the ground. She looked down to find that blood still covered her white dress. So she hadn't imagined Atris stabbing her.

And her death.

She drew in a deep breath. When she raised her gaze, a dragonfly buzzed around her before weaving within stalks of flowers that seemed to reach heaven itself.

Neve climbed to her feet and followed the dragonfly with its brilliant green and gold wings. The journey took her through lush plants and more vibrantly colored flowers than she'd ever seen before.

It was paradise.

Neve's feet halted when she saw the dragonfly land on the shoulder of a petite woman with coal—black hair that hung in glorious waves to her back.

Large, unique, lavender eyes watched Neve in a face too beautiful for words. And Neve had seen a lot of beauty as a Fae. Yet this woman put all of them to shame.

In contrast to the bright colors and life all around her, the woman was dressed in a magnificent gown of solid black. The skirts were full, but the edges didn't touch the ground. In fact, it looked like she was . . . floating.

Neve frowned as she let her gaze roam back up the dress. That's when she noticed there was a black paisley design a shade lighter on the black material. The bodice rose up to her neck but was sleeveless. The gown showed the woman's tiny waist and voluptuous curves.

"Who are you?"

"Death," the woman answered in a voice as soft and melodic as the breeze.

Neve cocked her head to the side. "Death?"

"Is it so hard to believe?"

"A little."

Death smiled, transforming her stunning face into one that left even Neve breathless. "Most assume Death is a man. I love to see reactions."

"What am I doing here?"

The smile dimmed. "I'm sorry about what happened. I'm sorry Bran pulled you into this war he began. It's my fault. I should've killed him, but I wanted him to suffer for breaking my rules and turning against the other

Reapers. So I threw him in the Netherworld."

"He escaped."

Death sighed, her lips compressing together for a moment. "That he did. Now, the Reapers are fighting him. You and your family were caught in the middle."

Neve eyed Death. "Did you bring me here because I figured out what the Reapers were?"

"No. That was brilliant, by the way. I hated that you found out, but I was immensely impressed."

"Hated because it meant my death?"

"Yes."

Neve knew she was already dead. Why else would Death be talking to her? And though she knew she could be thrown in the Netherworld, she still had questions she wanted Death to answer. "But not Jordyn or River?"

Lavender eyes narrowed on her. "You don't know the story."

"Did they learn of the Reapers?"

"Yes," she grudgingly admitted.

"But you didn't have them killed." No wonder Talin was so angry and ready to fight for her.

Death raised a black brow as her face became stony. "There is much you don't know, Neve Everwood. You've heard bits and pieces and came to your own conclusions."

"I'm not wrong. It's basic. Those two half—Fae

learned of the Reapers but they weren't killed."

"Actually, Bran killed Jordyn," Death stated in a harsh tone. "I gave her the choice to become a Reaper."

Well. That, Neve hadn't been prepared for. Perhaps she'd overstepped.

For long minutes, Death simply stared at her. "River isn't a Reaper. She is, however, carrying Kyran's child. She's also the only member left of her family that the Dark have hunted and killed for numerous generations. She has the ability to read long—dead Fae dialect in books that we're using to fight Bran."

"I see." Put that way, Neve brought absolutely nothing to the table.

"You think you're unworthy?"

Neve looked Death in the eye. "In the Fae world, I come from an influential, powerful, and wealthy family. I'm courted for my family, and my connections."

She took a deep breath and looked at the spectacular beauty around her, beauty she would never have thought to associate with Death. It proved that while Neve had learned her way around the Light Fae court, she knew nothing else.

"I'm not a warrior," she continued. "Not like Rhi. I can't read obscure Fae languages. I'm not carrying Talin's child. I have nothing. Why then, am I here?"

Death smiled at the dragonfly still perched on her

shoulder. It fluttered its wings before it flew off, zooming over Death, but never getting far. "I wanted to talk to you."

"I have no right to ask, but why didn't you help the Reapers when they battled Bran?"

Death sighed, her shoulders slumping slightly. "That's the problem. I can't. I want nothing more than to face Bran myself. He wouldn't stand a chance against me."

"I don't understand."

"What I'm about to tell you, the Reapers don't know yet. Bran is somehow draining my magic. He's weakening me."

Now Neve understood. "To kill you."

"Yes. I don't know how he's doing it, and I need to find out. Bran can't take over. It would put all the realms into chaos."

"The Reapers need to know."

"They will. Soon enough. Cael already suspects. He's too smart for his own good."

Neve found it curious that Death mumbled the last part, as if it were more her thoughts than something she wanted spoken aloud. But Neve didn't comment on it. She was too alarmed by what Death had just shared to do more than gawk at the entity.

"Enough of that." Death squared her shoulders as if she'd just shaken off bad thoughts. "I want to know what you would do for Talin."

"What I would do?" Neve repeated, unsure what Death was asking. "Anything. Everything."

"Yes, but *what*?"

Neve turned to the side and bent to smell a fragrant orange flower she'd never seen before. "Bran shared enough of his story that I realized why Talin hadn't told me who he was. I feared—still fear—that Talin might follow in Bran's footsteps."

"You think Talin loves you that much?"

Neve closed her eyes and heard Talin whisper of his love right before she'd died. Oddly, there hadn't been any pain. Why was she just now remembering that?

There had only been . . . peace.

Could Death be responsible for that? Neve recalled the feel of the blade sinking into her skin. There had been a terrible flash of pain, and then she'd been in Talin's arms, looking into his pale silver eyes.

Her lids lifted. "Talin is a man of honor. He'll feel responsible for what's happened to me and my family, though it isn't his fault. But yes, I do believe he loves me." She looked at Death. "Talin doesn't say something he doesn't mean."

"Talin does feel responsible. He's also incredibly angry right now. Would you leave Talin forever if it would make him better?"

Now Neve was really confused. "Leave? I'm dead. I've already left him."

"Not of your own will."

"I knew what was coming. I didn't want Talin to be the one to kill me. Nor did I want any of the Reapers to do it."

Death's lavender gaze softened as admiration filled them. "You asked Rhi to do it in order to save Talin."

"Talin could stay mad at Rhi, but I didn't want him angry at any of his brethren for doing what had to be done because of the rules."

"Answer my question."

Neve faced Death. She loved Talin more than she'd ever thought she could love anyone. He was the first thing she thought of when she woke, and the last thing on her mind before she fell asleep.

Everywhere she went, she searched for him. Even when she knew he wouldn't be there. Every minute spent with him bound her closer, tied her heart evermore to his.

His touch stirred her soul. His kisses roused her passion. And when their bodies were joined, she felt truly, completely whole.

Talin was the great love she'd waited her very, very long life for.

Neve blinked away the tears. All those times she'd

wanted to be like Rhi, and she was getting the one thing she hadn't wanted—the loss of her true love.

By the stars! Was this how Rhi felt? All the time? All those thousands upon thousands of years? Neve didn't know how Rhi stood it. The pain was ... unyielding, relentless.

"Neve," Death urged.

She nodded, sniffing. "Yes. I would walk away from Talin forever if I thought it would make him better."

"That's what I thought you'd say."

Neve was too shocked to do more than gape at Death.

Then Death smiled softly. "You say you bring nothing to the table, but, my dear, you bring loyalty, love, and honor. That is something to be proud of."

"I ... I don't understand." Why was Death saying all this? It was putting hope in Neve's heart, and that she couldn't take. Not now. Not after everything.

Death said, "I look for the greatest warriors of the Fae—both Light and Dark—for my Reapers. I kept it at seven always. Well, until recently. Every one of my Reapers was betrayed, and that betrayal brought about their deaths."

"Like me," Neve murmured.

"Exactly like you." Death's lips softened. "I'm giving you a choice. I can release your soul, and you'll find peace with your parents. Or you can accept my offer to become a Reaper and do my bidding."

Neve's heart nearly leapt from her chest in excitement at the offer. To be with Talin. For eternity! She opened her mouth to answer when Death held up a finger to stop her.

"I am judge and jury, Neve. The Reapers are executioners. Are you prepared to kill without knowing what the Fae did? Only on my word?"

Kill. Now that was something Neve hadn't thought about. Could she take someone's life again and again based just on Death's word? Someone had to be judge of the Fae. Talin and the others trusted Death. She could, as well.

Neve's heart sank. "As I said, I'm not a warrior. I know nothing of battle other than what I saw today."

"Is that a no?" Death asked with a quirk of her brow.

"I could do as you ask, but I'm not a—"

"I didn't ask if you were a warrior," Death interrupted her. "Bottom line. Do you want to be a Reaper?"

Neve smiled. "Yes."

"Good." Death closed the distance between them and laid her hand upon Neve's arm.

As she looked into Death's eyes, Neve saw what few ever had. Behind those lavender eyes was a soul weighted with responsibility, controlled by justice, and ruled by obligation. The universe rested on Death's shoulders, and she carried it with dignity and grace.

It was the loneliness she glimpsed that surprised Neve.

There wasn't time to think on it as she felt power—thick and pure—pour through her. Her magic increased, thrumming through her as it eagerly waited to be used.

The force of it all nearly brought Neve to her knees. She stood against it, her eyes closed and her teeth gritted. It felt like the entire universe was closing in on her, and just before she was crushed, everything exploded in a flash of dazzling lights that fell from the now dark sky like millions of stars.

Neve blinked up at the sky for the second time that day. Did Death control time, as well? Or had that passage of time actually occurred?

Then it didn't matter as the magic and power swirled through her, seeping into her bone and muscle to coat her. Neve lifted her hands and looked at them. Her fingertips tingled with the force of her magic.

She laughed, unable to believe what had just happened. She was a Reaper. A Reaper! Nothing would stand in the way of her being with Talin but Talin.

Neve turned her gaze to Death, who smiled in approval. "Thank you."

"You'll be a great addition to the team. And my name is Erith."

Neve twirled around. And that's when she realized she no longer had on her white dress. She now wore black pants that molded to her legs and tall black boots that ended over her knees.

The same slinky black material covered her torso and down her arms. A black leather corset covered her where dozens of small knife handles peeked out. From her elbows down to the first knuckles of her fingers were leather gauntlets, each holding another knife on the underside of her forearm.

She touched her hair to find it was now styled in five thick braids from her face to her neck before being weaved into one thick plait.

Death's smile widened when a sword appeared in Neve's right hand. Neve gaped at the curved blade. The pommel was black wood with silver swirled along it in thick, curvy designs.

"Welcome, Reaper," Erith said.

Chapter Twenty—two

"You doona belong here," the Dragon King stated angrily.

Talin grimaced. "I didn't mean to come."

"Fae?" the King bellowed at hearing his Irish accent. "You've got to be fucking kidding me."

Talin held up his hands. "I'm Light."

The King shot him a hard look with his sherry—colored eyes. "I'm no' daft. Who are you?"

"Talin," he replied without thinking about it. The Dragon Kings weren't likely to ever know he was a Reaper. "And you?"

The King stared before raking a hand through his short, sandy blond hair to dislodge the snow. "Roman. Now isna the time for you to be here."

"I know. I just needed some time alone."

"Your presence was felt the minute you went through our barrier."

Of course. Talin had forgotten that the Dragon Kings had a magical barrier up along their sixty thousand acres. It wasn't to keep humans out of their whisky distillery. It was to keep the Dark—or any Fae—out.

.

The only thing on Talin's side was the fact that the Dark released a video to the human world showing the Dragon Kings shifting from human to dragon and back again. That brought MI5, news crews, and others looking for a peek at them.

Which meant the Kings couldn't shift and fly as they normally would. That gave Talin a few minutes with Roman.

"I'll leave," Talin said.

Roman's face hardened. "And never return."

"The war between you and the Dark is heating up. I think you'd want the help of the Light."

"And that's why you're here? Instead of your queen?"

Roman had him there. Talin smiled and held up his hands. "I'm leaving."

He veiled himself but didn't leave. It was just a few seconds later that more Dragon Kings appeared. At the head was none other than Constantine, King of Kings.

"Who was it?" Con demanded.

Roman shrugged, still looking around. "He said his name was Talin."

"We should ask Rhi," said a King with aqua ringed dark blue eyes and long, wavy, dark hair.

Con sighed. "No' everything needs to be told to her, Rhys."

"She'll know," Rhys pointed out.

Con turned on his heel, ignoring the freezing temperatures and snow. "Fine. Ask her. We need to know why this Light was here."

Talin still wasn't sure how he'd ended up at Dreagan. He hadn't been thinking of the Dragon Kings. His thoughts had been on Neve.

He waited until all but Roman remained atop the mountain before Talin teleported to Inchmickery. To his shock, the others were already there.

Talin spotted Baylon, Jordyn, Kyran, and River combing through books, trying to find out where Eoghan might have been sent.

Fintan was in another room sharpening his sword while listening to the opera *Carmen*. Cael stood in his office with his back to the door and his gaze out the window.

Talin didn't need to ask what Cael was thinking about. Eoghan and Bran. It was the two things on everyone's minds.

He quietly walked to his chamber and opened the door. Talin stopped when he saw the bed, a bed he'd hoped to share with Neve. With each hour that passed without word from Death or Neve, Talin was coming to realize that Neve must've turned down the offer to become a Reaper.

Not that he could blame her. It wasn't an easy job. The

power and extra magic were amazing. The ability to remain veiled indefinitely among other attributes helped to soften the blow of what they did.

But it wasn't something any of them could forget.

He walked to the bed and touched it. Talin allowed himself to dream of a world with Neve in it. Having that snatched out of his grasp was heartbreaking. No wonder Bran had lost his mind.

Talin was close to doing the same himself. The only thing that stopped him was Neve telling him not to do what Bran had. Neve wouldn't want him to turn against those he considered family. He would hold it together.

Time would eventually heal his pain.

At least, he prayed it would.

He felt something behind him and whirled around. Talin's mouth fell open when he saw Neve. Her smile was wide, her silver eyes bright with happiness.

It was the black leather armor that had him eyeing her in approval. Was there anything this woman wore that didn't make him want to rip it off her and plunge into her body?

"Your eyes approve, but I don't hear any words," Neve said.

Talin took two steps and jerked her into his arms. He held her tightly. "I wasn't sure you'd say yes."

"I didn't think I was a warrior. Death thinks differently," Neve said with a chuckle.

Talin squeezed his eyes closed, happier than he'd ever been. "You're really here?"

"I'm really here."

"A Reaper?"

Neve nodded and slid her hands into his hair. "A Reaper. With all the responsibilities that you have."

"Neve—" he began.

She raised a brow and gave him a stern look. "It was my decision. Erith told me exactly what I would be doing. It's going to be hard at first, but I'm serving Death. I'm proud of that, even if I'm still hurting over how I came to be a Reaper. But," she hurried to say when he opened his mouth. "Now I'll get to hunt Bran along with you."

Talin didn't know what to say. He was both elated and sad that she was with him.

Neve stepped out of his arms. "Have your feelings for me changed?"

He jerked her back against him, shaking his head. "Never. I'm just wrapping my head around one of the leading Light Fae family members now being a Reaper."

"My parents are gone," she said in a soft voice. Her gaze lowered to his chest as she took a deep breath and released it. "Atris, though still alive, is also gone. I'll bring justice to Bran for my family."

"Aye, we will," Talin said.

Neve grinned as she looked back at him. "I can't wait to meet Jordyn and River."

The door slammed shut with a thought from Talin. He held Neve against him. "We have eternity with them. I want some time with you. Alone."

"Hmm. I like the sound of that."

Talin's heart was about to burst from happiness. "I . . . I . . ." He stopped and cleared his throat. Words had always come easily to him, but suddenly, now he couldn't get them out.

Neve put her hand over his heart and gazed up at him adoringly. He was the luckiest Fae in all the realms. The proof was the woman in his arms.

"I'm an arse for not telling you of my love sooner."

"Yes, you are," she agreed.

He paused for a moment. "I'm going to tell you every day."

"Yes, you are."

Talin smiled. "And you'll tell me every day."

"Damn right." Neve smiled.

Talin took a half—step back and held her hand between them. He gazed into her eyes. Nothing in their relationship had gone in sequence. Why should he start now? "From this moment through eternity I am yours."

Her eyes widened and her lips parted as she recognized the words of the marriage ceremony of the Fae. Neve swallowed and blinked hastily. "From this moment through eternity I am yours."

With those simple words, they were bound together as husband and wife.

She was his.

And he was hers.

Epilogue

Bran stared down at Searlas through the pouring rain in an alley in Dublin. The Dark was slowly dying. Part of Bran wanted to let him die for not killing Talin. Then again, the female Light Fae had ruined so much.

Bran knelt beside his lieutenant and easily healed him. He looked around the rain—soaked streets. "Find us a place. I want to know who that Light Fae was."

"Her name is Rhi."

His head jerked to Searlas. "How do you know her?"

"Everyone knows her." Searlas sat up, rubbing the spot where Kyran's sword had pierced his flesh. "She's a Queen's Guard. She also had an affair with a Dragon King."

Ah. The Dragon Kings. Bran hadn't paid them much attention before since he had bigger fish to fry—like Death. But Rhi was more powerful than he'd expected.

In fact, her power exceeded his. And that could put a wrench in his plans.

"We need to kill this Rhi."

Searlas frowned as he got to his feet. "It'd be better to

turn her to our side."

Bran slowly stood. This was the first smart thing Searlas had said in months. "Yes, she would make a fine addition to our ranks." And be a better lieutenant.

But Searlas didn't need to know that part yet.

"Recruit her," Bran ordered as he walked off into the night.

Searlas watched him. He owed everything to Bran, but he wasn't as stupid as Bran thought. Rhi was going to be harder to kill than the Reapers, and they hadn't had much luck in that department.

But the odds of Rhi coming to their side were next to nil. Besides, if she did, Searlas knew she would take his position. He hadn't killed and clawed his way to the top to move aside now.

With Bran occupied with the Reapers and Death, he'd never know if or when Searlas spoke with Rhi.

Searlas turned on his heel and went in the opposite direction to look for a new place for them to live. He hoped it was filled with humans because he had a need to kill.

Also by Donna Grant

The Sons of Texas series
    THE HERO
    THE PROTECTOR
    TH LEGEND
    The Dark King series
    DARK HEAT
    DARKEST FLAME
    FIRE RISING
    BURNING DESIRE
    HOT BLOODED
    NIGHT'S BLAZE
    SOUL SCORCHED
    PASSION IGNITES
    SMOLDERING HUNGER
    SMOKE AND FIRE
    The Dark Warrior series
    MIDNIGHT'S MASTER
    MIDNIGHT'S LOVER
    MIDNIGHT'S SEDUCTION
    MIDNIGHT'S WARRIOR
    MIDNIGHT'S KISS

MIDNIGHT'S CAPTIVE
MIDNIGHT'S TEMPTATION
MIDNIGHT'S PROMISE
MIDNIGHT'S SURRENDER
The Dark Sword series
DANGEROUS HIGHLANDER
FORBIDDEN HIGHLANDER
WICKED HIGHLANDER
UNTAMED HIGHLANDER
SHADOW HIGHLANDER
DARKEST HIGHLANDER

Tall, Dark, Deadly Alpha

About the Author

New York Times and *USA Today* bestselling author **Donna Grant** has been praised for her "totally addictive" and "unique and sensual" stories. She's the author of more than thirty novels spanning multiple genres of romance including the bestselling Dark King stories. THe acclaimed series features a thrilling combination of dragons, the Fae, and Highlanders who are dark, dangerous, and irresistible. She lives with her two children, a dog, and four cats in Texas.

Want to know when Donna's next book is available? You can sign up for her newsletter at www.DonnaGrant.com, follow her on Twitter

@donna_grant, or like her Facebook page at face-book.com/AuthorDonnaGrant.

CPSIA information can be obtained
at www.ICGtesting.com
Printed in the USA
LVOW11s0020210717
542039LV00002B/222/P

OFF

SCRABBLE
BRAND Crossword Game

WORDS

HarperCollins Publishers
Westerhill Road
Bishopbriggs
Glasgow
G64 2QT

Third edition 2012

Reprint 10 9 8 7 6 5 4 3 2 1 0

©HarperCollins Publishers 2004,
2005, 2006, 2007, 2011, 2012

ISBN 978-0-00-745911-7

SCRABBLE® and associated
trademarks and trade dress are
owned by, and used under licence
from, Mattel, Inc. SCRABBLE is a
registered trademark of J.W. Spear &
Sons Limited, a subsidiary of Mattel,
Inc. © 2012 Mattel, Inc.
All Rights Reserved.

Collins ® is a registered trademark of
HarperCollins Publishers Limited

www.collinslanguage.com

A catalogue record for this book is
available from the British Library

Typeset by
Davidson Publishing Solutions,
Glasgow

Printed in Great Britain by
Clays Ltd, St Ives plc

Scrabble Consultants
Darryl Francis
Allan Simmons

For the Publisher
Lucy Cooper
Kerry Ferguson
Elaine Higgleton

Computing Support
Thomas Callan

Introduction

A new edition of *Collins Official Scrabble Words* is always looked forward to with anticipation, and Darryl Francis and Allan Simmons of the Dictionary Committee of the World English-Language Scrabble Players Association (WESPA), together with their cohorts, have done a great compilation job on our behalf. It's great to see those words you have heard used for a year or two that are now playable on the Scrabble board like *blingy*, *mankini*, *moobs* and *mwah*. Then there's always the delicious search for new words that will increase your scoring power. Undoubtedly, the most used addition will be *qin* but others containing high scoring letters include *coxib*, *boxty*, *juvie*, *soz* and *fiqh*.

The sooner you can get down to analysing the changes, the better, as it will hopefully give you an advantage over players of similar ability who are lazier or less committed than you. There are some good high probability eight letter words this time, including *realtone* and *litreage*, plus 7's like *netroot*, *noilier*, and even *snotrag*!

Those words that have caught me out in the past are a personal bugbear. I won't be making errors with *airguns*, *beesting*, *costings*, *flob*, *strim*, *teabags*, *teenages*, and *ums* again but I expect I will find other ways of losing.

Personally speaking, when I'm not playing Scrabble, two of the essentials of life are food and cricket, and these are well represented. As a confirmed *foodie* (that's been there for some time), I've already consumed *chana*, *goji*, and *wagyu* and used *legside*, *jaffa*, and *paceman* whilst discussing our national summer game. In fact, with *offie*, *leggie*, and *quicky* also making the cut, I do wonder whether the proofs inadvertently passed across Aggers's desk.

There are, however, cuts as well as new additions. We have to say goodbye to 'addios' and farewell to 'ciaos' as, along with a handful of other words, they are no longer supported by the sources used. As one of the few people, outside Ireland, able to pronounce the high probability 'tanaiste' correctly I will miss this word the most. Such is the life of a Scrabble Promotions Manager.

I'd go as far as to say that you can't play Scrabble properly without *Official Scrabble Words*, so welcome to the club. Have a look at the following page for further Scrabble resources. I hope you enjoy using *Official Scrabble Words* as much as I do.

Philip Nelkon

two to nine
letter words

A

AA	ABANDON	ABAXIAL	ABDUCTEE	ABEYANCY
AAH	ABANDONED	ABAXILE	ABDUCTEES	ABEYANT
AAHED	ABANDONEE	ABAYA	ABDUCTING	ABFARAD
AAHING	ABANDONER	ABAYAS	ABDUCTION	ABFARADS
AAHS	ABANDONS	ABB	ABDUCTOR	ABHENRIES
AAL	ABANDS	ABBA	ABDUCTORS	ABHENRY
AALII	ABAPICAL	ABBACIES	ABDUCTS	ABHENRYS
AALIIS	ABAS	ABBACY	ABEAM	ABHOR
AALS	ABASE	ABBAS	ABEAR	ABHORRED
AARDVARK	ABASED	ABBATIAL	ABEARING	ABHORRENT
AARDVARKS	ABASEDLY	ABBE	ABEARS	ABHORRER
AARDWOLF	ABASEMENT	ABBED	ABED	ABHORRERS
AARGH	ABASER	ABBES	ABEGGING	ABHORRING
AARRGH	ABASERS	ABBESS	ABEIGH	ABHORS
AARRGHH	ABASES	ABBESSES	ABELE	ABID
AARTI	ABASH	ABBEY	ABELES	ABIDANCE
AARTIS	ABASHED	ABBEYS	ABELIA	ABIDANCES
AAS	ABASHEDLY	ABBOT	ABELIAN	ABIDDEN
AASVOGEL	ABASHES	ABBOTCIES	ABELIAS	ABIDE
AASVOGELS	ABASHING	ABBOTCY	ABELMOSK	ABIDED
AB	ABASHLESS	ABBOTS	ABELMOSKS	ABIDER
ABA	ABASHMENT	ABBOTSHIP	ABERNETHY	ABIDERS
ABAC	ABASIA	ABBS	ABERRANCE	ABIDES
ABACA	ABASIAS	ABCEE	ABERRANCY	ABIDING
ABACAS	ABASING	ABCEES	ABERRANT	ABIDINGLY
ABACI	ABASK	ABCOULOMB	ABERRANTS	ABIDINGS
ABACK	ABATABLE	ABDABS	ABERRATE	ABIES
ABACS	ABATE	ABDICABLE	ABERRATED	ABIETIC
ABACTINAL	ABATED	ABDICANT	ABERRATES	ABIGAIL
ABACTOR	ABATEMENT	ABDICATE	ABESSIVE	ABIGAILS
ABACTORS	ABATER	ABDICATED	ABESSIVES	ABILITIES
ABACUS	ABATERS	ABDICATES	ABET	ABILITY
ABACUSES	ABATES	ABDICATOR	ABETMENT	ABIOGENIC
ABAFT	ABATING	ABDOMEN	ABETMENTS	ABIOSES
ABAKA	ABATIS	ABDOMENS	ABETS	ABIOSIS
ABAKAS	ABATISES	ABDOMINA	ABETTAL	ABIOTIC
ABALONE	ABATOR	ABDOMINAL	ABETTALS	ABITUR
ABALONES	ABATORS	ABDUCE	ABETTED	ABITURS
ABAMP	ABATTIS	ABDUCED	ABETTER	ABJECT
ABAMPERE	ABATTISES	ABDUCENS	ABETTERS	ABJECTED
ABAMPERES	ABATTOIR	ABDUCENT	ABETTING	ABJECTING
ABAMPS	ABATTOIRS	ABDUCES	ABETTOR	ABJECTION
ABAND	ABATTU	ABDUCING	ABETTORS	ABJECTLY
ABANDED	ABATURE	ABDUCT	ABEYANCE	ABJECTS
ABANDING	ABATURES	ABDUCTED	ABEYANCES	ABJOINT

ABJOINTED
ABJOINTS
ABJURE
ABJURED
ABJURER
ABJURERS
ABJURES
ABJURING
ABLATE
ABLATED
ABLATES
ABLATING
ABLATION
ABLATIONS
ABLATIVAL
ABLATIVE
ABLATIVES
ABLATOR
ABLATORS
ABLAUT
ABLAUTS
ABLAZE
ABLE
ABLED
ABLEGATE
ABLEGATES
ABLEISM
ABLEISMS
ABLEIST
ABLEISTS
ABLER
ABLES
ABLEST
ABLET
ABLETS
ABLING
ABLINGS
ABLINS
ABLOOM
ABLOW
ABLUENT
ABLUENTS
ABLUSH
ABLUTED
ABLUTION
ABLUTIONS
ABLY

ABMHO
ABMHOS
ABNEGATE
ABNEGATED
ABNEGATES
ABNEGATOR
ABNORMAL
ABNORMALS
ABNORMITY
ABNORMOUS
ABO
ABOARD
ABODE
ABODED
ABODEMENT
ABODES
ABODING
ABOHM
ABOHMS
ABOIDEAU
ABOIDEAUS
ABOIDEAUX
ABOIL
ABOITEAU
ABOITEAUS
ABOITEAUX
ABOLISH
ABOLISHED
ABOLISHER
ABOLISHES
ABOLITION
ABOLLA
ABOLLAE
ABOLLAS
ABOMA
ABOMAS
ABOMASA
ABOMASAL
ABOMASI
ABOMASUM
ABOMASUS
ABOMINATE
ABONDANCE
ABOON
ABORAL
ABORALLY
ABORD

ABORDED
ABORDING
ABORDS
ABORE
ABORIGEN
ABORIGENS
ABORIGIN
ABORIGINE
ABORIGINS
ABORNE
ABORNING
ABORT
ABORTED
ABORTEE
ABORTEES
ABORTER
ABORTERS
ABORTING
ABORTION
ABORTIONS
ABORTIVE
ABORTS
ABORTUARY
ABORTUS
ABORTUSES
ABOS
ABOUGHT
ABOULIA
ABOULIAS
ABOULIC
ABOUND
ABOUNDED
ABOUNDING
ABOUNDS
ABOUT
ABOUTS
ABOVE
ABOVES
ABRACHIA
ABRACHIAS
ABRADABLE
ABRADANT
ABRADANTS
ABRADE
ABRADED
ABRADER
ABRADERS

ABRADES
ABRADING
ABRAID
ABRAIDED
ABRAIDING
ABRAIDS
ABRAM
ABRASAX
ABRASAXES
ABRASION
ABRASIONS
ABRASIVE
ABRASIVES
ABRAXAS
ABRAXASES
ABRAY
ABRAYED
ABRAYING
ABRAYS
ABRAZO
ABRAZOS
ABREACT
ABREACTED
ABREACTS
ABREAST
ABREGE
ABREGES
ABRI
ABRICOCK
ABRICOCKS
ABRIDGE
ABRIDGED
ABRIDGER
ABRIDGERS
ABRIDGES
ABRIDGING
ABRIM
ABRIN
ABRINS
ABRIS
ABROACH
ABROAD
ABROADS
ABROGABLE
ABROGATE
ABROGATED
ABROGATES

ABROGATOR
ABROOKE
ABROOKED
ABROOKES
ABROOKING
ABROSIA
ABROSIAS
ABRUPT
ABRUPTER
ABRUPTEST
ABRUPTION
ABRUPTLY
ABRUPTS
ABS
ABSCESS
ABSCESSED
ABSCESSES
ABSCIND
ABSCINDED
ABSCINDS
ABSCISE
ABSCISED
ABSCISES
ABSCISIC
ABSCISIN
ABSCISING
ABSCISINS
ABSCISS
ABSCISSA
ABSCISSAE
ABSCISSAS
ABSCISSE
ABSCISSES
ABSCISSIN
ABSCOND
ABSCONDED
ABSCONDER
ABSCONDS
ABSEIL
ABSEILED
ABSEILING
ABSEILS
ABSENCE
ABSENCES
ABSENT
ABSENTED
ABSENTEE

ABSENTEES	ABSTRUSER	ABUTTING	ACANTHIN	ACCEDES
ABSENTER	ABSURD	ABUZZ	ACANTHINE	ACCEDING
ABSENTERS	ABSURDER	ABVOLT	ACANTHINS	ACCEND
ABSENTING	ABSURDEST	ABVOLTS	ACANTHOID	ACCENDED
ABSENTLY	ABSURDISM	ABWATT	ACANTHOUS	ACCENDING
ABSENTS	ABSURDIST	ABWATTS	ACANTHS	ACCENDS
ABSEY	ABSURDITY	ABY	ACANTHUS	ACCENSION
ABSEYS	ABSURDLY	ABYE	ACAPNIA	ACCENT
ABSINTH	ABSURDS	ABYEING	ACAPNIAS	ACCENTED
ABSINTHE	ABTHANE	ABYES	ACARBOSE	ACCENTING
ABSINTHES	ABTHANES	ABYING	ACARBOSES	ACCENTOR
ABSINTHS	ABUBBLE	ABYS	ACARI	ACCENTORS
ABSIT	ABUILDING	ABYSM	ACARIAN	ACCENTS
ABSITS	ABULIA	ABYSMAL	ACARIASES	ACCENTUAL
ABSOLUTE	ABULIAS	ABYSMALLY	ACARIASIS	ACCEPT
ABSOLUTER	ABULIC	ABYSMS	ACARICIDE	ACCEPTANT
ABSOLUTES	ABUNA	ABYSS	ACARID	ACCEPTED
ABSOLVE	ABUNAS	ABYSSAL	ACARIDAN	ACCEPTEE
ABSOLVED	ABUNDANCE	ABYSSES	ACARIDANS	ACCEPTEES
ABSOLVENT	ABUNDANCY	ACACIA	ACARIDEAN	ACCEPTER
ABSOLVER	ABUNDANT	ACACIAS	ACARIDIAN	ACCEPTERS
ABSOLVERS	ABUNE	ACADEME	ACARIDS	ACCEPTING
ABSOLVES	ABURST	ACADEMES	ACARINE	ACCEPTIVE
ABSOLVING	ABUSABLE	ACADEMIA	ACARINES	ACCEPTOR
ABSONANT	ABUSAGE	ACADEMIAS	ACAROID	ACCEPTORS
ABSORB	ABUSAGES	ACADEMIC	ACAROLOGY	ACCEPTS
ABSORBANT	ABUSE	ACADEMICS	ACARPOUS	ACCESS
ABSORBATE	ABUSED	ACADEMIES	ACARUS	ACCESSARY
ABSORBED	ABUSER	ACADEMISM	ACATER	ACCESSED
ABSORBENT	ABUSERS	ACADEMIST	ACATERS	ACCESSES
ABSORBER	ABUSES	ACADEMY	ACATES	ACCESSING
ABSORBERS	ABUSING	ACAI	ACATHISIA	ACCESSION
ABSORBING	ABUSION	ACAIS	ACATOUR	ACCESSORY
ABSORBS	ABUSIONS	ACAJOU	ACATOURS	ACCIDENCE
ABSTAIN	ABUSIVE	ACAJOUS	ACAUDAL	ACCIDENT
ABSTAINED	ABUSIVELY	ACALCULIA	ACAUDATE	ACCIDENTS
ABSTAINER	ABUT	ACALEPH	ACAULINE	ACCIDIA
ABSTAINS	ABUTILON	ACALEPHAE	ACAULOSE	ACCIDIAS
ABSTERGE	ABUTILONS	ACALEPHAN	ACAULOUS	ACCIDIE
ABSTERGED	ABUTMENT	ACALEPHE	ACCA	ACCIDIES
ABSTERGES	ABUTMENTS	ACALEPHES	ACCABLE	ACCINGE
ABSTINENT	ABUTS	ACALEPHS	ACCAS	ACCINGED
ABSTRACT	ABUTTAL	ACANTH	ACCEDE	ACCINGES
ABSTRACTS	ABUTTALS	ACANTHA	ACCEDED	ACCINGING
ABSTRICT	ABUTTED	ACANTHAE	ACCEDENCE	ACCIPITER
ABSTRICTS	ABUTTER	ACANTHAS	ACCEDER	ACCITE
ABSTRUSE	ABUTTERS	ACANTHI	ACCEDERS	ACCITED

ACCITES	ACCOURTS	ACCUSER	ACETAMIDE	ACHIER
ACCITING	ACCOUTER	ACCUSERS	ACETAMIDS	ACHIEST
ACCLAIM	ACCOUTERS	ACCUSES	ACETATE	ACHIEVE
ACCLAIMED	ACCOUTRE	ACCUSING	ACETATED	ACHIEVED
ACCLAIMER	ACCOUTRED	ACCUSTOM	ACETATES	ACHIEVER
ACCLAIMS	ACCOUTRES	ACCUSTOMS	ACETIC	ACHIEVERS
ACCLIMATE	ACCOY	ACE	ACETIFIED	ACHIEVES
ACCLIVITY	ACCOYED	ACED	ACETIFIER	ACHIEVING
ACCLIVOUS	ACCOYING	ACEDIA	ACETIFIES	ACHILLEA
ACCLOY	ACCOYLD	ACEDIAS	ACETIFY	ACHILLEAS
ACCLOYED	ACCOYS	ACELDAMA	ACETIN	ACHIMENES
ACCLOYING	ACCREDIT	ACELDAMAS	ACETINS	ACHINESS
ACCLOYS	ACCREDITS	ACELLULAR	ACETONE	ACHING
ACCOAST	ACCRETE	ACENTRIC	ACETONES	ACHINGLY
ACCOASTED	ACCRETED	ACENTRICS	ACETONIC	ACHINGS
ACCOASTS	ACCRETES	ACEPHALIC	ACETOSE	ACHIOTE
ACCOIED	ACCRETING	ACEQUIA	ACETOUS	ACHIOTES
ACCOIL	ACCRETION	ACEQUIAS	ACETOXYL	ACHIRAL
ACCOILS	ACCRETIVE	ACER	ACETOXYLS	ACHKAN
ACCOLADE	ACCREW	ACERATE	ACETUM	ACHKANS
ACCOLADED	ACCREWED	ACERATED	ACETYL	ACHOLIA
ACCOLADES	ACCREWING	ACERB	ACETYLATE	ACHOLIAS
ACCOMPANY	ACCREWS	ACERBATE	ACETYLENE	ACHOO
ACCOMPT	ACCROIDES	ACERBATED	ACETYLIC	ACHROMAT
ACCOMPTED	ACCRUABLE	ACERBATES	ACETYLIDE	ACHROMATS
ACCOMPTS	ACCRUAL	ACERBER	ACETYLS	ACHROMIC
ACCORAGE	ACCRUALS	ACERBEST	ACH	ACHROMOUS
ACCORAGED	ACCRUE	ACERBIC	ACHAENIA	ACHY
ACCORAGES	ACCRUED	ACERBITY	ACHAENIUM	ACICLOVIR
ACCORD	ACCRUES	ACEROLA	ACHAGE	ACICULA
ACCORDANT	ACCRUING	ACEROLAS	ACHAGES	ACICULAE
ACCORDED	ACCUMBENT	ACEROSE	ACHALASIA	ACICULAR
ACCORDER	ACCURACY	ACEROUS	ACHAR	ACICULAS
ACCORDERS	ACCURATE	ACERS	ACHARNE	ACICULATE
ACCORDING	ACCURSE	ACERVATE	ACHARS	ACICULUM
ACCORDION	ACCURSED	ACERVULI	ACHARYA	ACICULUMS
ACCORDS	ACCURSES	ACERVULUS	ACHARYAS	ACID
ACCOST	ACCURSING	ACES	ACHARYAS	ACIDEMIA
ACCOSTED	ACCURST	ACESCENCE	ACHE	ACIDEMIAS
ACCOSTING	ACCUSABLE	ACESCENCY	ACHED	ACIDER
ACCOSTS	ACCUSABLY	ACESCENT	ACHENE	ACIDEST
ACCOUNT	ACCUSAL	ACESCENTS	ACHENES	ACIDHEAD
ACCOUNTED	ACCUSALS	ACETA	ACHENIA	ACIDHEADS
ACCOUNTS	ACCUSANT	ACETABULA	ACHENIAL	ACIDIC
ACCOURAGE	ACCUSANTS	ACETAL	ACHENIUM	ACIDIER
ACCOURT	ACCUSE	ACETALS	ACHENIUMS	ACIDIEST
ACCOURTED	ACCUSED	ACETAMID	ACHES	ACIDIFIED

ACIDIFIER	ACMITE	ACQUIREE	ACROGEN	ACTIN
ACIDIFIES	ACMITES	ACQUIREES	ACROGENIC	ACTINAL
ACIDIFY	ACNE	ACQUIRER	ACROGENS	ACTINALLY
ACIDITIES	ACNED	ACQUIRERS	ACROLECT	ACTING
ACIDITY	ACNES	ACQUIRES	ACROLECTS	ACTINGS
ACIDLY	ACNODAL	ACQUIRING	ACROLEIN	ACTINIA
ACIDNESS	ACNODE	ACQUIS	ACROLEINS	ACTINIAE
ACIDOPHIL	ACNODES	ACQUIST	ACROLITH	ACTINIAN
ACIDOSES	ACOCK	ACQUISTS	ACROLITHS	ACTINIANS
ACIDOSIS	ACOELOUS	ACQUIT	ACROMIA	ACTINIAS
ACIDOTIC	ACOEMETI	ACQUITE	ACROMIAL	ACTINIC
ACIDS	ACOLD	ACQUITES	ACROMION	ACTINIDE
ACIDULATE	ACOLUTHIC	ACQUITING	ACRONIC	ACTINIDES
ACIDULENT	ACOLYTE	ACQUITS	ACRONICAL	ACTINISM
ACIDULOUS	ACOLYTES	ACQUITTAL	ACRONYCAL	ACTINISMS
ACIDURIA	ACOLYTH	ACQUITTED	ACRONYM	ACTINIUM
ACIDURIAS	ACOLYTHS	ACQUITTER	ACRONYMIC	ACTINIUMS
ACIDY	ACONITE	ACRASIA	ACRONYMS	ACTINOID
ACIERAGE	ACONITES	ACRASIAS	ACROPETAL	ACTINOIDS
ACIERAGES	ACONITIC	ACRASIN	ACROPHOBE	ACTINON
ACIERATE	ACONITINE	ACRASINS	ACROPHONY	ACTINONS
ACIERATED	ACONITUM	ACRATIC	ACROPOLIS	ACTINOPOD
ACIERATES	ACONITUMS	ACRAWL	ACROSOMAL	ACTINS
ACIFORM	ACORN	ACRE	ACROSOME	ACTION
ACINAR	ACORNED	ACREAGE	ACROSOMES	ACTIONED
ACING	ACORNS	ACREAGES	ACROSPIRE	ACTIONER
ACINI	ACOSMISM	ACRED	ACROSS	ACTIONERS
ACINIC	ACOSMISMS	ACRES	ACROSTIC	ACTIONING
ACINIFORM	ACOSMIST	ACRID	ACROSTICS	ACTIONIST
ACINOSE	ACOSMISTS	ACRIDER	ACROTER	ACTIONS
ACINOUS	ACOUCHI	ACRIDEST	ACROTERIA	ACTIVATE
ACINUS	ACOUCHIES	ACRIDIN	ACROTERS	ACTIVATED
ACKEE	ACOUCHIS	ACRIDINE	ACROTIC	ACTIVATES
ACKEES	ACOUCHY	ACRIDINES	ACROTISM	ACTIVATOR
ACKER	ACOUSTIC	ACRIDINS	ACROTISMS	ACTIVE
ACKERS	ACOUSTICS	ACRIDITY	ACRYLATE	ACTIVELY
ACKNEW	ACQUAINT	ACRIDLY	ACRYLATES	ACTIVES
ACKNOW	ACQUAINTS	ACRIDNESS	ACRYLIC	ACTIVISE
ACKNOWING	ACQUEST	ACRIMONY	ACRYLICS	ACTIVISED
ACKNOWN	ACQUESTS	ACRITARCH	ACRYLYL	ACTIVISES
ACKNOWNE	ACQUIESCE	ACRITICAL	ACRYLYLS	ACTIVISM
ACKNOWS	ACQUIGHT	ACROBAT	ACT	ACTIVISMS
ACLINIC	ACQUIGHTS	ACROBATIC	ACTA	ACTIVIST
ACMATIC	ACQUIRAL	ACROBATS	ACTABLE	ACTIVISTS
ACME	ACQUIRALS	ACRODONT	ACTANT	ACTIVITY
ACMES	ACQUIRE	ACRODONTS	ACTANTS	ACTIVIZE
ACMIC	ACQUIRED	ACRODROME	ACTED	ACTIVIZED

ACTIVIZES	ACUTANCE	ADAWED	ADDOOMING	ADENYLS
ACTON	ACUTANCES	ADAWING	ADDOOMS	ADEPT
ACTONS	ACUTE	ADAWS	ADDORSED	ADEPTER
ACTOR	ACUTELY	ADAXIAL	ADDRESS	ADEPTEST
ACTORISH	ACUTENESS	ADAYS	ADDRESSED	ADEPTLY
ACTORLY	ACUTER	ADD	ADDRESSEE	ADEPTNESS
ACTORS	ACUTES	ADDABLE	ADDRESSER	ADEPTS
ACTRESS	ACUTEST	ADDAX	ADDRESSES	ADEQUACY
ACTRESSES	ACYCLIC	ADDAXES	ADDRESSOR	ADEQUATE
ACTRESSY	ACYCLOVIR	ADDEBTED	ADDREST	ADERMIN
ACTS	ACYL	ADDED	ADDS	ADERMINS
ACTUAL	ACYLATE	ADDEDLY	ADDUCE	ADESPOTA
ACTUALISE	ACYLATED	ADDEEM	ADDUCED	ADESSIVE
ACTUALIST	ACYLATES	ADDEEMED	ADDUCENT	ADESSIVES
ACTUALITE	ACYLATING	ADDEEMING	ADDUCER	ADHAN
ACTUALITY	ACYLATION	ADDEEMS	ADDUCERS	ADHANS
ACTUALIZE	ACYLOIN	ADDEND	ADDUCES	ADHARMA
ACTUALLY	ACYLOINS	ADDENDA	ADDUCIBLE	ADHARMAS
ACTUALS	ACYLS	ADDENDS	ADDUCING	ADHERABLE
ACTUARIAL	AD	ADDENDUM	ADDUCT	ADHERE
ACTUARIES	ADAGE	ADDENDUMS	ADDUCTED	ADHERED
ACTUARY	ADAGES	ADDER	ADDUCTING	ADHERENCE
ACTUATE	ADAGIAL	ADDERS	ADDUCTION	ADHEREND
ACTUATED	ADAGIO	ADDERWORT	ADDUCTIVE	ADHERENDS
ACTUATES	ADAGIOS	ADDIBLE	ADDUCTOR	ADHERENT
ACTUATING	ADAMANCE	ADDICT	ADDUCTORS	ADHERENTS
ACTUATION	ADAMANCES	ADDICTED	ADDUCTS	ADHERER
ACTUATOR	ADAMANCY	ADDICTING	ADDY	ADHERERS
ACTUATORS	ADAMANT	ADDICTION	ADEEM	ADHERES
ACTURE	ADAMANTLY	ADDICTIVE	ADEEMED	ADHERING
ACTURES	ADAMANTS	ADDICTS	ADEEMING	ADHESION
ACUATE	ADAMSITE	ADDIES	ADEEMS	ADHESIONS
ACUITIES	ADAMSITES	ADDING	ADEMPTION	ADHESIVE
ACUITY	ADAPT	ADDINGS	ADENINE	ADHESIVES
ACULEATE	ADAPTABLE	ADDIO	ADENINES	ADHIBIT
ACULEATED	ADAPTED	ADDITION	ADENITIS	ADHIBITED
ACULEATES	ADAPTER	ADDITIONS	ADENOID	ADHIBITS
ACULEI	ADAPTERS	ADDITIVE	ADENOIDAL	ADHOCRACY
ACULEUS	ADAPTING	ADDITIVES	ADENOIDS	ADIABATIC
ACUMEN	ADAPTION	ADDITORY	ADENOMA	ADIAPHORA
ACUMENS	ADAPTIONS	ADDLE	ADENOMAS	ADIEU
ACUMINATE	ADAPTIVE	ADDLED	ADENOMATA	ADIEUS
ACUMINOUS	ADAPTOGEN	ADDLEMENT	ADENOSES	ADIEUX
ACUPOINT	ADAPTOR	ADDLES	ADENOSINE	ADIOS
ACUPOINTS	ADAPTORS	ADDLING	ADENOSIS	ADIPIC
ACUSHLA	ADAPTS	ADDOOM	ADENYL	ADIPOCERE
ACUSHLAS	ADAW	ADDOOMED	ADENYLIC	ADIPOCYTE

ADIPOSE	ADJUSTORS	ADMIXTURE	ADORERS	ADUKI
ADIPOSES	ADJUSTS	ADMONISH	ADORES	ADUKIS
ADIPOSIS	ADJUTAGE	ADMONITOR	ADORING	ADULARIA
ADIPOSITY	ADJUTAGES	ADNASCENT	ADORINGLY	ADULARIAS
ADIPOUS	ADJUTANCY	ADNATE	ADORN	ADULATE
ADIPSIA	ADJUTANT	ADNATION	ADORNED	ADULATED
ADIPSIAS	ADJUTANTS	ADNATIONS	ADORNER	ADULATES
ADIT	ADJUVANCY	ADNEXA	ADORNERS	ADULATING
ADITS	ADJUVANT	ADNEXAL	ADORNING	ADULATION
ADJACENCE	ADJUVANTS	ADNOMINAL	ADORNMENT	ADULATOR
ADJACENCY	ADLAND	ADNOUN	ADORNS	ADULATORS
ADJACENT	ADLANDS	ADNOUNS	ADOS	ADULATORY
ADJACENTS	ADMAN	ADO	ADOWN	ADULT
ADJECTIVE	ADMASS	ADOBE	ADOZE	ADULTERER
ADJIGO	ADMASSES	ADOBELIKE	ADPRESS	ADULTERY
ADJIGOS	ADMEASURE	ADOBES	ADPRESSED	ADULTHOOD
ADJOIN	ADMEN	ADOBO	ADPRESSES	ADULTLIKE
ADJOINED	ADMIN	ADOBOS	ADRAD	ADULTLY
ADJOINING	ADMINICLE	ADONIS	ADREAD	ADULTNESS
ADJOINS	ADMINS	ADONISE	ADREADED	ADULTRESS
ADJOINT	ADMIRABLE	ADONISED	ADREADING	ADULTS
ADJOINTS	ADMIRABLY	ADONISES	ADREADS	ADUMBRAL
ADJOURN	ADMIRAL	ADONISING	ADRED	ADUMBRATE
ADJOURNED	ADMIRALS	ADONIZE	ADRENAL	ADUNC
ADJOURNS	ADMIRALTY	ADONIZED	ADRENALIN	ADUNCATE
ADJUDGE	ADMIRANCE	ADONIZES	ADRENALLY	ADUNCATED
ADJUDGED	ADMIRE	ADONIZING	ADRENALS	ADUNCITY
ADJUDGES	ADMIRED	ADOORS	ADRIFT	ADUNCOUS
ADJUDGING	ADMIRER	ADOPT	ADROIT	ADUST
ADJUNCT	ADMIRERS	ADOPTABLE	ADROITER	ADUSTED
ADJUNCTLY	ADMIRES	ADOPTED	ADROITEST	ADUSTING
ADJUNCTS	ADMIRING	ADOPTEE	ADROITLY	ADUSTS
ADJURE	ADMISSION	ADOPTEES	ADRY	ADVANCE
ADJURED	ADMISSIVE	ADOPTER	ADS	ADVANCED
ADJURER	ADMIT	ADOPTERS	ADSCRIPT	ADVANCER
ADJURERS	ADMITS	ADOPTING	ADSCRIPTS	ADVANCERS
ADJURES	ADMITTED	ADOPTION	ADSORB	ADVANCES
ADJURING	ADMITTEE	ADOPTIONS	ADSORBATE	ADVANCING
ADJUROR	ADMITTEES	ADOPTIOUS	ADSORBED	ADVANTAGE
ADJURORS	ADMITTER	ADOPTIVE	ADSORBENT	ADVECT
ADJUST	ADMITTERS	ADOPTS	ADSORBER	ADVECTED
ADJUSTED	ADMITTING	ADORABLE	ADSORBERS	ADVECTING
ADJUSTER	ADMIX	ADORABLY	ADSORBING	ADVECTION
ADJUSTERS	ADMIXED	ADORATION	ADSORBS	ADVECTIVE
ADJUSTING	ADMIXES	ADORE	ADSUKI	ADVECTS
ADJUSTIVE	ADMIXING	ADORED	ADSUKIS	ADVENE
ADJUSTOR	ADMIXT	ADORER	ADSUM	ADVENED

ADVENES	ADVOCATE	AEGIS	AEROBAT	AEROPHOBE
ADVENING	ADVOCATED	AEGISES	AEROBATIC	AEROPHONE
ADVENT	ADVOCATES	AEGLOGUE	AEROBATS	AEROPHORE
ADVENTIVE	ADVOCATOR	AEGLOGUES	AEROBE	AEROPHYTE
ADVENTS	ADVOUTRER	AEGROTAT	AEROBES	AEROPLANE
ADVENTURE	ADVOUTRY	AEGROTATS	AEROBIA	AEROPULSE
ADVERB	ADVOWSON	AEMULE	AEROBIC	AEROS
ADVERBIAL	ADVOWSONS	AEMULED	AEROBICS	AEROSAT
ADVERBS	ADWARD	AEMULES	AEROBIONT	AEROSATS
ADVERSARY	ADWARDED	AEMULING	AEROBIUM	AEROSCOPE
ADVERSE	ADWARDING	AENEOUS	AEROBOMB	AEROSHELL
ADVERSELY	ADWARDS	AENEUS	AEROBOMBS	AEROSOL
ADVERSER	ADWARE	AEOLIAN	AEROBOT	AEROSOLS
ADVERSEST	ADWARES	AEOLIPILE	AEROBOTS	AEROSPACE
ADVERSITY	ADWOMAN	AEOLIPYLE	AEROBRAKE	AEROSPIKE
ADVERT	ADWOMEN	AEON	AERODART	AEROSTAT
ADVERTED	ADYNAMIA	AEONIAN	AERODARTS	AEROSTATS
ADVERTENT	ADYNAMIAS	AEONIC	AERODROME	AEROTAXES
ADVERTING	ADYNAMIC	AEONS	AERODUCT	AEROTAXIS
ADVERTISE	ADYTA	AEPYORNIS	AERODUCTS	AEROTONE
ADVERTIZE	ADYTUM	AEQUORIN	AERODYNE	AEROTONES
ADVERTS	ADZ	AEQUORINS	AERODYNES	AEROTRAIN
ADVEW	ADZE	AERATE	AEROFOIL	AERUGO
ADVEWED	ADZED	AERATED	AEROFOILS	AERUGOS
ADVEWING	ADZES	AERATES	AEROGEL	AERY
ADVEWS	ADZING	AERATING	AEROGELS	AESC
ADVICE	ADZUKI	AERATION	AEROGRAM	AESCES
ADVICEFUL	ADZUKIS	AERATIONS	AEROGRAMS	AESCULIN
ADVICES	AE	AERATOR	AEROGRAPH	AESCULINS
ADVISABLE	AECIA	AERATORS	AEROLITE	AESIR
ADVISABLY	AECIAL	AERIAL	AEROLITES	AESTHESES
ADVISE	AECIDIA	AERIALIST	AEROLITH	AESTHESIA
ADVISED	AECIDIAL	AERIALITY	AEROLITHS	AESTHESIS
ADVISEDLY	AECIDIUM	AERIALLY	AEROLITIC	AESTHETE
ADVISEE	AECIUM	AERIALS	AEROLOGIC	AESTHETES
ADVISEES	AEDES	AERIE	AEROLOGY	AESTHETIC
ADVISER	AEDICULE	AERIED	AEROMANCY	AESTIVAL
ADVISERS	AEDICULES	AERIER	AEROMETER	AESTIVATE
ADVISES	AEDILE	AERIES	AEROMETRY	AETHER
ADVISING	AEDILES	AERIEST	AEROMOTOR	AETHEREAL
ADVISINGS	AEDINE	AERIFIED	AERONAUT	AETHERIC
ADVISOR	AEFALD	AERIFIES	AERONAUTS	AETHERS
ADVISORS	AEFAULD	AERIFORM	AERONOMER	AETIOLOGY
ADVISORY	AEGIRINE	AERIFY	AERONOMIC	AFALD
ADVOCAAT	AEGIRINES	AERIFYING	AERONOMY	AFAR
ADVOCAATS	AEGIRITE	AERILY	AEROPAUSE	AFARA
ADVOCACY	AEGIRITES	AERO	AEROPHAGY	AFARAS

AFARS	AFFINAL	AFFORDED	AFRAID	AGAINST
AFAWLD	AFFINE	AFFORDING	AFREET	AGALACTIA
AFEAR	AFFINED	AFFORDS	AFREETS	AGALLOCH
AFEARD	AFFINELY	AFFOREST	AFRESH	AGALLOCHS
AFEARED	AFFINES	AFFORESTS	AFRIT	AGALWOOD
AFEARING	AFFINITY	AFFRAP	AFRITS	AGALWOODS
AFEARS	AFFIRM	AFFRAPPED	AFRO	AGAMA
AFEBRILE	AFFIRMANT	AFFRAPS	AFRONT	AGAMAS
AFF	AFFIRMED	AFFRAY	AFROS	AGAMETE
AFFABLE	AFFIRMER	AFFRAYED	AFT	AGAMETES
AFFABLY	AFFIRMERS	AFFRAYER	AFTER	AGAMI
AFFAIR	AFFIRMING	AFFRAYERS	AFTERBODY	AGAMIC
AFFAIRE	AFFIRMS	AFFRAYING	AFTERCARE	AGAMID
AFFAIRES	AFFIX	AFFRAYS	AFTERCLAP	AGAMIDS
AFFAIRS	AFFIXABLE	AFFRENDED	AFTERDAMP	AGAMIS
AFFEAR	AFFIXAL	AFFRET	AFTERDECK	AGAMOGONY
AFFEARD	AFFIXED	AFFRETS	AFTEREYE	AGAMOID
AFFEARE	AFFIXER	AFFRICATE	AFTEREYED	AGAMOIDS
AFFEARED	AFFIXERS	AFFRIGHT	AFTEREYES	AGAMONT
AFFEARES	AFFIXES	AFFRIGHTS	AFTERGAME	AGAMONTS
AFFEARING	AFFIXIAL	AFFRONT	AFTERGLOW	AGAMOUS
AFFEARS	AFFIXING	AFFRONTE	AFTERHEAT	AGAPAE
AFFECT	AFFIXMENT	AFFRONTED	AFTERINGS	AGAPAI
AFFECTED	AFFIXTURE	AFFRONTEE	AFTERLIFE	AGAPE
AFFECTER	AFFLATED	AFFRONTS	AFTERMATH	AGAPEIC
AFFECTERS	AFFLATION	AFFUSION	AFTERMOST	AGAPES
AFFECTING	AFFLATUS	AFFUSIONS	AFTERNOON	AGAR
AFFECTION	AFFLICT	AFFY	AFTERPAIN	AGARIC
AFFECTIVE	AFFLICTED	AFFYDE	AFTERPEAK	AGARICS
AFFECTS	AFFLICTER	AFFYING	AFTERS	AGAROSE
AFFEER	AFFLICTS	AFGHAN	AFTERSHOW	AGAROSES
AFFEERED	AFFLUENCE	AFGHANI	AFTERSUN	AGARS
AFFEERING	AFFLUENCY	AFGHANIS	AFTERSUNS	AGAS
AFFEERS	AFFLUENT	AFGHANS	AFTERTAX	AGAST
AFFERENT	AFFLUENTS	AFIELD	AFTERTIME	AGATE
AFFERENTS	AFFLUENZA	AFIRE	AFTERWARD	AGATES
AFFIANCE	AFFLUX	AFLAJ	AFTERWORD	AGATEWARE
AFFIANCED	AFFLUXES	AFLAME	AFTMOST	AGATISE
AFFIANCES	AFFLUXION	AFLATOXIN	AFTOSA	AGATISED
AFFIANT	AFFOORD	AFLOAT	AFTOSAS	AGATISES
AFFIANTS	AFFOORDED	AFLUTTER	AG	AGATISING
AFFICHE	AFFOORDS	AFOOT	AGA	AGATIZE
AFFICHES	AFFORCE	AFORE	AGACANT	AGATIZED
AFFIDAVIT	AFFORCED	AFOREHAND	AGACANTE	AGATIZES
AFFIED	AFFORCES	AFORESAID	AGACERIE	AGATIZING
AFFIES	AFFORCING	AFORETIME	AGACERIES	AGATOID
AFFILIATE	AFFORD	AFOUL	AGAIN	AGAVE

AGAVES	AGENTING	AGGRIEVES	AGITATOR	AGNISES
AGAZE	AGENTINGS	AGGRO	AGITATORS	AGNISING
AGAZED	AGENTIVAL	AGGROS	AGITPOP	AGNIZE
AGE	AGENTIVE	AGGRY	AGITPOPS	AGNIZED
AGED	AGENTIVES	AGHA	AGITPROP	AGNIZES
AGEDLY	AGENTRIES	AGHAS	AGITPROPS	AGNIZING
AGEDNESS	AGENTRY	AGHAST	AGLARE	AGNOMEN
AGEE	AGENTS	AGILA	AGLEAM	AGNOMENS
AGEING	AGER	AGILAS	AGLEE	AGNOMINA
AGEINGS	AGERATUM	AGILE	AGLET	AGNOMINAL
AGEISM	AGERATUMS	AGILELY	AGLETS	AGNOSIA
AGEISMS	AGERS	AGILENESS	AGLEY	AGNOSIAS
AGEIST	AGES	AGILER	AGLIMMER	AGNOSIC
AGEISTS	AGEUSIA	AGILEST	AGLITTER	AGNOSTIC
AGELAST	AGEUSIAS	AGILITIES	AGLOO	AGNOSTICS
AGELASTIC	AGGADA	AGILITY	AGLOOS	AGO
AGELASTS	AGGADAH	AGIN	AGLOSSAL	AGOG
AGELESS	AGGADAHS	AGING	AGLOSSATE	AGOGE
AGELESSLY	AGGADAS	AGINGS	AGLOSSIA	AGOGES
AGELONG	AGGADIC	AGINNER	AGLOSSIAS	AGOGIC
AGEMATE	AGGADOT	AGINNERS	AGLOW	AGOGICS
AGEMATES	AGGADOTH	AGIO	AGLU	AGOING
AGEN	AGGER	AGIOS	AGLUS	AGON
AGENCIES	AGGERS	AGIOTAGE	AGLY	AGONAL
AGENCY	AGGIE	AGIOTAGES	AGLYCON	AGONE
AGENDA	AGGIES	AGISM	AGLYCONE	AGONES
AGENDAS	AGGRACE	AGISMS	AGLYCONES	AGONIC
AGENDUM	AGGRACED	AGIST	AGLYCONS	AGONIES
AGENDUMS	AGGRACES	AGISTED	AGMA	AGONISE
AGENE	AGGRACING	AGISTER	AGMAS	AGONISED
AGENES	AGGRADE	AGISTERS	AGMINATE	AGONISES
AGENESES	AGGRADED	AGISTING	AGNAIL	AGONISING
AGENESIA	AGGRADES	AGISTMENT	AGNAILS	AGONIST
AGENESIAS	AGGRADING	AGISTOR	AGNAME	AGONISTES
AGENESIS	AGGRATE	AGISTORS	AGNAMED	AGONISTIC
AGENETIC	AGGRATED	AGISTS	AGNAMES	AGONISTS
AGENISE	AGGRATES	AGITA	AGNATE	AGONIZE
AGENISED	AGGRATING	AGITABLE	AGNATES	AGONIZED
AGENISES	AGGRAVATE	AGITANS	AGNATHAN	AGONIZES
AGENISING	AGGREGATE	AGITAS	AGNATHANS	AGONIZING
AGENIZE	AGGRESS	AGITATE	AGNATHOUS	AGONS
AGENIZED	AGGRESSED	AGITATED	AGNATIC	AGONY
AGENIZES	AGGRESSES	AGITATES	AGNATICAL	AGOOD
AGENIZING	AGGRESSOR	AGITATING	AGNATION	AGORA
AGENT	AGGRI	AGITATION	AGNATIONS	AGORAE
AGENTED	AGGRIEVE	AGITATIVE	AGNISE	AGORAS
AGENTIAL	AGGRIEVED	AGITATO	AGNISED	AGOROT

AGOROTH	AGRIZING	AHENT	AIGAS	AIR
AGOUTA	AGRODOLCE	AHI	AIGHT	AIRBAG
AGOUTAS	AGROLOGIC	AHIGH	AIGLET	AIRBAGS
AGOUTI	AGROLOGY	AHIMSA	AIGLETS	AIRBASE
AGOUTIES	AGRONOMIC	AHIMSAS	AIGRET	AIRBASES
AGOUTIS	AGRONOMY	AHIND	AIGRETS	AIRBOARD
AGOUTY	AGROUND	AHING	AIGRETTE	AIRBOARDS
AGRAFE	AGRYPNIA	AHINT	AIGRETTES	AIRBOAT
AGRAFES	AGRYPNIAS	AHIS	AIGUILLE	AIRBOATS
AGRAFFE	AGRYZE	AHISTORIC	AIGUILLES	AIRBORNE
AGRAFFES	AGRYZED	AHOLD	AIKIDO	AIRBOUND
AGRAPHA	AGRYZES	AHOLDS	AIKIDOS	AIRBRICK
AGRAPHIA	AGRYZING	AHORSE	AIKONA	AIRBRICKS
AGRAPHIAS	AGS	AHOY	AIL	AIRBRUSH
AGRAPHIC	AGTERSKOT	AHS	AILANTHIC	AIRBURST
AGRAPHON	AGUACATE	AHULL	AILANTHUS	AIRBURSTS
AGRARIAN	AGUACATES	AHUNGERED	AILANTO	AIRBUS
AGRARIANS	AGUE	AHUNGRY	AILANTOS	AIRBUSES
AGRASTE	AGUED	AHURU	AILED	AIRBUSSES
AGRAVIC	AGUELIKE	AHURUHURU	AILERON	AIRCHECK
AGREE	AGUES	AHURUS	AILERONS	AIRCHECKS
AGREEABLE	AGUEWEED	AI	AILETTE	AIRCOACH
AGREEABLY	AGUEWEEDS	AIA	AILETTES	AIRCON
AGREED	AGUISE	AIAS	AILING	AIRCONS
AGREEING	AGUISED	AIBLINS	AILMENT	AIRCRAFT
AGREEMENT	AGUISES	AID	AILMENTS	AIRCREW
AGREES	AGUISH	AIDA	AILS	AIRCREWS
AGREGE	AGUISHLY	AIDANCE	AIM	AIRDATE
AGREGES	AGUISING	AIDANCES	AIMED	AIRDATES
AGREMENS	AGUIZE	AIDANT	AIMER	AIRDRAWN
AGREMENT	AGUIZED	AIDAS	AIMERS	AIRDROME
AGREMENTS	AGUIZES	AIDE	AIMFUL	AIRDROMES
AGRESTAL	AGUIZING	AIDED	AIMFULLY	AIRDROP
AGRESTIAL	AGUNA	AIDER	AIMING	AIRDROPS
AGRESTIC	AGUNAH	AIDERS	AIMLESS	AIRED
AGRIA	AGUNOT	AIDES	AIMLESSLY	AIRER
AGRIAS	AGUTI	AIDFUL	AIMS	AIRERS
AGRIMONY	AGUTIS	AIDING	AIN	AIREST
AGRIN	AH	AIDLESS	AINE	AIRFARE
AGRIOLOGY	AHA	AIDMAN	AINEE	AIRFARES
AGRISE	AHCHOO	AIDMEN	AINGA	AIRFIELD
AGRISED	AHEAD	AIDOI	AINGAS	AIRFIELDS
AGRISES	AHEAP	AIDOS	AINS	AIRFLOW
AGRISING	AHED	AIDS	AINSELL	AIRFLOWS
AGRIZE	AHEIGHT	AIERIES	AINSELLS	AIRFOIL
AGRIZED	AHEM	AIERY	AIOLI	AIRFOILS
AGRIZES	AHEMERAL	AIGA	AIOLIS	AIRFRAME

AIRFRAMES	AIRPORT	AIRTING	AKARYOTES	ALACHLOR
AIRGAP	AIRPORTS	AIRTS	AKARYOTIC	ALACHLORS
AIRGAPS	AIRPOST	AIRWARD	AKAS	ALACK
AIRGLOW	AIRPOSTS	AIRWARDS	AKATEA	ALACKADAY
AIRGLOWS	AIRPOWER	AIRWAVE	AKATEAS	ALACRITY
AIRGRAPH	AIRPOWERS	AIRWAVES	AKATHISIA	ALAE
AIRGRAPHS	AIRPROOF	AIRWAY	AKE	ALAIMENT
AIRGUN	AIRPROOFS	AIRWAYS	AKEAKE	ALAIMENTS
AIRGUNS	AIRPROX	AIRWISE	AKEAKES	ALALAGMOI
AIRHEAD	AIRPROXES	AIRWOMAN	AKED	ALALAGMOS
AIRHEADED	AIRS	AIRWOMEN	AKEDAH	ALALIA
AIRHEADS	AIRSCAPE	AIRWORTHY	AKEDAHS	ALALIAS
AIRHOLE	AIRSCAPES	AIRY	AKEE	ALAMEDA
AIRHOLES	AIRSCREW	AIS	AKEES	ALAMEDAS
AIRIER	AIRSCREWS	AISLE	AKELA	ALAMO
AIRIEST	AIRSHAFT	AISLED	AKELAS	ALAMODE
AIRILY	AIRSHAFTS	AISLELESS	AKENE	ALAMODES
AIRINESS	AIRSHED	AISLES	AKENES	ALAMORT
AIRING	AIRSHEDS	AISLEWAY	AKENIAL	ALAMOS
AIRINGS	AIRSHIP	AISLEWAYS	AKES	ALAN
AIRLESS	AIRSHIPS	AISLING	AKHARA	ALAND
AIRLIFT	AIRSHOT	AISLINGS	AKHARAS	ALANDS
AIRLIFTED	AIRSHOTS	AIT	AKIMBO	ALANE
AIRLIFTS	AIRSHOW	AITCH	AKIN	ALANG
AIRLIKE	AIRSHOWS	AITCHBONE	AKINESES	ALANGS
AIRLINE	AIRSICK	AITCHES	AKINESIA	ALANIN
AIRLINER	AIRSIDE	AITS	AKINESIAS	ALANINE
AIRLINERS	AIRSIDES	AITU	AKINESIS	ALANINES
AIRLINES	AIRSPACE	AITUS	AKINETIC	ALANINS
AIRLOCK	AIRSPACES	AIVER	AKING	ALANNAH
AIRLOCKS	AIRSPEED	AIVERS	AKIRAHO	ALANNAHS
AIRMAIL	AIRSPEEDS	AIZLE	AKIRAHOS	ALANS
AIRMAILED	AIRSTOP	AIZLES	AKITA	ALANT
AIRMAILS	AIRSTOPS	AJAR	AKITAS	ALANTS
AIRMAN	AIRSTREAM	AJEE	AKKAS	ALANYL
AIRMEN	AIRSTRIKE	AJIVA	AKOLUTHOS	ALANYLS
AIRMOBILE	AIRSTRIP	AJIVAS	AKRASIA	ALAP
AIRN	AIRSTRIPS	AJOWAN	AKRASIAS	ALAPA
AIRNED	AIRT	AJOWANS	AKRATIC	ALAPAS
AIRNING	AIRTED	AJUGA	AKVAVIT	ALAPS
AIRNS	AIRTH	AJUGAS	AKVAVITS	ALAR
AIRPARK	AIRTHED	AJUTAGE	AL	ALARM
AIRPARKS	AIRTHING	AJUTAGES	ALA	ALARMABLE
AIRPLANE	AIRTHS	AJWAN	ALAAP	ALARMED
AIRPLANES	AIRTIGHT	AJWANS	ALAAPS	ALARMEDLY
AIRPLAY	AIRTIME	AKA	ALABAMINE	ALARMING
AIRPLAYS	AIRTIMES	AKARYOTE	ALABASTER	ALARMISM

ALARMISMS	ALBESPINE	ALCAICS	ALDERMAN	ALEPINE
ALARMIST	ALBESPYNE	ALCAIDE	ALDERMEN	ALEPINES
ALARMISTS	ALBICORE	ALCAIDES	ALDERN	ALERCE
ALARMS	ALBICORES	ALCALDE	ALDERS	ALERCES
ALARUM	ALBINAL	ALCALDES	ALDICARB	ALERION
ALARUMED	ALBINESS	ALCARRAZA	ALDICARBS	ALERIONS
ALARUMING	ALBINIC	ALCATRAS	ALDOL	ALERT
ALARUMS	ALBINISM	ALCAYDE	ALDOLASE	ALERTED
ALARY	ALBINISMS	ALCAYDES	ALDOLASES	ALERTER
ALAS	ALBINO	ALCAZAR	ALDOLS	ALERTEST
ALASKA	ALBINOISM	ALCAZARS	ALDOSE	ALERTING
ALASKAS	ALBINOS	ALCHEMIC	ALDOSES	ALERTLY
ALASTOR	ALBINOTIC	ALCHEMIES	ALDOXIME	ALERTNESS
ALASTORS	ALBITE	ALCHEMISE	ALDOXIMES	ALERTS
ALASTRIM	ALBITES	ALCHEMIST	ALDRIN	ALES
ALASTRIMS	ALBITIC	ALCHEMIZE	ALDRINS	ALETHIC
ALATE	ALBITICAL	ALCHEMY	ALE	ALEURON
ALATED	ALBITISE	ALCHERA	ALEATORIC	ALEURONE
ALATES	ALBITISED	ALCHERAS	ALEATORY	ALEURONES
ALATION	ALBITISES	ALCHYMIES	ALEBENCH	ALEURONIC
ALATIONS	ALBITIZE	ALCHYMY	ALEC	ALEURONS
ALAY	ALBITIZED	ALCID	ALECITHAL	ALEVIN
ALAYED	ALBITIZES	ALCIDINE	ALECK	ALEVINS
ALAYING	ALBIZIA	ALCIDS	ALECKS	ALEW
ALAYS	ALBIZIAS	ALCO	ALECOST	ALEWASHED
ALB	ALBIZZIA	ALCOHOL	ALECOSTS	ALEWIFE
ALBA	ALBIZZIAS	ALCOHOLIC	ALECS	ALEWIVES
ALBACORE	ALBS	ALCOHOLS	ALEE	ALEWS
ALBACORES	ALBUGO	ALCOLOCK	ALEF	ALEXANDER
ALBARELLI	ALBUGOS	ALCOLOCKS	ALEFS	ALEXIA
ALBARELLO	ALBUM	ALCOOL	ALEFT	ALEXIAS
ALBAS	ALBUMEN	ALCOOLS	ALEGAR	ALEXIC
ALBATA	ALBUMENS	ALCOPOP	ALEGARS	ALEXIN
ALBATAS	ALBUMIN	ALCOPOPS	ALEGGE	ALEXINE
ALBATROSS	ALBUMINS	ALCORZA	ALEGGED	ALEXINES
ALBE	ALBUMOSE	ALCORZAS	ALEGGES	ALEXINIC
ALBEDO	ALBUMOSES	ALCOS	ALEGGING	ALEXINS
ALBEDOES	ALBUMS	ALCOVE	ALEHOUSE	ALEYE
ALBEDOS	ALBURNOUS	ALCOVED	ALEHOUSES	ALEYED
ALBEE	ALBURNUM	ALCOVES	ALEMBIC	ALEYES
ALBEIT	ALBURNUMS	ALDEA	ALEMBICS	ALEYING
ALBERGHI	ALBUTEROL	ALDEAS	ALEMBROTH	ALF
ALBERGO	ALCADE	ALDEHYDE	ALENCON	ALFA
ALBERT	ALCADES	ALDEHYDES	ALENCONS	ALFAKI
ALBERTITE	ALCAHEST	ALDEHYDIC	ALENGTH	ALFAKIS
ALBERTS	ALCAHESTS	ALDER	ALEPH	ALFALFA
ALBESCENT	ALCAIC	ALDERFLY	ALEPHS	ALFALFAS

ALFAQUI	ALGOID	ALIENISMS	ALISMAS	ALKANETS
ALFAQUIN	ALGOLOGY	ALIENIST	ALISON	ALKANNIN
ALFAQUINS	ALGOMETER	ALIENISTS	ALISONS	ALKANNINS
ALFAQUIS	ALGOMETRY	ALIENLY	ALIST	ALKENE
ALFAS	ALGOR	ALIENNESS	ALIT	ALKENES
ALFERECES	ALGORISM	ALIENOR	ALITERACY	ALKIE
ALFEREZ	ALGORISMS	ALIENORS	ALITERATE	ALKIES
ALFILARIA	ALGORITHM	ALIENS	ALIUNDE	ALKINE
ALFILERIA	ALGORS	ALIF	ALIVE	ALKINES
ALFORJA	ALGUACIL	ALIFORM	ALIVENESS	ALKO
ALFORJAS	ALGUACILS	ALIFS	ALIYA	ALKOS
ALFREDO	ALGUAZIL	ALIGARTA	ALIYAH	ALKOXIDE
ALFRESCO	ALGUAZILS	ALIGARTAS	ALIYAHS	ALKOXIDES
ALFS	ALGUM	ALIGHT	ALIYAS	ALKOXY
ALGA	ALGUMS	ALIGHTED	ALIYOS	ALKY
ALGAE	ALIAS	ALIGHTING	ALIYOT	ALKYD
ALGAECIDE	ALIASES	ALIGHTS	ALIYOTH	ALKYDS
ALGAL	ALIASING	ALIGN	ALIZARI	ALKYL
ALGAROBA	ALIASINGS	ALIGNED	ALIZARIN	ALKYLATE
ALGAROBAS	ALIBI	ALIGNER	ALIZARINE	ALKYLATED
ALGARROBA	ALIBIED	ALIGNERS	ALIZARINS	ALKYLATES
ALGARROBO	ALIBIES	ALIGNING	ALIZARIS	ALKYLIC
ALGAS	ALIBIING	ALIGNMENT	ALKAHEST	ALKYLS
ALGATE	ALIBIS	ALIGNS	ALKAHESTS	ALKYNE
ALGATES	ALIBLE	ALIKE	ALKALI	ALKYNES
ALGEBRA	ALICANT	ALIKENESS	ALKALIC	ALL
ALGEBRAIC	ALICANTS	ALIMENT	ALKALIES	ALLANITE
ALGEBRAS	ALICYCLIC	ALIMENTAL	ALKALIFY	ALLANITES
ALGERINE	ALIDAD	ALIMENTED	ALKALIN	ALLANTOIC
ALGERINES	ALIDADE	ALIMENTS	ALKALINE	ALLANTOID
ALGESES	ALIDADES	ALIMONIED	ALKALIS	ALLANTOIN
ALGESIA	ALIDADS	ALIMONIES	ALKALISE	ALLANTOIS
ALGESIAS	ALIEN	ALIMONY	ALKALISED	ALLATIVE
ALGESIC	ALIENABLE	ALINE	ALKALISER	ALLATIVES
ALGESIS	ALIENAGE	ALINED	ALKALISES	ALLAY
ALGETIC	ALIENAGES	ALINEMENT	ALKALIZE	ALLAYED
ALGICIDAL	ALIENATE	ALINER	ALKALIZED	ALLAYER
ALGICIDE	ALIENATED	ALINERS	ALKALIZER	ALLAYERS
ALGICIDES	ALIENATES	ALINES	ALKALIZES	ALLAYING
ALGID	ALIENATOR	ALINING	ALKALOID	ALLAYINGS
ALGIDITY	ALIENED	ALIPED	ALKALOIDS	ALLAYMENT
ALGIDNESS	ALIENEE	ALIPEDS	ALKALOSES	ALLAYS
ALGIN	ALIENEES	ALIPHATIC	ALKALOSIS	ALLCOMERS
ALGINATE	ALIENER	ALIQUANT	ALKALOTIC	ALLEDGE
ALGINATES	ALIENERS	ALIQUOT	ALKANE	ALLEDGED
ALGINIC	ALIENING	ALIQUOTS	ALKANES	ALLEDGES
ALGINS	ALIENISM	ALISMA	ALKANET	ALLEDGING

ALLEE	ALLEYED	ALLOMERIC	ALLOXANS	ALMANACK
ALLEES	ALLEYS	ALLOMETRY	ALLOY	ALMANACKS
ALLEGE	ALLEYWAY	ALLOMONE	ALLOYED	ALMANACS
ALLEGED	ALLEYWAYS	ALLOMONES	ALLOYING	ALMANDINE
ALLEGEDLY	ALLHEAL	ALLOMORPH	ALLOYS	ALMANDITE
ALLEGER	ALLHEALS	ALLONGE	ALLOZYME	ALMAS
ALLEGERS	ALLIABLE	ALLONGES	ALLOZYMES	ALME
ALLEGES	ALLIANCE	ALLONS	ALLS	ALMEH
ALLEGGE	ALLIANCES	ALLONYM	ALLSEED	ALMEHS
ALLEGGED	ALLICE	ALLONYMS	ALLSEEDS	ALMEMAR
ALLEGGES	ALLICES	ALLOPATH	ALLSORTS	ALMEMARS
ALLEGGING	ALLICHOLY	ALLOPATHS	ALLSPICE	ALMERIES
ALLEGIANT	ALLICIN	ALLOPATHY	ALLSPICES	ALMERY
ALLEGING	ALLICINS	ALLOPATRY	ALLUDE	ALMES
ALLEGORIC	ALLIED	ALLOPHANE	ALLUDED	ALMIGHTY
ALLEGORY	ALLIES	ALLOPHONE	ALLUDES	ALMIRAH
ALLEGRO	ALLIGARTA	ALLOPLASM	ALLUDING	ALMIRAHS
ALLEGROS	ALLIGATE	ALLOSAUR	ALLURE	ALMNER
ALLEL	ALLIGATED	ALLOSAURS	ALLURED	ALMNERS
ALLELE	ALLIGATES	ALLOSTERY	ALLURER	ALMOND
ALLELES	ALLIGATOR	ALLOT	ALLURERS	ALMONDS
ALLELIC	ALLIS	ALLOTMENT	ALLURES	ALMONDY
ALLELISM	ALLISES	ALLOTROPE	ALLURING	ALMONER
ALLELISMS	ALLIUM	ALLOTROPY	ALLUSION	ALMONERS
ALLELS	ALLIUMS	ALLOTS	ALLUSIONS	ALMONRIES
ALLELUIA	ALLNESS	ALLOTTED	ALLUSIVE	ALMONRY
ALLELUIAH	ALLNESSES	ALLOTTEE	ALLUVIA	ALMOST
ALLELUIAS	ALLNIGHT	ALLOTTEES	ALLUVIAL	ALMOUS
ALLEMANDE	ALLOBAR	ALLOTTER	ALLUVIALS	ALMS
ALLENARLY	ALLOBARS	ALLOTTERS	ALLUVION	ALMSGIVER
ALLERGEN	ALLOCABLE	ALLOTTERY	ALLUVIONS	ALMSHOUSE
ALLERGENS	ALLOCARPY	ALLOTTING	ALLUVIUM	ALMSMAN
ALLERGIC	ALLOCATE	ALLOTYPE	ALLUVIUMS	ALMSMEN
ALLERGICS	ALLOCATED	ALLOTYPES	ALLY	ALMSWOMAN
ALLERGIES	ALLOCATES	ALLOTYPIC	ALLYING	ALMSWOMEN
ALLERGIN	ALLOCATOR	ALLOTYPY	ALLYL	ALMUCE
ALLERGINS	ALLOD	ALLOVER	ALLYLIC	ALMUCES
ALLERGIST	ALLODIA	ALLOVERS	ALLYLS	ALMUD
ALLERGY	ALLODIAL	ALLOW	ALLYOU	ALMUDE
ALLERION	ALLODIUM	ALLOWABLE	ALMA	ALMUDES
ALLERIONS	ALLODIUMS	ALLOWABLY	ALMAGEST	ALMUDS
ALLETHRIN	ALLODS	ALLOWANCE	ALMAGESTS	ALMUG
ALLEVIANT	ALLODYNIA	ALLOWED	ALMAH	ALMUGS
ALLEVIATE	ALLOGAMY	ALLOWEDLY	ALMAHS	ALNAGE
ALLEY	ALLOGENIC	ALLOWING	ALMAIN	ALNAGER
ALLEYCAT	ALLOGRAFT	ALLOWS	ALMAINS	ALNAGERS
ALLEYCATS	ALLOGRAPH	ALLOXAN	ALMANAC	ALNAGES

ALNICO	ALPEEN	ALTERITY	ALULAS	AM
ALNICOS	ALPEENS	ALTERN	ALUM	AMA
ALOCASIA	ALPENGLOW	ALTERNANT	ALUMIN	AMABILE
ALOCASIAS	ALPENHORN	ALTERNAT	ALUMINA	AMADAVAT
ALOD	ALPHA	ALTERNATE	ALUMINAS	AMADAVATS
ALODIA	ALPHABET	ALTERNATS	ALUMINATE	AMADODA
ALODIAL	ALPHABETS	ALTERNE	ALUMINE	AMADOU
ALODIUM	ALPHAS	ALTERNES	ALUMINES	AMADOUS
ALODIUMS	ALPHASORT	ALTERS	ALUMINIC	AMAH
ALODS	ALPHATEST	ALTESSE	ALUMINISE	AMAHS
ALOE	ALPHORN	ALTESSES	ALUMINIUM	AMAIN
ALOED	ALPHORNS	ALTEZA	ALUMINIZE	AMAKOSI
ALOES	ALPHOSIS	ALTEZAS	ALUMINOUS	AMALGAM
ALOETIC	ALPHYL	ALTEZZA	ALUMINS	AMALGAMS
ALOETICS	ALPHYLS	ALTEZZAS	ALUMINUM	AMANDINE
ALOFT	ALPINE	ALTHAEA	ALUMINUMS	AMANDINES
ALOGIA	ALPINELY	ALTHAEAS	ALUMISH	AMANDLA
ALOGIAS	ALPINES	ALTHEA	ALUMIUM	AMANDLAS
ALOGICAL	ALPINISM	ALTHEAS	ALUMIUMS	AMANITA
ALOHA	ALPINISMS	ALTHO	ALUMNA	AMANITAS
ALOHAS	ALPINIST	ALTHORN	ALUMNAE	AMANITIN
ALOIN	ALPINISTS	ALTHORNS	ALUMNI	AMANITINS
ALOINS	ALPS	ALTHOUGH	ALUMNUS	AMARACUS
ALONE	ALREADY	ALTIGRAPH	ALUMROOT	AMARANT
ALONELY	ALRIGHT	ALTIMETER	ALUMROOTS	AMARANTH
ALONENESS	ALS	ALTIMETRY	ALUMS	AMARANTHS
ALONG	ALSIKE	ALTIPLANO	ALUMSTONE	AMARANTIN
ALONGSIDE	ALSIKES	ALTISSIMO	ALUNITE	AMARANTS
ALONGST	ALSO	ALTITUDE	ALUNITES	AMARELLE
ALOO	ALSOON	ALTITUDES	ALURE	AMARELLES
ALOOF	ALSOONE	ALTO	ALURES	AMARETTI
ALOOFLY	ALT	ALTOIST	ALUS	AMARETTO
ALOOFNESS	ALTAR	ALTOISTS	ALVEARIES	AMARETTOS
ALOOS	ALTARAGE	ALTOS	ALVEARY	AMARNA
ALOPECIA	ALTARAGES	ALTRICES	ALVEATED	AMARONE
ALOPECIAS	ALTARS	ALTRICIAL	ALVEOLAR	AMARONES
ALOPECIC	ALTARWISE	ALTRUISM	ALVEOLARS	AMARYLLID
ALOPECOID	ALTER	ALTRUISMS	ALVEOLATE	AMARYLLIS
ALOUD	ALTERABLE	ALTRUIST	ALVEOLE	AMAS
ALOW	ALTERABLY	ALTRUISTS	ALVEOLES	AMASS
ALOWE	ALTERANT	ALTS	ALVEOLI	AMASSABLE
ALP	ALTERANTS	ALU	ALVEOLUS	AMASSED
ALPACA	ALTERCATE	ALUDEL	ALVINE	AMASSER
ALPACAS	ALTERED	ALUDELS	ALWAY	AMASSERS
ALPACCA	ALTERER	ALULA	ALWAYS	AMASSES
ALPACCAS	ALTERERS	ALULAE	ALYSSUM	AMASSING
ALPARGATA	ALTERING	ALULAR	ALYSSUMS	AMASSMENT

AMATE	AMBEER	AMBOYNA	AMEIOSIS	AMETHYSTS
AMATED	AMBEERS	AMBOYNAS	AMELCORN	AMETROPIA
AMATES	AMBER	AMBRIES	AMELCORNS	AMETROPIC
AMATEUR	AMBERED	AMBROID	AMELIA	AMI
AMATEURS	AMBERGRIS	AMBROIDS	AMELIAS	AMIA
AMATING	AMBERIES	AMBROSIA	AMEN	AMIABLE
AMATION	AMBERINA	AMBROSIAL	AMENABLE	AMIABLY
AMATIONS	AMBERINAS	AMBROSIAN	AMENABLY	AMIANTHUS
AMATIVE	AMBERITE	AMBROSIAS	AMENAGE	AMIANTUS
AMATIVELY	AMBERITES	AMBROTYPE	AMENAGED	AMIAS
AMATOL	AMBERJACK	AMBRY	AMENAGES	AMICABLE
AMATOLS	AMBEROID	AMBSACE	AMENAGING	AMICABLY
AMATORIAL	AMBEROIDS	AMBSACES	AMENAUNCE	AMICE
AMATORIAN	AMBEROUS	AMBULACRA	AMEND	AMICES
AMATORY	AMBERS	AMBULANCE	AMENDABLE	AMICI
AMAUROSES	AMBERY	AMBULANT	AMENDE	AMICUS
AMAUROSIS	AMBIANCE	AMBULANTS	AMENDED	AMID
AMAUROTIC	AMBIANCES	AMBULATE	AMENDER	AMIDASE
AMAUT	AMBIENCE	AMBULATED	AMENDERS	AMIDASES
AMAUTS	AMBIENCES	AMBULATES	AMENDES	AMIDE
AMAZE	AMBIENT	AMBULATOR	AMENDING	AMIDES
AMAZED	AMBIENTS	AMBULETTE	AMENDMENT	AMIDIC
AMAZEDLY	AMBIGUITY	AMBUSCADE	AMENDS	AMIDIN
AMAZEMENT	AMBIGUOUS	AMBUSCADO	AMENE	AMIDINE
AMAZES	AMBIPOLAR	AMBUSH	AMENED	AMIDINES
AMAZING	AMBIT	AMBUSHED	AMENING	AMIDINS
AMAZINGLY	AMBITION	AMBUSHER	AMENITIES	AMIDMOST
AMAZON	AMBITIONS	AMBUSHERS	AMENITY	AMIDO
AMAZONIAN	AMBITIOUS	AMBUSHES	AMENS	AMIDOGEN
AMAZONITE	AMBITS	AMBUSHING	AMENT	AMIDOGENS
AMAZONS	AMBITTY	AME	AMENTA	AMIDOL
AMBACH	AMBIVERT	AMEARST	AMENTAL	AMIDOLS
AMBACHES	AMBIVERTS	AMEBA	AMENTIA	AMIDONE
AMBAGE	AMBLE	AMEBAE	AMENTIAS	AMIDONES
AMBAGES	AMBLED	AMEBAN	AMENTS	AMIDS
AMBAGIOUS	AMBLER	AMEBAS	AMENTUM	AMIDSHIP
AMBAN	AMBLERS	AMEBEAN	AMERCE	AMIDSHIPS
AMBANS	AMBLES	AMEBIASES	AMERCED	AMIDST
AMBARI	AMBLING	AMEBIASIS	AMERCER	AMIE
AMBARIES	AMBLINGS	AMEBIC	AMERCERS	AMIES
AMBARIS	AMBLYOPIA	AMEBOCYTE	AMERCES	AMIGA
AMBARY	AMBLYOPIC	AMEBOID	AMERCING	AMIGAS
AMBASSAGE	AMBO	AMEER	AMERICIUM	AMIGO
AMBASSIES	AMBOINA	AMEERATE	AMES	AMIGOS
AMBASSY	AMBOINAS	AMEERATES	AMESACE	AMILDAR
AMBATCH	AMBONES	AMEERS	AMESACES	AMILDARS
AMBATCHES	AMBOS	AMEIOSES	AMETHYST	AMIN

AMINE	AMMONIAS	AMOKURAS	AMORTIZE	AMPLE
AMINES	AMMONIATE	AMOLE	AMORTIZED	AMPLENESS
AMINIC	AMMONIC	AMOLES	AMORTIZES	AMPLER
AMINITIES	AMMONICAL	AMOMUM	AMOSITE	AMPLEST
AMINITY	AMMONIFY	AMOMUMS	AMOSITES	AMPLEXUS
AMINO	AMMONITE	AMONG	AMOTION	AMPLIDYNE
AMINS	AMMONITES	AMONGST	AMOTIONS	AMPLIFIED
AMIR	AMMONITIC	AMOOVE	AMOUNT	AMPLIFIER
AMIRATE	AMMONIUM	AMOOVED	AMOUNTED	AMPLIFIES
AMIRATES	AMMONIUMS	AMOOVES	AMOUNTING	AMPLIFY
AMIRS	AMMONO	AMOOVING	AMOUNTS	AMPLITUDE
AMIS	AMMONOID	AMORAL	AMOUR	AMPLOSOME
AMISES	AMMONOIDS	AMORALISM	AMOURETTE	AMPLY
AMISS	AMMONS	AMORALIST	AMOURS	AMPOULE
AMISSES	AMMOS	AMORALITY	AMOVE	AMPOULES
AMISSIBLE	AMNESIA	AMORALLY	AMOVED	AMPS
AMISSING	AMNESIAC	AMORANCE	AMOVES	AMPUL
AMITIES	AMNESIACS	AMORANCES	AMOVING	AMPULE
AMITOSES	AMNESIAS	AMORANT	AMOWT	AMPULES
AMITOSIS	AMNESIC	AMORCE	AMOWTS	AMPULLA
AMITOTIC	AMNESICS	AMORCES	AMP	AMPULLAE
AMITROLE	AMNESTIC	AMORET	AMPASSIES	AMPULLAR
AMITROLES	AMNESTIED	AMORETS	AMPASSY	AMPULLARY
AMITY	AMNESTIES	AMORETTI	AMPED	AMPULS
AMLA	AMNESTY	AMORETTO	AMPERAGE	AMPUTATE
AMLAS	AMNIA	AMORETTOS	AMPERAGES	AMPUTATED
AMMAN	AMNIC	AMORINI	AMPERE	AMPUTATES
AMMANS	AMNIO	AMORINO	AMPERES	AMPUTATOR
AMMETER	AMNION	AMORISM	AMPERSAND	AMPUTEE
AMMETERS	AMNIONIC	AMORISMS	AMPERZAND	AMPUTEES
AMMINE	AMNIONS	AMORIST	AMPHIBIA	AMREETA
AMMINES	AMNIOS	AMORISTIC	AMPHIBIAN	AMREETAS
AMMINO	AMNIOTE	AMORISTS	AMPHIBOLE	AMRIT
AMMIRAL	AMNIOTES	AMORNINGS	AMPHIBOLY	AMRITA
AMMIRALS	AMNIOTIC	AMOROSA	AMPHIGORY	AMRITAS
AMMO	AMNIOTOMY	AMOROSAS	AMPHIOXI	AMRITS
AMMOCETE	AMOEBA	AMOROSITY	AMPHIOXUS	AMSINCKIA
AMMOCETES	AMOEBAE	AMOROSO	AMPHIPATH	AMTMAN
AMMOCOETE	AMOEBAEAN	AMOROSOS	AMPHIPOD	AMTMANS
AMMON	AMOEBAN	AMOROUS	AMPHIPODS	AMTRAC
AMMONAL	AMOEBAS	AMOROUSLY	AMPHOLYTE	AMTRACK
AMMONALS	AMOEBEAN	AMORPHISM	AMPHORA	AMTRACKS
AMMONATE	AMOEBIC	AMORPHOUS	AMPHORAE	AMTRACS
AMMONATES	AMOEBOID	AMORT	AMPHORAL	AMU
AMMONIA	AMOK	AMORTISE	AMPHORAS	AMUCK
AMMONIAC	AMOKS	AMORTISED	AMPHORIC	AMUCKS
AMMONIACS	AMOKURA	AMORTISES	AMPING	AMULET

AMULETIC	AN	ANALCIMES	ANALYZE	ANARTHRIC
AMULETS	ANA	ANALCIMIC	ANALYZED	ANAS
AMUS	ANABAENA	ANALCITE	ANALYZER	ANASARCA
AMUSABLE	ANABAENAS	ANALCITES	ANALYZERS	ANASARCAS
AMUSE	ANABANTID	ANALECTA	ANALYZES	ANASTASES
AMUSEABLE	ANABAS	ANALECTIC	ANALYZING	ANASTASIS
AMUSED	ANABASES	ANALECTS	ANAMNESES	ANASTATIC
AMUSEDLY	ANABASIS	ANALEMMA	ANAMNESIS	ANATA
AMUSEMENT	ANABATIC	ANALEMMAS	ANAMNIOTE	ANATAS
AMUSER	ANABIOSES	ANALEPTIC	ANAN	ANATASE
AMUSERS	ANABIOSIS	ANALGESIA	ANANA	ANATASES
AMUSES	ANABIOTIC	ANALGESIC	ANANAS	ANATEXES
AMUSETTE	ANABLEPS	ANALGETIC	ANANASES	ANATEXIS
AMUSETTES	ANABOLIC	ANALGIA	ANANDROUS	ANATHEMA
AMUSIA	ANABOLISM	ANALGIAS	ANANKE	ANATHEMAS
AMUSIAS	ANABOLITE	ANALITIES	ANANKES	ANATMAN
AMUSIC	ANABRANCH	ANALITY	ANANTHOUS	ANATMANS
AMUSING	ANACHARIS	ANALLY	ANAPAEST	ANATOMIC
AMUSINGLY	ANACLINAL	ANALOG	ANAPAESTS	ANATOMIES
AMUSIVE	ANACLISES	ANALOGA	ANAPEST	ANATOMISE
AMYGDAL	ANACLISIS	ANALOGIC	ANAPESTS	ANATOMIST
AMYGDALA	ANACLITIC	ANALOGIES	ANAPESTIC	ANATOMIZE
AMYGDALAE	ANACONDA	ANALOGISE	ANAPESTS	ANATOMY
AMYGDALE	ANACONDAS	ANALOGISM	ANAPHASE	ANATOXIN
AMYGDALES	ANACRUSES	ANALOGIST	ANAPHASES	ANATOXINS
AMYGDALIN	ANACRUSIS	ANALOGIZE	ANAPHASIC	ANATROPY
AMYGDALS	ANADEM	ANALOGON	ANAPHOR	ANATTA
AMYGDULE	ANADEMS	ANALOGONS	ANAPHORA	ANATTAS
AMYGDULES	ANAEMIA	ANALOGOUS	ANAPHORAL	ANATTO
AMYL	ANAEMIAS	ANALOGS	ANAPHORAS	ANATTOS
AMYLASE	ANAEMIC	ANALOGUE	ANAPHORIC	ANAXIAL
AMYLASES	ANAEROBE	ANALOGUES	ANAPLASIA	ANBURIES
AMYLENE	ANAEROBES	ANALOGY	ANAPLASTY	ANBURY
AMYLENES	ANAEROBIA	ANALYSAND	ANAPTYXES	ANCE
AMYLIC	ANAEROBIC	ANALYSE	ANAPTYXIS	ANCESTOR
AMYLOGEN	ANAGLYPH	ANALYSED	ANARCH	ANCESTORS
AMYLOGENS	ANAGLYPHS	ANALYSER	ANARCHAL	ANCESTRAL
AMYLOID	ANAGLYPHY	ANALYSERS	ANARCHIAL	ANCESTRY
AMYLOIDAL	ANAGOGE	ANALYSES	ANARCHIC	ANCHO
AMYLOIDS	ANAGOGES	ANALYSING	ANARCHIES	ANCHOR
AMYLOPSIN	ANAGOGIC	ANALYSIS	ANARCHISE	ANCHORAGE
AMYLOSE	ANAGOGIES	ANALYST	ANARCHISM	ANCHORED
AMYLOSES	ANAGOGY	ANALYSTS	ANARCHIST	ANCHORESS
AMYLS	ANAGRAM	ANALYTE	ANARCHIZE	ANCHORET
AMYLUM	ANAGRAMS	ANALYTES	ANARCHS	ANCHORETS
AMYLUMS	ANAL	ANALYTIC	ANARCHY	ANCHORING
AMYOTONIA	ANALCIME	ANALYTICS	ANARTHRIA	ANCHORITE

ANCHORMAN	ANDESYTE	ANEMONE	ANGELED	ANGLICIZE
ANCHORMEN	ANDESYTES	ANEMONES	ANGELFISH	ANGLIFIED
ANCHORS	ANDIRON	ANEMOSES	ANGELHOOD	ANGLIFIES
ANCHOS	ANDIRONS	ANEMOSIS	ANGELIC	ANGLIFY
ANCHOVETA	ANDOUILLE	ANENST	ANGELICA	ANGLING
ANCHOVIES	ANDRADITE	ANENT	ANGELICAL	ANGLINGS
ANCHOVY	ANDRO	ANERGIA	ANGELICAS	ANGLIST
ANCHUSA	ANDROECIA	ANERGIAS	ANGELING	ANGLISTS
ANCHUSAS	ANDROGEN	ANERGIC	ANGELS	ANGLO
ANCHUSIN	ANDROGENS	ANERGIES	ANGELUS	ANGLOPHIL
ANCHUSINS	ANDROGYNE	ANERGY	ANGELUSES	ANGLOS
ANCHYLOSE	ANDROGYNY	ANERLY	ANGER	ANGOLA
ANCIENT	ANDROID	ANEROID	ANGERED	ANGOPHORA
ANCIENTER	ANDROIDS	ANEROIDS	ANGERING	ANGORA
ANCIENTLY	ANDROLOGY	ANES	ANGERLESS	ANGORAS
ANCIENTRY	ANDROMEDA	ANESTRA	ANGERLY	ANGOSTURA
ANCIENTS	ANDROS	ANESTRI	ANGERS	ANGRIER
ANCILE	ANDS	ANESTROUS	ANGICO	ANGRIES
ANCILIA	ANDVILE	ANESTRUM	ANGICOS	ANGRIEST
ANCILLA	ANDVILES	ANESTRUS	ANGINA	ANGRILY
ANCILLAE	ANE	ANETHOL	ANGINAL	ANGRINESS
ANCILLARY	ANEAR	ANETHOLE	ANGINAS	ANGRY
ANCILLAS	ANEARED	ANETHOLES	ANGINOSE	ANGST
ANCIPITAL	ANEARING	ANETHOLS	ANGINOUS	ANGSTIER
ANCLE	ANEARS	ANETIC	ANGIOGRAM	ANGSTIEST
ANCLES	ANEATH	ANEUPLOID	ANGIOLOGY	ANGSTROM
ANCOME	ANECDOTA	ANEURIN	ANGIOMA	ANGSTROMS
ANCOMES	ANECDOTAL	ANEURINS	ANGIOMAS	ANGSTS
ANCON	ANECDOTE	ANEURISM	ANGIOMATA	ANGSTY
ANCONAL	ANECDOTES	ANEURISMS	ANGKLUNG	ANGUIFORM
ANCONE	ANECDOTIC	ANEURYSM	ANGKLUNGS	ANGUINE
ANCONEAL	ANECDYSES	ANEURYSMS	ANGLE	ANGUIPED
ANCONES	ANECDYSIS	ANEW	ANGLED	ANGUIPEDE
ANCONOID	ANECHOIC	ANGA	ANGLEDUG	ANGUISH
ANCORA	ANELACE	ANGAKOK	ANGLEDUGS	ANGUISHED
ANCRESS	ANELACES	ANGAKOKS	ANGLEPOD	ANGUISHES
ANCRESSES	ANELASTIC	ANGARIA	ANGLEPODS	ANGULAR
AND	ANELE	ANGARIAS	ANGLER	ANGULARLY
ANDANTE	ANELED	ANGARIES	ANGLERS	ANGULATE
ANDANTES	ANELES	ANGARY	ANGLES	ANGULATED
ANDANTINI	ANELING	ANGAS	ANGLESITE	ANGULATES
ANDANTINO	ANELLI	ANGASHORE	ANGLEWISE	ANGULOSE
ANDESINE	ANEMIA	ANGEKKOK	ANGLEWORM	ANGULOUS
ANDESINES	ANEMIAS	ANGEKKOKS	ANGLICE	ANHEDONIA
ANDESITE	ANEMIC	ANGEKOK	ANGLICISE	ANHEDONIC
ANDESITES	ANEMOGRAM	ANGEKOKS	ANGLICISM	ANHEDRAL
ANDESITIC	ANEMOLOGY	ANGEL	ANGLICIST	ANHINGA

ANHINGAS

ANHINGAS	ANIMATERS	ANKLEBONE	ANNEALED	ANNUITIES
ANHUNGRED	ANIMATES	ANKLED	ANNEALER	ANNUITY
ANHYDRASE	ANIMATIC	ANKLES	ANNEALERS	ANNUL
ANHYDRIDE	ANIMATICS	ANKLET	ANNEALING	ANNULAR
ANHYDRITE	ANIMATING	ANKLETS	ANNEALS	ANNULARLY
ANHYDROUS	ANIMATION	ANKLING	ANNECTENT	ANNULARS
ANI	ANIMATISM	ANKLONG	ANNELID	ANNULATE
ANICCA	ANIMATIST	ANKLONGS	ANNELIDAN	ANNULATED
ANICCAS	ANIMATO	ANKLUNG	ANNELIDS	ANNULATES
ANICONIC	ANIMATOR	ANKLUNGS	ANNEX	ANNULET
ANICONISM	ANIMATORS	ANKUS	ANNEXABLE	ANNULETS
ANICONIST	ANIME	ANKUSES	ANNEXE	ANNULI
ANICUT	ANIMES	ANKUSH	ANNEXED	ANNULLED
ANICUTS	ANIMI	ANKUSHES	ANNEXES	ANNULLING
ANIDROSES	ANIMIS	ANKYLOSE	ANNEXING	ANNULMENT
ANIDROSIS	ANIMISM	ANKYLOSED	ANNEXION	ANNULOSE
ANIGH	ANIMISMS	ANKYLOSES	ANNEXIONS	ANNULS
ANIGHT	ANIMIST	ANKYLOSIS	ANNEXMENT	ANNULUS
ANIL	ANIMISTIC	ANKYLOTIC	ANNEXURE	ANNULUSES
ANILE	ANIMISTS	ANLACE	ANNEXURES	ANOA
ANILIN	ANIMOSITY	ANLACES	ANNICUT	ANOAS
ANILINE	ANIMUS	ANLAGE	ANNICUTS	ANOBIID
ANILINES	ANIMUSES	ANLAGEN	ANNO	ANOBIIDS
ANILINGUS	ANION	ANLAGES	ANNONA	ANODAL
ANILINS	ANIONIC	ANLAS	ANNONAS	ANODALLY
ANILITIES	ANIONS	ANLASES	ANNOTATE	ANODE
ANILITY	ANIRIDIA	ANN	ANNOTATED	ANODES
ANILS	ANIRIDIAS	ANNA	ANNOTATES	ANODIC
ANIMA	ANIRIDIC	ANNAL	ANNOTATOR	ANODISE
ANIMACIES	ANIS	ANNALISE	ANNOUNCE	ANODISED
ANIMACY	ANISE	ANNALISED	ANNOUNCED	ANODISES
ANIMAL	ANISEED	ANNALISES	ANNOUNCER	ANODISING
ANIMALIAN	ANISEEDS	ANNALIST	ANNOUNCES	ANODIZE
ANIMALIC	ANISES	ANNALISTS	ANNOY	ANODIZED
ANIMALIER	ANISETTE	ANNALIZE	ANNOYANCE	ANODIZES
ANIMALISE	ANISETTES	ANNALIZED	ANNOYED	ANODIZING
ANIMALISM	ANISIC	ANNALIZES	ANNOYER	ANODONTIA
ANIMALIST	ANISOGAMY	ANNALS	ANNOYERS	ANODYNE
ANIMALITY	ANISOLE	ANNAS	ANNOYING	ANODYNES
ANIMALIZE	ANISOLES	ANNAT	ANNOYS	ANODYNIC
ANIMALLY	ANKER	ANNATES	ANNS	ANOESES
ANIMALS	ANKERITE	ANNATS	ANNUAL	ANOESIS
ANIMAS	ANKERITES	ANNATTA	ANNUALISE	ANOESTRA
ANIMATE	ANKERS	ANNATTAS	ANNUALIZE	ANOESTRI
ANIMATED	ANKH	ANNATTO	ANNUALLY	ANOESTRUM
ANIMATELY	ANKHS	ANNATTOS	ANNUALS	ANOESTRUS
ANIMATER	ANKLE	ANNEAL	ANNUITANT	ANOETIC

ANOINT	ANOSMATIC	ANTBEARS	ANTHEMIA	ANTIBUG
ANOINTED	ANOSMIA	ANTBIRD	ANTHEMIC	ANTIBUSER
ANOINTER	ANOSMIAS	ANTBIRDS	ANTHEMING	ANTIC
ANOINTERS	ANOSMIC	ANTE	ANTHEMION	ANTICAL
ANOINTING	ANOTHER	ANTEATER	ANTHEMS	ANTICALLY
ANOINTS	ANOUGH	ANTEATERS	ANTHER	ANTICAR
ANOLE	ANOUROUS	ANTECEDE	ANTHERAL	ANTICHLOR
ANOLES	ANOVULANT	ANTECEDED	ANTHERID	ANTICISE
ANOLYTE	ANOVULAR	ANTECEDES	ANTHERIDS	ANTICISED
ANOLYTES	ANOW	ANTECHOIR	ANTHERS	ANTICISES
ANOMALIES	ANOXAEMIA	ANTED	ANTHESES	ANTICITY
ANOMALOUS	ANOXAEMIC	ANTEDATE	ANTHESIS	ANTICIVIC
ANOMALY	ANOXEMIA	ANTEDATED	ANTHILL	ANTICIZE
ANOMIC	ANOXEMIAS	ANTEDATES	ANTHILLS	ANTICIZED
ANOMIE	ANOXEMIC	ANTEED	ANTHOCARP	ANTICIZES
ANOMIES	ANOXIA	ANTEFIX	ANTHOCYAN	ANTICK
ANOMY	ANOXIAS	ANTEFIXA	ANTHODIA	ANTICKE
ANON	ANOXIC	ANTEFIXAE	ANTHODIUM	ANTICKED
ANONYM	ANS	ANTEFIXAL	ANTHOID	ANTICKING
ANONYMA	ANSA	ANTEFIXES	ANTHOLOGY	ANTICKS
ANONYMAS	ANSAE	ANTEING	ANTHOTAXY	ANTICLINE
ANONYMISE	ANSATE	ANTELOPE	ANTHOZOAN	ANTICLING
ANONYMITY	ANSATED	ANTELOPES	ANTHOZOIC	ANTICLY
ANONYMIZE	ANSERINE	ANTELUCAN	ANTHRACES	ANTICODON
ANONYMOUS	ANSERINES	ANTENATAL	ANTHRACIC	ANTICOLD
ANONYMS	ANSEROUS	ANTENATI	ANTHRAX	ANTICOUS
ANOOPSIA	ANSWER	ANTENNA	ANTHRAXES	ANTICRACK
ANOOPSIAS	ANSWERED	ANTENNAE	ANTHROPIC	ANTICRIME
ANOPHELES	ANSWERER	ANTENNAL	ANTHURIUM	ANTICS
ANOPIA	ANSWERERS	ANTENNARY	ANTI	ANTICULT
ANOPIAS	ANSWERING	ANTENNAS	ANTIABUSE	ANTICULTS
ANOPSIA	ANSWERS	ANTENNULE	ANTIACNE	ANTIDORA
ANOPSIAS	ANT	ANTEPAST	ANTIAGING	ANTIDOTAL
ANORAK	ANTA	ANTEPASTS	ANTIAIR	ANTIDOTE
ANORAKS	ANTACID	ANTERIOR	ANTIALIEN	ANTIDOTED
ANORECTAL	ANTACIDS	ANTEROOM	ANTIAR	ANTIDOTES
ANORECTIC	ANTAE	ANTEROOMS	ANTIARIN	ANTIDRAFT
ANORETIC	ANTALGIC	ANTES	ANTIARINS	ANTIDRUG
ANORETICS	ANTALGICS	ANTETYPE	ANTIARMOR	ANTIDUNE
ANOREXIA	ANTALKALI	ANTETYPES	ANTIARS	ANTIDUNES
ANOREXIAS	ANTAR	ANTEVERT	ANTIATOM	ANTIELITE
ANOREXIC	ANTARA	ANTEVERTS	ANTIATOMS	ANTIENT
ANOREXICS	ANTARAS	ANTHELIA	ANTIAUXIN	ANTIENTS
ANOREXIES	ANTARCTIC	ANTHELION	ANTIBIAS	ANTIFAT
ANOREXY	ANTARS	ANTHELIX	ANTIBLACK	ANTIFLU
ANORTHIC	ANTAS	ANTHEM	ANTIBODY	ANTIFOAM
ANORTHITE	ANTBEAR	ANTHEMED	ANTIBOSS	ANTIFOG

ANTIFRAUD	ANTINODE	ANTIRED	ANTITYPE	ANURANS
ANTIFUR	ANTINODES	ANTIRIOT	ANTITYPES	ANURESES
ANTIGANG	ANTINOISE	ANTIROCK	ANTITYPIC	ANURESIS
ANTIGAY	ANTINOME	ANTIROLL	ANTIULCER	ANURETIC
ANTIGEN	ANTINOMES	ANTIROYAL	ANTIUNION	ANURIA
ANTIGENE	ANTINOMIC	ANTIRUST	ANTIURBAN	ANURIAS
ANTIGENES	ANTINOMY	ANTIRUSTS	ANTIVENIN	ANURIC
ANTIGENIC	ANTINOVEL	ANTIS	ANTIVENOM	ANUROUS
ANTIGENS	ANTINUKE	ANTISAG	ANTIVIRAL	ANUS
ANTIGLARE	ANTINUKER	ANTISCIAN	ANTIVIRUS	ANUSES
ANTIGRAFT	ANTINUKES	ANTISENSE	ANTIWAR	ANVIL
ANTIGUN	ANTIPAPAL	ANTISERA	ANTIWEAR	ANVILED
ANTIHELIX	ANTIPARTY	ANTISERUM	ANTIWEED	ANVILING
ANTIHERO	ANTIPASTI	ANTISEX	ANTIWHITE	ANVILLED
ANTIHUMAN	ANTIPASTO	ANTISHAKE	ANTIWOMAN	ANVILLING
ANTIJAM	ANTIPATHY	ANTISHARK	ANTIWORLD	ANVILS
ANTIKING	ANTIPHON	ANTISHIP	ANTLER	ANVILTOP
ANTIKINGS	ANTIPHONS	ANTISHOCK	ANTLERED	ANVILTOPS
ANTIKNOCK	ANTIPHONY	ANTISKID	ANTLERS	ANXIETIES
ANTILABOR	ANTIPILL	ANTISLEEP	ANTLIA	ANXIETY
ANTILEAK	ANTIPODAL	ANTISLIP	ANTLIAE	ANXIOUS
ANTILEFT	ANTIPODE	ANTISMOG	ANTLIATE	ANXIOUSLY
ANTILIFE	ANTIPODES	ANTISMOKE	ANTLIKE	ANY
ANTILIFER	ANTIPOLAR	ANTISMUT	ANTLION	ANYBODIES
ANTILOCK	ANTIPOLE	ANTISNOB	ANTLIONS	ANYBODY
ANTILOG	ANTIPOLES	ANTISNOBS	ANTONYM	ANYHOW
ANTILOGS	ANTIPOPE	ANTISOLAR	ANTONYMIC	ANYMORE
ANTILOGY	ANTIPOPES	ANTISPAM	ANTONYMS	ANYON
ANTIMACHO	ANTIPORN	ANTISPAST	ANTONYMY	ANYONE
ANTIMALE	ANTIPOT	ANTISTAT	ANTPITTA	ANYONES
ANTIMAN	ANTIPRESS	ANTISTATE	ANTPITTAS	ANYONS
ANTIMASK	ANTIPYIC	ANTISTATS	ANTRA	ANYPLACE
ANTIMASKS	ANTIPYICS	ANTISTICK	ANTRAL	ANYROAD
ANTIMERE	ANTIQUARK	ANTISTORY	ANTRE	ANYTHING
ANTIMERES	ANTIQUARY	ANTISTYLE	ANTRES	ANYTHINGS
ANTIMERIC	ANTIQUATE	ANTITANK	ANTRORSE	ANYTIME
ANTIMINE	ANTIQUE	ANTITAX	ANTRUM	ANYWAY
ANTIMONIC	ANTIQUED	ANTITHEFT	ANTRUMS	ANYWAYS
ANTIMONY	ANTIQUELY	ANTITHET	ANTS	ANYWHEN
ANTIMONYL	ANTIQUER	ANTITHETS	ANTSIER	ANYWHERE
ANTIMUON	ANTIQUERS	ANTITOXIC	ANTSIEST	ANYWHERES
ANTIMUONS	ANTIQUES	ANTITOXIN	ANTSINESS	ANYWISE
ANTIMUSIC	ANTIQUEY	ANTITRADE	ANTSY	ANZIANI
ANTIMYCIN	ANTIQUING	ANTITRAGI	ANTWACKIE	AORIST
ANTING	ANTIQUITY	ANTITRUST	ANUCLEATE	AORISTIC
ANTINGS	ANTIRADAR	ANTITUMOR	ANURAL	AORISTS
ANTINODAL	ANTIRAPE	ANTITYPAL	ANURAN	AORTA

AORTAE	APEMAN	APHELION	APHTHAE	APLOMBS
AORTAL	APEMEN	APHELIONS	APHTHOUS	APLUSTRE
AORTAS	APEPSIA	APHERESES	APHYLLIES	APLUSTRES
AORTIC	APEPSIAS	APHERESIS	APHYLLOUS	APNEA
AORTITIS	APEPSIES	APHERETIC	APHYLLY	APNEAL
AOUDAD	APEPSY	APHESES	APIACEOUS	APNEAS
AOUDADS	APER	APHESIS	APIAN	APNEIC
APACE	APERCU	APHETIC	APIARIAN	APNEUSES
APACHE	APERCUS	APHETISE	APIARIANS	APNEUSIS
APACHES	APERIENT	APHETISED	APIARIES	APNEUSTIC
APADANA	APERIENTS	APHETISES	APIARIST	APNOEA
APADANAS	APERIES	APHETIZE	APIARISTS	APNOEAL
APAGE	APERIODIC	APHETIZED	APIARY	APNOEAS
APAGOGE	APERITIF	APHETIZES	APICAL	APNOEIC
APAGOGES	APERITIFS	APHICIDE	APICALLY	APO
APAGOGIC	APERITIVE	APHICIDES	APICALS	APOAPSES
APAID	APERS	APHID	APICES	APOAPSIS
APANAGE	APERT	APHIDES	APICIAN	APOCARP
APANAGED	APERTNESS	APHIDIAN	APICULATE	APOCARPS
APANAGES	APERTURAL	APHIDIANS	APICULI	APOCARPY
APAREJO	APERTURE	APHIDIOUS	APICULUS	APOCOPATE
APAREJOS	APERTURED	APHIDS	APIECE	APOCOPE
APART	APERTURES	APHIS	APIEZON	APOCOPES
APARTHEID	APERY	APHOLATE	APIMANIA	APOCOPIC
APARTMENT	APES	APHOLATES	APIMANIAS	APOCRINE
APARTNESS	APESHIT	APHONIA	APING	APOCRYPHA
APATETIC	APETALIES	APHONIAS	APIOL	APOD
APATHATON	APETALOUS	APHONIC	APIOLOGY	APODAL
APATHETIC	APETALY	APHONICS	APIOLS	APODE
APATHIES	APEX	APHONIES	APISH	APODES
APATHY	APEXES	APHONOUS	APISHLY	APODICTIC
APATITE	APGAR	APHONY	APISHNESS	APODOSES
APATITES	APHAGIA	APHORISE	APISM	APODOSIS
APATOSAUR	APHAGIAS	APHORISED	APISMS	APODOUS
APAY	APHAKIA	APHORISER	APIVOROUS	APODS
APAYD	APHAKIAS	APHORISES	APLANAT	APOENZYME
APAYING	APHANITE	APHORISM	APLANATIC	APOGAEIC
APAYS	APHANITES	APHORISMS	APLANATS	APOGAMIC
APE	APHANITIC	APHORIST	APLANETIC	APOGAMIES
APEAK	APHASIA	APHORISTS	APLASIA	APOGAMOUS
APED	APHASIAC	APHORIZE	APLASIAS	APOGAMY
APEDOM	APHASIACS	APHORIZED	APLASTIC	APOGEAL
APEDOMS	APHASIAS	APHORIZER	APLENTY	APOGEAN
APEEK	APHASIC	APHORIZES	APLITE	APOGEE
APEHOOD	APHASICS	APHOTIC	APLITES	APOGEES
APEHOODS	APHELIA	APHRODITE	APLITIC	APOGEIC
APELIKE	APHELIAN	APHTHA	APLOMB	APOGRAPH

APOGRAPHS	APOSITIAS	APPARELS	APPERILL	APPOINTED
APOLLO	APOSITIC	APPARENCY	APPERILLS	APPOINTEE
APOLLOS	APOSPORIC	APPARENT	APPERILS	APPOINTER
APOLOG	APOSPORY	APPARENTS	APPERTAIN	APPOINTOR
APOLOGAL	APOSTACY	APPARITOR	APPESTAT	APPOINTS
APOLOGIA	APOSTASY	APPAY	APPESTATS	APPORT
APOLOGIAE	APOSTATE	APPAYD	APPETENCE	APPORTION
APOLOGIAS	APOSTATES	APPAYING	APPETENCY	APPORTS
APOLOGIES	APOSTATIC	APPAYS	APPETENT	APPOSABLE
APOLOGISE	APOSTIL	APPEACH	APPETIBLE	APPOSE
APOLOGIST	APOSTILLE	APPEACHED	APPETISE	APPOSED
APOLOGIZE	APOSTILS	APPEACHES	APPETISED	APPOSER
APOLOGS	APOSTLE	APPEAL	APPETISER	APPOSERS
APOLOGUE	APOSTLES	APPEALED	APPETISES	APPOSES
APOLOGUES	APOSTOLIC	APPEALER	APPETITE	APPOSING
APOLOGY	APOTHECE	APPEALERS	APPETITES	APPOSITE
APOLUNE	APOTHECES	APPEALING	APPETIZE	APPRAISAL
APOLUNES	APOTHECIA	APPEALS	APPETIZED	APPRAISE
APOMICT	APOTHEGM	APPEAR	APPETIZER	APPRAISED
APOMICTIC	APOTHEGMS	APPEARED	APPETIZES	APPRAISEE
APOMICTS	APOTHEM	APPEARER	APPLAUD	APPRAISER
APOMIXES	APOTHEMS	APPEARERS	APPLAUDED	APPRAISES
APOMIXIS	APOZEM	APPEARING	APPLAUDER	APPREHEND
APOOP	APOZEMS	APPEARS	APPLAUDS	APPRESS
APOPHASES	APP	APPEASE	APPLAUSE	APPRESSED
APOPHASIS	APPAID	APPEASED	APPLAUSES	APPRESSES
APOPHATIC	APPAIR	APPEASER	APPLE	APPRISE
APOPHONY	APPAIRED	APPEASERS	APPLECART	APPRISED
APOPHYGE	APPAIRING	APPEASES	APPLEJACK	APPRISER
APOPHYGES	APPAIRS	APPEASING	APPLES	APPRISERS
APOPHYSES	APPAL	APPEL	APPLET	APPRISES
APOPHYSIS	APPALL	APPELLANT	APPLETS	APPRISING
APOPLAST	APPALLED	APPELLATE	APPLEY	APPRIZE
APOPLASTS	APPALLING	APPELLEE	APPLIABLE	APPRIZED
APOPLEX	APPALLS	APPELLEES	APPLIANCE	APPRIZER
APOPLEXED	APPALOOSA	APPELLOR	APPLICANT	APPRIZERS
APOPLEXES	APPALS	APPELLORS	APPLICATE	APPRIZES
APOPLEXY	APPALTI	APPELS	APPLIED	APPRIZING
APOPTOSES	APPALTO	APPEND	APPLIER	APPRO
APOPTOSIS	APPANAGE	APPENDAGE	APPLIERS	APPROACH
APOPTOTIC	APPANAGED	APPENDANT	APPLIES	APPROBATE
APORETIC	APPANAGES	APPENDED	APPLIQUE	APPROOF
APORIA	APPARAT	APPENDENT	APPLIQUED	APPROOFS
APORIAS	APPARATS	APPENDING	APPLIQUES	APPROS
APORT	APPARATUS	APPENDIX	APPLY	APPROVAL
APOS	APPAREL	APPENDS	APPLYING	APPROVALS
APOSITIA	APPARELED	APPERIL	APPOINT	APPROVE

APPROVED	APSIS	AQUANAUT	ARABIC	ARAPUNGA
APPROVER	APSO	AQUANAUTS	ARABICA	ARAPUNGAS
APPROVERS	APSOS	AQUAPHOBE	ARABICAS	ARAR
APPROVES	APT	AQUAPLANE	ARABICISE	ARAROBA
APPROVING	APTAMER	AQUAPORIN	ARABICIZE	ARAROBAS
APPS	APTAMERS	AQUARELLE	ARABILITY	ARARS
APPUI	APTED	AQUARIA	ARABIN	ARAUCARIA
APPUIED	APTER	AQUARIAL	ARABINOSE	ARAYSE
APPUIS	APTERAL	AQUARIAN	ARABINS	ARAYSED
APPULSE	APTERIA	AQUARIANS	ARABIS	ARAYSES
APPULSES	APTERISM	AQUARIIST	ARABISE	ARAYSING
APPULSIVE	APTERISMS	AQUARIST	ARABISED	ARB
APPUY	APTERIUM	AQUARISTS	ARABISES	ARBA
APPUYED	APTEROUS	AQUARIUM	ARABISING	ARBALEST
APPUYING	APTERYX	AQUARIUMS	ARABIZE	ARBALESTS
APPUYS	APTERYXES	AQUAROBIC	ARABIZED	ARBALIST
APRACTIC	APTEST	AQUAS	ARABIZES	ARBALISTS
APRAXIA	APTING	AQUASHOW	ARABIZING	ARBAS
APRAXIAS	APTITUDE	AQUASHOWS	ARABLE	ARBELEST
APRAXIC	APTITUDES	AQUATIC	ARABLES	ARBELESTS
APRES	APTLY	AQUATICS	ARACEOUS	ARBITER
APRICATE	APTNESS	AQUATINT	ARACHIS	ARBITERS
APRICATED	APTNESSES	AQUATINTA	ARACHISES	ARBITRAGE
APRICATES	APTOTE	AQUATINTS	ARACHNID	ARBITRAL
APRICOCK	APTOTES	AQUATONE	ARACHNIDS	ARBITRARY
APRICOCKS	APTOTIC	AQUATONES	ARACHNOID	ARBITRATE
APRICOT	APTS	AQUAVIT	ARAGONITE	ARBITRESS
APRICOTS	APYRASE	AQUAVITS	ARAISE	ARBITRIUM
APRIORISM	APYRASES	AQUEDUCT	ARAISED	ARBLAST
APRIORIST	APYRETIC	AQUEDUCTS	ARAISES	ARBLASTER
APRIORITY	APYREXIA	AQUEOUS	ARAISING	ARBLASTS
APRON	APYREXIAS	AQUEOUSLY	ARAK	ARBOR
APRONED	AQUA	AQUIFER	ARAKS	ARBOREAL
APRONFUL	AQUABATIC	AQUIFERS	ARALIA	ARBORED
APRONFULS	AQUABOARD	AQUILEGIA	ARALIAS	ARBOREOUS
APRONING	AQUACADE	AQUILINE	ARAME	ARBORES
APRONLIKE	AQUACADES	AQUILON	ARAMES	ARBORET
APRONS	AQUADROME	AQUILONS	ARAMID	ARBORETA
APROPOS	AQUAE	AQUIVER	ARAMIDS	ARBORETS
APROTIC	AQUAFARM	AR	ARANEID	ARBORETUM
APSARAS	AQUAFARMS	ARAARA	ARANEIDAN	ARBORIO
APSARASES	AQUAFER	ARAARAS	ARANEIDS	ARBORIOS
APSE	AQUAFERS	ARABA	ARANEOUS	ARBORISE
APSES	AQUAFIT	ARABAS	ARAPAIMA	ARBORISED
APSIDAL	AQUAFITS	ARABESK	ARAPAIMAS	ARBORISES
APSIDES	AQUALUNG	ARABESKS	ARAPONGA	ARBORIST
APSIDIOLE	AQUALUNGS	ARABESQUE	ARAPONGAS	ARBORISTS

ARBORIZE	ARCHAEUS	ARCHITYPE	ARCTOID	AREDE
ARBORIZED	ARCHAIC	ARCHIVAL	ARCTOPHIL	AREDES
ARBORIZES	ARCHAICAL	ARCHIVE	ARCUATE	AREDING
ARBOROUS	ARCHAISE	ARCHIVED	ARCUATED	AREFIED
ARBORS	ARCHAISED	ARCHIVES	ARCUATELY	AREFIES
ARBOUR	ARCHAISER	ARCHIVING	ARCUATION	AREFY
ARBOURED	ARCHAISES	ARCHIVIST	ARCUS	AREFYING
ARBOURS	ARCHAISM	ARCHIVOLT	ARCUSES	AREG
ARBOVIRAL	ARCHAISMS	ARCHLET	ARD	AREIC
ARBOVIRUS	ARCHAIST	ARCHLETS	ARDEB	ARENA
ARBS	ARCHAISTS	ARCHLUTE	ARDEBS	ARENAS
ARBUSCLE	ARCHAIZE	ARCHLUTES	ARDENCIES	ARENATION
ARBUSCLES	ARCHAIZED	ARCHLY	ARDENCY	ARENE
ARBUTE	ARCHAIZER	ARCHNESS	ARDENT	ARENES
ARBUTEAN	ARCHAIZES	ARCHOLOGY	ARDENTLY	ARENITE
ARBUTES	ARCHANGEL	ARCHON	ARDOR	ARENITES
ARBUTUS	ARCHDRUID	ARCHONS	ARDORS	ARENITIC
ARBUTUSES	ARCHDUCAL	ARCHONTIC	ARDOUR	ARENOSE
ARC	ARCHDUCHY	ARCHOSAUR	ARDOURS	ARENOUS
ARCADE	ARCHDUKE	ARCHRIVAL	ARDRI	AREOLA
ARCADED	ARCHDUKES	ARCHSTONE	ARDRIGH	AREOLAE
ARCADES	ARCHEAN	ARCHWAY	ARDRIGHS	AREOLAR
ARCADIA	ARCHED	ARCHWAYS	ARDRIS	AREOLAS
ARCADIAN	ARCHEI	ARCHWISE	ARDS	AREOLATE
ARCADIANS	ARCHENEMY	ARCIFORM	ARDUOUS	AREOLATED
ARCADIAS	ARCHER	ARCING	ARDUOUSLY	AREOLE
ARCADING	ARCHERESS	ARCINGS	ARE	AREOLES
ARCADINGS	ARCHERIES	ARCKED	AREA	AREOLOGY
ARCANA	ARCHERS	ARCKING	AREACH	AREOMETER
ARCANAS	ARCHERY	ARCKINGS	AREACHED	AREOSTYLE
ARCANE	ARCHES	ARCMIN	AREACHES	AREPA
ARCANELY	ARCHEST	ARCMINS	AREACHING	AREPAS
ARCANIST	ARCHETYPE	ARCMINUTE	AREAD	ARERE
ARCANISTS	ARCHEUS	ARCO	AREADING	ARES
ARCANUM	ARCHFIEND	ARCOGRAPH	AREADS	ARET
ARCANUMS	ARCHFOE	ARCOLOGY	AREAE	ARETE
ARCATURE	ARCHFOES	ARCOS	AREAL	ARETES
ARCATURES	ARCHICARP	ARCS	AREALLY	ARETHUSA
ARCCOSINE	ARCHIL	ARCSEC	AREAR	ARETHUSAS
ARCED	ARCHILOWE	ARCSECOND	AREAS	ARETS
ARCH	ARCHILS	ARCSECS	AREAWAY	ARETT
ARCHAEA	ARCHIMAGE	ARCSINE	AREAWAYS	ARETTED
ARCHAEAL	ARCHINE	ARCSINES	ARECA	ARETTING
ARCHAEAN	ARCHINES	ARCTIC	ARECAS	ARETTS
ARCHAEANS	ARCHING	ARCTICS	ARECOLINE	AREW
ARCHAEI	ARCHINGS	ARCTIID	ARED	ARF
ARCHAEON	ARCHITECT	ARCTIIDS	AREDD	ARFS

ARGAL	ARGOTS	ARIEL	ARKOSIC	ARMLET
ARGALA	ARGUABLE	ARIELS	ARKS	ARMLETS
ARGALAS	ARGUABLY	ARIETTA	ARLE	ARMLIKE
ARGALI	ARGUE	ARIETTAS	ARLED	ARMLOAD
ARGALIS	ARGUED	ARIETTE	ARLES	ARMLOADS
ARGALS	ARGUER	ARIETTES	ARLING	ARMLOCK
ARGAN	ARGUERS	ARIGHT	ARM	ARMLOCKED
ARGAND	ARGUES	ARIKI	ARMADA	ARMLOCKS
ARGANDS	ARGUFIED	ARIKIS	ARMADAS	ARMOIRE
ARGANS	ARGUFIER	ARIL	ARMADILLO	ARMOIRES
ARGEMONE	ARGUFIERS	ARILED	ARMAGNAC	ARMONICA
ARGEMONES	ARGUFIES	ARILLARY	ARMAGNACS	ARMONICAS
ARGENT	ARGUFY	ARILLATE	ARMAMENT	ARMOR
ARGENTAL	ARGUFYING	ARILLATED	ARMAMENTS	ARMORED
ARGENTIC	ARGUING	ARILLI	ARMATURE	ARMORER
ARGENTINE	ARGULI	ARILLODE	ARMATURED	ARMORERS
ARGENTITE	ARGULUS	ARILLODES	ARMATURES	ARMORIAL
ARGENTOUS	ARGUMENT	ARILLOID	ARMBAND	ARMORIALS
ARGENTS	ARGUMENTA	ARILLUS	ARMBANDS	ARMORIES
ARGENTUM	ARGUMENTS	ARILS	ARMCHAIR	ARMORING
ARGENTUMS	ARGUS	ARIOSE	ARMCHAIRS	ARMORIST
ARGH	ARGUSES	ARIOSI	ARMED	ARMORISTS
ARGHAN	ARGUTE	ARIOSO	ARMER	ARMORLESS
ARGHANS	ARGUTELY	ARIOSOS	ARMERS	ARMORS
ARGIL	ARGYLE	ARIOT	ARMET	ARMORY
ARGILLITE	ARGYLES	ARIPPLE	ARMETS	ARMOUR
ARGILS	ARGYLL	ARIS	ARMFUL	ARMOURED
ARGINASE	ARGYLLS	ARISE	ARMFULS	ARMOURER
ARGINASES	ARGYRIA	ARISEN	ARMGAUNT	ARMOURERS
ARGININE	ARGYRIAS	ARISES	ARMHOLE	ARMOURIES
ARGININES	ARGYRITE	ARISH	ARMHOLES	ARMOURING
ARGLE	ARGYRITES	ARISHES	ARMIES	ARMOURS
ARGLED	ARHAT	ARISING	ARMIGER	ARMOURY
ARGLES	ARHATS	ARISTA	ARMIGERAL	ARMOZEEN
ARGLING	ARHATSHIP	ARISTAE	ARMIGERO	ARMOZEENS
ARGOL	ARHYTHMIA	ARISTAS	ARMIGEROS	ARMOZINE
ARGOLS	ARHYTHMIC	ARISTATE	ARMIGERS	ARMOZINES
ARGON	ARIA	ARISTO	ARMIL	ARMPIT
ARGONAUT	ARIARY	ARISTOS	ARMILLA	ARMPITS
ARGONAUTS	ARIAS	ARISTOTLE	ARMILLAE	ARMREST
ARGONON	ARID	ARK	ARMILLARY	ARMRESTS
ARGONONS	ARIDER	ARKED	ARMILLAS	ARMS
ARGONS	ARIDEST	ARKING	ARMILS	ARMSFUL
ARGOSIES	ARIDITIES	ARKITE	ARMING	ARMURE
ARGOSY	ARIDITY	ARKITES	ARMINGS	ARMURES
ARGOT	ARIDLY	ARKOSE	ARMISTICE	ARMY
ARGOTIC	ARIDNESS	ARKOSES	ARMLESS	ARMYWORM

ARMYWORMS	ARPAS	ARREST	ARROGATED	ARSINE
ARNA	ARPEGGIO	ARRESTANT	ARROGATES	ARSINES
ARNAS	ARPEGGIOS	ARRESTED	ARROGATOR	ARSING
ARNATTO	ARPEN	ARRESTEE	ARROW	ARSINO
ARNATTOS	ARPENS	ARRESTEES	ARROWED	ARSIS
ARNICA	ARPENT	ARRESTER	ARROWHEAD	ARSON
ARNICAS	ARPENTS	ARRESTERS	ARROWING	ARSONIST
ARNOTTO	ARPILLERA	ARRESTING	ARROWLESS	ARSONISTS
ARNOTTOS	ARQUEBUS	ARRESTIVE	ARROWLIKE	ARSONITE
ARNUT	ARRACACHA	ARRESTOR	ARROWROOT	ARSONITES
ARNUTS	ARRACK	ARRESTORS	ARROWS	ARSONOUS
AROBA	ARRACKS	ARRESTS	ARROWWOOD	ARSONS
AROBAS	ARRAH	ARRET	ARROWWORM	ARSY
AROHA	ARRAIGN	ARRETS	ARROWY	ART
AROHAS	ARRAIGNED	ARRHIZAL	ARROYO	ARTAL
AROID	ARRAIGNER	ARRIAGE	ARROYOS	ARTEFACT
AROIDS	ARRAIGNS	ARRIAGES	ARS	ARTEFACTS
AROINT	ARRANGE	ARRIBA	ARSE	ARTEL
AROINTED	ARRANGED	ARRIDE	ARSED	ARTELS
AROINTING	ARRANGER	ARRIDED	ARSEHOLE	ARTEMISIA
AROINTS	ARRANGERS	ARRIDES	ARSEHOLED	ARTERIAL
AROLLA	ARRANGES	ARRIDING	ARSEHOLES	ARTERIALS
AROLLAS	ARRANGING	ARRIERE	ARSENAL	ARTERIES
AROMA	ARRANT	ARRIERO	ARSENALS	ARTERIOLE
AROMAS	ARRANTLY	ARRIEROS	ARSENATE	ARTERITIS
AROMATASE	ARRAS	ARRIS	ARSENATES	ARTERY
AROMATIC	ARRASED	ARRISES	ARSENIATE	ARTESIAN
AROMATICS	ARRASENE	ARRISH	ARSENIC	ARTFUL
AROMATISE	ARRASENES	ARRISHES	ARSENICAL	ARTFULLY
AROMATIZE	ARRASES	ARRIVAL	ARSENICS	ARTHOUSE
AROSE	ARRAUGHT	ARRIVALS	ARSENIDE	ARTHOUSES
AROUND	ARRAY	ARRIVANCE	ARSENIDES	ARTHRITIC
AROUSABLE	ARRAYAL	ARRIVANCY	ARSENIOUS	ARTHRITIS
AROUSAL	ARRAYALS	ARRIVE	ARSENITE	ARTHRODIA
AROUSALS	ARRAYED	ARRIVED	ARSENITES	ARTHROPOD
AROUSE	ARRAYER	ARRIVER	ARSENO	ARTHROSES
AROUSED	ARRAYERS	ARRIVERS	ARSENOUS	ARTHROSIS
AROUSER	ARRAYING	ARRIVES	ARSES	ARTI
AROUSERS	ARRAYMENT	ARRIVING	ARSEY	ARTIC
AROUSES	ARRAYS	ARRIVISME	ARSHEEN	ARTICHOKE
AROUSING	ARREAR	ARRIVISTE	ARSHEENS	ARTICLE
AROW	ARREARAGE	ARROBA	ARSHIN	ARTICLED
AROYNT	ARREARS	ARROBAS	ARSHINE	ARTICLES
AROYNTED	ARRECT	ARROGANCE	ARSHINES	ARTICLING
AROYNTING	ARREEDE	ARROGANCY	ARSHINS	ARTICS
AROYNTS	ARREEDES	ARROGANT	ARSIER	ARTICULAR
ARPA	ARREEDING	ARROGATE	ARSIEST	ARTIER

ARTIES	ARVOS	ASCIAN	ASHCAKE	ASIAGOS
ARTIEST	ARY	ASCIANS	ASHCAKES	ASIDE
ARTIFACT	ARYBALLOS	ASCIDIA	ASHCAN	ASIDES
ARTIFACTS	ARYL	ASCIDIAN	ASHCANS	ASINICO
ARTIFICE	ARYLS	ASCIDIANS	ASHED	ASINICOS
ARTIFICER	ARYTENOID	ASCIDIATE	ASHEN	ASININE
ARTIFICES	ARYTHMIA	ASCIDIUM	ASHERIES	ASININELY
ARTILLERY	ARYTHMIAS	ASCITES	ASHERY	ASININITY
ARTILY	ARYTHMIC	ASCITIC	ASHES	ASK
ARTINESS	AS	ASCITICAL	ASHET	ASKANCE
ARTIS	ASAFETIDA	ASCLEPIAD	ASHETS	ASKANCED
ARTISAN	ASANA	ASCLEPIAS	ASHFALL	ASKANCES
ARTISANAL	ASANAS	ASCOCARP	ASHFALLS	ASKANCING
ARTISANS	ASAR	ASCOCARPS	ASHIER	ASKANT
ARTIST	ASARUM	ASCOGONIA	ASHIEST	ASKANTED
ARTISTE	ASARUMS	ASCONCE	ASHINE	ASKANTING
ARTISTES	ASBESTIC	ASCORBATE	ASHINESS	ASKANTS
ARTISTIC	ASBESTINE	ASCORBIC	ASHING	ASKARI
ARTISTRY	ASBESTOS	ASCOSPORE	ASHIVER	ASKARIS
ARTISTS	ASBESTOUS	ASCOT	ASHKEY	ASKED
ARTLESS	ASBESTUS	ASCOTS	ASHKEYS	ASKER
ARTLESSLY	ASCARED	ASCRIBE	ASHLAR	ASKERS
ARTS	ASCARID	ASCRIBED	ASHLARED	ASKESES
ARTSIER	ASCARIDES	ASCRIBES	ASHLARING	ASKESIS
ARTSIES	ASCARIDS	ASCRIBING	ASHLARS	ASKEW
ARTSIEST	ASCARIS	ASCUS	ASHLER	ASKEWNESS
ARTSINESS	ASCAUNT	ASDIC	ASHLERED	ASKING
ARTSMAN	ASCEND	ASDICS	ASHLERING	ASKINGS
ARTSMEN	ASCENDANT	ASEA	ASHLERS	ASKLENT
ARTSY	ASCENDED	ASEISMIC	ASHLESS	ASKOI
ARTWORK	ASCENDENT	ASEITIES	ASHMAN	ASKOS
ARTWORKS	ASCENDER	ASEITY	ASHMEN	ASKS
ARTY	ASCENDERS	ASEPALOUS	ASHORE	ASLAKE
ARUGOLA	ASCENDEUR	ASEPSES	ASHPLANT	ASLAKED
ARUGOLAS	ASCENDING	ASEPSIS	ASHPLANTS	ASLAKES
ARUGULA	ASCENDS	ASEPTATE	ASHRAF	ASLAKING
ARUGULAS	ASCENSION	ASEPTIC	ASHRAM	ASLANT
ARUHE	ASCENSIVE	ASEPTICS	ASHRAMA	ASLEEP
ARUHES	ASCENT	ASEXUAL	ASHRAMAS	ASLOPE
ARUM	ASCENTS	ASEXUALLY	ASHRAMITE	ASLOSH
ARUMS	ASCERTAIN	ASH	ASHRAMS	ASMEAR
ARUSPEX	ASCESES	ASHAKE	ASHTANGA	ASMOULDER
ARUSPICES	ASCESIS	ASHAME	ASHTANGAS	ASOCIAL
ARVAL	ASCETIC	ASHAMED	ASHTRAY	ASOCIALS
ARVICOLE	ASCETICAL	ASHAMEDLY	ASHTRAYS	ASP
ARVICOLES	ASCETICS	ASHAMES	ASHY	ASPARAGUS
ARVO	ASCI	ASHAMING	ASIAGO	ASPARKLE

ASPARTAME	ASPHYXIA	ASRAMA	ASSENTER	ASSIGNEES
ASPARTATE	ASPHYXIAL	ASRAMAS	ASSENTERS	ASSIGNER
ASPARTIC	ASPHYXIAS	ASS	ASSENTING	ASSIGNERS
ASPECT	ASPHYXIES	ASSAGAI	ASSENTIVE	ASSIGNING
ASPECTED	ASPHYXY	ASSAGAIED	ASSENTOR	ASSIGNOR
ASPECTING	ASPIC	ASSAGAIS	ASSENTORS	ASSIGNORS
ASPECTS	ASPICK	ASSAI	ASSENTS	ASSIGNS
ASPECTUAL	ASPICKS	ASSAIL	ASSERT	ASSIST
ASPEN	ASPICS	ASSAILANT	ASSERTED	ASSISTANT
ASPENS	ASPIDIA	ASSAILED	ASSERTER	ASSISTED
ASPER	ASPIDIOID	ASSAILER	ASSERTERS	ASSISTER
ASPERATE	ASPIDIUM	ASSAILERS	ASSERTING	ASSISTERS
ASPERATED	ASPINE	ASSAILING	ASSERTION	ASSISTING
ASPERATES	ASPINES	ASSAILS	ASSERTIVE	ASSISTIVE
ASPERGE	ASPIRANT	ASSAIS	ASSERTOR	ASSISTOR
ASPERGED	ASPIRANTS	ASSAM	ASSERTORS	ASSISTORS
ASPERGER	ASPIRATA	ASSAMS	ASSERTORY	ASSISTS
ASPERGERS	ASPIRATAE	ASSART	ASSERTS	ASSIZE
ASPERGES	ASPIRATE	ASSARTED	ASSES	ASSIZED
ASPERGILL	ASPIRATED	ASSARTING	ASSESS	ASSIZER
ASPERGING	ASPIRATES	ASSARTS	ASSESSED	ASSIZERS
ASPERITY	ASPIRATOR	ASSASSIN	ASSESSES	ASSIZES
ASPERMIA	ASPIRE	ASSASSINS	ASSESSING	ASSIZING
ASPERMIAS	ASPIRED	ASSAULT	ASSESSOR	ASSLIKE
ASPEROUS	ASPIRER	ASSAULTED	ASSESSORS	ASSOCIATE
ASPERS	ASPIRERS	ASSAULTER	ASSET	ASSOIL
ASPERSE	ASPIRES	ASSAULTS	ASSETLESS	ASSOILED
ASPERSED	ASPIRIN	ASSAY	ASSETS	ASSOILING
ASPERSER	ASPIRING	ASSAYABLE	ASSEVER	ASSOILS
ASPERSERS	ASPIRINS	ASSAYED	ASSEVERED	ASSOILZIE
ASPERSES	ASPIS	ASSAYER	ASSEVERS	ASSONANCE
ASPERSING	ASPISES	ASSAYERS	ASSEZ	ASSONANT
ASPERSION	ASPISH	ASSAYING	ASSHOLE	ASSONANTS
ASPERSIVE	ASPLENIUM	ASSAYINGS	ASSHOLES	ASSONATE
ASPERSOIR	ASPORT	ASSAYS	ASSIDUITY	ASSONATED
ASPERSOR	ASPORTED	ASSEGAAI	ASSIDUOUS	ASSONATES
ASPERSORS	ASPORTING	ASSEGAAIS	ASSIEGE	ASSORT
ASPERSORY	ASPORTS	ASSEGAI	ASSIEGED	ASSORTED
ASPHALT	ASPOUT	ASSEGAIED	ASSIEGES	ASSORTER
ASPHALTED	ASPRAWL	ASSEGAIS	ASSIEGING	ASSORTERS
ASPHALTER	ASPREAD	ASSEMBLE	ASSIENTO	ASSORTING
ASPHALTIC	ASPRO	ASSEMBLED	ASSIENTOS	ASSORTIVE
ASPHALTS	ASPROS	ASSEMBLER	ASSIGN	ASSORTS
ASPHALTUM	ASPROUT	ASSEMBLES	ASSIGNAT	ASSOT
ASPHERIC	ASPS	ASSEMBLY	ASSIGNATS	ASSOTS
ASPHODEL	ASQUAT	ASSENT	ASSIGNED	ASSOTT
ASPHODELS	ASQUINT	ASSENTED	ASSIGNEE	ASSOTTED

ASSOTTING	ASTATIDES	ASTONE	ASTUNNED	ATACAMITE
ASSUAGE	ASTATINE	ASTONED	ASTUNNING	ATACTIC
ASSUAGED	ASTATINES	ASTONES	ASTUNS	ATAGHAN
ASSUAGER	ASTATKI	ASTONIED	ASTUTE	ATAGHANS
ASSUAGERS	ASTATKIS	ASTONIES	ASTUTELY	ATALAYA
ASSUAGES	ASTEISM	ASTONING	ASTUTER	ATALAYAS
ASSUAGING	ASTEISMS	ASTONISH	ASTUTEST	ATAMAN
ASSUASIVE	ASTELIC	ASTONY	ASTYLAR	ATAMANS
ASSUETUDE	ASTELIES	ASTONYING	ASUDDEN	ATAMASCO
ASSUMABLE	ASTELY	ASTOOP	ASUNDER	ATAMASCOS
ASSUMABLY	ASTER	ASTOUND	ASWARM	ATAP
ASSUME	ASTERIA	ASTOUNDED	ASWAY	ATAPS
ASSUMED	ASTERIAS	ASTOUNDS	ASWIM	ATARACTIC
ASSUMEDLY	ASTERID	ASTRACHAN	ASWING	ATARAXIA
ASSUMER	ASTERIDS	ASTRADDLE	ASWIRL	ATARAXIAS
ASSUMERS	ASTERISK	ASTRAGAL	ASWOON	ATARAXIC
ASSUMES	ASTERISKS	ASTRAGALI	ASYLA	ATARAXICS
ASSUMING	ASTERISM	ASTRAGALS	ASYLEE	ATARAXIES
ASSUMINGS	ASTERISMS	ASTRAKHAN	ASYLEES	ATARAXY
ASSUMPSIT	ASTERN	ASTRAL	ASYLLABIC	ATAVIC
ASSURABLE	ASTERNAL	ASTRALLY	ASYLUM	ATAVISM
ASSURANCE	ASTEROID	ASTRALS	ASYLUMS	ATAVISMS
ASSURE	ASTEROIDS	ASTRAND	ASYMMETRY	ATAVIST
ASSURED	ASTERS	ASTRANTIA	ASYMPTOTE	ATAVISTIC
ASSUREDLY	ASTERT	ASTRAY	ASYNAPSES	ATAVISTS
ASSUREDS	ASTERTED	ASTRICT	ASYNAPSIS	ATAXIA
ASSURER	ASTERTING	ASTRICTED	ASYNDETA	ATAXIAS
ASSURERS	ASTERTS	ASTRICTS	ASYNDETIC	ATAXIC
ASSURES	ASTHENIA	ASTRIDE	ASYNDETON	ATAXICS
ASSURGENT	ASTHENIAS	ASTRINGE	ASYNERGIA	ATAXIES
ASSURING	ASTHENIC	ASTRINGED	ASYNERGY	ATAXY
ASSUROR	ASTHENICS	ASTRINGER	ASYSTOLE	ATCHIEVE
ASSURORS	ASTHENIES	ASTRINGES	ASYSTOLES	ATCHIEVED
ASSWAGE	ASTHENY	ASTROCYTE	ASYSTOLIC	ATCHIEVES
ASSWAGED	ASTHMA	ASTRODOME	AT	ATE
ASSWAGES	ASTHMAS	ASTROFELL	ATAATA	ATEBRIN
ASSWAGING	ASTHMATIC	ASTROID	ATAATAS	ATEBRINS
ASTABLE	ASTHORE	ASTROIDS	ATABAL	ATECHNIC
ASTARE	ASTHORES	ASTROLABE	ATABALS	ATELIC
ASTART	ASTICHOUS	ASTROLOGY	ATABEG	ATELIER
ASTARTED	ASTIGMIA	ASTRONAUT	ATABEGS	ATELIERS
ASTARTING	ASTIGMIAS	ASTRONOMY	ATABEK	ATEMOYA
ASTARTS	ASTILBE	ASTROPHEL	ATABEKS	ATEMOYAS
ASTASIA	ASTILBES	ASTRUT	ATABRIN	ATEMPORAL
ASTASIAS	ASTIR	ASTUCIOUS	ATABRINE	ATENOLOL
ASTATIC	ASTOMATAL	ASTUCITY	ATABRINES	ATENOLOLS
ASTATIDE	ASTOMOUS	ASTUN	ATABRINS	ATES

ATHAME	ATHLETES	ATOLLS	ATONY	ATTACKED
ATHAMES	ATHLETIC	ATOM	ATOP	ATTACKER
ATHANASY	ATHLETICS	ATOMIC	ATOPIC	ATTACKERS
ATHANOR	ATHODYD	ATOMICAL	ATOPIES	ATTACKING
ATHANORS	ATHODYDS	ATOMICITY	ATOPY	ATTACKMAN
ATHEISE	ATHRILL	ATOMICS	ATRAMENT	ATTACKMEN
ATHEISED	ATHROB	ATOMIES	ATRAMENTS	ATTACKS
ATHEISES	ATHROCYTE	ATOMISE	ATRAZINE	ATTAGIRL
ATHEISING	ATHWART	ATOMISED	ATRAZINES	ATTAIN
ATHEISM	ATIGI	ATOMISER	ATREMBLE	ATTAINDER
ATHEISMS	ATIGIS	ATOMISERS	ATRESIA	ATTAINED
ATHEIST	ATILT	ATOMISES	ATRESIAS	ATTAINER
ATHEISTIC	ATIMIES	ATOMISING	ATRESIC	ATTAINERS
ATHEISTS	ATIMY	ATOMISM	ATRETIC	ATTAINING
ATHEIZE	ATINGLE	ATOMISMS	ATRIA	ATTAINS
ATHEIZED	ATISHOO	ATOMIST	ATRIAL	ATTAINT
ATHEIZES	ATISHOOS	ATOMISTIC	ATRIP	ATTAINTED
ATHEIZING	ATLANTES	ATOMISTS	ATRIUM	ATTAINTS
ATHELING	ATLAS	ATOMIZE	ATRIUMS	ATTAP
ATHELINGS	ATLASES	ATOMIZED	ATROCIOUS	ATTAPS
ATHEMATIC	ATLATL	ATOMIZER	ATROCITY	ATTAR
ATHENAEUM	ATLATLS	ATOMIZERS	ATROPHIA	ATTARS
ATHENEUM	ATMA	ATOMIZES	ATROPHIAS	ATTASK
ATHENEUMS	ATMAN	ATOMIZING	ATROPHIC	ATTASKED
ATHEOLOGY	ATMANS	ATOMS	ATROPHIED	ATTASKING
ATHEOUS	ATMAS	ATOMY	ATROPHIES	ATTASKS
ATHERINE	ATMOLOGY	ATONABLE	ATROPHY	ATTASKT
ATHERINES	ATMOLYSE	ATONAL	ATROPIA	ATTEMPER
ATHEROMA	ATMOLYSED	ATONALISM	ATROPIAS	ATTEMPERS
ATHEROMAS	ATMOLYSES	ATONALIST	ATROPIN	ATTEMPT
ATHETESES	ATMOLYSIS	ATONALITY	ATROPINE	ATTEMPTED
ATHETESIS	ATMOLYZE	ATONALLY	ATROPINES	ATTEMPTER
ATHETISE	ATMOLYZED	ATONE	ATROPINS	ATTEMPTS
ATHETISED	ATMOLYZES	ATONEABLE	ATROPISM	ATTEND
ATHETISES	ATMOMETER	ATONED	ATROPISMS	ATTENDANT
ATHETIZE	ATMOMETRY	ATONEMENT	ATROPOUS	ATTENDED
ATHETIZED	ATOC	ATONER	ATS	ATTENDEE
ATHETIZES	ATOCIA	ATONERS	ATT	ATTENDEES
ATHETOID	ATOCIAS	ATONES	ATTABOY	ATTENDER
ATHETOSES	ATOCS	ATONIA	ATTACH	ATTENDERS
ATHETOSIC	ATOK	ATONIAS	ATTACHE	ATTENDING
ATHETOSIS	ATOKAL	ATONIC	ATTACHED	ATTENDS
ATHETOTIC	ATOKE	ATONICITY	ATTACHER	ATTENT
ATHIRST	ATOKES	ATONICS	ATTACHERS	ATTENTAT
ATHLETA	ATOKOUS	ATONIES	ATTACHES	ATTENTATS
ATHLETAS	ATOKS	ATONING	ATTACHING	ATTENTION
ATHLETE	ATOLL	ATONINGLY	ATTACK	ATTENTIVE

ATTENTS	ATTRACT	AUBERGE	AUDITED	AUGUSTEST
ATTENUANT	ATTRACTED	AUBERGES	AUDITEE	AUGUSTLY
ATTENUATE	ATTRACTER	AUBERGINE	AUDITEES	AUGUSTS
ATTERCOP	ATTRACTOR	AUBRETIA	AUDITING	AUK
ATTERCOPS	ATTRACTS	AUBRETIAS	AUDITION	AUKLET
ATTEST	ATTRAHENS	AUBRIETA	AUDITIONS	AUKLETS
ATTESTANT	ATTRAHENT	AUBRIETAS	AUDITIVE	AUKS
ATTESTED	ATTRAP	AUBRIETIA	AUDITIVES	AULA
ATTESTER	ATTRAPPED	AUBURN	AUDITOR	AULARIAN
ATTESTERS	ATTRAPS	AUBURNS	AUDITORIA	AULARIANS
ATTESTING	ATTRIBUTE	AUCEPS	AUDITORS	AULAS
ATTESTOR	ATTRIST	AUCEPSES	AUDITORY	AULD
ATTESTORS	ATTRISTED	AUCTION	AUDITRESS	AULDER
ATTESTS	ATTRISTS	AUCTIONED	AUDITS	AULDEST
ATTIC	ATTRIT	AUCTIONS	AUE	AULIC
ATTICISE	ATTRITE	AUCTORIAL	AUF	AULNAGE
ATTICISED	ATTRITED	AUCUBA	AUFGABE	AULNAGER
ATTICISES	ATTRITES	AUCUBAS	AUFGABES	AULNAGERS
ATTICISM	ATTRITING	AUDACIOUS	AUFS	AULNAGES
ATTICISMS	ATTRITION	AUDACITY	AUGEND	AULOI
ATTICIST	ATTRITIVE	AUDAD	AUGENDS	AULOS
ATTICISTS	ATTRITS	AUDADS	AUGER	AUMAIL
ATTICIZE	ATTRITTED	AUDIAL	AUGERS	AUMAILED
ATTICIZED	ATTUENT	AUDIBLE	AUGHT	AUMAILING
ATTICIZES	ATTUITE	AUDIBLED	AUGHTS	AUMAILS
ATTICS	ATTUITED	AUDIBLES	AUGITE	AUMBRIES
ATTIRE	ATTUITES	AUDIBLING	AUGITES	AUMBRY
ATTIRED	ATTUITING	AUDIBLY	AUGITIC	AUMIL
ATTIRES	ATTUITION	AUDIENCE	AUGMENT	AUMILS
ATTIRING	ATTUITIVE	AUDIENCES	AUGMENTED	AUNE
ATTIRINGS	ATTUNE	AUDIENCIA	AUGMENTER	AUNES
ATTITUDE	ATTUNED	AUDIENT	AUGMENTOR	AUNT
ATTITUDES	ATTUNES	AUDIENTS	AUGMENTS	AUNTER
ATTOLASER	ATTUNING	AUDILE	AUGUR	AUNTERS
ATTOLLENS	ATUA	AUDILES	AUGURAL	AUNTHOOD
ATTOLLENT	ATUAS	AUDING	AUGURED	AUNTHOODS
ATTONCE	ATWAIN	AUDINGS	AUGURER	AUNTIE
ATTONE	ATWEEL	AUDIO	AUGURERS	AUNTIES
ATTONED	ATWEEN	AUDIOBOOK	AUGURIES	AUNTLIER
ATTONES	ATWITTER	AUDIOGRAM	AUGURING	AUNTLIEST
ATTONING	ATWIXT	AUDIOLOGY	AUGURS	AUNTLIKE
ATTORN	ATYPIC	AUDIOPHIL	AUGURSHIP	AUNTLY
ATTORNED	ATYPICAL	AUDIOS	AUGURY	AUNTS
ATTORNEY	AUA	AUDIOTAPE	AUGUST	AUNTY
ATTORNEYS	AUAS	AUDIPHONE	AUGUSTE	AURA
ATTORNING	AUBADE	AUDIT	AUGUSTER	AURAE
ATTORNS	AUBADES	AUDITABLE	AUGUSTES	AURAL

AURALITY	AURORALLY	AUTHORIAL	AUTOGENIC	AUTOPILOT
AURALLY	AURORAS	AUTHORING	AUTOGENY	AUTOPISTA
AURAR	AUROREAN	AUTHORISE	AUTOGIRO	AUTOPOINT
AURAS	AUROUS	AUTHORISH	AUTOGIROS	AUTOPSIA
AURATE	AURUM	AUTHORISM	AUTOGRAFT	AUTOPSIAS
AURATED	AURUMS	AUTHORITY	AUTOGRAPH	AUTOPSIC
AURATES	AUSFORM	AUTHORIZE	AUTOGUIDE	AUTOPSIED
AUREATE	AUSFORMED	AUTHORS	AUTOGYRO	AUTOPSIES
AUREATELY	AUSFORMS	AUTISM	AUTOGYROS	AUTOPSIST
AUREI	AUSLANDER	AUTISMS	AUTOHARP	AUTOPSY
AUREITIES	AUSPEX	AUTIST	AUTOHARPS	AUTOPTIC
AUREITY	AUSPICATE	AUTISTIC	AUTOICOUS	AUTOPUT
AURELIA	AUSPICE	AUTISTICS	AUTOING	AUTOPUTS
AURELIAN	AUSPICES	AUTISTS	AUTOLATRY	AUTOREPLY
AURELIANS	AUSTENITE	AUTO	AUTOLOGY	AUTOROUTE
AURELIAS	AUSTERE	AUTOBAHN	AUTOLYSE	AUTOS
AUREOLA	AUSTERELY	AUTOBAHNS	AUTOLYSED	AUTOSAVE
AUREOLAE	AUSTERER	AUTOBUS	AUTOLYSES	AUTOSAVED
AUREOLAS	AUSTEREST	AUTOBUSES	AUTOLYSIN	AUTOSAVES
AUREOLE	AUSTERITY	AUTOCADE	AUTOLYSIS	AUTOSCOPY
AUREOLED	AUSTRAL	AUTOCADES	AUTOLYTIC	AUTOSOMAL
AUREOLES	AUSTRALES	AUTOCAR	AUTOLYZE	AUTOSOME
AUREOLING	AUSTRALIS	AUTOCARP	AUTOLYZED	AUTOSOMES
AURES	AUSTRALS	AUTOCARPS	AUTOLYZES	AUTOSPORE
AUREUS	AUSUBO	AUTOCARS	AUTOMAGIC	AUTOTELIC
AURIC	AUSUBOS	AUTOCIDAL	AUTOMAKER	AUTOTEST
AURICLE	AUTACOID	AUTOCLAVE	AUTOMAN	AUTOTESTS
AURICLED	AUTACOIDS	AUTOCOID	AUTOMAT	AUTOTIMER
AURICLES	AUTARCH	AUTOCOIDS	AUTOMATA	AUTOTOMIC
AURICULA	AUTARCHIC	AUTOCRACY	AUTOMATE	AUTOTOMY
AURICULAE	AUTARCHS	AUTOCRAT	AUTOMATED	AUTOTOXIC
AURICULAR	AUTARCHY	AUTOCRATS	AUTOMATES	AUTOTOXIN
AURICULAS	AUTARKIC	AUTOCRIME	AUTOMATIC	AUTOTROPH
AURIFIED	AUTARKIES	AUTOCRINE	AUTOMATON	AUTOTUNE
AURIFIES	AUTARKIST	AUTOCROSS	AUTOMATS	AUTOTUNES
AURIFORM	AUTARKY	AUTOCUE	AUTOMEN	AUTOTYPE
AURIFY	AUTECIOUS	AUTOCUES	AUTOMETER	AUTOTYPED
AURIFYING	AUTECISM	AUTOCUTIE	AUTONOMIC	AUTOTYPES
AURIS	AUTECISMS	AUTOCYCLE	AUTONOMY	AUTOTYPIC
AURISCOPE	AUTEUR	AUTODYNE	AUTONYM	AUTOTYPY
AURIST	AUTEURISM	AUTODYNES	AUTONYMS	AUTOVAC
AURISTS	AUTEURIST	AUTOECISM	AUTOPEN	AUTOVACS
AUROCHS	AUTEURS	AUTOED	AUTOPENS	AUTUMN
AUROCHSES	AUTHENTIC	AUTOFLARE	AUTOPHAGY	AUTUMNAL
AURORA	AUTHOR	AUTOFOCUS	AUTOPHOBY	AUTUMNS
AURORAE	AUTHORED	AUTOGAMIC	AUTOPHONY	AUTUMNY
AURORAL	AUTHORESS	AUTOGAMY	AUTOPHYTE	AUTUNITE

AUTUNITES

AUTUNITES	AVAUNTED	AVERSIVE	AVIDLY	AVOIDER
AUXESES	AVAUNTING	AVERSIVES	AVIDNESS	AVOIDERS
AUXESIS	AVAUNTS	AVERT	AVIETTE	AVOIDING
AUXETIC	AVE	AVERTABLE	AVIETTES	AVOIDS
AUXETICS	AVEL	AVERTED	AVIFAUNA	AVOISION
AUXILIAR	AVELLAN	AVERTEDLY	AVIFAUNAE	AVOISIONS
AUXILIARS	AVELLANE	AVERTER	AVIFAUNAL	AVOPARCIN
AUXILIARY	AVELS	AVERTERS	AVIFAUNAS	AVOS
AUXIN	AVENGE	AVERTIBLE	AVIFORM	AVOSET
AUXINIC	AVENGED	AVERTING	AVIGATOR	AVOSETS
AUXINS	AVENGEFUL	AVERTS	AVIGATORS	AVOUCH
AUXOCYTE	AVENGER	AVES	AVINE	AVOUCHED
AUXOCYTES	AVENGERS	AVGAS	AVION	AVOUCHER
AUXOMETER	AVENGES	AVGASES	AVIONIC	AVOUCHERS
AUXOSPORE	AVENGING	AVGASSES	AVIONICS	AVOUCHES
AUXOTONIC	AVENIR	AVIAN	AVIONS	AVOUCHING
AUXOTROPH	AVENIRS	AVIANISE	AVIRULENT	AVOURE
AVA	AVENS	AVIANISED	AVISANDUM	AVOURES
AVADAVAT	AVENSES	AVIANISES	AVISE	AVOUTERER
AVADAVATS	AVENTAIL	AVIANIZE	AVISED	AVOUTRER
AVAIL	AVENTAILE	AVIANIZED	AVISEMENT	AVOUTRERS
AVAILABLE	AVENTAILS	AVIANIZES	AVISES	AVOUTRIES
AVAILABLY	AVENTRE	AVIANS	AVISING	AVOUTRY
AVAILE	AVENTRED	AVIARIES	AVISO	AVOW
AVAILED	AVENTRES	AVIARIST	AVISOS	AVOWABLE
AVAILES	AVENTRING	AVIARISTS	AVITAL	AVOWABLY
AVAILFUL	AVENTURE	AVIARY	AVIZANDUM	AVOWAL
AVAILING	AVENTURES	AVIATE	AVIZE	AVOWALS
AVAILS	AVENTURIN	AVIATED	AVIZED	AVOWED
AVAL	AVENUE	AVIATES	AVIZEFULL	AVOWEDLY
AVALANCHE	AVENUES	AVIATIC	AVIZES	AVOWER
AVALE	AVER	AVIATING	AVIZING	AVOWERS
AVALED	AVERAGE	AVIATION	AVO	AVOWING
AVALES	AVERAGED	AVIATIONS	AVOCADO	AVOWRIES
AVALING	AVERAGELY	AVIATOR	AVOCADOES	AVOWRY
AVANT	AVERAGES	AVIATORS	AVOCADOS	AVOWS
AVANTI	AVERAGING	AVIATRESS	AVOCATION	AVOYER
AVANTIST	AVERMENT	AVIATRICE	AVOCET	AVOYERS
AVANTISTS	AVERMENTS	AVIATRIX	AVOCETS	AVRUGA
AVARICE	AVERRABLE	AVICULAR	AVODIRE	AVRUGAS
AVARICES	AVERRED	AVID	AVODIRES	AVULSE
AVAS	AVERRING	AVIDER	AVOID	AVULSED
AVASCULAR	AVERS	AVIDEST	AVOIDABLE	AVULSES
AVAST	AVERSE	AVIDIN	AVOIDABLY	AVULSING
AVATAR	AVERSELY	AVIDINS	AVOIDANCE	AVULSION
AVATARS	AVERSION	AVIDITIES	AVOIDANT	AVULSIONS
AVAUNT	AVERSIONS	AVIDITY	AVOIDED	AVUNCULAR

AVYZE	AWAYDAY	AWL	AXIL	AXONS
AVYZED	AWAYDAYS	AWLBIRD	AXILE	AXOPLASM
AVYZES	AWAYES	AWLBIRDS	AXILEMMA	AXOPLASMS
AVYZING	AWAYNESS	AWLESS	AXILEMMAS	AXSEED
AW	AWAYS	AWLS	AXILLA	AXSEEDS
AWA	AWDL	AWLWORT	AXILLAE	AY
AWAIT	AWDLS	AWLWORTS	AXILLAR	AYAH
AWAITED	AWE	AWMOUS	AXILLARS	AYAHS
AWAITER	AWEARIED	AWMRIE	AXILLARY	AYAHUASCA
AWAITERS	AWEARY	AWMRIES	AXILLAS	AYAHUASCO
AWAITING	AWEATHER	AWMRY	AXILS	AYATOLLAH
AWAITS	AWED	AWN	AXING	AYE
AWAKE	AWEE	AWNED	AXINITE	AYELP
AWAKED	AWEEL	AWNER	AXINITES	AYENBITE
AWAKEN	AWEIGH	AWNERS	AXIOLOGY	AYENBITES
AWAKENED	AWEING	AWNIER	AXIOM	AYES
AWAKENER	AWELESS	AWNIEST	AXIOMATIC	AYGRE
AWAKENERS	AWES	AWNING	AXIOMS	AYIN
AWAKENING	AWESOME	AWNINGED	AXION	AYINS
AWAKENS	AWESOMELY	AWNINGS	AXIONS	AYONT
AWAKES	AWESTRUCK	AWNLESS	AXIS	AYRE
AWAKING	AWETO	AWNS	AXISED	AYRES
AWAKINGS	AWETOS	AWNY	AXISES	AYRIE
AWANTING	AWFUL	AWOKE	AXITE	AYRIES
AWARD	AWFULLER	AWOKEN	AXITES	AYS
AWARDABLE	AWFULLEST	AWOL	AXLE	AYU
AWARDED	AWFULLY	AWOLS	AXLED	AYURVEDA
AWARDEE	AWFULNESS	AWORK	AXLES	AYURVEDAS
AWARDEES	AWFY	AWRACK	AXLETREE	AYURVEDIC
AWARDER	AWHAPE	AWRONG	AXLETREES	AYUS
AWARDERS	AWHAPED	AWRY	AXLIKE	AYWORD
AWARDING	AWHAPES	AWSOME	AXMAN	AYWORDS
AWARDS	AWHAPING	AX	AXMEN	AZALEA
AWARE	AWHATO	AXAL	AXOID	AZALEAS
AWARENESS	AWHATOS	AXE	AXOIDS	AZAN
AWARER	AWHEEL	AXEBIRD	AXOLEMMA	AZANS
AWAREST	AWHEELS	AXEBIRDS	AXOLEMMAS	AZEDARACH
AWARN	AWHETO	AXED	AXOLOTL	AZEOTROPE
AWARNED	AWHETOS	AXEL	AXOLOTLS	AZEOTROPY
AWARNING	AWHILE	AXELS	AXON	AZERTY
AWARNS	AWHIRL	AXEMAN	AXONAL	AZIDE
AWASH	AWING	AXEMEN	AXONE	AZIDES
AWATCH	AWK	AXENIC	AXONEMAL	AZIDO
AWATO	AWKS	AXES	AXONEME	AZIMUTH
AWATOS	AWKWARD	AXIAL	AXONEMES	AZIMUTHAL
AWAVE	AWKWARDER	AXIALITY	AXONES	AZIMUTHS
AWAY	AWKWARDLY	AXIALLY	AXONIC	AZINE

AZINES	AZONIC	AZOTISE	AZULEJO	AZYGOSES
AZIONE	AZONS	AZOTISED	AZULEJOS	AZYGOUS
AZIONES	AZOTAEMIA	AZOTISES	AZURE	AZYGOUSLY
AZLON	AZOTAEMIC	AZOTISING	AZUREAN	AZYGY
AZLONS	AZOTE	AZOTIZE	AZURES	AZYM
AZO	AZOTED	AZOTIZED	AZURINE	AZYME
AZOIC	AZOTEMIA	AZOTIZES	AZURINES	AZYMES
AZOLE	AZOTEMIAS	AZOTIZING	AZURITE	AZYMITE
AZOLES	AZOTEMIC	AZOTOUS	AZURITES	AZYMITES
AZOLLA	AZOTES	AZOTURIA	AZURN	AZYMOUS
AZOLLAS	AZOTH	AZOTURIAS	AZURY	AZYMS
AZON	AZOTHS	AZUKI	AZYGIES	
AZONAL	AZOTIC	AZUKIS	AZYGOS	

B

BA	BABELDOM	BABUSHKAS	BACHARACH	BACKCOMBS
BAA	BABELDOMS	BABY	BACHAS	BACKCOURT
BAAED	BABELISH	BABYDOLL	BACHCHA	BACKCROSS
BAAING	BABELISM	BABYDOLLS	BACHCHAS	BACKDATE
BAAINGS	BABELISMS	BABYFOOD	BACHED	BACKDATED
BAAL	BABELS	BABYFOODS	BACHELOR	BACKDATES
BAALEBOS	BABES	BABYHOOD	BACHELORS	BACKDOOR
BAALIM	BABESIA	BABYHOODS	BACHES	BACKDOWN
BAALISM	BABESIAS	BABYING	BACHING	BACKDOWNS
BAALISMS	BABICHE	BABYISH	BACHS	BACKDRAFT
BAALS	BABICHES	BABYISHLY	BACILLAR	BACKDROP
BAAS	BABIED	BABYPROOF	BACILLARY	BACKDROPS
BAASES	BABIER	BABYSAT	BACILLI	BACKDROPT
BAASKAAP	BABIES	BABYSIT	BACILLUS	BACKED
BAASKAAPS	BABIEST	BABYSITS	BACK	BACKER
BAASKAP	BABIRUSA	BAC	BACKACHE	BACKERS
BAASKAPS	BABIRUSAS	BACALAO	BACKACHES	BACKET
BAASSKAP	BABIRUSSA	BACALAOS	BACKARE	BACKETS
BAASSKAPS	BABKA	BACCA	BACKBAND	BACKFALL
BABA	BABKAS	BACCAE	BACKBANDS	BACKFALLS
BABACO	BABLAH	BACCARA	BACKBEAT	BACKFIELD
BABACOOTE	BABLAHS	BACCARAS	BACKBEATS	BACKFILE
BABACOS	BABOO	BACCARAT	BACKBENCH	BACKFILES
BABALAS	BABOOL	BACCARATS	BACKBEND	BACKFILL
BABAS	BABOOLS	BACCARE	BACKBENDS	BACKFILLS
BABASSU	BABOON	BACCAS	BACKBIT	BACKFIRE
BABASSUS	BABOONERY	BACCATE	BACKBITE	BACKFIRED
BABBELAS	BABOONISH	BACCATED	BACKBITER	BACKFIRES
BABBITRY	BABOONS	BACCHANAL	BACKBITES	BACKFISCH
BABBITT	BABOOS	BACCHANT	BACKBLOCK	BACKFIT
BABBITTED	BABOOSH	BACCHANTE	BACKBOARD	BACKFITS
BABBITTRY	BABOOSHES	BACCHANTS	BACKBOND	BACKFLIP
BABBITTS	BABOUCHE	BACCHIAC	BACKBONDS	BACKFLIPS
BABBLE	BABOUCHES	BACCHIAN	BACKBONE	BACKFLOW
BABBLED	BABU	BACCHIC	BACKBONED	BACKFLOWS
BABBLER	BABUCHE	BACCHII	BACKBONES	BACKHAND
BABBLERS	BABUCHES	BACCHIUS	BACKBURN	BACKHANDS
BABBLES	BABUDOM	BACCIES	BACKBURNS	BACKHAUL
BABBLIER	BABUDOMS	BACCIFORM	BACKCAST	BACKHAULS
BABBLIEST	BABUISM	BACCO	BACKCASTS	BACKHOE
BABBLING	BABUISMS	BACCOES	BACKCHAT	BACKHOED
BABBLINGS	BABUL	BACCOS	BACKCHATS	BACKHOES
BABBLY	BABULS	BACCY	BACKCHECK	BACKHOUSE
BABE	BABUS	BACH	BACKCLOTH	BACKIE
BABEL	BABUSHKA	BACHA	BACKCOMB	BACKIES

two to nine letter words | 45

BACKING	BACKSLAP	BACON	BADIOUS	BAGGAGES
BACKINGS	BACKSLAPS	BACONER	BADLAND	BAGGED
BACKLAND	BACKSLASH	BACONERS	BADLANDS	BAGGER
BACKLANDS	BACKSLID	BACONS	BADLY	BAGGERS
BACKLASH	BACKSLIDE	BACS	BADMAN	BAGGIE
BACKLESS	BACKSPACE	BACTERIA	BADMASH	BAGGIER
BACKLIFT	BACKSPEER	BACTERIAL	BADMASHES	BAGGIES
BACKLIFTS	BACKSPEIR	BACTERIAN	BADMEN	BAGGIEST
BACKLIGHT	BACKSPIN	BACTERIAS	BADMINTON	BAGGILY
BACKLIST	BACKSPINS	BACTERIC	BADMOUTH	BAGGINESS
BACKLISTS	BACKSTAB	BACTERIN	BADMOUTHS	BAGGING
BACKLIT	BACKSTABS	BACTERINS	BADNESS	BAGGINGS
BACKLOAD	BACKSTAGE	BACTERISE	BADNESSES	BAGGIT
BACKLOADS	BACKSTAIR	BACTERIUM	BADS	BAGGITS
BACKLOG	BACKSTALL	BACTERIZE	BADWARE	BAGGY
BACKLOGS	BACKSTAMP	BACTEROID	BADWARES	BAGH
BACKLOT	BACKSTAY	BACULA	BAEL	BAGHOUSE
BACKLOTS	BACKSTAYS	BACULINE	BAELS	BAGHOUSES
BACKMOST	BACKSTOP	BACULITE	BAETYL	BAGHS
BACKOUT	BACKSTOPS	BACULITES	BAETYLS	BAGIE
BACKOUTS	BACKSTORY	BACULUM	BAFF	BAGIES
BACKPACK	BACKSWEPT	BACULUMS	BAFFED	BAGLESS
BACKPACKS	BACKSWING	BAD	BAFFIES	BAGLIKE
BACKPEDAL	BACKSWORD	BADASS	BAFFING	BAGMAN
BACKPIECE	BACKTRACK	BADASSED	BAFFLE	BAGMEN
BACKPLATE	BACKUP	BADASSES	BAFFLED	BAGNETTE
BACKRA	BACKUPS	BADDER	BAFFLEGAB	BAGNETTES
BACKRAS	BACKVELD	BADDEST	BAFFLER	BAGNIO
BACKREST	BACKVELDS	BADDIE	BAFFLERS	BAGNIOS
BACKRESTS	BACKWARD	BADDIES	BAFFLES	BAGPIPE
BACKROOM	BACKWARDS	BADDISH	BAFFLING	BAGPIPED
BACKROOMS	BACKWASH	BADDY	BAFFS	BAGPIPER
BACKRUSH	BACKWATER	BADE	BAFFY	BAGPIPERS
BACKS	BACKWOOD	BADGE	BAFT	BAGPIPES
BACKSAW	BACKWOODS	BADGED	BAFTS	BAGPIPING
BACKSAWS	BACKWORD	BADGELESS	BAG	BAGS
BACKSEAT	BACKWORDS	BADGER	BAGARRE	BAGSFUL
BACKSEATS	BACKWORK	BADGERED	BAGARRES	BAGUET
BACKSET	BACKWORKS	BADGERING	BAGASS	BAGUETS
BACKSETS	BACKWRAP	BADGERLY	BAGASSE	BAGUETTE
BACKSEY	BACKWRAPS	BADGERS	BAGASSES	BAGUETTES
BACKSEYS	BACKYARD	BADGES	BAGATELLE	BAGUIO
BACKSHISH	BACKYARDS	BADGING	BAGEL	BAGUIOS
BACKSHORE	BACLAVA	BADINAGE	BAGELS	BAGWASH
BACKSIDE	BACLAVAS	BADINAGED	BAGFUL	BAGWASHES
BACKSIDES	BACLOFEN	BADINAGES	BAGFULS	BAGWIG
BACKSIGHT	BACLOFENS	BADINERIE	BAGGAGE	BAGWIGS

BAGWORM	BAILSMEN	BAKEMEATS	BALBOAS	BALISAUR
BAGWORMS	BAININ	BAKEN	BALCONET	BALISAURS
BAH	BAININS	BAKEOFF	BALCONETS	BALISE
BAHADA	BAINITE	BAKEOFFS	BALCONIED	BALISES
BAHADAS	BAINITES	BAKER	BALCONIES	BALISTA
BAHADUR	BAIRN	BAKERIES	BALCONY	BALISTAE
BAHADURS	BAIRNISH	BAKERS	BALD	BALISTAS
BAHT	BAIRNLIER	BAKERY	BALDACHIN	BALK
BAHTS	BAIRNLIKE	BAKES	BALDAQUIN	BALKANISE
BAHU	BAIRNLY	BAKESHOP	BALDED	BALKANIZE
BAHUS	BAIRNS	BAKESHOPS	BALDER	BALKED
BAHUT	BAISEMAIN	BAKESTONE	BALDEST	BALKER
BAHUTS	BAIT	BAKEWARE	BALDFACED	BALKERS
BAHUVRIHI	BAITED	BAKEWARES	BALDHEAD	BALKIER
BAIDARKA	BAITER	BAKGAT	BALDHEADS	BALKIEST
BAIDARKAS	BAITERS	BAKHSHISH	BALDICOOT	BALKILY
BAIGNOIRE	BAITFISH	BAKING	BALDIE	BALKINESS
BAIL	BAITH	BAKINGS	BALDIER	BALKING
BAILABLE	BAITING	BAKKIE	BALDIES	BALKINGLY
BAILBOND	BAITINGS	BAKKIES	BALDIEST	BALKINGS
BAILBONDS	BAITS	BAKLAVA	BALDING	BALKLINE
BAILED	BAIZA	BAKLAVAS	BALDISH	BALKLINES
BAILEE	BAIZAS	BAKLAWA	BALDLY	BALKS
BAILEES	BAIZE	BAKLAWAS	BALDMONEY	BALKY
BAILER	BAIZED	BAKRA	BALDNESS	BALL
BAILERS	BAIZES	BAKRAS	BALDPATE	BALLABILE
BAILEY	BAIZING	BAKSHEESH	BALDPATED	BALLABILI
BAILEYS	BAJADA	BAKSHISH	BALDPATES	BALLAD
BAILIE	BAJADAS	BAL	BALDRIC	BALLADE
BAILIES	BAJAN	BALACLAVA	BALDRICK	BALLADED
BAILIFF	BAJANS	BALADIN	BALDRICKS	BALLADEER
BAILIFFS	BAJRA	BALADINE	BALDRICS	BALLADES
BAILING	BAJRAS	BALADINES	BALDS	BALLADIC
BAILIWICK	BAJREE	BALADINS	BALDY	BALLADIN
BAILLI	BAJREES	BALALAIKA	BALE	BALLADINE
BAILLIAGE	BAJRI	BALANCE	BALECTION	BALLADING
BAILLIE	BAJRIS	BALANCED	BALED	BALLADINS
BAILLIES	BAJU	BALANCER	BALEEN	BALLADIST
BAILLIS	BAJUS	BALANCERS	BALEENS	BALLADRY
BAILMENT	BAKE	BALANCES	BALEFIRE	BALLADS
BAILMENTS	BAKEAPPLE	BALANCING	BALEFIRES	BALLAN
BAILOR	BAKEBOARD	BALANITIS	BALEFUL	BALLANS
BAILORS	BAKED	BALAS	BALEFULLY	BALLANT
BAILOUT	BAKEHOUSE	BALASES	BALER	BALLANTED
BAILOUTS	BAKELITE	BALATA	BALERS	BALLANTS
BAILS	BAKELITES	BALATAS	BALES	BALLAST
BAILSMAN	BAKEMEAT	BALBOA	BALING	BALLASTED

BALLASTER	BALLOTER	BALS	BANALITY	BANDEROLS
BALLASTS	BALLOTERS	BALSA	BANALIZE	BANDERS
BALLAT	BALLOTING	BALSAM	BANALIZED	BANDFISH
BALLATED	BALLOTINI	BALSAMED	BANALIZES	BANDH
BALLATING	BALLOTS	BALSAMIC	BANALLY	BANDHS
BALLATS	BALLOW	BALSAMING	BANANA	BANDICOOT
BALLCLAY	BALLOWS	BALSAMS	BANANAS	BANDIED
BALLCLAYS	BALLPARK	BALSAMY	BANAUSIAN	BANDIER
BALLCOCK	BALLPARKS	BALSAS	BANAUSIC	BANDIES
BALLCOCKS	BALLPEEN	BALSAWOOD	BANC	BANDIEST
BALLED	BALLPOINT	BALTHASAR	BANCO	BANDINESS
BALLER	BALLROOM	BALTHAZAR	BANCOS	BANDING
BALLERINA	BALLROOMS	BALTI	BANCS	BANDINGS
BALLERINE	BALLS	BALTIC	BAND	BANDIT
BALLERS	BALLSIER	BALTIS	BANDA	BANDITO
BALLET	BALLSIEST	BALU	BANDAGE	BANDITOS
BALLETED	BALLSY	BALUN	BANDAGED	BANDITRY
BALLETIC	BALLUP	BALUNS	BANDAGER	BANDITS
BALLETING	BALLUPS	BALUS	BANDAGERS	BANDITTI
BALLETS	BALLUTE	BALUSTER	BANDAGES	BANDITTIS
BALLGAME	BALLUTES	BALUSTERS	BANDAGING	BANDMATE
BALLGAMES	BALLY	BALZARINE	BANDAID	BANDMATES
BALLHAWK	BALLYARD	BAM	BANDALORE	BANDOBAST
BALLHAWKS	BALLYARDS	BAMBI	BANDANA	BANDOBUST
BALLIES	BALLYHOO	BAMBINI	BANDANAS	BANDOG
BALLING	BALLYHOOS	BAMBINO	BANDANNA	BANDOGS
BALLINGS	BALLYRAG	BAMBINOS	BANDANNAS	BANDOLEER
BALLISTA	BALLYRAGS	BAMBIS	BANDAR	BANDOLEON
BALLISTAE	BALM	BAMBOO	BANDARI	BANDOLERO
BALLISTAS	BALMACAAN	BAMBOOS	BANDARIS	BANDOLIER
BALLISTIC	BALMED	BAMBOOZLE	BANDARS	BANDOLINE
BALLIUM	BALMIER	BAMMED	BANDAS	BANDONEON
BALLIUMS	BALMIEST	BAMMER	BANDBOX	BANDONION
BALLOCKS	BALMILY	BAMMERS	BANDBOXES	BANDOOK
BALLON	BALMINESS	BAMMING	BANDBRAKE	BANDOOKS
BALLONET	BALMING	BAMPOT	BANDEAU	BANDORA
BALLONETS	BALMLIKE	BAMPOTS	BANDEAUS	BANDORAS
BALLONNE	BALMORAL	BAMS	BANDEAUX	BANDORE
BALLONNES	BALMORALS	BAN	BANDED	BANDORES
BALLONS	BALMS	BANAK	BANDEIRA	BANDROL
BALLOON	BALMY	BANAKS	BANDEIRAS	BANDROLS
BALLOONED	BALNEAL	BANAL	BANDELET	BANDS
BALLOONS	BALNEARY	BANALER	BANDELETS	BANDSAW
BALLOT	BALONEY	BANALEST	BANDELIER	BANDSAWS
BALLOTED	BALONEYS	BANALISE	BANDER	BANDSHELL
BALLOTEE	BALOO	BANALISED	BANDEROL	BANDSMAN
BALLOTEES	BALOOS	BANALISES	BANDEROLE	BANDSMEN

B

BANDSTAND	BANISHER	BANNABLE	BANTING	BARASINGA
BANDSTER	BANISHERS	BANNED	BANTINGS	BARATHEA
BANDSTERS	BANISHES	BANNER	BANTLING	BARATHEAS
BANDURA	BANISHING	BANNERALL	BANTLINGS	BARATHRUM
BANDURAS	BANISTER	BANNERED	BANTS	BARAZA
BANDWAGON	BANISTERS	BANNERET	BANTU	BARAZAS
BANDWIDTH	BANJAX	BANNERETS	BANTUS	BARB
BANDY	BANJAXED	BANNERING	BANTY	BARBAL
BANDYING	BANJAXES	BANNEROL	BANXRING	BARBARIAN
BANDYINGS	BANJAXING	BANNEROLS	BANXRINGS	BARBARIC
BANDYMAN	BANJO	BANNERS	BANYA	BARBARISE
BANDYMEN	BANJOES	BANNET	BANYAN	BARBARISM
BANE	BANJOIST	BANNETS	BANYANS	BARBARITY
BANEBERRY	BANJOISTS	BANNING	BANYAS	BARBARIZE
BANED	BANJOS	BANNISTER	BANZAI	BARBAROUS
BANEFUL	BANJULELE	BANNOCK	BANZAIS	BARBASCO
BANEFULLY	BANK	BANNOCKS	BAOBAB	BARBASCOS
BANES	BANKABLE	BANNS	BAOBABS	BARBASTEL
BANG	BANKBOOK	BANOFFEE	BAP	BARBATE
BANGALAY	BANKBOOKS	BANOFFEES	BAPS	BARBATED
BANGALAYS	BANKCARD	BANOFFI	BAPTISE	BARBE
BANGALORE	BANKCARDS	BANOFFIS	BAPTISED	BARBECUE
BANGALOW	BANKED	BANQUET	BAPTISER	BARBECUED
BANGALOWS	BANKER	BANQUETED	BAPTISERS	BARBECUER
BANGED	BANKERLY	BANQUETER	BAPTISES	BARBECUES
BANGER	BANKERS	BANQUETS	BAPTISIA	BARBED
BANGERS	BANKET	BANQUETTE	BAPTISIAS	BARBEL
BANGING	BANKETS	BANS	BAPTISING	BARBELL
BANGKOK	BANKING	BANSELA	BAPTISM	BARBELLS
BANGKOKS	BANKINGS	BANSELAS	BAPTISMAL	BARBELS
BANGLE	BANKIT	BANSHEE	BAPTISMS	BARBEQUE
BANGLED	BANKITS	BANSHEES	BAPTIST	BARBEQUED
BANGLES	BANKNOTE	BANSHIE	BAPTISTRY	BARBEQUES
BANGS	BANKNOTES	BANSHIES	BAPTISTS	BARBER
BANGSRING	BANKROLL	BANT	BAPTIZE	BARBERED
BANGSTER	BANKROLLS	BANTAM	BAPTIZED	BARBERING
BANGSTERS	BANKRUPT	BANTAMS	BAPTIZER	BARBERRY
BANGTAIL	BANKRUPTS	BANTED	BAPTIZERS	BARBERS
BANGTAILS	BANKS	BANTENG	BAPTIZES	BARBES
BANI	BANKSIA	BANTENGS	BAPTIZING	BARBET
BANIA	BANKSIAS	BANTER	BAPU	BARBETS
BANIAN	BANKSIDE	BANTERED	BAPUS	BARBETTE
BANIANS	BANKSIDES	BANTERER	BAR	BARBETTES
BANIAS	BANKSMAN	BANTERERS	BARACAN	BARBICAN
BANING	BANKSMEN	BANTERING	BARACANS	BARBICANS
BANISH	BANLIEUE	BANTERS	BARACHOIS	BARBICEL
BANISHED	BANLIEUES	BANTIES	BARAGOUIN	BARBICELS

BARBIE	BARDSHIP	BARGELLO	BARKHAN	BARNS
BARBIES	BARDSHIPS	BARGELLOS	BARKHANS	BARNSTORM
BARBING	BARDY	BARGEMAN	BARKIER	BARNY
BARBITAL	BARE	BARGEMEN	BARKIEST	BARNYARD
BARBITALS	BAREBACK	BARGEPOLE	BARKING	BARNYARDS
BARBITONE	BAREBACKS	BARGES	BARKLESS	BAROCCO
BARBLESS	BAREBOAT	BARGEST	BARKS	BAROCCOS
BARBOLA	BAREBOATS	BARGESTS	BARKY	BAROCK
BARBOLAS	BAREBONE	BARGHEST	BARLEDUC	BAROCKS
BARBOTINE	BAREBONED	BARGHESTS	BARLEDUCS	BAROGRAM
BARBS	BAREBONES	BARGING	BARLESS	BAROGRAMS
BARBULE	BARED	BARGOON	BARLEY	BAROGRAPH
BARBULES	BAREFACED	BARGOONS	BARLEYS	BAROLO
BARBUT	BAREFIT	BARGOOSE	BARLOW	BAROLOS
BARBUTS	BAREFOOT	BARGUEST	BARLOWS	BAROMETER
BARBWIRE	BAREGE	BARGUESTS	BARM	BAROMETRY
BARBWIRES	BAREGES	BARHOP	BARMAID	BAROMETZ
BARBY	BAREGINE	BARHOPPED	BARMAIDS	BARON
BARCA	BAREGINES	BARHOPS	BARMAN	BARONAGE
BARCAROLE	BAREHAND	BARIATRIC	BARMBRACK	BARONAGES
BARCAS	BAREHANDS	BARIC	BARMEN	BARONESS
BARCHAN	BAREHEAD	BARILLA	BARMIE	BARONET
BARCHANE	BARELAND	BARILLAS	BARMIER	BARONETCY
BARCHANES	BARELY	BARING	BARMIEST	BARONETS
BARCHANS	BARENESS	BARISH	BARMINESS	BARONG
BARCODE	BARER	BARISTA	BARMKIN	BARONGS
BARCODED	BARES	BARISTAS	BARMKINS	BARONIAL
BARCODES	BARESARK	BARITE	BARMPOT	BARONIES
BARD	BARESARKS	BARITES	BARMPOTS	BARONNE
BARDASH	BAREST	BARITONAL	BARMS	BARONNES
BARDASHES	BARF	BARITONE	BARMY	BARONS
BARDE	BARFED	BARITONES	BARN	BARONY
BARDED	BARFING	BARIUM	BARNACLE	BAROPHILE
BARDES	BARFLIES	BARIUMS	BARNACLED	BAROQUE
BARDIC	BARFLY	BARK	BARNACLES	BAROQUELY
BARDIE	BARFS	BARKAN	BARNBRACK	BAROQUES
BARDIER	BARFUL	BARKANS	BARNED	BAROSAUR
BARDIES	BARGAIN	BARKED	BARNET	BAROSAURS
BARDIEST	BARGAINED	BARKEEP	BARNETS	BAROSCOPE
BARDING	BARGAINER	BARKEEPER	BARNEY	BAROSTAT
BARDISM	BARGAINS	BARKEEPS	BARNEYED	BAROSTATS
BARDISMS	BARGANDER	BARKEN	BARNEYING	BAROTITIS
BARDLING	BARGE	BARKENED	BARNEYS	BAROUCHE
BARDLINGS	BARGED	BARKENING	BARNIER	BAROUCHES
BARDO	BARGEE	BARKENS	BARNIEST	BARP
BARDOS	BARGEES	BARKER	BARNING	BARPERSON
BARDS	BARGEESE	BARKERS	BARNLIKE	BARPS

BARQUE	BARRENS	BARTERS	BASEBALLS	BASICALLY
BARQUES	BARRES	BARTISAN	BASEBAND	BASICITY
BARQUETTE	BARRET	BARTISANS	BASEBANDS	BASICS
BARRA	BARRETOR	BARTIZAN	BASEBOARD	BASIDIA
BARRABLE	BARRETORS	BARTIZANS	BASEBORN	BASIDIAL
BARRACAN	BARRETRY	BARTON	BASED	BASIDIUM
BARRACANS	BARRETS	BARTONS	BASEEJ	BASIFIED
BARRACE	BARRETTE	BARTSIA	BASELARD	BASIFIER
BARRACES	BARRETTER	BARTSIAS	BASELARDS	BASIFIERS
BARRACK	BARRETTES	BARWARE	BASELESS	BASIFIES
BARRACKED	BARRICADE	BARWARES	BASELINE	BASIFIXED
BARRACKER	BARRICADO	BARWOOD	BASELINER	BASIFUGAL
BARRACKS	BARRICO	BARWOODS	BASELINES	BASIFY'
BARRACOON	BARRICOES	BARYE	BASELY	BASIFYING
BARRACUDA	BARRICOS	BARYES	BASEMAN	BASIJ
BARRAGE	BARRIE	BARYON	BASEMEN	BASIL
BARRAGED	BARRIER	BARYONIC	BASEMENT	BASILAR
BARRAGES	BARRIERED	BARYONS	BASEMENTS	BASILARY
BARRAGING	BARRIERS	BARYTA	BASEN	BASILECT
BARRANCA	BARRIES	BARYTAS	BASENESS	BASILECTS
BARRANCAS	BARRIEST	BARYTE	BASENJI	BASILIC
BARRANCO	BARRING	BARYTES	BASENJIS	BASILICA
BARRANCOS	BARRINGS	BARYTIC	BASEPLATE	BASILICAE
BARRAS	BARRIO	BARYTON	BASER	BASILICAL
BARRAT	BARRIOS	BARYTONE	BASES	BASILICAN
BARRATER	BARRISTER	BARYTONES	BASEST	BASILICAS
BARRATERS	BARRO	BARYTONS	BASH	BASILICON
BARRATOR	BARROOM	BAS	BASHAW	BASILISK
BARRATORS	BARROOMS	BASAL	BASHAWISM	BASILISKS
BARRATRY	BARROW	BASALLY	BASHAWS	BASILS
BARRATS	BARROWFUL	BASALT	BASHED	BASIN
BARRE	BARROWS	BASALTES	BASHER	BASINAL
BARRED	BARRULET	BASALTIC	BASHERS	BASINED
BARREED	BARRULETS	BASALTINE	BASHES	BASINET
BARREFULL	BARRY	BASALTS	BASHFUL	BASINETS
BARREING	BARS	BASAN	BASHFULLY	BASINFUL
BARREL	BARSTOOL	BASANITE	BASHING	BASINFULS
BARRELAGE	BARSTOOLS	BASANITES	BASHINGS	BASING
BARRELED	BARTEND	BASANS	BASHLESS	BASINLIKE
BARRELFUL	BARTENDED	BASANT	BASHLIK	BASINS
BARRELING	BARTENDER	BASANTS	BASHLIKS	BASION
BARRELLED	BARTENDS	BASCINET	BASHLYK	BASIONS
BARRELS	BARTER	BASCINETS	BASHLYKS	BASIPETAL
BARREN	BARTERED	BASCULE	BASHMENT	BASIS
BARRENER	BARTERER	BASCULES	BASHMENTS	BASK
BARRENEST	BARTERERS	BASE	BASHO	BASKED
BARRENLY	BARTERING	BASEBALL	BASIC	BASKET

BASKETFUL	BASSOON	BATBOYS	BATHOS	BATTALIAS
BASKETRY	BASSOONS	BATCH	BATHOSES	BATTALION
BASKETS	BASSOS	BATCHED	BATHROBE	BATTAS
BASKING	BASSWOOD	BATCHER	BATHROBES	BATTEAU
BASKS	BASSWOODS	BATCHERS	BATHROOM	BATTEAUX
BASMATI	BASSY	BATCHES	BATHROOMS	BATTED
BASMATIS	BAST	BATCHING	BATHS	BATTEL
BASNET	BASTA	BATCHINGS	BATHTUB	BATTELED
BASNETS	BASTARD	BATE	BATHTUBS	BATTELER
BASOCHE	BASTARDLY	BATEAU	BATHWATER	BATTELERS
BASOCHES	BASTARDRY	BATEAUX	BATHYAL	BATTELING
BASON	BASTARDS	BATED	BATHYBIUS	BATTELLED
BASONS	BASTARDY	BATELESS	BATHYLITE	BATTELS
BASOPHIL	BASTE	BATELEUR	BATHYLITH	BATTEMENT
BASOPHILE	BASTED	BATELEURS	BATIK	BATTEN
BASOPHILS	BASTER	BATEMENT	BATIKED	BATTENED
BASQUE	BASTERS	BATEMENTS	BATIKING	BATTENER
BASQUED	BASTES	BATES	BATIKS	BATTENERS
BASQUES	BASTI	BATFISH	BATING	BATTENING
BASQUINE	BASTIDE	BATFISHES	BATISTE	BATTENS
BASQUINES	BASTIDES	BATFOWL	BATISTES	BATTER
BASS	BASTILE	BATFOWLED	BATLER	BATTERED
BASSE	BASTILES	BATFOWLER	BATLERS	BATTERER
BASSED	BASTILLE	BATFOWLS	BATLET	BATTERERS
BASSER	BASTILLES	BATGIRL	BATLETS	BATTERIE
BASSES	BASTINADE	BATGIRLS	BATLIKE	BATTERIES
BASSEST	BASTINADO	BATH	BATMAN	BATTERING
BASSET	BASTING	BATHCUBE	BATMEN	BATTERO
BASSETED	BASTINGS	BATHCUBES	BATOLOGY	BATTEROS
BASSETING	BASTION	BATHE	BATON	BATTERS
BASSETS	BASTIONED	BATHED	BATONED	BATTERY
BASSETT	BASTIONS	BATHER	BATONING	BATTIER
BASSETTED	BASTIS	BATHERS	BATONS	BATTIES
BASSETTS	BASTLE	BATHES	BATOON	BATTIEST
BASSI	BASTLES	BATHETIC	BATOONED	BATTIK
BASSIER	BASTO	BATHHOUSE	BATOONING	BATTIKS
BASSIEST	BASTOS	BATHING	BATOONS	BATTILL
BASSINET	BASTS	BATHLESS	BATRACHIA	BATTILLED
BASSINETS	BASUCO	BATHMAT	BATS	BATTILLS
BASSING	BASUCOS	BATHMATS	BATSMAN	BATTINESS
BASSIST	BAT	BATHMIC	BATSMEN	BATTING
BASSISTS	BATABLE	BATHMISM	BATSWING	BATTINGS
BASSLINE	BATATA	BATHMISMS	BATSWOMAN	BATTLE
BASSLINES	BATATAS	BATHOLITE	BATSWOMEN	BATTLEAX
BASSLY	BATAVIA	BATHOLITH	BATT	BATTLEAXE
BASSNESS	BATAVIAS	BATHORSE	BATTA	BATTLEBUS
BASSO	BATBOY	BATHORSES	BATTALIA	BATTLED

BATTLER	BAULKERS	BAWNEEN	BAZAZZ	BEADLEDOM
BATTLERS	BAULKIER	BAWNEENS	BAZAZZES	BEADLES
BATTLES	BAULKIEST	BAWNS	BAZILLION	BEADLIKE
BATTLING	BAULKILY	BAWR	BAZOO	BEADMAN
BATTOLOGY	BAULKING	BAWRS	BAZOOKA	BEADMEN
BATTS	BAULKS	BAWSUNT	BAZOOKAS	BEADROLL
BATTU	BAULKY	BAWTIE	BAZOOMS	BEADROLLS
BATTUE	BAUR	BAWTIES	BAZOOS	BEADS
BATTUES	BAURS	BAWTY	BAZOUKI	BEADSMAN
BATTUTA	BAUSOND	BAXTER	BAZOUKIS	BEADSMEN
BATTUTAS	BAUXITE	BAXTERS	BAZZAZZ	BEADWORK
BATTUTO	BAUXITES	BAY	BAZZAZZES	BEADWORKS
BATTUTOS	BAUXITIC	BAYADEER	BDELLIUM	BEADY
BATTY	BAVARDAGE	BAYADEERS	BDELLIUMS	BEAGLE
BATWING	BAVAROIS	BAYADERE	BE	BEAGLED
BATWOMAN	BAVIN	BAYADERES	BEACH	BEAGLER
BATWOMEN	BAVINS	BAYAMO	BEACHBALL	BEAGLERS
BAUBEE	BAWBEE	BAYAMOS	BEACHBOY	BEAGLES
BAUBEES	BAWBEES	BAYARD	BEACHBOYS	BEAGLING
BAUBLE	BAWBLE	BAYARDS	BEACHCOMB	BEAGLINGS
BAUBLES	BAWBLES	BAYBERRY	BEACHED	BEAK
BAUBLING	BAWCOCK	BAYE	BEACHES	BEAKED
BAUCHLE	BAWCOCKS	BAYED	BEACHGOER	BEAKER
BAUCHLED	BAWD	BAYES	BEACHHEAD	BEAKERFUL
BAUCHLES	BAWDIER	BAYING	BEACHIER	BEAKERS
BAUCHLING	BAWDIES	BAYLE	BEACHIEST	BEAKIER
BAUD	BAWDIEST	BAYLES	BEACHING	BEAKIEST
BAUDEKIN	BAWDILY	BAYMAN	BEACHSIDE	BEAKLESS
BAUDEKINS	BAWDINESS	BAYMEN	BEACHWEAR	BEAKLIKE
BAUDRIC	BAWDKIN	BAYONET	BEACHY	BEAKS
BAUDRICK	BAWDKINS	BAYONETED	BEACON	BEAKY
BAUDRICKE	BAWDRIC	BAYONETS	BEACONED	BEAM
BAUDRICKS	BAWDRICS	BAYOU	BEACONING	BEAMED
BAUDRICS	BAWDRIES	BAYOUS	BEACONS	BEAMER
BAUDRONS	BAWDRY	BAYS	BEAD	BEAMERS
BAUDS	BAWDS	BAYT	BEADBLAST	BEAMIER
BAUERA	BAWDY	BAYTED	BEADED	BEAMIEST
BAUERAS	BAWL	BAYTING	BEADER	BEAMILY
BAUHINIA	BAWLED	BAYTS	BEADERS	BEAMINESS
BAUHINIAS	BAWLER	BAYWOOD	BEADHOUSE	BEAMING
BAUK	BAWLERS	BAYWOODS	BEADIER	BEAMINGLY
BAUKED	BAWLEY	BAYYAN	BEADIEST	BEAMINGS
BAUKING	BAWLEYS	BAYYANS	BEADILY	BEAMISH
BAUKS	BAWLING	BAZAAR	BEADINESS	BEAMISHLY
BAULK	BAWLINGS	BAZAARS	BEADING	BEAMLESS
BAULKED	BAWLS	BAZAR	BEADINGS	BEAMLET
BAULKER	BAWN	BAZARS	BEADLE	BEAMLETS

BEAMLIKE	BEARHUG	BEATITUDE	BEBUNG	BECLAMOR
BEAMS	BEARHUGS	BEATLESS	BEBUNGS	BECLAMORS
BEAMY	BEARING	BEATNIK	BECALL	BECLASP
BEAN	BEARINGS	BEATNIKS	BECALLED	BECLASPED
BEANBAG	BEARISH	BEATS	BECALLING	BECLASPS
BEANBAGS	BEARISHLY	BEATY	BECALLS	BECLOAK
BEANBALL	BEARLIKE	BEAU	BECALM	BECLOAKED
BEANBALLS	BEARNAISE	BEAUCOUP	BECALMED	BECLOAKS
BEANED	BEARS	BEAUCOUPS	BECALMING	BECLOG
BEANERIES	BEARSKIN	BEAUFET	BECALMS	BECLOGGED
BEANERY	BEARSKINS	BEAUFETS	BECAME	BECLOGS
BEANFEAST	BEARWARD	BEAUFFET	BECAP	BECLOTHE
BEANIE	BEARWARDS	BEAUFFETS	BECAPPED	BECLOTHED
BEANIES	BEARWOOD	BEAUFIN	BECAPPING	BECLOTHES
BEANING	BEARWOODS	BEAUFINS	BECAPS	BECLOUD
BEANLIKE	BEAST	BEAUISH	BECARPET	BECLOUDED
BEANO	BEASTED	BEAUS	BECARPETS	BECLOUDS
BEANOS	BEASTHOOD	BEAUT	BECASSE	BECLOWN
BEANPOLE	BEASTIE	BEAUTEOUS	BECASSES	BECLOWNED
BEANPOLES	BEASTIES	BEAUTIED	BECAUSE	BECLOWNS
BEANS	BEASTILY	BEAUTIES	BECCACCIA	BECOME
BEANSTALK	BEASTING	BEAUTIFUL	BECCAFICO	BECOMES
BEANY	BEASTINGS	BEAUTIFY	BECHALK	BECOMING
BEAR	BEASTLIER	BEAUTS	BECHALKED	BECOMINGS
BEARABLE	BEASTLIKE	BEAUTY	BECHALKS	BECOWARD
BEARABLY	BEASTLY	BEAUTYING	BECHAMEL	BECOWARDS
BEARBERRY	BEASTS	BEAUX	BECHAMELS	BECQUEREL
BEARBINE	BEAT	BEAUXITE	BECHANCE	BECRAWL
BEARBINES	BEATABLE	BEAUXITES	BECHANCED	BECRAWLED
BEARCAT	BEATBOX	BEAVER	BECHANCES	BECRAWLS
BEARCATS	BEATBOXER	BEAVERED	BECHARM	BECRIME
BEARD	BEATBOXES	BEAVERIES	BECHARMED	BECRIMED
BEARDED	BEATEN	BEAVERING	BECHARMS	BECRIMES
BEARDIE	BEATER	BEAVERS	BECK	BECRIMING
BEARDIER	BEATERS	BEAVERY	BECKE	BECROWD
BEARDIES	BEATH	BEBEERINE	BECKED	BECROWDED
BEARDIEST	BEATHED	BEBEERU	BECKES	BECROWDS
BEARDING	BEATHING	BEBEERUS	BECKET	BECRUST
BEARDLESS	BEATHS	BEBLOOD	BECKETS	BECRUSTED
BEARDS	BEATIER	BEBLOODED	BECKING	BECRUSTS
BEARDY	BEATIEST	BEBLOODS	BECKON	BECUDGEL
BEARE	BEATIFIC	BEBOP	BECKONED	BECUDGELS
BEARED	BEATIFIED	BEBOPPED	BECKONER	BECURL
BEARER	BEATIFIES	BEBOPPER	BECKONERS	BECURLED
BEARERS	BEATIFY	BEBOPPERS	BECKONING	BECURLING
BEARES	BEATING	BEBOPPING	BECKONS	BECURLS
BEARGRASS	BEATINGS	BEBOPS	BECKS	BECURSE

BECURSED	BEDDER	BEDIM	BEDRIDDEN	BEDUCK
BECURSES	BEDDERS	BEDIMMED	BEDRIGHT	BEDUCKED
BECURSING	BEDDING	BEDIMMING	BEDRIGHTS	BEDUCKING
BECURST	BEDDINGS	BEDIMPLE	BEDRITE	BEDUCKS
BED	BEDE	BEDIMPLED	BEDRITES	BEDUIN
BEDABBLE	BEDEAFEN	BEDIMPLES	BEDRIVEL	BEDUINS
BEDABBLED	BEDEAFENS	BEDIMS	BEDRIVELS	BEDUMB
BEDABBLES	BEDECK	BEDIRTIED	BEDROCK	BEDUMBED
BEDAD	BEDECKED	BEDIRTIES	BEDROCKS	BEDUMBING
BEDAGGLE	BEDECKING	BEDIRTY	BEDROLL	BEDUMBS
BEDAGGLED	BEDECKS	BEDIZEN	BEDROLLS	BEDUNCE
BEDAGGLES	BEDEGUAR	BEDIZENED	BEDROOM	BEDUNCED
BEDAMN	BEDEGUARS	BEDIZENS	BEDROOMED	BEDUNCES
BEDAMNED	BEDEHOUSE	BEDLAM	BEDROOMS	BEDUNCING
BEDAMNING	BEDEL	BEDLAMISM	BEDROP	BEDUNG
BEDAMNS	BEDELL	BEDLAMITE	BEDROPPED	BEDUNGED
BEDARKEN	BEDELLS	BEDLAMP	BEDROPS	BEDUNGING
BEDARKENS	BEDELS	BEDLAMPS	BEDROPT	BEDUNGS
BEDASH	BEDELSHIP	BEDLAMS	BEDRUG	BEDUST
BEDASHED	BEDEMAN	BEDLESS	BEDRUGGED	BEDUSTED
BEDASHES	BEDEMEN	BEDLIKE	BEDRUGS	BEDUSTING
BEDASHING	BEDERAL	BEDMAKER	BEDS	BEDUSTS
BEDAUB	BEDERALS	BEDMAKERS	BEDSHEET	BEDWARD
BEDAUBED	BEDES	BEDMATE	BEDSHEETS	BEDWARDS
BEDAUBING	BEDESMAN	BEDMATES	BEDSIDE	BEDWARF
BEDAUBS	BEDESMEN	BEDOTTED	BEDSIDES	BEDWARFED
BEDAWIN	BEDEVIL	BEDOUIN	BEDSIT	BEDWARFS
BEDAWINS	BEDEVILED	BEDOUINS	BEDSITS	BEDWARMER
BEDAZE	BEDEVILS	BEDPAN	BEDSITTER	BEDWETTER
BEDAZED	BEDEW	BEDPANS	BEDSOCKS	BEDYDE
BEDAZES	BEDEWED	BEDPLATE	BEDSONIA	BEDYE
BEDAZING	BEDEWING	BEDPLATES	BEDSONIAS	BEDYED
BEDAZZLE	BEDEWS	BEDPOST	BEDSORE	BEDYEING
BEDAZZLED	BEDFAST	BEDPOSTS	BEDSORES	BEDYES
BEDAZZLES	BEDFELLOW	BEDQUILT	BEDSPREAD	BEE
BEDBATH	BEDFRAME	BEDQUILTS	BEDSPRING	BEEBEE
BEDBATHS	BEDFRAMES	BEDRAGGLE	BEDSTAND	BEEBEES
BEDBOARD	BEDGOWN	BEDRAIL	BEDSTANDS	BEEBREAD
BEDBOARDS	BEDGOWNS	BEDRAILS	BEDSTEAD	BEEBREADS
BEDBUG	BEDHEAD	BEDRAL	BEDSTEADS	BEECH
BEDBUGS	BEDHEADS	BEDRALS	BEDSTRAW	BEECHEN
BEDCHAIR	BEDIAPER	BEDRAPE	BEDSTRAWS	BEECHES
BEDCHAIRS	BEDIAPERS	BEDRAPED	BEDTICK	BEECHIER
BEDCOVER	BEDIDE	BEDRAPES	BEDTICKS	BEECHIEST
BEDCOVERS	BEDIGHT	BEDRAPING	BEDTIME	BEECHMAST
BEDDABLE	BEDIGHTED	BEDRENCH	BEDTIMES	BEECHNUT
BEDDED	BEDIGHTS	BEDRID	BEDU	BEECHNUTS

B

BEECHWOOD	BEERAGES	BEFFANAS	BEFRIENDS	BEGIFTS
BEECHY	BEERHALL	BEFINGER	BEFRINGE	BEGILD
BEEDI	BEERHALLS	BEFINGERS	BEFRINGED	BEGILDED
BEEDIE	BEERIER	BEFINNED	BEFRINGES	BEGILDING
BEEDIES	BEERIEST	BEFIT	BEFUDDLE	BEGILDS
BEEF	BEERILY	BEFITS	BEFUDDLED	BEGILT
BEEFALO	BEERINESS	BEFITTED	BEFUDDLES	BEGIN
BEEFALOES	BEERS	BEFITTING	BEG	BEGINNE
BEEFALOS	BEERY	BEFLAG	BEGAD	BEGINNER
BEEFCAKE	BEES	BEFLAGGED	BEGALL	BEGINNERS
BEEFCAKES	BEESOME	BEFLAGS	BEGALLED	BEGINNES
BEEFEATER	BEESTING	BEFLEA	BEGALLING	BEGINNING
BEEFED	BEESTINGS	BEFLEAED	BEGALLS	BEGINS
BEEFIER	BEESTUNG	BEFLEAING	BEGAN	BEGIRD
BEEFIEST	BEESWAX	BEFLEAS	BEGAR	BEGIRDED
BEEFILY	BEESWAXED	BEFLECK	BEGARS	BEGIRDING
BEEFINESS	BEESWAXES	BEFLECKED	BEGAT	BEGIRDLE
BEEFING	BEESWING	BEFLECKS	BEGAZE	BEGIRDLED
BEEFLESS	BEESWINGS	BEFLOWER	BEGAZED	BEGIRDLES
BEEFS	BEET	BEFLOWERS	BEGAZES	BEGIRDS
BEEFSTEAK	BEETED	BEFLUM	BEGAZING	BEGIRT
BEEFWOOD	BEETFLIES	BEFLUMMED	BEGEM	BEGLAD
BEEFWOODS	BEETFLY	BEFLUMS	BEGEMMED	BEGLADDED
BEEFY	BEETING	BEFOAM	BEGEMMING	BEGLADS
BEEGAH	BEETLE	BEFOAMED	BEGEMS	BEGLAMOR
BEEGAHS	BEETLED	BEFOAMING	BEGET	BEGLAMORS
BEEHIVE	BEETLER	BEFOAMS	BEGETS	BEGLAMOUR
BEEHIVES	BEETLERS	BEFOG	BEGETTER	BEGLERBEG
BEEKEEPER	BEETLES	BEFOGGED	BEGETTERS	BEGLOOM
BEELIKE	BEETLING	BEFOGGING	BEGETTING	BEGLOOMED
BEELINE	BEETROOT	BEFOGS	BEGGAR	BEGLOOMS
BEELINED	BEETROOTS	BEFOOL	BEGGARDOM	BEGNAW
BEELINES	BEETS	BEFOOLED	BEGGARED	BEGNAWED
BEELINING	BEEVES	BEFOOLING	BEGGARIES	BEGNAWING
BEEN	BEEYARD	BEFOOLS	BEGGARING	BEGNAWS
BEENAH	BEEYARDS	BEFORE	BEGGARLY	BEGO
BEENAHS	BEEZER	BEFORTUNE	BEGGARS	BEGOES
BEENTO	BEEZERS	BEFOUL	BEGGARY	BEGOGGLED
BEENTOS	BEFALL	BEFOULED	BEGGED	BEGOING
BEEP	BEFALLEN	BEFOULER	BEGGING	BEGONE
BEEPED	BEFALLING	BEFOULERS	BEGGINGLY	BEGONIA
BEEPER	BEFALLS	BEFOULING	BEGGINGS	BEGONIAS
BEEPERS	BEFANA	BEFOULS	BEGHARD	BEGORAH
BEEPING	BEFANAS	BEFRET	BEGHARDS	BEGORED
BEEPS	BEFELD	BEFRETS	BEGIFT	BEGORRA
BEER	BEFELL	BEFRETTED	BEGIFTED	BEGORRAH
BEERAGE	BEFFANA	BEFRIEND	BEGIFTING	BEGOT

BEGOTTEN	BEHAVES	BEIGE	BEKNAVING	BELCHES
BEGRIM	BEHAVING	BEIGEL	BEKNIGHT	BELCHING
BEGRIME	BEHAVIOR	BEIGELS	BEKNIGHTS	BELDAM
BEGRIMED	BEHAVIORS	BEIGES	BEKNOT	BELDAME
BEGRIMES	BEHAVIOUR	BEIGIER	BEKNOTS	BELDAMES
BEGRIMING	BEHEAD	BEIGIEST	BEKNOTTED	BELDAMS
BEGRIMMED	BEHEADAL	BEIGNE	BEKNOWN	BELEAGUER
BEGRIMS	BEHEADALS	BEIGNES	BEL	BELEAP
BEGROAN	BEHEADED	BEIGNET	BELABOR	BELEAPED
BEGROANED	BEHEADER	BEIGNETS	BELABORED	BELEAPING
BEGROANS	BEHEADERS	BEIGY	BELABORS	BELEAPS
BEGRUDGE	BEHEADING	BEIN	BELABOUR	BELEAPT
BEGRUDGED	BEHEADS	BEING	BELABOURS	BELEE
BEGRUDGER	BEHELD	BEINGLESS	BELACE	BELEED
BEGRUDGES	BEHEMOTH	BEINGNESS	BELACED	BELEEING
BEGS	BEHEMOTHS	BEINGS	BELACES	BELEES
BEGUILE	BEHEST	BEINKED	BELACING	BELEMNITE
BEGUILED	BEHESTS	BEINNESS	BELADIED	BELEMNOID
BEGUILER	BEHIGHT	BEJABBERS	BELADIES	BELFRIED
BEGUILERS	BEHIGHTS	BEJABERS	BELADY	BELFRIES
BEGUILES	BEHIND	BEJADE	BELADYING	BELFRY
BEGUILING	BEHINDS	BEJADED	BELAH	BELGA
BEGUIN	BEHOLD	BEJADES	BELAHS	BELGARD
BEGUINAGE	BEHOLDEN	BEJADING	BELAMIES	BELGARDS
BEGUINE	BEHOLDER	BEJANT	BELAMOURE	BELGAS
BEGUINES	BEHOLDERS	BEJANTS	BELAMY	BELIE
BEGUINS	BEHOLDING	BEJEEBERS	BELAR	BELIED
BEGULF	BEHOLDS	BEJEEZUS	BELARS	BELIEF
BEGULFED	BEHOOF	BEJESUIT	BELATE	BELIEFS
BEGULFING	BEHOOFS	BEJESUITS	BELATED	BELIER
BEGULFS	BEHOOVE	BEJESUS	BELATEDLY	BELIERS
BEGUM	BEHOOVED	BEJESUSES	BELATES	BELIES
BEGUMS	BEHOOVES	BEJEWEL	BELATING	BELIEVE
BEGUN	BEHOOVING	BEJEWELED	BELAUD	BELIEVED
BEGUNK	BEHOTE	BEJEWELS	BELAUDED	BELIEVER
BEGUNKED	BEHOTES	BEJUMBLE	BELAUDING	BELIEVERS
BEGUNKING	BEHOTING	BEJUMBLED	BELAUDS	BELIEVES
BEGUNKS	BEHOVE	BEJUMBLES	BELAY	BELIEVING
BEHALF	BEHOVED	BEKAH	BELAYED	BELIKE
BEHALVES	BEHOVEFUL	BEKAHS	BELAYER	BELIQUOR
BEHAPPEN	BEHOVELY	BEKISS	BELAYERS	BELIQUORS
BEHAPPENS	BEHOVES	BEKISSED	BELAYING	BELITTLE
BEHATTED	BEHOVING	BEKISSES	BELAYS	BELITTLED
BEHAVE	BEHOWL	BEKISSING	BELCH	BELITTLER
BEHAVED	BEHOWLED	BEKNAVE	BELCHED	BELITTLES
BEHAVER	BEHOWLING	BEKNAVED	BELCHER	BELIVE
BEHAVERS	BEHOWLS	BEKNAVES	BELCHERS	BELL

BELLBIND	BELOMANCY	BEMAUL	BEMOIL	BENCHY
BELLBINDS	BELON	BEMAULED	BEMOILED	BEND
BELLBIRD	BELONG	BEMAULING	BEMOILING	BENDABLE
BELLBIRDS	BELONGED	BEMAULS	BEMOILS	BENDAY
BELLBOY	BELONGER	BEMAZED	BEMONSTER	BENDAYED
BELLBOYS	BELONGERS	BEMBEX	BEMOUTH	BENDAYING
BELLCOTE	BELONGING	BEMBEXES	BEMOUTHED	BENDAYS
BELLCOTES	BELONGS	BEMBIX	BEMOUTHS	BENDED
BELLE	BELONS	BEMBIXES	BEMUD	BENDEE
BELLED	BELOVE	BEMEAN	BEMUDDED	BENDEES
BELLEEK	BELOVED	BEMEANED	BEMUDDING	BENDER
BELLEEKS	BELOVEDS	BEMEANING	BEMUDDLE	BENDERS
BELLES	BELOVES	BEMEANS	BEMUDDLED	BENDIER
BELLETER	BELOVING	BEMEANT	BEMUDDLES	BENDIEST
BELLETERS	BELOW	BEMEDAL	BEMUDS	BENDING
BELLHOP	BELOWS	BEMEDALED	BEMUFFLE	BENDINGLY
BELLHOPS	BELS	BEMEDALS	BEMUFFLED	BENDINGS
BELLIBONE	BELT	BEMETE	BEMUFFLES	BENDLET
BELLICOSE	BELTED	BEMETED	BEMURMUR	BENDLETS
BELLIED	BELTER	BEMETES	BEMURMURS	BENDS
BELLIES	BELTERS	BEMETING	BEMUSE	BENDWAYS
BELLING	BELTING	BEMINGLE	BEMUSED	BENDWISE
BELLINGS	BELTINGS	BEMINGLED	BEMUSEDLY	BENDY
BELLMAN	BELTLESS	BEMINGLES	BEMUSES	BENDYS
BELLMEN	BELTLINE	BEMIRE	BEMUSING	BENE
BELLOCK	BELTLINES	BEMIRED	BEMUZZLE	BENEATH
BELLOCKED	BELTMAN	BEMIRES	BEMUZZLED	BENEDICK
BELLOCKS	BELTMEN	BEMIRING	BEMUZZLES	BENEDICKS
BELLOW	BELTS	BEMIST	BEN	BENEDICT
BELLOWED	BELTWAY	BEMISTED	BENADRYL	BENEDICTS
BELLOWER	BELTWAYS	BEMISTING	BENADRYLS	BENEDIGHT
BELLOWERS	BELUGA	BEMISTS	BENAME	BENEFACT
BELLOWING	BELUGAS	BEMIX	BENAMED	BENEFACTS
BELLOWS	BELVEDERE	BEMIXED	BENAMES	BENEFIC
BELLPULL	BELYING	BEMIXES	BENAMING	BENEFICE
BELLPULLS	BEMA	BEMIXING	BENCH	BENEFICED
BELLS	BEMAD	BEMIXT	BENCHED	BENEFICES
BELLWORT	BEMADAM	BEMOAN	BENCHER	BENEFIT
BELLWORTS	BEMADAMED	BEMOANED	BENCHERS	BENEFITED
BELLY	BEMADAMS	BEMOANER	BENCHES	BENEFITER
BELLYACHE	BEMADDED	BEMOANERS	BENCHIER	BENEFITS
BELLYBAND	BEMADDEN	BEMOANING	BENCHIEST	BENEMPT
BELLYFUL	BEMADDENS	BEMOANS	BENCHING	BENEMPTED
BELLYFULS	BEMADDING	BEMOCK	BENCHLAND	BENES
BELLYING	BEMADS	BEMOCKED	BENCHLESS	BENET
BELLYINGS	BEMAS	BEMOCKING	BENCHMARK	BENETS
BELLYLIKE	BEMATA	BEMOCKS	BENCHTOP	BENETTED

BENETTING	BENTHOSES	BEPATCHED	BERASCAL	BERGENIA
BENGA	BENTIER	BEPATS	BERASCALS	BERGENIAS
BENGALINE	BENTIEST	BEPATTED	BERATE	BERGENS
BENGAS	BENTO	BEPATTING	BERATED	BERGERE
BENI	BENTONITE	BEPEARL	BERATES	BERGERES
BENIGHT	BENTOS	BEPEARLED	BERATING	BERGFALL
BENIGHTED	BENTS	BEPEARLS	BERAY	BERGFALLS
BENIGHTEN	BENTWOOD	BEPELT	BERAYED	BERGHAAN
BENIGHTER	BENTWOODS	BEPELTED	BERAYING	BERGHAANS
BENIGHTS	BENTY	BEPELTING	BERAYS	BERGMEHL
BENIGN	BENUMB	BEPELTS	BERBERE	BERGMEHLS
BENIGNANT	BENUMBED	BEPEPPER	BERBERES	BERGOMASK
BENIGNER	BENUMBING	BEPEPPERS	BERBERIN	BERGS
BENIGNEST	BENUMBS	BEPESTER	BERBERINE	BERGYLT
BENIGNITY	BENZAL	BEPESTERS	BERBERINS	BERGYLTS
BENIGNLY	BENZALS	BEPIMPLE	BERBERIS	BERHYME
BENIS	BENZENE	BEPIMPLED	BERBICE	BERHYMED
BENISEED	BENZENES	BEPIMPLES	BERCEAU	BERHYMES
BENISEEDS	BENZENOID	BEPITIED	BERCEAUX	BERHYMING
BENISON	BENZIDIN	BEPITIES	BERCEUSE	BERIBERI
BENISONS	BENZIDINE	BEPITY	BERCEUSES	BERIBERIS
BENITIER	BENZIDINS	BEPITYING	BERDACHE	BERIMBAU
BENITIERS	BENZIL	BEPLASTER	BERDACHES	BERIMBAUS
BENJ	BENZILS	BEPLUMED	BERDASH	BERIME
BENJAMIN	BENZIN	BEPOMMEL	BERDASHES	BERIMED
BENJAMINS	BENZINE	BEPOMMELS	BERE	BERIMES
BENJES	BENZINES	BEPOWDER	BEREAVE	BERIMING
BENNE	BENZINS	BEPOWDERS	BEREAVED	BERINGED
BENNES	BENZOATE	BEPRAISE	BEREAVEN	BERK
BENNET	BENZOATES	BEPRAISED	BEREAVER	BERKELIUM
BENNETS	BENZOIC	BEPRAISES	BEREAVERS	BERKO
BENNI	BENZOIN	BEPROSE	BEREAVES	BERKS
BENNIES	BENZOINS	BEPROSED	BEREAVING	BERLEY
BENNIS	BENZOL	BEPROSES	BEREFT	BERLEYED
BENNY	BENZOLE	BEPROSING	BERES	BERLEYING
BENOMYL	BENZOLES	BEPUFF	BERET	BERLEYS
BENOMYLS	BENZOLINE	BEPUFFED	BERETS	BERLIN
BENS	BENZOLS	BEPUFFING	BERETTA	BERLINE
BENT	BENZOYL	BEPUFFS	BERETTAS	BERLINES
BENTGRASS	BENZOYLS	BEQUEATH	BERG	BERLINS
BENTHAL	BENZYL	BEQUEATHS	BERGAMA	BERM
BENTHIC	BENZYLIC	BEQUEST	BERGAMAS	BERME
BENTHOAL	BENZYLS	BEQUESTS	BERGAMASK	BERMED
BENTHON	BEPAINT	BERAKE	BERGAMOT	BERMES
BENTHONIC	BEPAINTED	BERAKED	BERGAMOTS	BERMING
BENTHONS	BEPAINTS	BERAKES	BERGANDER	BERMS
BENTHOS	BEPAT	BERAKING	BERGEN	BERMUDAS

BERNICLE	BESANG	BESHOUT	BESMOKE	BESPECKLE
BERNICLES	BESAT	BESHOUTED	BESMOKED	BESPED
BEROB	BESAW	BESHOUTS	BESMOKES	BESPEED
BEROBBED	BESCATTER	BESHREW	BESMOKING	BESPEEDS
BEROBBING	BESCORCH	BESHREWED	BESMOOTH	BESPICE
BEROBED	BESCOUR	BESHREWS	BESMOOTHS	BESPICED
BEROBS	BESCOURED	BESHROUD	BESMUDGE	BESPICES
BEROUGED	BESCOURS	BESHROUDS	BESMUDGED	BESPICING
BERRET	BESCRAWL	BESIDE	BESMUDGES	BESPIT
BERRETS	BESCRAWLS	BESIDES	BESMUT	BESPITS
BERRETTA	BESCREEN	BESIEGE	BESMUTCH	BESPOKE
BERRETTAS	BESCREENS	BESIEGED	BESMUTS	BESPOKEN
BERRIED	BESEE	BESIEGER	BESMUTTED	BESPORT
BERRIES	BESEECH	BESIEGERS	BESNOW	BESPORTED
BERRIGAN	BESEECHED	BESIEGES	BESNOWED	BESPORTS
BERRIGANS	BESEECHER	BESIEGING	BESNOWING	BESPOT
BERRY	BESEECHES	BESIGH	BESNOWS	BESPOTS
BERRYING	BESEEING	BESIGHED	BESOGNIO	BESPOTTED
BERRYINGS	BESEEKE	BESIGHING	BESOGNIOS	BESPOUSE
BERRYLESS	BESEEKES	BESIGHS	BESOIN	BESPOUSED
BERRYLIKE	BESEEKING	BESING	BESOINS	BESPOUSES
BERSEEM	BESEEM	BESINGING	BESOM	BESPOUT
BERSEEMS	BESEEMED	BESINGS	BESOMED	BESPOUTED
BERSERK	BESEEMING	BESIT	BESOMING	BESPOUTS
BERSERKER	BESEEMLY	BESITS	BESOMS	BESPREAD
BERSERKLY	BESEEMS	BESITTING	BESONIAN	BESPREADS
BERSERKS	BESEEN	BESLAVE	BESONIANS	BESPRENT
BERTH	BESEES	BESLAVED	BESOOTHE	BEST
BERTHA	BESES	BESLAVER	BESOOTHED	BESTAD
BERTHAGE	BESET	BESLAVERS	BESOOTHES	BESTADDE
BERTHAGES	BESETMENT	BESLAVES	BESORT	BESTAIN
BERTHAS	BESETS	BESLAVING	BESORTED	BESTAINED
BERTHE	BESETTER	BESLIME	BESORTING	BESTAINS
BERTHED	BESETTERS	BESLIMED	BESORTS	BESTAR
BERTHES	BESETTING	BESLIMES	BESOT	BESTARRED
BERTHING	BESHADOW	BESLIMING	BESOTS	BESTARS
BERTHS	BESHADOWS	BESLOBBER	BESOTTED	BESTEAD
BERYL	BESHAME	BESLUBBER	BESOTTING	BESTEADED
BERYLINE	BESHAMED	BESMEAR	BESOUGHT	BESTEADS
BERYLLIA	BESHAMES	BESMEARED	BESOULED	BESTED
BERYLLIAS	BESHAMING	BESMEARER	BESPAKE	BESTI
BERYLLIUM	BESHINE	BESMEARS	BESPANGLE	BESTIAL
BERYLS	BESHINES	BESMILE	BESPAT	BESTIALLY
BES	BESHINING	BESMILED	BESPATE	BESTIALS
BESAINT	BESHIVER	BESMILES	BESPATTER	BESTIARY
BESAINTED	BESHIVERS	BESMILING	BESPEAK	BESTICK
BESAINTS	BESHONE	BESMIRCH	BESPEAKS	BESTICKS

BESTILL	BETAINE	BETHUMBS	BETREAD	BEVER
BESTILLED	BETAINES	BETHUMP	BETREADS	BEVERAGE
BESTILLS	BETAKE	BETHUMPED	BETRIM	BEVERAGES
BESTING	BETAKEN	BETHUMPS	BETRIMMED	BEVERS
BESTIR	BETAKES	BETHWACK	BETRIMS	BEVIES
BESTIRRED	BETAKING	BETHWACKS	BETROD	BEVOMIT
BESTIRS	BETAS	BETID	BETRODDEN	BEVOMITED
BESTIS	BETATOPIC	BETIDE	BETROTH	BEVOMITS
BESTORM	BETATRON	BETIDED	BETROTHAL	BEVOR
BESTORMED	BETATRONS	BETIDES	BETROTHED	BEVORS
BESTORMS	BETATTER	BETIDING	BETROTHS	BEVUE
BESTOW	BETATTERS	BETIGHT	BETS	BEVUES
BESTOWAL	BETAXED	BETIME	BETTA	BEVVIED
BESTOWALS	BETCHA	BETIMED	BETTAS	BEVVIES
BESTOWED	BETE	BETIMES	BETTED	BEVVY
BESTOWER	BETED	BETIMING	BETTER	BEVVYING
BESTOWERS	BETEEM	BETING	BETTERED	BEVY
BESTOWING	BETEEME	BETISE	BETTERING	BEWAIL
BESTOWS	BETEEMED	BETISES	BETTERS	BEWAILED
BESTREAK	BETEEMES	BETITLE	BETTIES	BEWAILER
BESTREAKS	BETEEMING	BETITLED	BETTING	BEWAILERS
BESTREW	BETEEMS	BETITLES	BETTINGS	BEWAILING
BESTREWED	BETEL	BETITLING	BETTONG	BEWAILS
BESTREWN	BETELNUT	BETOIL	BETTONGS	BEWARE
BESTREWS	BETELNUTS	BETOILED	BETTOR	BEWARED
BESTRID	BETELS	BETOILING	BETTORS	BEWARES
BESTRIDE	BETES	BETOILS	BETTY	BEWARING
BESTRIDES	BETH	BETOKEN	BETUMBLED	BEWEARIED
BESTRODE	BETHANK	BETOKENED	BETWEEN	BEWEARIES
BESTROW	BETHANKED	BETOKENS	BETWEENS	BEWEARY
BESTROWED	BETHANKIT	BETON	BETWIXT	BEWEEP
BESTROWN	BETHANKS	BETONIES	BEUNCLED	BEWEEPING
BESTROWS	BETHEL	BETONS	BEURRE	BEWEEPS
BESTS	BETHELS	BETONY	BEURRES	BEWENT
BESTUCK	BETHESDA	BETOOK	BEVATRON	BEWEPT
BESTUD	BETHESDAS	BETOSS	BEVATRONS	BEWET
BESTUDDED	BETHINK	BETOSSED	BEVEL	BEWETS
BESTUDS	BETHINKS	BETOSSES	BEVELED	BEWETTED
BESUITED	BETHORN	BETOSSING	BEVELER	BEWETTING
BESUNG	BETHORNED	BETRAY	BEVELERS	BEWHORE
BESWARM	BETHORNS	BETRAYAL	BEVELING	BEWHORED
BESWARMED	BETHOUGHT	BETRAYALS	BEVELLED	BEWHORES
BESWARMS	BETHRALL	BETRAYED	BEVELLER	BEWHORING
BET	BETHRALLS	BETRAYER	BEVELLERS	BEWIG
BETA	BETHS	BETRAYERS	BEVELLING	BEWIGGED
BETACISM	BETHUMB	BETRAYING	BEVELMENT	BEWIGGING
BETACISMS	BETHUMBED	BETRAYS	BEVELS	BEWIGS

BEWILDER	BEZONIAN	BHINDIS	BIAXIALLY	BICHIRS
BEWILDERS	BEZONIANS	BHISHTI	BIB	BICHORD
BEWINGED	BEZZANT	BHISHTIS	BIBACIOUS	BICHROME
BEWITCH	BEZZANTS	BHISTEE	BIBASIC	BICIPITAL
BEWITCHED	BEZZAZZ	BHISTEES	BIBATION	BICKER
BEWITCHER	BEZZAZZES	BHISTI	BIBATIONS	BICKERED
BEWITCHES	BEZZLE	BHISTIE	BIBB	BICKERER
BEWORM	BEZZLED	BHISTIES	BIBBED	BICKERERS
BEWORMED	BEZZLES	BHISTIS	BIBBER	BICKERING
BEWORMING	BEZZLING	BHOONA	BIBBERIES	BICKERS
BEWORMS	BHAGEE	BHOONAS	BIBBERS	BICKIE
BEWORRIED	BHAGEES	BHOOT	BIBBERY	BICKIES
BEWORRIES	BHAI	BHOOTS	BIBBING	BICOASTAL
BEWORRY	BHAIS	BHUNA	BIBBLE	BICOLOR
BEWRAP	BHAJAN	BHUNAS	BIBBLES	BICOLORED
BEWRAPPED	BHAJANS	BHUT	BIBBS	BICOLORS
BEWRAPS	BHAJEE	BHUTS	BIBCOCK	BICOLOUR
BEWRAPT	BHAJEES	BI	BIBCOCKS	BICOLOURS
BEWRAY	BHAJI	BIACETYL	BIBELOT	BICONCAVE
BEWRAYED	BHAJIA	BIACETYLS	BIBELOTS	BICONVEX
BEWRAYER	BHAJIS	BIACH	BIBFUL	BICORN
BEWRAYERS	BHAKTA	BIACHES	BIBFULS	BICORNATE
BEWRAYING	BHAKTAS	BIALI	BIBLE	BICORNE
BEWRAYS	BHAKTI	BIALIES	BIBLES	BICORNES
BEY	BHAKTIS	BIALIS	BIBLESS	BICORNS
BEYLIC	BHANG	BIALY	BIBLICAL	BICRON
BEYLICS	BHANGRA	BIALYS	BIBLICISM	BICRONS
BEYLIK	BHANGRAS	BIANNUAL	BIBLICIST	BICUSPID
BEYLIKS	BHANGS	BIANNUALS	BIBLIKE	BICUSPIDS
BEYOND	BHARAL	BIAS	BIBLIOTIC	BICYCLE
BEYONDS	BHARALS	BIASED	BIBLIST	BICYCLED
BEYS	BHAT	BIASEDLY	BIBLISTS	BICYCLER
BEZ	BHAVAN	BIASES	BIBS	BICYCLERS
BEZANT	BHAVANS	BIASING	BIBULOUS	BICYCLES
BEZANTS	BHAWAN	BIASINGS	BICAMERAL	BICYCLIC
BEZAZZ	BHAWANS	BIASNESS	BICARB	BICYCLING
BEZAZZES	BHEESTIE	BIASSED	BICARBS	BICYCLIST
BEZEL	BHEESTIES	BIASSEDLY	BICAUDAL	BID
BEZELS	BHEESTY	BIASSES	BICCIES	BIDARKA
BEZES	BHEL	BIASSING	BICCY	BIDARKAS
BEZIL	BHELPURI	BIATCH	BICE	BIDARKEE
BEZILS	BHELPURIS	BIATCHES	BICENTRIC	BIDARKEES
BEZIQUE	BHELS	BIATHLETE	BICEP	BIDDABLE
BEZIQUES	BHIKHU	BIATHLON	BICEPS	BIDDABLY
BEZOAR	BHIKHUS	BIATHLONS	BICEPSES	BIDDEN
BEZOARDIC	BHIKKHUNI	BIAXAL	BICES	BIDDER
BEZOARS	BHINDI	BIAXIAL	BICHIR	BIDDERS

B

BIDDIES	BIFFER	BIGENERS	BIGOTRIES	BILBOAS
BIDDING	BIFFERS	BIGEYE	BIGOTRY	BILBOES
BIDDINGS	BIFFIES	BIGEYES	BIGOTS	BILBOS
BIDDY	BIFFIN	BIGFEET	BIGS	BILBY
BIDE	BIFFING	BIGFOOT	BIGSTICK	BILE
BIDED	BIFFINS	BIGFOOTED	BIGTIME	BILECTION
BIDENT	BIFFO	BIGFOOTS	BIGUANIDE	BILED
BIDENTAL	BIFFOS	BIGG	BIGWIG	BILES
BIDENTALS	BIFFS	BIGGED	BIGWIGS	BILESTONE
BIDENTATE	BIFFY	BIGGER	BIHOURLY	BILEVEL
BIDENTS	BIFID	BIGGEST	BIJECTION	BILEVELS
BIDER	BIFIDITY	BIGGETY	BIJECTIVE	BILGE
BIDERS	BIFIDLY	BIGGIE	BIJOU	BILGED
BIDES	BIFILAR	BIGGIES	BIJOUS	BILGES
BIDET	BIFILARLY	BIGGIN	BIJOUX	BILGIER
BIDETS	BIFLEX	BIGGING	BIJUGATE	BILGIEST
BIDI	BIFOCAL	BIGGINGS	BIJUGOUS	BILGING
BIDING	BIFOCALED	BIGGINS	BIJWONER	BILGY
BIDINGS	BIFOCALS	BIGGISH	BIJWONERS	BILHARZIA
BIDIS	BIFOLD	BIGGITY	BIKE	BILIAN
BIDON	BIFOLIATE	BIGGON	BIKED	BILIANS
BIDONS	BIFORATE	BIGGONS	BIKER	BILIARIES
BIDS	BIFORKED	BIGGS	BIKERS	BILIARY
BIELD	BIFORM	BIGGY	BIKES	BILIMBI
BIELDED	BIFORMED	BIGHA	BIKEWAY	BILIMBING
BIELDIER	BIFTAH	BIGHAS	BIKEWAYS	BILIMBIS
BIELDIEST	BIFTAHS	BIGHEAD	BIKIE	BILINEAR
BIELDING	BIFTER	BIGHEADED	BIKIES	BILING
BIELDS	BIFTERS	BIGHEADS	BIKING	BILINGUAL
BIELDY	BIFURCATE	BIGHORN	BIKINGS	BILIOUS
BIEN	BIG	BIGHORNS	BIKINI	BILIOUSLY
BIENNALE	BIGA	BIGHT	BIKINIED	BILIRUBIN
BIENNALES	BIGAE	BIGHTED	BIKINIS	BILITERAL
BIENNIA	BIGAMIES	BIGHTING	BIKKIE	BILK
BIENNIAL	BIGAMIST	BIGHTS	BIKKIES	BILKED
BIENNIALS	BIGAMISTS	BIGLY	BILABIAL	BILKER
BIENNIUM	BIGAMOUS	BIGMOUTH	BILABIALS	BILKERS
BIENNIUMS	BIGAMY	BIGMOUTHS	BILABIATE	BILKING
BIER	BIGARADE	BIGNESS	BILANDER	BILKS
BIERS	BIGARADES	BIGNESSES	BILANDERS	BILL
BIESTINGS	BIGAROON	BIGNONIA	BILATERAL	BILLABLE
BIFACE	BIGAROONS	BIGNONIAS	BILAYER	BILLABONG
BIFACES	BIGARREAU	BIGOS	BILAYERS	BILLBOARD
BIFACIAL	BIGEMINAL	BIGOSES	BILBERRY	BILLBOOK
BIFARIOUS	BIGEMINY	BIGOT	BILBIES	BILLBOOKS
BIFF	BIGENER	BIGOTED	BILBO	BILLBUG
BIFFED	BIGENERIC	BIGOTEDLY	BILBOA	BILLBUGS

BILLED	BILLYOS	BINDABLE	BINKS	BIOFILM
BILLER	BILOBAR	BINDER	BINMAN	BIOFILMS
BILLERS	BILOBATE	BINDERIES	BINMEN	BIOFOULER
BILLET	BILOBATED	BINDERS	BINNACLE	BIOFUEL
BILLETED	BILOBED	BINDERY	BINNACLES	BIOFUELED
BILLETEE	BILOBULAR	BINDHI	BINNED	BIOFUELS
BILLETEES	BILOCULAR	BINDHIS	BINNING	BIOG
BILLETER	BILSTED	BINDI	BINOCLE	BIOGAS
BILLETERS	BILSTEDS	BINDING	BINOCLES	BIOGASES
BILLETING	BILTONG	BINDINGLY	BINOCS	BIOGASSES
BILLETS	BILTONGS	BINDINGS	BINOCULAR	BIOGEN
BILLFISH	BIMA	BINDIS	BINOMIAL	BIOGENIC
BILLFOLD	BIMAH	BINDLE	BINOMIALS	BIOGENIES
BILLFOLDS	BIMAHS	BINDLES	BINOMINAL	BIOGENOUS
BILLHEAD	BIMANAL	BINDS	BINOVULAR	BIOGENS
BILLHEADS	BIMANOUS	BINDWEED	BINS	BIOGENY
BILLHOOK	BIMANUAL	BINDWEEDS	BINT	BIOGRAPH
BILLHOOKS	BIMAS	BINE	BINTS	BIOGRAPHS
BILLIARD	BIMBASHI	BINER	BINTURONG	BIOGRAPHY
BILLIARDS	BIMBASHIS	BINERS	BINUCLEAR	BIOGS
BILLIE	BIMBETTE	BINERVATE	BIO	BIOHAZARD
BILLIES	BIMBETTES	BINES	BIOACTIVE	BIOHERM
BILLING	BIMBLE	BING	BIOASSAY	BIOHERMS
BILLINGS	BIMBO	BINGE	BIOASSAYS	BIOLOGIC
BILLION	BIMBOES	BINGED	BIOBANK	BIOLOGICS
BILLIONS	BIMBOS	BINGEING	BIOBANKS	BIOLOGIES
BILLIONTH	BIMENSAL	BINGER	BIOBLAST	BIOLOGISM
BILLMAN	BIMESTER	BINGERS	BIOBLASTS	BIOLOGIST
BILLMEN	BIMESTERS	BINGES	BIOCENOSE	BIOLOGY
BILLON	BIMETAL	BINGHI	BIOCHEMIC	BIOLYSES
BILLONS	BIMETALS	BINGHIS	BIOCHIP	BIOLYSIS
BILLOW	BIMETHYL	BINGIES	BIOCHIPS	BIOLYTIC
BILLOWED	BIMETHYLS	BINGING	BIOCIDAL	BIOMARKER
BILLOWIER	BIMODAL	BINGLE	BIOCIDE	BIOMASS
BILLOWING	BIMONTHLY	BINGLED	BIOCIDES	BIOMASSES
BILLOWS	BIMORPH	BINGLES	BIOCLEAN	BIOME
BILLOWY	BIMORPHS	BINGLING	BIOCYCLE	BIOMES
BILLS	BIN	BINGO	BIOCYCLES	BIOMETER
BILLY	BINAL	BINGOES	BIODATA	BIOMETERS
BILLYBOY	BINARIES	BINGOS	BIODIESEL	BIOMETRIC
BILLYBOYS	BINARISM	BINGS	BIODOT	BIOMETRY
BILLYCAN	BINARISMS	BINGY	BIODOTS	BIOMINING
BILLYCANS	BINARY	BINIOU	BIOENERGY	BIOMORPH
BILLYCOCK	BINATE	BINIOUS	BIOETHIC	BIOMORPHS
BILLYO	BINATELY	BINIT	BIOETHICS	BIONIC
BILLYOH	BINAURAL	BINITS	BIOFACT	BIONICS
BILLYOHS	BIND	BINK	BIOFACTS	BIONOMIC

BIONOMICS	BIOTIC	BIRAMOSE	BIRDSHOT	BIRSIEST
BIONOMIES	BIOTICAL	BIRAMOUS	BIRDSHOTS	BIRSLE
BIONOMIST	BIOTICS	BIRCH	BIRDSONG	BIRSLED
BIONOMY	BIOTIN	BIRCHBARK	BIRDSONGS	BIRSLES
BIONT	BIOTINS	BIRCHED	BIRDWATCH	BIRSLING
BIONTIC	BIOTITE	BIRCHEN	BIRDWING	BIRSY
BIONTS	BIOTITES	BIRCHES	BIRDWINGS	BIRTH
BIOPARENT	BIOTITIC	BIRCHING	BIREME	BIRTHDAY
BIOPHILIA	BIOTOPE	BIRCHIR	BIREMES	BIRTHDAYS
BIOPHOR	BIOTOPES	BIRCHIRS	BIRETTA	BIRTHDOM
BIOPHORE	BIOTOXIN	BIRD	BIRETTAS	BIRTHDOMS
BIOPHORES	BIOTOXINS	BIRDBATH	BIRIANI	BIRTHED
BIOPHORS	BIOTRON	BIRDBATHS	BIRIANIS	BIRTHING
BIOPIC	BIOTRONS	BIRDBRAIN	BIRIYANI	BIRTHINGS
BIOPICS	BIOTROPH	BIRDCAGE	BIRIYANIS	BIRTHMARK
BIOPIRACY	BIOTROPHS	BIRDCAGES	BIRK	BIRTHNAME
BIOPIRATE	BIOTURBED	BIRDCALL	BIRKEN	BIRTHRATE
BIOPLASM	BIOTYPE	BIRDCALLS	BIRKIE	BIRTHROOT
BIOPLASMS	BIOTYPES	BIRDDOG	BIRKIER	BIRTHS
BIOPLAST	BIOTYPIC	BIRDDOGS	BIRKIES	BIRTHWORT
BIOPLASTS	BIOVULAR	BIRDED	BIRKIEST	BIRYANI
BIOPSIC	BIOWEAPON	BIRDER	BIRKS	BIRYANIS
BIOPSIED	BIPACK	BIRDERS	BIRL	BIS
BIOPSIES	BIPACKS	BIRDFARM	BIRLE	BISCACHA
BIOPSY	BIPAROUS	BIRDFARMS	BIRLED	BISCACHAS
BIOPSYING	BIPARTED	BIRDFEED	BIRLER	BISCOTTI
BIOPTIC	BIPARTITE	BIRDFEEDS	BIRLERS	BISCOTTO
BIOREGION	BIPARTY	BIRDHOUSE	BIRLES	BISCUIT
BIORHYTHM	BIPED	BIRDIE	BIRLIEMAN	BISCUITS
BIOS	BIPEDAL	BIRDIED	BIRLIEMEN	BISCUITY
BIOSAFETY	BIPEDALLY	BIRDIEING	BIRLING	BISE
BIOSCOPE	BIPEDS	BIRDIES	BIRLINGS	BISECT
BIOSCOPES	BIPHASIC	BIRDING	BIRLINN	BISECTED
BIOSCOPY	BIPHENYL	BIRDINGS	BIRLINNS	BISECTING
BIOSENSOR	BIPHENYLS	BIRDLIFE	BIRLS	BISECTION
BIOSOCIAL	BIPINNATE	BIRDLIKE	BIRO	BISECTOR
BIOSOLID	BIPLANE	BIRDLIME	BIROS	BISECTORS
BIOSOLIDS	BIPLANES	BIRDLIMED	BIRR	BISECTRIX
BIOSPHERE	BIPOD	BIRDLIMES	BIRRED	BISECTS
BIOSTABLE	BIPODS	BIRDMAN	BIRRETTA	BISERIAL
BIOSTATIC	BIPOLAR	BIRDMEN	BIRRETTAS	BISERIATE
BIOSTROME	BIPRISM	BIRDS	BIRRING	BISERRATE
BIOTA	BIPRISMS	BIRDSEED	BIRROTCH	BISES
BIOTAS	BIPYRAMID	BIRDSEEDS	BIRRS	BISEXUAL
BIOTECH	BIRACIAL	BIRDSEYE	BIRSE	BISEXUALS
BIOTECHS	BIRADIAL	BIRDSEYES	BIRSES	BISH
BIOTERROR	BIRADICAL	BIRDSFOOT	BIRSIER	BISHES

BISHOP	BIT	BITTEN	BIVIUM	BLACKBOYS
BISHOPDOM	BITABLE	BITTER	BIVOUAC	BLACKBUCK
BISHOPED	BITCH	BITTERED	BIVOUACKS	BLACKBUTT
BISHOPESS	BITCHED	BITTERER	BIVOUACS	BLACKCAP
BISHOPING	BITCHEN	BITTEREST	BIVVIED	BLACKCAPS
BISHOPRIC	BITCHERY	BITTERING	BIVVIES	BLACKCOCK
BISHOPS	BITCHES	BITTERISH	BIVVY	BLACKDAMP
BISK	BITCHFEST	BITTERLY	BIVVYING	BLACKED
BISKS	BITCHIER	BITTERN	BIWEEKLY	BLACKEN
BISMAR	BITCHIEST	BITTERNS	BIYEARLY	BLACKENED
BISMARS	BITCHILY	BITTERNUT	BIZ	BLACKENER
BISMILLAH	BITCHING	BITTERS	BIZARRE	BLACKENS
BISMUTH	BITCHY	BITTIE	BIZARRELY	BLACKER
BISMUTHAL	BITE	BITTIER	BIZARRES	BLACKEST
BISMUTHIC	BITEABLE	BITTIES	BIZARRO	BLACKFACE
BISMUTHS	BITEPLATE	BITTIEST	BIZARROS	BLACKFIN
BISNAGA	BITER	BITTINESS	BIZAZZ	BLACKFINS
BISNAGAS	BITERS	BITTING	BIZAZZES	BLACKFISH
BISOM	BITES	BITTINGS	BIZCACHA	BLACKFLY
BISOMS	BITESIZE	BITTOCK	BIZCACHAS	BLACKGAME
BISON	BITEWING	BITTOCKS	BIZE	BLACKGUM
BISONS	BITEWINGS	BITTOR	BIZES	BLACKGUMS
BISONTINE	BITING	BITTORS	BIZNAGA	BLACKHEAD
BISPHENOL	BITINGLY	BITTOUR	BIZNAGAS	BLACKING
BISQUE	BITINGS	BITTOURS	BIZONAL	BLACKINGS
BISQUES	BITLESS	BITTS	BIZONE	BLACKISH
BISSON	BITMAP	BITTUR	BIZONES	BLACKJACK
BIST	BITMAPPED	BITTURS	BIZZES	BLACKLAND
BISTABLE	BITMAPS	BITTY	BIZZIES	BLACKLEAD
BISTABLES	BITO	BITUMED	BIZZO	BLACKLEG
BISTATE	BITONAL	BITUMEN	BIZZOS	BLACKLEGS
BISTER	BITOS	BITUMENS	BIZZY	BLACKLIST
BISTERED	BITOU	BIUNIQUE	BLAB	BLACKLY
BISTERS	BITS	BIVALENCE	BLABBED	BLACKMAIL
BISTORT	BITSER	BIVALENCY	BLABBER	BLACKNESS
BISTORTS	BITSERS	BIVALENT	BLABBERED	BLACKOUT
BISTOURY	BITSIER	BIVALENTS	BLABBERS	BLACKOUTS
BISTRE	BITSIEST	BIVALVATE	BLABBING	BLACKPOLL
BISTRED	BITSTOCK	BIVALVE	BLABBINGS	BLACKS
BISTRES	BITSTOCKS	BIVALVED	BLABBY	BLACKTAIL
BISTRO	BITSTREAM	BIVALVES	BLABS	BLACKTOP
BISTROIC	BITSY	BIVARIANT	BLACK	BLACKTOPS
BISTROS	BITT	BIVARIATE	BLACKBALL	BLACKWASH
BISULCATE	BITTACLE	BIVIA	BLACKBAND	BLACKWOOD
BISULFATE	BITTACLES	BIVINYL	BLACKBIRD	BLAD
BISULFIDE	BITTE	BIVINYLS	BLACKBODY	BLADDED
BISULFITE	BITTED	BIVIOUS	BLACKBOY	BLADDER

BLADDERED	BLAMABLE	BLARE	BLAT	BLAZONER
BLADDERS	BLAMABLY	BLARED	BLATANCY	BLAZONERS
BLADDERY	BLAME	BLARES	BLATANT	BLAZONING
BLADDING	BLAMEABLE	BLARING	BLATANTLY	BLAZONRY
BLADE	BLAMEABLY	BLARNEY	BLATE	BLAZONS
BLADED	BLAMED	BLARNEYED	BLATER	BLEACH
BLADELESS	BLAMEFUL	BLARNEYS	BLATEST	BLEACHED
BLADELIKE	BLAMELESS	BLART	BLATHER	BLEACHER
BLADER	BLAMER	BLARTED	BLATHERED	BLEACHERS
BLADERS	BLAMERS	BLARTING	BLATHERER	BLEACHERY
BLADES	BLAMES	BLARTS	BLATHERS	BLEACHES
BLADEWORK	BLAMING	BLASE	BLATS	BLEACHING
BLADIER	BLAMS	BLASH	BLATT	BLEAK
BLADIEST	BLANCH	BLASHES	BLATTANT	BLEAKER
BLADING	BLANCHED	BLASHIER	BLATTED	BLEAKEST
BLADINGS	BLANCHER	BLASHIEST	BLATTER	BLEAKISH
BLADS	BLANCHERS	BLASHY	BLATTERED	BLEAKLY
BLADY	BLANCHES	BLASPHEME	BLATTERS	BLEAKNESS
BLAE	BLANCHING	BLASPHEMY	BLATTING	BLEAKS
BLAEBERRY	BLANCO	BLAST	BLATTS	BLEAKY
BLAER	BLANCOED	BLASTED	BLAUBOK	BLEAR
BLAES	BLANCOING	BLASTEMA	BLAUBOKS	BLEARED
BLAEST	BLANCOS	BLASTEMAL	BLAUD	BLEARER
BLAFF	BLAND	BLASTEMAS	BLAUDED	BLEAREST
BLAFFS	BLANDED	BLASTEMIC	BLAUDING	BLEAREYED
BLAG	BLANDER	BLASTER	BLAUDS	BLEARIER
BLAGGED	BLANDEST	BLASTERS	BLAW	BLEARIEST
BLAGGER	BLANDING	BLASTIE	BLAWED	BLEARILY
BLAGGERS	BLANDISH	BLASTIER	BLAWING	BLEARING
BLAGGING	BLANDLY	BLASTIES	BLAWN	BLEARS
BLAGGINGS	BLANDNESS	BLASTIEST	BLAWORT	BLEARY
BLAGS	BLANDS	BLASTING	BLAWORTS	BLEAT
BLAGUE	BLANK	BLASTINGS	BLAWS	BLEATED
BLAGUER	BLANKED	BLASTMENT	BLAY	BLEATER
BLAGUERS	BLANKER	BLASTOFF	BLAYS	BLEATERS
BLAGUES	BLANKEST	BLASTOFFS	BLAZAR	BLEATING
BLAGUEUR	BLANKET	BLASTOID	BLAZARS	BLEATINGS
BLAGUEURS	BLANKETED	BLASTOIDS	BLAZE	BLEATS
BLAH	BLANKETS	BLASTOMA	BLAZED	BLEB
BLAHED	BLANKETY	BLASTOMAS	BLAZER	BLEBBIER
BLAHING	BLANKING	BLASTOPOR	BLAZERED	BLEBBIEST
BLAHS	BLANKINGS	BLASTS	BLAZERS	BLEBBING
BLAIN	BLANKLY	BLASTULA	BLAZES	BLEBBINGS
BLAINS	BLANKNESS	BLASTULAE	BLAZING	BLEBBY
BLAISE	BLANKS	BLASTULAR	BLAZINGLY	BLEBS
BLAIZE	BLANQUET	BLASTULAS	BLAZON	BLED
BLAM	BLANQUETS	BLASTY	BLAZONED	BLEE

BLEED

BLEED	BLESSEDER	BLINDEST	BLISSED	BLOBBING
BLEEDER	BLESSEDLY	BLINDFISH	BLISSES	BLOBBY
BLEEDERS	BLESSER	BLINDFOLD	BLISSFUL	BLOBS
BLEEDING	BLESSERS	BLINDGUT	BLISSING	BLOC
BLEEDINGS	BLESSES	BLINDGUTS	BLISSLESS	BLOCK
BLEEDS	BLESSING	BLINDING	BLIST	BLOCKABLE
BLEEP	BLESSINGS	BLINDINGS	BLISTER	BLOCKADE
BLEEPED	BLEST	BLINDLESS	BLISTERED	BLOCKADED
BLEEPER	BLET	BLINDLY	BLISTERS	BLOCKADER
BLEEPERS	BLETHER	BLINDNESS	BLISTERY	BLOCKADES
BLEEPING	BLETHERED	BLINDS	BLIT	BLOCKAGE
BLEEPS	BLETHERER	BLINDSIDE	BLITE	BLOCKAGES
BLEES	BLETHERS	BLINDWORM	BLITES	BLOCKBUST
BLELLUM	BLETS	BLING	BLITHE	BLOCKED
BLELLUMS	BLETTED	BLINGER	BLITHEFUL	BLOCKER
BLEMISH	BLETTING	BLINGEST	BLITHELY	BLOCKERS
BLEMISHED	BLEUATRE	BLINGIER	BLITHER	BLOCKHEAD
BLEMISHER	BLEW	BLINGIEST	BLITHERED	BLOCKHOLE
BLEMISHES	BLEWART	BLINGING	BLITHERS	BLOCKIE
BLENCH	BLEWARTS	BLINGLISH	BLITHEST	BLOCKIER
BLENCHED	BLEWITS	BLINGS	BLITS	BLOCKIES
BLENCHER	BLEWITSES	BLINGY	BLITTED	BLOCKIEST
BLENCHERS	BLEY	BLINI	BLITTER	BLOCKING
BLENCHES	BLEYS	BLINIS	BLITTERS	BLOCKINGS
BLENCHING	BLIGHT	BLINK	BLITTING	BLOCKISH
BLEND	BLIGHTED	BLINKARD	BLITZ	BLOCKS
BLENDE	BLIGHTER	BLINKARDS	BLITZED	BLOCKSHIP
BLENDED	BLIGHTERS	BLINKED	BLITZER	BLOCKWORK
BLENDER	BLIGHTIES	BLINKER	BLITZERS	BLOCKY
BLENDERS	BLIGHTING	BLINKERED	BLITZES	BLOCS
BLENDES	BLIGHTS	BLINKERS	BLITZING	BLOG
BLENDING	BLIGHTY	BLINKING	BLIVE	BLOGGED
BLENDINGS	BLIKSEM	BLINKS	BLIZZARD	BLOGGER
BLENDS	BLIMBING	BLINNED	BLIZZARDS	BLOGGERS
BLENNIES	BLIMBINGS	BLINNING	BLIZZARDY	BLOGGING
BLENNIOID	BLIMEY	BLINS	BLOAT	BLOGGINGS
BLENNY	BLIMP	BLINTZ	BLOATED	BLOGRING
BLENT	BLIMPISH	BLINTZE	BLOATER	BLOGRINGS
BLEOMYCIN	BLIMPS	BLINTZES	BLOATERS	BLOGROLL
BLERT	BLIMY	BLINY	BLOATING	BLOGROLLS
BLERTS	BLIN	BLIP	BLOATINGS	BLOGS
BLESBOK	BLIND	BLIPPED	BLOATS	BLOKART
BLESBOKS	BLINDAGE	BLIPPING	BLOATWARE	BLOKARTS
BLESBUCK	BLINDAGES	BLIPS	BLOB	BLOKE
BLESBUCKS	BLINDED	BLIPVERT	BLOBBED	BLOKEDOM
BLESS	BLINDER	BLIPVERTS	BLOBBIER	BLOKEDOMS
BLESSED	BLINDERS	BLISS	BLOBBIEST	BLOKEISH

BLOKES	BLOOK	BLOTTINGS	BLOWJOBS	BLUDGEONS
BLOKEY	BLOOKS	BLOTTO	BLOWLAMP	BLUDGER
BLOKIER	BLOOM	BLOTTY	BLOWLAMPS	BLUDGERS
BLOKIEST	BLOOMED	BLOUBOK	BLOWN	BLUDGES
BLOKISH	BLOOMER	BLOUBOKS	BLOWOFF	BLUDGING
BLONCKET	BLOOMERS	BLOUSE	BLOWOFFS	BLUDIE
BLOND	BLOOMERY	BLOUSED	BLOWOUT	BLUDIER
BLONDE	BLOOMIER	BLOUSES	BLOWOUTS	BLUDIEST
BLONDER	BLOOMIEST	BLOUSIER	BLOWPIPE	BLUDY
BLONDES	BLOOMING	BLOUSIEST	BLOWPIPES	BLUE
BLONDEST	BLOOMLESS	BLOUSILY	BLOWS	BLUEBACK
BLONDINE	BLOOMS	BLOUSING	BLOWSE	BLUEBACKS
BLONDINED	BLOOMY	BLOUSON	BLOWSED	BLUEBALL
BLONDINES	BLOOP	BLOUSONS	BLOWSES	BLUEBALLS
BLONDING	BLOOPED	BLOUSY	BLOWSIER	BLUEBEARD
BLONDINGS	BLOOPER	BLOVIATE	BLOWSIEST	BLUEBEAT
BLONDISH	BLOOPERS	BLOVIATED	BLOWSILY	BLUEBEATS
BLONDNESS	BLOOPING	BLOVIATES	BLOWSY	BLUEBELL
BLONDS	BLOOPS	BLOW	BLOWTORCH	BLUEBELLS
BLOOD	BLOOSME	BLOWBACK	BLOWTUBE	BLUEBERRY
BLOODBATH	BLOOSMED	BLOWBACKS	BLOWTUBES	BLUEBILL
BLOODED	BLOOSMES	BLOWBALL	BLOWUP	BLUEBILLS
BLOODFIN	BLOOSMING	BLOWBALLS	BLOWUPS	BLUEBIRD
BLOODFINS	BLOOTERED	BLOWBY	BLOWY	BLUEBIRDS
BLOODIED	BLOQUISTE	BLOWBYS	BLOWZE	BLUEBLOOD
BLOODIER	BLORE	BLOWDOWN	BLOWZED	BLUEBOOK
BLOODIES	BLORES	BLOWDOWNS	BLOWZES	BLUEBOOKS
BLOODIEST	BLOSSOM	BLOWED	BLOWZIER	BLUEBUCK
BLOODILY	BLOSSOMED	BLOWER	BLOWZIEST	BLUEBUCKS
BLOODING	BLOSSOMS	BLOWERS	BLOWZILY	BLUEBUSH
BLOODINGS	BLOSSOMY	BLOWFISH	BLOWZY	BLUECAP
BLOODLESS	BLOT	BLOWFLIES	BLUB	BLUECAPS
BLOODLIKE	BLOTCH	BLOWFLY	BLUBBED	BLUECOAT
BLOODLINE	BLOTCHED	BLOWGUN	BLUBBER	BLUECOATS
BLOODLUST	BLOTCHES	BLOWGUNS	BLUBBERED	BLUECURLS
BLOODRED	BLOTCHIER	BLOWHARD	BLUBBERER	BLUED
BLOODROOT	BLOTCHILY	BLOWHARDS	BLUBBERS	BLUEFIN
BLOODS	BLOTCHING	BLOWHOLE	BLUBBERY	BLUEFINS
BLOODSHED	BLOTCHY	BLOWHOLES	BLUBBING	BLUEFISH
BLOODSHOT	BLOTLESS	BLOWIE	BLUBS	BLUEGILL
BLOODWOOD	BLOTS	BLOWIER	BLUCHER	BLUEGILLS
BLOODWORM	BLOTTED	BLOWIES	BLUCHERS	BLUEGOWN
BLOODWORT	BLOTTER	BLOWIEST	BLUDE	BLUEGOWNS
BLOODY	BLOTTERS	BLOWINESS	BLUDES	BLUEGRASS
BLOODYING	BLOTTIER	BLOWING	BLUDGE	BLUEGUM
BLOOEY	BLOTTIEST	BLOWINGS	BLUDGED	BLUEGUMS
BLOOIE	BLOTTING	BLOWJOB	BLUDGEON	BLUEHEAD

BLUEHEADS	BLUFF	BLUNTHEAD	BLYPES	BOATER
BLUEING	BLUFFABLE	BLUNTING	BO	BOATERS
BLUEINGS	BLUFFED	BLUNTISH	BOA	BOATFUL
BLUEISH	BLUFFER	BLUNTLY	BOAB	BOATFULS
BLUEJACK	BLUFFERS	BLUNTNESS	BOABS	BOATHOOK
BLUEJACKS	BLUFFEST	BLUNTS	BOAK	BOATHOOKS
BLUEJAY	BLUFFING	BLUR	BOAKED	BOATHOUSE
BLUEJAYS	BLUFFLY	BLURB	BOAKING	BOATIE
BLUEJEANS	BLUFFNESS	BLURBED	BOAKS	BOATIES
BLUELINE	BLUFFS	BLURBING	BOAR	BOATING
BLUELINER	BLUGGIER	BLURBIST	BOARD	BOATINGS
BLUELINES	BLUGGIEST	BLURBISTS	BOARDABLE	BOATLIFT
BLUELY	BLUGGY	BLURBS	BOARDED	BOATLIFTS
BLUENESS	BLUID	BLURRED	BOARDER	BOATLIKE
BLUENOSE	BLUIDIER	BLURREDLY	BOARDERS	BOATLOAD
BLUENOSED	BLUIDIEST	BLURRIER	BOARDING	BOATLOADS
BLUENOSES	BLUIDS	BLURRIEST	BOARDINGS	BOATMAN
BLUEPOINT	BLUIDY	BLURRILY	BOARDLIKE	BOATMEN
BLUEPRINT	BLUIER	BLURRING	BOARDMAN	BOATNECK
BLUER	BLUIEST	BLURRY	BOARDMEN	BOATNECKS
BLUES	BLUING	BLURS	BOARDROOM	BOATS
BLUESHIFT	BLUINGS	BLURT	BOARDS	BOATSMAN
BLUESIER	BLUISH	BLURTED	BOARDWALK	BOATSMEN
BLUESIEST	BLUME	BLURTER	BOARFISH	BOATSWAIN
BLUESMAN	BLUMED	BLURTERS	BOARHOUND	BOATTAIL
BLUESMEN	BLUMES	BLURTING	BOARISH	BOATTAILS
BLUEST	BLUMING	BLURTINGS	BOARISHLY	BOATYARD
BLUESTEM	BLUNDER	BLURTS	BOARS	BOATYARDS
BLUESTEMS	BLUNDERED	BLUSH	BOART	BOB
BLUESTONE	BLUNDERER	BLUSHED	BOARTS	BOBA
BLUESY	BLUNDERS	BLUSHER	BOAS	BOBAC
BLUET	BLUNGE	BLUSHERS	BOAST	BOBACS
BLUETICK	BLUNGED	BLUSHES	BOASTED	BOBAK
BLUETICKS	BLUNGER	BLUSHET	BOASTER	BOBAKS
BLUETIT	BLUNGERS	BLUSHETS	BOASTERS	BOBAS
BLUETITS	BLUNGES	BLUSHFUL	BOASTFUL	BOBBED
BLUETS	BLUNGING	BLUSHING	BOASTING	BOBBEJAAN
BLUETTE	BLUNK	BLUSHINGS	BOASTINGS	BOBBER
BLUETTES	BLUNKED	BLUSHLESS	BOASTLESS	BOBBERIES
BLUEWEED	BLUNKER	BLUSTER	BOASTS	BOBBERS
BLUEWEEDS	BLUNKERS	BLUSTERED	BOAT	BOBBERY
BLUEWING	BLUNKING	BLUSTERER	BOATABLE	BOBBIES
BLUEWINGS	BLUNKS	BLUSTERS	BOATBILL	BOBBIN
BLUEWOOD	BLUNT	BLUSTERY	BOATBILLS	BOBBINET
BLUEWOODS	BLUNTED	BLUSTROUS	BOATED	BOBBINETS
BLUEY	BLUNTER	BLUTWURST	BOATEL	BOBBING
BLUEYS	BLUNTEST	BLYPE	BOATELS	BOBBINS

BOBBISH	BOBWIGS	BODGING	BOET	BOGGLING
BOBBITT	BOCACCIO	BODHI	BOETS	BOGGY
BOBBITTED	BOCACCIOS	BODHRAN	BOEUF	BOGIE
BOBBITTS	BOCAGE	BODHRANS	BOFF	BOGIED
BOBBLE	BOCAGES	BODICE	BOFFED	BOGIEING
BOBBLED	BOCCA	BODICES	BOFFIN	BOGIES
BOBBLES	BOCCAS	BODIED	BOFFING	BOGLAND
BOBBLIER	BOCCE	BODIES	BOFFINS	BOGLANDS
BOBBLIEST	BOCCES	BODIKIN	BOFFO	BOGLE
BOBBLING	BOCCI	BODIKINS	BOFFOLA	BOGLED
BOBBLY	BOCCIA	BODILESS	BOFFOLAS	BOGLES
BOBBY	BOCCIAS	BODILY	BOFFOS	BOGLING
BOBBYSOCK	BOCCIE	BODING	BOFFS	BOGMAN
BOBBYSOX	BOCCIES	BODINGLY	BOG	BOGMEN
BOBCAT	BOCCIS	BODINGS	BOGAN	BOGOAK
BOBCATS	BOCHE	BODKIN	BOGANS	BOGOAKS
BOBECHE	BOCHES	BODKINS	BOGART	BOGONG
BOBECHES	BOCK	BODLE	BOGARTED	BOGONGS
BOBFLOAT	BOCKED	BODLES	BOGARTING	BOGS
BOBFLOATS	BOCKEDY	BODRAG	BOGARTS	BOGUS
BOBLET	BOCKING	BODRAGS	BOGBEAN	BOGUSLY
BOBLETS	BOCKS	BODS	BOGBEANS	BOGUSNESS
BOBOL	BOCONCINI	BODY	BOGEY	BOGWOOD
BOBOLINK	BOD	BODYBOARD	BOGEYED	BOGWOODS
BOBOLINKS	BODACH	BODYCHECK	BOGEYING	BOGY
BOBOLLED	BODACHS	BODYGUARD	BOGEYISM	BOGYISM
BOBOLLING	BODACIOUS	BODYING	BOGEYISMS	BOGYISMS
BOBOLS	BODDLE	BODYLINE	BOGEYMAN	BOGYMAN
BOBOTIE	BODDLES	BODYLINES	BOGEYMEN	BOGYMEN
BOBOTIES	BODE	BODYSHELL	BOGEYS	BOH
BOBOWLER	BODED	BODYSUIT	BOGGARD	BOHEA
BOBOWLERS	BODEFUL	BODYSUITS	BOGGARDS	BOHEAS
BOBS	BODEGA	BODYSURF	BOGGART	BOHEMIA
BOBSLED	BODEGAS	BODYSURFS	BOGGARTS	BOHEMIAN
BOBSLEDS	BODEGUERO	BODYWORK	BOGGED	BOHEMIANS
BOBSLEIGH	BODEMENT	BODYWORKS	BOGGER	BOHEMIAS
BOBSTAY	BODEMENTS	BOEHMITE	BOGGERS	BOHO
BOBSTAYS	BODES	BOEHMITES	BOGGIER	BOHOS
BOBTAIL	BODGE	BOEP	BOGGIEST	BOHRIUM
BOBTAILED	BODGED	BOEPS	BOGGINESS	BOHRIUMS
BOBTAILS	BODGER	BOERBUL	BOGGING	BOHS
BOBWEIGHT	BODGERS	BOERBULL	BOGGISH	BOHUNK
BOBWHEEL	BODGES	BOERBULLS	BOGGLE	BOHUNKS
BOBWHEELS	BODGIE	BOERBULS	BOGGLED	BOI
BOBWHITE	BODGIER	BOEREWORS	BOGGLER	BOIL
BOBWHITES	BODGIES	BOERTJIE	BOGGLERS	BOILABLE
BOBWIG	BODGIEST	BOERTJIES	BOGGLES	BOILED

BOILER	BOLDLY	BOLLWORMS	BOMBARDE	BON
BOILERIES	BOLDNESS	BOLO	BOMBARDED	BONA
BOILERS	BOLDS	BOLOGNA	BOMBARDER	BONACI
BOILERY	BOLE	BOLOGNAS	BOMBARDES	BONACIS
BOILING	BOLECTION	BOLOGNESE	BOMBARDON	BONAMANI
BOILINGLY	BOLERO	BOLOGRAPH	BOMBARDS	BONAMANO
BOILINGS	BOLEROS	BOLOMETER	BOMBASINE	BONAMIA
BOILOFF	BOLES	BOLOMETRY	BOMBAST	BONAMIAS
BOILOFFS	BOLETE	BOLONEY	BOMBASTED	BONANZA
BOILOVER	BOLETES	BOLONEYS	BOMBASTER	BONANZAS
BOILOVERS	BOLETI	BOLOS	BOMBASTIC	BONASSUS
BOILS	BOLETUS	BOLSHEVIK	BOMBASTS	BONASUS
BOING	BOLETUSES	BOLSHIE	BOMBAX	BONASUSES
BOINGED	BOLIDE	BOLSHIER	BOMBAXES	BONBON
BOINGING	BOLIDES	BOLSHIES	BOMBAZINE	BONBONS
BOINGS	BOLINE	BOLSHIEST	BOMBE	BONCE
BOINK	BOLINES	BOLSHY	BOMBED	BONCES
BOINKED	BOLIVAR	BOLSON	BOMBER	BOND
BOINKING	BOLIVARES	BOLSONS	BOMBERS	BONDABLE
BOINKS	BOLIVARS	BOLSTER	BOMBES	BONDAGE
BOIS	BOLIVIA	BOLSTERED	BOMBESIN	BONDAGER
BOISERIE	BOLIVIANO	BOLSTERER	BOMBESINS	BONDAGERS
BOISERIES	BOLIVIAS	BOLSTERS	BOMBILATE	BONDAGES
BOITE	BOLIX	BOLT	BOMBINATE	BONDED
BOITES	BOLIXED	BOLTED	BOMBING	BONDER
BOK	BOLIXES	BOLTER	BOMBINGS	BONDERS
BOKE	BOLIXING	BOLTERS	BOMBLET	BONDING
BOKED	BOLL	BOLTHEAD	BOMBLETS	BONDINGS
BOKES	BOLLARD	BOLTHEADS	BOMBLOAD	BONDLESS
BOKING	BOLLARDS	BOLTHOLE	BOMBLOADS	BONDMAID
BOKO	BOLLED	BOLTHOLES	BOMBO	BONDMAIDS
BOKOS	BOLLEN	BOLTING	BOMBORA	BONDMAN
BOKS	BOLLETRIE	BOLTINGS	BOMBORAS	BONDMEN
BOLA	BOLLING	BOLTLESS	BOMBOS	BONDS
BOLAR	BOLLIX	BOLTLIKE	BOMBPROOF	BONDSMAN
BOLAS	BOLLIXED	BOLTONIA	BOMBS	BONDSMEN
BOLASES	BOLLIXES	BOLTONIAS	BOMBSHELL	BONDSTONE
BOLD	BOLLIXING	BOLTROPE	BOMBSIGHT	BONDUC
BOLDEN	BOLLOCK	BOLTROPES	BOMBSITE	BONDUCS
BOLDENED	BOLLOCKED	BOLTS	BOMBSITES	BONDWOMAN
BOLDENING	BOLLOCKS	BOLUS	BOMBYCID	BONDWOMEN
BOLDENS	BOLLOX	BOLUSES	BOMBYCIDS	BONE
BOLDER	BOLLOXED	BOMA	BOMBYCOID	BONEBLACK
BOLDEST	BOLLOXES	BOMAS	BOMBYX	BONED
BOLDFACE	BOLLOXING	BOMB	BOMBYXES	BONEFISH
BOLDFACED	BOLLS	BOMBABLE	BOMMIE	BONEHEAD
BOLDFACES	BOLLWORM	BOMBARD	BOMMIES	BONEHEADS

BONELESS	BONISMS	BONXIE	BOOFHEAD	BOOKER
BONEMEAL	BONIST	BONXIES	BOOFHEADS	BOOKERS
BONEMEALS	BONISTS	BONY	BOOFIER	BOOKFUL
BONER	BONITA	BONZA	BOOFIEST	BOOKFULS
BONERS	BONITAS	BONZE	BOOFY	BOOKIE
BONES	BONITO	BONZER	BOOGALOO	BOOKIER
BONESET	BONITOES	BONZES	BOOGALOOS	BOOKIES
BONESETS	BONITOS	BOO	BOOGER	BOOKIEST
BONETIRED	BONJOUR	BOOAI	BOOGERMAN	BOOKING
BONEY	BONK	BOOAIS	BOOGERMEN	BOOKINGS
BONEYARD	BONKED	BOOAY	BOOGERS	BOOKISH
BONEYARDS	BONKERS	BOOAYS	BOOGEY	BOOKISHLY
BONEYER	BONKING	BOOB	BOOGEYED	BOOKLAND
BONEYEST	BONKINGS	BOOBED	BOOGEYING	BOOKLANDS
BONFIRE	BONKS	BOOBHEAD	BOOGEYMAN	BOOKLESS
BONFIRES	BONNE	BOOBHEADS	BOOGEYMEN	BOOKLET
BONG	BONNES	BOOBIALLA	BOOGEYS	BOOKLETS
BONGED	BONNET	BOOBIE	BOOGIE	BOOKLICE
BONGING	BONNETED	BOOBIES	BOOGIED	BOOKLIGHT
BONGO	BONNETING	BOOBING	BOOGIEING	BOOKLORE
BONGOES	BONNETS	BOOBIRD	BOOGIEMAN	BOOKLORES
BONGOIST	BONNIBELL	BOOBIRDS	BOOGIEMEN	BOOKLOUSE
BONGOISTS	BONNIE	BOOBISH	BOOGIES	BOOKMAKER
BONGOS	BONNIER	BOOBOISIE	BOOGY	BOOKMAN
BONGRACE	BONNIES	BOOBOO	BOOGYING	BOOKMARK
BONGRACES	BONNIEST	BOOBOOK	BOOGYMAN	BOOKMARKS
BONGS	BONNILY	BOOBOOKS	BOOGYMEN	BOOKMEN
BONHAM	BONNINESS	BOOBOOS	BOOH	BOOKOO
BONHAMS	BONNOCK	BOOBS	BOOHAI	BOOKOOS
BONHOMIE	BONNOCKS	BOOBY	BOOHAIS	BOOKPLATE
BONHOMIES	BONNY	BOOBYISH	BOOHED	BOOKRACK
BONHOMMIE	BONOBO	BOOBYISM	BOOHING	BOOKRACKS
BONHOMOUS	BONOBOS	BOOBYISMS	BOOHOO	BOOKREST
BONIATO	BONSAI	BOOCOO	BOOHOOED	BOOKRESTS
BONIATOS	BONSELA	BOOCOOS	BOOHOOING	BOOKS
BONIBELL	BONSELAS	BOODIE	BOOHOOS	BOOKSHELF
BONIBELLS	BONSELLA	BOODIED	BOOHS	BOOKSHOP
BONIE	BONSELLAS	BOODIES	BOOING	BOOKSHOPS
BONIER	BONSOIR	BOODLE	BOOJUM	BOOKSIE
BONIEST	BONSPELL	BOODLED	BOOJUMS	BOOKSIER
BONIFACE	BONSPELLS	BOODLER	BOOK	BOOKSIEST
BONIFACES	BONSPIEL	BOODLERS	BOOKABLE	BOOKSTALL
BONILASSE	BONSPIELS	BOODLES	BOOKCASE	BOOKSTAND
BONINESS	BONTEBOK	BOODLING	BOOKCASES	BOOKSTORE
BONING	BONTEBOKS	BOODY	BOOKED	BOOKSY
BONINGS	BONUS	BOODYING	BOOKEND	BOOKWORK
BONISM	BONUSES	BOOED	BOOKENDS	BOOKWORKS

B

BOOKWORM	BOORISHLY	BOOTS	BORAZON	BORIC
BOOKWORMS	BOORKA	BOOTSTRAP	BORAZONS	BORIDE
BOOKY	BOORKAS	BOOTY	BORD	BORIDES
BOOL	BOORS	BOOZE	BORDAR	BORING
BOOLED	BOORTREE	BOOZED	BORDARS	BORINGLY
BOOLING	BOORTREES	BOOZER	BORDE	BORINGS
BOOLS	BOOS	BOOZERS	BORDEAUX	BORK
BOOM	BOOSE	BOOZES	BORDEL	BORKED
BOOMBOX	BOOSED	BOOZEY	BORDELLO	BORKING
BOOMBOXES	BOOSES	BOOZIER	BORDELLOS	BORKS
BOOMED	BOOSHIT	BOOZIEST	BORDELS	BORLOTTI
BOOMER	BOOSING	BOOZILY	BORDER	BORM
BOOMERANG	BOOST	BOOZINESS	BORDEREAU	BORMED
BOOMERS	BOOSTED	BOOZING	BORDERED	BORMING
BOOMIER	BOOSTER	BOOZINGS	BORDERER	BORMS
BOOMIEST	BOOSTERS	BOOZY	BORDERERS	BORN
BOOMING	BOOSTING	BOP	BORDERING	BORNA
BOOMINGLY	BOOSTS	BOPEEP	BORDERS	BORNE
BOOMINGS	BOOT	BOPEEPS	BORDES	BORNEOL
BOOMKIN	BOOTABLE	BOPPED	BORDS	BORNEOLS
BOOMKINS	BOOTBLACK	BOPPER	BORDURE	BORNITE
BOOMLET	BOOTCUT	BOPPERS	BORDURES	BORNITES
BOOMLETS	BOOTED	BOPPING	BORE	BORNITIC
BOOMS	BOOTEE	BOPS	BOREAL	BORNYL
BOOMSLANG	BOOTEES	BOR	BOREALIS	BORNYLS
BOOMTOWN	BOOTERIES	BORA	BOREAS	BORON
BOOMTOWNS	BOOTERY	BORACES	BOREASES	BORONIA
BOOMY	BOOTH	BORACHIO	BORECOLE	BORONIAS
BOON	BOOTHOSE	BORACHIOS	BORECOLES	BORONIC
BOONDOCK	BOOTHS	BORACIC	BORED	BORONS
BOONDOCKS	BOOTIE	BORACITE	BOREDOM	BOROUGH
BOONER	BOOTIES	BORACITES	BOREDOMS	BOROUGHS
BOONERS	BOOTIKIN	BORAGE	BOREE	BORREL
BOONG	BOOTIKINS	BORAGES	BOREEN	BORRELIA
BOONGA	BOOTING	BORAK	BOREENS	BORRELIAS
BOONGARY	BOOTJACK	BORAKS	BOREES	BORRELL
BOONGAS	BOOTJACKS	BORAL	BOREHOLE	BORROW
BOONGS	BOOTLACE	BORALS	BOREHOLES	BORROWED
BOONIES	BOOTLACES	BORANE	BOREL	BORROWER
BOONLESS	BOOTLAST	BORANES	BORER	BORROWERS
BOONS	BOOTLASTS	BORAS	BORERS	BORROWING
BOOR	BOOTLEG	BORATE	BORES	BORROWS
BOORD	BOOTLEGS	BORATED	BORESCOPE	BORS
BOORDE	BOOTLESS	BORATES	BORESOME	BORSCH
BOORDES	BOOTLICK	BORATING	BORGHETTO	BORSCHES
BOORDS	BOOTLICKS	BORAX	BORGO	BORSCHT
BOORISH	BOOTMAKER	BORAXES	BORGOS	BORSCHTS

BORSHCH	BOSKET	BOSTONS	BOTH	BOTTOMED
BORSHCHES	BOSKETS	BOSTRYX	BOTHAN	BOTTOMER
BORSHT	BOSKIER	BOSTRYXES	BOTHANS	BOTTOMERS
BORSHTS	BOSKIEST	BOSUN	BOTHER	BOTTOMING
BORSIC	BOSKINESS	BOSUNS	BOTHERED	BOTTOMRY
BORSICS	BOSKS	BOT	BOTHERING	BOTTOMS
BORSTAL	BOSKY	BOTA	BOTHERS	BOTTOMSET
BORSTALL	BOSOM	BOTANIC	BOTHIE	BOTTONY
BORSTALLS	BOSOMED	BOTANICA	BOTHIES	BOTTS
BORSTALS	BOSOMIER	BOTANICAL	BOTHOLE	BOTTY
BORT	BOSOMIEST	BOTANICAS	BOTHOLES	BOTULIN
BORTIER	BOSOMING	BOTANICS	BOTHRIA	BOTULINAL
BORTIEST	BOSOMS	BOTANIES	BOTHRIUM	BOTULINS
BORTS	BOSOMY	BOTANISE	BOTHRIUMS	BOTULINUM
BORTSCH	BOSON	BOTANISED	BOTHY	BOTULINUS
BORTSCHES	BOSONIC	BOTANISER	BOTHYMAN	BOTULISM
BORTY	BOSONS	BOTANISES	BOTHYMEN	BOTULISMS
BORTZ	BOSQUE	BOTANIST	BOTNET	BOUBOU
BORTZES	BOSQUES	BOTANISTS	BOTNETS	BOUBOUS
BORZOI	BOSQUET	BOTANIZE	BOTONE	BOUCHE
BORZOIS	BOSQUETS	BOTANIZED	BOTONEE	BOUCHEE
BOS	BOSS	BOTANIZER	BOTONNEE	BOUCHEES
BOSBERAAD	BOSSBOY	BOTANIZES	BOTRYOID	BOUCHES
BOSBOK	BOSSBOYS	BOTANY	BOTRYOSE	BOUCLE
BOSBOKS	BOSSDOM	BOTARGO	BOTRYTIS	BOUCLEE
BOSCAGE	BOSSDOMS	BOTARGOES	BOTS	BOUCLEES
BOSCAGES	BOSSED	BOTARGOS	BOTT	BOUCLES
BOSCHBOK	BOSSER	BOTAS	BOTTARGA	BOUDERIE
BOSCHBOKS	BOSSES	BOTCH	BOTTARGAS	BOUDERIES
BOSCHE	BOSSEST	BOTCHED	BOTTE	BOUDIN
BOSCHES	BOSSET	BOTCHEDLY	BOTTED	BOUDINS
BOSCHVARK	BOSSETS	BOTCHER	BOTTEGA	BOUDOIR
BOSCHVELD	BOSSIER	BOTCHERS	BOTTEGAS	BOUDOIRS
BOSH	BOSSIES	BOTCHERY	BOTTES	BOUFFANT
BOSHBOK	BOSSIEST	BOTCHES	BOTTIES	BOUFFANTS
BOSHBOKS	BOSSILY	BOTCHIER	BOTTINE	BOUFFE
BOSHES	BOSSINESS	BOTCHIEST	BOTTINES	BOUFFES
BOSHTA	BOSSING	BOTCHILY	BOTTING	BOUGE
BOSHTER	BOSSINGS	BOTCHING	BOTTLE	BOUGED
BOSHVARK	BOSSISM	BOTCHINGS	BOTTLED	BOUGES
BOSHVARKS	BOSSISMS	BOTCHY	BOTTLEFUL	BOUGET
BOSIE	BOSSY	BOTE	BOTTLER	BOUGETS
BOSIES	BOSTANGI	BOTEL	BOTTLERS	BOUGH
BOSK	BOSTANGIS	BOTELS	BOTTLES	BOUGHED
BOSKAGE	BOSTHOON	BOTES	BOTTLING	BOUGHLESS
BOSKAGES	BOSTHOONS	BOTFLIES	BOTTLINGS	BOUGHPOT
BOSKER	BOSTON	BOTFLY	BOTTOM	BOUGHPOTS

B

BOUGHS	BOUNDERS	BOURSIERS	BOWEL	BOWLINGS
BOUGHT	BOUNDING	BOURSIN	BOWELED	BOWLLIKE
BOUGHTEN	BOUNDLESS	BOURSINS	BOWELING	BOWLS
BOUGHTS	BOUNDNESS	BOURTREE	BOWELLED	BOWMAN
BOUGIE	BOUNDS	BOURTREES	BOWELLESS	BOWMEN
BOUGIES	BOUNED	BOUSE	BOWELLING	BOWNE
BOUGING	BOUNING	BOUSED	BOWELS	BOWNED
BOUILLI	BOUNS	BOUSES	BOWER	BOWNES
BOUILLIS	BOUNTEOUS	BOUSIER	BOWERBIRD	BOWNING
BOUILLON	BOUNTIED	BOUSIEST	BOWERED	BOWPOT
BOUILLONS	BOUNTIES	BOUSING	BOWERIES	BOWPOTS
BOUK	BOUNTIFUL	BOUSOUKI	BOWERING	BOWR
BOUKS	BOUNTREE	BOUSOUKIA	BOWERS	BOWRS
BOULDER	BOUNTREES	BOUSOUKIS	BOWERY	BOWS
BOULDERED	BOUNTY	BOUSY	BOWES	BOWSAW
BOULDERER	BOUNTYHED	BOUT	BOWET	BOWSAWS
BOULDERS	BOUQUET	BOUTADE	BOWETS	BOWSE
BOULDERY	BOUQUETS	BOUTADES	BOWFIN	BOWSED
BOULE	BOURASQUE	BOUTIQUE	BOWFINS	BOWSER
BOULES	BOURBON	BOUTIQUES	BOWFRONT	BOWSERS
BOULEVARD	BOURBONS	BOUTIQUEY	BOWGET	BOWSES
BOULLE	BOURD	BOUTON	BOWGETS	BOWSEY
BOULLES	BOURDER	BOUTONNE	BOWHEAD	BOWSEYS
BOULT	BOURDERS	BOUTONNEE	BOWHEADS	BOWSHOT
BOULTED	BOURDON	BOUTONS	BOWHUNTER	BOWSHOTS
BOULTER	BOURDONS	BOUTS	BOWIE	BOWSIE
BOULTERS	BOURDS	BOUVARDIA	BOWING	BOWSIES
BOULTING	BOURG	BOUVIER	BOWINGLY	BOWSING
BOULTINGS	BOURGEOIS	BOUVIERS	BOWINGS	BOWSPRIT
BOULTS	BOURGEON	BOUZOUKI	BOWKNOT	BOWSPRITS
BOUN	BOURGEONS	BOUZOUKIA	BOWKNOTS	BOWSTRING
BOUNCE	BOURGS	BOUZOUKIS	BOWL	BOWSTRUNG
BOUNCED	BOURKHA	BOVATE	BOWLDER	BOWWOW
BOUNCER	BOURKHAS	BOVATES	BOWLDERS	BOWWOWED
BOUNCERS	BOURLAW	BOVID	BOWLED	BOWWOWING
BOUNCES	BOURLAWS	BOVIDS	BOWLEG	BOWWOWS
BOUNCIER	BOURN	BOVINE	BOWLEGGED	BOWYANG
BOUNCIEST	BOURNE	BOVINELY	BOWLEGS	BOWYANGS
BOUNCILY	BOURNES	BOVINES	BOWLER	BOWYER
BOUNCING	BOURNS	BOVINITY	BOWLERS	BOWYERS
BOUNCY	BOURREE	BOVVER	BOWLESS	BOX
BOUND	BOURREES	BOVVERS	BOWLFUL	BOXBALL
BOUNDABLE	BOURRIDE	BOW	BOWLFULS	BOXBALLS
BOUNDARY	BOURRIDES	BOWAT	BOWLIKE	BOXBERRY
BOUNDED	BOURSE	BOWATS	BOWLINE	BOXBOARD
BOUNDEN	BOURSES	BOWBENT	BOWLINES	BOXBOARDS
BOUNDER	BOURSIER	BOWED	BOWLING	BOXCAR

BOXCARS	BOYCOTT	BRACE	BRACTS	BRAILLE
BOXED	BOYCOTTED	BRACED	BRAD	BRAILLED
BOXEN	BOYCOTTER	BRACELET	BRADAWL	BRAILLER
BOXER	BOYCOTTS	BRACELETS	BRADAWLS	BRAILLERS
BOXERCISE	BOYED	BRACER	BRADDED	BRAILLES
BOXERS	BOYF	BRACERO	BRADDING	BRAILLING
BOXES	BOYFRIEND	BRACEROS	BRADOON	BRAILLIST
BOXFISH	BOYFS	BRACERS	BRADOONS	BRAILS
BOXFISHES	BOYG	BRACES	BRADS	BRAIN
BOXFUL	BOYGS	BRACH	BRAE	BRAINBOX
BOXFULS	BOYHOOD	BRACHAH	BRAEHEID	BRAINCASE
BOXHAUL	BOYHOODS	BRACHAHS	BRAEHEIDS	BRAINDEAD
BOXHAULED	BOYING	BRACHES	BRAES	BRAINED
BOXHAULS	BOYISH	BRACHET	BRAG	BRAINFART
BOXIER	BOYISHLY	BRACHETS	BRAGGART	BRAINFOOD
BOXIEST	BOYKIE	BRACHIA	BRAGGARTS	BRAINIAC
BOXILY	BOYKIES	BRACHIAL	BRAGGED	BRAINIACS
BOXINESS	BOYLA	BRACHIALS	BRAGGER	BRAINIER
BOXING	BOYLAS	BRACHIATE	BRAGGERS	BRAINIEST
BOXINGS	BOYO	BRACHIUM	BRAGGEST	BRAINILY
BOXKEEPER	BOYOS	BRACHOT	BRAGGIER	BRAINING
BOXLIKE	BOYS	BRACHS	BRAGGIEST	BRAINISH
BOXPLOT	BOYSHORTS	BRACING	BRAGGING	BRAINLESS
BOXPLOTS	BOYSIER	BRACINGLY	BRAGGINGS	BRAINPAN
BOXROOM	BOYSIEST	BRACINGS	BRAGGY	BRAINPANS
BOXROOMS	BOYSY	BRACIOLA	BRAGLY	BRAINS
BOXTHORN	BOZO	BRACIOLAS	BRAGS	BRAINSICK
BOXTHORNS	BOZOS	BRACIOLE	BRAHMA	BRAINSTEM
BOXTIES	BOZZETTI	BRACIOLES	BRAHMAN	BRAINWASH
BOXTY	BOZZETTO	BRACK	BRAHMANI	BRAINWAVE
BOXWALLAH	BRA	BRACKEN	BRAHMANIS	BRAINY
BOXWOOD	BRAAI	BRACKENS	BRAHMANS	BRAIRD
BOXWOODS	BRAAIED	BRACKET	BRAHMAS	BRAIRDED
BOXY	BRAAIING	BRACKETED	BRAHMIN	BRAIRDING
BOY	BRAAIS	BRACKETS	BRAHMINS	BRAIRDS
BOYAR	BRAATA	BRACKISH	BRAID	BRAISE
BOYARD	BRAATAS	BRACKS	BRAIDE	BRAISED
BOYARDS	BRAATASES	BRACONID	BRAIDED	BRAISES
BOYARISM	BRABBLE	BRACONIDS	BRAIDER	BRAISING
BOYARISMS	BRABBLED	BRACT	BRAIDERS	BRAIZE
BOYARS	BRABBLER	BRACTEAL	BRAIDEST	BRAIZES
BOYAU	BRABBLERS	BRACTEATE	BRAIDING	BRAK
BOYAUX	BRABBLES	BRACTED	BRAIDINGS	BRAKE
BOYCHICK	BRABBLING	BRACTEOLE	BRAIDS	BRAKEAGE
BOYCHICKS	BRACCATE	BRACTLESS	BRAIL	BRAKEAGES
BOYCHIK	BRACCIA	BRACTLET	BRAILED	BRAKED
BOYCHIKS	BRACCIO	BRACTLETS	BRAILING	BRAKELESS

BRAKEMAN	BRANDISES	BRASHED	BRATLING	BRAVURE
BRAKEMEN	BRANDISH	BRASHER	BRATLINGS	BRAW
BRAKES	BRANDLESS	BRASHES	BRATPACK	BRAWER
BRAKESMAN	BRANDLING	BRASHEST	BRATPACKS	BRAWEST
BRAKESMEN	BRANDRETH	BRASHIER	BRATS	BRAWL
BRAKIER	BRANDS	BRASHIEST	BRATTICE	BRAWLED
BRAKIEST	BRANDY	BRASHING	BRATTICED	BRAWLER
BRAKING	BRANDYING	BRASHLY	BRATTICES	BRAWLERS
BRAKS	BRANE	BRASHNESS	BRATTIER	BRAWLIE
BRAKY	BRANES	BRASHY	BRATTIEST	BRAWLIER
BRALESS	BRANGLE	BRASIER	BRATTISH	BRAWLIEST
BRAMBLE	BRANGLED	BRASIERS	BRATTLE	BRAWLING
BRAMBLED	BRANGLES	BRASIL	BRATTLED	BRAWLINGS
BRAMBLES	BRANGLING	BRASILEIN	BRATTLES	BRAWLS
BRAMBLIER	BRANK	BRASILIN	BRATTLING	BRAWLY
BRAMBLING	BRANKED	BRASILINS	BRATTY	BRAWN
BRAMBLY	BRANKIER	BRASILS	BRATWURST	BRAWNED
BRAME	BRANKIEST	BRASS	BRAUNCH	BRAWNIER
BRAMES	BRANKING	BRASSAGE	BRAUNCHED	BRAWNIEST
BRAN	BRANKS	BRASSAGES	BRAUNCHES	BRAWNILY
BRANCARD	BRANKY	BRASSARD	BRAUNITE	BRAWNS
BRANCARDS	BRANLE	BRASSARDS	BRAUNITES	BRAWNY
BRANCH	BRANLES	BRASSART	BRAVA	BRAWS
BRANCHED	BRANNED	BRASSARTS	BRAVADO	BRAXIES
BRANCHER	BRANNER	BRASSED	BRAVADOED	BRAXY
BRANCHERS	BRANNERS	BRASSERIE	BRAVADOES	BRAY
BRANCHERY	BRANNIER	BRASSES	BRAVADOS	BRAYED
BRANCHES	BRANNIEST	BRASSET	BRAVAS	BRAYER
BRANCHIA	BRANNIGAN	BRASSETS	BRAVE	BRAYERS
BRANCHIAE	BRANNING	BRASSICA	BRAVED	BRAYING
BRANCHIAL	BRANNY	BRASSICAS	BRAVELY	BRAYS
BRANCHIER	BRANS	BRASSIE	BRAVENESS	BRAZA
BRANCHING	BRANSLE	BRASSIER	BRAVER	BRAZAS
BRANCHLET	BRANSLES	BRASSIERE	BRAVERIES	BRAZE
BRANCHY	BRANT	BRASSIES	BRAVERS	BRAZED
BRAND	BRANTAIL	BRASSIEST	BRAVERY	BRAZELESS
BRANDADE	BRANTAILS	BRASSILY	BRAVES	BRAZEN
BRANDADES	BRANTLE	BRASSING	BRAVEST	BRAZENED
BRANDED	BRANTLES	BRASSISH	BRAVI	BRAZENING
BRANDER	BRANTS	BRASSWARE	BRAVING	BRAZENLY
BRANDERED	BRAS	BRASSY	BRAVO	BRAZENRY
BRANDERS	BRASCO	BRAST	BRAVOED	BRAZENS
BRANDIED	BRASCOS	BRASTING	BRAVOES	BRAZER
BRANDIES	BRASERO	BRASTS	BRAVOING	BRAZERS
BRANDING	BRASEROS	BRAT	BRAVOS	BRAZES
BRANDINGS	BRASES	BRATCHET	BRAVURA	BRAZIER
BRANDISE	BRASH	BRATCHETS	BRAVURAS	BRAZIERS

BRAZIERY	BREAKOFFS	BREDIES	BREHONS	BREVETING
BRAZIL	BREAKOUT	BREDING	BREI	BREVETS
BRAZILEIN	BREAKOUTS	BREDREN	BREID	BREVETTED
BRAZILIN	BREAKS	BREDRENS	BREIDS	BREVIARY
BRAZILINS	BREAKTIME	BREDRIN	BREIING	BREVIATE
BRAZILS	BREAKUP	BREDRINS	BREINGE	BREVIATES
BRAZING	BREAKUPS	BREDS	BREINGED	BREVIER
BREACH	BREAKWALL	BREE	BREINGES	BREVIERS
BREACHED	BREAM	BREECH	BREINGING	BREVIS
BREACHER	BREAMED	BREECHED	BREIS	BREVISES
BREACHERS	BREAMING	BREECHES	BREIST	BREVITIES
BREACHES	BREAMS	BREECHING	BREISTS	BREVITY
BREACHING	BREARE	BREED	BREKKIES	BREW
BREAD	BREARES	BREEDER	BREKKY	BREWAGE
BREADBOX	BREASKIT	BREEDERS	BRELOQUE	BREWAGES
BREADED	BREASKITS	BREEDING	BRELOQUES	BREWED
BREADHEAD	BREAST	BREEDINGS	BREME	BREWER
BREADIER	BREASTED	BREEDS	BREN	BREWERIES
BREADIEST	BREASTFED	BREEKS	BRENNE	BREWERS
BREADING	BREASTING	BREEM	BRENNES	BREWERY
BREADLESS	BREASTPIN	BREENGE	BRENNING	BREWING
BREADLINE	BREASTS	BREENGED	BRENS	BREWINGS
BREADNUT	BREATH	BREENGES	BRENT	BREWIS
BREADNUTS	BREATHE	BREENGING	BRENTER	BREWISES
BREADROOM	BREATHED	BREER	BRENTEST	BREWPUB
BREADROOT	BREATHER	BREERED	BRENTS	BREWPUBS
BREADS	BREATHERS	BREERING	BRER	BREWS
BREADTH	BREATHES	BREERS	BRERE	BREWSKIES
BREADTHS	BREATHFUL	BREES	BRERES	BREWSKIES
BREADY	BREATHIER	BREESE	BRERS	BREWSKIS
BREAK	BREATHILY	BREESES	BRESAOLA	BREWSTER
BREAKABLE	BREATHING	BREEST	BRESAOLAS	BREWSTERS
BREAKAGE	BREATHS	BREESTS	BRETASCHE	BREY
BREAKAGES	BREATHY	BREEZE	BRETESSE	BREYED
BREAKAWAY	BRECCIA	BREEZED	BRETESSES	BREYING
BREAKBACK	BRECCIAL	BREEZES	BRETHREN	BREYS
BREAKBEAT	BRECCIAS	BREEZEWAY	BRETON	BRIAR
BREAKBONE	BRECCIATE	BREEZIER	BRETONS	BRIARD
BREAKDOWN	BRECHAM	BREEZIEST	BRETTICE	BRIARDS
BREAKER	BRECHAMS	BREEZILY	BRETTICED	BRIARED
BREAKERS	BRECHAN	BREEZING	BRETTICES	BRIARROOT
BREAKEVEN	BRECHANS	BREEZY	BREVE	BRIARS
BREAKFAST	BRED	BREGMA	BREVES	BRIARWOOD
BREAKING	BREDE	BREGMATA	BREVET	BRIARY
BREAKINGS	BREDED	BREGMATE	BREVETCY	BRIBABLE
BREAKNECK	BREDES	BREGMATIC	BREVETE	BRIBE
BREAKOFF	BREDIE	BREHON	BREVETED	BRIBEABLE

BRIBED	BRIDESMAN	BRIGADIER	BRINDED	BRISANCE
BRIBEE	BRIDESMEN	BRIGADING	BRINDISI	BRISANCES
BRIBEES	BRIDEWELL	BRIGALOW	BRINDISIS	BRISANT
BRIBER	BRIDGABLE	BRIGALOWS	BRINDLE	BRISE
BRIBERIES	BRIDGE	BRIGAND	BRINDLED	BRISES
BRIBERS	BRIDGED	BRIGANDRY	BRINDLES	BRISK
BRIBERY	BRIDGES	BRIGANDS	BRINE	BRISKED
BRIBES	BRIDGING	BRIGHT	BRINED	BRISKEN
BRIBING	BRIDGINGS	BRIGHTEN	BRINELESS	BRISKENED
BRICABRAC	BRIDIE	BRIGHTENS	BRINER	BRISKENS
BRICHT	BRIDIES	BRIGHTER	BRINERS	BRISKER
BRICHTER	BRIDING	BRIGHTEST	BRINES	BRISKEST
BRICHTEST	BRIDLE	BRIGHTISH	BRING	BRISKET
BRICK	BRIDLED	BRIGHTLY	BRINGDOWN	BRISKETS
BRICKBAT	BRIDLER	BRIGHTS	BRINGER	BRISKIER
BRICKBATS	BRIDLERS	BRIGS	BRINGERS	BRISKIEST
BRICKCLAY	BRIDLES	BRIGUE	BRINGING	BRISKING
BRICKED	BRIDLEWAY	BRIGUED	BRINGINGS	BRISKISH
BRICKEN	BRIDLING	BRIGUES	BRINGS	BRISKLY
BRICKIE	BRIDOON	BRIGUING	BRINIER	BRISKNESS
BRICKIER	BRIDOONS	BRIGUINGS	BRINIES	BRISKS
BRICKIES	BRIE	BRIK	BRINIEST	BRISKY
BRICKIEST	BRIEF	BRIKI	BRININESS	BRISLING
BRICKING	BRIEFCASE	BRIKIS	BRINING	BRISLINGS
BRICKINGS	BRIEFED	BRIKS	BRINISH	BRISS
BRICKKILN	BRIEFER	BRILL	BRINJAL	BRISSES
BRICKLE	BRIEFERS	BRILLER	BRINJALS	BRISTLE
BRICKLES	BRIEFEST	BRILLEST	BRINJARRY	BRISTLED
BRICKLIKE	BRIEFING	BRILLIANT	BRINK	BRISTLES
BRICKS	BRIEFINGS	BRILLO	BRINKMAN	BRISTLIER
BRICKWALL	BRIEFLESS	BRILLOS	BRINKMEN	BRISTLING
BRICKWORK	BRIEFLY	BRILLS	BRINKS	BRISTLY
BRICKY	BRIEFNESS	BRIM	BRINNIES	BRISTOL
BRICKYARD	BRIEFS	BRIMFUL	BRINNY	BRISTOLS
BRICOLAGE	BRIER	BRIMFULL	BRINS	BRISURE
BRICOLE	BRIERED	BRIMFULLY	BRINY	BRISURES
BRICOLES	BRIERIER	BRIMING	BRIO	BRIT
BRIDAL	BRIERIEST	BRIMINGS	BRIOCHE	BRITANNIA
BRIDALLY	BRIERROOT	BRIMLESS	BRIOCHES	BRITCHES
BRIDALS	BRIERS	BRIMMED	BRIOLETTE	BRITH
BRIDE	BRIERWOOD	BRIMMER	BRIONIES	BRITHS
BRIDECAKE	BRIERY	BRIMMERS	BRIONY	BRITS
BRIDED	BRIES	BRIMMING	BRIOS	BRITSCHKA
BRIDEMAID	BRIG	BRIMS	BRIQUET	BRITSKA
BRIDEMAN	BRIGADE	BRIMSTONE	BRIQUETS	BRITSKAS
BRIDEMEN	BRIGADED	BRIMSTONY	BRIQUETTE	BRITT
BRIDES	BRIGADES	BRIN	BRIS	BRITTANIA

BRITTLE	BROADWAYS	BRODEKINS	BROLLIES	BRONCHIAL
BRITTLED	BROADWISE	BRODKIN	BROLLY	BRONCHIUM
BRITTLELY	BROCADE	BRODKINS	BROMAL	BRONCHO
BRITTLER	BROCADED	BRODS	BROMALS	BRONCHOS
BRITTLES	BROCADES	BROEKIES	BROMATE	BRONCHUS
BRITTLEST	BROCADING	BROG	BROMATED	BRONCO
BRITTLING	BROCAGE	BROGAN	BROMATES	BRONCOS
BRITTLY	BROCAGES	BROGANS	BROMATING	BRONCS
BRITTS	BROCARD	BROGGED	BROME	BROND
BRITZKA	BROCARDS	BROGGING	BROMELAIN	BRONDS
BRITZKAS	BROCATEL	BROGH	BROMELIA	BRONDYRON
BRITZSKA	BROCATELS	BROGHS	BROMELIAD	BRONZE
BRITZSKAS	BROCCOLI	BROGS	BROMELIAS	BRONZED
BRIZE	BROCCOLIS	BROGUE	BROMELIN	BRONZEN
BRIZES	BROCH	BROGUEISH	BROMELINS	BRONZER
BRO	BROCHAN	BROGUERY	BROMEOSIN	BRONZERS
BROACH	BROCHANS	BROGUES	BROMES	BRONZES
BROACHED	BROCHE	BROGUISH	BROMIC	BRONZIER
BROACHER	BROCHED	BROIDER	BROMID	BRONZIEST
BROACHERS	BROCHES	BROIDERED	BROMIDE	BRONZIFY
BROACHES	BROCHETTE	BROIDERER	BROMIDES	BRONZING
BROACHING	BROCHING	BROIDERS	BROMIDIC	BRONZINGS
BROAD	BROCHO	BROIDERY	BROMIDS	BRONZITE
BROADAX	BROCHOS	BROIL	BROMIN	BRONZITES
BROADAXE	BROCHS	BROILED	BROMINATE	BRONZY
BROADAXES	BROCHURE	BROILER	BROMINE	BROO
BROADBAND	BROCHURES	BROILERS	BROMINES	BROOCH
BROADBEAN	BROCK	BROILING	BROMINISM	BROOCHED
BROADBILL	BROCKAGE	BROILS	BROMINS	BROOCHES
BROADBRIM	BROCKAGES	BROKAGE	BROMISE	BROOCHING
BROADCAST	BROCKED	BROKAGES	BROMISED	BROOD
BROADEN	BROCKET	BROKE	BROMISES	BROODED
BROADENED	BROCKETS	BROKED	BROMISING	BROODER
BROADENER	BROCKIT	BROKEN	BROMISM	BROODERS
BROADENS	BROCKRAM	BROKENLY	BROMISMS	BROODIER
BROADER	BROCKRAMS	BROKER	BROMIZE	BROODIEST
BROADEST	BROCKS	BROKERAGE	BROMIZED	BROODILY
BROADISH	BROCOLI	BROKERED	BROMIZES	BROODING
BROADLEAF	BROCOLIS	BROKERIES	BROMIZING	BROODINGS
BROADLINE	BROD	BROKERING	BROMMER	BROODLESS
BROADLOOM	BRODDED	BROKERS	BROMMERS	BROODMARE
BROADLY	BRODDING	BROKERY	BROMO	BROODS
BROADNESS	BRODDLE	BROKES	BROMOFORM	BROODY
BROADS	BRODDLED	BROKING	BROMOS	BROOK
BROADSIDE	BRODDLES	BROKINGS	BRONC	BROOKABLE
BROADTAIL	BRODDLING	BROLGA	BRONCHI	BROOKED
BROADWAY	BRODEKIN	BROLGAS	BRONCHIA	BROOKIE

BROOKIES	BROUGHTA	BRR	BRUME	BRUSKER
BROOKING	BROUGHTAS	BRRR	BRUMES	BRUSKEST
BROOKITE	BROUHAHA	BRU	BRUMMAGEM	BRUSQUE
BROOKITES	BROUHAHAS	BRUCELLA	BRUMMER	BRUSQUELY
BROOKLET	BROUZE	BRUCELLAE	BRUMMERS	BRUSQUER
BROOKLETS	BROUZES	BRUCELLAS	BRUMOUS	BRUSQUEST
BROOKLIKE	BROW	BRUCHID	BRUNCH	BRUSSELS
BROOKLIME	BROWALLIA	BRUCHIDS	BRUNCHED	BRUSSEN
BROOKS	BROWBAND	BRUCIN	BRUNCHER	BRUST
BROOKWEED	BROWBANDS	BRUCINE	BRUNCHERS	BRUSTING
BROOL	BROWBEAT	BRUCINES	BRUNCHES	BRUSTS
BROOLS	BROWBEATS	BRUCINS	BRUNCHING	BRUT
BROOM	BROWED	BRUCITE	BRUNET	BRUTAL
BROOMBALL	BROWLESS	BRUCITES	BRUNETS	BRUTALISE
BROOMCORN	BROWN	BRUCKLE	BRUNETTE	BRUTALISM
BROOMED	BROWNED	BRUGH	BRUNETTES	BRUTALIST
BROOMIER	BROWNER	BRUGHS	BRUNG	BRUTALITY
BROOMIEST	BROWNEST	BRUHAHA	BRUNIZEM	BRUTALIZE
BROOMING	BROWNIE	BRUHAHAS	BRUNIZEMS	BRUTALLY
BROOMRAPE	BROWNIER	BRUILZIE	BRUNT	BRUTE
BROOMS	BROWNIES	BRUILZIES	BRUNTED	BRUTED
BROOMY	BROWNIEST	BRUIN	BRUNTING	BRUTELIKE
BROOS	BROWNING	BRUINS	BRUNTS	BRUTELY
BROOSE	BROWNINGS	BRUISE	BRUS	BRUTENESS
BROOSES	BROWNISH	BRUISED	BRUSH	BRUTER
BROS	BROWNNESS	BRUISER	BRUSHBACK	BRUTERS
BROSE	BROWNNOSE	BRUISERS	BRUSHED	BRUTES
BROSES	BROWNOUT	BRUISES	BRUSHER	BRUTIFIED
BROSIER	BROWNOUTS	BRUISING	BRUSHERS	BRUTIFIES
BROSIEST	BROWNS	BRUISINGS	BRUSHES	BRUTIFY
BROSY	BROWNTAIL	BRUIT	BRUSHFIRE	BRUTING
BROTH	BROWNY	BRUITED	BRUSHIER	BRUTINGS
BROTHEL	BROWRIDGE	BRUITER	BRUSHIEST	BRUTISH
BROTHELS	BROWS	BRUITERS	BRUSHING	BRUTISHLY
BROTHER	BROWSABLE	BRUITING	BRUSHINGS	BRUTISM
BROTHERED	BROWSE	BRUITS	BRUSHLAND	BRUTISMS
BROTHERLY	BROWSED	BRULE	BRUSHLESS	BRUTS
BROTHERS	BROWSER	BRULES	BRUSHLIKE	BRUX
BROTHIER	BROWSERS	BRULOT	BRUSHMARK	BRUXED
BROTHIEST	BROWSES	BRULOTS	BRUSHOFF	BRUXES
BROTHS	BROWSIER	BRULYIE	BRUSHOFFS	BRUXING
BROTHY	BROWSIEST	BRULYIES	BRUSHUP	BRUXISM
BROUGH	BROWSING	BRULZIE	BRUSHUPS	BRUXISMS
BROUGHAM	BROWSINGS	BRULZIES	BRUSHWOOD	BRYOLOGY
BROUGHAMS	BROWST	BRUMAL	BRUSHWORK	BRYONIES
BROUGHS	BROWSTS	BRUMBIES	BRUSHY	BRYONY
BROUGHT	BROWSY	BRUMBY	BRUSK	BRYOPHYTE

BRYOZOAN	BUCCAL	BUCKLES	BUDDIES	BUFFALO
BRYOZOANS	BUCCALLY	BUCKLING	BUDDIEST	BUFFALOED
BUAT	BUCCANEER	BUCKLINGS	BUDDING	BUFFALOES
BUATS	BUCCANIER	BUCKO	BUDDINGS	BUFFALOS
BUAZE	BUCCINA	BUCKOES	BUDDLE	BUFFE
BUAZES	BUCCINAS	BUCKOS	BUDDLED	BUFFED
BUB	BUCELLAS	BUCKRA	BUDDLEIA	BUFFEL
BUBA	BUCENTAUR	BUCKRAKE	BUDDLEIAS	BUFFER
BUBAL	BUCHU	BUCKRAKES	BUDDLES	BUFFERED
BUBALE	BUCHUS	BUCKRAM	BUDDLING	BUFFERING
BUBALES	BUCK	BUCKRAMED	BUDDY	BUFFERS
BUBALINE	BUCKAROO	BUCKRAMS	BUDDYING	BUFFEST
BUBALIS	BUCKAROOS	BUCKRAS	BUDGE	BUFFET
BUBALISES	BUCKAYRO	BUCKS	BUDGED	BUFFETED
BUBALS	BUCKAYROS	BUCKSAW	BUDGER	BUFFETER
BUBAS	BUCKBEAN	BUCKSAWS	BUDGEREE	BUFFETERS
BUBBA	BUCKBEANS	BUCKSHEE	BUDGERO	BUFFETING
BUBBAS	BUCKBOARD	BUCKSHEES	BUDGEROS	BUFFETS
BUBBIES	BUCKBRUSH	BUCKSHISH	BUDGEROW	BUFFI
BUBBLE	BUCKED	BUCKSHOT	BUDGEROWS	BUFFIER
BUBBLED	BUCKEEN	BUCKSHOTS	BUDGERS	BUFFIEST
BUBBLEGUM	BUCKEENS	BUCKSKIN	BUDGES	BUFFING
BUBBLER	BUCKER	BUCKSKINS	BUDGET	BUFFINGS
BUBBLERS	BUCKEROO	BUCKSOM	BUDGETARY	BUFFO
BUBBLES	BUCKEROOS	BUCKTAIL	BUDGETED	BUFFOON
BUBBLIER	BUCKERS	BUCKTAILS	BUDGETEER	BUFFOONS
BUBBLIES	BUCKET	BUCKTEETH	BUDGETER	BUFFOS
BUBBLIEST	BUCKETED	BUCKTHORN	BUDGETERS	BUFFS
BUBBLING	BUCKETFUL	BUCKTOOTH	BUDGETING	BUFFY
BUBBLY	BUCKETING	BUCKU	BUDGETS	BUFO
BUBBY	BUCKETS	BUCKUS	BUDGIE	BUFOS
BUBINGA	BUCKEYE	BUCKWHEAT	BUDGIES	BUFOTALIN
BUBINGAS	BUCKEYES	BUCKYBALL	BUDGING	BUFTIE
BUBKES	BUCKHORN	BUCKYTUBE	BUDI	BUFTIES
BUBKIS	BUCKHORNS	BUCOLIC	BUDIS	BUFTY
BUBO	BUCKHOUND	BUCOLICAL	BUDLESS	BUG
BUBOED	BUCKIE	BUCOLICS	BUDLIKE	BUGABOO
BUBOES	BUCKIES	BUD	BUDMASH	BUGABOOS
BUBONIC	BUCKING	BUDA	BUDMASHES	BUGBANE
BUBS	BUCKINGS	BUDAS	BUDO	BUGBANES
BUBU	BUCKISH	BUDDED	BUDOS	BUGBEAR
BUBUKLE	BUCKISHLY	BUDDER	BUDS	BUGBEARS
BUBUKLES	BUCKLE	BUDDERS	BUDWORM	BUGEYE
BUBUS	BUCKLED	BUDDHA	BUDWORMS	BUGEYES
BUCARDO	BUCKLER	BUDDHAS	BUFF	BUGGAN
BUCARDOS	BUCKLERED	BUDDIED	BUFFA	BUGGANE
BUCATINI	BUCKLERS	BUDDIER	BUFFABLE	BUGGANES

BUGGANS	BUHRSTONE	BULBUL	BULLACES	BULLION
BUGGED	BUHUND	BULBULS	BULLAE	BULLIONS
BUGGER	BUHUNDS	BULGE	BULLARIES	BULLISH
BUGGERED	BUIBUI	BULGED	BULLARY	BULLISHLY
BUGGERIES	BUIBUIS	BULGER	BULLATE	BULLNECK
BUGGERING	BUIK	BULGERS	BULLBARS	BULLNECKS
BUGGERS	BUIKS	BULGES	BULLBAT	BULLNOSE
BUGGERY	BUILD	BULGHUR	BULLBATS	BULLNOSES
BUGGIER	BUILDABLE	BULGHURS	BULLBRIER	BULLOCK
BUGGIES	BUILDDOWN	BULGIER	BULLDOG	BULLOCKED
BUGGIEST	BUILDED	BULGIEST	BULLDOGS	BULLOCKS
BUGGIN	BUILDER	BULGINE	BULLDOZE	BULLOCKY
BUGGINESS	BUILDERS	BULGINES	BULLDOZED	BULLOSA
BUGGING	BUILDING	BULGINESS	BULLDOZER	BULLOUS
BUGGINGS	BUILDINGS	BULGING	BULLDOZES	BULLPEN
BUGGINS	BUILDS	BULGINGLY	BULLDUST	BULLPENS
BUGGY	BUILDUP	BULGUR	BULLDUSTS	BULLPOUT
BUGHOUSE	BUILDUPS	BULGURS	BULLDYKE	BULLPOUTS
BUGHOUSES	BUILT	BULGY	BULLDYKES	BULLRING
BUGLE	BUIRDLIER	BULIMIA	BULLED	BULLRINGS
BUGLED	BUIRDLY	BULIMIAC	BULLER	BULLRUSH
BUGLER	BUIST	BULIMIAS	BULLERED	BULLS
BUGLERS	BUISTED	BULIMIC	BULLERING	BULLSHAT
BUGLES	BUISTING	BULIMICS	BULLERS	BULLSHIT
BUGLET	BUISTS	BULIMIES	BULLET	BULLSHITS
BUGLETS	BUKE	BULIMUS	BULLETED	BULLSHOT
BUGLEWEED	BUKES	BULIMUSES	BULLETIN	BULLSHOTS
BUGLING	BUKKAKE	BULIMY	BULLETING	BULLSNAKE
BUGLOSS	BUKKAKES	BULK	BULLETINS	BULLWADDY
BUGLOSSES	BUKSHEE	BULKAGE	BULLETRIE	BULLWEED
BUGONG	BUKSHEES	BULKAGES	BULLETS	BULLWEEDS
BUGONGS	BUKSHI	BULKED	BULLFIGHT	BULLWHACK
BUGOUT	BUKSHIS	BULKER	BULLFINCH	BULLWHIP
BUGOUTS	BULB	BULKERS	BULLFROG	BULLWHIPS
BUGS	BULBAR	BULKHEAD	BULLFROGS	BULLY
BUGSEED	BULBED	BULKHEADS	BULLGINE	BULLYBOY
BUGSEEDS	BULBEL	BULKIER	BULLGINES	BULLYBOYS
BUGSHA	BULBELS	BULKIEST	BULLHEAD	BULLYCIDE
BUGSHAS	BULBIL	BULKILY	BULLHEADS	BULLYING
BUGWORT	BULBILS	BULKINESS	BULLHORN	BULLYISM
BUGWORTS	BULBING	BULKING	BULLHORNS	BULLYISMS
BUHL	BULBLET	BULKINGS	BULLIED	BULLYRAG
BUHLS	BULBLETS	BULKS	BULLIER	BULLYRAGS
BUHLWORK	BULBOSITY	BULKY	BULLIES	BULNBULN
BUHLWORKS	BULBOUS	BULL	BULLIEST	BULNBULNS
BUHR	BULBOUSLY	BULLA	BULLING	BULRUSH
BUHRS	BULBS	BULLACE	BULLINGS	BULRUSHES

BULRUSHY	BUMMED	BUNCHIER	BUNGALOWS	BUNKOING
BULSE	BUMMEL	BUNCHIEST	BUNGED	BUNKOS
BULSES	BUMMELS	BUNCHILY	BUNGEE	BUNKS
BULWADDEE	BUMMER	BUNCHING	BUNGEES	BUNKUM
BULWADDY	BUMMERS	BUNCHINGS	BUNGER	BUNKUMS
BULWARK	BUMMEST	BUNCHY	BUNGERS	BUNN
BULWARKED	BUMMING	BUNCING	BUNGEY	BUNNET
BULWARKS	BUMMLE	BUNCO	BUNGEYS	BUNNETS
BUM	BUMMLED	BUNCOED	BUNGHOLE	BUNNIA
BUMALO	BUMMLES	BUNCOING	BUNGHOLES	BUNNIAS
BUMALOTI	BUMMLING	BUNCOMBE	BUNGIE	BUNNIES
BUMALOTIS	BUMMOCK	BUNCOMBES	BUNGIES	BUNNS
BUMBAG	BUMMOCKS	BUNCOS	BUNGING	BUNNY
BUMBAGS	BUMP	BUND	BUNGLE	BUNODONT
BUMBAZE	BUMPED	BUNDE	BUNGLED	BUNRAKU
BUMBAZED	BUMPER	BUNDED	BUNGLER	BUNRAKUS
BUMBAZES	BUMPERED	BUNDH	BUNGLERS	BUNS
BUMBAZING	BUMPERING	BUNDHS	BUNGLES	BUNSEN
BUMBLE	BUMPERS	BUNDIED	BUNGLING	BUNSENS
BUMBLEBEE	BUMPH	BUNDIES	BUNGLINGS	BUNT
BUMBLED	BUMPHS	BUNDING	BUNGS	BUNTAL
BUMBLEDOM	BUMPIER	BUNDIST	BUNGWALL	BUNTALS
BUMBLER	BUMPIEST	BUNDISTS	BUNGWALLS	BUNTED
BUMBLERS	BUMPILY	BUNDLE	BUNGY	BUNTER
BUMBLES	BUMPINESS	BUNDLED	BUNIA	BUNTERS
BUMBLING	BUMPING	BUNDLER	BUNIAS	BUNTIER
BUMBLINGS	BUMPINGS	BUNDLERS	BUNION	BUNTIEST
BUMBO	BUMPKIN	BUNDLES	BUNIONS	BUNTING
BUMBOAT	BUMPKINLY	BUNDLING	BUNJE	BUNTINGS
BUMBOATS	BUMPKINS	BUNDLINGS	BUNJEE	BUNTLINE
BUMBOS	BUMPOLOGY	BUNDOBUST	BUNJEES	BUNTLINES
BUMELIA	BUMPS	BUNDOOK	BUNJES	BUNTS
BUMELIAS	BUMPTIOUS	BUNDOOKS	BUNJIE	BUNTY
BUMF	BUMPY	BUNDS	BUNJIES	BUNYA
BUMFLUFF	BUMS	BUNDT	BUNJY	BUNYAS
BUMFLUFFS	BUMSTER	BUNDTS	BUNK	BUNYIP
BUMFS	BUMSTERS	BUNDU	BUNKED	BUNYIPS
BUMFUCK	BUMSUCKER	BUNDUS	BUNKER	BUOY
BUMFUCKS	BUN	BUNDWALL	BUNKERED	BUOYAGE
BUMFUZZLE	BUNA	BUNDWALLS	BUNKERING	BUOYAGES
BUMKIN	BUNAS	BUNDY	BUNKERS	BUOYANCE
BUMKINS	BUNCE	BUNDYING	BUNKHOUSE	BUOYANCES
BUMMALO	BUNCED	BUNFIGHT	BUNKING	BUOYANCY
BUMMALOS	BUNCES	BUNFIGHTS	BUNKMATE	BUOYANT
BUMMALOTI	BUNCH	BUNG	BUNKMATES	BUOYANTLY
BUMMAREE	BUNCHED	BUNGALOID	BUNKO	BUOYED
BUMMAREES	BUNCHES	BUNGALOW	BUNKOED	BUOYING

BUOYS	BURDOCKS	BURGUNDY	BURLIEST	BURRAMYS
BUPKES	BURDS	BURHEL	BURLILY	BURRAWANG
BUPKIS	BUREAU	BURHELS	BURLINESS	BURRED
BUPKUS	BUREAUS	BURIAL	BURLING	BURREL
BUPLEVER	BUREAUX	BURIALS	BURLS	BURRELL
BUPLEVERS	BURET	BURIED	BURLY	BURRELLS
BUPPIE	BURETS	BURIER	BURN	BURRELS
BUPPIES	BURETTE	BURIERS	BURNABLE	BURRER
BUPPY	BURETTES	BURIES	BURNABLES	BURRERS
BUPRESTID	BURG	BURIN	BURNED	BURRHEL
BUPROPION	BURGAGE	BURINIST	BURNER	BURRHELS
BUQSHA	BURGAGES	BURINISTS	BURNERS	BURRIER
BUQSHAS	BURGANET	BURINS	BURNET	BURRIEST
BUR	BURGANETS	BURITI	BURNETS	BURRING
BURA	BURGEE	BURITIS	BURNIE	BURRITO
BURAN	BURGEES	BURK	BURNIES	BURRITOS
BURANS	BURGEON	BURKA	BURNING	BURRO
BURAS	BURGEONED	BURKAS	BURNINGLY	BURROS
BURB	BURGEONS	BURKE	BURNINGS	BURROW
BURBLE	BURGER	BURKED	BURNISH	BURROWED
BURBLED	BURGERS	BURKER	BURNISHED	BURROWER
BURBLER	BURGESS	BURKERS	BURNISHER	BURROWERS
BURBLERS	BURGESSES	BURKES	BURNISHES	BURROWING
BURBLES	BURGH	BURKHA	BURNOOSE	BURROWS
BURBLIER	BURGHAL	BURKHAS	BURNOOSED	BURRS
BURBLIEST	BURGHER	BURKING	BURNOOSES	BURRSTONE
BURBLING	BURGHERS	BURKITE	BURNOUS	BURRY
BURBLINGS	BURGHS	BURKITES	BURNOUSE	BURS
BURBLY	BURGHUL	BURKS	BURNOUSED	BURSA
BURBOT	BURGHULS	BURL	BURNOUSES	BURSAE
BURBOTS	BURGLAR	BURLADERO	BURNOUT	BURSAL
BURBS	BURGLARED	BURLAP	BURNOUTS	BURSAR
BURD	BURGLARS	BURLAPS	BURNS	BURSARIAL
BURDASH	BURGLARY	BURLED	BURNSIDE	BURSARIES
BURDASHES	BURGLE	BURLER	BURNSIDES	BURSARS
BURDEN	BURGLED	BURLERS	BURNT	BURSARY
BURDENED	BURGLES	BURLESK	BUROO	BURSAS
BURDENER	BURGLING	BURLESKS	BUROOS	BURSATE
BURDENERS	BURGONET	BURLESQUE	BURP	BURSE
BURDENING	BURGONETS	BURLETTA	BURPED	BURSEED
BURDENOUS	BURGOO	BURLETTAS	BURPEE	BURSEEDS
BURDENS	BURGOOS	BURLEY	BURPEES	BURSERA
BURDIE	BURGOUT	BURLEYCUE	BURPING	BURSES
BURDIES	BURGOUTS	BURLEYED	BURPS	BURSICON
BURDIZZO	BURGRAVE	BURLEYING	BURQA	BURSICONS
BURDIZZOS	BURGRAVES	BURLEYS	BURQAS	BURSIFORM
BURDOCK	BURGS	BURLIER	BURR	BURSITIS

BURST	BUSHER	BUSILY	BUSTIS	BUTEOS
BURSTED	BUSHERS	BUSINESS	BUSTLE	BUTES
BURSTEN	BUSHES	BUSINESSY	BUSTLED	BUTLE
BURSTER	BUSHFIRE	BUSING	BUSTLER	BUTLED
BURSTERS	BUSHFIRES	BUSINGS	BUSTLERS	BUTLER
BURSTING	BUSHFLIES	BUSK	BUSTLES	BUTLERAGE
BURSTONE	BUSHFLY	BUSKED	BUSTLINE	BUTLERED
BURSTONES	BUSHGOAT	BUSKER	BUSTLINES	BUTLERIES
BURSTS	BUSHGOATS	BUSKERS	BUSTLING	BUTLERING
BURTHEN	BUSHIDO	BUSKET	BUSTS	BUTLERS
BURTHENED	BUSHIDOS	BUSKETS	BUSTY	BUTLERY
BURTHENS	BUSHIE	BUSKIN	BUSULFAN	BUTLES
BURTON	BUSHIER	BUSKINED	BUSULFANS	BUTLING
BURTONS	BUSHIES	BUSKING	BUSUUTI	BUTMENT
BURWEED	BUSHIEST	BUSKINGS	BUSUUTIS	BUTMENTS
BURWEEDS	BUSHILY	BUSKINS	BUSY	BUTS
BURY	BUSHINESS	BUSKS	BUSYBODY	BUTSUDAN
BURYING	BUSHING	BUSKY	BUSYING	BUTSUDANS
BUS	BUSHINGS	BUSLOAD	BUSYNESS	BUTT
BUSBAR	BUSHLAND	BUSLOADS	BUSYWORK	BUTTALS
BUSBARS	BUSHLANDS	BUSMAN	BUSYWORKS	BUTTE
BUSBIES	BUSHLESS	BUSMEN	BUT	BUTTED
BUSBOY	BUSHLIKE	BUSS	BUTADIENE	BUTTER
BUSBOYS	BUSHMAN	BUSSED	BUTANE	BUTTERBUR
BUSBY	BUSHMEAT	BUSSES	BUTANES	BUTTERCUP
BUSED	BUSHMEATS	BUSSING	BUTANOIC	BUTTERED
BUSERA	BUSHMEN	BUSSINGS	BUTANOL	BUTTERFAT
BUSERAS	BUSHPIG	BUSSU	BUTANOLS	BUTTERFLY
BUSES	BUSHPIGS	BUSSUS	BUTANONE	BUTTERIER
BUSGIRL	BUSHTIT	BUST	BUTANONES	BUTTERIES
BUSGIRLS	BUSHTITS	BUSTARD	BUTCH	BUTTERINE
BUSH	BUSHVELD	BUSTARDS	BUTCHER	BUTTERING
BUSHBABY	BUSHVELDS	BUSTED	BUTCHERED	BUTTERNUT
BUSHBUCK	BUSHWA	BUSTEE	BUTCHERER	BUTTERS
BUSHBUCKS	BUSHWAH	BUSTEES	BUTCHERLY	BUTTERY
BUSHCRAFT	BUSHWAHS	BUSTER	BUTCHERS	BUTTES
BUSHED	BUSHWALK	BUSTERS	BUTCHERY	BUTTHEAD
BUSHEL	BUSHWALKS	BUSTI	BUTCHES	BUTTHEADS
BUSHELED	BUSHWAS	BUSTIC	BUTCHEST	BUTTIES
BUSHELER	BUSHWHACK	BUSTICATE	BUTCHING	BUTTING
BUSHELERS	BUSHWOMAN	BUSTICS	BUTCHINGS	BUTTINSKI
BUSHELING	BUSHWOMEN	BUSTIER	BUTCHNESS	BUTTINSKY
BUSHELLED	BUSHY	BUSTIERS	BUTE	BUTTLE
BUSHELLER	BUSIED	BUSTIEST	BUTENE	BUTTLED
BUSHELMAN	BUSIER	BUSTINESS	BUTENES	BUTTLES
BUSHELMEN	BUSIES	BUSTING	BUTEO	BUTTLING
BUSHELS	BUSIEST	BUSTINGS	BUTEONINE	BUTTOCK

BUTTOCKED	BUXOM	BUZZIEST	BYLANE	BYRLAWS
BUTTOCKS	BUXOMER	BUZZING	BYLANES	BYRLED
BUTTON	BUXOMEST	BUZZINGLY	BYLAW	BYRLING
BUTTONED	BUXOMLY	BUZZINGS	BYLAWS	BYRLS
BUTTONER	BUXOMNESS	BUZZKILL	BYLINE	BYRNIE
BUTTONERS	BUY	BUZZKILLS	BYLINED	BYRNIES
BUTTONING	BUYABLE	BUZZWIG	BYLINER	BYROAD
BUTTONS	BUYABLES	BUZZWIGS	BYLINERS	BYROADS
BUTTONY	BUYBACK	BUZZWORD	BYLINES	BYROOM
BUTTRESS	BUYBACKS	BUZZWORDS	BYLINING	BYROOMS
BUTTS	BUYER	BUZZY	BYLIVE	BYS
BUTTSTOCK	BUYERS	BWANA	BYNAME	BYSSAL
BUTTY	BUYING	BWANAS	BYNAMES	BYSSI
BUTTYMAN	BUYINGS	BWAZI	BYNEMPT	BYSSINE
BUTTYMEN	BUYOFF	BWAZIS	BYPASS	BYSSOID
BUTUT	BUYOFFS	BY	BYPASSED	BYSSUS
BUTUTS	BUYOUT	BYCATCH	BYPASSES	BYSSUSES
BUTYL	BUYOUTS	BYCATCHES	BYPASSING	BYSTANDER
BUTYLATE	BUYS	BYCOKET	BYPAST	BYSTREET
BUTYLATED	BUZKASHI	BYCOKETS	BYPATH	BYSTREETS
BUTYLATES	BUZKASHIS	BYDE	BYPATHS	BYTALK
BUTYLENE	BUZUKI	BYDED	BYPLACE	BYTALKS
BUTYLENES	BUZUKIA	BYDES	BYPLACES	BYTE
BUTYLS	BUZUKIS	BYDING	BYPLAY	BYTES
BUTYRAL	BUZZ	BYE	BYPLAYS	BYTOWNITE
BUTYRALS	BUZZARD	BYELAW	BYPRODUCT	BYWAY
BUTYRATE	BUZZARDS	BYELAWS	BYRE	BYWAYS
BUTYRATES	BUZZBAIT	BYES	BYREMAN	BYWONER
BUTYRIC	BUZZBAITS	BYGONE	BYREMEN	BYWONERS
BUTYRIN	BUZZCUT	BYGONES	BYRES	BYWORD
BUTYRINS	BUZZCUTS	BYKE	BYREWOMAN	BYWORDS
BUTYROUS	BUZZED	BYKED	BYREWOMEN	BYWORK
BUTYRYL	BUZZER	BYKES	BYRL	BYWORKS
BUTYRYLS	BUZZERS	BYKING	BYRLADY	BYZANT
BUVETTE	BUZZES	BYLANDER	BYRLAKIN	BYZANTINE
BUVETTES	BUZZIER	BYLANDERS	BYRLAW	BYZANTS

C

CAA	CABBY	CABOCHON	CACHALOT	CACOEPY
CAAED	CABDRIVER	CABOCHONS	CACHALOTS	CACOETHES
CAAING	CABER	CABOCS	CACHE	CACOETHIC
CAAS	CABERNET	CABOMBA	CACHECTIC	CACOGENIC
CAATINGA	CABERNETS	CABOMBAS	CACHED	CACOLET
CAATINGAS	CABERS	CABOODLE	CACHEPOT	CACOLETS
CAB	CABESTRO	CABOODLES	CACHEPOTS	CACOLOGY
CABA	CABESTROS	CABOOSE	CACHES	CACOMIXL
CABAL	CABEZON	CABOOSES	CACHET	CACOMIXLE
CABALA	CABEZONE	CABOSHED	CACHETED	CACOMIXLS
CABALAS	CABEZONES	CABOTAGE	CACHETING	CACONYM
CABALETTA	CABEZONS	CABOTAGES	CACHETS	CACONYMS
CABALETTE	CABILDO	CABOVER	CACHEXIA	CACONYMY
CABALISM	CABILDOS	CABRE	CACHEXIAS	CACOON
CABALISMS	CABIN	CABRESTA	CACHEXIC	CACOONS
CABALIST	CABINED	CABRESTAS	CACHEXIES	CACOPHONY
CABALISTS	CABINET	CABRESTO	CACHEXY	CACOTOPIA
CABALLED	CABINETRY	CABRESTOS	CACHING	CACTI
CABALLER	CABINETS	CABRETTA	CACHOLONG	CACTIFORM
CABALLERO	CABINING	CABRETTAS	CACHOLOT	CACTOID
CABALLERS	CABINMATE	CABRIE	CACHOLOTS	CACTUS
CABALLINE	CABINS	CABRIES	CACHOU	CACTUSES
CABALLING	CABLE	CABRILLA	CACHOUS	CACUMEN
CABALS	CABLECAST	CABRILLAS	CACHUCHA	CACUMINA
CABANA	CABLED	CABRIO	CACHUCHAS	CACUMINAL
CABANAS	CABLEGRAM	CABRIOLE	CACIQUE	CAD
CABARET	CABLER	CABRIOLES	CACIQUES	CADAGA
CABARETS	CABLERS	CABRIOLET	CACIQUISM	CADAGAS
CABAS	CABLES	CABRIOS	CACK	CADAGI
CABBAGE	CABLET	CABRIT	CACKIER	CADAGIS
CABBAGED	CABLETS	CABRITS	CACKIEST	CADASTER
CABBAGES	CABLEWAY	CABS	CACKLE	CADASTERS
CABBAGEY	CABLEWAYS	CABSTAND	CACKLED	CADASTRAL
CABBAGING	CABLING	CABSTANDS	CACKLER	CADASTRE
CABBAGY	CABLINGS	CACA	CACKLERS	CADASTRES
CABBALA	CABMAN	CACAFOGO	CACKLES	CADAVER
CABBALAH	CABMEN	CACAFOGOS	CACKLING	CADAVERIC
CABBALAHS	CABOB	CACAFUEGO	CACKS	CADAVERS
CABBALAS	CABOBBED	CACAO	CACKY	CADDICE
CABBALISM	CABOBBING	CACAOS	CACODEMON	CADDICES
CABBALIST	CABOBS	CACAS	CACODOXY	CADDIE
CABBED	CABOC	CACHACA	CACODYL	CADDIED
CABBIE	CABOCEER	CACHACAS	CACODYLIC	CADDIES
CABBIES	CABOCEERS	CACHAEMIA	CACODYLS	CADDIS
CABBING	CABOCHED	CACHAEMIC	CACOEPIES	CADDISED

CADDISES

CADDISES	CADRE	CAFFEINIC	CAHIERS	CAJOLES
CADDISFLY	CADRES	CAFFEINS	CAHOOT	CAJOLING
CADDISH	CADS	CAFFEISM	CAHOOTS	CAJON
CADDISHLY	CADUAC	CAFFEISMS	CAHOW	CAJONES
CADDY	CADUACS	CAFFILA	CAHOWS	CAJUN
CADDYING	CADUCEAN	CAFFILAS	CAID	CAJUPUT
CADDYSS	CADUCEI	CAFFS	CAIDS	CAJUPUTS
CADDYSSES	CADUCEUS	CAFILA	CAILLACH	CAKE
CADE	CADUCITY	CAFILAS	CAILLACHS	CAKED
CADEAU	CADUCOUS	CAFTAN	CAILLE	CAKES
CADEAUX	CAECA	CAFTANED	CAILLEACH	CAKEWALK
CADEE	CAECAL	CAFTANS	CAILLES	CAKEWALKS
CADEES	CAECALLY	CAG	CAILLIACH	CAKEY
CADELLE	CAECILIAN	CAGANER	CAIMAC	CAKIER
CADELLES	CAECITIS	CAGANERS	CAIMACAM	CAKIEST
CADENCE	CAECUM	CAGE	CAIMACAMS	CAKINESS
CADENCED	CAEOMA	CAGED	CAIMACS	CAKING
CADENCES	CAEOMAS	CAGEFUL	CAIMAN	CAKINGS
CADENCIES	CAERULE	CAGEFULS	CAIMANS	CAKY
CADENCING	CAERULEAN	CAGELIKE	CAIN	CALABASH
CADENCY	CAESAR	CAGELING	CAINS	CALABAZA
CADENT	CAESAREAN	CAGELINGS	CAIQUE	CALABAZAS
CADENTIAL	CAESARIAN	CAGER	CAIQUES	CALABOGUS
CADENZA	CAESARISM	CAGERS	CAIRD	CALABOOSE
CADENZAS	CAESARS	CAGES	CAIRDS	CALABRESE
CADES	CAESE	CAGEWORK	CAIRN	CALADIUM
CADET	CAESIOUS	CAGEWORKS	CAIRNED	CALADIUMS
CADETS	CAESIUM	CAGEY	CAIRNGORM	CALALOO
CADETSHIP	CAESIUMS	CAGEYNESS	CAIRNIER	CALALOOS
CADGE	CAESTUS	CAGIER	CAIRNIEST	CALALU
CADGED	CAESTUSES	CAGIEST	CAIRNS	CALALUS
CADGER	CAESURA	CAGILY	CAIRNY	CALAMANCO
CADGERS	CAESURAE	CAGINESS	CAISSON	CALAMAR
CADGES	CAESURAL	CAGING	CAISSONS	CALAMARI
CADGIER	CAESURAS	CAGMAG	CAITIFF	CALAMARIS
CADGIEST	CAESURIC	CAGMAGGED	CAITIFFS	CALAMARS
CADGING	CAFARD	CAGMAGS	CAITIVE	CALAMARY
CADGY	CAFARDS	CAGOT	CAITIVES	CALAMATA
CADI	CAFE	CAGOTS	CAJAPUT	CALAMATAS
CADIE	CAFES	CAGOUL	CAJAPUTS	CALAMI
CADIES	CAFETERIA	CAGOULE	CAJEPUT	CALAMINE
CADIS	CAFETIERE	CAGOULES	CAJEPUTS	CALAMINED
CADMIC	CAFETORIA	CAGOULS	CAJOLE	CALAMINES
CADMIUM	CAFF	CAGS	CAJOLED	CALAMINT
CADMIUMS	CAFFEIN	CAGY	CAJOLER	CALAMINTS
CADRANS	CAFFEINE	CAGYNESS	CAJOLERS	CALAMITE
CADRANSES	CAFFEINES	CAHIER	CAJOLERY	CALAMITES

CALAMITY CALCIUMS CALFLICKS CALISAYA CALLIPEES
CALAMUS CALCRETE CALFLIKE CALISAYAS CALLIPER
CALANDO CALCRETES CALFS CALIVER CALLIPERS
CALANDRIA CALCSPAR CALFSKIN CALIVERS CALLOP
CALANTHE CALCSPARS CALFSKINS CALIX CALLOPS
CALANTHES CALCTUFA CALIATOUR CALK CALLOSE
CALASH CALCTUFAS CALIBER CALKED CALLOSES
CALASHES CALCTUFF CALIBERED CALKER CALLOSITY
CALATHEA CALCTUFFS CALIBERS CALKERS CALLOUS
CALATHEAS CALCULAR CALIBRATE CALKIN CALLOUSED
CALATHI CALCULARY CALIBRE CALKING CALLOUSES
CALATHOS CALCULATE CALIBRED CALKINGS CALLOUSLY
CALATHUS CALCULI CALIBRES CALKINS CALLOW
CALAVANCE CALCULOSE CALICES CALKS CALLOWER
CALCANEA CALCULOUS CALICHE CALL CALLOWEST
CALCANEAL CALCULUS CALICHES CALLA CALLOWS
CALCANEAN CALDARIA CALICLE CALLABLE CALLS
CALCANEI CALDARIUM CALICLES CALLAIDES CALLTIME
CALCANEUM CALDERA CALICO CALLAIS CALLTIMES
CALCANEUS CALDERAS CALICOES CALLALOO CALLUNA
CALCAR CALDRON CALICOS CALLALOOS CALLUNAS
CALCARATE CALDRONS CALICULAR CALLAN CALLUS
CALCARIA CALECHE CALID CALLANS CALLUSED
CALCARINE CALECHES CALIDITY CALLANT CALLUSES
CALCARS CALEFIED CALIF CALLANTS CALLUSING
CALCEATE CALEFIES CALIFATE CALLAS CALM
CALCEATED CALEFY CALIFATES CALLBACK CALMANT
CALCEATES CALEFYING CALIFONT CALLBACKS CALMANTS
CALCED CALEMBOUR CALIFONTS CALLBOARD CALMATIVE
CALCEDONY CALENDAL CALIFS CALLBOY CALMED
CALCES CALENDAR CALIGO CALLBOYS CALMER
CALCIC CALENDARS CALIGOES CALLED CALMEST
CALCICOLE CALENDER CALIGOS CALLEE CALMIER
CALCIFIC CALENDERS CALIMA CALLEES CALMIEST
CALCIFIED CALENDRER CALIMAS CALLER CALMING
CALCIFIES CALENDRIC CALIMOCHO CALLERS CALMINGLY
CALCIFUGE CALENDRY CALIOLOGY CALLET CALMINGS
CALCIFY CALENDS CALIPASH CALLETS CALMLY
CALCIMINE CALENDULA CALIPEE CALLID CALMNESS
CALCINE CALENTURE CALIPEES CALLIDITY CALMS
CALCINED CALESA CALIPER CALLIGRAM CALMSTANE
CALCINES CALESAS CALIPERED CALLING CALMSTONE
CALCINING CALESCENT CALIPERS CALLINGS CALMY
CALCITE CALF CALIPH CALLIOPE CALO
CALCITES CALFDOZER CALIPHAL CALLIOPES CALOMEL
CALCITIC CALFLESS CALIPHATE CALLIPASH CALOMELS
CALCIUM CALFLICK CALIPHS CALLIPEE CALORIC

CALORICS	CALUMNY	CALZONES	CAMEL	CAMISE
CALORIE	CALUTRON	CALZONI	CAMELBACK	CAMISES
CALORIES	CALUTRONS	CAM	CAMELEER	CAMISIA
CALORIFIC	CALVADOS	CAMA	CAMELEERS	CAMISIAS
CALORISE	CALVARIA	CAMAIEU	CAMELEON	CAMISOLE
CALORISED	CALVARIAL	CAMAIEUX	CAMELEONS	CAMISOLES
CALORISES	CALVARIAN	CAMAIL	CAMELHAIR	CAMLET
CALORIST	CALVARIAS	CAMAILED	CAMELIA	CAMLETS
CALORISTS	CALVARIES	CAMAILS	CAMELIAS	CAMMED
CALORIZE	CALVARIUM	CAMAN	CAMELID	CAMMIE
CALORIZED	CALVARY	CAMANACHD	CAMELIDS	CAMMIES
CALORIZES	CALVE	CAMANS	CAMELINE	CAMMING
CALORY	CALVED	CAMARILLA	CAMELINES	CAMO
CALOS	CALVER	CAMARON	CAMELISH	CAMOGIE
CALOTTE	CALVERED	CAMARONS	CAMELLIA	CAMOGIES
CALOTTES	CALVERING	CAMAS	CAMELLIAS	CAMOMILE
CALOTYPE	CALVERS	CAMASES	CAMELLIKE	CAMOMILES
CALOTYPES	CALVES	CAMASH	CAMELOID	CAMOODI
CALOYER	CALVING	CAMASHES	CAMELOIDS	CAMOODIS
CALOYERS	CALVITIES	CAMASS	CAMELOT	CAMORRA
CALP	CALX	CAMASSES	CAMELOTS	CAMORRAS
CALPA	CALXES	CAMBER	CAMELRIES	CAMORRIST
CALPAC	CALYCATE	CAMBERED	CAMELRY	CAMOS
CALPACK	CALYCEAL	CAMBERING	CAMELS	CAMOTE
CALPACKS	CALYCES	CAMBERS	CAMEO	CAMOTES
CALPACS	CALYCINAL	CAMBIA	CAMEOED	CAMOUFLET
CALPAIN	CALYCINE	CAMBIAL	CAMEOING	CAMP
CALPAINS	CALYCLE	CAMBIFORM	CAMEOS	CAMPAGNA
CALPAS	CALYCLED	CAMBISM	CAMERA	CAMPAGNAS
CALPS	CALYCLES	CAMBISMS	CAMERAE	CAMPAGNE
CALQUE	CALYCOID	CAMBIST	CAMERAL	CAMPAIGN
CALQUED	CALYCULAR	CAMBISTRY	CAMERAMAN	CAMPAIGNS
CALQUES	CALYCULE	CAMBISTS	CAMERAMEN	CAMPANA
CALQUING	CALYCULES	CAMBIUM	CAMERAS	CAMPANAS
CALTHA	CALYCULI	CAMBIUMS	CAMERATED	CAMPANERO
CALTHAS	CALYCULUS	CAMBOGE	CAMES	CAMPANILE
CALTHROP	CALYPSO	CAMBOGES	CAMESE	CAMPANILI
CALTHROPS	CALYPSOES	CAMBOGIA	CAMESES	CAMPANIST
CALTRAP	CALYPSOS	CAMBOGIAS	CAMION	CAMPANULA
CALTRAPS	CALYPTER	CAMBOOSE	CAMIONS	CAMPCRAFT
CALTROP	CALYPTERA	CAMBOOSES	CAMIS	CAMPEACHY
CALTROPS	CALYPTERS	CAMBREL	CAMISA	CAMPEADOR
CALUMBA	CALYPTRA	CAMBRELS	CAMISADE	CAMPED
CALUMBAS	CALYPTRAS	CAMBRIC	CAMISADES	CAMPER
CALUMET	CALYX	CAMBRICS	CAMISADO	CAMPERIES
CALUMETS	CALYXES	CAMCORDER	CAMISADOS	CAMPERS
CALUMNIES	CALZONE	CAME	CAMISAS	CAMPERY

CAMPESINO	CAMPSTOOL	CANARD	CANDIDLY	CANEWARE
CAMPEST	CAMPUS	CANARDS	CANDIDS	CANEWARES
CAMPFIRE	CAMPUSED	CANARIED	CANDIE	CANFIELD
CAMPFIRES	CAMPUSES	CANARIES	CANDIED	CANFIELDS
CAMPHANE	CAMPUSING	CANARY	CANDIES	CANFUL
CAMPHANES	CAMPY	CANARYING	CANDIRU	CANFULS
CAMPHENE	CAMS	CANASTA	CANDIRUS	CANG
CAMPHENES	CAMSHAFT	CANASTAS	CANDLE	CANGLE
CAMPHINE	CAMSHAFTS	CANASTER	CANDLED	CANGLED
CAMPHINES	CAMSHO	CANASTERS	CANDLELIT	CANGLES
CAMPHIRE	CAMSHOCH	CANBANK	CANDLENUT	CANGLING
CAMPHIRES	CAMSTAIRY	CANBANKS	CANDLEPIN	CANGS
CAMPHOL	CAMSTANE	CANCAN	CANDLER	CANGUE
CAMPHOLS	CAMSTANES	CANCANS	CANDLERS	CANGUES
CAMPHONE	CAMSTEARY	CANCEL	CANDLES	CANICULAR
CAMPHONES	CAMSTONE	CANCELBOT	CANDLING	CANID
CAMPHOR	CAMSTONES	CANCELED	CANDOCK	CANIDS
CAMPHORIC	CAMUS	CANCELEER	CANDOCKS	CANIER
CAMPHORS	CAMUSES	CANCELER	CANDOR	CANIEST
CAMPI	CAMWOOD	CANCELERS	CANDORS	CANIKIN
CAMPIER	CAMWOODS	CANCELIER	CANDOUR	CANIKINS
CAMPIEST	CAN	CANCELING	CANDOURS	CANINE
CAMPILY	CANADA	CANCELLED	CANDY	CANINES
CAMPINESS	CANADAS	CANCELLER	CANDYGRAM	CANING
CAMPING	CANAIGRE	CANCELLI	CANDYING	CANINGS
CAMPINGS	CANAIGRES	CANCELS	CANDYMAN	CANINITY
CAMPION	CANAILLE	CANCER	CANDYMEN	CANISTEL
CAMPIONS	CANAILLES	CANCERATE	CANDYTUFT	CANISTELS
CAMPLE	CANAKIN	CANCERED	CANE	CANISTER
CAMPLED	CANAKINS	CANCEROUS	CANEBRAKE	CANISTERS
CAMPLES	CANAL	CANCERS	CANED	CANITIES
CAMPLING	CANALBOAT	CANCHA	CANEFRUIT	CANKER
CAMPLY	CANALED	CANCHAS	CANEGRUB	CANKERED
CAMPNESS	CANALING	CANCRINE	CANEGRUBS	CANKERING
CAMPO	CANALISE	CANCROID	CANEH	CANKEROUS
CAMPODEID	CANALISED	CANCROIDS	CANEHS	CANKERS
CAMPONG	CANALISES	CANDELA	CANELLA	CANKERY
CAMPONGS	CANALIZE	CANDELAS	CANELLAS	CANKLE
CAMPOREE	CANALIZED	CANDENT	CANELLINI	CANKLES
CAMPOREES	CANALIZES	CANDID	CANEPHOR	CANN
CAMPOS	CANALLED	CANDIDA	CANEPHORA	CANNA
CAMPOUT	CANALLER	CANDIDACY	CANEPHORE	CANNABIC
CAMPOUTS	CANALLERS	CANDIDAL	CANEPHORS	CANNABIN
CAMPS	CANALLING	CANDIDAS	CANER	CANNABINS
CAMPSHIRT	CANALS	CANDIDATE	CANERS	CANNABIS
CAMPSITE	CANAPE	CANDIDER	CANES	CANNACH
CAMPSITES	CANAPES	CANDIDEST	CANESCENT	CANNACHS

CANNAE	CANOEINGS	CANTALA	CANTING	CANVASERS
CANNAS	CANOEIST	CANTALAS	CANTINGLY	CANVASES
CANNED	CANOEISTS	CANTALOUP	CANTINGS	CANVASING
CANNEL	CANOER	CANTALS	CANTION	CANVASS
CANNELON	CANOERS	CANTAR	CANTIONS	CANVASSED
CANNELONI	CANOES	CANTARS	CANTLE	CANVASSER
CANNELONS	CANOEWOOD	CANTATA	CANTLED	CANVASSES
CANNELS	CANOLA	CANTATAS	CANTLES	CANY
CANNELURE	CANOLAS	CANTATE	CANTLET	CANYON
CANNER	CANON	CANTATES	CANTLETS	CANYONEER
CANNERIES	CANONESS	CANTDOG	CANTLING	CANYONING
CANNERS	CANONIC	CANTDOGS	CANTO	CANYONS
CANNERY	CANONICAL	CANTED	CANTON	CANZONA
CANNIBAL	CANONISE	CANTEEN	CANTONAL	CANZONAS
CANNIBALS	CANONISED	CANTEENS	CANTONED	CANZONE
CANNIE	CANONISER	CANTER	CANTONING	CANZONES
CANNIER	CANONISES	CANTERED	CANTONISE	CANZONET
CANNIEST	CANONIST	CANTERING	CANTONIZE	CANZONETS
CANNIKIN	CANONISTS	CANTERS	CANTONS	CANZONI
CANNIKINS	CANONIZE	CANTEST	CANTOR	CAP
CANNILY	CANONIZED	CANTHAL	CANTORIAL	CAPA
CANNINESS	CANONIZER	CANTHARI	CANTORIS	CAPABLE
CANNING	CANONIZES	CANTHARID	CANTORS	CAPABLER
CANNINGS	CANONRIES	CANTHARIS	CANTOS	CAPABLEST
CANNISTER	CANONRY	CANTHARUS	CANTRAIP	CAPABLY
CANNOLI	CANONS	CANTHI	CANTRAIPS	CAPACIOUS
CANNOLIS	CANOODLE	CANTHITIS	CANTRAP	CAPACITOR
CANNON	CANOODLED	CANTHOOK	CANTRAPS	CAPACITY
CANNONADE	CANOODLER	CANTHOOKS	CANTRED	CAPARISON
CANNONED	CANOODLES	CANTHUS	CANTREDS	CAPAS
CANNONEER	CANOPIC	CANTIC	CANTREF	CAPE
CANNONIER	CANOPIED	CANTICLE	CANTREFS	CAPED
CANNONING	CANOPIES	CANTICLES	CANTRIP	CAPELAN
CANNONRY	CANOPY	CANTICO	CANTRIPS	CAPELANS
CANNONS	CANOPYING	CANTICOED	CANTS	CAPELET
CANNOT	CANOROUS	CANTICOS	CANTUS	CAPELETS
CANNS	CANS	CANTICOY	CANTY	CAPELIN
CANNULA	CANSFUL	CANTICOYS	CANULA	CAPELINE
CANNULAE	CANSO	CANTICUM	CANULAE	CAPELINES
CANNULAR	CANSOS	CANTICUMS	CANULAR	CAPELINS
CANNULAS	CANST	CANTIER	CANULAS	CAPELLET
CANNULATE	CANSTICK	CANTIEST	CANULATE	CAPELLETS
CANNY	CANSTICKS	CANTILENA	CANULATED	CAPELLINE
CANOE	CANT	CANTILY	CANULATES	CAPELLINI
CANOEABLE	CANTABANK	CANTINA	CANVAS	CAPER
CANOED	CANTABILE	CANTINAS	CANVASED	CAPERED
CANOEING	CANTAL	CANTINESS	CANVASER	CAPERER

CAPERERS	CAPMAKER	CAPRIFIG	CAPSULISE	CARABIN
CAPERING	CAPMAKERS	CAPRIFIGS	CAPSULIZE	CARABINE
CAPERS	CAPO	CAPRIFOIL	CAPTAIN	CARABINER
CAPES	CAPOCCHIA	CAPRIFOLE	CAPTAINCY	CARABINES
CAPESKIN	CAPOEIRA	CAPRIFORM	CAPTAINED	CARABINS
CAPESKINS	CAPOEIRAS	CAPRIFY	CAPTAINRY	CARACAL
CAPEWORK	CAPON	CAPRINE	CAPTAINS	CARACALS
CAPEWORKS	CAPONATA	CAPRIOLE	CAPTAN	CARACARA
CAPEX	CAPONATAS	CAPRIOLED	CAPTANS	CARACARAS
CAPEXES	CAPONIER	CAPRIOLES	CAPTION	CARACK
CAPFUL	CAPONIERE	CAPRIS	CAPTIONED	CARACKS
CAPFULS	CAPONIERS	CAPROATE	CAPTIONS	CARACOL
CAPH	CAPONISE	CAPROATES	CAPTIOUS	CARACOLE
CAPHS	CAPONISED	CAPROCK	CAPTIVATE	CARACOLED
CAPI	CAPONISES	CAPROCKS	CAPTIVE	CARACOLER
CAPIAS	CAPONIZE	CAPROIC	CAPTIVED	CARACOLES
CAPIASES	CAPONIZED	CAPRYLATE	CAPTIVES	CARACOLS
CAPILLARY	CAPONIZES	CAPRYLIC	CAPTIVING	CARACT
CAPING	CAPONS	CAPS	CAPTIVITY	CARACTS
CAPITA	CAPORAL	CAPSAICIN	CAPTOPRIL	CARACUL
CAPITAL	CAPORALS	CAPSICIN	CAPTOR	CARACULS
CAPITALLY	CAPOS	CAPSICINS	CAPTORS	CARAFE
CAPITALS	CAPOT	CAPSICUM	CAPTURE	CARAFES
CAPITAN	CAPOTASTO	CAPSICUMS	CAPTURED	CARAGANA
CAPITANI	CAPOTE	CAPSID	CAPTURER	CARAGANAS
CAPITANO	CAPOTES	CAPSIDAL	CAPTURERS	CARAGEEN
CAPITANOS	CAPOTS	CAPSIDS	CAPTURES	CARAGEENS
CAPITANS	CAPOTTED	CAPSIZAL	CAPTURING	CARAMBA
CAPITATE	CAPOTTING	CAPSIZALS	CAPUCCIO	CARAMBOLA
CAPITATED	CAPOUCH	CAPSIZE	CAPUCCIOS	CARAMBOLE
CAPITAYN	CAPOUCHES	CAPSIZED	CAPUCHE	CARAMEL
CAPITAYNS	CAPPED	CAPSIZES	CAPUCHED	CARAMELS
CAPITELLA	CAPPER	CAPSIZING	CAPUCHES	CARANGID
CAPITOL	CAPPERS	CAPSOMER	CAPUCHIN	CARANGIDS
CAPITOLS	CAPPING	CAPSOMERE	CAPUCHINS	CARANGOID
CAPITULA	CAPPINGS	CAPSOMERS	CAPUERA	CARANNA
CAPITULAR	CAPRATE	CAPSTAN	CAPUERAS	CARANNAS
CAPITULUM	CAPRATES	CAPSTANS	CAPUL	CARAP
CAPIZ	CAPRIC	CAPSTONE	CAPULS	CARAPACE
CAPIZES	CAPRICCI	CAPSTONES	CAPUT	CARAPACED
CAPLE	CAPRICCIO	CAPSULAR	CAPYBARA	CARAPACES
CAPLES	CAPRICE	CAPSULARY	CAPYBARAS	CARAPAX
CAPLESS	CAPRICES	CAPSULATE	CAR	CARAPAXES
CAPLET	CAPRID	CAPSULE	CARABAO	CARAPS
CAPLETS	CAPRIDS	CAPSULED	CARABAOS	CARASSOW
CAPLIN	CAPRIFIED	CAPSULES	CARABID	CARASSOWS
CAPLINS	CAPRIFIES	CAPSULING	CARABIDS	CARAT

CARATE	CARBOLIZE	CARCINOMA	CARDPHONE	CARETAKES
CARATES	CARBON	CARD	CARDPUNCH	CARETOOK
CARATS	CARBONADE	CARDAMINE	CARDS	CARETS
CARAUNA	CARBONADO	CARDAMOM	CARDSHARP	CAREWARE
CARAUNAS	CARBONARA	CARDAMOMS	CARDUUS	CAREWARES
CARAVAN	CARBONATE	CARDAMON	CARDUUSES	CAREWORN
CARAVANCE	CARBONIC	CARDAMONS	CARDY	CAREX
CARAVANED	CARBONISE	CARDAMUM	CARE	CARFARE
CARAVANER	CARBONIUM	CARDAMUMS	CARED	CARFARES
CARAVANS	CARBONIZE	CARDAN	CAREEN	CARFAX
CARAVEL	CARBONOUS	CARDBOARD	CAREENAGE	CARFAXES
CARAVELLE	CARBONS	CARDCASE	CAREENED	CARFOX
CARAVELS	CARBONYL	CARDCASES	CAREENER	CARFOXES
CARAWAY	CARBONYLS	CARDECU	CAREENERS	CARFUFFLE
CARAWAYS	CARBORA	CARDECUE	CAREENING	CARFUL
CARB	CARBORAS	CARDECUES	CAREENS	CARFULS
CARBACHOL	CARBOS	CARDECUS	CAREER	CARGEESE
CARBAMATE	CARBOXYL	CARDED	CAREERED	CARGO
CARBAMIC	CARBOXYLS	CARDER	CAREERER	CARGOED
CARBAMIDE	CARBOY	CARDERS	CAREERERS	CARGOES
CARBAMINO	CARBOYED	CARDI	CAREERING	CARGOING
CARBAMOYL	CARBOYS	CARDIA	CAREERISM	CARGOOSE
CARBAMYL	CARBS	CARDIAC	CAREERIST	CARGOS
CARBAMYLS	CARBUNCLE	CARDIACAL	CAREERS	CARHOP
CARBANION	CARBURATE	CARDIACS	CAREFREE	CARHOPPED
CARBARN	CARBURET	CARDIAE	CAREFUL	CARHOPS
CARBARNS	CARBURETS	CARDIALGY	CAREFULLY	CARIACOU
CARBARYL	CARBURISE	CARDIAS	CAREGIVER	CARIACOUS
CARBARYLS	CARBURIZE	CARDIE	CARELESS	CARIAMA
CARBAZOLE	CARBY	CARDIES	CARELINE	CARIAMAS
CARBEEN	CARCAJOU	CARDIGAN	CARELINES	CARIBE
CARBEENS	CARCAJOUS	CARDIGANS	CAREME	CARIBES
CARBENE	CARCAKE	CARDINAL	CAREMES	CARIBOU
CARBENES	CARCAKES	CARDINALS	CARER	CARIBOUS
CARBIDE	CARCANET	CARDING	CARERS	CARICES
CARBIDES	CARCANETS	CARDINGS	CARES	CARIED
CARBIES	CARCASE	CARDIO	CARESS	CARIERE
CARBINE	CARCASED	CARDIOID	CARESSED	CARIERES
CARBINEER	CARCASES	CARDIOIDS	CARESSER	CARIES
CARBINES	CARCASING	CARDIOS	CARESSERS	CARILLON
CARBINIER	CARCASS	CARDIS	CARESSES	CARILLONS
CARBINOL	CARCASSED	CARDITIC	CARESSING	CARINA
CARBINOLS	CARCASSES	CARDITIS	CARESSIVE	CARINAE
CARBO	CARCEL	CARDON	CARET	CARINAL
CARBOLIC	CARCELS	CARDONS	CARETAKE	CARINAS
CARBOLICS	CARCERAL	CARDOON	CARETAKEN	CARINATE
CARBOLISE	CARCINOID	CARDOONS	CARETAKER	CARINATED

CARING	CARMINES	CARNYING	CAROUSES	CARRECTS
CARINGLY	CARN	CARNYX	CAROUSING	CARREFOUR
CARINGS	CARNAGE	CARNYXES	CARP	CARREL
CARIOCA	CARNAGES	CAROACH	CARPACCIO	CARRELL
CARIOCAS	CARNAHUBA	CAROACHES	CARPAL	CARRELLS
CARIOLE	CARNAL	CAROB	CARPALE	CARRELS
CARIOLES	CARNALISE	CAROBS	CARPALES	CARRIAGE
CARIOSE	CARNALISM	CAROCH	CARPALIA	CARRIAGES
CARIOSITY	CARNALIST	CAROCHE	CARPALS	CARRICK
CARIOUS	CARNALITY	CAROCHES	CARPED	CARRIED
CARITAS	CARNALIZE	CAROL	CARPEL	CARRIER
CARITASES	CARNALLED	CAROLED	CARPELS	CARRIERS
CARITATES	CARNALLY	CAROLER	CARPENTER	CARRIES
CARJACK	CARNALS	CAROLERS	CARPENTRY	CARRIOLE
CARJACKED	CARNAROLI	CAROLI	CARPER	CARRIOLES
CARJACKER	CARNATION	CAROLING	CARPERS	CARRION
CARJACKS	CARNAUBA	CAROLINGS	CARPET	CARRIONS
CARJACOU	CARNAUBAS	CAROLLED	CARPETBAG	CARRITCH
CARJACOUS	CARNELIAN	CAROLLER	CARPETED	CARROCH
CARK	CARNEOUS	CAROLLERS	CARPETING	CARROCHES
CARKED	CARNET	CAROLLING	CARPETS	CARROM
CARKING	CARNETS	CAROLS	CARPHONE	CARROMED
CARKS	CARNEY	CAROLUS	CARPHONES	CARROMING
CARL	CARNEYED	CAROLUSES	CARPI	CARROMS
CARLE	CARNEYING	CAROM	CARPING	CARRON
CARLES	CARNEYS	CAROMED	CARPINGLY	CARRONADE
CARLESS	CARNIE	CAROMEL	CARPINGS	CARROT
CARLIN	CARNIED	CAROMELS	CARPOLOGY	CARROTIER
CARLINE	CARNIER	CAROMING	CARPOOL	CARROTIN
CARLINES	CARNIES	CAROMS	CARPOOLED	CARROTINS
CARLING	CARNIEST	CARON	CARPOOLER	CARROTS
CARLINGS	CARNIFEX	CARONS	CARPOOLS	CARROTTOP
CARLINS	CARNIFIED	CAROTENE	CARPORT	CARROTY
CARLISH	CARNIFIES	CAROTENES	CARPORTS	CARROUSEL
CARLOAD	CARNIFY	CAROTID	CARPS	CARRS
CARLOADS	CARNITINE	CAROTIDAL	CARPUS	CARRY
CARLOCK	CARNIVAL	CAROTIDS	CARR	CARRYALL
CARLOCKS	CARNIVALS	CAROTIN	CARRACK	CARRYALLS
CARLOT	CARNIVORA	CAROTINS	CARRACKS	CARRYBACK
CARLOTS	CARNIVORE	CAROUSAL	CARRACT	CARRYCOT
CARLS	CARNIVORY	CAROUSALS	CARRACTS	CARRYCOTS
CARMAKER	CARNOSAUR	CAROUSE	CARRAGEEN	CARRYING
CARMAKERS	CARNOSE	CAROUSED	CARRAT	CARRYON
CARMAN	CARNOSITY	CAROUSEL	CARRATS	CARRYONS
CARMELITE	CARNOTITE	CAROUSELS	CARRAWAY	CARRYOUT
CARMEN	CARNS	CAROUSER	CARRAWAYS	CARRYOUTS
CARMINE	CARNY	CAROUSERS	CARRECT	CARRYOVER

CARRYTALE
CARS
CARSE
CARSES
CARSEY
CARSEYS
CARSHARE
CARSHARED
CARSHARES
CARSICK
CART
CARTA
CARTABLE
CARTAGE
CARTAGES
CARTAS
CARTE
CARTED
CARTEL
CARTELISE
CARTELISM
CARTELIST
CARTELIZE
CARTELS
CARTER
CARTERS
CARTES
CARTFUL
CARTFULS
CARTHORSE
CARTILAGE
CARTING
CARTLOAD
CARTLOADS
CARTOGRAM
CARTOLOGY
CARTON
CARTONAGE
CARTONED
CARTONING
CARTONS
CARTOON
CARTOONED
CARTOONS
CARTOONY
CARTOP
CARTOPPER

CARTOUCH
CARTOUCHE
CARTRIDGE
CARTROAD
CARTROADS
CARTS
CARTULARY
CARTWAY
CARTWAYS
CARTWHEEL
CARUCAGE
CARUCAGES
CARUCATE
CARUCATES
CARUNCLE
CARUNCLES
CARVACROL
CARVE
CARVED
CARVEL
CARVELS
CARVEN
CARVER
CARVERIES
CARVERS
CARVERY
CARVES
CARVIES
CARVING
CARVINGS
CARVY
CARWASH
CARWASHES
CARYATIC
CARYATID
CARYATIDS
CARYOPSES
CARYOPSIS
CARYOTIN
CARYOTINS
CASA
CASABA
CASABAS
CASAS
CASAVA
CASAVAS
CASBAH

CASBAHS
CASCABEL
CASCABELS
CASCABLE
CASCABLES
CASCADE
CASCADED
CASCADES
CASCADING
CASCADURA
CASCARA
CASCARAS
CASCHROM
CASCHROMS
CASCO
CASCOS
CASE
CASEASE
CASEASES
CASEATE
CASEATED
CASEATES
CASEATING
CASEATION
CASEBOOK
CASEBOOKS
CASEBOUND
CASED
CASEFIED
CASEFIES
CASEFY
CASEFYING
CASEIC
CASEIN
CASEINATE
CASEINS
CASELOAD
CASELOADS
CASEMAKER
CASEMAN
CASEMATE
CASEMATED
CASEMATES
CASEMEN
CASEMENT
CASEMENTS
CASEMIX

CASEMIXES
CASEOSE
CASEOSES
CASEOUS
CASERN
CASERNE
CASERNES
CASERNS
CASES
CASETTE
CASETTES
CASEVAC
CASEVACED
CASEVACS
CASEWORK
CASEWORKS
CASEWORM
CASEWORMS
CASH
CASHABLE
CASHAW
CASHAWS
CASHBACK
CASHBACKS
CASHBOOK
CASHBOOKS
CASHBOX
CASHBOXES
CASHED
CASHES
CASHEW
CASHEWS
CASHIER
CASHIERED
CASHIERER
CASHIERS
CASHING
CASHLESS
CASHMERE
CASHMERES
CASHOO
CASHOOS
CASHPOINT
CASIMERE
CASIMERES
CASIMIRE
CASIMIRES

CASING
CASINGS
CASINI
CASINO
CASINOS
CASITA
CASITAS
CASK
CASKED
CASKET
CASKETED
CASKETING
CASKETS
CASKIER
CASKIEST
CASKING
CASKS
CASKSTAND
CASKY
CASPASE
CASPASES
CASQUE
CASQUED
CASQUES
CASSABA
CASSABAS
CASSAREEP
CASSATA
CASSATAS
CASSATION
CASSAVA
CASSAVAS
CASSENA
CASSENAS
CASSENE
CASSENES
CASSEROLE
CASSETTE
CASSETTES
CASSIA
CASSIAS
CASSIMERE
CASSINA
CASSINAS
CASSINE
CASSINES
CASSINGLE

CASSINO	CASTRAL	CATALOS	CATBRIER	CATELOG
CASSINOS	CASTRATE	CATALPA	CATBRIERS	CATELOGS
CASSIS	CASTRATED	CATALPAS	CATCALL	CATENA
CASSISES	CASTRATER	CATALYSE	CATCALLED	CATENAE
CASSOCK	CASTRATES	CATALYSED	CATCALLER	CATENANE
CASSOCKED	CASTRATI	CATALYSER	CATCALLS	CATENANES
CASSOCKS	CASTRATO	CATALYSES	CATCH	CATENARY
CASSONADE	CASTRATOR	CATALYSIS	CATCHABLE	CATENAS
CASSONE	CASTRATOS	CATALYST	CATCHALL	CATENATE
CASSONES	CASTS	CATALYSTS	CATCHALLS	CATENATED
CASSOULET	CASUAL	CATALYTIC	CATCHCRY	CATENATES
CASSOWARY	CASUALISE	CATALYZE	CATCHED	CATENOID
CASSPIR	CASUALISM	CATALYZED	CATCHEN	CATENOIDS
CASSPIRS	CASUALIZE	CATALYZER	CATCHER	CATER
CAST	CASUALLY	CATALYZES	CATCHERS	CATERAN
CASTABLE	CASUALS	CATAMARAN	CATCHES	CATERANS
CASTANET	CASUALTY	CATAMENIA	CATCHFLY	CATERED
CASTANETS	CASUARINA	CATAMITE	CATCHIER	CATERER
CASTAWAY	CASUIST	CATAMITES	CATCHIEST	CATERERS
CASTAWAYS	CASUISTIC	CATAMOUNT	CATCHING	CATERESS
CASTE	CASUISTRY	CATAPAN	CATCHINGS	CATERING
CASTED	CASUISTS	CATAPANS	CATCHMENT	CATERINGS
CASTEISM	CASUS	CATAPHOR	CATCHPOLE	CATERS
CASTEISMS	CAT	CATAPHORA	CATCHPOLL	CATERWAUL
CASTELESS	CATABASES	CATAPHORS	CATCHT	CATES
CASTELLA	CATABASIS	CATAPHYLL	CATCHUP	CATFACE
CASTELLAN	CATABATIC	CATAPLASM	CATCHUPS	CATFACES
CASTELLUM	CATABOLIC	CATAPLEXY	CATCHWEED	CATFACING
CASTER	CATACLASM	CATAPULT	CATCHWORD	CATFALL
CASTERS	CATACLYSM	CATAPULTS	CATCHY	CATFALLS
CASTES	CATACOMB	CATARACT	CATCLAW	CATFIGHT
CASTIGATE	CATACOMBS	CATARACTS	CATCLAWS	CATFIGHTS
CASTING	CATAFALCO	CATARHINE	CATCON	CATFISH
CASTINGS	CATALASE	CATARRH	CATCONS	CATFISHES
CASTLE	CATALASES	CATARRHAL	CATE	CATFLAP
CASTLED	CATALATIC	CATARRHS	CATECHIN	CATFLAPS
CASTLES	CATALEPSY	CATASTA	CATECHINS	CATGUT
CASTLING	CATALEXES	CATASTAS	CATECHISE	CATGUTS
CASTOCK	CATALEXIS	CATATONIA	CATECHISM	CATHARISE
CASTOCKS	CATALO	CATATONIC	CATECHIST	CATHARIZE
CASTOFF	CATALOES	CATATONY	CATECHIZE	CATHARSES
CASTOFFS	CATALOG	CATAWBA	CATECHOL	CATHARSIS
CASTOR	CATALOGED	CATAWBAS	CATECHOLS	CATHARTIC
CASTOREUM	CATALOGER	CATBIRD	CATECHU	CATHEAD
CASTORIES	CATALOGIC	CATBIRDS	CATECHUS	CATHEADS
CASTORS	CATALOGS	CATBOAT	CATEGORIC	CATHECT
CASTORY	CATALOGUE	CATBOATS	CATEGORY	CATHECTED

CATHECTIC

CATHECTIC	CATNAPPER	CATWORM	CAULICLES	CAUSEYED
CATHECTS	CATNAPS	CATWORMS	CAULICULI	CAUSEYS
CATHEDRA	CATNEP	CAUCHEMAR	CAULIFORM	CAUSING
CATHEDRAE	CATNEPS	CAUCUS	CAULINARY	CAUSTIC
CATHEDRAL	CATNIP	CAUCUSED	CAULINE	CAUSTICAL
CATHEDRAS	CATNIPS	CAUCUSES	CAULIS	CAUSTICS
CATHEPSIN	CATOLYTE	CAUCUSING	CAULK	CAUTEL
CATHEPTIC	CATOLYTES	CAUCUSSED	CAULKED	CAUTELOUS
CATHETER	CATOPTRIC	CAUCUSSES	CAULKER	CAUTELS
CATHETERS	CATRIGGED	CAUDA	CAULKERS	CAUTER
CATHETUS	CATS	CAUDAD	CAULKING	CAUTERANT
CATHEXES	CATSKIN	CAUDAE	CAULKINGS	CAUTERIES
CATHEXIS	CATSKINS	CAUDAL	CAULKS	CAUTERISE
CATHISMA	CATSPAW	CAUDALLY	CAULOME	CAUTERISM
CATHISMAS	CATSPAWS	CAUDATE	CAULOMES	CAUTERIZE
CATHODAL	CATSUIT	CAUDATED	CAULS	CAUTERS
CATHODE	CATSUITS	CAUDATES	CAUM	CAUTERY
CATHODES	CATSUP	CAUDATION	CAUMED	CAUTION
CATHODIC	CATSUPS	CAUDEX	CAUMING	CAUTIONED
CATHOLE	CATTABU	CAUDEXES	CAUMS	CAUTIONER
CATHOLES	CATTABUS	CAUDICES	CAUMSTANE	CAUTIONRY
CATHOLIC	CATTAIL	CAUDICLE	CAUMSTONE	CAUTIONS
CATHOLICS	CATTAILS	CAUDICLES	CAUP	CAUTIOUS
CATHOLYTE	CATTALO	CAUDILLO	CAUPS	CAUVES
CATHOOD	CATTALOES	CAUDILLOS	CAUSA	CAVA
CATHOODS	CATTALOS	CAUDLE	CAUSABLE	CAVALCADE
CATHOUSE	CATTED	CAUDLED	CAUSAE	CAVALERO
CATHOUSES	CATTERIES	CAUDLES	CAUSAL	CAVALEROS
CATION	CATTERY	CAUDLING	CAUSALGIA	CAVALETTI
CATIONIC	CATTIE	CAUDRON	CAUSALGIC	CAVALIER
CATIONS	CATTIER	CAUDRONS	CAUSALITY	CAVALIERS
CATJANG	CATTIES	CAUF	CAUSALLY	CAVALLA
CATJANGS	CATTIEST	CAUGHT	CAUSALS	CAVALLAS
CATKIN	CATTILY	CAUK	CAUSATION	CAVALLIES
CATKINATE	CATTINESS	CAUKER	CAUSATIVE	CAVALLY
CATKINS	CATTING	CAUKERS	CAUSE	CAVALRIES
CATLIKE	CATTISH	CAUKS	CAUSED	CAVALRY
CATLIN	CATTISHLY	CAUL	CAUSELESS	CAVAS
CATLING	CATTLE	CAULD	CAUSEN	CAVASS
CATLINGS	CATTLEMAN	CAULDER	CAUSER	CAVASSES
CATLINS	CATTLEMEN	CAULDEST	CAUSERIE	CAVATINA
CATMINT	CATTLEYA	CAULDRIFE	CAUSERIES	CAVATINAS
CATMINTS	CATTLEYAS	CAULDRON	CAUSERS	CAVATINE
CATNAP	CATTY	CAULDRONS	CAUSES	CAVE
CATNAPER	CATWALK	CAULDS	CAUSEWAY	CAVEAT
CATNAPERS	CATWALKS	CAULES	CAUSEWAYS	CAVEATED
CATNAPPED	CATWORKS	CAULICLE	CAUSEY	CAVEATING

CAVEATOR	CAVINGS	CEAZE	CEIBAS	CELLARAGE
CAVEATORS	CAVITARY	CEAZED	CEIL	CELLARED
CAVEATS	CAVITATE	CEAZES	CEILED	CELLARER
CAVED	CAVITATED	CEAZING	CEILER	CELLARERS
CAVEFISH	CAVITATES	CEBADILLA	CEILERS	CELLARET
CAVEL	CAVITIED	CEBID	CEILI	CELLARETS
CAVELIKE	CAVITIES	CEBIDS	CEILIDH	CELLARING
CAVELS	CAVITY	CEBOID	CEILIDHS	CELLARIST
CAVEMAN	CAVORT	CEBOIDS	CEILING	CELLARMAN
CAVEMEN	CAVORTED	CECA	CEILINGED	CELLARMEN
CAVENDISH	CAVORTER	CECAL	CEILINGS	CELLAROUS
CAVER	CAVORTERS	CECALLY	CEILIS	CELLARS
CAVERN	CAVORTING	CECILS	CEILS	CELLARWAY
CAVERNED	CAVORTS	CECITIES	CEINTURE	CELLBLOCK
CAVERNING	CAVY	CECITIS	CEINTURES	CELLED
CAVERNOUS	CAW	CECITISES	CEL	CELLI
CAVERNS	CAWED	CECITY	CELADON	CELLING
CAVERS	CAWING	CECROPIA	CELADONS	CELLIST
CAVES	CAWINGS	CECROPIAS	CELANDINE	CELLISTS
CAVESSON	CAWK	CECROPIN	CELEB	CELLMATE
CAVESSONS	CAWKER	CECROPINS	CELEBRANT	CELLMATES
CAVETTI	CAWKERS	CECUM	CELEBRATE	CELLO
CAVETTO	CAWKS	CEDAR	CELEBRITY	CELLOIDIN
CAVETTOS	CAWS	CEDARBIRD	CELEBS	CELLOS
CAVIAR	CAXON	CEDARED	CELECOXIB	CELLOSE
CAVIARE	CAXONS	CEDARN	CELERIAC	CELLOSES
CAVIARES	CAY	CEDARS	CELERIACS	CELLPHONE
CAVIARIE	CAYENNE	CEDARWOOD	CELERIES	CELLS
CAVIARIES	CAYENNED	CEDARY	CELERITY	CELLULAR
CAVIARS	CAYENNES	CEDE	CELERY	CELLULARS
CAVICORN	CAYMAN	CEDED	CELESTA	CELLULASE
CAVICORNS	CAYMANS	CEDER	CELESTAS	CELLULE
CAVIE	CAYS	CEDERS	CELESTE	CELLULES
CAVIER	CAYUSE	CEDES	CELESTES	CELLULITE
CAVIERS	CAYUSES	CEDI	CELESTIAL	CELLULOID
CAVIES	CAZ	CEDILLA	CELESTINE	CELLULOSE
CAVIL	CAZIQUE	CEDILLAS	CELESTITE	CELLULOUS
CAVILED	CAZIQUES	CEDING	CELIAC	CELOM
CAVILER	CEANOTHUS	CEDIS	CELIACS	CELOMATA
CAVILERS	CEAS	CEDRATE	CELIBACY	CELOMIC
CAVILING	CEASE	CEDRATES	CELIBATE	CELOMS
CAVILLED	CEASED	CEDRINE	CELIBATES	CELOSIA
CAVILLER	CEASEFIRE	CEDULA	CELIBATIC	CELOSIAS
CAVILLERS	CEASELESS	CEDULAS	CELL	CELOTEX
CAVILLING	CEASES	CEE	CELLA	CELOTEXES
CAVILS	CEASING	CEES	CELLAE	CELS
CAVING	CEASINGS	CEIBA	CELLAR	CELSITUDE

CELT	CENSURED	CENTIPEDE	CENTURIAL	CERCARIA
CELTS	CENSURER	CENTNER	CENTURIES	CERCARIAE
CEMBALI	CENSURERS	CENTNERS	CENTURION	CERCARIAL
CEMBALIST	CENSURES	CENTO	CENTURY	CERCARIAN
CEMBALO	CENSURING	CENTOIST	CEORL	CERCARIAS
CEMBALOS	CENSUS	CENTOISTS	CEORLISH	CERCI
CEMBRA	CENSUSED	CENTONATE	CEORLS	CERCIS
CEMBRAS	CENSUSES	CENTONEL	CEP	CERCISES
CEMENT	CENSUSING	CENTONELL	CEPACEOUS	CERCOPID
CEMENTA	CENT	CENTONELS	CEPAGE	CERCOPIDS
CEMENTED	CENTAGE	CENTONES	CEPAGES	CERCUS
CEMENTER	CENTAGES	CENTONIST	CEPE	CERE
CEMENTERS	CENTAI	CENTOS	CEPES	CEREAL
CEMENTING	CENTAL	CENTRA	CEPHALAD	CEREALIST
CEMENTITE	CENTALS	CENTRAL	CEPHALATE	CEREALS
CEMENTS	CENTARE	CENTRALER	CEPHALIC	CEREBELLA
CEMENTUM	CENTARES	CENTRALLY	CEPHALICS	CEREBRA
CEMENTUMS	CENTAS	CENTRALS	CEPHALIN	CEREBRAL
CEMETERY	CENTAUR	CENTRE	CEPHALINS	CEREBRALS
CEMITARE	CENTAUREA	CENTRED	CEPHALOUS	CEREBRATE
CEMITARES	CENTAURIC	CENTREING	CEPHEID	CEREBRIC
CENACLE	CENTAURS	CENTRES	CEPHEIDS	CEREBROID
CENACLES	CENTAURY	CENTRIC	CEPS	CEREBRUM
CENDRE	CENTAVO	CENTRICAL	CERACEOUS	CEREBRUMS
CENOBITE	CENTAVOS	CENTRIES	CERAMAL	CERECLOTH
CENOBITES	CENTENARY	CENTRING	CERAMALS	CERED
CENOBITIC	CENTENIER	CENTRINGS	CERAMIC	CEREMENT
CENOTAPH	CENTER	CENTRIOLE	CERAMICS	CEREMENTS
CENOTAPHS	CENTERED	CENTRISM	CERAMIDE	CEREMONY
CENOTE	CENTERING	CENTRISMS	CERAMIDES	CEREOUS
CENOTES	CENTERS	CENTRIST	CERAMIST	CERES
CENOZOIC	CENTESES	CENTRISTS	CERAMISTS	CERESIN
CENS	CENTESIMI	CENTRODE	CERASIN	CERESINE
CENSE	CENTESIMO	CENTRODES	CERASINS	CERESINES
CENSED	CENTESIS	CENTROID	CERASTES	CERESINS
CENSER	CENTIARE	CENTROIDS	CERASTIUM	CEREUS
CENSERS	CENTIARES	CENTRUM	CERATE	CEREUSES
CENSES	CENTIGRAM	CENTRUMS	CERATED	CERGE
CENSING	CENTILE	CENTRY	CERATES	CERGES
CENSOR	CENTILES	CENTS	CERATIN	CERIA
CENSORED	CENTIME	CENTU	CERATINS	CERIAS
CENSORIAL	CENTIMES	CENTUM	CERATITIS	CERIC
CENSORIAN	CENTIMO	CENTUMS	CERATODUS	CERING
CENSORING	CENTIMOS	CENTUMVIR	CERATOID	CERIPH
CENSORS	CENTINEL	CENTUPLE	CERBEREAN	CERIPHS
CENSUAL	CENTINELL	CENTUPLED	CERBERIAN	CERISE
CENSURE	CENTINELS	CENTUPLES	CERCAL	CERISES

CERITE	CERUMENS	CESTODES	CHABUK	CHAFF
CERITES	CERUSE	CESTOI	CHABUKS	CHAFFED
CERIUM	CERUSES	CESTOID	CHACE	CHAFFER
CERIUMS	CERUSITE	CESTOIDS	CHACED	CHAFFERED
CERMET	CERUSITES	CESTOS	CHACES	CHAFFERER
CERMETS	CERUSSITE	CESTOSES	CHACHKA	CHAFFERS
CERNE	CERVELAS	CESTUI	CHACHKAS	CHAFFERY
CERNED	CERVELAT	CESTUIS	CHACING	CHAFFIER
CERNES	CERVELATS	CESTUS	CHACK	CHAFFIEST
CERNING	CERVEZA	CESTUSES	CHACKED	CHAFFINCH
CERNUOUS	CERVEZAS	CESURA	CHACKING	CHAFFING
CERO	CERVICAL	CESURAE	CHACKS	CHAFFINGS
CEROGRAPH	CERVICES	CESURAL	CHACMA	CHAFFRON
CEROMANCY	CERVICUM	CESURAS	CHACMAS	CHAFFRONS
CEROON	CERVICUMS	CESURE	CHACO	CHAFFS
CEROONS	CERVID	CESURES	CHACOES	CHAFFY
CEROS	CERVIDS	CETACEAN	CHACONINE	CHAFING
CEROTIC	CERVINE	CETACEANS	CHACONNE	CHAFT
CEROTYPE	CERVIX	CETACEOUS	CHACONNES	CHAFTS
CEROTYPES	CERVIXES	CETANE	CHACOS	CHAGAN
CEROUS	CESAREAN	CETANES	CHAD	CHAGANS
CERRADO	CESAREANS	CETE	CHADAR	CHAGRIN
CERRADOS	CESAREVNA	CETERACH	CHADARIM	CHAGRINED
CERRIAL	CESARIAN	CETERACHS	CHADARS	CHAGRINS
CERRIS	CESARIANS	CETES	CHADDAR	CHAI
CERRISES	CESIOUS	CETOLOGY	CHADDARS	CHAIN
CERT	CESIUM	CETRIMIDE	CHADDOR	CHAINE
CERTAIN	CESIUMS	CETUXIMAB	CHADDORS	CHAINED
CERTAINER	CESPITOSE	CETYL	CHADLESS	CHAINES
CERTAINLY	CESS	CETYLS	CHADO	CHAINFALL
CERTAINTY	CESSATION	CETYWALL	CHADOR	CHAINING
CERTES	CESSE	CETYWALLS	CHADORS	CHAINLESS
CERTIE	CESSED	CEVADILLA	CHADOS	CHAINLET
CERTIFIED	CESSER	CEVAPCICI	CHADRI	CHAINLETS
CERTIFIER	CESSERS	CEVICHE	CHADS	CHAINMAN
CERTIFIES	CESSES	CEVICHES	CHAEBOL	CHAINMEN
CERTIFY	CESSING	CEVITAMIC	CHAEBOLS	CHAINS
CERTITUDE	CESSION	CEYLANITE	CHAETA	CHAINSAW
CERTS	CESSIONS	CEYLONITE	CHAETAE	CHAINSAWS
CERTY	CESSPIT	CEZVE	CHAETAL	CHAINSHOT
CERULE	CESSPITS	CEZVES	CHAETODON	CHAINWORK
CERULEAN	CESSPOOL	CH	CHAETOPOD	CHAIR
CERULEANS	CESSPOOLS	CHA	CHAFE	CHAIRDAYS
CERULEIN	CESTA	CHABAZITE	CHAFED	CHAIRED
CERULEINS	CESTAS	CHABLIS	CHAFER	CHAIRING
CERULEOUS	CESTI	CHABOUK	CHAFERS	CHAIRLIFT
CERUMEN	CESTODE	CHABOUKS	CHAFES	CHAIRMAN

CHAIRMANS	CHALLAHS	CHAMFRONS	CHANCED	CHANOYUS
CHAIRMEN	CHALLAN	CHAMISA	CHANCEFUL	CHANSON
CHAIRS	CHALLANS	CHAMISAL	CHANCEL	CHANSONS
CHAIS	CHALLAS	CHAMISALS	CHANCELS	CHANT
CHAISE	CHALLENGE	CHAMISAS	CHANCER	CHANTABLE
CHAISES	CHALLIE	CHAMISE	CHANCERS	CHANTAGE
CHAKALAKA	CHALLIES	CHAMISES	CHANCERY	CHANTAGES
CHAKRA	CHALLIS	CHAMISO	CHANCES	CHANTED
CHAKRAS	CHALLISES	CHAMISOS	CHANCEY	CHANTER
CHAL	CHALLOT	CHAMLET	CHANCIER	CHANTERS
CHALAH	CHALLOTH	CHAMLETS	CHANCIEST	CHANTEUSE
CHALAHS	CHALLY	CHAMMIED	CHANCILY	CHANTEY
CHALAN	CHALONE	CHAMMIES	CHANCING	CHANTEYS
CHALANS	CHALONES	CHAMMY	CHANCRE	CHANTIE
CHALAZA	CHALONIC	CHAMMYING	CHANCRES	CHANTIES
CHALAZAE	CHALOT	CHAMOIS	CHANCROID	CHANTILLY
CHALAZAL	CHALOTH	CHAMOISED	CHANCROUS	CHANTING
CHALAZAS	CHALS	CHAMOISES	CHANCY	CHANTINGS
CHALAZIA	CHALUMEAU	CHAMOIX	CHANDELLE	CHANTOR
CHALAZION	CHALUPA	CHAMOMILE	CHANDLER	CHANTORS
CHALCID	CHALUPAS	CHAMP	CHANDLERS	CHANTRESS
CHALCIDS	CHALUTZ	CHAMPAC	CHANDLERY	CHANTRIES
CHALCOGEN	CHALUTZES	CHAMPACA	CHANFRON	CHANTRY
CHALDER	CHALUTZIM	CHAMPACAS	CHANFRONS	CHANTS
CHALDERS	CHALYBEAN	CHAMPACS	CHANG	CHANTY
CHALDRON	CHALYBITE	CHAMPAGNE	CHANGA	CHANUKIAH
CHALDRONS	CHAM	CHAMPAIGN	CHANGE	CHAO
CHALEH	CHAMADE	CHAMPAK	CHANGED	CHAOLOGY
CHALEHS	CHAMADES	CHAMPAKS	CHANGEFUL	CHAORDIC
CHALET	CHAMBER	CHAMPART	CHANGER	CHAOS
CHALETS	CHAMBERED	CHAMPARTS	CHANGERS	CHAOSES
CHALICE	CHAMBERER	CHAMPED	CHANGES	CHAOTIC
CHALICED	CHAMBERS	CHAMPER	CHANGEUP	CHAP
CHALICES	CHAMBRAY	CHAMPERS	CHANGEUPS	CHAPARRAL
CHALK	CHAMBRAYS	CHAMPERTY	CHANGING	CHAPATI
CHALKED	CHAMBRE	CHAMPIER	CHANGS	CHAPATIES
CHALKFACE	CHAMELEON	CHAMPIEST	CHANK	CHAPATIS
CHALKIER	CHAMELOT	CHAMPING	CHANKS	CHAPATTI
CHALKIEST	CHAMELOTS	CHAMPION	CHANNEL	CHAPATTIS
CHALKING	CHAMETZ	CHAMPIONS	CHANNELED	CHAPBOOK
CHALKLIKE	CHAMETZES	CHAMPLEVE	CHANNELER	CHAPBOOKS
CHALKPIT	CHAMFER	CHAMPS	CHANNELS	CHAPE
CHALKPITS	CHAMFERED	CHAMPY	CHANNER	CHAPEAU
CHALKS	CHAMFERER	CHAMS	CHANNERS	CHAPEAUS
CHALKY	CHAMFERS	CHANA	CHANOYO	CHAPEAUX
CHALLA	CHAMFRAIN	CHANAS	CHANOYOS	CHAPEL
CHALLAH	CHAMFRON	CHANCE	CHANOYU	CHAPELESS

CHAPELRY	CHARACID	CHARISMS	CHARQUIS	CHASMIEST
CHAPELS	CHARACIDS	CHARITIES	CHARR	CHASMS
CHAPERON	CHARACIN	CHARITY	CHARRED	CHASMY
CHAPERONE	CHARACINS	CHARIVARI	CHARRIER	CHASSE
CHAPERONS	CHARACT	CHARK	CHARRIEST	CHASSED
CHAPES	CHARACTER	CHARKA	CHARRING	CHASSEED
CHAPESS	CHARACTS	CHARKAS	CHARRO	CHASSEING
CHAPESSES	CHARADE	CHARKED	CHARROS	CHASSEPOT
CHAPITER	CHARADES	CHARKHA	CHARRS	CHASSES
CHAPITERS	CHARANGA	CHARKHAS	CHARRY	CHASSEUR
CHAPKA	CHARANGAS	CHARKING	CHARS	CHASSEURS
CHAPKAS	CHARANGO	CHARKS	CHART	CHASSIS
CHAPLAIN	CHARANGOS	CHARLADY	CHARTA	CHASTE
CHAPLAINS	CHARAS	CHARLATAN	CHARTABLE	CHASTELY
CHAPLESS	CHARASES	CHARLEY	CHARTAS	CHASTEN
CHAPLET	CHARBROIL	CHARLEYS	CHARTED	CHASTENED
CHAPLETED	CHARCOAL	CHARLIE	CHARTER	CHASTENER
CHAPLETS	CHARCOALS	CHARLIER	CHARTERED	CHASTENS
CHAPMAN	CHARCOALY	CHARLIES	CHARTERER	CHASTER
CHAPMEN	CHARD	CHARLOCK	CHARTERS	CHASTEST
CHAPPAL	CHARDS	CHARLOCKS	CHARTING	CHASTISE
CHAPPALS	CHARE	CHARLOTTE	CHARTISM	CHASTISED
CHAPPATI	CHARED	CHARM	CHARTISMS	CHASTISER
CHAPPATIS	CHARES	CHARMED	CHARTIST	CHASTISES
CHAPPED	CHARET	CHARMER	CHARTISTS	CHASTITY
CHAPPESS	CHARETS	CHARMERS	CHARTLESS	CHASUBLE
CHAPPIE	CHARGE	CHARMEUSE	CHARTS	CHASUBLES
CHAPPIER	CHARGED	CHARMFUL	CHARVER	CHAT
CHAPPIES	CHARGEFUL	CHARMING	CHARVERS	CHATBOT
CHAPPIEST	CHARGER	CHARMLESS	CHARWOMAN	CHATBOTS
CHAPPING	CHARGERS	CHARMONIA	CHARWOMEN	CHATCHKA
CHAPPY	CHARGES	CHARMS	CHARY	CHATCHKAS
CHAPRASSI	CHARGING	CHARNECO	CHAS	CHATCHKE
CHAPS	CHARGRILL	CHARNECOS	CHASE	CHATCHKES
CHAPSTICK	CHARIDEE	CHARNEL	CHASEABLE	CHATEAU
CHAPT	CHARIDEES	CHARNELS	CHASED	CHATEAUS
CHAPTER	CHARIER	CHAROSET	CHASEPORT	CHATEAUX
CHAPTERAL	CHARIEST	CHAROSETH	CHASER	CHATELAIN
CHAPTERED	CHARILY	CHAROSETS	CHASERS	CHATLINE
CHAPTERS	CHARINESS	CHARPAI	CHASES	CHATLINES
CHAPTREL	CHARING	CHARPAIS	CHASING	CHATON
CHAPTRELS	CHARIOT	CHARPIE	CHASINGS	CHATONS
CHAQUETA	CHARIOTED	CHARPIES	CHASM	CHATOYANT
CHAQUETAS	CHARIOTS	CHARPOY	CHASMAL	CHATROOM
CHAR	CHARISM	CHARPOYS	CHASMED	CHATROOMS
CHARA	CHARISMA	CHARQUI	CHASMIC	CHATS
CHARABANC	CHARISMAS	CHARQUID	CHASMIER	CHATTA

CHATTAS	CHAUSSES	CHEAPENER	CHECKOUT	CHEERIEST
CHATTED	CHAUSSURE	CHEAPENS	CHECKOUTS	CHEERILY
CHATTEL	CHAUVIN	CHEAPER	CHECKRAIL	CHEERING
CHATTELS	CHAUVINS	CHEAPEST	CHECKREIN	CHEERIO
CHATTER	CHAV	CHEAPIE	CHECKROOM	CHEERIOS
CHATTERED	CHAVE	CHEAPIES	CHECKROW	CHEERLEAD
CHATTERER	CHAVENDER	CHEAPING	CHECKROWS	CHEERLED
CHATTERS	CHAVETTE	CHEAPISH	CHECKS	CHEERLESS
CHATTERY	CHAVETTES	CHEAPJACK	CHECKSUM	CHEERLY
CHATTI	CHAVISH	CHEAPLY	CHECKSUMS	CHEERO
CHATTIER	CHAVS	CHEAPNESS	CHECKUP	CHEEROS
CHATTIES	CHAVVIER	CHEAPO	CHECKUPS	CHEERS
CHATTIEST	CHAVVIEST	CHEAPOS	CHECKY	CHEERY
CHATTILY	CHAVVY	CHEAPS	CHEDDAR	CHEESE
CHATTING	CHAW	CHEAPY	CHEDDARS	CHEESED
CHATTIS	CHAWBACON	CHEAT	CHEDDARY	CHEESES
CHATTY	CHAWDRON	CHEATABLE	CHEDDITE	CHEESEVAT
CHAUFE	CHAWDRONS	CHEATED	CHEDDITES	CHEESIER
CHAUFED	CHAWED	CHEATER	CHEDER	CHEESIEST
CHAUFER	CHAWER	CHEATERS	CHEDERS	CHEESILY
CHAUFERS	CHAWERS	CHEATERY	CHEDITE	CHEESING
CHAUFES	CHAWING	CHEATING	CHEDITES	CHEESY
CHAUFF	CHAWK	CHEATINGS	CHEECHAKO	CHEETAH
CHAUFFED	CHAWKS	CHEATS	CHEEK	CHEETAHS
CHAUFFER	CHAWS	CHEBEC	CHEEKBONE	CHEEWINK
CHAUFFERS	CHAY	CHEBECS	CHEEKED	CHEEWINKS
CHAUFFEUR	CHAYA	CHECHAKO	CHEEKFUL	CHEF
CHAUFFING	CHAYAS	CHECHAKOS	CHEEKFULS	CHEFDOM
CHAUFFS	CHAYOTE	CHECHAQUO	CHEEKIER	CHEFDOMS
CHAUFING	CHAYOTES	CHECHIA	CHEEKIEST	CHEFED
CHAUMER	CHAYROOT	CHECHIAS	CHEEKILY	CHEFFED
CHAUMERS	CHAYROOTS	CHECK	CHEEKING	CHEFFING
CHAUNCE	CHAYS	CHECKABLE	CHEEKLESS	CHEFING
CHAUNCED	CHAZAN	CHECKBOOK	CHEEKS	CHEFS
CHAUNCES	CHAZANIM	CHECKED	CHEEKY	CHEGOE
CHAUNCING	CHAZANS	CHECKER	CHEEP	CHEGOES
CHAUNGE	CHAZZAN	CHECKERED	CHEEPED	CHEILITIS
CHAUNGED	CHAZZANIM	CHECKERS	CHEEPER	CHEKA
CHAUNGES	CHAZZANS	CHECKIER	CHEEPERS	CHEKAS
CHAUNGING	CHAZZEN	CHECKIEST	CHEEPING	CHEKIST
CHAUNT	CHAZZENIM	CHECKING	CHEEPS	CHEKISTS
CHAUNTED	CHAZZENS	CHECKLESS	CHEER	CHELA
CHAUNTER	CHE	CHECKLIST	CHEERED	CHELAE
CHAUNTERS	CHEAP	CHECKMARK	CHEERER	CHELAS
CHAUNTING	CHEAPED	CHECKMATE	CHEERERS	CHELASHIP
CHAUNTRY	CHEAPEN	CHECKOFF	CHEERFUL	CHELATE
CHAUNTS	CHEAPENED	CHECKOFFS	CHEERIER	CHELATED

C

CHELATES	CHENARS	CHERUBINS	CHEVEREL	CHI
CHELATING	CHENET	CHERUBS	CHEVERELS	CHIA
CHELATION	CHENETS	CHERUP	CHEVERIL	CHIACK
CHELATOR	CHENILLE	CHERUPED	CHEVERILS	CHIACKED
CHELATORS	CHENILLES	CHERUPING	CHEVERON	CHIACKING
CHELICERA	CHENIX	CHERUPS	CHEVERONS	CHIACKS
CHELIFORM	CHENIXES	CHERVIL	CHEVERYE	CHIANTI
CHELIPED	CHENOPOD	CHERVILS	CHEVERYES	CHIANTIS
CHELIPEDS	CHENOPODS	CHESHIRE	CHEVET	CHIAO
CHELLUP	CHEONGSAM	CHESHIRES	CHEVETS	CHIAREZZA
CHELLUPS	CHEQUE	CHESIL	CHEVIED	CHIAREZZE
CHELOID	CHEQUER	CHESILS	CHEVIES	CHIAS
CHELOIDAL	CHEQUERED	CHESNUT	CHEVILLE	CHIASM
CHELOIDS	CHEQUERS	CHESNUTS	CHEVILLES	CHIASMA
CHELONE	CHEQUES	CHESS	CHEVIN	CHIASMAL
CHELONES	CHEQUIER	CHESSEL	CHEVINS	CHIASMAS
CHELONIAN	CHEQUIEST	CHESSELS	CHEVIOT	CHIASMATA
CHELP	CHEQUING	CHESSES	CHEVIOTS	CHIASMI
CHELPED	CHEQUY	CHESSMAN	CHEVRE	CHIASMIC
CHELPING	CHER	CHESSMEN	CHEVRES	CHIASMS
CHELPS	CHERALITE	CHEST	CHEVRET	CHIASMUS
CHEMIC	CHERE	CHESTED	CHEVRETS	CHIASTIC
CHEMICAL	CHERIMOYA	CHESTFUL	CHEVRETTE	CHIAUS
CHEMICALS	CHERISH	CHESTFULS	CHEVRON	CHIAUSED
CHEMICKED	CHERISHED	CHESTIER	CHEVRONED	CHIAUSES
CHEMICS	CHERISHER	CHESTIEST	CHEVRONS	CHIAUSING
CHEMISE	CHERISHES	CHESTILY	CHEVRONY	CHIB
CHEMISES	CHERMOULA	CHESTING	CHEVY	CHIBBED
CHEMISM	CHERNOZEM	CHESTNUT	CHEVYING	CHIBBING
CHEMISMS	CHEROOT	CHESTNUTS	CHEW	CHIBOL
CHEMISORB	CHEROOTS	CHESTS	CHEWABLE	CHIBOLS
CHEMIST	CHERRIED	CHESTY	CHEWED	CHIBOUK
CHEMISTRY	CHERRIER	CHETAH	CHEWER	CHIBOUKS
CHEMISTS	CHERRIES	CHETAHS	CHEWERS	CHIBOUQUE
CHEMITYPE	CHERRIEST	CHETH	CHEWET	CHIBS
CHEMITYPY	CHERRY	CHETHS	CHEWETS	CHIC
CHEMMIES	CHERRYING	CHETNIK	CHEWIE	CHICA
CHEMMY	CHERT	CHETNIKS	CHEWIER	CHICALOTE
CHEMO	CHERTIER	CHETRUM	CHEWIES	CHICANA
CHEMOKINE	CHERTIEST	CHETRUMS	CHEWIEST	CHICANAS
CHEMOS	CHERTS	CHEVAL	CHEWINESS	CHICANE
CHEMOSORB	CHERTY	CHEVALET	CHEWING	CHICANED
CHEMOSTAT	CHERUB	CHEVALETS	CHEWINK	CHICANER
CHEMPADUK	CHERUBIC	CHEVALIER	CHEWINKS	CHICANERS
CHEMURGIC	CHERUBIM	CHEVELURE	CHEWS	CHICANERY
CHEMURGY	CHERUBIMS	CHEVEN	CHEWY	CHICANES
CHENAR	CHERUBIN	CHEVENS	CHEZ	CHICANING

CHICANO	CHIDINGLY	CHILBLAIN	CHILLILY	CHIMP
CHICANOS	CHIDINGS	CHILD	CHILLING	CHIMPS
CHICAS	CHIDLINGS	CHILDBED	CHILLINGS	CHIN
CHICCORY	CHIEF	CHILDBEDS	CHILLIS	CHINA
CHICER	CHIEFDOM	CHILDCARE	CHILLNESS	CHINAMAN
CHICEST	CHIEFDOMS	CHILDE	CHILLS	CHINAMEN
CHICH	CHIEFER	CHILDED	CHILLUM	CHINAMPA
CHICHA	CHIEFERY	CHILDER	CHILLUMS	CHINAMPAS
CHICHAS	CHIEFESS	CHILDES	CHILLY	CHINAR
CHICHES	CHIEFEST	CHILDHOOD	CHILOPOD	CHINAROOT
CHICHI	CHIEFLESS	CHILDING	CHILOPODS	CHINARS
CHICHIER	CHIEFLING	CHILDISH	CHILTEPIN	CHINAS
CHICHIEST	CHIEFLY	CHILDLESS	CHIMAERA	CHINAWARE
CHICHIS	CHIEFRIES	CHILDLIER	CHIMAERAS	CHINBONE
CHICK	CHIEFRY	CHILDLIKE	CHIMAERIC	CHINBONES
CHICKADEE	CHIEFS	CHILDLY	CHIMAR	CHINCAPIN
CHICKAREE	CHIEFSHIP	CHILDNESS	CHIMARS	CHINCH
CHICKEE	CHIEFTAIN	CHILDREN	CHIMB	CHINCHES
CHICKEES	CHIEL	CHILDS	CHIMBLEY	CHINCHIER
CHICKEN	CHIELD	CHILE	CHIMBLEYS	CHINCHY
CHICKENED	CHIELDS	CHILES	CHIMBLIES	CHINCOUGH
CHICKENS	CHIELS	CHILI	CHIMBLY	CHINDIT
CHICKLING	CHIFFON	CHILIAD	CHIMBS	CHINDITS
CHICKORY	CHIFFONS	CHILIADAL	CHIME	CHINE
CHICKPEA	CHIFFONY	CHILIADIC	CHIMED	CHINED
CHICKPEAS	CHIGETAI	CHILIADS	CHIMER	CHINES
CHICKS	CHIGETAIS	CHILIAGON	CHIMERA	CHINESE
CHICKWEED	CHIGGA	CHILIARCH	CHIMERAS	CHINING
CHICLE	CHIGGAS	CHILIASM	CHIMERE	CHINK
CHICLES	CHIGGER	CHILIASMS	CHIMERES	CHINKAPIN
CHICLY	CHIGGERS	CHILIAST	CHIMERIC	CHINKARA
CHICNESS	CHIGNON	CHILIASTS	CHIMERID	CHINKARAS
CHICO	CHIGNONED	CHILIDOG	CHIMERIDS	CHINKED
CHICON	CHIGNONS	CHILIDOGS	CHIMERISM	CHINKIE
CHICONS	CHIGOE	CHILIES	CHIMERS	CHINKIER
CHICORIES	CHIGOES	CHILIS	CHIMES	CHINKIES
CHICORY	CHIGRE	CHILL	CHIMINEA	CHINKIEST
CHICOS	CHIGRES	CHILLADA	CHIMINEAS	CHINKING
CHICS	CHIHUAHUA	CHILLADAS	CHIMING	CHINKS
CHID	CHIK	CHILLED	CHIMLA	CHINKY
CHIDDEN	CHIKARA	CHILLER	CHIMLAS	CHINLESS
CHIDE	CHIKARAS	CHILLERS	CHIMLEY	CHINNED
CHIDED	CHIKHOR	CHILLEST	CHIMLEYS	CHINNING
CHIDER	CHIKHORS	CHILLI	CHIMNEY	CHINO
CHIDERS	CHIKOR	CHILLIER	CHIMNEYED	CHINONE
CHIDES	CHIKORS	CHILLIES	CHIMNEYS	CHINONES
CHIDING	CHIKS	CHILLIEST	CHIMO	CHINOOK

CHINOOKS	CHIRKEST	CHISELED	CHIVIES	CHLOROTIC
CHINOS	CHIRKING	CHISELER	CHIVING	CHLOROUS
CHINOVNIK	CHIRKS	CHISELERS	CHIVS	CHOANA
CHINS	CHIRL	CHISELING	CHIVVED	CHOANAE
CHINSTRAP	CHIRLED	CHISELLED	CHIVVIED	CHOBDAR
CHINTS	CHIRLING	CHISELLER	CHIVVIES	CHOBDARS
CHINTSES	CHIRLS	CHISELS	CHIVVING	CHOC
CHINTZ	CHIRM	CHIT	CHIVVY	CHOCCIER
CHINTZES	CHIRMED	CHITAL	CHIVVYING	CHOCCIES
CHINTZIER	CHIRMING	CHITALS	CHIVY	CHOCCIEST
CHINTZY	CHIRMS	CHITCHAT	CHIVYING	CHOCCY
CHINWAG	CHIRO	CHITCHATS	CHIYOGAMI	CHOCHO
CHINWAGS	CHIROLOGY	CHITIN	CHIZ	CHOCHOS
CHIP	CHIRONOMY	CHITINOID	CHIZZ	CHOCK
CHIPBOARD	CHIROPODY	CHITINOUS	CHIZZED	CHOCKED
CHIPMUCK	CHIROPTER	CHITINS	CHIZZES	CHOCKER
CHIPMUCKS	CHIROS	CHITLIN	CHIZZING	CHOCKFUL
CHIPMUNK	CHIRP	CHITLING	CHLAMYDES	CHOCKFULL
CHIPMUNKS	CHIRPED	CHITLINGS	CHLAMYDIA	CHOCKING
CHIPOCHIA	CHIRPER	CHITLINS	CHLAMYS	CHOCKO
CHIPOLATA	CHIRPERS	CHITON	CHLAMYSES	CHOCKOS
CHIPOTLE	CHIRPIER	CHITONS	CHLOASMA	CHOCKS
CHIPOTLES	CHIRPIEST	CHITOSAN	CHLOASMAS	CHOCO
CHIPPABLE	CHIRPILY	CHITOSANS	CHLORACNE	CHOCOLATE
CHIPPED	CHIRPING	CHITS	CHLORAL	CHOCOLATY
CHIPPER	CHIRPS	CHITTED	CHLORALS	CHOCOS
CHIPPERED	CHIRPY	CHITTER	CHLORATE	CHOCS
CHIPPERS	CHIRR	CHITTERED	CHLORATES	CHOCTAW
CHIPPIE	CHIRRE	CHITTERS	CHLORDAN	CHOCTAWS
CHIPPIER	CHIRRED	CHITTIER	CHLORDANE	CHODE
CHIPPIES	CHIRREN	CHITTIES	CHLORDANS	CHOENIX
CHIPPIEST	CHIRRES	CHITTIEST	CHLORELLA	CHOENIXES
CHIPPING	CHIRRING	CHITTING	CHLORIC	CHOG
CHIPPINGS	CHIRRS	CHITTY	CHLORID	CHOGS
CHIPPY	CHIRRUP	CHIV	CHLORIDE	CHOICE
CHIPS	CHIRRUPED	CHIVALRIC	CHLORIDES	CHOICEFUL
CHIPSET	CHIRRUPER	CHIVALRY	CHLORIDIC	CHOICELY
CHIPSETS	CHIRRUPS	CHIVAREE	CHLORIDS	CHOICER
CHIRAGRA	CHIRRUPY	CHIVAREED	CHLORIN	CHOICES
CHIRAGRAS	CHIRT	CHIVAREES	CHLORINE	CHOICEST
CHIRAGRIC	CHIRTED	CHIVARI	CHLORINES	CHOIR
CHIRAL	CHIRTING	CHIVARIED	CHLORINS	CHOIRBOY
CHIRALITY	CHIRTS	CHIVARIES	CHLORITE	CHOIRBOYS
CHIRIMOYA	CHIRU	CHIVE	CHLORITES	CHOIRED
CHIRK	CHIRUS	CHIVED	CHLORITIC	CHOIRGIRL
CHIRKED	CHIS	CHIVES	CHLOROSES	CHOIRING
CHIRKER	CHISEL	CHIVIED	CHLOROSIS	CHOIRLIKE

CHOIRMAN	CHOLERS	CHOOKS	CHORDATE	CHORISTS
CHOIRMEN	CHOLI	CHOOM	CHORDATES	CHORIZO
CHOIRS	CHOLIAMB	CHOOMS	CHORDED	CHORIZONT
CHOKE	CHOLIAMBS	CHOON	CHORDEE	CHORIZOS
CHOKEABLE	CHOLIC	CHOONS	CHORDEES	CHOROID
CHOKEBORE	CHOLINE	CHOOSE	CHORDING	CHOROIDAL
CHOKECOIL	CHOLINES	CHOOSER	CHORDINGS	CHOROIDS
CHOKED	CHOLIS	CHOOSERS	CHORDS	CHOROLOGY
CHOKEDAMP	CHOLLA	CHOOSES	CHORDWISE	CHORRIE
CHOKEHOLD	CHOLLAS	CHOOSEY	CHORE	CHORRIES
CHOKER	CHOLLERS	CHOOSIER	CHOREA	CHORTEN
CHOKERS	CHOLO	CHOOSIEST	CHOREAL	CHORTENS
CHOKES	CHOLOS	CHOOSING	CHOREAS	CHORTLE
CHOKEY	CHOLTRIES	CHOOSY	CHOREATIC	CHORTLED
CHOKEYS	CHOLTRY	CHOP	CHORED	CHORTLER
CHOKIDAR	CHOMETZ	CHOPHOUSE	CHOREE	CHORTLERS
CHOKIDARS	CHOMETZES	CHOPIN	CHOREES	CHORTLES
CHOKIER	CHOMMIE	CHOPINE	CHOREGI	CHORTLING
CHOKIES	CHOMMIES	CHOPINES	CHOREGIC	CHORUS
CHOKIEST	CHOMP	CHOPINS	CHOREGUS	CHORUSED
CHOKING	CHOMPED	CHOPLOGIC	CHOREIC	CHORUSES
CHOKINGLY	CHOMPER	CHOPPED	CHOREMAN	CHORUSING
CHOKO	CHOMPERS	CHOPPER	CHOREMEN	CHORUSSED
CHOKOS	CHOMPING	CHOPPERED	CHOREOID	CHORUSSES
CHOKRA	CHOMPS	CHOPPERS	CHORES	CHOSE
CHOKRAS	CHON	CHOPPIER	CHOREUS	CHOSEN
CHOKRI	CHONDRAL	CHOPPIEST	CHOREUSES	CHOSES
CHOKRIS	CHONDRE	CHOPPILY	CHORIA	CHOTA
CHOKY	CHONDRES	CHOPPING	CHORIAL	CHOTT
CHOLA	CHONDRI	CHOPPINGS	CHORIAMB	CHOTTS
CHOLAEMIA	CHONDRIFY	CHOPPY	CHORIAMBI	CHOU
CHOLAEMIC	CHONDRIN	CHOPS	CHORIAMBS	CHOUGH
CHOLAS	CHONDRINS	CHOPSOCKY	CHORIC	CHOUGHS
CHOLATE	CHONDRITE	CHOPSTICK	CHORINE	CHOULTRY
CHOLATES	CHONDROID	CHORAGI	CHORINES	CHOUNTER
CHOLECYST	CHONDROMA	CHORAGIC	CHORING	CHOUNTERS
CHOLELITH	CHONDRULE	CHORAGUS	CHORIOID	CHOUSE
CHOLEMIA	CHONDRUS	CHORAL	CHORIOIDS	CHOUSED
CHOLEMIAS	CHOOF	CHORALE	CHORION	CHOUSER
CHOLENT	CHOOFED	CHORALES	CHORIONIC	CHOUSERS
CHOLENTS	CHOOFING	CHORALIST	CHORIONS	CHOUSES
CHOLER	CHOOFS	CHORALLY	CHORISES	CHOUSH
CHOLERA	CHOOK	CHORALS	CHORISIS	CHOUSHES
CHOLERAIC	CHOOKED	CHORD	CHORISM	CHOUSING
CHOLERAS	CHOOKIE	CHORDA	CHORISMS	CHOUT
CHOLERIC	CHOOKIES	CHORDAE	CHORIST	CHOUTS
CHOLEROID	CHOOKING	CHORDAL	CHORISTER	CHOUX

CHOW	CHROMATIC	CHTHONIC	CHUGGED	CHUNKINGS
CHOWCHOW	CHROMATID	CHUB	CHUGGER	CHUNKS
CHOWCHOWS	CHROMATIN	CHUBASCO	CHUGGERS	CHUNKY
CHOWDER	CHROME	CHUBASCOS	CHUGGING	CHUNNEL
CHOWDERED	CHROMED	CHUBBIER	CHUGS	CHUNNELS
CHOWDERS	CHROMEL	CHUBBIEST	CHUKAR	CHUNNER
CHOWED	CHROMELS	CHUBBILY	CHUKARS	CHUNNERED
CHOWHOUND	CHROMENE	CHUBBY	CHUKKA	CHUNNERS
CHOWING	CHROMENES	CHUBS	CHUKKAR	CHUNTER
CHOWK	CHROMES	CHUCK	CHUKKARS	CHUNTERED
CHOWKIDAR	CHROMIC	CHUCKED	CHUKKAS	CHUNTERS
CHOWKS	CHROMIDE	CHUCKER	CHUKKER	CHUPATI
CHOWRI	CHROMIDES	CHUCKERS	CHUKKERS	CHUPATIS
CHOWRIES	CHROMIDIA	CHUCKHOLE	CHUKOR	CHUPATTI
CHOWRIS	CHROMIER	CHUCKIE	CHUKORS	CHUPATTIS
CHOWRY	CHROMIEST	CHUCKIES	CHUM	CHUPATTY
CHOWS	CHROMING	CHUCKING	CHUMASH	CHUPPA
CHOWSE	CHROMINGS	CHUCKLE	CHUMASHES	CHUPPAH
CHOWSED	CHROMISE	CHUCKLED	CHUMASHIM	CHUPPAHS
CHOWSES	CHROMISED	CHUCKLER	CHUMLEY	CHUPPAS
CHOWSING	CHROMISES	CHUCKLERS	CHUMLEYS	CHUPPOT
CHOWTIME	CHROMITE	CHUCKLES	CHUMMAGE	CHUPPOTH
CHOWTIMES	CHROMITES	CHUCKLING	CHUMMAGES	CHUPRASSY
CHRESARD	CHROMIUM	CHUCKS	CHUMMED	CHUR
CHRESARDS	CHROMIUMS	CHUCKY	CHUMMIER	CHURCH
CHRISM	CHROMIZE	CHUDDAH	CHUMMIES	CHURCHED
CHRISMA	CHROMIZED	CHUDDAHS	CHUMMIEST	CHURCHES
CHRISMAL	CHROMIZES	CHUDDAR	CHUMMILY	CHURCHIER
CHRISMALS	CHROMO	CHUDDARS	CHUMMING	CHURCHING
CHRISMON	CHROMOGEN	CHUDDER	CHUMMY	CHURCHISM
CHRISMONS	CHROMOS	CHUDDERS	CHUMP	CHURCHLY
CHRISMS	CHROMOUS	CHUDDIES	CHUMPED	CHURCHMAN
CHRISOM	CHROMY	CHUDDY	CHUMPING	CHURCHMEN
CHRISOMS	CHROMYL	CHUFA	CHUMPINGS	CHURCHWAY
CHRISTEN	CHROMYLS	CHUFAS	CHUMPS	CHURCHY
CHRISTENS	CHRONAXIE	CHUFF	CHUMS	CHURIDAR
CHRISTIAN	CHRONAXY	CHUFFED	CHUMSHIP	CHURIDARS
CHRISTIE	CHRONIC	CHUFFER	CHUMSHIPS	CHURINGA
CHRISTIES	CHRONICAL	CHUFFEST	CHUNDER	CHURINGAS
CHRISTOM	CHRONICLE	CHUFFIER	CHUNDERED	CHURL
CHRISTOMS	CHRONICS	CHUFFIEST	CHUNDERS	CHURLISH
CHRISTY	CHRONON	CHUFFING	CHUNK	CHURLS
CHROMA	CHRONONS	CHUFFS	CHUNKED	CHURN
CHROMAKEY	CHRYSALID	CHUFFY	CHUNKIER	CHURNED
CHROMAS	CHRYSALIS	CHUG	CHUNKIEST	CHURNER
CHROMATE	CHRYSANTH	CHUGALUG	CHUNKILY	CHURNERS
CHROMATES	CHTHONIAN	CHUGALUGS	CHUNKING	CHURNING

CHURNINGS
CHURNMILK
CHURNS
CHURR
CHURRED
CHURRING
CHURRO
CHURROS
CHURRS
CHURRUS
CHURRUSES
CHUSE
CHUSES
CHUSING
CHUT
CHUTE
CHUTED
CHUTES
CHUTING
CHUTIST
CHUTISTS
CHUTNEE
CHUTNEES
CHUTNEY
CHUTNEYS
CHUTZPA
CHUTZPAH
CHUTZPAHS
CHUTZPAS
CHYACK
CHYACKED
CHYACKING
CHYACKS
CHYLDE
CHYLE
CHYLES
CHYLIFIED
CHYLIFIES
CHYLIFY
CHYLOUS
CHYLURIA
CHYLURIAS
CHYME
CHYMES
CHYMIC
CHYMICS
CHYMIFIED

CHYMIFIES
CHYMIFY
CHYMIST
CHYMISTRY
CHYMISTS
CHYMOSIN
CHYMOSINS
CHYMOUS
CHYND
CHYPRE
CHYPRES
CHYTRID
CHYTRIDS
CIABATTA
CIABATTAS
CIABATTE
CIAO
CIBATION
CIBATIONS
CIBOL
CIBOLS
CIBORIA
CIBORIUM
CIBOULE
CIBOULES
CICADA
CICADAE
CICADAS
CICALA
CICALAS
CICALE
CICATRICE
CICATRISE
CICATRIX
CICATRIZE
CICELIES
CICELY
CICERO
CICERONE
CICERONED
CICERONES
CICERONI
CICEROS
CICHLID
CICHLIDAE
CICHLIDS
CICHLOID

CICINNUS
CICISBEI
CICISBEO
CICISBEOS
CICLATON
CICLATONS
CICLATOUN
CICOREE
CICOREES
CICUTA
CICUTAS
CICUTINE
CICUTINES
CID
CIDARIS
CIDARISES
CIDE
CIDED
CIDER
CIDERKIN
CIDERKINS
CIDERS
CIDERY
CIDES
CIDING
CIDS
CIEL
CIELED
CIELING
CIELINGS
CIELS
CIERGE
CIERGES
CIG
CIGAR
CIGARET
CIGARETS
CIGARETTE
CIGARILLO
CIGARLIKE
CIGARS
CIGGIE
CIGGIES
CIGGY
CIGS
CIGUATERA
CILANTRO

CILANTROS
CILIA
CILIARY
CILIATE
CILIATED
CILIATELY
CILIATES
CILIATION
CILICE
CILICES
CILICIOUS
CILIOLATE
CILIUM
CILL
CILLS
CIMAR
CIMARS
CIMBALOM
CIMBALOMS
CIMELIA
CIMEX
CIMICES
CIMIER
CIMIERS
CIMINITE
CIMINITES
CIMMERIAN
CIMOLITE
CIMOLITES
CINCH
CINCHED
CINCHES
CINCHING
CINCHINGS
CINCHONA
CINCHONAS
CINCHONIC
CINCINNUS
CINCT
CINCTURE
CINCTURED
CINCTURES
CINDER
CINDERED
CINDERING
CINDEROUS
CINDERS

CINDERY
CINE
CINEAST
CINEASTE
CINEASTES
CINEASTS
CINEMA
CINEMAS
CINEMATIC
CINEOL
CINEOLE
CINEOLES
CINEOLS
CINEPHILE
CINEPLEX
CINERAMIC
CINERARIA
CINERARY
CINERATOR
CINEREA
CINEREAL
CINEREAS
CINEREOUS
CINERIN
CINERINS
CINES
CINGULA
CINGULAR
CINGULATE
CINGULUM
CINNABAR
CINNABARS
CINNAMIC
CINNAMON
CINNAMONS
CINNAMONY
CINNAMYL
CINNAMYLS
CINQUAIN
CINQUAINS
CINQUE
CINQUES
CION
CIONS
CIOPPINO
CIOPPINOS
CIPHER

CIPHERED	CIRQUE	CISTRON	CITIZENS	CIVICISMS
CIPHERER	CIRQUES	CISTRONIC	CITO	CIVICS
CIPHERERS	CIRRATE	CISTRONS	CITOLA	CIVIE
CIPHERING	CIRRHOSED	CISTS	CITOLAS	CIVIES
CIPHERS	CIRRHOSES	CISTUS	CITOLE	CIVIL
CIPHONIES	CIRRHOSIS	CISTUSES	CITOLES	CIVILIAN
CIPHONY	CIRRHOTIC	CISTVAEN	CITRAL	CIVILIANS
CIPOLIN	CIRRI	CISTVAENS	CITRALS	CIVILISE
CIPOLINS	CIRRIFORM	CIT	CITRANGE	CIVILISED
CIPOLLINO	CIRRIPED	CITABLE	CITRANGES	CIVILISER
CIPPI	CIRRIPEDE	CITADEL	CITRATE	CIVILISES
CIPPUS	CIRRIPEDS	CITADELS	CITRATED	CIVILIST
CIRCA	CIRROSE	CITAL	CITRATES	CIVILISTS
CIRCADIAN	CIRROUS	CITALS	CITREOUS	CIVILITY
CIRCAR	CIRRUS	CITATION	CITRIC	CIVILIZE
CIRCARS	CIRSOID	CITATIONS	CITRIN	CIVILIZED
CIRCINATE	CIS	CITATOR	CITRINE	CIVILIZER
CIRCITER	CISALPINE	CITATORS	CITRINES	CIVILIZES
CIRCLE	CISCO	CITATORY	CITRININ	CIVILLY
CIRCLED	CISCOES	CITE	CITRININS	CIVILNESS
CIRCLER	CISCOS	CITEABLE	CITRINS	CIVILS
CIRCLERS	CISELEUR	CITED	CITRON	CIVISM
CIRCLES	CISELEURS	CITER	CITRONS	CIVISMS
CIRCLET	CISELURE	CITERS	CITROUS	CIVVIES
CIRCLETS	CISELURES	CITES	CITRUS	CIVVY
CIRCLING	CISLUNAR	CITESS	CITRUSES	CIZERS
CIRCLINGS	CISPADANE	CITESSES	CITRUSSY	CLABBER
CIRCLIP	CISPLATIN	CITHARA	CITRUSY	CLABBERED
CIRCLIPS	CISSIER	CITHARAS	CITS	CLABBERS
CIRCS	CISSIES	CITHARIST	CITTERN	CLACH
CIRCUIT	CISSIEST	CITHER	CITTERNS	CLACHAN
CIRCUITAL	CISSIFIED	CITHERN	CITY	CLACHANS
CIRCUITED	CISSING	CITHERNS	CITYFIED	CLACHS
CIRCUITRY	CISSINGS	CITHERS	CITYFIES	CLACK
CIRCUITS	CISSOID	CITHREN	CITYFY	CLACKBOX
CIRCUITY	CISSOIDS	CITHRENS	CITYFYING	CLACKDISH
CIRCULAR	CISSUS	CITIED	CITYSCAPE	CLACKED
CIRCULARS	CISSUSES	CITIES	CITYWARD	CLACKER
CIRCULATE	CISSY	CITIFIED	CITYWIDE	CLACKERS
CIRCUS	CIST	CITIFIES	CIVE	CLACKING
CIRCUSES	CISTED	CITIFY	CIVES	CLACKS
CIRCUSSY	CISTERN	CITIFYING	CIVET	CLAD
CIRCUSY	CISTERNA	CITIGRADE	CIVETLIKE	CLADDAGH
CIRE	CISTERNAE	CITING	CIVETS	CLADDAGHS
CIRES	CISTERNAL	CITIZEN	CIVIC	CLADDED
CIRL	CISTERNS	CITIZENLY	CIVICALLY	CLADDER
CIRLS	CISTIC	CITIZENRY	CIVICISM	CLADDERS

CLADDIE	CLAMES	CLANK	CLARIFIER	CLASSED
CLADDIES	CLAMLIKE	CLANKED	CLARIFIES	CLASSER
CLADDING	CLAMMED	CLANKIER	CLARIFY	CLASSERS
CLADDINGS	CLAMMER	CLANKIEST	CLARINET	CLASSES
CLADE	CLAMMERS	CLANKING	CLARINETS	CLASSIBLE
CLADES	CLAMMIER	CLANKINGS	CLARINI	CLASSIC
CLADISM	CLAMMIEST	CLANKS	CLARINO	CLASSICAL
CLADISMS	CLAMMILY	CLANKY	CLARINOS	CLASSICO
CLADIST	CLAMMING	CLANNISH	CLARION	CLASSICS
CLADISTIC	CLAMMY	CLANS	CLARIONED	CLASSIER
CLADISTS	CLAMOR	CLANSHIP	CLARIONET	CLASSIEST
CLADODE	CLAMORED	CLANSHIPS	CLARIONS	CLASSIFIC
CLADODES	CLAMORER	CLANSMAN	CLARITIES	CLASSIFY
CLADODIAL	CLAMORERS	CLANSMEN	CLARITY	CLASSILY
CLADOGRAM	CLAMORING	CLAP	CLARKIA	CLASSING
CLADS	CLAMOROUS	CLAPBOARD	CLARKIAS	CLASSINGS
CLAES	CLAMORS	CLAPBREAD	CLARO	CLASSIS
CLAFOUTI	CLAMOUR	CLAPDISH	CLAROES	CLASSISM
CLAFOUTIS	CLAMOURED	CLAPNET	CLAROS	CLASSISMS
CLAG	CLAMOURER	CLAPNETS	CLARSACH	CLASSIST
CLAGGED	CLAMOURS	CLAPPED	CLARSACHS	CLASSISTS
CLAGGIER	CLAMP	CLAPPER	CLART	CLASSLESS
CLAGGIEST	CLAMPDOWN	CLAPPERED	CLARTED	CLASSMAN
CLAGGING	CLAMPED	CLAPPERS	CLARTHEAD	CLASSMATE
CLAGGY	CLAMPER	CLAPPING	CLARTIER	CLASSMEN
CLAGS	CLAMPERED	CLAPPINGS	CLARTIEST	CLASSON
CLAIM	CLAMPERS	CLAPS	CLARTING	CLASSONS
CLAIMABLE	CLAMPING	CLAPT	CLARTS	CLASSROOM
CLAIMANT	CLAMPS	CLAPTRAP	CLARTY	CLASSWORK
CLAIMANTS	CLAMS	CLAPTRAPS	CLARY	CLASSY
CLAIMED	CLAMSHELL	CLAQUE	CLASH	CLAST
CLAIMER	CLAMWORM	CLAQUER	CLASHED	CLASTIC
CLAIMERS	CLAMWORMS	CLAQUERS	CLASHER	CLASTICS
CLAIMING	CLAN	CLAQUES	CLASHERS	CLASTS
CLAIMS	CLANG	CLAQUEUR	CLASHES	CLAT
CLAM	CLANGBOX	CLAQUEURS	CLASHING	CLATCH
CLAMANCY	CLANGED	CLARAIN	CLASHINGS	CLATCHED
CLAMANT	CLANGER	CLARAINS	CLASP	CLATCHES
CLAMANTLY	CLANGERS	CLARENCE	CLASPED	CLATCHING
CLAMBAKE	CLANGING	CLARENCES	CLASPER	CLATHRATE
CLAMBAKES	CLANGINGS	CLARENDON	CLASPERS	CLATS
CLAMBE	CLANGOR	CLARET	CLASPING	CLATTED
CLAMBER	CLANGORED	CLARETED	CLASPINGS	CLATTER
CLAMBERED	CLANGORS	CLARETING	CLASPS	CLATTERED
CLAMBERER	CLANGOUR	CLARETS	CLASPT	CLATTERER
CLAMBERS	CLANGOURS	CLARIES	CLASS	CLATTERS
CLAME	CLANGS	CLARIFIED	CLASSABLE	CLATTERY

CLATTING	CLAW	CLEANSERS	CLECKIEST	CLEPES
CLAUCHT	CLAWBACK	CLEANSES	CLECKING	CLEPING
CLAUCHTED	CLAWBACKS	CLEANSING	CLECKINGS	CLEPSYDRA
CLAUCHTS	CLAWED	CLEANSKIN	CLECKS	CLEPT
CLAUGHT	CLAWER	CLEANUP	CLECKY	CLERGIES
CLAUGHTED	CLAWERS	CLEANUPS	CLEEK	CLERGY
CLAUGHTS	CLAWING	CLEAR	CLEEKED	CLERGYMAN
CLAUSAL	CLAWLESS	CLEARABLE	CLEEKING	CLERGYMEN
CLAUSE	CLAWLIKE	CLEARAGE	CLEEKIT	CLERIC
CLAUSES	CLAWS	CLEARAGES	CLEEKS	CLERICAL
CLAUSTRA	CLAXON	CLEARANCE	CLEEP	CLERICALS
CLAUSTRAL	CLAXONS	CLEARCOLE	CLEEPED	CLERICATE
CLAUSTRUM	CLAY	CLEARCUT	CLEEPING	CLERICITY
CLAUSULA	CLAYBANK	CLEARCUTS	CLEEPS	CLERICS
CLAUSULAE	CLAYBANKS	CLEARED	CLEEVE	CLERID
CLAUSULAR	CLAYED	CLEARER	CLEEVES	CLERIDS
CLAUT	CLAYEY	CLEARERS	CLEF	CLERIHEW
CLAUTED	CLAYIER	CLEAREST	CLEFS	CLERIHEWS
CLAUTING	CLAYIEST	CLEAREYED	CLEFT	CLERISIES
CLAUTS	CLAYING	CLEARING	CLEFTED	CLERISY
CLAVATE	CLAYISH	CLEARINGS	CLEFTING	CLERK
CLAVATED	CLAYLIKE	CLEARLY	CLEFTS	CLERKDOM
CLAVATELY	CLAYMORE	CLEARNESS	CLEG	CLERKDOMS
CLAVATION	CLAYMORES	CLEARS	CLEGS	CLERKED
CLAVE	CLAYPAN	CLEARSKIN	CLEIDOIC	CLERKESS
CLAVECIN	CLAYPANS	CLEARWAY	CLEIK	CLERKING
CLAVECINS	CLAYS	CLEARWAYS	CLEIKS	CLERKISH
CLAVER	CLAYSTONE	CLEARWEED	CLEITHRAL	CLERKLIER
CLAVERED	CLAYTONIA	CLEARWING	CLEM	CLERKLIKE
CLAVERING	CLAYWARE	CLEAT	CLEMATIS	CLERKLING
CLAVERS	CLAYWARES	CLEATED	CLEMENCY	CLERKLY
CLAVES	CLEAN	CLEATING	CLEMENT	CLERKS
CLAVI	CLEANABLE	CLEATS	CLEMENTLY	CLERKSHIP
CLAVICLE	CLEANED	CLEAVABLE	CLEMMED	CLERUCH
CLAVICLES	CLEANER	CLEAVAGE	CLEMMING	CLERUCHIA
CLAVICORN	CLEANERS	CLEAVAGES	CLEMS	CLERUCHS
CLAVICULA	CLEANEST	CLEAVE	CLENCH	CLERUCHY
CLAVIE	CLEANING	CLEAVED	CLENCHED	CLEUCH
CLAVIER	CLEANINGS	CLEAVER	CLENCHER	CLEUCHS
CLAVIERS	CLEANLIER	CLEAVERS	CLENCHERS	CLEUGH
CLAVIES	CLEANLILY	CLEAVES	CLENCHES	CLEUGHS
CLAVIFORM	CLEANLY	CLEAVING	CLENCHING	CLEVE
CLAVIGER	CLEANNESS	CLEAVINGS	CLEOME	CLEVEITE
CLAVIGERS	CLEANS	CLECHE	CLEOMES	CLEVEITES
CLAVIS	CLEANSE	CLECK	CLEOPATRA	CLEVER
CLAVULATE	CLEANSED	CLECKED	CLEPE	CLEVERER
CLAVUS	CLEANSER	CLECKIER	CLEPED	CLEVEREST

CLEVERISH	CLIFTS	CLINGING	CLIQUIER	CLOCKED
CLEVERLY	CLIFTY	CLINGS	CLIQUIEST	CLOCKER
CLEVES	CLIMACTIC	CLINGY	CLIQUING	CLOCKERS
CLEVIS	CLIMATAL	CLINIC	CLIQUISH	CLOCKING
CLEVISES	CLIMATE	CLINICAL	CLIQUISM	CLOCKINGS
CLEW	CLIMATED	CLINICIAN	CLIQUISMS	CLOCKLIKE
CLEWED	CLIMATES	CLINICS	CLIQUY	CLOCKS
CLEWING	CLIMATIC	CLINIQUE	CLIT	CLOCKWISE
CLEWS	CLIMATING	CLINIQUES	CLITELLA	CLOCKWORK
CLIANTHUS	CLIMATISE	CLINK	CLITELLAR	CLOD
CLICHE	CLIMATIZE	CLINKED	CLITELLUM	CLODDED
CLICHED	CLIMATURE	CLINKER	CLITHRAL	CLODDIER
CLICHEED	CLIMAX	CLINKERED	CLITIC	CLODDIEST
CLICHES	CLIMAXED	CLINKERS	CLITICISE	CLODDING
CLICK	CLIMAXES	CLINKING	CLITICIZE	CLODDISH
CLICKABLE	CLIMAXING	CLINKS	CLITICS	CLODDY
CLICKED	CLIMB	CLINOAXES	CLITORAL	CLODLY
CLICKER	CLIMBABLE	CLINOAXIS	CLITORIC	CLODPATE
CLICKERS	CLIMBDOWN	CLINOSTAT	CLITORIS	CLODPATED
CLICKET	CLIMBED	CLINQUANT	CLITS	CLODPATES
CLICKETED	CLIMBER	CLINT	CLITTER	CLODPOLE
CLICKETS	CLIMBERS	CLINTONIA	CLITTERED	CLODPOLES
CLICKING	CLIMBING	CLINTS	CLITTERS	CLODPOLL
CLICKINGS	CLIMBINGS	CLIP	CLIVERS	CLODPOLLS
CLICKLESS	CLIMBS	CLIPART	CLIVIA	CLODS
CLICKS	CLIME	CLIPARTS	CLIVIAS	CLOFF
CLICKWRAP	CLIMES	CLIPBOARD	CLOACA	CLOFFS
CLIED	CLINAL	CLIPE	CLOACAE	CLOG
CLIENT	CLINALLY	CLIPED	CLOACAL	CLOGDANCE
CLIENTAGE	CLINAMEN	CLIPES	CLOACAS	CLOGGED
CLIENTAL	CLINAMENS	CLIPING	CLOACINAL	CLOGGER
CLIENTELE	CLINCH	CLIPPABLE	CLOACITIS	CLOGGERS
CLIENTS	CLINCHED	CLIPPED	CLOAK	CLOGGIER
CLIES	CLINCHER	CLIPPER	CLOAKED	CLOGGIEST
CLIFF	CLINCHERS	CLIPPERS	CLOAKING	CLOGGILY
CLIFFED	CLINCHES	CLIPPIE	CLOAKROOM	CLOGGING
CLIFFHANG	CLINCHING	CLIPPIES	CLOAKS	CLOGGINGS
CLIFFHUNG	CLINE	CLIPPING	CLOAM	CLOGGY
CLIFFIER	CLINES	CLIPPINGS	CLOAMS	CLOGS
CLIFFIEST	CLING	CLIPS	CLOBBER	CLOISON
CLIFFLIKE	CLINGED	CLIPSHEAR	CLOBBERED	CLOISONNE
CLIFFS	CLINGER	CLIPSHEET	CLOBBERS	CLOISONS
CLIFFY	CLINGERS	CLIPT	CLOCHARD	CLOISTER
CLIFT	CLINGFILM	CLIQUE	CLOCHARDS	CLOISTERS
CLIFTED	CLINGFISH	CLIQUED	CLOCHE	CLOISTRAL
CLIFTIER	CLINGIER	CLIQUES	CLOCHES	CLOKE
CLIFTIEST	CLINGIEST	CLIQUEY	CLOCK	CLOKED

CLOKES	CLOSENESS	CLOTTY	CLOWDERS	CLUBHAUL
CLOKING	CLOSEOUT	CLOTURE	CLOWN	CLUBHAULS
CLOMB	CLOSEOUTS	CLOTURED	CLOWNED	CLUBHEAD
CLOMP	CLOSER	CLOTURES	CLOWNERY	CLUBHEADS
CLOMPED	CLOSERS	CLOTURING	CLOWNFISH	CLUBHOUSE
CLOMPING	CLOSES	CLOU	CLOWNING	CLUBLAND
CLOMPS	CLOSEST	CLOUD	CLOWNINGS	CLUBLANDS
CLON	CLOSET	CLOUDAGE	CLOWNISH	CLUBMAN
CLONAL	CLOSETED	CLOUDAGES	CLOWNS	CLUBMEN
CLONALLY	CLOSETFUL	CLOUDED	CLOWS	CLUBROOM
CLONE	CLOSETING	CLOUDIER	CLOY	CLUBROOMS
CLONED	CLOSETS	CLOUDIEST	CLOYE	CLUBROOT
CLONER	CLOSEUP	CLOUDILY	CLOYED	CLUBROOTS
CLONERS	CLOSEUPS	CLOUDING	CLOYES	CLUBRUSH
CLONES	CLOSING	CLOUDINGS	CLOYING	CLUBS
CLONIC	CLOSINGS	CLOUDLAND	CLOYINGLY	CLUBWOMAN
CLONICITY	CLOSURE	CLOUDLESS	CLOYLESS	CLUBWOMEN
CLONIDINE	CLOSURED	CLOUDLET	CLOYMENT	CLUCK
CLONING	CLOSURES	CLOUDLETS	CLOYMENTS	CLUCKED
CLONINGS	CLOSURING	CLOUDLIKE	CLOYS	CLUCKIER
CLONISM	CLOT	CLOUDS	CLOYSOME	CLUCKIEST
CLONISMS	CLOTBUR	CLOUDTOWN	CLOZAPINE	CLUCKING
CLONK	CLOTBURS	CLOUDY	CLOZE	CLUCKS
CLONKED	CLOTE	CLOUGH	CLOZES	CLUCKY
CLONKING	CLOTES	CLOUGHS	CLUB	CLUDGIE
CLONKS	CLOTH	CLOUR	CLUBABLE	CLUDGIES
CLONS	CLOTHE	CLOURED	CLUBBABLE	CLUE
CLONUS	CLOTHED	CLOURING	CLUBBED	CLUED
CLONUSES	CLOTHES	CLOURS	CLUBBER	CLUEING
CLOOP	CLOTHIER	CLOUS	CLUBBERS	CLUELESS
CLOOPS	CLOTHIERS	CLOUT	CLUBBIER	CLUES
CLOOT	CLOTHING	CLOUTED	CLUBBIEST	CLUING
CLOOTIE	CLOTHINGS	CLOUTER	CLUBBILY	CLUMBER
CLOOTS	CLOTHLIKE	CLOUTERLY	CLUBBING	CLUMBERS
CLOP	CLOTHS	CLOUTERS	CLUBBINGS	CLUMP
CLOPPED	CLOTPOLL	CLOUTING	CLUBBISH	CLUMPED
CLOPPING	CLOTPOLLS	CLOUTS	CLUBBISM	CLUMPER
CLOPS	CLOTS	CLOVE	CLUBBISMS	CLUMPERS
CLOQUE	CLOTTED	CLOVEN	CLUBBIST	CLUMPIER
CLOQUES	CLOTTER	CLOVER	CLUBBISTS	CLUMPIEST
CLOSABLE	CLOTTERED	CLOVERED	CLUBBY	CLUMPING
CLOSE	CLOTTERS	CLOVERS	CLUBFACE	CLUMPISH
CLOSEABLE	CLOTTIER	CLOVERY	CLUBFACES	CLUMPLIKE
CLOSED	CLOTTIEST	CLOVES	CLUBFEET	CLUMPS
CLOSEDOWN	CLOTTING	CLOVIS	CLUBFOOT	CLUMPY
CLOSEHEAD	CLOTTINGS	CLOW	CLUBHAND	CLUMSIER
CLOSELY	CLOTTISH	CLOWDER	CLUBHANDS	CLUMSIEST

CLUMSILY	CNEMIS	COAGENT	COALLESS	COASTALLY
CLUMSY	CNIDA	COAGENTS	COALMAN	COASTED
CLUNCH	CNIDAE	COAGULA	COALMEN	COASTER
CLUNCHES	CNIDARIAN	COAGULANT	COALMINE	COASTERS
CLUNG	COACH	COAGULASE	COALMINER	COASTING
CLUNK	COACHABLE	COAGULATE	COALMINES	COASTINGS
CLUNKED	COACHDOG	COAGULUM	COALPIT	COASTLAND
CLUNKER	COACHDOGS	COAGULUMS	COALPITS	COASTLINE
CLUNKERS	COACHED	COAITA	COALS	COASTS
CLUNKIER	COACHEE	COAITAS	COALSACK	COASTWARD
CLUNKIEST	COACHEES	COAL	COALSACKS	COASTWISE
CLUNKING	COACHER	COALA	COALSHED	COAT
CLUNKS	COACHERS	COALAS	COALSHEDS	COATDRESS
CLUNKY	COACHES	COALBALL	COALY	COATE
CLUPEID	COACHIER	COALBALLS	COALYARD	COATED
CLUPEIDS	COACHIES	COALBIN	COALYARDS	COATEE
CLUPEOID	COACHIEST	COALBINS	COAMING	COATEES
CLUPEOIDS	COACHING	COALBOX	COAMINGS	COATER
CLUSIA	COACHINGS	COALBOXES	COANCHOR	COATERS
CLUSIAS	COACHLINE	COALED	COANCHORS	COATES
CLUSTER	COACHLOAD	COALER	COANNEX	COATI
CLUSTERED	COACHMAN	COALERS	COANNEXES	COATING
CLUSTERS	COACHMEN	COALESCE	COANNEXES	COATINGS
CLUSTERY	COACHWHIP	COALESCED	COAPPEAR	COATIS
CLUTCH	COACHWOOD	COALESCES	COAPPEARS	COATLESS
CLUTCHED	COACHWORK	COALFACE	COAPT	COATRACK
CLUTCHES	COACHY	COALFACES	COAPTED	COATRACKS
CLUTCHING	COACT	COALFIELD	COAPTING	COATROOM
CLUTCHY	COACTED	COALFISH	COAPTS	COATROOMS
CLUTTER	COACTING	COALHOLE	COARB	COATS
CLUTTERED	COACTION	COALHOLES	COARBS	COATSTAND
CLUTTERS	COACTIONS	COALHOUSE	COARCTATE	COATTAIL
CLUTTERY	COACTIVE	COALIER	COARSE	COATTAILS
CLY	COACTOR	COALIEST	COARSELY	COATTEND
CLYING	COACTORS	COALIFIED	COARSEN	COATTENDS
CLYPE	COACTS	COALIFIES	COARSENED	COATTEST
CLYPEAL	COADAPTED	COALIFY	COARSENS	COATTESTS
CLYPEATE	COADJUTOR	COALING	COARSER	COAUTHOR
CLYPED	COADMIRE	COALISE	COARSEST	COAUTHORS
CLYPEI	COADMIRED	COALISED	COARSISH	COAX
CLYPES	COADMIRES	COALISES	COASSIST	COAXAL
CLYPEUS	COADMIT	COALISING	COASSISTS	COAXED
CLYPING	COADMITS	COALITION	COASSUME	COAXER
CLYSTER	COADUNATE	COALIZE	COASSUMED	COAXERS
CLYSTERS	COAEVAL	COALIZED	COASSUMES	COAXES
CNEMIAL	COAEVALS	COALIZES	COAST	COAXIAL
CNEMIDES	COAGENCY	COALIZING	COASTAL	COAXIALLY

COAXING
COAXINGLY
COB
COBAEA
COBAEAS
COBALAMIN
COBALT
COBALTIC
COBALTINE
COBALTITE
COBALTOUS
COBALTS
COBB
COBBED
COBBER
COBBERS
COBBIER
COBBIEST
COBBING
COBBLE
COBBLED
COBBLER
COBBLERS
COBBLERY
COBBLES
COBBLING
COBBLINGS
COBBS
COBBY
COBIA
COBIAS
COBLE
COBLES
COBLOAF
COBLOAVES
COBNUT
COBNUTS
COBRA
COBRAS
COBRIC
COBRIFORM
COBS
COBURG
COBURGS
COBWEB
COBWEBBED
COBWEBBY

COBWEBS
COBZA
COBZAS
COCA
COCAIN
COCAINE
COCAINES
COCAINISE
COCAINISM
COCAINIST
COCAINIZE
COCAINS
COCAPTAIN
COCAS
COCCAL
COCCI
COCCIC
COCCID
COCCIDIA
COCCIDIUM
COCCIDS
COCCO
COCCOID
COCCOIDAL
COCCOIDS
COCCOLITE
COCCOLITH
COCCOS
COCCOUS
COCCUS
COCCYGEAL
COCCYGES
COCCYGIAN
COCCYX
COCCYXES
COCH
COCHAIR
COCHAIRED
COCHAIRS
COCHES
COCHIN
COCHINEAL
COCHINS
COCHLEA
COCHLEAE
COCHLEAR
COCHLEARE

COCHLEARS
COCHLEAS
COCHLEATE
COCINERA
COCINERAS
COCK
COCKADE
COCKADED
COCKADES
COCKAMAMY
COCKAPOO
COCKAPOOS
COCKATEEL
COCKATIEL
COCKATOO
COCKATOOS
COCKBILL
COCKBILLS
COCKBIRD
COCKBIRDS
COCKBOAT
COCKBOATS
COCKCROW
COCKCROWS
COCKED
COCKER
COCKERED
COCKEREL
COCKERELS
COCKERING
COCKERS
COCKET
COCKETS
COCKEYE
COCKEYED
COCKEYES
COCKFIGHT
COCKHORSE
COCKIER
COCKIES
COCKIEST
COCKILY
COCKINESS
COCKING
COCKISH
COCKLE
COCKLEBUR

COCKLED
COCKLEERT
COCKLEMAN
COCKLEMEN
COCKLER
COCKLERS
COCKLES
COCKLIKE
COCKLING
COCKLINGS
COCKLOFT
COCKLOFTS
COCKMATCH
COCKNEY
COCKNEYFY
COCKNEYS
COCKNIFY
COCKPIT
COCKPITS
COCKROACH
COCKS
COCKSCOMB
COCKSFOOT
COCKSHIES
COCKSHOT
COCKSHOTS
COCKSHUT
COCKSHUTS
COCKSHY
COCKSIER
COCKSIEST
COCKSPUR
COCKSPURS
COCKSURE
COCKSWAIN
COCKSY
COCKTAIL
COCKTAILS
COCKUP
COCKUPS
COCKY
COCO
COCOA
COCOANUT
COCOANUTS
COCOAS
COCOBOLA

COCOBOLAS
COCOBOLO
COCOBOLOS
COCOMAT
COCOMATS
COCONUT
COCONUTS
COCOON
COCOONED
COCOONERY
COCOONING
COCOONS
COCOPAN
COCOPANS
COCOPLUM
COCOPLUMS
COCOS
COCOTTE
COCOTTES
COCOUNSEL
COCOYAM
COCOYAMS
COCOZELLE
COCREATE
COCREATED
COCREATES
COCREATOR
COCTILE
COCTION
COCTIONS
COCULTURE
COCURATOR
COCUSWOOD
COD
CODA
CODABLE
CODAS
CODDED
CODDER
CODDERS
CODDING
CODDLE
CODDLED
CODDLER
CODDLERS
CODDLES
CODDLING

CODE	CODIFYING	COELOME	COERCING	COFFLING
CODEBOOK	CODILLA	COELOMES	COERCION	COFFRET
CODEBOOKS	CODILLAS	COELOMIC	COERCIONS	COFFRETS
CODEBTOR	CODILLE	COELOMS	COERCIVE	COFFS
CODEBTORS	CODILLES	COELOSTAT	COERECT	COFINANCE
CODEC	CODING	COEMBODY	COERECTED	COFIRING
CODECS	CODINGS	COEMPLOY	COERECTS	COFIRINGS
CODED	CODIRECT	COEMPLOYS	COESITE	COFOUND
CODEIA	CODIRECTS	COEMPT	COESITES	COFOUNDED
CODEIAS	CODIST	COEMPTED	COETERNAL	COFOUNDER
CODEIN	CODISTS	COEMPTING	COEVAL	COFOUNDS
CODEINA	CODLIN	COEMPTION	COEVALITY	COFT
CODEINAS	CODLING	COEMPTS	COEVALLY	COG
CODEINE	CODLINGS	COENACLE	COEVALS	COGENCE
CODEINES	CODLINS	COENACLES	COEVOLVE	COGENCES
CODEINS	CODOLOGY	COENACT	COEVOLVED	COGENCIES
CODELESS	CODOMAIN	COENACTED	COEVOLVES	COGENCY
CODEN	CODOMAINS	COENACTS	COEXERT	COGENER
CODENAME	CODON	COENAMOR	COEXERTED	COGENERS
CODENAMES	CODONS	COENAMORS	COEXERTS	COGENT
CODENS	CODPIECE	COENDURE	COEXIST	COGENTLY
CODER	CODPIECES	COENDURED	COEXISTED	COGGED
CODERIVE	CODRIVE	COENDURES	COEXISTS	COGGER
CODERIVED	CODRIVEN	COENOBIA	COEXTEND	COGGERS
CODERIVES	CODRIVER	COENOBITE	COEXTENDS	COGGIE
CODERS	CODRIVERS	COENOBIUM	COFACTOR	COGGIES
CODES	CODRIVES	COENOCYTE	COFACTORS	COGGING
CODESIGN	CODRIVING	COENOSARC	COFEATURE	COGGINGS
CODESIGNS	CODROVE	COENURE	COFF	COGGLE
CODETTA	CODS	COENURES	COFFED	COGGLED
CODETTAS	COED	COENURI	COFFEE	COGGLES
CODEVELOP	COEDIT	COENURUS	COFFEEPOT	COGGLIER
CODEWORD	COEDITED	COENZYME	COFFEES	COGGLIEST
CODEWORDS	COEDITING	COENZYMES	COFFER	COGGLING
CODEX	COEDITOR	COEQUAL	COFFERDAM	COGGLY
CODFISH	COEDITORS	COEQUALLY	COFFERED	COGIE
CODFISHES	COEDITS	COEQUALS	COFFERING	COGIES
CODGER	COEDS	COEQUATE	COFFERS	COGITABLE
CODGERS	COEFFECT	COEQUATED	COFFIN	COGITATE
CODICES	COEFFECTS	COEQUATES	COFFINED	COGITATED
CODICIL	COEHORN	COERCE	COFFING	COGITATES
CODICILS	COEHORNS	COERCED	COFFINING	COGITATOR
CODIFIED	COELIAC	COERCER	COFFINITE	COGITO
CODIFIER	COELIACS	COERCERS	COFFINS	COGITOS
CODIFIERS	COELOM	COERCES	COFFLE	COGNAC
CODIFIES	COELOMATA	COERCIBLE	COFFLED	COGNACS
CODIFY	COELOMATE	COERCIBLY	COFFLES	COGNATE

COGNATELY	COHEIR	COHYPONYM	COINMATES	COLA
COGNATES	COHEIRESS	COIF	COINOP	COLANDER
COGNATION	COHEIRS	COIFED	COINS	COLANDERS
COGNISANT	COHEN	COIFFE	COINSURE	COLAS
COGNISE	COHENS	COIFFED	COINSURED	COLBIES
COGNISED	COHERE	COIFFES	COINSURER	COLBY
COGNISER	COHERED	COIFFEUR	COINSURES	COLBYS
COGNISERS	COHERENCE	COIFFEURS	COINTER	COLCANNON
COGNISES	COHERENCY	COIFFEUSE	COINTERS	COLCHICA
COGNISING	COHERENT	COIFFING	COINTREAU	COLCHICUM
COGNITION	COHERER	COIFFURE	COINVENT	COLCOTHAR
COGNITIVE	COHERERS	COIFFURED	COINVENTS	COLD
COGNIZANT	COHERES	COIFFURES	COIR	COLDBLOOD
COGNIZE	COHERING	COIFING	COIRS	COLDCOCK
COGNIZED	COHERITOR	COIFS	COISTREL	COLDCOCKS
COGNIZER	COHESIBLE	COIGN	COISTRELS	COLDER
COGNIZERS	COHESION	COIGNE	COISTRIL	COLDEST
COGNIZES	COHESIONS	COIGNED	COISTRILS	COLDHOUSE
COGNIZING	COHESIVE	COIGNES	COIT	COLDIE
COGNOMEN	COHIBIT	COIGNING	COITAL	COLDIES
COGNOMENS	COHIBITED	COIGNS	COITALLY	COLDISH
COGNOMINA	COHIBITS	COIL	COITION	COLDLY
COGNOSCE	COHO	COILED	COITIONAL	COLDNESS
COGNOSCED	COHOBATE	COILER	COITIONS	COLDS
COGNOSCES	COHOBATED	COILERS	COITS	COLE
COGNOVIT	COHOBATES	COILING	COITUS	COLEAD
COGNOVITS	COHOE	COILS	COITUSES	COLEADER
COGON	COHOES	COIN	COJOIN	COLEADERS
COGONS	COHOG	COINABLE	COJOINED	COLEADING
COGS	COHOGS	COINAGE	COJOINING	COLEADS
COGUE	COHOLDER	COINAGES	COJOINS	COLECTOMY
COGUES	COHOLDERS	COINCIDE	COJONES	COLED
COGWAY	COHORN	COINCIDED	COKE	COLEOPTER
COGWAYS	COHORNS	COINCIDES	COKED	COLES
COGWHEEL	COHORT	COINED	COKEHEAD	COLESEED
COGWHEELS	COHORTS	COINER	COKEHEADS	COLESEEDS
COHAB	COHOS	COINERS	COKELIKE	COLESLAW
COHABIT	COHOSH	COINFECT	COKERNUT	COLESLAWS
COHABITED	COHOSHES	COINFECTS	COKERNUTS	COLESSEE
COHABITEE	COHOST	COINFER	COKES	COLESSEES
COHABITER	COHOSTED	COINFERS	COKESES	COLESSOR
COHABITS	COHOSTESS	COINHERE	COKIER	COLESSORS
COHABS	COHOSTING	COINHERED	COKIEST	COLETIT
COHEAD	COHOSTS	COINHERES	COKING	COLETITS
COHEADED	COHOUSING	COINING	COKULORIS	COLEUS
COHEADING	COHUNE	COININGS	COKY	COLEUSES
COHEADS	COHUNES	COINMATE	COL	COLEWORT

COLEWORTS	COLLARING	COLLINGS	COLOCATED	COLORED
COLEY	COLLARS	COLLINS	COLOCATES	COLOREDS
COLEYS	COLLATE	COLLINSES	COLOCYNTH	COLORER
COLIBRI	COLLATED	COLLINSIA	COLOG	COLORERS
COLIBRIS	COLLATES	COLLISION	COLOGNE	COLORFAST
COLIC	COLLATING	COLLOCATE	COLOGNED	COLORFUL
COLICIN	COLLATION	COLLODION	COLOGNES	COLORIFIC
COLICINE	COLLATIVE	COLLODIUM	COLOGS	COLORING
COLICINES	COLLATOR	COLLOGUE	COLOMBARD	COLORINGS
COLICINS	COLLATORS	COLLOGUED	COLON	COLORISE
COLICKIER	COLLEAGUE	COLLOGUES	COLONE	COLORISED
COLICKY	COLLECT	COLLOID	COLONEL	COLORISER
COLICROOT	COLLECTED	COLLOIDAL	COLONELCY	COLORISES
COLICS	COLLECTOR	COLLOIDS	COLONELS	COLORISM
COLICWEED	COLLECTS	COLLOP	COLONES	COLORISMS
COLIES	COLLED	COLLOPS	COLONI	COLORIST
COLIFORM	COLLEEN	COLLOQUE	COLONIAL	COLORISTS
COLIFORMS	COLLEENS	COLLOQUED	COLONIALS	COLORIZE
COLIN	COLLEGE	COLLOQUES	COLONIC	COLORIZED
COLINEAR	COLLEGER	COLLOQUIA	COLONICS	COLORIZER
COLINS	COLLEGERS	COLLOQUY	COLONIES	COLORIZES
COLIPHAGE	COLLEGES	COLLOTYPE	COLONISE	COLORLESS
COLISEUM	COLLEGIA	COLLOTYPY	COLONISED	COLORMAN
COLISEUMS	COLLEGIAL	COLLS	COLONISER	COLORMEN
COLISTIN	COLLEGIAN	COLLUDE	COLONISES	COLORS
COLISTINS	COLLEGIUM	COLLUDED	COLONIST	COLORWAY
COLITIC	COLLET	COLLUDER	COLONISTS	COLORWAYS
COLITIS	COLLETED	COLLUDERS	COLONITIS	COLORY
COLITISES	COLLETING	COLLUDES	COLONIZE	COLOSSAL
COLL	COLLETS	COLLUDING	COLONIZED	COLOSSEUM
COLLAGE	COLLICULI	COLLUSION	COLONIZER	COLOSSI
COLLAGED	COLLIDE	COLLUSIVE	COLONIZES	COLOSSUS
COLLAGEN	COLLIDED	COLLUVIA	COLONNADE	COLOSTOMY
COLLAGENS	COLLIDER	COLLUVIAL	COLONS	COLOSTRAL
COLLAGES	COLLIDERS	COLLUVIES	COLONUS	COLOSTRIC
COLLAGING	COLLIDES	COLLUVIUM	COLONY	COLOSTRUM
COLLAGIST	COLLIDING	COLLY	COLOPHON	COLOTOMY
COLLAPSAR	COLLIE	COLLYING	COLOPHONS	COLOUR
COLLAPSE	COLLIED	COLLYRIA	COLOPHONY	COLOURANT
COLLAPSED	COLLIER	COLLYRIUM	COLOR	COLOURED
COLLAPSES	COLLIERS	COLOBI	COLORABLE	COLOUREDS
COLLAR	COLLIERY	COLOBID	COLORABLY	COLOURER
COLLARD	COLLIES	COLOBOMA	COLORADO	COLOURERS
COLLARDS	COLLIGATE	COLOBOMAS	COLORANT	COLOURFUL
COLLARED	COLLIMATE	COLOBUS	COLORANTS	COLOURING
COLLARET	COLLINEAR	COLOBUSES	COLORBRED	COLOURISE
COLLARETS	COLLING	COLOCATE	COLORCAST	COLOURIST

COLOURIZE	COLURES	COMBIER	COMELIEST	COMITIAL
COLOURMAN	COLY	COMBIES	COMELILY	COMITIAS
COLOURMEN	COLZA	COMBIEST	COMELY	COMITIES
COLOURS	COLZAS	COMBINATE	COMEMBER	COMITY
COLOURWAY	COMA	COMBINE	COMEMBERS	COMIX
COLOURY	COMADE	COMBINED	COMEOVER	COMM
COLPITIS	COMAE	COMBINEDS	COMEOVERS	COMMA
COLPOTOMY	COMAKE	COMBINER	COMER	COMMAND
COLS	COMAKER	COMBINERS	COMERS	COMMANDED
COLT	COMAKERS	COMBINES	COMES	COMMANDER
COLTAN	COMAKES	COMBING	COMET	COMMANDO
COLTANS	COMAKING	COMBINGS	COMETARY	COMMANDOS
COLTED	COMAL	COMBINING	COMETH	COMMANDS
COLTER	COMANAGE	COMBIS	COMETHER	COMMAS
COLTERS	COMANAGED	COMBLE	COMETHERS	COMMATA
COLTING	COMANAGER	COMBLES	COMETIC	COMMENCE
COLTISH	COMANAGES	COMBLESS	COMETS	COMMENCED
COLTISHLY	COMARB	COMBLIKE	COMFIER	COMMENCER
COLTS	COMARBS	COMBO	COMFIEST	COMMENCES
COLTSFOOT	COMART	COMBOS	COMFINESS	COMMEND
COLTWOOD	COMARTS	COMBOVER	COMFIT	COMMENDAM
COLTWOODS	COMAS	COMBOVERS	COMFITS	COMMENDED
COLUBRIAD	COMATE	COMBRETUM	COMFITURE	COMMENDER
COLUBRID	COMATES	COMBS	COMFORT	COMMENDS
COLUBRIDS	COMATIC	COMBUST	COMFORTED	COMMENSAL
COLUBRINE	COMATIK	COMBUSTED	COMFORTER	COMMENT
COLUGO	COMATIKS	COMBUSTOR	COMFORTS	COMMENTED
COLUGOS	COMATOSE	COMBUSTS	COMFREY	COMMENTER
COLUMBARY	COMATULA	COMBWISE	COMFREYS	COMMENTOR
COLUMBATE	COMATULAE	COMBY	COMFY	COMMENTS
COLUMBIC	COMATULID	COME	COMIC	COMMER
COLUMBINE	COMB	COMEBACK	COMICAL	COMMERCE
COLUMBITE	COMBAT	COMEBACKS	COMICALLY	COMMERCED
COLUMBIUM	COMBATANT	COMEDDLE	COMICE	COMMERCES
COLUMBOUS	COMBATED	COMEDDLED	COMICES	COMMERE
COLUMEL	COMBATER	COMEDDLES	COMICS	COMMERES
COLUMELLA	COMBATERS	COMEDIAN	COMING	COMMERGE
COLUMELS	COMBATING	COMEDIANS	COMINGLE	COMMERGED
COLUMN	COMBATIVE	COMEDIC	COMINGLED	COMMERGES
COLUMNAL	COMBATS	COMEDIES	COMINGLES	COMMERS
COLUMNAR	COMBATTED	COMEDO	COMINGS	COMMIE
COLUMNEA	COMBE	COMEDONES	COMIQUE	COMMIES
COLUMNEAS	COMBED	COMEDOS	COMIQUES	COMMINATE
COLUMNED	COMBER	COMEDOWN	COMITADJI	COMMINGLE
COLUMNIST	COMBERS	COMEDOWNS	COMITAL	COMMINUTE
COLUMNS	COMBES	COMEDY	COMITATUS	COMMIS
COLURE	COMBI	COMELIER	COMITIA	COMMISSAR

COMMIT	COMMUNES	COMPARES	COMPLAINS	COMPOSITE
COMMITS	COMMUNING	COMPARING	COMPLAINT	COMPOST
COMMITTAL	COMMUNION	COMPART	COMPLEAT	COMPOSTED
COMMITTED	COMMUNISE	COMPARTED	COMPLECT	COMPOSTER
COMMITTEE	COMMUNISM	COMPARTS	COMPLECTS	COMPOSTS
COMMITTER	COMMUNIST	COMPAS	COMPLETE	COMPOSURE
COMMIX	COMMUNITY	COMPASS	COMPLETED	COMPOT
COMMIXED	COMMUNIZE	COMPASSED	COMPLETER	COMPOTE
COMMIXES	COMMUTATE	COMPASSES	COMPLETES	COMPOTES
COMMIXING	COMMUTE	COMPAST	COMPLEX	COMPOTIER
COMMIXT	COMMUTED	COMPEAR	COMPLEXED	COMPOTS
COMMO	COMMUTER	COMPEARED	COMPLEXER	COMPOUND
COMMODE	COMMUTERS	COMPEARS	COMPLEXES	COMPOUNDS
COMMODES	COMMUTES	COMPED	COMPLEXLY	COMPRADOR
COMMODIFY	COMMUTING	COMPEER	COMPLEXUS	COMPRESS
COMMODITY	COMMUTUAL	COMPEERED	COMPLIANT	COMPRINT
COMMODO	COMMY	COMPEERS	COMPLICE	COMPRINTS
COMMODORE	COMODO	COMPEL	COMPLICES	COMPRISAL
COMMON	COMONOMER	COMPELLED	COMPLICIT	COMPRISE
COMMONAGE	COMORBID	COMPELLER	COMPLIED	COMPRISED
COMMONED	COMOSE	COMPELS	COMPLIER	COMPRISES
COMMONER	COMOUS	COMPEND	COMPLIERS	COMPRIZE
COMMONERS	COMP	COMPENDIA	COMPLIES	COMPRIZED
COMMONEST	COMPACT	COMPENDS	COMPLIN	COMPRIZES
COMMONEY	COMPACTED	COMPER	COMPLINE	COMPS
COMMONEYS	COMPACTER	COMPERE	COMPLINES	COMPT
COMMONING	COMPACTLY	COMPERED	COMPLINS	COMPTABLE
COMMONLY	COMPACTOR	COMPERES	COMPLISH	COMPTED
COMMONS	COMPACTS	COMPERING	COMPLOT	COMPTER
COMMORANT	COMPADRE	COMPERS	COMPLOTS	COMPTERS
COMMOS	COMPADRES	COMPESCE	COMPLUVIA	COMPTIBLE
COMMOT	COMPAGE	COMPESCED	COMPLY	COMPTING
COMMOTE	COMPAGES	COMPESCES	COMPLYING	COMPTROLL
COMMOTES	COMPAND	COMPETE	COMPO	COMPTS
COMMOTION	COMPANDED	COMPETED	COMPONE	COMPULSE
COMMOTS	COMPANDER	COMPETENT	COMPONENT	COMPULSED
COMMOVE	COMPANDOR	COMPETES	COMPONY	COMPULSES
COMMOVED	COMPANDS	COMPETING	COMPORT	COMPUTANT
COMMOVES	COMPANIED	COMPILE	COMPORTED	COMPUTE
COMMOVING	COMPANIES	COMPILED	COMPORTS	COMPUTED
COMMS	COMPANING	COMPILER	COMPOS	COMPUTER
COMMUNAL	COMPANION	COMPILERS	COMPOSE	COMPUTERS
COMMUNARD	COMPANY	COMPILES	COMPOSED	COMPUTES
COMMUNE	COMPARE	COMPILING	COMPOSER	COMPUTING
COMMUNED	COMPARED	COMPING	COMPOSERS	COMPUTIST
COMMUNER	COMPARER	COMPITAL	COMPOSES	COMRADE
COMMUNERS	COMPARERS	COMPLAIN	COMPOSING	COMRADELY

COMRADERY	CONCEIVES	CONCISEST	CONDENSER	CONDYLAR
COMRADES	CONCENT	CONCISING	CONDENSES	CONDYLE
COMS	CONCENTER	CONCISION	CONDER	CONDYLES
COMSYMP	CONCENTRE	CONCLAVE	CONDERS	CONDYLOID
COMSYMPS	CONCENTS	CONCLAVES	CONDIDDLE	CONDYLOMA
COMTE	CONCENTUS	CONCLUDE	CONDIE	CONE
COMTES	CONCEPT	CONCLUDED	CONDIES	CONED
COMUS	CONCEPTI	CONCLUDER	CONDIGN	CONELRAD
COMUSES	CONCEPTS	CONCLUDES	CONDIGNLY	CONELRADS
CON	CONCEPTUS	CONCOCT	CONDIMENT	CONENOSE
CONACRE	CONCERN	CONCOCTED	CONDITION	CONENOSES
CONACRED	CONCERNED	CONCOCTER	CONDO	CONEPATE
CONACRES	CONCERNS	CONCOCTOR	CONDOES	CONEPATES
CONACRING	CONCERT	CONCOCTS	CONDOLE	CONEPATL
CONARIA	CONCERTED	CONCOLOR	CONDOLED	CONEPATLS
CONARIAL	CONCERTI	CONCORD	CONDOLENT	CONES
CONARIUM	CONCERTO	CONCORDAL	CONDOLER	CONEY
CONATION	CONCERTOS	CONCORDAT	CONDOLERS	CONEYS
CONATIONS	CONCERTS	CONCORDED	CONDOLES	CONF
CONATIVE	CONCETTI	CONCORDS	CONDOLING	CONFAB
CONATUS	CONCETTO	CONCOURS	CONDOM	CONFABBED
CONCAUSE	CONCH	CONCOURSE	CONDOMS	CONFABS
CONCAUSES	CONCHA	CONCREATE	CONDONE	CONFECT
CONCAVE	CONCHAE	CONCRETE	CONDONED	CONFECTED
CONCAVED	CONCHAL	CONCRETED	CONDONER	CONFECTS
CONCAVELY	CONCHAS	CONCRETES	CONDONERS	CONFER
CONCAVES	CONCHATE	CONCREW	CONDONES	CONFEREE
CONCAVING	CONCHE	CONCREWED	CONDONING	CONFEREES
CONCAVITY	CONCHED	CONCREWS	CONDOR	CONFERRAL
CONCEAL	CONCHES	CONCUBINE	CONDORES	CONFERRED
CONCEALED	CONCHIE	CONCUPIES	CONDORS	CONFERREE
CONCEALER	CONCHIES	CONCUPY	CONDOS	CONFERRER
CONCEALS	CONCHING	CONCUR	CONDUCE	CONFERS
CONCEDE	CONCHITIS	CONCURRED	CONDUCED	CONFERVA
CONCEDED	CONCHO	CONCURS	CONDUCER	CONFERVAE
CONCEDER	CONCHOID	CONCUSS	CONDUCERS	CONFERVAL
CONCEDERS	CONCHOIDS	CONCUSSED	CONDUCES	CONFERVAS
CONCEDES	CONCHOS	CONCUSSES	CONDUCING	CONFESS
CONCEDING	CONCHS	CONCYCLIC	CONDUCIVE	CONFESSED
CONCEDO	CONCHY	COND	CONDUCT	CONFESSES
CONCEIT	CONCIERGE	CONDEMN	CONDUCTED	CONFESSOR
CONCEITED	CONCILIAR	CONDEMNED	CONDUCTI	CONFEST
CONCEITS	CONCISE	CONDEMNER	CONDUCTOR	CONFESTLY
CONCEITY	CONCISED	CONDEMNOR	CONDUCTS	CONFETTI
CONCEIVE	CONCISELY	CONDEMNS	CONDUCTUS	CONFETTO
CONCEIVED	CONCISER	CONDENSE	CONDUIT	CONFIDANT
CONCEIVER	CONCISES	CONDENSED	CONDUITS	CONFIDE

CONFIDED	CONFRONT	CONGO	CONIOSES	CONNE
CONFIDENT	CONFRONTE	CONGOES	CONIOSIS	CONNECT
CONFIDER	CONFRONTS	CONGOS	CONIUM	CONNECTED
CONFIDERS	CONFS	CONGOU	CONIUMS	CONNECTER
CONFIDES	CONFUSE	CONGOUS	CONJECT	CONNECTOR
CONFIDING	CONFUSED	CONGRATS	CONJECTED	CONNECTS
CONFIGURE	CONFUSES	CONGREE	CONJECTS	CONNED
CONFINE	CONFUSING	CONGREED	CONJEE	CONNER
CONFINED	CONFUSION	CONGREES	CONJEED	CONNERS
CONFINER	CONFUTE	CONGREET	CONJEEING	CONNES
CONFINERS	CONFUTED	CONGREETS	CONJEES	CONNEXION
CONFINES	CONFUTER	CONGRESS	CONJOIN	CONNEXIVE
CONFINING	CONFUTERS	CONGRUE	CONJOINED	CONNIE
CONFIRM	CONFUTES	CONGRUED	CONJOINER	CONNIES
CONFIRMED	CONFUTING	CONGRUENT	CONJOINS	CONNING
CONFIRMEE	CONGA	CONGRUES	CONJOINT	CONNINGS
CONFIRMER	CONGAED	CONGRUING	CONJUGAL	CONNIVE
CONFIRMOR	CONGAING	CONGRUITY	CONJUGANT	CONNIVED
CONFIRMS	CONGAS	CONGRUOUS	CONJUGATE	CONNIVENT
CONFISEUR	CONGE	CONI	CONJUNCT	CONNIVER
CONFIT	CONGEAL	CONIA	CONJUNCTS	CONNIVERS
CONFITEOR	CONGEALED	CONIAS	CONJUNTO	CONNIVERY
CONFITS	CONGEALER	CONIC	CONJUNTOS	CONNIVES
CONFITURE	CONGEALS	CONICAL	CONJURE	CONNIVING
CONFIX	CONGED	CONICALLY	CONJURED	CONNOTATE
CONFIXED	CONGEE	CONICINE	CONJURER	CONNOTE
CONFIXES	CONGEED	CONICINES	CONJURERS	CONNOTED
CONFIXING	CONGEEING	CONICITY	CONJURES	CONNOTES
CONFLATE	CONGEES	CONICS	CONJURIES	CONNOTING
CONFLATED	CONGEING	CONIDIA	CONJURING	CONNOTIVE
CONFLATES	CONGENER	CONIDIAL	CONJUROR	CONNS
CONFLICT	CONGENERS	CONIDIAN	CONJURORS	CONNUBIAL
CONFLICTS	CONGENIAL	CONIDIUM	CONJURY	CONODONT
CONFLUENT	CONGENIC	CONIES	CONK	CONODONTS
CONFLUX	CONGER	CONIFER	CONKED	CONOID
CONFLUXES	CONGERIES	CONIFERS	CONKER	CONOIDAL
CONFOCAL	CONGERS	CONIFORM	CONKERS	CONOIDIC
CONFORM	CONGES	CONIINE	CONKIER	CONOIDS
CONFORMAL	CONGEST	CONIINES	CONKIEST	CONOMINEE
CONFORMED	CONGESTED	CONIMA	CONKING	CONQUER
CONFORMER	CONGESTS	CONIMAS	CONKS	CONQUERED
CONFORMS	CONGIARY	CONIN	CONKY	CONQUERER
CONFOUND	CONGII	CONINE	CONN	CONQUEROR
CONFOUNDS	CONGIUS	CONINES	CONNATE	CONQUERS
CONFRERE	CONGLOBE	CONING	CONNATELY	CONQUEST
CONFRERES	CONGLOBED	CONINS	CONNATION	CONQUESTS
CONFRERIE	CONGLOBES	CONIOLOGY	CONNATURE	CONQUIAN

CONQUIANS	CONSORTS	CONSUMPT	CONTEXT	CONTRIVES
CONS	CONSPIRE	CONSUMPTS	CONTEXTS	CONTROL
CONSCIENT	CONSPIRED	CONTACT	CONTICENT	CONTROLE
CONSCIOUS	CONSPIRER	CONTACTED	CONTINENT	CONTROLS
CONSCRIBE	CONSPIRES	CONTACTEE	CONTINUA	CONTROUL
CONSCRIPT	CONSPUE	CONTACTOR	CONTINUAL	CONTROULS
CONSEIL	CONSPUED	CONTACTS	CONTINUE	CONTUMACY
CONSEILS	CONSPUES	CONTADINA	CONTINUED	CONTUMELY
CONSENSUS	CONSPUING	CONTADINE	CONTINUER	CONTUND
CONSENT	CONSTABLE	CONTADINI	CONTINUES	CONTUNDED
CONSENTED	CONSTANCY	CONTADINO	CONTINUO	CONTUNDS
CONSENTER	CONSTANT	CONTAGIA	CONTINUOS	CONTUSE
CONSENTS	CONSTANTS	CONTAGION	CONTINUUM	CONTUSED
CONSERVE	CONSTATE	CONTAGIUM	CONTLINE	CONTUSES
CONSERVED	CONSTATED	CONTAIN	CONTLINES	CONTUSING
CONSERVER	CONSTATES	CONTAINED	CONTO	CONTUSION
CONSERVES	CONSTER	CONTAINER	CONTORNO	CONTUSIVE
CONSIDER	CONSTERED	CONTAINS	CONTORNOS	CONUNDRUM
CONSIDERS	CONSTERS	CONTANGO	CONTORT	CONURBAN
CONSIGN	CONSTRAIN	CONTANGOS	CONTORTED	CONURBIA
CONSIGNED	CONSTRICT	CONTE	CONTORTS	CONURBIAS
CONSIGNEE	CONSTRUAL	CONTECK	CONTOS	CONURE
CONSIGNER	CONSTRUCT	CONTECKS	CONTOUR	CONURES
CONSIGNOR	CONSTRUE	CONTEMN	CONTOURED	CONUS
CONSIGNS	CONSTRUED	CONTEMNED	CONTOURS	CONVECT
CONSIST	CONSTRUER	CONTEMNER	CONTRA	CONVECTED
CONSISTED	CONSTRUES	CONTEMNOR	CONTRACT	CONVECTOR
CONSISTS	CONSUL	CONTEMNS	CONTRACTS	CONVECTS
CONSOCIES	CONSULAGE	CONTEMPER	CONTRAIL	CONVENE
CONSOL	CONSULAR	CONTEMPO	CONTRAILS	CONVENED
CONSOLATE	CONSULARS	CONTEMPT	CONTRAIR	CONVENER
CONSOLE	CONSULATE	CONTEMPTS	CONTRALTI	CONVENERS
CONSOLED	CONSULS	CONTEND	CONTRALTO	CONVENES
CONSOLER	CONSULT	CONTENDED	CONTRARY	CONVENING
CONSOLERS	CONSULTA	CONTENDER	CONTRAS	CONVENOR
CONSOLES	CONSULTAS	CONTENDS	CONTRAST	CONVENORS
CONSOLING	CONSULTED	CONTENT	CONTRASTS	CONVENT
CONSOLS	CONSULTEE	CONTENTED	CONTRASTY	CONVENTED
CONSOLUTE	CONSULTER	CONTENTLY	CONTRAT	CONVENTS
CONSOMME	CONSULTOR	CONTENTS	CONTRATE	CONVERGE
CONSOMMES	CONSULTS	CONTES	CONTRATS	CONVERGED
CONSONANT	CONSUME	CONTESSA	CONTRIST	CONVERGES
CONSONOUS	CONSUMED	CONTESSAS	CONTRISTS	CONVERSE
CONSORT	CONSUMER	CONTEST	CONTRITE	CONVERSED
CONSORTED	CONSUMERS	CONTESTED	CONTRIVE	CONVERSER
CONSORTER	CONSUMES	CONTESTER	CONTRIVED	CONVERSES
CONSORTIA	CONSUMING	CONTESTS	CONTRIVER	CONVERSO

CONVERSOS	CONVOY	COOKOFF	COOMB	COOSENED
CONVERT	CONVOYED	COOKOFFS	COOMBE	COOSENING
CONVERTED	CONVOYING	COOKOUT	COOMBES	COOSENS
CONVERTER	CONVOYS	COOKOUTS	COOMBS	COOSER
CONVERTOR	CONVULSE	COOKROOM	COOMED	COOSERS
CONVERTS	CONVULSED	COOKROOMS	COOMIER	COOSIN
CONVEX	CONVULSES	COOKS	COOMIEST	COOSINED
CONVEXED	CONY	COOKSHACK	COOMING	COOSINING
CONVEXES	COO	COOKSHOP	COOMS	COOSINS
CONVEXING	COOCH	COOKSHOPS	COOMY	COOST
CONVEXITY	COOCHES	COOKSTOVE	COON	COOT
CONVEXLY	COOCOO	COOKTOP	COONCAN	COOTCH
CONVEY	COOED	COOKTOPS	COONCANS	COOTCHED
CONVEYAL	COOEE	COOKWARE	COONDOG	COOTCHES
CONVEYALS	COOEED	COOKWARES	COONDOGS	COOTCHING
CONVEYED	COOEEING	COOKY	COONHOUND	COOTER
CONVEYER	COOEES	COOL	COONS	COOTERS
CONVEYERS	COOER	COOLABAH	COONSKIN	COOTIE
CONVEYING	COOERS	COOLABAHS	COONSKINS	COOTIES
CONVEYOR	COOEY	COOLAMON	COONTIE	COOTIKIN
CONVEYORS	COOEYED	COOLAMONS	COONTIES	COOTIKINS
CONVEYS	COOEYING	COOLANT	COONTY	COOTS
CONVICT	COOEYS	COOLANTS	COOP	COOZE
CONVICTED	COOF	COOLDOWN	COOPED	COOZES
CONVICTS	COOFS	COOLDOWNS	COOPER	COP
CONVINCE	COOING	COOLED	COOPERAGE	COPACETIC
CONVINCED	COOINGLY	COOLER	COOPERATE	COPAIBA
CONVINCER	COOINGS	COOLERS	COOPERED	COPAIBAS
CONVINCES	COOK	COOLEST	COOPERIES	COPAIVA
CONVIVE	COOKABLE	COOLHOUSE	COOPERING	COPAIVAS
CONVIVED	COOKBOOK	COOLIBAH	COOPERS	COPAL
CONVIVES	COOKBOOKS	COOLIBAHS	COOPERY	COPALM
CONVIVIAL	COOKED	COOLIBAR	COOPING	COPALMS
CONVIVING	COOKER	COOLIBARS	COOPS	COPALS
CONVO	COOKERIES	COOLIE	COOPT	COPARCENY
CONVOCATE	COOKERS	COOLIES	COOPTED	COPARENT
CONVOKE	COOKERY	COOLING	COOPTING	COPARENTS
CONVOKED	COOKEY	COOLINGLY	COOPTION	COPARTNER
CONVOKER	COOKEYS	COOLINGS	COOPTIONS	COPASETIC
CONVOKERS	COOKHOUSE	COOLISH	COOPTS	COPASTOR
CONVOKES	COOKIE	COOLLY	COORDINAL	COPASTORS
CONVOKING	COOKIES	COOLNESS	COORIE	COPATAINE
CONVOLUTE	COOKING	COOLS	COORIED	COPATRIOT
CONVOLVE	COOKINGS	COOLTH	COORIEING	COPATRON
CONVOLVED	COOKLESS	COOLTHS	COORIES	COPATRONS
CONVOLVES	COOKMAID	COOLY	COOS	COPAY
CONVOS	COOKMAIDS	COOM	COOSEN	COPAYMENT

COPAYS	COPPERS	COPULA	COQUINA	CORD
COPE	COPPERY	COPULAE	COQUINAS	CORDAGE
COPECK	COPPICE	COPULAR	COQUITO	CORDAGES
COPECKS	COPPICED	COPULAS	COQUITOS	CORDATE
COPED	COPPICES	COPULATE	COR	CORDATELY
COPEMATE	COPPICING	COPULATED	CORACLE	CORDED
COPEMATES	COPPIES	COPULATES	CORACLES	CORDELLE
COPEN	COPPIN	COPURIFY	CORACOID	CORDELLED
COPENS	COPPING	COPY	CORACOIDS	CORDELLES
COPEPOD	COPPINS	COPYABLE	CORAGGIO	CORDER
COPEPODS	COPPLE	COPYBOOK	CORAL	CORDERS
COPER	COPPLES	COPYBOOKS	CORALLA	CORDGRASS
COPERED	COPPRA	COPYBOY	CORALLINE	CORDIAL
COPERING	COPPRAS	COPYBOYS	CORALLITE	CORDIALLY
COPERS	COPPY	COPYCAT	CORALLOID	CORDIALS
COPES	COPRA	COPYCATS	CORALLUM	CORDIFORM
COPESETIC	COPRAH	COPYDESK	CORALROOT	CORDINER
COPESTONE	COPRAHS	COPYDESKS	CORALS	CORDINERS
COPIED	COPRAS	COPYEDIT	CORALWORT	CORDING
COPIER	COPREMIA	COPYEDITS	CORAM	CORDINGS
COPIERS	COPREMIAS	COPYFIGHT	CORANACH	CORDITE
COPIES	COPREMIC	COPYGIRL	CORANACHS	CORDITES
COPIHUE	COPRESENT	COPYGIRLS	CORANTO	CORDLESS
COPIHUES	COPRINCE	COPYGRAPH	CORANTOES	CORDLIKE
COPILOT	COPRINCES	COPYHOLD	CORANTOS	CORDOBA
COPILOTS	COPRODUCE	COPYHOLDS	CORBAN	CORDOBAS
COPING	COPRODUCT	COPYING	CORBANS	CORDON
COPINGS	COPROLITE	COPYISM	CORBE	CORDONED
COPIOUS	COPROLITH	COPYISMS	CORBEAU	CORDONING
COPIOUSLY	COPROLOGY	COPYIST	CORBEAUS	CORDONNET
COPITA	COPROSMA	COPYISTS	CORBEIL	CORDONS
COPITAS	COPROSMAS	COPYLEFT	CORBEILLE	CORDOTOMY
COPLANAR	COPROZOIC	COPYLEFTS	CORBEILS	CORDOVAN
COPLOT	COPS	COPYREAD	CORBEL	CORDOVANS
COPLOTS	COPSE	COPYREADS	CORBELED	CORDS
COPLOTTED	COPSED	COPYRIGHT	CORBELING	CORDUROY
COPOLYMER	COPSES	COPYTAKER	CORBELLED	CORDUROYS
COPOUT	COPSEWOOD	COQUET	CORBELS	CORDWAIN
COPOUTS	COPSHOP	COQUETRY	CORBES	CORDWAINS
COPPED	COPSHOPS	COQUETS	CORBICULA	CORDWOOD
COPPER	COPSIER	COQUETTE	CORBIE	CORDWOODS
COPPERAH	COPSIEST	COQUETTED	CORBIES	CORDYLINE
COPPERAHS	COPSING	COQUETTES	CORBINA	CORE
COPPERAS	COPSY	COQUILLA	CORBINAS	CORED
COPPERED	COPTER	COQUILLAS	CORBY	COREDEEM
COPPERING	COPTERS	COQUILLE	CORCASS	COREDEEMS
COPPERISH	COPUBLISH	COQUILLES	CORCASSES	COREGENT

COREGENTS

COREGENTS
COREIGN
COREIGNS
CORELATE
CORELATED
CORELATES
CORELESS
CORELLA
CORELLAS
COREMIA
COREMIUM
COREOPSIS
CORER
CORERS
CORES
COREY
COREYS
CORF
CORFHOUSE
CORGI
CORGIS
CORIA
CORIANDER
CORIES
CORING
CORIOUS
CORIUM
CORIUMS
CORIVAL
CORIVALRY
CORIVALS
CORIXID
CORIXIDS
CORK
CORKAGE
CORKAGES
CORKBOARD
CORKBORER
CORKED
CORKER
CORKERS
CORKIER
CORKIEST
CORKINESS
CORKING
CORKIR
CORKIRS

CORKLIKE
CORKS
CORKSCREW
CORKTREE
CORKTREES
CORKWING
CORKWINGS
CORKWOOD
CORKWOODS
CORKY
CORM
CORMEL
CORMELS
CORMIDIA
CORMIDIUM
CORMLIKE
CORMOID
CORMORANT
CORMOUS
CORMS
CORMUS
CORMUSES
CORN
CORNACRE
CORNACRES
CORNAGE
CORNAGES
CORNBALL
CORNBALLS
CORNBORER
CORNBRAID
CORNBRASH
CORNBREAD
CORNCAKE
CORNCAKES
CORNCOB
CORNCOBS
CORNCRAKE
CORNCRIB
CORNCRIBS
CORNEA
CORNEAE
CORNEAL
CORNEAS
CORNED
CORNEITIS
CORNEL

CORNELIAN
CORNELS
CORNEMUSE
CORNEOUS
CORNER
CORNERED
CORNERING
CORNERMAN
CORNERMEN
CORNERS
CORNET
CORNETCY
CORNETIST
CORNETS
CORNETT
CORNETTI
CORNETTO
CORNETTS
CORNFED
CORNFIELD
CORNFLAG
CORNFLAGS
CORNFLAKE
CORNFLIES
CORNFLOUR
CORNFLY
CORNHUSK
CORNHUSKS
CORNI
CORNICE
CORNICED
CORNICES
CORNICHE
CORNICHES
CORNICHON
CORNICING
CORNICLE
CORNICLES
CORNICULA
CORNIER
CORNIEST
CORNIFIC
CORNIFIED
CORNIFIES
CORNIFORM
CORNIFY
CORNILY

CORNINESS
CORNING
CORNIST
CORNISTS
CORNLAND
CORNLANDS
CORNLOFT
CORNLOFTS
CORNMEAL
CORNMEALS
CORNMILL
CORNMILLS
CORNMOTH
CORNMOTHS
CORNO
CORNOPEAN
CORNPIPE
CORNPIPES
CORNPONE
CORNPONES
CORNROW
CORNROWED
CORNROWS
CORNS
CORNSTALK
CORNSTONE
CORNU
CORNUA
CORNUAL
CORNUS
CORNUSES
CORNUTE
CORNUTED
CORNUTES
CORNUTING
CORNUTO
CORNUTOS
CORNWORM
CORNWORMS
CORNY
COROCORE
COROCORES
COROCORO
COROCOROS
CORODIES
CORODY
COROLLA

COROLLARY
COROLLAS
COROLLATE
COROLLINE
CORONA
CORONACH
CORONACHS
CORONAE
CORONAL
CORONALLY
CORONALS
CORONARY
CORONAS
CORONATE
CORONATED
CORONATES
CORONEL
CORONELS
CORONER
CORONERS
CORONET
CORONETED
CORONETS
CORONIS
CORONISES
CORONIUM
CORONIUMS
CORONOID
COROTATE
COROTATED
COROTATES
COROZO
COROZOS
CORPORA
CORPORAL
CORPORALE
CORPORALS
CORPORAS
CORPORATE
CORPOREAL
CORPORIFY
CORPOSANT
CORPS
CORPSE
CORPSED
CORPSES
CORPSING

C

CORPSMAN	CORRUPTED	CORTINS	COS	COSMEA
CORPSMEN	CORRUPTER	CORTISOL	COSCRIPT	COSMEAS
CORPULENT	CORRUPTLY	CORTISOLS	COSCRIPTS	COSMESES
CORPUS	CORRUPTOR	CORTISONE	COSE	COSMESIS
CORPUSCLE	CORRUPTS	CORULER	COSEC	COSMETIC
CORPUSES	CORS	CORULERS	COSECANT	COSMETICS
CORRADE	CORSAC	CORUNDUM	COSECANTS	COSMIC
CORRADED	CORSACS	CORUNDUMS	COSECH	COSMICAL
CORRADES	CORSAGE	CORUSCANT	COSECHS	COSMID
CORRADING	CORSAGES	CORUSCATE	COSECS	COSMIDS
CORRAL	CORSAIR	CORVEE	COSED	COSMIN
CORRALLED	CORSAIRS	CORVEES	COSEISMAL	COSMINE
CORRALS	CORSE	CORVES	COSEISMIC	COSMINES
CORRASION	CORSELET	CORVET	COSES	COSMINS
CORRASIVE	CORSELETS	CORVETED	COSET	COSMISM
CORREA	CORSES	CORVETING	COSETS	COSMISMS
CORREAS	CORSET	CORVETS	COSEY	COSMIST
CORRECT	CORSETED	CORVETTE	COSEYS	COSMISTS
CORRECTED	CORSETIER	CORVETTED	COSH	COSMOCRAT
CORRECTER	CORSETING	CORVETTES	COSHED	COSMOGENY
CORRECTLY	CORSETRY	CORVID	COSHER	COSMOGONY
CORRECTOR	CORSETS	CORVIDS	COSHERED	COSMOID
CORRECTS	CORSEY	CORVINA	COSHERER	COSMOLINE
CORRELATE	CORSEYS	CORVINAS	COSHERERS	COSMOLOGY
CORRIDA	CORSIVE	CORVINE	COSHERIES	COSMONAUT
CORRIDAS	CORSIVES	CORVUS	COSHERING	COSMORAMA
CORRIDOR	CORSLET	CORVUSES	COSHERS	COSMOS
CORRIDORS	CORSLETED	CORY	COSHERY	COSMOSES
CORRIE	CORSLETS	CORYBANT	COSHES	COSMOTRON
CORRIES	CORSNED	CORYBANTS	COSHING	COSPHERED
CORRIGENT	CORSNEDS	CORYDALIS	COSIE	COSPONSOR
CORRIVAL	CORSO	CORYLUS	COSIED	COSS
CORRIVALS	CORSOS	CORYLUSES	COSIER	COSSACK
CORRODANT	CORTEGE	CORYMB	COSIERS	COSSACKS
CORRODE	CORTEGES	CORYMBED	COSIES	COSSES
CORRODED	CORTEX	CORYMBOSE	COSIEST	COSSET
CORRODENT	CORTEXES	CORYMBOUS	COSIGN	COSSETED
CORRODER	CORTICAL	CORYMBS	COSIGNED	COSSETING
CORRODERS	CORTICATE	CORYPHAEI	COSIGNER	COSSETS
CORRODES	CORTICES	CORYPHE	COSIGNERS	COSSIE
CORRODIES	CORTICOID	CORYPHEE	COSIGNING	COSSIES
CORRODING	CORTICOSE	CORYPHEES	COSIGNS	COST
CORRODY	CORTILE	CORYPHENE	COSILY	COSTA
CORROSION	CORTILI	CORYPHES	COSINE	COSTAE
CORROSIVE	CORTIN	CORYZA	COSINES	COSTAL
CORRUGATE	CORTINA	CORYZAL	COSINESS	COSTALGIA
CORRUPT	CORTINAS	CORYZAS	COSING	COSTALLY

COSTALS	COTEAU	COTTAGES	COUCHE	COUNCILOR
COSTAR	COTEAUX	COTTAGEY	COUCHED	COUNCILS
COSTARD	COTED	COTTAGING	COUCHEE	COUNSEL
COSTARDS	COTELETTE	COTTAR	COUCHEES	COUNSELED
COSTARRED	COTELINE	COTTARS	COUCHER	COUNSELEE
COSTARS	COTELINES	COTTAS	COUCHERS	COUNSELOR
COSTATE	COTENANCY	COTTED	COUCHES	COUNSELS
COSTATED	COTENANT	COTTER	COUCHETTE	COUNT
COSTE	COTENANTS	COTTERED	COUCHING	COUNTABLE
COSTEAN	COTERIE	COTTERING	COUCHINGS	COUNTABLY
COSTEANED	COTERIES	COTTERS	COUDE	COUNTBACK
COSTEANS	COTES	COTTID	COUGAN	COUNTDOWN
COSTED	COTH	COTTIDS	COUGANS	COUNTED
COSTER	COTHS	COTTIER	COUGAR	COUNTER
COSTERS	COTHURN	COTTIERS	COUGARS	COUNTERED
COSTES	COTHURNAL	COTTING	COUGH	COUNTERS
COSTING	COTHURNI	COTTISE	COUGHED	COUNTESS
COSTINGS	COTHURNS	COTTISED	COUGHER	COUNTIAN
COSTIVE	COTHURNUS	COTTISES	COUGHERS	COUNTIANS
COSTIVELY	COTICULAR	COTTISING	COUGHING	COUNTIES
COSTLESS	COTIDAL	COTTOID	COUGHINGS	COUNTING
COSTLIER	COTILLION	COTTON	COUGHS	COUNTLESS
COSTLIEST	COTILLON	COTTONADE	COUGUAR	COUNTLINE
COSTLY	COTILLONS	COTTONED	COUGUARS	COUNTRIES
COSTMARY	COTING	COTTONING	COULD	COUNTROL
COSTOTOMY	COTINGA	COTTONS	COULDEST	COUNTROLS
COSTREL	COTINGAS	COTTONY	COULDST	COUNTRY
COSTRELS	COTININE	COTTOWN	COULEE	COUNTS
COSTS	COTININES	COTTOWNS	COULEES	COUNTSHIP
COSTUME	COTISE	COTTS	COULIBIAC	COUNTY
COSTUMED	COTISED	COTTUS	COULIS	COUP
COSTUMER	COTISES	COTTUSES	COULISSE	COUPE
COSTUMERS	COTISING	COTURNIX	COULISSES	COUPED
COSTUMERY	COTLAND	COTWAL	COULOIR	COUPEE
COSTUMES	COTLANDS	COTWALS	COULOIRS	COUPEES
COSTUMEY	COTQUEAN	COTYLAE	COULOMB	COUPER
COSTUMIER	COTQUEANS	COTYLE	COULOMBIC	COUPERS
COSTUMING	COTRUSTEE	COTYLEDON	COULOMBS	COUPES
COSTUS	COTS	COTYLES	COULTER	COUPING
COSTUSES	COTT	COTYLOID	COULTERS	COUPLE
COSY	COTTA	COTYLOIDS	COUMARIC	COUPLED
COSYING	COTTABUS	COTYPE	COUMARIN	COUPLEDOM
COT	COTTAE	COTYPES	COUMARINS	COUPLER
COTAN	COTTAGE	COUCAL	COUMARONE	COUPLERS
COTANGENT	COTTAGED	COUCALS	COUMAROU	COUPLES
COTANS	COTTAGER	COUCH	COUMAROUS	COUPLET
COTE	COTTAGERS	COUCHANT	COUNCIL	COUPLETS

COUPLING	COURTED	COUTURES	COVERSINE	COWBIND
COUPLINGS	COURTEOUS	COUTURIER	COVERSLIP	COWBINDS
COUPON	COURTER	COUVADE	COVERT	COWBIRD
COUPONING	COURTERS	COUVADES	COVERTLY	COWBIRDS
COUPONS	COURTESAN	COUVERT	COVERTS	COWBOY
COUPS	COURTESY	COUVERTS	COVERTURE	COWBOYED
COUPURE	COURTEZAN	COUZIN	COVERUP	COWBOYING
COUPURES	COURTIER	COUZINS	COVERUPS	COWBOYS
COUR	COURTIERS	COVALENCE	COVES	COWED
COURAGE	COURTING	COVALENCY	COVET	COWEDLY
COURAGES	COURTINGS	COVALENT	COVETABLE	COWER
COURANT	COURTLET	COVARIANT	COVETED	COWERED
COURANTE	COURTLETS	COVARIATE	COVETER	COWERING
COURANTES	COURTLIER	COVARIED	COVETERS	COWERS
COURANTO	COURTLIKE	COVARIES	COVETING	COWFEEDER
COURANTOS	COURTLING	COVARY	COVETISE	COWFISH
COURANTS	COURTLY	COVARYING	COVETISES	COWFISHES
COURB	COURTROOM	COVE	COVETOUS	COWFLAP
COURBARIL	COURTS	COVED	COVETS	COWFLAPS
COURBED	COURTSHIP	COVELET	COVEY	COWFLOP
COURBETTE	COURTSIDE	COVELETS	COVEYS	COWFLOPS
COURBING	COURTYARD	COVELLINE	COVIN	COWGIRL
COURBS	COUSCOUS	COVELLITE	COVING	COWGIRLS
COURD	COUSIN	COVEN	COVINGS	COWGRASS
COURE	COUSINAGE	COVENANT	COVINOUS	COWHAGE
COURED	COUSINLY	COVENANTS	COVINS	COWHAGES
COURES	COUSINRY	COVENS	COVYNE	COWHAND
COURGETTE	COUSINS	COVENT	COVYNES	COWHANDS
COURIE	COUTA	COVENTS	COW	COWHEARD
COURIED	COUTAS	COVER	COWAGE	COWHEARDS
COURIEING	COUTEAU	COVERABLE	COWAGES	COWHEEL
COURIER	COUTEAUX	COVERAGE	COWAL	COWHEELS
COURIERED	COUTER	COVERAGES	COWALS	COWHERB
COURIERS	COUTERS	COVERALL	COWAN	COWHERBS
COURIES	COUTH	COVERALLS	COWANS	COWHERD
COURING	COUTHER	COVERED	COWARD	COWHERDS
COURLAN	COUTHEST	COVERER	COWARDED	COWHIDE
COURLANS	COUTHIE	COVERERS	COWARDICE	COWHIDED
COURS	COUTHIER	COVERING	COWARDING	COWHIDES
COURSE	COUTHIEST	COVERINGS	COWARDLY	COWHIDING
COURSED	COUTHS	COVERLESS	COWARDRY	COWHOUSE
COURSER	COUTHY	COVERLET	COWARDS	COWHOUSES
COURSERS	COUTIL	COVERLETS	COWBANE	COWIER
COURSES	COUTILLE	COVERLID	COWBANES	COWIEST
COURSING	COUTILLES	COVERLIDS	COWBELL	COWING
COURSINGS	COUTILS	COVERS	COWBELLS	COWINNER
COURT	COUTURE	COVERSED	COWBERRY	COWINNERS

COWISH	COWSHEDS	COYOTE	CRABBERS	CRACKUPS
COWITCH	COWSKIN	COYOTES	CRABBIER	CRACKY
COWITCHES	COWSKINS	COYOTILLO	CRABBIEST	CRACOWE
COWK	COWSLIP	COYPOU	CRABBILY	CRACOWES
COWKED	COWSLIPS	COYPOUS	CRABBING	CRADLE
COWKING	COWTREE	COYPU	CRABBIT	CRADLED
COWKS	COWTREES	COYPUS	CRABBY	CRADLER
COWL	COWY	COYS	CRABEATER	CRADLERS
COWLED	COX	COYSTREL	CRABGRASS	CRADLES
COWLICK	COXA	COYSTRELS	CRABLIKE	CRADLING
COWLICKS	COXAE	COYSTRIL	CRABMEAT	CRADLINGS
COWLING	COXAL	COYSTRILS	CRABMEATS	CRAFT
COWLINGS	COXALGIA	COZ	CRABS	CRAFTED
COWLS	COXALGIAS	COZE	CRABSTICK	CRAFTER
COWLSTAFF	COXALGIC	COZED	CRABWISE	CRAFTERS
COWMAN	COXALGIES	COZEN	CRABWOOD	CRAFTIER
COWMEN	COXALGY	COZENAGE	CRABWOODS	CRAFTIEST
COWORKER	COXCOMB	COZENAGES	CRACHACH	CRAFTILY
COWORKERS	COXCOMBIC	COZENED	CRACK	CRAFTING
COWP	COXCOMBRY	COZENER	CRACKA	CRAFTLESS
COWPAT	COXCOMBS	COZENERS	CRACKAS	CRAFTS
COWPATS	COXED	COZENING	CRACKBACK	CRAFTSMAN
COWPEA	COXES	COZENS	CRACKDOWN	CRAFTSMEN
COWPEAS	COXIB	COZES	CRACKED	CRAFTWORK
COWPED	COXIBS	COZEY	CRACKER	CRAFTY
COWPIE	COXIER	COZEYS	CRACKERS	CRAG
COWPIES	COXIEST	COZIE	CRACKET	CRAGFAST
COWPING	COXINESS	COZIED	CRACKETS	CRAGGED
COWPLOP	COXING	COZIER	CRACKHEAD	CRAGGIER
COWPLOPS	COXITIDES	COZIERS	CRACKING	CRAGGIEST
COWPOKE	COXITIS	COZIES	CRACKINGS	CRAGGILY
COWPOKES	COXLESS	COZIEST	CRACKJAW	CRAGGY
COWPOX	COXSWAIN	COZILY	CRACKJAWS	CRAGS
COWPOXES	COXSWAINS	COZINESS	CRACKLE	CRAGSMAN
COWPS	COXY	COZING	CRACKLED	CRAGSMEN
COWRIE	COY	COZY	CRACKLES	CRAIC
COWRIES	COYDOG	COZYING	CRACKLIER	CRAICS
COWRITE	COYDOGS	COZZES	CRACKLING	CRAIG
COWRITER	COYED	CRAAL	CRACKLY	CRAIGS
COWRITERS	COYER	CRAALED	CRACKNEL	CRAKE
COWRITES	COYEST	CRAALING	CRACKNELS	CRAKED
COWRITING	COYING	CRAALS	CRACKPOT	CRAKES
COWRITTEN	COYISH	CRAB	CRACKPOTS	CRAKING
COWROTE	COYISHLY	CRABAPPLE	CRACKS	CRAM
COWRY	COYLY	CRABBED	CRACKSMAN	CRAMBE
COWS	COYNESS	CRABBEDLY	CRACKSMEN	CRAMBES
COWSHED	COYNESSES	CRABBER	CRACKUP	CRAMBO

CRAMBOES	CRANES	CRAPELIKE	CRATERED	CRAWLWAY
CRAMBOS	CRANIA	CRAPES	CRATERING	CRAWLWAYS
CRAME	CRANIAL	CRAPIER	CRATERLET	CRAWLY
CRAMES	CRANIALLY	CRAPIEST	CRATEROUS	CRAWS
CRAMESIES	CRANIATE	CRAPING	CRATERS	CRAY
CRAMESY	CRANIATES	CRAPLE	CRATES	CRAYER
CRAMFULL	CRANING	CRAPLES	CRATHUR	CRAYERS
CRAMMABLE	CRANIUM	CRAPOLA	CRATHURS	CRAYFISH
CRAMMED	CRANIUMS	CRAPOLAS	CRATING	CRAYON
CRAMMER	CRANK	CRAPPED	CRATON	CRAYONED
CRAMMERS	CRANKCASE	CRAPPER	CRATONIC	CRAYONER
CRAMMING	CRANKED	CRAPPERS	CRATONS	CRAYONERS
CRAMOISIE	CRANKER	CRAPPIE	CRATUR	CRAYONING
CRAMOISY	CRANKEST	CRAPPIER	CRATURS	CRAYONIST
CRAMP	CRANKIER	CRAPPIES	CRAUNCH	CRAYONS
CRAMPBARK	CRANKIEST	CRAPPIEST	CRAUNCHED	CRAYS
CRAMPED	CRANKILY	CRAPPING	CRAUNCHES	CRAYTHUR
CRAMPER	CRANKING	CRAPPY	CRAUNCHY	CRAYTHURS
CRAMPERS	CRANKISH	CRAPS	CRAVAT	CRAZE
CRAMPET	CRANKLE	CRAPSHOOT	CRAVATS	CRAZED
CRAMPETS	CRANKLED	CRAPULENT	CRAVATTED	CRAZES
CRAMPFISH	CRANKLES	CRAPULOUS	CRAVE	CRAZIER
CRAMPIER	CRANKLING	CRAPY	CRAVED	CRAZIES
CRAMPIEST	CRANKLY	CRARE	CRAVEN	CRAZIEST
CRAMPING	CRANKNESS	CRARES	CRAVENED	CRAZILY
CRAMPIT	CRANKOUS	CRASES	CRAVENING	CRAZINESS
CRAMPITS	CRANKPIN	CRASH	CRAVENLY	CRAZING
CRAMPON	CRANKPINS	CRASHED	CRAVENS	CRAZY
CRAMPONED	CRANKS	CRASHER	CRAVER	CRAZYWEED
CRAMPONS	CRANKY	CRASHERS	CRAVERS	CREACH
CRAMPOON	CRANNIED	CRASHES	CRAVES	CREACHS
CRAMPOONS	CRANNIES	CRASHING	CRAVING	CREAGH
CRAMPS	CRANNOG	CRASHPAD	CRAVINGS	CREAGHS
CRAMPY	CRANNOGE	CRASHPADS	CRAW	CREAK
CRAMS	CRANNOGES	CRASIS	CRAWDAD	CREAKED
CRAN	CRANNOGS	CRASS	CRAWDADDY	CREAKIER
CRANACHAN	CRANNY	CRASSER	CRAWDADS	CREAKIEST
CRANAGE	CRANNYING	CRASSEST	CRAWFISH	CREAKILY
CRANAGES	CRANREUCH	CRASSLY	CRAWL	CREAKING
CRANBERRY	CRANS	CRASSNESS	CRAWLED	CREAKS
CRANCH	CRANTS	CRATCH	CRAWLER	CREAKY
CRANCHED	CRANTSES	CRATCHES	CRAWLERS	CREAM
CRANCHES	CRAP	CRATE	CRAWLIER	CREAMCUPS
CRANCHING	CRAPAUD	CRATED	CRAWLIEST	CREAMED
CRANE	CRAPAUDS	CRATEFUL	CRAWLING	CREAMER
CRANED	CRAPE	CRATEFULS	CRAWLINGS	CREAMERS
CRANEFLY	CRAPED	CRATER	CRAWLS	CREAMERY

CREAMIER	CRECHE	CREEPIES	CRENATELY	CREPITANT
CREAMIEST	CRECHES	CREEPIEST	CRENATION	CREPITATE
CREAMILY	CRED	CREEPILY	CRENATURE	CREPITUS
CREAMING	CREDAL	CREEPING	CRENEL	CREPOLINE
CREAMLAID	CREDENCE	CREEPS	CRENELATE	CREPON
CREAMLIKE	CREDENCES	CREEPY	CRENELED	CREPONS
CREAMPUFF	CREDENDA	CREES	CRENELING	CREPS
CREAMS	CREDENDUM	CREESE	CRENELLE	CREPT
CREAMWARE	CREDENT	CREESED	CRENELLED	CREPUSCLE
CREAMWOVE	CREDENZA	CREESES	CRENELLES	CREPY
CREAMY	CREDENZAS	CREESH	CRENELS	CRESCENDI
CREANCE	CREDIBLE	CREESHED	CRENSHAW	CRESCENDO
CREANCES	CREDIBLY	CREESHES	CRENSHAWS	CRESCENT
CREANT	CREDIT	CREESHIER	CRENULATE	CRESCENTS
CREASE	CREDITED	CREESHING	CREODONT	CRESCIVE
CREASED	CREDITING	CREESHY	CREODONTS	CRESOL
CREASER	CREDITOR	CREESING	CREOLE	CRESOLS
CREASERS	CREDITORS	CREM	CREOLES	CRESS
CREASES	CREDITS	CREMAINS	CREOLIAN	CRESSES
CREASIER	CREDO	CREMANT	CREOLIANS	CRESSET
CREASIEST	CREDOS	CREMASTER	CREOLISE	CRESSETS
CREASING	CREDS	CREMATE	CREOLISED	CRESSIER
CREASOTE	CREDULITY	CREMATED	CREOLISES	CRESSIEST
CREASOTED	CREDULOUS	CREMATES	CREOLIST	CRESSY
CREASOTES	CREE	CREMATING	CREOLISTS	CREST
CREASY	CREED	CREMATION	CREOLIZE	CRESTA
CREATABLE	CREEDAL	CREMATOR	CREOLIZED	CRESTAL
CREATE	CREEDS	CREMATORS	CREOLIZES	CRESTED
CREATED	CREEING	CREMATORY	CREOPHAGY	CRESTING
CREATES	CREEK	CREME	CREOSOL	CRESTINGS
CREATIC	CREEKIER	CREMES	CREOSOLS	CRESTLESS
CREATIN	CREEKIEST	CREMINI	CREOSOTE	CRESTON
CREATINE	CREEKS	CREMINIS	CREOSOTED	CRESTONS
CREATINES	CREEKY	CREMOCARP	CREOSOTES	CRESTS
CREATING	CREEL	CREMONA	CREOSOTIC	CRESYL
CREATINS	CREELED	CREMONAS	CREPANCE	CRESYLIC
CREATION	CREELING	CREMOR	CREPANCES	CRESYLS
CREATIONS	CREELS	CREMORNE	CREPE	CRETIC
CREATIVE	CREEP	CREMORNES	CREPED	CRETICS
CREATIVES	CREEPAGE	CREMORS	CREPERIE	CRETIN
CREATOR	CREEPAGES	CREMOSIN	CREPERIES	CRETINISE
CREATORS	CREEPED	CREMS	CREPES	CRETINISM
CREATRESS	CREEPER	CREMSIN	CREPEY	CRETINIZE
CREATRIX	CREEPERED	CRENA	CREPIER	CRETINOID
CREATURAL	CREEPERS	CRENAS	CREPIEST	CRETINOUS
CREATURE	CREEPIE	CRENATE	CREPINESS	CRETINS
CREATURES	CREEPIER	CRENATED	CREPING	CRETISM

CRETISMS	CRIBBLED	CRIMINIS	CRINOID	CRISSAL
CRETONNE	CRIBBLES	CRIMINOUS	CRINOIDAL	CRISSUM
CRETONNES	CRIBBLING	CRIMINY	CRINOIDS	CRISTA
CRETONS	CRIBELLA	CRIMMER	CRINOLINE	CRISTAE
CREUTZER	CRIBELLAR	CRIMMERS	CRINOSE	CRISTATE
CREUTZERS	CRIBELLUM	CRIMP	CRINUM	CRISTATED
CREVALLE	CRIBLE	CRIMPED	CRINUMS	CRIT
CREVALLES	CRIBRATE	CRIMPER	CRIOLLO	CRITERIA
CREVASSE	CRIBROSE	CRIMPERS	CRIOLLOS	CRITERIAL
CREVASSED	CRIBROUS	CRIMPIER	CRIOS	CRITERION
CREVASSES	CRIBS	CRIMPIEST	CRIOSES	CRITERIUM
CREVETTE	CRIBWORK	CRIMPING	CRIPE	CRITH
CREVETTES	CRIBWORKS	CRIMPLE	CRIPES	CRITHS
CREVICE	CRICETID	CRIMPLED	CRIPPLE	CRITIC
CREVICED	CRICETIDS	CRIMPLES	CRIPPLED	CRITICAL
CREVICES	CRICK	CRIMPLING	CRIPPLER	CRITICISE
CREW	CRICKED	CRIMPS	CRIPPLERS	CRITICISM
CREWCUT	CRICKET	CRIMPY	CRIPPLES	CRITICIZE
CREWCUTS	CRICKETED	CRIMS	CRIPPLING	CRITICS
CREWE	CRICKETER	CRIMSON	CRIS	CRITIQUE
CREWED	CRICKETS	CRIMSONED	CRISE	CRITIQUED
CREWEL	CRICKEY	CRIMSONS	CRISES	CRITIQUES
CREWELIST	CRICKING	CRINAL	CRISIC	CRITS
CREWELLED	CRICKS	CRINATE	CRISIS	CRITTER
CREWELS	CRICKY	CRINATED	CRISP	CRITTERS
CREWES	CRICOID	CRINE	CRISPATE	CRITTUR
CREWING	CRICOIDS	CRINED	CRISPATED	CRITTURS
CREWLESS	CRIED	CRINES	CRISPED	CRIVENS
CREWMAN	CRIER	CRINGE	CRISPEN	CRIVVENS
CREWMATE	CRIERS	CRINGED	CRISPENED	CROAK
CREWMATES	CRIES	CRINGER	CRISPENS	CROAKED
CREWMEN	CRIKEY	CRINGERS	CRISPER	CROAKER
CREWNECK	CRIM	CRINGES	CRISPERS	CROAKERS
CREWNECKS	CRIME	CRINGINGS	CRISPEST	CROAKIER
CREWS	CRIMED	CRINGLE	CRISPHEAD	CROAKIEST
CRIA	CRIMEFUL	CRINGLES	CRISPIER	CROAKILY
CRIANT	CRIMELESS	CRINING	CRISPIES	CROAKING
CRIAS	CRIMEN	CRINITE	CRISPIEST	CROAKINGS
CRIB	CRIMES	CRINITES	CRISPILY	CROAKS
CRIBBAGE	CRIMEWAVE	CRINKLE	CRISPIN	CROAKY
CRIBBAGES	CRIMINA	CRINKLED	CRISPING	CROC
CRIBBED	CRIMINAL	CRINKLES	CRISPINS	CROCEATE
CRIBBER	CRIMINALS	CRINKLIER	CRISPLY	CROCEIN
CRIBBERS	CRIMINATE	CRINKLIES	CRISPNESS	CROCEINE
CRIBBING	CRIMINE	CRINKLING	CRISPS	CROCEINES
CRIBBINGS	CRIMING	CRINKLY	CRISPY	CROCEINS
CRIBBLE	CRIMINI		CRISSA	CROCEOUS

CROCHE	CROMBED	CROONERS	CROSSBOW	CROTALA
CROCHES	CROMBING	CROONING	CROSSBOWS	CROTALINE
CROCHET	CROMBS	CROONINGS	CROSSBRED	CROTALISM
CROCHETED	CROME	CROONS	CROSSBUCK	CROTALS
CROCHETER	CROMED	CROOVE	CROSSCUT	CROTALUM
CROCHETS	CROMES	CROOVES	CROSSCUTS	CROTCH
CROCI	CROMING	CROP	CROSSE	CROTCHED
CROCINE	CROMLECH	CROPBOUND	CROSSED	CROTCHES
CROCK	CROMLECHS	CROPFUL	CROSSER	CROTCHET
CROCKED	CROMORNA	CROPFULL	CROSSERS	CROTCHETS
CROCKERY	CROMORNAS	CROPFULS	CROSSES	CROTCHETY
CROCKET	CROMORNE	CROPLAND	CROSSEST	CROTON
CROCKETED	CROMORNES	CROPLANDS	CROSSETTE	CROTONBUG
CROCKETS	CRONE	CROPLESS	CROSSFALL	CROTONIC
CROCKING	CRONES	CROPPED	CROSSFIRE	CROTONS
CROCKPOT	CRONET	CROPPER	CROSSFISH	CROTTLE
CROCKPOTS	CRONETS	CROPPERS	CROSSHAIR	CROTTLES
CROCKS	CRONIES	CROPPIE	CROSSHEAD	CROUCH
CROCODILE	CRONISH	CROPPIES	CROSSING	CROUCHED
CROCOITE	CRONK	CROPPING	CROSSINGS	CROUCHES
CROCOITES	CRONKER	CROPPINGS	CROSSISH	CROUCHING
CROCOSMIA	CRONKEST	CROPPY	CROSSJACK	CROUP
CROCS	CRONY	CROPS	CROSSLET	CROUPADE
CROCUS	CRONYISM	CROPSICK	CROSSLETS	CROUPADES
CROCUSES	CRONYISMS	CROQUANTE	CROSSLY	CROUPE
CROFT	CROODLE	CROQUET	CROSSNESS	CROUPED
CROFTED	CROODLED	CROQUETED	CROSSOVER	CROUPER
CROFTER	CROODLES	CROQUETS	CROSSROAD	CROUPERS
CROFTERS	CROODLING	CROQUETTE	CROSSRUFF	CROUPES
CROFTING	CROOK	CROQUIS	CROSSTALK	CROUPIER
CROFTINGS	CROOKBACK	CRORE	CROSSTIE	CROUPIERS
CROFTS	CROOKED	CROREPATI	CROSSTIED	CROUPIEST
CROG	CROOKEDER	CRORES	CROSSTIES	CROUPILY
CROGGED	CROOKEDLY	CROSIER	CROSSTOWN	CROUPING
CROGGIES	CROOKER	CROSIERED	CROSSTREE	CROUPON
CROGGING	CROOKERY	CROSIERS	CROSSWALK	CROUPONS
CROGGY	CROOKEST	CROSS	CROSSWAY	CROUPOUS
CROGS	CROOKING	CROSSABLE	CROSSWAYS	CROUPS
CROISSANT	CROOKNECK	CROSSARM	CROSSWIND	CROUPY
CROJIK	CROOKS	CROSSARMS	CROSSWISE	CROUSE
CROJIKS	CROOL	CROSSBAND	CROSSWORD	CROUSELY
CROKINOLE	CROOLED	CROSSBAR	CROSSWORT	CROUSTADE
CROMACK	CROOLING	CROSSBARS	CROST	CROUT
CROMACKS	CROOLS	CROSSBEAM	CROSTINI	CROUTE
CROMB	CROON	CROSSBILL	CROSTINIS	CROUTES
CROMBEC	CROONED	CROSSBIT	CROSTINO	CROUTON
CROMBECS	CROONER	CROSSBITE	CROTAL	CROUTONS

CROUTS	CROZER	CRUDS	CRUMBS	CRUNK
CROW	CROZERS	CRUDY	CRUMBUM	CRUNKED
CROWBAR	CROZES	CRUE	CRUMBUMS	CRUNKLE
CROWBARS	CROZIER	CRUEL	CRUMBY	CRUNKLED
CROWBERRY	CROZIERS	CRUELER	CRUMEN	CRUNKLES
CROWBOOT	CROZZLED	CRUELEST	CRUMENAL	CRUNKLING
CROWBOOTS	CRU	CRUELLER	CRUMENALS	CRUNKS
CROWD	CRUBEEN	CRUELLEST	CRUMENS	CRUNODAL
CROWDED	CRUBEENS	CRUELLS	CRUMHORN	CRUNODE
CROWDEDLY	CRUCES	CRUELLY	CRUMHORNS	CRUNODES
CROWDER	CRUCIAL	CRUELNESS	CRUMMACK	CRUOR
CROWDERS	CRUCIALLY	CRUELS	CRUMMACKS	CRUORES
CROWDIE	CRUCIAN	CRUELTIES	CRUMMIE	CRUORS
CROWDIES	CRUCIANS	CRUELTY	CRUMMIER	CRUPPER
CROWDING	CRUCIATE	CRUES	CRUMMIES	CRUPPERS
CROWDS	CRUCIATES	CRUET	CRUMMIEST	CRURA
CROWDY	CRUCIBLE	CRUETS	CRUMMOCK	CRURAL
CROWEA	CRUCIBLES	CRUISE	CRUMMOCKS	CRUS
CROWEAS	CRUCIFER	CRUISED	CRUMMY	CRUSADE
CROWED	CRUCIFERS	CRUISER	CRUMP	CRUSADED
CROWER	CRUCIFIED	CRUISERS	CRUMPED	CRUSADER
CROWERS	CRUCIFIER	CRUISES	CRUMPER	CRUSADERS
CROWFEET	CRUCIFIES	CRUISEWAY	CRUMPEST	CRUSADES
CROWFOOT	CRUCIFIX	CRUISIE	CRUMPET	CRUSADING
CROWFOOTS	CRUCIFORM	CRUISIES	CRUMPETS	CRUSADO
CROWING	CRUCIFY	CRUISING	CRUMPIER	CRUSADOES
CROWINGLY	CRUCK	CRUISINGS	CRUMPIEST	CRUSADOS
CROWN	CRUCKS	CRUIVE	CRUMPING	CRUSE
CROWNED	CRUD	CRUIVES	CRUMPLE	CRUSES
CROWNER	CRUDDED	CRUIZIE	CRUMPLED	CRUSET
CROWNERS	CRUDDIER	CRUIZIES	CRUMPLES	CRUSETS
CROWNET	CRUDDIEST	CRULLER	CRUMPLIER	CRUSH
CROWNETS	CRUDDING	CRULLERS	CRUMPLING	CRUSHABLE
CROWNING	CRUDDLE	CRUMB	CRUMPLY	CRUSHED
CROWNINGS	CRUDDLED	CRUMBED	CRUMPS	CRUSHER
CROWNLAND	CRUDDLES	CRUMBER	CRUMPY	CRUSHERS
CROWNLESS	CRUDDLING	CRUMBERS	CRUNCH	CRUSHES
CROWNLET	CRUDDY	CRUMBIER	CRUNCHED	CRUSHING
CROWNLETS	CRUDE	CRUMBIEST	CRUNCHER	CRUSIAN
CROWNS	CRUDELY	CRUMBING	CRUNCHERS	CRUSIANS
CROWNWORK	CRUDENESS	CRUMBLE	CRUNCHES	CRUSIE
CROWS	CRUDER	CRUMBLED	CRUNCHIE	CRUSIES
CROWSFEET	CRUDES	CRUMBLES	CRUNCHIER	CRUSILY
CROWSFOOT	CRUDEST	CRUMBLIER	CRUNCHIES	CRUST
CROWSTEP	CRUDITES	CRUMBLIES	CRUNCHILY	CRUSTA
CROWSTEPS	CRUDITIES	CRUMBLING	CRUNCHING	CRUSTACEA
CROZE	CRUDITY	CRUMBLY	CRUNCHY	CRUSTAE

CRUSTAL	CRYOMETRY	CUBBIEST	CUCKOLD	CUE
CRUSTATE	CRYONIC	CUBBING	CUCKOLDED	CUED
CRUSTATED	CRYONICS	CUBBINGS	CUCKOLDLY	CUEING
CRUSTED	CRYOPHYTE	CUBBISH	CUCKOLDOM	CUEINGS
CRUSTIER	CRYOPROBE	CUBBISHLY	CUCKOLDRY	CUEIST
CRUSTIES	CRYOSCOPE	CUBBY	CUCKOLDS	CUEISTS
CRUSTIEST	CRYOSCOPY	CUBBYHOLE	CUCKOO	CUES
CRUSTILY	CRYOSTAT	CUBE	CUCKOOED	CUESTA
CRUSTING	CRYOSTATS	CUBEB	CUCKOOING	CUESTAS
CRUSTLESS	CRYOTRON	CUBEBS	CUCKOOS	CUFF
CRUSTOSE	CRYOTRONS	CUBED	CUCULLATE	CUFFED
CRUSTS	CRYPT	CUBER	CUCUMBER	CUFFIN
CRUSTY	CRYPTADIA	CUBERS	CUCUMBERS	CUFFING
CRUSY	CRYPTAL	CUBES	CUCURBIT	CUFFINS
CRUTCH	CRYPTIC	CUBHOOD	CUCURBITS	CUFFLE
CRUTCHED	CRYPTICAL	CUBHOODS	CUD	CUFFLED
CRUTCHES	CRYPTO	CUBIC	CUDBEAR	CUFFLES
CRUTCHING	CRYPTOGAM	CUBICA	CUDBEARS	CUFFLESS
CRUVE	CRYPTON	CUBICAL	CUDDEN	CUFFLING
CRUVES	CRYPTONS	CUBICALLY	CUDDENS	CUFFLINK
CRUX	CRYPTONYM	CUBICAS	CUDDIE	CUFFLINKS
CRUXES	CRYPTOS	CUBICITY	CUDDIES	CUFFO
CRUZADO	CRYPTS	CUBICLE	CUDDIN	CUFFS
CRUZADOES	CRYSTAL	CUBICLES	CUDDINS	CUFFUFFLE
CRUZADOS	CRYSTALS	CUBICLY	CUDDLE	CUIF
CRUZEIRO	CSARDAS	CUBICS	CUDDLED	CUIFS
CRUZEIROS	CSARDASES	CUBICULA	CUDDLER	CUING
CRUZIE	CTENE	CUBICULUM	CUDDLERS	CUIRASS
CRUZIES	CTENES	CUBIFORM	CUDDLES	CUIRASSED
CRWTH	CTENIDIA	CUBING	CUDDLIER	CUIRASSES
CRWTHS	CTENIDIUM	CUBISM	CUDDLIEST	CUISH
CRY	CTENIFORM	CUBISMS	CUDDLING	CUISHES
CRYBABIES	CTENOID	CUBIST	CUDDLY	CUISINART
CRYBABY	CUADRILLA	CUBISTIC	CUDDY	CUISINE
CRYING	CUATRO	CUBISTS	CUDGEL	CUISINES
CRYINGLY	CUATROS	CUBIT	CUDGELED	CUISINIER
CRYINGS	CUB	CUBITAL	CUDGELER	CUISSE
CRYOBANK	CUBAGE	CUBITI	CUDGELERS	CUISSER
CRYOBANKS	CUBAGES	CUBITS	CUDGELING	CUISSERS
CRYOCABLE	CUBANE	CUBITUS	CUDGELLED	CUISSES
CRYOGEN	CUBANELLE	CUBITUSES	CUDGELLER	CUIT
CRYOGENIC	CUBANES	CUBLESS	CUDGELS	CUITER
CRYOGENS	CUBATURE	CUBOID	CUDGERIE	CUITERED
CRYOGENY	CUBATURES	CUBOIDAL	CUDGERIES	CUITERING
CRYOLITE	CUBBED	CUBOIDS	CUDS	CUITERS
CRYOLITES	CUBBIER	CUBS	CUDWEED	CUITIKIN
CRYOMETER	CUBBIES	CUCKING	CUDWEEDS	CUITIKINS

CUITS	CULMINA	CULTY	CUMULOSE	CUPFERRON
CUITTLE	CULMINANT	CULVER	CUMULOUS	CUPFUL
CUITTLED	CULMINATE	CULVERIN	CUMULUS	CUPFULS
CUITTLES	CULMING	CULVERINS	CUNABULA	CUPGALL
CUITTLING	CULMS	CULVERS	CUNCTATOR	CUPGALLS
CUKE	CULOTTE	CULVERT	CUNDIES	CUPHEAD
CUKES	CULOTTES	CULVERTS	CUNDUM	CUPHEADS
CULCH	CULPA	CUM	CUNDUMS	CUPID
CULCHES	CULPABLE	CUMACEAN	CUNDY	CUPIDITY
CULCHIE	CULPABLY	CUMACEANS	CUNEAL	CUPIDS
CULCHIES	CULPAE	CUMARIC	CUNEATE	CUPLIKE
CULET	CULPATORY	CUMARIN	CUNEATED	CUPMAN
CULETS	CULPRIT	CUMARINS	CUNEATELY	CUPMEN
CULEX	CULPRITS	CUMARONE	CUNEATIC	CUPOLA
CULEXES	CULT	CUMARONES	CUNEI	CUPOLAED
CULICES	CULTCH	CUMBENT	CUNEIFORM	CUPOLAING
CULICID	CULTCHES	CUMBER	CUNETTE	CUPOLAR
CULICIDS	CULTER	CUMBERED	CUNETTES	CUPOLAS
CULICINE	CULTERS	CUMBERER	CUNEUS	CUPOLATED
CULICINES	CULTI	CUMBERERS	CUNIFORM	CUPPA
CULINARY	CULTIC	CUMBERING	CUNIFORMS	CUPPAS
CULL	CULTIER	CUMBERS	CUNJEVOI	CUPPED
CULLAY	CULTIEST	CUMBIA	CUNJEVOIS	CUPPER
CULLAYS	CULTIGEN	CUMBIAS	CUNNER	CUPPERS
CULLED	CULTIGENS	CUMBRANCE	CUNNERS	CUPPIER
CULLENDER	CULTISH	CUMBROUS	CUNNING	CUPPIEST
CULLER	CULTISHLY	CUMBUNGI	CUNNINGER	CUPPING
CULLERS	CULTISM	CUMBUNGIS	CUNNINGLY	CUPPINGS
CULLET	CULTISMS	CUMEC	CUNNINGS	CUPPY
CULLETS	CULTIST	CUMECS	CUNT	CUPREOUS
CULLIED	CULTISTS	CUMIN	CUNTS	CUPRESSUS
CULLIES	CULTIVAR	CUMINS	CUP	CUPRIC
CULLING	CULTIVARS	CUMMER	CUPBEARER	CUPRITE
CULLINGS	CULTIVATE	CUMMERS	CUPBOARD	CUPRITES
CULLION	CULTLIKE	CUMMIN	CUPBOARDS	CUPROUS
CULLIONLY	CULTRATE	CUMMINS	CUPCAKE	CUPRUM
CULLIONS	CULTRATED	CUMQUAT	CUPCAKES	CUPRUMS
CULLIS	CULTS	CUMQUATS	CUPEL	CUPS
CULLISES	CULTURAL	CUMS	CUPELED	CUPSFUL
CULLS	CULTURATI	CUMSHAW	CUPELER	CUPULA
CULLY	CULTURE	CUMSHAWS	CUPELERS	CUPULAE
CULLYING	CULTURED	CUMULATE	CUPELING	CUPULAR
CULLYISM	CULTURES	CUMULATED	CUPELLED	CUPULATE
CULLYISMS	CULTURING	CUMULATES	CUPELLER	CUPULE
CULM	CULTURIST	CUMULET	CUPELLERS	CUPULES
CULMED	CULTUS	CUMULETS	CUPELLING	CUR
CULMEN	CULTUSES	CUMULI	CUPELS	CURABLE

CURABLY	CURBS	CURIA	CURNIEST	CURSEDLY
CURACAO	CURBSIDE	CURIAE	CURNS	CURSENARY
CURACAOS	CURBSIDES	CURIAL	CURNY	CURSER
CURACIES	CURBSTONE	CURIALISM	CURPEL	CURSERS
CURACOA	CURCH	CURIALIST	CURPELS	CURSES
CURACOAS	CURCHEF	CURIAS	CURR	CURSI
CURACY	CURCHEFS	CURIE	CURRACH	CURSING
CURAGH	CURCHES	CURIES	CURRACHS	CURSINGS
CURAGHS	CURCULIO	CURIET	CURRAGH	CURSITOR
CURANDERA	CURCULIOS	CURIETS	CURRAGHS	CURSITORS
CURANDERO	CURCUMA	CURING	CURRAJONG	CURSITORY
CURARA	CURCUMAS	CURIO	CURRAN	CURSIVE
CURARAS	CURCUMIN	CURIOS	CURRANS	CURSIVELY
CURARE	CURCUMINE	CURIOSA	CURRANT	CURSIVES
CURARES	CURCUMINS	CURIOSITY	CURRANTS	CURSOR
CURARI	CURD	CURIOUS	CURRANTY	CURSORARY
CURARINE	CURDED	CURIOUSER	CURRAWONG	CURSORES
CURARINES	CURDIER	CURIOUSLY	CURRED	CURSORIAL
CURARIS	CURDIEST	CURITE	CURREJONG	CURSORILY
CURARISE	CURDINESS	CURITES	CURRENCY	CURSORS
CURARISED	CURDING	CURIUM	CURRENT	CURSORY
CURARISES	CURDLE	CURIUMS	CURRENTLY	CURST
CURARIZE	CURDLED	CURL	CURRENTS	CURSTNESS
CURARIZED	CURDLER	CURLED	CURRICLE	CURSUS
CURARIZES	CURDLERS	CURLER	CURRICLES	CURT
CURASSOW	CURDLES	CURLERS	CURRICULA	CURTAIL
CURASSOWS	CURDLING	CURLEW	CURRIE	CURTAILED
CURAT	CURDS	CURLEWS	CURRIED	CURTAILER
CURATE	CURDY	CURLI	CURRIER	CURTAILS
CURATED	CURE	CURLICUE	CURRIERS	CURTAIN
CURATES	CURED	CURLICUED	CURRIERY	CURTAINED
CURATING	CURELESS	CURLICUES	CURRIES	CURTAINS
CURATIVE	CURER	CURLIER	CURRIJONG	CURTAL
CURATIVES	CURERS	CURLIES	CURRING	CURTALAX
CURATOR	CURES	CURLIEST	CURRISH	CURTALAXE
CURATORS	CURET	CURLILY	CURRISHLY	CURTALS
CURATORY	CURETS	CURLINESS	CURRS	CURTANA
CURATRIX	CURETTAGE	CURLING	CURRY	CURTANAS
CURATS	CURETTE	CURLINGS	CURRYCOMB	CURTATE
CURB	CURETTED	CURLPAPER	CURRYING	CURTATION
CURBABLE	CURETTES	CURLS	CURRYINGS	CURTAXE
CURBED	CURETTING	CURLY	CURS	CURTAXES
CURBER	CURF	CURLYCUE	CURSAL	CURTER
CURBERS	CURFEW	CURLYCUES	CURSE	CURTESIES
CURBING	CURFEWS	CURN	CURSED	CURTEST
CURBINGS	CURFS	CURNEY	CURSEDER	CURTESY
CURBLESS	CURFUFFLE	CURNIER	CURSEDEST	CURTILAGE

CURTLY	CUSHIER	CUSTOCKS	CUTEST	CUTTAGE
CURTNESS	CUSHIES	CUSTODE	CUTESY	CUTTAGES
CURTSEY	CUSHIEST	CUSTODES	CUTEY	CUTTER
CURTSEYED	CUSHILY	CUSTODIAL	CUTEYS	CUTTERS
CURTSEYS	CUSHINESS	CUSTODIAN	CUTGLASS	CUTTHROAT
CURTSIED	CUSHION	CUSTODIER	CUTGRASS	CUTTIER
CURTSIES	CUSHIONED	CUSTODIES	CUTICLE	CUTTIES
CURTSY	CUSHIONET	CUSTODY	CUTICLES	CUTTIEST
CURTSYING	CUSHIONS	CUSTOM	CUTICULA	CUTTING
CURULE	CUSHIONY	CUSTOMARY	CUTICULAE	CUTTINGLY
CURVATE	CUSHTY	CUSTOMED	CUTICULAR	CUTTINGS
CURVATED	CUSHY	CUSTOMER	CUTIE	CUTTLE
CURVATION	CUSK	CUSTOMERS	CUTIES	CUTTLED
CURVATIVE	CUSKS	CUSTOMISE	CUTIKIN	CUTTLES
CURVATURE	CUSP	CUSTOMIZE	CUTIKINS	CUTTLING
CURVE	CUSPAL	CUSTOMS	CUTIN	CUTTO
CURVEBALL	CUSPATE	CUSTOS	CUTINISE	CUTTOE
CURVED	CUSPATED	CUSTREL	CUTINISED	CUTTOES
CURVEDLY	CUSPED	CUSTRELS	CUTINISES	CUTTY
CURVES	CUSPID	CUSTUMAL	CUTINIZE	CUTUP
CURVESOME	CUSPIDAL	CUSTUMALS	CUTINIZED	CUTUPS
CURVET	CUSPIDATE	CUSTUMARY	CUTINIZES	CUTWATER
CURVETED	CUSPIDES	CUSUM	CUTINS	CUTWATERS
CURVETING	CUSPIDOR	CUSUMS	CUTIS	CUTWORK
CURVETS	CUSPIDORE	CUT	CUTISES	CUTWORKS
CURVETTED	CUSPIDORS	CUTANEOUS	CUTLAS	CUTWORM
CURVEY	CUSPIDS	CUTAWAY	CUTLASES	CUTWORMS
CURVIER	CUSPIER	CUTAWAYS	CUTLASS	CUVEE
CURVIEST	CUSPIEST	CUTBACK	CUTLASSES	CUVEES
CURVIFORM	CUSPIS	CUTBACKS	CUTLER	CUVETTE
CURVINESS	CUSPS	CUTBANK	CUTLERIES	CUVETTES
CURVING	CUSPY	CUTBANKS	CUTLERS	CUZ
CURVITAL	CUSS	CUTCH	CUTLERY	CUZZES
CURVITIES	CUSSED	CUTCHA	CUTLET	CUZZIE
CURVITY	CUSSEDLY	CUTCHERRY	CUTLETS	CUZZIES
CURVY	CUSSER	CUTCHERY	CUTLINE	CWM
CUSCUS	CUSSERS	CUTCHES	CUTLINES	CWMS
CUSCUSES	CUSSES	CUTDOWN	CUTOFF	CWTCH
CUSEC	CUSSING	CUTDOWNS	CUTOFFS	CWTCHED
CUSECS	CUSSO	CUTE	CUTOUT	CWTCHES
CUSH	CUSSOS	CUTELY	CUTOUTS	CWTCHING
CUSHAT	CUSSWORD	CUTENESS	CUTOVER	CYAN
CUSHATS	CUSSWORDS	CUTER	CUTOVERS	CYANAMID
CUSHAW	CUSTARD	CUTES	CUTPURSE	CYANAMIDE
CUSHAWS	CUSTARDS	CUTESIE	CUTPURSES	CYANAMIDS
CUSHES	CUSTARDY	CUTESIER	CUTS	CYANATE
CUSHIE	CUSTOCK	CUTESIEST	CUTTABLE	CYANATES

C

CYANIC	CYBERSEX	CYCLISTS	CYMAS	CYNODONT
CYANID	CYBERWAR	CYCLITOL	CYMATIA	CYNODONTS
CYANIDE	CYBERWARS	CYCLITOLS	CYMATICS	CYNOMOLGI
CYANIDED	CYBORG	CYCLIZE	CYMATIUM	CYNOSURAL
CYANIDES	CYBORGS	CYCLIZED	CYMBAL	CYNOSURE
CYANIDING	CYBRARIAN	CYCLIZES	CYMBALEER	CYNOSURES
CYANIDS	CYBRID	CYCLIZINE	CYMBALER	CYPHER
CYANIN	CYBRIDS	CYCLIZING	CYMBALERS	CYPHERED
CYANINE	CYCAD	CYCLO	CYMBALIST	CYPHERING
CYANINES	CYCADEOID	CYCLOGIRO	CYMBALO	CYPHERS
CYANINS	CYCADS	CYCLOID	CYMBALOES	CYPRES
CYANISE	CYCAS	CYCLOIDAL	CYMBALOM	CYPRESES
CYANISED	CYCASES	CYCLOIDS	CYMBALOMS	CYPRESS
CYANISES	CYCASIN	CYCLOLITH	CYMBALOS	CYPRESSES
CYANISING	CYCASINS	CYCLONAL	CYMBALS	CYPRIAN
CYANITE	CYCLAMATE	CYCLONE	CYMBIDIA	CYPRIANS
CYANITES	CYCLAMEN	CYCLONES	CYMBIDIUM	CYPRID
CYANITIC	CYCLAMENS	CYCLONIC	CYMBIFORM	CYPRIDES
CYANIZE	CYCLASE	CYCLONITE	CYMBLING	CYPRIDS
CYANIZED	CYCLASES	CYCLOPEAN	CYMBLINGS	CYPRINE
CYANIZES	CYCLE	CYCLOPES	CYME	CYPRINID
CYANIZING	CYCLECAR	CYCLOPIAN	CYMENE	CYPRINIDS
CYANO	CYCLECARS	CYCLOPIC	CYMENES	CYPRINOID
CYANOGEN	CYCLED	CYCLOPS	CYMES	CYPRIS
CYANOGENS	CYCLEPATH	CYCLORAMA	CYMLIN	CYPRUS
CYANOSED	CYCLER	CYCLOS	CYMLING	CYPRUSES
CYANOSES	CYCLERIES	CYCLOSES	CYMLINGS	CYPSELA
CYANOSIS	CYCLERS	CYCLOSIS	CYMLINS	CYPSELAE
CYANOTIC	CYCLERY	CYCLOTRON	CYMOGENE	CYST
CYANOTYPE	CYCLES	CYCLUS	CYMOGENES	CYSTEIN
CYANS	CYCLEWAY	CYCLUSES	CYMOGRAPH	CYSTEINE
CYANURATE	CYCLEWAYS	CYDER	CYMOID	CYSTEINES
CYANURET	CYCLIC	CYDERS	CYMOL	CYSTEINIC
CYANURETS	CYCLICAL	CYESES	CYMOLS	CYSTEINS
CYATHI	CYCLICALS	CYESIS	CYMOPHANE	CYSTIC
CYATHIA	CYCLICISM	CYGNET	CYMOSE	CYSTID
CYATHIUM	CYCLICITY	CYGNETS	CYMOSELY	CYSTIDEAN
CYATHUS	CYCLICLY	CYLICES	CYMOUS	CYSTIDS
CYBER	CYCLIN	CYLINDER	CYNANCHE	CYSTIFORM
CYBERCAFE	CYCLING	CYLINDERS	CYNANCHES	CYSTINE
CYBERCAST	CYCLINGS	CYLINDRIC	CYNEGETIC	CYSTINES
CYBERNATE	CYCLINS	CYLIX	CYNIC	CYSTITIS
CYBERNAUT	CYCLISE	CYMA	CYNICAL	CYSTOCARP
CYBERPET	CYCLISED	CYMAE	CYNICALLY	CYSTOCELE
CYBERPETS	CYCLISES	CYMAGRAPH	CYNICISM	CYSTOID
CYBERPORN	CYCLISING	CYMAR	CYNICISMS	CYSTOIDS
CYBERPUNK	CYCLIST	CYMARS	CYNICS	CYSTOLITH

CYSTOTOMY
CYSTS
CYTASE
CYTASES
CYTASTER
CYTASTERS
CYTE
CYTES
CYTIDINE
CYTIDINES
CYTIDYLIC
CYTISI
CYTISINE
CYTISINES

CYTISUS
CYTODE
CYTODES
CYTOGENY
CYTOID
CYTOKINE
CYTOKINES
CYTOKININ
CYTOLOGIC
CYTOLOGY
CYTOLYSES
CYTOLYSIN
CYTOLYSIS
CYTOLYTIC

CYTOMETER
CYTOMETRY
CYTON
CYTONS
CYTOPENIA
CYTOPLASM
CYTOPLAST
CYTOSINE
CYTOSINES
CYTOSOL
CYTOSOLIC
CYTOSOLS
CYTOSOME
CYTOSOMES

CYTOTAXES
CYTOTAXIS
CYTOTOXIC
CYTOTOXIN
CZAPKA
CZAPKAS
CZAR
CZARDAS
CZARDASES
CZARDOM
CZARDOMS
CZAREVICH
CZAREVNA
CZAREVNAS

CZARINA
CZARINAS
CZARISM
CZARISMS
CZARIST
CZARISTS
CZARITSA
CZARITSAS
CZARITZA
CZARITZAS
CZARS

C

D

DA	DACRON	DAEMONIC	DAGLOCKS	DAILYNESS
DAAL	DACRONS	DAEMONS	DAGO	DAIMEN
DAALS	DACTYL	DAES	DAGOBA	DAIMIO
DAB	DACTYLAR	DAFF	DAGOBAS	DAIMIOS
DABBA	DACTYLI	DAFFED	DAGOES	DAIMOKU
DABBAS	DACTYLIC	DAFFIER	DAGOS	DAIMOKUS
DABBED	DACTYLICS	DAFFIES	DAGS	DAIMON
DABBER	DACTYLIST	DAFFIEST	DAGWOOD	DAIMONES
DABBERS	DACTYLS	DAFFILY	DAGWOODS	DAIMONIC
DABBING	DACTYLUS	DAFFINESS	DAH	DAIMONS
DABBITIES	DAD	DAFFING	DAHABEAH	DAIMYO
DABBITY	DADA	DAFFINGS	DAHABEAHS	DAIMYOS
DABBLE	DADAH	DAFFODIL	DAHABEEAH	DAINE
DABBLED	DADAHS	DAFFODILS	DAHABIAH	DAINED
DABBLER	DADAISM	DAFFS	DAHABIAHS	DAINES
DABBLERS	DADAISMS	DAFFY	DAHABIEH	DAINING
DABBLES	DADAIST	DAFT	DAHABIEHS	DAINT
DABBLING	DADAISTIC	DAFTAR	DAHABIYA	DAINTIER
DABBLINGS	DADAISTS	DAFTARS	DAHABIYAH	DAINTIES
DABCHICK	DADAS	DAFTER	DAHABIYAS	DAINTIEST
DABCHICKS	DADDED	DAFTEST	DAHABIYEH	DAINTILY
DABS	DADDIES	DAFTIE	DAHL	DAINTY
DABSTER	DADDING	DAFTIES	DAHLIA	DAIQUIRI
DABSTERS	DADDLE	DAFTLY	DAHLIAS	DAIQUIRIS
DACE	DADDLED	DAFTNESS	DAHLS	DAIRIES
DACES	DADDLES	DAG	DAHOON	DAIRY
DACHA	DADDLING	DAGABA	DAHOONS	DAIRYING
DACHAS	DADDOCK	DAGABAS	DAHS	DAIRYINGS
DACHSHUND	DADDOCKS	DAGGA	DAIDLE	DAIRYMAID
DACITE	DADDY	DAGGAS	DAIDLED	DAIRYMAN
DACITES	DADGUM	DAGGED	DAIDLES	DAIRYMEN
DACK	DADO	DAGGER	DAIDLING	DAIS
DACKED	DADOED	DAGGERED	DAIDZEIN	DAISES
DACKER	DADOES	DAGGERING	DAIDZEINS	DAISHIKI
DACKERED	DADOING	DAGGERS	DAIKER	DAISHIKIS
DACKERING	DADOS	DAGGIER	DAIKERED	DAISIED
DACKERS	DADS	DAGGIEST	DAIKERING	DAISIES
DACKING	DAE	DAGGING	DAIKERS	DAISY
DACKS	DAEDAL	DAGGINGS	DAIKO	DAK
DACOIT	DAEDALEAN	DAGGLE	DAIKON	DAKER
DACOITAGE	DAEDALIAN	DAGGLED	DAIKONS	DAKERED
DACOITIES	DAEDALIC	DAGGLES	DAIKOS	DAKERHEN
DACOITS	DAEING	DAGGLING	DAILIES	DAKERHENS
DACOITY	DAEMON	DAGGY	DAILINESS	DAKERING
DACQUOISE	DAEMONES	DAGLOCK	DAILY	DAKERS

DAKOIT	DALTONISM	DAMNATION	DAN	DANDY
DAKOITI	DALTONS	DAMNATORY	DANAZOL	DANDYFUNK
DAKOITIES	DALTS	DAMNDEST	DANAZOLS	DANDYISH
DAKOITIS	DAM	DAMNDESTS	DANCE	DANDYISM
DAKOITS	DAMAGE	DAMNED	DANCEABLE	DANDYISMS
DAKOITY	DAMAGED	DAMNEDER	DANCED	DANDYPRAT
DAKS	DAMAGER	DAMNEDEST	DANCEHALL	DANEGELD
DAL	DAMAGERS	DAMNER	DANCER	DANEGELDS
DALAPON	DAMAGES	DAMNERS	DANCERS	DANEGELT
DALAPONS	DAMAGING	DAMNIFIED	DANCES	DANEGELTS
DALASI	DAMAN	DAMNIFIES	DANCETTE	DANELAGH
DALASIS	DAMANS	DAMNIFY	DANCETTEE	DANELAGHS
DALE	DAMAR	DAMNING	DANCETTES	DANELAW
DALED	DAMARS	DAMNINGLY	DANCETTY	DANELAWS
DALEDH	DAMASCENE	DAMNS	DANCEY	DANEWEED
DALEDHS	DAMASK	DAMOISEL	DANCICAL	DANEWEEDS
DALEDS	DAMASKED	DAMOISELS	DANCICALS	DANEWORT
DALES	DAMASKEEN	DAMOSEL	DANCIER	DANEWORTS
DALESMAN	DAMASKIN	DAMOSELS	DANCIEST	DANG
DALESMEN	DAMASKING	DAMOZEL	DANCING	DANGED
DALETH	DAMASKINS	DAMOZELS	DANCINGS	DANGER
DALETHS	DAMASKS	DAMP	DANCY	DANGERED
DALGYTE	DAMASQUIN	DAMPED	DANDELION	DANGERING
DALGYTES	DAMASSIN	DAMPEN	DANDER	DANGEROUS
DALI	DAMASSINS	DAMPENED	DANDERED	DANGERS
DALIS	DAMBOARD	DAMPENER	DANDERING	DANGING
DALLE	DAMBOARDS	DAMPENERS	DANDERS	DANGLE
DALLES	DAMBROD	DAMPENING	DANDIACAL	DANGLED
DALLIANCE	DAMBRODS	DAMPENS	DANDIER	DANGLER
DALLIED	DAME	DAMPER	DANDIES	DANGLERS
DALLIER	DAMES	DAMPERS	DANDIEST	DANGLES
DALLIERS	DAMEWORT	DAMPEST	DANDIFIED	DANGLIER
DALLIES	DAMEWORTS	DAMPIER	DANDIFIES	DANGLIEST
DALLOP	DAMFOOL	DAMPIEST	DANDIFY	DANGLING
DALLOPS	DAMIANA	DAMPING	DANDILY	DANGLINGS
DALLY	DAMIANAS	DAMPINGS	DANDIPRAT	DANGLY
DALLYING	DAMMAR	DAMPISH	DANDLE	DANGS
DALMAHOY	DAMMARS	DAMPLY	DANDLED	DANIO
DALMAHOYS	DAMME	DAMPNESS	DANDLER	DANIOS
DALMATIAN	DAMMED	DAMPS	DANDLERS	DANISH
DALMATIC	DAMMER	DAMPY	DANDLES	DANISHES
DALMATICS	DAMMERS	DAMS	DANDLING	DANK
DALS	DAMMING	DAMSEL	DANDRIFF	DANKER
DALT	DAMMIT	DAMSELFLY	DANDRIFFS	DANKEST
DALTON	DAMN	DAMSELS	DANDRUFF	DANKISH
DALTONIAN	DAMNABLE	DAMSON	DANDRUFFS	DANKLY
DALTONIC	DAMNABLY	DAMSONS	DANDRUFFY	DANKNESS

DANKS	DARBS	DARKLED	DARRED	DASTARD
DANNEBROG	DARCIES	DARKLES	DARRES	DASTARDLY
DANNIES	DARCY	DARKLIER	DARRING	DASTARDS
DANNY	DARCYS	DARKLIEST	DARSHAN	DASTARDY
DANS	DARE	DARKLING	DARSHANS	DASYMETER
DANSEUR	DARED	DARKLINGS	DART	DASYPOD
DANSEURS	DAREDEVIL	DARKLY	DARTBOARD	DASYPODS
DANSEUSE	DAREFUL	DARKMANS	DARTED	DASYURE
DANSEUSES	DARER	DARKNESS	DARTER	DASYURES
DANT	DARERS	DARKNET	DARTERS	DATA
DANTED	DARES	DARKNETS	DARTING	DATABANK
DANTHONIA	DARESAY	DARKROOM	DARTINGLY	DATABANKS
DANTING	DARG	DARKROOMS	DARTITIS	DATABASE
DANTON	DARGA	DARKS	DARTLE	DATABASED
DANTONED	DARGAH	DARKSOME	DARTLED	DATABASES
DANTONING	DARGAHS	DARKY	DARTLES	DATABLE
DANTONS	DARGAS	DARLING	DARTLING	DATABUS
DANTS	DARGLE	DARLINGLY	DARTRE	DATABUSES
DAP	DARGLES	DARLINGS	DARTRES	DATACARD
DAPHNE	DARGS	DARN	DARTROUS	DATACARDS
DAPHNES	DARI	DARNATION	DARTS	DATACOMMS
DAPHNIA	DARIC	DARNDEST	DARZI	DATAFLOW
DAPHNIAS	DARICS	DARNDESTS	DARZIS	DATAGLOVE
DAPHNID	DARING	DARNED	DAS	DATAGRAM
DAPHNIDS	DARINGLY	DARNEDER	DASH	DATAGRAMS
DAPPED	DARINGS	DARNEDEST	DASHBOARD	DATAL
DAPPER	DARIOLE	DARNEL	DASHED	DATALLER
DAPPERER	DARIOLES	DARNELS	DASHEEN	DATALLERS
DAPPEREST	DARIS	DARNER	DASHEENS	DATALS
DAPPERLY	DARK	DARNERS	DASHEKI	DATARIA
DAPPERS	DARKED	DARNING	DASHEKIS	DATARIAS
DAPPING	DARKEN	DARNINGS	DASHER	DATARIES
DAPPLE	DARKENED	DARNS	DASHERS	DATARY
DAPPLED	DARKENER	DAROGHA	DASHES	DATCHA
DAPPLES	DARKENERS	DAROGHAS	DASHI	DATCHAS
DAPPLING	DARKENING	DARRAIGN	DASHIER	DATE
DAPS	DARKENS	DARRAIGNE	DASHIEST	DATEABLE
DAPSONE	DARKER	DARRAIGNS	DASHIKI	DATEBOOK
DAPSONES	DARKEST	DARRAIN	DASHIKIS	DATEBOOKS
DAQUIRI	DARKEY	DARRAINE	DASHING	DATED
DAQUIRIS	DARKEYS	DARRAINED	DASHINGLY	DATEDLY
DARAF	DARKFIELD	DARRAINES	DASHIS	DATEDNESS
DARAFS	DARKIE	DARRAINS	DASHPOT	DATELESS
DARB	DARKIES	DARRAYN	DASHPOTS	DATELINE
DARBAR	DARKING	DARRAYNED	DASHY	DATELINED
DARBARS	DARKISH	DARRAYNS	DASSIE	DATELINES
DARBIES	DARKLE	DARRE	DASSIES	DATER

DATERS	DAUNDERED	DAWBRY	DAYBOOKS	DAYSIDES
DATES	DAUNDERS	DAWCOCK	DAYBOY	DAYSMAN
DATING	DAUNER	DAWCOCKS	DAYBOYS	DAYSMEN
DATINGS	DAUNERED	DAWD	DAYBREAK	DAYSPRING
DATIVAL	DAUNERING	DAWDED	DAYBREAKS	DAYSTAR
DATIVE	DAUNERS	DAWDING	DAYCARE	DAYSTARS
DATIVELY	DAUNT	DAWDLE	DAYCARES	DAYTALE
DATIVES	DAUNTED	DAWDLED	DAYCENTRE	DAYTALER
DATO	DAUNTER	DAWDLER	DAYCH	DAYTALERS
DATOLITE	DAUNTERS	DAWDLERS	DAYCHED	DAYTALES
DATOLITES	DAUNTING	DAWDLES	DAYCHES	DAYTIME
DATOS	DAUNTLESS	DAWDLING	DAYCHING	DAYTIMES
DATTO	DAUNTON	DAWDS	DAYDREAM	DAYWEAR
DATTOS	DAUNTONED	DAWED	DAYDREAMS	DAYWEARS
DATUM	DAUNTONS	DAWEN	DAYDREAMT	DAYWORK
DATUMS	DAUNTS	DAWING	DAYDREAMY	DAYWORKER
DATURA	DAUPHIN	DAWISH	DAYFLIES	DAYWORKS
DATURAS	DAUPHINE	DAWK	DAYFLOWER	DAZE
DATURIC	DAUPHINES	DAWKS	DAYFLY	DAZED
DATURINE	DAUPHINS	DAWN	DAYGIRL	DAZEDLY
DATURINES	DAUR	DAWNED	DAYGIRLS	DAZEDNESS
DAUB	DAURED	DAWNER	DAYGLO	DAZER
DAUBE	DAURING	DAWNERED	DAYGLOW	DAZERS
DAUBED	DAURS	DAWNERING	DAYGLOWS	DAZES
DAUBER	DAUT	DAWNERS	DAYLIGHT	DAZING
DAUBERIES	DAUTED	DAWNEY	DAYLIGHTS	DAZZLE
DAUBERS	DAUTIE	DAWNING	DAYLILIES	DAZZLED
DAUBERY	DAUTIES	DAWNINGS	DAYLILY	DAZZLER
DAUBES	DAUTING	DAWNLIKE	DAYLIT	DAZZLERS
DAUBIER	DAUTS	DAWNS	DAYLONG	DAZZLES
DAUBIEST	DAVEN	DAWS	DAYMARE	DAZZLING
DAUBING	DAVENED	DAWSONITE	DAYMARES	DAZZLINGS
DAUBINGLY	DAVENING	DAWT	DAYMARK	DE
DAUBINGS	DAVENPORT	DAWTED	DAYMARKS	DEACIDIFY
DAUBRIES	DAVENS	DAWTIE	DAYNT	DEACON
DAUBRY	DAVIDIA	DAWTIES	DAYPACK	DEACONED
DAUBS	DAVIDIAS	DAWTING	DAYPACKS	DEACONESS
DAUBY	DAVIES	DAWTS	DAYROOM	DEACONING
DAUD	DAVIT	DAY	DAYROOMS	DEACONRY
DAUDED	DAVITS	DAYAN	DAYS	DEACONS
DAUDING	DAVY	DAYANIM	DAYSACK	DEAD
DAUDS	DAW	DAYANS	DAYSACKS	DEADBEAT
DAUGHTER	DAWAH	DAYBED	DAYSAILER	DEADBEATS
DAUGHTERS	DAWAHS	DAYBEDS	DAYSAILOR	DEADBOLT
DAULT	DAWBAKE	DAYBOAT	DAYSHELL	DEADBOLTS
DAULTS	DAWBAKES	DAYBOATS	DAYSHELLS	DEADBOY
DAUNDER	DAWBRIES	DAYBOOK	DAYSIDE	DEADBOYS

DEADED	DEAFENS	DEARLING	DEAWS	DEBEAKED
DEADEN	DEAFER	DEARLINGS	DEAWY	DEBEAKING
DEADENED	DEAFEST	DEARLY	DEB	DEBEAKS
DEADENER	DEAFISH	DEARN	DEBACLE	DEBEARD
DEADENERS	DEAFLY	DEARNESS	DEBACLES	DEBEARDED
DEADENING	DEAFNESS	DEARNFUL	DEBAG	DEBEARDS
DEADENS	DEAIR	DEARNLY	DEBAGGED	DEBEL
DEADER	DEAIRED	DEARNS	DEBAGGING	DEBELLED
DEADERS	DEAIRING	DEARS	DEBAGS	DEBELLING
DEADEST	DEAIRS	DEARTH	DEBAR	DEBELS
DEADEYE	DEAL	DEARTHS	DEBARK	DEBENTURE
DEADEYES	DEALATE	DEARY	DEBARKED	DEBES
DEADFALL	DEALATED	DEASH	DEBARKER	DEBILE
DEADFALLS	DEALATES	DEASHED	DEBARKERS	DEBILITY
DEADHEAD	DEALATION	DEASHES	DEBARKING	DEBIT
DEADHEADS	DEALBATE	DEASHING	DEBARKS	DEBITED
DEADHOUSE	DEALER	DEASIL	DEBARMENT	DEBITING
DEADING	DEALERS	DEASILS	DEBARRASS	DEBITOR
DEADLIER	DEALFISH	DEASIUL	DEBARRED	DEBITORS
DEADLIEST	DEALING	DEASIULS	DEBARRING	DEBITS
DEADLIFT	DEALINGS	DEASOIL	DEBARS	DEBONAIR
DEADLIFTS	DEALS	DEASOILS	DEBASE	DEBONAIRE
DEADLIGHT	DEALT	DEATH	DEBASED	DEBONE
DEADLINE	DEAMINASE	DEATHBED	DEBASER	DEBONED
DEADLINED	DEAMINATE	DEATHBEDS	DEBASERS	DEBONER
DEADLINES	DEAMINISE	DEATHBLOW	DEBASES	DEBONERS
DEADLOCK	DEAMINIZE	DEATHCUP	DEBASING	DEBONES
DEADLOCKS	DEAN	DEATHCUPS	DEBATABLE	DEBONING
DEADLY	DEANED	DEATHFUL	DEBATABLY	DEBOSH
DEADMAN	DEANER	DEATHIER	DEBATE	DEBOSHED
DEADMEN	DEANERIES	DEATHIEST	DEBATED	DEBOSHES
DEADNESS	DEANERS	DEATHLESS	DEBATEFUL	DEBOSHING
DEADPAN	DEANERY	DEATHLIER	DEBATER	DEBOSS
DEADPANS	DEANING	DEATHLIKE	DEBATERS	DEBOSSED
DEADS	DEANS	DEATHLY	DEBATES	DEBOSSES
DEADSTOCK	DEANSHIP	DEATHS	DEBATING	DEBOSSING
DEADWOOD	DEANSHIPS	DEATHSMAN	DEBAUCH	DEBOUCH
DEADWOODS	DEAR	DEATHSMEN	DEBAUCHED	DEBOUCHE
DEAERATE	DEARE	DEATHTRAP	DEBAUCHEE	DEBOUCHED
DEAERATED	DEARED	DEATHWARD	DEBAUCHER	DEBOUCHES
DEAERATES	DEARER	DEATHY	DEBAUCHES	DEBRIDE
DEAERATOR	DEARES	DEAVE	DEBBIER	DEBRIDED
DEAF	DEAREST	DEAVED	DEBBIES	DEBRIDES
DEAFBLIND	DEARESTS	DEAVES	DEBBIEST	DEBRIDING
DEAFEN	DEARIE	DEAVING	DEBBY	DEBRIEF
DEAFENED	DEARIES	DEAW	DEBE	DEBRIEFED
DEAFENING	DEARING	DEAWIE	DEBEAK	DEBRIEFER

DEBRIEFS	DEBUTED	DECANI	DECEIVES	DECIDUATE
DEBRIS	DEBUTING	DECANOIC	DECEIVING	DECIDUOUS
DEBRUISE	DEBUTS	DECANT	DECELERON	DECIGRAM
DEBRUISED	DEBYE	DECANTATE	DECEMVIR	DECIGRAMS
DEBRUISES	DEBYES	DECANTED	DECEMVIRI	DECILE
DEBS	DECACHORD	DECANTER	DECEMVIRS	DECILES
DEBT	DECAD	DECANTERS	DECENARY	DECILITER
DEBTED	DECADAL	DECANTING	DECENCIES	DECILITRE
DEBTEE	DECADE	DECANTS	DECENCY	DECILLION
DEBTEES	DECADENCE	DECAPOD	DECENNARY	DECIMAL
DEBTLESS	DECADENCY	DECAPODAL	DECENNIA	DECIMALLY
DEBTOR	DECADENT	DECAPODAN	DECENNIAL	DECIMALS
DEBTORS	DECADENTS	DECAPODS	DECENNIUM	DECIMATE
DEBTS	DECADES	DECARB	DECENT	DECIMATED
DEBUD	DECADS	DECARBED	DECENTER	DECIMATES
DEBUDDED	DECAF	DECARBING	DECENTERS	DECIMATOR
DEBUDDING	DECAFF	DECARBS	DECENTEST	DECIME
DEBUDS	DECAFFS	DECARE	DECENTLY	DECIMES
DEBUG	DECAFS	DECARES	DECENTRE	DECIMETER
DEBUGGED	DECAGON	DECASTERE	DECENTRED	DECIMETRE
DEBUGGER	DECAGONAL	DECASTICH	DECENTRES	DECIPHER
DEBUGGERS	DECAGONS	DECASTYLE	DECEPTION	DECIPHERS
DEBUGGING	DECAGRAM	DECATHLON	DECEPTIVE	DECISION
DEBUGS	DECAGRAMS	DECAUDATE	DECEPTORY	DECISIONS
DEBUNK	DECAHEDRA	DECAY	DECERN	DECISIVE
DEBUNKED	DECAL	DECAYABLE	DECERNED	DECISORY
DEBUNKER	DECALCIFY	DECAYED	DECERNING	DECISTERE
DEBUNKERS	DECALED	DECAYER	DECERNS	DECK
DEBUNKING	DECALING	DECAYERS	DECERTIFY	DECKCHAIR
DEBUNKS	DECALITER	DECAYING	DECESSION	DECKED
DEBUR	DECALITRE	DECAYLESS	DECHEANCE	DECKEL
DEBURR	DECALLED	DECAYS	DECIARE	DECKELS
DEBURRED	DECALLING	DECCIE	DECIARES	DECKER
DEBURRING	DECALOG	DECCIES	DECIBEL	DECKERS
DEBURRS	DECALOGS	DECEASE	DECIBELS	DECKHAND
DEBURS	DECALOGUE	DECEASED	DECIDABLE	DECKHANDS
DEBUS	DECALS	DECEASES	DECIDE	DECKHOUSE
DEBUSED	DECAMETER	DECEASING	DECIDED	DECKING
DEBUSES	DECAMETRE	DECEDENT	DECIDEDLY	DECKINGS
DEBUSING	DECAMP	DECEDENTS	DECIDER	DECKLE
DEBUSSED	DECAMPED	DECEIT	DECIDERS	DECKLED
DEBUSSES	DECAMPING	DECEITFUL	DECIDES	DECKLES
DEBUSSING	DECAMPS	DECEITS	DECIDING	DECKO
DEBUT	DECANAL	DECEIVE	DECIDUA	DECKOED
DEBUTANT	DECANALLY	DECEIVED	DECIDUAE	DECKOING
DEBUTANTE	DECANE	DECEIVER	DECIDUAL	DECKOS
DEBUTANTS	DECANES	DECEIVERS	DECIDUAS	DECKS

DECLAIM	DECODING	DECREERS	DECURSION	DEEJAYED
DECLAIMED	DECOHERER	DECREES	DECURSIVE	DEEJAYING
DECLAIMER	DECOKE	DECREET	DECURVE	DEEJAYS
DECLAIMS	DECOKED	DECREETS	DECURVED	DEEK
DECLARANT	DECOKES	DECREMENT	DECURVES	DEELY
DECLARE	DECOKING	DECREPIT	DECURVING	DEEM
DECLARED	DECOLLATE	DECRETAL	DECURY	DEEMED
DECLARER	DECOLLETE	DECRETALS	DECUSSATE	DEEMING
DECLARERS	DECOLOR	DECRETIST	DEDAL	DEEMS
DECLARES	DECOLORED	DECRETIVE	DEDALIAN	DEEMSTER
DECLARING	DECOLORS	DECRETORY	DEDANS	DEEMSTERS
DECLASS	DECOLOUR	DECREW	DEDICANT	DEEN
DECLASSE	DECOLOURS	DECREWED	DEDICANTS	DEENS
DECLASSED	DECOMMIT	DECREWING	DEDICATE	DEEP
DECLASSEE	DECOMMITS	DECREWS	DEDICATED	DEEPEN
DECLASSES	DECOMPLEX	DECRIAL	DEDICATEE	DEEPENED
DECLAW	DECOMPOSE	DECRIALS	DEDICATES	DEEPENER
DECLAWED	DECONGEST	DECRIED	DEDICATOR	DEEPENERS
DECLAWING	DECONTROL	DECRIER	DEDIMUS	DEEPENING
DECLAWS	DECOR	DECRIERS	DEDIMUSES	DEEPENS
DECLINAL	DECORATE	DECRIES	DEDUCE	DEEPER
DECLINANT	DECORATED	DECROWN	DEDUCED	DEEPEST
DECLINATE	DECORATES	DECROWNED	DEDUCES	DEEPFELT
DECLINE	DECORATOR	DECROWNS	DEDUCIBLE	DEEPFROZE
DECLINED	DECOROUS	DECRY	DEDUCIBLY	DEEPIE
DECLINER	DECORS	DECRYING	DEDUCING	DEEPIES
DECLINERS	DECORUM	DECRYPT	DEDUCT	DEEPLY
DECLINES	DECORUMS	DECRYPTED	DEDUCTED	DEEPMOST
DECLINING	DECOS	DECRYPTS	DEDUCTING	DEEPNESS
DECLINIST	DECOUPAGE	DECTET	DEDUCTION	DEEPS
DECLIVITY	DECOUPLE	DECTETS	DEDUCTIVE	DEEPWATER
DECLIVOUS	DECOUPLED	DECUBITAL	DEDUCTS	DEER
DECLUTCH	DECOUPLER	DECUBITI	DEE	DEERBERRY
DECLUTTER	DECOUPLES	DECUBITUS	DEED	DEERE
DECO	DECOY	DECUMAN	DEEDED	DEERFLIES
DECOCT	DECOYED	DECUMANS	DEEDER	DEERFLY
DECOCTED	DECOYER	DECUMBENT	DEEDEST	DEERGRASS
DECOCTING	DECOYERS	DECUPLE	DEEDFUL	DEERHOUND
DECOCTION	DECOYING	DECUPLED	DEEDIER	DEERLET
DECOCTIVE	DECOYS	DECUPLES	DEEDIEST	DEERLETS
DECOCTS	DECREASE	DECUPLING	DEEDILY	DEERLIKE
DECOCTURE	DECREASED	DECURIA	DEEDING	DEERS
DECODE	DECREASES	DECURIAS	DEEDLESS	DEERSKIN
DECODED	DECREE	DECURIES	DEEDS	DEERSKINS
DECODER	DECREED	DECURION	DEEDY	DEERWEED
DECODERS	DECREEING	DECURIONS	DEEING	DEERWEEDS
DECODES	DECREER	DECURRENT	DEEJAY	DEERYARD

DEERYARDS	DEFEATISM	DEFFLY	DEFLECT	DEFORMS
DEES	DEFEATIST	DEFFO	DEFLECTED	DEFOUL
DEET	DEFEATS	DEFI	DEFLECTOR	DEFOULED
DEETS	DEFEATURE	DEFIANCE	DEFLECTS	DEFOULING
DEEV	DEFECATE	DEFIANCES	DEFLEX	DEFOULS
DEEVE	DEFECATED	DEFIANT	DEFLEXED	DEFRAG
DEEVED	DEFECATES	DEFIANTLY	DEFLEXES	DEFRAGGED
DEEVES	DEFECATOR	DEFICIENT	DEFLEXING	DEFRAGGER
DEEVING	DEFECT	DEFICIT	DEFLEXION	DEFRAGS
DEEVS	DEFECTED	DEFICITS	DEFLEXURE	DEFRAUD
DEEWAN	DEFECTING	DEFIED	DEFLORATE	DEFRAUDED
DEEWANS	DEFECTION	DEFIER	DEFLOWER	DEFRAUDER
DEF	DEFECTIVE	DEFIERS	DEFLOWERS	DEFRAUDS
DEFACE	DEFECTOR	DEFIES	DEFLUENT	DEFRAY
DEFACED	DEFECTORS	DEFILADE	DEFLUXION	DEFRAYAL
DEFACER	DEFECTS	DEFILADED	DEFO	DEFRAYALS
DEFACERS	DEFENCE	DEFILADES	DEFOAM	DEFRAYED
DEFACES	DEFENCED	DEFILE	DEFOAMED	DEFRAYER
DEFACING	DEFENCES	DEFILED	DEFOAMER	DEFRAYERS
DEFAECATE	DEFENCING	DEFILER	DEFOAMERS	DEFRAYING
DEFALCATE	DEFEND	DEFILERS	DEFOAMING	DEFRAYS
DEFAME	DEFENDANT	DEFILES	DEFOAMS	DEFREEZE
DEFAMED	DEFENDED	DEFILING	DEFOCUS	DEFREEZES
DEFAMER	DEFENDER	DEFINABLE	DEFOCUSED	DEFROCK
DEFAMERS	DEFENDERS	DEFINABLY	DEFOCUSES	DEFROCKED
DEFAMES	DEFENDING	DEFINE	DEFOG	DEFROCKS
DEFAMING	DEFENDS	DEFINED	DEFOGGED	DEFROST
DEFAMINGS	DEFENSE	DEFINER	DEFOGGER	DEFROSTED
DEFANG	DEFENSED	DEFINERS	DEFOGGERS	DEFROSTER
DEFANGED	DEFENSES	DEFINES	DEFOGGING	DEFROSTS
DEFANGING	DEFENSING	DEFINIENS	DEFOGS	DEFROZE
DEFANGS	DEFENSIVE	DEFINING	DEFOLIANT	DEFROZEN
DEFAST	DEFER	DEFINITE	DEFOLIATE	DEFT
DEFASTE	DEFERABLE	DEFIS	DEFORCE	DEFTER
DEFAT	DEFERENCE	DEFLATE	DEFORCED	DEFTEST
DEFATS	DEFERENT	DEFLATED	DEFORCER	DEFTLY
DEFATTED	DEFERENTS	DEFLATER	DEFORCERS	DEFTNESS
DEFATTING	DEFERMENT	DEFLATERS	DEFORCES	DEFUEL
DEFAULT	DEFERRAL	DEFLATES	DEFORCING	DEFUELED
DEFAULTED	DEFERRALS	DEFLATING	DEFOREST	DEFUELING
DEFAULTER	DEFERRED	DEFLATION	DEFORESTS	DEFUELLED
DEFAULTS	DEFERRER	DEFLATOR	DEFORM	DEFUELS
DEFEAT	DEFERRERS	DEFLATORS	DEFORMED	DEFUNCT
DEFEATED	DEFERRING	DEFLEA	DEFORMER	DEFUNCTS
DEFEATER	DEFERS	DEFLEAED	DEFORMERS	DEFUND
DEFEATERS	DEFFER	DEFLEAING	DEFORMING	DEFUNDED
DEFEATING	DEFFEST	DEFLEAS	DEFORMITY	DEFUNDING

DEFUNDS	DEGRADED	DEICERS	DEISM	DELAPSION
DEFUSE	DEGRADER	DEICES	DEISMS	DELATE
DEFUSED	DEGRADERS	DEICIDAL	DEIST	DELATED
DEFUSER	DEGRADES	DEICIDE	DEISTIC	DELATES
DEFUSERS	DEGRADING	DEICIDES	DEISTICAL	DELATING
DEFUSES	DEGRAS	DEICING	DEISTS	DELATION
DEFUSING	DEGREASE	DEICTIC	DEITIES	DELATIONS
DEFUZE	DEGREASED	DEICTICS	DEITY	DELATOR
DEFUZED	DEGREASER	DEID	DEIXES	DELATORS
DEFUZES	DEGREASES	DEIDER	DEIXIS	DELAY
DEFUZING	DEGREE	DEIDEST	DEIXISES	DELAYABLE
DEFY	DEGREED	DEIDS	DEJECT	DELAYED
DEFYING	DEGREES	DEIF	DEJECTA	DELAYER
DEG	DEGS	DEIFER	DEJECTED	DELAYERS
DEGAGE	DEGU	DEIFEST	DEJECTING	DELAYING
DEGAME	DEGUM	DEIFIC	DEJECTION	DELAYS
DEGAMES	DEGUMMED	DEIFICAL	DEJECTORY	DELE
DEGAMI	DEGUMMING	DEIFIED	DEJECTS	DELEAD
DEGAMIS	DEGUMS	DEIFIER	DEJEUNE	DELEADED
DEGARNISH	DEGUS	DEIFIERS	DEJEUNER	DELEADING
DEGAS	DEGUST	DEIFIES	DEJEUNERS	DELEADS
DEGASES	DEGUSTATE	DEIFORM	DEJEUNES	DELEAVE
DEGASSED	DEGUSTED	DEIFY	DEKAGRAM	DELEAVED
DEGASSER	DEGUSTING	DEIFYING	DEKAGRAMS	DELEAVES
DEGASSERS	DEGUSTS	DEIGN	DEKALITER	DELEAVING
DEGASSES	DEHISCE	DEIGNED	DEKALITRE	DELEBLE
DEGASSING	DEHISCED	DEIGNING	DEKALOGY	DELECTATE
DEGAUSS	DEHISCENT	DEIGNS	DEKAMETER	DELED
DEGAUSSED	DEHISCES	DEIL	DEKAMETRE	DELEGABLE
DEGAUSSER	DEHISCING	DEILS	DEKARE	DELEGACY
DEGAUSSES	DEHORN	DEINDEX	DEKARES	DELEGATE
DEGEARING	DEHORNED	DEINDEXED	DEKE	DELEGATED
DEGENDER	DEHORNER	DEINDEXES	DEKED	DELEGATEE
DEGENDERS	DEHORNERS	DEINOSAUR	DEKEING	DELEGATES
DEGERM	DEHORNING	DEIONISE	DEKES	DELEGATOR
DEGERMED	DEHORNS	DEIONISED	DEKING	DELEING
DEGERMING	DEHORT	DEIONISER	DEKKO	DELENDA
DEGERMS	DEHORTED	DEIONISES	DEKKOED	DELES
DEGGED	DEHORTER	DEIONIZE	DEKKOING	DELETABLE
DEGGING	DEHORTERS	DEIONIZED	DEKKOS	DELETE
DEGLAZE	DEHORTING	DEIONIZER	DEL	DELETED
DEGLAZED	DEHORTS	DEIONIZES	DELAINE	DELETES
DEGLAZES	DEHYDRATE	DEIPAROUS	DELAINES	DELETING
DEGLAZING	DEI	DEISEAL	DELAPSE	DELETION
DEGOUT	DEICE	DEISEALS	DELAPSED	DELETIONS
DEGOUTS	DEICED	DEISHEAL	DELAPSES	DELETIVE
DEGRADE	DEICER	DEISHEALS	DELAPSING	DELETORY

DELF	DELIVERS	DELUSION	DEMASTS	DEMIES
DELFS	DELIVERY	DELUSIONS	DEMAYNE	DEMIGOD
DELFT	DELL	DELUSIVE	DEMAYNES	DEMIGODS
DELFTS	DELLIES	DELUSORY	DEME	DEMIJOHN
DELFTWARE	DELLS	DELUSTER	DEMEAN	DEMIJOHNS
DELI	DELLY	DELUSTERS	DEMEANE	DEMILUNE
DELIBATE	DELO	DELUXE	DEMEANED	DEMILUNES
DELIBATED	DELOPE	DELVE	DEMEANES	DEMIMONDE
DELIBATES	DELOPED	DELVED	DEMEANING	DEMIPIQUE
DELIBLE	DELOPES	DELVER	DEMEANOR	DEMIREP
DELICACY	DELOPING	DELVERS	DEMEANORS	DEMIREPS
DELICATE	DELOS	DELVES	DEMEANOUR	DEMISABLE
DELICATES	DELOUSE	DELVING	DEMEANS	DEMISE
DELICE	DELOUSED	DEMAGOG	DEMENT	DEMISED
DELICES	DELOUSER	DEMAGOGED	DEMENTATE	DEMISES
DELICIOUS	DELOUSERS	DEMAGOGIC	DEMENTED	DEMISING
DELICT	DELOUSES	DEMAGOGS	DEMENTI	DEMISS
DELICTS	DELOUSING	DEMAGOGUE	DEMENTIA	DEMISSION
DELIGHT	DELPH	DEMAGOGY	DEMENTIAL	DEMISSIVE
DELIGHTED	DELPHIC	DEMAIN	DEMENTIAS	DEMISSLY
DELIGHTER	DELPHIN	DEMAINE	DEMENTING	DEMIST
DELIGHTS	DELPHINIA	DEMAINES	DEMENTIS	DEMISTED
DELIME	DELPHS	DEMAINS	DEMENTS	DEMISTER
DELIMED	DELS	DEMAN	DEMERARA	DEMISTERS
DELIMES	DELT	DEMAND	DEMERARAN	DEMISTING
DELIMING	DELTA	DEMANDANT	DEMERARAS	DEMISTS
DELIMIT	DELTAIC	DEMANDED	DEMERGE	DEMIT
DELIMITED	DELTAS	DEMANDER	DEMERGED	DEMITASSE
DELIMITER	DELTIC	DEMANDERS	DEMERGER	DEMITS
DELIMITS	DELTOID	DEMANDING	DEMERGERS	DEMITTED
DELINEATE	DELTOIDEI	DEMANDS	DEMERGES	DEMITTING
DELIQUIUM	DELTOIDS	DEMANNED	DEMERGING	DEMIURGE
DELIRIA	DELTS	DEMANNING	DEMERIT	DEMIURGES
DELIRIANT	DELUBRUM	DEMANS	DEMERITED	DEMIURGIC
DELIRIOUS	DELUBRUMS	DEMANTOID	DEMERITS	DEMIURGUS
DELIRIUM	DELUDABLE	DEMARCATE	DEMERSAL	DEMIVEG
DELIRIUMS	DELUDE	DEMARCHE	DEMERSE	DEMIVEGES
DELIS	DELUDED	DEMARCHES	DEMERSED	DEMIVOLT
DELISH	DELUDER	DEMARK	DEMERSES	DEMIVOLTE
DELIST	DELUDERS	DEMARKED	DEMERSING	DEMIVOLTS
DELISTED	DELUDES	DEMARKET	DEMERSION	DEMIWORLD
DELISTING	DELUDING	DEMARKETS	DEMES	DEMO
DELISTS	DELUGE	DEMARKING	DEMESNE	DEMOB
DELIVER	DELUGED	DEMARKS	DEMESNES	DEMOBBED
DELIVERED	DELUGES	DEMAST	DEMETON	DEMOBBING
DELIVERER	DELUGING	DEMASTED	DEMETONS	DEMOBS
DELIVERLY	DELUNDUNG	DEMASTING	DEMIC	DEMOCRACY

DEMOCRAT	DEMPT	DENERVATE	DENSELY	DENTITION
DEMOCRATS	DEMULCENT	DENES	DENSENESS	DENTOID
DEMOCRATY	DEMULSIFY	DENET	DENSER	DENTS
DEMODE	DEMUR	DENETS	DENSEST	DENTULOUS
DEMODED	DEMURE	DENETTED	DENSIFIED	DENTURAL
DEMOED	DEMURED	DENETTING	DENSIFIER	DENTURE
DEMOING	DEMURELY	DENGUE	DENSIFIES	DENTURES
DEMOLISH	DEMURER	DENGUES	DENSIFY	DENTURIST
DEMOLOGY	DEMURES	DENI	DENSITIES	DENUDATE
DEMON	DEMUREST	DENIABLE	DENSITY	DENUDATED
DEMONESS	DEMURING	DENIABLY	DENT	DENUDATES
DEMONIAC	DEMURRAGE	DENIAL	DENTAL	DENUDE
DEMONIACS	DEMURRAL	DENIALS	DENTALIA	DENUDED
DEMONIAN	DEMURRALS	DENIED	DENTALITY	DENUDER
DEMONIC	DEMURRED	DENIER	DENTALIUM	DENUDERS
DEMONICAL	DEMURRER	DENIERS	DENTALLY	DENUDES
DEMONISE	DEMURRERS	DENIES	DENTALS	DENUDING
DEMONISED	DEMURRING	DENIGRATE	DENTARIA	DENY
DEMONISES	DEMURS	DENIM	DENTARIAS	DENYING
DEMONISM	DEMY	DENIMED	DENTARIES	DENYINGLY
DEMONISMS	DEMYSHIP	DENIMS	DENTARY	DEODAND
DEMONIST	DEMYSHIPS	DENIS	DENTATE	DEODANDS
DEMONISTS	DEMYSTIFY	DENITRATE	DENTATED	DEODAR
DEMONIZE	DEN	DENITRIFY	DENTATELY	DEODARA
DEMONIZED	DENAR	DENIZEN	DENTATION	DEODARAS
DEMONIZES	DENARI	DENIZENED	DENTED	DEODARS
DEMONRIES	DENARIES	DENIZENS	DENTEL	DEODATE
DEMONRY	DENARII	DENNED	DENTELLE	DEODATES
DEMONS	DENARIUS	DENNET	DENTELLES	DEODORANT
DEMOS	DENARS	DENNETS	DENTELS	DEODORISE
DEMOSCENE	DENARY	DENNING	DENTEX	DEODORIZE
DEMOSES	DENATURE	DENOMINAL	DENTEXES	DEONTIC
DEMOTE	DENATURED	DENOTABLE	DENTICLE	DEONTICS
DEMOTED	DENATURES	DENOTATE	DENTICLES	DEORBIT
DEMOTES	DENAY	DENOTATED	DENTIFORM	DEORBITED
DEMOTIC	DENAYED	DENOTATES	DENTIL	DEORBITS
DEMOTICS	DENAYING	DENOTE	DENTILED	DEOXIDATE
DEMOTING	DENAYS	DENOTED	DENTILS	DEOXIDISE
DEMOTION	DENAZIFY	DENOTES	DENTIN	DEOXIDIZE
DEMOTIONS	DENDRIMER	DENOTING	DENTINAL	DEOXY
DEMOTIST	DENDRITE	DENOTIVE	DENTINE	DEPAINT
DEMOTISTS	DENDRITES	DENOUNCE	DENTINES	DEPAINTED
DEMOUNT	DENDRITIC	DENOUNCED	DENTING	DEPAINTS
DEMOUNTED	DENDROID	DENOUNCER	DENTINS	DEPANNEUR
DEMOUNTS	DENDRON	DENOUNCES	DENTIST	DEPART
DEMPSTER	DENDRONS	DENS	DENTISTRY	DEPARTED
DEMPSTERS	DENE	DENSE	DENTISTS	DEPARTEE

DEPARTEES	DEPLETERS	DEPOSITED	DEPUTISE	DERELICTS
DEPARTER	DEPLETES	DEPOSITOR	DEPUTISED	DEREPRESS
DEPARTERS	DEPLETING	DEPOSITS	DEPUTISES	DERES
DEPARTING	DEPLETION	DEPOT	DEPUTIZE	DERHAM
DEPARTS	DEPLETIVE	DEPOTS	DEPUTIZED	DERHAMS
DEPARTURE	DEPLETORY	DEPRAVE	DEPUTIZES	DERIDE
DEPASTURE	DEPLORE	DEPRAVED	DEPUTY	DERIDED
DEPECHE	DEPLORED	DEPRAVER	DEQUEUE	DERIDER
DEPECHES	DEPLORER	DEPRAVERS	DEQUEUED	DERIDERS
DEPEINCT	DEPLORERS	DEPRAVES	DEQUEUES	DERIDES
DEPEINCTS	DEPLORES	DEPRAVING	DEQUEUING	DERIDING
DEPEND	DEPLORING	DEPRAVITY	DERACINE	DERIG
DEPENDANT	DEPLOY	DEPRECATE	DERAIGN	DERIGGED
DEPENDED	DEPLOYED	DEPREDATE	DERAIGNED	DERIGGING
DEPENDENT	DEPLOYER	DEPREHEND	DERAIGNS	DERIGS
DEPENDING	DEPLOYERS	DEPRENYL	DERAIL	DERING
DEPENDS	DEPLOYING	DEPRENYLS	DERAILED	DERINGER
DEPEOPLE	DEPLOYS	DEPRESS	DERAILER	DERINGERS
DEPEOPLED	DEPLUME	DEPRESSED	DERAILERS	DERISIBLE
DEPEOPLES	DEPLUMED	DEPRESSES	DERAILING	DERISION
DEPERM	DEPLUMES	DEPRESSOR	DERAILS	DERISIONS
DEPERMED	DEPLUMING	DEPRIVAL	DERANGE	DERISIVE
DEPERMING	DEPOLISH	DEPRIVALS	DERANGED	DERISORY
DEPERMS	DEPONE	DEPRIVE	DERANGER	DERIVABLE
DEPICT	DEPONED	DEPRIVED	DERANGERS	DERIVABLY
DEPICTED	DEPONENT	DEPRIVER	DERANGES	DERIVATE
DEPICTER	DEPONENTS	DEPRIVERS	DERANGING	DERIVATES
DEPICTERS	DEPONES	DEPRIVES	DERAT	DERIVE
DEPICTING	DEPONING	DEPRIVING	DERATE	DERIVED
DEPICTION	DEPORT	DEPROGRAM	DERATED	DERIVER
DEPICTIVE	DEPORTED	DEPSIDE	DERATES	DERIVERS
DEPICTOR	DEPORTEE	DEPSIDES	DERATING	DERIVES
DEPICTORS	DEPORTEES	DEPTH	DERATINGS	DERIVING
DEPICTS	DEPORTER	DEPTHLESS	DERATION	DERM
DEPICTURE	DEPORTERS	DEPTHS	DERATIONS	DERMA
DEPIGMENT	DEPORTING	DEPURANT	DERATS	DERMAL
DEPILATE	DEPORTS	DEPURANTS	DERATTED	DERMAS
DEPILATED	DEPOSABLE	DEPURATE	DERATTING	DERMATIC
DEPILATES	DEPOSAL	DEPURATED	DERAY	DERMATOID
DEPILATOR	DEPOSALS	DEPURATES	DERAYED	DERMATOME
DEPLANE	DEPOSE	DEPURATOR	DERAYING	DERMESTID
DEPLANED	DEPOSED	DEPUTABLE	DERAYS	DERMIC
DEPLANES	DEPOSER	DEPUTE	DERBIES	DERMIS
DEPLANING	DEPOSERS	DEPUTED	DERBY	DERMISES
DEPLETE	DEPOSES	DEPUTES	DERE	DERMOID
DEPLETED	DEPOSING	DEPUTIES	DERED	DERMOIDS
DEPLETER	DEPOSIT	DEPUTING	DERELICT	DERMS

DERN	DESCENDED	DESI	DESKNOTES	DESPITED
DERNFUL	DESCENDER	DESICCANT	DESKS	DESPITES
DERNIER	DESCENDS	DESICCATE	DESKTOP	DESPITING
DERNLY	DESCENT	DESIGN	DESKTOPS	DESPOIL
DERNS	DESCENTS	DESIGNATE	DESMAN	DESPOILED
DERO	DESCHOOL	DESIGNED	DESMANS	DESPOILER
DEROGATE	DESCHOOLS	DESIGNEE	DESMID	DESPOILS
DEROGATED	DESCRIBE	DESIGNEES	DESMIDIAN	DESPOND
DEROGATES	DESCRIBED	DESIGNER	DESMIDS	DESPONDED
DEROS	DESCRIBER	DESIGNERS	DESMINE	DESPONDS
DERRICK	DESCRIBES	DESIGNFUL	DESMINES	DESPOT
DERRICKED	DESCRIED	DESIGNING	DESMODIUM	DESPOTAT
DERRICKS	DESCRIER	DESIGNS	DESMOID	DESPOTATE
DERRIERE	DESCRIERS	DESILVER	DESMOIDS	DESPOTATS
DERRIERES	DESCRIES	DESILVERS	DESMOSOME	DESPOTIC
DERRIES	DESCRIVE	DESINE	DESNOOD	DESPOTISM
DERRINGER	DESCRIVED	DESINED	DESNOODED	DESPOTS
DERRIS	DESCRIVES	DESINENCE	DESNOODS	DESPUMATE
DERRISES	DESCRY	DESINENT	DESOEUVRE	DESSE
DERRO	DESCRYING	DESINES	DESOLATE	DESSERT
DERROS	DESECRATE	DESINING	DESOLATED	DESSERTS
DERRY	DESEED	DESIPIENT	DESOLATER	DESSES
DERTH	DESEEDED	DESIRABLE	DESOLATES	DESTAIN
DERTHS	DESEEDING	DESIRABLY	DESOLATOR	DESTAINED
DERV	DESEEDS	DESIRE	DESORB	DESTAINS
DERVISH	DESELECT	DESIRED	DESORBED	DESTEMPER
DERVISHES	DESELECTS	DESIRER	DESORBING	DESTINATE
DERVS	DESERT	DESIRERS	DESORBS	DESTINE
DESALT	DESERTED	DESIRES	DESOXY	DESTINED
DESALTED	DESERTER	DESIRING	DESPAIR	DESTINES
DESALTER	DESERTERS	DESIROUS	DESPAIRED	DESTINIES
DESALTERS	DESERTIC	DESIST	DESPAIRER	DESTINING
DESALTING	DESERTIFY	DESISTED	DESPAIRS	DESTINY
DESALTS	DESERTING	DESISTING	DESPATCH	DESTITUTE
DESAND	DESERTION	DESISTS	DESPERADO	DESTOCK
DESANDED	DESERTS	DESK	DESPERATE	DESTOCKED
DESANDING	DESERVE	DESKBOUND	DESPIGHT	DESTOCKS
DESANDS	DESERVED	DESKFAST	DESPIGHTS	DESTRIER
DESCALE	DESERVER	DESKFASTS	DESPISAL	DESTRIERS
DESCALED	DESERVERS	DESKILL	DESPISALS	DESTROY
DESCALES	DESERVES	DESKILLED	DESPISE	DESTROYED
DESCALING	DESERVING	DESKILLS	DESPISED	DESTROYER
DESCANT	DESEX	DESKING	DESPISER	DESTROYS
DESCANTED	DESEXED	DESKINGS	DESPISERS	DESTRUCT
DESCANTER	DESEXES	DESKMAN	DESPISES	DESTRUCTO
DESCANTS	DESEXING	DESKMEN	DESPISING	DESTRUCTS
DESCEND	DESHI	DESKNOTE	DESPITE	DESUETUDE

DESUGAR	DETECTORS	DETINUE	DEUCE	DEVELS
DESUGARED	DETECTS	DETINUES	DEUCED	DEVERBAL
DESUGARS	DETENT	DETONABLE	DEUCEDLY	DEVERBALS
DESULFUR	DETENTE	DETONATE	DEUCES	DEVEST
DESULFURS	DETENTES	DETONATED	DEUCING	DEVESTED
DESULPHUR	DETENTION	DETONATES	DEUDDARN	DEVESTING
DESULTORY	DETENTIST	DETONATOR	DEUDDARNS	DEVESTS
DESYATIN	DETENTS	DETORSION	DEUS	DEVIANCE
DESYATINS	DETENU	DETORT	DEUTERATE	DEVIANCES
DESYNE	DETENUE	DETORTED	DEUTERIC	DEVIANCY
DESYNED	DETENUES	DETORTING	DEUTERIDE	DEVIANT
DESYNES	DETENUS	DETORTION	DEUTERIUM	DEVIANTS
DESYNING	DETER	DETORTS	DEUTERON	DEVIATE
DETACH	DETERGE	DETOUR	DEUTERONS	DEVIATED
DETACHED	DETERGED	DETOURED	DEUTON	DEVIATES
DETACHER	DETERGENT	DETOURING	DEUTONS	DEVIATING
DETACHERS	DETERGER	DETOURS	DEUTZIA	DEVIATION
DETACHES	DETERGERS	DETOX	DEUTZIAS	DEVIATIVE
DETACHING	DETERGES	DETOXED	DEV	DEVIATOR
DETAIL	DETERGING	DETOXES	DEVA	DEVIATORS
DETAILED	DETERMENT	DETOXIFY	DEVALL	DEVIATORY
DETAILER	DETERMINE	DETOXING	DEVALLED	DEVICE
DETAILERS	DETERRED	DETRACT	DEVALLING	DEVICEFUL
DETAILING	DETERRENT	DETRACTED	DEVALLS	DEVICES
DETAILS	DETERRER	DETRACTOR	DEVALUATE	DEVIL
DETAIN	DETERRERS	DETRACTS	DEVALUE	DEVILDOM
DETAINED	DETERRING	DETRAIN	DEVALUED	DEVILDOMS
DETAINEE	DETERS	DETRAINED	DEVALUES	DEVILED
DETAINEES	DETERSION	DETRAINS	DEVALUING	DEVILESS
DETAINER	DETERSIVE	DETRAQUE	DEVAS	DEVILET
DETAINERS	DETEST	DETRAQUEE	DEVASTATE	DEVILETS
DETAINING	DETESTED	DETRAQUES	DEVEIN	DEVILFISH
DETAINS	DETESTER	DETRIMENT	DEVEINED	DEVILING
DETANGLE	DETESTERS	DETRITAL	DEVEINING	DEVILINGS
DETANGLED	DETESTING	DETRITION	DEVEINS	DEVILISH
DETANGLER	DETESTS	DETRITUS	DEVEL	DEVILISM
DETANGLES	DETHATCH	DETRUDE	DEVELED	DEVILISMS
DETASSEL	DETHRONE	DETRUDED	DEVELING	DEVILKIN
DETASSELS	DETHRONED	DETRUDES	DEVELLED	DEVILKINS
DETECT	DETHRONER	DETRUDING	DEVELLING	DEVILLED
DETECTED	DETHRONES	DETRUSION	DEVELOP	DEVILLING
DETECTER	DETICK	DETRUSOR	DEVELOPE	DEVILMENT
DETECTERS	DETICKED	DETRUSORS	DEVELOPED	DEVILRIES
DETECTING	DETICKER	DETUNE	DEVELOPER	DEVILRY
DETECTION	DETICKERS	DETUNED	DEVELOPES	DEVILS
DETECTIVE	DETICKING	DETUNES	DEVELOPPE	DEVILSHIP
DETECTOR	DETICKS	DETUNING	DEVELOPS	DEVILTRY

DEVILWOOD	DEVOUR	DEWITTED	DEZINCED	DHURRIES
DEVIOUS	DEVOURED	DEWITTING	DEZINCING	DHUTI
DEVIOUSLY	DEVOURER	DEWITTS	DEZINCKED	DHUTIS
DEVISABLE	DEVOURERS	DEWLAP	DEZINCS	DI
DEVISAL	DEVOURING	DEWLAPPED	DHAK	DIABASE
DEVISALS	DEVOURS	DEWLAPS	DHAKS	DIABASES
DEVISE	DEVOUT	DEWLAPT	DHAL	DIABASIC
DEVISED	DEVOUTER	DEWLESS	DHALS	DIABETES
DEVISEE	DEVOUTEST	DEWOOL	DHAMMA	DIABETIC
DEVISEES	DEVOUTLY	DEWOOLED	DHAMMAS	DIABETICS
DEVISER	DEVS	DEWOOLING	DHANSAK	DIABLE
DEVISERS	DEVVEL	DEWOOLS	DHANSAKS	DIABLERIE
DEVISES	DEVVELLED	DEWORM	DHARMA	DIABLERY
DEVISING	DEVVELS	DEWORMED	DHARMAS	DIABLES
DEVISOR	DEW	DEWORMER	DHARMIC	DIABOLIC
DEVISORS	DEWAN	DEWORMERS	DHARMSALA	DIABOLISE
DEVITRIFY	DEWANI	DEWORMING	DHARNA	DIABOLISM
DEVLING	DEWANIS	DEWORMS	DHARNAS	DIABOLIST
DEVLINGS	DEWANNIES	DEWPOINT	DHIMMI	DIABOLIZE
DEVOICE	DEWANNY	DEWPOINTS	DHIMMIS	DIABOLO
DEVOICED	DEWANS	DEWS	DHOBI	DIABOLOGY
DEVOICES	DEWAR	DEWY	DHOBIS	DIABOLOS
DEVOICING	DEWARS	DEX	DHOL	DIACETYL
DEVOID	DEWATER	DEXES	DHOLE	DIACETYLS
DEVOIR	DEWATERED	DEXIE	DHOLES	DIACHRONY
DEVOIRS	DEWATERER	DEXIES	DHOLL	DIACHYLON
DEVOLVE	DEWATERS	DEXTER	DHOLLS	DIACHYLUM
DEVOLVED	DEWAX	DEXTERITY	DHOLS	DIACID
DEVOLVES	DEWAXED	DEXTEROUS	DHOOLIES	DIACIDIC
DEVOLVING	DEWAXES	DEXTERS	DHOOLY	DIACIDS
DEVON	DEWAXING	DEXTRAL	DHOORA	DIACODION
DEVONIAN	DEWBERRY	DEXTRALLY	DHOORAS	DIACODIUM
DEVONPORT	DEWCLAW	DEXTRAN	DHOOTI	DIACONAL
DEVONS	DEWCLAWED	DEXTRANS	DHOOTIE	DIACONATE
DEVORE	DEWCLAWS	DEXTRIN	DHOOTIES	DIACRITIC
DEVORES	DEWDROP	DEXTRINE	DHOOTIS	DIACT
DEVOT	DEWDROPS	DEXTRINES	DHOTI	DIACTINAL
DEVOTE	DEWED	DEXTRINS	DHOTIS	DIACTINE
DEVOTED	DEWFALL	DEXTRO	DHOURRA	DIACTINIC
DEVOTEDLY	DEWFALLS	DEXTRORSE	DHOURRAS	DIADEM
DEVOTEE	DEWFULL	DEXTROSE	DHOW	DIADEMED
DEVOTEES	DEWIER	DEXTROSES	DHOWS	DIADEMING
DEVOTES	DEWIEST	DEXTROUS	DHURNA	DIADEMS
DEVOTING	DEWILY	DEXY	DHURNAS	DIADOCHI
DEVOTION	DEWINESS	DEY	DHURRA	DIADOCHY
DEVOTIONS	DEWING	DEYS	DHURRAS	DIADROM
DEVOTS	DEWITT	DEZINC	DHURRIE	DIADROMS

DIAERESES	DIALOGISE	DIANE	DIARIST	DIATOMS
DIAERESIS	DIALOGISM	DIANODAL	DIARISTIC	DIATONIC
DIAERETIC	DIALOGIST	DIANOETIC	DIARISTS	DIATRETA
DIAGLYPH	DIALOGITE	DIANOIA	DIARIZE	DIATRETUM
DIAGLYPHS	DIALOGIZE	DIANOIAS	DIARIZED	DIATRIBE
DIAGNOSE	DIALOGS	DIANTHUS	DIARIZES	DIATRIBES
DIAGNOSED	DIALOGUE	DIAPASE	DIARIZING	DIATRON
DIAGNOSES	DIALOGUED	DIAPASES	DIARRHEA	DIATRONS
DIAGNOSIS	DIALOGUER	DIAPASON	DIARRHEAL	DIATROPIC
DIAGONAL	DIALOGUES	DIAPASONS	DIARRHEAS	DIAXON
DIAGONALS	DIALS	DIAPAUSE	DIARRHEIC	DIAXONS
DIAGRAM	DIALYSATE	DIAPAUSED	DIARRHOEA	DIAZEPAM
DIAGRAMED	DIALYSE	DIAPAUSES	DIARY	DIAZEPAMS
DIAGRAMS	DIALYSED	DIAPENTE	DIASCIA	DIAZEUXES
DIAGRAPH	DIALYSER	DIAPENTES	DIASCIAS	DIAZEUXIS
DIAGRAPHS	DIALYSERS	DIAPER	DIASCOPE	DIAZIN
DIAGRID	DIALYSES	DIAPERED	DIASCOPES	DIAZINE
DIAGRIDS	DIALYSING	DIAPERING	DIASPORA	DIAZINES
DIAL	DIALYSIS	DIAPERS	DIASPORAS	DIAZINON
DIALECT	DIALYTIC	DIAPHONE	DIASPORE	DIAZINONS
DIALECTAL	DIALYZATE	DIAPHONES	DIASPORES	DIAZINS
DIALECTIC	DIALYZE	DIAPHONIC	DIASPORIC	DIAZO
DIALECTS	DIALYZED	DIAPHONY	DIASTASE	DIAZOES
DIALED	DIALYZER	DIAPHRAGM	DIASTASES	DIAZOLE
DIALER	DIALYZERS	DIAPHYSES	DIASTASIC	DIAZOLES
DIALERS	DIALYZES	DIAPHYSIS	DIASTASIS	DIAZONIUM
DIALING	DIALYZING	DIAPIR	DIASTATIC	DIAZOS
DIALINGS	DIAMAGNET	DIAPIRIC	DIASTEM	DIAZOTISE
DIALIST	DIAMANTE	DIAPIRISM	DIASTEMA	DIAZOTIZE
DIALISTS	DIAMANTES	DIAPIRS	DIASTEMAS	DIB
DIALLAGE	DIAMETER	DIAPSID	DIASTEMS	DIBASIC
DIALLAGES	DIAMETERS	DIAPSIDS	DIASTER	DIBBED
DIALLAGIC	DIAMETRAL	DIAPYESES	DIASTERS	DIBBER
DIALLED	DIAMETRIC	DIAPYESIS	DIASTOLE	DIBBERS
DIALLEL	DIAMIDE	DIAPYETIC	DIASTOLES	DIBBING
DIALLER	DIAMIDES	DIARCH	DIASTOLIC	DIBBLE
DIALLERS	DIAMIN	DIARCHAL	DIASTRAL	DIBBLED
DIALLING	DIAMINE	DIARCHIC	DIASTYLE	DIBBLER
DIALLINGS	DIAMINES	DIARCHIES	DIASTYLES	DIBBLERS
DIALLIST	DIAMINS	DIARCHY	DIATHERMY	DIBBLES
DIALLISTS	DIAMOND	DIARIAL	DIATHESES	DIBBLING
DIALOG	DIAMONDED	DIARIAN	DIATHESIS	DIBBS
DIALOGED	DIAMONDS	DIARIES	DIATHETIC	DIBBUK
DIALOGER	DIAMYL	DIARISE	DIATOM	DIBBUKIM
DIALOGERS	DIANDRIES	DIARISED	DIATOMIC	DIBBUKKIM
DIALOGIC	DIANDROUS	DIARISES	DIATOMIST	DIBBUKS
DIALOGING	DIANDRY	DIARISING	DIATOMITE	DIBROMIDE

DIBS	DICKENSES	DICTIEST	DIDELPHIC	DIEOFF
DIBUTYL	DICKER	DICTING	DIDELPHID	DIEOFFS
DICACIOUS	DICKERED	DICTION	DIDICOI	DIERESES
DICACITY	DICKERING	DICTIONAL	DIDICOIS	DIERESIS
DICACODYL	DICKERS	DICTIONS	DIDICOY	DIERETIC
DICAMBA	DICKEY	DICTS	DIDICOYS	DIES
DICAMBAS	DICKEYS	DICTUM	DIDIE	DIESEL
DICAST	DICKHEAD	DICTUMS	DIDIES	DIESELED
DICASTERY	DICKHEADS	DICTY	DIDJERIDU	DIESELING
DICASTIC	DICKIE	DICTYOGEN	DIDO	DIESELISE
DICASTS	DICKIER	DICUMAROL	DIDOES	DIESELIZE
DICE	DICKIES	DICYCLIC	DIDOS	DIESELS
DICED	DICKIEST	DICYCLIES	DIDRACHM	DIESES
DICENTRA	DICKING	DICYCLY	DIDRACHMA	DIESINKER
DICENTRAS	DICKINGS	DID	DIDRACHMS	DIESIS
DICENTRIC	DICKS	DIDACT	DIDST	DIESTER
DICER	DICKTIER	DIDACTIC	DIDY	DIESTERS
DICERS	DICKTIEST	DIDACTICS	DIDYMIUM	DIESTOCK
DICES	DICKTY	DIDACTS	DIDYMIUMS	DIESTOCKS
DICEY	DICKY	DIDACTYL	DIDYMOUS	DIESTROUS
DICH	DICKYBIRD	DIDACTYLS	DIDYNAMY	DIESTRUM
DICHASIA	DICLINIES	DIDAKAI	DIE	DIESTRUMS
DICHASIAL	DICLINISM	DIDAKAIS	DIEB	DIESTRUS
DICHASIUM	DICLINOUS	DIDAKEI	DIEBACK	DIET
DICHOGAMY	DICLINY	DIDAKEIS	DIEBACKS	DIETARIAN
DICHONDRA	DICOT	DIDAPPER	DIEBS	DIETARIES
DICHOPTIC	DICOTS	DIDAPPERS	DIECIOUS	DIETARILY
DICHORD	DICOTYL	DIDDER	DIED	DIETARY
DICHORDS	DICOTYLS	DIDDERED	DIEDRAL	DIETED
DICHOTIC	DICROTAL	DIDDERING	DIEDRALS	DIETER
DICHOTOMY	DICROTIC	DIDDERS	DIEDRE	DIETERS
DICHROIC	DICROTISM	DIDDICOY	DIEDRES	DIETETIC
DICHROISM	DICROTOUS	DIDDICOYS	DIEGESES	DIETETICS
DICHROITE	DICT	DIDDIER	DIEGESIS	DIETHER
DICHROMAT	DICTA	DIDDIES	DIEGETIC	DIETHERS
DICHROMIC	DICTATE	DIDDIEST	DIEHARD	DIETHYL
DICHT	DICTATED	DIDDLE	DIEHARDS	DIETHYLS
DICHTED	DICTATES	DIDDLED	DIEING	DIETICIAN
DICHTING	DICTATING	DIDDLER	DIEL	DIETINE
DICHTS	DICTATION	DIDDLERS	DIELDRIN	DIETINES
DICIER	DICTATOR	DIDDLES	DIELDRINS	DIETING
DICIEST	DICTATORS	DIDDLEY	DIELYTRA	DIETINGS
DICING	DICTATORY	DIDDLEYS	DIELYTRAS	DIETIST
DICINGS	DICTATRIX	DIDDLIES	DIEMAKER	DIETISTS
DICK	DICTATURE	DIDDLING	DIEMAKERS	DIETITIAN
DICKED	DICTED	DIDDLY	DIENE	DIETS
DICKENS	DICTIER	DIDDY	DIENES	DIF

DIFF	DIGESTION	DIGLYPH	DIKTAT	DILUTEE
DIFFER	DIGESTIVE	DIGLYPHS	DIKTATS	DILUTEES
DIFFERED	DIGESTOR	DIGNIFIED	DILATABLE	DILUTER
DIFFERENT	DIGESTORS	DIGNIFIES	DILATABLY	DILUTERS
DIFFERING	DIGESTS	DIGNIFY	DILATANCY	DILUTES
DIFFERS	DIGGABLE	DIGNITARY	DILATANT	DILUTING
DIFFICILE	DIGGED	DIGNITIES	DILATANTS	DILUTION
DIFFICULT	DIGGER	DIGNITY	DILATATE	DILUTIONS
DIFFIDENT	DIGGERS	DIGONAL	DILATATOR	DILUTIVE
DIFFLUENT	DIGGING	DIGOXIN	DILATE	DILUTOR
DIFFORM	DIGGINGS	DIGOXINS	DILATED	DILUTORS
DIFFRACT	DIGHT	DIGRAPH	DILATER	DILUVIA
DIFFRACTS	DIGHTED	DIGRAPHIC	DILATERS	DILUVIAL
DIFFS	DIGHTING	DIGRAPHS	DILATES	DILUVIAN
DIFFUSE	DIGHTS	DIGRESS	DILATING	DILUVION
DIFFUSED	DIGICAM	DIGRESSED	DILATION	DILUVIONS
DIFFUSELY	DIGICAMS	DIGRESSER	DILATIONS	DILUVIUM
DIFFUSER	DIGIPACK	DIGRESSES	DILATIVE	DILUVIUMS
DIFFUSERS	DIGIPACKS	DIGS	DILATOR	DIM
DIFFUSES	DIGIT	DIGYNIAN	DILATORS	DIMBLE
DIFFUSING	DIGITAL	DIGYNOUS	DILATORY	DIMBLES
DIFFUSION	DIGITALIN	DIHEDRA	DILDO	DIME
DIFFUSIVE	DIGITALIS	DIHEDRAL	DILDOE	DIMENSION
DIFFUSOR	DIGITALLY	DIHEDRALS	DILDOES	DIMER
DIFFUSORS	DIGITALS	DIHEDRON	DILDOS	DIMERIC
DIFS	DIGITATE	DIHEDRONS	DILEMMA	DIMERISE
DIG	DIGITATED	DIHYBRID	DILEMMAS	DIMERISED
DIGAMIES	DIGITISE	DIHYBRIDS	DILEMMIC	DIMERISES
DIGAMIST	DIGITISED	DIHYDRIC	DILIGENCE	DIMERISM
DIGAMISTS	DIGITISER	DIKA	DILIGENT	DIMERISMS
DIGAMMA	DIGITISES	DIKAS	DILL	DIMERIZE
DIGAMMAS	DIGITIZE	DIKAST	DILLED	DIMERIZED
DIGAMOUS	DIGITIZED	DIKASTS	DILLI	DIMERIZES
DIGAMY	DIGITIZER	DIKDIK	DILLIER	DIMEROUS
DIGASTRIC	DIGITIZES	DIKDIKS	DILLIES	DIMERS
DIGENESES	DIGITONIN	DIKE	DILLIEST	DIMES
DIGENESIS	DIGITOXIN	DIKED	DILLING	DIMETER
DIGENETIC	DIGITRON	DIKER	DILLINGS	DIMETERS
DIGERATI	DIGITRONS	DIKERS	DILLIS	DIMETHYL
DIGEST	DIGITS	DIKES	DILLS	DIMETHYLS
DIGESTANT	DIGITULE	DIKETONE	DILLY	DIMETRIC
DIGESTED	DIGITULES	DIKEY	DILTIAZEM	DIMIDIATE
DIGESTER	DIGLOSSIA	DIKIER	DILUENT	DIMINISH
DIGESTERS	DIGLOSSIC	DIKIEST	DILUENTS	DIMISSORY
DIGESTIF	DIGLOT	DIKING	DILUTABLE	DIMITIES
DIGESTIFS	DIGLOTS	DIKKOP	DILUTE	DIMITY
DIGESTING	DIGLOTTIC	DIKKOPS	DILUTED	DIMLY

DIMMABLE	DINETTE	DINKIER	DIOECIOUS	DIP
DIMMED	DINETTES	DINKIES	DIOECISM	DIPCHICK
DIMMER	DINFUL	DINKIEST	DIOECISMS	DIPCHICKS
DIMMERS	DING	DINKING	DIOECY	DIPEPTIDE
DIMMEST	DINGBAT	DINKLY	DIOESTRUS	DIPHASE
DIMMING	DINGBATS	DINKS	DIOICOUS	DIPHASIC
DIMMINGS	DINGDONG	DINKUM	DIOL	DIPHENYL
DIMMISH	DINGDONGS	DINKUMS	DIOLEFIN	DIPHENYLS
DIMNESS	DINGE	DINKY	DIOLEFINS	DIPHONE
DIMNESSES	DINGED	DINMONT	DIOLS	DIPHONES
DIMORPH	DINGER	DINMONTS	DIONYSIAC	DIPHTHONG
DIMORPHIC	DINGERS	DINNA	DIONYSIAN	DIPHYSITE
DIMORPHS	DINGES	DINNAE	DIOPSIDE	DIPLEGIA
DIMOUT	DINGESES	DINNED	DIOPSIDES	DIPLEGIAS
DIMOUTS	DINGEY	DINNER	DIOPSIDIC	DIPLEGIC
DIMP	DINGEYS	DINNERED	DIOPTASE	DIPLEX
DIMPLE	DINGHIES	DINNERING	DIOPTASES	DIPLEXER
DIMPLED	DINGHY	DINNERS	DIOPTER	DIPLEXERS
DIMPLES	DINGIED	DINNING	DIOPTERS	DIPLOE
DIMPLIER	DINGIER	DINNLE	DIOPTRAL	DIPLOES
DIMPLIEST	DINGIES	DINNLED	DIOPTRATE	DIPLOGEN
DIMPLING	DINGIEST	DINNLES	DIOPTRE	DIPLOGENS
DIMPLY	DINGILY	DINNLING	DIOPTRES	DIPLOIC
DIMPS	DINGINESS	DINO	DIOPTRIC	DIPLOID
DIMPSIES	DINGING	DINOCERAS	DIOPTRICS	DIPLOIDIC
DIMPSY	DINGLE	DINOMANIA	DIORAMA	DIPLOIDS
DIMS	DINGLES	DINOS	DIORAMAS	DIPLOIDY
DIMWIT	DINGO	DINOSAUR	DIORAMIC	DIPLOMA
DIMWITS	DINGOED	DINOSAURS	DIORISM	DIPLOMACY
DIMWITTED	DINGOES	DINOTHERE	DIORISMS	DIPLOMAED
DIMYARIAN	DINGOING	DINS	DIORISTIC	DIPLOMAS
DIN	DINGS	DINT	DIORITE	DIPLOMAT
DINAR	DINGUS	DINTED	DIORITES	DIPLOMATA
DINARCHY	DINGUSES	DINTING	DIORITIC	DIPLOMATE
DINARS	DINGY	DINTLESS	DIOSGENIN	DIPLOMATS
DINDLE	DINGYING	DINTS	DIOTA	DIPLON
DINDLED	DINIC	DIOBOL	DIOTAS	DIPLONEMA
DINDLES	DINICS	DIOBOLON	DIOXAN	DIPLONS
DINDLING	DINING	DIOBOLONS	DIOXANE	DIPLONT
DINE	DINITRO	DIOBOLS	DIOXANES	DIPLONTIC
DINED	DINK	DIOCESAN	DIOXANS	DIPLONTS
DINER	DINKED	DIOCESANS	DIOXID	DIPLOPIA
DINERIC	DINKER	DIOCESE	DIOXIDE	DIPLOPIAS
DINERO	DINKEST	DIOCESES	DIOXIDES	DIPLOPIC
DINEROS	DINKEY	DIODE	DIOXIDS	DIPLOPOD
DINERS	DINKEYS	DIODES	DIOXIN	DIPLOPODS
DINES	DINKIE	DIOECIES	DIOXINS	DIPLOSES

DIPLOSIS	DIPTERON	DIRHEM	DISABUSAL	DISBARK
DIPLOTENE	DIPTERONS	DIRHEMS	DISABUSE	DISBARKED
DIPLOZOA	DIPTEROS	DIRIGE	DISABUSED	DISBARKS
DIPLOZOIC	DIPTEROUS	DIRIGENT	DISABUSES	DISBARRED
DIPLOZOON	DIPTYCA	DIRIGES	DISACCORD	DISBARS
DIPNET	DIPTYCAS	DIRIGIBLE	DISADORN	DISBELIEF
DIPNETS	DIPTYCH	DIRIGISM	DISADORNS	DISBENCH
DIPNETTED	DIPTYCHS	DIRIGISME	DISAFFECT	DISBODIED
DIPNOAN	DIQUARK	DIRIGISMS	DISAFFIRM	DISBOSOM
DIPNOANS	DIQUARKS	DIRIGISTE	DISAGREE	DISBOSOMS
DIPNOOUS	DIQUAT	DIRIMENT	DISAGREED	DISBOUND
DIPODIC	DIQUATS	DIRK	DISAGREES	DISBOWEL
DIPODIES	DIRAM	DIRKE	DISALLIED	DISBOWELS
DIPODY	DIRAMS	DIRKED	DISALLIES	DISBRANCH
DIPOLAR	DIRDAM	DIRKES	DISALLOW	DISBUD
DIPOLE	DIRDAMS	DIRKING	DISALLOWS	DISBUDDED
DIPOLES	DIRDUM	DIRKS	DISALLY	DISBUDS
DIPPABLE	DIRDUMS	DIRL	DISANCHOR	DISBURDEN
DIPPED	DIRE	DIRLED	DISANNEX	DISBURSAL
DIPPER	DIRECT	DIRLING	DISANNUL	DISBURSE
DIPPERFUL	DIRECTED	DIRLS	DISANNULS	DISBURSED
DIPPERS	DIRECTER	DIRNDL	DISANOINT	DISBURSER
DIPPIER	DIRECTEST	DIRNDLS	DISAPPEAR	DISBURSES
DIPPIEST	DIRECTING	DIRT	DISAPPLY	DISC
DIPPINESS	DIRECTION	DIRTBAG	DISARM	DISCAGE
DIPPING	DIRECTIVE	DIRTBAGS	DISARMED	DISCAGED
DIPPINGS	DIRECTLY	DIRTED	DISARMER	DISCAGES
DIPPY	DIRECTOR	DIRTIED	DISARMERS	DISCAGING
DIPROTIC	DIRECTORS	DIRTIER	DISARMING	DISCAL
DIPS	DIRECTORY	DIRTIES	DISARMS	DISCALCED
DIPSADES	DIRECTRIX	DIRTIEST	DISARRAY	DISCANDIE
DIPSAS	DIRECTS	DIRTILY	DISARRAYS	DISCANDY
DIPSHIT	DIREFUL	DIRTINESS	DISAS	DISCANT
DIPSHITS	DIREFULLY	DIRTING	DISASTER	DISCANTED
DIPSO	DIRELY	DIRTS	DISASTERS	DISCANTER
DIPSOS	DIREMPT	DIRTY	DISATTIRE	DISCANTS
DIPSTICK	DIREMPTED	DIRTYING	DISATTUNE	DISCARD
DIPSTICKS	DIREMPTS	DIS	DISAVOUCH	DISCARDED
DIPSWITCH	DIRENESS	DISA	DISAVOW	DISCARDER
DIPT	DIRER	DISABLE	DISAVOWAL	DISCARDS
DIPTERA	DIREST	DISABLED	DISAVOWED	DISCASE
DIPTERAL	DIRGE	DISABLER	DISAVOWER	DISCASED
DIPTERAN	DIRGEFUL	DISABLERS	DISAVOWS	DISCASES
DIPTERANS	DIRGELIKE	DISABLES	DISBAND	DISCASING
DIPTERAS	DIRGES	DISABLING	DISBANDED	DISCED
DIPTERIST	DIRHAM	DISABLISM	DISBANDS	DISCEPT
DIPTEROI	DIRHAMS	DISABLIST	DISBAR	DISCEPTED

DISCEPTS

DISCEPTS	DISCORDS	DISENDOWS	DISGUISER	DISHOUSED
DISCERN	DISCOS	DISENGAGE	DISGUISES	DISHOUSES
DISCERNED	DISCOUNT	DISENROL	DISGUST	DISHPAN
DISCERNER	DISCOUNTS	DISENROLS	DISGUSTED	DISHPANS
DISCERNS	DISCOURE	DISENTAIL	DISGUSTS	DISHRAG
DISCERP	DISCOURED	DISENTOMB	DISH	DISHRAGS
DISCERPED	DISCOURES	DISESTEEM	DISHABIT	DISHTOWEL
DISCERPS	DISCOURSE	DISEUR	DISHABITS	DISHUMOUR
DISCHARGE	DISCOVER	DISEURS	DISHABLE	DISHWARE
DISCHURCH	DISCOVERS	DISEUSE	DISHABLED	DISHWARES
DISCI	DISCOVERT	DISEUSES	DISHABLES	DISHWATER
DISCIDE	DISCOVERY	DISFAME	DISHALLOW	DISHY
DISCIDED	DISCREDIT	DISFAMES	DISHCLOTH	DISILLUDE
DISCIDES	DISCREET	DISFAVOR	DISHCLOUT	DISIMMURE
DISCIDING	DISCRETE	DISFAVORS	DISHDASH	DISINFECT
DISCIFORM	DISCRETER	DISFAVOUR	DISHDASHA	DISINFEST
DISCINCT	DISCROWN	DISFIGURE	DISHED	DISINFORM
DISCING	DISCROWNS	DISFLESH	DISHELM	DISINHUME
DISCIPLE	DISCS	DISFLUENT	DISHELMED	DISINTER
DISCIPLED	DISCUMBER	DISFOREST	DISHELMS	DISINTERS
DISCIPLES	DISCURE	DISFORM	DISHERIT	DISINURE
DISCLAIM	DISCURED	DISFORMED	DISHERITS	DISINURED
DISCLAIMS	DISCURES	DISFORMS	DISHES	DISINURES
DISCLIKE	DISCURING	DISFROCK	DISHEVEL	DISINVENT
DISCLIMAX	DISCURSUS	DISFROCKS	DISHEVELS	DISINVEST
DISCLOSE	DISCUS	DISGAVEL	DISHFUL	DISINVITE
DISCLOSED	DISCUSES	DISGAVELS	DISHFULS	DISJASKIT
DISCLOSER	DISCUSS	DISGEST	DISHIER	DISJECT
DISCLOSES	DISCUSSED	DISGESTED	DISHIEST	DISJECTED
DISCLOST	DISCUSSER	DISGESTS	DISHING	DISJECTS
DISCO	DISCUSSES	DISGODDED	DISHINGS	DISJOIN
DISCOBOLI	DISDAIN	DISGORGE	DISHLIKE	DISJOINED
DISCOED	DISDAINED	DISGORGED	DISHOME	DISJOINS
DISCOER	DISDAINS	DISGORGER	DISHOMED	DISJOINT
DISCOERS	DISEASE	DISGORGES	DISHOMES	DISJOINTS
DISCOID	DISEASED	DISGOWN	DISHOMING	DISJUNCT
DISCOIDAL	DISEASES	DISGOWNED	DISHONEST	DISJUNCTS
DISCOIDS	DISEASING	DISGOWNS	DISHONOR	DISJUNE
DISCOING	DISEDGE	DISGRACE	DISHONORS	DISJUNES
DISCOLOGY	DISEDGED	DISGRACED	DISHONOUR	DISK
DISCOLOR	DISEDGES	DISGRACER	DISHORN	DISKED
DISCOLORS	DISEDGING	DISGRADE	DISHORNED	DISKETTE
DISCOLOUR	DISEMBARK	DISGRADED	DISHORNS	DISKETTES
DISCOMFIT	DISEMBODY	DISGRADES	DISHORSE	DISKING
DISCOMMON	DISEMPLOY	DISGUISE	DISHORSED	DISKLESS
DISCORD	DISENABLE	DISGUISED	DISHORSES	DISKLIKE
DISCORDED	DISENDOW	DISGUISED	DISHOUSE	DISKS

DISLEAF	DISMASKED	DISPACED	DISPLAYER	DISPRIZE
DISLEAFED	DISMASKS	DISPACES	DISPLAYS	DISPRIZED
DISLEAFS	DISMAST	DISPACING	DISPLE	DISPRIZES
DISLEAL	DISMASTED	DISPARAGE	DISPLEASE	DISPROFIT
DISLEAVE	DISMASTS	DISPARATE	DISPLED	DISPROOF
DISLEAVED	DISMAY	DISPARITY	DISPLES	DISPROOFS
DISLEAVES	DISMAYD	DISPARK	DISPLING	DISPROOVE
DISLIKE	DISMAYED	DISPARKED	DISPLODE	DISPROVAL
DISLIKED	DISMAYFUL	DISPARKS	DISPLODED	DISPROVE
DISLIKEN	DISMAYING	DISPART	DISPLODES	DISPROVED
DISLIKENS	DISMAYL	DISPARTED	DISPLUME	DISPROVEN
DISLIKER	DISMAYLED	DISPARTS	DISPLUMED	DISPROVER
DISLIKERS	DISMAYLS	DISPATCH	DISPLUMES	DISPROVES
DISLIKES	DISMAYS	DISPATHY	DISPONDEE	DISPUNGE
DISLIKING	DISME	DISPAUPER	DISPONE	DISPUNGED
DISLIMB	DISMEMBER	DISPEACE	DISPONED	DISPUNGES
DISLIMBED	DISMES	DISPEACES	DISPONEE	DISPURSE
DISLIMBS	DISMISS	DISPEL	DISPONEES	DISPURSED
DISLIMN	DISMISSAL	DISPELLED	DISPONER	DISPURSES
DISLIMNED	DISMISSED	DISPELLER	DISPONERS	DISPURVEY
DISLIMNS	DISMISSES	DISPELS	DISPONES	DISPUTANT
DISLINK	DISMODED	DISPENCE	DISPONGE	DISPUTE
DISLINKED	DISMOUNT	DISPENCED	DISPONGED	DISPUTED
DISLINKS	DISMOUNTS	DISPENCES	DISPONGES	DISPUTER
DISLOAD	DISNEST	DISPEND	DISPONING	DISPUTERS
DISLOADED	DISNESTED	DISPENDED	DISPORT	DISPUTES
DISLOADS	DISNESTS	DISPENDS	DISPORTED	DISPUTING
DISLOCATE	DISOBEY	DISPENSE	DISPORTS	DISQUIET
DISLODGE	DISOBEYED	DISPENSED	DISPOSAL	DISQUIETS
DISLODGED	DISOBEYER	DISPENSER	DISPOSALS	DISRANK
DISLODGES	DISOBEYS	DISPENSES	DISPOSE	DISRANKED
DISLOIGN	DISOBLIGE	DISPEOPLE	DISPOSED	DISRANKS
DISLOIGNS	DISODIUM	DISPERSAL	DISPOSER	DISRATE
DISLOYAL	DISOMIC	DISPERSE	DISPOSERS	DISRATED
DISLUSTRE	DISOMIES	DISPERSED	DISPOSES	DISRATES
DISMAL	DISOMY	DISPERSER	DISPOSING	DISRATING
DISMALER	DISORBED	DISPERSES	DISPOST	DISREGARD
DISMALEST	DISORDER	DISPIRIT	DISPOSTED	DISRELISH
DISMALITY	DISORDERS	DISPIRITS	DISPOSTS	DISREPAIR
DISMALLER	DISORIENT	DISPLACE	DISPOSURE	DISREPUTE
DISMALLY	DISOWN	DISPLACED	DISPRAD	DISROBE
DISMALS	DISOWNED	DISPLACER	DISPRAISE	DISROBED
DISMAN	DISOWNER	DISPLACES	DISPREAD	DISROBER
DISMANNED	DISOWNERS	DISPLANT	DISPREADS	DISROBERS
DISMANS	DISOWNING	DISPLANTS	DISPRED	DISROBES
DISMANTLE	DISOWNS	DISPLAY	DISPREDS	DISROBING
DISMASK	DISPACE	DISPLAYED	DISPRISON	DISROOT

DISROOTED	DISSEVERS	DISTICHS	DISUNITE	DITHERING
DISROOTS	DISSHIVER	DISTIL	DISUNITED	DITHERS
DISRUPT	DISSIDENT	DISTILL	DISUNITER	DITHERY
DISRUPTED	DISSIGHT	DISTILLED	DISUNITES	DITHIOL
DISRUPTER	DISSIGHTS	DISTILLER	DISUNITY	DITHIONIC
DISRUPTOR	DISSIMILE	DISTILLS	DISUSAGE	DITHYRAMB
DISRUPTS	DISSING	DISTILS	DISUSAGES	DITING
DISS	DISSIPATE	DISTINCT	DISUSE	DITOKOUS
DISSAVE	DISSOCIAL	DISTINGUE	DISUSED	DITONE
DISSAVED	DISSOLUTE	DISTOME	DISUSES	DITONES
DISSAVES	DISSOLVE	DISTOMES	DISUSING	DITROCHEE
DISSAVING	DISSOLVED	DISTORT	DISVALUE	DITS
DISSEAT	DISSOLVER	DISTORTED	DISVALUED	DITSIER
DISSEATED	DISSOLVES	DISTORTER	DISVALUES	DITSIEST
DISSEATS	DISSONANT	DISTORTS	DISVOUCH	DITSINESS
DISSECT	DISSUADE	DISTRACT	DISYOKE	DITSY
DISSECTED	DISSUADED	DISTRACTS	DISYOKED	DITT
DISSECTOR	DISSUADER	DISTRAIL	DISYOKES	DITTANDER
DISSECTS	DISSUADES	DISTRAILS	DISYOKING	DITTANIES
DISSED	DISSUNDER	DISTRAIN	DIT	DITTANY
DISSEISE	DISTAFF	DISTRAINS	DITA	DITTAY
DISSEISED	DISTAFFS	DISTRAINT	DITAL	DITTAYS
DISSEISEE	DISTAIN	DISTRAIT	DITALS	DITTED
DISSEISES	DISTAINED	DISTRAITE	DITAS	DITTIED
DISSEISIN	DISTAINS	DISTRESS	DITCH	DITTIES
DISSEISOR	DISTAL	DISTRICT	DITCHED	DITTING
DISSEIZE	DISTALLY	DISTRICTS	DITCHER	DITTIT
DISSEIZED	DISTANCE	DISTRIX	DITCHERS	DITTO
DISSEIZEE	DISTANCED	DISTRIXES	DITCHES	DITTOED
DISSEIZES	DISTANCES	DISTRUST	DITCHING	DITTOING
DISSEIZIN	DISTANT	DISTRUSTS	DITCHLESS	DITTOLOGY
DISSEIZOR	DISTANTLY	DISTUNE	DITE	DITTOS
DISSEMBLE	DISTASTE	DISTUNED	DITED	DITTS
DISSEMBLY	DISTASTED	DISTUNES	DITES	DITTY
DISSENSUS	DISTASTES	DISTUNING	DITHECAL	DITTYING
DISSENT	DISTAVES	DISTURB	DITHECOUS	DITZ
DISSENTED	DISTEMPER	DISTURBED	DITHEISM	DITZES
DISSENTER	DISTEND	DISTURBER	DITHEISMS	DITZIER
DISSENTS	DISTENDED	DISTURBS	DITHEIST	DITZIEST
DISSERT	DISTENDER	DISTYLE	DITHEISTS	DITZINESS
DISSERTED	DISTENDS	DISTYLES	DITHELETE	DITZY
DISSERTS	DISTENT	DISULFATE	DITHELISM	DIURESES
DISSERVE	DISTHENE	DISULFID	DITHER	DIURESIS
DISSERVED	DISTHENES	DISULFIDE	DITHERED	DIURETIC
DISSERVES	DISTHRONE	DISULFIDS	DITHERER	DIURETICS
DISSES	DISTICH	DISUNION	DITHERERS	DIURNAL
DISSEVER	DISTICHAL	DISUNIONS	DITHERIER	DIURNALLY

DIURNALS	DIVESTING	DIVISIVE	DIYAS	DOBBED
DIURON	DIVESTS	DIVISOR	DIZAIN	DOBBER
DIURONS	DIVESTURE	DIVISORS	DIZAINS	DOBBERS
DIUTURNAL	DIVI	DIVNA	DIZEN	DOBBIE
DIV	DIVIDABLE	DIVO	DIZENED	DOBBIES
DIVA	DIVIDANT	DIVORCE	DIZENING	DOBBIN
DIVAGATE	DIVIDE	DIVORCED	DIZENMENT	DOBBING
DIVAGATED	DIVIDED	DIVORCEE	DIZENS	DOBBINS
DIVAGATES	DIVIDEDLY	DIVORCEES	DIZYGOTIC	DOBBY
DIVALENCE	DIVIDEND	DIVORCER	DIZYGOUS	DOBCHICK
DIVALENCY	DIVIDENDS	DIVORCERS	DIZZARD	DOBCHICKS
DIVALENT	DIVIDER	DIVORCES	DIZZARDS	DOBHASH
DIVALENTS	DIVIDERS	DIVORCING	DIZZIED	DOBHASHES
DIVAN	DIVIDES	DIVORCIVE	DIZZIER	DOBIE
DIVANS	DIVIDING	DIVOS	DIZZIES	DOBIES
DIVAS	DIVIDINGS	DIVOT	DIZZIEST	DOBLA
DIVE	DIVIDIVI	DIVOTS	DIZZILY	DOBLAS
DIVEBOMB	DIVIDIVIS	DIVS	DIZZINESS	DOBLON
DIVEBOMBS	DIVIDUAL	DIVULGATE	DIZZY	DOBLONES
DIVED	DIVIDUOUS	DIVULGE	DIZZYING	DOBLONS
DIVELLENT	DIVIED	DIVULGED	DJEBEL	DOBRA
DIVER	DIVINABLE	DIVULGER	DJEBELS	DOBRAS
DIVERGE	DIVINATOR	DIVULGERS	DJELLABA	DOBRO
DIVERGED	DIVINE	DIVULGES	DJELLABAH	DOBROS
DIVERGENT	DIVINED	DIVULGING	DJELLABAS	DOBS
DIVERGES	DIVINELY	DIVULSE	DJEMBE	DOBSON
DIVERGING	DIVINER	DIVULSED	DJEMBES	DOBSONFLY
DIVERS	DIVINERS	DIVULSES	DJIBBAH	DOBSONS
DIVERSE	DIVINES	DIVULSING	DJIBBAHS	DOBY
DIVERSED	DIVINEST	DIVULSION	DJIN	DOC
DIVERSELY	DIVING	DIVULSIVE	DJINN	DOCENT
DIVERSES	DIVINGS	DIVVIED	DJINNI	DOCENTS
DIVERSIFY	DIVINIFY	DIVVIER	DJINNS	DOCETIC
DIVERSING	DIVINING	DIVVIES	DJINNY	DOCHMIAC
DIVERSION	DIVINISE	DIVVIEST	DJINS	DOCHMII
DIVERSITY	DIVINISED	DIVVY	DO	DOCHMIUS
DIVERSLY	DIVINISES	DIVVYING	DOAB	DOCHT
DIVERT	DIVINITY	DIVYING	DOABLE	DOCIBLE
DIVERTED	DIVINIZE	DIWAN	DOABS	DOCILE
DIVERTER	DIVINIZED	DIWANS	DOAT	DOCILELY
DIVERTERS	DIVINIZES	DIXI	DOATED	DOCILER
DIVERTING	DIVIS	DIXIE	DOATER	DOCILEST
DIVERTIVE	DIVISIBLE	DIXIES	DOATERS	DOCILITY
DIVERTS	DIVISIBLY	DIXIT	DOATING	DOCIMASY
DIVES	DIVISIM	DIXITS	DOATINGS	DOCK
DIVEST	DIVISION	DIXY	DOATS	DOCKAGE
DIVESTED	DIVISIONS	DIYA	DOB	DOCKAGES

DOCKED	DOCTRINES	DODO	DOGESHIP	DOGHOLE
DOCKEN	DOCUDRAMA	DODOES	DOGESHIPS	DOGHOLES
DOCKENS	DOCUMENT	DODOISM	DOGEY	DOGHOUSE
DOCKER	DOCUMENTS	DODOISMS	DOGEYS	DOGHOUSES
DOCKERS	DOCUSOAP	DODOS	DOGFACE	DOGIE
DOCKET	DOCUSOAPS	DODS	DOGFACES	DOGIES
DOCKETED	DOD	DOE	DOGFIGHT	DOGLEG
DOCKETING	DODDARD	DOEK	DOGFIGHTS	DOGLEGGED
DOCKETS	DODDED	DOEKS	DOGFISH	DOGLEGS
DOCKHAND	DODDER	DOEN	DOGFISHES	DOGLIKE
DOCKHANDS	DODDERED	DOER	DOGFOUGHT	DOGMA
DOCKING	DODDERER	DOERS	DOGFOX	DOGMAN
DOCKINGS	DODDERERS	DOES	DOGFOXES	DOGMAS
DOCKISE	DODDERIER	DOESKIN	DOGGED	DOGMATA
DOCKISED	DODDERING	DOESKINS	DOGGEDER	DOGMATIC
DOCKISES	DODDERS	DOEST	DOGGEDEST	DOGMATICS
DOCKISING	DODDERY	DOETH	DOGGEDLY	DOGMATISE
DOCKIZE	DODDIER	DOF	DOGGER	DOGMATISM
DOCKIZED	DODDIES	DOFF	DOGGEREL	DOGMATIST
DOCKIZES	DODDIEST	DOFFED	DOGGERELS	DOGMATIZE
DOCKIZING	DODDING	DOFFER	DOGGERIES	DOGMATORY
DOCKLAND	DODDIPOLL	DOFFERS	DOGGERMAN	DOGMEN
DOCKLANDS	DODDLE	DOFFING	DOGGERMEN	DOGNAP
DOCKS	DODDLES	DOFFS	DOGGERS	DOGNAPED
DOCKSIDE	DODDY	DOG	DOGGERY	DOGNAPER
DOCKSIDES	DODDYPOLL	DOGARESSA	DOGGESS	DOGNAPERS
DOCKYARD	DODECAGON	DOGATE	DOGGESSES	DOGNAPING
DOCKYARDS	DODGE	DOGATES	DOGGIE	DOGNAPPED
DOCO	DODGEBALL	DOGBANE	DOGGIER	DOGNAPPER
DOCOS	DODGED	DOGBANES	DOGGIES	DOGNAPS
DOCQUET	DODGEM	DOGBERRY	DOGGIEST	DOGROBBER
DOCQUETED	DODGEMS	DOGBOLT	DOGGINESS	DOGS
DOCQUETS	DODGER	DOGBOLTS	DOGGING	DOGSBODY
DOCS	DODGERIES	DOGCART	DOGGINGS	DOGSHIP
DOCTOR	DODGERS	DOGCARTS	DOGGISH	DOGSHIPS
DOCTORAL	DODGERY	DOGDOM	DOGGISHLY	DOGSHORES
DOCTORAND	DODGES	DOGDOMS	DOGGO	DOGSKIN
DOCTORATE	DODGIER	DOGE	DOGGONE	DOGSKINS
DOCTORED	DODGIEST	DOGEAR	DOGGONED	DOGSLED
DOCTORESS	DODGINESS	DOGEARED	DOGGONER	DOGSLEDS
DOCTORIAL	DODGING	DOGEARING	DOGGONES	DOGSLEEP
DOCTORING	DODGINGS	DOGEARS	DOGGONEST	DOGSLEEPS
DOCTORLY	DODGY	DOGEATE	DOGGONING	DOGTEETH
DOCTORS	DODKIN	DOGEATES	DOGGREL	DOGTOOTH
DOCTRESS	DODKINS	DOGEDOM	DOGGRELS	DOGTOWN
DOCTRINAL	DODMAN	DOGEDOMS	DOGGY	DOGTOWNS
DOCTRINE	DODMANS	DOGES	DOGHANGED	DOGTROT

DOGTROTS	DOLICHOS	DOLOR	DOMIEST	DONATISMS
DOGVANE	DOLICHURI	DOLORIFIC	DOMINANCE	DONATIVE
DOGVANES	DOLINA	DOLOROSO	DOMINANCY	DONATIVES
DOGWATCH	DOLINAS	DOLOROUS	DOMINANT	DONATOR
DOGWOOD	DOLINE	DOLORS	DOMINANTS	DONATORS
DOGWOODS	DOLINES	DOLOS	DOMINATE	DONATORY
DOGY	DOLING	DOLOSSE	DOMINATED	DONDER
DOH	DOLIUM	DOLOSTONE	DOMINATES	DONDERED
DOHS	DOLL	DOLOUR	DOMINATOR	DONDERING
DOHYO	DOLLAR	DOLOURS	DOMINE	DONDERS
DOHYOS	DOLLARED	DOLPHIN	DOMINEE	DONE
DOILED	DOLLARISE	DOLPHINET	DOMINEER	DONEE
DOILIES	DOLLARIZE	DOLPHINS	DOMINEERS	DONEES
DOILT	DOLLARS	DOLS	DOMINEES	DONENESS
DOILTER	DOLLDOM	DOLT	DOMINES	DONEPEZIL
DOILTEST	DOLLDOMS	DOLTISH	DOMING	DONER
DOILY	DOLLED	DOLTISHLY	DOMINICAL	DONG
DOING	DOLLHOOD	DOLTS	DOMINICK	DONGA
DOINGS	DOLLHOODS	DOM	DOMINICKS	DONGAS
DOIT	DOLLHOUSE	DOMAIN	DOMINIE	DONGED
DOITED	DOLLIED	DOMAINAL	DOMINIES	DONGING
DOITIT	DOLLIER	DOMAINE	DOMINION	DONGLE
DOITKIN	DOLLIERS	DOMAINES	DOMINIONS	DONGLES
DOITKINS	DOLLIES	DOMAINS	DOMINIQUE	DONGOLA
DOITS	DOLLINESS	DOMAL	DOMINIUM	DONGOLAS
DOJO	DOLLING	DOMANIAL	DOMINIUMS	DONGS
DOJOS	DOLLISH	DOMATIA	DOMINO	DONING
DOL	DOLLISHLY	DOMATIUM	DOMINOES	DONINGS
DOLABRATE	DOLLOP	DOME	DOMINOS	DONJON
DOLCE	DOLLOPED	DOMED	DOMOIC	DONJONS
DOLCES	DOLLOPING	DOMELIKE	DOMS	DONKEY
DOLCETTO	DOLLOPS	DOMES	DOMY	DONKEYS
DOLCETTOS	DOLLS	DOMESDAY	DON	DONKO
DOLCI	DOLLY	DOMESDAYS	DONA	DONKOS
DOLDRUMS	DOLLYBIRD	DOMESTIC	DONAH	DONNA
DOLE	DOLLYING	DOMESTICS	DONAHS	DONNARD
DOLED	DOLMA	DOMETT	DONARIES	DONNART
DOLEFUL	DOLMADES	DOMETTS	DONARY	DONNAS
DOLEFULLY	DOLMAN	DOMIC	DONAS	DONNAT
DOLENT	DOLMANS	DOMICAL	DONATARY	DONNATS
DOLENTE	DOLMAS	DOMICALLY	DONATE	DONNE
DOLERITE	DOLMEN	DOMICIL	DONATED	DONNED
DOLERITES	DOLMENIC	DOMICILE	DONATES	DONNEE
DOLERITIC	DOLMENS	DOMICILED	DONATING	DONNEES
DOLES	DOLOMITE	DOMICILES	DONATION	DONNERD
DOLESOME	DOLOMITES	DOMICILS	DONATIONS	DONNERED
DOLIA	DOLOMITIC	DOMIER	DONATISM	DONNERT

DONNES	DOODAHS	DOOMSMAN	DOORYARD	DOPPINGS
DONNICKER	DOODIES	DOOMSMEN	DOORYARDS	DOPPIO
DONNIES	DOODLE	DOOMSTER	DOOS	DOPPIOS
DONNIKER	DOODLEBUG	DOOMSTERS	DOOSRA	DOPS
DONNIKERS	DOODLED	DOOMWATCH	DOOSRAS	DOPY
DONNING	DOODLER	DOOMY	DOOWOP	DOR
DONNISH	DOODLERS	DOON	DOOWOPS	DORAD
DONNISHLY	DOODLES	DOONA	DOOZER	DORADO
DONNISM	DOODLING	DOONAS	DOOZERS	DORADOS
DONNISMS	DOODOO	DOOR	DOOZIE	DORADS
DONNOT	DOODOOS	DOORBELL	DOOZIES	DORB
DONNOTS	DOODY	DOORBELLS	DOOZY	DORBA
DONNY	DOOFER	DOORCASE	DOP	DORBAS
DONOR	DOOFERS	DOORCASES	DOPA	DORBEETLE
DONORS	DOOFUS	DOORFRAME	DOPAMINE	DORBS
DONORSHIP	DOOFUSES	DOORJAMB	DOPAMINES	DORBUG
DONS	DOOHICKEY	DOORJAMBS	DOPANT	DORBUGS
DONSHIP	DOOK	DOORKNOB	DOPANTS	DORE
DONSHIPS	DOOKED	DOORKNOBS	DOPAS	DOREE
DONSIE	DOOKET	DOORKNOCK	DOPATTA	DOREES
DONSIER	DOOKETS	DOORLESS	DOPATTAS	DORES
DONSIEST	DOOKING	DOORMAN	DOPE	DORHAWK
DONSY	DOOKS	DOORMAT	DOPED	DORHAWKS
DONUT	DOOL	DOORMATS	DOPEHEAD	DORIC
DONUTS	DOOLALLY	DOORMEN	DOPEHEADS	DORIDOID
DONUTTED	DOOLAN	DOORN	DOPER	DORIDOIDS
DONUTTING	DOOLANS	DOORNAIL	DOPERS	DORIES
DONZEL	DOOLE	DOORNAILS	DOPES	DORIS
DONZELS	DOOLEE	DOORNBOOM	DOPESHEET	DORISE
DOO	DOOLEES	DOORNS	DOPESTER	DORISED
DOOB	DOOLES	DOORPLATE	DOPESTERS	DORISES
DOOBIE	DOOLIE	DOORPOST	DOPEY	DORISING
DOOBIES	DOOLIES	DOORPOSTS	DOPEYNESS	DORIZE
DOOBREY	DOOLS	DOORS	DOPIAZA	DORIZED
DOOBREYS	DOOLY	DOORSILL	DOPIAZAS	DORIZES
DOOBRIE	DOOM	DOORSILLS	DOPIER	DORIZING
DOOBRIES	DOOMED	DOORSMAN	DOPIEST	DORK
DOOBS	DOOMFUL	DOORSMEN	DOPILY	DORKIER
DOOCE	DOOMFULLY	DOORSTEP	DOPINESS	DORKIEST
DOOCED	DOOMIER	DOORSTEPS	DOPING	DORKINESS
DOOCES	DOOMIEST	DOORSTONE	DOPINGS	DORKISH
DOOCING	DOOMILY	DOORSTOP	DOPPED	DORKS
DOOCOT	DOOMING	DOORSTOPS	DOPPER	DORKY
DOOCOTS	DOOMS	DOORWAY	DOPPERS	DORLACH
DOODAD	DOOMSAYER	DOORWAYS	DOPPIE	DORLACHS
DOODADS	DOOMSDAY	DOORWOMAN	DOPPIES	DORM
DOODAH	DOOMSDAYS	DOORWOMEN	DOPPING	DORMANCY

DORMANT	DORTER	DOT	DOTY	DOUCHED
DORMANTS	DORTERS	DOTAGE	DOUANE	DOUCHES
DORMER	DORTIER	DOTAGES	DOUANES	DOUCHING
DORMERED	DORTIEST	DOTAL	DOUANIER	DOUCINE
DORMERS	DORTINESS	DOTANT	DOUANIERS	DOUCINES
DORMICE	DORTING	DOTANTS	DOUAR	DOUCS
DORMIE	DORTOUR	DOTARD	DOUARS	DOUGH
DORMIENT	DORTOURS	DOTARDLY	DOUBLE	DOUGHBALL
DORMIN	DORTS	DOTARDS	DOUBLED	DOUGHBOY
DORMINS	DORTY	DOTATION	DOUBLER	DOUGHBOYS
DORMITION	DORY	DOTATIONS	DOUBLERS	DOUGHFACE
DORMITIVE	DOS	DOTCOM	DOUBLES	DOUGHIER
DORMITORY	DOSAGE	DOTCOMMER	DOUBLET	DOUGHIEST
DORMOUSE	DOSAGES	DOTCOMS	DOUBLETON	DOUGHLIKE
DORMS	DOSE	DOTE	DOUBLETS	DOUGHNUT
DORMY	DOSED	DOTED	DOUBLING	DOUGHNUTS
DORNECK	DOSEH	DOTER	DOUBLINGS	DOUGHS
DORNECKS	DOSEHS	DOTERS	DOUBLOON	DOUGHT
DORNICK	DOSEMETER	DOTES	DOUBLOONS	DOUGHTIER
DORNICKS	DOSER	DOTH	DOUBLURE	DOUGHTILY
DORNOCK	DOSERS	DOTIER	DOUBLURES	DOUGHTY
DORNOCKS	DOSES	DOTIEST	DOUBLY	DOUGHY
DORONICUM	DOSH	DOTING	DOUBT	DOUK
DORP	DOSHES	DOTINGLY	DOUBTABLE	DOUKED
DORPER	DOSIMETER	DOTINGS	DOUBTABLY	DOUKING
DORPERS	DOSIMETRY	DOTISH	DOUBTED	DOUKS
DORPS	DOSING	DOTS	DOUBTER	DOULA
DORR	DOSIOLOGY	DOTTED	DOUBTERS	DOULAS
DORRED	DOSOLOGY	DOTTEL	DOUBTFUL	DOULEIA
DORRING	DOSS	DOTTELS	DOUBTFULS	DOULEIAS
DORRS	DOSSAL	DOTTER	DOUBTING	DOUM
DORS	DOSSALS	DOTTEREL	DOUBTINGS	DOUMA
DORSA	DOSSED	DOTTERELS	DOUBTLESS	DOUMAS
DORSAD	DOSSEL	DOTTERS	DOUBTS	DOUMS
DORSAL	DOSSELS	DOTTIER	DOUC	DOUN
DORSALLY	DOSSER	DOTTIEST	DOUCE	DOUP
DORSALS	DOSSERET	DOTTILY	DOUCELY	DOUPIONI
DORSE	DOSSERETS	DOTTINESS	DOUCENESS	DOUPIONIS
DORSEL	DOSSERS	DOTTING	DOUCEPERE	DOUPPIONI
DORSELS	DOSSES	DOTTLE	DOUCER	DOUPS
DORSER	DOSSHOUSE	DOTTLED	DOUCEST	DOUR
DORSERS	DOSSIER	DOTTLER	DOUCET	DOURA
DORSES	DOSSIERS	DOTTLES	DOUCETS	DOURAH
DORSIFLEX	DOSSIL	DOTTLEST	DOUCEUR	DOURAHS
DORSUM	DOSSILS	DOTTREL	DOUCEURS	DOURAS
DORT	DOSSING	DOTTRELS	DOUCHE	DOURER
DORTED	DOST	DOTTY	DOUCHEBAG	DOUREST

DOURINE	DOVING	DOWLIEST	DOWNLOADS	DOWNZONED
DOURINES	DOVISH	DOWLNE	DOWNMOST	DOWNZONES
DOURLY	DOW	DOWLNES	DOWNPIPE	DOWP
DOURNESS	DOWABLE	DOWLNEY	DOWNPIPES	DOWPS
DOUSE	DOWAGER	DOWLS	DOWNPLAY	DOWRIES
DOUSED	DOWAGERS	DOWLY	DOWNPLAYS	DOWRY
DOUSER	DOWAR	DOWN	DOWNPOUR	DOWS
DOUSERS	DOWARS	DOWNA	DOWNPOURS	DOWSABEL
DOUSES	DOWD	DOWNBEAT	DOWNRANGE	DOWSABELS
DOUSING	DOWDIER	DOWNBEATS	DOWNRIGHT	DOWSE
DOUT	DOWDIES	DOWNBOW	DOWNRIVER	DOWSED
DOUTED	DOWDIEST	DOWNBOWS	DOWNRUSH	DOWSER
DOUTER	DOWDILY	DOWNBURST	DOWNS	DOWSERS
DOUTERS	DOWDINESS	DOWNCAST	DOWNSCALE	DOWSES
DOUTING	DOWDS	DOWNCASTS	DOWNSHIFT	DOWSET
DOUTS	DOWDY	DOWNCOME	DOWNSIDE	DOWSETS
DOUX	DOWDYISH	DOWNCOMER	DOWNSIDES	DOWSING
DOUZEPER	DOWDYISM	DOWNCOMES	DOWNSIZE	DOWT
DOUZEPERS	DOWDYISMS	DOWNCOURT	DOWNSIZED	DOWTS
DOVE	DOWED	DOWNDRAFT	DOWNSIZER	DOXAPRAM
DOVECOT	DOWEL	DOWNED	DOWNSIZES	DOXAPRAMS
DOVECOTE	DOWELED	DOWNER	DOWNSLIDE	DOXASTIC
DOVECOTES	DOWELING	DOWNERS	DOWNSLOPE	DOXASTICS
DOVECOTS	DOWELINGS	DOWNFALL	DOWNSPIN	DOXIE
DOVED	DOWELLED	DOWNFALLS	DOWNSPINS	DOXIES
DOVEISH	DOWELLING	DOWNFIELD	DOWNSPOUT	DOXOLOGY
DOVEKEY	DOWELS	DOWNFLOW	DOWNSTAGE	DOXY
DOVEKEYS	DOWER	DOWNFLOWS	DOWNSTAIR	DOY
DOVEKIE	DOWERED	DOWNFORCE	DOWNSTATE	DOYEN
DOVEKIES	DOWERIES	DOWNGRADE	DOWNSWING	DOYENNE
DOVELET	DOWERING	DOWNHAUL	DOWNTHROW	DOYENNES
DOVELETS	DOWERLESS	DOWNHAULS	DOWNTICK	DOYENS
DOVELIKE	DOWERS	DOWNHILL	DOWNTICKS	DOYLEY
DOVEN	DOWERY	DOWNHILLS	DOWNTIME	DOYLEYS
DOVENED	DOWF	DOWNHOLE	DOWNTIMES	DOYLIES
DOVENING	DOWFNESS	DOWNIER	DOWNTOWN	DOYLY
DOVENS	DOWIE	DOWNIEST	DOWNTOWNS	DOYS
DOVER	DOWIER	DOWNINESS	DOWNTREND	DOZE
DOVERED	DOWIEST	DOWNING	DOWNTROD	DOZED
DOVERING	DOWING	DOWNLAND	DOWNTURN	DOZEN
DOVERS	DOWITCHER	DOWNLANDS	DOWNTURNS	DOZENED
DOVES	DOWL	DOWNLESS	DOWNWARD	DOZENING
DOVETAIL	DOWLAS	DOWNLIGHT	DOWNWARDS	DOZENS
DOVETAILS	DOWLASES	DOWNLIKE	DOWNWASH	DOZENTH
DOVIE	DOWLE	DOWNLINK	DOWNWIND	DOZENTHS
DOVIER	DOWLES	DOWNLINKS	DOWNY	DOZER
DOVIEST	DOWLIER	DOWNLOAD	DOWNZONE	DOZERS

DOZES	DRACONES	DRAGNETS	DRAMA	DRAPPIE
DOZIER	DRACONIAN	DRAGOMAN	DRAMADIES	DRAPPIES
DOZIEST	DRACONIC	DRAGOMANS	DRAMADY	DRAPPING
DOZILY	DRACONISM	DRAGOMEN	DRAMAS	DRAPPY
DOZINESS	DRACONTIC	DRAGON	DRAMATIC	DRAPS
DOZING	DRAD	DRAGONESS	DRAMATICS	DRASTIC
DOZINGS	DRAFF	DRAGONET	DRAMATISE	DRASTICS
DOZY	DRAFFIER	DRAGONETS	DRAMATIST	DRAT
DRAB	DRAFFIEST	DRAGONFLY	DRAMATIZE	DRATCHELL
DRABBED	DRAFFISH	DRAGONISE	DRAMATURG	DRATS
DRABBER	DRAFFS	DRAGONISH	DRAMEDIES	DRATTED
DRABBERS	DRAFFY	DRAGONISM	DRAMEDY	DRATTING
DRABBEST	DRAFT	DRAGONIZE	DRAMMACH	DRAUGHT
DRABBET	DRAFTABLE	DRAGONNE	DRAMMACHS	DRAUGHTED
DRABBETS	DRAFTED	DRAGONS	DRAMMED	DRAUGHTER
DRABBIER	DRAFTEE	DRAGOON	DRAMMING	DRAUGHTS
DRABBIEST	DRAFTEES	DRAGOONED	DRAMMOCK	DRAUGHTY
DRABBING	DRAFTER	DRAGOONS	DRAMMOCKS	DRAUNT
DRABBISH	DRAFTERS	DRAGROPE	DRAMS	DRAUNTED
DRABBLE	DRAFTIER	DRAGROPES	DRAMSHOP	DRAUNTING
DRABBLED	DRAFTIEST	DRAGS	DRAMSHOPS	DRAUNTS
DRABBLER	DRAFTILY	DRAGSMAN	DRANGWAY	DRAVE
DRABBLERS	DRAFTING	DRAGSMEN	DRANGWAYS	DRAW
DRABBLES	DRAFTINGS	DRAGSTER	DRANK	DRAWABLE
DRABBLING	DRAFTS	DRAGSTERS	DRANT	DRAWBACK
DRABBY	DRAFTSMAN	DRAGSTRIP	DRANTED	DRAWBACKS
DRABETTE	DRAFTSMEN	DRAIL	DRANTING	DRAWBAR
DRABETTES	DRAFTY	DRAILED	DRANTS	DRAWBARS
DRABLER	DRAG	DRAILING	DRAP	DRAWBORE
DRABLERS	DRAGEE	DRAILS	DRAPABLE	DRAWBORES
DRABLY	DRAGEES	DRAIN	DRAPE	DRAWDOWN
DRABNESS	DRAGGED	DRAINABLE	DRAPEABLE	DRAWDOWNS
DRABS	DRAGGER	DRAINAGE	DRAPED	DRAWEE
DRAC	DRAGGERS	DRAINAGES	DRAPER	DRAWEES
DRACAENA	DRAGGIER	DRAINED	DRAPERIED	DRAWER
DRACAENAS	DRAGGIEST	DRAINER	DRAPERIES	DRAWERFUL
DRACENA	DRAGGING	DRAINERS	DRAPERS	DRAWERS
DRACENAS	DRAGGINGS	DRAINING	DRAPERY	DRAWING
DRACHM	DRAGGLE	DRAINPIPE	DRAPES	DRAWINGS
DRACHMA	DRAGGLED	DRAINS	DRAPET	DRAWKNIFE
DRACHMAE	DRAGGLES	DRAISENE	DRAPETS	DRAWL
DRACHMAI	DRAGGLING	DRAISENES	DRAPEY	DRAWLED
DRACHMAS	DRAGGY	DRAISINE	DRAPIER	DRAWLER
DRACHMS	DRAGHOUND	DRAISINES	DRAPIERS	DRAWLERS
DRACK	DRAGLINE	DRAKE	DRAPIEST	DRAWLIER
DRACO	DRAGLINES	DRAKES	DRAPING	DRAWLIEST
DRACONE	DRAGNET	DRAM	DRAPPED	DRAWLING

DRAWLS	DREAMS	DREIGH	DRIBBLERS	DRINKABLE
DRAWLY	DREAMT	DREIGHER	DRIBBLES	DRINKABLY
DRAWN	DREAMTIME	DREIGHEST	DRIBBLET	DRINKER
DRAWNWORK	DREAMY	DREK	DRIBBLETS	DRINKERS
DRAWPLATE	DREAR	DREKS	DRIBBLIER	DRINKING
DRAWS	DREARE	DRENCH	DRIBBLING	DRINKINGS
DRAWSHAVE	DREARER	DRENCHED	DRIBBLY	DRINKS
DRAWTUBE	DREARES	DRENCHER	DRIBLET	DRIP
DRAWTUBES	DREAREST	DRENCHERS	DRIBLETS	DRIPLESS
DRAY	DREARIER	DRENCHES	DRIBS	DRIPPED
DRAYAGE	DREARIES	DRENCHING	DRICE	DRIPPER
DRAYAGES	DREARIEST	DRENT	DRICES	DRIPPERS
DRAYED	DREARILY	DREPANID	DRICKSIE	DRIPPIER
DRAYHORSE	DREARING	DREPANIDS	DRICKSIER	DRIPPIEST
DRAYING	DREARINGS	DREPANIUM	DRIED	DRIPPILY
DRAYMAN	DREARS	DRERE	DRIEGH	DRIPPING
DRAYMEN	DREARY	DRERES	DRIER	DRIPPINGS
DRAYS	DRECK	DRERIHEAD	DRIERS	DRIPPY
DRAZEL	DRECKIER	DRESS	DRIES	DRIPS
DRAZELS	DRECKIEST	DRESSAGE	DRIEST	DRIPSTONE
DREAD	DRECKS	DRESSAGES	DRIFT	DRIPT
DREADED	DRECKSILL	DRESSED	DRIFTAGE	DRISHEEN
DREADER	DRECKY	DRESSER	DRIFTAGES	DRISHEENS
DREADERS	DREDGE	DRESSERS	DRIFTED	DRIVABLE
DREADFUL	DREDGED	DRESSES	DRIFTER	DRIVE
DREADFULS	DREDGER	DRESSIER	DRIFTERS	DRIVEABLE
DREADING	DREDGERS	DRESSIEST	DRIFTIER	DRIVEL
DREADLESS	DREDGES	DRESSILY	DRIFTIEST	DRIVELED
DREADLOCK	DREDGING	DRESSING	DRIFTING	DRIVELER
DREADLY	DREDGINGS	DRESSINGS	DRIFTLESS	DRIVELERS
DREADS	DREE	DRESSMADE	DRIFTPIN	DRIVELINE
DREAM	DREED	DRESSMAKE	DRIFTPINS	DRIVELING
DREAMBOAT	DREEING	DRESSY	DRIFTS	DRIVELLED
DREAMED	DREES	DREST	DRIFTWOOD	DRIVELLER
DREAMER	DREG	DREVILL	DRIFTY	DRIVELS
DREAMERS	DREGGIER	DREVILLS	DRILL	DRIVEN
DREAMERY	DREGGIEST	DREW	DRILLABLE	DRIVER
DREAMFUL	DREGGISH	DREY	DRILLED	DRIVERS
DREAMHOLE	DREGGY	DREYS	DRILLER	DRIVES
DREAMIER	DREGS	DRIB	DRILLERS	DRIVEWAY
DREAMIEST	DREICH	DRIBBED	DRILLHOLE	DRIVEWAYS
DREAMILY	DREICHER	DRIBBER	DRILLING	DRIVING
DREAMING	DREICHEST	DRIBBERS	DRILLINGS	DRIVINGLY
DREAMINGS	DREIDEL	DRIBBING	DRILLS	DRIVINGS
DREAMLAND	DREIDELS	DRIBBLE	DRILLSHIP	DRIZZLE
DREAMLESS	DREIDL	DRIBBLED	DRILY	DRIZZLED
DREAMLIKE	DREIDLS	DRIBBLER	DRINK	DRIZZLES

DRIZZLIER	DROMONDS	DROOPY	DROSSY	DRUBBED
DRIZZLING	DROMONS	DROP	DROSTDIES	DRUBBER
DRIZZLY	DROMOS	DROPCLOTH	DROSTDY	DRUBBERS
DROGER	DRONE	DROPFLIES	DROSTDYS	DRUBBING
DROGERS	DRONED	DROPFLY	DROUGHT	DRUBBINGS
DROGHER	DRONER	DROPFORGE	DROUGHTS	DRUBS
DROGHERS	DRONERS	DROPHEAD	DROUGHTY	DRUCKEN
DROGUE	DRONES	DROPHEADS	DROUK	DRUDGE
DROGUES	DRONGO	DROPKICK	DROUKED	DRUDGED
DROGUET	DRONGOES	DROPKICKS	DROUKING	DRUDGER
DROGUETS	DRONGOS	DROPLET	DROUKINGS	DRUDGERS
DROICH	DRONIER	DROPLETS	DROUKIT	DRUDGERY
DROICHIER	DRONIEST	DROPLIGHT	DROUKS	DRUDGES
DROICHS	DRONING	DROPLOCK	DROUTH	DRUDGING
DROICHY	DRONINGLY	DROPOUT	DROUTHIER	DRUDGISM
DROID	DRONISH	DROPOUTS	DROUTHS	DRUDGISMS
DROIDS	DRONISHLY	DROPPABLE	DROUTHY	DRUG
DROIL	DRONKLAP	DROPPED	DROVE	DRUGGED
DROILED	DRONKLAPS	DROPPER	DROVED	DRUGGER
DROILING	DRONY	DROPPERS	DROVER	DRUGGERS
DROILS	DROOB	DROPPING	DROVERS	DRUGGET
DROIT	DROOBS	DROPPINGS	DROVES	DRUGGETS
DROITS	DROOG	DROPPLE	DROVING	DRUGGIE
DROLE	DROOGISH	DROPPLES	DROVINGS	DRUGGIER
DROLER	DROOGS	DROPS	DROW	DRUGGIES
DROLES	DROOK	DROPSHOT	DROWN	DRUGGIEST
DROLEST	DROOKED	DROPSHOTS	DROWND	DRUGGING
DROLL	DROOKING	DROPSICAL	DROWNDED	DRUGGIST
DROLLED	DROOKINGS	DROPSIED	DROWNDING	DRUGGISTS
DROLLER	DROOKIT	DROPSIES	DROWNDS	DRUGGY
DROLLERY	DROOKS	DROPSONDE	DROWNED	DRUGLORD
DROLLEST	DROOL	DROPSTONE	DROWNER	DRUGLORDS
DROLLING	DROOLED	DROPSY	DROWNERS	DRUGMAKER
DROLLINGS	DROOLIER	DROPT	DROWNING	DRUGS
DROLLISH	DROOLIEST	DROPWISE	DROWNINGS	DRUGSTORE
DROLLNESS	DROOLING	DROPWORT	DROWNS	DRUID
DROLLS	DROOLS	DROPWORTS	DROWS	DRUIDESS
DROLLY	DROOLY	DROSERA	DROWSE	DRUIDIC
DROME	DROOME	DROSERAS	DROWSED	DRUIDICAL
DROMEDARE	DROOMES	DROSHKIES	DROWSES	DRUIDISM
DROMEDARY	DROOP	DROSHKY	DROWSIER	DRUIDISMS
DROMES	DROOPED	DROSKIES	DROWSIEST	DRUIDRIES
DROMIC	DROOPIER	DROSKY	DROWSIHED	DRUIDRY
DROMICAL	DROOPIEST	DROSS	DROWSILY	DRUIDS
DROMOI	DROOPILY	DROSSES	DROWSING	DRUM
DROMON	DROOPING	DROSSIER	DROWSY	DRUMBEAT
DROMOND	DROOPS	DROSSIEST	DRUB	DRUMBEATS

DRUMBLE

DRUMBLE	DRUTHERS	DUADS	DUBITABLY	DUCKPINS
DRUMBLED	DRUXIER	DUAL	DUBITANCY	DUCKS
DRUMBLES	DRUXIEST	DUALIN	DUBITATE	DUCKSHOVE
DRUMBLING	DRUXY	DUALINS	DUBITATED	DUCKTAIL
DRUMFIRE	DRY	DUALISE	DUBITATES	DUCKTAILS
DRUMFIRES	DRYABLE	DUALISED	DUBNIUM	DUCKWALK
DRUMFISH	DRYAD	DUALISES	DUBNIUMS	DUCKWALKS
DRUMHEAD	DRYADES	DUALISING	DUBONNET	DUCKWEED
DRUMHEADS	DRYADIC	DUALISM	DUBONNETS	DUCKWEEDS
DRUMLIER	DRYADS	DUALISMS	DUBS	DUCKY
DRUMLIEST	DRYASDUST	DUALIST	DUBSTEP	DUCT
DRUMLIKE	DRYBEAT	DUALISTIC	DUBSTEPS	DUCTAL
DRUMLIN	DRYBEATEN	DUALISTS	DUCAL	DUCTED
DRUMLINS	DRYBEATS	DUALITIES	DUCALLY	DUCTILE
DRUMLY	DRYER	DUALITY	DUCAT	DUCTILELY
DRUMMED	DRYERS	DUALIZE	DUCATOON	DUCTILITY
DRUMMER	DRYEST	DUALIZED	DUCATOONS	DUCTING
DRUMMERS	DRYING	DUALIZES	DUCATS	DUCTINGS
DRUMMIES	DRYINGS	DUALIZING	DUCDAME	DUCTLESS
DRUMMING	DRYISH	DUALLED	DUCE	DUCTS
DRUMMOCK	DRYLAND	DUALLING	DUCES	DUCTULE
DRUMMOCKS	DRYLOT	DUALLY	DUCHESS	DUCTULES
DRUMMY	DRYLOTS	DUALS	DUCHESSE	DUCTWORK
DRUMROLL	DRYLY	DUAN	DUCHESSED	DUCTWORKS
DRUMROLLS	DRYMOUTH	DUANS	DUCHESSES	DUD
DRUMS	DRYMOUTHS	DUAR	DUCHIES	DUDDER
DRUMSTICK	DRYNESS	DUARCHIES	DUCHY	DUDDERIES
DRUNK	DRYNESSES	DUARCHY	DUCI	DUDDERS
DRUNKARD	DRYPOINT	DUARS	DUCK	DUDDERY
DRUNKARDS	DRYPOINTS	DUATHLON	DUCKBILL	DUDDIE
DRUNKEN	DRYS	DUATHLONS	DUCKBILLS	DUDDIER
DRUNKENLY	DRYSALTER	DUB	DUCKBOARD	DUDDIEST
DRUNKER	DRYSTONE	DUBBED	DUCKED	DUDDY
DRUNKEST	DRYSUIT	DUBBER	DUCKER	DUDE
DRUNKS	DRYSUITS	DUBBERS	DUCKERS	DUDED
DRUPE	DRYWALL	DUBBIN	DUCKFOOT	DUDEEN
DRUPEL	DRYWALLED	DUBBING	DUCKIE	DUDEENS
DRUPELET	DRYWALLS	DUBBINGS	DUCKIER	DUDES
DRUPELETS	DRYWELL	DUBBINS	DUCKIES	DUDGEON
DRUPELS	DRYWELLS	DUBBO	DUCKIEST	DUDGEONS
DRUPES	DSO	DUBBOS	DUCKING	DUDHEEN
DRUSE	DSOBO	DUBIETIES	DUCKINGS	DUDHEENS
DRUSEN	DSOBOS	DUBIETY	DUCKLING	DUDING
DRUSES	DSOMO	DUBIOSITY	DUCKLINGS	DUDISH
DRUSIER	DSOMOS	DUBIOUS	DUCKMOLE	DUDISHLY
DRUSIEST	DSOS	DUBIOUSLY	DUCKMOLES	DUDISM
DRUSY	DUAD	DUBITABLE	DUCKPIN	DUDISMS

DUDS	DUFF	DUKING	DULLY	DUMMIEST
DUE	DUFFED	DUKKA	DULNESS	DUMMINESS
DUECENTO	DUFFEL	DUKKAH	DULNESSES	DUMMKOPF
DUECENTOS	DUFFELS	DUKKAHS	DULOCRACY	DUMMKOPFS
DUED	DUFFER	DUKKAS	DULOSES	DUMMY
DUEFUL	DUFFERDOM	DUKKHA	DULOSIS	DUMMYING
DUEL	DUFFERISM	DUKKHAS	DULOTIC	DUMOSE
DUELED	DUFFERS	DULCAMARA	DULSE	DUMOSITY
DUELER	DUFFEST	DULCET	DULSES	DUMOUS
DUELERS	DUFFING	DULCETLY	DULY	DUMP
DUELING	DUFFINGS	DULCETS	DUMA	DUMPBIN
DUELIST	DUFFLE	DULCIAN	DUMAIST	DUMPBINS
DUELISTS	DUFFLES	DULCIANA	DUMAISTS	DUMPCART
DUELLED	DUFFS	DULCIANAS	DUMAS	DUMPCARTS
DUELLER	DUFUS	DULCIANS	DUMB	DUMPED
DUELLERS	DUFUSES	DULCIFIED	DUMBBELL	DUMPEE
DUELLI	DUG	DULCIFIES	DUMBBELLS	DUMPEES
DUELLING	DUGITE	DULCIFY	DUMBCANE	DUMPER
DUELLINGS	DUGITES	DULCIMER	DUMBCANES	DUMPERS
DUELLIST	DUGONG	DULCIMERS	DUMBED	DUMPIER
DUELLISTS	DUGONGS	DULCIMORE	DUMBER	DUMPIES
DUELLO	DUGOUT	DULCINEA	DUMBEST	DUMPIEST
DUELLOS	DUGOUTS	DULCINEAS	DUMBFOUND	DUMPILY
DUELS	DUGS	DULCITE	DUMBHEAD	DUMPINESS
DUELSOME	DUH	DULCITES	DUMBHEADS	DUMPING
DUENDE	DUHKHA	DULCITOL	DUMBING	DUMPINGS
DUENDES	DUHKHAS	DULCITOLS	DUMBLY	DUMPISH
DUENESS	DUI	DULCITUDE	DUMBNESS	DUMPISHLY
DUENESSES	DUIKER	DULCOSE	DUMBO	DUMPLE
DUENNA	DUIKERBOK	DULCOSES	DUMBOS	DUMPLED
DUENNAS	DUIKERS	DULE	DUMBS	DUMPLES
DUES	DUING	DULES	DUMBSHIT	DUMPLING
DUET	DUIT	DULIA	DUMBSHITS	DUMPLINGS
DUETED	DUITS	DULIAS	DUMBSHOW	DUMPS
DUETING	DUKA	DULL	DUMBSHOWS	DUMPSITE
DUETS	DUKAS	DULLARD	DUMDUM	DUMPSITES
DUETT	DUKE	DULLARDS	DUMDUMS	DUMPSTER
DUETTED	DUKED	DULLED	DUMELA	DUMPSTERS
DUETTI	DUKEDOM	DULLER	DUMFOUND	DUMPTRUCK
DUETTING	DUKEDOMS	DULLEST	DUMFOUNDS	DUMPY
DUETTINO	DUKELING	DULLIER	DUMKA	DUN
DUETTINOS	DUKELINGS	DULLIEST	DUMKY	DUNAM
DUETTIST	DUKERIES	DULLING	DUMMERER	DUNAMS
DUETTISTS	DUKERY	DULLISH	DUMMERERS	DUNCE
DUETTO	DUKES	DULLISHLY	DUMMIED	DUNCEDOM
DUETTOS	DUKESHIP	DULLNESS	DUMMIER	DUNCEDOMS
DUETTS	DUKESHIPS	DULLS	DUMMIES	DUNCELIKE

DUNCERIES	DUNKS	DUOMI	DURA	DURNEDER
DUNCERY	DUNLIN	DUOMO	DURABLE	DURNEDEST
DUNCES	DUNLINS	DUOMOS	DURABLES	DURNING
DUNCH	DUNNAGE	DUOPOLIES	DURABLY	DURNS
DUNCHED	DUNNAGES	DUOPOLY	DURAL	DURO
DUNCHES	DUNNAKIN	DUOPSONY	DURALS	DUROC
DUNCHING	DUNNAKINS	DUOS	DURALUMIN	DUROCS
DUNCICAL	DUNNART	DUOTONE	DURAMEN	DUROMETER
DUNCISH	DUNNARTS	DUOTONES	DURAMENS	DUROS
DUNCISHLY	DUNNED	DUP	DURANCE	DUROY
DUNDER	DUNNER	DUPABLE	DURANCES	DUROYS
DUNDERS	DUNNESS	DUPATTA	DURANT	DURR
DUNE	DUNNESSES	DUPATTAS	DURANTS	DURRA
DUNELAND	DUNNEST	DUPE	DURAS	DURRAS
DUNELANDS	DUNNIER	DUPED	DURATION	DURRIE
DUNELIKE	DUNNIES	DUPER	DURATIONS	DURRIES
DUNES	DUNNIEST	DUPERIES	DURATIVE	DURRS
DUNG	DUNNING	DUPERS	DURATIVES	DURRY
DUNGAREE	DUNNINGS	DUPERY	DURBAR	DURST
DUNGAREED	DUNNISH	DUPES	DURBARS	DURUKULI
DUNGAREES	DUNNITE	DUPING	DURDUM	DURUKULIS
DUNGED	DUNNITES	DUPION	DURDUMS	DURUM
DUNGEON	DUNNO	DUPIONS	DURE	DURUMS
DUNGEONED	DUNNOCK	DUPLE	DURED	DURZI
DUNGEONER	DUNNOCKS	DUPLET	DUREFUL	DURZIS
DUNGEONS	DUNNY	DUPLETS	DURES	DUSH
DUNGER	DUNS	DUPLEX	DURESS	DUSHED
DUNGERS	DUNSH	DUPLEXED	DURESSE	DUSHES
DUNGHEAP	DUNSHED	DUPLEXER	DURESSES	DUSHING
DUNGHEAPS	DUNSHES	DUPLEXERS	DURGAH	DUSK
DUNGHILL	DUNSHING	DUPLEXES	DURGAHS	DUSKED
DUNGHILLS	DUNT	DUPLEXING	DURGAN	DUSKEN
DUNGIER	DUNTED	DUPLEXITY	DURGANS	DUSKENED
DUNGIEST	DUNTING	DUPLICAND	DURGIER	DUSKENING
DUNGING	DUNTS	DUPLICATE	DURGIEST	DUSKENS
DUNGMERE	DUO	DUPLICITY	DURGY	DUSKER
DUNGMERES	DUOBINARY	DUPLIED	DURIAN	DUSKEST
DUNGS	DUODECIMO	DUPLIES	DURIANS	DUSKIER
DUNGY	DUODENA	DUPLY	DURICRUST	DUSKIEST
DUNITE	DUODENAL	DUPLYING	DURING	DUSKILY
DUNITES	DUODENARY	DUPONDII	DURION	DUSKINESS
DUNITIC	DUODENUM	DUPONDIUS	DURIONS	DUSKING
DUNK	DUODENUMS	DUPPED	DURMAST	DUSKISH
DUNKED	DUOLOG	DUPPIES	DURMASTS	DUSKISHLY
DUNKER	DUOLOGS	DUPPING	DURN	DUSKLY
DUNKERS	DUOLOGUE	DUPPY	DURNDEST	DUSKNESS
DUNKING	DUOLOGUES	DUPS	DURNED	DUSKS

DUSKY	DUTIFULLY	DWARFS	DYEINGS	DYNAMOS
DUST	DUTY	DWARVES	DYELINE	DYNAMOTOR
DUSTBIN	DUUMVIR	DWAUM	DYELINES	DYNAST
DUSTBINS	DUUMVIRAL	DWAUMED	DYER	DYNASTIC
DUSTCART	DUUMVIRI	DWAUMING	DYERS	DYNASTIES
DUSTCARTS	DUUMVIRS	DWAUMS	DYES	DYNASTS
DUSTCOAT	DUVET	DWEEB	DYESTER	DYNASTY
DUSTCOATS	DUVETINE	DWEEBIER	DYESTERS	DYNATRON
DUSTCOVER	DUVETINES	DWEEBIEST	DYESTUFF	DYNATRONS
DUSTED	DUVETS	DWEEBISH	DYESTUFFS	DYNE
DUSTER	DUVETYN	DWEEBS	DYEWEED	DYNEIN
DUSTERS	DUVETYNE	DWEEBY	DYEWEEDS	DYNEINS
DUSTHEAP	DUVETYNES	DWELL	DYEWOOD	DYNEL
DUSTHEAPS	DUVETYNS	DWELLED	DYEWOODS	DYNELS
DUSTIER	DUX	DWELLER	DYING	DYNES
DUSTIEST	DUXELLES	DWELLERS	DYINGLY	DYNODE
DUSTILY	DUXES	DWELLING	DYINGNESS	DYNODES
DUSTINESS	DUYKER	DWELLINGS	DYINGS	DYNORPHIN
DUSTING	DUYKERS	DWELLS	DYKE	DYSBINDIN
DUSTINGS	DVANDVA	DWELT	DYKED	DYSCHROA
DUSTLESS	DVANDVAS	DWILE	DYKES	DYSCHROAS
DUSTLIKE	DVORNIK	DWILES	DYKEY	DYSCHROIA
DUSTMAN	DVORNIKS	DWINDLE	DYKIER	DYSCRASIA
DUSTMEN	DWAAL	DWINDLED	DYKIEST	DYSCRASIC
DUSTOFF	DWAALS	DWINDLES	DYKING	DYSCRATIC
DUSTOFFS	DWALE	DWINDLING	DYKON	DYSENTERY
DUSTPAN	DWALES	DWINE	DYKONS	DYSGENIC
DUSTPANS	DWALM	DWINED	DYNAMETER	DYSGENICS
DUSTPROOF	DWALMED	DWINES	DYNAMIC	DYSLALIA
DUSTRAG	DWALMING	DWINING	DYNAMICAL	DYSLALIAS
DUSTRAGS	DWALMS	DYABLE	DYNAMICS	DYSLECTIC
DUSTS	DWAM	DYAD	DYNAMISE	DYSLEXIA
DUSTSHEET	DWAMMED	DYADIC	DYNAMISED	DYSLEXIAS
DUSTSTORM	DWAMMING	DYADICS	DYNAMISES	DYSLEXIC
DUSTUP	DWAMS	DYADS	DYNAMISM	DYSLEXICS
DUSTUPS	DWANG	DYARCHAL	DYNAMISMS	DYSLOGIES
DUSTY	DWANGS	DYARCHIC	DYNAMIST	DYSLOGY
DUTCH	DWARF	DYARCHIES	DYNAMISTS	DYSMELIA
DUTCHES	DWARFED	DYARCHY	DYNAMITE	DYSMELIAS
DUTCHMAN	DWARFER	DYBBUK	DYNAMITED	DYSMELIC
DUTCHMEN	DWARFEST	DYBBUKIM	DYNAMITER	DYSODIL
DUTEOUS	DWARFING	DYBBUKKIM	DYNAMITES	DYSODILE
DUTEOUSLY	DWARFISH	DYBBUKS	DYNAMITIC	DYSODILES
DUTIABLE	DWARFISM	DYE	DYNAMIZE	DYSODILS
DUTIED	DWARFISMS	DYEABLE	DYNAMIZED	DYSODYLE
DUTIES	DWARFLIKE	DYED	DYNAMIZES	DYSODYLES
DUTIFUL	DWARFNESS	DYEING	DYNAMO	DYSPATHY

DYSPEPSIA	DYSPLASIA	DYSTAXIA	DYSTONIC	DYVOUR
DYSPEPSY	DYSPNEA	DYSTAXIAS	DYSTOPIA	DYVOURIES
DYSPEPTIC	DYSPNEAL	DYSTECTIC	DYSTOPIAN	DYVOURS
DYSPHAGIA	DYSPNEAS	DYSTHESIA	DYSTOPIAS	DYVOURY
DYSPHAGIC	DYSPNEIC	DYSTHETIC	DYSTROPHY	DZEREN
DYSPHAGY	DYSPNOEA	DYSTHYMIA	DYSURIA	DZERENS
DYSPHASIA	DYSPNOEAL	DYSTHYMIC	DYSURIAS	DZHO
DYSPHASIC	DYSPNOEAS	DYSTOCIA	DYSURIC	DZHOS
DYSPHONIA	DYSPNOEIC	DYSTOCIAL	DYSURIES	DZIGGETAI
DYSPHONIC	DYSPNOIC	DYSTOCIAS	DYSURY	DZO
DYSPHORIA	DYSPRAXIA	DYSTONIA	DYTISCID	DZOS
DYSPHORIC	DYSPRAXIC	DYSTONIAS	DYTISCIDS	

E

EA	EARCONS	EARNEST	EARTHRISE	EAST
EACH	EARD	EARNESTLY	EARTHS	EASTABOUT
EACHWHERE	EARDED	EARNESTS	EARTHSET	EASTBOUND
EADISH	EARDING	EARNING	EARTHSETS	EASTED
EADISHES	EARDROP	EARNINGS	EARTHSTAR	EASTER
EAGER	EARDROPS	EARNS	EARTHWARD	EASTERLY
EAGERER	EARDRUM	EARPHONE	EARTHWAX	EASTERN
EAGEREST	EARDRUMS	EARPHONES	EARTHWOLF	EASTERNER
EAGERLY	EARDS	EARPICK	EARTHWORK	EASTERS
EAGERNESS	EARED	EARPICKS	EARTHWORM	EASTING
EAGERS	EARFLAP	EARPIECE	EARTHY	EASTINGS
EAGLE	EARFLAPS	EARPIECES	EARWAX	EASTLAND
EAGLED	EARFUL	EARPLUG	EARWAXES	EASTLANDS
EAGLEHAWK	EARFULS	EARPLUGS	EARWIG	EASTLIN
EAGLES	EARING	EARRING	EARWIGGED	EASTLING
EAGLET	EARINGS	EARRINGED	EARWIGGY	EASTLINGS
EAGLETS	EARL	EARRINGS	EARWIGS	EASTLINS
EAGLEWOOD	EARLAP	EARS	EARWORM	EASTMOST
EAGLING	EARLAPS	EARSHOT	EARWORMS	EASTS
EAGRE	EARLDOM	EARSHOTS	EAS	EASTWARD
EAGRES	EARLDOMS	EARST	EASE	EASTWARDS
EALDORMAN	EARLESS	EARSTONE	EASED	EASY
EALDORMEN	EARLIER	EARSTONES	EASEFUL	EASYGOING
EALE	EARLIES	EARTH	EASEFULLY	EASYING
EALES	EARLIEST	EARTHBORN	EASEL	EAT
EAN	EARLIKE	EARTHED	EASELED	EATABLE
EANED	EARLINESS	EARTHEN	EASELESS	EATABLES
EANING	EARLOBE	EARTHFALL	EASELS	EATAGE
EANLING	EARLOBES	EARTHFAST	EASEMENT	EATAGES
EANLINGS	EARLOCK	EARTHFLAX	EASEMENTS	EATCHE
EANS	EARLOCKS	EARTHIER	EASER	EATCHES
EAR	EARLS	EARTHIEST	EASERS	EATEN
EARACHE	EARLSHIP	EARTHILY	EASES	EATER
EARACHES	EARLSHIPS	EARTHING	EASIED	EATERIE
EARBALL	EARLY	EARTHLIER	EASIER	EATERIES
EARBALLS	EARLYWOOD	EARTHLIES	EASIES	EATERS
EARBASH	EARMARK	EARTHLIKE	EASIEST	EATERY
EARBASHED	EARMARKED	EARTHLING	EASILY	EATH
EARBASHER	EARMARKS	EARTHLY	EASINESS	EATHE
EARBASHES	EARMUFF	EARTHMAN	EASING	EATHLY
EARBOB	EARMUFFS	EARTHMEN	EASINGS	EATING
EARBOBS	EARN	EARTHNUT	EASLE	EATINGS
EARBUD	EARNED	EARTHNUTS	EASLES	EATS
EARBUDS	EARNER	EARTHPEA	EASSEL	EAU
EARCON	EARNERS	EARTHPEAS	EASSIL	EAUS

EAUX
EAVE
EAVED
EAVES
EAVESDRIP
EAVESDROP
EBAUCHE
EBAUCHES
EBAYER
EBAYERS
EBAYING
EBAYINGS
EBB
EBBED
EBBET
EBBETS
EBBING
EBBLESS
EBBS
EBENEZER
EBENEZERS
EBENISTE
EBENISTES
EBIONISE
EBIONISED
EBIONISES
EBIONISM
EBIONISMS
EBIONITIC
EBIONIZE
EBIONIZED
EBIONIZES
EBON
EBONICS
EBONIES
EBONISE
EBONISED
EBONISES
EBONISING
EBONIST
EBONISTS
EBONITE
EBONITES
EBONIZE
EBONIZED
EBONIZES
EBONIZING

EBONS
EBONY
EBOOK
EBOOKS
EBRIATE
EBRIATED
EBRIETIES
EBRIETY
EBRILLADE
EBRIOSE
EBRIOSITY
EBULLIENT
EBURNEAN
EBURNEOUS
ECAD
ECADS
ECARINATE
ECARTE
ECARTES
ECAUDATE
ECBOLE
ECBOLES
ECBOLIC
ECBOLICS
ECCE
ECCENTRIC
ECCLESIA
ECCLESIAE
ECCLESIAL
ECCO
ECCRINE
ECCRISES
ECCRISIS
ECCRITIC
ECCRITICS
ECDEMIC
ECDYSES
ECDYSIAL
ECDYSIAST
ECDYSIS
ECDYSON
ECDYSONE
ECDYSONES
ECDYSONS
ECESIC
ECESIS
ECESISES

ECH
ECHAPPE
ECHAPPES
ECHARD
ECHARDS
ECHE
ECHED
ECHELLE
ECHELLES
ECHELON
ECHELONED
ECHELONS
ECHES
ECHEVERIA
ECHIDNA
ECHIDNAE
ECHIDNAS
ECHIDNINE
ECHINACEA
ECHINATE
ECHINATED
ECHING
ECHINI
ECHINOID
ECHINOIDS
ECHINUS
ECHINUSES
ECHIUM
ECHIUMS
ECHIURAN
ECHIURANS
ECHIUROID
ECHO
ECHOED
ECHOER
ECHOERS
ECHOES
ECHOEY
ECHOGRAM
ECHOGRAMS
ECHOGRAPH
ECHOIC
ECHOIER
ECHOIEST
ECHOING
ECHOISE
ECHOISED

ECHOISES
ECHOISING
ECHOISM
ECHOISMS
ECHOIST
ECHOISTS
ECHOIZE
ECHOIZED
ECHOIZES
ECHOIZING
ECHOLALIA
ECHOLALIC
ECHOLESS
ECHOS
ECHOVIRUS
ECHT
ECLAIR
ECLAIRS
ECLAMPSIA
ECLAMPSY
ECLAMPTIC
ECLAT
ECLATS
ECLECTIC
ECLECTICS
ECLIPSE
ECLIPSED
ECLIPSER
ECLIPSERS
ECLIPSES
ECLIPSING
ECLIPSIS
ECLIPTIC
ECLIPTICS
ECLOGITE
ECLOGITES
ECLOGUE
ECLOGUES
ECLOSE
ECLOSED
ECLOSES
ECLOSING
ECLOSION
ECLOSIONS
ECO
ECOCIDAL
ECOCIDE

ECOCIDES
ECOD
ECOFREAK
ECOFREAKS
ECOLODGE
ECOLODGES
ECOLOGIC
ECOLOGIES
ECOLOGIST
ECOLOGY
ECOMAP
ECOMAPS
ECOMMERCE
ECONOBOX
ECONOMIC
ECONOMICS
ECONOMIES
ECONOMISE
ECONOMISM
ECONOMIST
ECONOMIZE
ECONOMY
ECONUT
ECONUTS
ECOPHOBIA
ECORCHE
ECORCHES
ECOREGION
ECOS
ECOSPHERE
ECOSSAISE
ECOSTATE
ECOSYSTEM
ECOTAGE
ECOTAGES
ECOTARIAN
ECOTONAL
ECOTONE
ECOTONES
ECOTOUR
ECOTOURS
ECOTOXIC
ECOTYPE
ECOTYPES
ECOTYPIC
ECPHRASES
ECPHRASIS

ECRASEUR	ECTOZOON	EDGED	EDITRIX	EELWORMS
ECRASEURS	ECTROPIC	EDGELESS	EDITRIXES	EELWRACK
ECRITOIRE	ECTROPION	EDGER	EDITS	EELWRACKS
ECRU	ECTROPIUM	EDGERS	EDS	EELY
ECRUS	ECTYPAL	EDGES	EDUCABLE	EEN
ECSTASES	ECTYPE	EDGEWAYS	EDUCABLES	EERIE
ECSTASIED	ECTYPES	EDGEWISE	EDUCATE	EERIER
ECSTASIES	ECU	EDGIER	EDUCATED	EERIEST
ECSTASIS	ECUELLE	EDGIEST	EDUCATES	EERILY
ECSTASISE	ECUELLES	EDGILY	EDUCATING	EERINESS
ECSTASIZE	ECUMENIC	EDGINESS	EDUCATION	EERY
ECSTASY	ECUMENICS	EDGING	EDUCATIVE	EEVEN
ECSTATIC	ECUMENISM	EDGINGS	EDUCATOR	EEVENS
ECSTATICS	ECUMENIST	EDGY	EDUCATORS	EEVN
ECTASES	ECURIE	EDH	EDUCATORY	EEVNING
ECTASIA	ECURIES	EDHS	EDUCE	EEVNINGS
ECTASIAS	ECUS	EDIBILITY	EDUCED	EEVNS
ECTASIS	ECZEMA	EDIBLE	EDUCEMENT	EF
ECTATIC	ECZEMAS	EDIBLES	EDUCES	EFF
ECTHYMA	ED	EDICT	EDUCIBLE	EFFABLE
ECTHYMAS	EDACIOUS	EDICTAL	EDUCING	EFFACE
ECTHYMATA	EDACITIES	EDICTALLY	EDUCT	EFFACED
ECTOBLAST	EDACITY	EDICTS	EDUCTION	EFFACER
ECTOCRINE	EDAMAME	EDIFICE	EDUCTIONS	EFFACERS
ECTODERM	EDAMAMES	EDIFICES	EDUCTIVE	EFFACES
ECTODERMS	EDAPHIC	EDIFICIAL	EDUCTOR	EFFACING
ECTOGENIC	EDDIED	EDIFIED	EDUCTORS	EFFECT
ECTOGENY	EDDIES	EDIFIER	EDUCTS	EFFECTED
ECTOMERE	EDDISH	EDIFIERS	EE	EFFECTER
ECTOMERES	EDDISHES	EDIFIES	EECH	EFFECTERS
ECTOMERIC	EDDO	EDIFY	EECHED	EFFECTING
ECTOMORPH	EDDOES	EDIFYING	EECHES	EFFECTIVE
ECTOPHYTE	EDDY	EDILE	EECHING	EFFECTOR
ECTOPIA	EDDYING	EDILES	EEJIT	EFFECTORS
ECTOPIAS	EDELWEISS	EDIT	EEJITS	EFFECTS
ECTOPIC	EDEMA	EDITABLE	EEK	EFFECTUAL
ECTOPIES	EDEMAS	EDITED	EEL	EFFED
ECTOPLASM	EDEMATA	EDITING	EELFARE	EFFEIR
ECTOPROCT	EDEMATOSE	EDITINGS	EELFARES	EFFEIRED
ECTOPY	EDEMATOUS	EDITION	EELGRASS	EFFEIRING
ECTOSARC	EDENIC	EDITIONED	EELIER	EFFEIRS
ECTOSARCS	EDENTAL	EDITIONS	EELIEST	EFFENDI
ECTOTHERM	EDENTATE	EDITOR	EELLIKE	EFFENDIS
ECTOZOA	EDENTATES	EDITORIAL	EELPOUT	EFFERE
ECTOZOAN	EDGE	EDITORS	EELPOUTS	EFFERED
ECTOZOANS	EDGEBONE	EDITRESS	EELS	EFFERENCE
ECTOZOIC	EDGEBONES	EDITRICES	EELWORM	EFFERENT

EFFERENTS	EFS	EGGING	EGOTISTIC	EIGHTS
EFFERES	EFT	EGGLER	EGOTISTS	EIGHTSMAN
EFFERING	EFTEST	EGGLERS	EGOTIZE	EIGHTSMEN
EFFETE	EFTS	EGGLESS	EGOTIZED	EIGHTSOME
EFFETELY	EFTSOON	EGGMASS	EGOTIZES	EIGHTVO
EFFICACY	EFTSOONS	EGGMASSES	EGOTIZING	EIGHTVOS
EFFICIENT	EGAD	EGGNOG	EGREGIOUS	EIGHTY
EFFIERCE	EGADS	EGGNOGS	EGRESS	EIGNE
EFFIERCED	EGAL	EGGPLANT	EGRESSED	EIK
EFFIERCES	EGALITE	EGGPLANTS	EGRESSES	EIKED
EFFIGIAL	EGALITES	EGGS	EGRESSING	EIKING
EFFIGIES	EGALITIES	EGGSHELL	EGRESSION	EIKON
EFFIGY	EGALITY	EGGSHELLS	EGRESSIVE	EIKONES
EFFING	EGALLY	EGGWASH	EGRET	EIKONS
EFFINGS	EGAREMENT	EGGWASHES	EGRETS	EIKS
EFFLUENCE	EGENCE	EGGWHISK	EGYPTIAN	EILD
EFFLUENT	EGENCES	EGGWHISKS	EGYPTIANS	EILDING
EFFLUENTS	EGENCIES	EGGY	EH	EILDINGS
EFFLUVIA	EGENCY	EGIS	EHED	EILDS
EFFLUVIAL	EGER	EGISES	EHING	EINA
EFFLUVIUM	EGERS	EGLANTINE	EHS	EINE
EFFLUX	EGEST	EGLATERE	EIDE	EINKORN
EFFLUXES	EGESTA	EGLATERES	EIDENT	EINKORNS
EFFLUXION	EGESTED	EGLOMISE	EIDER	EINSTEIN
EFFORCE	EGESTING	EGMA	EIDERDOWN	EINSTEINS
EFFORCED	EGESTION	EGMAS	EIDERS	EIRACK
EFFORCES	EGESTIONS	EGO	EIDETIC	EIRACKS
EFFORCING	EGESTIVE	EGOISM	EIDETICS	EIRENIC
EFFORT	EGESTS	EGOISMS	EIDOGRAPH	EIRENICAL
EFFORTFUL	EGG	EGOIST	EIDOLA	EIRENICON
EFFORTS	EGGAR	EGOISTIC	EIDOLIC	EISEGESES
EFFRAIDE	EGGARS	EGOISTS	EIDOLON	EISEGESIS
EFFRAY	EGGBEATER	EGOITIES	EIDOLONS	EISEL
EFFRAYS	EGGCUP	EGOITY	EIDOS	EISELL
EFFS	EGGCUPS	EGOLESS	EIGENMODE	EISELLS
EFFULGE	EGGED	EGOMANIA	EIGENTONE	EISELS
EFFULGED	EGGER	EGOMANIAC	EIGHT	EISH
EFFULGENT	EGGERIES	EGOMANIAS	EIGHTBALL	EISWEIN
EFFULGES	EGGERS	EGOS	EIGHTEEN	EISWEINS
EFFULGING	EGGERY	EGOTHEISM	EIGHTEENS	EITHER
EFFUSE	EGGFRUIT	EGOTISE	EIGHTFOIL	EJACULATE
EFFUSED	EGGFRUITS	EGOTISED	EIGHTFOLD	EJECT
EFFUSES	EGGHEAD	EGOTISES	EIGHTH	EJECTA
EFFUSING	EGGHEADED	EGOTISING	EIGHTHLY	EJECTABLE
EFFUSION	EGGHEADS	EGOTISM	EIGHTHS	EJECTED
EFFUSIONS	EGGIER	EGOTISMS	EIGHTIES	EJECTING
EFFUSIVE	EGGIEST	EGOTIST	EIGHTIETH	EJECTION

EJECTIONS	ELAPSES	ELDING	ELEGIAC	ELEVENTH
EJECTIVE	ELAPSING	ELDINGS	ELEGIACAL	ELEVENTHS
EJECTIVES	ELASTANCE	ELDINS	ELEGIACS	ELEVON
EJECTMENT	ELASTANE	ELDORADO	ELEGIAST	ELEVONS
EJECTOR	ELASTANES	ELDORADOS	ELEGIASTS	ELF
EJECTORS	ELASTASE	ELDRESS	ELEGIES	ELFED
EJECTS	ELASTASES	ELDRESSES	ELEGISE	ELFHOOD
EKE	ELASTIC	ELDRICH	ELEGISED	ELFHOODS
EKED	ELASTICS	ELDRITCH	ELEGISES	ELFIN
EKES	ELASTIN	ELDS	ELEGISING	ELFING
EKING	ELASTINS	ELECT	ELEGIST	ELFINS
EKISTIC	ELASTOMER	ELECTABLE	ELEGISTS	ELFISH
EKISTICAL	ELATE	ELECTED	ELEGIT	ELFISHLY
EKISTICS	ELATED	ELECTEE	ELEGITS	ELFLAND
EKKA	ELATEDLY	ELECTEES	ELEGIZE	ELFLANDS
EKKAS	ELATER	ELECTING	ELEGIZED	ELFLIKE
EKLOGITE	ELATERID	ELECTION	ELEGIZES	ELFLOCK
EKLOGITES	ELATERIDS	ELECTIONS	ELEGIZING	ELFLOCKS
EKPHRASES	ELATERIN	ELECTIVE	ELEGY	ELFS
EKPHRASIS	ELATERINS	ELECTIVES	ELEMENT	ELHI
EKPWELE	ELATERITE	ELECTOR	ELEMENTAL	ELIAD
EKPWELES	ELATERIUM	ELECTORAL	ELEMENTS	ELIADS
EKTEXINE	ELATERS	ELECTORS	ELEMI	ELICHE
EKTEXINES	ELATES	ELECTRESS	ELEMIS	ELICHES
EKUELE	ELATING	ELECTRET	ELENCH	ELICIT
EL	ELATION	ELECTRETS	ELENCHI	ELICITED
ELABORATE	ELATIONS	ELECTRIC	ELENCHIC	ELICITING
ELAEOLITE	ELATIVE	ELECTRICS	ELENCHS	ELICITOR
ELAIN	ELATIVES	ELECTRIFY	ELENCHTIC	ELICITORS
ELAINS	ELBOW	ELECTRISE	ELENCHUS	ELICITS
ELAIOSOME	ELBOWED	ELECTRIZE	ELENCTIC	ELIDE
ELAN	ELBOWING	ELECTRO	ELEOPTENE	ELIDED
ELANCE	ELBOWROOM	ELECTRODE	ELEPHANT	ELIDES
ELANCED	ELBOWS	ELECTROED	ELEPHANTS	ELIDIBLE
ELANCES	ELCHEE	ELECTRON	ELEUTHERI	ELIDING
ELANCING	ELCHEES	ELECTRONS	ELEVATE	ELIGIBLE
ELAND	ELCHI	ELECTROS	ELEVATED	ELIGIBLES
ELANDS	ELCHIS	ELECTRUM	ELEVATEDS	ELIGIBLY
ELANET	ELD	ELECTRUMS	ELEVATES	ELIMINANT
ELANETS	ELDER	ELECTS	ELEVATING	ELIMINATE
ELANS	ELDERCARE	ELECTUARY	ELEVATION	ELINT
ELAPHINE	ELDERLIES	ELEDOISIN	ELEVATOR	ELINTS
ELAPID	ELDERLY	ELEGANCE	ELEVATORS	ELISION
ELAPIDS	ELDERS	ELEGANCES	ELEVATORY	ELISIONS
ELAPINE	ELDERSHIP	ELEGANCY	ELEVEN	ELITE
ELAPSE	ELDEST	ELEGANT	ELEVENS	ELITES
ELAPSED	ELDIN	ELEGANTLY	ELEVENSES	ELITISM

ELITISMS	ELOIGNED	ELUDER	EMACIATES	EMBANKS
ELITIST	ELOIGNER	ELUDERS	EMACS	EMBAR
ELITISTS	ELOIGNERS	ELUDES	EMACSEN	EMBARGO
ELIXIR	ELOIGNING	ELUDIBLE	EMAIL	EMBARGOED
ELIXIRS	ELOIGNS	ELUDING	EMAILED	EMBARGOES
ELK	ELOIN	ELUENT	EMAILER	EMBARK
ELKHORN	ELOINED	ELUENTS	EMAILERS	EMBARKED
ELKHOUND	ELOINER	ELUSION	EMAILING	EMBARKING
ELKHOUNDS	ELOINERS	ELUSIONS	EMAILINGS	EMBARKS
ELKS	ELOINING	ELUSIVE	EMAILS	EMBARRASS
ELL	ELOINMENT	ELUSIVELY	EMANANT	EMBARRED
ELLAGIC	ELOINS	ELUSORY	EMANATE	EMBARRING
ELLIPSE	ELONGATE	ELUTE	EMANATED	EMBARS
ELLIPSES	ELONGATED	ELUTED	EMANATES	EMBASE
ELLIPSIS	ELONGATES	ELUTES	EMANATING	EMBASED
ELLIPSOID	ELOPE	ELUTING	EMANATION	EMBASES
ELLIPTIC	ELOPED	ELUTION	EMANATIST	EMBASING
ELLOPS	ELOPEMENT	ELUTIONS	EMANATIVE	EMBASSADE
ELLOPSES	ELOPER	ELUTOR	EMANATOR	EMBASSAGE
ELLS	ELOPERS	ELUTORS	EMANATORS	EMBASSIES
ELLWAND	ELOPES	ELUTRIATE	EMANATORY	EMBASSY
ELLWANDS	ELOPING	ELUVIA	EMBACE	EMBASTE
ELM	ELOPS	ELUVIAL	EMBACES	EMBATHE
ELMEN	ELOPSES	ELUVIATE	EMBACING	EMBATHED
ELMIER	ELOQUENCE	ELUVIATED	EMBAIL	EMBATHES
ELMIEST	ELOQUENT	ELUVIATES	EMBAILED	EMBATHING
ELMS	ELPEE	ELUVIUM	EMBAILING	EMBATTLE
ELMWOOD	ELPEES	ELUVIUMS	EMBAILS	EMBATTLED
ELMWOODS	ELS	ELVAN	EMBALE	EMBATTLES
ELMY	ELSE	ELVANITE	EMBALED	EMBAY
ELOCUTE	ELSEWHERE	ELVANITES	EMBALES	EMBAYED
ELOCUTED	ELSEWISE	ELVANS	EMBALING	EMBAYING
ELOCUTES	ELSHIN	ELVER	EMBALL	EMBAYLD
ELOCUTING	ELSHINS	ELVERS	EMBALLED	EMBAYMENT
ELOCUTION	ELSIN	ELVES	EMBALLING	EMBAYS
ELOCUTORY	ELSINS	ELVISH	EMBALLS	EMBED
ELODEA	ELT	ELVISHLY	EMBALM	EMBEDDED
ELODEAS	ELTCHI	ELYSIAN	EMBALMED	EMBEDDING
ELOGE	ELTCHIS	ELYTRA	EMBALMER	EMBEDMENT
ELOGES	ELTS	ELYTRAL	EMBALMERS	EMBEDS
ELOGIES	ELUANT	ELYTROID	EMBALMING	EMBELLISH
ELOGIST	ELUANTS	ELYTRON	EMBALMS	EMBER
ELOGISTS	ELUATE	ELYTROUS	EMBANK	EMBERS
ELOGIUM	ELUATES	ELYTRUM	EMBANKED	EMBEZZLE
ELOGIUMS	ELUCIDATE	EM	EMBANKER	EMBEZZLED
ELOGY	ELUDE	EMACIATE	EMBANKERS	EMBEZZLER
ELOIGN	ELUDED	EMACIATED	EMBANKING	EMBEZZLES

EMBITTER	EMBOLISE	EMBRACED	EMBRYONAL	EMERGENCE
EMBITTERS	EMBOLISED	EMBRACEOR	EMBRYONIC	EMERGENCY
EMBLAZE	EMBOLISES	EMBRACER	EMBRYONS	EMERGENT
EMBLAZED	EMBOLISM	EMBRACERS	EMBRYOS	EMERGENTS
EMBLAZER	EMBOLISMS	EMBRACERY	EMBRYOTIC	EMERGES
EMBLAZERS	EMBOLIZE	EMBRACES	EMBUS	EMERGING
EMBLAZES	EMBOLIZED	EMBRACING	EMBUSED	EMERIED
EMBLAZING	EMBOLIZES	EMBRACIVE	EMBUSES	EMERIES
EMBLAZON	EMBOLUS	EMBRAID	EMBUSIED	EMERITA
EMBLAZONS	EMBOLUSES	EMBRAIDED	EMBUSIES	EMERITAE
EMBLEM	EMBOLY	EMBRAIDS	EMBUSING	EMERITAS
EMBLEMA	EMBORDER	EMBRANGLE	EMBUSQUE	EMERITI
EMBLEMATA	EMBORDERS	EMBRASOR	EMBUSQUES	EMERITUS
EMBLEMED	EMBOSCATA	EMBRASORS	EMBUSSED	EMEROD
EMBLEMING	EMBOSK	EMBRASURE	EMBUSSES	EMERODS
EMBLEMISE	EMBOSKED	EMBRAVE	EMBUSSING	EMEROID
EMBLEMIZE	EMBOSKING	EMBRAVED	EMBUSY	EMEROIDS
EMBLEMS	EMBOSKS	EMBRAVES	EMBUSYING	EMERSE
EMBLIC	EMBOSOM	EMBRAVING	EMCEE	EMERSED
EMBLICS	EMBOSOMED	EMBRAZURE	EMCEED	EMERSION
EMBLOOM	EMBOSOMS	EMBREAD	EMCEEING	EMERSIONS
EMBLOOMED	EMBOSS	EMBREADED	EMCEES	EMERY
EMBLOOMS	EMBOSSED	EMBREADS	EMDASH	EMERYING
EMBLOSSOM	EMBOSSER	EMBREATHE	EMDASHES	EMES
EMBODIED	EMBOSSERS	EMBRITTLE	EME	EMESES
EMBODIER	EMBOSSES	EMBROCATE	EMEER	EMESIS
EMBODIERS	EMBOSSING	EMBROGLIO	EMEERATE	EMETIC
EMBODIES	EMBOST	EMBROIDER	EMEERATES	EMETICAL
EMBODY	EMBOUND	EMBROIL	EMEERS	EMETICS
EMBODYING	EMBOUNDED	EMBROILED	EMEND	EMETIN
EMBOG	EMBOUNDS	EMBROILER	EMENDABLE	EMETINE
EMBOGGED	EMBOW	EMBROILS	EMENDALS	EMETINES
EMBOGGING	EMBOWED	EMBROWN	EMENDATE	EMETINS
EMBOGS	EMBOWEL	EMBROWNED	EMENDATED	EMEU
EMBOGUE	EMBOWELED	EMBROWNS	EMENDATES	EMEUS
EMBOGUED	EMBOWELS	EMBRUE	EMENDATOR	EMEUTE
EMBOGUES	EMBOWER	EMBRUED	EMENDED	EMEUTES
EMBOGUING	EMBOWERED	EMBRUES	EMENDER	EMIC
EMBOIL	EMBOWERS	EMBRUING	EMENDERS	EMICANT
EMBOILED	EMBOWING	EMBRUTE	EMENDING	EMICATE
EMBOILING	EMBOWMENT	EMBRUTED	EMENDS	EMICATED
EMBOILS	EMBOWS	EMBRUTES	EMERALD	EMICATES
EMBOLDEN	EMBOX	EMBRUTING	EMERALDS	EMICATING
EMBOLDENS	EMBOXED	EMBRYO	EMERAUDE	EMICATION
EMBOLI	EMBOXES	EMBRYOID	EMERAUDES	EMICTION
EMBOLIC	EMBOXING	EMBRYOIDS	EMERGE	EMICTIONS
EMBOLIES	EMBRACE	EMBRYON	EMERGED	EMICTORY

EMIGRANT	EMMOVE	EMPALES	EMPERISH	EMPLOYERS
EMIGRANTS	EMMOVED	EMPALING	EMPERIZE	EMPLOYES
EMIGRATE	EMMOVES	EMPANADA	EMPERIZED	EMPLOYING
EMIGRATED	EMMOVING	EMPANADAS	EMPERIZES	EMPLOYS
EMIGRATES	EMMY	EMPANEL	EMPEROR	EMPLUME
EMIGRE	EMMYS	EMPANELED	EMPERORS	EMPLUMED
EMIGRES	EMO	EMPANELS	EMPERY	EMPLUMES
EMINENCE	EMODIN	EMPANOPLY	EMPHASES	EMPLUMING
EMINENCES	EMODINS	EMPARE	EMPHASIS	EMPOISON
EMINENCY	EMOLLIATE	EMPARED	EMPHASISE	EMPOISONS
EMINENT	EMOLLIENT	EMPARES	EMPHASIZE	EMPOLDER
EMINENTLY	EMOLUMENT	EMPARING	EMPHATIC	EMPOLDERS
EMIR	EMONG	EMPARL	EMPHATICS	EMPORIA
EMIRATE	EMONGES	EMPARLED	EMPHLYSES	EMPORIUM
EMIRATES	EMONGEST	EMPARLING	EMPHLYSIS	EMPORIUMS
EMIRS	EMONGST	EMPARLS	EMPHYSEMA	EMPOWER
EMISSARY	EMOS	EMPART	EMPIERCE	EMPOWERED
EMISSILE	EMOTE	EMPARTED	EMPIERCED	EMPOWERS
EMISSION	EMOTED	EMPARTING	EMPIERCES	EMPRESS
EMISSIONS	EMOTER	EMPARTS	EMPIGHT	EMPRESSE
EMISSIVE	EMOTERS	EMPATHIC	EMPIRE	EMPRESSES
EMIT	EMOTES	EMPATHIES	EMPIRES	EMPRISE
EMITS	EMOTICON	EMPATHISE	EMPIRIC	EMPRISES
EMITTANCE	EMOTICONS	EMPATHIST	EMPIRICAL	EMPRIZE
EMITTED	EMOTING	EMPATHIZE	EMPIRICS	EMPRIZES
EMITTER	EMOTION	EMPATHY	EMPLACE	EMPT
EMITTERS	EMOTIONAL	EMPATRON	EMPLACED	EMPTED
EMITTING	EMOTIONS	EMPATRONS	EMPLACES	EMPTIABLE
EMLETS	EMOTIVE	EMPAYRE	EMPLACING	EMPTIED
EMMA	EMOTIVELY	EMPAYRED	EMPLANE	EMPTIER
EMMARBLE	EMOTIVISM	EMPAYRES	EMPLANED	EMPTIERS
EMMARBLED	EMOTIVITY	EMPAYRING	EMPLANES	EMPTIES
EMMARBLES	EMOVE	EMPEACH	EMPLANING	EMPTIEST
EMMAS	EMOVED	EMPEACHED	EMPLASTER	EMPTILY
EMMER	EMOVES	EMPEACHES	EMPLASTIC	EMPTINESS
EMMERS	EMOVING	EMPENNAGE	EMPLEACH	EMPTING
EMMESH	EMPACKET	EMPEOPLE	EMPLECTON	EMPTINGS
EMMESHED	EMPACKETS	EMPEOPLED	EMPLECTUM	EMPTINS
EMMESHES	EMPAESTIC	EMPEOPLES	EMPLONGE	EMPTION
EMMESHING	EMPAIRE	EMPERCE	EMPLONGED	EMPTIONAL
EMMET	EMPAIRED	EMPERCED	EMPLONGES	EMPTIONS
EMMETROPE	EMPAIRES	EMPERCES	EMPLOY	EMPTS
EMMETS	EMPAIRING	EMPERCING	EMPLOYE	EMPTY
EMMEW	EMPALE	EMPERIES	EMPLOYED	EMPTYING
EMMEWED	EMPALED	EMPERISE	EMPLOYEE	EMPTYINGS
EMMEWING	EMPALER	EMPERISED	EMPLOYEES	EMPTYSES
EMMEWS	EMPALERS	EMPERISES	EMPLOYER	EMPTYSIS

EMPURPLE	EMULSOIDS	ENAMELING	ENCAPSULE	ENCHORIAL
EMPURPLED	EMULSOR	ENAMELIST	ENCARPUS	ENCHORIC
EMPURPLES	EMULSORS	ENAMELLED	ENCASE	ENCIERRO
EMPUSA	EMUNCTION	ENAMELLER	ENCASED	ENCIERROS
EMPUSAS	EMUNCTORY	ENAMELS	ENCASES	ENCINA
EMPUSE	EMUNGE	ENAMINE	ENCASH	ENCINAL
EMPUSES	EMUNGED	ENAMINES	ENCASHED	ENCINAS
EMPYEMA	EMUNGES	ENAMOR	ENCASHES	ENCIPHER
EMPYEMAS	EMUNGING	ENAMORADO	ENCASHING	ENCIPHERS
EMPYEMATA	EMURE	ENAMORED	ENCASING	ENCIRCLE
EMPYEMIC	EMURED	ENAMORING	ENCASTRE	ENCIRCLED
EMPYESES	EMURES	ENAMORS	ENCAUSTIC	ENCIRCLES
EMPYESIS	EMURING	ENAMOUR	ENCAVE	ENCLASP
EMPYREAL	EMUS	ENAMOURED	ENCAVED	ENCLASPED
EMPYREAN	EMYD	ENAMOURS	ENCAVES	ENCLASPS
EMPYREANS	EMYDE	ENANTHEMA	ENCAVING	ENCLAVE
EMPYREUMA	EMYDES	ENARCH	ENCEINTE	ENCLAVED
EMS	EMYDS	ENARCHED	ENCEINTES	ENCLAVES
EMU	EMYS	ENARCHES	ENCEPHALA	ENCLAVING
EMULATE	EN	ENARCHING	ENCHAFE	ENCLISES
EMULATED	ENABLE	ENARGITE	ENCHAFED	ENCLISIS
EMULATES	ENABLED	ENARGITES	ENCHAFES	ENCLITIC
EMULATING	ENABLER	ENARM	ENCHAFING	ENCLITICS
EMULATION	ENABLERS	ENARMED	ENCHAIN	ENCLOSE
EMULATIVE	ENABLES	ENARMING	ENCHAINED	ENCLOSED
EMULATOR	ENABLING	ENARMS	ENCHAINS	ENCLOSER
EMULATORS	ENACT	ENATE	ENCHANT	ENCLOSERS
EMULE	ENACTABLE	ENATES	ENCHANTED	ENCLOSES
EMULED	ENACTED	ENATIC	ENCHANTER	ENCLOSING
EMULES	ENACTING	ENATION	ENCHANTS	ENCLOSURE
EMULGE	ENACTION	ENATIONS	ENCHARGE	ENCLOTHE
EMULGED	ENACTIONS	ENAUNTER	ENCHARGED	ENCLOTHED
EMULGENCE	ENACTIVE	ENCAENIA	ENCHARGES	ENCLOTHES
EMULGENT	ENACTMENT	ENCAENIAS	ENCHARM	ENCLOUD
EMULGES	ENACTOR	ENCAGE	ENCHARMED	ENCLOUDED
EMULGING	ENACTORS	ENCAGED	ENCHARMS	ENCLOUDS
EMULING	ENACTORY	ENCAGES	ENCHASE	ENCODABLE
EMULOUS	ENACTS	ENCAGING	ENCHASED	ENCODE
EMULOUSLY	ENACTURE	ENCALM	ENCHASER	ENCODED
EMULSIBLE	ENACTURES	ENCALMED	ENCHASERS	ENCODER
EMULSIFY	ENALAPRIL	ENCALMING	ENCHASES	ENCODERS
EMULSIN	ENALLAGE	ENCALMS	ENCHASING	ENCODES
EMULSINS	ENALLAGES	ENCAMP	ENCHEASON	ENCODING
EMULSION	ENAMEL	ENCAMPED	ENCHEER	ENCOLOUR
EMULSIONS	ENAMELED	ENCAMPING	ENCHEERED	ENCOLOURS
EMULSIVE	ENAMELER	ENCAMPS	ENCHEERS	ENCOLPION
EMULSOID	ENAMELERS	ENCANTHIS	ENCHILADA	ENCOLPIUM

ENCOLURE	ENDAMEBAE	ENDGAMES	ENDOPOD	ENDPAPERS
ENCOLURES	ENDAMEBAS	ENDGATE	ENDOPODS	ENDPLATE
ENCOMIA	ENDAMEBIC	ENDGATES	ENDOPROCT	ENDPLATES
ENCOMIAST	ENDAMOEBA	ENDING	ENDORPHIN	ENDPLAY
ENCOMION	ENDANGER	ENDINGS	ENDORSE	ENDPLAYED
ENCOMIUM	ENDANGERS	ENDIRON	ENDORSED	ENDPLAYS
ENCOMIUMS	ENDARCH	ENDIRONS	ENDORSEE	ENDPOINT
ENCOMPASS	ENDARCHY	ENDITE	ENDORSEES	ENDPOINTS
ENCORE	ENDART	ENDITED	ENDORSER	ENDRIN
ENCORED	ENDARTED	ENDITES	ENDORSERS	ENDRINS
ENCORES	ENDARTING	ENDITING	ENDORSES	ENDS
ENCORING	ENDARTS	ENDIVE	ENDORSING	ENDSHIP
ENCOUNTER	ENDASH	ENDIVES	ENDORSIVE	ENDSHIPS
ENCOURAGE	ENDASHES	ENDLANG	ENDORSOR	ENDUE
ENCRADLE	ENDBRAIN	ENDLEAF	ENDORSORS	ENDUED
ENCRADLED	ENDBRAINS	ENDLEAFS	ENDOSARC	ENDUES
ENCRADLES	ENDEAR	ENDLEAVES	ENDOSARCS	ENDUING
ENCRATIES	ENDEARED	ENDLESS	ENDOSCOPE	ENDUNGEON
ENCRATY	ENDEARING	ENDLESSLY	ENDOSCOPY	ENDURABLE
ENCREASE	ENDEARS	ENDLONG	ENDOSMOS	ENDURABLY
ENCREASED	ENDEAVOR	ENDMOST	ENDOSMOSE	ENDURANCE
ENCREASES	ENDEAVORS	ENDNOTE	ENDOSOME	ENDURE
ENCRIMSON	ENDEAVOUR	ENDNOTES	ENDOSOMES	ENDURED
ENCRINAL	ENDECAGON	ENDOBLAST	ENDOSPERM	ENDURER
ENCRINIC	ENDED	ENDOCARP	ENDOSPORE	ENDURERS
ENCRINITE	ENDEICTIC	ENDOCARPS	ENDOSS	ENDURES
ENCROACH	ENDEIXES	ENDOCAST	ENDOSSED	ENDURING
ENCRUST	ENDEIXIS	ENDOCASTS	ENDOSSES	ENDURO
ENCRUSTED	ENDEMIAL	ENDOCRINE	ENDOSSING	ENDUROS
ENCRUSTS	ENDEMIC	ENDOCYTIC	ENDOSTEA	ENDWAYS
ENCRYPT	ENDEMICAL	ENDODERM	ENDOSTEAL	ENDWISE
ENCRYPTED	ENDEMICS	ENDODERMS	ENDOSTEUM	ENDYSES
ENCRYPTS	ENDEMISM	ENDODYNE	ENDOSTYLE	ENDYSIS
ENCUMBER	ENDEMISMS	ENDOERGIC	ENDOTHERM	ENDZONE
ENCUMBERS	ENDENIZEN	ENDOGAMIC	ENDOTOXIC	ENDZONES
ENCURTAIN	ENDER	ENDOGAMY	ENDOTOXIN	ENE
ENCYCLIC	ENDERMIC	ENDOGEN	ENDOW	ENEMA
ENCYCLICS	ENDERON	ENDOGENIC	ENDOWED	ENEMAS
ENCYST	ENDERONS	ENDOGENS	ENDOWER	ENEMATA
ENCYSTED	ENDERS	ENDOGENY	ENDOWERS	ENEMIES
ENCYSTING	ENDEW	ENDOLYMPH	ENDOWING	ENEMY
ENCYSTS	ENDEWED	ENDOMIXES	ENDOWMENT	ENERGETIC
END	ENDEWING	ENDOMIXIS	ENDOWS	ENERGIC
ENDAMAGE	ENDEWS	ENDOMORPH	ENDOZOA	ENERGID
ENDAMAGED	ENDEXINE	ENDOPHAGY	ENDOZOIC	ENERGIDS
ENDAMAGES	ENDEXINES	ENDOPHYTE	ENDOZOON	ENERGIES
ENDAMEBA	ENDGAME	ENDOPLASM	ENDPAPER	ENERGISE

ENERGISED	ENFILADE	ENFREES	ENGLISH	ENGRAMMIC
ENERGISER	ENFILADED	ENFREEZE	ENGLISHED	ENGRAMS
ENERGISES	ENFILADES	ENFREEZES	ENGLISHES	ENGRASP
ENERGIZE	ENFILED	ENFROSEN	ENGLOBE	ENGRASPED
ENERGIZED	ENFIRE	ENFROZE	ENGLOBED	ENGRASPS
ENERGIZER	ENFIRED	ENFROZEN	ENGLOBES	ENGRAVE
ENERGIZES	ENFIRES	ENG	ENGLOBING	ENGRAVED
ENERGUMEN	ENFIRING	ENGAGE	ENGLOOM	ENGRAVEN
ENERGY	ENFIX	ENGAGED	ENGLOOMED	ENGRAVER
ENERVATE	ENFIXED	ENGAGEDLY	ENGLOOMS	ENGRAVERS
ENERVATED	ENFIXES	ENGAGEE	ENGLUT	ENGRAVERY
ENERVATES	ENFIXING	ENGAGER	ENGLUTS	ENGRAVES
ENERVATOR	ENFLAME	ENGAGERS	ENGLUTTED	ENGRAVING
ENERVE	ENFLAMED	ENGAGES	ENGOBE	ENGRENAGE
ENERVED	ENFLAMES	ENGAGING	ENGOBES	ENGRIEVE
ENERVES	ENFLAMING	ENGAOL	ENGORE	ENGRIEVED
ENERVING	ENFLESH	ENGAOLED	ENGORED	ENGRIEVES
ENES	ENFLESHED	ENGAOLING	ENGORES	ENGROOVE
ENEW	ENFLESHES	ENGAOLS	ENGORGE	ENGROOVED
ENEWED	ENFLOWER	ENGARLAND	ENGORGED	ENGROOVES
ENEWING	ENFLOWERS	ENGENDER	ENGORGES	ENGROSS
ENEWS	ENFOLD	ENGENDERS	ENGORGING	ENGROSSED
ENFACE	ENFOLDED	ENGENDURE	ENGORING	ENGROSSER
ENFACED	ENFOLDER	ENGILD	ENGOULED	ENGROSSES
ENFACES	ENFOLDERS	ENGILDED	ENGOUMENT	ENGS
ENFACING	ENFOLDING	ENGILDING	ENGRACE	ENGUARD
ENFANT	ENFOLDS	ENGILDS	ENGRACED	ENGUARDED
ENFANTS	ENFORCE	ENGILT	ENGRACES	ENGUARDS
ENFEEBLE	ENFORCED	ENGINE	ENGRACING	ENGULF
ENFEEBLED	ENFORCER	ENGINED	ENGRAFF	ENGULFED
ENFEEBLER	ENFORCERS	ENGINEER	ENGRAFFED	ENGULFING
ENFEEBLES	ENFORCES	ENGINEERS	ENGRAFFS	ENGULFS
ENFELON	ENFORCING	ENGINER	ENGRAFT	ENGULPH
ENFELONED	ENFOREST	ENGINERS	ENGRAFTED	ENGULPHED
ENFELONS	ENFORESTS	ENGINERY	ENGRAFTS	ENGULPHS
ENFEOFF	ENFORM	ENGINES	ENGRAIL	ENGYSCOPE
ENFEOFFED	ENFORMED	ENGINING	ENGRAILED	ENHALO
ENFEOFFS	ENFORMING	ENGINOUS	ENGRAILS	ENHALOED
ENFESTED	ENFORMS	ENGIRD	ENGRAIN	ENHALOES
ENFETTER	ENFRAME	ENGIRDED	ENGRAINED	ENHALOING
ENFETTERS	ENFRAMED	ENGIRDING	ENGRAINER	ENHALOS
ENFEVER	ENFRAMES	ENGIRDLE	ENGRAINS	ENHANCE
ENFEVERED	ENFRAMING	ENGIRDLED	ENGRAM	ENHANCED
ENFEVERS	ENFREE	ENGIRDLES	ENGRAMMA	ENHANCER
ENFIERCE	ENFREED	ENGIRDS	ENGRAMMAS	ENHANCERS
ENFIERCED	ENFREEDOM	ENGIRT	ENGRAMME	ENHANCES
ENFIERCES	ENFREEING	ENGLACIAL	ENGRAMMES	ENHANCING

ENHANCIVE	ENLACED	ENMESHING	ENOLS	ENRANGE
ENHEARSE	ENLACES	ENMEW	ENOMOTIES	ENRANGED
ENHEARSED	ENLACING	ENMEWED	ENOMOTY	ENRANGES
ENHEARSES	ENLARD	ENMEWING	ENOPHILE	ENRANGING
ENHEARTEN	ENLARDED	ENMEWS	ENOPHILES	ENRANK
ENHUNGER	ENLARDING	ENMITIES	ENORM	ENRANKED
ENHUNGERS	ENLARDS	ENMITY	ENORMITY	ENRANKING
ENHYDRITE	ENLARGE	ENMOSSED	ENORMOUS	ENRANKS
ENHYDROS	ENLARGED	ENMOVE	ENOSES	ENRAPT
ENHYDROUS	ENLARGEN	ENMOVED	ENOSIS	ENRAPTURE
ENIAC	ENLARGENS	ENMOVES	ENOSISES	ENRAUNGE
ENIACS	ENLARGER	ENMOVING	ENOUGH	ENRAUNGED
ENIGMA	ENLARGERS	ENNAGE	ENOUGHS	ENRAUNGES
ENIGMAS	ENLARGES	ENNAGES	ENOUNCE	ENRAVISH
ENIGMATA	ENLARGING	ENNEAD	ENOUNCED	ENRHEUM
ENIGMATIC	ENLEVE	ENNEADIC	ENOUNCES	ENRHEUMED
ENISLE	ENLIGHT	ENNEADS	ENOUNCING	ENRHEUMS
ENISLED	ENLIGHTED	ENNEAGON	ENOW	ENRICH
ENISLES	ENLIGHTEN	ENNEAGONS	ENOWS	ENRICHED
ENISLING	ENLIGHTS	ENNEAGRAM	ENPLANE	ENRICHER
ENJAMB	ENLINK	ENNOBLE	ENPLANED	ENRICHERS
ENJAMBED	ENLINKED	ENNOBLED	ENPLANES	ENRICHES
ENJAMBING	ENLINKING	ENNOBLER	ENPLANING	ENRICHING
ENJAMBS	ENLINKS	ENNOBLERS	ENPRINT	ENRIDGED
ENJOIN	ENLIST	ENNOBLES	ENPRINTS	ENRING
ENJOINDER	ENLISTED	ENNOBLING	ENQUEUE	ENRINGED
ENJOINED	ENLISTEE	ENNOG	ENQUEUED	ENRINGING
ENJOINER	ENLISTEES	ENNOGS	ENQUEUES	ENRINGS
ENJOINERS	ENLISTER	ENNUI	ENQUEUING	ENRIVEN
ENJOINING	ENLISTERS	ENNUIED	ENQUIRE	ENROBE
ENJOINS	ENLISTING	ENNUIS	ENQUIRED	ENROBED
ENJOY	ENLISTS	ENNUYE	ENQUIRER	ENROBER
ENJOYABLE	ENLIT	ENNUYED	ENQUIRERS	ENROBERS
ENJOYABLY	ENLIVEN	ENNUYEE	ENQUIRES	ENROBES
ENJOYED	ENLIVENED	ENNUYING	ENQUIRIES	ENROBING
ENJOYER	ENLIVENER	ENODAL	ENQUIRING	ENROL
ENJOYERS	ENLIVENS	ENOKI	ENQUIRY	ENROLL
ENJOYING	ENLOCK	ENOKIDAKE	ENRACE	ENROLLED
ENJOYMENT	ENLOCKED	ENOKIS	ENRACED	ENROLLEE
ENJOYS	ENLOCKING	ENOKITAKE	ENRACES	ENROLLEES
ENKERNEL	ENLOCKS	ENOL	ENRACING	ENROLLER
ENKERNELS	ENLUMINE	ENOLASE	ENRAGE	ENROLLERS
ENKINDLE	ENLUMINED	ENOLASES	ENRAGED	ENROLLING
ENKINDLED	ENLUMINES	ENOLIC	ENRAGEDLY	ENROLLS
ENKINDLER	ENMESH	ENOLOGIES	ENRAGES	ENROLMENT
ENKINDLES	ENMESHED	ENOLOGIST	ENRAGING	ENROLS
ENLACE	ENMESHES	ENOLOGY	ENRANCKLE	ENROOT

ENROOTED	ENSHELTER	ENSOULING	ENTANGLED	ENTHRONED
ENROOTING	ENSHIELD	ENSOULS	ENTANGLER	ENTHRONES
ENROOTS	ENSHIELDS	ENSPHERE	ENTANGLES	ENTHUSE
ENROUGH	ENSHRINE	ENSPHERED	ENTASES	ENTHUSED
ENROUGHED	ENSHRINED	ENSPHERES	ENTASIA	ENTHUSES
ENROUGHS	ENSHRINEE	ENSTAMP	ENTASIAS	ENTHUSING
ENROUND	ENSHRINES	ENSTAMPED	ENTASIS	ENTHYMEME
ENROUNDED	ENSHROUD	ENSTAMPS	ENTASTIC	ENTIA
ENROUNDS	ENSHROUDS	ENSTATITE	ENTAYLE	ENTICE
ENS	ENSIFORM	ENSTEEP	ENTAYLED	ENTICED
ENSAMPLE	ENSIGN	ENSTEEPED	ENTAYLES	ENTICER
ENSAMPLED	ENSIGNCY	ENSTEEPS	ENTAYLING	ENTICERS
ENSAMPLES	ENSIGNED	ENSTYLE	ENTELECHY	ENTICES
ENSATE	ENSIGNING	ENSTYLED	ENTELLUS	ENTICING
ENSCONCE	ENSIGNS	ENSTYLES	ENTENDER	ENTICINGS
ENSCONCED	ENSILAGE	ENSTYLING	ENTENDERS	ENTIRE
ENSCONCES	ENSILAGED	ENSUE	ENTENTE	ENTIRELY
ENSCROLL	ENSILAGES	ENSUED	ENTENTES	ENTIRES
ENSCROLLS	ENSILE	ENSUES	ENTER	ENTIRETY
ENSEAL	ENSILED	ENSUING	ENTERA	ENTITIES
ENSEALED	ENSILES	ENSURE	ENTERABLE	ENTITLE
ENSEALING	ENSILING	ENSURED	ENTERAL	ENTITLED
ENSEALS	ENSKIED	ENSURER	ENTERALLY	ENTITLES
ENSEAM	ENSKIES	ENSURERS	ENTERATE	ENTITLING
ENSEAMED	ENSKY	ENSURES	ENTERED	ENTITY
ENSEAMING	ENSKYED	ENSURING	ENTERER	ENTOBLAST
ENSEAMS	ENSKYING	ENSWATHE	ENTERERS	ENTODERM
ENSEAR	ENSLAVE	ENSWATHED	ENTERIC	ENTODERMS
ENSEARED	ENSLAVED	ENSWATHES	ENTERICS	ENTOIL
ENSEARING	ENSLAVER	ENSWEEP	ENTERING	ENTOILED
ENSEARS	ENSLAVERS	ENSWEEPS	ENTERINGS	ENTOILING
ENSEMBLE	ENSLAVES	ENSWEPT	ENTERITIS	ENTOILS
ENSEMBLES	ENSLAVING	ENTAIL	ENTERON	ENTOMB
ENSERF	ENSNARE	ENTAILED	ENTERONS	ENTOMBED
ENSERFED	ENSNARED	ENTAILER	ENTERS	ENTOMBING
ENSERFING	ENSNARER	ENTAILERS	ENTERTAIN	ENTOMBS
ENSERFS	ENSNARERS	ENTAILING	ENTERTAKE	ENTOMIC
ENSEW	ENSNARES	ENTAILS	ENTERTOOK	ENTOPHYTE
ENSEWED	ENSNARING	ENTAME	ENTETE	ENTOPIC
ENSEWING	ENSNARL	ENTAMEBA	ENTETEE	ENTOPROCT
ENSEWS	ENSNARLED	ENTAMEBAE	ENTHALPY	ENTOPTIC
ENSHEATH	ENSNARLS	ENTAMEBAS	ENTHETIC	ENTOPTICS
ENSHEATHE	ENSORCEL	ENTAMED	ENTHRAL	ENTOTIC
ENSHEATHS	ENSORCELL	ENTAMES	ENTHRALL	ENTOURAGE
ENSHELL	ENSORCELS	ENTAMING	ENTHRALLS	ENTOZOA
ENSHELLED	ENSOUL	ENTAMOEBA	ENTHRALS	ENTOZOAL
ENSHELLS	ENSOULED	ENTANGLE	ENTHRONE	ENTOZOAN

ENTOZOANS	ENTROPIUM	ENVELOPER	ENWOMBED	EOSINE
ENTOZOIC	ENTROPY	ENVELOPES	ENWOMBING	EOSINES
ENTOZOON	ENTRUST	ENVELOPS	ENWOMBS	EOSINIC
ENTRAIL	ENTRUSTED	ENVENOM	ENWOUND	EOSINS
ENTRAILED	ENTRUSTS	ENVENOMED	ENWRAP	EOTHEN
ENTRAILS	ENTRY	ENVENOMS	ENWRAPPED	EPACRID
ENTRAIN	ENTRYISM	ENVERMEIL	ENWRAPS	EPACRIDS
ENTRAINED	ENTRYISMS	ENVIABLE	ENWREATH	EPACRIS
ENTRAINER	ENTRYIST	ENVIABLY	ENWREATHE	EPACRISES
ENTRAINS	ENTRYISTS	ENVIED	ENWREATHS	EPACT
ENTRALL	ENTRYWAY	ENVIER	ENZIAN	EPACTS
ENTRALLES	ENTRYWAYS	ENVIERS	ENZIANS	EPAENETIC
ENTRAMMEL	ENTWINE	ENVIES	ENZONE	EPAGOGE
ENTRANCE	ENTWINED	ENVIOUS	ENZONED	EPAGOGES
ENTRANCED	ENTWINES	ENVIOUSLY	ENZONES	EPAGOGIC
ENTRANCES	ENTWINING	ENVIRO	ENZONING	EPANODOS
ENTRANT	ENTWIST	ENVIRON	ENZOOTIC	EPARCH
ENTRANTS	ENTWISTED	ENVIRONED	ENZOOTICS	EPARCHATE
ENTRAP	ENTWISTS	ENVIRONS	ENZYM	EPARCHIAL
ENTRAPPED	ENUCLEATE	ENVIROS	ENZYMATIC	EPARCHIES
ENTRAPPER	ENUF	ENVISAGE	ENZYME	EPARCHS
ENTRAPS	ENUMERATE	ENVISAGED	ENZYMES	EPARCHY
ENTREAT	ENUNCIATE	ENVISAGES	ENZYMIC	EPATANT
ENTREATED	ENURE	ENVISION	ENZYMS	EPAULE
ENTREATS	ENURED	ENVISIONS	EOAN	EPAULES
ENTREATY	ENUREMENT	ENVOI	EOBIONT	EPAULET
ENTRECHAT	ENURES	ENVOIS	EOBIONTS	EPAULETS
ENTRECOTE	ENURESES	ENVOY	EOCENE	EPAULETTE
ENTREE	ENURESIS	ENVOYS	EOHIPPUS	EPAXIAL
ENTREES	ENURETIC	ENVOYSHIP	EOLIAN	EPAZOTE
ENTREMES	ENURETICS	ENVY	EOLIENNE	EPAZOTES
ENTREMETS	ENURING	ENVYING	EOLIENNES	EPEDAPHIC
ENTRENCH	ENURN	ENVYINGLY	EOLIPILE	EPEE
ENTREPOT	ENURNED	ENVYINGS	EOLIPILES	EPEEIST
ENTREPOTS	ENURNING	ENWALL	EOLITH	EPEEISTS
ENTRESOL	ENURNS	ENWALLED	EOLITHIC	EPEES
ENTRESOLS	ENVASSAL	ENWALLING	EOLITHS	EPEIRA
ENTREZ	ENVASSALS	ENWALLOW	EOLOPILE	EPEIRAS
ENTRIES	ENVAULT	ENWALLOWS	EOLOPILES	EPEIRIC
ENTRISM	ENVAULTED	ENWALLS	EON	EPEIRID
ENTRISMS	ENVAULTS	ENWHEEL	EONIAN	EPEIRIDS
ENTRIST	ENVEIGLE	ENWHEELED	EONISM	EPENDYMA
ENTRISTS	ENVEIGLED	ENWHEELS	EONISMS	EPENDYMAL
ENTROLD	ENVEIGLES	ENWIND	EONS	EPENDYMAS
ENTROPIC	ENVELOP	ENWINDING	EORL	EPEOLATRY
ENTROPIES	ENVELOPE	ENWINDS	EORLS	EPERDU
ENTROPION	ENVELOPED	ENWOMB	EOSIN	EPERDUE

EPERGNE	EPIC	EPIDEMICS	EPILATE	EPIPHYSIS
EPERGNES	EPICAL	EPIDERM	EPILATED	EPIPHYTAL
EPHA	EPICALLY	EPIDERMAL	EPILATES	EPIPHYTE
EPHAH	EPICALYX	EPIDERMIC	EPILATING	EPIPHYTES
EPHAHS	EPICANTHI	EPIDERMIS	EPILATION	EPIPHYTIC
EPHAS	EPICARDIA	EPIDERMS	EPILATOR	EPIPLOIC
EPHEBE	EPICARP	EPIDICTIC	EPILATORS	EPIPLOON
EPHEBES	EPICARPS	EPIDOSITE	EPILEPSY	EPIPLOONS
EPHEBI	EPICEDE	EPIDOTE	EPILEPTIC	EPIPOLIC
EPHEBIC	EPICEDES	EPIDOTES	EPILIMNIA	EPIPOLISM
EPHEBOI	EPICEDIA	EPIDOTIC	EPILITHIC	EPIROGENY
EPHEBOS	EPICEDIAL	EPIDURAL	EPILOBIUM	EPIRRHEMA
EPHEBUS	EPICEDIAN	EPIDURALS	EPILOG	EPISCIA
EPHEDRA	EPICEDIUM	EPIFAUNA	EPILOGIC	EPISCIAS
EPHEDRAS	EPICENE	EPIFAUNAE	EPILOGISE	EPISCOPAL
EPHEDRIN	EPICENES	EPIFAUNAL	EPILOGIST	EPISCOPE
EPHEDRINE	EPICENISM	EPIFAUNAS	EPILOGIZE	EPISCOPES
EPHEDRINS	EPICENTER	EPIFOCAL	EPILOGS	EPISCOPY
EPHELIDES	EPICENTRA	EPIGAEAL	EPILOGUE	EPISEMON
EPHELIS	EPICENTRE	EPIGAEAN	EPILOGUED	EPISEMONS
EPHEMERA	EPICIER	EPIGAEOUS	EPILOGUES	EPISODAL
EPHEMERAE	EPICIERS	EPIGAMIC	EPIMER	EPISODE
EPHEMERAL	EPICISM	EPIGEAL	EPIMERASE	EPISODES
EPHEMERAS	EPICISMS	EPIGEAN	EPIMERE	EPISODIAL
EPHEMERID	EPICIST	EPIGEIC	EPIMERES	EPISODIC
EPHEMERIS	EPICISTS	EPIGENE	EPIMERIC	EPISOMAL
EPHEMERON	EPICLESES	EPIGENIC	EPIMERISE	EPISOME
EPHIALTES	EPICLESIS	EPIGENIST	EPIMERISM	EPISOMES
EPHOD	EPICLIKE	EPIGENOUS	EPIMERIZE	EPISPERM
EPHODS	EPICORMIC	EPIGEOUS	EPIMERS	EPISPERMS
EPHOR	EPICOTYL	EPIGON	EPIMYSIA	EPISPORE
EPHORAL	EPICOTYLS	EPIGONE	EPIMYSIUM	EPISPORES
EPHORALTY	EPICRANIA	EPIGONES	EPINAOI	EPISTASES
EPHORATE	EPICRISES	EPIGONI	EPINAOS	EPISTASIS
EPHORATES	EPICRISIS	EPIGONIC	EPINASTIC	EPISTASY
EPHORI	EPICRITIC	EPIGONISM	EPINASTY	EPISTATIC
EPHORS	EPICS	EPIGONOUS	EPINEURAL	EPISTAXES
EPIBIOSES	EPICURE	EPIGONS	EPINEURIA	EPISTAXIS
EPIBIOSIS	EPICUREAN	EPIGONUS	EPINICIAN	EPISTEMIC
EPIBIOTIC	EPICURES	EPIGRAM	EPINICION	EPISTERNA
EPIBLAST	EPICURISE	EPIGRAMS	EPINIKIAN	EPISTLE
EPIBLASTS	EPICURISM	EPIGRAPH	EPINIKION	EPISTLED
EPIBLEM	EPICURIZE	EPIGRAPHS	EPINOSIC	EPISTLER
EPIBLEMS	EPICYCLE	EPIGRAPHY	EPIPHANIC	EPISTLERS
EPIBOLIC	EPICYCLES	EPIGYNIES	EPIPHANY	EPISTLES
EPIBOLIES	EPICYCLIC	EPIGYNOUS	EPIPHRAGM	EPISTLING
EPIBOLY	EPIDEMIC	EPIGYNY	EPIPHYSES	EPISTOLER

EPISTOLET

EPISTOLET	EPIZOANS	EPSOMITES	EQUATIVE	ERA
EPISTOLIC	EPIZOIC	EPUISE	EQUATOR	ERADIATE
EPISTOME	EPIZOISM	EPUISEE	EQUATORS	ERADIATED
EPISTOMES	EPIZOISMS	EPULARY	EQUERRIES	ERADIATES
EPISTYLE	EPIZOITE	EPULATION	EQUERRY	ERADICANT
EPISTYLES	EPIZOITES	EPULIDES	EQUID	ERADICATE
EPITAPH	EPIZOON	EPULIS	EQUIDS	ERAS
EPITAPHED	EPIZOOTIC	EPULISES	EQUIFINAL	ERASABLE
EPITAPHER	EPIZOOTY	EPULOTIC	EQUIMOLAL	ERASE
EPITAPHIC	EPOCH	EPULOTICS	EQUIMOLAR	ERASED
EPITAPHS	EPOCHA	EPURATE	EQUINAL	ERASEMENT
EPITASES	EPOCHAL	EPURATED	EQUINE	ERASER
EPITASIS	EPOCHALLY	EPURATES	EQUINELY	ERASERS
EPITAXES	EPOCHAS	EPURATING	EQUINES	ERASES
EPITAXIAL	EPOCHS	EPURATION	EQUINIA	ERASING
EPITAXIC	EPODE	EPYLLIA	EQUINIAS	ERASION
EPITAXIES	EPODES	EPYLLION	EQUINITY	ERASIONS
EPITAXIS	EPODIC	EPYLLIONS	EQUINOX	ERASURE
EPITAXY	EPONYM	EQUABLE	EQUINOXES	ERASURES
EPITHECA	EPONYMIC	EQUABLY	EQUIP	ERATHEM
EPITHECAE	EPONYMIES	EQUAL	EQUIPAGE	ERATHEMS
EPITHELIA	EPONYMOUS	EQUALED	EQUIPAGED	ERBIA
EPITHEM	EPONYMS	EQUALI	EQUIPAGES	ERBIAS
EPITHEMA	EPONYMY	EQUALING	EQUIPE	ERBIUM
EPITHEMS	EPOPEE	EQUALISE	EQUIPES	ERBIUMS
EPITHESES	EPOPEES	EQUALISED	EQUIPMENT	ERE
EPITHESIS	EPOPOEIA	EQUALISER	EQUIPOISE	ERECT
EPITHET	EPOPOEIAS	EQUALISES	EQUIPPED	ERECTABLE
EPITHETED	EPOPT	EQUALITY	EQUIPPER	ERECTED
EPITHETIC	EPOPTS	EQUALIZE	EQUIPPERS	ERECTER
EPITHETON	EPOS	EQUALIZED	EQUIPPING	ERECTERS
EPITHETS	EPOSES	EQUALIZER	EQUIPS	ERECTILE
EPITOME	EPOXIDE	EQUALIZES	EQUISETA	ERECTING
EPITOMES	EPOXIDES	EQUALLED	EQUISETIC	ERECTION
EPITOMIC	EPOXIDISE	EQUALLING	EQUISETUM	ERECTIONS
EPITOMISE	EPOXIDIZE	EQUALLY	EQUITABLE	ERECTIVE
EPITOMIST	EPOXIED	EQUALNESS	EQUITABLY	ERECTLY
EPITOMIZE	EPOXIES	EQUALS	EQUITANT	ERECTNESS
EPITONIC	EPOXY	EQUANT	EQUITES	ERECTOR
EPITOPE	EPOXYED	EQUANTS	EQUITIES	ERECTORS
EPITOPES	EPOXYING	EQUATABLE	EQUITY	ERECTS
EPITRITE	EPRIS	EQUATE	EQUIVALVE	ERED
EPITRITES	EPRISE	EQUATED	EQUIVOCAL	ERELONG
EPIZEUXES	EPSILON	EQUATES	EQUIVOKE	EREMIC
EPIZEUXIS	EPSILONIC	EQUATING	EQUIVOKES	EREMITAL
EPIZOA	EPSILONS	EQUATION	EQUIVOQUE	EREMITE
EPIZOAN	EPSOMITE	EQUATIONS	ER	EREMITES

EREMITIC	ERGOTIZED	ERNES	EROTIZE	ERUCTING
EREMITISH	ERGOTIZES	ERNING	EROTIZED	ERUCTS
EREMITISM	ERGOTS	ERNS	EROTIZES	ERUDITE
EREMURI	ERGS	ERODABLE	EROTIZING	ERUDITELY
EREMURUS	ERHU	ERODE	EROTOLOGY	ERUDITES
ERENOW	ERHUS	ERODED	ERR	ERUDITION
EREPSIN	ERIACH	ERODENT	ERRABLE	ERUGO
EREPSINS	ERIACHS	ERODENTS	ERRANCIES	ERUGOS
ERES	ERIC	ERODES	ERRANCY	ERUMPENT
ERETHIC	ERICA	ERODIBLE	ERRAND	ERUPT
ERETHISM	ERICAS	ERODING	ERRANDS	ERUPTED
ERETHISMS	ERICK	ERODIUM	ERRANT	ERUPTIBLE
ERETHITIC	ERICKS	ERODIUMS	ERRANTLY	ERUPTING
EREV	ERICOID	EROGENIC	ERRANTRY	ERUPTION
EREVS	ERICS	EROGENOUS	ERRANTS	ERUPTIONS
EREWHILE	ERIGERON	EROS	ERRATA	ERUPTIVE
EREWHILES	ERIGERONS	EROSE	ERRATAS	ERUPTIVES
ERF	ERING	EROSELY	ERRATIC	ERUPTS
ERG	ERINGO	EROSES	ERRATICAL	ERUV
ERGASTIC	ERINGOES	EROSIBLE	ERRATICS	ERUVIM
ERGATANER	ERINGOS	EROSION	ERRATUM	ERUVIN
ERGATE	ERINITE	EROSIONAL	ERRED	ERUVS
ERGATES	ERINITES	EROSIONS	ERRHINE	ERVALENTA
ERGATIVE	ERINUS	EROSIVE	ERRHINES	ERVEN
ERGATIVES	ERINUSES	EROSIVITY	ERRING	ERVIL
ERGATOID	ERIOMETER	EROSTRATE	ERRINGLY	ERVILS
ERGO	ERIONITE	EROTEMA	ERRINGS	ERYNGIUM
ERGODIC	ERIONITES	EROTEMAS	ERRONEOUS	ERYNGIUMS
ERGOGENIC	ERIOPHYID	EROTEME	ERROR	ERYNGO
ERGOGRAM	ERISTIC	EROTEMES	ERRORIST	ERYNGOES
ERGOGRAMS	ERISTICAL	EROTESES	ERRORISTS	ERYNGOS
ERGOGRAPH	ERISTICS	EROTESIS	ERRORLESS	ERYTHEMA
ERGOMANIA	ERK	EROTETIC	ERRORS	ERYTHEMAL
ERGOMETER	ERKS	EROTIC	ERRS	ERYTHEMAS
ERGOMETRY	ERLANG	EROTICA	ERS	ERYTHEMIC
ERGON	ERLANGS	EROTICAL	ERSATZ	ERYTHRINA
ERGONOMIC	ERLKING	EROTICISE	ERSATZES	ERYTHRISM
ERGONS	ERLKINGS	EROTICISM	ERSES	ERYTHRITE
ERGOS	ERM	EROTICIST	ERST	ERYTHROID
ERGOT	ERMELIN	EROTICIZE	ERSTWHILE	ERYTHRON
ERGOTIC	ERMELINS	EROTICS	ERUCIC	ERYTHRONS
ERGOTISE	ERMINE	EROTISE	ERUCIFORM	ES
ERGOTISED	ERMINED	EROTISED	ERUCT	ESCABECHE
ERGOTISES	ERMINES	EROTISES	ERUCTATE	ESCALADE
ERGOTISM	ERN	EROTISING	ERUCTATED	ESCALADED
ERGOTISMS	ERNE	EROTISM	ERUCTATES	ESCALADER
ERGOTIZE	ERNED	EROTISMS	ERUCTED	ESCALADES

ESCALADO	ESCHEATS	ESERINES	ESPIERS	ESSOINERS
ESCALATE	ESCHEW	ESES	ESPIES	ESSOINS
ESCALATED	ESCHEWAL	ESILE	ESPIONAGE	ESSONITE
ESCALATES	ESCHEWALS	ESILES	ESPLANADE	ESSONITES
ESCALATOR	ESCHEWED	ESKAR	ESPOUSAL	ESSOYNE
ESCALIER	ESCHEWER	ESKARS	ESPOUSALS	ESSOYNES
ESCALIERS	ESCHEWERS	ESKER	ESPOUSE	EST
ESCALLOP	ESCHEWING	ESKERS	ESPOUSED	ESTABLISH
ESCALLOPS	ESCHEWS	ESKIES	ESPOUSER	ESTACADE
ESCALOP	ESCLANDRE	ESKY	ESPOUSERS	ESTACADES
ESCALOPE	ESCOLAR	ESLOIN	ESPOUSES	ESTAFETTE
ESCALOPED	ESCOLARS	ESLOINED	ESPOUSING	ESTAMINET
ESCALOPES	ESCOPETTE	ESLOINING	ESPRESSO	ESTANCIA
ESCALOPS	ESCORT	ESLOINS	ESPRESSOS	ESTANCIAS
ESCAPABLE	ESCORTAGE	ESLOYNE	ESPRIT	ESTATE
ESCAPADE	ESCORTED	ESLOYNED	ESPRITS	ESTATED
ESCAPADES	ESCORTING	ESLOYNES	ESPUMOSO	ESTATES
ESCAPADO	ESCORTS	ESLOYNING	ESPUMOSOS	ESTATING
ESCAPE	ESCOT	ESNE	ESPY	ESTEEM
ESCAPED	ESCOTED	ESNECIES	ESPYING	ESTEEMED
ESCAPEE	ESCOTING	ESNECY	ESQUIRE	ESTEEMING
ESCAPEES	ESCOTS	ESNES	ESQUIRED	ESTEEMS
ESCAPER	ESCOTTED	ESOPHAGI	ESQUIRES	ESTER
ESCAPERS	ESCOTTING	ESOPHAGUS	ESQUIRESS	ESTERASE
ESCAPES	ESCRIBANO	ESOTERIC	ESQUIRING	ESTERASES
ESCAPING	ESCRIBE	ESOTERICA	ESQUISSE	ESTERIFY
ESCAPISM	ESCRIBED	ESOTERIES	ESQUISSES	ESTERS
ESCAPISMS	ESCRIBES	ESOTERISM	ESS	ESTHESES
ESCAPIST	ESCRIBING	ESOTERY	ESSAY	ESTHESIA
ESCAPISTS	ESCROC	ESOTROPIA	ESSAYED	ESTHESIAS
ESCAR	ESCROCS	ESOTROPIC	ESSAYER	ESTHESIS
ESCARGOT	ESCROL	ESPADA	ESSAYERS	ESTHETE
ESCARGOTS	ESCROLL	ESPADAS	ESSAYETTE	ESTHETES
ESCAROLE	ESCROLLS	ESPAGNOLE	ESSAYING	ESTHETIC
ESCAROLES	ESCROLS	ESPALIER	ESSAYISH	ESTHETICS
ESCARP	ESCROW	ESPALIERS	ESSAYIST	ESTIMABLE
ESCARPED	ESCROWED	ESPANOL	ESSAYISTS	ESTIMABLY
ESCARPING	ESCROWING	ESPANOLES	ESSAYS	ESTIMATE
ESCARPS	ESCROWS	ESPARTO	ESSE	ESTIMATED
ESCARS	ESCUAGE	ESPARTOS	ESSENCE	ESTIMATES
ESCHALOT	ESCUAGES	ESPECIAL	ESSENCES	ESTIMATOR
ESCHALOTS	ESCUDO	ESPERANCE	ESSENTIAL	ESTIVAL
ESCHAR	ESCUDOS	ESPIAL	ESSES	ESTIVATE
ESCHARS	ESCULENT	ESPIALS	ESSIVE	ESTIVATED
ESCHEAT	ESCULENTS	ESPIED	ESSIVES	ESTIVATES
ESCHEATED	ESEMPLASY	ESPIEGLE	ESSOIN	ESTIVATOR
ESCHEATOR	ESERINE	ESPIER	ESSOINER	ESTOC

ESTOCS	ESTRONES	ETCETERA	ETHEREAL	ETHMOIDAL
ESTOILE	ESTROS	ETCETERAS	ETHEREOUS	ETHMOIDS
ESTOILES	ESTROUS	ETCH	ETHERIAL	ETHNARCH
ESTOP	ESTRUAL	ETCHANT	ETHERIC	ETHNARCHS
ESTOPPAGE	ESTRUM	ETCHANTS	ETHERICAL	ETHNARCHY
ESTOPPED	ESTRUMS	ETCHED	ETHERIFY	ETHNIC
ESTOPPEL	ESTRUS	ETCHER	ETHERION	ETHNICAL
ESTOPPELS	ESTRUSES	ETCHERS	ETHERIONS	ETHNICISM
ESTOPPING	ESTS	ETCHES	ETHERISE	ETHNICITY
ESTOPS	ESTUARIAL	ETCHING	ETHERISED	ETHNICS
ESTOVER	ESTUARIAN	ETCHINGS	ETHERISER	ETHNOCIDE
ESTOVERS	ESTUARIES	ETEN	ETHERISES	ETHNOGENY
ESTRADE	ESTUARINE	ETENS	ETHERISH	ETHNOLOGY
ESTRADES	ESTUARY	ETERNAL	ETHERISM	ETHNONYM
ESTRADIOL	ESURIENCE	ETERNALLY	ETHERISMS	ETHNONYMS
ESTRAGON	ESURIENCY	ETERNALS	ETHERIST	ETHNOS
ESTRAGONS	ESURIENT	ETERNE	ETHERISTS	ETHNOSES
ESTRAL	ET	ETERNISE	ETHERIZE	ETHOGRAM
ESTRANGE	ETA	ETERNISED	ETHERIZED	ETHOGRAMS
ESTRANGED	ETACISM	ETERNISES	ETHERIZER	ETHOLOGIC
ESTRANGER	ETACISMS	ETERNITY	ETHERIZES	ETHOLOGY
ESTRANGES	ETAERIO	ETERNIZE	ETHERS	ETHONONE
ESTRAPADE	ETAERIOS	ETERNIZED	ETHIC	ETHONONES
ESTRAY	ETAGE	ETERNIZES	ETHICAL	ETHOS
ESTRAYED	ETAGERE	ETESIAN	ETHICALLY	ETHOSES
ESTRAYING	ETAGERES	ETESIANS	ETHICALS	ETHOXIDE
ESTRAYS	ETAGES	ETH	ETHICIAN	ETHOXIDES
ESTREAT	ETALAGE	ETHAL	ETHICIANS	ETHOXIES
ESTREATED	ETALAGES	ETHALS	ETHICISE	ETHOXY
ESTREATS	ETALON	ETHANAL	ETHICISED	ETHOXYL
ESTREPE	ETALONS	ETHANALS	ETHICISES	ETHOXYLS
ESTREPED	ETAMIN	ETHANE	ETHICISM	ETHS
ESTREPES	ETAMINE	ETHANES	ETHICISMS	ETHYL
ESTREPING	ETAMINES	ETHANOATE	ETHICIST	ETHYLATE
ESTRICH	ETAMINS	ETHANOIC	ETHICISTS	ETHYLATED
ESTRICHES	ETAPE	ETHANOL	ETHICIZE	ETHYLATES
ESTRIDGE	ETAPES	ETHANOLS	ETHICIZED	ETHYLENE
ESTRIDGES	ETAS	ETHANOYL	ETHICIZES	ETHYLENES
ESTRILDID	ETAT	ETHANOYLS	ETHICS	ETHYLENIC
ESTRIN	ETATISM	ETHE	ETHINYL	ETHYLIC
ESTRINS	ETATISME	ETHENE	ETHINYLS	ETHYLS
ESTRIOL	ETATISMES	ETHENES	ETHION	ETHYNE
ESTRIOLS	ETATISMS	ETHEPHON	ETHIONINE	ETHYNES
ESTRO	ETATIST	ETHEPHONS	ETHIONS	ETHYNYL
ESTROGEN	ETATISTE	ETHER	ETHIOPS	ETHYNYLS
ESTROGENS	ETATISTES	ETHERCAP	ETHIOPSES	ETIC
ESTRONE	ETATS	ETHERCAPS	ETHMOID	ETIOLATE

E

ETIOLATED	EUCALYPT	EUGENOL	EUNUCH	EUPHOTIC
ETIOLATES	EUCALYPTI	EUGENOLS	EUNUCHISE	EUPHRASIA
ETIOLIN	EUCALYPTS	EUGH	EUNUCHISM	EUPHRASY
ETIOLINS	EUCARYON	EUGHEN	EUNUCHIZE	EUPHROE
ETIOLOGIC	EUCARYONS	EUGHS	EUNUCHOID	EUPHROES
ETIOLOGY	EUCARYOT	EUGLENA	EUNUCHS	EUPHUISE
ETIQUETTE	EUCARYOTE	EUGLENAS	EUOI	EUPHUISED
ETNA	EUCARYOTS	EUGLENID	EUONYMIN	EUPHUISES
ETNAS	EUCHARIS	EUGLENIDS	EUONYMINS	EUPHUISM
ETOILE	EUCHLORIC	EUGLENOID	EUONYMUS	EUPHUISMS
ETOILES	EUCHLORIN	EUK	EUOUAE	EUPHUIST
ETOUFFEE	EUCHOLOGY	EUKARYON	EUOUAES	EUPHUISTS
ETOUFFEES	EUCHRE	EUKARYONS	EUPAD	EUPHUIZE
ETOURDI	EUCHRED	EUKARYOT	EUPADS	EUPHUIZED
ETOURDIE	EUCHRES	EUKARYOTE	EUPATRID	EUPHUIZES
ETRANGER	EUCHRING	EUKARYOTS	EUPATRIDS	EUPLASTIC
ETRANGERE	EUCLASE	EUKED	EUPEPSIA	EUPLOID
ETRANGERS	EUCLASES	EUKING	EUPEPSIAS	EUPLOIDS
ETRENNE	EUCLIDEAN	EUKS	EUPEPSIES	EUPLOIDY
ETRENNES	EUCLIDIAN	EULACHAN	EUPEPSY	EUPNEA
ETRIER	EUCRITE	EULACHANS	EUPEPTIC	EUPNEAS
ETRIERS	EUCRITES	EULACHON	EUPHAUSID	EUPNEIC
ETTERCAP	EUCRITIC	EULACHONS	EUPHEMISE	EUPNOEA
ETTERCAPS	EUCRYPHIA	EULOGIA	EUPHEMISM	EUPNOEAS
ETTIN	EUCYCLIC	EULOGIAE	EUPHEMIST	EUPNOEIC
ETTINS	EUDAEMON	EULOGIAS	EUPHEMIZE	EUREKA
ETTLE	EUDAEMONS	EULOGIES	EUPHENIC	EUREKAS
ETTLED	EUDAEMONY	EULOGISE	EUPHENICS	EURHYTHMY
ETTLES	EUDAIMON	EULOGISED	EUPHOBIA	EURIPI
ETTLING	EUDAIMONS	EULOGISER	EUPHOBIAS	EURIPUS
ETUDE	EUDEMON	EULOGISES	EUPHON	EURIPUSES
ETUDES	EUDEMONIA	EULOGIST	EUPHONIA	EURO
ETUI	EUDEMONIC	EULOGISTS	EUPHONIAS	EUROBOND
ETUIS	EUDEMONS	EULOGIUM	EUPHONIC	EUROBONDS
ETWEE	EUDIALYTE	EULOGIUMS	EUPHONIES	EUROCRAT
ETWEES	EUGARIE	EULOGIZE	EUPHONISE	EUROCRATS
ETYMA	EUGARIES	EULOGIZED	EUPHONISM	EUROCREEP
ETYMIC	EUGE	EULOGIZER	EUPHONIUM	EUROKIES
ETYMOLOGY	EUGENIA	EULOGIZES	EUPHONIZE	EUROKOUS
ETYMON	EUGENIAS	EULOGY	EUPHONS	EUROKY
ETYMONS	EUGENIC	EUMELANIN	EUPHONY	EURONOTE
ETYPIC	EUGENICAL	EUMERISM	EUPHORBIA	EURONOTES
ETYPICAL	EUGENICS	EUMERISMS	EUPHORIA	EUROPHILE
EUCAIN	EUGENISM	EUMONG	EUPHORIAS	EUROPIUM
EUCAINE	EUGENISMS	EUMONGS	EUPHORIC	EUROPIUMS
EUCAINES	EUGENIST	EUMUNG	EUPHORIES	EUROPOP
EUCAINS	EUGENISTS	EUMUNGS	EUPHORY	EUROPOPS

EUROS	EUTROPHY	EVASIONS	EVERTED	EVINCE
EURYBATH	EUTROPIC	EVASIVE	EVERTING	EVINCED
EURYBATHS	EUTROPIES	EVASIVELY	EVERTOR	EVINCES
EURYOKIES	EUTROPOUS	EVE	EVERTORS	EVINCIBLE
EURYOKOUS	EUTROPY	EVECTION	EVERTS	EVINCIBLY
EURYOKY	EUXENITE	EVECTIONS	EVERWHERE	EVINCING
EURYTHERM	EUXENITES	EVEJAR	EVERWHICH	EVINCIVE
EURYTHMIC	EVACUANT	EVEJARS	EVERY	EVIRATE
EURYTHMY	EVACUANTS	EVEN	EVERYBODY	EVIRATED
EURYTOPIC	EVACUATE	EVENED	EVERYDAY	EVIRATES
EUSOCIAL	EVACUATED	EVENEMENT	EVERYDAYS	EVIRATING
EUSOL	EVACUATES	EVENER	EVERYMAN	EVITABLE
EUSOLS	EVACUATOR	EVENERS	EVERYMEN	EVITATE
EUSTACIES	EVACUEE	EVENEST	EVERYONE	EVITATED
EUSTACY	EVACUEES	EVENFALL	EVERYWAY	EVITATES
EUSTASIES	EVADABLE	EVENFALLS	EVERYWHEN	EVITATING
EUSTASY	EVADE	EVENING	EVES	EVITATION
EUSTATIC	EVADED	EVENINGS	EVET	EVITE
EUSTELE	EVADER	EVENLY	EVETS	EVITED
EUSTELES	EVADERS	EVENNESS	EVHOE	EVITERNAL
EUSTYLE	EVADES	EVENS	EVICT	EVITES
EUSTYLES	EVADIBLE	EVENSONG	EVICTED	EVITING
EUTAXIA	EVADING	EVENSONGS	EVICTEE	EVO
EUTAXIAS	EVADINGLY	EVENT	EVICTEES	EVOCABLE
EUTAXIES	EVAGATION	EVENTED	EVICTING	EVOCATE
EUTAXITE	EVAGINATE	EVENTER	EVICTION	EVOCATED
EUTAXITES	EVALUABLE	EVENTERS	EVICTIONS	EVOCATES
EUTAXITIC	EVALUATE	EVENTFUL	EVICTOR	EVOCATING
EUTAXY	EVALUATED	EVENTIDE	EVICTORS	EVOCATION
EUTECTIC	EVALUATES	EVENTIDES	EVICTS	EVOCATIVE
EUTECTICS	EVALUATOR	EVENTING	EVIDENCE	EVOCATOR
EUTECTOID	EVANESCE	EVENTINGS	EVIDENCED	EVOCATORS
EUTEXIA	EVANESCED	EVENTLESS	EVIDENCES	EVOCATORY
EUTEXIAS	EVANESCES	EVENTRATE	EVIDENT	EVOE
EUTHANASE	EVANGEL	EVENTS	EVIDENTLY	EVOHE
EUTHANASY	EVANGELIC	EVENTUAL	EVIDENTS	EVOKE
EUTHANAZE	EVANGELS	EVENTUATE	EVIL	EVOKED
EUTHANISE	EVANGELY	EVER	EVILDOER	EVOKER
EUTHANIZE	EVANISH	EVERGLADE	EVILDOERS	EVOKERS
EUTHENICS	EVANISHED	EVERGREEN	EVILDOING	EVOKES
EUTHENIST	EVANISHES	EVERMORE	EVILER	EVOKING
EUTHERIAN	EVANITION	EVERNET	EVILEST	EVOLUE
EUTHYMIA	EVAPORATE	EVERNETS	EVILLER	EVOLUES
EUTHYMIAS	EVAPORITE	EVERSIBLE	EVILLEST	EVOLUTE
EUTHYROID	EVASIBLE	EVERSION	EVILLY	EVOLUTED
EUTRAPELY	EVASION	EVERSIONS	EVILNESS	EVOLUTES
EUTROPHIC	EVASIONAL	EVERT	EVILS	EVOLUTING

EVOLUTION	EXACTER	EXAPTED	EXCERPTED	EXCITON
EVOLUTIVE	EXACTERS	EXAPTIVE	EXCERPTER	EXCITONIC
EVOLVABLE	EXACTEST	EXARATE	EXCERPTOR	EXCITONS
EVOLVE	EXACTING	EXARATION	EXCERPTS	EXCITOR
EVOLVED	EXACTION	EXARCH	EXCERPTUM	EXCITORS
EVOLVENT	EXACTIONS	EXARCHAL	EXCESS	EXCLAIM
EVOLVER	EXACTLY	EXARCHATE	EXCESSED	EXCLAIMED
EVOLVERS	EXACTMENT	EXARCHIES	EXCESSES	EXCLAIMER
EVOLVES	EXACTNESS	EXARCHIST	EXCESSING	EXCLAIMS
EVOLVING	EXACTOR	EXARCHS	EXCESSIVE	EXCLAVE
EVONYMUS	EXACTORS	EXARCHY	EXCHANGE	EXCLAVES
EVOS	EXACTRESS	EXCAMB	EXCHANGED	EXCLOSURE
EVOVAE	EXACTS	EXCAMBED	EXCHANGER	EXCLUDE
EVOVAES	EXACUM	EXCAMBING	EXCHANGES	EXCLUDED
EVULGATE	EXACUMS	EXCAMBION	EXCHEAT	EXCLUDEE
EVULGATED	EXAHERTZ	EXCAMBIUM	EXCHEATS	EXCLUDEES
EVULGATES	EXALT	EXCAMBS	EXCHEQUER	EXCLUDER
EVULSE	EXALTED	EXCARNATE	EXCIDE	EXCLUDERS
EVULSED	EXALTEDLY	EXCAUDATE	EXCIDED	EXCLUDES
EVULSES	EXALTER	EXCAVATE	EXCIDES	EXCLUDING
EVULSING	EXALTERS	EXCAVATED	EXCIDING	EXCLUSION
EVULSION	EXALTING	EXCAVATES	EXCIMER	EXCLUSIVE
EVULSIONS	EXALTS	EXCAVATOR	EXCIMERS	EXCLUSORY
EVZONE	EXAM	EXCEED	EXCIPIENT	EXCORIATE
EVZONES	EXAMEN	EXCEEDED	EXCIPLE	EXCREMENT
EWE	EXAMENS	EXCEEDER	EXCIPLES	EXCRETA
EWER	EXAMINANT	EXCEEDERS	EXCISABLE	EXCRETAL
EWERS	EXAMINATE	EXCEEDING	EXCISE	EXCRETE
EWES	EXAMINE	EXCEEDS	EXCISED	EXCRETED
EWEST	EXAMINED	EXCEL	EXCISEMAN	EXCRETER
EWFTES	EXAMINEE	EXCELLED	EXCISEMEN	EXCRETERS
EWGHEN	EXAMINEES	EXCELLENT	EXCISES	EXCRETES
EWHOW	EXAMINER	EXCELLING	EXCISING	EXCRETING
EWK	EXAMINERS	EXCELS	EXCISION	EXCRETION
EWKED	EXAMINES	EXCELSIOR	EXCISIONS	EXCRETIVE
EWKING	EXAMINING	EXCENTRIC	EXCITABLE	EXCRETORY
EWKS	EXAMPLAR	EXCEPT	EXCITABLY	EXCUBANT
EWT	EXAMPLARS	EXCEPTANT	EXCITANCY	EXCUDIT
EWTS	EXAMPLE	EXCEPTED	EXCITANT	EXCULPATE
EX	EXAMPLED	EXCEPTING	EXCITANTS	EXCURRENT
EXABYTE	EXAMPLES	EXCEPTION	EXCITE	EXCURSE
EXABYTES	EXAMPLING	EXCEPTIVE	EXCITED	EXCURSED
EXACT	EXAMS	EXCEPTOR	EXCITEDLY	EXCURSES
EXACTA	EXANIMATE	EXCEPTORS	EXCITER	EXCURSING
EXACTABLE	EXANTHEM	EXCEPTS	EXCITERS	EXCURSION
EXACTAS	EXANTHEMA	EXCERPT	EXCITES	EXCURSIVE
EXACTED	EXANTHEMS	EXCERPTA	EXCITING	EXCURSUS

EXCUSABLE	EXEGETIC	EXHALABLE	EXILABLE	EXODOI
EXCUSABLY	EXEGETICS	EXHALANT	EXILE	EXODONTIA
EXCUSAL	EXEGETIST	EXHALANTS	EXILED	EXODOS
EXCUSALS	EXEME	EXHALE	EXILEMENT	EXODUS
EXCUSE	EXEMED	EXHALED	EXILER	EXODUSES
EXCUSED	EXEMES	EXHALENT	EXILERS	EXOENZYME
EXCUSER	EXEMING	EXHALENTS	EXILES	EXOERGIC
EXCUSERS	EXEMPLA	EXHALES	EXILIAN	EXOGAMIC
EXCUSES	EXEMPLAR	EXHALING	EXILIC	EXOGAMIES
EXCUSING	EXEMPLARS	EXHAUST	EXILING	EXOGAMOUS
EXCUSIVE	EXEMPLARY	EXHAUSTED	EXILITIES	EXOGAMY
EXEAT	EXEMPLE	EXHAUSTER	EXILITY	EXOGEN
EXEATS	EXEMPLES	EXHAUSTS	EXIMIOUS	EXOGENISM
EXEC	EXEMPLIFY	EXHEDRA	EXINE	EXOGENOUS
EXECRABLE	EXEMPLUM	EXHEDRAE	EXINES	EXOGENS
EXECRABLY	EXEMPT	EXHIBIT	EXING	EXOMION
EXECRATE	EXEMPTED	EXHIBITED	EXIST	EXOMIONS
EXECRATED	EXEMPTING	EXHIBITER	EXISTED	EXOMIS
EXECRATES	EXEMPTION	EXHIBITOR	EXISTENCE	EXOMISES
EXECRATOR	EXEMPTIVE	EXHIBITS	EXISTENT	EXON
EXECS	EXEMPTS	EXHORT	EXISTENTS	EXONERATE
EXECUTANT	EXEQUATUR	EXHORTED	EXISTING	EXONIC
EXECUTARY	EXEQUIAL	EXHORTER	EXISTS	EXONS
EXECUTE	EXEQUIES	EXHORTERS	EXIT	EXONUMIA
EXECUTED	EXEQUY	EXHORTING	EXITANCE	EXONUMIST
EXECUTER	EXERCISE	EXHORTS	EXITANCES	EXONYM
EXECUTERS	EXERCISED	EXHUMATE	EXITED	EXONYMS
EXECUTES	EXERCISER	EXHUMATED	EXITING	EXOPHAGY
EXECUTING	EXERCISES	EXHUMATES	EXITLESS	EXOPHORIC
EXECUTION	EXERCYCLE	EXHUME	EXITS	EXOPLANET
EXECUTIVE	EXERGIES	EXHUMED	EXO	EXOPLASM
EXECUTOR	EXERGONIC	EXHUMER	EXOCARP	EXOPLASMS
EXECUTORS	EXERGUAL	EXHUMERS	EXOCARPS	EXOPOD
EXECUTORY	EXERGUE	EXHUMES	EXOCRINE	EXOPODITE
EXECUTRIX	EXERGUES	EXHUMING	EXOCRINES	EXOPODS
EXECUTRY	EXERGY	EXIES	EXOCYCLIC	EXORABLE
EXED	EXERT	EXIGEANT	EXOCYTIC	EXORATION
EXEDRA	EXERTED	EXIGEANTE	EXOCYTOSE	EXORCISE
EXEDRAE	EXERTING	EXIGENCE	EXODE	EXORCISED
EXEEM	EXERTION	EXIGENCES	EXODERM	EXORCISER
EXEEMED	EXERTIONS	EXIGENCY	EXODERMAL	EXORCISES
EXEEMING	EXERTIVE	EXIGENT	EXODERMIS	EXORCISM
EXEEMS	EXERTS	EXIGENTLY	EXODERMS	EXORCISMS
EXEGESES	EXES	EXIGENTS	EXODES	EXORCIST
EXEGESIS	EXEUNT	EXIGIBLE	EXODIC	EXORCISTS
EXEGETE	EXFOLIANT	EXIGUITY	EXODIST	EXORCIZE
EXEGETES	EXFOLIATE	EXIGUOUS	EXODISTS	EXORCIZED

EXORCIZER	EXPECTED	EXPIRABLE	EXPORTERS	EXPUNGING
EXORCIZES	EXPECTER	EXPIRANT	EXPORTING	EXPURGATE
EXORDIA	EXPECTERS	EXPIRANTS	EXPORTS	EXPURGE
EXORDIAL	EXPECTING	EXPIRE	EXPOS	EXPURGED
EXORDIUM	EXPECTS	EXPIRED	EXPOSABLE	EXPURGES
EXORDIUMS	EXPEDIENT	EXPIRER	EXPOSAL	EXPURGING
EXOSMIC	EXPEDITE	EXPIRERS	EXPOSALS	EXQUISITE
EXOSMOSE	EXPEDITED	EXPIRES	EXPOSE	EXSCIND
EXOSMOSES	EXPEDITER	EXPIRIES	EXPOSED	EXSCINDED
EXOSMOSIS	EXPEDITES	EXPIRING	EXPOSER	EXSCINDS
EXOSMOTIC	EXPEDITOR	EXPIRY	EXPOSERS	EXSECANT
EXOSPHERE	EXPEL	EXPISCATE	EXPOSES	EXSECANTS
EXOSPORAL	EXPELLANT	EXPLAIN	EXPOSING	EXSECT
EXOSPORE	EXPELLED	EXPLAINED	EXPOSIT	EXSECTED
EXOSPORES	EXPELLEE	EXPLAINER	EXPOSITED	EXSECTING
EXOSPORIA	EXPELLEES	EXPLAINS	EXPOSITOR	EXSECTION
EXOSTOSES	EXPELLENT	EXPLANT	EXPOSITS	EXSECTS
EXOSTOSIS	EXPELLER	EXPLANTED	EXPOSTURE	EXSERT
EXOTERIC	EXPELLERS	EXPLANTS	EXPOSURE	EXSERTED
EXOTIC	EXPELLING	EXPLETIVE	EXPOSURES	EXSERTILE
EXOTICA	EXPELS	EXPLETORY	EXPOUND	EXSERTING
EXOTICISM	EXPEND	EXPLICATE	EXPOUNDED	EXSERTION
EXOTICIST	EXPENDED	EXPLICIT	EXPOUNDER	EXSERTS
EXOTICS	EXPENDER	EXPLICITS	EXPOUNDS	EXSICCANT
EXOTISM	EXPENDERS	EXPLODE	EXPRESS	EXSICCATE
EXOTISMS	EXPENDING	EXPLODED	EXPRESSED	EXSTROPHY
EXOTOXIC	EXPENDS	EXPLODER	EXPRESSER	EXSUCCOUS
EXOTOXIN	EXPENSE	EXPLODERS	EXPRESSES	EXTANT
EXOTOXINS	EXPENSED	EXPLODES	EXPRESSLY	EXTASIES
EXOTROPIA	EXPENSES	EXPLODING	EXPRESSO	EXTASY
EXOTROPIC	EXPENSING	EXPLOIT	EXPRESSOS	EXTATIC
EXPAND	EXPENSIVE	EXPLOITED	EXPUGN	EXTEMPORE
EXPANDED	EXPERT	EXPLOITER	EXPUGNED	EXTEND
EXPANDER	EXPERTED	EXPLOITS	EXPUGNING	EXTENDANT
EXPANDERS	EXPERTING	EXPLORE	EXPUGNS	EXTENDED
EXPANDING	EXPERTISE	EXPLORED	EXPULSE	EXTENDER
EXPANDOR	EXPERTISM	EXPLORER	EXPULSED	EXTENDERS
EXPANDORS	EXPERTIZE	EXPLORERS	EXPULSES	EXTENDING
EXPANDS	EXPERTLY	EXPLORES	EXPULSING	EXTENDS
EXPANSE	EXPERTS	EXPLORING	EXPULSION	EXTENSE
EXPANSES	EXPIABLE	EXPLOSION	EXPULSIVE	EXTENSILE
EXPANSILE	EXPIATE	EXPLOSIVE	EXPUNCT	EXTENSION
EXPANSION	EXPIATED	EXPO	EXPUNCTED	EXTENSITY
EXPANSIVE	EXPIATES	EXPONENT	EXPUNCTS	EXTENSIVE
EXPAT	EXPIATING	EXPONENTS	EXPUNGE	EXTENSOR
EXPATIATE	EXPIATION	EXPONIBLE	EXPUNGED	EXTENSORS
EXPATS	EXPIATOR	EXPORT	EXPUNGER	EXTENT
EXPECT	EXPIATORS	EXPORTED	EXPUNGERS	EXTENTS
EXPECTANT	EXPIATORY	EXPORTER	EXPUNGES	EXTENUATE

EXTERIOR	EXTRAIT	EXUDED	EYEBOLTS	EYES
EXTERIORS	EXTRAITS	EXUDES	EYEBRIGHT	EYESHADE
EXTERMINE	EXTRALITY	EXUDING	EYEBROW	EYESHADES
EXTERN	EXTRANET	EXUL	EYEBROWED	EYESHADOW
EXTERNAL	EXTRANETS	EXULS	EYEBROWS	EYESHINE
EXTERNALS	EXTRAPOSE	EXULT	EYECUP	EYESHINES
EXTERNAT	EXTRAS	EXULTANCE	EYECUPS	EYESHOT
EXTERNATS	EXTRAUGHT	EXULTANCY	EYED	EYESHOTS
EXTERNE	EXTRAVERT	EXULTANT	EYEDNESS	EYESIGHT
EXTERNES	EXTREAT	EXULTED	EYEDROPS	EYESIGHTS
EXTERNS	EXTREATS	EXULTING	EYEFOLD	EYESOME
EXTINCT	EXTREMA	EXULTS	EYEFOLDS	EYESORE
EXTINCTED	EXTREMAL	EXURB	EYEFUL	EYESORES
EXTINCTS	EXTREMALS	EXURBAN	EYEFULS	EYESPOT
EXTINE	EXTREME	EXURBIA	EYEGLASS	EYESPOTS
EXTINES	EXTREMELY	EXURBIAS	EYEHOLE	EYESTALK
EXTIRP	EXTREMER	EXURBS	EYEHOLES	EYESTALKS
EXTIRPATE	EXTREMES	EXUVIA	EYEHOOK	EYESTONE
EXTIRPED	EXTREMEST	EXUVIAE	EYEHOOKS	EYESTONES
EXTIRPING	EXTREMISM	EXUVIAL	EYEING	EYESTRAIN
EXTIRPS	EXTREMIST	EXUVIATE	EYELASH	EYETEETH
EXTOL	EXTREMITY	EXUVIATED	EYELASHES	EYETOOTH
EXTOLD	EXTREMUM	EXUVIATES	EYELESS	EYEWASH
EXTOLL	EXTRICATE	EXUVIUM	EYELET	EYEWASHES
EXTOLLED	EXTRINSIC	EYALET	EYELETED	EYEWATER
EXTOLLER	EXTRORSAL	EYALETS	EYELETEER	EYEWATERS
EXTOLLERS	EXTRORSE	EYAS	EYELETING	EYEWEAR
EXTOLLING	EXTROVERT	EYASES	EYELETS	EYEWEARS
EXTOLLS	EXTRUDE	EYASS	EYELETTED	EYEWINK
EXTOLMENT	EXTRUDED	EYASSES	EYELEVEL	EYEWINKS
EXTOLS	EXTRUDER	EYE	EYELIAD	EYING
EXTORSIVE	EXTRUDERS	EYEABLE	EYELIADS	EYLIAD
EXTORT	EXTRUDES	EYEBALL	EYELID	EYLIADS
EXTORTED	EXTRUDING	EYEBALLED	EYELIDS	EYNE
EXTORTER	EXTRUSILE	EYEBALLS	EYELIFT	EYOT
EXTORTERS	EXTRUSION	EYEBANK	EYELIFTS	EYOTS
EXTORTING	EXTRUSIVE	EYEBANKS	EYELIKE	EYRA
EXTORTION	EXTRUSORY	EYEBAR	EYELINER	EYRAS
EXTORTIVE	EXTUBATE	EYEBARS	EYELINERS	EYRE
EXTORTS	EXTUBATED	EYEBATH	EYEN	EYRES
EXTRA	EXTUBATES	EYEBATHS	EYEOPENER	EYRIE
EXTRABOLD	EXUBERANT	EYEBEAM	EYEPIECE	EYRIES
EXTRACT	EXUBERATE	EYEBEAMS	EYEPIECES	EYRIR
EXTRACTED	EXUDATE	EYEBLACK	EYEPOINT	EYRY
EXTRACTOR	EXUDATES	EYEBLACKS	EYEPOINTS	
EXTRACTS	EXUDATION	EYEBLINK	EYEPOPPER	
EXTRADITE	EXUDATIVE	EYEBLINKS	EYER	
EXTRADOS	EXUDE	EYEBOLT	EYERS	

F

FA	FACE	FACILE	FACULAE	FADING
FAA	FACEABLE	FACILELY	FACULAR	FADINGS
FAAING	FACEBAR	FACILITY	FACULTIES	FADLIKE
FAAN	FACEBARS	FACING	FACULTY	FADO
FAAS	FACEBOOK	FACINGS	FACUNDITY	FADOMETER
FAB	FACEBOOKS	FACONNE	FAD	FADOS
FABACEOUS	FACECLOTH	FACONNES	FADABLE	FADS
FABBER	FACED	FACSIMILE	FADAISE	FADY
FABBEST	FACEDOWN	FACT	FADAISES	FAE
FABBIER	FACEDOWNS	FACTFUL	FADDIER	FAECAL
FABBIEST	FACELESS	FACTICE	FADDIEST	FAECES
FABBY	FACELIFT	FACTICES	FADDINESS	FAENA
FABLE	FACELIFTS	FACTICITY	FADDISH	FAENAS
FABLED	FACEMAIL	FACTION	FADDISHLY	FAERIE
FABLER	FACEMAILS	FACTIONAL	FADDISM	FAERIES
FABLERS	FACEMAN	FACTIONS	FADDISMS	FAERY
FABLES	FACEMASK	FACTIOUS	FADDIST	FAFF
FABLIAU	FACEMASKS	FACTIS	FADDISTS	FAFFED
FABLIAUX	FACEMEN	FACTISES	FADDLE	FAFFING
FABLING	FACEPLATE	FACTITIVE	FADDLED	FAFFS
FABLINGS	FACEPRINT	FACTIVE	FADDLES	FAG
FABRIC	FACER	FACTOID	FADDLING	FAGACEOUS
FABRICANT	FACERS	FACTOIDAL	FADDY	FAGGED
FABRICATE	FACES	FACTOIDS	FADE	FAGGERIES
FABRICKED	FACET	FACTOR	FADEAWAY	FAGGERY
FABRICS	FACETE	FACTORAGE	FADEAWAYS	FAGGIER
FABS	FACETED	FACTORED	FADED	FAGGIEST
FABULAR	FACETELY	FACTORIAL	FADEDLY	FAGGING
FABULATE	FACETIAE	FACTORIES	FADEDNESS	FAGGINGS
FABULATED	FACETING	FACTORING	FADEIN	FAGGOT
FABULATES	FACETIOUS	FACTORISE	FADEINS	FAGGOTED
FABULATOR	FACETS	FACTORIZE	FADELESS	FAGGOTING
FABULISE	FACETTED	FACTORS	FADEOUT	FAGGOTRY
FABULISED	FACETTING	FACTORY	FADEOUTS	FAGGOTS
FABULISES	FACEUP	FACTOTUM	FADER	FAGGOTY
FABULIST	FACIA	FACTOTUMS	FADERS	FAGGY
FABULISTS	FACIAE	FACTS	FADES	FAGIN
FABULIZE	FACIAL	FACTSHEET	FADEUR	FAGINS
FABULIZED	FACIALIST	FACTUAL	FADEURS	FAGOT
FABULIZES	FACIALLY	FACTUALLY	FADGE	FAGOTED
FABULOUS	FACIALS	FACTUM	FADGED	FAGOTER
FABURDEN	FACIAS	FACTUMS	FADGES	FAGOTERS
FABURDENS	FACIEND	FACTURE	FADGING	FAGOTING
FACADE	FACIENDS	FACTURES	FADIER	FAGOTINGS
FACADES	FACIES	FACULA	FADIEST	FAGOTS

FAGOTTI	FAINS	FAITHERS	FALCHION	FALLOUT
FAGOTTIST	FAINT	FAITHFUL	FALCHIONS	FALLOUTS
FAGOTTO	FAINTED	FAITHFULS	FALCIFORM	FALLOW
FAGS	FAINTER	FAITHING	FALCON	FALLOWED
FAH	FAINTERS	FAITHLESS	FALCONER	FALLOWER
FAHLBAND	FAINTEST	FAITHS	FALCONERS	FALLOWEST
FAHLBANDS	FAINTIER	FAITOR	FALCONET	FALLOWING
FAHLERZ	FAINTIEST	FAITORS	FALCONETS	FALLOWS
FAHLERZES	FAINTING	FAITOUR	FALCONINE	FALLS
FAHLORE	FAINTINGS	FAITOURS	FALCONOID	FALSE
FAHLORES	FAINTISH	FAIX	FALCONRY	FALSED
FAHS	FAINTLY	FAJITA	FALCONS	FALSEFACE
FAIBLE	FAINTNESS	FAJITAS	FALCULA	FALSEHOOD
FAIBLES	FAINTS	FAKE	FALCULAE	FALSELY
FAIENCE	FAINTY	FAKED	FALCULAS	FALSENESS
FAIENCES	FAIR	FAKEER	FALCULATE	FALSER
FAIK	FAIRED	FAKEERS	FALDAGE	FALSERS
FAIKED	FAIRER	FAKEMENT	FALDAGES	FALSES
FAIKES	FAIREST	FAKEMENTS	FALDERAL	FALSEST
FAIKING	FAIRFACED	FAKER	FALDERALS	FALSETTO
FAIKS	FAIRGOER	FAKERIES	FALDEROL	FALSETTOS
FAIL	FAIRGOERS	FAKERS	FALDEROLS	FALSEWORK
FAILED	FAIRIES	FAKERY	FALDETTA	FALSIE
FAILING	FAIRILY	FAKES	FALDETTAS	FALSIES
FAILINGLY	FAIRING	FAKEY	FALDSTOOL	FALSIFIED
FAILINGS	FAIRINGS	FAKIE	FALL	FALSIFIER
FAILLE	FAIRISH	FAKIER	FALLACIES	FALSIFIES
FAILLES	FAIRISHLY	FAKIES	FALLACY	FALSIFY
FAILS	FAIRLEAD	FAKIEST	FALLAL	FALSING
FAILURE	FAIRLEADS	FAKING	FALLALERY	FALSISH
FAILURES	FAIRLY	FAKIR	FALLALISH	FALSISM
FAIN	FAIRNESS	FAKIRISM	FALLALS	FALSISMS
FAINE	FAIRS	FAKIRISMS	FALLAWAY	FALSITIES
FAINEANCE	FAIRWAY	FAKIRS	FALLAWAYS	FALSITY
FAINEANCY	FAIRWAYS	FALAFEL	FALLBACK	FALTBOAT
FAINEANT	FAIRY	FALAFELS	FALLBACKS	FALTBOATS
FAINEANTS	FAIRYDOM	FALAJ	FALLBOARD	FALTER
FAINED	FAIRYDOMS	FALANGISM	FALLEN	FALTERED
FAINER	FAIRYHOOD	FALANGIST	FALLER	FALTERER
FAINES	FAIRYISM	FALBALA	FALLERS	FALTERERS
FAINEST	FAIRYISMS	FALBALAS	FALLFISH	FALTERING
FAINING	FAIRYLAND	FALCADE	FALLIBLE	FALTERS
FAINITES	FAIRYLIKE	FALCADES	FALLIBLY	FALX
FAINLY	FAIRYTALE	FALCATE	FALLING	FAME
FAINNE	FAITH	FALCATED	FALLINGS	FAMED
FAINNES	FAITHED	FALCATION	FALLOFF	FAMELESS
FAINNESS	FAITHER	FALCES	FALLOFFS	FAMES

FAMILIAL	FANCYING	FANJETS	FANTASMIC	FARANDINE
FAMILIAR	FANCYWORK	FANK	FANTASMS	FARANDOLE
FAMILIARS	FAND	FANKLE	FANTASQUE	FARAWAY
FAMILIES	FANDANGLE	FANKLED	FANTAST	FARAWAYS
FAMILISM	FANDANGO	FANKLES	FANTASTIC	FARCE
FAMILISMS	FANDANGOS	FANKLING	FANTASTRY	FARCED
FAMILLE	FANDED	FANKS	FANTASTS	FARCEMEAT
FAMILLES	FANDING	FANLIGHT	FANTASY	FARCER
FAMILY	FANDOM	FANLIGHTS	FANTEEG	FARCERS
FAMINE	FANDOMS	FANLIKE	FANTEEGS	FARCES
FAMINES	FANDS	FANNED	FANTIGUE	FARCEUR
FAMING	FANE	FANNEL	FANTIGUES	FARCEURS
FAMISH	FANEGA	FANNELL	FANTOD	FARCEUSE
FAMISHED	FANEGADA	FANNELLS	FANTODS	FARCEUSES
FAMISHES	FANEGADAS	FANNELS	FANTOM	FARCI
FAMISHING	FANEGAS	FANNER	FANTOMS	FARCICAL
FAMOUS	FANES	FANNERS	FANTOOSH	FARCIE
FAMOUSED	FANFARADE	FANNIED	FANUM	FARCIED
FAMOUSES	FANFARE	FANNIES	FANUMS	FARCIES
FAMOUSING	FANFARED	FANNING	FANWISE	FARCIFIED
FAMOUSLY	FANFARES	FANNINGS	FANWORT	FARCIFIES
FAMULI	FANFARING	FANNY	FANWORTS	FARCIFY
FAMULUS	FANFARON	FANNYING	FANZINE	FARCIN
FAN	FANFARONA	FANO	FANZINES	FARCING
FANAL	FANFARONS	FANON	FAP	FARCINGS
FANALS	FANFIC	FANONS	FAQIR	FARCINS
FANATIC	FANFICS	FANOS	FAQIRS	FARCY
FANATICAL	FANFOLD	FANS	FAQUIR	FARD
FANATICS	FANFOLDED	FANSITE	FAQUIRS	FARDAGE
FANBASE	FANFOLDS	FANSITES	FAR	FARDAGES
FANBASES	FANG	FANSUB	FARAD	FARDED
FANBOY	FANGA	FANSUBS	FARADAIC	FARDEL
FANBOYS	FANGAS	FANTAD	FARADAY	FARDELS
FANCIABLE	FANGED	FANTADS	FARADAYS	FARDEN
FANCIED	FANGING	FANTAIL	FARADIC	FARDENS
FANCIER	FANGLE	FANTAILED	FARADISE	FARDING
FANCIERS	FANGLED	FANTAILS	FARADISED	FARDINGS
FANCIES	FANGLES	FANTASIA	FARADISER	FARDS
FANCIEST	FANGLESS	FANTASIAS	FARADISES	FARE
FANCIFIED	FANGLIKE	FANTASIE	FARADISM	FAREBOX
FANCIFIES	FANGLING	FANTASIED	FARADISMS	FAREBOXES
FANCIFUL	FANGO	FANTASIES	FARADIZE	FARED
FANCIFY	FANGOS	FANTASISE	FARADIZED	FARER
FANCILESS	FANGS	FANTASIST	FARADIZER	FARERS
FANCILY	FANION	FANTASIZE	FARADIZES	FARES
FANCINESS	FANIONS	FANTASM	FARADS	FAREWELL
FANCY	FANJET	FANTASMAL	FARAND	FAREWELLS

FARFAL	FAROLITO	FASCIAL	FASTEN	FATHOMED
FARFALLE	FAROLITOS	FASCIAS	FASTENED	FATHOMER
FARFALLES	FAROS	FASCIATE	FASTENER	FATHOMERS
FARFALS	FAROUCHE	FASCIATED	FASTENERS	FATHOMING
FARFEL	FARRAGO	FASCICLE	FASTENING	FATHOMS
FARFELS	FARRAGOES	FASCICLED	FASTENS	FATIDIC
FARFET	FARRAGOS	FASCICLES	FASTER	FATIDICAL
FARINA	FARRAND	FASCICULE	FASTERS	FATIGABLE
FARINAS	FARRANT	FASCICULI	FASTEST	FATIGATE
FARING	FARRED	FASCIITIS	FASTI	FATIGATED
FARINHA	FARREN	FASCINATE	FASTIE	FATIGATES
FARINHAS	FARRENS	FASCINE	FASTIES	FATIGUE
FARINOSE	FARRIER	FASCINES	FASTIGIUM	FATIGUED
FARL	FARRIERS	FASCIO	FASTING	FATIGUES
FARLE	FARRIERY	FASCIOLA	FASTINGS	FATIGUING
FARLES	FARRING	FASCIOLAS	FASTISH	FATING
FARLS	FARROW	FASCIOLE	FASTLY	FATISCENT
FARM	FARROWED	FASCIOLES	FASTNESS	FATLESS
FARMABLE	FARROWING	FASCIS	FASTS	FATLIKE
FARMED	FARROWS	FASCISM	FASTUOUS	FATLING
FARMER	FARRUCA	FASCISMI	FAT	FATLINGS
FARMERESS	FARRUCAS	FASCISMO	FATAL	FATLY
FARMERIES	FARS	FASCISMS	FATALISM	FATNESS
FARMERS	FARSE	FASCIST	FATALISMS	FATNESSES
FARMERY	FARSED	FASCISTA	FATALIST	FATS
FARMHAND	FARSEEING	FASCISTI	FATALISTS	FATSIA
FARMHANDS	FARSES	FASCISTIC	FATALITY	FATSIAS
FARMHOUSE	FARSIDE	FASCISTS	FATALLY	FATSO
FARMING	FARSIDES	FASCITIS	FATALNESS	FATSOES
FARMINGS	FARSING	FASH	FATBACK	FATSOS
FARMLAND	FART	FASHED	FATBACKS	FATSTOCK
FARMLANDS	FARTED	FASHERIES	FATBIRD	FATSTOCKS
FARMOST	FARTHEL	FASHERY	FATBIRDS	FATTED
FARMS	FARTHELS	FASHES	FATE	FATTEN
FARMSTEAD	FARTHER	FASHING	FATED	FATTENED
FARMWIFE	FARTHEST	FASHION	FATEFUL	FATTENER
FARMWIVES	FARTHING	FASHIONED	FATEFULLY	FATTENERS
FARMWORK	FARTHINGS	FASHIONER	FATES	FATTENING
FARMWORKS	FARTING	FASHIONS	FATHEAD	FATTENS
FARMYARD	FARTLEK	FASHIONY	FATHEADED	FATTER
FARMYARDS	FARTLEKS	FASHIOUS	FATHEADS	FATTEST
FARNARKEL	FARTS	FAST	FATHER	FATTIER
FARNESOL	FAS	FASTBACK	FATHERED	FATTIES
FARNESOLS	FASCES	FASTBACKS	FATHERING	FATTIEST
FARNESS	FASCI	FASTBALL	FATHERLY	FATTILY
FARNESSES	FASCIA	FASTBALLS	FATHERS	FATTINESS
FARO	FASCIAE	FASTED	FATHOM	FATTING

FATTISH	FAULTY	FAVEOLATE	FAX	FEARS
FATTISM	FAUN	FAVER	FAXED	FEARSOME
FATTISMS	FAUNA	FAVES	FAXES	FEART
FATTIST	FAUNAE	FAVEST	FAXING	FEASANCE
FATTISTS	FAUNAL	FAVICON	FAY	FEASANCES
FATTRELS	FAUNALLY	FAVICONS	FAYALITE	FEASE
FATTY	FAUNAS	FAVISM	FAYALITES	FEASED
FATUITIES	FAUNIST	FAVISMS	FAYED	FEASES
FATUITOUS	FAUNISTIC	FAVONIAN	FAYENCE	FEASIBLE
FATUITY	FAUNISTS	FAVOR	FAYENCES	FEASIBLY
FATUOUS	FAUNLIKE	FAVORABLE	FAYER	FEASING
FATUOUSLY	FAUNS	FAVORABLY	FAYEST	FEAST
FATWA	FAUNULA	FAVORED	FAYING	FEASTED
FATWAH	FAUNULAE	FAVORER	FAYNE	FEASTER
FATWAHED	FAUNULE	FAVORERS	FAYNED	FEASTERS
FATWAHING	FAUNULES	FAVORING	FAYNES	FEASTFUL
FATWAHS	FAUR	FAVORITE	FAYNING	FEASTING
FATWAING	FAURD	FAVORITES	FAYRE	FEASTINGS
FATWAS	FAURER	FAVORLESS	FAYRES	FEASTLESS
FATWOOD	FAUREST	FAVORS	FAYS	FEASTS
FATWOODS	FAUSTIAN	FAVOSE	FAZE	FEAT
FAUBOURG	FAUT	FAVOUR	FAZED	FEATED
FAUBOURGS	FAUTED	FAVOURED	FAZENDA	FEATEOUS
FAUCAL	FAUTEUIL	FAVOURER	FAZENDAS	FEATER
FAUCALS	FAUTEUILS	FAVOURERS	FAZES	FEATEST
FAUCES	FAUTING	FAVOURING	FAZING	FEATHER
FAUCET	FAUTOR	FAVOURITE	FE	FEATHERED
FAUCETS	FAUTORS	FAVOURS	FEAGUE	FEATHERS
FAUCHION	FAUTS	FAVOUS	FEAGUED	FEATHERY
FAUCHIONS	FAUVE	FAVRILE	FEAGUES	FEATING
FAUCHON	FAUVES	FAVRILES	FEAGUING	FEATLIER
FAUCHONS	FAUVETTE	FAVUS	FEAL	FEATLIEST
FAUCIAL	FAUVETTES	FAVUSES	FEALED	FEATLY
FAUGH	FAUVISM	FAW	FEALING	FEATOUS
FAULCHION	FAUVISMS	FAWN	FEALS	FEATS
FAULD	FAUVIST	FAWNED	FEALTIES	FEATUOUS
FAULDS	FAUVISTS	FAWNER	FEALTY	FEATURE
FAULT	FAUX	FAWNERS	FEAR	FEATURED
FAULTED	FAVA	FAWNIER	FEARE	FEATURELY
FAULTFUL	FAVAS	FAWNIEST	FEARED	FEATURES
FAULTIER	FAVE	FAWNING	FEARER	FEATURING
FAULTIEST	FAVEL	FAWNINGLY	FEARERS	FEAZE
FAULTILY	FAVELA	FAWNINGS	FEARES	FEAZED
FAULTING	FAVELAS	FAWNLIKE	FEARFUL	FEAZES
FAULTLESS	FAVELL	FAWNS	FEARFULLY	FEAZING
FAULTLINE	FAVELLA	FAWNY	FEARING	FEBLESSE
FAULTS	FAVELLAS	FAWS	FEARLESS	FEBLESSES

F

FEBRICITY	FEDERATED	FEELER	FEIGNS	FELINITY
FEBRICULA	FEDERATES	FEELERS	FEIJOA	FELL
FEBRICULE	FEDERATOR	FEELESS	FEIJOADA	FELLA
FEBRIFIC	FEDEX	FEELGOOD	FEIJOADAS	FELLABLE
FEBRIFUGE	FEDEXED	FEELING	FEIJOAS	FELLAH
FEBRILE	FEDEXES	FEELINGLY	FEINT	FELLAHEEN
FEBRILITY	FEDEXING	FEELINGS	FEINTED	FELLAHIN
FECAL	FEDORA	FEELS	FEINTER	FELLAHS
FECES	FEDORAS	FEEN	FEINTEST	FELLAS
FECHT	FEDS	FEENS	FEINTING	FELLATE
FECHTER	FEE	FEER	FEINTS	FELLATED
FECHTERS	FEEB	FEERED	FEIRIE	FELLATES
FECHTING	FEEBLE	FEERIE	FEIRIER	FELLATING
FECHTS	FEEBLED	FEERIES	FEIRIEST	FELLATIO
FECIAL	FEEBLER	FEERIN	FEIS	FELLATION
FECIALS	FEEBLES	FEERING	FEISEANNA	FELLATIOS
FECIT	FEEBLEST	FEERINGS	FEIST	FELLATOR
FECK	FEEBLING	FEERINS	FEISTIER	FELLATORS
FECKED	FEEBLISH	FEERS	FEISTIEST	FELLATRIX
FECKIN	FEEBLY	FEES	FEISTILY	FELLED
FECKING	FEEBS	FEESE	FEISTS	FELLER
FECKLESS	FEED	FEESED	FEISTY	FELLERS
FECKLY	FEEDABLE	FEESES	FELAFEL	FELLEST
FECKS	FEEDBACK	FEESING	FELAFELS	FELLIES
FECULA	FEEDBACKS	FEET	FELCH	FELLING
FECULAE	FEEDBAG	FEETFIRST	FELCHED	FELLINGS
FECULAS	FEEDBAGS	FEETLESS	FELCHES	FELLNESS
FECULENCE	FEEDBOX	FEEZE	FELCHING	FELLOE
FECULENCY	FEEDBOXES	FEEZED	FELDGRAU	FELLOES
FECULENT	FEEDER	FEEZES	FELDGRAUS	FELLOW
FECUND	FEEDERS	FEEZING	FELDSCHAR	FELLOWED
FECUNDATE	FEEDGRAIN	FEG	FELDSCHER	FELLOWING
FECUNDITY	FEEDHOLE	FEGARIES	FELDSHER	FELLOWLY
FED	FEEDHOLES	FEGARY	FELDSHERS	FELLOWMAN
FEDARIE	FEEDING	FEGS	FELDSPAR	FELLOWMEN
FEDARIES	FEEDINGS	FEH	FELDSPARS	FELLOWS
FEDAYEE	FEEDLOT	FEHM	FELDSPATH	FELLS
FEDAYEEN	FEEDLOTS	FEHME	FELICIA	FELLY
FEDELINI	FEEDS	FEHMIC	FELICIAS	FELON
FEDELINIS	FEEDSTOCK	FEHS	FELICIFIC	FELONIES
FEDERACY	FEEDSTUFF	FEIGN	FELICITER	FELONIOUS
FEDERAL	FEEDWATER	FEIGNED	FELICITY	FELONOUS
FEDERALLY	FEEDYARD	FEIGNEDLY	FELID	FELONRIES
FEDERALS	FEEDYARDS	FEIGNER	FELIDS	FELONRY
FEDERARIE	FEEING	FEIGNERS	FELINE	FELONS
FEDERARY	FEEL	FEIGNING	FELINELY	FELONY
FEDERATE	FEELBAD	FEIGNINGS	FELINES	FELSIC

F

FELSITE	FEMINISED	FENDING	FEOFFMENT	FERMIUMS
FELSITES	FEMINISES	FENDS	FEOFFOR	FERMS
FELSITIC	FEMINISM	FENDY	FEOFFORS	FERN
FELSPAR	FEMINISMS	FENESTRA	FEOFFS	FERNALLY
FELSPARS	FEMINIST	FENESTRAE	FER	FERNBIRD
FELSTONE	FEMINISTS	FENESTRAL	FERACIOUS	FERNBIRDS
FELSTONES	FEMINITY	FENESTRAS	FERACITY	FERNERIES
FELT	FEMINIZE	FENI	FERAL	FERNERY
FELTED	FEMINIZED	FENIS	FERALISED	FERNIER
FELTER	FEMINIZES	FENITAR	FERALIZED	FERNIEST
FELTERED	FEMITER	FENITARS	FERALS	FERNING
FELTERING	FEMITERS	FENKS	FERBAM	FERNINGS
FELTERS	FEMME	FENLAND	FERBAMS	FERNINST
FELTIER	FEMMES	FENLANDS	FERE	FERNLESS
FELTIEST	FEMMIER	FENMAN	FERER	FERNLIKE
FELTING	FEMMIEST	FENMEN	FERES	FERNS
FELTINGS	FEMMY	FENNEC	FEREST	FERNSHAW
FELTLIKE	FEMORA	FENNECS	FERETORY	FERNSHAWS
FELTS	FEMORAL	FENNEL	FERIA	FERNTICLE
FELTY	FEMS	FENNELS	FERIAE	FERNY
FELUCCA	FEMUR	FENNIER	FERIAL	FEROCIOUS
FELUCCAS	FEMURS	FENNIES	FERIAS	FEROCITY
FELWORT	FEN	FENNIEST	FERINE	FERRATE
FELWORTS	FENAGLE	FENNISH	FERITIES	FERRATES
FEM	FENAGLED	FENNY	FERITY	FERREL
FEMAL	FENAGLES	FENS	FERLIE	FERRELED
FEMALE	FENAGLING	FENT	FERLIED	FERRELING
FEMALES	FENCE	FENTANYL	FERLIER	FERRELLED
FEMALITY	FENCED	FENTANYLS	FERLIES	FERRELS
FEMALS	FENCELESS	FENTHION	FERLIEST	FERREOUS
FEME	FENCELIKE	FENTHIONS	FERLY	FERRET
FEMERALL	FENCER	FENTS	FERLYING	FERRETED
FEMERALLS	FENCEROW	FENUGREEK	FERM	FERRETER
FEMES	FENCEROWS	FENURON	FERMATA	FERRETERS
FEMETARY	FENCERS	FENURONS	FERMATAS	FERRETING
FEMICIDAL	FENCES	FEOD	FERMATE	FERRETS
FEMICIDE	FENCIBLE	FEODAL	FERMENT	FERRETY
FEMICIDES	FENCIBLES	FEODARIES	FERMENTED	FERRIAGE
FEMINACY	FENCING	FEODARY	FERMENTER	FERRIAGES
FEMINAL	FENCINGS	FEODS	FERMENTOR	FERRIC
FEMINAZI	FEND	FEOFF	FERMENTS	FERRIED
FEMINAZIS	FENDED	FEOFFED	FERMI	FERRIES
FEMINEITY	FENDER	FEOFFEE	FERMION	FERRITE
FEMINIE	FENDERED	FEOFFEES	FERMIONIC	FERRITES
FEMININE	FENDERS	FEOFFER	FERMIONS	FERRITIC
FEMININES	FENDIER	FEOFFERS	FERMIS	FERRITIN
FEMINISE	FENDIEST	FEOFFING	FERMIUM	FERRITINS

FERROCENE	FESCUES	FETERITA	FETTERING	FEVERFEW
FERROTYPE	FESS	FETERITAS	FETTERS	FEVERFEWS
FERROUS	FESSE	FETES	FETTING	FEVERING
FERRUGO	FESSED	FETIAL	FETTLE	FEVERISH
FERRUGOS	FESSES	FETIALES	FETTLED	FEVERLESS
FERRULE	FESSING	FETIALIS	FETTLER	FEVEROUS
FERRULED	FESSWISE	FETIALS	FETTLERS	FEVERROOT
FERRULES	FEST	FETICH	FETTLES	FEVERS
FERRULING	FESTA	FETICHE	FETTLING	FEVERWEED
FERRUM	FESTAL	FETICHES	FETTLINGS	FEVERWORT
FERRUMS	FESTALLY	FETICHISE	FETTS	FEW
FERRY	FESTALS	FETICHISM	FETTUCINE	FEWER
FERRYBOAT	FESTAS	FETICHIST	FETTUCINI	FEWEST
FERRYING	FESTER	FETICHIZE	FETUS	FEWMET
FERRYMAN	FESTERED	FETICIDAL	FETUSES	FEWMETS
FERRYMEN	FESTERING	FETICIDE	FETWA	FEWNESS
FERTIGATE	FESTERS	FETICIDES	FETWAS	FEWNESSES
FERTILE	FESTIER	FETID	FEU	FEWS
FERTILELY	FESTIEST	FETIDER	FEUAR	FEWTER
FERTILER	FESTILOGY	FETIDEST	FEUARS	FEWTERED
FERTILEST	FESTINATE	FETIDITY	FEUD	FEWTERING
FERTILISE	FESTIVAL	FETIDLY	FEUDAL	FEWTERS
FERTILITY	FESTIVALS	FETIDNESS	FEUDALISE	FEWTRILS
FERTILIZE	FESTIVE	FETING	FEUDALISM	FEY
FERULA	FESTIVELY	FETISH	FEUDALIST	FEYED
FERULAE	FESTIVITY	FETISHES	FEUDALITY	FEYER
FERULAS	FESTIVOUS	FETISHISE	FEUDALIZE	FEYEST
FERULE	FESTOLOGY	FETISHISM	FEUDALLY	FEYING
FERULED	FESTOON	FETISHIST	FEUDARIES	FEYLY
FERULES	FESTOONED	FETISHIZE	FEUDARY	FEYNESS
FERULING	FESTOONS	FETLOCK	FEUDATORY	FEYNESSES
FERVENCY	FESTS	FETLOCKED	FEUDED	FEYS
FERVENT	FESTY	FETLOCKS	FEUDING	FEZ
FERVENTER	FET	FETOLOGY	FEUDINGS	FEZES
FERVENTLY	FETA	FETOR	FEUDIST	FEZZED
FERVID	FETAL	FETORS	FEUDISTS	FEZZES
FERVIDER	FETAS	FETOSCOPE	FEUDS	FEZZY
FERVIDEST	FETATION	FETOSCOPY	FEUED	FIACRE
FERVIDITY	FETATIONS	FETS	FEUILLETE	FIACRES
FERVIDLY	FETCH	FETT	FEUING	FIANCE
FERVOR	FETCHED	FETTA	FEUS	FIANCEE
FERVOROUS	FETCHER	FETTAS	FEUTRE	FIANCEES
FERVORS	FETCHERS	FETTED	FEUTRED	FIANCES
FERVOUR	FETCHES	FETTER	FEUTRES	FIAR
FERVOURS	FETCHING	FETTERED	FEUTRING	FIARS
FES	FETE	FETTERER	FEVER	FIASCHI
FESCUE	FETED	FETTERERS	FEVERED	FIASCO

FIASCOES	FIBRINS	FICTION	FIDS	FIFERS
FIASCOS	FIBRO	FICTIONAL	FIDUCIAL	FIFES
FIAT	FIBROCYTE	FICTIONS	FIDUCIARY	FIFING
FIATED	FIBROID	FICTIVE	FIE	FIFTEEN
FIATING	FIBROIDS	FICTIVELY	FIEF	FIFTEENER
FIATS	FIBROIN	FICTOR	FIEFDOM	FIFTEENS
FIAUNT	FIBROINS	FICTORS	FIEFDOMS	FIFTEENTH
FIAUNTS	FIBROLINE	FICUS	FIEFS	FIFTH
FIB	FIBROLITE	FICUSES	FIELD	FIFTHLY
FIBBED	FIBROMA	FID	FIELDED	FIFTHS
FIBBER	FIBROMAS	FIDDIOUS	FIELDER	FIFTIES
FIBBERIES	FIBROMATA	FIDDLE	FIELDERS	FIFTIETH
FIBBERS	FIBROS	FIDDLED	FIELDFARE	FIFTIETHS
FIBBERY	FIBROSE	FIDDLER	FIELDING	FIFTY
FIBBING	FIBROSED	FIDDLERS	FIELDINGS	FIFTYISH
FIBER	FIBROSES	FIDDLES	FIELDMICE	FIG
FIBERED	FIBROSING	FIDDLEY	FIELDS	FIGEATER
FIBERFILL	FIBROSIS	FIDDLEYS	FIELDSMAN	FIGEATERS
FIBERISE	FIBROTIC	FIDDLIER	FIELDSMEN	FIGGED
FIBERISED	FIBROUS	FIDDLIEST	FIELDVOLE	FIGGERIES
FIBERISES	FIBROUSLY	FIDDLING	FIELDWARD	FIGGERY
FIBERIZE	FIBS	FIDDLY	FIELDWORK	FIGGING
FIBERIZED	FIBSTER	FIDEISM	FIEND	FIGHT
FIBERIZES	FIBSTERS	FIDEISMS	FIENDISH	FIGHTABLE
FIBERLESS	FIBULA	FIDEIST	FIENDLIKE	FIGHTBACK
FIBERLIKE	FIBULAE	FIDEISTIC	FIENDS	FIGHTER
FIBERS	FIBULAR	FIDEISTS	FIENT	FIGHTERS
FIBRANNE	FIBULAS	FIDELISMO	FIENTS	FIGHTING
FIBRANNES	FICE	FIDELISTA	FIER	FIGHTINGS
FIBRATE	FICES	FIDELITY	FIERCE	FIGHTS
FIBRATES	FICHE	FIDES	FIERCELY	FIGJAM
FIBRE	FICHES	FIDGE	FIERCER	FIGJAMS
FIBRED	FICHU	FIDGED	FIERCEST	FIGMENT
FIBREFILL	FICHUS	FIDGES	FIERE	FIGMENTS
FIBRELESS	FICIN	FIDGET	FIERES	FIGO
FIBRES	FICINS	FIDGETED	FIERIER	FIGOS
FIBRIFORM	FICKLE	FIDGETER	FIERIEST	FIGS
FIBRIL	FICKLED	FIDGETERS	FIERILY	FIGULINE
FIBRILAR	FICKLER	FIDGETIER	FIERINESS	FIGULINES
FIBRILLA	FICKLES	FIDGETING	FIERS	FIGURABLE
FIBRILLAE	FICKLEST	FIDGETS	FIERY	FIGURAL
FIBRILLAR	FICKLING	FIDGETY	FIEST	FIGURALLY
FIBRILLIN	FICKLY	FIDGING	FIESTA	FIGURANT
FIBRILS	FICO	FIDIBUS	FIESTAS	FIGURANTE
FIBRIN	FICOES	FIDIBUSES	FIFE	FIGURANTS
FIBRINOID	FICOS	FIDO	FIFED	FIGURATE
FIBRINOUS	FICTILE	FIDOS	FIFER	FIGURE

FIGURED	FILASSES	FILICIDES	FILMDOM	FILTRABLE
FIGUREDLY	FILATORY	FILIFORM	FILMDOMS	FILTRATE
FIGURER	FILATURE	FILIGRAIN	FILMED	FILTRATED
FIGURERS	FILATURES	FILIGRANE	FILMER	FILTRATES
FIGURES	FILAZER	FILIGREE	FILMERS	FILTRE
FIGURINE	FILAZERS	FILIGREED	FILMGOER	FILUM
FIGURINES	FILBERD	FILIGREES	FILMGOERS	FIMBLE
FIGURING	FILBERDS	FILII	FILMGOING	FIMBLES
FIGURIST	FILBERT	FILING	FILMI	FIMBRIA
FIGURISTS	FILBERTS	FILINGS	FILMIC	FIMBRIAE
FIGWORT	FILCH	FILIOQUE	FILMIER	FIMBRIAL
FIGWORTS	FILCHED	FILIOQUES	FILMIEST	FIMBRIATE
FIKE	FILCHER	FILISTER	FILMILY	FIN
FIKED	FILCHERS	FILISTERS	FILMINESS	FINABLE
FIKERIES	FILCHES	FILIUS	FILMING	FINAGLE
FIKERY	FILCHING	FILL	FILMIS	FINAGLED
FIKES	FILCHINGS	FILLABLE	FILMISH	FINAGLER
FIKIER	FILE	FILLAGREE	FILMLAND	FINAGLERS
FIKIEST	FILEABLE	FILLE	FILMLANDS	FINAGLES
FIKING	FILECARD	FILLED	FILMLESS	FINAGLING
FIKISH	FILECARDS	FILLER	FILMLIKE	FINAL
FIKY	FILED	FILLERS	FILMMAKER	FINALE
FIL	FILEFISH	FILLES	FILMS	FINALES
FILA	FILEMOT	FILLESTER	FILMSET	FINALIS
FILABEG	FILEMOTS	FILLET	FILMSETS	FINALISE
FILABEGS	FILENAME	FILLETED	FILMSTRIP	FINALISED
FILACEOUS	FILENAMES	FILLETING	FILMY	FINALISER
FILACER	FILER	FILLETS	FILO	FINALISES
FILACERS	FILERS	FILLIBEG	FILOPLUME	FINALISM
FILAGGRIN	FILES	FILLIBEGS	FILOPODIA	FINALISMS
FILAGREE	FILET	FILLIES	FILOS	FINALIST
FILAGREED	FILETED	FILLING	FILOSE	FINALISTS
FILAGREES	FILETING	FILLINGS	FILOSELLE	FINALITY
FILAMENT	FILETS	FILLIP	FILOVIRUS	FINALIZE
FILAMENTS	FILFOT	FILLIPED	FILS	FINALIZED
FILANDER	FILFOTS	FILLIPEEN	FILTER	FINALIZER
FILANDERS	FILIAL	FILLIPING	FILTERED	FINALIZES
FILAR	FILIALLY	FILLIPS	FILTERER	FINALLY
FILAREE	FILIATE	FILLISTER	FILTERERS	FINALS
FILAREES	FILIATED	FILLO	FILTERING	FINANCE
FILARIA	FILIATES	FILLOS	FILTERS	FINANCED
FILARIAE	FILIATING	FILLS	FILTH	FINANCES
FILARIAL	FILIATION	FILLY	FILTHIER	FINANCIAL
FILARIAN	FILIBEG	FILM	FILTHIEST	FINANCIER
FILARIID	FILIBEGS	FILMABLE	FILTHILY	FINANCING
FILARIIDS	FILICIDAL	FILMCARD	FILTHS	FINBACK
FILASSE	FILICIDE	FILMCARDS	FILTHY	FINBACKS

FINCA	FINGERERS	FINNACKS	FIREBACK	FIRELOCKS
FINCAS	FINGERING	FINNACS	FIREBACKS	FIREMAN
FINCH	FINGERS	FINNAN	FIREBALL	FIREMANIC
FINCHED	FINGERTIP	FINNANS	FIREBALLS	FIREMARK
FINCHES	FINI	FINNED	FIREBASE	FIREMARKS
FIND	FINIAL	FINNER	FIREBASES	FIREMEN
FINDABLE	FINIALED	FINNERS	FIREBIRD	FIREPAN
FINDER	FINIALS	FINNESKO	FIREBIRDS	FIREPANS
FINDERS	FINICAL	FINNICKY	FIREBOARD	FIREPINK
FINDING	FINICALLY	FINNIER	FIREBOAT	FIREPINKS
FINDINGS	FINICKETY	FINNIEST	FIREBOATS	FIREPLACE
FINDRAM	FINICKIER	FINNING	FIREBOMB	FIREPLUG
FINDRAMS	FINICKIN	FINNMARK	FIREBOMBS	FIREPLUGS
FINDS	FINICKING	FINNMARKS	FIREBOX	FIREPOT
FINE	FINICKY	FINNOCHIO	FIREBOXES	FIREPOTS
FINEABLE	FINIKIN	FINNOCK	FIREBRAND	FIREPOWER
FINED	FINIKING	FINNOCKS	FIREBRAT	FIREPROOF
FINEER	FINING	FINNSKO	FIREBRATS	FIRER
FINEERED	FININGS	FINNY	FIREBREAK	FIREROOM
FINEERING	FINIS	FINO	FIREBRICK	FIREROOMS
FINEERS	FINISES	FINOCCHIO	FIREBUG	FIRERS
FINEISH	FINISH	FINOCHIO	FIREBUGS	FIRES
FINELESS	FINISHED	FINOCHIOS	FIREBUSH	FIRESHIP
FINELY	FINISHER	FINOS	FIRECLAY	FIRESHIPS
FINENESS	FINISHERS	FINS	FIRECLAYS	FIRESIDE
FINER	FINISHES	FINSKO	FIRECREST	FIRESIDES
FINERIES	FINISHING	FIORATURA	FIRED	FIRESTONE
FINERS	FINITE	FIORD	FIREDAMP	FIRESTORM
FINERY	FINITELY	FIORDS	FIREDAMPS	FIRETHORN
FINES	FINITES	FIORIN	FIREDOG	FIRETRAP
FINESPUN	FINITISM	FIORINS	FIREDOGS	FIRETRAPS
FINESSE	FINITISMS	FIORITURA	FIREDRAKE	FIRETRUCK
FINESSED	FINITO	FIORITURE	FIREFANG	FIREWALL
FINESSER	FINITUDE	FIPPENCE	FIREFANGS	FIREWALLS
FINESSERS	FINITUDES	FIPPENCES	FIREFIGHT	FIREWATER
FINESSES	FINJAN	FIPPLE	FIREFLIES	FIREWEED
FINESSING	FINJANS	FIPPLES	FIREFLOAT	FIREWEEDS
FINEST	FINK	FIQH	FIREFLOOD	FIREWOMAN
FINFISH	FINKED	FIQHS	FIREFLY	FIREWOMEN
FINFISHES	FINKING	FIQUE	FIREGUARD	FIREWOOD
FINFOOT	FINKS	FIQUES	FIREHALL	FIREWOODS
FINFOOTS	FINLESS	FIR	FIREHALLS	FIREWORK
FINGAN	FINLIKE	FIRE	FIREHOUSE	FIREWORKS
FINGANS	FINMARK	FIREABLE	FIRELESS	FIREWORM
FINGER	FINMARKS	FIREARM	FIRELIGHT	FIREWORMS
FINGERED	FINNAC	FIREARMED	FIRELIT	FIRIE
FINGERER	FINNACK	FIREARMS	FIRELOCK	FIRIES

FIRING	FISCALLY	FISHMEAL	FIST	FITT
FIRINGS	FISCALS	FISHMEALS	FISTED	FITTABLE
FIRK	FISCS	FISHNET	FISTFIGHT	FITTE
FIRKED	FISGIG	FISHNETS	FISTFUL	FITTED
FIRKIN	FISGIGS	FISHPLATE	FISTFULS	FITTER
FIRKING	FISH	FISHPOLE	FISTIANA	FITTERS
FIRKINS	FISHABLE	FISHPOLES	FISTIC	FITTES
FIRKS	FISHBALL	FISHPOND	FISTICAL	FITTEST
FIRLOT	FISHBALLS	FISHPONDS	FISTICUFF	FITTING
FIRLOTS	FISHBOLT	FISHSKIN	FISTIER	FITTINGLY
FIRM	FISHBOLTS	FISHSKINS	FISTIEST	FITTINGS
FIRMAMENT	FISHBONE	FISHTAIL	FISTING	FITTS
FIRMAN	FISHBONES	FISHTAILS	FISTMELE	FIVE
FIRMANS	FISHBOWL	FISHWAY	FISTMELES	FIVEFOLD
FIRMED	FISHBOWLS	FISHWAYS	FISTNOTE	FIVEPENCE
FIRMER	FISHCAKE	FISHWIFE	FISTNOTES	FIVEPENNY
FIRMERS	FISHCAKES	FISHWIVES	FISTS	FIVEPIN
FIRMEST	FISHED	FISHWORM	FISTULA	FIVEPINS
FIRMING	FISHER	FISHWORMS	FISTULAE	FIVER
FIRMLESS	FISHERIES	FISHY	FISTULAR	FIVERS
FIRMLY	FISHERMAN	FISHYBACK	FISTULAS	FIVES
FIRMNESS	FISHERMEN	FISK	FISTULATE	FIX
FIRMS	FISHERS	FISKED	FISTULOSE	FIXABLE
FIRMWARE	FISHERY	FISKING	FISTULOUS	FIXATE
FIRMWARES	FISHES	FISKS	FISTY	FIXATED
FIRN	FISHEYE	FISNOMIE	FIT	FIXATES
FIRNS	FISHEYES	FISNOMIES	FITCH	FIXATIF
FIRRIER	FISHFUL	FISSATE	FITCHE	FIXATIFS
FIRRIEST	FISHGIG	FISSILE	FITCHEE	FIXATING
FIRRING	FISHGIGS	FISSILITY	FITCHES	FIXATION
FIRRINGS	FISHHOOK	FISSION	FITCHET	FIXATIONS
FIRRY	FISHHOOKS	FISSIONAL	FITCHETS	FIXATIVE
FIRS	FISHIER	FISSIONED	FITCHEW	FIXATIVES
FIRST	FISHIEST	FISSIONS	FITCHEWS	FIXATURE
FIRSTBORN	FISHIFIED	FISSIPED	FITCHY	FIXATURES
FIRSTHAND	FISHIFIES	FISSIPEDE	FITFUL	FIXED
FIRSTLING	FISHIFY	FISSIPEDS	FITFULLY	FIXEDLY
FIRSTLY	FISHILY	FISSIVE	FITLIER	FIXEDNESS
FIRSTNESS	FISHINESS	FISSLE	FITLIEST	FIXER
FIRSTS	FISHING	FISSLED	FITLY	FIXERS
FIRTH	FISHINGS	FISSLES	FITMENT	FIXES
FIRTHS	FISHKILL	FISSLING	FITMENTS	FIXING
FIRWOOD	FISHKILLS	FISSURAL	FITNA	FIXINGS
FIRWOODS	FISHLESS	FISSURE	FITNAS	FIXIT
FISC	FISHLIKE	FISSURED	FITNESS	FIXITIES
FISCAL	FISHLINE	FISSURES	FITNESSES	FIXITY
FISCALIST	FISHLINES	FISSURING	FITS	FIXIVE

FIXT	FLACKERED	FLAIL	FLAMFEWS	FLANNELS
FIXTURE	FLACKERS	FLAILED	FLAMIER	FLANNEN
FIXTURES	FLACKERY	FLAILING	FLAMIEST	FLANNENS
FIXURE	FLACKET	FLAILS	FLAMINES	FLANNIE
FIXURES	FLACKETS	FLAIR	FLAMING	FLANNIES
FIZ	FLACKING	FLAIRS	FLAMINGLY	FLANNY
FIZGIG	FLACKS	FLAK	FLAMINGO	FLANS
FIZGIGGED	FLACON	FLAKE	FLAMINGOS	FLAP
FIZGIGS	FLACONS	FLAKED	FLAMM	FLAPERON
FIZZ	FLAFF	FLAKER	FLAMMABLE	FLAPERONS
FIZZED	FLAFFED	FLAKERS	FLAMMED	FLAPJACK
FIZZEN	FLAFFER	FLAKES	FLAMMING	FLAPJACKS
FIZZENS	FLAFFERED	FLAKEY	FLAMMS	FLAPLESS
FIZZER	FLAFFERS	FLAKIER	FLAMMULE	FLAPPABLE
FIZZERS	FLAFFING	FLAKIES	FLAMMULES	FLAPPED
FIZZES	FLAFFS	FLAKIEST	FLAMS	FLAPPER
FIZZGIG	FLAG	FLAKILY	FLAMY	FLAPPERS
FIZZGIGS	FLAGELLA	FLAKINESS	FLAN	FLAPPIER
FIZZIER	FLAGELLAR	FLAKING	FLANCARD	FLAPPIEST
FIZZIEST	FLAGELLIN	FLAKS	FLANCARDS	FLAPPING
FIZZINESS	FLAGELLUM	FLAKY	FLANCH	FLAPPINGS
FIZZING	FLAGEOLET	FLAM	FLANCHED	FLAPPY
FIZZINGS	FLAGGED	FLAMBE	FLANCHES	FLAPS
FIZZLE	FLAGGER	FLAMBEAU	FLANCHING	FLAPTRACK
FIZZLED	FLAGGERS	FLAMBEAUS	FLANERIE	FLARE
FIZZLES	FLAGGIER	FLAMBEAUX	FLANERIES	FLAREBACK
FIZZLING	FLAGGIEST	FLAMBEE	FLANES	FLARED
FIZZY	FLAGGING	FLAMBEED	FLANEUR	FLARES
FJELD	FLAGGINGS	FLAMBEES	FLANEURS	FLAREUP
FJELDS	FLAGGY	FLAMBEING	FLANGE	FLAREUPS
FJORD	FLAGITATE	FLAMBES	FLANGED	FLARIER
FJORDIC	FLAGLESS	FLAME	FLANGER	FLARIEST
FJORDS	FLAGMAN	FLAMED	FLANGERS	FLARING
FLAB	FLAGMEN	FLAMELESS	FLANGES	FLARINGLY
FLABBIER	FLAGON	FLAMELET	FLANGING	FLARY
FLABBIEST	FLAGONS	FLAMELETS	FLANK	FLASER
FLABBILY	FLAGPOLE	FLAMELIKE	FLANKED	FLASERS
FLABBY	FLAGPOLES	FLAMEN	FLANKEN	FLASH
FLABELLA	FLAGRANCE	FLAMENCO	FLANKER	FLASHBACK
FLABELLUM	FLAGRANCY	FLAMENCOS	FLANKERED	FLASHBULB
FLABS	FLAGRANT	FLAMENS	FLANKERS	FLASHCARD
FLACCID	FLAGS	FLAMEOUT	FLANKING	FLASHCUBE
FLACCIDER	FLAGSHIP	FLAMEOUTS	FLANKS	FLASHED
FLACCIDLY	FLAGSHIPS	FLAMER	FLANNEL	FLASHER
FLACK	FLAGSTAFF	FLAMERS	FLANNELED	FLASHERS
FLACKED	FLAGSTICK	FLAMES	FLANNELET	FLASHES
FLACKER	FLAGSTONE	FLAMFEW	FLANNELLY	FLASHEST

FLASHGUN	FLATLONG	FLAUNCHED	FLAWED	FLECKERED
FLASHGUNS	FLATLY	FLAUNCHES	FLAWIER	FLECKERS
FLASHIER	FLATMATE	FLAUNE	FLAWIEST	FLECKIER
FLASHIEST	FLATMATES	FLAUNES	FLAWING	FLECKIEST
FLASHILY	FLATNESS	FLAUNT	FLAWLESS	FLECKING
FLASHING	FLATPACK	FLAUNTED	FLAWN	FLECKLESS
FLASHINGS	FLATPACKS	FLAUNTER	FLAWNS	FLECKS
FLASHLAMP	FLATS	FLAUNTERS	FLAWS	FLECKY
FLASHOVER	FLATSHARE	FLAUNTIER	FLAWY	FLECTION
FLASHTUBE	FLATSTICK	FLAUNTILY	FLAX	FLECTIONS
FLASHY	FLATTED	FLAUNTING	FLAXEN	FLED
FLASK	FLATTEN	FLAUNTS	FLAXES	FLEDGE
FLASKET	FLATTENED	FLAUNTY	FLAXIER	FLEDGED
FLASKETS	FLATTENER	FLAUTA	FLAXIEST	FLEDGES
FLASKS	FLATTENS	FLAUTAS	FLAXSEED	FLEDGIER
FLAT	FLATTER	FLAUTIST	FLAXSEEDS	FLEDGIEST
FLATBACK	FLATTERED	FLAUTISTS	FLAXY	FLEDGING
FLATBACKS	FLATTERER	FLAVA	FLAY	FLEDGLING
FLATBED	FLATTERS	FLAVANOL	FLAYED	FLEDGY
FLATBEDS	FLATTERY	FLAVANOLS	FLAYER	FLEE
FLATBOAT	FLATTEST	FLAVANONE	FLAYERS	FLEECE
FLATBOATS	FLATTIE	FLAVAS	FLAYING	FLEECED
FLATBREAD	FLATTIES	FLAVIN	FLAYS	FLEECER
FLATCAP	FLATTING	FLAVINE	FLAYSOME	FLEECERS
FLATCAPS	FLATTINGS	FLAVINES	FLEA	FLEECES
FLATCAR	FLATTISH	FLAVINS	FLEABAG	FLEECH
FLATCARS	FLATTOP	FLAVONE	FLEABAGS	FLEECHED
FLATETTE	FLATTOPS	FLAVONES	FLEABANE	FLEECHES
FLATETTES	FLATTY	FLAVONOID	FLEABANES	FLEECHING
FLATFEET	FLATULENT	FLAVONOL	FLEABITE	FLEECIE
FLATFISH	FLATUOUS	FLAVONOLS	FLEABITES	FLEECIER
FLATFOOT	FLATUS	FLAVOR	FLEADH	FLEECIES
FLATFOOTS	FLATUSES	FLAVORED	FLEADHS	FLEECIEST
FLATHEAD	FLATWARE	FLAVORER	FLEAM	FLEECILY
FLATHEADS	FLATWARES	FLAVORERS	FLEAMS	FLEECING
FLATIRON	FLATWASH	FLAVORFUL	FLEAPIT	FLEECY
FLATIRONS	FLATWAYS	FLAVORING	FLEAPITS	FLEEING
FLATLAND	FLATWISE	FLAVORIST	FLEAS	FLEER
FLATLANDS	FLATWORK	FLAVOROUS	FLEASOME	FLEERED
FLATLET	FLATWORKS	FLAVORS	FLEAWORT	FLEERER
FLATLETS	FLATWORM	FLAVORY	FLEAWORTS	FLEERERS
FLATLINE	FLATWORMS	FLAVOUR	FLECHE	FLEERING
FLATLINED	FLAUGHT	FLAVOURED	FLECHES	FLEERINGS
FLATLINER	FLAUGHTED	FLAVOURER	FLECHETTE	FLEERS
FLATLINES	FLAUGHTER	FLAVOURS	FLECK	FLEES
FLATLING	FLAUGHTS	FLAVOURY	FLECKED	FLEET
FLATLINGS	FLAUNCH	FLAW	FLECKER	FLEETED

FLEETER	FLESHLING	FLEXURE	FLINCHED	FLIRTED
FLEETEST	FLESHLY	FLEXURES	FLINCHER	FLIRTER
FLEETING	FLESHMENT	FLEY	FLINCHERS	FLIRTERS
FLEETLY	FLESHPOT	FLEYED	FLINCHES	FLIRTIER
FLEETNESS	FLESHPOTS	FLEYING	FLINCHING	FLIRTIEST
FLEETS	FLESHWORM	FLEYS	FLINDER	FLIRTING
FLEG	FLESHY	FLIBBERT	FLINDERS	FLIRTINGS
FLEGGED	FLETCH	FLIBBERTS	FLING	FLIRTISH
FLEGGING	FLETCHED	FLIC	FLINGER	FLIRTS
FLEGS	FLETCHER	FLICHTER	FLINGERS	FLIRTY
FLEHMEN	FLETCHERS	FLICHTERS	FLINGING	FLISK
FLEHMENED	FLETCHES	FLICK	FLINGS	FLISKED
FLEHMENS	FLETCHING	FLICKABLE	FLINKITE	FLISKIER
FLEISHIG	FLETTON	FLICKED	FLINKITES	FLISKIEST
FLEISHIK	FLETTONS	FLICKER	FLINT	FLISKING
FLEME	FLEURET	FLICKERED	FLINTED	FLISKS
FLEMES	FLEURETS	FLICKERS	FLINTHEAD	FLISKY
FLEMING	FLEURETTE	FLICKERY	FLINTIER	FLIT
FLEMISH	FLEURON	FLICKING	FLINTIEST	FLITCH
FLEMISHED	FLEURONS	FLICKS	FLINTIFY	FLITCHED
FLEMISHES	FLEURY	FLICS	FLINTILY	FLITCHES
FLEMIT	FLEW	FLIED	FLINTING	FLITCHING
FLENCH	FLEWED	FLIER	FLINTLIKE	FLITE
FLENCHED	FLEWS	FLIERS	FLINTLOCK	FLITED
FLENCHER	FLEX	FLIES	FLINTS	FLITES
FLENCHERS	FLEXAGON	FLIEST	FLINTY	FLITING
FLENCHES	FLEXAGONS	FLIGHT	FLIP	FLITS
FLENCHING	FLEXED	FLIGHTED	FLIPBOOK	FLITT
FLENSE	FLEXES	FLIGHTIER	FLIPBOOKS	FLITTED
FLENSED	FLEXIBLE	FLIGHTILY	FLIPFLOP	FLITTER
FLENSER	FLEXIBLY	FLIGHTING	FLIPFLOPS	FLITTERED
FLENSERS	FLEXILE	FLIGHTS	FLIPPANCY	FLITTERN
FLENSES	FLEXING	FLIGHTY	FLIPPANT	FLITTERNS
FLENSING	FLEXION	FLIM	FLIPPED	FLITTERS
FLESH	FLEXIONAL	FLIMFLAM	FLIPPER	FLITTING
FLESHED	FLEXIONS	FLIMFLAMS	FLIPPERS	FLITTINGS
FLESHER	FLEXITIME	FLIMP	FLIPPEST	FLIVVER
FLESHERS	FLEXO	FLIMPED	FLIPPIER	FLIVVERS
FLESHES	FLEXOR	FLIMPING	FLIPPIEST	FLIX
FLESHHOOD	FLEXORS	FLIMPS	FLIPPING	FLIXED
FLESHIER	FLEXOS	FLIMS	FLIPPY	FLIXES
FLESHIEST	FLEXTIME	FLIMSIER	FLIPS	FLIXING
FLESHILY	FLEXTIMER	FLIMSIES	FLIPSIDE	FLOAT
FLESHING	FLEXTIMES	FLIMSIEST	FLIPSIDES	FLOATABLE
FLESHINGS	FLEXUOSE	FLIMSILY	FLIR	FLOATAGE
FLESHLESS	FLEXUOUS	FLIMSY	FLIRS	FLOATAGES
FLESHLIER	FLEXURAL	FLINCH	FLIRT	FLOATANT

FLOATANTS	FLOGS	FLOPPERS	FLORULE	FLOURING
FLOATCUT	FLOKATI	FLOPPIER	FLORULES	FLOURISH
FLOATED	FLOKATIS	FLOPPIES	FLORY	FLOURISHY
FLOATEL	FLONG	FLOPPIEST	FLOSCULAR	FLOURLESS
FLOATELS	FLONGS	FLOPPILY	FLOSCULE	FLOURS
FLOATER	FLOOD	FLOPPING	FLOSCULES	FLOURY
FLOATERS	FLOODABLE	FLOPPY	FLOSH	FLOUSE
FLOATIER	FLOODED	FLOPS	FLOSHES	FLOUSED
FLOATIEST	FLOODER	FLOPTICAL	FLOSS	FLOUSES
FLOATING	FLOODERS	FLOR	FLOSSED	FLOUSH
FLOATINGS	FLOODGATE	FLORA	FLOSSER	FLOUSHED
FLOATS	FLOODING	FLORAE	FLOSSERS	FLOUSHES
FLOATY	FLOODINGS	FLORAL	FLOSSES	FLOUSHING
FLOB	FLOODLESS	FLORALLY	FLOSSIE	FLOUSING
FLOBBED	FLOODLIT	FLORALS	FLOSSIER	FLOUT
FLOBBING	FLOODMARK	FLORAS	FLOSSIES	FLOUTED
FLOBS	FLOODS	FLOREANT	FLOSSIEST	FLOUTER
FLOC	FLOODTIDE	FLOREAT	FLOSSILY	FLOUTERS
FLOCCED	FLOODWALL	FLOREATED	FLOSSING	FLOUTING
FLOCCI	FLOODWAY	FLORENCE	FLOSSINGS	FLOUTS
FLOCCING	FLOODWAYS	FLORENCES	FLOSSY	FLOW
FLOCCOSE	FLOOEY	FLORET	FLOTA	FLOWAGE
FLOCCULAR	FLOOIE	FLORETS	FLOTAGE	FLOWAGES
FLOCCULE	FLOOR	FLORIATED	FLOTAGES	FLOWCHART
FLOCCULES	FLOORAGE	FLORICANE	FLOTANT	FLOWED
FLOCCULI	FLOORAGES	FLORID	FLOTAS	FLOWER
FLOCCULUS	FLOORED	FLORIDEAN	FLOTATION	FLOWERAGE
FLOCCUS	FLOORER	FLORIDER	FLOTE	FLOWERBED
FLOCK	FLOORERS	FLORIDEST	FLOTEL	FLOWERED
FLOCKED	FLOORHEAD	FLORIDITY	FLOTELS	FLOWERER
FLOCKIER	FLOORING	FLORIDLY	FLOTES	FLOWERERS
FLOCKIEST	FLOORINGS	FLORIER	FLOTILLA	FLOWERET
FLOCKING	FLOORLESS	FLORIEST	FLOTILLAS	FLOWERETS
FLOCKINGS	FLOORS	FLORIFORM	FLOTSAM	FLOWERFUL
FLOCKLESS	FLOORSHOW	FLORIGEN	FLOTSAMS	FLOWERIER
FLOCKS	FLOOSIE	FLORIGENS	FLOUNCE	FLOWERILY
FLOCKY	FLOOSIES	FLORIN	FLOUNCED	FLOWERING
FLOCS	FLOOSY	FLORINS	FLOUNCES	FLOWERPOT
FLOE	FLOOZIE	FLORIST	FLOUNCIER	FLOWERS
FLOES	FLOOZIES	FLORISTIC	FLOUNCING	FLOWERY
FLOG	FLOOZY	FLORISTRY	FLOUNCY	FLOWING
FLOGGABLE	FLOP	FLORISTS	FLOUNDER	FLOWINGLY
FLOGGED	FLOPHOUSE	FLORS	FLOUNDERS	FLOWMETER
FLOGGER	FLOPOVER	FLORUIT	FLOUR	FLOWN
FLOGGERS	FLOPOVERS	FLORUITS	FLOURED	FLOWS
FLOGGING	FLOPPED	FLORULA	FLOURIER	FLOWSTONE
FLOGGINGS	FLOPPER	FLORULAE	FLOURIEST	FLOX

FLU	FLUIDAL	FLUNKED	FLUSHIER	FLUYTS
FLUATE	FLUIDALLY	FLUNKER	FLUSHIEST	FLY
FLUATES	FLUIDIC	FLUNKERS	FLUSHING	FLYABLE
FLUB	FLUIDICS	FLUNKEY	FLUSHINGS	FLYAWAY
FLUBBED	FLUIDIFY	FLUNKEYS	FLUSHNESS	FLYAWAYS
FLUBBER	FLUIDISE	FLUNKIE	FLUSHWORK	FLYBACK
FLUBBERS	FLUIDISED	FLUNKIES	FLUSHY	FLYBACKS
FLUBBING	FLUIDISER	FLUNKING	FLUSTER	FLYBANE
FLUBDUB	FLUIDISES	FLUNKS	FLUSTERED	FLYBANES
FLUBDUBS	FLUIDITY	FLUNKY	FLUSTERS	FLYBELT
FLUBS	FLUIDIZE	FLUNKYISM	FLUSTERY	FLYBELTS
FLUCTUANT	FLUIDIZED	FLUOR	FLUSTRATE	FLYBLEW
FLUCTUATE	FLUIDIZER	FLUORENE	FLUTE	FLYBLOW
FLUE	FLUIDIZES	FLUORENES	FLUTED	FLYBLOWN
FLUED	FLUIDLIKE	FLUORESCE	FLUTELIKE	FLYBLOWS
FLUELLEN	FLUIDLY	FLUORIC	FLUTER	FLYBOAT
FLUELLENS	FLUIDNESS	FLUORID	FLUTERS	FLYBOATS
FLUELLIN	FLUIDRAM	FLUORIDE	FLUTES	FLYBOOK
FLUELLINS	FLUIDRAMS	FLUORIDES	FLUTEY	FLYBOOKS
FLUENCE	FLUIDS	FLUORIDS	FLUTIER	FLYBOY
FLUENCES	FLUIER	FLUORIN	FLUTIEST	FLYBOYS
FLUENCIES	FLUIEST	FLUORINE	FLUTINA	FLYBRIDGE
FLUENCY	FLUISH	FLUORINES	FLUTINAS	FLYBY
FLUENT	FLUKE	FLUORINS	FLUTING	FLYBYS
FLUENTLY	FLUKED	FLUORITE	FLUTINGS	FLYER
FLUENTS	FLUKES	FLUORITES	FLUTIST	FLYERS
FLUERIC	FLUKEY	FLUOROSES	FLUTISTS	FLYEST
FLUERICS	FLUKIER	FLUOROSIS	FLUTTER	FLYHAND
FLUES	FLUKIEST	FLUOROTIC	FLUTTERED	FLYHANDS
FLUEWORK	FLUKILY	FLUORS	FLUTTERER	FLYING
FLUEWORKS	FLUKINESS	FLUORSPAR	FLUTTERS	FLYINGS
FLUEY	FLUKING	FLURR	FLUTTERY	FLYLEAF
FLUFF	FLUKY	FLURRED	FLUTY	FLYLEAVES
FLUFFED	FLUME	FLURRIED	FLUVIAL	FLYLESS
FLUFFER	FLUMED	FLURRIES	FLUVIATIC	FLYMAKER
FLUFFERS	FLUMES	FLURRING	FLUX	FLYMAKERS
FLUFFIER	FLUMING	FLURRS	FLUXED	FLYMAN
FLUFFIEST	FLUMMERY	FLURRY	FLUXES	FLYMEN
FLUFFILY	FLUMMOX	FLURRYING	FLUXGATE	FLYOFF
FLUFFING	FLUMMOXED	FLUS	FLUXGATES	FLYOFFS
FLUFFS	FLUMMOXES	FLUSH	FLUXING	FLYOVER
FLUFFY	FLUMP	FLUSHABLE	FLUXION	FLYOVERS
FLUGEL	FLUMPED	FLUSHED	FLUXIONAL	FLYPAPER
FLUGELMAN	FLUMPING	FLUSHER	FLUXIONS	FLYPAPERS
FLUGELMEN	FLUMPS	FLUSHERS	FLUXIVE	FLYPAST
FLUGELS	FLUNG	FLUSHES	FLUXMETER	FLYPASTS
FLUID	FLUNK	FLUSHEST	FLUYT	FLYPE

FLYPED	FOAMINGS	FOEMAN	FOGLE	FOLACIN
FLYPES	FOAMLESS	FOEMEN	FOGLES	FOLACINS
FLYPING	FOAMLIKE	FOEN	FOGLESS	FOLATE
FLYPITCH	FOAMS	FOES	FOGMAN	FOLATES
FLYPOSTER	FOAMY	FOETAL	FOGMEN	FOLD
FLYRODDER	FOB	FOETATION	FOGOU	FOLDABLE
FLYSCH	FOBBED	FOETICIDE	FOGOUS	FOLDAWAY
FLYSCHES	FOBBING	FOETID	FOGRAM	FOLDAWAYS
FLYSCREEN	FOBS	FOETIDER	FOGRAMITE	FOLDBACK
FLYSHEET	FOCACCIA	FOETIDEST	FOGRAMITY	FOLDBACKS
FLYSHEETS	FOCACCIAS	FOETIDLY	FOGRAMS	FOLDBOAT
FLYSPECK	FOCAL	FOETOR	FOGS	FOLDBOATS
FLYSPECKS	FOCALISE	FOETORS	FOGY	FOLDED
FLYSPRAY	FOCALISED	FOETUS	FOGYDOM	FOLDER
FLYSPRAYS	FOCALISES	FOETUSES	FOGYDOMS	FOLDEROL
FLYSTRIKE	FOCALIZE	FOG	FOGYISH	FOLDEROLS
FLYTE	FOCALIZED	FOGASH	FOGYISM	FOLDERS
FLYTED	FOCALIZES	FOGASHES	FOGYISMS	FOLDING
FLYTES	FOCALLY	FOGBOUND	FOH	FOLDINGS
FLYTIER	FOCI	FOGBOW	FOHN	FOLDOUT
FLYTIERS	FOCIMETER	FOGBOWS	FOHNS	FOLDOUTS
FLYTING	FOCOMETER	FOGDOG	FOIBLE	FOLDS
FLYTINGS	FOCUS	FOGDOGS	FOIBLES	FOLDUP
FLYTRAP	FOCUSABLE	FOGEY	FOID	FOLDUPS
FLYTRAPS	FOCUSED	FOGEYDOM	FOIDS	FOLEY
FLYWAY	FOCUSER	FOGEYDOMS	FOIL	FOLEYS
FLYWAYS	FOCUSERS	FOGEYISH	FOILABLE	FOLIA
FLYWEIGHT	FOCUSES	FOGEYISM	FOILBORNE	FOLIAGE
FLYWHEEL	FOCUSING	FOGEYISMS	FOILED	FOLIAGED
FLYWHEELS	FOCUSINGS	FOGEYS	FOILING	FOLIAGES
FOAL	FOCUSLESS	FOGFRUIT	FOILINGS	FOLIAR
FOALED	FOCUSSED	FOGFRUITS	FOILS	FOLIATE
FOALFOOT	FOCUSSES	FOGGAGE	FOILSMAN	FOLIATED
FOALFOOTS	FOCUSSING	FOGGAGES	FOILSMEN	FOLIATES
FOALING	FODDER	FOGGED	FOIN	FOLIATING
FOALS	FODDERED	FOGGER	FOINED	FOLIATION
FOAM	FODDERER	FOGGERS	FOINING	FOLIATURE
FOAMABLE	FODDERERS	FOGGIER	FOININGLY	FOLIC
FOAMED	FODDERING	FOGGIEST	FOINS	FOLIE
FOAMER	FODDERS	FOGGILY	FOISON	FOLIES
FOAMERS	FODGEL	FOGGINESS	FOISONS	FOLIO
FOAMIER	FOE	FOGGING	FOIST	FOLIOED
FOAMIEST	FOEDARIE	FOGGY	FOISTED	FOLIOING
FOAMILY	FOEDARIES	FOGHORN	FOISTER	FOLIOLATE
FOAMINESS	FOEDERATI	FOGHORNS	FOISTERS	FOLIOLE
FOAMING	FOEHN	FOGIE	FOISTING	FOLIOLES
FOAMINGLY	FOEHNS	FOGIES	FOISTS	FOLIOLOSE

FOLIOS	FOLLOWING	FONT	FOOTBAGS	FOOTMUFF
FOLIOSE	FOLLOWS	FONTAL	FOOTBALL	FOOTMUFFS
FOLIOUS	FOLLOWUP	FONTANEL	FOOTBALLS	FOOTNOTE
FOLIUM	FOLLOWUPS	FONTANELS	FOOTBAR	FOOTNOTED
FOLIUMS	FOLLY	FONTANGE	FOOTBARS	FOOTNOTES
FOLK	FOLLYING	FONTANGES	FOOTBATH	FOOTPACE
FOLKIE	FOMENT	FONTICULI	FOOTBATHS	FOOTPACES
FOLKIER	FOMENTED	FONTINA	FOOTBOARD	FOOTPAD
FOLKIES	FOMENTER	FONTINAS	FOOTBOY	FOOTPADS
FOLKIEST	FOMENTERS	FONTLET	FOOTBOYS	FOOTPAGE
FOLKISH	FOMENTING	FONTLETS	FOOTBRAKE	FOOTPAGES
FOLKLAND	FOMENTS	FONTS	FOOTCLOTH	FOOTPATH
FOLKLANDS	FOMES	FOOBAR	FOOTED	FOOTPATHS
FOLKLIFE	FOMITE	FOOD	FOOTER	FOOTPLATE
FOLKLIKE	FOMITES	FOODFUL	FOOTERED	FOOTPOST
FOLKLIVES	FON	FOODIE	FOOTERING	FOOTPOSTS
FOLKLORE	FOND	FOODIES	FOOTERS	FOOTPRINT
FOLKLORES	FONDA	FOODISM	FOOTFALL	FOOTPUMP
FOLKLORIC	FONDANT	FOODISMS	FOOTFALLS	FOOTPUMPS
FOLKMOOT	FONDANTS	FOODLESS	FOOTFAULT	FOOTRA
FOLKMOOTS	FONDAS	FOODS	FOOTGEAR	FOOTRACE
FOLKMOT	FONDED	FOODSTUFF	FOOTGEARS	FOOTRACES
FOLKMOTE	FONDER	FOODWAYS	FOOTHILL	FOOTRAS
FOLKMOTES	FONDEST	FOODY	FOOTHILLS	FOOTREST
FOLKMOTS	FONDING	FOOFARAW	FOOTHOLD	FOOTRESTS
FOLKS	FONDLE	FOOFARAWS	FOOTHOLDS	FOOTROPE
FOLKSIER	FONDLED	FOOL	FOOTIE	FOOTROPES
FOLKSIEST	FONDLER	FOOLED	FOOTIER	FOOTRULE
FOLKSILY	FONDLERS	FOOLERIES	FOOTIES	FOOTRULES
FOLKSONG	FONDLES	FOOLERY	FOOTIEST	FOOTS
FOLKSONGS	FONDLING	FOOLFISH	FOOTING	FOOTSIE
FOLKSY	FONDLINGS	FOOLHARDY	FOOTINGS	FOOTSIES
FOLKTALE	FONDLY	FOOLING	FOOTLE	FOOTSLOG
FOLKTALES	FONDNESS	FOOLINGS	FOOTLED	FOOTSLOGS
FOLKWAY	FONDS	FOOLISH	FOOTLER	FOOTSORE
FOLKWAYS	FONDU	FOOLISHER	FOOTLERS	FOOTSTALK
FOLKY	FONDUE	FOOLISHLY	FOOTLES	FOOTSTALL
FOLLES	FONDUED	FOOLPROOF	FOOTLESS	FOOTSTEP
FOLLICLE	FONDUEING	FOOLS	FOOTLIGHT	FOOTSTEPS
FOLLICLES	FONDUES	FOOLSCAP	FOOTLIKE	FOOTSTOCK
FOLLIED	FONDUING	FOOLSCAPS	FOOTLING	FOOTSTONE
FOLLIES	FONDUS	FOOSBALL	FOOTLINGS	FOOTSTOOL
FOLLIS	FONE	FOOSBALLS	FOOTLOOSE	FOOTSY
FOLLOW	FONLY	FOOT	FOOTMAN	FOOTWALL
FOLLOWED	FONNED	FOOTAGE	FOOTMARK	FOOTWALLS
FOLLOWER	FONNING	FOOTAGES	FOOTMARKS	FOOTWAY
FOLLOWERS	FONS	FOOTBAG	FOOTMEN	FOOTWAYS

FOOTWEAR	FORAYS	FORDID	FOREDOES	FORELAIN
FOOTWEARS	FORB	FORDING	FOREDOING	FORELAND
FOOTWEARY	FORBAD	FORDLESS	FOREDONE	FORELANDS
FOOTWELL	FORBADE	FORDO	FOREDOOM	FORELAY
FOOTWELLS	FORBARE	FORDOES	FOREDOOMS	FORELAYS
FOOTWORK	FORBEAR	FORDOING	FOREFACE	FORELEG
FOOTWORKS	FORBEARER	FORDONE	FOREFACES	FORELEGS
FOOTWORN	FORBEARS	FORDONNE	FOREFEEL	FORELEND
FOOTY	FORBID	FORDS	FOREFEELS	FORELENDS
FOOZLE	FORBIDAL	FORE	FOREFEET	FORELENT
FOOZLED	FORBIDALS	FOREANENT	FOREFELT	FORELIE
FOOZLER	FORBIDDAL	FOREARM	FOREFEND	FORELIES
FOOZLERS	FORBIDDEN	FOREARMED	FOREFENDS	FORELIFT
FOOZLES	FORBIDDER	FOREARMS	FOREFOOT	FORELIFTS
FOOZLING	FORBIDS	FOREBAY	FOREFRONT	FORELIMB
FOOZLINGS	FORBODE	FOREBAYS	FOREGLEAM	FORELIMBS
FOP	FORBODED	FOREBEAR	FOREGO	FORELOCK
FOPLING	FORBODES	FOREBEARS	FOREGOER	FORELOCKS
FOPLINGS	FORBODING	FOREBITT	FOREGOERS	FORELS
FOPPED	FORBORE	FOREBITTS	FOREGOES	FORELYING
FOPPERIES	FORBORNE	FOREBODE	FOREGOING	FOREMAN
FOPPERY	FORBS	FOREBODED	FOREGONE	FOREMAST
FOPPING	FORBY	FOREBODER	FOREGUT	FOREMASTS
FOPPISH	FORBYE	FOREBODES	FOREGUTS	FOREMEAN
FOPPISHLY	FORCAT	FOREBODY	FOREHAND	FOREMEANS
FOPS	FORCATS	FOREBOOM	FOREHANDS	FOREMEANT
FOR	FORCE	FOREBOOMS	FOREHEAD	FOREMEN
FORA	FORCEABLE	FOREBRAIN	FOREHEADS	FOREMILK
FORAGE	FORCED	FOREBY	FOREHENT	FOREMILKS
FORAGED	FORCEDLY	FOREBYE	FOREHENTS	FOREMOST
FORAGER	FORCEFUL	FORECABIN	FOREHOCK	FORENAME
FORAGERS	FORCELESS	FORECADDY	FOREHOCKS	FORENAMED
FORAGES	FORCEMEAT	FORECAR	FOREHOOF	FORENAMES
FORAGING	FORCEPS	FORECARS	FOREHOOFS	FORENIGHT
FORAM	FORCEPSES	FORECAST	FOREIGN	FORENOON
FORAMEN	FORCER	FORECASTS	FOREIGNER	FORENOONS
FORAMENS	FORCERS	FORECHECK	FOREIGNLY	FORENSIC
FORAMINA	FORCES	FORECLOSE	FOREJUDGE	FORENSICS
FORAMINAL	FORCIBLE	FORECLOTH	FOREKING	FOREPART
FORAMS	FORCIBLY	FORECOURT	FOREKINGS	FOREPARTS
FORANE	FORCING	FOREDATE	FOREKNEW	FOREPAST
FORASMUCH	FORCINGLY	FOREDATED	FOREKNOW	FOREPAW
FORAY	FORCIPATE	FOREDATES	FOREKNOWN	FOREPAWS
FORAYED	FORCIPES	FOREDECK	FOREKNOWS	FOREPEAK
FORAYER	FORD	FOREDECKS	FOREL	FOREPEAKS
FORAYERS	FORDABLE	FOREDID	FORELADY	FOREPLAN
FORAYING	FORDED	FOREDO	FORELAID	FOREPLANS

FOREPLAY

FOREPLAY	FORESPENT	FOREWOMEN	FORGIVEN	FORKHEADS
FOREPLAYS	FORESPOKE	FOREWORD	FORGIVER	FORKIER
FOREPOINT	FOREST	FOREWORDS	FORGIVERS	FORKIEST
FORERAN	FORESTAGE	FOREWORN	FORGIVES	FORKINESS
FORERANK	FORESTAIR	FOREX	FORGIVING	FORKING
FORERANKS	FORESTAL	FOREXES	FORGO	FORKLESS
FOREREACH	FORESTALL	FOREYARD	FORGOER	FORKLIFT
FOREREAD	FORESTAY	FOREYARDS	FORGOERS	FORKLIFTS
FOREREADS	FORESTAYS	FORFAIR	FORGOES	FORKLIKE
FORERUN	FORESTEAL	FORFAIRED	FORGOING	FORKS
FORERUNS	FORESTED	FORFAIRN	FORGONE	FORKSFUL
FORES	FORESTER	FORFAIRS	FORGOT	FORKTAIL
FORESAID	FORESTERS	FORFAITER	FORGOTTEN	FORKTAILS
FORESAIL	FORESTIAL	FORFAULT	FORHAILE	FORKY
FORESAILS	FORESTINE	FORFAULTS	FORHAILED	FORLANA
FORESAW	FORESTING	FORFEIT	FORHAILES	FORLANAS
FORESAY	FORESTRY	FORFEITED	FORHENT	FORLEND
FORESAYS	FORESTS	FORFEITER	FORHENTS	FORLENDS
FORESEE	FORESWEAR	FORFEITS	FORHOO	FORLENT
FORESEEN	FORESWORE	FORFEND	FORHOOED	FORLORN
FORESEER	FORESWORN	FORFENDED	FORHOOIE	FORLORNER
FORESEERS	FORETASTE	FORFENDS	FORHOOIED	FORLORNLY
FORESEES	FORETEACH	FORFEX	FORHOOIES	FORLORNS
FORESHANK	FORETEETH	FORFEXES	FORHOOING	FORM
FORESHEET	FORETELL	FORFICATE	FORHOOS	FORMABLE
FORESHEW	FORETELLS	FORFOCHEN	FORHOW	FORMABLY
FORESHEWN	FORETHINK	FORGAT	FORHOWED	FORMAL
FORESHEWS	FORETIME	FORGATHER	FORHOWING	FORMALIN
FORESHIP	FORETIMES	FORGAVE	FORHOWS	FORMALINS
FORESHIPS	FORETOKEN	FORGE	FORINSEC	FORMALISE
FORESHOCK	FORETOLD	FORGEABLE	FORINT	FORMALISM
FORESHORE	FORETOOTH	FORGED	FORINTS	FORMALIST
FORESHOW	FORETOP	FORGEMAN	FORJASKIT	FORMALITY
FORESHOWN	FORETOPS	FORGEMEN	FORJESKIT	FORMALIZE
FORESHOWS	FOREVER	FORGER	FORJUDGE	FORMALLY
FORESIDE	FOREVERS	FORGERIES	FORJUDGED	FORMALS
FORESIDES	FOREWARD	FORGERS	FORJUDGES	FORMAMIDE
FORESIGHT	FOREWARDS	FORGERY	FORK	FORMANT
FORESKIN	FOREWARN	FORGES	FORKBALL	FORMANTS
FORESKINS	FOREWARNS	FORGET	FORKBALLS	FORMAT
FORESKIRT	FOREWEIGH	FORGETFUL	FORKED	FORMATE
FORESLACK	FOREWENT	FORGETIVE	FORKEDLY	FORMATED
FORESLOW	FOREWIND	FORGETS	FORKER	FORMATES
FORESLOWS	FOREWINDS	FORGETTER	FORKERS	FORMATING
FORESPAKE	FOREWING	FORGING	FORKFUL	FORMATION
FORESPEAK	FOREWINGS	FORGINGS	FORKFULS	FORMATIVE
FORESPEND	FOREWOMAN	FORGIVE	FORKHEAD	FORMATS

FORMATTED	FORPINE	FORSWONCK	FORWARDER	FOSTERAGE
FORMATTER	FORPINED	FORSWORE	FORWARDLY	FOSTERED
FORME	FORPINES	FORSWORN	FORWARDS	FOSTERER
FORMED	FORPINING	FORSWUNK	FORWARN	FOSTERERS
FORMEE	FORPIT	FORSYTHIA	FORWARNED	FOSTERING
FORMER	FORPITS	FORT	FORWARNS	FOSTERS
FORMERLY	FORRAD	FORTALICE	FORWASTE	FOSTRESS
FORMERS	FORRADER	FORTE	FORWASTED	FOTHER
FORMES	FORRARDER	FORTED	FORWASTES	FOTHERED
FORMFUL	FORRAY	FORTES	FORWEARY	FOTHERING
FORMIATE	FORRAYED	FORTH	FORWENT	FOTHERS
FORMIATES	FORRAYING	FORTHCAME	FORWHY	FOU
FORMIC	FORRAYS	FORTHCOME	FORWORN	FOUAT
FORMICA	FORREN	FORTHINK	FORZA	FOUATS
FORMICANT	FORRIT	FORTHINKS	FORZANDI	FOUD
FORMICARY	FORSAID	FORTHWITH	FORZANDO	FOUDRIE
FORMICAS	FORSAKE	FORTHY	FORZANDOS	FOUDRIES
FORMICATE	FORSAKEN	FORTIES	FORZATI	FOUDS
FORMING	FORSAKER	FORTIETH	FORZATO	FOUER
FORMINGS	FORSAKERS	FORTIETHS	FORZATOS	FOUEST
FORMLESS	FORSAKES	FORTIFIED	FORZE	FOUET
FORMOL	FORSAKING	FORTIFIER	FOSCARNET	FOUETS
FORMOLS	FORSAY	FORTIFIES	FOSS	FOUETTE
FORMS	FORSAYING	FORTIFY	FOSSA	FOUETTES
FORMULA	FORSAYS	FORTILAGE	FOSSAE	FOUGADE
FORMULAE	FORSLACK	FORTING	FOSSAS	FOUGADES
FORMULAIC	FORSLACKS	FORTIS	FOSSATE	FOUGASSE
FORMULAR	FORSLOE	FORTITUDE	FOSSE	FOUGASSES
FORMULARY	FORSLOED	FORTLET	FOSSED	FOUGHT
FORMULAS	FORSLOES	FORTLETS	FOSSES	FOUGHTEN
FORMULATE	FORSLOW	FORTNIGHT	FOSSETTE	FOUGHTIER
FORMULISE	FORSLOWED	FORTRESS	FOSSETTES	FOUGHTY
FORMULISM	FORSLOWS	FORTS	FOSSICK	FOUL
FORMULIST	FORSOOK	FORTUITY	FOSSICKED	FOULARD
FORMULIZE	FORSOOTH	FORTUNATE	FOSSICKER	FOULARDS
FORMWORK	FORSPEAK	FORTUNE	FOSSICKS	FOULBROOD
FORMWORKS	FORSPEAKS	FORTUNED	FOSSIL	FOULDER
FORMYL	FORSPEND	FORTUNES	FOSSILISE	FOULDERED
FORMYLS	FORSPENDS	FORTUNING	FOSSILIZE	FOULDERS
FORNENST	FORSPENT	FORTUNIZE	FOSSILS	FOULE
FORNENT	FORSPOKE	FORTY	FOSSOR	FOULED
FORNICAL	FORSPOKEN	FORTYISH	FOSSORIAL	FOULER
FORNICATE	FORSWATT	FORUM	FOSSORS	FOULES
FORNICES	FORSWEAR	FORUMS	FOSSULA	FOULEST
FORNIX	FORSWEARS	FORWANDER	FOSSULAE	FOULIE
FORPET	FORSWINK	FORWARD	FOSSULATE	FOULIES
FORPETS	FORSWINKS	FORWARDED	FOSTER	FOULING

FOULINGS	FOURTHS	FOXBERRY	FOYNED	FRAGILELY
FOULLY	FOUS	FOXED	FOYNES	FRAGILER
FOULMART	FOUSSA	FOXES	FOYNING	FRAGILEST
FOULMARTS	FOUSSAS	FOXFIRE	FOYS	FRAGILITY
FOULNESS	FOUSTIER	FOXFIRES	FOZIER	FRAGMENT
FOULS	FOUSTIEST	FOXFISH	FOZIEST	FRAGMENTS
FOUMART	FOUSTY	FOXFISHES	FOZINESS	FRAGOR
FOUMARTS	FOUTER	FOXGLOVE	FOZY	FRAGORS
FOUND	FOUTERED	FOXGLOVES	FRA	FRAGRANCE
FOUNDED	FOUTERING	FOXHOLE	FRAB	FRAGRANCY
FOUNDER	FOUTERS	FOXHOLES	FRABBED	FRAGRANT
FOUNDERED	FOUTH	FOXHOUND	FRABBING	FRAGS
FOUNDERS	FOUTHS	FOXHOUNDS	FRABBIT	FRAICHEUR
FOUNDING	FOUTRA	FOXHUNT	FRABJOUS	FRAIL
FOUNDINGS	FOUTRAS	FOXHUNTED	FRABS	FRAILER
FOUNDLING	FOUTRE	FOXHUNTER	FRACAS	FRAILEST
FOUNDRESS	FOUTRED	FOXHUNTS	FRACASES	FRAILISH
FOUNDRIES	FOUTRES	FOXIE	FRACK	FRAILLY
FOUNDRY	FOUTRING	FOXIER	FRACKING	FRAILNESS
FOUNDS	FOVEA	FOXIES	FRACKINGS	FRAILS
FOUNT	FOVEAE	FOXIEST	FRACT	FRAILTEE
FOUNTAIN	FOVEAL	FOXILY	FRACTAL	FRAILTEES
FOUNTAINS	FOVEAS	FOXINESS	FRACTALS	FRAILTIES
FOUNTFUL	FOVEATE	FOXING	FRACTED	FRAILTY
FOUNTS	FOVEATED	FOXINGS	FRACTI	FRAIM
FOUR	FOVEIFORM	FOXLIKE	FRACTING	FRAIMS
FOURBALL	FOVEOLA	FOXSHARK	FRACTION	FRAISE
FOURBALLS	FOVEOLAE	FOXSHARKS	FRACTIONS	FRAISED
FOURCHEE	FOVEOLAR	FOXSHIP	FRACTIOUS	FRAISES
FOUREYED	FOVEOLAS	FOXSHIPS	FRACTS	FRAISING
FOURFOLD	FOVEOLATE	FOXSKIN	FRACTUR	FRAKTUR
FOURGON	FOVEOLE	FOXSKINS	FRACTURAL	FRAKTURS
FOURGONS	FOVEOLES	FOXTAIL	FRACTURE	FRAMABLE
FOURPENCE	FOVEOLET	FOXTAILS	FRACTURED	FRAMBESIA
FOURPENNY	FOVEOLETS	FOXTROT	FRACTURER	FRAMBOISE
FOURPLAY	FOWL	FOXTROTS	FRACTURES	FRAME
FOURPLAYS	FOWLED	FOXY	FRACTURS	FRAMEABLE
FOURPLEX	FOWLER	FOY	FRACTUS	FRAMED
FOURS	FOWLERS	FOYBOAT	FRAE	FRAMELESS
FOURSCORE	FOWLING	FOYBOATS	FRAENA	FRAMER
FOURSES	FOWLINGS	FOYER	FRAENUM	FRAMERS
FOURSOME	FOWLPOX	FOYERS	FRAENUMS	FRAMES
FOURSOMES	FOWLPOXES	FOYLE	FRAG	FRAMEWORK
FOURTEEN	FOWLS	FOYLED	FRAGGED	FRAMING
FOURTEENS	FOWTH	FOYLES	FRAGGING	FRAMINGS
FOURTH	FOWTHS	FOYLING	FRAGGINGS	FRAMPAL
FOURTHLY	FOX	FOYNE	FRAGILE	FRAMPLER

FRAMPLERS	FRAPPES	FRAYING	FREEDMAN	FREEZE
FRAMPOLD	FRAPPING	FRAYINGS	FREEDMEN	FREEZER
FRANC	FRAPS	FRAYS	FREEDOM	FREEZERS
FRANCHISE	FRAS	FRAZIL	FREEDOMS	FREEZES
FRANCISE	FRASCATI	FRAZILS	FREEFORM	FREEZING
FRANCISED	FRASCATIS	FRAZZLE	FREEGAN	FREEZINGS
FRANCISES	FRASS	FRAZZLED	FREEGANS	FREIGHT
FRANCIUM	FRASSES	FRAZZLES	FREEHAND	FREIGHTED
FRANCIUMS	FRAT	FRAZZLING	FREEHOLD	FREIGHTER
FRANCIZE	FRATCH	FREAK	FREEHOLDS	FREIGHTS
FRANCIZED	FRATCHES	FREAKED	FREEING	FREIT
FRANCIZES	FRATCHETY	FREAKERY	FREELANCE	FREITIER
FRANCO	FRATCHIER	FREAKFUL	FREELOAD	FREITIEST
FRANCOLIN	FRATCHING	FREAKIER	FREELOADS	FREITS
FRANCS	FRATCHY	FREAKIEST	FREELY	FREITY
FRANGER	FRATE	FREAKILY	FREEMAN	FREMD
FRANGERS	FRATER	FREAKING	FREEMASON	FREMDS
FRANGIBLE	FRATERIES	FREAKISH	FREEMEN	FREMIT
FRANGLAIS	FRATERNAL	FREAKOUT	FREENESS	FREMITS
FRANION	FRATERS	FREAKOUTS	FREEPHONE	FREMITUS
FRANIONS	FRATERY	FREAKS	FREER	FRENA
FRANK	FRATI	FREAKY	FREERIDE	FRENCH
FRANKABLE	FRATRIES	FRECKLE	FREERIDES	FRENCHED
FRANKED	FRATRY	FRECKLED	FREERS	FRENCHES
FRANKER	FRATS	FRECKLES	FREES	FRENCHIFY
FRANKERS	FRAU	FRECKLIER	FREESHEET	FRENCHING
FRANKEST	FRAUD	FRECKLING	FREESIA	FRENETIC
FRANKFORT	FRAUDFUL	FRECKLY	FREESIAS	FRENETICS
FRANKFURT	FRAUDS	FREDAINE	FREEST	FRENNE
FRANKING	FRAUDSMAN	FREDAINES	FREESTONE	FRENNES
FRANKLIN	FRAUDSMEN	FREE	FREESTYLE	FRENULA
FRANKLINS	FRAUDSTER	FREEBASE	FREET	FRENULAR
FRANKLY	FRAUGHAN	FREEBASED	FREETIER	FRENULUM
FRANKNESS	FRAUGHANS	FREEBASER	FREETIEST	FRENULUMS
FRANKS	FRAUGHT	FREEBASES	FREETS	FRENUM
FRANSERIA	FRAUGHTED	FREEBEE	FREETY	FRENUMS
FRANTIC	FRAUGHTER	FREEBEES	FREEWARE	FRENZICAL
FRANTICLY	FRAUGHTS	FREEBIE	FREEWARES	FRENZIED
FRANZIER	FRAULEIN	FREEBIES	FREEWAY	FRENZIES
FRANZIEST	FRAULEINS	FREEBOARD	FREEWAYS	FRENZILY
FRANZY	FRAUS	FREEBOOT	FREEWHEEL	FRENZY
FRAP	FRAUTAGE	FREEBOOTS	FREEWILL	FRENZYING
FRAPE	FRAUTAGES	FREEBOOTY	FREEWOMAN	FREQUENCE
FRAPPANT	FRAWZEY	FREEBORN	FREEWOMEN	FREQUENCY
FRAPPE	FRAWZEYS	FREECYCLE	FREEWRITE	FREQUENT
FRAPPED	FRAY	FREED	FREEWROTE	FREQUENTS
FRAPPEE	FRAYED	FREEDIVER	FREEZABLE	FRERE

FRERES	FRETTING	FRIENDS	FRILLY	FRISTING
FRESCADE	FRETTINGS	FRIER	FRINGE	FRISTS
FRESCADES	FRETTY	FRIERS	FRINGED	FRISURE
FRESCO	FRETWORK	FRIES	FRINGES	FRISURES
FRESCOED	FRETWORKS	FRIEZE	FRINGIER	FRIT
FRESCOER	FRIABLE	FRIEZED	FRINGIEST	FRITES
FRESCOERS	FRIAND	FRIEZES	FRINGING	FRITFLIES
FRESCOES	FRIANDE	FRIEZING	FRINGY	FRITFLY
FRESCOING	FRIANDES	FRIG	FRIPON	FRITH
FRESCOIST	FRIANDS	FRIGATE	FRIPONS	FRITHBORH
FRESCOS	FRIAR	FRIGATES	FRIPPER	FRITHS
FRESH	FRIARBIRD	FRIGATOON	FRIPPERER	FRITS
FRESHED	FRIARIES	FRIGES	FRIPPERS	FRITT
FRESHEN	FRIARLY	FRIGGED	FRIPPERY	FRITTATA
FRESHENED	FRIARS	FRIGGER	FRIPPET	FRITTATAS
FRESHENER	FRIARY	FRIGGERS	FRIPPETS	FRITTED
FRESHENS	FRIB	FRIGGING	FRIS	FRITTER
FRESHER	FRIBBLE	FRIGGINGS	FRISBEE	FRITTERED
FRESHERS	FRIBBLED	FRIGHT	FRISBEES	FRITTERER
FRESHES	FRIBBLER	FRIGHTED	FRISE	FRITTERS
FRESHEST	FRIBBLERS	FRIGHTEN	FRISEE	FRITTING
FRESHET	FRIBBLES	FRIGHTENS	FRISEES	FRITTS
FRESHETS	FRIBBLING	FRIGHTFUL	FRISES	FRITURE
FRESHIE	FRIBBLISH	FRIGHTING	FRISETTE	FRITURES
FRESHIES	FRIBS	FRIGHTS	FRISETTES	FRITZ
FRESHING	FRICADEL	FRIGID	FRISEUR	FRITZES
FRESHISH	FRICADELS	FRIGIDER	FRISEURS	FRIVOL
FRESHLY	FRICANDO	FRIGIDEST	FRISK	FRIVOLED
FRESHMAN	FRICASSEE	FRIGIDITY	FRISKA	FRIVOLER
FRESHMEN	FRICATIVE	FRIGIDLY	FRISKAS	FRIVOLERS
FRESHNESS	FRICHT	FRIGOT	FRISKED	FRIVOLING
FRESNEL	FRICHTED	FRIGOTS	FRISKER	FRIVOLITY
FRESNELS	FRICHTING	FRIGS	FRISKERS	FRIVOLLED
FRET	FRICHTS	FRIJOL	FRISKET	FRIVOLLER
FRETBOARD	FRICKING	FRIJOLE	FRISKETS	FRIVOLOUS
FRETFUL	FRICTION	FRIJOLES	FRISKFUL	FRIVOLS
FRETFULLY	FRICTIONS	FRIKKADEL	FRISKIER	FRIZ
FRETLESS	FRIDGE	FRILL	FRISKIEST	FRIZE
FRETS	FRIDGED	FRILLED	FRISKILY	FRIZED
FRETSAW	FRIDGES	FRILLER	FRISKING	FRIZER
FRETSAWS	FRIDGING	FRILLERS	FRISKINGS	FRIZERS
FRETSOME	FRIED	FRILLIER	FRISKS	FRIZES
FRETTED	FRIEDCAKE	FRILLIES	FRISKY	FRIZETTE
FRETTER	FRIEND	FRILLIEST	FRISSON	FRIZETTES
FRETTERS	FRIENDED	FRILLING	FRISSONS	FRIZING
FRETTIER	FRIENDING	FRILLINGS	FRIST	FRIZZ
FRETTIEST	FRIENDLY	FRILLS	FRISTED	FRIZZANTE

FRIZZED	FROGMARCH	FRONTLET	FROTHIER	FROWY
FRIZZER	FROGMEN	FRONTLETS	FROTHIEST	FROWZIER
FRIZZERS	FROGMOUTH	FRONTLINE	FROTHILY	FROWZIEST
FRIZZES	FROGS	FRONTLIST	FROTHING	FROWZILY
FRIZZIER	FROGSPAWN	FRONTMAN	FROTHLESS	FROWZY
FRIZZIES	FROIDEUR	FRONTMEN	FROTHS	FROZE
FRIZZIEST	FROIDEURS	FRONTON	FROTHY	FROZEN
FRIZZILY	FROING	FRONTONS	FROTTAGE	FROZENLY
FRIZZING	FROINGS	FRONTOON	FROTTAGES	FRUCTAN
FRIZZLE	FROISE	FRONTOONS	FROTTEUR	FRUCTANS
FRIZZLED	FROISES	FRONTPAGE	FROTTEURS	FRUCTED
FRIZZLER	FROLIC	FRONTS	FROUFROU	FRUCTIFY
FRIZZLERS	FROLICKED	FRONTWARD	FROUFROUS	FRUCTIVE
FRIZZLES	FROLICKER	FRONTWAYS	FROUGHIER	FRUCTOSE
FRIZZLIER	FROLICKY	FRONTWISE	FROUGHY	FRUCTOSES
FRIZZLING	FROLICS	FRORE	FROUNCE	FRUCTUARY
FRIZZLY	FROM	FROREN	FROUNCED	FRUCTUATE
FRIZZY	FROMAGE	FRORN	FROUNCES	FRUCTUOUS
FRO	FROMAGES	FRORNE	FROUNCING	FRUG
FROCK	FROMENTY	FRORY	FROUZIER	FRUGAL
FROCKED	FROND	FROS	FROUZIEST	FRUGALIST
FROCKING	FRONDAGE	FROSH	FROUZY	FRUGALITY
FROCKINGS	FRONDAGES	FROSHES	FROW	FRUGALLY
FROCKLESS	FRONDED	FROST	FROWARD	FRUGGED
FROCKS	FRONDENT	FROSTBIT	FROWARDLY	FRUGGING
FROE	FRONDEUR	FROSTBITE	FROWARDS	FRUGIVORE
FROES	FRONDEURS	FROSTED	FROWIE	FRUGS
FROG	FRONDLESS	FROSTEDS	FROWIER	FRUICT
FROGBIT	FRONDOSE	FROSTFISH	FROWIEST	FRUICTS
FROGBITS	FRONDOUS	FROSTIER	FROWN	FRUIT
FROGEYE	FRONDS	FROSTIEST	FROWNED	FRUITAGE
FROGEYED	FRONS	FROSTILY	FROWNER	FRUITAGES
FROGEYES	FRONT	FROSTING	FROWNERS	FRUITCAKE
FROGFISH	FRONTAGE	FROSTINGS	FROWNING	FRUITED
FROGGED	FRONTAGER	FROSTLESS	FROWNS	FRUITER
FROGGERY	FRONTAGES	FROSTLIKE	FROWS	FRUITERER
FROGGIER	FRONTAL	FROSTLINE	FROWSIER	FRUITERS
FROGGIEST	FRONTALLY	FROSTNIP	FROWSIEST	FRUITERY
FROGGING	FRONTALS	FROSTNIPS	FROWST	FRUITFUL
FROGGINGS	FRONTED	FROSTS	FROWSTED	FRUITIER
FROGGY	FRONTENIS	FROSTWORK	FROWSTER	FRUITIEST
FROGLET	FRONTER	FROSTY	FROWSTERS	FRUITILY
FROGLETS	FRONTES	FROTH	FROWSTIER	FRUITING
FROGLIKE	FRONTIER	FROTHED	FROWSTING	FRUITINGS
FROGLING	FRONTIERS	FROTHER	FROWSTS	FRUITION
FROGLINGS	FRONTING	FROTHERS	FROWSTY	FRUITIONS
FROGMAN	FRONTLESS	FROTHERY	FROWSY	FRUITIVE

FRUITLESS	FRYINGS	FUCUSED	FUGGED	FULFILS
FRUITLET	FRYPAN	FUCUSES	FUGGIER	FULGENCY
FRUITLETS	FRYPANS	FUD	FUGGIEST	FULGENT
FRUITLIKE	FUB	FUDDIES	FUGGILY	FULGENTLY
FRUITS	FUBAR	FUDDLE	FUGGINESS	FULGID
FRUITWOOD	FUBBED	FUDDLED	FUGGING	FULGOR
FRUITY	FUBBERIES	FUDDLER	FUGGY	FULGOROUS
FRUMENTY	FUBBERY	FUDDLERS	FUGHETTA	FULGORS
FRUMP	FUBBIER	FUDDLES	FUGHETTAS	FULGOUR
FRUMPED	FUBBIEST	FUDDLING	FUGIE	FULGOURS
FRUMPIER	FUBBING	FUDDLINGS	FUGIES	FULGURAL
FRUMPIEST	FUBBY	FUDDY	FUGIO	FULGURANT
FRUMPILY	FUBS	FUDGE	FUGIOS	FULGURATE
FRUMPING	FUBSIER	FUDGED	FUGITIVE	FULGURITE
FRUMPISH	FUBSIEST	FUDGES	FUGITIVES	FULGUROUS
FRUMPLE	FUBSY	FUDGING	FUGLE	FULHAM
FRUMPLED	FUCHSIA	FUDS	FUGLED	FULHAMS
FRUMPLES	FUCHSIAS	FUEHRER	FUGLEMAN	FULL
FRUMPLING	FUCHSIN	FUEHRERS	FUGLEMEN	FULLAGE
FRUMPS	FUCHSINE	FUEL	FUGLES	FULLAGES
FRUMPY	FUCHSINES	FUELED	FUGLIER	FULLAM
FRUSEMIDE	FUCHSINS	FUELER	FUGLIEST	FULLAMS
FRUSH	FUCHSITE	FUELERS	FUGLING	FULLAN
FRUSHED	FUCHSITES	FUELING	FUGLY	FULLANS
FRUSHES	FUCI	FUELLED	FUGS	FULLBACK
FRUSHING	FUCK	FUELLER	FUGU	FULLBACKS
FRUST	FUCKED	FUELLERS	FUGUE	FULLBLOOD
FRUSTA	FUCKER	FUELLING	FUGUED	FULLED
FRUSTRATE	FUCKERS	FUELS	FUGUELIKE	FULLER
FRUSTS	FUCKHEAD	FUELWOOD	FUGUES	FULLERED
FRUSTULE	FUCKHEADS	FUELWOODS	FUGUING	FULLERENE
FRUSTULES	FUCKING	FUERO	FUGUIST	FULLERIDE
FRUSTUM	FUCKINGS	FUEROS	FUGUISTS	FULLERIES
FRUSTUMS	FUCKOFF	FUFF	FUGUS	FULLERING
FRUTEX	FUCKOFFS	FUFFED	FUHRER	FULLERITE
FRUTICES	FUCKS	FUFFIER	FUHRERS	FULLERS
FRUTICOSE	FUCKUP	FUFFIEST	FUJI	FULLERY
FRUTIFIED	FUCKUPS	FUFFING	FUJIS	FULLEST
FRUTIFIES	FUCKWIT	FUFFS	FULCRA	FULLFACE
FRUTIFY	FUCKWITS	FUFFY	FULCRATE	FULLFACES
FRY	FUCOID	FUG	FULCRUM	FULLING
FRYABLE	FUCOIDAL	FUGACIOUS	FULCRUMS	FULLISH
FRYBREAD	FUCOIDS	FUGACITY	FULFIL	FULLNESS
FRYBREADS	FUCOSE	FUGAL	FULFILL	FULLS
FRYER	FUCOSES	FUGALLY	FULFILLED	FULLY
FRYERS	FUCOUS	FUGATO	FULFILLER	FULMAR
FRYING	FUCUS	FUGATOS	FULFILLS	FULMARS

FULMINANT	FUMET	FUNDS	FUNKHOLES	FURBELOWS
FULMINATE	FUMETS	FUNDUS	FUNKIA	FURBISH
FULMINE	FUMETTE	FUNDY	FUNKIAS	FURBISHED
FULMINED	FUMETTES	FUNEBRAL	FUNKIER	FURBISHER
FULMINES	FUMETTI	FUNEBRE	FUNKIEST	FURBISHES
FULMINIC	FUMETTO	FUNEBRIAL	FUNKILY	FURCA
FULMINING	FUMIER	FUNERAL	FUNKINESS	FURCAE
FULMINOUS	FUMIEST	FUNERALS	FUNKING	FURCAL
FULNESS	FUMIGANT	FUNERARY	FUNKS	FURCATE
FULNESSES	FUMIGANTS	FUNEREAL	FUNKSTER	FURCATED
FULSOME	FUMIGATE	FUNEST	FUNKSTERS	FURCATELY
FULSOMELY	FUMIGATED	FUNFAIR	FUNKY	FURCATES
FULSOMER	FUMIGATES	FUNFAIRS	FUNNED	FURCATING
FULSOMEST	FUMIGATOR	FUNFEST	FUNNEL	FURCATION
FULVID	FUMING	FUNFESTS	FUNNELED	FURCRAEA
FULVOUS	FUMINGLY	FUNG	FUNNELING	FURCRAEAS
FUM	FUMITORY	FUNGAL	FUNNELLED	FURCULA
FUMADO	FUMOSITY	FUNGALS	FUNNELS	FURCULAE
FUMADOES	FUMOUS	FUNGI	FUNNER	FURCULAR
FUMADOS	FUMS	FUNGIBLE	FUNNEST	FURCULUM
FUMAGE	FUMULI	FUNGIBLES	FUNNIER	FURDER
FUMAGES	FUMULUS	FUNGIC	FUNNIES	FUREUR
FUMARASE	FUMY	FUNGICIDE	FUNNIEST	FUREURS
FUMARASES	FUN	FUNGIFORM	FUNNILY	FURFAIR
FUMARATE	FUNBOARD	FUNGISTAT	FUNNINESS	FURFAIRS
FUMARATES	FUNBOARDS	FUNGO	FUNNING	FURFUR
FUMARIC	FUNCKIA	FUNGOES	FUNNY	FURFURAL
FUMAROLE	FUNCKIAS	FUNGOID	FUNNYMAN	FURFURALS
FUMAROLES	FUNCTION	FUNGOIDAL	FUNNYMEN	FURFURAN
FUMAROLIC	FUNCTIONS	FUNGOIDS	FUNPLEX	FURFURANS
FUMATORIA	FUNCTOR	FUNGOSITY	FUNPLEXES	FURFURES
FUMATORY	FUNCTORS	FUNGOUS	FUNS	FURFUROL
FUMBLE	FUND	FUNGS	FUNSTER	FURFUROLE
FUMBLED	FUNDABLE	FUNGUS	FUNSTERS	FURFUROLS
FUMBLER	FUNDAMENT	FUNGUSES	FUR	FURFUROUS
FUMBLERS	FUNDED	FUNHOUSE	FURACIOUS	FURFURS
FUMBLES	FUNDER	FUNHOUSES	FURACITY	FURIBUND
FUMBLING	FUNDERS	FUNICLE	FURAL	FURIES
FUME	FUNDI	FUNICLES	FURALS	FURIOSITY
FUMED	FUNDIC	FUNICULAR	FURAN	FURIOSO
FUMELESS	FUNDIE	FUNICULI	FURANE	FURIOSOS
FUMELIKE	FUNDIES	FUNICULUS	FURANES	FURIOUS
FUMER	FUNDING	FUNK	FURANOSE	FURIOUSLY
FUMEROLE	FUNDINGS	FUNKED	FURANOSES	FURKID
FUMEROLES	FUNDIS	FUNKER	FURANS	FURKIDS
FUMERS	FUNDLESS	FUNKERS	FURBEARER	FURL
FUMES	FUNDRAISE	FUNKHOLE	FURBELOW	FURLABLE

FURLANA

FURLANA	FURRINESS	FUSELAGES	FUSTIANS	FUTZES
FURLANAS	FURRING	FUSELESS	FUSTIC	FUTZING
FURLED	FURRINGS	FUSELIKE	FUSTICS	FUZE
FURLER	FURROW	FUSELS	FUSTIER	FUZED
FURLERS	FURROWED	FUSES	FUSTIEST	FUZEE
FURLESS	FURROWER	FUSHION	FUSTIGATE	FUZEES
FURLING	FURROWERS	FUSHIONS	FUSTILUGS	FUZES
FURLONG	FURROWING	FUSIBLE	FUSTILY	FUZIL
FURLONGS	FURROWS	FUSIBLY	FUSTINESS	FUZILS
FURLOUGH	FURROWY	FUSIDIC	FUSTING	FUZING
FURLOUGHS	FURRS	FUSIFORM	FUSTOC	FUZZ
FURLS	FURRY	FUSIL	FUSTOCS	FUZZBOX
FURMENTY	FURS	FUSILE	FUSTS	FUZZBOXES
FURMETIES	FURTH	FUSILEER	FUSTY	FUZZED
FURMETY	FURTHER	FUSILEERS	FUSULINID	FUZZES
FURMITIES	FURTHERED	FUSILIER	FUSUMA	FUZZIER
FURMITY	FURTHERER	FUSILIERS	FUTCHEL	FUZZIEST
FURNACE	FURTHERS	FUSILLADE	FUTCHELS	FUZZILY
FURNACED	FURTHEST	FUSILLI	FUTHARC	FUZZINESS
FURNACES	FURTIVE	FUSILLIS	FUTHARCS	FUZZING
FURNACING	FURTIVELY	FUSILS	FUTHARK	FUZZLE
FURNIMENT	FURUNCLE	FUSING	FUTHARKS	FUZZLED
FURNISH	FURUNCLES	FUSION	FUTHORC	FUZZLES
FURNISHED	FURY	FUSIONAL	FUTHORCS	FUZZLING
FURNISHER	FURZE	FUSIONISM	FUTHORK	FUZZTONE
FURNISHES	FURZES	FUSIONIST	FUTHORKS	FUZZTONES
FURNITURE	FURZIER	FUSIONS	FUTILE	FUZZY
FUROL	FURZIEST	FUSS	FUTILELY	FY
FUROLE	FURZY	FUSSBALL	FUTILER	FYCE
FUROLES	FUSAIN	FUSSBALLS	FUTILEST	FYCES
FUROLS	FUSAINS	FUSSED	FUTILITY	FYKE
FUROR	FUSARIA	FUSSER	FUTON	FYKED
FURORE	FUSARIUM	FUSSERS	FUTONS	FYKES
FURORES	FUSAROL	FUSSES	FUTSAL	FYKING
FURORS	FUSAROLE	FUSSIER	FUTSALS	FYLE
FURPHIES	FUSAROLES	FUSSIEST	FUTTOCK	FYLES
FURPHY	FUSAROLS	FUSSILY	FUTTOCKS	FYLFOT
FURR	FUSBALL	FUSSINESS	FUTURAL	FYLFOTS
FURRED	FUSBALLS	FUSSING	FUTURE	FYNBOS
FURRIER	FUSC	FUSSPOT	FUTURES	FYNBOSES
FURRIERS	FUSCOUS	FUSSPOTS	FUTURISM	FYRD
FURRIERY	FUSE	FUSSY	FUTURISMS	FYRDS
FURRIES	FUSED	FUST	FUTURIST	FYTTE
FURRIEST	FUSEE	FUSTED	FUTURISTS	FYTTES
FURRILY	FUSEES	FUSTET	FUTURITY	
FURRINER	FUSEL	FUSTETS	FUTZ	
FURRINERS	FUSELAGE	FUSTIAN	FUTZED	

G

GAB	GABLET	GADROONED	GAGGLE	GAIT
GABARDINE	GABLETS	GADROONS	GAGGLED	GAITA
GABBA	GABLING	GADS	GAGGLES	GAITAS
GABBARD	GABNASH	GADSMAN	GAGGLING	GAITED
GABBARDS	GABNASHES	GADSMEN	GAGGLINGS	GAITER
GABBART	GABOON	GADSO	GAGING	GAITERED
GABBARTS	GABOONS	GADWALL	GAGMAN	GAITERS
GABBAS	GABS	GADWALLS	GAGMEN	GAITING
GABBED	GABY	GADZOOKS	GAGS	GAITS
GABBER	GAD	GAE	GAGSTER	GAITT
GABBERS	GADABOUT	GAED	GAGSTERS	GAITTS
GABBIER	GADABOUTS	GAEING	GAHNITE	GAJO
GABBIEST	GADARENE	GAELICISE	GAHNITES	GAJOS
GABBINESS	GADDED	GAELICISM	GAID	GAK
GABBING	GADDER	GAELICIZE	GAIDS	GAKS
GABBLE	GADDERS	GAEN	GAIETIES	GAL
GABBLED	GADDI	GAES	GAIETY	GALA
GABBLER	GADDING	GAFF	GAIJIN	GALABEA
GABBLERS	GADDIS	GAFFE	GAILLARD	GALABEAH
GABBLES	GADE	GAFFED	GAILLARDE	GALABEAHS
GABBLING	GADES	GAFFER	GAILY	GALABEAS
GABBLINGS	GADFLIES	GAFFERS	GAIN	GALABIA
GABBRO	GADFLY	GAFFES	GAINABLE	GALABIAH
GABBROIC	GADGE	GAFFING	GAINED	GALABIAHS
GABBROID	GADGES	GAFFINGS	GAINER	GALABIAS
GABBROS	GADGET	GAFFS	GAINERS	GALABIEH
GABBY	GADGETEER	GAFFSAIL	GAINEST	GALABIEHS
GABELLE	GADGETRY	GAFFSAILS	GAINFUL	GALABIYA
GABELLED	GADGETS	GAG	GAINFULLY	GALABIYAH
GABELLER	GADGETY	GAGA	GAINING	GALABIYAS
GABELLERS	GADGIE	GAGAKU	GAININGS	GALACTIC
GABELLES	GADGIES	GAGAKUS	GAINLESS	GALACTOSE
GABERDINE	GADI	GAGE	GAINLIER	GALAGE
GABFEST	GADID	GAGEABLE	GAINLIEST	GALAGES
GABFESTS	GADIDS	GAGEABLY	GAINLY	GALAGO
GABIES	GADIS	GAGED	GAINS	GALAGOS
GABION	GADJE	GAGER	GAINSAID	GALAH
GABIONADE	GADJES	GAGERS	GAINSAY	GALAHS
GABIONAGE	GADJO	GAGES	GAINSAYER	GALANGA
GABIONED	GADLING	GAGGED	GAINSAYS	GALANGAL
GABIONS	GADLINGS	GAGGER	GAINST	GALANGALS
GABLE	GADOID	GAGGERIES	GAIR	GALANGAS
GABLED	GADOIDS	GAGGERS	GAIRFOWL	GALANT
GABLELIKE	GADOLINIC	GAGGERY	GAIRFOWLS	GALANTINE
GABLES	GADROON	GAGGING	GAIRS	GALANTY

G

GALAPAGO	GALLABEAS	GALLIED	GALLOWING	GALUTS
GALAPAGOS	GALLABIA	GALLIES	GALLOWS	GALVANIC
GALAS	GALLABIAH	GALLINAZO	GALLOWSES	GALVANISE
GALATEA	GALLABIAS	GALLING	GALLS	GALVANISM
GALATEAS	GALLABIEH	GALLINGLY	GALLSTONE	GALVANIST
GALAVANT	GALLABIYA	GALLINULE	GALLUMPH	GALVANIZE
GALAVANTS	GALLAMINE	GALLIOT	GALLUMPHS	GALVO
GALAX	GALLANT	GALLIOTS	GALLUS	GALVOS
GALAXES	GALLANTED	GALLIPOT	GALLUSED	GALYAC
GALAXIES	GALLANTER	GALLIPOTS	GALLUSES	GALYACS
GALAXY	GALLANTLY	GALLISE	GALLY	GALYAK
GALBANUM	GALLANTRY	GALLISED	GALLYING	GALYAKS
GALBANUMS	GALLANTS	GALLISES	GALOCHE	GAM
GALDRAGON	GALLATE	GALLISING	GALOCHED	GAMA
GALE	GALLATES	GALLISISE	GALOCHES	GAMAHUCHE
GALEA	GALLEASS	GALLISIZE	GALOCHING	GAMARUCHE
GALEAE	GALLED	GALLIUM	GALOOT	GAMAS
GALEAS	GALLEIN	GALLIUMS	GALOOTS	GAMASH
GALEATE	GALLEINS	GALLIVANT	GALOP	GAMASHES
GALEATED	GALLEON	GALLIVAT	GALOPADE	GAMAY
GALEIFORM	GALLEONS	GALLIVATS	GALOPADES	GAMAYS
GALENA	GALLERIA	GALLIWASP	GALOPED	GAMB
GALENAS	GALLERIAS	GALLIZE	GALOPIN	GAMBA
GALENGALE	GALLERIED	GALLIZED	GALOPING	GAMBADE
GALENIC	GALLERIES	GALLIZES	GALOPINS	GAMBADES
GALENICAL	GALLERIST	GALLIZING	GALOPPED	GAMBADO
GALENITE	GALLERY	GALLNUT	GALOPPING	GAMBADOED
GALENITES	GALLET	GALLNUTS	GALOPS	GAMBADOES
GALENOID	GALLETA	GALLOCK	GALORE	GAMBADOS
GALERE	GALLETAS	GALLON	GALORES	GAMBAS
GALERES	GALLETED	GALLONAGE	GALOSH	GAMBE
GALES	GALLETING	GALLONS	GALOSHE	GAMBES
GALETTE	GALLETS	GALLOON	GALOSHED	GAMBESON
GALETTES	GALLEY	GALLOONED	GALOSHES	GAMBESONS
GALILEE	GALLEYS	GALLOONS	GALOSHING	GAMBET
GALILEES	GALLFLIES	GALLOOT	GALOWSES	GAMBETS
GALINGALE	GALLFLY	GALLOOTS	GALRAVAGE	GAMBETTA
GALIONGEE	GALLIARD	GALLOP	GALS	GAMBETTAS
GALIOT	GALLIARDS	GALLOPADE	GALTONIA	GAMBIA
GALIOTS	GALLIASS	GALLOPED	GALTONIAS	GAMBIAS
GALIPOT	GALLIC	GALLOPER	GALUMPH	GAMBIER
GALIPOTS	GALLICA	GALLOPERS	GALUMPHED	GAMBIERS
GALIVANT	GALLICAN	GALLOPING	GALUMPHER	GAMBIR
GALIVANTS	GALLICAS	GALLOPS	GALUMPHS	GAMBIRS
GALL	GALLICISE	GALLOUS	GALUT	GAMBIST
GALLABEA	GALLICISM	GALLOW	GALUTH	GAMBISTS
GALLABEAH	GALLICIZE	GALLOWED	GALUTHS	GAMBIT

GAMBITED	GAMEST	GAMMONS	GANGLIER	GANS
GAMBITING	GAMESTER	GAMMY	GANGLIEST	GANSEY
GAMBITS	GAMESTERS	GAMODEME	GANGLING	GANSEYS
GAMBLE	GAMESY	GAMODEMES	GANGLION	GANT
GAMBLED	GAMETAL	GAMONE	GANGLIONS	GANTED
GAMBLER	GAMETE	GAMONES	GANGLY	GANTELOPE
GAMBLERS	GAMETES	GAMP	GANGPLANK	GANTING
GAMBLES	GAMETIC	GAMPISH	GANGPLOW	GANTLET
GAMBLING	GAMEY	GAMPS	GANGPLOWS	GANTLETED
GAMBLINGS	GAMEYNESS	GAMS	GANGREL	GANTLETS
GAMBO	GAMGEE	GAMUT	GANGRELS	GANTLINE
GAMBOES	GAMIC	GAMUTS	GANGRENE	GANTLINES
GAMBOGE	GAMIER	GAMY	GANGRENED	GANTLOPE
GAMBOGES	GAMIEST	GAMYNESS	GANGRENES	GANTLOPES
GAMBOGIAN	GAMILY	GAN	GANGS	GANTRIES
GAMBOGIC	GAMIN	GANACHE	GANGSHAG	GANTRY
GAMBOL	GAMINE	GANACHES	GANGSHAGS	GANTS
GAMBOLED	GAMINERIE	GANCH	GANGSMAN	GANYMEDE
GAMBOLING	GAMINES	GANCHED	GANGSMEN	GANYMEDES
GAMBOLLED	GAMINESS	GANCHES	GANGSTA	GAOL
GAMBOLS	GAMING	GANCHING	GANGSTAS	GAOLBIRD
GAMBREL	GAMINGS	GANDER	GANGSTER	GAOLBIRDS
GAMBRELS	GAMINS	GANDERED	GANGSTERS	GAOLBREAK
GAMBROON	GAMMA	GANDERING	GANGUE	GAOLED
GAMBROONS	GAMMADIA	GANDERISM	GANGUES	GAOLER
GAMBS	GAMMADION	GANDERS	GANGWAY	GAOLERESS
GAMBUSIA	GAMMAS	GANDY	GANGWAYS	GAOLERS
GAMBUSIAS	GAMMAT	GANE	GANISTER	GAOLING
GAME	GAMMATIA	GANEF	GANISTERS	GAOLLESS
GAMECOCK	GAMMATION	GANEFS	GANJA	GAOLS
GAMECOCKS	GAMMATS	GANEV	GANJAH	GAP
GAMED	GAMME	GANEVS	GANJAHS	GAPE
GAMELAN	GAMMED	GANG	GANJAS	GAPED
GAMELANS	GAMMER	GANGBANG	GANNED	GAPER
GAMELIKE	GAMMERS	GANGBANGS	GANNET	GAPERS
GAMELY	GAMMES	GANGBOARD	GANNETRY	GAPES
GAMENESS	GAMMIER	GANGED	GANNETS	GAPESEED
GAMEPLAY	GAMMIEST	GANGER	GANNING	GAPESEEDS
GAMEPLAYS	GAMMING	GANGERS	GANNISTER	GAPEWORM
GAMER	GAMMOCK	GANGING	GANOF	GAPEWORMS
GAMERS	GAMMOCKED	GANGINGS	GANOFS	GAPIER
GAMES	GAMMOCKS	GANGLAND	GANOID	GAPIEST
GAMESIER	GAMMON	GANGLANDS	GANOIDS	GAPING
GAMESIEST	GAMMONED	GANGLIA	GANOIN	GAPINGLY
GAMESMAN	GAMMONER	GANGLIAL	GANOINE	GAPINGS
GAMESMEN	GAMMONERS	GANGLIAR	GANOINES	GAPLESS
GAMESOME	GAMMONING	GANGLIATE	GANOINS	GAPO

G

GAPOS	GARBOIL	GARGOYLE	GAROTTED	GARTERS
GAPOSIS	GARBOILS	GARGOYLED	GAROTTER	GARTH
GAPOSISES	GARBOLOGY	GARGOYLES	GAROTTERS	GARTHS
GAPPED	GARBOS	GARI	GAROTTES	GARUDA
GAPPER	GARBS	GARIAL	GAROTTING	GARUDAS
GAPPERS	GARBURE	GARIALS	GAROUPA	GARUM
GAPPIER	GARBURES	GARIBALDI	GAROUPAS	GARUMS
GAPPIEST	GARCINIA	GARIGUE	GARPIKE	GARVEY
GAPPING	GARCINIAS	GARIGUES	GARPIKES	GARVEYS
GAPPINGS	GARCON	GARIS	GARRAN	GARVIE
GAPPY	GARCONS	GARISH	GARRANS	GARVIES
GAPS	GARDA	GARISHED	GARRE	GARVOCK
GAPY	GARDAI	GARISHES	GARRED	GARVOCKS
GAR	GARDANT	GARISHING	GARRES	GAS
GARAGE	GARDANTS	GARISHLY	GARRET	GASAHOL
GARAGED	GARDEN	GARJAN	GARRETED	GASAHOLS
GARAGEMAN	GARDENED	GARJANS	GARRETEER	GASALIER
GARAGEMEN	GARDENER	GARLAND	GARRETS	GASALIERS
GARAGES	GARDENERS	GARLANDED	GARRIGUE	GASBAG
GARAGEY	GARDENFUL	GARLANDRY	GARRIGUES	GASBAGGED
GARAGING	GARDENIA	GARLANDS	GARRING	GASBAGS
GARAGINGS	GARDENIAS	GARLIC	GARRISON	GASCON
GARAGIST	GARDENING	GARLICKED	GARRISONS	GASCONADE
GARAGISTE	GARDENS	GARLICKY	GARRON	GASCONISM
GARAGISTS	GARDEROBE	GARLICS	GARRONS	GASCONS
GARB	GARDYLOO	GARMENT	GARROT	GASEITIES
GARBAGE	GARDYLOOS	GARMENTED	GARROTE	GASEITY
GARBAGES	GARE	GARMENTS	GARROTED	GASELIER
GARBAGEY	GAREFOWL	GARNER	GARROTER	GASELIERS
GARBAGY	GAREFOWLS	GARNERED	GARROTERS	GASEOUS
GARBANZO	GARFISH	GARNERING	GARROTES	GASES
GARBANZOS	GARFISHES	GARNERS	GARROTING	GASFIELD
GARBE	GARGANEY	GARNET	GARROTS	GASFIELDS
GARBED	GARGANEYS	GARNETS	GARROTTE	GASH
GARBES	GARGANTUA	GARNI	GARROTTED	GASHED
GARBING	GARGARISE	GARNISH	GARROTTER	GASHER
GARBLE	GARGARISM	GARNISHED	GARROTTES	GASHES
GARBLED	GARGARIZE	GARNISHEE	GARRULITY	GASHEST
GARBLER	GARGET	GARNISHER	GARRULOUS	GASHFUL
GARBLERS	GARGETS	GARNISHES	GARRYA	GASHING
GARBLES	GARGETY	GARNISHRY	GARRYAS	GASHLY
GARBLESS	GARGLE	GARNITURE	GARRYOWEN	GASHOLDER
GARBLING	GARGLED	GAROTE	GARS	GASHOUSE
GARBLINGS	GARGLER	GAROTED	GART	GASHOUSES
GARBO	GARGLERS	GAROTES	GARTER	GASIFIED
GARBOARD	GARGLES	GAROTING	GARTERED	GASIFIER
GARBOARDS	GARGLING	GAROTTE	GARTERING	GASIFIERS

GASIFIES	GASSIEST	GATEMAN	GAUDILY	GAUNTLETS
GASIFORM	GASSILY	GATEMEN	GAUDINESS	GAUNTLY
GASIFY	GASSINESS	GATEPOST	GAUDING	GAUNTNESS
GASIFYING	GASSING	GATEPOSTS	GAUDS	GAUNTREE
GASKET	GASSINGS	GATER	GAUDY	GAUNTREES
GASKETS	GASSY	GATERS	GAUFER	GAUNTRIES
GASKIN	GAST	GATES	GAUFERS	GAUNTRY
GASKING	GASTED	GATEWAY	GAUFFER	GAUNTS
GASKINGS	GASTER	GATEWAYS	GAUFFERED	GAUP
GASKINS	GASTERS	GATH	GAUFFERS	GAUPED
GASLESS	GASTFULL	GATHER	GAUFRE	GAUPER
GASLIGHT	GASTIGHT	GATHERED	GAUFRES	GAUPERS
GASLIGHTS	GASTING	GATHERER	GAUGE	GAUPING
GASLIT	GASTNESS	GATHERERS	GAUGEABLE	GAUPS
GASMAN	GASTNESSE	GATHERING	GAUGEABLY	GAUPUS
GASMEN	GASTRAEA	GATHERS	GAUGED	GAUPUSES
GASOGENE	GASTRAEAS	GATHS	GAUGER	GAUR
GASOGENES	GASTRAEUM	GATING	GAUGERS	GAURS
GASOHOL	GASTRAL	GATINGS	GAUGES	GAUS
GASOHOLS	GASTREA	GATLING	GAUGING	GAUSS
GASOLENE	GASTREAS	GATOR	GAUGINGS	GAUSSES
GASOLENES	GASTRIC	GATORS	GAUJE	GAUSSIAN
GASOLIER	GASTRIN	GATS	GAUJES	GAUZE
GASOLIERS	GASTRINS	GATVOL	GAULEITER	GAUZELIKE
GASOLINE	GASTRITIC	GAU	GAULT	GAUZES
GASOLINES	GASTRITIS	GAUCHE	GAULTER	GAUZIER
GASOLINIC	GASTROPOD	GAUCHELY	GAULTERS	GAUZIEST
GASOMETER	GASTROPUB	GAUCHER	GAULTS	GAUZILY
GASOMETRY	GASTRULA	GAUCHERIE	GAUM	GAUZINESS
GASP	GASTRULAE	GAUCHESCO	GAUMED	GAUZY
GASPED	GASTRULAR	GAUCHEST	GAUMIER	GAVAGE
GASPER	GASTRULAS	GAUCHO	GAUMIEST	GAVAGES
GASPEREAU	GASTS	GAUCHOS	GAUMING	GAVE
GASPERS	GASWORKS	GAUCIE	GAUMLESS	GAVEL
GASPIER	GAT	GAUCIER	GAUMS	GAVELED
GASPIEST	GATE	GAUCIEST	GAUMY	GAVELING
GASPINESS	GATEAU	GAUCY	GAUN	GAVELKIND
GASPING	GATEAUS	GAUD	GAUNCH	GAVELLED
GASPINGLY	GATEAUX	GAUDEAMUS	GAUNCHED	GAVELLING
GASPINGS	GATECRASH	GAUDED	GAUNCHES	GAVELMAN
GASPS	GATED	GAUDERIES	GAUNCHING	GAVELMEN
GASPY	GATEFOLD	GAUDERY	GAUNT	GAVELOCK
GASSED	GATEFOLDS	GAUDGIE	GAUNTED	GAVELOCKS
GASSER	GATEHOUSE	GAUDGIES	GAUNTER	GAVELS
GASSERS	GATELEG	GAUDIER	GAUNTEST	GAVIAL
GASSES	GATELESS	GAUDIES	GAUNTING	GAVIALOID
GASSIER	GATELIKE	GAUDIEST	GAUNTLET	GAVIALS

GAVOT	GAYETIES	GAZOOKAS	GECKO	GEFILTE
GAVOTS	GAYETY	GAZOON	GECKOES	GEFUFFLE
GAVOTTE	GAYLY	GAZOONS	GECKOS	GEFUFFLED
GAVOTTED	GAYNESS	GAZOOS	GECKS	GEFUFFLES
GAVOTTES	GAYNESSES	GAZPACHO	GED	GEFULLTE
GAVOTTING	GAYS	GAZPACHOS	GEDACT	GEGGIE
GAW	GAYSOME	GAZUMP	GEDACTS	GEGGIES
GAWCIER	GAYWINGS	GAZUMPED	GEDDIT	GEHLENITE
GAWCIEST	GAZABO	GAZUMPER	GEDECKT	GEISHA
GAWCY	GAZABOES	GAZUMPERS	GEDECKTS	GEISHAS
GAWD	GAZABOS	GAZUMPING	GEDS	GEIST
GAWDS	GAZAL	GAZUMPS	GEE	GEISTS
GAWK	GAZALS	GAZUNDER	GEEBAG	GEIT
GAWKED	GAZANIA	GAZUNDERS	GEEBAGS	GEITS
GAWKER	GAZANIAS	GAZY	GEEBUNG	GEL
GAWKERS	GAZAR	GEAL	GEEBUNGS	GELABLE
GAWKIER	GAZARS	GEALED	GEECHEE	GELADA
GAWKIES	GAZE	GEALING	GEECHEES	GELADAS
GAWKIEST	GAZEBO	GEALOUS	GEED	GELANDE
GAWKIHOOD	GAZEBOES	GEALOUSY	GEEGAW	GELANT
GAWKILY	GAZEBOS	GEALS	GEEGAWS	GELANTS
GAWKINESS	GAZED	GEAN	GEEING	GELASTIC
GAWKING	GAZEFUL	GEANS	GEEK	GELATE
GAWKISH	GAZEHOUND	GEAR	GEEKDOM	GELATED
GAWKISHLY	GAZELLE	GEARBOX	GEEKDOMS	GELATES
GAWKS	GAZELLES	GEARBOXES	GEEKED	GELATI
GAWKY	GAZEMENT	GEARCASE	GEEKIER	GELATIN
GAWP	GAZEMENTS	GEARCASES	GEEKIEST	GELATINE
GAWPED	GAZER	GEARE	GEEKINESS	GELATINES
GAWPER	GAZERS	GEARED	GEEKS	GELATING
GAWPERS	GAZES	GEARES	GEEKSPEAK	GELATINS
GAWPING	GAZETTE	GEARHEAD	GEEKY	GELATION
GAWPS	GAZETTED	GEARHEADS	GEELBEK	GELATIONS
GAWPUS	GAZETTEER	GEARING	GEELBEKS	GELATIS
GAWPUSES	GAZETTES	GEARINGS	GEEP	GELATO
GAWS	GAZETTING	GEARLESS	GEEPOUND	GELATOS
GAWSIE	GAZIER	GEARS	GEEPOUNDS	GELCAP
GAWSIER	GAZIEST	GEARSHIFT	GEEPS	GELCAPS
GAWSIEST	GAZILLION	GEARWHEEL	GEES	GELD
GAWSY	GAZING	GEASON	GEESE	GELDED
GAY	GAZINGS	GEAT	GEEST	GELDER
GAYAL	GAZOGENE	GEATS	GEESTS	GELDERS
GAYALS	GAZOGENES	GEBUR	GEEZ	GELDING
GAYDAR	GAZON	GEBURS	GEEZAH	GELDINGS
GAYDARS	GAZONS	GECK	GEEZAHS	GELDS
GAYER	GAZOO	GECKED	GEEZER	GELEE
GAYEST	GAZOOKA	GECKING	GEEZERS	GELEES

GELID	GEMMATION	GENEALOGY	GENISTA	GENOMICS
GELIDER	GEMMATIVE	GENERA	GENISTAS	GENOMS
GELIDEST	GEMMED	GENERABLE	GENISTEIN	GENOTOXIC
GELIDITY	GEMMEN	GENERAL	GENITAL	GENOTYPE
GELIDLY	GEMMEOUS	GENERALCY	GENITALIA	GENOTYPES
GELIDNESS	GEMMERIES	GENERALE	GENITALIC	GENOTYPIC
GELIGNITE	GEMMERY	GENERALIA	GENITALLY	GENRE
GELLANT	GEMMIER	GENERALLY	GENITALS	GENRES
GELLANTS	GEMMIEST	GENERALS	GENITIVAL	GENRO
GELLED	GEMMILY	GENERANT	GENITIVE	GENROS
GELLIES	GEMMINESS	GENERANTS	GENITIVES	GENS
GELLING	GEMMING	GENERATE	GENITOR	GENSENG
GELLY	GEMMOLOGY	GENERATED	GENITORS	GENSENGS
GELOSIES	GEMMULE	GENERATES	GENITRIX	GENT
GELOSY	GEMMULES	GENERATOR	GENITURE	GENTEEL
GELS	GEMMY	GENERIC	GENITURES	GENTEELER
GELSEMIA	GEMOLOGY	GENERICAL	GENIUS	GENTEELLY
GELSEMINE	GEMONY	GENERICS	GENIUSES	GENTES
GELSEMIUM	GEMOT	GENEROUS	GENIZAH	GENTIAN
GELT	GEMOTE	GENES	GENIZAHS	GENTIANS
GELTS	GEMOTES	GENESES	GENIZOT	GENTIER
GEM	GEMOTS	GENESIS	GENIZOTH	GENTIEST
GEMATRIA	GEMS	GENET	GENLOCK	GENTIL
GEMATRIAS	GEMSBOK	GENETIC	GENLOCKS	GENTILE
GEMCLIP	GEMSBOKS	GENETICAL	GENNAKER	GENTILES
GEMCLIPS	GEMSBUCK	GENETICS	GENNAKERS	GENTILIC
GEMEL	GEMSBUCKS	GENETRIX	GENNED	GENTILISE
GEMELS	GEMSHORN	GENETS	GENNEL	GENTILISH
GEMFISH	GEMSHORNS	GENETTE	GENNELS	GENTILISM
GEMFISHES	GEMSTONE	GENETTES	GENNET	GENTILITY
GEMINAL	GEMSTONES	GENEVA	GENNETS	GENTILIZE
GEMINALLY	GEMUTLICH	GENEVAS	GENNIES	GENTLE
GEMINATE	GEN	GENIAL	GENNING	GENTLED
GEMINATED	GENA	GENIALISE	GENNY	GENTLEMAN
GEMINATES	GENAL	GENIALITY	GENOA	GENTLEMEN
GEMINI	GENAPPE	GENIALIZE	GENOAS	GENTLER
GEMINIES	GENAPPES	GENIALLY	GENOCIDAL	GENTLES
GEMINOUS	GENAS	GENIC	GENOCIDE	GENTLEST
GEMINY	GENDARME	GENICALLY	GENOCIDES	GENTLING
GEMLIKE	GENDARMES	GENICULAR	GENOGRAM	GENTLY
GEMMA	GENDER	GENIE	GENOGRAMS	GENTOO
GEMMAE	GENDERED	GENIES	GENOISE	GENTOOS
GEMMAN	GENDERING	GENII	GENOISES	GENTRICE
GEMMATE	GENDERISE	GENIP	GENOM	GENTRICES
GEMMATED	GENDERIZE	GENIPAP	GENOME	GENTRIES
GEMMATES	GENDERS	GENIPAPS	GENOMES	GENTRIFY
GEMMATING	GENE	GENIPS	GENOMIC	GENTRY

G

GENTS	GEOLOGIES	GERANIOLS	GERMINA	GESTATES
GENTY	GEOLOGISE	GERANIUM	GERMINAL	GESTATING
GENU	GEOLOGIST	GERANIUMS	GERMINANT	GESTATION
GENUA	GEOLOGIZE	GERARDIA	GERMINATE	GESTATIVE
GENUFLECT	GEOLOGY	GERARDIAS	GERMINESS	GESTATORY
GENUINE	GEOMANCER	GERBE	GERMING	GESTE
GENUINELY	GEOMANCY	GERBERA	GERMINS	GESTES
GENUS	GEOMANT	GERBERAS	GERMLIKE	GESTIC
GENUSES	GEOMANTIC	GERBES	GERMPLASM	GESTICAL
GEO	GEOMANTS	GERBIL	GERMPROOF	GESTS
GEOBOTANY	GEOMETER	GERBILLE	GERMS	GESTURAL
GEOCARPIC	GEOMETERS	GERBILLES	GERMY	GESTURE
GEOCARPY	GEOMETRIC	GERBILS	GERNE	GESTURED
GEOCORONA	GEOMETRID	GERE	GERNED	GESTURER
GEODE	GEOMETRY	GERENT	GERNES	GESTURERS
GEODES	GEOMYOID	GERENTS	GERNING	GESTURES
GEODESIC	GEOPHAGIA	GERENUK	GERONIMO	GESTURING
GEODESICS	GEOPHAGY	GERENUKS	GERONTIC	GET
GEODESIES	GEOPHILIC	GERES	GEROPIGA	GETA
GEODESIST	GEOPHONE	GERFALCON	GEROPIGAS	GETABLE
GEODESY	GEOPHONES	GERIATRIC	GERS	GETAS
GEODETIC	GEOPHYTE	GERLE	GERT	GETATABLE
GEODETICS	GEOPHYTES	GERLES	GERTCHA	GETAWAY
GEODIC	GEOPHYTIC	GERM	GERUND	GETAWAYS
GEODUCK	GEOPONIC	GERMAIN	GERUNDIAL	GETS
GEODUCKS	GEOPONICS	GERMAINE	GERUNDIVE	GETTABLE
GEOFACT	GEOPROBE	GERMAINES	GERUNDS	GETTER
GEOFACTS	GEOPROBES	GERMAINS	GESNERIA	GETTERED
GEOGENIES	GEORGETTE	GERMAN	GESNERIAD	GETTERING
GEOGENY	GEORGIC	GERMANDER	GESNERIAS	GETTERS
GEOGNOSES	GEORGICAL	GERMANE	GESSAMINE	GETTING
GEOGNOSIS	GEORGICS	GERMANELY	GESSE	GETTINGS
GEOGNOST	GEOS	GERMANIC	GESSED	GETUP
GEOGNOSTS	GEOSPHERE	GERMANISE	GESSES	GETUPS
GEOGNOSY	GEOSTATIC	GERMANITE	GESSING	GEUM
GEOGONIC	GEOTACTIC	GERMANIUM	GESSO	GEUMS
GEOGONIES	GEOTAXES	GERMANIZE	GESSOED	GEWGAW
GEOGONY	GEOTAXIS	GERMANOUS	GESSOES	GEWGAWED
GEOGRAPHY	GEOTHERM	GERMANS	GEST	GEWGAWS
GEOID	GEOTHERMS	GERMED	GESTALT	GEY
GEOIDAL	GEOTROPIC	GERMEN	GESTALTEN	GEYAN
GEOIDS	GER	GERMENS	GESTALTS	GEYER
GEOLATRY	GERAH	GERMFREE	GESTANT	GEYEST
GEOLOGER	GERAHS	GERMICIDE	GESTAPO	GEYSER
GEOLOGERS	GERANIAL	GERMIER	GESTAPOS	GEYSERITE
GEOLOGIAN	GERANIALS	GERMIEST	GESTATE	GEYSERS
GEOLOGIC	GERANIOL	GERMIN	GESTATED	GHARIAL

G

GHARIALS	GHIBLIS	GIB	GIDDINESS	GIGATON
GHARRI	GHILGAI	GIBBED	GIDDUP	GIGATONS
GHARRIES	GHILGAIS	GIBBER	GIDDY	GIGAWATT
GHARRIS	GHILLIE	GIBBERED	GIDDYAP	GIGAWATTS
GHARRY	GHILLIED	GIBBERING	GIDDYING	GIGGED
GHAST	GHILLIES	GIBBERISH	GIDDYUP	GIGGING
GHASTED	GHILLYING	GIBBERS	GIDGEE	GIGGIT
GHASTFUL	GHIS	GIBBET	GIDGEES	GIGGITED
GHASTING	GHOST	GIBBETED	GIDJEE	GIGGITING
GHASTLIER	GHOSTED	GIBBETING	GIDJEES	GIGGITS
GHASTLY	GHOSTIER	GIBBETS	GIDS	GIGGLE
GHASTNESS	GHOSTIEST	GIBBETTED	GIE	GIGGLED
GHASTS	GHOSTING	GIBBING	GIED	GIGGLER
GHAT	GHOSTINGS	GIBBON	GIEING	GIGGLERS
GHATS	GHOSTLIER	GIBBONS	GIEN	GIGGLES
GHAUT	GHOSTLIKE	GIBBOSE	GIES	GIGGLIER
GHAUTS	GHOSTLY	GIBBOSITY	GIF	GIGGLIEST
GHAZAL	GHOSTS	GIBBOUS	GIFT	GIGGLING
GHAZALS	GHOSTY	GIBBOUSLY	GIFTABLE	GIGGLINGS
GHAZEL	GHOUL	GIBBSITE	GIFTABLES	GIGGLY
GHAZELS	GHOULIE	GIBBSITES	GIFTED	GIGHE
GHAZI	GHOULIES	GIBE	GIFTEDLY	GIGLET
GHAZIES	GHOULISH	GIBED	GIFTEE	GIGLETS
GHAZIS	GHOULS	GIBEL	GIFTEES	GIGLOT
GHEE	GHRELIN	GIBELS	GIFTING	GIGLOTS
GHEES	GHRELINS	GIBER	GIFTLESS	GIGMAN
GHERAO	GHUBAR	GIBERS	GIFTS	GIGMANITY
GHERAOED	GHYLL	GIBES	GIFTSHOP	GIGMEN
GHERAOES	GHYLLS	GIBING	GIFTSHOPS	GIGOLO
GHERAOING	GI	GIBINGLY	GIFTWARE	GIGOLOS
GHERAOS	GIAMBEUX	GIBLET	GIFTWARES	GIGOT
GHERKIN	GIANT	GIBLETS	GIFTWRAP	GIGOTS
GHERKINS	GIANTESS	GIBLI	GIFTWRAPS	GIGS
GHESSE	GIANTHOOD	GIBLIS	GIG	GIGUE
GHESSED	GIANTISM	GIBS	GIGA	GIGUES
GHESSES	GIANTISMS	GIBSON	GIGABIT	GILA
GHESSING	GIANTLIER	GIBSONS	GIGABITS	GILAS
GHEST	GIANTLIKE	GIBUS	GIGABYTE	GILBERT
GHETTO	GIANTLY	GIBUSES	GIGABYTES	GILBERTS
GHETTOED	GIANTRIES	GID	GIGACYCLE	GILCUP
GHETTOES	GIANTRY	GIDDAP	GIGAFLOP	GILCUPS
GHETTOING	GIANTS	GIDDAY	GIGAFLOPS	GILD
GHETTOISE	GIANTSHIP	GIDDIED	GIGAHERTZ	GILDED
GHETTOIZE	GIAOUR	GIDDIER	GIGANTEAN	GILDEN
GHETTOS	GIAOURS	GIDDIES	GIGANTIC	GILDER
GHI	GIARDIA	GIDDIEST	GIGANTISM	GILDERS
GHIBLI	GIARDIAS	GIDDILY	GIGAS	GILDHALL

GILDHALLS	GIMBAL	GINGELIS	GINNIEST	GIRASOL
GILDING	GIMBALED	GINGELLI	GINNING	GIRASOLE
GILDINGS	GIMBALING	GINGELLIS	GINNINGS	GIRASOLES
GILDS	GIMBALLED	GINGELLY	GINNY	GIRASOLS
GILDSMAN	GIMBALS	GINGELY	GINORMOUS	GIRD
GILDSMEN	GIMCRACK	GINGER	GINS	GIRDED
GILET	GIMCRACKS	GINGERADE	GINSENG	GIRDER
GILETS	GIMEL	GINGERED	GINSENGS	GIRDERS
GILGAI	GIMELS	GINGERING	GINSHOP	GIRDING
GILGAIS	GIMLET	GINGERLY	GINSHOPS	GIRDINGLY
GILGIE	GIMLETED	GINGEROUS	GINZO	GIRDINGS
GILGIES	GIMLETING	GINGERS	GINZOES	GIRDLE
GILL	GIMLETS	GINGERY	GIO	GIRDLED
GILLAROO	GIMMAL	GINGES	GIOCOSO	GIRDLER
GILLAROOS	GIMMALLED	GINGHAM	GIOS	GIRDLERS
GILLED	GIMMALS	GINGHAMS	GIP	GIRDLES
GILLER	GIMME	GINGILI	GIPON	GIRDLING
GILLERS	GIMMER	GINGILIS	GIPONS	GIRDS
GILLET	GIMMERS	GINGILLI	GIPPED	GIRKIN
GILLETS	GIMMES	GINGILLIS	GIPPER	GIRKINS
GILLFLIRT	GIMMICK	GINGIVA	GIPPERS	GIRL
GILLIE	GIMMICKED	GINGIVAE	GIPPIES	GIRLHOOD
GILLIED	GIMMICKRY	GINGIVAL	GIPPING	GIRLHOODS
GILLIES	GIMMICKS	GINGKO	GIPPO	GIRLIE
GILLING	GIMMICKY	GINGKOES	GIPPOES	GIRLIER
GILLION	GIMMIE	GINGKOS	GIPPOS	GIRLIES
GILLIONS	GIMMIES	GINGLE	GIPPY	GIRLIEST
GILLNET	GIMMOR	GINGLES	GIPS	GIRLISH
GILLNETS	GIMMORS	GINGLYMI	GIPSEN	GIRLISHLY
GILLS	GIMP	GINGLYMUS	GIPSENS	GIRLOND
GILLY	GIMPED	GINGS	GIPSIED	GIRLONDS
GILLYING	GIMPIER	GINHOUSE	GIPSIES	GIRLS
GILLYVOR	GIMPIEST	GINHOUSES	GIPSY	GIRLY
GILLYVORS	GIMPING	GINK	GIPSYDOM	GIRN
GILPEY	GIMPS	GINKGO	GIPSYDOMS	GIRNED
GILPEYS	GIMPY	GINKGOES	GIPSYHOOD	GIRNEL
GILPIES	GIN	GINKGOS	GIPSYING	GIRNELS
GILPY	GING	GINKS	GIPSYISH	GIRNER
GILRAVAGE	GINGAL	GINN	GIPSYWORT	GIRNERS
GILSONITE	GINGALL	GINNED	GIRAFFE	GIRNIE
GILT	GINGALLS	GINNEL	GIRAFFES	GIRNIER
GILTCUP	GINGALS	GINNELS	GIRAFFID	GIRNIEST
GILTCUPS	GINGE	GINNER	GIRAFFINE	GIRNING
GILTHEAD	GINGELEY	GINNERIES	GIRAFFISH	GIRNS
GILTHEADS	GINGELEYS	GINNERS	GIRAFFOID	GIRO
GILTS	GINGELI	GINNERY	GIRANDOLA	GIROLLE
GILTWOOD	GINGELIES	GINNIER	GIRANDOLE	GIROLLES

GIRON	GIUST	GLACIALS	GLADWRAP	GLANCINGS
GIRONIC	GIUSTED	GLACIATE	GLADWRAPS	GLAND
GIRONNY	GIUSTING	GLACIATED	GLADY	GLANDERED
GIRONS	GIUSTO	GLACIATES	GLAIK	GLANDERS
GIROS	GIUSTS	GLACIER	GLAIKET	GLANDES
GIROSOL	GIVABLE	GLACIERED	GLAIKIT	GLANDLESS
GIROSOLS	GIVE	GLACIERS	GLAIKS	GLANDLIKE
GIRR	GIVEABLE	GLACIS	GLAIR	GLANDS
GIRRS	GIVEAWAY	GLACISES	GLAIRE	GLANDULAR
GIRSH	GIVEAWAYS	GLAD	GLAIRED	GLANDULE
GIRSHES	GIVEBACK	GLADDED	GLAIREOUS	GLANDULES
GIRT	GIVEBACKS	GLADDEN	GLAIRES	GLANS
GIRTED	GIVED	GLADDENED	GLAIRIER	GLARE
GIRTH	GIVEN	GLADDENER	GLAIRIEST	GLAREAL
GIRTHED	GIVENNESS	GLADDENS	GLAIRIN	GLARED
GIRTHING	GIVENS	GLADDER	GLAIRING	GLARELESS
GIRTHLINE	GIVER	GLADDEST	GLAIRINS	GLAREOUS
GIRTHS	GIVERS	GLADDIE	GLAIRS	GLARES
GIRTING	GIVES	GLADDIES	GLAIRY	GLARIER
GIRTLINE	GIVING	GLADDING	GLAIVE	GLARIEST
GIRTLINES	GIVINGS	GLADDON	GLAIVED	GLARINESS
GIRTS	GIZMO	GLADDONS	GLAIVES	GLARING
GIS	GIZMOLOGY	GLADE	GLAM	GLARINGLY
GISARME	GIZMOS	GLADELIKE	GLAMMED	GLARY
GISARMES	GIZZ	GLADES	GLAMMIER	GLASNOST
GISM	GIZZARD	GLADFUL	GLAMMIEST	GLASNOSTS
GISMO	GIZZARDS	GLADIATE	GLAMMING	GLASS
GISMOLOGY	GIZZEN	GLADIATOR	GLAMMY	GLASSED
GISMOS	GIZZENED	GLADIER	GLAMOR	GLASSEN
GISMS	GIZZENING	GLADIEST	GLAMORED	GLASSES
GIST	GIZZENS	GLADIOLA	GLAMORING	GLASSFUL
GISTS	GIZZES	GLADIOLAR	GLAMORISE	GLASSFULS
GIT	GJETOST	GLADIOLAS	GLAMORIZE	GLASSIE
GITANA	GJETOSTS	GLADIOLE	GLAMOROUS	GLASSIER
GITANAS	GJU	GLADIOLES	GLAMORS	GLASSIES
GITANO	GJUS	GLADIOLI	GLAMOUR	GLASSIEST
GITANOS	GLABELLA	GLADIOLUS	GLAMOURED	GLASSIFY
GITE	GLABELLAE	GLADIUS	GLAMOURS	GLASSILY
GITES	GLABELLAR	GLADIUSES	GLAMPING	GLASSINE
GITS	GLABRATE	GLADLIER	GLAMPINGS	GLASSINES
GITTARONE	GLABROUS	GLADLIEST	GLAMS	GLASSING
GITTED	GLACE	GLADLY	GLANCE	GLASSLESS
GITTERN	GLACEED	GLADNESS	GLANCED	GLASSLIKE
GITTERNED	GLACEING	GLADS	GLANCER	GLASSMAN
GITTERNS	GLACES	GLADSOME	GLANCERS	GLASSMEN
GITTIN	GLACIAL	GLADSOMER	GLANCES	GLASSWARE
GITTING	GLACIALLY	GLADSTONE	GLANCING	GLASSWORK

G

GLASSWORM

GLASSWORM
GLASSWORT
GLASSY
GLAUCOMA
GLAUCOMAS
GLAUCOUS
GLAUM
GLAUMED
GLAUMING
GLAUMS
GLAUR
GLAURIER
GLAURIEST
GLAURS
GLAURY
GLAZE
GLAZED
GLAZEN
GLAZER
GLAZERS
GLAZES
GLAZIER
GLAZIERS
GLAZIERY
GLAZIEST
GLAZILY
GLAZINESS
GLAZING
GLAZINGS
GLAZY
GLEAM
GLEAMED
GLEAMER
GLEAMERS
GLEAMIER
GLEAMIEST
GLEAMING
GLEAMINGS
GLEAMS
GLEAMY
GLEAN
GLEANABLE
GLEANED
GLEANER
GLEANERS
GLEANING
GLEANINGS

GLEANS
GLEAVE
GLEAVES
GLEBA
GLEBAE
GLEBE
GLEBELESS
GLEBES
GLEBIER
GLEBIEST
GLEBOUS
GLEBY
GLED
GLEDE
GLEDES
GLEDGE
GLEDGED
GLEDGES
GLEDGING
GLEDS
GLEE
GLEED
GLEEDS
GLEEFUL
GLEEFULLY
GLEEING
GLEEK
GLEEKED
GLEEKING
GLEEKS
GLEEMAN
GLEEMEN
GLEENIE
GLEENIES
GLEES
GLEESOME
GLEET
GLEETED
GLEETIER
GLEETIEST
GLEETING
GLEETS
GLEETY
GLEG
GLEGGER
GLEGGEST
GLEGLY

GLEGNESS
GLEI
GLEIS
GLEN
GLENGARRY
GLENLIKE
GLENOID
GLENOIDAL
GLENOIDS
GLENS
GLENT
GLENTED
GLENTING
GLENTS
GLEY
GLEYED
GLEYING
GLEYINGS
GLEYS
GLIA
GLIADIN
GLIADINE
GLIADINES
GLIADINS
GLIAL
GLIAS
GLIB
GLIBBED
GLIBBER
GLIBBERY
GLIBBEST
GLIBBING
GLIBLY
GLIBNESS
GLIBS
GLID
GLIDDER
GLIDDERY
GLIDDEST
GLIDE
GLIDED
GLIDEPATH
GLIDER
GLIDERS
GLIDES
GLIDING
GLIDINGLY

GLIDINGS
GLIFF
GLIFFING
GLIFFINGS
GLIFFS
GLIFT
GLIFTS
GLIKE
GLIKES
GLIM
GLIME
GLIMED
GLIMES
GLIMING
GLIMMER
GLIMMERED
GLIMMERS
GLIMMERY
GLIMPSE
GLIMPSED
GLIMPSER
GLIMPSERS
GLIMPSES
GLIMPSING
GLIMS
GLINT
GLINTED
GLINTIER
GLINTIEST
GLINTING
GLINTS
GLINTY
GLIOMA
GLIOMAS
GLIOMATA
GLIOSES
GLIOSIS
GLISK
GLISKS
GLISSADE
GLISSADED
GLISSADER
GLISSADES
GLISSANDI
GLISSANDO
GLISTEN
GLISTENED

GLISTENS
GLISTER
GLISTERED
GLISTERS
GLIT
GLITCH
GLITCHES
GLITCHIER
GLITCHY
GLITS
GLITTER
GLITTERED
GLITTERS
GLITTERY
GLITZ
GLITZED
GLITZES
GLITZIER
GLITZIEST
GLITZILY
GLITZING
GLITZY
GLOAM
GLOAMING
GLOAMINGS
GLOAMS
GLOAT
GLOATED
GLOATER
GLOATERS
GLOATING
GLOATS
GLOB
GLOBAL
GLOBALISE
GLOBALISM
GLOBALIST
GLOBALIZE
GLOBALLY
GLOBATE
GLOBATED
GLOBBIER
GLOBBIEST
GLOBBY
GLOBE
GLOBED
GLOBEFISH

GLOBELIKE
GLOBES
GLOBESITY
GLOBETROT
GLOBI
GLOBIN
GLOBING
GLOBINS
GLOBOID
GLOBOIDS
GLOBOSE
GLOBOSELY
GLOBOSITY
GLOBOUS
GLOBS
GLOBULAR
GLOBULARS
GLOBULE
GLOBULES
GLOBULET
GLOBULETS
GLOBULIN
GLOBULINS
GLOBULITE
GLOBULOUS
GLOBUS
GLOBY
GLOCHID
GLOCHIDIA
GLOCHIDS
GLODE
GLOGG
GLOGGS
GLOIRE
GLOIRES
GLOM
GLOMERA
GLOMERATE
GLOMERULE
GLOMERULI
GLOMMED
GLOMMING
GLOMS
GLOMUS
GLONOIN
GLONOINS
GLOOM

GLOOMED
GLOOMFUL
GLOOMIER
GLOOMIEST
GLOOMILY
GLOOMING
GLOOMINGS
GLOOMLESS
GLOOMS
GLOOMY
GLOOP
GLOOPED
GLOOPIER
GLOOPIEST
GLOOPING
GLOOPS
GLOOPY
GLOP
GLOPPED
GLOPPIER
GLOPPIEST
GLOPPING
GLOPPY
GLOPS
GLORIA
GLORIAS
GLORIED
GLORIES
GLORIFIED
GLORIFIER
GLORIFIES
GLORIFY
GLORIOLE
GLORIOLES
GLORIOSA
GLORIOSAS
GLORIOUS
GLORY
GLORYING
GLOSS
GLOSSA
GLOSSAE
GLOSSAL
GLOSSARY
GLOSSAS
GLOSSATOR
GLOSSED

GLOSSEME
GLOSSEMES
GLOSSER
GLOSSERS
GLOSSES
GLOSSIER
GLOSSIES
GLOSSIEST
GLOSSILY
GLOSSINA
GLOSSINAS
GLOSSING
GLOSSIST
GLOSSISTS
GLOSSITIC
GLOSSITIS
GLOSSLESS
GLOSSY
GLOST
GLOSTS
GLOTTAL
GLOTTIC
GLOTTIDES
GLOTTIS
GLOTTISES
GLOUT
GLOUTED
GLOUTING
GLOUTS
GLOVE
GLOVED
GLOVELESS
GLOVER
GLOVERS
GLOVES
GLOVING
GLOVINGS
GLOW
GLOWED
GLOWER
GLOWERED
GLOWERING
GLOWERS
GLOWFLIES
GLOWFLY
GLOWING
GLOWINGLY

GLOWLAMP
GLOWLAMPS
GLOWS
GLOWSTICK
GLOWWORM
GLOWWORMS
GLOXINIA
GLOXINIAS
GLOZE
GLOZED
GLOZES
GLOZING
GLOZINGS
GLUCAGON
GLUCAGONS
GLUCAN
GLUCANS
GLUCINA
GLUCINAS
GLUCINIC
GLUCINIUM
GLUCINUM
GLUCINUMS
GLUCONATE
GLUCOSE
GLUCOSES
GLUCOSIC
GLUCOSIDE
GLUE
GLUEBALL
GLUEBALLS
GLUED
GLUEING
GLUELIKE
GLUEPOT
GLUEPOTS
GLUER
GLUERS
GLUES
GLUEY
GLUEYNESS
GLUG
GLUGGABLE
GLUGGED
GLUGGING
GLUGS
GLUHWEIN

GLUHWEINS
GLUIER
GLUIEST
GLUILY
GLUINESS
GLUING
GLUISH
GLUM
GLUME
GLUMELIKE
GLUMELLA
GLUMELLAS
GLUMES
GLUMLY
GLUMMER
GLUMMEST
GLUMNESS
GLUMPIER
GLUMPIEST
GLUMPILY
GLUMPISH
GLUMPS
GLUMPY
GLUMS
GLUNCH
GLUNCHED
GLUNCHES
GLUNCHING
GLUON
GLUONS
GLURGE
GLURGES
GLUT
GLUTAEAL
GLUTAEI
GLUTAEUS
GLUTAMATE
GLUTAMIC
GLUTAMINE
GLUTE
GLUTEAL
GLUTEI
GLUTELIN
GLUTELINS
GLUTEN
GLUTENIN
GLUTENINS

G

G

GLUTENOUS	GLYCOSYLS	GNATWREN	GOADSMAN	GOBANGS
GLUTENS	GLYCYL	GNATWRENS	GOADSMEN	GOBANS
GLUTES	GLYCYLS	GNAW	GOADSTER	GOBAR
GLUTEUS	GLYPH	GNAWABLE	GOADSTERS	GOBBED
GLUTINOUS	GLYPHIC	GNAWED	GOAF	GOBBELINE
GLUTS	GLYPHS	GNAWER	GOAFS	GOBBET
GLUTTED	GLYPTAL	GNAWERS	GOAL	GOBBETS
GLUTTING	GLYPTALS	GNAWING	GOALBALL	GOBBI
GLUTTON	GLYPTIC	GNAWINGLY	GOALBALLS	GOBBIER
GLUTTONS	GLYPTICS	GNAWINGS	GOALED	GOBBIEST
GLUTTONY	GMELINITE	GNAWN	GOALIE	GOBBING
GLYCAEMIA	GNAMMA	GNAWS	GOALIES	GOBBLE
GLYCAEMIC	GNAR	GNEISS	GOALING	GOBBLED
GLYCAN	GNARL	GNEISSES	GOALLESS	GOBBLER
GLYCANS	GNARLED	GNEISSIC	GOALMOUTH	GOBBLERS
GLYCATION	GNARLIER	GNEISSOID	GOALPOST	GOBBLES
GLYCEMIA	GNARLIEST	GNEISSOSE	GOALPOSTS	GOBBLING
GLYCEMIAS	GNARLING	GNOCCHI	GOALS	GOBBO
GLYCEMIC	GNARLS	GNOMAE	GOALWARD	GOBBY
GLYCERIA	GNARLY	GNOME	GOALWARDS	GOBI
GLYCERIAS	GNARR	GNOMELIKE	GOANNA	GOBIES
GLYCERIC	GNARRED	GNOMES	GOANNAS	GOBIID
GLYCERIDE	GNARRING	GNOMIC	GOARY	GOBIIDS
GLYCERIN	GNARRS	GNOMICAL	GOAS	GOBIOID
GLYCERINE	GNARS	GNOMISH	GOAT	GOBIOIDS
GLYCERINS	GNASH	GNOMIST	GOATEE	GOBIS
GLYCEROL	GNASHED	GNOMISTS	GOATEED	GOBLET
GLYCEROLS	GNASHER	GNOMON	GOATEES	GOBLETS
GLYCERYL	GNASHERS	GNOMONIC	GOATFISH	GOBLIN
GLYCERYLS	GNASHES	GNOMONICS	GOATHERD	GOBLINS
GLYCIN	GNASHING	GNOMONS	GOATHERDS	GOBO
GLYCINE	GNASHINGS	GNOSES	GOATIER	GOBOES
GLYCINES	GNAT	GNOSIS	GOATIEST	GOBONEE
GLYCINS	GNATHAL	GNOSTIC	GOATISH	GOBONY
GLYCOCOLL	GNATHIC	GNOSTICAL	GOATISHLY	GOBOS
GLYCOGEN	GNATHION	GNOSTICS	GOATLIKE	GOBS
GLYCOGENS	GNATHIONS	GNOW	GOATLING	GOBSHITE
GLYCOL	GNATHITE	GNOWS	GOATLINGS	GOBSHITES
GLYCOLIC	GNATHITES	GNU	GOATS	GOBURRA
GLYCOLLIC	GNATHONIC	GNUS	GOATSKIN	GOBURRAS
GLYCOLS	GNATLIKE	GO	GOATSKINS	GOBY
GLYCONIC	GNATLING	GOA	GOATWEED	GOD
GLYCONICS	GNATLINGS	GOAD	GOATWEEDS	GODCHILD
GLYCOSE	GNATS	GOADED	GOATY	GODDAM
GLYCOSES	GNATTIER	GOADING	GOB	GODDAMMED
GLYCOSIDE	GNATTIEST	GOADLIKE	GOBAN	GODDAMN
GLYCOSYL	GNATTY	GOADS	GOBANG	GODDAMNED

GODDAMNS	GODSQUADS	GOHONZONS	GOLDSINNY	GOLLER
GODDAMS	GODWARD	GOIER	GOLDSIZE	GOLLERED
GODDED	GODWARDS	GOIEST	GOLDSIZES	GOLLERING
GODDEN	GODWIT	GOING	GOLDSMITH	GOLLERS
GODDENS	GODWITS	GOINGS	GOLDSPINK	GOLLIED
GODDESS	GOE	GOITER	GOLDSTICK	GOLLIES
GODDESSES	GOEL	GOITERED	GOLDSTONE	GOLLIWOG
GODDING	GOELS	GOITERS	GOLDTAIL	GOLLIWOGG
GODET	GOER	GOITRE	GOLDTONE	GOLLIWOGS
GODETIA	GOERS	GOITRED	GOLDURN	GOLLOP
GODETIAS	GOES	GOITRES	GOLDURNS	GOLLOPED
GODETS	GOEST	GOITROGEN	GOLDWORK	GOLLOPER
GODFATHER	GOETH	GOITROUS	GOLDWORKS	GOLLOPERS
GODHEAD	GOETHITE	GOJI	GOLDY	GOLLOPING
GODHEADS	GOETHITES	GOJIS	GOLE	GOLLOPS
GODHOOD	GOETIC	GOLCONDA	GOLEM	GOLLY
GODHOODS	GOETIES	GOLCONDAS	GOLEMS	GOLLYING
GODLESS	GOETY	GOLD	GOLES	GOLLYWOG
GODLESSLY	GOEY	GOLDARN	GOLF	GOLLYWOGS
GODLIER	GOFER	GOLDARNS	GOLFED	GOLOMYNKA
GODLIEST	GOFERS	GOLDBRICK	GOLFER	GOLOSH
GODLIKE	GOFF	GOLDBUG	GOLFERS	GOLOSHE
GODLILY	GOFFED	GOLDBUGS	GOLFIANA	GOLOSHED
GODLINESS	GOFFER	GOLDCREST	GOLFIANAS	GOLOSHES
GODLING	GOFFERED	GOLDEN	GOLFING	GOLOSHING
GODLINGS	GOFFERING	GOLDENED	GOLFINGS	GOLOSHOES
GODLY	GOFFERS	GOLDENER	GOLFS	GOLP
GODMOTHER	GOFFING	GOLDENEST	GOLGOTHA	GOLPE
GODOWN	GOFFS	GOLDENEYE	GOLGOTHAS	GOLPES
GODOWNS	GOGGA	GOLDENING	GOLIARD	GOLPS
GODPARENT	GOGGAS	GOLDENLY	GOLIARDIC	GOMBEEN
GODROON	GOGGLE	GOLDENROD	GOLIARDS	GOMBEENS
GODROONED	GOGGLEBOX	GOLDENS	GOLIARDY	GOMBO
GODROONS	GOGGLED	GOLDER	GOLIAS	GOMBOS
GODS	GOGGLER	GOLDEST	GOLIASED	GOMBRO
GODSEND	GOGGLERS	GOLDEYE	GOLIASES	GOMBROON
GODSENDS	GOGGLES	GOLDEYES	GOLIASING	GOMBROONS
GODSHIP	GOGGLIER	GOLDFIELD	GOLIATH	GOMBROS
GODSHIPS	GOGGLIEST	GOLDFINCH	GOLIATHS	GOMER
GODSLOT	GOGGLING	GOLDFINNY	GOLLAN	GOMERAL
GODSLOTS	GOGGLINGS	GOLDFISH	GOLLAND	GOMERALS
GODSO	GOGGLY	GOLDIER	GOLLANDS	GOMEREL
GODSON	GOGLET	GOLDIEST	GOLLANS	GOMERELS
GODSONS	GOGLETS	GOLDISH	GOLLAR	GOMERIL
GODSPEED	GOGO	GOLDLESS	GOLLARED	GOMERILS
GODSPEEDS	GOGOS	GOLDMINER	GOLLARING	GOMERS
GODSQUAD	GOHONZON	GOLDS	GOLLARS	GOMOKU

GOMOKUS	GONIFFS	GOODLIEST	GOOL	GOOSEGOBS
GOMPA	GONIFS	GOODLY	GOOLD	GOOSEGOG
GOMPAS	GONION	GOODMAN	GOOLDS	GOOSEGOGS
GOMPHOSES	GONIUM	GOODMEN	GOOLEY	GOOSEHERD
GOMPHOSIS	GONK	GOODNESS	GOOLEYS	GOOSENECK
GOMUTI	GONKS	GOODNIGHT	GOOLIE	GOOSERIES
GOMUTIS	GONNA	GOODS	GOOLIES	GOOSERY
GOMUTO	GONOCOCCI	GOODSIRE	GOOLS	GOOSES
GOMUTOS	GONOCYTE	GOODSIRES	GOOLY	GOOSEY
GON	GONOCYTES	GOODTIME	GOOMBAH	GOOSEYS
GONAD	GONODUCT	GOODWIFE	GOOMBAHS	GOOSIER
GONADAL	GONODUCTS	GOODWILL	GOOMBAY	GOOSIES
GONADIAL	GONOF	GOODWILLS	GOOMBAYS	GOOSIEST
GONADIC	GONOFS	GOODWIVES	GOON	GOOSINESS
GONADS	GONOPH	GOODY	GOONDA	GOOSING
GONDELAY	GONOPHORE	GOODYEAR	GOONDAS	GOOSY
GONDELAYS	GONOPHS	GOODYEARS	GOONEY	GOPAK
GONDOLA	GONOPOD	GOOEY	GOONEYS	GOPAKS
GONDOLAS	GONOPODS	GOOEYNESS	GOONIE	GOPHER
GONDOLIER	GONOPORE	GOOF	GOONIER	GOPHERED
GONE	GONOPORES	GOOFBALL	GOONIES	GOPHERING
GONEF	GONORRHEA	GOOFBALLS	GOONIEST	GOPHERS
GONEFS	GONOSOME	GOOFED	GOONS	GOPIK
GONENESS	GONOSOMES	GOOFIER	GOONY	GOPIKS
GONER	GONS	GOOFIEST	GOOP	GOPURA
GONERS	GONYS	GOOFILY	GOOPED	GOPURAM
GONFALON	GONYSES	GOOFINESS	GOOPIER	GOPURAMS
GONFALONS	GONZO	GOOFING	GOOPIEST	GOPURAS
GONFANON	GOO	GOOFS	GOOPINESS	GOR
GONFANONS	GOOBER	GOOFY	GOOPS	GORA
GONG	GOOBERS	GOOG	GOOPY	GORAL
GONGED	GOOBIES	GOOGLE	GOOR	GORALS
GONGING	GOOBY	GOOGLED	GOORAL	GORAMIES
GONGLIKE	GOOD	GOOGLES	GOORALS	GORAMY
GONGS	GOODBY	GOOGLIES	GOORIE	GORAS
GONGSTER	GOODBYE	GOOGLING	GOORIES	GORBELLY
GONGSTERS	GOODBYES	GOOGLY	GOOROO	GORBLIMEY
GONGYO	GOODBYS	GOOGOL	GOOROOS	GORBLIMY
GONGYOS	GOODFACED	GOOGOLS	GOORS	GORCOCK
GONIA	GOODFELLA	GOOGS	GOORY	GORCOCKS
GONIATITE	GOODIE	GOOIER	GOOS	GORCROW
GONIDIA	GOODIER	GOOIEST	GOOSANDER	GORCROWS
GONIDIAL	GOODIES	GOOILY	GOOSE	GORDITA
GONIDIC	GOODIEST	GOOINESS	GOOSED	GORDITAS
GONIDIUM	GOODINESS	GOOK	GOOSEFISH	GORE
GONIF	GOODISH	GOOKS	GOOSEFOOT	GORED
GONIFF	GOODLIER	GOOKY	GOOSEGOB	GOREHOUND

GORES	GORMLESS	GOSSAN	GOUGE	GOUTWEEDS
GORGE	GORMS	GOSSANS	GOUGED	GOUTWORT
GORGEABLE	GORMY	GOSSE	GOUGER	GOUTWORTS
GORGED	GORP	GOSSED	GOUGERE	GOUTY
GORGEDLY	GORPED	GOSSES	GOUGERES	GOV
GORGEOUS	GORPING	GOSSIB	GOUGERS	GOVERN
GORGER	GORPS	GOSSIBS	GOUGES	GOVERNALL
GORGERIN	GORSE	GOSSING	GOUGING	GOVERNED
GORGERINS	GORSEDD	GOSSIP	GOUJEERS	GOVERNESS
GORGERS	GORSEDDS	GOSSIPED	GOUJON	GOVERNING
GORGES	GORSES	GOSSIPER	GOUJONS	GOVERNOR
GORGET	GORSIER	GOSSIPERS	GOUK	GOVERNORS
GORGETED	GORSIEST	GOSSIPING	GOUKS	GOVERNS
GORGETS	GORSOON	GOSSIPPED	GOULASH	GOVS
GORGIA	GORSOONS	GOSSIPPER	GOULASHES	GOWAN
GORGIAS	GORSY	GOSSIPRY	GOURA	GOWANED
GORGING	GORY	GOSSIPS	GOURAMI	GOWANS
GORGIO	GOS	GOSSIPY	GOURAMIES	GOWANY
GORGIOS	GOSH	GOSSOON	GOURAMIS	GOWD
GORGON	GOSHAWK	GOSSOONS	GOURAS	GOWDER
GORGONEIA	GOSHAWKS	GOSSYPINE	GOURD	GOWDEST
GORGONIAN	GOSHT	GOSSYPOL	GOURDE	GOWDS
GORGONISE	GOSHTS	GOSSYPOLS	GOURDES	GOWDSPINK
GORGONIZE	GOSLARITE	GOSTER	GOURDIER	GOWF
GORGONS	GOSLET	GOSTERED	GOURDIEST	GOWFED
GORHEN	GOSLETS	GOSTERING	GOURDLIKE	GOWFER
GORHENS	GOSLING	GOSTERS	GOURDS	GOWFERS
GORI	GOSLINGS	GOT	GOURDY	GOWFING
GORIER	GOSPEL	GOTCHA	GOURMAND	GOWFS
GORIEST	GOSPELER	GOTCHAS	GOURMANDS	GOWK
GORILLA	GOSPELERS	GOTH	GOURMET	GOWKS
GORILLAS	GOSPELISE	GOTHIC	GOURMETS	GOWL
GORILLIAN	GOSPELIZE	GOTHICISE	GOUSTIER	GOWLAN
GORILLINE	GOSPELLED	GOTHICISM	GOUSTIEST	GOWLAND
GORILLOID	GOSPELLER	GOTHICIZE	GOUSTROUS	GOWLANDS
GORILY	GOSPELLY	GOTHICS	GOUSTY	GOWLANS
GORINESS	GOSPELS	GOTHITE	GOUT	GOWLED
GORING	GOSPODA	GOTHITES	GOUTFLIES	GOWLING
GORINGS	GOSPODAR	GOTHS	GOUTFLY	GOWLS
GORIS	GOSPODARS	GOTTA	GOUTIER	GOWN
GORM	GOSPODIN	GOTTEN	GOUTIEST	GOWNBOY
GORMAND	GOSPORT	GOUACHE	GOUTILY	GOWNBOYS
GORMANDS	GOSPORTS	GOUACHES	GOUTINESS	GOWNED
GORMED	GOSS	GOUCH	GOUTS	GOWNING
GORMIER	GOSSAMER	GOUCHED	GOUTTE	GOWNMAN
GORMIEST	GOSSAMERS	GOUCHES	GOUTTES	GOWNMEN
GORMING	GOSSAMERY	GOUCHING	GOUTWEED	GOWNS

G

G

GOWNSMAN	GRACIOSOS	GRAECISE	GRAITHING	GRANDAMES
GOWNSMEN	GRACIOUS	GRAECISED	GRAITHLY	GRANDAMS
GOWPEN	GRACKLE	GRAECISES	GRAITHS	GRANDAUNT
GOWPENFUL	GRACKLES	GRAECIZE	GRAKLE	GRANDBABY
GOWPENS	GRAD	GRAECIZED	GRAKLES	GRANDDAD
GOX	GRADABLE	GRAECIZES	GRALLOCH	GRANDDADS
GOXES	GRADABLES	GRAFF	GRALLOCHS	GRANDDAM
GOY	GRADATE	GRAFFED	GRAM	GRANDDAMS
GOYIM	GRADATED	GRAFFING	GRAMA	GRANDE
GOYISCH	GRADATES	GRAFFITI	GRAMARIES	GRANDEE
GOYISH	GRADATIM	GRAFFITIS	GRAMARY	GRANDEES
GOYLE	GRADATING	GRAFFITO	GRAMARYE	GRANDER
GOYLES	GRADATION	GRAFFS	GRAMARYES	GRANDEST
GOYS	GRADATORY	GRAFT	GRAMAS	GRANDEUR
GOZZAN	GRADDAN	GRAFTAGE	GRAMASH	GRANDEURS
GOZZANS	GRADDANED	GRAFTAGES	GRAMASHES	GRANDIOSE
GRAAL	GRADDANS	GRAFTED	GRAME	GRANDIOSO
GRAALS	GRADE	GRAFTER	GRAMERCY	GRANDKID
GRAB	GRADED	GRAFTERS	GRAMES	GRANDKIDS
GRABBABLE	GRADELESS	GRAFTING	GRAMMA	GRANDLY
GRABBED	GRADELIER	GRAFTINGS	GRAMMAGE	GRANDMA
GRABBER	GRADELY	GRAFTS	GRAMMAGES	GRANDMAMA
GRABBERS	GRADER	GRAHAM	GRAMMAR	GRANDMAS
GRABBIER	GRADERS	GRAHAMS	GRAMMARS	GRANDNESS
GRABBIEST	GRADES	GRAIL	GRAMMAS	GRANDPA
GRABBING	GRADIENT	GRAILE	GRAMMATIC	GRANDPAPA
GRABBLE	GRADIENTS	GRAILES	GRAMME	GRANDPAS
GRABBLED	GRADIN	GRAILS	GRAMMES	GRANDS
GRABBLER	GRADINE	GRAIN	GRAMOCHE	GRANDSIR
GRABBLERS	GRADINES	GRAINAGE	GRAMOCHES	GRANDSIRE
GRABBLES	GRADING	GRAINAGES	GRAMP	GRANDSIRS
GRABBLING	GRADINGS	GRAINE	GRAMPA	GRANDSON
GRABBY	GRADINI	GRAINED	GRAMPAS	GRANDSONS
GRABEN	GRADINO	GRAINER	GRAMPS	GRANFER
GRABENS	GRADINS	GRAINERS	GRAMPUS	GRANFERS
GRABS	GRADS	GRAINES	GRAMPUSES	GRANGE
GRACE	GRADUAL	GRAINIER	GRAMS	GRANGER
GRACED	GRADUALLY	GRAINIEST	GRAN	GRANGERS
GRACEFUL	GRADUALS	GRAINING	GRANA	GRANGES
GRACELESS	GRADUAND	GRAININGS	GRANARIES	GRANITA
GRACES	GRADUANDS	GRAINLESS	GRANARY	GRANITAS
GRACILE	GRADUATE	GRAINS	GRAND	GRANITE
GRACILES	GRADUATED	GRAINY	GRANDAD	GRANITES
GRACILIS	GRADUATES	GRAIP	GRANDADDY	GRANITIC
GRACILITY	GRADUATOR	GRAIPS	GRANDADS	GRANITISE
GRACING	GRADUS	GRAITH	GRANDAM	GRANITITE
GRACIOSO	GRADUSES	GRAITHED	GRANDAME	GRANITIZE

GRANITOID	GRAPESEED	GRASPER	GRATINGLY	GRAVIDITY
GRANIVORE	GRAPESHOT	GRASPERS	GRATINGS	GRAVIDLY
GRANNAM	GRAPETREE	GRASPING	GRATINS	GRAVIES
GRANNAMS	GRAPEVINE	GRASPLESS	GRATIS	GRAVING
GRANNIE	GRAPEY	GRASPS	GRATITUDE	GRAVINGS
GRANNIED	GRAPH	GRASS	GRATTOIR	GRAVIS
GRANNIES	GRAPHED	GRASSBIRD	GRATTOIRS	GRAVITAS
GRANNOM	GRAPHEME	GRASSED	GRATUITY	GRAVITATE
GRANNOMS	GRAPHEMES	GRASSER	GRATULANT	GRAVITIES
GRANNY	GRAPHEMIC	GRASSERS	GRATULATE	GRAVITINO
GRANNYING	GRAPHENE	GRASSES	GRAUNCH	GRAVITON
GRANNYISH	GRAPHENES	GRASSHOOK	GRAUNCHED	GRAVITONS
GRANOLA	GRAPHIC	GRASSIER	GRAUNCHER	GRAVITY
GRANOLAS	GRAPHICAL	GRASSIEST	GRAUNCHES	GRAVLAKS
GRANOLITH	GRAPHICLY	GRASSILY	GRAUPEL	GRAVLAX
GRANS	GRAPHICS	GRASSING	GRAUPELS	GRAVLAXES
GRANT	GRAPHING	GRASSINGS	GRAV	GRAVS
GRANTABLE	GRAPHITE	GRASSLAND	GRAVADLAX	GRAVURE
GRANTED	GRAPHITES	GRASSLESS	GRAVAMEN	GRAVURES
GRANTEE	GRAPHITIC	GRASSLIKE	GRAVAMENS	GRAVY
GRANTEES	GRAPHIUM	GRASSPLOT	GRAVAMINA	GRAY
GRANTER	GRAPHIUMS	GRASSQUIT	GRAVE	GRAYBACK
GRANTERS	GRAPHS	GRASSROOT	GRAVED	GRAYBACKS
GRANTING	GRAPIER	GRASSUM	GRAVEL	GRAYBEARD
GRANTOR	GRAPIEST	GRASSUMS	GRAVELED	GRAYED
GRANTORS	GRAPINESS	GRASSY	GRAVELESS	GRAYER
GRANTS	GRAPING	GRASTE	GRAVELIKE	GRAYEST
GRANTSMAN	GRAPLE	GRAT	GRAVELING	GRAYFISH
GRANTSMEN	GRAPLES	GRATE	GRAVELISH	GRAYFLIES
GRANULAR	GRAPLIN	GRATED	GRAVELLED	GRAYFLY
GRANULARY	GRAPLINE	GRATEFUL	GRAVELLY	GRAYHOUND
GRANULATE	GRAPLINES	GRATELESS	GRAVELS	GRAYING
GRANULE	GRAPLINS	GRATER	GRAVELY	GRAYISH
GRANULES	GRAPNEL	GRATERS	GRAVEN	GRAYLAG
GRANULITE	GRAPNELS	GRATES	GRAVENESS	GRAYLAGS
GRANULOMA	GRAPPA	GRATICULE	GRAVER	GRAYLE
GRANULOSE	GRAPPAS	GRATIFIED	GRAVERS	GRAYLES
GRANULOUS	GRAPPLE	GRATIFIER	GRAVES	GRAYLING
GRANUM	GRAPPLED	GRATIFIES	GRAVESIDE	GRAYLINGS
GRAPE	GRAPPLER	GRATIFY	GRAVESITE	GRAYLY
GRAPED	GRAPPLERS	GRATIN	GRAVEST	GRAYMAIL
GRAPELESS	GRAPPLES	GRATINATE	GRAVEWARD	GRAYMAILS
GRAPELICE	GRAPPLING	GRATINE	GRAVEYARD	GRAYNESS
GRAPELIKE	GRAPY	GRATINEE	GRAVID	GRAYOUT
GRAPERIES	GRASP	GRATINEED	GRAVIDA	GRAYOUTS
GRAPERY	GRASPABLE	GRATINEES	GRAVIDAE	GRAYS
GRAPES	GRASPED	GRATING	GRAVIDAS	GRAYSCALE

G

GRAYWACKE
GRAYWATER
GRAZABLE
GRAZE
GRAZEABLE
GRAZED
GRAZER
GRAZERS
GRAZES
GRAZIER
GRAZIERS
GRAZING
GRAZINGLY
GRAZINGS
GRAZIOSO
GREASE
GREASED
GREASER
GREASERS
GREASES
GREASIER
GREASIES
GREASIEST
GREASILY
GREASING
GREASY
GREAT
GREATCOAT
GREATEN
GREATENED
GREATENS
GREATER
GREATEST
GREATESTS
GREATLY
GREATNESS
GREATS
GREAVE
GREAVED
GREAVES
GREAVING
GREBE
GREBES
GREBO
GREBOS
GRECE
GRECES

GRECIAN
GRECIANS
GRECISE
GRECISED
GRECISES
GRECISING
GRECIZE
GRECIZED
GRECIZES
GRECIZING
GRECQUE
GRECQUES
GREE
GREEBO
GREEBOES
GREECE
GREECES
GREED
GREEDIER
GREEDIEST
GREEDILY
GREEDLESS
GREEDS
GREEDSOME
GREEDY
GREEGREE
GREEGREES
GREEING
GREEK
GREEKED
GREEKING
GREEKINGS
GREEN
GREENBACK
GREENBELT
GREENBONE
GREENBUG
GREENBUGS
GREENED
GREENER
GREENERS
GREENERY
GREENEST
GREENEYE
GREENEYES
GREENFLY
GREENGAGE

GREENHAND
GREENHEAD
GREENHORN
GREENIE
GREENIER
GREENIES
GREENIEST
GREENING
GREENINGS
GREENISH
GREENLET
GREENLETS
GREENLING
GREENLIT
GREENLY
GREENMAIL
GREENNESS
GREENROOM
GREENS
GREENSAND
GREENSICK
GREENSOME
GREENTH
GREENTHS
GREENWASH
GREENWAY
GREENWAYS
GREENWEED
GREENWING
GREENWOOD
GREENY
GREES
GREESE
GREESES
GREESING
GREESINGS
GREET
GREETE
GREETED
GREETER
GREETERS
GREETES
GREETING
GREETINGS
GREETS
GREFFIER
GREFFIERS

GREGALE
GREGALES
GREGARIAN
GREGARINE
GREGATIM
GREGE
GREGO
GREGOS
GREIGE
GREIGES
GREIN
GREINED
GREINING
GREINS
GREISEN
GREISENS
GREISLY
GREMIAL
GREMIALS
GREMLIN
GREMLINS
GREMMIE
GREMMIES
GREMMY
GREMOLATA
GREN
GRENACHE
GRENACHES
GRENADE
GRENADES
GRENADIER
GRENADINE
GRENNED
GRENNING
GRENS
GRESE
GRESES
GRESSING
GRESSINGS
GREVE
GREVES
GREVILLEA
GREW
GREWED
GREWHOUND
GREWING
GREWS

GREWSOME
GREWSOMER
GREX
GREXES
GREY
GREYBACK
GREYBACKS
GREYBEARD
GREYED
GREYER
GREYEST
GREYHEN
GREYHENS
GREYHOUND
GREYING
GREYINGS
GREYISH
GREYLAG
GREYLAGS
GREYLIST
GREYLISTS
GREYLY
GREYNESS
GREYS
GREYSCALE
GREYSTONE
GREYWACKE
GRIBBLE
GRIBBLES
GRICE
GRICED
GRICER
GRICERS
GRICES
GRICING
GRICINGS
GRID
GRIDDED
GRIDDER
GRIDDERS
GRIDDLE
GRIDDLED
GRIDDLES
GRIDDLING
GRIDE
GRIDED
GRIDELIN

GRIDELINS	GRIGGING	GRIMOIRES	GRIPPING	GRITS
GRIDES	GRIGRI	GRIMY	GRIPPLE	GRITSTONE
GRIDING	GRIGRIS	GRIN	GRIPPLES	GRITTED
GRIDIRON	GRIGS	GRINCH	GRIPPY	GRITTER
GRIDIRONS	GRIKE	GRINCHES	GRIPS	GRITTERS
GRIDLOCK	GRIKES	GRIND	GRIPSACK	GRITTEST
GRIDLOCKS	GRILL	GRINDED	GRIPSACKS	GRITTIER
GRIDS	GRILLADE	GRINDELIA	GRIPT	GRITTIEST
GRIECE	GRILLADES	GRINDER	GRIPTAPE	GRITTILY
GRIECED	GRILLAGE	GRINDERS	GRIPTAPES	GRITTING
GRIECES	GRILLAGES	GRINDERY	GRIPY	GRITTINGS
GRIEF	GRILLE	GRINDING	GRIS	GRITTY
GRIEFER	GRILLED	GRINDINGS	GRISAILLE	GRIVATION
GRIEFERS	GRILLER	GRINDS	GRISE	GRIVET
GRIEFFUL	GRILLERS	GRINGA	GRISED	GRIVETS
GRIEFLESS	GRILLERY	GRINGAS	GRISELY	GRIZE
GRIEFS	GRILLES	GRINGO	GRISEOUS	GRIZES
GRIESIE	GRILLING	GRINGOS	GRISES	GRIZZLE
GRIESLY	GRILLINGS	GRINNED	GRISETTE	GRIZZLED
GRIESY	GRILLION	GRINNER	GRISETTES	GRIZZLER
GRIEVANCE	GRILLIONS	GRINNERS	GRISGRIS	GRIZZLERS
GRIEVANT	GRILLROOM	GRINNING	GRISING	GRIZZLES
GRIEVANTS	GRILLS	GRINNINGS	GRISKIN	GRIZZLIER
GRIEVE	GRILLWORK	GRINS	GRISKINS	GRIZZLIES
GRIEVED	GRILSE	GRIOT	GRISLED	GRIZZLING
GRIEVER	GRILSES	GRIOTS	GRISLIER	GRIZZLY
GRIEVERS	GRIM	GRIP	GRISLIES	GROAN
GRIEVES	GRIMACE	GRIPE	GRISLIEST	GROANED
GRIEVING	GRIMACED	GRIPED	GRISLY	GROANER
GRIEVINGS	GRIMACER	GRIPER	GRISON	GROANERS
GRIEVOUS	GRIMACERS	GRIPERS	GRISONS	GROANFUL
GRIFF	GRIMACES	GRIPES	GRISSINI	GROANING
GRIFFE	GRIMACING	GRIPEY	GRISSINO	GROANINGS
GRIFFES	GRIMALKIN	GRIPIER	GRIST	GROANS
GRIFFIN	GRIME	GRIPIEST	GRISTER	GROAT
GRIFFINS	GRIMED	GRIPING	GRISTERS	GROATS
GRIFFON	GRIMES	GRIPINGLY	GRISTLE	GROCER
GRIFFONS	GRIMIER	GRIPLE	GRISTLES	GROCERIES
GRIFFS	GRIMIEST	GRIPMAN	GRISTLIER	GROCERS
GRIFT	GRIMILY	GRIPMEN	GRISTLY	GROCERY
GRIFTED	GRIMINESS	GRIPPE	GRISTMILL	GROCKED
GRIFTER	GRIMING	GRIPPED	GRISTS	GROCKING
GRIFTERS	GRIMLY	GRIPPER	GRISY	GROCKLE
GRIFTING	GRIMMER	GRIPPERS	GRIT	GROCKLES
GRIFTS	GRIMMEST	GRIPPES	GRITH	GRODIER
GRIG	GRIMNESS	GRIPPIER	GRITHS	GRODIEST
GRIGGED	GRIMOIRE	GRIPPIEST	GRITLESS	GRODY

G

GROG	GROOMING	GROSZY	GROUPIST	GROWINGS
GROGGED	GROOMINGS	GROT	GROUPISTS	GROWL
GROGGERY	GROOMS	GROTESQUE	GROUPLET	GROWLED
GROGGIER	GROOMSMAN	GROTS	GROUPLETS	GROWLER
GROGGIEST	GROOMSMEN	GROTTIER	GROUPOID	GROWLERS
GROGGILY	GROOVE	GROTTIEST	GROUPOIDS	GROWLERY
GROGGING	GROOVED	GROTTO	GROUPS	GROWLIER
GROGGY	GROOVER	GROTTOED	GROUPWARE	GROWLIEST
GROGRAM	GROOVERS	GROTTOES	GROUPWORK	GROWLING
GROGRAMS	GROOVES	GROTTOS	GROUPY	GROWLINGS
GROGS	GROOVIER	GROTTY	GROUSE	GROWLS
GROGSHOP	GROOVIEST	GROUCH	GROUSED	GROWLY
GROGSHOPS	GROOVILY	GROUCHED	GROUSER	GROWN
GROIN	GROOVING	GROUCHES	GROUSERS	GROWNUP
GROINED	GROOVY	GROUCHIER	GROUSES	GROWNUPS
GROINING	GROPE	GROUCHILY	GROUSEST	GROWS
GROININGS	GROPED	GROUCHING	GROUSING	GROWTH
GROINS	GROPER	GROUCHY	GROUT	GROWTHIER
GROK	GROPERS	GROUF	GROUTED	GROWTHIST
GROKED	GROPES	GROUFS	GROUTER	GROWTHS
GROKING	GROPING	GROUGH	GROUTERS	GROWTHY
GROKKED	GROPINGLY	GROUGHS	GROUTIER	GROYNE
GROKKING	GROSBEAK	GROUND	GROUTIEST	GROYNES
GROKS	GROSBEAKS	GROUNDAGE	GROUTING	GROZING
GROMA	GROSCHEN	GROUNDED	GROUTINGS	GRRL
GROMAS	GROSCHENS	GROUNDEN	GROUTS	GRRLS
GROMET	GROSER	GROUNDER	GROUTY	GRRRL
GROMETS	GROSERS	GROUNDERS	GROVE	GRRRLS
GROMMET	GROSERT	GROUNDHOG	GROVED	GRUB
GROMMETED	GROSERTS	GROUNDING	GROVEL	GRUBBED
GROMMETS	GROSET	GROUNDMAN	GROVELED	GRUBBER
GROMWELL	GROSETS	GROUNDMEN	GROVELER	GRUBBERS
GROMWELLS	GROSGRAIN	GROUNDNUT	GROVELERS	GRUBBIER
GRONE	GROSS	GROUNDOUT	GROVELESS	GRUBBIEST
GRONED	GROSSART	GROUNDS	GROVELING	GRUBBILY
GRONEFULL	GROSSARTS	GROUNDSEL	GROVELLED	GRUBBING
GRONES	GROSSED	GROUP	GROVELLER	GRUBBLE
GRONING	GROSSER	GROUPABLE	GROVELS	GRUBBLED
GROOF	GROSSERS	GROUPAGE	GROVES	GRUBBLES
GROOFS	GROSSES	GROUPAGES	GROVET	GRUBBLING
GROOLIER	GROSSEST	GROUPED	GROVETS	GRUBBY
GROOLIEST	GROSSING	GROUPER	GROW	GRUBS
GROOLY	GROSSLY	GROUPERS	GROWABLE	GRUBSTAKE
GROOM	GROSSNESS	GROUPIE	GROWER	GRUBWORM
GROOMED	GROSSULAR	GROUPIES	GROWERS	GRUBWORMS
GROOMER	GROSZ	GROUPING	GROWING	GRUDGE
GROOMERS	GROSZE	GROUPINGS	GROWINGLY	GRUDGED

GRUDGEFUL	GRUMBLERS	GRUNTED	GUAIACOL	GUARDANT
GRUDGER	GRUMBLES	GRUNTER	GUAIACOLS	GUARDANTS
GRUDGERS	GRUMBLIER	GRUNTERS	GUAIACS	GUARDDOG
GRUDGES	GRUMBLING	GRUNTING	GUAIACUM	GUARDDOGS
GRUDGING	GRUMBLY	GRUNTINGS	GUAIACUMS	GUARDED
GRUDGINGS	GRUME	GRUNTLE	GUAIOCUM	GUARDEDLY
GRUE	GRUMES	GRUNTLED	GUAIOCUMS	GUARDEE
GRUED	GRUMLY	GRUNTLES	GUAN	GUARDEES
GRUEING	GRUMMER	GRUNTLING	GUANA	GUARDER
GRUEL	GRUMMEST	GRUNTS	GUANABANA	GUARDERS
GRUELED	GRUMMET	GRUPPETTI	GUANACO	GUARDIAN
GRUELER	GRUMMETED	GRUPPETTO	GUANACOS	GUARDIANS
GRUELERS	GRUMMETS	GRUSHIE	GUANAS	GUARDING
GRUELING	GRUMNESS	GRUTCH	GUANASE	GUARDLESS
GRUELINGS	GRUMOSE	GRUTCHED	GUANASES	GUARDLIKE
GRUELLED	GRUMOUS	GRUTCHES	GUANAY	GUARDRAIL
GRUELLER	GRUMP	GRUTCHING	GUANAYS	GUARDROOM
GRUELLERS	GRUMPED	GRUTTEN	GUANAZOLO	GUARDS
GRUELLING	GRUMPH	GRUYERE	GUANGO	GUARDSHIP
GRUELS	GRUMPHED	GRUYERES	GUANGOS	GUARDSMAN
GRUES	GRUMPHIE	GRYCE	GUANIDIN	GUARDSMEN
GRUESOME	GRUMPHIES	GRYCES	GUANIDINE	GUARISH
GRUESOMER	GRUMPHING	GRYDE	GUANIDINS	GUARISHED
GRUFE	GRUMPHS	GRYDED	GUANIN	GUARISHES
GRUFES	GRUMPHY	GRYDES	GUANINE	GUARS
GRUFF	GRUMPIER	GRYDING	GUANINES	GUAVA
GRUFFED	GRUMPIEST	GRYESY	GUANINS	GUAVAS
GRUFFER	GRUMPILY	GRYFON	GUANO	GUAYABERA
GRUFFEST	GRUMPING	GRYFONS	GUANOS	GUAYULE
GRUFFIER	GRUMPISH	GRYKE	GUANOSINE	GUAYULES
GRUFFIEST	GRUMPS	GRYKES	GUANS	GUB
GRUFFILY	GRUMPY	GRYPE	GUANXI	GUBBAH
GRUFFING	GRUND	GRYPES	GUANXIS	GUBBAHS
GRUFFISH	GRUNDIES	GRYPHON	GUANYLIC	GUBBED
GRUFFLY	GRUNDLE	GRYPHONS	GUAR	GUBBING
GRUFFNESS	GRUNDLES	GRYPT	GUARANA	GUBBINS
GRUFFS	GRUNGE	GRYSBOK	GUARANAS	GUBBINSES
GRUFFY	GRUNGER	GRYSBOKS	GUARANI	GUBERNIYA
GRUFTED	GRUNGERS	GRYSELY	GUARANIES	GUBS
GRUGRU	GRUNGES	GRYSIE	GUARANIS	GUCK
GRUGRUS	GRUNGEY	GU	GUARANTEE	GUCKIER
GRUIFORM	GRUNGIER	GUACAMOLE	GUARANTOR	GUCKIEST
GRUING	GRUNGIEST	GUACHARO	GUARANTY	GUCKS
GRUM	GRUNGY	GUACHAROS	GUARD	GUCKY
GRUMBLE	GRUNION	GUACO	GUARDABLE	GUDDLE
GRUMBLED	GRUNIONS	GUACOS	GUARDAGE	GUDDLED
GRUMBLER	GRUNT	GUAIAC	GUARDAGES	GUDDLES

GUDDLING
GUDE
GUDEMAN
GUDEMEN
GUDES
GUDESIRE
GUDESIRES
GUDEWIFE
GUDEWIVES
GUDGEON
GUDGEONED
GUDGEONS
GUE
GUELDER
GUENON
GUENONS
GUERDON
GUERDONED
GUERDONER
GUERDONS
GUEREZA
GUEREZAS
GUERIDON
GUERIDONS
GUERILLA
GUERILLAS
GUERITE
GUERITES
GUERNSEY
GUERNSEYS
GUERRILLA
GUES
GUESS
GUESSABLE
GUESSED
GUESSER
GUESSERS
GUESSES
GUESSING
GUESSINGS
GUESSWORK
GUEST
GUESTBOOK
GUESTED
GUESTEN
GUESTENED
GUESTENS

GUESTING
GUESTS
GUESTWISE
GUFF
GUFFAW
GUFFAWED
GUFFAWING
GUFFAWS
GUFFIE
GUFFIES
GUFFS
GUGA
GUGAS
GUGGLE
GUGGLED
GUGGLES
GUGGLING
GUGLET
GUGLETS
GUICHET
GUICHETS
GUID
GUIDABLE
GUIDAGE
GUIDAGES
GUIDANCE
GUIDANCES
GUIDE
GUIDEBOOK
GUIDED
GUIDELESS
GUIDELINE
GUIDEPOST
GUIDER
GUIDERS
GUIDES
GUIDESHIP
GUIDEWAY
GUIDEWAYS
GUIDEWORD
GUIDING
GUIDINGS
GUIDON
GUIDONS
GUIDS
GUILD
GUILDER

GUILDERS
GUILDHALL
GUILDRIES
GUILDRY
GUILDS
GUILDSHIP
GUILDSMAN
GUILDSMEN
GUILE
GUILED
GUILEFUL
GUILELESS
GUILER
GUILERS
GUILES
GUILING
GUILLEMET
GUILLEMOT
GUILLOCHE
GUILT
GUILTIER
GUILTIEST
GUILTILY
GUILTLESS
GUILTS
GUILTY
GUIMBARD
GUIMBARDS
GUIMP
GUIMPE
GUIMPED
GUIMPES
GUIMPING
GUIMPS
GUINEA
GUINEAS
GUIPURE
GUIPURES
GUIRO
GUIROS
GUISARD
GUISARDS
GUISE
GUISED
GUISER
GUISERS
GUISES

GUISING
GUISINGS
GUITAR
GUITARIST
GUITARS
GUITGUIT
GUITGUITS
GUIZER
GUIZERS
GUL
GULA
GULAG
GULAGS
GULAR
GULAS
GULCH
GULCHED
GULCHES
GULCHING
GULDEN
GULDENS
GULE
GULES
GULET
GULETS
GULF
GULFED
GULFIER
GULFIEST
GULFING
GULFLIKE
GULFS
GULFWEED
GULFWEEDS
GULFY
GULL
GULLABLE
GULLABLY
GULLED
GULLER
GULLERIES
GULLERS
GULLERY
GULLET
GULLETS
GULLEY
GULLEYED

GULLEYING
GULLEYS
GULLIBLE
GULLIBLY
GULLIED
GULLIES
GULLING
GULLISH
GULLS
GULLWING
GULLY
GULLYING
GULOSITY
GULP
GULPED
GULPER
GULPERS
GULPH
GULPHS
GULPIER
GULPIEST
GULPING
GULPINGLY
GULPS
GULPY
GULS
GULY
GUM
GUMBALL
GUMBALLS
GUMBO
GUMBOIL
GUMBOILS
GUMBOOT
GUMBOOTS
GUMBOS
GUMBOTIL
GUMBOTILS
GUMDROP
GUMDROPS
GUMLANDS
GUMLESS
GUMLIKE
GUMLINE
GUMLINES
GUMMA
GUMMAS

GUMMATA	GUNDIES	GUNNEN	GUNYAH	GURRAHS
GUMMATOUS	GUNDOG	GUNNER	GUNYAHS	GURRIER
GUMMED	GUNDOGS	GUNNERA	GUP	GURRIERS
GUMMER	GUNDY	GUNNERAS	GUPPIES	GURRIES
GUMMERS	GUNFIGHT	GUNNERIES	GUPPY	GURRY
GUMMIER	GUNFIGHTS	GUNNERS	GUPS	GURS
GUMMIES	GUNFIRE	GUNNERY	GUQIN	GURSH
GUMMIEST	GUNFIRES	GUNNIES	GUQINS	GURSHES
GUMMILY	GUNFLINT	GUNNING	GUR	GURU
GUMMINESS	GUNFLINTS	GUNNINGS	GURAMI	GURUDOM
GUMMING	GUNFOUGHT	GUNNY	GURAMIS	GURUDOMS
GUMMINGS	GUNG	GUNNYBAG	GURDWARA	GURUISM
GUMMITE	GUNGE	GUNNYBAGS	GURDWARAS	GURUISMS
GUMMITES	GUNGED	GUNNYSACK	GURGE	GURUS
GUMMOSE	GUNGES	GUNPAPER	GURGED	GURUSHIP
GUMMOSES	GUNGIER	GUNPAPERS	GURGES	GURUSHIPS
GUMMOSIS	GUNGIEST	GUNPLAY	GURGING	GUS
GUMMOSITY	GUNGING	GUNPLAYS	GURGLE	GUSH
GUMMOUS	GUNGY	GUNPOINT	GURGLED	GUSHED
GUMMY	GUNHOUSE	GUNPOINTS	GURGLES	GUSHER
GUMNUT	GUNHOUSES	GUNPORT	GURGLET	GUSHERS
GUMNUTS	GUNITE	GUNPORTS	GURGLETS	GUSHES
GUMP	GUNITES	GUNPOWDER	GURGLING	GUSHIER
GUMPED	GUNK	GUNROOM	GURGOYLE	GUSHIEST
GUMPHION	GUNKHOLE	GUNROOMS	GURGOYLES	GUSHILY
GUMPHIONS	GUNKHOLED	GUNRUNNER	GURJUN	GUSHINESS
GUMPING	GUNKHOLES	GUNS	GURJUNS	GUSHING
GUMPS	GUNKIER	GUNSEL	GURL	GUSHINGLY
GUMPTION	GUNKIEST	GUNSELS	GURLED	GUSHY
GUMPTIONS	GUNKS	GUNSHIP	GURLET	GUSLA
GUMPTIOUS	GUNKY	GUNSHIPS	GURLETS	GUSLAR
GUMS	GUNLAYER	GUNSHOT	GURLIER	GUSLARS
GUMSHIELD	GUNLAYERS	GUNSHOTS	GURLIEST	GUSLAS
GUMSHOE	GUNLESS	GUNSIGHT	GURLING	GUSLE
GUMSHOED	GUNLOCK	GUNSIGHTS	GURLS	GUSLES
GUMSHOES	GUNLOCKS	GUNSMITH	GURLY	GUSLI
GUMSUCKER	GUNMAKER	GUNSMITHS	GURN	GUSLIS
GUMTREE	GUNMAKERS	GUNSTICK	GURNARD	GUSSET
GUMTREES	GUNMAN	GUNSTICKS	GURNARDS	GUSSETED
GUMWEED	GUNMEN	GUNSTOCK	GURNED	GUSSETING
GUMWEEDS	GUNMETAL	GUNSTOCKS	GURNET	GUSSETS
GUMWOOD	GUNMETALS	GUNSTONE	GURNETS	GUSSIE
GUMWOODS	GUNNAGE	GUNSTONES	GURNEY	GUSSIED
GUN	GUNNAGES	GUNTER	GURNEYS	GUSSIES
GUNBOAT	GUNNED	GUNTERS	GURNING	GUSSY
GUNBOATS	GUNNEL	GUNWALE	GURNS	GUSSYING
GUNCOTTON	GUNNELS	GUNWALES	GURRAH	GUST

GUSTABLE	GUTTATED	GUZZLER	GYMSLIPS	GYPSTER
GUSTABLES	GUTTATES	GUZZLERS	GYNAE	GYPSTERS
GUSTATION	GUTTATING	GUZZLES	GYNAECEA	GYPSUM
GUSTATIVE	GUTTATION	GUZZLING	GYNAECEUM	GYPSUMS
GUSTATORY	GUTTED	GWEDUC	GYNAECIA	GYPSY
GUSTED	GUTTER	GWEDUCK	GYNAECIUM	GYPSYDOM
GUSTFUL	GUTTERED	GWEDUCKS	GYNAECOID	GYPSYDOMS
GUSTIE	GUTTERING	GWEDUCS	GYNAES	GYPSYHOOD
GUSTIER	GUTTERS	GWINE	GYNANDRY	GYPSYING
GUSTIEST	GUTTERY	GWINIAD	GYNARCHIC	GYPSYISH
GUSTILY	GUTTIER	GWINIADS	GYNARCHY	GYPSYISM
GUSTINESS	GUTTIES	GWYNIAD	GYNECIA	GYPSYISMS
GUSTING	GUTTIEST	GWYNIADS	GYNECIC	GYPSYWORT
GUSTLESS	GUTTING	GYAL	GYNECIUM	GYRAL
GUSTO	GUTTLE	GYALS	GYNECOID	GYRALLY
GUSTOES	GUTTLED	GYBE	GYNIATRY	GYRANT
GUSTOS	GUTTLER	GYBED	GYNIE	GYRASE
GUSTS	GUTTLERS	GYBES	GYNIES	GYRASES
GUSTY	GUTTLES	GYBING	GYNNEY	GYRATE
GUT	GUTTLING	GYELD	GYNNEYS	GYRATED
GUTBUCKET	GUTTURAL	GYELDS	GYNNIES	GYRATES
GUTCHER	GUTTURALS	GYLDEN	GYNNY	GYRATING
GUTCHERS	GUTTY	GYM	GYNOCRACY	GYRATION
GUTFUL	GUTZER	GYMBAL	GYNOECIA	GYRATIONS
GUTFULS	GUTZERS	GYMBALS	GYNOECIUM	GYRATOR
GUTLESS	GUV	GYMKHANA	GYNOPHOBE	GYRATORS
GUTLESSLY	GUVS	GYMKHANAS	GYNOPHORE	GYRATORY
GUTLIKE	GUY	GYMMAL	GYNY	GYRE
GUTROT	GUYED	GYMMALS	GYOZA	GYRED
GUTROTS	GUYING	GYMNASIA	GYOZAS	GYRENE
GUTS	GUYLE	GYMNASIAL	GYP	GYRENES
GUTSED	GUYLED	GYMNASIC	GYPLURE	GYRES
GUTSER	GUYLER	GYMNASIEN	GYPLURES	GYRFALCON
GUTSERS	GUYLERS	GYMNASIUM	GYPPED	GYRI
GUTSES	GUYLES	GYMNAST	GYPPER	GYRING
GUTSFUL	GUYLINE	GYMNASTIC	GYPPERS	GYRO
GUTSFULS	GUYLINER	GYMNASTS	GYPPIE	GYROCAR
GUTSIER	GUYLINERS	GYMNIC	GYPPIES	GYROCARS
GUTSIEST	GUYLINES	GYMNOSOPH	GYPPING	GYRODYNE
GUTSILY	GUYLING	GYMP	GYPPO	GYRODYNES
GUTSINESS	GUYOT	GYMPED	GYPPOS	GYROIDAL
GUTSING	GUYOTS	GYMPIE	GYPPY	GYROLITE
GUTSY	GUYS	GYMPIES	GYPS	GYROLITES
GUTTA	GUYSE	GYMPING	GYPSEIAN	GYROMANCY
GUTTAE	GUYSES	GYMPS	GYPSEOUS	GYRON
GUTTAS	GUZZLE	GYMS	GYPSIED	GYRONIC
GUTTATE	GUZZLED	GYMSLIP	GYPSIES	GYRONNY

GYRONS	GYROSE	GYRUS	GYTRASHES	GYVES
GYROPILOT	GYROSTAT	GYRUSES	GYTTJA	GYVING
GYROPLANE	GYROSTATS	GYTE	GYTTJAS	
GYROS	GYROUS	GYTES	GYVE	
GYROSCOPE	GYROVAGUE	GYTRASH	GYVED	

G

H

HA	HACHIS	HACKSAW	HAEMAL	HAFTAROT
HAAF	HACHURE	HACKSAWED	HAEMATAL	HAFTAROTH
HAAFS	HACHURED	HACKSAWN	HAEMATEIN	HAFTED
HAANEPOOT	HACHURES	HACKSAWS	HAEMATIC	HAFTER
HAAR	HACHURING	HACKWORK	HAEMATICS	HAFTERS
HAARS	HACIENDA	HACKWORKS	HAEMATIN	HAFTING
HABANERA	HACIENDAS	HACQUETON	HAEMATINS	HAFTORAH
HABANERAS	HACK	HAD	HAEMATITE	HAFTORAHS
HABANERO	HACKABLE	HADAL	HAEMATOID	HAFTOROS
HABANEROS	HACKAMORE	HADARIM	HAEMATOMA	HAFTOROT
HABDABS	HACKBERRY	HADAWAY	HAEMIC	HAFTOROTH
HABDALAH	HACKBOLT	HADDEN	HAEMIN	HAFTS
HABDALAHS	HACKBOLTS	HADDEST	HAEMINS	HAG
HABERDINE	HACKBUT	HADDIE	HAEMOCOEL	HAGADIC
HABERGEON	HACKBUTS	HADDIES	HAEMOCYTE	HAGADIST
HABILABLE	HACKED	HADDING	HAEMOID	HAGADISTS
HABILE	HACKEE	HADDOCK	HAEMONIES	HAGBERRY
HABIT	HACKEES	HADDOCKS	HAEMONY	HAGBOLT
HABITABLE	HACKER	HADE	HAEMOSTAT	HAGBOLTS
HABITABLY	HACKERIES	HADED	HAEMS	HAGBORN
HABITAN	HACKERS	HADEDAH	HAEN	HAGBUSH
HABITANS	HACKERY	HADEDAHS	HAEREDES	HAGBUSHES
HABITANT	HACKETTE	HADES	HAEREMAI	HAGBUT
HABITANTS	HACKETTES	HADING	HAEREMAIS	HAGBUTEER
HABITAT	HACKIE	HADITH	HAERES	HAGBUTS
HABITATS	HACKIES	HADITHS	HAES	HAGBUTTER
HABITED	HACKING	HADJ	HAET	HAGDEN
HABITING	HACKINGS	HADJEE	HAETS	HAGDENS
HABITS	HACKLE	HADJEES	HAFF	HAGDON
HABITUAL	HACKLED	HADJES	HAFFET	HAGDONS
HABITUALS	HACKLER	HADJI	HAFFETS	HAGDOWN
HABITUATE	HACKLERS	HADJIS	HAFFIT	HAGDOWNS
HABITUDE	HACKLES	HADROME	HAFFITS	HAGFISH
HABITUDES	HACKLET	HADROMES	HAFFLIN	HAGFISHES
HABITUE	HACKLETS	HADRON	HAFFLINS	HAGG
HABITUES	HACKLIER	HADRONIC	HAFFS	HAGGADA
HABITUS	HACKLIEST	HADRONS	HAFIZ	HAGGADAH
HABLE	HACKLING	HADROSAUR	HAFIZES	HAGGADAHS
HABOOB	HACKLY	HADS	HAFNIUM	HAGGADAS
HABOOBS	HACKMAN	HADST	HAFNIUMS	HAGGADIC
HABU	HACKMEN	HAE	HAFT	HAGGADIST
HABUS	HACKNEY	HAECCEITY	HAFTARA	HAGGADOT
HACEK	HACKNEYED	HAED	HAFTARAH	HAGGADOTH
HACEKS	HACKNEYS	HAEING	HAFTARAHS	HAGGARD
HACENDADO	HACKS	HAEM	HAFTARAS	HAGGARDLY

HAGGARDS	HAILIER	HAIRINESS	HAKEAS	HALCYONIC
HAGGED	HAILIEST	HAIRING	HAKEEM	HALCYONS
HAGGING	HAILING	HAIRLESS	HAKEEMS	HALE
HAGGIS	HAILS	HAIRLIKE	HAKES	HALED
HAGGISES	HAILSHOT	HAIRLINE	HAKIM	HALENESS
HAGGISH	HAILSHOTS	HAIRLINES	HAKIMS	HALER
HAGGISHLY	HAILSTONE	HAIRLOCK	HAKU	HALERS
HAGGLE	HAILSTORM	HAIRLOCKS	HAKUS	HALERU
HAGGLED	HAILY	HAIRNET	HALACHA	HALES
HAGGLER	HAIMISH	HAIRNETS	HALACHAS	HALEST
HAGGLERS	HAIN	HAIRPIECE	HALACHIC	HALF
HAGGLES	HAINCH	HAIRPIN	HALACHIST	HALFA
HAGGLING	HAINCHED	HAIRPINS	HALACHOT	HALFAS
HAGGS	HAINCHES	HAIRS	HALACHOTH	HALFBACK
HAGIARCHY	HAINCHING	HAIRSPRAY	HALAKAH	HALFBACKS
HAGIOLOGY	HAINED	HAIRST	HALAKAHS	HALFBEAK
HAGLET	HAINING	HAIRSTED	HALAKHA	HALFBEAKS
HAGLETS	HAININGS	HAIRSTING	HALAKHAH	HALFEN
HAGLIKE	HAINS	HAIRSTS	HALAKHAHS	HALFLIFE
HAGRIDDEN	HAINT	HAIRSTYLE	HALAKHAS	HALFLIN
HAGRIDE	HAINTS	HAIRTAIL	HALAKHIC	HALFLING
HAGRIDER	HAIQUE	HAIRTAILS	HALAKHIST	HALFLINGS
HAGRIDERS	HAIQUES	HAIRWORK	HALAKHOT	HALFLINS
HAGRIDES	HAIR	HAIRWORKS	HALAKHOTH	HALFLIVES
HAGRIDING	HAIRBALL	HAIRWORM	HALAKIC	HALFNESS
HAGRODE	HAIRBALLS	HAIRWORMS	HALAKIST	HALFPACE
HAGS	HAIRBAND	HAIRY	HALAKISTS	HALFPACES
HAH	HAIRBANDS	HAIRYBACK	HALAKOTH	HALFPENCE
HAHA	HAIRBELL	HAITH	HALAL	HALFPENNY
HAHAS	HAIRBELLS	HAJ	HALALA	HALFPIPE
HAHNIUM	HAIRBRUSH	HAJES	HALALAH	HALFPIPES
HAHNIUMS	HAIRCAP	HAJI	HALALAHS	HALFS
HAHS	HAIRCAPS	HAJIS	HALALAS	HALFTIME
HAICK	HAIRCLOTH	HAJJ	HALALLED	HALFTIMES
HAICKS	HAIRCUT	HAJJAH	HALALLING	HALFTONE
HAIDUK	HAIRCUTS	HAJJAHS	HALALS	HALFTONES
HAIDUKS	HAIRDO	HAJJES	HALATION	HALFTRACK
HAIK	HAIRDOS	HAJJI	HALATIONS	HALFWAY
HAIKA	HAIRDRIER	HAJJIS	HALAVAH	HALFWIT
HAIKAI	HAIRDRYER	HAKA	HALAVAHS	HALFWITS
HAIKS	HAIRED	HAKAM	HALAZONE	HALIBUT
HAIKU	HAIRGRIP	HAKAMS	HALAZONES	HALIBUTS
HAIKUS	HAIRGRIPS	HAKARI	HALBERD	HALICORE
HAIL	HAIRIER	HAKARIS	HALBERDS	HALICORES
HAILED	HAIRIEST	HAKAS	HALBERT	HALID
HAILER	HAIRIF	HAKE	HALBERTS	HALIDE
HAILERS	HAIRIFS	HAKEA	HALCYON	HALIDES

H

HALIDOM	HALLOAING	HALOPHILE	HAMADRYAS	HAMMIER
HALIDOME	HALLOAS	HALOPHILY	HAMAL	HAMMIEST
HALIDOMES	HALLOED	HALOPHOBE	HAMALS	HAMMILY
HALIDOMS	HALLOES	HALOPHYTE	HAMAMELIS	HAMMINESS
HALIDS	HALLOING	HALOS	HAMARTIA	HAMMING
HALIEUTIC	HALLOO	HALOSERE	HAMARTIAS	HAMMOCK
HALIMOT	HALLOOED	HALOSERES	HAMATE	HAMMOCKS
HALIMOTE	HALLOOING	HALOTHANE	HAMATES	HAMMY
HALIMOTES	HALLOOS	HALOUMI	HAMAUL	HAMOSE
HALIMOTS	HALLOS	HALOUMIS	HAMAULS	HAMOUS
HALING	HALLOT	HALSE	HAMBA	HAMPER
HALIOTIS	HALLOTH	HALSED	HAMBLE	HAMPERED
HALITE	HALLOUMI	HALSER	HAMBLED	HAMPERER
HALITES	HALLOUMIS	HALSERS	HAMBLES	HAMPERERS
HALITOSES	HALLOW	HALSES	HAMBLING	HAMPERING
HALITOSIS	HALLOWED	HALSING	HAMBONE	HAMPERS
HALITOTIC	HALLOWER	HALT	HAMBONED	HAMPSTER
HALITOUS	HALLOWERS	HALTED	HAMBONES	HAMPSTERS
HALITUS	HALLOWING	HALTER	HAMBONING	HAMS
HALITUSES	HALLOWS	HALTERE	HAMBURG	HAMSTER
HALL	HALLS	HALTERED	HAMBURGER	HAMSTERS
HALLAH	HALLSTAND	HALTERES	HAMBURGS	HAMSTRING
HALLAHS	HALLUCAL	HALTERING	HAME	HAMSTRUNG
HALLAL	HALLUCES	HALTERS	HAMED	HAMULAR
HALLALI	HALLUX	HALTING	HAMES	HAMULATE
HALLALIS	HALLWAY	HALTINGLY	HAMEWITH	HAMULI
HALLALLED	HALLWAYS	HALTINGS	HAMFATTER	HAMULOSE
HALLALOO	HALLYON	HALTLESS	HAMING	HAMULOUS
HALLALOOS	HALLYONS	HALTS	HAMLET	HAMULUS
HALLALS	HALM	HALUTZ	HAMLETS	HAMZA
HALLAN	HALMA	HALUTZIM	HAMMADA	HAMZAH
HALLANS	HALMAS	HALVA	HAMMADAS	HAMZAHS
HALLEL	HALMS	HALVAH	HAMMAL	HAMZAS
HALLELS	HALO	HALVAHS	HAMMALS	HAN
HALLIAN	HALOBIONT	HALVAS	HAMMAM	HANAP
HALLIANS	HALOCLINE	HALVE	HAMMAMS	HANAPER
HALLIARD	HALOED	HALVED	HAMMED	HANAPERS
HALLIARDS	HALOES	HALVER	HAMMER	HANAPS
HALLING	HALOGEN	HALVERS	HAMMERED	HANCE
HALLINGS	HALOGENS	HALVES	HAMMERER	HANCES
HALLION	HALOGETON	HALVING	HAMMERERS	HANCH
HALLIONS	HALOID	HALYARD	HAMMERING	HANCHED
HALLMARK	HALOIDS	HALYARDS	HAMMERKOP	HANCHES
HALLMARKS	HALOING	HAM	HAMMERMAN	HANCHING
HALLO	HALOLIKE	HAMADA	HAMMERMEN	HAND
HALLOA	HALON	HAMADAS	HAMMERS	HANDAX
HALLOAED	HALONS	HAMADRYAD	HAMMERTOE	HANDAXES

HANDBAG	HANDISM	HANDSEL	HANGINGS	HANTED
HANDBAGS	HANDISMS	HANDSELED	HANGIS	HANTING
HANDBALL	HANDIWORK	HANDSELS	HANGMAN	HANTLE
HANDBALLS	HANDJAR	HANDSET	HANGMEN	HANTLES
HANDBELL	HANDJARS	HANDSETS	HANGNAIL	HANTS
HANDBELLS	HANDJOB	HANDSEWN	HANGNAILS	HANUKIAH
HANDBILL	HANDJOBS	HANDSFUL	HANGNEST	HANUKIAHS
HANDBILLS	HANDKNIT	HANDSHAKE	HANGNESTS	HANUMAN
HANDBLOWN	HANDKNITS	HANDSOME	HANGOUT	HANUMANS
HANDBOOK	HANDLE	HANDSOMER	HANGOUTS	HAO
HANDBOOKS	HANDLEBAR	HANDSOMES	HANGOVER	HAOLE
HANDBRAKE	HANDLED	HANDSPIKE	HANGOVERS	HAOLES
HANDCAR	HANDLER	HANDSTAFF	HANGS	HAOMA
HANDCARS	HANDLERS	HANDSTAMP	HANGTAG	HAOMAS
HANDCART	HANDLES	HANDSTAND	HANGTAGS	HAOS
HANDCARTS	HANDLESS	HANDSTURN	HANGUL	HAP
HANDCLAP	HANDLIKE	HANDTOWEL	HANGUP	HAPAX
HANDCLAPS	HANDLING	HANDWHEEL	HANGUPS	HAPAXES
HANDCLASP	HANDLINGS	HANDWORK	HANIWA	HAPHAZARD
HANDCRAFT	HANDLIST	HANDWORKS	HANJAR	HAPHTARA
HANDCUFF	HANDLISTS	HANDWOVEN	HANJARS	HAPHTARAH
HANDCUFFS	HANDLOOM	HANDWRIT	HANK	HAPHTARAS
HANDED	HANDLOOMS	HANDWRITE	HANKED	HAPHTAROT
HANDER	HANDMADE	HANDWROTE	HANKER	HAPKIDO
HANDERS	HANDMAID	HANDY	HANKERED	HAPKIDOS
HANDFAST	HANDMAIDS	HANDYMAN	HANKERER	HAPLESS
HANDFASTS	HANDOFF	HANDYMEN	HANKERERS	HAPLESSLY
HANDFED	HANDOFFS	HANDYWORK	HANKERING	HAPLITE
HANDFEED	HANDOUT	HANEPOOT	HANKERS	HAPLITES
HANDFEEDS	HANDOUTS	HANEPOOTS	HANKIE	HAPLITIC
HANDFUL	HANDOVER	HANG	HANKIES	HAPLOID
HANDFULS	HANDOVERS	HANGABLE	HANKING	HAPLOIDIC
HANDGRIP	HANDPASS	HANGAR	HANKS	HAPLOIDS
HANDGRIPS	HANDPHONE	HANGARED	HANKY	HAPLOIDY
HANDGUN	HANDPICK	HANGARING	HANSA	HAPLOLOGY
HANDGUNS	HANDPICKS	HANGARS	HANSAS	HAPLONT
HANDHELD	HANDPLAY	HANGBIRD	HANSE	HAPLONTIC
HANDHELDS	HANDPLAYS	HANGBIRDS	HANSEATIC	HAPLONTS
HANDHOLD	HANDPRESS	HANGDOG	HANSEL	HAPLOPIA
HANDHOLDS	HANDPRINT	HANGDOGS	HANSELED	HAPLOPIAS
HANDICAP	HANDRAIL	HANGED	HANSELING	HAPLOSES
HANDICAPS	HANDRAILS	HANGER	HANSELLED	HAPLOSIS
HANDIER	HANDROLL	HANGERS	HANSELS	HAPLOTYPE
HANDIEST	HANDROLLS	HANGFIRE	HANSES	HAPLY
HANDILY	HANDS	HANGFIRES	HANSOM	HAPPED
HANDINESS	HANDSAW	HANGI	HANSOMS	HAPPEN
HANDING	HANDSAWS	HANGING	HANT	HAPPENED

HAPPENING	HARASSED	HARDER	HARDTAIL	HARKED
HAPPENS	HARASSER	HARDEST	HARDTAILS	HARKEN
HAPPIED	HARASSERS	HARDFACE	HARDTOP	HARKENED
HAPPIER	HARASSES	HARDFACES	HARDTOPS	HARKENER
HAPPIES	HARASSING	HARDGOODS	HARDWARE	HARKENERS
HAPPIEST	HARBINGER	HARDGRASS	HARDWARES	HARKENING
HAPPILY	HARBOR	HARDHACK	HARDWIRE	HARKENS
HAPPINESS	HARBORAGE	HARDHACKS	HARDWIRED	HARKING
HAPPING	HARBORED	HARDHAT	HARDWIRES	HARKS
HAPPY	HARBORER	HARDHATS	HARDWOOD	HARL
HAPPYING	HARBORERS	HARDHEAD	HARDWOODS	HARLED
HAPS	HARBORFUL	HARDHEADS	HARDY	HARLEQUIN
HAPTEN	HARBORING	HARDIER	HARE	HARLING
HAPTENE	HARBOROUS	HARDIES	HAREBELL	HARLINGS
HAPTENES	HARBORS	HARDIEST	HAREBELLS	HARLOT
HAPTENIC	HARBOUR	HARDIHEAD	HARED	HARLOTRY
HAPTENS	HARBOURED	HARDIHOOD	HAREEM	HARLOTS
HAPTERON	HARBOURER	HARDILY	HAREEMS	HARLS
HAPTERONS	HARBOURS	HARDIMENT	HARELD	HARM
HAPTIC	HARD	HARDINESS	HARELDS	HARMALA
HAPTICAL	HARDASS	HARDISH	HARELIKE	HARMALAS
HAPTICS	HARDASSES	HARDLINE	HARELIP	HARMALIN
HAPU	HARDBACK	HARDLINER	HARELIPS	HARMALINE
HAPUKA	HARDBACKS	HARDLY	HAREM	HARMALINS
HAPUKAS	HARDBAKE	HARDMAN	HAREMS	HARMAN
HAPUKU	HARDBAKES	HARDMEN	HARES	HARMANS
HAPUKUS	HARDBALL	HARDNESS	HARESTAIL	HARMATTAN
HAPUS	HARDBALLS	HARDNOSE	HAREWOOD	HARMDOING
HAQUETON	HARDBEAM	HARDNOSED	HAREWOODS	HARMED
HAQUETONS	HARDBEAMS	HARDNOSES	HARIANA	HARMEL
HARAKEKE	HARDBOARD	HARDOKE	HARIANAS	HARMELS
HARAKEKES	HARDBOOT	HARDOKES	HARICOT	HARMER
HARAM	HARDBOOTS	HARDPACK	HARICOTS	HARMERS
HARAMBEE	HARDBOUND	HARDPACKS	HARIGALDS	HARMFUL
HARAMBEES	HARDCASE	HARDPAN	HARIGALS	HARMFULLY
HARAMDA	HARDCORE	HARDPANS	HARIJAN	HARMIN
HARAMDAS	HARDCORES	HARDPARTS	HARIJANS	HARMINE
HARAMDI	HARDCOURT	HARDROCK	HARIM	HARMINES
HARAMDIS	HARDCOVER	HARDROCKS	HARIMS	HARMING
HARAMS	HARDEDGE	HARDS	HARING	HARMINS
HARAMZADA	HARDEDGES	HARDSET	HARIOLATE	HARMLESS
HARAMZADI	HARDEN	HARDSHELL	HARIRA	HARMONIC
HARANGUE	HARDENED	HARDSHIP	HARIRAS	HARMONICA
HARANGUED	HARDENER	HARDSHIPS	HARISH	HARMONICS
HARANGUER	HARDENERS	HARDSTAND	HARISSA	HARMONIES
HARANGUES	HARDENING	HARDTACK	HARISSAS	HARMONISE
HARASS	HARDENS	HARDTACKS	HARK	HARMONIST

HARMONIUM	HARROWER	HASHED	HASTENER	HATER
HARMONIZE	HARROWERS	HASHEESH	HASTENERS	HATERENT
HARMONY	HARROWING	HASHES	HASTENING	HATERENTS
HARMOST	HARROWS	HASHHEAD	HASTENS	HATERS
HARMOSTS	HARRUMPH	HASHHEADS	HASTES	HATES
HARMOSTY	HARRUMPHS	HASHIER	HASTIER	HATFUL
HARMOTOME	HARRY	HASHIEST	HASTIEST	HATFULS
HARMS	HARRYING	HASHING	HASTILY	HATGUARD
HARN	HARSH	HASHINGS	HASTINESS	HATGUARDS
HARNESS	HARSHED	HASHISH	HASTING	HATH
HARNESSED	HARSHEN	HASHISHES	HASTINGS	HATHA
HARNESSER	HARSHENED	HASHMARK	HASTY	HATING
HARNESSES	HARSHENS	HASHMARKS	HAT	HATLESS
HARNS	HARSHER	HASHY	HATABLE	HATLIKE
HARO	HARSHES	HASK	HATBAND	HATMAKER
HAROS	HARSHEST	HASKS	HATBANDS	HATMAKERS
HAROSET	HARSHING	HASLET	HATBOX	HATPEG
HAROSETH	HARSHLY	HASLETS	HATBOXES	HATPEGS
HAROSETHS	HARSHNESS	HASP	HATBRUSH	HATPIN
HAROSETS	HARSLET	HASPED	HATCH	HATPINS
HARP	HARSLETS	HASPING	HATCHABLE	HATRACK
HARPED	HART	HASPS	HATCHBACK	HATRACKS
HARPER	HARTAL	HASS	HATCHECK	HATRED
HARPERS	HARTALS	HASSAR	HATCHECKS	HATREDS
HARPIES	HARTBEES	HASSARS	HATCHED	HATS
HARPIN	HARTBEEST	HASSEL	HATCHEL	HATSFUL
HARPING	HARTELY	HASSELS	HATCHELED	HATSTAND
HARPINGS	HARTEN	HASSES	HATCHELS	HATSTANDS
HARPINS	HARTENED	HASSIUM	HATCHER	HATTED
HARPIST	HARTENING	HASSIUMS	HATCHERS	HATTER
HARPISTS	HARTENS	HASSLE	HATCHERY	HATTERED
HARPOON	HARTLESSE	HASSLED	HATCHES	HATTERIA
HARPOONED	HARTS	HASSLES	HATCHET	HATTERIAS
HARPOONER	HARTSHORN	HASSLING	HATCHETS	HATTERING
HARPOONS	HARUMPH	HASSOCK	HATCHETY	HATTERS
HARPS	HARUMPHED	HASSOCKS	HATCHING	HATTING
HARPY	HARUMPHS	HASSOCKY	HATCHINGS	HATTINGS
HARPYLIKE	HARUSPEX	HAST	HATCHLING	HATTOCK
HARQUEBUS	HARUSPICY	HASTA	HATCHMENT	HATTOCKS
HARRIDAN	HARVEST	HASTATE	HATCHWAY	HAUBERK
HARRIDANS	HARVESTED	HASTATED	HATCHWAYS	HAUBERKS
HARRIED	HARVESTER	HASTATELY	HATE	HAUBOIS
HARRIER	HARVESTS	HASTE	HATEABLE	HAUD
HARRIERS	HAS	HASTED	HATED	HAUDING
HARRIES	HASBIAN	HASTEFUL	HATEFUL	HAUDS
HARROW	HASBIANS	HASTEN	HATEFULLY	HAUF
HARROWED	HASH	HASTENED	HATELESS	HAUFS

HAUGH	HAUSING	HAVOCKED	HAWMS	HAYRICK
HAUGHS	HAUSTELLA	HAVOCKER	HAWS	HAYRICKS
HAUGHT	HAUSTORIA	HAVOCKERS	HAWSE	HAYRIDE
HAUGHTIER	HAUT	HAVOCKING	HAWSED	HAYRIDES
HAUGHTILY	HAUTBOIS	HAVOCS	HAWSEHOLE	HAYS
HAUGHTY	HAUTBOY	HAW	HAWSEPIPE	HAYSEED
HAUL	HAUTBOYS	HAWALA	HAWSER	HAYSEEDS
HAULAGE	HAUTE	HAWALAS	HAWSERS	HAYSEL
HAULAGES	HAUTEUR	HAWBUCK	HAWSES	HAYSELS
HAULD	HAUTEURS	HAWBUCKS	HAWSING	HAYSTACK
HAULDS	HAUYNE	HAWED	HAWTHORN	HAYSTACKS
HAULED	HAUYNES	HAWFINCH	HAWTHORNS	HAYWARD
HAULER	HAVARTI	HAWING	HAWTHORNY	HAYWARDS
HAULERS	HAVARTIS	HAWK	HAY	HAYWIRE
HAULIER	HAVDALAH	HAWKBELL	HAYBAND	HAYWIRES
HAULIERS	HAVDALAHS	HAWKBELLS	HAYBANDS	HAZAN
HAULING	HAVDOLOH	HAWKBILL	HAYBOX	HAZANIM
HAULM	HAVDOLOHS	HAWKBILLS	HAYBOXES	HAZANS
HAULMIER	HAVE	HAWKBIT	HAYCOCK	HAZARD
HAULMIEST	HAVELOCK	HAWKBITS	HAYCOCKS	HAZARDED
HAULMS	HAVELOCKS	HAWKED	HAYED	HAZARDER
HAULMY	HAVEN	HAWKER	HAYER	HAZARDERS
HAULS	HAVENED	HAWKERS	HAYERS	HAZARDING
HAULST	HAVENING	HAWKEY	HAYEY	HAZARDIZE
HAULT	HAVENLESS	HAWKEYED	HAYFIELD	HAZARDOUS
HAULYARD	HAVENS	HAWKEYS	HAYFIELDS	HAZARDRY
HAULYARDS	HAVEOUR	HAWKIE	HAYFORK	HAZARDS
HAUNCH	HAVEOURS	HAWKIES	HAYFORKS	HAZE
HAUNCHED	HAVER	HAWKING	HAYIER	HAZED
HAUNCHES	HAVERED	HAWKINGS	HAYIEST	HAZEL
HAUNCHING	HAVEREL	HAWKISH	HAYING	HAZELHEN
HAUNT	HAVERELS	HAWKISHLY	HAYINGS	HAZELHENS
HAUNTED	HAVERING	HAWKIT	HAYLAGE	HAZELLY
HAUNTER	HAVERINGS	HAWKLIKE	HAYLAGES	HAZELNUT
HAUNTERS	HAVERS	HAWKMOTH	HAYLE	HAZELNUTS
HAUNTING	HAVERSACK	HAWKMOTHS	HAYLES	HAZELS
HAUNTINGS	HAVERSINE	HAWKNOSE	HAYLOFT	HAZER
HAUNTS	HAVES	HAWKNOSES	HAYLOFTS	HAZERS
HAURIANT	HAVILDAR	HAWKS	HAYMAKER	HAZES
HAURIENT	HAVILDARS	HAWKSBILL	HAYMAKERS	HAZIER
HAUSE	HAVING	HAWKSHAW	HAYMAKING	HAZIEST
HAUSED	HAVINGS	HAWKSHAWS	HAYMOW	HAZILY
HAUSEN	HAVIOR	HAWKWEED	HAYMOWS	HAZINESS
HAUSENS	HAVIORS	HAWKWEEDS	HAYRACK	HAZING
HAUSES	HAVIOUR	HAWM	HAYRACKS	HAZINGS
HAUSFRAU	HAVIOURS	HAWMED	HAYRAKE	HAZMAT
HAUSFRAUS	HAVOC	HAWMING	HAYRAKES	HAZMATS

HAZY	HEADINESS	HEADSAILS	HEALS	HEARTBEAT
HAZZAN	HEADING	HEADSCARF	HEALSOME	HEARTBURN
HAZZANIM	HEADINGS	HEADSET	HEALTH	HEARTED
HAZZANS	HEADLAMP	HEADSETS	HEALTHFUL	HEARTEN
HE	HEADLAMPS	HEADSHAKE	HEALTHIER	HEARTENED
HEAD	HEADLAND	HEADSHIP	HEALTHILY	HEARTENER
HEADACHE	HEADLANDS	HEADSHIPS	HEALTHISM	HEARTENS
HEADACHES	HEADLEASE	HEADSHOT	HEALTHS	HEARTFELT
HEADACHEY	HEADLESS	HEADSHOTS	HEALTHY	HEARTFREE
HEADACHY	HEADLIGHT	HEADSMAN	HEAME	HEARTH
HEADAGE	HEADLIKE	HEADSMEN	HEAP	HEARTHRUG
HEADAGES	HEADLINE	HEADSPACE	HEAPED	HEARTHS
HEADBAND	HEADLINED	HEADSTALL	HEAPER	HEARTIER
HEADBANDS	HEADLINER	HEADSTAND	HEAPERS	HEARTIES
HEADBANG	HEADLINES	HEADSTAY	HEAPIER	HEARTIEST
HEADBANGS	HEADLOCK	HEADSTAYS	HEAPIEST	HEARTIKIN
HEADBOARD	HEADLOCKS	HEADSTICK	HEAPING	HEARTILY
HEADCASE	HEADLONG	HEADSTOCK	HEAPS	HEARTING
HEADCASES	HEADMAN	HEADSTONE	HEAPSTEAD	HEARTLAND
HEADCHAIR	HEADMARK	HEADWALL	HEAPY	HEARTLESS
HEADCLOTH	HEADMARKS	HEADWALLS	HEAR	HEARTLET
HEADCOUNT	HEADMEN	HEADWARD	HEARABLE	HEARTLETS
HEADDRESS	HEADMOST	HEADWARDS	HEARD	HEARTLING
HEADED	HEADNOTE	HEADWATER	HEARDS	HEARTLY
HEADEND	HEADNOTES	HEADWAY	HEARE	HEARTPEA
HEADENDS	HEADPEACE	HEADWAYS	HEARER	HEARTPEAS
HEADER	HEADPHONE	HEADWIND	HEARERS	HEARTS
HEADERS	HEADPIECE	HEADWINDS	HEARES	HEARTSEED
HEADFAST	HEADPIN	HEADWORD	HEARIE	HEARTSICK
HEADFASTS	HEADPINS	HEADWORDS	HEARING	HEARTSINK
HEADFIRST	HEADRACE	HEADWORK	HEARINGS	HEARTSOME
HEADFISH	HEADRACES	HEADWORKS	HEARKEN	HEARTSORE
HEADFRAME	HEADRAIL	HEADY	HEARKENED	HEARTWOOD
HEADFUCK	HEADRAILS	HEAL	HEARKENER	HEARTWORM
HEADFUCKS	HEADREACH	HEALABLE	HEARKENS	HEARTY
HEADFUL	HEADREST	HEALD	HEARS	HEAST
HEADFULS	HEADRESTS	HEALDED	HEARSAY	HEASTE
HEADGATE	HEADRIG	HEALDING	HEARSAYS	HEASTES
HEADGATES	HEADRIGS	HEALDS	HEARSE	HEASTS
HEADGEAR	HEADRING	HEALED	HEARSED	HEAT
HEADGEARS	HEADRINGS	HEALEE	HEARSES	HEATABLE
HEADGUARD	HEADROOM	HEALEES	HEARSIER	HEATED
HEADHUNT	HEADROOMS	HEALER	HEARSIEST	HEATEDLY
HEADHUNTS	HEADROPE	HEALERS	HEARSING	HEATER
HEADIER	HEADROPES	HEALING	HEARSY	HEATERS
HEADIEST	HEADS	HEALINGLY	HEART	HEATH
HEADILY	HEADSAIL	HEALINGS	HEARTACHE	HEATHBIRD

H

HEATHCOCK	HEBEN	HECTORING	HEEDINESS	HEGEMON
HEATHEN	HEBENON	HECTORISM	HEEDING	HEGEMONIC
HEATHENRY	HEBENONS	HECTORLY	HEEDLESS	HEGEMONS
HEATHENS	HEBENS	HECTORS	HEEDS	HEGEMONY
HEATHER	HEBES	HEDDLE	HEEDY	HEGIRA
HEATHERED	HEBETANT	HEDDLED	HEEHAW	HEGIRAS
HEATHERS	HEBETATE	HEDDLES	HEEHAWED	HEGUMEN
HEATHERY	HEBETATED	HEDDLING	HEEHAWING	HEGUMENE
HEATHFOWL	HEBETATES	HEDER	HEEHAWS	HEGUMENES
HEATHIER	HEBETIC	HEDERA	HEEL	HEGUMENOI
HEATHIEST	HEBETUDE	HEDERAL	HEELBALL	HEGUMENOS
HEATHLAND	HEBETUDES	HEDERAS	HEELBALLS	HEGUMENS
HEATHLESS	HEBONA	HEDERATED	HEELBAR	HEGUMENY
HEATHLIKE	HEBONAS	HEDERS	HEELBARS	HEH
HEATHS	HEBRAISE	HEDGE	HEELED	HEHS
HEATHY	HEBRAISED	HEDGEBILL	HEELER	HEID
HEATING	HEBRAISES	HEDGED	HEELERS	HEIDS
HEATINGS	HEBRAIZE	HEDGEHOG	HEELING	HEIFER
HEATLESS	HEBRAIZED	HEDGEHOGS	HEELINGS	HEIFERS
HEATPROOF	HEBRAIZES	HEDGEHOP	HEELLESS	HEIGH
HEATS	HECATOMB	HEDGEHOPS	HEELPIECE	HEIGHT
HEATSPOT	HECATOMBS	HEDGEPIG	HEELPLATE	HEIGHTEN
HEATSPOTS	HECH	HEDGEPIGS	HEELPOST	HEIGHTENS
HEATWAVE	HECHT	HEDGER	HEELPOSTS	HEIGHTH
HEATWAVES	HECHTING	HEDGEROW	HEELS	HEIGHTHS
HEAUME	HECHTS	HEDGEROWS	HEELTAP	HEIGHTISM
HEAUMES	HECK	HEDGERS	HEELTAPS	HEIGHTS
HEAVE	HECKLE	HEDGES	HEEZE	HEIL
HEAVED	HECKLED	HEDGIER	HEEZED	HEILED
HEAVEN	HECKLER	HEDGIEST	HEEZES	HEILING
HEAVENLY	HECKLERS	HEDGING	HEEZIE	HEILS
HEAVENS	HECKLES	HEDGINGLY	HEEZIES	HEIMISH
HEAVER	HECKLING	HEDGINGS	HEEZING	HEINIE
HEAVERS	HECKLINGS	HEDGY	HEFT	HEINIES
HEAVES	HECKS	HEDONIC	HEFTE	HEINOUS
HEAVIER	HECOGENIN	HEDONICS	HEFTED	HEINOUSLY
HEAVIES	HECTARE	HEDONISM	HEFTER	HEIR
HEAVIEST	HECTARES	HEDONISMS	HEFTERS	HEIRDOM
HEAVILY	HECTIC	HEDONIST	HEFTIER	HEIRDOMS
HEAVINESS	HECTICAL	HEDONISTS	HEFTIEST	HEIRED
HEAVING	HECTICLY	HEDYPHANE	HEFTILY	HEIRESS
HEAVINGS	HECTICS	HEED	HEFTINESS	HEIRESSES
HEAVY	HECTOGRAM	HEEDED	HEFTING	HEIRING
HEAVYSET	HECTOR	HEEDER	HEFTS	HEIRLESS
HEBDOMAD	HECTORED	HEEDERS	HEFTY	HEIRLOOM
HEBDOMADS	HECTORER	HEEDFUL	HEGARI	HEIRLOOMS
HEBE	HECTORERS	HEEDFULLY	HEGARIS	HEIRS

HEIRSHIP	HELICONS	HELLENIZE	HELMSMEN	HEMATINE
HEIRSHIPS	HELICOPT	HELLER	HELO	HEMATINES
HEISHI	HELICOPTS	HELLERI	HELOPHYTE	HEMATINIC
HEIST	HELICTITE	HELLERIES	HELOS	HEMATINS
HEISTED	HELIDECK	HELLERIS	HELOT	HEMATITE
HEISTER	HELIDECKS	HELLERS	HELOTAGE	HEMATITES
HEISTERS	HELIDROME	HELLERY	HELOTAGES	HEMATITIC
HEISTING	HELILIFT	HELLFIRE	HELOTISM	HEMATOID
HEISTS	HELILIFTS	HELLFIRES	HELOTISMS	HEMATOMA
HEITIKI	HELIMAN	HELLHOLE	HELOTRIES	HEMATOMAS
HEITIKIS	HELIMEN	HELLHOLES	HELOTRY	HEMATOSES
HEJAB	HELING	HELLHOUND	HELOTS	HEMATOSIS
HEJABS	HELIO	HELLICAT	HELP	HEMATOZOA
HEJIRA	HELIODOR	HELLICATS	HELPABLE	HEMATURIA
HEJIRAS	HELIODORS	HELLIER	HELPDESK	HEMATURIC
HEJRA	HELIOGRAM	HELLIERS	HELPDESKS	HEME
HEJRAS	HELIOLOGY	HELLING	HELPED	HEMELYTRA
HEKETARA	HELIOS	HELLION	HELPER	HEMES
HEKETARAS	HELIOSES	HELLIONS	HELPERS	HEMIALGIA
HEKTARE	HELIOSIS	HELLISH	HELPFUL	HEMIC
HEKTARES	HELIOSTAT	HELLISHLY	HELPFULLY	HEMICYCLE
HEKTOGRAM	HELIOTYPE	HELLKITE	HELPING	HEMIHEDRY
HELCOID	HELIOTYPY	HELLKITES	HELPINGS	HEMIN
HELD	HELIOZOAN	HELLO	HELPLESS	HEMINA
HELE	HELIOZOIC	HELLOED	HELPLINE	HEMINAS
HELED	HELIPAD	HELLOES	HELPLINES	HEMINS
HELENIUM	HELIPADS	HELLOING	HELPMATE	HEMIOLA
HELENIUMS	HELIPILOT	HELLOS	HELPMATES	HEMIOLAS
HELES	HELIPORT	HELLOVA	HELPMEET	HEMIOLIA
HELIAC	HELIPORTS	HELLS	HELPMEETS	HEMIOLIAS
HELIACAL	HELISTOP	HELLUVA	HELPS	HEMIOLIC
HELIAST	HELISTOPS	HELLWARD	HELVE	HEMIONE
HELIASTS	HELIUM	HELLWARDS	HELVED	HEMIONES
HELIBORNE	HELIUMS	HELM	HELVES	HEMIONUS
HELIBUS	HELIX	HELMED	HELVETIUM	HEMIOPIA
HELIBUSES	HELIXES	HELMER	HELVING	HEMIOPIAS
HELICAL	HELL	HELMERS	HEM	HEMIOPIC
HELICALLY	HELLBENT	HELMET	HEMAGOG	HEMIOPSIA
HELICASE	HELLBOX	HELMETED	HEMAGOGS	HEMIPOD
HELICASES	HELLBOXES	HELMETING	HEMAGOGUE	HEMIPODE
HELICES	HELLBROTH	HELMETS	HEMAL	HEMIPODES
HELICITY	HELLCAT	HELMING	HEMATAL	HEMIPODS
HELICLINE	HELLCATS	HELMINTH	HEMATEIN	HEMIPTER
HELICOID	HELLDIVER	HELMINTHS	HEMATEINS	HEMIPTERS
HELICOIDS	HELLEBORE	HELMLESS	HEMATIC	HEMISPACE
HELICON	HELLED	HELMS	HEMATICS	HEMISTICH
HELICONIA	HELLENISE	HELMSMAN	HEMATIN	HEMITROPE

HEMITROPY	HENBIT	HENPECKED	HEPTARCH	HERBORIZE
HEMLINE	HENBITS	HENPECKS	HEPTARCHS	HERBOSE
HEMLINES	HENCE	HENRIES	HEPTARCHY	HERBOUS
HEMLOCK	HENCHMAN	HENRY	HEPTOSE	HERBS
HEMLOCKS	HENCHMEN	HENRYS	HEPTOSES	HERBY
HEMMED	HENCOOP	HENS	HER	HERCOGAMY
HEMMER	HENCOOPS	HENT	HERALD	HERCULEAN
HEMMERS	HEND	HENTED	HERALDED	HERCULES
HEMMING	HENDED	HENTING	HERALDIC	HERCYNITE
HEMOCOEL	HENDIADYS	HENTS	HERALDING	HERD
HEMOCOELS	HENDING	HEP	HERALDIST	HERDBOY
HEMOCYTE	HENDS	HEPAR	HERALDRY	HERDBOYS
HEMOCYTES	HENEQUEN	HEPARIN	HERALDS	HERDED
HEMOID	HENEQUENS	HEPARINS	HERB	HERDEN
HEMOLYMPH	HENEQUIN	HEPARS	HERBAGE	HERDENS
HEMOLYSE	HENEQUINS	HEPATIC	HERBAGED	HERDER
HEMOLYSED	HENGE	HEPATICA	HERBAGES	HERDERS
HEMOLYSES	HENGES	HEPATICAE	HERBAL	HERDESS
HEMOLYSIN	HENHOUSE	HEPATICAL	HERBALISM	HERDESSES
HEMOLYSIS	HENHOUSES	HEPATICAS	HERBALIST	HERDIC
HEMOLYTIC	HENIQUEN	HEPATICS	HERBALS	HERDICS
HEMOLYZE	HENIQUENS	HEPATISE	HERBAR	HERDING
HEMOLYZED	HENIQUIN	HEPATISED	HERBARIA	HERDLIKE
HEMOLYZES	HENIQUINS	HEPATISES	HERBARIAL	HERDMAN
HEMOPHILE	HENLEY	HEPATITE	HERBARIAN	HERDMEN
HEMOSTAT	HENLEYS	HEPATITES	HERBARIES	HERDS
HEMOSTATS	HENLIKE	HEPATITIS	HERBARIUM	HERDSMAN
HEMOTOXIC	HENNA	HEPATIZE	HERBARS	HERDSMEN
HEMOTOXIN	HENNAED	HEPATIZED	HERBARY	HERDWICK
HEMP	HENNAING	HEPATIZES	HERBED	HERDWICKS
HEMPEN	HENNAS	HEPATOMA	HERBELET	HERE
HEMPIE	HENNED	HEPATOMAS	HERBELETS	HEREABOUT
HEMPIER	HENNER	HEPCAT	HERBICIDE	HEREAFTER
HEMPIES	HENNERIES	HEPCATS	HERBIER	HEREAT
HEMPIEST	HENNERS	HEPPER	HERBIEST	HEREAWAY
HEMPLIKE	HENNERY	HEPPEST	HERBIST	HEREAWAYS
HEMPS	HENNIER	HEPS	HERBISTS	HEREBY
HEMPSEED	HENNIES	HEPSTER	HERBIVORA	HEREDES
HEMPSEEDS	HENNIEST	HEPSTERS	HERBIVORE	HEREDITY
HEMPWEED	HENNIN	HEPT	HERBIVORY	HEREFROM
HEMPWEEDS	HENNING	HEPTAD	HERBLESS	HEREIN
HEMPY	HENNINS	HEPTADS	HERBLET	HEREINTO
HEMS	HENNISH	HEPTAGON	HERBLETS	HERENESS
HEMSTITCH	HENNISHLY	HEPTAGONS	HERBLIKE	HEREOF
HEN	HENNY	HEPTANE	HERBOLOGY	HEREON
HENBANE	HENOTIC	HEPTANES	HERBORISE	HERES
HENBANES	HENPECK	HEPTAPODY	HERBORIST	HERESIES

HERESY	HERMS	HERPES	HESSIAN	HEUGH
HERETIC	HERN	HERPESES	HESSIANS	HEUGHS
HERETICAL	HERNIA	HERPETIC	HESSITE	HEUREKA
HERETICS	HERNIAE	HERPETICS	HESSITES	HEUREKAS
HERETO	HERNIAL	HERPETOID	HESSONITE	HEURETIC
HERETRIX	HERNIAS	HERPTILE	HEST	HEURETICS
HEREUNDER	HERNIATE	HERRIED	HESTERNAL	HEURISM
HEREUNTO	HERNIATED	HERRIES	HESTS	HEURISMS
HEREUPON	HERNIATES	HERRIMENT	HET	HEURISTIC
HEREWITH	HERNS	HERRING	HETAERA	HEVEA
HERIED	HERNSHAW	HERRINGER	HETAERAE	HEVEAS
HERIES	HERNSHAWS	HERRINGS	HETAERAS	HEW
HERIOT	HERO	HERRY	HETAERIC	HEWABLE
HERIOTS	HEROES	HERRYING	HETAERISM	HEWED
HERISSE	HEROIC	HERRYMENT	HETAERIST	HEWER
HERISSON	HEROICAL	HERS	HETAIRA	HEWERS
HERISSONS	HEROICISE	HERSALL	HETAIRAI	HEWGH
HERITABLE	HEROICIZE	HERSALLS	HETAIRAS	HEWING
HERITABLY	HEROICLY	HERSE	HETAIRIA	HEWINGS
HERITAGE	HEROICS	HERSED	HETAIRIAS	HEWN
HERITAGES	HEROIN	HERSELF	HETAIRIC	HEWS
HERITOR	HEROINE	HERSES	HETAIRISM	HEX
HERITORS	HEROINES	HERSHIP	HETAIRIST	HEXACHORD
HERITRESS	HEROINISM	HERSHIPS	HETE	HEXACT
HERITRIX	HEROINS	HERSTORY	HETERO	HEXACTS
HERKOGAMY	HEROISE	HERTZ	HETERODOX	HEXAD
HERL	HEROISED	HERTZES	HETERONYM	HEXADE
HERLING	HEROISES	HERY	HETEROPOD	HEXADES
HERLINGS	HEROISING	HERYE	HETEROS	HEXADIC
HERLS	HEROISM	HERYED	HETEROSES	HEXADS
HERM	HEROISMS	HERYES	HETEROSIS	HEXAFOIL
HERMA	HEROIZE	HERYING	HETEROTIC	HEXAFOILS
HERMAE	HEROIZED	HES	HETES	HEXAGON
HERMAEAN	HEROIZES	HESITANCE	HETH	HEXAGONAL
HERMAI	HEROIZING	HESITANCY	HETHER	HEXAGONS
HERMANDAD	HERON	HESITANT	HETHS	HEXAGRAM
HERMETIC	HERONRIES	HESITATE	HETING	HEXAGRAMS
HERMETICS	HERONRY	HESITATED	HETMAN	HEXAHEDRA
HERMETISM	HERONS	HESITATER	HETMANATE	HEXAMERAL
HERMETIST	HERONSEW	HESITATES	HETMANS	HEXAMETER
HERMIT	HERONSEWS	HESITATOR	HETS	HEXAMINE
HERMITAGE	HERONSHAW	HESP	HETTIE	HEXAMINES
HERMITESS	HEROON	HESPED	HETTIES	HEXANE
HERMITIC	HEROONS	HESPERID	HEUCH	HEXANES
HERMITISM	HEROS	HESPERIDS	HEUCHERA	HEXANOIC
HERMITRY	HEROSHIP	HESPING	HEUCHERAS	HEXAPLA
HERMITS	HEROSHIPS	HESPS	HEUCHS	HEXAPLAR

HEXAPLAS	HIBACHI	HIDE	HIGGLER	HIGHTAILS
HEXAPLOID	HIBACHIS	HIDEAWAY	HIGGLERS	HIGHTED
HEXAPOD	HIBAKUSHA	HIDEAWAYS	HIGGLES	HIGHTH
HEXAPODAL	HIBERNAL	HIDEBOUND	HIGGLING	HIGHTHS
HEXAPODIC	HIBERNATE	HIDED	HIGGLINGS	HIGHTING
HEXAPODS	HIBERNISE	HIDELESS	HIGH	HIGHTOP
HEXAPODY	HIBERNIZE	HIDEOSITY	HIGHBALL	HIGHTOPS
HEXARCH	HIBISCUS	HIDEOUS	HIGHBALLS	HIGHTS
HEXARCHY	HIC	HIDEOUSLY	HIGHBORN	HIGHVELD
HEXASTICH	HICATEE	HIDEOUT	HIGHBOY	HIGHVELDS
HEXASTYLE	HICATEES	HIDEOUTS	HIGHBOYS	HIGHWAY
HEXED	HICCATEE	HIDER	HIGHBRED	HIGHWAYS
HEXENE	HICCATEES	HIDERS	HIGHBROW	HIJAB
HEXENES	HICCOUGH	HIDES	HIGHBROWS	HIJABS
HEXER	HICCOUGHS	HIDING	HIGHBUSH	HIJACK
HEXEREI	HICCUP	HIDINGS	HIGHCHAIR	HIJACKED
HEXEREIS	HICCUPED	HIDLING	HIGHED	HIJACKER
HEXERS	HICCUPING	HIDLINGS	HIGHER	HIJACKERS
HEXES	HICCUPPED	HIDLINS	HIGHERED	HIJACKING
HEXING	HICCUPS	HIDROSES	HIGHERING	HIJACKS
HEXINGS	HICCUPY	HIDROSIS	HIGHERS	HIJINKS
HEXONE	HICK	HIDROTIC	HIGHEST	HIJRA
HEXONES	HICKEY	HIDROTICS	HIGHFLIER	HIJRAH
HEXOSAN	HICKEYS	HIE	HIGHFLYER	HIJRAHS
HEXOSANS	HICKIE	HIED	HIGHING	HIJRAS
HEXOSE	HICKIES	HIEING	HIGHISH	HIKE
HEXOSES	HICKISH	HIELAMAN	HIGHJACK	HIKED
HEXYL	HICKORIES	HIELAMANS	HIGHJACKS	HIKER
HEXYLENE	HICKORY	HIELAND	HIGHLAND	HIKERS
HEXYLENES	HICKS	HIEMAL	HIGHLANDS	HIKES
HEXYLIC	HICKWALL	HIEMS	HIGHLIFE	HIKING
HEXYLS	HICKWALLS	HIERACIUM	HIGHLIFES	HIKOI
HEY	HICKYMAL	HIERARCH	HIGHLIGHT	HIKOIED
HEYDAY	HICKYMALS	HIERARCHS	HIGHLY	HIKOIING
HEYDAYS	HID	HIERARCHY	HIGHMAN	HIKOIS
HEYDEY	HIDABLE	HIERATIC	HIGHMEN	HILA
HEYDEYS	HIDAGE	HIERATICA	HIGHMOST	HILAR
HEYDUCK	HIDAGES	HIERATICS	HIGHNESS	HILARIOUS
HEYDUCKS	HIDALGA	HIEROCRAT	HIGHRISE	HILARITY
HEYED	HIDALGAS	HIERODULE	HIGHRISES	HILCH
HEYING	HIDALGO	HIEROGRAM	HIGHROAD	HILCHED
HEYS	HIDALGOS	HIEROLOGY	HIGHROADS	HILCHES
HI	HIDDEN	HIERURGY	HIGHS	HILCHING
HIANT	HIDDENITE	HIES	HIGHSPOT	HILD
HIATAL	HIDDENLY	HIFALUTIN	HIGHSPOTS	HILDING
HIATUS	HIDDER	HIGGLE	HIGHT	HILDINGS
HIATUSES	HIDDERS	HIGGLED	HIGHTAIL	HILI

HILL	HIMBOS	HINKY	HIPPISH	HIRSEL
HILLBILLY	HIMS	HINNIED	HIPPO	HIRSELED
HILLCREST	HIMSELF	HINNIES	HIPPOCRAS	HIRSELING
HILLED	HIN	HINNY	HIPPODAME	HIRSELLED
HILLER	HINAHINA	HINNYING	HIPPOLOGY	HIRSELS
HILLERS	HINAHINAS	HINS	HIPPOS	HIRSLE
HILLFOLK	HINAU	HINT	HIPPURIC	HIRSLED
HILLFORT	HINAUS	HINTED	HIPPURITE	HIRSLES
HILLFORTS	HIND	HINTER	HIPPUS	HIRSLING
HILLIER	HINDBERRY	HINTERS	HIPPUSES	HIRSTIE
HILLIEST	HINDBRAIN	HINTING	HIPPY	HIRSUTE
HILLINESS	HINDCAST	HINTINGLY	HIPPYDOM	HIRSUTISM
HILLING	HINDCASTS	HINTINGS	HIPPYDOMS	HIRUDIN
HILLINGS	HINDER	HINTS	HIPS	HIRUDINS
HILLMEN	HINDERED	HIOI	HIPSHOT	HIRUNDINE
HILLO	HINDERER	HIOIS	HIPSTER	HIS
HILLOA	HINDERERS	HIP	HIPSTERS	HISH
HILLOAED	HINDERING	HIPBONE	HIPT	HISHED
HILLOAING	HINDERS	HIPBONES	HIRABLE	HISHES
HILLOAS	HINDFEET	HIPHUGGER	HIRAGANA	HISHING
HILLOCK	HINDFOOT	HIPLESS	HIRAGANAS	HISN
HILLOCKED	HINDGUT	HIPLIKE	HIRAGE	HISPANISM
HILLOCKS	HINDGUTS	HIPLINE	HIRAGES	HISPID
HILLOCKY	HINDHEAD	HIPLINES	HIRCINE	HISPIDITY
HILLOED	HINDHEADS	HIPLY	HIRCOSITY	HISS
HILLOES	HINDLEG	HIPNESS	HIRE	HISSED
HILLOING	HINDLEGS	HIPNESSES	HIREABLE	HISSELF
HILLOS	HINDMOST	HIPPARCH	HIREAGE	HISSER
HILLS	HINDRANCE	HIPPARCHS	HIREAGES	HISSERS
HILLSIDE	HINDS	HIPPED	HIRED	HISSES
HILLSIDES	HINDSHANK	HIPPEN	HIREE	HISSIER
HILLSLOPE	HINDSIGHT	HIPPENS	HIREES	HISSIES
HILLTOP	HINDWARD	HIPPER	HIRELING	HISSIEST
HILLTOPS	HINDWING	HIPPEST	HIRELINGS	HISSING
HILLY	HINDWINGS	HIPPIATRY	HIRER	HISSINGLY
HILT	HING	HIPPIC	HIRERS	HISSINGS
HILTED	HINGE	HIPPIE	HIRES	HISSY
HILTING	HINGED	HIPPIEDOM	HIRING	HIST
HILTLESS	HINGELESS	HIPPIEISH	HIRINGS	HISTAMIN
HILTS	HINGELIKE	HIPPIER	HIRLING	HISTAMINE
HILUM	HINGER	HIPPIES	HIRLINGS	HISTAMINS
HILUS	HINGERS	HIPPIEST	HIRPLE	HISTED
HIM	HINGES	HIPPIN	HIRPLED	HISTIDIN
HIMATIA	HINGING	HIPPINESS	HIRPLES	HISTIDINE
HIMATION	HINGS	HIPPING	HIRPLING	HISTIDINS
HIMATIONS	HINKIER	HIPPINGS	HIRRIENT	HISTIE
HIMBO	HINKIEST	HIPPINS	HIRRIENTS	HISTING

HISTIOID	HITTING	HOARINESS	HOBBYISMS	HOCUS
HISTOGEN	HIVE	HOARING	HOBBYIST	HOCUSED
HISTOGENS	HIVED	HOARS	HOBBYISTS	HOCUSES
HISTOGENY	HIVELESS	HOARSE	HOBBYLESS	HOCUSING
HISTOGRAM	HIVELIKE	HOARSELY	HOBDAY	HOCUSSED
HISTOID	HIVER	HOARSEN	HOBDAYED	HOCUSSES
HISTOLOGY	HIVERS	HOARSENED	HOBDAYING	HOCUSSING
HISTONE	HIVES	HOARSENS	HOBDAYS	HOD
HISTONES	HIVEWARD	HOARSER	HOBGOBLIN	HODAD
HISTORIAN	HIVEWARDS	HOARSEST	HOBJOB	HODADDIES
HISTORIC	HIVING	HOARY	HOBJOBBED	HODADDY
HISTORIED	HIYA	HOAS	HOBJOBBER	HODADS
HISTORIES	HIZEN	HOAST	HOBJOBS	HODDED
HISTORIFY	HIZENS	HOASTED	HOBLIKE	HODDEN
HISTORISM	HIZZ	HOASTING	HOBNAIL	HODDENS
HISTORY	HIZZED	HOASTMAN	HOBNAILED	HODDIN
HISTRIO	HIZZES	HOASTMEN	HOBNAILS	HODDING
HISTRION	HIZZING	HOASTS	HOBNOB	HODDINS
HISTRIONS	HIZZONER	HOATCHING	HOBNOBBED	HODDLE
HISTRIOS	HIZZONERS	HOATZIN	HOBNOBBER	HODDLED
HISTS	HM	HOATZINES	HOBNOBBY	HODDLES
HIT	HMM	HOATZINS	HOBNOBS	HODDLING
HITCH	HO	HOAX	HOBO	HODIERNAL
HITCHED	HOA	HOAXED	HOBODOM	HODJA
HITCHER	HOACTZIN	HOAXER	HOBODOMS	HODJAS
HITCHERS	HOACTZINS	HOAXERS	HOBOED	HODMAN
HITCHES	HOAED	HOAXES	HOBOES	HODMANDOD
HITCHHIKE	HOAGIE	HOAXING	HOBOING	HODMEN
HITCHIER	HOAGIES	HOB	HOBOISM	HODOGRAPH
HITCHIEST	HOAGY	HOBBED	HOBOISMS	HODOMETER
HITCHILY	HOAING	HOBBER	HOBOS	HODOMETRY
HITCHING	HOAR	HOBBERS	HOBS	HODOSCOPE
HITCHY	HOARD	HOBBIES	HOC	HODS
HITHE	HOARDED	HOBBING	HOCK	HOE
HITHER	HOARDER	HOBBISH	HOCKED	HOECAKE
HITHERED	HOARDERS	HOBBIT	HOCKER	HOECAKES
HITHERING	HOARDING	HOBBITRY	HOCKERS	HOED
HITHERS	HOARDINGS	HOBBITS	HOCKEY	HOEDOWN
HITHERTO	HOARDS	HOBBLE	HOCKEYS	HOEDOWNS
HITHES	HOARED	HOBBLED	HOCKING	HOEING
HITLESS	HOARFROST	HOBBLER	HOCKLE	HOELIKE
HITMAN	HOARHEAD	HOBBLERS	HOCKLED	HOER
HITMEN	HOARHEADS	HOBBLES	HOCKLES	HOERS
HITS	HOARHOUND	HOBBLING	HOCKLING	HOES
HITTABLE	HOARIER	HOBBLINGS	HOCKS	HOG
HITTER	HOARIEST	HOBBY	HOCKSHOP	HOGAN
HITTERS	HOARILY	HOBBYISM	HOCKSHOPS	HOGANS

HOGBACK	HOGWARD	HOKAS	HOLED	HOLLOAS
HOGBACKS	HOGWARDS	HOKE	HOLELESS	HOLLOED
HOGEN	HOGWASH	HOKED	HOLES	HOLLOES
HOGENS	HOGWASHES	HOKES	HOLESOM	HOLLOING
HOGFISH	HOGWEED	HOKEY	HOLESOME	HOLLOO
HOGFISHES	HOGWEEDS	HOKEYNESS	HOLEY	HOLLOOED
HOGG	HOH	HOKI	HOLEYER	HOLLOOING
HOGGED	HOHA	HOKIER	HOLEYEST	HOLLOOS
HOGGER	HOHED	HOKIEST	HOLIBUT	HOLLOS
HOGGEREL	HOHING	HOKILY	HOLIBUTS	HOLLOW
HOGGERELS	HOHS	HOKINESS	HOLIDAY	HOLLOWARE
HOGGERIES	HOI	HOKING	HOLIDAYED	HOLLOWED
HOGGERS	HOICK	HOKIS	HOLIDAYER	HOLLOWER
HOGGERY	HOICKED	HOKKU	HOLIDAYS	HOLLOWEST
HOGGET	HOICKING	HOKONUI	HOLIER	HOLLOWING
HOGGETS	HOICKS	HOKONUIS	HOLIES	HOLLOWLY
HOGGIN	HOICKSED	HOKUM	HOLIEST	HOLLOWS
HOGGING	HOICKSES	HOKUMS	HOLILY	HOLLY
HOGGINGS	HOICKSING	HOKYPOKY	HOLINESS	HOLLYHOCK
HOGGINS	HOIDEN	HOLANDRIC	HOLING	HOLM
HOGGISH	HOIDENED	HOLARCHY	HOLINGS	HOLMIA
HOGGISHLY	HOIDENING	HOLARD	HOLISM	HOLMIAS
HOGGS	HOIDENISH	HOLARDS	HOLISMS	HOLMIC
HOGH	HOIDENS	HOLD	HOLIST	HOLMIUM
HOGHOOD	HOIK	HOLDABLE	HOLISTIC	HOLMIUMS
HOGHOODS	HOIKED	HOLDALL	HOLISTS	HOLMS
HOGHS	HOIKING	HOLDALLS	HOLK	HOLOCAUST
HOGLIKE	HOIKS	HOLDBACK	HOLKED	HOLOCENE
HOGMANAY	HOING	HOLDBACKS	HOLKING	HOLOCRINE
HOGMANAYS	HOISE	HOLDDOWN	HOLKS	HOLOGAMY
HOGMANE	HOISED	HOLDDOWNS	HOLLA	HOLOGRAM
HOGMANES	HOISES	HOLDEN	HOLLAED	HOLOGRAMS
HOGMENAY	HOISIN	HOLDER	HOLLAING	HOLOGRAPH
HOGMENAYS	HOISING	HOLDERBAT	HOLLAND	HOLOGYNIC
HOGNOSE	HOISINS	HOLDERS	HOLLANDS	HOLOGYNY
HOGNOSED	HOIST	HOLDFAST	HOLLAS	HOLOHEDRA
HOGNOSES	HOISTED	HOLDFASTS	HOLLER	HOLON
HOGNUT	HOISTER	HOLDING	HOLLERED	HOLONIC
HOGNUTS	HOISTERS	HOLDINGS	HOLLERING	HOLONS
HOGS	HOISTING	HOLDOUT	HOLLERS	HOLOPHOTE
HOGSHEAD	HOISTINGS	HOLDOUTS	HOLLIDAM	HOLOPHYTE
HOGSHEADS	HOISTMAN	HOLDOVER	HOLLIDAMS	HOLOPTIC
HOGTIE	HOISTMEN	HOLDOVERS	HOLLIES	HOLOTYPE
HOGTIED	HOISTS	HOLDS	HOLLO	HOLOTYPES
HOGTIEING	HOISTWAY	HOLDUP	HOLLOA	HOLOTYPIC
HOGTIES	HOISTWAYS	HOLDUPS	HOLLOAED	HOLOZOIC
HOGTYING	HOKA	HOLE	HOLLOAING	HOLP

HOLPEN	HOMECRAFT	HOMESTEAD	HOMMOCK	HOMOTONY
HOLS	HOMED	HOMETOWN	HOMMOCKS	HOMOTYPAL
HOLSTEIN	HOMEFELT	HOMETOWNS	HOMMOS	HOMOTYPE
HOLSTEINS	HOMEGIRL	HOMEWARD	HOMMOSES	HOMOTYPES
HOLSTER	HOMEGIRLS	HOMEWARDS	HOMO	HOMOTYPIC
HOLSTERED	HOMEGROWN	HOMEWARE	HOMOCERCY	HOMOTYPY
HOLSTERS	HOMELAND	HOMEWARES	HOMODONT	HOMOUSIAN
HOLT	HOMELANDS	HOMEWORK	HOMODYNE	HOMS
HOLTS	HOMELESS	HOMEWORKS	HOMOEOBOX	HOMUNCLE
HOLY	HOMELIER	HOMEY	HOMOEOSES	HOMUNCLES
HOLYDAM	HOMELIEST	HOMEYNESS	HOMOEOSIS	HOMUNCULE
HOLYDAME	HOMELIKE	HOMEYS	HOMOEOTIC	HOMUNCULI
HOLYDAMES	HOMELILY	HOMICIDAL	HOMOGAMIC	HOMY
HOLYDAMS	HOMELY	HOMICIDE	HOMOGAMY	HON
HOLYDAY	HOMELYN	HOMICIDES	HOMOGENY	HONAN
HOLYDAYS	HOMELYNS	HOMIE	HOMOGONY	HONANS
HOLYSTONE	HOMEMADE	HOMIER	HOMOGRAFT	HONCHO
HOLYTIDE	HOMEMAKER	HOMIES	HOMOGRAPH	HONCHOED
HOLYTIDES	HOMEOBOX	HOMIEST	HOMOLOG	HONCHOING
HOM	HOMEOMERY	HOMILETIC	HOMOLOGIC	HONCHOS
HOMA	HOMEOPATH	HOMILIES	HOMOLOGS	HOND
HOMAGE	HOMEOSES	HOMILIST	HOMOLOGUE	HONDA
HOMAGED	HOMEOSIS	HOMILISTS	HOMOLOGY	HONDAS
HOMAGER	HOMEOTIC	HOMILY	HOMOLYSES	HONDLE
HOMAGERS	HOMEOWNER	HOMINES	HOMOLYSIS	HONDLED
HOMAGES	HOMEPAGE	HOMINESS	HOMOLYTIC	HONDLES
HOMAGING	HOMEPAGES	HOMING	HOMOMORPH	HONDLING
HOMALOID	HOMEPLACE	HOMINGS	HOMONYM	HONDS
HOMALOIDS	HOMEPORT	HOMINIAN	HOMONYMIC	HONE
HOMAS	HOMEPORTS	HOMINIANS	HOMONYMS	HONED
HOMBRE	HOMER	HOMINID	HOMONYMY	HONER
HOMBRES	HOMERED	HOMINIDS	HOMOPHILE	HONERS
HOMBURG	HOMERIC	HOMINIES	HOMOPHOBE	HONES
HOMBURGS	HOMERING	HOMININ	HOMOPHONE	HONEST
HOME	HOMEROOM	HOMININE	HOMOPHONY	HONESTER
HOMEBIRTH	HOMEROOMS	HOMININS	HOMOPHYLY	HONESTEST
HOMEBODY	HOMERS	HOMINISE	HOMOPLASY	HONESTIES
HOMEBOUND	HOMES	HOMINISED	HOMOPOLAR	HONESTLY
HOMEBOY	HOMESICK	HOMINISES	HOMOS	HONESTY
HOMEBOYS	HOMESITE	HOMINIZE	HOMOSEX	HONEWORT
HOMEBRED	HOMESITES	HOMINIZED	HOMOSEXES	HONEWORTS
HOMEBREDS	HOMESPUN	HOMINIZES	HOMOSPORY	HONEY
HOMEBREW	HOMESPUNS	HOMINOID	HOMOSTYLY	HONEYBEE
HOMEBREWS	HOMESTALL	HOMINOIDS	HOMOTAXES	HONEYBEES
HOMEBUILT	HOMESTAND	HOMINY	HOMOTAXIC	HONEYBUN
HOMEBUYER	HOMESTAY	HOMME	HOMOTAXIS	HONEYBUNS
HOMECOMER	HOMESTAYS	HOMMES	HOMOTONIC	HONEYCOMB

HONEYDEW	HONORING	HOOFBEATS	HOOLIES	HOOSHES
HONEYDEWS	HONORLESS	HOOFBOUND	HOOLIEST	HOOSHING
HONEYED	HONORS	HOOFED	HOOLIGAN	HOOT
HONEYEDLY	HONOUR	HOOFER	HOOLIGANS	HOOTCH
HONEYFUL	HONOURED	HOOFERS	HOOLOCK	HOOTCHES
HONEYING	HONOUREE	HOOFING	HOOLOCKS	HOOTED
HONEYLESS	HONOUREES	HOOFLESS	HOOLY	HOOTER
HONEYMOON	HONOURER	HOOFLIKE	HOON	HOOTERS
HONEYPOT	HONOURERS	HOOFPRINT	HOONED	HOOTIER
HONEYPOTS	HONOURING	HOOFROT	HOONING	HOOTIEST
HONEYS	HONOURS	HOOFROTS	HOONS	HOOTING
HONEYTRAP	HONS	HOOFS	HOOP	HOOTNANNY
HONG	HOO	HOOK	HOOPED	HOOTS
HONGI	HOOCH	HOOKA	HOOPER	HOOTY
HONGIED	HOOCHES	HOOKAH	HOOPERS	HOOVE
HONGIES	HOOCHIE	HOOKAHS	HOOPING	HOOVED
HONGIING	HOOCHIES	HOOKAS	HOOPLA	HOOVEN
HONGING	HOOD	HOOKCHECK	HOOPLAS	HOOVER
HONGIS	HOODED	HOOKED	HOOPLESS	HOOVERED
HONGS	HOODIA	HOOKER	HOOPLIKE	HOOVERING
HONIED	HOODIAS	HOOKERS	HOOPOE	HOOVERS
HONIEDLY	HOODIE	HOOKEY	HOOPOES	HOOVES
HONING	HOODIER	HOOKEYS	HOOPOO	HOOVING
HONK	HOODIES	HOOKIER	HOOPOOS	HOP
HONKED	HOODIEST	HOOKIES	HOOPS	HOPBIND
HONKER	HOODING	HOOKIEST	HOOPSKIRT	HOPBINDS
HONKERS	HOODLESS	HOOKING	HOOPSTER	HOPBINE
HONKEY	HOODLIKE	HOOKLESS	HOOPSTERS	HOPBINES
HONKEYS	HOODLUM	HOOKLET	HOOR	HOPDOG
HONKIE	HOODLUMS	HOOKLETS	HOORAH	HOPDOGS
HONKIES	HOODMAN	HOOKLIKE	HOORAHED	HOPE
HONKING	HOODMEN	HOOKNOSE	HOORAHING	HOPED
HONKS	HOODMOLD	HOOKNOSED	HOORAHS	HOPEFUL
HONKY	HOODMOLDS	HOOKNOSES	HOORAY	HOPEFULLY
HONOR	HOODOO	HOOKS	HOORAYED	HOPEFULS
HONORABLE	HOODOOED	HOOKUP	HOORAYING	HOPELESS
HONORABLY	HOODOOING	HOOKUPS	HOORAYS	HOPER
HONORAND	HOODOOISM	HOOKWORM	HOORD	HOPERS
HONORANDS	HOODOOS	HOOKWORMS	HOORDS	HOPES
HONORARIA	HOODS	HOOKY	HOOROO	HOPHEAD
HONORARY	HOODWINK	HOOLACHAN	HOORS	HOPHEADS
HONORED	HOODWINKS	HOOLEY	HOOSEGOW	HOPING
HONOREE	HOODY	HOOLEYS	HOOSEGOWS	HOPINGLY
HONOREES	HOOEY	HOOLICAN	HOOSGOW	HOPLITE
HONORER	HOOEYS	HOOLICANS	HOOSGOWS	HOPLITES
HONORERS	HOOF	HOOLIE	HOOSH	HOPLITIC
HONORIFIC	HOOFBEAT	HOOLIER	HOOSHED	HOPLOLOGY

HOPPED	HORKEYS	HORNLET	HORRIFIED	HORSTS
HOPPER	HORLICKS	HORNLETS	HORRIFIES	HORSY
HOPPERCAR	HORME	HORNLIKE	HORRIFY	HORTATION
HOPPERS	HORMES	HORNPIPE	HORROR	HORTATIVE
HOPPIER	HORMESES	HORNPIPES	HORRORS	HORTATORY
HOPPIEST	HORMESIS	HORNPOUT	HORS	HOS
HOPPING	HORMETIC	HORNPOUTS	HORSE	HOSANNA
HOPPINGS	HORMIC	HORNS	HORSEBACK	HOSANNAED
HOPPLE	HORMONAL	HORNSTONE	HORSEBEAN	HOSANNAH
HOPPLED	HORMONE	HORNTAIL	HORSEBOX	HOSANNAHS
HOPPLER	HORMONES	HORNTAILS	HORSECAR	HOSANNAS
HOPPLERS	HORMONIC	HORNWORK	HORSECARS	HOSE
HOPPLES	HORN	HORNWORKS	HORSED	HOSED
HOPPLING	HORNBAG	HORNWORM	HORSEFLY	HOSEL
HOPPUS	HORNBAGS	HORNWORMS	HORSEHAIR	HOSELIKE
HOPPY	HORNBEAK	HORNWORT	HORSEHIDE	HOSELS
HOPS	HORNBEAKS	HORNWORTS	HORSELESS	HOSEMAN
HOPSACK	HORNBEAM	HORNWRACK	HORSELIKE	HOSEMEN
HOPSACKS	HORNBEAMS	HORNY	HORSEMAN	HOSEN
HOPSCOTCH	HORNBILL	HORNYHEAD	HORSEMEAT	HOSEPIPE
HOPTOAD	HORNBILLS	HORNYWINK	HORSEMEN	HOSEPIPES
HOPTOADS	HORNBOOK	HOROEKA	HORSEMINT	HOSER
HORA	HORNBOOKS	HOROEKAS	HORSEPLAY	HOSERS
HORAH	HORNBUG	HOROKAKA	HORSEPOND	HOSES
HORAHS	HORNBUGS	HOROKAKAS	HORSEPOX	HOSEY
HORAL	HORNED	HOROLOGE	HORSERACE	HOSEYED
HORARY	HORNER	HOROLOGER	HORSES	HOSEYING
HORAS	HORNERS	HOROLOGES	HORSESHIT	HOSEYS
HORDE	HORNET	HOROLOGIA	HORSESHOD	HOSIER
HORDED	HORNETS	HOROLOGIC	HORSESHOE	HOSIERIES
HORDEIN	HORNFELS	HOROLOGY	HORSETAIL	HOSIERS
HORDEINS	HORNFUL	HOROMETRY	HORSEWAY	HOSIERY
HORDEOLA	HORNFULS	HOROPITO	HORSEWAYS	HOSING
HORDEOLUM	HORNGELD	HOROPITOS	HORSEWEED	HOSPICE
HORDES	HORNGELDS	HOROPTER	HORSEWHIP	HOSPICES
HORDING	HORNIER	HOROPTERS	HORSEY	HOSPITAGE
HORDOCK	HORNIEST	HOROSCOPE	HORSIER	HOSPITAL
HORDOCKS	HORNILY	HOROSCOPY	HORSIEST	HOSPITALE
HORE	HORNINESS	HORRENT	HORSILY	HOSPITALS
HOREHOUND	HORNING	HORRIBLE	HORSINESS	HOSPITIA
HORI	HORNINGS	HORRIBLES	HORSING	HOSPITIUM
HORIATIKI	HORNISH	HORRIBLY	HORSINGS	HOSPODAR
HORIS	HORNIST	HORRID	HORSON	HOSPODARS
HORIZON	HORNISTS	HORRIDER	HORSONS	HOSS
HORIZONAL	HORNITO	HORRIDEST	HORST	HOSSES
HORIZONS	HORNITOS	HORRIDLY	HORSTE	HOST
HORKEY	HORNLESS	HORRIFIC	HORSTES	HOSTA

HOSTAGE	HOTDOGGED	HOTTENTOT	HOURI	HOUSINGS
HOSTAGES	HOTDOGGER	HOTTER	HOURIS	HOUSLING
HOSTAS	HOTDOGS	HOTTERED	HOURLIES	HOUSTONIA
HOSTED	HOTE	HOTTERING	HOURLONG	HOUT
HOSTEL	HOTEL	HOTTERS	HOURLY	HOUTED
HOSTELED	HOTELDOM	HOTTEST	HOURPLATE	HOUTING
HOSTELER	HOTELDOMS	HOTTIE	HOURS	HOUTINGS
HOSTELERS	HOTELIER	HOTTIES	HOUSE	HOUTS
HOSTELING	HOTELIERS	HOTTING	HOUSEBOAT	HOVE
HOSTELLED	HOTELING	HOTTINGS	HOUSEBOY	HOVEA
HOSTELLER	HOTELINGS	HOTTISH	HOUSEBOYS	HOVEAS
HOSTELRY	HOTELLING	HOTTY	HOUSECARL	HOVED
HOSTELS	HOTELMAN	HOUDAH	HOUSECOAT	HOVEL
HOSTESS	HOTELMEN	HOUDAHS	HOUSED	HOVELED
HOSTESSED	HOTELS	HOUDAN	HOUSEFLY	HOVELING
HOSTESSES	HOTEN	HOUDANS	HOUSEFUL	HOVELLED
HOSTIE	HOTFOOT	HOUF	HOUSEFULS	HOVELLER
HOSTIES	HOTFOOTED	HOUFED	HOUSEHOLD	HOVELLERS
HOSTILE	HOTFOOTS	HOUFF	HOUSEKEEP	HOVELLING
HOSTILELY	HOTHEAD	HOUFFED	HOUSEKEPT	HOVELS
HOSTILES	HOTHEADED	HOUFFING	HOUSEL	HOVEN
HOSTILITY	HOTHEADS	HOUFFS	HOUSELED	HOVER
HOSTING	HOTHOUSE	HOUFING	HOUSELEEK	HOVERED
HOSTINGS	HOTHOUSED	HOUFS	HOUSELESS	HOVERER
HOSTLER	HOTHOUSES	HOUGH	HOUSELINE	HOVERERS
HOSTLERS	HOTLINE	HOUGHED	HOUSELING	HOVERFLY
HOSTLESSE	HOTLINES	HOUGHING	HOUSELLED	HOVERING
HOSTLY	HOTLINK	HOUGHS	HOUSELS	HOVERPORT
HOSTRIES	HOTLINKS	HOUHERE	HOUSEMAID	HOVERS
HOSTRY	HOTLY	HOUHERES	HOUSEMAN	HOVES
HOSTS	HOTNESS	HOUMMOS	HOUSEMATE	HOVING
HOT	HOTNESSES	HOUMMOSES	HOUSEMEN	HOW
HOTBED	HOTPLATE	HOUMOUS	HOUSER	HOWBE
HOTBEDS	HOTPLATES	HOUMOUSES	HOUSEROOM	HOWBEIT
HOTBLOOD	HOTPOT	HOUMUS	HOUSERS	HOWDAH
HOTBLOODS	HOTPOTS	HOUMUSES	HOUSES	HOWDAHS
HOTBOX	HOTPRESS	HOUND	HOUSESAT	HOWDIE
HOTBOXES	HOTROD	HOUNDED	HOUSESIT	HOWDIED
HOTCAKE	HOTRODS	HOUNDER	HOUSESITS	HOWDIES
HOTCAKES	HOTS	HOUNDERS	HOUSETOP	HOWDY
HOTCH	HOTSHOT	HOUNDFISH	HOUSETOPS	HOWDYING
HOTCHED	HOTSHOTS	HOUNDING	HOUSEWIFE	HOWE
HOTCHES	HOTSPOT	HOUNDS	HOUSEWORK	HOWES
HOTCHING	HOTSPOTS	HOUNGAN	HOUSEY	HOWEVER
HOTCHPOT	HOTSPUR	HOUNGANS	HOUSIER	HOWF
HOTCHPOTS	HOTSPURS	HOUR	HOUSIEST	HOWFED
HOTDOG	HOTTED	HOURGLASS	HOUSING	HOWFF

HOWFFED	HOYED	HUDDLE	HUGGING	HULLOO
HOWFFING	HOYING	HUDDLED	HUGGY	HULLOOED
HOWFFS	HOYLE	HUDDLER	HUGS	HULLOOING
HOWFING	HOYLES	HUDDLERS	HUGY	HULLOOS
HOWFS	HOYS	HUDDLES	HUH	HULLOS
HOWITZER	HRYVNA	HUDDLING	HUHU	HULLS
HOWITZERS	HRYVNAS	HUDDUP	HUHUS	HULLY
HOWK	HRYVNIA	HUDNA	HUI	HUM
HOWKED	HRYVNIAS	HUDNAS	HUIA	HUMA
HOWKER	HRYVNYA	HUDUD	HUIAS	HUMAN
HOWKERS	HRYVNYAS	HUDUDS	HUIC	HUMANE
HOWKING	HUANACO	HUE	HUIPIL	HUMANELY
HOWKS	HUANACOS	HUED	HUIPILES	HUMANER
HOWL	HUAQUERO	HUELESS	HUIPILS	HUMANEST
HOWLBACK	HUAQUEROS	HUER	HUIS	HUMANHOOD
HOWLBACKS	HUARACHE	HUERS	HUISACHE	HUMANISE
HOWLED	HUARACHES	HUES	HUISACHES	HUMANISED
HOWLER	HUARACHO	HUFF	HUISSIER	HUMANISER
HOWLERS	HUARACHOS	HUFFED	HUISSIERS	HUMANISES
HOWLET	HUB	HUFFER	HUITAIN	HUMANISM
HOWLETS	HUBBIES	HUFFERS	HUITAINS	HUMANISMS
HOWLING	HUBBLY	HUFFIER	HULA	HUMANIST
HOWLINGLY	HUBBUB	HUFFIEST	HULAS	HUMANISTS
HOWLINGS	HUBBUBOO	HUFFILY	HULE	HUMANITY
HOWLROUND	HUBBUBOOS	HUFFINESS	HULES	HUMANIZE
HOWLS	HUBBUBS	HUFFING	HULK	HUMANIZED
HOWRE	HUBBY	HUFFINGS	HULKED	HUMANIZER
HOWRES	HUBCAP	HUFFISH	HULKIER	HUMANIZES
HOWS	HUBCAPS	HUFFISHLY	HULKIEST	HUMANKIND
HOWSO	HUBRIS	HUFFKIN	HULKING	HUMANLIKE
HOWSOEVER	HUBRISES	HUFFKINS	HULKS	HUMANLY
HOWTOWDIE	HUBRISTIC	HUFFS	HULKY	HUMANNESS
HOWZAT	HUBS	HUFFY	HULL	HUMANOID
HOWZIT	HUCK	HUG	HULLED	HUMANOIDS
HOX	HUCKABACK	HUGE	HULLER	HUMANS
HOXED	HUCKED	HUGELY	HULLERS	HUMAS
HOXES	HUCKERY	HUGENESS	HULLIER	HUMATE
HOXING	HUCKING	HUGEOUS	HULLIEST	HUMATES
HOY	HUCKLE	HUGEOUSLY	HULLING	HUMBLE
HOYA	HUCKLED	HUGER	HULLO	HUMBLEBEE
HOYAS	HUCKLES	HUGEST	HULLOA	HUMBLED
HOYDEN	HUCKLING	HUGGABLE	HULLOAED	HUMBLER
HOYDENED	HUCKS	HUGGED	HULLOAING	HUMBLERS
HOYDENING	HUCKSTER	HUGGER	HULLOAS	HUMBLES
HOYDENISH	HUCKSTERS	HUGGERS	HULLOED	HUMBLESSE
HOYDENISM	HUCKSTERY	HUGGIER	HULLOES	HUMBLEST
HOYDENS	HUDDEN	HUGGIEST	HULLOING	HUMBLING

HUMBLINGS	HUMIDORS	HUMORING	HUNCHBACK	HUNTERS
HUMBLY	HUMIFIED	HUMORIST	HUNCHED	HUNTING
HUMBUCKER	HUMIFIES	HUMORISTS	HUNCHES	HUNTINGS
HUMBUG	HUMIFY	HUMORLESS	HUNCHING	HUNTRESS
HUMBUGGED	HUMIFYING	HUMOROUS	HUNDRED	HUNTS
HUMBUGGER	HUMILIANT	HUMORS	HUNDREDER	HUNTSMAN
HUMBUGS	HUMILIATE	HUMORSOME	HUNDREDOR	HUNTSMEN
HUMBUZZ	HUMILITY	HUMOUR	HUNDREDS	HUP
HUMBUZZES	HUMINT	HUMOURED	HUNDREDTH	HUPIRO
HUMDINGER	HUMINTS	HUMOURFUL	HUNG	HUPIROS
HUMDRUM	HUMITE	HUMOURING	HUNGAN	HUPPAH
HUMDRUMS	HUMITES	HUMOURS	HUNGANS	HUPPAHS
HUMECT	HUMITURE	HUMOUS	HUNGER	HUPPED
HUMECTANT	HUMITURES	HUMP	HUNGERED	HUPPING
HUMECTATE	HUMLIE	HUMPBACK	HUNGERFUL	HUPPOT
HUMECTED	HUMLIES	HUMPBACKS	HUNGERING	HUPPOTH
HUMECTING	HUMMABLE	HUMPED	HUNGERLY	HUPS
HUMECTIVE	HUMMAUM	HUMPEN	HUNGERS	HURCHEON
HUMECTS	HUMMAUMS	HUMPENS	HUNGOVER	HURCHEONS
HUMEFIED	HUMMED	HUMPER	HUNGRIER	HURDEN
HUMEFIES	HUMMEL	HUMPERS	HUNGRIEST	HURDENS
HUMEFY	HUMMELLED	HUMPH	HUNGRILY	HURDIES
HUMEFYING	HUMMELLER	HUMPHED	HUNGRY	HURDLE
HUMERAL	HUMMELS	HUMPHING	HUNH	HURDLED
HUMERALS	HUMMER	HUMPHS	HUNK	HURDLER
HUMERI	HUMMERS	HUMPIER	HUNKER	HURDLERS
HUMERUS	HUMMING	HUMPIES	HUNKERED	HURDLES
HUMF	HUMMINGS	HUMPIEST	HUNKERING	HURDLING
HUMFED	HUMMLE	HUMPINESS	HUNKERS	HURDLINGS
HUMFING	HUMMOCK	HUMPING	HUNKEY	HURDS
HUMFS	HUMMOCKED	HUMPLESS	HUNKEYS	HURL
HUMHUM	HUMMOCKS	HUMPLIKE	HUNKIE	HURLBAT
HUMHUMS	HUMMOCKY	HUMPS	HUNKIER	HURLBATS
HUMIC	HUMMUM	HUMPTIES	HUNKIES	HURLED
HUMICOLE	HUMMUMS	HUMPTY	HUNKIEST	HURLER
HUMICOLES	HUMMUS	HUMPY	HUNKS	HURLERS
HUMID	HUMMUSES	HUMS	HUNKSES	HURLEY
HUMIDER	HUMOGEN	HUMSTRUM	HUNKY	HURLEYS
HUMIDEST	HUMOGENS	HUMSTRUMS	HUNNISH	HURLIES
HUMIDEX	HUMONGOUS	HUMUNGOUS	HUNS	HURLING
HUMIDEXES	HUMOR	HUMUS	HUNT	HURLINGS
HUMIDICES	HUMORAL	HUMUSES	HUNTABLE	HURLS
HUMIDIFY	HUMORALLY	HUMUSY	HUNTAWAY	HURLY
HUMIDITY	HUMORED	HUMVEE	HUNTAWAYS	HURRA
HUMIDLY	HUMORESK	HUMVEES	HUNTED	HURRAED
HUMIDNESS	HUMORESKS	HUN	HUNTEDLY	HURRAH
HUMIDOR	HUMORFUL	HUNCH	HUNTER	HURRAHED

HURRAHING	HUSHERS	HUTCHIE	HYALOGENS	HYDRAZOIC
HURRAHS	HUSHES	HUTCHIES	HYALOID	HYDREMIA
HURRAING	HUSHFUL	HUTCHING	HYALOIDS	HYDREMIAS
HURRAS	HUSHIER	HUTIA	HYALONEMA	HYDRIA
HURRAY	HUSHIEST	HUTIAS	HYBRID	HYDRIAE
HURRAYED	HUSHING	HUTLIKE	HYBRIDISE	HYDRIC
HURRAYING	HUSHPUPPY	HUTMENT	HYBRIDISM	HYDRID
HURRAYS	HUSHY	HUTMENTS	HYBRIDIST	HYDRIDE
HURRICANE	HUSK	HUTS	HYBRIDITY	HYDRIDES
HURRICANO	HUSKED	HUTTED	HYBRIDIZE	HYDRIDS
HURRIED	HUSKER	HUTTING	HYBRIDOMA	HYDRILLA
HURRIEDLY	HUSKERS	HUTTINGS	HYBRIDOUS	HYDRILLAS
HURRIER	HUSKIER	HUTZPA	HYBRIDS	HYDRIODIC
HURRIERS	HUSKIES	HUTZPAH	HYBRIS	HYDRO
HURRIES	HUSKIEST	HUTZPAHS	HYBRISES	HYDROCAST
HURRY	HUSKILY	HUTZPAS	HYBRISTIC	HYDROCELE
HURRYING	HUSKINESS	HUZOOR	HYDANTOIN	HYDROFOIL
HURRYINGS	HUSKING	HUZOORS	HYDATHODE	HYDROGEL
HURST	HUSKINGS	HUZZA	HYDATID	HYDROGELS
HURSTS	HUSKLIKE	HUZZAED	HYDATIDS	HYDROGEN
HURT	HUSKS	HUZZAH	HYDATOID	HYDROGENS
HURTER	HUSKY	HUZZAHED	HYDRA	HYDROID
HURTERS	HUSO	HUZZAHING	HYDRACID	HYDROIDS
HURTFUL	HUSOS	HUZZAHS	HYDRACIDS	HYDROLASE
HURTFULLY	HUSS	HUZZAING	HYDRAE	HYDROLOGY
HURTING	HUSSAR	HUZZAS	HYDRAEMIA	HYDROLYSE
HURTLE	HUSSARS	HUZZIES	HYDRAGOG	HYDROLYTE
HURTLED	HUSSES	HUZZY	HYDRAGOGS	HYDROLYZE
HURTLES	HUSSIES	HWAN	HYDRANGEA	HYDROMA
HURTLESS	HUSSIF	HWYL	HYDRANT	HYDROMAS
HURTLING	HUSSIFS	HWYLS	HYDRANTH	HYDROMATA
HURTS	HUSSY	HYACINE	HYDRANTHS	HYDROMEL
HUSBAND	HUSTINGS	HYACINES	HYDRANTS	HYDROMELS
HUSBANDED	HUSTLE	HYACINTH	HYDRAS	HYDRONAUT
HUSBANDER	HUSTLED	HYACINTHS	HYDRASE	HYDRONIC
HUSBANDLY	HUSTLER	HYAENA	HYDRASES	HYDRONIUM
HUSBANDRY	HUSTLERS	HYAENAS	HYDRASTIS	HYDROPATH
HUSBANDS	HUSTLES	HYAENIC	HYDRATE	HYDROPIC
HUSH	HUSTLING	HYALIN	HYDRATED	HYDROPS
HUSHABIED	HUSTLINGS	HYALINE	HYDRATES	HYDROPSES
HUSHABIES	HUSWIFE	HYALINES	HYDRATING	HYDROPSY
HUSHABY	HUSWIFES	HYALINISE	HYDRATION	HYDROPTIC
HUSHED	HUSWIVES	HYALINIZE	HYDRATOR	HYDROPULT
HUSHEDLY	HUT	HYALINS	HYDRATORS	HYDROS
HUSHER	HUTCH	HYALITE	HYDRAULIC	HYDROSERE
HUSHERED	HUTCHED	HYALITES	HYDRAZIDE	HYDROSKI
HUSHERING	HUTCHES	HYALOGEN	HYDRAZINE	HYDROSKIS

HYDROSOL	HYKE	HYMNIC	HYPERNYMY	HYPNOTEES
HYDROSOLS	HYKES	HYMNING	HYPERON	HYPNOTIC
HYDROSOMA	HYLA	HYMNIST	HYPERONS	HYPNOTICS
HYDROSOME	HYLAS	HYMNISTS	HYPEROPE	HYPNOTISE
HYDROSTAT	HYLDING	HYMNLESS	HYPEROPES	HYPNOTISM
HYDROUS	HYLDINGS	HYMNLIKE	HYPEROPIA	HYPNOTIST
HYDROVANE	HYLE	HYMNODIES	HYPEROPIC	HYPNOTIZE
HYDROXIDE	HYLEG	HYMNODIST	HYPERPNEA	HYPNOTOID
HYDROXY	HYLEGS	HYMNODY	HYPERPURE	HYPNUM
HYDROXYL	HYLES	HYMNOLOGY	HYPERREAL	HYPNUMS
HYDROXYLS	HYLIC	HYMNS	HYPERS	HYPO
HYDROZOA	HYLICISM	HYNDE	HYPERTEXT	HYPOACID
HYDROZOAN	HYLICISMS	HYNDES	HYPES	HYPOBARIC
HYDROZOON	HYLICIST	HYOID	HYPESTER	HYPOBLAST
HYDYNE	HYLICISTS	HYOIDAL	HYPESTERS	HYPOBOLE
HYDYNES	HYLISM	HYOIDEAN	HYPETHRAL	HYPOBOLES
HYE	HYLISMS	HYOIDS	HYPHA	HYPOCAUST
HYED	HYLIST	HYOSCINE	HYPHAE	HYPOCIST
HYEING	HYLISTS	HYOSCINES	HYPHAL	HYPOCISTS
HYEN	HYLOBATE	HYP	HYPHEMIA	HYPOCOTYL
HYENA	HYLOBATES	HYPALGIA	HYPHEMIAS	HYPOCRISY
HYENAS	HYLOIST	HYPALGIAS	HYPHEN	HYPOCRITE
HYENIC	HYLOISTS	HYPALLAGE	HYPHENATE	HYPODERM
HYENINE	HYLOPHYTE	HYPANTHIA	HYPHENED	HYPODERMA
HYENOID	HYLOZOIC	HYPATE	HYPHENIC	HYPODERMS
HYENS	HYLOZOISM	HYPATES	HYPHENING	HYPOED
HYES	HYLOZOIST	HYPE	HYPHENISE	HYPOGAEA
HYETAL	HYMEN	HYPED	HYPHENISM	HYPOGAEAL
HYETOLOGY	HYMENAEAL	HYPER	HYPHENIZE	HYPOGAEAN
HYGEIST	HYMENAEAN	HYPERACID	HYPHENS	HYPOGAEUM
HYGEISTS	HYMENAL	HYPERARID	HYPHIES	HYPOGEA
HYGIEIST	HYMENEAL	HYPERBOLA	HYPHY	HYPOGEAL
HYGIEISTS	HYMENEALS	HYPERBOLE	HYPING	HYPOGEAN
HYGIENE	HYMENEAN	HYPERCUBE	HYPINGS	HYPOGENE
HYGIENES	HYMENIA	HYPEREMIA	HYPINOSES	HYPOGENIC
HYGIENIC	HYMENIAL	HYPEREMIC	HYPINOSIS	HYPOGEOUS
HYGIENICS	HYMENIUM	HYPERFINE	HYPNIC	HYPOGEUM
HYGIENIST	HYMENIUMS	HYPERGAMY	HYPNICS	HYPOGYNY
HYGRISTOR	HYMENS	HYPERGOL	HYPNOGENY	HYPOID
HYGRODEIK	HYMN	HYPERGOLS	HYPNOID	HYPOING
HYGROLOGY	HYMNAL	HYPERICIN	HYPNOIDAL	HYPOMANIA
HYGROMA	HYMNALS	HYPERICUM	HYPNOLOGY	HYPOMANIC
HYGROMAS	HYMNARIES	HYPERLINK	HYPNONE	HYPOMORPH
HYGROMATA	HYMNARY	HYPERMART	HYPNONES	HYPONASTY
HYGROPHIL	HYMNBOOK	HYPERNOVA	HYPNOSES	HYPONEA
HYGROSTAT	HYMNBOOKS	HYPERNYM	HYPNOSIS	HYPONEAS
HYING	HYMNED	HYPERNYMS	HYPNOTEE	HYPONOIA

HYPONOIAS

HYPONOIAS	HYPOPYON	HYPOTONIA	HYPURAL	HYSTERIA
HYPONYM	HYPOPYONS	HYPOTONIC	HYRACES	HYSTERIAS
HYPONYMS	HYPOS	HYPOXEMIA	HYRACOID	HYSTERIC
HYPONYMY	HYPOSTOME	HYPOXEMIC	HYRACOIDS	HYSTERICS
HYPOPHYGE	HYPOSTYLE	HYPOXIA	HYRAX	HYSTEROID
HYPOPLOID	HYPOTAXES	HYPOXIAS	HYRAXES	HYTE
HYPOPNEA	HYPOTAXIS	HYPOXIC	HYSON	HYTHE
HYPOPNEAS	HYPOTHEC	HYPPED	HYSONS	HYTHES
HYPOPNEIC	HYPOTHECA	HYPPING	HYSSOP	
HYPOPNOEA	HYPOTHECS	HYPS	HYSSOPS	

I

IAMB	ICEFALL	ICIER	ICTERUSES	IDENT
IAMBI	ICEFALLS	ICIEST	ICTIC	IDENTIC
IAMBIC	ICEFIELD	ICILY	ICTUS	IDENTICAL
IAMBICS	ICEFIELDS	ICINESS	ICTUSES	IDENTIFY
IAMBIST	ICEHOUSE	ICINESSES	ICY	IDENTIKIT
IAMBISTS	ICEHOUSES	ICING	ID	IDENTITY
IAMBS	ICEKHANA	ICINGS	IDANT	IDENTS
IAMBUS	ICEKHANAS	ICK	IDANTS	IDEOGRAM
IAMBUSES	ICELESS	ICKER	IDE	IDEOGRAMS
IANTHINE	ICELIKE	ICKERS	IDEA	IDEOGRAPH
IATRIC	ICEMAKER	ICKIER	IDEAED	IDEOLOGIC
IATRICAL	ICEMAKERS	ICKIEST	IDEAL	IDEOLOGUE
IATROGENY	ICEMAN	ICKILY	IDEALESS	IDEOLOGY
IBADAH	ICEMEN	ICKINESS	IDEALISE	IDEOMOTOR
IBADAT	ICEPACK	ICKLE	IDEALISED	IDEOPHONE
IBERIS	ICEPACKS	ICKLER	IDEALISER	IDEOPOLIS
IBERISES	ICER	ICKLEST	IDEALISES	IDES
IBEX	ICERS	ICKY	IDEALISM	IDIOBLAST
IBEXES	ICES	ICON	IDEALISMS	IDIOCIES
IBICES	ICESTONE	ICONES	IDEALIST	IDIOCY
IBIDEM	ICESTONES	ICONIC	IDEALISTS	IDIOGRAM
IBIS	ICEWINE	ICONICAL	IDEALITY	IDIOGRAMS
IBISES	ICEWINES	ICONICITY	IDEALIZE	IDIOGRAPH
IBOGAINE	ICH	ICONIFIED	IDEALIZED	IDIOLECT
IBOGAINES	ICHABOD	ICONIFIES	IDEALIZER	IDIOLECTS
IBRIK	ICHED	ICONIFY	IDEALIZES	IDIOM
IBRIKS	ICHES	ICONISE	IDEALLESS	IDIOMATIC
IBUPROFEN	ICHING	ICONISED	IDEALLY	IDIOMS
ICE	ICHNEUMON	ICONISES	IDEALNESS	IDIOPATHY
ICEBALL	ICHNITE	ICONISING	IDEALOGUE	IDIOPHONE
ICEBALLS	ICHNITES	ICONIZE	IDEALOGY	IDIOPLASM
ICEBERG	ICHNOLITE	ICONIZED	IDEALS	IDIOT
ICEBERGS	ICHNOLOGY	ICONIZES	IDEAS	IDIOTCIES
ICEBLINK	ICHOR	ICONIZING	IDEATA	IDIOTCY
ICEBLINKS	ICHOROUS	ICONOLOGY	IDEATE	IDIOTIC
ICEBOAT	ICHORS	ICONOSTAS	IDEATED	IDIOTICAL
ICEBOATER	ICHS	ICONS	IDEATES	IDIOTICON
ICEBOATS	ICHTHIC	ICTAL	IDEATING	IDIOTISH
ICEBOUND	ICHTHYIC	ICTERIC	IDEATION	IDIOTISM
ICEBOX	ICHTHYOID	ICTERICAL	IDEATIONS	IDIOTISMS
ICEBOXES	ICHTHYS	ICTERICS	IDEATIVE	IDIOTS
ICECAP	ICHTHYSES	ICTERID	IDEATUM	IDIOTYPE
ICECAPPED	ICICLE	ICTERIDS	IDEE	IDIOTYPES
ICECAPS	ICICLED	ICTERINE	IDEES	IDIOTYPIC
ICED	ICICLES	ICTERUS	IDEM	IDLE

IDLED	IDYLLIAN	IGNITION	ILEITIDES	ILLINIUMS
IDLEHOOD	IDYLLIC	IGNITIONS	ILEITIS	ILLIPE
IDLEHOODS	IDYLLIST	IGNITOR	ILEITISES	ILLIPES
IDLENESS	IDYLLISTS	IGNITORS	ILEOSTOMY	ILLIQUID
IDLER	IDYLLS	IGNITRON	ILEUM	ILLISION
IDLERS	IDYLS	IGNITRONS	ILEUS	ILLISIONS
IDLES	IF	IGNOBLE	ILEUSES	ILLITE
IDLESSE	IFF	IGNOBLER	ILEX	ILLITES
IDLESSES	IFFIER	IGNOBLEST	ILEXES	ILLITIC
IDLEST	IFFIEST	IGNOBLY	ILIA	ILLNESS
IDLING	IFFINESS	IGNOMIES	ILIAC	ILLNESSES
IDLY	IFFY	IGNOMINY	ILIACUS	ILLOGIC
IDOCRASE	IFS	IGNOMY	ILIACUSES	ILLOGICAL
IDOCRASES	IFTAR	IGNORABLE	ILIAD	ILLOGICS
IDOL	IFTARS	IGNORAMI	ILIADS	ILLS
IDOLA	IGAD	IGNORAMUS	ILIAL	ILLTH
IDOLATER	IGAPO	IGNORANCE	ILICES	ILLTHS
IDOLATERS	IGAPOS	IGNORANT	ILIUM	ILLUDE
IDOLATOR	IGARAPE	IGNORANTS	ILK	ILLUDED
IDOLATORS	IGARAPES	IGNORE	ILKA	ILLUDES
IDOLATRY	IGG	IGNORED	ILKADAY	ILLUDING
IDOLISE	IGGED	IGNORER	ILKADAYS	ILLUME
IDOLISED	IGGING	IGNORERS	ILKS	ILLUMED
IDOLISER	IGGS	IGNORES	ILL	ILLUMES
IDOLISERS	IGLOO	IGNORING	ILLAPSE	ILLUMINE
IDOLISES	IGLOOS	IGUANA	ILLAPSED	ILLUMINED
IDOLISING	IGLU	IGUANAS	ILLAPSES	ILLUMINER
IDOLISM	IGLUS	IGUANIAN	ILLAPSING	ILLUMINES
IDOLISMS	IGNARO	IGUANIANS	ILLATION	ILLUMING
IDOLIST	IGNAROES	IGUANID	ILLATIONS	ILLUPI
IDOLISTS	IGNAROS	IGUANIDS	ILLATIVE	ILLUPIS
IDOLIZE	IGNATIA	IGUANODON	ILLATIVES	ILLUSION
IDOLIZED	IGNATIAS	IHRAM	ILLAWARRA	ILLUSIONS
IDOLIZER	IGNEOUS	IHRAMS	ILLEGAL	ILLUSIVE
IDOLIZERS	IGNESCENT	IJTIHAD	ILLEGALLY	ILLUSORY
IDOLIZES	IGNIFIED	IJTIHADS	ILLEGALS	ILLUVIA
IDOLIZING	IGNIFIES	IKAN	ILLEGIBLE	ILLUVIAL
IDOLON	IGNIFY	IKANS	ILLEGIBLY	ILLUVIATE
IDOLS	IGNIFYING	IKAT	ILLER	ILLUVIUM
IDOLUM	IGNITABLE	IKATS	ILLEST	ILLUVIUMS
IDONEITY	IGNITE	IKEBANA	ILLIAD	ILLY
IDONEOUS	IGNITED	IKEBANAS	ILLIADS	ILMENITE
IDS	IGNITER	IKON	ILLIBERAL	ILMENITES
IDYL	IGNITERS	IKONS	ILLICIT	IMAGE
IDYLIST	IGNITES	ILEA	ILLICITLY	IMAGEABLE
IDYLISTS	IGNITIBLE	ILEAC	ILLIMITED	IMAGED
IDYLL	IGNITING	ILEAL	ILLINIUM	IMAGELESS

IMAGER	IMBARRED	IMBOSS	IMITANT	IMMESHES
IMAGERIES	IMBARRING	IMBOSSED	IMITANTS	IMMESHING
IMAGERS	IMBARS	IMBOSSES	IMITATE	IMMEW
IMAGERY	IMBASE	IMBOSSING	IMITATED	IMMEWED
IMAGES	IMBASED	IMBOWER	IMITATES	IMMEWING
IMAGINAL	IMBASES	IMBOWERED	IMITATING	IMMEWS
IMAGINARY	IMBASING	IMBOWERS	IMITATION	IMMIES
IMAGINE	IMBATHE	IMBRANGLE	IMITATIVE	IMMIGRANT
IMAGINED	IMBATHED	IMBRAST	IMITATOR	IMMIGRATE
IMAGINEER	IMBATHES	IMBREX	IMITATORS	IMMINENCE
IMAGINER	IMBATHING	IMBRICATE	IMMANACLE	IMMINENCY
IMAGINERS	IMBECILE	IMBRICES	IMMANE	IMMINENT
IMAGINES	IMBECILES	IMBROGLIO	IMMANELY	IMMINGLE
IMAGING	IMBECILIC	IMBROWN	IMMANENCE	IMMINGLED
IMAGINGS	IMBED	IMBROWNED	IMMANENCY	IMMINGLES
IMAGINING	IMBEDDED	IMBROWNS	IMMANENT	IMMINUTE
IMAGINIST	IMBEDDING	IMBRUE	IMMANITY	IMMISSION
IMAGISM	IMBEDS	IMBRUED	IMMANTLE	IMMIT
IMAGISMS	IMBIBE	IMBRUES	IMMANTLED	IMMITS
IMAGIST	IMBIBED	IMBRUING	IMMANTLES	IMMITTED
IMAGISTIC	IMBIBER	IMBRUTE	IMMASK	IMMITTING
IMAGISTS	IMBIBERS	IMBRUTED	IMMASKED	IMMIX
IMAGO	IMBIBES	IMBRUTES	IMMASKING	IMMIXED
IMAGOES	IMBIBING	IMBRUTING	IMMASKS	IMMIXES
IMAGOS	IMBITTER	IMBUE	IMMATURE	IMMIXING
IMAM	IMBITTERS	IMBUED	IMMATURES	IMMIXTURE
IMAMATE	IMBIZO	IMBUEMENT	IMMEDIACY	IMMOBILE
IMAMATES	IMBIZOS	IMBUES	IMMEDIATE	IMMODEST
IMAMS	IMBLAZE	IMBUING	IMMENSE	IMMODESTY
IMARET	IMBLAZED	IMBURSE	IMMENSELY	IMMOLATE
IMARETS	IMBLAZES	IMBURSED	IMMENSER	IMMOLATED
IMARI	IMBLAZING	IMBURSES	IMMENSEST	IMMOLATES
IMARIS	IMBODIED	IMBURSING	IMMENSITY	IMMOLATOR
IMAUM	IMBODIES	IMID	IMMERGE	IMMOMENT
IMAUMS	IMBODY	IMIDAZOLE	IMMERGED	IMMORAL
IMBALANCE	IMBODYING	IMIDE	IMMERGES	IMMORALLY
IMBALM	IMBOLDEN	IMIDES	IMMERGING	IMMORTAL
IMBALMED	IMBOLDENS	IMIDIC	IMMERSE	IMMORTALS
IMBALMER	IMBORDER	IMIDO	IMMERSED	IMMOTILE
IMBALMERS	IMBORDERS	IMIDS	IMMERSER	IMMOVABLE
IMBALMING	IMBOSK	IMINAZOLE	IMMERSERS	IMMOVABLY
IMBALMS	IMBOSKED	IMINE	IMMERSES	IMMUNE
IMBAR	IMBOSKING	IMINES	IMMERSING	IMMUNES
IMBARK	IMBOSKS	IMINO	IMMERSION	IMMUNISE
IMBARKED	IMBOSOM	IMINOUREA	IMMERSIVE	IMMUNISED
IMBARKING	IMBOSOMED	IMITABLE	IMMESH	IMMUNISER
IMBARKS	IMBOSOMS	IMITANCY	IMMESHED	IMMUNISES

IMMUNITY	IMPANELS	IMPEARLED	IMPHEES	IMPLICITY
IMMUNIZE	IMPANNEL	IMPEARLS	IMPI	IMPLIED
IMMUNIZED	IMPANNELS	IMPECCANT	IMPIES	IMPLIEDLY
IMMUNIZER	IMPARITY	IMPED	IMPIETIES	IMPLIES
IMMUNIZES	IMPARK	IMPEDANCE	IMPIETY	IMPLODE
IMMUNOGEN	IMPARKED	IMPEDE	IMPING	IMPLODED
IMMURE	IMPARKING	IMPEDED	IMPINGE	IMPLODENT
IMMURED	IMPARKS	IMPEDER	IMPINGED	IMPLODES
IMMURES	IMPARL	IMPEDERS	IMPINGENT	IMPLODING
IMMURING	IMPARLED	IMPEDES	IMPINGER	IMPLORE
IMMUTABLE	IMPARLING	IMPEDING	IMPINGERS	IMPLORED
IMMUTABLY	IMPARLS	IMPEDOR	IMPINGES	IMPLORER
IMMY	IMPART	IMPEDORS	IMPINGING	IMPLORERS
IMP	IMPARTED	IMPEL	IMPINGS	IMPLORES
IMPACABLE	IMPARTER	IMPELLED	IMPIOUS	IMPLORING
IMPACT	IMPARTERS	IMPELLENT	IMPIOUSLY	IMPLOSION
IMPACTED	IMPARTIAL	IMPELLER	IMPIS	IMPLOSIVE
IMPACTER	IMPARTING	IMPELLERS	IMPISH	IMPLUNGE
IMPACTERS	IMPARTS	IMPELLING	IMPISHLY	IMPLUNGED
IMPACTFUL	IMPASSE	IMPELLOR	IMPLANT	IMPLUNGES
IMPACTING	IMPASSES	IMPELLORS	IMPLANTED	IMPLUVIA
IMPACTION	IMPASSION	IMPELS	IMPLANTER	IMPLUVIUM
IMPACTITE	IMPASSIVE	IMPEND	IMPLANTS	IMPLY
IMPACTIVE	IMPASTE	IMPENDED	IMPLATE	IMPLYING
IMPACTOR	IMPASTED	IMPENDENT	IMPLATED	IMPOCKET
IMPACTORS	IMPASTES	IMPENDING	IMPLATES	IMPOCKETS
IMPACTS	IMPASTING	IMPENDS	IMPLATING	IMPOLDER
IMPAINT	IMPASTO	IMPENNATE	IMPLEACH	IMPOLDERS
IMPAINTED	IMPASTOED	IMPERATOR	IMPLEAD	IMPOLICY
IMPAINTS	IMPASTOS	IMPERFECT	IMPLEADED	IMPOLITE
IMPAIR	IMPATIENS	IMPERIA	IMPLEADER	IMPOLITER
IMPAIRED	IMPATIENT	IMPERIAL	IMPLEADS	IMPOLITIC
IMPAIRER	IMPAVE	IMPERIALS	IMPLED	IMPONE
IMPAIRERS	IMPAVED	IMPERIL	IMPLEDGE	IMPONED
IMPAIRING	IMPAVES	IMPERILED	IMPLEDGED	IMPONENT
IMPAIRS	IMPAVID	IMPERILS	IMPLEDGES	IMPONENTS
IMPALA	IMPAVIDLY	IMPERIOUS	IMPLEMENT	IMPONES
IMPALAS	IMPAVING	IMPERIUM	IMPLETE	IMPONING
IMPALE	IMPAWN	IMPERIUMS	IMPLETED	IMPOROUS
IMPALED	IMPAWNED	IMPETICOS	IMPLETES	IMPORT
IMPALER	IMPAWNING	IMPETIGO	IMPLETING	IMPORTANT
IMPALERS	IMPAWNS	IMPETIGOS	IMPLETION	IMPORTED
IMPALES	IMPEACH	IMPETRATE	IMPLEX	IMPORTER
IMPALING	IMPEACHED	IMPETUOUS	IMPLEXES	IMPORTERS
IMPANATE	IMPEACHER	IMPETUS	IMPLEXION	IMPORTING
IMPANEL	IMPEACHES	IMPETUSES	IMPLICATE	IMPORTS
IMPANELED	IMPEARL	IMPHEE	IMPLICIT	IMPORTUNE

IMPOSABLE	IMPREST	IMPURPLED	INAUGURAL	INCAVED
IMPOSE	IMPRESTS	IMPURPLES	INAURATE	INCAVES
IMPOSED	IMPRIMIS	IMPUTABLE	INBEING	INCAVI
IMPOSER	IMPRINT	IMPUTABLY	INBEINGS	INCAVING
IMPOSERS	IMPRINTED	IMPUTE	INBENT	INCAVO
IMPOSES	IMPRINTER	IMPUTED	INBOARD	INCEDE
IMPOSEX	IMPRINTS	IMPUTER	INBOARDS	INCEDED
IMPOSEXES	IMPRISON	IMPUTERS	INBORN	INCEDES
IMPOSING	IMPRISONS	IMPUTES	INBOUND	INCEDING
IMPOST	IMPROBITY	IMPUTING	INBOUNDED	INCENSE
IMPOSTED	IMPROMPTU	IMSHI	INBOUNDS	INCENSED
IMPOSTER	IMPROPER	IMSHY	INBOX	INCENSER
IMPOSTERS	IMPROV	IN	INBOXES	INCENSERS
IMPOSTING	IMPROVE	INABILITY	INBREAK	INCENSES
IMPOSTOR	IMPROVED	INACTION	INBREAKS	INCENSING
IMPOSTORS	IMPROVER	INACTIONS	INBREATHE	INCENSOR
IMPOSTS	IMPROVERS	INACTIVE	INBRED	INCENSORS
IMPOSTUME	IMPROVES	INAIDABLE	INBREDS	INCENSORY
IMPOSTURE	IMPROVING	INAMORATA	INBREED	INCENT
IMPOT	IMPROVISE	INAMORATO	INBREEDER	INCENTED
IMPOTENCE	IMPROVS	INANE	INBREEDS	INCENTER
IMPOTENCY	IMPRUDENT	INANELY	INBRING	INCENTERS
IMPOTENT	IMPS	INANENESS	INBRINGS	INCENTING
IMPOTENTS	IMPSONITE	INANER	INBROUGHT	INCENTIVE
IMPOTS	IMPUDENCE	INANES	INBUILT	INCENTRE
IMPOUND	IMPUDENCY	INANEST	INBURNING	INCENTRES
IMPOUNDED	IMPUDENT	INANGA	INBURST	INCENTS
IMPOUNDER	IMPUGN	INANGAS	INBURSTS	INCEPT
IMPOUNDS	IMPUGNED	INANIMATE	INBY	INCEPTED
IMPOWER	IMPUGNER	INANITIES	INBYE	INCEPTING
IMPOWERED	IMPUGNERS	INANITION	INCAGE	INCEPTION
IMPOWERS	IMPUGNING	INANITY	INCAGED	INCEPTIVE
IMPRECATE	IMPUGNS	INAPT	INCAGES	INCEPTOR
IMPRECISE	IMPULSE	INAPTLY	INCAGING	INCEPTORS
IMPREGN	IMPULSED	INAPTNESS	INCANT	INCEPTS
IMPREGNED	IMPULSES	INARABLE	INCANTED	INCERTAIN
IMPREGNS	IMPULSING	INARCH	INCANTING	INCESSANT
IMPRESA	IMPULSION	INARCHED	INCANTS	INCEST
IMPRESARI	IMPULSIVE	INARCHES	INCAPABLE	INCESTS
IMPRESAS	IMPUNDULU	INARCHING	INCAPABLY	INCH
IMPRESE	IMPUNITY	INARM	INCARNATE	INCHASE
IMPRESES	IMPURE	INARMED	INCASE	INCHASED
IMPRESS	IMPURELY	INARMING	INCASED	INCHASES
IMPRESSE	IMPURER	INARMS	INCASES	INCHASING
IMPRESSED	IMPUREST	INASMUCH	INCASING	INCHED
IMPRESSER	IMPURITY	INAUDIBLE	INCAUTION	INCHER
IMPRESSES	IMPURPLE	INAUDIBLY	INCAVE	INCHERS

INCHES	INCLES	INCREASE	INCURVING	INDEWS
INCHING	INCLINE	INCREASED	INCURVITY	INDEX
INCHMEAL	INCLINED	INCREASER	INCUS	INDEXABLE
INCHOATE	INCLINER	INCREASES	INCUSE	INDEXAL
INCHOATED	INCLINERS	INCREATE	INCUSED	INDEXED
INCHOATES	INCLINES	INCREMATE	INCUSES	INDEXER
INCHPIN	INCLINING	INCREMENT	INCUSING	INDEXERS
INCHPINS	INCLIP	INCRETION	INCUT	INDEXES
INCHWORM	INCLIPPED	INCRETORY	INDABA	INDEXICAL
INCHWORMS	INCLIPS	INCROSS	INDABAS	INDEXING
INCIDENCE	INCLOSE	INCROSSED	INDAGATE	INDEXINGS
INCIDENT	INCLOSED	INCROSSES	INDAGATED	INDEXLESS
INCIDENTS	INCLOSER	INCRUST	INDAGATES	INDIA
INCIPIENT	INCLOSERS	INCRUSTED	INDAGATOR	INDIAS
INCIPIT	INCLOSES	INCRUSTS	INDAMIN	INDICAN
INCIPITS	INCLOSING	INCUBATE	INDAMINE	INDICANS
INCISAL	INCLOSURE	INCUBATED	INDAMINES	INDICANT
INCISE	INCLUDE	INCUBATES	INDAMINS	INDICANTS
INCISED	INCLUDED	INCUBATOR	INDART	INDICATE
INCISES	INCLUDES	INCUBI	INDARTED	INDICATED
INCISING	INCLUDING	INCUBOUS	INDARTING	INDICATES
INCISION	INCLUSION	INCUBUS	INDARTS	INDICATOR
INCISIONS	INCLUSIVE	INCUBUSES	INDEBTED	INDICES
INCISIVE	INCOG	INCUDAL	INDECENCY	INDICIA
INCISOR	INCOGNITA	INCUDATE	INDECENT	INDICIAL
INCISORS	INCOGNITO	INCUDES	INDECORUM	INDICIAS
INCISORY	INCOGS	INCULCATE	INDEED	INDICIUM
INCISURAL	INCOME	INCULPATE	INDELIBLE	INDICIUMS
INCISURE	INCOMER	INCULT	INDELIBLY	INDICT
INCISURES	INCOMERS	INCUMBENT	INDEMNIFY	INDICTED
INCITABLE	INCOMES	INCUMBER	INDEMNITY	INDICTEE
INCITANT	INCOMING	INCUMBERS	INDENE	INDICTEES
INCITANTS	INCOMINGS	INCUNABLE	INDENES	INDICTER
INCITE	INCOMMODE	INCUR	INDENT	INDICTERS
INCITED	INCOMPACT	INCURABLE	INDENTED	INDICTING
INCITER	INCONDITE	INCURABLY	INDENTER	INDICTION
INCITERS	INCONIE	INCURIOUS	INDENTERS	INDICTOR
INCITES	INCONNU	INCURRED	INDENTING	INDICTORS
INCITING	INCONNUE	INCURRENT	INDENTION	INDICTS
INCIVIL	INCONNUES	INCURRING	INDENTOR	INDIE
INCIVISM	INCONNUS	INCURS	INDENTORS	INDIES
INCIVISMS	INCONY	INCURSION	INDENTS	INDIGEN
INCLASP	INCORPSE	INCURSIVE	INDENTURE	INDIGENCE
INCLASPED	INCORPSED	INCURVATE	INDEVOUT	INDIGENCY
INCLASPS	INCORPSES	INCURVE	INDEW	INDIGENE
INCLE	INCORRECT	INCURVED	INDEWED	INDIGENES
INCLEMENT	INCORRUPT	INCURVES	INDEWING	INDIGENS

INDIGENT	INDORSING	INDULGING	INERM	INFANTINE
INDIGENTS	INDORSOR	INDULIN	INERMOUS	INFANTRY
INDIGEST	INDORSORS	INDULINE	INERRABLE	INFANTS
INDIGESTS	INDOW	INDULINES	INERRABLY	INFARCT
INDIGN	INDOWED	INDULINS	INERRANCY	INFARCTED
INDIGNANT	INDOWING	INDULT	INERRANT	INFARCTS
INDIGNIFY	INDOWS	INDULTS	INERT	INFARE
INDIGNITY	INDOXYL	INDUMENTA	INERTER	INFARES
INDIGNLY	INDOXYLS	INDUNA	INERTEST	INFATUATE
INDIGO	INDRAFT	INDUNAS	INERTIA	INFAUNA
INDIGOES	INDRAFTS	INDURATE	INERTIAE	INFAUNAE
INDIGOID	INDRAUGHT	INDURATED	INERTIAL	INFAUNAL
INDIGOIDS	INDRAWN	INDURATES	INERTIAS	INFAUNAS
INDIGOS	INDRENCH	INDUSIA	INERTLY	INFAUST
INDIGOTIC	INDRI	INDUSIAL	INERTNESS	INFECT
INDIGOTIN	INDRIS	INDUSIATE	INERTS	INFECTANT
INDINAVIR	INDRISES	INDUSIUM	INERUDITE	INFECTED
INDIRECT	INDUBIOUS	INDUSTRY	INESSIVE	INFECTER
INDIRUBIN	INDUCE	INDUVIAE	INESSIVES	INFECTERS
INDISPOSE	INDUCED	INDUVIAL	INEXACT	INFECTING
INDITE	INDUCER	INDUVIATE	INEXACTLY	INFECTION
INDITED	INDUCERS	INDWELL	INEXPERT	INFECTIVE
INDITER	INDUCES	INDWELLER	INEXPERTS	INFECTOR
INDITERS	INDUCIAE	INDWELLS	INFALL	INFECTORS
INDITES	INDUCIBLE	INDWELT	INFALLING	INFECTS
INDITING	INDUCING	INEARTH	INFALLS	INFECUND
INDIUM	INDUCT	INEARTHED	INFAME	INFEFT
INDIUMS	INDUCTED	INEARTHS	INFAMED	INFEFTED
INDIVIDUA	INDUCTEE	INEBRIANT	INFAMES	INFEFTING
INDOCIBLE	INDUCTEES	INEBRIATE	INFAMIES	INFEFTS
INDOCILE	INDUCTILE	INEBRIETY	INFAMING	INFELT
INDOL	INDUCTING	INEBRIOUS	INFAMISE	INFEOFF
INDOLE	INDUCTION	INEDIBLE	INFAMISED	INFEOFFED
INDOLENCE	INDUCTIVE	INEDIBLY	INFAMISES	INFEOFFS
INDOLENCY	INDUCTOR	INEDITA	INFAMIZE	INFER
INDOLENT	INDUCTORS	INEDITED	INFAMIZED	INFERABLE
INDOLES	INDUCTS	INEFFABLE	INFAMIZES	INFERABLY
INDOLS	INDUE	INEFFABLY	INFAMOUS	INFERE
INDOOR	INDUED	INELASTIC	INFAMY	INFERENCE
INDOORS	INDUES	INELEGANT	INFANCIES	INFERIAE
INDORSE	INDUING	INEPT	INFANCY	INFERIBLE
INDORSED	INDULGE	INEPTER	INFANT	INFERIOR
INDORSEE	INDULGED	INEPTEST	INFANTA	INFERIORS
INDORSEES	INDULGENT	INEPTLY	INFANTAS	INFERNAL
INDORSER	INDULGER	INEPTNESS	INFANTE	INFERNO
INDORSERS	INDULGERS	INEQUABLE	INFANTES	INFERNOS
INDORSES	INDULGES	INEQUITY	INFANTILE	INFERRED

INFERRER	INFLAME	INFOLDING	INFUSORY	INGRAFTED
INFERRERS	INFLAMED	INFOLDS	ING	INGRAFTS
INFERRING	INFLAMER	INFOMANIA	INGAN	INGRAIN
INFERS	INFLAMERS	INFORCE	INGANS	INGRAINED
INFERTILE	INFLAMES	INFORCED	INGATE	INGRAINER
INFEST	INFLAMING	INFORCES	INGATES	INGRAINS
INFESTANT	INFLATE	INFORCING	INGATHER	INGRAM
INFESTED	INFLATED	INFORM	INGATHERS	INGRATE
INFESTER	INFLATER	INFORMAL	INGENER	INGRATELY
INFESTERS	INFLATERS	INFORMANT	INGENERS	INGRATES
INFESTING	INFLATES	INFORMED	INGENIOUS	INGRESS
INFESTS	INFLATING	INFORMER	INGENIUM	INGRESSES
INFICETE	INFLATION	INFORMERS	INGENIUMS	INGROOVE
INFIDEL	INFLATIVE	INFORMING	INGENU	INGROOVED
INFIDELIC	INFLATOR	INFORMS	INGENUE	INGROOVES
INFIDELS	INFLATORS	INFORTUNE	INGENUES	INGROSS
INFIELD	INFLATUS	INFOS	INGENUITY	INGROSSED
INFIELDER	INFLECT	INFOTECH	INGENUOUS	INGROSSES
INFIELDS	INFLECTED	INFOTECHS	INGENUS	INGROUND
INFIGHT	INFLECTOR	INFOUGHT	INGEST	INGROUP
INFIGHTER	INFLECTS	INFRA	INGESTA	INGROUPS
INFIGHTS	INFLEXED	INFRACT	INGESTED	INGROWING
INFILL	INFLEXION	INFRACTED	INGESTING	INGROWN
INFILLED	INFLEXURE	INFRACTOR	INGESTION	INGROWTH
INFILLING	INFLICT	INFRACTS	INGESTIVE	INGROWTHS
INFILLS	INFLICTED	INFRARED	INGESTS	INGRUM
INFIMA	INFLICTER	INFRAREDS	INGINE	INGS
INFIMUM	INFLICTOR	INFRINGE	INGINES	INGUINAL
INFIMUMS	INFLICTS	INFRINGED	INGLE	INGULF
INFINITE	INFLIGHT	INFRINGER	INGLENEUK	INGULFED
INFINITES	INFLOW	INFRINGES	INGLENOOK	INGULFING
INFINITY	INFLOWING	INFRUGAL	INGLES	INGULFS
INFIRM	INFLOWS	INFULA	INGLOBE	INGULPH
INFIRMARY	INFLUENCE	INFULAE	INGLOBED	INGULPHED
INFIRMED	INFLUENT	INFURIATE	INGLOBES	INGULPHS
INFIRMER	INFLUENTS	INFUSCATE	INGLOBING	INHABIT
INFIRMEST	INFLUENZA	INFUSE	INGLUVIAL	INHABITED
INFIRMING	INFLUX	INFUSED	INGLUVIES	INHABITER
INFIRMITY	INFLUXES	INFUSER	INGO	INHABITOR
INFIRMLY	INFLUXION	INFUSERS	INGOES	INHABITS
INFIRMS	INFO	INFUSES	INGOING	INHALANT
INFIX	INFOBAHN	INFUSIBLE	INGOINGS	INHALANTS
INFIXED	INFOBAHNS	INFUSING	INGOT	INHALATOR
INFIXES	INFOLD	INFUSION	INGOTED	INHALE
INFIXING	INFOLDED	INFUSIONS	INGOTING	INHALED
INFIXION	INFOLDER	INFUSIVE	INGOTS	INHALER
INFIXIONS	INFOLDERS	INFUSORIA	INGRAFT	INHALERS

INHALES	INHUMATE	INJURABLE	INKSTONES	INNED
INHALING	INHUMATED	INJURE	INKWELL	INNER
INHARMONY	INHUMATES	INJURED	INKWELLS	INNERLY
INHAUL	INHUME	INJURER	INKWOOD	INNERMOST
INHAULER	INHUMED	INJURERS	INKWOODS	INNERNESS
INHAULERS	INHUMER	INJURES	INKY	INNERS
INHAULS	INHUMERS	INJURIES	INLACE	INNERSOLE
INHAUST	INHUMES	INJURING	INLACED	INNERVATE
INHAUSTED	INHUMING	INJURIOUS	INLACES	INNERVE
INHAUSTS	INIA	INJURY	INLACING	INNERVED
INHEARSE	INIMICAL	INJUSTICE	INLAID	INNERVES
INHEARSED	INION	INK	INLAND	INNERVING
INHEARSES	INIONS	INKBERRY	INLANDER	INNERWEAR
INHERCE	INIQUITY	INKBLOT	INLANDERS	INNING
INHERCED	INISLE	INKBLOTS	INLANDS	INNINGS
INHERCES	INISLED	INKED	INLAY	INNIT
INHERCING	INISLES	INKER	INLAYER	INNKEEPER
INHERE	INISLING	INKERS	INLAYERS	INNLESS
INHERED	INITIAL	INKHOLDER	INLAYING	INNOCENCE
INHERENCE	INITIALED	INKHORN	INLAYINGS	INNOCENCY
INHERENCY	INITIALER	INKHORNS	INLAYS	INNOCENT
INHERENT	INITIALLY	INKHOSI	INLET	INNOCENTS
INHERES	INITIALS	INKHOSIS	INLETS	INNOCUITY
INHERING	INITIATE	INKIER	INLETTING	INNOCUOUS
INHERIT	INITIATED	INKIEST	INLIER	INNOVATE
INHERITED	INITIATES	INKINESS	INLIERS	INNOVATED
INHERITOR	INITIATOR	INKING	INLOCK	INNOVATES
INHERITS	INJECT	INKJET	INLOCKED	INNOVATOR
INHESION	INJECTANT	INKLE	INLOCKING	INNOXIOUS
INHESIONS	INJECTED	INKLED	INLOCKS	INNS
INHIBIN	INJECTING	INKLES	INLY	INNUENDO
INHIBINS	INJECTION	INKLESS	INLYING	INNUENDOS
INHIBIT	INJECTIVE	INKLIKE	INMATE	INNYARD
INHIBITED	INJECTOR	INKLING	INMATES	INNYARDS
INHIBITER	INJECTORS	INKLINGS	INMESH	INOCULA
INHIBITOR	INJECTS	INKOSI	INMESHED	INOCULANT
INHIBITS	INJELLIED	INKOSIS	INMESHES	INOCULATE
INHOLDER	INJELLIES	INKPAD	INMESHING	INOCULUM
INHOLDERS	INJELLY	INKPADS	INMIGRANT	INOCULUMS
INHOLDING	INJERA	INKPOT	INMOST	INODOROUS
INHOOP	INJERAS	INKPOTS	INN	INOPINATE
INHOOPED	INJOINT	INKS	INNAGE	INORB
INHOOPING	INJOINTED	INKSPOT	INNAGES	INORBED
INHOOPS	INJOINTS	INKSPOTS	INNARDS	INORBING
INHUMAN	INJUNCT	INKSTAND	INNATE	INORBS
INHUMANE	INJUNCTED	INKSTANDS	INNATELY	INORGANIC
INHUMANLY	INJUNCTS	INKSTONE	INNATIVE	INORNATE

INOSINE	INRUNS	INSELBERG	INSIPIENT	INSPHERES
INOSINES	INRUSH	INSENSATE	INSIST	INSPIRE
INOSITE	INRUSHES	INSERT	INSISTED	INSPIRED
INOSITES	INRUSHING	INSERTED	INSISTENT	INSPIRER
INOSITOL	INS	INSERTER	INSISTER	INSPIRERS
INOSITOLS	INSANE	INSERTERS	INSISTERS	INSPIRES
INOTROPIC	INSANELY	INSERTING	INSISTING	INSPIRING
INPATIENT	INSANER	INSERTION	INSISTS	INSPIRIT
INPAYMENT	INSANEST	INSERTS	INSNARE	INSPIRITS
INPHASE	INSANIE	INSET	INSNARED	INSTABLE
INPOUR	INSANIES	INSETS	INSNARER	INSTAL
INPOURED	INSANITY	INSETTED	INSNARERS	INSTALL
INPOURING	INSATIATE	INSETTER	INSNARES	INSTALLED
INPOURS	INSATIETY	INSETTERS	INSNARING	INSTALLER
INPUT	INSCAPE	INSETTING	INSOFAR	INSTALLS
INPUTS	INSCAPES	INSHALLAH	INSOLATE	INSTALS
INPUTTED	INSCIENCE	INSHEATH	INSOLATED	INSTANCE
INPUTTER	INSCIENT	INSHEATHE	INSOLATES	INSTANCED
INPUTTERS	INSCONCE	INSHEATHS	INSOLE	INSTANCES
INPUTTING	INSCONCED	INSHELL	INSOLENCE	INSTANCY
INQILAB	INSCONCES	INSHELLED	INSOLENT	INSTANT
INQILABS	INSCRIBE	INSHELLS	INSOLENTS	INSTANTER
INQUERE	INSCRIBED	INSHELTER	INSOLES	INSTANTLY
INQUERED	INSCRIBER	INSHIP	INSOLUBLE	INSTANTS
INQUERES	INSCRIBES	INSHIPPED	INSOLUBLY	INSTAR
INQUERING	INSCROLL	INSHIPS	INSOLVENT	INSTARRED
INQUEST	INSCROLLS	INSHORE	INSOMNIA	INSTARS
INQUESTS	INSCULP	INSHRINE	INSOMNIAC	INSTATE
INQUIET	INSCULPED	INSHRINED	INSOMNIAS	INSTATED
INQUIETED	INSCULPS	INSHRINES	INSOMUCH	INSTATES
INQUIETLY	INSCULPT	INSIDE	INSOOTH	INSTATING
INQUIETS	INSEAM	INSIDER	INSOUL	INSTEAD
INQUILINE	INSEAMED	INSIDERS	INSOULED	INSTEP
INQUINATE	INSEAMING	INSIDES	INSOULING	INSTEPS
INQUIRE	INSEAMS	INSIDIOUS	INSOULS	INSTIGATE
INQUIRED	INSECT	INSIGHT	INSOURCE	INSTIL
INQUIRER	INSECTAN	INSIGHTS	INSOURCED	INSTILL
INQUIRERS	INSECTARY	INSIGNE	INSOURCES	INSTILLED
INQUIRES	INSECTEAN	INSIGNIA	INSPAN	INSTILLER
INQUIRIES	INSECTILE	INSIGNIAS	INSPANNED	INSTILLS
INQUIRING	INSECTION	INSINCERE	INSPANS	INSTILS
INQUIRY	INSECTS	INSINEW	INSPECT	INSTINCT
INQUORATE	INSECURE	INSINEWED	INSPECTED	INSTINCTS
INRO	INSEEM	INSINEWS	INSPECTOR	INSTITUTE
INROAD	INSEEMED	INSINUATE	INSPECTS	INSTRESS
INROADS	INSEEMING	INSIPID	INSPHERE	INSTROKE
INRUN	INSEEMS	INSIPIDLY	INSPHERED	INSTROKES

INSTRUCT	INTAGLIO	INTERARCH	INTERLAY	INTERROW
INSTRUCTS	INTAGLIOS	INTERBANK	INTERLAYS	INTERRUPT
INSUCKEN	INTAKE	INTERBED	INTERLEAF	INTERS
INSULA	INTAKES	INTERBEDS	INTERLEND	INTERSECT
INSULAE	INTARSIA	INTERBRED	INTERLENT	INTERSERT
INSULANT	INTARSIAS	INTERCEDE	INTERLINE	INTERSEX
INSULANTS	INTEGER	INTERCELL	INTERLINK	INTERTERM
INSULAR	INTEGERS	INTERCEPT	INTERLOAN	INTERTEXT
INSULARLY	INTEGRAL	INTERCITY	INTERLOCK	INTERTIE
INSULARS	INTEGRALS	INTERCLAN	INTERLOOP	INTERTIES
INSULATE	INTEGRAND	INTERCLUB	INTERLOPE	INTERTILL
INSULATED	INTEGRANT	INTERCOM	INTERLUDE	INTERUNIT
INSULATES	INTEGRATE	INTERCOMS	INTERMALE	INTERVAL
INSULATOR	INTEGRIN	INTERCROP	INTERMAT	INTERVALE
INSULIN	INTEGRINS	INTERCUT	INTERMATS	INTERVALS
INSULINS	INTEGRITY	INTERCUTS	INTERMENT	INTERVEIN
INSULSE	INTEL	INTERDASH	INTERMESH	INTERVENE
INSULSITY	INTELLECT	INTERDEAL	INTERMIT	INTERVIEW
INSULT	INTELS	INTERDICT	INTERMITS	INTERWAR
INSULTANT	INTENABLE	INTERDINE	INTERMIX	INTERWEB
INSULTED	INTEND	INTERESS	INTERMONT	INTERWEBS
INSULTER	INTENDANT	INTERESSE	INTERMURE	INTERWIND
INSULTERS	INTENDED	INTEREST	INTERN	INTERWORK
INSULTING	INTENDEDS	INTERESTS	INTERNAL	INTERWOVE
INSULTS	INTENDER	INTERFACE	INTERNALS	INTERZONE
INSURABLE	INTENDERS	INTERFERE	INTERNE	INTESTACY
INSURANCE	INTENDING	INTERFILE	INTERNED	INTESTATE
INSURANT	INTENDS	INTERFIRM	INTERNEE	INTESTINE
INSURANTS	INTENIBLE	INTERFLOW	INTERNEES	INTHRAL
INSURE	INTENSATE	INTERFOLD	INTERNES	INTHRALL
INSURED	INTENSE	INTERFUSE	INTERNET	INTHRALLS
INSUREDS	INTENSELY	INTERGANG	INTERNETS	INTHRALS
INSURER	INTENSER	INTERGREW	INTERNING	INTHRONE
INSURERS	INTENSEST	INTERGROW	INTERNIST	INTHRONED
INSURES	INTENSIFY	INTERIM	INTERNODE	INTHRONES
INSURGENT	INTENSION	INTERIMS	INTERNS	INTI
INSURING	INTENSITY	INTERIOR	INTERPAGE	INTIFADA
INSWATHE	INTENSIVE	INTERIORS	INTERPLAY	INTIFADAH
INSWATHED	INTENT	INTERJECT	INTERPLED	INTIFADAS
INSWATHES	INTENTION	INTERJOIN	INTERPONE	INTIFADEH
INSWEPT	INTENTIVE	INTERKNIT	INTERPOSE	INTIL
INSWING	INTENTLY	INTERKNOT	INTERPRET	INTIMA
INSWINGER	INTENTS	INTERLACE	INTERRACE	INTIMACY
INSWINGS	INTER	INTERLAID	INTERRAIL	INTIMAE
INTACT	INTERACT	INTERLAP	INTERRED	INTIMAL
INTACTLY	INTERACTS	INTERLAPS	INTERREX	INTIMAS
INTAGLI	INTERAGE	INTERLARD	INTERRING	INTIMATE

INTIMATED	INTRA	INTRUDING	INUREMENT	INVENT
INTIMATER	INTRACITY	INTRUSION	INURES	INVENTED
INTIMATES	INTRADA	INTRUSIVE	INURING	INVENTER
INTIME	INTRADAS	INTRUST	INURN	INVENTERS
INTIMISM	INTRADAY	INTRUSTED	INURNED	INVENTING
INTIMISMS	INTRADOS	INTRUSTS	INURNING	INVENTION
INTIMIST	INTRANET	INTUBATE	INURNMENT	INVENTIVE
INTIMISTE	INTRANETS	INTUBATED	INURNS	INVENTOR
INTIMISTS	INTRANT	INTUBATES	INUSITATE	INVENTORS
INTIMITY	INTRANTS	INTUIT	INUST	INVENTORY
INTINE	INTREAT	INTUITED	INUSTION	INVENTS
INTINES	INTREATED	INTUITING	INUSTIONS	INVERITY
INTIRE	INTREATS	INTUITION	INUTILE	INVERNESS
INTIS	INTRENCH	INTUITIVE	INUTILELY	INVERSE
INTITLE	INTREPID	INTUITS	INUTILITY	INVERSED
INTITLED	INTRICACY	INTUMESCE	INVADABLE	INVERSELY
INTITLES	INTRICATE	INTURN	INVADE	INVERSES
INTITLING	INTRIGANT	INTURNED	INVADED	INVERSING
INTITULE	INTRIGUE	INTURNS	INVADER	INVERSION
INTITULED	INTRIGUED	INTUSE	INVADERS	INVERSIVE
INTITULES	INTRIGUER	INTUSES	INVADES	INVERT
INTO	INTRIGUES	INTWINE	INVADING	INVERTASE
INTOED	INTRINCE	INTWINED	INVALID	INVERTED
INTOMB	INTRINSIC	INTWINES	INVALIDED	INVERTER
INTOMBED	INTRO	INTWINING	INVALIDLY	INVERTERS
INTOMBING	INTRODUCE	INTWIST	INVALIDS	INVERTIN
INTOMBS	INTROFIED	INTWISTED	INVAR	INVERTING
INTONACO	INTROFIES	INTWISTS	INVARIANT	INVERTINS
INTONACOS	INTROFY	INUKSHUIT	INVARS	INVERTOR
INTONATE	INTROIT	INUKSHUK	INVASION	INVERTORS
INTONATED	INTROITAL	INUKSHUKS	INVASIONS	INVERTS
INTONATES	INTROITS	INULA	INVASIVE	INVEST
INTONATOR	INTROITUS	INULAS	INVEAGLE	INVESTED
INTONE	INTROJECT	INULASE	INVEAGLED	INVESTING
INTONED	INTROLD	INULASES	INVEAGLES	INVESTOR
INTONER	INTROMIT	INULIN	INVECKED	INVESTORS
INTONERS	INTROMITS	INULINS	INVECTED	INVESTS
INTONES	INTRON	INUMBRATE	INVECTIVE	INVEXED
INTONING	INTRONS	INUNCTION	INVEIGH	INVIABLE
INTONINGS	INTRORSE	INUNDANT	INVEIGHED	INVIABLY
INTORSION	INTROS	INUNDATE	INVEIGHER	INVIDIOUS
INTORT	INTROVERT	INUNDATED	INVEIGHS	INVIOLACY
INTORTED	INTRUDE	INUNDATES	INVEIGLE	INVIOLATE
INTORTING	INTRUDED	INUNDATOR	INVEIGLED	INVIOUS
INTORTION	INTRUDER	INURBANE	INVEIGLER	INVIRILE
INTORTS	INTRUDERS	INURE	INVEIGLES	INVISCID
INTOWN	INTRUDES	INURED	INVENIT	INVISIBLE

INVISIBLY	INWEAVES	IODISED	IONIZING	IRENOLOGY
INVITAL	INWEAVING	IODISER	IONOGEN	IRES
INVITE	INWICK	IODISERS	IONOGENIC	IRID
INVITED	INWICKED	IODISES	IONOGENS	IRIDAL
INVITEE	INWICKING	IODISING	IONOMER	IRIDEAL
INVITEES	INWICKS	IODISM	IONOMERS	IRIDES
INVITER	INWIND	IODISMS	IONONE	IRIDIAL
INVITERS	INWINDING	IODIZE	IONONES	IRIDIAN
INVITES	INWINDS	IODIZED	IONOPAUSE	IRIDIC
INVITING	INWIT	IODIZER	IONOPHORE	IRIDISE
INVITINGS	INWITH	IODIZERS	IONOSONDE	IRIDISED
INVOCABLE	INWITS	IODIZES	IONOTROPY	IRIDISES
INVOCATE	INWORK	IODIZING	IONS	IRIDISING
INVOCATED	INWORKED	IODOFORM	IOPANOIC	IRIDIUM
INVOCATES	INWORKING	IODOFORMS	IOS	IRIDIUMS
INVOCATOR	INWORKS	IODOMETRY	IOTA	IRIDIZE
INVOICE	INWORN	IODOPHILE	IOTACISM	IRIDIZED
INVOICED	INWOUND	IODOPHOR	IOTACISMS	IRIDIZES
INVOICES	INWOVE	IODOPHORS	IOTAS	IRIDIZING
INVOICING	INWOVEN	IODOPSIN	IPECAC	IRIDOCYTE
INVOKE	INWRAP	IODOPSINS	IPECACS	IRIDOLOGY
INVOKED	INWRAPPED	IODOUS	IPOMOEA	IRIDOTOMY
INVOKER	INWRAPS	IODURET	IPOMOEAS	IRIDS
INVOKERS	INWREATHE	IODURETS	IPPON	IRING
INVOKES	INWROUGHT	IODYRITE	IPPONS	IRIS
INVOKING	INYALA	IODYRITES	IPRINDOLE	IRISATE
INVOLUCEL	INYALAS	IOLITE	IRACUND	IRISATED
INVOLUCRA	IO	IOLITES	IRADE	IRISATES
INVOLUCRE	IODATE	ION	IRADES	IRISATING
INVOLUTE	IODATED	IONIC	IRASCIBLE	IRISATION
INVOLUTED	IODATES	IONICITY	IRASCIBLY	IRISCOPE
INVOLUTES	IODATING	IONICS	IRATE	IRISCOPES
INVOLVE	IODATION	IONISABLE	IRATELY	IRISED
INVOLVED	IODATIONS	IONISE	IRATENESS	IRISES
INVOLVER	IODIC	IONISED	IRATER	IRISING
INVOLVERS	IODID	IONISER	IRATEST	IRITIC
INVOLVES	IODIDE	IONISERS	IRE	IRITIS
INVOLVING	IODIDES	IONISES	IRED	IRITISES
INWALL	IODIDS	IONISING	IREFUL	IRK
INWALLED	IODIN	IONIUM	IREFULLY	IRKED
INWALLING	IODINATE	IONIUMS	IRELESS	IRKING
INWALLS	IODINATED	IONIZABLE	IRENIC	IRKS
INWARD	IODINATES	IONIZE	IRENICAL	IRKSOME
INWARDLY	IODINE	IONIZED	IRENICISM	IRKSOMELY
INWARDS	IODINES	IONIZER	IRENICON	IROKO
INWEAVE	IODINS	IONIZERS	IRENICONS	IROKOS
INWEAVED	IODISE	IONIZES	IRENICS	IRON

IRONBARK	IRONY	ISATIN	ISMATICAL	ISOCRYMES
IRONBARKS	IRRADIANT	ISATINE	ISMS	ISOCYANIC
IRONBOUND	IRRADIATE	ISATINES	ISNA	ISOCYCLIC
IRONCLAD	IRREAL	ISATINIC	ISNAE	ISODICA
IRONCLADS	IRREALITY	ISATINS	ISO	ISODICON
IRONE	IRREDENTA	ISBA	ISOAMYL	ISODOMA
IRONED	IRREGULAR	ISBAS	ISOAMYLS	ISODOMON
IRONER	IRRELATED	ISCHAEMIA	ISOBAR	ISODOMOUS
IRONERS	IRRIDENTA	ISCHAEMIC	ISOBARE	ISODOMUM
IRONES	IRRIGABLE	ISCHEMIA	ISOBARES	ISODONT
IRONIC	IRRIGABLY	ISCHEMIAS	ISOBARIC	ISODONTAL
IRONICAL	IRRIGATE	ISCHEMIC	ISOBARISM	ISODONTS
IRONIER	IRRIGATED	ISCHIA	ISOBARS	ISODOSE
IRONIES	IRRIGATES	ISCHIADIC	ISOBASE	ISODOSES
IRONIEST	IRRIGATOR	ISCHIAL	ISOBASES	ISOENZYME
IRONING	IRRIGUOUS	ISCHIATIC	ISOBATH	ISOETES
IRONINGS	IRRISION	ISCHIUM	ISOBATHIC	ISOFORM
IRONISE	IRRISIONS	ISCHURIA	ISOBATHS	ISOFORMS
IRONISED	IRRISORY	ISCHURIAS	ISOBRONT	ISOGAMETE
IRONISES	IRRITABLE	ISEIKONIA	ISOBRONTS	ISOGAMIC
IRONISING	IRRITABLY	ISEIKONIC	ISOBUTANE	ISOGAMIES
IRONIST	IRRITANCY	ISENERGIC	ISOBUTENE	ISOGAMOUS
IRONISTS	IRRITANT	ISH	ISOBUTYL	ISOGAMY
IRONIZE	IRRITANTS	ISHES	ISOBUTYLS	ISOGENEIC
IRONIZED	IRRITATE	ISINGLASS	ISOCHASM	ISOGENIC
IRONIZES	IRRITATED	ISIT	ISOCHASMS	ISOGENIES
IRONIZING	IRRITATES	ISLAND	ISOCHEIM	ISOGENOUS
IRONLESS	IRRITATOR	ISLANDED	ISOCHEIMS	ISOGENY
IRONLIKE	IRRUPT	ISLANDER	ISOCHIMAL	ISOGLOSS
IRONMAN	IRRUPTED	ISLANDERS	ISOCHIME	ISOGON
IRONMEN	IRRUPTING	ISLANDING	ISOCHIMES	ISOGONAL
IRONNESS	IRRUPTION	ISLANDS	ISOCHOR	ISOGONALS
IRONS	IRRUPTIVE	ISLE	ISOCHORE	ISOGONE
IRONSIDE	IRRUPTS	ISLED	ISOCHORES	ISOGONES
IRONSIDES	IRUKANDJI	ISLELESS	ISOCHORIC	ISOGONIC
IRONSMITH	IS	ISLEMAN	ISOCHORS	ISOGONICS
IRONSTONE	ISABEL	ISLEMEN	ISOCHRON	ISOGONIES
IRONWARE	ISABELLA	ISLES	ISOCHRONE	ISOGONS
IRONWARES	ISABELLAS	ISLESMAN	ISOCHRONS	ISOGONY
IRONWEED	ISABELS	ISLESMEN	ISOCLINAL	ISOGRAFT
IRONWEEDS	ISAGOGE	ISLET	ISOCLINE	ISOGRAFTS
IRONWOMAN	ISAGOGES	ISLETED	ISOCLINES	ISOGRAM
IRONWOMEN	ISAGOGIC	ISLETS	ISOCLINIC	ISOGRAMS
IRONWOOD	ISAGOGICS	ISLING	ISOCRACY	ISOGRAPH
IRONWOODS	ISALLOBAR	ISLOMANIA	ISOCRATIC	ISOGRAPHS
IRONWORK	ISARITHM	ISM	ISOCRYMAL	ISOGRIV
IRONWORKS	ISARITHMS	ISMATIC	ISOCRYME	ISOGRIVS

ISOHEL	ISONOMIC	ISOTONIC	ITACONIC	ITINERANT
ISOHELS	ISONOMIES	ISOTOPE	ITALIC	ITINERARY
ISOHYDRIC	ISONOMOUS	ISOTOPES	ITALICISE	ITINERATE
ISOHYET	ISONOMY	ISOTOPIC	ITALICIZE	ITS
ISOHYETAL	ISOOCTANE	ISOTOPIES	ITALICS	ITSELF
ISOHYETS	ISOPACH	ISOTOPY	ITAS	IURE
ISOKONT	ISOPACHS	ISOTRON	ITCH	IVIED
ISOKONTAN	ISOPHONE	ISOTRONS	ITCHED	IVIES
ISOKONTS	ISOPHONES	ISOTROPIC	ITCHES	IVORIED
ISOLABLE	ISOPHOTAL	ISOTROPY	ITCHIER	IVORIES
ISOLATE	ISOPHOTE	ISOTYPE	ITCHIEST	IVORIST
ISOLATED	ISOPHOTES	ISOTYPES	ITCHILY	IVORISTS
ISOLATES	ISOPLETH	ISOTYPIC	ITCHINESS	IVORY
ISOLATING	ISOPLETHS	ISOZYME	ITCHING	IVORYBILL
ISOLATION	ISOPOD	ISOZYMES	ITCHINGS	IVORYLIKE
ISOLATIVE	ISOPODAN	ISOZYMIC	ITCHWEED	IVORYWOOD
ISOLATOR	ISOPODANS	ISPAGHULA	ITCHWEEDS	IVRESSE
ISOLATORS	ISOPODOUS	ISSEI	ITCHY	IVRESSES
ISOLEAD	ISOPODS	ISSEIS	ITEM	IVY
ISOLEADS	ISOPOLITY	ISSUABLE	ITEMED	IVYLIKE
ISOLEX	ISOPRENE	ISSUABLY	ITEMING	IWI
ISOLEXES	ISOPRENES	ISSUANCE	ITEMISE	IWIS
ISOLINE	ISOPROPYL	ISSUANCES	ITEMISED	IXIA
ISOLINES	ISOPTERAN	ISSUANT	ITEMISER	IXIAS
ISOLOG	ISOPYCNAL	ISSUE	ITEMISERS	IXODIASES
ISOLOGOUS	ISOPYCNIC	ISSUED	ITEMISES	IXODIASIS
ISOLOGS	ISOS	ISSUELESS	ITEMISING	IXODID
ISOLOGUE	ISOSCELES	ISSUER	ITEMIZE	IXODIDS
ISOLOGUES	ISOSMOTIC	ISSUERS	ITEMIZED	IXORA
ISOMER	ISOSPIN	ISSUES	ITEMIZER	IXORAS
ISOMERASE	ISOSPINS	ISSUING	ITEMIZERS	IXTLE
ISOMERE	ISOSPORY	ISTANA	ITEMIZES	IXTLES
ISOMERES	ISOSTACY	ISTANAS	ITEMIZING	IZAR
ISOMERIC	ISOSTASY	ISTHMI	ITEMS	IZARD
ISOMERISE	ISOSTATIC	ISTHMIAN	ITERANCE	IZARDS
ISOMERISM	ISOSTERIC	ISTHMIANS	ITERANCES	IZARS
ISOMERIZE	ISOTACH	ISTHMIC	ITERANT	IZVESTIA
ISOMEROUS	ISOTACHS	ISTHMOID	ITERATE	IZVESTIAS
ISOMERS	ISOTACTIC	ISTHMUS	ITERATED	IZVESTIYA
ISOMETRIC	ISOTHERAL	ISTHMUSES	ITERATES	IZZARD
ISOMETRY	ISOTHERE	ISTLE	ITERATING	IZZARDS
ISOMORPH	ISOTHERES	ISTLES	ITERATION	IZZAT
ISOMORPHS	ISOTHERM	IT	ITERATIVE	IZZATS
ISONIAZID	ISOTHERMS	ITA	ITERUM	
ISONOME	ISOTONE	ITACISM	ITHER	
ISONOMES	ISOTONES	ITACISMS	ITINERACY	

J

JA	JACKAROO	JACKSTONE	JAGER	JAILHOUSE
JAAP	JACKAROOS	JACKSTRAW	JAGERS	JAILING
JAAPS	JACKASS	JACKSY	JAGG	JAILLESS
JAB	JACKASSES	JACKY	JAGGARIES	JAILOR
JABBED	JACKBOOT	JACOBIN	JAGGARY	JAILORESS
JABBER	JACKBOOTS	JACOBINS	JAGGED	JAILORS
JABBERED	JACKDAW	JACOBUS	JAGGEDER	JAILS
JABBERER	JACKDAWS	JACOBUSES	JAGGEDEST	JAK
JABBERERS	JACKED	JACONET	JAGGEDLY	JAKE
JABBERING	JACKEEN	JACONETS	JAGGER	JAKES
JABBERS	JACKEENS	JACQUARD	JAGGERIES	JAKESES
JABBING	JACKER	JACQUARDS	JAGGERS	JAKEY
JABBINGLY	JACKEROO	JACQUERIE	JAGGERY	JAKEYS
JABBLE	JACKEROOS	JACTATION	JAGGHERY	JAKFRUIT
JABBLED	JACKERS	JACULATE	JAGGIER	JAKFRUITS
JABBLES	JACKET	JACULATED	JAGGIES	JAKS
JABBLING	JACKETED	JACULATES	JAGGIEST	JALABIB
JABERS	JACKETING	JACULATOR	JAGGING	JALAP
JABIRU	JACKETS	JACUZZI	JAGGS	JALAPENO
JABIRUS	JACKFISH	JACUZZIS	JAGGY	JALAPENOS
JABORANDI	JACKFRUIT	JADE	JAGHIR	JALAPIC
JABOT	JACKIES	JADED	JAGHIRDAR	JALAPIN
JABOTS	JACKING	JADEDLY	JAGHIRE	JALAPINS
JABS	JACKINGS	JADEDNESS	JAGHIRES	JALAPS
JACAL	JACKKNIFE	JADEITE	JAGHIRS	JALFREZI
JACALES	JACKLEG	JADEITES	JAGIR	JALOP
JACALS	JACKLEGS	JADELIKE	JAGIRS	JALOPIES
JACAMAR	JACKLIGHT	JADERIES	JAGLESS	JALOPPIES
JACAMARS	JACKMAN	JADERY	JAGRA	JALOPPY
JACANA	JACKMEN	JADES	JAGRAS	JALOPS
JACANAS	JACKPLANE	JADING	JAGS	JALOPY
JACARANDA	JACKPOT	JADISH	JAGUAR	JALOUSE
JACARE	JACKPOTS	JADISHLY	JAGUARS	JALOUSED
JACARES	JACKROLL	JADITIC	JAI	JALOUSES
JACCHUS	JACKROLLS	JAEGER	JAIL	JALOUSIE
JACCHUSES	JACKS	JAEGERS	JAILABLE	JALOUSIED
JACENT	JACKSCREW	JAFA	JAILBAIT	JALOUSIES
JACINTH	JACKSHAFT	JAFAS	JAILBAITS	JALOUSING
JACINTHE	JACKSIE	JAFFA	JAILBIRD	JAM
JACINTHES	JACKSIES	JAFFAS	JAILBIRDS	JAMAAT
JACINTHS	JACKSMELT	JAG	JAILBREAK	JAMAATS
JACK	JACKSMITH	JAGA	JAILED	JAMADAR
JACKAL	JACKSNIPE	JAGAED	JAILER	JAMADARS
JACKALLED	JACKSTAY	JAGAING	JAILERESS	JAMB
JACKALS	JACKSTAYS	JAGAS	JAILERS	JAMBALAYA

JAMBART	JAMMERS	JANNY	JARGONELS	JARUL
JAMBARTS	JAMMIER	JANSKY	JARGONING	JARULS
JAMBE	JAMMIES	JANSKYS	JARGONISE	JARVEY
JAMBEAU	JAMMIEST	JANTEE	JARGONISH	JARVEYS
JAMBEAUX	JAMMING	JANTIER	JARGONIST	JARVIE
JAMBED	JAMMINGS	JANTIES	JARGONIZE	JARVIES
JAMBEE	JAMMY	JANTIEST	JARGONS	JASEY
JAMBEES	JAMON	JANTY	JARGONY	JASEYS
JAMBER	JAMPACKED	JAP	JARGOON	JASIES
JAMBERS	JAMPAN	JAPAN	JARGOONS	JASMIN
JAMBES	JAMPANEE	JAPANISE	JARHEAD	JASMINE
JAMBEUX	JAMPANEES	JAPANISED	JARHEADS	JASMINES
JAMBIER	JAMPANI	JAPANISES	JARINA	JASMINS
JAMBIERS	JAMPANIS	JAPANIZE	JARINAS	JASMONATE
JAMBING	JAMPANS	JAPANIZED	JARK	JASP
JAMBIYA	JAMPOT	JAPANIZES	JARKMAN	JASPE
JAMBIYAH	JAMPOTS	JAPANNED	JARKMEN	JASPER
JAMBIYAHS	JAMS	JAPANNER	JARKS	JASPERISE
JAMBIYAS	JANE	JAPANNERS	JARL	JASPERIZE
JAMBO	JANES	JAPANNING	JARLDOM	JASPEROUS
JAMBOK	JANGLE	JAPANS	JARLDOMS	JASPERS
JAMBOKKED	JANGLED	JAPE	JARLS	JASPERY
JAMBOKS	JANGLER	JAPED	JARLSBERG	JASPES
JAMBOLAN	JANGLERS	JAPER	JAROOL	JASPIDEAN
JAMBOLANA	JANGLES	JAPERIES	JAROOLS	JASPILITE
JAMBOLANS	JANGLIER	JAPERS	JAROSITE	JASPIS
JAMBONE	JANGLIEST	JAPERY	JAROSITES	JASPISES
JAMBONES	JANGLING	JAPES	JAROVISE	JASPS
JAMBOOL	JANGLINGS	JAPING	JAROVISED	JASS
JAMBOOLS	JANGLY	JAPINGLY	JAROVISES	JASSES
JAMBOREE	JANIFORM	JAPINGS	JAROVIZE	JASSID
JAMBOREES	JANISARY	JAPONICA	JAROVIZED	JASSIDS
JAMBS	JANISSARY	JAPONICAS	JAROVIZES	JASY
JAMBU	JANITOR	JAPPED	JARP	JATAKA
JAMBUL	JANITORS	JAPPING	JARPED	JATAKAS
JAMBULS	JANITRESS	JAPS	JARPING	JATO
JAMBUS	JANITRIX	JAR	JARPS	JATOS
JAMDANI	JANIZAR	JARARACA	JARRAH	JATROPHA
JAMDANIS	JANIZARS	JARARACAS	JARRAHS	JATROPHAS
JAMES	JANIZARY	JARARAKA	JARRED	JAUK
JAMESES	JANKER —	JARARAKAS	JARRING	JAUKED
JAMJAR	JANKERS	JARFUL	JARRINGLY	JAUKING
JAMJARS	JANN	JARFULS	JARRINGS	JAUKS
JAMLIKE	JANNIES	JARGON	JARS	JAUNCE
JAMMABLE	JANNOCK	JARGONED	JARSFUL	JAUNCED
JAMMED	JANNOCKS	JARGONEER	JARTA	JAUNCES
JAMMER	JANNS	JARGONEL	JARTAS	JAUNCING

JAUNDICE	JAWFALLS	JAZZY	JEEZ	JELUTONG
JAUNDICED	JAWHOLE	JEALOUS	JEFE	JELUTONGS
JAUNDICES	JAWHOLES	JEALOUSE	JEFES	JEMADAR
JAUNSE	JAWING	JEALOUSED	JEFF	JEMADARS
JAUNSED	JAWINGS	JEALOUSES	JEFFED	JEMBE
JAUNSES	JAWLESS	JEALOUSLY	JEFFING	JEMBES
JAUNSING	JAWLIKE	JEALOUSY	JEFFS	JEMIDAR
JAUNT	JAWLINE	JEAN	JEHAD	JEMIDARS
JAUNTED	JAWLINES	JEANED	JEHADEEN	JEMIMA
JAUNTEE	JAWS	JEANETTE	JEHADI	JEMIMAS
JAUNTIE	JAXIE	JEANETTES	JEHADIS	JEMMIED
JAUNTIER	JAXIES	JEANS	JEHADISM	JEMMIER
JAUNTIES	JAXY	JEAT	JEHADISMS	JEMMIES
JAUNTIEST	JAY	JEATS	JEHADIST	JEMMIEST
JAUNTILY	JAYBIRD	JEBEL	JEHADISTS	JEMMINESS
JAUNTING	JAYBIRDS	JEBELS	JEHADS	JEMMY
JAUNTS	JAYCEE	JEDI	JEHU	JEMMYING
JAUNTY	JAYCEES	JEDIS	JEHUS	JENNET
JAUP	JAYGEE	JEE	JEJUNA	JENNETING
JAUPED	JAYGEES	JEED	JEJUNAL	JENNETS
JAUPING	JAYHAWKER	JEEING	JEJUNE	JENNIES
JAUPS	JAYS	JEEL	JEJUNELY	JENNY
JAVA	JAYVEE	JEELED	JEJUNITY	JEOFAIL
JAVAS	JAYVEES	JEELIE	JEJUNUM	JEOFAILS
JAVEL	JAYWALK	JEELIED	JELAB	JEON
JAVELIN	JAYWALKED	JEELIEING	JELABS	JEOPARD
JAVELINA	JAYWALKER	JEELIES	JELL	JEOPARDED
JAVELINAS	JAYWALKS	JEELING	JELLABA	JEOPARDER
JAVELINED	JAZERANT	JEELS	JELLABAH	JEOPARDS
JAVELINS	JAZERANTS	JEELY	JELLABAHS	JEOPARDY
JAVELS	JAZIES	JEELYING	JELLABAS	JEQUERITY
JAW	JAZY	JEEP	JELLED	JEQUIRITY
JAWAN	JAZZ	JEEPED	JELLIED	JERBIL
JAWANS	JAZZBO	JEEPERS	JELLIES	JERBILS
JAWARI	JAZZBOS	JEEPING	JELLIFIED	JERBOA
JAWARIS	JAZZED	JEEPNEY	JELLIFIES	JERBOAS
JAWBATION	JAZZER	JEEPNEYS	JELLIFY	JEREED
JAWBONE	JAZZERS	JEEPS	JELLING	JEREEDS
JAWBONED	JAZZES	JEER	JELLO	JEREMIAD
JAWBONER	JAZZIER	JEERED	JELLOS	JEREMIADS
JAWBONERS	JAZZIEST	JEERER	JELLS	JEREPIGO
JAWBONES	JAZZILY	JEERERS	JELLY	JEREPIGOS
JAWBONING	JAZZINESS	JEERING	JELLYBEAN	JERFALCON
JAWBOX	JAZZING	JEERINGLY	JELLYFISH	JERID
JAWBOXES	JAZZLIKE	JEERINGS	JELLYING	JERIDS
JAWED	JAZZMAN	JEERS	JELLYLIKE	JERK
JAWFALL	JAZZMEN	JEES	JELLYROLL	JERKED

JERKER	JESSIES	JETTIED	JHATKA	JIGGERED
JERKERS	JESSING	JETTIER	JHATKAS	JIGGERING
JERKIER	JEST	JETTIES	JIAO	JIGGERS
JERKIES	JESTBOOK	JETTIEST	JIAOS	JIGGIER
JERKIEST	JESTBOOKS	JETTINESS	JIB	JIGGIEST
JERKILY	JESTED	JETTING	JIBB	JIGGING
JERKIN	JESTEE	JETTISON	JIBBA	JIGGINGS
JERKINESS	JESTEES	JETTISONS	JIBBAH	JIGGISH
JERKING	JESTER	JETTON	JIBBAHS	JIGGLE
JERKINGLY	JESTERS	JETTONS	JIBBAS	JIGGLED
JERKINGS	JESTFUL	JETTY	JIBBED	JIGGLES
JERKINS	JESTING	JETTYING	JIBBER	JIGGLIER
JERKS	JESTINGLY	JETWAY	JIBBERED	JIGGLIEST
JERKWATER	JESTINGS	JETWAYS	JIBBERING	JIGGLING
JERKY	JESTS	JEU	JIBBERS	JIGGLY
JEROBOAM	JESUIT	JEUNE	JIBBING	JIGGUMBOB
JEROBOAMS	JESUITIC	JEUX	JIBBINGS	JIGGY
JERQUE	JESUITISM	JEW	JIBBONS	JIGJIG
JERQUED	JESUITRY	JEWED	JIBBOOM	JIGJIGGED
JERQUER	JESUITS	JEWEL	JIBBOOMS	JIGJIGS
JERQUERS	JESUS	JEWELED	JIBBS	JIGLIKE
JERQUES	JET	JEWELER	JIBE	JIGOT
JERQUING	JETBEAD	JEWELERS	JIBED	JIGOTS
JERQUINGS	JETBEADS	JEWELFISH	JIBER	JIGS
JERREED	JETE	JEWELING	JIBERS	JIGSAW
JERREEDS	JETES	JEWELLED	JIBES	JIGSAWED
JERRICAN	JETFOIL	JEWELLER	JIBING	JIGSAWING
JERRICANS	JETFOILS	JEWELLERS	JIBINGLY	JIGSAWN
JERRID	JETLAG	JEWELLERY	JIBS	JIGSAWS
JERRIDS	JETLAGS	JEWELLIKE	JICAMA	JIHAD
JERRIES	JETLIKE	JEWELLING	JICAMAS	JIHADEEN
JERRY	JETLINER	JEWELRIES	JICKAJOG	JIHADI
JERRYCAN	JETLINERS	JEWELRY	JICKAJOGS	JIHADIS
JERRYCANS	JETON	JEWELS	JIFF	JIHADISM
JERSEY	JETONS	JEWELWEED	JIFFIES	JIHADISMS
JERSEYED	JETPORT	JEWFISH	JIFFS	JIHADIST
JERSEYS	JETPORTS	JEWFISHES	JIFFY	JIHADISTS
JESS	JETS	JEWIE	JIG	JIHADS
JESSAMIES	JETSAM	JEWIES	JIGABOO	JILBAB
JESSAMINE	JETSAMS	JEWING	JIGABOOS	JILBABS
JESSAMY	JETSOM	JEWS	JIGAJIG	JILGIE
JESSANT	JETSOMS	JEZAIL	JIGAJIGS	JILGIES
JESSE	JETSON	JEZAILS	JIGAJOG	JILL
JESSED	JETSONS	JEZEBEL	JIGAJOGS	JILLAROO
JESSERANT	JETSTREAM	JEZEBELS	JIGAMAREE	JILLAROOS
JESSES	JETTATURA	JHALA	JIGGED	JILLET
JESSIE	JETTED	JHALAS	JIGGER	JILLETS

JILLFLIRT	JINGLETS	JIRKINETS	JOBBERY	JODELLING
JILLION	JINGLIER	JIRRE	JOBBIE	JODELS
JILLIONS	JINGLIEST	JISM	JOBBIES	JODHPUR
JILLIONTH	JINGLING	JISMS	JOBBING	JODHPURS
JILLS	JINGLY	JISSOM	JOBBINGS	JOE
JILT	JINGO	JISSOMS	JOBCENTRE	JOES
JILTED	JINGOES	JITNEY	JOBE	JOEY
JILTER	JINGOISH	JITNEYS	JOBED	JOEYS
JILTERS	JINGOISM	JITTER	JOBERNOWL	JOG
JILTING	JINGOISMS	JITTERBUG	JOBES	JOGGED
JILTS	JINGOIST	JITTERED	JOBHOLDER	JOGGER
JIMCRACK	JINGOISTS	JITTERIER	JOBING	JOGGERS
JIMCRACKS	JINJILI	JITTERING	JOBLESS	JOGGING
JIMINY	JINJILIS	JITTERS	JOBNAME	JOGGINGS
JIMJAM	JINK	JITTERY	JOBNAMES	JOGGLE
JIMJAMS	JINKED	JIUJITSU	JOBS	JOGGLED
JIMMIE	JINKER	JIUJITSUS	JOBSEEKER	JOGGLER
JIMMIED	JINKERED	JIUJUTSU	JOBSHARE	JOGGLERS
JIMMIES	JINKERING	JIUJUTSUS	JOBSHARES	JOGGLES
JIMMINY	JINKERS	JIVE	JOBSWORTH	JOGGLING
JIMMY	JINKING	JIVEASS	JOCK	JOGPANTS
JIMMYING	JINKS	JIVED	JOCKETTE	JOGS
JIMP	JINN	JIVER	JOCKETTES	JOGTROT
JIMPER	JINNE	JIVERS	JOCKEY	JOGTROTS
JIMPEST	JINNEE	JIVES	JOCKEYED	JOHANNES
JIMPIER	JINNI	JIVEY	JOCKEYING	JOHN
JIMPIEST	JINNIS	JIVIER	JOCKEYISH	JOHNBOAT
JIMPLY	JINNS	JIVIEST	JOCKEYISM	JOHNBOATS
JIMPNESS	JINRIKSHA	JIVING	JOCKEYS	JOHNNIE
JIMPSON	JINS	JIVY	JOCKISH	JOHNNIES
JIMPY	JINX	JIZ	JOCKO	JOHNNY
JIMSON	JINXED	JIZZ	JOCKOS	JOHNS
JIN	JINXES	JIZZES	JOCKS	JOHNSON
JINGAL	JINXING	JNANA	JOCKSTRAP	JOHNSONS
JINGALL	JIPIJAPA	JNANAS	JOCKTELEG	JOIN
JINGALLS	JIPIJAPAS	JO	JOCO	JOINABLE
JINGALS	JIPYAPA	JOANNA	JOCOSE	JOINDER
JINGBANG	JIPYAPAS	JOANNAS	JOCOSELY	JOINDERS
JINGBANGS	JIRBLE	JOANNES	JOCOSITY	JOINED
JINGKO	JIRBLED	JOANNESES	JOCULAR	JOINER
JINGKOES	JIRBLES	JOB	JOCULARLY	JOINERIES
JINGLE	JIRBLING	JOBATION	JOCULATOR	JOINERS
JINGLED	JIRD	JOBATIONS	JOCUND	JOINERY
JINGLER	JIRDS	JOBBED	JOCUNDITY	JOINING
JINGLERS	JIRGA	JOBBER	JOCUNDLY	JOININGS
JINGLES	JIRGAS	JOBBERIES	JODEL	JOINS
JINGLET	JIRKINET	JOBBERS	JODELLED	JOINT

JOINTED	JOLLED	JOMON	JOSSERS	JOURNAL
JOINTEDLY	JOLLER	JOMOS	JOSSES	JOURNALED
JOINTER	JOLLERS	JONCANOE	JOSTLE	JOURNALS
JOINTERS	JOLLEY	JONCANOES	JOSTLED	JOURNEY
JOINTING	JOLLEYER	JONES	JOSTLER	JOURNEYED
JOINTINGS	JOLLEYERS	JONESED	JOSTLERS	JOURNEYER
JOINTLESS	JOLLEYING	JONESES	JOSTLES	JOURNEYS
JOINTLY	JOLLEYS	JONESING	JOSTLING	JOURNO
JOINTNESS	JOLLIED	JONG	JOSTLINGS	JOURNOS
JOINTRESS	JOLLIER	JONGLEUR	JOT	JOURS
JOINTS	JOLLIERS	JONGLEURS	JOTA	JOUST
JOINTURE	JOLLIES	JONGS	JOTAS	JOUSTED
JOINTURED	JOLLIEST	JONNOCK	JOTS	JOUSTER
JOINTURES	JOLLIFIED	JONNYCAKE	JOTTED	JOUSTERS
JOINTWEED	JOLLIFIES	JONQUIL	JOTTER	JOUSTING
JOINTWORM	JOLLIFY	JONQUILS	JOTTERS	JOUSTS
JOIST	JOLLILY	JONTIES	JOTTIER	JOVIAL
JOISTED	JOLLIMENT	JONTY	JOTTIEST	JOVIALITY
JOISTING	JOLLINESS	JOOK	JOTTING	JOVIALLY
JOISTS	JOLLING	JOOKED	JOTTINGS	JOVIALTY
JOJOBA	JOLLITIES	JOOKERIES	JOTTY	JOW
JOJOBAS	JOLLITY	JOOKERY	JOTUN	JOWAR
JOKE	JOLLOP	JOOKING	JOTUNN	JOWARI
JOKED	JOLLOPS	JOOKS	JOTUNNS	JOWARIS
JOKER	JOLLS	JOR	JOTUNS	JOWARS
JOKERS	JOLLY	JORAM	JOUAL	JOWED
JOKES	JOLLYBOAT	JORAMS	JOUALS	JOWING
JOKESMITH	JOLLYER	JORDAN	JOUGS	JOWL
JOKESOME	JOLLYERS	JORDANS	JOUISANCE	JOWLED
JOKESTER	JOLLYHEAD	JORDELOO	JOUK	JOWLER
JOKESTERS	JOLLYING	JORDELOOS	JOUKED	JOWLERS
JOKEY	JOLLYINGS	JORS	JOUKERIES	JOWLIER
JOKIER	JOLS	JORUM	JOUKERY	JOWLIEST
JOKIEST	JOLT	JORUMS	JOUKING	JOWLINESS
JOKILY	JOLTED	JOSEPH	JOUKS	JOWLING
JOKINESS	JOLTER	JOSEPHS	JOULE	JOWLS
JOKING	JOLTERS	JOSH	JOULED	JOWLY
JOKINGLY	JOLTHEAD	JOSHED	JOULES	JOWS
JOKOL	JOLTHEADS	JOSHER	JOULING	JOY
JOKY	JOLTIER	JOSHERS	JOUNCE	JOYANCE
JOL	JOLTIEST	JOSHES	JOUNCED	JOYANCES
JOLE	JOLTILY	JOSHING	JOUNCES	JOYED
JOLED	JOLTING	JOSHINGLY	JOUNCIER	JOYFUL
JOLES	JOLTINGLY	JOSKIN	JOUNCIEST	JOYFULLER
JOLING	JOLTS	JOSKINS	JOUNCING	JOYFULLY
JOLIOTIUM	JOLTY	JOSS	JOUNCY	JOYING
JOLL	JOMO	JOSSER	JOUR	JOYLESS

J

JOYLESSLY	JUDDERY	JUGGLERS	JUKEBOXES	JUMELLE
JOYOUS	JUDGE	JUGGLERY	JUKED	JUMELLES
JOYOUSLY	JUDGEABLE	JUGGLES	JUKES	JUMP
JOYPAD	JUDGED	JUGGLING	JUKING	JUMPABLE
JOYPADS	JUDGELESS	JUGGLINGS	JUKSKEI	JUMPED
JOYPOP	JUDGELIKE	JUGHEAD	JUKSKEIS	JUMPER
JOYPOPPED	JUDGEMENT	JUGHEADS	JUKU	JUMPERS
JOYPOPPER	JUDGER	JUGLET	JUKUS	JUMPIER
JOYPOPS	JUDGERS	JUGLETS	JULEP	JUMPIEST
JOYRIDDEN	JUDGES	JUGS	JULEPS	JUMPILY
JOYRIDE	JUDGESHIP	JUGSFUL	JULIENNE	JUMPINESS
JOYRIDER	JUDGING	JUGULA	JULIENNED	JUMPING
JOYRIDERS	JUDGINGLY	JUGULAR	JULIENNES	JUMPINGLY
JOYRIDES	JUDGMATIC	JUGULARS	JULIET	JUMPINGS
JOYRIDING	JUDGMENT	JUGULATE	JULIETS	JUMPOFF
JOYRODE	JUDGMENTS	JUGULATED	JUMAR	JUMPOFFS
JOYS	JUDICABLE	JUGULATES	JUMARED	JUMPS
JOYSTICK	JUDICATOR	JUGULUM	JUMARING	JUMPSUIT
JOYSTICKS	JUDICIAL	JUGUM	JUMARRED	JUMPSUITS
JUBA	JUDICIARY	JUGUMS	JUMARRING	JUMPY
JUBAS	JUDICIOUS	JUICE	JUMARS	JUN
JUBATE	JUDIES	JUICED	JUMART	JUNCATE
JUBBAH	JUDO	JUICEHEAD	JUMARTS	JUNCATES
JUBBAHS	JUDOGI	JUICELESS	JUMBAL	JUNCO
JUBE	JUDOGIS	JUICER	JUMBALS	JUNCOES
JUBES	JUDOIST	JUICERS	JUMBIE	JUNCOS
JUBHAH	JUDOISTS	JUICES	JUMBIES	JUNCTION
JUBHAHS	JUDOKA	JUICIER	JUMBLE	JUNCTIONS
JUBILANCE	JUDOKAS	JUICIEST	JUMBLED	JUNCTURAL
JUBILANCY	JUDOS	JUICILY	JUMBLER	JUNCTURE
JUBILANT	JUDS	JUICINESS	JUMBLERS	JUNCTURES
JUBILATE	JUDY	JUICING	JUMBLES	JUNCUS
JUBILATED	JUG	JUICY	JUMBLIER	JUNCUSES
JUBILATES	JUGA	JUJITSU	JUMBLIEST	JUNEATING
JUBILE	JUGAL	JUJITSUS	JUMBLING	JUNGLE
JUBILEE	JUGALS	JUJU	JUMBLY	JUNGLED
JUBILEES	JUGATE	JUJUBE	JUMBO	JUNGLEGYM
JUBILES	JUGFUL	JUJUBES	JUMBOISE	JUNGLES
JUCO	JUGFULS	JUJUISM	JUMBOISED	JUNGLI
JUCOS	JUGGED	JUJUISMS	JUMBOISES	JUNGLIER
JUD	JUGGING	JUJUIST	JUMBOIZE	JUNGLIEST
JUDAS	JUGGINGS	JUJUISTS	JUMBOIZED	JUNGLIS
JUDASES	JUGGINS	JUJUS	JUMBOIZES	JUNGLIST
JUDDER	JUGGINSES	JUJUTSU	JUMBOS	JUNGLISTS
JUDDERED	JUGGLE	JUJUTSUS	JUMBUCK	JUNGLY
JUDDERING	JUGGLED	JUKE	JUMBUCKS	JUNIOR
JUDDERS	JUGGLER	JUKEBOX	JUMBY	JUNIORATE

JUNIORITY	JUNKMAN	JURE	JUSTED	JUTS
JUNIORS	JUNKMEN	JUREL	JUSTER	JUTTED
JUNIPER	JUNKS	JURELS	JUSTERS	JUTTIED
JUNIPERS	JUNKY	JURIDIC	JUSTEST	JUTTIES
JUNK	JUNKYARD	JURIDICAL	JUSTICE	JUTTING
JUNKANOO	JUNKYARDS	JURIED	JUSTICER	JUTTINGLY
JUNKANOOS	JUNTA	JURIES	JUSTICERS	JUTTY
JUNKED	JUNTAS	JURIST	JUSTICES	JUTTYING
JUNKER	JUNTO	JURISTIC	JUSTICIAR	JUVE
JUNKERS	JUNTOS	JURISTS	JUSTIFIED	JUVENAL
JUNKET	JUPATI	JUROR	JUSTIFIER	JUVENALS
JUNKETED	JUPATIS	JURORS	JUSTIFIES	JUVENILE
JUNKETEER	JUPE	JURY	JUSTIFY	JUVENILES
JUNKETER	JUPES	JURYING	JUSTING	JUVENILIA
JUNKETERS	JUPON	JURYLESS	JUSTLE	JUVES
JUNKETING	JUPONS	JURYMAN	JUSTLED	JUVIE
JUNKETS	JURA	JURYMAST	JUSTLES	JUVIES
JUNKETTED	JURAL	JURYMASTS	JUSTLING	JUXTAPOSE
JUNKETTER	JURALLY	JURYMEN	JUSTLY	JYMOLD
JUNKIE	JURANT	JURYWOMAN	JUSTNESS	JYNX
JUNKIER	JURANTS	JURYWOMEN	JUSTS	JYNXES
JUNKIES	JURASSIC	JUS	JUT	
JUNKIEST	JURAT	JUSSIVE	JUTE	
JUNKINESS	JURATORY	JUSSIVES	JUTELIKE	
JUNKING	JURATS	JUST	JUTES	

J

K

KA	KACCHAS	KAGU	KAINITS	KALENDS
KAAL	KACHA	KAGUS	KAINS	KALES
KAAMA	KACHAHRI	KAHAL	KAIROMONE	KALEWIFE
KAAMAS	KACHAHRIS	KAHALS	KAIS	KALEWIVES
KAAS	KACHCHA	KAHAWAI	KAISER	KALEYARD
KAB	KACHERI	KAHAWAIS	KAISERDOM	KALEYARDS
KABAB	KACHERIS	KAHIKATEA	KAISERIN	KALI
KABABBED	KACHINA	KAHIKATOA	KAISERINS	KALIAN
KABABBING	KACHINAS	KAHUNA	KAISERISM	KALIANS
KABABS	KACK	KAHUNAS	KAISERS	KALIF
KABADDI	KACKS	KAI	KAIZEN	KALIFATE
KABADDIS	KADAITCHA	KAIAK	KAIZENS	KALIFATES
KABAKA	KADDISH	KAIAKED	KAJAWAH	KALIFS
KABAKAS	KADDISHES	KAIAKING	KAJAWAHS	KALIMBA
KABALA	KADDISHIM	KAIAKS	KAJEPUT	KALIMBAS
KABALAS	KADE	KAID	KAJEPUTS	KALINITE
KABALISM	KADES	KAIDS	KAK	KALINITES
KABALISMS	KADI	KAIE	KAKA	KALIPH
KABALIST	KADIS	KAIES	KAKAPO	KALIPHATE
KABALISTS	KAE	KAIF	KAKAPOS	KALIPHS
KABAR	KAED	KAIFS	KAKARIKI	KALIS
KABARS	KAEING	KAIK	KAKARIKIS	KALIUM
KABAYA	KAES	KAIKA	KAKAS	KALIUMS
KABAYAS	KAF	KAIKAI	KAKEMONO	KALLIDIN
KABBALA	KAFFIR	KAIKAIS	KAKEMONOS	KALLIDINS
KABBALAH	KAFFIRS	KAIKAS	KAKI	KALLITYPE
KABBALAHS	KAFFIYAH	KAIKAWAKA	KAKIEMON	KALMIA
KABBALAS	KAFFIYAHS	KAIKOMAKO	KAKIEMONS	KALMIAS
KABBALISM	KAFFIYEH	KAIKS	KAKIS	KALONG
KABBALIST	KAFFIYEHS	KAIL	KAKODYL	KALONGS
KABELE	KAFILA	KAILS	KAKODYLS	KALOOKI
KABELES	KAFILAS	KAILYAIRD	KAKS	KALOOKIE
KABELJOU	KAFIR	KAILYARD	KAKURO	KALOOKIES
KABELJOUS	KAFIRS	KAILYARDS	KAKUROS	KALOOKIS
KABELJOUW	KAFS	KAIM	KALAM	KALOTYPE
KABIKI	KAFTAN	KAIMAKAM	KALAMATA	KALOTYPES
KABIKIS	KAFTANS	KAIMAKAMS	KALAMATAS	KALPA
KABOB	KAGO	KAIMS	KALAMDAN	KALPAC
KABOBBED	KAGOOL	KAIN	KALAMDANS	KALPACS
KABOBBING	KAGOOLS	KAING	KALAMKARI	KALPAK
KABOBS	KAGOS	KAINGA	KALAMS	KALPAKS
KABS	KAGOUL	KAINGAS	KALANCHOE	KALPAS
KABUKI	KAGOULE	KAINIT	KALE	KALPIS
KABUKIS	KAGOULES	KAINITE	KALENDAR	KALPISES
KACCHA	KAGOULS	KAINITES	KALENDARS	KALSOMINE

KALUKI	KAMSINS	KANZUS	KARATE	KARTINGS
KALUKIS	KANA	KAOLIANG	KARATEIST	KARTS
KALUMPIT	KANAE	KAOLIANGS	KARATEKA	KARYOGAMY
KALUMPITS	KANAES	KAOLIN	KARATEKAS	KARYOGRAM
KALYPTRA	KANAKA	KAOLINE	KARATES	KARYOLOGY
KALYPTRAS	KANAKAS	KAOLINES	KARATS	KARYON
KAM	KANAMYCIN	KAOLINIC	KAREAREA	KARYONS
KAMA	KANAS	KAOLINISE	KAREAREAS	KARYOSOME
KAMAAINA	KANBAN	KAOLINITE	KARENGO	KARYOTIN
KAMAAINAS	KANBANS	KAOLINIZE	KARENGOS	KARYOTINS
KAMACITE	KANDIES	KAOLINS	KARITE	KARYOTYPE
KAMACITES	KANDY	KAON	KARITES	KARZIES
KAMAHI	KANE	KAONIC	KARK	KARZY
KAMAHIS	KANEH	KAONS	KARKED	KAS
KAMALA	KANEHS	KAPA	KARKING	KASBAH
KAMALAS	KANES	KAPAS	KARKS	KASBAHS
KAMAS	KANG	KAPH	KARMA	KASHA
KAME	KANGA	KAPHS	KARMAS	KASHAS
KAMEES	KANGAROO	KAPOK	KARMIC	KASHER
KAMEESES	KANGAROOS	KAPOKS	KARN	KASHERED
KAMEEZ	KANGAS	KAPPA	KARNS	KASHERING
KAMEEZES	KANGHA	KAPPAS	KARO	KASHERS
KAMELA	KANGHAS	KAPUKA	KAROO	KASHMIR
KAMELAS	KANGS	KAPUKAS	KAROOS	KASHMIRS
KAMERAD	KANJI	KAPUT	KARORO	KASHRUS
KAMERADED	KANJIS	KAPUTT	KAROROS	KASHRUSES
KAMERADS	KANS	KARA	KAROS	KASHRUT
KAMES	KANSES	KARABINER	KAROSHI	KASHRUTH
KAMI	KANT	KARAISM	KAROSHIS	KASHRUTHS
KAMICHI	KANTAR	KARAISMS	KAROSS	KASHRUTS
KAMICHIS	KANTARS	KARAIT	KAROSSES	KASME
KAMIK	KANTED	KARAITS	KARRI	KAT
KAMIKAZE	KANTELA	KARAKA	KARRIS	KATA
KAMIKAZES	KANTELAS	KARAKAS	KARROO	KATABASES
KAMIKS	KANTELE	KARAKIA	KARROOS	KATABASIS
KAMILA	KANTELES	KARAKIAS	KARSEY	KATABATIC
KAMILAS	KANTEN	KARAKUL	KARSEYS	KATABOLIC
KAMIS	KANTENS	KARAKULS	KARSIES	KATAKANA
KAMISES	KANTHA	KARAMU	KARST	KATAKANAS
KAMME	KANTHAS	KARAMUS	KARSTIC	KATAL
KAMOKAMO	KANTIKOY	KARANGA	KARSTIFY	KATALS
KAMOKAMOS	KANTIKOYS	KARANGAED	KARSTS	KATANA
KAMPONG	KANTING	KARANGAS	KARSY	KATANAS
KAMPONGS	KANTS	KARAOKE	KART	KATAS
KAMSEEN	KANUKA	KARAOKES	KARTER	KATCHINA
KAMSEENS	KANUKAS	KARAS	KARTERS	KATCHINAS
KAMSIN	KANZU	KARAT	KARTING	KATCINA

K

KATCINAS

KATCINAS	KAWAKAWA	KEB	KEDGIEST	KEENINGS
KATHAK	KAWAKAWAS	KEBAB	KEDGING	KEENLY
KATHAKALI	KAWAS	KEBABBED	KEDGY	KEENNESS
KATHAKS	KAWAU	KEBABBING	KEDS	KEENO
KATHARSES	KAWAUS	KEBABS	KEECH	KEENOS
KATHARSIS	KAWED	KEBAR	KEECHES	KEENS
KATHODAL	KAWING	KEBARS	KEEF	KEEP
KATHODE	KAWS	KEBBED	KEEFS	KEEPABLE
KATHODES	KAY	KEBBIE	KEEK	KEEPER
KATHODIC	KAYAK	KEBBIES	KEEKED	KEEPERS
KATI	KAYAKED	KEBBING	KEEKER	KEEPING
KATION	KAYAKER	KEBBOCK	KEEKERS	KEEPINGS
KATIONS	KAYAKERS	KEBBOCKS	KEEKING	KEEPNET
KATIPO	KAYAKING	KEBBUCK	KEEKS	KEEPNETS
KATIPOS	KAYAKINGS	KEBBUCKS	KEEL	KEEPS
KATIS	KAYAKS	KEBELE	KEELAGE	KEEPSAKE
KATORGA	KAYLE	KEBELES	KEELAGES	KEEPSAKES
KATORGAS	KAYLES	KEBLAH	KEELBOAT	KEEPSAKY
KATS	KAYLIED	KEBLAHS	KEELBOATS	KEESHOND
KATSURA	KAYO	KEBOB	KEELED	KEESHONDS
KATSURAS	KAYOED	KEBOBBED	KEELER	KEESTER
KATTI	KAYOES	KEBOBBING	KEELERS	KEESTERS
KATTIS	KAYOING	KEBOBS	KEELHALE	KEET
KATYDID	KAYOINGS	KEBS	KEELHALED	KEETS
KATYDIDS	KAYOS	KECK	KEELHALES	KEEVE
KAUGH	KAYS	KECKED	KEELHAUL	KEEVES
KAUGHS	KAZACHKI	KECKING	KEELHAULS	KEF
KAUMATUA	KAZACHOC	KECKLE	KEELIE	KEFFEL
KAUMATUAS	KAZACHOCS	KECKLED	KEELIES	KEFFELS
KAUPAPA	KAZACHOK	KECKLES	KEELING	KEFFIYAH
KAUPAPAS	KAZATSKI	KECKLING	KEELINGS	KEFFIYAHS
KAURI	KAZATSKY	KECKLINGS	KEELIVINE	KEFFIYEH
KAURIES	KAZATZKA	KECKS	KEELLESS	KEFFIYEHS
KAURIS	KAZATZKAS	KECKSES	KEELMAN	KEFIR
KAURU	KAZI	KECKSIES	KEELMEN	KEFIRS
KAURUS	KAZILLION	KECKSY	KEELS	KEFS
KAURY	KAZIS	KED	KEELSON	KEFTEDES
KAVA	KAZOO	KEDDAH	KEELSONS	KEFUFFLE
KAVAKAVA	KAZOOS	KEDDAHS	KEELYVINE	KEFUFFLED
KAVAKAVAS	KBAR	KEDGE	KEEMA	KEFUFFLES
KAVAL	KBARS	KEDGED	KEEMAS	KEG
KAVALS	KEA	KEDGER	KEEN	KEGELER
KAVAS	KEAS	KEDGEREE	KEENED	KEGELERS
KAVASS	KEASAR	KEDGEREES	KEENER	KEGGED
KAVASSES	KEASARS	KEDGERS	KEENERS	KEGGER
KAW	KEAVIE	KEDGES	KEENEST	KEGGERS
KAWA	KEAVIES	KEDGIER	KEENING	KEGGING

KEGLER	KELPY	KENNELMAN	KERAMIC	KERMISES
KEGLERS	KELSON	KENNELMEN	KERAMICS	KERN
KEGLING	KELSONS	KENNELS	KERATIN	KERNE
KEGLINGS	KELT	KENNER	KERATINS	KERNED
KEGS	KELTER	KENNERS	KERATITIS	KERNEL
KEHUA	KELTERS	KENNET	KERATOID	KERNELED
KEHUAS	KELTIE	KENNETS	KERATOMA	KERNELING
KEIGHT	KELTIES	KENNETT	KERATOMAS	KERNELLED
KEIR	KELTS	KENNETTED	KERATOSE	KERNELLY
KEIREN	KELTY	KENNETTS	KERATOSES	KERNELS
KEIRENS	KELVIN	KENNING	KERATOSIC	KERNES
KEIRETSU	KELVINS	KENNINGS	KERATOSIS	KERNING
KEIRETSUS	KEMB	KENO	KERATOTIC	KERNINGS
KEIRIN	KEMBED	KENOS	KERB	KERNISH
KEIRINS	KEMBING	KENOSES	KERBAYA	KERNITE
KEIRS	KEMBLA	KENOSIS	KERBAYAS	KERNITES
KEISTER	KEMBLAS	KENOSISES	KERBED	KERNS
KEISTERS	KEMBO	KENOTIC	KERBING	KERO
KEITLOA	KEMBOED	KENOTICS	KERBINGS	KEROGEN
KEITLOAS	KEMBOING	KENOTRON	KERBS	KEROGENS
KEKENO	KEMBOS	KENOTRONS	KERBSIDE	KEROS
KEKENOS	KEMBS	KENS	KERBSIDES	KEROSENE
KEKERENGU	KEMP	KENSPECK	KERBSTONE	KEROSENES
KEKS	KEMPED	KENT	KERCHIEF	KEROSINE
KEKSYE	KEMPER	KENTE	KERCHIEFS	KEROSINES
KEKSYES	KEMPERS	KENTED	KERCHOO	KERPLUNK
KELEP	KEMPIER	KENTES	KEREL	KERPLUNKS
KELEPS	KEMPIEST	KENTIA	KERELS	KERRIA
KELIM	KEMPING	KENTIAS	KERERU	KERRIAS
KELIMS	KEMPINGS	KENTING	KERERUS	KERRIES
KELL	KEMPLE	KENTLEDGE	KERF	KERRY
KELLAUT	KEMPLES	KENTS	KERFED	KERSEY
KELLAUTS	KEMPS	KEP	KERFING	KERSEYS
KELLIES	KEMPT	KEPHALIC	KERFLOOEY	KERVE
KELLS	KEMPY	KEPHALICS	KERFS	KERVED
KELLY	KEN	KEPHALIN	KERFUFFLE	KERVES
KELOID	KENAF	KEPHALINS	KERKIER	KERVING
KELOIDAL	KENAFS	KEPHIR	KERKIEST	KERYGMA
KELOIDS	KENCH	KEPHIRS	KERKY	KERYGMAS
KELP	KENCHES	KEPI	KERMA	KERYGMATA
KELPED	KENDO	KEPIS	KERMAS	KESAR
KELPER	KENDOS	KEPPED	KERMES	KESARS
KELPERS	KENNED	KEPPEN	KERMESITE	KESH
KELPIE	KENNEL	KEPPING	KERMESS	KESHES
KELPIES	KENNELED	KEPPIT	KERMESSE	KEST
KELPING	KENNELING	KEPS	KERMESSES	KESTING
KELPS	KENNELLED	KEPT	KERMIS	KESTREL

KESTRELS	KEWLEST	KEYWORKER	KHATS	KHOUM
KESTS	KEWPIE	KGOTLA	KHAYA	KHOUMS
KET	KEWPIES	KGOTLAS	KHAYAL	KHUD
KETA	KEX	KHADDAR	KHAYALS	KHUDS
KETAMINE	KEXES	KHADDARS	KHAYAS	KHURTA
KETAMINES	KEY	KHADI	KHAZEN	KHURTAS
KETAS	KEYBOARD	KHADIS	KHAZENIM	KHUSKHUS
KETCH	KEYBOARDS	KHAF	KHAZENS	KHUTBAH
KETCHES	KEYBUGLE	KHAFS	KHAZI	KHUTBAHS
KETCHING	KEYBUGLES	KHAKI	KHAZIS	KI
KETCHUP	KEYBUTTON	KHAKILIKE	KHEDA	KIAAT
KETCHUPS	KEYCARD	KHAKIS	KHEDAH	KIAATS
KETE	KEYCARDS	KHALAT	KHEDAHS	KIANG
KETENE	KEYED	KHALATS	KHEDAS	KIANGS
KETENES	KEYHOLE	KHALIF	KHEDIVA	KIAUGH
KETES	KEYHOLES	KHALIFA	KHEDIVAL	KIAUGHS
KETMIA	KEYING	KHALIFAH	KHEDIVAS	KIBBE
KETMIAS	KEYINGS	KHALIFAHS	KHEDIVATE	KIBBEH
KETO	KEYLESS	KHALIFAS	KHEDIVE	KIBBEHS
KETOGENIC	KEYLINE	KHALIFAT	KHEDIVES	KIBBES
KETOL	KEYLINES	KHALIFATE	KHEDIVIAL	KIBBI
KETOLS	KEYLOGGER	KHALIFATS	KHET	KIBBIS
KETONE	KEYNOTE	KHALIFS	KHETH	KIBBITZ
KETONEMIA	KEYNOTED	KHAMSEEN	KHETHS	KIBBITZED
KETONES	KEYNOTER	KHAMSEENS	KHETS	KIBBITZER
KETONIC	KEYNOTERS	KHAMSIN	KHI	KIBBITZES
KETONURIA	KEYNOTES	KHAMSINS	KHILAFAT	KIBBLE
KETOSE	KEYNOTING	KHAN	KHILAFATS	KIBBLED
KETOSES	KEYPAD	KHANATE	KHILAT	KIBBLES
KETOSIS	KEYPADS	KHANATES	KHILATS	KIBBLING
KETOTIC	KEYPAL	KHANDA	KHILIM	KIBBUTZ
KETOXIME	KEYPALS	KHANDAS	KHILIMS	KIBBUTZIM
KETOXIMES	KEYPUNCH	KHANGA	KHIMAR	KIBE
KETS	KEYRING	KHANGAS	KHIMARS	KIBEI
KETTLE	KEYS	KHANJAR	KHIRKAH	KIBEIS
KETTLEFUL	KEYSET	KHANJARS	KHIRKAHS	KIBES
KETTLES	KEYSETS	KHANS	KHIS	KIBITKA
KETUBAH	KEYSTER	KHANSAMA	KHODJA	KIBITKAS
KETUBAHS	KEYSTERS	KHANSAMAH	KHODJAS	KIBITZ
KETUBOT	KEYSTONE	KHANSAMAS	KHOJA	KIBITZED
KETUBOTH	KEYSTONED	KHANUM	KHOJAS	KIBITZER
KEVEL	KEYSTONES	KHANUMS	KHOR	KIBITZERS
KEVELS	KEYSTROKE	KHAPH	KHORS	KIBITZES
KEVIL	KEYWAY	KHAPHS	KHOTBAH	KIBITZING
KEVILS	KEYWAYS	KHARIF	KHOTBAHS	KIBLA
KEWL	KEYWORD	KHARIFS	KHOTBEH	KIBLAH
KEWLER	KEYWORDS	KHAT	KHOTBEHS	KIBLAHS

KIBLAS	KIDDIES	KIDVIDS	KILLASES	KILOGRAM
KIBOSH	KIDDING	KIEF	KILLCOW	KILOGRAMS
KIBOSHED	KIDDINGLY	KIEFS	KILLCOWS	KILOGRAY
KIBOSHES	KIDDISH	KIEKIE	KILLCROP	KILOGRAYS
KIBOSHING	KIDDLE	KIEKIES	KILLCROPS	KILOHERTZ
KICK	KIDDLES	KIELBASA	KILLDEE	KILOJOULE
KICKABLE	KIDDO	KIELBASAS	KILLDEER	KILOLITER
KICKABOUT	KIDDOES	KIELBASI	KILLDEERS	KILOLITRE
KICKBACK	KIDDOS	KIELBASY	KILLDEES	KILOMETER
KICKBACKS	KIDDUSH	KIER	KILLED	KILOMETRE
KICKBALL	KIDDUSHES	KIERIE	KILLER	KILOMOLE
KICKBALLS	KIDDY	KIERIES	KILLERS	KILOMOLES
KICKBOARD	KIDDYING	KIERS	KILLICK	KILOPOND
KICKBOX	KIDDYWINK	KIESELGUR	KILLICKS	KILOPONDS
KICKBOXED	KIDEL	KIESERITE	KILLIE	KILORAD
KICKBOXER	KIDELS	KIESTER	KILLIES	KILORADS
KICKBOXES	KIDGE	KIESTERS	KILLIFISH	KILOS
KICKDOWN	KIDGIE	KIEV	KILLING	KILOTON
KICKDOWNS	KIDGIER	KIEVE	KILLINGLY	KILOTONNE
KICKED	KIDGIEST	KIEVES	KILLINGS	KILOTONS
KICKER	KIDGLOVE	KIEVS	KILLJOY	KILOVOLT
KICKERS	KIDLET	KIF	KILLJOYS	KILOVOLTS
KICKFLIP	KIDLETS	KIFF	KILLOCK	KILOWATT
KICKFLIPS	KIDLIKE	KIFS	KILLOCKS	KILOWATTS
KICKIER	KIDLING	KIGHT	KILLOGIE	KILP
KICKIEST	KIDLINGS	KIGHTS	KILLOGIES	KILPS
KICKING	KIDNAP	KIKE	KILLS	KILT
KICKOFF	KIDNAPED	KIKES	KILLUT	KILTED
KICKOFFS	KIDNAPEE	KIKOI	KILLUTS	KILTER
KICKOUT	KIDNAPEES	KIKOIS	KILN	KILTERS
KICKOUTS	KIDNAPER	KIKUMON	KILNED	KILTIE
KICKS	KIDNAPERS	KIKUMONS	KILNING	KILTIES
KICKSHAW	KIDNAPING	KIKUYU	KILNS	KILTING
KICKSHAWS	KIDNAPPED	KIKUYUS	KILO	KILTINGS
KICKSTAND	KIDNAPPEE	KILD	KILOBAR	KILTLIKE
KICKSTART	KIDNAPPER	KILDERKIN	KILOBARS	KILTS
KICKUP	KIDNAPS	KILERG	KILOBASE	KILTY
KICKUPS	KIDNEY	KILERGS	KILOBASES	KIMBO
KICKY	KIDNEYS	KILEY	KILOBAUD	KIMBOED
KID	KIDOLOGY	KILEYS	KILOBAUDS	KIMBOING
KIDDED	KIDS	KILIM	KILOBIT	KIMBOS
KIDDER	KIDSKIN	KILIMS	KILOBITS	KIMCHEE
KIDDERS	KIDSKINS	KILL	KILOBYTE	KIMCHEES
KIDDIE	KIDSTAKES	KILLABLE	KILOBYTES	KIMCHI
KIDDIED	KIDULT	KILLADAR	KILOCURIE	KIMCHIS
KIDDIER	KIDULTS	KILLADARS	KILOCYCLE	KIMMER
KIDDIERS	KIDVID	KILLAS	KILOGAUSS	KIMMERS

KIMONO	KINESCOPE	KINGSHIP	KIPPA	KIRNING
KIMONOED	KINESES	KINGSHIPS	KIPPAGE	KIRNS
KIMONOS	KINESIC	KINGSIDE	KIPPAGES	KIRPAN
KIN	KINESICS	KINGSIDES	KIPPAS	KIRPANS
KINA	KINESIS	KINGSNAKE	KIPPED	KIRRI
KINAKINA	KINETIC	KINGWOOD	KIPPEN	KIRRIS
KINAKINAS	KINETICAL	KINGWOODS	KIPPER	KIRS
KINARA	KINETICS	KININ	KIPPERED	KIRSCH
KINARAS	KINETIN	KININS	KIPPERER	KIRSCHES
KINAS	KINETINS	KINK	KIPPERERS	KIRTAN
KINASE	KINFOLK	KINKAJOU	KIPPERING	KIRTANS
KINASES	KINFOLKS	KINKAJOUS	KIPPERS	KIRTLE
KINCHIN	KING	KINKED	KIPPING	KIRTLED
KINCHINS	KINGBIRD	KINKIER	KIPPS	KIRTLES
KINCOB	KINGBIRDS	KINKIEST	KIPS	KIS
KINCOBS	KINGBOLT	KINKILY	KIPSKIN	KISAN
KIND	KINGBOLTS	KINKINESS	KIPSKINS	KISANS
KINDA	KINGCRAFT	KINKING	KIPUNJI	KISH
KINDED	KINGCUP	KINKLE	KIPUNJIS	KISHES
KINDER	KINGCUPS	KINKLES	KIR	KISHKA
KINDERS	KINGDOM	KINKS	KIRANA	KISHKAS
KINDEST	KINGDOMED	KINKY	KIRANAS	KISHKE
KINDIE	KINGDOMS	KINLESS	KIRBEH	KISHKES
KINDIES	KINGED	KINO	KIRBEHS	KISMAT
KINDING	KINGFISH	KINONE	KIRBIGRIP	KISMATS
KINDLE	KINGHOOD	KINONES	KIRBY	KISMET
KINDLED	KINGHOODS	KINOS	KIRIGAMI	KISMETIC
KINDLER	KINGING	KINRED	KIRIGAMIS	KISMETS
KINDLERS	KINGKLIP	KINREDS	KIRIMON	KISS
KINDLES	KINGKLIPS	KINS	KIRIMONS	KISSABLE
KINDLESS	KINGLE	KINSFOLK	KIRK	KISSABLY
KINDLIER	KINGLES	KINSFOLKS	KIRKED	KISSAGRAM
KINDLIEST	KINGLESS	KINSHIP	KIRKING	KISSED
KINDLILY	KINGLET	KINSHIPS	KIRKINGS	KISSEL
KINDLING	KINGLETS	KINSMAN	KIRKMAN	KISSELS
KINDLINGS	KINGLIER	KINSMEN	KIRKMEN	KISSER
KINDLY	KINGLIEST	KINSWOMAN	KIRKS	KISSERS
KINDNESS	KINGLIKE	KINSWOMEN	KIRKTON	KISSES
KINDRED	KINGLING	KINTLEDGE	KIRKTONS	KISSIER
KINDREDS	KINGLINGS	KIORE	KIRKWARD	KISSIEST
KINDS	KINGLY	KIORES	KIRKYAIRD	KISSING
KINDY	KINGMAKER	KIOSK	KIRKYARD	KISSINGS
KINE	KINGPIN	KIOSKS	KIRKYARDS	KISSOGRAM
KINEMA	KINGPINS	KIP	KIRMESS	KISSY
KINEMAS	KINGPOST	KIPE	KIRMESSES	KIST
KINEMATIC	KINGPOSTS	KIPES	KIRN	KISTED
KINES	KINGS	KIPP	KIRNED	KISTFUL

KISTFULS	KITTENED	KLEENEX	KLUDGEY	KNAPWEED
KISTING	KITTENING	KLEENEXES	KLUDGIER	KNAPWEEDS
KISTS	KITTENISH	KLENDUSIC	KLUDGIEST	KNAR
KISTVAEN	KITTENS	KLEPHT	KLUDGING	KNARL
KISTVAENS	KITTENY	KLEPHTIC	KLUDGY	KNARLIER
KIT	KITTIES	KLEPHTISM	KLUGE	KNARLIEST
KITBAG	KITTING	KLEPHTS	KLUGED	KNARLS
KITBAGS	KITTIWAKE	KLEPTO	KLUGES	KNARLY
KITCHEN	KITTLE	KLEPTOS	KLUGING	KNARRED
KITCHENED	KITTLED	KLETT	KLUTZ	KNARRIER
KITCHENER	KITTLER	KLETTS	KLUTZES	KNARRIEST
KITCHENET	KITTLES	KLEZMER	KLUTZIER	KNARRING
KITCHENS	KITTLEST	KLEZMERS	KLUTZIEST	KNARRY
KITE	KITTLIER	KLEZMORIM	KLUTZY	KNARS
KITEBOARD	KITTLIEST	KLICK	KLYSTRON	KNAUR
KITED	KITTLING	KLICKS	KLYSTRONS	KNAURS
KITELIKE	KITTLY	KLIEG	KNACK	KNAVE
KITENGE	KITTUL	KLIK	KNACKED	KNAVERIES
KITENGES	KITTULS	KLIKS	KNACKER	KNAVERY
KITER	KITTY	KLINKER	KNACKERED	KNAVES
KITERS	KITUL	KLINKERS	KNACKERS	KNAVESHIP
KITES	KITULS	KLINOSTAT	KNACKERY	KNAVISH
KITH	KIVA	KLIPDAS	KNACKIER	KNAVISHLY
KITHARA	KIVAS	KLIPDASES	KNACKIEST	KNAWE
KITHARAS	KIWI	KLISTER	KNACKING	KNAWEL
KITHE	KIWIFRUIT	KLISTERS	KNACKISH	KNAWELS
KITHED	KIWIS	KLONDIKE	KNACKS	KNAWES
KITHES	KLANG	KLONDIKED	KNACKY	KNEAD
KITHING	KLANGS	KLONDIKER	KNAG	KNEADABLE
KITHS	KLAP	KLONDIKES	KNAGGIER	KNEADED
KITING	KLAPPED	KLONDYKE	KNAGGIEST	KNEADER
KITINGS	KLAPPING	KLONDYKED	KNAGGY	KNEADERS
KITLING	KLAPS	KLONDYKER	KNAGS	KNEADING
KITLINGS	KLATCH	KLONDYKES	KNAIDEL	KNEADS
KITS	KLATCHES	KLONG	KNAIDLACH	KNEE
KITSCH	KLATSCH	KLONGS	KNAP	KNEECAP
KITSCHES	KLATSCHES	KLOOCH	KNAPPED	KNEECAPS
KITSCHIER	KLAVERN	KLOOCHES	KNAPPER	KNEED
KITSCHIFY	KLAVERNS	KLOOCHMAN	KNAPPERS	KNEEHOLE
KITSCHILY	KLAVIER	KLOOCHMEN	KNAPPING	KNEEHOLES
KITSCHY	KLAVIERS	KLOOF	KNAPPLE	KNEEING
KITSET	KLAXON	KLOOFS	KNAPPLED	KNEEJERK
KITSETS	KLAXONED	KLOOTCH	KNAPPLES	KNEEL
KITTED	KLAXONING	KLOOTCHES	KNAPPLING	KNEELED
KITTEL	KLAXONS	KLUDGE	KNAPS	KNEELER
KITTELS	KLEAGLE	KLUDGED	KNAPSACK	KNEELERS
KITTEN	KLEAGLES	KLUDGES	KNAPSACKS	KNEELING

K

KNEELS
KNEEPAD
KNEEPADS
KNEEPAN
KNEEPANS
KNEEPIECE
KNEES
KNEESIES
KNEESOCK
KNEESOCKS
KNEIDEL
KNEIDELS
KNEIDLACH
KNELL
KNELLED
KNELLING
KNELLS
KNELT
KNESSET
KNESSETS
KNEVELL
KNEVELLED
KNEVELLS
KNEW
KNICKER
KNICKERED
KNICKERS
KNICKS
KNIFE
KNIFED
KNIFELESS
KNIFELIKE
KNIFEMAN
KNIFEMEN
KNIFER
KNIFEREST
KNIFERS
KNIFES
KNIFING
KNIFINGS
KNIGHT
KNIGHTAGE
KNIGHTED
KNIGHTING
KNIGHTLY
KNIGHTS
KNIPHOFIA

KNISH
KNISHES
KNIT
KNITCH
KNITCHES
KNITS
KNITTABLE
KNITTED
KNITTER
KNITTERS
KNITTING
KNITTINGS
KNITTLE
KNITTLES
KNITWEAR
KNITWEARS
KNIVE
KNIVED
KNIVES
KNIVING
KNOB
KNOBBED
KNOBBER
KNOBBERS
KNOBBIER
KNOBBIEST
KNOBBING
KNOBBLE
KNOBBLED
KNOBBLES
KNOBBLIER
KNOBBLING
KNOBBLY
KNOBBY
KNOBHEAD
KNOBHEADS
KNOBLIKE
KNOBS
KNOBSTICK
KNOCK
KNOCKDOWN
KNOCKED
KNOCKER
KNOCKERS
KNOCKING
KNOCKINGS
KNOCKLESS

KNOCKOFF
KNOCKOFFS
KNOCKOUT
KNOCKOUTS
KNOCKS
KNOLL
KNOLLED
KNOLLER
KNOLLERS
KNOLLIER
KNOLLIEST
KNOLLING
KNOLLS
KNOLLY
KNOP
KNOPPED
KNOPS
KNOSP
KNOSPS
KNOT
KNOTGRASS
KNOTHOLE
KNOTHOLES
KNOTLESS
KNOTLIKE
KNOTS
KNOTTED
KNOTTER
KNOTTERS
KNOTTIER
KNOTTIEST
KNOTTILY
KNOTTING
KNOTTINGS
KNOTTY
KNOTWEED
KNOTWEEDS
KNOTWORK
KNOTWORKS
KNOUT
KNOUTED
KNOUTING
KNOUTS
KNOW
KNOWABLE
KNOWE
KNOWER

KNOWERS
KNOWES
KNOWHOW
KNOWHOWS
KNOWING
KNOWINGER
KNOWINGLY
KNOWINGS
KNOWLEDGE
KNOWN
KNOWNS
KNOWS
KNUB
KNUBBIER
KNUBBIEST
KNUBBLE
KNUBBLED
KNUBBLES
KNUBBLIER
KNUBBLING
KNUBBLY
KNUBBY
KNUBS
KNUCKLE
KNUCKLED
KNUCKLER
KNUCKLERS
KNUCKLES
KNUCKLIER
KNUCKLING
KNUCKLY
KNUR
KNURL
KNURLED
KNURLIER
KNURLIEST
KNURLING
KNURLINGS
KNURLS
KNURLY
KNURR
KNURRS
KNURS
KNUT
KNUTS
KO
KOA

KOALA
KOALAS
KOAN
KOANS
KOAP
KOAPS
KOAS
KOB
KOBAN
KOBANG
KOBANGS
KOBANS
KOBO
KOBOLD
KOBOLDS
KOBOS
KOBS
KOCHIA
KOCHIAS
KOEKOEA
KOEKOEAS
KOEL
KOELS
KOFF
KOFFS
KOFTA
KOFTAS
KOFTGAR
KOFTGARI
KOFTGARIS
KOFTGARS
KOFTWORK
KOFTWORKS
KOGAL
KOGALS
KOHA
KOHANIM
KOHAS
KOHEKOHE
KOHEKOHES
KOHEN
KOHL
KOHLRABI
KOHLRABIS
KOHLS
KOI
KOINE

K

KOINES	KOMATIKS	KOORI	KORORAS	KOUMYSES
KOIS	KOMBU	KOORIES	KOROS	KOUMYSS
KOJI	KOMBUS	KOORIS	KOROWAI	KOUMYSSES
KOJIS	KOMISSAR	KOP	KOROWAIS	KOUPREY
KOKA	KOMISSARS	KOPASETIC	KORS	KOUPREYS
KOKAKO	KOMITAJI	KOPECK	KORU	KOURA
KOKAKOS	KOMITAJIS	KOPECKS	KORUN	KOURAS
KOKANEE	KOMONDOR	KOPEK	KORUNA	KOURBASH
KOKANEES	KOMONDORS	KOPEKS	KORUNAS	KOUROI
KOKAS	KON	KOPH	KORUNY	KOUROS
KOKER	KONAKI	KOPHS	KORUS	KOUSKOUS
KOKERS	KONAKIS	KOPIYKA	KOS	KOUSSO
KOKIRI	KONBU	KOPIYKAS	KOSES	KOUSSOS
KOKIRIS	KONBUS	KOPIYOK	KOSHER	KOW
KOKOBEH	KOND	KOPJE	KOSHERED	KOWHAI
KOKOPU	KONDO	KOPJES	KOSHERING	KOWHAIS
KOKOPUS	KONDOS	KOPPA	KOSHERS	KOWS
KOKOWAI	KONEKE	KOPPAS	KOSMOS	KOWTOW
KOKOWAIS	KONEKES	KOPPIE	KOSMOSES	KOWTOWED
KOKRA	KONFYT	KOPPIES	KOSS	KOWTOWER
KOKRAS	KONFYTS	KOPS	KOSSES	KOWTOWERS
KOKUM	KONGONI	KOR	KOTARE	KOWTOWING
KOKUMS	KONIMETER	KORA	KOTARES	KOWTOWS
KOLA	KONINI	KORAI	KOTCH	KRAAL
KOLACKY	KONINIS	KORARI	KOTCHED	KRAALED
KOLAS	KONIOLOGY	KORARIS	KOTCHES	KRAALING
KOLBASI	KONISCOPE	KORAS	KOTCHING	KRAALS
KOLBASIS	KONK	KORAT	KOTO	KRAB
KOLBASSI	KONKED	KORATS	KOTOS	KRABS
KOLBASSIS	KONKING	KORE	KOTOW	KRAFT
KOLHOZ	KONKS	KORERO	KOTOWED	KRAFTS
KOLHOZES	KONNING	KOREROED	KOTOWER	KRAIT
KOLHOZY	KONS	KOREROING	KOTOWERS	KRAITS
KOLINSKI	KOODOO	KOREROS	KOTOWING	KRAKEN
KOLINSKY	KOODOOS	KORES	KOTOWS	KRAKENS
KOLKHOS	KOOK	KORFBALL	KOTTABOS	KRAKOWIAK
KOLKHOSES	KOOKED	KORFBALLS	KOTUKU	KRAMERIA
KOLKHOSY	KOOKIE	KORIMAKO	KOTUKUS	KRAMERIAS
KOLKHOZ	KOOKIER	KORIMAKOS	KOTWAL	KRANG
KOLKHOZES	KOOKIEST	KORKIR	KOTWALS	KRANGS
KOLKHOZY	KOOKILY	KORKIRS	KOULAN	KRANS
KOLKOZ	KOOKINESS	KORMA	KOULANS	KRANSES
KOLKOZES	KOOKING	KORMAS	KOUMIS	KRANTZ
KOLKOZY	KOOKS	KORO	KOUMISES	KRANTZES
KOLO	KOOKY	KOROMIKO	KOUMISS	KRANZ
KOLOS	KOOLAH	KOROMIKOS	KOUMISSES	KRANZES
KOMATIK	KOOLAHS	KORORA	KOUMYS	KRATER

KRATERS	KRUBI	KUEH	KUNA	KUTUS
KRAUT	KRUBIS	KUES	KUNDALINI	KUVASZ
KRAUTS	KRUBUT	KUFI	KUNE	KUVASZOK
KREASOTE	KRUBUTS	KUFIS	KUNEKUNE	KUZU
KREASOTED	KRULLER	KUFIYAH	KUNEKUNES	KUZUS
KREASOTES	KRULLERS	KUFIYAHS	KUNJOOS	KVAS
KREATINE	KRUMHORN	KUGEL	KUNKAR	KVASES
KREATINES	KRUMHORNS	KUGELS	KUNKARS	KVASS
KREEP	KRUMKAKE	KUIA	KUNKUR	KVASSES
KREEPS	KRUMKAKES	KUIAS	KUNKURS	KVELL
KREESE	KRUMMHOLZ	KUKRI	KUNZITE	KVELLED
KREESED	KRUMMHORN	KUKRIS	KUNZITES	KVELLING
KREESES	KRUMPER	KUKU	KURBASH	KVELLS
KREESING	KRUMPERS	KUKUS	KURBASHED	KVETCH
KREMLIN	KRUMPING	KULA	KURBASHES	KVETCHED
KREMLINS	KRUMPINGS	KULAK	KURFUFFLE	KVETCHER
KRENG	KRUNK	KULAKI	KURGAN	KVETCHERS
KRENGS	KRUNKED	KULAKS	KURGANS	KVETCHES
KREOSOTE	KRUNKS	KULAN	KURI	KVETCHIER
KREOSOTED	KRYOLITE	KULANS	KURIS	KVETCHILY
KREOSOTES	KRYOLITES	KULAS	KURRAJONG	KVETCHING
KREPLACH	KRYOLITH	KULBASA	KURRE	KVETCHY
KREPLECH	KRYOLITHS	KULBASAS	KURRES	KWACHA
KREUTZER	KRYOMETER	KULFI	KURSAAL	KWACHAS
KREUTZERS	KRYPSES	KULFIS	KURSAALS	KWAITO
KREUZER	KRYPSIS	KULTUR	KURTA	KWAITOS
KREUZERS	KRYPTON	KULTURS	KURTAS	KWANZA
KREWE	KRYPTONS	KUMARA	KURTOSES	KWANZAS
KREWES	KRYTRON	KUMARAHOU	KURTOSIS	KWELA
KRILL	KRYTRONS	KUMARAS	KURU	KWELAS
KRILLS	KSAR	KUMARI	KURUS	KY
KRIMMER	KSARS	KUMARIS	KURVEY	KYACK
KRIMMERS	KUCCHA	KUMBALOI	KURVEYED	KYACKS
KRIS	KUCCHAS	KUMERA	KURVEYING	KYAK
KRISED	KUCHCHA	KUMERAS	KURVEYOR	KYAKS
KRISES	KUCHEN	KUMIKUMI	KURVEYORS	KYANG
KRISING	KUCHENS	KUMIKUMIS	KURVEYS	KYANGS
KROMESKY	KUDLIK	KUMISS	KUSSO	KYANISE
KRONA	KUDLIKS	KUMISSES	KUSSOS	KYANISED
KRONE	KUDO	KUMITE	KUTA	KYANISES
KRONEN	KUDOS	KUMITES	KUTAS	KYANISING
KRONER	KUDOSES	KUMMEL	KUTCH	KYANITE
KRONOR	KUDU	KUMMELS	KUTCHA	KYANITES
KRONUR	KUDUS	KUMQUAT	KUTCHES	KYANITIC
KROON	KUDZU	KUMQUATS	KUTI	KYANIZE
KROONI	KUDZUS	KUMYS	KUTIS	KYANIZED
KROONS	KUE	KUMYSES	KUTU	KYANIZES

KYANIZING	KYE	KYLLOSIS	KYNE	KYTE
KYAR	KYES	KYLOE	KYOGEN	KYTES
KYARS	KYLE	KYLOES	KYOGENS	KYTHE
KYAT	KYLES	KYMOGRAM	KYPE	KYTHED
KYATS	KYLICES	KYMOGRAMS	KYPES	KYTHES
KYBO	KYLIE	KYMOGRAPH	KYPHOSES	KYTHING
KYBOS	KYLIES	KYND	KYPHOSIS	KYU
KYBOSH	KYLIKES	KYNDE	KYPHOTIC	KYUS
KYBOSHED	KYLIN	KYNDED	KYRIE	
KYBOSHES	KYLINS	KYNDES	KYRIELLE	
KYBOSHING	KYLIX	KYNDING	KYRIELLES	
KYDST	KYLLOSES	KYNDS	KYRIES	

LA	LABILITY	LABURNUM	LACK	LACTATES
LAAGER	LABIS	LABURNUMS	LACKADAY	LACTATING
LAAGERED	LABISES	LABYRINTH	LACKED	LACTATION
LAAGERING	LABIUM	LAC	LACKER	LACTEAL
LAAGERS	LABLAB	LACCOLITE	LACKERED	LACTEALLY
LAARI	LABLABS	LACCOLITH	LACKERING	LACTEALS
LAARIS	LABOR	LACE	LACKERS	LACTEAN
LAB	LABORED	LACEBARK	LACKEY	LACTEOUS
LABARA	LABOREDLY	LACEBARKS	LACKEYED	LACTIC
LABARUM	LABORER	LACED	LACKEYING	LACTIFIC
LABARUMS	LABORERS	LACELESS	LACKEYS	LACTIVISM
LABDA	LABORING	LACELIKE	LACKING	LACTIVIST
LABDACISM	LABORIOUS	LACER	LACKLAND	LACTONE
LABDANUM	LABORISM	LACERABLE	LACKLANDS	LACTONES
LABDANUMS	LABORISMS	LACERANT	LACKS	LACTONIC
LABDAS	LABORIST	LACERATE	LACMUS	LACTOSE
LABEL	LABORISTS	LACERATED	LACMUSES	LACTOSES
LABELABLE	LABORITE	LACERATES	LACONIC	LACUNA
LABELED	LABORITES	LACERS	LACONICAL	LACUNAE
LABELER	LABORS	LACERTIAN	LACONISM	LACUNAL
LABELERS	LABOUR	LACERTID	LACONISMS	LACUNAR
LABELING	LABOURED	LACERTIDS	LACQUER	LACUNARIA
LABELLA	LABOURER	LACERTINE	LACQUERED	LACUNARS
LABELLATE	LABOURERS	LACES	LACQUERER	LACUNARY
LABELLED	LABOURING	LACET	LACQUERS	LACUNAS
LABELLER	LABOURISM	LACETS	LACQUEY	LACUNATE
LABELLERS	LABOURIST	LACEWING	LACQUEYED	LACUNE
LABELLING	LABOURS	LACEWINGS	LACQUEYS	LACUNES
LABELLIST	LABRA	LACEWOOD	LACRIMAL	LACUNOSE
LABELLOID	LABRADOR	LACEWOODS	LACRIMALS	LACY
LABELLUM	LABRADORS	LACEWORK	LACRIMARY	LAD
LABELMATE	LABRAL	LACEWORKS	LACRIMOSO	LADANUM
LABELS	LABRET	LACEY	LACROSSE	LADANUMS
LABIA	LABRETS	LACHES	LACROSSES	LADDER
LABIAL	LABRID	LACHESES	LACRYMAL	LADDERED
LABIALISE	LABRIDS	LACHRYMAL	LACRYMALS	LADDERING
LABIALISM	LABROID	LACIER	LACS	LADDERS
LABIALITY	LABROIDS	LACIEST	LACTAM	LADDERY
LABIALIZE	LABROSE	LACILY	LACTAMS	LADDIE
LABIALLY	LABRUM	LACINESS	LACTARIAN	LADDIES
LABIALS	LABRUMS	LACING	LACTARY	LADDISH
LABIATE	LABRUSCA	LACINGS	LACTASE	LADDISM
LABIATED	LABRYS	LACINIA	LACTASES	LADDISMS
LABIATES	LABRYSES	LACINIAE	LACTATE	LADE
LABILE	LABS	LACINIATE	LACTATED	LADED

LADEN	LADYFY	LAGGER	LAIGH	LAKEBED
LADENED	LADYFYING	LAGGERS	LAIGHER	LAKEBEDS
LADENING	LADYHOOD	LAGGIN	LAIGHEST	LAKED
LADENS	LADYHOODS	LAGGING	LAIGHS	LAKEFRONT
LADER	LADYISH	LAGGINGLY	LAIK	LAKELAND
LADERS	LADYISM	LAGGINGS	LAIKA	LAKELANDS
LADES	LADYISMS	LAGGINS	LAIKAS	LAKELET
LADETTE	LADYKIN	LAGNAPPE	LAIKED	LAKELETS
LADETTES	LADYKINS	LAGNAPPES	LAIKER	LAKELIKE
LADHOOD	LADYLIKE	LAGNIAPPE	LAIKERS	LAKEPORT
LADHOODS	LADYLOVE	LAGOMORPH	LAIKING	LAKEPORTS
LADIES	LADYLOVES	LAGOON	LAIKS	LAKER
LADIFIED	LADYPALM	LAGOONAL	LAIN	LAKERS
LADIFIES	LADYPALMS	LAGOONS	LAIPSE	LAKES
LADIFY	LADYSHIP	LAGRIMOSO	LAIPSED	LAKESHORE
LADIFYING	LADYSHIPS	LAGS	LAIPSES	LAKESIDE
LADING	LAER	LAGUNA	LAIPSING	LAKESIDES
LADINGS	LAERED	LAGUNAS	LAIR	LAKH
LADINO	LAERING	LAGUNE	LAIRAGE	LAKHS
LADINOS	LAERS	LAGUNES	LAIRAGES	LAKIER
LADLE	LAESIE	LAH	LAIRD	LAKIEST
LADLED	LAETARE	LAHAR	LAIRDLY	LAKIN
LADLEFUL	LAETARES	LAHARS	LAIRDS	LAKING
LADLEFULS	LAETRILE	LAHS	LAIRDSHIP	LAKINGS
LADLER	LAETRILES	LAIC	LAIRED	LAKINS
LADLERS	LAEVIGATE	LAICAL	LAIRIER	LAKISH
LADLES	LAEVO	LAICALLY	LAIRIEST	LAKSA
LADLING	LAEVULIN	LAICH	LAIRING	LAKSAS
LADRON	LAEVULINS	LAICHS	LAIRISE	LAKY
LADRONE	LAEVULOSE	LAICISE	LAIRISED	LALANG
LADRONES	LAG	LAICISED	LAIRISES	LALANGS
LADRONS	LAGAN	LAICISES	LAIRISING	LALDIE
LADS	LAGANS	LAICISING	LAIRIZE	LALDIES
LADY	LAGENA	LAICISM	LAIRIZED	LALDY
LADYBIRD	LAGENAS	LAICISMS	LAIRIZES	LALIQUE
LADYBIRDS	LAGEND	LAICITIES	LAIRIZING	LALIQUES
LADYBOY	LAGENDS	LAICITY	LAIRS	LALL
LADYBOYS	LAGER	LAICIZE	LAIRY	LALLAN
LADYBUG	LAGERED	LAICIZED	LAISSE	LALLAND
LADYBUGS	LAGERING	LAICIZES	LAISSES	LALLANDS
LADYCOW	LAGERS	LAICIZING	LAITANCE	LALLANS
LADYCOWS	LAGGARD	LAICS	LAITANCES	LALLATION
LADYFIED	LAGGARDLY	LAID	LAITH	LALLED
LADYFIES	LAGGARDS	LAIDED	LAITHLY	LALLING
LADYFISH	LAGGED	LAIDING	LAITIES	LALLINGS
LADYFLIES	LAGGEN	LAIDLY	LAITY	LALLS
LADYFLY	LAGGENS	LAIDS	LAKE	LALLYGAG

LALLYGAGS

LALLYGAGS	LAMBY	LAMINGTON	LAMPOONED	LANCING
LAM	LAME	LAMININ	LAMPOONER	LAND
LAMA	LAMEBRAIN	LAMININS	LAMPOONS	LANDAMMAN
LAMAISTIC	LAMED	LAMINITIS	LAMPPOST	LANDAU
LAMANTIN	LAMEDH	LAMINOSE	LAMPPOSTS	LANDAULET
LAMANTINS	LAMEDHS	LAMINOUS	LAMPREY	LANDAUS
LAMAS	LAMEDS	LAMISH	LAMPREYS	LANDBOARD
LAMASERAI	LAMELLA	LAMISTER	LAMPS	LANDDAMNE
LAMASERY	LAMELLAE	LAMISTERS	LAMPSHADE	LANDDROS
LAMB	LAMELLAR	LAMITER	LAMPSHELL	LANDDROST
LAMBADA	LAMELLAS	LAMITERS	LAMPUKA	LANDE
LAMBADAS	LAMELLATE	LAMMED	LAMPUKAS	LANDED
LAMBAST	LAMELLOID	LAMMER	LAMPUKI	LANDER
LAMBASTE	LAMELLOSE	LAMMERS	LAMPUKIS	LANDERS
LAMBASTED	LAMELY	LAMMIE	LAMPYRID	LANDES
LAMBASTES	LAMENESS	LAMMIES	LAMPYRIDS	LANDFALL
LAMBASTS	LAMENT	LAMMIGER	LAMS	LANDFALLS
LAMBDA	LAMENTED	LAMMIGERS	LAMSTER	LANDFILL
LAMBDAS	LAMENTER	LAMMING	LAMSTERS	LANDFILLS
LAMBDOID	LAMENTERS	LAMMINGS	LANA	LANDFORCE
LAMBED	LAMENTING	LAMMY	LANAI	LANDFORM
LAMBENCY	LAMENTS	LAMP	LANAIS	LANDFORMS
LAMBENT	LAMER	LAMPAD	LANAS	LANDGRAB
LAMBENTLY	LAMES	LAMPADARY	LANATE	LANDGRABS
LAMBER	LAMEST	LAMPADIST	LANATED	LANDGRAVE
LAMBERS	LAMETER	LAMPADS	LANCE	LANDING
LAMBERT	LAMETERS	LAMPAS	LANCED	LANDINGS
LAMBERTS	LAMIA	LAMPASES	LANCEGAY	LANDLADY
LAMBIE	LAMIAE	LAMPASSE	LANCEGAYS	LANDLER
LAMBIER	LAMIAS	LAMPASSES	LANCEJACK	LANDLERS
LAMBIES	LAMIGER	LAMPBLACK	LANCELET	LANDLESS
LAMBIEST	LAMIGERS	LAMPBRUSH	LANCELETS	LANDLINE
LAMBING	LAMINA	LAMPED	LANCEOLAR	LANDLINES
LAMBINGS	LAMINABLE	LAMPER	LANCER	LANDLOPER
LAMBITIVE	LAMINAE	LAMPERN	LANCERS	LANDLORD
LAMBKILL	LAMINAL	LAMPERNS	LANCES	LANDLORDS
LAMBKILLS	LAMINALS	LAMPERS	LANCET	LANDMAN
LAMBKIN	LAMINAR	LAMPERSES	LANCETED	LANDMARK
LAMBKINS	LAMINARIA	LAMPHOLE	LANCETS	LANDMARKS
LAMBLIKE	LAMINARIN	LAMPHOLES	LANCEWOOD	LANDMASS
LAMBLING	LAMINARY	LAMPING	LANCH	LANDMEN
LAMBLINGS	LAMINAS	LAMPINGS	LANCHED	LANDMINE
LAMBOYS	LAMINATE	LAMPION	LANCHES	LANDMINED
LAMBRUSCO	LAMINATED	LAMPIONS	LANCHING	LANDMINES
LAMBS	LAMINATES	LAMPLIGHT	LANCIERS	LANDOWNER
LAMBSKIN	LAMINATOR	LAMPLIT	LANCIFORM	LANDRACE
LAMBSKINS	LAMING	LAMPOON	LANCINATE	LANDRACES

326 | two to nine letter words

LANDRAIL	LANGSPELS	LANOLINS	LAPILLI	LAR
LANDRAILS	LANGSPIEL	LANOSE	LAPILLUS	LARBOARD
LANDS	LANGSYNE	LANOSITY	LAPIN	LARBOARDS
LANDSCAPE	LANGSYNES	LANT	LAPINS	LARCENER
LANDSHARK	LANGUAGE	LANTANA	LAPIS	LARCENERS
LANDSIDE	LANGUAGED	LANTANAS	LAPISES	LARCENIES
LANDSIDES	LANGUAGES	LANTERLOO	LAPJE	LARCENIST
LANDSKIP	LANGUE	LANTERN	LAPJES	LARCENOUS
LANDSKIPS	LANGUED	LANTERNED	LAPPED	LARCENY
LANDSLEIT	LANGUES	LANTERNS	LAPPEL	LARCH
LANDSLID	LANGUET	LANTHANON	LAPPELS	LARCHEN
LANDSLIDE	LANGUETS	LANTHANUM	LAPPER	LARCHES
LANDSLIP	LANGUETTE	LANTHORN	LAPPERED	LARD
LANDSLIPS	LANGUID	LANTHORNS	LAPPERING	LARDALITE
LANDSMAN	LANGUIDLY	LANTS	LAPPERS	LARDED
LANDSMEN	LANGUISH	LANTSKIP	LAPPET	LARDER
LANDWARD	LANGUOR	LANTSKIPS	LAPPETED	LARDERER
LANDWARDS	LANGUORS	LANUGO	LAPPETS	LARDERERS
LANDWIND	LANGUR	LANUGOS	LAPPIE	LARDERS
LANDWINDS	LANGURS	LANX	LAPPIES	LARDIER
LANE	LANIARD	LANYARD	LAPPING	LARDIEST
LANELY	LANIARDS	LANYARDS	LAPPINGS	LARDING
LANES	LANIARIES	LAODICEAN	LAPS	LARDLIKE
LANEWAY	LANIARY	LAOGAI	LAPSABLE	LARDON
LANEWAYS	LANITAL	LAOGAIS	LAPSANG	LARDONS
LANG	LANITALS	LAP	LAPSANGS	LARDOON
LANGAHA	LANK	LAPBOARD	LAPSE	LARDOONS
LANGAHAS	LANKED	LAPBOARDS	LAPSED	LARDS
LANGAR	LANKER	LAPDOG	LAPSER	LARDY
LANGARS	LANKEST	LAPDOGS	LAPSERS	LARE
LANGER	LANKIER	LAPEL	LAPSES	LAREE
LANGERED	LANKIEST	LAPELED	LAPSIBLE	LAREES
LANGERS	LANKILY	LAPELLED	LAPSING	LARES
LANGEST	LANKINESS	LAPELS	LAPSTONE	LARGANDO
LANGLAUF	LANKING	LAPFUL	LAPSTONES	LARGE
LANGLAUFS	LANKLY	LAPFULS	LAPSTRAKE	LARGELY
LANGLEY	LANKNESS	LAPHELD	LAPSTREAK	LARGEN
LANGLEYS	LANKS	LAPIDARY	LAPSUS	LARGENED
LANGOUSTE	LANKY	LAPIDATE	LAPTOP	LARGENESS
LANGRAGE	LANNER	LAPIDATED	LAPTOPS	LARGENING
LANGRAGES	LANNERET	LAPIDATES	LAPTRAY	LARGENS
LANGREL	LANNERETS	LAPIDEOUS	LAPTRAYS	LARGER
LANGRELS	LANNERS	LAPIDES	LAPWING	LARGES
LANGRIDGE	LANOLATED	LAPIDIFIC	LAPWINGS	LARGESS
LANGSHAN	LANOLIN	LAPIDIFY	LAPWORK	LARGESSE
LANGSHANS	LANOLINE	LAPIDIST	LAPWORKS	LARGESSES
LANGSPEL	LANOLINES	LAPIDISTS	LAQUEARIA	LARGEST

LARGHETTO	LARRUPING	LASINGS	LATCHING	LATEXES
LARGISH	LARRUPS	LASKET	LATCHKEY	LATH
LARGITION	LARS	LASKETS	LATCHKEYS	LATHE
LARGO	LARUM	LASQUE	LATE	LATHED
LARGOS	LARUMS	LASQUES	LATECOMER	LATHEE
LARI	LARVA	LASS	LATED	LATHEES
LARIAT	LARVAE	LASSES	LATEEN	LATHEN
LARIATED	LARVAL	LASSI	LATEENER	LATHER
LARIATING	LARVAS	LASSIE	LATEENERS	LATHERED
LARIATS	LARVATE	LASSIES	LATEENS	LATHERER
LARINE	LARVATED	LASSIS	LATELY	LATHERERS
LARIS	LARVICIDE	LASSITUDE	LATEN	LATHERIER
LARK	LARVIFORM	LASSLORN	LATENCE	LATHERING
LARKED	LARVIKITE	LASSO	LATENCES	LATHERS
LARKER	LARYNGAL	LASSOCK	LATENCIES	LATHERY
LARKERS	LARYNGALS	LASSOCKS	LATENCY	LATHES
LARKIER	LARYNGEAL	LASSOED	LATENED	LATHI
LARKIEST	LARYNGES	LASSOER	LATENESS	LATHIER
LARKINESS	LARYNX	LASSOERS	LATENING	LATHIEST
LARKING	LARYNXES	LASSOES	LATENS	LATHING
LARKISH	LAS	LASSOING	LATENT	LATHINGS
LARKS	LASAGNA	LASSOS	LATENTLY	LATHIS
LARKSOME	LASAGNAS	LASSU	LATENTS	LATHLIKE
LARKSPUR	LASAGNE	LASSUS	LATER	LATHS
LARKSPURS	LASAGNES	LAST	LATERAD	LATHWORK
LARKY	LASCAR	LASTAGE	LATERAL	LATHWORKS
LARMIER	LASCARS	LASTAGES	LATERALED	LATHY
LARMIERS	LASE	LASTBORN	LATERALLY	LATHYRISM
LARN	LASED	LASTBORNS	LATERALS	LATHYRUS
LARNAKES	LASER	LASTED	LATERBORN	LATI
LARNAX	LASERDISC	LASTER	LATERISE	LATICES
LARNED	LASERDISK	LASTERS	LATERISED	LATICIFER
LARNEY	LASERS	LASTING	LATERISES	LATICLAVE
LARNEYS	LASERWORT	LASTINGLY	LATERITE	LATIFONDI
LARNIER	LASES	LASTINGS	LATERITES	LATIGO
LARNIEST	LASH	LASTLY	LATERITIC	LATIGOES
LARNING	LASHED	LASTS	LATERIZE	LATIGOS
LARNS	LASHER	LAT	LATERIZED	LATILLA
LAROID	LASHERS	LATAH	LATERIZES	LATILLAS
LARRIGAN	LASHES	LATAHS	LATESCENT	LATIMERIA
LARRIGANS	LASHING	LATAKIA	LATEST	LATINA
LARRIKIN	LASHINGLY	LATAKIAS	LATESTS	LATINAS
LARRIKINS	LASHINGS	LATCH	LATEWAKE	LATINISE
LARRUP	LASHINS	LATCHED	LATEWAKES	LATINISED
LARRUPED	LASHKAR	LATCHES	LATEWOOD	LATINISES
LARRUPER	LASHKARS	LATCHET	LATEWOODS	LATINITY
LARRUPERS	LASING	LATCHETS	LATEX	LATINIZE

LATINIZED	LAUDABLE	LAUNDERER	LAVED	LAWFUL
LATINIZES	LAUDABLY	LAUNDERS	LAVEER	LAWFULLY
LATINO	LAUDANUM	LAUNDRESS	LAVEERED	LAWGIVER
LATINOS	LAUDANUMS	LAUNDRIES	LAVEERING	LAWGIVERS
LATISH	LAUDATION	LAUNDRY	LAVEERS	LAWGIVING
LATITANCY	LAUDATIVE	LAUNDS	LAVEMENT	LAWIN
LATITANT	LAUDATOR	LAURA	LAVEMENTS	LAWINE
LATITAT	LAUDATORS	LAURAE	LAVENDER	LAWINES
LATITATS	LAUDATORY	LAURAS	LAVENDERS	LAWING
LATITUDE	LAUDED	LAUREATE	LAVER	LAWINGS
LATITUDES	LAUDER	LAUREATED	LAVEROCK	LAWINS
LATKE	LAUDERS	LAUREATES	LAVEROCKS	LAWK
LATKES	LAUDING	LAUREL	LAVERS	LAWKS
LATOSOL	LAUDS	LAURELED	LAVES	LAWLAND
LATOSOLIC	LAUF	LAURELING	LAVING	LAWLANDS
LATOSOLS	LAUFS	LAURELLED	LAVISH	LAWLESS
LATRANT	LAUGH	LAURELS	LAVISHED	LAWLESSLY
LATRATION	LAUGHABLE	LAURIC	LAVISHER	LAWLIKE
LATRIA	LAUGHABLY	LAURYL	LAVISHERS	LAWMAKER
LATRIAS	LAUGHED	LAURYLS	LAVISHES	LAWMAKERS
LATRINE	LAUGHER	LAUWINE	LAVISHEST	LAWMAKING
LATRINES	LAUGHERS	LAUWINES	LAVISHING	LAWMAN
LATROCINY	LAUGHFUL	LAV	LAVISHLY	LAWMEN
LATRON	LAUGHIER	LAVA	LAVOLT	LAWMONGER
LATRONS	LAUGHIEST	LAVABO	LAVOLTA	LAWN
LATS	LAUGHING	LAVABOES	LAVOLTAED	LAWNED
LATTE	LAUGHINGS	LAVABOS	LAVOLTAS	LAWNIER
LATTEN	LAUGHLINE	LAVAFORM	LAVOLTED	LAWNIEST
LATTENS	LAUGHS	LAVAGE	LAVOLTING	LAWNMOWER
LATTER	LAUGHSOME	LAVAGES	LAVOLTS	LAWNS
LATTERLY	LAUGHTER	LAVALAVA	LAVRA	LAWNY
LATTES	LAUGHTERS	LAVALAVAS	LAVRAS	LAWS
LATTICE	LAUGHY	LAVALIER	LAVROCK	LAWSUIT
LATTICED	LAUNCE	LAVALIERE	LAVROCKS	LAWSUITS
LATTICES	LAUNCED	LAVALIERS	LAVS	LAWYER
LATTICING	LAUNCES	LAVALIKE	LAVVIES	LAWYERED
LATTICINI	LAUNCH	LAVANDIN	LAVVY	LAWYERING
LATTICINO	LAUNCHED	LAVANDINS	LAW	LAWYERLY
LATTIN	LAUNCHER	LAVAS	LAWBOOK	LAWYERS
LATTINS	LAUNCHERS	LAVASH	LAWBOOKS	LAX
LATU	LAUNCHES	LAVASHES	LAWCOURT	LAXATION
LAUAN	LAUNCHING	LAVATERA	LAWCOURTS	LAXATIONS
LAUANS	LAUNCHPAD	LAVATERAS	LAWED	LAXATIVE
LAUCH	LAUNCING	LAVATION	LAWER	LAXATIVES
LAUCHING	LAUND	LAVATIONS	LAWEST	LAXATOR
LAUCHS	LAUNDER	LAVATORY	LAWFARE	LAXATORS
LAUD	LAUNDERED	LAVE	LAWFARES	LAXER

LAXES

LAXES
LAXEST
LAXISM
LAXISMS
LAXIST
LAXISTS
LAXITIES
LAXITY
LAXLY
LAXNESS
LAXNESSES
LAY
LAYABOUT
LAYABOUTS
LAYAWAY
LAYAWAYS
LAYBACK
LAYBACKED
LAYBACKS
LAYDEEZ
LAYED
LAYER
LAYERAGE
LAYERAGES
LAYERED
LAYERING
LAYERINGS
LAYERS
LAYETTE
LAYETTES
LAYIN
LAYING
LAYINGS
LAYINS
LAYLOCK
LAYLOCKS
LAYMAN
LAYMEN
LAYOFF
LAYOFFS
LAYOUT
LAYOUTS
LAYOVER
LAYOVERS
LAYPEOPLE
LAYPERSON
LAYS

LAYSHAFT
LAYSHAFTS
LAYSTALL
LAYSTALLS
LAYTIME
LAYTIMES
LAYUP
LAYUPS
LAYWOMAN
LAYWOMEN
LAZAR
LAZARET
LAZARETS
LAZARETTE
LAZARETTO
LAZARS
LAZE
LAZED
LAZES
LAZIED
LAZIER
LAZIES
LAZIEST
LAZILY
LAZINESS
LAZING
LAZO
LAZOED
LAZOES
LAZOING
LAZOS
LAZULI
LAZULIS
LAZULITE
LAZULITES
LAZURITE
LAZURITES
LAZY
LAZYBONES
LAZYING
LAZYISH
LAZZARONE
LAZZARONI
LAZZI
LAZZO
LEA
LEACH

LEACHABLE
LEACHATE
LEACHATES
LEACHED
LEACHER
LEACHERS
LEACHES
LEACHIER
LEACHIEST
LEACHING
LEACHINGS
LEACHOUR
LEACHOURS
LEACHY
LEAD
LEADED
LEADEN
LEADENED
LEADENING
LEADENLY
LEADENS
LEADER
LEADERENE
LEADERS
LEADIER
LEADIEST
LEADING
LEADINGLY
LEADINGS
LEADLESS
LEADMAN
LEADMEN
LEADOFF
LEADOFFS
LEADPLANT
LEADS
LEADSCREW
LEADSMAN
LEADSMEN
LEADWORK
LEADWORKS
LEADWORT
LEADWORTS
LEADY
LEAF
LEAFAGE
LEAFAGES

LEAFBUD
LEAFBUDS
LEAFED
LEAFERIES
LEAFERY
LEAFIER
LEAFIEST
LEAFINESS
LEAFING
LEAFLESS
LEAFLET
LEAFLETED
LEAFLETER
LEAFLETS
LEAFLIKE
LEAFS
LEAFSTALK
LEAFWORM
LEAFWORMS
LEAFY
LEAGUE
LEAGUED
LEAGUER
LEAGUERED
LEAGUERS
LEAGUES
LEAGUING
LEAK
LEAKAGE
LEAKAGES
LEAKED
LEAKER
LEAKERS
LEAKIER
LEAKIEST
LEAKILY
LEAKINESS
LEAKING
LEAKLESS
LEAKPROOF
LEAKS
LEAKY
LEAL
LEALER
LEALEST
LEALLY
LEALTIES

LEALTY
LEAM
LEAMED
LEAMING
LEAMS
LEAN
LEANED
LEANER
LEANERS
LEANEST
LEANING
LEANINGS
LEANLY
LEANNESS
LEANS
LEANT
LEANY
LEAP
LEAPED
LEAPER
LEAPEROUS
LEAPERS
LEAPFROG
LEAPFROGS
LEAPING
LEAPOROUS
LEAPROUS
LEAPS
LEAPT
LEAR
LEARE
LEARED
LEARES
LEARIER
LEARIEST
LEARINESS
LEARING
LEARN
LEARNABLE
LEARNED
LEARNEDLY
LEARNER
LEARNERS
LEARNING
LEARNINGS
LEARNS
LEARNT

LEARS	LEAVIEST	LECTURER	LEERED	LEGAL
LEARY	LEAVING	LECTURERS	LEERIER	LEGALESE
LEAS	LEAVINGS	LECTURES	LEERIEST	LEGALESES
LEASABLE	LEAVY	LECTURING	LEERILY	LEGALISE
LEASE	LEAZE	LECTURN	LEERINESS	LEGALISED
LEASEBACK	LEAZES	LECTURNS	LEERING	LEGALISER
LEASED	LEBBEK	LECYTHI	LEERINGLY	LEGALISES
LEASEHOLD	LEBBEKS	LECYTHIS	LEERINGS	LEGALISM
LEASER	LEBEN	LECYTHUS	LEERS	LEGALISMS
LEASERS	LEBENS	LED	LEERY	LEGALIST
LEASES	LEBKUCHEN	LEDDEN	LEES	LEGALISTS
LEASH	LECANORA	LEDDENS	LEESE	LEGALITY
LEASHED	LECANORAS	LEDGE	LEESES	LEGALIZE
LEASHES	LECCIES	LEDGED	LEESING	LEGALIZED
LEASHING	LECCY	LEDGER	LEET	LEGALIZER
LEASING	LECH	LEDGERED	LEETLE	LEGALIZES
LEASINGS	LECHAIM	LEDGERING	LEETS	LEGALLY
LEASOW	LECHAIMS	LEDGERS	LEETSPEAK	LEGALS
LEASOWE	LECHAYIM	LEDGES	LEEWARD	LEGATARY
LEASOWED	LECHAYIMS	LEDGIER	LEEWARDLY	LEGATE
LEASOWES	LECHED	LEDGIEST	LEEWARDS	LEGATED
LEASOWING	LECHER	LEDGY	LEEWAY	LEGATEE
LEASOWS	LECHERED	LEDUM	LEEWAYS	LEGATEES
LEAST	LECHERIES	LEDUMS	LEEZE	LEGATES
LEASTS	LECHERING	LEE	LEFT	LEGATINE
LEASTWAYS	LECHEROUS	LEEAR	LEFTE	LEGATING
LEASTWISE	LECHERS	LEEARS	LEFTER	LEGATION
LEASURE	LECHERY	LEEBOARD	LEFTEST	LEGATIONS
LEASURES	LECHES	LEEBOARDS	LEFTIE	LEGATO
LEAT	LECHING	LEECH	LEFTIES	LEGATOR
LEATHER	LECHWE	LEECHDOM	LEFTISH	LEGATORS
LEATHERED	LECHWES	LEECHDOMS	LEFTISM	LEGATOS
LEATHERN	LECITHIN	LEECHED	LEFTISMS	LEGEND
LEATHERS	LECITHINS	LEECHEE	LEFTIST	LEGENDARY
LEATHERY	LECTERN	LEECHEES	LEFTISTS	LEGENDISE
LEATS	LECTERNS	LEECHES	LEFTMOST	LEGENDIST
LEAVE	LECTIN	LEECHING	LEFTMOSTS	LEGENDIZE
LEAVED	LECTINS	LEECHLIKE	LEFTOVER	LEGENDRY
LEAVEN	LECTION	LEED	LEFTOVERS	LEGENDS
LEAVENED	LECTIONS	LEEING	LEFTS	LEGER
LEAVENING	LECTOR	LEEK	LEFTWARD	LEGERING
LEAVENOUS	LECTORATE	LEEKS	LEFTWARDS	LEGERINGS
LEAVENS	LECTORS	LEEP	LEFTWING	LEGERITY
LEAVER	LECTOTYPE	LEEPED	LEFTY	LEGERS
LEAVERS	LECTRESS	LEEPING	LEG	LEGES
LEAVES	LECTURE	LEEPS	LEGACIES	LEGGE
LEAVIER	LECTURED	LEER	LEGACY	LEGGED

LEGGER	LEGROOMS	LEISURE	LEMONIEST	LENIENTLY
LEGGERS	LEGS	LEISURED	LEMONING	LENIENTS
LEGGES	LEGSIDE	LEISURELY	LEMONISH	LENIFIED
LEGGIE	LEGSIDES	LEISURES	LEMONLIKE	LENIFIES
LEGGIER	LEGUAAN	LEISURING	LEMONS	LENIFY
LEGGIERO	LEGUAANS	LEITMOTIF	LEMONWOOD	LENIFYING
LEGGIES	LEGUAN	LEITMOTIV	LEMONY	LENIS
LEGGIEST	LEGUANS	LEK	LEMPIRA	LENITE
LEGGIN	LEGUME	LEKE	LEMPIRAS	LENITED
LEGGINESS	LEGUMES	LEKGOTLA	LEMUR	LENITES
LEGGING	LEGUMIN	LEKGOTLAS	LEMURES	LENITIES
LEGGINGED	LEGUMINS	LEKKED	LEMURIAN	LENITING
LEGGINGS	LEGWARMER	LEKKER	LEMURIANS	LENITION
LEGGINS	LEGWEAR	LEKKING	LEMURINE	LENITIONS
LEGGISM	LEGWEARS	LEKKINGS	LEMURINES	LENITIVE
LEGGISMS	LEGWORK	LEKS	LEMURLIKE	LENITIVES
LEGGY	LEGWORKS	LEKU	LEMUROID	LENITY
LEGHORN	LEHAIM	LEKVAR	LEMUROIDS	LENO
LEGHORNS	LEHAIMS	LEKVARS	LEMURS	LENOS
LEGIBLE	LEHAYIM	LEKYTHI	LEND	LENS
LEGIBLY	LEHAYIMS	LEKYTHOI	LENDABLE	LENSE
LEGION	LEHR	LEKYTHOS	LENDER	LENSED
LEGIONARY	LEHRJAHRE	LEKYTHUS	LENDERS	LENSES
LEGIONED	LEHRS	LEMAN	LENDING	LENSING
LEGIONS	LEHUA	LEMANS	LENDINGS	LENSLESS
LEGISLATE	LEHUAS	LEME	LENDS	LENSMAN
LEGIST	LEI	LEMED	LENES	LENSMEN
LEGISTS	LEIDGER	LEMEL	LENG	LENT
LEGIT	LEIDGERS	LEMELS	LENGED	LENTANDO
LEGITIM	LEIGER	LEMES	LENGER	LENTEN
LEGITIMS	LEIGERS	LEMING	LENGEST	LENTI
LEGITS	LEIOMYOMA	LEMMA	LENGING	LENTIC
LEGLAN	LEIPOA	LEMMAS	LENGS	LENTICEL
LEGLANS	LEIPOAS	LEMMATA	LENGTH	LENTICELS
LEGLEN	LEIR	LEMMATISE	LENGTHEN	LENTICLE
LEGLENS	LEIRED	LEMMATIZE	LENGTHENS	LENTICLES
LEGLESS	LEIRING	LEMMING	LENGTHFUL	LENTICULE
LEGLET	LEIRS	LEMMINGS	LENGTHIER	LENTIFORM
LEGLETS	LEIS	LEMNISCAL	LENGTHILY	LENTIGO
LEGLIKE	LEISH	LEMNISCI	LENGTHMAN	LENTIL
LEGLIN	LEISHER	LEMNISCUS	LENGTHMEN	LENTILS
LEGLINS	LEISHEST	LEMON	LENGTHS	LENTISC
LEGMAN	LEISLER	LEMONADE	LENGTHY	LENTISCS
LEGMEN	LEISLERS	LEMONADES	LENIENCE	LENTISK
LEGONG	LEISTER	LEMONED	LENIENCES	LENTISKS
LEGONGS	LEISTERED	LEMONFISH	LENIENCY	LENTO
LEGROOM	LEISTERS	LEMONIER	LENIENT	LENTOID

LENTOIDS	LEPTOPHOS	LETCHINGS	LEUCINE	LEVE
LENTOR	LEPTOSOME	LETDOWN	LEUCINES	LEVEE
LENTORS	LEPTOTENE	LETDOWNS	LEUCINS	LEVEED
LENTOS	LEQUEAR	LETHAL	LEUCISTIC	LEVEEING
LENTOUS	LEQUEARS	LETHALITY	LEUCITE	LEVEES
LENVOY	LERE	LETHALLY	LEUCITES	LEVEL
LENVOYS	LERED	LETHALS	LEUCITIC	LEVELED
LEONE	LERES	LETHARGIC	LEUCO	LEVELER
LEONES	LERING	LETHARGY	LEUCOCYTE	LEVELERS
LEONINE	LERP	LETHE	LEUCOMA	LEVELING
LEOPARD	LERPS	LETHEAN	LEUCOMAS	LEVELLED
LEOPARDS	LES	LETHEE	LEUCOSIN	LEVELLER
LEOTARD	LESBIAN	LETHEES	LEUCOSINS	LEVELLERS
LEOTARDED	LESBIANS	LETHES	LEUCOTOME	LEVELLEST
LEOTARDS	LESBIC	LETHIED	LEUCOTOMY	LEVELLING
LEP	LESBO	LETS	LEUD	LEVELLY
LEPER	LESBOS	LETTABLE	LEUDES	LEVELNESS
LEPERS	LESES	LETTED	LEUDS	LEVELS
LEPID	LESION	LETTER	LEUGH	LEVER
LEPIDOTE	LESIONED	LETTERBOX	LEUGHEN	LEVERAGE
LEPIDOTES	LESIONING	LETTERED	LEUKAEMIA	LEVERAGED
LEPORID	LESIONS	LETTERER	LEUKEMIA	LEVERAGES
LEPORIDAE	LESPEDEZA	LETTERERS	LEUKEMIAS	LEVERED
LEPORIDS	LESS	LETTERING	LEUKEMIC	LEVERET
LEPORINE	LESSEE	LETTERMAN	LEUKEMICS	LEVERETS
LEPPED	LESSEES	LETTERMEN	LEUKEMOID	LEVERING
LEPPING	LESSEN	LETTERN	LEUKOCYTE	LEVERS
LEPRA	LESSENED	LETTERNS	LEUKOMA	LEVES
LEPRAS	LESSENING	LETTERS	LEUKOMAS	LEVIABLE
LEPROSE	LESSENS	LETTERSET	LEUKON	LEVIATHAN
LEPROSERY	LESSER	LETTING	LEUKONS	LEVIED
LEPROSIES	LESSES	LETTINGS	LEUKOSES	LEVIER
LEPROSITY	LESSON	LETTRE	LEUKOSIS	LEVIERS
LEPROSY	LESSONED	LETTRES	LEUKOTIC	LEVIES
LEPROTIC	LESSONING	LETTUCE	LEUKOTOMY	LEVIGABLE
LEPROUS	LESSONS	LETTUCES	LEV	LEVIGATE
LEPROUSLY	LESSOR	LETUP	LEVA	LEVIGATED
LEPS	LESSORS	LETUPS	LEVANT	LEVIGATES
LEPT	LEST	LEU	LEVANTED	LEVIGATOR
LEPTA	LESTED	LEUCAEMIA	LEVANTER	LEVIN
LEPTIN	LESTING	LEUCAEMIC	LEVANTERS	LEVINS
LEPTINS	LESTS	LEUCEMIA	LEVANTINE	LEVIRATE
LEPTOME	LET	LEUCEMIAS	LEVANTING	LEVIRATES
LEPTOMES	LETCH	LEUCEMIC	LEVANTS	LEVIRATIC
LEPTON	LETCHED	LEUCH	LEVATOR	LEVIS
LEPTONIC	LETCHES	LEUCHEN	LEVATORES	LEVITATE
LEPTONS	LETCHING	LEUCIN	LEVATORS	LEVITATED

LEVITATES

LEVITATES	LEXIGRAMS	LIBATING	LIBERTINE	LICENSOR
LEVITATOR	LEXIS	LIBATION	LIBERTY	LICENSORS
LEVITE	LEXISES	LIBATIONS	LIBIDINAL	LICENSURE
LEVITES	LEY	LIBATORY	LIBIDO	LICENTE
LEVITIC	LEYLANDI	LIBBARD	LIBIDOS	LICH
LEVITICAL	LEYLANDII	LIBBARDS	LIBKEN	LICHANOS
LEVITIES	LEYLANDIS	LIBBED	LIBKENS	LICHEE
LEVITY	LEYS	LIBBER	LIBLAB	LICHEES
LEVO	LEZ	LIBBERS	LIBLABS	LICHEN
LEVODOPA	LEZES	LIBBING	LIBRA	LICHENED
LEVODOPAS	LEZZ	LIBECCHIO	LIBRAE	LICHENIN
LEVOGYRE	LEZZA	LIBECCIO	LIBRAIRE	LICHENING
LEVULIN	LEZZAS	LIBECCIOS	LIBRAIRES	LICHENINS
LEVULINS	LEZZES	LIBEL	LIBRAIRIE	LICHENISM
LEVULOSE	LEZZIE	LIBELANT	LIBRARIAN	LICHENIST
LEVULOSES	LEZZIES	LIBELANTS	LIBRARIES	LICHENOID
LEVY	LEZZY	LIBELED	LIBRARY	LICHENOSE
LEVYING	LI	LIBELEE	LIBRAS	LICHENOUS
LEW	LIABILITY	LIBELEES	LIBRATE	LICHENS
LEWD	LIABLE	LIBELER	LIBRATED	LICHES
LEWDER	LIAISE	LIBELERS	LIBRATES	LICHGATE
LEWDEST	LIAISED	LIBELING	LIBRATING	LICHGATES
LEWDLY	LIAISES	LIBELINGS	LIBRATION	LICHI
LEWDNESS	LIAISING	LIBELIST	LIBRATORY	LICHIS
LEWDSBIES	LIAISON	LIBELISTS	LIBRETTI	LICHT
LEWDSBY	LIAISONS	LIBELLANT	LIBRETTO	LICHTED
LEWDSTER	LIANA	LIBELLED	LIBRETTOS	LICHTER
LEWDSTERS	LIANAS	LIBELLEE	LIBRI	LICHTEST
LEWIS	LIANE	LIBELLEES	LIBRIFORM	LICHTING
LEWISES	LIANES	LIBELLER	LIBS	LICHTLIED
LEWISIA	LIANG	LIBELLERS	LICE	LICHTLIES
LEWISIAS	LIANGS	LIBELLING	LICENCE	LICHTLY
LEWISITE	LIANOID	LIBELLOUS	LICENCED	LICHTS
LEWISITES	LIAR	LIBELOUS	LICENCEE	LICHWAKE
LEWISSON	LIARD	LIBELS	LICENCEES	LICHWAKES
LEWISSONS	LIARDS	LIBER	LICENCER	LICHWAY
LEX	LIARS	LIBERAL	LICENCERS	LICHWAYS
LEXEME	LIART	LIBERALLY	LICENCES	LICIT
LEXEMES	LIAS	LIBERALS	LICENCING	LICITLY
LEXEMIC	LIASES	LIBERATE	LICENSE	LICITNESS
LEXES	LIATRIS	LIBERATED	LICENSED	LICK
LEXICA	LIATRISES	LIBERATES	LICENSEE	LICKED
LEXICAL	LIB	LIBERATOR	LICENSEES	LICKER
LEXICALLY	LIBANT	LIBERO	LICENSER	LICKERISH
LEXICON	LIBATE	LIBEROS	LICENSERS	LICKERS
LEXICONS	LIBATED	LIBERS	LICENSES	LICKING
LEXIGRAM	LIBATES	LIBERTIES	LICENSING	LICKINGS

LICKPENNY	LIERS	LIFTBOY	LIGHTENER	LIGROINES
LICKS	LIES	LIFTBOYS	LIGHTENS	LIGROINS
LICKSPIT	LIEU	LIFTED	LIGHTER	LIGS
LICKSPITS	LIEUS	LIFTER	LIGHTERED	LIGULA
LICORICE	LIEVE	LIFTERS	LIGHTERS	LIGULAE
LICORICES	LIEVER	LIFTGATE	LIGHTEST	LIGULAR
LICTOR	LIEVES	LIFTGATES	LIGHTFACE	LIGULAS
LICTORIAN	LIEVEST	LIFTING	LIGHTFAST	LIGULATE
LICTORS	LIFE	LIFTMAN	LIGHTFUL	LIGULATED
LID	LIFEBELT	LIFTMEN	LIGHTING	LIGULE
LIDAR	LIFEBELTS	LIFTOFF	LIGHTINGS	LIGULES
LIDARS	LIFEBLOOD	LIFTOFFS	LIGHTISH	LIGULOID
LIDDED	LIFEBOAT	LIFTS	LIGHTLESS	LIGURE
LIDDING	LIFEBOATS	LIFULL	LIGHTLIED	LIGURES
LIDGER	LIFEBUOY	LIG	LIGHTLIES	LIKABLE
LIDGERS	LIFEBUOYS	LIGAMENT	LIGHTLY	LIKABLY
LIDLESS	LIFECARE	LIGAMENTS	LIGHTNESS	LIKE
LIDO	LIFECARES	LIGAN	LIGHTNING	LIKEABLE
LIDOCAINE	LIFEFUL	LIGAND	LIGHTS	LIKEABLY
LIDOS	LIFEGUARD	LIGANDS	LIGHTSHIP	LIKED
LIDS	LIFEHACK	LIGANS	LIGHTSOME	LIKELIER
LIE	LIFEHACKS	LIGASE	LIGHTWAVE	LIKELIEST
LIED	LIFEHOLD	LIGASES	LIGHTWOOD	LIKELY
LIEDER	LIFELESS	LIGATE	LIGNAGE	LIKEN
LIEF	LIFELIKE	LIGATED	LIGNAGES	LIKENED
LIEFER	LIFELINE	LIGATES	LIGNALOES	LIKENESS
LIEFEST	LIFELINES	LIGATING	LIGNAN	LIKENING
LIEFLY	LIFELONG	LIGATION	LIGNANS	LIKENS
LIEFS	LIFER	LIGATIONS	LIGNE	LIKER
LIEGE	LIFERS	LIGATIVE	LIGNEOUS	LIKERS
LIEGEDOM	LIFES	LIGATURE	LIGNES	LIKES
LIEGEDOMS	LIFESAVER	LIGATURED	LIGNICOLE	LIKEST
LIEGELESS	LIFESOME	LIGATURES	LIGNIFIED	LIKEWAKE
LIEGEMAN	LIFESPAN	LIGER	LIGNIFIES	LIKEWAKES
LIEGEMEN	LIFESPANS	LIGERS	LIGNIFORM	LIKEWALK
LIEGER	LIFESTYLE	LIGGE	LIGNIFY	LIKEWALKS
LIEGERS	LIFETIME	LIGGED	LIGNIN	LIKEWISE
LIEGES	LIFETIMES	LIGGER	LIGNINS	LIKIN
LIEN	LIFEWAY	LIGGERS	LIGNITE	LIKING
LIENABLE	LIFEWAYS	LIGGES	LIGNITES	LIKINGS
LIENAL	LIFEWORK	LIGGING	LIGNITIC	LIKINS
LIENS	LIFEWORKS	LIGGINGS	LIGNOSE	LIKUTA
LIENTERIC	LIFEWORLD	LIGHT	LIGNOSES	LILAC
LIENTERY	LIFT	LIGHTBULB	LIGNUM	LILACS
LIER	LIFTABLE	LIGHTED	LIGNUMS	LILANGENI
LIERNE	LIFTBACK	LIGHTEN	LIGROIN	LILIED
LIERNES	LIFTBACKS	LIGHTENED	LIGROINE	LILIES

LILL	LIMBI	LIMITEDLY	LIMPING	LINDWORMS
LILLED	LIMBIC	LIMITEDS	LIMPINGLY	LINDY
LILLING	LIMBIER	LIMITER	LIMPINGS	LINE
LILLIPUT	LIMBIEST	LIMITERS	LIMPKIN	LINEABLE
LILLIPUTS	LIMBING	LIMITES	LIMPKINS	LINEAGE
LILLS	LIMBLESS	LIMITING	LIMPLY	LINEAGES
LILO	LIMBMEAL	LIMITINGS	LIMPNESS	LINEAL
LILOS	LIMBO	LIMITLESS	LIMPS	LINEALITY
LILT	LIMBOS	LIMITS	LIMPSEY	LINEALLY
LILTED	LIMBOUS	LIMMA	LIMPSIER	LINEAMENT
LILTING	LIMBS	LIMMAS	LIMPSIEST	LINEAR
LILTINGLY	LIMBUS	LIMMER	LIMPSY	LINEARISE
LILTS	LIMBUSES	LIMMERS	LIMULI	LINEARITY
LILY	LIMBY	LIMN	LIMULOID	LINEARIZE
LILYLIKE	LIME	LIMNAEID	LIMULOIDS	LINEARLY
LIMA	LIMEADE	LIMNAEIDS	LIMULUS	LINEATE
LIMACEL	LIMEADES	LIMNED	LIMULUSES	LINEATED
LIMACELS	LIMED	LIMNER	LIMY	LINEATION
LIMACEOUS	LIMEKILN	LIMNERS	LIN	LINEBRED
LIMACES	LIMEKILNS	LIMNETIC	LINABLE	LINECUT
LIMACINE	LIMELESS	LIMNIC	LINAC	LINECUTS
LIMACON	LIMELIGHT	LIMNING	LINACS	LINED
LIMACONS	LIMELIT	LIMNOLOGY	LINAGE	LINELESS
LIMAIL	LIMEN	LIMNS	LINAGES	LINELIKE
LIMAILS	LIMENS	LIMO	LINALOL	LINEMAN
LIMAN	LIMEPIT	LIMONENE	LINALOLS	LINEMEN
LIMANS	LIMEPITS	LIMONENES	LINALOOL	LINEN
LIMAS	LIMERICK	LIMONITE	LINALOOLS	LINENS
LIMATION	LIMERICKS	LIMONITES	LINCH	LINENY
LIMATIONS	LIMES	LIMONITIC	LINCHES	LINEOLATE
LIMAX	LIMESCALE	LIMOS	LINCHET	LINER
LIMB	LIMESTONE	LIMOSES	LINCHETS	LINERLESS
LIMBA	LIMEWASH	LIMOSIS	LINCHPIN	LINERS
LIMBAS	LIMEWATER	LIMOUS	LINCHPINS	LINES
LIMBATE	LIMEY	LIMOUSINE	LINCRUSTA	LINESMAN
LIMBEC	LIMEYS	LIMP	LINCTURE	LINESMEN
LIMBECK	LIMIER	LIMPA	LINCTURES	LINEUP
LIMBECKS	LIMIEST	LIMPAS	LINCTUS	LINEUPS
LIMBECS	LIMINA	LIMPED	LINCTUSES	LINEY
LIMBED	LIMINAL	LIMPER	LIND	LING
LIMBER	LIMINESS	LIMPERS	LINDANE	LINGA
LIMBERED	LIMING	LIMPEST	LINDANES	LINGAM
LIMBERER	LIMINGS	LIMPET	LINDEN	LINGAMS
LIMBEREST	LIMIT	LIMPETS	LINDENS	LINGAS
LIMBERING	LIMITABLE	LIMPID	LINDIES	LINGBERRY
LIMBERLY	LIMITARY	LIMPIDITY	LINDS	LINGCOD
LIMBERS	LIMITED	LIMPIDLY	LINDWORM	LINGCODS

LINGEL	LINIMENT	LINNIES	LINUM	LIPECTOMY
LINGELS	LINIMENTS	LINNING	LINUMS	LIPEMIA
LINGER	LININ	LINNS	LINURON	LIPEMIAS
LINGERED	LINING	LINNY	LINURONS	LIPID
LINGERER	LININGS	LINO	LINUX	LIPIDE
LINGERERS	LININS	LINOCUT	LINUXES	LIPIDES
LINGERIE	LINISH	LINOCUTS	LINY	LIPIDIC
LINGERIES	LINISHED	LINOLEATE	LION	LIPIDS
LINGERING	LINISHER	LINOLEIC	LIONCEL	LIPIN
LINGERS	LINISHERS	LINOLENIC	LIONCELLE	LIPINS
LINGIER	LINISHES	LINOLEUM	LIONCELS	LIPLESS
LINGIEST	LINISHING	LINOLEUMS	LIONEL	LIPLIKE
LINGLE	LINK	LINOS	LIONELS	LIPO
LINGLES	LINKABLE	LINOTYPE	LIONESS	LIPOCYTE
LINGO	LINKAGE	LINOTYPED	LIONESSES	LIPOCYTES
LINGOES	LINKAGES	LINOTYPER	LIONET	LIPOGRAM
LINGOT	LINKBOY	LINOTYPES	LIONETS	LIPOGRAMS
LINGOTS	LINKBOYS	LINS	LIONFISH	LIPOIC
LINGS	LINKED	LINSANG	LIONHEAD	LIPOID
LINGSTER	LINKER	LINSANGS	LIONHEADS	LIPOIDAL
LINGSTERS	LINKERS	LINSEED	LIONISE	LIPOIDS
LINGUA	LINKIER	LINSEEDS	LIONISED	LIPOLITIC
LINGUAE	LINKIEST	LINSEY	LIONISER	LIPOLYSES
LINGUAL	LINKING	LINSEYS	LIONISERS	LIPOLYSIS
LINGUALLY	LINKMAN	LINSTOCK	LIONISES	LIPOLYTIC
LINGUALS	LINKMEN	LINSTOCKS	LIONISING	LIPOMA
LINGUAS	LINKROT	LINT	LIONISM	LIPOMAS
LINGUICA	LINKROTS	LINTED	LIONISMS	LIPOMATA
LINGUICAS	LINKS	LINTEL	LIONIZE	LIPOPLAST
LINGUINE	LINKSLAND	LINTELLED	LIONIZED	LIPOS
LINGUINES	LINKSMAN	LINTELS	LIONIZER	LIPOSOMAL
LINGUINI	LINKSMEN	LINTER	LIONIZERS	LIPOSOME
LINGUINIS	LINKSPAN	LINTERS	LIONIZES	LIPOSOMES
LINGUISA	LINKSPANS	LINTIE	LIONIZING	LIPOSUCK
LINGUISAS	LINKSTER	LINTIER	LIONLIKE	LIPOSUCKS
LINGUIST	LINKSTERS	LINTIES	LIONLY	LIPOTROPY
LINGUISTS	LINKUP	LINTIEST	LIONS	LIPPED
LINGULA	LINKUPS	LINTING	LIP	LIPPEN
LINGULAE	LINKWORK	LINTLESS	LIPA	LIPPENED
LINGULAR	LINKWORKS	LINTOL	LIPAEMIA	LIPPENING
LINGULAS	LINKY	LINTOLS	LIPAEMIAS	LIPPENS
LINGULATE	LINN	LINTS	LIPARITE	LIPPER
LINGY	LINNED	LINTSEED	LIPARITES	LIPPERED
LINHAY	LINNET	LINTSEEDS	LIPAS	LIPPERING
LINHAYS	LINNETS	LINTSTOCK	LIPASE	LIPPERS
LINIER	LINNEY	LINTWHITE	LIPASES	LIPPIE
LINIEST	LINNEYS	LINTY	LIPE	LIPPIER

LIPPIES	LIQUORING	LISTEL	LITH	LITIGANT
LIPPIEST	LIQUORISH	LISTELS	LITHARGE	LITIGANTS
LIPPINESS	LIQUORS	LISTEN	LITHARGES	LITIGATE
LIPPING	LIRA	LISTENED	LITHATE	LITIGATED
LIPPINGS	LIRAS	LISTENER	LITHATES	LITIGATES
LIPPITUDE	LIRE	LISTENERS	LITHE	LITIGATOR
LIPPY	LIRI	LISTENING	LITHED	LITIGIOUS
LIPREAD	LIRIOPE	LISTENS	LITHELY	LITING
LIPREADER	LIRIOPES	LISTER	LITHEMIA	LITMUS
LIPREADS	LIRIPIPE	LISTERIA	LITHEMIAS	LITMUSES
LIPS	LIRIPIPES	LISTERIAL	LITHEMIC	LITORAL
LIPSALVE	LIRIPOOP	LISTERIAS	LITHENESS	LITOTES
LIPSALVES	LIRIPOOPS	LISTERS	LITHER	LITOTIC
LIPSTICK	LIRK	LISTETH	LITHERLY	LITRE
LIPSTICKS	LIRKED	LISTFUL	LITHES	LITREAGE
LIPURIA	LIRKING	LISTING	LITHESOME	LITREAGES
LIPURIAS	LIRKS	LISTINGS	LITHEST	LITRES
LIQUABLE	LIROT	LISTLESS	LITHIA	LITS
LIQUATE	LIROTH	LISTS	LITHIAS	LITTEN
LIQUATED	LIS	LISTSERV	LITHIASES	LITTER
LIQUATES	LISENTE	LISTSERVS	LITHIASIS	LITTERBAG
LIQUATING	LISK	LIT	LITHIC	LITTERBUG
LIQUATION	LISKS	LITAI	LITHIFIED	LITTERED
LIQUEFIED	LISLE	LITANIES	LITHIFIES	LITTERER
LIQUEFIER	LISLES	LITANY	LITHIFY	LITTERERS
LIQUEFIES	LISP	LITAS	LITHING	LITTERING
LIQUEFY	LISPED	LITCHI	LITHISTID	LITTERS
LIQUESCE	LISPER	LITCHIS	LITHITE	LITTERY
LIQUESCED	LISPERS	LITE	LITHITES	LITTLE
LIQUESCES	LISPING	LITED	LITHIUM	LITTLER
LIQUEUR	LISPINGLY	LITENESS	LITHIUMS	LITTLES
LIQUEURED	LISPINGS	LITER	LITHO	LITTLEST
LIQUEURS	LISPOUND	LITERACY	LITHOCYST	LITTLIE
LIQUID	LISPOUNDS	LITERAL	LITHOED	LITTLIES
LIQUIDATE	LISPS	LITERALLY	LITHOID	LITTLIN
LIQUIDISE	LISPUND	LITERALS	LITHOIDAL	LITTLING
LIQUIDITY	LISPUNDS	LITERARY	LITHOING	LITTLINGS
LIQUIDIZE	LISSES	LITERATE	LITHOLOGY	LITTLINS
LIQUIDLY	LISSOM	LITERATES	LITHOPONE	LITTLISH
LIQUIDS	LISSOME	LITERATI	LITHOPS	LITTORAL
LIQUIDUS	LISSOMELY	LITERATIM	LITHOS	LITTORALS
LIQUIFIED	LISSOMLY	LITERATO	LITHOSOL	LITU
LIQUIFIES	LIST	LITERATOR	LITHOSOLS	LITURGIC
LIQUIFY	LISTABLE	LITERATUS	LITHOTOME	LITURGICS
LIQUOR	LISTED	LITEROSE	LITHOTOMY	LITURGIES
LIQUORED	LISTEE	LITERS	LITHS	LITURGISM
LIQUORICE	LISTEES	LITES	LITIGABLE	LITURGIST

LITURGY	LIVEYERE	LOADERS	LOATHEST	LOBELINES
LITUUS	LIVEYERES	LOADING	LOATHFUL	LOBES
LITUUSES	LIVEYERS	LOADINGS	LOATHING	LOBI
LIVABLE	LIVID	LOADS	LOATHINGS	LOBING
LIVE	LIVIDER	LOADSPACE	LOATHLY	LOBINGS
LIVEABLE	LIVIDEST	LOADSTAR	LOATHNESS	LOBIPED
LIVED	LIVIDITY	LOADSTARS	LOATHSOME	LOBLOLLY
LIVEDO	LIVIDLY	LOADSTONE	LOATHY	LOBO
LIVEDOS	LIVIDNESS	LOAF	LOAVE	LOBOLA
LIVELIER	LIVIER	LOAFED	LOAVED	LOBOLAS
LIVELIEST	LIVIERS	LOAFER	LOAVES	LOBOLO
LIVELILY	LIVING	LOAFERISH	LOAVING	LOBOLOS
LIVELOD	LIVINGLY	LOAFERS	LOB	LOBOS
LIVELODS	LIVINGS	LOAFING	LOBAR	LOBOSE
LIVELONG	LIVOR	LOAFINGS	LOBATE	LOBOTOMY
LIVELONGS	LIVORS	LOAFS	LOBATED	LOBS
LIVELOOD	LIVRAISON	LOAM	LOBATELY	LOBSCOUSE
LIVELOODS	LIVRE	LOAMED	LOBATION	LOBSTER
LIVELY	LIVRES	LOAMIER	LOBATIONS	LOBSTERED
LIVEN	LIVYER	LOAMIEST	LOBBED	LOBSTERER
LIVENED	LIVYERS	LOAMINESS	LOBBER	LOBSTERS
LIVENER	LIXIVIA	LOAMING	LOBBERS	LOBSTICK
LIVENERS	LIXIVIAL	LOAMLESS	LOBBIED	LOBSTICKS
LIVENESS	LIXIVIATE	LOAMS	LOBBIES	LOBULAR
LIVENING	LIXIVIOUS	LOAMY	LOBBING	LOBULARLY
LIVENS	LIXIVIUM	LOAN	LOBBY	LOBULATE
LIVER	LIXIVIUMS	LOANABLE	LOBBYER	LOBULATED
LIVERED	LIZARD	LOANBACK	LOBBYERS	LOBULE
LIVERIED	LIZARDS	LOANBACKS	LOBBYGOW	LOBULES
LIVERIES	LIZZIE	LOANED	LOBBYGOWS	LOBULI
LIVERING	LIZZIES	LOANEE	LOBBYING	LOBULOSE
LIVERISH	LLAMA	LOANEES	LOBBYINGS	LOBULUS
LIVERLEAF	LLAMAS	LOANER	LOBBYISM	LOBUS
LIVERLESS	LLANERO	LOANERS	LOBBYISMS	LOBWORM
LIVERS	LLANEROS	LOANING	LOBBYIST	LOBWORMS
LIVERWORT	LLANO	LOANINGS	LOBBYISTS	LOCA
LIVERY	LLANOS	LOANS	LOBE	LOCAL
LIVERYMAN	LO	LOANSHIFT	LOBECTOMY	LOCALE
LIVERYMEN	LOACH	LOANWORD	LOBED	LOCALES
LIVES	LOACHES	LOANWORDS	LOBEFIN	LOCALISE
LIVEST	LOAD	LOAST	LOBEFINS	LOCALISED
LIVESTOCK	LOADED	LOATH	LOBELESS	LOCALISER
LIVETRAP	LOADEN	LOATHE	LOBELET	LOCALISES
LIVETRAPS	LOADENED	LOATHED	LOBELETS	LOCALISM
LIVEWARE	LOADENING	LOATHER	LOBELIA	LOCALISMS
LIVEWARES	LOADENS	LOATHERS	LOBELIAS	LOCALIST
LIVEYER	LOADER	LOATHES	LOBELINE	LOCALISTS

LOCALITE	LOCKFUL	LOCULAR	LODICULES	LOGGIEST
LOCALITES	LOCKFULS	LOCULATE	LODS	LOGGING
LOCALITY	LOCKHOUSE	LOCULATED	LOERIE	LOGGINGS
LOCALIZE	LOCKING	LOCULE	LOERIES	LOGGISH
LOCALIZED	LOCKINGS	LOCULED	LOESS	LOGGY
LOCALIZER	LOCKJAW	LOCULES	LOESSAL	LOGIA
LOCALIZES	LOCKJAWS	LOCULI	LOESSES	LOGIC
LOCALLY	LOCKLESS	LOCULUS	LOESSIAL	LOGICAL
LOCALNESS	LOCKMAKER	LOCUM	LOESSIC	LOGICALLY
LOCALS	LOCKMAN	LOCUMS	LOFT	LOGICIAN
LOCATABLE	LOCKMEN	LOCUPLETE	LOFTED	LOGICIANS
LOCATE	LOCKNUT	LOCUS	LOFTER	LOGICISE
LOCATED	LOCKNUTS	LOCUST	LOFTERS	LOGICISED
LOCATER	LOCKOUT	LOCUSTA	LOFTIER	LOGICISES
LOCATERS	LOCKOUTS	LOCUSTAE	LOFTIEST	LOGICISM
LOCATES	LOCKPICK	LOCUSTAL	LOFTILY	LOGICISMS
LOCATING	LOCKPICKS	LOCUSTED	LOFTINESS	LOGICIST
LOCATION	LOCKRAM	LOCUSTING	LOFTING	LOGICISTS
LOCATIONS	LOCKRAMS	LOCUSTS	LOFTLESS	LOGICIZE
LOCATIVE	LOCKS	LOCUTION	LOFTLIKE	LOGICIZED
LOCATIVES	LOCKSET	LOCUTIONS	LOFTS	LOGICIZES
LOCATOR	LOCKSETS	LOCUTORY	LOFTSMAN	LOGICLESS
LOCATORS	LOCKSMAN	LOD	LOFTSMEN	LOGICS
LOCELLATE	LOCKSMEN	LODE	LOFTY	LOGIE
LOCH	LOCKSMITH	LODEN	LOG	LOGIER
LOCHAN	LOCKSTEP	LODENS	LOGAN	LOGIES
LOCHANS	LOCKSTEPS	LODES	LOGANIA	LOGIEST
LOCHIA	LOCKUP	LODESMAN	LOGANIAS	LOGILY
LOCHIAL	LOCKUPS	LODESMEN	LOGANS	LOGIN
LOCHS	LOCO	LODESTAR	LOGAOEDIC	LOGINESS
LOCI	LOCOED	LODESTARS	LOGARITHM	LOGINS
LOCK	LOCOES	LODESTONE	LOGBOARD	LOGION
LOCKABLE	LOCOFOCO	LODGE	LOGBOARDS	LOGIONS
LOCKAGE	LOCOFOCOS	LODGEABLE	LOGBOOK	LOGISTIC
LOCKAGES	LOCOING	LODGED	LOGBOOKS	LOGISTICS
LOCKAWAY	LOCOISM	LODGEMENT	LOGE	LOGJAM
LOCKAWAYS	LOCOISMS	LODGEPOLE	LOGES	LOGJAMMED
LOCKBOX	LOCOMAN	LODGER	LOGGAT	LOGJAMS
LOCKBOXES	LOCOMEN	LODGERS	LOGGATS	LOGJUICE
LOCKDOWN	LOCOMOTE	LODGES	LOGGED	LOGJUICES
LOCKDOWNS	LOCOMOTED	LODGING	LOGGER	LOGLINE
LOCKED	LOCOMOTES	LODGINGS	LOGGERS	LOGLINES
LOCKER	LOCOMOTOR	LODGMENT	LOGGETS	LOGLOG
LOCKERS	LOCOPLANT	LODGMENTS	LOGGIA	LOGLOGS
LOCKET	LOCOS	LODICULA	LOGGIAS	LOGNORMAL
LOCKETS	LOCOWEED	LODICULAE	LOGGIE	LOGO
LOCKFAST	LOCOWEEDS	LODICULE	LOGGIER	LOGOFF

LOGOFFS	LOITERERS	LONE	LONGINGLY	LOOFFUL
LOGOGRAM	LOITERING	LONELIER	LONGINGS	LOOFFULS
LOGOGRAMS	LOITERS	LONELIEST	LONGISH	LOOFS
LOGOGRAPH	LOKE	LONELILY	LONGITUDE	LOOIE
LOGOGRIPH	LOKES	LONELY	LONGJUMP	LOOIES
LOGOI	LOKSHEN	LONENESS	LONGJUMPS	LOOING
LOGOMACH	LOLIGO	LONER	LONGLEAF	LOOK
LOGOMACHS	LOLIGOS	LONERS	LONGLINE	LOOKALIKE
LOGOMACHY	LOLIUM	LONESOME	LONGLINES	LOOKDOWN
LOGON	LOLIUMS	LONESOMES	LONGLIST	LOOKDOWNS
LOGONS	LOLL	LONG	LONGLISTS	LOOKED
LOGOPEDIC	LOLLED	LONGA	LONGLY	LOOKER
LOGOPHILE	LOLLER	LONGAEVAL	LONGNECK	LOOKERS
LOGORRHEA	LOLLERS	LONGAN	LONGNECKS	LOOKING
LOGOS	LOLLIES	LONGANS	LONGNESS	LOOKISM
LOGOTHETE	LOLLING	LONGAS	LONGS	LOOKISMS
LOGOTYPE	LOLLINGLY	LONGBOARD	LONGSHIP	LOOKIST
LOGOTYPES	LOLLIPOP	LONGBOAT	LONGSHIPS	LOOKISTS
LOGOTYPY	LOLLIPOPS	LONGBOATS	LONGSHORE	LOOKOUT
LOGOUT	LOLLOP	LONGBOW	LONGSOME	LOOKOUTS
LOGOUTS	LOLLOPED	LONGBOWS	LONGSPUR	LOOKOVER
LOGROLL	LOLLOPING	LONGCASE	LONGSPURS	LOOKOVERS
LOGROLLED	LOLLOPS	LONGCLOTH	LONGTIME	LOOKS
LOGROLLER	LOLLOPY	LONGE	LONGUEUR	LOOKSISM
LOGROLLS	LOLLS	LONGED	LONGUEURS	LOOKSISMS
LOGS	LOLLY	LONGEING	LONGWALL	LOOKUP
LOGWAY	LOLLYGAG	LONGER	LONGWALLS	LOOKUPS
LOGWAYS	LOLLYGAGS	LONGERON	LONGWAYS	LOOM
LOGWOOD	LOLLYPOP	LONGERONS	LONGWISE	LOOMED
LOGWOODS	LOLLYPOPS	LONGERS	LONGWORM	LOOMING
LOGY	LOLOG	LONGES	LONGWORMS	LOOMS
LOHAN	LOLOGS	LONGEST	LONICERA	LOON
LOHANS	LOMA	LONGEVAL	LONICERAS	LOONEY
LOID	LOMAS	LONGEVITY	LOO	LOONEYS
LOIDED	LOMATA	LONGEVOUS	LOOBIER	LOONIE
LOIDING	LOME	LONGHAIR	LOOBIES	LOONIER
LOIDS	LOMED	LONGHAIRS	LOOBIEST	LOONIES
LOIN	LOMEIN	LONGHAND	LOOBILY	LOONIEST
LOINCLOTH	LOMEINS	LONGHANDS	LOOBY	LOONILY
LOINS	LOMENT	LONGHEAD	LOOED	LOONINESS
LOIPE	LOMENTA	LONGHEADS	LOOEY	LOONING
LOIPEN	LOMENTS	LONGHORN	LOOEYS	LOONINGS
LOIR	LOMENTUM	LONGHORNS	LOOF	LOONS
LOIRS	LOMENTUMS	LONGHOUSE	LOOFA	LOONY
LOITER	LOMES	LONGICORN	LOOFAH	LOOP
LOITERED	LOMING	LONGIES	LOOFAHS	LOOPED
LOITERER	LOMPISH	LONGING	LOOFAS	LOOPER

LOOPERS	LOPERS	LORDOMA	LOSABLE	LOTS
LOOPHOLE	LOPES	LORDOMAS	LOSE	LOTTE
LOOPHOLED	LOPGRASS	LORDOSES	LOSED	LOTTED
LOOPHOLES	LOPHODONT	LORDOSIS	LOSEL	LOTTER
LOOPIER	LOPING	LORDOTIC	LOSELS	LOTTERIES
LOOPIEST	LOPOLITH	LORDS	LOSEN	LOTTERS
LOOPILY	LOPOLITHS	LORDSHIP	LOSER	LOTTERY
LOOPINESS	LOPPED	LORDSHIPS	LOSERS	LOTTES
LOOPING	LOPPER	LORDY	LOSES	LOTTING
LOOPINGS	LOPPERED	LORE	LOSH	LOTTO
LOOPS	LOPPERING	LOREAL	LOSING	LOTTOS
LOOPY	LOPPERS	LOREL	LOSINGLY	LOTUS
LOOR	LOPPIER	LORELS	LOSINGS	LOTUSES
LOORD	LOPPIES	LORES	LOSLYF	LOTUSLAND
LOORDS	LOPPIEST	LORETTE	LOSLYFS	LOU
LOOS	LOPPING	LORETTES	LOSS	LOUCHE
LOOSE	LOPPINGS	LORGNETTE	LOSSES	LOUCHELY
LOOSEBOX	LOPPY	LORGNON	LOSSIER	LOUCHER
LOOSED	LOPS	LORGNONS	LOSSIEST	LOUCHEST
LOOSELY	LOPSIDED	LORIC	LOSSLESS	LOUD
LOOSEN	LOPSTICK	LORICA	LOSSMAKER	LOUDEN
LOOSENED	LOPSTICKS	LORICAE	LOSSY	LOUDENED
LOOSENER	LOQUACITY	LORICATE	LOST	LOUDENING
LOOSENERS	LOQUAT	LORICATED	LOSTNESS	LOUDENS
LOOSENESS	LOQUATS	LORICATES	LOT	LOUDER
LOOSENING	LOQUITUR	LORICS	LOTA	LOUDEST
LOOSENS	LOR	LORIES	LOTAH	LOUDISH
LOOSER	LORAL	LORIKEET	LOTAHS	LOUDLIER
LOOSES	LORAN	LORIKEETS	LOTAS	LOUDLIEST
LOOSEST	LORANS	LORIMER	LOTE	LOUDLY
LOOSIE	LORATE	LORIMERS	LOTES	LOUDMOUTH
LOOSIES	LORAZEPAM	LORINER	LOTH	LOUDNESS
LOOSING	LORCHA	LORINERS	LOTHARIO	LOUED
LOOSINGS	LORCHAS	LORING	LOTHARIOS	LOUGH
LOOT	LORD	LORINGS	LOTHEFULL	LOUGHS
LOOTED	LORDED	LORIOT	LOTHER	LOUIE
LOOTEN	LORDING	LORIOTS	LOTHEST	LOUIES
LOOTER	LORDINGS	LORIS	LOTHFULL	LOUING
LOOTERS	LORDKIN	LORISES	LOTHNESS	LOUIS
LOOTING	LORDKINS	LORN	LOTHSOME	LOUMA
LOOTINGS	LORDLESS	LORNNESS	LOTI	LOUMAS
LOOTS	LORDLIER	LORRELL	LOTIC	LOUN
LOOVES	LORDLIEST	LORRELLS	LOTION	LOUND
LOP	LORDLIKE	LORRIES	LOTIONS	LOUNDED
LOPE	LORDLING	LORRY	LOTO	LOUNDER
LOPED	LORDLINGS	LORY	LOTOS	LOUNDERED
LOPER	LORDLY	LOS	LOTOSES	LOUNDERS

LOUNDING	LOUSINESS	LOVERED	LOWINGS	LOWSIT
LOUNDS	LOUSING	LOVERLESS	LOWISH	LOWT
LOUNED	LOUSY	LOVERLY	LOWLAND	LOWTED
LOUNGE	LOUT	LOVERS	LOWLANDER	LOWTING
LOUNGED	LOUTED	LOVES	LOWLANDS	LOWTS
LOUNGER	LOUTING	LOVESEAT	LOWLIER	LOWVELD
LOUNGERS	LOUTISH	LOVESEATS	LOWLIEST	LOWVELDS
LOUNGES	LOUTISHLY	LOVESICK	LOWLIFE	LOX
LOUNGEY	LOUTS	LOVESOME	LOWLIFER	LOXED
LOUNGIER	LOUVAR	LOVEVINE	LOWLIFERS	LOXES
LOUNGIEST	LOUVARS	LOVEVINES	LOWLIFES	LOXING
LOUNGING	LOUVER	LOVEY	LOWLIGHT	LOXODROME
LOUNGINGS	LOUVERED	LOVEYS	LOWLIGHTS	LOXODROMY
LOUNGY	LOUVERS	LOVING	LOWLIHEAD	LOXYGEN
LOUNING	LOUVRE	LOVINGLY	LOWLILY	LOXYGENS
LOUNS	LOUVRED	LOVINGS	LOWLINESS	LOY
LOUP	LOUVRES	LOW	LOWLIVES	LOYAL
LOUPE	LOVABLE	LOWAN	LOWLY	LOYALER
LOUPED	LOVABLY	LOWANS	LOWN	LOYALEST
LOUPEN	LOVAGE	LOWBALL	LOWND	LOYALISM
LOUPES	LOVAGES	LOWBALLED	LOWNDED	LOYALISMS
LOUPING	LOVAT	LOWBALLS	LOWNDING	LOYALIST
LOUPIT	LOVATS	LOWBORN	LOWNDS	LOYALISTS
LOUPS	LOVE	LOWBOY	LOWNE	LOYALLER
LOUR	LOVEABLE	LOWBOYS	LOWNED	LOYALLEST
LOURE	LOVEABLY	LOWBRED	LOWNES	LOYALLY
LOURED	LOVEBIRD	LOWBROW	LOWNESS	LOYALNESS
LOURES	LOVEBIRDS	LOWBROWED	LOWNESSES	LOYALTIES
LOURIE	LOVEBITE	LOWBROWS	LOWNING	LOYALTY
LOURIER	LOVEBITES	LOWDOWN	LOWNS	LOYS
LOURIES	LOVEBUG	LOWDOWNS	LOWP	LOZELL
LOURIEST	LOVEBUGS	LOWE	LOWPED	LOZELLS
LOURING	LOVED	LOWED	LOWPING	LOZEN
LOURINGLY	LOVEFEST	LOWER	LOWPS	LOZENGE
LOURINGS	LOVEFESTS	LOWERABLE	LOWRIDER	LOZENGED
LOURS	LOVELESS	LOWERCASE	LOWRIDERS	LOZENGES
LOURY	LOVELIER	LOWERED	LOWRIE	LOZENGY
LOUS	LOVELIES	LOWERIER	LOWRIES	LOZENS
LOUSE	LOVELIEST	LOWERIEST	LOWRY	LUACH
LOUSED	LOVELIGHT	LOWERING	LOWS	LUAU
LOUSER	LOVELILY	LOWERINGS	LOWSE	LUAUS
LOUSERS	LOVELOCK	LOWERMOST	LOWSED	LUBBARD
LOUSES	LOVELOCKS	LOWERS	LOWSENING	LUBBARDS
LOUSEWORT	LOVELORN	LOWERY	LOWSER	LUBBER
LOUSIER	LOVELY	LOWES	LOWSES	LUBBERLY
LOUSIEST	LOVEMAKER	LOWEST	LOWSEST	LUBBERS
LOUSILY	LOVER	LOWING	LOWSING	LUBE

LUBED	LUCKIES	LUGER	LUMBARS	LUMPFISH
LUBES	LUCKIEST	LUGERS	LUMBER	LUMPIER
LUBFISH	LUCKILY	LUGES	LUMBERED	LUMPIEST
LUBFISHES	LUCKINESS	LUGGABLE	LUMBERER	LUMPILY
LUBING	LUCKING	LUGGABLES	LUMBERERS	LUMPINESS
LUBRA	LUCKLESS	LUGGAGE	LUMBERING	LUMPING
LUBRAS	LUCKPENNY	LUGGAGES	LUMBERLY	LUMPINGLY
LUBRIC	LUCKS	LUGGED	LUMBERMAN	LUMPISH
LUBRICAL	LUCKY	LUGGER	LUMBERMEN	LUMPISHLY
LUBRICANT	LUCRATIVE	LUGGERS	LUMBERS	LUMPKIN
LUBRICATE	LUCRE	LUGGIE	LUMBRICAL	LUMPKINS
LUBRICITY	LUCRES	LUGGIES	LUMBRICI	LUMPS
LUBRICOUS	LUCTATION	LUGGING	LUMBRICUS	LUMPY
LUCARNE	LUCUBRATE	LUGHOLE	LUMEN	LUMS
LUCARNES	LUCULENT	LUGHOLES	LUMENAL	LUNA
LUCE	LUCUMA	LUGING	LUMENS	LUNACIES
LUCENCE	LUCUMAS	LUGINGS	LUMINA	LUNACY
LUCENCES	LUCUMO	LUGS	LUMINAIRE	LUNANAUT
LUCENCIES	LUCUMONES	LUGSAIL	LUMINAL	LUNANAUTS
LUCENCY	LUCUMOS	LUGSAILS	LUMINANCE	LUNAR
LUCENT	LUD	LUGWORM	LUMINANT	LUNARIAN
LUCENTLY	LUDE	LUGWORMS	LUMINANTS	LUNARIANS
LUCERN	LUDERICK	LUIT	LUMINARIA	LUNARIES
LUCERNE	LUDERICKS	LUITEN	LUMINARY	LUNARIST
LUCERNES	LUDES	LUKE	LUMINE	LUNARISTS
LUCERNS	LUDIC	LUKEWARM	LUMINED	LUNARNAUT
LUCES	LUDICALLY	LULIBUB	LUMINES	LUNARS
LUCHOT	LUDICROUS	LULIBUBS	LUMINESCE	LUNARY
LUCHOTH	LUDO	LULL	LUMINING	LUNAS
LUCID	LUDOS	LULLABIED	LUMINISM	LUNATE
LUCIDER	LUDS	LULLABIES	LUMINISMS	LUNATED
LUCIDEST	LUDSHIP	LULLABY	LUMINIST	LUNATELY
LUCIDITY	LUDSHIPS	LULLED	LUMINISTS	LUNATES
LUCIDLY	LUES	LULLER	LUMINOUS	LUNATIC
LUCIDNESS	LUETIC	LULLERS	LUMME	LUNATICAL
LUCIFER	LUETICS	LULLING	LUMMIER	LUNATICS
LUCIFERIN	LUFF	LULLS	LUMMIEST	LUNATION
LUCIFERS	LUFFA	LULU	LUMMOX	LUNATIONS
LUCIGEN	LUFFAS	LULUS	LUMMOXES	LUNCH
LUCIGENS	LUFFED	LUM	LUMMY	LUNCHBOX
LUCITE	LUFFING	LUMA	LUMP	LUNCHED
LUCITES	LUFFS	LUMAS	LUMPED	LUNCHEON
LUCK	LUG	LUMBAGO	LUMPEN	LUNCHEONS
LUCKED	LUGE	LUMBAGOS	LUMPENLY	LUNCHER
LUCKEN	LUGED	LUMBANG	LUMPENS	LUNCHERS
LUCKIE	LUGEING	LUMBANGS	LUMPER	LUNCHES
LUCKIER	LUGEINGS	LUMBAR	LUMPERS	LUNCHING

LUNCHMEAT	LUNKS	LURES	LUSKS	LUTEFISKS
LUNCHROOM	LUNT	LUREX	LUST	LUTEIN
LUNCHTIME	LUNTED	LUREXES	LUSTED	LUTEINISE
LUNE	LUNTING	LURGI	LUSTER	LUTEINIZE
LUNES	LUNTS	LURGIES	LUSTERED	LUTEINS
LUNET	LUNULA	LURGIS	LUSTERING	LUTENIST
LUNETS	LUNULAE	LURGY	LUSTERS	LUTENISTS
LUNETTE	LUNULAR	LURID	LUSTFUL	LUTEOLIN
LUNETTES	LUNULATE	LURIDER	LUSTFULLY	LUTEOLINS
LUNG	LUNULATED	LURIDEST	LUSTICK	LUTEOLOUS
LUNGAN	LUNULE	LURIDLY	LUSTIER	LUTEOUS
LUNGANS	LUNULES	LURIDNESS	LUSTIEST	LUTER
LUNGE	LUNY	LURING	LUSTIHEAD	LUTERS
LUNGED	LUNYIE	LURINGLY	LUSTIHOOD	LUTES
LUNGEE	LUNYIES	LURINGS	LUSTILY	LUTESCENT
LUNGEES	LUPANAR	LURK	LUSTINESS	LUTETIUM
LUNGEING	LUPANARS	LURKED	LUSTING	LUTETIUMS
LUNGER	LUPIN	LURKER	LUSTIQUE	LUTEUM
LUNGERS	LUPINE	LURKERS	LUSTLESS	LUTFISK
LUNGES	LUPINES	LURKING	LUSTRA	LUTFISKS
LUNGFISH	LUPINS	LURKINGLY	LUSTRAL	LUTHERN
LUNGFUL	LUPOID	LURKINGS	LUSTRATE	LUTHERNS
LUNGFULS	LUPOUS	LURKS	LUSTRATED	LUTHIER
LUNGI	LUPPEN	LURRIES	LUSTRATES	LUTHIERS
LUNGIE	LUPULIN	LURRY	LUSTRE	LUTING
LUNGIES	LUPULINE	LURS	LUSTRED	LUTINGS
LUNGING	LUPULINIC	LURVE	LUSTRES	LUTIST
LUNGIS	LUPULINS	LURVES	LUSTRINE	LUTISTS
LUNGLESS	LUPUS	LUSCIOUS	LUSTRINES	LUTITE
LUNGS	LUPUSES	LUSER	LUSTRING	LUTITES
LUNGWORM	LUR	LUSERS	LUSTRINGS	LUTTEN
LUNGWORMS	LURCH	LUSH	LUSTROUS	LUTZ
LUNGWORT	LURCHED	LUSHED	LUSTRUM	LUTZES
LUNGWORTS	LURCHER	LUSHER	LUSTRUMS	LUV
LUNGYI	LURCHERS	LUSHERS	LUSTS	LUVS
LUNGYIS	LURCHES	LUSHES	LUSTY	LUVVIE
LUNIER	LURCHING	LUSHEST	LUSUS	LUVVIEDOM
LUNIES	LURDAN	LUSHIER	LUSUSES	LUVVIES
LUNIEST	LURDANE	LUSHIEST	LUTANIST	LUVVY
LUNINESS	LURDANES	LUSHING	LUTANISTS	LUX
LUNISOLAR	LURDANS	LUSHLY	LUTE	LUXATE
LUNITIDAL	LURDEN	LUSHNESS	LUTEA	LUXATED
LUNK	LURDENS	LUSHY	LUTEAL	LUXATES
LUNKER	LURE	LUSK	LUTECIUM	LUXATING
LUNKERS	LURED	LUSKED	LUTECIUMS	LUXATION
LUNKHEAD	LURER	LUSKING	LUTED	LUXATIONS
LUNKHEADS	LURERS	LUSKISH	LUTEFISK	LUXE

LUXES	LYCHGATES	LYMS	LYRE	LYSIN
LUXMETER	LYCHNIS	LYNAGE	LYREBIRD	LYSINE
LUXMETERS	LYCHNISES	LYNAGES	LYREBIRDS	LYSINES
LUXURIANT	LYCOPENE	LYNCEAN	LYRES	LYSING
LUXURIATE	LYCOPENES	LYNCH	LYRIC	LYSINS
LUXURIES	LYCOPOD	LYNCHED	LYRICAL	LYSIS
LUXURIOUS	LYCOPODS	LYNCHER	LYRICALLY	LYSOGEN
LUXURIST	LYCRA	LYNCHERS	LYRICISE	LYSOGENIC
LUXURISTS	LYCRAS	LYNCHES	LYRICISED	LYSOGENS
LUXURY	LYDDITE	LYNCHET	LYRICISES	LYSOGENY
LUZ	LYDDITES	LYNCHETS	LYRICISM	LYSOL
LUZERN	LYE	LYNCHING	LYRICISMS	LYSOLS
LUZERNS	LYES	LYNCHINGS	LYRICIST	LYSOSOMAL
LUZZES	LYFULL	LYNCHPIN	LYRICISTS	LYSOSOME
LWEI	LYING	LYNCHPINS	LYRICIZE	LYSOSOMES
LWEIS	LYINGLY	LYNE	LYRICIZED	LYSOZYME
LYAM	LYINGS	LYNES	LYRICIZES	LYSOZYMES
LYAMS	LYKEWAKE	LYNX	LYRICON	LYSSA
LYARD	LYKEWAKES	LYNXES	LYRICONS	LYSSAS
LYART	LYKEWALK	LYNXLIKE	LYRICS	LYTE
LYASE	LYKEWALKS	LYOLYSES	LYRIFORM	LYTED
LYASES	LYM	LYOLYSIS	LYRISM	LYTES
LYCAENID	LYME	LYOMEROUS	LYRISMS	LYTHE
LYCAENIDS	LYMES	LYONNAISE	LYRIST	LYTHES
LYCEA	LYMITER	LYOPHIL	LYRISTS	LYTIC
LYCEE	LYMITERS	LYOPHILE	LYSATE	LYTICALLY
LYCEES	LYMPH	LYOPHILED	LYSATES	LYTING
LYCEUM	LYMPHAD	LYOPHILIC	LYSE	LYTTA
LYCEUMS	LYMPHADS	LYOPHOBE	LYSED	LYTTAE
LYCH	LYMPHATIC	LYOPHOBIC	LYSERGIC	LYTTAS
LYCHEE	LYMPHOID	LYRA	LYSERGIDE	
LYCHEES	LYMPHOMA	LYRATE	LYSES	
LYCHES	LYMPHOMAS	LYRATED	LYSIGENIC	
LYCHGATE	LYMPHS	LYRATELY	LYSIMETER	

M

MA	MACAWS	MACHISMOS	MACROLIDE	MADCAPS
MAA	MACCABAW	MACHMETER	MACROLOGY	MADDED
MAAED	MACCABAWS	MACHO	MACROMERE	MADDEN
MAAING	MACCABOY	MACHOISM	MACROMOLE	MADDENED
MAAR	MACCABOYS	MACHOISMS	MACRON	MADDENING
MAARE	MACCARONI	MACHOS	MACRONS	MADDENS
MAARS	MACCHIA	MACHREE	MACROPOD	MADDER
MAAS	MACCHIATO	MACHREES	MACROPODS	MADDERS
MAASES	MACCHIE	MACHS	MACROPSIA	MADDEST
MAATJES	MACCOBOY	MACHZOR	MACROS	MADDING
MABE	MACCOBOYS	MACHZORIM	MACROTOUS	MADDINGLY
MABELA	MACE	MACHZORS	MACRURAL	MADDISH
MABELAS	MACED	MACING	MACRURAN	MADDOCK
MABES	MACEDOINE	MACINTOSH	MACRURANS	MADDOCKS
MAC	MACER	MACK	MACRUROID	MADE
MACABER	MACERAL	MACKEREL	MACRUROUS	MADEFIED
MACABRE	MACERALS	MACKERELS	MACS	MADEFIES
MACABRELY	MACERATE	MACKINAW	MACTATION	MADEFY
MACACO	MACERATED	MACKINAWS	MACULA	MADEFYING
MACACOS	MACERATER	MACKLE	MACULAE	MADEIRA
MACADAM	MACERATES	MACKLED	MACULAR	MADEIRAS
MACADAMIA	MACERATOR	MACKLES	MACULAS	MADELEINE
MACADAMS	MACERS	MACKLING	MACULATE	MADERISE
MACAHUBA	MACES	MACKS	MACULATED	MADERISED
MACAHUBAS	MACH	MACLE	MACULATES	MADERISES
MACALLUM	MACHAIR	MACLED	MACULE	MADERIZE
MACALLUMS	MACHAIRS	MACLES	MACULED	MADERIZED
MACAQUE	MACHAN	MACON	MACULES	MADERIZES
MACAQUES	MACHANS	MACONS	MACULING	MADGE
MACARISE	MACHE	MACOYA	MACULOSE	MADGES
MACARISED	MACHER	MACOYAS	MACUMBA	MADHOUSE
MACARISES	MACHERS	MACRAME	MACUMBAS	MADHOUSES
MACARISM	MACHES	MACRAMES	MAD	MADID
MACARISMS	MACHETE	MACRAMI	MADAFU	MADISON
MACARIZE	MACHETES	MACRAMIS	MADAFUS	MADISONS
MACARIZED	MACHI	MACRO	MADAM	MADLING
MACARIZES	MACHINATE	MACROBIAN	MADAME	MADLINGS
MACARONI	MACHINE	MACROCODE	MADAMED	MADLY
MACARONIC	MACHINED	MACROCOPY	MADAMES	MADMAN
MACARONIS	MACHINERY	MACROCOSM	MADAMING	MADMEN
MACAROON	MACHINES	MACROCYST	MADAMS	MADNESS
MACAROONS	MACHINIMA	MACROCYTE	MADAROSES	MADNESSES
MACASSAR	MACHINING	MACRODOME	MADAROSIS	MADONNA
MACASSARS	MACHINIST	MACRODONT	MADBRAIN	MADONNAS
MACAW	MACHISMO	MACROGLIA	MADCAP	MADOQUA

MADOQUAS	MAESTRI	MAGGOTIER	MAGNETICS	MAHATMA
MADRAS	MAESTRO	MAGGOTS	MAGNETISE	MAHATMAS
MADRASA	MAESTROS	MAGGOTY	MAGNETISM	MAHEWU
MADRASAH	MAFFIA	MAGGS	MAGNETIST	MAHEWUS
MADRASAHS	MAFFIAS	MAGI	MAGNETITE	MAHIMAHI
MADRASAS	MAFFICK	MAGIAN	MAGNETIZE	MAHIMAHIS
MADRASES	MAFFICKED	MAGIANISM	MAGNETO	MAHJONG
MADRASSA	MAFFICKER	MAGIANS	MAGNETON	MAHJONGG
MADRASSAH	MAFFICKS	MAGIC	MAGNETONS	MAHJONGGS
MADRASSAS	MAFFLED	MAGICAL	MAGNETOS	MAHJONGS
MADRE	MAFFLIN	MAGICALLY	MAGNETRON	MAHLSTICK
MADREPORE	MAFFLING	MAGICIAN	MAGNETS	MAHMAL
MADRES	MAFFLINGS	MAGICIANS	MAGNIFIC	MAHMALS
MADRIGAL	MAFFLINS	MAGICKED	MAGNIFICO	MAHOE
MADRIGALS	MAFIA	MAGICKING	MAGNIFIED	MAHOES
MADRILENE	MAFIAS	MAGICS	MAGNIFIER	MAHOGANY
MADRONA	MAFIC	MAGILP	MAGNIFIES	MAHONIA
MADRONAS	MAFICS	MAGILPS	MAGNIFY	MAHONIAS
MADRONE	MAFIOSI	MAGISM	MAGNITUDE	MAHOUT
MADRONES	MAFIOSO	MAGISMS	MAGNOLIA	MAHOUTS
MADRONO	MAFIOSOS	MAGISTER	MAGNOLIAS	MAHSEER
MADRONOS	MAFTED	MAGISTERS	MAGNON	MAHSEERS
MADS	MAFTIR	MAGISTERY	MAGNONS	MAHSIR
MADTOM	MAFTIRS	MAGISTRAL	MAGNOX	MAHSIRS
MADTOMS	MAG	MAGLEV	MAGNOXES	MAHUA
MADURO	MAGAININ	MAGLEVS	MAGNUM	MAHUANG
MADUROS	MAGAININS	MAGMA	MAGNUMS	MAHUANGS
MADWOMAN	MAGALOG	MAGMAS	MAGNUS	MAHUAS
MADWOMEN	MAGALOGS	MAGMATA	MAGOT	MAHWA
MADWORT	MAGALOGUE	MAGMATIC	MAGOTS	MAHWAS
MADWORTS	MAGAZINE	MAGMATISM	MAGPIE	MAHZOR
MADZOON	MAGAZINES	MAGNALIUM	MAGPIES	MAHZORIM
MADZOONS	MAGDALEN	MAGNATE	MAGS	MAHZORS
MAE	MAGDALENE	MAGNATES	MAGSMAN	MAIASAUR
MAELID	MAGDALENS	MAGNES	MAGSMEN	MAIASAURA
MAELIDS	MAGE	MAGNESES	MAGUEY	MAIASAURS
MAELSTROM	MAGENTA	MAGNESIA	MAGUEYS	MAID
MAENAD	MAGENTAS	MAGNESIAL	MAGUS	MAIDAN
MAENADES	MAGES	MAGNESIAN	MAGYAR	MAIDANS
MAENADIC	MAGESHIP	MAGNESIAS	MAHA	MAIDED
MAENADISM	MAGESHIPS	MAGNESIC	MAHARAJA	MAIDEN
MAENADS	MAGG	MAGNESITE	MAHARAJAH	MAIDENISH
MAERL	MAGGED	MAGNESIUM	MAHARAJAS	MAIDENLY
MAERLS	MAGGIE	MAGNET	MAHARANEE	MAIDENS
MAES	MAGGIES	MAGNETAR	MAHARANI	MAIDHOOD
MAESTOSO	MAGGING	MAGNETARS	MAHARANIS	MAIDHOODS
MAESTOSOS	MAGGOT	MAGNETIC	MAHARISHI	MAIDING

MAIDISH	MAILSHOT	MAINYARDS	MAKEABLE	MALANDERS
MAIDISM	MAILSHOTS	MAIOLICA	MAKEBATE	MALANGA
MAIDISMS	MAILVAN	MAIOLICAS	MAKEBATES	MALANGAS
MAIDLESS	MAILVANS	MAIR	MAKEFAST	MALAPERT
MAIDS	MAIM	MAIRE	MAKEFASTS	MALAPERTS
MAIEUTIC	MAIMED	MAIREHAU	MAKELESS	MALAPROP
MAIEUTICS	MAIMER	MAIREHAUS	MAKEOVER	MALAPROPS
MAIGRE	MAIMERS	MAIRES	MAKEOVERS	MALAR
MAIGRES	MAIMING	MAIRS	MAKER	MALARIA
MAIHEM	MAIMINGS	MAISE	MAKEREADY	MALARIAL
MAIHEMS	MAIMS	MAISES	MAKERS	MALARIAN
MAIK	MAIN	MAIST	MAKES	MALARIAS
MAIKO	MAINBOOM	MAISTER	MAKESHIFT	MALARIOUS
MAIKOS	MAINBOOMS	MAISTERED	MAKEUP	MALARKEY
MAIKS	MAINBRACE	MAISTERS	MAKEUPS	MALARKEYS
MAIL	MAINDOOR	MAISTRIES	MAKI	MALARKIES
MAILABLE	MAINDOORS	MAISTRING	MAKIMONO	MALARKY
MAILBAG	MAINED	MAISTRY	MAKIMONOS	MALAROMA
MAILBAGS	MAINER	MAISTS	MAKING	MALAROMAS
MAILBOX	MAINEST	MAIZE	MAKINGS	MALARS
MAILBOXES	MAINFRAME	MAIZES	MAKIS	MALAS
MAILCAR	MAINING	MAJAGUA	MAKO	MALATE
MAILCARS	MAINLAND	MAJAGUAS	MAKOS	MALATES
MAILCOACH	MAINLANDS	MAJESTIC	MAKS	MALATHION
MAILE	MAINLINE	MAJESTIES	MAKUTA	MALAX
MAILED	MAINLINED	MAJESTY	MAKUTU	MALAXAGE
MAILER	MAINLINER	MAJLIS	MAKUTUED	MALAXAGES
MAILERS	MAINLINES	MAJLISES	MAKUTUING	MALAXATE
MAILES	MAINLY	MAJOLICA	MAKUTUS	MALAXATED
MAILGRAM	MAINMAST	MAJOLICAS	MAL	MALAXATES
MAILGRAMS	MAINMASTS	MAJOR	MALA	MALAXATOR
MAILING	MAINOR	MAJORAT	MALACCA	MALAXED
MAILINGS	MAINORS	MAJORATS	MALACCAS	MALAXES
MAILL	MAINOUR	MAJORDOMO	MALACHITE	MALAXING
MAILLESS	MAINOURS	MAJORED	MALACIA	MALE
MAILLOT	MAINPRISE	MAJORETTE	MALACIAS	MALEATE
MAILLOTS	MAINS	MAJORING	MALADIES	MALEATES
MAILLS	MAINSAIL	MAJORITY	MALADROIT	MALEDICT
MAILMAN	MAINSAILS	MAJORLY	MALADY	MALEDICTS
MAILMEN	MAINSHEET	MAJORS	MALAGUENA	MALEFFECT
MAILMERGE	MAINSTAY	MAJORSHIP	MALAISE	MALEFIC
MAILPOUCH	MAINSTAYS	MAJUSCULE	MALAISES	MALEFICE
MAILROOM	MAINTAIN	MAK	MALAM	MALEFICES
MAILROOMS	MAINTAINS	MAKABLE	MALAMS	MALEIC
MAILS	MAINTOP	MAKAR	MALAMUTE	MALEMIUT
MAILSACK	MAINTOPS	MAKARS	MALAMUTES	MALEMIUTS
MAILSACKS	MAINYARD	MAKE	MALANDER	MALEMUTE

MALEMUTES	MALL	MALONATE	MALWARES	MAMMALITY
MALENESS	MALLAM	MALONATES	MALWAS	MAMMALOGY
MALENGINE	MALLAMS	MALONIC	MAM	MAMMALS
MALES	MALLANDER	MALOTI	MAMA	MAMMARY
MALFED	MALLARD	MALPIGHIA	MAMAGUY	MAMMAS
MALFORMED	MALLARDS	MALPOSED	MAMAGUYED	MAMMATE
MALGRADO	MALLCORE	MALS	MAMAGUYS	MAMMATI
MALGRE	MALLCORES	MALSTICK	MAMAKAU	MAMMATUS
MALGRED	MALLEABLE	MALSTICKS	MAMAKAUS	MAMMEE
MALGRES	MALLEABLY	MALT	MAMAKO	MAMMEES
MALGRING	MALLEATE	MALTALENT	MAMAKOS	MAMMER
MALI	MALLEATED	MALTASE	MAMAKU	MAMMERED
MALIBU	MALLEATES	MALTASES	MAMAKUS	MAMMERING
MALIC	MALLECHO	MALTED	MAMALIGA	MAMMERS
MALICE	MALLECHOS	MALTEDS	MAMALIGAS	MAMMET
MALICED	MALLED	MALTESE	MAMAS	MAMMETRY
MALICES	MALLEE	MALTHA	MAMBA	MAMMETS
MALICHO	MALLEES	MALTHAS	MAMBAS	MAMMEY
MALICHOS	MALLEI	MALTIER	MAMBO	MAMMEYS
MALICING	MALLEMUCK	MALTIEST	MAMBOED	MAMMIE
MALICIOUS	MALLENDER	MALTINESS	MAMBOES	MAMMIES
MALIGN	MALLEOLAR	MALTING	MAMBOING	MAMMIFER
MALIGNANT	MALLEOLI	MALTINGS	MAMBOS	MAMMIFERS
MALIGNED	MALLEOLUS	MALTMAN	MAMEE	MAMMIFORM
MALIGNER	MALLET	MALTMEN	MAMEES	MAMMILLA
MALIGNERS	MALLETS	MALTOL	MAMELON	MAMMILLAE
MALIGNING	MALLEUS	MALTOLS	MAMELONS	MAMMITIS
MALIGNITY	MALLEUSES	MALTOSE	MAMELUCO	MAMMOCK
MALIGNLY	MALLING	MALTOSES	MAMELUCOS	MAMMOCKED
MALIGNS	MALLINGS	MALTREAT	MAMELUKE	MAMMOCKS
MALIHINI	MALLOW	MALTREATS	MAMELUKES	MAMMOGRAM
MALIHINIS	MALLOWS	MALTS	MAMEY	MAMMON
MALIK	MALLS	MALTSTER	MAMEYES	MAMMONISH
MALIKS	MALM	MALTSTERS	MAMEYS	MAMMONISM
MALINE	MALMAG	MALTWORM	MAMIE	MAMMONIST
MALINES	MALMAGS	MALTWORMS	MAMIES	MAMMONITE
MALINGER	MALMIER	MALTY	MAMILLA	MAMMONS
MALINGERS	MALMIEST	MALVA	MAMILLAE	MAMMOTH
MALINGERY	MALMS	MALVAS	MAMILLAR	MAMMOTHS
MALIS	MALMSEY	MALVASIA	MAMILLARY	MAMMY
MALISM	MALMSEYS	MALVASIAN	MAMILLATE	MAMPARA
MALISMS	MALMSTONE	MALVASIAS	MAMLUK	MAMPARAS
MALISON	MALMY	MALVESIE	MAMLUKS	MAMPOER
MALISONS	MALODOR	MALVESIES	MAMMA	MAMPOERS
MALIST	MALODORS	MALVOISIE	MAMMAE	MAMS
MALKIN	MALODOUR	MALWA	MAMMAL	MAMSELLE
MALKINS	MALODOURS	MALWARE	MAMMALIAN	MAMSELLES

MAMZER	MANDALAS	MANDUCATE	MANGILY	MANIFESTO
MAMZERIM	MANDALIC	MANDYLION	MANGINESS	MANIFESTS
MAMZERS	MANDAMUS	MANE	MANGING	MANIFOLD
MAN	MANDARIN	MANED	MANGLE	MANIFOLDS
MANA	MANDARINE	MANEGE	MANGLED	MANIFORM
MANACLE	MANDARINS	MANEGED	MANGLER	MANIHOC
MANACLED	MANDATARY	MANEGES	MANGLERS	MANIHOCS
MANACLES	MANDATE	MANEGING	MANGLES	MANIHOT
MANACLING	MANDATED	MANEH	MANGLING	MANIHOTS
MANAGE	MANDATES	MANEHS	MANGO	MANIKIN
MANAGED	MANDATING	MANELESS	MANGOES	MANIKINS
MANAGER	MANDATOR	MANENT	MANGOLD	MANILA
MANAGERS	MANDATORS	MANES	MANGOLDS	MANILAS
MANAGES	MANDATORY	MANET	MANGONEL	MANILLA
MANAGING	MANDI	MANEUVER	MANGONELS	MANILLAS
MANAIA	MANDIBLE	MANEUVERS	MANGOS	MANILLE
MANAIAS	MANDIBLES	MANFUL	MANGOSTAN	MANILLES
MANAKIN	MANDILION	MANFULLY	MANGOUSTE	MANIOC
MANAKINS	MANDIOC	MANG	MANGROVE	MANIOCA
MANANA	MANDIOCA	MANGA	MANGROVES	MANIOCAS
MANANAS	MANDIOCAS	MANGABEY	MANGS	MANIOCS
MANAS	MANDIOCCA	MANGABEYS	MANGULATE	MANIPLE
MANAT	MANDIOCS	MANGABIES	MANGY	MANIPLES
MANATEE	MANDIR	MANGABY	MANHANDLE	MANIPLIES
MANATEES	MANDIRA	MANGAL	MANHATTAN	MANIPULAR
MANATI	MANDIRAS	MANGALS	MANHOLE	MANIS
MANATIS	MANDIRS	MANGANATE	MANHOLES	MANITO
MANATOID	MANDIS	MANGANESE	MANHOOD	MANITOS
MANATS	MANDOLA	MANGANIC	MANHOODS	MANITOU
MANATU	MANDOLAS	MANGANIN	MANHUNT	MANITOUS
MANATUS	MANDOLIN	MANGANINS	MANHUNTER	MANITU
MANAWA	MANDOLINE	MANGANITE	MANHUNTS	MANITUS
MANAWAS	MANDOLINS	MANGANOUS	MANI	MANJACK
MANCALA	MANDOM	MANGAS	MANIA	MANJACKS
MANCALAS	MANDOMS	MANGE	MANIAC	MANKIER
MANCANDO	MANDORA	MANGEAO	MANIACAL	MANKIEST
MANCHE	MANDORAS	MANGEAOS	MANIACS	MANKIND
MANCHES	MANDORLA	MANGED	MANIAS	MANKINDS
MANCHET	MANDORLAS	MANGEL	MANIC	MANKINI
MANCHETS	MANDRAKE	MANGELS	MANICALLY	MANKINIS
MANCIPATE	MANDRAKES	MANGER	MANICOTTI	MANKY
MANCIPLE	MANDREL	MANGERS	MANICS	MANLESS
MANCIPLES	MANDRELS	MANGES	MANICURE	MANLIER
MANCUS	MANDRIL	MANGETOUT	MANICURED	MANLIEST
MANCUSES	MANDRILL	MANGEY	MANICURES	MANLIKE
MAND	MANDRILLS	MANGIER	MANIES	MANLIKELY
MANDALA	MANDRILS	MANGIEST	MANIFEST	MANLILY

M

MANLINESS	MANRIDER	MANTLETS	MANYATA	MARA
MANLY	MANRIDERS	MANTLING	MANYATAS	MARABI
MANMADE	MANRIDING	MANTLINGS	MANYATTA	MARABIS
MANNA	MANROPE	MANTO	MANYATTAS	MARABOU
MANNAN	MANROPES	MANTOES	MANYFOLD	MARABOUS
MANNANS	MANS	MANTOS	MANYPLIES	MARABOUT
MANNAS	MANSARD	MANTRA	MANZANITA	MARABOUTS
MANNED	MANSARDED	MANTRAM	MANZELLO	MARABUNTA
MANNEQUIN	MANSARDS	MANTRAMS	MANZELLOS	MARACA
MANNER	MANSE	MANTRAP	MAOMAO	MARACAS
MANNERED	MANSES	MANTRAPS	MAOMAOS	MARAE
MANNERISM	MANSHIFT	MANTRAS	MAORMOR	MARAES
MANNERIST	MANSHIFTS	MANTRIC	MAORMORS	MARAGING
MANNERLY	MANSION	MANTUA	MAP	MARAGINGS
MANNERS	MANSIONS	MANTUAS	MAPAU	MARAH
MANNIKIN	MANSLAYER	MANTY	MAPAUS	MARAHS
MANNIKINS	MANSONRY	MANUAL	MAPLE	MARANATHA
MANNING	MANSUETE	MANUALLY	MAPLELIKE	MARANTA
MANNISH	MANSWORN	MANUALS	MAPLES	MARANTAS
MANNISHLY	MANTA	MANUARY	MAPLESS	MARARI
MANNITE	MANTAS	MANUBRIA	MAPLIKE	MARARIS
MANNITES	MANTEAU	MANUBRIAL	MAPMAKER	MARAS
MANNITIC	MANTEAUS	MANUBRIUM	MAPMAKERS	MARASCA
MANNITOL	MANTEAUX	MANUHIRI	MAPMAKING	MARASCAS
MANNITOLS	MANTEEL	MANUHIRIS	MAPPABLE	MARASMIC
MANNOSE	MANTEELS	MANUKA	MAPPED	MARASMOID
MANNOSES	MANTEL	MANUKAS	MAPPEMOND	MARASMUS
MANO	MANTELET	MANUL	MAPPER	MARATHON
MANOAO	MANTELETS	MANULS	MAPPERIES	MARATHONS
MANOAOS	MANTELS	MANUMEA	MAPPERS	MARAUD
MANOEUVRE	MANTES	MANUMEAS	MAPPERY	MARAUDED
MANOMETER	MANTIC	MANUMIT	MAPPING	MARAUDER
MANOMETRY	MANTICORA	MANUMITS	MAPPINGS	MARAUDERS
MANOR	MANTICORE	MANURANCE	MAPPIST	MARAUDING
MANORIAL	MANTID	MANURE	MAPPISTS	MARAUDS
MANORS	MANTIDS	MANURED	MAPS	MARAVEDI
MANOS	MANTIES	MANURER	MAPSTICK	MARAVEDIS
MANOSCOPY	MANTILLA	MANURERS	MAPSTICKS	MARBELISE
MANPACK	MANTILLAS	MANURES	MAPWISE	MARBELIZE
MANPACKS	MANTIS	MANURIAL	MAQUETTE	MARBLE
MANPOWER	MANTISES	MANURING	MAQUETTES	MARBLED
MANPOWERS	MANTISSA	MANURINGS	MAQUI	MARBLEISE
MANQUE	MANTISSAS	MANUS	MAQUILA	MARBLEIZE
MANRED	MANTLE	MANWARD	MAQUILAS	MARBLER
MANREDS	MANTLED	MANWARDS	MAQUIS	MARBLERS
MANRENT	MANTLES	MANWISE	MAQUISARD	MARBLES
MANRENTS	MANTLET	MANY	MAR	MARBLIER

MARBLIEST	MAREROS	MARINADE	MARKHOORS	MARMOSES
MARBLING	MARES	MARINADED	MARKHOR	MARMOSET
MARBLINGS	MARESCHAL	MARINADES	MARKHORS	MARMOSETS
MARBLY	MARG	MARINARA	MARKING	MARMOT
MARC	MARGARIC	MARINARAS	MARKINGS	MARMOTS
MARCASITE	MARGARIN	MARINAS	MARKKA	MARMS
MARCATO	MARGARINE	MARINATE	MARKKAA	MAROCAIN
MARCATOS	MARGARINS	MARINATED	MARKKAS	MAROCAINS
MARCEL	MARGARITA	MARINATES	MARKMAN	MARON
MARCELLA	MARGARITE	MARINE	MARKMEN	MARONS
MARCELLAS	MARGAY	MARINER	MARKS	MAROON
MARCELLED	MARGAYS	MARINERA	MARKSMAN	MAROONED
MARCELLER	MARGE	MARINERAS	MARKSMEN	MAROONER
MARCELS	MARGENT	MARINERS	MARKUP	MAROONERS
MARCH	MARGENTED	MARINES	MARKUPS	MAROONING
MARCHED	MARGENTS	MARINIERE	MARL	MAROONS
MARCHEN	MARGES	MARIPOSA	MARLE	MAROQUIN
MARCHER	MARGIN	MARIPOSAS	MARLED	MAROQUINS
MARCHERS	MARGINAL	MARISCHAL	MARLES	MAROR
MARCHES	MARGINALS	MARISH	MARLIER	MARORS
MARCHESA	MARGINATE	MARISHES	MARLIEST	MARPLOT
MARCHESAS	MARGINED	MARITAGE	MARLIN	MARPLOTS
MARCHESE	MARGINING	MARITAGES	MARLINE	MARQUE
MARCHESI	MARGINS	MARITAL	MARLINES	MARQUEE
MARCHING	MARGOSA	MARITALLY	MARLING	MARQUEES
MARCHLAND	MARGOSAS	MARITIME	MARLINGS	MARQUES
MARCHLIKE	MARGRAVE	MARJORAM	MARLINS	MARQUESS
MARCHMAN	MARGRAVES	MARJORAMS	MARLITE	MARQUETRY
MARCHMEN	MARGS	MARK	MARLITES	MARQUIS
MARCHPANE	MARIA	MARKA	MARLITIC	MARQUISE
MARCONI	MARIACHI	MARKAS	MARLS	MARQUISES
MARCONIED	MARIACHIS	MARKDOWN	MARLSTONE	MARRAM
MARCONIS	MARIALITE	MARKDOWNS	MARLY	MARRAMS
MARCS	MARID	MARKED	MARM	MARRANO
MARD	MARIDS	MARKEDLY	MARMALADE	MARRANOS
MARDIED	MARIES	MARKER	MARMALISE	MARRED
MARDIER	MARIGOLD	MARKERS	MARMALIZE	MARRELS
MARDIES	MARIGOLDS	MARKET	MARMARISE	MARRER
MARDIEST	MARIGRAM	MARKETED	MARMARIZE	MARRERS
MARDY	MARIGRAMS	MARKETEER	MARMELISE	MARRI
MARDYING	MARIGRAPH	MARKETER	MARMELIZE	MARRIAGE
MARE	MARIHUANA	MARKETERS	MARMEM	MARRIAGES
MAREMMA	MARIJUANA	MARKETING	MARMITE	MARRIED
MAREMMAS	MARIMBA	MARKETISE	MARMITES	MARRIEDS
MAREMME	MARIMBAS	MARKETIZE	MARMOREAL	MARRIER
MARENGO	MARIMBIST	MARKETS	MARMOREAN	MARRIERS
MARERO	MARINA	MARKHOOR	MARMOSE	MARRIES

MARRING	MARTAGON	MARVERED	MASHGIHIM	MASONING
MARRIS	MARTAGONS	MARVERING	MASHIACH	MASONITE
MARRON	MARTED	MARVERS	MASHIACHS	MASONITES
MARRONS	MARTEL	MARVIER	MASHIE	MASONRIED
MARROW	MARTELLED	MARVIEST	MASHIER	MASONRIES
MARROWED	MARTELLO	MARVY	MASHIES	MASONRY
MARROWFAT	MARTELLOS	MARXISANT	MASHIEST	MASONS
MARROWING	MARTELS	MARY	MASHING	MASOOLAH
MARROWISH	MARTEN	MARYBUD	MASHINGS	MASOOLAHS
MARROWS	MARTENS	MARYBUDS	MASHLAM	MASQUE
MARROWSKY	MARTEXT	MARYJANE	MASHLAMS	MASQUER
MARROWY	MARTEXTS	MARYJANES	MASHLIM	MASQUERS
MARRUM	MARTIAL	MARZIPAN	MASHLIMS	MASQUES
MARRUMS	MARTIALLY	MARZIPANS	MASHLIN	MASS
MARRY	MARTIALS	MAS	MASHLINS	MASSA
MARRYING	MARTIAN	MASA	MASHLOCH	MASSACRE
MARRYINGS	MARTIANS	MASALA	MASHLOCHS	MASSACRED
MARS	MARTIN	MASALAS	MASHLUM	MASSACRER
MARSALA	MARTINET	MASAS	MASHLUMS	MASSACRES
MARSALAS	MARTINETS	MASCARA	MASHMAN	MASSAGE
MARSE	MARTING	MASCARAED	MASHMEN	MASSAGED
MARSEILLE	MARTINGAL	MASCARAS	MASHUA	MASSAGER
MARSES	MARTINI	MASCARON	MASHUAS	MASSAGERS
MARSH	MARTINIS	MASCARONS	MASHUP	MASSAGES
MARSHAL	MARTINS	MASCLE	MASHUPS	MASSAGING
MARSHALCY	MARTLET	MASCLED	MASHY	MASSAGIST
MARSHALED	MARTLETS	MASCLES	MASING	MASSAS
MARSHALER	MARTS	MASCON	MASJID	MASSCULT
MARSHALL	MARTYR	MASCONS	MASJIDS	MASSCULTS
MARSHALLS	MARTYRDOM	MASCOT	MASK	MASSE
MARSHALS	MARTYRED	MASCOTS	MASKABLE	MASSED
MARSHBUCK	MARTYRIA	MASCULINE	MASKED	MASSEDLY
MARSHES	MARTYRIES	MASCULIST	MASKEG	MASSES
MARSHIER	MARTYRING	MASCULY	MASKEGS	MASSETER
MARSHIEST	MARTYRISE	MASE	MASKER	MASSETERS
MARSHLAND	MARTYRISM	MASED	MASKERS	MASSEUR
MARSHLIKE	MARTYRIUM	MASER	MASKING	MASSEURS
MARSHWORT	MARTYRIZE	MASERS	MASKINGS	MASSEUSE
MARSHY	MARTYRLY	MASES	MASKLIKE	MASSEUSES
MARSPORT	MARTYRS	MASH	MASKS	MASSICOT
MARSPORTS	MARTYRY	MASHALLAH	MASLIN	MASSICOTS
MARSQUAKE	MARVEL	MASHED	MASLINS	MASSIER
MARSUPIA	MARVELED	MASHER	MASOCHISM	MASSIEST
MARSUPIAL	MARVELING	MASHERS	MASOCHIST	MASSIF
MARSUPIAN	MARVELLED	MASHES	MASON	MASSIFS
MARSUPIUM	MARVELOUS	MASHGIACH	MASONED	MASSINESS
MART	MARVELS	MASHGIAH	MASONIC	MASSING

MASSIVE	MASTIXES	MATCHETS	MATILDA	MATSAH
MASSIVELY	MASTLESS	MATCHING	MATILDAS	MATSAHS
MASSIVES	MASTLIKE	MATCHLESS	MATILY	MATSURI
MASSLESS	MASTODON	MATCHLOCK	MATIN	MATSURIS
MASSOOLA	MASTODONS	MATCHMADE	MATINAL	MATSUTAKE
MASSOOLAS	MASTODONT	MATCHMAKE	MATINEE	MATT
MASSTIGE	MASTOID	MATCHMARK	MATINEES	MATTAMORE
MASSTIGES	MASTOIDAL	MATCHPLAY	MATINESS	MATTE
MASSY	MASTOIDS	MATCHUP	MATING	MATTED
MASSYMORE	MASTOPEXY	MATCHUPS	MATINGS	MATTEDLY
MAST	MASTS	MATCHWOOD	MATINS	MATTER
MASTABA	MASTY	MATE	MATIPO	MATTERED
MASTABAH	MASU	MATED	MATIPOS	MATTERFUL
MASTABAHS	MASULA	MATELASSE	MATJES	MATTERING
MASTABAS	MASULAS	MATELESS	MATLESS	MATTERS
MASTED	MASURIUM	MATELOT	MATLO	MATTERY
MASTER	MASURIUMS	MATELOTE	MATLOS	MATTES
MASTERATE	MASUS	MATELOTES	MATLOW	MATTIE
MASTERDOM	MAT	MATELOTS	MATLOWS	MATTIES
MASTERED	MATACHIN	MATELOTTE	MATOKE	MATTIFIED
MASTERFUL	MATACHINA	MATER	MATOKES	MATTIFIES
MASTERIES	MATACHINI	MATERIAL	MATOOKE	MATTIFY
MASTERING	MATADOR	MATERIALS	MATOOKES	MATTIN
MASTERLY	MATADORA	MATERIEL	MATRASS	MATTING
MASTERS	MATADORAS	MATERIELS	MATRASSES	MATTINGS
MASTERY	MATADORE	MATERNAL	MATRES	MATTINS
MASTFUL	MATADORES	MATERNITY	MATRIARCH	MATTOCK
MASTHEAD	MATADORS	MATERS	MATRIC	MATTOCKS
MASTHEADS	MATAGOURI	MATES	MATRICE	MATTOID
MASTHOUSE	MATAI	MATESHIP	MATRICES	MATTOIDS
MASTIC	MATAIS	MATESHIPS	MATRICIDE	MATTRASS
MASTICATE	MATAMATA	MATEY	MATRICS	MATTRESS
MASTICH	MATAMATAS	MATEYNESS	MATRICULA	MATTS
MASTICHE	MATAMBALA	MATEYS	MATRILINY	MATURABLE
MASTICHES	MATATA	MATFELLON	MATRIMONY	MATURATE
MASTICHS	MATATAS	MATFELON	MATRIX	MATURATED
MASTICOT	MATATU	MATFELONS	MATRIXES	MATURATES
MASTICOTS	MATATUS	MATGRASS	MATRON	MATURE
MASTICS	MATCH	MATH	MATRONAGE	MATURED
MASTIER	MATCHABLE	MATHESES	MATRONAL	MATURELY
MASTIEST	MATCHBOOK	MATHESIS	MATRONISE	MATURER
MASTIFF	MATCHBOX	MATHS	MATRONIZE	MATURERS
MASTIFFS	MATCHED	MATICO	MATRONLY	MATURES
MASTING	MATCHER	MATICOS	MATRONS	MATUREST
MASTITIC	MATCHERS	MATIER	MATROSS	MATURING
MASTITIS	MATCHES	MATIES	MATROSSES	MATURITY
MASTIX	MATCHET	MATIEST	MATS	MATUTINAL

M

MATUTINE	MAUNDERED	MAWED	MAXIMISES	MAYOR
MATWEED	MAUNDERER	MAWGER	MAXIMIST	MAYORAL
MATWEEDS	MAUNDERS	MAWING	MAXIMISTS	MAYORALTY
MATY	MAUNDIES	MAWK	MAXIMITE	MAYORESS
MATZA	MAUNDING	MAWKIER	MAXIMITES	MAYORS
MATZAH	MAUNDS	MAWKIEST	MAXIMIZE	MAYORSHIP
MATZAHS	MAUNDY	MAWKIN	MAXIMIZED	MAYOS
MATZAS	MAUNGIER	MAWKINS	MAXIMIZER	MAYPOLE
MATZO	MAUNGIEST	MAWKISH	MAXIMIZES	MAYPOLES
MATZOH	MAUNGY	MAWKISHLY	MAXIMS	MAYPOP
MATZOHS	MAUNNA	MAWKS	MAXIMUM	MAYPOPS
MATZOON	MAURI	MAWKY	MAXIMUMLY	MAYS
MATZOONS	MAURIS	MAWMET	MAXIMUMS	MAYST
MATZOS	MAUSOLEA	MAWMETRY	MAXIMUS	MAYSTER
MATZOT	MAUSOLEAN	MAWMETS	MAXIMUSES	MAYSTERS
MATZOTH	MAUSOLEUM	MAWN	MAXING	MAYVIN
MAUBIES	MAUT	MAWPUS	MAXIS	MAYVINS
MAUBY	MAUTHER	MAWPUSES	MAXIXE	MAYWEED
MAUD	MAUTHERS	MAWR	MAXIXES	MAYWEEDS
MAUDLIN	MAUTS	MAWRS	MAXWELL	MAZAEDIA
MAUDLINLY	MAUVAIS	MAWS	MAXWELLS	MAZAEDIUM
MAUDS	MAUVAISE	MAWSEED	MAY	MAZARD
MAUGER	MAUVE	MAWSEEDS	MAYA	MAZARDS
MAUGRE	MAUVEIN	MAWTHER	MAYAN	MAZARINE
MAUGRED	MAUVEINE	MAWTHERS	MAYAPPLE	MAZARINES
MAUGRES	MAUVEINES	MAX	MAYAPPLES	MAZE
MAUGRING	MAUVEINS	MAXED	MAYAS	MAZED
MAUL	MAUVER	MAXES	MAYBE	MAZEDLY
MAULED	MAUVES	MAXI	MAYBES	MAZEDNESS
MAULER	MAUVEST	MAXICOAT	MAYBIRD	MAZEFUL
MAULERS	MAUVIN	MAXICOATS	MAYBIRDS	MAZELIKE
MAULGRE	MAUVINE	MAXILLA	MAYBUSH	MAZELTOV
MAULGRED	MAUVINES	MAXILLAE	MAYBUSHES	MAZEMENT
MAULGRES	MAUVINS	MAXILLAR	MAYDAY	MAZEMENTS
MAULGRING	MAVEN	MAXILLARY	MAYDAYS	MAZER
MAULING	MAVENS	MAXILLAS	MAYED	MAZERS
MAULS	MAVERICK	MAXILLULA	MAYEST	MAZES
MAULSTICK	MAVERICKS	MAXIM	MAYFLIES	MAZEY
MAULVI	MAVIE	MAXIMA	MAYFLOWER	MAZHBI
MAULVIS	MAVIES	MAXIMAL	MAYFLY	MAZHBIS
MAUMET	MAVIN	MAXIMALLY	MAYHAP	MAZIER
MAUMETRY	MAVINS	MAXIMALS	MAYHAPPEN	MAZIEST
MAUMETS	MAVIS	MAXIMIN	MAYHEM	MAZILY
MAUN	MAVISES	MAXIMINS	MAYHEMS	MAZINESS
MAUND	MAVOURNIN	MAXIMISE	MAYING	MAZING
MAUNDED	MAW	MAXIMISED	MAYINGS	MAZOURKA
MAUNDER	MAWBOUND	MAXIMISER	MAYO	MAZOURKAS

MAZOUT
MAZOUTS
MAZUMA
MAZUMAS
MAZURKA
MAZURKAS
MAZUT
MAZUTS
MAZY
MAZZARD
MAZZARDS
MBAQANGA
MBAQANGAS
MBIRA
MBIRAS
ME
MEACOCK
MEACOCKS
MEAD
MEADOW
MEADOWS
MEADOWY
MEADS
MEAGER
MEAGERLY
MEAGRE
MEAGRELY
MEAGRER
MEAGRES
MEAGREST
MEAL
MEALED
MEALER
MEALERS
MEALIE
MEALIER
MEALIES
MEALIEST
MEALINESS
MEALING
MEALLESS
MEALS
MEALTIME
MEALTIMES
MEALWORM
MEALWORMS
MEALY

MEALYBUG
MEALYBUGS
MEAN
MEANDER
MEANDERED
MEANDERER
MEANDERS
MEANDRIAN
MEANDROUS
MEANE
MEANED
MEANER
MEANERS
MEANES
MEANEST
MEANIE
MEANIES
MEANING
MEANINGLY
MEANINGS
MEANLY
MEANNESS
MEANS
MEANT
MEANTIME
MEANTIMES
MEANWHILE
MEANY
MEARE
MEARES
MEARING
MEASE
MEASED
MEASES
MEASING
MEASLE
MEASLED
MEASLES
MEASLIER
MEASLIEST
MEASLING
MEASLY
MEASURE
MEASURED
MEASURER
MEASURERS
MEASURES

MEASURING
MEAT
MEATAL
MEATAXE
MEATAXES
MEATBALL
MEATBALLS
MEATED
MEATH
MEATHE
MEATHEAD
MEATHEADS
MEATHES
MEATHS
MEATIER
MEATIEST
MEATILY
MEATINESS
MEATLESS
MEATLOAF
MEATMAN
MEATMEN
MEATS
MEATSPACE
MEATUS
MEATUSES
MEATY
MEAWES
MEAZEL
MEAZELS
MEBOS
MEBOSES
MECCA
MECCAS
MECHANIC
MECHANICS
MECHANISE
MECHANISM
MECHANIST
MECHANIZE
MECHITZA
MECHITZAS
MECHITZOT
MECK
MECKS
MECLIZINE
MECONATE

MECONATES
MECONIC
MECONIN
MECONINS
MECONIUM
MECONIUMS
MED
MEDACCA
MEDACCAS
MEDAILLON
MEDAKA
MEDAKAS
MEDAL
MEDALED
MEDALET
MEDALETS
MEDALING
MEDALIST
MEDALISTS
MEDALLED
MEDALLIC
MEDALLING
MEDALLION
MEDALLIST
MEDALPLAY
MEDALS
MEDCINAL
MEDDLE
MEDDLED
MEDDLER
MEDDLERS
MEDDLES
MEDDLING
MEDDLINGS
MEDEVAC
MEDEVACED
MEDEVACS
MEDFLIES
MEDFLY
MEDIA
MEDIACIES
MEDIACY
MEDIAD
MEDIAE
MEDIAEVAL
MEDIAL
MEDIALLY

MEDIALS
MEDIAN
MEDIANLY
MEDIANS
MEDIANT
MEDIANTS
MEDIAS
MEDIATE
MEDIATED
MEDIATELY
MEDIATES
MEDIATING
MEDIATION
MEDIATISE
MEDIATIVE
MEDIATIZE
MEDIATOR
MEDIATORS
MEDIATORY
MEDIATRIX
MEDIC
MEDICABLE
MEDICABLY
MEDICAID
MEDICAIDS
MEDICAL
MEDICALLY
MEDICALS
MEDICANT
MEDICANTS
MEDICARE
MEDICARES
MEDICATE
MEDICATED
MEDICATES
MEDICIDE
MEDICIDES
MEDICINAL
MEDICINE
MEDICINED
MEDICINER
MEDICINES
MEDICK
MEDICKS
MEDICO
MEDICOS
MEDICS

M

MEDIEVAL	MEE	MEGADEAL	MEGATONIC	MEISTERS
MEDIEVALS	MEED	MEGADEALS	MEGATONS	MEITH
MEDIGAP	MEEDS	MEGADEATH	MEGAVOLT	MEITHS
MEDIGAPS	MEEK	MEGADOSE	MEGAVOLTS	MEJLIS
MEDII	MEEKEN	MEGADOSES	MEGAWATT	MEJLISES
MEDINA	MEEKENED	MEGADYNE	MEGAWATTS	MEKKA
MEDINAS	MEEKENING	MEGADYNES	MEGILLA	MEKKAS
MEDIOCRE	MEEKENS	MEGAFARAD	MEGILLAH	MEKOMETER
MEDITATE	MEEKER	MEGAFAUNA	MEGILLAHS	MEL
MEDITATED	MEEKEST	MEGAFLOP	MEGILLAS	MELA
MEDITATES	MEEKLY	MEGAFLOPS	MEGILLOTH	MELALEUCA
MEDITATOR	MEEKNESS	MEGAFLORA	MEGILP	MELAMDIM
MEDIUM	MEEMIE	MEGAFOG	MEGILPH	MELAMED
MEDIUMS	MEEMIES	MEGAFOGS	MEGILPHS	MELAMINE
MEDIUS	MEER	MEGAGAUSS	MEGILPS	MELAMINES
MEDIUSES	MEERCAT	MEGAHERTZ	MEGOHM	MELAMPODE
MEDIVAC	MEERCATS	MEGAHIT	MEGOHMS	MELANGE
MEDIVACED	MEERED	MEGAHITS	MEGRIM	MELANGES
MEDIVACS	MEERING	MEGAJOULE	MEGRIMS	MELANIAN
MEDLAR	MEERKAT	MEGALITH	MEGS	MELANIC
MEDLARS	MEERKATS	MEGALITHS	MEH	MELANICS
MEDLE	MEERS	MEGALITRE	MEHNDI	MELANIN
MEDLED	MEES	MEGALOPIC	MEHNDIS	MELANINS
MEDLES	MEET	MEGALOPS	MEIBOMIAN	MELANISE
MEDLEY	MEETER	MEGAPHONE	MEIKLE	MELANISED
MEDLEYS	MEETERS	MEGAPHYLL	MEIN	MELANISES
MEDLING	MEETEST	MEGAPIXEL	MEINED	MELANISM
MEDRESA	MEETING	MEGAPLEX	MEINEY	MELANISMS
MEDRESAS	MEETINGS	MEGAPOD	MEINEYS	MELANIST
MEDRESE	MEETLY	MEGAPODE	MEINIE	MELANISTS
MEDRESES	MEETNESS	MEGAPODES	MEINIES	MELANITE
MEDRESSEH	MEETS	MEGAPODS	MEINING	MELANITES
MEDS	MEFF	MEGARA	MEINS	MELANITIC
MEDULLA	MEFFS	MEGARAD	MEINT	MELANIZE
MEDULLAE	MEG	MEGARADS	MEINY	MELANIZED
MEDULLAR	MEGA	MEGARON	MEIOCYTE	MELANIZES
MEDULLARY	MEGABAR	MEGARONS	MEIOCYTES	MELANO
MEDULLAS	MEGABARS	MEGASCOPE	MEIOFAUNA	MELANOID
MEDULLATE	MEGABIT	MEGASPORE	MEIONITE	MELANOIDS
MEDUSA	MEGABITS	MEGASS	MEIONITES	MELANOMA
MEDUSAE	MEGABUCK	MEGASSE	MEIOSES	MELANOMAS
MEDUSAL	MEGABUCKS	MEGASSES	MEIOSIS	MELANOS
MEDUSAN	MEGABYTE	MEGASTAR	MEIOSPORE	MELANOSES
MEDUSANS	MEGABYTES	MEGASTARS	MEIOTIC	MELANOSIS
MEDUSAS	MEGACITY	MEGASTORE	MEISHI	MELANOTIC
MEDUSOID	MEGACURIE	MEGATHERE	MEISHIS	MELANOUS
MEDUSOIDS	MEGACYCLE	MEGATON	MEISTER	MELANURIA

MELANURIC	MELLOW	MELTAGE	MEMORIALS	MENDS
MELAPHYRE	MELLOWED	MELTAGES	MEMORIES	MENE
MELAS	MELLOWER	MELTDOWN	MEMORISE	MENED
MELASTOME	MELLOWEST	MELTDOWNS	MEMORISED	MENEER
MELATONIN	MELLOWING	MELTED	MEMORISER	MENEERS
MELBA	MELLOWLY	MELTEMI	MEMORISES	MENES
MELD	MELLOWS	MELTEMIS	MEMORITER	MENFOLK
MELDED	MELLOWY	MELTER	MEMORIZE	MENFOLKS
MELDER	MELLS	MELTERS	MEMORIZED	MENG
MELDERS	MELOCOTON	MELTIER	MEMORIZER	MENGE
MELDING	MELODEON	MELTIEST	MEMORIZES	MENGED
MELDS	MELODEONS	MELTING	MEMORY	MENGES
MELEE	MELODIA	MELTINGLY	MEMOS	MENGING
MELEES	MELODIAS	MELTINGS	MEMS	MENGS
MELENA	MELODIC	MELTITH	MEMSAHIB	MENHADEN
MELENAS	MELODICA	MELTITHS	MEMSAHIBS	MENHADENS
MELIC	MELODICAS	MELTON	MEN	MENHIR
MELICK	MELODICS	MELTONS	MENACE	MENHIRS
MELICKS	MELODIES	MELTS	MENACED	MENIAL
MELICS	MELODION	MELTWATER	MENACER	MENIALLY
MELIK	MELODIONS	MELTY	MENACERS	MENIALS
MELIKS	MELODIOUS	MELUNGEON	MENACES	MENILITE
MELILITE	MELODISE	MEM	MENACING	MENILITES
MELILITES	MELODISED	MEMBER	MENAD	MENING
MELILOT	MELODISER	MEMBERED	MENADIONE	MENINGEAL
MELILOTS	MELODISES	MEMBERS	MENADS	MENINGES
MELINITE	MELODIST	MEMBRAL	MENAGE	MENINX
MELINITES	MELODISTS	MEMBRANAL	MENAGED	MENISCAL
MELIORATE	MELODIZE	MEMBRANE	MENAGERIE	MENISCATE
MELIORISM	MELODIZED	MEMBRANED	MENAGES	MENISCI
MELIORIST	MELODIZER	MEMBRANES	MENAGING	MENISCOID
MELIORITY	MELODIZES	MEME	MENARCHE	MENISCUS
MELISMA	MELODRAMA	MEMENTO	MENARCHES	MENO
MELISMAS	MELODRAME	MEMENTOES	MENAZON	MENOLOGY
MELISMATA	MELODY	MEMENTOS	MENAZONS	MENOMINEE
MELITTIN	MELOID	MEMES	MEND	MENOMINI
MELITTINS	MELOIDS	MEMETIC	MENDABLE	MENOMINIS
MELL	MELOMANIA	MEMETICS	MENDACITY	MENOPAUSE
MELLAY	MELOMANIC	MEMO	MENDED	MENOPOLIS
MELLAYS	MELON	MEMOIR	MENDER	MENOPOME
MELLED	MELONGENE	MEMOIRISM	MENDERS	MENOPOMES
MELLIFIC	MELONS	MEMOIRIST	MENDICANT	MENORAH
MELLING	MELOXICAM	MEMOIRS	MENDICITY	MENORAHS
MELLITE	MELPHALAN	MEMORABLE	MENDIGO	MENORRHEA
MELLITES	MELS	MEMORABLY	MENDIGOS	MENSA
MELLITIC	MELT	MEMORANDA	MENDING	MENSAE
MELLOTRON	MELTABLE	MEMORIAL	MENDINGS	MENSAL

M

MENSAS	MENTORING	MERCIES	MERGING	MERMAIDEN
MENSCH	MENTORS	MERCIFIDE	MERGINGS	MERMAIDS
MENSCHEN	MENTOS	MERCIFIED	MERI	MERMAN
MENSCHES	MENTUM	MERCIFIES	MERICARP	MERMEN
MENSCHY	MENU	MERCIFUL	MERICARPS	MEROCRINE
MENSE	MENUDO	MERCIFY	MERIDIAN	MEROGONY
MENSED	MENUDOS	MERCILESS	MERIDIANS	MEROISTIC
MENSEFUL	MENUISIER	MERCS	MERIL	MEROME
MENSELESS	MENUS	MERCURATE	MERILS	MEROMES
MENSES	MENYIE	MERCURIAL	MERIMAKE	MERONYM
MENSH	MENYIES	MERCURIC	MERIMAKES	MERONYMS
MENSHED	MEOU	MERCURIES	MERING	MERONYMY
MENSHEN	MEOUED	MERCURISE	MERINGS	MEROPIA
MENSHES	MEOUING	MERCURIZE	MERINGUE	MEROPIAS
MENSHING	MEOUS	MERCUROUS	MERINGUES	MEROPIC
MENSING	MEOW	MERCURY	MERINO	MEROPIDAN
MENSTRUA	MEOWED	MERCY	MERINOS	MEROSOME
MENSTRUAL	MEOWING	MERDE	MERIS	MEROSOMES
MENSTRUUM	MEOWS	MERDES	MERISES	MEROZOITE
MENSUAL	MEPACRINE	MERE	MERISIS	MERPEOPLE
MENSURAL	MEPHITIC	MERED	MERISM	MERRIER
MENSWEAR	MEPHITIS	MEREL	MERISMS	MERRIES
MENSWEARS	MEPHITISM	MERELL	MERISTEM	MERRIEST
MENT	MERANTI	MERELLS	MERISTEMS	MERRILY
MENTA	MERANTIS	MERELS	MERISTIC	MERRIMENT
MENTAL	MERBROMIN	MERELY	MERIT	MERRINESS
MENTALESE	MERC	MERENGUE	MERITED	MERRY
MENTALISM	MERCAPTAN	MERENGUES	MERITING	MERRYMAN
MENTALIST	MERCAPTO	MEREOLOGY	MERITLESS	MERRYMEN
MENTALITY	MERCAT	MERER	MERITS	MERSALYL
MENTALLY	MERCATS	MERES	MERK	MERSALYLS
MENTATION	MERCENARY	MERESMAN	MERKIN	MERSE
MENTEE	MERCER	MERESMEN	MERKINS	MERSES
MENTEES	MERCERIES	MEREST	MERKS	MERSION
MENTHENE	MERCERISE	MERESTONE	MERL	MERSIONS
MENTHENES	MERCERIZE	MERFOLK	MERLE	MERYCISM
MENTHOL	MERCERS	MERFOLKS	MERLES	MERYCISMS
MENTHOLS	MERCERY	MERGANSER	MERLIN	MES
MENTICIDE	MERCES	MERGE	MERLING	MESA
MENTION	MERCH	MERGED	MERLINGS	MESAIL
MENTIONED	MERCHANT	MERGEE	MERLINS	MESAILS
MENTIONER	MERCHANTS	MERGEES	MERLON	MESAL
MENTIONS	MERCHES	MERGENCE	MERLONS	MESALLY
MENTO	MERCHET	MERGENCES	MERLOT	MESARAIC
MENTOR	MERCHETS	MERGER	MERLOTS	MESARCH
MENTORED	MERCHILD	MERGERS	MERLS	MESAS
MENTORIAL	MERCIABLE	MERGES	MERMAID	MESCAL

MESCALIN	MESMERISM	MESQUITS	MESTOME	METAMALE
MESCALINE	MESMERIST	MESS	MESTOMES	METAMALES
MESCALINS	MESMERIZE	MESSAGE	MESTOMS	METAMER
MESCALISM	MESNALTY	MESSAGED	MESTRANOL	METAMERAL
MESCALS	MESNE	MESSAGES	MET	METAMERE
MESCLUM	MESNES	MESSAGING	META	METAMERES
MESCLUMS	MESOBLAST	MESSALINE	METABASES	METAMERIC
MESCLUN	MESOCARP	MESSAN	METABASIS	METAMERS
MESCLUNS	MESOCARPS	MESSANS	METABATIC	METAMICT
MESDAMES	MESOCRANY	MESSED	METABOLIC	METANOIA
MESE	MESODERM	MESSENGER	METABOLY	METANOIAS
MESEEMED	MESODERMS	MESSES	METACARPI	METAPELET
MESEEMETH	MESOGLEA	MESSIAH	METADATA	METAPHASE
MESEEMS	MESOGLEAL	MESSIAHS	METAFILE	METAPHOR
MESEL	MESOGLEAS	MESSIANIC	METAFILES	METAPHORS
MESELED	MESOGLOEA	MESSIAS	METAGE	METAPLASM
MESELS	MESOLITE	MESSIASES	METAGENIC	METAPLOT
MESENTERA	MESOLITES	MESSIER	METAGES	METARCHON
MESENTERY	MESOMERE	MESSIEST	METAIRIE	METASOMA
MESES	MESOMERES	MESSIEURS	METAIRIES	METASOMAS
MESETA	MESOMORPH	MESSILY	METAL	METATAG
MESETAS	MESON	MESSINESS	METALED	METATAGS
MESH	MESONIC	MESSING	METALHEAD	METATARSI
MESHED	MESONS	MESSMAN	METALING	METATE
MESHES	MESOPAUSE	MESSMATE	METALISE	METATES
MESHIER	MESOPHILE	MESSMATES	METALISED	METAVERSE
MESHIEST	MESOPHYL	MESSMEN	METALISES	METAXYLEM
MESHING	MESOPHYLL	MESSUAGE	METALIST	METAYAGE
MESHINGS	MESOPHYLS	MESSUAGES	METALISTS	METAYAGES
MESHUGA	MESOPHYTE	MESSY	METALIZE	METAYER
MESHUGAAS	MESOSCALE	MESTEE	METALIZED	METAYERS
MESHUGAH	MESOSOME	MESTEES	METALIZES	METAZOA
MESHUGAS	MESOSOMES	MESTER	METALLED	METAZOAL
MESHUGGA	MESOTRON	MESTERS	METALLIC	METAZOAN
MESHUGGAH	MESOTRONS	MESTESO	METALLICS	METAZOANS
MESHUGGE	MESOZOAN	MESTESOES	METALLIKE	METAZOIC
MESHWORK	MESOZOANS	MESTESOS	METALLINE	METAZOON
MESHWORKS	MESOZOIC	MESTINO	METALLING	METCAST
MESHY	MESPRISE	MESTINOES	METALLISE	METCASTS
MESIAD	MESPRISES	MESTINOS	METALLIST	METE
MESIAL	MESPRIZE	MESTIZA	METALLIZE	METED
MESIALLY	MESPRIZES	MESTIZAS	METALLOID	METEOR
MESIAN	MESQUIN	MESTIZO	METALLY	METEORIC
MESIC	MESQUINE	MESTIZOES	METALMARK	METEORISM
MESICALLY	MESQUIT	MESTIZOS	METALS	METEORIST
MESMERIC	MESQUITE	MESTO	METALWARE	METEORITE
MESMERISE	MESQUITES	MESTOM	METALWORK	METEOROID

METEOROUS	METHYLAL	METRICATE	MEWLS	MIAOWED
METEORS	METHYLALS	METRICIAN	MEWS	MIAOWING
METEPA	METHYLASE	METRICISE	MEWSED	MIAOWS
METEPAS	METHYLATE	METRICISM	MEWSES	MIASM
METER	METHYLENE	METRICIST	MEWSING	MIASMA
METERAGE	METHYLIC	METRICIZE	MEYNT	MIASMAL
METERAGES	METHYLS	METRICS	MEZAIL	MIASMAS
METERED	METHYSES	METRIFIED	MEZAILS	MIASMATA
METERING	METHYSIS	METRIFIER	MEZCAL	MIASMATIC
METERS	METHYSTIC	METRIFIES	MEZCALINE	MIASMIC
METES	METIC	METRIFY	MEZCALS	MIASMOUS
METESTICK	METICAIS	METRING	MEZE	MIASMS
METESTRUS	METICAL	METRIST	MEZEREON	MIAUL
METEWAND	METICALS	METRISTS	MEZEREONS	MIAULED
METEWANDS	METICS	METRITIS	MEZEREUM	MIAULING
METEYARD	METIER	METRO	MEZEREUMS	MIAULS
METEYARDS	METIERS	METROLOGY	MEZES	MIB
METFORMIN	METIF	METRONOME	MEZQUIT	MIBS
METH	METIFS	METROPLEX	MEZQUITE	MIBUNA
METHADON	METING	METROS	MEZQUITES	MIBUNAS
METHADONE	METIS	METS	MEZQUITS	MIC
METHADONS	METISSE	METTLE	MEZUZA	MICA
METHANAL	METISSES	METTLED	MEZUZAH	MICACEOUS
METHANALS	METOL	METTLES	MEZUZAHS	MICAS
METHANE	METOLS	METUMP	MEZUZAS	MICATE
METHANES	METONYM	METUMPS	MEZUZOT	MICATED
METHANOIC	METONYMIC	MEU	MEZUZOTH	MICATES
METHANOL	METONYMS	MEUNIERE	MEZZ	MICATING
METHANOLS	METONYMY	MEUS	MEZZALUNA	MICAWBER
METHEGLIN	METOPAE	MEUSE	MEZZANINE	MICAWBERS
METHINK	METOPE	MEUSED	MEZZE	MICE
METHINKS	METOPES	MEUSES	MEZZES	MICELL
METHO	METOPIC	MEUSING	MEZZO	MICELLA
METHOD	METOPISM	MEVE	MEZZOS	MICELLAE
METHODIC	METOPISMS	MEVED	MEZZOTINT	MICELLAR
METHODISE	METOPON	MEVES	MGANGA	MICELLAS
METHODISM	METOPONS	MEVING	MGANGAS	MICELLE
METHODIST	METOPRYL	MEVROU	MHO	MICELLES
METHODIZE	METOPRYLS	MEVROUS	MHORR	MICELLS
METHODS	METRALGIA	MEW	MHORRS	MICH
METHOS	METRAZOL	MEWED	MHOS	MICHAEL
METHOUGHT	METRAZOLS	MEWING	MI	MICHAELS
METHOXIDE	METRE	MEWL	MIAOU	MICHE
METHOXY	METRED	MEWLED	MIAOUED	MICHED
METHOXYL	METRES	MEWLER	MIAOUING	MICHER
METHS	METRIC	MEWLERS	MIAOUS	MICHERS
METHYL	METRICAL	MEWLING	MIAOW	MICHES

MICHIGAN	MICRODONT	MIDAIR	MIDLANDER	MIDTERMS
MICHIGANS	MICRODOT	MIDAIRS	MIDLANDS	MIDTOWN
MICHING	MICRODOTS	MIDBAND	MIDLEG	MIDTOWNS
MICHINGS	MICROFILM	MIDBRAIN	MIDLEGS	MIDWATCH
MICHT	MICROFORM	MIDBRAINS	MIDLIFE	MIDWAY
MICHTS	MICROGLIA	MIDCAP	MIDLIFER	MIDWAYS
MICK	MICROGRAM	MIDCOURSE	MIDLIFERS	MIDWEEK
MICKERIES	MICROHM	MIDCULT	MIDLINE	MIDWEEKLY
MICKERY	MICROHMS	MIDCULTS	MIDLINES	MIDWEEKS
MICKEY	MICROINCH	MIDDAY	MIDLIST	MIDWIFE
MICKEYED	MICROJET	MIDDAYS	MIDLISTS	MIDWIFED
MICKEYING	MICROJETS	MIDDEN	MIDLIVES	MIDWIFERY
MICKEYS	MICROLITE	MIDDENS	MIDMONTH	MIDWIFES
MICKIES	MICROLITH	MIDDEST	MIDMONTHS	MIDWIFING
MICKLE	MICROLOAN	MIDDIE	MIDMOST	MIDWINTER
MICKLER	MICROLOGY	MIDDIES	MIDMOSTS	MIDWIVE
MICKLES	MICROLUX	MIDDLE	MIDNIGHT	MIDWIVED
MICKLEST	MICROMERE	MIDDLED	MIDNIGHTS	MIDWIVES
MICKS	MICROMESH	MIDDLEMAN	MIDNOON	MIDWIVING
MICKY	MICROMHO	MIDDLEMEN	MIDNOONS	MIDYEAR
MICO	MICROMHOS	MIDDLER	MIDPOINT	MIDYEARS
MICOS	MICROMINI	MIDDLERS	MIDPOINTS	MIELIE
MICRA	MICROMOLE	MIDDLES	MIDRANGE	MIELIES
MICRIFIED	MICRON	MIDDLING	MIDRANGES	MIEN
MICRIFIES	MICRONISE	MIDDLINGS	MIDRASH	MIENS
MICRIFY	MICRONIZE	MIDDORSAL	MIDRASHIC	MIEVE
MICRO	MICRONS	MIDDY	MIDRASHIM	MIEVED
MICROBAR	MICROPORE	MIDFIELD	MIDRASHOT	MIEVES
MICROBARS	MICROPSIA	MIDFIELDS	MIDRIB	MIEVING
MICROBE	MICROPUMP	MIDGE	MIDRIBS	MIFF
MICROBEAM	MICROPYLE	MIDGES	MIDRIFF	MIFFED
MICROBES	MICROS	MIDGET	MIDRIFFS	MIFFIER
MICROBIAL	MICROSITE	MIDGETS	MIDS	MIFFIEST
MICROBIAN	MICROSOME	MIDGIE	MIDSHIP	MIFFILY
MICROBIC	MICROTOME	MIDGIER	MIDSHIPS	MIFFINESS
MICROBLOG	MICROTOMY	MIDGIES	MIDSIZE	MIFFING
MICROBREW	MICROTONE	MIDGIEST	MIDSIZED	MIFFS
MICROBUS	MICROVOLT	MIDGUT	MIDSOLE	MIFFY
MICROCAP	MICROWATT	MIDGUTS	MIDSOLES	MIFTY
MICROCAR	MICROWAVE	MIDGY	MIDSPACE	MIG
MICROCARD	MICROWIRE	MIDI	MIDSPACES	MIGG
MICROCARS	MICRURGY	MIDINETTE	MIDST	MIGGLE
MICROCHIP	MICS	MIDIRON	MIDSTORY	MIGGLES
MICROCODE	MICTION	MIDIRONS	MIDSTREAM	MIGGS
MICROCOPY	MICTIONS	MIDIS	MIDSTS	MIGHT
MICROCOSM	MICTURATE	MIDISKIRT	MIDSUMMER	MIGHTEST
MICROCYTE	MID	MIDLAND	MIDTERM	MIGHTFUL

MIGHTIER	MIKVOS	MILIARIA	MILKTOAST	MILLIGAL
MIGHTIEST	MIKVOT	MILIARIAL	MILKWEED	MILLIGALS
MIGHTILY	MIKVOTH	MILIARIAS	MILKWEEDS	MILLIGRAM
MIGHTS	MIL	MILIARY	MILKWOOD	MILLILUX
MIGHTST	MILADI	MILIEU	MILKWOODS	MILLIME
MIGHTY	MILADIES	MILIEUS	MILKWORT	MILLIMES
MIGMATITE	MILADIS	MILIEUX	MILKWORTS	MILLIMHO
MIGNON	MILADY	MILITANCE	MILKY	MILLIMHOS
MIGNONNE	MILAGE	MILITANCY	MILL	MILLIMOLE
MIGNONNES	MILAGES	MILITANT	MILLABLE	MILLINE
MIGNONS	MILCH	MILITANTS	MILLAGE	MILLINER
MIGRAINE	MILCHIG	MILITAR	MILLAGES	MILLINERS
MIGRAINES	MILCHIK	MILITARIA	MILLBOARD	MILLINERY
MIGRANT	MILD	MILITARY	MILLCAKE	MILLINES
MIGRANTS	MILDED	MILITATE	MILLCAKES	MILLING
MIGRATE	MILDEN	MILITATED	MILLDAM	MILLINGS
MIGRATED	MILDENED	MILITATES	MILLDAMS	MILLIOHM
MIGRATES	MILDENING	MILITIA	MILLE	MILLIOHMS
MIGRATING	MILDENS	MILITIAS	MILLED	MILLION
MIGRATION	MILDER	MILIUM	MILLENARY	MILLIONS
MIGRATOR	MILDEST	MILK	MILLENNIA	MILLIONTH
MIGRATORS	MILDEW	MILKED	MILLEPED	MILLIPED
MIGRATORY	MILDEWED	MILKEN	MILLEPEDE	MILLIPEDE
MIGS	MILDEWING	MILKER	MILLEPEDS	MILLIPEDS
MIHA	MILDEWS	MILKERS	MILLEPORE	MILLIREM
MIHAS	MILDEWY	MILKFISH	MILLER	MILLIREMS
MIHI	MILDING	MILKIER	MILLERITE	MILLIVOLT
MIHIED	MILDLY	MILKIEST	MILLERS	MILLIWATT
MIHIING	MILDNESS	MILKILY	MILLES	MILLOCRAT
MIHIS	MILDS	MILKINESS	MILLET	MILLPOND
MIHRAB	MILE	MILKING	MILLETS	MILLPONDS
MIHRABS	MILEAGE	MILKINGS	MILLHAND	MILLRACE
MIJNHEER	MILEAGES	MILKLESS	MILLHANDS	MILLRACES
MIJNHEERS	MILEPOST	MILKLIKE	MILLHOUSE	MILLRIND
MIKADO	MILEPOSTS	MILKMAID	MILLIARD	MILLRINDS
MIKADOS	MILER	MILKMAIDS	MILLIARDS	MILLRUN
MIKE	MILERS	MILKMAN	MILLIARE	MILLRUNS
MIKED	MILES	MILKMEN	MILLIARES	MILLS
MIKES	MILESIAN	MILKO	MILLIARY	MILLSCALE
MIKING	MILESIMO	MILKOS	MILLIBAR	MILLSTONE
MIKRA	MILESIMOS	MILKS	MILLIBARS	MILLTAIL
MIKRON	MILESTONE	MILKSHAKE	MILLIE	MILLTAILS
MIKRONS	MILF	MILKSHED	MILLIEME	MILLWHEEL
MIKVAH	MILFOIL	MILKSHEDS	MILLIEMES	MILLWORK
MIKVAHS	MILFOILS	MILKSOP	MILLIER	MILLWORKS
MIKVEH	MILFS	MILKSOPPY	MILLIERS	MILNEB
MIKVEHS	MILIA	MILKSOPS	MILLIES	MILNEBS

MILO	MIMETITES	MINCIER	MINGING	MINIKIN
MILOMETER	MIMIC	MINCIEST	MINGLE	MINIKINS
MILOR	MIMICAL	MINCING	MINGLED	MINILAB
MILORD	MIMICKED	MINCINGLY	MINGLER	MINILABS
MILORDS	MIMICKER	MINCY	MINGLERS	MINIM
MILORS	MIMICKERS	MIND	MINGLES	MINIMA
MILOS	MIMICKING	MINDED	MINGLING	MINIMAL
MILPA	MIMICRIES	MINDER	MINGLINGS	MINIMALLY
MILPAS	MIMICRY	MINDERS	MINGS	MINIMALS
MILREIS	MIMICS	MINDFUCK	MINGY	MINIMART
MILS	MIMING	MINDFUCKS	MINI	MINIMARTS
MILSEY	MIMIVIRUS	MINDFUL	MINIATE	MINIMAX
MILSEYS	MIMMER	MINDFULLY	MINIATED	MINIMAXED
MILT	MIMMEST	MINDING	MINIATES	MINIMAXES
MILTED	MIMMICK	MINDINGS	MINIATING	MINIMENT
MILTER	MIMMICKED	MINDLESS	MINIATION	MINIMENTS
MILTERS	MIMMICKS	MINDS	MINIATURE	MINIMILL
MILTIER	MIMOSA	MINDSET	MINIBAR	MINIMILLS
MILTIEST	MIMOSAE	MINDSETS	MINIBARS	MINIMISE
MILTING	MIMOSAS	MINDSHARE	MINIBIKE	MINIMISED
MILTONIA	MIMSEY	MINE	MINIBIKER	MINIMISER
MILTONIAS	MIMSIER	MINEABLE	MINIBIKES	MINIMISES
MILTS	MIMSIEST	MINED	MINIBREAK	MINIMISM
MILTY	MIMSY	MINEFIELD	MINIBUS	MINIMISMS
MILTZ	MIMULUS	MINELAYER	MINIBUSES	MINIMIST
MILTZES	MIMULUSES	MINEOLA	MINICAB	MINIMISTS
MILVINE	MINA	MINEOLAS	MINICABS	MINIMIZE
MIM	MINABLE	MINER	MINICAM	MINIMIZED
MIMBAR	MINACIOUS	MINERAL	MINICAMP	MINIMIZER
MIMBARS	MINACITY	MINERALS	MINICAMPS	MINIMIZES
MIME	MINAE	MINERS	MINICAMS	MINIMOTO
MIMED	MINAR	MINES	MINICAR	MINIMOTOS
MIMEO	MINARET	MINESHAFT	MINICARS	MINIMS
MIMEOED	MINARETED	MINESTONE	MINICOM	MINIMUM
MIMEOING	MINARETS	MINETTE	MINICOMS	MINIMUMS
MIMEOS	MINARS	MINETTES	MINIDISC	MINIMUS
MIMER	MINAS	MINEVER	MINIDISCS	MINIMUSES
MIMERS	MINATORY	MINEVERS	MINIDISH	MINING
MIMES	MINBAR	MING	MINIDISK	MININGS
MIMESES	MINBARS	MINGE	MINIDISKS	MINION
MIMESIS	MINCE	MINGED	MINIDRESS	MINIONS
MIMESISES	MINCED	MINGER	MINIER	MINIPARK
MIMESTER	MINCEMEAT	MINGERS	MINIEST	MINIPARKS
MIMESTERS	MINCER	MINGES	MINIFIED	MINIPILL
MIMETIC	MINCERS	MINGIER	MINIFIES	MINIPILLS
MIMETICAL	MINCES	MINGIEST	MINIFY	MINIRUGBY
MIMETITE	MINCEUR	MINGINESS	MINIFYING	MINIS

MINISCULE	MINORSHIP	MINYANS	MIRKEST	MISAGENT
MINISH	MINOS	MIOCENE	MIRKIER	MISAGENTS
MINISHED	MINOTAUR	MIOMBO	MIRKIEST	MISAIM
MINISHES	MINOXIDIL	MIOMBOS	MIRKILY	MISAIMED
MINISHING	MINSHUKU	MIOSES	MIRKINESS	MISAIMING
MINISKI	MINSHUKUS	MIOSIS	MIRKS	MISAIMS
MINISKIRT	MINSTER	MIOTIC	MIRKY	MISALIGN
MINISKIS	MINSTERS	MIOTICS	MIRLIER	MISALIGNS
MINISTATE	MINSTREL	MIPS	MIRLIEST	MISALLEGE
MINISTER	MINSTRELS	MIQUELET	MIRLIGOES	MISALLIED
MINISTERS	MINT	MIQUELETS	MIRLITON	MISALLIES
MINISTRY	MINTAGE	MIR	MIRLITONS	MISALLOT
MINITOWER	MINTAGES	MIRABELLE	MIRLY	MISALLOTS
MINITRACK	MINTED	MIRABILIA	MIRO	MISALLY
MINIUM	MINTER	MIRABILIS	MIROMIRO	MISALTER
MINIUMS	MINTERS	MIRABLE	MIROMIROS	MISALTERS
MINIVAN	MINTIER	MIRACIDIA	MIROS	MISANDRY
MINIVANS	MINTIEST	MIRACLE	MIRROR	MISAPPLY
MINIVER	MINTING	MIRACLES	MIRRORED	MISARRAY
MINIVERS	MINTS	MIRADOR	MIRRORING	MISARRAYS
MINIVET	MINTY	MIRADORS	MIRRORS	MISASSAY
MINIVETS	MINUEND	MIRAGE	MIRS	MISASSAYS
MINK	MINUENDS	MIRAGES	MIRTH	MISASSIGN
MINKE	MINUET	MIRANDISE	MIRTHFUL	MISATE
MINKES	MINUETS	MIRANDIZE	MIRTHLESS	MISATONE
MINKS	MINUS	MIRBANE	MIRTHS	MISATONED
MINNEOLA	MINUSCULE	MIRBANES	MIRV	MISATONES
MINNEOLAS	MINUSES	MIRCHI	MIRVED	MISAUNTER
MINNICK	MINUTE	MIRE	MIRVING	MISAVER
MINNICKED	MINUTED	MIRED	MIRVS	MISAVERS
MINNICKS	MINUTELY	MIREPOIX	MIRY	MISAVISED
MINNIE	MINUTEMAN	MIRES	MIRZA	MISAWARD
MINNIES	MINUTEMEN	MIREX	MIRZAS	MISAWARDS
MINNOCK	MINUTER	MIREXES	MIS	MISBECAME
MINNOCKED	MINUTES	MIRI	MISACT	MISBECOME
MINNOCKS	MINUTEST	MIRIER	MISACTED	MISBEGAN
MINNOW	MINUTIA	MIRIEST	MISACTING	MISBEGIN
MINNOWS	MINUTIAE	MIRIFIC	MISACTS	MISBEGINS
MINNY	MINUTIAL	MIRIFICAL	MISADAPT	MISBEGOT
MINO	MINUTING	MIRIN	MISADAPTS	MISBEGUN
MINOR	MINUTIOSE	MIRINESS	MISADD	MISBEHAVE
MINORCA	MINX	MIRING	MISADDED	MISBELIEF
MINORCAS	MINXES	MIRINS	MISADDING	MISBESEEM
MINORED	MINXISH	MIRITI	MISADDS	MISBESTOW
MINORING	MINY	MIRITIS	MISADJUST	MISBIAS
MINORITY	MINYAN	MIRK	MISADVICE	MISBIASED
MINORS	MINYANIM	MIRKER	MISADVISE	MISBIASES

MISBILL	MISCODING	MISDID	MISERERE	MISFRAMED
MISBILLED	MISCOIN	MISDIET	MISERERES	MISFRAMES
MISBILLS	MISCOINED	MISDIETS	MISERES	MISGAUGE
MISBIND	MISCOINS	MISDIGHT	MISERIES	MISGAUGED
MISBINDS	MISCOLOR	MISDIRECT	MISERLIER	MISGAUGES
MISBIRTH	MISCOLORS	MISDIVIDE	MISERLY	MISGAVE
MISBIRTHS	MISCOLOUR	MISDO	MISERS	MISGIVE
MISBORN	MISCOOK	MISDOER	MISERY	MISGIVEN
MISBOUND	MISCOOKED	MISDOERS	MISES	MISGIVES
MISBRAND	MISCOOKS	MISDOES	MISESTEEM	MISGIVING
MISBRANDS	MISCOPIED	MISDOING	MISEVENT	MISGO
MISBUILD	MISCOPIES	MISDOINGS	MISEVENTS	MISGOES
MISBUILDS	MISCOPY	MISDONE	MISFAITH	MISGOING
MISBUILT	MISCOUNT	MISDONNE	MISFAITHS	MISGONE
MISBUTTON	MISCOUNTS	MISDOUBT	MISFALL	MISGOTTEN
MISCALL	MISCREANT	MISDOUBTS	MISFALLEN	MISGOVERN
MISCALLED	MISCREATE	MISDRAW	MISFALLS	MISGRADE
MISCALLER	MISCREDIT	MISDRAWN	MISFALNE	MISGRADED
MISCALLS	MISCREED	MISDRAWS	MISFARE	MISGRADES
MISCARRY	MISCREEDS	MISDREAD	MISFARED	MISGRAFF
MISCAST	MISCUE	MISDREADS	MISFARES	MISGRAFT
MISCASTS	MISCUED	MISDRIVE	MISFARING	MISGRAFTS
MISCEGEN	MISCUEING	MISDRIVEN	MISFEASOR	MISGREW
MISCEGENE	MISCUES	MISDRIVES	MISFED	MISGROW
MISCEGENS	MISCUING	MISDROVE	MISFEED	MISGROWN
MISCEGINE	MISCUT	MISE	MISFEEDS	MISGROWS
MISCH	MISCUTS	MISEASE	MISFEIGN	MISGROWTH
MISCHANCE	MISDATE	MISEASES	MISFEIGNS	MISGUESS
MISCHANCY	MISDATED	MISEAT	MISFELL	MISGUGGLE
MISCHARGE	MISDATES	MISEATEN	MISFIELD	MISGUIDE
MISCHIEF	MISDATING	MISEATING	MISFIELDS	MISGUIDED
MISCHIEFS	MISDEAL	MISEATS	MISFILE	MISGUIDER
MISCHOICE	MISDEALER	MISEDIT	MISFILED	MISGUIDES
MISCHOOSE	MISDEALS	MISEDITED	MISFILES	MISHANDLE
MISCHOSE	MISDEALT	MISEDITS	MISFILING	MISHANTER
MISCHOSEN	MISDEED	MISEMPLOY	MISFIRE	MISHAP
MISCIBLE	MISDEEDS	MISENROL	MISFIRED	MISHAPPED
MISCITE	MISDEEM	MISENROLL	MISFIRES	MISHAPPEN
MISCITED	MISDEEMED	MISENROLS	MISFIRING	MISHAPS
MISCITES	MISDEEMS	MISENTER	MISFIT	MISHAPT
MISCITING	MISDEFINE	MISENTERS	MISFITS	MISHEAR
MISCLAIM	MISDEMEAN	MISENTRY	MISFITTED	MISHEARD
MISCLAIMS	MISDEMPT	MISER	MISFOCUS	MISHEARS
MISCLASS	MISDESERT	MISERABLE	MISFORM	MISHEGAAS
MISCODE	MISDIAL	MISERABLY	MISFORMED	MISHEGOSS
MISCODED	MISDIALED	MISERE	MISFORMS	MISHIT
MISCODES	MISDIALS	MISERE	MISFRAME	MISHITS

M

MISHMASH	MISLAYERS	MISMARKS	MISPARTED	MISRAISES
MISHMEE	MISLAYING	MISMARRY	MISPARTS	MISRATE
MISHMEES	MISLAYS	MISMATCH	MISPATCH	MISRATED
MISHMI	MISLEAD	MISMATE	MISPEN	MISRATES
MISHMIS	MISLEADER	MISMATED	MISPENNED	MISRATING
MISHMOSH	MISLEADS	MISMATES	MISPENS	MISREAD
MISINFER	MISLEARED	MISMATING	MISPHRASE	MISREADS
MISINFERS	MISLEARN	MISMEET	MISPICKEL	MISRECKON
MISINFORM	MISLEARNS	MISMEETS	MISPLACE	MISRECORD
MISINTEND	MISLEARNT	MISMET	MISPLACED	MISREFER
MISINTER	MISLED	MISMETRE	MISPLACES	MISREFERS
MISINTERS	MISLEEKE	MISMETRED	MISPLAN	MISREGARD
MISJOIN	MISLEEKED	MISMETRES	MISPLANS	MISRELATE
MISJOINED	MISLEEKES	MISMOVE	MISPLANT	MISRELIED
MISJOINS	MISLETOE	MISMOVED	MISPLANTS	MISRELIES
MISJUDGE	MISLETOES	MISMOVES	MISPLAY	MISRELY
MISJUDGED	MISLIE	MISMOVING	MISPLAYED	MISRENDER
MISJUDGER	MISLIES	MISNAME	MISPLAYS	MISREPORT
MISJUDGES	MISLIGHT	MISNAMED	MISPLEAD	MISRHYMED
MISKAL	MISLIGHTS	MISNAMES	MISPLEADS	MISROUTE
MISKALS	MISLIKE	MISNAMING	MISPLEASE	MISROUTED
MISKEEP	MISLIKED	MISNOMER	MISPLED	MISROUTES
MISKEEPS	MISLIKER	MISNOMERS	MISPOINT	MISRULE
MISKEN	MISLIKERS	MISNUMBER	MISPOINTS	MISRULED
MISKENNED	MISLIKES	MISO	MISPOISE	MISRULES
MISKENS	MISLIKING	MISOCLERE	MISPOISED	MISRULING
MISKENT	MISLIPPEN	MISOGAMIC	MISPOISES	MISS
MISKEPT	MISLIT	MISOGAMY	MISPRAISE	MISSA
MISKEY	MISLIVE	MISOGYNIC	MISPRICE	MISSABLE
MISKEYED	MISLIVED	MISOGYNY	MISPRICED	MISSAE
MISKEYING	MISLIVES	MISOLOGY	MISPRICES	MISSAID
MISKEYS	MISLIVING	MISONEISM	MISPRINT	MISSAL
MISKICK	MISLOCATE	MISONEIST	MISPRINTS	MISSALS
MISKICKED	MISLODGE	MISORDER	MISPRISE	MISSAW
MISKICKS	MISLODGED	MISORDERS	MISPRISED	MISSAY
MISKNEW	MISLODGES	MISORIENT	MISPRISES	MISSAYING
MISKNOW	MISLUCK	MISOS	MISPRIZE	MISSAYS
MISKNOWN	MISLUCKED	MISPAGE	MISPRIZED	MISSEAT
MISKNOWS	MISLUCKS	MISPAGED	MISPRIZER	MISSEATED
MISLABEL	MISLYING	MISPAGES	MISPRIZES	MISSEATS
MISLABELS	MISMADE	MISPAGING	MISPROUD	MISSED
MISLABOR	MISMAKE	MISPAINT	MISQUOTE	MISSEE
MISLABORS	MISMAKES	MISPAINTS	MISQUOTED	MISSEEING
MISLAID	MISMAKING	MISPARSE	MISQUOTER	MISSEEM
MISLAIN	MISMANAGE	MISPARSED	MISQUOTES	MISSEEMED
MISLAY	MISMARK	MISPARSES	MISRAISE	MISSEEMS
MISLAYER	MISMARKED	MISPART	MISRAISED	MISSEEN

MISSEES	MISSOUT	MISTALS	MISTLES	MISVALUE
MISSEL	MISSOUTS	MISTAUGHT	MISTLETOE	MISVALUED
MISSELL	MISSPACE	MISTBOW	MISTLING	MISVALUES
MISSELLS	MISSPACED	MISTBOWS	MISTOLD	MISWEEN
MISSELS	MISSPACES	MISTEACH	MISTOOK	MISWEENED
MISSEND	MISSPEAK	MISTED	MISTOUCH	MISWEENS
MISSENDS	MISSPEAKS	MISTELL	MISTRACE	MISWEND
MISSENSE	MISSPELL	MISTELLS	MISTRACED	MISWENDS
MISSENSES	MISSPELLS	MISTEMPER	MISTRACES	MISWENT
MISSENT	MISSPELT	MISTEND	MISTRAIN	MISWORD
MISSES	MISSPEND	MISTENDED	MISTRAINS	MISWORDED
MISSET	MISSPENDS	MISTENDS	MISTRAL	MISWORDS
MISSETS	MISSPENT	MISTER	MISTRALS	MISWRIT
MISSHAPE	MISSPOKE	MISTERED	MISTREAT	MISWRITE
MISSHAPED	MISSPOKEN	MISTERIES	MISTREATS	MISWRITES
MISSHAPEN	MISSTAMP	MISTERING	MISTRESS	MISWROTE
MISSHAPER	MISSTAMPS	MISTERM	MISTRIAL	MISYOKE
MISSHAPES	MISSTART	MISTERMED	MISTRIALS	MISYOKED
MISSHOD	MISSTARTS	MISTERMS	MISTRUST	MISYOKES
MISSHOOD	MISSTATE	MISTERS	MISTRUSTS	MISYOKING
MISSHOODS	MISSTATED	MISTERY	MISTRUTH	MITCH
MISSIER	MISSTATES	MISTEUK	MISTRUTHS	MITCHED
MISSIES	MISSTEER	MISTFUL	MISTRYST	MITCHES
MISSIEST	MISSTEERS	MISTHINK	MISTRYSTS	MITCHING
MISSILE	MISSTEP	MISTHINKS	MISTS	MITE
MISSILEER	MISSTEPS	MISTHREW	MISTUNE	MITER
MISSILERY	MISSTOP	MISTHROW	MISTUNED	MITERED
MISSILES	MISSTOPS	MISTHROWN	MISTUNES	MITERER
MISSILRY	MISSTRIKE	MISTHROWS	MISTUNING	MITERERS
MISSING	MISSTRUCK	MISTICO	MISTUTOR	MITERING
MISSINGLY	MISSTYLE	MISTICOS	MISTUTORS	MITERS
MISSION	MISSTYLED	MISTIER	MISTY	MITERWORT
MISSIONAL	MISSTYLES	MISTIEST	MISTYPE	MITES
MISSIONED	MISSUIT	MISTIGRIS	MISTYPED	MITHER
MISSIONER	MISSUITED	MISTILY	MISTYPES	MITHERED
MISSIONS	MISSUITS	MISTIME	MISTYPING	MITHERING
MISSIS	MISSUS	MISTIMED	MISUNION	MITHERS
MISSISES	MISSUSES	MISTIMES	MISUNIONS	MITICIDAL
MISSISH	MISSY	MISTIMING	MISUSAGE	MITICIDE
MISSIVE	MIST	MISTINESS	MISUSAGES	MITICIDES
MISSIVES	MISTAKE	MISTING	MISUSE	MITIER
MISSOLD	MISTAKEN	MISTINGS	MISUSED	MITIEST
MISSORT	MISTAKER	MISTITLE	MISUSER	MITIGABLE
MISSORTED	MISTAKERS	MISTITLED	MISUSERS	MITIGANT
MISSORTS	MISTAKES	MISTITLES	MISUSES	MITIGATE
MISSOUND	MISTAKING	MISTLE	MISUSING	MITIGATED
MISSOUNDS	MISTAL	MISTLED	MISUST	MITIGATES

MITIGATOR	MIXIBLE	MNEMONS	MOBIES	MOCK
MITIS	MIXIER	MO	MOBILE	MOCKABLE
MITISES	MIXIEST	MOA	MOBILES	MOCKADO
MITOGEN	MIXING	MOAI	MOBILISE	MOCKADOES
MITOGENIC	MIXMASTER	MOAN	MOBILISED	MOCKAGE
MITOGENS	MIXOLOGY	MOANED	MOBILISER	MOCKAGES
MITOMYCIN	MIXT	MOANER	MOBILISES	MOCKED
MITOSES	MIXTE	MOANERS	MOBILITY	MOCKER
MITOSIS	MIXTION	MOANFUL	MOBILIZE	MOCKERED
MITOTIC	MIXTIONS	MOANFULLY	MOBILIZED	MOCKERIES
MITRAILLE	MIXTURE	MOANING	MOBILIZER	MOCKERING
MITRAL	MIXTURES	MOANINGLY	MOBILIZES	MOCKERNUT
MITRE	MIXUP	MOANINGS	MOBLE	MOCKERS
MITRED	MIXUPS	MOANS	MOBLED	MOCKERY
MITRES	MIXY	MOAS	MOBLES	MOCKING
MITREWORT	MIZ	MOAT	MOBLING	MOCKINGLY
MITRIFORM	MIZEN	MOATED	MOBLOG	MOCKINGS
MITRING	MIZENMAST	MOATING	MOBLOGGER	MOCKNEY
MITSVAH	MIZENS	MOATLIKE	MOBLOGS	MOCKNEYS
MITSVAHS	MIZMAZE	MOATS	MOBOCRACY	MOCKS
MITSVOTH	MIZMAZES	MOB	MOBOCRAT	MOCKTAIL
MITT	MIZUNA	MOBBED	MOBOCRATS	MOCKTAILS
MITTEN	MIZUNAS	MOBBER	MOBS	MOCKUP
MITTENED	MIZZ	MOBBERS	MOBSMAN	MOCKUPS
MITTENS	MIZZEN	MOBBIE	MOBSMEN	MOCOCK
MITTIMUS	MIZZENS	MOBBIES	MOBSTER	MOCOCKS
MITTS	MIZZES	MOBBING	MOBSTERS	MOCS
MITUMBA	MIZZLE	MOBBINGS	MOBY	MOCUCK
MITUMBAS	MIZZLED	MOBBISH	MOC	MOCUCKS
MITY	MIZZLES	MOBBISHLY	MOCASSIN	MOCUDDUM
MITZVAH	MIZZLIER	MOBBISM	MOCASSINS	MOCUDDUMS
MITZVAHS	MIZZLIEST	MOBBISMS	MOCCASIN	MOD
MITZVOTH	MIZZLING	MOBBLE	MOCCASINS	MODAFINIL
MIURUS	MIZZLINGS	MOBBLED	MOCCIES	MODAL
MIURUSES	MIZZLY	MOBBLES	MOCH	MODALISM
MIX	MIZZONITE	MOBBLING	MOCHA	MODALISMS
MIXABLE	MIZZY	MOBBY	MOCHAS	MODALIST
MIXDOWN	MM	MOBCAP	MOCHELL	MODALISTS
MIXDOWNS	MNA	MOBCAPS	MOCHELLS	MODALITY
MIXED	MNAS	MOBCAST	MOCHIE	MODALLY
MIXEDLY	MNEME	MOBCASTED	MOCHIER	MODALS
MIXEDNESS	MNEMES	MOBCASTS	MOCHIEST	MODDED
MIXEN	MNEMIC	MOBE	MOCHILA	MODDER
MIXENS	MNEMON	MOBES	MOCHILAS	MODDERS
MIXER	MNEMONIC	MOBEY	MOCHINESS	MODDING
MIXERS	MNEMONICS	MOBEYS	MOCHS	MODDINGS
MIXES	MNEMONIST	MOBIE	MOCHY	MODE

MODEL	MODESTLY	MOER	MOIDERED	MOJO
MODELED	MODESTY	MOERED	MOIDERING	MOJOES
MODELER	MODGE	MOERING	MOIDERS	MOJOS
MODELERS	MODGED	MOERS	MOIDORE	MOKADDAM
MODELING	MODGES	MOES	MOIDORES	MOKADDAMS
MODELINGS	MODGING	MOFETTE	MOIETIES	MOKE
MODELIST	MODI	MOFETTES	MOIETY	MOKES
MODELISTS	MODICA	MOFFETTE	MOIL	MOKI
MODELLED	MODICUM	MOFFETTES	MOILED	MOKIHI
MODELLER	MODICUMS	MOFFIE	MOILER	MOKIHIS
MODELLERS	MODIFIED	MOFFIES	MOILERS	MOKIS
MODELLI	MODIFIER	MOFO	MOILING	MOKO
MODELLING	MODIFIERS	MOFOS	MOILINGLY	MOKOMOKO
MODELLO	MODIFIES	MOFUSSIL	MOILS	MOKOMOKOS
MODELLOS	MODIFY	MOFUSSILS	MOINEAU	MOKOPUNA
MODELS	MODIFYING	MOG	MOINEAUS	MOKOPUNAS
MODEM	MODII	MOGGAN	MOIRA	MOKORO
MODEMED	MODILLION	MOGGANS	MOIRAI	MOKOROS
MODEMING	MODIOLAR	MOGGED	MOIRE	MOKOS
MODEMS	MODIOLI	MOGGIE	MOIRES	MOKSHA
MODENA	MODIOLUS	MOGGIES	MOISER	MOKSHAS
MODENAS	MODISH	MOGGING	MOISERS	MOL
MODER	MODISHLY	MOGGY	MOIST	MOLA
MODERATE	MODIST	MOGHUL	MOISTED	MOLAL
MODERATED	MODISTE	MOGHULS	MOISTEN	MOLALITY
MODERATES	MODISTES	MOGS	MOISTENED	MOLAR
MODERATO	MODISTS	MOGUL	MOISTENER	MOLARITY
MODERATOR	MODIUS	MOGULED	MOISTENS	MOLARS
MODERATOS	MODIWORT	MOGULS	MOISTER	MOLAS
MODERN	MODIWORTS	MOHAIR	MOISTEST	MOLASSE
MODERNE	MODS	MOHAIRS	MOISTFUL	MOLASSES
MODERNER	MODULAR	MOHALIM	MOISTIFY	MOLD
MODERNES	MODULARLY	MOHAWK	MOISTING	MOLDABLE
MODERNEST	MODULARS	MOHAWKS	MOISTLY	MOLDAVITE
MODERNISE	MODULATE	MOHEL	MOISTNESS	MOLDBOARD
MODERNISM	MODULATED	MOHELIM	MOISTS	MOLDED
MODERNIST	MODULATES	MOHELS	MOISTURE	MOLDER
MODERNITY	MODULATOR	MOHICAN	MOISTURES	MOLDERED
MODERNIZE	MODULE	MOHICANS	MOIT	MOLDERING
MODERNLY	MODULES	MOHR	MOITHER	MOLDERS
MODERNS	MODULI	MOHRS	MOITHERED	MOLDIER
MODERS	MODULO	MOHUA	MOITHERS	MOLDIEST
MODES	MODULUS	MOHUAS	MOITS	MOLDINESS
MODEST	MODUS	MOHUR	MOJARRA	MOLDING
MODESTER	MOE	MOHURS	MOJARRAS	MOLDINGS
MODESTEST	MOELLON	MOI	MOJITO	MOLDS
MODESTIES	MOELLONS	MOIDER	MOJITOS	MOLDWARP

M

MOLDWARPS	MOLLUSKS	MOMMY	MONAXIAL	MONG
MOLDY	MOLLY	MOMS	MONAXON	MONGCORN
MOLE	MOLLYHAWK	MOMSER	MONAXONIC	MONGCORNS
MOLECAST	MOLLYMAWK	MOMSERS	MONAXONS	MONGED
MOLECASTS	MOLOCH	MOMUS	MONAZITE	MONGEESE
MOLECULAR	MOLOCHISE	MOMUSES	MONAZITES	MONGER
MOLECULE	MOLOCHIZE	MOMZER	MONDAIN	MONGERED
MOLECULES	MOLOCHS	MOMZERIM	MONDAINE	MONGERIES
MOLEHILL	MOLOSSI	MOMZERS	MONDAINES	MONGERING
MOLEHILLS	MOLOSSUS	MON	MONDAINS	MONGERS
MOLES	MOLS	MONA	MONDE	MONGERY
MOLESKIN	MOLT	MONACHAL	MONDES	MONGO
MOLESKINS	MOLTED	MONACHISM	MONDIAL	MONGOE
MOLEST	MOLTEN	MONACHIST	MONDO	MONGOES
MOLESTED	MOLTENLY	MONACID	MONDOS	MONGOL
MOLESTER	MOLTER	MONACIDIC	MONECIAN	MONGOLIAN
MOLESTERS	MOLTERS	MONACIDS	MONECIOUS	MONGOLISM
MOLESTFUL	MOLTING	MONACT	MONELLIN	MONGOLOID
MOLESTING	MOLTO	MONACTINE	MONELLINS	MONGOLS
MOLESTS	MOLTS	MONAD	MONEME	MONGOOSE
MOLIES	MOLY	MONADAL	MONEMES	MONGOOSES
MOLIMEN	MOLYBDATE	MONADES	MONER	MONGOS
MOLIMENS	MOLYBDIC	MONADIC	MONERA	MONGREL
MOLINE	MOLYBDOUS	MONADICAL	MONERAN	MONGRELLY
MOLINES	MOM	MONADISM	MONERANS	MONGRELS
MOLINET	MOME	MONADISMS	MONERGISM	MONGS
MOLINETS	MOMENT	MONADNOCK	MONERON	MONGST
MOLL	MOMENTA	MONADS	MONETARY	MONIAL
MOLLA	MOMENTANY	MONAL	MONETH	MONIALS
MOLLAH	MOMENTARY	MONALS	MONETHS	MONICKER
MOLLAHS	MOMENTLY	MONANDRY	MONETISE	MONICKERS
MOLLAS	MOMENTO	MONARCH	MONETISED	MONIE
MOLLIE	MOMENTOES	MONARCHAL	MONETISES	MONIED
MOLLIES	MOMENTOS	MONARCHIC	MONETIZE	MONIES
MOLLIFIED	MOMENTOUS	MONARCHS	MONETIZED	MONIKER
MOLLIFIER	MOMENTS	MONARCHY	MONETIZES	MONIKERS
MOLLIFIES	MOMENTUM	MONARDA	MONEY	MONILIA
MOLLIFY	MOMENTUMS	MONARDAS	MONEYBAG	MONILIAL
MOLLITIES	MOMES	MONAS	MONEYBAGS	MONILIAS
MOLLS	MOMI	MONASES	MONEYED	MONIMENT
MOLLUSC	MOMISM	MONASTERY	MONEYER	MONIMENTS
MOLLUSCA	MOMISMS	MONASTIC	MONEYERS	MONIPLIES
MOLLUSCAN	MOMMA	MONASTICS	MONEYLESS	MONISH
MOLLUSCS	MOMMAS	MONATOMIC	MONEYMAN	MONISHED
MOLLUSCUM	MOMMET	MONAUL	MONEYMEN	MONISHES
MOLLUSK	MOMMETS	MONAULS	MONEYS	MONISHING
MOLLUSKAN	MOMMIES	MONAURAL	MONEYWORT	MONISM

MONISMS	MONOCOQUE	MONOLATER	MONORHINE	MONSTERAS
MONIST	MONOCOT	MONOLATRY	MONORHYME	MONSTERED
MONISTIC	MONOCOTS	MONOLAYER	MONOS	MONSTERS
MONISTS	MONOCOTYL	MONOLINE	MONOSEMY	MONSTROUS
MONITION	MONOCRACY	MONOLITH	MONOSES	MONTADALE
MONITIONS	MONOCRAT	MONOLITHS	MONOSIES	MONTAGE
MONITIVE	MONOCRATS	MONOLOG	MONOSIS	MONTAGED
MONITOR	MONOCULAR	MONOLOGIC	MONOSKI	MONTAGES
MONITORED	MONOCYCLE	MONOLOGS	MONOSKIED	MONTAGING
MONITORS	MONOCYTE	MONOLOGUE	MONOSKIER	MONTAN
MONITORY	MONOCYTES	MONOLOGY	MONOSKIS	MONTANE
MONITRESS	MONOCYTIC	MONOMACHY	MONOSOME	MONTANES
MONK	MONODIC	MONOMANIA	MONOSOMES	MONTANT
MONKERIES	MONODICAL	MONOMARK	MONOSOMIC	MONTANTO
MONKERY	MONODIES	MONOMARKS	MONOSOMY	MONTANTOS
MONKEY	MONODIST	MONOMER	MONOSTELE	MONTANTS
MONKEYED	MONODISTS	MONOMERIC	MONOSTELY	MONTARIA
MONKEYING	MONODONT	MONOMERS	MONOSTICH	MONTARIAS
MONKEYISH	MONODRAMA	MONOMETER	MONOSTOME	MONTE
MONKEYISM	MONODY	MONOMIAL	MONOSTYLE	MONTEITH
MONKEYPOD	MONOECIES	MONOMIALS	MONOSY	MONTEITHS
MONKEYPOT	MONOECISM	MONOMODE	MONOTASK	MONTEM
MONKEYS	MONOECY	MONONYM	MONOTASKS	MONTEMS
MONKFISH	MONOESTER	MONONYMS	MONOTINT	MONTERO
MONKHOOD	MONOFIL	MONOPHAGY	MONOTINTS	MONTEROS
MONKHOODS	MONOFILS	MONOPHASE	MONOTONE	MONTES
MONKISH	MONOFUEL	MONOPHONY	MONOTONED	MONTH
MONKISHLY	MONOFUELS	MONOPHYLY	MONOTONES	MONTHLIES
MONKS	MONOGAMIC	MONOPITCH	MONOTONIC	MONTHLING
MONKSHOOD	MONOGAMY	MONOPLANE	MONOTONY	MONTHLONG
MONO	MONOGENIC	MONOPLOID	MONOTREME	MONTHLY
MONOACID	MONOGENY	MONOPOD	MONOTROCH	MONTHS
MONOACIDS	MONOGERM	MONOPODE	MONOTYPE	MONTICLE
MONOAMINE	MONOGLOT	MONOPODES	MONOTYPES	MONTICLES
MONOAO	MONOGLOTS	MONOPODIA	MONOTYPIC	MONTICULE
MONOAOS	MONOGONY	MONOPODS	MONOVULAR	MONTIES
MONOBASIC	MONOGRAM	MONOPODY	MONOXIDE	MONTRE
MONOBROW	MONOGRAMS	MONOPOLE	MONOXIDES	MONTRES
MONOBROWS	MONOGRAPH	MONOPOLES	MONOXYLON	MONTURE
MONOCARP	MONOGYNY	MONOPOLY	MONS	MONTURES
MONOCARPS	MONOHULL	MONOPSONY	MONSIEUR	MONTY
MONOCEROS	MONOHULLS	MONOPTERA	MONSIGNOR	MONUMENT
MONOCHORD	MONOICOUS	MONOPTOTE	MONSOON	MONUMENTS
MONOCLE	MONOKINE	MONOPULSE	MONSOONAL	MONURON
MONOCLED	MONOKINES	MONORAIL	MONSOONS	MONURONS
MONOCLES	MONOKINI	MONORAILS	MONSTER	MONY
MONOCLINE	MONOKINIS	MONORCHID	MONSTERA	MONYPLIES

M

MONZONITE	MOONBEAM	MOONSAIL	MOORLOGS	MOPEY
MOO	MOONBEAMS	MOONSAILS	MOORMAN	MOPHEAD
MOOBS	MOONBLIND	MOONSCAPE	MOORMEN	MOPHEADS
MOOCH	MOONBOW	MOONSEED	MOORS	MOPIER
MOOCHED	MOONBOWS	MOONSEEDS	MOORVA	MOPIEST
MOOCHER	MOONCAKE	MOONSET	MOORVAS	MOPILY
MOOCHERS	MOONCAKES	MOONSETS	MOORWORT	MOPINESS
MOOCHES	MOONCALF	MOONSHEE	MOORWORTS	MOPING
MOOCHING	MOONCHILD	MOONSHEES	MOORY	MOPINGLY
MOOD	MOONDUST	MOONSHINE	MOOS	MOPISH
MOODIED	MOONDUSTS	MOONSHINY	MOOSE	MOPISHLY
MOODIER	MOONED	MOONSHOT	MOOSEBIRD	MOPOKE
MOODIES	MOONER	MOONSHOTS	MOOSEWOOD	MOPOKES
MOODIEST	MOONERS	MOONSTONE	MOOSEYARD	MOPPED
MOODILY	MOONEYE	MOONWALK	MOOT	MOPPER
MOODINESS	MOONEYES	MOONWALKS	MOOTABLE	MOPPERS
MOODS	MOONFACE	MOONWARD	MOOTED	MOPPET
MOODY	MOONFACED	MOONWARDS	MOOTER	MOPPETS
MOODYING	MOONFACES	MOONWORT	MOOTERS	MOPPIER
MOOED	MOONFISH	MOONWORTS	MOOTEST	MOPPIEST
MOOI	MOONG	MOONY	MOOTING	MOPPING
MOOING	MOONIER	MOOP	MOOTINGS	MOPPY
MOOK	MOONIES	MOOPED	MOOTMAN	MOPS
MOOKS	MOONIEST	MOOPING	MOOTMEN	MOPSIES
MOOKTAR	MOONILY	MOOPS	MOOTNESS	MOPSTICK
MOOKTARS	MOONINESS	MOOR	MOOTS	MOPSTICKS
MOOL	MOONING	MOORAGE	MOOVE	MOPSY
MOOLA	MOONISH	MOORAGES	MOOVED	MOPUS
MOOLAH	MOONISHLY	MOORBURN	MOOVES	MOPUSES
MOOLAHS	MOONLESS	MOORBURNS	MOOVING	MOPY
MOOLAS	MOONLET	MOORCOCK	MOP	MOQUETTE
MOOLED	MOONLETS	MOORCOCKS	MOPANE	MOQUETTES
MOOLEY	MOONLIGHT	MOORED	MOPANES	MOR
MOOLEYS	MOONLIKE	MOORFOWL	MOPANI	MORA
MOOLI	MOONLIT	MOORFOWLS	MOPANIS	MORACEOUS
MOOLIES	MOONPHASE	MOORHEN	MOPBOARD	MORAE
MOOLING	MOONPORT	MOORHENS	MOPBOARDS	MORAINAL
MOOLIS	MOONPORTS	MOORIER	MOPE	MORAINE
MOOLOO	MOONQUAKE	MOORIEST	MOPED	MORAINES
MOOLOOS	MOONRAKER	MOORILL	MOPEDS	MORAINIC
MOOLS	MOONRISE	MOORILLS	MOPEHAWK	MORAL
MOOLVI	MOONRISES	MOORING	MOPEHAWKS	MORALE
MOOLVIE	MOONROCK	MOORINGS	MOPER	MORALES
MOOLVIES	MOONROCKS	MOORISH	MOPERIES	MORALISE
MOOLVIS	MOONROOF	MOORLAND	MOPERS	MORALISED
MOOLY	MOONROOFS	MOORLANDS	MOPERY	MORALISER
MOON	MOONS	MOORLOG	MOPES	MORALISES

MORALISM	MORDENTS	MORNAYS	MORRAS	MORTGAGEE
MORALISMS	MORE	MORNE	MORRELL	MORTGAGER
MORALIST	MOREEN	MORNED	MORRELLS	MORTGAGES
MORALISTS	MOREENS	MORNES	MORRHUA	MORTGAGOR
MORALITY	MOREISH	MORNING	MORRHUAS	MORTICE
MORALIZE	MOREL	MORNINGS	MORRICE	MORTICED
MORALIZED	MORELLE	MORNS	MORRICES	MORTICER
MORALIZER	MORELLES	MOROCCO	MORRION	MORTICERS
MORALIZES	MORELLO	MOROCCOS	MORRIONS	MORTICES
MORALL	MORELLOS	MORON	MORRIS	MORTICIAN
MORALLED	MORELS	MORONIC	MORRISED	MORTICING
MORALLER	MORENDO	MORONISM	MORRISES	MORTIFIC
MORALLERS	MORENESS	MORONISMS	MORRISING	MORTIFIED
MORALLING	MOREOVER	MORONITY	MORRO	MORTIFIER
MORALLS	MOREPORK	MORONS	MORROS	MORTIFIES
MORALLY	MOREPORKS	MOROSE	MORROW	MORTIFY
MORALS	MORES	MOROSELY	MORROWS	MORTISE
MORAS	MORESQUE	MOROSER	MORS	MORTISED
MORASS	MORESQUES	MOROSEST	MORSAL	MORTISER
MORASSES	MORGAN	MOROSITY	MORSE	MORTISERS
MORASSY	MORGANITE	MORPH	MORSEL	MORTISES
MORAT	MORGANS	MORPHEAN	MORSELED	MORTISING
MORATORIA	MORGAY	MORPHED	MORSELING	MORTLING
MORATORY	MORGAYS	MORPHEME	MORSELLED	MORTLINGS
MORATS	MORGEN	MORPHEMES	MORSELS	MORTMAIN
MORAY	MORGENS	MORPHEMIC	MORSES	MORTMAINS
MORAYS	MORGUE	MORPHETIC	MORSURE	MORTS
MORBID	MORGUES	MORPHEW	MORSURES	MORTSAFE
MORBIDER	MORIA	MORPHEWS	MORT	MORTSAFES
MORBIDEST	MORIAS	MORPHIA	MORTAL	MORTUARY
MORBIDITY	MORIBUND	MORPHIAS	MORTALISE	MORULA
MORBIDLY	MORICHE	MORPHIC	MORTALITY	MORULAE
MORBIFIC	MORICHES	MORPHIN	MORTALIZE	MORULAR
MORBILLI	MORION	MORPHINE	MORTALLY	MORULAS
MORBUS	MORIONS	MORPHINES	MORTALS	MORWONG
MORBUSES	MORISCO	MORPHING	MORTAR	MORWONGS
MORCEAU	MORISCOES	MORPHINGS	MORTARED	MORYAH
MORCEAUX	MORISCOS	MORPHINIC	MORTARING	MOS
MORCHA	MORISH	MORPHINS	MORTARMAN	MOSAIC
MORCHAS	MORKIN	MORPHO	MORTARMEN	MOSAICISM
MORDACITY	MORKINS	MORPHOGEN	MORTARS	MOSAICIST
MORDANCY	MORLING	MORPHOS	MORTARY	MOSAICKED
MORDANT	MORLINGS	MORPHOSES	MORTBELL	MOSAICS
MORDANTED	MORMAOR	MORPHOSIS	MORTBELLS	MOSASAUR
MORDANTLY	MORMAORS	MORPHOTIC	MORTCLOTH	MOSASAURI
MORDANTS	MORN	MORPHS	MORTGAGE	MOSASAURS
MORDENT	MORNAY	MORRA	MORTGAGED	MOSCHATE

M

MOSCHATEL	MOSSY	MOTILES	MOTORINGS	MOTZA
MOSE	MOST	MOTILITY	MOTORISE	MOTZAS
MOSED	MOSTE	MOTION	MOTORISED	MOU
MOSELLE	MOSTEST	MOTIONAL	MOTORISES	MOUCH
MOSELLES	MOSTESTS	MOTIONED	MOTORIST	MOUCHARD
MOSES	MOSTLY	MOTIONER	MOTORISTS	MOUCHARDS
MOSEY	MOSTS	MOTIONERS	MOTORIUM	MOUCHED
MOSEYED	MOSTWHAT	MOTIONING	MOTORIUMS	MOUCHER
MOSEYING	MOT	MOTIONIST	MOTORIZE	MOUCHERS
MOSEYS	MOTE	MOTIONS	MOTORIZED	MOUCHES
MOSH	MOTED	MOTIS	MOTORIZES	MOUCHING
MOSHAV	MOTEL	MOTIVATE	MOTORLESS	MOUCHOIR
MOSHAVIM	MOTELIER	MOTIVATED	MOTORMAN	MOUCHOIRS
MOSHED	MOTELIERS	MOTIVATES	MOTORMEN	MOUDIWART
MOSHER	MOTELS	MOTIVATOR	MOTORS	MOUDIWORT
MOSHERS	MOTEN	MOTIVE	MOTORSHIP	MOUE
MOSHES	MOTES	MOTIVED	MOTORWAY	MOUES
MOSHING	MOTET	MOTIVES	MOTORWAYS	MOUFFLON
MOSHINGS	MOTETS	MOTIVIC	MOTORY	MOUFFLONS
MOSING	MOTETT	MOTIVING	MOTOSCAFI	MOUFLON
MOSK	MOTETTIST	MOTIVITY	MOTOSCAFO	MOUFLONS
MOSKONFYT	MOTETTS	MOTLEY	MOTS	MOUGHT
MOSKS	MOTEY	MOTLEYER	MOTSER	MOUILLE
MOSLINGS	MOTH	MOTLEYEST	MOTSERS	MOUJIK
MOSQUE	MOTHBALL	MOTLEYS	MOTT	MOUJIKS
MOSQUES	MOTHBALLS	MOTLIER	MOTTE	MOULAGE
MOSQUITO	MOTHED	MOTLIEST	MOTTES	MOULAGES
MOSQUITOS	MOTHER	MOTMOT	MOTTIER	MOULD
MOSS	MOTHERED	MOTMOTS	MOTTIES	MOULDABLE
MOSSBACK	MOTHERESE	MOTOCROSS	MOTTIEST	MOULDED
MOSSBACKS	MOTHERING	MOTOR	MOTTLE	MOULDER
MOSSED	MOTHERLY	MOTORABLE	MOTTLED	MOULDERED
MOSSER	MOTHERS	MOTORAIL	MOTTLER	MOULDERS
MOSSERS	MOTHERY	MOTORAILS	MOTTLERS	MOULDIER
MOSSES	MOTHIER	MOTORBIKE	MOTTLES	MOULDIEST
MOSSGROWN	MOTHIEST	MOTORBOAT	MOTTLING	MOULDING
MOSSIE	MOTHLIKE	MOTORBUS	MOTTLINGS	MOULDINGS
MOSSIER	MOTHPROOF	MOTORCADE	MOTTO	MOULDS
MOSSIES	MOTHS	MOTORCAR	MOTTOED	MOULDWARP
MOSSIEST	MOTHY	MOTORCARS	MOTTOES	MOULDY
MOSSINESS	MOTI	MOTORDOM	MOTTOS	MOULIN
MOSSING	MOTIER	MOTORDOMS	MOTTS	MOULINET
MOSSLAND	MOTIEST	MOTORED	MOTTY	MOULINETS
MOSSLANDS	MOTIF	MOTORHOME	MOTU	MOULINS
MOSSLIKE	MOTIFIC	MOTORIAL	MOTUCA	MOULS
MOSSO	MOTIFS	MOTORIC	MOTUCAS	MOULT
MOSSPLANT	MOTILE	MOTORING	MOTUS	MOULTED

MOULTEN	MOUSELIKE	MOUTERERS	MOVIES	MOZO
MOULTER	MOUSEMAT	MOUTERING	MOVING	MOZOS
MOULTERS	MOUSEMATS	MOUTERS	MOVINGLY	MOZZ
MOULTING	MOUSEOVER	MOUTH	MOVIOLA	MOZZES
MOULTINGS	MOUSEPAD	MOUTHABLE	MOVIOLAS	MOZZETTA
MOULTS	MOUSEPADS	MOUTHED	MOW	MOZZETTAS
MOUND	MOUSER	MOUTHER	MOWA	MOZZETTE
MOUNDBIRD	MOUSERIES	MOUTHERS	MOWAS	MOZZIE
MOUNDED	MOUSERS	MOUTHFEEL	MOWBURN	MOZZIES
MOUNDING	MOUSERY	MOUTHFUL	MOWBURNED	MOZZLE
MOUNDS	MOUSES	MOUTHFULS	MOWBURNS	MOZZLES
MOUNSEER	MOUSETAIL	MOUTHIER	MOWBURNT	MPRET
MOUNSEERS	MOUSETRAP	MOUTHIEST	MOWDIE	MPRETS
MOUNT	MOUSEY	MOUTHILY	MOWDIES	MRIDAMGAM
MOUNTABLE	MOUSIE	MOUTHING	MOWED	MRIDANG
MOUNTAIN	MOUSIER	MOUTHLESS	MOWER	MRIDANGA
MOUNTAINS	MOUSIES	MOUTHLIKE	MOWERS	MRIDANGAM
MOUNTAINY	MOUSIEST	MOUTHPART	MOWING	MRIDANGAS
MOUNTANT	MOUSILY	MOUTHS	MOWINGS	MRIDANGS
MOUNTANTS	MOUSINESS	MOUTHWASH	MOWN	MU
MOUNTED	MOUSING	MOUTHY	MOWRA	MUCATE
MOUNTER	MOUSINGS	MOUTON	MOWRAS	MUCATES
MOUNTERS	MOUSLE	MOUTONNEE	MOWS	MUCH
MOUNTING	MOUSLED	MOUTONS	MOXA	MUCHACHA
MOUNTINGS	MOUSLES	MOVABLE	MOXAS	MUCHACHAS
MOUNTS	MOUSLING	MOVABLES	MOXIE	MUCHACHO
MOUP	MOUSME	MOVABLY	MOXIES	MUCHACHOS
MOUPED	MOUSMEE	MOVE	MOY	MUCHEL
MOUPING	MOUSMEES	MOVEABLE	MOYA	MUCHELL
MOUPS	MOUSMES	MOVEABLES	MOYAS	MUCHELLS
MOURN	MOUSSAKA	MOVEABLY	MOYITIES	MUCHELS
MOURNED	MOUSSAKAS	MOVED	MOYITY	MUCHES
MOURNER	MOUSSE	MOVELESS	MOYL	MUCHLY
MOURNERS	MOUSSED	MOVEMENT	MOYLE	MUCHNESS
MOURNFUL	MOUSSES	MOVEMENTS	MOYLED	MUCHO
MOURNING	MOUSSING	MOVER	MOYLES	MUCIC
MOURNINGS	MOUST	MOVERS	MOYLING	MUCID
MOURNIVAL	MOUSTACHE	MOVES	MOYLS	MUCIDITY
MOURNS	MOUSTED	MOVIE	MOYS	MUCIDNESS
MOUS	MOUSTING	MOVIEDOM	MOZ	MUCIGEN
MOUSAKA	MOUSTS	MOVIEDOMS	MOZE	MUCIGENS
MOUSAKAS	MOUSY	MOVIEGOER	MOZED	MUCILAGE
MOUSE	MOUTAN	MOVIELAND	MOZES	MUCILAGES
MOUSEBIRD	MOUTANS	MOVIEOKE	MOZETTA	MUCIN
MOUSED	MOUTER	MOVIEOKES	MOZETTAS	MUCINOGEN
MOUSEKIN	MOUTERED	MOVIEOLA	MOZETTE	MUCINOID
MOUSEKINS	MOUTERER	MOVIEOLAS	MOZING	MUCINOUS

MUCINS	MUCRONATE	MUDFLATS	MUDWORTS	MUGGING
MUCK	MUCRONES	MUDFLOW	MUEDDIN	MUGGINGS
MUCKAMUCK	MUCROS	MUDFLOWS	MUEDDINS	MUGGINS
MUCKED	MUCULENT	MUDGE	MUENSTER	MUGGINSES
MUCKENDER	MUCUS	MUDGED	MUENSTERS	MUGGISH
MUCKER	MUCUSES	MUDGER	MUESLI	MUGGS
MUCKERED	MUD	MUDGERS	MUESLIS	MUGGUR
MUCKERING	MUDBATH	MUDGES	MUEZZIN	MUGGURS
MUCKERISH	MUDBATHS	MUDGING	MUEZZINS	MUGGY
MUCKERS	MUDBUG	MUDGUARD	MUFF	MUGHAL
MUCKHEAP	MUDBUGS	MUDGUARDS	MUFFED	MUGHALS
MUCKHEAPS	MUDCAP	MUDHEN	MUFFETTEE	MUGS
MUCKIER	MUDCAPPED	MUDHENS	MUFFIN	MUGSHOT
MUCKIEST	MUDCAPS	MUDHOLE	MUFFINEER	MUGSHOTS
MUCKILY	MUDCAT	MUDHOLES	MUFFING	MUGWORT
MUCKINESS	MUDCATS	MUDHOOK	MUFFINS	MUGWORTS
MUCKING	MUDDED	MUDHOOKS	MUFFISH	MUGWUMP
MUCKLE	MUDDER	MUDHOPPER	MUFFLE	MUGWUMPS
MUCKLES	MUDDERS	MUDIR	MUFFLED	MUHLIES
MUCKLUCK	MUDDIED	MUDIRIA	MUFFLER	MUHLY
MUCKLUCKS	MUDDIER	MUDIRIAS	MUFFLERED	MUID
MUCKRAKE	MUDDIES	MUDIRIEH	MUFFLERS	MUIDS
MUCKRAKED	MUDDIEST	MUDIRIEHS	MUFFLES	MUIL
MUCKRAKER	MUDDILY	MUDIRS	MUFFLING	MUILS
MUCKRAKES	MUDDINESS	MUDLARK	MUFFS	MUIR
MUCKS	MUDDING	MUDLARKED	MUFLON	MUIRBURN
MUCKSWEAT	MUDDLE	MUDLARKS	MUFLONS	MUIRBURNS
MUCKWORM	MUDDLED	MUDLOGGER	MUFTI	MUIRS
MUCKWORMS	MUDDLER	MUDPACK	MUFTIS	MUIST
MUCKY	MUDDLERS	MUDPACKS	MUG	MUISTED
MUCKYMUCK	MUDDLES	MUDPUPPY	MUGEARITE	MUISTING
MUCLUC	MUDDLIER	MUDRA	MUGFUL	MUISTS
MUCLUCS	MUDDLIEST	MUDRAS	MUGFULS	MUJAHEDIN
MUCOID	MUDDLING	MUDROCK	MUGG	MUJAHIDIN
MUCOIDAL	MUDDLINGS	MUDROCKS	MUGGA	MUJIK
MUCOIDS	MUDDLY	MUDROOM	MUGGAR	MUJIKS
MUCOLYTIC	MUDDY	MUDROOMS	MUGGARS	MUKHTAR
MUCOR	MUDDYING	MUDS	MUGGAS	MUKHTARS
MUCORS	MUDEJAR	MUDSCOW	MUGGED	MUKLUK
MUCOSA	MUDEJARES	MUDSCOWS	MUGGEE	MUKLUKS
MUCOSAE	MUDEYE	MUDSILL	MUGGEES	MUKTUK
MUCOSAL	MUDEYES	MUDSILLS	MUGGER	MUKTUKS
MUCOSAS	MUDFISH	MUDSLIDE	MUGGERS	MULATTA
MUCOSE	MUDFISHES	MUDSLIDES	MUGGIER	MULATTAS
MUCOSITY	MUDFLAP	MUDSTONE	MUGGIEST	MULATTO
MUCOUS	MUDFLAPS	MUDSTONES	MUGGILY	MULATTOES
MUCRO	MUDFLAT	MUDWORT	MUGGINESS	MULATTOS

MULBERRY	MULLEY	MULTIGRID	MULTURES	MUMSIEST
MULCH	MULLEYS	MULTIGYM	MULTURING	MUMSY
MULCHED	MULLIGAN	MULTIGYMS	MUM	MUMU
MULCHES	MULLIGANS	MULTIHUED	MUMBLE	MUMUS
MULCHING	MULLING	MULTIHULL	MUMBLED	MUN
MULCT	MULLION	MULTIJET	MUMBLER	MUNCH
MULCTED	MULLIONED	MULTILANE	MUMBLERS	MUNCHABLE
MULCTING	MULLIONS	MULTILINE	MUMBLES	MUNCHED
MULCTS	MULLITE	MULTILOBE	MUMBLIER	MUNCHER
MULE	MULLITES	MULTIMODE	MUMBLIEST	MUNCHERS
MULED	MULLOCK	MULTIPACK	MUMBLING	MUNCHES
MULES	MULLOCKS	MULTIPAGE	MUMBLINGS	MUNCHIES
MULESED	MULLOCKY	MULTIPARA	MUMBLY	MUNCHING
MULESES	MULLOWAY	MULTIPART	MUMCHANCE	MUNCHKIN
MULESING	MULLOWAYS	MULTIPATH	MUMM	MUNCHKINS
MULESINGS	MULLS	MULTIPED	MUMMED	MUNDANE
MULETA	MULMUL	MULTIPEDE	MUMMER	MUNDANELY
MULETAS	MULMULL	MULTIPEDS	MUMMERIES	MUNDANER
MULETEER	MULMULLS	MULTIPION	MUMMERS	MUNDANEST
MULETEERS	MULMULS	MULTIPLE	MUMMERY	MUNDANITY
MULEY	MULSE	MULTIPLES	MUMMIA	MUNDIC
MULEYS	MULSES	MULTIPLET	MUMMIAS	MUNDICS
MULGA	MULSH	MULTIPLEX	MUMMICHOG	MUNDIFIED
MULGAS	MULSHED	MULTIPLY	MUMMIED	MUNDIFIES
MULING	MULSHES	MULTIPOLE	MUMMIES	MUNDIFY
MULISH	MULSHING	MULTIPORT	MUMMIFIED	MUNDUNGO
MULISHLY	MULTEITY	MULTIROLE	MUMMIFIES	MUNDUNGOS
MULL	MULTIAGE	MULTIROOM	MUMMIFORM	MUNDUNGUS
MULLA	MULTIATOM	MULTISITE	MUMMIFY	MUNG
MULLAH	MULTIBAND	MULTISIZE	MUMMING	MUNGA
MULLAHED	MULTIBANK	MULTISTEP	MUMMINGS	MUNGAS
MULLAHING	MULTICAR	MULTITASK	MUMMOCK	MUNGCORN
MULLAHISM	MULTICAST	MULTITON	MUMMOCKS	MUNGCORNS
MULLAHS	MULTICELL	MULTITONE	MUMMS	MUNGE
MULLARKY	MULTICIDE	MULTITOOL	MUMMY	MUNGED
MULLAS	MULTICITY	MULTITUDE	MUMMYING	MUNGES
MULLED	MULTICOPY	MULTIUNIT	MUMP	MUNGING
MULLEIN	MULTIDAY	MULTIUSE	MUMPED	MUNGO
MULLEINS	MULTIDISC	MULTIUSER	MUMPER	MUNGOES
MULLEN	MULTIDRUG	MULTIWALL	MUMPERS	MUNGOOSE
MULLENS	MULTIFID	MULTIYEAR	MUMPING	MUNGOOSES
MULLER	MULTIFIL	MULTUM	MUMPISH	MUNGOS
MULLERED	MULTIFILS	MULTUMS	MUMPISHLY	MUNGS
MULLERING	MULTIFOIL	MULTURE	MUMPS	MUNI
MULLERS	MULTIFOLD	MULTURED	MUMPSIMUS	MUNICIPAL
MULLET	MULTIFORM	MULTURER	MUMS	MUNIFIED
MULLETS	MULTIGERM	MULTURERS	MUMSIER	MUNIFIES

MUNIFY	MURAENIDS	MURKER	MURREES	MUSCAT
MUNIFYING	MURAGE	MURKEST	MURRELET	MUSCATEL
MUNIMENT	MURAGES	MURKIER	MURRELETS	MUSCATELS
MUNIMENTS	MURAL	MURKIEST	MURREN	MUSCATS
MUNIS	MURALED	MURKILY	MURRENS	MUSCAVADO
MUNITE	MURALIST	MURKINESS	MURRES	MUSCID
MUNITED	MURALISTS	MURKISH	MURREY	MUSCIDS
MUNITES	MURALLED	MURKLY	MURREYS	MUSCLE
MUNITING	MURALS	MURKS	MURRHA	MUSCLED
MUNITION	MURAS	MURKSOME	MURRHAS	MUSCLEMAN
MUNITIONS	MURDABAD	MURKY	MURRHINE	MUSCLEMEN
MUNNION	MURDER	MURL	MURRHINES	MUSCLES
MUNNIONS	MURDERED	MURLAIN	MURRI	MUSCLIER
MUNS	MURDEREE	MURLAINS	MURRIES	MUSCLIEST
MUNSHI	MURDEREES	MURLAN	MURRIN	MUSCLING
MUNSHIS	MURDERER	MURLANS	MURRINE	MUSCLINGS
MUNSTER	MURDERERS	MURLED	MURRINES	MUSCLY
MUNSTERS	MURDERESS	MURLIER	MURRINS	MUSCOID
MUNT	MURDERING	MURLIEST	MURRION	MUSCOLOGY
MUNTER	MURDEROUS	MURLIN	MURRIONS	MUSCONE
MUNTERS	MURDERS	MURLING	MURRIS	MUSCONES
MUNTIN	MURE	MURLINS	MURRS	MUSCOSE
MUNTING	MURED	MURLS	MURRY	MUSCOVADO
MUNTINGS	MUREIN	MURLY	MURTHER	MUSCOVITE
MUNTINS	MUREINS	MURMUR	MURTHERED	MUSCOVY
MUNTJAC	MURENA	MURMURED	MURTHERER	MUSCULAR
MUNTJACS	MURENAS	MURMURER	MURTHERS	MUSCULOUS
MUNTJAK	MURES	MURMURERS	MURTI	MUSE
MUNTJAKS	MUREX	MURMURING	MURTIS	MUSED
MUNTRIE	MUREXES	MURMUROUS	MURVA	MUSEFUL
MUNTRIES	MURGEON	MURMURS	MURVAS	MUSEFULLY
MUNTS	MURGEONED	MURPHIES	MUS	MUSEOLOGY
MUNTU	MURGEONS	MURPHY	MUSACEOUS	MUSER
MUNTUS	MURIATE	MURR	MUSANG	MUSERS
MUON	MURIATED	MURRA	MUSANGS	MUSES
MUONIC	MURIATES	MURRAGH	MUSAR	MUSET
MUONIUM	MURIATIC	MURRAGHS	MUSARS	MUSETS
MUONIUMS	MURICATE	MURRAIN	MUSCA	MUSETTE
MUONS	MURICATED	MURRAINED	MUSCADEL	MUSETTES
MUPPET	MURICES	MURRAINS	MUSCADELS	MUSEUM
MUPPETS	MURID	MURRAM	MUSCADET	MUSEUMS
MUQADDAM	MURIDS	MURRAMS	MUSCADETS	MUSH
MUQADDAMS	MURIFORM	MURRAS	MUSCADIN	MUSHA
MURA	MURINE	MURRAY	MUSCADINE	MUSHED
MURAENA	MURINES	MURRAYS	MUSCADINS	MUSHER
MURAENAS	MURING	MURRE	MUSCAE	MUSHERS
MURAENID	MURK	MURREE	MUSCARINE	MUSHES

MUSHIER	MUSKIEST	MUST	MUTATION	MUTTER
MUSHIEST	MUSKILY	MUSTACHE	MUTATIONS	MUTTERED
MUSHILY	MUSKINESS	MUSTACHED	MUTATIVE	MUTTERER
MUSHINESS	MUSKING	MUSTACHES	MUTATORY	MUTTERERS
MUSHING	MUSKIT	MUSTACHIO	MUTCH	MUTTERING
MUSHMOUTH	MUSKITS	MUSTANG	MUTCHED	MUTTERS
MUSHROOM	MUSKLE	MUSTANGS	MUTCHES	MUTTON
MUSHROOMS	MUSKLES	MUSTARD	MUTCHING	MUTTONS
MUSHY	MUSKMELON	MUSTARDS	MUTCHKIN	MUTTONY
MUSIC	MUSKONE	MUSTARDY	MUTCHKINS	MUTTS
MUSICAL	MUSKONES	MUSTED	MUTE	MUTUAL
MUSICALE	MUSKOX	MUSTEE	MUTED	MUTUALISE
MUSICALES	MUSKOXEN	MUSTEES	MUTEDLY	MUTUALISM
MUSICALLY	MUSKRAT	MUSTELID	MUTELY	MUTUALIST
MUSICALS	MUSKRATS	MUSTELIDS	MUTENESS	MUTUALITY
MUSICIAN	MUSKROOT	MUSTELINE	MUTER	MUTUALIZE
MUSICIANS	MUSKROOTS	MUSTER	MUTES	MUTUALLY
MUSICK	MUSKS	MUSTERED	MUTEST	MUTUALS
MUSICKED	MUSKY	MUSTERER	MUTHA	MUTUCA
MUSICKER	MUSLIN	MUSTERERS	MUTHAS	MUTUCAS
MUSICKERS	MUSLINED	MUSTERING	MUTI	MUTUEL
MUSICKING	MUSLINET	MUSTERS	MUTICATE	MUTUELS
MUSICKS	MUSLINETS	MUSTH	MUTICOUS	MUTULAR
MUSICLESS	MUSLINS	MUSTHS	MUTILATE	MUTULE
MUSICS	MUSMON	MUSTIER	MUTILATED	MUTULES
MUSIMON	MUSMONS	MUSTIEST	MUTILATES	MUTUUM
MUSIMONS	MUSO	MUSTILY	MUTILATOR	MUTUUMS
MUSING	MUSOS	MUSTINESS	MUTINE	MUUMUU
MUSINGLY	MUSPIKE	MUSTING	MUTINED	MUUMUUS
MUSINGS	MUSPIKES	MUSTS	MUTINEER	MUX
MUSIT	MUSQUASH	MUSTY	MUTINEERS	MUXED
MUSITS	MUSROL	MUT	MUTINES	MUXES
MUSIVE	MUSROLS	MUTABLE	MUTING	MUXING
MUSJID	MUSS	MUTABLY	MUTINIED	MUZAKY
MUSJIDS	MUSSE	MUTAGEN	MUTINIES	MUZHIK
MUSK	MUSSED	MUTAGENIC	MUTINING	MUZHIKS
MUSKED	MUSSEL	MUTAGENS	MUTINOUS	MUZJIK
MUSKEG	MUSSELLED	MUTANDA	MUTINY	MUZJIKS
MUSKEGS	MUSSELS	MUTANDUM	MUTINYING	MUZZ
MUSKET	MUSSES	MUTANT	MUTIS	MUZZED
MUSKETEER	MUSSIER	MUTANTS	MUTISM	MUZZES
MUSKETOON	MUSSIEST	MUTASE	MUTISMS	MUZZIER
MUSKETRY	MUSSILY	MUTASES	MUTON	MUZZIEST
MUSKETS	MUSSINESS	MUTATE	MUTONS	MUZZILY
MUSKIE	MUSSING	MUTATED	MUTOSCOPE	MUZZINESS
MUSKIER	MUSSITATE	MUTATES	MUTS	MUZZING
MUSKIES	MUSSY	MUTATING	MUTT	MUZZLE

M

MUZZLED	MYCOTOXIN	MYOGEN	MYOTOME	MYSTERIES
MUZZLER	MYCOVIRUS	MYOGENIC	MYOTOMES	MYSTERY
MUZZLERS	MYCS	MYOGENS	MYOTONIA	MYSTIC
MUZZLES	MYDRIASES	MYOGLOBIN	MYOTONIAS	MYSTICAL
MUZZLING	MYDRIASIS	MYOGRAM	MYOTONIC	MYSTICETE
MUZZY	MYDRIATIC	MYOGRAMS	MYOTUBE	MYSTICISM
MVULE	MYELIN	MYOGRAPH	MYOTUBES	MYSTICLY
MVULES	MYELINE	MYOGRAPHS	MYRBANE	MYSTICS
MWAH	MYELINES	MYOGRAPHY	MYRBANES	MYSTIFIED
MWALIMU	MYELINIC	MYOID	MYRIAD	MYSTIFIER
MWALIMUS	MYELINS	MYOLOGIC	MYRIADS	MYSTIFIES
MY	MYELITIS	MYOLOGIES	MYRIADTH	MYSTIFY
MYAL	MYELOCYTE	MYOLOGIST	MYRIADTHS	MYSTIQUE
MYALGIA	MYELOGRAM	MYOLOGY	MYRIAPOD	MYSTIQUES
MYALGIAS	MYELOID	MYOMA	MYRIAPODS	MYTH
MYALGIC	MYELOMA	MYOMANCY	MYRICA	MYTHI
MYALISM	MYELOMAS	MYOMANTIC	MYRICAS	MYTHIC
MYALISMS	MYELOMATA	MYOMAS	MYRINGA	MYTHICAL
MYALIST	MYELON	MYOMATA	MYRINGAS	MYTHICISE
MYALISTS	MYELONS	MYOMATOUS	MYRIOPOD	MYTHICISM
MYALL	MYGALE	MYONEURAL	MYRIOPODS	MYTHICIST
MYALLS	MYGALES	MYOPATHIC	MYRIORAMA	MYTHICIZE
MYASES	MYIASES	MYOPATHY	MYRISTIC	MYTHIER
MYASIS	MYIASIS	MYOPE	MYRMECOID	MYTHIEST
MYC	MYIOPHILY	MYOPES	MYRMIDON	MYTHISE
MYCELE	MYLAR	MYOPHILY	MYRMIDONS	MYTHISED
MYCELES	MYLARS	MYOPIA	MYROBALAN	MYTHISES
MYCELIA	MYLODON	MYOPIAS	MYRRH	MYTHISING
MYCELIAL	MYLODONS	MYOPIC	MYRRHIC	MYTHISM
MYCELIAN	MYLODONT	MYOPICS	MYRRHINE	MYTHISMS
MYCELIUM	MYLODONTS	MYOPIES	MYRRHOL	MYTHIST
MYCELLA	MYLOHYOID	MYOPS	MYRRHOLS	MYTHISTS
MYCELLAS	MYLONITE	MYOPSES	MYRRHS	MYTHIZE
MYCELOID	MYLONITES	MYOPY	MYRTLE	MYTHIZED
MYCETES	MYLONITIC	MYOSCOPE	MYRTLES	MYTHIZES
MYCETOMA	MYNA	MYOSCOPES	MYSELF	MYTHIZING
MYCETOMAS	MYNAH	MYOSES	MYSID	MYTHMAKER
MYCOBIONT	MYNAHS	MYOSIN	MYSIDS	MYTHOI
MYCOFLORA	MYNAS	MYOSINS	MYSOST	MYTHOLOGY
MYCOLOGIC	MYNHEER	MYOSIS	MYSOSTS	MYTHOMANE
MYCOLOGY	MYNHEERS	MYOSITIS	MYSPACE	MYTHOPEIC
MYCOPHAGY	MYOBLAST	MYOSOTE	MYSPACED	MYTHOPOET
MYCOPHILE	MYOBLASTS	MYOSOTES	MYSPACES	MYTHOS
MYCORHIZA	MYOCARDIA	MYOSOTIS	MYSPACING	MYTHS
MYCOSES	MYOCLONIC	MYOSTATIN	MYSTAGOG	MYTHUS
MYCOSIS	MYOCLONUS	MYOTIC	MYSTAGOGS	MYTHY
MYCOTIC	MYOFIBRIL	MYOTICS	MYSTAGOGY	MYTILOID

MYXAMEBA	MYXEDEMAS	MYXOEDEMA	MYXOS	MZUNGU
MYXAMEBAE	MYXEDEMIC	MYXOID	MYXOVIRAL	MZUNGUS
MYXAMEBAS	MYXO	MYXOMA	MYXOVIRUS	
MYXAMOEBA	MYXOCYTE	MYXOMAS	MZEE	
MYXEDEMA	MYXOCYTES	MYXOMATA	MZEES	

M

N

NA	NACRES	NAGGINGS	NAINSOOK	NAMAYCUSH
NAAM	NACRITE	NAGGY	NAINSOOKS	NAME
NAAMS	NACRITES	NAGMAAL	NAIRA	NAMEABLE
NAAN	NACROUS	NAGMAALS	NAIRAS	NAMECHECK
NAANS	NADA	NAGOR	NAIRU	NAMED
NAARTJE	NADAS	NAGORS	NAIRUS	NAMELESS
NAARTJES	NADIR	NAGS	NAISSANCE	NAMELY
NAARTJIE	NADIRAL	NAH	NAISSANT	NAMEPLATE
NAARTJIES	NADIRS	NAHAL	NAIVE	NAMER
NAB	NADORS	NAHALS	NAIVELY	NAMERS
NABBED	NADS	NAIAD	NAIVENESS	NAMES
NABBER	NAE	NAIADES	NAIVER	NAMESAKE
NABBERS	NAEBODIES	NAIADS	NAIVES	NAMESAKES
NABBING	NAEBODY	NAIANT	NAIVEST	NAMETAG
NABE	NAETHING	NAIF	NAIVETE	NAMETAGS
NABES	NAETHINGS	NAIFER	NAIVETES	NAMETAPE
NABIS	NAEVE	NAIFEST	NAIVETIES	NAMETAPES
NABK	NAEVES	NAIFLY	NAIVETY	NAMING
NABKS	NAEVI	NAIFNESS	NAIVIST	NAMINGS
NABLA	NAEVOID	NAIFS	NAKED	NAMMA
NABLAS	NAEVUS	NAIK	NAKEDER	NAMS
NABOB	NAFF	NAIKS	NAKEDEST	NAMU
NABOBERY	NAFFED	NAIL	NAKEDLY	NAMUS
NABOBESS	NAFFER	NAILBITER	NAKEDNESS	NAN
NABOBISH	NAFFEST	NAILBRUSH	NAKER	NANA
NABOBISM	NAFFING	NAILED	NAKERS	NANAS
NABOBISMS	NAFFLY	NAILER	NAKFA	NANCE
NABOBS	NAFFNESS	NAILERIES	NAKFAS	NANCES
NABS	NAFFS	NAILERS	NALA	NANCIES
NACARAT	NAG	NAILERY	NALAS	NANCIFIED
NACARATS	NAGA	NAILFILE	NALED	NANCY
NACELLE	NAGANA	NAILFILES	NALEDS	NANDIN
NACELLES	NAGANAS	NAILFOLD	NALIDIXIC	NANDINA
NACH	NAGAPIE	NAILFOLDS	NALLA	NANDINAS
NACHAS	NAGAPIES	NAILHEAD	NALLAH	NANDINE
NACHE	NAGARI	NAILHEADS	NALLAHS	NANDINES
NACHES	NAGARIS	NAILING	NALLAS	NANDINS
NACHO	NAGAS	NAILINGS	NALOXONE	NANDOO
NACHOS	NAGGED	NAILLESS	NALOXONES	NANDOOS
NACHTMAAL	NAGGER	NAILS	NAM	NANDU
NACKET	NAGGERS	NAILSET	NAMABLE	NANDUS
NACKETS	NAGGIER	NAILSETS	NAMASKAR	NANE
NACRE	NAGGIEST	NAIN	NAMASKARS	NANG
NACRED	NAGGING	NAINSELL	NAMASTE	NANISM
NACREOUS	NAGGINGLY	NAINSELLS	NAMASTES	NANISMS

NANITE	NAP	NAPRON	NARGHILES	NARTHEXES
NANITES	NAPA	NAPRONS	NARGHILLY	NARTJIE
NANKEEN	NAPALM	NAPROXEN	NARGHILY	NARTJIES
NANKEENS	NAPALMED	NAPROXENS	NARGILE	NARWAL
NANKIN	NAPALMING	NAPS	NARGILEH	NARWALS
NANKINS	NAPALMS	NARAS	NARGILEHS	NARWHAL
NANNA	NAPAS	NARASES	NARGILES	NARWHALE
NANNAS	NAPE	NARC	NARGILIES	NARWHALES
NANNIE	NAPED	NARCEEN	NARGILY	NARWHALS
NANNIED	NAPERIES	NARCEENS	NARGUILEH	NARY
NANNIES	NAPERY	NARCEIN	NARIAL	NAS
NANNY	NAPES	NARCEINE	NARIC	NASAL
NANNYGAI	NAPHTHA	NARCEINES	NARICORN	NASALISE
NANNYGAIS	NAPHTHAS	NARCEINS	NARICORNS	NASALISED
NANNYING	NAPHTHENE	NARCISM	NARINE	NASALISES
NANNYISH	NAPHTHOL	NARCISMS	NARIS	NASALISM
NANOBE	NAPHTHOLS	NARCISSI	NARK	NASALISMS
NANOBES	NAPHTHOUS	NARCISSUS	NARKED	NASALITY
NANOBOT	NAPHTHYL	NARCIST	NARKIER	NASALIZE
NANOBOTS	NAPHTHYLS	NARCISTIC	NARKIEST	NASALIZED
NANODOT	NAPHTOL	NARCISTS	NARKING	NASALIZES
NANODOTS	NAPHTOLS	NARCO	NARKS	NASALLY
NANOGRAM	NAPIFORM	NARCOMA	NARKY	NASALS
NANOGRAMS	NAPING	NARCOMAS	NARQUOIS	NASARD
NANOMETER	NAPKIN	NARCOMATA	NARRAS	NASARDS
NANOMETRE	NAPKINS	NARCOS	NARRASES	NASCENCE
NANOOK	NAPLESS	NARCOSE	NARRATE	NASCENCES
NANOOKS	NAPOLEON	NARCOSES	NARRATED	NASCENCY
NANOPORE	NAPOLEONS	NARCOSIS	NARRATER	NASCENT
NANOPORES	NAPOO	NARCOTIC	NARRATERS	NASEBERRY
NANOSCALE	NAPOOED	NARCOTICS	NARRATES	NASHGAB
NANOTECH	NAPOOING	NARCOTINE	NARRATING	NASHGABS
NANOTECHS	NAPOOS	NARCOTISE	NARRATION	NASHI
NANOTESLA	NAPPA	NARCOTISM	NARRATIVE	NASHIS
NANOTUBE	NAPPAS	NARCOTIST	NARRATOR	NASIAL
NANOTUBES	NAPPE	NARCOTIZE	NARRATORS	NASION
NANOWATT	NAPPED	NARCS	NARRATORY	NASIONS
NANOWATTS	NAPPER	NARD	NARRE	NASSELLA
NANOWIRE	NAPPERS	NARDED	NARROW	NASTALIK
NANOWIRES	NAPPES	NARDINE	NARROWED	NASTALIKS
NANOWORLD	NAPPIE	NARDING	NARROWER	NASTIC
NANS	NAPPIER	NARDOO	NARROWEST	NASTIER
NANUA	NAPPIES	NARDOOS	NARROWING	NASTIES
NANUAS	NAPPIEST	NARDS	NARROWISH	NASTIEST
NAOI	NAPPINESS	NARE	NARROWLY	NASTILY
NAOS	NAPPING	NARES	NARROWS	NASTINESS
NAOSES	NAPPY	NARGHILE	NARTHEX	NASTY

NASUTE	NATTILY	NAUTILOID	NAYS	NEARSHORE
NASUTES	NATTINESS	NAUTILUS	NAYSAID	NEARSIDE
NAT	NATTY	NAVAID	NAYSAY	NEARSIDES
NATAL	NATURA	NAVAIDS	NAYSAYER	NEAT
NATALITY	NATURAE	NAVAL	NAYSAYERS	NEATEN
NATANT	NATURAL	NAVALISM	NAYSAYING	NEATENED
NATANTLY	NATURALLY	NAVALISMS	NAYSAYS	NEATENING
NATATION	NATURALS	NAVALLY	NAYTHLES	NEATENS
NATATIONS	NATURE	NAVAR	NAYWARD	NEATER
NATATORIA	NATURED	NAVARCH	NAYWARDS	NEATEST
NATATORY	NATURES	NAVARCHS	NAYWORD	NEATH
NATCH	NATURING	NAVARCHY	NAYWORDS	NEATHERD
NATCHES	NATURISM	NAVARHO	NAZE	NEATHERDS
NATES	NATURISMS	NAVARHOS	NAZES	NEATLY
NATHELESS	NATURIST	NAVARIN	NAZI	NEATNESS
NATHEMO	NATURISTS	NAVARINS	NAZIFIED	NEATNIK
NATHEMORE	NAUCH	NAVARS	NAZIFIES	NEATNIKS
NATHLESS	NAUCHES	NAVE	NAZIFY	NEATS
NATIFORM	NAUGAHYDE	NAVEL	NAZIFYING	NEB
NATION	NAUGHT	NAVELS	NAZIR	NEBBED
NATIONAL	NAUGHTIER	NAVELWORT	NAZIRS	NEBBICH
NATIONALS	NAUGHTIES	NAVES	NAZIS	NEBBICHS
NATIONS	NAUGHTILY	NAVETTE	NE	NEBBING
NATIS	NAUGHTS	NAVETTES	NEAFE	NEBBISH
NATIVE	NAUGHTY	NAVEW	NEAFES	NEBBISHE
NATIVELY	NAUMACHIA	NAVEWS	NEAFFE	NEBBISHER
NATIVES	NAUMACHY	NAVICERT	NEAFFES	NEBBISHES
NATIVISM	NAUNT	NAVICERTS	NEAL	NEBBISHY
NATIVISMS	NAUNTS	NAVICULA	NEALED	NEBBUK
NATIVIST	NAUPLIAL	NAVICULAR	NEALING	NEBBUKS
NATIVISTS	NAUPLII	NAVICULAS	NEALS	NEBECK
NATIVITY	NAUPLIOID	NAVIES	NEANIC	NEBECKS
NATRIUM	NAUPLIUS	NAVIGABLE	NEAP	NEBEK
NATRIUMS	NAUSEA	NAVIGABLY	NEAPED	NEBEKS
NATROLITE	NAUSEANT	NAVIGATE	NEAPING	NEBEL
NATRON	NAUSEANTS	NAVIGATED	NEAPS	NEBELS
NATRONS	NAUSEAS	NAVIGATES	NEAR	NEBENKERN
NATS	NAUSEATE	NAVIGATOR	NEARBY	NEBISH
NATTER	NAUSEATED	NAVVIED	NEARED	NEBISHES
NATTERED	NAUSEATES	NAVVIES	NEARER	NEBRIS
NATTERER	NAUSEOUS	NAVVY	NEAREST	NEBRISES
NATTERERS	NAUTCH	NAVVYING	NEARING	NEBS
NATTERING	NAUTCHES	NAVY	NEARLIER	NEBULA
NATTERS	NAUTIC	NAW	NEARLIEST	NEBULAE
NATTERY	NAUTICAL	NAWAB	NEARLY	NEBULAR
NATTIER	NAUTICS	NAWABS	NEARNESS	NEBULAS
NATTIEST	NAUTILI	NAY	NEARS	NEBULE

NEBULES	NECKWEED	NEEDILY	NEGATERS	NEIGH
NEBULISE	NECKWEEDS	NEEDINESS	NEGATES	NEIGHBOR
NEBULISED	NECROLOGY	NEEDING	NEGATING	NEIGHBORS
NEBULISER	NECROPHIL	NEEDLE	NEGATION	NEIGHBOUR
NEBULISES	NECROPOLI	NEEDLED	NEGATIONS	NEIGHED
NEBULIUM	NECROPSY	NEEDLEFUL	NEGATIVE	NEIGHING
NEBULIUMS	NECROSE	NEEDLER	NEGATIVED	NEIGHS
NEBULIZE	NECROSED	NEEDLERS	NEGATIVES	NEINEI
NEBULIZED	NECROSES	NEEDLES	NEGATON	NEINEIS
NEBULIZER	NECROSING	NEEDLESS	NEGATONS	NEIST
NEBULIZES	NECROSIS	NEEDLIER	NEGATOR	NEITHER
NEBULOSE	NECROTIC	NEEDLIEST	NEGATORS	NEIVE
NEBULOUS	NECROTISE	NEEDLING	NEGATORY	NEIVES
NEBULY	NECROTIZE	NEEDLINGS	NEGATRON	NEK
NECESSARY	NECROTOMY	NEEDLY	NEGATRONS	NEKS
NECESSITY	NECTAR	NEEDMENT	NEGLECT	NEKTON
NECK	NECTAREAL	NEEDMENTS	NEGLECTED	NEKTONIC
NECKATEE	NECTAREAN	NEEDS	NEGLECTER	NEKTONS
NECKATEES	NECTARED	NEEDY	NEGLECTOR	NELIES
NECKBAND	NECTARIAL	NEELD	NEGLECTS	NELIS
NECKBANDS	NECTARIED	NEELDS	NEGLIGE	NELLIE
NECKBEEF	NECTARIES	NEELE	NEGLIGEE	NELLIES
NECKBEEFS	NECTARINE	NEELES	NEGLIGEES	NELLY
NECKCLOTH	NECTAROUS	NEEM	NEGLIGENT	NELSON
NECKED	NECTARS	NEEMB	NEGLIGES	NELSONS
NECKER	NECTARY	NEEMBS	NEGOCIANT	NELUMBIUM
NECKERS	NED	NEEMS	NEGOTIANT	NELUMBO
NECKGEAR	NEDDIER	NEEP	NEGOTIATE	NELUMBOS
NECKGEARS	NEDDIES	NEEPS	NEGRESS	NEMA
NECKING	NEDDIEST	NEESBERRY	NEGRESSES	NEMAS
NECKINGS	NEDDISH	NEESE	NEGRITUDE	NEMATIC
NECKLACE	NEDDY	NEESED	NEGRO	NEMATODE
NECKLACED	NEDETTE	NEESES	NEGROES	NEMATODES
NECKLACES	NEDETTES	NEESING	NEGROHEAD	NEMATOID
NECKLESS	NEDS	NEEZE	NEGROID	NEMERTEAN
NECKLET	NEE	NEEZED	NEGROIDAL	NEMERTIAN
NECKLETS	NEED	NEEZES	NEGROIDS	NEMERTINE
NECKLIKE	NEEDED	NEEZING	NEGROISM	NEMESES
NECKLINE	NEEDER	NEF	NEGROISMS	NEMESIA
NECKLINES	NEEDERS	NEFANDOUS	NEGRONI	NEMESIAS
NECKPIECE	NEEDFIRE	NEFARIOUS	NEGRONIS	NEMESIS
NECKS	NEEDFIRES	NEFAST	NEGROPHIL	NEMN
NECKTIE	NEEDFUL	NEFS	NEGS	NEMNED
NECKTIES	NEEDFULLY	NEG	NEGUS	NEMNING
NECKVERSE	NEEDFULS	NEGATE	NEGUSES	NEMNS
NECKWEAR	NEEDIER	NEGATED	NEIF	NEMOPHILA
NECKWEARS	NEEDIEST	NEGATER	NEIFS	NEMORAL

N

NEMOROUS	NEOPHYTE	NEPHRISMS	NEROLIS	NESTFUL
NEMPT	NEOPHYTES	NEPHRITE	NEROLS	NESTFULS
NENE	NEOPHYTIC	NEPHRITES	NERTS	NESTING
NENES	NEOPILINA	NEPHRITIC	NERTZ	NESTINGS
NENNIGAI	NEOPLASIA	NEPHRITIS	NERVAL	NESTLE
NENNIGAIS	NEOPLASM	NEPHROID	NERVATE	NESTLED
NENUPHAR	NEOPLASMS	NEPHRON	NERVATION	NESTLER
NENUPHARS	NEOPLASTY	NEPHRONS	NERVATURE	NESTLERS
NEOBLAST	NEOPRENE	NEPHROSES	NERVE	NESTLES
NEOBLASTS	NEOPRENES	NEPHROSIS	NERVED	NESTLIKE
NEOCON	NEOSOUL	NEPHROTIC	NERVELESS	NESTLING
NEOCONS	NEOSOULS	NEPIONIC	NERVELET	NESTLINGS
NEOCORTEX	NEOTEINIA	NEPIT	NERVELETS	NESTOR
NEODYMIUM	NEOTENIC	NEPITS	NERVER	NESTORS
NEOGENE	NEOTENIES	NEPOTIC	NERVERS	NESTS
NEOGOTHIC	NEOTENOUS	NEPOTISM	NERVES	NET
NEOLITH	NEOTENY	NEPOTISMS	NERVIER	NETBALL
NEOLITHIC	NEOTERIC	NEPOTIST	NERVIEST	NETBALLER
NEOLITHS	NEOTERICS	NEPOTISTS	NERVILY	NETBALLS
NEOLOGIAN	NEOTERISE	NEPS	NERVINE	NETE
NEOLOGIC	NEOTERISM	NEPTUNIUM	NERVINES	NETES
NEOLOGIES	NEOTERIST	NERAL	NERVINESS	NETFUL
NEOLOGISE	NEOTERIZE	NERALS	NERVING	NETFULS
NEOLOGISM	NEOTOXIN	NERD	NERVINGS	NETHEAD
NEOLOGIST	NEOTOXINS	NERDIC	NERVOSITY	NETHEADS
NEOLOGIZE	NEOTROPIC	NERDICS	NERVOUS	NETHELESS
NEOLOGY	NEOTYPE	NERDIER	NERVOUSLY	NETHER
NEOMORPH	NEOTYPES	NERDIEST	NERVULAR	NETIZEN
NEOMORPHS	NEP	NERDINESS	NERVULE	NETIZENS
NEOMYCIN	NEPENTHE	NERDISH	NERVULES	NETLESS
NEOMYCINS	NEPENTHES	NERDS	NERVURE	NETLIKE
NEON	NEPER	NERDY	NERVURES	NETMINDER
NEONATAL	NEPERS	NEREID	NERVY	NETOP
NEONATE	NEPETA	NEREIDES	NESCIENCE	NETOPS
NEONATES	NEPETAS	NEREIDS	NESCIENT	NETROOT
NEONED	NEPHALISM	NEREIS	NESCIENTS	NETROOTS
NEONOMIAN	NEPHALIST	NERINE	NESH	NETS
NEONS	NEPHELINE	NERINES	NESHER	NETSPEAK
NEOPAGAN	NEPHELITE	NERITE	NESHEST	NETSPEAKS
NEOPAGANS	NEPHEW	NERITES	NESHNESS	NETSUKE
NEOPHILE	NEPHEWS	NERITIC	NESS	NETSUKES
NEOPHILES	NEPHOGRAM	NERK	NESSES	NETT
NEOPHILIA	NEPHOLOGY	NERKA	NEST	NETTABLE
NEOPHOBE	NEPHRALGY	NERKAS	NESTABLE	NETTED
NEOPHOBES	NEPHRIC	NERKS	NESTED	NETTER
NEOPHOBIA	NEPHRIDIA	NEROL	NESTER	NETTERS
NEOPHOBIC	NEPHRISM	NEROLI	NESTERS	NETTIE

NETTIER	NEUROGLIA	NEVELLING	NEWSCASTS	NEXTS
NETTIES	NEUROGRAM	NEVELS	NEWSDESK	NEXUS
NETTIEST	NEUROID	NEVER	NEWSDESKS	NEXUSES
NETTING	NEUROLOGY	NEVERMIND	NEWSED	NGAI
NETTINGS	NEUROMA	NEVERMORE	NEWSES	NGAIO
NETTLE	NEUROMAS	NEVES	NEWSFLASH	NGAIOS
NETTLED	NEUROMAST	NEVI	NEWSGIRL	NGANA
NETTLER	NEUROMATA	NEVOID	NEWSGIRLS	NGANAS
NETTLERS	NEURON	NEVUS	NEWSGROUP	NGARARA
NETTLES	NEURONAL	NEW	NEWSHAWK	NGARARAS
NETTLIER	NEURONE	NEWBIE	NEWSHAWKS	NGATI
NETTLIEST	NEURONES	NEWBIES	NEWSHOUND	NGATIS
NETTLING	NEURONIC	NEWBORN	NEWSIE	NGOMA
NETTLY	NEURONS	NEWBORNS	NEWSIER	NGOMAS
NETTS	NEUROPATH	NEWCOME	NEWSIES	NGULTRUM
NETTY	NEUROPIL	NEWCOMER	NEWSIEST	NGULTRUMS
NETWORK	NEUROPILS	NEWCOMERS	NEWSINESS	NGWEE
NETWORKED	NEUROSAL	NEWED	NEWSING	NHANDU
NETWORKER	NEUROSES	NEWEL	NEWSLESS	NHANDUS
NETWORKS	NEUROSIS	NEWELL	NEWSMAKER	NIACIN
NEUK	NEUROTIC	NEWELLED	NEWSMAN	NIACINS
NEUKS	NEUROTICS	NEWELLS	NEWSMEN	NIAISERIE
NEUM	NEUROTOMY	NEWELS	NEWSPAPER	NIALAMIDE
NEUMATIC	NEURULA	NEWER	NEWSPEAK	NIB
NEUME	NEURULAE	NEWEST	NEWSPEAKS	NIBBED
NEUMES	NEURULAR	NEWFANGLE	NEWSPRINT	NIBBING
NEUMIC	NEURULAS	NEWFOUND	NEWSREEL	NIBBLE
NEUMS	NEUSTIC	NEWIE	NEWSREELS	NIBBLED
NEURAL	NEUSTON	NEWIES	NEWSROOM	NIBBLER
NEURALGIA	NEUSTONIC	NEWING	NEWSROOMS	NIBBLERS
NEURALGIC	NEUSTONS	NEWISH	NEWSSTAND	NIBBLES
NEURALLY	NEUTER	NEWISHLY	NEWSTRADE	NIBBLING
NEURATION	NEUTERED	NEWLY	NEWSWIRE	NIBBLINGS
NEURAXON	NEUTERING	NEWLYWED	NEWSWIRES	NIBLICK
NEURAXONS	NEUTERS	NEWLYWEDS	NEWSWOMAN	NIBLICKS
NEURILITY	NEUTRAL	NEWMARKET	NEWSWOMEN	NIBLIKE
NEURINE	NEUTRALLY	NEWMOWN	NEWSY	NIBS
NEURINES	NEUTRALS	NEWNESS	NEWT	NICAD
NEURISM	NEUTRETTO	NEWNESSES	NEWTON	NICADS
NEURISMS	NEUTRINO	NEWS	NEWTONS	NICCOLITE
NEURITE	NEUTRINOS	NEWSAGENT	NEWTS	NICE
NEURITES	NEUTRON	NEWSBEAT	NEWWAVER	NICEISH
NEURITIC	NEUTRONIC	NEWSBEATS	NEWWAVERS	NICELY
NEURITICS	NEUTRONS	NEWSBOY	NEXT	NICENESS
NEURITIS	NEVE	NEWSBOYS	NEXTDOOR	NICER
NEUROCHIP	NEVEL	NEWSBREAK	NEXTLY	NICEST
NEUROCOEL	NEVELLED	NEWSCAST	NEXTNESS	NICETIES

NICETY	NICOL	NIDOROUS	NIGER	NIGHTJARS
NICHE	NICOLS	NIDORS	NIGERS	NIGHTLESS
NICHED	NICOMPOOP	NIDS	NIGGARD	NIGHTLIFE
NICHER	NICOTIAN	NIDUS	NIGGARDED	NIGHTLIKE
NICHERED	NICOTIANA	NIDUSES	NIGGARDLY	NIGHTLONG
NICHERING	NICOTIANS	NIE	NIGGARDS	NIGHTLY
NICHERS	NICOTIN	NIECE	NIGGER	NIGHTMARE
NICHES	NICOTINE	NIECES	NIGGERDOM	NIGHTMARY
NICHING	NICOTINED	NIED	NIGGERED	NIGHTS
NICHT	NICOTINES	NIEF	NIGGERING	NIGHTSIDE
NICHTS	NICOTINIC	NIEFS	NIGGERISH	NIGHTSPOT
NICISH	NICOTINS	NIELLATED	NIGGERISM	NIGHTTIDE
NICK	NICTATE	NIELLI	NIGGERS	NIGHTTIME
NICKAR	NICTATED	NIELLIST	NIGGERY	NIGHTWARD
NICKARS	NICTATES	NIELLISTS	NIGGLE	NIGHTWEAR
NICKED	NICTATING	NIELLO	NIGGLED	NIGHTY
NICKEL	NICTATION	NIELLOED	NIGGLER	NIGIRI
NICKELED	NICTITANT	NIELLOING	NIGGLERS	NIGIRIS
NICKELIC	NICTITATE	NIELLOS	NIGGLES	NIGRICANT
NICKELINE	NID	NIES	NIGGLIER	NIGRIFIED
NICKELING	NIDAL	NIEVE	NIGGLIEST	NIGRIFIES
NICKELISE	NIDAMENTA	NIEVEFUL	NIGGLING	NIGRIFY
NICKELIZE	NIDATE	NIEVEFULS	NIGGLINGS	NIGRITUDE
NICKELLED	NIDATED	NIEVES	NIGGLY	NIGROSIN
NICKELOUS	NIDATES	NIFE	NIGH	NIGROSINE
NICKELS	NIDATING	NIFES	NIGHED	NIGROSINS
NICKER	NIDATION	NIFF	NIGHER	NIHIL
NICKERED	NIDATIONS	NIFFED	NIGHEST	NIHILISM
NICKERING	NIDDERING	NIFFER	NIGHING	NIHILISMS
NICKERS	NIDDICK	NIFFERED	NIGHLY	NIHILIST
NICKING	NIDDICKS	NIFFERING	NIGHNESS	NIHILISTS
NICKLE	NIDE	NIFFERS	NIGHS	NIHILITY
NICKLED	NIDED	NIFFIER	NIGHT	NIHILS
NICKLES	NIDERING	NIFFIEST	NIGHTBIRD	NIHONGA
NICKLING	NIDERINGS	NIFFING	NIGHTCAP	NIHONGAS
NICKNACK	NIDERLING	NIFFNAFF	NIGHTCAPS	NIKAB
NICKNACKS	NIDES	NIFFNAFFS	NIGHTCLUB	NIKABS
NICKNAME	NIDGET	NIFFS	NIGHTED	NIKAH
NICKNAMED	NIDGETS	NIFFY	NIGHTFALL	NIKAHS
NICKNAMER	NIDI	NIFTIER	NIGHTFIRE	NIKAU
NICKNAMES	NIDIFIED	NIFTIES	NIGHTGEAR	NIKAUS
NICKPOINT	NIDIFIES	NIFTIEST	NIGHTGLOW	NIL
NICKS	NIDIFY	NIFTILY	NIGHTGOWN	NILGAI
NICKSTICK	NIDIFYING	NIFTINESS	NIGHTHAWK	NILGAIS
NICKUM	NIDING	NIFTY	NIGHTIE	NILGAU
NICKUMS	NIDINGS	NIGELLA	NIGHTIES	NILGAUS
NICOISE	NIDOR	NIGELLAS	NIGHTJAR	NILGHAI

NILGHAIS	NINEPENCE	NIPPINESS	NITERY	NITROGEN
NILGHAU	NINEPENNY	NIPPING	NITES	NITROGENS
NILGHAUS	NINEPIN	NIPPINGLY	NITHER	NITROLIC
NILL	NINEPINS	NIPPLE	NITHERED	NITROS
NILLED	NINES	NIPPLED	NITHERING	NITROSO
NILLING	NINESCORE	NIPPLES	NITHERS	NITROSYL
NILLS	NINETEEN	NIPPLING	NITHING	NITROSYLS
NILPOTENT	NINETEENS	NIPPY	NITHINGS	NITROUS
NILS	NINETIES	NIPS	NITID	NITROX
NIM	NINETIETH	NIPTER	NITINOL	NITROXES
NIMB	NINETY	NIPTERS	NITINOLS	NITROXYL
NIMBED	NINHYDRIN	NIQAB	NITON	NITROXYLS
NIMBI	NINJA	NIQABS	NITONS	NITRY
NIMBLE	NINJAS	NIRAMIAI	NITPICK	NITRYL
NIMBLER	NINJITSU	NIRAMIAIS	NITPICKED	NITRYLS
NIMBLESSE	NINJITSUS	NIRL	NITPICKER	NITS
NIMBLEST	NINJUTSU	NIRLED	NITPICKS	NITTIER
NIMBLEWIT	NINJUTSUS	NIRLIE	NITPICKY	NITTIEST
NIMBLY	NINNIES	NIRLIER	NITRAMINE	NITTY
NIMBS	NINNY	NIRLIEST	NITRATE	NITWIT
NIMBUS	NINNYISH	NIRLING	NITRATED	NITWITS
NIMBUSED	NINON	NIRLIT	NITRATES	NITWITTED
NIMBUSES	NINONS	NIRLS	NITRATINE	NIVAL
NIMBYISM	NINTH	NIRLY	NITRATING	NIVATION
NIMBYISMS	NINTHLY	NIRVANA	NITRATION	NIVATIONS
NIMBYNESS	NINTHS	NIRVANAS	NITRATOR	NIVEOUS
NIMIETIES	NIOBATE	NIRVANIC	NITRATORS	NIX
NIMIETY	NIOBATES	NIS	NITRE	NIXE
NIMIOUS	NIOBIC	NISBERRY	NITRES	NIXED
NIMMED	NIOBITE	NISEI	NITRIC	NIXER
NIMMER	NIOBITES	NISEIS	NITRID	NIXERS
NIMMERS	NIOBIUM	NISGUL	NITRIDE	NIXES
NIMMING	NIOBIUMS	NISGULS	NITRIDED	NIXIE
NIMONIC	NIOBOUS	NISH	NITRIDES	NIXIES
NIMPS	NIP	NISHES	NITRIDING	NIXING
NIMROD	NIPA	NISI	NITRIDS	NIXY
NIMRODS	NIPAS	NISSE	NITRIFIED	NIZAM
NIMS	NIPCHEESE	NISSES	NITRIFIER	NIZAMATE
NINCOM	NIPPED	NISUS	NITRIFIES	NIZAMATES
NINCOMS	NIPPER	NIT	NITRIFY	NIZAMS
NINCUM	NIPPERED	NITCHIE	NITRIL	NKOSI
NINCUMS	NIPPERING	NITCHIES	NITRILE	NKOSIS
NINE	NIPPERKIN	NITE	NITRILES	NO
NINEBARK	NIPPERS	NITER	NITRILS	NOAH
NINEBARKS	NIPPIER	NITERIE	NITRITE	NOAHS
NINEFOLD	NIPPIEST	NITERIES	NITRITES	NOB
NINEHOLES	NIPPILY	NITERS	NITRO	NOBBIER

N

NOBBIEST	NOCTILUCA	NODI	NOIRS	NOMBLES
NOBBILY	NOCTUA	NODICAL	NOISE	NOMBRIL
NOBBINESS	NOCTUARY	NODOSE	NOISED	NOMBRILS
NOBBLE	NOCTUAS	NODOSITY	NOISEFUL	NOME
NOBBLED	NOCTUID	NODOUS	NOISELESS	NOMEN
NOBBLER	NOCTUIDS	NODS	NOISENIK	NOMES
NOBBLERS	NOCTULE	NODULAR	NOISENIKS	NOMIC
NOBBLES	NOCTULES	NODULATED	NOISES	NOMINA
NOBBLING	NOCTUOID	NODULE	NOISETTE	NOMINABLE
NOBBUT	NOCTURIA	NODULED	NOISETTES	NOMINAL
NOBBY	NOCTURIAS	NODULES	NOISIER	NOMINALLY
NOBELIUM	NOCTURN	NODULOSE	NOISIEST	NOMINALS
NOBELIUMS	NOCTURNAL	NODULOUS	NOISILY	NOMINATE
NOBILESSE	NOCTURNE	NODUS	NOISINESS	NOMINATED
NOBILIARY	NOCTURNES	NOEL	NOISING	NOMINATES
NOBILITY	NOCTURNS	NOELS	NOISOME	NOMINATOR
NOBLE	NOCUOUS	NOES	NOISOMELY	NOMINEE
NOBLEMAN	NOCUOUSLY	NOESES	NOISY	NOMINEES
NOBLEMEN	NOD	NOESIS	NOLE	NOMISM
NOBLENESS	NODAL	NOESISES	NOLES	NOMISMS
NOBLER	NODALISE	NOETIC	NOLITION	NOMISTIC
NOBLES	NODALISED	NOG	NOLITIONS	NOMOCRACY
NOBLESSE	NODALISES	NOGAKU	NOLL	NOMOGENY
NOBLESSES	NODALITY	NOGG	NOLLS	NOMOGRAM
NOBLEST	NODALIZE	NOGGED	NOLO	NOMOGRAMS
NOBLY	NODALIZED	NOGGIN	NOLOS	NOMOGRAPH
NOBODIES	NODALIZES	NOGGING	NOM	NOMOI
NOBODY	NODALLY	NOGGINGS	NOMA	NOMOLOGIC
NOBS	NODATED	NOGGINS	NOMAD	NOMOLOGY
NOCAKE	NODATION	NOGGS	NOMADE	NOMOS
NOCAKES	NODATIONS	NOGS	NOMADES	NOMOTHETE
NOCENT	NODDED	NOH	NOMADIC	NOMS
NOCENTLY	NODDER	NOHOW	NOMADIES	NON
NOCENTS	NODDERS	NOHOWISH	NOMADISE	NONA
NOCHEL	NODDIER	NOIL	NOMADISED	NONACID
NOCHELED	NODDIES	NOILIER	NOMADISES	NONACIDIC
NOCHELING	NODDIEST	NOILIEST	NOMADISM	NONACIDS
NOCHELLED	NODDING	NOILS	NOMADISMS	NONACTING
NOCHELS	NODDINGLY	NOILY	NOMADIZE	NONACTION
NOCK	NODDINGS	NOINT	NOMADIZED	NONACTIVE
NOCKED	NODDLE	NOINTED	NOMADIZES	NONACTOR
NOCKET	NODDLED	NOINTER	NOMADS	NONACTORS
NOCKETS	NODDLES	NOINTERS	NOMADY	NONADDICT
NOCKING	NODDLING	NOINTING	NOMARCH	NONADULT
NOCKS	NODDY	NOINTS	NOMARCHS	NONADULTS
NOCTILIO	NODE	NOIR	NOMARCHY	NONAGE
NOCTILIOS	NODES	NOIRISH	NOMAS	NONAGED

NONAGES	NONCOITAL	NONET	NONGLARES	NONLEAFY
NONAGON	NONCOKING	NONETHNIC	NONGLAZED	NONLEAGUE
NONAGONAL	NONCOLA	NONETS	NONGLOSSY	NONLEGAL
NONAGONS	NONCOLAS	NONETTE	NONGOLFER	NONLEGUME
NONANE	NONCOLOR	NONETTES	NONGRADED	NONLETHAL
NONANES	NONCOLORS	NONETTI	NONGREASY	NONLEVEL
NONANIMAL	NONCOM	NONETTO	NONGREEN	NONLIABLE
NONANOIC	NONCOMBAT	NONETTOS	NONGROWTH	NONLIFE
NONANSWER	NONCOMS	NONEVENT	NONGS	NONLINEAL
NONARABLE	NONCONCUR	NONEVENTS	NONGUEST	NONLINEAR
NONART	NONCORE	NONEXEMPT	NONGUESTS	NONLIQUID
NONARTIST	NONCOUNTY	NONEXOTIC	NONGUILT	NONLIVES
NONARTS	NONCREDIT	NONEXPERT	NONGUILTS	NONLIVING
NONARY	NONCRIME	NONEXTANT	NONHARDY	NONLOCAL
NONAS	NONCRIMES	NONFACT	NONHEME	NONLOCALS
NONATOMIC	NONCRISES	NONFACTOR	NONHERO	NONLOVING
NONAUTHOR	NONCRISIS	NONFACTS	NONHEROES	NONLOYAL
NONBANK	NONCYCLIC	NONFADING	NONHEROIC	NONLYRIC
NONBANKS	NONDAIRY	NONFAMILY	NONHOME	NONMAJOR
NONBASIC	NONDANCE	NONFAN	NONHUMAN	NONMAJORS
NONBEING	NONDANCER	NONFANS	NONHUMANS	NONMAN
NONBEINGS	NONDANCES	NONFARM	NONHUNTER	NONMANUAL
NONBELIEF	NONDEGREE	NONFARMER	NONI	NONMARKET
NONBINARY	NONDEMAND	NONFAT	NONIDEAL	NONMATURE
NONBITING	NONDESERT	NONFATAL	NONILLION	NONMEAT
NONBLACK	NONDOCTOR	NONFATTY	NONIMAGE	NONMEMBER
NONBLACKS	NONDOLLAR	NONFEUDAL	NONIMAGES	NONMEN
NONBODIES	NONDRIP	NONFILIAL	NONIMMUNE	NONMENTAL
NONBODY	NONDRIVER	NONFINAL	NONIMPACT	NONMETAL
NONBONDED	NONDRUG	NONFINITE	NONINERT	NONMETALS
NONBOOK	NONDRYING	NONFISCAL	NONINJURY	NONMETRIC
NONBOOKS	NONE	NONFLUID	NONINSECT	NONMETRO
NONBRAND	NONEDIBLE	NONFLUIDS	NONIONIC	NONMOBILE
NONBUYING	NONEGO	NONFLYING	NONIRON	NONMODAL
NONCAKING	NONEGOS	NONFOCAL	NONIS	NONMODERN
NONCAMPUS	NONELECT	NONFOOD	NONISSUE	NONMONEY
NONCAREER	NONELITE	NONFORMAL	NONISSUES	NONMORAL
NONCASH	NONEMPTY	NONFOSSIL	NONJOINER	NONMORTAL
NONCASUAL	NONENDING	NONFROZEN	NONJURIES	NONMOTILE
NONCAUSAL	NONENERGY	NONFUEL	NONJURING	NONMOVING
NONCE	NONENTITY	NONFUNDED	NONJUROR	NONMUSIC
NONCEREAL	NONENTRY	NONG	NONJURORS	NONMUSICS
NONCES	NONEQUAL	NONGAME	NONJURY	NONMUTANT
NONCHURCH	NONEQUALS	NONGAY	NONKOSHER	NONMUTUAL
NONCLASS	NONEROTIC	NONGAYS	NONLABOR	NONNASAL
NONCLING	NONES	NONGHETTO	NONLAWYER	NONNATIVE
NONCODING	NONESUCH	NONGLARE	NONLEADED	NONNAVAL

N

NONNEURAL	NONPROFIT	NONSTATIC	NONUSING	NOODLES
NONNEWS	NONPROS	NONSTEADY	NONVACANT	NOODLING
NONNIES	NONPROVEN	NONSTICK	NONVALID	NOODLINGS
NONNOBLE	NONPUBLIC	NONSTICKY	NONVECTOR	NOOGIE
NONNORMAL	NONQUOTA	NONSTOP	NONVENOUS	NOOGIES
NONNOVEL	NONRACIAL	NONSTOPS	NONVERBAL	NOOIT
NONNOVELS	NONRANDOM	NONSTORY	NONVESTED	NOOK
NONNY	NONRATED	NONSTYLE	NONVIABLE	NOOKIE
NONOBESE	NONREADER	NONSTYLES	NONVIEWER	NOOKIER
NONOHMIC	NONRETURN	NONSUCH	NONVIRAL	NOOKIES
NONOILY	NONRHOTIC	NONSUCHES	NONVIRGIN	NOOKIEST
NONORAL	NONRIGID	NONSUGAR	NONVIRILE	NOOKLIKE
NONORALLY	NONRIOTER	NONSUGARS	NONVISUAL	NOOKS
NONOWNER	NONRIVAL	NONSUIT	NONVITAL	NOOKY
NONOWNERS	NONRIVALS	NONSUITED	NONVOCAL	NOOLOGIES
NONPAGAN	NONROYAL	NONSUITS	NONVOCALS	NOOLOGY
NONPAGANS	NONRUBBER	NONSYSTEM	NONVOTER	NOOMETRY
NONPAID	NONRULING	NONTALKER	NONVOTERS	NOON
NONPAPAL	NONRURAL	NONTARGET	NONVOTING	NOONDAY
NONPAPIST	NONSACRED	NONTARIFF	NONWAGE	NOONDAYS
NONPAR	NONSALINE	NONTAX	NONWAR	NOONED
NONPAREIL	NONSCHOOL	NONTAXES	NONWARS	NOONER
NONPARENT	NONSECRET	NONTHEIST	NONWHITE	NOONERS
NONPARITY	NONSECURE	NONTIDAL	NONWHITES	NOONING
NONPAROUS	NONSELF	NONTITLE	NONWINGED	NOONINGS
NONPARTY	NONSELVES	NONTONAL	NONWOODY	NOONS
NONPAST	NONSENSE	NONTONIC	NONWOOL	NOONTIDE
NONPASTS	NONSENSES	NONTOXIC	NONWORD	NOONTIDES
NONPAYING	NONSERIAL	NONTRAGIC	NONWORDS	NOONTIME
NONPEAK	NONSEXIST	NONTRIBAL	NONWORK	NOONTIMES
NONPERSON	NONSEXUAL	NONTRUMP	NONWORKER	NOOP
NONPLANAR	NONSHRINK	NONTRUTH	NONWOVEN	NOOPS
NONPLAY	NONSIGNER	NONTRUTHS	NONWOVENS	NOOSE
NONPLAYER	NONSKATER	NONUNION	NONWRITER	NOOSED
NONPLAYS	NONSKED	NONUNIONS	NONYL	NOOSER
NONPLIANT	NONSKEDS	NONUNIQUE	NONYLS	NOOSERS
NONPLUS	NONSKID	NONUPLE	NONZERO	NOOSES
NONPLUSED	NONSKIER	NONUPLES	NOO	NOOSING
NONPLUSES	NONSKIERS	NONUPLET	NOOB	NOOSPHERE
NONPOETIC	NONSLIP	NONUPLETS	NOOBS	NOOTROPIC
NONPOINT	NONSMOKER	NONURBAN	NOODGE	NOPAL
NONPOLAR	NONSOCIAL	NONURGENT	NOODGED	NOPALES
NONPOLICE	NONSOLAR	NONUSABLE	NOODGES	NOPALITO
NONPOOR	NONSOLID	NONUSE	NOODGING	NOPALITOS
NONPOROUS	NONSOLIDS	NONUSER	NOODLE	NOPALS
NONPOSTAL	NONSPEECH	NONUSERS	NOODLED	NOPE
NONPRINT	NONSTAPLE	NONUSES	NOODLEDOM	NOPLACE

NOR	NORTHERN	NOSHES	NOTARIZES	NOTICERS
NORDIC	NORTHERNS	NOSHING	NOTARY	NOTICES
NORI	NORTHERS	NOSIER	NOTATE	NOTICING
NORIA	NORTHING	NOSIES	NOTATED	NOTIFIED
NORIAS	NORTHINGS	NOSIEST	NOTATES	NOTIFIER
NORIMON	NORTHLAND	NOSILY	NOTATING	NOTIFIERS
NORIMONS	NORTHMOST	NOSINESS	NOTATION	NOTIFIES
NORIS	NORTHS	NOSING	NOTATIONS	NOTIFY
NORITE	NORTHWARD	NOSINGS	NOTCH	NOTIFYING
NORITES	NORTHWEST	NOSODE	NOTCHBACK	NOTING
NORITIC	NORWARD	NOSODES	NOTCHED	NOTION
NORK	NORWARDS	NOSOLOGIC	NOTCHEL	NOTIONAL
NORKS	NOS	NOSOLOGY	NOTCHELED	NOTIONIST
NORLAND	NOSE	NOSTALGIA	NOTCHELS	NOTIONS
NORLANDS	NOSEAN	NOSTALGIC	NOTCHER	NOTITIA
NORM	NOSEANS	NOSTOC	NOTCHERS	NOTITIAE
NORMA	NOSEBAG	NOSTOCS	NOTCHES	NOTITIAS
NORMAL	NOSEBAGS	NOSTOI	NOTCHIER	NOTOCHORD
NORMALCY	NOSEBAND	NOSTOLOGY	NOTCHIEST	NOTORIETY
NORMALISE	NOSEBANDS	NOSTOS	NOTCHING	NOTORIOUS
NORMALITY	NOSEBLEED	NOSTRIL	NOTCHINGS	NOTORNIS
NORMALIZE	NOSED	NOSTRILS	NOTCHY	NOTOUR
NORMALLY	NOSEDIVE	NOSTRO	NOTE	NOTT
NORMALS	NOSEDIVED	NOSTRUM	NOTEBOOK	NOTTURNI
NORMAN	NOSEDIVES	NOSTRUMS	NOTEBOOKS	NOTTURNO
NORMANDE	NOSEDOVE	NOSY	NOTECARD	NOTUM
NORMANS	NOSEGAY	NOT	NOTECARDS	NOUGAT
NORMAS	NOSEGAYS	NOTA	NOTECASE	NOUGATINE
NORMATIVE	NOSEGUARD	NOTABILIA	NOTECASES	NOUGATS
NORMED	NOSELESS	NOTABLE	NOTED	NOUGHT
NORMLESS	NOSELIKE	NOTABLES	NOTEDLY	NOUGHTIES
NORMS	NOSELITE	NOTABLY	NOTEDNESS	NOUGHTS
NOROVIRUS	NOSELITES	NOTAEUM	NOTELESS	NOUL
NORSEL	NOSEPIECE	NOTAEUMS	NOTELET	NOULD
NORSELLED	NOSER	NOTAIRE	NOTELETS	NOULDE
NORSELLER	NOSERS	NOTAIRES	NOTEPAD	NOULE
NORSELS	NOSES	NOTAL	NOTEPADS	NOULES
NORTENA	NOSEWHEEL	NOTANDA	NOTEPAPER	NOULS
NORTENAS	NOSEY	NOTANDUM	NOTER	NOUMENA
NORTENO	NOSEYS	NOTAPHILY	NOTERS	NOUMENAL
NORTENOS	NOSH	NOTARIAL	NOTES	NOUMENON
NORTH	NOSHED	NOTARIES	NOTHER	NOUN
NORTHEAST	NOSHER	NOTARISE	NOTHING	NOUNAL
NORTHED	NOSHERIE	NOTARISED	NOTHINGS	NOUNALLY
NORTHER	NOSHERIES	NOTARISES	NOTICE	NOUNIER
NORTHERED	NOSHERS	NOTARIZE	NOTICED	NOUNIEST
NORTHERLY	NOSHERY	NOTARIZED	NOTICER	NOUNLESS

NOUNS	NOVELISED	NOWHERES	NUBBIEST	NUCLEOID
NOUNY	NOVELISER	NOWHITHER	NUBBIN	NUCLEOIDS
NOUP	NOVELISES	NOWISE	NUBBINESS	NUCLEOLAR
NOUPS	NOVELISH	NOWL	NUBBING	NUCLEOLE
NOURICE	NOVELISM	NOWLS	NUBBINS	NUCLEOLES
NOURICES	NOVELISMS	NOWN	NUBBLE	NUCLEOLI
NOURISH	NOVELIST	NOWNESS	NUBBLED	NUCLEOLUS
NOURISHED	NOVELISTS	NOWNESSES	NUBBLES	NUCLEON
NOURISHER	NOVELIZE	NOWS	NUBBLIER	NUCLEONIC
NOURISHES	NOVELIZED	NOWT	NUBBLIEST	NUCLEONS
NOURITURE	NOVELIZER	NOWTIER	NUBBLING	NUCLEUS
NOURSLE	NOVELIZES	NOWTIEST	NUBBLY	NUCLEUSES
NOURSLED	NOVELLA	NOWTS	NUBBY	NUCLIDE
NOURSLES	NOVELLAE	NOWTY	NUBECULA	NUCLIDES
NOURSLING	NOVELLAS	NOWY	NUBECULAE	NUCLIDIC
NOUS	NOVELLE	NOX	NUBIA	NUCULE
NOUSELL	NOVELLY	NOXAL	NUBIAS	NUCULES
NOUSELLED	NOVELS	NOXES	NUBIFORM	NUDATION
NOUSELLS	NOVELTIES	NOXIOUS	NUBILE	NUDATIONS
NOUSES	NOVELTY	NOXIOUSLY	NUBILITY	NUDDIES
NOUSLE	NOVEMBER	NOY	NUBILOSE	NUDDY
NOUSLED	NOVEMBERS	NOYADE	NUBILOUS	NUDE
NOUSLES	NOVENA	NOYADES	NUBS	NUDELY
NOUSLING	NOVENAE	NOYANCE	NUBUCK	NUDENESS
NOUT	NOVENARY	NOYANCES	NUBUCKS	NUDER
NOUVEAU	NOVENAS	NOYAU	NUCELLAR	NUDES
NOUVEAUX	NOVENNIAL	NOYAUS	NUCELLI	NUDEST
NOUVELLE	NOVERCAL	NOYED	NUCELLUS	NUDGE
NOUVELLES	NOVERINT	NOYES	NUCHA	NUDGED
NOVA	NOVERINTS	NOYESES	NUCHAE	NUDGER
NOVAE	NOVICE	NOYING	NUCHAL	NUDGERS
NOVALIA	NOVICES	NOYOUS	NUCHALS	NUDGES
NOVALIKE	NOVICIATE	NOYS	NUCLEAL	NUDGING
NOVAS	NOVITIATE	NOYSOME	NUCLEAR	NUDICAUL
NOVATE	NOVITIES	NOZZER	NUCLEASE	NUDIE
NOVATED	NOVITY	NOZZERS	NUCLEASES	NUDIES
NOVATES	NOVOCAINE	NOZZLE	NUCLEATE	NUDISM
NOVATING	NOVODAMUS	NOZZLES	NUCLEATED	NUDISMS
NOVATION	NOVUM	NTH	NUCLEATES	NUDIST
NOVATIONS	NOVUMS	NU	NUCLEATOR	NUDISTS
NOVEL	NOW	NUANCE	NUCLEI	NUDITIES
NOVELDOM	NOWADAYS	NUANCED	NUCLEIC	NUDITY
NOVELDOMS	NOWAY	NUANCES	NUCLEIDE	NUDNICK
NOVELESE	NOWAYS	NUANCING	NUCLEIDES	NUDNICKS
NOVELESES	NOWED	NUB	NUCLEIN	NUDNIK
NOVELETTE	NOWHENCE	NUBBED	NUCLEINIC	NUDNIKS
NOVELISE	NOWHERE	NUBBIER	NUCLEINS	NUDZH

NUDZHED	NUMBERED	NUMSKULLS	NURHAGS	NUTCASES
NUDZHES	NUMBERER	NUN	NURL	NUTGALL
NUDZHING	NUMBERERS	NUNATAK	NURLED	NUTGALLS
NUFF	NUMBERING	NUNATAKER	NURLING	NUTGRASS
NUFFIN	NUMBERS	NUNATAKS	NURLS	NUTHATCH
NUFFINS	NUMBEST	NUNCHAKU	NURR	NUTHOUSE
NUFFS	NUMBFISH	NUNCHAKUS	NURRS	NUTHOUSES
NUGAE	NUMBING	NUNCHEON	NURS	NUTJOB
NUGATORY	NUMBINGLY	NUNCHEONS	NURSE	NUTJOBBER
NUGGAR	NUMBLES	NUNCHUCKS	NURSED	NUTJOBS
NUGGARS	NUMBLY	NUNCIO	NURSELIKE	NUTLET
NUGGET	NUMBNESS	NUNCIOS	NURSELING	NUTLETS
NUGGETED	NUMBS	NUNCLE	NURSEMAID	NUTLIKE
NUGGETING	NUMBSKULL	NUNCLES	NURSER	NUTMEAL
NUGGETS	NUMCHUCK	NUNCUPATE	NURSERIES	NUTMEALS
NUGGETTED	NUMCHUCKS	NUNDINAL	NURSERS	NUTMEAT
NUGGETY	NUMDAH	NUNDINE	NURSERY	NUTMEATS
NUISANCE	NUMDAHS	NUNDINES	NURSES	NUTMEG
NUISANCER	NUMEN	NUNHOOD	NURSING	NUTMEGGED
NUISANCES	NUMERABLE	NUNHOODS	NURSINGS	NUTMEGGY
NUKE	NUMERABLY	NUNLIKE	NURSLE	NUTMEGS
NUKED	NUMERACY	NUNNATION	NURSLED	NUTPECKER
NUKES	NUMERAIRE	NUNNERIES	NURSLES	NUTPICK
NUKING	NUMERAL	NUNNERY	NURSLING	NUTPICKS
NULL	NUMERALLY	NUNNISH	NURSLINGS	NUTRIA
NULLA	NUMERALS	NUNNY	NURTURAL	NUTRIAS
NULLAH	NUMERARY	NUNS	NURTURANT	NUTRIENT
NULLAHS	NUMERATE	NUNSHIP	NURTURE	NUTRIENTS
NULLAS	NUMERATED	NUNSHIPS	NURTURED	NUTRIMENT
NULLED	NUMERATES	NUPTIAL	NURTURER	NUTRITION
NULLIFIED	NUMERATOR	NUPTIALLY	NURTURERS	NUTRITIVE
NULLIFIER	NUMERIC	NUPTIALS	NURTURES	NUTS
NULLIFIES	NUMERICAL	NUR	NURTURING	NUTSEDGE
NULLIFY	NUMERICS	NURAGHE	NUS	NUTSEDGES
NULLING	NUMEROUS	NURAGHI	NUT	NUTSHELL
NULLINGS	NUMINA	NURAGHIC	NUTANT	NUTSHELLS
NULLIPARA	NUMINOUS	NURD	NUTARIAN	NUTSIER
NULLIPORE	NUMMARY	NURDIER	NUTARIANS	NUTSIEST
NULLITIES	NUMMULAR	NURDIEST	NUTATE	NUTSO
NULLITY	NUMMULARY	NURDISH	NUTATED	NUTSY
NULLNESS	NUMMULINE	NURDLE	NUTATES	NUTTED
NULLS	NUMMULITE	NURDLED	NUTATING	NUTTER
NUMB	NUMNAH	NURDLES	NUTATION	NUTTERIES
NUMBAT	NUMNAHS	NURDLING	NUTATIONS	NUTTERS
NUMBATS	NUMPTIES	NURDS	NUTBROWN	NUTTERY
NUMBED	NUMPTY	NURDY	NUTBUTTER	NUTTIER
NUMBER	NUMSKULL	NURHAG	NUTCASE	NUTTIEST

NUTTILY	NUZZLING	NYCTALOPS	NYMPHAEA	NYMPHO
NUTTINESS	NY	NYE	NYMPHAEUM	NYMPHOS
NUTTING	NYAFF	NYED	NYMPHAL	NYMPHS
NUTTINGS	NYAFFED	NYES	NYMPHALID	NYS
NUTTY	NYAFFING	NYING	NYMPHEAN	NYSSA
NUTWOOD	NYAFFS	NYLGHAI	NYMPHET	NYSSAS
NUTWOODS	NYALA	NYLGHAIS	NYMPHETIC	NYSTAGMIC
NUZZER	NYALAS	NYLGHAU	NYMPHETS	NYSTAGMUS
NUZZERS	NYANZA	NYLGHAUS	NYMPHETTE	NYSTATIN
NUZZLE	NYANZAS	NYLON	NYMPHIC	NYSTATINS
NUZZLED	NYAS	NYLONS	NYMPHICAL	
NUZZLER	NYASES	NYMPH	NYMPHISH	
NUZZLERS	NYBBLE	NYMPHA	NYMPHLIKE	
NUZZLES	NYBBLES	NYMPHAE	NYMPHLY	

O

OAF	OASES	OBEAHISMS	OBFUSCATE	OBLIGATED
OAFISH	OASIS	OBEAHS	OBI	OBLIGATES
OAFISHLY	OAST	OBECHE	OBIA	OBLIGATI
OAFS	OASTHOUSE	OBECHES	OBIAS	OBLIGATO
OAK	OASTS	OBEDIENCE	OBIED	OBLIGATOR
OAKED	OAT	OBEDIENT	OBIING	OBLIGATOS
OAKEN	OATCAKE	OBEISANCE	OBIISM	OBLIGE
OAKENSHAW	OATCAKES	OBEISANT	OBIISMS	OBLIGED
OAKER	OATEN	OBEISM	OBIIT	OBLIGEE
OAKERS	OATER	OBEISMS	OBIS	OBLIGEES
OAKIER	OATERS	OBELI	OBIT	OBLIGER
OAKIES	OATH	OBELIA	OBITAL	OBLIGERS
OAKIEST	OATHABLE	OBELIAS	OBITER	OBLIGES
OAKLIKE	OATHS	OBELION	OBITS	OBLIGING
OAKLING	OATIER	OBELISCAL	OBITUAL	OBLIGOR
OAKLINGS	OATIEST	OBELISE	OBITUARY	OBLIGORS
OAKMOSS	OATLIKE	OBELISED	OBJECT	OBLIQUE
OAKMOSSES	OATMEAL	OBELISES	OBJECTED	OBLIQUED
OAKS	OATMEALS	OBELISING	OBJECTIFY	OBLIQUELY
OAKUM	OATS	OBELISK	OBJECTING	OBLIQUER
OAKUMS	OATY	OBELISKS	OBJECTION	OBLIQUES
OAKY	OAVES	OBELISM	OBJECTIVE	OBLIQUEST
OANSHAGH	OB	OBELISMS	OBJECTOR	OBLIQUID
OANSHAGHS	OBA	OBELIZE	OBJECTORS	OBLIQUING
OAR	OBANG	OBELIZED	OBJECTS	OBLIQUITY
OARAGE	OBANGS	OBELIZES	OBJET	OBLIVION
OARAGES	OBAS	OBELIZING	OBJETS	OBLIVIONS
OARED	OBBLIGATI	OBELUS	OBJURE	OBLIVIOUS
OARFISH	OBBLIGATO	OBENTO	OBJURED	OBLONG
OARFISHES	OBCONIC	OBENTOS	OBJURES	OBLONGLY
OARIER	OBCONICAL	OBES	OBJURGATE	OBLONGS
OARIEST	OBCORDATE	OBESE	OBJURING	OBLOQUIAL
OARING	OBDURACY	OBESELY	OBLAST	OBLOQUIES
OARLESS	OBDURATE	OBESENESS	OBLASTI	OBLOQUY
OARLIKE	OBDURATED	OBESER	OBLASTS	OBNOXIOUS
OARLOCK	OBDURATES	OBESEST	OBLATE	OBO
OARLOCKS	OBDURE	OBESITIES	OBLATELY	OBOE
OARS	OBDURED	OBESITY	OBLATES	OBOES
OARSMAN	OBDURES	OBEY	OBLATION	OBOIST
OARSMEN	OBDURING	OBEYABLE	OBLATIONS	OBOISTS
OARSWOMAN	OBE	OBEYED	OBLATORY	OBOL
OARSWOMEN	OBEAH	OBEYER	OBLIGABLE	OBOLARY
OARWEED	OBEAHED	OBEYERS	OBLIGANT	OBOLE
OARWEEDS	OBEAHING	OBEYING	OBLIGANTS	OBOLES
OARY	OBEAHISM	OBEYS	OBLIGATE	OBOLI

O

OBOLS	OBSIGNATE	OBTUNDITY	OCCIPITA	OCEANAUTS
OBOLUS	OBSIGNED	OBTUNDS	OCCIPITAL	OCEANIC
OBOS	OBSIGNING	OBTURATE	OCCIPUT	OCEANID
OBOVATE	OBSIGNS	OBTURATED	OCCIPUTS	OCEANIDES
OBOVATELY	OBSOLESCE	OBTURATES	OCCLUDE	OCEANIDS
OBOVOID	OBSOLETE	OBTURATOR	OCCLUDED	OCEANS
OBREPTION	OBSOLETED	OBTUSE	OCCLUDENT	OCELLAR
OBS	OBSOLETES	OBTUSELY	OCCLUDER	OCELLATE
OBSCENE	OBSTACLE	OBTUSER	OCCLUDERS	OCELLATED
OBSCENELY	OBSTACLES	OBTUSEST	OCCLUDES	OCELLI
OBSCENER	OBSTETRIC	OBTUSITY	OCCLUDING	OCELLUS
OBSCENEST	OBSTINACY	OBUMBRATE	OCCLUSAL	OCELOID
OBSCENITY	OBSTINATE	OBVENTION	OCCLUSION	OCELOT
OBSCURANT	OBSTRUCT	OBVERSE	OCCLUSIVE	OCELOTS
OBSCURE	OBSTRUCTS	OBVERSELY	OCCLUSOR	OCH
OBSCURED	OBSTRUENT	OBVERSES	OCCLUSORS	OCHE
OBSCURELY	OBTAIN	OBVERSION	OCCULT	OCHER
OBSCURER	OBTAINED	OBVERT	OCCULTED	OCHERED
OBSCURERS	OBTAINER	OBVERTED	OCCULTER	OCHERING
OBSCURES	OBTAINERS	OBVERTING	OCCULTERS	OCHEROUS
OBSCUREST	OBTAINING	OBVERTS	OCCULTING	OCHERS
OBSCURING	OBTAINS	OBVIABLE	OCCULTISM	OCHERY
OBSCURITY	OBTECT	OBVIATE	OCCULTIST	OCHES
OBSECRATE	OBTECTED	OBVIATED	OCCULTLY	OCHIDORE
OBSEQUENT	OBTEMPER	OBVIATES	OCCULTS	OCHIDORES
OBSEQUIAL	OBTEMPERS	OBVIATING	OCCUPANCE	OCHLOCRAT
OBSEQUIE	OBTEND	OBVIATION	OCCUPANCY	OCHONE
OBSEQUIES	OBTENDED	OBVIATOR	OCCUPANT	OCHRE
OBSEQUY	OBTENDING	OBVIATORS	OCCUPANTS	OCHREA
OBSERVANT	OBTENDS	OBVIOUS	OCCUPATE	OCHREAE
OBSERVE	OBTENTION	OBVIOUSLY	OCCUPATED	OCHREATE
OBSERVED	OBTEST	OBVOLUTE	OCCUPATES	OCHRED
OBSERVER	OBTESTED	OBVOLUTED	OCCUPIED	OCHREOUS
OBSERVERS	OBTESTING	OBVOLVENT	OCCUPIER	OCHRES
OBSERVES	OBTESTS	OCA	OCCUPIERS	OCHREY
OBSERVING	OBTRUDE	OCARINA	OCCUPIES	OCHRING
OBSESS	OBTRUDED	OCARINAS	OCCUPY	OCHROID
OBSESSED	OBTRUDER	OCAS	OCCUPYING	OCHROUS
OBSESSES	OBTRUDERS	OCCAM	OCCUR	OCHRY
OBSESSING	OBTRUDES	OCCAMIES	OCCURRED	OCICAT
OBSESSION	OBTRUDING	OCCAMS	OCCURRENT	OCICATS
OBSESSIVE	OBTRUSION	OCCAMY	OCCURRING	OCKER
OBSESSOR	OBTRUSIVE	OCCASION	OCCURS	OCKERISM
OBSESSORS	OBTUND	OCCASIONS	OCCY	OCKERISMS
OBSIDIAN	OBTUNDED	OCCIDENT	OCEAN	OCKERS
OBSIDIANS	OBTUNDENT	OCCIDENTS	OCEANARIA	OCKODOLS
OBSIGN	OBTUNDING	OCCIES	OCEANAUT	OCOTILLO

OCOTILLOS	OCTETTE	ODA	ODOGRAPH	ODYSSEY
OCREA	OCTETTES	ODAH	ODOGRAPHS	ODYSSEYS
OCREAE	OCTETTS	ODAHS	ODOMETER	ODZOOKS
OCREATE	OCTILLION	ODAL	ODOMETERS	OE
OCTA	OCTOFID	ODALIQUE	ODOMETRY	OECIST
OCTACHORD	OCTOHEDRA	ODALIQUES	ODONATE	OECISTS
OCTAD	OCTONARII	ODALISK	ODONATES	OECOLOGIC
OCTADIC	OCTONARY	ODALISKS	ODONATIST	OECOLOGY
OCTADS	OCTOPI	ODALISQUE	ODONTALGY	OECUMENIC
OCTAGON	OCTOPLOID	ODALLER	ODONTIC	OEDEMA
OCTAGONAL	OCTOPOD	ODALLERS	ODONTIST	OEDEMAS
OCTAGONS	OCTOPODAN	ODALS	ODONTISTS	OEDEMATA
OCTAHEDRA	OCTOPODES	ODAS	ODONTOID	OEDIPAL
OCTAL	OCTOPODS	ODD	ODONTOIDS	OEDIPALLY
OCTALS	OCTOPOID	ODDBALL	ODONTOMA	OEDIPEAN
OCTAMETER	OCTOPUS	ODDBALLS	ODONTOMAS	OEDOMETER
OCTAN	OCTOPUSES	ODDER	ODOR	OEILLADE
OCTANE	OCTOPUSH	ODDEST	ODORANT	OEILLADES
OCTANES	OCTOROON	ODDISH	ODORANTS	OENANTHIC
OCTANGLE	OCTOROONS	ODDITIES	ODORATE	OENOLOGY
OCTANGLES	OCTOSTYLE	ODDITY	ODORED	OENOMANCY
OCTANOL	OCTOTHORP	ODDLY	ODORFUL	OENOMANIA
OCTANOLS	OCTROI	ODDMENT	ODORISE	OENOMEL
OCTANS	OCTROIS	ODDMENTS	ODORISED	OENOMELS
OCTANT	OCTUOR	ODDNESS	ODORISES	OENOMETER
OCTANTAL	OCTUORS	ODDNESSES	ODORISING	OENOPHIL
OCTANTS	OCTUPLE	ODDS	ODORIZE	OENOPHILE
OCTAPLA	OCTUPLED	ODDSMAKER	ODORIZED	OENOPHILS
OCTAPLAS	OCTUPLES	ODDSMAN	ODORIZES	OENOPHILY
OCTAPLOID	OCTUPLET	ODDSMEN	ODORIZING	OENOTHERA
OCTAPODIC	OCTUPLETS	ODE	ODORLESS	OERLIKON
OCTAPODY	OCTUPLEX	ODEA	ODOROUS	OERLIKONS
OCTARCHY	OCTUPLING	ODEON	ODOROUSLY	OERSTED
OCTAROON	OCTUPLY	ODEONS	ODORS	OERSTEDS
OCTAROONS	OCTYL	ODES	ODOUR	OES
OCTAS	OCTYLS	ODEUM	ODOURED	OESOPHAGI
OCTASTICH	OCULAR	ODEUMS	ODOURFUL	OESTRAL
OCTASTYLE	OCULARIST	ODIC	ODOURLESS	OESTRIN
OCTAVAL	OCULARLY	ODIFEROUS	ODOURS	OESTRINS
OCTAVE	OCULARS	ODIOUS	ODS	OESTRIOL
OCTAVES	OCULATE	ODIOUSLY	ODSO	OESTRIOLS
OCTAVO	OCULATED	ODISM	ODYL	OESTROGEN
OCTAVOS	OCULI	ODISMS	ODYLE	OESTRONE
OCTENNIAL	OCULIST	ODIST	ODYLES	OESTRONES
OCTET	OCULISTS	ODISTS	ODYLISM	OESTROUS
OCTETS	OCULUS	ODIUM	ODYLISMS	OESTRUM
OCTETT	OD	ODIUMS	ODYLS	OESTRUMS

O

OESTRUS	OFFICES	OFFTAKES	OGRISH	OILGAS
OESTRUSES	OFFICIAL	OFFTRACK	OGRISHLY	OILGASES
OEUVRE	OFFICIALS	OFFY	OGRISM	OILHOLE
OEUVRES	OFFICIANT	OFLAG	OGRISMS	OILHOLES
OF	OFFICIARY	OFLAGS	OH	OILIER
OFAY	OFFICIATE	OFT	OHED	OILIEST
OFAYS	OFFICINAL	OFTEN	OHIA	OILILY
OFF	OFFICIOUS	OFTENER	OHIAS	OILINESS
OFFAL	OFFIE	OFTENEST	OHING	OILING
OFFALS	OFFIES	OFTENNESS	OHM	OILLET
OFFBEAT	OFFING	OFTER	OHMAGE	OILLETS
OFFBEATS	OFFINGS	OFTEST	OHMAGES	OILMAN
OFFCAST	OFFISH	OFTTIMES	OHMIC	OILMEN
OFFCASTS	OFFISHLY	OGAM	OHMICALLY	OILNUT
OFFCUT	OFFKEY	OGAMIC	OHMMETER	OILNUTS
OFFCUTS	OFFLINE	OGAMS	OHMMETERS	OILPAPER
OFFED	OFFLOAD	OGDOAD	OHMS	OILPAPERS
OFFENCE	OFFLOADED	OGDOADS	OHO	OILPROOF
OFFENCES	OFFLOADS	OGEE	OHONE	OILS
OFFEND	OFFPEAK	OGEED	OHS	OILSEED
OFFENDED	OFFPRINT	OGEES	OI	OILSEEDS
OFFENDER	OFFPRINTS	OGGIN	OIDIA	OILSKIN
OFFENDERS	OFFPUT	OGGINS	OIDIOID	OILSKINS
OFFENDING	OFFPUTS	OGHAM	OIDIUM	OILSTONE
OFFENDS	OFFRAMP	OGHAMIC	OIK	OILSTONES
OFFENSE	OFFRAMPS	OGHAMIST	OIKIST	OILTIGHT
OFFENSES	OFFS	OGHAMISTS	OIKISTS	OILWAY
OFFENSIVE	OFFSADDLE	OGHAMS	OIKS	OILWAYS
OFFER	OFFSCREEN	OGIVAL	OIL	OILY
OFFERABLE	OFFSCUM	OGIVE	OILBIRD	OINK
OFFERED	OFFSCUMS	OGIVES	OILBIRDS	OINKED
OFFEREE	OFFSEASON	OGLE	OILCAMP	OINKING
OFFEREES	OFFSET	OGLED	OILCAMPS	OINKS
OFFERER	OFFSETS	OGLER	OILCAN	OINOLOGY
OFFERERS	OFFSHOOT	OGLERS	OILCANS	OINOMEL
OFFERING	OFFSHOOTS	OGLES	OILCLOTH	OINOMELS
OFFERINGS	OFFSHORE	OGLING	OILCLOTHS	OINT
OFFEROR	OFFSHORED	OGLINGS	OILCUP	OINTED
OFFERORS	OFFSHORES	OGMIC	OILCUPS	OINTING
OFFERS	OFFSIDE	OGRE	OILED	OINTMENT
OFFERTORY	OFFSIDER	OGREISH	OILER	OINTMENTS
OFFHAND	OFFSIDERS	OGREISHLY	OILERIES	OINTS
OFFHANDED	OFFSIDES	OGREISM	OILERS	OIS
OFFICE	OFFSPRING	OGREISMS	OILERY	OITICICA
OFFICER	OFFSTAGE	OGRES	OILFIELD	OITICICAS
OFFICERED	OFFSTAGES	OGRESS	OILFIELDS	OJIME
OFFICERS	OFFTAKE	OGRESSES	OILFIRED	OJIMES

OKA	OLEANDERS	OLIGEMIA	OLOGOAN	OMENTUMS
OKAPI	OLEARIA	OLIGEMIAS	OLOGOANED	OMER
OKAPIS	OLEARIAS	OLIGEMIC	OLOGOANS	OMERS
OKAS	OLEASTER	OLIGIST	OLOGY	OMERTA
OKAY	OLEASTERS	OLIGISTS	OLOLIUQUI	OMERTAS
OKAYED	OLEATE	OLIGOCENE	OLOROSO	OMICRON
OKAYING	OLEATES	OLIGOGENE	OLOROSOS	OMICRONS
OKAYS	OLECRANAL	OLIGOMER	OLPAE	OMIGOD
OKE	OLECRANON	OLIGOMERS	OLPE	OMIKRON
OKEH	OLEFIANT	OLIGOPOLY	OLPES	OMIKRONS
OKEHS	OLEFIN	OLIGURIA	OLYCOOK	OMINOUS
OKES	OLEFINE	OLIGURIAS	OLYCOOKS	OMINOUSLY
OKEYDOKE	OLEFINES	OLIGURIC	OLYKOEK	OMISSIBLE
OKEYDOKEY	OLEFINIC	OLINGO	OLYKOEKS	OMISSION
OKIMONO	OLEFINS	OLINGOS	OLYMPIAD	OMISSIONS
OKIMONOS	OLEIC	OLIO	OLYMPIADS	OMISSIVE
OKRA	OLEIN	OLIOS	OLYMPICS	OMIT
OKRAS	OLEINE	OLIPHANT	OM	OMITS
OKTA	OLEINES	OLIPHANTS	OMADHAUN	OMITTANCE
OKTAS	OLEINS	OLITORIES	OMADHAUNS	OMITTED
OLD	OLENT	OLITORY	OMASA	OMITTER
OLDE	OLEO	OLIVARY	OMASAL	OMITTERS
OLDEN	OLEOGRAPH	OLIVE	OMASUM	OMITTING
OLDENED	OLEORESIN	OLIVENITE	OMBER	OMLAH
OLDENING	OLEOS	OLIVER	OMBERS	OMLAHS
OLDENS	OLES	OLIVERS	OMBRE	OMMATEA
OLDER	OLESTRA	OLIVES	OMBRELLA	OMMATEUM
OLDEST	OLESTRAS	OLIVET	OMBRELLAS	OMMATIDIA
OLDIE	OLEUM	OLIVETS	OMBRES	OMNEITIES
OLDIES	OLEUMS	OLIVINE	OMBROPHIL	OMNEITY
OLDISH	OLFACT	OLIVINES	OMBU	OMNIANA
OLDNESS	OLFACTED	OLIVINIC	OMBUDSMAN	OMNIARCH
OLDNESSES	OLFACTING	OLLA	OMBUDSMEN	OMNIARCHS
OLDS	OLFACTION	OLLAMH	OMBUS	OMNIBUS
OLDSQUAW	OLFACTIVE	OLLAMHS	OMEGA	OMNIBUSES
OLDSQUAWS	OLFACTORY	OLLAS	OMEGAS	OMNIETIES
OLDSTER	OLFACTS	OLLAV	OMELET	OMNIETY
OLDSTERS	OLIBANUM	OLLAVS	OMELETS	OMNIFIC
OLDSTYLE	OLIBANUMS	OLLER	OMELETTE	OMNIFIED
OLDSTYLES	OLICOOK	OLLERS	OMELETTES	OMNIFIES
OLDWIFE	OLICOOKS	OLLIE	OMEN	OMNIFORM
OLDWIVES	OLID	OLLIES	OMENED	OMNIFY
OLDY	OLIGAEMIA	OLM	OMENING	OMNIFYING
OLE	OLIGAEMIC	OLMS	OMENS	OMNIMODE
OLEA	OLIGARCH	OLOGIES	OMENTA	OMNIRANGE
OLEACEOUS	OLIGARCHS	OLOGIST	OMENTAL	OMNIUM
OLEANDER	OLIGARCHY	OLOGISTS	OMENTUM	OMNIUMS

O

OMNIVORA	ONCOLOGY	ONFLOW	ONSETTERS	OOFIER
OMNIVORE	ONCOLYSES	ONFLOWS	ONSETTING	OOFIEST
OMNIVORES	ONCOLYSIS	ONGAONGA	ONSHORE	OOFS
OMNIVORY	ONCOLYTIC	ONGAONGAS	ONSHORING	OOFTISH
OMOHYOID	ONCOME	ONGOING	ONSIDE	OOFTISHES
OMOHYOIDS	ONCOMES	ONGOINGS	ONSIDES	OOFY
OMOPHAGIA	ONCOMETER	ONIE	ONSLAUGHT	OOGAMETE
OMOPHAGIC	ONCOMING	ONION	ONST	OOGAMETES
OMOPHAGY	ONCOMINGS	ONIONED	ONSTAGE	OOGAMIES
OMOPHORIA	ONCOST	ONIONIER	ONSTEAD	OOGAMOUS
OMOPLATE	ONCOSTMAN	ONIONIEST	ONSTEADS	OOGAMY
OMOPLATES	ONCOSTMEN	ONIONING	ONSTREAM	OOGENESES
OMOV	ONCOSTS	ONIONS	ONTIC	OOGENESIS
OMOVS	ONCOTOMY	ONIONSKIN	ONTICALLY	OOGENETIC
OMPHACITE	ONCOVIRUS	ONIONY	ONTO	OOGENIES
OMPHALI	ONCUS	ONIRIC	ONTOGENIC	OOGENY
OMPHALIC	ONDATRA	ONISCOID	ONTOGENY	OOGONIA
OMPHALOID	ONDATRAS	ONIUM	ONTOLOGIC	OOGONIAL
OMPHALOS	ONDINE	ONIUMS	ONTOLOGY	OOGONIUM
OMRAH	ONDINES	ONKUS	ONUS	OOGONIUMS
OMRAHS	ONDING	ONLAY	ONUSES	OOH
OMS	ONDINGS	ONLAYS	ONWARD	OOHED
ON	ONDOGRAM	ONLIEST	ONWARDLY	OOHING
ONAGER	ONDOGRAMS	ONLINE	ONWARDS	OOHS
ONAGERS	ONDOGRAPH	ONLINER	ONY	OOIDAL
ONAGRI	ONE	ONLINERS	ONYCHA	OOLACHAN
ONANISM	ONEFOLD	ONLOAD	ONYCHAS	OOLACHANS
ONANISMS	ONEIRIC	ONLOADED	ONYCHIA	OOLAKAN
ONANIST	ONELY	ONLOADING	ONYCHIAS	OOLAKANS
ONANISTIC	ONENESS	ONLOADS	ONYCHITE	OOLITE
ONANISTS	ONENESSES	ONLOOKER	ONYCHITES	OOLITES
ONBEAT	ONER	ONLOOKERS	ONYCHITIS	OOLITH
ONBEATS	ONERIER	ONLOOKING	ONYCHIUM	OOLITHS
ONBOARD	ONERIEST	ONLY	ONYCHIUMS	OOLITIC
ONCE	ONEROUS	ONNED	ONYMOUS	OOLOGIC
ONCER	ONEROUSLY	ONNING	ONYX	OOLOGICAL
ONCERS	ONERS	ONO	ONYXES	OOLOGIES
ONCES	ONERY	ONOMASTIC	OO	OOLOGIST
ONCET	ONES	ONOS	OOBIT	OOLOGISTS
ONCIDIUM	ONESELF	ONRUSH	OOBITS	OOLOGY
ONCIDIUMS	ONETIME	ONRUSHES	OOCYST	OOLONG
ONCOGEN	ONEYER	ONRUSHING	OOCYSTS	OOLONGS
ONCOGENE	ONEYERS	ONS	OOCYTE	OOM
ONCOGENES	ONEYRE	ONSCREEN	OOCYTES	OOMIAC
ONCOGENIC	ONEYRES	ONSET	OODLES	OOMIACK
ONCOGENS	ONFALL	ONSETS	OODLINS	OOMIACKS
ONCOLOGIC	ONFALLS	ONSETTER	OOF	OOMIACS

OOMIAK	OOTHECA	OPENABLE	OPERETTAS	OPORICE
OOMIAKS	OOTHECAE	OPENCAST	OPERON	OPORICES
OOMPAH	OOTHECAL	OPENED	OPERONS	OPOSSUM
OOMPAHED	OOTID	OPENER	OPEROSE	OPOSSUMS
OOMPAHING	OOTIDS	OPENERS	OPEROSELY	OPPIDAN
OOMPAHS	OOTS	OPENEST	OPEROSITY	OPPIDANS
OOMPH	OOZE	OPENING	OPES	OPPILANT
OOMPHS	OOZED	OPENINGS	OPGEFOK	OPPILATE
OOMS	OOZES	OPENLY	OPHIDIAN	OPPILATED
OOMYCETE	OOZIER	OPENNESS	OPHIDIANS	OPPILATES
OOMYCETES	OOZIEST	OPENS	OPHIOLITE	OPPO
OON	OOZILY	OPENSIDE	OPHIOLOGY	OPPONENCY
OONS	OOZINESS	OPENSIDES	OPHITE	OPPONENT
OONT	OOZING	OPENWORK	OPHITES	OPPONENTS
OONTS	OOZY	OPENWORKS	OPHITIC	OPPORTUNE
OOP	OP	OPEPE	OPHIURA	OPPOS
OOPED	OPACIFIED	OPEPES	OPHIURAN	OPPOSABLE
OOPHORON	OPACIFIER	OPERA	OPHIURANS	OPPOSABLY
OOPHORONS	OPACIFIES	OPERABLE	OPHIURAS	OPPOSE
OOPHYTE	OPACIFY	OPERABLY	OPHIURID	OPPOSED
OOPHYTES	OPACITIES	OPERAGOER	OPHIURIDS	OPPOSER
OOPHYTIC	OPACITY	OPERAND	OPHIUROID	OPPOSERS
OOPING	OPACOUS	OPERANDS	OPIATE	OPPOSES
OOPS	OPAH	OPERANT	OPIATED	OPPOSING
OOR	OPAHS	OPERANTLY	OPIATES	OPPOSITE
OORALI	OPAL	OPERANTS	OPIATING	OPPOSITES
OORALIS	OPALED	OPERAS	OPIFICER	OPPRESS
OORIAL	OPALESCE	OPERATE	OPIFICERS	OPPRESSED
OORIALS	OPALESCED	OPERATED	OPINABLE	OPPRESSES
OORIE	OPALESCES	OPERATES	OPINE	OPPRESSOR
OORIER	OPALINE	OPERATIC	OPINED	OPPUGN
OORIEST	OPALINES	OPERATICS	OPINES	OPPUGNANT
OOS	OPALISED	OPERATING	OPING	OPPUGNED
OOSE	OPALIZED	OPERATION	OPINICUS	OPPUGNER
OOSES	OPALS	OPERATISE	OPINING	OPPUGNERS
OOSIER	OPAQUE	OPERATIVE	OPINION	OPPUGNING
OOSIEST	OPAQUED	OPERATIZE	OPINIONED	OPPUGNS
OOSPERM	OPAQUELY	OPERATOR	OPINIONS	OPS
OOSPERMS	OPAQUER	OPERATORS	OPIOID	OPSIMATH
OOSPHERE	OPAQUES	OPERCELE	OPIOIDS	OPSIMATHS
OOSPHERES	OPAQUEST	OPERCELES	OPIUM	OPSIMATHY
OOSPORE	OPAQUING	OPERCULA	OPIUMISM	OPSIN
OOSPORES	OPCODE	OPERCULAR	OPIUMISMS	OPSINS
OOSPORIC	OPCODES	OPERCULE	OPIUMS	OPSOMANIA
OOSPOROUS	OPE	OPERCULES	OPOBALSAM	OPSONIC
OOSY	OPED	OPERCULUM	OPODELDOC	OPSONIFY
OOT	OPEN	OPERETTA	OPOPANAX	OPSONIN

OPSONINS

OPSONINS	OPTION	ORAD	ORATORS	ORCHIDS
OPSONISE	OPTIONAL	ORAGIOUS	ORATORY	ORCHIL
OPSONISED	OPTIONALS	ORAL	ORATRESS	ORCHILLA
OPSONISES	OPTIONED	ORALISM	ORATRICES	ORCHILLAS
OPSONIUM	OPTIONEE	ORALISMS	ORATRIX	ORCHILS
OPSONIUMS	OPTIONEES	ORALIST	ORATRIXES	ORCHIS
OPSONIZE	OPTIONING	ORALISTS	ORB	ORCHISES
OPSONIZED	OPTIONS	ORALITIES	ORBED	ORCHITIC
OPSONIZES	OPTOLOGY	ORALITY	ORBICULAR	ORCHITIS
OPT	OPTOMETER	ORALLY	ORBIER	ORCIN
OPTANT	OPTOMETRY	ORALS	ORBIEST	ORCINE
OPTANTS	OPTOPHONE	ORANG	ORBING	ORCINES
OPTATIVE	OPTRONICS	ORANGE	ORBIT	ORCINOL
OPTATIVES	OPTS	ORANGEADE	ORBITA	ORCINOLS
OPTED	OPULENCE	ORANGER	ORBITAL	ORCINS
OPTER	OPULENCES	ORANGERIE	ORBITALLY	ORCS
OPTERS	OPULENCY	ORANGERY	ORBITALS	ORD
OPTIC	OPULENT	ORANGES	ORBITAS	ORDAIN
OPTICAL	OPULENTLY	ORANGEST	ORBITED	ORDAINED
OPTICALLY	OPULUS	ORANGEY	ORBITER	ORDAINER
OPTICIAN	OPULUSES	ORANGIER	ORBITERS	ORDAINERS
OPTICIANS	OPUNTIA	ORANGIEST	ORBITIES	ORDAINING
OPTICIST	OPUNTIAS	ORANGISH	ORBITING	ORDAINS
OPTICISTS	OPUS	ORANGS	ORBITS	ORDALIAN
OPTICS	OPUSCLE	ORANGUTAN	ORBITY	ORDALIUM
OPTIMA	OPUSCLES	ORANGY	ORBLESS	ORDALIUMS
OPTIMAL	OPUSCULA	ORANT	ORBS	ORDEAL
OPTIMALLY	OPUSCULAR	ORANTS	ORBY	ORDEALS
OPTIMATE	OPUSCULE	ORARIA	ORC	ORDER
OPTIMATES	OPUSCULES	ORARIAN	ORCA	ORDERABLE
OPTIME	OPUSCULUM	ORARIANS	ORCAS	ORDERED
OPTIMES	OPUSES	ORARION	ORCEIN	ORDERER
OPTIMISE	OQUASSA	ORARIONS	ORCEINS	ORDERERS
OPTIMISED	OQUASSAS	ORARIUM	ORCHARD	ORDERING
OPTIMISER	OR	ORARIUMS	ORCHARDS	ORDERINGS
OPTIMISES	ORA	ORATE	ORCHAT	ORDERLESS
OPTIMISM	ORACH	ORATED	ORCHATS	ORDERLIES
OPTIMISMS	ORACHE	ORATES	ORCHEL	ORDERLY
OPTIMIST	ORACHES	ORATING	ORCHELLA	ORDERS
OPTIMISTS	ORACIES	ORATION	ORCHELLAS	ORDINAIRE
OPTIMIZE	ORACLE	ORATIONS	ORCHELS	ORDINAL
OPTIMIZED	ORACLED	ORATOR	ORCHESES	ORDINALLY
OPTIMIZER	ORACLES	ORATORIAL	ORCHESIS	ORDINALS
OPTIMIZES	ORACLING	ORATORIAN	ORCHESTIC	ORDINANCE
OPTIMUM	ORACULAR	ORATORIES	ORCHESTRA	ORDINAND
OPTIMUMS	ORACULOUS	ORATORIO	ORCHID	ORDINANDS
OPTING	ORACY	ORATORIOS	ORCHIDIST	ORDINANT

ORDINANTS	ORGANA	ORGILLOUS	ORIGINS	OROGENS
ORDINAR	ORGANDIE	ORGONE	ORIHOU	OROGENY
ORDINARS	ORGANDIES	ORGONES	ORIHOUS	OROGRAPHY
ORDINARY	ORGANDY	ORGUE	ORILLION	OROIDE
ORDINATE	ORGANELLE	ORGUES	ORILLIONS	OROIDES
ORDINATED	ORGANIC	ORGULOUS	ORINASAL	OROLOGIES
ORDINATES	ORGANICAL	ORGY	ORINASALS	OROLOGIST
ORDINEE	ORGANICS	ORIBATID	ORIOLE	OROLOGY
ORDINEES	ORGANISE	ORIBATIDS	ORIOLES	OROMETER
ORDINES	ORGANISED	ORIBI	ORISHA	OROMETERS
ORDNANCE	ORGANISER	ORIBIS	ORISHAS	ORONASAL
ORDNANCES	ORGANISES	ORICALCHE	ORISON	OROPESA
ORDO	ORGANISM	ORICHALC	ORISONS	OROPESAS
ORDOS	ORGANISMS	ORICHALCS	ORIXA	OROTUND
ORDS	ORGANIST	ORIEL	ORIXAS	ORPHAN
ORDURE	ORGANISTS	ORIELLED	ORLE	ORPHANAGE
ORDURES	ORGANITY	ORIELS	ORLEANS	ORPHANED
ORDUROUS	ORGANIZE	ORIENCIES	ORLEANSES	ORPHANING
ORE	ORGANIZED	ORIENCY	ORLES	ORPHANISM
OREAD	ORGANIZER	ORIENT	ORLISTAT	ORPHANS
OREADES	ORGANIZES	ORIENTAL	ORLISTATS	ORPHARION
OREADS	ORGANON	ORIENTALS	ORLON	ORPHIC
ORECTIC	ORGANONS	ORIENTATE	ORLONS	ORPHICAL
ORECTIVE	ORGANOSOL	ORIENTED	ORLOP	ORPHISM
OREGANO	ORGANOTIN	ORIENTEER	ORLOPS	ORPHISMS
OREGANOS	ORGANS	ORIENTER	ORMER	ORPHREY
OREIDE	ORGANUM	ORIENTERS	ORMERS	ORPHREYED
OREIDES	ORGANUMS	ORIENTING	ORMOLU	ORPHREYS
OREODONT	ORGANZA	ORIENTS	ORMOLUS	ORPIMENT
OREODONTS	ORGANZAS	ORIFEX	ORNAMENT	ORPIMENTS
OREOLOGY	ORGANZINE	ORIFEXES	ORNAMENTS	ORPIN
OREPEARCH	ORGASM	ORIFICE	ORNATE	ORPINE
ORES	ORGASMED	ORIFICES	ORNATELY	ORPINES
ORESTUNCK	ORGASMIC	ORIFICIAL	ORNATER	ORPINS
OREWEED	ORGASMING	ORIFLAMME	ORNATEST	ORRA
OREWEEDS	ORGASMS	ORIGAMI	ORNERIER	ORRAMAN
OREXIN	ORGASTIC	ORIGAMIS	ORNERIEST	ORRAMEN
OREXINS	ORGEAT	ORIGAN	ORNERY	ORRERIES
OREXIS	ORGEATS	ORIGANE	ORNIS	ORRERY
OREXISES	ORGIA	ORIGANES	ORNISES	ORRICE
ORF	ORGIAC	ORIGANS	ORNITHES	ORRICES
ORFE	ORGIAS	ORIGANUM	ORNITHIC	ORRIS
ORFES	ORGIAST	ORIGANUMS	ORNITHINE	ORRISES
ORFRAY	ORGIASTIC	ORIGIN	ORNITHOID	ORRISROOT
ORFRAYS	ORGIASTS	ORIGINAL	OROGEN	ORS
ORFS	ORGIC	ORIGINALS	OROGENIC	ORSEILLE
ORGAN	ORGIES	ORIGINATE	OROGENIES	ORSEILLES

O

ORSELLIC	OSCITANT	OSMOSING	OSTEITIS	OSTRACEAN
ORT	OSCITATE	OSMOSIS	OSTENSIVE	OSTRACISE
ORTANIQUE	OSCITATED	OSMOTIC	OSTENSORY	OSTRACISM
ORTHIAN	OSCITATES	OSMOUS	OSTENT	OSTRACIZE
ORTHICON	OSCULA	OSMUND	OSTENTS	OSTRACOD
ORTHICONS	OSCULANT	OSMUNDA	OSTEOCYTE	OSTRACODE
ORTHO	OSCULAR	OSMUNDAS	OSTEODERM	OSTRACODS
ORTHOAXES	OSCULATE	OSMUNDINE	OSTEOGEN	OSTRACON
ORTHOAXIS	OSCULATED	OSMUNDS	OSTEOGENS	OSTRAKA
ORTHODOX	OSCULATES	OSNABURG	OSTEOGENY	OSTRAKON
ORTHODOXY	OSCULE	OSNABURGS	OSTEOID	OSTREGER
ORTHOEPIC	OSCULES	OSPREY	OSTEOIDS	OSTREGERS
ORTHOEPY	OSCULUM	OSPREYS	OSTEOLOGY	OSTRICH
ORTHOPEDY	OSE	OSSA	OSTEOMA	OSTRICHES
ORTHOPOD	OSES	OSSARIUM	OSTEOMAS	OTAKU
ORTHOPODS	OSETRA	OSSARIUMS	OSTEOMATA	OTALGIA
ORTHOPTER	OSETRAS	OSSATURE	OSTEOPATH	OTALGIAS
ORTHOPTIC	OSHAC	OSSATURES	OSTEOSES	OTALGIC
ORTHOS	OSHACS	OSSEIN	OSTEOSIS	OTALGIES
ORTHOSES	OSIER	OSSEINS	OSTEOTOME	OTALGY
ORTHOSIS	OSIERED	OSSELET	OSTEOTOMY	OTARIES
ORTHOTIC	OSIERIES	OSSELETS	OSTIA	OTARINE
ORTHOTICS	OSIERS	OSSEOUS	OSTIAL	OTARY
ORTHOTIST	OSIERY	OSSEOUSLY	OSTIARIES	OTHER
ORTHOTONE	OSMATE	OSSETER	OSTIARY	OTHERNESS
ORTHROS	OSMATES	OSSETERS	OSTIATE	OTHERS
ORTHROSES	OSMATIC	OSSETRA	OSTINATI	OTHERWISE
ORTOLAN	OSMETERIA	OSSETRAS	OSTINATO	OTIC
ORTOLANS	OSMIATE	OSSIA	OSTINATOS	OTIOSE
ORTS	OSMIATES	OSSICLE	OSTIOLAR	OTIOSELY
ORVAL	OSMIC	OSSICLES	OSTIOLATE	OTIOSITY
ORVALS	OSMICALLY	OSSICULAR	OSTIOLE	OTITIC
ORYX	OSMICS	OSSIFIC	OSTIOLES	OTITIDES
ORYXES	OSMIOUS	OSSIFIED	OSTIUM	OTITIS
ORZO	OSMIUM	OSSIFIER	OSTLER	OTITISES
ORZOS	OSMIUMS	OSSIFIERS	OSTLERESS	OTOCYST
OS	OSMOL	OSSIFIES	OSTLERS	OTOCYSTIC
OSAR	OSMOLAL	OSSIFRAGA	OSTMARK	OTOCYSTS
OSCAR	OSMOLAR	OSSIFRAGE	OSTMARKS	OTOLITH
OSCARS	OSMOLE	OSSIFY	OSTOMATE	OTOLITHIC
OSCHEAL	OSMOLES	OSSIFYING	OSTOMATES	OTOLITHS
OSCILLATE	OSMOLS	OSSOBUCO	OSTOMIES	OTOLOGIES
OSCINE	OSMOMETER	OSSOBUCOS	OSTOMY	OTOLOGIST
OSCINES	OSMOMETRY	OSSUARIES	OSTOSES	OTOLOGY
OSCININE	OSMOSE	OSSUARY	OSTOSIS	OTOPLASTY
OSCITANCE	OSMOSED	OSTEAL	OSTOSISES	OTORRHOEA
OSCITANCY	OSMOSES	OSTEITIC	OSTRACA	OTOSCOPE

OTOSCOPES	OUGLIE	OURIE	OUTBAKING	OUTBRAVES
OTOSCOPIC	OUGLIED	OURIER	OUTBAR	OUTBRAWL
OTOSCOPY	OUGLIEING	OURIEST	OUTBARK	OUTBRAWLS
OTOTOXIC	OUGLIES	OURN	OUTBARKED	OUTBRAZEN
OTTAR	OUGUIYA	OUROBOROS	OUTBARKS	OUTBREAK
OTTARS	OUGUIYAS	OUROLOGY	OUTBARRED	OUTBREAKS
OTTAVA	OUIJA	OUROSCOPY	OUTBARS	OUTBRED
OTTAVAS	OUIJAS	OURS	OUTBAWL	OUTBREED
OTTAVINO	OUISTITI	OURSELF	OUTBAWLED	OUTBREEDS
OTTAVINOS	OUISTITIS	OURSELVES	OUTBAWLS	OUTBRIBE
OTTER	OUK	OUS	OUTBEAM	OUTBRIBED
OTTERED	OUKS	OUSEL	OUTBEAMED	OUTBRIBES
OTTERING	OULACHON	OUSELS	OUTBEAMS	OUTBROKE
OTTERS	OULACHONS	OUST	OUTBEG	OUTBROKEN
OTTO	OULAKAN	OUSTED	OUTBEGGED	OUTBUILD
OTTOMAN	OULAKANS	OUSTER	OUTBEGS	OUTBUILDS
OTTOMANS	OULD	OUSTERS	OUTBID	OUTBUILT
OTTOS	OULDER	OUSTING	OUTBIDDEN	OUTBULGE
OTTRELITE	OULDEST	OUSTITI	OUTBIDDER	OUTBULGED
OU	OULK	OUSTITIS	OUTBIDS	OUTBULGES
OUABAIN	OULKS	OUSTS	OUTBITCH	OUTBULK
OUABAINS	OULONG	OUT	OUTBLAZE	OUTBULKED
OUAKARI	OULONGS	OUTACT	OUTBLAZED	OUTBULKS
OUAKARIS	OUMA	OUTACTED	OUTBLAZES	OUTBULLY
OUBAAS	OUMAS	OUTACTING	OUTBLEAT	OUTBURN
OUBAASES	OUNCE	OUTACTS	OUTBLEATS	OUTBURNED
OUBIT	OUNCES	OUTADD	OUTBLESS	OUTBURNS
OUBITS	OUNDY	OUTADDED	OUTBLOOM	OUTBURNT
OUBLIETTE	OUP	OUTADDING	OUTBLOOMS	OUTBURST
OUCH	OUPA	OUTADDS	OUTBLUFF	OUTBURSTS
OUCHED	OUPAS	OUTAGE	OUTBLUFFS	OUTBUY
OUCHES	OUPED	OUTAGES	OUTBLUSH	OUTBUYING
OUCHING	OUPH	OUTARGUE	OUTBOARD	OUTBUYS
OUCHT	OUPHE	OUTARGUED	OUTBOARDS	OUTBY
OUCHTS	OUPHES	OUTARGUES	OUTBOAST	OUTBYE
OUD	OUPHS	OUTASIGHT	OUTBOASTS	OUTCALL
OUDS	OUPING	OUTASK	OUTBOUGHT	OUTCALLS
OUENS	OUPS	OUTASKED	OUTBOUND	OUTCAPER
OUGHLIED	OUR	OUTASKING	OUTBOUNDS	OUTCAPERS
OUGHLIES	OURALI	OUTASKS	OUTBOX	OUTCAST
OUGHLY	OURALIS	OUTATE	OUTBOXED	OUTCASTE
OUGHLYING	OURANG	OUTBACK	OUTBOXES	OUTCASTED
OUGHT	OURANGS	OUTBACKER	OUTBOXING	OUTCASTES
OUGHTED	OURARI	OUTBACKS	OUTBRAG	OUTCASTS
OUGHTING	OURARIS	OUTBAKE	OUTBRAGS	OUTCATCH
OUGHTNESS	OUREBI	OUTBAKED	OUTBRAVE	OUTCAUGHT
OUGHTS	OUREBIS	OUTBAKES	OUTBRAVED	OUTCAVIL

O

OUTCAVILS	OUTDARE	OUTDURE	OUTFENCES	OUTFROWN
OUTCHARGE	OUTDARED	OUTDURED	OUTFIELD	OUTFROWNS
OUTCHARM	OUTDARES	OUTDURES	OUTFIELDS	OUTFUMBLE
OUTCHARMS	OUTDARING	OUTDURING	OUTFIGHT	OUTGAIN
OUTCHEAT	OUTDATE	OUTDWELL	OUTFIGHTS	OUTGAINED
OUTCHEATS	OUTDATED	OUTDWELLS	OUTFIGURE	OUTGAINS
OUTCHID	OUTDATES	OUTDWELT	OUTFIND	OUTGALLOP
OUTCHIDE	OUTDATING	OUTEARN	OUTFINDS	OUTGAMBLE
OUTCHIDED	OUTDAZZLE	OUTEARNED	OUTFIRE	OUTGAS
OUTCHIDES	OUTDEBATE	OUTEARNS	OUTFIRED	OUTGASES
OUTCITIES	OUTDESIGN	OUTEAT	OUTFIRES	OUTGASSED
OUTCITY	OUTDID	OUTEATEN	OUTFIRING	OUTGASSES
OUTCLASS	OUTDO	OUTEATING	OUTFISH	OUTGATE
OUTCLIMB	OUTDODGE	OUTEATS	OUTFISHED	OUTGATES
OUTCLIMBS	OUTDODGED	OUTECHO	OUTFISHES	OUTGAVE
OUTCLOMB	OUTDODGES	OUTECHOED	OUTFIT	OUTGAZE
OUTCOACH	OUTDOER	OUTECHOES	OUTFITS	OUTGAZED
OUTCOME	OUTDOERS	OUTED	OUTFITTED	OUTGAZES
OUTCOMES	OUTDOES	OUTEDGE	OUTFITTER	OUTGAZING
OUTCOOK	OUTDOING	OUTEDGES	OUTFLANK	OUTGIVE
OUTCOOKED	OUTDONE	OUTER	OUTFLANKS	OUTGIVEN
OUTCOOKS	OUTDOOR	OUTERCOAT	OUTFLASH	OUTGIVES
OUTCOUNT	OUTDOORS	OUTERMOST	OUTFLEW	OUTGIVING
OUTCOUNTS	OUTDOORSY	OUTERS	OUTFLIES	OUTGLARE
OUTCRAFTY	OUTDRAG	OUTERWEAR	OUTFLING	OUTGLARED
OUTCRAWL	OUTDRAGS	OUTFABLE	OUTFLINGS	OUTGLARES
OUTCRAWLS	OUTDRANK	OUTFABLED	OUTFLOAT	OUTGLEAM
OUTCRIED	OUTDRAW	OUTFABLES	OUTFLOATS	OUTGLEAMS
OUTCRIES	OUTDRAWN	OUTFACE	OUTFLOW	OUTGLOW
OUTCROP	OUTDRAWS	OUTFACED	OUTFLOWED	OUTGLOWED
OUTCROPS	OUTDREAM	OUTFACES	OUTFLOWN	OUTGLOWS
OUTCROSS	OUTDREAMS	OUTFACING	OUTFLOWS	OUTGNAW
OUTCROW	OUTDREAMT	OUTFALL	OUTFLUSH	OUTGNAWED
OUTCROWD	OUTDRESS	OUTFALLS	OUTFLY	OUTGNAWN
OUTCROWDS	OUTDREW	OUTFAST	OUTFLYING	OUTGNAWS
OUTCROWED	OUTDRINK	OUTFASTED	OUTFOOL	OUTGO
OUTCROWS	OUTDRINKS	OUTFASTS	OUTFOOLED	OUTGOER
OUTCRY	OUTDRIVE	OUTFAWN	OUTFOOLS	OUTGOERS
OUTCRYING	OUTDRIVEN	OUTFAWNED	OUTFOOT	OUTGOES
OUTCURSE	OUTDRIVES	OUTFAWNS	OUTFOOTED	OUTGOING
OUTCURSED	OUTDROP	OUTFEAST	OUTFOOTS	OUTGOINGS
OUTCURSES	OUTDROPS	OUTFEASTS	OUTFOUGHT	OUTGONE
OUTCURVE	OUTDROVE	OUTFEEL	OUTFOUND	OUTGREW
OUTCURVES	OUTDRUNK	OUTFEELS	OUTFOX	OUTGRIN
OUTDANCE	OUTDUEL	OUTFELT	OUTFOXED	OUTGRINS
OUTDANCED	OUTDUELED	OUTFENCE	OUTFOXES	OUTGROSS
OUTDANCES	OUTDUELS	OUTFENCED	OUTFOXING	OUTGROUP

OUTGROUPS	OUTHYRING	OUTLAWING	OUTMAN	OUTPITIES
OUTGROW	OUTING	OUTLAWRY	OUTMANNED	OUTPITY
OUTGROWN	OUTINGS	OUTLAWS	OUTMANS	OUTPLACE
OUTGROWS	OUTJEST	OUTLAY	OUTMANTLE	OUTPLACED
OUTGROWTH	OUTJESTED	OUTLAYING	OUTMARCH	OUTPLACER
OUTGUARD	OUTJESTS	OUTLAYS	OUTMASTER	OUTPLACES
OUTGUARDS	OUTJET	OUTLEAD	OUTMATCH	OUTPLAN
OUTGUESS	OUTJETS	OUTLEADS	OUTMODE	OUTPLANS
OUTGUIDE	OUTJINX	OUTLEAP	OUTMODED	OUTPLAY
OUTGUIDED	OUTJINXED	OUTLEAPED	OUTMODES	OUTPLAYED
OUTGUIDES	OUTJINXES	OUTLEAPS	OUTMODING	OUTPLAYS
OUTGUN	OUTJOCKEY	OUTLEAPT	OUTMOST	OUTPLOD
OUTGUNNED	OUTJUGGLE	OUTLEARN	OUTMOVE	OUTPLODS
OUTGUNS	OUTJUMP	OUTLEARNS	OUTMOVED	OUTPLOT
OUTGUSH	OUTJUMPED	OUTLEARNT	OUTMOVES	OUTPLOTS
OUTGUSHED	OUTJUMPS	OUTLED	OUTMOVING	OUTPOINT
OUTGUSHES	OUTJUT	OUTLER	OUTMUSCLE	OUTPOINTS
OUTHANDLE	OUTJUTS	OUTLERS	OUTNAME	OUTPOLL
OUTHAUL	OUTJUTTED	OUTLET	OUTNAMED	OUTPOLLED
OUTHAULER	OUTKEEP	OUTLETS	OUTNAMES	OUTPOLLS
OUTHAULS	OUTKEEPS	OUTLIE	OUTNAMING	OUTPORT
OUTHEAR	OUTKEPT	OUTLIED	OUTNESS	OUTPORTER
OUTHEARD	OUTKICK	OUTLIER	OUTNESSES	OUTPORTS
OUTHEARS	OUTKICKED	OUTLIERS	OUTNIGHT	OUTPOST
OUTHER	OUTKICKS	OUTLIES	OUTNIGHTS	OUTPOSTS
OUTHIRE	OUTKILL	OUTLINE	OUTNUMBER	OUTPOUR
OUTHIRED	OUTKILLED	OUTLINEAR	OUTOFFICE	OUTPOURED
OUTHIRES	OUTKILLS	OUTLINED	OUTPACE	OUTPOURER
OUTHIRING	OUTKISS	OUTLINER	OUTPACED	OUTPOURS
OUTHIT	OUTKISSED	OUTLINERS	OUTPACES	OUTPOWER
OUTHITS	OUTKISSES	OUTLINES	OUTPACING	OUTPOWERS
OUTHOMER	OUTLAID	OUTLINING	OUTPAINT	OUTPRAY
OUTHOMERS	OUTLAIN	OUTLIVE	OUTPAINTS	OUTPRAYED
OUTHOUSE	OUTLAND	OUTLIVED	OUTPART	OUTPRAYS
OUTHOUSES	OUTLANDER	OUTLIVER	OUTPARTS	OUTPREACH
OUTHOWL	OUTLANDS	OUTLIVERS	OUTPASS	OUTPREEN
OUTHOWLED	OUTLASH	OUTLIVES	OUTPASSED	OUTPREENS
OUTHOWLS	OUTLASHES	OUTLIVING	OUTPASSES	OUTPRESS
OUTHUMOR	OUTLAST	OUTLOOK	OUTPEEP	OUTPRICE
OUTHUMORS	OUTLASTED	OUTLOOKED	OUTPEEPED	OUTPRICED
OUTHUNT	OUTLASTS	OUTLOOKS	OUTPEEPS	OUTPRICES
OUTHUNTED	OUTLAUGH	OUTLOVE	OUTPEER	OUTPRIZE
OUTHUNTS	OUTLAUGHS	OUTLOVED	OUTPEERED	OUTPRIZED
OUTHUSTLE	OUTLAUNCE	OUTLOVES	OUTPEERS	OUTPRIZES
OUTHYRE	OUTLAUNCH	OUTLOVING	OUTPEOPLE	OUTPULL
OUTHYRED	OUTLAW	OUTLUSTRE	OUTPITCH	OUTPULLED
OUTHYRES	OUTLAWED	OUTLYING	OUTPITIED	OUTPULLS

OUTPUNCH	OUTRECKON	OUTROW	OUTSETS	OUTSMILES
OUTPUPIL	OUTRED	OUTROWED	OUTSHAME	OUTSMOKE
OUTPUPILS	OUTREDDED	OUTROWING	OUTSHAMED	OUTSMOKED
OUTPURSUE	OUTREDDEN	OUTROWS	OUTSHAMES	OUTSMOKES
OUTPUSH	OUTREDS	OUTRUN	OUTSHINE	OUTSNORE
OUTPUSHED	OUTREIGN	OUTRUNG	OUTSHINED	OUTSNORED
OUTPUSHES	OUTREIGNS	OUTRUNNER	OUTSHINES	OUTSNORES
OUTPUT	OUTRELIEF	OUTRUNS	OUTSHONE	OUTSOAR
OUTPUTS	OUTREMER	OUTRUSH	OUTSHOOT	OUTSOARED
OUTPUTTED	OUTREMERS	OUTRUSHED	OUTSHOOTS	OUTSOARS
OUTQUOTE	OUTRIDDEN	OUTRUSHES	OUTSHOT	OUTSOLD
OUTQUOTED	OUTRIDE	OUTS	OUTSHOTS	OUTSOLE
OUTQUOTES	OUTRIDER	OUTSAID	OUTSHOUT	OUTSOLES
OUTRACE	OUTRIDERS	OUTSAIL	OUTSHOUTS	OUTSOURCE
OUTRACED	OUTRIDES	OUTSAILED	OUTSIDE	OUTSPAN
OUTRACES	OUTRIDING	OUTSAILS	OUTSIDER	OUTSPANS
OUTRACING	OUTRIG	OUTSANG	OUTSIDERS	OUTSPEAK
OUTRAGE	OUTRIGGED	OUTSAT	OUTSIDES	OUTSPEAKS
OUTRAGED	OUTRIGGER	OUTSAVOR	OUTSIGHT	OUTSPED
OUTRAGES	OUTRIGHT	OUTSAVORS	OUTSIGHTS	OUTSPEED
OUTRAGING	OUTRIGS	OUTSAW	OUTSIN	OUTSPEEDS
OUTRAISE	OUTRING	OUTSAY	OUTSING	OUTSPELL
OUTRAISED	OUTRINGS	OUTSAYING	OUTSINGS	OUTSPELLS
OUTRAISES	OUTRIVAL	OUTSAYS	OUTSINNED	OUTSPELT
OUTRAN	OUTRIVALS	OUTSCHEME	OUTSINS	OUTSPEND
OUTRANCE	OUTRO	OUTSCOLD	OUTSIT	OUTSPENDS
OUTRANCES	OUTROAR	OUTSCOLDS	OUTSITS	OUTSPENT
OUTRANG	OUTROARED	OUTSCOOP	OUTSIZE	OUTSPOKE
OUTRANGE	OUTROARS	OUTSCOOPS	OUTSIZED	OUTSPOKEN
OUTRANGED	OUTROCK	OUTSCORE	OUTSIZES	OUTSPORT
OUTRANGES	OUTROCKED	OUTSCORED	OUTSKATE	OUTSPORTS
OUTRANK	OUTROCKS	OUTSCORES	OUTSKATED	OUTSPRANG
OUTRANKED	OUTRODE	OUTSCORN	OUTSKATES	OUTSPREAD
OUTRANKS	OUTROLL	OUTSCORNS	OUTSKIRT	OUTSPRING
OUTRATE	OUTROLLED	OUTSCREAM	OUTSKIRTS	OUTSPRINT
OUTRATED	OUTROLLS	OUTSEE	OUTSLEEP	OUTSPRUNG
OUTRATES	OUTROOP	OUTSEEING	OUTSLEEPS	OUTSTAND
OUTRATING	OUTROOPER	OUTSEEN	OUTSLEPT	OUTSTANDS
OUTRAVE	OUTROOPS	OUTSEES	OUTSLICK	OUTSTARE
OUTRAVED	OUTROOT	OUTSELL	OUTSLICKS	OUTSTARED
OUTRAVES	OUTROOTED	OUTSELLS	OUTSMART	OUTSTARES
OUTRAVING	OUTROOTS	OUTSERT	OUTSMARTS	OUTSTART
OUTRE	OUTROPE	OUTSERTS	OUTSMELL	OUTSTARTS
OUTREACH	OUTROPER	OUTSERVE	OUTSMELLS	OUTSTATE
OUTREAD	OUTROPERS	OUTSERVED	OUTSMELT	OUTSTATED
OUTREADS	OUTROPES	OUTSERVES	OUTSMILE	OUTSTATES
OUTREASON	OUTROS	OUTSET	OUTSMILED	OUTSTAY

OUTSTAYED	OUTTAKING	OUTVENOMS	OUTWHIRL	OUTYELPED
OUTSTAYS	OUTTALK	OUTVIE	OUTWHIRLS	OUTYELPS
OUTSTEER	OUTTALKED	OUTVIED	OUTWICK	OUTYIELD
OUTSTEERS	OUTTALKS	OUTVIES	OUTWICKED	OUTYIELDS
OUTSTEP	OUTTASK	OUTVOICE	OUTWICKS	OUVERT
OUTSTEPS	OUTTASKED	OUTVOICED	OUTWILE	OUVERTE
OUTSTOOD	OUTTASKS	OUTVOICES	OUTWILED	OUVRAGE
OUTSTRAIN	OUTTELL	OUTVOTE	OUTWILES	OUVRAGES
OUTSTRIDE	OUTTELLS	OUTVOTED	OUTWILING	OUVRIER
OUTSTRIKE	OUTTHANK	OUTVOTER	OUTWILL	OUVRIERE
OUTSTRIP	OUTTHANKS	OUTVOTERS	OUTWILLED	OUVRIERES
OUTSTRIPS	OUTTHIEVE	OUTVOTES	OUTWILLS	OUVRIERS
OUTSTRIVE	OUTTHINK	OUTVOTING	OUTWIN	OUZEL
OUTSTRODE	OUTTHINKS	OUTVYING	OUTWIND	OUZELS
OUTSTROKE	OUTTHREW	OUTWAIT	OUTWINDED	OUZO
OUTSTROVE	OUTTHROB	OUTWAITED	OUTWINDS	OUZOS
OUTSTRUCK	OUTTHROBS	OUTWAITS	OUTWING	OVA
OUTSTUDY	OUTTHROW	OUTWALK	OUTWINGED	OVAL
OUTSTUNT	OUTTHROWN	OUTWALKED	OUTWINGS	OVALBUMIN
OUTSTUNTS	OUTTHROWS	OUTWALKS	OUTWINS	OVALITIES
OUTSULK	OUTTHRUST	OUTWAR	OUTWISH	OVALITY
OUTSULKED	OUTTOLD	OUTWARD	OUTWISHED	OVALLY
OUTSULKS	OUTTONGUE	OUTWARDLY	OUTWISHES	OVALNESS
OUTSUM	OUTTOOK	OUTWARDS	OUTWIT	OVALS
OUTSUMMED	OUTTOP	OUTWARRED	OUTWITH	OVARIAL
OUTSUMS	OUTTOPPED	OUTWARS	OUTWITS	OVARIAN
OUTSUNG	OUTTOPS	OUTWASH	OUTWITTED	OVARIES
OUTSWAM	OUTTOWER	OUTWASHES	OUTWON	OVARIOLE
OUTSWARE	OUTTOWERS	OUTWASTE	OUTWORE	OVARIOLES
OUTSWEAR	OUTTRADE	OUTWASTED	OUTWORK	OVARIOUS
OUTSWEARS	OUTTRADED	OUTWASTES	OUTWORKED	OVARITIS
OUTSWEEP	OUTTRADES	OUTWATCH	OUTWORKER	OVARY
OUTSWEEPS	OUTTRAVEL	OUTWEAR	OUTWORKS	OVATE
OUTSWELL	OUTTRICK	OUTWEARS	OUTWORN	OVATED
OUTSWELLS	OUTTRICKS	OUTWEARY	OUTWORTH	OVATELY
OUTSWEPT	OUTTROT	OUTWEED	OUTWORTHS	OVATES
OUTSWIM	OUTTROTS	OUTWEEDED	OUTWOUND	OVATING
OUTSWIMS	OUTTRUMP	OUTWEEDS	OUTWREST	OVATION
OUTSWING	OUTTRUMPS	OUTWEEP	OUTWRESTS	OVATIONAL
OUTSWINGS	OUTTURN	OUTWEEPS	OUTWRIT	OVATIONS
OUTSWORE	OUTTURNS	OUTWEIGH	OUTWRITE	OVATOR
OUTSWORN	OUTVALUE	OUTWEIGHS	OUTWRITES	OVATORS
OUTSWUM	OUTVALUED	OUTWELL	OUTWROTE	OVEL
OUTSWUNG	OUTVALUES	OUTWELLED	OUTYELL	OVELS
OUTTAKE	OUTVAUNT	OUTWELLS	OUTYELLED	OVEN
OUTTAKEN	OUTVAUNTS	OUTWENT	OUTYELLS	OVENABLE
OUTTAKES	OUTVENOM	OUTWEPT	OUTYELP	OVENBIRD

OVENBIRDS	OVERBIG	OVERCATCH	OVERDARED	OVEREATER
OVENED	OVERBILL	OVERCHEAP	OVERDARES	OVEREATS
OVENING	OVERBILLS	OVERCHECK	OVERDATED	OVERED
OVENLIKE	OVERBITE	OVERCHILL	OVERDEAR	OVEREDIT
OVENPROOF	OVERBITES	OVERCIVIL	OVERDECK	OVEREDITS
OVENS	OVERBLEW	OVERCLAD	OVERDECKS	OVEREGG
OVENWARE	OVERBLOW	OVERCLAIM	OVERDID	OVEREGGED
OVENWARES	OVERBLOWN	OVERCLASS	OVERDIGHT	OVEREGGS
OVENWOOD	OVERBLOWS	OVERCLEAN	OVERDO	OVEREMOTE
OVENWOODS	OVERBOARD	OVERCLEAR	OVERDOER	OVEREXERT
OVER	OVERBOIL	OVERCLOCK	OVERDOERS	OVEREYE
OVERABLE	OVERBOILS	OVERCLOSE	OVERDOES	OVEREYED
OVERACT	OVERBOLD	OVERCLOUD	OVERDOG	OVEREYES
OVERACTED	OVERBOOK	OVERCLOY	OVERDOGS	OVEREYING
OVERACTS	OVERBOOKS	OVERCLOYS	OVERDOING	OVERFALL
OVERACUTE	OVERBOOT	OVERCLUB	OVERDONE	OVERFALLS
OVERAGE	OVERBOOTS	OVERCLUBS	OVERDOSE	OVERFAR
OVERAGED	OVERBORE	OVERCOACH	OVERDOSED	OVERFAST
OVERAGES	OVERBORN	OVERCOAT	OVERDOSES	OVERFAT
OVERALERT	OVERBORNE	OVERCOATS	OVERDRAFT	OVERFAVOR
OVERALL	OVERBOUND	OVERCOLD	OVERDRANK	OVERFEAR
OVERALLED	OVERBRAKE	OVERCOLOR	OVERDRAW	OVERFEARS
OVERALLS	OVERBRED	OVERCOME	OVERDRAWN	OVERFED
OVERAPT	OVERBREED	OVERCOMER	OVERDRAWS	OVERFEED
OVERARCH	OVERBRIEF	OVERCOMES	OVERDRESS	OVERFEEDS
OVERARM	OVERBRIM	OVERCOOK	OVERDREW	OVERFELL
OVERARMED	OVERBRIMS	OVERCOOKS	OVERDRIED	OVERFILL
OVERARMS	OVERBROAD	OVERCOOL	OVERDRIES	OVERFILLS
OVERATE	OVERBROW	OVERCOOLS	OVERDRINK	OVERFINE
OVERAWE	OVERBROWS	OVERCOUNT	OVERDRIVE	OVERFISH
OVERAWED	OVERBUILD	OVERCOVER	OVERDROVE	OVERFIT
OVERAWES	OVERBUILT	OVERCOY	OVERDRUNK	OVERFLEW
OVERAWING	OVERBULK	OVERCRAM	OVERDRY	OVERFLIES
OVERBAKE	OVERBULKS	OVERCRAMS	OVERDUB	OVERFLOOD
OVERBAKED	OVERBURN	OVERCRAW	OVERDUBS	OVERFLOW
OVERBAKES	OVERBURNS	OVERCRAWS	OVERDUE	OVERFLOWN
OVERBANK	OVERBURNT	OVERCROP	OVERDUST	OVERFLOWS
OVERBANKS	OVERBUSY	OVERCROPS	OVERDUSTS	OVERFLUSH
OVERBEAR	OVERBUY	OVERCROW	OVERDYE	OVERFLY
OVERBEARS	OVERBUYS	OVERCROWD	OVERDYED	OVERFOCUS
OVERBEAT	OVERBY	OVERCROWS	OVERDYER	OVERFOLD
OVERBEATS	OVERCALL	OVERCURE	OVERDYERS	OVERFOLDS
OVERBED	OVERCALLS	OVERCURED	OVERDYES	OVERFOND
OVERBET	OVERCAME	OVERCURES	OVEREAGER	OVERFOUL
OVERBETS	OVERCARRY	OVERCUT	OVEREASY	OVERFRANK
OVERBID	OVERCAST	OVERCUTS	OVEREAT	OVERFREE
OVERBIDS	OVERCASTS	OVERDARE	OVEREATEN	OVERFULL

OVERFUND	OVERHALES	OVERJOY	OVERLIER	OVERNAME
OVERFUNDS	OVERHAND	OVERJOYED	OVERLIERS	OVERNAMED
OVERFUSSY	OVERHANDS	OVERJOYS	OVERLIES	OVERNAMES
OVERGALL	OVERHANG	OVERJUMP	OVERLIGHT	OVERNEAR
OVERGALLS	OVERHANGS	OVERJUMPS	OVERLIT	OVERNEAT
OVERGANG	OVERHAPPY	OVERJUST	OVERLIVE	OVERNET
OVERGANGS	OVERHARD	OVERKEEN	OVERLIVED	OVERNETS
OVERGAVE	OVERHASTE	OVERKEEP	OVERLIVES	OVERNEW
OVERGEAR	OVERHASTY	OVERKEEPS	OVERLOAD	OVERNICE
OVERGEARS	OVERHATE	OVERKEPT	OVERLOADS	OVERNIGHT
OVERGET	OVERHATED	OVERKEST	OVERLOCK	OVERPACK
OVERGETS	OVERHATES	OVERKILL	OVERLOCKS	OVERPACKS
OVERGILD	OVERHAUL	OVERKILLS	OVERLONG	OVERPAGE
OVERGILDS	OVERHAULS	OVERKIND	OVERLOOK	OVERPAID
OVERGILT	OVERHEAD	OVERKING	OVERLOOKS	OVERPAINT
OVERGIRD	OVERHEADS	OVERKINGS	OVERLORD	OVERPART
OVERGIRDS	OVERHEAP	OVERKNEE	OVERLORDS	OVERPARTS
OVERGIRT	OVERHEAPS	OVERLABOR	OVERLOUD	OVERPASS
OVERGIVE	OVERHEAR	OVERLADE	OVERLOVE	OVERPAST
OVERGIVEN	OVERHEARD	OVERLADED	OVERLOVED	OVERPAY
OVERGIVES	OVERHEARS	OVERLADEN	OVERLOVES	OVERPAYS
OVERGLAD	OVERHEAT	OVERLADES	OVERLUSH	OVERPEDAL
OVERGLAZE	OVERHEATS	OVERLAID	OVERLUSTY	OVERPEER
OVERGLOOM	OVERHELD	OVERLAIN	OVERLY	OVERPEERS
OVERGO	OVERHENT	OVERLAND	OVERLYING	OVERPERCH
OVERGOAD	OVERHENTS	OVERLANDS	OVERMAN	OVERPERT
OVERGOADS	OVERHIGH	OVERLAP	OVERMANS	OVERPITCH
OVERGOES	OVERHIT	OVERLAPS	OVERMANY	OVERPLAID
OVERGOING	OVERHITS	OVERLARD	OVERMAST	OVERPLAN
OVERGONE	OVERHOLD	OVERLARDS	OVERMASTS	OVERPLANS
OVERGORGE	OVERHOLDS	OVERLARGE	OVERMATCH	OVERPLANT
OVERGOT	OVERHOLY	OVERLATE	OVERMEEK	OVERPLAST
OVERGRADE	OVERHONOR	OVERLAX	OVERMELT	OVERPLAY
OVERGRAIN	OVERHOPE	OVERLAY	OVERMELTS	OVERPLAYS
OVERGRASS	OVERHOPED	OVERLAYS	OVERMEN	OVERPLIED
OVERGRAZE	OVERHOPES	OVERLEAF	OVERMERRY	OVERPLIES
OVERGREAT	OVERHOT	OVERLEAP	OVERMILD	OVERPLOT
OVERGREEN	OVERHUNG	OVERLEAPS	OVERMILK	OVERPLOTS
OVERGREW	OVERHUNT	OVERLEAPT	OVERMILKS	OVERPLUS
OVERGROW	OVERHUNTS	OVERLEARN	OVERMINE	OVERPLY
OVERGROWN	OVERHYPE	OVERLEND	OVERMINED	OVERPOISE
OVERGROWS	OVERHYPED	OVERLENDS	OVERMINES	OVERPOST
OVERHAILE	OVERHYPES	OVERLENT	OVERMIX	OVERPOSTS
OVERHAIR	OVERIDLE	OVERLET	OVERMIXED	OVERPOWER
OVERHAIRS	OVERING	OVERLETS	OVERMIXES	OVERPRESS
OVERHALE	OVERINKED	OVERLEWD	OVERMOUNT	OVERPRICE
OVERHALED	OVERISSUE	OVERLIE	OVERMUCH	OVERPRINT

OVERPRIZE	OVERSAILS	OVERSKIP	OVERSTREW	OVERTIMID
OVERPROOF	OVERSALE	OVERSKIPS	OVERSTUDY	OVERTIP
OVERPROUD	OVERSALES	OVERSKIRT	OVERSTUFF	OVERTIPS
OVERPUMP	OVERSALT	OVERSLEEP	OVERSTUNK	OVERTIRE
OVERPUMPS	OVERSALTS	OVERSLEPT	OVERSUDS	OVERTIRED
OVERQUICK	OVERSAUCE	OVERSLIP	OVERSUP	OVERTIRES
OVERRACK	OVERSAVE	OVERSLIPS	OVERSUPS	OVERTLY
OVERRACKS	OVERSAVED	OVERSLIPT	OVERSURE	OVERTNESS
OVERRAKE	OVERSAVES	OVERSLOW	OVERSWAM	OVERTOIL
OVERRAKED	OVERSAW	OVERSMAN	OVERSWAY	OVERTOILS
OVERRAKES	OVERSCALE	OVERSMEN	OVERSWAYS	OVERTONE
OVERRAN	OVERSCORE	OVERSMOKE	OVERSWEAR	OVERTONES
OVERRANK	OVERSEA	OVERSOAK	OVERSWEET	OVERTOOK
OVERRASH	OVERSEAS	OVERSOAKS	OVERSWELL	OVERTOP
OVERRATE	OVERSEE	OVERSOFT	OVERSWIM	OVERTOPS
OVERRATED	OVERSEED	OVERSOLD	OVERSWIMS	OVERTOWER
OVERRATES	OVERSEEDS	OVERSOON	OVERSWING	OVERTRADE
OVERREACH	OVERSEEN	OVERSOUL	OVERSWORE	OVERTRAIN
OVERREACT	OVERSEER	OVERSOULS	OVERSWORN	OVERTREAT
OVERREAD	OVERSEERS	OVERSOW	OVERSWUM	OVERTRICK
OVERREADS	OVERSEES	OVERSOWED	OVERSWUNG	OVERTRIM
OVERRED	OVERSELL	OVERSOWN	OVERT	OVERTRIMS
OVERREDS	OVERSELLS	OVERSOWS	OVERTAKE	OVERTRIP
OVERREN	OVERSET	OVERSPEND	OVERTAKEN	OVERTRIPS
OVERRENS	OVERSETS	OVERSPENT	OVERTAKES	OVERTRUMP
OVERRICH	OVERSEW	OVERSPICE	OVERTALK	OVERTRUST
OVERRIDE	OVERSEWED	OVERSPILL	OVERTALKS	OVERTURE
OVERRIDER	OVERSEWN	OVERSPILT	OVERTAME	OVERTURED
OVERRIDES	OVERSEWS	OVERSPIN	OVERTART	OVERTURES
OVERRIFE	OVERSEXED	OVERSPINS	OVERTASK	OVERTURN
OVERRIGID	OVERSHADE	OVERSTAFF	OVERTASKS	OVERTURNS
OVERRIPE	OVERSHARP	OVERSTAIN	OVERTAX	OVERTYPE
OVERRIPEN	OVERSHINE	OVERSTAND	OVERTAXED	OVERTYPED
OVERROAST	OVERSHIRT	OVERSTANK	OVERTAXES	OVERTYPES
OVERRODE	OVERSHOE	OVERSTARE	OVERTEACH	OVERURGE
OVERRUDE	OVERSHOES	OVERSTATE	OVERTEEM	OVERURGED
OVERRUFF	OVERSHONE	OVERSTAY	OVERTEEMS	OVERURGES
OVERRUFFS	OVERSHOOT	OVERSTAYS	OVERTHICK	OVERUSE
OVERRULE	OVERSHOT	OVERSTEER	OVERTHIN	OVERUSED
OVERRULED	OVERSHOTS	OVERSTEP	OVERTHINK	OVERUSES
OVERRULER	OVERSICK	OVERSTEPS	OVERTHREW	OVERUSING
OVERRULES	OVERSIDE	OVERSTINK	OVERTHROW	OVERVALUE
OVERRUN	OVERSIDES	OVERSTIR	OVERTIGHT	OVERVEIL
OVERRUNS	OVERSIGHT	OVERSTIRS	OVERTIME	OVERVEILS
OVERS	OVERSIZE	OVERSTOCK	OVERTIMED	OVERVIEW
OVERSAD	OVERSIZED	OVERSTOOD	OVERTIMER	OVERVIEWS
OVERSAIL	OVERSIZES	OVERSTORY	OVERTIMES	OVERVIVID

O

OVERVOTE	OVICIDE	OWED	OWT	OXIDATED
OVERVOTED	OVICIDES	OWELTIES	OWTS	OXIDATES
OVERVOTES	OVIDUCAL	OWELTY	OX	OXIDATING
OVERWARM	OVIDUCT	OWER	OXACILLIN	OXIDATION
OVERWARMS	OVIDUCTAL	OWERBY	OXALATE	OXIDATIVE
OVERWARY	OVIDUCTS	OWERLOUP	OXALATED	OXIDE
OVERWASH	OVIFEROUS	OWERLOUPS	OXALATES	OXIDES
OVERWATCH	OVIFORM	OWES	OXALATING	OXIDIC
OVERWATER	OVIGEROUS	OWING	OXALIC	OXIDISE
OVERWEAK	OVINE	OWL	OXALIS	OXIDISED
OVERWEAR	OVINES	OWLED	OXALISES	OXIDISER
OVERWEARS	OVIPARA	OWLER	OXAZEPAM	OXIDISERS
OVERWEARY	OVIPARITY	OWLERIES	OXAZEPAMS	OXIDISES
OVERWEEN	OVIPAROUS	OWLERS	OXAZINE	OXIDISING
OVERWEENS	OVIPOSIT	OWLERY	OXAZINES	OXIDIZE
OVERWEIGH	OVIPOSITS	OWLET	OXBLOOD	OXIDIZED
OVERWENT	OVIRAPTOR	OWLETS	OXBLOODS	OXIDIZER
OVERWET	OVISAC	OWLIER	OXBOW	OXIDIZERS
OVERWETS	OVISACS	OWLIEST	OXBOWS	OXIDIZES
OVERWHELM	OVIST	OWLING	OXCART	OXIDIZING
OVERWIDE	OVISTS	OWLISH	OXCARTS	OXIDS
OVERWILY	OVOID	OWLISHLY	OXEN	OXIES
OVERWIND	OVOIDAL	OWLLIKE	OXER	OXIM
OVERWINDS	OVOIDALS	OWLS	OXERS	OXIME
OVERWING	OVOIDS	OWLY	OXES	OXIMES
OVERWINGS	OVOLI	OWN	OXEYE	OXIMETER
OVERWISE	OVOLO	OWNABLE	OXEYES	OXIMETERS
OVERWORD	OVOLOS	OWNED	OXFORD	OXIMETRY
OVERWORDS	OVONIC	OWNER	OXFORDS	OXIMS
OVERWORE	OVONICS	OWNERLESS	OXGANG	OXLAND
OVERWORK	OVOTESTES	OWNERS	OXGANGS	OXLANDS
OVERWORKS	OVOTESTIS	OWNERSHIP	OXGATE	OXLIKE
OVERWORN	OVULAR	OWNING	OXGATES	OXLIP
OVERWOUND	OVULARY	OWNS	OXHEAD	OXLIPS
OVERWRAP	OVULATE	OWRE	OXHEADS	OXO
OVERWRAPS	OVULATED	OWRECOME	OXHEART	OXONIUM
OVERWREST	OVULATES	OWRECOMES	OXHEARTS	OXONIUMS
OVERWRITE	OVULATING	OWRELAY	OXHIDE	OXPECKER
OVERWROTE	OVULATION	OWRELAYS	OXHIDES	OXPECKERS
OVERYEAR	OVULATORY	OWRES	OXID	OXSLIP
OVERYEARS	OVULE	OWREWORD	OXIDABLE	OXSLIPS
OVERZEAL	OVULES	OWREWORDS	OXIDANT	OXTAIL
OVERZEALS	OVUM	OWRIE	OXIDANTS	OXTAILS
OVIBOS	OW	OWRIER	OXIDASE	OXTER
OVIBOSES	OWCHE	OWRIEST	OXIDASES	OXTERED
OVIBOVINE	OWCHES	OWSE	OXIDASIC	OXTERING
OVICIDAL	OWE	OWSEN	OXIDATE	OXTERS

O

OXTONGUE	OXYMORONS	OY	OYSTRIGE	OZONIDE
OXTONGUES	OXYNTIC	OYE	OYSTRIGES	OZONIDES
OXY	OXYPHIL	OYER	OZAENA	OZONISE
OXYACID	OXYPHILE	OYERS	OZAENAS	OZONISED
OXYACIDS	OXYPHILES	OYES	OZALID	OZONISER
OXYCODONE	OXYPHILIC	OYESES	OZALIDS	OZONISERS
OXYGEN	OXYPHILS	OYESSES	OZEKI	OZONISES
OXYGENASE	OXYSALT	OYEZ	OZEKIS	OZONISING
OXYGENATE	OXYSALTS	OYEZES	OZOCERITE	OZONIZE
OXYGENIC	OXYSOME	OYS	OZOKERITE	OZONIZED
OXYGENISE	OXYSOMES	OYSTER	OZONATE	OZONIZER
OXYGENIZE	OXYTOCIC	OYSTERED	OZONATED	OZONIZERS
OXYGENOUS	OXYTOCICS	OYSTERER	OZONATES	OZONIZES
OXYGENS	OXYTOCIN	OYSTERERS	OZONATING	OZONIZING
OXYMEL	OXYTOCINS	OYSTERING	OZONATION	OZONOUS
OXYMELS	OXYTONE	OYSTERMAN	OZONE	OZZIE
OXYMORA	OXYTONES	OYSTERMEN	OZONES	OZZIES
OXYMORON	OXYTONIC	OYSTERS	OZONIC	

O

P

PA	PACHUCOS	PACKMULE	PADDY	PAEDO
PAAL	PACHYDERM	PACKMULES	PADDYWACK	PAEDOLOGY
PAALS	PACHYTENE	PACKNESS	PADELLA	PAEDOS
PAAN	PACIER	PACKS	PADELLAS	PAELLA
PAANS	PACIEST	PACKSACK	PADEMELON	PAELLAS
PABLUM	PACIFIC	PACKSACKS	PADERERO	PAENULA
PABLUMS	PACIFICAE	PACKSHEET	PADEREROS	PAENULAE
PABOUCHE	PACIFICAL	PACKSTAFF	PADI	PAENULAS
PABOUCHES	PACIFIED	PACKWAX	PADIS	PAEON
PABULAR	PACIFIER	PACKWAXES	PADISHAH	PAEONIC
PABULOUS	PACIFIERS	PACKWAY	PADISHAHS	PAEONICS
PABULUM	PACIFIES	PACKWAYS	PADKOS	PAEONIES
PABULUMS	PACIFISM	PACO	PADLE	PAEONS
PAC	PACIFISMS	PACOS	PADLES	PAEONY
PACA	PACIFIST	PACS	PADLOCK	PAESAN
PACABLE	PACIFISTS	PACT	PADLOCKED	PAESANI
PACAS	PACIFY	PACTA	PADLOCKS	PAESANO
PACATION	PACIFYING	PACTION	PADMA	PAESANOS
PACATIONS	PACING	PACTIONAL	PADMAS	PAESANS
PACE	PACK	PACTIONED	PADNAG	PAGAN
PACED	PACKABLE	PACTIONS	PADNAGS	PAGANDOM
PACEMAKER	PACKAGE	PACTS	PADOUK	PAGANDOMS
PACEMAN	PACKAGED	PACTUM	PADOUKS	PAGANISE
PACEMEN	PACKAGER	PACY	PADRE	PAGANISED
PACER	PACKAGERS	PAD	PADRES	PAGANISER
PACERS	PACKAGES	PADANG	PADRI	PAGANISES
PACES	PACKAGING	PADANGS	PADRONE	PAGANISH
PACEWAY	PACKBOARD	PADAUK	PADRONES	PAGANISM
PACEWAYS	PACKCLOTH	PADAUKS	PADRONI	PAGANISMS
PACEY	PACKED	PADDED	PADRONISM	PAGANIST
PACHA	PACKER	PADDER	PADS	PAGANISTS
PACHADOM	PACKERS	PADDERS	PADSAW	PAGANIZE
PACHADOMS	PACKET	PADDIES	PADSAWS	PAGANIZED
PACHAK	PACKETED	PADDING	PADSHAH	PAGANIZER
PACHAKS	PACKETING	PADDINGS	PADSHAHS	PAGANIZES
PACHALIC	PACKETS	PADDLE	PADUASOY	PAGANS
PACHALICS	PACKFONG	PADDLED	PADUASOYS	PAGE
PACHAS	PACKFONGS	PADDLER	PADYMELON	PAGEANT
PACHINKO	PACKFRAME	PADDLERS	PAEAN	PAGEANTRY
PACHINKOS	PACKHORSE	PADDLES	PAEANISM	PAGEANTS
PACHISI	PACKING	PADDLING	PAEANISMS	PAGEBOY
PACHISIS	PACKINGS	PADDLINGS	PAEANS	PAGEBOYS
PACHOULI	PACKLY	PADDOCK	PAEDERAST	PAGED
PACHOULIS	PACKMAN	PADDOCKED	PAEDEUTIC	PAGEFUL
PACHUCO	PACKMEN	PADDOCKS	PAEDIATRY	PAGEFULS

PAGEHOOD	PAILLARDS	PAIRIALS	PALABRAS	PALEAL
PAGEHOODS	PAILLASSE	PAIRING	PALACE	PALEATE
PAGER	PAILLETTE	PAIRINGS	PALACED	PALEBUCK
PAGERS	PAILLON	PAIRS	PALACES	PALEBUCKS
PAGES	PAILLONS	PAIRWISE	PALADIN	PALED
PAGEVIEW	PAILS	PAIS	PALADINS	PALEFACE
PAGEVIEWS	PAILSFUL	PAISA	PALAESTRA	PALEFACES
PAGINAL	PAIN	PAISAN	PALAFITTE	PALELY
PAGINATE	PAINCH	PAISANA	PALAGI	PALEMPORE
PAGINATED	PAINCHES	PAISANAS	PALAGIS	PALENESS
PAGINATES	PAINED	PAISANO	PALAIS	PALEOCENE
PAGING	PAINFUL	PAISANOS	PALAMA	PALEOGENE
PAGINGS	PAINFULLY	PAISANS	PALAMAE	PALEOLITH
PAGLE	PAINIM	PAISAS	PALAMATE	PALEOLOGY
PAGLES	PAINIMS	PAISE	PALAMINO	PALEOSOL
PAGOD	PAINING	PAISLEY	PALAMINOS	PALEOSOLS
PAGODA	PAINLESS	PAISLEYS	PALAMPORE	PALEOZOIC
PAGODAS	PAINS	PAITRICK	PALANKEEN	PALER
PAGODS	PAINT	PAITRICKS	PALANQUIN	PALES
PAGRI	PAINTABLE	PAJAMA	PALAPA	PALEST
PAGRIS	PAINTBALL	PAJAMAED	PALAPAS	PALESTRA
PAGURIAN	PAINTBOX	PAJAMAS	PALAS	PALESTRAE
PAGURIANS	PAINTED	PAJOCK	PALASES	PALESTRAL
PAGURID	PAINTER	PAJOCKE	PALATABLE	PALESTRAS
PAGURIDS	PAINTERLY	PAJOCKES	PALATABLY	PALET
PAH	PAINTERS	PAJOCKS	PALATAL	PALETOT
PAHAUTEA	PAINTIER	PAKAHI	PALATALLY	PALETOTS
PAHAUTEAS	PAINTIEST	PAKAHIS	PALATALS	PALETS
PAHLAVI	PAINTING	PAKAPOO	PALATE	PALETTE
PAHLAVIS	PAINTINGS	PAKAPOOS	PALATED	PALETTES
PAHOEHOE	PAINTRESS	PAKEHA	PALATES	PALEWAYS
PAHOEHOES	PAINTS	PAKEHAS	PALATIAL	PALEWISE
PAHS	PAINTURE	PAKFONG	PALATINE	PALFREY
PAID	PAINTURES	PAKFONGS	PALATINES	PALFREYED
PAIDEUTIC	PAINTWORK	PAKIHI	PALATING	PALFREYS
PAIDLE	PAINTY	PAKIHIS	PALAVER	PALIER
PAIDLES	PAIOCK	PAKKA	PALAVERED	PALIEST
PAIGLE	PAIOCKE	PAKOKO	PALAVERER	PALIFORM
PAIGLES	PAIOCKES	PAKOKOS	PALAVERS	PALIKAR
PAIK	PAIOCKS	PAKORA	PALAY	PALIKARS
PAIKED	PAIR	PAKORAS	PALAYS	PALILALIA
PAIKING	PAIRE	PAKTHONG	PALAZZI	PALILLOGY
PAIKS	PAIRED	PAKTHONGS	PALAZZO	PALIMONY
PAIL	PAIRER	PAKTONG	PALAZZOS	PALING
PAILFUL	PAIRES	PAKTONGS	PALE	PALINGS
PAILFULS	PAIREST	PAL	PALEA	PALINKA
PAILLARD	PAIRIAL	PALABRA	PALEAE	PALINKAS

PALINODE	PALLIES	PALMITINS	PALSTAFFS	PAMS
PALINODES	PALLIEST	PALMLIKE	PALSTAVE	PAN
PALINODY	PALLING	PALMS	PALSTAVES	PANACEA
PALINOPIA	PALLIUM	PALMTOP	PALSY	PANACEAN
PALISADE	PALLIUMS	PALMTOPS	PALSYING	PANACEAS
PALISADED	PALLONE	PALMY	PALSYLIKE	PANACHAEA
PALISADES	PALLONES	PALMYRA	PALTER	PANACHE
PALISADO	PALLOR	PALMYRAS	PALTERED	PANACHES
PALISH	PALLORS	PALOLO	PALTERER	PANADA
PALKEE	PALLS	PALOLOS	PALTERERS	PANADAS
PALKEES	PALLY	PALOMINO	PALTERING	PANAMA
PALKI	PALLYING	PALOMINOS	PALTERS	PANAMAS
PALKIS	PALM	PALOOKA	PALTRIER	PANARIES
PALL	PALMAR	PALOOKAS	PALTRIEST	PANARY
PALLA	PALMARIAN	PALOVERDE	PALTRILY	PANATELA
PALLADIA	PALMARY	PALP	PALTRY	PANATELAS
PALLADIC	PALMATE	PALPABLE	PALUDAL	PANATELLA
PALLADIUM	PALMATED	PALPABLY	PALUDIC	PANAX
PALLADOUS	PALMATELY	PALPAL	PALUDINAL	PANAXES
PALLAE	PALMATION	PALPATE	PALUDINE	PANBROIL
PALLAH	PALMED	PALPATED	PALUDISM	PANBROILS
PALLAHS	PALMER	PALPATES	PALUDISMS	PANCAKE
PALLED	PALMERS	PALPATING	PALUDOSE	PANCAKED
PALLET	PALMETTE	PALPATION	PALUDOUS	PANCAKES
PALLETED	PALMETTES	PALPATOR	PALUSTRAL	PANCAKING
PALLETING	PALMETTO	PALPATORS	PALY	PANCE
PALLETISE	PALMETTOS	PALPATORY	PAM	PANCES
PALLETIZE	PALMFUL	PALPEBRA	PAMPA	PANCETTA
PALLETS	PALMFULS	PALPEBRAE	PAMPAS	PANCETTAS
PALLETTE	PALMHOUSE	PALPEBRAL	PAMPASES	PANCHAX
PALLETTES	PALMIE	PALPEBRAS	PAMPEAN	PANCHAXES
PALLIA	PALMIER	PALPED	PAMPEANS	PANCHAYAT
PALLIAL	PALMIES	PALPI	PAMPER	PANCHEON
PALLIARD	PALMIEST	PALPING	PAMPERED	PANCHEONS
PALLIARDS	PALMIET	PALPITANT	PAMPERER	PANCHION
PALLIASSE	PALMIETS	PALPITATE	PAMPERERS	PANCHIONS
PALLIATE	PALMING	PALPS	PAMPERING	PANCOSMIC
PALLIATED	PALMIPED	PALPUS	PAMPERO	PANCRATIA
PALLIATES	PALMIPEDE	PALS	PAMPEROS	PANCRATIC
PALLIATOR	PALMIPEDS	PALSGRAVE	PAMPERS	PANCREAS
PALLID	PALMIST	PALSHIP	PAMPHLET	PAND
PALLIDER	PALMISTER	PALSHIPS	PAMPHLETS	PANDA
PALLIDEST	PALMISTRY	PALSIED	PAMPHREY	PANDANI
PALLIDITY	PALMISTS	PALSIER	PAMPHREYS	PANDANUS
PALLIDLY	PALMITATE	PALSIES	PAMPOEN	PANDAR
PALLIED	PALMITIC	PALSIEST	PAMPOENS	PANDARED
PALLIER	PALMITIN	PALSTAFF	PAMPOOTIE	PANDARING

PANDARS	PANEITY	PANHUMAN	PANNICLES	PANTALONS
PANDAS	PANEL	PANIC	PANNIER	PANTALOON
PANDATION	PANELED	PANICALLY	PANNIERED	PANTDRESS
PANDECT	PANELESS	PANICK	PANNIERS	PANTED
PANDECTS	PANELING	PANICKED	PANNIKEL	PANTER
PANDEMIA	PANELINGS	PANICKIER	PANNIKELL	PANTERS
PANDEMIAN	PANELISED	PANICKING	PANNIKELS	PANTHEISM
PANDEMIAS	PANELIST	PANICKS	PANNIKIN	PANTHEIST
PANDEMIC	PANELISTS	PANICKY	PANNIKINS	PANTHENOL
PANDEMICS	PANELIZED	PANICLE	PANNING	PANTHEON
PANDER	PANELLED	PANICLED	PANNINGS	PANTHEONS
PANDERED	PANELLING	PANICLES	PANNOSE	PANTHER
PANDERER	PANELLIST	PANICS	PANNUS	PANTHERS
PANDERERS	PANELS	PANICUM	PANNUSES	PANTIE
PANDERESS	PANES	PANICUMS	PANOCHA	PANTIES
PANDERING	PANETELA	PANIER	PANOCHAS	PANTIHOSE
PANDERISM	PANETELAS	PANIERS	PANOCHE	PANTILE
PANDERLY	PANETELLA	PANIM	PANOCHES	PANTILED
PANDEROUS	PANETTONE	PANIMS	PANOISTIC	PANTILES
PANDERS	PANETTONI	PANING	PANOPLIED	PANTILING
PANDIED	PANFISH	PANINI	PANOPLIES	PANTINE
PANDIES	PANFISHES	PANINIS	PANOPLY	PANTINES
PANDIT	PANFRIED	PANINO	PANOPTIC	PANTING
PANDITS	PANFRIES	PANISC	PANORAMA	PANTINGLY
PANDOOR	PANFRY	PANISCS	PANORAMAS	PANTINGS
PANDOORS	PANFRYING	PANISK	PANORAMIC	PANTLER
PANDORA	PANFUL	PANISKS	PANPIPE	PANTLERS
PANDORAS	PANFULS	PANJANDRA	PANPIPES	PANTO
PANDORE	PANG	PANKO	PANS	PANTOFFLE
PANDORES	PANGA	PANKOS	PANSEXUAL	PANTOFLE
PANDOUR	PANGAMIC	PANLOGISM	PANSIED	PANTOFLES
PANDOURS	PANGAMIES	PANMICTIC	PANSIES	PANTOMIME
PANDOWDY	PANGAMY	PANMIXES	PANSOPHIC	PANTON
PANDS	PANGAS	PANMIXIA	PANSOPHY	PANTONS
PANDURA	PANGED	PANMIXIAS	PANSPERMY	PANTOS
PANDURAS	PANGEN	PANMIXIS	PANSTICK	PANTOUFLE
PANDURATE	PANGENE	PANNAGE	PANSTICKS	PANTOUM
PANDY	PANGENES	PANNAGES	PANSY	PANTOUMS
PANDYING	PANGENS	PANNE	PANT	PANTRIES
PANE	PANGING	PANNED	PANTABLE	PANTROPIC
PANED	PANGLESS	PANNELLED	PANTABLES	PANTRY
PANEER	PANGOLIN	PANNER	PANTAGAMY	PANTRYMAN
PANEERS	PANGOLINS	PANNERS	PANTALEON	PANTRYMEN
PANEGOISM	PANGRAM	PANNES	PANTALET	PANTS
PANEGYRIC	PANGRAMS	PANNICK	PANTALETS	PANTSUIT
PANEGYRY	PANGS	PANNICKS	PANTALON	PANTSUITS
PANEITIES	PANHANDLE	PANNICLE	PANTALONE	PANTUN

PANTUNS	PAPERBOY	PAPPADAMS	PARABOLAS	PARAFOIL
PANTY	PAPERBOYS	PAPPADOM	PARABOLE	PARAFOILS
PANTYHOSE	PAPERCLIP	PAPPADOMS	PARABOLES	PARAFORM
PANZER	PAPERED	PAPPED	PARABOLIC	PARAFORMS
PANZERS	PAPERER	PAPPI	PARABRAKE	PARAGE
PANZOOTIC	PAPERERS	PAPPIER	PARACHOR	PARAGES
PAOLI	PAPERGIRL	PAPPIES	PARACHORS	PARAGLIDE
PAOLO	PAPERIER	PAPPIEST	PARACHUTE	PARAGOGE
PAP	PAPERIEST	PAPPING	PARACLETE	PARAGOGES
PAPA	PAPERING	PAPPOOSE	PARACME	PARAGOGIC
PAPABLE	PAPERINGS	PAPPOOSES	PARACMES	PARAGOGUE
PAPACIES	PAPERLESS	PAPPOSE	PARACRINE	PARAGON
PAPACY	PAPERS	PAPPOUS	PARACUSES	PARAGONED
PAPADAM	PAPERWARE	PAPPUS	PARACUSIS	PARAGONS
PAPADAMS	PAPERWORK	PAPPUSES	PARADE	PARAGRAM
PAPADOM	PAPERY	PAPPY	PARADED	PARAGRAMS
PAPADOMS	PAPES	PAPRICA	PARADER	PARAGRAPH
PAPADUM	PAPETERIE	PAPRICAS	PARADERS	PARAKEET
PAPADUMS	PAPHIAN	PAPRIKA	PARADES	PARAKEETS
PAPAIN	PAPHIANS	PAPRIKAS	PARADIGM	PARAKELIA
PAPAINS	PAPILIO	PAPS	PARADIGMS	PARAKITE
PAPAL	PAPILIOS	PAPULA	PARADING	PARAKITES
PAPALISE	PAPILLA	PAPULAE	PARADISAL	PARALALIA
PAPALISED	PAPILLAE	PAPULAR	PARADISE	PARALEGAL
PAPALISES	PAPILLAR	PAPULE	PARADISES	PARALEXIA
PAPALISM	PAPILLARY	PAPULES	PARADISIC	PARALEXIC
PAPALISMS	PAPILLATE	PAPULOSE	PARADOR	PARALLAX
PAPALIST	PAPILLOMA	PAPULOUS	PARADORES	PARALLEL
PAPALISTS	PAPILLON	PAPYRAL	PARADORS	PARALLELS
PAPALIZE	PAPILLONS	PAPYRI	PARADOS	PARALOGIA
PAPALIZED	PAPILLOSE	PAPYRIAN	PARADOSES	PARALOGUE
PAPALIZES	PAPILLOTE	PAPYRINE	PARADOX	PARALOGY
PAPALLY	PAPILLOUS	PAPYRUS	PARADOXAL	PARALYSE
PAPARAZZI	PAPILLULE	PAPYRUSES	PARADOXER	PARALYSED
PAPARAZZO	PAPISH	PAR	PARADOXES	PARALYSER
PAPAS	PAPISHER	PARA	PARADOXY	PARALYSES
PAPAUMA	PAPISHERS	PARABASES	PARADROP	PARALYSIS
PAPAUMAS	PAPISHES	PARABASIS	PARADROPS	PARALYTIC
PAPAW	PAPISM	PARABEMA	PARAE	PARALYZE
PAPAWS	PAPISMS	PARABEN	PARAFFIN	PARALYZED
PAPAYA	PAPIST	PARABENS	PARAFFINE	PARALYZER
PAPAYAN	PAPISTIC	PARABLAST	PARAFFINS	PARALYZES
PAPAYAS	PAPISTRY	PARABLE	PARAFFINY	PARAMATTA
PAPE	PAPISTS	PARABLED	PARAFFLE	PARAMECIA
PAPER	PAPOOSE	PARABLES	PARAFFLES	PARAMEDIC
PAPERBACK	PAPOOSES	PARABLING	PARAFLE	PARAMENT
PAPERBARK	PAPPADAM	PARABOLA	PARAFLES	PARAMENTA

PARAMENTS

PARAMENTS	PARASAILS	PARCELS	PAREGORIC	PARGETING
PARAMESE	PARASANG	PARCENARY	PAREIRA	PARGETS
PARAMESES	PARASANGS	PARCENER	PAREIRAS	PARGETTED
PARAMETER	PARASCEVE	PARCENERS	PARELLA	PARGETTER
PARAMO	PARASHAH	PARCH	PARELLAS	PARGING
PARAMORPH	PARASHAHS	PARCHED	PARELLE	PARGINGS
PARAMOS	PARASHOT	PARCHEDLY	PARELLES	PARGO
PARAMOUNT	PARASHOTH	PARCHEESI	PARENESES	PARGOS
PARAMOUR	PARASITE	PARCHES	PARENESIS	PARGYLINE
PARAMOURS	PARASITES	PARCHESI	PARENT	PARHELIA
PARAMYLUM	PARASITIC	PARCHESIS	PARENTAGE	PARHELIC
PARANETE	PARASOL	PARCHING	PARENTAL	PARHELION
PARANETES	PARASOLED	PARCHISI	PARENTED	PARHYPATE
PARANG	PARASOLS	PARCHISIS	PARENTING	PARIAH
PARANGS	PARATAXES	PARCHMENT	PARENTS	PARIAHS
PARANOEA	PARATAXIS	PARCIMONY	PAREO	PARIAL
PARANOEAS	PARATHA	PARCLOSE	PAREOS	PARIALS
PARANOEIC	PARATHAS	PARCLOSES	PARER	PARIAN
PARANOIA	PARATHION	PARD	PARERA	PARIANS
PARANOIAC	PARATONIC	PARDAH	PARERAS	PARIES
PARANOIAS	PARATROOP	PARDAHS	PARERGA	PARIETAL
PARANOIC	PARAVAIL	PARDAL	PARERGON	PARIETALS
PARANOICS	PARAVANE	PARDALE	PARERS	PARIETIES
PARANOID	PARAVANES	PARDALES	PARES	PARING
PARANOIDS	PARAVANT	PARDALIS	PARESES	PARINGS
PARANYM	PARAVAUNT	PARDALOTE	PARESIS	PARIS
PARANYMPH	PARAWING	PARDALS	PARETIC	PARISCHAN
PARANYMS	PARAWINGS	PARDED	PARETICS	PARISES
PARAPARA	PARAXIAL	PARDEE	PAREU	PARISH
PARAPARAS	PARAZOA	PARDI	PAREUS	PARISHAD
PARAPENTE	PARAZOAN	PARDIE	PAREV	PARISHADS
PARAPET	PARAZOANS	PARDINE	PAREVE	PARISHEN
PARAPETED	PARAZOON	PARDNER	PARFAIT	PARISHENS
PARAPETS	PARBAKE	PARDNERS	PARFAITS	PARISHES
PARAPH	PARBAKED	PARDON	PARFLECHE	PARISON
PARAPHED	PARBAKES	PARDONED	PARFLESH	PARISONS
PARAPHING	PARBAKING	PARDONER	PARFOCAL	PARITIES
PARAPHS	PARBOIL	PARDONERS	PARGANA	PARITOR
PARAPODIA	PARBOILED	PARDONING	PARGANAS	PARITORS
PARAQUAT	PARBOILS	PARDONS	PARGASITE	PARITY
PARAQUATS	PARBREAK	PARDS	PARGE	PARK
PARAQUET	PARBREAKS	PARDY	PARGED	PARKA
PARAQUETS	PARBUCKLE	PARE	PARGES	PARKADE
PARAQUITO	PARCEL	PARECIOUS	PARGET	PARKADES
PARARHYME	PARCELED	PARECISM	PARGETED	PARKAS
PARAS	PARCELING	PARECISMS	PARGETER	PARKED
PARASAIL	PARCELLED	PARED	PARGETERS	PARKEE

PARKEES	PARLIES	PAROSMIA	PARRIED	PARSONS
PARKER	PARLING	PAROSMIAS	PARRIER	PART
PARKERS	PARLOR	PAROTIC	PARRIERS	PARTAKE
PARKETTE	PARLORS	PAROTID	PARRIES	PARTAKEN
PARKETTES	PARLOUR	PAROTIDES	PARRING	PARTAKER
PARKI	PARLOURS	PAROTIDS	PARRITCH	PARTAKERS
PARKIE	PARLOUS	PAROTIS	PARROCK	PARTAKES
PARKIER	PARLOUSLY	PAROTITIC	PARROCKED	PARTAKING
PARKIES	PARLY	PAROTITIS	PARROCKS	PARTAN
PARKIEST	PARMESAN	PAROTOID	PARROKET	PARTANS
PARKIN	PARMESANS	PAROTOIDS	PARROKETS	PARTED
PARKING	PAROCHIAL	PAROUS	PARROQUET	PARTER
PARKINGS	PAROCHIN	PAROUSIA	PARROT	PARTERRE
PARKINS	PAROCHINE	PAROUSIAS	PARROTED	PARTERRES
PARKIS	PAROCHINS	PAROXYSM	PARROTER	PARTERS
PARKISH	PARODIC	PAROXYSMS	PARROTERS	PARTI
PARKLAND	PARODICAL	PARP	PARROTING	PARTIAL
PARKLANDS	PARODIED	PARPANE	PARROTRY	PARTIALLY
PARKLIKE	PARODIES	PARPANES	PARROTS	PARTIALS
PARKLY	PARODIST	PARPED	PARROTY	PARTIBLE
PARKOUR	PARODISTS	PARPEN	PARRS	PARTICLE
PARKOURS	PARODOI	PARPEND	PARRY	PARTICLES
PARKS	PARODOS	PARPENDS	PARRYING	PARTIED
PARKWARD	PARODY	PARPENS	PARS	PARTIER
PARKWARDS	PARODYING	PARPENT	PARSABLE	PARTIERS
PARKWAY	PAROEMIA	PARPENTS	PARSE	PARTIES
PARKWAYS	PAROEMIAC	PARPING	PARSEC	PARTIM
PARKY	PAROEMIAL	PARPOINT	PARSECS	PARTING
PARLANCE	PAROEMIAS	PARPOINTS	PARSED	PARTINGS
PARLANCES	PAROICOUS	PARPS	PARSER	PARTIS
PARLANDO	PAROL	PARQUET	PARSERS	PARTISAN
PARLANTE	PAROLABLE	PARQUETED	PARSES	PARTISANS
PARLAY	PAROLE	PARQUETRY	PARSIMONY	PARTITA
PARLAYED	PAROLED	PARQUETS	PARSING	PARTITAS
PARLAYING	PAROLEE	PARR	PARSINGS	PARTITE
PARLAYS	PAROLEES	PARRA	PARSLEY	PARTITION
PARLE	PAROLES	PARRAKEET	PARSLEYED	PARTITIVE
PARLED	PAROLING	PARRAL	PARSLEYS	PARTITURA
PARLEMENT	PAROLS	PARRALS	PARSLIED	PARTIZAN
PARLES	PARONYM	PARRAS	PARSNEP	PARTIZANS
PARLEY	PARONYMIC	PARRED	PARSNEPS	PARTLET
PARLEYED	PARONYMS	PARREL	PARSNIP	PARTLETS
PARLEYER	PARONYMY	PARRELS	PARSNIPS	PARTLY
PARLEYERS	PAROQUET	PARRHESIA	PARSON	PARTNER
PARLEYING	PAROQUETS	PARRICIDE	PARSONAGE	PARTNERED
PARLEYS	PARORE	PARRIDGE	PARSONIC	PARTNERS
PARLEYVOO	PARORES	PARRIDGES	PARSONISH	PARTON

P

PARTONS	PASEARING	PASSAGING	PASSMENTS	PASTINESS
PARTOOK	PASEARS	PASSALONG	PASSOUT	PASTING
PARTRIDGE	PASELA	PASSAMENT	PASSOUTS	PASTINGS
PARTS	PASELAS	PASSANT	PASSOVER	PASTIS
PARTURE	PASEO	PASSATA	PASSOVERS	PASTISES
PARTURES	PASEOS	PASSATAS	PASSPORT	PASTITSIO
PARTWAY	PASES	PASSBAND	PASSPORTS	PASTITSO
PARTWORK	PASH	PASSBANDS	PASSUS	PASTITSOS
PARTWORKS	PASHA	PASSBOOK	PASSUSES	PASTLESS
PARTY	PASHADOM	PASSBOOKS	PASSWORD	PASTNESS
PARTYER	PASHADOMS	PASSE	PASSWORDS	PASTOR
PARTYERS	PASHALIC	PASSED	PAST	PASTORAL
PARTYGOER	PASHALICS	PASSEE	PASTA	PASTORALE
PARTYING	PASHALIK	PASSEL	PASTALIKE	PASTORALI
PARTYISM	PASHALIKS	PASSELS	PASTANCE	PASTORALS
PARTYISMS	PASHAS	PASSEMENT	PASTANCES	PASTORATE
PARULIDES	PASHED	PASSENGER	PASTAS	PASTORED
PARULIS	PASHES	PASSEPIED	PASTE	PASTORING
PARULISES	PASHIM	PASSER	PASTED	PASTORIUM
PARURA	PASHIMS	PASSERBY	PASTEDOWN	PASTORLY
PARURAS	PASHING	PASSERINE	PASTEL	PASTORS
PARURE	PASHKA	PASSERS	PASTELIST	PASTRAMI
PARURES	PASHKAS	PASSERSBY	PASTELS	PASTRAMIS
PARURESES	PASHM	PASSES	PASTER	PASTRIES
PARURESIS	PASHMINA	PASSIBLE	PASTERN	PASTROMI
PARVE	PASHMINAS	PASSIBLY	PASTERNS	PASTROMIS
PARVENU	PASHMS	PASSIM	PASTERS	PASTRY
PARVENUE	PASODOBLE	PASSING	PASTES	PASTS
PARVENUES	PASPALUM	PASSINGLY	PASTEUP	PASTURAGE
PARVENUS	PASPALUMS	PASSINGS	PASTEUPS	PASTURAL
PARVIS	PASPIES	PASSION	PASTICCI	PASTURE
PARVISE	PASPY	PASSIONAL	PASTICCIO	PASTURED
PARVISES	PASQUIL	PASSIONED	PASTICHE	PASTURER
PARVO	PASQUILER	PASSIONS	PASTICHES	PASTURERS
PARVOLIN	PASQUILS	PASSIVATE	PASTIE	PASTURES
PARVOLINE	PASS	PASSIVE	PASTIER	PASTURING
PARVOLINS	PASSABLE	PASSIVELY	PASTIES	PASTY
PARVOS	PASSABLY	PASSIVES	PASTIEST	PAT
PAS	PASSADE	PASSIVISM	PASTIL	PATACA
PASCAL	PASSADES	PASSIVIST	PASTILLE	PATACAS
PASCALS	PASSADO	PASSIVITY	PASTILLES	PATAGIA
PASCHAL	PASSADOES	PASSKEY	PASTILS	PATAGIAL
PASCHALS	PASSADOS	PASSKEYS	PASTILY	PATAGIUM
PASCUAL	PASSAGE	PASSLESS	PASTIME	PATAKA
PASE	PASSAGED	PASSMAN	PASTIMES	PATAKAS
PASEAR	PASSAGER	PASSMEN	PASTINA	PATAMAR
PASEARED	PASSAGES	PASSMENT	PASTINAS	PATAMARS

P

PATBALL	PATERS	PATINIZE	PATRONLY	PATZERS
PATBALLS	PATES	PATINIZED	PATRONNE	PAUA
PATCH	PATH	PATINIZES	PATRONNES	PAUAS
PATCHABLE	PATHED	PATINS	PATRONS	PAUCAL
PATCHED	PATHETIC	PATIO	PATROON	PAUCALS
PATCHER	PATHETICS	PATIOS	PATROONS	PAUCITIES
PATCHERS	PATHIC	PATISSIER	PATS	PAUCITY
PATCHERY	PATHICS	PATKA	PATSIES	PAUGHTIER
PATCHES	PATHING	PATKAS	PATSY	PAUGHTY
PATCHIER	PATHLESS	PATLY	PATTAMAR	PAUL
PATCHIEST	PATHNAME	PATNESS	PATTAMARS	PAULDRON
PATCHILY	PATHNAMES	PATNESSES	PATTE	PAULDRONS
PATCHING	PATHOGEN	PATOIS	PATTED	PAULIN
PATCHINGS	PATHOGENE	PATONCE	PATTEE	PAULINS
PATCHOCKE	PATHOGENS	PATOOTIE	PATTEN	PAULOWNIA
PATCHOULI	PATHOGENY	PATOOTIES	PATTENED	PAULS
PATCHOULY	PATHOLOGY	PATRIAL	PATTENING	PAUNCE
PATCHWORK	PATHOS	PATRIALS	PATTENS	PAUNCES
PATCHY	PATHOSES	PATRIARCH	PATTER	PAUNCH
PATE	PATHS	PATRIATE	PATTERED	PAUNCHED
PATED	PATHWAY	PATRIATED	PATTERER	PAUNCHES
PATELLA	PATHWAYS	PATRIATES	PATTERERS	PAUNCHIER
PATELLAE	PATIBLE	PATRICIAN	PATTERING	PAUNCHING
PATELLAR	PATIENCE	PATRICIDE	PATTERN	PAUNCHY
PATELLAS	PATIENCES	PATRICK	PATTERNED	PAUPER
PATELLATE	PATIENT	PATRICKS	PATTERNS	PAUPERED
PATEN	PATIENTED	PATRICO	PATTERS	PAUPERESS
PATENCIES	PATIENTER	PATRICOES	PATTES	PAUPERING
PATENCY	PATIENTLY	PATRILINY	PATTIE	PAUPERISE
PATENS	PATIENTS	PATRIMONY	PATTIES	PAUPERISM
PATENT	PATIKI	PATRIOT	PATTING	PAUPERIZE
PATENTED	PATIKIS	PATRIOTIC	PATTLE	PAUPERS
PATENTEE	PATIN	PATRIOTS	PATTLES	PAUPIETTE
PATENTEES	PATINA	PATRISTIC	PATTRESS	PAUROPOD
PATENTING	PATINAE	PATROL	PATTY	PAUROPODS
PATENTLY	PATINAED	PATROLLED	PATTYPAN	PAUSAL
PATENTOR	PATINAS	PATROLLER	PATTYPANS	PAUSE
PATENTORS	PATINATE	PATROLMAN	PATU	PAUSED
PATENTS	PATINATED	PATROLMEN	PATULENT	PAUSEFUL
PATER	PATINATES	PATROLOGY	PATULIN	PAUSELESS
PATERA	PATINE	PATROLS	PATULINS	PAUSER
PATERAE	PATINED	PATRON	PATULOUS	PAUSERS
PATERCOVE	PATINES	PATRONAGE	PATUS	PAUSES
PATERERO	PATINING	PATRONAL	PATUTUKI	PAUSING
PATEREROS	PATINISE	PATRONESS	PATUTUKIS	PAUSINGLY
PATERNAL	PATINISED	PATRONISE	PATY	PAUSINGS
PATERNITY	PATINISES	PATRONIZE	PATZER	PAV

P

PAVAGE
PAVAGES
PAVAN
PAVANE
PAVANES
PAVANS
PAVE
PAVED
PAVEED
PAVEMENT
PAVEMENTS
PAVEN
PAVENS
PAVER
PAVERS
PAVES
PAVID
PAVILION
PAVILIONS
PAVILLON
PAVILLONS
PAVIN
PAVING
PAVINGS
PAVINS
PAVIOR
PAVIORS
PAVIOUR
PAVIOURS
PAVIS
PAVISE
PAVISER
PAVISERS
PAVISES
PAVISSE
PAVISSES
PAVLOVA
PAVLOVAS
PAVONAZZO
PAVONE
PAVONES
PAVONIAN
PAVONINE
PAVS
PAW
PAWA
PAWAS

PAWAW
PAWAWED
PAWAWING
PAWAWS
PAWED
PAWER
PAWERS
PAWING
PAWK
PAWKIER
PAWKIEST
PAWKILY
PAWKINESS
PAWKS
PAWKY
PAWL
PAWLS
PAWN
PAWNABLE
PAWNAGE
PAWNAGES
PAWNCE
PAWNCES
PAWNED
PAWNEE
PAWNEES
PAWNER
PAWNERS
PAWNING
PAWNOR
PAWNORS
PAWNS
PAWNSHOP
PAWNSHOPS
PAWPAW
PAWPAWS
PAWS
PAX
PAXES
PAXIUBA
PAXIUBAS
PAXWAX
PAXWAXES
PAY
PAYABLE
PAYABLES
PAYABLY

PAYBACK
PAYBACKS
PAYCHECK
PAYCHECKS
PAYDAY
PAYDAYS
PAYED
PAYEE
PAYEES
PAYER
PAYERS
PAYFONE
PAYFONES
PAYGRADE
PAYGRADES
PAYING
PAYINGS
PAYLIST
PAYLISTS
PAYLOAD
PAYLOADS
PAYMASTER
PAYMENT
PAYMENTS
PAYNIM
PAYNIMRY
PAYNIMS
PAYOFF
PAYOFFS
PAYOLA
PAYOLAS
PAYOR
PAYORS
PAYOUT
PAYOUTS
PAYPHONE
PAYPHONES
PAYROLL
PAYROLLS
PAYS
PAYSAGE
PAYSAGES
PAYSAGIST
PAYSD
PAYSLIP
PAYSLIPS
PAZAZZ

PAZAZZES
PAZZAZZ
PAZZAZZES
PE
PEA
PEABERRY
PEACE
PEACEABLE
PEACEABLY
PEACED
PEACEFUL
PEACELESS
PEACENIK
PEACENIKS
PEACES
PEACETIME
PEACH
PEACHBLOW
PEACHED
PEACHER
PEACHERS
PEACHES
PEACHIER
PEACHIEST
PEACHILY
PEACHING
PEACHY
PEACING
PEACOAT
PEACOATS
PEACOCK
PEACOCKED
PEACOCKS
PEACOCKY
PEACOD
PEACODS
PEAFOWL
PEAFOWLS
PEAG
PEAGE
PEAGES
PEAGS
PEAHEN
PEAHENS
PEAK
PEAKED
PEAKIER

PEAKIEST
PEAKING
PEAKISH
PEAKLESS
PEAKLIKE
PEAKS
PEAKY
PEAL
PEALED
PEALIKE
PEALING
PEALS
PEAN
PEANED
PEANING
PEANS
PEANUT
PEANUTS
PEAPOD
PEAPODS
PEAR
PEARCE
PEARCED
PEARCES
PEARCING
PEARE
PEARES
PEARL
PEARLASH
PEARLED
PEARLER
PEARLERS
PEARLIER
PEARLIES
PEARLIEST
PEARLIN
PEARLING
PEARLINGS
PEARLINS
PEARLISED
PEARLITE
PEARLITES
PEARLITIC
PEARLIZED
PEARLS
PEARLWORT
PEARLY

PEARMAIN	PEAZED	PECORINO	PEDALED	PEDIATRIC
PEARMAINS	PEAZES	PECORINOS	PEDALER	PEDICAB
PEARS	PEAZING	PECS	PEDALERS	PEDICABS
PEARST	PEBA	PECTASE	PEDALFER	PEDICEL
PEART	PEBAS	PECTASES	PEDALFERS	PEDICELS
PEARTER	PEBBLE	PECTATE	PEDALIER	PEDICLE
PEARTEST	PEBBLED	PECTATES	PEDALIERS	PEDICLED
PEARTLY	PEBBLES	PECTEN	PEDALING	PEDICLES
PEARTNESS	PEBBLIER	PECTENS	PEDALLED	PEDICULAR
PEARWOOD	PEBBLIEST	PECTIC	PEDALLER	PEDICULI
PEARWOODS	PEBBLING	PECTIN	PEDALLERS	PEDICULUS
PEAS	PEBBLINGS	PECTINAL	PEDALLING	PEDICURE
PEASANT	PEBBLY	PECTINATE	PEDALO	PEDICURED
PEASANTRY	PEBRINE	PECTINEAL	PEDALOES	PEDICURES
PEASANTS	PEBRINES	PECTINES	PEDALOS	PEDIFORM
PEASANTY	PEC	PECTINOUS	PEDALS	PEDIGREE
PEASCOD	PECAN	PECTINS	PEDANT	PEDIGREED
PEASCODS	PECANS	PECTISE	PEDANTIC	PEDIGREES
PEASE	PECCABLE	PECTISED	PEDANTISE	PEDIMENT
PEASECOD	PECCANCY	PECTISES	PEDANTISM	PEDIMENTS
PEASECODS	PECCANT	PECTISING	PEDANTIZE	PEDIPALP
PEASED	PECCANTLY	PECTIZE	PEDANTRY	PEDIPALPI
PEASEN	PECCARIES	PECTIZED	PEDANTS	PEDIPALPS
PEASES	PECCARY	PECTIZES	PEDATE	PEDLAR
PEASING	PECCAVI	PECTIZING	PEDATELY	PEDLARIES
PEASON	PECCAVIS	PECTOLITE	PEDATIFID	PEDLARS
PEASOUPER	PECH	PECTORAL	PEDDER	PEDLARY
PEAT	PECHAN	PECTORALS	PEDDERS	PEDLER
PEATARIES	PECHANS	PECTOSE	PEDDLE	PEDLERIES
PEATARY	PECHED	PECTOSES	PEDDLED	PEDLERS
PEATERIES	PECHING	PECULATE	PEDDLER	PEDLERY
PEATERY	PECHS	PECULATED	PEDDLERS	PEDOCAL
PEATIER	PECK	PECULATES	PEDDLERY	PEDOCALIC
PEATIEST	PECKE	PECULATOR	PEDDLES	PEDOCALS
PEATLAND	PECKED	PECULIA	PEDDLING	PEDOGENIC
PEATLANDS	PECKER	PECULIAR	PEDDLINGS	PEDOLOGIC
PEATMAN	PECKERS	PECULIARS	PEDERAST	PEDOLOGY
PEATMEN	PECKES	PECULIUM	PEDERASTS	PEDOMETER
PEATS	PECKIER	PECUNIARY	PEDERASTY	PEDOPHILE
PEATSHIP	PECKIEST	PECUNIOUS	PEDERERO	PEDORTHIC
PEATSHIPS	PECKING	PED	PEDEREROS	PEDRAIL
PEATY	PECKINGS	PEDAGOG	PEDES	PEDRAILS
PEAVEY	PECKISH	PEDAGOGIC	PEDESES	PEDRERO
PEAVEYS	PECKISHLY	PEDAGOGS	PEDESIS	PEDREROES
PEAVIES	PECKS	PEDAGOGUE	PEDESTAL	PEDREROS
PEAVY	PECKY	PEDAGOGY	PEDESTALS	PEDRO
PEAZE	PECORINI	PEDAL	PEDETIC	PEDROS

P

PEDS	PEEPHOLES	PEGGING	PEKINS	PELLITORY
PEDUNCLE	PEEPING	PEGGINGS	PEKOE	PELLMELL
PEDUNCLED	PEEPS	PEGGY	PEKOES	PELLMELLS
PEDUNCLES	PEEPSHOW	PEGH	PEL	PELLOCK
PEE	PEEPSHOWS	PEGHED	PELA	PELLOCKS
PEEBEEN	PEEPUL	PEGHING	PELAGE	PELLS
PEEBEENS	PEEPULS	PEGHS	PELAGES	PELLUCID
PEECE	PEER	PEGLEGGED	PELAGIAL	PELLUM
PEECES	PEERAGE	PEGLESS	PELAGIAN	PELLUMS
PEED	PEERAGES	PEGLIKE	PELAGIANS	PELMA
PEEING	PEERED	PEGMATITE	PELAGIC	PELMANISM
PEEK	PEERESS	PEGS	PELAGICS	PELMAS
PEEKABO	PEERESSES	PEH	PELAS	PELMATIC
PEEKABOO	PEERIE	PEHS	PELE	PELMET
PEEKABOOS	PEERIER	PEIGNOIR	PELECYPOD	PELMETS
PEEKABOS	PEERIES	PEIGNOIRS	PELERINE	PELOID
PEEKAPOO	PEERIEST	PEIN	PELERINES	PELOIDS
PEEKAPOOS	PEERING	PEINCT	PELES	PELOLOGY
PEEKED	PEERLESS	PEINCTED	PELF	PELON
PEEKING	PEERS	PEINCTING	PELFS	PELORIA
PEEKS	PEERY	PEINCTS	PELHAM	PELORIAN
PEEL	PEES	PEINED	PELHAMS	PELORIAS
PEELABLE	PEESWEEP	PEINING	PELICAN	PELORIC
PEELED	PEESWEEPS	PEINS	PELICANS	PELORIES
PEELER	PEETWEET	PEIRASTIC	PELISSE	PELORISED
PEELERS	PEETWEETS	PEISE	PELISSES	PELORISM
PEELING	PEEVE	PEISED	PELITE	PELORISMS
PEELINGS	PEEVED	PEISES	PELITES	PELORIZED
PEELS	PEEVER	PEISHWA	PELITIC	PELORUS
PEEN	PEEVERS	PEISHWAH	PELL	PELORUSES
PEENED	PEEVES	PEISHWAHS	PELLACH	PELORY
PEENGE	PEEVING	PEISHWAS	PELLACHS	PELOTA
PEENGED	PEEVISH	PEISING	PELLACK	PELOTAS
PEENGEING	PEEVISHLY	PEIZE	PELLACKS	PELOTON
PEENGES	PEEWEE	PEIZED	PELLAGRA	PELOTONS
PEENGING	PEEWEES	PEIZES	PELLAGRAS	PELS
PEENING	PEEWIT	PEIZING	PELLAGRIN	PELT
PEENS	PEEWITS	PEJORATE	PELLET	PELTA
PEEOY	PEG	PEJORATED	PELLETAL	PELTAE
PEEOYS	PEGASUS	PEJORATES	PELLETED	PELTAS
PEEP	PEGASUSES	PEKAN	PELLETIFY	PELTAST
PEEPE	PEGBOARD	PEKANS	PELLETING	PELTASTS
PEEPED	PEGBOARDS	PEKE	PELLETISE	PELTATE
PEEPER	PEGBOX	PEKEPOO	PELLETIZE	PELTATELY
PEEPERS	PEGBOXES	PEKEPOOS	PELLETS	PELTATION
PEEPES	PEGGED	PEKES	PELLICLE	PELTED
PEEPHOLE	PEGGIES	PEKIN	PELLICLES	PELTER

PELTERED	PENATES	PENETRATE	PENNANTS	PENSEES
PELTERING	PENCE	PENFOLD	PENNATE	PENSEL
PELTERS	PENCEL	PENFOLDS	PENNATED	PENSELS
PELTING	PENCELS	PENFUL	PENNATULA	PENSIL
PELTINGLY	PENCES	PENFULS	PENNE	PENSILE
PELTINGS	PENCHANT	PENGO	PENNED	PENSILITY
PELTLESS	PENCHANTS	PENGOS	PENNEECH	PENSILS
PELTRIES	PENCIL	PENGUIN	PENNEECHS	PENSION
PELTRY	PENCILED	PENGUINRY	PENNEECK	PENSIONE
PELTS	PENCILER	PENGUINS	PENNEECKS	PENSIONED
PELVES	PENCILERS	PENHOLDER	PENNER	PENSIONER
PELVIC	PENCILING	PENI	PENNERS	PENSIONES
PELVICS	PENCILLED	PENIAL	PENNES	PENSIONS
PELVIFORM	PENCILLER	PENICIL	PENNI	PENSIVE
PELVIS	PENCILS	PENICILS	PENNIA	PENSIVELY
PELVISES	PENCRAFT	PENIE	PENNIED	PENSTEMON
PEMBINA	PENCRAFTS	PENIES	PENNIES	PENSTER
PEMBINAS	PEND	PENILE	PENNIFORM	PENSTERS
PEMBROKE	PENDANT	PENILL	PENNILESS	PENSTOCK
PEMBROKES	PENDANTLY	PENILLION	PENNILL	PENSTOCKS
PEMICAN	PENDANTS	PENING	PENNINE	PENSUM
PEMICANS	PENDED	PENINSULA	PENNINES	PENSUMS
PEMMICAN	PENDENCY	PENIS	PENNING	PENT
PEMMICANS	PENDENT	PENISES	PENNINITE	PENTACLE
PEMOLINE	PENDENTLY	PENISTONE	PENNIS	PENTACLES
PEMOLINES	PENDENTS	PENITENCE	PENNON	PENTACT
PEMPHIGUS	PENDICLE	PENITENCY	PENNONCEL	PENTACTS
PEMPHIX	PENDICLER	PENITENT	PENNONED	PENTAD
PEMPHIXES	PENDICLES	PENITENTS	PENNONS	PENTADIC
PEN	PENDING	PENK	PENNY	PENTADS
PENAL	PENDRAGON	PENKNIFE	PENNYBOY	PENTAGON
PENALISE	PENDS	PENKNIVES	PENNYBOYS	PENTAGONS
PENALISED	PENDU	PENKS	PENNYFEE	PENTAGRAM
PENALISES	PENDULAR	PENLIGHT	PENNYFEES	PENTALOGY
PENALITY	PENDULATE	PENLIGHTS	PENNYLAND	PENTALPHA
PENALIZE	PENDULE	PENLITE	PENNYWISE	PENTAMERY
PENALIZED	PENDULES	PENLITES	PENNYWORT	PENTANE
PENALIZES	PENDULINE	PENMAN	PENOCHE	PENTANES
PENALLY	PENDULOUS	PENMEN	PENOCHES	PENTANGLE
PENALTIES	PENDULUM	PENNA	PENOLOGY	PENTANOIC
PENALTY	PENDULUMS	PENNAE	PENONCEL	PENTANOL
PENANCE	PENE	PENNAL	PENONCELS	PENTANOLS
PENANCED	PENED	PENNALISM	PENPOINT	PENTAPODY
PENANCES	PENEPLAIN	PENNALS	PENPOINTS	PENTARCH
PENANCING	PENEPLANE	PENNAME	PENPUSHER	PENTARCHS
PENANG	PENES	PENNAMES	PENS	PENTARCHY
PENANGS	PENETRANT	PENNANT	PENSEE	PENTATHLA

P

PENTENE
PENTENES
PENTHIA
PENTHIAS
PENTHOUSE
PENTICE
PENTICED
PENTICES
PENTICING
PENTISE
PENTISED
PENTISES
PENTISING
PENTITI
PENTITO
PENTODE
PENTODES
PENTOMIC
PENTOSAN
PENTOSANE
PENTOSANS
PENTOSE
PENTOSES
PENTOSIDE
PENTOXIDE
PENTROOF
PENTROOFS
PENTS
PENTYL
PENTYLENE
PENTYLS
PENUCHE
PENUCHES
PENUCHI
PENUCHIS
PENUCHLE
PENUCHLES
PENUCKLE
PENUCKLES
PENULT
PENULTIMA
PENULTS
PENUMBRA
PENUMBRAE
PENUMBRAL
PENUMBRAS
PENURIES

PENURIOUS
PENURY
PENWOMAN
PENWOMEN
PEON
PEONAGE
PEONAGES
PEONES
PEONIES
PEONISM
PEONISMS
PEONS
PEONY
PEOPLE
PEOPLED
PEOPLER
PEOPLERS
PEOPLES
PEOPLING
PEP
PEPERINO
PEPERINOS
PEPEROMIA
PEPERONI
PEPERONIS
PEPFUL
PEPINO
PEPINOS
PEPLA
PEPLOS
PEPLOSES
PEPLUM
PEPLUMED
PEPLUMS
PEPLUS
PEPLUSES
PEPO
PEPONIDA
PEPONIDAS
PEPONIUM
PEPONIUMS
PEPOS
PEPPED
PEPPER
PEPPERBOX
PEPPERED
PEPPERER

PEPPERERS
PEPPERIER
PEPPERING
PEPPERONI
PEPPERS
PEPPERY
PEPPIER
PEPPIEST
PEPPILY
PEPPINESS
PEPPING
PEPPY
PEPS
PEPSIN
PEPSINATE
PEPSINE
PEPSINES
PEPSINS
PEPTALK
PEPTALKED
PEPTALKS
PEPTIC
PEPTICITY
PEPTICS
PEPTID
PEPTIDASE
PEPTIDE
PEPTIDES
PEPTIDIC
PEPTIDS
PEPTISE
PEPTISED
PEPTISER
PEPTISERS
PEPTISES
PEPTISING
PEPTIZE
PEPTIZED
PEPTIZER
PEPTIZERS
PEPTIZES
PEPTIZING
PEPTONE
PEPTONES
PEPTONIC
PEPTONISE
PEPTONIZE

PEQUISTE
PEQUISTES
PER
PERACID
PERACIDS
PERACUTE
PERAEA
PERAEON
PERAEONS
PERAEOPOD
PERAI
PERAIS
PERBORATE
PERCALE
PERCALES
PERCALINE
PERCASE
PERCE
PERCEABLE
PERCEANT
PERCED
PERCEIVE
PERCEIVED
PERCEIVER
PERCEIVES
PERCEN
PERCENT
PERCENTAL
PERCENTS
PERCEPT
PERCEPTS
PERCES
PERCH
PERCHANCE
PERCHED
PERCHER
PERCHERON
PERCHERS
PERCHERY
PERCHES
PERCHING
PERCHINGS
PERCIFORM
PERCINE
PERCING
PERCOCT
PERCOID

PERCOIDS
PERCOLATE
PERCOLIN
PERCOLINS
PERCUSS
PERCUSSED
PERCUSSES
PERCUSSOR
PERDENDO
PERDIE
PERDITION
PERDU
PERDUE
PERDUES
PERDURE
PERDURED
PERDURES
PERDURING
PERDUS
PERDY
PERE
PEREA
PEREGAL
PEREGALS
PEREGRIN
PEREGRINE
PEREGRINS
PEREIA
PEREION
PEREIONS
PEREIOPOD
PEREIRA
PEREIRAS
PERENNATE
PERENNIAL
PERENNITY
PERENTIE
PERENTIES
PERENTY
PEREON
PEREONS
PEREOPOD
PEREOPODS
PERES
PERFAY
PERFECT
PERFECTA

P

PERFECTAS	PERI	PERIGON	PERIPETIA	PERKILY
PERFECTED	PERIAGUA	PERIGONE	PERIPETY	PERKIN
PERFECTER	PERIAGUAS	PERIGONES	PERIPHERY	PERKINESS
PERFECTI	PERIAKTOI	PERIGONIA	PERIPLASM	PERKING
PERFECTLY	PERIAKTOS	PERIGONS	PERIPLAST	PERKINS
PERFECTO	PERIANTH	PERIGYNY	PERIPLUS	PERKISH
PERFECTOR	PERIANTHS	PERIHELIA	PERIPROCT	PERKS
PERFECTOS	PERIAPSES	PERIKARYA	PERIPTER	PERKY
PERFECTS	PERIAPSIS	PERIL	PERIPTERS	PERLEMOEN
PERFERVID	PERIAPT	PERILED	PERIPTERY	PERLITE
PERFERVOR	PERIAPTS	PERILING	PERIQUE	PERLITES
PERFET	PERIBLAST	PERILLA	PERIQUES	PERLITIC
PERFIDIES	PERIBLEM	PERILLAS	PERIS	PERLOUS
PERFIDY	PERIBLEMS	PERILLED	PERISARC	PERM
PERFIN	PERIBOLI	PERILLING	PERISARCS	PERMALINK
PERFING	PERIBOLOI	PERILOUS	PERISCIAN	PERMALLOY
PERFINGS	PERIBOLOS	PERILS	PERISCOPE	PERMANENT
PERFINS	PERIBOLUS	PERILUNE	PERISH	PERMATAN
PERFORANS	PERICARP	PERILUNES	PERISHED	PERMATANS
PERFORANT	PERICARPS	PERILYMPH	PERISHER	PERMEABLE
PERFORATE	PERICLASE	PERIMETER	PERISHERS	PERMEABLY
PERFORCE	PERICLINE	PERIMETRY	PERISHES	PERMEANCE
PERFORM	PERICON	PERIMORPH	PERISHING	PERMEANT
PERFORMED	PERICONES	PERIMYSIA	PERISPERM	PERMEANTS
PERFORMER	PERICOPAE	PERINAEUM	PERISTOME	PERMEASE
PERFORMS	PERICOPAL	PERINATAL	PERISTYLE	PERMEASES
PERFUME	PERICOPE	PERINEA	PERITI	PERMEATE
PERFUMED	PERICOPES	PERINEAL	PERITONEA	PERMEATED
PERFUMER	PERICOPIC	PERINEUM	PERITRACK	PERMEATES
PERFUMERS	PERICYCLE	PERINEUMS	PERITRICH	PERMEATOR
PERFUMERY	PERIDERM	PERIOD	PERITUS	PERMED
PERFUMES	PERIDERMS	PERIODATE	PERIWIG	PERMIAN
PERFUMIER	PERIDIA	PERIODED	PERIWIGS	PERMIE
PERFUMING	PERIDIAL	PERIODIC	PERJINK	PERMIES
PERFUMY	PERIDINIA	PERIODID	PERJURE	PERMING
PERFUSATE	PERIDIUM	PERIODIDE	PERJURED	PERMIT
PERFUSE	PERIDIUMS	PERIODIDS	PERJURER	PERMITS
PERFUSED	PERIDOT	PERIODING	PERJURES	PERMITTED
PERFUSES	PERIDOTE	PERIODISE	PERJURIES	PERMITTEE
PERFUSING	PERIDOTES	PERIODIZE	PERJURING	PERMITTER
PERFUSION	PERIDOTIC	PERIODS	PERJUROUS	PERMS
PERFUSIVE	PERIDOTS	PERIOST	PERJURY	PERMUTATE
PERGOLA	PERIDROME	PERIOSTEA	PERK	PERMUTE
PERGOLAS	PERIGEAL	PERIOSTS	PERKED	PERMUTED
PERGUNNAH	PERIGEAN	PERIOTIC	PERKIER	PERMUTES
PERHAPS	PERIGEE	PERIOTICS	PERKIEST	PERMUTING
PERHAPSES	PERIGEES	PERIPATUS		PERN

PERNANCY	PERRUQUE	PERSUADER	PERUSERS	PESKILY
PERNIO	PERRUQUES	PERSUADES	PERUSES	PESKINESS
PERNIONES	PERRY	PERSUE	PERUSING	PESKY
PERNOD	PERSALT	PERSUED	PERV	PESO
PERNODS	PERSALTS	PERSUES	PERVADE	PESOS
PERNS	PERSANT	PERSUING	PERVADED	PESSARIES
PEROGI	PERSAUNT	PERSWADE	PERVADER	PESSARY
PEROGIES	PERSE	PERSWADED	PERVADERS	PESSIMA
PERONE	PERSECUTE	PERSWADES	PERVADES	PESSIMAL
PERONEAL	PERSEITY	PERT	PERVADING	PESSIMISM
PERONES	PERSELINE	PERTAIN	PERVASION	PESSIMIST
PERONEUS	PERSES	PERTAINED	PERVASIVE	PESSIMUM
PERORAL	PERSEVERE	PERTAINS	PERVE	PEST
PERORALLY	PERSICO	PERTAKE	PERVED	PESTER
PERORATE	PERSICOS	PERTAKEN	PERVERSE	PESTERED
PERORATED	PERSICOT	PERTAKES	PERVERSER	PESTERER
PERORATES	PERSICOTS	PERTAKING	PERVERT	PESTERERS
PERORATOR	PERSIENNE	PERTER	PERVERTED	PESTERING
PEROVSKIA	PERSIMMON	PERTEST	PERVERTER	PESTEROUS
PEROXID	PERSING	PERTHITE	PERVERTS	PESTERS
PEROXIDE	PERSIST	PERTHITES	PERVES	PESTFUL
PEROXIDED	PERSISTED	PERTHITIC	PERVIATE	PESTHOLE
PEROXIDES	PERSISTER	PERTINENT	PERVIATED	PESTHOLES
PEROXIDIC	PERSISTS	PERTLY	PERVIATES	PESTHOUSE
PEROXIDS	PERSON	PERTNESS	PERVICACY	PESTICIDE
PEROXO	PERSONA	PERTOOK	PERVIER	PESTIER
PEROXY	PERSONAE	PERTS	PERVIEST	PESTIEST
PERP	PERSONAGE	PERTURB	PERVING	PESTILENT
PERPEND	PERSONAL	PERTURBED	PERVIOUS	PESTLE
PERPENDED	PERSONALS	PERTURBER	PERVS	PESTLED
PERPENDS	PERSONAS	PERTURBS	PERVY	PESTLES
PERPENT	PERSONATE	PERTUSATE	PES	PESTLING
PERPENTS	PERSONIFY	PERTUSE	PESADE	PESTO
PERPETUAL	PERSONISE	PERTUSED	PESADES	PESTOLOGY
PERPLEX	PERSONIZE	PERTUSION	PESANT	PESTOS
PERPLEXED	PERSONNED	PERTUSSAL	PESANTE	PESTS
PERPLEXER	PERSONNEL	PERTUSSES	PESANTS	PESTY
PERPLEXES	PERSONS	PERTUSSIS	PESAUNT	PET
PERPS	PERSPEX	PERUKE	PESAUNTS	PETABYTE
PERRADIAL	PERSPEXES	PERUKED	PESETA	PETABYTES
PERRADII	PERSPIRE	PERUKES	PESETAS	PETAFLOP
PERRADIUS	PERSPIRED	PERUSABLE	PESEWA	PETAFLOPS
PERRIER	PERSPIRES	PERUSAL	PESEWAS	PETAHERTZ
PERRIERS	PERSPIRY	PERUSALS	PESHWA	PETAL
PERRIES	PERST	PERUSE	PESHWAS	PETALED
PERRON	PERSUADE	PERUSED	PESKIER	PETALINE
PERRONS	PERSUADED	PERUSER	PESKIEST	PETALISM

PETALISMS	PETIT	PETTEDLY	PEYOTIST	PHALLI
PETALLED	PETITE	PETTER	PEYOTISTS	PHALLIC
PETALLIKE	PETITES	PETTERS	PEYOTL	PHALLIN
PETALODIC	PETITION	PETTI	PEYOTLS	PHALLINS
PETALODY	PETITIONS	PETTICOAT	PEYSE	PHALLISM
PETALOID	PETITORY	PETTIER	PEYSED	PHALLISMS
PETALOUS	PETNAP	PETTIES	PEYSES	PHALLIST
PETALS	PETNAPER	PETTIEST	PEYSING	PHALLISTS
PETANQUE	PETNAPERS	PETTIFOG	PEYTRAL	PHALLOID
PETANQUES	PETNAPING	PETTIFOGS	PEYTRALS	PHALLUS
PETAR	PETNAPPED	PETTILY	PEYTREL	PHALLUSES
PETARA	PETNAPPER	PETTINESS	PEYTRELS	PHANG
PETARAS	PETNAPS	PETTING	PEZANT	PHANGED
PETARD	PETRALE	PETTINGS	PEZANTS	PHANGING
PETARDS	PETRALES	PETTISH	PEZIZOID	PHANGS
PETARIES	PETRARIES	PETTISHLY	PFENNIG	PHANSIGAR
PETARS	PETRARY	PETTITOES	PFENNIGE	PHANTASIM
PETARY	PETRE	PETTLE	PFENNIGS	PHANTASM
PETASOS	PETREL	PETTLED	PFENNING	PHANTASMA
PETASOSES	PETRELS	PETTLES	PFENNINGS	PHANTASMS
PETASUS	PETRES	PETTLING	PFFT	PHANTAST
PETASUSES	PETRI	PETTO	PFUI	PHANTASTS
PETAURINE	PETRIFIC	PETTY	PHACELIA	PHANTASY
PETAURIST	PETRIFIED	PETULANCE	PHACELIAS	PHANTOM
PETCHARY	PETRIFIER	PETULANCY	PHACOID	PHANTOMS
PETCOCK	PETRIFIES	PETULANT	PHACOIDAL	PHANTOMY
PETCOCKS	PETRIFY	PETUNIA	PHACOLITE	PHANTOSME
PETECHIA	PETROGENY	PETUNIAS	PHACOLITH	PHARAOH
PETECHIAE	PETROGRAM	PETUNTSE	PHAEIC	PHARAOHS
PETECHIAL	PETROL	PETUNTSES	PHAEISM	PHARAONIC
PETER	PETROLAGE	PETUNTZE	PHAEISMS	PHARE
PETERED	PETROLEUM	PETUNTZES	PHAENOGAM	PHARES
PETERING	PETROLEUR	PEW	PHAETON	PHARISAIC
PETERMAN	PETROLIC	PEWEE	PHAETONS	PHARISEE
PETERMEN	PETROLLED	PEWEES	PHAGE	PHARISEES
PETERS	PETROLOGY	PEWHOLDER	PHAGEDENA	PHARM
PETERSHAM	PETROLS	PEWIT	PHAGES	PHARMA
PETHER	PETRONEL	PEWITS	PHAGOCYTE	PHARMACY
PETHERS	PETRONELS	PEWS	PHAGOSOME	PHARMAS
PETHIDINE	PETROSAL	PEWTER	PHALANGAL	PHARMED
PETILLANT	PETROSALS	PEWTERER	PHALANGE	PHARMING
PETIOLAR	PETROUS	PEWTERERS	PHALANGER	PHARMINGS
PETIOLATE	PETS	PEWTERS	PHALANGES	PHARMS
PETIOLE	PETSAI	PEYOTE	PHALANGID	PHAROS
PETIOLED	PETSAIS	PEYOTES	PHALANX	PHAROSES
PETIOLES	PETTABLE	PEYOTISM	PHALANXES	PHARYNGAL
PETIOLULE	PETTED	PEYOTISMS	PHALAROPE	PHARYNGES

P

PHARYNX	PHENAKITE	PHEW	PHIZES	PHONATES
PHARYNXES	PHENATE	PHI	PHIZOG	PHONATHON
PHASE	PHENATES	PHIAL	PHIZOGS	PHONATING
PHASEAL	PHENAZIN	PHIALLED	PHIZZES	PHONATION
PHASED	PHENAZINE	PHIALLING	PHLEBITIC	PHONATORY
PHASEDOWN	PHENAZINS	PHIALS	PHLEBITIS	PHONE
PHASELESS	PHENE	PHILABEG	PHLEGM	PHONECAM
PHASEOLIN	PHENES	PHILABEGS	PHLEGMIER	PHONECAMS
PHASEOUT	PHENETIC	PHILAMOT	PHLEGMON	PHONECARD
PHASEOUTS	PHENETICS	PHILAMOTS	PHLEGMONS	PHONED
PHASES	PHENETOL	PHILANDER	PHLEGMS	PHONEME
PHASIC	PHENETOLE	PHILATELY	PHLEGMY	PHONEMES
PHASING	PHENETOLS	PHILHORSE	PHLOEM	PHONEMIC
PHASINGS	PHENGITE	PHILIBEG	PHLOEMS	PHONEMICS
PHASIS	PHENGITES	PHILIBEGS	PHLOMIS	PHONER
PHASMID	PHENIC	PHILIPPIC	PHLOMISES	PHONERS
PHASMIDS	PHENIX	PHILISTIA	PHLORIZIN	PHONES
PHASOR	PHENIXES	PHILLABEG	PHLOX	PHONETIC
PHASORS	PHENOCOPY	PHILLIBEG	PHLOXES	PHONETICS
PHAT	PHENOGAM	PHILOGYNY	PHLYCTENA	PHONETISE
PHATIC	PHENOGAMS	PHILOLOGY	PHO	PHONETISM
PHATTER	PHENOL	PHILOMATH	PHOBIA	PHONETIST
PHATTEST	PHENOLATE	PHILOMEL	PHOBIAS	PHONETIZE
PHEASANT	PHENOLIC	PHILOMELA	PHOBIC	PHONEY
PHEASANTS	PHENOLICS	PHILOMELS	PHOBICS	PHONEYED
PHEAZAR	PHENOLOGY	PHILOMOT	PHOBISM	PHONEYING
PHEAZARS	PHENOLS	PHILOMOTS	PHOBISMS	PHONEYS
PHEER	PHENOM	PHILOPENA	PHOBIST	PHONIC
PHEERE	PHENOMENA	PHILTER	PHOBISTS	PHONICS
PHEERES	PHENOMS	PHILTERED	PHOCA	PHONIED
PHEERS	PHENOTYPE	PHILTERS	PHOCAE	PHONIER
PHEESE	PHENOXIDE	PHILTRA	PHOCAS	PHONIES
PHEESED	PHENOXY	PHILTRE	PHOCINE	PHONIEST
PHEESES	PHENYL	PHILTRED	PHOCOMELY	PHONILY
PHEESING	PHENYLENE	PHILTRES	PHOEBE	PHONINESS
PHEEZE	PHENYLIC	PHILTRING	PHOEBES	PHONING
PHEEZED	PHENYLS	PHILTRUM	PHOEBUS	PHONMETER
PHEEZES	PHENYTOIN	PHIMOSES	PHOEBUSES	PHONO
PHEEZING	PHEON	PHIMOSIS	PHOENIX	PHONOGRAM
PHELLEM	PHEONS	PHIMOTIC	PHOENIXES	PHONOLITE
PHELLEMS	PHERESES	PHINNOCK	PHOH	PHONOLOGY
PHELLOGEN	PHERESIS	PHINNOCKS	PHOLADES	PHONON
PHELLOID	PHEROMONE	PHIS	PHOLAS	PHONONS
PHELONIA	PHESE	PHISHING	PHON	PHONOPORE
PHELONION	PHESED	PHISHINGS	PHONAL	PHONOS
PHENACITE	PHESES	PHISNOMY	PHONATE	PHONOTYPE
PHENAKISM	PHESING	PHIZ	PHONATED	PHONOTYPY

PHONS	PHOTOGENS	PHRATRAL	PHYLARCH	PHYSICKY
PHONY	PHOTOGENY	PHRATRIC	PHYLARCHS	PHYSICS
PHONYING	PHOTOGRAM	PHRATRIES	PHYLARCHY	PHYSIO
PHOOEY	PHOTOGS	PHRATRY	PHYLAXIS	PHYSIOS
PHORATE	PHOTOING	PHREAK	PHYLE	PHYSIQUE
PHORATES	PHOTOLYSE	PHREAKED	PHYLESES	PHYSIQUED
PHORESIES	PHOTOLYZE	PHREAKER	PHYLESIS	PHYSIQUES
PHORESY	PHOTOMAP	PHREAKERS	PHYLETIC	PHYSIS
PHORMINX	PHOTOMAPS	PHREAKING	PHYLETICS	PHYTANE
PHORMIUM	PHOTOMASK	PHREAKS	PHYLIC	PHYTANES
PHORMIUMS	PHOTON	PHREATIC	PHYLLARY	PHYTIN
PHORONID	PHOTONIC	PHRENESES	PHYLLID	PHYTINS
PHORONIDS	PHOTONICS	PHRENESIS	PHYLLIDS	PHYTOGENY
PHOS	PHOTONS	PHRENETIC	PHYLLITE	PHYTOID
PHOSGENE	PHOTOPHIL	PHRENIC	PHYLLITES	PHYTOL
PHOSGENES	PHOTOPIA	PHRENICS	PHYLLITIC	PHYTOLITH
PHOSPHATE	PHOTOPIAS	PHRENISM	PHYLLO	PHYTOLOGY
PHOSPHENE	PHOTOPIC	PHRENISMS	PHYLLODE	PHYTOLS
PHOSPHID	PHOTOPLAY	PHRENITIC	PHYLLODES	PHYTON
PHOSPHIDE	PHOTOPSIA	PHRENITIS	PHYLLODIA	PHYTONIC
PHOSPHIDS	PHOTOPSY	PHRENSIED	PHYLLODY	PHYTONS
PHOSPHIN	PHOTOS	PHRENSIES	PHYLLOID	PHYTOSES
PHOSPHINE	PHOTOSCAN	PHRENSY	PHYLLOIDS	PHYTOSIS
PHOSPHINS	PHOTOSET	PHRENTICK	PHYLLOME	PHYTOTOMY
PHOSPHITE	PHOTOSETS	PHRYGANA	PHYLLOMES	PHYTOTRON
PHOSPHOR	PHOTOSHOP	PHRYGANAS	PHYLLOMIC	PI
PHOSPHORE	PHOTOSTAT	PHT	PHYLLOPOD	PIA
PHOSPHORI	PHOTOTAXY	PHTHALATE	PHYLLOS	PIACEVOLE
PHOSPHORS	PHOTOTUBE	PHTHALEIN	PHYLOGENY	PIACULAR
PHOSSY	PHOTOTYPE	PHTHALIC	PHYLON	PIAFFE
PHOT	PHOTOTYPY	PHTHALIN	PHYLUM	PIAFFED
PHOTIC	PHOTS	PHTHALINS	PHYSALIA	PIAFFER
PHOTICS	PHPHT	PHTHISES	PHYSALIAS	PIAFFERS
PHOTINIA	PHRASAL	PHTHISIC	PHYSALIS	PIAFFES
PHOTINIAS	PHRASALLY	PHTHISICS	PHYSED	PIAFFING
PHOTISM	PHRASE	PHTHISIS	PHYSEDS	PIAL
PHOTISMS	PHRASED	PHUT	PHYSES	PIAN
PHOTO	PHRASEMAN	PHUTS	PHYSETER	PIANETTE
PHOTOCARD	PHRASEMEN	PHUTTED	PHYSETERS	PIANETTES
PHOTOCELL	PHRASER	PHUTTING	PHYSIATRY	PIANI
PHOTOCOPY	PHRASERS	PHWOAH	PHYSIC	PIANIC
PHOTOED	PHRASES	PHWOAR	PHYSICAL	PIANINO
PHOTOFIT	PHRASIER	PHYCOCYAN	PHYSICALS	PIANINOS
PHOTOFITS	PHRASIEST	PHYCOLOGY	PHYSICIAN	PIANISM
PHOTOG	PHRASING	PHYLA	PHYSICISM	PIANISMS
PHOTOGEN	PHRASINGS	PHYLAE	PHYSICIST	PIANIST
PHOTOGENE	PHRASY	PHYLAR	PHYSICKED	PIANISTE

P

PIANISTES	PICARO	PICKERIES	PICOGRAMS	PICTURIZE
PIANISTIC	PICAROON	PICKERS	PICOLIN	PICUL
PIANISTS	PICAROONS	PICKERY	PICOLINE	PICULET
PIANO	PICAROS	PICKET	PICOLINES	PICULETS
PIANOLIST	PICAS	PICKETED	PICOLINIC	PICULS
PIANOS	PICAYUNE	PICKETER	PICOLINS	PIDDLE
PIANS	PICAYUNES	PICKETERS	PICOMETER	PIDDLED
PIARIST	PICCADILL	PICKETING	PICOMETRE	PIDDLER
PIARISTS	PICCANIN	PICKETS	PICOMOLE	PIDDLERS
PIAS	PICCANINS	PICKIER	PICOMOLES	PIDDLES
PIASABA	PICCATA	PICKIEST	PICONG	PIDDLIER
PIASABAS	PICCIES	PICKILY	PICONGS	PIDDLIEST
PIASAVA	PICCOLO	PICKIN	PICOT	PIDDLING
PIASAVAS	PICCOLOS	PICKINESS	PICOTE	PIDDLY
PIASSABA	PICCY	PICKING	PICOTED	PIDDOCK
PIASSABAS	PICE	PICKINGS	PICOTEE	PIDDOCKS
PIASSAVA	PICENE	PICKINS	PICOTEES	PIDGEON
PIASSAVAS	PICENES	PICKLE	PICOTING	PIDGEONS
PIASTER	PICEOUS	PICKLED	PICOTITE	PIDGIN
PIASTERS	PICHOLINE	PICKLER	PICOTITES	PIDGINISE
PIASTRE	PICHURIM	PICKLERS	PICOTS	PIDGINIZE
PIASTRES	PICHURIMS	PICKLES	PICOWAVE	PIDGINS
PIAZZA	PICIFORM	PICKLING	PICOWAVED	PIE
PIAZZAS	PICINE	PICKLOCK	PICOWAVES	PIEBALD
PIAZZE	PICK	PICKLOCKS	PICQUET	PIEBALDS
PIAZZIAN	PICKABACK	PICKMAW	PICQUETED	PIECE
PIBAL	PICKABLE	PICKMAWS	PICQUETS	PIECED
PIBALS	PICKADIL	PICKOFF	PICRA	PIECELESS
PIBROCH	PICKADILL	PICKOFFS	PICRAS	PIECEMEAL
PIBROCHS	PICKADILS	PICKPROOF	PICRATE	PIECEN
PIC	PICKAPACK	PICKS	PICRATED	PIECENED
PICA	PICKAROON	PICKTHANK	PICRATES	PIECENER
PICACHO	PICKAX	PICKUP	PICRIC	PIECENERS
PICACHOS	PICKAXE	PICKUPS	PICRITE	PIECENING
PICADILLO	PICKAXED	PICKWICK	PICRITES	PIECENS
PICADOR	PICKAXES	PICKWICKS	PICRITIC	PIECER
PICADORES	PICKAXING	PICKY	PICS	PIECERS
PICADORS	PICKBACK	PICLORAM	PICTARNIE	PIECES
PICAL	PICKBACKS	PICLORAMS	PICTOGRAM	PIECEWISE
PICAMAR	PICKED	PICNIC	PICTORIAL	PIECEWORK
PICAMARS	PICKEER	PICNICKED	PICTURAL	PIECING
PICANINNY	PICKEERED	PICNICKER	PICTURALS	PIECINGS
PICANTE	PICKEERER	PICNICKY	PICTURE	PIECRUST
PICARA	PICKEERS	PICNICS	PICTURED	PIECRUSTS
PICARAS	PICKER	PICOCURIE	PICTURES	PIED
PICARIAN	PICKEREL	PICOFARAD	PICTURING	PIEDFORT
PICARIANS	PICKERELS	PICOGRAM	PICTURISE	PIEDFORTS

PIEDISH	PIETIES	PIGGISHLY	PIGSNIES	PILAFFS
PIEDISHES	PIETISM	PIGGY	PIGSNY	PILAFS
PIEDMONT	PIETISMS	PIGGYBACK	PIGSTICK	PILAO
PIEDMONTS	PIETIST	PIGHEADED	PIGSTICKS	PILAOS
PIEDNESS	PIETISTIC	PIGHT	PIGSTIES	PILAR
PIEFORT	PIETISTS	PIGHTED	PIGSTUCK	PILASTER
PIEFORTS	PIETS	PIGHTING	PIGSTY	PILASTERS
PIEHOLE	PIETY	PIGHTLE	PIGSWILL	PILAU
PIEHOLES	PIEZO	PIGHTLES	PIGSWILLS	PILAUS
PIEING	PIFFERARI	PIGHTS	PIGTAIL	PILAW
PIEMAN	PIFFERARO	PIGLET	PIGTAILED	PILAWS
PIEMEN	PIFFERO	PIGLETS	PIGTAILS	PILCH
PIEND	PIFFEROS	PIGLIKE	PIGWASH	PILCHARD
PIENDS	PIFFLE	PIGLING	PIGWASHES	PILCHARDS
PIEPLANT	PIFFLED	PIGLINGS	PIGWEED	PILCHER
PIEPLANTS	PIFFLER	PIGMAEAN	PIGWEEDS	PILCHERS
PIEPOWDER	PIFFLERS	PIGMEAN	PIHOIHOI	PILCHES
PIER	PIFFLES	PIGMEAT	PIHOIHOIS	PILCORN
PIERAGE	PIFFLING	PIGMEATS	PIING	PILCORNS
PIERAGES	PIG	PIGMENT	PIKA	PILCROW
PIERCE	PIGBOAT	PIGMENTAL	PIKAKE	PILCROWS
PIERCED	PIGBOATS	PIGMENTED	PIKAKES	PILE
PIERCER	PIGEON	PIGMENTS	PIKAS	PILEA
PIERCERS	PIGEONED	PIGMIES	PIKAU	PILEAS
PIERCES	PIGEONING	PIGMOID	PIKAUS	PILEATE
PIERCING	PIGEONITE	PIGMY	PIKE	PILEATED
PIERCINGS	PIGEONRY	PIGNERATE	PIKED	PILED
PIERHEAD	PIGEONS	PIGNOLI	PIKELET	PILEI
PIERHEADS	PIGFACE	PIGNOLIA	PIKELETS	PILELESS
PIERID	PIGFACES	PIGNOLIAS	PIKEMAN	PILEOUS
PIERIDINE	PIGFEED	PIGNOLIS	PIKEMEN	PILER
PIERIDS	PIGFEEDS	PIGNORA	PIKEPERCH	PILERS
PIERIS	PIGFISH	PIGNORATE	PIKER	PILES
PIERISES	PIGFISHES	PIGNUS	PIKERS	PILEUM
PIEROGI	PIGGED	PIGNUT	PIKES	PILEUP
PIEROGIES	PIGGERIES	PIGNUTS	PIKESTAFF	PILEUPS
PIERRETTE	PIGGERY	PIGOUT	PIKEY	PILEUS
PIERROT	PIGGIE	PIGOUTS	PIKEYS	PILEWORK
PIERROTS	PIGGIER	PIGPEN	PIKI	PILEWORKS
PIERS	PIGGIES	PIGPENS	PIKING	PILEWORT
PIERST	PIGGIEST	PIGS	PIKINGS	PILEWORTS
PIERT	PIGGIN	PIGSCONCE	PIKIS	PILFER
PIERTS	PIGGINESS	PIGSKIN	PIKUL	PILFERAGE
PIES	PIGGING	PIGSKINS	PIKULS	PILFERED
PIET	PIGGINGS	PIGSNEY	PILA	PILFERER
PIETA	PIGGINS	PIGSNEYS	PILAF	PILFERERS
PIETAS	PIGGISH	PIGSNIE	PILAFF	PILFERIES

P

PILFERING	PILLORY	PIMENTON	PINCERS	PINETUM
PILFERS	PILLOW	PIMENTONS	PINCH	PINEWOOD
PILFERY	PILLOWED	PIMENTOS	PINCHBECK	PINEWOODS
PILGARLIC	PILLOWING	PIMENTS	PINCHBUG	PINEY
PILGRIM	PILLOWS	PIMIENTO	PINCHBUGS	PINFALL
PILGRIMER	PILLOWY	PIMIENTOS	PINCHCOCK	PINFALLS
PILGRIMS	PILLS	PIMP	PINCHECK	PINFISH
PILI	PILLWORM	PIMPED	PINCHECKS	PINFISHES
PILIFORM	PILLWORMS	PIMPERNEL	PINCHED	PINFOLD
PILING	PILLWORT	PIMPING	PINCHER	PINFOLDED
PILINGS	PILLWORTS	PIMPINGS	PINCHERS	PINFOLDS
PILINUT	PILOMOTOR	PIMPLE	PINCHES	PING
PILINUTS	PILONIDAL	PIMPLED	PINCHFIST	PINGED
PILIS	PILOSE	PIMPLES	PINCHGUT	PINGER
PILL	PILOSITY	PIMPLIER	PINCHGUTS	PINGERS
PILLAGE	PILOT	PIMPLIEST	PINCHING	PINGING
PILLAGED	PILOTAGE	PIMPLY	PINCHINGS	PINGLE
PILLAGER	PILOTAGES	PIMPS	PINDAN	PINGLED
PILLAGERS	PILOTED	PIN	PINDANS	PINGLER
PILLAGES	PILOTFISH	PINA	PINDAREE	PINGLERS
PILLAGING	PILOTING	PINACEOUS	PINDAREES	PINGLES
PILLAR	PILOTINGS	PINACOID	PINDARI	PINGLING
PILLARED	PILOTIS	PINACOIDS	PINDARIS	PINGO
PILLARING	PILOTLESS	PINAFORE	PINDER	PINGOES
PILLARIST	PILOTMAN	PINAFORED	PINDERS	PINGOS
PILLARS	PILOTMEN	PINAFORES	PINDLING	PINGPONG
PILLAU	PILOTS	PINAKOID	PINDOWN	PINGPONGS
PILLAUS	PILOUS	PINAKOIDS	PINDOWNS	PINGRASS
PILLBOX	PILOW	PINANG	PINE	PINGS
PILLBOXES	PILOWS	PINANGS	PINEAL	PINGUEFY
PILLED	PILSENER	PINAS	PINEALS	PINGUID
PILLHEAD	PILSENERS	PINASTER	PINEAPPLE	PINGUIN
PILLHEADS	PILSNER	PINASTERS	PINECONE	PINGUINS
PILLICOCK	PILSNERS	PINATA	PINECONES	PINHEAD
PILLIE	PILULA	PINATAS	PINED	PINHEADED
PILLIES	PILULAE	PINBALL	PINEDROPS	PINHEADS
PILLING	PILULAR	PINBALLED	PINELAND	PINHOLE
PILLINGS	PILULAS	PINBALLS	PINELANDS	PINHOLES
PILLION	PILULE	PINBOARD	PINELIKE	PINHOOKER
PILLIONED	PILULES	PINBOARDS	PINENE	PINIER
PILLIONS	PILUM	PINBONE	PINENES	PINIES
PILLOCK	PILUS	PINBONES	PINERIES	PINIEST
PILLOCKS	PILY	PINCASE	PINERY	PINING
PILLORIED	PIMA	PINCASES	PINES	PINION
PILLORIES	PIMAS	PINCER	PINESAP	PINIONED
PILLORISE	PIMENT	PINCERED	PINESAPS	PINIONING
PILLORIZE	PIMENTO	PINCERING	PINETA	PINIONS

PINITE	PINNATION	PINSWELL	PIONED	PIPER
PINITES	PINNED	PINSWELLS	PIONEER	PIPERIC
PINITOL	PINNER	PINT	PIONEERED	PIPERINE
PINITOLS	PINNERS	PINTA	PIONEERS	PIPERINES
PINK	PINNET	PINTABLE	PIONER	PIPERONAL
PINKED	PINNETS	PINTABLES	PIONERS	PIPERS
PINKEN	PINNIE	PINTADA	PIONEY	PIPES
PINKENED	PINNIES	PINTADAS	PIONEYS	PIPESTEM
PINKENING	PINNING	PINTADERA	PIONIC	PIPESTEMS
PINKENS	PINNINGS	PINTADO	PIONIES	PIPESTONE
PINKER	PINNIPED	PINTADOES	PIONING	PIPET
PINKERS	PINNIPEDE	PINTADOS	PIONINGS	PIPETS
PINKERTON	PINNIPEDS	PINTAIL	PIONS	PIPETTE
PINKEST	PINNOCK	PINTAILED	PIONY	PIPETTED
PINKEY	PINNOCKS	PINTAILS	PIOPIO	PIPETTES
PINKEYE	PINNOED	PINTANO	PIOPIOS	PIPETTING
PINKEYES	PINNULA	PINTANOS	PIOSITIES	PIPEWORK
PINKEYS	PINNULAE	PINTAS	PIOSITY	PIPEWORKS
PINKIE	PINNULAR	PINTLE	PIOTED	PIPEWORT
PINKIER	PINNULAS	PINTLES	PIOUS	PIPEWORTS
PINKIES	PINNULATE	PINTO	PIOUSLY	PIPI
PINKIEST	PINNULE	PINTOES	PIOUSNESS	PIPIER
PINKINESS	PINNULES	PINTOS	PIOY	PIPIEST
PINKING	PINNY	PINTS	PIOYE	PIPINESS
PINKINGS	PINOCHLE	PINTSIZE	PIOYES	PIPING
PINKISH	PINOCHLES	PINTSIZED	PIOYS	PIPINGLY
PINKLY	PINOCLE	PINUP	PIP	PIPINGS
PINKNESS	PINOCLES	PINUPS	PIPA	PIPIS
PINKO	PINOCYTIC	PINWALE	PIPAGE	PIPISTREL
PINKOES	PINOLE	PINWALES	PIPAGES	PIPIT
PINKOS	PINOLES	PINWEED	PIPAL	PIPITS
PINKROOT	PINON	PINWEEDS	PIPALS	PIPKIN
PINKROOTS	PINONES	PINWHEEL	PIPAS	PIPKINS
PINKS	PINONS	PINWHEELS	PIPE	PIPLESS
PINKY	PINOT	PINWORK	PIPEAGE	PIPPED
PINNA	PINOTAGE	PINWORKS	PIPEAGES	PIPPIER
PINNACE	PINOTAGES	PINWORM	PIPECLAY	PIPPIEST
PINNACES	PINOTS	PINWORMS	PIPECLAYS	PIPPIN
PINNACLE	PINPOINT	PINWRENCH	PIPED	PIPPING
PINNACLED	PINPOINTS	PINXIT	PIPEFISH	PIPPINS
PINNACLES	PINPRICK	PINY	PIPEFUL	PIPPY
PINNAE	PINPRICKS	PINYIN	PIPEFULS	PIPS
PINNAL	PINS	PINYON	PIPELESS	PIPSQUEAK
PINNAS	PINSCHER	PINYONS	PIPELIKE	PIPUL
PINNATE	PINSCHERS	PIOLET	PIPELINE	PIPULS
PINNATED	PINSETTER	PIOLETS	PIPELINED	PIPY
PINNATELY	PINSTRIPE	PION	PIPELINES	PIQUANCE

PIQUANCES	PIROG	PISIFORM	PISTOU	PITHIER
PIQUANCY	PIROGEN	PISIFORMS	PISTOUS	PITHIEST
PIQUANT	PIROGHI	PISKIES	PIT	PITHILY
PIQUANTLY	PIROGI	PISKY	PITA	PITHINESS
PIQUE	PIROGIES	PISMIRE	PITAHAYA	PITHING
PIQUED	PIROGUE	PISMIRES	PITAHAYAS	PITHLESS
PIQUES	PIROGUES	PISO	PITAPAT	PITHLIKE
PIQUET	PIROJKI	PISOLITE	PITAPATS	PITHOI
PIQUETED	PIROPLASM	PISOLITES	PITARA	PITHOS
PIQUETING	PIROQUE	PISOLITH	PITARAH	PITHS
PIQUETS	PIROQUES	PISOLITHS	PITARAHS	PITHY
PIQUILLO	PIROSHKI	PISOLITIC	PITARAS	PITIABLE
PIQUILLOS	PIROUETTE	PISOS	PITAS	PITIABLY
PIQUING	PIROZHKI	PISS	PITAYA	PITIED
PIR	PIROZHOK	PISSANT	PITAYAS	PITIER
PIRACETAM	PIRS	PISSANTS	PITCH	PITIERS
PIRACIES	PIS	PISSED	PITCHBEND	PITIES
PIRACY	PISCARIES	PISSER	PITCHED	PITIETH
PIRAGUA	PISCARY	PISSERS	PITCHER	PITIFUL
PIRAGUAS	PISCATOR	PISSES	PITCHERS	PITIFULLY
PIRAI	PISCATORS	PISSHEAD	PITCHES	PITIKINS
PIRAIS	PISCATORY	PISSHEADS	PITCHFORK	PITILESS
PIRANA	PISCATRIX	PISSING	PITCHIER	PITMAN
PIRANAS	PISCIFORM	PISSOIR	PITCHIEST	PITMANS
PIRANHA	PISCINA	PISSOIRS	PITCHILY	PITMEN
PIRANHAS	PISCINAE	PISTACHE	PITCHING	PITON
PIRARUCU	PISCINAL	PISTACHES	PITCHINGS	PITONS
PIRARUCUS	PISCINAS	PISTACHIO	PITCHMAN	PITPROP
PIRATE	PISCINE	PISTAREEN	PITCHMEN	PITPROPS
PIRATED	PISCINES	PISTE	PITCHOUT	PITS
PIRATES	PISCIVORE	PISTES	PITCHOUTS	PITSAW
PIRATIC	PISCO	PISTIL	PITCHPINE	PITSAWS
PIRATICAL	PISCOS	PISTILS	PITCHPIPE	PITTA
PIRATING	PISE	PISTOL	PITCHPOLE	PITTANCE
PIRAYA	PISES	PISTOLE	PITCHY	PITTANCES
PIRAYAS	PISH	PISTOLED	PITEOUS	PITTAS
PIRIFORM	PISHED	PISTOLEER	PITEOUSLY	PITTED
PIRL	PISHEOG	PISTOLERO	PITFALL	PITTEN
PIRLICUE	PISHEOGS	PISTOLES	PITFALLS	PITTER
PIRLICUED	PISHER	PISTOLET	PITH	PITTERED
PIRLICUES	PISHERS	PISTOLETS	PITHBALL	PITTERING
PIRLS	PISHES	PISTOLIER	PITHBALLS	PITTERS
PIRN	PISHING	PISTOLING	PITHEAD	PITTING
PIRNIE	PISHOGE	PISTOLLED	PITHEADS	PITTINGS
PIRNIES	PISHOGES	PISTOLS	PITHECOID	PITTITE
PIRNIT	PISHOGUE	PISTON	PITHED	PITTITES
PIRNS	PISHOGUES	PISTONS	PITHFUL	PITUITA

PITUITARY	PIZZAIOLA	PLACENTA	PLAGUY	PLANARITY
PITUITAS	PIZZALIKE	PLACENTAE	PLAICE	PLANATE
PITUITE	PIZZAS	PLACENTAL	PLAICES	PLANATION
PITUITES	PIZZAZ	PLACENTAS	PLAID	PLANCH
PITUITRIN	PIZZAZES	PLACER	PLAIDED	PLANCHE
PITURI	PIZZAZZ	PLACERS	PLAIDING	PLANCHED
PITURIS	PIZZAZZES	PLACES	PLAIDINGS	PLANCHES
PITY	PIZZAZZY	PLACET	PLAIDMAN	PLANCHET
PITYING	PIZZELLE	PLACETS	PLAIDMEN	PLANCHETS
PITYINGLY	PIZZELLES	PLACID	PLAIDS	PLANCHING
PITYROID	PIZZERIA	PLACIDER	PLAIN	PLANE
PIU	PIZZERIAS	PLACIDEST	PLAINANT	PLANED
PIUM	PIZZICATI	PLACIDITY	PLAINANTS	PLANELOAD
PIUMS	PIZZICATO	PLACIDLY	PLAINED	PLANENESS
PIUPIU	PIZZLE	PLACING	PLAINER	PLANER
PIUPIUS	PIZZLES	PLACINGS	PLAINEST	PLANERS
PIVOT	PLAAS	PLACIT	PLAINFUL	PLANES
PIVOTABLE	PLAASES	PLACITA	PLAINING	PLANESIDE
PIVOTAL	PLACABLE	PLACITORY	PLAININGS	PLANET
PIVOTALLY	PLACABLY	PLACITS	PLAINISH	PLANETARY
PIVOTED	PLACARD	PLACITUM	PLAINLY	PLANETIC
PIVOTER	PLACARDED	PLACK	PLAINNESS	PLANETOID
PIVOTERS	PLACARDS	PLACKET	PLAINS	PLANETS
PIVOTING	PLACATE	PLACKETS	PLAINSMAN	PLANFORM
PIVOTINGS	PLACATED	PLACKLESS	PLAINSMEN	PLANFORMS
PIVOTMAN	PLACATER	PLACKS	PLAINSONG	PLANGENCY
PIVOTMEN	PLACATERS	PLACODERM	PLAINT	PLANGENT
PIVOTS	PLACATES	PLACOID	PLAINTEXT	PLANING
PIX	PLACATING	PLACOIDS	PLAINTFUL	PLANISH
PIXEL	PLACATION	PLAFOND	PLAINTIFF	PLANISHED
PIXELS	PLACATIVE	PLAFONDS	PLAINTIVE	PLANISHER
PIXES	PLACATORY	PLAGAL	PLAINTS	PLANISHES
PIXIE	PLACCAT	PLAGE	PLAINWORK	PLANK
PIXIEISH	PLACCATE	PLAGES	PLAISTER	PLANKED
PIXIES	PLACCATES	PLAGIARY	PLAISTERS	PLANKING
PIXILATED	PLACCATS	PLAGIUM	PLAIT	PLANKINGS
PIXINESS	PLACE	PLAGIUMS	PLAITED	PLANKS
PIXY	PLACEABLE	PLAGUE	PLAITER	PLANKTER
PIXYISH	PLACEBO	PLAGUED	PLAITERS	PLANKTERS
PIZAZZ	PLACEBOES	PLAGUER	PLAITING	PLANKTON
PIZAZZES	PLACEBOS	PLAGUERS	PLAITINGS	PLANKTONS
PIZAZZY	PLACED	PLAGUES	PLAITS	PLANLESS
PIZE	PLACEKICK	PLAGUEY	PLAN	PLANNED
PIZED	PLACELESS	PLAGUIER	PLANAR	PLANNER
PIZES	PLACEMAN	PLAGUIEST	PLANARIA	PLANNERS
PIZING	PLACEMEN	PLAGUILY	PLANARIAN	PLANNING
PIZZA	PLACEMENT	PLAGUING	PLANARIAS	PLANNINGS

PLANOSOL	PLASHED	PLASTRUMS	PLATINUMS	PLAYDAYS
PLANOSOLS	PLASHER	PLAT	PLATITUDE	PLAYDOUGH
PLANS	PLASHERS	PLATAN	PLATONIC	PLAYDOWN
PLANT	PLASHES	PLATANE	PLATONICS	PLAYDOWNS
PLANTA	PLASHET	PLATANES	PLATONISM	PLAYED
PLANTABLE	PLASHETS	PLATANNA	PLATOON	PLAYER
PLANTAE	PLASHIER	PLATANNAS	PLATOONED	PLAYERS
PLANTAGE	PLASHIEST	PLATANS	PLATOONS	PLAYFIELD
PLANTAGES	PLASHING	PLATBAND	PLATS	PLAYFUL
PLANTAIN	PLASHINGS	PLATBANDS	PLATTED	PLAYFULLY
PLANTAINS	PLASHY	PLATE	PLATTER	PLAYGIRL
PLANTAR	PLASM	PLATEASM	PLATTERS	PLAYGIRLS
PLANTAS	PLASMA	PLATEASMS	PLATTING	PLAYGOER
PLANTED	PLASMAGEL	PLATEAU	PLATTINGS	PLAYGOERS
PLANTER	PLASMAS	PLATEAUED	PLATY	PLAYGOING
PLANTERS	PLASMASOL	PLATEAUS	PLATYFISH	PLAYGROUP
PLANTING	PLASMATIC	PLATEAUX	PLATYPI	PLAYHOUSE
PLANTINGS	PLASMIC	PLATED	PLATYPUS	PLAYING
PLANTLESS	PLASMID	PLATEFUL	PLATYS	PLAYLAND
PLANTLET	PLASMIDS	PLATEFULS	PLATYSMA	PLAYLANDS
PLANTLETS	PLASMIN	PLATELET	PLATYSMAS	PLAYLESS
PLANTLIKE	PLASMINS	PLATELETS	PLAUDIT	PLAYLET
PLANTLING	PLASMODIA	PLATELIKE	PLAUDITE	PLAYLETS
PLANTS	PLASMOID	PLATEMAN	PLAUDITS	PLAYLIKE
PLANTSMAN	PLASMOIDS	PLATEMARK	PLAUSIBLE	PLAYLIST
PLANTSMEN	PLASMON	PLATEMEN	PLAUSIBLY	PLAYLISTS
PLANTULE	PLASMONS	PLATEN	PLAUSIVE	PLAYMAKER
PLANTULES	PLASMS	PLATENS	PLAUSTRAL	PLAYMATE
PLANULA	PLAST	PLATER	PLAY	PLAYMATES
PLANULAE	PLASTE	PLATERS	PLAYA	PLAYOFF
PLANULAR	PLASTER	PLATES	PLAYABLE	PLAYOFFS
PLANULATE	PLASTERED	PLATESFUL	PLAYACT	PLAYPEN
PLANULOID	PLASTERER	PLATFORM	PLAYACTED	PLAYPENS
PLANURIA	PLASTERS	PLATFORMS	PLAYACTOR	PLAYROOM
PLANURIAS	PLASTERY	PLATIER	PLAYACTS	PLAYROOMS
PLANURIES	PLASTIC	PLATIES	PLAYAS	PLAYS
PLANURY	PLASTICKY	PLATIEST	PLAYBACK	PLAYSLIP
PLANXTIES	PLASTICLY	PLATINA	PLAYBACKS	PLAYSLIPS
PLANXTY	PLASTICS	PLATINAS	PLAYBILL	PLAYSOME
PLAP	PLASTID	PLATING	PLAYBILLS	PLAYSUIT
PLAPPED	PLASTIDS	PLATINGS	PLAYBOOK	PLAYSUITS
PLAPPING	PLASTIQUE	PLATINIC	PLAYBOOKS	PLAYTHING
PLAPS	PLASTISOL	PLATINISE	PLAYBOY	PLAYTIME
PLAQUE	PLASTRAL	PLATINIZE	PLAYBOYS	PLAYTIMES
PLAQUES	PLASTRON	PLATINOID	PLAYDATE	PLAYWEAR
PLAQUETTE	PLASTRONS	PLATINOUS	PLAYDATES	PLAZA
PLASH	PLASTRUM	PLATINUM	PLAYDAY	PLAZAS

PLEA	PLEBE	PLENIPOES	PLEUGHED	PLIGHT
PLEACH	PLEBEAN	PLENIPOS	PLEUGHING	PLIGHTED
PLEACHED	PLEBEIAN	PLENISH	PLEUGHS	PLIGHTER
PLEACHES	PLEBEIANS	PLENISHED	PLEURA	PLIGHTERS
PLEACHING	PLEBES	PLENISHER	PLEURAE	PLIGHTFUL
PLEAD	PLEBIFIED	PLENISHES	PLEURAL	PLIGHTING
PLEADABLE	PLEBIFIES	PLENISM	PLEURAS	PLIGHTS
PLEADED	PLEBIFY	PLENISMS	PLEURISY	PLIM
PLEADER	PLEBS	PLENIST	PLEURITIC	PLIMMED
PLEADERS	PLECTRA	PLENISTS	PLEURITIS	PLIMMING
PLEADING	PLECTRE	PLENITUDE	PLEURON	PLIMS
PLEADINGS	PLECTRES	PLENTEOUS	PLEURONIA	PLIMSOL
PLEADS	PLECTRON	PLENTIES	PLEUSTON	PLIMSOLE
PLEAED	PLECTRONS	PLENTIFUL	PLEUSTONS	PLIMSOLES
PLEAING	PLECTRUM	PLENTY	PLEW	PLIMSOLL
PLEAS	PLECTRUMS	PLENUM	PLEWS	PLIMSOLLS
PLEASABLE	PLED	PLENUMS	PLEX	PLIMSOLS
PLEASANCE	PLEDGABLE	PLEON	PLEXAL	PLING
PLEASANT	PLEDGE	PLEONAL	PLEXES	PLINGS
PLEASE	PLEDGED	PLEONASM	PLEXIFORM	PLINK
PLEASED	PLEDGEE	PLEONASMS	PLEXOR	PLINKED
PLEASEDLY	PLEDGEES	PLEONAST	PLEXORS	PLINKER
PLEASEMAN	PLEDGEOR	PLEONASTE	PLEXURE	PLINKERS
PLEASEMEN	PLEDGEORS	PLEONASTS	PLEXURES	PLINKIER
PLEASER	PLEDGER	PLEONEXIA	PLEXUS	PLINKIEST
PLEASERS	PLEDGERS	PLEONIC	PLEXUSES	PLINKING
PLEASES	PLEDGES	PLEONS	PLIABLE	PLINKINGS
PLEASETH	PLEDGET	PLEOPOD	PLIABLY	PLINKS
PLEASING	PLEDGETS	PLEOPODS	PLIANCIES	PLINKY
PLEASINGS	PLEDGING	PLERION	PLIANCY	PLINTH
PLEASURE	PLEDGOR	PLERIONS	PLIANT	PLINTHS
PLEASURED	PLEDGORS	PLEROMA	PLIANTLY	PLIOCENE
PLEASURER	PLEIAD	PLEROMAS	PLICA	PLIOFILM
PLEASURES	PLEIADES	PLEROME	PLICAE	PLIOFILMS
PLEAT	PLEIADS	PLEROMES	PLICAL	PLIOSAUR
PLEATED	PLEIOCENE	PLESH	PLICATE	PLIOSAURS
PLEATER	PLEIOMERY	PLESHES	PLICATED	PLIOTRON
PLEATERS	PLEIOTAXY	PLESSOR	PLICATELY	PLIOTRONS
PLEATHER	PLENA	PLESSORS	PLICATES	PLISKIE
PLEATHERS	PLENARIES	PLETHORA	PLICATING	PLISKIES
PLEATING	PLENARILY	PLETHORAS	PLICATION	PLISKY
PLEATLESS	PLENARTY	PLETHORIC	PLICATURE	PLISSE
PLEATS	PLENARY	PLEUCH	PLIE	PLISSES
PLEB	PLENCH	PLEUCHED	PLIED	PLOAT
PLEBBIER	PLENCHES	PLEUCHING	PLIER	PLOATED
PLEBBIEST	PLENILUNE	PLEUCHS	PLIERS	PLOATING
PLEBBY	PLENIPO	PLEUGH	PLIES	PLOATS

PLOD	PLOTFUL	PLOWBOY	PLUGGING	PLUMERIA
PLODDED	PLOTLESS	PLOWBOYS	PLUGGINGS	PLUMERIAS
PLODDER	PLOTLINE	PLOWED	PLUGHOLE	PLUMERIES
PLODDERS	PLOTLINES	PLOWER	PLUGHOLES	PLUMERY
PLODDING	PLOTS	PLOWERS	PLUGLESS	PLUMES
PLODDINGS	PLOTTAGE	PLOWHEAD	PLUGOLA	PLUMIER
PLODGE	PLOTTAGES	PLOWHEADS	PLUGOLAS	PLUMIEST
PLODGED	PLOTTED	PLOWING	PLUGS	PLUMING
PLODGES	PLOTTER	PLOWLAND	PLUGUGLY	PLUMIPED
PLODGING	PLOTTERED	PLOWLANDS	PLUM	PLUMIPEDS
PLODS	PLOTTERS	PLOWMAN	PLUMAGE	PLUMIST
PLOIDIES	PLOTTIE	PLOWMEN	PLUMAGED	PLUMISTS
PLOIDY	PLOTTIER	PLOWS	PLUMAGES	PLUMLIKE
PLONG	PLOTTIES	PLOWSHARE	PLUMATE	PLUMMER
PLONGD	PLOTTIEST	PLOWSTAFF	PLUMB	PLUMMEST
PLONGE	PLOTTING	PLOWTER	PLUMBABLE	PLUMMET
PLONGED	PLOTTINGS	PLOWTERED	PLUMBAGO	PLUMMETED
PLONGES	PLOTTY	PLOWTERS	PLUMBAGOS	PLUMMETS
PLONGING	PLOTZ	PLOY	PLUMBATE	PLUMMIER
PLONGS	PLOTZED	PLOYED	PLUMBATES	PLUMMIEST
PLONK	PLOTZES	PLOYING	PLUMBED	PLUMMY
PLONKED	PLOTZING	PLOYS	PLUMBEOUS	PLUMOSE
PLONKER	PLOUGH	PLU	PLUMBER	PLUMOSELY
PLONKERS	PLOUGHBOY	PLUCK	PLUMBERS	PLUMOSITY
PLONKIER	PLOUGHED	PLUCKED	PLUMBERY	PLUMOUS
PLONKIEST	PLOUGHER	PLUCKER	PLUMBIC	PLUMP
PLONKING	PLOUGHERS	PLUCKERS	PLUMBING	PLUMPED
PLONKINGS	PLOUGHING	PLUCKIER	PLUMBINGS	PLUMPEN
PLONKO	PLOUGHMAN	PLUCKIEST	PLUMBISM	PLUMPENED
PLONKOS	PLOUGHMEN	PLUCKILY	PLUMBISMS	PLUMPENS
PLONKS	PLOUGHS	PLUCKING	PLUMBITE	PLUMPER
PLONKY	PLOUK	PLUCKS	PLUMBITES	PLUMPERS
PLOOK	PLOUKIE	PLUCKY	PLUMBLESS	PLUMPEST
PLOOKIE	PLOUKIER	PLUE	PLUMBNESS	PLUMPIE
PLOOKIER	PLOUKIEST	PLUES	PLUMBOUS	PLUMPIER
PLOOKIEST	PLOUKS	PLUFF	PLUMBS	PLUMPIEST
PLOOKS	PLOUKY	PLUFFED	PLUMBUM	PLUMPING
PLOOKY	PLOUTER	PLUFFIER	PLUMBUMS	PLUMPISH
PLOP	PLOUTERED	PLUFFIEST	PLUMCOT	PLUMPLY
PLOPPED	PLOUTERS	PLUFFING	PLUMCOTS	PLUMPNESS
PLOPPING	PLOVER	PLUFFS	PLUMDAMAS	PLUMPS
PLOPS	PLOVERS	PLUFFY	PLUME	PLUMPY
PLOSION	PLOVERY	PLUG	PLUMED	PLUMS
PLOSIONS	PLOW	PLUGBOARD	PLUMELESS	PLUMULA
PLOSIVE	PLOWABLE	PLUGGED	PLUMELET	PLUMULAE
PLOSIVES	PLOWBACK	PLUGGER	PLUMELETS	PLUMULAR
PLOT	PLOWBACKS	PLUGGERS	PLUMELIKE	PLUMULATE

PLUMULE	PLUSHILY	POACHER	POCKY	PODITE
PLUMULES	PLUSHLY	POACHERS	POCO	PODITES
PLUMULOSE	PLUSHNESS	POACHES	POCOSEN	PODITIC
PLUMY	PLUSHY	POACHIER	POCOSENS	PODIUM
PLUNDER	PLUSING	POACHIEST	POCOSIN	PODIUMS
PLUNDERED	PLUSSAGE	POACHING	POCOSINS	PODLEY
PLUNDERER	PLUSSAGES	POACHINGS	POCOSON	PODLEYS
PLUNDERS	PLUSSED	POACHY	POCOSONS	PODLIKE
PLUNGE	PLUSSES	POAKA	POD	PODOCARP
PLUNGED	PLUSSING	POAKAS	PODAGRA	PODOCARPS
PLUNGER	PLUTEAL	POAKE	PODAGRAL	PODOLOGY
PLUNGERS	PLUTEI	POAKES	PODAGRAS	PODOMERE
PLUNGES	PLUTEUS	POAS	PODAGRIC	PODOMERES
PLUNGING	PLUTEUSES	POBLANO	PODAGROUS	PODS
PLUNGINGS	PLUTOCRAT	POBLANOS	PODAL	PODSOL
PLUNK	PLUTOLOGY	POBOY	PODALIC	PODSOLIC
PLUNKED	PLUTON	POBOYS	PODARGUS	PODSOLISE
PLUNKER	PLUTONIAN	POCHARD	PODCAST	PODSOLIZE
PLUNKERS	PLUTONIC	POCHARDS	PODCASTED	PODSOLS
PLUNKIER	PLUTONISM	POCHAY	PODCASTER	PODZOL
PLUNKIEST	PLUTONIUM	POCHAYS	PODCASTS	PODZOLIC
PLUNKING	PLUTONOMY	POCHETTE	PODDED	PODZOLISE
PLUNKS	PLUTONS	POCHETTES	PODDIE	PODZOLIZE
PLUNKY	PLUVIAL	POCHOIR	PODDIER	PODZOLS
PLURAL	PLUVIALS	POCHOIRS	PODDIES	POECHORE
PLURALISE	PLUVIAN	POCK	PODDIEST	POECHORES
PLURALISM	PLUVIOSE	POCKARD	PODDING	POEM
PLURALIST	PLUVIOUS	POCKARDS	PODDLE	POEMATIC
PLURALITY	PLUVIUS	POCKED	PODDLED	POEMS
PLURALIZE	PLY	POCKET	PODDLES	POENOLOGY
PLURALLY	PLYER	POCKETED	PODDLING	POEP
PLURALS	PLYERS	POCKETER	PODDY	POEPOL
PLURIPARA	PLYING	POCKETERS	PODESTA	POEPOLS
PLURISIE	PLYINGLY	POCKETFUL	PODESTAS	POEPS
PLURISIES	PLYWOOD	POCKETING	PODEX	POESIED
PLURRY	PLYWOODS	POCKETS	PODEXES	POESIES
PLUS	PNEUMA	POCKIER	PODGE	POESY
PLUSAGE	PNEUMAS	POCKIES	PODGES	POESYING
PLUSAGES	PNEUMATIC	POCKIEST	PODGIER	POET
PLUSED	PNEUMONIA	POCKILY	PODGIEST	POETASTER
PLUSES	PNEUMONIC	POCKING	PODGILY	POETASTRY
PLUSH	PO	POCKMANKY	PODGINESS	POETESS
PLUSHER	POA	POCKMARK	PODGY	POETESSES
PLUSHES	POACEOUS	POCKMARKS	PODIA	POETIC
PLUSHEST	POACH	POCKPIT	PODIAL	POETICAL
PLUSHIER	POACHABLE	POCKPITS	PODIATRIC	POETICALS
PLUSHIEST	POACHED	POCKS	PODIATRY	POETICISE

POETICISM	POH	POISERS	POL	POLER
POETICIZE	POHIRI	POISES	POLACCA	POLERS
POETICS	POHIRIS	POISHA	POLACCAS	POLES
POETICULE	POI	POISING	POLACRE	POLESTAR
POETISE	POIGNADO	POISON	POLACRES	POLESTARS
POETISED	POIGNANCE	POISONED	POLAR	POLEWARD
POETISER	POIGNANCY	POISONER	POLARISE	POLEY
POETISERS	POIGNANT	POISONERS	POLARISED	POLEYN
POETISES	POILU	POISONING	POLARISER	POLEYNS
POETISING	POILUS	POISONOUS	POLARISES	POLEYS
POETIZE	POINADO	POISONS	POLARITY	POLIANITE
POETIZED	POINADOES	POISSON	POLARIZE	POLICE
POETIZER	POINCIANA	POISSONS	POLARIZED	POLICED
POETIZERS	POIND	POITIN	POLARIZER	POLICEMAN
POETIZES	POINDED	POITINS	POLARIZES	POLICEMEN
POETIZING	POINDER	POITREL	POLARON	POLICER
POETLESS	POINDERS	POITRELS	POLARONS	POLICERS
POETLIKE	POINDING	POITRINE	POLARS	POLICES
POETRESSE	POINDINGS	POITRINES	POLDER	POLICIES
POETRIES	POINDS	POKABLE	POLDERED	POLICING
POETRY	POINT	POKAL	POLDERING	POLICINGS
POETS	POINTABLE	POKALS	POLDERS	POLICY
POETSHIP	POINTE	POKE	POLE	POLIES
POETSHIPS	POINTED	POKEBERRY	POLEAX	POLING
POFFLE	POINTEDLY	POKED	POLEAXE	POLINGS
POFFLES	POINTEL	POKEFUL	POLEAXED	POLIO
POGEY	POINTELLE	POKEFULS	POLEAXES	POLIOS
POGEYS	POINTELS	POKELOGAN	POLEAXING	POLIS
POGGE	POINTER	POKER	POLECAT	POLISES
POGGES	POINTERS	POKERISH	POLECATS	POLISH
POGIES	POINTES	POKEROOT	POLED	POLISHED
POGO	POINTIER	POKEROOTS	POLEIS	POLISHER
POGOED	POINTIEST	POKERS	POLELESS	POLISHERS
POGOER	POINTILLE	POKERWORK	POLEMARCH	POLISHES
POGOERS	POINTING	POKES	POLEMIC	POLISHING
POGOING	POINTINGS	POKEWEED	POLEMICAL	POLITBURO
POGONIA	POINTLESS	POKEWEEDS	POLEMICS	POLITE
POGONIAS	POINTMAN	POKEY	POLEMISE	POLITELY
POGONIP	POINTMEN	POKEYS	POLEMISED	POLITER
POGONIPS	POINTS	POKIE	POLEMISES	POLITESSE
POGOS	POINTSMAN	POKIER	POLEMIST	POLITEST
POGROM	POINTSMEN	POKIES	POLEMISTS	POLITIC
POGROMED	POINTY	POKIEST	POLEMIZE	POLITICAL
POGROMING	POIS	POKILY	POLEMIZED	POLITICK
POGROMIST	POISE	POKINESS	POLEMIZES	POLITICKS
POGROMS	POISED	POKING	POLENTA	POLITICLY
POGY	POISER	POKY	POLENTAS	POLITICO

POLITICOS	POLLINGS	POLONISM	POLYGALA	POLYPARIA
POLITICS	POLLINIA	POLONISMS	POLYGALAS	POLYPARY
POLITIES	POLLINIC	POLONIUM	POLYGAM	POLYPE
POLITIQUE	POLLINISE	POLONIUMS	POLYGAMIC	POLYPED
POLITY	POLLINIUM	POLONIZE	POLYGAMS	POLYPEDS
POLJE	POLLINIZE	POLONIZED	POLYGAMY	POLYPES
POLJES	POLLIST	POLONIZES	POLYGENE	POLYPHAGY
POLK	POLLISTS	POLONY	POLYGENES	POLYPHASE
POLKA	POLLIWIG	POLOS	POLYGENIC	POLYPHON
POLKAED	POLLIWIGS	POLS	POLYGENY	POLYPHONE
POLKAING	POLLIWOG	POLT	POLYGLOT	POLYPHONS
POLKAS	POLLIWOGS	POLTED	POLYGLOTS	POLYPHONY
POLKED	POLLMAN	POLTFEET	POLYGLOTT	POLYPI
POLKING	POLLMEN	POLTFOOT	POLYGON	POLYPIDE
POLKS	POLLOCK	POLTING	POLYGONAL	POLYPIDES
POLL	POLLOCKS	POLTROON	POLYGONS	POLYPIDOM
POLLACK	POLLS	POLTROONS	POLYGONUM	POLYPILL
POLLACKS	POLLSTER	POLTS	POLYGONY	POLYPILLS
POLLAN	POLLSTERS	POLVERINE	POLYGRAPH	POLYPINE
POLLANS	POLLTAKER	POLY	POLYGYNY	POLYPITE
POLLARD	POLLUCITE	POLYACID	POLYHEDRA	POLYPITES
POLLARDED	POLLUSION	POLYACT	POLYIMIDE	POLYPLOID
POLLARDS	POLLUTANT	POLYADIC	POLYLEMMA	POLYPNEA
POLLAXE	POLLUTE	POLYAMIDE	POLYMASTY	POLYPNEAS
POLLAXED	POLLUTED	POLYAMINE	POLYMATH	POLYPNEIC
POLLAXES	POLLUTER	POLYAMORY	POLYMATHS	POLYPOD
POLLAXING	POLLUTERS	POLYANDRY	POLYMATHY	POLYPODS
POLLED	POLLUTES	POLYANTHA	POLYMER	POLYPODY
POLLEE	POLLUTING	POLYANTHI	POLYMERIC	POLYPOID
POLLEES	POLLUTION	POLYARCH	POLYMERS	POLYPORE
POLLEN	POLLUTIVE	POLYARCHY	POLYMERY	POLYPORES
POLLENATE	POLLY	POLYAXIAL	POLYMORPH	POLYPOSES
POLLENED	POLLYANNA	POLYAXON	POLYMYXIN	POLYPOSIS
POLLENING	POLLYWIG	POLYAXONS	POLYNIA	POLYPOUS
POLLENS	POLLYWIGS	POLYBASIC	POLYNIAS	POLYPS
POLLENT	POLLYWOG	POLYBRID	POLYNYA	POLYPTYCH
POLLER	POLLYWOGS	POLYBRIDS	POLYNYAS	POLYPUS
POLLERS	POLO	POLYCARPY	POLYNYI	POLYPUSES
POLLEX	POLOIDAL	POLYCHETE	POLYOL	POLYS
POLLICAL	POLOIST	POLYCONIC	POLYOLS	POLYSEME
POLLICES	POLOISTS	POLYCOT	POLYOMA	POLYSEMES
POLLICIE	POLONAISE	POLYCOTS	POLYOMAS	POLYSEMIC
POLLICIES	POLONIE	POLYDEMIC	POLYOMINO	POLYSEMY
POLLICY	POLONIES	POLYENE	POLYONYM	POLYSOME
POLLIES	POLONISE	POLYENES	POLYONYMS	POLYSOMES
POLLINATE	POLONISED	POLYENIC	POLYONYMY	POLYSOMIC
POLLING	POLONISES	POLYESTER	POLYP	POLYSOMY

POLYSTYLE	POMMELE	PONCEAUX	PONGING	PONTOONS
POLYTENE	POMMELED	PONCED	PONGO	PONTS
POLYTENY	POMMELING	PONCES	PONGOES	PONTY
POLYTHENE	POMMELLED	PONCEY	PONGOS	PONY
POLYTONAL	POMMELS	PONCHO	PONGS	PONYING
POLYTYPE	POMMETTY	PONCHOED	PONGY	PONYSKIN
POLYTYPES	POMMIE	PONCHOS	PONIARD	PONYSKINS
POLYTYPIC	POMMIES	PONCIER	PONIARDED	PONYTAIL
POLYURIA	POMMY	PONCIEST	PONIARDS	PONYTAILS
POLYURIAS	POMO	PONCING	PONIED	PONZU
POLYURIC	POMOERIUM	PONCY	PONIES	PONZUS
POLYVINYL	POMOLOGY	POND	PONK	POO
POLYWATER	POMOS	PONDAGE	PONKED	POOCH
POLYZOA	POMP	PONDAGES	PONKING	POOCHED
POLYZOAN	POMPADOUR	PONDED	PONKS	POOCHES
POLYZOANS	POMPANO	PONDER	PONS	POOCHING
POLYZOARY	POMPANOS	PONDERAL	PONT	POOD
POLYZOIC	POMPELO	PONDERATE	PONTAGE	POODLE
POLYZONAL	POMPELOS	PONDERED	PONTAGES	POODLES
POLYZOOID	POMPEY	PONDERER	PONTAL	POODS
POLYZOON	POMPEYED	PONDERERS	PONTES	POOED
POM	POMPEYING	PONDERING	PONTIANAC	POOF
POMACE	POMPEYS	PONDEROSA	PONTIANAK	POOFIER
POMACEOUS	POMPHOLYX	PONDEROUS	PONTIC	POOFIEST
POMACES	POMPIER	PONDERS	PONTIE	POOFS
POMADE	POMPILID	PONDING	PONTIES	POOFTAH
POMADED	POMPILIDS	PONDOK	PONTIFEX	POOFTAHS
POMADES	POMPION	PONDOKKIE	PONTIFF	POOFTER
POMADING	POMPIONS	PONDOKS	PONTIFFS	POOFTERS
POMANDER	POMPOM	PONDS	PONTIFIC	POOFY
POMANDERS	POMPOMS	PONDWEED	PONTIFICE	POOGYE
POMATO	POMPON	PONDWEEDS	PONTIFIED	POOGYES
POMATOES	POMPONS	PONE	PONTIFIES	POOH
POMATUM	POMPOON	PONENT	PONTIFY	POOHED
POMATUMS	POMPOONS	PONES	PONTIL	POOHING
POMBE	POMPOSITY	PONEY	PONTILE	POOHS
POMBES	POMPOUS	PONEYS	PONTILES	POOING
POME	POMPOUSLY	PONG	PONTILS	POOJA
POMELO	POMPS	PONGA	PONTINE	POOJAH
POMELOS	POMROY	PONGAS	PONTLEVIS	POOJAHS
POMEROY	POMROYS	PONGED	PONTON	POOJAS
POMEROYS	POMS	PONGEE	PONTONEER	POOK
POMES	POMWATER	PONGEES	PONTONIER	POOKA
POMFRET	POMWATERS	PONGID	PONTONS	POOKAS
POMFRETS	PONCE	PONGIDS	PONTOON	POOKING
POMMEE	PONCEAU	PONGIER	PONTOONED	POOKIT
POMMEL	PONCEAUS	PONGIEST	PONTOONER	POOKS

POOL	POOT	POPINJAYS	POPRIN	PORGED
POOLED	POOTED	POPISH	POPS	PORGES
POOLER	POOTER	POPISHLY	POPSICLE	PORGIE
POOLERS	POOTERS	POPJOY	POPSICLES	PORGIES
POOLHALL	POOTING	POPJOYED	POPSIE	PORGING
POOLHALLS	POOTLE	POPJOYING	POPSIES	PORGY
POOLING	POOTLED	POPJOYS	POPSOCK	PORIER
POOLROOM	POOTLES	POPLAR	POPSOCKS	PORIEST
POOLROOMS	POOTLING	POPLARS	POPSTER	PORIFER
POOLS	POOTS	POPLIN	POPSTERS	PORIFERAL
POOLSIDE	POOVE	POPLINS	POPSTREL	PORIFERAN
POOLSIDES	POOVERIES	POPLITEAL	POPSTRELS	PORIFERS
POON	POOVERY	POPLITEI	POPSY	PORINA
POONAC	POOVES	POPLITEUS	POPULACE	PORINAS
POONACS	POOVIER	POPLITIC	POPULACES	PORINESS
POONCE	POOVIEST	POPOVER	POPULAR	PORING
POONCED	POOVY	POPOVERS	POPULARLY	PORISM
POONCES	POP	POPPA	POPULARS	PORISMS
POONCING	POPADUM	POPPADOM	POPULATE	PORISTIC
POONS	POPADUMS	POPPADOMS	POPULATED	PORK
POONTANG	POPCORN	POPPADUM	POPULATES	PORKED
POONTANGS	POPCORNS	POPPADUMS	POPULISM	PORKER
POOP	POPE	POPPAS	POPULISMS	PORKERS
POOPED	POPEDOM	POPPED	POPULIST	PORKIER
POOPER	POPEDOMS	POPPER	POPULISTS	PORKIES
POOPERS	POPEHOOD	POPPERING	POPULOUS	PORKIEST
POOPING	POPEHOODS	POPPERS	PORAE	PORKINESS
POOPS	POPELESS	POPPET	PORAES	PORKING
POOR	POPELIKE	POPPETS	PORAL	PORKLING
POORER	POPELING	POPPIED	PORANGI	PORKLINGS
POOREST	POPELINGS	POPPIER	PORBEAGLE	PORKPIE
POORHOUSE	POPERA	POPPIES	PORCELAIN	PORKPIES
POORI	POPERAS	POPPIEST	PORCH	PORKS
POORIS	POPERIES	POPPING	PORCHES	PORKWOOD
POORISH	POPERIN	POPPISH	PORCHETTA	PORKWOODS
POORLIER	POPERINS	POPPIT	PORCINE	PORKY
POORLIEST	POPERY	POPPITS	PORCINI	PORLOCK
POORLY	POPES	POPPLE	PORCINIS	PORLOCKED
POORMOUTH	POPESEYE	POPPLED	PORCINO	PORLOCKS
POORNESS	POPESHIP	POPPLES	PORCUPINE	PORN
POORT	POPESHIPS	POPPLIER	PORCUPINY	PORNIER
POORTITH	POPETTE	POPPLIEST	PORE	PORNIEST
POORTITHS	POPETTES	POPPLING	PORED	PORNO
POORTS	POPEYED	POPPLY	PORER	PORNOS
POORWILL	POPGUN	POPPY	PORERS	PORNS
POORWILLS	POPGUNS	POPPYCOCK	PORES	PORNY
POOS	POPINJAY	POPPYHEAD	PORGE	POROGAMIC

POROGAMY	PORTANCES	PORTION	POSED	POSOLES
POROMERIC	PORTAPACK	PORTIONED	POSER	POSOLOGIC
POROSCOPE	PORTAPAK	PORTIONER	POSERISH	POSOLOGY
POROSCOPY	PORTAPAKS	PORTIONS	POSERS	POSS
POROSE	PORTAS	PORTLAND	POSES	POSSE
POROSES	PORTASES	PORTLANDS	POSEUR	POSSED
POROSIS	PORTATE	PORTLAST	POSEURS	POSSER
POROSITY	PORTATILE	PORTLASTS	POSEUSE	POSSERS
POROUS	PORTATIVE	PORTLESS	POSEUSES	POSSES
POROUSLY	PORTED	PORTLIER	POSEY	POSSESS
PORPESS	PORTEND	PORTLIEST	POSH	POSSESSED
PORPESSE	PORTENDED	PORTLY	POSHED	POSSESSES
PORPESSES	PORTENDS	PORTMAN	POSHER	POSSESSOR
PORPHYRIA	PORTENT	PORTMEN	POSHES	POSSET
PORPHYRIC	PORTENTS	PORTOISE	POSHEST	POSSETED
PORPHYRIN	PORTEOUS	PORTOISES	POSHING	POSSETING
PORPHYRIO	PORTER	PORTOLAN	POSHLY	POSSETS
PORPHYRY	PORTERAGE	PORTOLANI	POSHNESS	POSSIBLE
PORPOISE	PORTERED	PORTOLANO	POSHO	POSSIBLER
PORPOISED	PORTERESS	PORTOLANS	POSHOS	POSSIBLES
PORPOISES	PORTERING	PORTOUS	POSHTEEN	POSSIBLY
PORPORATE	PORTERLY	PORTOUSES	POSHTEENS	POSSIE
PORRECT	PORTERS	PORTRAIT	POSIER	POSSIES
PORRECTED	PORTESS	PORTRAITS	POSIES	POSSING
PORRECTS	PORTESSE	PORTRAY	POSIEST	POSSUM
PORRENGER	PORTESSES	PORTRAYAL	POSIGRADE	POSSUMED
PORRIDGE	PORTFIRE	PORTRAYED	POSING	POSSUMING
PORRIDGES	PORTFIRES	PORTRAYER	POSINGLY	POSSUMS
PORRIDGY	PORTFOLIO	PORTRAYS	POSINGS	POST
PORRIGO	PORTHOLE	PORTREEVE	POSIT	POSTAGE
PORRIGOS	PORTHOLES	PORTRESS	POSITED	POSTAGES
PORRINGER	PORTHORS	PORTS	POSITIF	POSTAL
PORT	PORTHOS	PORTSIDE	POSITIFS	POSTALLY
PORTA	PORTHOSES	PORTULACA	POSITING	POSTALS
PORTABLE	PORTHOUSE	PORTULAN	POSITION	POSTANAL
PORTABLES	PORTICO	PORTULANS	POSITIONS	POSTAXIAL
PORTABLY	PORTICOED	PORTY	POSITIVE	POSTBAG
PORTAGE	PORTICOES	PORWIGGLE	POSITIVER	POSTBAGS
PORTAGED	PORTICOS	PORY	POSITIVES	POSTBASE
PORTAGES	PORTIER	POS	POSITON	POSTBOX
PORTAGING	PORTIERE	POSABLE	POSITONS	POSTBOXES
PORTAGUE	PORTIERED	POSADA	POSITRON	POSTBOY
PORTAGUES	PORTIERES	POSADAS	POSITRONS	POSTBOYS
PORTAL	PORTIEST	POSAUNE	POSITS	POSTBURN
PORTALED	PORTIGUE	POSAUNES	POSNET	POSTBUS
PORTALS	PORTIGUES	POSE	POSNETS	POSTBUSES
PORTANCE	PORTING	POSEABLE	POSOLE	POSTCARD

POSTCARDS	POSTHOUSE	POSTSYNCS	POTATION	POTHERB
POSTCAVA	POSTICAL	POSTTAX	POTATIONS	POTHERBS
POSTCAVAE	POSTICHE	POSTTEEN	POTATO	POTHERED
POSTCAVAL	POSTICHES	POSTTEENS	POTATOBUG	POTHERING
POSTCAVAS	POSTICOUS	POSTTEST	POTATOES	POTHERS
POSTCODE	POSTIE	POSTTESTS	POTATORY	POTHERY
POSTCODED	POSTIES	POSTTRIAL	POTBELLY	POTHOLDER
POSTCODES	POSTIL	POSTULANT	POTBOIL	POTHOLE
POSTCOUP	POSTILED	POSTULATA	POTBOILED	POTHOLED
POSTCRASH	POSTILING	POSTULATE	POTBOILER	POTHOLER
POSTDATE	POSTILION	POSTURAL	POTBOILS	POTHOLERS
POSTDATED	POSTILLED	POSTURE	POTBOUND	POTHOLES
POSTDATES	POSTILLER	POSTURED	POTBOY	POTHOLING
POSTDIVE	POSTILS	POSTURER	POTBOYS	POTHOOK
POSTDOC	POSTIN	POSTURERS	POTCH	POTHOOKS
POSTDOCS	POSTING	POSTURES	POTCHE	POTHOS
POSTDRUG	POSTINGS	POSTURING	POTCHED	POTHOUSE
POSTED	POSTINS	POSTURISE	POTCHER	POTHOUSES
POSTEEN	POSTIQUE	POSTURIST	POTCHERS	POTHUNTER
POSTEENS	POSTIQUES	POSTURIZE	POTCHES	POTICARY
POSTER	POSTLUDE	POSTVIRAL	POTCHING	POTICHE
POSTERED	POSTLUDES	POSTWAR	POTE	POTICHES
POSTERING	POSTMAN	POSTWOMAN	POTED	POTIN
POSTERIOR	POSTMARK	POSTWOMEN	POTEEN	POTING
POSTERITY	POSTMARKS	POSY	POTEENS	POTINS
POSTERN	POSTMEN	POT	POTENCE	POTION
POSTERNS	POSTNASAL	POTABLE	POTENCES	POTIONS
POSTERS	POSTNATAL	POTABLES	POTENCIES	POTJIE
POSTFACE	POSTNATI	POTAE	POTENCY	POTJIES
POSTFACES	POSTOP	POTAES	POTENT	POTLACH
POSTFAULT	POSTOPS	POTAGE	POTENTATE	POTLACHE
POSTFIRE	POSTORAL	POTAGER	POTENTIAL	POTLACHES
POSTFIX	POSTPAID	POTAGERS	POTENTISE	POTLATCH
POSTFIXAL	POSTPONE	POTAGES	POTENTIZE	POTLIKE
POSTFIXED	POSTPONED	POTALE	POTENTLY	POTLINE
POSTFIXES	POSTPONER	POTALES	POTENTS	POTLINES
POSTFORM	POSTPONES	POTAMIC	POTES	POTLUCK
POSTFORMS	POSTPOSE	POTASH	POTFUL	POTLUCKS
POSTGAME	POSTPOSED	POTASHED	POTFULS	POTMAN
POSTGRAD	POSTPOSES	POTASHES	POTGUN	POTMEN
POSTGRADS	POSTPUNK	POTASHING	POTGUNS	POTOMETER
POSTHASTE	POSTRACE	POTASS	POTHEAD	POTOO
POSTHEAT	POSTRIDER	POTASSA	POTHEADS	POTOOS
POSTHEATS	POSTRIOT	POTASSAS	POTHECARY	POTOROO
POSTHOLE	POSTS	POTASSES	POTHEEN	POTOROOS
POSTHOLES	POSTSHOW	POTASSIC	POTHEENS	POTPIE
POSTHORSE	POSTSYNC	POTASSIUM	POTHER	POTPIES

POTPOURRI

POTPOURRI	POTZERS	POULDRON	POURED	POUTS
POTS	POUCH	POULDRONS	POURER	POUTY
POTSHARD	POUCHED	POULE	POURERS	POVERTIES
POTSHARDS	POUCHES	POULES	POURIE	POVERTY
POTSHARE	POUCHFUL	POULP	POURIES	POW
POTSHARES	POUCHFULS	POULPE	POURING	POWAN
POTSHERD	POUCHIER	POULPES	POURINGLY	POWANS
POTSHERDS	POUCHIEST	POULPS	POURINGS	POWDER
POTSHOP	POUCHING	POULT	POURPOINT	POWDERED
POTSHOPS	POUCHY	POULTER	POURS	POWDERER
POTSHOT	POUDER	POULTERER	POURSEW	POWDERERS
POTSHOTS	POUDERS	POULTERERS	POURSEWED	POWDERIER
POTSIE	POUDRE	POULTICE	POURSEWS	POWDERING
POTSIES	POUDRES	POULTICED	POURSUE	POWDERS
POTSTONE	POUF	POULTICES	POURSUED	POWDERY
POTSTONES	POUFED	POULTRIES	POURSUES	POWELLISE
POTSY	POUFF	POULTRY	POURSUING	POWELLITE
POTT	POUFFE	POULTS	POURSUIT	POWELLIZE
POTTABLE	POUFFED	POUNCE	POURSUITS	POWER
POTTAGE	POUFFES	POUNCED	POURTRAY	POWERBOAT
POTTAGES	POUFFIER	POUNCER	POURTRAYD	POWERED
POTTED	POUFFIEST	POUNCERS	POURTRAYS	POWERFUL
POTTEEN	POUFFING	POUNCES	POUSADA	POWERING
POTTEENS	POUFFS	POUNCET	POUSADAS	POWERLESS
POTTER	POUFFY	POUNCETS	POUSOWDIE	POWERPLAY
POTTERED	POUFING	POUNCHING	POUSSE	POWERS
POTTERER	POUFS	POUNCING	POUSSES	POWFAGGED
POTTERERS	POUFTAH	POUND	POUSSETTE	POWHIRI
POTTERIES	POUFTAHS	POUNDAGE	POUSSIE	POWHIRIS
POTTERING	POUFTER	POUNDAGES	POUSSIES	POWIN
POTTERS	POUFTERS	POUNDAL	POUSSIN	POWINS
POTTERY	POUK	POUNDALS	POUSSINS	POWN
POTTIER	POUKE	POUNDCAKE	POUT	POWND
POTTIES	POUKES	POUNDED	POUTED	POWNDED
POTTIEST	POUKING	POUNDER	POUTER	POWNDING
POTTINESS	POUKIT	POUNDERS	POUTERS	POWNDS
POTTING	POUKS	POUNDING	POUTFUL	POWNEY
POTTINGAR	POULAINE	POUNDINGS	POUTHER	POWNEYS
POTTINGER	POULAINES	POUNDS	POUTHERED	POWNIE
POTTLE	POULARD	POUPE	POUTHERS	POWNIES
POTTLES	POULARDE	POUPED	POUTIER	POWNS
POTTO	POULARDES	POUPES	POUTIEST	POWNY
POTTOS	POULARDS	POUPING	POUTINE	POWRE
POTTS	POULDER	POUPT	POUTINES	POWRED
POTTY	POULDERS	POUR	POUTING	POWRES
POTWALLER	POULDRE	POURABLE	POUTINGLY	POWRING
POTZER	POULDRES	POURBOIRE	POUTINGS	POWS

POWSOWDY	PRACTIC	PRAISES	PRAOS	PRAWNING
POWTER	PRACTICAL	PRAISING	PRASE	PRAWNS
POWTERED	PRACTICE	PRAISINGS	PRASES	PRAXES
POWTERING	PRACTICED	PRAJNA	PRAT	PRAXIS
POWTERS	PRACTICER	PRAJNAS	PRATE	PRAXISES
POWWAW	PRACTICES	PRALINE	PRATED	PRAY
POWWOW	PRACTICK	PRALINES	PRATER	PRAYED
POWWOWED	PRACTICKS	PRAM	PRATERS	PRAYER
POWWOWING	PRACTICS	PRAMS	PRATES	PRAYERFUL
POWWOWS	PRACTICUM	PRANA	PRATFALL	PRAYERS
POX	PRACTIQUE	PRANAS	PRATFALLS	PRAYING
POXED	PRACTISE	PRANAYAMA	PRATFELL	PRAYINGLY
POXES	PRACTISED	PRANCE	PRATIE	PRAYINGS
POXIER	PRACTISER	PRANCED	PRATIES	PRAYS
POXIEST	PRACTISES	PRANCER	PRATING	PRE
POXING	PRACTIVE	PRANCERS	PRATINGLY	PREABSORB
POXVIRUS	PRACTOLOL	PRANCES	PRATINGS	PREACCUSE
POXY	PRAD	PRANCING	PRATIQUE	PREACE
POYNANT	PRADS	PRANCINGS	PRATIQUES	PREACED
POYNT	PRAEAMBLE	PRANCK	PRATS	PREACES
POYNTED	PRAECIPE	PRANCKE	PRATT	PREACH
POYNTING	PRAECIPES	PRANCKED	PRATTED	PREACHED
POYNTS	PRAECOCES	PRANCKES	PRATTING	PREACHER
POYOU	PRAEDIAL	PRANCKING	PRATTLE	PREACHERS
POYOUS	PRAEDIALS	PRANCKS	PRATTLED	PREACHES
POYSE	PRAEFECT	PRANDIAL	PRATTLER	PREACHIER
POYSED	PRAEFECTS	PRANG	PRATTLERS	PREACHIFY
POYSES	PRAELECT	PRANGED	PRATTLES	PREACHILY
POYSING	PRAELECTS	PRANGING	PRATTLING	PREACHING
POYSON	PRAELUDIA	PRANGS	PRATTS	PREACHY
POYSONED	PRAENOMEN	PRANK	PRATY	PREACING
POYSONING	PRAESES	PRANKED	PRAU	PREACT
POYSONS	PRAESIDIA	PRANKFUL	PRAUNCE	PREACTED
POZ	PRAETOR	PRANKIER	PRAUNCED	PREACTING
POZOLE	PRAETORS	PRANKIEST	PRAUNCES	PREACTS
POZOLES	PRAGMATIC	PRANKING	PRAUNCING	PREADAMIC
POZZ	PRAHU	PRANKINGS	PRAUS	PREADAPT
POZZIES	PRAHUS	PRANKISH	PRAVITIES	PREADAPTS
POZZOLAN	PRAIRIE	PRANKLE	PRAVITY	PREADJUST
POZZOLANA	PRAIRIED	PRANKLED	PRAWLE	PREADMIT
POZZOLANS	PRAIRIES	PRANKLES	PRAWLES	PREADMITS
POZZY	PRAISE	PRANKLING	PRAWLIN	PREADOPT
PRAAM	PRAISEACH	PRANKS	PRAWLINS	PREADOPTS
PRAAMS	PRAISED	PRANKSOME	PRAWN	PREADULT
PRABBLE	PRAISEFUL	PRANKSTER	PRAWNED	PREADULTS
PRABBLES	PRAISER	PRANKY	PRAWNER	PREAGED
PRACHARAK	PRAISERS	PRAO	PRAWNERS	PREALLOT

PREALLOTS	PREBIND	PRECEPIT	PRECODED	PREDELLE
PREALTER	PREBINDS	PRECEPITS	PRECODES	PREDESIGN
PREALTERS	PREBIOTIC	PRECEPT	PRECODING	PREDEVOTE
PREAMBLE	PREBIRTH	PRECEPTOR	PRECOITAL	PREDIAL
PREAMBLED	PREBIRTHS	PRECEPTS	PRECONISE	PREDIALS
PREAMBLES	PREBLESS	PRECES	PRECONIZE	PREDICANT
PREAMP	PREBOARD	PRECESS	PRECOOK	PREDICATE
PREAMPS	PREBOARDS	PRECESSED	PRECOOKED	PREDICT
PREANAL	PREBOIL	PRECESSES	PRECOOKER	PREDICTED
PREAPPLY	PREBOILED	PRECHARGE	PRECOOKS	PREDICTER
PREARM	PREBOILS	PRECHECK	PRECOOL	PREDICTOR
PREARMED	PREBOOK	PRECHECKS	PRECOOLED	PREDICTS
PREARMING	PREBOOKED	PRECHILL	PRECOOLS	PREDIED
PREARMS	PREBOOKS	PRECHILLS	PRECOUP	PREDIES
PREASE	PREBOOM	PRECHOOSE	PRECRASH	PREDIGEST
PREASED	PREBORN	PRECHOSE	PRECREASE	PREDIKANT
PREASES	PREBOUGHT	PRECHOSEN	PRECRISIS	PREDILECT
PREASING	PREBOUND	PRECIEUSE	PRECURE	PREDINNER
PREASSE	PREBUDGET	PRECIEUX	PRECURED	PREDIVE
PREASSED	PREBUILD	PRECINCT	PRECURES	PREDOOM
PREASSES	PREBUILDS	PRECINCTS	PRECURING	PREDOOMED
PREASSIGN	PREBUILT	PRECIOUS	PRECURRER	PREDOOMS
PREASSING	PREBUTTAL	PRECIPE	PRECURSE	PREDRAFT
PREASSURE	PREBUY	PRECIPES	PRECURSES	PREDRIED
PREATOMIC	PREBUYING	PRECIPICE	PRECURSOR	PREDRIES
PREATTUNE	PREBUYS	PRECIS	PRECUT	PREDRILL
PREAUDIT	PRECANCEL	PRECISE	PRECUTS	PREDRILLS
PREAUDITS	PRECANCER	PRECISED	PREDACITY	PREDRY
PREAVER	PRECAST	PRECISELY	PREDATE	PREDRYING
PREAVERS	PRECASTS	PRECISER	PREDATED	PREDUSK
PREAXIAL	PRECATIVE	PRECISES	PREDATES	PREDUSKS
PREBADE	PRECATORY	PRECISEST	PREDATING	PREDY
PREBAKE	PRECAUDAL	PRECISIAN	PREDATION	PREDYING
PREBAKED	PRECAVA	PRECISING	PREDATISM	PREE
PREBAKES	PRECAVAE	PRECISION	PREDATIVE	PREED
PREBAKING	PRECAVAL	PRECISIVE	PREDATOR	PREEDIT
PREBASAL	PRECEDE	PRECITED	PREDATORS	PREEDITED
PREBATTLE	PRECEDED	PRECLEAN	PREDATORY	PREEDITS
PREBEND	PRECEDENT	PRECLEANS	PREDAWN	PREEING
PREBENDAL	PRECEDES	PRECLEAR	PREDAWNS	PREELECT
PREBENDS	PRECEDING	PRECLEARS	PREDEATH	PREELECTS
PREBID	PRECEESE	PRECLUDE	PREDEATHS	PREEMIE
PREBIDDEN	PRECENSOR	PRECLUDED	PREDEBATE	PREEMIES
PREBIDS	PRECENT	PRECLUDES	PREDEDUCT	PREEMPT
PREBILL	PRECENTED	PRECOCIAL	PREDEFINE	PREEMPTED
PREBILLED	PRECENTOR	PRECOCITY	PREDELLA	PREEMPTOR
PREBILLS	PRECENTS	PRECODE	PREDELLAS	PREEMPTS

PREEN	PREFILED	PREHEATED	PRELECTOR	PREMIES
PREENACT	PREFILES	PREHEATER	PRELECTS	PREMISE
PREENACTS	PREFILING	PREHEATS	PRELEGAL	PREMISED
PREENED	PREFILLED	PREHEND	PRELIFE	PREMISES
PREENER	PREFIRE	PREHENDED	PRELIM	PREMISING
PREENERS	PREFIRED	PREHENDS	PRELIMIT	PREMISS
PREENING	PREFIRES	PREHENSOR	PRELIMITS	PREMISSED
PREENS	PREFIRING	PREHIRING	PRELIMS	PREMISSES
PREERECT	PREFIX	PREHNITE	PRELIVES	PREMIUM
PREERECTS	PREFIXAL	PREHNITES	PRELOAD	PREMIUMS
PREES	PREFIXED	PREHUMAN	PRELOADED	PREMIX
PREEVE	PREFIXES	PREHUMANS	PRELOADS	PREMIXED
PREEVED	PREFIXING	PREIF	PRELOCATE	PREMIXES
PREEVES	PREFIXION	PREIFE	PRELOVED	PREMIXING
PREEVING	PREFLAME	PREIFES	PRELUDE	PREMIXT
PREEXCITE	PREFLIGHT	PREIFS	PRELUDED	PREMODERN
PREEXEMPT	PREFOCUS	PREIMPOSE	PRELUDER	PREMODIFY
PREEXILIC	PREFORM	PREINFORM	PRELUDERS	PREMOLAR
PREEXIST	PREFORMAT	PREINSERT	PRELUDES	PREMOLARS
PREEXISTS	PREFORMED	PREINVITE	PRELUDI	PREMOLD
PREEXPOSE	PREFORMS	PREJINK	PRELUDIAL	PREMOLDED
PREFAB	PREFRANK	PREJUDGE	PRELUDING	PREMOLDS
PREFABBED	PREFRANKS	PREJUDGED	PRELUDIO	PREMOLT
PREFABS	PREFREEZE	PREJUDGER	PRELUNCH	PREMONISH
PREFACE	PREFROZE	PREJUDGES	PRELUSION	PREMORAL
PREFACED	PREFROZEN	PREJUDICE	PRELUSIVE	PREMORSE
PREFACER	PREFUND	PREJUDIZE	PRELUSORY	PREMOSAIC
PREFACERS	PREFUNDED	PRELACIES	PREM	PREMOTION
PREFACES	PREFUNDS	PRELACY	PREMADE	PREMOVE
PREFACIAL	PREGAME	PRELATE	PREMAN	PREMOVED
PREFACING	PREGAMES	PRELATES	PREMARKET	PREMOVES
PREFADE	PREGGERS	PRELATESS	PREMATURE	PREMOVING
PREFADED	PREGGIER	PRELATIAL	PREMEAL	PREMS
PREFADES	PREGGIEST	PRELATIC	PREMED	PREMUNE
PREFADING	PREGGY	PRELATIES	PREMEDIC	PREMY
PREFARD	PREGNABLE	PRELATION	PREMEDICS	PRENAME
PREFATORY	PREGNANCE	PRELATISE	PREMEDS	PRENAMES
PREFECT	PREGNANCY	PRELATISH	PREMEET	PRENASAL
PREFECTS	PREGNANT	PRELATISM	PREMEN	PRENASALS
PREFER	PREGROWTH	PRELATIST	PREMERGER	PRENATAL
PREFERRED	PREGUIDE	PRELATIZE	PREMIA	PRENATALS
PREFERRER	PREGUIDED	PRELATURE	PREMIE	PRENEED
PREFERS	PREGUIDES	PRELATY	PREMIER	PRENOMEN
PREFEUDAL	PREHALLUX	PRELAUNCH	PREMIERE	PRENOMENS
PREFIGHT	PREHANDLE	PRELAW	PREMIERED	PRENOMINA
PREFIGURE	PREHARDEN	PRELECT	PREMIERES	PRENOON
PREFILE	PREHEAT	PRELECTED	PREMIERS	PRENOTIFY

P

PRENOTION	PREPENSE	PREPUPAS	PRESEASON	PRESIFTS
PRENT	PREPENSED	PREPUTIAL	PRESELECT	PRESIGNAL
PRENTED	PREPENSES	PREQUEL	PRESELL	PRESLEEP
PRENTICE	PREPILL	PREQUELS	PRESELLS	PRESLICE
PRENTICED	PREPLACE	PRERACE	PRESENCE	PRESLICED
PRENTICES	PREPLACED	PRERADIO	PRESENCES	PRESLICES
PRENTING	PREPLACES	PRERECORD	PRESENILE	PRESOAK
PRENTS	PREPLAN	PRERECTAL	PRESENT	PRESOAKED
PRENUBILE	PREPLANS	PREREFORM	PRESENTED	PRESOAKS
PRENUMBER	PREPLANT	PRERENAL	PRESENTEE	PRESOLD
PRENUP	PREPOLLEX	PRERETURN	PRESENTER	PRESOLVE
PRENUPS	PREPONE	PREREVIEW	PRESENTLY	PRESOLVED
PRENZIE	PREPONED	PRERINSE	PRESENTS	PRESOLVES
PREOBTAIN	PREPONES	PRERINSED	PRESERVE	PRESONG
PREOCCUPY	PREPONING	PRERINSES	PRESERVED	PRESORT
PREOCULAR	PREPOSE	PRERIOT	PRESERVER	PRESORTED
PREON	PREPOSED	PREROCK	PRESERVES	PRESORTS
PREONS	PREPOSES	PRERUPT	PRESES	PRESPLIT
PREOP	PREPOSING	PRESA	PRESET	PRESS
PREOPS	PREPOSTOR	PRESAGE	PRESETS	PRESSED
PREOPTION	PREPOTENT	PRESAGED	PRESETTLE	PRESSER
PREORAL	PREPPED	PRESAGER	PRESHAPE	PRESSERS
PREORDAIN	PREPPIE	PRESAGERS	PRESHAPED	PRESSES
PREORDER	PREPPIER	PRESAGES	PRESHAPES	PRESSFAT
PREORDERS	PREPPIES	PRESAGING	PRESHIP	PRESSFATS
PREOWNED	PREPPIEST	PRESALE	PRESHIPS	PRESSFUL
PREP	PREPPILY	PRESALES	PRESHOW	PRESSFULS
PREPACK	PREPPING	PRESBYOPE	PRESHOWED	PRESSGANG
PREPACKED	PREPPY	PRESBYOPY	PRESHOWN	PRESSIE
PREPACKS	PREPREG	PRESBYTE	PRESHOWS	PRESSIES
PREPAID	PREPREGS	PRESBYTER	PRESHRANK	PRESSING
PREPARE	PREPRESS	PRESBYTES	PRESHRINK	PRESSINGS
PREPARED	PREPRICE	PRESBYTIC	PRESHRUNK	PRESSION
PREPARER	PREPRICED	PRESCHOOL	PRESIDE	PRESSIONS
PREPARERS	PREPRICES	PRESCIENT	PRESIDED	PRESSMAN
PREPARES	PREPRINT	PRESCIND	PRESIDENT	PRESSMARK
PREPARING	PREPRINTS	PRESCINDS	PRESIDER	PRESSMEN
PREPASTE	PREPS	PRESCIOUS	PRESIDERS	PRESSOR
PREPASTED	PREPUBES	PRESCORE	PRESIDES	PRESSORS
PREPASTES	PREPUBIS	PRESCORED	PRESIDIA	PRESSROOM
PREPAVE	PREPUCE	PRESCORES	PRESIDIAL	PRESSRUN
PREPAVED	PREPUCES	PRESCREEN	PRESIDING	PRESSRUNS
PREPAVES	PREPUEBLO	PRESCRIBE	PRESIDIO	PRESSURE
PREPAVING	PREPUNCH	PRESCRIPT	PRESIDIOS	PRESSURED
PREPAY	PREPUPA	PRESCUTA	PRESIDIUM	PRESSURES
PREPAYING	PREPUPAE	PRESCUTUM	PRESIFT	PRESSWORK
PREPAYS	PREPUPAL	PRESE	PRESIFTED	PREST

PRESTAMP	PRETERITE	PREVAIL	PREWARNED	PRICED
PRESTAMPS	PRETERITS	PREVAILED	PREWARNS	PRICELESS
PRESTED	PRETERM	PREVAILER	PREWASH	PRICER
PRESTER	PRETERMIT	PREVAILS	PREWASHED	PRICERS
PRESTERNA	PRETERMS	PREVALENT	PREWASHES	PRICES
PRESTERS	PRETEST	PREVALUE	PREWEIGH	PRICEY
PRESTIGE	PRETESTED	PREVALUED	PREWEIGHS	PRICIER
PRESTIGES	PRETESTS	PREVALUES	PREWIRE	PRICIEST
PRESTING	PRETEXT	PREVE	PREWIRED	PRICILY
PRESTO	PRETEXTED	PREVED	PREWIRES	PRICINESS
PRESTORE	PRETEXTS	PREVENE	PREWIRING	PRICING
PRESTORED	PRETOLD	PREVENED	PREWORK	PRICINGS
PRESTORES	PRETONIC	PREVENES	PREWORKED	PRICK
PRESTOS	PRETOR	PREVENING	PREWORKS	PRICKED
PRESTRESS	PRETORIAL	PREVENT	PREWORN	PRICKER
PRESTRIKE	PRETORIAN	PREVENTED	PREWRAP	PRICKERS
PRESTS	PRETORS	PREVENTER	PREWRAPS	PRICKET
PRESUME	PRETRAIN	PREVENTS	PREWYN	PRICKETS
PRESUMED	PRETRAINS	PREVERB	PREWYNS	PRICKIER
PRESUMER	PRETRAVEL	PREVERBAL	PREX	PRICKIEST
PRESUMERS	PRETREAT	PREVERBS	PREXES	PRICKING
PRESUMES	PRETREATS	PREVES	PREXIES	PRICKINGS
PRESUMING	PRETRIAL	PREVIABLE	PREXY	PRICKLE
PRESUMMIT	PRETRIALS	PREVIEW	PREY	PRICKLED
PRESURVEY	PRETRIM	PREVIEWED	PREYED	PRICKLES
PRETAPE	PRETRIMS	PREVIEWER	PREYER	PRICKLIER
PRETAPED	PRETTIED	PREVIEWS	PREYERS	PRICKLING
PRETAPES	PRETTIER	PREVING	PREYFUL	PRICKLY
PRETAPING	PRETTIES	PREVIOUS	PREYING	PRICKS
PRETASTE	PRETTIEST	PREVISE	PREYS	PRICKWOOD
PRETASTED	PRETTIFY	PREVISED	PREZ	PRICKY
PRETASTES	PRETTILY	PREVISES	PREZES	PRICY
PRETAX	PRETTY	PREVISING	PREZZIE	PRIDE
PRETEEN	PRETTYING	PREVISION	PREZZIES	PRIDED
PRETEENS	PRETTYISH	PREVISIT	PRIAL	PRIDEFUL
PRETELL	PRETTYISM	PREVISITS	PRIALS	PRIDELESS
PRETELLS	PRETYPE	PREVISOR	PRIAPEAN	PRIDES
PRETENCE	PRETYPED	PREVISORS	PRIAPI	PRIDIAN
PRETENCES	PRETYPES	PREVUE	PRIAPIC	PRIDING
PRETEND	PRETYPING	PREVUED	PRIAPISM	PRIED
PRETENDED	PRETZEL	PREVUES	PRIAPISMS	PRIEDIEU
PRETENDER	PRETZELS	PREVUING	PRIAPUS	PRIEDIEUS
PRETENDS	PREUNION	PREWAR	PRIAPUSES	PRIEDIEUX
PRETENSE	PREUNIONS	PREWARM	PRIBBLE	PRIEF
PRETENSES	PREUNITE	PREWARMED	PRIBBLES	PRIEFE
PRETERIST	PREUNITED	PREWARMS	PRICE	PRIEFES
PRETERIT	PREUNITES	PREWARN	PRICEABLE	PRIEFS

PRIER	PRIMATIC	PRIMULA	PRIORATE	PRIVADO
PRIERS	PRIMAVERA	PRIMULAS	PRIORATES	PRIVADOES
PRIES	PRIME	PRIMULINE	PRIORESS	PRIVADOS
PRIEST	PRIMED	PRIMUS	PRIORIES	PRIVATE
PRIESTED	PRIMELY	PRIMUSES	PRIORITY	PRIVATEER
PRIESTESS	PRIMENESS	PRIMY	PRIORLY	PRIVATELY
PRIESTING	PRIMER	PRINCE	PRIORS	PRIVATER
PRIESTLY	PRIMERO	PRINCED	PRIORSHIP	PRIVATES
PRIESTS	PRIMEROS	PRINCEDOM	PRIORY	PRIVATEST
PRIEVE	PRIMERS	PRINCEKIN	PRISAGE	PRIVATION
PRIEVED	PRIMES	PRINCELET	PRISAGES	PRIVATISE
PRIEVES	PRIMETIME	PRINCELY	PRISE	PRIVATISM
PRIEVING	PRIMEUR	PRINCES	PRISED	PRIVATIST
PRIG	PRIMEURS	PRINCESS	PRISER	PRIVATIVE
PRIGGED	PRIMEVAL	PRINCESSE	PRISERE	PRIVATIZE
PRIGGER	PRIMI	PRINCING	PRISERES	PRIVET
PRIGGERS	PRIMINE	PRINCIPAL	PRISERS	PRIVETS
PRIGGERY	PRIMINES	PRINCIPE	PRISES	PRIVIER
PRIGGING	PRIMING	PRINCIPI	PRISING	PRIVIES
PRIGGINGS	PRIMINGS	PRINCIPIA	PRISM	PRIVIEST
PRIGGISH	PRIMIPARA	PRINCIPLE	PRISMATIC	PRIVILEGE
PRIGGISM	PRIMITIAE	PRINCOCK	PRISMOID	PRIVILY
PRIGGISMS	PRIMITIAL	PRINCOCKS	PRISMOIDS	PRIVITIES
PRIGS	PRIMITIAS	PRINCOX	PRISMS	PRIVITY
PRILL	PRIMITIVE	PRINCOXES	PRISMY	PRIVY
PRILLED	PRIMLY	PRINK	PRISON	PRIZABLE
PRILLING	PRIMMED	PRINKED	PRISONED	PRIZE
PRILLS	PRIMMER	PRINKER	PRISONER	PRIZED
PRIM	PRIMMERS	PRINKERS	PRISONERS	PRIZEMAN
PRIMA	PRIMMEST	PRINKING	PRISONING	PRIZEMEN
PRIMACIES	PRIMMING	PRINKS	PRISONOUS	PRIZER
PRIMACY	PRIMNESS	PRINT	PRISONS	PRIZERS
PRIMAEVAL	PRIMO	PRINTABLE	PRISS	PRIZES
PRIMAGE	PRIMORDIA	PRINTED	PRISSED	PRIZING
PRIMAGES	PRIMOS	PRINTER	PRISSES	PRO
PRIMAL	PRIMP	PRINTERS	PRISSIER	PROA
PRIMALITY	PRIMPED	PRINTERY	PRISSIES	PROACTION
PRIMALLY	PRIMPING	PRINTHEAD	PRISSIEST	PROACTIVE
PRIMARIES	PRIMPS	PRINTING	PRISSILY	PROAS
PRIMARILY	PRIMROSE	PRINTINGS	PRISSING	PROB
PRIMARY	PRIMROSED	PRINTLESS	PRISSY	PROBABLE
PRIMAS	PRIMROSES	PRINTOUT	PRISTANE	PROBABLES
PRIMATAL	PRIMROSY	PRINTOUTS	PRISTANES	PROBABLY
PRIMATALS	PRIMS	PRINTS	PRISTINE	PROBALL
PRIMATE	PRIMSIE	PRION	PRITHEE	PROBAND
PRIMATES	PRIMSIER	PRIONS	PRIVACIES	PROBANDS
PRIMATIAL	PRIMSIEST	PRIOR	PRIVACY	PROBANG

PROBANGS	PROCIDENT	PRODROMES	PROFILING	PROHIBITS
PROBATE	PROCINCT	PRODROMI	PROFILIST	PROIGN
PROBATED	PROCINCTS	PRODROMIC	PROFIT	PROIGNED
PROBATES	PROCLAIM	PRODROMUS	PROFITED	PROIGNING
PROBATING	PROCLAIMS	PRODRUG	PROFITEER	PROIGNS
PROBATION	PROCLISES	PRODRUGS	PROFITER	PROIN
PROBATIVE	PROCLISIS	PRODS	PROFITERS	PROINE
PROBATORY	PROCLITIC	PRODUCE	PROFITING	PROINED
PROBE	PROCLIVE	PRODUCED	PROFITS	PROINES
PROBEABLE	PROCONSUL	PRODUCER	PROFLUENT	PROINING
PROBED	PROCREANT	PRODUCERS	PROFORMA	PROINS
PROBER	PROCREATE	PRODUCES	PROFOUND	PROJECT
PROBERS	PROCTAL	PRODUCING	PROFOUNDS	PROJECTED
PROBES	PROCTITIS	PRODUCT	PROFS	PROJECTOR
PROBING	PROCTODEA	PRODUCTS	PROFUSE	PROJECTS
PROBINGLY	PROCTOR	PROEM	PROFUSELY	PROJET
PROBIOTIC	PROCTORED	PROEMBRYO	PROFUSER	PROJETS
PROBIT	PROCTORS	PROEMIAL	PROFUSERS	PROKARYON
PROBITIES	PROCURACY	PROEMS	PROFUSION	PROKARYOT
PROBITS	PROCURAL	PROENZYME	PROFUSIVE	PROKE
PROBITY	PROCURALS	PROESTRUS	PROG	PROKED
PROBLEM	PROCURE	PROETTE	PROGENIES	PROKER
PROBLEMS	PROCURED	PROETTES	PROGENY	PROKERS
PROBOSCIS	PROCURER	PROF	PROGERIA	PROKES
PROBS	PROCURERS	PROFACE	PROGERIAS	PROKING
PROCACITY	PROCURES	PROFAMILY	PROGESTIN	PROLABOR
PROCAINE	PROCURESS	PROFANE	PROGGED	PROLACTIN
PROCAINES	PROCUREUR	PROFANED	PROGGER	PROLAMIN
PROCAMBIA	PROCURING	PROFANELY	PROGGERS	PROLAMINE
PROCARP	PROCYONID	PROFANER	PROGGING	PROLAMINS
PROCARPS	PROD	PROFANERS	PROGGINS	PROLAN
PROCARYON	PRODDED	PROFANES	PROGNOSE	PROLANS
PROCEDURE	PRODDER	PROFANING	PROGNOSED	PROLAPSE
PROCEED	PRODDERS	PROFANITY	PROGNOSES	PROLAPSED
PROCEEDED	PRODDING	PROFESS	PROGNOSIS	PROLAPSES
PROCEEDER	PRODIGAL	PROFESSED	PROGRADE	PROLAPSUS
PROCEEDS	PRODIGALS	PROFESSES	PROGRADED	PROLATE
PROCERITY	PRODIGIES	PROFESSOR	PROGRADES	PROLATED
PROCESS	PRODIGY	PROFFER	PROGRAM	PROLATELY
PROCESSED	PRODITOR	PROFFERED	PROGRAMED	PROLATES
PROCESSER	PRODITORS	PROFFERER	PROGRAMER	PROLATING
PROCESSES	PRODITORY	PROFFERS	PROGRAMME	PROLATION
PROCESSOR	PRODNOSE	PROFILE	PROGRAMS	PROLATIVE
PROCHAIN	PRODNOSED	PROFILED	PROGRESS	PROLE
PROCHEIN	PRODNOSES	PROFILER	PROGS	PROLED
PROCHOICE	PRODROMAL	PROFILERS	PROGUN	PROLEG
PROCHURCH	PRODROME	PROFILES	PROHIBIT	PROLEGS

PROLEPSES

PROLEPSES	PROMINES	PRONATED	PROOFS	PROPHASE
PROLEPSIS	PROMISE	PRONATES	PROOTIC	PROPHASES
PROLEPTIC	PROMISED	PRONATING	PROOTICS	PROPHASIC
PROLER	PROMISEE	PRONATION	PROP	PROPHECY
PROLERS	PROMISEES	PRONATOR	PROPAGATE	PROPHESY
PROLES	PROMISER	PRONATORS	PROPAGE	PROPHET
PROLETARY	PROMISERS	PRONE	PROPAGED	PROPHETIC
PROLICIDE	PROMISES	PRONELY	PROPAGES	PROPHETS
PROLIFIC	PROMISING	PRONENESS	PROPAGING	PROPHYLL
PROLINE	PROMISOR	PRONEPHRA	PROPAGULA	PROPHYLLS
PROLINES	PROMISORS	PRONER	PROPAGULE	PROPINE
PROLING	PROMISSOR	PRONES	PROPALE	PROPINED
PROLIX	PROMMER	PRONEST	PROPALED	PROPINES
PROLIXITY	PROMMERS	PRONEUR	PROPALES	PROPINING
PROLIXLY	PROMO	PRONEURS	PROPALING	PROPIONIC
PROLL	PROMODERN	PRONG	PROPANE	PROPJET
PROLLED	PROMOED	PRONGBUCK	PROPANES	PROPJETS
PROLLER	PROMOING	PRONGED	PROPANOIC	PROPMAN
PROLLERS	PROMOS	PRONGHORN	PROPANOL	PROPMEN
PROLLING	PROMOTE	PRONGING	PROPANOLS	PROPODEON
PROLLS	PROMOTED	PRONGS	PROPANONE	PROPODEUM
PROLOG	PROMOTER	PRONK	PROPEL	PROPOLIS
PROLOGED	PROMOTERS	PRONKED	PROPELLED	PROPONE
PROLOGING	PROMOTES	PRONKING	PROPELLER	PROPONED
PROLOGISE	PROMOTING	PRONKINGS	PROPELLOR	PROPONENT
PROLOGIST	PROMOTION	PRONKS	PROPELS	PROPONES
PROLOGIZE	PROMOTIVE	PRONOTA	PROPENAL	PROPONING
PROLOGS	PROMOTOR	PRONOTAL	PROPENALS	PROPOSAL
PROLOGUE	PROMOTORS	PRONOTUM	PROPEND	PROPOSALS
PROLOGUED	PROMPT	PRONOUN	PROPENDED	PROPOSE
PROLOGUES	PROMPTED	PRONOUNCE	PROPENDS	PROPOSED
PROLONG	PROMPTER	PRONOUNS	PROPENE	PROPOSER
PROLONGE	PROMPTERS	PRONTO	PROPENES	PROPOSERS
PROLONGED	PROMPTEST	PRONUCLEI	PROPENOIC	PROPOSES
PROLONGER	PROMPTING	PRONUNCIO	PROPENOL	PROPOSING
PROLONGES	PROMPTLY	PROO	PROPENOLS	PROPOSITA
PROLONGS	PROMPTS	PROOEMION	PROPENSE	PROPOSITI
PROLUSION	PROMPTURE	PROOEMIUM	PROPENYL	PROPOUND
PROLUSORY	PROMS	PROOF	PROPER	PROPOUNDS
PROM	PROMULGE	PROOFED	PROPERDIN	PROPPANT
PROMACHOS	PROMULGED	PROOFER	PROPERER	PROPPANTS
PROMENADE	PROMULGES	PROOFERS	PROPEREST	PROPPED
PROMETAL	PROMUSCES	PROOFING	PROPERLY	PROPPING
PROMETALS	PROMUSCIS	PROOFINGS	PROPERS	PROPRETOR
PROMETRIC	PRONAOI	PROOFLESS	PROPERTY	PROPRIA
PROMINE	PRONAOS	PROOFREAD	PROPHAGE	PROPRIETY
PROMINENT	PRONATE	PROOFROOM	PROPHAGES	PROPRIUM

PROPS	PROSELYTE	PROSTIE	PROTEOMIC	PROTOZOIC
PROPTOSES	PROSEMAN	PROSTIES	PROTEOSE	PROTOZOON
PROPTOSIS	PROSEMEN	PROSTOMIA	PROTEOSES	PROTRACT
PROPULSOR	PROSER	PROSTRATE	PROTEST	PROTRACTS
PROPYL	PROSERS	PROSTYLE	PROTESTED	PROTRADE
PROPYLA	PROSES	PROSTYLES	PROTESTER	PROTRUDE
PROPYLAEA	PROSEUCHA	PROSUMER	PROTESTOR	PROTRUDED
PROPYLENE	PROSEUCHE	PROSUMERS	PROTESTS	PROTRUDES
PROPYLIC	PROSIER	PROSY	PROTEUS	PROTYL
PROPYLITE	PROSIEST	PROTAMIN	PROTEUSES	PROTYLE
PROPYLON	PROSIFIED	PROTAMINE	PROTHALLI	PROTYLES
PROPYLONS	PROSIFIES	PROTAMINS	PROTHESES	PROTYLS
PROPYLS	PROSIFY	PROTANDRY	PROTHESIS	PROUD
PRORATE	PROSILY	PROTANOPE	PROTHETIC	PROUDER
PRORATED	PROSIMIAN	PROTASES	PROTHORAX	PROUDEST
PRORATES	PROSINESS	PROTASIS	PROTHYL	PROUDFUL
PRORATING	PROSING	PROTATIC	PROTHYLS	PROUDISH
PRORATION	PROSINGS	PROTEA	PROTIST	PROUDLY
PRORE	PROSIT	PROTEAN	PROTISTAN	PROUDNESS
PRORECTOR	PROSO	PROTEANS	PROTISTIC	PROUL
PROREFORM	PROSODIAL	PROTEAS	PROTISTS	PROULED
PRORES	PROSODIAN	PROTEASE	PROTIUM	PROULER
PROROGATE	PROSODIC	PROTEASES	PROTIUMS	PROULERS
PROROGUE	PROSODIES	PROTECT	PROTO	PROULING
PROROGUED	PROSODIST	PROTECTED	PROTOAVIS	PROULS
PROROGUES	PROSODY	PROTECTER	PROTOCOL	PROUNION
PROS	PROSOMA	PROTECTOR	PROTOCOLS	PROUSTITE
PROSAIC	PROSOMAL	PROTECTS	PROTODERM	PROVABLE
PROSAICAL	PROSOMAS	PROTEGE	PROTOGINE	PROVABLY
PROSAISM	PROSOMATA	PROTEGEE	PROTOGYNY	PROVAND
PROSAISMS	PROSOPON	PROTEGEES	PROTON	PROVANDS
PROSAIST	PROSOPONS	PROTEGES	PROTONATE	PROVANT
PROSAISTS	PROSOS	PROTEI	PROTONEMA	PROVE
PROSATEUR	PROSPECT	PROTEID	PROTONIC	PROVEABLE
PROSCENIA	PROSPECTS	PROTEIDE	PROTONS	PROVEABLY
PROSCRIBE	PROSPER	PROTEIDES	PROTOPOD	PROVED
PROSCRIPT	PROSPERED	PROTEIDS	PROTOPODS	PROVEDOR
PROSE	PROSPERS	PROTEIN	PROTORE	PROVEDORE
PROSECCO	PROSS	PROTEINIC	PROTORES	PROVEDORS
PROSECCOS	PROSSES	PROTEINS	PROTOSTAR	PROVEN
PROSECT	PROSSIE	PROTEND	PROTOTYPE	PROVEND
PROSECTED	PROSSIES	PROTENDED	PROTOXID	PROVENDER
PROSECTOR	PROST	PROTENDS	PROTOXIDE	PROVENDS
PROSECTS	PROSTATE	PROTENSE	PROTOXIDS	PROVENLY
PROSECUTE	PROSTATES	PROTENSES	PROTOZOA	PROVER
PROSED	PROSTATIC	PROTEOME	PROTOZOAL	PROVERB
PROSELIKE	PROSTERNA	PROTEOMES	PROTOZOAN	PROVERBED

PROVERBS	PROWESSES	PRUNELLES	PSALMED	PSILOSIS
PROVERS	PROWEST	PRUNELLO	PSALMIC	PSILOTIC
PROVES	PROWL	PRUNELLOS	PSALMING	PSION
PROVIANT	PROWLED	PRUNER	PSALMIST	PSIONIC
PROVIANTS	PROWLER	PRUNERS	PSALMISTS	PSIONICS
PROVIDE	PROWLERS	PRUNES	PSALMODIC	PSIONS
PROVIDED	PROWLING	PRUNING	PSALMODY	PSIS
PROVIDENT	PROWLINGS	PRUNINGS	PSALMS	PSOAE
PROVIDER	PROWLS	PRUNT	PSALTER	PSOAI
PROVIDERS	PROWS	PRUNTED	PSALTERIA	PSOAS
PROVIDES	PROXEMIC	PRUNTS	PSALTERS	PSOASES
PROVIDING	PROXEMICS	PRUNUS	PSALTERY	PSOATIC
PROVIDOR	PROXIES	PRUNUSES	PSALTRESS	PSOCID
PROVIDORS	PROXIMAL	PRURIENCE	PSALTRIES	PSOCIDS
PROVINCE	PROXIMATE	PRURIENCY	PSALTRY	PSORA
PROVINCES	PROXIMITY	PRURIENT	PSAMMITE	PSORALEA
PROVINE	PROXIMO	PRURIGO	PSAMMITES	PSORALEAS
PROVINED	PROXY	PRURIGOS	PSAMMITIC	PSORALEN
PROVINES	PROYN	PRURITIC	PSAMMON	PSORALENS
PROVING	PROYNE	PRURITUS	PSAMMONS	PSORAS
PROVINGS	PROYNED	PRUSIK	PSCHENT	PSORIASES
PROVINING	PROYNES	PRUSIKED	PSCHENTS	PSORIASIS
PROVIRAL	PROYNING	PRUSIKING	PSELLISM	PSORIATIC
PROVIRUS	PROYNS	PRUSIKS	PSELLISMS	PSORIC
PROVISION	PROZYMITE	PRUSSIAN	PSEPHISM	PSST
PROVISO	PRUDE	PRUSSIATE	PSEPHISMS	PST
PROVISOES	PRUDENCE	PRUSSIC	PSEPHITE	PSYCH
PROVISOR	PRUDENCES	PRUTA	PSEPHITES	PSYCHE
PROVISORS	PRUDENT	PRUTAH	PSEPHITIC	PSYCHED
PROVISORY	PRUDENTLY	PRUTOT	PSEUD	PSYCHES
PROVISOS	PRUDERIES	PRUTOTH	PSEUDAXES	PSYCHIC
PROVOCANT	PRUDERY	PRY	PSEUDAXIS	PSYCHICAL
PROVOKE	PRUDES	PRYER	PSEUDERY	PSYCHICS
PROVOKED	PRUDISH	PRYERS	PSEUDISH	PSYCHING
PROVOKER	PRUDISHLY	PRYING	PSEUDO	PSYCHISM
PROVOKERS	PRUH	PRYINGLY	PSEUDONYM	PSYCHISMS
PROVOKES	PRUINA	PRYINGS	PSEUDOPOD	PSYCHIST
PROVOKING	PRUINAS	PRYS	PSEUDOS	PSYCHISTS
PROVOLONE	PRUINE	PRYSE	PSEUDS	PSYCHO
PROVOST	PRUINES	PRYSED	PSHAW	PSYCHOGAS
PROVOSTRY	PRUINOSE	PRYSES	PSHAWED	PSYCHOID
PROVOSTS	PRUNABLE	PRYSING	PSHAWING	PSYCHOIDS
PROW	PRUNE	PRYTANEA	PSHAWS	PSYCHOS
PROWAR	PRUNED	PRYTANEUM	PSI	PSYCHOSES
PROWER	PRUNELLA	PRYTHEE	PSILOCIN	PSYCHOSIS
PROWESS	PRUNELLAS	PSALM	PSILOCINS	PSYCHOTIC
PROWESSED	PRUNELLE	PSALMBOOK	PSILOSES	PSYCHS

PSYLLA	PTYALISM	PUCER	PUDDOCKS	PUFFED
PSYLLAS	PTYALISMS	PUCES	PUDDY	PUFFER
PSYLLID	PTYALIZE	PUCEST	PUDENCIES	PUFFERIES
PSYLLIDS	PTYALIZED	PUCK	PUDENCY	PUFFERS
PSYLLIUM	PTYALIZES	PUCKA	PUDENDA	PUFFERY
PSYLLIUMS	PTYXES	PUCKED	PUDENDAL	PUFFIER
PSYOP	PTYXIS	PUCKER	PUDENDOUS	PUFFIEST
PSYOPS	PTYXISES	PUCKERED	PUDENDUM	PUFFILY
PSYWAR	PUB	PUCKERER	PUDENT	PUFFIN
PSYWARS	PUBBED	PUCKERERS	PUDGE	PUFFINESS
PTARMIC	PUBBING	PUCKERIER	PUDGES	PUFFING
PTARMICS	PUBBINGS	PUCKERING	PUDGIER	PUFFINGLY
PTARMIGAN	PUBCO	PUCKERS	PUDGIEST	PUFFINGS
PTERIA	PUBCOS	PUCKERY	PUDGILY	PUFFINS
PTERIDINE	PUBE	PUCKFIST	PUDGINESS	PUFFS
PTERIN	PUBERAL	PUCKFISTS	PUDGY	PUFFY
PTERINS	PUBERTAL	PUCKING	PUDIBUND	PUFTALOON
PTERION	PUBERTIES	PUCKISH	PUDIC	PUG
PTEROIC	PUBERTY	PUCKISHLY	PUDICITY	PUGAREE
PTEROPOD	PUBES	PUCKLE	PUDOR	PUGAREES
PTEROPODS	PUBESCENT	PUCKLES	PUDORS	PUGGAREE
PTEROSAUR	PUBIC	PUCKOUT	PUDS	PUGGAREES
PTERYGIA	PUBIS	PUCKOUTS	PUDSEY	PUGGED
PTERYGIAL	PUBISES	PUCKS	PUDSIER	PUGGERIES
PTERYGIUM	PUBLIC	PUD	PUDSIEST	PUGGERY
PTERYGOID	PUBLICAN	PUDDEN	PUDSY	PUGGIE
PTERYLA	PUBLICANS	PUDDENING	PUDU	PUGGIER
PTERYLAE	PUBLICISE	PUDDENS	PUDUS	PUGGIES
PTILOSES	PUBLICIST	PUDDER	PUEBLO	PUGGIEST
PTILOSIS	PUBLICITY	PUDDERED	PUEBLOS	PUGGINESS
PTISAN	PUBLICIZE	PUDDERING	PUER	PUGGING
PTISANS	PUBLICLY	PUDDERS	PUERED	PUGGINGS
PTOMAIN	PUBLICS	PUDDIES	PUERILE	PUGGISH
PTOMAINE	PUBLISH	PUDDING	PUERILELY	PUGGLE
PTOMAINES	PUBLISHED	PUDDINGS	PUERILISM	PUGGLED
PTOMAINIC	PUBLISHER	PUDDINGY	PUERILITY	PUGGLES
PTOMAINS	PUBLISHES	PUDDLE	PUERING	PUGGLING
PTOOEY	PUBS	PUDDLED	PUERPERA	PUGGREE
PTOSES	PUCAN	PUDDLER	PUERPERAE	PUGGREES
PTOSIS	PUCANS	PUDDLERS	PUERPERAL	PUGGRIES
PTOTIC	PUCCOON	PUDDLES	PUERPERIA	PUGGRY
PTUI	PUCCOONS	PUDDLIER	PUERS	PUGGY
PTYALIN	PUCE	PUDDLIEST	PUFF	PUGH
PTYALINS	PUCELAGE	PUDDLING	PUFFBALL	PUGIL
PTYALISE	PUCELAGES	PUDDLINGS	PUFFBALLS	PUGILISM
PTYALISED	PUCELLE	PUDDLY	PUFFBIRD	PUGILISMS
PTYALISES	PUCELLES	PUDDOCK	PUFFBIRDS	PUGILIST

PUGILISTS	PUL	PULLOVERS	PULPY	PULVERINE
PUGILS	PULA	PULLS	PULQUE	PULVERING
PUGMARK	PULAO	PULLULATE	PULQUES	PULVERISE
PUGMARKS	PULAOS	PULLUP	PULS	PULVERIZE
PUGNACITY	PULAS	PULLUPS	PULSANT	PULVEROUS
PUGREE	PULDRON	PULLUS	PULSAR	PULVERS
PUGREES	PULDRONS	PULMO	PULSARS	PULVIL
PUGS	PULE	PULMONARY	PULSATE	PULVILIO
PUH	PULED	PULMONATE	PULSATED	PULVILIOS
PUHA	PULER	PULMONES	PULSATES	PULVILLAR
PUHAS	PULERS	PULMONIC	PULSATILE	PULVILLE
PUIR	PULES	PULMONICS	PULSATING	PULVILLED
PUIRER	PULI	PULMOTOR	PULSATION	PULVILLES
PUIREST	PULICENE	PULMOTORS	PULSATIVE	PULVILLI
PUIRTITH	PULICIDE	PULP	PULSATOR	PULVILLIO
PUIRTITHS	PULICIDES	PULPAL	PULSATORS	PULVILLUS
PUISNE	PULIER	PULPALLY	PULSATORY	PULVILS
PUISNES	PULIEST	PULPBOARD	PULSE	PULVINAR
PUISNY	PULIK	PULPED	PULSED	PULVINARS
PUISSANCE	PULING	PULPER	PULSEJET	PULVINATE
PUISSANT	PULINGLY	PULPERS	PULSEJETS	PULVINI
PUISSAUNT	PULINGS	PULPIER	PULSELESS	PULVINULE
PUJA	PULIS	PULPIEST	PULSER	PULVINUS
PUJAH	PULK	PULPIFIED	PULSERS	PULWAR
PUJAHS	PULKA	PULPIFIES	PULSES	PULWARS
PUJARI	PULKAS	PULPIFY	PULSIDGE	PULY
PUJARIS	PULKHA	PULPILY	PULSIDGES	PUMA
PUJAS	PULKHAS	PULPINESS	PULSIFIC	PUMAS
PUKA	PULKS	PULPING	PULSING	PUMELO
PUKAS	PULL	PULPIT	PULSION	PUMELOS
PUKATEA	PULLBACK	PULPITAL	PULSIONS	PUMICATE
PUKATEAS	PULLBACKS	PULPITED	PULSOJET	PUMICATED
PUKE	PULLED	PULPITEER	PULSOJETS	PUMICATES
PUKED	PULLER	PULPITER	PULTAN	PUMICE
PUKEKO	PULLERS	PULPITERS	PULTANS	PUMICED
PUKEKOS	PULLET	PULPITRY	PULTON	PUMICEOUS
PUKER	PULLETS	PULPITS	PULTONS	PUMICER
PUKERS	PULLEY	PULPITUM	PULTOON	PUMICERS
PUKES	PULLEYS	PULPITUMS	PULTOONS	PUMICES
PUKEY	PULLI	PULPLESS	PULTUN	PUMICING
PUKIER	PULLING	PULPMILL	PULTUNS	PUMICITE
PUKIEST	PULLMAN	PULPMILLS	PULTURE	PUMICITES
PUKING	PULLMANS	PULPOUS	PULTURES	PUMIE
PUKKA	PULLORUM	PULPS	PULU	PUMIES
PUKU	PULLOUT	PULPSTONE	PULUS	PUMMEL
PUKUS	PULLOUTS	PULPWOOD	PULVER	PUMMELED
PUKY	PULLOVER	PULPWOODS	PULVERED	PUMMELING

PUMMELLED	PUNCHIEST	PUNISHER	PUNTEES	PUPPODUM
PUMMELO	PUNCHILY	PUNISHERS	PUNTER	PUPPODUMS
PUMMELOS	PUNCHING	PUNISHES	PUNTERS	PUPPY
PUMMELS	PUNCHLESS	PUNISHING	PUNTIES	PUPPYDOM
PUMP	PUNCHLINE	PUNITION	PUNTING	PUPPYDOMS
PUMPED	PUNCHY	PUNITIONS	PUNTO	PUPPYHOOD
PUMPER	PUNCING	PUNITIVE	PUNTOS	PUPPYING
PUMPERS	PUNCTA	PUNITORY	PUNTS	PUPPYISH
PUMPHOOD	PUNCTATE	PUNJI	PUNTSMAN	PUPPYISM
PUMPHOODS	PUNCTATED	PUNJIS	PUNTSMEN	PUPPYISMS
PUMPING	PUNCTATOR	PUNK	PUNTY	PUPPYLIKE
PUMPINGS	PUNCTILIO	PUNKA	PUNY	PUPS
PUMPION	PUNCTO	PUNKAH	PUP	PUPU
PUMPIONS	PUNCTOS	PUNKAHS	PUPA	PUPUNHA
PUMPKIN	PUNCTUAL	PUNKAS	PUPAE	PUPUNHAS
PUMPKING	PUNCTUATE	PUNKER	PUPAL	PUPUS
PUMPKINGS	PUNCTULE	PUNKERS	PUPARIA	PUR
PUMPKINS	PUNCTULES	PUNKEST	PUPARIAL	PURANA
PUMPLESS	PUNCTUM	PUNKEY	PUPARIUM	PURANAS
PUMPLIKE	PUNCTURE	PUNKEYS	PUPAS	PURANIC
PUMPS	PUNCTURED	PUNKIE	PUPATE	PURBLIND
PUMY	PUNCTURER	PUNKIER	PUPATED	PURCHASE
PUN	PUNCTURES	PUNKIES	PUPATES	PURCHASED
PUNA	PUNDIT	PUNKIEST	PUPATING	PURCHASER
PUNAANI	PUNDITIC	PUNKIN	PUPATION	PURCHASES
PUNAANY	PUNDITRY	PUNKINESS	PUPATIONS	PURDA
PUNALUA	PUNDITS	PUNKINS	PUPFISH	PURDAH
PUNALUAN	PUNDONOR	PUNKISH	PUPFISHES	PURDAHED
PUNALUAS	PUNG	PUNKS	PUPIL	PURDAHS
PUNANI	PUNGA	PUNKY	PUPILAGE	PURDAS
PUNANY	PUNGAS	PUNNED	PUPILAGES	PURDONIUM
PUNAS	PUNGENCE	PUNNER	PUPILAR	PURE
PUNCE	PUNGENCES	PUNNERS	PUPILARY	PUREBLOOD
PUNCED	PUNGENCY	PUNNET	PUPILLAGE	PUREBRED
PUNCES	PUNGENT	PUNNETS	PUPILLAR	PUREBREDS
PUNCH	PUNGENTLY	PUNNIER	PUPILLARY	PURED
PUNCHBAG	PUNGLE	PUNNIEST	PUPILLATE	PUREE
PUNCHBAGS	PUNGLED	PUNNING	PUPILS	PUREED
PUNCHBALL	PUNGLES	PUNNINGLY	PUPILSHIP	PUREEING
PUNCHBOWL	PUNGLING	PUNNINGS	PUPPED	PUREES
PUNCHED	PUNGS	PUNNY	PUPPET	PURELY
PUNCHEON	PUNIER	PUNS	PUPPETEER	PURENESS
PUNCHEONS	PUNIEST	PUNSTER	PUPPETRY	PURER
PUNCHER	PUNILY	PUNSTERS	PUPPETS	PURES
PUNCHERS	PUNINESS	PUNT	PUPPIED	PUREST
PUNCHES	PUNISH	PUNTED	PUPPIES	PURFLE
PUNCHIER	PUNISHED	PUNTEE	PUPPING	PURFLED

P

PURFLER	PURLICUED	PURRED	PURULENCE	PUSLED
PURFLERS	PURLICUES	PURRING	PURULENCY	PUSLES
PURFLES	PURLIEU	PURRINGLY	PURULENT	PUSLEY
PURFLING	PURLIEUS	PURRINGS	PURVEY	PUSLEYS
PURFLINGS	PURLIN	PURRS	PURVEYED	PUSLIKE
PURFLY	PURLINE	PURS	PURVEYING	PUSLING
PURGATION	PURLINES	PURSE	PURVEYOR	PUSS
PURGATIVE	PURLING	PURSED	PURVEYORS	PUSSEL
PURGATORY	PURLINGS	PURSEFUL	PURVEYS	PUSSELS
PURGE	PURLINS	PURSEFULS	PURVIEW	PUSSER
PURGEABLE	PURLOIN	PURSELIKE	PURVIEWS	PUSSERS
PURGED	PURLOINED	PURSER	PUS	PUSSES
PURGER	PURLOINER	PURSERS	PUSES	PUSSIER
PURGERS	PURLOINS	PURSES	PUSH	PUSSIES
PURGES	PURLS	PURSEW	PUSHBALL	PUSSIEST
PURGING	PUROMYCIN	PURSEWED	PUSHBALLS	PUSSLEY
PURGINGS	PURPIE	PURSEWING	PUSHBIKE	PUSSLEYS
PURI	PURPIES	PURSEWS	PUSHBIKES	PUSSLIES
PURIFIED	PURPLE	PURSIER	PUSHCART	PUSSLIKE
PURIFIER	PURPLED	PURSIEST	PUSHCARTS	PUSSLY
PURIFIERS	PURPLER	PURSILY	PUSHCHAIR	PUSSY
PURIFIES	PURPLES	PURSINESS	PUSHDOWN	PUSSYCAT
PURIFY	PURPLEST	PURSING	PUSHDOWNS	PUSSYCATS
PURIFYING	PURPLIER	PURSLAIN	PUSHED	PUSSYFOOT
PURIN	PURPLIEST	PURSLAINS	PUSHER	PUSSYTOES
PURINE	PURPLING	PURSLANE	PUSHERS	PUSTULANT
PURINES	PURPLISH	PURSLANES	PUSHES	PUSTULAR
PURING	PURPLY	PURSUABLE	PUSHFUL	PUSTULATE
PURINS	PURPORT	PURSUAL	PUSHFULLY	PUSTULE
PURIRI	PURPORTED	PURSUALS	PUSHIER	PUSTULED
PURIRIS	PURPORTS	PURSUANCE	PUSHIEST	PUSTULES
PURIS	PURPOSE	PURSUANT	PUSHILY	PUSTULOUS
PURISM	PURPOSED	PURSUE	PUSHINESS	PUT
PURISMS	PURPOSELY	PURSUED	PUSHING	PUTAMEN
PURIST	PURPOSES	PURSUER	PUSHINGLY	PUTAMINA
PURISTIC	PURPOSING	PURSUERS	PUSHOVER	PUTATIVE
PURISTS	PURPOSIVE	PURSUES	PUSHOVERS	PUTCHEON
PURITAN	PURPURA	PURSUING	PUSHPIN	PUTCHEONS
PURITANIC	PURPURAS	PURSUINGS	PUSHPINS	PUTCHER
PURITANS	PURPURE	PURSUIT	PUSHPIT	PUTCHERS
PURITIES	PURPUREAL	PURSUITS	PUSHPITS	PUTCHOCK
PURITY	PURPURES	PURSY	PUSHROD	PUTCHOCKS
PURL	PURPURIC	PURTIER	PUSHRODS	PUTCHUK
PURLED	PURPURIN	PURTIEST	PUSHUP	PUTCHUKS
PURLER	PURPURINS	PURTRAID	PUSHUPS	PUTDOWN
PURLERS	PURPY	PURTRAYD	PUSHY	PUTDOWNS
PURLICUE	PURR	PURTY	PUSLE	PUTEAL

PUTEALS	PUTTINGS	PYCNOSIS	PYKNOTIC	PYRANOSE
PUTELI	PUTTO	PYCNOTIC	PYLON	PYRANOSES
PUTELIS	PUTTOCK	PYE	PYLONS	PYRANS
PUTID	PUTTOCKS	PYEBALD	PYLORI	PYRAZOLE
PUTLOCK	PUTTS	PYEBALDS	PYLORIC	PYRAZOLES
PUTLOCKS	PUTTY	PYEING	PYLORUS	PYRE
PUTLOG	PUTTYING	PYELITIC	PYLORUSES	PYRENE
PUTLOGS	PUTTYLESS	PYELITIS	PYNE	PYRENEITE
PUTOFF	PUTTYLIKE	PYELOGRAM	PYNED	PYRENES
PUTOFFS	PUTTYROOT	PYEMIA	PYNES	PYRENOID
PUTOIS	PUTURE	PYEMIAS	PYNING	PYRENOIDS
PUTON	PUTURES	PYEMIC	PYODERMA	PYRES
PUTONGHUA	PUTZ	PYENGADU	PYODERMAS	PYRETHRIN
PUTONS	PUTZED	PYENGADUS	PYODERMIC	PYRETHRUM
PUTOUT	PUTZES	PYES	PYOGENIC	PYRETIC
PUTOUTS	PUTZING	PYET	PYOID	PYREX
PUTREFIED	PUY	PYETS	PYONER	PYREXES
PUTREFIER	PUYS	PYGAL	PYONERS	PYREXIA
PUTREFIES	PUZEL	PYGALS	PYONINGS	PYREXIAL
PUTREFY	PUZELS	PYGARG	PYORRHEA	PYREXIAS
PUTRID	PUZZEL	PYGARGS	PYORRHEAL	PYREXIC
PUTRIDER	PUZZELS	PYGIDIA	PYORRHEAS	PYRIC
PUTRIDEST	PUZZLE	PYGIDIAL	PYORRHEIC	PYRIDIC
PUTRIDITY	PUZZLED	PYGIDIUM	PYORRHOEA	PYRIDINE
PUTRIDLY	PUZZLEDLY	PYGIDIUMS	PYOSES	PYRIDINES
PUTS	PUZZLEDOM	PYGMAEAN	PYOSIS	PYRIDOXAL
PUTSCH	PUZZLER	PYGMEAN	PYOT	PYRIDOXIN
PUTSCHES	PUZZLERS	PYGMIES	PYOTS	PYRIFORM
PUTSCHIST	PUZZLES	PYGMOID	PYRACANTH	PYRITE
PUTT	PUZZLING	PYGMY	PYRAL	PYRITES
PUTTED	PUZZOLANA	PYGMYISH	PYRALID	PYRITIC
PUTTEE	PYA	PYGMYISM	PYRALIDID	PYRITICAL
PUTTEES	PYAEMIA	PYGMYISMS	PYRALIDS	PYRITISE
PUTTEN	PYAEMIAS	PYGOSTYLE	PYRALIS	PYRITISED
PUTTER	PYAEMIC	PYIC	PYRALISES	PYRITISES
PUTTERED	PYAS	PYIN	PYRAMID	PYRITIZE
PUTTERER	PYAT	PYINKADO	PYRAMIDAL	PYRITIZED
PUTTERERS	PYATS	PYINKADOS	PYRAMIDED	PYRITIZES
PUTTERING	PYCNIC	PYINS	PYRAMIDES	PYRITOUS
PUTTERS	PYCNIDIA	PYJAMA	PYRAMIDIA	PYRO
PUTTI	PYCNIDIAL	PYJAMAED	PYRAMIDIC	PYROCERAM
PUTTIE	PYCNIDIUM	PYJAMAS	PYRAMIDON	PYROCLAST
PUTTIED	PYCNITE	PYKNIC	PYRAMIDS	PYROGEN
PUTTIER	PYCNITES	PYKNICS	PYRAMIS	PYROGENIC
PUTTIERS	PYCNON	PYKNOSES	PYRAMISES	PYROGENS
PUTTIES	PYCNONS	PYKNOSIS	PYRAN	PYROLA
PUTTING	PYCNOSES	PYKNOSOME	PYRANOID	PYROLAS

PYROLATER

PYROLATER
PYROLATRY
PYROLISE
PYROLISED
PYROLISES
PYROLIZE
PYROLIZED
PYROLIZES
PYROLOGY
PYROLYSE
PYROLYSED
PYROLYSER
PYROLYSES
PYROLYSIS
PYROLYTIC
PYROLYZE

PYROLYZED
PYROLYZER
PYROLYZES
PYROMANCY
PYROMANIA
PYROMETER
PYROMETRY
PYRONE
PYRONES
PYRONINE
PYRONINES
PYROPE
PYROPES
PYROPHONE
PYROPUS
PYROPUSES

PYROS
PYROSCOPE
PYROSES
PYROSIS
PYROSISES
PYROSOME
PYROSOMES
PYROSTAT
PYROSTATS
PYROXENE
PYROXENES
PYROXENIC
PYROXYLE
PYROXYLES
PYROXYLIC
PYROXYLIN

PYRRHIC
PYRRHICS
PYRRHOUS
PYRROL
PYRROLE
PYRROLES
PYRROLIC
PYRROLS
PYRUVATE
PYRUVATES
PYRUVIC
PYTHIUM
PYTHIUMS
PYTHON
PYTHONESS
PYTHONIC

PYTHONS
PYURIA
PYURIAS
PYX
PYXED
PYXES
PYXIDES
PYXIDIA
PYXIDIUM
PYXIE
PYXIES
PYXING
PYXIS
PZAZZ
PZAZZES

P

Q

QABALA	QORMA	QUADRIGAS	QUAIGHS	QUANDANG
QABALAH	QORMAS	QUADRILLE	QUAIL	QUANDANGS
QABALAHS	QUA	QUADRIVIA	QUAILED	QUANDARY
QABALAS	QUAALUDE	QUADROON	QUAILING	QUANDONG
QABALISM	QUAALUDES	QUADROONS	QUAILINGS	QUANDONGS
QABALISMS	QUACK	QUADRUMAN	QUAILS	QUANGO
QABALIST	QUACKED	QUADRUPED	QUAINT	QUANGOS
QABALISTS	QUACKER	QUADRUPLE	QUAINTER	QUANNET
QADI	QUACKERS	QUADRUPLY	QUAINTEST	QUANNETS
QADIS	QUACKERY	QUADS	QUAINTLY	QUANT
QAID	QUACKIER	QUAERE	QUAIR	QUANTA
QAIDS	QUACKIEST	QUAERED	QUAIRS	QUANTAL
QAIMAQAM	QUACKING	QUAEREING	QUAIS	QUANTALLY
QAIMAQAMS	QUACKISH	QUAERES	QUAKE	QUANTED
QALAMDAN	QUACKISM	QUAERITUR	QUAKED	QUANTIC
QALAMDANS	QUACKISMS	QUAESITUM	QUAKER	QUANTICAL
QANAT	QUACKLE	QUAESTOR	QUAKERS	QUANTICS
QANATS	QUACKLED	QUAESTORS	QUAKES	QUANTIFY
QASIDA	QUACKLES	QUAFF	QUAKIER	QUANTILE
QASIDAS	QUACKLING	QUAFFABLE	QUAKIEST	QUANTILES
QAT	QUACKS	QUAFFED	QUAKILY	QUANTING
QATS	QUACKY	QUAFFER	QUAKINESS	QUANTISE
QAWWAL	QUAD	QUAFFERS	QUAKING	QUANTISED
QAWWALI	QUADDED	QUAFFING	QUAKINGLY	QUANTISER
QAWWALIS	QUADDING	QUAFFS	QUAKINGS	QUANTISES
QAWWALS	QUADPLAY	QUAG	QUAKY	QUANTITY
QI	QUADPLAYS	QUAGGA	QUALE	QUANTIZE
QIBLA	QUADPLEX	QUAGGAS	QUALIA	QUANTIZED
QIBLAS	QUADRANS	QUAGGIER	QUALIFIED	QUANTIZER
QIGONG	QUADRANT	QUAGGIEST	QUALIFIER	QUANTIZES
QIGONGS	QUADRANTS	QUAGGY	QUALIFIES	QUANTONG
QIN	QUADRAT	QUAGMIRE	QUALIFY	QUANTONGS
QINDAR	QUADRATE	QUAGMIRED	QUALITIED	QUANTS
QINDARKA	QUADRATED	QUAGMIRES	QUALITIES	QUANTUM
QINDARS	QUADRATES	QUAGMIRY	QUALITY	QUANTUMS
QINGHAOSU	QUADRATIC	QUAGS	QUALM	QUARE
QINS	QUADRATS	QUAHAUG	QUALMIER	QUARENDEN
QINTAR	QUADRATUS	QUAHAUGS	QUALMIEST	QUARENDER
QINTARKA	QUADRELLA	QUAHOG	QUALMING	QUARER
QINTARS	QUADRIC	QUAHOGS	QUALMISH	QUAREST
QIS	QUADRICEP	QUAI	QUALMLESS	QUARK
QIVIUT	QUADRICS	QUAICH	QUALMS	QUARKS
QIVIUTS	QUADRIFID	QUAICHES	QUALMY	QUARREL
QOPH	QUADRIGA	QUAICHS	QUAMASH	QUARRELED
QOPHS	QUADRIGAE	QUAIGH	QUAMASHES	QUARRELER

QUARRELS	QUARTZY	QUAYSIDE	QUEENS	QUERCETIC
QUARRIAN	QUASAR	QUAYSIDES	QUEENSHIP	QUERCETIN
QUARRIANS	QUASARS	QUAZZIER	QUEENSIDE	QUERCETUM
QUARRIED	QUASH	QUAZZIEST	QUEENY	QUERCINE
QUARRIER	QUASHED	QUAZZY	QUEER	QUERCITIN
QUARRIERS	QUASHEE	QUBIT	QUEERDOM	QUERIDA
QUARRIES	QUASHEES	QUBITS	QUEERDOMS	QUERIDAS
QUARRION	QUASHER	QUBYTE	QUEERED	QUERIED
QUARRIONS	QUASHERS	QUBYTES	QUEERER	QUERIER
QUARRY	QUASHES	QUEACH	QUEEREST	QUERIERS
QUARRYING	QUASHIE	QUEACHES	QUEERING	QUERIES
QUARRYMAN	QUASHIES	QUEACHIER	QUEERISH	QUERIMONY
QUARRYMEN	QUASHING	QUEACHY	QUEERITY	QUERIST
QUART	QUASI	QUEAN	QUEERLY	QUERISTS
QUARTAN	QUASS	QUEANS	QUEERNESS	QUERN
QUARTANS	QUASSES	QUEASIER	QUEERS	QUERNS
QUARTE	QUASSIA	QUEASIEST	QUEEST	QUERULOUS
QUARTER	QUASSIAS	QUEASILY	QUEESTS	QUERY
QUARTERED	QUASSIN	QUEASY	QUEINT	QUERYING
QUARTERER	QUASSINS	QUEAZIER	QUELCH	QUERYINGS
QUARTERLY	QUAT	QUEAZIEST	QUELCHED	QUEST
QUARTERN	QUATCH	QUEAZY	QUELCHES	QUESTANT
QUARTERNS	QUATCHED	QUEBEC	QUELCHING	QUESTANTS
QUARTERS	QUATCHES	QUEBECS	QUELEA	QUESTED
QUARTES	QUATCHING	QUEBRACHO	QUELEAS	QUESTER
QUARTET	QUATE	QUEECHIER	QUELL	QUESTERS
QUARTETS	QUATORZE	QUEECHY	QUELLABLE	QUESTING
QUARTETT	QUATORZES	QUEEN	QUELLED	QUESTINGS
QUARTETTE	QUATRAIN	QUEENCAKE	QUELLER	QUESTION
QUARTETTI	QUATRAINS	QUEENDOM	QUELLERS	QUESTIONS
QUARTETTO	QUATRE	QUEENDOMS	QUELLING	QUESTOR
QUARTETTS	QUATRES	QUEENED	QUELLS	QUESTORS
QUARTIC	QUATS	QUEENFISH	QUEME	QUESTRIST
QUARTICS	QUAVER	QUEENHOOD	QUEMED	QUESTS
QUARTIER	QUAVERED	QUEENIE	QUEMES	QUETCH
QUARTIERS	QUAVERER	QUEENIER	QUEMING	QUETCHED
QUARTILE	QUAVERERS	QUEENIES	QUENA	QUETCHES
QUARTILES	QUAVERIER	QUEENIEST	QUENAS	QUETCHING
QUARTO	QUAVERING	QUEENING	QUENCH	QUETHE
QUARTOS	QUAVERS	QUEENINGS	QUENCHED	QUETHES
QUARTS	QUAVERY	QUEENITE	QUENCHER	QUETHING
QUARTZ	QUAY	QUEENITES	QUENCHERS	QUETSCH
QUARTZES	QUAYAGE	QUEENLESS	QUENCHES	QUETSCHES
QUARTZIER	QUAYAGES	QUEENLET	QUENCHING	QUETZAL
QUARTZITE	QUAYD	QUEENLETS	QUENELLE	QUETZALES
QUARTZOSE	QUAYLIKE	QUEENLIER	QUENELLES	QUETZALS
QUARTZOUS	QUAYS	QUEENLY	QUEP	QUEUE

Q

QUEUED	QUICKSTEP	QUIETUS	QUINCHES	QUINTAINS
QUEUEING	QUICKY	QUIETUSES	QUINCHING	QUINTAL
QUEUEINGS	QUID	QUIFF	QUINCUNX	QUINTALS
QUEUER	QUIDAM	QUIFFS	QUINE	QUINTAN
QUEUERS	QUIDAMS	QUIGHT	QUINELA	QUINTANS
QUEUES	QUIDDANY	QUIGHTED	QUINELAS	QUINTAR
QUEUING	QUIDDIT	QUIGHTING	QUINELLA	QUINTARS
QUEUINGS	QUIDDITCH	QUIGHTS	QUINELLAS	QUINTAS
QUEY	QUIDDITS	QUILL	QUINES	QUINTE
QUEYN	QUIDDITY	QUILLAI	QUINIC	QUINTES
QUEYNIE	QUIDDLE	QUILLAIA	QUINIDINE	QUINTET
QUEYNIES	QUIDDLED	QUILLAIAS	QUINIE	QUINTETS
QUEYNS	QUIDDLER	QUILLAIS	QUINIELA	QUINTETT
QUEYS	QUIDDLERS	QUILLAJA	QUINIELAS	QUINTETTE
QUEZAL	QUIDDLES	QUILLAJAS	QUINIES	QUINTETTI
QUEZALES	QUIDDLING	QUILLBACK	QUININ	QUINTETTO
QUEZALS	QUIDNUNC	QUILLED	QUININA	QUINTETTS
QUIBBLE	QUIDNUNCS	QUILLET	QUININAS	QUINTIC
QUIBBLED	QUIDS	QUILLETS	QUININE	QUINTICS
QUIBBLER	QUIESCE	QUILLING	QUININES	QUINTILE
QUIBBLERS	QUIESCED	QUILLINGS	QUININS	QUINTILES
QUIBBLES	QUIESCENT	QUILLMAN	QUINNAT	QUINTIN
QUIBBLING	QUIESCES	QUILLMEN	QUINNATS	QUINTINS
QUIBLIN	QUIESCING	QUILLON	QUINO	QUINTROON
QUIBLINS	QUIET	QUILLONS	QUINOA	QUINTS
QUICH	QUIETED	QUILLS	QUINOAS	QUINTUPLE
QUICHE	QUIETEN	QUILLWORK	QUINOID	QUINTUPLY
QUICHED	QUIETENED	QUILLWORT	QUINOIDAL	QUINZE
QUICHES	QUIETENER	QUILT	QUINOIDS	QUINZES
QUICHING	QUIETENS	QUILTED	QUINOL	QUIP
QUICK	QUIETER	QUILTER	QUINOLIN	QUIPO
QUICKBEAM	QUIETERS	QUILTERS	QUINOLINE	QUIPOS
QUICKEN	QUIETEST	QUILTING	QUINOLINS	QUIPPED
QUICKENED	QUIETING	QUILTINGS	QUINOLONE	QUIPPER
QUICKENER	QUIETINGS	QUILTS	QUINOLS	QUIPPERS
QUICKENS	QUIETISM	QUIM	QUINONE	QUIPPIER
QUICKER	QUIETISMS	QUIMS	QUINONES	QUIPPIEST
QUICKEST	QUIETIST	QUIN	QUINONOID	QUIPPING
QUICKIE	QUIETISTS	QUINA	QUINOS	QUIPPISH
QUICKIES	QUIETIVE	QUINARIES	QUINQUINA	QUIPPU
QUICKLIME	QUIETIVES	QUINARY	QUINS	QUIPPUS
QUICKLY	QUIETLY	QUINAS	QUINSIED	QUIPPY
QUICKNESS	QUIETNESS	QUINATE	QUINSIES	QUIPS
QUICKS	QUIETS	QUINCE	QUINSY	QUIPSTER
QUICKSAND	QUIETSOME	QUINCES	QUINT	QUIPSTERS
QUICKSET	QUIETUDE	QUINCHE	QUINTA	QUIPU
QUICKSETS	QUIETUDES	QUINCHED	QUINTAIN	QUIPUS

Q

QUIRE	QUITES	QUIZZED	QUOIT	QUOTATIVE
QUIRED	QUITING	QUIZZER	QUOITED	QUOTE
QUIRES	QUITRENT	QUIZZERS	QUOITER	QUOTED
QUIRING	QUITRENTS	QUIZZERY	QUOITERS	QUOTER
QUIRISTER	QUITS	QUIZZES	QUOITING	QUOTERS
QUIRK	QUITTAL	QUIZZICAL	QUOITS	QUOTES
QUIRKED	QUITTALS	QUIZZIFY	QUOKKA	QUOTH
QUIRKIER	QUITTANCE	QUIZZING	QUOKKAS	QUOTHA
QUIRKIEST	QUITTED	QUIZZINGS	QUOLL	QUOTIDIAN
QUIRKILY	QUITTER	QUOAD	QUOLLS	QUOTIENT
QUIRKING	QUITTERS	QUOD	QUOMODO	QUOTIENTS
QUIRKISH	QUITTING	QUODDED	QUOMODOS	QUOTING
QUIRKS	QUITTOR	QUODDING	QUONDAM	QUOTITION
QUIRKY	QUITTORS	QUODLIBET	QUONK	QUOTUM
QUIRT	QUIVER	QUODLIN	QUONKED	QUOTUMS
QUIRTED	QUIVERED	QUODLINS	QUONKING	QURSH
QUIRTING	QUIVERER	QUODS	QUONKS	QURSHES
QUIRTS	QUIVERERS	QUOHOG	QUOOKE	QURUSH
QUISLING	QUIVERFUL	QUOHOGS	QUOP	QURUSHES
QUISLINGS	QUIVERIER	QUOIF	QUOPPED	QUYTE
QUIST	QUIVERING	QUOIFED	QUOPPING	QUYTED
QUISTS	QUIVERISH	QUOIFING	QUOPS	QUYTES
QUIT	QUIVERS	QUOIFS	QUORATE	QUYTING
QUITCH	QUIVERY	QUOIN	QUORUM	QWERTIES
QUITCHED	QUIXOTE	QUOINED	QUORUMS	QWERTY
QUITCHES	QUIXOTES	QUOINING	QUOTA	QWERTYS
QUITCHING	QUIXOTIC	QUOININGS	QUOTABLE	
QUITCLAIM	QUIXOTISM	QUOINS	QUOTABLY	
QUITE	QUIXOTRY	QUOIST	QUOTAS	
QUITED	QUIZ	QUOISTS	QUOTATION	

R

RABANNA	RABBLES	RACEMOID	RACINOS	RADARS
RABANNAS	RABBLING	RACEMOSE	RACISM	RADDED
RABAT	RABBLINGS	RACEMOUS	RACISMS	RADDER
RABATINE	RABBONI	RACEPATH	RACIST	RADDEST
RABATINES	RABBONIS	RACEPATHS	RACISTS	RADDING
RABATMENT	RABI	RACER	RACK	RADDLE
RABATO	RABIC	RACERS	RACKED	RADDLED
RABATOES	RABID	RACES	RACKER	RADDLEMAN
RABATOS	RABIDER	RACETRACK	RACKERS	RADDLEMEN
RABATS	RABIDEST	RACEWALK	RACKET	RADDLES
RABATTE	RABIDITY	RACEWALKS	RACKETED	RADDLING
RABATTED	RABIDLY	RACEWAY	RACKETEER	RADDOCKE
RABATTES	RABIDNESS	RACEWAYS	RACKETER	RADDOCKES
RABATTING	RABIES	RACH	RACKETERS	RADE
RABBET	RABIETIC	RACHE	RACKETIER	RADGE
RABBETED	RABIS	RACHES	RACKETING	RADGER
RABBETING	RACA	RACHET	RACKETRY	RADGES
RABBETS	RACAHOUT	RACHETED	RACKETS	RADGEST
RABBI	RACAHOUTS	RACHETING	RACKETT	RADIABLE
RABBIES	RACCAHOUT	RACHETS	RACKETTS	RADIAL
RABBIN	RACCOON	RACHIAL	RACKETY	RADIALE
RABBINATE	RACCOONS	RACHIDES	RACKFUL	RADIALIA
RABBINIC	RACE	RACHIDIAL	RACKFULS	RADIALISE
RABBINICS	RACEABLE	RACHIDIAN	RACKING	RADIALITY
RABBINISM	RACECARD	RACHILLA	RACKINGLY	RADIALIZE
RABBINIST	RACECARDS	RACHILLAE	RACKINGS	RADIALLY
RABBINITE	RACED	RACHILLAS	RACKLE	RADIALS
RABBINS	RACEGOER	RACHIS	RACKS	RADIAN
RABBIS	RACEGOERS	RACHISES	RACKWORK	RADIANCE
RABBIT	RACEGOING	RACHITIC	RACKWORKS	RADIANCES
RABBITED	RACEHORSE	RACHITIS	RACLETTE	RADIANCY
RABBITER	RACEMATE	RACIAL	RACLETTES	RADIANS
RABBITERS	RACEMATES	RACIALISE	RACLOIR	RADIANT
RABBITING	RACEME	RACIALISM	RACLOIRS	RADIANTLY
RABBITO	RACEMED	RACIALIST	RACON	RADIANTS
RABBITOH	RACEMES	RACIALIZE	RACONS	RADIATA
RABBITOHS	RACEMIC	RACIALLY	RACONTEUR	RADIATAS
RABBITOS	RACEMISE	RACIATION	RACOON	RADIATE
RABBITRY	RACEMISED	RACIER	RACOONS	RADIATED
RABBITS	RACEMISES	RACIEST	RACQUET	RADIATELY
RABBITY	RACEMISM	RACILY	RACQUETED	RADIATES
RABBLE	RACEMISMS	RACINESS	RACQUETS	RADIATING
RABBLED	RACEMIZE	RACING	RACY	RADIATION
RABBLER	RACEMIZED	RACINGS	RAD	RADIATIVE
RABBLERS	RACEMIZES	RACINO	RADAR	RADIATOR

RADIATORS	RADULAR	RAGEFUL	RAGOUTS	RAIL
RADIATORY	RADULAS	RAGER	RAGPICKER	RAILAGE
RADICAL	RADULATE	RAGERS	RAGS	RAILAGES
RADICALLY	RADWASTE	RAGES	RAGSTONE	RAILBED
RADICALS	RADWASTES	RAGG	RAGSTONES	RAILBEDS
RADICAND	RAFALE	RAGGA	RAGTAG	RAILBIRD
RADICANDS	RAFALES	RAGGAS	RAGTAGS	RAILBIRDS
RADICANT	RAFF	RAGGED	RAGTIME	RAILBUS
RADICATE	RAFFIA	RAGGEDER	RAGTIMER	RAILBUSES
RADICATED	RAFFIAS	RAGGEDEST	RAGTIMERS	RAILCAR
RADICATES	RAFFINATE	RAGGEDIER	RAGTIMES	RAILCARD
RADICCHIO	RAFFINOSE	RAGGEDLY	RAGTOP	RAILCARDS
RADICEL	RAFFISH	RAGGEDY	RAGTOPS	RAILCARS
RADICELS	RAFFISHLY	RAGGEE	RAGU	RAILE
RADICES	RAFFLE	RAGGEES	RAGULED	RAILED
RADICLE	RAFFLED	RAGGERIES	RAGULY	RAILER
RADICLES	RAFFLER	RAGGERY	RAGUS	RAILERS
RADICULAR	RAFFLERS	RAGGIER	RAGWEED	RAILES
RADICULE	RAFFLES	RAGGIES	RAGWEEDS	RAILHEAD
RADICULES	RAFFLESIA	RAGGIEST	RAGWHEEL	RAILHEADS
RADII	RAFFLING	RAGGING	RAGWHEELS	RAILING
RADIO	RAFFS	RAGGINGS	RAGWORK	RAILINGLY
RADIOED	RAFT	RAGGLE	RAGWORKS	RAILINGS
RADIOGOLD	RAFTED	RAGGLED	RAGWORM	RAILLERY
RADIOGRAM	RAFTER	RAGGLES	RAGWORMS	RAILLESS
RADIOING	RAFTERED	RAGGLING	RAGWORT	RAILLIES
RADIOLOGY	RAFTERING	RAGGS	RAGWORTS	RAILLY
RADIOMAN	RAFTERS	RAGGY	RAH	RAILMAN
RADIOMEN	RAFTING	RAGHEAD	RAHED	RAILMEN
RADIONICS	RAFTINGS	RAGHEADS	RAHING	RAILROAD
RADIOS	RAFTMAN	RAGI	RAHS	RAILROADS
RADIOTHON	RAFTMEN	RAGING	RAHUI	RAILS
RADISH	RAFTS	RAGINGLY	RAHUIS	RAILWAY
RADISHES	RAFTSMAN	RAGINGS	RAI	RAILWAYS
RADIUM	RAFTSMEN	RAGINI	RAIA	RAILWOMAN
RADIUMS	RAG	RAGINIS	RAIAS	RAILWOMEN
RADIUS	RAGA	RAGIS	RAID	RAIMENT
RADIUSES	RAGAS	RAGLAN	RAIDED	RAIMENTS
RADIX	RAGBAG	RAGLANS	RAIDER	RAIN
RADIXES	RAGBAGS	RAGMAN	RAIDERS	RAINBAND
RADOME	RAGBOLT	RAGMANS	RAIDING	RAINBANDS
RADOMES	RAGBOLTS	RAGMEN	RAIDINGS	RAINBIRD
RADON	RAGDE	RAGMENT	RAIDS	RAINBIRDS
RADONS	RAGE	RAGMENTS	RAIK	RAINBOW
RADS	RAGED	RAGOUT	RAIKED	RAINBOWED
RADULA	RAGEE	RAGOUTED	RAIKING	RAINBOWS
RADULAE	RAGEES	RAGOUTING	RAIKS	RAINBOWY

RAINCHECK	RAIT	RAKUS	RAMENTA	RAMPAGED
RAINCOAT	RAITA	RALE	RAMENTUM	RAMPAGER
RAINCOATS	RAITAS	RALES	RAMEOUS	RAMPAGERS
RAINDATE	RAITED	RALLIED	RAMEQUIN	RAMPAGES
RAINDATES	RAITING	RALLIER	RAMEQUINS	RAMPAGING
RAINDROP	RAITS	RALLIERS	RAMET	RAMPANCY
RAINDROPS	RAIYAT	RALLIES	RAMETS	RAMPANT
RAINE	RAIYATS	RALLIFORM	RAMI	RAMPANTLY
RAINED	RAJ	RALLINE	RAMIE	RAMPART
RAINES	RAJA	RALLY	RAMIES	RAMPARTED
RAINFALL	RAJAH	RALLYE	RAMIFIED	RAMPARTS
RAINFALLS	RAJAHS	RALLYES	RAMIFIES	RAMPAUGE
RAINIER	RAJAHSHIP	RALLYING	RAMIFORM	RAMPAUGED
RAINIEST	RAJAS	RALLYINGS	RAMIFY	RAMPAUGES
RAINILY	RAJASHIP	RALLYIST	RAMIFYING	RAMPED
RAININESS	RAJASHIPS	RALLYISTS	RAMILIE	RAMPER
RAINING	RAJES	RALPH	RAMILIES	RAMPERS
RAINLESS	RAKE	RALPHED	RAMILLIE	RAMPICK
RAINMAKER	RAKED	RALPHING	RAMILLIES	RAMPICKED
RAINOUT	RAKEE	RALPHS	RAMIN	RAMPICKS
RAINOUTS	RAKEES	RAM	RAMINS	RAMPIKE
RAINPROOF	RAKEHELL	RAMADA	RAMIS	RAMPIKES
RAINS	RAKEHELLS	RAMADAS	RAMJET	RAMPING
RAINSPOUT	RAKEHELLY	RAMAKIN	RAMJETS	RAMPINGS
RAINSTORM	RAKEOFF	RAMAKINS	RAMMED	RAMPION
RAINTIGHT	RAKEOFFS	RAMAL	RAMMEL	RAMPIONS
RAINWASH	RAKER	RAMATE	RAMMELS	RAMPIRE
RAINWATER	RAKERIES	RAMBLA	RAMMER	RAMPIRED
RAINWEAR	RAKERS	RAMBLAS	RAMMERS	RAMPIRES
RAINWEARS	RAKERY	RAMBLE	RAMMIER	RAMPOLE
RAINY	RAKES	RAMBLED	RAMMIES	RAMPOLES
RAIRD	RAKESHAME	RAMBLER	RAMMIEST	RAMPS
RAIRDS	RAKI	RAMBLERS	RAMMING	RAMPSMAN
RAIS	RAKIA	RAMBLES	RAMMISH	RAMPSMEN
RAISABLE	RAKIAS	RAMBLING	RAMMISHLY	RAMROD
RAISE	RAKIJA	RAMBLINGS	RAMMLE	RAMRODDED
RAISEABLE	RAKIJAS	RAMBUTAN	RAMMLES	RAMRODS
RAISED	RAKING	RAMBUTANS	RAMMY	RAMS
RAISER	RAKINGS	RAMCAT	RAMONA	RAMSHORN
RAISERS	RAKIS	RAMCATS	RAMONAS	RAMSHORNS
RAISES	RAKISH	RAMEAL	RAMOSE	RAMSON
RAISIN	RAKISHLY	RAMEE	RAMOSELY	RAMSONS
RAISING	RAKSHAS	RAMEES	RAMOSITY	RAMSTAM
RAISINGS	RAKSHASA	RAMEKIN	RAMOUS	RAMTIL
RAISINS	RAKSHASAS	RAMEKINS	RAMOUSLY	RAMTILLA
RAISINY	RAKSHASES	RAMEN	RAMP	RAMTILLAS
RAISONNE	RAKU	RAMENS	RAMPAGE	RAMTILS

R

RAMULAR	RAND	RANGOLIS	RANTERISM	RAPINE
RAMULI	RANDAN	RANGY	RANTERS	RAPINES
RAMULOSE	RANDANS	RANI	RANTING	RAPING
RAMULOUS	RANDED	RANID	RANTINGLY	RAPINI
RAMULUS	RANDEM	RANIDS	RANTINGS	RAPIST
RAMUS	RANDEMS	RANIFORM	RANTIPOLE	RAPISTS
RAN	RANDIE	RANINE	RANTS	RAPLOCH
RANA	RANDIER	RANIS	RANULA	RAPLOCHS
RANARIAN	RANDIES	RANK	RANULAR	RAPPAREE
RANARIUM	RANDIEST	RANKE	RANULAS	RAPPAREES
RANARIUMS	RANDILY	RANKED	RANUNCULI	RAPPE
RANAS	RANDINESS	RANKER	RANZEL	RAPPED
RANCE	RANDING	RANKERS	RANZELMAN	RAPPEE
RANCED	RANDLORD	RANKES	RANZELMEN	RAPPEES
RANCEL	RANDLORDS	RANKEST	RANZELS	RAPPEL
RANCELS	RANDOM	RANKING	RAOULIA	RAPPELED
RANCES	RANDOMISE	RANKINGS	RAOULIAS	RAPPELING
RANCH	RANDOMIZE	RANKISH	RAP	RAPPELLED
RANCHED	RANDOMLY	RANKISM	RAPACIOUS	RAPPELS
RANCHER	RANDOMS	RANKISMS	RAPACITY	RAPPEN
RANCHERIA	RANDON	RANKLE	RAPE	RAPPER
RANCHERIE	RANDONS	RANKLED	RAPED	RAPPERS
RANCHERO	RANDS	RANKLES	RAPER	RAPPES
RANCHEROS	RANDY	RANKLESS	RAPERS	RAPPING
RANCHERS	RANEE	RANKLING	RAPES	RAPPINGS
RANCHES	RANEES	RANKLY	RAPESEED	RAPPINI
RANCHING	RANG	RANKNESS	RAPESEEDS	RAPPORT
RANCHINGS	RANGA	RANKS	RAPHAE	RAPPORTS
RANCHLESS	RANGAS	RANKSHIFT	RAPHANIA	RAPS
RANCHLIKE	RANGATIRA	RANPIKE	RAPHANIAS	RAPT
RANCHMAN	RANGE	RANPIKES	RAPHE	RAPTLY
RANCHMEN	RANGED	RANSACK	RAPHES	RAPTNESS
RANCHO	RANGELAND	RANSACKED	RAPHIA	RAPTOR
RANCHOS	RANGER	RANSACKER	RAPHIAS	RAPTORIAL
RANCID	RANGERS	RANSACKS	RAPHIDE	RAPTORS
RANCIDER	RANGES	RANSEL	RAPHIDES	RAPTURE
RANCIDEST	RANGI	RANSELS	RAPHIS	RAPTURED
RANCIDITY	RANGIER	RANSHAKLE	RAPID	RAPTURES
RANCIDLY	RANGIEST	RANSOM	RAPIDER	RAPTURING
RANCING	RANGILY	RANSOMED	RAPIDEST	RAPTURISE
RANCOR	RANGINESS	RANSOMER	RAPIDITY	RAPTURIST
RANCORED	RANGING	RANSOMERS	RAPIDLY	RAPTURIZE
RANCOROUS	RANGINGS	RANSOMING	RAPIDNESS	RAPTUROUS
RANCORS	RANGIORA	RANSOMS	RAPIDS	RARE
RANCOUR	RANGIORAS	RANT	RAPIER	RAREBIT
RANCOURED	RANGIS	RANTED	RAPIERED	RAREBITS
RANCOURS	RANGOLI	RANTER	RAPIERS	RARED

RAREE	RASHERS	RAT	RATH	RATOO
RAREFIED	RASHES	RATA	RATHA	RATOON
RAREFIER	RASHEST	RATABLE	RATHAS	RATOONED
RAREFIERS	RASHIE	RATABLES	RATHE	RATOONER
RAREFIES	RASHIES	RATABLY	RATHER	RATOONERS
RAREFY	RASHING	RATAFEE	RATHEREST	RATOONING
RAREFYING	RASHLIKE	RATAFEES	RATHERIPE	RATOONS
RARELY	RASHLY	RATAFIA	RATHERISH	RATOOS
RARENESS	RASHNESS	RATAFIAS	RATHEST	RATOS
RARER	RASING	RATAL	RATHOLE	RATPACK
RARERIPE	RASMALAI	RATALS	RATHOLES	RATPACKS
RARERIPES	RASMALAIS	RATAN	RATHOUSE	RATPROOF
RARES	RASORIAL	RATANIES	RATHOUSES	RATS
RAREST	RASP	RATANS	RATHRIPE	RATSBANE
RARIFIED	RASPATORY	RATANY	RATHRIPES	RATSBANES
RARIFIES	RASPBERRY	RATAPLAN	RATHS	RATTAIL
RARIFY	RASPED	RATAPLANS	RATICIDE	RATTAILED
RARIFYING	RASPER	RATAS	RATICIDES	RATTAILS
RARING	RASPERS	RATATAT	RATIFIED	RATTAN
RARITIES	RASPIER	RATATATS	RATIFIER	RATTANS
RARITY	RASPIEST	RATBAG	RATIFIERS	RATTED
RARK	RASPINESS	RATBAGS	RATIFIES	RATTEEN
RARKED	RASPING	RATBITE	RATIFY	RATTEENS
RARKING	RASPINGLY	RATCH	RATIFYING	RATTEN
RARKS	RASPINGS	RATCHED	RATINE	RATTENED
RAS	RASPISH	RATCHES	RATINES	RATTENER
RASBORA	RASPS	RATCHET	RATING	RATTENERS
RASBORAS	RASPY	RATCHETED	RATINGS	RATTENING
RASCAILLE	RASSE	RATCHETS	RATIO	RATTENS
RASCAL	RASSES	RATCHING	RATION	RATTER
RASCALDOM	RASSLE	RATE	RATIONAL	RATTERIES
RASCALISM	RASSLED	RATEABLE	RATIONALE	RATTERS
RASCALITY	RASSLES	RATEABLY	RATIONALS	RATTERY
RASCALLY	RASSLING	RATED	RATIONED	RATTIER
RASCALS	RAST	RATEEN	RATIONING	RATTIEST
RASCASSE	RASTA	RATEENS	RATIONS	RATTILY
RASCASSES	RASTAFARI	RATEL	RATIOS	RATTINESS
RASCHEL	RASTER	RATELS	RATITE	RATTING
RASCHELS	RASTERED	RATEMETER	RATITES	RATTINGS
RASE	RASTERING	RATEPAYER	RATLIKE	RATTISH
RASED	RASTERISE	RATER	RATLIN	RATTLE
RASER	RASTERIZE	RATERS	RATLINE	RATTLEBAG
RASERS	RASTERS	RATES	RATLINES	RATTLEBOX
RASES	RASTRUM	RATFINK	RATLING	RATTLED
RASH	RASTRUMS	RATFINKS	RATLINGS	RATTLER
RASHED	RASURE	RATFISH	RATLINS	RATTLERS
RASHER	RASURES	RATFISHES	RATO	RATTLES

R

RATTLIER	RAUWOLFIA	RAVINING	RAYING	RAZZLES
RATTLIEST	RAV	RAVINS	RAYLE	RE
RATTLIN	RAVAGE	RAVIOLI	RAYLED	REABSORB
RATTLINE	RAVAGED	RAVIOLIS	RAYLES	REABSORBS
RATTLINES	RAVAGER	RAVISH	RAYLESS	REACCEDE
RATTLING	RAVAGERS	RAVISHED	RAYLESSLY	REACCEDED
RATTLINGS	RAVAGES	RAVISHER	RAYLET	REACCEDES
RATTLINS	RAVAGING	RAVISHERS	RAYLETS	REACCENT
RATTLY	RAVE	RAVISHES	RAYLIKE	REACCENTS
RATTON	RAVED	RAVISHING	RAYLING	REACCEPT
RATTONS	RAVEL	RAVS	RAYNE	REACCEPTS
RATTOON	RAVELED	RAW	RAYNES	REACCLAIM
RATTOONED	RAVELER	RAWARU	RAYON	REACCUSE
RATTOONS	RAVELERS	RAWARUS	RAYONS	REACCUSED
RATTRAP	RAVELIN	RAWBONE	RAYS	REACCUSES
RATTRAPS	RAVELING	RAWBONED	RAZE	REACH
RATTY	RAVELINGS	RAWER	RAZED	REACHABLE
RATU	RAVELINS	RAWEST	RAZEE	REACHED
RATUS	RAVELLED	RAWHEAD	RAZEED	REACHER
RAUCID	RAVELLER	RAWHEADS	RAZEEING	REACHERS
RAUCITIES	RAVELLERS	RAWHIDE	RAZEES	REACHES
RAUCITY	RAVELLING	RAWHIDED	RAZER	REACHING
RAUCLE	RAVELLY	RAWHIDES	RAZERS	REACHLESS
RAUCLER	RAVELMENT	RAWHIDING	RAZES	REACQUIRE
RAUCLEST	RAVELS	RAWIN	RAZING	REACT
RAUCOUS	RAVEN	RAWING	RAZMATAZ	REACTANCE
RAUCOUSLY	RAVENED	RAWINGS	RAZOO	REACTANT
RAUGHT	RAVENER	RAWINS	RAZOOS	REACTANTS
RAUN	RAVENERS	RAWISH	RAZOR	REACTED
RAUNCH	RAVENING	RAWLY	RAZORABLE	REACTING
RAUNCHED	RAVENINGS	RAWMAISH	RAZORBACK	REACTION
RAUNCHES	RAVENLIKE	RAWN	RAZORBILL	REACTIONS
RAUNCHIER	RAVENOUS	RAWNESS	RAZORCLAM	REACTIVE
RAUNCHILY	RAVENS	RAWNESSES	RAZORED	REACTOR
RAUNCHING	RAVER	RAWNS	RAZORFISH	REACTORS
RAUNCHY	RAVERS	RAWS	RAZORING	REACTS
RAUNGE	RAVES	RAX	RAZORS	REACTUATE
RAUNGED	RAVIGOTE	RAXED	RAZURE	READ
RAUNGES	RAVIGOTES	RAXES	RAZURES	READABLE
RAUNGING	RAVIGOTTE	RAXING	RAZZ	READABLY
RAUNS	RAVIN	RAY	RAZZBERRY	READAPT
RAUPATU	RAVINE	RAYA	RAZZED	READAPTED
RAUPATUS	RAVINED	RAYAH	RAZZES	READAPTS
RAUPO	RAVINES	RAYAHS	RAZZIA	READD
RAUPOS	RAVING	RAYAS	RAZZIAS	READDED
RAURIKI	RAVINGLY	RAYED	RAZZING	READDICT
RAURIKIS	RAVINGS	RAYGRASS	RAZZLE	READDICTS

READDING	REAGINS	REALS	REAPPEAR	REASONED
READDRESS	REAK	REALTER	REAPPEARS	REASONER
READDS	REAKED	REALTERED	REAPPLIED	REASONERS
READER	REAKING	REALTERS	REAPPLIES	REASONING
READERLY	REAKS	REALTIE	REAPPLY	REASONS
READERS	REAL	REALTIES	REAPPOINT	REASSAIL
READIED	REALER	REALTIME	REAPPROVE	REASSAILS
READIER	REALES	REALTONE	REAPS	REASSERT
READIES	REALEST	REALTONES	REAR	REASSERTS
READIEST	REALGAR	REALTOR	REARED	REASSESS
READILY	REALGARS	REALTORS	REARER	REASSIGN
READINESS	REALIA	REALTY	REARERS	REASSIGNS
READING	REALIGN	REAM	REARGUARD	REASSORT
READINGS	REALIGNED	REAME	REARGUE	REASSORTS
READJUST	REALIGNS	REAMED	REARGUED	REASSUME
READJUSTS	REALISE	REAMEND	REARGUES	REASSUMED
README	REALISED	REAMENDED	REARGUING	REASSUMES
READMIT	REALISER	REAMENDS	REARHORSE	REASSURE
READMITS	REALISERS	REAMER	REARING	REASSURED
READOPT	REALISES	REAMERS	REARISE	REASSURER
READOPTED	REALISING	REAMES	REARISEN	REASSURES
READOPTS	REALISM	REAMIER	REARISES	REAST
READORN	REALISMS	REAMIEST	REARISING	REASTED
READORNED	REALIST	REAMING	REARLY	REASTIER
READORNS	REALISTIC	REAMS	REARM	REASTIEST
READOUT	REALISTS	REAMY	REARMED	REASTING
READOUTS	REALITIES	REAN	REARMICE	REASTS
READS	REALITY	REANALYSE	REARMING	REASTY
READVANCE	REALIZE	REANALYZE	REARMOST	REATA
READVISE	REALIZED	REANIMATE	REARMOUSE	REATAS
READVISED	REALIZER	REANNEX	REARMS	REATE
READVISES	REALIZERS	REANNEXED	REAROSE	REATES
READY	REALIZES	REANNEXES	REAROUSAL	REATTACH
READYING	REALIZING	REANOINT	REAROUSE	REATTACK
READYMADE	REALLIE	REANOINTS	REAROUSED	REATTACKS
REAEDIFY	REALLIED	REANS	REAROUSES	REATTAIN
REAEDIFYE	REALLIES	REANSWER	REARRANGE	REATTAINS
REAFFIRM	REALLOT	REANSWERS	REARREST	REATTEMPT
REAFFIRMS	REALLOTS	REAP	REARRESTS	REAVAIL
REAFFIX	REALLY	REAPABLE	REARS	REAVAILED
REAFFIXED	REALLYING	REAPED	REARWARD	REAVAILS
REAFFIXES	REALM	REAPER	REARWARDS	REAVE
REAGENCY	REALMLESS	REAPERS	REASCEND	REAVED
REAGENT	REALMS	REAPHOOK	REASCENDS	REAVER
REAGENTS	REALNESS	REAPHOOKS	REASCENT	REAVERS
REAGIN	REALO	REAPING	REASCENTS	REAVES
REAGINIC	REALOS	REAPPAREL	REASON	REAVING

REAVOW	REBECS	REBOARDS	REBREEDS	RECALLING
REAVOWED	REBEGAN	REBOATION	REBS	RECALLS
REAVOWING	REBEGIN	REBODIED	REBUFF	RECALMENT
REAVOWS	REBEGINS	REBODIES	REBUFFED	RECALS
REAWAKE	REBEGUN	REBODY	REBUFFING	RECAMIER
REAWAKED	REBEL	REBODYING	REBUFFS	RECAMIERS
REAWAKEN	REBELDOM	REBOIL	REBUILD	RECANE
REAWAKENS	REBELDOMS	REBOILED	REBUILDED	RECANED
REAWAKES	REBELLED	REBOILING	REBUILDS	RECANES
REAWAKING	REBELLER	REBOILS	REBUILT	RECANING
REAWOKE	REBELLERS	REBOOK	REBUKABLE	RECANT
REAWOKEN	REBELLING	REBOOKED	REBUKE	RECANTED
REB	REBELLION	REBOOKING	REBUKED	RECANTER
REBACK	REBELLOW	REBOOKS	REBUKEFUL	RECANTERS
REBACKED	REBELLOWS	REBOOT	REBUKER	RECANTING
REBACKING	REBELS	REBOOTED	REBUKERS	RECANTS
REBACKS	REBID	REBOOTING	REBUKES	RECAP
REBADGE	REBIDDEN	REBOOTS	REBUKING	RECAPPED
REBADGED	REBIDDING	REBOP	REBURIAL	RECAPPING
REBADGES	REBIDS	REBOPS	REBURIALS	RECAPS
REBADGING	REBILL	REBORE	REBURIED	RECAPTION
REBAIT	REBILLED	REBORED	REBURIES	RECAPTOR
REBAITED	REBILLING	REBORES	REBURY	RECAPTORS
REBAITING	REBILLS	REBORING	REBURYING	RECAPTURE
REBAITS	REBIND	REBORN	REBUS	RECARPET
REBALANCE	REBINDING	REBORROW	REBUSES	RECARPETS
REBAPTISE	REBINDS	REBORROWS	REBUT	RECARRIED
REBAPTISM	REBIRTH	REBOTTLE	REBUTMENT	RECARRIES
REBAPTIZE	REBIRTHER	REBOTTLED	REBUTS	RECARRY
REBAR	REBIRTHS	REBOTTLES	REBUTTAL	RECAST
REBARS	REBIT	REBOUGHT	REBUTTALS	RECASTING
REBATABLE	REBITE	REBOUND	REBUTTED	RECASTS
REBATE	REBITES	REBOUNDED	REBUTTER	RECATALOG
REBATED	REBITING	REBOUNDER	REBUTTERS	RECATCH
REBATER	REBITTEN	REBOUNDS	REBUTTING	RECATCHES
REBATERS	REBLEND	REBOZO	REBUTTON	RECAUGHT
REBATES	REBLENDED	REBOZOS	REBUTTONS	RECAUTION
REBATING	REBLENDS	REBRACE	REBUY	RECCE
REBATO	REBLENT	REBRACED	REBUYING	RECCED
REBATOES	REBLOCHON	REBRACES	REBUYS	RECCEED
REBATOS	REBLOOM	REBRACING	REC	RECCEING
REBBE	REBLOOMED	REBRANCH	RECAL	RECCES
REBBES	REBLOOMS	REBRAND	RECALESCE	RECCIED
REBBETZIN	REBLOSSOM	REBRANDED	RECALL	RECCIES
REBEC	REBOANT	REBRANDS	RECALLED	RECCO
REBECK	REBOARD	REBRED	RECALLER	RECCOS
REBECKS	REBOARDED	REBREED	RECALLERS	RECCY

RECCYING	RECESSIVE	RECITALS	RECLOSE	RECOLORED
RECEDE	RECHANGE	RECITE	RECLOSED	RECOLORS
RECEDED	RECHANGED	RECITED	RECLOSES	RECOMB
RECEDES	RECHANGES	RECITER	RECLOSING	RECOMBED
RECEDING	RECHANNEL	RECITERS	RECLOTHE	RECOMBINE
RECEIPT	RECHARGE	RECITES	RECLOTHED	RECOMBING
RECEIPTED	RECHARGED	RECITING	RECLOTHES	RECOMBS
RECEIPTOR	RECHARGER	RECITS	RECLUSE	RECOMFORT
RECEIPTS	RECHARGES	RECK	RECLUSELY	RECOMMEND
RECEIVAL	RECHART	RECKAN	RECLUSES	RECOMMIT
RECEIVALS	RECHARTED	RECKED	RECLUSION	RECOMMITS
RECEIVE	RECHARTER	RECKING	RECLUSIVE	RECOMPACT
RECEIVED	RECHARTS	RECKLESS	RECLUSORY	RECOMPILE
RECEIVER	RECHATE	RECKLING	RECOAL	RECOMPOSE
RECEIVERS	RECHATES	RECKLINGS	RECOALED	RECOMPUTE
RECEIVES	RECHAUFFE	RECKON	RECOALING	RECON
RECEIVING	RECHEAT	RECKONED	RECOALS	RECONCILE
RECEMENT	RECHEATED	RECKONER	RECOAT	RECONDITE
RECEMENTS	RECHEATS	RECKONERS	RECOATED	RECONDUCT
RECENCIES	RECHECK	RECKONING	RECOATING	RECONFER
RECENCY	RECHECKED	RECKONS	RECOATS	RECONFERS
RECENSE	RECHECKS	RECKS	RECOCK	RECONFINE
RECENSED	RECHERCHE	RECLAD	RECOCKED	RECONFIRM
RECENSES	RECHEW	RECLADDED	RECOCKING	RECONNECT
RECENSING	RECHEWED	RECLADS	RECOCKS	RECONNED
RECENSION	RECHEWING	RECLAIM	RECODE	RECONNING
RECENSOR	RECHEWS	RECLAIMED	RECODED	RECONQUER
RECENSORS	RECHIE	RECLAIMER	RECODES	RECONS
RECENT	RECHIP	RECLAIMS	RECODIFY	RECONSIGN
RECENTER	RECHIPPED	RECLAME	RECODING	RECONSOLE
RECENTEST	RECHIPS	RECLAMES	RECOGNISE	RECONSULT
RECENTLY	RECHLESSE	RECLASP	RECOGNIZE	RECONTACT
RECENTRE	RECHOOSE	RECLASPED	RECOIL	RECONTOUR
RECENTRED	RECHOOSES	RECLASPS	RECOILED	RECONVENE
RECENTRES	RECHOSE	RECLEAN	RECOILER	RECONVERT
RECEPT	RECHOSEN	RECLEANED	RECOILERS	RECONVEY
RECEPTION	RECIPE	RECLEANS	RECOILING	RECONVEYS
RECEPTIVE	RECIPES	RECLIMB	RECOILS	RECONVICT
RECEPTOR	RECIPIENT	RECLIMBED	RECOIN	RECOOK
RECEPTORS	RECIRCLE	RECLIMBS	RECOINAGE	RECOOKED
RECEPTS	RECIRCLED	RECLINATE	RECOINED	RECOOKING
RECERTIFY	RECIRCLES	RECLINE	RECOINING	RECOOKS
RECESS	RECISION	RECLINED	RECOINS	RECOPIED
RECESSED	RECISIONS	RECLINER	RECOLLECT	RECOPIES
RECESSES	RECIT	RECLINERS	RECOLLET	RECOPY
RECESSING	RECITABLE	RECLINES	RECOLLETS	RECOPYING
RECESSION	RECITAL	RECLINING	RECOLOR	RECORD

R

RECORDED	RECRATING	RECTRESS	RECYCLER	REDCOAT
RECORDER	RECREANCE	RECTRICES	RECYCLERS	REDCOATS
RECORDERS	RECREANCY	RECTRIX	RECYCLES	REDD
RECORDING	RECREANT	RECTUM	RECYCLING	REDDED
RECORDIST	RECREANTS	RECTUMS	RECYCLIST	REDDEN
RECORDS	RECREATE	RECTUS	RED	REDDENDA
RECORK	RECREATED	RECUILE	REDACT	REDDENDO
RECORKED	RECREATES	RECUILED	REDACTED	REDDENDOS
RECORKING	RECREATOR	RECUILES	REDACTING	REDDENDUM
RECORKS	RECREMENT	RECUILING	REDACTION	REDDENED
RECOUNT	RECROSS	RECULE	REDACTOR	REDDENING
RECOUNTAL	RECROSSED	RECULED	REDACTORS	REDDENS
RECOUNTED	RECROSSES	RECULES	REDACTS	REDDER
RECOUNTER	RECROWN	RECULING	REDAMAGE	REDDERS
RECOUNTS	RECROWNED	RECUMBENT	REDAMAGED	REDDEST
RECOUP	RECROWNS	RECUR	REDAMAGES	REDDIER
RECOUPE	RECRUIT	RECURE	REDAN	REDDIEST
RECOUPED	RECRUITAL	RECURED	REDANS	REDDING
RECOUPING	RECRUITED	RECURES	REDARGUE	REDDINGS
RECOUPLE	RECRUITER	RECURING	REDARGUED	REDDISH
RECOUPLED	RECRUITS	RECURRED	REDARGUES	REDDISHLY
RECOUPLES	RECS	RECURRENT	REDATE	REDDLE
RECOUPS	RECTA	RECURRING	REDATED	REDDLED
RECOURE	RECTAL	RECURS	REDATES	REDDLEMAN
RECOURED	RECTALLY	RECURSION	REDATING	REDDLEMEN
RECOURES	RECTANGLE	RECURSIVE	REDBACK	REDDLES
RECOURING	RECTI	RECURVATE	REDBACKS	REDDLING
RECOURSE	RECTIFIED	RECURVE	REDBAIT	REDDS
RECOURSED	RECTIFIER	RECURVED	REDBAITED	REDDY
RECOURSES	RECTIFIES	RECURVES	REDBAITER	REDE
RECOVER	RECTIFY	RECURVING	REDBAITS	REDEAL
RECOVERED	RECTION	RECUSAL	REDBAY	REDEALING
RECOVEREE	RECTIONS	RECUSALS	REDBAYS	REDEALS
RECOVERER	RECTITIC	RECUSANCE	REDBELLY	REDEALT
RECOVEROR	RECTITIS	RECUSANCY	REDBIRD	REDEAR
RECOVERS	RECTITUDE	RECUSANT	REDBIRDS	REDEARS
RECOVERY	RECTO	RECUSANTS	REDBONE	REDECIDE
RECOWER	RECTOCELE	RECUSE	REDBONES	REDECIDED
RECOWERED	RECTOR	RECUSED	REDBREAST	REDECIDES
RECOWERS	RECTORAL	RECUSES	REDBRICK	REDECRAFT
RECOYLE	RECTORATE	RECUSING	REDBRICKS	REDED
RECOYLED	RECTORESS	RECUT	REDBUD	REDEEM
RECOYLES	RECTORIAL	RECUTS	REDBUDS	REDEEMED
RECOYLING	RECTORIES	RECUTTING	REDBUG	REDEEMER
RECRATE	RECTORS	RECYCLATE	REDBUGS	REDEEMERS
RECRATED	RECTORY	RECYCLE	REDCAP	REDEEMING
RECRATES	RECTOS	RECYCLED	REDCAPS	REDEEMS

REDEFEAT	REDIALS	REDOING	REDREW	REDUCTANT
REDEFEATS	REDIAS	REDOLENCE	REDRIED	REDUCTASE
REDEFECT	REDICTATE	REDOLENCY	REDRIES	REDUCTION
REDEFECTS	REDID	REDOLENT	REDRILL	REDUCTIVE
REDEFIED	REDIGEST	REDON	REDRILLED	REDUCTOR
REDEFIES	REDIGESTS	REDONE	REDRILLS	REDUCTORS
REDEFINE	REDIGRESS	REDONNED	REDRIVE	REDUIT
REDEFINED	REDING	REDONNING	REDRIVEN	REDUITS
REDEFINES	REDINGOTE	REDONS	REDRIVES	REDUNDANT
REDEFY	REDIP	REDOS	REDRIVING	REDUVIID
REDEFYING	REDIPPED	REDOUBLE	REDROOT	REDUVIIDS
REDELESS	REDIPPING	REDOUBLED	REDROOTS	REDUX
REDELIVER	REDIPS	REDOUBLER	REDROVE	REDWARE
REDEMAND	REDIPT	REDOUBLES	REDRY	REDWARES
REDEMANDS	REDIRECT	REDOUBT	REDRYING	REDWATER
REDENIED	REDIRECTS	REDOUBTED	REDS	REDWATERS
REDENIES	REDISCUSS	REDOUBTS	REDSEAR	REDWING
REDENY	REDISPLAY	REDOUND	REDSHANK	REDWINGS
REDENYING	REDISPOSE	REDOUNDED	REDSHANKS	REDWOOD
REDEPLOY	REDISTIL	REDOUNDS	REDSHARE	REDWOODS
REDEPLOYS	REDISTILL	REDOUT	REDSHIFT	REDYE
REDEPOSIT	REDISTILS	REDOUTS	REDSHIFTS	REDYED
REDES	REDIVIDE	REDOWA	REDSHIRE	REDYEING
REDESCEND	REDIVIDED	REDOWAS	REDSHIRT	REDYES
REDESIGN	REDIVIDES	REDOX	REDSHIRTS	REE
REDESIGNS	REDIVIVUS	REDOXES	REDSHORT	REEARN
REDEVELOP	REDIVORCE	REDPOLL	REDSKIN	REEARNED
REDEYE	REDLEG	REDPOLLS	REDSKINS	REEARNING
REDEYES	REDLEGS	REDRAFT	REDSTART	REEARNS
REDFIN	REDLINE	REDRAFTED	REDSTARTS	REEBOK
REDFINS	REDLINED	REDRAFTS	REDSTREAK	REEBOKS
REDFISH	REDLINER	REDRAW	REDTAIL	REECH
REDFISHES	REDLINERS	REDRAWER	REDTAILS	REECHED
REDFOOT	REDLINES	REDRAWERS	REDTOP	REECHES
REDFOOTS	REDLINING	REDRAWING	REDTOPS	REECHIE
REDHANDED	REDLY	REDRAWN	REDUB	REECHIER
REDHEAD	REDNECK	REDRAWS	REDUBBED	REECHIEST
REDHEADED	REDNECKED	REDREAM	REDUBBING	REECHING
REDHEADS	REDNECKS	REDREAMED	REDUBS	REECHO
REDHORSE	REDNESS	REDREAMS	REDUCE	REECHOED
REDHORSES	REDNESSES	REDREAMT	REDUCED	REECHOES
REDIA	REDO	REDRESS	REDUCER	REECHOING
REDIAE	REDOCK	REDRESSAL	REDUCERS	REECHY
REDIAL	REDOCKED	REDRESSED	REDUCES	REED
REDIALED	REDOCKING	REDRESSER	REDUCIBLE	REEDBED
REDIALING	REDOCKS	REDRESSES	REDUCIBLY	REEDBEDS
REDIALLED	REDOES	REDRESSOR	REDUCING	REEDBIRD

R

REEDBIRDS	REEKER	REENGAGES	REEXPORTS	REFERENDA
REEDBUCK	REEKERS	REENGRAVE	REEXPOSE	REFERENT
REEDBUCKS	REEKIE	REENJOY	REEXPOSED	REFERENTS
REEDE	REEKIER	REENJOYED	REEXPOSES	REFERRAL
REEDED	REEKIEST	REENJOYS	REEXPRESS	REFERRALS
REEDEN	REEKING	REENLARGE	REF	REFERRED
REEDER	REEKINGLY	REENLIST	REFACE	REFERRER
REEDERS	REEKS	REENLISTS	REFACED	REFERRERS
REEDES	REEKY	REENROLL	REFACES	REFERRING
REEDIER	REEL	REENROLLS	REFACING	REFERS
REEDIEST	REELABLE	REENS	REFALL	REFFED
REEDIFIED	REELECT	REENSLAVE	REFALLEN	REFFING
REEDIFIES	REELECTED	REENTER	REFALLING	REFFO
REEDIFY	REELECTS	REENTERED	REFALLS	REFFOS
REEDILY	REELED	REENTERS	REFASHION	REFIGHT
REEDINESS	REELER	REENTRANT	REFASTEN	REFIGHTS
REEDING	REELERS	REENTRIES	REFASTENS	REFIGURE
REEDINGS	REELEVATE	REENTRY	REFECT	REFIGURED
REEDIT	REELING	REEQUIP	REFECTED	REFIGURES
REEDITED	REELINGLY	REEQUIPS	REFECTING	REFILE
REEDITING	REELINGS	REERECT	REFECTION	REFILED
REEDITION	REELMAN	REERECTED	REFECTIVE	REFILES
REEDITS	REELMEN	REERECTS	REFECTORY	REFILING
REEDLIKE	REELS	REES	REFECTS	REFILL
REEDLING	REEMBARK	REEST	REFED	REFILLED
REEDLINGS	REEMBARKS	REESTED	REFEED	REFILLING
REEDMAN	REEMBODY	REESTIER	REFEEDING	REFILLS
REEDMEN	REEMBRACE	REESTIEST	REFEEDS	REFILM
REEDS	REEMERGE	REESTING	REFEEL	REFILMED
REEDUCATE	REEMERGED	REESTS	REFEELING	REFILMING
REEDY	REEMERGES	REESTY	REFEELS	REFILMS
REEF	REEMIT	REEVE	REFEL	REFILTER
REEFABLE	REEMITS	REEVED	REFELL	REFILTERS
REEFED	REEMITTED	REEVES	REFELLED	REFINABLE
REEFER	REEMPLOY	REEVING	REFELLING	REFINANCE
REEFERS	REEMPLOYS	REEVOKE	REFELS	REFIND
REEFIER	REEN	REEVOKED	REFELT	REFINDING
REEFIEST	REENACT	REEVOKES	REFENCE	REFINDS
REEFING	REENACTED	REEVOKING	REFENCED	REFINE
REEFINGS	REENACTOR	REEXAMINE	REFENCES	REFINED
REEFS	REENACTS	REEXECUTE	REFENCING	REFINEDLY
REEFY	REENDOW	REEXHIBIT	REFER	REFINER
REEJECT	REENDOWED	REEXPEL	REFERABLE	REFINERS
REEJECTED	REENDOWS	REEXPELS	REFEREE	REFINERY
REEJECTS	REENFORCE	REEXPLAIN	REFEREED	REFINES
REEK	REENGAGE	REEXPLORE	REFEREES	REFINING
REEKED	REENGAGED	REEXPORT	REFERENCE	REFININGS

R

REFINISH	REFLOWERS	REFOUNDS	REFULGENT	REGALIAN
REFIRE	REFLOWING	REFRACT	REFUND	REGALIAS
REFIRED	REFLOWN	REFRACTED	REFUNDED	REGALING
REFIRES	REFLOWS	REFRACTOR	REFUNDER	REGALISM
REFIRING	REFLUENCE	REFRACTS	REFUNDERS	REGALISMS
REFIT	REFLUENT	REFRAIN	REFUNDING	REGALIST
REFITMENT	REFLUX	REFRAINED	REFUNDS	REGALISTS
REFITS	REFLUXED	REFRAINER	REFURBISH	REGALITY
REFITTED	REFLUXES	REFRAINS	REFURNISH	REGALLY
REFITTING	REFLUXING	REFRAME	REFUSABLE	REGALNESS
REFIX	REFLY	REFRAMED	REFUSAL	REGALS
REFIXED	REFLYING	REFRAMES	REFUSALS	REGAR
REFIXES	REFOCUS	REFRAMING	REFUSE	REGARD
REFIXING	REFOCUSED	REFREEZE	REFUSED	REGARDANT
REFLAG	REFOCUSES	REFREEZES	REFUSENIK	REGARDED
REFLAGGED	REFOLD	REFRESH	REFUSER	REGARDER
REFLAGS	REFOLDED	REFRESHED	REFUSERS	REGARDERS
REFLATE	REFOLDING	REFRESHEN	REFUSES	REGARDFUL
REFLATED	REFOLDS	REFRESHER	REFUSING	REGARDING
REFLATES	REFOOT	REFRESHES	REFUSION	REGARDS
REFLATING	REFOOTED	REFRIED	REFUSIONS	REGARS
REFLATION	REFOOTING	REFRIES	REFUSNIK	REGATHER
REFLECT	REFOOTS	REFRINGE	REFUSNIKS	REGATHERS
REFLECTED	REFOREST	REFRINGED	REFUTABLE	REGATTA
REFLECTER	REFORESTS	REFRINGES	REFUTABLY	REGATTAS
REFLECTOR	REFORGE	REFRONT	REFUTAL	REGAUGE
REFLECTS	REFORGED	REFRONTED	REFUTALS	REGAUGED
REFLET	REFORGES	REFRONTS	REFUTE	REGAUGES
REFLETS	REFORGING	REFROZE	REFUTED	REGAUGING
REFLEW	REFORM	REFROZEN	REFUTER	REGAVE
REFLEX	REFORMADE	REFRY	REFUTERS	REGEAR
REFLEXED	REFORMADO	REFRYING	REFUTES	REGEARED
REFLEXES	REFORMAT	REFS	REFUTING	REGEARING
REFLEXING	REFORMATE	REFT	REG	REGEARS
REFLEXION	REFORMATS	REFUEL	REGAIN	REGELATE
REFLEXIVE	REFORMED	REFUELED	REGAINED	REGELATED
REFLEXLY	REFORMER	REFUELING	REGAINER	REGELATES
REFLIES	REFORMERS	REFUELLED	REGAINERS	REGENCE
REFLOAT	REFORMING	REFUELS	REGAINING	REGENCES
REFLOATED	REFORMISM	REFUGE	REGAINS	REGENCIES
REFLOATS	REFORMIST	REFUGED	REGAL	REGENCY
REFLOOD	REFORMS	REFUGEE	REGALE	REGENT
REFLOODED	REFORTIFY	REFUGEES	REGALED	REGENTAL
REFLOODS	REFOUGHT	REFUGES	REGALER	REGENTS
REFLOW	REFOUND	REFUGIA	REGALERS	REGES
REFLOWED	REFOUNDED	REFUGING	REGALES	REGEST
REFLOWER	REFOUNDER	REFUGIUM	REGALIA	REGESTS

R

REGGAE	REGLAZES	REGRATER	REGULABLE	REHEARING
REGGAES	REGLAZING	REGRATERS	REGULAE	REHEARS
REGGAETON	REGLET	REGRATES	REGULAR	REHEARSAL
REGGO	REGLETS	REGRATING	REGULARLY	REHEARSE
REGGOS	REGLORIFY	REGRATOR	REGULARS	REHEARSED
REGICIDAL	REGLOSS	REGRATORS	REGULATE	REHEARSER
REGICIDE	REGLOSSED	REGREDE	REGULATED	REHEARSES
REGICIDES	REGLOSSES	REGREDED	REGULATES	REHEAT
REGIE	REGLOW	REGREDES	REGULATOR	REHEATED
REGIES	REGLOWED	REGREDING	REGULI	REHEATER
REGIFT	REGLOWING	REGREEN	REGULINE	REHEATERS
REGIFTED	REGLOWS	REGREENED	REGULISE	REHEATING
REGIFTING	REGLUE	REGREENS	REGULISED	REHEATS
REGIFTS	REGLUED	REGREET	REGULISES	REHEEL
REGILD	REGLUES	REGREETED	REGULIZE	REHEELED
REGILDED	REGLUING	REGREETS	REGULIZED	REHEELING
REGILDING	REGMA	REGRESS	REGULIZES	REHEELS
REGILDS	REGMAKER	REGRESSED	REGULO	REHEM
REGILT	REGMAKERS	REGRESSES	REGULOS	REHEMMED
REGIME	REGMATA	REGRESSOR	REGULUS	REHEMMING
REGIMEN	REGNA	REGRET	REGULUSES	REHEMS
REGIMENS	REGNAL	REGRETFUL	REGUR	REHINGE
REGIMENT	REGNANCY	REGRETS	REGURS	REHINGED
REGIMENTS	REGNANT	REGRETTED	REH	REHINGES
REGIMES	REGNUM	REGRETTER	REHAB	REHINGING
REGIMINAL	REGO	REGREW	REHABBED	REHIRE
REGINA	REGOLITH	REGRIND	REHABBER	REHIRED
REGINAE	REGOLITHS	REGRINDS	REHABBERS	REHIRES
REGINAL	REGORGE	REGROOM	REHABBING	REHIRING
REGINAS	REGORGED	REGROOMED	REHABS	REHOBOAM
REGION	REGORGES	REGROOMS	REHAMMER	REHOBOAMS
REGIONAL	REGORGING	REGROOVE	REHAMMERS	REHOME
REGIONALS	REGOS	REGROOVED	REHANDLE	REHOMED
REGIONARY	REGOSOL	REGROOVES	REHANDLED	REHOMES
REGIONS	REGOSOLS	REGROUND	REHANDLES	REHOMING
REGISSEUR	REGRADE	REGROUP	REHANG	REHOUSE
REGISTER	REGRADED	REGROUPED	REHANGED	REHOUSED
REGISTERS	REGRADES	REGROUPS	REHANGING	REHOUSES
REGISTRAR	REGRADING	REGROW	REHANGS	REHOUSING
REGISTRY	REGRAFT	REGROWING	REHARDEN	REHS
REGIUS	REGRAFTED	REGROWN	REHARDENS	REHUNG
REGIVE	REGRAFTS	REGROWS	REHASH	REHYDRATE
REGIVEN	REGRANT	REGROWTH	REHASHED	REI
REGIVES	REGRANTED	REGROWTHS	REHASHES	REIF
REGIVING	REGRANTS	REGS	REHASHING	REIFIED
REGLAZE	REGRATE	REGUERDON	REHEAR	REIFIER
REGLAZED	REGRATED	REGULA	REHEARD	REIFIERS

REIFIES	REINDUCT	REINVADE	REJECTER	REKINDLE
REIFS	REINDUCTS	REINVADED	REJECTERS	REKINDLED
REIFY	REINED	REINVADES	REJECTING	REKINDLES
REIFYING	REINETTE	REINVENT	REJECTION	REKING
REIGN	REINETTES	REINVENTS	REJECTIVE	REKNIT
REIGNED	REINFECT	REINVEST	REJECTOR	REKNITS
REIGNING	REINFECTS	REINVESTS	REJECTORS	REKNITTED
REIGNITE	REINFLAME	REINVITE	REJECTS	REKNOT
REIGNITED	REINFLATE	REINVITED	REJIG	REKNOTS
REIGNITES	REINFORCE	REINVITES	REJIGGED	REKNOTTED
REIGNS	REINFORM	REINVOKE	REJIGGER	RELABEL
REIK	REINFORMS	REINVOKED	REJIGGERS	RELABELED
REIKI	REINFUND	REINVOKES	REJIGGING	RELABELS
REIKIS	REINFUNDS	REINVOLVE	REJIGS	RELACE
REIKS	REINFUSE	REIRD	REJOICE	RELACED
REILLUME	REINFUSED	REIRDS	REJOICED	RELACES
REILLUMED	REINFUSES	REIS	REJOICER	RELACHE
REILLUMES	REINHABIT	REISES	REJOICERS	RELACHES
REIMAGE	REINING	REISSUE	REJOICES	RELACING
REIMAGED	REINJECT	REISSUED	REJOICING	RELACQUER
REIMAGES	REINJECTS	REISSUER	REJOIN	RELAID
REIMAGINE	REINJURE	REISSUERS	REJOINDER	RELAND
REIMAGING	REINJURED	REISSUES	REJOINED	RELANDED
REIMBURSE	REINJURES	REISSUING	REJOINING	RELANDING
REIMMERSE	REINJURY	REIST	REJOINS	RELANDS
REIMPLANT	REINK	REISTAFEL	REJON	RELAPSE
REIMPORT	REINKED	REISTED	REJONEO	RELAPSED
REIMPORTS	REINKING	REISTING	REJONEOS	RELAPSER
REIMPOSE	REINKS	REISTS	REJONES	RELAPSERS
REIMPOSED	REINLESS	REITBOK	REJOURN	RELAPSES
REIMPOSES	REINS	REITBOKS	REJOURNED	RELAPSING
REIN	REINSERT	REITER	REJOURNS	RELATA
REINCITE	REINSERTS	REITERANT	REJUDGE	RELATABLE
REINCITED	REINSMAN	REITERATE	REJUDGED	RELATE
REINCITES	REINSMEN	REITERS	REJUDGES	RELATED
REINCUR	REINSPECT	REIVE	REJUDGING	RELATEDLY
REINCURS	REINSPIRE	REIVED	REJUGGLE	RELATER
REINDEER	REINSTAL	REIVER	REJUGGLED	RELATERS
REINDEERS	REINSTALL	REIVERS	REJUGGLES	RELATES
REINDEX	REINSTALS	REIVES	REJUSTIFY	RELATING
REINDEXED	REINSTATE	REIVING	REKE	RELATION
REINDEXES	REINSURE	REJACKET	REKED	RELATIONS
REINDICT	REINSURED	REJACKETS	REKES	RELATIVAL
REINDICTS	REINSURER	REJECT	REKEY	RELATIVE
REINDUCE	REINSURES	REJECTED	REKEYED	RELATIVES
REINDUCED	REINTER	REJECTEE	REKEYING	RELATOR
REINDUCES	REINTERS	REJECTEES	REKEYS	RELATORS

R

RELATUM
RELAUNCH
RELAUNDER
RELAX
RELAXABLE
RELAXANT
RELAXANTS
RELAXED
RELAXEDLY
RELAXER
RELAXERS
RELAXES
RELAXIN
RELAXING
RELAXINS
RELAY
RELAYED
RELAYING
RELAYS
RELEARN
RELEARNED
RELEARNS
RELEARNT
RELEASE
RELEASED
RELEASEE
RELEASEES
RELEASER
RELEASERS
RELEASES
RELEASING
RELEASOR
RELEASORS
RELEGABLE
RELEGATE
RELEGATED
RELEGATES
RELEND
RELENDING
RELENDS
RELENT
RELENTED
RELENTING
RELENTS
RELET
RELETS
RELETTER

RELETTERS
RELETTING
RELEVANCE
RELEVANCY
RELEVANT
RELEVE
RELEVES
RELIABLE
RELIABLES
RELIABLY
RELIANCE
RELIANCES
RELIANT
RELIANTLY
RELIC
RELICENSE
RELICS
RELICT
RELICTION
RELICTS
RELIDE
RELIE
RELIED
RELIEF
RELIEFS
RELIER
RELIERS
RELIES
RELIEVE
RELIEVED
RELIEVER
RELIEVERS
RELIEVES
RELIEVING
RELIEVO
RELIEVOS
RELIGHT
RELIGHTED
RELIGHTS
RELIGIEUX
RELIGION
RELIGIONS
RELIGIOSE
RELIGIOSO
RELIGIOUS
RELINE
RELINED

RELINES
RELINING
RELINK
RELINKED
RELINKING
RELINKS
RELIQUARY
RELIQUE
RELIQUEFY
RELIQUES
RELIQUIAE
RELISH
RELISHED
RELISHES
RELISHING
RELIST
RELISTED
RELISTING
RELISTS
RELIT
RELIVABLE
RELIVE
RELIVED
RELIVER
RELIVERED
RELIVERS
RELIVES
RELIVING
RELLENO
RELLENOS
RELLIE
RELLIES
RELLISH
RELLISHED
RELLISHES
RELOAD
RELOADED
RELOADER
RELOADERS
RELOADING
RELOADS
RELOAN
RELOANED
RELOANING
RELOANS
RELOCATE
RELOCATED

RELOCATEE
RELOCATES
RELOCATOR
RELOCK
RELOCKED
RELOCKING
RELOCKS
RELOOK
RELOOKED
RELOOKING
RELOOKS
RELUCENT
RELUCT
RELUCTANT
RELUCTATE
RELUCTED
RELUCTING
RELUCTS
RELUME
RELUMED
RELUMES
RELUMINE
RELUMINED
RELUMINES
RELUMING
RELY
RELYING
REM
REMADE
REMADES
REMAIL
REMAILED
REMAILING
REMAILS
REMAIN
REMAINDER
REMAINED
REMAINING
REMAINS
REMAKE
REMAKER
REMAKERS
REMAKES
REMAKING
REMAN
REMAND
REMANDED

REMANDING
REMANDS
REMANENCE
REMANENCY
REMANENT
REMANENTS
REMANET
REMANETS
REMANIE
REMANIES
REMANNED
REMANNING
REMANS
REMAP
REMAPPED
REMAPPING
REMAPS
REMARK
REMARKED
REMARKER
REMARKERS
REMARKET
REMARKETS
REMARKING
REMARKS
REMARQUE
REMARQUED
REMARQUES
REMARRIED
REMARRIES
REMARRY
REMASTER
REMASTERS
REMATCH
REMATCHED
REMATCHES
REMATE
REMATED
REMATES
REMATING
REMBLAI
REMBLAIS
REMBLE
REMBLED
REMBLES
REMBLING
REMEAD

REMEADED	REMIGIAL	REMODELED	REMUDA	RENEGADOS
REMEADING	REMIGRATE	REMODELER	REMUDAS	RENEGATE
REMEADS	REMIND	REMODELS	REMUEUR	RENEGATES
REMEASURE	REMINDED	REMODIFY	REMUEURS	RENEGE
REMEDE	REMINDER	REMOISTEN	REMURMUR	RENEGED
REMEDED	REMINDERS	REMOLADE	REMURMURS	RENEGER
REMEDES	REMINDFUL	REMOLADES	REN	RENEGERS
REMEDIAL	REMINDING	REMOLD	RENAGUE	RENEGES
REMEDIAT	REMINDS	REMOLDED	RENAGUED	RENEGING
REMEDIATE	REMINISCE	REMOLDING	RENAGUES	RENEGUE
REMEDIED	REMINT	REMOLDS	RENAGUING	RENEGUED
REMEDIES	REMINTED	REMONTANT	RENAIL	RENEGUER
REMEDING	REMINTING	REMONTOIR	RENAILED	RENEGUERS
REMEDY	REMINTS	REMORA	RENAILING	RENEGUES
REMEDYING	REMISE	REMORAS	RENAILS	RENEGUING
REMEET	REMISED	REMORID	RENAL	RENEST
REMEETING	REMISES	REMORSE	RENAME	RENESTED
REMEETS	REMISING	REMORSES	RENAMED	RENESTING
REMEID	REMISS	REMOTE	RENAMES	RENESTS
REMEIDED	REMISSION	REMOTELY	RENAMING	RENEW
REMEIDING	REMISSIVE	REMOTER	RENASCENT	RENEWABLE
REMEIDS	REMISSLY	REMOTES	RENATURE	RENEWABLY
REMELT	REMISSORY	REMOTEST	RENATURED	RENEWAL
REMELTED	REMIT	REMOTION	RENATURES	RENEWALS
REMELTING	REMITMENT	REMOTIONS	RENAY	RENEWED
REMELTS	REMITS	REMOUD	RENAYED	RENEWEDLY
REMEMBER	REMITTAL	REMOULADE	RENAYING	RENEWER
REMEMBERS	REMITTALS	REMOULD	RENAYS	RENEWERS
REMEN	REMITTED	REMOULDED	RENCONTRE	RENEWING
REMEND	REMITTEE	REMOULDS	REND	RENEWINGS
REMENDED	REMITTEES	REMOUNT	RENDED	RENEWS
REMENDING	REMITTENT	REMOUNTED	RENDER	RENEY
REMENDS	REMITTER	REMOUNTS	RENDERED	RENEYED
REMENS	REMITTERS	REMOVABLE	RENDERER	RENEYING
REMERCIED	REMITTING	REMOVABLY	RENDERERS	RENEYS
REMERCIES	REMITTOR	REMOVAL	RENDERING	RENFIERST
REMERCY	REMITTORS	REMOVALS	RENDERS	RENFORCE
REMERGE	REMIX	REMOVE	RENDIBLE	RENFORCED
REMERGED	REMIXED	REMOVED	RENDING	RENFORCES
REMERGES	REMIXES	REMOVEDLY	RENDITION	RENFORST
REMERGING	REMIXING	REMOVER	RENDS	RENGA
REMET	REMIXT	REMOVERS	RENDZINA	RENGAS
REMEX	REMIXTURE	REMOVES	RENDZINAS	RENIED
REMIGATE	REMNANT	REMOVING	RENEGADE	RENIES
REMIGATED	REMNANTAL	REMS	RENEGADED	RENIFORM
REMIGATES	REMNANTS	REMUAGE	RENEGADES	RENIG
REMIGES	REMODEL	REMUAGES	RENEGADO	RENIGGED

R

RENIGGING	RENTED	REOPPOSED	REPARKS	REPELLENT
RENIGS	RENTER	REOPPOSES	REPARTEE	REPELLER
RENIN	RENTERS	REORDAIN	REPARTEED	REPELLERS
RENINS	RENTES	REORDAINS	REPARTEES	REPELLING
RENITENCE	RENTIER	REORDER	REPASS	REPELS
RENITENCY	RENTIERS	REORDERED	REPASSAGE	REPENT
RENITENT	RENTING	REORDERS	REPASSED	REPENTANT
RENK	RENTINGS	REORIENT	REPASSES	REPENTED
RENKER	RENTS	REORIENTS	REPASSING	REPENTER
RENKEST	RENUMBER	REOS	REPAST	REPENTERS
RENMINBI	RENUMBERS	REOUTFIT	REPASTED	REPENTING
RENMINBIS	RENVERSE	REOUTFITS	REPASTING	REPENTS
RENNASE	RENVERSED	REOVIRUS	REPASTS	REPEOPLE
RENNASES	RENVERSES	REOXIDISE	REPASTURE	REPEOPLED
RENNE	RENVERST	REOXIDIZE	REPATCH	REPEOPLES
RENNED	RENVOI	REP	REPATCHED	REPERCUSS
RENNES	RENVOIS	REPACIFY	REPATCHES	REPEREPE
RENNET	RENVOY	REPACK	REPATTERN	REPEREPES
RENNETS	RENVOYS	REPACKAGE	REPAVE	REPERK
RENNIN	RENY	REPACKED	REPAVED	REPERKED
RENNING	RENYING	REPACKING	REPAVES	REPERKING
RENNINGS	REO	REPACKS	REPAVING	REPERKS
RENNINS	REOBJECT	REPAID	REPAY	REPERTORY
RENOGRAM	REOBJECTS	REPAINT	REPAYABLE	REPERUSAL
RENOGRAMS	REOBSERVE	REPAINTED	REPAYING	REPERUSE
RENOTIFY	REOBTAIN	REPAINTS	REPAYMENT	REPERUSED
RENOUNCE	REOBTAINS	REPAIR	REPAYS	REPERUSES
RENOUNCED	REOCCUPY	REPAIRED	REPEAL	REPETEND
RENOUNCER	REOCCUR	REPAIRER	REPEALED	REPETENDS
RENOUNCES	REOCCURS	REPAIRERS	REPEALER	REPHRASE
RENOVATE	REOFFEND	REPAIRING	REPEALERS	REPHRASED
RENOVATED	REOFFENDS	REPAIRMAN	REPEALING	REPHRASES
RENOVATES	REOFFER	REPAIRMEN	REPEALS	REPIGMENT
RENOVATOR	REOFFERED	REPAIRS	REPEAT	REPIN
RENOWN	REOFFERS	REPAND	REPEATED	REPINE
RENOWNED	REOIL	REPANDLY	REPEATER	REPINED
RENOWNER	REOILED	REPANEL	REPEATERS	REPINER
RENOWNERS	REOILING	REPANELED	REPEATING	REPINERS
RENOWNING	REOILS	REPANELS	REPEATS	REPINES
RENOWNS	REOPEN	REPAPER	REPECHAGE	REPINING
RENS	REOPENED	REPAPERED	REPEG	REPININGS
RENT	REOPENER	REPAPERS	REPEGGED	REPINNED
RENTABLE	REOPENERS	REPARABLE	REPEGGING	REPINNING
RENTAL	REOPENING	REPARABLY	REPEGS	REPINS
RENTALLER	REOPENS	REPARK	REPEL	REPIQUE
RENTALS	REOPERATE	REPARKED	REPELLANT	REPIQUED
RENTE	REOPPOSE	REPARKING	REPELLED	REPIQUES

REPIQUING	REPLICATE	REPOSALL	REPRESSER	REPROGRAM
REPLA	REPLICON	REPOSALLS	REPRESSES	REPROOF
REPLACE	REPLICONS	REPOSALS	REPRESSOR	REPROOFED
REPLACED	REPLIED	REPOSE	REPRICE	REPROOFS
REPLACER	REPLIER	REPOSED	REPRICED	REPROS
REPLACERS	REPLIERS	REPOSEDLY	REPRICES	REPROVAL
REPLACES	REPLIES	REPOSEFUL	REPRICING	REPROVALS
REPLACING	REPLOT	REPOSER	REPRIEFE	REPROVE
REPLAN	REPLOTS	REPOSERS	REPRIEFES	REPROVED
REPLANNED	REPLOTTED	REPOSES	REPRIEVAL	REPROVER
REPLANS	REPLOW	REPOSING	REPRIEVE	REPROVERS
REPLANT	REPLOWED	REPOSIT	REPRIEVED	REPROVES
REPLANTED	REPLOWING	REPOSITED	REPRIEVER	REPROVING
REPLANTS	REPLOWS	REPOSITOR	REPRIEVES	REPRYVE
REPLASTER	REPLUM	REPOSITS	REPRIMAND	REPRYVED
REPLATE	REPLUMB	REPOSSESS	REPRIME	REPRYVES
REPLATED	REPLUMBED	REPOST	REPRIMED	REPRYVING
REPLATES	REPLUMBS	REPOSTED	REPRIMES	REPS
REPLATING	REPLUNGE	REPOSTING	REPRIMING	REPTANT
REPLAY	REPLUNGED	REPOSTS	REPRINT	REPTATION
REPLAYED	REPLUNGES	REPOSURE	REPRINTED	REPTILE
REPLAYING	REPLY	REPOSURES	REPRINTER	REPTILES
REPLAYS	REPLYING	REPOT	REPRINTS	REPTILIA
REPLEAD	REPO	REPOTS	REPRISAL	REPTILIAN
REPLEADED	REPOINT	REPOTTED	REPRISALS	REPTILIUM
REPLEADER	REPOINTED	REPOTTING	REPRISE	REPTILOID
REPLEADS	REPOINTS	REPOUR	REPRISED	REPUBLIC
REPLED	REPOLISH	REPOURED	REPRISES	REPUBLICS
REPLEDGE	REPOLL	REPOURING	REPRISING	REPUBLISH
REPLEDGED	REPOLLED	REPOURS	REPRIVE	REPUDIATE
REPLEDGES	REPOLLING	REPOUSSE	REPRIVED	REPUGN
REPLENISH	REPOLLS	REPOUSSES	REPRIVES	REPUGNANT
REPLETE	REPOMAN	REPOWER	REPRIVING	REPUGNED
REPLETED	REPOMEN	REPOWERED	REPRIZE	REPUGNING
REPLETELY	REPONE	REPOWERS	REPRIZED	REPUGNS
REPLETES	REPONED	REPP	REPRIZES	REPULP
REPLETING	REPONES	REPPED	REPRIZING	REPULPED
REPLETION	REPONING	REPPING	REPRO	REPULPING
REPLEVIED	REPORT	REPPINGS	REPROACH	REPULPS
REPLEVIES	REPORTAGE	REPPS	REPROBACY	REPULSE
REPLEVIN	REPORTED	REPREEVE	REPROBATE	REPULSED
REPLEVINS	REPORTER	REPREEVED	REPROBE	REPULSER
REPLEVY	REPORTERS	REPREEVES	REPROBED	REPULSERS
REPLICA	REPORTING	REPREHEND	REPROBES	REPULSES
REPLICANT	REPORTS	REPRESENT	REPROBING	REPULSING
REPLICAS	REPOS	REPRESS	REPROCESS	REPULSION
REPLICASE	REPOSAL	REPRESSED	REPRODUCE	REPULSIVE

R

REPUMP	REQUIT	REREMOUSE	RESAILING	RESCULPT
REPUMPED	REQUITAL	RERENT	RESAILS	RESCULPTS
REPUMPING	REQUITALS	RERENTED	RESALABLE	RESEAL
REPUMPS	REQUITE	RERENTING	RESALE	RESEALED
REPUNIT	REQUITED	RERENTS	RESALES	RESEALING
REPUNITS	REQUITER	REREPEAT	RESALGAR	RESEALS
REPURE	REQUITERS	REREPEATS	RESALGARS	RESEARCH
REPURED	REQUITES	REREVIEW	RESALUTE	RESEASON
REPURES	REQUITING	REREVIEWS	RESALUTED	RESEASONS
REPURIFY	REQUITS	REREVISE	RESALUTES	RESEAT
REPURING	REQUITTED	REREVISED	RESAMPLE	RESEATED
REPURPOSE	REQUOTE	REREVISES	RESAMPLED	RESEATING
REPURSUE	REQUOTED	REREWARD	RESAMPLES	RESEATS
REPURSUED	REQUOTES	REREWARDS	RESAT	RESEAU
REPURSUES	REQUOTING	RERIG	RESAW	RESEAUS
REPUTABLE	REQUOYLE	RERIGGED	RESAWED	RESEAUX
REPUTABLY	REQUOYLED	RERIGGING	RESAWING	RESECT
REPUTE	REQUOYLES	RERIGS	RESAWN	RESECTED
REPUTED	RERACK	RERISE	RESAWS	RESECTING
REPUTEDLY	RERACKED	RERISEN	RESAY	RESECTION
REPUTES	RERACKING	RERISES	RESAYING	RESECTS
REPUTING	RERACKS	RERISING	RESAYS	RESECURE
REPUTINGS	RERADIATE	REROLL	RESCALE	RESECURED
REQUALIFY	RERAIL	REROLLED	RESCALED	RESECURES
REQUERE	RERAILED	REROLLER	RESCALES	RESEDA
REQUERED	RERAILING	REROLLERS	RESCALING	RESEDAS
REQUERES	RERAILS	REROLLING	RESCHOOL	RESEE
REQUERING	RERAISE	REROLLS	RESCHOOLS	RESEED
REQUEST	RERAISED	REROOF	RESCIND	RESEEDED
REQUESTED	RERAISES	REROOFED	RESCINDED	RESEEDING
REQUESTER	RERAISING	REROOFING	RESCINDER	RESEEDS
REQUESTOR	RERAN	REROOFS	RESCINDS	RESEEING
REQUESTS	REREAD	REROSE	RESCORE	RESEEK
REQUICKEN	REREADING	REROUTE	RESCORED	RESEEKING
REQUIEM	REREADS	REROUTED	RESCORES	RESEEKS
REQUIEMS	REREBRACE	REROUTES	RESCORING	RESEEN
REQUIGHT	RERECORD	REROUTING	RESCREEN	RESEES
REQUIGHTS	RERECORDS	RERUN	RESCREENS	RESEIZE
REQUIN	REREDOS	RERUNNING	RESCRIPT	RESEIZED
REQUINS	REREDOSES	RERUNS	RESCRIPTS	RESEIZES
REQUIRE	REREDOSSE	RES	RESCUABLE	RESEIZING
REQUIRED	RERELEASE	RESADDLE	RESCUE	RESEIZURE
REQUIRER	REREMAI	RESADDLED	RESCUED	RESELECT
REQUIRERS	REREMAIS	RESADDLES	RESCUER	RESELECTS
REQUIRES	REREMICE	RESAID	RESCUERS	RESELL
REQUIRING	REREMIND	RESAIL	RESCUES	RESELLER
REQUISITE	REREMINDS	RESAILED	RESCUING	RESELLERS

RESELLING	RESHAPES	RESIDERS	RESINISED	RESKUING
RESELLS	RESHAPING	RESIDES	RESINISES	RESLATE
RESEMBLE	RESHARPEN	RESIDING	RESINIZE	RESLATED
RESEMBLED	RESHAVE	RESIDS	RESINIZED	RESLATES
RESEMBLER	RESHAVED	RESIDUA	RESINIZES	RESLATING
RESEMBLES	RESHAVEN	RESIDUAL	RESINLIKE	RESMELT
RESEND	RESHAVES	RESIDUALS	RESINOID	RESMELTED
RESENDING	RESHAVING	RESIDUARY	RESINOIDS	RESMELTS
RESENDS	RESHES	RESIDUE	RESINOSES	RESMOOTH
RESENT	RESHINE	RESIDUES	RESINOSIS	RESMOOTHS
RESENTED	RESHINED	RESIDUOUS	RESINOUS	RESNATRON
RESENTER	RESHINES	RESIDUUM	RESINS	RESOAK
RESENTERS	RESHINGLE	RESIDUUMS	RESINY	RESOAKED
RESENTFUL	RESHINING	RESIFT	RESIST	RESOAKING
RESENTING	RESHIP	RESIFTED	RESISTANT	RESOAKS
RESENTIVE	RESHIPPED	RESIFTING	RESISTED	RESOD
RESENTS	RESHIPPER	RESIFTS	RESISTENT	RESODDED
RESERPINE	RESHIPS	RESIGHT	RESISTER	RESODDING
RESERVE	RESHOD	RESIGHTED	RESISTERS	RESODS
RESERVED	RESHOE	RESIGHTS	RESISTING	RESOFTEN
RESERVER	RESHOED	RESIGN	RESISTIVE	RESOFTENS
RESERVERS	RESHOEING	RESIGNED	RESISTOR	RESOJET
RESERVES	RESHOES	RESIGNER	RESISTORS	RESOJETS
RESERVICE	RESHONE	RESIGNERS	RESISTS	RESOLD
RESERVING	RESHOOT	RESIGNING	RESIT	RESOLDER
RESERVIST	RESHOOTS	RESIGNS	RESITE	RESOLDERS
RESERVOIR	RESHOT	RESILE	RESITED	RESOLE
RESES	RESHOW	RESILED	RESITES	RESOLED
RESET	RESHOWED	RESILES	RESITING	RESOLES
RESETS	RESHOWER	RESILIENT	RESITS	RESOLING
RESETTED	RESHOWERS	RESILIN	RESITTING	RESOLUBLE
RESETTER	RESHOWING	RESILING	RESITUATE	RESOLUTE
RESETTERS	RESHOWN	RESILINS	RESIZE	RESOLUTER
RESETTING	RESHOWS	RESILVER	RESIZED	RESOLUTES
RESETTLE	RESHUFFLE	RESILVERS	RESIZES	RESOLVE
RESETTLED	RESIANCE	RESIN	RESIZING	RESOLVED
RESETTLES	RESIANCES	RESINATA	RESKETCH	RESOLVENT
RESEW	RESIANT	RESINATAS	RESKEW	RESOLVER
RESEWED	RESIANTS	RESINATE	RESKEWED	RESOLVERS
RESEWING	RESID	RESINATED	RESKEWING	RESOLVES
RESEWN	RESIDE	RESINATES	RESKEWS	RESOLVING
RESEWS	RESIDED	RESINED	RESKILL	RESONANCE
RESH	RESIDENCE	RESINER	RESKILLED	RESONANT
RESHAPE	RESIDENCY	RESINERS	RESKILLS	RESONANTS
RESHAPED	RESIDENT	RESINIFY	RESKUE	RESONATE
RESHAPER	RESIDENTS	RESINING	RESKUED	RESONATED
RESHAPERS	RESIDER	RESINISE	RESKUES	RESONATES

R

RESONATOR	RESPIRES	RESTACK	RESTOKES	RESUBMIT
RESORB	RESPIRING	RESTACKED	RESTOKING	RESUBMITS
RESORBED	RESPITE	RESTACKS	RESTORAL	RESULT
RESORBENT	RESPITED	RESTAFF	RESTORALS	RESULTANT
RESORBING	RESPITES	RESTAFFED	RESTORE	RESULTED
RESORBS	RESPITING	RESTAFFS	RESTORED	RESULTFUL
RESORCIN	RESPLEND	RESTAGE	RESTORER	RESULTING
RESORCINS	RESPLENDS	RESTAGED	RESTORERS	RESULTS
RESORT	RESPLICE	RESTAGES	RESTORES	RESUMABLE
RESORTED	RESPLICED	RESTAGING	RESTORING	RESUME
RESORTER	RESPLICES	RESTAMP	RESTOS	RESUMED
RESORTERS	RESPLIT	RESTAMPED	RESTRAIN	RESUMER
RESORTING	RESPLITS	RESTAMPS	RESTRAINS	RESUMERS
RESORTS	RESPOKE	RESTART	RESTRAINT	RESUMES
RESOUGHT	RESPOKEN	RESTARTED	RESTRESS	RESUMING
RESOUND	RESPOND	RESTARTER	RESTRETCH	RESUMMON
RESOUNDED	RESPONDED	RESTARTS	RESTRICT	RESUMMONS
RESOUNDS	RESPONDER	RESTATE	RESTRICTS	RESUPINE
RESOURCE	RESPONDS	RESTATED	RESTRIKE	RESUPPLY
RESOURCED	RESPONSA	RESTATES	RESTRIKES	RESURFACE
RESOURCES	RESPONSE	RESTATING	RESTRING	RESURGE
RESOW	RESPONSER	RESTATION	RESTRINGE	RESURGED
RESOWED	RESPONSES	RESTED	RESTRINGS	RESURGENT
RESOWING	RESPONSOR	RESTEM	RESTRIVE	RESURGES
RESOWN	RESPONSUM	RESTEMMED	RESTRIVEN	RESURGING
RESOWS	RESPOOL	RESTEMS	RESTRIVES	RESURRECT
RESPACE	RESPOOLED	RESTER	RESTROOM	RESURVEY
RESPACED	RESPOOLS	RESTERS	RESTROOMS	RESURVEYS
RESPACES	RESPOT	RESTFUL	RESTROVE	RESUSPEND
RESPACING	RESPOTS	RESTFULLY	RESTRUCK	RESWALLOW
RESPADE	RESPOTTED	RESTIER	RESTRUNG	RET
RESPADED	RESPRANG	RESTIEST	RESTS	RETABLE
RESPADES	RESPRAY	RESTIFF	RESTUDIED	RETABLES
RESPADING	RESPRAYED	RESTIFORM	RESTUDIES	RETACK
RESPEAK	RESPRAYS	RESTING	RESTUDY	RETACKED
RESPEAKS	RESPREAD	RESTINGS	RESTUFF	RETACKING
RESPECIFY	RESPREADS	RESTITCH	RESTUFFED	RETACKLE
RESPECT	RESPRING	RESTITUTE	RESTUFFS	RETACKLED
RESPECTED	RESPRINGS	RESTIVE	RESTUMP	RETACKLES
RESPECTER	RESPROUT	RESTIVELY	RESTUMPED	RETACKS
RESPECTS	RESPROUTS	RESTLESS	RESTUMPS	RETAG
RESPELL	RESPRUNG	RESTO	RESTY	RETAGGED
RESPELLED	RESSALDAR	RESTOCK	RESTYLE	RETAGGING
RESPELLS	REST	RESTOCKED	RESTYLED	RETAGS
RESPELT	RESTABLE	RESTOCKS	RESTYLES	RETAIL
RESPIRE	RESTABLED	RESTOKE	RESTYLING	RETAILED
RESPIRED	RESTABLES	RESTOKED	RESUBJECT	RETAILER

RETAILERS	RETCH	RETICENCY	RETINULA	RETOURED
RETAILING	RETCHED	RETICENT	RETINULAE	RETOURING
RETAILOR	RETCHES	RETICLE	RETINULAR	RETOURS
RETAILORS	RETCHING	RETICLES	RETINULAS	RETRACE
RETAILS	RETCHLESS	RETICULA	RETIRACY	RETRACED
RETAIN	RETE	RETICULAR	RETIRAL	RETRACER
RETAINED	RETEACH	RETICULE	RETIRALS	RETRACERS
RETAINER	RETEACHES	RETICULES	RETIRANT	RETRACES
RETAINERS	RETEAM	RETICULUM	RETIRANTS	RETRACING
RETAINING	RETEAMED	RETIE	RETIRE	RETRACK
RETAINS	RETEAMING	RETIED	RETIRED	RETRACKED
RETAKE	RETEAMS	RETIEING	RETIREDLY	RETRACKS
RETAKEN	RETEAR	RETIES	RETIREE	RETRACT
RETAKER	RETEARING	RETIFORM	RETIREES	RETRACTED
RETAKERS	RETEARS	RETIGHTEN	RETIRER	RETRACTOR
RETAKES	RETELL	RETILE	RETIRERS	RETRACTS
RETAKING	RETELLER	RETILED	RETIRES	RETRAICT
RETAKINGS	RETELLERS	RETILES	RETIRING	RETRAICTS
RETALIATE	RETELLING	RETILING	RETITLE	RETRAIN
RETALLIED	RETELLS	RETIME	RETITLED	RETRAINED
RETALLIES	RETEM	RETIMED	RETITLES	RETRAINEE
RETALLY	RETEMPER	RETIMES	RETITLING	RETRAINS
RETAMA	RETEMPERS	RETIMING	RETOLD	RETRAIT
RETAMAS	RETEMS	RETINA	RETOOK	RETRAITE
RETAPE	RETENE	RETINAE	RETOOL	RETRAITES
RETAPED	RETENES	RETINAL	RETOOLED	RETRAITS
RETAPES	RETENTION	RETINALS	RETOOLING	RETRAITT
RETAPING	RETENTIVE	RETINAS	RETOOLS	RETRAITTS
RETARD	RETEST	RETINE	RETORE	RETRAL
RETARDANT	RETESTED	RETINENE	RETORN	RETRALLY
RETARDATE	RETESTIFY	RETINENES	RETORSION	RETRATE
RETARDED	RETESTING	RETINES	RETORT	RETRATED
RETARDER	RETESTS	RETINITE	RETORTED	RETRATES
RETARDERS	RETEXTURE	RETINITES	RETORTER	RETRATING
RETARDING	RETHINK	RETINITIS	RETORTERS	RETREAD
RETARDS	RETHINKER	RETINOIC	RETORTING	RETREADED
RETARGET	RETHINKS	RETINOID	RETORTION	RETREADS
RETARGETS	RETHOUGHT	RETINOIDS	RETORTIVE	RETREAT
RETASTE	RETHREAD	RETINOL	RETORTS	RETREATED
RETASTED	RETHREADS	RETINOLS	RETOTAL	RETREATER
RETASTES	RETIA	RETINT	RETOTALED	RETREATS
RETASTING	RETIAL	RETINTED	RETOTALS	RETREE
RETAUGHT	RETIARII	RETINTING	RETOUCH	RETREES
RETAX	RETIARIUS	RETINTS	RETOUCHED	RETRENCH
RETAXED	RETIARY	RETINUE	RETOUCHER	RETRIAL
RETAXES	RETICELLA	RETINUED	RETOUCHES	RETRIALS
RETAXING	RETICENCE	RETINUES	RETOUR	RETRIBUTE

R

RETRIED	RETURFED	REUTTER	REVENGER	REVERTANT
RETRIES	RETURFING	REUTTERED	REVENGERS	REVERTED
RETRIEVAL	RETURFS	REUTTERS	REVENGES	REVERTER
RETRIEVE	RETURN	REV	REVENGING	REVERTERS
RETRIEVED	RETURNED	REVALENTA	REVENGIVE	REVERTING
RETRIEVER	RETURNEE	REVALUATE	REVENUAL	REVERTIVE
RETRIEVES	RETURNEES	REVALUE	REVENUE	REVERTS
RETRIM	RETURNER	REVALUED	REVENUED	REVERY
RETRIMMED	RETURNERS	REVALUES	REVENUER	REVEST
RETRIMS	RETURNIK	REVALUING	REVENUERS	REVESTED
RETRO	RETURNIKS	REVAMP	REVENUES	REVESTING
RETROACT	RETURNING	REVAMPED	REVERABLE	REVESTRY
RETROACTS	RETURNS	REVAMPER	REVERB	REVESTS
RETROCEDE	RETUSE	REVAMPERS	REVERBED	REVET
RETROD	RETWIST	REVAMPING	REVERBING	REVETMENT
RETRODDEN	RETWISTED	REVAMPS	REVERBS	REVETS
RETRODICT	RETWISTS	REVANCHE	REVERE	REVETTED
RETROFIRE	RETYING	REVANCHES	REVERED	REVETTING
RETROFIT	RETYPE	REVARNISH	REVERENCE	REVEUR
RETROFITS	RETYPED	REVEAL	REVEREND	REVEURS
RETROFLEX	RETYPES	REVEALED	REVERENDS	REVEUSE
RETROJECT	RETYPING	REVEALER	REVERENT	REVEUSES
RETRONYM	REUNIFIED	REVEALERS	REVERER	REVIBRATE
RETRONYMS	REUNIFIES	REVEALING	REVERERS	REVICTUAL
RETROPACK	REUNIFY	REVEALS	REVERES	REVIE
RETRORSE	REUNION	REVEHENT	REVERIE	REVIED
RETROS	REUNIONS	REVEILLE	REVERIES	REVIES
RETROUSSE	REUNITE	REVEILLES	REVERIFY	REVIEW
RETROVERT	REUNITED	REVEL	REVERING	REVIEWAL
RETRY	REUNITER	REVELATOR	REVERIST	REVIEWALS
RETRYING	REUNITERS	REVELED	REVERISTS	REVIEWED
RETS	REUNITES	REVELER	REVERS	REVIEWER
RETSINA	REUNITING	REVELERS	REVERSAL	REVIEWERS
RETSINAS	REUPTAKE	REVELING	REVERSALS	REVIEWING
RETTED	REUPTAKES	REVELLED	REVERSE	REVIEWS
RETTERIES	REURGE	REVELLER	REVERSED	REVILE
RETTERY	REURGED	REVELLERS	REVERSELY	REVILED
RETTING	REURGES	REVELLING	REVERSER	REVILER
RETUND	REURGING	REVELMENT	REVERSERS	REVILERS
RETUNDED	REUSABLE	REVELRIES	REVERSES	REVILES
RETUNDING	REUSABLES	REVELROUS	REVERSI	REVILING
RETUNDS	REUSE	REVELRY	REVERSING	REVILINGS
RETUNE	REUSED	REVELS	REVERSION	REVIOLATE
RETUNED	REUSES	REVENANT	REVERSIS	REVISABLE
RETUNES	REUSING	REVENANTS	REVERSO	REVISAL
RETUNING	REUTILISE	REVENGE	REVERSOS	REVISALS
RETURF	REUTILIZE	REVENGED	REVERT	REVISE

REVISED	REVOLUTE	REWASHING	REWIRING	REZONING
REVISER	REVOLVE	REWATER	REWOKE	REZZES
REVISERS	REVOLVED	REWATERED	REWOKEN	RHABDOID
REVISES	REVOLVER	REWATERS	REWON	RHABDOIDS
REVISING	REVOLVERS	REWAX	REWORD	RHABDOM
REVISION	REVOLVES	REWAXED	REWORDED	RHABDOMAL
REVISIONS	REVOLVING	REWAXES	REWORDING	RHABDOME
REVISIT	REVOTE	REWAXING	REWORDS	RHABDOMES
REVISITED	REVOTED	REWEAR	REWORE	RHABDOMS
REVISITS	REVOTES	REWEARING	REWORK	RHABDUS
REVISOR	REVOTING	REWEARS	REWORKED	RHABDUSES
REVISORS	REVS	REWEAVE	REWORKING	RHACHIAL
REVISORY	REVUE	REWEAVED	REWORKS	RHACHIDES
REVIVABLE	REVUES	REWEAVES	REWORN	RHACHILLA
REVIVABLY	REVUIST	REWEAVING	REWOUND	RHACHIS
REVIVAL	REVUISTS	REWED	REWOVE	RHACHISES
REVIVALS	REVULSED	REWEDDED	REWOVEN	RHACHITIS
REVIVE	REVULSION	REWEDDING	REWRAP	RHAGADES
REVIVED	REVULSIVE	REWEDS	REWRAPPED	RHAMNOSE
REVIVER	REVVED	REWEIGH	REWRAPS	RHAMNOSES
REVIVERS	REVVING	REWEIGHED	REWRAPT	RHAMNUS
REVIVES	REVYING	REWEIGHS	REWRITE	RHAMNUSES
REVIVIFY	REW	REWELD	REWRITER	RHAMPHOID
REVIVING	REWAKE	REWELDED	REWRITERS	RHANJA
REVIVINGS	REWAKED	REWELDING	REWRITES	RHANJAS
REVIVOR	REWAKEN	REWELDS	REWRITING	RHAPHAE
REVIVORS	REWAKENED	REWET	REWRITTEN	RHAPHE
REVOCABLE	REWAKENS	REWETS	REWROTE	RHAPHES
REVOCABLY	REWAKES	REWETTED	REWROUGHT	RHAPHIDE
REVOICE	REWAKING	REWETTING	REWS	RHAPHIDES
REVOICED	REWAN	REWIDEN	REWTH	RHAPHIS
REVOICES	REWARD	REWIDENED	REWTHS	RHAPONTIC
REVOICING	REWARDED	REWIDENS	REX	RHAPSODE
REVOKABLE	REWARDER	REWILDING	REXES	RHAPSODES
REVOKABLY	REWARDERS	REWIN	REXINE	RHAPSODIC
REVOKE	REWARDFUL	REWIND	REXINES	RHAPSODY
REVOKED	REWARDING	REWINDED	REYNARD	RHATANIES
REVOKER	REWARDS	REWINDER	REYNARDS	RHATANY
REVOKERS	REWAREWA	REWINDERS	REZ	RHEA
REVOKES	REWAREWAS	REWINDING	REZERO	RHEAS
REVOKING	REWARM	REWINDS	REZEROED	RHEBOK
REVOLT	REWARMED	REWINNING	REZEROES	RHEBOKS
REVOLTED	REWARMING	REWINS	REZEROING	RHEMATIC
REVOLTER	REWARMS	REWIRABLE	REZEROS	RHEME
REVOLTERS	REWASH	REWIRE	REZONE	RHEMES
REVOLTING	REWASHED	REWIRED	REZONED	RHENIUM
REVOLTS	REWASHES	REWIRES	REZONES	RHENIUMS

R

RHEOBASE	RHINITIS	RHODOPSIN	RHYMELESS	RIBALDLY
RHEOBASES	RHINO	RHODORA	RHYMER	RIBALDRY
RHEOBASIC	RHINOCERI	RHODORAS	RHYMERS	RIBALDS
RHEOCHORD	RHINOLITH	RHODOUS	RHYMES	RIBAND
RHEOCORD	RHINOLOGY	RHODY	RHYMESTER	RIBANDS
RHEOCORDS	RHINOS	RHOEADINE	RHYMING	RIBAS
RHEOLOGIC	RHIPIDATE	RHOMB	RHYMIST	RIBATTUTA
RHEOLOGY	RHIPIDION	RHOMBI	RHYMISTS	RIBAUD
RHEOMETER	RHIPIDIUM	RHOMBIC	RHYNE	RIBAUDRED
RHEOMETRY	RHIZIC	RHOMBICAL	RHYNES	RIBAUDRY
RHEOPHIL	RHIZINE	RHOMBOI	RHYOLITE	RIBAUDS
RHEOPHILE	RHIZINES	RHOMBOID	RHYOLITES	RIBAVIRIN
RHEOSTAT	RHIZOBIA	RHOMBOIDS	RHYOLITIC	RIBBAND
RHEOSTATS	RHIZOBIAL	RHOMBOS	RHYTA	RIBBANDS
RHEOTAXES	RHIZOBIUM	RHOMBS	RHYTHM	RIBBED
RHEOTAXIS	RHIZOCARP	RHOMBUS	RHYTHMAL	RIBBER
RHEOTOME	RHIZOCAUL	RHOMBUSES	RHYTHMED	RIBBERS
RHEOTOMES	RHIZOID	RHONCHAL	RHYTHMI	RIBBIER
RHEOTROPE	RHIZOIDAL	RHONCHI	RHYTHMIC	RIBBIEST
RHESUS	RHIZOIDS	RHONCHIAL	RHYTHMICS	RIBBING
RHESUSES	RHIZOMA	RHONCHUS	RHYTHMISE	RIBBINGS
RHETOR	RHIZOMATA	RHONE	RHYTHMIST	RIBBON
RHETORIC	RHIZOME	RHONES	RHYTHMIZE	RIBBONED
RHETORICS	RHIZOMES	RHOPALIC	RHYTHMS	RIBBONING
RHETORISE	RHIZOMIC	RHOPALISM	RHYTHMUS	RIBBONRY
RHETORIZE	RHIZOPI	RHOS	RHYTIDOME	RIBBONS
RHETORS	RHIZOPOD	RHOTACISE	RHYTINA	RIBBONY
RHEUM	RHIZOPODS	RHOTACISM	RHYTINAS	RIBBY
RHEUMATIC	RHIZOPUS	RHOTACIST	RHYTON	RIBCAGE
RHEUMATIZ	RHIZOTOMY	RHOTACIZE	RHYTONS	RIBCAGES
RHEUMED	RHO	RHOTIC	RIA	RIBES
RHEUMIC	RHODAMIN	RHOTICITY	RIAD	RIBEYE
RHEUMIER	RHODAMINE	RHUBARB	RIADS	RIBEYES
RHEUMIEST	RHODAMINS	RHUBARBED	RIAL	RIBGRASS
RHEUMS	RHODANATE	RHUBARBS	RIALS	RIBIBE
RHEUMY	RHODANIC	RHUBARBY	RIALTO	RIBIBES
RHEXES	RHODANISE	RHUMB	RIALTOS	RIBIBLE
RHEXIS	RHODANIZE	RHUMBA	RIANCIES	RIBIBLES
RHEXISES	RHODIC	RHUMBAED	RIANCY	RIBIER
RHIES	RHODIE	RHUMBAING	RIANT	RIBIERS
RHIGOLENE	RHODIES	RHUMBAS	RIANTLY	RIBLESS
RHIME	RHODINAL	RHUMBS	RIAS	RIBLET
RHIMES	RHODINALS	RHUS	RIATA	RIBLETS
RHINAL	RHODIUM	RHUSES	RIATAS	RIBLIKE
RHINE	RHODIUMS	RHY	RIB	RIBOSE
RHINES	RHODOLITE	RHYME	RIBA	RIBOSES
RHINITIC	RHODONITE	RHYMED	RIBALD	RIBOSOMAL

RIBOSOME	RICHWEED	RIDABLE	RIDGLING	RIFFOLA
RIBOSOMES	RICHWEEDS	RIDDANCE	RIDGLINGS	RIFFOLAS
RIBOZYMAL	RICIER	RIDDANCES	RIDGY	RIFFRAFF
RIBOZYME	RICIEST	RIDDED	RIDICULE	RIFFRAFFS
RIBOZYMES	RICIN	RIDDEN	RIDICULED	RIFFS
RIBS	RICING	RIDDER	RIDICULER	RIFLE
RIBSTON	RICINS	RIDDERS	RIDICULES	RIFLEBIRD
RIBSTONE	RICINUS	RIDDING	RIDING	RIFLED
RIBSTONES	RICINUSES	RIDDLE	RIDINGS	RIFLEMAN
RIBSTONS	RICK	RIDDLED	RIDLEY	RIFLEMEN
RIBWORK	RICKED	RIDDLER	RIDLEYS	RIFLER
RIBWORKS	RICKER	RIDDLERS	RIDOTTO	RIFLERIES
RIBWORT	RICKERS	RIDDLES	RIDOTTOS	RIFLERS
RIBWORTS	RICKET	RIDDLING	RIDS	RIFLERY
RICE	RICKETIER	RIDDLINGS	RIEL	RIFLES
RICEBIRD	RICKETILY	RIDE	RIELS	RIFLING
RICEBIRDS	RICKETS	RIDEABLE	RIEM	RIFLINGS
RICED	RICKETTY	RIDENT	RIEMPIE	RIFLIP
RICER	RICKETY	RIDER	RIEMPIES	RIFLIPS
RICERCAR	RICKEY	RIDERED	RIEMS	RIFS
RICERCARE	RICKEYS	RIDERLESS	RIESLING	RIFT
RICERCARI	RICKING	RIDERS	RIESLINGS	RIFTE
RICERCARS	RICKLE	RIDERSHIP	RIEVE	RIFTED
RICERCATA	RICKLES	RIDES	RIEVER	RIFTIER
RICERS	RICKLY	RIDGE	RIEVERS	RIFTIEST
RICES	RICKRACK	RIDGEBACK	RIEVES	RIFTING
RICEY	RICKRACKS	RIDGED	RIEVING	RIFTLESS
RICH	RICKS	RIDGEL	RIF	RIFTS
RICHED	RICKSHA	RIDGELIKE	RIFAMPIN	RIFTY
RICHEN	RICKSHAS	RIDGELINE	RIFAMPINS	RIG
RICHENED	RICKSHAW	RIDGELING	RIFAMYCIN	RIGADOON
RICHENING	RICKSHAWS	RIDGELS	RIFE	RIGADOONS
RICHENS	RICKSTAND	RIDGEPOLE	RIFELY	RIGATONI
RICHER	RICKSTICK	RIDGER	RIFENESS	RIGATONIS
RICHES	RICKYARD	RIDGERS	RIFER	RIGAUDON
RICHESSE	RICKYARDS	RIDGES	RIFEST	RIGAUDONS
RICHESSES	RICOCHET	RIDGETOP	RIFF	RIGG
RICHEST	RICOCHETS	RIDGETOPS	RIFFAGE	RIGGALD
RICHING	RICOTTA	RIDGETREE	RIFFAGES	RIGGALDS
RICHLY	RICOTTAS	RIDGEWAY	RIFFED	RIGGED
RICHNESS	RICRAC	RIDGEWAYS	RIFFING	RIGGER
RICHT	RICRACS	RIDGIER	RIFFLE	RIGGERS
RICHTED	RICTAL	RIDGIEST	RIFFLED	RIGGING
RICHTER	RICTUS	RIDGIL	RIFFLER	RIGGINGS
RICHTEST	RICTUSES	RIDGILS	RIFFLERS	RIGGISH
RICHTING	RICY	RIDGING	RIFFLES	RIGGS
RICHTS	RID	RIDGINGS	RIFFLING	RIGHT

R

RIGHTABLE	RIGOL	RIMAE	RINDLESS	RINGTAWS
RIGHTABLY	RIGOLL	RIMAYE	RINDS	RINGTONE
RIGHTED	RIGOLLS	RIMAYES	RINDY	RINGTONES
RIGHTEN	RIGOLS	RIME	RINE	RINGTOSS
RIGHTENED	RIGOR	RIMED	RINES	RINGWAY
RIGHTENS	RIGORISM	RIMELESS	RING	RINGWAYS
RIGHTEOUS	RIGORISMS	RIMER	RINGBARK	RINGWISE
RIGHTER	RIGORIST	RIMERS	RINGBARKS	RINGWOMB
RIGHTERS	RIGORISTS	RIMES	RINGBIT	RINGWOMBS
RIGHTEST	RIGOROUS	RIMESTER	RINGBITS	RINGWORK
RIGHTFUL	RIGORS	RIMESTERS	RINGBOLT	RINGWORKS
RIGHTIES	RIGOUR	RIMFIRE	RINGBOLTS	RINGWORM
RIGHTING	RIGOURS	RIMFIRES	RINGBONE	RINGWORMS
RIGHTINGS	RIGOUT	RIMIER	RINGBONES	RINK
RIGHTISH	RIGOUTS	RIMIEST	RINGDOVE	RINKED
RIGHTISM	RIGS	RIMINESS	RINGDOVES	RINKHALS
RIGHTISMS	RIGSDALER	RIMING	RINGED	RINKING
RIGHTIST	RIGWIDDIE	RIMLAND	RINGENT	RINKS
RIGHTISTS	RIGWOODIE	RIMLANDS	RINGER	RINNING
RIGHTLESS	RIJSTAFEL	RIMLESS	RINGERS	RINS
RIGHTLY	RIKISHA	RIMMED	RINGETTE	RINSABLE
RIGHTMOST	RIKISHAS	RIMMER	RINGETTES	RINSE
RIGHTNESS	RIKISHI	RIMMERS	RINGGIT	RINSEABLE
RIGHTO	RIKSHAW	RIMMING	RINGGITS	RINSED
RIGHTS	RIKSHAWS	RIMMINGS	RINGHALS	RINSER
RIGHTSIZE	RILE	RIMOSE	RINGING	RINSERS
RIGHTWARD	RILED	RIMOSELY	RINGINGLY	RINSES
RIGHTY	RILES	RIMOSITY	RINGINGS	RINSIBLE
RIGID	RILEY	RIMOUS	RINGLESS	RINSING
RIGIDER	RILIER	RIMPLE	RINGLET	RINSINGS
RIGIDEST	RILIEST	RIMPLED	RINGLETED	RIOJA
RIGIDIFY	RILIEVI	RIMPLES	RINGLETS	RIOJAS
RIGIDISE	RILIEVO	RIMPLING	RINGLIKE	RIOT
RIGIDISED	RILING	RIMROCK	RINGMAN	RIOTED
RIGIDISES	RILL	RIMROCKS	RINGMEN	RIOTER
RIGIDITY	RILLE	RIMS	RINGNECK	RIOTERS
RIGIDIZE	RILLED	RIMSHOT	RINGNECKS	RIOTING
RIGIDIZED	RILLES	RIMSHOTS	RINGS	RIOTINGS
RIGIDIZES	RILLET	RIMU	RINGSIDE	RIOTISE
RIGIDLY	RILLETS	RIMUS	RINGSIDER	RIOTISES
RIGIDNESS	RILLETTES	RIMY	RINGSIDES	RIOTIZE
RIGIDS	RILLING	RIN	RINGSTAND	RIOTIZES
RIGLIN	RILLMARK	RIND	RINGSTER	RIOTOUS
RIGLING	RILLMARKS	RINDED	RINGSTERS	RIOTOUSLY
RIGLINGS	RILLS	RINDIER	RINGTAIL	RIOTRIES
RIGLINS	RIM	RINDIEST	RINGTAILS	RIOTRY
RIGMAROLE	RIMA	RINDING	RINGTAW	RIOTS

RIZARDS

RIP	RIPPLER	RISKIEST	RITUALISE	RIVERBANK
RIPARIAL	RIPPLERS	RISKILY	RITUALISM	RIVERBED
RIPARIAN	RIPPLES	RISKINESS	RITUALIST	RIVERBEDS
RIPARIANS	RIPPLET	RISKING	RITUALIZE	RIVERBOAT
RIPCORD	RIPPLETS	RISKLESS	RITUALLY	RIVERED
RIPCORDS	RIPPLIER	RISKS	RITUALS	RIVERET
RIPE	RIPPLIEST	RISKY	RITUXIMAB	RIVERETS
RIPECK	RIPPLING	RISOLUTO	RITZ	RIVERHEAD
RIPECKS	RIPPLINGS	RISORII	RITZES	RIVERINE
RIPED	RIPPLY	RISORIUS	RITZIER	RIVERLESS
RIPELY	RIPPS	RISOTTO	RITZIEST	RIVERLIKE
RIPEN	RIPRAP	RISOTTOS	RITZILY	RIVERMAN
RIPENED	RIPRAPPED	RISP	RITZINESS	RIVERMEN
RIPENER	RIPRAPS	RISPED	RITZY	RIVERS
RIPENERS	RIPS	RISPETTI	RIVA	RIVERSIDE
RIPENESS	RIPSAW	RISPETTO	RIVAGE	RIVERWARD
RIPENING	RIPSAWED	RISPING	RIVAGES	RIVERWAY
RIPENS	RIPSAWING	RISPINGS	RIVAL	RIVERWAYS
RIPER	RIPSAWN	RISPS	RIVALED	RIVERWEED
RIPERS	RIPSAWS	RISQUE	RIVALESS	RIVERY
RIPES	RIPSTOP	RISQUES	RIVALING	RIVES
RIPEST	RIPSTOPS	RISSOLE	RIVALISE	RIVET
RIPIENI	RIPT	RISSOLES	RIVALISED	RIVETED
RIPIENIST	RIPTIDE	RISTRA	RIVALISES	RIVETER
RIPIENO	RIPTIDES	RISTRAS	RIVALITY	RIVETERS
RIPIENOS	RIRORIRO	RISUS	RIVALIZE	RIVETING
RIPING	RIRORIROS	RISUSES	RIVALIZED	RIVETINGS
RIPOFF	RISALDAR	RIT	RIVALIZES	RIVETS
RIPOFFS	RISALDARS	RITARD	RIVALLED	RIVETTED
RIPOST	RISE	RITARDS	RIVALLESS	RIVETTING
RIPOSTE	RISEN	RITE	RIVALLING	RIVIERA
RIPOSTED	RISER	RITELESS	RIVALRIES	RIVIERAS
RIPOSTES	RISERS	RITENUTO	RIVALROUS	RIVIERE
RIPOSTING	RISES	RITENUTOS	RIVALRY	RIVIERES
RIPOSTS	RISHI	RITES	RIVALS	RIVING
RIPP	RISHIS	RITONAVIR	RIVALSHIP	RIVLIN
RIPPABLE	RISIBLE	RITORNEL	RIVAS	RIVLINS
RIPPED	RISIBLES	RITORNELL	RIVE	RIVO
RIPPER	RISIBLY	RITORNELS	RIVED	RIVULET
RIPPERS	RISING	RITS	RIVEL	RIVULETS
RIPPIER	RISINGS	RITT	RIVELLED	RIVULOSE
RIPPIERS	RISK	RITTED	RIVELLING	RIYAL
RIPPING	RISKED	RITTER	RIVELS	RIYALS
RIPPINGLY	RISKER	RITTERS	RIVEN	RIZ
RIPPINGS	RISKERS	RITTING	RIVER	RIZA
RIPPLE	RISKFUL	RITTS	RIVERAIN	RIZARD
RIPPLED	RISKIER	RITUAL	RIVERAINS	RIZARDS

RIZAS	ROADWAYS	ROBBERY	ROCHETS	ROCKSLIDE
RIZZAR	ROADWORK	ROBBIN	ROCK	ROCKWATER
RIZZARED	ROADWORKS	ROBBING	ROCKABIES	ROCKWEED
RIZZARING	ROAM	ROBBINS	ROCKABLE	ROCKWEEDS
RIZZARS	ROAMED	ROBE	ROCKABY	ROCKWORK
RIZZART	ROAMER	ROBED	ROCKABYE	ROCKWORKS
RIZZARTS	ROAMERS	ROBES	ROCKABYES	ROCKY
RIZZER	ROAMING	ROBIN	ROCKAWAY	ROCOCO
RIZZERED	ROAMINGS	ROBING	ROCKAWAYS	ROCOCOS
RIZZERING	ROAMS	ROBINGS	ROCKBOUND	ROCQUET
RIZZERS	ROAN	ROBINIA	ROCKED	ROCQUETS
RIZZOR	ROANPIPE	ROBINIAS	ROCKER	ROCS
RIZZORED	ROANPIPES	ROBINS	ROCKERIES	ROD
RIZZORING	ROANS	ROBLE	ROCKERS	RODDED
RIZZORS	ROAR	ROBLES	ROCKERY	RODDING
ROACH	ROARED	ROBORANT	ROCKET	RODDINGS
ROACHED	ROARER	ROBORANTS	ROCKETED	RODE
ROACHES	ROARERS	ROBOT	ROCKETEER	RODED
ROACHING	ROARIE	ROBOTIC	ROCKETER	RODENT
ROAD	ROARIER	ROBOTICS	ROCKETERS	RODENTS
ROADBED	ROARIEST	ROBOTISE	ROCKETING	RODEO
ROADBEDS	ROARING	ROBOTISED	ROCKETRY	RODEOED
ROADBLOCK	ROARINGLY	ROBOTISES	ROCKETS	RODEOING
ROADCRAFT	ROARINGS	ROBOTISM	ROCKFALL	RODEOS
ROADEO	ROARMING	ROBOTISMS	ROCKFALLS	RODES
ROADEOS	ROARS	ROBOTIZE	ROCKFISH	RODEWAY
ROADHOUSE	ROARY	ROBOTIZED	ROCKHOUND	RODEWAYS
ROADIE	ROAST	ROBOTIZES	ROCKIER	RODFISHER
ROADIES	ROASTED	ROBOTRIES	ROCKIERS	RODGERSIA
ROADING	ROASTER	ROBOTRY	ROCKIEST	RODING
ROADINGS	ROASTERS	ROBOTS	ROCKILY	RODINGS
ROADKILL	ROASTING	ROBS	ROCKINESS	RODLESS
ROADKILLS	ROASTINGS	ROBURITE	ROCKING	RODLIKE
ROADLESS	ROASTS	ROBURITES	ROCKINGLY	RODMAN
ROADMAN	ROATE	ROBUST	ROCKINGS	RODMEN
ROADMEN	ROATED	ROBUSTA	ROCKLAY	RODS
ROADS	ROATES	ROBUSTAS	ROCKLAYS	RODSMAN
ROADSHOW	ROATING	ROBUSTER	ROCKLESS	RODSMEN
ROADSHOWS	ROB	ROBUSTEST	ROCKLIKE	RODSTER
ROADSIDE	ROBALO	ROBUSTLY	ROCKLING	RODSTERS
ROADSIDES	ROBALOS	ROC	ROCKLINGS	ROE
ROADSMAN	ROBAND	ROCAILLE	ROCKOON	ROEBUCK
ROADSMEN	ROBANDS	ROCAILLES	ROCKOONS	ROEBUCKS
ROADSTEAD	ROBBED	ROCAMBOLE	ROCKROSE	ROED
ROADSTER	ROBBER	ROCH	ROCKROSES	ROEMER
ROADSTERS	ROBBERIES	ROCHES	ROCKS	ROEMERS
ROADWAY	ROBBERS	ROCHET	ROCKSHAFT	ROENTGEN

ROENTGENS	ROISTERER	ROLLICKED	ROMANS	RONEO
ROES	ROISTERS	ROLLICKS	ROMANTIC	RONEOED
ROESTI	ROISTING	ROLLICKY	ROMANTICS	RONEOING
ROESTIS	ROISTS	ROLLING	ROMANZA	RONEOS
ROESTONE	ROJAK	ROLLINGS	ROMANZAS	RONEPIPE
ROESTONES	ROJAKS	ROLLMOP	ROMAUNT	RONEPIPES
ROGALLO	ROJI	ROLLMOPS	ROMAUNTS	RONES
ROGALLOS	ROJIS	ROLLNECK	ROMCOM	RONG
ROGATION	ROK	ROLLNECKS	ROMCOMS	RONGGENG
ROGATIONS	ROKE	ROLLOCK	ROMELDALE	RONGGENGS
ROGATORY	ROKED	ROLLOCKS	ROMEO	RONIN
ROGER	ROKELAY	ROLLOUT	ROMEOS	RONINS
ROGERED	ROKELAYS	ROLLOUTS	ROMNEYA	RONION
ROGERING	ROKER	ROLLOVER	ROMNEYAS	RONIONS
ROGERINGS	ROKERS	ROLLOVERS	ROMP	RONNE
ROGERS	ROKES	ROLLS	ROMPED	RONNEL
ROGNON	ROKIER	ROLLTOP	ROMPER	RONNELS
ROGNONS	ROKIEST	ROLLWAY	ROMPERS	RONNIE
ROGUE	ROKING	ROLLWAYS	ROMPING	RONNIES
ROGUED	ROKKAKU	ROM	ROMPINGLY	RONNING
ROGUEING	ROKS	ROMA	ROMPISH	RONT
ROGUER	ROKY	ROMAGE	ROMPISHLY	RONTE
ROGUERIES	ROLAG	ROMAGES	ROMPS	RONTES
ROGUERS	ROLAGS	ROMAIKA	ROMS	RONTGEN
ROGUERY	ROLAMITE	ROMAIKAS	RONCADOR	RONTGENS
ROGUES	ROLAMITES	ROMAINE	RONCADORS	RONTS
ROGUESHIP	ROLE	ROMAINES	RONDACHE	RONYON
ROGUING	ROLES	ROMAJI	RONDACHES	RONYONS
ROGUISH	ROLF	ROMAJIS	RONDAVEL	RONZ
ROGUISHLY	ROLFED	ROMAL	RONDAVELS	RONZER
ROGUY	ROLFER	ROMALS	RONDE	RONZERS
ROIL	ROLFERS	ROMAN	RONDEAU	ROO
ROILED	ROLFING	ROMANCE	RONDEAUX	ROOD
ROILIER	ROLFINGS	ROMANCED	RONDEL	ROODS
ROILIEST	ROLFS	ROMANCER	RONDELET	ROOF
ROILING	ROLL	ROMANCERS	RONDELETS	ROOFED
ROILS	ROLLABLE	ROMANCES	RONDELLE	ROOFER
ROILY	ROLLAWAY	ROMANCING	RONDELLES	ROOFERS
ROIN	ROLLAWAYS	ROMANESCO	RONDELS	ROOFIE
ROINED	ROLLBACK	ROMANISE	RONDES	ROOFIER
ROINING	ROLLBACKS	ROMANISED	RONDINO	ROOFIES
ROINISH	ROLLBAR	ROMANISES	RONDINOS	ROOFIEST
ROINS	ROLLBARS	ROMANIZE	RONDO	ROOFING
ROIST	ROLLED	ROMANIZED	RONDOS	ROOFINGS
ROISTED	ROLLER	ROMANIZES	RONDURE	ROOFLESS
ROISTER	ROLLERS	ROMANO	RONDURES	ROOFLIKE
ROISTERED	ROLLICK	ROMANOS	RONE	ROOFLINE

R

ROOFLINES	ROOP	ROOTLE	ROQUETTE	ROSEATE
ROOFS	ROOPED	ROOTLED	ROQUETTES	ROSEATELY
ROOFSCAPE	ROOPIER	ROOTLES	RORAL	ROSEBAY
ROOFTOP	ROOPIEST	ROOTLESS	RORE	ROSEBAYS
ROOFTOPS	ROOPING	ROOTLET	RORES	ROSEBOWL
ROOFTREE	ROOPIT	ROOTLETS	RORIC	ROSEBOWLS
ROOFTREES	ROOPS	ROOTLIKE	RORID	ROSEBUD
ROOFY	ROOPY	ROOTLING	RORIE	ROSEBUDS
ROOIBOS	ROORBACH	ROOTS	RORIER	ROSEBUSH
ROOIKAT	ROORBACHS	ROOTSIER	RORIEST	ROSED
ROOIKATS	ROORBACK	ROOTSIEST	RORQUAL	ROSEFINCH
ROOINEK	ROORBACKS	ROOTSTALK	RORQUALS	ROSEFISH
ROOINEKS	ROOS	ROOTSTOCK	RORT	ROSEHIP
ROOK	ROOSA	ROOTSY	RORTED	ROSEHIPS
ROOKED	ROOSAS	ROOTWORM	RORTER	ROSELESS
ROOKERIES	ROOSE	ROOTWORMS	RORTERS	ROSELIKE
ROOKERY	ROOSED	ROOTY	RORTIER	ROSELLA
ROOKIE	ROOSER	ROPABLE	RORTIEST	ROSELLAS
ROOKIER	ROOSERS	ROPE	RORTING	ROSELLE
ROOKIES	ROOSES	ROPEABLE	RORTINGS	ROSELLES
ROOKIEST	ROOSING	ROPED	RORTS	ROSEMARY
ROOKING	ROOST	ROPELIKE	RORTY	ROSEOLA
ROOKISH	ROOSTED	ROPER	RORY	ROSEOLAR
ROOKS	ROOSTER	ROPERIES	ROSACE	ROSEOLAS
ROOKY	ROOSTERS	ROPERS	ROSACEA	ROSERIES
ROOM	ROOSTING	ROPERY	ROSACEAS	ROSEROOT
ROOMED	ROOSTS	ROPES	ROSACEOUS	ROSEROOTS
ROOMER	ROOT	ROPEWALK	ROSACES	ROSERY
ROOMERS	ROOTAGE	ROPEWALKS	ROSAKER	ROSES
ROOMETTE	ROOTAGES	ROPEWAY	ROSAKERS	ROSESLUG
ROOMETTES	ROOTBOUND	ROPEWAYS	ROSALIA	ROSESLUGS
ROOMFUL	ROOTCAP	ROPEWORK	ROSALIAS	ROSET
ROOMFULS	ROOTCAPS	ROPEWORKS	ROSANILIN	ROSETED
ROOMIE	ROOTED	ROPEY	ROSARIA	ROSETING
ROOMIER	ROOTEDLY	ROPIER	ROSARIAN	ROSETS
ROOMIES	ROOTER	ROPIEST	ROSARIANS	ROSETTE
ROOMIEST	ROOTERS	ROPILY	ROSARIES	ROSETTED
ROOMILY	ROOTHOLD	ROPINESS	ROSARIUM	ROSETTES
ROOMINESS	ROOTHOLDS	ROPING	ROSARIUMS	ROSETTING
ROOMING	ROOTIER	ROPINGS	ROSARY	ROSETTY
ROOMMATE	ROOTIES	ROPY	ROSBIF	ROSETY
ROOMMATES	ROOTIEST	ROQUE	ROSBIFS	ROSEWATER
ROOMS	ROOTINESS	ROQUES	ROSCID	ROSEWOOD
ROOMSOME	ROOTING	ROQUET	ROSCOE	ROSEWOODS
ROOMY	ROOTINGS	ROQUETED	ROSCOES	ROSHI
ROON	ROOTKIT	ROQUETING	ROSE	ROSHIS
ROONS	ROOTKITS	ROQUETS	ROSEAL	ROSIED

R

ROSIER	ROSTRALLY	ROTENONES	ROTULA	ROUGHING
ROSIERE	ROSTRATE	ROTES	ROTULAE	ROUGHISH
ROSIERES	ROSTRATED	ROTGRASS	ROTULAS	ROUGHLEG
ROSIERS	ROSTRUM	ROTGUT	ROTUND	ROUGHLEGS
ROSIES	ROSTRUMS	ROTGUTS	ROTUNDA	ROUGHLY
ROSIEST	ROSTS	ROTHER	ROTUNDAS	ROUGHNECK
ROSILY	ROSULA	ROTHERS	ROTUNDATE	ROUGHNESS
ROSIN	ROSULAS	ROTI	ROTUNDED	ROUGHS
ROSINATE	ROSULATE	ROTIFER	ROTUNDER	ROUGHSHOD
ROSINATES	ROSY	ROTIFERAL	ROTUNDEST	ROUGHT
ROSINED	ROSYING	ROTIFERAN	ROTUNDING	ROUGHY
ROSINER	ROT	ROTIFERS	ROTUNDITY	ROUGING
ROSINERS	ROTA	ROTIFORM	ROTUNDLY	ROUILLE
ROSINESS	ROTACHUTE	ROTING	ROTUNDS	ROUILLES
ROSING	ROTAL	ROTIS	ROTURIER	ROUL
ROSINING	ROTAMETER	ROTL	ROTURIERS	ROULADE
ROSINOL	ROTAN	ROTLS	ROUBLE	ROULADES
ROSINOLS	ROTANS	ROTO	ROUBLES	ROULE
ROSINOUS	ROTAPLANE	ROTOGRAPH	ROUCHE	ROULEAU
ROSINS	ROTARIES	ROTOLO	ROUCHES	ROULEAUS
ROSINWEED	ROTARY	ROTOLOS	ROUCOU	ROULEAUX
ROSINY	ROTAS	ROTON	ROUCOUS	ROULES
ROSIT	ROTATABLE	ROTONS	ROUE	ROULETTE
ROSITED	ROTATE	ROTOR	ROUEN	ROULETTED
ROSITING	ROTATED	ROTORS	ROUENS	ROULETTES
ROSITS	ROTATES	ROTOS	ROUES	ROULS
ROSMARINE	ROTATING	ROTOSCOPE	ROUGE	ROUM
ROSOGLIO	ROTATION	ROTOTILL	ROUGED	ROUMING
ROSOGLIOS	ROTATIONS	ROTOTILLS	ROUGES	ROUMINGS
ROSOLIO	ROTATIVE	ROTOVATE	ROUGH	ROUMS
ROSOLIOS	ROTATOR	ROTOVATED	ROUGHAGE	ROUNCE
ROSSER	ROTATORES	ROTOVATES	ROUGHAGES	ROUNCES
ROSSERS	ROTATORS	ROTOVATOR	ROUGHBACK	ROUNCEVAL
ROST	ROTATORY	ROTS	ROUGHCAST	ROUNCIES
ROSTED	ROTAVATE	ROTTAN	ROUGHDRY	ROUNCY
ROSTELLA	ROTAVATED	ROTTANS	ROUGHED	ROUND
ROSTELLAR	ROTAVATES	ROTTE	ROUGHEN	ROUNDARCH
ROSTELLUM	ROTAVATOR	ROTTED	ROUGHENED	ROUNDBALL
ROSTER	ROTAVIRUS	ROTTEN	ROUGHENS	ROUNDED
ROSTERED	ROTCH	ROTTENER	ROUGHER	ROUNDEDLY
ROSTERING	ROTCHE	ROTTENEST	ROUGHERS	ROUNDEL
ROSTERS	ROTCHES	ROTTENLY	ROUGHEST	ROUNDELAY
ROSTI	ROTCHIE	ROTTENS	ROUGHHEW	ROUNDELS
ROSTING	ROTCHIES	ROTTER	ROUGHHEWN	ROUNDER
ROSTIS	ROTE	ROTTERS	ROUGHHEWS	ROUNDERS
ROSTRA	ROTED	ROTTES	ROUGHIE	ROUNDEST
ROSTRAL	ROTENONE	ROTTING	ROUGHIES	ROUNDHAND

ROUNDHEEL	ROUSTS	ROWDEDOWS	ROYALISE	RUBACE
ROUNDING	ROUT	ROWDIER	ROYALISED	RUBACES
ROUNDINGS	ROUTE	ROWDIES	ROYALISES	RUBAI
ROUNDISH	ROUTED	ROWDIEST	ROYALISM	RUBAIYAT
ROUNDLE	ROUTEING	ROWDILY	ROYALISMS	RUBASSE
ROUNDLES	ROUTEMAN	ROWDINESS	ROYALIST	RUBASSES
ROUNDLET	ROUTEMEN	ROWDY	ROYALISTS	RUBATI
ROUNDLETS	ROUTER	ROWDYDOW	ROYALIZE	RUBATO
ROUNDLY	ROUTERS	ROWDYDOWS	ROYALIZED	RUBATOS
ROUNDNESS	ROUTES	ROWDYISH	ROYALIZES	RUBBABOO
ROUNDS	ROUTEWAY	ROWDYISM	ROYALLER	RUBBABOOS
ROUNDSMAN	ROUTEWAYS	ROWDYISMS	ROYALLEST	RUBBED
ROUNDSMEN	ROUTH	ROWED	ROYALLY	RUBBER
ROUNDTRIP	ROUTHIE	ROWEL	ROYALMAST	RUBBERED
ROUNDUP	ROUTHIER	ROWELED	ROYALS	RUBBERIER
ROUNDUPS	ROUTHIEST	ROWELING	ROYALTIES	RUBBERING
ROUNDURE	ROUTHS	ROWELLED	ROYALTY	RUBBERISE
ROUNDURES	ROUTINE	ROWELLING	ROYNE	RUBBERIZE
ROUNDWOOD	ROUTINEER	ROWELS	ROYNED	RUBBERS
ROUNDWORM	ROUTINELY	ROWEN	ROYNES	RUBBERY
ROUP	ROUTINES	ROWENS	ROYNING	RUBBET
ROUPED	ROUTING	ROWER	ROYNISH	RUBBIDIES
ROUPET	ROUTINGS	ROWERS	ROYST	RUBBIDY
ROUPIER	ROUTINISE	ROWING	ROYSTED	RUBBIES
ROUPIEST	ROUTINISM	ROWINGS	ROYSTER	RUBBING
ROUPILY	ROUTINIST	ROWLOCK	ROYSTERED	RUBBINGS
ROUPING	ROUTINIZE	ROWLOCKS	ROYSTERER	RUBBISH
ROUPIT	ROUTOUS	ROWME	ROYSTERS	RUBBISHED
ROUPS	ROUTOUSLY	ROWMES	ROYSTING	RUBBISHES
ROUPY	ROUTS	ROWND	ROYSTS	RUBBISHLY
ROUSANT	ROUX	ROWNDED	ROZELLE	RUBBISHY
ROUSE	ROVE	ROWNDELL	ROZELLES	RUBBIT
ROUSED	ROVED	ROWNDELLS	ROZET	RUBBITIES
ROUSEMENT	ROVEN	ROWNDING	ROZETED	RUBBITY
ROUSER	ROVER	ROWNDS	ROZETING	RUBBLE
ROUSERS	ROVERS	ROWOVER	ROZETS	RUBBLED
ROUSES	ROVES	ROWOVERS	ROZIT	RUBBLES
ROUSING	ROVING	ROWS	ROZITED	RUBBLIER
ROUSINGLY	ROVINGLY	ROWT	ROZITING	RUBBLIEST
ROUSSEAU	ROVINGS	ROWTED	ROZITS	RUBBLING
ROUSSEAUS	ROW	ROWTH	ROZZER	RUBBLY
ROUSSETTE	ROWABLE	ROWTHS	ROZZERS	RUBBOARD
ROUST	ROWAN	ROWTING	RUANA	RUBBOARDS
ROUSTED	ROWANS	ROWTS	RUANAS	RUBBY
ROUSTER	ROWBOAT	ROYAL	RUB	RUBDOWN
ROUSTERS	ROWBOATS	ROYALET	RUBABOO	RUBDOWNS
ROUSTING	ROWDEDOW	ROYALETS	RUBABOOS	RUBE

RUBEFIED	RUBRICAL	RUDDER	RUELLES	RUGGEDLY
RUBEFIES	RUBRICATE	RUDDERS	RUELLIA	RUGGELACH
RUBEFY	RUBRICIAN	RUDDIED	RUELLIAS	RUGGER
RUBEFYING	RUBRICS	RUDDIER	RUER	RUGGERS
RUBEL	RUBS	RUDDIES	RUERS	RUGGIER
RUBELLA	RUBSTONE	RUDDIEST	RUES	RUGGIEST
RUBELLAN	RUBSTONES	RUDDILY	RUFESCENT	RUGGING
RUBELLANS	RUBUS	RUDDINESS	RUFF	RUGGINGS
RUBELLAS	RUBY	RUDDING	RUFFE	RUGGY
RUBELLITE	RUBYING	RUDDLE	RUFFED	RUGLIKE
RUBELS	RUBYLIKE	RUDDLED	RUFFES	RUGOLA
RUBEOLA	RUC	RUDDLEMAN	RUFFIAN	RUGOLAS
RUBEOLAR	RUCHE	RUDDLEMEN	RUFFIANED	RUGOSA
RUBEOLAS	RUCHED	RUDDLES	RUFFIANLY	RUGOSAS
RUBES	RUCHES	RUDDLING	RUFFIANS	RUGOSE
RUBESCENT	RUCHING	RUDDOCK	RUFFIN	RUGOSELY
RUBICELLE	RUCHINGS	RUDDOCKS	RUFFING	RUGOSITY
RUBICON	RUCK	RUDDS	RUFFINS	RUGOUS
RUBICONED	RUCKED	RUDDY	RUFFLE	RUGS
RUBICONS	RUCKING	RUDDYING	RUFFLED	RUGULOSE
RUBICUND	RUCKLE	RUDE	RUFFLER	RUIN
RUBIDIC	RUCKLED	RUDELY	RUFFLERS	RUINABLE
RUBIDIUM	RUCKLES	RUDENESS	RUFFLES	RUINATE
RUBIDIUMS	RUCKLING	RUDER	RUFFLIER	RUINATED
RUBIED	RUCKMAN	RUDERAL	RUFFLIEST	RUINATES
RUBIER	RUCKMEN	RUDERALS	RUFFLIKE	RUINATING
RUBIES	RUCKS	RUDERIES	RUFFLING	RUINATION
RUBIEST	RUCKSACK	RUDERY	RUFFLINGS	RUINED
RUBIFIED	RUCKSACKS	RUDES	RUFFLY	RUINER
RUBIFIES	RUCKSEAT	RUDESBIES	RUFFS	RUINERS
RUBIFY	RUCKSEATS	RUDESBY	RUFIYAA	RUING
RUBIFYING	RUCKUS	RUDEST	RUFIYAAS	RUINGS
RUBIGO	RUCKUSES	RUDIE	RUFOUS	RUINING
RUBIGOS	RUCOLA	RUDIES	RUG	RUININGS
RUBIN	RUCOLAS	RUDIMENT	RUGA	RUINOUS
RUBINE	RUCS	RUDIMENTS	RUGAE	RUINOUSLY
RUBINEOUS	RUCTATION	RUDISH	RUGAL	RUINS
RUBINES	RUCTION	RUDS	RUGALACH	RUKH
RUBINS	RUCTIONS	RUE	RUGATE	RUKHS
RUBIOUS	RUCTIOUS	RUED	RUGBIES	RULABLE
RUBLE	RUD	RUEDA	RUGBY	RULE
RUBLES	RUDACEOUS	RUEDAS	RUGELACH	RULED
RUBOFF	RUDAS	RUEFUL	RUGGED	RULELESS
RUBOFFS	RUDASES	RUEFULLY	RUGGEDER	RULER
RUBOUT	RUDBECKIA	RUEING	RUGGEDEST	RULERED
RUBOUTS	RUDD	RUEINGS	RUGGEDISE	RULERING
RUBRIC	RUDDED	RUELLE	RUGGEDIZE	RULERS

R

RULERSHIP	RUMKIN	RUMPUS	RUNLESS	RUPTURE
RULES	RUMKINS	RUMPUSES	RUNLET	RUPTURED
RULESSE	RUMLY	RUMPY	RUNLETS	RUPTURES
RULIER	RUMMAGE	RUMRUNNER	RUNNABLE	RUPTURING
RULIEST	RUMMAGED	RUMS	RUNNEL	RURAL
RULING	RUMMAGER	RUN	RUNNELS	RURALISE
RULINGS	RUMMAGERS	RUNABOUT	RUNNER	RURALISED
RULLION	RUMMAGES	RUNABOUTS	RUNNERS	RURALISES
RULLIONS	RUMMAGING	RUNAGATE	RUNNET	RURALISM
RULLOCK	RUMMER	RUNAGATES	RUNNETS	RURALISMS
RULLOCKS	RUMMERS	RUNANGA	RUNNIER	RURALIST
RULY	RUMMEST	RUNANGAS	RUNNIEST	RURALISTS
RUM	RUMMIER	RUNAROUND	RUNNINESS	RURALITE
RUMAKI	RUMMIES	RUNAWAY	RUNNING	RURALITES
RUMAKIS	RUMMIEST	RUNAWAYS	RUNNINGLY	RURALITY
RUMAL	RUMMILY	RUNBACK	RUNNINGS	RURALIZE
RUMALS	RUMMINESS	RUNBACKS	RUNNION	RURALIZED
RUMBA	RUMMISH	RUNCH	RUNNIONS	RURALIZES
RUMBAED	RUMMY	RUNCHES	RUNNY	RURALLY
RUMBAING	RUMNESS	RUNCIBLE	RUNOFF	RURALNESS
RUMBAS	RUMNESSES	RUNCINATE	RUNOFFS	RURALS
RUMBELOW	RUMOR	RUND	RUNOUT	RURBAN
RUMBELOWS	RUMORED	RUNDALE	RUNOUTS	RURP
RUMBLE	RUMORING	RUNDALES	RUNOVER	RURPS
RUMBLED	RUMOROUS	RUNDLE	RUNOVERS	RURU
RUMBLER	RUMORS	RUNDLED	RUNRIG	RURUS
RUMBLERS	RUMOUR	RUNDLES	RUNRIGS	RUSA
RUMBLES	RUMOURED	RUNDLET	RUNROUND	RUSALKA
RUMBLIER	RUMOURER	RUNDLETS	RUNROUNDS	RUSALKAS
RUMBLIEST	RUMOURERS	RUNDOWN	RUNS	RUSAS
RUMBLING	RUMOURING	RUNDOWNS	RUNT	RUSCUS
RUMBLINGS	RUMOURS	RUNDS	RUNTED	RUSCUSES
RUMBLY	RUMP	RUNE	RUNTIER	RUSE
RUMBO	RUMPED	RUNECRAFT	RUNTIEST	RUSES
RUMBOS	RUMPIES	RUNED	RUNTINESS	RUSH
RUME	RUMPING	RUNELIKE	RUNTISH	RUSHED
RUMEN	RUMPLE	RUNES	RUNTISHLY	RUSHEE
RUMENS	RUMPLED	RUNFLAT	RUNTS	RUSHEES
RUMES	RUMPLES	RUNFLATS	RUNTY	RUSHEN
RUMINA	RUMPLESS	RUNG	RUNWAY	RUSHER
RUMINAL	RUMPLIER	RUNGLESS	RUNWAYS	RUSHERS
RUMINANT	RUMPLIEST	RUNGS	RUPEE	RUSHES
RUMINANTS	RUMPLING	RUNIC	RUPEES	RUSHIER
RUMINATE	RUMPLY	RUNKLE	RUPIA	RUSHIEST
RUMINATED	RUMPO	RUNKLED	RUPIAH	RUSHINESS
RUMINATES	RUMPOS	RUNKLES	RUPIAHS	RUSHING
RUMINATOR	RUMPS	RUNKLING	RUPIAS	RUSHINGS

RUSHLIGHT	RUSTED	RUSTLINGS	RUTTER	RYES
RUSHLIKE	RUSTIC	RUSTPROOF	RUTTERS	RYFE
RUSHY	RUSTICAL	RUSTRE	RUTTIER	RYKE
RUSINE	RUSTICALS	RUSTRED	RUTTIEST	RYKED
RUSK	RUSTICANA	RUSTRES	RUTTILY	RYKES
RUSKS	RUSTICATE	RUSTS	RUTTINESS	RYKING
RUSMA	RUSTICIAL	RUSTY	RUTTING	RYMME
RUSMAS	RUSTICISE	RUT	RUTTINGS	RYMMED
RUSSE	RUSTICISM	RUTABAGA	RUTTISH	RYMMES
RUSSEL	RUSTICITY	RUTABAGAS	RUTTISHLY	RYMMING
RUSSELS	RUSTICIZE	RUTACEOUS	RUTTY	RYND
RUSSET	RUSTICLY	RUTH	RYA	RYNDS
RUSSETED	RUSTICS	RUTHENIC	RYAL	RYOKAN
RUSSETING	RUSTIER	RUTHENIUM	RYALS	RYOKANS
RUSSETS	RUSTIEST	RUTHFUL	RYAS	RYOT
RUSSETY	RUSTILY	RUTHFULLY	RYBAT	RYOTS
RUSSIA	RUSTINESS	RUTHLESS	RYBATS	RYOTWARI
RUSSIAS	RUSTING	RUTHS	RYBAUDRYE	RYOTWARIS
RUSSIFIED	RUSTINGS	RUTILANT	RYE	RYPE
RUSSIFIES	RUSTLE	RUTILATED	RYEBREAD	RYPECK
RUSSIFY	RUSTLED	RUTILE	RYEBREADS	RYPECKS
RUSSULA	RUSTLER	RUTILES	RYEFLOUR	RYPER
RUSSULAE	RUSTLERS	RUTIN	RYEFLOURS	
RUSSULAS	RUSTLES	RUTINS	RYEGRASS	
RUST	RUSTLESS	RUTS	RYEPECK	
RUSTABLE	RUSTLING	RUTTED	RYEPECKS	

R

S

SAAG	SABKHAS	SACCIFORM	SACRALITY	SADDLES
SAAGS	SABKHAT	SACCOI	SACRALIZE	SADDLING
SAB	SABKHATS	SACCOS	SACRALS	SADDO
SABADILLA	SABLE	SACCOSES	SACRAMENT	SADDOES
SABAL	SABLED	SACCULAR	SACRARIA	SADDOS
SABALS	SABLEFISH	SACCULATE	SACRARIAL	SADE
SABATON	SABLES	SACCULE	SACRARIUM	SADES
SABATONS	SABLING	SACCULES	SACRED	SADHANA
SABAYON	SABOT	SACCULI	SACREDLY	SADHANAS
SABAYONS	SABOTAGE	SACCULUS	SACRIFICE	SADHE
SABBAT	SABOTAGED	SACELLA	SACRIFIDE	SADHES
SABBATH	SABOTAGES	SACELLUM	SACRIFIED	SADHU
SABBATHS	SABOTEUR	SACHEM	SACRIFIES	SADHUS
SABBATIC	SABOTEURS	SACHEMDOM	SACRIFY	SADI
SABBATICS	SABOTIER	SACHEMIC	SACRILEGE	SADIRON
SABBATINE	SABOTIERS	SACHEMS	SACRING	SADIRONS
SABBATISE	SABOTS	SACHET	SACRINGS	SADIS
SABBATISM	SABRA	SACHETED	SACRIST	SADISM
SABBATIZE	SABRAS	SACHETS	SACRISTAN	SADISMS
SABBATS	SABRE	SACK	SACRISTS	SADIST
SABBED	SABRED	SACKABLE	SACRISTY	SADISTIC
SABBING	SABRES	SACKAGE	SACRUM	SADISTS
SABBINGS	SABREUR	SACKAGES	SACRUMS	SADLY
SABE	SABREURS	SACKBUT	SACS	SADNESS
SABED	SABREWING	SACKBUTS	SAD	SADNESSES
SABEING	SABRING	SACKCLOTH	SADDED	SADO
SABELLA	SABS	SACKED	SADDEN	SADOS
SABELLAS	SABULINE	SACKER	SADDENED	SADS
SABER	SABULOSE	SACKERS	SADDENING	SADZA
SABERED	SABULOUS	SACKFUL	SADDENS	SADZAS
SABERING	SABURRA	SACKFULS	SADDER	SAE
SABERLIKE	SABURRAL	SACKING	SADDEST	SAECULUM
SABERS	SABURRAS	SACKINGS	SADDHU	SAECULUMS
SABES	SAC	SACKLESS	SADDHUS	SAETER
SABHA	SACATON	SACKLIKE	SADDIE	SAETERS
SABHAS	SACATONS	SACKS	SADDIES	SAFARI
SABIN	SACBUT	SACKSFUL	SADDING	SAFARIED
SABINE	SACBUTS	SACLESS	SADDISH	SAFARIING
SABINES	SACCADE	SACLIKE	SADDLE	SAFARIS
SABINS	SACCADES	SACQUE	SADDLEBAG	SAFARIST
SABIR	SACCADIC	SACQUES	SADDLEBOW	SAFARISTS
SABIRS	SACCATE	SACRA	SADDLED	SAFE
SABKHA	SACCHARIC	SACRAL	SADDLER	SAFED
SABKHAH	SACCHARIN	SACRALGIA	SADDLERS	SAFEGUARD
SABKHAHS	SACCHARUM	SACRALISE	SADDLERY	SAFELIGHT

SAFELY	SAGEBRUSH	SAGUIN	SAILMAKER	SAIRING
SAFENESS	SAGELY	SAGUINS	SAILOR	SAIRS
SAFER	SAGENE	SAGUM	SAILORING	SAIS
SAFES	SAGENES	SAGY	SAILORLY	SAIST
SAFEST	SAGENESS	SAHEB	SAILORS	SAITH
SAFETIED	SAGENITE	SAHEBS	SAILPLANE	SAITHE
SAFETIES	SAGENITES	SAHIB	SAILROOM	SAITHES
SAFETY	SAGENITIC	SAHIBA	SAILROOMS	SAITHS
SAFETYING	SAGER	SAHIBAH	SAILS	SAIYID
SAFETYMAN	SAGES	SAHIBAHS	SAIM	SAIYIDS
SAFETYMEN	SAGEST	SAHIBAS	SAIMIN	SAJOU
SAFFIAN	SAGGAR	SAHIBS	SAIMINS	SAJOUS
SAFFIANS	SAGGARD	SAHIWAL	SAIMIRI	SAKAI
SAFFLOWER	SAGGARDS	SAHIWALS	SAIMIRIS	SAKAIS
SAFFRON	SAGGARED	SAHUARO	SAIMS	SAKE
SAFFRONED	SAGGARING	SAHUAROS	SAIN	SAKER
SAFFRONS	SAGGARS	SAI	SAINE	SAKERET
SAFFRONY	SAGGED	SAIBLING	SAINED	SAKERETS
SAFING	SAGGER	SAIBLINGS	SAINFOIN	SAKERS
SAFRANIN	SAGGERED	SAIC	SAINFOINS	SAKES
SAFRANINE	SAGGERING	SAICE	SAINING	SAKI
SAFRANINS	SAGGERS	SAICES	SAINS	SAKIA
SAFROL	SAGGIER	SAICK	SAINT	SAKIAS
SAFROLE	SAGGIEST	SAICKS	SAINTDOM	SAKIEH
SAFROLES	SAGGING	SAICS	SAINTDOMS	SAKIEHS
SAFROLS	SAGGINGS	SAID	SAINTED	SAKIS
SAFRONAL	SAGGY	SAIDEST	SAINTESS	SAKIYEH
SAFRONALS	SAGIER	SAIDS	SAINTFOIN	SAKIYEHS
SAFT	SAGIEST	SAIDST	SAINTHOOD	SAKKOI
SAFTER	SAGINATE	SAIGA	SAINTING	SAKKOS
SAFTEST	SAGINATED	SAIGAS	SAINTISH	SAKKOSES
SAG	SAGINATES	SAIKEI	SAINTISM	SAKSAUL
SAGA	SAGITTA	SAIKEIS	SAINTISMS	SAKSAULS
SAGACIOUS	SAGITTAL	SAIKLESS	SAINTLESS	SAL
SAGACITY	SAGITTARY	SAIL	SAINTLIER	SALAAM
SAGAMAN	SAGITTAS	SAILABLE	SAINTLIKE	SALAAMED
SAGAMEN	SAGITTATE	SAILBOARD	SAINTLILY	SALAAMING
SAGAMORE	SAGO	SAILBOAT	SAINTLING	SALAAMS
SAGAMORES	SAGOIN	SAILBOATS	SAINTLY	SALABLE
SAGANASH	SAGOINS	SAILCLOTH	SAINTS	SALABLY
SAGAPENUM	SAGOS	SAILED	SAINTSHIP	SALACIOUS
SAGAS	SAGOUIN	SAILER	SAIQUE	SALACITY
SAGATHIES	SAGOUINS	SAILERS	SAIQUES	SALAD
SAGATHY	SAGRADA	SAILFISH	SAIR	SALADANG
SAGBUT	SAGS	SAILING	SAIRED	SALADANGS
SAGBUTS	SAGUARO	SAILINGS	SAIRER	SALADE
SAGE	SAGUAROS	SAILLESS	SAIREST	SALADES

SALADING	SALICES	SALLAL	SALPA	SALTEST
SALADINGS	SALICET	SALLALS	SALPAE	SALTFISH
SALADS	SALICETA	SALLE	SALPAS	SALTIE
SALAL	SALICETS	SALLEE	SALPIAN	SALTIER
SALALS	SALICETUM	SALLEES	SALPIANS	SALTIERS
SALAMI	SALICIN	SALLES	SALPICON	SALTIES
SALAMIS	SALICINE	SALLET	SALPICONS	SALTIEST
SALAMON	SALICINES	SALLETS	SALPID	SALTILY
SALAMONS	SALICINS	SALLIED	SALPIDS	SALTINE
SALANGANE	SALICYLIC	SALLIER	SALPIFORM	SALTINES
SALARIAT	SALIENCE	SALLIERS	SALPINGES	SALTINESS
SALARIATS	SALIENCES	SALLIES	SALPINX	SALTING
SALARIED	SALIENCY	SALLOW	SALPINXES	SALTINGS
SALARIES	SALIENT	SALLOWED	SALPS	SALTIRE
SALARY	SALIENTLY	SALLOWER	SALS	SALTIRES
SALARYING	SALIENTS	SALLOWEST	SALSA	SALTISH
SALARYMAN	SALIFIED	SALLOWING	SALSAED	SALTISHLY
SALARYMEN	SALIFIES	SALLOWISH	SALSAING	SALTLESS
SALBAND	SALIFY	SALLOWLY	SALSAS	SALTLIKE
SALBANDS	SALIFYING	SALLOWS	SALSE	SALTLY
SALCHOW	SALIGOT	SALLOWY	SALSES	SALTNESS
SALCHOWS	SALIGOTS	SALLY	SALSIFIES	SALTO
SALE	SALIMETER	SALLYING	SALSIFY	SALTOED
SALEABLE	SALIMETRY	SALLYPORT	SALSILLA	SALTOING
SALEABLY	SALINA	SALMI	SALSILLAS	SALTOS
SALEP	SALINAS	SALMIS	SALT	SALTPAN
SALEPS	SALINE	SALMON	SALTANDO	SALTPANS
SALERATUS	SALINES	SALMONET	SALTANT	SALTPETER
SALERING	SALINISE	SALMONETS	SALTANTS	SALTPETRE
SALERINGS	SALINISED	SALMONID	SALTATE	SALTS
SALEROOM	SALINISES	SALMONIDS	SALTATED	SALTUS
SALEROOMS	SALINITY	SALMONOID	SALTATES	SALTUSES
SALES	SALINIZE	SALMONS	SALTATING	SALTWATER
SALESGIRL	SALINIZED	SALMONY	SALTATION	SALTWORK
SALESLADY	SALINIZES	SALOL	SALTATO	SALTWORKS
SALESMAN	SALIVA	SALOLS	SALTATORY	SALTWORT
SALESMEN	SALIVAL	SALOMETER	SALTBOX	SALTWORTS
SALESROOM	SALIVARY	SALON	SALTBOXES	SALTY
SALET	SALIVAS	SALONS	SALTBUSH	SALUBRITY
SALETS	SALIVATE	SALOON	SALTCAT	SALUE
SALEWD	SALIVATED	SALOONS	SALTCATS	SALUED
SALEYARD	SALIVATES	SALOOP	SALTCHUCK	SALUES
SALEYARDS	SALIVATOR	SALOOPS	SALTED	SALUING
SALFERN	SALIX	SALOP	SALTER	SALUKI
SALFERNS	SALL	SALOPIAN	SALTERN	SALUKIS
SALIAUNCE	SALLAD	SALOPS	SALTERNS	SALURETIC
SALIC	SALLADS	SALP	SALTERS	SALUTARY

SALUTE	SAMANS	SAMIER	SAMSARAS	SANDBURR
SALUTED	SAMARA	SAMIEST	SAMSARIC	SANDBURRS
SALUTER	SAMARAS	SAMISEN	SAMSHOO	SANDBURS
SALUTERS	SAMARITAN	SAMISENS	SAMSHOOS	SANDCRACK
SALUTES	SAMARIUM	SAMITE	SAMSHU	SANDDAB
SALUTING	SAMARIUMS	SAMITES	SAMSHUS	SANDDABS
SALVABLE	SAMAS	SAMITHI	SAMURAI	SANDED
SALVABLY	SAMBA	SAMITHIS	SAMURAIS	SANDEK
SALVAGE	SAMBAED	SAMITI	SAN	SANDEKS
SALVAGED	SAMBAING	SAMITIS	SANATIVE	SANDER
SALVAGEE	SAMBAL	SAMIZDAT	SANATORIA	SANDERS
SALVAGEES	SAMBALS	SAMIZDATS	SANATORY	SANDERSES
SALVAGER	SAMBAR	SAMLET	SANBENITO	SANDFISH
SALVAGERS	SAMBARS	SAMLETS	SANCAI	SANDFLIES
SALVAGES	SAMBAS	SAMLOR	SANCAIS	SANDFLY
SALVAGING	SAMBHAR	SAMLORS	SANCHO	SANDGLASS
SALVARSAN	SAMBHARS	SAMMED	SANCHOS	SANDHEAP
SALVATION	SAMBHUR	SAMMIES	SANCTA	SANDHEAPS
SALVATORY	SAMBHURS	SAMMING	SANCTIFY	SANDHI
SALVE	SAMBO	SAMMY	SANCTION	SANDHILL
SALVED	SAMBOS	SAMNITIS	SANCTIONS	SANDHILLS
SALVER	SAMBUCA	SAMOSA	SANCTITY	SANDHIS
SALVERS	SAMBUCAS	SAMOSAS	SANCTUARY	SANDHOG
SALVES	SAMBUKE	SAMOVAR	SANCTUM	SANDHOGS
SALVETE	SAMBUKES	SAMOVARS	SANCTUMS	SANDIER
SALVETES	SAMBUR	SAMOYED	SAND	SANDIEST
SALVIA	SAMBURS	SAMOYEDS	SANDABLE	SANDINESS
SALVIAS	SAME	SAMP	SANDAL	SANDING
SALVIFIC	SAMECH	SAMPAN	SANDALED	SANDINGS
SALVING	SAMECHS	SAMPANS	SANDALING	SANDIVER
SALVINGS	SAMEK	SAMPHIRE	SANDALLED	SANDIVERS
SALVO	SAMEKH	SAMPHIRES	SANDALS	SANDLESS
SALVOED	SAMEKHS	SAMPI	SANDARAC	SANDLIKE
SALVOES	SAMEKS	SAMPIRE	SANDARACH	SANDLING
SALVOING	SAMEL	SAMPIRES	SANDARACS	SANDLINGS
SALVOR	SAMELY	SAMPIS	SANDBAG	SANDLOT
SALVORS	SAMEN	SAMPLE	SANDBAGS	SANDLOTS
SALVOS	SAMENESS	SAMPLED	SANDBANK	SANDMAN
SALWAR	SAMES	SAMPLER	SANDBANKS	SANDMEN
SALWARS	SAMEY	SAMPLERS	SANDBAR	SANDPAPER
SAM	SAMEYNESS	SAMPLERY	SANDBARS	SANDPEEP
SAMA	SAMFOO	SAMPLES	SANDBLAST	SANDPEEPS
SAMAAN	SAMFOOS	SAMPLING	SANDBOX	SANDPILE
SAMAANS	SAMFU	SAMPLINGS	SANDBOXES	SANDPILES
SAMADHI	SAMFUS	SAMPS	SANDBOY	SANDPIPER
SAMADHIS	SAMIEL	SAMS	SANDBOYS	SANDPIT
SAMAN	SAMIELS	SAMSARA	SANDBUR	SANDPITS

S

SANDPUMP	SANGOMA	SANNUPS	SANTOS	SAPONATED
SANDPUMPS	SANGOMAS	SANNYASI	SANTOUR	SAPONIFY
SANDS	SANGOS	SANNYASIN	SANTOURS	SAPONIN
SANDSHOE	SANGRIA	SANNYASIS	SANTS	SAPONINE
SANDSHOES	SANGRIAS	SANPAN	SANTUR	SAPONINES
SANDSOAP	SANGS	SANPANS	SANTURS	SAPONINS
SANDSOAPS	SANGUIFY	SANPRO	SANYASI	SAPONITE
SANDSPOUT	SANGUINE	SANPROS	SANYASIS	SAPONITES
SANDSPUR	SANGUINED	SANS	SAOLA	SAPOR
SANDSPURS	SANGUINES	SANSA	SAOLAS	SAPORIFIC
SANDSTONE	SANICLE	SANSAR	SAOUARI	SAPOROUS
SANDSTORM	SANICLES	SANSARS	SAOUARIS	SAPORS
SANDWICH	SANIDINE	SANSAS	SAP	SAPOTA
SANDWORM	SANIDINES	SANSEI	SAPAJOU	SAPOTAS
SANDWORMS	SANIES	SANSEIS	SAPAJOUS	SAPOTE
SANDWORT	SANIFIED	SANSERIF	SAPAN	SAPOTES
SANDWORTS	SANIFIES	SANSERIFS	SAPANS	SAPOUR
SANDY	SANIFY	SANT	SAPANWOOD	SAPOURS
SANDYISH	SANIFYING	SANTAL	SAPEGO	SAPPAN
SANE	SANING	SANTALIC	SAPEGOES	SAPPANS
SANED	SANIOUS	SANTALIN	SAPELE	SAPPED
SANELY	SANITARIA	SANTALINS	SAPELES	SAPPER
SANENESS	SANITARY	SANTALOL	SAPFUL	SAPPERS
SANER	SANITATE	SANTALOLS	SAPHEAD	SAPPHIC
SANES	SANITATED	SANTALS	SAPHEADED	SAPPHICS
SANEST	SANITATES	SANTERA	SAPHEADS	SAPPHIRE
SANG	SANITIES	SANTERAS	SAPHENA	SAPPHIRED
SANGA	SANITISE	SANTERIA	SAPHENAE	SAPPHIRES
SANGAR	SANITISED	SANTERIAS	SAPHENAS	SAPPHISM
SANGAREE	SANITISER	SANTERO	SAPHENOUS	SAPPHISMS
SANGAREES	SANITISES	SANTEROS	SAPID	SAPPHIST
SANGARS	SANITIZE	SANTIMI	SAPIDITY	SAPPHISTS
SANGAS	SANITIZED	SANTIMS	SAPIDLESS	SAPPIER
SANGEET	SANITIZER	SANTIMU	SAPIDNESS	SAPPIEST
SANGEETS	SANITIZES	SANTIR	SAPIENCE	SAPPILY
SANGER	SANITORIA	SANTIRS	SAPIENCES	SAPPINESS
SANGERS	SANITY	SANTO	SAPIENCY	SAPPING
SANGFROID	SANJAK	SANTOL	SAPIENS	SAPPLE
SANGH	SANJAKS	SANTOLINA	SAPIENT	SAPPLED
SANGHA	SANK	SANTOLS	SAPIENTLY	SAPPLES
SANGHAS	SANKO	SANTON	SAPIENTS	SAPPLING
SANGHAT	SANKOS	SANTONICA	SAPLESS	SAPPY
SANGHATS	SANNIE	SANTONIN	SAPLING	SAPRAEMIA
SANGHS	SANNIES	SANTONINS	SAPLINGS	SAPRAEMIC
SANGLIER	SANNOP	SANTONS	SAPODILLA	SAPREMIA
SANGLIERS	SANNOPS	SANTOOR	SAPOGENIN	SAPREMIAS
SANGO	SANNUP	SANTOORS	SAPONARIA	SAPREMIC

S

SAPROBE	SARCOMERE	SARKINESS	SARTORS	SASTRUGA
SAPROBES	SARCONET	SARKING	SARUS	SASTRUGI
SAPROBIAL	SARCONETS	SARKINGS	SARUSES	SAT
SAPROBIC	SARCOPTIC	SARKS	SASARARA	SATAI
SAPROLITE	SARCOSOME	SARKY	SASARARAS	SATAIS
SAPROPEL	SARCOUS	SARMENT	SASER	SATANG
SAPROPELS	SARD	SARMENTA	SASERS	SATANGS
SAPROZOIC	SARDANA	SARMENTS	SASH	SATANIC
SAPS	SARDANAS	SARMENTUM	SASHAY	SATANICAL
SAPSAGO	SARDAR	SARMIE	SASHAYED	SATANISM
SAPSAGOS	SARDARS	SARMIES	SASHAYING	SATANISMS
SAPSUCKER	SARDEL	SARNEY	SASHAYS	SATANIST
SAPUCAIA	SARDELLE	SARNEYS	SASHED	SATANISTS
SAPUCAIAS	SARDELLES	SARNIE	SASHES	SATANITY
SAPWOOD	SARDELS	SARNIES	SASHIMI	SATARA
SAPWOODS	SARDINE	SAROD	SASHIMIS	SATARAS
SAR	SARDINED	SARODE	SASHING	SATAY
SARABAND	SARDINES	SARODES	SASHLESS	SATAYS
SARABANDE	SARDINING	SARODIST	SASIN	SATCHEL
SARABANDS	SARDIUS	SARODISTS	SASINE	SATCHELED
SARAFAN	SARDIUSES	SARODS	SASINES	SATCHELS
SARAFANS	SARDONIAN	SARONG	SASINS	SATE
SARAN	SARDONIC	SARONGS	SASKATOON	SATED
SARANGI	SARDONYX	SARONIC	SASQUATCH	SATEDNESS
SARANGIS	SARDS	SAROS	SASS	SATEEN
SARANS	SARED	SAROSES	SASSABIES	SATEENS
SARAPE	SAREE	SARPANCH	SASSABY	SATELESS
SARAPES	SAREES	SARRASIN	SASSAFRAS	SATELLES
SARBACANE	SARGASSO	SARRASINS	SASSARARA	SATELLITE
SARCASM	SARGASSOS	SARRAZIN	SASSE	SATEM
SARCASMS	SARGASSUM	SARRAZINS	SASSED	SATES
SARCASTIC	SARGE	SARS	SASSES	SATI
SARCENET	SARGES	SARSAR	SASSIER	SATIABLE
SARCENETS	SARGO	SARSARS	SASSIES	SATIABLY
SARCINA	SARGOS	SARSDEN	SASSIEST	SATIATE
SARCINAE	SARGOSES	SARSDENS	SASSILY	SATIATED
SARCINAS	SARGUS	SARSEN	SASSINESS	SATIATES
SARCOCARP	SARGUSES	SARSENET	SASSING	SATIATING
SARCODE	SARI	SARSENETS	SASSOLIN	SATIATION
SARCODES	SARIN	SARSENS	SASSOLINS	SATIETIES
SARCODIC	SARING	SARSNET	SASSOLITE	SATIETY
SARCOID	SARINS	SARSNETS	SASSWOOD	SATIN
SARCOIDS	SARIS	SARTOR	SASSWOODS	SATINED
SARCOLOGY	SARK	SARTORIAL	SASSY	SATINET
SARCOMA	SARKIER	SARTORIAN	SASSYWOOD	SATINETS
SARCOMAS	SARKIEST	SARTORII	SASTRA	SATINETTA
SARCOMATA	SARKILY	SARTORIUS	SASTRAS	SATINETTE

S

SATING	SATURNINE	SAUGER	SAUTOIRE	SAVINGLY
SATINING	SATURNISM	SAUGERS	SAUTOIRES	SAVINGS
SATINPOD	SATURNIST	SAUGH	SAUTOIRS	SAVINS
SATINPODS	SATYR	SAUGHS	SAUTS	SAVIOR
SATINS	SATYRA	SAUGHY	SAV	SAVIORS
SATINWOOD	SATYRAL	SAUL	SAVABLE	SAVIOUR
SATINY	SATYRALS	SAULGE	SAVAGE	SAVIOURS
SATIRE	SATYRAS	SAULGES	SAVAGED	SAVOR
SATIRES	SATYRESS	SAULIE	SAVAGEDOM	SAVORED
SATIRIC	SATYRIC	SAULIES	SAVAGELY	SAVORER
SATIRICAL	SATYRICAL	SAULS	SAVAGER	SAVORERS
SATIRISE	SATYRID	SAULT	SAVAGERY	SAVORIER
SATIRISED	SATYRIDS	SAULTS	SAVAGES	SAVORIES
SATIRISER	SATYRISK	SAUNA	SAVAGEST	SAVORIEST
SATIRISES	SATYRISKS	SAUNAED	SAVAGING	SAVORILY
SATIRIST	SATYRLIKE	SAUNAING	SAVAGISM	SAVORING
SATIRISTS	SATYRS	SAUNAS	SAVAGISMS	SAVORLESS
SATIRIZE	SAU	SAUNT	SAVANNA	SAVOROUS
SATIRIZED	SAUBA	SAUNTED	SAVANNAH	SAVORS
SATIRIZER	SAUBAS	SAUNTER	SAVANNAHS	SAVORY
SATIRIZES	SAUCE	SAUNTERED	SAVANNAS	SAVOUR
SATIS	SAUCEBOAT	SAUNTERER	SAVANT	SAVOURED
SATISFICE	SAUCEBOX	SAUNTERS	SAVANTE	SAVOURER
SATISFIED	SAUCED	SAUNTING	SAVANTES	SAVOURERS
SATISFIER	SAUCELESS	SAUNTS	SAVANTS	SAVOURIER
SATISFIES	SAUCEPAN	SAUREL	SAVARIN	SAVOURIES
SATISFY	SAUCEPANS	SAURELS	SAVARINS	SAVOURILY
SATIVE	SAUCEPOT	SAURIAN	SAVATE	SAVOURING
SATORI	SAUCEPOTS	SAURIANS	SAVATES	SAVOURLY
SATORIS	SAUCER	SAURIES	SAVE	SAVOURS
SATRAP	SAUCERFUL	SAUROID	SAVEABLE	SAVOURY
SATRAPAL	SAUCERS	SAUROPOD	SAVED	SAVOY
SATRAPIES	SAUCES	SAUROPODS	SAVEGARD	SAVOYARD
SATRAPS	SAUCH	SAURY	SAVEGARDS	SAVOYARDS
SATRAPY	SAUCHS	SAUSAGE	SAVELOY	SAVOYS
SATSUMA	SAUCIER	SAUSAGES	SAVELOYS	SAVS
SATSUMAS	SAUCIERS	SAUT	SAVER	SAVVEY
SATURABLE	SAUCIEST	SAUTE	SAVERS	SAVVEYED
SATURANT	SAUCILY	SAUTED	SAVES	SAVVEYING
SATURANTS	SAUCINESS	SAUTEED	SAVEY	SAVVEYS
SATURATE	SAUCING	SAUTEEING	SAVEYED	SAVVIED
SATURATED	SAUCISSE	SAUTEING	SAVEYING	SAVVIER
SATURATER	SAUCISSES	SAUTERNE	SAVEYS	SAVVIES
SATURATES	SAUCISSON	SAUTERNES	SAVIN	SAVVIEST
SATURATOR	SAUCY	SAUTES	SAVINE	SAVVILY
SATURNIC	SAUFGARD	SAUTING	SAVINES	SAVVINESS
SATURNIID	SAUFGARDS	SAUTOIR	SAVING	SAVVY

S

SAVVYING	SAWYER	SBIRRI	SCAITHING	SCALEUP
SAW	SAWYERS	SBIRRO	SCAITHS	SCALEUPS
SAWAH	SAX	SCAB	SCALA	SCALEWORK
SAWAHS	SAXATILE	SCABBARD	SCALABLE	SCALIER
SAWBILL	SAXAUL	SCABBARDS	SCALABLY	SCALIEST
SAWBILLS	SAXAULS	SCABBED	SCALADE	SCALINESS
SAWBLADE	SAXE	SCABBIER	SCALADES	SCALING
SAWBLADES	SAXES	SCABBIEST	SCALADO	SCALINGS
SAWBONES	SAXHORN	SCABBILY	SCALADOS	SCALL
SAWBUCK	SAXHORNS	SCABBING	SCALAE	SCALLAWAG
SAWBUCKS	SAXICOLE	SCABBLE	SCALAGE	SCALLED
SAWDER	SAXIFRAGE	SCABBLED	SCALAGES	SCALLIES
SAWDERED	SAXITOXIN	SCABBLES	SCALAR	SCALLION
SAWDERING	SAXONIES	SCABBLING	SCALARE	SCALLIONS
SAWDERS	SAXONITE	SCABBY	SCALARES	SCALLOP
SAWDUST	SAXONITES	SCABIES	SCALARS	SCALLOPED
SAWDUSTED	SAXONY	SCABIETIC	SCALATION	SCALLOPER
SAWDUSTS	SAXOPHONE	SCABIOSA	SCALAWAG	SCALLOPS
SAWDUSTY	SAXTUBA	SCABIOSAS	SCALAWAGS	SCALLS
SAWED	SAXTUBAS	SCABIOUS	SCALD	SCALLY
SAWER	SAY	SCABLAND	SCALDED	SCALLYWAG
SAWERS	SAYABLE	SCABLANDS	SCALDER	SCALOGRAM
SAWFISH	SAYED	SCABLIKE	SCALDERS	SCALP
SAWFISHES	SAYEDS	SCABRID	SCALDFISH	SCALPED
SAWFLIES	SAYER	SCABROUS	SCALDHEAD	SCALPEL
SAWFLY	SAYERS	SCABS	SCALDIC	SCALPELS
SAWGRASS	SAYEST	SCAD	SCALDING	SCALPER
SAWHORSE	SAYID	SCADS	SCALDINGS	SCALPERS
SAWHORSES	SAYIDS	SCAFF	SCALDINI	SCALPING
SAWING	SAYING	SCAFFIE	SCALDINO	SCALPINGS
SAWINGS	SAYINGS	SCAFFIES	SCALDS	SCALPINS
SAWLIKE	SAYNE	SCAFFOLD	SCALDSHIP	SCALPLESS
SAWLOG	SAYON	SCAFFOLDS	SCALE	SCALPRUM
SAWLOGS	SAYONARA	SCAFFS	SCALEABLE	SCALPRUMS
SAWMILL	SAYONARAS	SCAG	SCALEABLY	SCALPS
SAWMILLS	SAYONS	SCAGGED	SCALED	SCALY
SAWN	SAYS	SCAGGING	SCALELESS	SCAM
SAWNEY	SAYST	SCAGLIA	SCALELIKE	SCAMBLE
SAWNEYS	SAYYID	SCAGLIAS	SCALENE	SCAMBLED
SAWPIT	SAYYIDS	SCAGLIOLA	SCALENI	SCAMBLER
SAWPITS	SAZ	SCAGS	SCALENUS	SCAMBLERS
SAWS	SAZERAC	SCAIL	SCALEPAN	SCAMBLES
SAWSHARK	SAZERACS	SCAILED	SCALEPANS	SCAMBLING
SAWSHARKS	SAZES	SCAILING	SCALER	SCAMEL
SAWTEETH	SAZHEN	SCAILS	SCALERS	SCAMELS
SAWTIMBER	SAZHENS	SCAITH	SCALES	SCAMMED
SAWTOOTH	SAZZES	SCAITHED	SCALETAIL	SCAMMER

S

SCAMMERS	SCANTIEST	SCARCE	SCARPAING	SCATOLOGY
SCAMMING	SCANTILY	SCARCELY	SCARPAS	SCATS
SCAMMONY	SCANTING	SCARCER	SCARPED	SCATT
SCAMP	SCANTITY	SCARCEST	SCARPER	SCATTED
SCAMPED	SCANTLE	SCARCITY	SCARPERED	SCATTER
SCAMPER	SCANTLED	SCARE	SCARPERS	SCATTERED
SCAMPERED	SCANTLES	SCARECROW	SCARPETTI	SCATTERER
SCAMPERER	SCANTLING	SCARED	SCARPETTO	SCATTERS
SCAMPERS	SCANTLY	SCAREDER	SCARPH	SCATTERY
SCAMPI	SCANTNESS	SCAREDEST	SCARPHED	SCATTIER
SCAMPIES	SCANTS	SCAREHEAD	SCARPHING	SCATTIEST
SCAMPING	SCANTY	SCARER	SCARPHS	SCATTILY
SCAMPINGS	SCAPA	SCARERS	SCARPINES	SCATTING
SCAMPIS	SCAPAED	SCARES	SCARPING	SCATTINGS
SCAMPISH	SCAPAING	SCAREY	SCARPINGS	SCATTS
SCAMPS	SCAPAS	SCARF	SCARPS	SCATTY
SCAMS	SCAPE	SCARFED	SCARRE	SCAUD
SCAMSTER	SCAPED	SCARFER	SCARRED	SCAUDED
SCAMSTERS	SCAPEGOAT	SCARFERS	SCARRES	SCAUDING
SCAMTO	SCAPELESS	SCARFING	SCARRIER	SCAUDS
SCAMTOS	SCAPEMENT	SCARFINGS	SCARRIEST	SCAUP
SCAN	SCAPES	SCARFISH	SCARRING	SCAUPED
SCAND	SCAPHOID	SCARFPIN	SCARRINGS	SCAUPER
SCANDAL	SCAPHOIDS	SCARFPINS	SCARRY	SCAUPERS
SCANDALED	SCAPHOPOD	SCARFS	SCARS	SCAUPING
SCANDALS	SCAPI	SCARFSKIN	SCART	SCAUPS
SCANDENT	SCAPING	SCARFWISE	SCARTED	SCAUR
SCANDIA	SCAPOLITE	SCARIER	SCARTH	SCAURED
SCANDIAS	SCAPOSE	SCARIEST	SCARTHS	SCAURIES
SCANDIC	SCAPPLE	SCARIFIED	SCARTING	SCAURING
SCANDIUM	SCAPPLED	SCARIFIER	SCARTS	SCAURS
SCANDIUMS	SCAPPLES	SCARIFIES	SCARVES	SCAURY
SCANNABLE	SCAPPLING	SCARIFY	SCARY	SCAVAGE
SCANNED	SCAPULA	SCARILY	SCAT	SCAVAGER
SCANNER	SCAPULAE	SCARINESS	SCATBACK	SCAVAGERS
SCANNERS	SCAPULAR	SCARING	SCATBACKS	SCAVAGES
SCANNING	SCAPULARS	SCARIOSE	SCATCH	SCAVENGE
SCANNINGS	SCAPULARY	SCARIOUS	SCATCHES	SCAVENGED
SCANS	SCAPULAS	SCARLESS	SCATH	SCAVENGER
SCANSION	SCAPUS	SCARLET	SCATHE	SCAVENGES
SCANSIONS	SCAR	SCARLETED	SCATHED	SCAW
SCANT	SCARAB	SCARLETS	SCATHEFUL	SCAWS
SCANTED	SCARABAEI	SCARMOGE	SCATHES	SCAWTITE
SCANTER	SCARABEE	SCARMOGES	SCATHING	SCAWTITES
SCANTEST	SCARABEES	SCARP	SCATHS	SCAZON
SCANTIER	SCARABOID	SCARPA	SCATOLE	SCAZONS
SCANTIES	SCARABS	SCARPAED	SCATOLES	SCAZONTES

SCAZONTIC	SCEPTERS	SCHEMER	SCHLEPPY	SCHMOOSE
SCEAT	SCEPTIC	SCHEMERS	SCHLEPS	SCHMOOSED
SCEATT	SCEPTICAL	SCHEMES	SCHLICH	SCHMOOSES
SCEATTAS	SCEPTICS	SCHEMIE	SCHLICHS	SCHMOOZ
SCEDULE	SCEPTRAL	SCHEMIES	SCHLIERE	SCHMOOZE
SCEDULED	SCEPTRE	SCHEMING	SCHLIEREN	SCHMOOZED
SCEDULES	SCEPTRED	SCHEMINGS	SCHLIERIC	SCHMOOZER
SCEDULING	SCEPTRES	SCHERZI	SCHLOCK	SCHMOOZES
SCELERAT	SCEPTRING	SCHERZO	SCHLOCKER	SCHMOOZY
SCELERATE	SCEPTRY	SCHERZOS	SCHLOCKS	SCHMOS
SCELERATS	SCERNE	SCHIAVONE	SCHLOCKY	SCHMUCK
SCENA	SCERNED	SCHIEDAM	SCHLONG	SCHMUCKS
SCENARIES	SCERNES	SCHIEDAMS	SCHLONGS	SCHMUTTER
SCENARIO	SCERNING	SCHILLER	SCHLOSS	SCHNAPPER
SCENARIOS	SCHANSE	SCHILLERS	SCHLOSSES	SCHNAPPS
SCENARISE	SCHANSES	SCHILLING	SCHLUB	SCHNAPS
SCENARIST	SCHANTZE	SCHIMMEL	SCHLUBS	SCHNAPSES
SCENARIZE	SCHANTZES	SCHIMMELS	SCHLUMP	SCHNAUZER
SCENARY	SCHANZE	SCHISM	SCHLUMPED	SCHNECKE
SCENAS	SCHANZES	SCHISMA	SCHLUMPS	SCHNECKEN
SCEND	SCHAPPE	SCHISMAS	SCHLUMPY	SCHNELL
SCENDED	SCHAPPED	SCHISMS	SCHMALTZ	SCHNITZEL
SCENDING	SCHAPPES	SCHIST	SCHMALTZY	SCHNOOK
SCENDS	SCHAPSKA	SCHISTOSE	SCHMALZ	SCHNOOKS
SCENE	SCHAPSKAS	SCHISTOUS	SCHMALZES	SCHNORKEL
SCENED	SCHATCHEN	SCHISTS	SCHMALZY	SCHNORR
SCENEMAN	SCHAV	SCHIZIER	SCHMATTE	SCHNORRED
SCENEMEN	SCHAVS	SCHIZIEST	SCHMATTES	SCHNORRER
SCENERIES	SCHECHITA	SCHIZO	SCHMEAR	SCHNORRS
SCENERY	SCHEDULAR	SCHIZOID	SCHMEARED	SCHNOZ
SCENES	SCHEDULE	SCHIZOIDS	SCHMEARS	SCHNOZES
SCENESTER	SCHEDULED	SCHIZONT	SCHMECK	SCHNOZZ
SCENIC	SCHEDULER	SCHIZONTS	SCHMECKS	SCHNOZZES
SCENICAL	SCHEDULES	SCHIZOPOD	SCHMEER	SCHNOZZLE
SCENICS	SCHEELITE	SCHIZOS	SCHMEERED	SCHOLAR
SCENING	SCHELLIES	SCHIZY	SCHMEERS	SCHOLARCH
SCENT	SCHELLUM	SCHIZZIER	SCHMELZ	SCHOLARLY
SCENTED	SCHELLUMS	SCHIZZY	SCHMELZE	SCHOLARS
SCENTFUL	SCHELLY	SCHLAGER	SCHMELZES	SCHOLIA
SCENTING	SCHELM	SCHLAGERS	SCHMICK	SCHOLIAST
SCENTINGS	SCHELMS	SCHLEMIEL	SCHMICKER	SCHOLION
SCENTLESS	SCHEMA	SCHLEMIHL	SCHMO	SCHOLIUM
SCENTS	SCHEMAS	SCHLEP	SCHMOCK	SCHOLIUMS
SCEPSIS	SCHEMATA	SCHLEPP	SCHMOCKS	SCHOOL
SCEPSISES	SCHEMATIC	SCHLEPPED	SCHMOE	SCHOOLBAG
SCEPTER	SCHEME	SCHLEPPER	SCHMOES	SCHOOLBOY
SCEPTERED	SCHEMED	SCHLEPPS	SCHMOOS	SCHOOLDAY

SCHOOLE	SCHWAS	SCIROCCO	SCLERITE	SCOLDINGS
SCHOOLED	SCIAENID	SCIROCCOS	SCLERITES	SCOLDS
SCHOOLERY	SCIAENIDS	SCIROCS	SCLERITIC	SCOLECES
SCHOOLES	SCIAENOID	SCIRRHI	SCLERITIS	SCOLECID
SCHOOLIE	SCIAMACHY	SCIRRHOID	SCLEROID	SCOLECIDS
SCHOOLIES	SCIARID	SCIRRHOUS	SCLEROMA	SCOLECITE
SCHOOLING	SCIARIDS	SCIRRHUS	SCLEROMAS	SCOLECOID
SCHOOLKID	SCIATIC	SCISSEL	SCLEROSAL	SCOLEX
SCHOOLMAN	SCIATICA	SCISSELS	SCLEROSE	SCOLIA
SCHOOLMEN	SCIATICAL	SCISSIL	SCLEROSED	SCOLICES
SCHOOLS	SCIATICAS	SCISSILE	SCLEROSES	SCOLIOMA
SCHOONER	SCIATICS	SCISSILS	SCLEROSIS	SCOLIOMAS
SCHOONERS	SCIENCE	SCISSION	SCLEROTAL	SCOLION
SCHORL	SCIENCED	SCISSIONS	SCLEROTIA	SCOLIOSES
SCHORLS	SCIENCES	SCISSOR	SCLEROTIC	SCOLIOSIS
SCHOUT	SCIENT	SCISSORED	SCLEROTIN	SCOLIOTIC
SCHOUTS	SCIENTER	SCISSORER	SCLEROUS	SCOLLOP
SCHRIK	SCIENTIAL	SCISSORS	SCLIFF	SCOLLOPED
SCHRIKS	SCIENTISE	SCISSURE	SCLIFFS	SCOLLOPS
SCHROD	SCIENTISM	SCISSURES	SCLIM	SCOLYTID
SCHRODS	SCIENTIST	SCIURID	SCLIMMED	SCOLYTIDS
SCHTICK	SCIENTIZE	SCIURIDS	SCLIMMING	SCOLYTOID
SCHTICKS	SCILICET	SCIURINE	SCLIMS	SCOMBRID
SCHTIK	SCILLA	SCIURINES	SCODIER	SCOMBRIDS
SCHTIKS	SCILLAS	SCIUROID	SCODIEST	SCOMBROID
SCHTOOK	SCIMETAR	SCLAFF	SCODY	SCOMFISH
SCHTOOKS	SCIMETARS	SCLAFFED	SCOFF	SCONCE
SCHTOOM	SCIMITAR	SCLAFFER	SCOFFED	SCONCED
SCHTUCK	SCIMITARS	SCLAFFERS	SCOFFER	SCONCES
SCHTUCKS	SCIMITER	SCLAFFING	SCOFFERS	SCONCHEON
SCHTUM	SCIMITERS	SCLAFFS	SCOFFING	SCONCING
SCHUIT	SCINCOID	SCLATE	SCOFFINGS	SCONE
SCHUITS	SCINCOIDS	SCLATES	SCOFFLAW	SCONES
SCHUL	SCINTILLA	SCLAUNDER	SCOFFLAWS	SCONTION
SCHULN	SCIOLISM	SCLAVE	SCOFFS	SCONTIONS
SCHULS	SCIOLISMS	SCLAVES	SCOG	SCOOBIES
SCHUSS	SCIOLIST	SCLERA	SCOGGED	SCOOBY
SCHUSSED	SCIOLISTS	SCLERAE	SCOGGING	SCOOCH
SCHUSSER	SCIOLOUS	SCLERAL	SCOGS	SCOOCHED
SCHUSSERS	SCIOLTO	SCLERAS	SCOINSON	SCOOCHES
SCHUSSES	SCIOMACHY	SCLERE	SCOINSONS	SCOOCHING
SCHUSSING	SCIOMANCY	SCLEREID	SCOLD	SCOOG
SCHUYT	SCION	SCLEREIDE	SCOLDABLE	SCOOGED
SCHUYTS	SCIONS	SCLEREIDS	SCOLDED	SCOOGING
SCHVARTZE	SCIOPHYTE	SCLEREMA	SCOLDER	SCOOGS
SCHWA	SCIOSOPHY	SCLEREMAS	SCOLDERS	SCOOP
SCHWARTZE	SCIROC	SCLERES	SCOLDING	SCOOPABLE

S

SCOOPED	SCORE	SCOTERS	SCOUSERS	SCRABBLES
SCOOPER	SCORECARD	SCOTIA	SCOUSES	SCRABBLY
SCOOPERS	SCORED	SCOTIAS	SCOUT	SCRABS
SCOOPFUL	SCORELESS	SCOTOMA	SCOUTED	SCRAE
SCOOPFULS	SCORELINE	SCOTOMAS	SCOUTER	SCRAES
SCOOPING	SCOREPAD	SCOTOMATA	SCOUTERS	SCRAG
SCOOPINGS	SCOREPADS	SCOTOMIA	SCOUTH	SCRAGGED
SCOOPS	SCORER	SCOTOMIAS	SCOUTHER	SCRAGGIER
SCOOPSFUL	SCORERS	SCOTOMIES	SCOUTHERS	SCRAGGILY
SCOOSH	SCORES	SCOTOMY	SCOUTHERY	SCRAGGING
SCOOSHED	SCORIA	SCOTOPHIL	SCOUTHS	SCRAGGLY
SCOOSHES	SCORIAC	SCOTOPIA	SCOUTING	SCRAGGY
SCOOSHING	SCORIAE	SCOTOPIAS	SCOUTINGS	SCRAGS
SCOOT	SCORIFIED	SCOTOPIC	SCOUTS	SCRAICH
SCOOTCH	SCORIFIER	SCOTS	SCOW	SCRAICHED
SCOOTCHED	SCORIFIES	SCOTTIE	SCOWDER	SCRAICHS
SCOOTCHES	SCORIFY	SCOTTIES	SCOWDERED	SCRAIGH
SCOOTED	SCORING	SCOUG	SCOWDERS	SCRAIGHED
SCOOTER	SCORINGS	SCOUGED	SCOWED	SCRAIGHS
SCOOTERS	SCORIOUS	SCOUGING	SCOWING	SCRAM
SCOOTING	SCORN	SCOUGS	SCOWL	SCRAMB
SCOOTS	SCORNED	SCOUNDREL	SCOWLED	SCRAMBED
SCOP	SCORNER	SCOUP	SCOWLER	SCRAMBING
SCOPA	SCORNERS	SCOUPED	SCOWLERS	SCRAMBLE
SCOPAE	SCORNFUL	SCOUPING	SCOWLING	SCRAMBLED
SCOPATE	SCORNING	SCOUPS	SCOWLS	SCRAMBLER
SCOPE	SCORNINGS	SCOUR	SCOWP	SCRAMBLES
SCOPED	SCORNS	SCOURED	SCOWPED	SCRAMBS
SCOPELID	SCORODITE	SCOURER	SCOWPING	SCRAMJET
SCOPELIDS	SCORPER	SCOURERS	SCOWPS	SCRAMJETS
SCOPELOID	SCORPERS	SCOURGE	SCOWRER	SCRAMMED
SCOPES	SCORPIOID	SCOURGED	SCOWRERS	SCRAMMING
SCOPING	SCORPION	SCOURGER	SCOWRIE	SCRAMS
SCOPOLINE	SCORPIONS	SCOURGERS	SCOWRIES	SCRAN
SCOPS	SCORRENDO	SCOURGES	SCOWS	SCRANCH
SCOPULA	SCORSE	SCOURGING	SCOWTH	SCRANCHED
SCOPULAE	SCORSED	SCOURIE	SCOWTHER	SCRANCHES
SCOPULAS	SCORSER	SCOURIES	SCOWTHERS	SCRANNEL
SCOPULATE	SCORSERS	SCOURING	SCOWTHS	SCRANNELS
SCORBUTIC	SCORSES	SCOURINGS	SCOZZA	SCRANNIER
SCORCH	SCORSING	SCOURS	SCOZZAS	SCRANNY
SCORCHED	SCOT	SCOURSE	SCRAB	SCRANS
SCORCHER	SCOTCH	SCOURSED	SCRABBED	SCRAP
SCORCHERS	SCOTCHED	SCOURSES	SCRABBING	SCRAPABLE
SCORCHES	SCOTCHES	SCOURSING	SCRABBLE	SCRAPBOOK
SCORCHING	SCOTCHING	SCOUSE	SCRABBLED	SCRAPE
SCORDATO	SCOTER	SCOUSER	SCRABBLER	SCRAPED

S

SCRAPEGUT
SCRAPER
SCRAPERS
SCRAPES
SCRAPHEAP
SCRAPIE
SCRAPIES
SCRAPING
SCRAPINGS
SCRAPPAGE
SCRAPPED
SCRAPPER
SCRAPPERS
SCRAPPIER
SCRAPPILY
SCRAPPING
SCRAPPLE
SCRAPPLES
SCRAPPY
SCRAPS
SCRAPYARD
SCRAT
SCRATCH
SCRATCHED
SCRATCHER
SCRATCHES
SCRATCHIE
SCRATCHY
SCRATS
SCRATTED
SCRATTING
SCRATTLE
SCRATTLED
SCRATTLES
SCRAUCH
SCRAUCHED
SCRAUCHS
SCRAUGH
SCRAUGHED
SCRAUGHS
SCRAW
SCRAWL
SCRAWLED
SCRAWLER
SCRAWLERS
SCRAWLIER
SCRAWLING

SCRAWLS
SCRAWLY
SCRAWM
SCRAWMED
SCRAWMING
SCRAWMS
SCRAWNIER
SCRAWNILY
SCRAWNY
SCRAWP
SCRAWPED
SCRAWPING
SCRAWPS
SCRAWS
SCRAY
SCRAYE
SCRAYES
SCRAYS
SCREAK
SCREAKED
SCREAKIER
SCREAKING
SCREAKS
SCREAKY
SCREAM
SCREAMED
SCREAMER
SCREAMERS
SCREAMING
SCREAMO
SCREAMOS
SCREAMS
SCREE
SCREECH
SCREECHED
SCREECHER
SCREECHES
SCREECHY
SCREED
SCREEDED
SCREEDER
SCREEDERS
SCREEDING
SCREEDS
SCREEN
SCREENED
SCREENER

SCREENERS
SCREENFUL
SCREENIE
SCREENIES
SCREENING
SCREENS
SCREES
SCREET
SCREETED
SCREETING
SCREETS
SCREEVE
SCREEVED
SCREEVER
SCREEVERS
SCREEVES
SCREEVING
SCREICH
SCREICHED
SCREICHS
SCREIGH
SCREIGHED
SCREIGHS
SCREW
SCREWABLE
SCREWBALL
SCREWBEAN
SCREWED
SCREWER
SCREWERS
SCREWIER
SCREWIEST
SCREWING
SCREWINGS
SCREWLIKE
SCREWS
SCREWTOP
SCREWTOPS
SCREWUP
SCREWUPS
SCREWWORM
SCREWY
SCRIBABLE
SCRIBAL
SCRIBBLE
SCRIBBLED
SCRIBBLER

SCRIBBLES
SCRIBBLY
SCRIBE
SCRIBED
SCRIBER
SCRIBERS
SCRIBES
SCRIBING
SCRIBINGS
SCRIBISM
SCRIBISMS
SCRIECH
SCRIECHED
SCRIECHS
SCRIED
SCRIENE
SCRIENES
SCRIES
SCRIEVE
SCRIEVED
SCRIEVES
SCRIEVING
SCRIGGLE
SCRIGGLED
SCRIGGLES
SCRIGGLY
SCRIKE
SCRIKED
SCRIKES
SCRIKING
SCRIM
SCRIMMAGE
SCRIMP
SCRIMPED
SCRIMPER
SCRIMPERS
SCRIMPIER
SCRIMPILY
SCRIMPING
SCRIMPIT
SCRIMPLY
SCRIMPS
SCRIMPY
SCRIMS
SCRIMSHAW
SCRIMURE
SCRIMURES

SCRINE
SCRINES
SCRIP
SCRIPPAGE
SCRIPS
SCRIPT
SCRIPTED
SCRIPTER
SCRIPTERS
SCRIPTING
SCRIPTORY
SCRIPTS
SCRIPTURE
SCRITCH
SCRITCHED
SCRITCHES
SCRIVE
SCRIVED
SCRIVENER
SCRIVES
SCRIVING
SCROBBLE
SCROBBLED
SCROBBLES
SCROBE
SCROBES
SCROD
SCRODDLED
SCRODS
SCROFULA
SCROFULAS
SCROG
SCROGGIE
SCROGGIER
SCROGGIN
SCROGGINS
SCROGGY
SCROGS
SCROLL
SCROLLED
SCROLLER
SCROLLERS
SCROLLING
SCROLLS
SCROME
SCROMED
SCROMES

SCROMING	SCRUBBER	SCRUPLING	SCUFFLER	SCULTCH
SCROOCH	SCRUBBERS	SCRUTABLE	SCUFFLERS	SCULTCHES
SCROOCHED	SCRUBBIER	SCRUTATOR	SCUFFLES	SCUM
SCROOCHES	SCRUBBILY	SCRUTINY	SCUFFLING	SCUMBAG
SCROOGE	SCRUBBING	SCRUTO	SCUFFS	SCUMBAGS
SCROOGED	SCRUBBY	SCRUTOIRE	SCUFT	SCUMBER
SCROOGES	SCRUBLAND	SCRUTOS	SCUFTS	SCUMBERED
SCROOGING	SCRUBS	SCRUZE	SCUG	SCUMBERS
SCROOP	SCRUFF	SCRUZED	SCUGGED	SCUMBLE
SCROOPED	SCRUFFIER	SCRUZES	SCUGGING	SCUMBLED
SCROOPING	SCRUFFILY	SCRUZING	SCUGS	SCUMBLES
SCROOPS	SCRUFFS	SCRY	SCUL	SCUMBLING
SCROOTCH	SCRUFFY	SCRYDE	SCULCH	SCUMFISH
SCRORP	SCRUM	SCRYER	SCULCHES	SCUMLESS
SCRORPS	SCRUMDOWN	SCRYERS	SCULK	SCUMLIKE
SCROTA	SCRUMMAGE	SCRYING	SCULKED	SCUMMED
SCROTAL	SCRUMMED	SCRYINGS	SCULKER	SCUMMER
SCROTE	SCRUMMIE	SCRYNE	SCULKERS	SCUMMERS
SCROTES	SCRUMMIER	SCRYNES	SCULKING	SCUMMIER
SCROTUM	SCRUMMIES	SCUBA	SCULKS	SCUMMIEST
SCROTUMS	SCRUMMING	SCUBAED	SCULL	SCUMMILY
SCROUGE	SCRUMMY	SCUBAING	SCULLE	SCUMMING
SCROUGED	SCRUMP	SCUBAS	SCULLED	SCUMMINGS
SCROUGER	SCRUMPED	SCUCHIN	SCULLER	SCUMMY
SCROUGERS	SCRUMPIES	SCUCHINS	SCULLERS	SCUMS
SCROUGES	SCRUMPING	SCUD	SCULLERY	SCUNCHEON
SCROUGING	SCRUMPLE	SCUDDALER	SCULLES	SCUNDERED
SCROUNGE	SCRUMPLED	SCUDDED	SCULLING	SCUNGE
SCROUNGED	SCRUMPLES	SCUDDER	SCULLINGS	SCUNGED
SCROUNGER	SCRUMPOX	SCUDDERS	SCULLION	SCUNGES
SCROUNGES	SCRUMPS	SCUDDING	SCULLIONS	SCUNGIER
SCROUNGY	SCRUMPY	SCUDDLE	SCULLS	SCUNGIEST
SCROW	SCRUMS	SCUDDLED	SCULP	SCUNGILLI
SCROWDGE	SCRUNCH	SCUDDLES	SCULPED	SCUNGING
SCROWDGED	SCRUNCHED	SCUDDLING	SCULPIN	SCUNGY
SCROWDGES	SCRUNCHES	SCUDI	SCULPING	SCUNNER
SCROWL	SCRUNCHIE	SCUDLER	SCULPINS	SCUNNERED
SCROWLE	SCRUNCHY	SCUDLERS	SCULPS	SCUNNERS
SCROWLED	SCRUNT	SCUDO	SCULPSIT	SCUP
SCROWLES	SCRUNTIER	SCUDS	SCULPT	SCUPPAUG
SCROWLING	SCRUNTS	SCUFF	SCULPTED	SCUPPAUGS
SCROWLS	SCRUNTY	SCUFFED	SCULPTING	SCUPPER
SCROWS	SCRUPLE	SCUFFER	SCULPTOR	SCUPPERED
SCROYLE	SCRUPLED	SCUFFERS	SCULPTORS	SCUPPERS
SCROYLES	SCRUPLER	SCUFFING	SCULPTS	SCUPS
SCRUB	SCRUPLERS	SCUFFLE	SCULPTURE	SCUR
SCRUBBED	SCRUPLES	SCUFFLED	SCULS	SCURF

SCURFIER	SCUTS	SDEIGN	SEAFOODS	SEALYHAMS
SCURFIEST	SCUTTER	SDEIGNE	SEAFOWL	SEAM
SCURFS	SCUTTERED	SDEIGNED	SEAFOWLS	SEAMAID
SCURFY	SCUTTERS	SDEIGNES	SEAFRONT	SEAMAIDS
SCURRED	SCUTTLE	SDEIGNING	SEAFRONTS	SEAMAN
SCURRIED	SCUTTLED	SDEIGNS	SEAGIRT	SEAMANLY
SCURRIER	SCUTTLER	SDEIN	SEAGOING	SEAMARK
SCURRIERS	SCUTTLERS	SDEINED	SEAGULL	SEAMARKS
SCURRIES	SCUTTLES	SDEINING	SEAGULLS	SEAME
SCURRIL	SCUTTLING	SDEINS	SEAHAWK	SEAMED
SCURRILE	SCUTUM	SEA	SEAHAWKS	SEAMEN
SCURRING	SCUTWORK	SEABAG	SEAHOG	SEAMER
SCURRIOUR	SCUTWORKS	SEABAGS	SEAHOGS	SEAMERS
SCURRY	SCUZZ	SEABANK	SEAHORSE	SEAMES
SCURRYING	SCUZZBAG	SEABANKS	SEAHORSES	SEAMFREE
SCURS	SCUZZBAGS	SEABEACH	SEAHOUND	SEAMIER
SCURVIER	SCUZZBALL	SEABED	SEAHOUNDS	SEAMIEST
SCURVIES	SCUZZES	SEABEDS	SEAKALE	SEAMINESS
SCURVIEST	SCUZZIER	SEABIRD	SEAKALES	SEAMING
SCURVILY	SCUZZIEST	SEABIRDS	SEAL	SEAMINGS
SCURVY	SCUZZY	SEABLITE	SEALABLE	SEAMLESS
SCUSE	SCYBALA	SEABLITES	SEALANT	SEAMLIKE
SCUSED	SCYBALOUS	SEABOARD	SEALANTS	SEAMOUNT
SCUSES	SCYBALUM	SEABOARDS	SEALCH	SEAMOUNTS
SCUSING	SCYE	SEABOOT	SEALCHS	SEAMS
SCUT	SCYES	SEABOOTS	SEALED	SEAMSET
SCUTA	SCYPHATE	SEABORNE	SEALER	SEAMSETS
SCUTAGE	SCYPHI	SEABOTTLE	SEALERIES	SEAMSTER
SCUTAGES	SCYPHUS	SEACOAST	SEALERS	SEAMSTERS
SCUTAL	SCYTALE	SEACOASTS	SEALERY	SEAMY
SCUTATE	SCYTALES	SEACOCK	SEALGH	SEAN
SCUTATION	SCYTHE	SEACOCKS	SEALGHS	SEANCE
SCUTCH	SCYTHED	SEACRAFT	SEALIFT	SEANCES
SCUTCHED	SCYTHEMAN	SEACRAFTS	SEALIFTED	SEANED
SCUTCHEON	SCYTHEMEN	SEACUNNY	SEALIFTS	SEANING
SCUTCHER	SCYTHER	SEADOG	SEALINE	SEANNACHY
SCUTCHERS	SCYTHERS	SEADOGS	SEALINES	SEANS
SCUTCHES	SCYTHES	SEADROME	SEALING	SEAPIECE
SCUTCHING	SCYTHING	SEADROMES	SEALINGS	SEAPIECES
SCUTE	SDAINE	SEAFARER	SEALLIKE	SEAPLANE
SCUTELLA	SDAINED	SEAFARERS	SEALPOINT	SEAPLANES
SCUTELLAR	SDAINES	SEAFARING	SEALS	SEAPORT
SCUTELLUM	SDAINING	SEAFLOOR	SEALSKIN	SEAPORTS
SCUTES	SDAYN	SEAFLOORS	SEALSKINS	SEAQUAKE
SCUTIFORM	SDAYNED	SEAFOLK	SEALWAX	SEAQUAKES
SCUTIGER	SDAYNING	SEAFOLKS	SEALWAXES	SEAQUARIA
SCUTIGERS	SDAYNS	SEAFOOD	SEALYHAM	SEAR

S

SEARAT	SEASONS	SEAWORM	SECHS	SECRETIVE
SEARATS	SEASPEAK	SEAWORMS	SECKEL	SECRETLY
SEARCE	SEASPEAKS	SEAWORTHY	SECKELS	SECRETOR
SEARCED	SEASTRAND	SEAZE	SECKLE	SECRETORS
SEARCES	SEASURE	SEAZED	SECKLES	SECRETORY
SEARCH	SEASURES	SEAZES	SECLUDE	SECRETS
SEARCHED	SEAT	SEAZING	SECLUDED	SECS
SEARCHER	SEATBACK	SEBACEOUS	SECLUDES	SECT
SEARCHERS	SEATBACKS	SEBACIC	SECLUDING	SECTARIAL
SEARCHES	SEATBELT	SEBASIC	SECLUSION	SECTARIAN
SEARCHING	SEATBELTS	SEBATE	SECLUSIVE	SECTARIES
SEARCING	SEATED	SEBATES	SECO	SECTARY
SEARE	SEATER	SEBESTEN	SECODONT	SECTATOR
SEARED	SEATERS	SEBESTENS	SECODONTS	SECTATORS
SEARER	SEATING	SEBIFIC	SECONAL	SECTILE
SEAREST	SEATINGS	SEBORRHEA	SECONALS	SECTILITY
SEARING	SEATLESS	SEBUM	SECOND	SECTION
SEARINGLY	SEATMATE	SEBUMS	SECONDARY	SECTIONAL
SEARINGS	SEATMATES	SEBUNDIES	SECONDE	SECTIONED
SEARNESS	SEATRAIN	SEBUNDY	SECONDED	SECTIONS
SEAROBIN	SEATRAINS	SEC	SECONDEE	SECTOR
SEAROBINS	SEATROUT	SECALOSE	SECONDEES	SECTORAL
SEARS	SEATROUTS	SECALOSES	SECONDER	SECTORED
SEAS	SEATS	SECANT	SECONDERS	SECTORIAL
SEASCAPE	SEATWORK	SECANTLY	SECONDES	SECTORING
SEASCAPES	SEATWORKS	SECANTS	SECONDI	SECTORISE
SEASCOUT	SEAWALL	SECATEUR	SECONDING	SECTORIZE
SEASCOUTS	SEAWALLS	SECATEURS	SECONDLY	SECTORS
SEASE	SEAWAN	SECCO	SECONDO	SECTS
SEASED	SEAWANS	SECCOS	SECONDS	SECULAR
SEASES	SEAWANT	SECEDE	SECPAR	SECULARLY
SEASHELL	SEAWANTS	SECEDED	SECPARS	SECULARS
SEASHELLS	SEAWARD	SECEDER	SECRECIES	SECULUM
SEASHORE	SEAWARDLY	SECEDERS	SECRECY	SECULUMS
SEASHORES	SEAWARDS	SECEDES	SECRET	SECUND
SEASICK	SEAWARE	SECEDING	SECRETA	SECUNDINE
SEASICKER	SEAWARES	SECERN	SECRETAGE	SECUNDLY
SEASIDE	SEAWATER	SECERNED	SECRETARY	SECUNDUM
SEASIDES	SEAWATERS	SECERNENT	SECRETE	SECURABLE
SEASING	SEAWAY	SECERNING	SECRETED	SECURANCE
SEASON	SEAWAYS	SECERNS	SECRETER	SECURE
SEASONAL	SEAWEED	SECESH	SECRETES	SECURED
SEASONALS	SEAWEEDS	SECESHER	SECRETEST	SECURELY
SEASONED	SEAWIFE	SECESHERS	SECRETIN	SECURER
SEASONER	SEAWIVES	SECESHES	SECRETING	SECURERS
SEASONERS	SEAWOMAN	SECESSION	SECRETINS	SECURES
SEASONING	SEAWOMEN	SECH	SECRETION	SECUREST

S

SECURING	SEDUCINGS	SEEDTIME	SEERS	SEI
SECURITAN	SEDUCIVE	SEEDTIMES	SEES	SEICENTO
SECURITY	SEDUCTION	SEEDY	SEESAW	SEICENTOS
SED	SEDUCTIVE	SEEING	SEESAWED	SEICHE
SEDAN	SEDUCTOR	SEEINGS	SEESAWING	SEICHES
SEDANS	SEDUCTORS	SEEK	SEESAWS	SEIDEL
SEDARIM	SEDULITY	SEEKER	SEETHE	SEIDELS
SEDATE	SEDULOUS	SEEKERS	SEETHED	SEIF
SEDATED	SEDUM	SEEKING	SEETHER	SEIFS
SEDATELY	SEDUMS	SEEKS	SEETHERS	SEIGNEUR
SEDATER	SEE	SEEL	SEETHES	SEIGNEURS
SEDATES	SEEABLE	SEELD	SEETHING	SEIGNEURY
SEDATEST	SEECATCH	SEELED	SEETHINGS	SEIGNIOR
SEDATING	SEED	SEELIE	SEEWING	SEIGNIORS
SEDATION	SEEDBED	SEELIER	SEFER	SEIGNIORY
SEDATIONS	SEEDBEDS	SEELIEST	SEG	SEIGNORAL
SEDATIVE	SEEDBOX	SEELING	SEGAR	SEIGNORY
SEDATIVES	SEEDBOXES	SEELINGS	SEGARS	SEIK
SEDENT	SEEDCAKE	SEELS	SEGETAL	SEIKER
SEDENTARY	SEEDCAKES	SEELY	SEGGAR	SEIKEST
SEDER	SEEDCASE	SEEM	SEGGARS	SEIL
SEDERS	SEEDCASES	SEEMED	SEGHOL	SEILED
SEDERUNT	SEEDEATER	SEEMER	SEGHOLATE	SEILING
SEDERUNTS	SEEDED	SEEMERS	SEGHOLS	SEILS
SEDES	SEEDER	SEEMING	SEGMENT	SEINE
SEDGE	SEEDERS	SEEMINGLY	SEGMENTAL	SEINED
SEDGED	SEEDIER	SEEMINGS	SEGMENTED	SEINER
SEDGELAND	SEEDIEST	SEEMLESS	SEGMENTS	SEINERS
SEDGES	SEEDILY	SEEMLIER	SEGNI	SEINES
SEDGIER	SEEDINESS	SEEMLIEST	SEGNO	SEINING
SEDGIEST	SEEDING	SEEMLIHED	SEGNOS	SEININGS
SEDGY	SEEDINGS	SEEMLY	SEGO	SEIR
SEDILE	SEEDLESS	SEEMLYHED	SEGOL	SEIRS
SEDILIA	SEEDLIKE	SEEMS	SEGOLATE	SEIS
SEDILIUM	SEEDLING	SEEN	SEGOLATES	SEISABLE
SEDIMENT	SEEDLINGS	SEEP	SEGOLS	SEISE
SEDIMENTS	SEEDLIP	SEEPAGE	SEGOS	SEISED
SEDITION	SEEDLIPS	SEEPAGES	SEGREANT	SEISER
SEDITIONS	SEEDMAN	SEEPED	SEGREGANT	SEISERS
SEDITIOUS	SEEDMEN	SEEPIER	SEGREGATE	SEISES
SEDUCE	SEEDNESS	SEEPIEST	SEGS	SEISIN
SEDUCED	SEEDPOD	SEEPING	SEGUE	SEISING
SEDUCER	SEEDPODS	SEEPS	SEGUED	SEISINGS
SEDUCERS	SEEDS	SEEPY	SEGUEING	SEISINS
SEDUCES	SEEDSMAN	SEER	SEGUES	SEISM
SEDUCIBLE	SEEDSMEN	SEERESS	SEHRI	SEISMAL
SEDUCING	SEEDSTOCK	SEERESSES	SEHRIS	SEISMIC

SEISMICAL	SELDSHOWN	SELFIST	SEMANTEME	SEMIDOME
SEISMISM	SELE	SELFISTS	SEMANTIC	SEMIDOMED
SEISMISMS	SELECT	SELFLESS	SEMANTICS	SEMIDOMES
SEISMS	SELECTA	SELFNESS	SEMANTIDE	SEMIDRY
SEISOR	SELECTAS	SELFS	SEMANTRA	SEMIDWARF
SEISORS	SELECTED	SELFSAME	SEMANTRON	SEMIE
SEISURE	SELECTEE	SELFWARD	SEMAPHORE	SEMIERECT
SEISURES	SELECTEES	SELFWARDS	SEMATIC	SEMIES
SEITAN	SELECTING	SELICTAR	SEMBLABLE	SEMIFINAL
SEITANS	SELECTION	SELICTARS	SEMBLABLY	SEMIFIT
SEITEN	SELECTIVE	SELKIE	SEMBLANCE	SEMIFLUID
SEITENS	SELECTLY	SELKIES	SEMBLANT	SEMIGALA
SEITIES	SELECTMAN	SELL	SEMBLANTS	SEMIGLOSS
SEITY	SELECTMEN	SELLA	SEMBLE	SEMIGROUP
SEIZABLE	SELECTOR	SELLABLE	SEMBLED	SEMIHARD
SEIZE	SELECTORS	SELLAE	SEMBLES	SEMIHIGH
SEIZED	SELECTS	SELLAS	SEMBLING	SEMIHOBO
SEIZER	SELENATE	SELLE	SEME	SEMIHOBOS
SEIZERS	SELENATES	SELLER	SEMEE	SEMILLON
SEIZES	SELENIAN	SELLERS	SEMEED	SEMILLONS
SEIZIN	SELENIC	SELLES	SEMEIA	SEMILOG
SEIZING	SELENIDE	SELLING	SEMEION	SEMILUNAR
SEIZINGS	SELENIDES	SELLINGS	SEMEIOTIC	SEMILUNE
SEIZINS	SELENIOUS	SELLOFF	SEMEME	SEMILUNES
SEIZOR	SELENITE	SELLOFFS	SEMEMES	SEMIMAT
SEIZORS	SELENITES	SELLOTAPE	SEMEMIC	SEMIMATT
SEIZURE	SELENITIC	SELLOUT	SEMEN	SEMIMATTE
SEIZURES	SELENIUM	SELLOUTS	SEMENS	SEMIMETAL
SEJANT	SELENIUMS	SELLS	SEMES	SEMIMICRO
SEJEANT	SELENOSES	SELS	SEMESTER	SEMIMILD
SEKOS	SELENOSIS	SELSYN	SEMESTERS	SEMIMOIST
SEKOSES	SELENOUS	SELSYNS	SEMESTRAL	SEMIMUTE
SEKT	SELES	SELTZER	SEMI	SEMINA
SEKTS	SELF	SELTZERS	SEMIANGLE	SEMINAL
SEL	SELFDOM	SELVA	SEMIARID	SEMINALLY
SELACHIAN	SELFDOMS	SELVAGE	SEMIBALD	SEMINAR
SELADANG	SELFED	SELVAGED	SEMIBOLD	SEMINARS
SELADANGS	SELFHEAL	SELVAGEE	SEMIBOLDS	SEMINARY
SELAH	SELFHEALS	SELVAGEES	SEMIBREVE	SEMINATE
SELAHS	SELFHOOD	SELVAGES	SEMIBULL	SEMINATED
SELAMLIK	SELFHOODS	SELVAGING	SEMIBULLS	SEMINATES
SELAMLIKS	SELFING	SELVAS	SEMICOLON	SEMINOMA
SELCOUTH	SELFINGS	SELVEDGE	SEMICOMA	SEMINOMAD
SELD	SELFISH	SELVEDGED	SEMICOMAS	SEMINOMAS
SELDOM	SELFISHLY	SELVEDGES	SEMICURED	SEMINUDE
SELDOMLY	SELFISM	SELVES	SEMIDEAF	SEMIOLOGY
SELDSEEN	SELFISMS	SEMAINIER	SEMIDEIFY	SEMIOPEN

S

SEMIOSES	SEMPLEST	SENGREEN	SENSEIS	SENTIMO
SEMIOSIS	SEMPLICE	SENGREENS	SENSELESS	SENTIMOS
SEMIOTIC	SEMPRE	SENHOR	SENSES	SENTINEL
SEMIOTICS	SEMPSTER	SENHORA	SENSI	SENTINELS
SEMIOVAL	SEMPSTERS	SENHORAS	SENSIBLE	SENTING
SEMIPED	SEMSEM	SENHORES	SENSIBLER	SENTRIES
SEMIPEDS	SEMSEMS	SENHORITA	SENSIBLES	SENTRY
SEMIPIOUS	SEMUNCIA	SENHORS	SENSIBLY	SENTS
SEMIPLUME	SEMUNCIAE	SENILE	SENSILE	SENVIES
SEMIPOLAR	SEMUNCIAL	SENILELY	SENSILLA	SENVY
SEMIPRO	SEMUNCIAS	SENILES	SENSILLAE	SENZA
SEMIPROS	SEN	SENILITY	SENSILLUM	SEPAD
SEMIRAW	SENA	SENIOR	SENSING	SEPADDED
SEMIRIGID	SENARIES	SENIORITY	SENSINGS	SEPADDING
SEMIROUND	SENARII	SENIORS	SENSIS	SEPADS
SEMIRURAL	SENARIUS	SENITI	SENSISM	SEPAL
SEMIS	SENARY	SENNA	SENSISMS	SEPALED
SEMISES	SENAS	SENNACHIE	SENSIST	SEPALINE
SEMISOFT	SENATE	SENNAS	SENSISTS	SEPALLED
SEMISOLID	SENATES	SENNET	SENSITISE	SEPALODY
SEMISOLUS	SENATOR	SENNETS	SENSITIVE	SEPALOID
SEMISTIFF	SENATORS	SENNIGHT	SENSITIZE	SEPALOUS
SEMISWEET	SEND	SENNIGHTS	SENSOR	SEPALS
SEMITAR	SENDABLE	SENNIT	SENSORIA	SEPARABLE
SEMITARS	SENDAL	SENNITS	SENSORIAL	SEPARABLY
SEMITAUR	SENDALS	SENOPIA	SENSORILY	SEPARATA
SEMITAURS	SENDED	SENOPIAS	SENSORIUM	SEPARATE
SEMITIST	SENDER	SENOR	SENSORS	SEPARATED
SEMITISTS	SENDERS	SENORA	SENSORY	SEPARATES
SEMITONAL	SENDING	SENORAS	SENSUAL	SEPARATOR
SEMITONE	SENDINGS	SENORES	SENSUALLY	SEPARATUM
SEMITONES	SENDOFF	SENORITA	SENSUM	SEPHEN
SEMITONIC	SENDOFFS	SENORITAS	SENSUOUS	SEPHENS
SEMITRUCK	SENDS	SENORS	SENT	SEPIA
SEMIURBAN	SENDUP	SENRYU	SENTE	SEPIAS
SEMIVOCAL	SENDUPS	SENS	SENTED	SEPIC
SEMIVOWEL	SENE	SENSA	SENTENCE	SEPIMENT
SEMIWATER	SENECA	SENSATE	SENTENCED	SEPIMENTS
SEMIWILD	SENECAS	SENSATED	SENTENCER	SEPIOLITE
SEMIWORKS	SENECIO	SENSATELY	SENTENCES	SEPIOST
SEMMIT	SENECIOS	SENSATES	SENTENTIA	SEPIOSTS
SEMMITS	SENEGA	SENSATING	SENTI	SEPIUM
SEMOLINA	SENEGAS	SENSATION	SENTIENCE	SEPIUMS
SEMOLINAS	SENES	SENSE	SENTIENCY	SEPMAG
SEMPER	SENESCENT	SENSED	SENTIENT	SEPOY
SEMPLE	SENESCHAL	SENSEFUL	SENTIENTS	SEPOYS
SEMPLER	SENGI	SENSEI	SENTIMENT	SEPPUKU

SEPPUKUS	SEQUELA	SERAPHIN	SERGED	SERIOUSLY
SEPS	SEQUELAE	SERAPHINE	SERGER	SERIPH
SEPSES	SEQUELISE	SERAPHINS	SERGERS	SERIPHS
SEPSIS	SEQUELIZE	SERAPHS	SERGES	SERJEANCY
SEPT	SEQUELS	SERASKIER	SERGING	SERJEANT
SEPTA	SEQUENCE	SERDAB	SERGINGS	SERJEANTS
SEPTAGE	SEQUENCED	SERDABS	SERIAL	SERJEANTY
SEPTAGES	SEQUENCER	SERE	SERIALISE	SERK
SEPTAL	SEQUENCES	SERED	SERIALISM	SERKALI
SEPTARIA	SEQUENCY	SEREIN	SERIALIST	SERKALIS
SEPTARIAN	SEQUENT	SEREINS	SERIALITY	SERKS
SEPTARIUM	SEQUENTLY	SERENADE	SERIALIZE	SERMON
SEPTATE	SEQUENTS	SERENADED	SERIALLY	SERMONED
SEPTATION	SEQUESTER	SERENADER	SERIALS	SERMONEER
SEPTEMFID	SEQUESTRA	SERENADES	SERIATE	SERMONER
SEPTEMVIR	SEQUIN	SERENATA	SERIATED	SERMONERS
SEPTENARY	SEQUINED	SERENATAS	SERIATELY	SERMONET
SEPTENNIA	SEQUINING	SERENATE	SERIATES	SERMONETS
SEPTET	SEQUINNED	SERENATES	SERIATIM	SERMONIC
SEPTETS	SEQUINS	SERENE	SERIATING	SERMONING
SEPTETTE	SEQUITUR	SERENED	SERIATION	SERMONISE
SEPTETTES	SEQUITURS	SERENELY	SERIC	SERMONIZE
SEPTIC	SEQUOIA	SERENER	SERICEOUS	SERMONS
SEPTICAL	SEQUOIAS	SERENES	SERICIN	SEROGROUP
SEPTICITY	SER	SERENEST	SERICINS	SEROLOGIC
SEPTICS	SERA	SERENING	SERICITE	SEROLOGY
SEPTIFORM	SERAC	SERENITY	SERICITES	SERON
SEPTIMAL	SERACS	SERER	SERICITIC	SERONS
SEPTIME	SERAFILE	SERES	SERICON	SEROON
SEPTIMES	SERAFILES	SEREST	SERICONS	SEROONS
SEPTIMOLE	SERAFIN	SERF	SERIEMA	SEROPUS
SEPTLEVA	SERAFINS	SERFAGE	SERIEMAS	SEROPUSES
SEPTLEVAS	SERAGLIO	SERFAGES	SERIES	SEROSA
SEPTS	SERAGLIOS	SERFDOM	SERIF	SEROSAE
SEPTUM	SERAI	SERFDOMS	SERIFED	SEROSAL
SEPTUMS	SERAIL	SERFHOOD	SERIFFED	SEROSAS
SEPTUOR	SERAILS	SERFHOODS	SERIFS	SEROSITY
SEPTUORS	SERAIS	SERFISH	SERIGRAPH	SEROTINAL
SEPTUPLE	SERAL	SERFLIKE	SERIN	SEROTINE
SEPTUPLED	SERANG	SERFS	SERINE	SEROTINES
SEPTUPLES	SERANGS	SERFSHIP	SERINES	SEROTINY
SEPTUPLET	SERAPE	SERFSHIPS	SERINETTE	SEROTONIN
SEPULCHER	SERAPES	SERGE	SERING	SEROTYPE
SEPULCHRE	SERAPH	SERGEANCY	SERINGA	SEROTYPED
SEPULTURE	SERAPHIC	SERGEANT	SERINGAS	SEROTYPES
SEQUACITY	SERAPHIM	SERGEANTS	SERINS	SEROTYPIC
SEQUEL	SERAPHIMS	SERGEANTY	SERIOUS	SEROUS

S

SEROVAR	SERUEWE	SERVOS	SETBACKS	SETWALLS
SEROVARS	SERUEWED	SERVQUAL	SETENANT	SEVEN
SEROW	SERUEWES	SERVQUALS	SETENANTS	SEVENFOLD
SEROWS	SERUEWING	SESAME	SETIFORM	SEVENS
SERPENT	SERUM	SESAMES	SETLINE	SEVENTEEN
SERPENTRY	SERUMAL	SESAMOID	SETLINES	SEVENTH
SERPENTS	SERUMS	SESAMOIDS	SETNESS	SEVENTHLY
SERPIGO	SERVABLE	SESE	SETNESSES	SEVENTHS
SERPIGOES	SERVAL	SESELI	SETOFF	SEVENTIES
SERPIGOS	SERVALS	SESELIS	SETOFFS	SEVENTY
SERPULID	SERVANT	SESEY	SETON	SEVER
SERPULIDS	SERVANTED	SESH	SETONS	SEVERABLE
SERPULITE	SERVANTRY	SESHES	SETOSE	SEVERAL
SERR	SERVANTS	SESS	SETOUS	SEVERALLY
SERRA	SERVE	SESSA	SETOUT	SEVERALS
SERRAE	SERVEABLE	SESSES	SETOUTS	SEVERALTY
SERRAN	SERVED	SESSILE	SETS	SEVERANCE
SERRANID	SERVER	SESSILITY	SETSCREW	SEVERE
SERRANIDS	SERVERIES	SESSION	SETSCREWS	SEVERED
SERRANO	SERVERS	SESSIONAL	SETT	SEVERELY
SERRANOID	SERVERY	SESSIONS	SETTEE	SEVERER
SERRANOS	SERVES	SESSPOOL	SETTEES	SEVEREST
SERRANS	SERVEWE	SESSPOOLS	SETTER	SEVERIES
SERRAS	SERVEWED	SESTERCE	SETTERED	SEVERING
SERRATE	SERVEWES	SESTERCES	SETTERING	SEVERITY
SERRATED	SERVEWING	SESTERTIA	SETTERS	SEVERS
SERRATES	SERVICE	SESTERTII	SETTING	SEVERY
SERRATI	SERVICED	SESTET	SETTINGS	SEVICHE
SERRATING	SERVICER	SESTETS	SETTLE	SEVICHES
SERRATION	SERVICERS	SESTETT	SETTLED	SEVRUGA
SERRATURE	SERVICES	SESTETTE	SETTLER	SEVRUGAS
SERRATUS	SERVICING	SESTETTES	SETTLERS	SEW
SERRE	SERVIENT	SESTETTO	SETTLES	SEWABLE
SERRED	SERVIETTE	SESTETTOS	SETTLING	SEWAGE
SERREFILE	SERVILE	SESTETTS	SETTLINGS	SEWAGES
SERRES	SERVILELY	SESTINA	SETTLOR	SEWAN
SERRICORN	SERVILES	SESTINAS	SETTLORS	SEWANS
SERRIED	SERVILISM	SESTINE	SETTS	SEWAR
SERRIEDLY	SERVILITY	SESTINES	SETUALE	SEWARS
SERRIES	SERVING	SESTON	SETUALES	SEWED
SERRIFORM	SERVINGS	SESTONS	SETULE	SEWEL
SERRING	SERVITOR	SET	SETULES	SEWELLEL
SERRS	SERVITORS	SETA	SETULOSE	SEWELLELS
SERRULATE	SERVITUDE	SETACEOUS	SETULOUS	SEWELS
SERRY	SERVLET	SETAE	SETUP	SEWEN
SERRYING	SERVLETS	SETAL	SETUPS	SEWENS
SERS	SERVO	SETBACK	SETWALL	SEWER

SEWERAGE	SEXTAN	SFERICS	SHADER	SHAGGIEST
SEWERAGES	SEXTANS	SFORZANDI	SHADERS	SHAGGILY
SEWERED	SEXTANSES	SFORZANDO	SHADES	SHAGGING
SEWERING	SEXTANT	SFORZATI	SHADFLIES	SHAGGY
SEWERINGS	SEXTANTAL	SFORZATO	SHADFLY	SHAGPILE
SEWERLESS	SEXTANTS	SFORZATOS	SHADIER	SHAGREEN
SEWERLIKE	SEXTARII	SFUMATO	SHADIEST	SHAGREENS
SEWERS	SEXTARIUS	SFUMATOS	SHADILY	SHAGROON
SEWIN	SEXTET	SGRAFFITI	SHADINESS	SHAGROONS
SEWING	SEXTETS	SGRAFFITO	SHADING	SHAGS
SEWINGS	SEXTETT	SH	SHADINGS	SHAH
SEWINS	SEXTETTE	SHA	SHADKHAN	SHAHADA
SEWN	SEXTETTES	SHABASH	SHADKHANS	SHAHADAS
SEWS	SEXTETTS	SHABBATOT	SHADOOF	SHAHDOM
SEX	SEXTILE	SHABBIER	SHADOOFS	SHAHDOMS
SEXAHOLIC	SEXTILES	SHABBIEST	SHADOW	SHAHEED
SEXED	SEXTO	SHABBILY	SHADOWBOX	SHAHEEDS
SEXENNIAL	SEXTOLET	SHABBLE	SHADOWED	SHAHID
SEXER	SEXTOLETS	SHABBLES	SHADOWER	SHAHIDS
SEXERCISE	SEXTON	SHABBY	SHADOWERS	SHAHS
SEXERS	SEXTONESS	SHABRACK	SHADOWIER	SHAHTOOSH
SEXES	SEXTONS	SHABRACKS	SHADOWILY	SHAIKH
SEXFID	SEXTOS	SHACK	SHADOWING	SHAIKHS
SEXFOIL	SEXTS	SHACKED	SHADOWS	SHAIRD
SEXFOILS	SEXTUOR	SHACKING	SHADOWY	SHAIRDS
SEXIER	SEXTUORS	SHACKLE	SHADRACH	SHAIRN
SEXIEST	SEXTUPLE	SHACKLED	SHADRACHS	SHAIRNS
SEXILY	SEXTUPLED	SHACKLER	SHADS	SHAITAN
SEXINESS	SEXTUPLES	SHACKLERS	SHADUF	SHAITANS
SEXING	SEXTUPLET	SHACKLES	SHADUFS	SHAKABLE
SEXINGS	SEXTUPLY	SHACKLING	SHADY	SHAKE
SEXISM	SEXUAL	SHACKO	SHAFT	SHAKEABLE
SEXISMS	SEXUALISE	SHACKOES	SHAFTED	SHAKED
SEXIST	SEXUALISM	SHACKOS	SHAFTER	SHAKEDOWN
SEXISTS	SEXUALIST	SHACKS	SHAFTERS	SHAKEN
SEXLESS	SEXUALITY	SHAD	SHAFTING	SHAKEOUT
SEXLESSLY	SEXUALIZE	SHADBERRY	SHAFTINGS	SHAKEOUTS
SEXLINKED	SEXUALLY	SHADBLOW	SHAFTLESS	SHAKER
SEXOLOGIC	SEXVALENT	SHADBLOWS	SHAFTS	SHAKERS
SEXOLOGY	SEXY	SHADBUSH	SHAG	SHAKES
SEXPERT	SEY	SHADCHAN	SHAGBARK	SHAKEUP
SEXPERTS	SEYEN	SHADCHANS	SHAGBARKS	SHAKEUPS
SEXPOT	SEYENS	SHADDOCK	SHAGGABLE	SHAKIER
SEXPOTS	SEYS	SHADDOCKS	SHAGGED	SHAKIEST
SEXT	SEYSURE	SHADE	SHAGGER	SHAKILY
SEXTAIN	SEYSURES	SHADED	SHAGGERS	SHAKINESS
SEXTAINS	SEZ	SHADELESS	SHAGGIER	SHAKING

S

SHAKINGS
SHAKO
SHAKOES
SHAKOS
SHAKT
SHAKUDO
SHAKUDOS
SHAKY
SHALE
SHALED
SHALELIKE
SHALES
SHALEY
SHALIER
SHALIEST
SHALING
SHALL
SHALLI
SHALLIS
SHALLON
SHALLONS
SHALLOON
SHALLOONS
SHALLOP
SHALLOPS
SHALLOT
SHALLOTS
SHALLOW
SHALLOWED
SHALLOWER
SHALLOWLY
SHALLOWS
SHALM
SHALMS
SHALOM
SHALOMS
SHALOT
SHALOTS
SHALT
SHALWAR
SHALWARS
SHALY
SHAM
SHAMA
SHAMABLE
SHAMABLY
SHAMAL

SHAMALS
SHAMAN
SHAMANIC
SHAMANISM
SHAMANIST
SHAMANS
SHAMAS
SHAMATEUR
SHAMBA
SHAMBAS
SHAMBLE
SHAMBLED
SHAMBLES
SHAMBLIER
SHAMBLING
SHAMBLY
SHAMBOLIC
SHAME
SHAMEABLE
SHAMEABLY
SHAMED
SHAMEFAST
SHAMEFUL
SHAMELESS
SHAMER
SHAMERS
SHAMES
SHAMIANA
SHAMIANAH
SHAMIANAS
SHAMINA
SHAMINAS
SHAMING
SHAMISEN
SHAMISENS
SHAMMAS
SHAMMASH
SHAMMASIM
SHAMMED
SHAMMER
SHAMMERS
SHAMMES
SHAMMIED
SHAMMIES
SHAMMING
SHAMMOS
SHAMMOSIM

SHAMMY
SHAMMYING
SHAMOIS
SHAMOS
SHAMOSIM
SHAMOY
SHAMOYED
SHAMOYING
SHAMOYS
SHAMPOO
SHAMPOOED
SHAMPOOER
SHAMPOOS
SHAMROCK
SHAMROCKS
SHAMS
SHAMUS
SHAMUSES
SHAN
SHANACHIE
SHAND
SHANDIES
SHANDRIES
SHANDRY
SHANDS
SHANDY
SHANGHAI
SHANGHAIS
SHANK
SHANKBONE
SHANKED
SHANKING
SHANKS
SHANNIES
SHANNY
SHANS
SHANTEY
SHANTEYS
SHANTI
SHANTIES
SHANTIH
SHANTIHS
SHANTIS
SHANTUNG
SHANTUNGS
SHANTY
SHANTYMAN

SHANTYMEN
SHAPABLE
SHAPEABLE
SHAPE
SHAPEABLE
SHAPED
SHAPELESS
SHAPELIER
SHAPELY
SHAPEN
SHAPER
SHAPERS
SHAPES
SHAPEUP
SHAPEUPS
SHAPEWEAR
SHAPING
SHAPINGS
SHAPS
SHARABLE
SHARD
SHARDED
SHARDS
SHARE
SHAREABLE
SHARECROP
SHARED
SHAREMAN
SHAREMEN
SHARER
SHARERS
SHARES
SHARESMAN
SHARESMEN
SHAREWARE
SHARIA
SHARIAH
SHARIAHS
SHARIAS
SHARIAT
SHARIATS
SHARIF
SHARIFIAN
SHARIFS
SHARING
SHARINGS
SHARK
SHARKED

SHARKER
SHARKERS
SHARKING
SHARKINGS
SHARKLIKE
SHARKS
SHARKSKIN
SHARN
SHARNIER
SHARNIEST
SHARNS
SHARNY
SHARON
SHARP
SHARPED
SHARPEN
SHARPENED
SHARPENER
SHARPENS
SHARPER
SHARPERS
SHARPEST
SHARPIE
SHARPIES
SHARPING
SHARPINGS
SHARPISH
SHARPLY
SHARPNESS
SHARPS
SHARPY
SHASH
SHASHED
SHASHES
SHASHING
SHASHLICK
SHASHLIK
SHASHLIKS
SHASLIK
SHASLIKS
SHASTER
SHASTERS
SHASTRA
SHASTRAS
SHAT
SHATOOSH
SHATTER

S

SHATTERED	SHAYAS	SHEAVED	SHEEPCOT	SHEEVES
SHATTERER	SHAYS	SHEAVES	SHEEPCOTE	SHEGETZ
SHATTERS	SHAZAM	SHEAVING	SHEEPCOTS	SHEHITA
SHATTERY	SHCHI	SHEBANG	SHEEPDOG	SHEHITAH
SHAUCHLE	SHCHIS	SHEBANGS	SHEEPDOGS	SHEHITAHS
SHAUCHLED	SHE	SHEBEAN	SHEEPFOLD	SHEHITAS
SHAUCHLES	SHEA	SHEBEANS	SHEEPHEAD	SHEIK
SHAUCHLY	SHEADING	SHEBEEN	SHEEPIER	SHEIKDOM
SHAUGH	SHEADINGS	SHEBEENED	SHEEPIEST	SHEIKDOMS
SHAUGHS	SHEAF	SHEBEENER	SHEEPISH	SHEIKH
SHAUL	SHEAFED	SHEBEENS	SHEEPLE	SHEIKHA
SHAULED	SHEAFIER	SHECHITA	SHEEPLIKE	SHEIKHAS
SHAULING	SHEAFIEST	SHECHITAH	SHEEPMAN	SHEIKHDOM
SHAULS	SHEAFING	SHECHITAS	SHEEPMEN	SHEIKHS
SHAVABLE	SHEAFLIKE	SHED	SHEEPO	SHEIKS
SHAVE	SHEAFS	SHEDABLE	SHEEPOS	SHEILA
SHAVEABLE	SHEAFY	SHEDDABLE	SHEEPSKIN	SHEILAS
SHAVED	SHEAL	SHEDDED	SHEEPWALK	SHEILING
SHAVELING	SHEALED	SHEDDER	SHEEPY	SHEILINGS
SHAVEN	SHEALING	SHEDDERS	SHEER	SHEITAN
SHAVER	SHEALINGS	SHEDDING	SHEERED	SHEITANS
SHAVERS	SHEALS	SHEDDINGS	SHEERER	SHEKALIM
SHAVES	SHEAR	SHEDFUL	SHEEREST	SHEKEL
SHAVETAIL	SHEARED	SHEDFULS	SHEERING	SHEKELIM
SHAVIE	SHEARER	SHEDHAND	SHEERLEG	SHEKELS
SHAVIES	SHEARERS	SHEDHANDS	SHEERLEGS	SHELDDUCK
SHAVING	SHEARING	SHEDLIKE	SHEERLY	SHELDRAKE
SHAVINGS	SHEARINGS	SHEDLOAD	SHEERNESS	SHELDUCK
SHAW	SHEARLEG	SHEDLOADS	SHEERS	SHELDUCKS
SHAWED	SHEARLEGS	SHEDS	SHEESH	SHELF
SHAWING	SHEARLING	SHEEL	SHEESHA	SHELFED
SHAWL	SHEARMAN	SHEELED	SHEESHAS	SHELFFUL
SHAWLED	SHEARMEN	SHEELING	SHEET	SHELFFULS
SHAWLEY	SHEARS	SHEELS	SHEETED	SHELFIER
SHAWLEYS	SHEAS	SHEEN	SHEETER	SHELFIEST
SHAWLIE	SHEATFISH	SHEENED	SHEETERS	SHELFING
SHAWLIES	SHEATH	SHEENEY	SHEETFED	SHELFLIKE
SHAWLING	SHEATHE	SHEENEYS	SHEETIER	SHELFROOM
SHAWLINGS	SHEATHED	SHEENFUL	SHEETIEST	SHELFS
SHAWLLESS	SHEATHER	SHEENIE	SHEETING	SHELFY
SHAWLS	SHEATHERS	SHEENIER	SHEETINGS	SHELL
SHAWM	SHEATHES	SHEENIES	SHEETLESS	SHELLAC
SHAWMS	SHEATHIER	SHEENIEST	SHEETLIKE	SHELLACK
SHAWN	SHEATHING	SHEENING	SHEETROCK	SHELLACKS
SHAWS	SHEATHS	SHEENS	SHEETS	SHELLACS
SHAY	SHEATHY	SHEENY	SHEETY	SHELLBACK
SHAYA	SHEAVE	SHEEP	SHEEVE	SHELLBARK

S

SHELLDUCK	SHEQEL	SHEUGHS	SHIFT	SHIM
SHELLED	SHEQELS	SHEVA	SHIFTABLE	SHIMAAL
SHELLER	SHERANG	SHEVAS	SHIFTED	SHIMAALS
SHELLERS	SHERANGS	SHEW	SHIFTER	SHIMMED
SHELLFIRE	SHERBERT	SHEWBREAD	SHIFTERS	SHIMMER
SHELLFISH	SHERBERTS	SHEWED	SHIFTIER	SHIMMERED
SHELLFUL	SHERBET	SHEWEL	SHIFTIEST	SHIMMERS
SHELLFULS	SHERBETS	SHEWELS	SHIFTILY	SHIMMERY
SHELLIER	SHERD	SHEWER	SHIFTING	SHIMMEY
SHELLIEST	SHERDS	SHEWERS	SHIFTINGS	SHIMMEYS
SHELLING	SHERE	SHEWING	SHIFTLESS	SHIMMIED
SHELLINGS	SHEREEF	SHEWN	SHIFTS	SHIMMIES
SHELLS	SHEREEFS	SHEWS	SHIFTWORK	SHIMMING
SHELLWORK	SHERIA	SHH	SHIFTY	SHIMMY
SHELLY	SHERIAS	SHIAI	SHIGELLA	SHIMMYING
SHELTA	SHERIAT	SHIAIS	SHIGELLAE	SHIMOZZLE
SHELTAS	SHERIATS	SHIATSU	SHIGELLAS	SHIMS
SHELTER	SHERIF	SHIATSUS	SHIITAKE	SHIN
SHELTERED	SHERIFF	SHIATZU	SHIITAKES	SHINBONE
SHELTERER	SHERIFFS	SHIATZUS	SHIKAR	SHINBONES
SHELTERS	SHERIFIAN	SHIBAH	SHIKAREE	SHINDIES
SHELTERY	SHERIFS	SHIBAHS	SHIKAREES	SHINDIG
SHELTIE	SHERLOCK	SHIBUICHI	SHIKARI	SHINDIGS
SHELTIES	SHERLOCKS	SHICKER	SHIKARIS	SHINDY
SHELTY	SHEROOT	SHICKERED	SHIKARRED	SHINDYS
SHELVE	SHEROOTS	SHICKERS	SHIKARS	SHINE
SHELVED	SHERPA	SHICKSA	SHIKKER	SHINED
SHELVER	SHERPAS	SHICKSAS	SHIKKERS	SHINELESS
SHELVERS	SHERRIES	SHIDDER	SHIKSA	SHINER
SHELVES	SHERRIS	SHIDDERS	SHIKSAS	SHINERS
SHELVIER	SHERRISES	SHIDDUCH	SHIKSE	SHINES
SHELVIEST	SHERRY	SHIED	SHIKSEH	SHINESS
SHELVING	SHERWANI	SHIEL	SHIKSEHS	SHINESSES
SHELVINGS	SHERWANIS	SHIELD	SHIKSES	SHINGLE
SHELVY	SHES	SHIELDED	SHILINGI	SHINGLED
SHEMALE	SHET	SHIELDER	SHILL	SHINGLER
SHEMALES	SHETLAND	SHIELDERS	SHILLABER	SHINGLERS
SHEMOZZLE	SHETLANDS	SHIELDING	SHILLALA	SHINGLES
SHEND	SHETS	SHIELDS	SHILLALAH	SHINGLIER
SHENDING	SHETTING	SHIELED	SHILLALAS	SHINGLING
SHENDS	SHEUCH	SHIELING	SHILLELAH	SHINGLY
SHENT	SHEUCHED	SHIELINGS	SHILLING	SHINGUARD
SHEOL	SHEUCHING	SHIELS	SHILLINGS	SHINIER
SHEOLS	SHEUCHS	SHIER	SHILLS	SHINIES
SHEPHERD	SHEUGH	SHIERS	SHILPIT	SHINIEST
SHEPHERDS	SHEUGHED	SHIES	SHILY	SHINILY
SHEQALIM	SHEUGHING	SHIEST		SHININESS

S

SHINING	SHIPPER	SHIRTBAND	SHITTING	SHLOCKY
SHININGLY	SHIPPERS	SHIRTED	SHITTY	SHLOSHIM
SHINJU	SHIPPIE	SHIRTIER	SHITZU	SHLOSHIMS
SHINJUS	SHIPPIES	SHIRTIEST	SHITZUS	SHLUB
SHINKIN	SHIPPING	SHIRTILY	SHIUR	SHLUBS
SHINKINS	SHIPPINGS	SHIRTING	SHIURIM	SHLUMP
SHINLEAF	SHIPPO	SHIRTINGS	SHIV	SHLUMPED
SHINLEAFS	SHIPPON	SHIRTLESS	SHIVA	SHLUMPING
SHINNE	SHIPPONS	SHIRTS	SHIVAH	SHLUMPS
SHINNED	SHIPPOS	SHIRTTAIL	SHIVAHS	SHLUMPY
SHINNERY	SHIPPOUND	SHIRTY	SHIVAREE	SHMALTZ
SHINNES	SHIPS	SHISH	SHIVAREED	SHMALTZES
SHINNEY	SHIPSHAPE	SHISHA	SHIVAREES	SHMALTZY
SHINNEYED	SHIPSIDE	SHISHAS	SHIVAS	SHMATTE
SHINNEYS	SHIPSIDES	SHISO	SHIVE	SHMATTES
SHINNIED	SHIPWAY	SHISOS	SHIVER	SHMEAR
SHINNIES	SHIPWAYS	SHIST	SHIVERED	SHMEARS
SHINNING	SHIPWORM	SHISTS	SHIVERER	SHMEK
SHINNY	SHIPWORMS	SHIT	SHIVERERS	SHMEKS
SHINNYING	SHIPWRECK	SHITAKE	SHIVERIER	SHMO
SHINS	SHIPYARD	SHITAKES	SHIVERING	SHMOCK
SHINTIED	SHIPYARDS	SHITE	SHIVERS	SHMOCKS
SHINTIES	SHIR	SHITED	SHIVERY	SHMOES
SHINTY	SHIRALEE	SHITES	SHIVES	SHMOOSE
SHINTYING	SHIRALEES	SHITFACE	SHIVITI	SHMOOSED
SHINY	SHIRE	SHITFACED	SHIVITIS	SHMOOSES
SHIP	SHIRED	SHITFACES	SHIVOO	SHMOOSING
SHIPBOARD	SHIREMAN	SHITHEAD	SHIVOOS	SHMOOZE
SHIPBORNE	SHIREMEN	SHITHEADS	SHIVS	SHMOOZED
SHIPFUL	SHIRES	SHITHOLE	SHIVVED	SHMOOZER
SHIPFULS	SHIRING	SHITHOLES	SHIVVING	SHMOOZERS
SHIPLAP	SHIRK	SHITHOUSE	SHKOTZIM	SHMOOZES
SHIPLAPS	SHIRKED	SHITING	SHLEMIEHL	SHMOOZIER
SHIPLESS	SHIRKER	SHITLESS	SHLEMIEL	SHMOOZING
SHIPLOAD	SHIRKERS	SHITLIST	SHLEMIELS	SHMOOZY
SHIPLOADS	SHIRKING	SHITLISTS	SHLEP	SHMUCK
SHIPMAN	SHIRKS	SHITLOAD	SHLEPP	SHMUCKS
SHIPMATE	SHIRR	SHITLOADS	SHLEPPED	SHNAPPS
SHIPMATES	SHIRRA	SHITS	SHLEPPER	SHNAPS
SHIPMEN	SHIRRALEE	SHITTAH	SHLEPPERS	SHNOOK
SHIPMENT	SHIRRAS	SHITTAHS	SHLEPPING	SHNOOKS
SHIPMENTS	SHIRRED	SHITTED	SHLEPPS	SHNORRER
SHIPOWNER	SHIRRING	SHITTIER	SHLEPS	SHNORRERS
SHIPPABLE	SHIRRINGS	SHITTIEST	SHLIMAZEL	SHOAL
SHIPPED	SHIRRS	SHITTILY	SHLOCK	SHOALED
SHIPPEN	SHIRS	SHITTIM	SHLOCKIER	SHOALER
SHIPPENS	SHIRT	SHITTIMS	SHLOCKS	SHOALEST

S

SHOALIER	SHOEPACS	SHOOGLES	SHOPMEN	SHORTED
SHOALIEST	SHOER	SHOOGLIER	SHOPPE	SHORTEN
SHOALING	SHOERS	SHOOGLING	SHOPPED	SHORTENED
SHOALINGS	SHOES	SHOOGLY	SHOPPER	SHORTENER
SHOALNESS	SHOESHINE	SHOOING	SHOPPERS	SHORTENS
SHOALS	SHOETREE	SHOOK	SHOPPES	SHORTER
SHOALWISE	SHOETREES	SHOOKS	SHOPPIER	SHORTEST
SHOALY	SHOFAR	SHOOL	SHOPPIEST	SHORTFALL
SHOAT	SHOFARS	SHOOLE	SHOPPING	SHORTGOWN
SHOATS	SHOFROTH	SHOOLED	SHOPPINGS	SHORTHAIR
SHOCHET	SHOG	SHOOLES	SHOPPY	SHORTHAND
SHOCHETIM	SHOGGED	SHOOLING	SHOPS	SHORTHEAD
SHOCHETS	SHOGGING	SHOOLS	SHOPTALK	SHORTHOLD
SHOCK	SHOGGLE	SHOON	SHOPTALKS	SHORTHORN
SHOCKABLE	SHOGGLED	SHOORA	SHOPWOMAN	SHORTIA
SHOCKED	SHOGGLES	SHOORAS	SHOPWOMEN	SHORTIAS
SHOCKER	SHOGGLIER	SHOOS	SHOPWORN	SHORTIE
SHOCKERS	SHOGGLING	SHOOT	SHORAN	SHORTIES
SHOCKING	SHOGGLY	SHOOTABLE	SHORANS	SHORTING
SHOCKS	SHOGI	SHOOTDOWN	SHORE	SHORTISH
SHOD	SHOGIS	SHOOTER	SHOREBIRD	SHORTLIST
SHODDEN	SHOGS	SHOOTERS	SHORED	SHORTLY
SHODDIER	SHOGUN	SHOOTING	SHORELESS	SHORTNESS
SHODDIES	SHOGUNAL	SHOOTINGS	SHORELINE	SHORTS
SHODDIEST	SHOGUNATE	SHOOTIST	SHOREMAN	SHORTSTOP
SHODDILY	SHOGUNS	SHOOTISTS	SHOREMEN	SHORTWAVE
SHODDY	SHOJI	SHOOTOUT	SHORER	SHORTY
SHODER	SHOJIS	SHOOTOUTS	SHORERS	SHOT
SHODERS	SHOLA	SHOOTS	SHORES	SHOTE
SHOE	SHOLAS	SHOP	SHORESIDE	SHOTES
SHOEBILL	SHOLOM	SHOPBOARD	SHORESMAN	SHOTFIRER
SHOEBILLS	SHOLOMS	SHOPBOT	SHORESMEN	SHOTGUN
SHOEBLACK	SHONE	SHOPBOTS	SHOREWARD	SHOTGUNS
SHOEBOX	SHONEEN	SHOPBOY	SHOREWEED	SHOTHOLE
SHOEBOXES	SHONEENS	SHOPBOYS	SHORING	SHOTHOLES
SHOED	SHONKIER	SHOPE	SHORINGS	SHOTMAKER
SHOEHORN	SHONKIEST	SHOPFRONT	SHORL	SHOTPROOF
SHOEHORNS	SHONKY	SHOPFUL	SHORLS	SHOTS
SHOEING	SHOO	SHOPFULS	SHORN	SHOTT
SHOEINGS	SHOOED	SHOPGIRL	SHORT	SHOTTE
SHOELACE	SHOOFLIES	SHOPGIRLS	SHORTAGE	SHOTTED
SHOELACES	SHOOFLY	SHOPHAR	SHORTAGES	SHOTTEN
SHOELESS	SHOOGIE	SHOPHARS	SHORTARM	SHOTTES
SHOEMAKER	SHOOGIED	SHOPHROTH	SHORTARSE	SHOTTING
SHOEPAC	SHOOGIES	SHOPLIFT	SHORTCAKE	SHOTTLE
SHOEPACK	SHOOGLE	SHOPLIFTS	SHORTCUT	SHOTTLES
SHOEPACKS	SHOOGLED	SHOPMAN	SHORTCUTS	SHOTTS

SHOUGH	SHOWCASE	SHOWYARD	SHRIEKIER	SHRITCHES
SHOUGHS	SHOWCASED	SHOWYARDS	SHRIEKING	SHRIVE
SHOULD	SHOWCASES	SHOYU	SHRIEKS	SHRIVED
SHOULDER	SHOWD	SHOYUS	SHRIEKY	SHRIVEL
SHOULDERS	SHOWDED	SHRADDHA	SHRIEVAL	SHRIVELED
SHOULDEST	SHOWDING	SHRADDHAS	SHRIEVE	SHRIVELS
SHOULDST	SHOWDOWN	SHRANK	SHRIEVED	SHRIVEN
SHOUSE	SHOWDOWNS	SHRAPNEL	SHRIEVES	SHRIVER
SHOUSES	SHOWDS	SHRAPNELS	SHRIEVING	SHRIVERS
SHOUT	SHOWED	SHRED	SHRIFT	SHRIVES
SHOUTED	SHOWER	SHREDDED	SHRIFTS	SHRIVING
SHOUTER	SHOWERED	SHREDDER	SHRIGHT	SHRIVINGS
SHOUTERS	SHOWERER	SHREDDERS	SHRIGHTS	SHROFF
SHOUTHER	SHOWERERS	SHREDDIER	SHRIKE	SHROFFAGE
SHOUTHERS	SHOWERFUL	SHREDDING	SHRIKED	SHROFFED
SHOUTIER	SHOWERIER	SHREDDY	SHRIKES	SHROFFING
SHOUTIEST	SHOWERING	SHREDLESS	SHRIKING	SHROFFS
SHOUTING	SHOWERS	SHREDS	SHRILL	SHROOM
SHOUTINGS	SHOWERY	SHREEK	SHRILLED	SHROOMED
SHOUTLINE	SHOWGHE	SHREEKED	SHRILLER	SHROOMER
SHOUTS	SHOWGHES	SHREEKING	SHRILLEST	SHROOMERS
SHOUTY	SHOWGIRL	SHREEKS	SHRILLIER	SHROOMING
SHOVE	SHOWGIRLS	SHREIK	SHRILLING	SHROOMS
SHOVED	SHOWIER	SHREIKED	SHRILLS	SHROUD
SHOVEL	SHOWIEST	SHREIKING	SHRILLY	SHROUDED
SHOVELED	SHOWILY	SHREIKS	SHRIMP	SHROUDIER
SHOVELER	SHOWINESS	SHREW	SHRIMPED	SHROUDING
SHOVELERS	SHOWING	SHREWD	SHRIMPER	SHROUDS
SHOVELFUL	SHOWINGS	SHREWDER	SHRIMPERS	SHROUDY
SHOVELING	SHOWJUMP	SHREWDEST	SHRIMPIER	SHROVE
SHOVELLED	SHOWJUMPS	SHREWDIE	SHRIMPING	SHROVED
SHOVELLER	SHOWMAN	SHREWDIES	SHRIMPS	SHROVES
SHOVELS	SHOWMANLY	SHREWDLY	SHRIMPY	SHROVING
SHOVER	SHOWMEN	SHREWED	SHRINAL	SHROW
SHOVERS	SHOWN	SHREWING	SHRINE	SHROWD
SHOVES	SHOWOFF	SHREWISH	SHRINED	SHROWED
SHOVING	SHOWOFFS	SHREWLIKE	SHRINES	SHROWING
SHOVINGS	SHOWPIECE	SHREWMICE	SHRINING	SHROWS
SHOW	SHOWPLACE	SHREWS	SHRINK	SHRUB
SHOWABLE	SHOWRING	SHRI	SHRINKAGE	SHRUBBED
SHOWBIZ	SHOWRINGS	SHRIECH	SHRINKER	SHRUBBERY
SHOWBIZZY	SHOWROOM	SHRIECHED	SHRINKERS	SHRUBBIER
SHOWBOAT	SHOWROOMS	SHRIECHES	SHRINKING	SHRUBBING
SHOWBOATS	SHOWS	SHRIEK	SHRINKS	SHRUBBY
SHOWBOX	SHOWTIME	SHRIEKED	SHRIS	SHRUBLAND
SHOWBOXES	SHOWTIMES	SHRIEKER	SHRITCH	SHRUBLESS
SHOWBREAD	SHOWY	SHRIEKERS	SHRITCHED	SHRUBLIKE

S

SHRUBS	SHUFFLES	SHUTE	SIALIC	SICCED
SHRUG	SHUFFLING	SHUTED	SIALID	SICCING
SHRUGGED	SHUFTI	SHUTES	SIALIDAN	SICCITIES
SHRUGGING	SHUFTIES	SHUTEYE	SIALIDANS	SICCITY
SHRUGS	SHUFTIS	SHUTEYES	SIALIDS	SICE
SHRUNK	SHUFTY	SHUTING	SIALOGRAM	SICES
SHRUNKEN	SHUGGIES	SHUTOFF	SIALOID	SICH
SHTCHI	SHUGGY	SHUTOFFS	SIALOLITH	SICHT
SHTCHIS	SHUL	SHUTOUT	SIALON	SICHTED
SHTETEL	SHULE	SHUTOUTS	SIALONS	SICHTING
SHTETELS	SHULED	SHUTS	SIALS	SICHTS
SHTETL	SHULES	SHUTTER	SIAMANG	SICILIANA
SHTETLACH	SHULING	SHUTTERED	SIAMANGS	SICILIANE
SHTETLS	SHULN	SHUTTERS	SIAMESE	SICILIANO
SHTICK	SHULS	SHUTTING	SIAMESED	SICK
SHTICKIER	SHUN	SHUTTLE	SIAMESES	SICKBAY
SHTICKS	SHUNLESS	SHUTTLED	SIAMESING	SICKBAYS
SHTICKY	SHUNNABLE	SHUTTLER	SIAMEZE	SICKBED
SHTIK	SHUNNED	SHUTTLERS	SIAMEZED	SICKBEDS
SHTIKS	SHUNNER	SHUTTLES	SIAMEZES	SICKED
SHTOOK	SHUNNERS	SHUTTLING	SIAMEZING	SICKEE
SHTOOKS	SHUNNING	SHVARTZE	SIB	SICKEES
SHTOOM	SHUNPIKE	SHVARTZES	SIBB	SICKEN
SHTUCK	SHUNPIKED	SHWA	SIBBS	SICKENED
SHTUCKS	SHUNPIKER	SHWANPAN	SIBILANCE	SICKENER
SHTUM	SHUNPIKES	SHWANPANS	SIBILANCY	SICKENERS
SHTUMM	SHUNS	SHWAS	SIBILANT	SICKENING
SHTUP	SHUNT	SHWESHWE	SIBILANTS	SICKENS
SHTUPPED	SHUNTED	SHWESHWES	SIBILATE	SICKER
SHTUPPING	SHUNTER	SHY	SIBILATED	SICKERLY
SHTUPS	SHUNTERS	SHYER	SIBILATES	SICKEST
SHUBUNKIN	SHUNTING	SHYERS	SIBILATOR	SICKIE
SHUCK	SHUNTINGS	SHYEST	SIBILOUS	SICKIES
SHUCKED	SHUNTS	SHYING	SIBLING	SICKING
SHUCKER	SHURA	SHYISH	SIBLINGS	SICKISH
SHUCKERS	SHURAS	SHYLOCK	SIBS	SICKISHLY
SHUCKING	SHURIKEN	SHYLOCKED	SIBSHIP	SICKLE
SHUCKINGS	SHURIKENS	SHYLOCKS	SIBSHIPS	SICKLED
SHUCKS	SHUSH	SHYLY	SIBYL	SICKLEMAN
SHUDDER	SHUSHED	SHYNESS	SIBYLIC	SICKLEMEN
SHUDDERED	SHUSHER	SHYNESSES	SIBYLLIC	SICKLEMIA
SHUDDERS	SHUSHERS	SHYPOO	SIBYLLINE	SICKLEMIC
SHUDDERY	SHUSHES	SHYPOOS	SIBYLS	SICKLES
SHUFFLE	SHUSHING	SHYSTER	SIC	SICKLIED
SHUFFLED	SHUT	SHYSTERS	SICCAN	SICKLIER
SHUFFLER	SHUTDOWN	SI	SICCAR	SICKLIES
SHUFFLERS	SHUTDOWNS	SIAL	SICCATIVE	SICKLIEST

SICKLILY	SIDELIGHT	SIDEWALL	SIETH	SIGHTING
SICKLING	SIDELINE	SIDEWALLS	SIETHS	SIGHTINGS
SICKLY	SIDELINED	SIDEWARD	SIEUR	SIGHTLESS
SICKLYING	SIDELINER	SIDEWARDS	SIEURS	SIGHTLIER
SICKNESS	SIDELINES	SIDEWAY	SIEVE	SIGHTLINE
SICKNURSE	SIDELING	SIDEWAYS	SIEVED	SIGHTLY
SICKO	SIDELOCK	SIDEWHEEL	SIEVELIKE	SIGHTS
SICKOS	SIDELOCKS	SIDEWISE	SIEVERT	SIGHTSAW
SICKOUT	SIDELONG	SIDH	SIEVERTS	SIGHTSEE
SICKOUTS	SIDEMAN	SIDHA	SIEVES	SIGHTSEEN
SICKROOM	SIDEMEN	SIDHAS	SIEVING	SIGHTSEER
SICKROOMS	SIDENOTE	SIDHE	SIF	SIGHTSEES
SICKS	SIDENOTES	SIDING	SIFAKA	SIGHTSMAN
SICLIKE	SIDEPATH	SIDINGS	SIFAKAS	SIGHTSMEN
SICS	SIDEPATHS	SIDLE	SIFFLE	SIGIL
SIDA	SIDEPIECE	SIDLED	SIFFLED	SIGILLARY
SIDALCEA	SIDER	SIDLER	SIFFLES	SIGILLATE
SIDALCEAS	SIDERAL	SIDLERS	SIFFLEUR	SIGILS
SIDAS	SIDERATE	SIDLES	SIFFLEURS	SIGISBEI
SIDDHA	SIDERATED	SIDLING	SIFFLEUSE	SIGISBEO
SIDDHAS	SIDERATES	SIDLINGLY	SIFFLING	SIGLA
SIDDHI	SIDEREAL	SIECLE	SIFREI	SIGLAS
SIDDHIS	SIDERITE	SIECLES	SIFT	SIGLOI
SIDDHUISM	SIDERITES	SIEGE	SIFTED	SIGLOS
SIDDUR	SIDERITIC	SIEGED	SIFTER	SIGLUM
SIDDURIM	SIDEROAD	SIEGER	SIFTERS	SIGMA
SIDDURS	SIDEROADS	SIEGERS	SIFTING	SIGMAS
SIDE	SIDEROSES	SIEGES	SIFTINGLY	SIGMATE
SIDEARM	SIDEROSIS	SIEGING	SIFTINGS	SIGMATED
SIDEARMS	SIDEROTIC	SIELD	SIFTS	SIGMATES
SIDEBAND	SIDERS	SIEMENS	SIGANID	SIGMATIC
SIDEBANDS	SIDES	SIEN	SIGANIDS	SIGMATING
SIDEBAR	SIDESHOOT	SIENITE	SIGH	SIGMATION
SIDEBARS	SIDESHOW	SIENITES	SIGHED	SIGMATISM
SIDEBOARD	SIDESHOWS	SIENNA	SIGHER	SIGMATRON
SIDEBONES	SIDESLIP	SIENNAS	SIGHERS	SIGMOID
SIDEBURNS	SIDESLIPS	SIENS	SIGHFUL	SIGMOIDAL
SIDECAR	SIDESMAN	SIENT	SIGHING	SIGMOIDS
SIDECARS	SIDESMEN	SIENTS	SIGHINGLY	SIGN
SIDECHECK	SIDESPIN	SIEROZEM	SIGHLESS	SIGNA
SIDED	SIDESPINS	SIEROZEMS	SIGHLIKE	SIGNABLE
SIDEDNESS	SIDESTEP	SIERRA	SIGHS	SIGNAGE
SIDEDRESS	SIDESTEPS	SIERRAN	SIGHT	SIGNAGES
SIDEHILL	SIDESWIPE	SIERRAS	SIGHTABLE	SIGNAL
SIDEHILLS	SIDETRACK	SIES	SIGHTED	SIGNALED
SIDEKICK	SIDEWALK	SIESTA	SIGHTER	SIGNALER
SIDEKICKS	SIDEWALKS	SIESTAS	SIGHTERS	SIGNALERS

S

SIGNALING	SIGNORIAS	SILENTLY	SILKALINE	SILPHIA
SIGNALISE	SIGNORIES	SILENTS	SILKED	SILPHIUM
SIGNALIZE	SIGNORINA	SILENUS	SILKEN	SILPHIUMS
SIGNALLED	SIGNORINE	SILER	SILKENED	SILT
SIGNALLER	SIGNORINE	SILERS	SILKENING	SILTATION
SIGNALLY	SIGNORINI	SILES	SILKENS	SILTED
SIGNALMAN	SIGNORINO	SILESIA	SILKIE	SILTIER
SIGNALMEN	SIGNORS	SILESIAS	SILKIER	SILTIEST
SIGNALS	SIGNORY	SILEX	SILKIES	SILTING
SIGNARIES	SIGNPOST	SILEXES	SILKIEST	SILTS
SIGNARY	SIGNPOSTS	SILICA	SILKILY	SILTSTONE
SIGNATORY	SIGNS	SILICAS	SILKINESS	SILTY
SIGNATURE	SIJO	SILICATE	SILKING	SILURIAN
SIGNBOARD	SIJOS	SILICATED	SILKLIKE	SILURID
SIGNED	SIK	SILICATES	SILKOLINE	SILURIDS
SIGNEE	SIKA	SILICEOUS	SILKS	SILURIST
SIGNEES	SIKAS	SILICIC	SILKTAIL	SILURISTS
SIGNER	SIKE	SILICIDE	SILKTAILS	SILUROID
SIGNERS	SIKER	SILICIDES	SILKWEED	SILUROIDS
SIGNET	SIKES	SILICIFY	SILKWEEDS	SILVA
SIGNETED	SIKORSKY	SILICIOUS	SILKWORM	SILVAE
SIGNETING	SILAGE	SILICIUM	SILKWORMS	SILVAN
SIGNETS	SILAGED	SILICIUMS	SILKY	SILVANS
SIGNEUR	SILAGEING	SILICLE	SILL	SILVAS
SIGNEURIE	SILAGES	SILICLES	SILLABUB	SILVATIC
SIGNIEUR	SILAGING	SILICON	SILLABUBS	SILVER
SIGNIEURS	SILANE	SILICONE	SILLADAR	SILVERED
SIGNIFICS	SILANES	SILICONES	SILLADARS	SILVERER
SIGNIFIED	SILASTIC	SILICONS	SILLER	SILVERERS
SIGNIFIER	SILASTICS	SILICOSES	SILLERS	SILVEREYE
SIGNIFIES	SILD	SILICOSIS	SILLIBUB	SILVERIER
SIGNIFY	SILDS	SILICOTIC	SILLIBUBS	SILVERING
SIGNING	SILE	SILICULA	SILLIER	SILVERISE
SIGNINGS	SILED	SILICULAE	SILLIES	SILVERIZE
SIGNIOR	SILEN	SILICULAS	SILLIEST	SILVERLY
SIGNIORI	SILENCE	SILICULE	SILLILY	SILVERN
SIGNIORS	SILENCED	SILICULES	SILLINESS	SILVERS
SIGNIORY	SILENCER	SILING	SILLOCK	SILVERY
SIGNLESS	SILENCERS	SILIQUA	SILLOCKS	SILVEX
SIGNOR	SILENCES	SILIQUAE	SILLS	SILVEXES
SIGNORA	SILENCING	SILIQUAS	SILLY	SILVICAL
SIGNORAS	SILENE	SILIQUE	SILO	SILVICS
SIGNORE	SILENES	SILIQUES	SILOED	SILYMARIN
SIGNORES	SILENI	SILIQUOSE	SILOING	SIM
SIGNORI	SILENS	SILIQUOUS	SILOS	SIMA
SIGNORIA	SILENT	SILK	SILOXANE	SIMAR
SIGNORIAL	SILENTER	SILKALENE	SILOXANES	SIMAROUBA

SIMARRE	SIMONIOUS	SIMPLISTS	SINEW	SINHS
SIMARRES	SIMONISE	SIMPLY	SINEWED	SINICAL
SIMARS	SIMONISED	SIMPS	SINEWIER	SINICISE
SIMARUBA	SIMONISES	SIMS	SINEWIEST	SINICISED
SIMARUBAS	SIMONIST	SIMUL	SINEWING	SINICISES
SIMAS	SIMONISTS	SIMULACRA	SINEWLESS	SINICIZE
SIMATIC	SIMONIZE	SIMULACRE	SINEWS	SINICIZED
SIMAZINE	SIMONIZED	SIMULANT	SINEWY	SINICIZES
SIMAZINES	SIMONIZES	SIMULANTS	SINFONIA	SINING
SIMBA	SIMONY	SIMULAR	SINFONIAS	SINISTER
SIMBAS	SIMOOM	SIMULARS	SINFONIE	SINISTRAL
SIMI	SIMOOMS	SIMULATE	SINFUL	SINK
SIMIAL	SIMOON	SIMULATED	SINFULLY	SINKABLE
SIMIAN	SIMOONS	SIMULATES	SING	SINKAGE
SIMIANS	SIMORG	SIMULATOR	SINGABLE	SINKAGES
SIMILAR	SIMORGS	SIMULCAST	SINGALONG	SINKER
SIMILARLY	SIMP	SIMULIUM	SINGE	SINKERS
SIMILE	SIMPAI	SIMULIUMS	SINGED	SINKHOLE
SIMILES	SIMPAIS	SIMULS	SINGEING	SINKHOLES
SIMILISE	SIMPATICO	SIMURG	SINGER	SINKIER
SIMILISED	SIMPER	SIMURGH	SINGERS	SINKIEST
SIMILISES	SIMPERED	SIMURGHS	SINGES	SINKING
SIMILIZE	SIMPERER	SIMURGS	SINGING	SINKINGS
SIMILIZED	SIMPERERS	SIN	SINGINGLY	SINKS
SIMILIZES	SIMPERING	SINAPISM	SINGINGS	SINKY
SIMILOR	SIMPERS	SINAPISMS	SINGLE	SINLESS
SIMILORS	SIMPKIN	SINCE	SINGLED	SINLESSLY
SIMIOID	SIMPKINS	SINCERE	SINGLEDOM	SINNED
SIMIOUS	SIMPLE	SINCERELY	SINGLES	SINNER
SIMIS	SIMPLED	SINCERER	SINGLET	SINNERED
SIMITAR	SIMPLER	SINCEREST	SINGLETON	SINNERING
SIMITARS	SIMPLERS	SINCERITY	SINGLETS	SINNERS
SIMKIN	SIMPLES	SINCIPITA	SINGLING	SINNET
SIMKINS	SIMPLESSE	SINCIPUT	SINGLINGS	SINNETS
SIMLIN	SIMPLEST	SINCIPUTS	SINGLY	SINNING
SIMLINS	SIMPLETON	SIND	SINGS	SINNINGIA
SIMMER	SIMPLEX	SINDED	SINGSONG	SINOLOGUE
SIMMERED	SIMPLEXES	SINDING	SINGSONGS	SINOLOGY
SIMMERING	SIMPLICES	SINDINGS	SINGSONGY	SINOPIA
SIMMERS	SIMPLICIA	SINDON	SINGSPIEL	SINOPIAS
SIMNEL	SIMPLIFY	SINDONS	SINGULAR	SINOPIE
SIMNELS	SIMPLING	SINDS	SINGULARS	SINOPIS
SIMOLEON	SIMPLINGS	SINE	SINGULARY	SINOPISES
SIMOLEONS	SIMPLISM	SINECURE	SINGULT	SINOPITE
SIMONIAC	SIMPLISMS	SINECURES	SINGULTS	SINOPITES
SIMONIACS	SIMPLIST	SINED	SINGULTUS	SINS
SIMONIES	SIMPLISTE	SINES	SINH	SINSYNE

S

SINTER	SIPPLING	SIRONISED	SISTER	SITTELLAS
SINTERED	SIPPY	SIRONISES	SISTERED	SITTEN
SINTERING	SIPS	SIRONIZE	SISTERING	SITTER
SINTERS	SIR	SIRONIZED	SISTERLY	SITTERS
SINTERY	SIRCAR	SIRONIZES	SISTERS	SITTINE
SINUATE	SIRCARS	SIROSET	SISTING	SITTING
SINUATED	SIRDAR	SIRRA	SISTRA	SITTINGS
SINUATELY	SIRDARS	SIRRAH	SISTROID	SITUATE
SINUATES	SIRE	SIRRAHS	SISTRUM	SITUATED
SINUATING	SIRED	SIRRAS	SISTRUMS	SITUATES
SINUATION	SIREE	SIRRED	SISTS	SITUATING
SINUITIS	SIREES	SIRREE	SIT	SITUATION
SINUOSE	SIREN	SIRREES	SITAR	SITULA
SINUOSITY	SIRENIAN	SIRRING	SITARIST	SITULAE
SINUOUS	SIRENIANS	SIRS	SITARISTS	SITUP
SINUOUSLY	SIRENIC	SIRTUIN	SITARS	SITUPS
SINUS	SIRENISE	SIRTUINS	SITATUNGA	SITUS
SINUSES	SIRENISED	SIRUP	SITCOM	SITUSES
SINUSITIS	SIRENISES	SIRUPED	SITCOMS	SITUTUNGA
SINUSLIKE	SIRENIZE	SIRUPIER	SITE	SITZ
SINUSOID	SIRENIZED	SIRUPIEST	SITED	SITZKRIEG
SINUSOIDS	SIRENIZES	SIRUPING	SITELLA	SITZMARK
SIP	SIRENS	SIRUPS	SITELLAS	SITZMARKS
SIPE	SIRES	SIRUPY	SITES	SIVER
SIPED	SIRGANG	SIRVENTE	SITFAST	SIVERS
SIPES	SIRGANGS	SIRVENTES	SITFASTS	SIWASH
SIPHON	SIRI	SIS	SITH	SIWASHED
SIPHONAGE	SIRIASES	SISAL	SITHE	SIWASHES
SIPHONAL	SIRIASIS	SISALS	SITHED	SIWASHING
SIPHONATE	SIRIH	SISERARY	SITHEE	SIX
SIPHONED	SIRIHS	SISES	SITHEN	SIXAIN
SIPHONET	SIRING	SISKIN	SITHENCE	SIXAINE
SIPHONETS	SIRINGS	SISKINS	SITHENS	SIXAINES
SIPHONIC	SIRIS	SISS	SITHES	SIXAINS
SIPHONING	SIRKAR	SISSES	SITHING	SIXER
SIPHONS	SIRKARS	SISSIER	SITING	SIXERS
SIPHUNCLE	SIRLOIN	SISSIES	SITIOLOGY	SIXES
SIPING	SIRLOINS	SISSIEST	SITKA	SIXFOLD
SIPPED	SIRNAME	SISSIFIED	SITKAMER	SIXMO
SIPPER	SIRNAMED	SISSINESS	SITKAMERS	SIXMOS
SIPPERS	SIRNAMES	SISSOO	SITOLOGY	SIXPENCE
SIPPET	SIRNAMING	SISSOOS	SITREP	SIXPENCES
SIPPETS	SIROC	SISSY	SITREPS	SIXPENNY
SIPPING	SIROCCO	SISSYISH	SITS	SIXSCORE
SIPPLE	SIROCCOS	SISSYNESS	SITTAR	SIXSCORES
SIPPLED	SIROCS	SIST	SITTARS	SIXTE
SIPPLES	SIRONISE	SISTED	SITTELLA	SIXTEEN

SIXTEENER	SIZZLINGS	SKATOLE	SKEGGERS	SKENNED
SIXTEENMO	SJAMBOK	SKATOLES	SKEGGS	SKENNING
SIXTEENS	SJAMBOKED	SKATOLS	SKEGS	SKENS
SIXTEENTH	SJAMBOKS	SKATS	SKEIGH	SKEO
SIXTES	SJOE	SKATT	SKEIGHER	SKEOS
SIXTH	SKA	SKATTS	SKEIGHEST	SKEP
SIXTHLY	SKAG	SKAW	SKEIN	SKEPFUL
SIXTHS	SKAGS	SKAWS	SKEINED	SKEPFULS
SIXTIES	SKAIL	SKEAN	SKEINING	SKEPPED
SIXTIETH	SKAILED	SKEANE	SKEINS	SKEPPING
SIXTIETHS	SKAILING	SKEANES	SKELDER	SKEPS
SIXTY	SKAILS	SKEANS	SKELDERED	SKEPSIS
SIXTYISH	SKAITH	SKEAR	SKELDERS	SKEPSISES
SIZABLE	SKAITHED	SKEARED	SKELETAL	SKEPTIC
SIZABLY	SKAITHING	SKEARIER	SKELETON	SKEPTICAL
SIZAR	SKAITHS	SKEARIEST	SKELETONS	SKEPTICS
SIZARS	SKALD	SKEARING	SKELF	SKER
SIZARSHIP	SKALDIC	SKEARS	SKELFS	SKERRED
SIZE	SKALDS	SKEARY	SKELL	SKERRICK
SIZEABLE	SKALDSHIP	SKEDADDLE	SKELLIE	SKERRICKS
SIZEABLY	SKANGER	SKEE	SKELLIED	SKERRIES
SIZED	SKANGERS	SKEECHAN	SKELLIER	SKERRING
SIZEISM	SKANK	SKEECHANS	SKELLIES	SKERRY
SIZEISMS	SKANKED	SKEED	SKELLIEST	SKERS
SIZEIST	SKANKER	SKEEF	SKELLOCH	SKET
SIZEISTS	SKANKERS	SKEEING	SKELLOCHS	SKETCH
SIZEL	SKANKIER	SKEELIER	SKELLS	SKETCHED
SIZELS	SKANKIEST	SKEELIEST	SKELLUM	SKETCHER
SIZER	SKANKING	SKEELY	SKELLUMS	SKETCHERS
SIZERS	SKANKINGS	SKEEN	SKELLY	SKETCHES
SIZES	SKANKS	SKEENS	SKELLYING	SKETCHIER
SIZIER	SKANKY	SKEER	SKELM	SKETCHILY
SIZIEST	SKART	SKEERED	SKELMS	SKETCHING
SIZINESS	SKARTH	SKEERIER	SKELP	SKETCHPAD
SIZING	SKARTHS	SKEERIEST	SKELPED	SKETCHY
SIZINGS	SKARTS	SKEERING	SKELPING	SKETS
SIZISM	SKAS	SKEERS	SKELPINGS	SKETTED
SIZISMS	SKAT	SKEERY	SKELPIT	SKETTING
SIZIST	SKATE	SKEES	SKELPS	SKEW
SIZISTS	SKATED	SKEESICKS	SKELTER	SKEWBACK
SIZY	SKATEPARK	SKEET	SKELTERED	SKEWBACKS
SIZZLE	SKATER	SKEETER	SKELTERS	SKEWBALD
SIZZLED	SKATERS	SKEETERS	SKELUM	SKEWBALDS
SIZZLER	SKATES	SKEETS	SKELUMS	SKEWED
SIZZLERS	SKATING	SKEG	SKEN	SKEWER
SIZZLES	SKATINGS	SKEGG	SKENE	SKEWERED
SIZZLING	SKATOL	SKEGGER	SKENES	SKEWERING

SKEWERS

SKEWERS	SKIEY	SKIMPED	SKIPLANE	SKITTER
SKEWEST	SKIEYER	SKIMPIER	SKIPLANES	SKITTERED
SKEWING	SKIEYEST	SKIMPIEST	SKIPPABLE	SKITTERS
SKEWNESS	SKIFF	SKIMPILY	SKIPPED	SKITTERY
SKEWS	SKIFFED	SKIMPING	SKIPPER	SKITTISH
SKEWWHIFF	SKIFFING	SKIMPS	SKIPPERED	SKITTLE
SKI	SKIFFLE	SKIMPY	SKIPPERS	SKITTLED
SKIABLE	SKIFFLED	SKIMS	SKIPPET	SKITTLES
SKIAGRAM	SKIFFLES	SKIN	SKIPPETS	SKITTLING
SKIAGRAMS	SKIFFLESS	SKINCARE	SKIPPIER	SKIVE
SKIAGRAPH	SKIFFLING	SKINCARES	SKIPPIEST	SKIVED
SKIAMACHY	SKIFFS	SKINFLICK	SKIPPING	SKIVER
SKIASCOPE	SKIING	SKINFLINT	SKIPPINGS	SKIVERED
SKIASCOPY	SKIINGS	SKINFOOD	SKIPPY	SKIVERING
SKIATRON	SKIJORER	SKINFOODS	SKIPS	SKIVERS
SKIATRONS	SKIJORERS	SKINFUL	SKIRL	SKIVES
SKIBOB	SKIJORING	SKINFULS	SKIRLED	SKIVIE
SKIBOBBED	SKILFUL	SKINHEAD	SKIRLING	SKIVIER
SKIBOBBER	SKILFULLY	SKINHEADS	SKIRLINGS	SKIVIEST
SKIBOBS	SKILL	SKINK	SKIRLS	SKIVING
SKID	SKILLED	SKINKED	SKIRMISH	SKIVINGS
SKIDDED	SKILLESS	SKINKER	SKIRR	SKIVVIED
SKIDDER	SKILLET	SKINKERS	SKIRRED	SKIVVIES
SKIDDERS	SKILLETS	SKINKING	SKIRRET	SKIVVY
SKIDDIER	SKILLFUL	SKINKS	SKIRRETS	SKIVVYING
SKIDDIEST	SKILLIER	SKINLESS	SKIRRING	SKIVY
SKIDDING	SKILLIES	SKINLIKE	SKIRRS	SKIWEAR
SKIDDOO	SKILLIEST	SKINNED	SKIRT	SKLATE
SKIDDOOED	SKILLING	SKINNER	SKIRTED	SKLATED
SKIDDOOS	SKILLINGS	SKINNERS	SKIRTER	SKLATES
SKIDDY	SKILLION	SKINNIER	SKIRTERS	SKLATING
SKIDLID	SKILLIONS	SKINNIES	SKIRTING	SKLENT
SKIDLIDS	SKILLS	SKINNIEST	SKIRTINGS	SKLENTED
SKIDOO	SKILLY	SKINNING	SKIRTLESS	SKLENTING
SKIDOOED	SKIM	SKINNY	SKIRTLIKE	SKLENTS
SKIDOOING	SKIMBOARD	SKINS	SKIRTS	SKLIFF
SKIDOOS	SKIMMED	SKINT	SKIS	SKLIFFS
SKIDPAN	SKIMMER	SKINTER	SKIT	SKLIM
SKIDPANS	SKIMMERS	SKINTEST	SKITCH	SKLIMMED
SKIDPROOF	SKIMMIA	SKINTIGHT	SKITCHED	SKLIMMING
SKIDS	SKIMMIAS	SKIO	SKITCHES	SKLIMS
SKIDWAY	SKIMMING	SKIORING	SKITCHING	SKOAL
SKIDWAYS	SKIMMINGS	SKIORINGS	SKITE	SKOALED
SKIED	SKIMO	SKIOS	SKITED	SKOALING
SKIER	SKIMOBILE	SKIP	SKITES	SKOALS
SKIERS	SKIMOS	SKIPJACK	SKITING	SKOFF
SKIES	SKIMP	SKIPJACKS	SKITS	SKOFFED

SKOFFING	SKRIKS	SKUNKING	SKYJACKED	SKYWRITE
SKOFFS	SKRIMMAGE	SKUNKS	SKYJACKER	SKYWRITER
SKOKIAAN	SKRIMP	SKUNKWEED	SKYJACKS	SKYWRITES
SKOKIAANS	SKRIMPED	SKUNKY	SKYLAB	SKYWROTE
SKOL	SKRIMPING	SKURRIED	SKYLABS	SLAB
SKOLIA	SKRIMPS	SKURRIES	SKYLARK	SLABBED
SKOLION	SKRONK	SKURRY	SKYLARKED	SLABBER
SKOLLED	SKRONKS	SKURRYING	SKYLARKER	SLABBERED
SKOLLIE	SKRUMP	SKUTTLE	SKYLARKS	SLABBERER
SKOLLIES	SKRUMPED	SKUTTLED	SKYLESS	SLABBERS
SKOLLING	SKRUMPING	SKUTTLES	SKYLIGHT	SLABBERY
SKOLLY	SKRUMPS	SKUTTLING	SKYLIGHTS	SLABBIER
SKOLS	SKRY	SKY	SKYLIKE	SLABBIEST
SKOOKUM	SKRYER	SKYBOARD	SKYLINE	SLABBING
SKOOL	SKRYERS	SKYBOARDS	SKYLINES	SLABBY
SKOOLS	SKRYING	SKYBORN	SKYLIT	SLABLIKE
SKOOSH	SKUA	SKYBORNE	SKYMAN	SLABS
SKOOSHED	SKUAS	SKYBOX	SKYMEN	SLABSTONE
SKOOSHES	SKUDLER	SKYBOXES	SKYPHOI	SLACK
SKOOSHING	SKUDLERS	SKYBRIDGE	SKYPHOS	SLACKED
SKORT	SKUG	SKYCAP	SKYR	SLACKEN
SKORTS	SKUGGED	SKYCAPS	SKYRE	SLACKENED
SKOSH	SKUGGING	SKYCLAD	SKYRED	SLACKENER
SKOSHES	SKUGS	SKYDIVE	SKYRES	SLACKENS
SKRAN	SKULK	SKYDIVED	SKYRING	SLACKER
SKRANS	SKULKED	SKYDIVER	SKYRMION	SLACKERS
SKREEGH	SKULKER	SKYDIVERS	SKYRMIONS	SLACKEST
SKREEGHED	SKULKERS	SKYDIVES	SKYROCKET	SLACKING
SKREEGHS	SKULKING	SKYDIVING	SKYRS	SLACKLY
SKREEN	SKULKINGS	SKYDOVE	SKYSAIL	SLACKNESS
SKREENS	SKULKS	SKYED	SKYSAILS	SLACKS
SKREIGH	SKULL	SKYER	SKYSCAPE	SLADANG
SKREIGHED	SKULLCAP	SKYERS	SKYSCAPES	SLADANGS
SKREIGHS	SKULLCAPS	SKYEY	SKYSURF	SLADE
SKRIECH	SKULLED	SKYF	SKYSURFED	SLADES
SKRIECHED	SKULLING	SKYFED	SKYSURFER	SLAE
SKRIECHS	SKULLS	SKYFING	SKYSURFS	SLAES
SKRIED	SKULPIN	SKYFS	SKYTE	SLAG
SKRIEGH	SKULPINS	SKYHOME	SKYTED	SLAGGED
SKRIEGHED	SKUMMER	SKYHOMES	SKYTES	SLAGGIER
SKRIEGHS	SKUMMERED	SKYHOOK	SKYTING	SLAGGIEST
SKRIES	SKUMMERS	SKYHOOKS	SKYWALK	SLAGGING
SKRIK	SKUNK	SKYIER	SKYWALKS	SLAGGINGS
SKRIKE	SKUNKBIRD	SKYIEST	SKYWARD	SLAGGY
SKRIKED	SKUNKED	SKYING	SKYWARDS	SLAGS
SKRIKES	SKUNKIER	SKYISH	SKYWAY	SLAID
SKRIKING	SKUNKIEST	SKYJACK	SKYWAYS	SLAIN

SLAINTE	SLANGINGS	SLAT	SLAVOPHIL	SLEEKED
SLAIRG	SLANGISH	SLATCH	SLAW	SLEEKEN
SLAIRGED	SLANGS	SLATCHES	SLAWS	SLEEKENED
SLAIRGING	SLANGUAGE	SLATE	SLAY	SLEEKENS
SLAIRGS	SLANGULAR	SLATED	SLAYABLE	SLEEKER
SLAISTER	SLANGY	SLATELIKE	SLAYED	SLEEKERS
SLAISTERS	SLANK	SLATER	SLAYER	SLEEKEST
SLAISTERY	SLANT	SLATERS	SLAYERS	SLEEKIER
SLAKABLE	SLANTED	SLATES	SLAYING	SLEEKIEST
SLAKE	SLANTER	SLATEY	SLAYS	SLEEKING
SLAKEABLE	SLANTERS	SLATHER	SLEAVE	SLEEKINGS
SLAKED	SLANTIER	SLATHERED	SLEAVED	SLEEKIT
SLAKELESS	SLANTIEST	SLATHERS	SLEAVES	SLEEKLY
SLAKER	SLANTING	SLATIER	SLEAVING	SLEEKNESS
SLAKERS	SLANTLY	SLATIEST	SLEAZE	SLEEKS
SLAKES	SLANTS	SLATINESS	SLEAZEBAG	SLEEKY
SLAKING	SLANTWAYS	SLATING	SLEAZES	SLEEP
SLALOM	SLANTWISE	SLATINGS	SLEAZIER	SLEEPAWAY
SLALOMED	SLANTY	SLATS	SLEAZIEST	SLEEPER
SLALOMER	SLAP	SLATTED	SLEAZILY	SLEEPERS
SLALOMERS	SLAPDASH	SLATTER	SLEAZO	SLEEPERY
SLALOMING	SLAPHAPPY	SLATTERED	SLEAZOID	SLEEPIER
SLALOMIST	SLAPHEAD	SLATTERN	SLEAZOIDS	SLEEPIEST
SLALOMS	SLAPHEADS	SLATTERNS	SLEAZY	SLEEPILY
SLAM	SLAPJACK	SLATTERS	SLEB	SLEEPING
SLAMDANCE	SLAPJACKS	SLATTERY	SLEBS	SLEEPINGS
SLAMMAKIN	SLAPPED	SLATTING	SLED	SLEEPLESS
SLAMMED	SLAPPER	SLATTINGS	SLEDDED	SLEEPLIKE
SLAMMER	SLAPPERS	SLATY	SLEDDER	SLEEPOUT
SLAMMERS	SLAPPING	SLAUGHTER	SLEDDERS	SLEEPOUTS
SLAMMING	SLAPPINGS	SLAVE	SLEDDING	SLEEPOVER
SLAMMINGS	SLAPS	SLAVED	SLEDDINGS	SLEEPRY
SLAMS	SLAPSHOT	SLAVER	SLEDED	SLEEPS
SLANDER	SLAPSHOTS	SLAVERED	SLEDGE	SLEEPSUIT
SLANDERED	SLAPSTICK	SLAVERER	SLEDGED	SLEEPWALK
SLANDERER	SLART	SLAVERERS	SLEDGER	SLEEPWEAR
SLANDERS	SLARTED	SLAVERIES	SLEDGERS	SLEEPY
SLANE	SLARTING	SLAVERING	SLEDGES	SLEER
SLANES	SLARTS	SLAVERS	SLEDGING	SLEEST
SLANG	SLASH	SLAVERY	SLEDGINGS	SLEET
SLANGED	SLASHED	SLAVES	SLEDS	SLEETED
SLANGER	SLASHER	SLAVEY	SLEE	SLEETIER
SLANGERS	SLASHERS	SLAVEYS	SLEECH	SLEETIEST
SLANGIER	SLASHES	SLAVING	SLEECHES	SLEETING
SLANGIEST	SLASHFEST	SLAVISH	SLEECHIER	SLEETS
SLANGILY	SLASHING	SLAVISHLY	SLEECHY	SLEETY
SLANGING	SLASHINGS	SLAVOCRAT	SLEEK	SLEEVE

SLEEVED	SLICKEN	SLIMDOWN	SLINTER	SLIPUPS
SLEEVEEN	SLICKENED	SLIMDOWNS	SLINTERS	SLIPWARE
SLEEVEENS	SLICKENER	SLIME	SLIOTAR	SLIPWARES
SLEEVELET	SLICKENS	SLIMEBALL	SLIOTARS	SLIPWAY
SLEEVER	SLICKER	SLIMED	SLIP	SLIPWAYS
SLEEVERS	SLICKERED	SLIMES	SLIPCASE	SLISH
SLEEVES	SLICKERS	SLIMIER	SLIPCASED	SLISHES
SLEEVING	SLICKEST	SLIMIEST	SLIPCASES	SLIT
SLEEVINGS	SLICKING	SLIMILY	SLIPCOVER	SLITHER
SLEEZIER	SLICKINGS	SLIMINESS	SLIPDRESS	SLITHERED
SLEEZIEST	SLICKLY	SLIMING	SLIPE	SLITHERS
SLEEZY	SLICKNESS	SLIMLINE	SLIPED	SLITHERY
SLEIDED	SLICKROCK	SLIMLY	SLIPES	SLITLESS
SLEIGH	SLICKS	SLIMMED	SLIPFORM	SLITLIKE
SLEIGHED	SLICKSTER	SLIMMER	SLIPFORMS	SLITS
SLEIGHER	SLID	SLIMMERS	SLIPING	SLITTED
SLEIGHERS	SLIDABLE	SLIMMEST	SLIPKNOT	SLITTER
SLEIGHING	SLIDDEN	SLIMMING	SLIPKNOTS	SLITTERS
SLEIGHS	SLIDDER	SLIMMINGS	SLIPLESS	SLITTIER
SLEIGHT	SLIDDERED	SLIMMISH	SLIPNOOSE	SLITTIEST
SLEIGHTS	SLIDDERS	SLIMNESS	SLIPOUT	SLITTING
SLENDER	SLIDDERY	SLIMPSIER	SLIPOUTS	SLITTY
SLENDERER	SLIDE	SLIMPSY	SLIPOVER	SLIVE
SLENDERLY	SLIDED	SLIMS	SLIPOVERS	SLIVED
SLENTER	SLIDER	SLIMSIER	SLIPPAGE	SLIVEN
SLENTERS	SLIDERS	SLIMSIEST	SLIPPAGES	SLIVER
SLEPT	SLIDES	SLIMSY	SLIPPED	SLIVERED
SLEUTH	SLIDEWAY	SLIMY	SLIPPER	SLIVERER
SLEUTHED	SLIDEWAYS	SLING	SLIPPERED	SLIVERERS
SLEUTHING	SLIDING	SLINGBACK	SLIPPERS	SLIVERING
SLEUTHS	SLIDINGLY	SLINGER	SLIPPERY	SLIVERS
SLEW	SLIDINGS	SLINGERS	SLIPPIER	SLIVES
SLEWED	SLIER	SLINGING	SLIPPIEST	SLIVING
SLEWING	SLIEST	SLINGS	SLIPPILY	SLIVOVIC
SLEWS	SLIEVE	SLINGSHOT	SLIPPING	SLIVOVICA
SLEY	SLIEVES	SLINK	SLIPPY	SLIVOVITZ
SLEYS	SLIGHT	SLINKED	SLIPRAIL	SLIVOWITZ
SLICE	SLIGHTED	SLINKER	SLIPRAILS	SLOAN
SLICEABLE	SLIGHTER	SLINKERS	SLIPS	SLOANS
SLICED	SLIGHTERS	SLINKIER	SLIPSHEET	SLOB
SLICER	SLIGHTEST	SLINKIEST	SLIPSHOD	SLOBBER
SLICERS	SLIGHTING	SLINKILY	SLIPSLOP	SLOBBERED
SLICES	SLIGHTISH	SLINKING	SLIPSLOPS	SLOBBERER
SLICING	SLIGHTLY	SLINKS	SLIPSOLE	SLOBBERS
SLICINGS	SLIGHTS	SLINKSKIN	SLIPSOLES	SLOBBERY
SLICK	SLILY	SLINKWEED	SLIPT	SLOBBIER
SLICKED	SLIM	SLINKY	SLIPUP	SLOBBIEST

S

SLOBBISH	SLOOSHING	SLOTTERS	SLUBBED	SLUICIER
SLOBBY	SLOOT	SLOTTING	SLUBBER	SLUICIEST
SLOBLAND	SLOOTS	SLOUCH	SLUBBERED	SLUICING
SLOBLANDS	SLOP	SLOUCHED	SLUBBERS	SLUICY
SLOBS	SLOPE	SLOUCHER	SLUBBIER	SLUING
SLOCKEN	SLOPED	SLOUCHERS	SLUBBIEST	SLUIT
SLOCKENED	SLOPER	SLOUCHES	SLUBBING	SLUITS
SLOCKENS	SLOPERS	SLOUCHIER	SLUBBINGS	SLUM
SLOE	SLOPES	SLOUCHILY	SLUBBS	SLUMBER
SLOEBUSH	SLOPEWISE	SLOUCHING	SLUBBY	SLUMBERED
SLOES	SLOPIER	SLOUCHY	SLUBS	SLUMBERER
SLOETHORN	SLOPIEST	SLOUGH	SLUDGE	SLUMBERS
SLOETREE	SLOPING	SLOUGHED	SLUDGED	SLUMBERY
SLOETREES	SLOPINGLY	SLOUGHI	SLUDGES	SLUMBROUS
SLOG	SLOPPED	SLOUGHIER	SLUDGIER	SLUMBRY
SLOGAN	SLOPPIER	SLOUGHING	SLUDGIEST	SLUMGUM
SLOGANEER	SLOPPIEST	SLOUGHIS	SLUDGING	SLUMGUMS
SLOGANISE	SLOPPILY	SLOUGHS	SLUDGY	SLUMISM
SLOGANIZE	SLOPPING	SLOUGHY	SLUE	SLUMISMS
SLOGANS	SLOPPY	SLOVE	SLUED	SLUMLORD
SLOGGED	SLOPS	SLOVEN	SLUEING	SLUMLORDS
SLOGGER	SLOPWORK	SLOVENLY	SLUES	SLUMMED
SLOGGERS	SLOPWORKS	SLOVENRY	SLUFF	SLUMMER
SLOGGING	SLOPY	SLOVENS	SLUFFED	SLUMMERS
SLOGS	SLORM	SLOW	SLUFFING	SLUMMIER
SLOID	SLORMED	SLOWBACK	SLUFFS	SLUMMIEST
SLOIDS	SLORMING	SLOWBACKS	SLUG	SLUMMING
SLOJD	SLORMS	SLOWCOACH	SLUGABED	SLUMMINGS
SLOJDS	SLOSH	SLOWDOWN	SLUGABEDS	SLUMMOCK
SLOKEN	SLOSHED	SLOWDOWNS	SLUGFEST	SLUMMOCKS
SLOKENED	SLOSHES	SLOWED	SLUGFESTS	SLUMMY
SLOKENING	SLOSHIER	SLOWER	SLUGGABED	SLUMP
SLOKENS	SLOSHIEST	SLOWEST	SLUGGARD	SLUMPED
SLOMMOCK	SLOSHING	SLOWING	SLUGGARDS	SLUMPIER
SLOMMOCKS	SLOSHINGS	SLOWINGS	SLUGGED	SLUMPIEST
SLOOM	SLOSHY	SLOWISH	SLUGGER	SLUMPING
SLOOMED	SLOT	SLOWLY	SLUGGERS	SLUMPS
SLOOMIER	SLOTBACK	SLOWNESS	SLUGGING	SLUMPY
SLOOMIEST	SLOTBACKS	SLOWPOKE	SLUGGISH	SLUMS
SLOOMING	SLOTH	SLOWPOKES	SLUGHORN	SLUNG
SLOOMS	SLOTHED	SLOWS	SLUGHORNE	SLUNGSHOT
SLOOMY	SLOTHFUL	SLOWWORM	SLUGHORNS	SLUNK
SLOOP	SLOTHING	SLOWWORMS	SLUGS	SLUR
SLOOPS	SLOTHS	SLOYD	SLUICE	SLURB
SLOOSH	SLOTS	SLOYDS	SLUICED	SLURBAN
SLOOSHED	SLOTTED	SLUB	SLUICES	SLURBS
SLOOSHES	SLOTTER	SLUBB	SLUICEWAY	SLURP

SLURPED	SLYPES	SMALTS	SMATTERED	SMELLABLE
SLURPER	SMA	SMARAGD	SMATTERER	SMELLED
SLURPERS	SMAAK	SMARAGDE	SMATTERS	SMELLER
SLURPIER	SMAAKED	SMARAGDES	SMAZE	SMELLERS
SLURPIEST	SMAAKING	SMARAGDS	SMAZES	SMELLIER
SLURPING	SMAAKS	SMARM	SMEAR	SMELLIES
SLURPS	SMACK	SMARMED	SMEARCASE	SMELLIEST
SLURPY	SMACKDOWN	SMARMIER	SMEARED	SMELLING
SLURRED	SMACKED	SMARMIEST	SMEARER	SMELLINGS
SLURRIED	SMACKER	SMARMILY	SMEARERS	SMELLS
SLURRIES	SMACKERS	SMARMING	SMEARIER	SMELLY
SLURRING	SMACKHEAD	SMARMS	SMEARIEST	SMELT
SLURRY	SMACKING	SMARMY	SMEARILY	SMELTED
SLURRYING	SMACKINGS	SMART	SMEARING	SMELTER
SLURS	SMACKS	SMARTARSE	SMEARS	SMELTERS
SLUSE	SMAIK	SMARTASS	SMEARY	SMELTERY
SLUSES	SMAIKS	SMARTED	SMEATH	SMELTING
SLUSH	SMALL	SMARTEN	SMEATHS	SMELTINGS
SLUSHED	SMALLAGE	SMARTENED	SMECTIC	SMELTS
SLUSHES	SMALLAGES	SMARTENS	SMECTITE	SMERK
SLUSHIER	SMALLBOY	SMARTER	SMECTITES	SMERKED
SLUSHIES	SMALLBOYS	SMARTEST	SMECTITIC	SMERKING
SLUSHIEST	SMALLED	SMARTIE	SMEDDUM	SMERKS
SLUSHILY	SMALLER	SMARTIES	SMEDDUMS	SMEUSE
SLUSHING	SMALLEST	SMARTING	SMEE	SMEUSES
SLUSHY	SMALLING	SMARTISH	SMEECH	SMEW
SLUT	SMALLISH	SMARTLY	SMEECHED	SMEWS
SLUTCH	SMALLNESS	SMARTNESS	SMEECHES	SMICKER
SLUTCHES	SMALLPOX	SMARTS	SMEECHING	SMICKERED
SLUTCHIER	SMALLS	SMARTWEED	SMEEK	SMICKERS
SLUTCHY	SMALLSAT	SMARTY	SMEEKED	SMICKET
SLUTS	SMALLSATS	SMASH	SMEEKING	SMICKETS
SLUTTERY	SMALLTIME	SMASHABLE	SMEEKS	SMICKLY
SLUTTIER	SMALM	SMASHED	SMEES	SMIDDIED
SLUTTIEST	SMALMED	SMASHER	SMEETH	SMIDDIES
SLUTTILY	SMALMILY	SMASHEROO	SMEETHS	SMIDDY
SLUTTISH	SMALMING	SMASHERS	SMEGMA	SMIDDYING
SLUTTY	SMALMS	SMASHES	SMEGMAS	SMIDGE
SLY	SMALMY	SMASHING	SMEIK	SMIDGEN
SLYBOOTS	SMALT	SMASHINGS	SMEIKED	SMIDGENS
SLYER	SMALTI	SMASHUP	SMEIKING	SMIDGEON
SLYEST	SMALTINE	SMASHUPS	SMEIKS	SMIDGEONS
SLYISH	SMALTINES	SMATCH	SMEKE	SMIDGES
SLYLY	SMALTITE	SMATCHED	SMEKED	SMIDGIN
SLYNESS	SMALTITES	SMATCHES	SMEKES	SMIDGINS
SLYNESSES	SMALTO	SMATCHING	SMEKING	SMIERCASE
SLYPE	SMALTOS	SMATTER	SMELL	SMIGHT

S

SMIGHTING	SMIRTING	SMOKEJACK	SMOOSHES	SMOUSING
SMIGHTS	SMIRTINGS	SMOKELESS	SMOOSHING	SMOUT
SMILAX	SMIT	SMOKELIKE	SMOOT	SMOUTED
SMILAXES	SMITE	SMOKEPOT	SMOOTED	SMOUTING
SMILE	SMITER	SMOKEPOTS	SMOOTH	SMOUTS
SMILED	SMITERS	SMOKER	SMOOTHED	SMOWT
SMILEFUL	SMITES	SMOKERS	SMOOTHEN	SMOWTS
SMILELESS	SMITH	SMOKES	SMOOTHENS	SMOYLE
SMILER	SMITHED	SMOKEY	SMOOTHER	SMOYLED
SMILERS	SMITHERS	SMOKIE	SMOOTHERS	SMOYLES
SMILES	SMITHERY	SMOKIER	SMOOTHES	SMOYLING
SMILET	SMITHIED	SMOKIES	SMOOTHEST	SMRITI
SMILETS	SMITHIES	SMOKIEST	SMOOTHIE	SMRITIS
SMILEY	SMITHING	SMOKILY	SMOOTHIES	SMUDGE
SMILEYS	SMITHS	SMOKINESS	SMOOTHING	SMUDGED
SMILIER	SMITHY	SMOKING	SMOOTHISH	SMUDGEDLY
SMILIEST	SMITHYING	SMOKINGS	SMOOTHLY	SMUDGER
SMILING	SMITING	SMOKO	SMOOTHS	SMUDGERS
SMILINGLY	SMITS	SMOKOS	SMOOTHY	SMUDGES
SMILINGS	SMITTED	SMOKY	SMOOTING	SMUDGIER
SMILODON	SMITTEN	SMOLDER	SMOOTS	SMUDGIEST
SMILODONS	SMITTING	SMOLDERED	SMORBROD	SMUDGILY
SMIR	SMITTLE	SMOLDERS	SMORBRODS	SMUDGING
SMIRCH	SMOCK	SMOLT	SMORE	SMUDGINGS
SMIRCHED	SMOCKED	SMOLTS	SMORED	SMUDGY
SMIRCHER	SMOCKING	SMOOCH	SMORES	SMUG
SMIRCHERS	SMOCKINGS	SMOOCHED	SMORING	SMUGGED
SMIRCHES	SMOCKLIKE	SMOOCHER	SMORZANDO	SMUGGER
SMIRCHING	SMOCKS	SMOOCHERS	SMORZATO	SMUGGERY
SMIRK	SMOG	SMOOCHES	SMOTE	SMUGGEST
SMIRKED	SMOGGIER	SMOOCHIER	SMOTHER	SMUGGING
SMIRKER	SMOGGIEST	SMOOCHING	SMOTHERED	SMUGGLE
SMIRKERS	SMOGGY	SMOOCHY	SMOTHERER	SMUGGLED
SMIRKIER	SMOGLESS	SMOODGE	SMOTHERS	SMUGGLER
SMIRKIEST	SMOGS	SMOODGED	SMOTHERY	SMUGGLERS
SMIRKILY	SMOILE	SMOODGES	SMOUCH	SMUGGLES
SMIRKING	SMOILED	SMOODGING	SMOUCHED	SMUGGLING
SMIRKS	SMOILES	SMOOGE	SMOUCHES	SMUGLY
SMIRKY	SMOILING	SMOOGED	SMOUCHING	SMUGNESS
SMIRR	SMOKABLE	SMOOGES	SMOULDER	SMUGS
SMIRRED	SMOKE	SMOOGING	SMOULDERS	SMUR
SMIRRIER	SMOKEABLE	SMOOR	SMOULDRY	SMURFING
SMIRRIEST	SMOKEBOX	SMOORED	SMOUSE	SMURFINGS
SMIRRING	SMOKED	SMOORING	SMOUSED	SMURRED
SMIRRS	SMOKEHO	SMOORS	SMOUSER	SMURRIER
SMIRRY	SMOKEHOOD	SMOOSH	SMOUSERS	SMURRIEST
SMIRS	SMOKEHOS	SMOOSHED	SMOUSES	SMURRING

S

SMURRY	SNAGGING	SNAPPER	SNARLY	SNEAKSBY
SMURS	SNAGGY	SNAPPERED	SNARRED	SNEAKY
SMUSH	SNAGLIKE	SNAPPERS	SNARRING	SNEAP
SMUSHED	SNAGS	SNAPPIER	SNARS	SNEAPED
SMUSHES	SNAIL	SNAPPIEST	SNARY	SNEAPING
SMUSHING	SNAILED	SNAPPILY	SNASH	SNEAPS
SMUT	SNAILERY	SNAPPING	SNASHED	SNEATH
SMUTCH	SNAILFISH	SNAPPINGS	SNASHES	SNEATHS
SMUTCHED	SNAILIER	SNAPPISH	SNASHING	SNEB
SMUTCHES	SNAILIEST	SNAPPY	SNASTE	SNEBBE
SMUTCHIER	SNAILING	SNAPS	SNASTES	SNEBBED
SMUTCHING	SNAILLIKE	SNAPSHOT	SNATCH	SNEBBES
SMUTCHY	SNAILS	SNAPSHOTS	SNATCHED	SNEBBING
SMUTS	SNAILY	SNAPTIN	SNATCHER	SNEBS
SMUTTED	SNAKE	SNAPTINS	SNATCHERS	SNECK
SMUTTIER	SNAKEBIRD	SNAPWEED	SNATCHES	SNECKED
SMUTTIEST	SNAKEBIT	SNAPWEEDS	SNATCHIER	SNECKING
SMUTTILY	SNAKEBITE	SNAR	SNATCHILY	SNECKS
SMUTTING	SNAKED	SNARE	SNATCHING	SNED
SMUTTY	SNAKEFISH	SNARED	SNATCHY	SNEDDED
SMYTRIE	SNAKEHEAD	SNARELESS	SNATH	SNEDDING
SMYTRIES	SNAKELIKE	SNARER	SNATHE	SNEDS
SNAB	SNAKEPIT	SNARERS	SNATHES	SNEE
SNABBLE	SNAKEPITS	SNARES	SNATHS	SNEED
SNABBLED	SNAKEROOT	SNARF	SNAW	SNEEING
SNABBLES	SNAKES	SNARFED	SNAWED	SNEER
SNABBLING	SNAKESKIN	SNARFING	SNAWING	SNEERED
SNABS	SNAKEWEED	SNARFS	SNAWS	SNEERER
SNACK	SNAKEWISE	SNARIER	SNAZZIER	SNEERERS
SNACKED	SNAKEWOOD	SNARIEST	SNAZZIEST	SNEERFUL
SNACKER	SNAKEY	SNARING	SNAZZILY	SNEERIER
SNACKERS	SNAKIER	SNARINGS	SNAZZY	SNEERIEST
SNACKETTE	SNAKIEST	SNARK	SNEAD	SNEERING
SNACKING	SNAKILY	SNARKIER	SNEADS	SNEERINGS
SNACKS	SNAKINESS	SNARKIEST	SNEAK	SNEERS
SNAFFLE	SNAKING	SNARKILY	SNEAKED	SNEERY
SNAFFLED	SNAKISH	SNARKS	SNEAKER	SNEES
SNAFFLES	SNAKY	SNARKY	SNEAKERED	SNEESH
SNAFFLING	SNAP	SNARL	SNEAKERS	SNEESHAN
SNAFU	SNAPBACK	SNARLED	SNEAKEUP	SNEESHANS
SNAFUED	SNAPBACKS	SNARLER	SNEAKEUPS	SNEESHES
SNAFUING	SNAPHANCE	SNARLERS	SNEAKIER	SNEESHIN
SNAFUS	SNAPLESS	SNARLIER	SNEAKIEST	SNEESHING
SNAG	SNAPLINK	SNARLIEST	SNEAKILY	SNEESHINS
SNAGGED	SNAPLINKS	SNARLING	SNEAKING	SNEEZE
SNAGGIER	SNAPPABLE	SNARLINGS	SNEAKISH	SNEEZED
SNAGGIEST	SNAPPED	SNARLS	SNEAKS	SNEEZER

S

SNEEZERS	SNIFFIEST	SNIPERS	SNOBBIER	SNOOPIER
SNEEZES	SNIFFILY	SNIPES	SNOBBIEST	SNOOPIEST
SNEEZIER	SNIFFING	SNIPIER	SNOBBILY	SNOOPILY
SNEEZIEST	SNIFFINGS	SNIPIEST	SNOBBISH	SNOOPING
SNEEZING	SNIFFISH	SNIPING	SNOBBISM	SNOOPS
SNEEZINGS	SNIFFLE	SNIPINGS	SNOBBISMS	SNOOPY
SNEEZY	SNIFFLED	SNIPPED	SNOBBY	SNOOT
SNELL	SNIFFLER	SNIPPER	SNOBLING	SNOOTED
SNELLED	SNIFFLERS	SNIPPERS	SNOBLINGS	SNOOTFUL
SNELLER	SNIFFLES	SNIPPET	SNOBS	SNOOTFULS
SNELLEST	SNIFFLIER	SNIPPETS	SNOD	SNOOTIER
SNELLING	SNIFFLING	SNIPPETY	SNODDED	SNOOTIEST
SNELLS	SNIFFLY	SNIPPIER	SNODDER	SNOOTILY
SNELLY	SNIFFS	SNIPPIEST	SNODDEST	SNOOTING
SNIB	SNIFFY	SNIPPILY	SNODDING	SNOOTS
SNIBBED	SNIFT	SNIPPING	SNODDIT	SNOOTY
SNIBBING	SNIFTED	SNIPPINGS	SNODS	SNOOZE
SNIBS	SNIFTER	SNIPPY	SNOEK	SNOOZED
SNICK	SNIFTERED	SNIPS	SNOEKS	SNOOZER
SNICKED	SNIFTERS	SNIPY	SNOEP	SNOOZERS
SNICKER	SNIFTIER	SNIRT	SNOG	SNOOZES
SNICKERED	SNIFTIEST	SNIRTLE	SNOGGED	SNOOZIER
SNICKERER	SNIFTING	SNIRTLED	SNOGGING	SNOOZIEST
SNICKERS	SNIFTS	SNIRTLES	SNOGS	SNOOZING
SNICKERY	SNIFTY	SNIRTLING	SNOKE	SNOOZLE
SNICKET	SNIG	SNIRTS	SNOKED	SNOOZLED
SNICKETS	SNIGGED	SNIT	SNOKES	SNOOZLES
SNICKING	SNIGGER	SNITCH	SNOKING	SNOOZLING
SNICKS	SNIGGERED	SNITCHED	SNOOD	SNOOZY
SNIDE	SNIGGERER	SNITCHER	SNOODED	SNORE
SNIDED	SNIGGERS	SNITCHERS	SNOODING	SNORED
SNIDELY	SNIGGING	SNITCHES	SNOODS	SNORER
SNIDENESS	SNIGGLE	SNITCHIER	SNOOK	SNORERS
SNIDER	SNIGGLED	SNITCHING	SNOOKED	SNORES
SNIDES	SNIGGLER	SNITCHY	SNOOKER	SNORING
SNIDEST	SNIGGLERS	SNITS	SNOOKERED	SNORINGS
SNIDEY	SNIGGLES	SNIVEL	SNOOKERS	SNORKEL
SNIDIER	SNIGGLING	SNIVELED	SNOOKING	SNORKELED
SNIDIEST	SNIGLET	SNIVELER	SNOOKS	SNORKELER
SNIDING	SNIGLETS	SNIVELERS	SNOOL	SNORKELS
SNIES	SNIGS	SNIVELING	SNOOLED	SNORT
SNIFF	SNIP	SNIVELLED	SNOOLING	SNORTED
SNIFFABLE	SNIPE	SNIVELLER	SNOOLS	SNORTER
SNIFFED	SNIPED	SNIVELLY	SNOOP	SNORTERS
SNIFFER	SNIPEFISH	SNIVELS	SNOOPED	SNORTIER
SNIFFERS	SNIPELIKE	SNOB	SNOOPER	SNORTIEST
SNIFFIER	SNIPER	SNOBBERY	SNOOPERS	SNORTING

SNORTINGS	SNOWBUSH	SNOWSCAPE	SNUFFLERS	SOAP
SNORTS	SNOWCAP	SNOWSHED	SNUFFLES	SOAPBARK
SNORTY	SNOWCAPS	SNOWSHEDS	SNUFFLIER	SOAPBARKS
SNOT	SNOWCAT	SNOWSHOE	SNUFFLING	SOAPBERRY
SNOTRAG	SNOWCATS	SNOWSHOED	SNUFFLY	SOAPBOX
SNOTRAGS	SNOWCLONE	SNOWSHOER	SNUFFS	SOAPBOXED
SNOTS	SNOWDOME	SNOWSHOES	SNUFFY	SOAPBOXES
SNOTTED	SNOWDOMES	SNOWSLIDE	SNUG	SOAPED
SNOTTER	SNOWDRIFT	SNOWSLIP	SNUGGED	SOAPER
SNOTTERED	SNOWDROP	SNOWSLIPS	SNUGGER	SOAPERS
SNOTTERS	SNOWDROPS	SNOWSTORM	SNUGGERIE	SOAPIE
SNOTTERY	SNOWED	SNOWSUIT	SNUGGERY	SOAPIER
SNOTTIE	SNOWFALL	SNOWSUITS	SNUGGEST	SOAPIES
SNOTTIER	SNOWFALLS	SNOWY	SNUGGIES	SOAPIEST
SNOTTIES	SNOWFIELD	SNUB	SNUGGING	SOAPILY
SNOTTIEST	SNOWFLAKE	SNUBBE	SNUGGLE	SOAPINESS
SNOTTILY	SNOWFLECK	SNUBBED	SNUGGLED	SOAPING
SNOTTING	SNOWFLICK	SNUBBER	SNUGGLES	SOAPLAND
SNOTTY	SNOWGLOBE	SNUBBERS	SNUGGLING	SOAPLANDS
SNOUT	SNOWIER	SNUBBES	SNUGLY	SOAPLESS
SNOUTED	SNOWIEST	SNUBBIER	SNUGNESS	SOAPLIKE
SNOUTIER	SNOWILY	SNUBBIEST	SNUGS	SOAPROOT
SNOUTIEST	SNOWINESS	SNUBBING	SNUSH	SOAPROOTS
SNOUTING	SNOWING	SNUBBINGS	SNUSHED	SOAPS
SNOUTISH	SNOWISH	SNUBBISH	SNUSHES	SOAPSTONE
SNOUTLESS	SNOWK	SNUBBY	SNUSHING	SOAPSUDS
SNOUTLIKE	SNOWKED	SNUBFIN	SNUZZLE	SOAPSUDSY
SNOUTS	SNOWKING	SNUBNESS	SNUZZLED	SOAPWORT
SNOUTY	SNOWKS	SNUBS	SNUZZLES	SOAPWORTS
SNOW	SNOWLAND	SNUCK	SNUZZLING	SOAPY
SNOWBALL	SNOWLANDS	SNUDGE	SNY	SOAR
SNOWBALLS	SNOWLESS	SNUDGED	SNYE	SOARAWAY
SNOWBANK	SNOWLIKE	SNUDGES	SNYES	SOARE
SNOWBANKS	SNOWLINE	SNUDGING	SO	SOARED
SNOWBELL	SNOWLINES	SNUFF	SOAK	SOARER
SNOWBELLS	SNOWMAKER	SNUFFBOX	SOAKAGE	SOARERS
SNOWBELT	SNOWMAN	SNUFFED	SOAKAGES	SOARES
SNOWBELTS	SNOWMELT	SNUFFER	SOAKAWAY	SOARING
SNOWBERRY	SNOWMELTS	SNUFFERS	SOAKAWAYS	SOARINGLY
SNOWBIRD	SNOWMEN	SNUFFIER	SOAKED	SOARINGS
SNOWBIRDS	SNOWMOLD	SNUFFIEST	SOAKEN	SOARS
SNOWBLINK	SNOWMOLDS	SNUFFILY	SOAKER	SOAVE
SNOWBOARD	SNOWPACK	SNUFFING	SOAKERS	SOAVES
SNOWBOOT	SNOWPACKS	SNUFFINGS	SOAKING	SOB
SNOWBOOTS	SNOWPLOW	SNUFFLE	SOAKINGLY	SOBA
SNOWBOUND	SNOWPLOWS	SNUFFLED	SOAKINGS	SOBAS
SNOWBRUSH	SNOWS	SNUFFLER	SOAKS	SOBBED

S

SOBBER	SOCIALLY	SODAS	SOFT	SOGGY
SOBBERS	SOCIALS	SODBUSTER	SOFTA	SOGS
SOBBING	SOCIATE	SODDED	SOFTAS	SOH
SOBBINGLY	SOCIATES	SODDEN	SOFTBACK	SOHO
SOBBINGS	SOCIATION	SODDENED	SOFTBACKS	SOHS
SOBEIT	SOCIATIVE	SODDENING	SOFTBALL	SOHUR
SOBER	SOCIETAL	SODDENLY	SOFTBALLS	SOHURS
SOBERED	SOCIETIES	SODDENS	SOFTBOUND	SOIGNE
SOBERER	SOCIETY	SODDIER	SOFTCORE	SOIGNEE
SOBEREST	SOCIOGRAM	SODDIES	SOFTCOVER	SOIL
SOBERING	SOCIOLECT	SODDIEST	SOFTED	SOILAGE
SOBERISE	SOCIOLOGY	SODDING	SOFTEN	SOILAGES
SOBERISED	SOCIOPATH	SODDY	SOFTENED	SOILBORNE
SOBERISES	SOCK	SODGER	SOFTENER	SOILED
SOBERIZE	SOCKED	SODGERED	SOFTENERS	SOILIER
SOBERIZED	SOCKET	SODGERING	SOFTENING	SOILIEST
SOBERIZES	SOCKETED	SODGERS	SOFTENS	SOILINESS
SOBERLY	SOCKETING	SODIC	SOFTER	SOILING
SOBERNESS	SOCKETS	SODICITY	SOFTEST	SOILINGS
SOBERS	SOCKETTE	SODIUM	SOFTGOODS	SOILLESS
SOBFUL	SOCKETTES	SODIUMS	SOFTHEAD	SOILS
SOBOLE	SOCKEYE	SODOM	SOFTHEADS	SOILURE
SOBOLES	SOCKEYES	SODOMIES	SOFTIE	SOILURES
SOBRIETY	SOCKING	SODOMISE	SOFTIES	SOILY
SOBRIQUET	SOCKLESS	SODOMISED	SOFTING	SOIREE
SOBS	SOCKMAN	SODOMISES	SOFTISH	SOIREES
SOC	SOCKMEN	SODOMIST	SOFTLING	SOJA
SOCA	SOCKO	SODOMISTS	SOFTLINGS	SOJAS
SOCAGE	SOCKS	SODOMITE	SOFTLY	SOJOURN
SOCAGER	SOCLE	SODOMITES	SOFTNESS	SOJOURNED
SOCAGERS	SOCLES	SODOMITIC	SOFTS	SOJOURNER
SOCAGES	SOCMAN	SODOMIZE	SOFTSHELL	SOJOURNS
SOCAS	SOCMEN	SODOMIZED	SOFTWARE	SOKAH
SOCCAGE	SOCS	SODOMIZES	SOFTWARES	SOKAHS
SOCCAGES	SOD	SODOMS	SOFTWOOD	SOKAIYA
SOCCER	SODA	SODOMY	SOFTWOODS	SOKE
SOCCERS	SODAIC	SODS	SOFTY	SOKEMAN
SOCIABLE	SODAIN	SOEVER	SOG	SOKEMANRY
SOCIABLES	SODAINE	SOFA	SOGER	SOKEMEN
SOCIABLY	SODALESS	SOFABED	SOGERS	SOKEN
SOCIAL	SODALIST	SOFABEDS	SOGGED	SOKENS
SOCIALISE	SODALISTS	SOFAR	SOGGIER	SOKES
SOCIALISM	SODALITE	SOFARS	SOGGIEST	SOKOL
SOCIALIST	SODALITES	SOFAS	SOGGILY	SOKOLS
SOCIALITE	SODALITY	SOFFIONI	SOGGINESS	SOL
SOCIALITY	SODAMIDE	SOFFIT	SOGGING	SOLA
SOCIALIZE	SODAMIDES	SOFFITS	SOGGINGS	SOLACE

SOLACED	SOLDADO	SOLENODON	SOLIDNESS	SOLSTICES
SOLACER	SOLDADOS	SOLENOID	SOLIDS	SOLUBLE
SOLACERS	SOLDAN	SOLENOIDS	SOLIDUM	SOLUBLES
SOLACES	SOLDANS	SOLEPLATE	SOLIDUMS	SOLUBLY
SOLACING	SOLDE	SOLEPRINT	SOLIDUS	SOLUM
SOLACIOUS	SOLDER	SOLER	SOLILOQUY	SOLUMS
SOLAH	SOLDERED	SOLERA	SOLING	SOLUNAR
SOLAHS	SOLDERER	SOLERAS	SOLION	SOLUS
SOLAN	SOLDERERS	SOLERET	SOLIONS	SOLUTAL
SOLAND	SOLDERING	SOLERETS	SOLIPED	SOLUTE
SOLANDER	SOLDERS	SOLERS	SOLIPEDS	SOLUTES
SOLANDERS	SOLDES	SOLES	SOLIPSISM	SOLUTION
SOLANDS	SOLDI	SOLEUS	SOLIPSIST	SOLUTIONS
SOLANIN	SOLDIER	SOLEUSES	SOLIQUID	SOLUTIVE
SOLANINE	SOLDIERED	SOLFATARA	SOLIQUIDS	SOLVABLE
SOLANINES	SOLDIERLY	SOLFEGE	SOLITAIRE	SOLVATE
SOLANINS	SOLDIERS	SOLFEGES	SOLITARY	SOLVATED
SOLANO	SOLDIERY	SOLFEGGI	SOLITO	SOLVATES
SOLANOS	SOLDO	SOLFEGGIO	SOLITON	SOLVATING
SOLANS	SOLDS	SOLFERINO	SOLITONS	SOLVATION
SOLANUM	SOLE	SOLGEL	SOLITUDE	SOLVE
SOLANUMS	SOLECISE	SOLI	SOLITUDES	SOLVED
SOLAR	SOLECISED	SOLICIT	SOLIVE	SOLVENCY
SOLARIA	SOLECISES	SOLICITED	SOLIVES	SOLVENT
SOLARISE	SOLECISM	SOLICITOR	SOLLAR	SOLVENTLY
SOLARISED	SOLECISMS	SOLICITS	SOLLARS	SOLVENTS
SOLARISES	SOLECIST	SOLICITY	SOLLER	SOLVER
SOLARISM	SOLECISTS	SOLID	SOLLERET	SOLVERS
SOLARISMS	SOLECIZE	SOLIDAGO	SOLLERETS	SOLVES
SOLARIST	SOLECIZED	SOLIDAGOS	SOLLERS	SOLVING
SOLARISTS	SOLECIZES	SOLIDARE	SOLLICKER	SOM
SOLARIUM	SOLED	SOLIDARES	SOLO	SOMA
SOLARIUMS	SOLEI	SOLIDARY	SOLOED	SOMAN
SOLARIZE	SOLEIN	SOLIDATE	SOLOING	SOMANS
SOLARIZED	SOLELESS	SOLIDATED	SOLOIST	SOMAS
SOLARIZES	SOLELY	SOLIDATES	SOLOISTIC	SOMASCOPE
SOLARS	SOLEMN	SOLIDER	SOLOISTS	SOMATA
SOLAS	SOLEMNER	SOLIDEST	SOLON	SOMATIC
SOLATE	SOLEMNESS	SOLIDI	SOLONCHAK	SOMATISM
SOLATED	SOLEMNEST	SOLIDIFY	SOLONETS	SOMATISMS
SOLATES	SOLEMNIFY	SOLIDISH	SOLONETZ	SOMATIST
SOLATIA	SOLEMNISE	SOLIDISM	SOLONS	SOMATISTS
SOLATING	SOLEMNITY	SOLIDISMS	SOLOS	SOMBER
SOLATION	SOLEMNIZE	SOLIDIST	SOLPUGID	SOMBERED
SOLATIONS	SOLEMNLY	SOLIDISTS	SOLPUGIDS	SOMBERER
SOLATIUM	SOLENESS	SOLIDITY	SOLS	SOMBEREST
SOLD	SOLENETTE	SOLIDLY	SOLSTICE	SOMBERING

S

SOMBERLY	SOMONI	SONGLESS	SONSE	SOOPSTAKE
SOMBERS	SOMS	SONGLIKE	SONSES	SOOT
SOMBRE	SOMY	SONGMAN	SONSHIP	SOOTE
SOMBRED	SON	SONGMEN	SONSHIPS	SOOTED
SOMBRELY	SONANCE	SONGOLOLO	SONSIE	SOOTERKIN
SOMBRER	SONANCES	SONGS	SONSIER	SOOTES
SOMBRERO	SONANCIES	SONGSMITH	SONSIEST	SOOTFLAKE
SOMBREROS	SONANCY	SONGSTER	SONSY	SOOTH
SOMBRES	SONANT	SONGSTERS	SONTAG	SOOTHE
SOMBREST	SONANTAL	SONHOOD	SONTAGS	SOOTHED
SOMBRING	SONANTIC	SONHOODS	SONTIES	SOOTHER
SOMBROUS	SONANTS	SONIC	SOOCHONG	SOOTHERED
SOME	SONAR	SONICALLY	SOOCHONGS	SOOTHERS
SOMEBODY	SONARMAN	SONICATE	SOOEY	SOOTHES
SOMEDAY	SONARMEN	SONICATED	SOOGEE	SOOTHEST
SOMEDEAL	SONARS	SONICATES	SOOGEED	SOOTHFAST
SOMEDELE	SONATA	SONICATOR	SOOGEEING	SOOTHFUL
SOMEGATE	SONATAS	SONICS	SOOGEES	SOOTHING
SOMEHOW	SONATINA	SONLESS	SOOGIE	SOOTHINGS
SOMEONE	SONATINAS	SONLIKE	SOOGIED	SOOTHLICH
SOMEONES	SONATINE	SONLY	SOOGIEING	SOOTHLY
SOMEPLACE	SONCE	SONNE	SOOGIES	SOOTHS
SOMERSET	SONCES	SONNES	SOOJEY	SOOTHSAID
SOMERSETS	SONDAGE	SONNET	SOOJEYS	SOOTHSAY
SOMETHING	SONDAGES	SONNETARY	SOOK	SOOTHSAYS
SOMETIME	SONDE	SONNETED	SOOKED	SOOTIER
SOMETIMES	SONDELI	SONNETEER	SOOKING	SOOTIEST
SOMEWAY	SONDELIS	SONNETING	SOOKS	SOOTILY
SOMEWAYS	SONDER	SONNETISE	SOOL	SOOTINESS
SOMEWHAT	SONDERS	SONNETIZE	SOOLE	SOOTING
SOMEWHATS	SONDES	SONNETS	SOOLED	SOOTLESS
SOMEWHEN	SONE	SONNETTED	SOOLES	SOOTS
SOMEWHERE	SONERI	SONNIES	SOOLING	SOOTY
SOMEWHILE	SONERIS	SONNY	SOOLS	SOP
SOMEWHY	SONES	SONOBUOY	SOOM	SOPAPILLA
SOMEWISE	SONG	SONOBUOYS	SOOMED	SOPH
SOMITAL	SONGBIRD	SONOGRAM	SOOMING	SOPHERIC
SOMITE	SONGBIRDS	SONOGRAMS	SOOMS	SOPHERIM
SOMITES	SONGBOOK	SONOGRAPH	SOON	SOPHIES
SOMITIC	SONGBOOKS	SONOMETER	SOONER	SOPHISM
SOMMELIER	SONGCRAFT	SONORANT	SOONERS	SOPHISMS
SOMNIAL	SONGFEST	SONORANTS	SOONEST	SOPHIST
SOMNIATE	SONGFESTS	SONORITY	SOOP	SOPHISTER
SOMNIATED	SONGFUL	SONOROUS	SOOPED	SOPHISTIC
SOMNIATES	SONGFULLY	SONOVOX	SOOPING	SOPHISTRY
SOMNIFIC	SONGKOK	SONOVOXES	SOOPINGS	SOPHISTS
SOMNOLENT	SONGKOKS	SONS	SOOPS	SOPHOMORE

SOPHS	SORBITIC	SORELS	SOROSISES	SOS
SOPHY	SORBITISE	SORELY	SORPTION	SOSATIE
SOPITE	SORBITIZE	SORENESS	SORPTIONS	SOSATIES
SOPITED	SORBITOL	SORER	SORPTIVE	SOSS
SOPITES	SORBITOLS	SORES	SORRA	SOSSED
SOPITING	SORBO	SOREST	SORRAS	SOSSES
SOPOR	SORBOSE	SOREX	SORREL	SOSSING
SOPORIFIC	SORBOSES	SOREXES	SORRELS	SOSSINGS
SOPOROSE	SORBS	SORGHO	SORRIER	SOSTENUTI
SOPOROUS	SORBUS	SORGHOS	SORRIEST	SOSTENUTO
SOPORS	SORBUSES	SORGHUM	SORRILY	SOT
SOPPED	SORCERER	SORGHUMS	SORRINESS	SOTERIAL
SOPPIER	SORCERERS	SORGO	SORROW	SOTH
SOPPIEST	SORCERESS	SORGOS	SORROWED	SOTHS
SOPPILY	SORCERIES	SORI	SORROWER	SOTOL
SOPPINESS	SORCEROUS	SORICINE	SORROWERS	SOTOLS
SOPPING	SORCERY	SORICOID	SORROWFUL	SOTS
SOPPINGS	SORD	SORING	SORROWING	SOTTED
SOPPY	SORDA	SORINGS	SORROWS	SOTTEDLY
SOPRA	SORDES	SORITES	SORRY	SOTTING
SOPRANI	SORDID	SORITIC	SORRYISH	SOTTINGS
SOPRANINI	SORDIDER	SORITICAL	SORT	SOTTISH
SOPRANINO	SORDIDEST	SORN	SORTA	SOTTISHLY
SOPRANIST	SORDIDLY	SORNED	SORTABLE	SOTTISIER
SOPRANO	SORDINE	SORNER	SORTABLY	SOU
SOPRANOS	SORDINES	SORNERS	SORTAL	SOUARI
SOPS	SORDINI	SORNING	SORTALS	SOUARIS
SORA	SORDINO	SORNINGS	SORTANCE	SOUBISE
SORAGE	SORDO	SORNS	SORTANCES	SOUBISES
SORAGES	SORDOR	SOROBAN	SORTATION	SOUBRETTE
SORAL	SORDORS	SOROBANS	SORTED	SOUCAR
SORAS	SORDS	SOROCHE	SORTER	SOUCARS
SORB	SORE	SOROCHES	SORTERS	SOUCE
SORBABLE	SORED	SORORAL	SORTES	SOUCED
SORBARIA	SOREDIA	SORORALLY	SORTIE	SOUCES
SORBARIAS	SOREDIAL	SORORATE	SORTIED	SOUCHONG
SORBATE	SOREDIATE	SORORATES	SORTIEING	SOUCHONGS
SORBATES	SOREDIUM	SORORIAL	SORTIES	SOUCING
SORBED	SOREE	SORORISE	SORTILEGE	SOUCT
SORBENT	SOREES	SORORISED	SORTILEGY	SOUDAN
SORBENTS	SOREHEAD	SORORISES	SORTING	SOUDANS
SORBET	SOREHEADS	SORORITY	SORTINGS	SOUFFLE
SORBETS	SOREHON	SORORIZE	SORTITION	SOUFFLED
SORBIC	SOREHONS	SORORIZED	SORTMENT	SOUFFLEED
SORBING	SOREL	SORORIZES	SORTMENTS	SOUFFLES
SORBITE	SORELL	SOROSES	SORTS	SOUGH
SORBITES	SORELLS	SOROSIS	SORUS	SOUGHED

S

SOUGHING	SOUPCONS	SOURVELD	SOUTIES	SOWDER
SOUGHS	SOUPED	SOURVELDS	SOUTPIEL	SOWDERS
SOUGHT	SOUPER	SOURWOOD	SOUTPIELS	SOWED
SOUK	SOUPERS	SOURWOODS	SOUTS	SOWENS
SOUKED	SOUPFIN	SOUS	SOUVENIR	SOWER
SOUKING	SOUPFINS	SOUSE	SOUVENIRS	SOWERS
SOUKOUS	SOUPIER	SOUSED	SOUVLAKI	SOWF
SOUKOUSES	SOUPIEST	SOUSES	SOUVLAKIA	SOWFED
SOUKS	SOUPING	SOUSING	SOUVLAKIS	SOWFF
SOUL	SOUPLE	SOUSINGS	SOV	SOWFFED
SOULDAN	SOUPLED	SOUSLIK	SOVENANCE	SOWFFING
SOULDANS	SOUPLES	SOUSLIKS	SOVEREIGN	SOWFFS
SOULDIER	SOUPLESS	SOUT	SOVIET	SOWFING
SOULDIERS	SOUPLIKE	SOUTACHE	SOVIETIC	SOWFS
SOULED	SOUPLING	SOUTACHES	SOVIETISE	SOWING
SOULFUL	SOUPS	SOUTANE	SOVIETISM	SOWINGS
SOULFULLY	SOUPSPOON	SOUTANES	SOVIETIST	SOWL
SOULLESS	SOUPY	SOUTAR	SOVIETIZE	SOWLE
SOULLIKE	SOUR	SOUTARS	SOVIETS	SOWLED
SOULMATE	SOURBALL	SOUTENEUR	SOVKHOZ	SOWLES
SOULMATES	SOURBALLS	SOUTER	SOVKHOZES	SOWLING
SOULS	SOURCE	SOUTERLY	SOVKHOZY	SOWLS
SOUM	SOURCED	SOUTERS	SOVRAN	SOWM
SOUMED	SOURCEFUL	SOUTH	SOVRANLY	SOWMED
SOUMING	SOURCES	SOUTHEAST	SOVRANS	SOWMING
SOUMINGS	SOURCING	SOUTHED	SOVRANTY	SOWMS
SOUMS	SOURCINGS	SOUTHER	SOVS	SOWN
SOUND	SOURDINE	SOUTHERED	SOW	SOWND
SOUNDABLE	SOURDINES	SOUTHERLY	SOWABLE	SOWNDED
SOUNDBITE	SOURDOUGH	SOUTHERN	SOWANS	SOWNDING
SOUNDBOX	SOURED	SOUTHERNS	SOWAR	SOWNDS
SOUNDCARD	SOURER	SOUTHERS	SOWARREE	SOWNE
SOUNDED	SOUREST	SOUTHING	SOWARREES	SOWNES
SOUNDER	SOURING	SOUTHINGS	SOWARRIES	SOWP
SOUNDERS	SOURINGS	SOUTHLAND	SOWARRY	SOWPS
SOUNDEST	SOURISH	SOUTHMOST	SOWARS	SOWS
SOUNDING	SOURISHLY	SOUTHPAW	SOWBACK	SOWSE
SOUNDINGS	SOURLY	SOUTHPAWS	SOWBACKS	SOWSED
SOUNDLESS	SOURNESS	SOUTHRON	SOWBELLY	SOWSES
SOUNDLY	SOUROCK	SOUTHRONS	SOWBREAD	SOWSING
SOUNDMAN	SOUROCKS	SOUTHS	SOWBREADS	SOWSSE
SOUNDMEN	SOURPUSS	SOUTHSAID	SOWCAR	SOWSSED
SOUNDNESS	SOURS	SOUTHSAY	SOWCARS	SOWSSES
SOUNDPOST	SOURSE	SOUTHSAYS	SOWCE	SOWSSING
SOUNDS	SOURSES	SOUTHWARD	SOWCED	SOWTER
SOUP	SOURSOP	SOUTHWEST	SOWCES	SOWTERS
SOUPCON	SOURSOPS	SOUTIE	SOWCING	SOWTH

SOWTHED	SPACIALLY	SPAEINGS	SPALLE	SPANGING
SOWTHING	SPACIER	SPAEMAN	SPALLED	SPANGLE
SOWTHS	SPACIEST	SPAEMEN	SPALLER	SPANGLED
SOX	SPACINESS	SPAER	SPALLERS	SPANGLER
SOY	SPACING	SPAERS	SPALLES	SPANGLERS
SOYA	SPACINGS	SPAES	SPALLING	SPANGLES
SOYAS	SPACIOUS	SPAETZLE	SPALLINGS	SPANGLET
SOYBEAN	SPACKLE	SPAETZLES	SPALLS	SPANGLETS
SOYBEANS	SPACKLED	SPAEWIFE	SPALPEEN	SPANGLIER
SOYLE	SPACKLES	SPAEWIVES	SPALPEENS	SPANGLING
SOYLES	SPACKLING	SPAG	SPALT	SPANGLY
SOYMILK	SPACY	SPAGERIC	SPALTED	SPANGS
SOYMILKS	SPADASSIN	SPAGGED	SPALTING	SPANIEL
SOYS	SPADE	SPAGGING	SPALTS	SPANIELS
SOYUZ	SPADED	SPAGHETTI	SPAM	SPANING
SOYUZES	SPADEFISH	SPAGIRIC	SPAMBOT	SPANK
SOZ	SPADEFUL	SPAGS	SPAMBOTS	SPANKED
SOZIN	SPADEFULS	SPAGYRIC	SPAMMED	SPANKER
SOZINE	SPADELIKE	SPAGYRICS	SPAMMER	SPANKERS
SOZINES	SPADEMAN	SPAGYRIST	SPAMMERS	SPANKING
SOZINS	SPADEMEN	SPAHEE	SPAMMIE	SPANKINGS
SOZZLE	SPADER	SPAHEES	SPAMMIER	SPANKS
SOZZLED	SPADERS	SPAHI	SPAMMIES	SPANLESS
SOZZLES	SPADES	SPAHIS	SPAMMIEST	SPANNED
SOZZLIER	SPADESMAN	SPAIL	SPAMMING	SPANNER
SOZZLIEST	SPADESMEN	SPAILS	SPAMMINGS	SPANNERS
SOZZLING	SPADEWORK	SPAIN	SPAMMY	SPANNING
SOZZLY	SPADGER	SPAINED	SPAMS	SPANS
SPA	SPADGERS	SPAING	SPAN	SPANSPEK
SPACE	SPADICES	SPAINGS	SPANAEMIA	SPANSPEKS
SPACEBAND	SPADILLE	SPAINING	SPANAEMIC	SPANSULE
SPACED	SPADILLES	SPAINS	SPANCEL	SPANSULES
SPACELAB	SPADILLIO	SPAIRGE	SPANCELED	SPANWORM
SPACELABS	SPADILLO	SPAIRGED	SPANCELS	SPANWORMS
SPACELESS	SPADILLOS	SPAIRGES	SPANDEX	SPAR
SPACEMAN	SPADING	SPAIRGING	SPANDEXES	SPARABLE
SPACEMEN	SPADIX	SPAIT	SPANDREL	SPARABLES
SPACEPORT	SPADIXES	SPAITS	SPANDRELS	SPARAXIS
SPACER	SPADO	SPAKE	SPANDRIL	SPARD
SPACERS	SPADOES	SPALD	SPANDRILS	SPARE
SPACES	SPADONES	SPALDEEN	SPANE	SPAREABLE
SPACESHIP	SPADOS	SPALDEENS	SPANED	SPARED
SPACESUIT	SPADROON	SPALDS	SPANES	SPARELESS
SPACEWALK	SPADROONS	SPALE	SPANG	SPARELY
SPACEWARD	SPAE	SPALES	SPANGED	SPARENESS
SPACEY	SPAED	SPALL	SPANGHEW	SPARER
SPACIAL	SPAEING	SPALLABLE	SPANGHEWS	SPARERIB

S

SPARERIBS	SPARRE	SPATHAL	SPAWNIEST	SPEARLIKE
SPARERS	SPARRED	SPATHE	SPAWNING	SPEARMAN
SPARES	SPARRER	SPATHED	SPAWNINGS	SPEARMEN
SPAREST	SPARRERS	SPATHES	SPAWNS	SPEARMINT
SPARGE	SPARRES	SPATHIC	SPAWNY	SPEARS
SPARGED	SPARRIER	SPATHOSE	SPAWS	SPEARWORT
SPARGER	SPARRIEST	SPATIAL	SPAY	SPEARY
SPARGERS	SPARRING	SPATIALLY	SPAYAD	SPEAT
SPARGES	SPARRINGS	SPATLESE	SPAYADS	SPEATS
SPARGING	SPARROW	SPATLESEN	SPAYD	SPEC
SPARID	SPARROWS	SPATLESES	SPAYDS	SPECCED
SPARIDS	SPARRY	SPATS	SPAYED	SPECCIES
SPARING	SPARS	SPATTED	SPAYING	SPECCING
SPARINGLY	SPARSE	SPATTEE	SPAYS	SPECCY
SPARK	SPARSEDLY	SPATTEES	SPAZ	SPECIAL
SPARKE	SPARSELY	SPATTER	SPAZA	SPECIALER
SPARKED	SPARSER	SPATTERED	SPAZZ	SPECIALLY
SPARKER	SPARSEST	SPATTERS	SPAZZED	SPECIALS
SPARKERS	SPARSITY	SPATTING	SPAZZES	SPECIALTY
SPARKES	SPART	SPATULA	SPAZZING	SPECIATE
SPARKIE	SPARTAN	SPATULAR	SPEAK	SPECIATED
SPARKIER	SPARTANS	SPATULAS	SPEAKABLE	SPECIATES
SPARKIES	SPARTEINE	SPATULATE	SPEAKEASY	SPECIE
SPARKIEST	SPARTERIE	SPATULE	SPEAKER	SPECIES
SPARKILY	SPARTH	SPATULES	SPEAKERS	SPECIFIC
SPARKING	SPARTHE	SPATZLE	SPEAKING	SPECIFICS
SPARKISH	SPARTHES	SPATZLES	SPEAKINGS	SPECIFIED
SPARKLE	SPARTHS	SPAUL	SPEAKOUT	SPECIFIER
SPARKLED	SPARTICLE	SPAULD	SPEAKOUTS	SPECIFIES
SPARKLER	SPARTINA	SPAULDS	SPEAKS	SPECIFY
SPARKLERS	SPARTINAS	SPAULS	SPEAL	SPECIMEN
SPARKLES	SPARTS	SPAVIE	SPEALS	SPECIMENS
SPARKLESS	SPAS	SPAVIES	SPEAN	SPECIOUS
SPARKLET	SPASM	SPAVIET	SPEANED	SPECK
SPARKLETS	SPASMATIC	SPAVIN	SPEANING	SPECKED
SPARKLIER	SPASMED	SPAVINED	SPEANS	SPECKIER
SPARKLIES	SPASMIC	SPAVINS	SPEAR	SPECKIEST
SPARKLING	SPASMING	SPAW	SPEARED	SPECKING
SPARKLY	SPASMODIC	SPAWL	SPEARER	SPECKLE
SPARKPLUG	SPASMS	SPAWLED	SPEARERS	SPECKLED
SPARKS	SPASTIC	SPAWLING	SPEARFISH	SPECKLES
SPARKY	SPASTICS	SPAWLS	SPEARGUN	SPECKLESS
SPARLIKE	SPAT	SPAWN	SPEARGUNS	SPECKLING
SPARLING	SPATE	SPAWNED	SPEARHEAD	SPECKS
SPARLINGS	SPATES	SPAWNER	SPEARIER	SPECKY
SPAROID	SPATFALL	SPAWNERS	SPEARIEST	SPECS
SPAROIDS	SPATFALLS	SPAWNIER	SPEARING	SPECTACLE

SPECTATE	SPEEDWAYS	SPELKS	SPERMARIA	SPHAGNUM
SPECTATED	SPEEDWELL	SPELL	SPERMARY	SPHAGNUMS
SPECTATES	SPEEDY	SPELLABLE	SPERMATIA	SPHAIREE
SPECTATOR	SPEEL	SPELLBIND	SPERMATIC	SPHAIREES
SPECTER	SPEELED	SPELLDOWN	SPERMATID	SPHEAR
SPECTERS	SPEELER	SPELLED	SPERMIC	SPHEARE
SPECTRA	SPEELERS	SPELLER	SPERMINE	SPHEARES
SPECTRAL	SPEELING	SPELLERS	SPERMINES	SPHEARS
SPECTRE	SPEELS	SPELLFUL	SPERMOUS	SPHENDONE
SPECTRES	SPEER	SPELLICAN	SPERMS	SPHENE
SPECTRIN	SPEERED	SPELLING	SPERRE	SPHENES
SPECTRINS	SPEERING	SPELLINGS	SPERRED	SPHENIC
SPECTRUM	SPEERINGS	SPELLS	SPERRES	SPHENODON
SPECTRUMS	SPEERS	SPELT	SPERRING	SPHENOID
SPECULA	SPEIL	SPELTER	SPERSE	SPHENOIDS
SPECULAR	SPEILED	SPELTERS	SPERSED	SPHERAL
SPECULATE	SPEILING	SPELTS	SPERSES	SPHERE
SPECULUM	SPEILS	SPELTZ	SPERSING	SPHERED
SPECULUMS	SPEIR	SPELTZES	SPERST	SPHERES
SPED	SPEIRED	SPELUNK	SPERTHE	SPHERIC
SPEECH	SPEIRING	SPELUNKED	SPERTHES	SPHERICAL
SPEECHED	SPEIRINGS	SPELUNKER	SPET	SPHERICS
SPEECHES	SPEIRS	SPELUNKS	SPETCH	SPHERIER
SPEECHFUL	SPEISE	SPENCE	SPETCHES	SPHERIEST
SPEECHIFY	SPEISES	SPENCER	SPETS	SPHERING
SPEECHING	SPEISS	SPENCERS	SPETSNAZ	SPHEROID
SPEED	SPEISSES	SPENCES	SPETTING	SPHEROIDS
SPEEDBALL	SPEK	SPEND	SPETZNAZ	SPHERULAR
SPEEDBOAT	SPEKBOOM	SPENDABLE	SPEUG	SPHERULE
SPEEDED	SPEKBOOMS	SPENDALL	SPEUGS	SPHERULES
SPEEDER	SPEKS	SPENDALLS	SPEW	SPHERY
SPEEDERS	SPELAEAN	SPENDER	SPEWED	SPHINCTER
SPEEDFUL	SPELD	SPENDERS	SPEWER	SPHINGES
SPEEDIER	SPELDED	SPENDIER	SPEWERS	SPHINGID
SPEEDIEST	SPELDER	SPENDIEST	SPEWIER	SPHINGIDS
SPEEDILY	SPELDERED	SPENDING	SPEWIEST	SPHINX
SPEEDING	SPELDERS	SPENDINGS	SPEWINESS	SPHINXES
SPEEDINGS	SPELDIN	SPENDS	SPEWING	SPHYGMIC
SPEEDLESS	SPELDING	SPENDY	SPEWS	SPHYGMOID
SPEEDO	SPELDINGS	SPENSE	SPEWY	SPHYGMUS
SPEEDOS	SPELDINS	SPENSES	SPHACELUS	SPHYNX
SPEEDREAD	SPELDRIN	SPENT	SPHAER	SPHYNXES
SPEEDS	SPELDRING	SPEOS	SPHAERE	SPIAL
SPEEDSTER	SPELDRINS	SPEOSES	SPHAERES	SPIALS
SPEEDUP	SPELDS	SPERLING	SPHAERITE	SPIC
SPEEDUPS	SPELEAN	SPERLINGS	SPHAERS	SPICA
SPEEDWAY	SPELK	SPERM	SPHAGNOUS	SPICAE

S

SPICAS	SPIED	SPIKES	SPINAGES	SPINNIES
SPICATE	SPIEGEL	SPIKEY	SPINAL	SPINNING
SPICATED	SPIEGELS	SPIKIER	SPINALLY	SPINNINGS
SPICCATO	SPIEL	SPIKIEST	SPINALS	SPINNY
SPICCATOS	SPIELED	SPIKILY	SPINAR	SPINODE
SPICE	SPIELER	SPIKINESS	SPINARS	SPINODES
SPICEBUSH	SPIELERS	SPIKING	SPINAS	SPINOFF
SPICED	SPIELING	SPIKS	SPINATE	SPINOFFS
SPICELESS	SPIELS	SPIKY	SPINDLE	SPINONE
SPICER	SPIER	SPILE	SPINDLED	SPINONI
SPICERIES	SPIERED	SPILED	SPINDLER	SPINOR
SPICERS	SPIERING	SPILES	SPINDLERS	SPINORS
SPICERY	SPIERS	SPILIKIN	SPINDLES	SPINOSE
SPICES	SPIES	SPILIKINS	SPINDLIER	SPINOSELY
SPICEY	SPIF	SPILING	SPINDLING	SPINOSITY
SPICIER	SPIFF	SPILINGS	SPINDLY	SPINOUS
SPICIEST	SPIFFED	SPILITE	SPINDRIFT	SPINOUT
SPICILEGE	SPIFFIED	SPILITES	SPINE	SPINOUTS
SPICILY	SPIFFIER	SPILITIC	SPINED	SPINS
SPICINESS	SPIFFIES	SPILL	SPINEL	SPINSTER
SPICING	SPIFFIEST	SPILLABLE	SPINELESS	SPINSTERS
SPICK	SPIFFILY	SPILLAGE	SPINELIKE	SPINTEXT
SPICKER	SPIFFING	SPILLAGES	SPINELLE	SPINTEXTS
SPICKEST	SPIFFS	SPILLED	SPINELLES	SPINTO
SPICKNEL	SPIFFY	SPILLER	SPINELS	SPINTOS
SPICKNELS	SPIFFYING	SPILLERS	SPINES	SPINULA
SPICKS	SPIFS	SPILLIKIN	SPINET	SPINULAE
SPICS	SPIGHT	SPILLING	SPINETS	SPINULATE
SPICULA	SPIGHTED	SPILLINGS	SPINETTE	SPINULE
SPICULAE	SPIGHTING	SPILLOVER	SPINETTES	SPINULES
SPICULAR	SPIGHTS	SPILLS	SPINIER	SPINULOSE
SPICULATE	SPIGNEL	SPILLWAY	SPINIEST	SPINULOUS
SPICULE	SPIGNELS	SPILLWAYS	SPINIFEX	SPINY
SPICULES	SPIGOT	SPILOSITE	SPINIFORM	SPIRACLE
SPICULUM	SPIGOTS	SPILT	SPININESS	SPIRACLES
SPICY	SPIK	SPILTH	SPINK	SPIRACULA
SPIDE	SPIKE	SPILTHS	SPINKS	SPIRAEA
SPIDER	SPIKED	SPIM	SPINLESS	SPIRAEAS
SPIDERIER	SPIKEFISH	SPIMS	SPINNAKER	SPIRAL
SPIDERISH	SPIKELET	SPIN	SPINNER	SPIRALED
SPIDERMAN	SPIKELETS	SPINA	SPINNERET	SPIRALING
SPIDERMEN	SPIKELIKE	SPINACENE	SPINNERS	SPIRALISM
SPIDERS	SPIKENARD	SPINACH	SPINNERY	SPIRALIST
SPIDERWEB	SPIKER	SPINACHES	SPINNET	SPIRALITY
SPIDERY	SPIKERIES	SPINACHY	SPINNETS	SPIRALLED
SPIDES	SPIKERS	SPINAE	SPINNEY	SPIRALLY
SPIE	SPIKERY	SPINAGE	SPINNEYS	SPIRALS

SPIRANT	SPIRTLE	SPLASHIER	SPLICING	SPLOTCHES
SPIRANTS	SPIRTLES	SPLASHILY	SPLICINGS	SPLOTCHY
SPIRASTER	SPIRTS	SPLASHING	SPLIFF	SPLURGE
SPIRATED	SPIRULA	SPLASHY	SPLIFFS	SPLURGED
SPIRATION	SPIRULAE	SPLAT	SPLINE	SPLURGER
SPIRE	SPIRULAS	SPLATCH	SPLINED	SPLURGERS
SPIREA	SPIRULINA	SPLATCHED	SPLINES	SPLURGES
SPIREAS	SPIRY	SPLATCHES	SPLINING	SPLURGIER
SPIRED	SPIT	SPLATS	SPLINT	SPLURGING
SPIRELESS	SPITAL	SPLATTED	SPLINTED	SPLURGY
SPIRELET	SPITALS	SPLATTER	SPLINTER	SPLUTTER
SPIRELETS	SPITBALL	SPLATTERS	SPLINTERS	SPLUTTERS
SPIREM	SPITBALLS	SPLATTING	SPLINTERY	SPLUTTERY
SPIREME	SPITCHER	SPLAY	SPLINTING	SPOD
SPIREMES	SPITE	SPLAYED	SPLINTS	SPODDIER
SPIREMS	SPITED	SPLAYFEET	SPLISH	SPODDIEST
SPIRES	SPITEFUL	SPLAYFOOT	SPLISHED	SPODDY
SPIREWISE	SPITES	SPLAYING	SPLISHES	SPODE
SPIRIC	SPITFIRE	SPLAYS	SPLISHING	SPODES
SPIRICS	SPITFIRES	SPLEEN	SPLIT	SPODIUM
SPIRIER	SPITING	SPLEENFUL	SPLITS	SPODIUMS
SPIRIEST	SPITS	SPLEENIER	SPLITTED	SPODOGRAM
SPIRILLA	SPITTED	SPLEENISH	SPLITTER	SPODOSOL
SPIRILLAR	SPITTEN	SPLEENS	SPLITTERS	SPODOSOLS
SPIRILLUM	SPITTER	SPLEENY	SPLITTING	SPODS
SPIRING	SPITTERS	SPLENDENT	SPLITTISM	SPODUMENE
SPIRIT	SPITTING	SPLENDID	SPLITTIST	SPOFFISH
SPIRITED	SPITTINGS	SPLENDOR	SPLODGE	SPOFFY
SPIRITFUL	SPITTLE	SPLENDORS	SPLODGED	SPOIL
SPIRITING	SPITTLES	SPLENDOUR	SPLODGES	SPOILABLE
SPIRITISM	SPITTOON	SPLENETIC	SPLODGIER	SPOILAGE
SPIRITIST	SPITTOONS	SPLENIA	SPLODGILY	SPOILAGES
SPIRITOSO	SPITZ	SPLENIAL	SPLODGING	SPOILED
SPIRITOUS	SPITZES	SPLENIC	SPLODGY	SPOILER
SPIRITS	SPIV	SPLENII	SPLOG	SPOILERS
SPIRITUAL	SPIVS	SPLENITIS	SPLOGS	SPOILFIVE
SPIRITUEL	SPIVVERY	SPLENIUM	SPLOOSH	SPOILFUL
SPIRITUS	SPIVVIER	SPLENIUMS	SPLOOSHED	SPOILING
SPIRITY	SPIVVIEST	SPLENIUS	SPLOOSHES	SPOILS
SPIRLING	SPIVVY	SPLENT	SPLORE	SPOILSMAN
SPIRLINGS	SPLAKE	SPLENTS	SPLORES	SPOILSMEN
SPIROGRAM	SPLAKES	SPLEUCHAN	SPLOSH	SPOILT
SPIROGYRA	SPLASH	SPLICE	SPLOSHED	SPOKE
SPIROID	SPLASHED	SPLICED	SPLOSHES	SPOKED
SPIRT	SPLASHER	SPLICER	SPLOSHING	SPOKEN
SPIRTED	SPLASHERS	SPLICERS	SPLOTCH	SPOKES
SPIRTING	SPLASHES	SPLICES	SPLOTCHED	SPOKESMAN

S

SPOKESMEN	SPOOFER	SPOONWAYS	SPORTIER	SPOUT
SPOKEWISE	SPOOFERS	SPOONWISE	SPORTIES	SPOUTED
SPOKING	SPOOFERY	SPOONWORM	SPORTIEST	SPOUTER
SPOLIATE	SPOOFIER	SPOONY	SPORTIF	SPOUTERS
SPOLIATED	SPOOFIEST	SPOOR	SPORTILY	SPOUTIER
SPOLIATES	SPOOFING	SPOORED	SPORTING	SPOUTIEST
SPOLIATOR	SPOOFINGS	SPOORER	SPORTIVE	SPOUTING
SPONDAIC	SPOOFS	SPOORERS	SPORTLESS	SPOUTINGS
SPONDAICS	SPOOFY	SPOORING	SPORTS	SPOUTLESS
SPONDEE	SPOOK	SPOORS	SPORTSMAN	SPOUTS
SPONDEES	SPOOKED	SPOOT	SPORTSMEN	SPOUTY
SPONDULIX	SPOOKERY	SPOOTS	SPORTY	SPRACK
SPONDYL	SPOOKIER	SPORADIC	SPORULAR	SPRACKLE
SPONDYLS	SPOOKIEST	SPORAL	SPORULATE	SPRACKLED
SPONGE	SPOOKILY	SPORANGIA	SPORULE	SPRACKLES
SPONGEBAG	SPOOKING	SPORE	SPORULES	SPRAD
SPONGED	SPOOKISH	SPORED	SPOSH	SPRADDLE
SPONGEOUS	SPOOKS	SPORES	SPOSHES	SPRADDLED
SPONGER	SPOOKY	SPORICIDE	SPOSHIER	SPRADDLES
SPONGERS	SPOOL	SPORIDESM	SPOSHIEST	SPRAG
SPONGES	SPOOLED	SPORIDIA	SPOSHY	SPRAGGED
SPONGIER	SPOOLER	SPORIDIAL	SPOT	SPRAGGING
SPONGIEST	SPOOLERS	SPORIDIUM	SPOTLESS	SPRAGS
SPONGILY	SPOOLING	SPORING	SPOTLIGHT	SPRAID
SPONGIN	SPOOLINGS	SPORK	SPOTLIT	SPRAIN
SPONGING	SPOOLS	SPORKS	SPOTS	SPRAINED
SPONGINS	SPOOM	SPOROCARP	SPOTTABLE	SPRAINING
SPONGIOSE	SPOOMED	SPOROCYST	SPOTTED	SPRAINS
SPONGIOUS	SPOOMING	SPOROCYTE	SPOTTER	SPRAINT
SPONGOID	SPOOMS	SPOROGENY	SPOTTERS	SPRAINTS
SPONGY	SPOON	SPOROGONY	SPOTTIE	SPRANG
SPONSAL	SPOONBAIT	SPOROID	SPOTTIER	SPRANGLE
SPONSALIA	SPOONBILL	SPOROPHYL	SPOTTIES	SPRANGLED
SPONSIBLE	SPOONED	SPOROZOA	SPOTTIEST	SPRANGLES
SPONSING	SPOONEY	SPOROZOAL	SPOTTILY	SPRANGS
SPONSINGS	SPOONEYS	SPOROZOAN	SPOTTING	SPRAT
SPONSION	SPOONFED	SPOROZOIC	SPOTTINGS	SPRATS
SPONSIONS	SPOONFUL	SPOROZOON	SPOTTY	SPRATTLE
SPONSON	SPOONFULS	SPORRAN	SPOUSAGE	SPRATTLED
SPONSONS	SPOONHOOK	SPORRANS	SPOUSAGES	SPRATTLES
SPONSOR	SPOONIER	SPORT	SPOUSAL	SPRAUCHLE
SPONSORED	SPOONIES	SPORTABLE	SPOUSALLY	SPRAUNCY
SPONSORS	SPOONIEST	SPORTANCE	SPOUSALS	SPRAWL
SPONTOON	SPOONILY	SPORTED	SPOUSE	SPRAWLED
SPONTOONS	SPOONING	SPORTER	SPOUSED	SPRAWLER
SPOOF	SPOONS	SPORTERS	SPOUSES	SPRAWLERS
SPOOFED	SPOONSFUL	SPORTFUL	SPOUSING	SPRAWLIER

S

SPRAWLING	SPREEZING	SPRINTS	SPRUIT	SPULZIE
SPRAWLS	SPREKELIA	SPRIT	SPRUITS	SPULZIED
SPRAWLY	SPRENT	SPRITE	SPRUNG	SPULZIES
SPRAY	SPREW	SPRITEFUL	SPRUSH	SPUMANTE
SPRAYED	SPREWS	SPRITELY	SPRUSHED	SPUMANTES
SPRAYER	SPRIER	SPRITES	SPRUSHES	SPUME
SPRAYERS	SPRIEST	SPRITS	SPRUSHING	SPUMED
SPRAYEY	SPRIG	SPRITSAIL	SPRY	SPUMES
SPRAYIER	SPRIGGED	SPRITZ	SPRYER	SPUMIER
SPRAYIEST	SPRIGGER	SPRITZED	SPRYEST	SPUMIEST
SPRAYING	SPRIGGERS	SPRITZER	SPRYLY	SPUMING
SPRAYINGS	SPRIGGIER	SPRITZERS	SPRYNESS	SPUMONE
SPRAYS	SPRIGGING	SPRITZES	SPUD	SPUMONES
SPREAD	SPRIGGY	SPRITZIG	SPUDDED	SPUMONI
SPREADER	SPRIGHT	SPRITZIGS	SPUDDER	SPUMONIS
SPREADERS	SPRIGHTED	SPRITZING	SPUDDERS	SPUMOUS
SPREADING	SPRIGHTLY	SPROCKET	SPUDDIER	SPUMY
SPREADS	SPRIGHTS	SPROCKETS	SPUDDIEST	SPUN
SPREAGH	SPRIGS	SPROD	SPUDDING	SPUNGE
SPREAGHS	SPRIGTAIL	SPRODS	SPUDDINGS	SPUNGES
SPREATHE	SPRING	SPROG	SPUDDLE	SPUNK
SPREATHED	SPRINGAL	SPROGS	SPUDDLES	SPUNKED
SPREATHES	SPRINGALD	SPRONG	SPUDDY	SPUNKIE
SPREAZE	SPRINGALS	SPROUT	SPUDS	SPUNKIER
SPREAZED	SPRINGBOK	SPROUTED	SPUE	SPUNKIES
SPREAZES	SPRINGE	SPROUTING	SPUED	SPUNKIEST
SPREAZING	SPRINGED	SPROUTS	SPUEING	SPUNKILY
SPRECHERY	SPRINGER	SPRUCE	SPUER	SPUNKING
SPRECKLED	SPRINGERS	SPRUCED	SPUERS	SPUNKS
SPRED	SPRINGES	SPRUCELY	SPUES	SPUNKY
SPREDD	SPRINGIER	SPRUCER	SPUG	SPUNYARN
SPREDDE	SPRINGILY	SPRUCES	SPUGGIES	SPUNYARNS
SPREDDEN	SPRINGING	SPRUCEST	SPUGGY	SPUR
SPREDDES	SPRINGLE	SPRUCIER	SPUGS	SPURGALL
SPREDDING	SPRINGLES	SPRUCIEST	SPUILZIE	SPURGALLS
SPREDDS	SPRINGLET	SPRUCING	SPUILZIED	SPURGE
SPREDS	SPRINGS	SPRUCY	SPUILZIES	SPURGES
SPREE	SPRINGY	SPRUE	SPUING	SPURIAE
SPREED	SPRINKLE	SPRUES	SPULE	SPURIOUS
SPREEING	SPRINKLED	SPRUG	SPULES	SPURLESS
SPREES	SPRINKLER	SPRUGS	SPULYE	SPURLING
SPREETHE	SPRINKLES	SPRUIK	SPULYED	SPURLINGS
SPREETHED	SPRINT	SPRUIKED	SPULYEING	SPURN
SPREETHES	SPRINTED	SPRUIKER	SPULYES	SPURNE
SPREEZE	SPRINTER	SPRUIKERS	SPULYIE	SPURNED
SPREEZED	SPRINTERS	SPRUIKING	SPULYIED	SPURNER
SPREEZES	SPRINTING	SPRUIKS	SPULYIES	SPURNERS

SPURNES	SPYPLANE	SQUALLIER	SQUASHILY	SQUEALING
SPURNING	SPYPLANES	SQUALLING	SQUASHING	SQUEALS
SPURNINGS	SPYRE	SQUALLISH	SQUASHY	SQUEAMISH
SPURNS	SPYRES	SQUALLS	SQUAT	SQUEEGEE
SPURRED	SPYWARE	SQUALLY	SQUATLY	SQUEEGEED
SPURRER	SPYWARES	SQUALOID	SQUATNESS	SQUEEGEES
SPURRERS	SQUAB	SQUALOR	SQUATS	SQUEEZE
SPURREY	SQUABASH	SQUALORS	SQUATTED	SQUEEZED
SPURREYS	SQUABBED	SQUAMA	SQUATTER	SQUEEZER
SPURRIER	SQUABBER	SQUAMAE	SQUATTERS	SQUEEZERS
SPURRIERS	SQUABBEST	SQUAMATE	SQUATTEST	SQUEEZES
SPURRIES	SQUABBIER	SQUAMATES	SQUATTIER	SQUEEZIER
SPURRIEST	SQUABBING	SQUAME	SQUATTILY	SQUEEZING
SPURRING	SQUABBISH	SQUAMELLA	SQUATTING	SQUEEZY
SPURRINGS	SQUABBLE	SQUAMES	SQUATTLE	SQUEG
SPURRY	SQUABBLED	SQUAMOSAL	SQUATTLED	SQUEGGED
SPURS	SQUABBLER	SQUAMOSE	SQUATTLES	SQUEGGER
SPURT	SQUABBLES	SQUAMOUS	SQUATTY	SQUEGGERS
SPURTED	SQUABBY	SQUAMULA	SQUAW	SQUEGGING
SPURTER	SQUABS	SQUAMULAS	SQUAWBUSH	SQUEGS
SPURTERS	SQUACCO	SQUAMULE	SQUAWFISH	SQUELCH
SPURTING	SQUACCOS	SQUAMULES	SQUAWK	SQUELCHED
SPURTLE	SQUAD	SQUANDER	SQUAWKED	SQUELCHER
SPURTLES	SQUADDED	SQUANDERS	SQUAWKER	SQUELCHES
SPURTS	SQUADDIE	SQUARE	SQUAWKERS	SQUELCHY
SPURWAY	SQUADDIES	SQUARED	SQUAWKIER	SQUIB
SPURWAYS	SQUADDING	SQUARELY	SQUAWKING	SQUIBBED
SPUTA	SQUADDY	SQUARER	SQUAWKS	SQUIBBING
SPUTNIK	SQUADRON	SQUARERS	SQUAWKY	SQUIBS
SPUTNIKS	SQUADRONE	SQUARES	SQUAWMAN	SQUID
SPUTTER	SQUADRONS	SQUAREST	SQUAWMEN	SQUIDDED
SPUTTERED	SQUADS	SQUARIAL	SQUAWROOT	SQUIDDING
SPUTTERER	SQUAIL	SQUARIALS	SQUAWS	SQUIDGE
SPUTTERS	SQUAILED	SQUARING	SQUEAK	SQUIDGED
SPUTTERY	SQUAILER	SQUARINGS	SQUEAKED	SQUIDGES
SPUTUM	SQUAILERS	SQUARISH	SQUEAKER	SQUIDGIER
SPY	SQUAILING	SQUARK	SQUEAKERS	SQUIDGING
SPYAL	SQUAILS	SQUARKS	SQUEAKERY	SQUIDGY
SPYALS	SQUALENE	SQUARROSE	SQUEAKIER	SQUIDS
SPYCAM	SQUALENES	SQUARSON	SQUEAKILY	SQUIER
SPYCAMS	SQUALID	SQUARSONS	SQUEAKING	SQUIERS
SPYGLASS	SQUALIDER	SQUASH	SQUEAKS	SQUIFF
SPYHOLE	SQUALIDLY	SQUASHED	SQUEAKY	SQUIFFED
SPYHOLES	SQUALL	SQUASHER	SQUEAL	SQUIFFER
SPYING	SQUALLED	SQUASHERS	SQUEALED	SQUIFFERS
SPYINGS	SQUALLER	SQUASHES	SQUEALER	SQUIFFIER
SPYMASTER	SQUALLERS	SQUASHIER	SQUEALERS	SQUIFFY

S

SQUIGGLE	SQUIRESS	SRADHA	STACKROOM	STAGGARDS
SQUIGGLED	SQUIRING	SRADHAS	STACKS	STAGGART
SQUIGGLER	SQUIRISH	SRI	STACKUP	STAGGARTS
SQUIGGLES	SQUIRM	SRIS	STACKUPS	STAGGED
SQUIGGLY	SQUIRMED	ST	STACKYARD	STAGGER
SQUILGEE	SQUIRMER	STAB	STACTE	STAGGERED
SQUILGEED	SQUIRMERS	STABBED	STACTES	STAGGERER
SQUILGEES	SQUIRMIER	STABBER	STADDA	STAGGERS
SQUILL	SQUIRMING	STABBERS	STADDAS	STAGGERY
SQUILLA	SQUIRMS	STABBING	STADDLE	STAGGIE
SQUILLAE	SQUIRMY	STABBINGS	STADDLES	STAGGIER
SQUILLAS	SQUIRR	STABILATE	STADE	STAGGIES
SQUILLION	SQUIRRED	STABILE	STADES	STAGGIEST
SQUILLS	SQUIRREL	STABILES	STADIA	STAGGING
SQUINANCY	SQUIRRELS	STABILISE	STADIAL	STAGGY
SQUINCH	SQUIRRELY	STABILITY	STADIALS	STAGHORN
SQUINCHED	SQUIRRING	STABILIZE	STADIAS	STAGHORNS
SQUINCHES	SQUIRRS	STABLE	STADIUM	STAGHOUND
SQUINIED	SQUIRT	STABLEBOY	STADIUMS	STAGIER
SQUINIES	SQUIRTED	STABLED	STAFF	STAGIEST
SQUINNIED	SQUIRTER	STABLEMAN	STAFFAGE	STAGILY
SQUINNIER	SQUIRTERS	STABLEMEN	STAFFAGES	STAGINESS
SQUINNIES	SQUIRTING	STABLER	STAFFED	STAGING
SQUINNY	SQUIRTS	STABLERS	STAFFER	STAGINGS
SQUINT	SQUISH	STABLES	STAFFERS	STAGNANCE
SQUINTED	SQUISHED	STABLEST	STAFFING	STAGNANCY
SQUINTER	SQUISHES	STABLING	STAFFMAN	STAGNANT
SQUINTERS	SQUISHIER	STABLINGS	STAFFMEN	STAGNATE
SQUINTEST	SQUISHING	STABLISH	STAFFROOM	STAGNATED
SQUINTIER	SQUISHY	STABLY	STAFFS	STAGNATES
SQUINTING	SQUIT	STABS	STAG	STAGS
SQUINTS	SQUITCH	STACATION	STAGE	STAGY
SQUINTY	SQUITCHES	STACCATI	STAGEABLE	STAID
SQUINY	SQUITS	STACCATO	STAGED	STAIDER
SQUINYING	SQUITTERS	STACCATOS	STAGEFUL	STAIDEST
SQUIRAGE	SQUIZ	STACHYS	STAGEFULS	STAIDLY
SQUIRAGES	SQUIZZES	STACHYSES	STAGEHAND	STAIDNESS
SQUIRALTY	SQUOOSH	STACK	STAGELIKE	STAIG
SQUIRARCH	SQUOOSHED	STACKABLE	STAGER	STAIGS
SQUIRE	SQUOOSHES	STACKED	STAGERIES	STAIN
SQUIREAGE	SQUOOSHY	STACKER	STAGERS	STAINABLE
SQUIRED	SQUUSH	STACKERS	STAGERY	STAINED
SQUIREDOM	SQUUSHED	STACKET	STAGES	STAINER
SQUIREEN	SQUUSHES	STACKETS	STAGETTE	STAINERS
SQUIREENS	SQUUSHING	STACKING	STAGETTES	STAINING
SQUIRELY	SRADDHA	STACKINGS	STAGEY	STAININGS
SQUIRES	SRADDHAS	STACKLESS	STAGGARD	STAINLESS

S

STAINS

STAINS	STALKING	STAMPEDO	STANDUP	STAPEDIAL
STAIR	STALKINGS	STAMPEDOS	STANDUPS	STAPEDII
STAIRCASE	STALKLESS	STAMPER	STANE	STAPEDIUS
STAIRED	STALKLIKE	STAMPERS	STANED	STAPELIA
STAIRFOOT	STALKO	STAMPING	STANES	STAPELIAS
STAIRHEAD	STALKOES	STAMPINGS	STANG	STAPES
STAIRLESS	STALKS	STAMPLESS	STANGED	STAPH
STAIRLIFT	STALKY	STAMPS	STANGING	STAPHS
STAIRLIKE	STALL	STANCE	STANGS	STAPLE
STAIRS	STALLAGE	STANCES	STANHOPE	STAPLED
STAIRSTEP	STALLAGES	STANCH	STANHOPES	STAPLER
STAIRWAY	STALLED	STANCHED	STANIEL	STAPLERS
STAIRWAYS	STALLING	STANCHEL	STANIELS	STAPLES
STAIRWELL	STALLINGS	STANCHELS	STANINE	STAPLING
STAIRWISE	STALLION	STANCHER	STANINES	STAPLINGS
STAIRWORK	STALLIONS	STANCHERS	STANING	STAPPED
STAITH	STALLMAN	STANCHES	STANK	STAPPING
STAITHE	STALLMEN	STANCHEST	STANKED	STAPPLE
STAITHES	STALLS	STANCHING	STANKING	STAPPLES
STAITHS	STALWART	STANCHION	STANKS	STAPS
STAKE	STALWARTS	STANCHLY	STANNARY	STAR
STAKED	STALWORTH	STANCK	STANNATE	STARAGEN
STAKEOUT	STAMEN	STAND	STANNATES	STARAGENS
STAKEOUTS	STAMENED	STANDARD	STANNATOR	STARBOARD
STAKES	STAMENS	STANDARDS	STANNEL	STARBURST
STAKING	STAMINA	STANDAWAY	STANNELS	STARCH
STALACTIC	STAMINAL	STANDBY	STANNIC	STARCHED
STALAG	STAMINAS	STANDBYS	STANNITE	STARCHER
STALAGMA	STAMINATE	STANDDOWN	STANNITES	STARCHERS
STALAGMAS	STAMINEAL	STANDEE	STANNOUS	STARCHES
STALAGS	STAMINODE	STANDEES	STANNUM	STARCHIER
STALE	STAMINODY	STANDEN	STANNUMS	STARCHILY
STALED	STAMINOID	STANDER	STANOL	STARCHING
STALELY	STAMMEL	STANDERS	STANOLS	STARCHY
STALEMATE	STAMMELS	STANDFAST	STANYEL	STARDOM
STALENESS	STAMMER	STANDGALE	STANYELS	STARDOMS
STALER	STAMMERED	STANDING	STANZA	STARDRIFT
STALES	STAMMERER	STANDINGS	STANZAED	STARDUST
STALEST	STAMMERS	STANDISH	STANZAIC	STARDUSTS
STALING	STAMNOI	STANDOFF	STANZAS	STARE
STALK	STAMNOS	STANDOFFS	STANZE	STARED
STALKED	STAMP	STANDOUT	STANZES	STARER
STALKER	STAMPED	STANDOUTS	STANZO	STARERS
STALKERS	STAMPEDE	STANDOVER	STANZOES	STARES
STALKIER	STAMPEDED	STANDPAT	STANZOS	STARETS
STALKIEST	STAMPEDER	STANDPIPE	STAP	STARETSES
STALKILY	STAMPEDES	STANDS	STAPEDES	STARETZ

STARETZES	STARRING	STASIDION	STATISTS	STAYAWAYS
STARFISH	STARRINGS	STASIMA	STATIVE	STAYED
STARFRUIT	STARRS	STASIMON	STATIVES	STAYER
STARGAZE	STARRY	STASIS	STATOCYST	STAYERS
STARGAZED	STARS	STAT	STATOLITH	STAYING
STARGAZER	STARSHINE	STATABLE	STATOR	STAYLESS
STARGAZES	STARSHIP	STATAL	STATORS	STAYMAKER
STARGAZEY	STARSHIPS	STATANT	STATS	STAYNE
STARING	STARSPOT	STATE	STATTO	STAYNED
STARINGLY	STARSPOTS	STATEABLE	STATTOS	STAYNES
STARINGS	STARSTONE	STATED	STATUA	STAYNING
STARK	START	STATEDLY	STATUARY	STAYRE
STARKED	STARTED	STATEHOOD	STATUAS	STAYRES
STARKEN	STARTER	STATELESS	STATUE	STAYS
STARKENED	STARTERS	STATELET	STATUED	STAYSAIL
STARKENS	STARTFUL	STATELETS	STATUES	STAYSAILS
STARKER	STARTING	STATELIER	STATUETTE	STEAD
STARKERS	STARTINGS	STATELILY	STATURE	STEADED
STARKEST	STARTISH	STATELILY	STATURED	STEADFAST
STARKING	STARTLE	STATELY	STATURES	STEADIED
STARKLY	STARTLED	STATEMENT	STATUS	STEADIER
STARKNESS	STARTLER	STATER	STATUSES	STEADIERS
STARKS	STARTLERS	STATEROOM	STATUSY	STEADIES
STARLESS	STARTLES	STATERS	STATUTE	STEADIEST
STARLET	STARTLING	STATES	STATUTES	STEADILY
STARLETS	STARTLISH	STATESIDE	STATUTORY	STEADING
STARLIGHT	STARTLY	STATESMAN	STAUMREL	STEADINGS
STARLIKE	STARTS	STATESMEN	STAUMRELS	STEADS
STARLING	STARTSY	STATEWIDE	STAUN	STEADY
STARLINGS	STARTUP	STATIC	STAUNCH	STEADYING
STARLIT	STARTUPS	STATICAL	STAUNCHED	STEAK
STARN	STARVE	STATICE	STAUNCHER	STEAKS
STARNED	STARVED	STATICES	STAUNCHES	STEAL
STARNIE	STARVER	STATICKY	STAUNCHLY	STEALABLE
STARNIES	STARVERS	STATICS	STAUNING	STEALAGE
STARNING	STARVES	STATIM	STAUNS	STEALAGES
STARNOSE	STARVING	STATIN	STAVE	STEALE
STARNOSES	STARVINGS	STATING	STAVED	STEALED
STARNS	STARWORT	STATINS	STAVES	STEALER
STAROSTA	STARWORTS	STATION	STAVING	STEALERS
STAROSTAS	STASES	STATIONAL	STAVUDINE	STEALES
STAROSTY	STASH	STATIONED	STAW	STEALING
STARR	STASHED	STATIONER	STAWED	STEALINGS
STARRED	STASHES	STATIONS	STAWING	STEALS
STARRIER	STASHIE	STATISM	STAWS	STEALT
STARRIEST	STASHIES	STATISMS	STAY	STEALTH
STARRILY	STASHING	STATISTIC	STAYAWAY	STEALTHED

S

STEALTHS	STEATITES	STEELING	STEERAGE	STELIC
STEALTHY	STEATITIC	STEELINGS	STEERAGES	STELL
STEAM	STEATOMA	STEELMAN	STEERED	STELLA
STEAMBOAT	STEATOMAS	STEELMEN	STEERER	STELLAR
STEAMED	STEATOSES	STEELS	STEERERS	STELLAS
STEAMER	STEATOSIS	STEELWARE	STEERIES	STELLATE
STEAMERED	STED	STEELWORK	STEERING	STELLATED
STEAMERS	STEDD	STEELY	STEERINGS	STELLED
STEAMIE	STEDDE	STEELYARD	STEERLING	STELLERID
STEAMIER	STEDDED	STEEM	STEERS	STELLIFY
STEAMIES	STEDDES	STEEMED	STEERSMAN	STELLING
STEAMIEST	STEDDIED	STEEMING	STEERSMEN	STELLIO
STEAMILY	STEDDIES	STEEMS	STEERY	STELLION
STEAMING	STEDDING	STEEN	STEEVE	STELLIONS
STEAMINGS	STEDDS	STEENBOK	STEEVED	STELLITE
STEAMROLL	STEDDY	STEENBOKS	STEEVELY	STELLITES
STEAMS	STEDDYING	STEENBRAS	STEEVER	STELLS
STEAMSHIP	STEDE	STEENBUCK	STEEVES	STELLULAR
STEAMY	STEDED	STEENED	STEEVEST	STEM
STEAN	STEDES	STEENING	STEEVING	STEMBOK
STEANE	STEDFAST	STEENINGS	STEEVINGS	STEMBOKS
STEANED	STEDING	STEENKIRK	STEGNOSES	STEMBUCK
STEANES	STEDS	STEENS	STEGNOSIS	STEMBUCKS
STEANING	STEED	STEEP	STEGNOTIC	STEME
STEANINGS	STEEDED	STEEPED	STEGODON	STEMED
STEANS	STEEDIED	STEEPEN	STEGODONS	STEMES
STEAPSIN	STEEDIES	STEEPENED	STEGODONT	STEMHEAD
STEAPSINS	STEEDING	STEEPENS	STEGOMYIA	STEMHEADS
STEAR	STEEDLIKE	STEEPER	STEGOSAUR	STEMING
STEARAGE	STEEDS	STEEPERS	STEIL	STEMLESS
STEARAGES	STEEDY	STEEPEST	STEILS	STEMLET
STEARATE	STEEDYING	STEEPEUP	STEIN	STEMLETS
STEARATES	STEEK	STEEPIER	STEINBOCK	STEMLIKE
STEARD	STEEKED	STEEPIEST	STEINBOK	STEMMA
STEARE	STEEKING	STEEPING	STEINBOKS	STEMMAS
STEARED	STEEKIT	STEEPISH	STEINED	STEMMATA
STEARES	STEEKS	STEEPLE	STEINING	STEMMATIC
STEARIC	STEEL	STEEPLED	STEININGS	STEMME
STEARIN	STEELBOW	STEEPLES	STEINKIRK	STEMMED
STEARINE	STEELBOWS	STEEPLING	STEINS	STEMMER
STEARINES	STEELD	STEEPLY	STELA	STEMMERS
STEARING	STEELED	STEEPNESS	STELAE	STEMMERY
STEARINS	STEELHEAD	STEEPS	STELAI	STEMMES
STEARS	STEELIE	STEEPUP	STELAR	STEMMIER
STEARSMAN	STEELIER	STEEPY	STELE	STEMMIEST
STEARSMEN	STEELIES	STEER	STELENE	STEMMING
STEATITE	STEELIEST	STEERABLE	STELES	STEMMINGS

STEMMY	STENTED	STERILE	STET	STIBIUMS
STEMPEL	STENTING	STERILELY	STETS	STIBNITE
STEMPELS	STENTOR	STERILISE	STETSON	STIBNITES
STEMPLE	STENTORS	STERILITY	STETSONS	STICCADO
STEMPLES	STENTOUR	STERILIZE	STETTED	STICCADOS
STEMS	STENTOURS	STERLET	STETTING	STICCATO
STEMSON	STENTS	STERLETS	STEVEDORE	STICCATOS
STEMSONS	STEP	STERLING	STEVEN	STICH
STEMWARE	STEPBAIRN	STERLINGS	STEVENS	STICHARIA
STEMWARES	STEPCHILD	STERN	STEW	STICHERA
STEN	STEPDAME	STERNA	STEWABLE	STICHERON
STENCH	STEPDAMES	STERNAGE	STEWARD	STICHIC
STENCHED	STEPHANE	STERNAGES	STEWARDED	STICHIDIA
STENCHES	STEPHANES	STERNAL	STEWARDRY	STICHOI
STENCHFUL	STEPLIKE	STERNEBRA	STEWARDS	STICHOS
STENCHIER	STEPNEY	STERNED	STEWARTRY	STICHS
STENCHING	STEPNEYS	STERNER	STEWBUM	STICK
STENCHY	STEPOVER	STERNEST	STEWBUMS	STICKABLE
STENCIL	STEPOVERS	STERNFAST	STEWED	STICKBALL
STENCILED	STEPPE	STERNING	STEWER	STICKED
STENCILER	STEPPED	STERNITE	STEWERS	STICKER
STENCILS	STEPPER	STERNITES	STEWIER	STICKERED
STEND	STEPPERS	STERNITIC	STEWIEST	STICKERS
STENDED	STEPPES	STERNLY	STEWING	STICKFUL
STENDING	STEPPING	STERNMOST	STEWINGS	STICKFULS
STENDS	STEPS	STERNNESS	STEWPAN	STICKIED
STENGAH	STEPSON	STERNPORT	STEWPANS	STICKIER
STENGAHS	STEPSONS	STERNPOST	STEWPOND	STICKIES
STENLOCK	STEPSTOOL	STERNS	STEWPONDS	STICKIEST
STENLOCKS	STEPT	STERNSON	STEWPOT	STICKILY
STENNED	STEPWISE	STERNSONS	STEWPOTS	STICKING
STENNING	STERADIAN	STERNUM	STEWS	STICKINGS
STENO	STERCORAL	STERNUMS	STEWY	STICKIT
STENOBATH	STERCULIA	STERNWARD	STEY	STICKJAW
STENOKIES	STERE	STERNWAY	STEYER	STICKJAWS
STENOKOUS	STEREO	STERNWAYS	STEYEST	STICKLE
STENOKY	STEREOED	STEROID	STHENIA	STICKLED
STENOPAIC	STEREOING	STEROIDAL	STHENIAS	STICKLER
STENOS	STEREOME	STEROIDS	STHENIC	STICKLERS
STENOSED	STEREOMES	STEROL	STIBBLE	STICKLES
STENOSES	STEREOS	STEROLS	STIBBLER	STICKLIKE
STENOSIS	STERES	STERTOR	STIBBLERS	STICKLING
STENOTIC	STERIC	STERTORS	STIBBLES	STICKMAN
STENOTYPE	STERICAL	STERVE	STIBIAL	STICKMEN
STENOTYPY	STERIGMA	STERVED	STIBINE	STICKOUT
STENS	STERIGMAS	STERVES	STIBINES	STICKOUTS
STENT	STERILANT	STERVING	STIBIUM	STICKPIN

S

STICKPINS	STIGMA	STILTIER	STINKBUGS	STIPULATE
STICKS	STIGMAL	STILTIEST	STINKER	STIPULE
STICKSEED	STIGMAS	STILTING	STINKEROO	STIPULED
STICKUM	STIGMATA	STILTINGS	STINKERS	STIPULES
STICKUMS	STIGMATIC	STILTISH	STINKHORN	STIR
STICKUP	STIGME	STILTS	STINKIER	STIRABOUT
STICKUPS	STIGMES	STILTY	STINKIEST	STIRE
STICKWEED	STILB	STIM	STINKING	STIRED
STICKWORK	STILBENE	STIME	STINKO	STIRES
STICKY	STILBENES	STIMED	STINKPOT	STIRING
STICKYING	STILBITE	STIMES	STINKPOTS	STIRK
STICTION	STILBITES	STIMIE	STINKS	STIRKS
STICTIONS	STILBS	STIMIED	STINKWEED	STIRLESS
STIDDIE	STILE	STIMIES	STINKWOOD	STIRP
STIDDIED	STILED	STIMING	STINKY	STIRPES
STIDDIES	STILES	STIMS	STINT	STIRPS
STIE	STILET	STIMULANT	STINTED	STIRRA
STIED	STILETS	STIMULATE	STINTEDLY	STIRRABLE
STIES	STILETTO	STIMULI	STINTER	STIRRAH
STIEVE	STILETTOS	STIMULUS	STINTERS	STIRRAHS
STIEVELY	STILING	STIMY	STINTIER	STIRRAS
STIEVER	STILL	STIMYING	STINTIEST	STIRRE
STIEVEST	STILLAGE	STING	STINTING	STIRRED
STIFF	STILLAGES	STINGAREE	STINTINGS	STIRRER
STIFFED	STILLBORN	STINGBULL	STINTLESS	STIRRERS
STIFFEN	STILLED	STINGED	STINTS	STIRRES
STIFFENED	STILLER	STINGER	STINTY	STIRRING
STIFFENER	STILLERS	STINGERS	STIPA	STIRRINGS
STIFFENS	STILLEST	STINGFISH	STIPAS	STIRRUP
STIFFER	STILLIER	STINGIER	STIPE	STIRRUPS
STIFFEST	STILLIEST	STINGIES	STIPED	STIRS
STIFFIE	STILLING	STINGIEST	STIPEL	STISHIE
STIFFIES	STILLINGS	STINGILY	STIPELS	STISHIES
STIFFING	STILLION	STINGING	STIPEND	STITCH
STIFFISH	STILLIONS	STINGINGS	STIPENDS	STITCHED
STIFFLY	STILLMAN	STINGLESS	STIPES	STITCHER
STIFFNESS	STILLMEN	STINGO	STIPIFORM	STITCHERS
STIFFS	STILLNESS	STINGOS	STIPITATE	STITCHERY
STIFFWARE	STILLROOM	STINGRAY	STIPITES	STITCHES
STIFFY	STILLS	STINGRAYS	STIPPLE	STITCHING
STIFLE	STILLY	STINGS	STIPPLED	STITHIED
STIFLED	STILT	STINGY	STIPPLER	STITHIES
STIFLER	STILTBIRD	STINK	STIPPLERS	STITHY
STIFLERS	STILTED	STINKARD	STIPPLES	STITHYING
STIFLES	STILTEDLY	STINKARDS	STIPPLING	STIVE
STIFLING	STILTER	STINKBIRD	STIPULAR	STIVED
STIFLINGS	STILTERS	STINKBUG	STIPULARY	STIVER

S

STIVERS	STOCKMEN	STOKES	STOMODEAL	STONINESS
STIVES	STOCKPILE	STOKESIA	STOMODEUM	STONING
STIVIER	STOCKPOT	STOKESIAS	STOMP	STONINGS
STIVIEST	STOCKPOTS	STOKING	STOMPED	STONISH
STIVING	STOCKROOM	STOKVEL	STOMPER	STONISHED
STIVY	STOCKS	STOKVELS	STOMPERS	STONISHES
STOA	STOCKTAKE	STOLE	STOMPIE	STONK
STOAE	STOCKTOOK	STOLED	STOMPIES	STONKED
STOAI	STOCKWORK	STOLEN	STOMPING	STONKER
STOAS	STOCKY	STOLES	STOMPS	STONKERED
STOAT	STOCKYARD	STOLID	STONABLE	STONKERS
STOATS	STODGE	STOLIDER	STOND	STONKING
STOB	STODGED	STOLIDEST	STONDS	STONKS
STOBBED	STODGER	STOLIDITY	STONE	STONN
STOBBING	STODGERS	STOLIDLY	STONEABLE	STONNE
STOBIE	STODGES	STOLLEN	STONEBOAT	STONNED
STOBS	STODGIER	STOLLENS	STONECAST	STONNES
STOCCADO	STODGIEST	STOLN	STONECHAT	STONNING
STOCCADOS	STODGILY	STOLON	STONECROP	STONNS
STOCCATA	STODGING	STOLONATE	STONED	STONY
STOCCATAS	STODGY	STOLONIC	STONEFISH	STONYING
STOCIOUS	STOEP	STOLONS	STONEFLY	STOOD
STOCK	STOEPS	STOLPORT	STONEHAND	STOODEN
STOCKADE	STOGEY	STOLPORTS	STONELESS	STOOGE
STOCKADED	STOGEYS	STOMA	STONELIKE	STOOGED
STOCKADES	STOGIE	STOMACH	STONEN	STOOGES
STOCKAGE	STOGIES	STOMACHAL	STONER	STOOGING
STOCKAGES	STOGY	STOMACHED	STONERAG	STOOK
STOCKCAR	STOIC	STOMACHER	STONERAGS	STOOKED
STOCKCARS	STOICAL	STOMACHIC	STONERAW	STOOKER
STOCKED	STOICALLY	STOMACHS	STONERAWS	STOOKERS
STOCKER	STOICISM	STOMACHY	STONERN	STOOKIE
STOCKERS	STOICISMS	STOMACK	STONERS	STOOKIES
STOCKFISH	STOICS	STOMACKS	STONES	STOOKING
STOCKIER	STOIT	STOMAL	STONESHOT	STOOKS
STOCKIEST	STOITED	STOMAS	STONEWALL	STOOL
STOCKILY	STOITER	STOMATA	STONEWARE	STOOLBALL
STOCKINET	STOITERED	STOMATAL	STONEWASH	STOOLED
STOCKING	STOITERS	STOMATE	STONEWORK	STOOLIE
STOCKINGS	STOITING	STOMATES	STONEWORT	STOOLIES
STOCKISH	STOITS	STOMATIC	STONEY	STOOLING
STOCKIST	STOKE	STOMATOUS	STONG	STOOLS
STOCKISTS	STOKED	STOMIA	STONIED	STOOP
STOCKLESS	STOKEHOLD	STOMIUM	STONIER	STOOPBALL
STOCKLIST	STOKEHOLE	STOMIUMS	STONIES	STOOPE
STOCKLOCK	STOKER	STOMODAEA	STONIEST	STOOPED
STOCKMAN	STOKERS	STOMODEA	STONILY	STOOPER

S

STOOPERS	STOPPLING	STORMLIKE	STOURY	STOWND
STOOPES	STOPS	STORMS	STOUSH	STOWNDED
STOOPING	STOPT	STORMY	STOUSHED	STOWNDING
STOOPS	STOPWATCH	STORNELLI	STOUSHES	STOWNDS
STOOR	STOPWORD	STORNELLO	STOUSHIE	STOWNLINS
STOORS	STOPWORDS	STORY	STOUSHIES	STOWP
STOOSHIE	STORABLE	STORYBOOK	STOUSHING	STOWPS
STOOSHIES	STORABLES	STORYETTE	STOUT	STOWRE
STOOZE	STORAGE	STORYING	STOUTEN	STOWRES
STOOZED	STORAGES	STORYINGS	STOUTENED	STOWS
STOOZER	STORAX	STORYLINE	STOUTENS	STRABISM
STOOZERS	STORAXES	STOSS	STOUTER	STRABISMS
STOOZES	STORE	STOSSES	STOUTEST	STRACK
STOOZING	STORED	STOT	STOUTH	STRAD
STOOZINGS	STOREMAN	STOTIN	STOUTHS	STRADDLE
STOP	STOREMEN	STOTINKA	STOUTISH	STRADDLED
STOPBANK	STORER	STOTINKI	STOUTLY	STRADDLER
STOPBANKS	STOREROOM	STOTINOV	STOUTNESS	STRADDLES
STOPCOCK	STORERS	STOTINS	STOUTS	STRADIOT
STOPCOCKS	STORES	STOTIOUS	STOVAINE	STRADIOTS
STOPE	STORESHIP	STOTS	STOVAINES	STRADS
STOPED	STOREWIDE	STOTT	STOVE	STRAE
STOPER	STOREY	STOTTED	STOVED	STRAES
STOPERS	STOREYED	STOTTER	STOVEPIPE	STRAFE
STOPES	STOREYS	STOTTERED	STOVER	STRAFED
STOPGAP	STORGE	STOTTERS	STOVERS	STRAFER
STOPGAPS	STORGES	STOTTIE	STOVES	STRAFERS
STOPING	STORIATED	STOTTIES	STOVETOP	STRAFES
STOPINGS	STORIED	STOTTING	STOVETOPS	STRAFF
STOPLESS	STORIES	STOTTS	STOVIES	STRAFFED
STOPLIGHT	STORIETTE	STOTTY	STOVING	STRAFFING
STOPOFF	STORING	STOUN	STOVINGS	STRAFFS
STOPOFFS	STORK	STOUND	STOW	STRAFING
STOPOVER	STORKS	STOUNDED	STOWABLE	STRAG
STOPOVERS	STORM	STOUNDING	STOWAGE	STRAGGLE
STOPPABLE	STORMBIRD	STOUNDS	STOWAGES	STRAGGLED
STOPPAGE	STORMCOCK	STOUNING	STOWAWAY	STRAGGLER
STOPPAGES	STORMED	STOUNS	STOWAWAYS	STRAGGLES
STOPPED	STORMER	STOUP	STOWDOWN	STRAGGLY
STOPPER	STORMERS	STOUPS	STOWDOWNS	STRAGS
STOPPERED	STORMFUL	STOUR	STOWED	STRAICHT
STOPPERS	STORMIER	STOURE	STOWER	STRAIGHT
STOPPING	STORMIEST	STOURES	STOWERS	STRAIGHTS
STOPPINGS	STORMILY	STOURIE	STOWING	STRAIK
STOPPLE	STORMING	STOURIER	STOWINGS	STRAIKED
STOPPLED	STORMINGS	STOURIEST	STOWLINS	STRAIKING
STOPPLES	STORMLESS	STOURS	STOWN	STRAIKS

STRAIN	STRANGLES	STRAWHAT	STREEL	STRETTOS
STRAINED	STRANGURY	STRAWIER	STREELED	STREUSEL
STRAINER	STRAP	STRAWIEST	STREELING	STREUSELS
STRAINERS	STRAPHANG	STRAWING	STREELS	STREW
STRAINING	STRAPHUNG	STRAWLESS	STREET	STREWAGE
STRAINS	STRAPLESS	STRAWLIKE	STREETAGE	STREWAGES
STRAINT	STRAPLINE	STRAWN	STREETBOY	STREWED
STRAINTS	STRAPPADO	STRAWS	STREETCAR	STREWER
STRAIT	STRAPPED	STRAWWORM	STREETED	STREWERS
STRAITED	STRAPPER	STRAWY	STREETFUL	STREWING
STRAITEN	STRAPPERS	STRAY	STREETIER	STREWINGS
STRAITENS	STRAPPIER	STRAYED	STREETING	STREWMENT
STRAITER	STRAPPING	STRAYER	STREETS	STREWN
STRAITEST	STRAPPY	STRAYERS	STREETY	STREWS
STRAITING	STRAPS	STRAYING	STREIGHT	STREWTH
STRAITLY	STRAPWORT	STRAYINGS	STREIGHTS	STRIA
STRAITS	STRASS	STRAYLING	STREIGNE	STRIAE
STRAK	STRASSES	STRAYS	STREIGNED	STRIATA
STRAKE	STRATA	STRAYVE	STREIGNES	STRIATE
STRAKED	STRATAGEM	STRAYVED	STRELITZ	STRIATED
STRAKES	STRATAL	STRAYVES	STRELITZI	STRIATES
STRAMACON	STRATAS	STRAYVING	STRENE	STRIATING
STRAMASH	STRATEGIC	STREAK	STRENES	STRIATION
STRAMAZON	STRATEGY	STREAKED	STRENGTH	STRIATUM
STRAMMEL	STRATH	STREAKER	STRENGTHS	STRIATUMS
STRAMMELS	STRATHS	STREAKERS	STRENUITY	STRIATURE
STRAMONY	STRATI	STREAKIER	STRENUOUS	STRICH
STRAMP	STRATIFY	STREAKILY	STREP	STRICHES
STRAMPED	STRATONIC	STREAKING	STREPENT	STRICK
STRAMPING	STRATOSE	STREAKS	STREPS	STRICKEN
STRAMPS	STRATOUS	STREAKY	STRESS	STRICKLE
STRAND	STRATUM	STREAM	STRESSED	STRICKLED
STRANDED	STRATUMS	STREAMBED	STRESSES	STRICKLES
STRANDER	STRATUS	STREAMED	STRESSFUL	STRICKS
STRANDERS	STRAUCHT	STREAMER	STRESSING	STRICT
STRANDING	STRAUCHTS	STREAMERS	STRESSOR	STRICTER
STRANDS	STRAUGHT	STREAMIER	STRESSORS	STRICTEST
STRANG	STRAUGHTS	STREAMING	STRETCH	STRICTION
STRANGE	STRAUNGE	STREAMLET	STRETCHED	STRICTISH
STRANGELY	STRAVAGE	STREAMS	STRETCHER	STRICTLY
STRANGER	STRAVAGED	STREAMY	STRETCHES	STRICTURE
STRANGERS	STRAVAGES	STREEK	STRETCHY	STRIDDEN
STRANGES	STRAVAIG	STREEKED	STRETTA	STRIDDLE
STRANGEST	STRAVAIGS	STREEKER	STRETTAS	STRIDDLED
STRANGLE	STRAW	STREEKERS	STRETTE	STRIDDLES
STRANGLED	STRAWED	STREEKING	STRETTI	STRIDE
STRANGLER	STRAWEN	STREEKS	STRETTO	STRIDENCE

STRIDENCY	STRINKLED	STROBINGS	STRONTIAS	STROYING
STRIDENT	STRINKLES	STRODDLE	STRONTIC	STROYS
STRIDER	STRIP	STRODDLED	STRONTIUM	STRUCK
STRIDERS	STRIPE	STRODDLES	STROOK	STRUCKEN
STRIDES	STRIPED	STRODE	STROOKE	STRUCTURE
STRIDING	STRIPER	STRODLE	STROOKEN	STRUDEL
STRIDLING	STRIPERS	STRODLED	STROOKES	STRUDELS
STRIDOR	STRIPES	STRODLES	STROP	STRUGGLE
STRIDORS	STRIPEY	STRODLING	STROPHE	STRUGGLED
STRIFE	STRIPIER	STROKABLE	STROPHES	STRUGGLER
STRIFEFUL	STRIPIEST	STROKE	STROPHIC	STRUGGLES
STRIFES	STRIPING	STROKED	STROPHOID	STRUM
STRIFT	STRIPINGS	STROKEN	STROPHULI	STRUMA
STRIFTS	STRIPLING	STROKER	STROPPED	STRUMAE
STRIG	STRIPPED	STROKERS	STROPPER	STRUMAS
STRIGA	STRIPPER	STROKES	STROPPERS	STRUMATIC
STRIGAE	STRIPPERS	STROKING	STROPPIER	STRUMITIS
STRIGATE	STRIPPING	STROKINGS	STROPPILY	STRUMMED
STRIGGED	STRIPS	STROLL	STROPPING	STRUMMEL
STRIGGING	STRIPT	STROLLED	STROPPY	STRUMMELS
STRIGIL	STRIPY	STROLLER	STROPS	STRUMMER
STRIGILS	STRIVE	STROLLERS	STROSSERS	STRUMMERS
STRIGINE	STRIVED	STROLLING	STROUD	STRUMMING
STRIGOSE	STRIVEN	STROLLS	STROUDING	STRUMOSE
STRIGS	STRIVER	STROMA	STROUDS	STRUMOUS
STRIKE	STRIVERS	STROMAL	STROUP	STRUMPET
STRIKEOUT	STRIVES	STROMATA	STROUPACH	STRUMPETS
STRIKER	STRIVING	STROMATIC	STROUPAN	STRUMS
STRIKERS	STRIVINGS	STROMB	STROUPANS	STRUNG
STRIKES	STROAM	STROMBS	STROUPS	STRUNT
STRIKING	STROAMED	STROMBUS	STROUT	STRUNTED
STRIKINGS	STROAMING	STROND	STROUTED	STRUNTING
STRIM	STROAMS	STRONDS	STROUTING	STRUNTS
STRIMMED	STROBE	STRONG	STROUTS	STRUT
STRIMMING	STROBED	STRONGARM	STROVE	STRUTS
STRIMS	STROBES	STRONGBOX	STROW	STRUTTED
STRING	STROBIC	STRONGER	STROWED	STRUTTER
STRINGED	STROBIL	STRONGEST	STROWER	STRUTTERS
STRINGENT	STROBILA	STRONGISH	STROWERS	STRUTTING
STRINGER	STROBILAE	STRONGLY	STROWING	STRYCHNIA
STRINGERS	STROBILAR	STRONGMAN	STROWINGS	STRYCHNIC
STRINGIER	STROBILE	STRONGMEN	STROWN	STUB
STRINGILY	STROBILES	STRONGYL	STROWS	STUBBED
STRINGING	STROBILI	STRONGYLE	STROY	STUBBIE
STRINGS	STROBILS	STRONGYLS	STROYED	STUBBIER
STRINGY	STROBILUS	STRONTIA	STROYER	STUBBIES
STRINKLE	STROBING	STRONTIAN	STROYERS	STUBBIEST

STUBBILY	STUDIOUS	STUMMING	STUPIDEST	STYLEE
STUBBING	STUDLIER	STUMP	STUPIDITY	STYLEES
STUBBLE	STUDLIEST	STUMPAGE	STUPIDLY	STYLELESS
STUBBLED	STUDLY	STUMPAGES	STUPIDS	STYLER
STUBBLES	STUDS	STUMPED	STUPING	STYLERS
STUBBLIER	STUDWORK	STUMPER	STUPOR	STYLES
STUBBLY	STUDWORKS	STUMPERS	STUPOROUS	STYLET
STUBBORN	STUDY	STUMPIER	STUPORS	STYLETS
STUBBORNS	STUDYING	STUMPIES	STUPRATE	STYLI
STUBBY	STUFF	STUMPIEST	STUPRATED	STYLIE
STUBS	STUFFED	STUMPILY	STUPRATES	STYLIER
STUCCO	STUFFER	STUMPING	STURDIED	STYLIEST
STUCCOED	STUFFERS	STUMPINGS	STURDIER	STYLIFORM
STUCCOER	STUFFIER	STUMPS	STURDIES	STYLING
STUCCOERS	STUFFIEST	STUMPWORK	STURDIEST	STYLINGS
STUCCOES	STUFFILY	STUMPY	STURDILY	STYLISE
STUCCOING	STUFFING	STUMS	STURDY	STYLISED
STUCCOS	STUFFINGS	STUN	STURE	STYLISER
STUCK	STUFFLESS	STUNG	STURGEON	STYLISERS
STUCKS	STUFFS	STUNK	STURGEONS	STYLISES
STUD	STUFFY	STUNKARD	STURMER	STYLISH
STUDBOOK	STUGGIER	STUNNED	STURMERS	STYLISHLY
STUDBOOKS	STUGGIEST	STUNNER	STURNINE	STYLISING
STUDDED	STUGGY	STUNNERS	STURNOID	STYLIST
STUDDEN	STUIVER	STUNNING	STURNUS	STYLISTIC
STUDDIE	STUIVERS	STUNNINGS	STURNUSES	STYLISTS
STUDDIES	STUKKEND	STUNS	STURT	STYLITE
STUDDING	STULL	STUNSAIL	STURTED	STYLITES
STUDDINGS	STULLS	STUNSAILS	STURTING	STYLITIC
STUDDLE	STULM	STUNT	STURTS	STYLITISM
STUDDLES	STULMS	STUNTED	STUSHIE	STYLIZE
STUDE	STULTIFY	STUNTING	STUSHIES	STYLIZED
STUDENT	STUM	STUNTMAN	STUTTER	STYLIZER
STUDENTRY	STUMBLE	STUNTMEN	STUTTERED	STYLIZERS
STUDENTS	STUMBLED	STUNTS	STUTTERER	STYLIZES
STUDENTY	STUMBLER	STUPA	STUTTERS	STYLIZING
STUDFARM	STUMBLERS	STUPAS	STY	STYLO
STUDFARMS	STUMBLES	STUPE	STYE	STYLOBATE
STUDFISH	STUMBLIER	STUPED	STYED	STYLOID
STUDHORSE	STUMBLING	STUPEFIED	STYES	STYLOIDS
STUDIED	STUMBLY	STUPEFIER	STYGIAN	STYLOLITE
STUDIEDLY	STUMER	STUPEFIES	STYING	STYLOPES
STUDIER	STUMERS	STUPEFY	STYLAR	STYLOPISE
STUDIERS	STUMM	STUPENT	STYLATE	STYLOPIZE
STUDIES	STUMMED	STUPES	STYLE	STYLOPS
STUDIO	STUMMEL	STUPID	STYLEBOOK	STYLOS
STUDIOS	STUMMELS	STUPIDER	STYLED	STYLUS

S

STYLUSES	SUBABBOT	SUBBASS	SUBCOSTA	SUBDWARF
STYME	SUBABBOTS	SUBBASSES	SUBCOSTAE	SUBDWARFS
STYMED	SUBACID	SUBBED	SUBCOSTAL	SUBECHO
STYMES	SUBACIDLY	SUBBIE	SUBCOUNTY	SUBECHOES
STYMIE	SUBACRID	SUBBIES	SUBCRUST	SUBEDAR
STYMIED	SUBACT	SUBBING	SUBCRUSTS	SUBEDARS
STYMIEING	SUBACTED	SUBBINGS	SUBCULT	SUBEDIT
STYMIES	SUBACTING	SUBBLOCK	SUBCULTS	SUBEDITED
STYMING	SUBACTION	SUBBLOCKS	SUBCUTES	SUBEDITOR
STYMY	SUBACTS	SUBBRANCH	SUBCUTIS	SUBEDITS
STYMYING	SUBACUTE	SUBBREED	SUBDEACON	SUBENTIRE
STYPSIS	SUBADAR	SUBBREEDS	SUBDEALER	SUBENTRY
STYPSISES	SUBADARS	SUBBUREAU	SUBDEAN	SUBEPOCH
STYPTIC	SUBADULT	SUBBY	SUBDEANS	SUBEPOCHS
STYPTICAL	SUBADULTS	SUBCANTOR	SUBDEB	SUBEQUAL
STYPTICS	SUBAERIAL	SUBCASTE	SUBDEBS	SUBER
STYRAX	SUBAGENCY	SUBCASTES	SUBDEPOT	SUBERATE
STYRAXES	SUBAGENT	SUBCAUDAL	SUBDEPOTS	SUBERATES
STYRE	SUBAGENTS	SUBCAUSE	SUBDEPUTY	SUBERECT
STYRED	SUBAH	SUBCAUSES	SUBDERMAL	SUBEREOUS
STYRENE	SUBAHDAR	SUBCAVITY	SUBDEW	SUBERIC
STYRENES	SUBAHDARS	SUBCELL	SUBDEWED	SUBERIN
STYRES	SUBAHDARY	SUBCELLAR	SUBDEWING	SUBERINS
STYRING	SUBAHS	SUBCELLS	SUBDEWS	SUBERISE
STYROFOAM	SUBAHSHIP	SUBCENTER	SUBDIVIDE	SUBERISED
STYTE	SUBALAR	SUBCHASER	SUBDOLOUS	SUBERISES
STYTED	SUBALPINE	SUBCHIEF	SUBDORSAL	SUBERIZE
STYTES	SUBALTERN	SUBCHIEFS	SUBDUABLE	SUBERIZED
STYTING	SUBAPICAL	SUBCHORD	SUBDUABLY	SUBERIZES
SUABILITY	SUBAQUA	SUBCHORDS	SUBDUAL	SUBEROSE
SUABLE	SUBARCTIC	SUBCLAIM	SUBDUALS	SUBEROUS
SUABLY	SUBAREA	SUBCLAIMS	SUBDUCE	SUBERS
SUASIBLE	SUBAREAS	SUBCLAN	SUBDUCED	SUBFAMILY
SUASION	SUBARID	SUBCLANS	SUBDUCES	SUBFEU
SUASIONS	SUBAS	SUBCLASS	SUBDUCING	SUBFEUED
SUASIVE	SUBASTRAL	SUBCLAUSE	SUBDUCT	SUBFEUING
SUASIVELY	SUBATOM	SUBCLERK	SUBDUCTED	SUBFEUS
SUASORY	SUBATOMIC	SUBCLERKS	SUBDUCTS	SUBFIELD
SUAVE	SUBATOMS	SUBCLIMAX	SUBDUE	SUBFIELDS
SUAVELY	SUBAUDIO	SUBCODE	SUBDUED	SUBFILE
SUAVENESS	SUBAURAL	SUBCODES	SUBDUEDLY	SUBFILES
SUAVER	SUBAXIAL	SUBCOLONY	SUBDUER	SUBFIX
SUAVEST	SUBBASAL	SUBCONSUL	SUBDUERS	SUBFIXES
SUAVITIES	SUBBASE	SUBCOOL	SUBDUES	SUBFLOOR
SUAVITY	SUBBASES	SUBCOOLED	SUBDUING	SUBFLOORS
SUB	SUBBASIN	SUBCOOLS	SUBDUPLE	SUBFLUID
SUBA	SUBBASINS	SUBCORTEX	SUBDURAL	SUBFOSSIL

SUBFRAME	SUBJECTS	SUBMATRIX	SUBORNS	SUBSCALES
SUBFRAMES	SUBJOIN	SUBMEN	SUBOSCINE	SUBSCHEMA
SUBFUSC	SUBJOINED	SUBMENTA	SUBOVAL	SUBSCRIBE
SUBFUSCS	SUBJOINS	SUBMENTAL	SUBOVATE	SUBSCRIPT
SUBFUSK	SUBJUGATE	SUBMENTUM	SUBOXIDE	SUBSEA
SUBFUSKS	SUBLATE	SUBMENU	SUBOXIDES	SUBSECIVE
SUBGENERA	SUBLATED	SUBMENUS	SUBPANEL	SUBSECT
SUBGENRE	SUBLATES	SUBMERGE	SUBPANELS	SUBSECTOR
SUBGENRES	SUBLATING	SUBMERGED	SUBPAR	SUBSECTS
SUBGENUS	SUBLATION	SUBMERGES	SUBPART	SUBSELLIA
SUBGOAL	SUBLEASE	SUBMERSE	SUBPARTS	SUBSENSE
SUBGOALS	SUBLEASED	SUBMERSED	SUBPENA	SUBSENSES
SUBGRADE	SUBLEASES	SUBMERSES	SUBPENAED	SUBSERE
SUBGRADES	SUBLESSEE	SUBMICRON	SUBPENAS	SUBSERES
SUBGRAPH	SUBLESSOR	SUBMISS	SUBPERIOD	SUBSERIES
SUBGRAPHS	SUBLET	SUBMISSLY	SUBPHASE	SUBSERVE
SUBGROUP	SUBLETHAL	SUBMIT	SUBPHASES	SUBSERVED
SUBGROUPS	SUBLETS	SUBMITS	SUBPHYLA	SUBSERVES
SUBGUM	SUBLETTER	SUBMITTAL	SUBPHYLAR	SUBSET
SUBGUMS	SUBLEVEL	SUBMITTED	SUBPHYLUM	SUBSETS
SUBHA	SUBLEVELS	SUBMITTER	SUBPLOT	SUBSHAFT
SUBHAS	SUBLIMATE	SUBMUCOSA	SUBPLOTS	SUBSHAFTS
SUBHEAD	SUBLIME	SUBMUCOUS	SUBPOENA	SUBSHELL
SUBHEADS	SUBLIMED	SUBNASAL	SUBPOENAS	SUBSHELLS
SUBHEDRAL	SUBLIMELY	SUBNET	SUBPOLAR	SUBSHRUB
SUBHUMAN	SUBLIMER	SUBNETS	SUBPOTENT	SUBSHRUBS
SUBHUMANS	SUBLIMERS	SUBNEURAL	SUBPRIME	SUBSIDE
SUBHUMID	SUBLIMES	SUBNICHE	SUBPRIMES	SUBSIDED
SUBIDEA	SUBLIMEST	SUBNICHES	SUBPRIOR	SUBSIDER
SUBIDEAS	SUBLIMING	SUBNIVEAL	SUBPRIORS	SUBSIDERS
SUBIMAGO	SUBLIMISE	SUBNIVEAN	SUBPUBIC	SUBSIDES
SUBIMAGOS	SUBLIMIT	SUBNODAL	SUBRACE	SUBSIDIES
SUBINCISE	SUBLIMITS	SUBNORMAL	SUBRACES	SUBSIDING
SUBINDEX	SUBLIMITY	SUBNUCLEI	SUBREGION	SUBSIDISE
SUBINFEUD	SUBLIMIZE	SUBOCEAN	SUBRENT	SUBSIDIZE
SUBITEM	SUBLINE	SUBOCTAVE	SUBRENTS	SUBSIDY
SUBITEMS	SUBLINEAR	SUBOCULAR	SUBRING	SUBSIST
SUBITISE	SUBLINES	SUBOFFICE	SUBRINGS	SUBSISTED
SUBITISED	SUBLOT	SUBOPTIC	SUBROGATE	SUBSISTER
SUBITISES	SUBLOTS	SUBORAL	SUBRULE	SUBSISTS
SUBITIZE	SUBLUNAR	SUBORDER	SUBRULES	SUBSITE
SUBITIZED	SUBLUNARY	SUBORDERS	SUBS	SUBSITES
SUBITIZES	SUBLUNATE	SUBORN	SUBSACRAL	SUBSIZAR
SUBITO	SUBLUXATE	SUBORNED	SUBSALE	SUBSIZARS
SUBJACENT	SUBMAN	SUBORNER	SUBSALES	SUBSKILL
SUBJECT	SUBMARINE	SUBORNERS	SUBSAMPLE	SUBSKILLS
SUBJECTED	SUBMARKET	SUBORNING	SUBSCALE	SUBSOCIAL

S

SUBSOIL	SUBTEXT	SUBTUNIC	SUBZONAL	SUCCUBINE
SUBSOILED	SUBTEXTS	SUBTUNICS	SUBZONE	SUCCUBOUS
SUBSOILER	SUBTHEME	SUBTYPE	SUBZONES	SUCCUBUS
SUBSOILS	SUBTHEMES	SUBTYPES	SUCCADE	SUCCULENT
SUBSOLAR	SUBTIDAL	SUBUCULA	SUCCADES	SUCCUMB
SUBSONG	SUBTIL	SUBUCULAS	SUCCAH	SUCCUMBED
SUBSONGS	SUBTILE	SUBULATE	SUCCAHS	SUCCUMBER
SUBSONIC	SUBTILELY	SUBUNIT	SUCCEDENT	SUCCUMBS
SUBSPACE	SUBTILER	SUBUNITS	SUCCEED	SUCCURSAL
SUBSPACES	SUBTILEST	SUBURB	SUCCEEDED	SUCCUS
SUBSTAGE	SUBTILIN	SUBURBAN	SUCCEEDER	SUCCUSS
SUBSTAGES	SUBTILINS	SUBURBANS	SUCCEEDS	SUCCUSSED
SUBSTANCE	SUBTILISE	SUBURBED	SUCCENTOR	SUCCUSSES
SUBSTATE	SUBTILITY	SUBURBIA	SUCCES	SUCH
SUBSTATES	SUBTILIZE	SUBURBIAS	SUCCESS	SUCHLIKE
SUBSTRACT	SUBTILTY	SUBURBS	SUCCESSES	SUCHNESS
SUBSTRATA	SUBTITLE	SUBURSINE	SUCCESSOR	SUCHWISE
SUBSTRATE	SUBTITLED	SUBVASSAL	SUCCI	SUCK
SUBSTRUCT	SUBTITLES	SUBVENE	SUCCINATE	SUCKED
SUBSTYLAR	SUBTLE	SUBVENED	SUCCINCT	SUCKEN
SUBSTYLE	SUBTLER	SUBVENES	SUCCINIC	SUCKENER
SUBSTYLES	SUBTLEST	SUBVENING	SUCCINITE	SUCKENERS
SUBSULTUS	SUBTLETY	SUBVERSAL	SUCCINYL	SUCKENS
SUBSUME	SUBTLY	SUBVERSE	SUCCINYLS	SUCKER
SUBSUMED	SUBTONE	SUBVERSED	SUCCISE	SUCKERED
SUBSUMES	SUBTONES	SUBVERSES	SUCCOR	SUCKERING
SUBSUMING	SUBTONIC	SUBVERST	SUCCORED	SUCKERS
SUBSYSTEM	SUBTONICS	SUBVERT	SUCCORER	SUCKET
SUBTACK	SUBTOPIA	SUBVERTED	SUCCORERS	SUCKETS
SUBTACKS	SUBTOPIAN	SUBVERTER	SUCCORIES	SUCKFISH
SUBTALAR	SUBTOPIAS	SUBVERTS	SUCCORING	SUCKHOLE
SUBTASK	SUBTOPIC	SUBVICAR	SUCCORS	SUCKHOLES
SUBTASKS	SUBTOPICS	SUBVICARS	SUCCORY	SUCKIER
SUBTAXA	SUBTORRID	SUBVIRAL	SUCCOS	SUCKIEST
SUBTAXON	SUBTOTAL	SUBVIRUS	SUCCOSE	SUCKING
SUBTAXONS	SUBTOTALS	SUBVISUAL	SUCCOT	SUCKINGS
SUBTEEN	SUBTRACT	SUBVOCAL	SUCCOTASH	SUCKLE
SUBTEENS	SUBTRACTS	SUBWARDEN	SUCCOTH	SUCKLED
SUBTENANT	SUBTREND	SUBWAY	SUCCOUR	SUCKLER
SUBTEND	SUBTRENDS	SUBWAYED	SUCCOURED	SUCKLERS
SUBTENDED	SUBTRIBE	SUBWAYING	SUCCOURER	SUCKLES
SUBTENDS	SUBTRIBES	SUBWAYS	SUCCOURS	SUCKLESS
SUBTENSE	SUBTRIST	SUBWOOFER	SUCCOUS	SUCKLING
SUBTENSES	SUBTROPIC	SUBWORLD	SUCCUBA	SUCKLINGS
SUBTENURE	SUBTRUDE	SUBWORLDS	SUCCUBAE	SUCKS
SUBTEST	SUBTRUDED	SUBWRITER	SUCCUBAS	SUCKY
SUBTESTS	SUBTRUDES	SUBZERO	SUCCUBI	SUCRALOSE

SUCRASE	SUDSER	SUFFIXAL	SUGHED	SUJEE
SUCRASES	SUDSERS	SUFFIXED	SUGHING	SUJEES
SUCRE	SUDSES	SUFFIXES	SUGHS	SUK
SUCRES	SUDSIER	SUFFIXING	SUGO	SUKH
SUCRIER	SUDSIEST	SUFFIXION	SUGOS	SUKHS
SUCRIERS	SUDSING	SUFFLATE	SUGS	SUKIYAKI
SUCROSE	SUDSLESS	SUFFLATED	SUHUR	SUKIYAKIS
SUCROSES	SUDSY	SUFFLATES	SUHURS	SUKKAH
SUCTION	SUE	SUFFOCATE	SUI	SUKKAHS
SUCTIONAL	SUEABLE	SUFFRAGAN	SUICIDAL	SUKKOS
SUCTIONED	SUED	SUFFRAGE	SUICIDE	SUKKOT
SUCTIONS	SUEDE	SUFFRAGES	SUICIDED	SUKKOTH
SUCTORIAL	SUEDED	SUFFUSE	SUICIDES	SUKS
SUCTORIAN	SUEDES	SUFFUSED	SUICIDING	SUKUK
SUCURUJU	SUEDETTE	SUFFUSES	SUID	SUKUKS
SUCURUJUS	SUEDETTES	SUFFUSING	SUIDIAN	SULCAL
SUD	SUEDING	SUFFUSION	SUIDIANS	SULCALISE
SUDAMEN	SUENT	SUFFUSIVE	SUIDS	SULCALIZE
SUDAMINA	SUER	SUG	SUILLINE	SULCATE
SUDAMINAL	SUERS	SUGAN	SUING	SULCATED
SUDARIA	SUES	SUGANS	SUINGS	SULCATION
SUDARIES	SUET	SUGAR	SUINT	SULCI
SUDARIUM	SUETIER	SUGARALLY	SUINTS	SULCUS
SUDARY	SUETIEST	SUGARBUSH	SUIPLAP	SULDAN
SUDATE	SUETS	SUGARCANE	SUIPLAPS	SULDANS
SUDATED	SUETTIER	SUGARCOAT	SUIT	SULFA
SUDATES	SUETTIEST	SUGARED	SUITABLE	SULFAS
SUDATING	SUETTY	SUGARER	SUITABLY	SULFATASE
SUDATION	SUETY	SUGARERS	SUITCASE	SULFATE
SUDATIONS	SUFFARI	SUGARIER	SUITCASES	SULFATED
SUDATORIA	SUFFARIS	SUGARIEST	SUITE	SULFATES
SUDATORY	SUFFECT	SUGARING	SUITED	SULFATIC
SUDD	SUFFER	SUGARINGS	SUITER	SULFATING
SUDDEN	SUFFERED	SUGARLESS	SUITERS	SULFATION
SUDDENLY	SUFFERER	SUGARLIKE	SUITES	SULFID
SUDDENS	SUFFERERS	SUGARLOAF	SUITING	SULFIDE
SUDDENTY	SUFFERING	SUGARPLUM	SUITINGS	SULFIDES
SUDDER	SUFFERS	SUGARS	SUITLIKE	SULFIDS
SUDDERS	SUFFETE	SUGARY	SUITOR	SULFINYL
SUDDS	SUFFETES	SUGGED	SUITORED	SULFINYLS
SUDOR	SUFFICE	SUGGEST	SUITORING	SULFITE
SUDORAL	SUFFICED	SUGGESTED	SUITORS	SULFITES
SUDORIFIC	SUFFICER	SUGGESTER	SUITRESS	SULFITIC
SUDOROUS	SUFFICERS	SUGGESTS	SUITS	SULFO
SUDORS	SUFFICES	SUGGING	SUIVANTE	SULFONATE
SUDS	SUFFICING	SUGGINGS	SUIVANTES	SULFONE
SUDSED	SUFFIX	SUGH	SUIVEZ	SULFONES

S

SULFONIC	SULPHATED	SUMMAND	SUMOIST	SUNBIRDS
SULFONIUM	SULPHATES	SUMMANDS	SUMOISTS	SUNBLIND
SULFONYL	SULPHATIC	SUMMAR	SUMOS	SUNBLINDS
SULFONYLS	SULPHID	SUMMARIES	SUMOTORI	SUNBLOCK
SULFOXIDE	SULPHIDE	SUMMARILY	SUMOTORIS	SUNBLOCKS
SULFUR	SULPHIDES	SUMMARISE	SUMP	SUNBONNET
SULFURATE	SULPHIDS	SUMMARIST	SUMPH	SUNBOW
SULFURED	SULPHINYL	SUMMARIZE	SUMPHISH	SUNBOWS
SULFURET	SULPHITE	SUMMARY	SUMPHS	SUNBRIGHT
SULFURETS	SULPHITES	SUMMAS	SUMPIT	SUNBURN
SULFURIC	SULPHITIC	SUMMAT	SUMPITAN	SUNBURNED
SULFURING	SULPHONE	SUMMATE	SUMPITANS	SUNBURNS
SULFURISE	SULPHONES	SUMMATED	SUMPITS	SUNBURNT
SULFURIZE	SULPHONIC	SUMMATES	SUMPS	SUNBURST
SULFUROUS	SULPHONYL	SUMMATING	SUMPSIMUS	SUNBURSTS
SULFURS	SULPHS	SUMMATION	SUMPTER	SUNCHOKE
SULFURY	SULPHUR	SUMMATIVE	SUMPTERS	SUNCHOKES
SULFURYL	SULPHURED	SUMMATS	SUMPTUARY	SUNDAE
SULFURYLS	SULPHURET	SUMMED	SUMPTUOUS	SUNDAES
SULK	SULPHURIC	SUMMER	SUMPWEED	SUNDARI
SULKED	SULPHURS	SUMMERED	SUMPWEEDS	SUNDARIS
SULKER	SULPHURY	SUMMERIER	SUMS	SUNDECK
SULKERS	SULPHURYL	SUMMERING	SUMY	SUNDECKS
SULKIER	SULTAN	SUMMERLY	SUN	SUNDER
SULKIES	SULTANA	SUMMERS	SUNBACK	SUNDERED
SULKIEST	SULTANAS	SUMMERSET	SUNBAKE	SUNDERER
SULKILY	SULTANATE	SUMMERY	SUNBAKED	SUNDERERS
SULKINESS	SULTANESS	SUMMING	SUNBAKES	SUNDERING
SULKING	SULTANIC	SUMMINGS	SUNBAKING	SUNDERS
SULKS	SULTANS	SUMMIST	SUNBATH	SUNDEW
SULKY	SULTRIER	SUMMISTS	SUNBATHE	SUNDEWS
SULLAGE	SULTRIEST	SUMMIT	SUNBATHED	SUNDIAL
SULLAGES	SULTRILY	SUMMITAL	SUNBATHER	SUNDIALS
SULLEN	SULTRY	SUMMITED	SUNBATHES	SUNDOG
SULLENER	SULU	SUMMITEER	SUNBATHS	SUNDOGS
SULLENEST	SULUS	SUMMITING	SUNBEAM	SUNDOWN
SULLENLY	SUM	SUMMITRY	SUNBEAMED	SUNDOWNED
SULLENS	SUMAC	SUMMITS	SUNBEAMS	SUNDOWNER
SULLIABLE	SUMACH	SUMMON	SUNBEAMY	SUNDOWNS
SULLIED	SUMACHS	SUMMONED	SUNBEAT	SUNDRA
SULLIES	SUMACS	SUMMONER	SUNBEATEN	SUNDRAS
SULLY	SUMATRA	SUMMONERS	SUNBED	SUNDRESS
SULLYING	SUMATRAS	SUMMONING	SUNBEDS	SUNDRI
SULPH	SUMLESS	SUMMONS	SUNBELT	SUNDRIES
SULPHA	SUMMA	SUMMONSED	SUNBELTS	SUNDRILY
SULPHAS	SUMMABLE	SUMMONSES	SUNBERRY	SUNDRIS
SULPHATE	SUMMAE	SUMO	SUNBIRD	SUNDROPS

S

SUNDRY	SUNNINESS	SUP	SUPERFAST	SUPERMOTO
SUNFAST	SUNNING	SUPAWN	SUPERFINE	SUPERNAL
SUNFISH	SUNNS	SUPAWNS	SUPERFIRM	SUPERNATE
SUNFISHES	SUNNY	SUPE	SUPERFIT	SUPERNOVA
SUNFLOWER	SUNPORCH	SUPER	SUPERFIX	SUPERPIMP
SUNG	SUNPROOF	SUPERABLE	SUPERFLUX	SUPERPLUS
SUNGAR	SUNRAY	SUPERABLY	SUPERFOOD	SUPERPORT
SUNGARS	SUNRAYS	SUPERADD	SUPERFUND	SUPERPOSE
SUNGAZER	SUNRISE	SUPERADDS	SUPERFUSE	SUPERPRO
SUNGAZERS	SUNRISES	SUPERATE	SUPERGENE	SUPERPROS
SUNGAZING	SUNRISING	SUPERATED	SUPERGLUE	SUPERRACE
SUNGLASS	SUNROOF	SUPERATES	SUPERGOOD	SUPERREAL
SUNGLOW	SUNROOFS	SUPERATOM	SUPERGUN	SUPERRICH
SUNGLOWS	SUNROOM	SUPERB	SUPERGUNS	SUPERROAD
SUNGREBE	SUNROOMS	SUPERBAD	SUPERHEAT	SUPERS
SUNGREBES	SUNS	SUPERBANK	SUPERHERO	SUPERSAFE
SUNHAT	SUNSCALD	SUPERBER	SUPERHET	SUPERSALE
SUNHATS	SUNSCALDS	SUPERBEST	SUPERHETS	SUPERSALT
SUNI	SUNSCREEN	SUPERBIKE	SUPERHIGH	SUPERSAUR
SUNIS	SUNSEEKER	SUPERBITY	SUPERHIT	SUPERSEDE
SUNK	SUNSET	SUPERBLY	SUPERHITS	SUPERSELL
SUNKEN	SUNSETS	SUPERBOLD	SUPERHIVE	SUPERSEX
SUNKET	SUNSHADE	SUPERBOMB	SUPERHOT	SUPERSHOW
SUNKETS	SUNSHADES	SUPERBRAT	SUPERHYPE	SUPERSIZE
SUNKIE	SUNSHINE	SUPERBUG	SUPERING	SUPERSOFT
SUNKIES	SUNSHINES	SUPERBUGS	SUPERIOR	SUPERSOLD
SUNKS	SUNSHINY	SUPERCAR	SUPERIORS	SUPERSPY
SUNLAMP	SUNSPOT	SUPERCARS	SUPERJET	SUPERSTAR
SUNLAMPS	SUNSPOTS	SUPERCEDE	SUPERJETS	SUPERSTUD
SUNLAND	SUNSTAR	SUPERCHIC	SUPERJOCK	SUPERTAX
SUNLANDS	SUNSTARS	SUPERCITY	SUPERLAIN	SUPERTHIN
SUNLESS	SUNSTONE	SUPERCLUB	SUPERLAY	SUPERTRAM
SUNLESSLY	SUNSTONES	SUPERCOIL	SUPERLIE	SUPERVENE
SUNLIGHT	SUNSTROKE	SUPERCOLD	SUPERLIES	SUPERVISE
SUNLIGHTS	SUNSTRUCK	SUPERCOOL	SUPERLOAD	SUPERWAIF
SUNLIKE	SUNSUIT	SUPERCOP	SUPERLONG	SUPERWAVE
SUNLIT	SUNSUITS	SUPERCOPS	SUPERLOO	SUPERWEED
SUNN	SUNTAN	SUPERCOW	SUPERLOOS	SUPERWIDE
SUNNA	SUNTANNED	SUPERCOWS	SUPERMALE	SUPERWIFE
SUNNAH	SUNTANS	SUPERCUTE	SUPERMAN	SUPES
SUNNAHS	SUNTRAP	SUPERED	SUPERMART	SUPINATE
SUNNAS	SUNTRAPS	SUPEREGO	SUPERMAX	SUPINATED
SUNNED	SUNUP	SUPEREGOS	SUPERMEN	SUPINATES
SUNNIER	SUNUPS	SUPERETTE	SUPERMIND	SUPINATOR
SUNNIES	SUNWARD	SUPERFAN	SUPERMINI	SUPINE
SUNNIEST	SUNWARDS	SUPERFANS	SUPERMOM	SUPINELY
SUNNILY	SUNWISE	SUPERFARM	SUPERMOMS	SUPINES

SUPLEX	SUPREME	SURCULUS	SURFMEN	SURMOUNTS
SUPLEXES	SUPREMELY	SURD	SURFPERCH	SURMULLET
SUPPAWN	SUPREMER	SURDITIES	SURFRIDER	SURNAME
SUPPAWNS	SUPREMES	SURDITY	SURFS	SURNAMED
SUPPEAGO	SUPREMEST	SURDS	SURFSIDE	SURNAMER
SUPPED	SUPREMITY	SURE	SURFY	SURNAMERS
SUPPER	SUPREMO	SURED	SURGE	SURNAMES
SUPPERED	SUPREMOS	SUREFIRE	SURGED	SURNAMING
SUPPERING	SUPREMUM	SURELY	SURGEFUL	SURPASS
SUPPERS	SUPREMUMS	SURENESS	SURGELESS	SURPASSED
SUPPING	SUPS	SURER	SURGENT	SURPASSER
SUPPLANT	SUQ	SURES	SURGEON	SURPASSES
SUPPLANTS	SUQS	SUREST	SURGEONCY	SURPLICE
SUPPLE	SUR	SURETIED	SURGEONS	SURPLICED
SUPPLED	SURA	SURETIES	SURGER	SURPLICES
SUPPLELY	SURAH	SURETY	SURGERIES	SURPLUS
SUPPLER	SURAHS	SURETYING	SURGERS	SURPLUSED
SUPPLES	SURAL	SURF	SURGERY	SURPLUSES
SUPPLEST	SURAMIN	SURFABLE	SURGES	SURPRINT
SUPPLIAL	SURAMINS	SURFACE	SURGICAL	SURPRINTS
SUPPLIALS	SURANCE	SURFACED	SURGIER	SURPRISAL
SUPPLIANT	SURANCES	SURFACER	SURGIEST	SURPRISE
SUPPLICAT	SURAS	SURFACERS	SURGING	SURPRISED
SUPPLIED	SURAT	SURFACES	SURGINGS	SURPRISER
SUPPLIER	SURATS	SURFACING	SURGY	SURPRISES
SUPPLIERS	SURBAHAR	SURFBIRD	SURICATE	SURPRIZE
SUPPLIES	SURBAHARS	SURFBIRDS	SURICATES	SURPRIZED
SUPPLING	SURBASE	SURFBOARD	SURIMI	SURPRIZES
SUPPLY	SURBASED	SURFBOAT	SURIMIS	SURQUEDRY
SUPPLYING	SURBASES	SURFBOATS	SURING	SURQUEDY
SUPPORT	SURBATE	SURFED	SURLIER	SURRA
SUPPORTED	SURBATED	SURFEIT	SURLIEST	SURRAS
SUPPORTER	SURBATES	SURFEITED	SURLILY	SURREAL
SUPPORTS	SURBATING	SURFEITER	SURLINESS	SURREALLY
SUPPOSAL	SURBED	SURFEITS	SURLOIN	SURREALS
SUPPOSALS	SURBEDDED	SURFER	SURLOINS	SURREBUT
SUPPOSE	SURBEDS	SURFERS	SURLY	SURREBUTS
SUPPOSED	SURBET	SURFFISH	SURMASTER	SURREINED
SUPPOSER	SURCEASE	SURFICIAL	SURMISAL	SURREJOIN
SUPPOSERS	SURCEASED	SURFIE	SURMISALS	SURRENDER
SUPPOSES	SURCEASES	SURFIER	SURMISE	SURRENDRY
SUPPOSING	SURCHARGE	SURFIES	SURMISED	SURREY
SUPPRESS	SURCINGLE	SURFIEST	SURMISER	SURREYS
SUPPURATE	SURCOAT	SURFING	SURMISERS	SURROGACY
SUPRA	SURCOATS	SURFINGS	SURMISES	SURROGATE
SUPREMA	SURCULI	SURFLIKE	SURMISING	SURROUND
SUPREMACY	SURCULOSE	SURFMAN	SURMOUNT	SURROUNDS

SURROYAL	SUSPECTER	SUTTEES	SWAG	SWAMP
SURROYALS	SUSPECTS	SUTTLE	SWAGE	SWAMPED
SURTAX	SUSPENCE	SUTTLED	SWAGED	SWAMPER
SURTAXED	SUSPEND	SUTTLES	SWAGER	SWAMPERS
SURTAXES	SUSPENDED	SUTTLETIE	SWAGERS	SWAMPIER
SURTAXING	SUSPENDER	SUTTLING	SWAGES	SWAMPIEST
SURTITLE	SUSPENDS	SUTTLY	SWAGGED	SWAMPING
SURTITLES	SUSPENS	SUTURAL	SWAGGER	SWAMPISH
SURTOUT	SUSPENSE	SUTURALLY	SWAGGERED	SWAMPLAND
SURTOUTS	SUSPENSER	SUTURE	SWAGGERER	SWAMPLESS
SURUCUCU	SUSPENSES	SUTURED	SWAGGERS	SWAMPS
SURUCUCUS	SUSPENSOR	SUTURES	SWAGGIE	SWAMPY
SURVEIL	SUSPICION	SUTURING	SWAGGIES	SWAMY
SURVEILED	SUSPIRE	SUZERAIN	SWAGGING	SWAN
SURVEILLE	SUSPIRED	SUZERAINS	SWAGING	SWANG
SURVEILS	SUSPIRES	SVARAJ	SWAGMAN	SWANHERD
SURVEY	SUSPIRING	SVARAJES	SWAGMEN	SWANHERDS
SURVEYAL	SUSS	SVASTIKA	SWAGS	SWANK
SURVEYALS	SUSSED	SVASTIKAS	SWAGSHOP	SWANKED
SURVEYED	SUSSES	SVEDBERG	SWAGSHOPS	SWANKER
SURVEYING	SUSSING	SVEDBERGS	SWAGSMAN	SWANKERS
SURVEYOR	SUSTAIN	SVELTE	SWAGSMEN	SWANKEST
SURVEYORS	SUSTAINED	SVELTELY	SWAIL	SWANKEY
SURVEYS	SUSTAINER	SVELTER	SWAILS	SWANKEYS
SURVIEW	SUSTAINS	SVELTEST	SWAIN	SWANKIE
SURVIEWED	SUSTINENT	SWAB	SWAINING	SWANKIER
SURVIEWS	SUSU	SWABBED	SWAININGS	SWANKIES
SURVIVAL	SUSURRANT	SWABBER	SWAINISH	SWANKIEST
SURVIVALS	SUSURRATE	SWABBERS	SWAINS	SWANKILY
SURVIVE	SUSURROUS	SWABBIE	SWALE	SWANKING
SURVIVED	SUSURRUS	SWABBIES	SWALED	SWANKPOT
SURVIVER	SUSUS	SWABBING	SWALES	SWANKPOTS
SURVIVERS	SUTILE	SWABBY	SWALIER	SWANKS
SURVIVES	SUTLER	SWABS	SWALIEST	SWANKY
SURVIVING	SUTLERIES	SWACK	SWALING	SWANLIKE
SURVIVOR	SUTLERS	SWACKED	SWALINGS	SWANNED
SURVIVORS	SUTLERY	SWAD	SWALLET	SWANNERY
SUS	SUTOR	SWADDIE	SWALLETS	SWANNIE
SUSCEPTOR	SUTORIAL	SWADDIES	SWALLOW	SWANNIER
SUSCITATE	SUTORIAN	SWADDLE	SWALLOWED	SWANNIES
SUSES	SUTORS	SWADDLED	SWALLOWER	SWANNIEST
SUSHI	SUTRA	SWADDLER	SWALLOWS	SWANNING
SUSHIS	SUTRAS	SWADDLERS	SWALY	SWANNINGS
SUSLIK	SUTTA	SWADDLES	SWAM	SWANNY
SUSLIKS	SUTTAS	SWADDLING	SWAMI	SWANPAN
SUSPECT	SUTTEE	SWADDY	SWAMIES	SWANPANS
SUSPECTED	SUTTEEISM	SWADS	SWAMIS	SWANS

S

SWANSDOWN	SWARVED	SWAYED	SWEDE	SWEETLIPS
SWANSKIN	SWARVES	SWAYER	SWEDES	SWEETLY
SWANSKINS	SWARVING	SWAYERS	SWEDGER	SWEETMAN
SWANSONG	SWASH	SWAYFUL	SWEDGERS	SWEETMEAL
SWANSONGS	SWASHED	SWAYING	SWEE	SWEETMEAT
SWAP	SWASHER	SWAYINGS	SWEED	SWEETMEN
SWAPPED	SWASHERS	SWAYL	SWEEING	SWEETNESS
SWAPPER	SWASHES	SWAYLED	SWEEL	SWEETS
SWAPPERS	SWASHIER	SWAYLING	SWEELED	SWEETSHOP
SWAPPING	SWASHIEST	SWAYLINGS	SWEELING	SWEETSOP
SWAPPINGS	SWASHING	SWAYLS	SWEELS	SWEETSOPS
SWAPS	SWASHINGS	SWAYS	SWEENEY	SWEETVELD
SWAPT	SWASHWORK	SWAZZLE	SWEENEYS	SWEETWOOD
SWAPTION	SWASHY	SWAZZLES	SWEENIES	SWEETY
SWAPTIONS	SWASTICA	SWEAL	SWEENY	SWEIR
SWARAJ	SWASTICAS	SWEALED	SWEEP	SWEIRED
SWARAJES	SWASTIKA	SWEALING	SWEEPBACK	SWEIRER
SWARAJISM	SWASTIKAS	SWEALINGS	SWEEPER	SWEIREST
SWARAJIST	SWAT	SWEALS	SWEEPERS	SWEIRING
SWARD	SWATCH	SWEAR	SWEEPIER	SWEIRNESS
SWARDED	SWATCHES	SWEARD	SWEEPIEST	SWEIRS
SWARDIER	SWATH	SWEARDS	SWEEPING	SWEIRT
SWARDIEST	SWATHABLE	SWEARER	SWEEPINGS	SWELCHIE
SWARDING	SWATHE	SWEARERS	SWEEPS	SWELCHIES
SWARDS	SWATHED	SWEARIER	SWEEPY	SWELL
SWARDY	SWATHER	SWEARIEST	SWEER	SWELLDOM
SWARE	SWATHERS	SWEARING	SWEERED	SWELLDOMS
SWARF	SWATHES	SWEARINGS	SWEERING	SWELLED
SWARFED	SWATHIER	SWEARS	SWEERS	SWELLER
SWARFING	SWATHIEST	SWEARWORD	SWEERT	SWELLERS
SWARFS	SWATHING	SWEARY	SWEES	SWELLEST
SWARM	SWATHS	SWEAT	SWEET	SWELLFISH
SWARMED	SWATHY	SWEATBAND	SWEETCORN	SWELLHEAD
SWARMER	SWATS	SWEATBOX	SWEETED	SWELLING
SWARMERS	SWATTED	SWEATED	SWEETEN	SWELLINGS
SWARMING	SWATTER	SWEATER	SWEETENED	SWELLISH
SWARMINGS	SWATTERED	SWEATERS	SWEETENER	SWELLS
SWARMS	SWATTERS	SWEATIER	SWEETENS	SWELT
SWART	SWATTIER	SWEATIEST	SWEETER	SWELTED
SWARTH	SWATTIEST	SWEATILY	SWEETEST	SWELTER
SWARTHIER	SWATTING	SWEATING	SWEETFISH	SWELTERED
SWARTHILY	SWATTINGS	SWEATINGS	SWEETIE	SWELTERS
SWARTHS	SWATTY	SWEATLESS	SWEETIES	SWELTING
SWARTHY	SWAY	SWEATS	SWEETING	SWELTRIER
SWARTNESS	SWAYABLE	SWEATSHOP	SWEETINGS	SWELTRY
SWARTY	SWAYBACK	SWEATSUIT	SWEETISH	SWELTS
SWARVE	SWAYBACKS	SWEATY	SWEETLIP	SWEPT

SWEPTBACK	SWILLER	SWINGBYS	SWIRES	SWIVELING
SWEPTWING	SWILLERS	SWINGE	SWIRL	SWIVELLED
SWERF	SWILLING	SWINGED	SWIRLED	SWIVELS
SWERFED	SWILLINGS	SWINGEING	SWIRLIER	SWIVES
SWERFING	SWILLS	SWINGER	SWIRLIEST	SWIVET
SWERFS	SWIM	SWINGERS	SWIRLING	SWIVETS
SWERVABLE	SWIMMABLE	SWINGES	SWIRLS	SWIVING
SWERVE	SWIMMER	SWINGIER	SWIRLY	SWIZ
SWERVED	SWIMMERET	SWINGIEST	SWISH	SWIZZ
SWERVER	SWIMMERS	SWINGING	SWISHED	SWIZZED
SWERVERS	SWIMMIER	SWINGINGS	SWISHER	SWIZZES
SWERVES	SWIMMIEST	SWINGISM	SWISHERS	SWIZZING
SWERVING	SWIMMILY	SWINGISMS	SWISHES	SWIZZLE
SWERVINGS	SWIMMING	SWINGLE	SWISHEST	SWIZZLED
SWEVEN	SWIMMINGS	SWINGLED	SWISHIER	SWIZZLER
SWEVENS	SWIMMY	SWINGLES	SWISHIEST	SWIZZLERS
SWEY	SWIMS	SWINGLING	SWISHING	SWIZZLES
SWEYED	SWIMSUIT	SWINGMAN	SWISHINGS	SWIZZLING
SWEYING	SWIMSUITS	SWINGMEN	SWISHY	SWOB
SWEYS	SWIMWEAR	SWINGS	SWISS	SWOBBED
SWIDDEN	SWIMWEARS	SWINGTAIL	SWISSES	SWOBBER
SWIDDENS	SWINDGE	SWINGTREE	SWISSING	SWOBBERS
SWIES	SWINDGED	SWINGY	SWISSINGS	SWOBBING
SWIFT	SWINDGES	SWINISH	SWITCH	SWOBS
SWIFTED	SWINDGING	SWINISHLY	SWITCHED	SWOFFER
SWIFTER	SWINDLE	SWINK	SWITCHEL	SWOFFERS
SWIFTERS	SWINDLED	SWINKED	SWITCHELS	SWOFFING
SWIFTEST	SWINDLER	SWINKER	SWITCHER	SWOFFINGS
SWIFTIE	SWINDLERS	SWINKERS	SWITCHERS	SWOLLEN
SWIFTIES	SWINDLES	SWINKING	SWITCHES	SWOLLENLY
SWIFTING	SWINDLING	SWINKS	SWITCHIER	SWOLN
SWIFTLET	SWINE	SWINNEY	SWITCHING	SWOON
SWIFTLETS	SWINEHERD	SWINNEYS	SWITCHMAN	SWOONED
SWIFTLY	SWINEHOOD	SWIPE	SWITCHMEN	SWOONER
SWIFTNESS	SWINELIKE	SWIPED	SWITCHY	SWOONERS
SWIFTS	SWINEPOX	SWIPER	SWITH	SWOONIER
SWIFTY	SWINERIES	SWIPERS	SWITHE	SWOONIEST
SWIG	SWINERY	SWIPES	SWITHER	SWOONING
SWIGGED	SWINES	SWIPEY	SWITHERED	SWOONINGS
SWIGGER	SWING	SWIPIER	SWITHERS	SWOONS
SWIGGERS	SWINGARM	SWIPIEST	SWITHLY	SWOONY
SWIGGING	SWINGARMS	SWIPING	SWITS	SWOOP
SWIGS	SWINGBEAT	SWIPLE	SWITSES	SWOOPED
SWILER	SWINGBIN	SWIPLES	SWIVE	SWOOPER
SWILERS	SWINGBINS	SWIPPLE	SWIVED	SWOOPERS
SWILL	SWINGBOAT	SWIPPLES	SWIVEL	SWOOPIER
SWILLED	SWINGBY	SWIRE	SWIVELED	SWOOPIEST

S

SWOOPING

SWOOPING
SWOOPS
SWOOPY
SWOOSH
SWOOSHED
SWOOSHES
SWOOSHING
SWOP
SWOPPED
SWOPPER
SWOPPERS
SWOPPING
SWOPPINGS
SWOPS
SWOPT
SWORD
SWORDBILL
SWORDED
SWORDER
SWORDERS
SWORDFISH
SWORDING
SWORDLESS
SWORDLIKE
SWORDMAN
SWORDMEN
SWORDPLAY
SWORDS
SWORDSMAN
SWORDSMEN
SWORDTAIL
SWORE
SWORN
SWOT
SWOTS
SWOTTED
SWOTTER
SWOTTERS
SWOTTIER
SWOTTIEST
SWOTTING
SWOTTINGS
SWOTTY
SWOUN
SWOUND
SWOUNDED
SWOUNDING

SWOUNDS
SWOUNE
SWOUNED
SWOUNES
SWOUNING
SWOUNS
SWOWND
SWOWNDS
SWOWNE
SWOWNES
SWOZZLE
SWOZZLES
SWUM
SWUNG
SWY
SYBARITE
SYBARITES
SYBARITIC
SYBBE
SYBBES
SYBIL
SYBILS
SYBO
SYBOE
SYBOES
SYBOTIC
SYBOTISM
SYBOTISMS
SYBOW
SYBOWS
SYCAMINE
SYCAMINES
SYCAMORE
SYCAMORES
SYCE
SYCEE
SYCEES
SYCES
SYCOMORE
SYCOMORES
SYCONIA
SYCONIUM
SYCOPHANT
SYCOSES
SYCOSIS
SYE
SYED

SYEING
SYEN
SYENITE
SYENITES
SYENITIC
SYENS
SYES
SYKE
SYKER
SYKES
SYLI
SYLIS
SYLLABARY
SYLLABI
SYLLABIC
SYLLABICS
SYLLABIFY
SYLLABISE
SYLLABISM
SYLLABIZE
SYLLABLE
SYLLABLED
SYLLABLES
SYLLABUB
SYLLABUBS
SYLLABUS
SYLLEPSES
SYLLEPSIS
SYLLEPTIC
SYLLOGE
SYLLOGES
SYLLOGISE
SYLLOGISM
SYLLOGIST
SYLLOGIZE
SYLPH
SYLPHIC
SYLPHID
SYLPHIDE
SYLPHIDES
SYLPHIDS
SYLPHIER
SYLPHIEST
SYLPHINE
SYLPHISH
SYLPHLIKE
SYLPHS

SYLPHY
SYLVA
SYLVAE
SYLVAN
SYLVANER
SYLVANERS
SYLVANITE
SYLVANS
SYLVAS
SYLVATIC
SYLVIA
SYLVIAS
SYLVIINE
SYLVIN
SYLVINE
SYLVINES
SYLVINITE
SYLVINS
SYLVITE
SYLVITES
SYMAR
SYMARS
SYMBION
SYMBIONS
SYMBIONT
SYMBIONTS
SYMBIOSES
SYMBIOSIS
SYMBIOT
SYMBIOTE
SYMBIOTES
SYMBIOTIC
SYMBIOTS
SYMBOL
SYMBOLE
SYMBOLED
SYMBOLES
SYMBOLIC
SYMBOLICS
SYMBOLING
SYMBOLISE
SYMBOLISM
SYMBOLIST
SYMBOLIZE
SYMBOLLED
SYMBOLOGY
SYMBOLS

SYMITAR
SYMITARE
SYMITARES
SYMITARS
SYMMETRAL
SYMMETRIC
SYMMETRY
SYMPATHIN
SYMPATHY
SYMPATICO
SYMPATRIC
SYMPATRY
SYMPETALY
SYMPHILE
SYMPHILES
SYMPHILY
SYMPHONIC
SYMPHONY
SYMPHYSES
SYMPHYSIS
SYMPHYTIC
SYMPLAST
SYMPLASTS
SYMPLOCE
SYMPLOCES
SYMPODIA
SYMPODIAL
SYMPODIUM
SYMPOSIA
SYMPOSIAC
SYMPOSIAL
SYMPOSIUM
SYMPTOM
SYMPTOMS
SYMPTOSES
SYMPTOSIS
SYMPTOTIC
SYN
SYNAGOG
SYNAGOGAL
SYNAGOGS
SYNAGOGUE
SYNALEPHA
SYNANDRIA
SYNANGIA
SYNANGIUM
SYNANON

SYNANONS	SYNCOPTIC	SYNERGIST	SYNOPSISE	SYNURA
SYNANTHIC	SYNCRETIC	SYNERGIZE	SYNOPSIZE	SYNURAE
SYNANTHY	SYNCS	SYNERGY	SYNOPTIC	SYPE
SYNAPHEA	SYNCYTIA	SYNES	SYNOPTICS	SYPED
SYNAPHEAS	SYNCYTIAL	SYNESES	SYNOPTIST	SYPES
SYNAPHEIA	SYNCYTIUM	SYNESIS	SYNOVIA	SYPH
SYNAPSE	SYND	SYNESISES	SYNOVIAL	SYPHER
SYNAPSED	SYNDACTYL	SYNFUEL	SYNOVIAS	SYPHERED
SYNAPSES	SYNDED	SYNFUELS	SYNOVITIC	SYPHERING
SYNAPSID	SYNDESES	SYNGAMIC	SYNOVITIS	SYPHERS
SYNAPSIDS	SYNDESIS	SYNGAMIES	SYNROC	SYPHILIS
SYNAPSING	SYNDET	SYNGAMOUS	SYNROCS	SYPHILISE
SYNAPSIS	SYNDETIC	SYNGAMY	SYNTACTIC	SYPHILIZE
SYNAPTASE	SYNDETON	SYNGAS	SYNTAGM	SYPHILOID
SYNAPTE	SYNDETONS	SYNGASES	SYNTAGMA	SYPHILOMA
SYNAPTES	SYNDETS	SYNGASSES	SYNTAGMAS	SYPHON
SYNAPTIC	SYNDIC	SYNGENEIC	SYNTAGMIC	SYPHONED
SYNARCHY	SYNDICAL	SYNGENIC	SYNTAGMS	SYPHONING
SYNASTRY	SYNDICATE	SYNGRAPH	SYNTAN	SYPHONS
SYNAXARIA	SYNDICS	SYNGRAPHS	SYNTANS	SYPHS
SYNAXES	SYNDING	SYNING	SYNTAX	SYPING
SYNAXIS	SYNDINGS	SYNIZESES	SYNTAXES	SYRAH
SYNC	SYNDROME	SYNIZESIS	SYNTECTIC	SYRAHS
SYNCARP	SYNDROMES	SYNKARYA	SYNTENIC	SYREN
SYNCARPS	SYNDROMIC	SYNKARYON	SYNTENIES	SYRENS
SYNCARPY	SYNDS	SYNOD	SYNTENY	SYRETTE
SYNCED	SYNE	SYNODAL	SYNTEXIS	SYRETTES
SYNCH	SYNECHIA	SYNODALS	SYNTH	SYRINGA
SYNCHED	SYNECHIAS	SYNODIC	SYNTHASE	SYRINGAS
SYNCHING	SYNECIOUS	SYNODICAL	SYNTHASES	SYRINGE
SYNCHRO	SYNECTIC	SYNODS	SYNTHESES	SYRINGEAL
SYNCHRONY	SYNECTICS	SYNODSMAN	SYNTHESIS	SYRINGED
SYNCHROS	SYNED	SYNODSMEN	SYNTHETIC	SYRINGES
SYNCHS	SYNEDRIA	SYNOECETE	SYNTHON	SYRINGING
SYNCHYSES	SYNEDRIAL	SYNOECISE	SYNTHONS	SYRINX
SYNCHYSIS	SYNEDRION	SYNOECISM	SYNTHPOP	SYRINXES
SYNCING	SYNEDRIUM	SYNOECIZE	SYNTHPOPS	SYRPHIAN
SYNCLINAL	SYNERESES	SYNOEKETE	SYNTHRONI	SYRPHIANS
SYNCLINE	SYNERESIS	SYNOICOUS	SYNTHS	SYRPHID
SYNCLINES	SYNERGIA	SYNONYM	SYNTONIC	SYRPHIDS
SYNCOM	SYNERGIAS	SYNONYME	SYNTONIES	SYRTES
SYNCOMS	SYNERGIC	SYNONYMES	SYNTONIN	SYRTIS
SYNCOPAL	SYNERGID	SYNONYMIC	SYNTONINS	SYRUP
SYNCOPATE	SYNERGIDS	SYNONYMS	SYNTONISE	SYRUPED
SYNCOPE	SYNERGIES	SYNONYMY	SYNTONIZE	SYRUPIER
SYNCOPES	SYNERGISE	SYNOPSES	SYNTONOUS	SYRUPIEST
SYNCOPIC	SYNERGISM	SYNOPSIS	SYNTONY	SYRUPING

S

SYRUPLIKE
SYRUPS
SYRUPY
SYSADMIN
SYSADMINS
SYSOP
SYSOPS

SYSSITIA
SYSSITIAS
SYSTALTIC
SYSTEM
SYSTEMED
SYSTEMIC
SYSTEMICS

SYSTEMISE
SYSTEMIZE
SYSTEMS
SYSTOLE
SYSTOLES
SYSTOLIC
SYSTYLE

SYSTYLES
SYTHE
SYTHES
SYVER
SYVERS
SYZYGAL
SYZYGETIC

SYZYGIAL
SYZYGIES
SYZYGY

T

TA	TABETIC	TABOR	TABUN	TACKETS
TAAL	TABETICS	TABORED	TABUNS	TACKETY
TAALS	TABI	TABORER	TABUS	TACKEY
TAATA	TABID	TABORERS	TACAHOUT	TACKIER
TAATAS	TABINET	TABORET	TACAHOUTS	TACKIES
TAB	TABINETS	TABORETS	TACAMAHAC	TACKIEST
TABANID	TABLA	TABORIN	TACAN	TACKIFIED
TABANIDS	TABLAS	TABORINE	TACANS	TACKIFIER
TABARD	TABLATURE	TABORINES	TACE	TACKIFIES
TABARDED	TABLE	TABORING	TACES	TACKIFY
TABARDS	TABLEAU	TABORINS	TACET	TACKILY
TABARET	TABLEAUS	TABORS	TACH	TACKINESS
TABARETS	TABLEAUX	TABOULEH	TACHE	TACKING
TABASHEER	TABLED	TABOULEHS	TACHES	TACKINGS
TABASHIR	TABLEFUL	TABOULI	TACHINA	TACKLE
TABASHIRS	TABLEFULS	TABOULIS	TACHINID	TACKLED
TABBED	TABLELAND	TABOUR	TACHINIDS	TACKLER
TABBIED	TABLELESS	TABOURED	TACHISM	TACKLERS
TABBIES	TABLEMATE	TABOURER	TACHISME	TACKLES
TABBINET	TABLES	TABOURERS	TACHISMES	TACKLESS
TABBINETS	TABLESFUL	TABOURET	TACHISMS	TACKLING
TABBING	TABLET	TABOURETS	TACHIST	TACKLINGS
TABBIS	TABLETED	TABOURIN	TACHISTE	TACKS
TABBISES	TABLETING	TABOURING	TACHISTES	TACKSMAN
TABBOULEH	TABLETOP	TABOURINS	TACHISTS	TACKSMEN
TABBOULI	TABLETOPS	TABOURS	TACHO	TACKY
TABBOULIS	TABLETS	TABRERE	TACHOGRAM	TACMAHACK
TABBY	TABLETTED	TABRERES	TACHOS	TACNODE
TABBYHOOD	TABLEWARE	TABRET	TACHS	TACNODES
TABBYING	TABLEWISE	TABRETS	TACHYLITE	TACO
TABEFIED	TABLIER	TABS	TACHYLYTE	TACONITE
TABEFIES	TABLIERS	TABU	TACHYON	TACONITES
TABEFY	TABLING	TABUED	TACHYONIC	TACOS
TABEFYING	TABLINGS	TABUING	TACHYONS	TACRINE
TABELLION	TABLOID	TABULA	TACHYPNEA	TACRINES
TABER	TABLOIDS	TABULABLE	TACIT	TACT
TABERD	TABLOIDY	TABULAE	TACITLY	TACTFUL
TABERDAR	TABOGGAN	TABULAR	TACITNESS	TACTFULLY
TABERDARS	TABOGGANS	TABULARLY	TACITURN	TACTIC
TABERDS	TABOO	TABULATE	TACK	TACTICAL
TABERED	TABOOED	TABULATED	TACKBOARD	TACTICIAN
TABERING	TABOOING	TABULATES	TACKED	TACTICITY
TABERS	TABOOLEY	TABULATOR	TACKER	TACTICS
TABES	TABOOLEYS	TABULI	TACKERS	TACTILE
TABESCENT	TABOOS	TABULIS	TACKET	TACTILELY

TACTILIST	TAG	TAHR	TAILING	TAINTURE
TACTILITY	TAGALONG	TAHRS	TAILINGS	TAINTURES
TACTION	TAGALONGS	TAHSIL	TAILLAMP	TAIPAN
TACTIONS	TAGAREEN	TAHSILDAR	TAILLAMPS	TAIPANS
TACTISM	TAGAREENS	TAHSILS	TAILLE	TAIRA
TACTISMS	TAGBOARD	TAI	TAILLES	TAIRAS
TACTLESS	TAGBOARDS	TAIAHA	TAILLESS	TAIS
TACTS	TAGETES	TAIAHAS	TAILLEUR	TAISCH
TACTUAL	TAGGANT	TAIG	TAILLEURS	TAISCHES
TACTUALLY	TAGGANTS	TAIGA	TAILLIE	TAISH
TAD	TAGGED	TAIGAS	TAILLIES	TAISHES
TADDIE	TAGGEE	TAIGLACH	TAILLIGHT	TAIT
TADDIES	TAGGEES	TAIGLE	TAILLIKE	TAITS
TADPOLE	TAGGER	TAIGLED	TAILOR	TAIVER
TADPOLES	TAGGERS	TAIGLES	TAILORED	TAIVERED
TADS	TAGGIER	TAIGLING	TAILORESS	TAIVERING
TAE	TAGGIEST	TAIGS	TAILORING	TAIVERS
TAED	TAGGING	TAIHOA	TAILORS	TAIVERT
TAEDIUM	TAGGINGS	TAIKO	TAILPIECE	TAJ
TAEDIUMS	TAGGY	TAIKONAUT	TAILPIPE	TAJES
TAEING	TAGHAIRM	TAIKOS	TAILPIPED	TAJINE
TAEKWONDO	TAGHAIRMS	TAIL	TAILPIPES	TAJINES
TAEL	TAGINE	TAILARD	TAILPLANE	TAK
TAELS	TAGINES	TAILARDS	TAILRACE	TAKA
TAENIA	TAGLESS	TAILBACK	TAILRACES	TAKABLE
TAENIAE	TAGLIKE	TAILBACKS	TAILS	TAKAHE
TAENIAS	TAGLINE	TAILBOARD	TAILSKID	TAKAHES
TAENIASES	TAGLINES	TAILBONE	TAILSKIDS	TAKAMAKA
TAENIASIS	TAGLIONI	TAILBONES	TAILSLIDE	TAKAMAKAS
TAENIATE	TAGLIONIS	TAILCOAT	TAILSPIN	TAKAS
TAENIOID	TAGMA	TAILCOATS	TAILSPINS	TAKE
TAES	TAGMATA	TAILED	TAILSTOCK	TAKEABLE
TAFFAREL	TAGMEME	TAILENDER	TAILWATER	TAKEAWAY
TAFFARELS	TAGMEMES	TAILER	TAILWHEEL	TAKEAWAYS
TAFFEREL	TAGMEMIC	TAILERON	TAILWIND	TAKEDOWN
TAFFERELS	TAGMEMICS	TAILERONS	TAILWINDS	TAKEDOWNS
TAFFETA	TAGRAG	TAILERS	TAILYE	TAKEN
TAFFETAS	TAGRAGS	TAILFAN	TAILYES	TAKEOFF
TAFFETY	TAGS	TAILFANS	TAILZIE	TAKEOFFS
TAFFIA	TAGUAN	TAILFIN	TAILZIES	TAKEOUT
TAFFIAS	TAGUANS	TAILFINS	TAIN	TAKEOUTS
TAFFIES	TAHA	TAILFLIES	TAINS	TAKEOVER
TAFFRAIL	TAHAS	TAILFLY	TAINT	TAKEOVERS
TAFFRAILS	TAHINA	TAILGATE	TAINTED	TAKER
TAFFY	TAHINAS	TAILGATED	TAINTING	TAKERS
TAFIA	TAHINI	TAILGATER	TAINTLESS	TAKES
TAFIAS	TAHINIS	TAILGATES	TAINTS	TAKEUP

TAKEUPS	TALCS	TALKIE	TALLITOT	TAM
TAKHI	TALCUM	TALKIER	TALLITOTH	TAMABLE
TAKHIS	TALCUMS	TALKIES	TALLITS	TAMAL
TAKI	TALCY	TALKIEST	TALLNESS	TAMALE
TAKIER	TALE	TALKINESS	TALLOL	TAMALES
TAKIEST	TALEA	TALKING	TALLOLS	TAMALS
TAKIN	TALEAE	TALKINGS	TALLOT	TAMANDU
TAKING	TALEFUL	TALKS	TALLOTS	TAMANDUA
TAKINGLY	TALEGALLA	TALKTIME	TALLOW	TAMANDUAS
TAKINGS	TALEGGIO	TALKTIMES	TALLOWED	TAMANDUS
TAKINS	TALEGGIOS	TALKY	TALLOWING	TAMANOIR
TAKIS	TALENT	TALL	TALLOWISH	TAMANOIRS
TAKKIES	TALENTED	TALLAGE	TALLOWS	TAMANU
TAKS	TALENTS	TALLAGED	TALLOWY	TAMANUS
TAKY	TALER	TALLAGES	TALLS	TAMARA
TALA	TALERS	TALLAGING	TALLY	TAMARACK
TALAK	TALES	TALLAISIM	TALLYHO	TAMARACKS
TALAKS	TALESMAN	TALLAT	TALLYHOED	TAMARAO
TALANT	TALESMEN	TALLATS	TALLYHOS	TAMARAOS
TALANTS	TALEYSIM	TALLBOY	TALLYING	TAMARAS
TALAPOIN	TALI	TALLBOYS	TALLYMAN	TAMARAU
TALAPOINS	TALIGRADE	TALLENT	TALLYMEN	TAMARAUS
TALAQ	TALION	TALLENTS	TALLYSHOP	TAMARI
TALAQS	TALIONIC	TALLER	TALMA	TAMARILLO
TALAR	TALIONS	TALLEST	TALMAS	TAMARIN
TALARIA	TALIPAT	TALLET	TALMUD	TAMARIND
TALARS	TALIPATS	TALLETS	TALMUDIC	TAMARINDS
TALAS	TALIPED	TALLGRASS	TALMUDISM	TAMARINS
TALAUNT	TALIPEDS	TALLIABLE	TALMUDS	TAMARIS
TALAUNTS	TALIPES	TALLIATE	TALON	TAMARISK
TALAYOT	TALIPOT	TALLIATED	TALONED	TAMARISKS
TALAYOTS	TALIPOTS	TALLIATES	TALONS	TAMASHA
TALBOT	TALISMAN	TALLIED	TALOOKA	TAMASHAS
TALBOTS	TALISMANS	TALLIER	TALOOKAS	TAMBAC
TALBOTYPE	TALK	TALLIERS	TALPA	TAMBACS
TALC	TALKABLE	TALLIES	TALPAE	TAMBAK
TALCED	TALKATHON	TALLIS	TALPAS	TAMBAKS
TALCIER	TALKATIVE	TALLISES	TALUK	TAMBALA
TALCIEST	TALKBACK	TALLISH	TALUKA	TAMBALAS
TALCING	TALKBACKS	TALLISIM	TALUKAS	TAMBER
TALCKED	TALKBOX	TALLIT	TALUKDAR	TAMBERS
TALCKIER	TALKBOXES	TALLITES	TALUKDARS	TAMBOUR
TALCKIEST	TALKED	TALLITH	TALUKS	TAMBOURA
TALCKING	TALKER	TALLITHES	TALUS	TAMBOURAS
TALCKY	TALKERS	TALLITHIM	TALUSES	TAMBOURED
TALCOSE	TALKFEST	TALLITHS	TALWEG	TAMBOURER
TALCOUS	TALKFESTS	TALLITIM	TALWEGS	TAMBOURIN

T

TAMBOURS	TAMPERS	TANGENTS	TANKA	TANNINS
TAMBUR	TAMPING	TANGERINE	TANKAGE	TANNISH
TAMBURA	TAMPINGS	TANGHIN	TANKAGES	TANNOY
TAMBURAS	TAMPION	TANGHININ	TANKARD	TANNOYED
TAMBURIN	TAMPIONS	TANGHINS	TANKARDS	TANNOYING
TAMBURINS	TAMPON	TANGI	TANKAS	TANNOYS
TAMBURS	TAMPONADE	TANGIBLE	TANKED	TANOREXIC
TAME	TAMPONAGE	TANGIBLES	TANKER	TANREC
TAMEABLE	TAMPONED	TANGIBLY	TANKERS	TANRECS
TAMED	TAMPONING	TANGIE	TANKFUL	TANS
TAMEIN	TAMPONS	TANGIER	TANKFULS	TANSIES
TAMEINS	TAMPS	TANGIES	TANKIA	TANSY
TAMELESS	TAMS	TANGIEST	TANKIAS	TANTALATE
TAMELY	TAMWORTH	TANGINESS	TANKIES	TANTALIC
TAMENESS	TAMWORTHS	TANGING	TANKING	TANTALISE
TAMER	TAN	TANGIS	TANKINGS	TANTALISM
TAMERS	TANA	TANGLE	TANKINI	TANTALITE
TAMES	TANADAR	TANGLED	TANKINIS	TANTALIZE
TAMEST	TANADARS	TANGLER	TANKLESS	TANTALOUS
TAMIN	TANAGER	TANGLERS	TANKLIKE	TANTALUM
TAMINE	TANAGERS	TANGLES	TANKS	TANTALUMS
TAMINES	TANAGRA	TANGLIER	TANKSHIP	TANTALUS
TAMING	TANAGRAS	TANGLIEST	TANKSHIPS	TANTARA
TAMINGS	TANAGRINE	TANGLING	TANKY	TANTARARA
TAMINS	TANALISED	TANGLINGS	TANLING	TANTARAS
TAMIS	TANALIZED	TANGLY	TANLINGS	TANTI
TAMISE	TANAS	TANGO	TANNA	TANTIVIES
TAMISES	TANBARK	TANGOED	TANNABLE	TANTIVY
TAMMAR	TANBARKS	TANGOING	TANNAGE	TANTO
TAMMARS	TANDEM	TANGOIST	TANNAGES	TANTONIES
TAMMIE	TANDEMS	TANGOISTS	TANNAH	TANTONY
TAMMIED	TANDOOR	TANGOLIKE	TANNAHS	TANTRA
TAMMIES	TANDOORI	TANGOS	TANNAS	TANTRAS
TAMMY	TANDOORIS	TANGRAM	TANNATE	TANTRIC
TAMMYING	TANDOORS	TANGRAMS	TANNATES	TANTRISM
TAMOXIFEN	TANE	TANGS	TANNED	TANTRISMS
TAMP	TANG	TANGUN	TANNER	TANTRUM
TAMPALA	TANGA	TANGUNS	TANNERIES	TANTRUMS
TAMPALAS	TANGAS	TANGY	TANNERS	TANUKI
TAMPAN	TANGED	TANH	TANNERY	TANUKIS
TAMPANS	TANGELO	TANHS	TANNEST	TANYARD
TAMPED	TANGELOS	TANIST	TANNIC	TANYARDS
TAMPER	TANGENCE	TANISTRY	TANNIE	TANZANITE
TAMPERED	TANGENCES	TANISTS	TANNIES	TAO
TAMPERER	TANGENCY	TANIWHA	TANNIN	TAONGA
TAMPERERS	TANGENT	TANIWHAS	TANNING	TAONGAS
TAMPERING	TANGENTAL	TANK	TANNINGS	TAOS

TAP	TAPHOUSES	TARA	TARGES	TARRAGONS
TAPA	TAPING	TARAIRE	TARGET	TARRAS
TAPACOLO	TAPIOCA	TARAIRES	TARGETED	TARRASES
TAPACOLOS	TAPIOCAS	TARAKIHI	TARGETEER	TARRE
TAPACULO	TAPIR	TARAKIHIS	TARGETING	TARRED
TAPACULOS	TAPIROID	TARAMA	TARGETS	TARRES
TAPADERA	TAPIRS	TARAMAS	TARGING	TARRIANCE
TAPADERAS	TAPIS	TARAMEA	TARIFF	TARRIED
TAPADERO	TAPISES	TARAMEAS	TARIFFED	TARRIER
TAPADEROS	TAPIST	TARAND	TARIFFING	TARRIERS
TAPALO	TAPISTS	TARANDS	TARIFFS	TARRIES
TAPALOS	TAPLASH	TARANTARA	TARING	TARRIEST
TAPAS	TAPLASHES	TARANTAS	TARINGS	TARRINESS
TAPE	TAPPA	TARANTASS	TARLATAN	TARRING
TAPEABLE	TAPPABLE	TARANTISM	TARLATANS	TARRINGS
TAPED	TAPPAS	TARANTIST	TARLETAN	TARROCK
TAPELESS	TAPPED	TARANTULA	TARLETANS	TARROCKS
TAPELIKE	TAPPER	TARAS	TARMAC	TARROW
TAPELINE	TAPPERS	TARAXACUM	TARMACKED	TARROWED
TAPELINES	TAPPET	TARBOGGIN	TARMACS	TARROWING
TAPEN	TAPPETS	TARBOOSH	TARN	TARROWS
TAPENADE	TAPPICE	TARBOUCHE	TARNAL	TARRY
TAPENADES	TAPPICED	TARBOUSH	TARNALLY	TARRYING
TAPER	TAPPICES	TARBOY	TARNATION	TARS
TAPERED	TAPPICING	TARBOYS	TARNISH	TARSAL
TAPERER	TAPPING	TARBUSH	TARNISHED	TARSALGIA
TAPERERS	TAPPINGS	TARBUSHES	TARNISHER	TARSALS
TAPERING	TAPPIT	TARCEL	TARNISHES	TARSEAL
TAPERINGS	TAPROOM	TARCELS	TARNS	TARSEALS
TAPERNESS	TAPROOMS	TARDIED	TARO	TARSEL
TAPERS	TAPROOT	TARDIER	TAROC	TARSELS
TAPERWISE	TAPROOTED	TARDIES	TAROCS	TARSI
TAPES	TAPROOTS	TARDIEST	TAROK	TARSIA
TAPESTRY	TAPS	TARDILY	TAROKS	TARSIAS
TAPET	TAPSMAN	TARDINESS	TAROS	TARSIER
TAPETA	TAPSMEN	TARDIVE	TAROT	TARSIERS
TAPETAL	TAPSTER	TARDO	TAROTS	TARSIOID
TAPETI	TAPSTERS	TARDY	TARP	TARSIPED
TAPETIS	TAPSTRESS	TARDYING	TARPAN	TARSIPEDS
TAPETS	TAPSTRY	TARDYON	TARPANS	TARSUS
TAPETUM	TAPU	TARDYONS	TARPAPER	TART
TAPEWORM	TAPUED	TARE	TARPAPERS	TARTAN
TAPEWORMS	TAPUING	TARED	TARPAULIN	TARTANA
TAPHOLE	TAPUS	TARES	TARPON	TARTANAS
TAPHOLES	TAQUERIA	TARGA	TARPONS	TARTANE
TAPHONOMY	TAQUERIAS	TARGE	TARPS	TARTANED
TAPHOUSE	TAR	TARGED	TARRAGON	TARTANES

TARTANRY	TASBIH	TASTER	TATTIEST	TAUON
TARTANS	TASBIHS	TASTERS	TATTILY	TAUONS
TARTAR	TASER	TASTES	TATTINESS	TAUPATA
TARTARE	TASERED	TASTEVIN	TATTING	TAUPATAS
TARTARES	TASERING	TASTEVINS	TATTINGS	TAUPE
TARTARIC	TASERS	TASTIER	TATTLE	TAUPES
TARTARISE	TASH	TASTIEST	TATTLED	TAUPIE
TARTARIZE	TASHED	TASTILY	TATTLER	TAUPIES
TARTARLY	TASHES	TASTINESS	TATTLERS	TAUREAN
TARTAROUS	TASHING	TASTING	TATTLES	TAURIC
TARTARS	TASIMETER	TASTINGS	TATTLING	TAURIFORM
TARTED	TASIMETRY	TASTY	TATTLINGS	TAURINE
TARTER	TASK	TAT	TATTOO	TAURINES
TARTEST	TASKBAR	TATAHASH	TATTOOED	TAUS
TARTIER	TASKBARS	TATAMI	TATTOOER	TAUT
TARTIEST	TASKED	TATAMIS	TATTOOERS	TAUTAUG
TARTILY	TASKER	TATAR	TATTOOING	TAUTAUGS
TARTINE	TASKERS	TATARS	TATTOOIST	TAUTED
TARTINES	TASKING	TATE	TATTOOS	TAUTEN
TARTINESS	TASKINGS	TATER	TATTOW	TAUTENED
TARTING	TASKLESS	TATERS	TATTOWED	TAUTENING
TARTISH	TASKS	TATES	TATTOWING	TAUTENS
TARTISHLY	TASKWORK	TATH	TATTOWS	TAUTER
TARTLET	TASKWORKS	TATHED	TATTS	TAUTEST
TARTLETS	TASLET	TATHING	TATTY	TAUTING
TARTLY	TASLETS	TATHS	TATU	TAUTIT
TARTNESS	TASS	TATIE	TATUED	TAUTLY
TARTRATE	TASSE	TATIES	TATUING	TAUTNESS
TARTRATED	TASSEL	TATLER	TATUS	TAUTOG
TARTRATES	TASSELED	TATLERS	TAU	TAUTOGS
TARTS	TASSELING	TATOU	TAUBE	TAUTOLOGY
TARTUFE	TASSELL	TATOUAY	TAUBES	TAUTOMER
TARTUFES	TASSELLED	TATOUAYS	TAUGHT	TAUTOMERS
TARTUFFE	TASSELLS	TATOUS	TAUHINU	TAUTONYM
TARTUFFES	TASSELLY	TATS	TAUHINUS	TAUTONYMS
TARTUFO	TASSELS	TATSOI	TAUHOU	TAUTONYMY
TARTUFOS	TASSES	TATSOIS	TAUHOUS	TAUTS
TARTY	TASSET	TATT	TAUIWI	TAV
TARWEED	TASSETS	TATTED	TAUIWIS	TAVA
TARWEEDS	TASSIE	TATTER	TAULD	TAVAH
TARWHINE	TASSIES	TATTERED	TAUNT	TAVAHS
TARWHINES	TASTABLE	TATTERING	TAUNTED	TAVAS
TARZAN	TASTE	TATTERS	TAUNTER	TAVER
TARZANS	TASTEABLE	TATTERY	TAUNTERS	TAVERED
TAS	TASTED	TATTIE	TAUNTING	TAVERING
TASAR	TASTEFUL	TATTIER	TAUNTINGS	TAVERN
TASARS	TASTELESS	TATTIES	TAUNTS	TAVERNA

T

TAVERNAS	TAWTED	TAXMEN	TEACARTS	TEAMS
TAVERNER	TAWTIE	TAXOL	TEACH	TEAMSTER
TAVERNERS	TAWTIER	TAXOLS	TEACHABLE	TEAMSTERS
TAVERNS	TAWTIEST	TAXON	TEACHABLY	TEAMWISE
TAVERS	TAWTING	TAXONOMER	TEACHER	TEAMWORK
TAVERT	TAWTS	TAXONOMIC	TEACHERLY	TEAMWORKS
TAVS	TAX	TAXONOMY	TEACHERS	TEAPOT
TAW	TAXA	TAXONS	TEACHES	TEAPOTS
TAWA	TAXABLE	TAXOR	TEACHIE	TEAPOY
TAWAI	TAXABLES	TAXORS	TEACHING	TEAPOYS
TAWAIS	TAXABLY	TAXPAID	TEACHINGS	TEAR
TAWAS	TAXACEOUS	TAXPAYER	TEACHLESS	TEARABLE
TAWDRIER	TAXAMETER	TAXPAYERS	TEACUP	TEARAWAY
TAWDRIES	TAXATION	TAXPAYING	TEACUPFUL	TEARAWAYS
TAWDRIEST	TAXATIONS	TAXUS	TEACUPS	TEARDOWN
TAWDRILY	TAXATIVE	TAXWISE	TEAD	TEARDOWNS
TAWDRY	TAXED	TAXYING	TEADE	TEARDROP
TAWED	TAXEME	TAY	TEADES	TEARDROPS
TAWER	TAXEMES	TAYASSUID	TEADS	TEARED
TAWERIES	TAXEMIC	TAYBERRY	TEAED	TEARER
TAWERS	TAXER	TAYRA	TEAGLE	TEARERS
TAWERY	TAXERS	TAYRAS	TEAGLED	TEARFUL
TAWHAI	TAXES	TAYS	TEAGLES	TEARFULLY
TAWHAIS	TAXI	TAZZA	TEAGLING	TEARGAS
TAWHIRI	TAXIARCH	TAZZAS	TEAHOUSE	TEARGASES
TAWHIRIS	TAXIARCHS	TAZZE	TEAHOUSES	TEARIER
TAWIE	TAXICAB	TCHICK	TEAING	TEARIEST
TAWIER	TAXICABS	TCHICKED	TEAK	TEARILY
TAWIEST	TAXIDERMY	TCHICKING	TEAKETTLE	TEARINESS
TAWING	TAXIED	TCHICKS	TEAKS	TEARING
TAWINGS	TAXIES	TCHOTCHKE	TEAKWOOD	TEARLESS
TAWNEY	TAXIING	TE	TEAKWOODS	TEAROOM
TAWNEYS	TAXIMAN	TEA	TEAL	TEAROOMS
TAWNIER	TAXIMEN	TEABAG	TEALIGHT	TEARS
TAWNIES	TAXIMETER	TEABAGS	TEALIGHTS	TEARSHEET
TAWNIEST	TAXING	TEABERRY	TEALIKE	TEARSTAIN
TAWNILY	TAXINGLY	TEABOARD	TEALS	TEARSTRIP
TAWNINESS	TAXINGS	TEABOARDS	TEAM	TEARY
TAWNY	TAXIPLANE	TEABOWL	TEAMAKER	TEAS
TAWPIE	TAXIS	TEABOWLS	TEAMAKERS	TEASABLE
TAWPIES	TAXITE	TEABOX	TEAMED	TEASE
TAWS	TAXITES	TEABOXES	TEAMER	TEASED
TAWSE	TAXITIC	TEABREAD	TEAMERS	TEASEL
TAWSED	TAXIWAY	TEABREADS	TEAMING	TEASELED
TAWSES	TAXIWAYS	TEACAKE	TEAMINGS	TEASELER
TAWSING	TAXLESS	TEACAKES	TEAMMATE	TEASELERS
TAWT	TAXMAN	TEACART	TEAMMATES	TEASELING

T

TEASELLED	TECHNICS	TEEK	TEERS	TEGUMEN
TEASELLER	TECHNIKON	TEEL	TEES	TEGUMENT
TEASELS	TECHNIQUE	TEELS	TEETER	TEGUMENTS
TEASER	TECHNO	TEEM	TEETERED	TEGUMINA
TEASERS	TECHNOPOP	TEEMED	TEETERING	TEGUS
TEASES	TECHNOS	TEEMER	TEETERS	TEHR
TEASHOP	TECHS	TEEMERS	TEETH	TEHRS
TEASHOPS	TECHY	TEEMFUL	TEETHE	TEHSIL
TEASING	TECKEL	TEEMING	TEETHED	TEHSILDAR
TEASINGLY	TECKELS	TEEMINGLY	TEETHER	TEHSILS
TEASINGS	TECS	TEEMLESS	TEETHERS	TEIGLACH
TEASPOON	TECTA	TEEMS	TEETHES	TEIID
TEASPOONS	TECTAL	TEEN	TEETHING	TEIIDS
TEAT	TECTIFORM	TEENAGE	TEETHINGS	TEIL
TEATASTER	TECTITE	TEENAGED	TEETHLESS	TEILS
TEATED	TECTITES	TEENAGER	TEETOTAL	TEIN
TEATIME	TECTONIC	TEENAGERS	TEETOTALS	TEIND
TEATIMES	TECTONICS	TEENAGES	TEETOTUM	TEINDED
TEATS	TECTONISM	TEEND	TEETOTUMS	TEINDING
TEAWARE	TECTORIAL	TEENDED	TEF	TEINDS
TEAWARES	TECTRICES	TEENDING	TEFF	TEINS
TEAZE	TECTRIX	TEENDS	TEFFS	TEKKIE
TEAZED	TECTUM	TEENE	TEFILLAH	TEKKIES
TEAZEL	TECTUMS	TEENED	TEFILLIN	TEKNONYMY
TEAZELED	TED	TEENER	TEFLON	TEKTITE
TEAZELING	TEDDED	TEENERS	TEFLONS	TEKTITES
TEAZELLED	TEDDER	TEENES	TEFS	TEKTITIC
TEAZELS	TEDDERED	TEENFUL	TEG	TEL
TEAZES	TEDDERING	TEENIER	TEGG	TELA
TEAZING	TEDDERS	TEENIEST	TEGGS	TELAE
TEAZLE	TEDDIE	TEENING	TEGMEN	TELAMON
TEAZLED	TEDDIES	TEENS	TEGMENTA	TELAMONES
TEAZLES	TEDDING	TEENSIER	TEGMENTAL	TELAMONS
TEAZLING	TEDDY	TEENSIEST	TEGMENTUM	TELARY
TEBBAD	TEDIER	TEENSY	TEGMINA	TELCO
TEBBADS	TEDIEST	TEENTIER	TEGMINAL	TELCOS
TEC	TEDIOSITY	TEENTIEST	TEGS	TELD
TECH	TEDIOUS	TEENTSIER	TEGU	TELE
TECHED	TEDIOUSLY	TEENTSY	TEGUA	TELECAST
TECHIE	TEDISOME	TEENTY	TEGUAS	TELECASTS
TECHIER	TEDIUM	TEENY	TEGUEXIN	TELECHIR
TECHIES	TEDIUMS	TEENYBOP	TEGUEXINS	TELECHIRS
TECHIEST	TEDS	TEEPEE	TEGULA	TELECINE
TECHILY	TEDY	TEEPEES	TEGULAE	TELECINES
TECHINESS	TEE	TEER	TEGULAR	TELECOM
TECHNIC	TEED	TEERED	TEGULARLY	TELECOMS
TECHNICAL	TEEING	TEERING	TEGULATED	TELEDU

TELEDUS	TELESALES	TELIAL	TELOME	TEMPLAR
TELEFAX	TELESCOPE	TELIC	TELOMERE	TEMPLARS
TELEFAXED	TELESCOPY	TELICALLY	TELOMERES	TEMPLATE
TELEFAXES	TELESEME	TELIUM	TELOMES	TEMPLATES
TELEFILM	TELESEMES	TELL	TELOMIC	TEMPLE
TELEFILMS	TELESES	TELLABLE	TELOPHASE	TEMPLED
TELEGA	TELESHOP	TELLAR	TELOS	TEMPLES
TELEGAS	TELESHOPS	TELLARED	TELOTAXES	TEMPLET
TELEGENIC	TELESIS	TELLARING	TELOTAXIS	TEMPLETS
TELEGONIC	TELESM	TELLARS	TELPHER	TEMPO
TELEGONY	TELESMS	TELLEN	TELPHERED	TEMPORAL
TELEGRAM	TELESTIC	TELLENS	TELPHERIC	TEMPORALS
TELEGRAMS	TELESTICH	TELLER	TELPHERS	TEMPORARY
TELEGRAPH	TELESTICS	TELLERED	TELS	TEMPORE
TELEMAN	TELETEX	TELLERING	TELSON	TEMPORISE
TELEMARK	TELETEXES	TELLERS	TELSONIC	TEMPORIZE
TELEMARKS	TELETEXT	TELLIES	TELSONS	TEMPOS
TELEMATIC	TELETEXTS	TELLIN	TELT	TEMPS
TELEMEN	TELETHON	TELLING	TEMAZEPAM	TEMPT
TELEMETER	TELETHONS	TELLINGLY	TEMBLOR	TEMPTABLE
TELEMETRY	TELETRON	TELLINGS	TEMBLORES	TEMPTED
TELEOLOGY	TELETRONS	TELLINOID	TEMBLORS	TEMPTER
TELEONOMY	TELETYPE	TELLINS	TEME	TEMPTERS
TELEOSAUR	TELETYPED	TELLS	TEMED	TEMPTING
TELEOST	TELETYPES	TELLTALE	TEMENE	TEMPTINGS
TELEOSTS	TELEVIEW	TELLTALES	TEMENOS	TEMPTRESS
TELEPATH	TELEVIEWS	TELLURAL	TEMERITY	TEMPTS
TELEPATHS	TELEVISE	TELLURATE	TEMEROUS	TEMPURA
TELEPATHY	TELEVISED	TELLURIAN	TEMES	TEMPURAS
TELEPHEME	TELEVISER	TELLURIC	TEMP	TEMS
TELEPHONE	TELEVISES	TELLURIDE	TEMPED	TEMSE
TELEPHONY	TELEVISOR	TELLURION	TEMPEH	TEMSED
TELEPHOTO	TELEWORK	TELLURISE	TEMPEHS	TEMSES
TELEPIC	TELEWORKS	TELLURITE	TEMPER	TEMSING
TELEPICS	TELEX	TELLURIUM	TEMPERA	TEMULENCE
TELEPLAY	TELEXED	TELLURIZE	TEMPERAS	TEMULENCY
TELEPLAYS	TELEXES	TELLUROUS	TEMPERATE	TEMULENT
TELEPOINT	TELEXING	TELLUS	TEMPERED	TEN
TELEPORT	TELFER	TELLUSES	TEMPERER	TENABLE
TELEPORTS	TELFERAGE	TELLY	TEMPERERS	TENABLY
TELERAN	TELFERED	TELLYS	TEMPERING	TENACE
TELERANS	TELFERIC	TELNET	TEMPERS	TENACES
TELERGIC	TELFERING	TELNETED	TEMPEST	TENACIOUS
TELERGIES	TELFERS	TELNETING	TEMPESTED	TENACITY
TELERGY	TELFORD	TELNETS	TEMPESTS	TENACULA
TELES	TELFORDS	TELNETTED	TEMPI	TENACULUM
TELESALE	TELIA	TELOI	TEMPING	TENAIL

TENAILLE

TENAILLE	TENE	TENONS	TENSORS	TENURES
TENAILLES	TENEBRAE	TENOR	TENT	TENURIAL
TENAILLON	TENEBRIO	TENORIST	TENTACLE	TENURING
TENAILS	TENEBRIOS	TENORISTS	TENTACLED	TENUTI
TENANCIES	TENEBRISM	TENORITE	TENTACLES	TENUTO
TENANCY	TENEBRIST	TENORITES	TENTACULA	TENUTOS
TENANT	TENEBRITY	TENORLESS	TENTAGE	TENZON
TENANTED	TENEBROSE	TENOROON	TENTAGES	TENZONS
TENANTING	TENEBROUS	TENOROONS	TENTATION	TEOCALLI
TENANTRY	TENEMENT	TENORS	TENTATIVE	TEOCALLIS
TENANTS	TENEMENTS	TENOTOMY	TENTED	TEOPAN
TENCH	TENENDUM	TENOUR	TENTER	TEOPANS
TENCHES	TENENDUMS	TENOURS	TENTERED	TEOSINTE
TEND	TENES	TENPENCE	TENTERING	TEOSINTES
TENDANCE	TENESMIC	TENPENCES	TENTERS	TEPA
TENDANCES	TENESMUS	TENPENNY	TENTFUL	TEPAL
TENDED	TENET	TENPIN	TENTFULS	TEPALS
TENDENCE	TENETS	TENPINS	TENTH	TEPAS
TENDENCES	TENFOLD	TENREC	TENTHLY	TEPEE
TENDENCIES	TENFOLDS	TENRECS	TENTHS	TEPEES
TENDENCY	TENGE	TENS	TENTIE	TEPEFIED
TENDENZ	TENGES	TENSE	TENTIER	TEPEFIES
TENDENZEN	TENIA	TENSED	TENTIEST	TEPEFY
TENDER	TENIACIDE	TENSELESS	TENTIGO	TEPEFYING
TENDERED	TENIAE	TENSELY	TENTIGOS	TEPHIGRAM
TENDERER	TENIAFUGE	TENSENESS	TENTING	TEPHILLAH
TENDERERS	TENIAS	TENSER	TENTINGS	TEPHILLIN
TENDEREST	TENIASES	TENSES	TENTLESS	TEPHRA
TENDERING	TENIASIS	TENSEST	TENTLIKE	TEPHRAS
TENDERISE	TENIOID	TENSIBLE	TENTMAKER	TEPHRITE
TENDERIZE	TENNE	TENSIBLY	TENTORIA	TEPHRITES
TENDERLY	TENNER	TENSILE	TENTORIAL	TEPHRITIC
TENDERS	TENNERS	TENSILELY	TENTORIUM	TEPHROITE
TENDING	TENNES	TENSILITY	TENTS	TEPID
TENDINOUS	TENNIES	TENSING	TENTWISE	TEPIDARIA
TENDON	TENNIS	TENSION	TENTY	TEPIDER
TENDONS	TENNISES	TENSIONAL	TENUE	TEPIDEST
TENDRE	TENNIST	TENSIONED	TENUES	TEPIDITY
TENDRES	TENNISTS	TENSIONER	TENUIOUS	TEPIDLY
TENDRESSE	TENNO	TENSIONS	TENUIS	TEPIDNESS
TENDRIL	TENNOS	TENSITIES	TENUITIES	TEPOY
TENDRILED	TENNY	TENSITY	TENUITY	TEPOYS
TENDRILS	TENON	TENSIVE	TENUOUS	TEQUILA
TENDRON	TENONED	TENSON	TENUOUSLY	TEQUILAS
TENDRONS	TENONER	TENSONS	TENURABLE	TEQUILLA
TENDS	TENONERS	TENSOR	TENURE	TEQUILLAS
TENDU	TENONING	TENSORIAL	TENURED	TERABYTE

TERABYTES	TEREBRAS	TERMS	TERRELLAS	TERTIUM
TERAFLOP	TEREBRATE	TERMTIME	TERRENE	TERTIUS
TERAFLOPS	TEREDINES	TERMTIMES	TERRENELY	TERTIUSES
TERAGLIN	TEREDO	TERN	TERRENES	TERTS
TERAGLINS	TEREDOS	TERNAL	TERRET	TERVALENT
TERAHERTZ	TEREFA	TERNARIES	TERRETS	TERYLENE
TERAI	TEREFAH	TERNARY	TERRIBLE	TERYLENES
TERAIS	TEREK	TERNATE	TERRIBLES	TERZETTA
TERAKIHI	TEREKS	TERNATELY	TERRIBLY	TERZETTAS
TERAKIHIS	TERES	TERNE	TERRICOLE	TERZETTI
TERAOHM	TERETE	TERNED	TERRIER	TERZETTO
TERAOHMS	TERETES	TERNES	TERRIERS	TERZETTOS
TERAPH	TERF	TERNING	TERRIES	TES
TERAPHIM	TERFE	TERNION	TERRIFIC	TESLA
TERAPHIMS	TERFES	TERNIONS	TERRIFIED	TESLAS
TERAS	TERFS	TERNS	TERRIFIER	TESSELATE
TERATA	TERGA	TERPENE	TERRIFIES	TESSELLA
TERATISM	TERGAL	TERPENES	TERRIFY	TESSELLAE
TERATISMS	TERGITE	TERPENIC	TERRINE	TESSELLAR
TERATOGEN	TERGITES	TERPENOID	TERRINES	TESSERA
TERATOID	TERGUM	TERPINEOL	TERRIT	TESSERACT
TERATOMA	TERIYAKI	TERPINOL	TERRITORY	TESSERAE
TERATOMAS	TERIYAKIS	TERPINOLS	TERRITS	TESSERAL
TERAWATT	TERM	TERRA	TERROIR	TESSITURA
TERAWATTS	TERMAGANT	TERRACE	TERROIRS	TESSITURE
TERBIA	TERMED	TERRACED	TERROR	TEST
TERBIAS	TERMER	TERRACES	TERRORFUL	TESTA
TERBIC	TERMERS	TERRACING	TERRORISE	TESTABLE
TERBIUM	TERMINAL	TERRAE	TERRORISM	TESTACEAN
TERBIUMS	TERMINALS	TERRAFORM	TERRORIST	TESTACIES
TERCE	TERMINATE	TERRAIN	TERRORIZE	TESTACY
TERCEL	TERMINER	TERRAINS	TERRORS	TESTAE
TERCELET	TERMINERS	TERRAMARA	TERRY	TESTAMENT
TERCELETS	TERMING	TERRAMARE	TERSE	TESTAMUR
TERCELS	TERMINI	TERRANE	TERSELY	TESTAMURS
TERCES	TERMINISM	TERRANES	TERSENESS	TESTATE
TERCET	TERMINIST	TERRAPIN	TERSER	TESTATES
TERCETS	TERMINUS	TERRAPINS	TERSEST	TESTATION
TERCIO	TERMITARY	TERRARIA	TERSION	TESTATOR
TERCIOS	TERMITE	TERRARIUM	TERSIONS	TESTATORS
TEREBENE	TERMITES	TERRAS	TERTIA	TESTATRIX
TEREBENES	TERMITIC	TERRASES	TERTIAL	TESTATUM
TEREBIC	TERMLESS	TERRAZZO	TERTIALS	TESTATUMS
TEREBINTH	TERMLIES	TERRAZZOS	TERTIAN	TESTCROSS
TEREBRA	TERMLY	TERREEN	TERTIANS	TESTE
TEREBRAE	TERMOR	TERREENS	TERTIARY	TESTED
TEREBRANT	TERMORS	TERRELLA	TERTIAS	TESTEE

TESTEES	TETANUSES	TETRONAL	TEXTBOOK	THALLIUM
TESTER	TETANY	TETRONALS	TEXTBOOKS	THALLIUMS
TESTERN	TETCHED	TETROXID	TEXTED	THALLOID
TESTERNED	TETCHIER	TETROXIDE	TEXTER	THALLOUS
TESTERNS	TETCHIEST	TETROXIDS	TEXTERS	THALLUS
TESTERS	TETCHILY	TETRYL	TEXTILE	THALLUSES
TESTES	TETCHY	TETRYLS	TEXTILES	THALWEG
TESTICLE	TETE	TETS	TEXTING	THALWEGS
TESTICLES	TETES	TETTER	TEXTINGS	THAN
TESTIER	TETH	TETTERED	TEXTLESS	THANA
TESTIEST	TETHER	TETTERING	TEXTORIAL	THANADAR
TESTIFIED	TETHERED	TETTEROUS	TEXTPHONE	THANADARS
TESTIFIER	TETHERING	TETTERS	TEXTS	THANAGE
TESTIFIES	TETHERS	TETTIX	TEXTUAL	THANAGES
TESTIFY	TETHS	TETTIXES	TEXTUALLY	THANAH
TESTILY	TETOTUM	TEUCH	TEXTUARY	THANAHS
TESTIMONY	TETOTUMS	TEUCHAT	TEXTURAL	THANAS
TESTINESS	TETRA	TEUCHATS	TEXTURE	THANATISM
TESTING	TETRACID	TEUCHER	TEXTURED	THANATIST
TESTINGS	TETRACIDS	TEUCHEST	TEXTURES	THANATOID
TESTIS	TETRACT	TEUCHTER	TEXTURING	THANATOS
TESTON	TETRACTS	TEUCHTERS	TEXTURISE	THANE
TESTONS	TETRAD	TEUGH	TEXTURIZE	THANEDOM
TESTOON	TETRADIC	TEUGHER	THACK	THANEDOMS
TESTOONS	TETRADITE	TEUGHEST	THACKED	THANEHOOD
TESTRIL	TETRADS	TEUGHLY	THACKING	THANES
TESTRILL	TETRAGON	TEUTONISE	THACKS	THANESHIP
TESTRILLS	TETRAGONS	TEUTONIZE	THAE	THANG
TESTRILS	TETRAGRAM	TEVATRON	THAGI	THANGKA
TESTS	TETRALOGY	TEVATRONS	THAGIS	THANGKAS
TESTUDO	TETRAMER	TEW	THAIM	THANGS
TESTUDOS	TETRAMERS	TEWART	THAIRM	THANK
TESTY	TETRAPLA	TEWARTS	THAIRMS	THANKED
TET	TETRAPLAS	TEWED	THALAMI	THANKEE
TETANAL	TETRAPOD	TEWEL	THALAMIC	THANKER
TETANIC	TETRAPODS	TEWELS	THALAMUS	THANKERS
TETANICAL	TETRAPODY	TEWHIT	THALASSIC	THANKFUL
TETANICS	TETRARCH	TEWHITS	THALE	THANKING
TETANIES	TETRARCHS	TEWING	THALER	THANKINGS
TETANISE	TETRARCHY	TEWIT	THALERS	THANKIT
TETANISED	TETRAS	TEWITS	THALI	THANKLESS
TETANISES	TETRAXON	TEWS	THALIAN	THANKS
TETANIZE	TETRAXONS	TEX	THALIS	THANKYOU
TETANIZED	TETRI	TEXAS	THALLI	THANKYOUS
TETANIZES	TETRIS	TEXASES	THALLIC	THANNA
TETANOID	TETRODE	TEXES	THALLINE	THANNAH
TETANUS	TETRODES	TEXT	THALLIOUS	THANNAHS

THANNAS	THEBES	THEMATA	THEORIC	THEREUPON
THANS	THECA	THEMATIC	THEORICS	THEREWITH
THAR	THECAE	THEMATICS	THEORIES	THERIAC
THARM	THECAL	THEME	THEORIQUE	THERIACA
THARMS	THECATE	THEMED	THEORISE	THERIACAL
THARS	THECODONT	THEMELESS	THEORISED	THERIACAS
THAT	THEE	THEMES	THEORISER	THERIACS
THATAWAY	THEED	THEMING	THEORISES	THERIAN
THATCH	THEEING	THEMSELF	THEORIST	THERIANS
THATCHED	THEEK	THEN	THEORISTS	THERM
THATCHER	THEEKED	THENABOUT	THEORIZE	THERMAE
THATCHERS	THEEKING	THENAGE	THEORIZED	THERMAL
THATCHES	THEEKS	THENAGES	THEORIZER	THERMALLY
THATCHIER	THEELIN	THENAL	THEORIZES	THERMALS
THATCHING	THEELINS	THENAR	THEORY	THERME
THATCHT	THEELOL	THENARS	THEOSOPH	THERMEL
THATCHY	THEELOLS	THENCE	THEOSOPHS	THERMELS
THATNESS	THEES	THENS	THEOSOPHY	THERMES
THAUMATIN	THEFT	THEOCON	THEOTOKOI	THERMETTE
THAW	THEFTLESS	THEOCONS	THEOTOKOS	THERMIC
THAWED	THEFTS	THEOCRACY	THEOW	THERMICAL
THAWER	THEFTUOUS	THEOCRASY	THEOWS	THERMIDOR
THAWERS	THEGITHER	THEOCRAT	THERALITE	THERMION
THAWIER	THEGN	THEOCRATS	THERAPIES	THERMIONS
THAWIEST	THEGNLY	THEODICY	THERAPIST	THERMIT
THAWING	THEGNS	THEOGONIC	THERAPSID	THERMITE
THAWINGS	THEIC	THEOGONY	THERAPY	THERMITES
THAWLESS	THEICS	THEOLOG	THERBLIG	THERMITS
THAWS	THEIN	THEOLOGER	THERBLIGS	THERMOS
THAWY	THEINE	THEOLOGIC	THERE	THERMOSES
THE	THEINES	THEOLOGS	THEREAT	THERMOSET
THEACEOUS	THEINS	THEOLOGUE	THEREAWAY	THERMOTIC
THEANDRIC	THEIR	THEOLOGY	THEREBY	THERMS
THEARCHIC	THEIRS	THEOMACHY	THEREFOR	THEROID
THEARCHY	THEIRSELF	THEOMANCY	THEREFORE	THEROLOGY
THEATER	THEISM	THEOMANIA	THEREFROM	THEROPOD
THEATERS	THEISMS	THEONOMY	THEREIN	THEROPODS
THEATRAL	THEIST	THEOPATHY	THEREINTO	THESAURAL
THEATRE	THEISTIC	THEOPHAGY	THEREMIN	THESAURI
THEATRES	THEISTS	THEOPHANY	THEREMINS	THESAURUS
THEATRIC	THELEMENT	THEORBIST	THERENESS	THESE
THEATRICS	THELF	THEORBO	THEREOF	THESES
THEAVE	THELITIS	THEORBOS	THEREON	THESIS
THEAVES	THELVES	THEOREM	THEREOUT	THESP
THEBAINE	THELYTOKY	THEOREMIC	THERES	THESPIAN
THEBAINES	THEM	THEOREMS	THERETO	THESPIANS
THEBE	THEMA	THEORETIC	THEREUNTO	THESPS

T

THETA

THETA
THETAS
THETCH
THETCHED
THETCHES
THETCHING
THETE
THETES
THETHER
THETIC
THETICAL
THEURGIC
THEURGIES
THEURGIST
THEURGY
THEW
THEWED
THEWES
THEWIER
THEWIEST
THEWLESS
THEWS
THEWY
THEY
THIAMIN
THIAMINE
THIAMINES
THIAMINS
THIASUS
THIASUSES
THIAZIDE
THIAZIDES
THIAZIN
THIAZINE
THIAZINES
THIAZINS
THIAZOL
THIAZOLE
THIAZOLES
THIAZOLS
THIBET
THIBETS
THIBLE
THIBLES
THICK
THICKED
THICKEN

THICKENED
THICKENER
THICKENS
THICKER
THICKEST
THICKET
THICKETED
THICKETS
THICKETY
THICKHEAD
THICKIE
THICKIES
THICKING
THICKISH
THICKLEAF
THICKLY
THICKNESS
THICKO
THICKOES
THICKOS
THICKS
THICKSET
THICKSETS
THICKSKIN
THICKY
THIEF
THIEFLIKE
THIEVE
THIEVED
THIEVERY
THIEVES
THIEVING
THIEVINGS
THIEVISH
THIG
THIGGER
THIGGERS
THIGGING
THIGGINGS
THIGGIT
THIGH
THIGHBONE
THIGHED
THIGHS
THIGS
THILK
THILL

THILLER
THILLERS
THILLS
THIMBLE
THIMBLED
THIMBLES
THIMBLING
THIN
THINCLAD
THINCLADS
THINDOWN
THINDOWNS
THINE
THING
THINGAMY
THINGHOOD
THINGIER
THINGIES
THINGIEST
THINGNESS
THINGS
THINGUMMY
THINGY
THINK
THINKABLE
THINKABLY
THINKER
THINKERS
THINKING
THINKINGS
THINKS
THINLY
THINNED
THINNER
THINNERS
THINNESS
THINNEST
THINNING
THINNINGS
THINNISH
THINS
THIO
THIOFURAN
THIOL
THIOLIC
THIOLS
THIONATE

THIONATES
THIONIC
THIONIN
THIONINE
THIONINES
THIONINS
THIONYL
THIONYLS
THIOPHEN
THIOPHENE
THIOPHENS
THIOPHIL
THIOTEPA
THIOTEPAS
THIOUREA
THIOUREAS
THIR
THIRAM
THIRAMS
THIRD
THIRDED
THIRDHAND
THIRDING
THIRDINGS
THIRDLY
THIRDS
THIRDSMAN
THIRDSMEN
THIRL
THIRLAGE
THIRLAGES
THIRLED
THIRLING
THIRLS
THIRST
THIRSTED
THIRSTER
THIRSTERS
THIRSTFUL
THIRSTIER
THIRSTILY
THIRSTING
THIRSTS
THIRSTY
THIRTEEN
THIRTEENS
THIRTIES

THIRTIETH
THIRTY
THIRTYISH
THIS
THISAWAY
THISNESS
THISTLE
THISTLES
THISTLIER
THISTLY
THITHER
THITHERTO
THIVEL
THIVELS
THLIPSES
THLIPSIS
THO
THOFT
THOFTS
THOLE
THOLED
THOLEIITE
THOLEPIN
THOLEPINS
THOLES
THOLI
THOLING
THOLOBATE
THOLOI
THOLOS
THOLUS
THON
THONDER
THONG
THONGED
THONGS
THORACAL
THORACES
THORACIC
THORAX
THORAXES
THORIA
THORIAS
THORIC
THORITE
THORITES
THORIUM

THORIUMS	THRALDOMS	THREAT	THRIDACES	THROATY
THORN	THRALL	THREATED	THRIDDED	THROB
THORNBACK	THRALLDOM	THREATEN	THRIDDING	THROBBED
THORNBILL	THRALLED	THREATENS	THRIDS	THROBBER
THORNBIRD	THRALLING	THREATFUL	THRIFT	THROBBERS
THORNBUSH	THRALLS	THREATING	THRIFTIER	THROBBING
THORNED	THRANG	THREATS	THRIFTILY	THROBLESS
THORNIER	THRANGED	THREAVE	THRIFTS	THROBS
THORNIEST	THRANGING	THREAVES	THRIFTY	THROE
THORNILY	THRANGS	THREE	THRILL	THROED
THORNING	THRAPPLE	THREEFOLD	THRILLANT	THROEING
THORNLESS	THRAPPLED	THREENESS	THRILLED	THROES
THORNLIKE	THRAPPLES	THREEP	THRILLER	THROMBI
THORNS	THRASH	THREEPEAT	THRILLERS	THROMBIN
THORNSET	THRASHED	THREEPED	THRILLIER	THROMBINS
THORNTREE	THRASHER	THREEPER	THRILLING	THROMBOSE
THORNY	THRASHERS	THREEPERS	THRILLS	THROMBUS
THORO	THRASHES	THREEPING	THRILLY	THRONE
THORON	THRASHING	THREEPIT	THRIMSA	THRONED
THORONS	THRASONIC	THREEPS	THRIMSAS	THRONES
THOROUGH	THRAVE	THREES	THRIP	THRONG
THOROUGHS	THRAVES	THREESOME	THRIPS	THRONGED
THORP	THRAW	THRENE	THRIPSES	THRONGFUL
THORPE	THRAWARD	THRENES	THRISSEL	THRONGING
THORPES	THRAWART	THRENETIC	THRISSELS	THRONGS
THORPS	THRAWED	THRENODE	THRIST	THRONING
THOSE	THRAWING	THRENODES	THRISTED	THRONNER
THOTHER	THRAWN	THRENODIC	THRISTING	THRONNERS
THOU	THRAWNLY	THRENODY	THRISTLE	THROPPLE
THOUED	THRAWS	THRENOS	THRISTLES	THROPPLED
THOUGH	THREAD	THRENOSES	THRISTS	THROPPLES
THOUGHT	THREADED	THREONINE	THRISTY	THROSTLE
THOUGHTED	THREADEN	THRESH	THRIVE	THROSTLES
THOUGHTEN	THREADER	THRESHED	THRIVED	THROTTLE
THOUGHTS	THREADERS	THRESHEL	THRIVEN	THROTTLED
THOUING	THREADFIN	THRESHELS	THRIVER	THROTTLER
THOUS	THREADIER	THRESHER	THRIVERS	THROTTLES
THOUSAND	THREADING	THRESHERS	THRIVES	THROUGH
THOUSANDS	THREADS	THRESHES	THRIVING	THROUGHLY
THOWEL	THREADY	THRESHING	THRIVINGS	THROVE
THOWELS	THREAP	THRESHOLD	THRO	THROW
THOWL	THREAPED	THRETTIES	THROAT	THROWAWAY
THOWLESS	THREAPER	THRETTY	THROATED	THROWBACK
THOWLS	THREAPERS	THREW	THROATIER	THROWDOWN
THRAE	THREAPING	THRICE	THROATILY	THROWE
THRAIPING	THREAPIT	THRID	THROATING	THROWER
THRALDOM	THREAPS	THRIDACE	THROATS	THROWERS

THROWES	THUGGO	THURIBLES	THYMOCYTE	TICHIER
THROWING	THUGGOS	THURIFER	THYMOL	TICHIEST
THROWINGS	THUGS	THURIFERS	THYMOLS	TICHY
THROWN	THUJA	THURIFIED	THYMOSIN	TICING
THROWS	THUJAS	THURIFIES	THYMOSINS	TICK
THROWSTER	THULIA	THURIFY	THYMUS	TICKED
THRU	THULIAS	THURL	THYMUSES	TICKEN
THRUM	THULITE	THURLS	THYMY	TICKENS
THRUMMED	THULITES	THUS	THYRATRON	TICKER
THRUMMER	THULIUM	THUSES	THYREOID	TICKERS
THRUMMERS	THULIUMS	THUSLY	THYREOIDS	TICKET
THRUMMIER	THUMB	THUSNESS	THYRISTOR	TICKETED
THRUMMING	THUMBED	THUSWISE	THYROID	TICKETING
THRUMMY	THUMBHOLE	THUYA	THYROIDAL	TICKETS
THRUMS	THUMBIER	THUYAS	THYROIDS	TICKEY
THRUPENNY	THUMBIEST	THWACK	THYROXIN	TICKEYS
THRUPUT	THUMBING	THWACKED	THYROXINE	TICKIES
THRUPUTS	THUMBKIN	THWACKER	THYROXINS	TICKING
THRUSH	THUMBKINS	THWACKERS	THYRSE	TICKINGS
THRUSHES	THUMBLESS	THWACKING	THYRSES	TICKLACE
THRUST	THUMBLIKE	THWACKS	THYRSI	TICKLACES
THRUSTED	THUMBLING	THWAITE	THYRSOID	TICKLE
THRUSTER	THUMBNAIL	THWAITES	THYRSUS	TICKLED
THRUSTERS	THUMBNUT	THWART	THYSELF	TICKLER
THRUSTFUL	THUMBNUTS	THWARTED	TI	TICKLERS
THRUSTING	THUMBPOT	THWARTER	TIAN	TICKLES
THRUSTOR	THUMBPOTS	THWARTERS	TIANS	TICKLIER
THRUSTORS	THUMBS	THWARTING	TIAR	TICKLIEST
THRUSTS	THUMBTACK	THWARTLY	TIARA	TICKLING
THRUTCH	THUMBY	THWARTS	TIARAED	TICKLINGS
THRUTCHED	THUMP	THY	TIARAS	TICKLISH
THRUTCHES	THUMPED	THYINE	TIARS	TICKLY
THRUWAY	THUMPER	THYLACINE	TIBIA	TICKS
THRUWAYS	THUMPERS	THYLAKOID	TIBIAE	TICKSEED
THRYMSA	THUMPING	THYLOSE	TIBIAL	TICKSEEDS
THRYMSAS	THUMPS	THYLOSES	TIBIAS	TICKTACK
THUD	THUNDER	THYLOSIS	TIC	TICKTACKS
THUDDED	THUNDERED	THYME	TICAL	TICKTOCK
THUDDING	THUNDERER	THYMES	TICALS	TICKTOCKS
THUDS	THUNDERS	THYMEY	TICCA	TICKY
THUG	THUNDERY	THYMI	TICCED	TICS
THUGGEE	THUNDROUS	THYMIC	TICCING	TICTAC
THUGGEES	THUNK	THYMIDINE	TICE	TICTACKED
THUGGERY	THUNKED	THYMIER	TICED	TICTACS
THUGGISH	THUNKING	THYMIEST	TICES	TICTOC
THUGGISM	THUNKS	THYMINE	TICH	TICTOCKED
THUGGISMS	THURIBLE	THYMINES	TICHES	TICTOCS

TID	TIDIEST	TIFFINED	TIGLONS	TILINGS
TIDAL	TIDILY	TIFFING	TIGON	TILL
TIDALLY	TIDINESS	TIFFINGS	TIGONS	TILLABLE
TIDBIT	TIDING	TIFFINING	TIGRESS	TILLAGE
TIDBITS	TIDINGS	TIFFINS	TIGRESSES	TILLAGES
TIDDIER	TIDIVATE	TIFFS	TIGRIDIA	TILLED
TIDDIES	TIDIVATED	TIFOSI	TIGRIDIAS	TILLER
TIDDIEST	TIDIVATES	TIFOSO	TIGRINE	TILLERED
TIDDLE	TIDS	TIFT	TIGRISH	TILLERING
TIDDLED	TIDY	TIFTED	TIGRISHLY	TILLERMAN
TIDDLER	TIDYING	TIFTING	TIGROID	TILLERMEN
TIDDLERS	TIDYTIPS	TIFTS	TIGS	TILLERS
TIDDLES	TIE	TIG	TIK	TILLICUM
TIDDLEY	TIEBACK	TIGE	TIKA	TILLICUMS
TIDDLEYS	TIEBACKS	TIGER	TIKANGA	TILLIER
TIDDLIER	TIEBREAK	TIGEREYE	TIKANGAS	TILLIEST
TIDDLIES	TIEBREAKS	TIGEREYES	TIKAS	TILLING
TIDDLIEST	TIECLASP	TIGERISH	TIKE	TILLINGS
TIDDLING	TIECLASPS	TIGERISM	TIKES	TILLITE
TIDDLY	TIED	TIGERISMS	TIKI	TILLITES
TIDDY	TIEING	TIGERLIKE	TIKIED	TILLS
TIDE	TIELESS	TIGERLY	TIKIING	TILLY
TIDED	TIEPIN	TIGERS	TIKIS	TILS
TIDELAND	TIEPINS	TIGERWOOD	TIKKA	TILT
TIDELANDS	TIER	TIGERY	TIKKAS	TILTABLE
TIDELESS	TIERCE	TIGES	TIKOLOSHE	TILTED
TIDELIKE	TIERCED	TIGGED	TIKS	TILTER
TIDELINE	TIERCEL	TIGGING	TIKTAALIK	TILTERS
TIDELINES	TIERCELET	TIGHT	TIL	TILTH
TIDEMARK	TIERCELS	TIGHTASS	TILAK	TILTHS
TIDEMARKS	TIERCERON	TIGHTEN	TILAKS	TILTING
TIDEMILL	TIERCES	TIGHTENED	TILAPIA	TILTINGS
TIDEMILLS	TIERCET	TIGHTENER	TILAPIAS	TILTMETER
TIDERIP	TIERCETS	TIGHTENS	TILBURIES	TILTROTOR
TIDERIPS	TIERED	TIGHTER	TILBURY	TILTS
TIDES	TIERING	TIGHTEST	TILDE	TILTYARD
TIDESMAN	TIERS	TIGHTISH	TILDES	TILTYARDS
TIDESMEN	TIES	TIGHTKNIT	TILE	TIMARAU
TIDEWATER	TIETAC	TIGHTLY	TILED	TIMARAUS
TIDEWAVE	TIETACK	TIGHTNESS	TILEFISH	TIMARIOT
TIDEWAVES	TIETACKS	TIGHTROPE	TILELIKE	TIMARIOTS
TIDEWAY	TIETACS	TIGHTS	TILER	TIMBAL
TIDEWAYS	TIFF	TIGHTWAD	TILERIES	TIMBALE
TIDIED	TIFFANIES	TIGHTWADS	TILERS	TIMBALES
TIDIER	TIFFANY	TIGHTWIRE	TILERY	TIMBALS
TIDIERS	TIFFED	TIGLIC	TILES	TIMBER
TIDIES	TIFFIN	TIGLON	TILING	TIMBERED

TIMBERING	TIMIDLY	TINDED	TINKED	TINSELLED
TIMBERMAN	TIMIDNESS	TINDER	TINKER	TINSELLY
TIMBERMEN	TIMING	TINDERBOX	TINKERED	TINSELRY
TIMBERS	TIMINGS	TINDERS	TINKERER	TINSELS
TIMBERY	TIMIST	TINDERY	TINKERERS	TINSEY
TIMBO	TIMISTS	TINDING	TINKERING	TINSEYS
TIMBOS	TIMOCRACY	TINDS	TINKERMAN	TINSMITH
TIMBRAL	TIMOLOL	TINE	TINKERMEN	TINSMITHS
TIMBRE	TIMOLOLS	TINEA	TINKERS	TINSNIPS
TIMBREL	TIMON	TINEAL	TINKERTOY	TINSTONE
TIMBRELS	TIMONEER	TINEAS	TINKING	TINSTONES
TIMBRES	TIMONEERS	TINED	TINKLE	TINT
TIME	TIMONS	TINEID	TINKLED	TINTACK
TIMEBOMB	TIMOROUS	TINEIDS	TINKLER	TINTACKS
TIMEBOMBS	TIMORSOME	TINES	TINKLERS	TINTED
TIMECARD	TIMOTHIES	TINFOIL	TINKLES	TINTER
TIMECARDS	TIMOTHY	TINFOILS	TINKLIER	TINTERS
TIMED	TIMOUS	TINFUL	TINKLIEST	TINTIER
TIMEFRAME	TIMOUSLY	TINFULS	TINKLING	TINTIEST
TIMELESS	TIMPANA	TING	TINKLINGS	TINTINESS
TIMELIER	TIMPANI	TINGE	TINKLY	TINTING
TIMELIEST	TIMPANIST	TINGED	TINKS	TINTINGS
TIMELINE	TIMPANO	TINGEING	TINLIKE	TINTLESS
TIMELINES	TIMPANUM	TINGES	TINMAN	TINTOOKIE
TIMELY	TIMPANUMS	TINGING	TINMEN	TINTS
TIMENOGUY	TIMPS	TINGLE	TINNED	TINTY
TIMEOUS	TIN	TINGLED	TINNER	TINTYPE
TIMEOUSLY	TINA	TINGLER	TINNERS	TINTYPES
TIMEOUT	TINAJA	TINGLERS	TINNIE	TINWARE
TIMEOUTS	TINAJAS	TINGLES	TINNIER	TINWARES
TIMEPASS	TINAMOU	TINGLIER	TINNIES	TINWORK
TIMEPIECE	TINAMOUS	TINGLIEST	TINNIEST	TINWORKS
TIMER	TINAS	TINGLING	TINNILY	TINY
TIMERS	TINCAL	TINGLINGS	TINNINESS	TIP
TIMES	TINCALS	TINGLISH	TINNING	TIPCART
TIMESAVER	TINCHEL	TINGLY	TINNINGS	TIPCARTS
TIMESCALE	TINCHELS	TINGS	TINNITUS	TIPCAT
TIMESHARE	TINCT	TINGUAITE	TINNY	TIPCATS
TIMESTAMP	TINCTED	TINHORN	TINPLATE	TIPI
TIMETABLE	TINCTING	TINHORNS	TINPLATED	TIPIS
TIMEWORK	TINCTS	TINIER	TINPLATES	TIPLESS
TIMEWORKS	TINCTURE	TINIES	TINPOT	TIPOFF
TIMEWORN	TINCTURED	TINIEST	TINPOTS	TIPOFFS
TIMID	TINCTURES	TINILY	TINS	TIPPABLE
TIMIDER	TIND	TININESS	TINSEL	TIPPED
TIMIDEST	TINDAL	TINING	TINSELED	TIPPEE
TIMIDITY	TINDALS	TINK	TINSELING	TIPPEES

TIPPER	TIPUNAS	TISICK	TITHES	TITTER
TIPPERS	TIRADE	TISICKS	TITHING	TITTERED
TIPPET	TIRADES	TISSUAL	TITHINGS	TITTERER
TIPPETS	TIRAGE	TISSUE	TITHONIA	TITTERERS
TIPPIER	TIRAGES	TISSUED	TITHONIAS	TITTERING
TIPPIEST	TIRAMISU	TISSUES	TITI	TITTERS
TIPPING	TIRAMISUS	TISSUEY	TITIAN	TITTIE
TIPPINGS	TIRASSE	TISSUING	TITIANS	TITTIES
TIPPLE	TIRASSES	TISSULAR	TITILLATE	TITTING
TIPPLED	TIRE	TISWAS	TITIS	TITTISH
TIPPLER	TIRED	TISWASES	TITIVATE	TITTIVATE
TIPPLERS	TIREDER	TIT	TITIVATED	TITTLE
TIPPLES	TIREDEST	TITAN	TITIVATES	TITTLEBAT
TIPPLING	TIREDLY	TITANATE	TITIVATOR	TITTLED
TIPPY	TIREDNESS	TITANATES	TITLARK	TITTLES
TIPPYTOE	TIRELESS	TITANESS	TITLARKS	TITTLING
TIPPYTOED	TIRELING	TITANIA	TITLE	TITTUP
TIPPYTOES	TIRELINGS	TITANIAS	TITLED	TITTUPED
TIPS	TIRES	TITANIC	TITLELESS	TITTUPING
TIPSHEET	TIRESOME	TITANIS	TITLER	TITTUPPED
TIPSHEETS	TIREWOMAN	TITANISES	TITLERS	TITTUPPY
TIPSIER	TIREWOMEN	TITANISM	TITLES	TITTUPS
TIPSIEST	TIRING	TITANISMS	TITLING	TITTUPY
TIPSIFIED	TIRINGS	TITANITE	TITLINGS	TITTY
TIPSIFIES	TIRITI	TITANITES	TITLIST	TITUBANCY
TIPSIFY	TIRITIS	TITANIUM	TITLISTS	TITUBANT
TIPSILY	TIRL	TITANIUMS	TITMAN	TITUBATE
TIPSINESS	TIRLED	TITANOUS	TITMEN	TITUBATED
TIPSTAFF	TIRLING	TITANS	TITMICE	TITUBATES
TIPSTAFFS	TIRLS	TITBIT	TITMOSE	TITULAR
TIPSTAVES	TIRO	TITBITS	TITMOUSE	TITULARLY
TIPSTER	TIROES	TITCH	TITOKI	TITULARS
TIPSTERS	TIRONIC	TITCHES	TITOKIS	TITULARY
TIPSTOCK	TIROS	TITCHIER	TITRABLE	TITULE
TIPSTOCKS	TIRR	TITCHIEST	TITRANT	TITULED
TIPSY	TIRRED	TITCHY	TITRANTS	TITULES
TIPT	TIRRING	TITE	TITRATE	TITULI
TIPTOE	TIRRIT	TITELY	TITRATED	TITULING
TIPTOED	TIRRITS	TITER	TITRATES	TITULUS
TIPTOEING	TIRRIVEE	TITERS	TITRATING	TITUP
TIPTOES	TIRRIVEES	TITFER	TITRATION	TITUPED
TIPTOP	TIRRIVIE	TITFERS	TITRATOR	TITUPING
TIPTOPS	TIRRIVIES	TITHABLE	TITRATORS	TITUPPED
TIPTRONIC	TIRRS	TITHE	TITRE	TITUPPING
TIPULA	TIS	TITHED	TITRES	TITUPS
TIPULAS	TISANE	TITHER	TITS	TITUPY
TIPUNA	TISANES	TITHERS	TITTED	TIVY

TIX	TOAZES	TODDLES	TOFFISH	TOILER
TIYIN	TOAZING	TODDLING	TOFFS	TOILERS
TIYINS	TOBACCO	TODDY	TOFFY	TOILES
TIZWAS	TOBACCOES	TODGER	TOFORE	TOILET
TIZWASES	TOBACCOS	TODGERS	TOFT	TOILETED
TIZZ	TOBIES	TODIES	TOFTS	TOILETING
TIZZES	TOBOGGAN	TODS	TOFU	TOILETRY
TIZZIES	TOBOGGANS	TODY	TOFUS	TOILETS
TIZZY	TOBOGGIN	TOE	TOFUTTI	TOILETTE
TJANTING	TOBOGGINS	TOEA	TOFUTTIS	TOILETTES
TJANTINGS	TOBY	TOEAS	TOG	TOILFUL
TMESES	TOC	TOEBIE	TOGA	TOILFULLY
TMESIS	TOCCATA	TOEBIES	TOGAE	TOILINET
TO	TOCCATAS	TOECAP	TOGAED	TOILINETS
TOAD	TOCCATE	TOECAPS	TOGAS	TOILING
TOADEATER	TOCCATINA	TOECLIP	TOGATE	TOILINGS
TOADFISH	TOCHER	TOECLIPS	TOGATED	TOILLESS
TOADFLAX	TOCHERED	TOED	TOGAVIRUS	TOILS
TOADGRASS	TOCHERING	TOEHOLD	TOGE	TOILSOME
TOADIED	TOCHERS	TOEHOLDS	TOGED	TOILWORN
TOADIES	TOCK	TOEIER	TOGES	TOING
TOADISH	TOCKED	TOEIEST	TOGETHER	TOINGS
TOADLESS	TOCKIER	TOEING	TOGGED	TOISE
TOADLIKE	TOCKIEST	TOELESS	TOGGER	TOISEACH
TOADRUSH	TOCKING	TOELIKE	TOGGERED	TOISEACHS
TOADS	TOCKLEY	TOENAIL	TOGGERIES	TOISECH
TOADSTONE	TOCKLEYS	TOENAILED	TOGGERING	TOISECHS
TOADSTOOL	TOCKS	TOENAILS	TOGGERS	TOISES
TOADY	TOCKY	TOEPIECE	TOGGERY	TOISON
TOADYING	TOCO	TOEPIECES	TOGGING	TOISONS
TOADYISH	TOCOLOGY	TOEPLATE	TOGGLE	TOIT
TOADYISM	TOCOS	TOEPLATES	TOGGLED	TOITED
TOADYISMS	TOCS	TOERAG	TOGGLER	TOITING
TOAST	TOCSIN	TOERAGGER	TOGGLERS	TOITOI
TOASTED	TOCSINS	TOERAGS	TOGGLES	TOITOIS
TOASTER	TOD	TOES	TOGGLING	TOITS
TOASTERS	TODAY	TOESHOE	TOGS	TOKAMAK
TOASTIE	TODAYS	TOESHOES	TOGUE	TOKAMAKS
TOASTIER	TODDE	TOETOE	TOGUES	TOKAY
TOASTIES	TODDED	TOETOES	TOHEROA	TOKAYS
TOASTIEST	TODDES	TOEY	TOHEROAS	TOKE
TOASTING	TODDIES	TOFF	TOHO	TOKED
TOASTINGS	TODDING	TOFFEE	TOHUNGA	TOKEN
TOASTS	TODDLE	TOFFEES	TOHUNGAS	TOKENED
TOASTY	TODDLED	TOFFIER	TOIL	TOKENING
TOAZE	TODDLER	TOFFIES	TOILE	TOKENISM
TOAZED	TODDLERS	TOFFIEST	TOILED	TOKENISMS

TOKENS	TOLIDINES	TOLUIDE	TOMBOLOS	TON
TOKER	TOLIDINS	TOLUIDES	TOMBOY	TONAL
TOKERS	TOLING	TOLUIDIDE	TOMBOYISH	TONALITE
TOKES	TOLINGS	TOLUIDIN	TOMBOYS	TONALITES
TOKING	TOLL	TOLUIDINE	TOMBS	TONALITIC
TOKO	TOLLABLE	TOLUIDINS	TOMBSTONE	TONALITY
TOKOLOGY	TOLLAGE	TOLUIDS	TOMCAT	TONALLY
TOKOLOSHE	TOLLAGES	TOLUOL	TOMCATS	TONANT
TOKOLOSHI	TOLLBAR	TOLUOLE	TOMCATTED	TONDI
TOKOMAK	TOLLBARS	TOLUOLES	TOMCOD	TONDINI
TOKOMAKS	TOLLBOOTH	TOLUOLS	TOMCODS	TONDINO
TOKONOMA	TOLLDISH	TOLUS	TOME	TONDINOS
TOKONOMAS	TOLLED	TOLUYL	TOMENTA	TONDO
TOKOS	TOLLER	TOLUYLS	TOMENTOSE	TONDOS
TOKOTOKO	TOLLERS	TOLYL	TOMENTOUS	TONE
TOKOTOKOS	TOLLEY	TOLYLS	TOMENTUM	TONEARM
TOKTOKKIE	TOLLEYS	TOLZEY	TOMES	TONEARMS
TOLA	TOLLGATE	TOLZEYS	TOMFOOL	TONED
TOLAN	TOLLGATES	TOM	TOMFOOLED	TONELESS
TOLANE	TOLLHOUSE	TOMAHAWK	TOMFOOLS	TONEME
TOLANES	TOLLIE	TOMAHAWKS	TOMIA	TONEMES
TOLANS	TOLLIES	TOMALLEY	TOMIAL	TONEMIC
TOLAR	TOLLING	TOMALLEYS	TOMIUM	TONEPAD
TOLARJEV	TOLLINGS	TOMAN	TOMMED	TONEPADS
TOLARJI	TOLLMAN	TOMANS	TOMMIED	TONER
TOLARS	TOLLMEN	TOMATILLO	TOMMIES	TONERS
TOLAS	TOLLS	TOMATO	TOMMING	TONES
TOLBOOTH	TOLLWAY	TOMATOES	TOMMY	TONETIC
TOLBOOTHS	TOLLWAYS	TOMATOEY	TOMMYING	TONETICS
TOLD	TOLLY	TOMB	TOMMYROT	TONETTE
TOLE	TOLSEL	TOMBAC	TOMMYROTS	TONETTES
TOLED	TOLSELS	TOMBACK	TOMO	TONEY
TOLEDO	TOLSEY	TOMBACKS	TOMOGRAM	TONG
TOLEDOS	TOLSEYS	TOMBACS	TOMOGRAMS	TONGA
TOLERABLE	TOLT	TOMBAK	TOMOGRAPH	TONGAS
TOLERABLY	TOLTER	TOMBAKS	TOMORROW	TONGED
TOLERANCE	TOLTERED	TOMBAL	TOMORROWS	TONGER
TOLERANT	TOLTERING	TOMBED	TOMOS	TONGERS
TOLERATE	TOLTERS	TOMBIC	TOMPION	TONGING
TOLERATED	TOLTS	TOMBING	TOMPIONS	TONGMAN
TOLERATES	TOLU	TOMBLESS	TOMPON	TONGMEN
TOLERATOR	TOLUATE	TOMBLIKE	TOMPONED	TONGS
TOLES	TOLUATES	TOMBOC	TOMPONING	TONGSTER
TOLEWARE	TOLUENE	TOMBOCS	TOMPONS	TONGSTERS
TOLEWARES	TOLUENES	TOMBOLA	TOMS	TONGUE
TOLIDIN	TOLUIC	TOMBOLAS	TOMTIT	TONGUED
TOLIDINE	TOLUID	TOMBOLO	TOMTITS	TONGUELET

TONGUES

TONGUES	TONSILAR	TOOLSET	TOOTLERS	TOPICAL
TONGUING	TONSILLAR	TOOLSETS	TOOTLES	TOPICALLY
TONGUINGS	TONSILS	TOOLSHED	TOOTLING	TOPICS
TONIC	TONSOR	TOOLSHEDS	TOOTS	TOPING
TONICALLY	TONSORIAL	TOOM	TOOTSED	TOPIS
TONICITY	TONSORS	TOOMED	TOOTSES	TOPKICK
TONICS	TONSURE	TOOMER	TOOTSIE	TOPKICKS
TONIER	TONSURED	TOOMEST	TOOTSIES	TOPKNOT
TONIES	TONSURES	TOOMING	TOOTSING	TOPKNOTS
TONIEST	TONSURING	TOOMS	TOOTSY	TOPLESS
TONIGHT	TONTINE	TOON	TOP	TOPLINE
TONIGHTS	TONTINER	TOONIE	TOPALGIA	TOPLINED
TONING	TONTINERS	TOONIES	TOPALGIAS	TOPLINER
TONINGS	TONTINES	TOONS	TOPARCH	TOPLINERS
TONISH	TONUS	TOORIE	TOPARCHS	TOPLINES
TONISHLY	TONUSES	TOORIES	TOPARCHY	TOPLINING
TONITE	TONY	TOOSHIE	TOPAZ	TOPLOFTY
TONITES	TOO	TOOSHIER	TOPAZES	TOPMAKER
TONK	TOOART	TOOSHIEST	TOPAZINE	TOPMAKERS
TONKA	TOOARTS	TOOT	TOPCOAT	TOPMAKING
TONKED	TOOK	TOOTED	TOPCOATS	TOPMAN
TONKER	TOOL	TOOTER	TOPCROSS	TOPMAST
TONKERS	TOOLBAG	TOOTERS	TOPE	TOPMASTS
TONKING	TOOLBAGS	TOOTH	TOPECTOMY	TOPMEN
TONKS	TOOLBAR	TOOTHACHE	TOPED	TOPMINNOW
TONLET	TOOLBARS	TOOTHCOMB	TOPEE	TOPMOST
TONLETS	TOOLBOX	TOOTHED	TOPEES	TOPNOTCH
TONNAG	TOOLBOXES	TOOTHFISH	TOPEK	TOPO
TONNAGE	TOOLED	TOOTHFUL	TOPEKS	TOPOGRAPH
TONNAGES	TOOLER	TOOTHFULS	TOPER	TOPOI
TONNAGS	TOOLERS	TOOTHIER	TOPERS	TOPOLOGIC
TONNE	TOOLHEAD	TOOTHIEST	TOPES	TOPOLOGY
TONNEAU	TOOLHEADS	TOOTHILY	TOPFLIGHT	TOPONYM
TONNEAUS	TOOLHOUSE	TOOTHING	TOPFUL	TOPONYMAL
TONNEAUX	TOOLIE	TOOTHINGS	TOPFULL	TOPONYMIC
TONNELL	TOOLIES	TOOTHLESS	TOPH	TOPONYMS
TONNELLS	TOOLING	TOOTHLIKE	TOPHE	TOPONYMY
TONNER	TOOLINGS	TOOTHPICK	TOPHES	TOPOS
TONNERS	TOOLKIT	TOOTHS	TOPHI	TOPOTYPE
TONNES	TOOLKITS	TOOTHSOME	TOPHS	TOPOTYPES
TONNISH	TOOLLESS	TOOTHWASH	TOPHUS	TOPPED
TONNISHLY	TOOLMAKER	TOOTHWORT	TOPI	TOPPER
TONOMETER	TOOLMAN	TOOTHY	TOPIARIAN	TOPPERS
TONOMETRY	TOOLMEN	TOOTING	TOPIARIES	TOPPIER
TONOPLAST	TOOLROOM	TOOTLE	TOPIARIST	TOPPIEST
TONS	TOOLROOMS	TOOTLED	TOPIARY	TOPPING
TONSIL	TOOLS	TOOTLER	TOPIC	TOPPINGLY

TOPPINGS	TORCHABLE	TORMINAL	TORREFIES	TORTONI
TOPPLE	TORCHED	TORMINOUS	TORREFY	TORTONIS
TOPPLED	TORCHER	TORN	TORRENT	TORTRICES
TOPPLES	TORCHERE	TORNADE	TORRENTS	TORTRICID
TOPPLING	TORCHERES	TORNADES	TORRET	TORTRIX
TOPPY	TORCHERS	TORNADIC	TORRETS	TORTRIXES
TOPS	TORCHES	TORNADO	TORRID	TORTS
TOPSAIL	TORCHIER	TORNADOES	TORRIDER	TORTUOUS
TOPSAILS	TORCHIERE	TORNADOS	TORRIDEST	TORTURE
TOPSCORE	TORCHIERS	TORNILLO	TORRIDITY	TORTURED
TOPSCORED	TORCHIEST	TORNILLOS	TORRIDLY	TORTURER
TOPSCORES	TORCHING	TORO	TORRIFIED	TORTURERS
TOPSIDE	TORCHINGS	TOROID	TORRIFIES	TORTURES
TOPSIDER	TORCHLIKE	TOROIDAL	TORRIFY	TORTURING
TOPSIDERS	TORCHON	TOROIDS	TORRS	TORTUROUS
TOPSIDES	TORCHONS	TOROS	TORS	TORULA
TOPSMAN	TORCHWOOD	TOROSE	TORSADE	TORULAE
TOPSMEN	TORCHY	TOROSITY	TORSADES	TORULAS
TOPSOIL	TORCS	TOROT	TORSE	TORULI
TOPSOILED	TORCULAR	TOROTH	TORSEL	TORULIN
TOPSOILS	TORCULARS	TOROUS	TORSELS	TORULINS
TOPSPIN	TORDION	TORPEDO	TORSES	TORULOSE
TOPSPINS	TORDIONS	TORPEDOED	TORSI	TORULOSES
TOPSTITCH	TORE	TORPEDOER	TORSION	TORULOSIS
TOPSTONE	TOREADOR	TORPEDOES	TORSIONAL	TORULUS
TOPSTONES	TOREADORS	TORPEDOS	TORSIONS	TORUS
TOPWORK	TORERO	TORPEFIED	TORSIVE	TORY
TOPWORKED	TOREROS	TORPEFIES	TORSK	TOSA
TOPWORKS	TORES	TORPEFY	TORSKS	TOSAS
TOQUE	TOREUTIC	TORPID	TORSO	TOSE
TOQUES	TOREUTICS	TORPIDITY	TORSOS	TOSED
TOQUET	TORGOCH	TORPIDLY	TORT	TOSES
TOQUETS	TORGOCHS	TORPIDS	TORTA	TOSH
TOQUILLA	TORI	TORPITUDE	TORTAS	TOSHACH
TOQUILLAS	TORIC	TORPOR	TORTE	TOSHACHS
TOR	TORICS	TORPORS	TORTELLI	TOSHED
TORA	TORIES	TORQUATE	TORTEN	TOSHER
TORAH	TORII	TORQUATED	TORTES	TOSHERS
TORAHS	TORMENT	TORQUE	TORTILE	TOSHES
TORAN	TORMENTA	TORQUED	TORTILITY	TOSHIER
TORANA	TORMENTED	TORQUER	TORTILLA	TOSHIEST
TORANAS	TORMENTER	TORQUERS	TORTILLAS	TOSHING
TORANS	TORMENTIL	TORQUES	TORTILLON	TOSHY
TORAS	TORMENTOR	TORQUESES	TORTIOUS	TOSING
TORBANITE	TORMENTS	TORQUING	TORTIVE	TOSS
TORC	TORMENTUM	TORR	TORTOISE	TOSSED
TORCH	TORMINA	TORREFIED	TORTOISES	TOSSEN

T

TOSSER	TOTED	TOUCHES	TOURED	TOUTIER
TOSSERS	TOTEM	TOUCHHOLE	TOURER	TOUTIEST
TOSSES	TOTEMIC	TOUCHIER	TOURERS	TOUTING
TOSSIER	TOTEMISM	TOUCHIEST	TOURIE	TOUTS
TOSSIEST	TOTEMISMS	TOUCHILY	TOURIES	TOUZE
TOSSILY	TOTEMIST	TOUCHING	TOURING	TOUZED
TOSSING	TOTEMISTS	TOUCHINGS	TOURINGS	TOUZES
TOSSINGS	TOTEMITE	TOUCHLESS	TOURISM	TOUZIER
TOSSPOT	TOTEMITES	TOUCHLINE	TOURISMS	TOUZIEST
TOSSPOTS	TOTEMS	TOUCHMARK	TOURIST	TOUZING
TOSSUP	TOTER	TOUCHPAD	TOURISTA	TOUZLE
TOSSUPS	TOTERS	TOUCHPADS	TOURISTAS	TOUZLED
TOSSY	TOTES	TOUCHTONE	TOURISTED	TOUZLES
TOST	TOTHER	TOUCHUP	TOURISTIC	TOUZLING
TOSTADA	TOTIENT	TOUCHUPS	TOURISTS	TOUZY
TOSTADAS	TOTIENTS	TOUCHWOOD	TOURISTY	TOVARICH
TOSTADO	TOTING	TOUCHY	TOURNEDOS	TOVARISCH
TOSTADOS	TOTITIVE	TOUGH	TOURNEY	TOVARISH
TOT	TOTITIVES	TOUGHED	TOURNEYED	TOW
TOTABLE	TOTS	TOUGHEN	TOURNEYER	TOWABLE
TOTAL	TOTTED	TOUGHENED	TOURNEYS	TOWAGE
TOTALED	TOTTER	TOUGHENER	TOURNURE	TOWAGES
TOTALING	TOTTERED	TOUGHENS	TOURNURES	TOWARD
TOTALISE	TOTTERER	TOUGHER	TOURS	TOWARDLY
TOTALISED	TOTTERERS	TOUGHEST	TOURTIERE	TOWARDS
TOTALISER	TOTTERING	TOUGHIE	TOUSE	TOWAWAY
TOTALISES	TOTTERS	TOUGHIES	TOUSED	TOWAWAYS
TOTALISM	TOTTERY	TOUGHING	TOUSER	TOWBAR
TOTALISMS	TOTTIE	TOUGHISH	TOUSERS	TOWBARS
TOTALIST	TOTTIER	TOUGHLY	TOUSES	TOWBOAT
TOTALISTS	TOTTIES	TOUGHNESS	TOUSIER	TOWBOATS
TOTALITY	TOTTIEST	TOUGHS	TOUSIEST	TOWED
TOTALIZE	TOTTING	TOUGHY	TOUSING	TOWEL
TOTALIZED	TOTTINGS	TOUK	TOUSINGS	TOWELED
TOTALIZER	TOTTY	TOUKED	TOUSLE	TOWELETTE
TOTALIZES	TOUCAN	TOUKING	TOUSLED	TOWELHEAD
TOTALLED	TOUCANET	TOUKS	TOUSLES	TOWELING
TOTALLING	TOUCANETS	TOUN	TOUSLING	TOWELINGS
TOTALLY	TOUCANS	TOUNS	TOUSTIE	TOWELLED
TOTALS	TOUCH	TOUPEE	TOUSTIER	TOWELLING
TOTANUS	TOUCHABLE	TOUPEED	TOUSTIEST	TOWELS
TOTANUSES	TOUCHBACK	TOUPEES	TOUSY	TOWER
TOTAQUINE	TOUCHDOWN	TOUPET	TOUT	TOWERED
TOTARA	TOUCHE	TOUPETS	TOUTED	TOWERIER
TOTARAS	TOUCHED	TOUR	TOUTER	TOWERIEST
TOTE	TOUCHER	TOURACO	TOUTERS	TOWERING
TOTEABLE	TOUCHERS	TOURACOS	TOUTIE	TOWERLESS

TOWERLIKE	TOWNS	TOXEMIC	TOZE	TRACKABLE
TOWERS	TOWNSCAPE	TOXIC	TOZED	TRACKAGE
TOWERY	TOWNSFOLK	TOXICAL	TOZES	TRACKAGES
TOWHEAD	TOWNSHIP	TOXICALLY	TOZIE	TRACKBALL
TOWHEADED	TOWNSHIPS	TOXICANT	TOZIES	TRACKBED
TOWHEADS	TOWNSKIP	TOXICANTS	TOZING	TRACKBEDS
TOWHEE	TOWNSKIPS	TOXICITY	TRABEATE	TRACKED
TOWHEES	TOWNSMAN	TOXICOSES	TRABEATED	TRACKER
TOWIE	TOWNSMEN	TOXICOSIS	TRABECULA	TRACKERS
TOWIER	TOWNWEAR	TOXICS	TRABS	TRACKING
TOWIES	TOWNY	TOXIGENIC	TRACE	TRACKINGS
TOWIEST	TOWPATH	TOXIN	TRACEABLE	TRACKLESS
TOWING	TOWPATHS	TOXINE	TRACEABLY	TRACKMAN
TOWINGS	TOWPLANE	TOXINES	TRACED	TRACKMEN
TOWKAY	TOWPLANES	TOXINS	TRACELESS	TRACKPAD
TOWKAYS	TOWROPE	TOXOCARA	TRACER	TRACKPADS
TOWLINE	TOWROPES	TOXOCARAL	TRACERIED	TRACKROAD
TOWLINES	TOWS	TOXOCARAS	TRACERIES	TRACKS
TOWMON	TOWSACK	TOXOID	TRACERS	TRACKSIDE
TOWMOND	TOWSACKS	TOXOIDS	TRACERY	TRACKSUIT
TOWMONDS	TOWSE	TOXOPHILY	TRACES	TRACKWAY
TOWMONS	TOWSED	TOY	TRACEUR	TRACKWAYS
TOWMONT	TOWSER	TOYED	TRACEURS	TRACT
TOWMONTS	TOWSERS	TOYER	TRACHEA	TRACTABLE
TOWN	TOWSES	TOYERS	TRACHEAE	TRACTABLY
TOWNEE	TOWSIER	TOYETIC	TRACHEAL	TRACTATE
TOWNEES	TOWSIEST	TOYING	TRACHEARY	TRACTATES
TOWNFOLK	TOWSING	TOYINGS	TRACHEAS	TRACTATOR
TOWNHALL	TOWSY	TOYISH	TRACHEATE	TRACTED
TOWNHOME	TOWT	TOYISHLY	TRACHEID	TRACTILE
TOWNHOMES	TOWTED	TOYLESOME	TRACHEIDE	TRACTING
TOWNHOUSE	TOWTING	TOYLESS	TRACHEIDS	TRACTION
TOWNIE	TOWTS	TOYLIKE	TRACHEOLE	TRACTIONS
TOWNIER	TOWY	TOYLSOM	TRACHINUS	TRACTIVE
TOWNIES	TOWZE	TOYMAN	TRACHITIS	TRACTOR
TOWNIEST	TOWZED	TOYMEN	TRACHLE	TRACTORS
TOWNISH	TOWZES	TOYO	TRACHLED	TRACTRIX
TOWNLAND	TOWZIER	TOYON	TRACHLES	TRACTS
TOWNLANDS	TOWZIEST	TOYONS	TRACHLING	TRACTUS
TOWNLESS	TOWZING	TOYOS	TRACHOMA	TRACTUSES
TOWNLET	TOWZY	TOYS	TRACHOMAS	TRAD
TOWNLETS	TOXAEMIA	TOYSHOP	TRACHYTE	TRADABLE
TOWNLIER	TOXAEMIAS	TOYSHOPS	TRACHYTES	TRADE
TOWNLIEST	TOXAEMIC	TOYSOME	TRACHYTIC	TRADEABLE
TOWNLING	TOXAPHENE	TOYTOWN	TRACING	TRADED
TOWNLINGS	TOXEMIA	TOYWOMAN	TRACINGS	TRADEFUL
TOWNLY	TOXEMIAS	TOYWOMEN	TRACK	TRADELESS

TRADEMARK	TRAIKS	TRAMEL	TRANCEDLY	TRANSFORM
TRADENAME	TRAIL	TRAMELED	TRANCES	TRANSFUSE
TRADEOFF	TRAILABLE	TRAMELING	TRANCEY	TRANSGENE
TRADEOFFS	TRAILED	TRAMELL	TRANCHE	TRANSHIP
TRADER	TRAILER	TRAMELLED	TRANCHES	TRANSHIPS
TRADERS	TRAILERED	TRAMELLS	TRANCHET	TRANSHUME
TRADES	TRAILERS	TRAMELS	TRANCHETS	TRANSIENT
TRADESMAN	TRAILHEAD	TRAMLESS	TRANCIER	TRANSIRE
TRADESMEN	TRAILING	TRAMLINE	TRANCIEST	TRANSIRES
TRADING	TRAILLESS	TRAMLINED	TRANCING	TRANSIT
TRADINGS	TRAILS	TRAMLINES	TRANECT	TRANSITED
TRADITION	TRAILSIDE	TRAMMED	TRANECTS	TRANSITS
TRADITIVE	TRAIN	TRAMMEL	TRANGAM	TRANSLATE
TRADITOR	TRAINABLE	TRAMMELED	TRANGAMS	TRANSMEW
TRADITORS	TRAINBAND	TRAMMELER	TRANGLE	TRANSMEWS
TRADS	TRAINED	TRAMMELS	TRANGLES	TRANSMIT
TRADUCE	TRAINEE	TRAMMIE	TRANK	TRANSMITS
TRADUCED	TRAINEES	TRAMMIES	TRANKS	TRANSMOVE
TRADUCER	TRAINER	TRAMMING	TRANKUM	TRANSMUTE
TRADUCERS	TRAINERS	TRAMP	TRANKUMS	TRANSOM
TRADUCES	TRAINFUL	TRAMPED	TRANNIE	TRANSOMED
TRADUCIAN	TRAINFULS	TRAMPER	TRANNIES	TRANSOMS
TRADUCING	TRAINING	TRAMPERS	TRANNY	TRANSONIC
TRAFFIC	TRAININGS	TRAMPET	TRANQ	TRANSPIRE
TRAFFICKY	TRAINLESS	TRAMPETS	TRANQS	TRANSPORT
TRAFFICS	TRAINLOAD	TRAMPETTE	TRANQUIL	TRANSPOSE
TRAGAL	TRAINMAN	TRAMPIER	TRANS	TRANSSHIP
TRAGEDIAN	TRAINMEN	TRAMPIEST	TRANSACT	TRANSUDE
TRAGEDIES	TRAINS	TRAMPING	TRANSACTS	TRANSUDED
TRAGEDY	TRAINWAY	TRAMPINGS	TRANSAXLE	TRANSUDES
TRAGELAPH	TRAINWAYS	TRAMPISH	TRANSCEND	TRANSUME
TRAGI	TRAIPSE	TRAMPLE	TRANSCODE	TRANSUMED
TRAGIC	TRAIPSED	TRAMPLED	TRANSDUCE	TRANSUMES
TRAGICAL	TRAIPSES	TRAMPLER	TRANSE	TRANSUMPT
TRAGICS	TRAIPSING	TRAMPLERS	TRANSECT	TRANSVEST
TRAGOPAN	TRAIT	TRAMPLES	TRANSECTS	TRANT
TRAGOPANS	TRAITOR	TRAMPLING	TRANSENNA	TRANTED
TRAGULE	TRAITORLY	TRAMPOLIN	TRANSEPT	TRANTER
TRAGULES	TRAITORS	TRAMPS	TRANSEPTS	TRANTERS
TRAGULINE	TRAITRESS	TRAMPY	TRANSES	TRANTING
TRAGUS	TRAITS	TRAMROAD	TRANSEUNT	TRANTS
TRAHISON	TRAJECT	TRAMROADS	TRANSFARD	TRAP
TRAHISONS	TRAJECTED	TRAMS	TRANSFECT	TRAPAN
TRAIK	TRAJECTS	TRAMWAY	TRANSFER	TRAPANNED
TRAIKED	TRAM	TRAMWAYS	TRANSFERS	TRAPANNER
TRAIKING	TRAMCAR	TRANCE	TRANSFIX	TRAPANS
TRAIKIT	TRAMCARS	TRANCED	TRANSFIXT	TRAPBALL

TRAPBALLS	TRASHCANS	TRAVERSES	TREADLE	TREDDLES
TRAPDOOR	TRASHED	TRAVERTIN	TREADLED	TREDDLING
TRAPDOORS	TRASHER	TRAVES	TREADLER	TREDILLE
TRAPE	TRASHERS	TRAVESTY	TREADLERS	TREDILLES
TRAPED	TRASHERY	TRAVIS	TREADLES	TREDRILLE
TRAPES	TRASHES	TRAVISES	TREADLESS	TREE
TRAPESED	TRASHIER	TRAVOIS	TREADLING	TREED
TRAPESES	TRASHIEST	TRAVOISE	TREADMILL	TREEHOUSE
TRAPESING	TRASHILY	TRAVOISES	TREADS	TREEING
TRAPEZE	TRASHING	TRAWL	TREAGUE	TREELAWN
TRAPEZED	TRASHMAN	TRAWLED	TREAGUES	TREELAWNS
TRAPEZES	TRASHMEN	TRAWLER	TREASON	TREELESS
TRAPEZIA	TRASHTRIE	TRAWLERS	TREASONS	TREELIKE
TRAPEZIAL	TRASHY	TRAWLEY	TREASURE	TREEN
TRAPEZII	TRASS	TRAWLEYS	TREASURED	TREENAIL
TRAPEZING	TRASSES	TRAWLING	TREASURER	TREENAILS
TRAPEZIST	TRAT	TRAWLINGS	TREASURES	TREENS
TRAPEZIUM	TRATS	TRAWLNET	TREASURY	TREENWARE
TRAPEZIUS	TRATT	TRAWLNETS	TREAT	TREES
TRAPEZOID	TRATTORIA	TRAWLS	TREATABLE	TREESHIP
TRAPFALL	TRATTORIE	TRAY	TREATED	TREESHIPS
TRAPFALLS	TRATTS	TRAYBIT	TREATER	TREETOP
TRAPING	TRAUCHLE	TRAYBITS	TREATERS	TREETOPS
TRAPLIKE	TRAUCHLED	TRAYFUL	TREATIES	TREEWARE
TRAPLINE	TRAUCHLES	TRAYFULS	TREATING	TREEWARES
TRAPLINES	TRAUMA	TRAYNE	TREATINGS	TREEWAX
TRAPNEST	TRAUMAS	TRAYNED	TREATISE	TREEWAXES
TRAPNESTS	TRAUMATA	TRAYNES	TREATISES	TREF
TRAPPEAN	TRAUMATIC	TRAYNING	TREATMENT	TREFA
TRAPPED	TRAVAIL	TRAYS	TREATS	TREFAH
TRAPPER	TRAVAILED	TRAZODONE	TREATY	TREFOIL
TRAPPERS	TRAVAILS	TREACHER	TREBBIANO	TREFOILED
TRAPPIER	TRAVE	TREACHERS	TREBLE	TREFOILS
TRAPPIEST	TRAVEL	TREACHERY	TREBLED	TREGETOUR
TRAPPING	TRAVELED	TREACHOUR	TREBLES	TREHALA
TRAPPINGS	TRAVELER	TREACLE	TREBLING	TREHALAS
TRAPPOSE	TRAVELERS	TREACLED	TREBLY	TREHALOSE
TRAPPOUS	TRAVELING	TREACLES	TREBUCHET	TREIF
TRAPPY	TRAVELLED	TREACLIER	TREBUCKET	TREIFA
TRAPROCK	TRAVELLER	TREACLING	TRECENTO	TREILLAGE
TRAPROCKS	TRAVELOG	TREACLY	TRECENTOS	TREILLE
TRAPS	TRAVELOGS	TREAD	TRECK	TREILLES
TRAPT	TRAVELS	TREADED	TRECKED	TREK
TRAPUNTO	TRAVERSAL	TREADER	TRECKING	TREKKED
TRAPUNTOS	TRAVERSE	TREADERS	TRECKS	TREKKER
TRASH	TRAVERSED	TREADING	TREDDLE	TREKKERS
TRASHCAN	TRAVERSER	TREADINGS	TREDDLED	TREKKING

TREKKINGS	TRENDIES	TRESTS	TRIALLED	TRIBESMEN
TREKS	TRENDIEST	TRET	TRIALLING	TRIBLET
TRELLIS	TRENDIFY	TRETINOIN	TRIALLIST	TRIBLETS
TRELLISED	TRENDILY	TRETS	TRIALOGUE	TRIBOLOGY
TRELLISES	TRENDING	TREVALLY	TRIALS	TRIBRACH
TREMA	TRENDOID	TREVALLYS	TRIALWARE	TRIBRACHS
TREMAS	TRENDOIDS	TREVET	TRIANGLE	TRIBULATE
TREMATIC	TRENDS	TREVETS	TRIANGLED	TRIBUNAL
TREMATODE	TRENDY	TREVIS	TRIANGLES	TRIBUNALS
TREMATOID	TRENDYISM	TREVISES	TRIAPSAL	TRIBUNARY
TREMBLANT	TRENISE	TREVISS	TRIARCH	TRIBUNATE
TREMBLE	TRENISES	TREVISSES	TRIARCHS	TRIBUNE
TREMBLED	TRENTAL	TREW	TRIARCHY	TRIBUNES
TREMBLER	TRENTALS	TREWS	TRIASSIC	TRIBUTARY
TREMBLERS	TREPAN	TREWSMAN	TRIATHLON	TRIBUTE
TREMBLES	TREPANG	TREWSMEN	TRIATIC	TRIBUTER
TREMBLIER	TREPANGS	TREY	TRIATICS	TRIBUTERS
TREMBLING	TREPANNED	TREYBIT	TRIATOMIC	TRIBUTES
TREMBLY	TREPANNER	TREYBITS	TRIAXIAL	TRICAR
TREMIE	TREPANS	TREYS	TRIAXIALS	TRICARS
TREMIES	TREPHINE	TREZ	TRIAXON	TRICE
TREMOLANT	TREPHINED	TREZES	TRIAXONS	TRICED
TREMOLITE	TREPHINER	TRIABLE	TRIAZIN	TRICEP
TREMOLO	TREPHINES	TRIAC	TRIAZINE	TRICEPS
TREMOLOS	TREPID	TRIACID	TRIAZINES	TRICEPSES
TREMOR	TREPIDANT	TRIACIDS	TRIAZINS	TRICERION
TREMORED	TREPONEMA	TRIACS	TRIAZOLE	TRICES
TREMORING	TREPONEME	TRIACT	TRIAZOLES	TRICHINA
TREMOROUS	TRES	TRIACTINE	TRIAZOLIC	TRICHINAE
TREMORS	TRESPASS	TRIAD	TRIBADE	TRICHINAL
TREMULANT	TRESS	TRIADIC	TRIBADES	TRICHINAS
TREMULATE	TRESSED	TRIADICS	TRIBADIC	TRICHITE
TREMULOUS	TRESSEL	TRIADISM	TRIBADIES	TRICHITES
TRENAIL	TRESSELS	TRIADISMS	TRIBADISM	TRICHITIC
TRENAILS	TRESSES	TRIADIST	TRIBADY	TRICHOID
TRENCH	TRESSIER	TRIADISTS	TRIBAL	TRICHOME
TRENCHAND	TRESSIEST	TRIADS	TRIBALISM	TRICHOMES
TRENCHANT	TRESSING	TRIAGE	TRIBALIST	TRICHOMIC
TRENCHARD	TRESSOUR	TRIAGED	TRIBALLY	TRICHORD
TRENCHED	TRESSOURS	TRIAGES	TRIBALS	TRICHORDS
TRENCHER	TRESSURE	TRIAGING	TRIBASIC	TRICHOSES
TRENCHERS	TRESSURED	TRIAL	TRIBBLE	TRICHOSIS
TRENCHES	TRESSURES	TRIALISM	TRIBBLES	TRICHROIC
TRENCHING	TRESSY	TRIALISMS	TRIBE	TRICHROME
TREND	TREST	TRIALIST	TRIBELESS	TRICING
TRENDED	TRESTLE	TRIALISTS	TRIBES	TRICK
TRENDIER	TRESTLES	TRIALITY	TRIBESMAN	TRICKED

TRICKER	TRICYCLER	TRIFLED	TRIGYNIAN	TRIMARANS
TRICKERS	TRICYCLES	TRIFLER	TRIGYNOUS	TRIMER
TRICKERY	TRICYCLIC	TRIFLERS	TRIHEDRA	TRIMERIC
TRICKIE	TRIDACNA	TRIFLES	TRIHEDRAL	TRIMERISM
TRICKIER	TRIDACNAS	TRIFLING	TRIHEDRON	TRIMEROUS
TRICKIEST	TRIDACTYL	TRIFLINGS	TRIHYBRID	TRIMERS
TRICKILY	TRIDARN	TRIFOCAL	TRIHYDRIC	TRIMESTER
TRICKING	TRIDARNS	TRIFOCALS	TRIJET	TRIMETER
TRICKINGS	TRIDE	TRIFOLD	TRIJETS	TRIMETERS
TRICKISH	TRIDENT	TRIFOLIES	TRIJUGATE	TRIMETHYL
TRICKLE	TRIDENTAL	TRIFOLIUM	TRIJUGOUS	TRIMETRIC
TRICKLED	TRIDENTED	TRIFOLY	TRIKE	TRIMIX
TRICKLES	TRIDENTS	TRIFORIA	TRIKES	TRIMIXES
TRICKLESS	TRIDUAN	TRIFORIAL	TRILBIES	TRIMLY
TRICKLET	TRIDUUM	TRIFORIUM	TRILBY	TRIMMED
TRICKLETS	TRIDUUMS	TRIFORM	TRILBYS	TRIMMER
TRICKLIER	TRIDYMITE	TRIFORMED	TRILD	TRIMMERS
TRICKLING	TRIE	TRIG	TRILEMMA	TRIMMEST
TRICKLY	TRIECIOUS	TRIGAMIES	TRILEMMAS	TRIMMING
TRICKS	TRIED	TRIGAMIST	TRILINEAR	TRIMMINGS
TRICKSIER	TRIELLA	TRIGAMOUS	TRILITH	TRIMNESS
TRICKSILY	TRIELLAS	TRIGAMY	TRILITHIC	TRIMORPH
TRICKSOME	TRIENE	TRIGEMINI	TRILITHON	TRIMORPHS
TRICKSTER	TRIENES	TRIGGED	TRILITHS	TRIMOTOR
TRICKSY	TRIENNIA	TRIGGER	TRILL	TRIMOTORS
TRICKY	TRIENNIAL	TRIGGERED	TRILLED	TRIMS
TRICLAD	TRIENNIUM	TRIGGERS	TRILLER	TRIMTAB
TRICLADS	TRIENS	TRIGGEST	TRILLERS	TRIMTABS
TRICLINIA	TRIENTES	TRIGGING	TRILLING	TRIN
TRICLINIC	TRIER	TRIGLOT	TRILLINGS	TRINAL
TRICLOSAN	TRIERARCH	TRIGLOTS	TRILLION	TRINARY
TRICOLOR	TRIERS	TRIGLY	TRILLIONS	TRINDLE
TRICOLORS	TRIES	TRIGLYPH	TRILLIUM	TRINDLED
TRICOLOUR	TRIETERIC	TRIGLYPHS	TRILLIUMS	TRINDLES
TRICORN	TRIETHYL	TRIGNESS	TRILLO	TRINDLING
TRICORNE	TRIFACIAL	TRIGO	TRILLOES	TRINE
TRICORNES	TRIFECTA	TRIGON	TRILLS	TRINED
TRICORNS	TRIFECTAS	TRIGONAL	TRILOBAL	TRINES
TRICOT	TRIFF	TRIGONIC	TRILOBATE	TRINGLE
TRICOTINE	TRIFFER	TRIGONOUS	TRILOBE	TRINGLES
TRICOTS	TRIFFEST	TRIGONS	TRILOBED	TRINING
TRICROTIC	TRIFFIC	TRIGOS	TRILOBES	TRINITIES
TRICTRAC	TRIFFID	TRIGRAM	TRILOBITE	TRINITRIN
TRICTRACS	TRIFFIDS	TRIGRAMS	TRILOGIES	TRINITY
TRICUSPID	TRIFFIDY	TRIGRAPH	TRILOGY	TRINKET
TRICYCLE	TRIFID	TRIGRAPHS	TRIM	TRINKETED
TRICYCLED	TRIFLE	TRIGS	TRIMARAN	TRINKETER

TRINKETRY	TRIPLANES	TRIPS	TRISOMIES	TRIUMPH
TRINKETS	TRIPLE	TRIPSES	TRISOMY	TRIUMPHAL
TRINKUM	TRIPLED	TRIPSIS	TRIST	TRIUMPHED
TRINKUMS	TRIPLES	TRIPTAN	TRISTATE	TRIUMPHER
TRINODAL	TRIPLET	TRIPTANE	TRISTE	TRIUMPHS
TRINOMIAL	TRIPLETS	TRIPTANES	TRISTESSE	TRIUMVIR
TRINS	TRIPLEX	TRIPTANS	TRISTEZA	TRIUMVIRI
TRIO	TRIPLEXES	TRIPTOTE	TRISTEZAS	TRIUMVIRS
TRIODE	TRIPLIED	TRIPTOTES	TRISTFUL	TRIUMVIRY
TRIODES	TRIPLIES	TRIPTYCA	TRISTICH	TRIUNE
TRIOL	TRIPLING	TRIPTYCAS	TRISTICHS	TRIUNES
TRIOLEIN	TRIPLINGS	TRIPTYCH	TRISUL	TRIUNITY
TRIOLEINS	TRIPLITE	TRIPTYCHS	TRISULA	TRIVALENT
TRIOLET	TRIPLITES	TRIPTYQUE	TRISULAS	TRIVALVE
TRIOLETS	TRIPLOID	TRIPUDIA	TRISULS	TRIVALVED
TRIOLS	TRIPLOIDS	TRIPUDIUM	TRITANOPE	TRIVALVES
TRIONES	TRIPLOIDY	TRIPWIRE	TRITE	TRIVET
TRIONYM	TRIPLY	TRIPWIRES	TRITELY	TRIVETS
TRIONYMAL	TRIPLYING	TRIPY	TRITENESS	TRIVIA
TRIONYMS	TRIPOD	TRIQUETRA	TRITER	TRIVIAL
TRIOR	TRIPODAL	TRIRADIAL	TRITES	TRIVIALLY
TRIORS	TRIPODIC	TRIREME	TRITEST	TRIVIUM
TRIOS	TRIPODIES	TRIREMES	TRITHEISM	TRIVIUMS
TRIOSE	TRIPODS	TRISAGION	TRITHEIST	TRIWEEKLY
TRIOSES	TRIPODY	TRISCELE	TRITHING	TRIZONAL
TRIOXID	TRIPOLI	TRISCELES	TRITHINGS	TRIZONE
TRIOXIDE	TRIPOLIS	TRISECT	TRITIATE	TRIZONES
TRIOXIDES	TRIPOS	TRISECTED	TRITIATED	TROAD
TRIOXIDS	TRIPOSES	TRISECTOR	TRITIATES	TROADE
TRIOXYGEN	TRIPPANT	TRISECTS	TRITICAL	TROADES
TRIP	TRIPPED	TRISEME	TRITICALE	TROADS
TRIPACK	TRIPPER	TRISEMES	TRITICISM	TROAK
TRIPACKS	TRIPPERS	TRISEMIC	TRITICUM	TROAKED
TRIPART	TRIPPERY	TRISERIAL	TRITICUMS	TROAKING
TRIPE	TRIPPET	TRISHAW	TRITIDE	TROAKS
TRIPEDAL	TRIPPETS	TRISHAWS	TRITIDES	TROAT
TRIPERIES	TRIPPIER	TRISKELE	TRITIUM	TROATED
TRIPERY	TRIPPIEST	TRISKELES	TRITIUMS	TROATING
TRIPES	TRIPPING	TRISKELIA	TRITOMA	TROATS
TRIPEY	TRIPPINGS	TRISMIC	TRITOMAS	TROCAR
TRIPHASE	TRIPPLE	TRISMUS	TRITON	TROCARS
TRIPHONE	TRIPPLED	TRISMUSES	TRITONE	TROCHAIC
TRIPHONES	TRIPPLER	TRISODIUM	TRITONES	TROCHAICS
TRIPIER	TRIPPLERS	TRISOME	TRITONIA	TROCHAL
TRIPIEST	TRIPPLES	TRISOMES	TRITONIAS	TROCHAR
TRIPITAKA	TRIPPLING	TRISOMIC	TRITONS	TROCHARS
TRIPLANE	TRIPPY	TRISOMICS	TRITURATE	TROCHE

TROCHEE	TROILIST	TRONA	TROPISMS	TROUNCER
TROCHEES	TROILISTS	TRONAS	TROPIST	TROUNCERS
TROCHES	TROILITE	TRONC	TROPISTIC	TROUNCES
TROCHI	TROILITES	TRONCS	TROPISTS	TROUNCING
TROCHIL	TROILUS	TRONE	TROPOLOGY	TROUPE
TROCHILI	TROILUSES	TRONES	TROPONIN	TROUPED
TROCHILIC	TROIS	TRONK	TROPONINS	TROUPER
TROCHILS	TROKE	TRONKS	TROPPO	TROUPERS
TROCHILUS	TROKED	TRONS	TROSSERS	TROUPES
TROCHISK	TROKES	TROOLIE	TROT	TROUPIAL
TROCHISKS	TROKING	TROOLIES	TROTH	TROUPIALS
TROCHITE	TROLAND	TROOP	TROTHED	TROUPING
TROCHITES	TROLANDS	TROOPED	TROTHFUL	TROUSE
TROCHLEA	TROLL	TROOPER	TROTHING	TROUSER
TROCHLEAE	TROLLED	TROOPERS	TROTHLESS	TROUSERED
TROCHLEAR	TROLLER	TROOPIAL	TROTHS	TROUSERS
TROCHLEAS	TROLLERS	TROOPIALS	TROTLINE	TROUSES
TROCHOID	TROLLEY	TROOPING	TROTLINES	TROUSSEAU
TROCHOIDS	TROLLEYED	TROOPS	TROTS	TROUT
TROCHUS	TROLLEYS	TROOPSHIP	TROTTED	TROUTER
TROCHUSES	TROLLIED	TROOSTITE	TROTTER	TROUTERS
TROCK	TROLLIES	TROOZ	TROTTERS	TROUTFUL
TROCKED	TROLLING	TROP	TROTTING	TROUTIER
TROCKEN	TROLLINGS	TROPAEOLA	TROTTINGS	TROUTIEST
TROCKING	TROLLIUS	TROPARIA	TROTTOIR	TROUTING
TROCKS	TROLLOP	TROPARION	TROTTOIRS	TROUTINGS
TROD	TROLLOPED	TROPE	TROTYL	TROUTLESS
TRODDEN	TROLLOPEE	TROPED	TROTYLS	TROUTLET
TRODE	TROLLOPS	TROPEOLIN	TROUBLE	TROUTLETS
TRODES	TROLLOPY	TROPES	TROUBLED	TROUTLING
TRODS	TROLLS	TROPHESY	TROUBLER	TROUTS
TROELIE	TROLLY	TROPHI	TROUBLERS	TROUTY
TROELIES	TROLLYING	TROPHIC	TROUBLES	TROUVERE
TROELY	TROMBONE	TROPHIED	TROUBLING	TROUVERES
TROFFER	TROMBONES	TROPHIES	TROUBLOUS	TROUVEUR
TROFFERS	TROMINO	TROPHY	TROUCH	TROUVEURS
TROG	TROMINOES	TROPHYING	TROUCHES	TROVE
TROGGED	TROMINOS	TROPIC	TROUGH	TROVER
TROGGING	TROMMEL	TROPICAL	TROUGHED	TROVERS
TROGGS	TROMMELS	TROPICALS	TROUGHING	TROVES
TROGON	TROMP	TROPICS	TROUGHS	TROW
TROGONS	TROMPE	TROPIN	TROULE	TROWED
TROGS	TROMPED	TROPINE	TROULED	TROWEL
TROIKA	TROMPES	TROPINES	TROULES	TROWELED
TROIKAS	TROMPING	TROPING	TROULING	TROWELER
TROILISM	TROMPS	TROPINS	TROUNCE	TROWELERS
TROILISMS	TRON	TROPISM	TROUNCED	TROWELING

TROWELLED

TROWELLED	TRUCKLINE	TRUISMS	TRUSS	TRYP
TROWELLER	TRUCKLING	TRUISTIC	TRUSSED	TRYPAN
TROWELS	TRUCKLOAD	TRULL	TRUSSER	TRYPS
TROWING	TRUCKMAN	TRULLS	TRUSSERS	TRYPSIN
TROWS	TRUCKMEN	TRULY	TRUSSES	TRYPSINS
TROWSERS	TRUCKS	TRUMEAU	TRUSSING	TRYPTIC
TROWTH	TRUCKSTOP	TRUMEAUX	TRUSSINGS	TRYSAIL
TROWTHS	TRUCULENT	TRUMP	TRUST	TRYSAILS
TROY	TRUDGE	TRUMPED	TRUSTABLE	TRYST
TROYS	TRUDGED	TRUMPERY	TRUSTED	TRYSTE
TRUANCIES	TRUDGEN	TRUMPET	TRUSTEE	TRYSTED
TRUANCY	TRUDGENS	TRUMPETED	TRUSTEED	TRYSTER
TRUANT	TRUDGEON	TRUMPETER	TRUSTEES	TRYSTERS
TRUANTED	TRUDGEONS	TRUMPETS	TRUSTER	TRYSTES
TRUANTING	TRUDGER	TRUMPING	TRUSTERS	TRYSTING
TRUANTLY	TRUDGERS	TRUMPINGS	TRUSTFUL	TRYSTS
TRUANTRY	TRUDGES	TRUMPLESS	TRUSTIER	TRYWORKS
TRUANTS	TRUDGING	TRUMPS	TRUSTIES	TSADDIK
TRUCAGE	TRUDGINGS	TRUNCAL	TRUSTIEST	TSADDIKIM
TRUCAGES	TRUE	TRUNCATE	TRUSTILY	TSADDIKS
TRUCE	TRUEBLUE	TRUNCATED	TRUSTING	TSADDIQ
TRUCED	TRUEBLUES	TRUNCATES	TRUSTLESS	TSADDIQIM
TRUCELESS	TRUEBORN	TRUNCHEON	TRUSTOR	TSADDIQS
TRUCES	TRUEBRED	TRUNDLE	TRUSTORS	TSADE
TRUCHMAN	TRUED	TRUNDLED	TRUSTS	TSADES
TRUCHMANS	TRUEING	TRUNDLER	TRUSTY	TSADI
TRUCHMEN	TRUELOVE	TRUNDLERS	TRUTH	TSADIS
TRUCIAL	TRUELOVES	TRUNDLES	TRUTHFUL	TSAMBA
TRUCING	TRUEMAN	TRUNDLING	TRUTHIER	TSAMBAS
TRUCK	TRUEMEN	TRUNK	TRUTHIEST	TSANTSA
TRUCKABLE	TRUENESS	TRUNKED	TRUTHLESS	TSANTSAS
TRUCKAGE	TRUEPENNY	TRUNKFISH	TRUTHLIKE	TSAR
TRUCKAGES	TRUER	TRUNKFUL	TRUTHS	TSARDOM
TRUCKED	TRUES	TRUNKFULS	TRUTHY	TSARDOMS
TRUCKER	TRUEST	TRUNKING	TRY	TSAREVICH
TRUCKERS	TRUFFE	TRUNKINGS	TRYE	TSAREVNA
TRUCKFUL	TRUFFES	TRUNKLESS	TRYER	TSAREVNAS
TRUCKFULS	TRUFFLE	TRUNKS	TRYERS	TSARINA
TRUCKIE	TRUFFLED	TRUNKWORK	TRYING	TSARINAS
TRUCKIES	TRUFFLES	TRUNNEL	TRYINGLY	TSARISM
TRUCKING	TRUFFLING	TRUNNELS	TRYINGS	TSARISMS
TRUCKINGS	TRUG	TRUNNION	TRYKE	TSARIST
TRUCKLE	TRUGO	TRUNNIONS	TRYKES	TSARISTS
TRUCKLED	TRUGOS	TRUQUAGE	TRYMA	TSARITSA
TRUCKLER	TRUGS	TRUQUAGES	TRYMATA	TSARITSAS
TRUCKLERS	TRUING	TRUQUEUR	TRYOUT	TSARITZA
TRUCKLES	TRUISM	TRUQUEURS	TRYOUTS	TSARITZAS

TSARS	TUATUAS	TUBEWORMS	TUCKETS	TUGRAS
TSATSKE	TUB	TUBFAST	TUCKING	TUGRIK
TSATSKES	TUBA	TUBFASTS	TUCKS	TUGRIKS
TSESSEBE	TUBAE	TUBFISH	TUCKSHOP	TUGS
TSESSEBES	TUBAGE	TUBFISHES	TUCKSHOPS	TUI
TSETSE	TUBAGES	TUBFUL	TUCOTUCO	TUILLE
TSETSES	TUBAIST	TUBFULS	TUCOTUCOS	TUILLES
TSIGANE	TUBAISTS	TUBICOLAR	TUCUTUCO	TUILLETTE
TSIGANES	TUBAL	TUBICOLE	TUCUTUCOS	TUILYIE
TSIMMES	TUBAR	TUBICOLES	TUCUTUCU	TUILYIED
TSITSITH	TUBAS	TUBIFEX	TUCUTUCUS	TUILYIES
TSK	TUBATE	TUBIFEXES	TUFA	TUILZIE
TSKED	TUBBABLE	TUBIFICID	TUFACEOUS	TUILZIED
TSKING	TUBBED	TUBIFORM	TUFAS	TUILZIES
TSKS	TUBBER	TUBING	TUFF	TUINA
TSKTSK	TUBBERS	TUBINGS	TUFFE	TUINAS
TSKTSKED	TUBBIER	TUBIST	TUFFES	TUIS
TSKTSKING	TUBBIEST	TUBISTS	TUFFET	TUISM
TSKTSKS	TUBBINESS	TUBLIKE	TUFFETS	TUISMS
TSOORIS	TUBBING	TUBS	TUFFS	TUITION
TSORES	TUBBINGS	TUBULAR	TUFOLI	TUITIONAL
TSORIS	TUBBISH	TUBULARLY	TUFT	TUITIONS
TSORRISS	TUBBY	TUBULATE	TUFTED	TUKTOO
TSOTSI	TUBE	TUBULATED	TUFTER	TUKTOOS
TSOTSIS	TUBECTOMY	TUBULATES	TUFTERS	TUKTU
TSOURIS	TUBED	TUBULATOR	TUFTIER	TUKTUS
TSOURISES	TUBEFUL	TUBULE	TUFTIEST	TULADI
TSUBA	TUBEFULS	TUBULES	TUFTILY	TULADIS
TSUBAS	TUBELESS	TUBULIN	TUFTING	TULAREMIA
TSUNAMI	TUBELIKE	TUBULINS	TUFTINGS	TULAREMIC
TSUNAMIC	TUBENOSE	TUBULOSE	TUFTS	TULBAN
TSUNAMIS	TUBENOSES	TUBULOUS	TUFTY	TULBANS
TSURIS	TUBER	TUBULURE	TUG	TULCHAN
TSURISES	TUBERCLE	TUBULURES	TUGBOAT	TULCHANS
TSUTSUMU	TUBERCLED	TUCHUN	TUGBOATS	TULE
TSUTSUMUS	TUBERCLES	TUCHUNS	TUGGED	TULES
TUAN	TUBERCULA	TUCK	TUGGER	TULIP
TUANS	TUBERCULE	TUCKAHOE	TUGGERS	TULIPANT
TUART	TUBEROID	TUCKAHOES	TUGGING	TULIPANTS
TUARTS	TUBEROSE	TUCKED	TUGGINGLY	TULIPLIKE
TUATARA	TUBEROSES	TUCKER	TUGGINGS	TULIPS
TUATARAS	TUBEROUS	TUCKERBAG	TUGHRA	TULIPWOOD
TUATERA	TUBERS	TUCKERBOX	TUGHRAS	TULLE
TUATERAS	TUBES	TUCKERED	TUGHRIK	TULLES
TUATH	TUBEWORK	TUCKERING	TUGHRIKS	TULLIBEE
TUATHS	TUBEWORKS	TUCKERS	TUGLESS	TULLIBEES
TUATUA	TUBEWORM	TUCKET	TUGRA	TULPA

T

TULPAS	TUMPING	TUNEUPS	TUPIK	TURBO
TULWAR	TUMPLINE	TUNG	TUPIKS	TURBOCAR
TULWARS	TUMPLINES	TUNGS	TUPLE	TURBOCARS
TUM	TUMPS	TUNGSTATE	TUPLES	TURBOFAN
TUMBLE	TUMPY	TUNGSTEN	TUPPED	TURBOFANS
TUMBLEBUG	TUMS	TUNGSTENS	TUPPENCE	TURBOJET
TUMBLED	TUMSHIE	TUNGSTIC	TUPPENCES	TURBOJETS
TUMBLER	TUMSHIES	TUNGSTITE	TUPPENNY	TURBOND
TUMBLERS	TUMULAR	TUNGSTOUS	TUPPING	TURBONDS
TUMBLES	TUMULARY	TUNIC	TUPS	TURBOPROP
TUMBLESET	TUMULI	TUNICA	TUPTOWING	TURBOS
TUMBLING	TUMULOSE	TUNICAE	TUPUNA	TURBOT
TUMBLINGS	TUMULOUS	TUNICATE	TUPUNAS	TURBOTS
TUMBREL	TUMULT	TUNICATED	TUQUE	TURBULENT
TUMBRELS	TUMULTED	TUNICATES	TUQUES	TURCOPOLE
TUMBRIL	TUMULTING	TUNICIN	TURACIN	TURD
TUMBRILS	TUMULTS	TUNICINS	TURACINS	TURDINE
TUMEFIED	TUMULUS	TUNICKED	TURACO	TURDION
TUMEFIES	TUMULUSES	TUNICLE	TURACOS	TURDIONS
TUMEFY	TUN	TUNICLES	TURACOU	TURDOID
TUMEFYING	TUNA	TUNICS	TURACOUS	TURDS
TUMESCE	TUNABLE	TUNIER	TURBAN	TURDUCKEN
TUMESCED	TUNABLY	TUNIEST	TURBAND	TUREEN
TUMESCENT	TUNAS	TUNING	TURBANDS	TUREENS
TUMESCES	TUNBELLY	TUNINGS	TURBANED	TURF
TUMESCING	TUND	TUNNAGE	TURBANNED	TURFED
TUMID	TUNDED	TUNNAGES	TURBANS	TURFEN
TUMIDITY	TUNDING	TUNNED	TURBANT	TURFGRASS
TUMIDLY	TUNDISH	TUNNEL	TURBANTS	TURFIER
TUMIDNESS	TUNDISHES	TUNNELED	TURBARIES	TURFIEST
TUMMIES	TUNDRA	TUNNELER	TURBARY	TURFINESS
TUMMLER	TUNDRAS	TUNNELERS	TURBETH	TURFING
TUMMLERS	TUNDS	TUNNELING	TURBETHS	TURFINGS
TUMMY	TUNDUN	TUNNELLED	TURBID	TURFITE
TUMOR	TUNDUNS	TUNNELLER	TURBIDITE	TURFITES
TUMORAL	TUNE	TUNNELS	TURBIDITY	TURFLESS
TUMORLIKE	TUNEABLE	TUNNIES	TURBIDLY	TURFLIKE
TUMOROUS	TUNEABLY	TUNNING	TURBINAL	TURFMAN
TUMORS	TUNED	TUNNINGS	TURBINALS	TURFMEN
TUMOUR	TUNEFUL	TUNNY	TURBINATE	TURFS
TUMOURS	TUNEFULLY	TUNS	TURBINE	TURFSKI
TUMP	TUNELESS	TUNY	TURBINED	TURFSKIS
TUMPED	TUNER	TUP	TURBINES	TURFY
TUMPHIES	TUNERS	TUPEK	TURBIT	TURGENCY
TUMPHY	TUNES	TUPEKS	TURBITH	TURGENT
TUMPIER	TUNESMITH	TUPELO	TURBITHS	TURGENTLY
TUMPIEST	TUNEUP	TUPELOS	TURBITS	TURGID

TURGIDER	TURNED	TURRETED	TUSSEH	TUTORING
TURGIDEST	TURNER	TURRETS	TUSSEHS	TUTORINGS
TURGIDITY	TURNERIES	TURRIBANT	TUSSER	TUTORISE
TURGIDLY	TURNERS	TURRICAL	TUSSERS	TUTORISED
TURGITE	TURNERY	TURTLE	TUSSES	TUTORISES
TURGITES	TURNHALL	TURTLED	TUSSIS	TUTORISM
TURGOR	TURNHALLS	TURTLER	TUSSISES	TUTORISMS
TURGORS	TURNING	TURTLERS	TUSSIVE	TUTORIZE
TURION	TURNINGS	TURTLES	TUSSLE	TUTORIZED
TURIONS	TURNIP	TURTLING	TUSSLED	TUTORIZES
TURISTA	TURNIPED	TURTLINGS	TUSSLES	TUTORS
TURISTAS	TURNIPING	TURVES	TUSSLING	TUTORSHIP
TURK	TURNIPS	TUSCHE	TUSSOCK	TUTOYED
TURKEY	TURNIPY	TUSCHES	TUSSOCKED	TUTOYER
TURKEYS	TURNKEY	TUSH	TUSSOCKS	TUTOYERED
TURKIES	TURNKEYS	TUSHED	TUSSOCKY	TUTOYERS
TURKIESES	TURNOFF	TUSHERIES	TUSSOR	TUTRESS
TURKIS	TURNOFFS	TUSHERY	TUSSORE	TUTRESSES
TURKISES	TURNON	TUSHES	TUSSORES	TUTRICES
TURKOIS	TURNONS	TUSHIE	TUSSORS	TUTRIX
TURKOISES	TURNOUT	TUSHIES	TUSSUCK	TUTRIXES
TURKS	TURNOUTS	TUSHING	TUSSUCKS	TUTS
TURLOUGH	TURNOVER	TUSHKAR	TUSSUR	TUTSAN
TURLOUGHS	TURNOVERS	TUSHKARS	TUSSURS	TUTSANS
TURM	TURNPIKE	TUSHKER	TUT	TUTSED
TURME	TURNPIKES	TUSHKERS	TUTANIA	TUTSES
TURMERIC	TURNROUND	TUSHY	TUTANIAS	TUTSING
TURMERICS	TURNS	TUSK	TUTEE	TUTTED
TURMES	TURNSKIN	TUSKAR	TUTEES	TUTTI
TURMOIL	TURNSKINS	TUSKARS	TUTELAGE	TUTTIES
TURMOILED	TURNSOLE	TUSKED	TUTELAGES	TUTTING
TURMOILS	TURNSOLES	TUSKER	TUTELAR	TUTTINGS
TURMS	TURNSPIT	TUSKERS	TUTELARS	TUTTIS
TURN	TURNSPITS	TUSKIER	TUTELARY	TUTTY
TURNABLE	TURNSTILE	TUSKIEST	TUTENAG	TUTU
TURNABOUT	TURNSTONE	TUSKING	TUTENAGS	TUTUED
TURNAGAIN	TURNTABLE	TUSKINGS	TUTIORISM	TUTUS
TURNBACK	TURNUP	TUSKLESS	TUTIORIST	TUTWORK
TURNBACKS	TURNUPS	TUSKLIKE	TUTMAN	TUTWORKER
TURNCOAT	TUROPHILE	TUSKS	TUTMEN	TUTWORKS
TURNCOATS	TURPETH	TUSKY	TUTOR	TUX
TURNCOCK	TURPETHS	TUSSAC	TUTORAGE	TUXEDO
TURNCOCKS	TURPITUDE	TUSSAH	TUTORAGES	TUXEDOED
TURNDOWN	TURPS	TUSSAHS	TUTORED	TUXEDOES
TURNDOWNS	TURQUOIS	TUSSAL	TUTORESS	TUXEDOS
TURNDUN	TURQUOISE	TUSSAR	TUTORIAL	TUXES
TURNDUNS	TURRET	TUSSARS	TUTORIALS	TUYER

TUYERE	TWASOME	TWEENIE	TWIDDLER	TWINBERRY
TUYERES	TWASOMES	TWEENIES	TWIDDLERS	TWINBORN
TUYERS	TWAT	TWEENS	TWIDDLES	TWINE
TUZZ	TWATS	TWEENY	TWIDDLIER	TWINED
TUZZES	TWATTLE	TWEER	TWIDDLING	TWINER
TWA	TWATTLED	TWEERED	TWIDDLY	TWINERS
TWADDLE	TWATTLER	TWEERING	TWIER	TWINES
TWADDLED	TWATTLERS	TWEERS	TWIERS	TWINGE
TWADDLER	TWATTLES	TWEEST	TWIFOLD	TWINGED
TWADDLERS	TWATTLING	TWEET	TWIFORKED	TWINGEING
TWADDLES	TWAY	TWEETED	TWIFORMED	TWINGES
TWADDLIER	TWAYBLADE	TWEETER	TWIG	TWINGING
TWADDLING	TWAYS	TWEETERS	TWIGGED	TWINIER
TWADDLY	TWEAK	TWEETING	TWIGGEN	TWINIEST
TWAE	TWEAKED	TWEETS	TWIGGER	TWINIGHT
TWAES	TWEAKER	TWEEZE	TWIGGERS	TWINING
TWAFALD	TWEAKERS	TWEEZED	TWIGGIER	TWININGLY
TWAIN	TWEAKIER	TWEEZER	TWIGGIEST	TWININGS
TWAINS	TWEAKIEST	TWEEZERS	TWIGGING	TWINJET
TWAITE	TWEAKING	TWEEZES	TWIGGY	TWINJETS
TWAITES	TWEAKINGS	TWEEZING	TWIGHT	TWINK
TWAL	TWEAKS	TWELFTH	TWIGHTED	TWINKED
TWALPENNY	TWEAKY	TWELFTHLY	TWIGHTING	TWINKIE
TWALS	TWEE	TWELFTHS	TWIGHTS	TWINKIES
TWANG	TWEED	TWELVE	TWIGLESS	TWINKING
TWANGED	TWEEDIER	TWELVEMO	TWIGLET	TWINKLE
TWANGER	TWEEDIEST	TWELVEMOS	TWIGLETS	TWINKLED
TWANGERS	TWEEDILY	TWELVES	TWIGLIKE	TWINKLER
TWANGIER	TWEEDLE	TWENTIES	TWIGLOO	TWINKLERS
TWANGIEST	TWEEDLED	TWENTIETH	TWIGLOOS	TWINKLES
TWANGING	TWEEDLER	TWENTY	TWIGS	TWINKLING
TWANGINGS	TWEEDLERS	TWENTYISH	TWIGSOME	TWINKLY
TWANGLE	TWEEDLES	TWERP	TWILIGHT	TWINKS
TWANGLED	TWEEDLING	TWERPIER	TWILIGHTS	TWINLING
TWANGLER	TWEEDS	TWERPIEST	TWILIT	TWINLINGS
TWANGLERS	TWEEDY	TWERPS	TWILL	TWINNED
TWANGLES	TWEEL	TWERPY	TWILLED	TWINNING
TWANGLING	TWEELED	TWIBIL	TWILLIES	TWINNINGS
TWANGS	TWEELING	TWIBILL	TWILLING	TWINS
TWANGY	TWEELS	TWIBILLS	TWILLINGS	TWINSET
TWANK	TWEELY	TWIBILS	TWILLS	TWINSETS
TWANKAY	TWEEN	TWICE	TWILLY	TWINSHIP
TWANKAYS	TWEENAGE	TWICER	TWILT	TWINSHIPS
TWANKIES	TWEENAGER	TWICERS	TWILTED	TWINTER
TWANKS	TWEENER	TWICHILD	TWILTING	TWINTERS
TWANKY	TWEENERS	TWIDDLE	TWILTS	TWINY
TWAS	TWEENESS	TWIDDLED	TWIN	TWIRE

TWIRED	TWITTENS	TWYFOLD	TYMPANO	TYPHUSES
TWIRES	TWITTER	TYCHISM	TYMPANS	TYPIC
TWIRING	TWITTERED	TYCHISMS	TYMPANUM	TYPICAL
TWIRL	TWITTERER	TYCOON	TYMPANUMS	TYPICALLY
TWIRLED	TWITTERS	TYCOONATE	TYMPANY	TYPIER
TWIRLER	TWITTERY	TYCOONERY	TYMPS	TYPIEST
TWIRLERS	TWITTING	TYCOONS	TYND	TYPIFIED
TWIRLIER	TWITTINGS	TYDE	TYNDE	TYPIFIER
TWIRLIEST	TWIXT	TYE	TYNE	TYPIFIERS
TWIRLING	TWIZZLE	TYED	TYNED	TYPIFIES
TWIRLS	TWIZZLED	TYEE	TYNES	TYPIFY
TWIRLY	TWIZZLES	TYEES	TYNING	TYPIFYING
TWIRP	TWIZZLING	TYEING	TYPABLE	TYPING
TWIRPIER	TWO	TYER	TYPAL	TYPINGS
TWIRPIEST	TWOCCER	TYERS	TYPE	TYPIST
TWIRPS	TWOCCERS	TYES	TYPEABLE	TYPISTS
TWIRPY	TWOCCING	TYG	TYPEBAR	TYPO
TWISCAR	TWOCCINGS	TYGS	TYPEBARS	TYPOGRAPH
TWISCARS	TWOCKER	TYIN	TYPECASE	TYPOLOGIC
TWIST	TWOCKERS	TYING	TYPECASES	TYPOLOGY
TWISTABLE	TWOCKING	TYIYN	TYPECAST	TYPOMANIA
TWISTED	TWOCKINGS	TYIYNS	TYPECASTS	TYPOS
TWISTER	TWOER	TYKE	TYPED	TYPP
TWISTERS	TWOERS	TYKES	TYPEFACE	TYPPS
TWISTIER	TWOFER	TYKISH	TYPEFACES	TYPTO
TWISTIEST	TWOFERS	TYLECTOMY	TYPES	TYPTOED
TWISTING	TWOFOLD	TYLER	TYPESET	TYPTOING
TWISTINGS	TWOFOLDS	TYLERS	TYPESETS	TYPTOS
TWISTOR	TWONESS	TYLOPOD	TYPESTYLE	TYPY
TWISTORS	TWONESSES	TYLOPODS	TYPEWRITE	TYRAMINE
TWISTS	TWONIE	TYLOSES	TYPEWROTE	TYRAMINES
TWISTY	TWONIES	TYLOSIN	TYPEY	TYRAN
TWIT	TWOONIE	TYLOSINS	TYPHLITIC	TYRANED
TWITCH	TWOONIES	TYLOSIS	TYPHLITIS	TYRANING
TWITCHED	TWOPENCE	TYLOTE	TYPHOID	TYRANNE
TWITCHER	TWOPENCES	TYLOTES	TYPHOIDAL	TYRANNED
TWITCHERS	TWOPENNY	TYMBAL	TYPHOIDIN	TYRANNES
TWITCHES	TWOS	TYMBALS	TYPHOIDS	TYRANNESS
TWITCHIER	TWOSEATER	TYMP	TYPHON	TYRANNIC
TWITCHILY	TWOSOME	TYMPAN	TYPHONIAN	TYRANNIES
TWITCHING	TWOSOMES	TYMPANA	TYPHONIC	TYRANNING
TWITCHY	TWOSTROKE	TYMPANAL	TYPHONS	TYRANNIS
TWITE	TWP	TYMPANI	TYPHOON	TYRANNISE
TWITES	TWYER	TYMPANIC	TYPHOONS	TYRANNIZE
TWITS	TWYERE	TYMPANICS	TYPHOSE	TYRANNOUS
TWITTED	TWYERES	TYMPANIES	TYPHOUS	TYRANNY
TWITTEN	TWYERS	TYMPANIST	TYPHUS	TYRANS

TYRANT

TYRANT	TYRONIC	TZADDIK	TZARINAS	TZETZES
TYRANTED	TYROPITTA	TZADDIKIM	TZARISM	TZIGANE
TYRANTING	TYROS	TZADDIKS	TZARISMS	TZIGANES
TYRANTS	TYROSINE	TZADDIQ	TZARIST	TZIGANIES
TYRE	TYROSINES	TZADDIQIM	TZARISTS	TZIGANY
TYRED	TYSTIE	TZADDIQS	TZARITZA	TZIMMES
TYRELESS	TYSTIES	TZADDIS	TZARITZAS	TZITZIS
TYRES	TYTE	TZAR	TZARS	TZITZIT
TYRING	TYTHE	TZARDOM	TZATZIKI	TZITZITH
TYRO	TYTHED	TZARDOMS	TZATZIKIS	TZURIS
TYROCIDIN	TYTHES	TZAREVNA	TZETSE	
TYROES	TYTHING	TZAREVNAS	TZETSES	
TYRONES	TZADDI	TZARINA	TZETZE	

U

UAKARI	UGLIED	ULCERED	ULTERIOR	ULULATED
UAKARIS	UGLIER	ULCERING	ULTIMA	ULULATES
UBEROUS	UGLIES	ULCEROUS	ULTIMACY	ULULATING
UBERTIES	UGLIEST	ULCERS	ULTIMAS	ULULATION
UBERTY	UGLIFIED	ULE	ULTIMATA	ULUS
UBIETIES	UGLIFIER	ULEMA	ULTIMATE	ULVA
UBIETY	UGLIFIERS	ULEMAS	ULTIMATED	ULVAS
UBIQUE	UGLIFIES	ULES	ULTIMATES	ULYIE
UBIQUITIN	UGLIFY	ULEX	ULTIMATUM	ULYIES
UBIQUITY	UGLIFYING	ULEXES	ULTIMO	ULZIE
UBUNTU	UGLILY	ULEXITE	ULTION	ULZIES
UBUNTUS	UGLINESS	ULEXITES	ULTIONS	UM
UCKERS	UGLY	ULICES	ULTRA	UMAMI
UDAL	UGLYING	ULICON	ULTRACHIC	UMAMIS
UDALLER	UGS	ULICONS	ULTRACOLD	UMANGITE
UDALLERS	UGSOME	ULIGINOSE	ULTRACOOL	UMANGITES
UDALS	UH	ULIGINOUS	ULTRADRY	UMBEL
UDDER	UHLAN	ULIKON	ULTRAFAST	UMBELED
UDDERED	UHLANS	ULIKONS	ULTRAFINE	UMBELLAR
UDDERFUL	UHURU	ULITIS	ULTRAHEAT	UMBELLATE
UDDERLESS	UHURUS	ULITISES	ULTRAHIGH	UMBELLED
UDDERS	UILLEAN	ULLAGE	ULTRAHIP	UMBELLET
UDO	UILLEANN	ULLAGED	ULTRAHOT	UMBELLETS
UDOMETER	UINTAHITE	ULLAGES	ULTRAISM	UMBELLULE
UDOMETERS	UINTAITE	ULLAGING	ULTRAISMS	UMBELS
UDOMETRIC	UINTAITES	ULLING	ULTRAIST	UMBER
UDOMETRY	UITLANDER	ULLINGS	ULTRAISTS	UMBERED
UDON	UJAMAA	ULMACEOUS	ULTRALEFT	UMBERING
UDONS	UJAMAAS	ULMIN	ULTRALOW	UMBERS
UDOS	UKASE	ULMINS	ULTRAPOSH	UMBERY
UDS	UKASES	ULNA	ULTRAPURE	UMBILICAL
UEY	UKE	ULNAD	ULTRARARE	UMBILICI
UEYS	UKELELE	ULNAE	ULTRARED	UMBILICUS
UFO	UKELELES	ULNAR	ULTRAREDS	UMBLE
UFOLOGIES	UKES	ULNARE	ULTRARICH	UMBLES
UFOLOGIST	UKULELE	ULNARIA	ULTRAS	UMBO
UFOLOGY	UKULELES	ULNAS	ULTRASAFE	UMBONAL
UFOS	ULAMA	ULOSES	ULTRASLOW	UMBONATE
UG	ULAMAS	ULOSIS	ULTRASOFT	UMBONES
UGALI	ULAN	ULOTRICHY	ULTRATHIN	UMBONIC
UGALIS	ULANS	ULPAN	ULTRATINY	UMBOS
UGGED	ULCER	ULPANIM	ULTRAWIDE	UMBRA
UGGING	ULCERATE	ULSTER	ULU	UMBRACULA
UGH	ULCERATED	ULSTERED	ULULANT	UMBRAE
UGHS	ULCERATES	ULSTERS	ULULATE	UMBRAGE

UMBRAGED	UMMED	UNACHING	UNAMENDED	UNAWAKED
UMBRAGES	UMMING	UNACIDIC	UNAMERCED	UNAWARDED
UMBRAGING	UMP	UNACTABLE	UNAMIABLE	UNAWARE
UMBRAL	UMPED	UNACTED	UNAMUSED	UNAWARELY
UMBRAS	UMPH	UNACTIVE	UNAMUSING	UNAWARES
UMBRATED	UMPIE	UNADAPTED	UNANCHOR	UNAWED
UMBRATIC	UMPIES	UNADDED	UNANCHORS	UNAWESOME
UMBRATILE	UMPING	UNADEPT	UNANELED	UNAXED
UMBRE	UMPIRAGE	UNADEPTLY	UNANIMITY	UNBACKED
UMBREL	UMPIRAGES	UNADMIRED	UNANIMOUS	UNBAFFLED
UMBRELLA	UMPIRE	UNADOPTED	UNANNEXED	UNBAG
UMBRELLAS	UMPIRED	UNADORED	UNANNOYED	UNBAGGED
UMBRELLO	UMPIRES	UNADORNED	UNANXIOUS	UNBAGGING
UMBRELLOS	UMPIRING	UNADULT	UNAPPAREL	UNBAGS
UMBRELS	UMPS	UNADVISED	UNAPPLIED	UNBAITED
UMBRERE	UMPTEEN	UNAFRAID	UNAPT	UNBAKED
UMBRERES	UMPTEENTH	UNAGED	UNAPTLY	UNBALANCE
UMBRES	UMPTIETH	UNAGEING	UNAPTNESS	UNBALE
UMBRETTE	UMPTY	UNAGILE	UNARCHED	UNBALED
UMBRETTES	UMPY	UNAGING	UNARGUED	UNBALES
UMBRIERE	UMQUHILE	UNAGREED	UNARISEN	UNBALING
UMBRIERES	UMRA	UNAI	UNARM	UNBAN
UMBRIL	UMRAH	UNAIDABLE	UNARMED	UNBANDAGE
UMBRILS	UMRAHS	UNAIDED	UNARMING	UNBANDED
UMBROSE	UMRAS	UNAIDEDLY	UNARMORED	UNBANKED
UMBROUS	UMS	UNAIMED	UNARMS	UNBANNED
UMFAZI	UMTEENTH	UNAIRED	UNAROUSED	UNBANNING
UMFAZIS	UMU	UNAIS	UNARRAYED	UNBANS
UMIAC	UMUS	UNAKIN	UNARTFUL	UNBAPTISE
UMIACK	UMWELT	UNAKING	UNARY	UNBAPTIZE
UMIACKS	UMWELTS	UNAKITE	UNASHAMED	UNBAR
UMIACS	UMWHILE	UNAKITES	UNASKED	UNBARBED
UMIAK	UN	UNALARMED	UNASSAYED	UNBARE
UMIAKS	UNABASHED	UNALERTED	UNASSUMED	UNBARED
UMIAQ	UNABATED	UNALIGNED	UNASSURED	UNBARES
UMIAQS	UNABATING	UNALIKE	UNATONED	UNBARING
UMLAUT	UNABETTED	UNALIST	UNATTIRED	UNBARK
UMLAUTED	UNABIDING	UNALISTS	UNATTUNED	UNBARKED
UMLAUTING	UNABJURED	UNALIVE	UNAU	UNBARKING
UMLAUTS	UNABLE	UNALLAYED	UNAUDITED	UNBARKS
UMLUNGU	UNABORTED	UNALLEGED	UNAUS	UNBARRED
UMLUNGUS	UNABRADED	UNALLIED	UNAVENGED	UNBARRING
UMM	UNABUSED	UNALLOWED	UNAVERAGE	UNBARS
UMMA	UNABUSIVE	UNALLOYED	UNAVERTED	UNBASED
UMMAH	UNACCRUED	UNALTERED	UNAVOIDED	UNBASHFUL
UMMAHS	UNACCUSED	UNAMASSED	UNAVOWED	UNBASTED
UMMAS	UNACERBIC	UNAMAZED	UNAWAKE	UNBATED

UNBATHED	UNBIASSED	UNBONE	UNBRIDGED	UNCAKED
UNBE	UNBIASSES	UNBONED	UNBRIDLE	UNCAKES
UNBEAR	UNBID	UNBONES	UNBRIDLED	UNCAKING
UNBEARDED	UNBIDDEN	UNBONING	UNBRIDLES	UNCALLED
UNBEARED	UNBIGOTED	UNBONNET	UNBRIEFED	UNCANDID
UNBEARING	UNBILLED	UNBONNETS	UNBRIGHT	UNCANDLED
UNBEARS	UNBIND	UNBOOKED	UNBRIZZED	UNCANDOUR
UNBEATEN	UNBINDING	UNBOOKISH	UNBROILED	UNCANNED
UNBED	UNBINDS	UNBOOT	UNBROKE	UNCANNIER
UNBEDDED	UNBISHOP	UNBOOTED	UNBROKEN	UNCANNILY
UNBEDDING	UNBISHOPS	UNBOOTING	UNBROWNED	UNCANNY
UNBEDS	UNBITT	UNBOOTS	UNBRUISED	UNCANONIC
UNBEEN	UNBITTED	UNBORE	UNBRUSED	UNCAP
UNBEGET	UNBITTEN	UNBORN	UNBRUSHED	UNCAPABLE
UNBEGETS	UNBITTER	UNBORNE	UNBUCKLE	UNCAPE
UNBEGGED	UNBITTING	UNBOSOM	UNBUCKLED	UNCAPED
UNBEGOT	UNBITTS	UNBOSOMED	UNBUCKLES	UNCAPES
UNBEGUILE	UNBLAMED	UNBOSOMER	UNBUDDED	UNCAPING
UNBEGUN	UNBLENDED	UNBOSOMS	UNBUDGING	UNCAPPED
UNBEING	UNBLENT	UNBOTTLE	UNBUILD	UNCAPPING
UNBEINGS	UNBLESS	UNBOTTLED	UNBUILDS	UNCAPS
UNBEKNOWN	UNBLESSED	UNBOTTLES	UNBUILT	UNCARDED
UNBELIEF	UNBLESSES	UNBOUGHT	UNBULKY	UNCARED
UNBELIEFS	UNBLEST	UNBOUNCY	UNBUNDLE	UNCAREFUL
UNBELIEVE	UNBLIND	UNBOUND	UNBUNDLED	UNCARING
UNBELOVED	UNBLINDED	UNBOUNDED	UNBUNDLER	UNCART
UNBELT	UNBLINDS	UNBOWED	UNBUNDLES	UNCARTED
UNBELTED	UNBLOCK	UNBOWING	UNBURDEN	UNCARTING
UNBELTING	UNBLOCKED	UNBOX	UNBURDENS	UNCARTS
UNBELTS	UNBLOCKS	UNBOXED	UNBURIED	UNCARVED
UNBEMUSED	UNBLOODED	UNBOXES	UNBURIES	UNCASE
UNBEND	UNBLOODY	UNBOXING	UNBURNED	UNCASED
UNBENDED	UNBLOTTED	UNBRACE	UNBURNT	UNCASES
UNBENDING	UNBLOWED	UNBRACED	UNBURROW	UNCASHED
UNBENDS	UNBLOWN	UNBRACES	UNBURROWS	UNCASING
UNBENIGN	UNBLUNTED	UNBRACING	UNBURTHEN	UNCASKED
UNBENT	UNBLURRED	UNBRAID	UNBURY	UNCAST
UNBEREFT	UNBOARDED	UNBRAIDED	UNBURYING	UNCATCHY
UNBERUFEN	UNBOBBED	UNBRAIDS	UNBUSTED	UNCATE
UNBESEEM	UNBODIED	UNBRAKE	UNBUSY	UNCATERED
UNBESEEMS	UNBODING	UNBRAKED	UNBUTTON	UNCAUGHT
UNBESPEAK	UNBOILED	UNBRAKES	UNBUTTONS	UNCAUSED
UNBESPOKE	UNBOLT	UNBRAKING	UNCAGE	UNCE
UNBIAS	UNBOLTED	UNBRANDED	UNCAGED	UNCEASING
UNBIASED	UNBOLTING	UNBRASTE	UNCAGES	UNCEDED
UNBIASES	UNBOLTS	UNBRED	UNCAGING	UNCERTAIN
UNBIASING	UNBONDED	UNBREECH	UNCAKE	UNCES

U

UNCESSANT	UNCIFORMS	UNCLIPPED	UNCOLTED	UNCOWLED
UNCHAIN	UNCINAL	UNCLIPS	UNCOLTING	UNCOWLING
UNCHAINED	UNCINARIA	UNCLIPT	UNCOLTS	UNCOWLS
UNCHAINS	UNCINATE	UNCLOAK	UNCOMBED	UNCOY
UNCHAIR	UNCINATED	UNCLOAKED	UNCOMBINE	UNCOYNED
UNCHAIRED	UNCINI	UNCLOAKS	UNCOMELY	UNCRACKED
UNCHAIRS	UNCINUS	UNCLOG	UNCOMFIER	UNCRATE
UNCHANCY	UNCIPHER	UNCLOGGED	UNCOMFY	UNCRATED
UNCHANGED	UNCIPHERS	UNCLOGS	UNCOMIC	UNCRATES
UNCHARGE	UNCITED	UNCLOSE	UNCOMMON	UNCRATING
UNCHARGED	UNCIVIL	UNCLOSED	UNCONCERN	UNCRAZY
UNCHARGES	UNCIVILLY	UNCLOSES	UNCONFINE	UNCREATE
UNCHARITY	UNCLAD	UNCLOSING	UNCONFORM	UNCREATED
UNCHARM	UNCLAIMED	UNCLOTHE	UNCONFUSE	UNCREATES
UNCHARMED	UNCLAMP	UNCLOTHED	UNCONGEAL	UNCREWED
UNCHARMS	UNCLAMPED	UNCLOTHES	UNCOOKED	UNCROPPED
UNCHARNEL	UNCLAMPS	UNCLOUD	UNCOOL	UNCROSS
UNCHARRED	UNCLARITY	UNCLOUDED	UNCOOLED	UNCROSSED
UNCHARTED	UNCLASP	UNCLOUDS	UNCOPE	UNCROSSES
UNCHARY	UNCLASPED	UNCLOUDY	UNCOPED	UNCROWDED
UNCHASTE	UNCLASPS	UNCLOVEN	UNCOPES	UNCROWN
UNCHASTER	UNCLASSED	UNCLOYED	UNCOPING	UNCROWNED
UNCHECK	UNCLASSY	UNCLOYING	UNCORD	UNCROWNS
UNCHECKED	UNCLAWED	UNCLUTCH	UNCORDED	UNCRUDDED
UNCHECKS	UNCLE	UNCLUTTER	UNCORDIAL	UNCRUMPLE
UNCHEERED	UNCLEAN	UNCO	UNCORDING	UNCRUSHED
UNCHEWED	UNCLEANED	UNCOATED	UNCORDS	UNCTION
UNCHIC	UNCLEANER	UNCOATING	UNCORK	UNCTIONS
UNCHICLY	UNCLEANLY	UNCOBBLED	UNCORKED	UNCTUOUS
UNCHILD	UNCLEAR	UNCOCK	UNCORKING	UNCUFF
UNCHILDED	UNCLEARED	UNCOCKED	UNCORKS	UNCUFFED
UNCHILDS	UNCLEARER	UNCOCKING	UNCORRUPT	UNCUFFING
UNCHILLED	UNCLEARLY	UNCOCKS	UNCOS	UNCUFFS
UNCHOKE	UNCLED	UNCODED	UNCOSTLY	UNCULLED
UNCHOKED	UNCLEFT	UNCOER	UNCOUNTED	UNCURABLE
UNCHOKES	UNCLENCH	UNCOERCED	UNCOUPLE	UNCURABLY
UNCHOKING	UNCLES	UNCOES	UNCOUPLED	UNCURB
UNCHOSEN	UNCLESHIP	UNCOEST	UNCOUPLER	UNCURBED
UNCHRISOM	UNCLEW	UNCOFFIN	UNCOUPLES	UNCURBING
UNCHURCH	UNCLEWED	UNCOFFINS	UNCOURTLY	UNCURBS
UNCI	UNCLEWING	UNCOIL	UNCOUTH	UNCURDLED
UNCIA	UNCLEWS	UNCOILED	UNCOUTHER	UNCURED
UNCIAE	UNCLICHED	UNCOILING	UNCOUTHLY	UNCURIOUS
UNCIAL	UNCLIMBED	UNCOILS	UNCOVER	UNCURL
UNCIALLY	UNCLINCH	UNCOINED	UNCOVERED	UNCURLED
UNCIALS	UNCLING	UNCOLORED	UNCOVERS	UNCURLING
UNCIFORM	UNCLIP	UNCOLT	UNCOWL	UNCURLS

UNCURRENT	UNDECKS	UNDERCLAD	UNDERIVED	UNDERRUN
UNCURSE	UNDEE	UNDERCLAY	UNDERJAW	UNDERRUNS
UNCURSED	UNDEEDED	UNDERCLUB	UNDERJAWS	UNDERSAID
UNCURSES	UNDEFACED	UNDERCOAT	UNDERKEEP	UNDERSAY
UNCURSING	UNDEFIDE	UNDERCOOK	UNDERKEPT	UNDERSAYS
UNCURTAIN	UNDEFIED	UNDERCOOL	UNDERKILL	UNDERSEA
UNCURVED	UNDEFILED	UNDERCUT	UNDERKING	UNDERSEAL
UNCUS	UNDEFINED	UNDERCUTS	UNDERLAID	UNDERSEAS
UNCUT	UNDEIFIED	UNDERDAKS	UNDERLAIN	UNDERSELF
UNCUTE	UNDEIFIES	UNDERDECK	UNDERLAP	UNDERSELL
UNCYNICAL	UNDEIFY	UNDERDID	UNDERLAPS	UNDERSET
UNDAM	UNDELAYED	UNDERDO	UNDERLAY	UNDERSETS
UNDAMAGED	UNDELETE	UNDERDOER	UNDERLAYS	UNDERSHOT
UNDAMMED	UNDELETED	UNDERDOES	UNDERLEAF	UNDERSIDE
UNDAMMING	UNDELETES	UNDERDOG	UNDERLET	UNDERSIGN
UNDAMNED	UNDELIGHT	UNDERDOGS	UNDERLETS	UNDERSIZE
UNDAMPED	UNDELUDED	UNDERDONE	UNDERLIE	UNDERSKY
UNDAMS	UNDENIED	UNDERDOSE	UNDERLIER	UNDERSOIL
UNDARING	UNDENTED	UNDERDRAW	UNDERLIES	UNDERSOLD
UNDASHED	UNDER	UNDERDREW	UNDERLINE	UNDERSONG
UNDATABLE	UNDERACT	UNDEREAT	UNDERLING	UNDERSPIN
UNDATE	UNDERACTS	UNDEREATS	UNDERLIP	UNDERTAKE
UNDATED	UNDERAGE	UNDERFED	UNDERLIPS	UNDERTANE
UNDAUNTED	UNDERAGED	UNDERFEED	UNDERLIT	UNDERTAX
UNDAWNING	UNDERAGES	UNDERFELT	UNDERLOAD	UNDERTIME
UNDAZZLE	UNDERARM	UNDERFIRE	UNDERMAN	UNDERTINT
UNDAZZLED	UNDERARMS	UNDERFISH	UNDERMANS	UNDERTONE
UNDAZZLES	UNDERATE	UNDERFLOW	UNDERMEN	UNDERTOOK
UNDE	UNDERBAKE	UNDERFONG	UNDERMINE	UNDERTOW
UNDEAD	UNDERBEAR	UNDERFOOT	UNDERMOST	UNDERTOWS
UNDEAF	UNDERBID	UNDERFUND	UNDERN	UNDERUSE
UNDEAFED	UNDERBIDS	UNDERFUR	UNDERNOTE	UNDERUSED
UNDEAFING	UNDERBIT	UNDERFURS	UNDERNS	UNDERUSES
UNDEAFS	UNDERBITE	UNDERGIRD	UNDERPAID	UNDERVEST
UNDEALT	UNDERBODY	UNDERGIRT	UNDERPART	UNDERVOTE
UNDEAR	UNDERBORE	UNDERGO	UNDERPASS	UNDERWAY
UNDEBASED	UNDERBOSS	UNDERGOD	UNDERPAY	UNDERWEAR
UNDEBATED	UNDERBRED	UNDERGODS	UNDERPAYS	UNDERWENT
UNDECAGON	UNDERBRIM	UNDERGOER	UNDERPEEP	UNDERWING
UNDECAYED	UNDERBUD	UNDERGOES	UNDERPIN	UNDERWIRE
UNDECEIVE	UNDERBUDS	UNDERGONE	UNDERPINS	UNDERWIT
UNDECENT	UNDERBUSH	UNDERGOWN	UNDERPLAY	UNDERWITS
UNDECIDED	UNDERBUY	UNDERGRAD	UNDERPLOT	UNDERWOOD
UNDECIMAL	UNDERBUYS	UNDERHAIR	UNDERPROP	UNDERWOOL
UNDECK	UNDERCARD	UNDERHAND	UNDERRAN	UNDERWORK
UNDECKED	UNDERCART	UNDERHEAT	UNDERRATE	UNDESERT
UNDECKING	UNDERCAST	UNDERHUNG	UNDERRIPE	UNDESERTS

U

UNDESERVE	UNDREAMED	UNEASILY	UNEXCUSED	UNFENCED
UNDESIRED	UNDREAMT	UNEASY	UNEXOTIC	UNFENCES
UNDEVOUT	UNDRESS	UNEATABLE	UNEXPERT	UNFENCING
UNDID	UNDRESSED	UNEATEN	UNEXPIRED	UNFERTILE
UNDIES	UNDRESSES	UNEATH	UNEXPOSED	UNFETTER
UNDIGHT	UNDREST	UNEATHES	UNEXTINCT	UNFETTERS
UNDIGHTS	UNDREW	UNEDGE	UNEXTREME	UNFEUDAL
UNDIGNIFY	UNDRIED	UNEDGED	UNEYED	UNFEUED
UNDILUTED	UNDRILLED	UNEDGES	UNFABLED	UNFIGURED
UNDIMMED	UNDRIVEN	UNEDGING	UNFACT	UNFILDE
UNDINE	UNDROSSY	UNEDIBLE	UNFACTS	UNFILED
UNDINES	UNDROWNED	UNEDITED	UNFADABLE	UNFILIAL
UNDINISM	UNDRUNK	UNEFFACED	UNFADED	UNFILLED
UNDINISMS	UNDUBBED	UNELATED	UNFADING	UNFILMED
UNDINTED	UNDUE	UNELECTED	UNFAILING	UNFINE
UNDIPPED	UNDUG	UNEMPTIED	UNFAIR	UNFIRED
UNDIVIDED	UNDULANCE	UNENDED	UNFAIRED	UNFIRM
UNDIVINE	UNDULANCY	UNENDING	UNFAIRER	UNFISHED
UNDO	UNDULANT	UNENDOWED	UNFAIREST	UNFIT
UNDOABLE	UNDULAR	UNENGAGED	UNFAIRING	UNFITLY
UNDOCILE	UNDULATE	UNENJOYED	UNFAIRLY	UNFITNESS
UNDOCK	UNDULATED	UNENSURED	UNFAIRS	UNFITS
UNDOCKED	UNDULATES	UNENTERED	UNFAITH	UNFITTED
UNDOCKING	UNDULATOR	UNENVIED	UNFAITHS	UNFITTER
UNDOCKS	UNDULLED	UNENVIOUS	UNFAKED	UNFITTEST
UNDOER	UNDULOSE	UNENVYING	UNFALLEN	UNFITTING
UNDOERS	UNDULOUS	UNEQUABLE	UNFAMED	UNFIX
UNDOES	UNDULY	UNEQUAL	UNFAMOUS	UNFIXED
UNDOING	UNDUTEOUS	UNEQUALED	UNFANCIED	UNFIXES
UNDOINGS	UNDUTIFUL	UNEQUALLY	UNFANCY	UNFIXING
UNDONE	UNDY	UNEQUALS	UNFANNED	UNFIXITY
UNDOOMED	UNDYED	UNERASED	UNFASTEN	UNFIXT
UNDOTTED	UNDYING	UNEROTIC	UNFASTENS	UNFLAPPED
UNDOUBLE	UNDYINGLY	UNERRING	UNFAULTY	UNFLASHY
UNDOUBLED	UNDYNAMIC	UNESPIED	UNFAVORED	UNFLAWED
UNDOUBLES	UNEAGER	UNESSAYED	UNFAZED	UNFLEDGED
UNDOUBTED	UNEAGERLY	UNESSENCE	UNFEARED	UNFLESH
UNDRAINED	UNEARED	UNETH	UNFEARFUL	UNFLESHED
UNDRAPE	UNEARNED	UNETHICAL	UNFEARING	UNFLESHES
UNDRAPED	UNEARTH	UNEVADED	UNFED	UNFLESHLY
UNDRAPES	UNEARTHED	UNEVEN	UNFEED	UNFLEXED
UNDRAPING	UNEARTHLY	UNEVENER	UNFEELING	UNFLOORED
UNDRAW	UNEARTHS	UNEVENEST	UNFEIGNED	UNFLUSH
UNDRAWING	UNEASE	UNEVENLY	UNFELLED	UNFLUSHED
UNDRAWN	UNEASES	UNEVOLVED	UNFELT	UNFLUSHES
UNDRAWS	UNEASIER	UNEXALTED	UNFELTED	UNFLUTED
UNDREADED	UNEASIEST	UNEXCITED	UNFENCE	UNFLYABLE

UNFOCUSED UNFROZEN UNGILD UNGREASED UNHALLOWS
UNFOILED UNFUELLED UNGILDED UNGREEDY UNHALSED
UNFOLD UNFUMED UNGILDING UNGREEN UNHALVED
UNFOLDED UNFUNDED UNGILDS UNGROOMED UNHAND
UNFOLDER UNFUNNIER UNGILT UNGROUND UNHANDED
UNFOLDERS UNFUNNY UNGIRD UNGROUPED UNHANDIER
UNFOLDING UNFURL UNGIRDED UNGROWN UNHANDILY
UNFOLDS UNFURLED UNGIRDING UNGRUDGED UNHANDING
UNFOND UNFURLING UNGIRDS UNGUAL UNHANDLED
UNFOOL UNFURLS UNGIRT UNGUARD UNHANDS
UNFOOLED UNFURNISH UNGIRTH UNGUARDED UNHANDY
UNFOOLING UNFURRED UNGIRTHED UNGUARDS UNHANG
UNFOOLS UNFUSED UNGIRTHS UNGUENT UNHANGED
UNFOOTED UNFUSSIER UNGIVING UNGUENTA UNHANGING
UNFORBID UNFUSSILY UNGLAD UNGUENTS UNHANGS
UNFORCED UNFUSSY UNGLAZED UNGUENTUM UNHAPPIED
UNFORGED UNGAG UNGLOSSED UNGUES UNHAPPIER
UNFORGOT UNGAGGED UNGLOVE UNGUESSED UNHAPPIES
UNFORKED UNGAGGING UNGLOVED UNGUIDED UNHAPPILY
UNFORM UNGAGS UNGLOVES UNGUIFORM UNHAPPY
UNFORMAL UNGAIN UNGLOVING UNGUILTY UNHARBOUR
UNFORMED UNGAINFUL UNGLUE UNGUINOUS UNHARDY
UNFORMING UNGAINLY UNGLUED UNGUIS UNHARMED
UNFORMS UNGALLANT UNGLUES UNGULA UNHARMFUL
UNFORTUNE UNGALLED UNGLUING UNGULAE UNHARMING
UNFOUGHT UNGARBED UNGOD UNGULAR UNHARNESS
UNFOUND UNGARBLED UNGODDED UNGULATE UNHARRIED
UNFOUNDED UNGATED UNGODDING UNGULATES UNHASP
UNFRAMED UNGAUGED UNGODLIER UNGULED UNHASPED
UNFRANKED UNGAZED UNGODLIKE UNGUM UNHASPING
UNFRAUGHT UNGAZING UNGODLILY UNGUMMED UNHASPS
UNFREE UNGEAR UNGODLY UNGUMMING UNHASTING
UNFREED UNGEARED UNGODS UNGUMS UNHASTY
UNFREEDOM UNGEARING UNGORD UNGYVE UNHAT
UNFREEING UNGEARS UNGORED UNGYVED UNHATCHED
UNFREEMAN UNGELDED UNGORGED UNGYVES UNHATS
UNFREEMEN UNGENIAL UNGOT UNGYVING UNHATTED
UNFREES UNGENTEEL UNGOTTEN UNHABLE UNHATTING
UNFREEZE UNGENTLE UNGOWN UNHACKED UNHAUNTED
UNFREEZES UNGENTLY UNGOWNED UNHAILED UNHEAD
UNFRETTED UNGENUINE UNGOWNING UNHAIR UNHEADED
UNFRIEND UNGERMANE UNGOWNS UNHAIRED UNHEADING
UNFRIENDS UNGET UNGRACED UNHAIRER UNHEADS
UNFROCK UNGETS UNGRADED UNHAIRERS UNHEAL
UNFROCKED UNGETTING UNGRASSED UNHAIRING UNHEALED
UNFROCKS UNGHOSTLY UNGRAVELY UNHAIRS UNHEALING
UNFROZE UNGIFTED UNGRAZED UNHALLOW UNHEALS

UNHEALTH	UNHIVING	UNI	UNINSURED	UNIT
UNHEALTHS	UNHOARD	UNIALGAL	UNINURED	UNITAGE
UNHEALTHY	UNHOARDED	UNIAXIAL	UNINVITED	UNITAGES
UNHEARD	UNHOARDS	UNIBODY	UNINVOKED	UNITAL
UNHEARSE	UNHOLIER	UNIBROW	UNION	UNITARD
UNHEARSED	UNHOLIEST	UNIBROWS	UNIONISE	UNITARDS
UNHEARSES	UNHOLILY	UNICITIES	UNIONISED	UNITARIAN
UNHEART	UNHOLPEN	UNICITY	UNIONISER	UNITARILY
UNHEARTED	UNHOLY	UNICOLOR	UNIONISES	UNITARY
UNHEARTS	UNHOMELY	UNICOLOUR	UNIONISM	UNITE
UNHEATED	UNHONEST	UNICORN	UNIONISMS	UNITED
UNHEDGED	UNHONORED	UNICORNS	UNIONIST	UNITEDLY
UNHEEDED	UNHOOD	UNICYCLE	UNIONISTS	UNITER
UNHEEDFUL	UNHOODED	UNICYCLED	UNIONIZE	UNITERS
UNHEEDILY	UNHOODING	UNICYCLES	UNIONIZED	UNITES
UNHEEDING	UNHOODS	UNIDEAED	UNIONIZER	UNITIES
UNHEEDY	UNHOOK	UNIDEAL	UNIONIZES	UNITING
UNHELE	UNHOOKED	UNIFACE	UNIONS	UNITINGS
UNHELED	UNHOOKING	UNIFACES	UNIPAROUS	UNITION
UNHELES	UNHOOKS	UNIFIABLE	UNIPED	UNITIONS
UNHELING	UNHOOP	UNIFIC	UNIPEDS	UNITISE
UNHELM	UNHOOPED	UNIFIED	UNIPLANAR	UNITISED
UNHELMED	UNHOOPING	UNIFIER	UNIPOD	UNITISER
UNHELMING	UNHOOPS	UNIFIERS	UNIPODS	UNITISERS
UNHELMS	UNHOPED	UNIFIES	UNIPOLAR	UNITISES
UNHELPED	UNHOPEFUL	UNIFILAR	UNIPOTENT	UNITISING
UNHELPFUL	UNHORSE	UNIFORM	UNIQUE	UNITIVE
UNHEPPEN	UNHORSED	UNIFORMED	UNIQUELY	UNITIVELY
UNHEROIC	UNHORSES	UNIFORMER	UNIQUER	UNITIZE
UNHERST	UNHORSING	UNIFORMLY	UNIQUES	UNITIZED
UNHEWN	UNHOSTILE	UNIFORMS	UNIQUEST	UNITIZER
UNHIDDEN	UNHOUSE	UNIFY	UNIRAMOSE	UNITIZERS
UNHINGE	UNHOUSED	UNIFYING	UNIRAMOUS	UNITIZES
UNHINGED	UNHOUSES	UNIFYINGS	UNIRONED	UNITIZING
UNHINGES	UNHOUSING	UNIJUGATE	UNIRONIC	UNITRUST
UNHINGING	UNHUMAN	UNILINEAL	UNIS	UNITRUSTS
UNHIP	UNHUMANLY	UNILINEAR	UNISERIAL	UNITS
UNHIPPER	UNHUMBLED	UNILLUMED	UNISEX	UNITY
UNHIPPEST	UNHUNG	UNILOBAR	UNISEXES	UNIVALENT
UNHIRABLE	UNHUNTED	UNILOBED	UNISEXUAL	UNIVALVE
UNHIRED	UNHURRIED	UNIMBUED	UNISIZE	UNIVALVED
UNHITCH	UNHURT	UNIMPEDED	UNISON	UNIVALVES
UNHITCHED	UNHURTFUL	UNIMPOSED	UNISONAL	UNIVERSAL
UNHITCHES	UNHUSK	UNINCITED	UNISONANT	UNIVERSE
UNHIVE	UNHUSKED	UNINDEXED	UNISONOUS	UNIVERSES
UNHIVED	UNHUSKING	UNINJURED	UNISONS	UNIVOCAL
UNHIVES	UNHUSKS	UNINSTALL	UNISSUED	UNIVOCALS

UNJADED	UNKNELLED	UNLEADS	UNLISTED	UNMADE
UNJAM	UNKNIGHT	UNLEAL	UNLIT	UNMAILED
UNJAMMED	UNKNIGHTS	UNLEARN	UNLIVABLE	UNMAIMED
UNJAMMING	UNKNIT	UNLEARNED	UNLIVE	UNMAKABLE
UNJAMS	UNKNITS	UNLEARNS	UNLIVED	UNMAKE
UNJEALOUS	UNKNITTED	UNLEARNT	UNLIVELY	UNMAKER
UNJOINED	UNKNOT	UNLEASED	UNLIVES	UNMAKERS
UNJOINT	UNKNOTS	UNLEASH	UNLIVING	UNMAKES
UNJOINTED	UNKNOTTED	UNLEASHED	UNLOAD	UNMAKING
UNJOINTS	UNKNOWING	UNLEASHES	UNLOADED	UNMAKINGS
UNJOYFUL	UNKNOWN	UNLED	UNLOADER	UNMAN
UNJOYOUS	UNKNOWNS	UNLESS	UNLOADERS	UNMANACLE
UNJUDGED	UNKOSHER	UNLET	UNLOADING	UNMANAGED
UNJUST	UNLABELED	UNLETHAL	UNLOADS	UNMANFUL
UNJUSTER	UNLABORED	UNLETTED	UNLOBED	UNMANLIER
UNJUSTEST	UNLACE	UNLEVEL	UNLOCATED	UNMANLIKE
UNJUSTLY	UNLACED	UNLEVELED	UNLOCK	UNMANLY
UNKED	UNLACES	UNLEVELS	UNLOCKED	UNMANNED
UNKEELED	UNLACING	UNLEVIED	UNLOCKING	UNMANNING
UNKEMPT	UNLADE	UNLICH	UNLOCKS	UNMANNISH
UNKEMPTLY	UNLADED	UNLICKED	UNLOGICAL	UNMANS
UNKEND	UNLADEN	UNLID	UNLOOKED	UNMANTLE
UNKENNED	UNLADES	UNLIDDED	UNLOOSE	UNMANTLED
UNKENNEL	UNLADING	UNLIDDING	UNLOOSED	UNMANTLES
UNKENNELS	UNLADINGS	UNLIDS	UNLOOSEN	UNMANURED
UNKENT	UNLAID	UNLIGHTED	UNLOOSENS	UNMAPPED
UNKEPT	UNLASH	UNLIKABLE	UNLOOSES	UNMARD
UNKET	UNLASHED	UNLIKE	UNLOOSING	UNMARKED
UNKID	UNLASHES	UNLIKED	UNLOPPED	UNMARRED
UNKIND	UNLASHING	UNLIKELY	UNLORD	UNMARRIED
UNKINDER	UNLAST	UNLIKES	UNLORDED	UNMARRIES
UNKINDEST	UNLASTE	UNLIMBER	UNLORDING	UNMARRY
UNKINDLED	UNLATCH	UNLIMBERS	UNLORDLY	UNMASK
UNKINDLY	UNLATCHED	UNLIME	UNLORDS	UNMASKED
UNKING	UNLATCHES	UNLIMED	UNLOSABLE	UNMASKER
UNKINGED	UNLAW	UNLIMES	UNLOST	UNMASKERS
UNKINGING	UNLAWED	UNLIMING	UNLOVABLE	UNMASKING
UNKINGLY	UNLAWFUL	UNLIMITED	UNLOVE	UNMASKS
UNKINGS	UNLAWING	UNLINE	UNLOVED	UNMATCHED
UNKINK	UNLAWS	UNLINEAL	UNLOVELY	UNMATED
UNKINKED	UNLAY	UNLINED	UNLOVES	UNMATTED
UNKINKING	UNLAYING	UNLINES	UNLOVING	UNMATURED
UNKINKS	UNLAYS	UNLINING	UNLUCKIER	UNMEANING
UNKISS	UNLEAD	UNLINK	UNLUCKILY	UNMEANT
UNKISSED	UNLEADED	UNLINKED	UNLUCKY	UNMEEK
UNKISSES	UNLEADEDS	UNLINKING	UNLYRICAL	UNMEET
UNKISSING	UNLEADING	UNLINKS	UNMACHO	UNMEETLY

U

UNMELLOW	UNMONIED	UNNESTING	UNPANGED	UNPILING
UNMELTED	UNMOOR	UNNESTS	UNPANNEL	UNPILOTED
UNMENDED	UNMOORED	UNNETHES	UNPANNELS	UNPIN
UNMERITED	UNMOORING	UNNETTED	UNPAPER	UNPINKED
UNMERRY	UNMOORS	UNNOBLE	UNPAPERED	UNPINKT
UNMESH	UNMORAL	UNNOBLED	UNPAPERS	UNPINNED
UNMESHED	UNMORALLY	UNNOBLES	UNPARED	UNPINNING
UNMESHES	UNMORTISE	UNNOBLING	UNPARTED	UNPINS
UNMESHING	UNMOTIVED	UNNOISY	UNPARTIAL	UNPITIED
UNMET	UNMOULD	UNNOTED	UNPATCHED	UNPITIFUL
UNMETED	UNMOULDED	UNNOTICED	UNPATHED	UNPITTED
UNMEW	UNMOULDS	UNNUANCED	UNPAVED	UNPITYING
UNMEWED	UNMOUNT	UNOAKED	UNPAY	UNPLACE
UNMEWING	UNMOUNTED	UNOBEYED	UNPAYABLE	UNPLACED
UNMEWS	UNMOUNTS	UNOBVIOUS	UNPAYING	UNPLACES
UNMILKED	UNMOURNED	UNOFFERED	UNPAYS	UNPLACING
UNMILLED	UNMOVABLE	UNOFTEN	UNPEELED	UNPLAGUED
UNMINDED	UNMOVABLY	UNOILED	UNPEERED	UNPLAINED
UNMINDFUL	UNMOVED	UNOPEN	UNPEG	UNPLAIT
UNMINED	UNMOVEDLY	UNOPENED	UNPEGGED	UNPLAITED
UNMINGLE	UNMOVING	UNOPPOSED	UNPEGGING	UNPLAITS
UNMINGLED	UNMOWN	UNORDER	UNPEGS	UNPLANKED
UNMINGLES	UNMUFFLE	UNORDERED	UNPEN	UNPLANNED
UNMIRY	UNMUFFLED	UNORDERLY	UNPENNED	UNPLANTED
UNMISSED	UNMUFFLES	UNORDERS	UNPENNIED	UNPLAYED
UNMITER	UNMUSICAL	UNORNATE	UNPENNING	UNPLEASED
UNMITERED	UNMUZZLE	UNOWED	UNPENS	UNPLEATED
UNMITERS	UNMUZZLED	UNOWNED	UNPENT	UNPLEDGED
UNMITRE	UNMUZZLES	UNPACED	UNPEOPLE	UNPLIABLE
UNMITRED	UNNAIL	UNPACK	UNPEOPLED	UNPLIABLY
UNMITRES	UNNAILED	UNPACKED	UNPEOPLES	UNPLIANT
UNMITRING	UNNAILING	UNPACKER	UNPERCH	UNPLOWED
UNMIX	UNNAILS	UNPACKERS	UNPERCHED	UNPLUCKED
UNMIXABLE	UNNAMABLE	UNPACKING	UNPERCHES	UNPLUG
UNMIXED	UNNAMED	UNPACKS	UNPERFECT	UNPLUGGED
UNMIXEDLY	UNNANELD	UNPADDED	UNPERPLEX	UNPLUGS
UNMIXES	UNNATIVE	UNPAGED	UNPERSON	UNPLUMB
UNMIXING	UNNATURAL	UNPAID	UNPERSONS	UNPLUMBED
UNMIXT	UNNEATH	UNPAINED	UNPERVERT	UNPLUMBS
UNMOANED	UNNEEDED	UNPAINFUL	UNPICK	UNPLUME
UNMODISH	UNNEEDFUL	UNPAINT	UNPICKED	UNPLUMED
UNMOLD	UNNERVE	UNPAINTED	UNPICKING	UNPLUMES
UNMOLDED	UNNERVED	UNPAINTS	UNPICKS	UNPLUMING
UNMOLDING	UNNERVES	UNPAIRED	UNPIERCED	UNPOETIC
UNMOLDS	UNNERVING	UNPALSIED	UNPILE	UNPOINTED
UNMOLTEN	UNNEST	UNPANEL	UNPILED	UNPOISED
UNMONEYED	UNNESTED	UNPANELS	UNPILES	UNPOISON

UNPOISONS	UNPUCKERS	UNREADILY	UNRESERVE	UNROBED
UNPOLICED	UNPULLED	UNREADY	UNREST	UNROBES
UNPOLISH	UNPURE	UNREAL	UNRESTED	UNROBING
UNPOLITE	UNPURELY	UNREALISE	UNRESTFUL	UNROLL
UNPOLITIC	UNPURGED	UNREALISM	UNRESTING	UNROLLED
UNPOLLED	UNPURSE	UNREALITY	UNRESTS	UNROLLING
UNPOPE	UNPURSED	UNREALIZE	UNRETIRE	UNROLLS
UNPOPED	UNPURSES	UNREALLY	UNRETIRED	UNROOF
UNPOPES	UNPURSING	UNREAPED	UNRETIRES	UNROOFED
UNPOPING	UNPURSUED	UNREASON	UNREVISED	UNROOFING
UNPOPULAR	UNPUZZLE	UNREASONS	UNREVOKED	UNROOFS
UNPOSED	UNPUZZLED	UNREAVE	UNRHYMED	UNROOST
UNPOSTED	UNPUZZLES	UNREAVED	UNRIBBED	UNROOSTED
UNPOTABLE	UNQUAKING	UNREAVES	UNRID	UNROOSTS
UNPOTTED	UNQUALIFY	UNREAVING	UNRIDABLE	UNROOT
UNPRAISE	UNQUEEN	UNREBATED	UNRIDDEN	UNROOTED
UNPRAISED	UNQUEENED	UNREBUKED	UNRIDDLE	UNROOTING
UNPRAISES	UNQUEENLY	UNRECKED	UNRIDDLED	UNROOTS
UNPRAY	UNQUEENS	UNRED	UNRIDDLER	UNROPE
UNPRAYED	UNQUELLED	UNREDREST	UNRIDDLES	UNROPED
UNPRAYING	UNQUIET	UNREDUCED	UNRIFLED	UNROPES
UNPRAYS	UNQUIETED	UNREDY	UNRIG	UNROPING
UNPREACH	UNQUIETER	UNREEL	UNRIGGED	UNROSINED
UNPRECISE	UNQUIETLY	UNREELED	UNRIGGING	UNROTTED
UNPREDICT	UNQUIETS	UNREELER	UNRIGHT	UNROTTEN
UNPREPARE	UNQUOTE	UNREELERS	UNRIGHTS	UNROUGED
UNPRESSED	UNQUOTED	UNREELING	UNRIGS	UNROUGH
UNPRETTY	UNQUOTES	UNREELS	UNRIMED	UNROUND
UNPRICED	UNQUOTING	UNREEVE	UNRINGED	UNROUNDED
UNPRIEST	UNRACED	UNREEVED	UNRINSED	UNROUNDS
UNPRIESTS	UNRACKED	UNREEVES	UNRIP	UNROUSED
UNPRIMED	UNRAISED	UNREEVING	UNRIPE	UNROVE
UNPRINTED	UNRAKE	UNREFINED	UNRIPELY	UNROVEN
UNPRISON	UNRAKED	UNREFUTED	UNRIPENED	UNROYAL
UNPRISONS	UNRAKES	UNREIN	UNRIPER	UNROYALLY
UNPRIZED	UNRAKING	UNREINED	UNRIPEST	UNRUBBED
UNPROBED	UNRANKED	UNREINING	UNRIPPED	UNRUDE
UNPROP	UNRATED	UNREINS	UNRIPPING	UNRUFFE
UNPROPER	UNRAVAGED	UNRELATED	UNRIPS	UNRUFFLE
UNPROPPED	UNRAVEL	UNRELAXED	UNRISEN	UNRUFFLED
UNPROPS	UNRAVELED	UNREMOVED	UNRIVALED	UNRUFFLES
UNPROVED	UNRAVELS	UNRENEWED	UNRIVEN	UNRULE
UNPROVEN	UNRAZED	UNRENT	UNRIVET	UNRULED
UNPROVIDE	UNRAZORED	UNRENTED	UNRIVETED	UNRULES
UNPROVOKE	UNREACHED	UNREPAID	UNRIVETS	UNRULIER
UNPRUNED	UNREAD	UNREPAIR	UNROASTED	UNRULIEST
UNPUCKER	UNREADIER	UNREPAIRS	UNROBE	UNRULY

UNRUMPLED

UNRUMPLED	UNSCENTED	UNSELVES	UNSHAVEN	UNSIGHTLY
UNRUSHED	UNSCOURED	UNSENSE	UNSHEATHE	UNSIGHTS
UNRUSTED	UNSCREW	UNSENSED	UNSHED	UNSIGNED
UNS	UNSCREWED	UNSENSES	UNSHELL	UNSILENT
UNSADDLE	UNSCREWS	UNSENSING	UNSHELLED	UNSIMILAR
UNSADDLED	UNSCYTHED	UNSENT	UNSHELLS	UNSINEW
UNSADDLES	UNSEAL	UNSERIOUS	UNSHENT	UNSINEWED
UNSAFE	UNSEALED	UNSERVED	UNSHEWN	UNSINEWS
UNSAFELY	UNSEALING	UNSET	UNSHIFT	UNSINFUL
UNSAFER	UNSEALS	UNSETS	UNSHIFTED	UNSISTING
UNSAFEST	UNSEAM	UNSETTING	UNSHIFTS	UNSIZABLE
UNSAFETY	UNSEAMED	UNSETTLE	UNSHIP	UNSIZED
UNSAID	UNSEAMING	UNSETTLED	UNSHIPPED	UNSKILFUL
UNSAILED	UNSEAMS	UNSETTLES	UNSHIPS	UNSKILLED
UNSAINED	UNSEARED	UNSEVERED	UNSHIRTED	UNSKIMMED
UNSAINT	UNSEASON	UNSEW	UNSHOCKED	UNSKINNED
UNSAINTED	UNSEASONS	UNSEWED	UNSHOD	UNSLAIN
UNSAINTLY	UNSEAT	UNSEWING	UNSHOE	UNSLAKED
UNSAINTS	UNSEATED	UNSEWN	UNSHOED	UNSLICED
UNSALABLE	UNSEATING	UNSEWS	UNSHOEING	UNSLICK
UNSALABLY	UNSEATS	UNSEX	UNSHOES	UNSLING
UNSALTED	UNSECRET	UNSEXED	UNSHOOT	UNSLINGS
UNSALUTED	UNSECULAR	UNSEXES	UNSHOOTED	UNSLUICE
UNSAMPLED	UNSECURED	UNSEXING	UNSHOOTS	UNSLUICED
UNSAPPED	UNSEDUCED	UNSEXIST	UNSHORN	UNSLUICES
UNSASHED	UNSEEABLE	UNSEXUAL	UNSHOT	UNSLUNG
UNSATABLE	UNSEEDED	UNSEXY	UNSHOUT	UNSMART
UNSATED	UNSEEING	UNSHACKLE	UNSHOUTED	UNSMILING
UNSATIATE	UNSEEL	UNSHADED	UNSHOUTS	UNSMITTEN
UNSATING	UNSEELED	UNSHADOW	UNSHOWN	UNSMOKED
UNSAVED	UNSEELIE	UNSHADOWS	UNSHOWY	UNSMOOTH
UNSAVORY	UNSEELING	UNSHAKED	UNSHRIVED	UNSMOOTHS
UNSAVOURY	UNSEELS	UNSHAKEN	UNSHRIVEN	UNSMOTE
UNSAWED	UNSEEMING	UNSHALE	UNSHROUD	UNSNAG
UNSAWN	UNSEEMLY	UNSHALED	UNSHROUDS	UNSNAGGED
UNSAY	UNSEEN	UNSHALES	UNSHRUBD	UNSNAGS
UNSAYABLE	UNSEENS	UNSHALING	UNSHRUNK	UNSNAP
UNSAYING	UNSEIZED	UNSHAMED	UNSHUNNED	UNSNAPPED
UNSAYS	UNSELDOM	UNSHAPE	UNSHUT	UNSNAPS
UNSCALE	UNSELF	UNSHAPED	UNSHUTS	UNSNARL
UNSCALED	UNSELFED	UNSHAPELY	UNSHUTTER	UNSNARLED
UNSCALES	UNSELFING	UNSHAPEN	UNSICKER	UNSNARLS
UNSCALING	UNSELFISH	UNSHAPES	UNSICKLED	UNSNECK
UNSCANNED	UNSELFS	UNSHAPING	UNSIFTED	UNSNECKED
UNSCARRED	UNSELL	UNSHARED	UNSIGHING	UNSNECKS
UNSCARY	UNSELLING	UNSHARP	UNSIGHT	UNSNUFFED
UNSCATHED	UNSELLS	UNSHAVED	UNSIGHTED	UNSOAKED

UNSOAPED	UNSPELLS	UNSTEPPED	UNSUITING	UNTANGLES
UNSOBER	UNSPENT	UNSTEPS	UNSUITS	UNTANNED
UNSOBERLY	UNSPHERE	UNSTERILE	UNSULLIED	UNTAPPED
UNSOCIAL	UNSPHERED	UNSTICK	UNSUMMED	UNTARRED
UNSOCKET	UNSPHERES	UNSTICKS	UNSUNG	UNTASTED
UNSOCKETS	UNSPIDE	UNSTIFLED	UNSUNK	UNTAUGHT
UNSOD	UNSPIED	UNSTILLED	UNSUNNED	UNTAX
UNSODDEN	UNSPILLED	UNSTINTED	UNSUNNY	UNTAXED
UNSOFT	UNSPILT	UNSTIRRED	UNSUPPLE	UNTAXES
UNSOILED	UNSPLIT	UNSTITCH	UNSURE	UNTAXING
UNSOLACED	UNSPOILED	UNSTOCK	UNSURED	UNTEACH
UNSOLD	UNSPOILT	UNSTOCKED	UNSURELY	UNTEACHES
UNSOLDER	UNSPOKE	UNSTOCKS	UNSURER	UNTEAM
UNSOLDERS	UNSPOKEN	UNSTONED	UNSUREST	UNTEAMED
UNSOLEMN	UNSPOOL	UNSTOP	UNSUSPECT	UNTEAMING
UNSOLID	UNSPOOLED	UNSTOPPED	UNSWADDLE	UNTEAMS
UNSOLIDLY	UNSPOOLS	UNSTOPPER	UNSWATHE	UNTEMPER
UNSOLVED	UNSPOTTED	UNSTOPS	UNSWATHED	UNTEMPERS
UNSONCY	UNSPRAYED	UNSTOW	UNSWATHES	UNTEMPTED
UNSONSIE	UNSPRUNG	UNSTOWED	UNSWAYED	UNTENABLE
UNSONSY	UNSPUN	UNSTOWING	UNSWEAR	UNTENABLY
UNSOOTE	UNSQUARED	UNSTOWS	UNSWEARS	UNTENANT
UNSOOTHED	UNSTABLE	UNSTRAP	UNSWEET	UNTENANTS
UNSORTED	UNSTABLER	UNSTRAPS	UNSWEPT	UNTENDED
UNSOUGHT	UNSTABLY	UNSTRESS	UNSWOLLEN	UNTENDER
UNSOUL	UNSTACK	UNSTRING	UNSWORE	UNTENT
UNSOULED	UNSTACKED	UNSTRINGS	UNSWORN	UNTENTED
UNSOULING	UNSTACKS	UNSTRIP	UNTACK	UNTENTING
UNSOULS	UNSTAID	UNSTRIPED	UNTACKED	UNTENTS
UNSOUND	UNSTAINED	UNSTRIPS	UNTACKING	UNTENTY
UNSOUNDED	UNSTALKED	UNSTRUCK	UNTACKLE	UNTENURED
UNSOUNDER	UNSTAMPED	UNSTRUNG	UNTACKLED	UNTESTED
UNSOUNDLY	UNSTARCH	UNSTUCK	UNTACKLES	UNTETHER
UNSOURCED	UNSTARRED	UNSTUDIED	UNTACKS	UNTETHERS
UNSOURED	UNSTARRY	UNSTUFFED	UNTACTFUL	UNTHANKED
UNSOWED	UNSTATE	UNSTUFFY	UNTAGGED	UNTHATCH
UNSOWN	UNSTATED	UNSTUFT	UNTAILED	UNTHAW
UNSPAR	UNSTATES	UNSTUNG	UNTAINTED	UNTHAWED
UNSPARED	UNSTATING	UNSTYLISH	UNTAKEN	UNTHAWING
UNSPARING	UNSTAYED	UNSUBDUED	UNTAMABLE	UNTHAWS
UNSPARRED	UNSTAYING	UNSUBJECT	UNTAMABLY	UNTHINK
UNSPARS	UNSTEADY	UNSUBTLE	UNTAME	UNTHINKS
UNSPEAK	UNSTEEL	UNSUBTLY	UNTAMED	UNTHOUGHT
UNSPEAKS	UNSTEELED	UNSUCCESS	UNTAMES	UNTHREAD
UNSPED	UNSTEELS	UNSUCKED	UNTAMING	UNTHREADS
UNSPELL	UNSTEMMED	UNSUIT	UNTANGLE	UNTHRIFT
UNSPELLED	UNSTEP	UNSUITED	UNTANGLED	UNTHRIFTS

U

UNTHRIFTY	UNTRACED	UNTUNEFUL	UNVEIL	UNWARPED
UNTHRONE	UNTRACES	UNTUNES	UNVEILED	UNWARY
UNTHRONED	UNTRACING	UNTUNING	UNVEILER	UNWASHED
UNTHRONES	UNTRACK	UNTURBID	UNVEILERS	UNWASHEDS
UNTIDIED	UNTRACKED	UNTURF	UNVEILING	UNWASHEN
UNTIDIER	UNTRACKS	UNTURFED	UNVEILS	UNWASTED
UNTIDIES	UNTRADED	UNTURFING	UNVEINED	UNWASTING
UNTIDIEST	UNTRAINED	UNTURFS	UNVENTED	UNWATCHED
UNTIDILY	UNTRAPPED	UNTURN	UNVERSED	UNWATER
UNTIDY	UNTREAD	UNTURNED	UNVESTED	UNWATERED
UNTIDYING	UNTREADED	UNTURNING	UNVETTED	UNWATERS
UNTIE	UNTREADS	UNTURNS	UNVEXED	UNWATERY
UNTIED	UNTREATED	UNTUTORED	UNVEXT	UNWAXED
UNTIEING	UNTRENDY	UNTWILLED	UNVIABLE	UNWAYED
UNTIES	UNTRESSED	UNTWINE	UNVIEWED	UNWEAL
UNTIL	UNTRIDE	UNTWINED	UNVIRTUE	UNWEALS
UNTILE	UNTRIED	UNTWINES	UNVIRTUES	UNWEANED
UNTILED	UNTRIM	UNTWINING	UNVISITED	UNWEAPON
UNTILES	UNTRIMMED	UNTWIST	UNVISOR	UNWEAPONS
UNTILING	UNTRIMS	UNTWISTED	UNVISORED	UNWEARIED
UNTILLED	UNTROD	UNTWISTS	UNVISORS	UNWEARY
UNTILTED	UNTRODDEN	UNTYING	UNVITAL	UNWEAVE
UNTIMED	UNTRUE	UNTYINGS	UNVIZARD	UNWEAVES
UNTIMELY	UNTRUER	UNTYPABLE	UNVIZARDS	UNWEAVING
UNTIMEOUS	UNTRUEST	UNTYPICAL	UNVOCAL	UNWEBBED
UNTIN	UNTRUISM	UNUNBIUM	UNVOICE	UNWED
UNTINGED	UNTRUISMS	UNUNBIUMS	UNVOICED	UNWEDDED
UNTINNED	UNTRULY	UNUNITED	UNVOICES	UNWEEDED
UNTINNING	UNTRUSS	UNUNUNIUM	UNVOICING	UNWEENED
UNTINS	UNTRUSSED	UNURGED	UNVULGAR	UNWEETING
UNTIPPED	UNTRUSSER	UNUSABLE	UNWAGED	UNWEIGHED
UNTIRABLE	UNTRUSSES	UNUSABLY	UNWAKED	UNWEIGHT
UNTIRED	UNTRUST	UNUSED	UNWAKENED	UNWEIGHTS
UNTIRING	UNTRUSTS	UNUSEFUL	UNWALLED	UNWELCOME
UNTITLED	UNTRUSTY	UNUSHERED	UNWANING	UNWELDED
UNTO	UNTRUTH	UNUSUAL	UNWANTED	UNWELDY
UNTOILING	UNTRUTHS	UNUSUALLY	UNWARDED	UNWELL
UNTOLD	UNTUCK	UNUTTERED	UNWARE	UNWEPT
UNTOMB	UNTUCKED	UNVAIL	UNWARELY	UNWET
UNTOMBED	UNTUCKING	UNVAILE	UNWARES	UNWETTED
UNTOMBING	UNTUCKS	UNVAILED	UNWARIE	UNWHIPPED
UNTOMBS	UNTUFTED	UNVAILES	UNWARIER	UNWHIPT
UNTONED	UNTUMBLED	UNVAILING	UNWARIEST	UNWHITE
UNTORN	UNTUNABLE	UNVAILS	UNWARILY	UNWIELDLY
UNTOUCHED	UNTUNABLY	UNVALUED	UNWARLIKE	UNWIELDY
UNTOWARD	UNTUNE	UNVARIED	UNWARMED	UNWIFELY
UNTRACE	UNTUNED	UNVARYING	UNWARNED	UNWIGGED

UNWILFUL	UNWONT	UPAITHRIC	UPBUILT	UPDATE
UNWILL	UNWONTED	UPAS	UPBURNING	UPDATED
UNWILLED	UNWOODED	UPASES	UPBURST	UPDATER
UNWILLING	UNWOOED	UPBEAR	UPBURSTS	UPDATERS
UNWILLS	UNWORDED	UPBEARER	UPBY	UPDATES
UNWIND	UNWORK	UPBEARERS	UPBYE	UPDATING
UNWINDER	UNWORKED	UPBEARING	UPCAST	UPDIVE
UNWINDERS	UNWORKING	UPBEARS	UPCASTING	UPDIVED
UNWINDING	UNWORKS	UPBEAT	UPCASTS	UPDIVES
UNWINDS	UNWORLDLY	UPBEATS	UPCATCH	UPDIVING
UNWINGED	UNWORMED	UPBIND	UPCATCHES	UPDO
UNWINKING	UNWORN	UPBINDING	UPCAUGHT	UPDOS
UNWIPED	UNWORRIED	UPBINDS	UPCHEER	UPDOVE
UNWIRE	UNWORTH	UPBLEW	UPCHEERED	UPDRAFT
UNWIRED	UNWORTHS	UPBLOW	UPCHEERS	UPDRAFTS
UNWIRES	UNWORTHY	UPBLOWING	UPCHUCK	UPDRAG
UNWIRING	UNWOUND	UPBLOWN	UPCHUCKED	UPDRAGGED
UNWISDOM	UNWOUNDED	UPBLOWS	UPCHUCKS	UPDRAGS
UNWISDOMS	UNWOVE	UPBOIL	UPCLIMB	UPDRAUGHT
UNWISE	UNWOVEN	UPBOILED	UPCLIMBED	UPDRAW
UNWISELY	UNWRAP	UPBOILING	UPCLIMBS	UPDRAWING
UNWISER	UNWRAPPED	UPBOILS	UPCLOSE	UPDRAWN
UNWISEST	UNWRAPS	UPBORE	UPCLOSED	UPDRAWS
UNWISH	UNWREAKED	UPBORNE	UPCLOSES	UPDREW
UNWISHED	UNWREATHE	UPBOUND	UPCLOSING	UPDRIED
UNWISHES	UNWRINKLE	UPBOUNDEN	UPCOAST	UPDRIES
UNWISHFUL	UNWRITE	UPBOW	UPCOIL	UPDRY
UNWISHING	UNWRITES	UPBOWS	UPCOILED	UPDRYING
UNWIST	UNWRITING	UPBRAID	UPCOILING	UPEND
UNWIT	UNWRITTEN	UPBRAIDED	UPCOILS	UPENDED
UNWITCH	UNWROTE	UPBRAIDER	UPCOME	UPENDING
UNWITCHED	UNWROUGHT	UPBRAIDS	UPCOMES	UPENDS
UNWITCHES	UNWRUNG	UPBRAST	UPCOMING	UPFIELD
UNWITS	UNYEANED	UPBRAY	UPCOUNTRY	UPFILL
UNWITTED	UNYOKE	UPBRAYED	UPCOURT	UPFILLED
UNWITTILY	UNYOKED	UPBRAYING	UPCURL	UPFILLING
UNWITTING	UNYOKES	UPBRAYS	UPCURLED	UPFILLS
UNWITTY	UNYOKING	UPBREAK	UPCURLING	UPFLING
UNWIVE	UNYOUNG	UPBREAKS	UPCURLS	UPFLINGS
UNWIVED	UNZEALOUS	UPBRING	UPCURVE	UPFLOW
UNWIVES	UNZIP	UPBRINGS	UPCURVED	UPFLOWED
UNWIVING	UNZIPPED	UPBROKE	UPCURVES	UPFLOWING
UNWOMAN	UNZIPPING	UPBROKEN	UPCURVING	UPFLOWS
UNWOMANED	UNZIPS	UPBROUGHT	UPDART	UPFLUNG
UNWOMANLY	UNZONED	UPBUILD	UPDARTED	UPFOLD
UNWOMANS	UP	UPBUILDER	UPDARTING	UPFOLDED
UNWON	UPADAISY	UPBUILDS	UPDARTS	UPFOLDING

UPFOLDS	UPHAUD	UPKEEP	UPLOCK	UPRAN
UPFOLLOW	UPHAUDING	UPKEEPS	UPLOCKED	UPRATE
UPFOLLOWS	UPHAUDS	UPKNIT	UPLOCKING	UPRATED
UPFRONT	UPHEAP	UPKNITS	UPLOCKS	UPRATES
UPFURL	UPHEAPED	UPKNITTED	UPLOOK	UPRATING
UPFURLED	UPHEAPING	UPLAID	UPLOOKED	UPREACH
UPFURLING	UPHEAPS	UPLAND	UPLOOKING	UPREACHED
UPFURLS	UPHEAVAL	UPLANDER	UPLOOKS	UPREACHES
UPGANG	UPHEAVALS	UPLANDERS	UPLYING	UPREAR
UPGANGS	UPHEAVE	UPLANDISH	UPMAKE	UPREARED
UPGATHER	UPHEAVED	UPLANDS	UPMAKER	UPREARING
UPGATHERS	UPHEAVER	UPLAY	UPMAKERS	UPREARS
UPGAZE	UPHEAVERS	UPLAYING	UPMAKES	UPREST
UPGAZED	UPHEAVES	UPLAYS	UPMAKING	UPRESTS
UPGAZES	UPHEAVING	UPLEAD	UPMAKINGS	UPRIGHT
UPGAZING	UPHELD	UPLEADING	UPMANSHIP	UPRIGHTED
UPGIRD	UPHILD	UPLEADS	UPMARKET	UPRIGHTLY
UPGIRDED	UPHILL	UPLEAN	UPMARKETS	UPRIGHTS
UPGIRDING	UPHILLS	UPLEANED	UPMOST	UPRISAL
UPGIRDS	UPHOARD	UPLEANING	UPO	UPRISALS
UPGIRT	UPHOARDED	UPLEANS	UPON	UPRISE
UPGO	UPHOARDS	UPLEANT	UPPED	UPRISEN
UPGOES	UPHOIST	UPLEAP	UPPER	UPRISER
UPGOING	UPHOISTED	UPLEAPED	UPPERCASE	UPRISERS
UPGOINGS	UPHOISTS	UPLEAPING	UPPERCUT	UPRISES
UPGONE	UPHOLD	UPLEAPS	UPPERCUTS	UPRISING
UPGRADE	UPHOLDER	UPLEAPT	UPPERMOST	UPRISINGS
UPGRADED	UPHOLDERS	UPLED	UPPERPART	UPRIST
UPGRADER	UPHOLDING	UPLIFT	UPPERS	UPRISTS
UPGRADERS	UPHOLDS	UPLIFTED	UPPILE	UPRIVER
UPGRADES	UPHOLSTER	UPLIFTER	UPPILED	UPRIVERS
UPGRADING	UPHOORD	UPLIFTERS	UPPILES	UPROAR
UPGREW	UPHOORDED	UPLIFTING	UPPILING	UPROARED
UPGROW	UPHOORDS	UPLIFTS	UPPING	UPROARING
UPGROWING	UPHOVE	UPLIGHT	UPPINGS	UPROARS
UPGROWN	UPHROE	UPLIGHTED	UPPISH	UPROLL
UPGROWS	UPHROES	UPLIGHTER	UPPISHLY	UPROLLED
UPGROWTH	UPHUDDEN	UPLIGHTS	UPPITY	UPROLLING
UPGROWTHS	UPHUNG	UPLINK	UPPROP	UPROLLS
UPGUSH	UPHURL	UPLINKED	UPPROPPED	UPROOT
UPGUSHED	UPHURLED	UPLINKING	UPPROPS	UPROOTAL
UPGUSHES	UPHURLING	UPLINKS	UPRAISE	UPROOTALS
UPGUSHING	UPHURLS	UPLIT	UPRAISED	UPROOTED
UPHAND	UPJET	UPLOAD	UPRAISER	UPROOTER
UPHANG	UPJETS	UPLOADED	UPRAISERS	UPROOTERS
UPHANGING	UPJETTED	UPLOADING	UPRAISES	UPROOTING
UPHANGS	UPJETTING	UPLOADS	UPRAISING	UPROOTS

UPROSE	UPSITTING	UPSTAY	UPTEARS	UPVALUE
UPROUSE	UPSIZE	UPSTAYED	UPTEMPO	UPVALUED
UPROUSED	UPSIZED	UPSTAYING	UPTEMPOS	UPVALUES
UPROUSES	UPSIZES	UPSTAYS	UPTER	UPVALUING
UPROUSING	UPSIZING	UPSTEP	UPTHREW	UPWAFT
UPRUN	UPSKILL	UPSTEPPED	UPTHROW	UPWAFTED
UPRUNNING	UPSKILLED	UPSTEPS	UPTHROWN	UPWAFTING
UPRUNS	UPSKILLS	UPSTIR	UPTHROWS	UPWAFTS
UPRUSH	UPSLOPE	UPSTIRRED	UPTHRUST	UPWARD
UPRUSHED	UPSOAR	UPSTIRS	UPTHRUSTS	UPWARDLY
UPRUSHES	UPSOARED	UPSTOOD	UPTHUNDER	UPWARDS
UPRUSHING	UPSOARING	UPSTREAM	UPTICK	UPWELL
UPRYST	UPSOARS	UPSTREAMS	UPTICKS	UPWELLED
UPS	UPSOLD	UPSTROKE	UPTIE	UPWELLING
UPSADAISY	UPSPAKE	UPSTROKES	UPTIED	UPWELLS
UPSCALE	UPSPEAK	UPSURGE	UPTIES	UPWENT
UPSCALED	UPSPEAKS	UPSURGED	UPTIGHT	UPWHIRL
UPSCALES	UPSPEAR	UPSURGES	UPTIGHTER	UPWHIRLED
UPSCALING	UPSPEARED	UPSURGING	UPTILT	UPWHIRLS
UPSEE	UPSPEARS	UPSWAY	UPTILTED	UPWIND
UPSEES	UPSPOKE	UPSWAYED	UPTILTING	UPWINDING
UPSELL	UPSPOKEN	UPSWAYING	UPTILTS	UPWINDS
UPSELLING	UPSPRANG	UPSWAYS	UPTIME	UPWOUND
UPSELLS	UPSPRING	UPSWEEP	UPTIMES	UPWRAP
UPSEND	UPSPRINGS	UPSWEEPS	UPTITLING	UPWRAPS
UPSENDING	UPSPRUNG	UPSWELL	UPTOOK	UPWROUGHT
UPSENDS	UPSTAGE	UPSWELLED	UPTORE	UR
UPSENT	UPSTAGED	UPSWELLS	UPTORN	URACHI
UPSET	UPSTAGER	UPSWEPT	UPTOSS	URACHUS
UPSETS	UPSTAGERS	UPSWING	UPTOSSED	URACHUSES
UPSETTER	UPSTAGES	UPSWINGS	UPTOSSES	URACIL
UPSETTERS	UPSTAGING	UPSWOLLEN	UPTOSSING	URACILS
UPSETTING	UPSTAIR	UPSWUNG	UPTOWN	URAEI
UPSEY	UPSTAIRS	UPSY	UPTOWNER	URAEMIA
UPSEYS	UPSTAND	UPTA	UPTOWNERS	URAEMIAS
UPSHIFT	UPSTANDS	UPTAK	UPTOWNS	URAEMIC
UPSHIFTED	UPSTARE	UPTAKE	UPTRAIN	URAEUS
UPSHIFTS	UPSTARED	UPTAKEN	UPTRAINED	URAEUSES
UPSHOOT	UPSTARES	UPTAKES	UPTRAINS	URALI
UPSHOOTS	UPSTARING	UPTAKING	UPTREND	URALIS
UPSHOT	UPSTART	UPTAKS	UPTRENDS	URALITE
UPSHOTS	UPSTARTED	UPTALK	UPTRILLED	URALITES
UPSIDE	UPSTARTS	UPTALKED	UPTURN	URALITIC
UPSIDES	UPSTATE	UPTALKING	UPTURNED	URALITISE
UPSIES	UPSTATER	UPTALKS	UPTURNING	URALITIZE
UPSILON	UPSTATERS	UPTEAR	UPTURNS	URANIA
UPSILONS	UPSTATES	UPTEARING	UPTYING	URANIAN

URANIAS	URBANITY	URESIS	URINATOR	UROLOGIST
URANIC	URBANIZE	URETER	URINATORS	UROLOGY
URANIDE	URBANIZED	URETERAL	URINE	UROMERE
URANIDES	URBANIZES	URETERIC	URINED	UROMERES
URANIN	URBIA	URETERS	URINEMIA	UROPOD
URANINITE	URBIAS	URETHAN	URINEMIAS	UROPODAL
URANINS	URBS	URETHANE	URINEMIC	UROPODOUS
URANISCI	URCEOLATE	URETHANES	URINES	UROPODS
URANISCUS	URCEOLI	URETHANS	URINING	UROPYGIA
URANISM	URCEOLUS	URETHRA	URINOLOGY	UROPYGIAL
URANISMS	URCHIN	URETHRAE	URINOSE	UROPYGIUM
URANITE	URCHINS	URETHRAL	URINOUS	UROSCOPIC
URANITES	URD	URETHRAS	URITE	UROSCOPY
URANITIC	URDE	URETIC	URITES	UROSES
URANIUM	URDEE	URGE	URMAN	UROSIS
URANIUMS	URDS	URGED	URMANS	UROSOME
URANOLOGY	URDY	URGENCE	URN	UROSOMES
URANOUS	URE	URGENCES	URNAL	UROSTEGE
URANYL	UREA	URGENCIES	URNED	UROSTEGES
URANYLIC	UREAL	URGENCY	URNFIELD	UROSTOMY
URANYLS	UREAS	URGENT	URNFIELDS	UROSTYLE
URAO	UREASE	URGENTLY	URNFUL	UROSTYLES
URAOS	UREASES	URGER	URNFULS	URP
URARE	UREDIA	URGERS	URNING	URPED
URARES	UREDIAL	URGES	URNINGS	URPING
URARI	UREDINE	URGING	URNLIKE	URPS
URARIS	UREDINES	URGINGLY	URNS	URSA
URASE	UREDINIA	URGINGS	UROBILIN	URSAE
URASES	UREDINIAL	URIAL	UROBILINS	URSID
URATE	UREDINIUM	URIALS	UROBOROS	URSIDS
URATES	UREDINOUS	URIC	UROCHORD	URSIFORM
URATIC	UREDIUM	URICASE	UROCHORDS	URSINE
URB	UREDO	URICASES	UROCHROME	URSON
URBAN	UREDOS	URIDINE	URODELAN	URSONS
URBANE	UREDOSORI	URIDINES	URODELANS	URTEXT
URBANELY	UREIC	URIDYLIC	URODELE	URTEXTS
URBANER	UREIDE	URINAL	URODELES	URTICA
URBANEST	UREIDES	URINALS	URODELOUS	URTICANT
URBANISE	UREMIA	URINANT	UROGENOUS	URTICANTS
URBANISED	UREMIAS	URINARIES	UROGRAPHY	URTICARIA
URBANISES	UREMIC	URINARY	UROKINASE	URTICAS
URBANISM	URENA	URINATE	UROLAGNIA	URTICATE
URBANISMS	URENAS	URINATED	UROLITH	URTICATED
URBANIST	URENT	URINATES	UROLITHIC	URTICATES
URBANISTS	UREOTELIC	URINATING	UROLITHS	URUBU
URBANITE	URES	URINATION	UROLOGIC	URUBUS
URBANITES	URESES	URINATIVE	UROLOGIES	URUS

URUSES	USHERING	USURIOUS	UTILISING	UTTERERS
URUSHIOL	USHERINGS	USUROUS	UTILITIES	UTTEREST
URUSHIOLS	USHERS	USURP	UTILITY	UTTERING
URVA	USHERSHIP	USURPED	UTILIZE	UTTERINGS
URVAS	USING	USURPEDLY	UTILIZED	UTTERLESS
US	USNEA	USURPER	UTILIZER	UTTERLY
USABILITY	USNEAS	USURPERS	UTILIZERS	UTTERMOST
USABLE	USQUABAE	USURPING	UTILIZES	UTTERNESS
USABLY	USQUABAES	USURPINGS	UTILIZING	UTTERS
USAGE	USQUE	USURPS	UTIS	UTU
USAGER	USQUEBAE	USURY	UTISES	UTUS
USAGERS	USQUEBAES	USWARD	UTMOST	UVA
USAGES	USQUES	USWARDS	UTMOSTS	UVAE
USANCE	USTION	UT	UTOPIA	UVAROVITE
USANCES	USTIONS	UTA	UTOPIAN	UVAS
USAUNCE	USTULATE	UTAS	UTOPIANS	UVEA
USAUNCES	USUAL	UTASES	UTOPIAS	UVEAL
USE	USUALLY	UTE	UTOPIAST	UVEAS
USEABLE	USUALNESS	UTENSIL	UTOPIASTS	UVEITIC
USEABLY	USUALS	UTENSILS	UTOPISM	UVEITIS
USED	USUCAPION	UTERI	UTOPISMS	UVEITISES
USEFUL	USUCAPT	UTERINE	UTOPIST	UVEOUS
USEFULLY	USUCAPTED	UTERITIS	UTOPISTIC	UVULA
USEFULS	USUCAPTS	UTEROTOMY	UTOPISTS	UVULAE
USELESS	USUFRUCT	UTERUS	UTRICLE	UVULAR
USELESSLY	USUFRUCTS	UTERUSES	UTRICLES	UVULARLY
USER	USURE	UTES	UTRICULAR	UVULARS
USERNAME	USURED	UTILE	UTRICULI	UVULAS
USERNAMES	USURER	UTILIDOR	UTRICULUS	UVULITIS
USERS	USURERS	UTILIDORS	UTS	UXORIAL
USES	USURES	UTILISE	UTTER	UXORIALLY
USHER	USURESS	UTILISED	UTTERABLE	UXORICIDE
USHERED	USURESSES	UTILISER	UTTERANCE	UXORIOUS
USHERESS	USURIES	UTILISERS	UTTERED	
USHERETTE	USURING	UTILISES	UTTERER	

U

V

VAC	VACUOLAR	VAGINULES	VAKAS	VALIDATE
VACANCE	VACUOLATE	VAGITUS	VAKASES	VALIDATED
VACANCES	VACUOLE	VAGITUSES	VAKEEL	VALIDATES
VACANCIES	VACUOLES	VAGOTOMY	VAKEELS	VALIDER
VACANCY	VACUOUS	VAGOTONIA	VAKIL	VALIDEST
VACANT	VACUOUSLY	VAGOTONIC	VAKILS	VALIDITY
VACANTLY	VACUUM	VAGRANCY	VALANCE	VALIDLY
VACATABLE	VACUUMED	VAGRANT	VALANCED	VALIDNESS
VACATE	VACUUMING	VAGRANTLY	VALANCES	VALINE
VACATED	VACUUMS	VAGRANTS	VALANCING	VALINES
VACATES	VADE	VAGROM	VALE	VALIS
VACATING	VADED	VAGS	VALENCE	VALISE
VACATION	VADES	VAGUE	VALENCES	VALISES
VACATIONS	VADING	VAGUED	VALENCIA	VALIUM
VACATUR	VADOSE	VAGUELY	VALENCIAS	VALKYR
VACATURS	VAE	VAGUENESS	VALENCIES	VALKYRIE
VACCINA	VAES	VAGUER	VALENCY	VALKYRIES
VACCINAL	VAG	VAGUES	VALENTINE	VALKYRS
VACCINAS	VAGABOND	VAGUEST	VALERATE	VALLAR
VACCINATE	VAGABONDS	VAGUING	VALERATES	VALLARY
VACCINE	VAGAL	VAGUS	VALERIAN	VALLATE
VACCINEE	VAGALLY	VAHANA	VALERIANS	VALLATION
VACCINEES	VAGARIES	VAHANAS	VALERIC	VALLECULA
VACCINES	VAGARIOUS	VAHINE	VALES	VALLEY
VACCINIA	VAGARISH	VAHINES	VALET	VALLEYED
VACCINIAL	VAGARY	VAIL	VALETA	VALLEYS
VACCINIAS	VAGGED	VAILED	VALETAS	VALLHUND
VACCINIUM	VAGGING	VAILING	VALETE	VALLHUNDS
VACHERIN	VAGI	VAILS	VALETED	VALLONIA
VACHERINS	VAGILE	VAIN	VALETES	VALLONIAS
VACILLANT	VAGILITY	VAINER	VALETING	VALLUM
VACILLATE	VAGINA	VAINESSE	VALETINGS	VALLUMS
VACKED	VAGINAE	VAINESSES	VALETS	VALONEA
VACKING	VAGINAL	VAINEST	VALGOID	VALONEAS
VACS	VAGINALLY	VAINGLORY	VALGOUS	VALONIA
VACUA	VAGINANT	VAINLY	VALGUS	VALONIAS
VACUATE	VAGINAS	VAINNESS	VALGUSES	VALOR
VACUATED	VAGINATE	VAIR	VALI	VALORISE
VACUATES	VAGINATED	VAIRE	VALIANCE	VALORISED
VACUATING	VAGINITIS	VAIRIER	VALIANCES	VALORISES
VACUATION	VAGINOSES	VAIRIEST	VALIANCY	VALORIZE
VACUIST	VAGINOSIS	VAIRS	VALIANT	VALORIZED
VACUISTS	VAGINULA	VAIRY	VALIANTLY	VALORIZES
VACUITIES	VAGINULAE	VAIVODE	VALIANTS	VALOROUS
VACUITY	VAGINULE	VAIVODES	VALID	VALORS

VALOUR	VAMOOSE	VANDALS	VANS	VAPOURS
VALOURS	VAMOOSED	VANDAS	VANT	VAPOURY
VALPROATE	VAMOOSES	VANDYKE	VANTAGE	VAPULATE
VALPROIC	VAMOOSING	VANDYKED	VANTAGED	VAPULATED
VALSE	VAMOSE	VANDYKES	VANTAGES	VAPULATES
VALSED	VAMOSED	VANDYKING	VANTAGING	VAQUERO
VALSES	VAMOSES	VANE	VANTBRACE	VAQUEROS
VALSING	VAMOSING	VANED	VANTBRASS	VAR
VALUABLE	VAMP	VANELESS	VANTS	VARA
VALUABLES	VAMPED	VANES	VANWARD	VARACTOR
VALUABLY	VAMPER	VANESSA	VAPID	VARACTORS
VALUATE	VAMPERS	VANESSAS	VAPIDER	VARAN
VALUATED	VAMPIER	VANESSID	VAPIDEST	VARANS
VALUATES	VAMPIEST	VANESSIDS	VAPIDITY	VARAS
VALUATING	VAMPING	VANG	VAPIDLY	VARDIES
VALUATION	VAMPINGS	VANGS	VAPIDNESS	VARDY
VALUATOR	VAMPIRE	VANGUARD	VAPOR	VARE
VALUATORS	VAMPIRED	VANGUARDS	VAPORABLE	VAREC
VALUE	VAMPIRES	VANILLA	VAPORED	VARECH
VALUED	VAMPIRIC	VANILLAS	VAPORER	VARECHS
VALUELESS	VAMPIRING	VANILLIC	VAPORERS	VARECS
VALUER	VAMPIRISE	VANILLIN	VAPORETTI	VARES
VALUERS	VAMPIRISH	VANILLINS	VAPORETTO	VAREUSE
VALUES	VAMPIRISM	VANISH	VAPORIFIC	VAREUSES
VALUING	VAMPIRIZE	VANISHED	VAPORING	VARGUENO
VALUTA	VAMPISH	VANISHER	VAPORINGS	VARGUENOS
VALUTAS	VAMPISHLY	VANISHERS	VAPORISE	VARIA
VALVAL	VAMPLATE	VANISHES	VAPORISED	VARIABLE
VALVAR	VAMPLATES	VANISHING	VAPORISER	VARIABLES
VALVASSOR	VAMPS	VANITAS	VAPORISES	VARIABLY
VALVATE	VAMPY	VANITASES	VAPORISH	VARIANCE
VALVE	VAN	VANITIED	VAPORIZE	VARIANCES
VALVED	VANADATE	VANITIES	VAPORIZED	VARIANT
VALVELESS	VANADATES	VANITORY	VAPORIZER	VARIANTS
VALVELET	VANADIATE	VANITY	VAPORIZES	VARIAS
VALVELETS	VANADIC	VANLOAD	VAPORLESS	VARIATE
VALVELIKE	VANADIUM	VANLOADS	VAPORLIKE	VARIATED
VALVES	VANADIUMS	VANMAN	VAPOROUS	VARIATES
VALVING	VANADOUS	VANMEN	VAPORS	VARIATING
VALVULA	VANASPATI	VANNED	VAPORWARE	VARIATION
VALVULAE	VANDA	VANNER	VAPORY	VARIATIVE
VALVULAR	VANDAL	VANNERS	VAPOUR	VARICEAL
VALVULE	VANDALIC	VANNING	VAPOURED	VARICELLA
VALVULES	VANDALISE	VANNINGS	VAPOURER	VARICES
VAMBRACE	VANDALISH	VANPOOL	VAPOURERS	VARICOID
VAMBRACED	VANDALISM	VANPOOLS	VAPOURING	VARICOSE
VAMBRACES	VANDALIZE	VANQUISH	VAPOURISH	VARICOSED

VARICOSES	VARNISH	VASOVAGAL	VAUDOO	VAVASORY
VARICOSIS	VARNISHED	VASSAIL	VAUDOOS	VAVASOUR
VARIED	VARNISHER	VASSAILS	VAUDOUX	VAVASOURS
VARIEDLY	VARNISHES	VASSAL	VAULT	VAVASSOR
VARIEGATE	VARNISHY	VASSALAGE	VAULTAGE	VAVASSORS
VARIER	VAROOM	VASSALESS	VAULTAGES	VAVS
VARIERS	VAROOMED	VASSALISE	VAULTED	VAW
VARIES	VAROOMING	VASSALIZE	VAULTER	VAWARD
VARIETAL	VAROOMS	VASSALLED	VAULTERS	VAWARDS
VARIETALS	VARROA	VASSALRY	VAULTIER	VAWNTIE
VARIETIES	VARROAS	VASSALS	VAULTIEST	VAWNTIER
VARIETY	VARS	VAST	VAULTING	VAWNTIEST
VARIFOCAL	VARSAL	VASTER	VAULTINGS	VAWS
VARIFORM	VARSITIES	VASTEST	VAULTLIKE	VAWTE
VARIOLA	VARSITY	VASTIDITY	VAULTS	VAWTED
VARIOLAR	VARTABED	VASTIER	VAULTY	VAWTES
VARIOLAS	VARTABEDS	VASTIEST	VAUNCE	VAWTING
VARIOLATE	VARUS	VASTITIES	VAUNCED	VEAL
VARIOLE	VARUSES	VASTITUDE	VAUNCES	VEALE
VARIOLES	VARVE	VASTITY	VAUNCING	VEALED
VARIOLITE	VARVED	VASTLY	VAUNT	VEALER
VARIOLOID	VARVEL	VASTNESS	VAUNTAGE	VEALERS
VARIOLOUS	VARVELLED	VASTS	VAUNTAGES	VEALES
VARIORUM	VARVELS	VASTY	VAUNTED	VEALIER
VARIORUMS	VARVES	VAT	VAUNTER	VEALIEST
VARIOUS	VARY	VATABLE	VAUNTERS	VEALING
VARIOUSLY	VARYING	VATFUL	VAUNTERY	VEALS
VARISCITE	VARYINGLY	VATFULS	VAUNTFUL	VEALY
VARISIZED	VARYINGS	VATIC	VAUNTIE	VECTOR
VARISTOR	VAS	VATICAL	VAUNTIER	VECTORED
VARISTORS	VASA	VATICIDE	VAUNTIEST	VECTORIAL
VARITYPE	VASAL	VATICIDES	VAUNTING	VECTORING
VARITYPED	VASCULA	VATICINAL	VAUNTINGS	VECTORISE
VARITYPES	VASCULAR	VATMAN	VAUNTS	VECTORIZE
VARIX	VASCULUM	VATMEN	VAUNTY	VECTORS
VARLET	VASCULUMS	VATS	VAURIEN	VEDALIA
VARLETESS	VASE	VATTED	VAURIENS	VEDALIAS
VARLETRY	VASECTOMY	VATTER	VAUS	VEDETTE
VARLETS	VASELIKE	VATTERS	VAUT	VEDETTES
VARLETTO	VASELINE	VATTING	VAUTE	VEDUTA
VARLETTOS	VASELINES	VATU	VAUTED	VEDUTE
VARMENT	VASES	VATUS	VAUTES	VEDUTISTA
VARMENTS	VASIFORM	VAU	VAUTING	VEDUTISTI
VARMINT	VASOMOTOR	VAUCH	VAUTS	VEE
VARMINTS	VASOSPASM	VAUCHED	VAV	VEEJAY
VARNA	VASOTOCIN	VAUCHES	VAVASOR	VEEJAYS
VARNAS	VASOTOMY	VAUCHING	VAVASORS	VEENA

V

VEENAS	VEGIES	VEINULETS	VELOCITY	VENDERS
VEEP	VEGO	VEINY	VELODROME	VENDETTA
VEEPEE	VEGOS	VELA	VELOUR	VENDETTAS
VEEPEES	VEHEMENCE	VELAMEN	VELOURS	VENDEUSE
VEEPS	VEHEMENCY	VELAMINA	VELOUTE	VENDEUSES
VEER	VEHEMENT	VELAR	VELOUTES	VENDIBLE
VEERED	VEHICLE	VELARIA	VELOUTINE	VENDIBLES
VEERIES	VEHICLES	VELARIC	VELSKOEN	VENDIBLY
VEERING	VEHICULAR	VELARISE	VELSKOENS	VENDING
VEERINGLY	VEHM	VELARISED	VELUM	VENDINGS
VEERINGS	VEHME	VELARISES	VELURE	VENDIS
VEERS	VEHMIC	VELARIUM	VELURED	VENDISES
VEERY	VEHMIQUE	VELARIZE	VELURES	VENDISS
VEES	VEIL	VELARIZED	VELURING	VENDISSES
VEG	VEILED	VELARIZES	VELVERET	VENDITION
VEGA	VEILEDLY	VELARS	VELVERETS	VENDOR
VEGAN	VEILER	VELATE	VELVET	VENDORS
VEGANIC	VEILERS	VELATED	VELVETED	VENDS
VEGANISM	VEILIER	VELATURA	VELVETEEN	VENDUE
VEGANISMS	VEILIEST	VELATURAS	VELVETIER	VENDUES
VEGANS	VEILING	VELCRO	VELVETING	VENEER
VEGAS	VEILINGS	VELCROS	VELVETS	VENEERED
VEGELATE	VEILLESS	VELD	VELVETY	VENEERER
VEGELATES	VEILLEUSE	VELDS	VENA	VENEERERS
VEGEMITE	VEILLIKE	VELDSKOEN	VENAE	VENEERING
VEGEMITES	VEILS	VELDT	VENAL	VENEERS
VEGES	VEILY	VELDTS	VENALITY	VENEFIC
VEGETABLE	VEIN	VELE	VENALLY	VENEFICAL
VEGETABLY	VEINAL	VELES	VENATIC	VENENATE
VEGETAL	VEINED	VELETA	VENATICAL	VENENATED
VEGETALLY	VEINER	VELETAS	VENATION	VENENATES
VEGETALS	VEINERS	VELIGER	VENATIONS	VENENE
VEGETANT	VEINIER	VELIGERS	VENATOR	VENENES
VEGETATE	VEINIEST	VELITES	VENATORS	VENENOSE
VEGETATED	VEINING	VELL	VEND	VENERABLE
VEGETATES	VEININGS	VELLEITY	VENDABLE	VENERABLY
VEGETE	VEINLESS	VELLENAGE	VENDABLES	VENERATE
VEGETIST	VEINLET	VELLET	VENDACE	VENERATED
VEGETISTS	VEINLETS	VELLETS	VENDACES	VENERATES
VEGETIVE	VEINLIKE	VELLICATE	VENDAGE	VENERATOR
VEGETIVES	VEINOUS	VELLON	VENDAGES	VENEREAL
VEGGED	VEINS	VELLONS	VENDANGE	VENEREAN
VEGGES	VEINSTONE	VELLS	VENDANGES	VENEREANS
VEGGIE	VEINSTUFF	VELLUM	VENDED	VENEREOUS
VEGGIES	VEINULE	VELLUMS	VENDEE	VENERER
VEGGING	VEINULES	VELLUS	VENDEES	VENERERS
VEGIE	VEINULET	VELOCE	VENDER	VENERIES

VENERY	VENOMS	VENTURERS	VERBENAS	VERDURED
VENETIAN	VENOSE	VENTURES	VERBERATE	VERDURES
VENETIANS	VENOSITY	VENTURI	VERBIAGE	VERDUROUS
VENEWE	VENOUS	VENTURING	VERBIAGES	VERECUND
VENEWES	VENOUSLY	VENTURIS	VERBICIDE	VERGE
VENEY	VENT	VENTUROUS	VERBID	VERGED
VENEYS	VENTAGE	VENUE	VERBIDS	VERGENCE
VENGE	VENTAGES	VENUES	VERBIFIED	VERGENCES
VENGEABLE	VENTAIL	VENULAR	VERBIFIES	VERGENCY
VENGEABLY	VENTAILE	VENULE	VERBIFY	VERGER
VENGEANCE	VENTAILES	VENULES	VERBILE	VERGERS
VENGED	VENTAILS	VENULOSE	VERBILES	VERGES
VENGEFUL	VENTANA	VENULOUS	VERBING	VERGING
VENGEMENT	VENTANAS	VENUS	VERBINGS	VERGLAS
VENGER	VENTAYLE	VENUSES	VERBLESS	VERGLASES
VENGERS	VENTAYLES	VENVILLE	VERBOSE	VERIDIC
VENGES	VENTED	VENVILLES	VERBOSELY	VERIDICAL
VENGING	VENTER	VERA	VERBOSER	VERIER
VENIAL	VENTERS	VERACIOUS	VERBOSEST	VERIEST
VENIALITY	VENTIDUCT	VERACITY	VERBOSITY	VERIFIED
VENIALLY	VENTIFACT	VERANDA	VERBOTEN	VERIFIER
VENIDIUM	VENTIGE	VERANDAED	VERBS	VERIFIERS
VENIDIUMS	VENTIGES	VERANDAH	VERD	VERIFIES
VENIN	VENTIL	VERANDAHS	VERDANCY	VERIFY
VENINE	VENTILATE	VERANDAS	VERDANT	VERIFYING
VENINES	VENTILS	VERAPAMIL	VERDANTLY	VERILY
VENINS	VENTING	VERATRIA	VERDELHO	VERISM
VENIRE	VENTINGS	VERATRIAS	VERDELHOS	VERISMO
VENIREMAN	VENTLESS	VERATRIN	VERDERER	VERISMOS
VENIREMEN	VENTOSE	VERATRINE	VERDERERS	VERISMS
VENIRES	VENTOSITY	VERATRINS	VERDEROR	VERIST
VENISON	VENTOUSE	VERATRUM	VERDERORS	VERISTIC
VENISONS	VENTOUSES	VERATRUMS	VERDET	VERISTS
VENITE	VENTRAL	VERB	VERDETS	VERITABLE
VENITES	VENTRALLY	VERBAL	VERDICT	VERITABLY
VENNEL	VENTRALS	VERBALISE	VERDICTS	VERITAS
VENNELS	VENTRE	VERBALISM	VERDIGRIS	VERITATES
VENOGRAM	VENTRED	VERBALIST	VERDIN	VERITE
VENOGRAMS	VENTRES	VERBALITY	VERDINS	VERITES
VENOLOGY	VENTRICLE	VERBALIZE	VERDIT	VERITIES
VENOM	VENTRING	VERBALLED	VERDITE	VERITY
VENOMED	VENTRINGS	VERBALLY	VERDITER	VERJUICE
VENOMER	VENTROUS	VERBALS	VERDITERS	VERJUICED
VENOMERS	VENTS	VERBARIAN	VERDITES	VERJUICES
VENOMING	VENTURE	VERBASCUM	VERDITS	VERKRAMP
VENOMLESS	VENTURED	VERBATIM	VERDOY	VERLAN
VENOMOUS	VENTURER	VERBENA	VERDURE	VERLANS

VERLIG	VERNIX	VERSIN	VERVELLED	VESTIBULA
VERLIGTE	VERNIXES	VERSINE	VERVELS	VESTIBULE
VERLIGTES	VERONAL	VERSINES	VERVEN	VESTIGE
VERMAL	VERONALS	VERSING	VERVENS	VESTIGES
VERMEIL	VERONICA	VERSINGS	VERVES	VESTIGIA
VERMEILED	VERONICAS	VERSINS	VERVET	VESTIGIAL
VERMEILLE	VERONIQUE	VERSION	VERVETS	VESTIGIUM
VERMEILS	VERQUERE	VERSIONAL	VERY	VESTIMENT
VERMELL	VERQUERES	VERSIONER	VESICA	VESTING
VERMELLS	VERQUIRE	VERSIONS	VESICAE	VESTINGS
VERMES	VERQUIRES	VERSO	VESICAL	VESTITURE
VERMIAN	VERRA	VERSOS	VESICANT	VESTLESS
VERMICIDE	VERREL	VERST	VESICANTS	VESTLIKE
VERMICULE	VERRELS	VERSTE	VESICATE	VESTMENT
VERMIFORM	VERREY	VERSTES	VESICATED	VESTMENTS
VERMIFUGE	VERRUCA	VERSTS	VESICATES	VESTRAL
VERMIL	VERRUCAE	VERSUS	VESICLE	VESTRIES
VERMILIES	VERRUCAS	VERSUTE	VESICLES	VESTRY
VERMILION	VERRUCOSE	VERT	VESICULA	VESTRYMAN
VERMILLED	VERRUCOUS	VERTEBRA	VESICULAE	VESTRYMEN
VERMILS	VERRUGA	VERTEBRAE	VESICULAR	VESTS
VERMILY	VERRUGAS	VERTEBRAL	VESPA	VESTURAL
VERMIN	VERRY	VERTEBRAS	VESPAS	VESTURE
VERMINATE	VERS	VERTED	VESPER	VESTURED
VERMINED	VERSAL	VERTEX	VESPERAL	VESTURER
VERMINOUS	VERSALS	VERTEXES	VESPERALS	VESTURERS
VERMINS	VERSANT	VERTICAL	VESPERS	VESTURES
VERMINY	VERSANTS	VERTICALS	VESPIARY	VESTURING
VERMIS	VERSATILE	VERTICES	VESPID	VESUVIAN
VERMOULU	VERSE	VERTICIL	VESPIDS	VESUVIANS
VERMOUTH	VERSED	VERTICILS	VESPINE	VET
VERMOUTHS	VERSELET	VERTICITY	VESPOID	VETCH
VERMUTH	VERSELETS	VERTIGO	VESSAIL	VETCHES
VERMUTHS	VERSEMAN	VERTIGOES	VESSAILS	VETCHIER
VERNACLE	VERSEMEN	VERTIGOS	VESSEL	VETCHIEST
VERNACLES	VERSER	VERTING	VESSELED	VETCHLING
VERNAL	VERSERS	VERTIPORT	VESSELS	VETCHY
VERNALISE	VERSES	VERTS	VEST	VETERAN
VERNALITY	VERSET	VERTU	VESTA	VETERANS
VERNALIZE	VERSETS	VERTUE	VESTAL	VETIVER
VERNALLY	VERSICLE	VERTUES	VESTALLY	VETIVERS
VERNANT	VERSICLES	VERTUOUS	VESTALS	VETIVERT
VERNATION	VERSIFIED	VERTUS	VESTAS	VETIVERTS
VERNICLE	VERSIFIER	VERVAIN	VESTED	VETKOEK
VERNICLES	VERSIFIES	VERVAINS	VESTEE	VETKOEKS
VERNIER	VERSIFORM	VERVE	VESTEES	VETO
VERNIERS	VERSIFY	VERVEL	VESTIARY	VETOED

VETOER	VIALED	VIBRATOR	VICHIES	VIDEODISC
VETOERS	VIALFUL	VIBRATORS	VICHY	VIDEODISK
VETOES	VIALFULS	VIBRATORY	VICIATE	VIDEOED
VETOING	VIALING	VIBRATOS	VICIATED	VIDEOFIT
VETOLESS	VIALLED	VIBRIO	VICIATES	VIDEOFITS
VETS	VIALLING	VIBRIOID	VICIATING	VIDEOGRAM
VETTED	VIALS	VIBRION	VICINAGE	VIDEOING
VETTER	VIAMETER	VIBRIONIC	VICINAGES	VIDEOLAND
VETTERS	VIAMETERS	VIBRIONS	VICINAL	VIDEOS
VETTING	VIAND	VIBRIOS	VICING	VIDEOTAPE
VETTINGS	VIANDS	VIBRIOSES	VICINITY	VIDEOTEX
VETTURA	VIAS	VIBRIOSIS	VICIOSITY	VIDEOTEXT
VETTURAS	VIATIC	VIBRISSA	VICIOUS	VIDETTE
VETTURINI	VIATICA	VIBRISSAE	VICIOUSLY	VIDETTES
VETTURINO	VIATICAL	VIBRISSAL	VICOMTE	VIDICON
VEX	VIATICALS	VIBRONIC	VICOMTES	VIDICONS
VEXATION	VIATICUM	VIBS	VICTIM	VIDIMUS
VEXATIONS	VIATICUMS	VIBURNUM	VICTIMISE	VIDIMUSES
VEXATIOUS	VIATOR	VIBURNUMS	VICTIMIZE	VIDS
VEXATORY	VIATORES	VICAR	VICTIMS	VIDUAGE
VEXED	VIATORIAL	VICARAGE	VICTOR	VIDUAGES
VEXEDLY	VIATORS	VICARAGES	VICTORESS	VIDUAL
VEXEDNESS	VIBE	VICARATE	VICTORIA	VIDUITIES
VEXER	VIBES	VICARATES	VICTORIAS	VIDUITY
VEXERS	VIBEX	VICARESS	VICTORIES	VIDUOUS
VEXES	VIBEY	VICARIAL	VICTORINE	VIE
VEXIL	VIBICES	VICARIANT	VICTORS	VIED
VEXILLA	VIBIER	VICARIATE	VICTORY	VIELLE
VEXILLAR	VIBIEST	VICARIES	VICTRESS	VIELLES
VEXILLARY	VIBIST	VICARIOUS	VICTRIX	VIENNA
VEXILLATE	VIBISTS	VICARLY	VICTRIXES	VIER
VEXILLUM	VIBRACULA	VICARS	VICTUAL	VIERS
VEXILS	VIBRAHARP	VICARSHIP	VICTUALED	VIES
VEXING	VIBRANCE	VICARY	VICTUALER	VIEW
VEXINGLY	VIBRANCES	VICE	VICTUALS	VIEWABLE
VEXINGS	VIBRANCY	VICED	VICUGNA	VIEWDATA
VEXT	VIBRANT	VICEGERAL	VICUGNAS	VIEWDATAS
VEZIR	VIBRANTLY	VICELESS	VICUNA	VIEWED
VEZIRS	VIBRANTS	VICELIKE	VICUNAS	VIEWER
VIA	VIBRATE	VICENARY	VID	VIEWERS
VIABILITY	VIBRATED	VICENNIAL	VIDAME	VIEWIER
VIABLE	VIBRATES	VICEREGAL	VIDAMES	VIEWIEST
VIABLY	VIBRATILE	VICEREINE	VIDE	VIEWINESS
VIADUCT	VIBRATING	VICEROY	VIDELICET	VIEWING
VIADUCTS	VIBRATION	VICEROYS	VIDENDA	VIEWINGS
VIAE	VIBRATIVE	VICES	VIDENDUM	VIEWLESS
VIAL	VIBRATO	VICESIMAL	VIDEO	VIEWLY

VIEWPHONE	VILELY	VILLIACO	VINER	VIOL
VIEWPOINT	VILENESS	VILLIACOS	VINERIES	VIOLA
VIEWS	VILER	VILLIAGO	VINERS	VIOLABLE
VIEWY	VILEST	VILLIAGOS	VINERY	VIOLABLY
VIFDA	VILIACO	VILLIFORM	VINES	VIOLAS
VIFDAS	VILIACOES	VILLOSE	VINEW	VIOLATE
VIG	VILIACOS	VILLOSITY	VINEWED	VIOLATED
VIGA	VILIAGO	VILLOUS	VINEWING	VIOLATER
VIGAS	VILIAGOES	VILLOUSLY	VINEWS	VIOLATERS
VIGESIMAL	VILIAGOS	VILLS	VINEYARD	VIOLATES
VIGIA	VILIFIED	VILLUS	VINEYARDS	VIOLATING
VIGIAS	VILIFIER	VIM	VINIC	VIOLATION
VIGIL	VILIFIERS	VIMANA	VINIER	VIOLATIVE
VIGILANCE	VILIFIES	VIMANAS	VINIEST	VIOLATOR
VIGILANT	VILIFY	VIMEN	VINIFERA	VIOLATORS
VIGILANTE	VILIFYING	VIMINA	VINIFERAS	VIOLD
VIGILS	VILIPEND	VIMINAL	VINIFIED	VIOLENCE
VIGNERON	VILIPENDS	VIMINEOUS	VINIFIES	VIOLENCES
VIGNERONS	VILL	VIMS	VINIFY	VIOLENT
VIGNETTE	VILLA	VIN	VINIFYING	VIOLENTED
VIGNETTED	VILLADOM	VINA	VINING	VIOLENTLY
VIGNETTER	VILLADOMS	VINACEOUS	VINO	VIOLENTS
VIGNETTES	VILLAE	VINAL	VINOLENT	VIOLER
VIGOR	VILLAGE	VINALS	VINOLOGY	VIOLERS
VIGORISH	VILLAGER	VINAS	VINOS	VIOLET
VIGORO	VILLAGERS	VINASSE	VINOSITY	VIOLETS
VIGOROS	VILLAGERY	VINASSES	VINOUS	VIOLIN
VIGOROSO	VILLAGES	VINCA	VINOUSLY	VIOLINIST
VIGOROUS	VILLAGIO	VINCAS	VINS	VIOLINS
VIGORS	VILLAGIOS	VINCIBLE	VINT	VIOLIST
VIGOUR	VILLAGREE	VINCIBLY	VINTAGE	VIOLISTS
VIGOURS	VILLAIN	VINCULA	VINTAGED	VIOLONE
VIGS	VILLAINS	VINCULUM	VINTAGER	VIOLONES
VIHARA	VILLAINY	VINCULUMS	VINTAGERS	VIOLS
VIHARAS	VILLAN	VINDALOO	VINTAGES	VIOMYCIN
VIHUELA	VILLANAGE	VINDALOOS	VINTAGING	VIOMYCINS
VIHUELAS	VILLANIES	VINDEMIAL	VINTED	VIOSTEROL
VIKING	VILLANOUS	VINDICATE	VINTING	VIPER
VIKINGISM	VILLANS	VINE	VINTNER	VIPERFISH
VIKINGS	VILLANY	VINEAL	VINTNERS	VIPERINE
VILAYET	VILLAR	VINED	VINTRIES	VIPERISH
VILAYETS	VILLAS	VINEGAR	VINTRY	VIPEROUS
VILD	VILLATIC	VINEGARED	VINTS	VIPERS
VILDE	VILLEIN	VINEGARS	VINY	VIRAEMIA
VILDLY	VILLEINS	VINEGARY	VINYL	VIRAEMIAS
VILDNESS	VILLENAGE	VINELESS	VINYLIC	VIRAEMIC
VILE	VILLI	VINELIKE	VINYLS	VIRAGO

VIRAGOES	VIRGULATE	VIRTUOSAS	VISCOSES	VISITEES
VIRAGOISH	VIRGULE	VIRTUOSE	VISCOSITY	VISITER
VIRAGOS	VIRGULES	VIRTUOSI	VISCOUNT	VISITERS
VIRAL	VIRICIDAL	VIRTUOSIC	VISCOUNTS	VISITES
VIRALLY	VIRICIDE	VIRTUOSO	VISCOUNTY	VISITING
VIRANDA	VIRICIDES	VIRTUOSOS	VISCOUS	VISITINGS
VIRANDAS	VIRID	VIRTUOUS	VISCOUSLY	VISITOR
VIRANDO	VIRIDIAN	VIRTUS	VISCUM	VISITORS
VIRANDOS	VIRIDIANS	VIRUCIDAL	VISCUMS	VISITRESS
VIRE	VIRIDITE	VIRUCIDE	VISCUS	VISITS
VIRED	VIRIDITES	VIRUCIDES	VISE	VISIVE
VIRELAI	VIRIDITY	VIRULENCE	VISED	VISNE
VIRELAIS	VIRILE	VIRULENCY	VISEED	VISNES
VIRELAY	VIRILELY	VIRULENT	VISEING	VISNOMIE
VIRELAYS	VIRILISE	VIRUS	VISELIKE	VISNOMIES
VIREMENT	VIRILISED	VIRUSES	VISES	VISNOMY
VIREMENTS	VIRILISES	VIRUSLIKE	VISHING	VISON
VIREMIA	VIRILISM	VIRUSOID	VISHINGS	VISONS
VIREMIAS	VIRILISMS	VIRUSOIDS	VISIBLE	VISOR
VIREMIC	VIRILITY	VIS	VISIBLES	VISORED
VIRENT	VIRILIZE	VISA	VISIBLY	VISORING
VIREO	VIRILIZED	VISAED	VISIE	VISORLESS
VIREONINE	VIRILIZES	VISAGE	VISIED	VISORS
VIREOS	VIRILOCAL	VISAGED	VISIEING	VISTA
VIRES	VIRING	VISAGES	VISIER	VISTAED
VIRESCENT	VIRINO	VISAGIST	VISIERS	VISTAING
VIRETOT	VIRINOS	VISAGISTE	VISIES	VISTAL
VIRETOTS	VIRION	VISAGISTS	VISILE	VISTALESS
VIRGA	VIRIONS	VISAING	VISILES	VISTAS
VIRGAS	VIRL	VISARD	VISING	VISTO
VIRGATE	VIRLS	VISARDS	VISION	VISTOS
VIRGATES	VIROGENE	VISAS	VISIONAL	VISUAL
VIRGE	VIROGENES	VISCACHA	VISIONARY	VISUALISE
VIRGER	VIROID	VISCACHAS	VISIONED	VISUALIST
VIRGERS	VIROIDS	VISCARIA	VISIONER	VISUALITY
VIRGES	VIROLOGIC	VISCARIAS	VISIONERS	VISUALIZE
VIRGIN	VIROLOGY	VISCERA	VISIONING	VISUALLY
VIRGINAL	VIROSE	VISCERAL	VISIONIST	VISUALS
VIRGINALS	VIROSES	VISCERATE	VISIONS	VITA
VIRGINED	VIROSIS	VISCID	VISIT	VITACEOUS
VIRGINIA	VIROUS	VISCIDITY	VISITABLE	VITAE
VIRGINIAS	VIRTU	VISCIDLY	VISITANT	VITAL
VIRGINING	VIRTUAL	VISCIN	VISITANTS	VITALISE
VIRGINITY	VIRTUALLY	VISCINS	VISITATOR	VITALISED
VIRGINIUM	VIRTUE	VISCOID	VISITE	VITALISER
VIRGINLY	VIRTUES	VISCOIDAL	VISITED	VITALISES
VIRGINS	VIRTUOSA	VISCOSE	VISITEE	VITALISM

VITALISMS	VITIOUS	VIVATS	VIZIED	VOCALICS
VITALIST	VITRAGE	VIVDA	VIZIER	VOCALION
VITALISTS	VITRAGES	VIVDAS	VIZIERATE	VOCALIONS
VITALITY	VITRAIL	VIVE	VIZIERIAL	VOCALISE
VITALIZE	VITRAIN	VIVELY	VIZIERS	VOCALISED
VITALIZED	VITRAINS	VIVENCIES	VIZIES	VOCALISER
VITALIZER	VITRAUX	VIVENCY	VIZIR	VOCALISES
VITALIZES	VITREOUS	VIVER	VIZIRATE	VOCALISM
VITALLY	VITREUM	VIVERRA	VIZIRATES	VOCALISMS
VITALNESS	VITREUMS	VIVERRAS	VIZIRIAL	VOCALIST
VITALS	VITRIC	VIVERRID	VIZIRS	VOCALISTS
VITAMER	VITRICS	VIVERRIDS	VIZIRSHIP	VOCALITY
VITAMERS	VITRIFIED	VIVERRINE	VIZOR	VOCALIZE
VITAMIN	VITRIFIES	VIVERS	VIZORED	VOCALIZED
VITAMINE	VITRIFORM	VIVES	VIZORING	VOCALIZER
VITAMINES	VITRIFY	VIVIANITE	VIZORLESS	VOCALIZES
VITAMINIC	VITRINE	VIVID	VIZORS	VOCALLY
VITAMINS	VITRINES	VIVIDER	VIZSLA	VOCALNESS
VITAS	VITRIOL	VIVIDEST	VIZSLAS	VOCALS
VITASCOPE	VITRIOLED	VIVIDITY	VIZY	VOCATION
VITATIVE	VITRIOLIC	VIVIDLY	VIZYING	VOCATIONS
VITE	VITRIOLS	VIVIDNESS	VIZZIE	VOCATIVE
VITELLARY	VITTA	VIVIFIC	VIZZIED	VOCATIVES
VITELLI	VITTAE	VIVIFIED	VIZZIEING	VOCES
VITELLIN	VITTATE	VIVIFIER	VIZZIES	VOCODER
VITELLINE	VITTLE	VIVIFIERS	VLEI	VOCODERS
VITELLINS	VITTLED	VIVIFIES	VLEIS	VOCULAR
VITELLUS	VITTLES	VIVIFY	VLIES	VOCULE
VITESSE	VITTLING	VIVIFYING	VLOG	VOCULES
VITESSES	VITULAR	VIVIPARA	VLOGGER	VODCAST
VITEX	VITULINE	VIVIPARY	VLOGGERS	VODCASTED
VITEXES	VIVA	VIVISECT	VLOGGING	VODCASTER
VITIABLE	VIVACE	VIVISECTS	VLOGGINGS	VODCASTS
VITIATE	VIVACES	VIVO	VLOGS	VODDIES
VITIATED	VIVACIOUS	VIVRES	VLY	VODDY
VITIATES	VIVACITY	VIXEN	VOAR	VODKA
VITIATING	VIVAED	VIXENISH	VOARS	VODKAS
VITIATION	VIVAING	VIXENLY	VOCAB	VODOU
VITIATOR	VIVAMENTE	VIXENS	VOCABLE	VODOUN
VITIATORS	VIVANDIER	VIZAMENT	VOCABLES	VODOUNS
VITICETA	VIVARIA	VIZAMENTS	VOCABLY	VODOUS
VITICETUM	VIVARIES	VIZARD	VOCABS	VODUN
VITICIDE	VIVARIUM	VIZARDED	VOCABULAR	VODUNS
VITICIDES	VIVARIUMS	VIZARDING	VOCAL	VOE
VITILIGO	VIVARY	VIZARDS	VOCALESE	VOEMA
VITILIGOS	VIVAS	VIZCACHA	VOCALESES	VOEMAS
VITIOSITY	VIVAT	VIZCACHAS	VOCALIC	VOERTSAK

VOERTSEK	VOILES	VOLITION	VOLUMINAL	VOMITINGS
VOES	VOIP	VOLITIONS	VOLUMING	VOMITIVE
VOETSAK	VOIPS	VOLITIVE	VOLUMISE	VOMITIVES
VOETSEK	VOISINAGE	VOLITIVES	VOLUMISED	VOMITO
VOGIE	VOITURE	VOLK	VOLUMISER	VOMITORIA
VOGIER	VOITURES	VOLKS	VOLUMISES	VOMITORY
VOGIEST	VOITURIER	VOLKSLIED	VOLUMIST	VOMITOS
VOGUE	VOIVODE	VOLKSRAAD	VOLUMISTS	VOMITOUS
VOGUED	VOIVODES	VOLLEY	VOLUMIZE	VOMITS
VOGUEING	VOL	VOLLEYED	VOLUMIZED	VOMITUS
VOGUEINGS	VOLA	VOLLEYER	VOLUMIZER	VOMITUSES
VOGUER	VOLABLE	VOLLEYERS	VOLUMIZES	VONGOLE
VOGUERS	VOLAE	VOLLEYING	VOLUNTARY	VOODOO
VOGUES	VOLAGE	VOLLEYS	VOLUNTEER	VOODOOED
VOGUEY	VOLANT	VOLOST	VOLUSPA	VOODOOING
VOGUIER	VOLANTE	VOLOSTS	VOLUSPAS	VOODOOISM
VOGUIEST	VOLANTES	VOLPINO	VOLUTE	VOODOOIST
VOGUING	VOLAR	VOLPINOS	VOLUTED	VOODOOS
VOGUINGS	VOLARIES	VOLPLANE	VOLUTES	VOORKAMER
VOGUISH	VOLARY	VOLPLANED	VOLUTIN	VOORSKOT
VOGUISHLY	VOLATIC	VOLPLANES	VOLUTINS	VOORSKOTS
VOICE	VOLATILE	VOLS	VOLUTION	VOR
VOICED	VOLATILES	VOLT	VOLUTIONS	VORACIOUS
VOICEFUL	VOLCANIAN	VOLTA	VOLUTOID	VORACITY
VOICELESS	VOLCANIC	VOLTAGE	VOLVA	VORAGO
VOICEMAIL	VOLCANICS	VOLTAGES	VOLVAE	VORAGOES
VOICEOVER	VOLCANISE	VOLTAIC	VOLVAS	VORANT
VOICER	VOLCANISM	VOLTAISM	VOLVATE	VORLAGE
VOICERS	VOLCANIST	VOLTAISMS	VOLVE	VORLAGES
VOICES	VOLCANIZE	VOLTE	VOLVED	VORPAL
VOICING	VOLCANO	VOLTED	VOLVES	VORRED
VOICINGS	VOLCANOES	VOLTES	VOLVING	VORRING
VOID	VOLCANOS	VOLTI	VOLVOX	VORS
VOIDABLE	VOLE	VOLTIGEUR	VOLVOXES	VORTEX
VOIDANCE	VOLED	VOLTING	VOLVULI	VORTEXES
VOIDANCES	VOLENS	VOLTINISM	VOLVULUS	VORTICAL
VOIDED	VOLERIES	VOLTMETER	VOMER	VORTICES
VOIDEE	VOLERY	VOLTS	VOMERINE	VORTICISM
VOIDEES	VOLES	VOLUBIL	VOMERS	VORTICIST
VOIDER	VOLET	VOLUBLE	VOMICA	VORTICITY
VOIDERS	VOLETS	VOLUBLY	VOMICAE	VORTICOSE
VOIDING	VOLING	VOLUCRINE	VOMICAS	VOSTRO
VOIDINGS	VOLITANT	VOLUME	VOMIT	VOTABLE
VOIDNESS	VOLITATE	VOLUMED	VOMITED	VOTARESS
VOIDS	VOLITATED	VOLUMES	VOMITER	VOTARIES
VOILA	VOLITATES	VOLUMETER	VOMITERS	VOTARIST
VOILE	VOLITIENT	VOLUMETRY	VOMITING	VOTARISTS

VOTARY	VOUGES	VOYAGED	VUGH	VULPICIDE
VOTE	VOULGE	VOYAGER	VUGHIER	VULPINE
VOTEABLE	VOULGES	VOYAGERS	VUGHIEST	VULPINISM
VOTED	VOULU	VOYAGES	VUGHS	VULPINITE
VOTEEN	VOUSSOIR	VOYAGEUR	VUGHY	VULSELLA
VOTEENS	VOUSSOIRS	VOYAGEURS	VUGS	VULSELLAE
VOTELESS	VOUTSAFE	VOYAGING	VULCAN	VULSELLUM
VOTER	VOUTSAFED	VOYEUR	VULCANIAN	VULTURE
VOTERS	VOUTSAFES	VOYEURISM	VULCANIC	VULTURES
VOTES	VOUVRAY	VOYEURS	VULCANISE	VULTURINE
VOTING	VOUVRAYS	VOZHD	VULCANISM	VULTURISH
VOTINGS	VOW	VOZHDS	VULCANIST	VULTURISM
VOTIVE	VOWED	VRAIC	VULCANITE	VULTURN
VOTIVELY	VOWEL	VRAICKER	VULCANIZE	VULTURNS
VOTIVES	VOWELISE	VRAICKERS	VULCANS	VULTUROUS
VOTRESS	VOWELISED	VRAICKING	VULGAR	VULVA
VOTRESSES	VOWELISES	VRAICS	VULGARER	VULVAE
VOUCH	VOWELIZE	VRIL	VULGAREST	VULVAL
VOUCHED	VOWELIZED	VRILS	VULGARIAN	VULVAR
VOUCHEE	VOWELIZES	VROOM	VULGARISE	VULVAS
VOUCHEES	VOWELLED	VROOMED	VULGARISM	VULVATE
VOUCHER	VOWELLESS	VROOMING	VULGARITY	VULVIFORM
VOUCHERED	VOWELLING	VROOMS	VULGARIZE	VULVITIS
VOUCHERS	VOWELLY	VROT	VULGARLY	VUM
VOUCHES	VOWELS	VROU	VULGARS	VUMMED
VOUCHING	VOWER	VROUS	VULGATE	VUMMING
VOUCHSAFE	VOWERS	VROUW	VULGATES	VUMS
VOUDON	VOWESS	VROUWS	VULGO	VUTTIER
VOUDONS	VOWESSES	VROW	VULGUS	VUTTIEST
VOUDOU	VOWING	VROWS	VULGUSES	VUTTY
VOUDOUED	VOWLESS	VUG	VULN	VUVUZELA
VOUDOUING	VOWS	VUGG	VULNED	VUVUZELAS
VOUDOUN	VOX	VUGGIER	VULNERARY	VYING
VOUDOUNS	VOXEL	VUGGIEST	VULNERATE	VYINGLY
VOUDOUS	VOXELS	VUGGS	VULNING	VYINGS
VOUGE	VOYAGE	VUGGY	VULNS	

W

WAAC	WADDLE	WAENESS	WAGERER	WAGONLOAD
WAACS	WADDLED	WAENESSES	WAGERERS	WAGONS
WAB	WADDLER	WAES	WAGERING	WAGS
WABAIN	WADDLERS	WAESOME	WAGERS	WAGSOME
WABAINS	WADDLES	WAESUCK	WAGES	WAGTAIL
WABBIT	WADDLIER	WAESUCKS	WAGGA	WAGTAILS
WABBLE	WADDLIEST	WAFER	WAGGAS	WAGYU
WABBLED	WADDLING	WAFERED	WAGGED	WAGYUS
WABBLER	WADDLY	WAFERING	WAGGER	WAHCONDA
WABBLERS	WADDS	WAFERS	WAGGERIES	WAHCONDAS
WABBLES	WADDY	WAFERY	WAGGERS	WAHINE
WABBLIER	WADDYING	WAFF	WAGGERY	WAHINES
WABBLIEST	WADE	WAFFED	WAGGING	WAHOO
WABBLING	WADEABLE	WAFFIE	WAGGISH	WAHOOS
WABBLY	WADED	WAFFIES	WAGGISHLY	WAI
WABOOM	WADER	WAFFING	WAGGLE	WAIATA
WABOOMS	WADERS	WAFFLE	WAGGLED	WAIATAS
WABS	WADES	WAFFLED	WAGGLER	WAID
WABSTER	WADI	WAFFLER	WAGGLERS	WAIDE
WABSTERS	WADIES	WAFFLERS	WAGGLES	WAIF
WACK	WADING	WAFFLES	WAGGLIER	WAIFED
WACKE	WADINGS	WAFFLIER	WAGGLIEST	WAIFING
WACKER	WADIS	WAFFLIEST	WAGGLING	WAIFISH
WACKERS	WADMAAL	WAFFLING	WAGGLY	WAIFLIKE
WACKES	WADMAALS	WAFFLINGS	WAGGON	WAIFS
WACKEST	WADMAL	WAFFLY	WAGGONED	WAIFT
WACKIER	WADMALS	WAFFS	WAGGONER	WAIFTS
WACKIEST	WADMEL	WAFT	WAGGONERS	WAIL
WACKILY	WADMELS	WAFTAGE	WAGGONING	WAILED
WACKINESS	WADMOL	WAFTAGES	WAGGONS	WAILER
WACKO	WADMOLL	WAFTED	WAGHALTER	WAILERS
WACKOS	WADMOLLS	WAFTER	WAGING	WAILFUL
WACKS	WADMOLS	WAFTERS	WAGMOIRE	WAILFULLY
WACKY	WADS	WAFTING	WAGMOIRES	WAILING
WAD	WADSET	WAFTINGS	WAGON	WAILINGLY
WADABLE	WADSETS	WAFTS	WAGONAGE	WAILINGS
WADD	WADSETT	WAFTURE	WAGONAGES	WAILS
WADDED	WADSETTED	WAFTURES	WAGONED	WAILSOME
WADDER	WADSETTER	WAG	WAGONER	WAIN
WADDERS	WADSETTS	WAGE	WAGONERS	WAINAGE
WADDIE	WADT	WAGED	WAGONETTE	WAINAGES
WADDIED	WADTS	WAGELESS	WAGONFUL	WAINED
WADDIES	WADY	WAGENBOOM	WAGONFULS	WAINING
WADDING	WAE	WAGER	WAGONING	WAINS
WADDINGS	WAEFUL	WAGERED	WAGONLESS	WAINSCOT

WAINSCOTS	WAIVING	WALE	WALLAROOS	WALTZ
WAIR	WAIVODE	WALED	WALLAS	WALTZED
WAIRED	WAIVODES	WALER	WALLBOARD	WALTZER
WAIRING	WAIWODE	WALERS	WALLCHART	WALTZERS
WAIRS	WAIWODES	WALES	WALLED	WALTZES
WAIRSH	WAKA	WALI	WALLER	WALTZING
WAIRSHER	WAKAME	WALIER	WALLERS	WALTZINGS
WAIRSHEST	WAKAMES	WALIES	WALLET	WALTZLIKE
WAIRUA	WAKANDA	WALIEST	WALLETS	WALY
WAIRUAS	WAKANDAS	WALING	WALLEYE	WAMBENGER
WAIS	WAKAS	WALIS	WALLEYED	WAMBLE
WAIST	WAKE	WALISE	WALLEYES	WAMBLED
WAISTBAND	WAKEBOARD	WALISES	WALLFISH	WAMBLES
WAISTBELT	WAKED	WALK	WALLIE	WAMBLIER
WAISTCOAT	WAKEFUL	WALKABLE	WALLIER	WAMBLIEST
WAISTED	WAKEFULLY	WALKABOUT	WALLIES	WAMBLING
WAISTER	WAKELESS	WALKATHON	WALLIEST	WAMBLINGS
WAISTERS	WAKEMAN	WALKAWAY	WALLING	WAMBLY
WAISTING	WAKEMEN	WALKAWAYS	WALLINGS	WAME
WAISTINGS	WAKEN	WALKED	WALLOP	WAMED
WAISTLESS	WAKENED	WALKER	WALLOPED	WAMEFOU
WAISTLINE	WAKENER	WALKERS	WALLOPER	WAMEFOUS
WAISTS	WAKENERS	WALKIES	WALLOPERS	WAMEFUL
WAIT	WAKENING	WALKING	WALLOPING	WAMEFULS
WAITE	WAKENINGS	WALKINGS	WALLOPS	WAMES
WAITED	WAKENS	WALKMILL	WALLOW	WAMMUL
WAITER	WAKER	WALKMILLS	WALLOWED	WAMMULS
WAITERAGE	WAKERIFE	WALKOUT	WALLOWER	WAMMUS
WAITERED	WAKERS	WALKOUTS	WALLOWERS	WAMMUSES
WAITERING	WAKES	WALKOVER	WALLOWING	WAMPEE
WAITERS	WAKF	WALKOVERS	WALLOWS	WAMPEES
WAITES	WAKFS	WALKS	WALLPAPER	WAMPISH
WAITING	WAKIKI	WALKUP	WALLS	WAMPISHED
WAITINGLY	WAKIKIS	WALKUPS	WALLSEND	WAMPISHES
WAITINGS	WAKING	WALKWAY	WALLSENDS	WAMPUM
WAITLIST	WAKINGS	WALKWAYS	WALLWORT	WAMPUMS
WAITLISTS	WALD	WALKYRIE	WALLWORTS	WAMPUS
WAITRESS	WALDFLUTE	WALKYRIES	WALLY	WAMPUSES
WAITRON	WALDGRAVE	WALL	WALLYBALL	WAMUS
WAITRONS	WALDHORN	WALLA	WALLYDRAG	WAMUSES
WAITS	WALDHORNS	WALLABA	WALNUT	WAN
WAITSTAFF	WALDO	WALLABAS	WALNUTS	WANCHANCY
WAIVE	WALDOES	WALLABIES	WALRUS	WAND
WAIVED	WALDOS	WALLABY	WALRUSES	WANDER
WAIVER	WALDRAPP	WALLAH	WALTIER	WANDERED
WAIVERS	WALDRAPPS	WALLAHS	WALTIEST	WANDERER
WAIVES	WALDS	WALLAROO	WALTY	WANDERERS

WANDERING	WANKY	WANWORTHS	WARDED	WARFARINS
WANDEROO	WANLE	WANY	WARDEN	WARHABLE
WANDEROOS	WANLY	WANZE	WARDENED	WARHEAD
WANDERS	WANNA	WANZED	WARDENING	WARHEADS
WANDLE	WANNABE	WANZES	WARDENRY	WARHORSE
WANDLIKE	WANNABEE	WANZING	WARDENS	WARHORSES
WANDOO	WANNABEES	WAP	WARDER	WARIBASHI
WANDOOS	WANNABES	WAPENSHAW	WARDERED	WARIER
WANDS	WANNED	WAPENTAKE	WARDERING	WARIEST
WANE	WANNEL	WAPINSHAW	WARDERS	WARILY
WANED	WANNER	WAPITI	WARDIAN	WARIMENT
WANES	WANNESS	WAPITIS	WARDING	WARIMENTS
WANEY	WANNESSES	WAPPED	WARDINGS	WARINESS
WANG	WANNEST	WAPPEND	WARDLESS	WARING
WANGAN	WANNIGAN	WAPPER	WARDMOTE	WARISON
WANGANS	WANNIGANS	WAPPERED	WARDMOTES	WARISONS
WANGLE	WANNING	WAPPERING	WARDOG	WARK
WANGLED	WANNION	WAPPERS	WARDOGS	WARKED
WANGLER	WANNIONS	WAPPING	WARDRESS	WARKING
WANGLERS	WANNISH	WAPS	WARDROBE	WARKS
WANGLES	WANS	WAQF	WARDROBED	WARLESS
WANGLING	WANT	WAQFS	WARDROBER	WARLIKE
WANGLINGS	WANTAGE	WAR	WARDROBES	WARLING
WANGS	WANTAGES	WARAGI	WARDROOM	WARLINGS
WANGUN	WANTAWAY	WARAGIS	WARDROOMS	WARLOCK
WANGUNS	WANTAWAYS	WARATAH	WARDROP	WARLOCKRY
WANHOPE	WANTED	WARATAHS	WARDROPS	WARLOCKS
WANHOPES	WANTER	WARB	WARDS	WARLORD
WANIER	WANTERS	WARBIER	WARDSHIP	WARLORDS
WANIEST	WANTHILL	WARBIEST	WARDSHIPS	WARM
WANIGAN	WANTHILLS	WARBIRD	WARE	WARMAKER
WANIGANS	WANTIES	WARBIRDS	WARED	WARMAKERS
WANING	WANTING	WARBLE	WAREHOU	WARMAN
WANINGS	WANTON	WARBLED	WAREHOUS	WARMBLOOD
WANION	WANTONED	WARBLER	WAREHOUSE	WARMED
WANIONS	WANTONER	WARBLERS	WARELESS	WARMEN
WANK	WANTONERS	WARBLES	WAREROOM	WARMER
WANKED	WANTONEST	WARBLING	WAREROOMS	WARMERS
WANKER	WANTONING	WARBLINGS	WARES	WARMEST
WANKERS	WANTONISE	WARBONNET	WAREZ	WARMING
WANKIER	WANTONIZE	WARBS	WARFARE	WARMINGS
WANKIEST	WANTONLY	WARBY	WARFARED	WARMISH
WANKING	WANTONS	WARCRAFT	WARFARER	WARMLY
WANKLE	WANTS	WARCRAFTS	WARFARERS	WARMNESS
WANKS	WANTY	WARD	WARFARES	WARMONGER
WANKSTA	WANWORDY	WARDCORN	WARFARIN	WARMOUTH
WANKSTAS	WANWORTH	WARDCORNS	WARFARING	WARMOUTHS

WARMS	WARRANTS	WARTIME	WASHES	WASSAILER
WARMTH	WARRANTY	WARTIMES	WASHHAND	WASSAILRY
WARMTHS	WARRAY	WARTLESS	WASHHOUSE	WASSAILS
WARMUP	WARRAYED	WARTLIKE	WASHIER	WASSERMAN
WARMUPS	WARRAYING	WARTS	WASHIEST	WASSERMEN
WARN	WARRAYS	WARTWEED	WASHILY	WASSUP
WARNED	WARRE	WARTWEEDS	WASHIN	WAST
WARNER	WARRED	WARTWORT	WASHINESS	WASTABLE
WARNERS	WARREN	WARTWORTS	WASHING	WASTAGE
WARNING	WARRENER	WARTY	WASHINGS	WASTAGES
WARNINGLY	WARRENERS	WARWOLF	WASHINS	WASTE
WARNINGS	WARRENS	WARWOLVES	WASHLAND	WASTED
WARNS	WARREY	WARWORK	WASHLANDS	WASTEFUL
WARP	WARREYED	WARWORKS	WASHOUT	WASTEL
WARPAGE	WARREYING	WARWORN	WASHOUTS	WASTELAND
WARPAGES	WARREYS	WARY	WASHPOT	WASTELOT
WARPATH	WARRIGAL	WARZONE	WASHPOTS	WASTELOTS
WARPATHS	WARRIGALS	WARZONES	WASHRAG	WASTELS
WARPED	WARRING	WAS	WASHRAGS	WASTENESS
WARPER	WARRIOR	WASABI	WASHROOM	WASTER
WARPERS	WARRIORS	WASABIS	WASHROOMS	WASTERED
WARPING	WARRISON	WASE	WASHSTAND	WASTERFUL
WARPINGS	WARRISONS	WASES	WASHTUB	WASTERIE
WARPLANE	WARS	WASH	WASHTUBS	WASTERIES
WARPLANES	WARSAW	WASHABLE	WASHUP	WASTERING
WARPOWER	WARSAWS	WASHABLES	WASHUPS	WASTERS
WARPOWERS	WARSHIP	WASHAWAY	WASHWIPE	WASTERY
WARPS	WARSHIPS	WASHAWAYS	WASHWIPES	WASTES
WARPWISE	WARSLE	WASHBALL	WASHWOMAN	WASTEWAY
WARRAGAL	WARSLED	WASHBALLS	WASHWOMEN	WASTEWAYS
WARRAGALS	WARSLER	WASHBASIN	WASHY	WASTEWEIR
WARRAGLE	WARSLERS	WASHBOARD	WASP	WASTFULL
WARRAGLES	WARSLES	WASHBOWL	WASPIE	WASTING
WARRAGUL	WARSLING	WASHBOWLS	WASPIER	WASTINGLY
WARRAGULS	WARST	WASHCLOTH	WASPIES	WASTINGS
WARRAN	WARSTLE	WASHDAY	WASPIEST	WASTNESS
WARRAND	WARSTLED	WASHDAYS	WASPILY	WASTREL
WARRANDED	WARSTLER	WASHED	WASPINESS	WASTRELS
WARRANDS	WARSTLERS	WASHEN	WASPISH	WASTRIE
WARRANED	WARSTLES	WASHER	WASPISHLY	WASTRIES
WARRANING	WARSTLING	WASHERED	WASPLIKE	WASTRIFE
WARRANS	WART	WASHERIES	WASPNEST	WASTRIFES
WARRANT	WARTED	WASHERING	WASPNESTS	WASTRY
WARRANTED	WARTHOG	WASHERMAN	WASPS	WASTS
WARRANTEE	WARTHOGS	WASHERMEN	WASPY	WAT
WARRANTER	WARTIER	WASHERS	WASSAIL	WATAP
WARRANTOR	WARTIEST	WASHERY	WASSAILED	WATAPE

WATAPES	WATERILY	WATTS	WAVEFORM	WAWLED
WATAPS	WATERING	WAUCHT	WAVEFORMS	WAWLING
WATCH	WATERINGS	WAUCHTED	WAVEFRONT	WAWLINGS
WATCHABLE	WATERISH	WAUCHTING	WAVEGUIDE	WAWLS
WATCHBAND	WATERJET	WAUCHTS	WAVELESS	WAWS
WATCHBOX	WATERJETS	WAUFF	WAVELET	WAX
WATCHCASE	WATERLEAF	WAUFFED	WAVELETS	WAXABLE
WATCHCRY	WATERLESS	WAUFFING	WAVELIKE	WAXBERRY
WATCHDOG	WATERLILY	WAUFFS	WAVELLITE	WAXBILL
WATCHDOGS	WATERLINE	WAUGH	WAVEMETER	WAXBILLS
WATCHED	WATERLOG	WAUGHED	WAVEOFF	WAXCLOTH
WATCHER	WATERLOGS	WAUGHING	WAVEOFFS	WAXCLOTHS
WATCHERS	WATERLOO	WAUGHS	WAVER	WAXED
WATCHES	WATERLOOS	WAUGHT	WAVERED	WAXEN
WATCHET	WATERMAN	WAUGHTED	WAVERER	WAXER
WATCHETS	WATERMARK	WAUGHTING	WAVERERS	WAXERS
WATCHEYE	WATERMEN	WAUGHTS	WAVERIER	WAXES
WATCHEYES	WATERPOX	WAUK	WAVERIEST	WAXEYE
WATCHFUL	WATERS	WAUKED	WAVERING	WAXEYES
WATCHING	WATERSHED	WAUKER	WAVERINGS	WAXFLOWER
WATCHLIST	WATERSIDE	WAUKERS	WAVEROUS	WAXIER
WATCHMAN	WATERSKI	WAUKING	WAVERS	WAXIEST
WATCHMEN	WATERSKIS	WAUKMILL	WAVERY	WAXILY
WATCHOUT	WATERWAY	WAUKMILLS	WAVES	WAXINESS
WATCHOUTS	WATERWAYS	WAUKRIFE	WAVESHAPE	WAXING
WATCHWORD	WATERWEED	WAUKS	WAVESON	WAXINGS
WATE	WATERWORK	WAUL	WAVESONS	WAXLIKE
WATER	WATERWORN	WAULED	WAVEY	WAXPLANT
WATERAGE	WATERY	WAULING	WAVEYS	WAXPLANTS
WATERAGES	WATERZOOI	WAULINGS	WAVICLE	WAXWEED
WATERBED	WATS	WAULK	WAVICLES	WAXWEEDS
WATERBEDS	WATT	WAULKED	WAVIER	WAXWING
WATERBIRD	WATTAGE	WAULKER	WAVIES	WAXWINGS
WATERBUCK	WATTAGES	WAULKERS	WAVIEST	WAXWORK
WATERBUS	WATTAPE	WAULKING	WAVILY	WAXWORKER
WATERDOG	WATTAPES	WAULKMILL	WAVINESS	WAXWORKS
WATERDOGS	WATTER	WAULKS	WAVING	WAXWORM
WATERED	WATTEST	WAULS	WAVINGS	WAXWORMS
WATERER	WATTHOUR	WAUR	WAVY	WAXY
WATERERS	WATTHOURS	WAURED	WAW	WAY
WATERFALL	WATTLE	WAURING	WAWA	WAYBILL
WATERFOWL	WATTLED	WAURS	WAWAED	WAYBILLS
WATERHEAD	WATTLES	WAURST	WAWAING	WAYBOARD
WATERHEN	WATTLESS	WAVE	WAWAS	WAYBOARDS
WATERHENS	WATTLING	WAVEBAND	WAWE	WAYBREAD
WATERIER	WATTLINGS	WAVEBANDS	WAWES	WAYBREADS
WATERIEST	WATTMETER	WAVED	WAWL	WAYED

WAYFARE	WAZZOCK	WEANLINGS	WEATHER	WEBISODE
WAYFARED	WAZZOCKS	WEANS	WEATHERED	WEBISODES
WAYFARER	WE	WEAPON	WEATHERER	WEBLESS
WAYFARERS	WEAK	WEAPONED	WEATHERLY	WEBLIKE
WAYFARES	WEAKEN	WEAPONEER	WEATHERS	WEBLISH
WAYFARING	WEAKENED	WEAPONING	WEAVE	WEBLISHES
WAYGOING	WEAKENER	WEAPONISE	WEAVED	WEBLOG
WAYGOINGS	WEAKENERS	WEAPONIZE	WEAVER	WEBLOGGER
WAYGONE	WEAKENING	WEAPONRY	WEAVERS	WEBLOGS
WAYGOOSE	WEAKENS	WEAPONS	WEAVES	WEBMAIL
WAYGOOSES	WEAKER	WEAR	WEAVING	WEBMAILS
WAYING	WEAKEST	WEARABLE	WEAVINGS	WEBMASTER
WAYLAID	WEAKFISH	WEARABLES	WEAZAND	WEBPAGE
WAYLAY	WEAKISH	WEARED	WEAZANDS	WEBPAGES
WAYLAYER	WEAKISHLY	WEARER	WEAZEN	WEBRING
WAYLAYERS	WEAKLIER	WEARERS	WEAZENED	WEBRINGS
WAYLAYING	WEAKLIEST	WEARIED	WEAZENING	WEBS
WAYLAYS	WEAKLING	WEARIER	WEAZENS	WEBSITE
WAYLEAVE	WEAKLINGS	WEARIES	WEB	WEBSITES
WAYLEAVES	WEAKLY	WEARIEST	WEBBED	WEBSTER
WAYLEGGO	WEAKNESS	WEARIFUL	WEBBIE	WEBSTERS
WAYLESS	WEAKON	WEARILESS	WEBBIER	WEBWHEEL
WAYMARK	WEAKONS	WEARILY	WEBBIES	WEBWHEELS
WAYMARKED	WEAKSIDE	WEARINESS	WEBBIEST	WEBWORK
WAYMARKS	WEAKSIDES	WEARING	WEBBING	WEBWORKS
WAYMENT	WEAL	WEARINGLY	WEBBINGS	WEBWORM
WAYMENTED	WEALD	WEARINGS	WEBBY	WEBWORMS
WAYMENTS	WEALDS	WEARISH	WEBCAM	WEBZINE
WAYPOINT	WEALS	WEARISOME	WEBCAMS	WEBZINES
WAYPOINTS	WEALSMAN	WEARPROOF	WEBCAST	WECHT
WAYPOST	WEALSMEN	WEARS	WEBCASTED	WECHTS
WAYPOSTS	WEALTH	WEARY	WEBCASTER	WED
WAYS	WEALTHIER	WEARYING	WEBCASTS	WEDDED
WAYSIDE	WEALTHILY	WEASAND	WEBER	WEDDER
WAYSIDES	WEALTHS	WEASANDS	WEBERS	WEDDERED
WAYWARD	WEALTHY	WEASEL	WEBFED	WEDDERING
WAYWARDLY	WEAMB	WEASELED	WEBFEET	WEDDERS
WAYWISER	WEAMBS	WEASELER	WEBFOOT	WEDDING
WAYWISERS	WEAN	WEASELERS	WEBFOOTED	WEDDINGS
WAYWODE	WEANED	WEASELING	WEBHEAD	WEDEL
WAYWODES	WEANEL	WEASELLED	WEBHEADS	WEDELED
WAYWORN	WEANELS	WEASELLER	WEBIFIED	WEDELING
WAYZGOOSE	WEANER	WEASELLY	WEBIFIES	WEDELN
WAZIR	WEANERS	WEASELS	WEBIFY	WEDELNED
WAZIRS	WEANING	WEASELY	WEBIFYING	WEDELNING
WAZOO	WEANINGS	WEASON	WEBINAR	WEDELNS
WAZOOS	WEANLING	WEASONS	WEBINARS	WEDELS

W

WEDGE	WEEKS	WEEVERS	WEIGHTY	WELD
WEDGED	WEEL	WEEVIL	WEIL	WELDABLE
WEDGELIKE	WEELS	WEEVILED	WEILS	WELDED
WEDGES	WEEM	WEEVILLED	WEINER	WELDER
WEDGEWISE	WEEMS	WEEVILLY	WEINERS	WELDERS
WEDGIE	WEEN	WEEVILS	WEIR	WELDING
WEDGIER	WEENED	WEEVILY	WEIRD	WELDINGS
WEDGIES	WEENIE	WEEWEE	WEIRDED	WELDLESS
WEDGIEST	WEENIER	WEEWEED	WEIRDER	WELDMENT
WEDGING	WEENIES	WEEWEEING	WEIRDEST	WELDMENTS
WEDGINGS	WEENIEST	WEEWEES	WEIRDIE	WELDOR
WEDGY	WEENING	WEFT	WEIRDIES	WELDORS
WEDLOCK	WEENS	WEFTAGE	WEIRDING	WELDS
WEDLOCKS	WEENSIER	WEFTAGES	WEIRDLY	WELFARE
WEDS	WEENSIEST	WEFTE	WEIRDNESS	WELFARES
WEE	WEENSY	WEFTED	WEIRDO	WELFARISM
WEED	WEENY	WEFTES	WEIRDOES	WELFARIST
WEEDED	WEEP	WEFTING	WEIRDOS	WELK
WEEDER	WEEPER	WEFTS	WEIRDS	WELKE
WEEDERIES	WEEPERS	WEFTWISE	WEIRDY	WELKED
WEEDERS	WEEPHOLE	WEID	WEIRED	WELKES
WEEDERY	WEEPHOLES	WEIDS	WEIRING	WELKIN
WEEDICIDE	WEEPIE	WEIGELA	WEIRS	WELKING
WEEDIER	WEEPIER	WEIGELAS	WEISE	WELKINS
WEEDIEST	WEEPIES	WEIGELIA	WEISED	WELKS
WEEDILY	WEEPIEST	WEIGELIAS	WEISES	WELKT
WEEDINESS	WEEPILY	WEIGH	WEISING	WELL
WEEDING	WEEPINESS	WEIGHABLE	WEIZE	WELLADAY
WEEDINGS	WEEPING	WEIGHAGE	WEIZED	WELLADAYS
WEEDLESS	WEEPINGLY	WEIGHAGES	WEIZES	WELLANEAR
WEEDLIKE	WEEPINGS	WEIGHED	WEIZING	WELLAWAY
WEEDS	WEEPS	WEIGHER	WEKA	WELLAWAYS
WEEDY	WEEPY	WEIGHERS	WEKAS	WELLBEING
WEEING	WEER	WEIGHING	WELAWAY	WELLBORN
WEEK	WEES	WEIGHINGS	WELCH	WELLCURB
WEEKDAY	WEEST	WEIGHMAN	WELCHED	WELLCURBS
WEEKDAYS	WEET	WEIGHMEN	WELCHER	WELLCURBS
WEEKE	WEETE	WEIGHS	WELCHERS	WELLDOER
WEEKEND	WEETED	WEIGHT	WELCHES	WELLDOERS
WEEKENDED	WEETEN	WEIGHTAGE	WELCHING	WELLED
WEEKENDER	WEETER	WEIGHTED	WELCOME	WELLHEAD
WEEKENDS	WEETEST	WEIGHTER	WELCOMED	WELLHEADS
WEEKES	WEETING	WEIGHTERS	WELCOMELY	WELLHOLE
WEEKLIES	WEETINGLY	WEIGHTIER	WELCOMER	WELLHOLES
WEEKLONG	WEETLESS	WEIGHTILY	WELCOMERS	WELLHOUSE
WEEKLY	WEETS	WEIGHTING	WELCOMES	WELLIE
WEEKNIGHT	WEEVER	WEIGHTS	WELCOMING	WELLIES
				WELLING

W

WELLINGS	WENT	WESTLINS	WHACKER	WHAMPLE
WELLNESS	WENTS	WESTMOST	WHACKERS	WHAMPLES
WELLS	WEPT	WESTS	WHACKIER	WHAMS
WELLSITE	WERE	WESTWARD	WHACKIEST	WHANAU
WELLSITES	WEREGILD	WESTWARDS	WHACKING	WHANAUS
WELLY	WEREGILDS	WET	WHACKINGS	WHANG
WELS	WEREWOLF	WETA	WHACKO	WHANGAM
WELSH	WERGELD	WETAS	WHACKOES	WHANGAMS
WELSHED	WERGELDS	WETBACK	WHACKOS	WHANGED
WELSHER	WERGELT	WETBACKS	WHACKS	WHANGEE
WELSHERS	WERGELTS	WETHER	WHACKY	WHANGEES
WELSHES	WERGILD	WETHERS	WHAE	WHANGING
WELSHING	WERGILDS	WETLAND	WHAISLE	WHANGS
WELT	WERNERITE	WETLANDS	WHAISLED	WHAP
WELTED	WERO	WETLY	WHAISLES	WHAPPED
WELTER	WEROS	WETNESS	WHAISLING	WHAPPER
WELTERED	WERRIS	WETNESSES	WHAIZLE	WHAPPERS
WELTERING	WERRISES	WETPROOF	WHAIZLED	WHAPPING
WELTERS	WERSH	WETS	WHAIZLES	WHAPS
WELTING	WERSHER	WETSUIT	WHAIZLING	WHARE
WELTINGS	WERSHEST	WETSUITS	WHAKAIRO	WHARENUI
WELTS	WERT	WETTABLE	WHAKAIROS	WHARENUIS
WEM	WERWOLF	WETTED	WHAKAPAPA	WHAREPUNI
WEMB	WERWOLVES	WETTER	WHALE	WHARES
WEMBS	WESAND	WETTERS	WHALEBACK	WHARF
WEMS	WESANDS	WETTEST	WHALEBOAT	WHARFAGE
WEN	WESKIT	WETTIE	WHALEBONE	WHARFAGES
WENA	WESKITS	WETTIES	WHALED	WHARFED
WENCH	WESSAND	WETTING	WHALELIKE	WHARFIE
WENCHED	WESSANDS	WETTINGS	WHALEMAN	WHARFIES
WENCHER	WEST	WETTISH	WHALEMEN	WHARFING
WENCHERS	WESTABOUT	WETWARE	WHALER	WHARFINGS
WENCHES	WESTBOUND	WETWARES	WHALERIES	WHARFS
WENCHING	WESTED	WEX	WHALERS	WHARVE
WEND	WESTER	WEXE	WHALERY	WHARVES
WENDED	WESTERED	WEXED	WHALES	WHAT
WENDIGO	WESTERING	WEXES	WHALING	WHATA
WENDIGOS	WESTERLY	WEXING	WHALINGS	WHATAS
WENDING	WESTERN	WEY	WHALLY	WHATEN
WENDS	WESTERNER	WEYARD	WHAM	WHATEVER
WENGE	WESTERNS	WEYS	WHAMMED	WHATNA
WENGES	WESTERS	WEYWARD	WHAMMIES	WHATNESS
WENNIER	WESTIE	WEZAND	WHAMMING	WHATNOT
WENNIEST	WESTIES	WEZANDS	WHAMMO	WHATNOTS
WENNISH	WESTING	WHA	WHAMMOS	WHATS
WENNY	WESTINGS	WHACK	WHAMMY	WHATSIS
WENS	WESTLIN	WHACKED	WHAMO	WHATSISES

WHATSIT	WHEELLESS	WHELKED	WHEREUPON	WHICKERS
WHATSITS	WHEELMAN	WHELKIER	WHEREVER	WHID
WHATSO	WHEELMEN	WHELKIEST	WHEREWITH	WHIDAH
WHATTEN	WHEELS	WHELKS	WHERRET	WHIDAHS
WHAUP	WHEELSMAN	WHELKY	WHERRETED	WHIDDED
WHAUPS	WHEELSMEN	WHELM	WHERRETS	WHIDDER
WHAUR	WHEELWORK	WHELMED	WHERRIED	WHIDDERED
WHAURS	WHEELY	WHELMING	WHERRIES	WHIDDERS
WHEAL	WHEEN	WHELMS	WHERRIT	WHIDDING
WHEALS	WHEENGE	WHELP	WHERRITED	WHIDS
WHEAR	WHEENGED	WHELPED	WHERRITS	WHIFF
WHEARE	WHEENGES	WHELPING	WHERRY	WHIFFED
WHEAT	WHEENGING	WHELPLESS	WHERRYING	WHIFFER
WHEATEAR	WHEENS	WHELPS	WHERRYMAN	WHIFFERS
WHEATEARS	WHEEP	WHEMMLE	WHERRYMEN	WHIFFET
WHEATEN	WHEEPED	WHEMMLED	WHERVE	WHIFFETS
WHEATENS	WHEEPING	WHEMMLES	WHERVES	WHIFFIER
WHEATIER	WHEEPLE	WHEMMLING	WHET	WHIFFIEST
WHEATIEST	WHEEPLED	WHEN	WHETHER	WHIFFING
WHEATLAND	WHEEPLES	WHENAS	WHETS	WHIFFINGS
WHEATLESS	WHEEPLING	WHENCE	WHETSTONE	WHIFFLE
WHEATMEAL	WHEEPS	WHENCES	WHETTED	WHIFFLED
WHEATS	WHEESH	WHENCEVER	WHETTER	WHIFFLER
WHEATWORM	WHEESHED	WHENEVER	WHETTERS	WHIFFLERS
WHEATY	WHEESHES	WHENS	WHETTING	WHIFFLERY
WHEE	WHEESHING	WHENUA	WHEUGH	WHIFFLES
WHEECH	WHEESHT	WHENUAS	WHEUGHED	WHIFFLING
WHEECHED	WHEESHTED	WHENWE	WHEUGHING	WHIFFS
WHEECHING	WHEESHTS	WHENWES	WHEUGHS	WHIFFY
WHEECHS	WHEEZE	WHERE	WHEW	WHIFT
WHEEDLE	WHEEZED	WHEREAS	WHEWED	WHIFTS
WHEEDLED	WHEEZER	WHEREASES	WHEWING	WHIG
WHEEDLER	WHEEZERS	WHEREAT	WHEWS	WHIGGED
WHEEDLERS	WHEEZES	WHEREBY	WHEY	WHIGGING
WHEEDLES	WHEEZIER	WHEREFOR	WHEYEY	WHIGS
WHEEDLING	WHEEZIEST	WHEREFORE	WHEYFACE	WHILE
WHEEL	WHEEZILY	WHEREFROM	WHEYFACED	WHILED
WHEELBASE	WHEEZING	WHEREIN	WHEYFACES	WHILERE
WHEELED	WHEEZINGS	WHEREINTO	WHEYIER	WHILES
WHEELER	WHEEZLE	WHERENESS	WHEYIEST	WHILING
WHEELERS	WHEEZLED	WHEREOF	WHEYISH	WHILK
WHEELIE	WHEEZLES	WHEREON	WHEYLIKE	WHILLIED
WHEELIER	WHEEZLING	WHEREOUT	WHEYS	WHILLIES
WHEELIES	WHEEZY	WHERES	WHICH	WHILLY
WHEELIEST	WHEFT	WHERESO	WHICHEVER	WHILLYING
WHEELING	WHEFTS	WHERETO	WHICKER	WHILLYWHA
WHEELINGS	WHELK	WHEREUNTO	WHICKERED	WHILOM

WHILST	WHINGING	WHIPRAYS	WHIRTLE	WHITEBEAM
WHIM	WHINGY	WHIPS	WHIRTLES	WHITECAP
WHIMBERRY	WHINIARD	WHIPSAW	WHISH	WHITECAPS
WHIMBREL	WHINIARDS	WHIPSAWED	WHISHED	WHITECOAT
WHIMBRELS	WHINIER	WHIPSAWN	WHISHES	WHITECOMB
WHIMMED	WHINIEST	WHIPSAWS	WHISHING	WHITED
WHIMMIER	WHININESS	WHIPSNAKE	WHISHT	WHITEDAMP
WHIMMIEST	WHINING	WHIPSTAFF	WHISHTED	WHITEFACE
WHIMMING	WHININGLY	WHIPSTALL	WHISHTING	WHITEFISH
WHIMMY	WHININGS	WHIPSTER	WHISHTS	WHITEFLY
WHIMPER	WHINNIED	WHIPSTERS	WHISK	WHITEHEAD
WHIMPERED	WHINNIER	WHIPSTOCK	WHISKED	WHITELIST
WHIMPERER	WHINNIES	WHIPT	WHISKER	WHITELY
WHIMPERS	WHINNIEST	WHIPTAIL	WHISKERED	WHITEN
WHIMPLE	WHINNY	WHIPTAILS	WHISKERS	WHITENED
WHIMPLED	WHINNYING	WHIPWORM	WHISKERY	WHITENER
WHIMPLES	WHINS	WHIPWORMS	WHISKET	WHITENERS
WHIMPLING	WHINSTONE	WHIR	WHISKETS	WHITENESS
WHIMS	WHINY	WHIRL	WHISKEY	WHITENING
WHIMSEY	WHINYARD	WHIRLBAT	WHISKEYS	WHITENS
WHIMSEYS	WHINYARDS	WHIRLBATS	WHISKIES	WHITEOUT
WHIMSICAL	WHIO	WHIRLED	WHISKING	WHITEOUTS
WHIMSIED	WHIOS	WHIRLER	WHISKS	WHITEPOT
WHIMSIER	WHIP	WHIRLERS	WHISKY	WHITEPOTS
WHIMSIES	WHIPBIRD	WHIRLIER	WHISPER	WHITER
WHIMSIEST	WHIPBIRDS	WHIRLIES	WHISPERED	WHITES
WHIMSILY	WHIPCAT	WHIRLIEST	WHISPERER	WHITEST
WHIMSY	WHIPCATS	WHIRLIGIG	WHISPERS	WHITETAIL
WHIN	WHIPCORD	WHIRLING	WHISPERY	WHITEWALL
WHINBERRY	WHIPCORDS	WHIRLINGS	WHISS	WHITEWARE
WHINCHAT	WHIPCORDY	WHIRLPOOL	WHISSED	WHITEWASH
WHINCHATS	WHIPJACK	WHIRLS	WHISSES	WHITEWING
WHINE	WHIPJACKS	WHIRLWIND	WHISSING	WHITEWOOD
WHINED	WHIPLASH	WHIRLY	WHIST	WHITEY
WHINER	WHIPLESS	WHIRR	WHISTED	WHITEYS
WHINERS	WHIPLIKE	WHIRRED	WHISTING	WHITHER
WHINES	WHIPPED	WHIRRET	WHISTLE	WHITHERED
WHINEY	WHIPPER	WHIRRETED	WHISTLED	WHITHERS
WHINGDING	WHIPPERS	WHIRRETS	WHISTLER	WHITIER
WHINGE	WHIPPET	WHIRRIED	WHISTLERS	WHITIES
WHINGED	WHIPPETS	WHIRRIES	WHISTLES	WHITIEST
WHINGEING	WHIPPIER	WHIRRING	WHISTLING	WHITING
WHINGER	WHIPPIEST	WHIRRINGS	WHISTS	WHITINGS
WHINGERS	WHIPPING	WHIRRS	WHIT	WHITISH
WHINGES	WHIPPINGS	WHIRRY	WHITE	WHITLING
WHINGIER	WHIPPY	WHIRRYING	WHITEBAIT	WHITLINGS
WHINGIEST	WHIPRAY	WHIRS	WHITEBASS	WHITLOW

WHITLOWS	WHOLEFOOD	WHOOPS	WHUMMLE	WICKETS
WHITRACK	WHOLEMEAL	WHOOPSIE	WHUMMLED	WICKIES
WHITRACKS	WHOLENESS	WHOOPSIES	WHUMMLES	WICKING
WHITRET	WHOLES	WHOOSH	WHUMMLING	WICKINGS
WHITRETS	WHOLESALE	WHOOSHED	WHUMP	WICKIUP
WHITRICK	WHOLESOME	WHOOSHES	WHUMPED	WICKIUPS
WHITRICKS	WHOLISM	WHOOSHING	WHUMPING	WICKLESS
WHITS	WHOLISMS	WHOOSIS	WHUMPS	WICKS
WHITSTER	WHOLIST	WHOOSISES	WHUNSTANE	WICKTHING
WHITSTERS	WHOLISTIC	WHOOT	WHUP	WICKY
WHITTAW	WHOLISTS	WHOOTED	WHUPPED	WICKYUP
WHITTAWER	WHOLLY	WHOOTING	WHUPPING	WICKYUPS
WHITTAWS	WHOLPHIN	WHOOTS	WHUPPINGS	WICOPIES
WHITTER	WHOLPHINS	WHOP	WHUPS	WICOPY
WHITTERED	WHOM	WHOPPED	WHY	WIDDER
WHITTERS	WHOMBLE	WHOPPER	WHYDAH	WIDDERS
WHITTLE	WHOMBLED	WHOPPERS	WHYDAHS	WIDDIE
WHITTLED	WHOMBLES	WHOPPING	WHYDUNIT	WIDDIES
WHITTLER	WHOMBLING	WHOPPINGS	WHYDUNITS	WIDDLE
WHITTLERS	WHOMEVER	WHOPS	WHYDUNNIT	WIDDLED
WHITTLES	WHOMMLE	WHORE	WHYEVER	WIDDLES
WHITTLING	WHOMMLED	WHORED	WHYS	WIDDLING
WHITTRET	WHOMMLES	WHOREDOM	WIBBLE	WIDDY
WHITTRETS	WHOMMLING	WHOREDOMS	WIBBLED	WIDE
WHITY	WHOMP	WHORES	WIBBLES	WIDEAWAKE
WHIZ	WHOMPED	WHORESON	WIBBLING	WIDEBAND
WHIZBANG	WHOMPING	WHORESONS	WICCA	WIDEBODY
WHIZBANGS	WHOMPS	WHORING	WICCAN	WIDELY
WHIZZ	WHOMSO	WHORISH	WICCANS	WIDEN
WHIZZBANG	WHOOBUB	WHORISHLY	WICCAS	WIDENED
WHIZZED	WHOOBUBS	WHORL	WICE	WIDENER
WHIZZER	WHOOF	WHORLBAT	WICH	WIDENERS
WHIZZERS	WHOOFED	WHORLBATS	WICHES	WIDENESS
WHIZZES	WHOOFING	WHORLED	WICK	WIDENING
WHIZZIER	WHOOFS	WHORLS	WICKAPE	WIDENS
WHIZZIEST	WHOOP	WHORT	WICKAPES	WIDEOUT
WHIZZING	WHOOPED	WHORTLE	WICKED	WIDEOUTS
WHIZZINGS	WHOOPEE	WHORTLES	WICKEDER	WIDER
WHIZZO	WHOOPEES	WHORTS	WICKEDEST	WIDES
WHIZZY	WHOOPER	WHOSE	WICKEDLY	WIDEST
WHO	WHOOPERS	WHOSEVER	WICKEDS	WIDGEON
WHOA	WHOOPIE	WHOSIS	WICKEN	WIDGEONS
WHODUNIT	WHOOPIES	WHOSISES	WICKENS	WIDGET
WHODUNITS	WHOOPING	WHOSO	WICKER	WIDGETS
WHODUNNIT	WHOOPINGS	WHOSOEVER	WICKERED	WIDGIE
WHOEVER	WHOOPLA	WHOT	WICKERS	WIDGIES
WHOLE	WHOOPLAS	WHOW	WICKET	WIDISH

WIDOW	WIFIE	WIGWAGS	WILIER	WILLYARD
WIDOWBIRD	WIFIES	WIGWAM	WILIEST	WILLYART
WIDOWED	WIFING	WIGWAMS	WILILY	WILLYING
WIDOWER	WIFTIER	WIKI	WILINESS	WILLYWAW
WIDOWERED	WIFTIEST	WIKIS	WILING	WILLYWAWS
WIDOWERS	WIFTY	WIKIUP	WILIS	WILT
WIDOWHOOD	WIG	WIKIUPS	WILJA	WILTED
WIDOWING	WIGAN	WILCO	WILJAS	WILTING
WIDOWMAN	WIGANS	WILD	WILL	WILTJA
WIDOWMEN	WIGEON	WILDCARD	WILLABLE	WILTJAS
WIDOWS	WIGEONS	WILDCARDS	WILLED	WILTS
WIDTH	WIGGA	WILDCAT	WILLEMITE	WILY
WIDTHS	WIGGAS	WILDCATS	WILLER	WIMBLE
WIDTHWAY	WIGGED	WILDED	WILLERS	WIMBLED
WIDTHWAYS	WIGGER	WILDER	WILLEST	WIMBLES
WIDTHWISE	WIGGERIES	WILDERED	WILLET	WIMBLING
WIEL	WIGGERS	WILDERING	WILLETS	WIMBREL
WIELD	WIGGERY	WILDERS	WILLEY	WIMBRELS
WIELDABLE	WIGGIER	WILDEST	WILLEYED	WIMMIN
WIELDED	WIGGIEST	WILDFIRE	WILLEYING	WIMP
WIELDER	WIGGING	WILDFIRES	WILLEYS	WIMPED
WIELDERS	WIGGINGS	WILDFOWL	WILLFUL	WIMPIER
WIELDIER	WIGGLE	WILDFOWLS	WILLFULLY	WIMPIEST
WIELDIEST	WIGGLED	WILDGRAVE	WILLIAM	WIMPINESS
WIELDING	WIGGLER	WILDING	WILLIAMS	WIMPING
WIELDLESS	WIGGLERS	WILDINGS	WILLIE	WIMPISH
WIELDS	WIGGLES	WILDISH	WILLIED	WIMPISHLY
WIELDY	WIGGLIER	WILDLAND	WILLIES	WIMPLE
WIELS	WIGGLIEST	WILDLANDS	WILLING	WIMPLED
WIENER	WIGGLING	WILDLIFE	WILLINGER	WIMPLES
WIENERS	WIGGLY	WILDLIFES	WILLINGLY	WIMPLING
WIENIE	WIGGY	WILDLING	WILLIWAU	WIMPS
WIENIES	WIGHT	WILDLINGS	WILLIWAUS	WIMPY
WIFE	WIGHTED	WILDLY	WILLIWAW	WIN
WIFED	WIGHTING	WILDNESS	WILLIWAWS	WINCE
WIFEDOM	WIGHTLY	WILDS	WILLOW	WINCED
WIFEDOMS	WIGHTS	WILDWOOD	WILLOWED	WINCER
WIFEHOOD	WIGLESS	WILDWOODS	WILLOWER	WINCERS
WIFEHOODS	WIGLET	WILE	WILLOWERS	WINCES
WIFELESS	WIGLETS	WILED	WILLOWIER	WINCEY
WIFELIER	WIGLIKE	WILEFUL	WILLOWING	WINCEYS
WIFELIEST	WIGMAKER	WILES	WILLOWISH	WINCH
WIFELIKE	WIGMAKERS	WILFUL	WILLOWS	WINCHED
WIFELY	WIGS	WILFULLY	WILLOWY	WINCHER
WIFES	WIGWAG	WILGA	WILLPOWER	WINCHERS
WIFEY	WIGWAGGED	WILGAS	WILLS	WINCHES
WIFEYS	WIGWAGGER	WILI	WILLY	WINCHING

WINCHMAN	WINDINESS	WINDWARD	WINGLIKE	WINNOW
WINCHMEN	WINDING	WINDWARDS	WINGMAN	WINNOWED
WINCING	WINDINGLY	WINDWAY	WINGMEN	WINNOWER
WINCINGS	WINDINGS	WINDWAYS	WINGOVER	WINNOWERS
WINCOPIPE	WINDLASS	WINDY	WINGOVERS	WINNOWING
WIND	WINDLE	WINE	WINGS	WINNOWS
WINDABLE	WINDLED	WINEBERRY	WINGSPAN	WINNS
WINDAC	WINDLES	WINED	WINGSPANS	WINO
WINDACS	WINDLESS	WINEGLASS	WINGSUIT	WINOES
WINDAGE	WINDLING	WINELESS	WINGSUITS	WINOS
WINDAGES	WINDLINGS	WINEMAKER	WINGTIP	WINS
WINDAS	WINDMILL	WINEPRESS	WINGTIPS	WINSEY
WINDASES	WINDMILLS	WINERIES	WINGY	WINSEYS
WINDBAG	WINDOCK	WINERY	WINIER	WINSOME
WINDBAGS	WINDOCKS	WINES	WINIEST	WINSOMELY
WINDBELL	WINDORE	WINESAP	WINING	WINSOMER
WINDBELLS	WINDORES	WINESAPS	WINISH	WINSOMEST
WINDBILL	WINDOW	WINESHOP	WINK	WINTER
WINDBILLS	WINDOWED	WINESHOPS	WINKED	WINTERED
WINDBLAST	WINDOWING	WINESKIN	WINKER	WINTERER
WINDBLOW	WINDOWS	WINESKINS	WINKERS	WINTERERS
WINDBLOWN	WINDOWY	WINESOP	WINKING	WINTERFED
WINDBLOWS	WINDPIPE	WINESOPS	WINKINGLY	WINTERIER
WINDBORNE	WINDPIPES	WINEY	WINKINGS	WINTERING
WINDBOUND	WINDPROOF	WING	WINKLE	WINTERISE
WINDBREAK	WINDRING	WINGBACK	WINKLED	WINTERISH
WINDBURN	WINDROW	WINGBACKS	WINKLER	WINTERIZE
WINDBURNS	WINDROWED	WINGBEAT	WINKLERS	WINTERLY
WINDBURNT	WINDROWER	WINGBEATS	WINKLES	WINTERS
WINDCHILL	WINDROWS	WINGBOW	WINKLING	WINTERY
WINDED	WINDS	WINGBOWS	WINKS	WINTLE
WINDER	WINDSAIL	WINGCHAIR	WINLESS	WINTLED
WINDERS	WINDSAILS	WINGDING	WINN	WINTLES
WINDFALL	WINDSES	WINGDINGS	WINNA	WINTLING
WINDFALLS	WINDSHAKE	WINGE	WINNABLE	WINTRIER
WINDFLAW	WINDSHIP	WINGED	WINNARD	WINTRIEST
WINDFLAWS	WINDSHIPS	WINGEDLY	WINNARDS	WINTRILY
WINDGALL	WINDSOCK	WINGEING	WINNED	WINTRY
WINDGALLS	WINDSOCKS	WINGER	WINNER	WINY
WINDGUN	WINDSTORM	WINGERS	WINNERS	WINZE
WINDGUNS	WINDSURF	WINGES	WINNING	WINZES
WINDHOVER	WINDSURFS	WINGIER	WINNINGLY	WIPE
WINDIER	WINDSWEPT	WINGIEST	WINNINGS	WIPEABLE
WINDIEST	WINDTHROW	WINGING	WINNLE	WIPED
WINDIGO	WINDTIGHT	WINGLESS	WINNLES	WIPEOUT
WINDIGOS	WINDUP	WINGLET	WINNOCK	WIPEOUTS
WINDILY	WINDUPS	WINGLETS	WINNOCKS	WIPER

W

WIPERS	WIRY	WISPIER	WITED	WITLINGS
WIPES	WIS	WISPIEST	WITELESS	WITLOOF
WIPING	WISARD	WISPILY	WITES	WITLOOFS
WIPINGS	WISARDS	WISPINESS	WITGAT	WITNESS
WIPPEN	WISDOM	WISPING	WITGATS	WITNESSED
WIPPENS	WISDOMS	WISPISH	WITH	WITNESSER
WIRABLE	WISE	WISPLIKE	WITHAL	WITNESSES
WIRE	WISEACRE	WISPS	WITHDRAW	WITNEY
WIRED	WISEACRES	WISPY	WITHDRAWN	WITNEYS
WIREDRAW	WISEASS	WISS	WITHDRAWS	WITS
WIREDRAWN	WISEASSES	WISSED	WITHDREW	WITTED
WIREDRAWS	WISECRACK	WISSES	WITHE	WITTER
WIREDREW	WISED	WISSING	WITHED	WITTERED
WIREFRAME	WISEGUY	WIST	WITHER	WITTERING
WIREGRASS	WISEGUYS	WISTARIA	WITHERED	WITTERS
WIREHAIR	WISELIER	WISTARIAS	WITHERER	WITTICISM
WIREHAIRS	WISELIEST	WISTED	WITHERERS	WITTIER
WIRELESS	WISELING	WISTERIA	WITHERING	WITTIEST
WIRELIKE	WISELINGS	WISTERIAS	WITHERITE	WITTILY
WIREMAN	WISELY	WISTFUL	WITHEROD	WITTINESS
WIREMEN	WISENESS	WISTFULLY	WITHERODS	WITTING
WIREPHOTO	WISENT	WISTING	WITHERS	WITTINGLY
WIRER	WISENTS	WISTITI	WITHES	WITTINGS
WIRERS	WISER	WISTITIS	WITHHAULT	WITTOL
WIRES	WISES	WISTLY	WITHHELD	WITTOLLY
WIRETAP	WISEST	WISTS	WITHHOLD	WITTOLS
WIRETAPS	WISEWOMAN	WIT	WITHHOLDS	WITTY
WIREWAY	WISEWOMEN	WITAN	WITHIER	WITWALL
WIREWAYS	WISH	WITANS	WITHIES	WITWALLS
WIREWORK	WISHA	WITBLITS	WITHIEST	WITWANTON
WIREWORKS	WISHBONE	WITCH	WITHIN	WIVE
WIREWORM	WISHBONES	WITCHED	WITHING	WIVED
WIREWORMS	WISHED	WITCHEN	WITHINS	WIVEHOOD
WIREWOVE	WISHER	WITCHENS	WITHOUT	WIVEHOODS
WIRIER	WISHERS	WITCHERY	WITHOUTEN	WIVER
WIRIEST	WISHES	WITCHES	WITHOUTS	WIVERN
WIRILDA	WISHFUL	WITCHETTY	WITHS	WIVERNS
WIRILDAS	WISHFULLY	WITCHHOOD	WITHSTAND	WIVERS
WIRILY	WISHING	WITCHIER	WITHSTOOD	WIVES
WIRINESS	WISHINGS	WITCHIEST	WITHWIND	WIVING
WIRING	WISHLESS	WITCHING	WITHWINDS	WIZ
WIRINGS	WISHT	WITCHINGS	WITHY	WIZARD
WIRRA	WISING	WITCHKNOT	WITHYWIND	WIZARDLY
WIRRAH	WISKET	WITCHLIKE	WITING	WIZARDRY
WIRRAHS	WISKETS	WITCHWEED	WITLESS	WIZARDS
WIRRICOW	WISP	WITCHY	WITLESSLY	WIZEN
WIRRICOWS	WISPED	WITE	WITLING	WIZENED

WIZENING	WOFULLEST	WOLVES	WOMMITS	WOODBINDS
WIZENS	WOFULLY	WOLVING	WOMYN	WOODBINE
WIZES	WOFULNESS	WOLVINGS	WON	WOODBINES
WIZIER	WOG	WOLVISH	WONDER	WOODBINS
WIZIERS	WOGGISH	WOLVISHLY	WONDERED	WOODBLOCK
WIZZEN	WOGGLE	WOMAN	WONDERER	WOODBORER
WIZZENS	WOGGLES	WOMANED	WONDERERS	WOODBOX
WIZZES	WOGS	WOMANHOOD	WONDERFUL	WOODBOXES
WO	WOIWODE	WOMANING	WONDERING	WOODCHAT
WOAD	WOIWODES	WOMANISE	WONDERKID	WOODCHATS
WOADED	WOK	WOMANISED	WONDEROUS	WOODCHIP
WOADS	WOKE	WOMANISER	WONDERS	WOODCHIPS
WOADWAX	WOKEN	WOMANISES	WONDRED	WOODCHOP
WOADWAXEN	WOKKA	WOMANISH	WONDROUS	WOODCHOPS
WOADWAXES	WOKS	WOMANISM	WONGA	WOODCHUCK
WOALD	WOLD	WOMANISMS	WONGAS	WOODCOCK
WOALDS	WOLDS	WOMANIST	WONGI	WOODCOCKS
WOBBEGONG	WOLF	WOMANISTS	WONGIED	WOODCRAFT
WOBBLE	WOLFBERRY	WOMANIZE	WONGIING	WOODCUT
WOBBLED	WOLFED	WOMANIZED	WONGIS	WOODCUTS
WOBBLER	WOLFER	WOMANIZER	WONING	WOODED
WOBBLERS	WOLFERS	WOMANIZES	WONINGS	WOODEN
WOBBLES	WOLFFISH	WOMANKIND	WONK	WOODENED
WOBBLIER	WOLFHOUND	WOMANLESS	WONKIER	WOODENER
WOBBLIES	WOLFING	WOMANLIER	WONKIEST	WOODENEST
WOBBLIEST	WOLFINGS	WOMANLIKE	WONKS	WOODENING
WOBBLING	WOLFISH	WOMANLY	WONKY	WOODENLY
WOBBLINGS	WOLFISHLY	WOMANNESS	WONNED	WOODENS
WOBBLY	WOLFKIN	WOMANS	WONNER	WOODENTOP
WOBEGONE	WOLFKINS	WOMB	WONNERS	WOODFREE
WOCK	WOLFLIKE	WOMBAT	WONNING	WOODGRAIN
WOCKS	WOLFLING	WOMBATS	WONNINGS	WOODHEN
WODGE	WOLFLINGS	WOMBED	WONS	WOODHENS
WODGES	WOLFRAM	WOMBIER	WONT	WOODHOLE
WOE	WOLFRAMS	WOMBIEST	WONTED	WOODHOLES
WOEBEGONE	WOLFS	WOMBING	WONTEDLY	WOODHORSE
WOEFUL	WOLFSBANE	WOMBLIKE	WONTING	WOODHOUSE
WOEFULLER	WOLFSKIN	WOMBS	WONTLESS	WOODIE
WOEFULLY	WOLFSKINS	WOMBY	WONTON	WOODIER
WOENESS	WOLLIES	WOMEN	WONTONS	WOODIES
WOENESSES	WOLLY	WOMENFOLK	WONTS	WOODIEST
WOES	WOLVE	WOMENKIND	WOO	WOODINESS
WOESOME	WOLVED	WOMERA	WOOBUT	WOODING
WOF	WOLVER	WOMERAS	WOOBUTS	WOODLAND
WOFS	WOLVERENE	WOMMERA	WOOD	WOODLANDS
WOFUL	WOLVERINE	WOMMERAS	WOODBIN	WOODLARK
WOFULLER	WOLVERS	WOMMIT	WOODBIND	WOODLARKS

WOODLESS	WOODWALES	WOOLERS	WOOPS	WORDINESS
WOODLICE	WOODWARD	WOOLFAT	WOOPSED	WORDING
WOODLORE	WOODWARDS	WOOLFATS	WOOPSES	WORDINGS
WOODLORES	WOODWAX	WOOLFELL	WOOPSING	WORDISH
WOODLOT	WOODWAXEN	WOOLFELLS	WOORALI	WORDLESS
WOODLOTS	WOODWAXES	WOOLHAT	WOORALIS	WORDLORE
WOODLOUSE	WOODWIND	WOOLHATS	WOORARA	WORDLORES
WOODMAN	WOODWINDS	WOOLIE	WOORARAS	WORDPLAY
WOODMEAL	WOODWORK	WOOLIER	WOORARI	WORDPLAYS
WOODMEALS	WOODWORKS	WOOLIES	WOORARIS	WORDS
WOODMEN	WOODWORM	WOOLIEST	WOOS	WORDSMITH
WOODMICE	WOODWORMS	WOOLINESS	WOOSE	WORDY
WOODMOUSE	WOODWOSE	WOOLLED	WOOSEL	WORE
WOODNESS	WOODWOSES	WOOLLEN	WOOSELL	WORK
WOODNOTE	WOODY	WOOLLENS	WOOSELLS	WORKABLE
WOODNOTES	WOODYARD	WOOLLIER	WOOSELS	WORKABLY
WOODPILE	WOODYARDS	WOOLLIES	WOOSES	WORKADAY
WOODPILES	WOOED	WOOLLIEST	WOOSH	WORKADAYS
WOODPRINT	WOOER	WOOLLIKE	WOOSHED	WORKBAG
WOODRAT	WOOERS	WOOLLILY	WOOSHES	WORKBAGS
WOODRATS	WOOF	WOOLLY	WOOSHING	WORKBENCH
WOODREEVE	WOOFED	WOOLMAN	WOOT	WORKBOAT
WOODROOF	WOOFER	WOOLMEN	WOOTZ	WORKBOATS
WOODROOFS	WOOFERS	WOOLPACK	WOOTZES	WORKBOOK
WOODRUFF	WOOFIER	WOOLPACKS	WOOZIER	WORKBOOKS
WOODRUFFS	WOOFIEST	WOOLS	WOOZIEST	WORKBOX
WOODRUSH	WOOFING	WOOLSACK	WOOZILY	WORKBOXES
WOODS	WOOFS	WOOLSACKS	WOOZINESS	WORKDAY
WOODSCREW	WOOFTER	WOOLSEY	WOOZY	WORKDAYS
WOODSHED	WOOFTERS	WOOLSEYS	WOP	WORKED
WOODSHEDS	WOOFY	WOOLSHED	WOPPED	WORKER
WOODSHOCK	WOOHOO	WOOLSHEDS	WOPPING	WORKERIST
WOODSIA	WOOING	WOOLSKIN	WOPS	WORKERS
WOODSIAS	WOOINGLY	WOOLSKINS	WORCESTER	WORKFARE
WOODSIER	WOOINGS	WOOLWARD	WORD	WORKFARES
WOODSIEST	WOOL	WOOLWORK	WORDAGE	WORKFLOW
WOODSKIN	WOOLD	WOOLWORKS	WORDAGES	WORKFLOWS
WOODSKINS	WOOLDED	WOOLY	WORDBOOK	WORKFOLK
WOODSMAN	WOOLDER	WOOMERA	WORDBOOKS	WORKFOLKS
WOODSMEN	WOOLDERS	WOOMERANG	WORDBOUND	WORKFORCE
WOODSPITE	WOOLDING	WOOMERAS	WORDBREAK	WORKFUL
WOODSTONE	WOOLDINGS	WOON	WORDED	WORKGIRL
WOODSTOVE	WOOLDS	WOONED	WORDGAME	WORKGIRLS
WOODSY	WOOLED	WOONING	WORDGAMES	WORKGROUP
WOODTONE	WOOLEN	WOONS	WORDIER	WORKHORSE
WOODTONES	WOOLENS	WOOPIE	WORDIEST	WORKHOUR
WOODWALE	WOOLER	WOOPIES	WORDILY	WORKHOURS

WORKHOUSE	WORMED	WORRYCOWS	WOTCHER	WRANG
WORKING	WORMER	WORRYGUTS	WOTS	WRANGED
WORKINGS	WORMERIES	WORRYING	WOTTED	WRANGING
WORKLESS	WORMERS	WORRYINGS	WOTTEST	WRANGLE
WORKLOAD	WORMERY	WORRYWART	WOTTETH	WRANGLED
WORKLOADS	WORMFLIES	WORSE	WOTTING	WRANGLER
WORKMAN	WORMFLY	WORSED	WOUBIT	WRANGLERS
WORKMANLY	WORMGEAR	WORSEN	WOUBITS	WRANGLES
WORKMATE	WORMGEARS	WORSENED	WOULD	WRANGLING
WORKMATES	WORMHOLE	WORSENESS	WOULDEST	WRANGS
WORKMEN	WORMHOLED	WORSENING	WOULDS	WRAP
WORKOUT	WORMHOLES	WORSENS	WOULDST	WRAPOVER
WORKOUTS	WORMIER	WORSER	WOUND	WRAPOVERS
WORKPIECE	WORMIEST	WORSES	WOUNDABLE	WRAPPAGE
WORKPLACE	WORMIL	WORSET	WOUNDED	WRAPPAGES
WORKPRINT	WORMILS	WORSETS	WOUNDEDLY	WRAPPED
WORKROOM	WORMINESS	WORSHIP	WOUNDER	WRAPPER
WORKROOMS	WORMING	WORSHIPED	WOUNDERS	WRAPPERED
WORKS	WORMISH	WORSHIPER	WOUNDILY	WRAPPERS
WORKSAFE	WORMLIKE	WORSHIPS	WOUNDING	WRAPPING
WORKSHEET	WORMROOT	WORSING	WOUNDINGS	WRAPPINGS
WORKSHOP	WORMROOTS	WORST	WOUNDLESS	WRAPROUND
WORKSHOPS	WORMS	WORSTED	WOUNDS	WRAPS
WORKSHY	WORMSEED	WORSTEDS	WOUNDWORT	WRAPT
WORKSOME	WORMSEEDS	WORSTING	WOUNDY	WRASSE
WORKSPACE	WORMWOOD	WORSTS	WOURALI	WRASSES
WORKTABLE	WORMWOODS	WORT	WOURALIS	WRASSLE
WORKTOP	WORMY	WORTH	WOVE	WRASSLED
WORKTOPS	WORN	WORTHED	WOVEN	WRASSLES
WORKUP	WORNNESS	WORTHFUL	WOVENS	WRASSLING
WORKUPS	WORRAL	WORTHIED	WOW	WRAST
WORKWEAR	WORRALS	WORTHIER	WOWED	WRASTED
WORKWEARS	WORREL	WORTHIES	WOWEE	WRASTING
WORKWEEK	WORRELS	WORTHIEST	WOWF	WRASTLE
WORKWEEKS	WORRICOW	WORTHILY	WOWFER	WRASTLED
WORKWOMAN	WORRICOWS	WORTHING	WOWFEST	WRASTLES
WORKWOMEN	WORRIED	WORTHLESS	WOWING	WRASTLING
WORLD	WORRIEDLY	WORTHS	WOWS	WRASTS
WORLDBEAT	WORRIER	WORTHY	WOWSER	WRATE
WORLDED	WORRIERS	WORTHYING	WOWSERS	WRATH
WORLDLIER	WORRIES	WORTLE	WOX	WRATHED
WORLDLING	WORRIMENT	WORTLES	WOXEN	WRATHFUL
WORLDLY	WORRISOME	WORTS	WRACK	WRATHIER
WORLDS	WORRIT	WOS	WRACKED	WRATHIEST
WORLDVIEW	WORRITED	WOSBIRD	WRACKFUL	WRATHILY
WORLDWIDE	WORRITING	WOSBIRDS	WRACKING	WRATHING
WORM	WORRITS	WOST	WRACKS	WRATHLESS
WORMCAST	WORRY	WOT	WRAITH	WRATHS
WORMCASTS	WORRYCOW	WOTCHA	WRAITHS	WRATHY

WRAWL	WREST	WRINKLIES	WRONGING	WURSTS
WRAWLED	WRESTED	WRINKLING	WRONGLY	WURTZITE
WRAWLING	WRESTER	WRINKLY	WRONGNESS	WURTZITES
WRAWLS	WRESTERS	WRIST	WRONGOUS	WURZEL
WRAXLE	WRESTING	WRISTBAND	WRONGS	WURZELS
WRAXLED	WRESTLE	WRISTIER	WROOT	WUS
WRAXLES	WRESTLED	WRISTIEST	WROOTED	WUSES
WRAXLING	WRESTLER	WRISTLET	WROOTING	WUSHU
WRAXLINGS	WRESTLERS	WRISTLETS	WROOTS	WUSHUS
WREAK	WRESTLES	WRISTLOCK	WROTE	WUSS
WREAKED	WRESTLING	WRISTS	WROTH	WUSSES
WREAKER	WRESTS	WRISTY	WROTHFUL	WUSSIER
WREAKERS	WRETCH	WRIT	WROUGHT	WUSSIES
WREAKFUL	WRETCHED	WRITABLE	WRUNG	WUSSIEST
WREAKING	WRETCHES	WRITATIVE	WRY	WUSSY
WREAKLESS	WRETHE	WRITE	WRYBILL	WUTHER
WREAKS	WRETHED	WRITEABLE	WRYBILLS	WUTHERED
WREATH	WRETHES	WRITER	WRYER	WUTHERING
WREATHE	WRETHING	WRITERESS	WRYEST	WUTHERS
WREATHED	WRICK	WRITERLY	WRYING	WUXIA
WREATHEN	WRICKED	WRITERS	WRYLY	WUXIAS
WREATHER	WRICKING	WRITES	WRYNECK	WUZZLE
WREATHERS	WRICKS	WRITHE	WRYNECKS	WUZZLED
WREATHES	WRIED	WRITHED	WRYNESS	WUZZLES
WREATHIER	WRIER	WRITHEN	WRYNESSES	WUZZLING
WREATHING	WRIES	WRITHER	WRYTHEN	WYANDOTTE
WREATHS	WRIEST	WRITHERS	WUD	WYCH
WREATHY	WRIGGLE	WRITHES	WUDDED	WYCHES
WRECK	WRIGGLED	WRITHING	WUDDING	WYE
WRECKAGE	WRIGGLER	WRITHINGS	WUDJULA	WYES
WRECKAGES	WRIGGLERS	WRITHLED	WUDJULAS	WYLE
WRECKED	WRIGGLES	WRITING	WUDS	WYLED
WRECKER	WRIGGLIER	WRITINGS	WUDU	WYLES
WRECKERS	WRIGGLING	WRITS	WUDUS	WYLIECOAT
WRECKFISH	WRIGGLY	WRITTEN	WUKKAS	WYLING
WRECKFUL	WRIGHT	WRIZLED	WULFENITE	WYN
WRECKING	WRIGHTS	WROATH	WULL	WYND
WRECKINGS	WRING	WROATHS	WULLED	WYNDS
WRECKS	WRINGED	WROKE	WULLING	WYNN
WREN	WRINGER	WROKEN	WULLS	WYNNS
WRENCH	WRINGERS	WRONG	WUNNER	WYNS
WRENCHED	WRINGING	WRONGDOER	WUNNERS	WYTE
WRENCHER	WRINGS	WRONGED	WURLEY	WYTED
WRENCHERS	WRINKLE	WRONGER	WURLEYS	WYTES
WRENCHES	WRINKLED	WRONGERS	WURLIE	WYTING
WRENCHING	WRINKLES	WRONGEST	WURLIES	WYVERN
WRENS	WRINKLIER	WRONGFUL	WURST	WYVERNS

X

XANTHAM
XANTHAMS
XANTHAN
XANTHANS
XANTHATE
XANTHATES
XANTHEIN
XANTHEINS
XANTHENE
XANTHENES
XANTHIC
XANTHIN
XANTHINE
XANTHINES
XANTHINS
XANTHISM
XANTHISMS
XANTHOMA
XANTHOMAS
XANTHONE
XANTHONES
XANTHOUS
XANTHOXYL
XEBEC
XEBECS
XENIA
XENIAL
XENIAS
XENIC
XENIUM

XENOBLAST
XENOCRYST
XENOGAMY
XENOGENIC
XENOGENY
XENOGRAFT
XENOLITH
XENOLITHS
XENOMANIA
XENOMENIA
XENON
XENONS
XENOPHILE
XENOPHOBE
XENOPHOBY
XENOPHYA
XENOPUS
XENOPUSES
XENOTIME
XENOTIMES
XENURINE
XERAFIN
XERAFINS
XERANSES
XERANSIS
XERANTIC
XERAPHIN
XERAPHINS
XERARCH
XERASIA

XERASIAS
XERIC
XERICALLY
XERISCAPE
XEROCHASY
XERODERMA
XEROMA
XEROMAS
XEROMATA
XEROMORPH
XEROPHAGY
XEROPHILE
XEROPHILY
XEROPHYTE
XEROSERE
XEROSERES
XEROSES
XEROSIS
XEROSTOMA
XEROTES
XEROTIC
XEROX
XEROXED
XEROXES
XEROXING
XERUS
XERUSES
XI
XIPHOID
XIPHOIDAL

XIPHOIDS
XIPHOPAGI
XIS
XOANA
XOANON
XRAY
XRAYS
XU
XYLAN
XYLANS
XYLEM
XYLEMS
XYLENE
XYLENES
XYLENOL
XYLENOLS
XYLIC
XYLIDIN
XYLIDINE
XYLIDINES
XYLIDINS
XYLITOL
XYLITOLS
XYLOCARP
XYLOCARPS
XYLOGEN
XYLOGENS
XYLOGRAPH
XYLOID
XYLOIDIN

XYLOIDINE
XYLOIDINS
XYLOL
XYLOLOGY
XYLOLS
XYLOMA
XYLOMAS
XYLOMATA
XYLOMETER
XYLONIC
XYLONITE
XYLONITES
XYLOPHAGE
XYLOPHONE
XYLORIMBA
XYLOSE
XYLOSES
XYLOTOMY
XYLYL
XYLYLS
XYST
XYSTER
XYSTERS
XYSTI
XYSTOI
XYSTOS
XYSTS
XYSTUS

Y

YA	YAFFLE	YAMENS	YAPPIES	YARKED
YAAR	YAFFLES	YAMMER	YAPPIEST	YARKING
YAARS	YAFFS	YAMMERED	YAPPING	YARKS
YABA	YAG	YAMMERER	YAPPINGLY	YARMELKE
YABAS	YAGER	YAMMERERS	YAPPS	YARMELKES
YABBA	YAGERS	YAMMERING	YAPPY	YARMULKA
YABBAS	YAGGER	YAMMERS	YAPS	YARMULKAS
YABBER	YAGGERS	YAMPIES	YAPSTER	YARMULKE
YABBERED	YAGI	YAMPY	YAPSTERS	YARMULKES
YABBERING	YAGIS	YAMS	YAQONA	YARN
YABBERS	YAGS	YAMULKA	YAQONAS	YARNED
YABBIE	YAH	YAMULKAS	YAR	YARNER
YABBIED	YAHOO	YAMUN	YARCO	YARNERS
YABBIES	YAHOOISM	YAMUNS	YARCOS	YARNING
YABBY	YAHOOISMS	YANG	YARD	YARNS
YABBYING	YAHOOS	YANGS	YARDAGE	YARPHA
YACCA	YAHRZEIT	YANK	YARDAGES	YARPHAS
YACCAS	YAHRZEITS	YANKED	YARDANG	YARR
YACHT	YAHS	YANKEE	YARDANGS	YARRAMAN
YACHTED	YAIRD	YANKEES	YARDARM	YARRAMANS
YACHTER	YAIRDS	YANKER	YARDARMS	YARRAMEN
YACHTERS	YAK	YANKERS	YARDBIRD	YARRAN
YACHTIE	YAKHDAN	YANKIE	YARDBIRDS	YARRANS
YACHTIES	YAKHDANS	YANKIES	YARDED	YARROW
YACHTING	YAKIMONO	YANKING	YARDER	YARROWS
YACHTINGS	YAKIMONOS	YANKS	YARDERS	YARRS
YACHTMAN	YAKITORI	YANQUI	YARDING	YARTA
YACHTMEN	YAKITORIS	YANQUIS	YARDINGS	YARTAS
YACHTS	YAKKA	YANTRA	YARDLAND	YARTO
YACHTSMAN	YAKKAS	YANTRAS	YARDLANDS	YARTOS
YACHTSMEN	YAKKED	YAOURT	YARDMAN	YASHMAC
YACK	YAKKER	YAOURTS	YARDMEN	YASHMACS
YACKA	YAKKERS	YAP	YARDS	YASHMAK
YACKAS	YAKKING	YAPOCK	YARDSTICK	YASHMAKS
YACKED	YAKOW	YAPOCKS	YARDWAND	YASMAK
YACKER	YAKOWS	YAPOK	YARDWANDS	YASMAKS
YACKERS	YAKS	YAPOKS	YARDWORK	YATAGAN
YACKING	YAKUZA	YAPON	YARDWORKS	YATAGANS
YACKS	YALD	YAPONS	YARE	YATAGHAN
YAD	YALE	YAPP	YARELY	YATAGHANS
YADS	YALES	YAPPED	YARER	YATE
YAE	YAM	YAPPER	YAREST	YATES
YAFF	YAMALKA	YAPPERS	YARFA	YATTER
YAFFED	YAMALKAS	YAPPIE	YARFAS	YATTERED
YAFFING	YAMEN	YAPPIER	YARK	YATTERING

YATTERS	YBET	YEARLIES	YELD	YENTA
YAUD	YBLENT	YEARLING	YELDRING	YENTAS
YAUDS	YBORE	YEARLINGS	YELDRINGS	YENTE
YAULD	YBOUND	YEARLONG	YELDROCK	YENTES
YAUP	YBOUNDEN	YEARLY	YELDROCKS	YEOMAN
YAUPED	YBRENT	YEARN	YELK	YEOMANLY
YAUPER	YCLAD	YEARNED	YELKS	YEOMANRY
YAUPERS	YCLED	YEARNER	YELL	YEOMEN
YAUPING	YCLEEPE	YEARNERS	YELLED	YEP
YAUPON	YCLEEPED	YEARNING	YELLER	YEPS
YAUPONS	YCLEEPES	YEARNINGS	YELLERS	YERBA
YAUPS	YCLEEPING	YEARNS	YELLING	YERBAS
YAUTIA	YCLEPED	YEARS	YELLINGS	YERD
YAUTIAS	YCLEPT	YEAS	YELLOCH	YERDED
YAW	YCOND	YEASAYER	YELLOCHED	YERDING
YAWED	YDRAD	YEASAYERS	YELLOCHS	YERDS
YAWEY	YDRED	YEAST	YELLOW	YERK
YAWING	YE	YEASTED	YELLOWED	YERKED
YAWL	YEA	YEASTIER	YELLOWER	YERKING
YAWLED	YEAD	YEASTIEST	YELLOWEST	YERKS
YAWLING	YEADING	YEASTILY	YELLOWFIN	YERSINIA
YAWLS	YEADS	YEASTING	YELLOWIER	YERSINIAE
YAWMETER	YEAH	YEASTLESS	YELLOWING	YERSINIAS
YAWMETERS	YEAHS	YEASTLIKE	YELLOWISH	YES
YAWN	YEALDON	YEASTS	YELLOWLY	YESES
YAWNED	YEALDONS	YEASTY	YELLOWS	YESHIVA
YAWNER	YEALING	YEBO	YELLOWY	YESHIVAH
YAWNERS	YEALINGS	YECCH	YELLS	YESHIVAHS
YAWNIER	YEALM	YECCHS	YELM	YESHIVAS
YAWNIEST	YEALMED	YECH	YELMED	YESHIVOT
YAWNING	YEALMING	YECHIER	YELMING	YESHIVOTH
YAWNINGLY	YEALMS	YECHIEST	YELMS	YESK
YAWNINGS	YEAN	YECHS	YELP	YESKED
YAWNS	YEANED	YECHY	YELPED	YESKING
YAWNSOME	YEANING	YEDE	YELPER	YESKS
YAWNY	YEANLING	YEDES	YELPERS	YESSED
YAWP	YEANLINGS	YEDING	YELPING	YESSES
YAWPED	YEANS	YEED	YELPINGS	YESSING
YAWPER	YEAR	YEEDING	YELPS	YEST
YAWPERS	YEARBOOK	YEEDS	YELT	YESTER
YAWPING	YEARBOOKS	YEELIN	YELTS	YESTERDAY
YAWPINGS	YEARD	YEELINS	YEMMER	YESTEREVE
YAWPS	YEARDED	YEGG	YEMMERS	YESTERN
YAWS	YEARDING	YEGGMAN	YEN	YESTREEN
YAWY	YEARDS	YEGGMEN	YENNED	YESTREENS
YAY	YEAREND	YEGGS	YENNING	YESTS
YAYS	YEARENDS	YEH	YENS	YESTY

YET	YIKED	YLIKE	YODS	YOKERING
YETI	YIKES	YLKE	YOGA	YOKERS
YETIS	YIKING	YLKES	YOGAS	YOKES
YETT	YIKKER	YMOLT	YOGEE	YOKING
YETTIE	YIKKERED	YMOLTEN	YOGEES	YOKINGS
YETTIES	YIKKERING	YMPE	YOGH	YOKKED
YETTS	YIKKERS	YMPES	YOGHOURT	YOKKING
YEUK	YILL	YMPING	YOGHOURTS	YOKOZUNA
YEUKED	YILLS	YMPT	YOGHS	YOKOZUNAS
YEUKIER	YIN	YNAMBU	YOGHURT	YOKS
YEUKIEST	YINCE	YNAMBUS	YOGHURTS	YOKUL
YEUKING	YINDIE	YO	YOGI	YOLD
YEUKS	YINDIES	YOB	YOGIC	YOLDRING
YEUKY	YINS	YOBBERIES	YOGIN	YOLDRINGS
YEVE	YIP	YOBBERY	YOGINI	YOLK
YEVEN	YIPE	YOBBISH	YOGINIS	YOLKED
YEVES	YIPES	YOBBISHLY	YOGINS	YOLKIER
YEVING	YIPPED	YOBBISM	YOGIS	YOLKIEST
YEW	YIPPEE	YOBBISMS	YOGISM	YOLKLESS
YEWEN	YIPPER	YOBBO	YOGISMS	YOLKS
YEWS	YIPPERS	YOBBOES	YOGURT	YOLKY
YEX	YIPPIE	YOBBOS	YOGURTS	YOM
YEXED	YIPPIES	YOBS	YOHIMBE	YOMIM
YEXES	YIPPING	YOCK	YOHIMBES	YOMP
YEXING	YIPPY	YOCKED	YOHIMBINE	YOMPED
YFERE	YIPS	YOCKING	YOICK	YOMPING
YGLAUNST	YIRD	YOCKS	YOICKED	YOMPS
YGO	YIRDED	YOD	YOICKING	YON
YGOE	YIRDING	YODE	YOICKS	YOND
YIBBLES	YIRDS	YODEL	YOICKSED	YONDER
YICKER	YIRK	YODELED	YOICKSES	YONDERLY
YICKERED	YIRKED	YODELER	YOICKSING	YONDERS
YICKERING	YIRKING	YODELERS	YOJAN	YONI
YICKERS	YIRKS	YODELING	YOJANA	YONIC
YID	YIRR	YODELLED	YOJANAS	YONIS
YIDAKI	YIRRED	YODELLER	YOJANS	YONKER
YIDAKIS	YIRRING	YODELLERS	YOK	YONKERS
YIDS	YIRRS	YODELLING	YOKE	YONKS
YIELD	YIRTH	YODELS	YOKED	YONNIE
YIELDABLE	YIRTHS	YODH	YOKEL	YONNIES
YIELDED	YITE	YODHS	YOKELESS	YONT
YIELDER	YITES	YODLE	YOKELISH	YOOF
YIELDERS	YITIE	YODLED	YOKELS	YOOFS
YIELDING	YITIES	YODLER	YOKEMATE	YOOP
YIELDINGS	YITTEN	YODLERS	YOKEMATES	YOOPS
YIELDS	YLEM	YODLES	YOKER	YORE
YIKE	YLEMS	YODLING	YOKERED	YORES

YORK	YOURT	YPSILON	YUCKIEST	YUMMIEST
YORKED	YOURTS	YPSILONS	YUCKINESS	YUMMINESS
YORKER	YOUS	YRAPT	YUCKING	YUMMO
YORKERS	YOUSE	YRAVISHED	YUCKO	YUMMY
YORKIE	YOUTH	YRENT	YUCKS	YUMP
YORKIES	YOUTHEN	YRIVD	YUCKY	YUMPED
YORKING	YOUTHENED	YRNEH	YUFT	YUMPIE
YORKS	YOUTHENS	YRNEHS	YUFTS	YUMPIES
YORLING	YOUTHFUL	YSAME	YUG	YUMPING
YORLINGS	YOUTHHEAD	YSHEND	YUGA	YUMPS
YORP	YOUTHHOOD	YSHENDING	YUGARIE	YUNX
YORPED	YOUTHIER	YSHENDS	YUGARIES	YUNXES
YORPING	YOUTHIEST	YSHENT	YUGAS	YUP
YORPS	YOUTHLESS	YSLAKED	YUGS	YUPON
YOTTABYTE	YOUTHLY	YTOST	YUK	YUPONS
YOU	YOUTHS	YTTERBIA	YUKATA	YUPPIE
YOUK	YOUTHSOME	YTTERBIAS	YUKATAS	YUPPIEDOM
YOUKED	YOUTHY	YTTERBIC	YUKE	YUPPIEISH
YOUKING	YOW	YTTERBITE	YUKED	YUPPIES
YOUKS	YOWE	YTTERBIUM	YUKES	YUPPIFIED
YOUNG	YOWED	YTTERBOUS	YUKIER	YUPPIFIES
YOUNGER	YOWES	YTTRIA	YUKIEST	YUPPIFY
YOUNGERS	YOWIE	YTTRIAS	YUKING	YUPPY
YOUNGEST	YOWIES	YTTRIC	YUKKED	YUPS
YOUNGISH	YOWING	YTTRIOUS	YUKKIER	YUPSTER
YOUNGLING	YOWL	YTTRIUM	YUKKIEST	YUPSTERS
YOUNGLY	YOWLED	YTTRIUMS	YUKKING	YURT
YOUNGNESS	YOWLER	YU	YUKKY	YURTA
YOUNGS	YOWLERS	YUAN	YUKO	YURTAS
YOUNGSTER	YOWLEY	YUANS	YUKOS	YURTS
YOUNGTH	YOWLEYS	YUCA	YUKS	YUS
YOUNGTHLY	YOWLING	YUCAS	YUKY	YUTZ
YOUNGTHS	YOWLINGS	YUCCA	YULAN	YUTZES
YOUNKER	YOWLS	YUCCAS	YULANS	YUZU
YOUNKERS	YOWS	YUCCH	YULE	YUZUS
YOUPON	YPERITE	YUCH	YULES	YWIS
YOUPONS	YPERITES	YUCK	YULETIDE	YWROKE
YOUR	YPIGHT	YUCKED	YULETIDES	
YOURN	YPLAST	YUCKER	YUM	
YOURS	YPLIGHT	YUCKERS	YUMMIER	
YOURSELF	YPSILOID	YUCKIER	YUMMIES	

Y

Z

ZA	ZAMAN	ZANJERO	ZARIS	ZEBRASSES
ZABAIONE	ZAMANG	ZANJEROS	ZARNEC	ZEBRAWOOD
ZABAIONES	ZAMANGS	ZANTE	ZARNECS	ZEBRINA
ZABAJONE	ZAMANS	ZANTES	ZARNICH	ZEBRINAS
ZABAJONES	ZAMARRA	ZANTHOXYL	ZARNICHS	ZEBRINE
ZABETA	ZAMARRAS	ZANY	ZARZUELA	ZEBRINES
ZABETAS	ZAMARRO	ZANYING	ZARZUELAS	ZEBRINNY
ZABRA	ZAMARROS	ZANYISH	ZAS	ZEBROID
ZABRAS	ZAMBO	ZANYISM	ZASTRUGA	ZEBRULA
ZABTIEH	ZAMBOMBA	ZANYISMS	ZASTRUGI	ZEBRULAS
ZABTIEHS	ZAMBOMBAS	ZANZA	ZATI	ZEBRULE
ZACATON	ZAMBOORAK	ZANZAS	ZATIS	ZEBRULES
ZACATONS	ZAMBOS	ZANZE	ZAX	ZEBU
ZACK	ZAMBUCK	ZANZES	ZAXES	ZEBUB
ZACKS	ZAMBUCKS	ZAP	ZAYIN	ZEBUBS
ZADDICK	ZAMBUK	ZAPATA	ZAYINS	ZEBUS
ZADDIK	ZAMBUKS	ZAPATEADO	ZAZEN	ZECCHIN
ZADDIKIM	ZAMIA	ZAPATEO	ZAZENS	ZECCHINE
ZADDIKS	ZAMIAS	ZAPATEOS	ZEA	ZECCHINES
ZAFFAR	ZAMINDAR	ZAPOTILLA	ZEAL	ZECCHINI
ZAFFARS	ZAMINDARI	ZAPPED	ZEALANT	ZECCHINO
ZAFFER	ZAMINDARS	ZAPPER	ZEALANTS	ZECCHINOS
ZAFFERS	ZAMINDARY	ZAPPERS	ZEALFUL	ZECCHINS
ZAFFIR	ZAMOUSE	ZAPPIER	ZEALLESS	ZECHIN
ZAFFIRS	ZAMOUSES	ZAPPIEST	ZEALOT	ZECHINS
ZAFFRE	ZAMPOGNA	ZAPPING	ZEALOTISM	ZED
ZAFFRES	ZAMPOGNAS	ZAPPY	ZEALOTRY	ZEDOARIES
ZAFTIG	ZAMPONE	ZAPS	ZEALOTS	ZEDOARY
ZAG	ZAMPONI	ZAPTIAH	ZEALOUS	ZEDS
ZAGGED	ZAMZAWED	ZAPTIAHS	ZEALOUSLY	ZEE
ZAGGING	ZANAMIVIR	ZAPTIEH	ZEALS	ZEES
ZAGS	ZANANA	ZAPTIEHS	ZEAS	ZEIN
ZAIBATSU	ZANANAS	ZARAPE	ZEATIN	ZEINS
ZAIKAI	ZANDER	ZARAPES	ZEATINS	ZEITGEBER
ZAIKAIS	ZANDERS	ZARATITE	ZEBEC	ZEITGEIST
ZAIRE	ZANELLA	ZARATITES	ZEBECK	ZEK
ZAIRES	ZANELLAS	ZAREBA	ZEBECKS	ZEKS
ZAITECH	ZANIED	ZAREBAS	ZEBECS	ZEL
ZAITECHS	ZANIER	ZAREEBA	ZEBRA	ZELANT
ZAKAT	ZANIES	ZAREEBAS	ZEBRAFISH	ZELANTS
ZAKATS	ZANIEST	ZARF	ZEBRAIC	ZELATOR
ZAKOUSKA	ZANILY	ZARFS	ZEBRANO	ZELATORS
ZAKOUSKI	ZANINESS	ZARI	ZEBRANOS	ZELATRICE
ZAKUSKA	ZANJA	ZARIBA	ZEBRAS	ZELATRIX
ZAKUSKI	ZANJAS	ZARIBAS	ZEBRASS	ZELKOVA

Z

ZELKOVAS	ZERUMBETS	ZIGANS	ZINCITES	ZINKIFIES
ZELOSO	ZEST	ZIGGED	ZINCKED	ZINKIFY
ZELOTYPIA	ZESTED	ZIGGING	ZINCKIER	ZINKING
ZELS	ZESTER	ZIGGURAT	ZINCKIEST	ZINKY
ZEMINDAR	ZESTERS	ZIGGURATS	ZINCKIFY	ZINNIA
ZEMINDARI	ZESTFUL	ZIGS	ZINCKING	ZINNIAS
ZEMINDARS	ZESTFULLY	ZIGZAG	ZINCKY	ZINS
ZEMINDARY	ZESTIER	ZIGZAGGED	ZINCO	ZIP
ZEMSTVA	ZESTIEST	ZIGZAGGER	ZINCODE	ZIPLESS
ZEMSTVO	ZESTILY	ZIGZAGGY	ZINCODES	ZIPLOCK
ZEMSTVOS	ZESTING	ZIGZAGS	ZINCOID	ZIPLOCKED
ZENAIDA	ZESTLESS	ZIKKURAT	ZINCOS	ZIPLOCKS
ZENAIDAS	ZESTS	ZIKKURATS	ZINCOUS	ZIPPED
ZENANA	ZESTY	ZIKURAT	ZINCS	ZIPPER
ZENANAS	ZETA	ZIKURATS	ZINCY	ZIPPERED
ZENDIK	ZETAS	ZILA	ZINDABAD	ZIPPERING
ZENDIKS	ZETETIC	ZILAS	ZINE	ZIPPERS
ZENITH	ZETETICS	ZILCH	ZINEB	ZIPPIER
ZENITHAL	ZETTABYTE	ZILCHES	ZINEBS	ZIPPIEST
ZENITHS	ZEUGMA	ZILL	ZINES	ZIPPING
ZEOLITE	ZEUGMAS	ZILLA	ZINFANDEL	ZIPPO
ZEOLITES	ZEUGMATIC	ZILLAH	ZING	ZIPPOS
ZEOLITIC	ZEUXITE	ZILLAHS	ZINGANI	ZIPPY
ZEP	ZEUXITES	ZILLAS	ZINGANO	ZIPS
ZEPHYR	ZEX	ZILLION	ZINGARA	ZIPTOP
ZEPHYRS	ZEXES	ZILLIONS	ZINGARE	ZIRAM
ZEPPELIN	ZEZE	ZILLIONTH	ZINGARI	ZIRAMS
ZEPPELINS	ZEZES	ZILLS	ZINGARO	ZIRCALLOY
ZEPPOLE	ZHO	ZIMB	ZINGED	ZIRCALOY
ZEPPOLES	ZHOMO	ZIMBI	ZINGEL	ZIRCALOYS
ZEPPOLI	ZHOMOS	ZIMBIS	ZINGELS	ZIRCON
ZEPS	ZHOS	ZIMBS	ZINGER	ZIRCONIA
ZERDA	ZIBELINE	ZIMOCCA	ZINGERS	ZIRCONIAS
ZERDAS	ZIBELINES	ZIMOCCAS	ZINGIBER	ZIRCONIC
ZEREBA	ZIBELLINE	ZIN	ZINGIBERS	ZIRCONIUM
ZEREBAS	ZIBET	ZINC	ZINGIER	ZIRCONS
ZERIBA	ZIBETH	ZINCATE	ZINGIEST	ZIT
ZERIBAS	ZIBETHS	ZINCATES	ZINGING	ZITE
ZERK	ZIBETS	ZINCED	ZINGS	ZITHER
ZERKS	ZIFF	ZINCIC	ZINGY	ZITHERIST
ZERO	ZIFFIUS	ZINCIER	ZINKE	ZITHERN
ZEROED	ZIFFIUSES	ZINCIEST	ZINKED	ZITHERNS
ZEROES	ZIFFS	ZINCIFIED	ZINKENITE	ZITHERS
ZEROING	ZIG	ZINCIFIES	ZINKES	ZITI
ZEROS	ZIGAN	ZINCIFY	ZINKIER	ZITIS
ZEROTH	ZIGANKA	ZINCING	ZINKIEST	ZITS
ZERUMBET	ZIGANKAS	ZINCITE	ZINKIFIED	ZIZ

ZIZANIA	ZOECIUM	ZONERS	ZOOGLEAL	ZOON
ZIZANIAS	ZOEFORM	ZONES	ZOOGLEAS	ZOONAL
ZIZEL	ZOETIC	ZONETIME	ZOOGLOEA	ZOONED
ZIZELS	ZOETROPE	ZONETIMES	ZOOGLOEAE	ZOONIC
ZIZIT	ZOETROPES	ZONING	ZOOGLOEAL	ZOONING
ZIZITH	ZOETROPIC	ZONINGS	ZOOGLOEAS	ZOONITE
ZIZYPHUS	ZOFTIG	ZONK	ZOOGLOEIC	ZOONITES
ZIZZ	ZOIATRIA	ZONKED	ZOOGONIES	ZOONITIC
ZIZZED	ZOIATRIAS	ZONKING	ZOOGONOUS	ZOONOMIA
ZIZZES	ZOIATRICS	ZONKS	ZOOGONY	ZOONOMIAS
ZIZZING	ZOIC	ZONOID	ZOOGRAFT	ZOONOMIC
ZIZZLE	ZOISITE	ZONULA	ZOOGRAFTS	ZOONOMIES
ZIZZLED	ZOISITES	ZONULAE	ZOOGRAPHY	ZOONOMIST
ZIZZLES	ZOISM	ZONULAR	ZOOID	ZOONOMY
ZIZZLING	ZOISMS	ZONULAS	ZOOIDAL	ZOONOSES
ZLOTE	ZOIST	ZONULE	ZOOIDS	ZOONOSIS
ZLOTIES	ZOISTS	ZONULES	ZOOIER	ZOONOTIC
ZLOTY	ZOL	ZONULET	ZOOIEST	ZOONS
ZLOTYCH	ZOLPIDEM	ZONULETS	ZOOKEEPER	ZOOPATHY
ZLOTYS	ZOLPIDEMS	ZONURE	ZOOKS	ZOOPERAL
ZO	ZOLS	ZONURES	ZOOLATER	ZOOPERIES
ZOA	ZOMBI	ZOO	ZOOLATERS	ZOOPERIST
ZOAEA	ZOMBIE	ZOOBIOTIC	ZOOLATRIA	ZOOPERY
ZOAEAE	ZOMBIES	ZOOBLAST	ZOOLATRY	ZOOPHAGAN
ZOAEAS	ZOMBIFIED	ZOOBLASTS	ZOOLITE	ZOOPHAGY
ZOARIA	ZOMBIFIES	ZOOCHORE	ZOOLITES	ZOOPHILE
ZOARIAL	ZOMBIFY	ZOOCHORES	ZOOLITH	ZOOPHILES
ZOARIUM	ZOMBIISM	ZOOCHORY	ZOOLITHIC	ZOOPHILIA
ZOBO	ZOMBIISMS	ZOOCYTIA	ZOOLITHS	ZOOPHILIC
ZOBOS	ZOMBIS	ZOOCYTIUM	ZOOLITIC	ZOOPHILY
ZOBU	ZOMBORUK	ZOOEA	ZOOLOGIC	ZOOPHOBE
ZOBUS	ZOMBORUKS	ZOOEAE	ZOOLOGIES	ZOOPHOBES
ZOCALO	ZONA	ZOOEAL	ZOOLOGIST	ZOOPHOBIA
ZOCALOS	ZONAE	ZOOEAS	ZOOLOGY	ZOOPHORI
ZOCCO	ZONAL	ZOOECIA	ZOOM	ZOOPHORIC
ZOCCOLO	ZONALLY	ZOOECIUM	ZOOMANCY	ZOOPHORUS
ZOCCOLOS	ZONARY	ZOOEY	ZOOMANIA	ZOOPHYTE
ZOCCOS	ZONATE	ZOOGAMETE	ZOOMANIAS	ZOOPHYTES
ZODIAC	ZONATED	ZOOGAMIES	ZOOMANTIC	ZOOPHYTIC
ZODIACAL	ZONATION	ZOOGAMOUS	ZOOMED	ZOOPLASTY
ZODIACS	ZONATIONS	ZOOGAMY	ZOOMETRIC	ZOOS
ZOEA	ZONDA	ZOOGENIC	ZOOMETRY	ZOOSCOPIC
ZOEAE	ZONDAS	ZOOGENIES	ZOOMING	ZOOSCOPY
ZOEAL	ZONE	ZOOGENOUS	ZOOMORPH	ZOOSPERM
ZOEAS	ZONED	ZOOGENY	ZOOMORPHS	ZOOSPERMS
ZOECHROME	ZONELESS	ZOOGLEA	ZOOMORPHY	ZOOSPORE
ZOECIA	ZONER	ZOOGLEAE	ZOOMS	ZOOSPORES

Z

ZOOSPORIC	ZORBING	ZUCCHINI	ZYGAL	ZYMOGEN
ZOOSTEROL	ZORBINGS	ZUCCHINIS	ZYGANTRA	ZYMOGENE
ZOOT	ZORBONAUT	ZUCHETTA	ZYGANTRUM	ZYMOGENES
ZOOTAXIES	ZORGITE	ZUCHETTAS	ZYGOCACTI	ZYMOGENIC
ZOOTAXY	ZORGITES	ZUCHETTO	ZYGODONT	ZYMOGENS
ZOOTECHNY	ZORI	ZUCHETTOS	ZYGOID	ZYMOGRAM
ZOOTHECIA	ZORIL	ZUFFOLI	ZYGOMA	ZYMOGRAMS
ZOOTHEISM	ZORILLA	ZUFFOLO	ZYGOMAS	ZYMOID
ZOOTHOME	ZORILLAS	ZUFOLI	ZYGOMATA	ZYMOLOGIC
ZOOTHOMES	ZORILLE	ZUFOLO	ZYGOMATIC	ZYMOLOGY
ZOOTIER	ZORILLES	ZUGZWANG	ZYGON	ZYMOLYSES
ZOOTIEST	ZORILLO	ZUGZWANGS	ZYGOPHYTE	ZYMOLYSIS
ZOOTOMIC	ZORILLOS	ZULU	ZYGOSE	ZYMOLYTIC
ZOOTOMIES	ZORILS	ZULUS	ZYGOSES	ZYMOME
ZOOTOMIST	ZORINO	ZUMBOORUK	ZYGOSIS	ZYMOMES
ZOOTOMY	ZORINOS	ZUPA	ZYGOSITY	ZYMOMETER
ZOOTOXIC	ZORIS	ZUPAN	ZYGOSPERM	ZYMOSAN
ZOOTOXIN	ZORRO	ZUPANS	ZYGOSPORE	ZYMOSANS
ZOOTOXINS	ZORROS	ZUPAS	ZYGOTE	ZYMOSES
ZOOTROPE	ZOS	ZURF	ZYGOTENE	ZYMOSIS
ZOOTROPES	ZOSTER	ZURFS	ZYGOTENES	ZYMOTIC
ZOOTROPHY	ZOSTERS	ZUZ	ZYGOTES	ZYMOTICS
ZOOTY	ZOUAVE	ZUZIM	ZYGOTIC	ZYMURGIES
ZOOTYPE	ZOUAVES	ZUZZIM	ZYLONITE	ZYMURGY
ZOOTYPES	ZOUK	ZWANZIGER	ZYLONITES	ZYTHUM
ZOOTYPIC	ZOUKS	ZWIEBACK	ZYMASE	ZYTHUMS
ZOOZOO	ZOUNDS	ZWIEBACKS	ZYMASES	ZYZZYVA
ZOOZOOS	ZOWIE	ZYDECO	ZYME	ZYZZYVAS
ZOPILOTE	ZOYSIA	ZYDECOS	ZYMES	ZZZ
ZOPILOTES	ZOYSIAS	ZYGA	ZYMIC	ZZZS
ZOPPA	ZUCCHETTI	ZYGAENID	ZYMITE	
ZOPPO	ZUCCHETTO	ZYGAENOID	ZYMITES	

ten to fifteen
letter words

AARDWOLVES	ABERRANCIES	ABLATIVELY	ABORIGINALLY	ABSCISSIONS
ABACTERIAL	ABERRANTLY	ABLUTIONARY	ABORIGINALS	ABSCONDENCE
ABACTINALLY	ABERRATING	ABLUTOMANE	ABORIGINES	ABSCONDENCES
ABANDONEDLY	ABERRATION	ABLUTOMANES	ABORTICIDE	ABSCONDERS
ABANDONEES	ABERRATIONAL	ABNEGATING	ABORTICIDES	ABSCONDING
ABANDONERS	ABERRATIONS	ABNEGATION	ABORTIFACIENT	ABSEILINGS
ABANDONING	ABEYANCIES	ABNEGATIONS	ABORTIFACIENTS	ABSENTEEISM
ABANDONMENT	ABHOMINABLE	ABNEGATORS	ABORTIONAL	ABSENTEEISMS
ABANDONMENTS	ABHORRENCE	ABNORMALISM	ABORTIONIST	ABSENTMINDED
ABANDONWARE	ABHORRENCES	ABNORMALISMS	ABORTIONISTS	ABSENTMINDEDLY
ABANDONWARES	ABHORRENCIES	ABNORMALITIES	ABORTIVELY	ABSINTHIATED
ABASEMENTS	ABHORRENCY	ABNORMALITY	ABORTIVENESS	ABSINTHISM
ABASHMENTS	ABHORRENTLY	ABNORMALLY	ABORTIVENESSES	ABSINTHISMS
ABATEMENTS	ABHORRINGS	ABNORMITIES	ABORTUARIES	ABSOLUTELY
ABBOTSHIPS	ABIOGENESES	ABODEMENTS	ABOVEBOARD	ABSOLUTENESS
ABBREVIATE	ABIOGENESIS	ABOLISHABLE	ABOVEGROUND	ABSOLUTENESSES
ABBREVIATED	ABIOGENETIC	ABOLISHERS	ABRACADABRA	ABSOLUTEST
ABBREVIATES	ABIOGENETICALLY	ABOLISHING	ABRACADABRAS	ABSOLUTION
ABBREVIATING	ABIOGENICALLY	ABOLISHMENT	ABRANCHIAL	ABSOLUTIONS
ABBREVIATION	ABIOGENIST	ABOLISHMENTS	ABRANCHIATE	ABSOLUTISE
ABBREVIATIONS	ABIOGENISTS	ABOLITIONAL	ABRASIVELY	ABSOLUTISED
ABBREVIATOR	ABIOLOGICAL	ABOLITIONARY	ABRASIVENESS	ABSOLUTISES
ABBREVIATORS	ABIOTICALLY	ABOLITIONISM	ABRASIVENESSES	ABSOLUTISING
ABBREVIATORY	ABIOTROPHIC	ABOLITIONISMS	ABREACTING	ABSOLUTISM
ABBREVIATURE	ABIOTROPHIES	ABOLITIONIST	ABREACTION	ABSOLUTISMS
ABBREVIATURES	ABIOTROPHY	ABOLITIONISTS	ABREACTIONS	ABSOLUTIST
ABCOULOMBS	ABIRRITANT	ABOLITIONS	ABREACTIVE	ABSOLUTISTIC
ABDICATING	ABIRRITANTS	ABOMINABLE	ABRIDGABLE	ABSOLUTISTS
ABDICATION	ABIRRITATE	ABOMINABLENESS	ABRIDGEABLE	ABSOLUTIVE
ABDICATIONS	ABIRRITATED	ABOMINABLY	ABRIDGEMENT	ABSOLUTIZE
ABDICATIVE	ABIRRITATES	ABOMINATED	ABRIDGEMENTS	ABSOLUTIZED
ABDICATORS	ABIRRITATING	ABOMINATES	ABRIDGMENT	ABSOLUTIZES
ABDOMINALLY	ABITURIENT	ABOMINATING	ABRIDGMENTS	ABSOLUTIZING
ABDOMINALS	ABITURIENTS	ABOMINATION	ABROGATING	ABSOLUTORY
ABDOMINOPLASTY	ABJECTIONS	ABOMINATIONS	ABROGATION	ABSOLVABLE
ABDOMINOUS	ABJECTNESS	ABOMINATOR	ABROGATIONS	ABSOLVENTS
ABDUCENTES	ABJECTNESSES	ABOMINATORS	ABROGATIVE	ABSOLVITOR
ABDUCTIONS	ABJOINTING	ABONDANCES	ABROGATORS	ABSOLVITORS
ABDUCTORES	ABJUNCTION	ABONNEMENT	ABRUPTIONS	ABSORBABILITIES
ABECEDARIAN	ABJUNCTIONS	ABONNEMENTS	ABRUPTNESS	ABSORBABILITY
ABECEDARIANS	ABJURATION	ABORIGINAL	ABRUPTNESSES	ABSORBABLE
ABERDEVINE	ABJURATIONS	ABORIGINALISM	ABSCESSING	ABSORBANCE
ABERDEVINES	ABLACTATION	ABORIGINALISMS	ABSCINDING	ABSORBANCES
ABERNETHIES	ABLACTATIONS	ABORIGINALITIES	ABSCISSINS	ABSORBANCIES
ABERRANCES	ABLATITIOUS	ABORIGINALITY	ABSCISSION	ABSORBANCY

ABSORBANTS
ABSORBATES
ABSORBEDLY
ABSORBEFACIENT
ABSORBEFACIENTS
ABSORBENCIES
ABSORBENCY
ABSORBENTS
ABSORBINGLY
ABSORPTANCE
ABSORPTANCES
ABSORPTIOMETER
ABSORPTIOMETERS
ABSORPTION
ABSORPTIONS
ABSORPTIVE
ABSORPTIVENESS
ABSORPTIVITIES
ABSORPTIVITY
ABSQUATULATE
ABSQUATULATED
ABSQUATULATES
ABSQUATULATING
ABSTAINERS
ABSTAINING
ABSTEMIOUS
ABSTEMIOUSLY
ABSTEMIOUSNESS
ABSTENTION
ABSTENTIONISM
ABSTENTIONISMS
ABSTENTIONIST
ABSTENTIONISTS
ABSTENTIONS
ABSTENTIOUS
ABSTERGENT
ABSTERGENTS
ABSTERGING
ABSTERSION
ABSTERSIONS
ABSTERSIVE
ABSTERSIVES
ABSTINENCE
ABSTINENCES
ABSTINENCIES
ABSTINENCY
ABSTINENTLY

ABSTRACTABLE
ABSTRACTED
ABSTRACTEDLY
ABSTRACTEDNESS
ABSTRACTER
ABSTRACTERS
ABSTRACTEST
ABSTRACTING
ABSTRACTION
ABSTRACTIONAL
ABSTRACTIONISM
ABSTRACTIONISMS
ABSTRACTIONIST
ABSTRACTIONISTS
ABSTRACTIONS
ABSTRACTIVE
ABSTRACTIVELY
ABSTRACTIVES
ABSTRACTLY
ABSTRACTNESS
ABSTRACTNESSES
ABSTRACTOR
ABSTRACTORS
ABSTRICTED
ABSTRICTING
ABSTRICTION
ABSTRICTIONS
ABSTRUSELY
ABSTRUSENESS
ABSTRUSENESSES
ABSTRUSEST
ABSTRUSITIES
ABSTRUSITY
ABSURDISMS
ABSURDISTS
ABSURDITIES
ABSURDNESS
ABSURDNESSES
ABUNDANCES
ABUNDANCIES
ABUNDANTLY
ABUSIVENESS
ABUSIVENESSES
ABYSSOPELAGIC
ACADEMICAL
ACADEMICALISM
ACADEMICALISMS

ACADEMICALLY
ACADEMICALS
ACADEMICIAN
ACADEMICIANS
ACADEMICISM
ACADEMICISMS
ACADEMISMS
ACADEMISTS
ACALCULIAS
ACALEPHANS
ACANACEOUS
ACANTHACEOUS
ACANTHOCEPHALAN
ACANTHUSES
ACARICIDAL
ACARICIDES
ACARIDEANS
ACARIDIANS
ACARIDOMATIA
ACARIDOMATIUM
ACARODOMATIA
ACARODOMATIUM
ACAROLOGIES
ACAROLOGIST
ACAROLOGISTS
ACAROPHILIES
ACAROPHILY
ACARPELLOUS
ACARPELOUS
ACATALECTIC
ACATALECTICS
ACATALEPSIES
ACATALEPSY
ACATALEPTIC
ACATALEPTICS
ACATAMATHESIA
ACATAMATHESIAS
ACATHISIAS
ACAULESCENT
ACCEDENCES
ACCELERABLE
ACCELERANDO
ACCELERANDOS
ACCELERANT
ACCELERANTS
ACCELERATE
ACCELERATED

ACCELERATES
ACCELERATING
ACCELERATINGLY
ACCELERATION
ACCELERATIONS
ACCELERATIVE
ACCELERATOR
ACCELERATORS
ACCELERATORY
ACCELEROMETER
ACCELEROMETERS
ACCENSIONS
ACCENTLESS
ACCENTUALITIES
ACCENTUALITY
ACCENTUALLY
ACCENTUATE
ACCENTUATED
ACCENTUATES
ACCENTUATING
ACCENTUATION
ACCENTUATIONS
ACCEPTABILITIES
ACCEPTABILITY
ACCEPTABLE
ACCEPTABLENESS
ACCEPTABLY
ACCEPTANCE
ACCEPTANCES
ACCEPTANCIES
ACCEPTANCY
ACCEPTANTS
ACCEPTATION
ACCEPTATIONS
ACCEPTEDLY
ACCEPTILATION
ACCEPTILATIONS
ACCEPTINGLY
ACCEPTINGNESS
ACCEPTINGNESSES
ACCEPTIVITIES
ACCEPTIVITY
ACCESSARIES
ACCESSARILY
ACCESSARINESS
ACCESSARINESSES
ACCESSIBILITIES

ACCESSIBILITY
ACCESSIBLE
ACCESSIBLENESS
ACCESSIBLY
ACCESSIONAL
ACCESSIONED
ACCESSIONING
ACCESSIONS
ACCESSORIAL
ACCESSORIES
ACCESSORII
ACCESSORILY
ACCESSORINESS
ACCESSORINESSES
ACCESSORISE
ACCESSORISED
ACCESSORISES
ACCESSORISING
ACCESSORIUS
ACCESSORIZE
ACCESSORIZED
ACCESSORIZES
ACCESSORIZING
ACCIACCATURA
ACCIACCATURAS
ACCIACCATURE
ACCIDENCES
ACCIDENTAL
ACCIDENTALISM
ACCIDENTALISMS
ACCIDENTALITIES
ACCIDENTALITY
ACCIDENTALLY
ACCIDENTALNESS
ACCIDENTALS
ACCIDENTED
ACCIDENTLY
ACCIDENTOLOGIES
ACCIDENTOLOGY
ACCIPITERS
ACCIPITRAL
ACCIPITRINE
ACCIPITRINES
ACCLAIMERS
ACCLAIMING
ACCLAMATION
ACCLAMATIONS

ACCLAMATORY	ACCOMPANIST	ACCOUNTANTSHIPS	ACCUMULATING	ACETALDEHYDES
ACCLIMATABLE	ACCOMPANISTS	ACCOUNTING	ACCUMULATION	ACETAMIDES
ACCLIMATATION	ACCOMPANYING	ACCOUNTINGS	ACCUMULATIONS	ACETAMINOPHEN
ACCLIMATATIONS	ACCOMPANYIST	ACCOUPLEMENT	ACCUMULATIVE	ACETAMINOPHENS
ACCLIMATED	ACCOMPANYISTS	ACCOUPLEMENTS	ACCUMULATIVELY	ACETANILID
ACCLIMATES	ACCOMPLICE	ACCOURAGED	ACCUMULATOR	ACETANILIDE
ACCLIMATING	ACCOMPLICES	ACCOURAGES	ACCUMULATORS	ACETANILIDES
ACCLIMATION	ACCOMPLISH	ACCOURAGING	ACCURACIES	ACETANILIDS
ACCLIMATIONS	ACCOMPLISHABLE	ACCOURTING	ACCURATELY	ACETAZOLAMIDE
ACCLIMATISABLE	ACCOMPLISHED	ACCOUSTREMENT	ACCURATENESS	ACETAZOLAMIDES
ACCLIMATISATION	ACCOMPLISHER	ACCOUSTREMENTS	ACCURATENESSES	ACETIFICATION
ACCLIMATISE	ACCOMPLISHERS	ACCOUTERED	ACCURSEDLY	ACETIFICATIONS
ACCLIMATISED	ACCOMPLISHES	ACCOUTERING	ACCURSEDNESS	ACETIFIERS
ACCLIMATISER	ACCOMPLISHING	ACCOUTERMENT	ACCURSEDNESSES	ACETIFYING
ACCLIMATISERS	ACCOMPLISHMENT	ACCOUTERMENTS	ACCUSATION	ACETOMETER
ACCLIMATISES	ACCOMPLISHMENTS	ACCOUTREMENT	ACCUSATIONS	ACETOMETERS
ACCLIMATISING	ACCOMPTABLE	ACCOUTREMENTS	ACCUSATIVAL	ACETONAEMIA
ACCLIMATIZABLE	ACCOMPTANT	ACCOUTRING	ACCUSATIVE	ACETONAEMIAS
ACCLIMATIZATION	ACCOMPTANTS	ACCREDITABLE	ACCUSATIVELY	ACETONEMIA
ACCLIMATIZE	ACCOMPTING	ACCREDITATION	ACCUSATIVES	ACETONEMIAS
ACCLIMATIZED	ACCORAGING	ACCREDITATIONS	ACCUSATORIAL	ACETONITRILE
ACCLIMATIZER	ACCORDABLE	ACCREDITED	ACCUSATORY	ACETONITRILES
ACCLIMATIZERS	ACCORDANCE	ACCREDITING	ACCUSEMENT	ACETONURIA
ACCLIMATIZES	ACCORDANCES	ACCRESCENCE	ACCUSEMENTS	ACETONURIAS
ACCLIMATIZING	ACCORDANCIES	ACCRESCENCES	ACCUSINGLY	ACETOPHENETIDIN
ACCLIVITIES	ACCORDANCY	ACCRESCENT	ACCUSTOMARY	ACETYLATED
ACCLIVITOUS	ACCORDANTLY	ACCRETIONARY	ACCUSTOMATION	ACETYLATES
ACCOASTING	ACCORDINGLY	ACCRETIONS	ACCUSTOMATIONS	ACETYLATING
ACCOLADING	ACCORDIONIST	ACCRUEMENT	ACCUSTOMED	ACETYLATION
ACCOMMODABLE	ACCORDIONISTS	ACCRUEMENTS	ACCUSTOMEDNESS	ACETYLATIONS
ACCOMMODATE	ACCORDIONS	ACCUBATION	ACCUSTOMING	ACETYLATIVE
ACCOMMODATED	ACCOSTABLE	ACCUBATIONS	ACCUSTREMENT	ACETYLCHOLINE
ACCOMMODATES	ACCOUCHEMENT	ACCULTURAL	ACCUSTREMENTS	ACETYLCHOLINES
ACCOMMODATING	ACCOUCHEMENTS	ACCULTURATE	ACEPHALOUS	ACETYLENES
ACCOMMODATINGLY	ACCOUCHEUR	ACCULTURATED	ACERACEOUS	ACETYLENIC
ACCOMMODATION	ACCOUCHEURS	ACCULTURATES	ACERBATING	ACETYLIDES
ACCOMMODATIONAL	ACCOUCHEUSE	ACCULTURATING	ACERBICALLY	ACETYLSALICYLIC
ACCOMMODATIONS	ACCOUCHEUSES	ACCULTURATION	ACERBITIES	ACHAENIUMS
ACCOMMODATIVE	ACCOUNTABILITY	ACCULTURATIONAL	ACERVATELY	ACHAENOCARP
ACCOMMODATOR	ACCOUNTABLE	ACCULTURATIONS	ACERVATION	ACHAENOCARPS
ACCOMMODATORS	ACCOUNTABLENESS	ACCULTURATIVE	ACERVATIONS	ACHALASIAS
ACCOMPANIED	ACCOUNTABLY	ACCUMBENCIES	ACESCENCES	ACHIEVABLE
ACCOMPANIER	ACCOUNTANCIES	ACCUMBENCY	ACESCENCIES	ACHIEVEMENT
ACCOMPANIERS	ACCOUNTANCY	ACCUMULABLE	ACETABULAR	ACHIEVEMENTS
ACCOMPANIES	ACCOUNTANT	ACCUMULATE	ACETABULUM	ACHINESSES
ACCOMPANIMENT	ACCOUNTANTS	ACCUMULATED	ACETABULUMS	ACHLAMYDEOUS
ACCOMPANIMENTS	ACCOUNTANTSHIP	ACCUMULATES	ACETALDEHYDE	ACHLORHYDRIA

ACHLORHYDRIAS	ACIDOMETER	ACOUSTICIANS	ACRITARCHS	ACRYLAMIDES
ACHLORHYDRIC	ACIDOMETERS	ACQUAINTANCE	ACROAMATIC	ACRYLONITRILE
ACHONDRITE	ACIDOPHILE	ACQUAINTANCES	ACROAMATICAL	ACRYLONITRILES
ACHONDRITES	ACIDOPHILES	ACQUAINTED	ACROBATICALLY	ACTABILITIES
ACHONDRITIC	ACIDOPHILIC	ACQUAINTING	ACROBATICS	ACTABILITY
ACHONDROPLASIA	ACIDOPHILOUS	ACQUIESCED	ACROBATISM	ACTINICALLY
ACHONDROPLASIAS	ACIDOPHILS	ACQUIESCENCE	ACROBATISMS	ACTINIFORM
ACHONDROPLASTIC	ACIDOPHILUS	ACQUIESCENCES	ACROCARPOUS	ACTINOBACILLI
ACHROMATIC	ACIDOPHILUSES	ACQUIESCENT	ACROCENTRIC	ACTINOBACILLUS
ACHROMATICALLY	ACIDULATED	ACQUIESCENTLY	ACROCENTRICS	ACTINOBIOLOGIES
ACHROMATICITIES	ACIDULATES	ACQUIESCENTS	ACROCYANOSES	ACTINOBIOLOGY
ACHROMATICITY	ACIDULATING	ACQUIESCES	ACROCYANOSIS	ACTINOCHEMISTRY
ACHROMATIN	ACIDULATION	ACQUIESCING	ACRODROMOUS	ACTINOLITE
ACHROMATINS	ACIDULATIONS	ACQUIESCINGLY	ACROGENOUS	ACTINOLITES
ACHROMATISATION	ACIERATING	ACQUIGHTING	ACROGENOUSLY	ACTINOMERE
ACHROMATISE	ACIERATION	ACQUIRABILITIES	ACROLITHIC	ACTINOMERES
ACHROMATISED	ACIERATIONS	ACQUIRABILITY	ACROMEGALIC	ACTINOMETER
ACHROMATISES	ACINACEOUS	ACQUIRABLE	ACROMEGALICS	ACTINOMETERS
ACHROMATISING	ACINACIFORM	ACQUIREMENT	ACROMEGALIES	ACTINOMETRIC
ACHROMATISM	ACINETOBACTER	ACQUIREMENTS	ACROMEGALY	ACTINOMETRICAL
ACHROMATISMS	ACINETOBACTERS	ACQUISITION	ACRONICALLY	ACTINOMETRIES
ACHROMATIZATION	ACKNOWLEDGE	ACQUISITIONAL	ACRONYCALLY	ACTINOMETRY
ACHROMATIZE	ACKNOWLEDGEABLE	ACQUISITIONS	ACRONYCHAL	ACTINOMORPHIC
ACHROMATIZED	ACKNOWLEDGEABLY	ACQUISITIVE	ACRONYCHALLY	ACTINOMORPHIES
ACHROMATIZES	ACKNOWLEDGED	ACQUISITIVELY	ACRONYMANIA	ACTINOMORPHOUS
ACHROMATIZING	ACKNOWLEDGEDLY	ACQUISITIVENESS	ACRONYMANIAS	ACTINOMORPHY
ACHROMATOPSIA	ACKNOWLEDGEMENT	ACQUISITOR	ACRONYMICALLY	ACTINOMYCES
ACHROMATOPSIAS	ACKNOWLEDGER	ACQUISITORS	ACRONYMOUS	ACTINOMYCETE
ACHROMATOUS	ACKNOWLEDGERS	ACQUITMENT	ACROPARESTHESIA	ACTINOMYCETES
ACICLOVIRS	ACKNOWLEDGES	ACQUITMENTS	ACROPETALLY	ACTINOMYCETOUS
ACICULATED	ACKNOWLEDGING	ACQUITTALS	ACROPHOBES	ACTINOMYCIN
ACIDANTHERA	ACKNOWLEDGMENT	ACQUITTANCE	ACROPHOBIA	ACTINOMYCINS
ACIDANTHERAS	ACKNOWLEDGMENTS	ACQUITTANCED	ACROPHOBIAS	ACTINOMYCOSES
ACIDICALLY	ACOELOMATE	ACQUITTANCES	ACROPHOBIC	ACTINOMYCOSIS
ACIDIFIABLE	ACOELOMATES	ACQUITTANCING	ACROPHOBICS	ACTINOMYCOTIC
ACIDIFICATION	ACOLOUTHIC	ACQUITTERS	ACROPHONETIC	ACTINOPODS
ACIDIFICATIONS	ACOLOUTHITE	ACQUITTING	ACROPHONIC	ACTINOTHERAPIES
ACIDIFIERS	ACOLOUTHITES	ACRIDITIES	ACROPHONIES	ACTINOTHERAPY
ACIDIFYING	ACOLOUTHOS	ACRIDNESSES	ACROPOLISES	ACTINOURANIUM
ACIDIMETER	ACOLOUTHOSES	ACRIFLAVIN	ACROSPIRES	ACTINOURANIUMS
ACIDIMETERS	ACONITINES	ACRIFLAVINE	ACROSTICAL	ACTINOZOAN
ACIDIMETRIC	ACOTYLEDON	ACRIFLAVINES	ACROSTICALLY	ACTIONABLE
ACIDIMETRICAL	ACOTYLEDONOUS	ACRIFLAVINS	ACROTERIAL	ACTIONABLY
ACIDIMETRICALLY	ACOTYLEDONS	ACRIMONIES	ACROTERION	ACTIONISTS
ACIDIMETRIES	ACOUSTICAL	ACRIMONIOUS	ACROTERIUM	ACTIONLESS
ACIDIMETRY	ACOUSTICALLY	ACRIMONIOUSLY	ACROTERIUMS	ACTIVATING
ACIDNESSES	ACOUSTICIAN	ACRIMONIOUSNESS	ACRYLAMIDE	ACTIVATION

ACTIVATIONS	ADAPTABLENESSES	ADENOCARCINOMA	ADJACENCES	ADMINICULATE
ACTIVATORS	ADAPTATION	ADENOCARCINOMAS	ADJACENCIES	ADMINICULATED
ACTIVENESS	ADAPTATIONAL	ADENOHYPOPHYSES	ADJACENTLY	ADMINICULATES
ACTIVENESSES	ADAPTATIONALLY	ADENOHYPOPHYSIS	ADJECTIVAL	ADMINICULATING
ACTIVISING	ADAPTATIONS	ADENOIDECTOMIES	ADJECTIVALLY	ADMINISTER
ACTIVISTIC	ADAPTATIVE	ADENOIDECTOMY	ADJECTIVELY	ADMINISTERED
ACTIVITIES	ADAPTEDNESS	ADENOMATOUS	ADJECTIVES	ADMINISTERING
ACTIVIZING	ADAPTEDNESSES	ADENOPATHIES	ADJOURNING	ADMINISTERS
ACTOMYOSIN	ADAPTIVELY	ADENOPATHY	ADJOURNMENT	ADMINISTRABLE
ACTOMYOSINS	ADAPTIVENESS	ADENOSINES	ADJOURNMENTS	ADMINISTRANT
ACTUALISATION	ADAPTIVENESSES	ADENOVIRAL	ADJUDGEMENT	ADMINISTRANTS
ACTUALISATIONS	ADAPTIVITIES	ADENOVIRUS	ADJUDGEMENTS	ADMINISTRATE
ACTUALISED	ADAPTIVITY	ADENOVIRUSES	ADJUDGMENT	ADMINISTRATED
ACTUALISES	ADAPTOGENIC	ADEPTNESSES	ADJUDGMENTS	ADMINISTRATES
ACTUALISING	ADAPTOGENS	ADEQUACIES	ADJUDICATE	ADMINISTRATING
ACTUALISTS	ADDERSTONE	ADEQUATELY	ADJUDICATED	ADMINISTRATION
ACTUALITES	ADDERSTONES	ADEQUATENESS	ADJUDICATES	ADMINISTRATIONS
ACTUALITIES	ADDERWORTS	ADEQUATENESSES	ADJUDICATING	ADMINISTRATIVE
ACTUALIZATION	ADDICTEDNESS	ADEQUATIVE	ADJUDICATION	ADMINISTRATOR
ACTUALIZATIONS	ADDICTEDNESSES	ADHERENCES	ADJUDICATIONS	ADMINISTRATORS
ACTUALIZED	ADDICTIONS	ADHERENTLY	ADJUDICATIVE	ADMINISTRATRIX
ACTUALIZES	ADDITAMENT	ADHESIONAL	ADJUDICATOR	ADMIRABILITIES
ACTUALIZING	ADDITAMENTS	ADHESIVELY	ADJUDICATORS	ADMIRABILITY
ACTUARIALLY	ADDITIONAL	ADHESIVENESS	ADJUDICATORY	ADMIRABLENESS
ACTUATIONS	ADDITIONALITIES	ADHESIVENESSES	ADJUNCTION	ADMIRABLENESSES
ACUMINATED	ADDITIONALITY	ADHIBITING	ADJUNCTIONS	ADMIRALSHIP
ACUMINATES	ADDITIONALLY	ADHIBITION	ADJUNCTIVE	ADMIRALSHIPS
ACUMINATING	ADDITITIOUS	ADHIBITIONS	ADJUNCTIVELY	ADMIRALTIES
ACUMINATION	ADDITIVELY	ADHOCRACIES	ADJURATION	ADMIRANCES
ACUMINATIONS	ADDITIVITIES	ADIABATICALLY	ADJURATIONS	ADMIRATION
ACUPRESSURE	ADDITIVITY	ADIABATICS	ADJURATORY	ADMIRATIONS
ACUPRESSURES	ADDLEMENTS	ADIACTINIC	ADJUSTABILITIES	ADMIRATIVE
ACUPUNCTURAL	ADDLEPATED	ADIAPHORISM	ADJUSTABILITY	ADMIRAUNCE
ACUPUNCTURE	ADDRESSABILITY	ADIAPHORISMS	ADJUSTABLE	ADMIRAUNCES
ACUPUNCTURES	ADDRESSABLE	ADIAPHORIST	ADJUSTABLY	ADMIRINGLY
ACUPUNCTURIST	ADDRESSEES	ADIAPHORISTIC	ADJUSTMENT	ADMISSIBILITIES
ACUPUNCTURISTS	ADDRESSERS	ADIAPHORISTS	ADJUSTMENTAL	ADMISSIBILITY
ACUTENESSES	ADDRESSING	ADIAPHORON	ADJUSTMENTS	ADMISSIBLE
ACYCLOVIRS	ADDRESSORS	ADIAPHOROUS	ADJUTANCIES	ADMISSIBLENESS
ACYLATIONS	ADDUCEABLE	ADIATHERMANCIES	ADJUVANCIES	ADMISSIONS
ADACTYLOUS	ADDUCTIONS	ADIATHERMANCY	ADMEASURED	ADMITTABLE
ADAMANCIES	ADELANTADO	ADIATHERMANOUS	ADMEASUREMENT	ADMITTANCE
ADAMANTEAN	ADELANTADOS	ADIATHERMIC	ADMEASUREMENTS	ADMITTANCES
ADAMANTINE	ADEMPTIONS	ADIPOCERES	ADMEASURES	ADMITTEDLY
ADAPTABILITIES	ADENECTOMIES	ADIPOCEROUS	ADMEASURING	ADMIXTURES
ADAPTABILITY	ADENECTOMY	ADIPOCYTES	ADMINICLES	ADMONISHED
ADAPTABLENESS	ADENITISES	ADIPOSITIES	ADMINICULAR	ADMONISHER

ADMONISHERS	ADRENOCORTICAL	ADULTHOODS	ADVERBIALISING	ADVISEDNESSES
ADMONISHES	ADROITNESS	ADULTNESSES	ADVERBIALIZE	ADVISEMENT
ADMONISHING	ADROITNESSES	ADULTRESSES	ADVERBIALIZED	ADVISEMENTS
ADMONISHINGLY	ADSCITITIOUS	ADUMBRATED	ADVERBIALIZES	ADVISERSHIP
ADMONISHMENT	ADSCITITIOUSLY	ADUMBRATES	ADVERBIALIZING	ADVISERSHIPS
ADMONISHMENTS	ADSCRIPTION	ADUMBRATING	ADVERBIALLY	ADVISORATE
ADMONITION	ADSCRIPTIONS	ADUMBRATION	ADVERBIALS	ADVISORATES
ADMONITIONS	ADSORBABILITIES	ADUMBRATIONS	ADVERSARIA	ADVISORIES
ADMONITIVE	ADSORBABILITY	ADUMBRATIVE	ADVERSARIAL	ADVOCACIES
ADMONITORILY	ADSORBABLE	ADUMBRATIVELY	ADVERSARIES	ADVOCATING
ADMONITORS	ADSORBATES	ADUNCITIES	ADVERSARINESS	ADVOCATION
ADMONITORY	ADSORBENTS	ADVANCEMENT	ADVERSARINESSES	ADVOCATIONS
ADNOMINALS	ADSORPTION	ADVANCEMENTS	ADVERSATIVE	ADVOCATIVE
ADOLESCENCE	ADSORPTIONS	ADVANCINGLY	ADVERSATIVELY	ADVOCATORS
ADOLESCENCES	ADSORPTIVE	ADVANTAGEABLE	ADVERSATIVES	ADVOCATORY
ADOLESCENT	ADULARESCENCE	ADVANTAGED	ADVERSENESS	ADVOUTRERS
ADOLESCENTLY	ADULARESCENCES	ADVANTAGEOUS	ADVERSENESSES	ADVOUTRIES
ADOLESCENTS	ADULARESCENT	ADVANTAGEOUSLY	ADVERSITIES	AECIDIOSPORE
ADOPTABILITIES	ADULATIONS	ADVANTAGES	ADVERTENCE	AECIDIOSPORES
ADOPTABILITY	ADULTERANT	ADVANTAGING	ADVERTENCES	AECIDOSPORE
ADOPTIANISM	ADULTERANTS	ADVECTIONS	ADVERTENCIES	AECIDOSPORES
ADOPTIANISMS	ADULTERATE	ADVENTITIA	ADVERTENCY	AECIOSPORE
ADOPTIANIST	ADULTERATED	ADVENTITIAL	ADVERTENTLY	AECIOSPORES
ADOPTIANISTS	ADULTERATES	ADVENTITIAS	ADVERTISED	AEDILESHIP
ADOPTIONISM	ADULTERATING	ADVENTITIOUS	ADVERTISEMENT	AEDILESHIPS
ADOPTIONISMS	ADULTERATION	ADVENTITIOUSLY	ADVERTISEMENTS	AEOLIPILES
ADOPTIONIST	ADULTERATIONS	ADVENTIVES	ADVERTISER	AEOLIPYLES
ADOPTIONISTS	ADULTERATOR	ADVENTURED	ADVERTISERS	AEOLOTROPIC
ADOPTIVELY	ADULTERATORS	ADVENTUREFUL	ADVERTISES	AEOLOTROPIES
ADORABILITIES	ADULTERERS	ADVENTURER	ADVERTISING	AEOLOTROPY
ADORABILITY	ADULTERESS	ADVENTURERS	ADVERTISINGS	AEPYORNISES
ADORABLENESS	ADULTERESSES	ADVENTURES	ADVERTIZED	AERENCHYMA
ADORABLENESSES	ADULTERIES	ADVENTURESOME	ADVERTIZEMENT	AERENCHYMAS
ADORATIONS	ADULTERINE	ADVENTURESS	ADVERTIZEMENTS	AERENCHYMATOUS
ADORNMENTS	ADULTERINES	ADVENTURESSES	ADVERTIZER	AERIALISTS
ADPRESSING	ADULTERISE	ADVENTURING	ADVERTIZERS	AERIALITIES
ADRENALECTOMIES	ADULTERISED	ADVENTURISM	ADVERTIZES	AERIFICATION
ADRENALECTOMY	ADULTERISES	ADVENTURISMS	ADVERTIZING	AERIFICATIONS
ADRENALINE	ADULTERISING	ADVENTURIST	ADVERTIZINGS	AEROACOUSTICS
ADRENALINES	ADULTERIZE	ADVENTURISTIC	ADVERTORIAL	AEROBALLISTICS
ADRENALINS	ADULTERIZED	ADVENTURISTS	ADVERTORIALS	AEROBATICS
ADRENALISED	ADULTERIZES	ADVENTUROUS	ADVISABILITIES	AEROBICALLY
ADRENALIZED	ADULTERIZING	ADVENTUROUSLY	ADVISABILITY	AEROBICISE
ADRENERGIC	ADULTEROUS	ADVENTUROUSNESS	ADVISABLENESS	AEROBICISED
ADRENERGICALLY	ADULTEROUSLY	ADVERBIALISE	ADVISABLENESSES	AEROBICISES
ADRENOCHROME	ADULTESCENT	ADVERBIALISED	ADVISATORY	AEROBICISING
ADRENOCHROMES	ADULTESCENTS	ADVERBIALISES	ADVISEDNESS	AEROBICIST

AEROBICISTS	AEROLOGIST	AEROSOLISED	AESTIVATED	AFFERENTLY
AEROBICIZE	AEROLOGISTS	AEROSOLISES	AESTIVATES	AFFETTUOSO
AEROBICIZED	AEROMAGNETIC	AEROSOLISING	AESTIVATING	AFFIANCING
AEROBICIZES	AEROMANCIES	AEROSOLIZATION	AESTIVATION	AFFICIONADO
AEROBICIZING	AEROMECHANIC	AEROSOLIZATIONS	AESTIVATIONS	AFFICIONADOS
AEROBIOLOGICAL	AEROMECHANICAL	AEROSOLIZE	AESTIVATOR	AFFIDAVITS
AEROBIOLOGIES	AEROMECHANICS	AEROSOLIZED	AESTIVATORS	AFFILIABLE
AEROBIOLOGIST	AEROMEDICAL	AEROSOLIZES	AETHEREALITIES	AFFILIATED
AEROBIOLOGISTS	AEROMEDICINE	AEROSOLIZING	AETHEREALITY	AFFILIATES
AEROBIOLOGY	AEROMEDICINES	AEROSPACES	AETHEREALLY	AFFILIATING
AEROBIONTS	AEROMETERS	AEROSPHERE	AETHRIOSCOPE	AFFILIATION
AEROBIOSES	AEROMETRIC	AEROSPHERES	AETHRIOSCOPES	AFFILIATIONS
AEROBIOSIS	AEROMETRIES	AEROSPIKES	AETIOLOGICAL	AFFINITIES
AEROBIOTIC	AEROMOTORS	AEROSTATIC	AETIOLOGICALLY	AFFINITIVE
AEROBIOTICALLY	AERONAUTIC	AEROSTATICAL	AETIOLOGIES	AFFIRMABLE
AEROBRAKED	AERONAUTICAL	AEROSTATICS	AETIOLOGIST	AFFIRMANCE
AEROBRAKES	AERONAUTICALLY	AEROSTATION	AETIOLOGISTS	AFFIRMANCES
AEROBRAKING	AERONAUTICS	AEROSTATIONS	AFFABILITIES	AFFIRMANTS
AEROBRAKINGS	AERONEUROSES	AEROSTRUCTURE	AFFABILITY	AFFIRMATION
AERODIGESTIVE	AERONEUROSIS	AEROSTRUCTURES	AFFECTABILITIES	AFFIRMATIONS
AERODONETICS	AERONOMERS	AEROTACTIC	AFFECTABILITY	AFFIRMATIVE
AERODROMES	AERONOMICAL	AEROTRAINS	AFFECTABLE	AFFIRMATIVELY
AERODYNAMIC	AERONOMIES	AEROTROPIC	AFFECTATION	AFFIRMATIVES
AERODYNAMICAL	AERONOMIST	AEROTROPISM	AFFECTATIONS	AFFIRMATORY
AERODYNAMICALLY	AERONOMISTS	AEROTROPISMS	AFFECTEDLY	AFFIRMINGLY
AERODYNAMICIST	AEROPAUSES	AERUGINOUS	AFFECTEDNESS	AFFIXATION
AERODYNAMICISTS	AEROPHAGIA	AESTHESIAS	AFFECTEDNESSES	AFFIXATIONS
AERODYNAMICS	AEROPHAGIAS	AESTHESIOGEN	AFFECTINGLY	AFFIXMENTS
AEROELASTIC	AEROPHAGIES	AESTHESIOGENIC	AFFECTIONAL	AFFIXTURES
AEROELASTICIAN	AEROPHOBES	AESTHESIOGENS	AFFECTIONALLY	AFFLATIONS
AEROELASTICIANS	AEROPHOBIA	AESTHETICAL	AFFECTIONATE	AFFLATUSES
AEROELASTICITY	AEROPHOBIAS	AESTHETICALLY	AFFECTIONATELY	AFFLICTERS
AEROEMBOLISM	AEROPHOBIC	AESTHETICIAN	AFFECTIONED	AFFLICTING
AEROEMBOLISMS	AEROPHONES	AESTHETICIANS	AFFECTIONING	AFFLICTINGS
AEROGENERATOR	AEROPHORES	AESTHETICISE	AFFECTIONLESS	AFFLICTION
AEROGENERATORS	AEROPHYTES	AESTHETICISED	AFFECTIONS	AFFLICTIONS
AEROGRAMME	AEROPLANES	AESTHETICISES	AFFECTIVELY	AFFLICTIVE
AEROGRAMMES	AEROPLANKTON	AESTHETICISING	AFFECTIVENESS	AFFLICTIVELY
AEROGRAPHIES	AEROPLANKTONS	AESTHETICISM	AFFECTIVENESSES	AFFLUENCES
AEROGRAPHS	AEROPULSES	AESTHETICISMS	AFFECTIVITIES	AFFLUENCIES
AEROGRAPHY	AEROSCOPES	AESTHETICIST	AFFECTIVITY	AFFLUENTIAL
AEROHYDROPLANE	AEROSHELLS	AESTHETICISTS	AFFECTLESS	AFFLUENTIALS
AEROHYDROPLANES	AEROSIDERITE	AESTHETICIZE	AFFECTLESSNESS	AFFLUENTLY
AEROLITHOLOGIES	AEROSIDERITES	AESTHETICIZED	AFFEERMENT	AFFLUENTNESS
AEROLITHOLOGY	AEROSOLISATION	AESTHETICIZES	AFFEERMENTS	AFFLUENTNESSES
AEROLOGICAL	AEROSOLISATIONS	AESTHETICIZING	AFFENPINSCHER	AFFLUENZAS
AEROLOGIES	AEROSOLISE	AESTHETICS	AFFENPINSCHERS	AFFLUXIONS

AFFOORDING	AFORETHOUGHT	AFTERSHAFT	AGGLOMERATES	AGGREGATENESS
AFFORCEMENT	AFORETHOUGHTS	AFTERSHAFTS	AGGLOMERATING	AGGREGATENESSES
AFFORCEMENTS	AFRORMOSIA	AFTERSHAVE	AGGLOMERATION	AGGREGATES
AFFORDABILITIES	AFRORMOSIAS	AFTERSHAVES	AGGLOMERATIONS	AGGREGATING
AFFORDABILITY	AFTERBIRTH	AFTERSHOCK	AGGLOMERATIVE	AGGREGATION
AFFORDABLE	AFTERBIRTHS	AFTERSHOCKS	AGGLUTINABILITY	AGGREGATIONAL
AFFORDABLY	AFTERBODIES	AFTERSHOWS	AGGLUTINABLE	AGGREGATIONS
AFFORESTABLE	AFTERBRAIN	AFTERSUPPER	AGGLUTINANT	AGGREGATIVE
AFFORESTATION	AFTERBRAINS	AFTERSUPPERS	AGGLUTINANTS	AGGREGATIVELY
AFFORESTATIONS	AFTERBURNER	AFTERSWARM	AGGLUTINATE	AGGREGATOR
AFFORESTED	AFTERBURNERS	AFTERSWARMS	AGGLUTINATED	AGGREGATORS
AFFORESTING	AFTERBURNING	AFTERTASTE	AGGLUTINATES	AGGRESSING
AFFRANCHISE	AFTERBURNINGS	AFTERTASTES	AGGLUTINATING	AGGRESSION
AFFRANCHISED	AFTERCARES	AFTERTHOUGHT	AGGLUTINATION	AGGRESSIONS
AFFRANCHISEMENT	AFTERCLAPS	AFTERTHOUGHTS	AGGLUTINATIONS	AGGRESSIVE
AFFRANCHISES	AFTERDAMPS	AFTERTIMES	AGGLUTINATIVE	AGGRESSIVELY
AFFRANCHISING	AFTERDECKS	AFTERWARDS	AGGLUTININ	AGGRESSIVENESS
AFFRAPPING	AFTEREFFECT	AFTERWORDS	AGGLUTININS	AGGRESSIVITIES
AFFREIGHTMENT	AFTEREFFECTS	AFTERWORLD	AGGLUTINOGEN	AGGRESSIVITY
AFFREIGHTMENTS	AFTEREYEING	AFTERWORLDS	AGGLUTINOGENIC	AGGRESSORS
AFFRICATED	AFTEREYING	AGALACTIAS	AGGLUTINOGENS	AGGRIEVEDLY
AFFRICATES	AFTERGAMES	AGALMATOLITE	AGGRADATION	AGGRIEVEMENT
AFFRICATING	AFTERGLOWS	AGALMATOLITES	AGGRADATIONS	AGGRIEVEMENTS
AFFRICATION	AFTERGRASS	AGAMICALLY	AGGRANDISE	AGGRIEVING
AFFRICATIONS	AFTERGRASSES	AGAMOGENESES	AGGRANDISED	AGILENESSES
AFFRICATIVE	AFTERGROWTH	AGAMOGENESIS	AGGRANDISEMENT	AGISTMENTS
AFFRICATIVES	AFTERGROWTHS	AGAMOGENETIC	AGGRANDISEMENTS	AGITATEDLY
AFFRIGHTED	AFTERGUARD	AGAMOGONIES	AGGRANDISER	AGITATIONAL
AFFRIGHTEDLY	AFTERGUARDS	AGAMOSPERMIES	AGGRANDISERS	AGITATIONS
AFFRIGHTEN	AFTERHEATS	AGAMOSPERMY	AGGRANDISES	AGNATICALLY
AFFRIGHTENED	AFTERIMAGE	AGAPANTHUS	AGGRANDISING	AGNOIOLOGIES
AFFRIGHTENING	AFTERIMAGES	AGAPANTHUSES	AGGRANDIZE	AGNOIOLOGY
AFFRIGHTENS	AFTERLIFES	AGARICACEOUS	AGGRANDIZED	AGNOSTICISM
AFFRIGHTFUL	AFTERLIVES	AGATEWARES	AGGRANDIZEMENT	AGNOSTICISMS
AFFRIGHTING	AFTERMARKET	AGATHODAIMON	AGGRANDIZEMENTS	AGONISEDLY
AFFRIGHTMENT	AFTERMARKETS	AGATHODAIMONS	AGGRANDIZER	AGONISINGLY
AFFRIGHTMENTS	AFTERMATHS	AGEDNESSES	AGGRANDIZERS	AGONISTICAL
AFFRONTING	AFTERNOONS	AGELESSNESS	AGGRANDIZES	AGONISTICALLY
AFFRONTINGLY	AFTERPAINS	AGELESSNESSES	AGGRANDIZING	AGONISTICS
AFFRONTINGS	AFTERPARTIES	AGENDALESS	AGGRAVATED	AGONIZEDLY
AFFRONTIVE	AFTERPARTY	AGENTIVITIES	AGGRAVATES	AGONIZINGLY
AFICIONADA	AFTERPEAKS	AGENTIVITY	AGGRAVATING	AGONOTHETES
AFICIONADAS	AFTERPIECE	AGGIORNAMENTI	AGGRAVATINGLY	AGORAPHOBE
AFICIONADO	AFTERPIECES	AGGIORNAMENTO	AGGRAVATION	AGORAPHOBES
AFICIONADOS	AFTERSALES	AGGIORNAMENTOS	AGGRAVATIONS	AGORAPHOBIA
AFLATOXINS	AFTERSENSATION	AGGLOMERATE	AGGREGATED	AGORAPHOBIAS
AFOREMENTIONED	AFTERSENSATIONS	AGGLOMERATED	AGGREGATELY	AGORAPHOBIC

AGORAPHOBICS	AGROFORESTER	AILOUROPHILIA	AIRMANSHIP	ALBUMENISE
AGRANULOCYTE	AGROFORESTERS	AILOUROPHILIAS	AIRMANSHIPS	ALBUMENISED
AGRANULOCYTES	AGROFORESTRIES	AILOUROPHILIC	AIRPROOFED	ALBUMENISES
AGRANULOCYTOSES	AGROFORESTRY	AILOUROPHOBE	AIRPROOFING	ALBUMENISING
AGRANULOCYTOSIS	AGROINDUSTRIAL	AILOUROPHOBES	AIRSICKNESS	ALBUMENIZE
AGRANULOSES	AGROINDUSTRIES	AILOUROPHOBIA	AIRSICKNESSES	ALBUMENIZED
AGRANULOSIS	AGROINDUSTRY	AILOUROPHOBIAS	AIRSTREAMS	ALBUMENIZES
AGRARIANISM	AGROLOGICAL	AILOUROPHOBIC	AIRSTRIKES	ALBUMENIZING
AGRARIANISMS	AGROLOGIES	AILUROPHILE	AIRTIGHTNESS	ALBUMINATE
AGREEABILITIES	AGROLOGIST	AILUROPHILES	AIRTIGHTNESSES	ALBUMINATES
AGREEABILITY	AGROLOGISTS	AILUROPHILIA	AIRWORTHIER	ALBUMINISE
AGREEABLENESS	AGRONOMIAL	AILUROPHILIAS	AIRWORTHIEST	ALBUMINISED
AGREEABLENESSES	AGRONOMICAL	AILUROPHILIC	AIRWORTHINESS	ALBUMINISES
AGREEMENTS	AGRONOMICALLY	AILUROPHOBE	AIRWORTHINESSES	ALBUMINISING
AGREGATION	AGRONOMICS	AILUROPHOBES	AITCHBONES	ALBUMINIZE
AGREGATIONS	AGRONOMIES	AILUROPHOBIA	AKATHISIAS	ALBUMINIZED
AGRIBUSINESS	AGRONOMIST	AILUROPHOBIAS	AKOLOUTHOS	ALBUMINIZES
AGRIBUSINESSES	AGRONOMISTS	AILUROPHOBIC	AKOLOUTHOSES	ALBUMINIZING
AGRIBUSINESSMAN	AGROSTEMMA	AIMLESSNESS	AKOLUTHOSES	ALBUMINOID
AGRIBUSINESSMEN	AGROSTEMMAS	AIMLESSNESSES	ALABAMINES	ALBUMINOIDS
AGRICHEMICAL	AGROSTEMMATA	AIRBOARDING	ALABANDINE	ALBUMINOUS
AGRICHEMICALS	AGROSTOLOGICAL	AIRBOARDINGS	ALABANDINES	ALBUMINURIA
AGRICULTURAL	AGROSTOLOGIES	AIRBRUSHED	ALABANDITE	ALBUMINURIAS
AGRICULTURALIST	AGROSTOLOGIST	AIRBRUSHES	ALABANDITES	ALBUMINURIC
AGRICULTURALLY	AGROSTOLOGISTS	AIRBRUSHING	ALABASTERS	ALBUTEROLS
AGRICULTURE	AGROSTOLOGY	AIRBURSTED	ALABASTRINE	ALCAICERIA
AGRICULTURES	AGROTERRORISM	AIRBURSTING	ALABLASTER	ALCAICERIAS
AGRICULTURIST	AGROTERRORISMS	AIRCOACHES	ALABLASTERS	ALCARRAZAS
AGRICULTURISTS	AGROTOURISM	AIRCRAFTMAN	ALACRITIES	ALCATRASES
AGRIMONIES	AGROTOURISMS	AIRCRAFTMEN	ALACRITOUS	ALCHEMICAL
AGRIOLOGIES	AGROTOURIST	AIRCRAFTSMAN	ALARMINGLY	ALCHEMICALLY
AGRIPRODUCT	AGROTOURISTS	AIRCRAFTSMEN	ALBARELLOS	ALCHEMISED
AGRIPRODUCTS	AGRYPNOTIC	AIRCRAFTSWOMAN	ALBATROSSES	ALCHEMISES
AGRITOURISM	AGRYPNOTICS	AIRCRAFTSWOMEN	ALBERTITES	ALCHEMISING
AGRITOURISMS	AGTERSKOTS	AIRCRAFTWOMAN	ALBESCENCE	ALCHEMISTIC
AGRITOURIST	AGUARDIENTE	AIRCRAFTWOMEN	ALBESCENCES	ALCHEMISTICAL
AGRITOURISTS	AGUARDIENTES	AIRDROPPED	ALBESPINES	ALCHEMISTS
AGROBIOLOGICAL	AHISTORICAL	AIRDROPPING	ALBESPYNES	ALCHEMIZED
AGROBIOLOGIES	AHORSEBACK	AIRFREIGHT	ALBINESSES	ALCHEMIZES
AGROBIOLOGIST	AHURUHURUS	AIRFREIGHTED	ALBINISTIC	ALCHEMIZING
AGROBIOLOGISTS	AICHMOPHOBIA	AIRFREIGHTING	ALBINOISMS	ALCHERINGA
AGROBIOLOGY	AICHMOPHOBIAS	AIRFREIGHTS	ALBITISING	ALCHERINGAS
AGROBUSINESS	AIGUILLETTE	AIRINESSES	ALBITIZING	ALCOHOLICALLY
AGROBUSINESSES	AIGUILLETTES	AIRLESSNESS	ALBUGINEOUS	ALCOHOLICITIES
AGROCHEMICAL	AILANTHUSES	AIRLESSNESSES	ALBUMBLATT	ALCOHOLICITY
AGROCHEMICALS	AILOUROPHILE	AIRLIFTING	ALBUMBLATTER	ALCOHOLICS
AGRODOLCES	AILOUROPHILES	AIRMAILING	ALBUMBLATTS	ALCOHOLISATION

ALCOHOLISATIONS	ALEMBICATED	ALIENABILITY	ALKALINIZATIONS	ALLEGORIZER
ALCOHOLISE	ALEMBICATION	ALIENATING	ALKALINIZE	ALLEGORIZERS
ALCOHOLISED	ALEMBICATIONS	ALIENATION	ALKALINIZED	ALLEGORIZES
ALCOHOLISES	ALEMBROTHS	ALIENATIONS	ALKALINIZES	ALLEGORIZING
ALCOHOLISING	ALERTNESSES	ALIENATORS	ALKALINIZING	ALLEGRETTO
ALCOHOLISM	ALEXANDERS	ALIENNESSES	ALKALISABLE	ALLEGRETTOS
ALCOHOLISMS	ALEXANDERSES	ALIGHTMENT	ALKALISERS	ALLELOMORPH
ALCOHOLIZATION	ALEXANDRINE	ALIGHTMENTS	ALKALISING	ALLELOMORPHIC
ALCOHOLIZATIONS	ALEXANDRINES	ALIGNMENTS	ALKALIZABLE	ALLELOMORPHISM
ALCOHOLIZE	ALEXANDRITE	ALIKENESSES	ALKALIZERS	ALLELOMORPHISMS
ALCOHOLIZED	ALEXANDRITES	ALIMENTARY	ALKALIZING	ALLELOMORPHS
ALCOHOLIZES	ALEXIPHARMAKON	ALIMENTATION	ALKALOIDAL	ALLELOPATHIC
ALCOHOLIZING	ALEXIPHARMAKONS	ALIMENTATIONS	ALKYLATING	ALLELOPATHIES
ALCOHOLOMETER	ALEXIPHARMIC	ALIMENTATIVE	ALKYLATION	ALLELOPATHY
ALCOHOLOMETERS	ALEXIPHARMICS	ALIMENTING	ALKYLATIONS	ALLELUIAHS
ALCOHOLOMETRIES	ALFILARIAS	ALIMENTIVENESS	ALLANTOIDAL	ALLEMANDES
ALCOHOLOMETRY	ALFILERIAS	ALINEATION	ALLANTOIDES	ALLERGENIC
ALCYONARIAN	ALGAECIDES	ALINEATIONS	ALLANTOIDS	ALLERGENICITIES
ALCYONARIANS	ALGARROBAS	ALINEMENTS	ALLANTOINS	ALLERGENICITY
ALDERFLIES	ALGARROBOS	ALISMACEOUS	ALLANTOISES	ALLERGISTS
ALDERMANIC	ALGEBRAICAL	ALITERACIES	ALLARGANDO	ALLETHRINS
ALDERMANITIES	ALGEBRAICALLY	ALITERATES	ALLAYMENTS	ALLEVIANTS
ALDERMANITY	ALGEBRAIST	ALIVENESSES	ALLEGATION	ALLEVIATED
ALDERMANLIKE	ALGEBRAISTS	ALIZARINES	ALLEGATIONS	ALLEVIATES
ALDERMANLY	ALGIDITIES	ALKAHESTIC	ALLEGEANCE	ALLEVIATING
ALDERMANRIES	ALGIDNESSES	ALKALESCENCE	ALLEGEANCES	ALLEVIATION
ALDERMANRY	ALGOLAGNIA	ALKALESCENCES	ALLEGIANCE	ALLEVIATIONS
ALDERMANSHIP	ALGOLAGNIAC	ALKALESCENCIES	ALLEGIANCES	ALLEVIATIVE
ALDERMANSHIPS	ALGOLAGNIACS	ALKALESCENCY	ALLEGIANTS	ALLEVIATOR
ALDERWOMAN	ALGOLAGNIAS	ALKALESCENT	ALLEGORICAL	ALLEVIATORS
ALDERWOMEN	ALGOLAGNIC	ALKALIFIED	ALLEGORICALLY	ALLEVIATORY
ALDOHEXOSE	ALGOLAGNIST	ALKALIFIES	ALLEGORICALNESS	ALLHALLOND
ALDOHEXOSES	ALGOLAGNISTS	ALKALIFYING	ALLEGORIES	ALLHALLOWEN
ALDOLISATION	ALGOLOGICAL	ALKALIMETER	ALLEGORISATION	ALLHALLOWN
ALDOLISATIONS	ALGOLOGICALLY	ALKALIMETERS	ALLEGORISATIONS	ALLHOLLOWN
ALDOLIZATION	ALGOLOGIES	ALKALIMETRIC	ALLEGORISE	ALLIACEOUS
ALDOLIZATIONS	ALGOLOGIST	ALKALIMETRIES	ALLEGORISED	ALLICHOLIES
ALDOPENTOSE	ALGOLOGISTS	ALKALIMETRY	ALLEGORISER	ALLIGARTAS
ALDOPENTOSES	ALGOMETERS	ALKALINISATION	ALLEGORISERS	ALLIGATING
ALDOSTERONE	ALGOMETRIES	ALKALINISATIONS	ALLEGORISES	ALLIGATION
ALDOSTERONES	ALGOPHOBIA	ALKALINISE	ALLEGORISING	ALLIGATIONS
ALDOSTERONISM	ALGOPHOBIAS	ALKALINISED	ALLEGORIST	ALLIGATORS
ALDOSTERONISMS	ALGORISMIC	ALKALINISES	ALLEGORISTS	ALLINEATION
ALEATORIES	ALGORITHMIC	ALKALINISING	ALLEGORIZATION	ALLINEATIONS
ALEBENCHES	ALGORITHMICALLY	ALKALINITIES	ALLEGORIZATIONS	ALLITERATE
ALEGGEAUNCE	ALGORITHMS	ALKALINITY	ALLEGORIZE	ALLITERATED
ALEGGEAUNCES	ALIENABILITIES	ALKALINIZATION	ALLEGORIZED	ALLITERATES

ALLITERATING	ALLOPATHIST	ALLUREMENTS	ALPHABETISES	ALTERNANTS
ALLITERATION	ALLOPATHISTS	ALLURINGLY	ALPHABETISING	ALTERNATED
ALLITERATIONS	ALLOPATRIC	ALLUSIVELY	ALPHABETIZATION	ALTERNATELY
ALLITERATIVE	ALLOPATRICALLY	ALLUSIVENESS	ALPHABETIZE	ALTERNATES
ALLITERATIVELY	ALLOPATRIES	ALLUSIVENESSES	ALPHABETIZED	ALTERNATIM
ALLNIGHTER	ALLOPHANES	ALLWEATHER	ALPHABETIZER	ALTERNATING
ALLNIGHTERS	ALLOPHONES	ALLWEATHERS	ALPHABETIZERS	ALTERNATION
ALLOANTIBODIES	ALLOPHONIC	ALLYCHOLLIES	ALPHABETIZES	ALTERNATIONS
ALLOANTIBODY	ALLOPLASMIC	ALLYCHOLLY	ALPHABETIZING	ALTERNATIVE
ALLOANTIGEN	ALLOPLASMS	ALMACANTAR	ALPHAMERIC	ALTERNATIVELY
ALLOANTIGENS	ALLOPLASTIC	ALMACANTARS	ALPHAMERICAL	ALTERNATIVENESS
ALLOCARPIES	ALLOPOLYPLOID	ALMANDINES	ALPHAMERICALLY	ALTERNATIVES
ALLOCATABLE	ALLOPOLYPLOIDS	ALMANDITES	ALPHAMETIC	ALTERNATOR
ALLOCATING	ALLOPOLYPLOIDY	ALMIGHTILY	ALPHAMETICS	ALTERNATORS
ALLOCATION	ALLOPURINOL	ALMIGHTINESS	ALPHANUMERIC	ALTIGRAPHS
ALLOCATIONS	ALLOPURINOLS	ALMIGHTINESSES	ALPHANUMERICAL	ALTIMETERS
ALLOCATORS	ALLOSAURUS	ALMSGIVERS	ALPHANUMERICS	ALTIMETRICAL
ALLOCHEIRIA	ALLOSAURUSES	ALMSGIVING	ALPHASORTED	ALTIMETRICALLY
ALLOCHEIRIAS	ALLOSTERIC	ALMSGIVINGS	ALPHASORTING	ALTIMETRIES
ALLOCHIRIA	ALLOSTERICALLY	ALMSHOUSES	ALPHASORTS	ALTIPLANOS
ALLOCHIRIAS	ALLOSTERIES	ALMUCANTAR	ALPHATESTED	ALTISONANT
ALLOCHTHONOUS	ALLOTETRAPLOID	ALMUCANTARS	ALPHATESTING	ALTISSIMOS
ALLOCUTION	ALLOTETRAPLOIDS	ALOGICALLY	ALPHATESTS	ALTITONANT
ALLOCUTIONS	ALLOTETRAPLOIDY	ALONENESSES	ALPHOSISES	ALTITUDINAL
ALLODYNIAS	ALLOTHEISM	ALONGSHORE	ALSTROEMERIA	ALTITUDINARIAN
ALLOGAMIES	ALLOTHEISMS	ALONGSHOREMAN	ALSTROEMERIAS	ALTITUDINARIANS
ALLOGAMOUS	ALLOTMENTS	ALONGSHOREMEN	ALTALTISSIMO	ALTITUDINOUS
ALLOGENEIC	ALLOTRIOMORPHIC	ALOOFNESSES	ALTALTISSIMOS	ALTOCUMULI
ALLOGRAFTED	ALLOTROPES	ALPARGATAS	ALTARPIECE	ALTOCUMULUS
ALLOGRAFTING	ALLOTROPIC	ALPENGLOWS	ALTARPIECES	ALTOGETHER
ALLOGRAFTS	ALLOTROPICALLY	ALPENHORNS	ALTAZIMUTH	ALTOGETHERS
ALLOGRAPHIC	ALLOTROPIES	ALPENSTOCK	ALTAZIMUTHS	ALTORUFFLED
ALLOGRAPHS	ALLOTROPISM	ALPENSTOCKS	ALTERABILITIES	ALTOSTRATI
ALLOIOSTROPHOS	ALLOTROPISMS	ALPESTRINE	ALTERABILITY	ALTOSTRATUS
ALLOMERISM	ALLOTROPOUS	ALPHABETARIAN	ALTERATION	ALTRICIALS
ALLOMERISMS	ALLOTTERIES	ALPHABETARIANS	ALTERATIONS	ALTRUISTIC
ALLOMEROUS	ALLOTYPICALLY	ALPHABETED	ALTERATIVE	ALTRUISTICALLY
ALLOMETRIC	ALLOTYPIES	ALPHABETIC	ALTERATIVES	ALUMINATES
ALLOMETRIES	ALLOWABILITIES	ALPHABETICAL	ALTERCATED	ALUMINIFEROUS
ALLOMORPHIC	ALLOWABILITY	ALPHABETICALLY	ALTERCATES	ALUMINISED
ALLOMORPHISM	ALLOWABLENESS	ALPHABETIFORM	ALTERCATING	ALUMINISES
ALLOMORPHISMS	ALLOWABLENESSES	ALPHABETING	ALTERCATION	ALUMINISING
ALLOMORPHS	ALLOWABLES	ALPHABETISATION	ALTERCATIONS	ALUMINIUMS
ALLONYMOUS	ALLOWANCED	ALPHABETISE	ALTERCATIVE	ALUMINIZED
ALLOPATHIC	ALLOWANCES	ALPHABETISED	ALTERITIES	ALUMINIZES
ALLOPATHICALLY	ALLOWANCING	ALPHABETISER	ALTERNANCE	ALUMINIZING
ALLOPATHIES	ALLUREMENT	ALPHABETISERS	ALTERNANCES	ALUMINOSILICATE

ALUMINOSITIES	AMAZEDNESSES	AMBIVALENTLY	AMELIORATORS	AMINOACIDURIAS
ALUMINOSITY	AMAZEMENTS	AMBIVERSION	AMELIORATORY	AMINOBENZOIC
ALUMINOTHERMIES	AMAZONIANS	AMBIVERSIONS	AMELOBLAST	AMINOBUTENE
ALUMINOTHERMY	AMAZONITES	AMBLYGONITE	AMELOBLASTS	AMINOBUTENES
ALUMSTONES	AMAZONSTONE	AMBLYGONITES	AMELOGENESES	AMINOPEPTIDASE
ALVEOLARLY	AMAZONSTONES	AMBLYOPIAS	AMELOGENESIS	AMINOPEPTIDASES
ALVEOLATION	AMBAGITORY	AMBOCEPTOR	AMENABILITIES	AMINOPHENAZONE
ALVEOLATIONS	AMBASSADOR	AMBOCEPTORS	AMENABILITY	AMINOPHENAZONES
ALVEOLITIS	AMBASSADORIAL	AMBOSEXUAL	AMENABLENESS	AMINOPHENOL
ALVEOLITISES	AMBASSADORS	AMBROSIALLY	AMENABLENESSES	AMINOPHENOLS
ALYCOMPAINE	AMBASSADORSHIP	AMBROTYPES	AMENAUNCES	AMINOPHYLLINE
ALYCOMPAINES	AMBASSADORSHIPS	AMBULACRAL	AMENDATORY	AMINOPHYLLINES
AMAKWEREKWERE	AMBASSADRESS	AMBULACRUM	AMENDMENTS	AMINOPTERIN
AMALGAMATE	AMBASSADRESSES	AMBULANCEMAN	AMENORRHEA	AMINOPTERINS
AMALGAMATED	AMBASSAGES	AMBULANCEMEN	AMENORRHEAS	AMINOPYRINE
AMALGAMATES	AMBERGRISES	AMBULANCES	AMENORRHEIC	AMINOPYRINES
AMALGAMATING	AMBERJACKS	AMBULANCEWOMAN	AMENORRHOEA	AMISSIBILITIES
AMALGAMATION	AMBIDENTATE	AMBULANCEWOMEN	AMENORRHOEAS	AMISSIBILITY
AMALGAMATIONS	AMBIDEXTER	AMBULATING	AMENTACEOUS	AMITOTICALLY
AMALGAMATIVE	AMBIDEXTERITIES	AMBULATION	AMENTIFEROUS	AMITRIPTYLINE
AMALGAMATOR	AMBIDEXTERITY	AMBULATIONS	AMERCEABLE	AMITRIPTYLINES
AMALGAMATORS	AMBIDEXTEROUS	AMBULATORIES	AMERCEMENT	AMITRYPTYLINE
AMANTADINE	AMBIDEXTERS	AMBULATORILY	AMERCEMENTS	AMITRYPTYLINES
AMANTADINES	AMBIDEXTROUS	AMBULATORS	AMERCIABLE	AMMOCOETES
AMANUENSES	AMBIDEXTROUSLY	AMBULATORY	AMERCIAMENT	AMMONIACAL
AMANUENSIS	AMBIGUITIES	AMBULETTES	AMERCIAMENTS	AMMONIACUM
AMARACUSES	AMBIGUOUSLY	AMBUSCADED	AMERICIUMS	AMMONIACUMS
AMARANTACEOUS	AMBIGUOUSNESS	AMBUSCADER	AMETABOLIC	AMMONIATED
AMARANTHACEOUS	AMBIGUOUSNESSES	AMBUSCADERS	AMETABOLISM	AMMONIATES
AMARANTHINE	AMBILATERAL	AMBUSCADES	AMETABOLISMS	AMMONIATING
AMARANTINE	AMBIOPHONIES	AMBUSCADING	AMETABOLOUS	AMMONIATION
AMARYLLIDACEOUS	AMBIOPHONY	AMBUSCADOES	AMETHYSTINE	AMMONIATIONS
AMARYLLIDS	AMBISEXUAL	AMBUSCADOS	AMETROPIAS	AMMONIFICATION
AMARYLLISES	AMBISEXUALITIES	AMBUSHMENT	AMIABILITIES	AMMONIFICATIONS
AMASSMENTS	AMBISEXUALITY	AMBUSHMENTS	AMIABILITY	AMMONIFIED
AMATEURISH	AMBISEXUALS	AMEBOCYTES	AMIABLENESS	AMMONIFIES
AMATEURISHLY	AMBITIONED	AMELIORABLE	AMIABLENESSES	AMMONIFYING
AMATEURISHNESS	AMBITIONING	AMELIORANT	AMIANTHINE	AMMONOLYSES
AMATEURISM	AMBITIONLESS	AMELIORANTS	AMIANTHOID	AMMONOLYSIS
AMATEURISMS	AMBITIOUSLY	AMELIORATE	AMIANTHOIDAL	AMMOPHILOUS
AMATEURSHIP	AMBITIOUSNESS	AMELIORATED	AMIANTHUSES	AMMUNITION
AMATEURSHIPS	AMBITIOUSNESSES	AMELIORATES	AMIANTUSES	AMMUNITIONED
AMATIVENESS	AMBIVALENCE	AMELIORATING	AMICABILITIES	AMMUNITIONING
AMATIVENESSES	AMBIVALENCES	AMELIORATION	AMICABILITY	AMMUNITIONS
AMATORIALLY	AMBIVALENCIES	AMELIORATIONS	AMICABLENESS	AMNESTYING
AMATORIOUS	AMBIVALENCY	AMELIORATIVE	AMICABLENESSES	AMNIOCENTESES
AMAZEDNESS	AMBIVALENT	AMELIORATOR	AMINOACIDURIA	AMNIOCENTESIS

AMNIOTOMIES	AMPHIARTHROSIS	AMPHIOXUSES	AMPLIDYNES	ANABAPTISE
AMOBARBITAL	AMPHIASTER	AMPHIPATHIC	AMPLIFIABLE	ANABAPTISED
AMOBARBITALS	AMPHIASTERS	AMPHIPHILE	AMPLIFICATION	ANABAPTISES
AMOEBIASES	AMPHIBIANS	AMPHIPHILES	AMPLIFICATIONS	ANABAPTISING
AMOEBIASIS	AMPHIBIOTIC	AMPHIPHILIC	AMPLIFIERS	ANABAPTISM
AMOEBIFORM	AMPHIBIOUS	AMPHIPLOID	AMPLIFYING	ANABAPTISMS
AMOEBOCYTE	AMPHIBIOUSLY	AMPHIPLOIDIES	AMPLITUDES	ANABAPTIST
AMOEBOCYTES	AMPHIBIOUSNESS	AMPHIPLOIDS	AMPLOSOMES	ANABAPTISTIC
AMONTILLADO	AMPHIBLASTIC	AMPHIPLOIDY	AMPULLACEAL	ANABAPTISTS
AMONTILLADOS	AMPHIBLASTULA	AMPHIPODOUS	AMPULLACEOUS	ANABAPTIZE
AMORALISMS	AMPHIBLASTULAE	AMPHIPROSTYLAR	AMPULLOSITIES	ANABAPTIZED
AMORALISTS	AMPHIBOLES	AMPHIPROSTYLE	AMPULLOSITY	ANABAPTIZES
AMORALITIES	AMPHIBOLIC	AMPHIPROSTYLES	AMPUTATING	ANABAPTIZING
AMOROSITIES	AMPHIBOLIES	AMPHIPROTIC	AMPUTATION	ANABLEPSES
AMOROUSNESS	AMPHIBOLITE	AMPHISBAENA	AMPUTATIONS	ANABOLISMS
AMOROUSNESSES	AMPHIBOLITES	AMPHISBAENAE	AMPUTATORS	ANABOLITES
AMORPHISMS	AMPHIBOLOGICAL	AMPHISBAENAS	AMRITATTVA	ANABOLITIC
AMORPHOUSLY	AMPHIBOLOGIES	AMPHISBAENIC	AMRITATTVAS	ANABRANCHES
AMORPHOUSNESS	AMPHIBOLOGY	AMPHISCIAN	AMSINCKIAS	ANACARDIACEOUS
AMORPHOUSNESSES	AMPHIBOLOUS	AMPHISCIANS	AMUSEMENTS	ANACARDIUM
AMORTISABLE	AMPHIBRACH	AMPHISTOMATAL	AMUSINGNESS	ANACARDIUMS
AMORTISATION	AMPHIBRACHIC	AMPHISTOMATIC	AMUSINGNESSES	ANACATHARSES
AMORTISATIONS	AMPHIBRACHS	AMPHISTOMOUS	AMUSIVENESS	ANACATHARSIS
AMORTISEMENT	AMPHICHROIC	AMPHISTYLAR	AMUSIVENESSES	ANACATHARTIC
AMORTISEMENTS	AMPHICHROMATIC	AMPHISTYLARS	AMYGDALACEOUS	ANACATHARTICS
AMORTISING	AMPHICOELOUS	AMPHITHEATER	AMYGDALATE	ANACHARISES
AMORTIZABLE	AMPHICTYON	AMPHITHEATERS	AMYGDALINE	ANACHORISM
AMORTIZATION	AMPHICTYONIC	AMPHITHEATRAL	AMYGDALINS	ANACHORISMS
AMORTIZATIONS	AMPHICTYONIES	AMPHITHEATRE	AMYGDALOID	ANACHRONIC
AMORTIZEMENT	AMPHICTYONS	AMPHITHEATRES	AMYGDALOIDAL	ANACHRONICAL
AMORTIZEMENTS	AMPHICTYONY	AMPHITHEATRIC	AMYGDALOIDS	ANACHRONICALLY
AMORTIZING	AMPHIDENTATE	AMPHITHEATRICAL	AMYLACEOUS	ANACHRONISM
AMOURETTES	AMPHIDIPLOID	AMPHITHECIA	AMYLOIDOSES	ANACHRONISMS
AMOXICILLIN	AMPHIDIPLOIDIES	AMPHITHECIUM	AMYLOIDOSIS	ANACHRONISTIC
AMOXICILLINS	AMPHIDIPLOIDS	AMPHITRICHA	AMYLOLYSES	ANACHRONOUS
AMOXYCILLIN	AMPHIDIPLOIDY	AMPHITRICHOUS	AMYLOLYSIS	ANACHRONOUSLY
AMOXYCILLINS	AMPHIGASTRIA	AMPHITROPOUS	AMYLOLYTIC	ANACLASTIC
AMPELOGRAPHIES	AMPHIGASTRIUM	AMPHOLYTES	AMYLOPECTIN	ANACOLUTHA
AMPELOGRAPHY	AMPHIGORIC	AMPHOTERIC	AMYLOPECTINS	ANACOLUTHIA
AMPELOPSES	AMPHIGORIES	AMPICILLIN	AMYLOPLAST	ANACOLUTHIAS
AMPELOPSIS	AMPHIGOURI	AMPICILLINS	AMYLOPLASTS	ANACOLUTHIC
AMPEROMETRIC	AMPHIGOURIS	AMPLENESSES	AMYLOPSINS	ANACOLUTHICALLY
AMPERSANDS	AMPHIMACER	AMPLEXICAUL	AMYOTONIAS	ANACOLUTHON
AMPERZANDS	AMPHIMACERS	AMPLEXUSES	AMYOTROPHIC	ANACOLUTHONS
AMPHETAMINE	AMPHIMICTIC	AMPLIATION	AMYOTROPHIES	ANACOUSTIC
AMPHETAMINES	AMPHIMIXES	AMPLIATIONS	AMYOTROPHY	ANACREONTIC
AMPHIARTHROSES	AMPHIMIXIS	AMPLIATIVE	ANABANTIDS	ANACREONTICALLY

ANACREONTICS	ANAGRAMMATISES	ANALYTICITIES	ANAPTYCTICAL	ANATOMISED
ANACRUSTIC	ANAGRAMMATISING	ANALYTICITY	ANARCHICAL	ANATOMISER
ANADIPLOSES	ANAGRAMMATISM	ANALYZABILITIES	ANARCHICALLY	ANATOMISERS
ANADIPLOSIS	ANAGRAMMATISMS	ANALYZABILITY	ANARCHISED	ANATOMISES
ANADROMOUS	ANAGRAMMATIST	ANALYZABLE	ANARCHISES	ANATOMISING
ANADYOMENE	ANAGRAMMATISTS	ANALYZATION	ANARCHISING	ANATOMISTS
ANAEMICALLY	ANAGRAMMATIZE	ANALYZATIONS	ANARCHISMS	ANATOMIZATION
ANAEROBICALLY	ANAGRAMMATIZED	ANAMNESTIC	ANARCHISTIC	ANATOMIZATIONS
ANAEROBIONT	ANAGRAMMATIZES	ANAMNESTICALLY	ANARCHISTICALLY	ANATOMIZED
ANAEROBIONTS	ANAGRAMMATIZING	ANAMNIOTES	ANARCHISTS	ANATOMIZER
ANAEROBIOSES	ANAGRAMMED	ANAMNIOTIC	ANARCHIZED	ANATOMIZERS
ANAEROBIOSIS	ANAGRAMMER	ANAMORPHIC	ANARCHIZES	ANATOMIZES
ANAEROBIOTIC	ANAGRAMMERS	ANAMORPHISM	ANARCHIZING	ANATOMIZING
ANAEROBIUM	ANAGRAMMING	ANAMORPHISMS	ANARTHRIAS	ANATROPIES
ANAESTHESES	ANALEMMATA	ANAMORPHOSCOPE	ANARTHROUS	ANATROPOUS
ANAESTHESIA	ANALEMMATIC	ANAMORPHOSCOPES	ANARTHROUSLY	ANCESTORED
ANAESTHESIAS	ANALEPTICS	ANAMORPHOSES	ANARTHROUSNESS	ANCESTORIAL
ANAESTHESIOLOGY	ANALGESIAS	ANAMORPHOSIS	ANASARCOUS	ANCESTORING
ANAESTHESIS	ANALGESICS	ANAMORPHOUS	ANASTIGMAT	ANCESTRALLY
ANAESTHETIC	ANALGETICS	ANANDAMIDE	ANASTIGMATIC	ANCESTRALS
ANAESTHETICALLY	ANALOGICAL	ANANDAMIDES	ANASTIGMATISM	ANCESTRESS
ANAESTHETICS	ANALOGICALLY	ANAPAESTIC	ANASTIGMATISMS	ANCESTRESSES
ANAESTHETISE	ANALOGISED	ANAPAESTICAL	ANASTIGMATS	ANCESTRIES
ANAESTHETISED	ANALOGISES	ANAPESTICS	ANASTOMOSE	ANCHORAGES
ANAESTHETISES	ANALOGISING	ANAPHORESES	ANASTOMOSED	ANCHORESSES
ANAESTHETISING	ANALOGISMS	ANAPHORESIS	ANASTOMOSES	ANCHORETIC
ANAESTHETIST	ANALOGISTS	ANAPHORICAL	ANASTOMOSING	ANCHORETICAL
ANAESTHETISTS	ANALOGIZED	ANAPHORICALLY	ANASTOMOSIS	ANCHORETTE
ANAESTHETIZE	ANALOGIZES	ANAPHRODISIA	ANASTOMOTIC	ANCHORETTES
ANAESTHETIZED	ANALOGIZING	ANAPHRODISIAC	ANASTROPHE	ANCHORITES
ANAESTHETIZES	ANALOGOUSLY	ANAPHRODISIACS	ANASTROPHES	ANCHORITIC
ANAESTHETIZING	ANALOGOUSNESS	ANAPHRODISIAS	ANASTROZOLE	ANCHORITICAL
ANAGENESES	ANALOGOUSNESSES	ANAPHYLACTIC	ANASTROZOLES	ANCHORITICALLY
ANAGENESIS	ANALPHABET	ANAPHYLACTOID	ANATHEMATA	ANCHORLESS
ANAGLYPHIC	ANALPHABETE	ANAPHYLAXES	ANATHEMATICAL	ANCHORPEOPLE
ANAGLYPHICAL	ANALPHABETES	ANAPHYLAXIES	ANATHEMATISE	ANCHORPERSON
ANAGLYPHIES	ANALPHABETIC	ANAPHYLAXIS	ANATHEMATISED	ANCHORPERSONS
ANAGLYPTIC	ANALPHABETICS	ANAPHYLAXY	ANATHEMATISES	ANCHORWOMAN
ANAGLYPTICAL	ANALPHABETISM	ANAPLASIAS	ANATHEMATISING	ANCHORWOMEN
ANAGNORISES	ANALPHABETISMS	ANAPLASMOSES	ANATHEMATIZE	ANCHOVETAS
ANAGNORISIS	ANALPHABETS	ANAPLASMOSIS	ANATHEMATIZED	ANCHOVETTA
ANAGOGICAL	ANALYSABLE	ANAPLASTIC	ANATHEMATIZES	ANCHOVETTAS
ANAGOGICALLY	ANALYSANDS	ANAPLASTIES	ANATHEMATIZING	ANCHYLOSED
ANAGRAMMATIC	ANALYSATION	ANAPLEROSES	ANATOMICAL	ANCHYLOSES
ANAGRAMMATICAL	ANALYSATIONS	ANAPLEROSIS	ANATOMICALLY	ANCHYLOSING
ANAGRAMMATISE	ANALYTICAL	ANAPLEROTIC	ANATOMISATION	ANCHYLOSIS
ANAGRAMMATISED	ANALYTICALLY	ANAPTYCTIC	ANATOMISATIONS	ANCHYLOTIC

A

ANCIENTEST	ANDROPAUSES	ANENCEPHALIC	ANGIOGENIC	ANGLOMANIAS
ANCIENTNESS	ANDROPHORE	ANENCEPHALIES	ANGIOGRAMS	ANGLOPHILE
ANCIENTNESSES	ANDROPHORES	ANENCEPHALY	ANGIOGRAPHIC	ANGLOPHILES
ANCIENTRIES	ANDROSPHINGES	ANESTHESIA	ANGIOGRAPHIES	ANGLOPHILIA
ANCILLARIES	ANDROSPHINX	ANESTHESIAS	ANGIOGRAPHY	ANGLOPHILIAS
ANCIPITOUS	ANDROSPHINXES	ANESTHESIOLOGY	ANGIOLOGIES	ANGLOPHILIC
ANCYLOSTOMIASES	ANDROSTERONE	ANESTHETIC	ANGIOMATOUS	ANGLOPHILS
ANCYLOSTOMIASIS	ANDROSTERONES	ANESTHETICALLY	ANGIOPLASTIES	ANGLOPHOBE
ANDALUSITE	ANECDOTAGE	ANESTHETICS	ANGIOPLASTY	ANGLOPHOBES
ANDALUSITES	ANECDOTAGES	ANESTHETISE	ANGIOSARCOMA	ANGLOPHOBIA
ANDANTINOS	ANECDOTALISM	ANESTHETISED	ANGIOSARCOMAS	ANGLOPHOBIAC
ANDOUILLES	ANECDOTALISMS	ANESTHETISES	ANGIOSARCOMATA	ANGLOPHOBIAS
ANDOUILLETTE	ANECDOTALIST	ANESTHETISING	ANGIOSPERM	ANGLOPHOBIC
ANDOUILLETTES	ANECDOTALISTS	ANESTHETIST	ANGIOSPERMAL	ANGLOPHONE
ANDRADITES	ANECDOTALLY	ANESTHETISTS	ANGIOSPERMOUS	ANGLOPHONES
ANDROCENTRIC	ANECDOTICAL	ANESTHETIZATION	ANGIOSPERMS	ANGLOPHONIC
ANDROCENTRISM	ANECDOTICALLY	ANESTHETIZE	ANGIOSTOMATOUS	ANGOPHORAS
ANDROCENTRISMS	ANECDOTIST	ANESTHETIZED	ANGIOSTOMOUS	ANGOSTURAS
ANDROCEPHALOUS	ANECDOTISTS	ANESTHETIZES	ANGIOTENSIN	ANGRINESSES
ANDROCLINIA	ANELASTICITIES	ANESTHETIZING	ANGIOTENSINS	ANGUIFAUNA
ANDROCLINIUM	ANELASTICITY	ANEUPLOIDIES	ANGLEBERRIES	ANGUIFAUNAE
ANDRODIOECIOUS	ANEMICALLY	ANEUPLOIDS	ANGLEBERRY	ANGUIFAUNAS
ANDRODIOECISM	ANEMOCHORE	ANEUPLOIDY	ANGLEDOZER	ANGUILLIFORM
ANDRODIOECISMS	ANEMOCHORES	ANEURISMAL	ANGLEDOZERS	ANGUISHING
ANDROECIAL	ANEMOCHOROUS	ANEURISMALLY	ANGLERFISH	ANGULARITIES
ANDROECIUM	ANEMOGRAMS	ANEURISMATIC	ANGLERFISHES	ANGULARITY
ANDROECIUMS	ANEMOGRAPH	ANEURYSMAL	ANGLESITES	ANGULARNESS
ANDROGENESES	ANEMOGRAPHIC	ANEURYSMALLY	ANGLETWITCH	ANGULARNESSES
ANDROGENESIS	ANEMOGRAPHIES	ANEURYSMATIC	ANGLETWITCHES	ANGULATING
ANDROGENETIC	ANEMOGRAPHS	ANFRACTUOSITIES	ANGLEWORMS	ANGULATION
ANDROGENIC	ANEMOGRAPHY	ANFRACTUOSITY	ANGLICISATION	ANGULATIONS
ANDROGENOUS	ANEMOLOGIES	ANFRACTUOUS	ANGLICISATIONS	ANGUSTIFOLIATE
ANDROGYNES	ANEMOMETER	ANGASHORES	ANGLICISED	ANGUSTIROSTRATE
ANDROGYNIES	ANEMOMETERS	ANGELFISHES	ANGLICISES	ANGWANTIBO
ANDROGYNOPHORE	ANEMOMETRIC	ANGELHOODS	ANGLICISING	ANGWANTIBOS
ANDROGYNOPHORES	ANEMOMETRICAL	ANGELICALLY	ANGLICISMS	ANHARMONIC
ANDROGYNOUS	ANEMOMETRIES	ANGELOLATRIES	ANGLICISTS	ANHEDONIAS
ANDROLOGIES	ANEMOMETRY	ANGELOLATRY	ANGLICIZATION	ANHELATION
ANDROLOGIST	ANEMOPHILIES	ANGELOLOGIES	ANGLICIZATIONS	ANHELATIONS
ANDROLOGISTS	ANEMOPHILOUS	ANGELOLOGIST	ANGLICIZED	ANHIDROSES
ANDROMEDAS	ANEMOPHILY	ANGELOLOGISTS	ANGLICIZES	ANHIDROSIS
ANDROMEDOTOXIN	ANEMOPHOBIA	ANGELOLOGY	ANGLICIZING	ANHIDROTIC
ANDROMEDOTOXINS	ANEMOPHOBIAS	ANGELOPHANIES	ANGLIFYING	ANHIDROTICS
ANDROMONOECIOUS	ANEMOSCOPE	ANGELOPHANY	ANGLISTICS	ANHUNGERED
ANDROMONOECISM	ANEMOSCOPES	ANGIOCARPOUS	ANGLOMANIA	ANHYDRASES
ANDROMONOECISMS	ANENCEPHALIA	ANGIOGENESES	ANGLOMANIAC	ANHYDRIDES
ANDROPAUSE	ANENCEPHALIAS	ANGIOGENESIS	ANGLOMANIACS	ANHYDRITES

ANICONISMS

ANICONISMS	ANIMATRONICS	ANNEXATIONISTS	ANNUNCIATIONS	ANOVULATIONS
ANICONISTS	ANIMOSITIES	ANNEXATIONS	ANNUNCIATIVE	ANOVULATORY
ANILINCTUS	ANISEIKONIA	ANNEXMENTS	ANNUNCIATOR	ANOXAEMIAS
ANILINCTUSES	ANISEIKONIAS	ANNIHILABLE	ANNUNCIATORS	ANSWERABILITIES
ANILINGUSES	ANISEIKONIC	ANNIHILATE	ANNUNCIATORY	ANSWERABILITY
ANIMADVERSION	ANISOCERCAL	ANNIHILATED	ANNUNTIATE	ANSWERABLE
ANIMADVERSIONS	ANISODACTYL	ANNIHILATES	ANNUNTIATED	ANSWERABLENESS
ANIMADVERT	ANISODACTYLOUS	ANNIHILATING	ANNUNTIATES	ANSWERABLY
ANIMADVERTED	ANISODACTYLS	ANNIHILATION	ANNUNTIATING	ANSWERLESS
ANIMADVERTER	ANISOGAMIES	ANNIHILATIONISM	ANODICALLY	ANSWERPHONE
ANIMADVERTERS	ANISOGAMOUS	ANNIHILATIONS	ANODISATION	ANSWERPHONES
ANIMADVERTING	ANISOMERIC	ANNIHILATIVE	ANODISATIONS	ANTAGONISABLE
ANIMADVERTS	ANISOMEROUS	ANNIHILATOR	ANODIZATION	ANTAGONISATION
ANIMALCULA	ANISOMETRIC	ANNIHILATORS	ANODIZATIONS	ANTAGONISATIONS
ANIMALCULAR	ANISOMETROPIA	ANNIHILATORY	ANODONTIAS	ANTAGONISE
ANIMALCULE	ANISOMETROPIAS	ANNIVERSARIES	ANOESTROUS	ANTAGONISED
ANIMALCULES	ANISOMETROPIC	ANNIVERSARY	ANOINTMENT	ANTAGONISES
ANIMALCULISM	ANISOMORPHIC	ANNOTATABLE	ANOINTMENTS	ANTAGONISING
ANIMALCULISMS	ANISOPHYLLIES	ANNOTATING	ANOMALISTIC	ANTAGONISM
ANIMALCULIST	ANISOPHYLLOUS	ANNOTATION	ANOMALISTICAL	ANTAGONISMS
ANIMALCULISTS	ANISOPHYLLY	ANNOTATIONS	ANOMALISTICALLY	ANTAGONIST
ANIMALCULUM	ANISOTROPIC	ANNOTATIVE	ANOMALOUSLY	ANTAGONISTIC
ANIMALIERS	ANISOTROPICALLY	ANNOTATORS	ANOMALOUSNESS	ANTAGONISTS
ANIMALISATION	ANISOTROPIES	ANNOUNCEMENT	ANOMALOUSNESSES	ANTAGONIZABLE
ANIMALISATIONS	ANISOTROPISM	ANNOUNCEMENTS	ANONACEOUS	ANTAGONIZATION
ANIMALISED	ANISOTROPISMS	ANNOUNCERS	ANONYMISED	ANTAGONIZATIONS
ANIMALISES	ANISOTROPY	ANNOUNCING	ANONYMISES	ANTAGONIZE
ANIMALISING	ANKLEBONES	ANNOYANCES	ANONYMISING	ANTAGONIZED
ANIMALISMS	ANKYLOSAUR	ANNOYINGLY	ANONYMITIES	ANTAGONIZES
ANIMALISTIC	ANKYLOSAURS	ANNUALISED	ANONYMIZED	ANTAGONIZING
ANIMALISTS	ANKYLOSAURUS	ANNUALISES	ANONYMIZES	ANTALKALIES
ANIMALITIES	ANKYLOSAURUSES	ANNUALISING	ANONYMIZING	ANTALKALINE
ANIMALIZATION	ANKYLOSING	ANNUALIZED	ANONYMOUSLY	ANTALKALINES
ANIMALIZATIONS	ANKYLOSTOMIASES	ANNUALIZES	ANONYMOUSNESS	ANTALKALIS
ANIMALIZED	ANKYLOSTOMIASIS	ANNUALIZING	ANONYMOUSNESSES	ANTAPHRODISIAC
ANIMALIZES	ANNABERGITE	ANNUITANTS	ANOPHELINE	ANTAPHRODISIACS
ANIMALIZING	ANNABERGITES	ANNULARITIES	ANOPHELINES	ANTARTHRITIC
ANIMALLIKE	ANNALISING	ANNULARITY	ANORECTICS	ANTARTHRITICS
ANIMATEDLY	ANNALISTIC	ANNULATION	ANOREXIGENIC	ANTASTHMATIC
ANIMATENESS	ANNALIZING	ANNULATIONS	ANORTHITES	ANTASTHMATICS
ANIMATENESSES	ANNEALINGS	ANNULLABLE	ANORTHITIC	ANTEBELLUM
ANIMATINGLY	ANNELIDANS	ANNULMENTS	ANORTHOSITE	ANTECEDENCE
ANIMATIONS	ANNEXATION	ANNUNCIATE	ANORTHOSITES	ANTECEDENCES
ANIMATISMS	ANNEXATIONAL	ANNUNCIATED	ANORTHOSITIC	ANTECEDENT
ANIMATISTS	ANNEXATIONISM	ANNUNCIATES	ANOTHERGUESS	ANTECEDENTLY
ANIMATRONIC	ANNEXATIONISMS	ANNUNCIATING	ANOVULANTS	ANTECEDENTS
ANIMATRONICALLY	ANNEXATIONIST	ANNUNCIATION	ANOVULATION	ANTECEDING

ANTICHLORS

A

ANTECESSOR	ANTHELMINTIC	ANTHOZOANS	ANTHROPOPATHY	ANTIAUTHORITY
ANTECESSORS	ANTHELMINTICS	ANTHRACENE	ANTHROPOPHAGI	ANTIAUXINS
ANTECHAMBER	ANTHEMWISE	ANTHRACENES	ANTHROPOPHAGIC	ANTIBACCHII
ANTECHAMBERS	ANTHERIDIA	ANTHRACITE	ANTHROPOPHAGIES	ANTIBACCHIUS
ANTECHAPEL	ANTHERIDIAL	ANTHRACITES	ANTHROPOPHAGITE	ANTIBACKLASH
ANTECHAPELS	ANTHERIDIUM	ANTHRACITIC	ANTHROPOPHAGOUS	ANTIBACTERIAL
ANTECHOIRS	ANTHEROZOID	ANTHRACNOSE	ANTHROPOPHAGUS	ANTIBACTERIALS
ANTEDATING	ANTHEROZOIDS	ANTHRACNOSES	ANTHROPOPHAGY	ANTIBALLISTIC
ANTEDILUVIAL	ANTHEROZOOID	ANTHRACOID	ANTHROPOPHOBIA	ANTIBARBARUS
ANTEDILUVIALLY	ANTHEROZOOIDS	ANTHRACOSES	ANTHROPOPHOBIAS	ANTIBARBARUSES
ANTEDILUVIAN	ANTHERSMUT	ANTHRACOSIS	ANTHROPOPHOBIC	ANTIBARYON
ANTEDILUVIANS	ANTHERSMUTS	ANTHRANILATE	ANTHROPOPHOBICS	ANTIBARYONS
ANTEMERIDIAN	ANTHOCARPOUS	ANTHRANILATES	ANTHROPOPHUISM	ANTIBILIOUS
ANTEMORTEM	ANTHOCARPS	ANTHRAQUINONE	ANTHROPOPHUISMS	ANTIBILLBOARD
ANTEMUNDANE	ANTHOCHLORE	ANTHRAQUINONES	ANTHROPOPHYTE	ANTIBIOSES
ANTENATALLY	ANTHOCHLORES	ANTHROPICAL	ANTHROPOPHYTES	ANTIBIOSIS
ANTENATALS	ANTHOCYANIN	ANTHROPOBIOLOGY	ANTHROPOPSYCHIC	ANTIBIOTIC
ANTENNIFEROUS	ANTHOCYANINS	ANTHROPOCENTRIC	ANTHROPOSOPHIC	ANTIBIOTICALLY
ANTENNIFORM	ANTHOCYANS	ANTHROPOGENESES	ANTHROPOSOPHIES	ANTIBIOTICS
ANTENNULAR	ANTHOLOGICAL	ANTHROPOGENESIS	ANTHROPOSOPHIST	ANTIBLACKISM
ANTENNULES	ANTHOLOGIES	ANTHROPOGENETIC	ANTHROPOSOPHY	ANTIBLACKISMS
ANTENUPTIAL	ANTHOLOGISE	ANTHROPOGENIC	ANTHROPOTOMIES	ANTIBODIES
ANTEORBITAL	ANTHOLOGISED	ANTHROPOGENIES	ANTHROPOTOMY	ANTIBOURGEOIS
ANTEPENDIA	ANTHOLOGISER	ANTHROPOGENY	ANTHURIUMS	ANTIBOYCOTT
ANTEPENDIUM	ANTHOLOGISERS	ANTHROPOGONIES	ANTIABORTION	ANTIBURGLAR
ANTEPENDIUMS	ANTHOLOGISES	ANTHROPOGONY	ANTIABORTIONIST	ANTIBURGLARY
ANTEPENULT	ANTHOLOGISING	ANTHROPOGRAPHY	ANTIACADEMIC	ANTIBUSERS
ANTEPENULTIMA	ANTHOLOGIST	ANTHROPOID	ANTIADITIS	ANTIBUSINESS
ANTEPENULTIMAS	ANTHOLOGISTS	ANTHROPOIDAL	ANTIADITISES	ANTIBUSING
ANTEPENULTIMATE	ANTHOLOGIZE	ANTHROPOIDS	ANTIAGGRESSION	ANTICAKING
ANTEPENULTS	ANTHOLOGIZED	ANTHROPOLATRIES	ANTIAIRCRAFT	ANTICANCER
ANTEPOSITION	ANTHOLOGIZER	ANTHROPOLATRY	ANTIAIRCRAFTS	ANTICAPITALISM
ANTEPOSITIONS	ANTHOLOGIZERS	ANTHROPOLOGICAL	ANTIALCOHOL	ANTICAPITALISMS
ANTEPRANDIAL	ANTHOLOGIZES	ANTHROPOLOGIES	ANTIALCOHOLISM	ANTICAPITALIST
ANTERIORITIES	ANTHOLOGIZING	ANTHROPOLOGIST	ANTIALLERGENIC	ANTICAPITALISTS
ANTERIORITY	ANTHOMANIA	ANTHROPOLOGISTS	ANTIANEMIA	ANTICARCINOGEN
ANTERIORLY	ANTHOMANIAC	ANTHROPOLOGY	ANTIANXIETY	ANTICARCINOGENS
ANTEROGRADE	ANTHOMANIACS	ANTHROPOMETRIC	ANTIAPARTHEID	ANTICARIES
ANTEVERSION	ANTHOMANIAS	ANTHROPOMETRIES	ANTIAPHRODISIAC	ANTICATALYST
ANTEVERSIONS	ANTHOPHILOUS	ANTHROPOMETRIST	ANTIARRHYTHMIC	ANTICATALYSTS
ANTEVERTED	ANTHOPHORE	ANTHROPOMETRY	ANTIARRHYTHMICS	ANTICATHODE
ANTEVERTING	ANTHOPHORES	ANTHROPOMORPH	ANTIARTHRITIC	ANTICATHODES
ANTHELICES	ANTHOPHYLLITE	ANTHROPOMORPHIC	ANTIARTHRITICS	ANTICATHOLIC
ANTHELIONS	ANTHOPHYLLITES	ANTHROPOMORPHS	ANTIARTHRITIS	ANTICELLULITE
ANTHELIXES	ANTHOTAXIES	ANTHROPOPATHIC	ANTIASTHMA	ANTICENSORSHIP
ANTHELMINTHIC	ANTHOXANTHIN	ANTHROPOPATHIES	ANTIASTHMATIC	ANTICHLORISTIC
ANTHELMINTHICS	ANTHOXANTHINS	ANTHROPOPATHISM	ANTIASTHMATICS	ANTICHLORS

ANTICHOICE	ANTICLOTTING	ANTIDIURETIC	ANTIFERTILITY	ANTIHUMANISMS
ANTICHOICER	ANTICOAGULANT	ANTIDIURETICS	ANTIFILIBUSTER	ANTIHUMANISTIC
ANTICHOICERS	ANTICOAGULANTS	ANTIDOGMATIC	ANTIFOAMING	ANTIHUNTER
ANTICHOLESTEROL	ANTICODONS	ANTIDOTALLY	ANTIFOGGING	ANTIHUNTING
ANTICHOLINERGIC	ANTICOINCIDENCE	ANTIDOTING	ANTIFORECLOSURE	ANTIHYDROGEN
ANTICHRIST	ANTICOLLISION	ANTIDROMIC	ANTIFOREIGN	ANTIHYDROGENS
ANTICHRISTIAN	ANTICOLONIAL	ANTIDROMICALLY	ANTIFOREIGNER	ANTIHYSTERIC
ANTICHRISTIANLY	ANTICOLONIALISM	ANTIDUMPING	ANTIFORMALIST	ANTIHYSTERICS
ANTICHRISTS	ANTICOLONIALIST	ANTIECONOMIC	ANTIFOULING	ANTIJACOBIN
ANTICHTHONES	ANTICOMMERCIAL	ANTIEDUCATIONAL	ANTIFOULINGS	ANTIJACOBINS
ANTICHURCH	ANTICOMMUNISM	ANTIEGALITARIAN	ANTIFREEZE	ANTIJAMMING
ANTICIGARETTE	ANTICOMMUNISMS	ANTIELECTRON	ANTIFREEZES	ANTIJAMMINGS
ANTICIPANT	ANTICOMMUNIST	ANTIELECTRONS	ANTIFRICTION	ANTIKICKBACK
ANTICIPANTS	ANTICOMMUNISTS	ANTIELITES	ANTIFUNGAL	ANTIKNOCKS
ANTICIPATABLE	ANTICOMPETITIVE	ANTIELITISM	ANTIFUNGALS	ANTILEGOMENA
ANTICIPATE	ANTICONSUMER	ANTIELITISMS	ANTIGAMBLING	ANTILEPROSY
ANTICIPATED	ANTICONVULSANT	ANTIELITIST	ANTIGENICALLY	ANTILEPTON
ANTICIPATES	ANTICONVULSANTS	ANTIEMETIC	ANTIGENICITIES	ANTILEPTONS
ANTICIPATING	ANTICONVULSIVE	ANTIEMETICS	ANTIGENICITY	ANTILEUKEMIC
ANTICIPATION	ANTICONVULSIVES	ANTIENTROPIC	ANTIGLOBULIN	ANTILIBERAL
ANTICIPATIONS	ANTICORPORATE	ANTIEPILEPSY	ANTIGLOBULINS	ANTILIBERALISM
ANTICIPATIVE	ANTICORROSION	ANTIEPILEPTIC	ANTIGOVERNMENT	ANTILIBERALISMS
ANTICIPATIVELY	ANTICORROSIVE	ANTIEPILEPTICS	ANTIGRAVITIES	ANTILIBERALS
ANTICIPATOR	ANTICORROSIVES	ANTIEROTIC	ANTIGRAVITY	ANTILIBERTARIAN
ANTICIPATORILY	ANTICORRUPTION	ANTIESTROGEN	ANTIGROPELOES	ANTILIFERS
ANTICIPATORS	ANTICREATIVE	ANTIESTROGENS	ANTIGROPELOS	ANTILITERATE
ANTICIPATORY	ANTICRUELTY	ANTIEVOLUTION	ANTIGROWTH	ANTILITTER
ANTICISING	ANTICULTURAL	ANTIFAMILY	ANTIGUERRILLA	ANTILITTERING
ANTICIVISM	ANTICYCLONE	ANTIFASCISM	ANTIHALATION	ANTILOGARITHM
ANTICIVISMS	ANTICYCLONES	ANTIFASCISMS	ANTIHALATIONS	ANTILOGARITHMIC
ANTICIZING	ANTICYCLONIC	ANTIFASCIST	ANTIHELICES	ANTILOGARITHMS
ANTICLASSICAL	ANTIDANDRUFF	ANTIFASCISTS	ANTIHELIXES	ANTILOGICAL
ANTICLASTIC	ANTIDAZZLE	ANTIFASHION	ANTIHELMINTHIC	ANTILOGIES
ANTICLERICAL	ANTIDEFAMATION	ANTIFASHIONABLE	ANTIHELMINTHICS	ANTILOGOUS
ANTICLERICALISM	ANTIDEMOCRATIC	ANTIFASHIONS	ANTIHEROES	ANTILOPINE
ANTICLERICALS	ANTIDEPRESSANT	ANTIFATIGUE	ANTIHEROIC	ANTILYNCHING
ANTICLIMACTIC	ANTIDEPRESSANTS	ANTIFEBRILE	ANTIHEROINE	ANTIMACASSAR
ANTICLIMACTICAL	ANTIDEPRESSION	ANTIFEBRILES	ANTIHEROINES	ANTIMACASSARS
ANTICLIMAX	ANTIDERIVATIVE	ANTIFEDERALIST	ANTIHERPES	ANTIMAGNETIC
ANTICLIMAXES	ANTIDERIVATIVES	ANTIFEDERALISTS	ANTIHIJACK	ANTIMALARIA
ANTICLINAL	ANTIDESICCANT	ANTIFEMALE	ANTIHISTAMINE	ANTIMALARIAL
ANTICLINALS	ANTIDESICCANTS	ANTIFEMININE	ANTIHISTAMINES	ANTIMALARIALS
ANTICLINES	ANTIDEVELOPMENT	ANTIFEMINISM	ANTIHISTAMINIC	ANTIMANAGEMENT
ANTICLINORIA	ANTIDIABETIC	ANTIFEMINISMS	ANTIHISTAMINICS	ANTIMARIJUANA
ANTICLINORIUM	ANTIDIARRHEAL	ANTIFEMINIST	ANTIHISTORICAL	ANTIMARKET
ANTICLINORIUMS	ANTIDIARRHEALS	ANTIFEMINISTS	ANTIHOMOSEXUAL	ANTIMASQUE
ANTICLOCKWISE	ANTIDILUTION	ANTIFERROMAGNET	ANTIHUMANISM	ANTIMASQUES

ANTIMATERIALISM	ANTIMONOPOLIST	ANTIODONTALGICS	ANTIPIRACY	ANTIQUITARIANS
ANTIMATERIALIST	ANTIMONOPOLISTS	ANTIOXIDANT	ANTIPLAGUE	ANTIQUITIES
ANTIMATTER	ANTIMONOPOLY	ANTIOXIDANTS	ANTIPLAQUE	ANTIRABIES
ANTIMATTERS	ANTIMONOUS	ANTIOZONANT	ANTIPLEASURE	ANTIRACHITIC
ANTIMECHANIST	ANTIMONYLS	ANTIOZONANTS	ANTIPOACHING	ANTIRACHITICS
ANTIMECHANISTS	ANTIMOSQUITO	ANTIPARALLEL	ANTIPODALS	ANTIRACISM
ANTIMERGER	ANTIMUSICAL	ANTIPARALLELS	ANTIPODEAN	ANTIRACISMS
ANTIMERISM	ANTIMUSICS	ANTIPARASITIC	ANTIPODEANS	ANTIRACIST
ANTIMERISMS	ANTIMUTAGEN	ANTIPARTICLE	ANTIPOETIC	ANTIRACISTS
ANTIMETABOLE	ANTIMUTAGENS	ANTIPARTICLES	ANTIPOLICE	ANTIRADARS
ANTIMETABOLES	ANTIMYCINS	ANTIPARTIES	ANTIPOLITICAL	ANTIRADICAL
ANTIMETABOLIC	ANTIMYCOTIC	ANTIPASTOS	ANTIPOLITICS	ANTIRADICALISM
ANTIMETABOLITE	ANTINARRATIVE	ANTIPATHETIC	ANTIPOLLUTION	ANTIRADICALISMS
ANTIMETABOLITES	ANTINARRATIVES	ANTIPATHETICAL	ANTIPOLLUTIONS	ANTIRATIONAL
ANTIMETATHESES	ANTINATIONAL	ANTIPATHIC	ANTIPOPULAR	ANTIRATIONALISM
ANTIMETATHESIS	ANTINATIONALIST	ANTIPATHIES	ANTIPORNOGRAPHY	ANTIRATIONALIST
ANTIMICROBIAL	ANTINATURAL	ANTIPATHIST	ANTIPOVERTY	ANTIRATIONALITY
ANTIMICROBIALS	ANTINATURE	ANTIPATHISTS	ANTIPREDATOR	ANTIREALISM
ANTIMILITARISM	ANTINAUSEA	ANTIPERIODIC	ANTIPROGRESSIVE	ANTIREALISMS
ANTIMILITARISMS	ANTINEOPLASTIC	ANTIPERIODICS	ANTIPROTON	ANTIREALIST
ANTIMILITARIST	ANTINEPHRITIC	ANTIPERISTALSES	ANTIPROTONS	ANTIREALISTS
ANTIMILITARISTS	ANTINEPHRITICS	ANTIPERISTALSIS	ANTIPRURITIC	ANTIRECESSION
ANTIMILITARY	ANTINEPOTISM	ANTIPERISTALTIC	ANTIPRURITICS	ANTIREFLECTION
ANTIMISSILE	ANTINEUTRINO	ANTIPERISTASES	ANTIPSYCHIATRY	ANTIREFLECTIVE
ANTIMISSILES	ANTINEUTRINOS	ANTIPERISTASIS	ANTIPSYCHOTIC	ANTIREFORM
ANTIMITOTIC	ANTINEUTRON	ANTIPERSONNEL	ANTIPSYCHOTICS	ANTIREGULATORY
ANTIMITOTICS	ANTINEUTRONS	ANTIPERSPIRANT	ANTIPYRESES	ANTIREJECTION
ANTIMNEMONIC	ANTINOISES	ANTIPERSPIRANTS	ANTIPYRESIS	ANTIRELIGION
ANTIMNEMONICS	ANTINOMIAN	ANTIPESTICIDE	ANTIPYRETIC	ANTIRELIGIOUS
ANTIMODERN	ANTINOMIANISM	ANTIPETALOUS	ANTIPYRETICS	ANTIREPUBLICAN
ANTIMODERNIST	ANTINOMIANISMS	ANTIPHLOGISTIC	ANTIPYRINE	ANTIREPUBLICANS
ANTIMODERNISTS	ANTINOMIANS	ANTIPHLOGISTICS	ANTIPYRINES	ANTIRETROVIRAL
ANTIMONARCHICAL	ANTINOMICAL	ANTIPHONAL	ANTIQUARIAN	ANTIRETROVIRALS
ANTIMONARCHIST	ANTINOMICALLY	ANTIPHONALLY	ANTIQUARIANISM	ANTIRHEUMATIC
ANTIMONARCHISTS	ANTINOMIES	ANTIPHONALS	ANTIQUARIANISMS	ANTIRHEUMATICS
ANTIMONATE	ANTINOVELIST	ANTIPHONARIES	ANTIQUARIANS	ANTIRITUALISM
ANTIMONATES	ANTINOVELISTS	ANTIPHONARY	ANTIQUARIES	ANTIRITUALISMS
ANTIMONIAL	ANTINOVELS	ANTIPHONER	ANTIQUARKS	ANTIROMANTIC
ANTIMONIALS	ANTINUCLEAR	ANTIPHONERS	ANTIQUATED	ANTIROMANTICISM
ANTIMONIATE	ANTINUCLEARIST	ANTIPHONIC	ANTIQUATEDNESS	ANTIROMANTICS
ANTIMONIATES	ANTINUCLEARISTS	ANTIPHONICAL	ANTIQUATES	ANTIROYALIST
ANTIMONIDE	ANTINUCLEON	ANTIPHONICALLY	ANTIQUATING	ANTIROYALISTS
ANTIMONIDES	ANTINUCLEONS	ANTIPHONIES	ANTIQUATION	ANTIRRHINUM
ANTIMONIES	ANTINUKERS	ANTIPHRASES	ANTIQUATIONS	ANTIRRHINUMS
ANTIMONIOUS	ANTIOBESITY	ANTIPHRASIS	ANTIQUENESS	ANTISATELLITE
ANTIMONITE	ANTIOBSCENITY	ANTIPHRASTIC	ANTIQUENESSES	ANTISCIANS
ANTIMONITES	ANTIODONTALGIC	ANTIPHRASTICAL	ANTIQUITARIAN	ANTISCIENCE

ANTISCIENCES	ANTISOCIALITY	ANTITHETIC	ANTONYMOUS	APHIDICIDE
ANTISCIENTIFIC	ANTISOCIALLY	ANTITHETICAL	ANTRORSELY	APHIDICIDES
ANTISCORBUTIC	ANTISPASMODIC	ANTITHETICALLY	ANTSINESSES	APHORISERS
ANTISCORBUTICS	ANTISPASMODICS	ANTITHROMBIN	ANUCLEATED	APHORISING
ANTISCRIPTURAL	ANTISPASTIC	ANTITHROMBINS	ANXIOLYTIC	APHORISTIC
ANTISECRECY	ANTISPASTS	ANTITHROMBOTIC	ANXIOLYTICS	APHORISTICALLY
ANTISEGREGATION	ANTISPECULATION	ANTITHROMBOTICS	ANXIOUSNESS	APHORIZERS
ANTISEIZURE	ANTISPECULATIVE	ANTITHYROID	ANXIOUSNESSES	APHORIZING
ANTISENTIMENTAL	ANTISPENDING	ANTITOBACCO	ANYTHINGARIAN	APHRODISIA
ANTISEPALOUS	ANTISTATIC	ANTITOXINS	ANYTHINGARIANS	APHRODISIAC
ANTISEPARATIST	ANTISTATICS	ANTITRADES	ANYWHITHER	APHRODISIACAL
ANTISEPARATISTS	ANTISTORIES	ANTITRADITIONAL	AORISTICALLY	APHRODISIACS
ANTISEPSES	ANTISTRESS	ANTITRAGUS	AORTITISES	APHRODISIAS
ANTISEPSIS	ANTISTRIKE	ANTITRANSPIRANT	AORTOGRAPHIC	APHRODITES
ANTISEPTIC	ANTISTROPHE	ANTITRINITARIAN	AORTOGRAPHIES	APICULTURAL
ANTISEPTICALLY	ANTISTROPHES	ANTITRUSTER	AORTOGRAPHY	APICULTURE
ANTISEPTICISE	ANTISTROPHIC	ANTITRUSTERS	APAGOGICAL	APICULTURES
ANTISEPTICISED	ANTISTROPHON	ANTITUBERCULAR	APAGOGICALLY	APICULTURIST
ANTISEPTICISES	ANTISTROPHONS	ANTITUBERCULOUS	APARTHEIDS	APICULTURISTS
ANTISEPTICISING	ANTISTUDENT	ANTITUMORAL	APARTHOTEL	APIOLOGIES
ANTISEPTICISM	ANTISTYLES	ANTITUMORS	APARTHOTELS	APISHNESSES
ANTISEPTICISMS	ANTISUBMARINE	ANTITUSSIVE	APARTMENTAL	APITHERAPIES
ANTISEPTICIZE	ANTISUBSIDY	ANTITUSSIVES	APARTMENTS	APITHERAPY
ANTISEPTICIZED	ANTISUBVERSION	ANTITYPHOID	APARTNESSES	APLACENTAL
ANTISEPTICIZES	ANTISUBVERSIVE	ANTITYPICAL	APATHATONS	APLANATICALLY
ANTISEPTICIZING	ANTISUICIDE	ANTITYPICALLY	APATHETICAL	APLANATISM
ANTISEPTICS	ANTISYMMETRIC	ANTIUNIVERSITY	APATHETICALLY	APLANATISMS
ANTISERUMS	ANTISYPHILITIC	ANTIVENENE	APATOSAURS	APLANOGAMETE
ANTISEXIST	ANTISYPHILITICS	ANTIVENENES	APATOSAURUS	APLANOGAMETES
ANTISEXISTS	ANTISYZYGIES	ANTIVENINS	APATOSAURUSES	APLANOSPORE
ANTISEXUAL	ANTISYZYGY	ANTIVENOMS	APERIODICALLY	APLANOSPORES
ANTISEXUALITIES	ANTITAKEOVER	ANTIVIOLENCE	APERIODICITIES	APOAPSIDES
ANTISEXUALITY	ANTITARNISH	ANTIVIRALS	APERIODICITY	APOCALYPSE
ANTISHAKES	ANTITECHNOLOGY	ANTIVIRUSES	APERITIVES	APOCALYPSES
ANTISHOCKS	ANTITERRORISM	ANTIVITAMIN	APERTNESSES	APOCALYPTIC
ANTISHOPLIFTING	ANTITERRORISMS	ANTIVITAMINS	APHAERESES	APOCALYPTICAL
ANTISLAVERY	ANTITERRORIST	ANTIVIVISECTION	APHAERESIS	APOCALYPTICALLY
ANTISMOKER	ANTITERRORISTS	ANTIWELFARE	APHAERETIC	APOCALYPTICISM
ANTISMOKERS	ANTITHALIAN	ANTIWHALING	APHANIPTEROUS	APOCALYPTICISMS
ANTISMOKING	ANTITHEISM	ANTIWORLDS	APHELANDRA	APOCALYPTISM
ANTISMUGGLING	ANTITHEISMS	ANTIWRINKLE	APHELANDRAS	APOCALYPTISMS
ANTISOCIAL	ANTITHEIST	ANTONINIANUS	APHELIOTROPIC	APOCALYPTIST
ANTISOCIALISM	ANTITHEISTIC	ANTONINIANUSES	APHELIOTROPISM	APOCALYPTISTS
ANTISOCIALISMS	ANTITHEISTS	ANTONOMASIA	APHELIOTROPISMS	APOCARPIES
ANTISOCIALIST	ANTITHEORETICAL	ANTONOMASIAS	APHETICALLY	APOCARPOUS
ANTISOCIALISTS	ANTITHESES	ANTONOMASTIC	APHETISING	APOCATASTASES
ANTISOCIALITIES	ANTITHESIS	ANTONYMIES	APHETIZING	APOCATASTASIS

APOCHROMAT	APOLOGISER	APOSPORIES	APOTHECIAL	APPARITORS
APOCHROMATIC	APOLOGISERS	APOSPOROUS	APOTHECIUM	APPARTEMENT
APOCHROMATISM	APOLOGISES	APOSTACIES	APOTHEGMATIC	APPARTEMENTS
APOCHROMATISMS	APOLOGISING	APOSTASIES	APOTHEGMATICAL	APPASSIONATO
APOCHROMATS	APOLOGISTS	APOSTATICAL	APOTHEGMATISE	APPEACHING
APOCOPATED	APOLOGIZED	APOSTATISE	APOTHEGMATISED	APPEACHMENT
APOCOPATES	APOLOGIZER	APOSTATISED	APOTHEGMATISES	APPEACHMENTS
APOCOPATING	APOLOGIZERS	APOSTATISES	APOTHEGMATISING	APPEALABILITIES
APOCOPATION	APOLOGIZES	APOSTATISING	APOTHEGMATIST	APPEALABILITY
APOCOPATIONS	APOLOGIZING	APOSTATIZE	APOTHEGMATISTS	APPEALABLE
APOCRYPHAL	APOMICTICAL	APOSTATIZED	APOTHEGMATIZE	APPEALINGLY
APOCRYPHALLY	APOMICTICALLY	APOSTATIZES	APOTHEGMATIZED	APPEALINGNESS
APOCRYPHALNESS	APOMORPHIA	APOSTATIZING	APOTHEGMATIZES	APPEALINGNESSES
APOCRYPHON	APOMORPHIAS	APOSTILLES	APOTHEGMATIZING	APPEARANCE
APOCYNACEOUS	APOMORPHINE	APOSTLESHIP	APOTHEOSES	APPEARANCES
APOCYNTHION	APOMORPHINES	APOSTLESHIPS	APOTHEOSIS	APPEASABLE
APOCYNTHIONS	APONEUROSES	APOSTOLATE	APOTHEOSISE	APPEASEMENT
APODEICTIC	APONEUROSIS	APOSTOLATES	APOTHEOSISED	APPEASEMENTS
APODEICTICAL	APONEUROTIC	APOSTOLICAL	APOTHEOSISES	APPEASINGLY
APODEICTICALLY	APOPEMPTIC	APOSTOLICALLY	APOTHEOSISING	APPELLANTS
APODICTICAL	APOPHLEGMATIC	APOSTOLICISM	APOTHEOSIZE	APPELLATION
APODICTICALLY	APOPHLEGMATICS	APOSTOLICISMS	APOTHEOSIZED	APPELLATIONAL
APODYTERIUM	APOPHONIES	APOSTOLICITIES	APOTHEOSIZES	APPELLATIONS
APODYTERIUMS	APOPHTHEGM	APOSTOLICITY	APOTHEOSIZING	APPELLATIVE
APOENZYMES	APOPHTHEGMATIC	APOSTOLISE	APOTROPAIC	APPELLATIVELY
APOGAMOUSLY	APOPHTHEGMATISE	APOSTOLISED	APOTROPAICALLY	APPELLATIVES
APOGEOTROPIC	APOPHTHEGMATIST	APOSTOLISES	APOTROPAISM	APPENDAGES
APOGEOTROPISM	APOPHTHEGMATIZE	APOSTOLISING	APOTROPAISMS	APPENDANTS
APOGEOTROPISMS	APOPHTHEGMS	APOSTOLIZE	APOTROPOUS	APPENDECTOMIES
APOLAUSTIC	APOPHYLLITE	APOSTOLIZED	APPALLINGLY	APPENDECTOMY
APOLAUSTICS	APOPHYLLITES	APOSTOLIZES	APPALOOSAS	APPENDENTS
APOLIPOPROTEIN	APOPHYSATE	APOSTOLIZING	APPARATCHIK	APPENDICECTOMY
APOLIPOPROTEINS	APOPHYSEAL	APOSTROPHE	APPARATCHIKI	APPENDICES
APOLITICAL	APOPHYSEAL	APOSTROPHES	APPARATCHIKS	APPENDICITIS
APOLITICALITIES	APOPHYSIAL	APOSTROPHIC	APPARATUSES	APPENDICITISES
APOLITICALITY	APOPLECTIC	APOSTROPHISE	APPARELING	APPENDICLE
APOLITICALLY	APOPLECTICAL	APOSTROPHISED	APPARELLED	APPENDICLES
APOLITICISM	APOPLECTICALLY	APOSTROPHISES	APPARELLING	APPENDICULAR
APOLITICISMS	APOPLECTICS	APOSTROPHISING	APPARELMENT	APPENDICULARIAN
APOLLONIAN	APOPLEXIES	APOSTROPHIZE	APPARELMENTS	APPENDICULATE
APOLLONICON	APOPLEXING	APOSTROPHIZED	APPARENCIES	APPENDIXES
APOLLONICONS	APOPROTEIN	APOSTROPHIZES	APPARENTLY	APPERCEIVE
APOLOGETIC	APOPROTEINS	APOSTROPHIZING	APPARENTNESS	APPERCEIVED
APOLOGETICAL	APOSEMATIC	APOSTROPHUS	APPARENTNESSES	APPERCEIVES
APOLOGETICALLY	APOSEMATICALLY	APOSTROPHUSES	APPARITION	APPERCEIVING
APOLOGETICS	APOSIOPESES	APOTHECARIES	APPARITIONAL	APPERCEPTION
APOLOGISED	APOSIOPESIS	APOTHECARY	APPARITIONS	APPERCEPTIONS

APPERCEPTIVE	APPLICANTS	APPRECIABLY	APPROBATIVE	APRICATION
APPERCIPIENT	APPLICATION	APPRECIATE	APPROBATORY	APRICATIONS
APPERTAINANCE	APPLICATIONS	APPRECIATED	APPROPINQUATE	APRIORISMS
APPERTAINANCES	APPLICATIVE	APPRECIATES	APPROPINQUATED	APRIORISTS
APPERTAINED	APPLICATIVELY	APPRECIATING	APPROPINQUATES	APRIORITIES
APPERTAINING	APPLICATOR	APPRECIATION	APPROPINQUATING	APSIDIOLES
APPERTAINMENT	APPLICATORS	APPRECIATIONS	APPROPINQUATION	APTERYGIAL
APPERTAINMENTS	APPLICATORY	APPRECIATIVE	APPROPINQUE	APTITUDINAL
APPERTAINS	APPLIQUEING	APPRECIATIVELY	APPROPINQUED	APTITUDINALLY
APPERTINENT	APPOGGIATURA	APPRECIATOR	APPROPINQUES	AQUABATICS
APPERTINENTS	APPOGGIATURAS	APPRECIATORILY	APPROPINQUING	AQUABOARDS
APPETEEZEMENT	APPOGGIATURE	APPRECIATORS	APPROPINQUITIES	AQUACEUTICAL
APPETEEZEMENTS	APPOINTEES	APPRECIATORY	APPROPINQUITY	AQUACEUTICALS
APPETENCES	APPOINTERS	APPREHENDED	APPROPRIABLE	AQUACULTURAL
APPETENCIES	APPOINTING	APPREHENDING	APPROPRIACIES	AQUACULTURE
APPETISEMENT	APPOINTIVE	APPREHENDS	APPROPRIACY	AQUACULTURES
APPETISEMENTS	APPOINTMENT	APPREHENSIBLE	APPROPRIATE	AQUACULTURIST
APPETISERS	APPOINTMENTS	APPREHENSIBLY	APPROPRIATED	AQUACULTURISTS
APPETISING	APPOINTORS	APPREHENSION	APPROPRIATELY	AQUADROMES
APPETISINGLY	APPORTIONABLE	APPREHENSIONS	APPROPRIATENESS	AQUAEROBICS
APPETITION	APPORTIONED	APPREHENSIVE	APPROPRIATES	AQUAFARMED
APPETITIONS	APPORTIONER	APPREHENSIVELY	APPROPRIATING	AQUAFARMING
APPETITIVE	APPORTIONERS	APPRENTICE	APPROPRIATION	AQUAFITNESS
APPETIZERS	APPORTIONING	APPRENTICED	APPROPRIATIONS	AQUAFITNESSES
APPETIZING	APPORTIONMENT	APPRENTICEHOOD	APPROPRIATIVE	AQUAFORTIS
APPETIZINGLY	APPORTIONMENTS	APPRENTICEHOODS	APPROPRIATOR	AQUAFORTISES
APPLAUDABLE	APPORTIONS	APPRENTICEMENT	APPROPRIATORS	AQUAFORTIST
APPLAUDABLY	APPOSITELY	APPRENTICEMENTS	APPROVABLE	AQUAFORTISTS
APPLAUDERS	APPOSITENESS	APPRENTICES	APPROVABLY	AQUALEATHER
APPLAUDING	APPOSITENESSES	APPRENTICESHIP	APPROVANCE	AQUALEATHERS
APPLAUDINGLY	APPOSITION	APPRENTICESHIPS	APPROVANCES	AQUAMANALE
APPLAUSIVE	APPOSITIONAL	APPRENTICING	APPROVINGLY	AQUAMANALES
APPLAUSIVELY	APPOSITIONS	APPRESSING	APPROXIMAL	AQUAMANILE
APPLECARTS	APPOSITIVE	APPRESSORIA	APPROXIMATE	AQUAMANILES
APPLEDRAIN	APPOSITIVELY	APPRESSORIUM	APPROXIMATED	AQUAMARINE
APPLEDRAINS	APPOSITIVES	APPRISINGS	APPROXIMATELY	AQUAMARINES
APPLEJACKS	APPRAISABLE	APPRIZINGS	APPROXIMATES	AQUANAUTICS
APPLERINGIE	APPRAISALS	APPROACHABILITY	APPROXIMATING	AQUAPHOBES
APPLERINGIES	APPRAISEES	APPROACHABLE	APPROXIMATION	AQUAPHOBIA
APPLESAUCE	APPRAISEMENT	APPROACHED	APPROXIMATIONS	AQUAPHOBIAS
APPLESAUCES	APPRAISEMENTS	APPROACHES	APPROXIMATIVE	AQUAPHOBIC
APPLIANCES	APPRAISERS	APPROACHING	APPULSIVELY	AQUAPHOBICS
APPLICABILITIES	APPRAISING	APPROBATED	APPURTENANCE	AQUAPLANED
APPLICABILITY	APPRAISINGLY	APPROBATES	APPURTENANCES	AQUAPLANER
APPLICABLE	APPRAISIVE	APPROBATING	APPURTENANT	AQUAPLANERS
APPLICABLENESS	APPRAISIVELY	APPROBATION	APPURTENANTS	AQUAPLANES
APPLICABLY	APPRECIABLE	APPROBATIONS	APRICATING	AQUAPLANING

AQUAPLANINGS	ARACHNIDANS	ARBITRARINESSES	ARCHAEOLOGIES	ARCHEGONIUM
AQUAPORINS	ARACHNOIDAL	ARBITRATED	ARCHAEOLOGIST	ARCHENEMIES
AQUARELLES	ARACHNOIDITIS	ARBITRATES	ARCHAEOLOGISTS	ARCHENTERA
AQUARELLIST	ARACHNOIDITISES	ARBITRATING	ARCHAEOLOGY	ARCHENTERIC
AQUARELLISTS	ARACHNOIDS	ARBITRATION	ARCHAEOMETRIC	ARCHENTERON
AQUARIISTS	ARACHNOLOGICAL	ARBITRATIONAL	ARCHAEOMETRIES	ARCHENTERONS
AQUAROBICS	ARACHNOLOGIES	ARBITRATIONS	ARCHAEOMETRIST	ARCHEOASTRONOMY
AQUATICALLY	ARACHNOLOGIST	ARBITRATIVE	ARCHAEOMETRISTS	ARCHEOBOTANIES
AQUATINTAS	ARACHNOLOGISTS	ARBITRATOR	ARCHAEOMETRY	ARCHEOBOTANIST
AQUATINTED	ARACHNOLOGY	ARBITRATORS	ARCHAEOPTERYX	ARCHEOBOTANISTS
AQUATINTER	ARACHNOPHOBE	ARBITRATRICES	ARCHAEOPTERYXES	ARCHEOBOTANY
AQUATINTERS	ARACHNOPHOBES	ARBITRATRIX	ARCHAEORNIS	ARCHEOLOGICAL
AQUATINTING	ARACHNOPHOBIA	ARBITRATRIXES	ARCHAEORNISES	ARCHEOLOGICALLY
AQUATINTIST	ARACHNOPHOBIAS	ARBITREMENT	ARCHAEOZOOLOGY	ARCHEOLOGIES
AQUATINTISTS	ARACHNOPHOBIC	ARBITREMENTS	ARCHAEZOOLOGIES	ARCHEOLOGIST
AQUICULTURAL	ARACHNOPHOBICS	ARBITRESSES	ARCHAEZOOLOGY	ARCHEOLOGISTS
AQUICULTURE	ARAEOMETER	ARBITRIUMS	ARCHAICALLY	ARCHEOLOGY
AQUICULTURES	ARAEOMETERS	ARBLASTERS	ARCHAICISM	ARCHEOMAGNETISM
AQUICULTURIST	ARAEOMETRIC	ARBORACEOUS	ARCHAICISMS	ARCHEOMETRIES
AQUICULTURISTS	ARAEOMETRICAL	ARBOREALLY	ARCHAISERS	ARCHEOMETRY
AQUIFEROUS	ARAEOMETRIES	ARBORESCENCE	ARCHAISING	ARCHEOZOOLOGIES
AQUIFOLIACEOUS	ARAEOMETRY	ARBORESCENCES	ARCHAISTIC	ARCHEOZOOLOGIST
AQUILEGIAS	ARAEOSTYLE	ARBORESCENT	ARCHAIZERS	ARCHEOZOOLOGY
AQUILINITIES	ARAEOSTYLES	ARBORETUMS	ARCHAIZING	ARCHERESSES
AQUILINITY	ARAEOSYSTYLE	ARBORICULTURAL	ARCHANGELIC	ARCHERFISH
ARABESQUED	ARAEOSYSTYLES	ARBORICULTURE	ARCHANGELS	ARCHERFISHES
ARABESQUES	ARAGONITES	ARBORICULTURES	ARCHBISHOP	ARCHESPORE
ARABICISATION	ARAGONITIC	ARBORICULTURIST	ARCHBISHOPRIC	ARCHESPORES
ARABICISATIONS	ARALIACEOUS	ARBORISATION	ARCHBISHOPRICS	ARCHESPORIA
ARABICISED	ARAUCARIAN	ARBORISATIONS	ARCHBISHOPS	ARCHESPORIAL
ARABICISES	ARAUCARIAS	ARBORISING	ARCHDEACON	ARCHESPORIUM
ARABICISING	ARBALESTER	ARBORIZATION	ARCHDEACONRIES	ARCHETYPAL
ARABICIZATION	ARBALESTERS	ARBORIZATIONS	ARCHDEACONRY	ARCHETYPALLY
ARABICIZATIONS	ARBALISTER	ARBORIZING	ARCHDEACONS	ARCHETYPES
ARABICIZED	ARBALISTERS	ARBORVITAE	ARCHDIOCESAN	ARCHETYPICAL
ARABICIZES	ARBITRABLE	ARBORVITAES	ARCHDIOCESE	ARCHETYPICALLY
ARABICIZING	ARBITRAGED	ARBOVIRUSES	ARCHDIOCESES	ARCHFIENDS
ARABILITIES	ARBITRAGER	ARBUSCULAR	ARCHDRUIDS	ARCHGENETHLIAC
ARABINOSES	ARBITRAGERS	ARCANENESS	ARCHDUCHESS	ARCHGENETHLIACS
ARABINOSIDE	ARBITRAGES	ARCANENESSES	ARCHDUCHESSES	ARCHICARPS
ARABINOSIDES	ARBITRAGEUR	ARCCOSINES	ARCHDUCHIES	ARCHIDIACONAL
ARABISATION	ARBITRAGEURS	ARCHAEBACTERIA	ARCHDUKEDOM	ARCHIDIACONATE
ARABISATIONS	ARBITRAGING	ARCHAEBACTERIUM	ARCHDUKEDOMS	ARCHIDIACONATES
ARABIZATION	ARBITRAMENT	ARCHAEOBOTANIES	ARCHEGONIA	ARCHIEPISCOPACY
ARABIZATIONS	ARBITRAMENTS	ARCHAEOBOTANIST	ARCHEGONIAL	ARCHIEPISCOPAL
ARACHIDONIC	ARBITRARILY	ARCHAEOBOTANY	ARCHEGONIATE	ARCHIEPISCOPATE
ARACHNIDAN	ARBITRARINESS	ARCHAEOLOGICAL	ARCHEGONIATES	ARCHILOWES

ARCHIMAGES	ARCMINUTES	ARGONAUTIC	ARMIGEROUS	ARRAIGNINGS
ARCHIMANDRITE	ARCOGRAPHS	ARGUMENTATION	ARMILLARIA	ARRAIGNMENT
ARCHIMANDRITES	ARCOLOGIES	ARGUMENTATIONS	ARMILLARIAS	ARRAIGNMENTS
ARCHIPELAGIAN	ARCSECONDS	ARGUMENTATIVE	ARMIPOTENCE	ARRANGEABLE
ARCHIPELAGIC	ARCTANGENT	ARGUMENTATIVELY	ARMIPOTENCES	ARRANGEMENT
ARCHIPELAGO	ARCTANGENTS	ARGUMENTIVE	ARMIPOTENT	ARRANGEMENTS
ARCHIPELAGOES	ARCTICALLY	ARGUMENTUM	ARMISTICES	ARRAYMENTS
ARCHIPELAGOS	ARCTOPHILE	ARGUMENTUMS	ARMLOCKING	ARREARAGES
ARCHIPHONEME	ARCTOPHILES	ARGUTENESS	ARMORIALLY	ARRESTABLE
ARCHIPHONEMES	ARCTOPHILIA	ARGUTENESSES	ARMOURLESS	ARRESTANTS
ARCHIPLASM	ARCTOPHILIAS	ARGYRODITE	AROMATASES	ARRESTATION
ARCHIPLASMIC	ARCTOPHILIES	ARGYRODITES	AROMATHERAPIES	ARRESTATIONS
ARCHIPLASMS	ARCTOPHILIST	ARHATSHIPS	AROMATHERAPIST	ARRESTINGLY
ARCHITECTED	ARCTOPHILISTS	ARHYTHMIAS	AROMATHERAPISTS	ARRESTMENT
ARCHITECTING	ARCTOPHILS	ARIBOFLAVINOSES	AROMATHERAPY	ARRESTMENTS
ARCHITECTONIC	ARCTOPHILY	ARIBOFLAVINOSIS	AROMATICALLY	ARRHENOTOKIES
ARCHITECTONICS	ARCUATIONS	ARIDNESSES	AROMATICITIES	ARRHENOTOKY
ARCHITECTS	ARCUBALIST	ARISTOCRACIES	AROMATICITY	ARRHYTHMIA
ARCHITECTURAL	ARCUBALISTS	ARISTOCRACY	AROMATISATION	ARRHYTHMIAS
ARCHITECTURALLY	ARDUOUSNESS	ARISTOCRAT	AROMATISATIONS	ARRHYTHMIC
ARCHITECTURE	ARDUOUSNESSES	ARISTOCRATIC	AROMATISED	ARRIVANCES
ARCHITECTURES	ARECOLINES	ARISTOCRATICAL	AROMATISES	ARRIVANCIES
ARCHITRAVE	AREFACTION	ARISTOCRATISM	AROMATISING	ARRIVEDERCI
ARCHITRAVED	AREFACTIONS	ARISTOCRATISMS	AROMATIZATION	ARRIVISMES
ARCHITRAVES	ARENACEOUS	ARISTOCRATS	AROMATIZATIONS	ARRIVISTES
ARCHITYPES	ARENATIONS	ARISTOLOCHIA	AROMATIZED	ARROGANCES
ARCHIVISTS	ARENICOLOUS	ARISTOLOCHIAS	AROMATIZES	ARROGANCIES
ARCHIVOLTS	AREOCENTRIC	ARISTOLOGIES	AROMATIZING	ARROGANTLY
ARCHNESSES	AREOGRAPHIC	ARISTOLOGY	ARPEGGIATE	ARROGATING
ARCHOLOGIES	AREOGRAPHIES	ARISTOTLES	ARPEGGIATED	ARROGATION
ARCHONSHIP	AREOGRAPHY	ARITHMETIC	ARPEGGIATES	ARROGATIONS
ARCHONSHIPS	AREOLATION	ARITHMETICAL	ARPEGGIATING	ARROGATIVE
ARCHONTATE	AREOLATIONS	ARITHMETICALLY	ARPEGGIATION	ARROGATORS
ARCHONTATES	AREOLOGIES	ARITHMETICIAN	ARPEGGIATIONS	ARRONDISSEMENT
ARCHOPLASM	AREOMETERS	ARITHMETICIANS	ARPEGGIONE	ARRONDISSEMENTS
ARCHOPLASMIC	AREOSTYLES	ARITHMETICS	ARPEGGIONES	ARROWGRASS
ARCHOPLASMS	AREOSYSTILE	ARITHMOMANIA	ARPILLERAS	ARROWGRASSES
ARCHOSAURIAN	AREOSYSTILES	ARITHMOMANIAS	ARQUEBUSADE	ARROWHEADS
ARCHOSAURS	ARFVEDSONITE	ARITHMOMETER	ARQUEBUSADES	ARROWROOTS
ARCHPRIEST	ARFVEDSONITES	ARITHMOMETERS	ARQUEBUSES	ARROWWOODS
ARCHPRIESTHOOD	ARGENTIFEROUS	ARITHMOPHOBIA	ARQUEBUSIER	ARROWWORMS
ARCHPRIESTHOODS	ARGENTINES	ARITHMOPHOBIAS	ARQUEBUSIERS	ARSENIATES
ARCHPRIESTS	ARGENTITES	ARMADILLOS	ARRACACHAS	ARSENICALS
ARCHPRIESTSHIP	ARGILLACEOUS	ARMAMENTARIA	ARRAGONITE	ARSENOPYRITE
ARCHPRIESTSHIPS	ARGILLIFEROUS	ARMAMENTARIUM	ARRAGONITES	ARSENOPYRITES
ARCHRIVALS	ARGILLITES	ARMAMENTARIUMS	ARRAIGNERS	ARSMETRICK
ARCHSTONES	ARGILLITIC	ARMATURING	ARRAIGNING	ARSMETRICKS

ARSPHENAMINE	ARTHROMERES	ARTIFICIALIZING	ASCENDANTS	ASEPTICIZES
ARSPHENAMINES	ARTHROMERIC	ARTIFICIALLY	ASCENDENCE	ASEPTICIZING
ARTEFACTUAL	ARTHROPATHIES	ARTIFICIALNESS	ASCENDENCES	ASEXUALITIES
ARTEMISIAS	ARTHROPATHY	ARTILLERIES	ASCENDENCIES	ASEXUALITY
ARTEMISININ	ARTHROPLASTIES	ARTILLERIST	ASCENDENCY	ASHAMEDNESS
ARTEMISININS	ARTHROPLASTY	ARTILLERISTS	ASCENDENTS	ASHAMEDNESSES
ARTERIALISATION	ARTHROPODAL	ARTILLERYMAN	ASCENDEURS	ASHINESSES
ARTERIALISE	ARTHROPODAN	ARTILLERYMEN	ASCENDIBLE	ASHLARINGS
ARTERIALISED	ARTHROPODOUS	ARTINESSES	ASCENSIONAL	ASHLERINGS
ARTERIALISES	ARTHROPODS	ARTIODACTYL	ASCENSIONIST	ASHRAMITES
ARTERIALISING	ARTHROSCOPE	ARTIODACTYLOUS	ASCENSIONISTS	ASININITIES
ARTERIALIZATION	ARTHROSCOPES	ARTIODACTYLS	ASCENSIONS	ASKEWNESSES
ARTERIALIZE	ARTHROSCOPIC	ARTISANSHIP	ASCERTAINABLE	ASPARAGINASE
ARTERIALIZED	ARTHROSCOPIES	ARTISANSHIPS	ASCERTAINABLY	ASPARAGINASES
ARTERIALIZES	ARTHROSCOPY	ARTISTICAL	ASCERTAINED	ASPARAGINE
ARTERIALIZING	ARTHROSPORE	ARTISTICALLY	ASCERTAINING	ASPARAGINES
ARTERIALLY	ARTHROSPORES	ARTISTRIES	ASCERTAINMENT	ASPARAGUSES
ARTERIOGRAM	ARTHROSPORIC	ARTLESSNESS	ASCERTAINMENTS	ASPARTAMES
ARTERIOGRAMS	ARTHROSPOROUS	ARTLESSNESSES	ASCERTAINS	ASPARTATES
ARTERIOGRAPHIC	ARTICHOKES	ARTOCARPUS	ASCETICALLY	ASPECTABLE
ARTERIOGRAPHIES	ARTICULABLE	ARTOCARPUSES	ASCETICISM	ASPERATING
ARTERIOGRAPHY	ARTICULACIES	ARTSINESSES	ASCETICISMS	ASPERGATION
ARTERIOLAR	ARTICULACY	ARUNDINACEOUS	ASCITITIOUS	ASPERGATIONS
ARTERIOLES	ARTICULATE	ARVICOLINE	ASCLEPIADACEOUS	ASPERGILLA
ARTERIOTOMIES	ARTICULATED	ARYBALLOID	ASCLEPIADS	ASPERGILLI
ARTERIOTOMY	ARTICULATELY	ARYBALLOSES	ASCLEPIASES	ASPERGILLOSES
ARTERIOVENOUS	ARTICULATENESS	ARYTAENOID	ASCOCARPIC	ASPERGILLOSIS
ARTERITIDES	ARTICULATES	ARYTAENOIDS	ASCOGONIUM	ASPERGILLS
ARTERITISES	ARTICULATING	ARYTENOIDAL	ASCOMYCETE	ASPERGILLUM
ARTFULNESS	ARTICULATION	ARYTENOIDS	ASCOMYCETES	ASPERGILLUMS
ARTFULNESSES	ARTICULATIONS	ASAFETIDAS	ASCOMYCETOUS	ASPERGILLUS
ARTHRALGIA	ARTICULATIVE	ASAFOETIDA	ASCORBATES	ASPERITIES
ARTHRALGIAS	ARTICULATOR	ASAFOETIDAS	ASCOSPORES	ASPERSIONS
ARTHRALGIC	ARTICULATORS	ASARABACCA	ASCOSPORIC	ASPERSIVELY
ARTHRECTOMIES	ARTICULATORY	ASARABACCAS	ASCRIBABLE	ASPERSOIRS
ARTHRECTOMY	ARTIFACTUAL	ASBESTIFORM	ASCRIPTION	ASPERSORIA
ARTHRITICALLY	ARTIFICERS	ASBESTOSES	ASCRIPTIONS	ASPERSORIES
ARTHRITICS	ARTIFICIAL	ASBESTOSIS	ASCRIPTIVE	ASPERSORIUM
ARTHRITIDES	ARTIFICIALISE	ASBESTUSES	ASEPTICALLY	ASPERSORIUMS
ARTHRITISES	ARTIFICIALISED	ASCARIASES	ASEPTICISE	ASPHALTERS
ARTHRODESES	ARTIFICIALISES	ASCARIASIS	ASEPTICISED	ASPHALTING
ARTHRODESIS	ARTIFICIALISING	ASCENDABLE	ASEPTICISES	ASPHALTITE
ARTHRODIAE	ARTIFICIALITIES	ASCENDANCE	ASEPTICISING	ASPHALTITES
ARTHRODIAL	ARTIFICIALITY	ASCENDANCES	ASEPTICISM	ASPHALTUMS
ARTHROGRAPHIES	ARTIFICIALIZE	ASCENDANCIES	ASEPTICISMS	ASPHERICAL
ARTHROGRAPHY	ARTIFICIALIZED	ASCENDANCY	ASEPTICIZE	ASPHETERISE
ARTHROMERE	ARTIFICIALIZES	ASCENDANTLY	ASEPTICIZED	ASPHETERISED

ASPHETERISES	ASSASSINATIONS	ASSESSORIAL	ASSISTANCES	ASSUEFACTION
ASPHETERISING	ASSASSINATOR	ASSESSORSHIP	ASSISTANTS	ASSUEFACTIONS
ASPHETERISM	ASSASSINATORS	ASSESSORSHIPS	ASSISTANTSHIP	ASSUETUDES
ASPHETERISMS	ASSAULTERS	ASSEVERATE	ASSISTANTSHIPS	ASSUMABILITIES
ASPHETERIZE	ASSAULTING	ASSEVERATED	ASSOCIABILITIES	ASSUMABILITY
ASPHETERIZED	ASSAULTIVE	ASSEVERATES	ASSOCIABILITY	ASSUMINGLY
ASPHETERIZES	ASSAULTIVELY	ASSEVERATING	ASSOCIABLE	ASSUMPSITS
ASPHETERIZING	ASSAULTIVENESS	ASSEVERATINGLY	ASSOCIATED	ASSUMPTION
ASPHYXIANT	ASSEGAAIED	ASSEVERATION	ASSOCIATES	ASSUMPTIONS
ASPHYXIANTS	ASSEGAAIING	ASSEVERATIONS	ASSOCIATESHIP	ASSUMPTIVE
ASPHYXIATE	ASSEGAIING	ASSEVERATIVE	ASSOCIATESHIPS	ASSUMPTIVELY
ASPHYXIATED	ASSEMBLAGE	ASSEVERING	ASSOCIATING	ASSURANCES
ASPHYXIATES	ASSEMBLAGES	ASSIBILATE	ASSOCIATION	ASSUREDNESS
ASPHYXIATING	ASSEMBLAGIST	ASSIBILATED	ASSOCIATIONAL	ASSUREDNESSES
ASPHYXIATION	ASSEMBLAGISTS	ASSIBILATES	ASSOCIATIONISM	ASSURGENCIES
ASPHYXIATIONS	ASSEMBLANCE	ASSIBILATING	ASSOCIATIONISMS	ASSURGENCY
ASPHYXIATOR	ASSEMBLANCES	ASSIBILATION	ASSOCIATIONIST	ASSYTHMENT
ASPHYXIATORS	ASSEMBLAUNCE	ASSIBILATIONS	ASSOCIATIONISTS	ASSYTHMENTS
ASPIDISTRA	ASSEMBLAUNCES	ASSIDUITIES	ASSOCIATIONS	ASTACOLOGICAL
ASPIDISTRAS	ASSEMBLERS	ASSIDUOUSLY	ASSOCIATIVE	ASTACOLOGIES
ASPIRATING	ASSEMBLIES	ASSIDUOUSNESS	ASSOCIATIVELY	ASTACOLOGIST
ASPIRATION	ASSEMBLING	ASSIDUOUSNESSES	ASSOCIATIVITIES	ASTACOLOGISTS
ASPIRATIONAL	ASSEMBLYMAN	ASSIGNABILITIES	ASSOCIATIVITY	ASTACOLOGY
ASPIRATIONS	ASSEMBLYMEN	ASSIGNABILITY	ASSOCIATOR	ASTARBOARD
ASPIRATORS	ASSEMBLYWOMAN	ASSIGNABLE	ASSOCIATORS	ASTATICALLY
ASPIRATORY	ASSEMBLYWOMEN	ASSIGNABLY	ASSOCIATORY	ASTATICISM
ASPIRINGLY	ASSENTANEOUS	ASSIGNATION	ASSOILMENT	ASTATICISMS
ASPIRINGNESS	ASSENTATION	ASSIGNATIONS	ASSOILMENTS	ASTEREOGNOSES
ASPIRINGNESSES	ASSENTATIONS	ASSIGNMENT	ASSOILZIED	ASTEREOGNOSIS
ASPLANCHNIC	ASSENTATOR	ASSIGNMENTS	ASSOILZIEING	ASTERIATED
ASPLENIUMS	ASSENTATORS	ASSIMILABILITY	ASSOILZIES	ASTERIDIAN
ASPORTATION	ASSENTIENT	ASSIMILABLE	ASSONANCES	ASTERIDIANS
ASPORTATIONS	ASSENTIENTS	ASSIMILABLY	ASSONANTAL	ASTERISKED
ASSAFETIDA	ASSENTINGLY	ASSIMILATE	ASSONATING	ASTERISKING
ASSAFETIDAS	ASSENTIVENESS	ASSIMILATED	ASSORTATIVE	ASTERISKLESS
ASSAFOETIDA	ASSENTIVENESSES	ASSIMILATES	ASSORTATIVELY	ASTEROIDAL
ASSAFOETIDAS	ASSERTABLE	ASSIMILATING	ASSORTEDNESS	ASTEROIDEAN
ASSAGAIING	ASSERTEDLY	ASSIMILATION	ASSORTEDNESSES	ASTEROIDEANS
ASSAILABLE	ASSERTIBLE	ASSIMILATIONISM	ASSORTMENT	ASTHENOPIA
ASSAILANTS	ASSERTIONS	ASSIMILATIONIST	ASSORTMENTS	ASTHENOPIAS
ASSAILMENT	ASSERTIVELY	ASSIMILATIONS	ASSUAGEMENT	ASTHENOPIC
ASSAILMENTS	ASSERTIVENESS	ASSIMILATIVE	ASSUAGEMENTS	ASTHENOSPHERE
ASSASSINATE	ASSERTIVENESSES	ASSIMILATIVELY	ASSUAGINGS	ASTHENOSPHERES
ASSASSINATED	ASSERTORIC	ASSIMILATOR	ASSUBJUGATE	ASTHENOSPHERIC
ASSASSINATES	ASSESSABLE	ASSIMILATORS	ASSUBJUGATED	ASTHMATICAL
ASSASSINATING	ASSESSMENT	ASSIMILATORY	ASSUBJUGATES	ASTHMATICALLY
ASSASSINATION	ASSESSMENTS	ASSISTANCE	ASSUBJUGATING	ASTHMATICS

ASTIGMATIC	ASTROCHEMISTRY	ASTRONOMISE	ASYNCHRONOUS	ATHWARTSHIPS
ASTIGMATICALLY	ASTROCOMPASS	ASTRONOMISED	ASYNCHRONOUSLY	ATMOLOGIES
ASTIGMATICS	ASTROCOMPASSES	ASTRONOMISES	ASYNCHRONY	ATMOLOGIST
ASTIGMATISM	ASTROCYTES	ASTRONOMISING	ASYNDETICALLY	ATMOLOGISTS
ASTIGMATISMS	ASTROCYTIC	ASTRONOMIZE	ASYNDETONS	ATMOLYSING
ASTOMATOUS	ASTROCYTOMA	ASTRONOMIZED	ASYNERGIAS	ATMOLYZING
ASTONISHED	ASTROCYTOMAS	ASTRONOMIZES	ASYNERGIES	ATMOMETERS
ASTONISHES	ASTROCYTOMATA	ASTRONOMIZING	ASYNTACTIC	ATMOMETRIES
ASTONISHING	ASTRODOMES	ASTROPHELS	ASYSTOLISM	ATMOSPHERE
ASTONISHINGLY	ASTRODYNAMICIST	ASTROPHOBIA	ASYSTOLISMS	ATMOSPHERED
ASTONISHMENT	ASTRODYNAMICS	ASTROPHOBIAS	ATACAMITES	ATMOSPHERES
ASTONISHMENTS	ASTROFELLS	ASTROPHOBIC	ATARACTICS	ATMOSPHERIC
ASTOUNDING	ASTROGEOLOGIES	ASTROPHOTOGRAPH	ATAVISTICALLY	ATMOSPHERICAL
ASTOUNDINGLY	ASTROGEOLOGIST	ASTROPHYSICAL	ATCHIEVING	ATMOSPHERICALLY
ASTOUNDMENT	ASTROGEOLOGISTS	ASTROPHYSICALLY	ATELECTASES	ATMOSPHERICS
ASTOUNDMENTS	ASTROGEOLOGY	ASTROPHYSICIST	ATELECTASIS	ATOMICALLY
ASTRACHANS	ASTROHATCH	ASTROPHYSICISTS	ATELECTATIC	ATOMICITIES
ASTRAGALUS	ASTROHATCHES	ASTROPHYSICS	ATELEIOSES	ATOMISATION
ASTRAKHANS	ASTROLABES	ASTROSPHERE	ATELEIOSIS	ATOMISATIONS
ASTRANTIAS	ASTROLATRIES	ASTROSPHERES	ATHANASIES	ATOMISTICAL
ASTRAPHOBIA	ASTROLATRY	ASTROTOURISM	ATHEISTICAL	ATOMISTICALLY
ASTRAPHOBIAS	ASTROLOGER	ASTROTOURISMS	ATHEISTICALLY	ATOMIZATION
ASTRAPHOBIC	ASTROLOGERS	ASTROTOURIST	ATHEMATICALLY	ATOMIZATIONS
ASTRAPOPHOBIA	ASTROLOGIC	ASTROTOURISTS	ATHENAEUMS	ATONALISMS
ASTRAPOPHOBIAS	ASTROLOGICAL	ASTROTURFER	ATHEOLOGICAL	ATONALISTS
ASTRICTING	ASTROLOGICALLY	ASTROTURFERS	ATHEOLOGIES	ATONALITIES
ASTRICTION	ASTROLOGIES	ASTROTURFING	ATHEORETICAL	ATONEMENTS
ASTRICTIONS	ASTROLOGIST	ASTROTURFINGS	ATHERMANCIES	ATONICITIES
ASTRICTIVE	ASTROLOGISTS	ASTUCIOUSLY	ATHERMANCY	ATRABILIAR
ASTRICTIVELY	ASTROMETRIC	ASTUCITIES	ATHERMANOUS	ATRABILIOUS
ASTRINGENCE	ASTROMETRICAL	ASTUTENESS	ATHEROGENESES	ATRABILIOUSNESS
ASTRINGENCES	ASTROMETRIES	ASTUTENESSES	ATHEROGENESIS	ATRACURIUM
ASTRINGENCIES	ASTROMETRY	ASYMMETRIC	ATHEROGENIC	ATRACURIUMS
ASTRINGENCY	ASTRONAUTIC	ASYMMETRICAL	ATHEROMATA	ATRAMENTAL
ASTRINGENT	ASTRONAUTICAL	ASYMMETRICALLY	ATHEROMATOUS	ATRAMENTOUS
ASTRINGENTLY	ASTRONAUTICALLY	ASYMMETRIES	ATHEROSCLEROSES	ATROCIOUSLY
ASTRINGENTS	ASTRONAUTICS	ASYMPTOMATIC	ATHEROSCLEROSIS	ATROCIOUSNESS
ASTRINGERS	ASTRONAUTS	ASYMPTOTES	ATHEROSCLEROTIC	ATROCIOUSNESSES
ASTRINGING	ASTRONAVIGATION	ASYMPTOTIC	ATHETISING	ATROCITIES
ASTROBIOLOGIES	ASTRONAVIGATOR	ASYMPTOTICAL	ATHETIZING	ATROPHYING
ASTROBIOLOGIST	ASTRONAVIGATORS	ASYMPTOTICALLY	ATHLETICALLY	ATTACHABLE
ASTROBIOLOGISTS	ASTRONOMER	ASYNARTETE	ATHLETICISM	ATTACHMENT
ASTROBIOLOGY	ASTRONOMERS	ASYNARTETES	ATHLETICISMS	ATTACHMENTS
ASTROBLEME	ASTRONOMIC	ASYNARTETIC	ATHROCYTES	ATTACKABLE
ASTROBLEMES	ASTRONOMICAL	ASYNCHRONIES	ATHROCYTOSES	ATTAINABILITIES
ASTROBOTANIES	ASTRONOMICALLY	ASYNCHRONISM	ATHROCYTOSIS	ATTAINABILITY
ASTROBOTANY	ASTRONOMIES	ASYNCHRONISMS	ATHWARTSHIP	ATTAINABLE

ATTAINABLENESS	ATTICISING	ATTRACTIVE	AUDIBILITIES	AUDITORIES
ATTAINDERS	ATTICIZING	ATTRACTIVELY	AUDIBILITY	AUDITORILY
ATTAINMENT	ATTIREMENT	ATTRACTIVENESS	AUDIBLENESS	AUDITORIUM
ATTAINMENTS	ATTIREMENTS	ATTRACTORS	AUDIBLENESSES	AUDITORIUMS
ATTAINTING	ATTITUDINAL	ATTRAHENTS	AUDIENCIAS	AUDITORSHIP
ATTAINTMENT	ATTITUDINALLY	ATTRAPPING	AUDIOBOOKS	AUDITORSHIPS
ATTAINTMENTS	ATTITUDINARIAN	ATTRIBUTABLE	AUDIOCASSETTE	AUDITRESSES
ATTAINTURE	ATTITUDINARIANS	ATTRIBUTED	AUDIOCASSETTES	AUGMENTABLE
ATTAINTURES	ATTITUDINISE	ATTRIBUTER	AUDIOGENIC	AUGMENTATION
ATTEMPERED	ATTITUDINISED	ATTRIBUTERS	AUDIOGRAMS	AUGMENTATIONS
ATTEMPERING	ATTITUDINISER	ATTRIBUTES	AUDIOGRAPH	AUGMENTATIVE
ATTEMPERMENT	ATTITUDINISERS	ATTRIBUTING	AUDIOGRAPHS	AUGMENTATIVELY
ATTEMPERMENTS	ATTITUDINISES	ATTRIBUTION	AUDIOLOGIC	AUGMENTATIVES
ATTEMPTABILITY	ATTITUDINISING	ATTRIBUTIONAL	AUDIOLOGICAL	AUGMENTERS
ATTEMPTABLE	ATTITUDINISINGS	ATTRIBUTIONS	AUDIOLOGICALLY	AUGMENTING
ATTEMPTERS	ATTITUDINIZE	ATTRIBUTIVE	AUDIOLOGIES	AUGMENTORS
ATTEMPTING	ATTITUDINIZED	ATTRIBUTIVELY	AUDIOLOGIST	AUGURSHIPS
ATTENDANCE	ATTITUDINIZER	ATTRIBUTIVENESS	AUDIOLOGISTS	AUGUSTNESS
ATTENDANCES	ATTITUDINIZERS	ATTRIBUTIVES	AUDIOMETER	AUGUSTNESSES
ATTENDANCIES	ATTITUDINIZES	ATTRIBUTOR	AUDIOMETERS	AURALITIES
ATTENDANCY	ATTITUDINIZING	ATTRIBUTORS	AUDIOMETRIC	AUREATENESS
ATTENDANTS	ATTITUDINIZINGS	ATTRISTING	AUDIOMETRICALLY	AUREATENESSES
ATTENDEMENT	ATTOLASERS	ATTRITIONAL	AUDIOMETRICIAN	AURICULARLY
ATTENDEMENTS	ATTOLLENTS	ATTRITIONS	AUDIOMETRICIANS	AURICULARS
ATTENDINGS	ATTOPHYSICS	ATTRITTING	AUDIOMETRIES	AURICULATE
ATTENDMENT	ATTORNEYDOM	ATTUITIONAL	AUDIOMETRIST	AURICULATED
ATTENDMENTS	ATTORNEYDOMS	ATTUITIONS	AUDIOMETRISTS	AURICULATELY
ATTENTIONAL	ATTORNEYED	ATTUITIVELY	AUDIOMETRY	AURIFEROUS
ATTENTIONS	ATTORNEYING	ATTUNEMENT	AUDIOPHILE	AURISCOPES
ATTENTIVELY	ATTORNEYISM	ATTUNEMENTS	AUDIOPHILES	AURISCOPIC
ATTENTIVENESS	ATTORNEYISMS	ATYPICALITIES	AUDIOPHILS	AUSCULTATE
ATTENTIVENESSES	ATTORNEYSHIP	ATYPICALITY	AUDIOTAPED	AUSCULTATED
ATTENUANTS	ATTORNEYSHIPS	ATYPICALLY	AUDIOTAPES	AUSCULTATES
ATTENUATED	ATTORNMENT	AUBERGINES	AUDIOTAPING	AUSCULTATING
ATTENUATES	ATTORNMENTS	AUBERGISTE	AUDIOTYPING	AUSCULTATION
ATTENUATING	ATTRACTABLE	AUBERGISTES	AUDIOTYPINGS	AUSCULTATIONS
ATTENUATION	ATTRACTANCE	AUBRIETIAS	AUDIOTYPIST	AUSCULTATIVE
ATTENUATIONS	ATTRACTANCES	AUCTIONARY	AUDIOTYPISTS	AUSCULTATOR
ATTENUATOR	ATTRACTANCIES	AUCTIONEER	AUDIOVISUAL	AUSCULTATORS
ATTENUATORS	ATTRACTANCY	AUCTIONEERED	AUDIOVISUALLY	AUSCULTATORY
ATTESTABLE	ATTRACTANT	AUCTIONEERING	AUDIOVISUALS	AUSFORMING
ATTESTANTS	ATTRACTANTS	AUCTIONEERS	AUDIPHONES	AUSLANDERS
ATTESTATION	ATTRACTERS	AUCTIONING	AUDITIONED	AUSPICATED
ATTESTATIONS	ATTRACTING	AUDACIOUSLY	AUDITIONER	AUSPICATES
ATTESTATIVE	ATTRACTINGLY	AUDACIOUSNESS	AUDITIONERS	AUSPICATING
ATTESTATOR	ATTRACTION	AUDACIOUSNESSES	AUDITIONING	AUSPICIOUS
ATTESTATORS	ATTRACTIONS	AUDACITIES	AUDITORIAL	AUSPICIOUSLY

AUSPICIOUSNESS	AUTHORISMS	AUTOCHTHONES	AUTOGENESES	AUTOLYZATE
AUSTENITES	AUTHORITARIAN	AUTOCHTHONIC	AUTOGENESIS	AUTOLYZATES
AUSTENITIC	AUTHORITARIANS	AUTOCHTHONIES	AUTOGENETIC	AUTOLYZING
AUSTERENESS	AUTHORITATIVE	AUTOCHTHONISM	AUTOGENICS	AUTOMAGICALLY
AUSTERENESSES	AUTHORITATIVELY	AUTOCHTHONISMS	AUTOGENIES	AUTOMAKERS
AUSTERITIES	AUTHORITIES	AUTOCHTHONOUS	AUTOGENOUS	AUTOMATABLE
AUSTRALITE	AUTHORIZABLE	AUTOCHTHONOUSLY	AUTOGENOUSLY	AUTOMATICAL
AUSTRALITES	AUTHORIZATION	AUTOCHTHONS	AUTOGRAFTED	AUTOMATICALLY
AUSTRINGER	AUTHORIZATIONS	AUTOCHTHONY	AUTOGRAFTING	AUTOMATICITIES
AUSTRINGERS	AUTHORIZED	AUTOCLAVED	AUTOGRAFTS	AUTOMATICITY
AUTARCHICAL	AUTHORIZER	AUTOCLAVES	AUTOGRAPHED	AUTOMATICS
AUTARCHIES	AUTHORIZERS	AUTOCLAVING	AUTOGRAPHIC	AUTOMATING
AUTARCHIST	AUTHORIZES	AUTOCOPROPHAGY	AUTOGRAPHICAL	AUTOMATION
AUTARCHISTS	AUTHORIZING	AUTOCORRELATION	AUTOGRAPHICALLY	AUTOMATIONS
AUTARKICAL	AUTHORLESS	AUTOCRACIES	AUTOGRAPHIES	AUTOMATISATION
AUTARKISTS	AUTHORSHIP	AUTOCRATIC	AUTOGRAPHING	AUTOMATISATIONS
AUTECOLOGIC	AUTHORSHIPS	AUTOCRATICAL	AUTOGRAPHS	AUTOMATISE
AUTECOLOGICAL	AUTISTICALLY	AUTOCRATICALLY	AUTOGRAPHY	AUTOMATISED
AUTECOLOGIES	AUTOALLOGAMIES	AUTOCRIMES	AUTOGRAVURE	AUTOMATISES
AUTECOLOGY	AUTOALLOGAMY	AUTOCRITIQUE	AUTOGRAVURES	AUTOMATISING
AUTEURISMS	AUTOANTIBODIES	AUTOCRITIQUES	AUTOGUIDES	AUTOMATISM
AUTEURISTS	AUTOANTIBODY	AUTOCROSSES	AUTOHYPNOSES	AUTOMATISMS
AUTHENTICAL	AUTOBAHNEN	AUTOCUTIES	AUTOHYPNOSIS	AUTOMATIST
AUTHENTICALLY	AUTOBIOGRAPHER	AUTOCYCLES	AUTOHYPNOTIC	AUTOMATISTS
AUTHENTICATE	AUTOBIOGRAPHERS	AUTODESTRUCT	AUTOIMMUNE	AUTOMATIZATION
AUTHENTICATED	AUTOBIOGRAPHIC	AUTODESTRUCTED	AUTOIMMUNITIES	AUTOMATIZATIONS
AUTHENTICATES	AUTOBIOGRAPHIES	AUTODESTRUCTING	AUTOIMMUNITY	AUTOMATIZE
AUTHENTICATING	AUTOBIOGRAPHY	AUTODESTRUCTIVE	AUTOINFECTION	AUTOMATIZED
AUTHENTICATION	AUTOBUSSES	AUTODESTRUCTS	AUTOINFECTIONS	AUTOMATIZES
AUTHENTICATIONS	AUTOCATALYSE	AUTODIDACT	AUTOINOCULATION	AUTOMATIZING
AUTHENTICATOR	AUTOCATALYSED	AUTODIDACTIC	AUTOIONISATION	AUTOMATONS
AUTHENTICATORS	AUTOCATALYSES	AUTODIDACTICISM	AUTOIONISATIONS	AUTOMATOUS
AUTHENTICITIES	AUTOCATALYSING	AUTODIDACTS	AUTOIONIZATION	AUTOMETERS
AUTHENTICITY	AUTOCATALYSIS	AUTOECIOUS	AUTOIONIZATIONS	AUTOMOBILE
AUTHIGENIC	AUTOCATALYTIC	AUTOECIOUSLY	AUTOJUMBLE	AUTOMOBILED
AUTHORCRAFT	AUTOCATALYZE	AUTOECISMS	AUTOJUMBLES	AUTOMOBILES
AUTHORCRAFTS	AUTOCATALYZED	AUTOEROTIC	AUTOKINESES	AUTOMOBILIA
AUTHORESSES	AUTOCATALYZES	AUTOEROTICISM	AUTOKINESIS	AUTOMOBILING
AUTHORINGS	AUTOCATALYZING	AUTOEROTICISMS	AUTOKINETIC	AUTOMOBILISM
AUTHORISABLE	AUTOCEPHALIC	AUTOEROTISM	AUTOLATRIES	AUTOMOBILISMS
AUTHORISATION	AUTOCEPHALIES	AUTOEROTISMS	AUTOLOADING	AUTOMOBILIST
AUTHORISATIONS	AUTOCEPHALOUS	AUTOEXPOSURE	AUTOLOGIES	AUTOMOBILISTS
AUTHORISED	AUTOCEPHALY	AUTOEXPOSURES	AUTOLOGOUS	AUTOMOBILITIES
AUTHORISER	AUTOCHANGER	AUTOFLARES	AUTOLYSATE	AUTOMOBILITY
AUTHORISERS	AUTOCHANGERS	AUTOFOCUSES	AUTOLYSATES	AUTOMORPHIC
AUTHORISES	AUTOCHTHON	AUTOGAMIES	AUTOLYSING	AUTOMORPHICALLY
AUTHORISING	AUTOCHTHONAL	AUTOGAMOUS	AUTOLYSINS	AUTOMORPHISM

AUTOMORPHISMS	AUTOROTATION	AUTOTOMOUS	AVASCULARITIES	AVOCATIONAL
AUTOMOTIVE	AUTOROTATIONS	AUTOTOXAEMIA	AVASCULARITY	AVOCATIONALLY
AUTONOMICAL	AUTOROUTES	AUTOTOXAEMIAS	AVENACEOUS	AVOCATIONS
AUTONOMICALLY	AUTOSAVING	AUTOTOXEMIA	AVENGEMENT	AVOIDANCES
AUTONOMICS	AUTOSCHEDIASM	AUTOTOXEMIAS	AVENGEMENTS	AVOIRDUPOIS
AUTONOMIES	AUTOSCHEDIASMS	AUTOTOXINS	AVENGERESS	AVOIRDUPOISES
AUTONOMIST	AUTOSCHEDIASTIC	AUTOTRANSFORMER	AVENGERESSES	AVOPARCINS
AUTONOMISTS	AUTOSCHEDIAZE	AUTOTRANSFUSION	AVENTAILES	AVOUCHABLE
AUTONOMOUS	AUTOSCHEDIAZED	AUTOTROPHIC	AVENTURINE	AVOUCHMENT
AUTONOMOUSLY	AUTOSCHEDIAZES	AUTOTROPHICALLY	AVENTURINES	AVOUCHMENTS
AUTOPHAGIA	AUTOSCHEDIAZING	AUTOTROPHIES	AVENTURINS	AVOUTERERS
AUTOPHAGIAS	AUTOSCOPIC	AUTOTROPHS	AVERAGENESS	AVOWABLENESS
AUTOPHAGIES	AUTOSCOPIES	AUTOTROPHY	AVERAGENESSES	AVOWABLENESSES
AUTOPHAGOUS	AUTOSEXING	AUTOTYPIES	AVERAGINGS	AVUNCULARITIES
AUTOPHANOUS	AUTOSOMALLY	AUTOTYPING	AVERRUNCATE	AVUNCULARITY
AUTOPHOBIA	AUTOSPORES	AUTOTYPOGRAPHY	AVERRUNCATED	AVUNCULARLY
AUTOPHOBIAS	AUTOSTABILITIES	AUTOWINDER	AVERRUNCATES	AVUNCULATE
AUTOPHOBIES	AUTOSTABILITY	AUTOWINDERS	AVERRUNCATING	AVUNCULATES
AUTOPHONIES	AUTOSTRADA	AUTOWORKER	AVERRUNCATION	AVVOGADORE
AUTOPHYTES	AUTOSTRADAS	AUTOWORKERS	AVERRUNCATIONS	AVVOGADORES
AUTOPHYTIC	AUTOSTRADE	AUTOXIDATION	AVERRUNCATOR	AWAKENINGS
AUTOPHYTICALLY	AUTOSUGGEST	AUTOXIDATIONS	AVERRUNCATORS	AWARENESSES
AUTOPILOTS	AUTOSUGGESTED	AUTUMNALLY	AVERSENESS	AWAYNESSES
AUTOPISTAS	AUTOSUGGESTING	AUXANOMETER	AVERSENESSES	AWELESSNESS
AUTOPLASTIC	AUTOSUGGESTION	AUXANOMETERS	AVERSIVELY	AWELESSNESSES
AUTOPLASTIES	AUTOSUGGESTIONS	AUXILIARIES	AVERSIVENESS	AWESOMENESS
AUTOPLASTY	AUTOSUGGESTIVE	AUXOCHROME	AVERSIVENESSES	AWESOMENESSES
AUTOPOINTS	AUTOSUGGESTS	AUXOCHROMES	AVERTIMENT	AWESTRICKEN
AUTOPOLYPLOID	AUTOTELLER	AUXOMETERS	AVERTIMENTS	AWFULNESSES
AUTOPOLYPLOIDS	AUTOTELLERS	AUXOSPORES	AVGOLEMONO	AWKWARDEST
AUTOPOLYPLOIDY	AUTOTETRAPLOID	AUXOTROPHIC	AVGOLEMONOS	AWKWARDISH
AUTOPSISTS	AUTOTETRAPLOIDS	AUXOTROPHIES	AVIANISING	AWKWARDNESS
AUTOPSYING	AUTOTETRAPLOIDY	AUXOTROPHS	AVIANIZING	AWKWARDNESSES
AUTOPTICAL	AUTOTHEISM	AUXOTROPHY	AVIATRESSES	AXENICALLY
AUTOPTICALLY	AUTOTHEISMS	AVAILABILITIES	AVIATRICES	AXEROPHTHOL
AUTORADIOGRAM	AUTOTHEIST	AVAILABILITY	AVIATRIXES	AXEROPHTHOLS
AUTORADIOGRAMS	AUTOTHEISTS	AVAILABLENESS	AVICULTURE	AXIALITIES
AUTORADIOGRAPH	AUTOTIMERS	AVAILABLENESSES	AVICULTURES	AXILLARIES
AUTORADIOGRAPHS	AUTOTOMIES	AVAILINGLY	AVICULTURIST	AXINOMANCIES
AUTORADIOGRAPHY	AUTOTOMISE	AVALANCHED	AVICULTURISTS	AXINOMANCY
AUTOREPLIES	AUTOTOMISED	AVALANCHES	AVIDNESSES	AXIOLOGICAL
AUTORICKSHAW	AUTOTOMISES	AVALANCHING	AVISANDUMS	AXIOLOGICALLY
AUTORICKSHAWS	AUTOTOMISING	AVANTURINE	AVISEMENTS	AXIOLOGIES
AUTOROTATE	AUTOTOMIZE	AVANTURINES	AVITAMINOSES	AXIOLOGIST
AUTOROTATED	AUTOTOMIZED	AVARICIOUS	AVITAMINOSIS	AXIOLOGISTS
AUTOROTATES	AUTOTOMIZES	AVARICIOUSLY	AVITAMINOTIC	AXIOMATICAL
AUTOROTATING	AUTOTOMIZING	AVARICIOUSNESS	AVIZANDUMS	AXIOMATICALLY

AXIOMATICS	AXIOMATIZED	AXONOMETRY	AZEDARACHS	AZOOSPERMIAS
AXIOMATISATION	AXIOMATIZES	AXOPLASMIC	AZEOTROPES	AZOOSPERMIC
AXIOMATISATIONS	AXIOMATIZING	AYAHUASCAS	AZEOTROPIC	AZOTAEMIAS
AXIOMATISE	AXISYMMETRIC	AYAHUASCOS	AZEOTROPIES	AZOTOBACTER
AXIOMATISED	AXISYMMETRICAL	AYATOLLAHS	AZIDOTHYMIDINE	AZOTOBACTERS
AXIOMATISES	AXISYMMETRIES	AYUNTAMIENTO	AZIDOTHYMIDINES	AZYGOSPORE
AXIOMATISING	AXISYMMETRY	AYUNTAMIENTOS	AZIMUTHALLY	AZYGOSPORES
AXIOMATIZATION	AXOLEMMATA	AYURVEDICS	AZOBENZENE	
AXIOMATIZATIONS	AXONOMETRIC	AZATHIOPRINE	AZOBENZENES	
AXIOMATIZE	AXONOMETRIES	AZATHIOPRINES	AZOOSPERMIA	

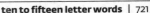

B

BAALEBATIM
BABACOOTES
BABBITRIES
BABBITTING
BABBITTRIES
BABBLATIVE
BABBLEMENT
BABBLEMENTS
BABELESQUE
BABESIASES
BABESIASIS
BABESIOSES
BABESIOSIS
BABINGTONITE
BABINGTONITES
BABIROUSSA
BABIROUSSAS
BABIRUSSAS
BABOONERIES
BABYPROOFED
BABYPROOFING
BABYPROOFS
BABYSITTING
BACCALAUREAN
BACCALAUREATE
BACCALAUREATES
BACCHANALIA
BACCHANALIAN
BACCHANALIANISM
BACCHANALIANS
BACCHANALS
BACCHANTES
BACCIFEROUS
BACCIVOROUS
BACHARACHS
BACHELORDOM
BACHELORDOMS
BACHELORETTE
BACHELORETTES
BACHELORHOOD
BACHELORHOODS
BACHELORISM
BACHELORISMS
BACHELORSHIP
BACHELORSHIPS

BACILLAEMIA
BACILLAEMIAS
BACILLEMIA
BACILLEMIAS
BACILLICIDE
BACILLICIDES
BACILLIFORM
BACILLURIA
BACILLURIAS
BACITRACIN
BACITRACINS
BACKBENCHER
BACKBENCHERS
BACKBENCHES
BACKBITERS
BACKBITING
BACKBITINGS
BACKBITTEN
BACKBLOCKER
BACKBLOCKERS
BACKBLOCKS
BACKBOARDS
BACKBONELESS
BACKBREAKER
BACKBREAKERS
BACKBREAKING
BACKBURNED
BACKBURNING
BACKCASTING
BACKCHATTED
BACKCHATTING
BACKCHECKED
BACKCHECKING
BACKCHECKS
BACKCLOTHS
BACKCOMBED
BACKCOMBING
BACKCOUNTRIES
BACKCOUNTRY
BACKCOURTMAN
BACKCOURTMEN
BACKCOURTS
BACKCROSSED
BACKCROSSES
BACKCROSSING

BACKDATING
BACKDRAFTS
BACKDRAUGHT
BACKDRAUGHTS
BACKDROPPED
BACKDROPPING
BACKFIELDS
BACKFILLED
BACKFILLING
BACKFILLINGS
BACKFIRING
BACKFISCHES
BACKFITTED
BACKFITTING
BACKFITTINGS
BACKFLIPPED
BACKFLIPPING
BACKGAMMON
BACKGAMMONED
BACKGAMMONING
BACKGAMMONS
BACKGROUND
BACKGROUNDED
BACKGROUNDER
BACKGROUNDERS
BACKGROUNDING
BACKGROUNDS
BACKHANDED
BACKHANDEDLY
BACKHANDEDNESS
BACKHANDER
BACKHANDERS
BACKHANDING
BACKHAULED
BACKHAULING
BACKHOEING
BACKHOUSES
BACKLASHED
BACKLASHER
BACKLASHERS
BACKLASHES
BACKLASHING
BACKLIGHTED
BACKLIGHTING
BACKLIGHTS

BACKLISTED
BACKLISTING
BACKLOADED
BACKLOADING
BACKLOGGED
BACKLOGGING
BACKMARKER
BACKMARKERS
BACKPACKED
BACKPACKER
BACKPACKERS
BACKPACKING
BACKPACKINGS
BACKPEDALED
BACKPEDALING
BACKPEDALLED
BACKPEDALLING
BACKPEDALS
BACKPIECES
BACKPLATES
BACKRUSHES
BACKSCATTER
BACKSCATTERED
BACKSCATTERING
BACKSCATTERINGS
BACKSCATTERS
BACKSCRATCH
BACKSCRATCHED
BACKSCRATCHER
BACKSCRATCHERS
BACKSCRATCHES
BACKSCRATCHING
BACKSCRATCHINGS
BACKSHEESH
BACKSHEESHED
BACKSHEESHES
BACKSHEESHING
BACKSHISHED
BACKSHISHES
BACKSHISHING
BACKSHORES
BACKSIGHTS
BACKSLAPPED
BACKSLAPPER
BACKSLAPPERS

BACKSLAPPING
BACKSLASHES
BACKSLIDDEN
BACKSLIDER
BACKSLIDERS
BACKSLIDES
BACKSLIDING
BACKSLIDINGS
BACKSPACED
BACKSPACER
BACKSPACERS
BACKSPACES
BACKSPACING
BACKSPEERED
BACKSPEERING
BACKSPEERS
BACKSPEIRED
BACKSPEIRING
BACKSPEIRS
BACKSPLASH
BACKSPLASHES
BACKSTABBED
BACKSTABBER
BACKSTABBERS
BACKSTABBING
BACKSTABBINGS
BACKSTAGES
BACKSTAIRS
BACKSTALLS
BACKSTAMPED
BACKSTAMPING
BACKSTAMPS
BACKSTARTING
BACKSTITCH
BACKSTITCHED
BACKSTITCHES
BACKSTITCHING
BACKSTOPPED
BACKSTOPPING
BACKSTORIES
BACKSTREET
BACKSTREETS
BACKSTRETCH
BACKSTRETCHES
BACKSTROKE

BACKSTROKES	BACTERIOLOGY	BADMOUTHING	BALCONETTES	BALLERINAS
BACKSWINGS	BACTERIOLYSES	BAFFLEGABS	BALDACHINO	BALLETICALLY
BACKSWORDMAN	BACTERIOLYSIN	BAFFLEMENT	BALDACHINOS	BALLETOMANE
BACKSWORDMEN	BACTERIOLYSINS	BAFFLEMENTS	BALDACHINS	BALLETOMANES
BACKSWORDS	BACTERIOLYSIS	BAFFLINGLY	BALDAQUINS	BALLETOMANIA
BACKSWORDSMAN	BACTERIOLYTIC	BAGASSOSES	BALDERDASH	BALLETOMANIAS
BACKSWORDSMEN	BACTERIOPHAGE	BAGASSOSIS	BALDERDASHES	BALLFLOWER
BACKTRACKED	BACTERIOPHAGES	BAGATELLES	BALDERLOCKS	BALLFLOWERS
BACKTRACKING	BACTERIOPHAGIC	BAGGINESSES	BALDERLOCKSES	BALLHANDLING
BACKTRACKINGS	BACTERIOPHAGIES	BAGPIPINGS	BALDHEADED	BALLHANDLINGS
BACKTRACKS	BACTERIOPHAGOUS	BAGSWINGER	BALDICOOTS	BALLICATTER
BACKVELDER	BACTERIOPHAGY	BAGSWINGERS	BALDMONEYS	BALLICATTERS
BACKVELDERS	BACTERIOSES	BAHUVRIHIS	BALDNESSES	BALLISTICALLY
BACKWARDATION	BACTERIOSIS	BAIGNOIRES	BALECTIONS	BALLISTICS
BACKWARDATIONS	BACTERIOSTASES	BAILIESHIP	BALEFULNESS	BALLISTITE
BACKWARDLY	BACTERIOSTASIS	BAILIESHIPS	BALEFULNESSES	BALLISTITES
BACKWARDNESS	BACTERIOSTAT	BAILIFFSHIP	BALIBUNTAL	BALLISTOSPORE
BACKWARDNESSES	BACTERIOSTATIC	BAILIFFSHIPS	BALIBUNTALS	BALLISTOSPORES
BACKWASHED	BACTERIOSTATS	BAILIWICKS	BALKANISATION	BALLOCKSED
BACKWASHES	BACTERIOTOXIN	BAILLIAGES	BALKANISATIONS	BALLOCKSES
BACKWASHING	BACTERIOTOXINS	BAILLIESHIP	BALKANISED	BALLOCKSING
BACKWATERS	BACTERISATION	BAILLIESHIPS	BALKANISES	BALLOONING
BACKWOODSMAN	BACTERISATIONS	BAIRNLIEST	BALKANISING	BALLOONINGS
BACKWOODSMEN	BACTERISED	BAISEMAINS	BALKANIZATION	BALLOONIST
BACKWOODSY	BACTERISES	BAITFISHES	BALKANIZATIONS	BALLOONISTS
BACKWORKER	BACTERISING	BAKEAPPLES	BALKANIZED	BALLOTTEMENT
BACKWORKERS	BACTERIURIA	BAKEBOARDS	BALKANIZES	BALLOTTEMENTS
BACTERAEMIA	BACTERIURIAS	BAKEHOUSES	BALKANIZING	BALLPLAYER
BACTERAEMIAS	BACTERIZATION	BAKESTONES	BALKINESSES	BALLPLAYERS
BACTEREMIA	BACTERIZATIONS	BAKHSHISHED	BALLABILES	BALLPOINTS
BACTEREMIAS	BACTERIZED	BAKHSHISHES	BALLADEERED	BALLSINESS
BACTEREMIC	BACTERIZES	BAKHSHISHING	BALLADEERING	BALLSINESSES
BACTERIALLY	BACTERIZING	BAKSHEESHED	BALLADEERS	BALLYHOOED
BACTERIALS	BACTEROIDS	BAKSHEESHES	BALLADINES	BALLYHOOING
BACTERICIDAL	BACTERURIA	BAKSHEESHING	BALLADISTS	BALLYRAGGED
BACTERICIDALLY	BACTERURIAS	BAKSHISHED	BALLADMONGER	BALLYRAGGING
BACTERICIDE	BACULIFORM	BAKSHISHES	BALLADMONGERS	BALMACAANS
BACTERICIDES	BACULOVIRUS	BAKSHISHING	BALLADRIES	BALMINESSES
BACTERIOCIN	BACULOVIRUSES	BALACLAVAS	BALLANTING	BALMORALITIES
BACTERIOCINS	BADDELEYITE	BALALAIKAS	BALLANWRASSE	BALMORALITY
BACTERIOID	BADDELEYITES	BALANCEABLE	BALLANWRASSES	BALNEARIES
BACTERIOIDS	BADDERLOCK	BALANCINGS	BALLASTERS	BALNEATION
BACTERIOLOGIC	BADDERLOCKS	BALANITISES	BALLASTING	BALNEATIONS
BACTERIOLOGICAL	BADINAGING	BALBRIGGAN	BALLBREAKER	BALNEOLOGICAL
BACTERIOLOGIES	BADINERIES	BALBRIGGANS	BALLBREAKERS	BALNEOLOGIES
BACTERIOLOGIST	BADMINTONS	BALBUTIENT	BALLCARRIER	BALNEOLOGIST
BACTERIOLOGISTS	BADMOUTHED	BALCONETTE	BALLCARRIERS	BALNEOLOGISTS

BALNEOLOGY	BANDINESSES	BANQUETEER	BARBASTELS	BARKEEPERS
BALNEOTHERAPIES	BANDITRIES	BANQUETEERS	BARBECUERS	BARKENTINE
BALNEOTHERAPY	BANDLEADER	BANQUETERS	BARBECUING	BARKENTINES
BALSAMIFEROUS	BANDLEADERS	BANQUETING	BARBELLATE	BARLEYCORN
BALSAMINACEOUS	BANDMASTER	BANQUETINGS	BARBEQUING	BARLEYCORNS
BALSAWOODS	BANDMASTERS	BANQUETTES	BARBERRIES	BARMBRACKS
BALTHASARS	BANDOBASTS	BANTAMWEIGHT	BARBERSHOP	BARMINESSES
BALTHAZARS	BANDOBUSTS	BANTAMWEIGHTS	BARBERSHOPS	BARMITSVAH
BALUSTERED	BANDOLEERED	BANTERINGLY	BARBITONES	BARMITSVAHS
BALUSTRADE	BANDOLEERS	BANTERINGS	BARBITURATE	BARMITZVAH
BALUSTRADED	BANDOLEONS	BANTINGISM	BARBITURATES	BARMITZVAHS
BALUSTRADES	BANDOLEROS	BANTINGISMS	BARBITURIC	BARNBRACKS
BALZARINES	BANDOLIERED	BAPHOMETIC	BARBOTINES	BARNSBREAKING
BAMBOOZLED	BANDOLIERS	BAPTISMALLY	BARCAROLES	BARNSBREAKINGS
BAMBOOZLEMENT	BANDOLINED	BAPTISTERIES	BARCAROLLE	BARNSTORMED
BAMBOOZLEMENTS	BANDOLINES	BAPTISTERY	BARCAROLLES	BARNSTORMER
BAMBOOZLER	BANDOLINING	BAPTISTRIES	BARDOLATER	BARNSTORMERS
BAMBOOZLERS	BANDONEONS	BARAESTHESIA	BARDOLATERS	BARNSTORMING
BAMBOOZLES	BANDONIONS	BARAESTHESIAS	BARDOLATRIES	BARNSTORMINGS
BAMBOOZLING	BANDSHELLS	BARAGOUINS	BARDOLATROUS	BARNSTORMS
BANALISATION	BANDSPREADING	BARASINGAS	BARDOLATRY	BAROCEPTOR
BANALISATIONS	BANDSPREADINGS	BARASINGHA	BAREBACKED	BAROCEPTORS
BANALISING	BANDSTANDS	BARASINGHAS	BAREBACKING	BARODYNAMICS
BANALITIES	BANDWAGONS	BARATHRUMS	BAREFACEDLY	BAROGNOSES
BANALIZATION	BANDWIDTHS	BARBARESQUE	BAREFACEDNESS	BAROGNOSIS
BANALIZATIONS	BANEBERRIES	BARBARIANISM	BAREFACEDNESSES	BAROGRAPHIC
BANALIZING	BANEFULNESS	BARBARIANISMS	BAREFOOTED	BAROGRAPHS
BANCASSURANCE	BANEFULNESSES	BARBARIANS	BAREHANDED	BAROMETERS
BANCASSURANCES	BANGSRINGS	BARBARICALLY	BAREHANDING	BAROMETRIC
BANCASSURER	BANISHMENT	BARBARISATION	BAREHEADED	BAROMETRICAL
BANCASSURERS	BANISHMENTS	BARBARISATIONS	BARELEGGED	BAROMETRICALLY
BANDALORES	BANISTERED	BARBARISED	BARENESSES	BAROMETRIES
BANDBRAKES	BANJULELES	BARBARISES	BARESTHESIA	BAROMETZES
BANDEIRANTE	BANKABILITIES	BARBARISING	BARESTHESIAS	BARONESSES
BANDEIRANTES	BANKABILITY	BARBARISMS	BARGAINERS	BARONETAGE
BANDELIERS	BANKROLLED	BARBARITIES	BARGAINING	BARONETAGES
BANDERILLA	BANKROLLER	BARBARIZATION	BARGAININGS	BARONETCIES
BANDERILLAS	BANKROLLERS	BARBARIZATIONS	BARGANDERS	BARONETESS
BANDERILLERO	BANKROLLING	BARBARIZED	BARGEBOARD	BARONETESSES
BANDERILLEROS	BANKRUPTCIES	BARBARIZES	BARGEBOARDS	BARONETICAL
BANDEROLES	BANKRUPTCY	BARBARIZING	BARGEMASTER	BAROPHILES
BANDERSNATCH	BANKRUPTED	BARBAROUSLY	BARGEMASTERS	BAROPHILIC
BANDERSNATCHES	BANKRUPTING	BARBAROUSNESS	BARGEPOLES	BAROPHORESES
BANDFISHES	BANNERALLS	BARBAROUSNESSES	BARHOPPING	BAROPHORESIS
BANDICOOTED	BANNERETTE	BARBASCOES	BARIATRICS	BARORECEPTOR
BANDICOOTING	BANNERETTES	BARBASTELLE	BARKANTINE	BARORECEPTORS
BANDICOOTS	BANNISTERS	BARBASTELLES	BARKANTINES	BAROSCOPES

BAROSCOPIC	BARRICADOED	BASIDIOMYCETE	BASTARDRIES	BATHYMETERS
BAROTITISES	BARRICADOES	BASIDIOMYCETES	BASTINADED	BATHYMETRIC
BAROTRAUMA	BARRICADOING	BASIDIOMYCETOUS	BASTINADES	BATHYMETRICAL
BAROTRAUMAS	BARRICADOS	BASIDIOSPORE	BASTINADING	BATHYMETRICALLY
BAROTRAUMATA	BARRIERING	BASIDIOSPORES	BASTINADOED	BATHYMETRIES
BARPERSONS	BARRISTERIAL	BASIDIOSPOROUS	BASTINADOES	BATHYMETRY
BARQUANTINE	BARRISTERS	BASIFICATION	BASTINADOING	BATHYPELAGIC
BARQUANTINES	BARRISTERSHIP	BASIFICATIONS	BASTNAESITE	BATHYSCAPE
BARQUENTINE	BARRISTERSHIPS	BASILICONS	BASTNAESITES	BATHYSCAPES
BARQUENTINES	BARROWFULS	BASIPETALLY	BASTNASITE	BATHYSCAPH
BARQUETTES	BARTENDERS	BASKETBALL	BASTNASITES	BATHYSCAPHE
BARRACKERS	BARTENDING	BASKETBALLS	BATFOWLERS	BATHYSCAPHES
BARRACKING	BARTIZANED	BASKETFULS	BATFOWLING	BATHYSCAPHS
BARRACKINGS	BARYCENTRE	BASKETLIKE	BATFOWLINGS	BATHYSPHERE
BARRACOONS	BARYCENTRES	BASKETRIES	BATHETICALLY	BATHYSPHERES
BARRACOUTA	BARYCENTRIC	BASKETSFUL	BATHHOUSES	BATMITZVAH
BARRACOUTAS	BARYSPHERE	BASKETWEAVE	BATHMITSVAH	BATMITZVAHS
BARRACUDAS	BARYSPHERES	BASKETWEAVER	BATHMITSVAHS	BATOLOGICAL
BARRAMUNDA	BASALTWARE	BASKETWEAVERS	BATHMITZVAH	BATOLOGIES
BARRAMUNDAS	BASALTWARES	BASKETWEAVES	BATHMITZVAHS	BATOLOGIST
BARRAMUNDI	BASEBALLER	BASKETWORK	BATHMIZVAH	BATOLOGISTS
BARRAMUNDIES	BASEBALLERS	BASKETWORKS	BATHMIZVAHS	BATRACHIAN
BARRAMUNDIS	BASEBOARDS	BASMITZVAH	BATHOCHROME	BATRACHIANS
BARRATRIES	BASEBURNER	BASMITZVAHS	BATHOCHROMES	BATRACHOPHOBIA
BARRATROUS	BASEBURNERS	BASOPHILES	BATHOCHROMIC	BATRACHOPHOBIAS
BARRATROUSLY	BASELESSLY	BASOPHILIA	BATHOLITES	BATRACHOPHOBIC
BARRELAGES	BASELESSNESS	BASOPHILIAS	BATHOLITHIC	BATSMANSHIP
BARRELFULS	BASELESSNESSES	BASOPHILIC	BATHOLITHS	BATSMANSHIPS
BARRELHEAD	BASELINERS	BASSETTING	BATHOLITIC	BATTAILOUS
BARRELHEADS	BASEMENTLESS	BASSNESSES	BATHOMETER	BATTALIONS
BARRELHOUSE	BASENESSES	BASSOONIST	BATHOMETERS	BATTEILANT
BARRELHOUSES	BASEPLATES	BASSOONISTS	BATHOMETRIC	BATTELLING
BARRELLING	BASERUNNER	BASTARDIES	BATHOMETRICALLY	BATTEMENTS
BARRELSFUL	BASERUNNERS	BASTARDISATION	BATHOMETRIES	BATTENINGS
BARRENNESS	BASERUNNING	BASTARDISATIONS	BATHOMETRY	BATTERINGS
BARRENNESSES	BASERUNNINGS	BASTARDISE	BATHOPHILOUS	BATTILLING
BARRENWORT	BASHAWISMS	BASTARDISED	BATHOPHOBIA	BATTINESSES
BARRENWORTS	BASHAWSHIP	BASTARDISES	BATHOPHOBIAS	BATTLEAXES
BARRETRIES	BASHAWSHIPS	BASTARDISING	BATHWATERS	BATTLEBUSES
BARRETROUS	BASHFULNESS	BASTARDISM	BATHYBIUSES	BATTLEBUSSES
BARRETROUSLY	BASHFULNESSES	BASTARDISMS	BATHYGRAPHICAL	BATTLEDOOR
BARRETTERS	BASHIBAZOUK	BASTARDIZATION	BATHYLIMNETIC	BATTLEDOORS
BARRICADED	BASHIBAZOUKS	BASTARDIZATIONS	BATHYLITES	BATTLEDORE
BARRICADER	BASICITIES	BASTARDIZE	BATHYLITHIC	BATTLEDORES
BARRICADERS	BASICRANIAL	BASTARDIZED	BATHYLITHS	BATTLEDRESS
BARRICADES	BASIDIOCARP	BASTARDIZES	BATHYLITIC	BATTLEDRESSES
BARRICADING	BASIDIOCARPS	BASTARDIZING	BATHYMETER	BATTLEFIELD

B

BATTLEFIELDS	BEADBLASTING	BEAUMONTAGE	BECQUERELS	BEDRAGGLING
BATTLEFRONT	BEADBLASTS	BEAUMONTAGES	BECRAWLING	BEDRENCHED
BATTLEFRONTS	BEADHOUSES	BEAUMONTAGUE	BECROWDING	BEDRENCHES
BATTLEGROUND	BEADINESSES	BEAUMONTAGUES	BECRUSTING	BEDRENCHING
BATTLEGROUNDS	BEADLEDOMS	BEAUTEOUSLY	BECUDGELED	BEDRIVELED
BATTLEMENT	BEADLEHOOD	BEAUTEOUSNESS	BECUDGELING	BEDRIVELING
BATTLEMENTED	BEADLEHOODS	BEAUTEOUSNESSES	BECUDGELLED	BEDRIVELLED
BATTLEMENTS	BEADLESHIP	BEAUTICIAN	BECUDGELLING	BEDRIVELLING
BATTLEPIECE	BEADLESHIPS	BEAUTICIANS	BEDABBLING	BEDROPPING
BATTLEPIECES	BEADSWOMAN	BEAUTIFICATION	BEDAGGLING	BEDRUGGING
BATTLEPLANE	BEADSWOMEN	BEAUTIFICATIONS	BEDARKENED	BEDSITTERS
BATTLEPLANES	BEAKERFULS	BEAUTIFIED	BEDARKENING	BEDSITTING
BATTLESHIP	BEAMINESSES	BEAUTIFIER	BEDAZZLEMENT	BEDSPREADS
BATTLESHIPS	BEANFEASTS	BEAUTIFIERS	BEDAZZLEMENTS	BEDSPRINGS
BATTLEWAGON	BEANSTALKS	BEAUTIFIES	BEDAZZLING	BEDWARFING
BATTLEWAGONS	BEARABILITIES	BEAUTIFULLER	BEDCHAMBER	BEDWARMERS
BATTOLOGICAL	BEARABILITY	BEAUTIFULLEST	BEDCHAMBERS	BEDWETTERS
BATTOLOGIES	BEARABLENESS	BEAUTIFULLY	BEDCLOTHES	BEECHDROPS
BAUDRICKES	BEARABLENESSES	BEAUTIFULNESS	BEDCOVERING	BEECHMASTS
BAUDRONSES	BEARBAITING	BEAUTIFULNESSES	BEDCOVERINGS	BEECHWOODS
BAULKINESS	BEARBAITINGS	BEAUTIFYING	BEDEAFENED	BEEFBURGER
BAULKINESSES	BEARBERRIES	BEAVERBOARD	BEDEAFENING	BEEFBURGERS
BAVARDAGES	BEARDEDNESS	BEAVERBOARDS	BEDEHOUSES	BEEFEATERS
BAVAROISES	BEARDEDNESSES	BEBEERINES	BEDELLSHIP	BEEFINESSES
BAWDINESSES	BEARDLESSNESS	BEBLOODING	BEDELLSHIPS	BEEFSTEAKS
BAWDYHOUSE	BEARDLESSNESSES	BEBLUBBERED	BEDELSHIPS	BEEKEEPERS
BAWDYHOUSES	BEARDTONGUE	BECARPETED	BEDEVILING	BEEKEEPING
BAYBERRIES	BEARDTONGUES	BECARPETING	BEDEVILLED	BEEKEEPINGS
BAYONETING	BEARGRASSES	BECCACCIAS	BEDEVILLING	BEERINESSES
BAYONETTED	BEARISHNESS	BECCAFICOS	BEDEVILMENT	BEESWAXING
BAYONETTING	BEARISHNESSES	BECHALKING	BEDEVILMENTS	BEESWINGED
BAZILLIONS	BEARNAISES	BECHANCING	BEDFELLOWS	BEETLEBRAIN
BEACHBALLS	BEASTHOODS	BECHARMING	BEDIAPERED	BEETLEBRAINED
BEACHCOMBED	BEASTLIEST	BECKONINGS	BEDIAPERING	BEETLEBRAINS
BEACHCOMBER	BEASTLINESS	BECLAMORED	BEDIGHTING	BEETLEHEAD
BEACHCOMBERS	BEASTLINESSES	BECLAMORING	BEDIMMINGS	BEETLEHEADED
BEACHCOMBING	BEATBOXERS	BECLASPING	BEDIMPLING	BEETLEHEADS
BEACHCOMBINGS	BEATBOXING	BECLOAKING	BEDIRTYING	BEETMASTER
BEACHCOMBS	BEATBOXINGS	BECLOGGING	BEDIZENING	BEETMASTERS
BEACHFRONT	BEATIFICAL	BECLOTHING	BEDIZENMENT	BEETMISTER
BEACHFRONTS	BEATIFICALLY	BECLOUDING	BEDIZENMENTS	BEETMISTERS
BEACHGOERS	BEATIFICATION	BECLOWNING	BEDLAMISMS	BEFINGERED
BEACHHEADS	BEATIFICATIONS	BECOMINGLY	BEDLAMITES	BEFINGERING
BEACHWEARS	BEATIFYING	BECOMINGNESS	BEDPRESSER	BEFITTINGLY
BEADBLASTED	BEATITUDES	BECOMINGNESSES	BEDPRESSERS	BEFLAGGING
BEADBLASTER	BEAUJOLAIS	BECOWARDED	BEDRAGGLED	BEFLECKING
BEADBLASTERS	BEAUJOLAISES	BECOWARDING	BEDRAGGLES	BEFLOWERED

BEFLOWERING	BEHAPPENED	BELIEVABLE	BELLWETHERS	BENCHWARMERS
BEFLUMMING	BEHAPPENING	BELIEVABLY	BELLYACHED	BENEDICITE
BEFOREHAND	BEHAVIORAL	BELIEVINGLY	BELLYACHER	BENEDICITES
BEFORETIME	BEHAVIORALLY	BELIEVINGS	BELLYACHERS	BENEDICTION
BEFORTUNED	BEHAVIORISM	BELIQUORED	BELLYACHES	BENEDICTIONAL
BEFORTUNES	BEHAVIORISMS	BELIQUORING	BELLYACHING	BENEDICTIONS
BEFORTUNING	BEHAVIORIST	BELITTLEMENT	BELLYBANDS	BENEDICTIVE
BEFOULMENT	BEHAVIORISTIC	BELITTLEMENTS	BELLYBUTTON	BENEDICTORY
BEFOULMENTS	BEHAVIORISTS	BELITTLERS	BELLYBUTTONS	BENEDICTUS
BEFRETTING	BEHAVIOURAL	BELITTLING	BELOMANCIES	BENEDICTUSES
BEFRIENDED	BEHAVIOURALLY	BELITTLINGLY	BELONGINGNESS	BENEFACTED
BEFRIENDER	BEHAVIOURISM	BELLADONNA	BELONGINGNESSES	BENEFACTING
BEFRIENDERS	BEHAVIOURISMS	BELLADONNAS	BELONGINGS	BENEFACTION
BEFRIENDING	BEHAVIOURIST	BELLAMOURE	BELOWDECKS	BENEFACTIONS
BEFRINGING	BEHAVIOURISTIC	BELLAMOURES	BELOWGROUND	BENEFACTOR
BEFUDDLEMENT	BEHAVIOURISTS	BELLARMINE	BELOWSTAIRS	BENEFACTORS
BEFUDDLEMENTS	BEHAVIOURS	BELLARMINES	BELSHAZZAR	BENEFACTORY
BEFUDDLING	BEHEADINGS	BELLETRISM	BELSHAZZARS	BENEFACTRESS
BEGGARDOMS	BEHIGHTING	BELLETRISMS	BELTCOURSE	BENEFACTRESSES
BEGGARHOOD	BEHINDHAND	BELLETRIST	BELTCOURSES	BENEFICENCE
BEGGARHOODS	BEHOLDINGS	BELLETRISTIC	BELVEDERES	BENEFICENCES
BEGGARLINESS	BEINGNESSES	BELLETRISTICAL	BEMADAMING	BENEFICENT
BEGGARLINESSES	BEINNESSES	BELLETRISTS	BEMADDENED	BENEFICENTIAL
BEGGARWEED	BEJESUITED	BELLETTRIST	BEMADDENING	BENEFICENTLY
BEGGARWEEDS	BEJESUITING	BELLETTRISTS	BEMEDALLED	BENEFICIAL
BEGINNINGLESS	BEJEWELING	BELLFLOWER	BEMEDALLING	BENEFICIALLY
BEGINNINGS	BEJEWELLED	BELLFLOWERS	BEMINGLING	BENEFICIALNESS
BEGIRDLING	BEJEWELLING	BELLFOUNDER	BEMOANINGS	BENEFICIALS
BEGLADDING	BEJUMBLING	BELLFOUNDERS	BEMONSTERED	BENEFICIARIES
BEGLAMORED	BEKNIGHTED	BELLFOUNDRIES	BEMONSTERING	BENEFICIARY
BEGLAMORING	BEKNIGHTING	BELLFOUNDRY	BEMONSTERS	BENEFICIATE
BEGLAMOURED	BEKNOTTING	BELLHANGER	BEMOUTHING	BENEFICIATED
BEGLAMOURING	BELABORING	BELLHANGERS	BEMUDDLING	BENEFICIATES
BEGLAMOURS	BELABOURED	BELLIBONES	BEMUFFLING	BENEFICIATING
BEGLERBEGS	BELABOURING	BELLICOSELY	BEMURMURED	BENEFICIATION
BEGLOOMING	BELAMOURES	BELLICOSITIES	BEMURMURING	BENEFICIATIONS
BEGRIMMING	BELATEDNESS	BELLICOSITY	BEMUSEMENT	BENEFICING
BEGROANING	BELATEDNESSES	BELLIGERATI	BEMUSEMENTS	BENEFITERS
BEGRUDGERIES	BELEAGUERED	BELLIGERENCE	BEMUZZLING	BENEFITING
BEGRUDGERS	BELEAGUERING	BELLIGERENCES	BENCHERSHIP	BENEFITTED
BEGRUDGERY	BELEAGUERMENT	BELLIGERENCIES	BENCHERSHIPS	BENEFITTING
BEGRUDGING	BELEAGUERMENTS	BELLIGERENCY	BENCHLANDS	BENEPLACITO
BEGRUDGINGLY	BELEAGUERS	BELLIGERENT	BENCHMARKED	BENEVOLENCE
BEGUILEMENT	BELEMNITES	BELLIGERENTLY	BENCHMARKING	BENEVOLENCES
BEGUILEMENTS	BELIEFLESS	BELLIGERENTS	BENCHMARKINGS	BENEVOLENT
BEGUILINGLY	BELIEVABILITIES	BELLOCKING	BENCHMARKS	BENEVOLENTLY
BEGUINAGES	BELIEVABILITY	BELLWETHER	BENCHWARMER	BENEVOLENTNESS

BENGALINES	BENZOPHENONES	BERSAGLIERE	BESLAVERING	BESTAINING
BENIGHTEDLY	BENZOQUINONE	BERSAGLIERI	BESLOBBERED	BESTARRING
BENIGHTEDNESS	BENZOQUINONES	BERSERKERS	BESLOBBERING	BESTEADING
BENIGHTEDNESSES	BENZPYRENE	BERTILLONAGE	BESLOBBERS	BESTIALISE
BENIGHTENED	BENZPYRENES	BERTILLONAGES	BESLUBBERED	BESTIALISED
BENIGHTENING	BENZYLIDINE	BERYLLIOSES	BESLUBBERING	BESTIALISES
BENIGHTENINGS	BENZYLIDINES	BERYLLIOSIS	BESLUBBERS	BESTIALISING
BENIGHTENS	BEPAINTING	BERYLLIUMS	BESMEARERS	BESTIALISM
BENIGHTERS	BEPEARLING	BESAINTING	BESMEARING	BESTIALISMS
BENIGHTING	BEPEPPERED	BESCATTERED	BESMIRCHED	BESTIALITIES
BENIGHTINGS	BEPEPPERING	BESCATTERING	BESMIRCHES	BESTIALITY
BENIGHTMENT	BEPESTERED	BESCATTERS	BESMIRCHING	BESTIALIZE
BENIGHTMENTS	BEPESTERING	BESCORCHED	BESMOOTHED	BESTIALIZED
BENIGNANCIES	BEPIMPLING	BESCORCHES	BESMOOTHING	BESTIALIZES
BENIGNANCY	BEPLASTERED	BESCORCHING	BESMUDGING	BESTIALIZING
BENIGNANTLY	BEPLASTERING	BESCOURING	BESMUTCHED	BESTIARIES
BENIGNITIES	BEPLASTERS	BESCRAWLED	BESMUTCHES	BESTICKING
BENTGRASSES	BEPOMMELLED	BESCRAWLING	BESMUTCHING	BESTILLING
BENTHOPELAGIC	BEPOMMELLING	BESCREENED	BESMUTTING	BESTIRRING
BENTHOSCOPE	BEPOWDERED	BESCREENING	BESOOTHING	BESTORMING
BENTHOSCOPES	BEPOWDERING	BESCRIBBLE	BESOTTEDLY	BESTOWMENT
BENTONITES	BEPRAISING	BESCRIBBLED	BESOTTEDNESS	BESTOWMENTS
BENTONITIC	BEQUEATHABLE	BESCRIBBLES	BESOTTEDNESSES	BESTRADDLE
BENUMBEDNESS	BEQUEATHAL	BESCRIBBLING	BESPANGLED	BESTRADDLED
BENUMBEDNESSES	BEQUEATHALS	BESEECHERS	BESPANGLES	BESTRADDLES
BENUMBINGLY	BEQUEATHED	BESEECHING	BESPANGLING	BESTRADDLING
BENUMBMENT	BEQUEATHER	BESEECHINGLY	BESPATTERED	BESTRAUGHT
BENUMBMENTS	BEQUEATHERS	BESEECHINGNESS	BESPATTERING	BESTREAKED
BENZALDEHYDE	BEQUEATHING	BESEECHINGS	BESPATTERS	BESTREAKING
BENZALDEHYDES	BEQUEATHMENT	BESEEMINGLY	BESPEAKING	BESTREWING
BENZANTHRACENE	BEQUEATHMENTS	BESEEMINGNESS	BESPECKLED	BESTRIDABLE
BENZANTHRACENES	BERASCALED	BESEEMINGNESSES	BESPECKLES	BESTRIDDEN
BENZENECARBONYL	BERASCALING	BESEEMINGS	BESPECKLING	BESTRIDING
BENZENOIDS	BERBERIDACEOUS	BESETMENTS	BESPECTACLED	BESTROWING
BENZIDINES	BERBERINES	BESHADOWED	BESPEEDING	BESTSELLER
BENZIMIDAZOLE	BERBERISES	BESHADOWING	BESPITTING	BESTSELLERDOM
BENZIMIDAZOLES	BEREAVEMENT	BESHIVERED	BESPORTING	BESTSELLERDOMS
BENZOAPYRENE	BEREAVEMENTS	BESHIVERING	BESPOTTEDNESS	BESTSELLERS
BENZOAPYRENES	BERGAMASKS	BESHOUTING	BESPOTTEDNESSES	BESTSELLING
BENZOCAINE	BERGANDERS	BESHREWING	BESPOTTING	BESTUDDING
BENZOCAINES	BERGOMASKS	BESHROUDED	BESPOUSING	BESWARMING
BENZODIAZEPINE	BERGSCHRUND	BESHROUDING	BESPOUTING	BETACAROTENE
BENZODIAZEPINES	BERGSCHRUNDS	BESIEGEMENT	BESPREADING	BETACAROTENES
BENZOFURAN	BERIBBONED	BESIEGEMENTS	BESPRINKLE	BETACYANIN
BENZOFURANS	BERKELIUMS	BESIEGINGLY	BESPRINKLED	BETACYANINS
BENZOLINES	BERRYFRUIT	BESIEGINGS	BESPRINKLES	BETATTERED
BENZOPHENONE	BERRYFRUITS	BESLAVERED	BESPRINKLING	BETATTERING

BETHANKING	BEWILDERMENT	BIBLIOMANIAS	BICAMERALISTS	BIENSEANCE
BETHANKITS	BEWILDERMENTS	BIBLIOPEGIC	BICAPSULAR	BIENSEANCES
BETHINKING	BEWITCHERIES	BIBLIOPEGIES	BICARBONATE	BIERKELLER
BETHORNING	BEWITCHERS	BIBLIOPEGIST	BICARBONATES	BIERKELLERS
BETHRALLED	BEWITCHERY	BIBLIOPEGISTS	BICARPELLARY	BIFACIALLY
BETHRALLING	BEWITCHING	BIBLIOPEGY	BICENTENARIES	BIFARIOUSLY
BETHUMBING	BEWITCHINGLY	BIBLIOPHAGIST	BICENTENARY	BIFIDITIES
BETHUMPING	BEWITCHMENT	BIBLIOPHAGISTS	BICENTENNIAL	BIFLAGELLATE
BETHWACKED	BEWITCHMENTS	BIBLIOPHIL	BICENTENNIALS	BIFOLIOLATE
BETHWACKING	BEWORRYING	BIBLIOPHILE	BICEPHALOUS	BIFUNCTIONAL
BETOKENING	BEWRAPPING	BIBLIOPHILES	BICHLORIDE	BIFURCATED
BETREADING	BHIKKHUNIS	BIBLIOPHILIC	BICHLORIDES	BIFURCATES
BETRIMMING	BIANNUALLY	BIBLIOPHILIES	BICHROMATE	BIFURCATING
BETROTHALS	BIANNULATE	BIBLIOPHILISM	BICHROMATED	BIFURCATION
BETROTHEDS	BIASNESSES	BIBLIOPHILISMS	BICHROMATES	BIFURCATIONS
BETROTHING	BIATHLETES	BIBLIOPHILIST	BICKERINGS	BIGAMOUSLY
BETROTHMENT	BIAURICULAR	BIBLIOPHILISTIC	BICOLLATERAL	BIGARREAUS
BETROTHMENTS	BIAURICULATE	BIBLIOPHILISTS	BICOLOURED	BIGEMINIES
BETTERINGS	BIBLICALLY	BIBLIOPHILS	BICOMPONENT	BIGFOOTING
BETTERMENT	BIBLICISMS	BIBLIOPHILY	BICONCAVITIES	BIGHEADEDLY
BETTERMENTS	BIBLICISTS	BIBLIOPHOBIA	BICONCAVITY	BIGHEADEDNESS
BETTERMOST	BIBLIOGRAPHER	BIBLIOPHOBIAS	BICONDITIONAL	BIGHEADEDNESSES
BETTERNESS	BIBLIOGRAPHERS	BIBLIOPOLE	BICONDITIONALS	BIGHEARTED
BETTERNESSES	BIBLIOGRAPHIC	BIBLIOPOLES	BICONVEXITIES	BIGHEARTEDLY
BETULACEOUS	BIBLIOGRAPHICAL	BIBLIOPOLIC	BICONVEXITY	BIGHEARTEDNESS
BETWEENBRAIN	BIBLIOGRAPHIES	BIBLIOPOLICAL	BICORNUATE	BIGMOUTHED
BETWEENBRAINS	BIBLIOGRAPHY	BIBLIOPOLIES	BICORPORATE	BIGNONIACEOUS
BETWEENITIES	BIBLIOLATER	BIBLIOPOLIST	BICULTURAL	BIGUANIDES
BETWEENITY	BIBLIOLATERS	BIBLIOPOLISTS	BICULTURALISM	BIJECTIONS
BETWEENNESS	BIBLIOLATRIES	BIBLIOPOLY	BICULTURALISMS	BIJOUTERIE
BETWEENNESSES	BIBLIOLATRIST	BIBLIOTHECA	BICUSPIDATE	BIJOUTERIES
BETWEENTIME	BIBLIOLATRISTS	BIBLIOTHECAE	BICUSPIDATES	BILATERALISM
BETWEENTIMES	BIBLIOLATROUS	BIBLIOTHECAL	BICYCLICAL	BILATERALISMS
BETWEENWHILES	BIBLIOLATRY	BIBLIOTHECARIES	BICYCLISTS	BILATERALLY
BEVELLINGS	BIBLIOLOGICAL	BIBLIOTHECARY	BIDDABILITIES	BILBERRIES
BEVELMENTS	BIBLIOLOGIES	BIBLIOTHECAS	BIDDABILITY	BILDUNGSROMAN
BEVOMITING	BIBLIOLOGIST	BIBLIOTHERAPIES	BIDDABLENESS	BILDUNGSROMANS
BEWAILINGLY	BIBLIOLOGISTS	BIBLIOTHERAPY	BIDDABLENESSES	BILECTIONS
BEWAILINGS	BIBLIOLOGY	BIBLIOTICS	BIDENTATED	BILESTONES
BEWEARYING	BIBLIOMANCIES	BIBLIOTIST	BIDIALECTAL	BILGEWATER
BEWELTERED	BIBLIOMANCY	BIBLIOTISTS	BIDIALECTALISM	BILGEWATERS
BEWHISKERED	BIBLIOMANE	BIBULOUSLY	BIDIALECTALISMS	BILHARZIAL
BEWILDERED	BIBLIOMANES	BIBULOUSNESS	BIDIRECTIONAL	BILHARZIAS
BEWILDEREDLY	BIBLIOMANIA	BIBULOUSNESSES	BIDIRECTIONALLY	BILHARZIASES
BEWILDEREDNESS	BIBLIOMANIAC	BICAMERALISM	BIDONVILLE	BILHARZIASIS
BEWILDERING	BIBLIOMANIACAL	BICAMERALISMS	BIDONVILLES	BILHARZIOSES
BEWILDERINGLY	BIBLIOMANIACS	BICAMERALIST	BIENNIALLY	BILHARZIOSIS

BILIMBINGS
BILINGUALISM
BILINGUALISMS
BILINGUALLY
BILINGUALS
BILINGUIST
BILINGUISTS
BILIOUSNESS
BILIOUSNESSES
BILIRUBINS
BILIVERDIN
BILIVERDINS
BILLABONGS
BILLBOARDED
BILLBOARDING
BILLBOARDS
BILLFISHES
BILLINGSGATE
BILLINGSGATES
BILLIONAIRE
BILLIONAIRES
BILLIONTHS
BILLOWIEST
BILLOWINESS
BILLOWINESSES
BILLOWINGS
BILLPOSTER
BILLPOSTERS
BILLPOSTING
BILLPOSTINGS
BILLSTICKER
BILLSTICKERS
BILLSTICKING
BILLSTICKINGS
BILLYCOCKS
BILOCATION
BILOCATIONS
BILOCULATE
BIMANUALLY
BIMESTRIAL
BIMESTRIALLY
BIMETALLIC
BIMETALLICS
BIMETALLISM
BIMETALLISMS
BIMETALLIST
BIMETALLISTIC

BIMETALLISTS
BIMILLENARIES
BIMILLENARY
BIMILLENNIA
BIMILLENNIAL
BIMILLENNIALS
BIMILLENNIUM
BIMILLENNIUMS
BIMODALITIES
BIMODALITY
BIMOLECULAR
BIMOLECULARLY
BIMONTHLIES
BIMORPHEMIC
BINATIONAL
BINAURALLY
BINDINGNESS
BINDINGNESSES
BINOCULARITIES
BINOCULARITY
BINOCULARLY
BINOCULARS
BINOMIALLY
BINOMINALS
BINTURONGS
BINUCLEATE
BINUCLEATED
BIOACCUMULATE
BIOACCUMULATED
BIOACCUMULATES
BIOACCUMULATING
BIOACCUMULATION
BIOACOUSTICS
BIOACTIVITIES
BIOACTIVITY
BIOAERATION
BIOAERATIONS
BIOAERONAUTICS
BIOASSAYED
BIOASSAYING
BIOASTRONAUTICS
BIOAVAILABILITY
BIOAVAILABLE
BIOCATALYST
BIOCATALYSTS
BIOCATALYTIC
BIOCELLATE

BIOCENOLOGIES
BIOCENOLOGY
BIOCENOSES
BIOCENOSIS
BIOCENOTIC
BIOCHEMICAL
BIOCHEMICALLY
BIOCHEMICALS
BIOCHEMIST
BIOCHEMISTRIES
BIOCHEMISTRY
BIOCHEMISTS
BIOCLASTIC
BIOCLIMATIC
BIOCLIMATOLOGY
BIOCOENOLOGIES
BIOCOENOLOGY
BIOCOENOSES
BIOCOENOSIS
BIOCOENOTIC
BIOCOMPATIBLE
BIOCOMPUTING
BIOCOMPUTINGS
BIOCONTROL
BIOCONTROLS
BIOCONVERSION
BIOCONVERSIONS
BIODEGRADABLE
BIODEGRADATION
BIODEGRADATIONS
BIODEGRADE
BIODEGRADED
BIODEGRADES
BIODEGRADING
BIODESTRUCTIBLE
BIODIESELS
BIODIVERSITIES
BIODIVERSITY
BIODYNAMIC
BIODYNAMICAL
BIODYNAMICS
BIOECOLOGICAL
BIOECOLOGICALLY
BIOECOLOGIES
BIOECOLOGIST
BIOECOLOGISTS
BIOECOLOGY

BIOELECTRIC
BIOELECTRICAL
BIOELECTRICITY
BIOENERGETIC
BIOENERGETICS
BIOENERGIES
BIOENGINEER
BIOENGINEERED
BIOENGINEERING
BIOENGINEERINGS
BIOENGINEERS
BIOETHANOL
BIOETHANOLS
BIOETHICAL
BIOETHICIST
BIOETHICISTS
BIOFEEDBACK
BIOFEEDBACKS
BIOFLAVONOID
BIOFLAVONOIDS
BIOFOULERS
BIOFOULING
BIOFOULINGS
BIOGENESES
BIOGENESIS
BIOGENETIC
BIOGENETICAL
BIOGENETICALLY
BIOGENETICS
BIOGEOCHEMICAL
BIOGEOCHEMICALS
BIOGEOCHEMISTRY
BIOGEOGRAPHER
BIOGEOGRAPHERS
BIOGEOGRAPHIC
BIOGEOGRAPHICAL
BIOGEOGRAPHIES
BIOGEOGRAPHY
BIOGRAPHED
BIOGRAPHEE
BIOGRAPHEES
BIOGRAPHER
BIOGRAPHERS
BIOGRAPHIC
BIOGRAPHICAL
BIOGRAPHICALLY
BIOGRAPHIES

BIOGRAPHING
BIOGRAPHISE
BIOGRAPHISED
BIOGRAPHISES
BIOGRAPHISING
BIOGRAPHIZE
BIOGRAPHIZED
BIOGRAPHIZES
BIOGRAPHIZING
BIOHAZARDOUS
BIOHAZARDS
BIOINDUSTRIES
BIOINDUSTRY
BIOINFORMATICS
BIOLOGICAL
BIOLOGICALLY
BIOLOGICALS
BIOLOGISMS
BIOLOGISTIC
BIOLOGISTS
BIOLUMINESCENCE
BIOLUMINESCENT
BIOMAGNETICS
BIOMARKERS
BIOMATERIAL
BIOMATERIALS
BIOMATHEMATICAL
BIOMATHEMATICS
BIOMECHANICAL
BIOMECHANICALLY
BIOMECHANICS
BIOMEDICAL
BIOMEDICINE
BIOMEDICINES
BIOMETEOROLOGY
BIOMETRICAL
BIOMETRICALLY
BIOMETRICIAN
BIOMETRICIANS
BIOMETRICS
BIOMETRIES
BIOMIMETIC
BIOMIMETICS
BIOMIMICRIES
BIOMIMICRY
BIOMININGS
BIOMOLECULAR

B

BIOMOLECULE	BIOSCIENTIFIC	BIPEDALISM	BIRDWATCHERS	BISSEXTILES
BIOMOLECULES	BIOSCIENTIST	BIPEDALISMS	BIRDWATCHES	BISTOURIES
BIOMORPHIC	BIOSCIENTISTS	BIPEDALITIES	BIRDWATCHING	BISULFATES
BIONOMICALLY	BIOSCOPIES	BIPEDALITY	BIRDWATCHINGS	BISULFIDES
BIONOMISTS	BIOSENSORS	BIPETALOUS	BIREFRINGENCE	BISULFITES
BIOPARENTS	BIOSOCIALLY	BIPINNARIA	BIREFRINGENCES	BISULPHATE
BIOPESTICIDAL	BIOSPHERES	BIPINNARIAS	BIREFRINGENT	BISULPHATES
BIOPESTICIDE	BIOSPHERIC	BIPINNATELY	BIROSTRATE	BISULPHIDE
BIOPESTICIDES	BIOSTATICALLY	BIPOLARISATION	BIRTHMARKS	BISULPHIDES
BIOPHILIAS	BIOSTATICS	BIPOLARISATIONS	BIRTHNAMES	BISULPHITE
BIOPHYSICAL	BIOSTATISTICAL	BIPOLARISE	BIRTHNIGHT	BISULPHITES
BIOPHYSICALLY	BIOSTATISTICIAN	BIPOLARISED	BIRTHNIGHTS	BISYMMETRIC
BIOPHYSICIST	BIOSTATISTICS	BIPOLARISES	BIRTHPLACE	BISYMMETRICAL
BIOPHYSICISTS	BIOSTRATIGRAPHY	BIPOLARISING	BIRTHPLACES	BISYMMETRICALLY
BIOPHYSICS	BIOSTROMES	BIPOLARITIES	BIRTHRATES	BISYMMETRIES
BIOPIRACIES	BIOSURGERIES	BIPOLARITY	BIRTHRIGHT	BISYMMETRY
BIOPIRATES	BIOSURGERY	BIPOLARIZATION	BIRTHRIGHTS	BITARTRATE
BIOPLASMIC	BIOSYNTHESES	BIPOLARIZATIONS	BIRTHROOTS	BITARTRATES
BIOPOIESES	BIOSYNTHESIS	BIPOLARIZE	BIRTHSTONE	BITCHERIES
BIOPOIESIS	BIOSYNTHETIC	BIPOLARIZED	BIRTHSTONES	BITCHFESTS
BIOPOLYMER	BIOSYSTEMATIC	BIPOLARIZES	BIRTHWORTS	BITCHINESS
BIOPOLYMERS	BIOSYSTEMATICS	BIPOLARIZING	BISECTIONAL	BITCHINESSES
BIOPROSPECTING	BIOSYSTEMATIST	BIPROPELLANT	BISECTIONALLY	BITEPLATES
BIOPROSPECTINGS	BIOSYSTEMATISTS	BIPROPELLANTS	BISECTIONS	BITMAPPING
BIOPSYCHOLOGIES	BIOTECHNICAL	BIPYRAMIDAL	BISECTRICES	BITONALITIES
BIOPSYCHOLOGY	BIOTECHNOLOGIES	BIPYRAMIDS	BISEXUALISM	BITONALITY
BIOREACTOR	BIOTECHNOLOGIST	BIQUADRATE	BISEXUALISMS	BITSTREAMS
BIOREACTORS	BIOTECHNOLOGY	BIQUADRATES	BISEXUALITIES	BITTERBARK
BIOREAGENT	BIOTELEMETRIC	BIQUADRATIC	BISEXUALITY	BITTERBARKS
BIOREAGENTS	BIOTELEMETRIES	BIQUADRATICS	BISEXUALLY	BITTERBRUSH
BIOREGIONAL	BIOTELEMETRY	BIQUARTERLY	BISHOPBIRD	BITTERBRUSHES
BIOREGIONALISM	BIOTERRORS	BIQUINTILE	BISHOPBIRDS	BITTERCRESS
BIOREGIONALISMS	BIOTICALLY	BIQUINTILES	BISHOPDOMS	BITTERCRESSES
BIOREGIONALIST	BIOTURBATION	BIRACIALISM	BISHOPESSES	BITTERLING
BIOREGIONALISTS	BIOTURBATIONS	BIRACIALISMS	BISHOPRICS	BITTERLINGS
BIOREGIONS	BIOWEAPONS	BIRACIALLY	BISHOPWEED	BITTERNESS
BIOREMEDIATION	BIPARENTAL	BIRADICALS	BISHOPWEEDS	BITTERNESSES
BIOREMEDIATIONS	BIPARENTALLY	BIRCHBARKS	BISMUTHINITE	BITTERNUTS
BIORHYTHMIC	BIPARIETAL	BIRDBRAINED	BISMUTHINITES	BITTERROOT
BIORHYTHMICALLY	BIPARTISAN	BIRDBRAINS	BISMUTHOUS	BITTERROOTS
BIORHYTHMICS	BIPARTISANISM	BIRDDOGGED	BISOCIATION	BITTERSWEET
BIORHYTHMS	BIPARTISANISMS	BIRDDOGGING	BISOCIATIONS	BITTERSWEETLY
BIOSAFETIES	BIPARTISANSHIP	BIRDHOUSES	BISOCIATIVE	BITTERSWEETNESS
BIOSATELLITE	BIPARTISANSHIPS	BIRDLIMING	BISPHENOLS	BITTERSWEETS
BIOSATELLITES	BIPARTITELY	BIRDSFOOTS	BISPHOSPHONATE	BITTERWEED
BIOSCIENCE	BIPARTITION	BIRDWATCHED	BISPHOSPHONATES	BITTERWEEDS
BIOSCIENCES	BIPARTITIONS	BIRDWATCHER	BISSEXTILE	BITTERWOOD

BITTERWOODS	BLACKBERRYINGS	BLACKLISTERS	BLAMELESSLY	BLASTOCYST
BITTINESSES	BLACKBIRDED	BLACKLISTING	BLAMELESSNESS	BLASTOCYSTS
BITUMINATE	BLACKBIRDER	BLACKLISTINGS	BLAMELESSNESSES	BLASTODERM
BITUMINATED	BLACKBIRDERS	BLACKLISTS	BLAMEWORTHINESS	BLASTODERMIC
BITUMINATES	BLACKBIRDING	BLACKMAILED	BLAMEWORTHY	BLASTODERMS
BITUMINATING	BLACKBIRDINGS	BLACKMAILER	BLANCHISSEUSE	BLASTODISC
BITUMINISATION	BLACKBIRDS	BLACKMAILERS	BLANCHISSEUSES	BLASTODISCS
BITUMINISATIONS	BLACKBOARD	BLACKMAILING	BLANCMANGE	BLASTOGENESES
BITUMINISE	BLACKBOARDS	BLACKMAILS	BLANCMANGES	BLASTOGENESIS
BITUMINISED	BLACKBODIES	BLACKNESSES	BLANDISHED	BLASTOGENETIC
BITUMINISES	BLACKBUCKS	BLACKPOLLS	BLANDISHER	BLASTOGENIC
BITUMINISING	BLACKBUTTS	BLACKSMITH	BLANDISHERS	BLASTOMATA
BITUMINIZATION	BLACKCOCKS	BLACKSMITHING	BLANDISHES	BLASTOMERE
BITUMINIZATIONS	BLACKCURRANT	BLACKSMITHINGS	BLANDISHING	BLASTOMERES
BITUMINIZE	BLACKCURRANTS	BLACKSMITHS	BLANDISHMENT	BLASTOMERIC
BITUMINIZED	BLACKDAMPS	BLACKSNAKE	BLANDISHMENTS	BLASTOMYCOSES
BITUMINIZES	BLACKENERS	BLACKSNAKES	BLANDNESSES	BLASTOMYCOSIS
BITUMINIZING	BLACKENING	BLACKSTRAP	BLANKETFLOWER	BLASTOPORAL
BITUMINOUS	BLACKENINGS	BLACKTAILS	BLANKETFLOWERS	BLASTOPORE
BIUNIQUENESS	BLACKFACED	BLACKTHORN	BLANKETING	BLASTOPORES
BIUNIQUENESSES	BLACKFACES	BLACKTHORNS	BLANKETINGS	BLASTOPORIC
BIVALENCES	BLACKFISHES	BLACKTOPPED	BLANKETLIKE	BLASTOPORS
BIVALENCIES	BLACKFLIES	BLACKTOPPING	BLANKETWEED	BLASTOSPHERE
BIVALVULAR	BLACKGAMES	BLACKWASHED	BLANKETWEEDS	BLASTOSPHERES
BIVARIANTS	BLACKGUARD	BLACKWASHES	BLANKNESSES	BLASTOSPORE
BIVARIATES	BLACKGUARDED	BLACKWASHING	BLANQUETTE	BLASTOSPORES
BIVOUACKED	BLACKGUARDING	BLACKWATER	BLANQUETTES	BLASTULATION
BIVOUACKING	BLACKGUARDISM	BLACKWATERS	BLARNEYING	BLASTULATIONS
BIWEEKLIES	BLACKGUARDISMS	BLACKWOODS	BLASPHEMED	BLATANCIES
BIZARRENESS	BLACKGUARDLY	BLADDERLIKE	BLASPHEMER	BLATHERERS
BIZARRENESSES	BLACKGUARDS	BLADDERNOSE	BLASPHEMERS	BLATHERING
BIZARRERIE	BLACKHANDER	BLADDERNOSES	BLASPHEMES	BLATHERSKITE
BIZARRERIES	BLACKHANDERS	BLADDERNUT	BLASPHEMIES	BLATHERSKITES
BLABBERING	BLACKHEADED	BLADDERNUTS	BLASPHEMING	BLATTERING
BLABBERMOUTH	BLACKHEADS	BLADDERWORT	BLASPHEMOUS	BLAXPLOITATION
BLABBERMOUTHS	BLACKHEART	BLADDERWORTS	BLASPHEMOUSLY	BLAXPLOITATIONS
BLACKAMOOR	BLACKHEARTS	BLADDERWRACK	BLASPHEMOUSNESS	BLAZONINGS
BLACKAMOORS	BLACKISHLY	BLADDERWRACKS	BLASTEMATA	BLAZONRIES
BLACKBALLED	BLACKJACKED	BLADEWORKS	BLASTEMATIC	BLEACHABLE
BLACKBALLING	BLACKJACKING	BLAEBERRIES	BLASTMENTS	BLEACHERIES
BLACKBALLINGS	BLACKJACKS	BLAMABLENESS	BLASTOCHYLE	BLEACHERITE
BLACKBALLS	BLACKLANDS	BLAMABLENESSES	BLASTOCHYLES	BLEACHERITES
BLACKBANDS	BLACKLEADS	BLAMEABLENESS	BLASTOCOEL	BLEACHINGS
BLACKBERRIED	BLACKLEGGED	BLAMEABLENESSES	BLASTOCOELE	BLEAKNESSES
BLACKBERRIES	BLACKLEGGING	BLAMEFULLY	BLASTOCOELES	BLEARINESS
BLACKBERRY	BLACKLISTED	BLAMEFULNESS	BLASTOCOELIC	BLEARINESSES
BLACKBERRYING	BLACKLISTER	BLAMEFULNESSES	BLASTOCOELS	BLEMISHERS

BLEMISHING	BLINDSTOREY	BLOCKISHNESSES	BLOODSTOCKS	BLUEBERRIES
BLEMISHMENT	BLINDSTOREYS	BLOCKSHIPS	BLOODSTONE	BLUEBLOODS
BLEMISHMENTS	BLINDSTORIES	BLOCKWORKS	BLOODSTONES	BLUEBONNET
BLENNIOIDS	BLINDSTORY	BLOGGERATI	BLOODSTREAM	BLUEBONNETS
BLENNORRHEA	BLINDWORMS	BLOGOSPHERE	BLOODSTREAMS	BLUEBOTTLE
BLENNORRHEAS	BLINGLISHES	BLOGOSPHERES	BLOODSUCKER	BLUEBOTTLES
BLENNORRHOEA	BLINKERING	BLOGSTREAM	BLOODSUCKERS	BLUEBREAST
BLENNORRHOEAS	BLISSFULLY	BLOGSTREAMS	BLOODSUCKING	BLUEBREASTS
BLEOMYCINS	BLISSFULNESS	BLOKARTING	BLOODTHIRSTIER	BLUEBUSHES
BLEPHARISM	BLISSFULNESSES	BLOKARTINGS	BLOODTHIRSTIEST	BLUEFISHES
BLEPHARISMS	BLISTERIER	BLOKEISHNESS	BLOODTHIRSTILY	BLUEGRASSES
BLEPHARITIC	BLISTERIEST	BLOKEISHNESSES	BLOODTHIRSTY	BLUEISHNESS
BLEPHARITIS	BLISTERING	BLOKISHNESS	BLOODWOODS	BLUEISHNESSES
BLEPHARITISES	BLISTERINGLY	BLOKISHNESSES	BLOODWORMS	BLUEJACKET
BLEPHAROPLAST	BLITHENESS	BLONDENESS	BLOODWORTS	BLUEJACKETS
BLEPHAROPLASTS	BLITHENESSES	BLONDENESSES	BLOOMERIES	BLUEJACKING
BLEPHAROPLASTY	BLITHERING	BLONDINING	BLOQUISTES	BLUEJACKINGS
BLEPHAROSPASM	BLITHESOME	BLONDNESSES	BLOSSOMING	BLUELINERS
BLEPHAROSPASMS	BLITHESOMELY	BLOODBATHS	BLOSSOMINGS	BLUENESSES
BLESSEDEST	BLITHESOMENESS	BLOODCURDLING	BLOSSOMLESS	BLUEPOINTS
BLESSEDNESS	BLITZKRIEG	BLOODCURDLINGLY	BLOTCHIEST	BLUEPRINTED
BLESSEDNESSES	BLITZKRIEGS	BLOODGUILT	BLOTCHINESS	BLUEPRINTING
BLETHERANSKATE	BLIZZARDLY	BLOODGUILTINESS	BLOTCHINESSES	BLUEPRINTS
BLETHERANSKATES	BLOATEDNESS	BLOODGUILTS	BLOTCHINGS	BLUESHIFTED
BLETHERATION	BLOATEDNESSES	BLOODGUILTY	BLOTTESQUE	BLUESHIFTS
BLETHERATIONS	BLOATWARES	BLOODHOUND	BLOTTESQUES	BLUESNARFING
BLETHERERS	BLOCKADERS	BLOODHOUNDS	BLOVIATING	BLUESNARFINGS
BLETHERING	BLOCKADING	BLOODINESS	BLOVIATION	BLUESTOCKING
BLETHERINGS	BLOCKBOARD	BLOODINESSES	BLOVIATIONS	BLUESTOCKINGS
BLETHERSKATE	BLOCKBOARDS	BLOODLESSLY	BLOWFISHES	BLUESTONES
BLETHERSKATES	BLOCKBUSTED	BLOODLESSNESS	BLOWINESSES	BLUETHROAT
BLIGHTINGLY	BLOCKBUSTER	BLOODLESSNESSES	BLOWSINESS	BLUETHROATS
BLIGHTINGS	BLOCKBUSTERS	BLOODLETTER	BLOWSINESSES	BLUETONGUE
BLIMPISHLY	BLOCKBUSTING	BLOODLETTERS	BLOWTORCHED	BLUETONGUES
BLIMPISHNESS	BLOCKBUSTINGS	BLOODLETTING	BLOWTORCHES	BLUFFNESSES
BLIMPISHNESSES	BLOCKBUSTS	BLOODLETTINGS	BLOWTORCHING	BLUISHNESS
BLINDFISHES	BLOCKHEADED	BLOODLINES	BLOWZINESS	BLUISHNESSES
BLINDFOLDED	BLOCKHEADEDLY	BLOODLUSTS	BLOWZINESSES	BLUNDERBUSS
BLINDFOLDING	BLOCKHEADEDNESS	BLOODMOBILE	BLUBBERERS	BLUNDERBUSSES
BLINDFOLDS	BLOCKHEADS	BLOODMOBILES	BLUBBERIER	BLUNDERERS
BLINDINGLY	BLOCKHOLES	BLOODROOTS	BLUBBERIEST	BLUNDERING
BLINDNESSES	BLOCKHOUSE	BLOODSHEDS	BLUBBERING	BLUNDERINGLY
BLINDSIDED	BLOCKHOUSES	BLOODSPRENT	BLUDGEONED	BLUNDERINGS
BLINDSIDES	BLOCKINESS	BLOODSTAIN	BLUDGEONER	BLUNTHEADS
BLINDSIDING	BLOCKINESSES	BLOODSTAINED	BLUDGEONERS	BLUNTNESSES
BLINDSIGHT	BLOCKISHLY	BLOODSTAINS	BLUDGEONING	BLURREDNESS
BLINDSIGHTS	BLOCKISHNESS	BLOODSTOCK	BLUEBEARDS	BLURREDNESSES

B

BLURRINESS	BOBSLEDDERS	BOHEMIANISMS	BOMBARDMENTS	BONILASSES
BLURRINESSES	BOBSLEDDING	BOILERMAKER	BOMBARDONS	BONINESSES
BLURRINGLY	BOBSLEDDINGS	BOILERMAKERS	BOMBASINES	BONKBUSTER
BLUSHINGLY	BOBSLEIGHED	BOILERPLATE	BOMBASTERS	BONKBUSTERS
BLUSHLESSLY	BOBSLEIGHING	BOILERPLATED	BOMBASTICALLY	BONNIBELLS
BLUSTERERS	BOBSLEIGHS	BOILERPLATES	BOMBASTING	BONNILASSE
BLUSTERIER	BOBTAILING	BOILERPLATING	BOMBAZINES	BONNILASSES
BLUSTERIEST	BOBWEIGHTS	BOILERSUIT	BOMBILATED	BONNINESSES
BLUSTERING	BOCCONCINI	BOILERSUITS	BOMBILATES	BONNYCLABBER
BLUSTERINGLY	BODACIOUSLY	BOISTEROUS	BOMBILATING	BONNYCLABBERS
BLUSTERINGS	BODDHISATTVA	BOISTEROUSLY	BOMBILATION	BOOBIALLAS
BLUSTEROUS	BODDHISATTVAS	BOISTEROUSNESS	BOMBILATIONS	BOOBOISIES
BLUSTEROUSLY	BODEGUEROS	BOKMAKIERIE	BOMBINATED	BOOGALOOED
BLUTWURSTS	BODHISATTVA	BOKMAKIERIES	BOMBINATES	BOOGALOOING
BOARDINGHOUSE	BODHISATTVAS	BOLDFACING	BOMBINATING	BOOKBINDER
BOARDINGHOUSES	BODYBOARDED	BOLDNESSES	BOMBINATION	BOOKBINDERIES
BOARDROOMS	BODYBOARDING	BOLECTIONS	BOMBINATIONS	BOOKBINDERS
BOARDSAILING	BODYBOARDINGS	BOLIVIANOS	BOMBPROOFED	BOOKBINDERY
BOARDSAILINGS	BODYBOARDS	BOLLETRIES	BOMBPROOFING	BOOKBINDING
BOARDSAILOR	BODYBUILDER	BOLLOCKING	BOMBPROOFS	BOOKBINDINGS
BOARDSAILORS	BODYBUILDERS	BOLLOCKINGS	BOMBSHELLS	BOOKCROSSING
BOARDWALKS	BODYBUILDING	BOLLOCKSED	BOMBSIGHTS	BOOKCROSSINGS
BOARFISHES	BODYBUILDINGS	BOLLOCKSES	BONAMIASES	BOOKISHNESS
BOARHOUNDS	BODYCHECKED	BOLLOCKSING	BONAMIASIS	BOOKISHNESSES
BOARISHNESS	BODYCHECKING	BOLOGNESES	BONASSUSES	BOOKKEEPER
BOARISHNESSES	BODYCHECKS	BOLOGRAPHS	BONBONNIERE	BOOKKEEPERS
BOASTFULLY	BODYGUARDED	BOLOMETERS	BONBONNIERES	BOOKKEEPING
BOASTFULNESS	BODYGUARDING	BOLOMETRIC	BONDHOLDER	BOOKKEEPINGS
BOASTFULNESSES	BODYGUARDS	BOLOMETRICALLY	BONDHOLDERS	BOOKLIGHTS
BOASTINGLY	BODYSHELLS	BOLOMETRIES	BONDMANSHIP	BOOKMAKERS
BOATBUILDER	BODYSURFED	BOLSHEVIKI	BONDMANSHIPS	BOOKMAKING
BOATBUILDERS	BODYSURFER	BOLSHEVIKS	BONDSERVANT	BOOKMAKINGS
BOATBUILDING	BODYSURFERS	BOLSHEVISM	BONDSERVANTS	BOOKMARKED
BOATBUILDINGS	BODYSURFING	BOLSHEVISMS	BONDSTONES	BOOKMARKER
BOATHOUSES	BODYSURFINGS	BOLSHEVIZE	BONDSWOMAN	BOOKMARKERS
BOATLIFTED	BODYWORKER	BOLSHEVIZED	BONDSWOMEN	BOOKMARKING
BOATLIFTING	BODYWORKERS	BOLSHEVIZES	BONEBLACKS	BOOKMOBILE
BOATSWAINS	BOEREMUSIEK	BOLSHEVIZING	BONEFISHES	BOOKMOBILES
BOBBEJAANS	BOEREMUSIEKS	BOLSTERERS	BONEFISHING	BOOKPLATES
BOBBITTING	BOEREWORSES	BOLSTERING	BONEFISHINGS	BOOKSELLER
BOBBLEHEAD	BOGGINESSES	BOLSTERINGS	BONEHEADED	BOOKSELLERS
BOBBLEHEADS	BOGTROTTER	BOMBACACEOUS	BONEHEADEDNESS	BOOKSELLING
BOBBYSOCKS	BOGTROTTERS	BOMBARDERS	BONESETTER	BOOKSELLINGS
BOBBYSOXER	BOGTROTTING	BOMBARDIER	BONESETTERS	BOOKSHELVES
BOBBYSOXERS	BOGTROTTINGS	BOMBARDIERS	BONESHAKER	BOOKSTALLS
BOBSLEDDED	BOGUSNESSES	BOMBARDING	BONESHAKERS	BOOKSTANDS
BOBSLEDDER	BOHEMIANISM	BOMBARDMENT	BONHOMMIES	BOOKSTORES

BOOMERANGED	BORDERLANDS	BOTTOMLAND	BOUNTIFULLY	BOWDLERIZING
BOOMERANGING	BORDERLESS	BOTTOMLANDS	BOUNTIFULNESS	BOWERBIRDS
BOOMERANGS	BORDERLINE	BOTTOMLESS	BOUNTIFULNESSES	BOWERWOMAN
BOOMSLANGS	BORDERLINES	BOTTOMLESSLY	BOUNTYHEDS	BOWERWOMEN
BOONDOGGLE	BORDRAGING	BOTTOMLESSNESS	BOUQUETIERE	BOWHUNTERS
BOONDOGGLED	BORDRAGINGS	BOTTOMMOST	BOUQUETIERES	BOWSTRINGED
BOONDOGGLER	BORESCOPES	BOTTOMNESS	BOURASQUES	BOWSTRINGING
BOONDOGGLERS	BORGHETTOS	BOTTOMNESSES	BOURBONISM	BOWSTRINGS
BOONDOGGLES	BORINGNESS	BOTTOMRIES	BOURBONISMS	BOXBERRIES
BOONDOGGLING	BORINGNESSES	BOTULINUMS	BOURGEOISE	BOXERCISES
BOONGARIES	BOROHYDRIDE	BOTULINUSES	BOURGEOISES	BOXHAULING
BOORISHNESS	BOROHYDRIDES	BOUGAINVILIA	BOURGEOISIE	BOXINESSES
BOORISHNESSES	BOROSILICATE	BOUGAINVILIAS	BOURGEOISIES	BOXKEEPERS
BOOSTERISH	BOROSILICATES	BOUGAINVILLAEA	BOURGEOISIFIED	BOXWALLAHS
BOOSTERISM	BORROWINGS	BOUGAINVILLAEAS	BOURGEOISIFIES	BOYCOTTERS
BOOSTERISMS	BOSBERAADS	BOUGAINVILLEA	BOURGEOISIFY	BOYCOTTING
BOOTBLACKS	BOSCHVARKS	BOUGAINVILLEAS	BOURGEOISIFYING	BOYFRIENDS
BOOTLEGGED	BOSCHVELDS	BOUILLABAISSE	BOURGEONED	BOYISHNESS
BOOTLEGGER	BOSKINESSES	BOUILLABAISSES	BOURGEONING	BOYISHNESSES
BOOTLEGGERS	BOSSINESSES	BOUILLOTTE	BOURGUIGNON	BOYSENBERRIES
BOOTLEGGING	BOSSYBOOTS	BOUILLOTTES	BOURGUIGNONNE	BOYSENBERRY
BOOTLEGGINGS	BOTANICALLY	BOULDERERS	BOUSINGKEN	BRAAIVLEIS
BOOTLESSLY	BOTANICALS	BOULDERING	BOUSINGKENS	BRAAIVLEISES
BOOTLESSNESS	BOTANISERS	BOULDERINGS	BOUSTROPHEDON	BRABBLEMENT
BOOTLESSNESSES	BOTANISING	BOULEVARDIER	BOUSTROPHEDONIC	BRABBLEMENTS
BOOTLICKED	BOTANIZERS	BOULEVARDIERS	BOUSTROPHEDONS	BRACHIATED
BOOTLICKER	BOTANIZING	BOULEVARDS	BOUTONNIERE	BRACHIATES
BOOTLICKERS	BOTANOMANCIES	BOULEVERSEMENT	BOUTONNIERES	BRACHIATING
BOOTLICKING	BOTANOMANCY	BOULEVERSEMENTS	BOUVARDIAS	BRACHIATION
BOOTLICKINGS	BOTCHERIES	BOULLEWORK	BOVINITIES	BRACHIATIONS
BOOTLOADER	BOTCHINESS	BOULLEWORKS	BOWDLERISATION	BRACHIATOR
BOOTLOADERS	BOTCHINESSES	BOUNCEDOWN	BOWDLERISATIONS	BRACHIATORS
BOOTMAKERS	BOTHERATION	BOUNCEDOWNS	BOWDLERISE	BRACHIOCEPHALIC
BOOTMAKING	BOTHERATIONS	BOUNCINESS	BOWDLERISED	BRACHIOPOD
BOOTMAKINGS	BOTHERSOME	BOUNCINESSES	BOWDLERISER	BRACHIOPODS
BOOTSTRAPPED	BOTRYOIDAL	BOUNCINGLY	BOWDLERISERS	BRACHIOSAURUS
BOOTSTRAPPING	BOTRYTISES	BOUNDARIES	BOWDLERISES	BRACHIOSAURUSES
BOOTSTRAPS	BOTTLEBRUSH	BOUNDEDNESS	BOWDLERISING	BRACHISTOCHRONE
BOOTYLICIOUS	BOTTLEBRUSHES	BOUNDEDNESSES	BOWDLERISM	BRACHYAXES
BOOZINESSES	BOTTLEFULS	BOUNDERISH	BOWDLERISMS	BRACHYAXIS
BORAGINACEOUS	BOTTLENECK	BOUNDLESSLY	BOWDLERIZATION	BRACHYCEPHAL
BORBORYGMAL	BOTTLENECKED	BOUNDLESSNESS	BOWDLERIZATIONS	BRACHYCEPHALIC
BORBORYGMI	BOTTLENECKING	BOUNDLESSNESSES	BOWDLERIZE	BRACHYCEPHALICS
BORBORYGMIC	BOTTLENECKS	BOUNDNESSES	BOWDLERIZED	BRACHYCEPHALIES
BORBORYGMUS	BOTTLENOSE	BOUNTEOUSLY	BOWDLERIZER	BRACHYCEPHALISM
BORDEREAUX	BOTTLENOSES	BOUNTEOUSNESS	BOWDLERIZERS	BRACHYCEPHALOUS
BORDERLAND	BOTTOMINGS	BOUNTEOUSNESSES	BOWDLERIZES	BRACHYCEPHALS

BRACHYCEPHALY	BRADYSEISM	BRAINTEASERS	BRASSIERES	BREADLINES
BRACHYCEROUS	BRADYSEISMS	BRAINWASHED	BRASSINESS	BREADROOMS
BRACHYDACTYL	BRAGADISME	BRAINWASHER	BRASSINESSES	BREADROOTS
BRACHYDACTYLIC	BRAGADISMES	BRAINWASHERS	BRASSWARES	BREADSTICK
BRACHYDACTYLIES	BRAGGADOCIO	BRAINWASHES	BRATPACKER	BREADSTICKS
BRACHYDACTYLISM	BRAGGADOCIOS	BRAINWASHING	BRATPACKERS	BREADSTUFF
BRACHYDACTYLOUS	BRAGGADOCIOUS	BRAINWASHINGS	BRATTICING	BREADSTUFFS
BRACHYDACTYLY	BRAGGARTISM	BRAINWAVES	BRATTICINGS	BREADTHWAYS
BRACHYDIAGONAL	BRAGGARTISMS	BRAMBLIEST	BRATTINESS	BREADTHWISE
BRACHYDIAGONALS	BRAGGARTLY	BRAMBLINGS	BRATTINESSES	BREADWINNER
BRACHYDOME	BRAGGINGLY	BRANCHERIES	BRATTISHED	BREADWINNERS
BRACHYDOMES	BRAHMANISM	BRANCHIATE	BRATTISHES	BREADWINNING
BRACHYGRAPHIES	BRAHMANISMS	BRANCHIEST	BRATTISHING	BREADWINNINGS
BRACHYGRAPHY	BRAHMANIST	BRANCHINGS	BRATTISHINGS	BREAKABLENESS
BRACHYLOGIES	BRAHMANISTS	BRANCHIOPOD	BRATTLINGS	BREAKABLENESSES
BRACHYLOGOUS	BRAHMINISM	BRANCHIOPODS	BRATWURSTS	BREAKABLES
BRACHYLOGY	BRAHMINISMS	BRANCHIOSTEGAL	BRAUNCHING	BREAKAWAYS
BRACHYODONT	BRAHMINIST	BRANCHLESS	BRAUNSCHWEIGER	BREAKBEATS
BRACHYPINAKOID	BRAHMINISTS	BRANCHLETS	BRAUNSCHWEIGERS	BREAKDANCE
BRACHYPINAKOIDS	BRAILLEWRITER	BRANCHLIKE	BRAVADOING	BREAKDANCED
BRACHYPRISM	BRAILLEWRITERS	BRANCHLINE	BRAVENESSES	BREAKDANCER
BRACHYPRISMS	BRAILLISTS	BRANCHLINES	BRAVISSIMO	BREAKDANCERS
BRACHYPTERISM	BRAINBOXES	BRANDERING	BRAWNINESS	BREAKDANCES
BRACHYPTERISMS	BRAINCASES	BRANDISHED	BRAWNINESSES	BREAKDANCING
BRACHYPTEROUS	BRAINCHILD	BRANDISHER	BRAZENNESS	BREAKDANCINGS
BRACHYTHERAPIES	BRAINCHILDREN	BRANDISHERS	BRAZENNESSES	BREAKDOWNS
BRACHYTHERAPY	BRAINFARTS	BRANDISHES	BRAZENRIES	BREAKEVENS
BRACHYURAL	BRAINFOODS	BRANDISHING	BRAZIERIES	BREAKFASTED
BRACHYURAN	BRAININESS	BRANDLINGS	BRAZILEINS	BREAKFASTER
BRACHYURANS	BRAININESSES	BRANDRETHS	BRAZILWOOD	BREAKFASTERS
BRACHYUROUS	BRAINLESSLY	BRANFULNESS	BRAZILWOODS	BREAKFASTING
BRACKETING	BRAINLESSNESS	BRANFULNESSES	BREADBASKET	BREAKFASTS
BRACKETINGS	BRAINLESSNESSES	BRANGLINGS	BREADBASKETS	BREAKFRONT
BRACKISHNESS	BRAINPOWER	BRANKURSINE	BREADBERRIES	BREAKFRONTS
BRACKISHNESSES	BRAINPOWERS	BRANKURSINES	BREADBERRY	BREAKPOINT
BRACTEATES	BRAINSICKLY	BRANNIGANS	BREADBOARD	BREAKPOINTS
BRACTEOLATE	BRAINSICKNESS	BRASHINESS	BREADBOARDED	BREAKTHROUGH
BRACTEOLES	BRAINSICKNESSES	BRASHINESSES	BREADBOARDING	BREAKTHROUGHS
BRADYCARDIA	BRAINSTEMS	BRASHNESSES	BREADBOARDS	BREAKTIMES
BRADYCARDIAC	BRAINSTORM	BRASILEINS	BREADBOXES	BREAKWALLS
BRADYCARDIAS	BRAINSTORMED	BRASSBOUND	BREADCRUMB	BREAKWATER
BRADYKINESIA	BRAINSTORMER	BRASSERIES	BREADCRUMBED	BREAKWATERS
BRADYKINESIAS	BRAINSTORMERS	BRASSFOUNDER	BREADCRUMBING	BREASTBONE
BRADYKININ	BRAINSTORMING	BRASSFOUNDERS	BREADCRUMBS	BREASTBONES
BRADYKININS	BRAINSTORMINGS	BRASSFOUNDING	BREADFRUIT	BREASTFEED
BRADYPEPTIC	BRAINSTORMS	BRASSFOUNDINGS	BREADFRUITS	BREASTFEEDING
BRADYPEPTICS	BRAINTEASER	BRASSICACEOUS	BREADHEADS	BREASTFEEDINGS

BROKERINGS

B

BREASTFEEDS	BRECCIATION	BRICKMAKING	BRIGHTWORKS	BROADBANDS
BREASTPINS	BRECCIATIONS	BRICKMAKINGS	BRILLIANCE	BROADBEANS
BREASTPLATE	BREECHBLOCK	BRICKWALLS	BRILLIANCES	BROADBILLS
BREASTPLATES	BREECHBLOCKS	BRICKWORKS	BRILLIANCIES	BROADBRIMS
BREASTPLOUGH	BREECHCLOTH	BRICKYARDS	BRILLIANCY	BROADBRUSH
BREASTPLOUGHS	BREECHCLOTHS	BRICOLAGES	BRILLIANTE	BROADCASTED
BREASTRAIL	BREECHCLOUT	BRIDECAKES	BRILLIANTED	BROADCASTER
BREASTRAILS	BREECHCLOUTS	BRIDEGROOM	BRILLIANTINE	BROADCASTERS
BREASTSTROKE	BREECHINGS	BRIDEGROOMS	BRILLIANTINES	BROADCASTING
BREASTSTROKER	BREECHLESS	BRIDEMAIDEN	BRILLIANTING	BROADCASTINGS
BREASTSTROKERS	BREECHLOADER	BRIDEMAIDENS	BRILLIANTLY	BROADCASTS
BREASTSTROKES	BREECHLOADERS	BRIDEMAIDS	BRILLIANTNESS	BROADCLOTH
BREASTSUMMER	BREEZELESS	BRIDESMAID	BRILLIANTNESSES	BROADCLOTHS
BREASTSUMMERS	BREEZEWAYS	BRIDESMAIDS	BRILLIANTS	BROADENERS
BREASTWORK	BREEZINESS	BRIDEWEALTH	BRIMFULLNESS	BROADENING
BREASTWORKS	BREEZINESSES	BRIDEWEALTHS	BRIMFULLNESSES	BROADLEAVES
BREATHABILITIES	BREMSSTRAHLUNG	BRIDEWELLS	BRIMFULNESS	BROADLINES
BREATHABILITY	BREMSSTRAHLUNGS	BRIDGEABLE	BRIMFULNESSES	BROADLOOMS
BREATHABLE	BRESSUMMER	BRIDGEBOARD	BRIMSTONES	BROADNESSES
BREATHALYSE	BRESSUMMERS	BRIDGEBOARDS	BRINELLING	BROADPIECE
BREATHALYSED	BRETASCHES	BRIDGEHEAD	BRINELLINGS	BROADPIECES
BREATHALYSER	BRETTICING	BRIDGEHEADS	BRINGDOWNS	BROADSCALE
BREATHALYSERS	BREUNNERITE	BRIDGELESS	BRININESSES	BROADSHEET
BREATHALYSES	BREUNNERITES	BRIDGEWORK	BRINJARRIES	BROADSHEETS
BREATHALYSING	BREVETCIES	BRIDGEWORKS	BRINKMANSHIP	BROADSIDED
BREATHALYZE	BREVETTING	BRIDLEWAYS	BRINKMANSHIPS	BROADSIDES
BREATHALYZED	BREVIARIES	BRIDLEWISE	BRINKSMANSHIP	BROADSIDING
BREATHALYZER	BREVIPENNATE	BRIEFCASES	BRINKSMANSHIPS	BROADSWORD
BREATHALYZERS	BREWMASTER	BRIEFNESSES	BRIOLETTES	BROADSWORDS
BREATHALYZES	BREWMASTERS	BRIERROOTS	BRIQUETTED	BROADTAILS
BREATHALYZING	BRIARROOTS	BRIERWOODS	BRIQUETTES	BROBDINGNAGIAN
BREATHARIAN	BRIARWOODS	BRIGADIERS	BRIQUETTING	BROCATELLE
BREATHARIANISM	BRICABRACS	BRIGANDAGE	BRISKENING	BROCATELLES
BREATHARIANISMS	BRICKCLAYS	BRIGANDAGES	BRISKNESSES	BROCCOLINI
BREATHARIANS	BRICKEARTH	BRIGANDINE	BRISTLECONE	BROCCOLINIS
BREATHIEST	BRICKEARTHS	BRIGANDINES	BRISTLECONES	BROCHETTES
BREATHINESS	BRICKFIELD	BRIGANDRIES	BRISTLELIKE	BROGUERIES
BREATHINESSES	BRICKFIELDER	BRIGANTINE	BRISTLETAIL	BROIDERERS
BREATHINGS	BRICKFIELDERS	BRIGANTINES	BRISTLETAILS	BROIDERIES
BREATHLESS	BRICKFIELDS	BRIGHTENED	BRISTLIEST	BROIDERING
BREATHLESSLY	BRICKKILNS	BRIGHTENER	BRISTLINESS	BROIDERINGS
BREATHLESSNESS	BRICKLAYER	BRIGHTENERS	BRISTLINESSES	BROKENHEARTED
BREATHTAKING	BRICKLAYERS	BRIGHTENING	BRITANNIAS	BROKENHEARTEDLY
BREATHTAKINGLY	BRICKLAYING	BRIGHTNESS	BRITSCHKAS	BROKENNESS
BRECCIATED	BRICKLAYINGS	BRIGHTNESSES	BRITTANIAS	BROKENNESSES
BRECCIATES	BRICKMAKER	BRIGHTSOME	BRITTLENESS	BROKERAGES
BRECCIATING	BRICKMAKERS	BRIGHTWORK	BRITTLENESSES	BROKERINGS

BROMEGRASS
BROMEGRASSES
BROMELAINS
BROMELIACEOUS
BROMELIADS
BROMEOSINS
BROMHIDROSES
BROMHIDROSIS
BROMIDROSES
BROMIDROSIS
BROMINATED
BROMINATES
BROMINATING
BROMINATION
BROMINATIONS
BROMINISMS
BROMOCRIPTINE
BROMOCRIPTINES
BROMOFORMS
BROMOURACIL
BROMOURACILS
BRONCHIALLY
BRONCHIECTASES
BRONCHIECTASIS
BRONCHIOLAR
BRONCHIOLE
BRONCHIOLES
BRONCHIOLITIS
BRONCHIOLITISES
BRONCHITIC
BRONCHITICS
BRONCHITIS
BRONCHITISES
BRONCHODILATOR
BRONCHODILATORS
BRONCHOGENIC
BRONCHOGRAPHIES
BRONCHOGRAPHY
BRONCHOSCOPE
BRONCHOSCOPES
BRONCHOSCOPIC
BRONCHOSCOPICAL
BRONCHOSCOPIES
BRONCHOSCOPIST
BRONCHOSCOPISTS
BRONCHOSCOPY
BRONCHOSPASM

BRONCHOSPASMS
BRONCHOSPASTIC
BRONCOBUSTER
BRONCOBUSTERS
BRONDYRONS
BRONTOBYTE
BRONTOBYTES
BRONTOSAUR
BRONTOSAURS
BRONTOSAURUS
BRONTOSAURUSES
BRONZIFIED
BRONZIFIES
BRONZIFYING
BROODINESS
BROODINESSES
BROODINGLY
BROODMARES
BROOKLIMES
BROOKWEEDS
BROOMBALLER
BROOMBALLERS
BROOMBALLS
BROOMCORNS
BROOMRAPES
BROOMSTAFF
BROOMSTAFFS
BROOMSTICK
BROOMSTICKS
BROTHERHOOD
BROTHERHOODS
BROTHERING
BROTHERLIKE
BROTHERLINESS
BROTHERLINESSES
BROUGHTASES
BROWALLIAS
BROWBEATEN
BROWBEATER
BROWBEATERS
BROWBEATING
BROWBEATINGS
BROWNFIELD
BROWNFIELDS
BROWNNESSES
BROWNNOSED
BROWNNOSER

BROWNNOSERS
BROWNNOSES
BROWNNOSING
BROWNSHIRT
BROWNSHIRTS
BROWNSTONE
BROWNSTONES
BROWRIDGES
BROWSABLES
BRUCELLOSES
BRUCELLOSIS
BRUGMANSIA
BRUGMANSIAS
BRUMMAGEMS
BRUSCHETTA
BRUSCHETTAS
BRUSCHETTE
BRUSHABILITIES
BRUSHABILITY
BRUSHBACKS
BRUSHFIRES
BRUSHLANDS
BRUSHMARKS
BRUSHWHEEL
BRUSHWHEELS
BRUSHWOODS
BRUSHWORKS
BRUSQUENESS
BRUSQUENESSES
BRUSQUERIE
BRUSQUERIES
BRUTALISATION
BRUTALISATIONS
BRUTALISED
BRUTALISES
BRUTALISING
BRUTALISMS
BRUTALISTS
BRUTALITIES
BRUTALIZATION
BRUTALIZATIONS
BRUTALIZED
BRUTALIZES
BRUTALIZING
BRUTENESSES
BRUTIFYING
BRUTISHNESS

BRUTISHNESSES
BRYOLOGICAL
BRYOLOGIES
BRYOLOGIST
BRYOLOGISTS
BRYOPHYLLUM
BRYOPHYLLUMS
BRYOPHYTES
BRYOPHYTIC
BUBBLEGUMS
BUBBLEHEAD
BUBBLEHEADED
BUBBLEHEADS
BUBONOCELE
BUBONOCELES
BUCCANEERED
BUCCANEERING
BUCCANEERINGS
BUCCANEERISH
BUCCANEERS
BUCCANIERED
BUCCANIERING
BUCCANIERS
BUCCINATOR
BUCCINATORS
BUCCINATORY
BUCELLASES
BUCENTAURS
BUCKBOARDS
BUCKBRUSHES
BUCKETFULS
BUCKETINGS
BUCKETSFUL
BUCKHOUNDS
BUCKJUMPER
BUCKJUMPERS
BUCKJUMPING
BUCKJUMPINGS
BUCKLERING
BUCKRAMING
BUCKSHISHED
BUCKSHISHES
BUCKSHISHING
BUCKSKINNED
BUCKTHORNS
BUCKTOOTHED
BUCKWHEATS

BUCKYBALLS
BUCKYTUBES
BUCOLICALLY
BUDGERIGAR
BUDGERIGARS
BUDGETEERS
BUFFALOBERRIES
BUFFALOBERRY
BUFFALOFISH
BUFFALOFISHES
BUFFALOING
BUFFETINGS
BUFFLEHEAD
BUFFLEHEADS
BUFFOONERIES
BUFFOONERY
BUFFOONISH
BUFOTALINS
BUFOTENINE
BUFOTENINES
BUGGINESSES
BUGLEWEEDS
BUHRSTONES
BUILDDOWNS
BUIRDLIEST
BULBIFEROUS
BULBOSITIES
BULBOUSNESS
BULBOUSNESSES
BULGINESSES
BULKINESSES
BULLBAITING
BULLBAITINGS
BULLBRIERS
BULLDOGGED
BULLDOGGER
BULLDOGGERS
BULLDOGGING
BULLDOGGINGS
BULLDOZERS
BULLDOZING
BULLETINED
BULLETINING
BULLETPROOF
BULLETPROOFED
BULLETPROOFING
BULLETPROOFS

BULLETRIES	BUMBERSHOOT	BUREAUCRATESE	BURNETTIZED	BUSHWALKINGS
BULLETWOOD	BUMBERSHOOTS	BUREAUCRATESES	BURNETTIZES	BUSHWHACKED
BULLETWOODS	BUMBLEBEES	BUREAUCRATIC	BURNETTIZING	BUSHWHACKER
BULLFIGHTER	BUMBLEBERRIES	BUREAUCRATISE	BURNISHABLE	BUSHWHACKERS
BULLFIGHTERS	BUMBLEBERRY	BUREAUCRATISED	BURNISHERS	BUSHWHACKING
BULLFIGHTING	BUMBLEDOMS	BUREAUCRATISES	BURNISHING	BUSHWHACKINGS
BULLFIGHTINGS	BUMBLINGLY	BUREAUCRATISING	BURNISHINGS	BUSHWHACKS
BULLFIGHTS	BUMFREEZER	BUREAUCRATISM	BURNISHMENT	BUSINESSES
BULLFINCHES	BUMFREEZERS	BUREAUCRATISMS	BURNISHMENTS	BUSINESSLIKE
BULLHEADED	BUMFUZZLED	BUREAUCRATIST	BURRAMUNDI	BUSINESSMAN
BULLHEADEDLY	BUMFUZZLES	BUREAUCRATISTS	BURRAMUNDIS	BUSINESSMEN
BULLHEADEDNESS	BUMFUZZLING	BUREAUCRATIZE	BURRAMYSES	BUSINESSPEOPLE
BULLIONIST	BUMMALOTIS	BUREAUCRATIZED	BURRAWANGS	BUSINESSPERSON
BULLIONISTS	BUMPINESSES	BUREAUCRATIZES	BURROWSTOWN	BUSINESSPERSONS
BULLISHNESS	BUMPKINISH	BUREAUCRATIZING	BURROWSTOWNS	BUSINESSWOMAN
BULLISHNESSES	BUMPOLOGIES	BUREAUCRATS	BURRSTONES	BUSINESSWOMEN
BULLMASTIFF	BUMPSADAISY	BURGEONING	BURSARSHIP	BUSTICATED
BULLMASTIFFS	BUMPTIOUSLY	BURGLARIES	BURSARSHIPS	BUSTICATES
BULLNECKED	BUMPTIOUSNESS	BURGLARING	BURSERACEOUS	BUSTICATING
BULLOCKIES	BUMPTIOUSNESSES	BURGLARIOUS	BURSICULATE	BUSTINESSES
BULLOCKING	BUMSUCKERS	BURGLARIOUSLY	BURSITISES	BUSTLINGLY
BULLROARER	BUMSUCKING	BURGLARISE	BURTHENING	BUSYBODIED
BULLROARERS	BUMSUCKINGS	BURGLARISED	BURTHENSOME	BUSYBODIES
BULLRUSHES	BUNCHBERRIES	BURGLARISES	BUSHBABIES	BUSYBODYING
BULLSHITTED	BUNCHBERRY	BURGLARISING	BUSHBASHING	BUSYBODYINGS
BULLSHITTER	BUNCHGRASS	BURGLARIZE	BUSHBASHINGS	BUSYNESSES
BULLSHITTERS	BUNCHGRASSES	BURGLARIZED	BUSHCRAFTS	BUTADIENES
BULLSHITTING	BUNCHINESS	BURGLARIZES	BUSHELLERS	BUTCHERBIRD
BULLSHITTINGS	BUNCHINESSES	BURGLARIZING	BUSHELLING	BUTCHERBIRDS
BULLSNAKES	BUNDOBUSTS	BURGLARPROOF	BUSHELLINGS	BUTCHERERS
BULLTERRIER	BUNGALOIDS	BURGOMASTER	BUSHELWOMAN	BUTCHERIES
BULLTERRIERS	BUNGLESOME	BURGOMASTERS	BUSHELWOMEN	BUTCHERING
BULLWADDIE	BUNGLINGLY	BURGUNDIES	BUSHHAMMER	BUTCHERINGS
BULLWADDIES	BUNKHOUSES	BURLADEROS	BUSHHAMMERS	BUTCHNESSES
BULLWHACKED	BUOYANCIES	BURLESQUED	BUSHINESSES	BUTENEDIOIC
BULLWHACKING	BUOYANTNESS	BURLESQUELY	BUSHMANSHIP	BUTEONINES
BULLWHACKS	BUOYANTNESSES	BURLESQUER	BUSHMANSHIPS	BUTLERAGES
BULLWHIPPED	BUPIVACAINE	BURLESQUERS	BUSHMASTER	BUTLERSHIP
BULLWHIPPING	BUPIVACAINES	BURLESQUES	BUSHMASTERS	BUTLERSHIPS
BULLYCIDES	BUPRENORPHINE	BURLESQUING	BUSHRANGER	BUTTERBALL
BULLYRAGGED	BUPRENORPHINES	BURLEYCUES	BUSHRANGERS	BUTTERBALLS
BULLYRAGGING	BUPRESTIDS	BURLINESSES	BUSHRANGING	BUTTERBURS
BULWADDEES	BUPROPIONS	BURNETTISE	BUSHRANGINGS	BUTTERCUPS
BULWADDIES	BURDENSOME	BURNETTISED	BUSHWALKED	BUTTERDOCK
BULWARKING	BUREAUCRACIES	BURNETTISES	BUSHWALKER	BUTTERDOCKS
BUMBAILIFF	BUREAUCRACY	BURNETTISING	BUSHWALKERS	BUTTERFATS
BUMBAILIFFS	BUREAUCRAT	BURNETTIZE	BUSHWALKING	BUTTERFINGERED

BUTTERFINGERS
BUTTERFISH
BUTTERFISHES
BUTTERFLIED
BUTTERFLIES
BUTTERFLYER
BUTTERFLYERS
BUTTERFLYING
BUTTERIEST
BUTTERINES
BUTTERINESS
BUTTERINESSES
BUTTERLESS
BUTTERMILK

BUTTERMILKS
BUTTERNUTS
BUTTERSCOTCH
BUTTERSCOTCHES
BUTTERWEED
BUTTERWEEDS
BUTTERWORT
BUTTERWORTS
BUTTINSKIES
BUTTINSKIS
BUTTOCKING
BUTTONBALL
BUTTONBALLS
BUTTONBUSH

BUTTONBUSHES
BUTTONHELD
BUTTONHOLD
BUTTONHOLDING
BUTTONHOLDS
BUTTONHOLE
BUTTONHOLED
BUTTONHOLER
BUTTONHOLERS
BUTTONHOLES
BUTTONHOLING
BUTTONHOOK
BUTTONHOOKED
BUTTONHOOKING

BUTTONHOOKS
BUTTONLESS
BUTTONMOULD
BUTTONMOULDS
BUTTONWOOD
BUTTONWOODS
BUTTRESSED
BUTTRESSES
BUTTRESSING
BUTTSTOCKS
BUTYLATING
BUTYLATION
BUTYLATIONS
BUTYRACEOUS

BUTYRALDEHYDE
BUTYRALDEHYDES
BUTYROPHENONE
BUTYROPHENONES
BUXOMNESSES
BUZZKILLER
BUZZKILLERS
BYPRODUCTS
BYSSACEOUS
BYSSINOSES
BYSSINOSIS
BYSTANDERS
BYTOWNITES

C

CABALETTAS	CACKLEBERRY	CADDISWORM	CALABOOSES	CALCIMINES
CABALISTIC	CACODAEMON	CADDISWORMS	CALABRESES	CALCIMINING
CABALISTICAL	CACODAEMONS	CADETSHIPS	CALAMANCOES	CALCINABLE
CABALLEROS	CACODEMONIC	CADUCITIES	CALAMANCOS	CALCINATION
CABBAGETOWN	CACODEMONS	CAECILIANS	CALAMANDER	CALCINATIONS
CABBAGETOWNS	CACODOXIES	CAECITISES	CALAMANDERS	CALCINOSES
CABBAGEWORM	CACOEPISTIC	CAENOGENESES	CALAMARIES	CALCINOSIS
CABBAGEWORMS	CACOGASTRIC	CAENOGENESIS	CALAMINING	CALCITONIN
CABBALISMS	CACOGENICS	CAENOGENETIC	CALAMITIES	CALCITONINS
CABBALISTIC	CACOGRAPHER	CAESALPINOID	CALAMITOUS	CALCSINTER
CABBALISTICAL	CACOGRAPHERS	CAESAREANS	CALAMITOUSLY	CALCSINTERS
CABBALISTS	CACOGRAPHIC	CAESARIANS	CALAMITOUSNESS	CALCULABILITIES
CABDRIVERS	CACOGRAPHICAL	CAESARISMS	CALAMONDIN	CALCULABILITY
CABINETMAKER	CACOGRAPHIES	CAESAROPAPISM	CALAMONDINS	CALCULABLE
CABINETMAKERS	CACOGRAPHY	CAESAROPAPISMS	CALANDRIAS	CALCULABLY
CABINETMAKING	CACOLOGIES	CAESPITOSE	CALAVANCES	CALCULATED
CABINETMAKINGS	CACOMISTLE	CAESPITOSELY	CALAVERITE	CALCULATEDLY
CABINETRIES	CACOMISTLES	CAFETERIAS	CALAVERITES	CALCULATEDNESS
CABINETWORK	CACOMIXLES	CAFETIERES	CALCAREOUS	CALCULATES
CABINETWORKS	CACONYMIES	CAFETORIUM	CALCAREOUSLY	CALCULATING
CABINMATES	CACOPHONIC	CAFETORIUMS	CALCARIFEROUS	CALCULATINGLY
CABLECASTED	CACOPHONICAL	CAFFEINATED	CALCARIFORM	CALCULATION
CABLECASTING	CACOPHONICALLY	CAFFEINISM	CALCEAMENTA	CALCULATIONAL
CABLECASTS	CACOPHONIES	CAFFEINISMS	CALCEAMENTUM	CALCULATIONS
CABLEGRAMS	CACOPHONIOUS	CAGEYNESSES	CALCEATING	CALCULATIVE
CABLEVISION	CACOPHONOUS	CAGINESSES	CALCEDONIES	CALCULATOR
CABLEVISIONS	CACOPHONOUSLY	CAGMAGGING	CALCEDONIO	CALCULATORS
CABRIOLETS	CACOTOPIAN	CAGYNESSES	CALCEDONIOS	CALCULUSES
CACAFUEGOS	CACOTOPIAS	CAILLEACHS	CALCEIFORM	CALEFACIENT
CACCIATORA	CACOTROPHIES	CAILLIACHS	CALCEOLARIA	CALEFACIENTS
CACCIATORE	CACOTROPHY	CAINOGENESES	CALCEOLARIAS	CALEFACTION
CACHAEMIAS	CACTACEOUS	CAINOGENESIS	CALCEOLATE	CALEFACTIONS
CACHECTICAL	CACTOBLASTES	CAINOGENETIC	CALCICOLES	CALEFACTIVE
CACHINNATE	CACTOBLASTIS	CAIRNGORMS	CALCICOLOUS	CALEFACTOR
CACHINNATED	CACUMINALS	CAJOLEMENT	CALCIFEROL	CALEFACTORIES
CACHINNATES	CACUMINOUS	CAJOLEMENTS	CALCIFEROLS	CALEFACTORS
CACHINNATING	CADASTRALLY	CAJOLERIES	CALCIFEROUS	CALEFACTORY
CACHINNATION	CADAVERINE	CAJOLINGLY	CALCIFICATION	CALEMBOURS
CACHINNATIONS	CADAVERINES	CAKEWALKED	CALCIFICATIONS	CALENDARED
CACHINNATORY	CADAVEROUS	CAKEWALKER	CALCIFUGAL	CALENDARER
CACHOLONGS	CADAVEROUSLY	CAKEWALKERS	CALCIFUGES	CALENDARERS
CACIQUISMS	CADAVEROUSNESS	CAKEWALKING	CALCIFUGOUS	CALENDARING
CACKERMANDER	CADDISFLIES	CAKINESSES	CALCIFYING	CALENDARISATION
CACKERMANDERS	CADDISHNESS	CALABASHES	CALCIGEROUS	CALENDARISE
CACKLEBERRIES	CADDISHNESSES	CALABOGUSES	CALCIMINED	CALENDARISED

CALENDARISES	CALLIATURES	CALORIFICATIONS	CAMELBACKS	CAMPANOLOGY
CALENDARISING	CALLIDITIES	CALORIFIER	CAMELEOPARD	CAMPANULACEOUS
CALENDARIST	CALLIGRAMME	CALORIFIERS	CAMELEOPARDS	CAMPANULAR
CALENDARISTS	CALLIGRAMMES	CALORIMETER	CAMELHAIRS	CAMPANULAS
CALENDARIZATION	CALLIGRAMS	CALORIMETERS	CAMELOPARD	CAMPANULATE
CALENDARIZE	CALLIGRAPHER	CALORIMETRIC	CAMELOPARDS	CAMPCRAFTS
CALENDARIZED	CALLIGRAPHERS	CALORIMETRICAL	CAMERAPERSON	CAMPEADORS
CALENDARIZES	CALLIGRAPHIC	CALORIMETRIES	CAMERAPERSONS	CAMPESINOS
CALENDARIZING	CALLIGRAPHICAL	CALORIMETRY	CAMERATION	CAMPESTRAL
CALENDERED	CALLIGRAPHIES	CALORISING	CAMERATIONS	CAMPESTRIAN
CALENDERER	CALLIGRAPHIST	CALORIZING	CAMERAWOMAN	CAMPGROUND
CALENDERERS	CALLIGRAPHISTS	CALOTYPIST	CAMERAWOMEN	CAMPGROUNDS
CALENDERING	CALLIGRAPHY	CALOTYPISTS	CAMERAWORK	CAMPHORACEOUS
CALENDERINGS	CALLIOPSIS	CALUMNIABLE	CAMERAWORKS	CAMPHORATE
CALENDRERS	CALLIPASHES	CALUMNIATE	CAMERLENGO	CAMPHORATED
CALENDRICAL	CALLIPERED	CALUMNIATED	CAMERLENGOS	CAMPHORATES
CALENDRIES	CALLIPERING	CALUMNIATES	CAMERLINGO	CAMPHORATING
CALENDULAS	CALLIPYGEAN	CALUMNIATING	CAMERLINGOS	CAMPIMETRIES
CALENTURES	CALLIPYGIAN	CALUMNIATION	CAMIKNICKERS	CAMPIMETRY
CALESCENCE	CALLIPYGOUS	CALUMNIATIONS	CAMIKNICKS	CAMPINESSES
CALESCENCES	CALLISTEMON	CALUMNIATOR	CAMISADOES	CAMPNESSES
CALFDOZERS	CALLISTEMONS	CALUMNIATORS	CAMORRISTA	CAMPODEIDS
CALIATOURS	CALLISTHENIC	CALUMNIATORY	CAMORRISTI	CAMPODEIFORM
CALIBRATED	CALLISTHENICS	CALUMNIOUS	CAMORRISTS	CAMPSHIRTS
CALIBRATER	CALLITHUMP	CALUMNIOUSLY	CAMOUFLAGE	CAMPSTOOLS
CALIBRATERS	CALLITHUMPIAN	CALVADOSES	CAMOUFLAGEABLE	CAMPYLOBACTER
CALIBRATES	CALLITHUMPS	CALVARIUMS	CAMOUFLAGED	CAMPYLOBACTERS
CALIBRATING	CALLOSITIES	CALYCANTHEMIES	CAMOUFLAGES	CAMPYLOTROPOUS
CALIBRATION	CALLOUSING	CALYCANTHEMY	CAMOUFLAGIC	CAMSTEERIE
CALIBRATIONS	CALLOUSNESS	CALYCANTHUS	CAMOUFLAGING	CANALBOATS
CALIBRATOR	CALLOUSNESSES	CALYCANTHUSES	CAMOUFLETS	CANALICULAR
CALIBRATORS	CALLOWNESS	CALYCIFORM	CAMOUFLEUR	CANALICULATE
CALIDITIES	CALLOWNESSES	CALYCOIDEOUS	CAMOUFLEURS	CANALICULATED
CALIFORNIUM	CALMATIVES	CALYCULATE	CAMPAIGNED	CANALICULI
CALIFORNIUMS	CALMNESSES	CALYPSONIAN	CAMPAIGNER	CANALICULUS
CALIGINOSITIES	CALMODULIN	CALYPSONIANS	CAMPAIGNERS	CANALISATION
CALIGINOSITY	CALMODULINS	CALYPTERAS	CAMPAIGNING	CANALISATIONS
CALIGINOUS	CALMSTANES	CALYPTRATE	CAMPANEROS	CANALISING
CALIMOCHOS	CALMSTONES	CALYPTROGEN	CAMPANIFORM	CANALIZATION
CALIOLOGIES	CALORESCENCE	CALYPTROGENS	CAMPANILES	CANALIZATIONS
CALIPASHES	CALORESCENCES	CAMANACHDS	CAMPANISTS	CANALIZING
CALIPERING	CALORESCENT	CAMARADERIE	CAMPANOLOGER	CANCELABLE
CALIPHATES	CALORICALLY	CAMARADERIES	CAMPANOLOGERS	CANCELATION
CALISTHENIC	CALORICITIES	CAMARILLAS	CAMPANOLOGICAL	CANCELATIONS
CALISTHENICS	CALORICITY	CAMBERINGS	CAMPANOLOGIES	CANCELBOTS
CALLBOARDS	CALORIFICALLY	CAMBISTRIES	CAMPANOLOGIST	CANCELEERED
CALLIATURE	CALORIFICATION	CAMCORDERS	CAMPANOLOGISTS	CANCELEERING

CANCELEERS	CANDIDIASIS	CANISTERIZE	CANNULATIONS	CANTHARIDINS
CANCELIERED	CANDIDNESS	CANISTERIZED	CANOEWOODS	CANTHARIDS
CANCELIERING	CANDIDNESSES	CANISTERIZES	CANONESSES	CANTHAXANTHIN
CANCELIERS	CANDLEBERRIES	CANISTERIZING	CANONICALLY	CANTHAXANTHINE
CANCELLABLE	CANDLEBERRY	CANKEREDLY	CANONICALS	CANTHAXANTHINES
CANCELLARIAL	CANDLEFISH	CANKEREDNESS	CANONICATE	CANTHAXANTHINS
CANCELLARIAN	CANDLEFISHES	CANKEREDNESSES	CANONICATES	CANTHITISES
CANCELLARIATE	CANDLEHOLDER	CANKERWORM	CANONICITIES	CANTICOING
CANCELLARIATES	CANDLEHOLDERS	CANKERWORMS	CANONICITY	CANTICOYED
CANCELLATE	CANDLELIGHT	CANNABINOID	CANONISATION	CANTICOYING
CANCELLATED	CANDLELIGHTED	CANNABINOIDS	CANONISATIONS	CANTILENAS
CANCELLATION	CANDLELIGHTER	CANNABINOL	CANONISERS	CANTILEVER
CANCELLATIONS	CANDLELIGHTERS	CANNABINOLS	CANONISING	CANTILEVERED
CANCELLERS	CANDLELIGHTS	CANNABISES	CANONISTIC	CANTILEVERING
CANCELLING	CANDLENUTS	CANNELLINI	CANONIZATION	CANTILEVERS
CANCELLOUS	CANDLEPINS	CANNELLONI	CANONIZATIONS	CANTILLATE
CANCERATED	CANDLEPOWER	CANNELURES	CANONIZERS	CANTILLATED
CANCERATES	CANDLEPOWERS	CANNIBALISATION	CANONIZING	CANTILLATES
CANCERATING	CANDLESNUFFER	CANNIBALISE	CANOODLERS	CANTILLATING
CANCERATION	CANDLESNUFFERS	CANNIBALISED	CANOODLING	CANTILLATION
CANCERATIONS	CANDLESTICK	CANNIBALISES	CANOPHILIA	CANTILLATIONS
CANCEROPHOBIA	CANDLESTICKS	CANNIBALISING	CANOPHILIAS	CANTILLATORY
CANCEROPHOBIAS	CANDLEWICK	CANNIBALISM	CANOPHILIST	CANTINESSES
CANCEROUSLY	CANDLEWICKS	CANNIBALISMS	CANOPHILISTS	CANTONISATION
CANCERPHOBIA	CANDLEWOOD	CANNIBALISTIC	CANOPHOBIA	CANTONISATIONS
CANCERPHOBIAS	CANDLEWOODS	CANNIBALIZATION	CANOPHOBIAS	CANTONISED
CANCIONERO	CANDYFLOSS	CANNIBALIZE	CANOROUSLY	CANTONISES
CANCIONEROS	CANDYFLOSSES	CANNIBALIZED	CANOROUSNESS	CANTONISING
CANCRIFORM	CANDYGRAMS	CANNIBALIZES	CANOROUSNESSES	CANTONIZATION
CANCRIZANS	CANDYTUFTS	CANNIBALIZING	CANTABANKS	CANTONIZATIONS
CANDELABRA	CANEBRAKES	CANNIBALLY	CANTABILES	CANTONIZED
CANDELABRAS	CANEFRUITS	CANNINESSES	CANTALOUPE	CANTONIZES
CANDELABRUM	CANEPHORAS	CANNISTERS	CANTALOUPES	CANTONIZING
CANDELABRUMS	CANEPHORES	CANNONADED	CANTALOUPS	CANTONMENT
CANDELILLA	CANEPHORUS	CANNONADES	CANTANKEROUS	CANTONMENTS
CANDELILLAS	CANEPHORUSES	CANNONADING	CANTANKEROUSLY	CANULATING
CANDESCENCE	CANESCENCE	CANNONBALL	CANTATRICE	CANULATION
CANDESCENCES	CANESCENCES	CANNONBALLED	CANTATRICES	CANULATIONS
CANDESCENT	CANINITIES	CANNONBALLING	CANTATRICI	CANVASBACK
CANDESCENTLY	CANISTERED	CANNONBALLS	CANTERBURIES	CANVASBACKS
CANDIDACIES	CANISTERING	CANNONEERS	CANTERBURY	CANVASLIKE
CANDIDATES	CANISTERISATION	CANNONIERS	CANTERBURYS	CANVASSERS
CANDIDATESHIP	CANISTERISE	CANNONRIES	CANTHARIDAL	CANVASSING
CANDIDATESHIPS	CANISTERISED	CANNULATED	CANTHARIDES	CANVASSINGS
CANDIDATURE	CANISTERISES	CANNULATES	CANTHARIDIAN	CANYONEERS
CANDIDATURES	CANISTERISING	CANNULATING	CANTHARIDIC	CANYONINGS
CANDIDIASES	CANISTERIZATION	CANNULATION	CANTHARIDIN	CANZONETTA

CANZONETTAS	CAPITALISATION	CAPPARIDACEOUS	CAPTIVATED	CARAVANCES
CANZONETTE	CAPITALISATIONS	CAPPELLETTI	CAPTIVATES	CARAVANEER
CAOUTCHOUC	CAPITALISE	CAPPERNOITIES	CAPTIVATING	CARAVANEERS
CAOUTCHOUCS	CAPITALISED	CAPPERNOITY	CAPTIVATINGLY	CARAVANERS
CAPABILITIES	CAPITALISES	CAPPUCCINI	CAPTIVATION	CARAVANETTE
CAPABILITY	CAPITALISING	CAPPUCCINO	CAPTIVATIONS	CARAVANETTES
CAPABLENESS	CAPITALISM	CAPPUCCINOS	CAPTIVATOR	CARAVANING
CAPABLENESSES	CAPITALISMS	CAPREOLATE	CAPTIVATORS	CARAVANINGS
CAPACIOUSLY	CAPITALIST	CAPRICCIOS	CAPTIVAUNCE	CARAVANNED
CAPACIOUSNESS	CAPITALISTIC	CAPRICCIOSO	CAPTIVAUNCES	CARAVANNER
CAPACIOUSNESSES	CAPITALISTS	CAPRICIOUS	CAPTIVITIES	CARAVANNERS
CAPACITANCE	CAPITALIZATION	CAPRICIOUSLY	CAPTOPRILS	CARAVANNING
CAPACITANCES	CAPITALIZATIONS	CAPRICIOUSNESS	CARABINEER	CARAVANNINGS
CAPACITATE	CAPITALIZE	CAPRIFICATION	CARABINEERS	CARAVANSARAI
CAPACITATED	CAPITALIZED	CAPRIFICATIONS	CARABINERO	CARAVANSARAIS
CAPACITATES	CAPITALIZES	CAPRIFOILS	CARABINEROS	CARAVANSARIES
CAPACITATING	CAPITALIZING	CAPRIFOLES	CARABINERS	CARAVANSARY
CAPACITATION	CAPITATION	CAPRIFOLIACEOUS	CARABINIER	CARAVANSERAI
CAPACITATIONS	CAPITATIONS	CAPRIFYING	CARABINIERE	CARAVANSERAIS
CAPACITIES	CAPITATIVE	CAPRIOLING	CARABINIERI	CARAVELLES
CAPACITIVE	CAPITELLUM	CAPROLACTAM	CARABINIERS	CARBACHOLS
CAPACITIVELY	CAPITOLIAN	CAPROLACTAMS	CARACOLERS	CARBAMATES
CAPACITORS	CAPITOLINE	CAPRYLATES	CARACOLING	CARBAMAZEPINE
CAPARISONED	CAPITULANT	CAPSAICINS	CARACOLLED	CARBAMAZEPINES
CAPARISONING	CAPITULANTS	CAPSIZABLE	CARACOLLING	CARBAMIDES
CAPARISONS	CAPITULARIES	CAPSOMERES	CARAGEENAN	CARBAMIDINE
CAPELLINES	CAPITULARLY	CAPSULATED	CARAGEENANS	CARBAMIDINES
CAPELLMEISTER	CAPITULARS	CAPSULATION	CARAMBOLAS	CARBAMOYLS
CAPELLMEISTERS	CAPITULARY	CAPSULATIONS	CARAMBOLED	CARBANIONS
CAPERCAILLIE	CAPITULATE	CAPSULISED	CARAMBOLES	CARBAZOLES
CAPERCAILLIES	CAPITULATED	CAPSULISES	CARAMBOLING	CARBIMAZOLE
CAPERCAILZIE	CAPITULATES	CAPSULISING	CARAMELISATION	CARBIMAZOLES
CAPERCAILZIES	CAPITULATING	CAPSULIZED	CARAMELISATIONS	CARBINEERS
CAPERINGLY	CAPITULATION	CAPSULIZES	CARAMELISE	CARBINIERS
CAPERNOITED	CAPITULATIONS	CAPSULIZING	CARAMELISED	CARBOCYCLIC
CAPERNOITIE	CAPITULATOR	CAPTAINCIES	CARAMELISES	CARBOHYDRASE
CAPERNOITIES	CAPITULATORS	CAPTAINING	CARAMELISING	CARBOHYDRASES
CAPERNOITY	CAPITULATORY	CAPTAINRIES	CARAMELIZATION	CARBOHYDRATE
CAPILLACEOUS	CAPNOMANCIES	CAPTAINSHIP	CARAMELIZATIONS	CARBOHYDRATES
CAPILLAIRE	CAPNOMANCY	CAPTAINSHIPS	CARAMELIZE	CARBOLATED
CAPILLAIRES	CAPOCCHIAS	CAPTIONING	CARAMELIZED	CARBOLISED
CAPILLARIES	CAPODASTRO	CAPTIONLESS	CARAMELIZES	CARBOLISES
CAPILLARITIES	CAPODASTROS	CAPTIOUSLY	CARAMELIZING	CARBOLISING
CAPILLARITY	CAPONIERES	CAPTIOUSNESS	CARAMELLED	CARBOLIZED
CAPILLITIA	CAPONISING	CAPTIOUSNESSES	CARAMELLING	CARBOLIZES
CAPILLITIUM	CAPONIZING	CAPTIVANCE	CARANGOIDS	CARBOLIZING
CAPILLITIUMS	CAPOTASTOS	CAPTIVANCES	CARAPACIAL	CARBONACEOUS

C

CARBONADES	CARBOXYLATION	CARCINOLOGIST	CARDIOLOGIST	CARETAKERS
CARBONADOED	CARBOXYLATIONS	CARCINOLOGISTS	CARDIOLOGISTS	CARETAKING
CARBONADOES	CARBOXYLIC	CARCINOLOGY	CARDIOLOGY	CARETAKINGS
CARBONADOING	CARBUNCLED	CARCINOMAS	CARDIOMEGALIES	CAREWORKER
CARBONADOS	CARBUNCLES	CARCINOMATA	CARDIOMEGALY	CAREWORKERS
CARBONARAS	CARBUNCULAR	CARCINOMATOID	CARDIOMOTOR	CARFUFFLED
CARBONATED	CARBURATED	CARCINOMATOSES	CARDIOMYOPATHY	CARFUFFLES
CARBONATES	CARBURATES	CARCINOMATOSIS	CARDIOPATHIES	CARFUFFLING
CARBONATING	CARBURATING	CARCINOMATOUS	CARDIOPATHY	CARHOPPING
CARBONATION	CARBURATION	CARCINOSARCOMA	CARDIOPLEGIA	CARICATURA
CARBONATIONS	CARBURATIONS	CARCINOSARCOMAS	CARDIOPLEGIAS	CARICATURAL
CARBONATITE	CARBURETED	CARCINOSES	CARDIOPULMONARY	CARICATURAS
CARBONATITES	CARBURETER	CARCINOSIS	CARDIOTHORACIC	CARICATURE
CARBONETTE	CARBURETERS	CARDAMINES	CARDIOTONIC	CARICATURED
CARBONETTES	CARBURETING	CARDBOARDS	CARDIOTONICS	CARICATURES
CARBONIFEROUS	CARBURETION	CARDBOARDY	CARDIOVASCULAR	CARICATURING
CARBONISATION	CARBURETIONS	CARDHOLDER	CARDITISES	CARICATURIST
CARBONISATIONS	CARBURETOR	CARDHOLDERS	CARDOPHAGI	CARICATURISTS
CARBONISED	CARBURETORS	CARDIALGIA	CARDOPHAGUS	CARILLONED
CARBONISER	CARBURETTED	CARDIALGIAS	CARDPHONES	CARILLONING
CARBONISERS	CARBURETTER	CARDIALGIC	CARDPLAYER	CARILLONIST
CARBONISES	CARBURETTERS	CARDIALGIES	CARDPLAYERS	CARILLONISTS
CARBONISING	CARBURETTING	CARDIGANED	CARDPUNCHES	CARILLONNED
CARBONIUMS	CARBURETTOR	CARDINALATE	CARDSHARPER	CARILLONNEUR
CARBONIZATION	CARBURETTORS	CARDINALATES	CARDSHARPERS	CARILLONNEURS
CARBONIZATIONS	CARBURISATION	CARDINALATIAL	CARDSHARPING	CARILLONNING
CARBONIZED	CARBURISATIONS	CARDINALITIAL	CARDSHARPINGS	CARIOGENIC
CARBONIZER	CARBURISED	CARDINALITIES	CARDSHARPS	CARIOSITIES
CARBONIZERS	CARBURISES	CARDINALITY	CARDUACEOUS	CARIOUSNESS
CARBONIZES	CARBURISING	CARDINALLY	CAREENAGES	CARIOUSNESSES
CARBONIZING	CARBURIZATION	CARDINALSHIP	CAREERISMS	CARJACKERS
CARBONLESS	CARBURIZATIONS	CARDINALSHIPS	CAREERISTS	CARJACKING
CARBONNADE	CARBURIZED	CARDIOCENTESES	CAREFREENESS	CARJACKINGS
CARBONNADES	CARBURIZES	CARDIOCENTESIS	CAREFREENESSES	CARMAGNOLE
CARBONYLATE	CARBURIZING	CARDIOGENIC	CAREFULLER	CARMAGNOLES
CARBONYLATED	CARBYLAMINE	CARDIOGRAM	CAREFULLEST	CARMELITES
CARBONYLATES	CARBYLAMINES	CARDIOGRAMS	CAREFULNESS	CARMINATIVE
CARBONYLATING	CARCASSING	CARDIOGRAPH	CAREFULNESSES	CARMINATIVES
CARBONYLATION	CARCINOGEN	CARDIOGRAPHER	CAREGIVERS	CARNAHUBAS
CARBONYLATIONS	CARCINOGENESES	CARDIOGRAPHERS	CAREGIVING	CARNALISED
CARBONYLIC	CARCINOGENESIS	CARDIOGRAPHIC	CAREGIVINGS	CARNALISES
CARBOXYLASE	CARCINOGENIC	CARDIOGRAPHICAL	CARELESSLY	CARNALISING
CARBOXYLASES	CARCINOGENICITY	CARDIOGRAPHIES	CARELESSNESS	CARNALISMS
CARBOXYLATE	CARCINOGENS	CARDIOGRAPHS	CARELESSNESSES	CARNALISTS
CARBOXYLATED	CARCINOIDS	CARDIOGRAPHY	CARESSINGLY	CARNALITIES
CARBOXYLATES	CARCINOLOGICAL	CARDIOLOGICAL	CARESSINGS	CARNALIZED
CARBOXYLATING	CARCINOLOGIES	CARDIOLOGIES	CARESSIVELY	CARNALIZES

CARNALIZING	CARPETBAGGERIES	CARRONADES	CARTOONISH	CASEWORKER
CARNALLING	CARPETBAGGERS	CARROTIEST	CARTOONISHLY	CASEWORKERS
CARNALLITE	CARPETBAGGERY	CARROTTOPPED	CARTOONIST	CASHIERERS
CARNALLITES	CARPETBAGGING	CARROTTOPS	CARTOONISTS	CASHIERING
CARNAPTIOUS	CARPETBAGS	CARROUSELS	CARTOONLIKE	CASHIERINGS
CARNAROLIS	CARPETINGS	CARRYBACKS	CARTOPHILE	CASHIERMENT
CARNASSIAL	CARPETMONGER	CARRYFORWARD	CARTOPHILES	CASHIERMENTS
CARNASSIALS	CARPETMONGERS	CARRYFORWARDS	CARTOPHILIC	CASHPOINTS
CARNATIONED	CARPETWEED	CARRYOVERS	CARTOPHILIES	CASINGHEAD
CARNATIONS	CARPETWEEDS	CARRYTALES	CARTOPHILIST	CASINGHEADS
CARNELIANS	CARPHOLOGIES	CARSHARING	CARTOPHILISTS	CASKSTANDS
CARNIFEXES	CARPHOLOGY	CARSHARINGS	CARTOPHILY	CASSAREEPS
CARNIFICATION	CARPOGONIA	CARSICKNESS	CARTOPPERS	CASSATIONS
CARNIFICATIONS	CARPOGONIAL	CARSICKNESSES	CARTOUCHES	CASSEROLED
CARNIFICIAL	CARPOGONIUM	CARTELISATION	CARTRIDGES	CASSEROLES
CARNIFYING	CARPOLOGICAL	CARTELISATIONS	CARTULARIES	CASSEROLING
CARNITINES	CARPOLOGIES	CARTELISED	CARTWHEELED	CASSIMERES
CARNIVALESQUE	CARPOLOGIST	CARTELISES	CARTWHEELER	CASSINGLES
CARNIVORES	CARPOLOGISTS	CARTELISING	CARTWHEELERS	CASSIOPEIUM
CARNIVORIES	CARPOMETACARPI	CARTELISMS	CARTWHEELING	CASSIOPEIUMS
CARNIVOROUS	CARPOMETACARPUS	CARTELISTS	CARTWHEELS	CASSITERITE
CARNIVOROUSLY	CARPOOLERS	CARTELIZATION	CARTWRIGHT	CASSITERITES
CARNIVOROUSNESS	CARPOOLING	CARTELIZATIONS	CARTWRIGHTS	CASSOLETTE
CARNOSAURS	CARPOOLINGS	CARTELIZED	CARUNCULAR	CASSOLETTES
CARNOSITIES	CARPOPHAGOUS	CARTELIZES	CARUNCULATE	CASSONADES
CARNOTITES	CARPOPHORE	CARTELIZING	CARUNCULATED	CASSOULETS
CAROLLINGS	CARPOPHORES	CARTHAMINE	CARUNCULOUS	CASSOWARIES
CAROMELLED	CARPOSPORE	CARTHAMINES	CARVACROLS	CASSUMUNAR
CAROMELLING	CARPOSPORES	CARTHORSES	CARYATIDAL	CASSUMUNARS
CAROTENOID	CARRAGEENAN	CARTILAGES	CARYATIDEAN	CASTABILITIES
CAROTENOIDS	CARRAGEENANS	CARTILAGINOUS	CARYATIDES	CASTABILITY
CAROTINOID	CARRAGEENIN	CARTOGRAMS	CARYATIDIC	CASTANOSPERMINE
CAROTINOIDS	CARRAGEENINS	CARTOGRAPHER	CARYOPSIDES	CASTELLANS
CAROUSINGLY	CARRAGEENS	CARTOGRAPHERS	CARYOPTERIS	CASTELLATED
CAROUSINGS	CARRAGHEEN	CARTOGRAPHIC	CARYOPTERISES	CASTELLATION
CARPACCIOS	CARRAGHEENAN	CARTOGRAPHICAL	CASCADURAS	CASTELLATIONS
CARPELLARY	CARRAGHEENANS	CARTOGRAPHIES	CASCARILLA	CASTELLUMS
CARPELLATE	CARRAGHEENIN	CARTOGRAPHY	CASCARILLAS	CASTIGATED
CARPELLATES	CARRAGHEENINS	CARTOLOGICAL	CASEATIONS	CASTIGATES
CARPENTARIA	CARRAGHEENS	CARTOLOGIES	CASEBEARER	CASTIGATING
CARPENTARIAS	CARREFOURS	CARTOMANCIES	CASEBEARERS	CASTIGATION
CARPENTERED	CARRIAGEABLE	CARTOMANCY	CASEINATES	CASTIGATIONS
CARPENTERING	CARRIAGEWAY	CARTONAGES	CASEINOGEN	CASTIGATOR
CARPENTERS	CARRIAGEWAYS	CARTONNAGE	CASEINOGENS	CASTIGATORS
CARPENTRIES	CARRITCHES	CARTONNAGES	CASEMAKERS	CASTIGATORY
CARPETBAGGED	CARRIWITCHET	CARTOONING	CASEMENTED	CASTOREUMS
CARPETBAGGER	CARRIWITCHETS	CARTOONINGS	CASEVACING	CASTRAMETATION

C

CASTRAMETATIONS	CATACLASMS	CATALOGUIZES	CATASTROPHE	CATECHISTS
CASTRATERS	CATACLASTIC	CATALOGUIZING	CATASTROPHES	CATECHIZATION
CASTRATING	CATACLINAL	CATALYSERS	CATASTROPHIC	CATECHIZATIONS
CASTRATION	CATACLYSMAL	CATALYSING	CATASTROPHISM	CATECHIZED
CASTRATIONS	CATACLYSMIC	CATALYTICAL	CATASTROPHISMS	CATECHIZER
CASTRATORS	CATACLYSMICALLY	CATALYTICALLY	CATASTROPHIST	CATECHIZERS
CASTRATORY	CATACLYSMS	CATALYZERS	CATASTROPHISTS	CATECHIZES
CASUALISATION	CATACOUSTICS	CATALYZING	CATATONIAS	CATECHIZING
CASUALISATIONS	CATACUMBAL	CATAMARANS	CATATONICALLY	CATECHIZINGS
CASUALISED	CATADIOPTRIC	CATAMENIAL	CATATONICS	CATECHOLAMINE
CASUALISES	CATADIOPTRICAL	CATAMOUNTAIN	CATATONIES	CATECHOLAMINES
CASUALISING	CATADROMOUS	CATAMOUNTAINS	CATCALLERS	CATECHUMEN
CASUALISMS	CATAFALCOES	CATAMOUNTS	CATCALLING	CATECHUMENAL
CASUALIZATION	CATAFALQUE	CATANANCHE	CATCHCRIES	CATECHUMENATE
CASUALIZATIONS	CATAFALQUES	CATANANCHES	CATCHFLIES	CATECHUMENATES
CASUALIZED	CATALECTIC	CATAPHONIC	CATCHINESS	CATECHUMENICAL
CASUALIZES	CATALECTICS	CATAPHONICS	CATCHINESSES	CATECHUMENISM
CASUALIZING	CATALEPSIES	CATAPHORAS	CATCHMENTS	CATECHUMENISMS
CASUALNESS	CATALEPTIC	CATAPHORESES	CATCHPENNIES	CATECHUMENS
CASUALNESSES	CATALEPTICALLY	CATAPHORESIS	CATCHPENNY	CATECHUMENSHIP
CASUALTIES	CATALEPTICS	CATAPHORETIC	CATCHPHRASE	CATECHUMENSHIPS
CASUARINAS	CATALLACTIC	CATAPHORIC	CATCHPHRASES	CATEGOREMATIC
CASUISTICAL	CATALLACTICALLY	CATAPHORICALLY	CATCHPOLES	CATEGORIAL
CASUISTICALLY	CATALLACTICS	CATAPHRACT	CATCHPOLLS	CATEGORIALLY
CASUISTRIES	CATALOGERS	CATAPHRACTIC	CATCHWATER	CATEGORICAL
CATABOLICALLY	CATALOGING	CATAPHRACTS	CATCHWEEDS	CATEGORICALLY
CATABOLISE	CATALOGISE	CATAPHYLLARY	CATCHWEIGHT	CATEGORICALNESS
CATABOLISED	CATALOGISED	CATAPHYLLS	CATCHWORDS	CATEGORIES
CATABOLISES	CATALOGISES	CATAPHYSICAL	CATECHESES	CATEGORISATION
CATABOLISING	CATALOGISING	CATAPLASIA	CATECHESIS	CATEGORISATIONS
CATABOLISM	CATALOGIZE	CATAPLASIAS	CATECHETIC	CATEGORISE
CATABOLISMS	CATALOGIZED	CATAPLASMS	CATECHETICAL	CATEGORISED
CATABOLITE	CATALOGIZES	CATAPLASTIC	CATECHETICALLY	CATEGORISES
CATABOLITES	CATALOGIZING	CATAPLECTIC	CATECHETICS	CATEGORISING
CATABOLIZE	CATALOGUED	CATAPLEXIES	CATECHISATION	CATEGORIST
CATABOLIZED	CATALOGUER	CATAPULTED	CATECHISATIONS	CATEGORISTS
CATABOLIZES	CATALOGUERS	CATAPULTIC	CATECHISED	CATEGORIZATION
CATABOLIZING	CATALOGUES	CATAPULTIER	CATECHISER	CATEGORIZATIONS
CATACAUSTIC	CATALOGUING	CATAPULTIERS	CATECHISERS	CATEGORIZE
CATACAUSTICS	CATALOGUISE	CATAPULTING	CATECHISES	CATEGORIZED
CATACHRESES	CATALOGUISED	CATARACTOUS	CATECHISING	CATEGORIZES
CATACHRESIS	CATALOGUISES	CATARRHALLY	CATECHISINGS	CATEGORIZING
CATACHRESTIC	CATALOGUISING	CATARRHINE	CATECHISMAL	CATENACCIO
CATACHRESTICAL	CATALOGUIST	CATARRHINES	CATECHISMS	CATENACCIOS
CATACLASES	CATALOGUISTS	CATARRHOUS	CATECHISTIC	CATENARIAN
CATACLASIS	CATALOGUIZE	CATASTASES	CATECHISTICAL	CATENARIES
CATACLASMIC	CATALOGUIZED	CATASTASIS	CATECHISTICALLY	CATENATING

CATENATION	CATHODOGRAPHER	CAULIFLORIES	CAUTIONERS	CELEBRATING
CATENATIONS	CATHODOGRAPHERS	CAULIFLOROUS	CAUTIONING	CELEBRATION
CATENULATE	CATHODOGRAPHIES	CAULIFLORY	CAUTIONRIES	CELEBRATIONS
CATERCORNER	CATHODOGRAPHS	CAULIFLOWER	CAUTIOUSLY	CELEBRATIVE
CATERCORNERED	CATHODOGRAPHY	CAULIFLOWERET	CAUTIOUSNESS	CELEBRATOR
CATERESSES	CATHOLICALLY	CAULIFLOWERETS	CAUTIOUSNESSES	CELEBRATORS
CATERPILLAR	CATHOLICATE	CAULIFLOWERS	CAVALCADED	CELEBRATORY
CATERPILLARS	CATHOLICATES	CAULIGENOUS	CAVALCADES	CELEBRITIES
CATERWAULED	CATHOLICISATION	CAUMSTANES	CAVALCADING	CELEBUTANTE
CATERWAULER	CATHOLICISE	CAUMSTONES	CAVALIERED	CELEBUTANTES
CATERWAULERS	CATHOLICISED	CAUSABILITIES	CAVALIERING	CELECOXIBS
CATERWAULING	CATHOLICISES	CAUSABILITY	CAVALIERISH	CELERITIES
CATERWAULINGS	CATHOLICISING	CAUSALGIAS	CAVALIERISM	CELESTIALLY
CATERWAULS	CATHOLICISM	CAUSALITIES	CAVALIERISMS	CELESTIALS
CATFACINGS	CATHOLICISMS	CAUSATIONAL	CAVALIERLY	CELESTINES
CATHARISED	CATHOLICITIES	CAUSATIONISM	CAVALLETTI	CELESTITES
CATHARISES	CATHOLICITY	CAUSATIONISMS	CAVALRYMAN	CELIBACIES
CATHARISING	CATHOLICIZATION	CAUSATIONIST	CAVALRYMEN	CELIBATARIAN
CATHARIZED	CATHOLICIZE	CAUSATIONISTS	CAVEFISHES	CELLARAGES
CATHARIZES	CATHOLICIZED	CAUSATIONS	CAVENDISHES	CELLARETTE
CATHARIZING	CATHOLICIZES	CAUSATIVELY	CAVERNICOLOUS	CELLARETTES
CATHARTICAL	CATHOLICIZING	CAUSATIVENESS	CAVERNOUSLY	CELLARISTS
CATHARTICALLY	CATHOLICLY	CAUSATIVENESSES	CAVERNULOUS	CELLARWAYS
CATHARTICS	CATHOLICOI	CAUSATIVES	CAVILLATION	CELLBLOCKS
CATHECTING	CATHOLICON	CAUSELESSLY	CAVILLATIONS	CELLENTANI
CATHEDRALS	CATHOLICONS	CAUSELESSNESS	CAVILLINGS	CELLENTANIS
CATHEDRATIC	CATHOLICOS	CAUSELESSNESSES	CAVITATING	CELLIFEROUS
CATHEPSINS	CATHOLICOSES	CAUSEWAYED	CAVITATION	CELLOBIOSE
CATHETERISATION	CATHOLYTES	CAUSEWAYING	CAVITATIONS	CELLOBIOSES
CATHETERISE	CATIONICALLY	CAUSTICALLY	CEANOTHUSES	CELLOIDINS
CATHETERISED	CATNAPPERS	CAUSTICITIES	CEASEFIRES	CELLOPHANE
CATHETERISES	CATNAPPING	CAUSTICITY	CEASELESSLY	CELLOPHANES
CATHETERISING	CATOPTRICAL	CAUSTICNESS	CEASELESSNESS	CELLPHONES
CATHETERISM	CATOPTRICS	CAUSTICNESSES	CEASELESSNESSES	CELLULARITIES
CATHETERISMS	CATTINESSES	CAUTERANTS	CEBADILLAS	CELLULARITY
CATHETERIZATION	CATTISHNESS	CAUTERISATION	CECUTIENCIES	CELLULASES
CATHETERIZE	CATTISHNESSES	CAUTERISATIONS	CECUTIENCY	CELLULATED
CATHETERIZED	CAUCHEMARS	CAUTERISED	CEDARBIRDS	CELLULIFEROUS
CATHETERIZES	CAUCUSSING	CAUTERISES	CEDARWOODS	CELLULITES
CATHETERIZING	CAUDATIONS	CAUTERISING	CEDRELACEOUS	CELLULITIS
CATHETOMETER	CAUDILLISMO	CAUTERISMS	CEILOMETER	CELLULITISES
CATHETOMETERS	CAUDILLISMOS	CAUTERIZATION	CEILOMETERS	CELLULOIDS
CATHETUSES	CAULESCENT	CAUTERIZATIONS	CELANDINES	CELLULOLYTIC
CATHODALLY	CAULICOLOUS	CAUTERIZED	CELEBRANTS	CELLULOSES
CATHODICAL	CAULICULATE	CAUTERIZES	CELEBRATED	CELLULOSIC
CATHODICALLY	CAULICULUS	CAUTERIZING	CELEBRATEDNESS	CELLULOSICS
CATHODOGRAPH	CAULICULUSES	CAUTIONARY	CELEBRATES	CELSITUDES

CEMBALISTS	CENTERFOLDS	CENTRALISMS	CENTRIPETALISM	CEPHALOCHORDATE
CEMENTATION	CENTERINGS	CENTRALIST	CENTRIPETALISMS	CEPHALOMETER
CEMENTATIONS	CENTERLESS	CENTRALISTIC	CENTRIPETALLY	CEPHALOMETERS
CEMENTATORY	CENTERLINE	CENTRALISTS	CENTROBARIC	CEPHALOMETRIC
CEMENTITES	CENTERLINES	CENTRALITIES	CENTROCLINAL	CEPHALOMETRIES
CEMENTITIOUS	CENTERPIECE	CENTRALITY	CENTROIDAL	CEPHALOMETRY
CEMETERIES	CENTERPIECES	CENTRALIZATION	CENTROLECITHAL	CEPHALOPOD
CENESTHESES	CENTESIMAL	CENTRALIZATIONS	CENTROMERE	CEPHALOPODAN
CENESTHESIA	CENTESIMALLY	CENTRALIZE	CENTROMERES	CEPHALOPODANS
CENESTHESIAS	CENTESIMALS	CENTRALIZED	CENTROMERIC	CEPHALOPODIC
CENESTHESIS	CENTESIMOS	CENTRALIZER	CENTROSOME	CEPHALOPODOUS
CENESTHETIC	CENTIGRADE	CENTRALIZERS	CENTROSOMES	CEPHALOPODS
CENOBITICAL	CENTIGRADES	CENTRALIZES	CENTROSOMIC	CEPHALORIDINE
CENOGENESES	CENTIGRAMME	CENTRALIZING	CENTROSPHERE	CEPHALORIDINES
CENOGENESIS	CENTIGRAMMES	CENTREBOARD	CENTROSPHERES	CEPHALOSPORIN
CENOGENETIC	CENTIGRAMS	CENTREBOARDS	CENTROSYMMETRIC	CEPHALOSPORINS
CENOGENETICALLY	CENTILITER	CENTREFOLD	CENTUMVIRATE	CEPHALOTHIN
CENOSPECIES	CENTILITERS	CENTREFOLDS	CENTUMVIRATES	CEPHALOTHINS
CENOTAPHIC	CENTILITRE	CENTREINGS	CENTUMVIRI	CEPHALOTHORACES
CENSORABLE	CENTILITRES	CENTRELINE	CENTUPLICATE	CEPHALOTHORACIC
CENSORIOUS	CENTILLION	CENTRELINES	CENTUPLICATED	CEPHALOTHORAX
CENSORIOUSLY	CENTILLIONS	CENTREPIECE	CENTUPLICATES	CEPHALOTHORAXES
CENSORIOUSNESS	CENTILLIONTH	CENTREPIECES	CENTUPLICATING	CEPHALOTOMIES
CENSORSHIP	CENTILLIONTHS	CENTRICALLY	CENTUPLICATION	CEPHALOTOMY
CENSORSHIPS	CENTIMETER	CENTRICALNESS	CENTUPLICATIONS	CERAMICIST
CENSURABILITIES	CENTIMETERS	CENTRICALNESSES	CENTUPLING	CERAMICISTS
CENSURABILITY	CENTIMETRE	CENTRICITIES	CENTURIATION	CERAMOGRAPHIES
CENSURABLE	CENTIMETRES	CENTRICITY	CENTURIATIONS	CERAMOGRAPHY
CENSURABLENESS	CENTIMETRIC	CENTRIFUGAL	CENTURIATOR	CERARGYRITE
CENSURABLY	CENTIMORGAN	CENTRIFUGALISE	CENTURIATORS	CERARGYRITES
CENTAUREAS	CENTIMORGANS	CENTRIFUGALISED	CENTURIONS	CERASTIUMS
CENTAURIAN	CENTINELLS	CENTRIFUGALISES	CEPHALAGRA	CERATITISES
CENTAURIES	CENTIPEDES	CENTRIFUGALIZE	CEPHALAGRAS	CERATODUSES
CENTENARIAN	CENTIPOISE	CENTRIFUGALIZED	CEPHALALGIA	CERATOPSIAN
CENTENARIANISM	CENTIPOISES	CENTRIFUGALIZES	CEPHALALGIAS	CERATOPSIANS
CENTENARIANISMS	CENTONELLS	CENTRIFUGALLY	CEPHALALGIC	CERATOPSID
CENTENARIANS	CENTONISTS	CENTRIFUGALS	CEPHALEXIN	CERATOPSIDS
CENTENARIES	CENTRALEST	CENTRIFUGATION	CEPHALEXINS	CERCARIANS
CENTENIERS	CENTRALISATION	CENTRIFUGATIONS	CEPHALICALLY	CERCOPITHECID
CENTENNIAL	CENTRALISATIONS	CENTRIFUGE	CEPHALISATION	CERCOPITHECIDS
CENTENNIALLY	CENTRALISE	CENTRIFUGED	CEPHALISATIONS	CERCOPITHECOID
CENTENNIALS	CENTRALISED	CENTRIFUGENCE	CEPHALITIS	CERCOPITHECOIDS
CENTERBOARD	CENTRALISER	CENTRIFUGENCES	CEPHALITISES	CEREALISTS
CENTERBOARDS	CENTRALISERS	CENTRIFUGES	CEPHALIZATION	CEREBELLAR
CENTEREDNESS	CENTRALISES	CENTRIFUGING	CEPHALIZATIONS	CEREBELLIC
CENTEREDNESSES	CENTRALISING	CENTRIOLES	CEPHALOCELE	CEREBELLOUS
CENTERFOLD	CENTRALISM	CENTRIPETAL	CEPHALOCELES	CEREBELLUM

C

CEREBELLUMS	CERTIFIABLY	CEYLANITES	CHALAZIONS	CHALYBITES
CEREBRALISM	CERTIFICATE	CEYLONITES	CHALAZOGAMIC	CHAMAELEON
CEREBRALISMS	CERTIFICATED	CHABAZITES	CHALAZOGAMIES	CHAMAELEONS
CEREBRALIST	CERTIFICATES	CHACONINES	CHALAZOGAMY	CHAMAEPHYTE
CEREBRALISTS	CERTIFICATING	CHAENOMELES	CHALCANTHITE	CHAMAEPHYTES
CEREBRALLY	CERTIFICATION	CHAENOMELESES	CHALCANTHITES	CHAMBERERS
CEREBRATED	CERTIFICATIONS	CHAETIFEROUS	CHALCEDONIC	CHAMBERHAND
CEREBRATES	CERTIFICATORIES	CHAETODONS	CHALCEDONIES	CHAMBERHANDS
CEREBRATING	CERTIFICATORY	CHAETOGNATH	CHALCEDONY	CHAMBERING
CEREBRATION	CERTIFIERS	CHAETOGNATHS	CHALCEDONYX	CHAMBERINGS
CEREBRATIONS	CERTIFYING	CHAETOPODS	CHALCEDONYXES	CHAMBERLAIN
CEREBRIFORM	CERTIORARI	CHAFFERERS	CHALCOCITE	CHAMBERLAINS
CEREBRITIS	CERTIORARIS	CHAFFERIES	CHALCOCITES	CHAMBERLAINSHIP
CEREBRITISES	CERTITUDES	CHAFFERING	CHALCOGENIDE	CHAMBERMAID
CEREBROSIDE	CERULOPLASMIN	CHAFFINCHES	CHALCOGENIDES	CHAMBERMAIDS
CEREBROSIDES	CERULOPLASMINS	CHAFFINGLY	CHALCOGENS	CHAMBERPOT
CEREBROSPINAL	CERUMINOUS	CHAGRINING	CHALCOGRAPHER	CHAMBERPOTS
CEREBROTONIA	CERUSSITES	CHAGRINNED	CHALCOGRAPHERS	CHAMBRANLE
CEREBROTONIAS	CERVELASES	CHAGRINNING	CHALCOGRAPHIC	CHAMBRANLES
CEREBROTONIC	CERVICITIS	CHAINBRAKE	CHALCOGRAPHICAL	CHAMELEONIC
CEREBROVASCULAR	CERVICITISES	CHAINBRAKES	CHALCOGRAPHIES	CHAMELEONLIKE
CERECLOTHS	CERVICOGRAPHIES	CHAINFALLS	CHALCOGRAPHIST	CHAMELEONS
CEREMONIAL	CERVICOGRAPHY	CHAINPLATE	CHALCOGRAPHISTS	CHAMFERERS
CEREMONIALISM	CESAREVICH	CHAINPLATES	CHALCOGRAPHY	CHAMFERING
CEREMONIALISMS	CESAREVICHES	CHAINSAWED	CHALCOLITHIC	CHAMFRAINS
CEREMONIALIST	CESAREVITCH	CHAINSAWING	CHALCOPYRITE	CHAMOISING
CEREMONIALISTS	CESAREVITCHES	CHAINSHOTS	CHALCOPYRITES	CHAMOMILES
CEREMONIALLY	CESAREVNAS	CHAINSTITCH	CHALICOTHERE	CHAMPAGNES
CEREMONIALS	CESAREWICH	CHAINSTITCHES	CHALICOTHERES	CHAMPAIGNS
CEREMONIES	CESAREWICHES	CHAINWHEEL	CHALKBOARD	CHAMPERTIES
CEREMONIOUS	CESAREWITCH	CHAINWHEELS	CHALKBOARDS	CHAMPERTOUS
CEREMONIOUSLY	CESAREWITCHES	CHAINWORKS	CHALKFACES	CHAMPIGNON
CEREMONIOUSNESS	CESPITOSELY	CHAIRBORNE	CHALKINESS	CHAMPIGNONS
CERIFEROUS	CESSATIONS	CHAIRBOUND	CHALKINESSES	CHAMPIONED
CEROGRAPHIC	CESSIONARIES	CHAIRLIFTS	CHALKSTONE	CHAMPIONESS
CEROGRAPHICAL	CESSIONARY	CHAIRMANED	CHALKSTONES	CHAMPIONESSES
CEROGRAPHIES	CESTOIDEAN	CHAIRMANING	CHALLENGEABLE	CHAMPIONING
CEROGRAPHIST	CESTOIDEANS	CHAIRMANNED	CHALLENGED	CHAMPIONSHIP
CEROGRAPHISTS	CETEOSAURUS	CHAIRMANNING	CHALLENGER	CHAMPIONSHIPS
CEROGRAPHS	CETEOSAURUSES	CHAIRMANSHIP	CHALLENGERS	CHAMPLEVES
CEROGRAPHY	CETOLOGICAL	CHAIRMANSHIPS	CHALLENGES	CHANCELESS
CEROMANCIES	CETOLOGIES	CHAIRPERSON	CHALLENGING	CHANCELLERIES
CEROPLASTIC	CETOLOGIST	CHAIRPERSONS	CHALLENGINGLY	CHANCELLERY
CEROPLASTICS	CETOLOGISTS	CHAIRWOMAN	CHALUMEAUS	CHANCELLOR
CERTAINEST	CETRIMIDES	CHAIRWOMEN	CHALUMEAUX	CHANCELLORIES
CERTAINTIES	CETUXIMABS	CHAISELESS	CHALYBEATE	CHANCELLORS
CERTIFIABLE	CEVADILLAS	CHAKALAKAS	CHALYBEATES	CHANCELLORSHIP

CHANCELLORSHIPS	CHANNELIZING	CHAPSTICKS	CHARBROILING	CHARLESTON
CHANCELLORY	CHANNELLED	CHAPTALISATION	CHARBROILS	CHARLESTONED
CHANCERIES	CHANNELLER	CHAPTALISATIONS	CHARCOALED	CHARLESTONING
CHANCINESS	CHANNELLERS	CHAPTALISE	CHARCOALING	CHARLESTONS
CHANCINESSES	CHANNELLING	CHAPTALISED	CHARCUTERIE	CHARLOTTES
CHANCROIDAL	CHANSONETTE	CHAPTALISES	CHARCUTERIES	CHARMEUSES
CHANCROIDS	CHANSONETTES	CHAPTALISING	CHARDONNAY	CHARMINGER
CHANDELIER	CHANSONNIER	CHAPTALIZATION	CHARDONNAYS	CHARMINGEST
CHANDELIERED	CHANSONNIERS	CHAPTALIZATIONS	CHARGEABILITIES	CHARMINGLY
CHANDELIERS	CHANTARELLE	CHAPTALIZE	CHARGEABILITY	CHARMLESSLY
CHANDELLED	CHANTARELLES	CHAPTALIZED	CHARGEABLE	CHARMONIUM
CHANDELLES	CHANTECLER	CHAPTALIZES	CHARGEABLENESS	CHAROSETHS
CHANDELLING	CHANTECLERS	CHAPTALIZING	CHARGEABLY	CHARTACEOUS
CHANDLERIES	CHANTERELLE	CHAPTERHOUSE	CHARGEBACK	CHARTERERS
CHANDLERING	CHANTERELLES	CHAPTERHOUSES	CHARGEBACKS	CHARTERING
CHANDLERINGS	CHANTEUSES	CHAPTERING	CHARGEHAND	CHARTERPARTIES
CHANDLERLY	CHANTICLEER	CHARABANCS	CHARGEHANDS	CHARTERPARTY
CHANGEABILITIES	CHANTICLEERS	CHARACINOID	CHARGELESS	CHARTHOUSE
CHANGEABILITY	CHANTINGLY	CHARACTERED	CHARGESHEET	CHARTHOUSES
CHANGEABLE	CHANTRESSES	CHARACTERFUL	CHARGESHEETS	CHARTOGRAPHER
CHANGEABLENESS	CHANUKIAHS	CHARACTERIES	CHARGRILLED	CHARTOGRAPHERS
CHANGEABLY	CHAOLOGIES	CHARACTERING	CHARGRILLING	CHARTOGRAPHIC
CHANGEFULLY	CHAOLOGIST	CHARACTERISABLE	CHARGRILLS	CHARTOGRAPHICAL
CHANGEFULNESS	CHAOLOGISTS	CHARACTERISE	CHARINESSES	CHARTOGRAPHIES
CHANGEFULNESSES	CHAOTICALLY	CHARACTERISED	CHARIOTEER	CHARTOGRAPHY
CHANGELESS	CHAPARAJOS	CHARACTERISER	CHARIOTEERED	CHARTREUSE
CHANGELESSLY	CHAPAREJOS	CHARACTERISERS	CHARIOTEERING	CHARTREUSES
CHANGELESSNESS	CHAPARRALS	CHARACTERISES	CHARIOTEERS	CHARTULARIES
CHANGELING	CHAPATTIES	CHARACTERISING	CHARIOTING	CHARTULARY
CHANGELINGS	CHAPELRIES	CHARACTERISM	CHARISMATA	CHASEPORTS
CHANGEOVER	CHAPERONAGE	CHARACTERISMS	CHARISMATIC	CHASMOGAMIC
CHANGEOVERS	CHAPERONAGES	CHARACTERISTIC	CHARISMATICS	CHASMOGAMIES
CHANGEROUND	CHAPERONED	CHARACTERISTICS	CHARITABLE	CHASMOGAMOUS
CHANGEROUNDS	CHAPERONES	CHARACTERIZABLE	CHARITABLENESS	CHASMOGAMY
CHANNELERS	CHAPERONING	CHARACTERIZE	CHARITABLY	CHASSEPOTS
CHANNELING	CHAPFALLEN	CHARACTERIZED	CHARIVARIED	CHASTENERS
CHANNELISATION	CHAPLAINCIES	CHARACTERIZER	CHARIVARIING	CHASTENESS
CHANNELISATIONS	CHAPLAINCY	CHARACTERIZERS	CHARIVARIS	CHASTENESSES
CHANNELISE	CHAPLAINRIES	CHARACTERIZES	CHARLADIES	CHASTENING
CHANNELISED	CHAPLAINRY	CHARACTERIZING	CHARLATANIC	CHASTENINGLY
CHANNELISES	CHAPLAINSHIP	CHARACTERLESS	CHARLATANICAL	CHASTENMENT
CHANNELISING	CHAPLAINSHIPS	CHARACTEROLOGY	CHARLATANISM	CHASTENMENTS
CHANNELIZATION	CHAPMANSHIP	CHARACTERS	CHARLATANISMS	CHASTISABLE
CHANNELIZATIONS	CHAPMANSHIPS	CHARACTERY	CHARLATANISTIC	CHASTISEMENT
CHANNELIZE	CHAPPESSES	CHARBROILED	CHARLATANRIES	CHASTISEMENTS
CHANNELIZED	CHAPRASSIES	CHARBROILER	CHARLATANRY	CHASTISERS
CHANNELIZES	CHAPRASSIS	CHARBROILERS	CHARLATANS	CHASTISING

CHASTITIES	CHEAPENING	CHEEKINESSES	CHEESESTEAKS	CHEMOAUTROPH
CHATEAUBRIAND	CHEAPISHLY	CHEEKPIECE	CHEESETASTER	CHEMOAUTROPHS
CHATEAUBRIANDS	CHEAPJACKS	CHEEKPIECES	CHEESETASTERS	CHEMOCEPTOR
CHATELAINE	CHEAPNESSES	CHEEKPOUCH	CHEESEVATS	CHEMOCEPTORS
CHATELAINES	CHEAPSKATE	CHEEKPOUCHES	CHEESEWIRE	CHEMOKINES
CHATELAINS	CHEAPSKATES	CHEEKTEETH	CHEESEWIRES	CHEMOKINESES
CHATOYANCE	CHEATERIES	CHEEKTOOTH	CHEESEWOOD	CHEMOKINESIS
CHATOYANCES	CHEATINGLY	CHEERFULLER	CHEESEWOODS	CHEMOLITHOTROPH
CHATOYANCIES	CHECHAKOES	CHEERFULLEST	CHEESEWRING	CHEMONASTIES
CHATOYANCY	CHECHAQUOS	CHEERFULLY	CHEESEWRINGS	CHEMONASTY
CHATOYANTS	CHECKBOOKS	CHEERFULNESS	CHEESINESS	CHEMOPSYCHIATRY
CHATTERATI	CHECKCLERK	CHEERFULNESSES	CHEESINESSES	CHEMORECEPTION
CHATTERBOX	CHECKCLERKS	CHEERINESS	CHEILITISES	CHEMORECEPTIONS
CHATTERBOXES	CHECKERBERRIES	CHEERINESSES	CHELASHIPS	CHEMORECEPTIVE
CHATTERERS	CHECKERBERRY	CHEERINGLY	CHELATABLE	CHEMORECEPTOR
CHATTERING	CHECKERBLOOM	CHEERISHNESS	CHELATIONS	CHEMORECEPTORS
CHATTERINGS	CHECKERBLOOMS	CHEERISHNESSES	CHELICERAE	CHEMOSMOSES
CHATTINESS	CHECKERBOARD	CHEERLEADER	CHELICERAL	CHEMOSMOSIS
CHATTINESSES	CHECKERBOARDS	CHEERLEADERS	CHELICERATE	CHEMOSMOTIC
CHAUDFROID	CHECKERING	CHEERLEADING	CHELICERATES	CHEMOSORBED
CHAUDFROIDS	CHECKLATON	CHEERLEADS	CHELIFEROUS	CHEMOSORBING
CHAUFFEURED	CHECKLATONS	CHEERLESSLY	CHELONIANS	CHEMOSORBS
CHAUFFEURING	CHECKLISTED	CHEERLESSNESS	CHELUVIATION	CHEMOSPHERE
CHAUFFEURS	CHECKLISTING	CHEERLESSNESSES	CHELUVIATIONS	CHEMOSPHERES
CHAUFFEUSE	CHECKLISTS	CHEESEBOARD	CHEMAUTOTROPH	CHEMOSPHERIC
CHAUFFEUSED	CHECKMARKED	CHEESEBOARDS	CHEMAUTOTROPHIC	CHEMOSTATS
CHAUFFEUSES	CHECKMARKING	CHEESEBURGER	CHEMAUTOTROPHS	CHEMOSURGERIES
CHAUFFEUSING	CHECKMARKS	CHEESEBURGERS	CHEMIATRIC	CHEMOSURGERY
CHAULMOOGRA	CHECKMATED	CHEESECAKE	CHEMICALLY	CHEMOSURGICAL
CHAULMOOGRAS	CHECKMATES	CHEESECAKES	CHEMICKING	CHEMOSYNTHESES
CHAULMUGRA	CHECKMATING	CHEESECLOTH	CHEMIOSMOSES	CHEMOSYNTHESIS
CHAULMUGRAS	CHECKPOINT	CHEESECLOTHS	CHEMIOSMOSIS	CHEMOSYNTHETIC
CHAUNTRESS	CHECKPOINTS	CHEESECUTTER	CHEMIOSMOTIC	CHEMOTACTIC
CHAUNTRESSES	CHECKRAILS	CHEESECUTTERS	CHEMISETTE	CHEMOTACTICALLY
CHAUNTRIES	CHECKREINS	CHEESEHOPPER	CHEMISETTES	CHEMOTAXES
CHAUSSURES	CHECKROOMS	CHEESEHOPPERS	CHEMISORBED	CHEMOTAXIS
CHAUTAUQUA	CHECKROWED	CHEESEMITE	CHEMISORBING	CHEMOTAXONOMIC
CHAUTAUQUAS	CHECKROWING	CHEESEMITES	CHEMISORBS	CHEMOTAXONOMIES
CHAUVINISM	CHECKWEIGHER	CHEESEMONGER	CHEMISORPTION	CHEMOTAXONOMIST
CHAUVINISMS	CHECKWEIGHERS	CHEESEMONGERS	CHEMISORPTIONS	CHEMOTAXONOMY
CHAUVINIST	CHEECHAKOES	CHEESEPARER	CHEMISTRIES	CHEMOTHERAPIES
CHAUVINISTIC	CHEECHAKOS	CHEESEPARERS	CHEMITYPES	CHEMOTHERAPIST
CHAUVINISTS	CHEECHALKO	CHEESEPARING	CHEMITYPIES	CHEMOTHERAPISTS
CHAVENDERS	CHEECHALKOES	CHEESEPARINGS	CHEMOATTRACTANT	CHEMOTHERAPY
CHAVTASTIC	CHEECHALKOS	CHEESEPRESS	CHEMOAUTOTROPH	CHEMOTROPIC
CHAWBACONS	CHEEKBONES	CHEESEPRESSES	CHEMOAUTOTROPHS	CHEMOTROPICALLY
CHEAPENERS	CHEEKINESS	CHEESESTEAK	CHEMOAUTOTROPHY	CHEMOTROPISM

CHEMOTROPISMS	CHESTINESS	CHIEFTAINESS	CHILIARCHS	CHINOISERIE
CHEMPADUKS	CHESTINESSES	CHIEFTAINESSES	CHILIARCHY	CHINOISERIES
CHEMURGICAL	CHEVALIERS	CHIEFTAINRIES	CHILIASTIC	CHINOVNIKS
CHEMURGIES	CHEVELURES	CHIEFTAINRY	CHILLINESS	CHINQUAPIN
CHENOPODIACEOUS	CHEVESAILE	CHIEFTAINS	CHILLINESSES	CHINQUAPINS
CHEONGSAMS	CHEVESAILES	CHIEFTAINSHIP	CHILLINGLY	CHINSTRAPS
CHEQUEBOOK	CHEVISANCE	CHIEFTAINSHIPS	CHILLNESSES	CHINTZIEST
CHEQUEBOOKS	CHEVISANCES	CHIFFCHAFF	CHILOPODAN	CHINWAGGED
CHEQUERBOARD	CHEVRETTES	CHIFFCHAFFS	CHILOPODANS	CHINWAGGING
CHEQUERBOARDS	CHEVROTAIN	CHIFFONADE	CHILOPODOUS	CHIONODOXA
CHEQUERING	CHEVROTAINS	CHIFFONADES	CHILTEPINS	CHIONODOXAS
CHEQUERWISE	CHEWINESSES	CHIFFONIER	CHIMAERISM	CHIPBOARDS
CHEQUERWORK	CHIACKINGS	CHIFFONIERS	CHIMAERISMS	CHIPOCHIAS
CHEQUERWORKS	CHIAROSCURISM	CHIFFONNIER	CHIMERICAL	CHIPOLATAS
CHERALITES	CHIAROSCURISMS	CHIFFONNIERS	CHIMERICALLY	CHIPPERING
CHERIMOYAS	CHIAROSCURIST	CHIFFOROBE	CHIMERICALNESS	CHIPPINESS
CHERIMOYER	CHIAROSCURISTS	CHIFFOROBES	CHIMERISMS	CHIPPINESSES
CHERIMOYERS	CHIAROSCURO	CHIHUAHUAS	CHIMICHANGA	CHIQUICHIQUI
CHERISHABLE	CHIAROSCUROS	CHILBLAINED	CHIMICHANGAS	CHIQUICHIQUIS
CHERISHERS	CHIASMATIC	CHILBLAINS	CHIMNEYBOARD	CHIRAGRICAL
CHERISHING	CHIASTOLITE	CHILDBEARING	CHIMNEYBOARDS	CHIRALITIES
CHERISHINGLY	CHIASTOLITES	CHILDBEARINGS	CHIMNEYBREAST	CHIRIMOYAS
CHERISHMENT	CHIBOUQUES	CHILDBIRTH	CHIMNEYBREASTS	CHIROGNOMIES
CHERISHMENTS	CHICALOTES	CHILDBIRTHS	CHIMNEYING	CHIROGNOMY
CHERMOULAS	CHICANERIES	CHILDCARES	CHIMNEYLIKE	CHIROGRAPH
CHERNOZEMIC	CHICANINGS	CHILDCROWING	CHIMNEYPIECE	CHIROGRAPHER
CHERNOZEMS	CHICCORIES	CHILDCROWINGS	CHIMNEYPIECES	CHIROGRAPHERS
CHERRYLIKE	CHICKABIDDIES	CHILDERMAS	CHIMNEYPOT	CHIROGRAPHIC
CHERRYSTONE	CHICKABIDDY	CHILDERMASES	CHIMNEYPOTS	CHIROGRAPHICAL
CHERRYSTONES	CHICKADEES	CHILDHOODS	CHIMPANZEE	CHIROGRAPHIES
CHERSONESE	CHICKAREES	CHILDISHLY	CHIMPANZEES	CHIROGRAPHIST
CHERSONESES	CHICKENHEARTED	CHILDISHNESS	CHINABERRIES	CHIROGRAPHISTS
CHERUBICAL	CHICKENING	CHILDISHNESSES	CHINABERRY	CHIROGRAPHS
CHERUBICALLY	CHICKENPOX	CHILDLESSNESS	CHINACHINA	CHIROGRAPHY
CHERUBIMIC	CHICKENPOXES	CHILDLESSNESSES	CHINACHINAS	CHIROLOGIES
CHERUBLIKE	CHICKENSHIT	CHILDLIEST	CHINAROOTS	CHIROLOGIST
CHERVONETS	CHICKENSHITS	CHILDLIKENESS	CHINAWARES	CHIROLOGISTS
CHESSBOARD	CHICKLINGS	CHILDLIKENESSES	CHINCAPINS	CHIROMANCER
CHESSBOARDS	CHICKORIES	CHILDMINDER	CHINCHERINCHEE	CHIROMANCERS
CHESSBOXING	CHICKWEEDS	CHILDMINDERS	CHINCHERINCHEES	CHIROMANCIES
CHESSBOXINGS	CHICNESSES	CHILDNESSES	CHINCHIEST	CHIROMANCY
CHESSPIECE	CHIEFERIES	CHILDPROOF	CHINCHILLA	CHIROMANTIC
CHESSPIECES	CHIEFESSES	CHILIAGONS	CHINCHILLAS	CHIROMANTICAL
CHESSYLITE	CHIEFLINGS	CHILIAHEDRA	CHINCOUGHS	CHIRONOMER
CHESSYLITES	CHIEFSHIPS	CHILIAHEDRON	CHINKAPINS	CHIRONOMERS
CHESTERFIELD	CHIEFTAINCIES	CHILIAHEDRONS	CHINKERINCHEE	CHIRONOMIC
CHESTERFIELDS	CHIEFTAINCY	CHILIARCHIES	CHINKERINCHEES	CHIRONOMID

CHIRONOMIDS	CHLAMYDIAL	CHLORINATED	CHLOROMETRY	CHOIRGIRLS
CHIRONOMIES	CHLAMYDIAS	CHLORINATES	CHLOROPHYL	CHOIRMASTER
CHIROPODIAL	CHLAMYDOMONADES	CHLORINATING	CHLOROPHYLL	CHOIRMASTERS
CHIROPODIES	CHLAMYDOMONAS	CHLORINATION	CHLOROPHYLLOID	CHOIRSCREEN
CHIROPODIST	CHLAMYDOSPORE	CHLORINATIONS	CHLOROPHYLLOUS	CHOIRSCREENS
CHIROPODISTS	CHLAMYDOSPORES	CHLORINATOR	CHLOROPHYLLS	CHOIRSTALLS
CHIROPRACTIC	CHLOANTHITE	CHLORINATORS	CHLOROPHYLS	CHOKEBERRIES
CHIROPRACTICS	CHLOANTHITES	CHLORINISE	CHLOROPHYTUM	CHOKEBERRY
CHIROPRACTOR	CHLOASMATA	CHLORINISED	CHLOROPHYTUMS	CHOKEBORES
CHIROPRACTORS	CHLORACETIC	CHLORINISES	CHLOROPICRIN	CHOKECHERRIES
CHIROPTERAN	CHLORACNES	CHLORINISING	CHLOROPICRINS	CHOKECHERRY
CHIROPTERANS	CHLORALISM	CHLORINITIES	CHLOROPLAST	CHOKECOILS
CHIROPTEROUS	CHLORALISMS	CHLORINITY	CHLOROPLASTAL	CHOKEDAMPS
CHIROPTERS	CHLORALOSE	CHLORINIZE	CHLOROPLASTIC	CHOKEHOLDS
CHIRPINESS	CHLORALOSED	CHLORINIZED	CHLOROPLASTS	CHOLAEMIAS
CHIRPINESSES	CHLORALOSES	CHLORINIZES	CHLOROPRENE	CHOLAGOGIC
CHIRRUPERS	CHLORAMBUCIL	CHLORINIZING	CHLOROPRENES	CHOLAGOGUE
CHIRRUPING	CHLORAMBUCILS	CHLORITISATION	CHLOROQUIN	CHOLAGOGUES
CHIRURGEON	CHLORAMINE	CHLORITISATIONS	CHLOROQUINE	CHOLANGIOGRAM
CHIRURGEONLY	CHLORAMINES	CHLORITIZATION	CHLOROQUINES	CHOLANGIOGRAMS
CHIRURGEONS	CHLORAMPHENICOL	CHLORITIZATIONS	CHLOROQUINS	CHOLANGIOGRAPHY
CHIRURGERIES	CHLORARGYRITE	CHLOROACETIC	CHLOROTHIAZIDE	CHOLECALCIFEROL
CHIRURGERY	CHLORARGYRITES	CHLOROARGYRITE	CHLOROTHIAZIDES	CHOLECYSTECTOMY
CHIRURGICAL	CHLORDANES	CHLOROBENZENE	CHLORPICRIN	CHOLECYSTITIS
CHISELLERS	CHLORELLAS	CHLOROBENZENES	CHLORPICRINS	CHOLECYSTITISES
CHISELLING	CHLORENCHYMA	CHLOROBROMIDE	CHLORPROMAZINE	CHOLECYSTOKININ
CHISELLINGS	CHLORENCHYMAS	CHLOROBROMIDES	CHLORPROMAZINES	CHOLECYSTOSTOMY
CHITARRONE	CHLORHEXIDINE	CHLOROCRUORIN	CHLORPROPAMIDE	CHOLECYSTOTOMY
CHITARRONI	CHLORHEXIDINES	CHLOROCRUORINS	CHLORPROPAMIDES	CHOLECYSTS
CHITCHATTED	CHLORIDATE	CHLORODYNE	CHLORTHALIDONE	CHOLELITHIASES
CHITCHATTING	CHLORIDATED	CHLORODYNES	CHLORTHALIDONES	CHOLELITHIASIS
CHITTAGONG	CHLORIDATES	CHLOROFORM	CHOANOCYTE	CHOLELITHS
CHITTAGONGS	CHLORIDATING	CHLOROFORMED	CHOANOCYTES	CHOLERICALLY
CHITTERING	CHLORIDISE	CHLOROFORMER	CHOCAHOLIC	CHOLERICLY
CHITTERINGS	CHLORIDISED	CHLOROFORMERS	CHOCAHOLICS	CHOLESTASES
CHITTERLING	CHLORIDISES	CHLOROFORMING	CHOCKABLOCK	CHOLESTASIS
CHITTERLINGS	CHLORIDISING	CHLOROFORMIST	CHOCKSTONE	CHOLESTATIC
CHIVALRIES	CHLORIDIZE	CHLOROFORMISTS	CHOCKSTONES	CHOLESTERIC
CHIVALROUS	CHLORIDIZED	CHLOROFORMS	CHOCOHOLIC	CHOLESTERIN
CHIVALROUSLY	CHLORIDIZES	CHLOROHYDRIN	CHOCOHOLICS	CHOLESTERINS
CHIVALROUSNESS	CHLORIDIZING	CHLOROHYDRINS	CHOCOLATES	CHOLESTEROL
CHIVAREEING	CHLORIMETER	CHLOROMETER	CHOCOLATEY	CHOLESTEROLEMIA
CHIVARIING	CHLORIMETERS	CHLOROMETERS	CHOCOLATIER	CHOLESTEROLS
CHIYOGAMIS	CHLORIMETRIC	CHLOROMETHANE	CHOCOLATIERS	CHOLESTYRAMINE
CHLAMYDATE	CHLORIMETRIES	CHLOROMETHANES	CHOCOLATIEST	CHOLESTYRAMINES
CHLAMYDEOUS	CHLORIMETRY	CHLOROMETRIC	CHOICENESS	CHOLIAMBIC
CHLAMYDIAE	CHLORINATE	CHLOROMETRIES	CHOICENESSES	CHOLIAMBICS

C

CHOLINERGIC	CHORAGUSES	CHORIZATIONS	CHRISTENER	CHROMATOSPHERES
CHOLINERGICALLY	CHORALISTS	CHORIZONTIST	CHRISTENERS	CHROMATYPE
CHOLINESTERASE	CHORDAMESODERM	CHORIZONTISTS	CHRISTENING	CHROMATYPES
CHOLINESTERASES	CHORDAMESODERMS	CHORIZONTS	CHRISTENINGS	CHROMIDIUM
CHOMOPHYTE	CHORDOPHONE	CHOROGRAPHER	CHRISTIANIA	CHROMINANCE
CHOMOPHYTES	CHORDOPHONES	CHOROGRAPHERS	CHRISTIANIAS	CHROMINANCES
CHONDRICHTHYAN	CHORDOPHONIC	CHOROGRAPHIC	CHRISTIANS	CHROMISING
CHONDRICHTHYANS	CHORDOTOMIES	CHOROGRAPHICAL	CHRISTOPHANIES	CHROMIZING
CHONDRIFICATION	CHORDOTOMY	CHOROGRAPHIES	CHRISTOPHANY	CHROMOCENTER
CHONDRIFIED	CHOREGRAPH	CHOROGRAPHY	CHROMAFFIN	CHROMOCENTERS
CHONDRIFIES	CHOREGRAPHED	CHOROIDITIS	CHROMAKEYS	CHROMODYNAMICS
CHONDRIFYING	CHOREGRAPHER	CHOROIDITISES	CHROMATICALLY	CHROMOGENIC
CHONDRIOSOMAL	CHOREGRAPHERS	CHOROLOGICAL	CHROMATICISM	CHROMOGENS
CHONDRIOSOME	CHOREGRAPHIC	CHOROLOGIES	CHROMATICISMS	CHROMOGRAM
CHONDRIOSOMES	CHOREGRAPHIES	CHOROLOGIST	CHROMATICITIES	CHROMOGRAMS
CHONDRITES	CHOREGRAPHING	CHOROLOGISTS	CHROMATICITY	CHROMOMERE
CHONDRITIC	CHOREGRAPHS	CHOROPLETH	CHROMATICNESS	CHROMOMERES
CHONDRITIS	CHOREGRAPHY	CHOROPLETHS	CHROMATICNESSES	CHROMOMERIC
CHONDRITISES	CHOREGUSES	CHORUSMASTER	CHROMATICS	CHROMONEMA
CHONDROBLAST	CHOREIFORM	CHORUSMASTERS	CHROMATIDS	CHROMONEMAL
CHONDROBLASTS	CHOREODRAMA	CHORUSSING	CHROMATINIC	CHROMONEMATA
CHONDROCRANIA	CHOREODRAMAS	CHOUCROUTE	CHROMATINS	CHROMONEMATIC
CHONDROCRANIUM	CHOREOGRAPH	CHOUCROUTES	CHROMATIST	CHROMONEMIC
CHONDROCRANIUMS	CHOREOGRAPHED	CHOULTRIES	CHROMATISTS	CHROMOPHIL
CHONDROGENESES	CHOREOGRAPHER	CHOUNTERED	CHROMATOGRAM	CHROMOPHILIC
CHONDROGENESIS	CHOREOGRAPHERS	CHOUNTERING	CHROMATOGRAMS	CHROMOPHOBE
CHONDROITIN	CHOREOGRAPHIC	CHOWDERHEAD	CHROMATOGRAPH	CHROMOPHORE
CHONDROITINS	CHOREOGRAPHIES	CHOWDERHEADED	CHROMATOGRAPHED	CHROMOPHORES
CHONDROMAS	CHOREOGRAPHING	CHOWDERHEADS	CHROMATOGRAPHER	CHROMOPHORIC
CHONDROMATA	CHOREOGRAPHS	CHOWDERING	CHROMATOGRAPHIC	CHROMOPHOROUS
CHONDROMATOSES	CHOREOGRAPHY	CHOWHOUNDS	CHROMATOGRAPHS	CHROMOPLAST
CHONDROMATOSIS	CHOREOLOGIES	CHOWKIDARS	CHROMATOGRAPHY	CHROMOPLASTS
CHONDROMATOUS	CHOREOLOGIST	CHREMATIST	CHROMATOID	CHROMOPROTEIN
CHONDROPHORINE	CHOREOLOGISTS	CHREMATISTIC	CHROMATOLOGIES	CHROMOPROTEINS
CHONDROPHORINES	CHOREOLOGY	CHREMATISTICS	CHROMATOLOGIST	CHROMOSCOPE
CHONDROSKELETON	CHOREPISCOPAL	CHREMATISTS	CHROMATOLOGISTS	CHROMOSCOPES
CHONDROSTIAN	CHORIAMBIC	CHRESTOMATHIC	CHROMATOLOGY	CHROMOSOMAL
CHONDROSTIANS	CHORIAMBICS	CHRESTOMATHICAL	CHROMATOLYSES	CHROMOSOMALLY
CHONDRULES	CHORIAMBUS	CHRESTOMATHIES	CHROMATOLYSIS	CHROMOSOME
CHOPFALLEN	CHORIAMBUSES	CHRESTOMATHY	CHROMATOLYTIC	CHROMOSOMES
CHOPHOUSES	CHORIOALLANTOIC	CHRISMATION	CHROMATOPHORE	CHROMOSPHERE
CHOPLOGICS	CHORIOALLANTOIS	CHRISMATIONS	CHROMATOPHORES	CHROMOSPHERES
CHOPPERING	CHORIOCARCINOMA	CHRISMATORIES	CHROMATOPHORIC	CHROMOSPHERIC
CHOPPINESS	CHORISATION	CHRISMATORY	CHROMATOPHOROUS	CHROMOTHERAPIES
CHOPPINESSES	CHORISATIONS	CHRISTCROSS	CHROMATOPSIA	CHROMOTHERAPY
CHOPSOCKIES	CHORISTERS	CHRISTCROSSES	CHROMATOPSIAS	CHROMOTYPE
CHOPSTICKS	CHORIZATION	CHRISTENED	CHROMATOSPHERE	CHROMOTYPES

C

CHROMOXYLOGRAPH	CHRONOSCOPE	CHUCKLINGS	CHURNMILKS	CICATRIZING
CHRONAXIES	CHRONOSCOPES	CHUCKWALLA	CHURRIGUERESCO	CICERONEING
CHRONICALLY	CHRONOSCOPIC	CHUCKWALLAS	CHURRIGUERESQUE	CICHORACEOUS
CHRONICITIES	CHRONOTHERAPIES	CHUFFINESS	CHYLACEOUS	CICINNUSES
CHRONICITY	CHRONOTHERAPY	CHUFFINESSES	CHYLIFEROUS	CICISBEISM
CHRONICLED	CHRONOTRON	CHUGALUGGED	CHYLIFICATION	CICISBEISMS
CHRONICLER	CHRONOTRONS	CHUGALUGGING	CHYLIFICATIONS	CICLATOUNS
CHRONICLERS	CHRYSALIDAL	CHUMMINESS	CHYLIFYING	CICLOSPORIN
CHRONICLES	CHRYSALIDES	CHUMMINESSES	CHYLOMICRON	CICLOSPORINS
CHRONICLING	CHRYSALIDS	CHUNDERING	CHYLOMICRONS	CIGARETTES
CHRONOBIOLOGIC	CHRYSALISES	CHUNDEROUS	CHYMIFEROUS	CIGARILLOS
CHRONOBIOLOGIES	CHRYSANTHEMUM	CHUNKINESS	CHYMIFICATION	CIGUATERAS
CHRONOBIOLOGIST	CHRYSANTHEMUMS	CHUNKINESSES	CHYMIFICATIONS	CILIATIONS
CHRONOBIOLOGY	CHRYSANTHS	CHUNNERING	CHYMIFYING	CIMETIDINE
CHRONOGRAM	CHRYSAROBIN	CHUNTERING	CHYMISTRIES	CIMETIDINES
CHRONOGRAMMATIC	CHRYSAROBINS	CHUPATTIES	CHYMOTRYPSIN	CINCHONACEOUS
CHRONOGRAMS	CHRYSOBERYL	CHUPRASSIES	CHYMOTRYPSINS	CINCHONIDINE
CHRONOGRAPH	CHRYSOBERYLS	CHURCHGOER	CHYMOTRYPTIC	CINCHONIDINES
CHRONOGRAPHER	CHRYSOCOLLA	CHURCHGOERS	CIBACHROME	CINCHONINE
CHRONOGRAPHERS	CHRYSOCOLLAS	CHURCHGOING	CIBACHROMES	CINCHONINES
CHRONOGRAPHIC	CHRYSOCRACIES	CHURCHGOINGS	CICADELLID	CINCHONINIC
CHRONOGRAPHIES	CHRYSOCRACY	CHURCHIANITIES	CICADELLIDS	CINCHONISATION
CHRONOGRAPHS	CHRYSOLITE	CHURCHIANITY	CICATRICES	CINCHONISATIONS
CHRONOGRAPHY	CHRYSOLITES	CHURCHIEST	CICATRICHULE	CINCHONISE
CHRONOLOGER	CHRYSOLITIC	CHURCHINGS	CICATRICHULES	CINCHONISED
CHRONOLOGERS	CHRYSOMELID	CHURCHISMS	CICATRICIAL	CINCHONISES
CHRONOLOGIC	CHRYSOMELIDS	CHURCHLESS	CICATRICLE	CINCHONISING
CHRONOLOGICAL	CHRYSOPHAN	CHURCHLIER	CICATRICLES	CINCHONISM
CHRONOLOGICALLY	CHRYSOPHANS	CHURCHLIEST	CICATRICOSE	CINCHONISMS
CHRONOLOGIES	CHRYSOPHILITE	CHURCHLINESS	CICATRICULA	CINCHONIZATION
CHRONOLOGISE	CHRYSOPHILITES	CHURCHLINESSES	CICATRICULAS	CINCHONIZATIONS
CHRONOLOGISED	CHRYSOPHYTE	CHURCHMANLY	CICATRISANT	CINCHONIZE
CHRONOLOGISES	CHRYSOPHYTES	CHURCHMANSHIP	CICATRISATION	CINCHONIZED
CHRONOLOGISING	CHRYSOPRASE	CHURCHMANSHIPS	CICATRISATIONS	CINCHONIZES
CHRONOLOGIST	CHRYSOPRASES	CHURCHPEOPLE	CICATRISED	CINCHONIZING
CHRONOLOGISTS	CHRYSOTILE	CHURCHWARD	CICATRISER	CINCINNATE
CHRONOLOGIZE	CHRYSOTILES	CHURCHWARDEN	CICATRISERS	CINCINNUSES
CHRONOLOGIZED	CHUBBINESS	CHURCHWARDENS	CICATRISES	CINCTURING
CHRONOLOGIZES	CHUBBINESSES	CHURCHWARDS	CICATRISING	CINEANGIOGRAPHY
CHRONOLOGIZING	CHUCKAWALLA	CHURCHWAYS	CICATRIXES	CINEMAGOER
CHRONOLOGY	CHUCKAWALLAS	CHURCHWOMAN	CICATRIZANT	CINEMAGOERS
CHRONOMETER	CHUCKHOLES	CHURCHWOMEN	CICATRIZATION	CINEMATHEQUE
CHRONOMETERS	CHUCKLEHEAD	CHURCHYARD	CICATRIZATIONS	CINEMATHEQUES
CHRONOMETRIC	CHUCKLEHEADED	CHURCHYARDS	CICATRIZED	CINEMATICALLY
CHRONOMETRICAL	CHUCKLEHEADS	CHURLISHLY	CICATRIZER	CINEMATISE
CHRONOMETRIES	CHUCKLESOME	CHURLISHNESS	CICATRIZERS	CINEMATISED
CHRONOMETRY	CHUCKLINGLY	CHURLISHNESSES	CICATRIZES	CINEMATISES

CINEMATISING	CIRCUITIES	CIRCUMAMBULATOR	CIRCUMFUSED	CIRCUMPOSING
CINEMATIZE	CIRCUITING	CIRCUMBENDIBUS	CIRCUMFUSES	CIRCUMPOSITION
CINEMATIZED	CIRCUITOUS	CIRCUMCENTER	CIRCUMFUSILE	CIRCUMPOSITIONS
CINEMATIZES	CIRCUITOUSLY	CIRCUMCENTERS	CIRCUMFUSING	CIRCUMSCISSILE
CINEMATIZING	CIRCUITOUSNESS	CIRCUMCENTRE	CIRCUMFUSION	CIRCUMSCRIBABLE
CINEMATOGRAPH	CIRCUITRIES	CIRCUMCENTRES	CIRCUMFUSIONS	CIRCUMSCRIBE
CINEMATOGRAPHED	CIRCULABLE	CIRCUMCIRCLE	CIRCUMGYRATE	CIRCUMSCRIBED
CINEMATOGRAPHER	CIRCULARISATION	CIRCUMCIRCLES	CIRCUMGYRATED	CIRCUMSCRIBER
CINEMATOGRAPHIC	CIRCULARISE	CIRCUMCISE	CIRCUMGYRATES	CIRCUMSCRIBERS
CINEMATOGRAPHS	CIRCULARISED	CIRCUMCISED	CIRCUMGYRATING	CIRCUMSCRIBES
CINEMATOGRAPHY	CIRCULARISER	CIRCUMCISER	CIRCUMGYRATION	CIRCUMSCRIBING
CINEMICROGRAPHY	CIRCULARISERS	CIRCUMCISERS	CIRCUMGYRATIONS	CIRCUMSCRIPTION
CINEPHILES	CIRCULARISES	CIRCUMCISES	CIRCUMGYRATORY	CIRCUMSCRIPTIVE
CINEPLEXES	CIRCULARISING	CIRCUMCISING	CIRCUMINCESSION	CIRCUMSOLAR
CINERARIAS	CIRCULARITIES	CIRCUMCISION	CIRCUMINSESSION	CIRCUMSPECT
CINERARIUM	CIRCULARITY	CIRCUMCISIONS	CIRCUMJACENCIES	CIRCUMSPECTION
CINERATION	CIRCULARIZATION	CIRCUMDUCE	CIRCUMJACENCY	CIRCUMSPECTIONS
CINERATIONS	CIRCULARIZE	CIRCUMDUCED	CIRCUMJACENT	CIRCUMSPECTIVE
CINERATORS	CIRCULARIZED	CIRCUMDUCES	CIRCUMLITTORAL	CIRCUMSPECTLY
CINERITIOUS	CIRCULARIZER	CIRCUMDUCING	CIRCUMLOCUTE	CIRCUMSPECTNESS
CINGULATED	CIRCULARIZERS	CIRCUMDUCT	CIRCUMLOCUTED	CIRCUMSTANCE
CINNABARIC	CIRCULARIZES	CIRCUMDUCTED	CIRCUMLOCUTES	CIRCUMSTANCED
CINNABARINE	CIRCULARIZING	CIRCUMDUCTING	CIRCUMLOCUTING	CIRCUMSTANCES
CINNAMONIC	CIRCULARLY	CIRCUMDUCTION	CIRCUMLOCUTION	CIRCUMSTANCING
CINNARIZINE	CIRCULARNESS	CIRCUMDUCTIONS	CIRCUMLOCUTIONS	CIRCUMSTANTIAL
CINNARIZINES	CIRCULARNESSES	CIRCUMDUCTORY	CIRCUMLOCUTORY	CIRCUMSTANTIALS
CINQUECENTIST	CIRCULATABLE	CIRCUMDUCTS	CIRCUMLUNAR	CIRCUMSTANTIATE
CINQUECENTISTS	CIRCULATED	CIRCUMFERENCE	CIRCUMMURE	CIRCUMSTELLAR
CINQUECENTO	CIRCULATES	CIRCUMFERENCES	CIRCUMMURED	CIRCUMVALLATE
CINQUECENTOS	CIRCULATING	CIRCUMFERENTIAL	CIRCUMMURES	CIRCUMVALLATED
CINQUEFOIL	CIRCULATINGS	CIRCUMFERENTOR	CIRCUMMURING	CIRCUMVALLATES
CINQUEFOILS	CIRCULATION	CIRCUMFERENTORS	CIRCUMNAVIGABLE	CIRCUMVALLATING
CIPHERINGS	CIRCULATIONS	CIRCUMFLECT	CIRCUMNAVIGATE	CIRCUMVALLATION
CIPHERTEXT	CIRCULATIVE	CIRCUMFLECTED	CIRCUMNAVIGATED	CIRCUMVENT
CIPHERTEXTS	CIRCULATOR	CIRCUMFLECTING	CIRCUMNAVIGATES	CIRCUMVENTED
CIPOLLINOS	CIRCULATORS	CIRCUMFLECTS	CIRCUMNAVIGATOR	CIRCUMVENTER
CIPROFLOXACIN	CIRCULATORY	CIRCUMFLEX	CIRCUMNUTATE	CIRCUMVENTERS
CIPROFLOXACINS	CIRCUMAMBAGES	CIRCUMFLEXES	CIRCUMNUTATED	CIRCUMVENTING
CIRCASSIAN	CIRCUMAMBAGIOUS	CIRCUMFLEXION	CIRCUMNUTATES	CIRCUMVENTION
CIRCASSIANS	CIRCUMAMBIENCE	CIRCUMFLEXIONS	CIRCUMNUTATING	CIRCUMVENTIONS
CIRCASSIENNE	CIRCUMAMBIENCES	CIRCUMFLUENCE	CIRCUMNUTATION	CIRCUMVENTIVE
CIRCASSIENNES	CIRCUMAMBIENCY	CIRCUMFLUENCES	CIRCUMNUTATIONS	CIRCUMVENTOR
CIRCENSIAL	CIRCUMAMBIENT	CIRCUMFLUENT	CIRCUMNUTATORY	CIRCUMVENTORS
CIRCENSIAN	CIRCUMAMBIENTLY	CIRCUMFLUOUS	CIRCUMPOLAR	CIRCUMVENTS
CIRCINATELY	CIRCUMAMBULATE	CIRCUMFORANEAN	CIRCUMPOSE	CIRCUMVOLUTION
CIRCUITEER	CIRCUMAMBULATED	CIRCUMFORANEOUS	CIRCUMPOSED	CIRCUMVOLUTIONS
CIRCUITEERS	CIRCUMAMBULATES	CIRCUMFUSE	CIRCUMPOSES	CIRCUMVOLUTORY

CIRCUMVOLVE
CIRCUMVOLVED
CIRCUMVOLVES
CIRCUMVOLVING
CIRRHIPEDE
CIRRHIPEDES
CIRRHOTICS
CIRRIGRADE
CIRRIPEDES
CIRROCUMULI
CIRROCUMULUS
CIRROSTRATI
CIRROSTRATIVE
CIRROSTRATUS
CISMONTANE
CISPLATINS
CISPONTINE
CISTACEOUS
CITATIONAL
CITHARISTIC
CITHARISTS
CITIFICATION
CITIFICATIONS
CITIZENESS
CITIZENESSES
CITIZENISE
CITIZENISED
CITIZENISES
CITIZENISING
CITIZENIZE
CITIZENIZED
CITIZENIZES
CITIZENIZING
CITIZENRIES
CITIZENSHIP
CITIZENSHIPS
CITRICULTURE
CITRICULTURES
CITRICULTURIST
CITRICULTURISTS
CITRONELLA
CITRONELLAL
CITRONELLALS
CITRONELLAS
CITRONELLOL
CITRONELLOLS
CITRULLINE

CITRULLINES
CITYFICATION
CITYFICATIONS
CITYSCAPES
CIVILIANISATION
CIVILIANISE
CIVILIANISED
CIVILIANISES
CIVILIANISING
CIVILIANIZATION
CIVILIANIZE
CIVILIANIZED
CIVILIANIZES
CIVILIANIZING
CIVILISABLE
CIVILISATION
CIVILISATIONAL
CIVILISATIONS
CIVILISERS
CIVILISING
CIVILITIES
CIVILIZABLE
CIVILIZATION
CIVILIZATIONAL
CIVILIZATIONS
CIVILIZERS
CIVILIZING
CIVILNESSES
CLABBERING
CLACKBOXES
CLACKDISHES
CLADISTICALLY
CLADISTICS
CLADOCERAN
CLADOCERANS
CLADOGENESES
CLADOGENESIS
CLADOGENETIC
CLADOGRAMS
CLADOPHYLL
CLADOPHYLLS
CLADOSPORIA
CLADOSPORIUM
CLADOSPORIUMS
CLAIRAUDIENCE
CLAIRAUDIENCES
CLAIRAUDIENT

CLAIRAUDIENTLY
CLAIRAUDIENTS
CLAIRCOLLE
CLAIRCOLLES
CLAIRSCHACH
CLAIRSCHACHS
CLAIRVOYANCE
CLAIRVOYANCES
CLAIRVOYANCIES
CLAIRVOYANCY
CLAIRVOYANT
CLAIRVOYANTLY
CLAIRVOYANTS
CLAMANCIES
CLAMATORIAL
CLAMBERERS
CLAMBERING
CLAMJAMFRIES
CLAMJAMFRY
CLAMJAMPHRIE
CLAMJAMPHRIES
CLAMMINESS
CLAMMINESSES
CLAMOROUSLY
CLAMOROUSNESS
CLAMOROUSNESSES
CLAMOURERS
CLAMOURING
CLAMPDOWNS
CLAMPERING
CLAMSHELLS
CLANDESTINE
CLANDESTINELY
CLANDESTINENESS
CLANDESTINITIES
CLANDESTINITY
CLANGBOXES
CLANGORING
CLANGOROUS
CLANGOROUSLY
CLANGOURED
CLANGOURING
CLANJAMFRAY
CLANJAMFRAYS
CLANKINGLY
CLANNISHLY
CLANNISHNESS

CLANNISHNESSES
CLANSWOMAN
CLANSWOMEN
CLAPBOARDED
CLAPBOARDING
CLAPBOARDS
CLAPBREADS
CLAPDISHES
CLAPOMETER
CLAPOMETERS
CLAPPERBOARD
CLAPPERBOARDS
CLAPPERBOY
CLAPPERBOYS
CLAPPERCLAW
CLAPPERCLAWED
CLAPPERCLAWER
CLAPPERCLAWERS
CLAPPERCLAWING
CLAPPERCLAWS
CLAPPERING
CLAPPERINGS
CLAPTRAPPERIES
CLAPTRAPPERY
CLARABELLA
CLARABELLAS
CLARENDONS
CLARIBELLA
CLARIBELLAS
CLARICHORD
CLARICHORDS
CLARIFICATION
CLARIFICATIONS
CLARIFIERS
CLARIFYING
CLARINETIST
CLARINETISTS
CLARINETTIST
CLARINETTISTS
CLARIONETS
CLARIONING
CLARTHEADS
CLASHINGLY
CLASSICALISM
CLASSICALISMS
CLASSICALIST
CLASSICALISTS

CLASSICALITIES
CLASSICALITY
CLASSICALLY
CLASSICALNESS
CLASSICALNESSES
CLASSICALS
CLASSICISE
CLASSICISED
CLASSICISES
CLASSICISING
CLASSICISM
CLASSICISMS
CLASSICIST
CLASSICISTIC
CLASSICISTS
CLASSICIZE
CLASSICIZED
CLASSICIZES
CLASSICIZING
CLASSIFIABLE
CLASSIFICATION
CLASSIFICATIONS
CLASSIFICATORY
CLASSIFIED
CLASSIFIER
CLASSIFIERS
CLASSIFIES
CLASSIFYING
CLASSINESS
CLASSINESSES
CLASSLESSNESS
CLASSLESSNESSES
CLASSMATES
CLASSROOMS
CLASSWORKS
CLATHRATES
CLATTERERS
CLATTERING
CLATTERINGLY
CLAUCHTING
CLAUDICATION
CLAUDICATIONS
CLAUGHTING
CLAUSTRATION
CLAUSTRATIONS
CLAUSTROPHOBE
CLAUSTROPHOBES

CLAUSTROPHOBIA	CLEARNESSES	CLERKLINESS	CLIMATOLOGICAL	CLINTONIAS
CLAUSTROPHOBIAS	CLEARSKINS	CLERKLINESSES	CLIMATOLOGIES	CLIOMETRIC
CLAUSTROPHOBIC	CLEARSTORIED	CLERKLINGS	CLIMATOLOGIST	CLIOMETRICAL
CLAVATIONS	CLEARSTORIES	CLERKSHIPS	CLIMATOLOGISTS	CLIOMETRICIAN
CLAVECINIST	CLEARSTORY	CLEROMANCIES	CLIMATOLOGY	CLIOMETRICIANS
CLAVECINISTS	CLEARWEEDS	CLEROMANCY	CLIMATURES	CLIOMETRICS
CLAVICEMBALO	CLEARWINGS	CLERUCHIAL	CLIMAXLESS	CLIPBOARDS
CLAVICEMBALOS	CLEAVABILITIES	CLERUCHIAS	CLIMBDOWNS	CLIPSHEARS
CLAVICHORD	CLEAVABILITY	CLERUCHIES	CLINANDRIA	CLIPSHEETS
CLAVICHORDIST	CLEAVABLENESS	CLEVERALITIES	CLINANDRIUM	CLIQUINESS
CLAVICHORDISTS	CLEAVABLENESSES	CLEVERALITY	CLINCHINGLY	CLIQUINESSES
CLAVICHORDS	CLEISTOGAMIC	CLEVERDICK	CLINDAMYCIN	CLIQUISHLY
CLAVICORNS	CLEISTOGAMIES	CLEVERDICKS	CLINDAMYCINS	CLIQUISHNESS
CLAVICULAE	CLEISTOGAMOUS	CLEVERNESS	CLINGFILMS	CLIQUISHNESSES
CLAVICULAR	CLEISTOGAMOUSLY	CLEVERNESSES	CLINGFISHES	CLISHMACLAVER
CLAVICULATE	CLEISTOGAMY	CLIANTHUSES	CLINGINESS	CLISHMACLAVERS
CLAVICYTHERIA	CLEMATISES	CLICKETING	CLINGINESSES	CLISTOGAMIES
CLAVICYTHERIUM	CLEMENCIES	CLICKSTREAM	CLINGINGLY	CLISTOGAMY
CLAVIERIST	CLEMENTINE	CLICKSTREAMS	CLINGINGNESS	CLITICISED
CLAVIERISTIC	CLEMENTINES	CLICKWRAPS	CLINGINGNESSES	CLITICISES
CLAVIERISTS	CLENBUTEROL	CLIENTAGES	CLINGSTONE	CLITICISING
CLAVIGEROUS	CLENBUTEROLS	CLIENTELES	CLINGSTONES	CLITICIZED
CLAWHAMMER	CLEOPATRAS	CLIENTLESS	CLINICALLY	CLITICIZES
CLAYMATION	CLEPSYDRAE	CLIENTSHIP	CLINICALNESS	CLITICIZING
CLAYMATIONS	CLEPSYDRAS	CLIENTSHIPS	CLINICALNESSES	CLITORECTOMIES
CLAYSTONES	CLEPTOCRACIES	CLIFFHANGER	CLINICIANS	CLITORECTOMY
CLAYTONIAS	CLEPTOCRACY	CLIFFHANGERS	CLINKERING	CLITORIDECTOMY
CLEANABILITIES	CLEPTOMANIA	CLIFFHANGING	CLINKSTONE	CLITORIDES
CLEANABILITY	CLEPTOMANIAC	CLIFFHANGINGS	CLINKSTONES	CLITORISES
CLEANHANDED	CLEPTOMANIACS	CLIFFHANGS	CLINOCHLORE	CLITTERING
CLEANLIEST	CLEPTOMANIAS	CLIMACTERIC	CLINOCHLORES	CLOACALINE
CLEANLINESS	CLERESTORIED	CLIMACTERICAL	CLINODIAGONAL	CLOACITISES
CLEANLINESSES	CLERESTORIES	CLIMACTERICALLY	CLINODIAGONALS	CLOAKROOMS
CLEANNESSES	CLERESTORY	CLIMACTERICS	CLINOMETER	CLOBBERING
CLEANSABLE	CLERGIABLE	CLIMACTICAL	CLINOMETERS	CLOCKMAKER
CLEANSINGS	CLERGYABLE	CLIMACTICALLY	CLINOMETRIC	CLOCKMAKERS
CLEANSKINS	CLERGYWOMAN	CLIMATICAL	CLINOMETRICAL	CLOCKWORKS
CLEARANCES	CLERGYWOMEN	CLIMATICALLY	CLINOMETRIES	CLODDISHLY
CLEARCOLED	CLERICALISM	CLIMATISED	CLINOMETRY	CLODDISHNESS
CLEARCOLES	CLERICALISMS	CLIMATISES	CLINOPINACOID	CLODDISHNESSES
CLEARCOLING	CLERICALIST	CLIMATISING	CLINOPINACOIDS	CLODHOPPER
CLEARCUTTING	CLERICALISTS	CLIMATIZED	CLINOPINAKOID	CLODHOPPERS
CLEARHEADED	CLERICALLY	CLIMATIZES	CLINOPINAKOIDS	CLODHOPPING
CLEARHEADEDLY	CLERICATES	CLIMATIZING	CLINOPYROXENE	CLOFIBRATE
CLEARHEADEDNESS	CLERICITIES	CLIMATOGRAPHIES	CLINOPYROXENES	CLOFIBRATES
CLEARINGHOUSE	CLERKESSES	CLIMATOGRAPHY	CLINOSTATS	CLOGDANCES
CLEARINGHOUSES	CLERKLIEST	CLIMATOLOGIC	CLINQUANTS	CLOGGINESS

C

CLOGGINESSES	CLOUDINESS	CNIDOBLASTS	COAGULABLE	COARSENING
CLOISONNAGE	CLOUDINESSES	COACERVATE	COAGULANTS	COASSISTED
CLOISONNAGES	CLOUDLANDS	COACERVATED	COAGULASES	COASSISTING
CLOISONNES	CLOUDLESSLY	COACERVATES	COAGULATED	COASSUMING
CLOISTERED	CLOUDLESSNESS	COACERVATING	COAGULATES	COASTEERING
CLOISTERER	CLOUDLESSNESSES	COACERVATION	COAGULATING	COASTEERINGS
CLOISTERERS	CLOUDSCAPE	COACERVATIONS	COAGULATION	COASTGUARD
CLOISTERING	CLOUDSCAPES	COACHBUILDER	COAGULATIONS	COASTGUARDMAN
CLOISTRESS	CLOUDTOWNS	COACHBUILDERS	COAGULATIVE	COASTGUARDMEN
CLOISTRESSES	CLOVERGRASS	COACHBUILDING	COAGULATOR	COASTGUARDS
CLOMIPHENE	CLOVERGRASSES	COACHBUILDINGS	COAGULATORS	COASTGUARDSMAN
CLOMIPHENES	CLOVERLEAF	COACHBUILT	COAGULATORY	COASTGUARDSMEN
CLONAZEPAM	CLOVERLEAFS	COACHLINES	COALESCENCE	COASTLANDS
CLONAZEPAMS	CLOVERLEAVES	COACHLOADS	COALESCENCES	COASTLINES
CLONICITIES	CLOWNERIES	COACHWHIPS	COALESCENT	COASTWARDS
CLONIDINES	CLOWNFISHES	COACHWOODS	COALESCING	COATDRESSES
CLOSEDOWNS	CLOWNISHLY	COACHWORKS	COALFIELDS	COATIMUNDI
CLOSEFISTED	CLOWNISHNESS	COACTIVELY	COALFISHES	COATIMUNDIS
CLOSEHEADS	CLOWNISHNESSES	COACTIVITIES	COALHOUSES	COATSTANDS
CLOSEMOUTHED	CLOXACILLIN	COACTIVITY	COALIFICATION	COATTENDED
CLOSENESSES	CLOXACILLINS	COADAPTATION	COALIFICATIONS	COATTENDING
CLOSESTOOL	CLOZAPINES	COADAPTATIONS	COALIFYING	COATTESTED
CLOSESTOOLS	CLUBABILITIES	COADJACENCIES	COALITIONAL	COATTESTING
CLOSETFULS	CLUBABILITY	COADJACENCY	COALITIONER	COAUTHORED
CLOSTRIDIA	CLUBBABILITIES	COADJACENT	COALITIONERS	COAUTHORING
CLOSTRIDIAL	CLUBBABILITY	COADJUTANT	COALITIONISM	COAUTHORSHIP
CLOSTRIDIAN	CLUBBINESS	COADJUTANTS	COALITIONISMS	COAUTHORSHIPS
CLOSTRIDIUM	CLUBBINESSES	COADJUTORS	COALITIONIST	COBALAMINS
CLOSTRIDIUMS	CLUBFOOTED	COADJUTORSHIP	COALITIONISTS	COBALTIFEROUS
CLOTHBOUND	CLUBHAULED	COADJUTORSHIPS	COALITIONS	COBALTINES
CLOTHESHORSE	CLUBHAULING	COADJUTRESS	COALMASTER	COBALTITES
CLOTHESHORSES	CLUBHOUSES	COADJUTRESSES	COALMASTERS	COBBLERIES
CLOTHESLINE	CLUBMANSHIP	COADJUTRICES	COALMINERS	COBBLESTONE
CLOTHESLINED	CLUBMANSHIPS	COADJUTRIX	COANCHORED	COBBLESTONED
CLOTHESLINES	CLUBMASTER	COADJUTRIXES	COANCHORING	COBBLESTONES
CLOTHESLINING	CLUBMASTERS	COADMIRING	COANNEXING	COBBLESTONING
CLOTHESPIN	CLUBRUSHES	COADMITTED	COAPPEARED	COBELLIGERENT
CLOTHESPINS	CLUMPINESS	COADMITTING	COAPPEARING	COBELLIGERENTS
CLOTHESPRESS	CLUMPINESSES	COADUNATED	COAPTATION	COBWEBBERIES
CLOTHESPRESSES	CLUMSINESS	COADUNATES	COAPTATIONS	COBWEBBERY
CLOTTERING	CLUMSINESSES	COADUNATING	COARCTATED	COBWEBBIER
CLOTTINESS	CLUSTERING	COADUNATION	COARCTATES	COBWEBBIEST
CLOTTINESSES	CLUSTERINGLY	COADUNATIONS	COARCTATING	COBWEBBING
CLOUDBERRIES	CLUTTERING	COADUNATIVE	COARCTATION	COCAINISATION
CLOUDBERRY	CLYPEIFORM	COAGENCIES	COARCTATIONS	COCAINISATIONS
CLOUDBURST	CNIDARIANS	COAGULABILITIES	COARSENESS	COCAINISED
CLOUDBURSTS	CNIDOBLAST	COAGULABILITY	COARSENESSES	COCAINISES

C

COCAINISING	COCKATIELS	COCKSUCKER	CODEFENDANT	COEDUCATIONS
COCAINISMS	COCKATRICE	COCKSUCKERS	CODEFENDANTS	COEFFICIENT
COCAINISTS	COCKATRICES	COCKSURELY	CODEPENDENCE	COEFFICIENTS
COCAINIZATION	COCKBILLED	COCKSURENESS	CODEPENDENCES	COELACANTH
COCAINIZATIONS	COCKBILLING	COCKSURENESSES	CODEPENDENCIES	COELACANTHIC
COCAINIZED	COCKCHAFER	COCKSWAINED	CODEPENDENCY	COELACANTHS
COCAINIZES	COCKCHAFERS	COCKSWAINING	CODEPENDENT	COELANAGLYPHIC
COCAINIZING	COCKCROWING	COCKSWAINS	CODEPENDENTS	COELENTERA
COCAPTAINED	COCKCROWINGS	COCKTAILED	CODERIVING	COELENTERATE
COCAPTAINING	COCKERNONIES	COCKTAILING	CODESIGNED	COELENTERATES
COCAPTAINS	COCKERNONY	COCKTEASER	CODESIGNING	COELENTERIC
COCARBOXYLASE	COCKEYEDLY	COCKTEASERS	CODETERMINATION	COELENTERON
COCARBOXYLASES	COCKEYEDNESS	COCKTHROWING	CODEVELOPED	COELOMATES
COCARCINOGEN	COCKEYEDNESSES	COCKTHROWINGS	CODEVELOPER	COELOMATIC
COCARCINOGENIC	COCKFIGHTING	COCKYLEEKIES	CODEVELOPERS	COELOSTATS
COCARCINOGENS	COCKFIGHTINGS	COCKYLEEKY	CODEVELOPING	COELUROSAUR
COCATALYST	COCKFIGHTS	COCOMPOSER	CODEVELOPS	COELUROSAURS
COCATALYSTS	COCKHORSES	COCOMPOSERS	CODICILLARY	COEMBODIED
COCCIDIOSES	COCKIELEEKIE	COCONSCIOUS	CODICOLOGICAL	COEMBODIES
COCCIDIOSIS	COCKIELEEKIES	COCONSCIOUSES	CODICOLOGIES	COEMBODYING
COCCIDIOSTAT	COCKINESSES	COCONSCIOUSNESS	CODICOLOGY	COEMPLOYED
COCCIDIOSTATS	COCKLEBOAT	COCONSPIRATOR	CODIFIABILITIES	COEMPLOYING
COCCIFEROUS	COCKLEBOATS	COCONSPIRATORS	CODIFIABILITY	COEMPTIONS
COCCINEOUS	COCKLEBURS	COCOONERIES	CODIFICATION	COENACTING
COCCOLITES	COCKLEERTS	COCOONINGS	CODIFICATIONS	COENAESTHESES
COCCOLITHS	COCKLESHELL	COCOUNSELED	CODIRECTED	COENAESTHESIA
COCHAIRING	COCKLESHELLS	COCOUNSELING	CODIRECTING	COENAESTHESIAS
COCHAIRMAN	COCKMATCHES	COCOUNSELLED	CODIRECTION	COENAESTHESIS
COCHAIRMEN	COCKNEYDOM	COCOUNSELLING	CODIRECTIONS	COENAMORED
COCHAIRPERSON	COCKNEYDOMS	COCOUNSELS	CODIRECTOR	COENAMORING
COCHAIRPERSONS	COCKNEYFICATION	COCOZELLES	CODIRECTORS	COENDURING
COCHAIRWOMAN	COCKNEYFIED	COCREATING	CODISCOVER	COENENCHYMA
COCHAIRWOMEN	COCKNEYFIES	COCREATORS	CODISCOVERED	COENENCHYMAS
COCHAMPION	COCKNEYFYING	COCULTIVATE	CODISCOVERER	COENENCHYMATA
COCHAMPIONS	COCKNEYISH	COCULTIVATED	CODISCOVERERS	COENESTHESES
COCHINEALS	COCKNEYISM	COCULTIVATES	CODISCOVERING	COENESTHESIA
COCHLEARES	COCKNEYISMS	COCULTIVATING	CODISCOVERS	COENESTHESIAS
COCHLEARIFORM	COCKNIFICATION	COCULTIVATION	CODOLOGIES	COENESTHESIS
COCHLEATED	COCKNIFICATIONS	COCULTIVATIONS	CODOMINANCE	COENESTHETIC
COCKABULLIES	COCKNIFIED	COCULTURED	CODOMINANCES	COENOBITES
COCKABULLY	COCKNIFIES	COCULTURES	CODOMINANT	COENOBITIC
COCKALEEKIE	COCKNIFYING	COCULTURING	CODOMINANTS	COENOBITICAL
COCKALEEKIES	COCKROACHES	COCURATORS	CODSWALLOP	COENOBITISM
COCKALORUM	COCKSCOMBS	COCURRICULAR	CODSWALLOPS	COENOBITISMS
COCKALORUMS	COCKSFOOTS	COCUSWOODS	COEDUCATION	COENOCYTES
COCKAMAMIE	COCKSINESS	CODECLINATION	COEDUCATIONAL	COENOCYTIC
COCKATEELS	COCKSINESSES	CODECLINATIONS	COEDUCATIONALLY	COENOSARCS

C

COENOSPECIES	COEXTENSION	COGNITIVITIES	COHOSTESSES	COLATITUDES
COENOSTEUM	COEXTENSIONS	COGNITIVITY	COHOSTESSING	COLCANNONS
COENOSTEUMS	COEXTENSIVE	COGNIZABLE	COHOUSINGS	COLCHICINE
COENZYMATIC	COEXTENSIVELY	COGNIZABLY	COHYPONYMS	COLCHICINES
COENZYMATICALLY	COFAVORITE	COGNIZANCE	COIFFEUSES	COLCHICUMS
COEQUALITIES	COFAVORITES	COGNIZANCES	COIFFURING	COLCOTHARS
COEQUALITY	COFEATURED	COGNOMINAL	COILABILITIES	COLDBLOODS
COEQUALNESS	COFEATURES	COGNOMINALLY	COILABILITY	COLDCOCKED
COEQUALNESSES	COFEATURING	COGNOMINATE	COINCIDENCE	COLDCOCKING
COEQUATING	COFFEEHOUSE	COGNOMINATED	COINCIDENCES	COLDHEARTED
COERCIMETER	COFFEEHOUSES	COGNOMINATES	COINCIDENCIES	COLDHEARTEDLY
COERCIMETERS	COFFEEMAKER	COGNOMINATING	COINCIDENCY	COLDHEARTEDNESS
COERCIONIST	COFFEEMAKERS	COGNOMINATION	COINCIDENT	COLDHOUSES
COERCIONISTS	COFFEEPOTS	COGNOMINATIONS	COINCIDENTAL	COLDNESSES
COERCIVELY	COFFERDAMS	COGNOSCENTE	COINCIDENTALLY	COLECTOMIES
COERCIVENESS	COFFINITES	COGNOSCENTI	COINCIDENTLY	COLEMANITE
COERCIVENESSES	COFINANCED	COGNOSCIBLE	COINCIDING	COLEMANITES
COERCIVITIES	COFINANCES	COGNOSCING	COINFECTED	COLEOPTERA
COERCIVITY	COFINANCING	COHABITANT	COINFECTING	COLEOPTERAL
COERECTING	COFOUNDERS	COHABITANTS	COINFERRED	COLEOPTERAN
COESSENTIAL	COFOUNDING	COHABITATION	COINFERRING	COLEOPTERANS
COESSENTIALITY	COFUNCTION	COHABITATIONS	COINHERENCE	COLEOPTERIST
COESSENTIALLY	COFUNCTIONS	COHABITEES	COINHERENCES	COLEOPTERISTS
COESSENTIALNESS	COGENERATION	COHABITERS	COINHERING	COLEOPTERON
COETANEOUS	COGENERATIONS	COHABITING	COINHERITANCE	COLEOPTERONS
COETANEOUSLY	COGENERATOR	COHEIRESSES	COINHERITANCES	COLEOPTEROUS
COETANEOUSNESS	COGENERATORS	COHERENCES	COINHERITOR	COLEOPTERS
COETERNALLY	COGITATING	COHERENCIES	COINHERITORS	COLEOPTILE
COETERNITIES	COGITATINGLY	COHERENTLY	COINSTANTANEITY	COLEOPTILES
COETERNITY	COGITATION	COHERITORS	COINSTANTANEOUS	COLEORHIZA
COEVALITIES	COGITATIONS	COHESIBILITIES	COINSURANCE	COLEORHIZAE
COEVOLUTION	COGITATIVE	COHESIBILITY	COINSURANCES	COLEORHIZAS
COEVOLUTIONARY	COGITATIVELY	COHESIONLESS	COINSURERS	COLEORRHIZA
COEVOLUTIONS	COGITATIVENESS	COHESIVELY	COINSURING	COLEORRHIZAE
COEVOLVING	COGITATORS	COHESIVENESS	COINTERRED	COLEORRHIZAS
COEXECUTOR	COGNATENESS	COHESIVENESSES	COINTERRING	COLESTIPOL
COEXECUTORS	COGNATENESSES	COHIBITING	COINTREAUS	COLESTIPOLS
COEXECUTRICES	COGNATIONS	COHIBITION	COINVENTED	COLICKIEST
COEXECUTRIX	COGNISABLE	COHIBITIONS	COINVENTING	COLICROOTS
COEXECUTRIXES	COGNISABLY	COHIBITIVE	COINVENTOR	COLICWEEDS
COEXERTING	COGNISANCE	COHOBATING	COINVENTORS	COLINEARITIES
COEXISTENCE	COGNISANCES	COHOMOLOGICAL	COINVESTIGATOR	COLINEARITY
COEXISTENCES	COGNITIONAL	COHOMOLOGIES	COINVESTIGATORS	COLIPHAGES
COEXISTENT	COGNITIONS	COHOMOLOGY	COINVESTOR	COLLABORATE
COEXISTING	COGNITIVELY	COHORTATIVE	COINVESTORS	COLLABORATED
COEXTENDED	COGNITIVISM	COHORTATIVES	COKULORISES	COLLABORATES
COEXTENDING	COGNITIVISMS	COHOSTESSED	COLATITUDE	COLLABORATING

COLLABORATION	COLLECTEDNESS	COLLENCHYMA	COLLOCUTORS	COLOGARITHM
COLLABORATIONS	COLLECTEDNESSES	COLLENCHYMAS	COLLOCUTORY	COLOGARITHMS
COLLABORATIVE	COLLECTIBLE	COLLENCHYMATA	COLLODIONS	COLOMBARDS
COLLABORATIVELY	COLLECTIBLES	COLLENCHYMATOUS	COLLODIUMS	COLONELCIES
COLLABORATIVES	COLLECTING	COLLETERIAL	COLLOGUING	COLONELLING
COLLABORATOR	COLLECTINGS	COLLICULUS	COLLOIDALITIES	COLONELLINGS
COLLABORATORS	COLLECTION	COLLIERIES	COLLOIDALITY	COLONELSHIP
COLLAGENASE	COLLECTIONS	COLLIESHANGIE	COLLOIDALLY	COLONELSHIPS
COLLAGENASES	COLLECTIVE	COLLIESHANGIES	COLLOQUIAL	COLONIALISE
COLLAGENIC	COLLECTIVELY	COLLIGATED	COLLOQUIALISM	COLONIALISED
COLLAGENOUS	COLLECTIVENESS	COLLIGATES	COLLOQUIALISMS	COLONIALISES
COLLAGISTS	COLLECTIVES	COLLIGATING	COLLOQUIALIST	COLONIALISING
COLLAPSABILITY	COLLECTIVISE	COLLIGATION	COLLOQUIALISTS	COLONIALISM
COLLAPSABLE	COLLECTIVISED	COLLIGATIONS	COLLOQUIALITIES	COLONIALISMS
COLLAPSARS	COLLECTIVISES	COLLIGATIVE	COLLOQUIALITY	COLONIALIST
COLLAPSIBILITY	COLLECTIVISING	COLLIMATED	COLLOQUIALLY	COLONIALISTIC
COLLAPSIBLE	COLLECTIVISM	COLLIMATES	COLLOQUIALNESS	COLONIALISTS
COLLAPSING	COLLECTIVISMS	COLLIMATING	COLLOQUIALS	COLONIALIZE
COLLARBONE	COLLECTIVIST	COLLIMATION	COLLOQUIED	COLONIALIZED
COLLARBONES	COLLECTIVISTIC	COLLIMATIONS	COLLOQUIES	COLONIALIZES
COLLARETTE	COLLECTIVISTS	COLLIMATOR	COLLOQUING	COLONIALIZING
COLLARETTES	COLLECTIVITIES	COLLIMATORS	COLLOQUISE	COLONIALLY
COLLARLESS	COLLECTIVITY	COLLINEARITIES	COLLOQUISED	COLONIALNESS
COLLATABLE	COLLECTIVIZE	COLLINEARITY	COLLOQUISES	COLONIALNESSES
COLLATERAL	COLLECTIVIZED	COLLINEARLY	COLLOQUISING	COLONISABLE
COLLATERALISE	COLLECTIVIZES	COLLINSIAS	COLLOQUIST	COLONISATION
COLLATERALISED	COLLECTIVIZING	COLLIQUABLE	COLLOQUISTS	COLONISATIONIST
COLLATERALISES	COLLECTORATE	COLLIQUANT	COLLOQUIUM	COLONISATIONS
COLLATERALISING	COLLECTORATES	COLLIQUATE	COLLOQUIUMS	COLONISERS
COLLATERALITIES	COLLECTORS	COLLIQUATED	COLLOQUIZE	COLONISING
COLLATERALITY	COLLECTORSHIP	COLLIQUATES	COLLOQUIZED	COLONITISES
COLLATERALIZE	COLLECTORSHIPS	COLLIQUATING	COLLOQUIZES	COLONIZABLE
COLLATERALIZED	COLLEGIALISM	COLLIQUATION	COLLOQUIZING	COLONIZATION
COLLATERALIZES	COLLEGIALISMS	COLLIQUATIONS	COLLOQUYING	COLONIZATIONIST
COLLATERALIZING	COLLEGIALITIES	COLLIQUATIVE	COLLOTYPES	COLONIZATIONS
COLLATERALLY	COLLEGIALITY	COLLIQUESCENCE	COLLOTYPIC	COLONIZERS
COLLATERALS	COLLEGIALLY	COLLIQUESCENCES	COLLOTYPIES	COLONIZING
COLLATIONS	COLLEGIANER	COLLISIONAL	COLLUCTATION	COLONNADED
COLLEAGUED	COLLEGIANERS	COLLISIONALLY	COLLUCTATIONS	COLONNADES
COLLEAGUES	COLLEGIANS	COLLISIONS	COLLUSIONS	COLONOSCOPE
COLLEAGUESHIP	COLLEGIATE	COLLOCATED	COLLUSIVELY	COLONOSCOPES
COLLEAGUESHIPS	COLLEGIATELY	COLLOCATES	COLLUVIUMS	COLONOSCOPIES
COLLEAGUING	COLLEGIATES	COLLOCATING	COLLYRIUMS	COLONOSCOPY
COLLECTABLE	COLLEGIUMS	COLLOCATION	COLLYWOBBLES	COLOPHONIES
COLLECTABLES	COLLEMBOLAN	COLLOCATIONAL	COLOBOMATA	COLOQUINTIDA
COLLECTANEA	COLLEMBOLANS	COLLOCATIONS	COLOCATING	COLOQUINTIDAS
COLLECTEDLY	COLLEMBOLOUS	COLLOCUTOR	COLOCYNTHS	COLORATION

COLORATIONS	COLOURABLE	COLTISHNESSES	COMBRETUMS	COMINGLING
COLORATURA	COLOURABLENESS	COLTSFOOTS	COMBURGESS	COMITADJIS
COLORATURAS	COLOURABLY	COLUBRIADS	COMBURGESSES	COMITATIVE
COLORATURE	COLOURANTS	COLUBRIFORM	COMBUSTIBILITY	COMITATIVES
COLORATURES	COLOURATION	COLUMBARIA	COMBUSTIBLE	COMITATUSES
COLORBREED	COLOURATIONS	COLUMBARIES	COMBUSTIBLENESS	COMMANDABLE
COLORBREEDING	COLOURFAST	COLUMBARIUM	COMBUSTIBLES	COMMANDANT
COLORBREEDS	COLOURFASTNESS	COLUMBATES	COMBUSTIBLY	COMMANDANTS
COLORCASTED	COLOURFULLY	COLUMBINES	COMBUSTING	COMMANDANTSHIP
COLORCASTING	COLOURFULNESS	COLUMBITES	COMBUSTION	COMMANDANTSHIPS
COLORCASTS	COLOURFULNESSES	COLUMBIUMS	COMBUSTIONS	COMMANDEER
COLORECTAL	COLOURINGS	COLUMELLAE	COMBUSTIOUS	COMMANDEERED
COLORFASTNESS	COLOURISATION	COLUMELLAR	COMBUSTIVE	COMMANDEERING
COLORFASTNESSES	COLOURISATIONS	COLUMNARITIES	COMBUSTIVES	COMMANDEERS
COLORFULLY	COLOURISED	COLUMNARITY	COMBUSTORS	COMMANDERIES
COLORFULNESS	COLOURISES	COLUMNATED	COMEDDLING	COMMANDERS
COLORFULNESSES	COLOURISING	COLUMNIATED	COMEDICALLY	COMMANDERSHIP
COLORIMETER	COLOURISTIC	COLUMNIATION	COMEDIENNE	COMMANDERSHIPS
COLORIMETERS	COLOURISTS	COLUMNIATIONS	COMEDIENNES	COMMANDERY
COLORIMETRIC	COLOURIZATION	COLUMNISTIC	COMEDIETTA	COMMANDING
COLORIMETRICAL	COLOURIZATIONS	COLUMNISTS	COMEDIETTAS	COMMANDINGLY
COLORIMETRIES	COLOURIZED	COMANAGEMENT	COMEDOGENIC	COMMANDMENT
COLORIMETRY	COLOURIZES	COMANAGEMENTS	COMELINESS	COMMANDMENTS
COLORISATION	COLOURIZING	COMANAGERS	COMELINESSES	COMMANDOES
COLORISATIONS	COLOURLESS	COMANAGING	COMESTIBLE	COMMEASURABLE
COLORISERS	COLOURLESSLY	COMANCHERO	COMESTIBLES	COMMEASURE
COLORISING	COLOURLESSNESS	COMANCHEROS	COMETOGRAPHIES	COMMEASURED
COLORISTIC	COLOURPOINT	COMATOSELY	COMETOGRAPHY	COMMEASURES
COLORISTICALLY	COLOURPOINTS	COMATULIDS	COMETOLOGIES	COMMEASURING
COLORIZATION	COLOURWASH	COMBATABLE	COMETOLOGY	COMMEMORABLE
COLORIZATIONS	COLOURWASHED	COMBATANTS	COMEUPPANCE	COMMEMORATE
COLORIZERS	COLOURWASHES	COMBATIVELY	COMEUPPANCES	COMMEMORATED
COLORIZING	COLOURWASHING	COMBATIVENESS	COMFINESSES	COMMEMORATES
COLORLESSLY	COLOURWAYS	COMBATIVENESSES	COMFITURES	COMMEMORATING
COLORLESSNESS	COLPITISES	COMBATTING	COMFORTABLE	COMMEMORATION
COLORLESSNESSES	COLPORTAGE	COMBINABILITIES	COMFORTABLENESS	COMMEMORATIONAL
COLORPOINT	COLPORTAGES	COMBINABILITY	COMFORTABLY	COMMEMORATIONS
COLORPOINTS	COLPORTEUR	COMBINABLE	COMFORTERS	COMMEMORATIVE
COLOSSALLY	COLPORTEURS	COMBINATION	COMFORTING	COMMEMORATIVELY
COLOSSEUMS	COLPOSCOPE	COMBINATIONAL	COMFORTINGLY	COMMEMORATIVES
COLOSSUSES	COLPOSCOPES	COMBINATIONS	COMFORTLESS	COMMEMORATOR
COLOSTOMIES	COLPOSCOPICAL	COMBINATIVE	COMFORTLESSLY	COMMEMORATORS
COLOSTROUS	COLPOSCOPICALLY	COMBINATORIAL	COMFORTLESSNESS	COMMEMORATORY
COLOSTRUMS	COLPOSCOPIES	COMBINATORIALLY	COMICALITIES	COMMENCEMENT
COLOTOMIES	COLPOSCOPY	COMBINATORICS	COMICALITY	COMMENCEMENTS
COLOURABILITIES	COLPOTOMIES	COMBINATORY	COMICALNESS	COMMENCERS
COLOURABILITY	COLTISHNESS	COMBININGS	COMICALNESSES	COMMENCING

COMMENDABLE
COMMENDABLENESS
COMMENDABLY
COMMENDAMS
COMMENDATION
COMMENDATIONS
COMMENDATOR
COMMENDATORS
COMMENDATORY
COMMENDERS
COMMENDING
COMMENSALISM
COMMENSALISMS
COMMENSALITIES
COMMENSALITY
COMMENSALLY
COMMENSALS
COMMENSURABLE
COMMENSURABLY
COMMENSURATE
COMMENSURATELY
COMMENSURATION
COMMENSURATIONS
COMMENTARIAL
COMMENTARIAT
COMMENTARIATS
COMMENTARIES
COMMENTARY
COMMENTATE
COMMENTATED
COMMENTATES
COMMENTATING
COMMENTATION
COMMENTATIONS
COMMENTATOR
COMMENTATORIAL
COMMENTATORS
COMMENTERS
COMMENTING
COMMENTORS
COMMERCIAL
COMMERCIALESE
COMMERCIALESES
COMMERCIALISE
COMMERCIALISED
COMMERCIALISES
COMMERCIALISING

COMMERCIALISM
COMMERCIALISMS
COMMERCIALIST
COMMERCIALISTIC
COMMERCIALISTS
COMMERCIALITIES
COMMERCIALITY
COMMERCIALIZE
COMMERCIALIZED
COMMERCIALIZES
COMMERCIALIZING
COMMERCIALLY
COMMERCIALS
COMMERCING
COMMERGING
COMMINATED
COMMINATES
COMMINATING
COMMINATION
COMMINATIONS
COMMINATIVE
COMMINATORY
COMMINGLED
COMMINGLES
COMMINGLING
COMMINUTED
COMMINUTES
COMMINUTING
COMMINUTION
COMMINUTIONS
COMMISERABLE
COMMISERATE
COMMISERATED
COMMISERATES
COMMISERATING
COMMISERATINGLY
COMMISERATION
COMMISERATIONS
COMMISERATIVE
COMMISERATIVELY
COMMISERATOR
COMMISERATORS
COMMISSAIRE
COMMISSAIRES
COMMISSARIAL
COMMISSARIAT
COMMISSARIATS

COMMISSARIES
COMMISSARS
COMMISSARY
COMMISSARYSHIP
COMMISSARYSHIPS
COMMISSION
COMMISSIONAIRE
COMMISSIONAIRES
COMMISSIONAL
COMMISSIONARY
COMMISSIONED
COMMISSIONER
COMMISSIONERS
COMMISSIONING
COMMISSIONS
COMMISSURAL
COMMISSURE
COMMISSURES
COMMITMENT
COMMITMENTS
COMMITTABLE
COMMITTALS
COMMITTEEMAN
COMMITTEEMEN
COMMITTEES
COMMITTEESHIP
COMMITTEESHIPS
COMMITTEEWOMAN
COMMITTEEWOMEN
COMMITTERS
COMMITTING
COMMIXTION
COMMIXTIONS
COMMIXTURE
COMMIXTURES
COMMODIFICATION
COMMODIFIED
COMMODIFIES
COMMODIFYING
COMMODIOUS
COMMODIOUSLY
COMMODIOUSNESS
COMMODITIES
COMMODITISE
COMMODITISED
COMMODITISES
COMMODITISING

COMMODITIZE
COMMODITIZED
COMMODITIZES
COMMODITIZING
COMMODORES
COMMONABLE
COMMONAGES
COMMONALITIES
COMMONALITY
COMMONALTIES
COMMONALTY
COMMONHOLD
COMMONHOLDS
COMMONINGS
COMMONNESS
COMMONNESSES
COMMONPLACE
COMMONPLACED
COMMONPLACENESS
COMMONPLACES
COMMONPLACING
COMMONSENSE
COMMONSENSIBLE
COMMONSENSICAL
COMMONWEAL
COMMONWEALS
COMMONWEALTH
COMMONWEALTHS
COMMORANTS
COMMORIENTES
COMMOTIONAL
COMMOTIONS
COMMUNALISATION
COMMUNALISE
COMMUNALISED
COMMUNALISER
COMMUNALISERS
COMMUNALISES
COMMUNALISING
COMMUNALISM
COMMUNALISMS
COMMUNALIST
COMMUNALISTIC
COMMUNALISTS
COMMUNALITIES
COMMUNALITY
COMMUNALIZATION

COMMUNALIZE
COMMUNALIZED
COMMUNALIZER
COMMUNALIZERS
COMMUNALIZES
COMMUNALIZING
COMMUNALLY
COMMUNARDS
COMMUNAUTAIRE
COMMUNAUTAIRES
COMMUNICABILITY
COMMUNICABLE
COMMUNICABLY
COMMUNICANT
COMMUNICANTS
COMMUNICATE
COMMUNICATED
COMMUNICATEE
COMMUNICATEES
COMMUNICATES
COMMUNICATING
COMMUNICATION
COMMUNICATIONAL
COMMUNICATIONS
COMMUNICATIVE
COMMUNICATIVELY
COMMUNICATOR
COMMUNICATORS
COMMUNICATORY
COMMUNINGS
COMMUNIONAL
COMMUNIONALLY
COMMUNIONS
COMMUNIQUE
COMMUNIQUES
COMMUNISATION
COMMUNISATIONS
COMMUNISED
COMMUNISES
COMMUNISING
COMMUNISMS
COMMUNISTIC
COMMUNISTICALLY
COMMUNISTS
COMMUNITAIRE
COMMUNITAIRES
COMMUNITARIAN

C

COMMUNITARIANS	COMPANDERS	COMPASSIONATE	COMPENSATIONAL	COMPLANATE
COMMUNITIES	COMPANDING	COMPASSIONATED	COMPENSATIONS	COMPLANATION
COMMUNIZATION	COMPANDORS	COMPASSIONATELY	COMPENSATIVE	COMPLANATIONS
COMMUNIZATIONS	COMPANIABLE	COMPASSIONATES	COMPENSATOR	COMPLECTED
COMMUNIZED	COMPANIONABLE	COMPASSIONATING	COMPENSATORS	COMPLECTING
COMMUNIZES	COMPANIONABLY	COMPASSIONED	COMPENSATORY	COMPLEMENT
COMMUNIZING	COMPANIONATE	COMPASSIONING	COMPESCING	COMPLEMENTAL
COMMUTABILITIES	COMPANIONED	COMPASSIONLESS	COMPETENCE	COMPLEMENTALLY
COMMUTABILITY	COMPANIONHOOD	COMPASSIONS	COMPETENCES	COMPLEMENTARIES
COMMUTABLE	COMPANIONHOODS	COMPATIBILITIES	COMPETENCIES	COMPLEMENTARILY
COMMUTABLENESS	COMPANIONING	COMPATIBILITY	COMPETENCY	COMPLEMENTARITY
COMMUTATED	COMPANIONLESS	COMPATIBLE	COMPETENTLY	COMPLEMENTARY
COMMUTATES	COMPANIONS	COMPATIBLENESS	COMPETENTNESS	COMPLEMENTATION
COMMUTATING	COMPANIONSHIP	COMPATIBLES	COMPETENTNESSES	COMPLEMENTED
COMMUTATION	COMPANIONSHIPS	COMPATIBLY	COMPETITION	COMPLEMENTING
COMMUTATIONS	COMPANIONWAY	COMPATRIOT	COMPETITIONS	COMPLEMENTISER
COMMUTATIVE	COMPANIONWAYS	COMPATRIOTIC	COMPETITIVE	COMPLEMENTISERS
COMMUTATIVELY	COMPANYING	COMPATRIOTISM	COMPETITIVELY	COMPLEMENTIZER
COMMUTATIVITIES	COMPARABILITIES	COMPATRIOTISMS	COMPETITIVENESS	COMPLEMENTIZERS
COMMUTATIVITY	COMPARABILITY	COMPATRIOTS	COMPETITOR	COMPLEMENTS
COMMUTATOR	COMPARABLE	COMPEARANCE	COMPETITORS	COMPLETABLE
COMMUTATORS	COMPARABLENESS	COMPEARANCES	COMPILATION	COMPLETELY
COMONOMERS	COMPARABLY	COMPEARANT	COMPILATIONS	COMPLETENESS
COMPACTEDLY	COMPARATIST	COMPEARANTS	COMPILATOR	COMPLETENESSES
COMPACTEDNESS	COMPARATISTS	COMPEARING	COMPILATORS	COMPLETERS
COMPACTEDNESSES	COMPARATIVE	COMPEERING	COMPILATORY	COMPLETEST
COMPACTERS	COMPARATIVELY	COMPELLABLE	COMPILEMENT	COMPLETING
COMPACTEST	COMPARATIVENESS	COMPELLABLY	COMPILEMENTS	COMPLETION
COMPACTIBLE	COMPARATIVES	COMPELLATION	COMPLACENCE	COMPLETIONS
COMPACTIFIED	COMPARATIVIST	COMPELLATIONS	COMPLACENCES	COMPLETIST
COMPACTIFIES	COMPARATIVISTS	COMPELLATIVE	COMPLACENCIES	COMPLETISTS
COMPACTIFY	COMPARATOR	COMPELLATIVES	COMPLACENCY	COMPLETIVE
COMPACTIFYING	COMPARATORS	COMPELLERS	COMPLACENT	COMPLETORY
COMPACTING	COMPARISON	COMPELLING	COMPLACENTLY	COMPLEXATION
COMPACTION	COMPARISONS	COMPELLINGLY	COMPLAINANT	COMPLEXATIONS
COMPACTIONS	COMPARTING	COMPENDIOUS	COMPLAINANTS	COMPLEXEDNESS
COMPACTNESS	COMPARTMENT	COMPENDIOUSLY	COMPLAINED	COMPLEXEDNESSES
COMPACTNESSES	COMPARTMENTAL	COMPENDIOUSNESS	COMPLAINER	COMPLEXEST
COMPACTORS	COMPARTMENTALLY	COMPENDIUM	COMPLAINERS	COMPLEXIFIED
COMPACTURE	COMPARTMENTED	COMPENDIUMS	COMPLAINING	COMPLEXIFIES
COMPACTURES	COMPARTMENTING	COMPENSABILITY	COMPLAININGLY	COMPLEXIFY
COMPAGINATE	COMPARTMENTS	COMPENSABLE	COMPLAININGS	COMPLEXIFYING
COMPAGINATED	COMPASSABLE	COMPENSATE	COMPLAINTS	COMPLEXING
COMPAGINATES	COMPASSING	COMPENSATED	COMPLAISANCE	COMPLEXION
COMPAGINATING	COMPASSINGS	COMPENSATES	COMPLAISANCES	COMPLEXIONAL
COMPAGINATION	COMPASSION	COMPENSATING	COMPLAISANT	COMPLEXIONED
COMPAGINATIONS	COMPASSIONABLE	COMPENSATION	COMPLAISANTLY	COMPLEXIONLESS

COMPLEXIONS	COMPLOTTER	COMPOTATORS	COMPRISING	COMPUTABILITIES
COMPLEXITIES	COMPLOTTERS	COMPOTATORY	COMPRIZING	COMPUTABILITY
COMPLEXITY	COMPLOTTING	COMPOTIERS	COMPROMISE	COMPUTABLE
COMPLEXNESS	COMPLUVIUM	COMPOUNDABLE	COMPROMISED	COMPUTANTS
COMPLEXNESSES	COMPLUVIUMS	COMPOUNDED	COMPROMISER	COMPUTATION
COMPLEXOMETRIC	COMPONENCIES	COMPOUNDER	COMPROMISERS	COMPUTATIONAL
COMPLEXONE	COMPONENCY	COMPOUNDERS	COMPROMISES	COMPUTATIONALLY
COMPLEXONES	COMPONENTAL	COMPOUNDING	COMPROMISING	COMPUTATIONS
COMPLEXUSES	COMPONENTIAL	COMPRADORE	COMPROMISINGLY	COMPUTATIVE
COMPLIABLE	COMPONENTS	COMPRADORES	COMPROVINCIAL	COMPUTATOR
COMPLIABLENESS	COMPORTANCE	COMPRADORS	COMPTROLLED	COMPUTATORS
COMPLIABLY	COMPORTANCES	COMPREHEND	COMPTROLLER	COMPUTERATE
COMPLIANCE	COMPORTING	COMPREHENDED	COMPTROLLERS	COMPUTERDOM
COMPLIANCES	COMPORTMENT	COMPREHENDIBLE	COMPTROLLERSHIP	COMPUTERDOMS
COMPLIANCIES	COMPORTMENTS	COMPREHENDING	COMPTROLLING	COMPUTERESE
COMPLIANCY	COMPOSEDLY	COMPREHENDS	COMPTROLLS	COMPUTERESES
COMPLIANTLY	COMPOSEDNESS	COMPREHENSIBLE	COMPULSATIVE	COMPUTERISABLE
COMPLIANTNESS	COMPOSEDNESSES	COMPREHENSIBLY	COMPULSATORY	COMPUTERISATION
COMPLIANTNESSES	COMPOSITED	COMPREHENSION	COMPULSING	COMPUTERISE
COMPLICACIES	COMPOSITELY	COMPREHENSIONS	COMPULSION	COMPUTERISED
COMPLICACY	COMPOSITENESS	COMPREHENSIVE	COMPULSIONIST	COMPUTERISES
COMPLICANT	COMPOSITENESSES	COMPREHENSIVELY	COMPULSIONISTS	COMPUTERISING
COMPLICATE	COMPOSITES	COMPREHENSIVES	COMPULSIONS	COMPUTERIST
COMPLICATED	COMPOSITING	COMPREHENSIVISE	COMPULSITOR	COMPUTERISTS
COMPLICATEDLY	COMPOSITION	COMPREHENSIVIZE	COMPULSITORS	COMPUTERIZABLE
COMPLICATEDNESS	COMPOSITIONAL	COMPRESSED	COMPULSIVE	COMPUTERIZATION
COMPLICATES	COMPOSITIONALLY	COMPRESSEDLY	COMPULSIVELY	COMPUTERIZE
COMPLICATING	COMPOSITIONS	COMPRESSES	COMPULSIVENESS	COMPUTERIZED
COMPLICATION	COMPOSITIVE	COMPRESSIBILITY	COMPULSIVES	COMPUTERIZES
COMPLICATIONS	COMPOSITOR	COMPRESSIBLE	COMPULSIVITIES	COMPUTERIZING
COMPLICATIVE	COMPOSITORIAL	COMPRESSIBLY	COMPULSIVITY	COMPUTERLESS
COMPLICITIES	COMPOSITORS	COMPRESSING	COMPULSORIES	COMPUTERLIKE
COMPLICITOUS	COMPOSITOUS	COMPRESSION	COMPULSORILY	COMPUTERNIK
COMPLICITY	COMPOSSIBILITY	COMPRESSIONAL	COMPULSORINESS	COMPUTERNIKS
COMPLIMENT	COMPOSSIBLE	COMPRESSIONS	COMPULSORY	COMPUTERPHOBE
COMPLIMENTAL	COMPOSTABLE	COMPRESSIVE	COMPUNCTION	COMPUTERPHOBES
COMPLIMENTARILY	COMPOSTERS	COMPRESSIVELY	COMPUNCTIONS	COMPUTERPHOBIA
COMPLIMENTARY	COMPOSTING	COMPRESSOR	COMPUNCTIOUS	COMPUTERPHOBIAS
COMPLIMENTED	COMPOSTURE	COMPRESSORS	COMPUNCTIOUSLY	COMPUTERPHOBIC
COMPLIMENTER	COMPOSTURED	COMPRESSURE	COMPURGATION	COMPUTINGS
COMPLIMENTERS	COMPOSTURES	COMPRESSURES	COMPURGATIONS	COMPUTISTS
COMPLIMENTING	COMPOSTURING	COMPRIMARIO	COMPURGATOR	COMRADELINESS
COMPLIMENTS	COMPOSURES	COMPRIMARIOS	COMPURGATORIAL	COMRADELINESSES
COMPLISHED	COMPOTATION	COMPRINTED	COMPURGATORS	COMRADERIES
COMPLISHES	COMPOTATIONS	COMPRINTING	COMPURGATORY	COMRADESHIP
COMPLISHING	COMPOTATIONSHIP	COMPRISABLE	COMPURSION	COMRADESHIPS
COMPLOTTED	COMPOTATOR	COMPRISALS	COMPURSIONS	COMSTOCKER

C

COMSTOCKERIES	CONCENTERING	CONCEPTUALIZING	CONCESSIONAIRE	CONCINNOUS
COMSTOCKERS	CONCENTERS	CONCEPTUALLY	CONCESSIONAIRES	CONCIPIENCIES
COMSTOCKERY	CONCENTRATE	CONCEPTUSES	CONCESSIONAL	CONCIPIENCY
COMSTOCKISM	CONCENTRATED	CONCERNANCIES	CONCESSIONARIES	CONCIPIENT
COMSTOCKISMS	CONCENTRATEDLY	CONCERNANCY	CONCESSIONARY	CONCISENESS
CONACREISM	CONCENTRATES	CONCERNEDLY	CONCESSIONER	CONCISENESSES
CONACREISMS	CONCENTRATING	CONCERNEDNESS	CONCESSIONERS	CONCISIONS
CONATIONAL	CONCENTRATION	CONCERNEDNESSES	CONCESSIONIST	CONCLAMATION
CONCANAVALIN	CONCENTRATIONS	CONCERNING	CONCESSIONISTS	CONCLAMATIONS
CONCANAVALINS	CONCENTRATIVE	CONCERNMENT	CONCESSIONNAIRE	CONCLAVIST
CONCATENATE	CONCENTRATIVELY	CONCERNMENTS	CONCESSIONS	CONCLAVISTS
CONCATENATED	CONCENTRATOR	CONCERTANTE	CONCESSIVE	CONCLUDERS
CONCATENATES	CONCENTRATORS	CONCERTANTES	CONCESSIVELY	CONCLUDING
CONCATENATING	CONCENTRED	CONCERTANTI	CONCETTISM	CONCLUSION
CONCATENATION	CONCENTRES	CONCERTEDLY	CONCETTISMS	CONCLUSIONARY
CONCATENATIONS	CONCENTRIC	CONCERTEDNESS	CONCETTIST	CONCLUSIONS
CONCAVENESS	CONCENTRICAL	CONCERTEDNESSES	CONCETTISTS	CONCLUSIVE
CONCAVENESSES	CONCENTRICALLY	CONCERTGOER	CONCHIFEROUS	CONCLUSIVELY
CONCAVITIES	CONCENTRICITIES	CONCERTGOERS	CONCHIFORM	CONCLUSIVENESS
CONCEALABLE	CONCENTRICITY	CONCERTGOING	CONCHIGLIE	CONCLUSORY
CONCEALERS	CONCENTRING	CONCERTGOINGS	CONCHIOLIN	CONCOCTERS
CONCEALING	CONCEPTACLE	CONCERTINA	CONCHIOLINS	CONCOCTING
CONCEALINGLY	CONCEPTACLES	CONCERTINAED	CONCHITISES	CONCOCTION
CONCEALMENT	CONCEPTION	CONCERTINAING	CONCHOIDAL	CONCOCTIONS
CONCEALMENTS	CONCEPTIONAL	CONCERTINAS	CONCHOIDALLY	CONCOCTIVE
CONCEDEDLY	CONCEPTIONS	CONCERTING	CONCHOLOGICAL	CONCOCTORS
CONCEITEDLY	CONCEPTIOUS	CONCERTINI	CONCHOLOGIES	CONCOLORATE
CONCEITEDNESS	CONCEPTIVE	CONCERTINIST	CONCHOLOGIST	CONCOLOROUS
CONCEITEDNESSES	CONCEPTUAL	CONCERTINISTS	CONCHOLOGISTS	CONCOMITANCE
CONCEITFUL	CONCEPTUALISE	CONCERTINO	CONCHOLOGY	CONCOMITANCES
CONCEITING	CONCEPTUALISED	CONCERTINOS	CONCIERGES	CONCOMITANCIES
CONCEITLESS	CONCEPTUALISER	CONCERTISE	CONCILIABLE	CONCOMITANCY
CONCEIVABILITY	CONCEPTUALISERS	CONCERTISED	CONCILIARLY	CONCOMITANT
CONCEIVABLE	CONCEPTUALISES	CONCERTISES	CONCILIARY	CONCOMITANTLY
CONCEIVABLENESS	CONCEPTUALISING	CONCERTISING	CONCILIATE	CONCOMITANTS
CONCEIVABLY	CONCEPTUALISM	CONCERTIZE	CONCILIATED	CONCORDANCE
CONCEIVERS	CONCEPTUALISMS	CONCERTIZED	CONCILIATES	CONCORDANCES
CONCEIVING	CONCEPTUALIST	CONCERTIZES	CONCILIATING	CONCORDANT
CONCELEBRANT	CONCEPTUALISTIC	CONCERTIZING	CONCILIATION	CONCORDANTLY
CONCELEBRANTS	CONCEPTUALISTS	CONCERTMASTER	CONCILIATIONS	CONCORDATS
CONCELEBRATE	CONCEPTUALITIES	CONCERTMASTERS	CONCILIATIVE	CONCORDIAL
CONCELEBRATED	CONCEPTUALITY	CONCERTMEISTER	CONCILIATOR	CONCORDING
CONCELEBRATES	CONCEPTUALIZE	CONCERTMEISTERS	CONCILIATORILY	CONCORPORATE
CONCELEBRATING	CONCEPTUALIZED	CONCERTSTUCK	CONCILIATORS	CONCORPORATED
CONCELEBRATION	CONCEPTUALIZER	CONCERTSTUCKS	CONCILIATORY	CONCORPORATES
CONCELEBRATIONS	CONCEPTUALIZERS	CONCESSIBLE	CONCINNITIES	CONCORPORATING
CONCENTERED	CONCEPTUALIZES	CONCESSION	CONCINNITY	CONCOURSES

C

CONCREATED	CONCURRENCE	CONDIDDLED	CONDUCTIBILITY	CONFECTIONERS
CONCREATES	CONCURRENCES	CONDIDDLES	CONDUCTIBLE	CONFECTIONERY
CONCREATING	CONCURRENCIES	CONDIDDLING	CONDUCTIMETRIC	CONFECTIONS
CONCREMATION	CONCURRENCY	CONDIGNNESS	CONDUCTING	CONFEDERACIES
CONCREMATIONS	CONCURRENT	CONDIGNNESSES	CONDUCTIOMETRIC	CONFEDERACY
CONCRESCENCE	CONCURRENTLY	CONDIMENTAL	CONDUCTION	CONFEDERAL
CONCRESCENCES	CONCURRENTS	CONDIMENTED	CONDUCTIONAL	CONFEDERATE
CONCRESCENT	CONCURRING	CONDIMENTING	CONDUCTIONS	CONFEDERATED
CONCRETELY	CONCURRINGLY	CONDIMENTS	CONDUCTIVE	CONFEDERATES
CONCRETENESS	CONCUSSING	CONDISCIPLE	CONDUCTIVELY	CONFEDERATING
CONCRETENESSES	CONCUSSION	CONDISCIPLES	CONDUCTIVITIES	CONFEDERATION
CONCRETING	CONCUSSIONS	CONDITIONABLE	CONDUCTIVITY	CONFEDERATIONS
CONCRETION	CONCUSSIVE	CONDITIONAL	CONDUCTOMETRIC	CONFEDERATIVE
CONCRETIONARY	CONCYCLICALLY	CONDITIONALITY	CONDUCTORIAL	CONFERENCE
CONCRETIONS	CONDEMNABLE	CONDITIONALLY	CONDUCTORS	CONFERENCES
CONCRETISATION	CONDEMNABLY	CONDITIONALS	CONDUCTORSHIP	CONFERENCIER
CONCRETISATIONS	CONDEMNATION	CONDITIONATE	CONDUCTORSHIPS	CONFERENCIERS
CONCRETISE	CONDEMNATIONS	CONDITIONATED	CONDUCTRESS	CONFERENCING
CONCRETISED	CONDEMNATORY	CONDITIONATES	CONDUCTRESSES	CONFERENCINGS
CONCRETISES	CONDEMNERS	CONDITIONATING	CONDUPLICATE	CONFERENTIAL
CONCRETISING	CONDEMNING	CONDITIONED	CONDUPLICATION	CONFERMENT
CONCRETISM	CONDEMNINGLY	CONDITIONER	CONDUPLICATIONS	CONFERMENTS
CONCRETISMS	CONDEMNORS	CONDITIONERS	CONDYLOMAS	CONFERRABLE
CONCRETIST	CONDENSABILITY	CONDITIONING	CONDYLOMATA	CONFERRALS
CONCRETISTS	CONDENSABLE	CONDITIONINGS	CONDYLOMATOUS	CONFERREES
CONCRETIVE	CONDENSATE	CONDITIONS	CONEFLOWER	CONFERRENCE
CONCRETIVELY	CONDENSATED	CONDOLATORY	CONEFLOWERS	CONFERRENCES
CONCRETIZATION	CONDENSATES	CONDOLEMENT	CONFABBING	CONFERRERS
CONCRETIZATIONS	CONDENSATING	CONDOLEMENTS	CONFABULAR	CONFERRING
CONCRETIZE	CONDENSATION	CONDOLENCE	CONFABULATE	CONFERVOID
CONCRETIZED	CONDENSATIONAL	CONDOLENCES	CONFABULATED	CONFERVOIDS
CONCRETIZES	CONDENSATIONS	CONDOLINGLY	CONFABULATES	CONFESSABLE
CONCRETIZING	CONDENSERIES	CONDOMINIUM	CONFABULATING	CONFESSANT
CONCREWING	CONDENSERS	CONDOMINIUMS	CONFABULATION	CONFESSANTS
CONCUBINAGE	CONDENSERY	CONDONABLE	CONFABULATIONS	CONFESSEDLY
CONCUBINAGES	CONDENSIBILITY	CONDONATION	CONFABULATOR	CONFESSING
CONCUBINARIES	CONDENSIBLE	CONDONATIONS	CONFABULATORS	CONFESSION
CONCUBINARY	CONDENSING	CONDOTTIERE	CONFABULATORY	CONFESSIONAL
CONCUBINES	CONDESCEND	CONDOTTIERI	CONFARREATE	CONFESSIONALISM
CONCUBITANCIES	CONDESCENDED	CONDUCEMENT	CONFARREATION	CONFESSIONALIST
CONCUBITANCY	CONDESCENDENCE	CONDUCEMENTS	CONFARREATIONS	CONFESSIONALLY
CONCUBITANT	CONDESCENDENCES	CONDUCIBLE	CONFECTING	CONFESSIONALS
CONCUBITANTS	CONDESCENDING	CONDUCINGLY	CONFECTION	CONFESSIONARIES
CONCUPISCENCE	CONDESCENDINGLY	CONDUCIVENESS	CONFECTIONARIES	CONFESSIONARY
CONCUPISCENCES	CONDESCENDS	CONDUCIVENESSES	CONFECTIONARY	CONFESSIONS
CONCUPISCENT	CONDESCENSION	CONDUCTANCE	CONFECTIONER	CONFESSORESS
CONCUPISCIBLE	CONDESCENSIONS	CONDUCTANCES	CONFECTIONERIES	CONFESSORESSES

CONFESSORS

C

CONFESSORS	CONFIRMATORY	CONFLUENTLY	CONFUSABLES	CONGLOBATIONS
CONFESSORSHIP	CONFIRMEDLY	CONFLUENTS	CONFUSEDLY	CONGLOBING
CONFESSORSHIPS	CONFIRMEDNESS	CONFOCALLY	CONFUSEDNESS	CONGLOBULATE
CONFIDANTE	CONFIRMEDNESSES	CONFORMABILITY	CONFUSEDNESSES	CONGLOBULATED
CONFIDANTES	CONFIRMEES	CONFORMABLE	CONFUSIBLE	CONGLOBULATES
CONFIDANTS	CONFIRMERS	CONFORMABLENESS	CONFUSIBLES	CONGLOBULATING
CONFIDENCE	CONFIRMING	CONFORMABLY	CONFUSINGLY	CONGLOBULATION
CONFIDENCES	CONFIRMINGS	CONFORMANCE	CONFUSIONAL	CONGLOBULATIONS
CONFIDENCIES	CONFIRMORS	CONFORMANCES	CONFUSIONS	CONGLOMERATE
CONFIDENCY	CONFISCABLE	CONFORMATION	CONFUTABLE	CONGLOMERATED
CONFIDENTIAL	CONFISCATABLE	CONFORMATIONAL	CONFUTATION	CONGLOMERATES
CONFIDENTIALITY	CONFISCATE	CONFORMATIONS	CONFUTATIONS	CONGLOMERATEUR
CONFIDENTIALLY	CONFISCATED	CONFORMERS	CONFUTATIVE	CONGLOMERATEURS
CONFIDENTLY	CONFISCATES	CONFORMING	CONFUTEMENT	CONGLOMERATIC
CONFIDENTS	CONFISCATING	CONFORMINGLY	CONFUTEMENTS	CONGLOMERATING
CONFIDINGLY	CONFISCATION	CONFORMISM	CONGEALABLE	CONGLOMERATION
CONFIDINGNESS	CONFISCATIONS	CONFORMISMS	CONGEALABLENESS	CONGLOMERATIONS
CONFIDINGNESSES	CONFISCATOR	CONFORMIST	CONGEALERS	CONGLOMERATIVE
CONFIGURATE	CONFISCATORS	CONFORMISTS	CONGEALING	CONGLOMERATOR
CONFIGURATED	CONFISCATORY	CONFORMITIES	CONGEALMENT	CONGLOMERATORS
CONFIGURATES	CONFISERIE	CONFORMITY	CONGEALMENTS	CONGLUTINANT
CONFIGURATING	CONFISERIES	CONFOUNDABLE	CONGELATION	CONGLUTINATE
CONFIGURATION	CONFISEURS	CONFOUNDED	CONGELATIONS	CONGLUTINATED
CONFIGURATIONAL	CONFITEORS	CONFOUNDEDLY	CONGENERIC	CONGLUTINATES
CONFIGURATIONS	CONFITURES	CONFOUNDEDNESS	CONGENERICAL	CONGLUTINATING
CONFIGURATIVE	CONFLAGRANT	CONFOUNDER	CONGENERICS	CONGLUTINATION
CONFIGURED	CONFLAGRATE	CONFOUNDERS	CONGENEROUS	CONGLUTINATIONS
CONFIGURES	CONFLAGRATED	CONFOUNDING	CONGENETIC	CONGLUTINATIVE
CONFIGURING	CONFLAGRATES	CONFOUNDINGLY	CONGENIALITIES	CONGLUTINATOR
CONFINABLE	CONFLAGRATING	CONFRATERNAL	CONGENIALITY	CONGLUTINATORS
CONFINEABLE	CONFLAGRATION	CONFRATERNITIES	CONGENIALLY	CONGRATTERS
CONFINEDLY	CONFLAGRATIONS	CONFRATERNITY	CONGENIALNESS	CONGRATULABLE
CONFINEDNESS	CONFLAGRATIVE	CONFRERIES	CONGENIALNESSES	CONGRATULANT
CONFINEDNESSES	CONFLATING	CONFRONTAL	CONGENITAL	CONGRATULANTS
CONFINELESS	CONFLATION	CONFRONTALS	CONGENITALLY	CONGRATULATE
CONFINEMENT	CONFLATIONS	CONFRONTATION	CONGENITALNESS	CONGRATULATED
CONFINEMENTS	CONFLICTED	CONFRONTATIONAL	CONGESTIBLE	CONGRATULATES
CONFIRMABILITY	CONFLICTFUL	CONFRONTATIONS	CONGESTING	CONGRATULATING
CONFIRMABLE	CONFLICTING	CONFRONTED	CONGESTION	CONGRATULATION
CONFIRMAND	CONFLICTINGLY	CONFRONTER	CONGESTIONS	CONGRATULATIONS
CONFIRMANDS	CONFLICTION	CONFRONTERS	CONGESTIVE	CONGRATULATIVE
CONFIRMATION	CONFLICTIONS	CONFRONTING	CONGIARIES	CONGRATULATOR
CONFIRMATIONAL	CONFLICTIVE	CONFRONTMENT	CONGLOBATE	CONGRATULATORS
CONFIRMATIONS	CONFLICTORY	CONFRONTMENTS	CONGLOBATED	CONGRATULATORY
CONFIRMATIVE	CONFLICTUAL	CONFUSABILITIES	CONGLOBATES	CONGREEING
CONFIRMATOR	CONFLUENCE	CONFUSABILITY	CONGLOBATING	CONGREETED
CONFIRMATORS	CONFLUENCES	CONFUSABLE	CONGLOBATION	CONGREETING

C

CONGREGANT	CONJECTURE	CONJURATOR	CONNIPTION	CONQUERINGLY
CONGREGANTS	CONJECTURED	CONJURATORS	CONNIPTIONS	CONQUERORS
CONGREGATE	CONJECTURER	CONJUREMENT	CONNIVANCE	CONQUISTADOR
CONGREGATED	CONJECTURERS	CONJUREMENTS	CONNIVANCES	CONQUISTADORES
CONGREGATES	CONJECTURES	CONJURINGS	CONNIVANCIES	CONQUISTADORS
CONGREGATING	CONJECTURING	CONNASCENCE	CONNIVANCY	CONSANGUINE
CONGREGATION	CONJOINERS	CONNASCENCES	CONNIVENCE	CONSANGUINEOUS
CONGREGATIONAL	CONJOINING	CONNASCENCIES	CONNIVENCES	CONSANGUINITIES
CONGREGATIONS	CONJOINTLY	CONNASCENCY	CONNIVENCIES	CONSANGUINITY
CONGREGATIVE	CONJUGABLE	CONNASCENT	CONNIVENCY	CONSCIENCE
CONGREGATOR	CONJUGALITIES	CONNATENESS	CONNIVENTLY	CONSCIENCELESS
CONGREGATORS	CONJUGALITY	CONNATENESSES	CONNIVERIES	CONSCIENCES
CONGRESSED	CONJUGALLY	CONNATIONS	CONNIVINGLY	CONSCIENTIOUS
CONGRESSES	CONJUGANTS	CONNATURAL	CONNOISSEUR	CONSCIENTIOUSLY
CONGRESSING	CONJUGATED	CONNATURALISE	CONNOISSEURS	CONSCIENTISE
CONGRESSIONAL	CONJUGATELY	CONNATURALISED	CONNOISSEURSHIP	CONSCIENTISED
CONGRESSIONALLY	CONJUGATENESS	CONNATURALISES	CONNOTATED	CONSCIENTISES
CONGRESSMAN	CONJUGATENESSES	CONNATURALISING	CONNOTATES	CONSCIENTISING
CONGRESSMEN	CONJUGATES	CONNATURALITIES	CONNOTATING	CONSCIENTIZE
CONGRESSPEOPLE	CONJUGATING	CONNATURALITY	CONNOTATION	CONSCIENTIZED
CONGRESSPERSON	CONJUGATINGS	CONNATURALIZE	CONNOTATIONAL	CONSCIENTIZES
CONGRESSPERSONS	CONJUGATION	CONNATURALIZED	CONNOTATIONS	CONSCIENTIZING
CONGRESSWOMAN	CONJUGATIONAL	CONNATURALIZES	CONNOTATIVE	CONSCIONABLE
CONGRESSWOMEN	CONJUGATIONALLY	CONNATURALIZING	CONNOTATIVELY	CONSCIONABLY
CONGRUENCE	CONJUGATIONS	CONNATURALLY	CONNOTIVELY	CONSCIOUSES
CONGRUENCES	CONJUGATIVE	CONNATURALNESS	CONNUBIALISM	CONSCIOUSLY
CONGRUENCIES	CONJUGATOR	CONNATURES	CONNUBIALISMS	CONSCIOUSNESS
CONGRUENCY	CONJUGATORS	CONNECTABLE	CONNUBIALITIES	CONSCIOUSNESSES
CONGRUENTLY	CONJUNCTION	CONNECTEDLY	CONNUBIALITY	CONSCRIBED
CONGRUITIES	CONJUNCTIONAL	CONNECTEDNESS	CONNUBIALLY	CONSCRIBES
CONGRUOUSLY	CONJUNCTIONALLY	CONNECTEDNESSES	CONNUMERATE	CONSCRIBING
CONGRUOUSNESS	CONJUNCTIONS	CONNECTERS	CONNUMERATED	CONSCRIPTED
CONGRUOUSNESSES	CONJUNCTIVA	CONNECTIBLE	CONNUMERATES	CONSCRIPTING
CONICITIES	CONJUNCTIVAE	CONNECTING	CONNUMERATING	CONSCRIPTION
CONIDIOPHORE	CONJUNCTIVAL	CONNECTION	CONNUMERATION	CONSCRIPTIONAL
CONIDIOPHORES	CONJUNCTIVAS	CONNECTIONAL	CONNUMERATIONS	CONSCRIPTIONIST
CONIDIOPHOROUS	CONJUNCTIVE	CONNECTIONISM	CONOIDALLY	CONSCRIPTIONS
CONIDIOSPORE	CONJUNCTIVELY	CONNECTIONISMS	CONOIDICAL	CONSCRIPTS
CONIDIOSPORES	CONJUNCTIVENESS	CONNECTIONS	CONOMINEES	CONSECRATE
CONIFEROUS	CONJUNCTIVES	CONNECTIVE	CONOSCENTE	CONSECRATED
CONIOLOGIES	CONJUNCTIVITIS	CONNECTIVELY	CONOSCENTI	CONSECRATEDNESS
CONIROSTRAL	CONJUNCTLY	CONNECTIVES	CONQUERABLE	CONSECRATES
CONJECTING	CONJUNCTURAL	CONNECTIVITIES	CONQUERABLENESS	CONSECRATING
CONJECTURABLE	CONJUNCTURE	CONNECTIVITY	CONQUERERS	CONSECRATION
CONJECTURABLY	CONJUNCTURES	CONNECTORS	CONQUERESS	CONSECRATIONS
CONJECTURAL	CONJURATION	CONNEXIONAL	CONQUERESSES	CONSECRATIVE
CONJECTURALLY	CONJURATIONS	CONNEXIONS	CONQUERING	CONSECRATOR

CONSECRATORS CONSERVATISED CONSIGLIERI CONSOLATING CONSPIRACIES
CONSECRATORY CONSERVATISES CONSIGNABLE CONSOLATION CONSPIRACY
CONSECTANEOUS CONSERVATISING CONSIGNATION CONSOLATIONS CONSPIRANT
CONSECTARIES CONSERVATISM CONSIGNATIONS CONSOLATORIES CONSPIRATION
CONSECTARY CONSERVATISMS CONSIGNATORIES CONSOLATORY CONSPIRATIONAL
CONSECUTION CONSERVATIVE CONSIGNATORY CONSOLATRICES CONSPIRATIONS
CONSECUTIONS CONSERVATIVELY CONSIGNEES CONSOLATRIX CONSPIRATOR
CONSECUTIVE CONSERVATIVES CONSIGNERS CONSOLATRIXES CONSPIRATORIAL
CONSECUTIVELY CONSERVATIZE CONSIGNIFIED CONSOLEMENT CONSPIRATORS
CONSECUTIVENESS CONSERVATIZED CONSIGNIFIES CONSOLEMENTS CONSPIRATORY
CONSENESCENCE CONSERVATIZES CONSIGNIFY CONSOLIDATE CONSPIRATRESS
CONSENESCENCES CONSERVATIZING CONSIGNIFYING CONSOLIDATED CONSPIRATRESSES
CONSENESCENCIES CONSERVATOIRE CONSIGNING CONSOLIDATES CONSPIRERS
CONSENESCENCY CONSERVATOIRES CONSIGNMENT CONSOLIDATING CONSPIRING
CONSENSION CONSERVATOR CONSIGNMENTS CONSOLIDATION CONSPIRINGLY
CONSENSIONS CONSERVATORIA CONSIGNORS CONSOLIDATIONS CONSPURCATION
CONSENSUAL CONSERVATORIAL CONSILIENCE CONSOLIDATIVE CONSPURCATIONS
CONSENSUALLY CONSERVATORIES CONSILIENCES CONSOLIDATOR CONSTABLES
CONSENSUSES CONSERVATORIUM CONSILIENT CONSOLIDATORS CONSTABLESHIP
CONSENTANEITIES CONSERVATORIUMS CONSIMILAR CONSOLINGLY CONSTABLESHIPS
CONSENTANEITY CONSERVATORS CONSIMILARITIES CONSONANCE CONSTABLEWICK
CONSENTANEOUS CONSERVATORSHIP CONSIMILARITY CONSONANCES CONSTABLEWICKS
CONSENTANEOUSLY CONSERVATORY CONSIMILITIES CONSONANCIES CONSTABULARIES
CONSENTERS CONSERVATRICES CONSIMILITUDE CONSONANCY CONSTABULARY
CONSENTIENCE CONSERVATRIX CONSIMILITUDES CONSONANTAL CONSTANCIES
CONSENTIENCES CONSERVATRIXES CONSIMILITY CONSONANTALLY CONSTANTAN
CONSENTIENT CONSERVERS CONSISTENCE CONSONANTLY CONSTANTANS
CONSENTING CONSERVING CONSISTENCES CONSONANTS CONSTANTLY
CONSENTINGLY CONSIDERABLE CONSISTENCIES CONSORTABLE CONSTATATION
CONSEQUENCE CONSIDERABLES CONSISTENCY CONSORTERS CONSTATATIONS
CONSEQUENCED CONSIDERABLY CONSISTENT CONSORTIAL CONSTATING
CONSEQUENCES CONSIDERANCE CONSISTENTLY CONSORTING CONSTATIVE
CONSEQUENCING CONSIDERANCES CONSISTING CONSORTISM CONSTATIVES
CONSEQUENT CONSIDERATE CONSISTORIAL CONSORTISMS CONSTELLATE
CONSEQUENTIAL CONSIDERATELY CONSISTORIAN CONSORTIUM CONSTELLATED
CONSEQUENTIALLY CONSIDERATENESS CONSISTORIES CONSORTIUMS CONSTELLATES
CONSEQUENTLY CONSIDERATION CONSISTORY CONSPECIFIC CONSTELLATING
CONSEQUENTS CONSIDERATIONS CONSOCIATE CONSPECIFICS CONSTELLATION
CONSERVABLE CONSIDERATIVE CONSOCIATED CONSPECTUITIES CONSTELLATIONAL
CONSERVANCIES CONSIDERATIVELY CONSOCIATES CONSPECTUITY CONSTELLATIONS
CONSERVANCY CONSIDERED CONSOCIATING CONSPECTUS CONSTELLATORY
CONSERVANT CONSIDERER CONSOCIATION CONSPECTUSES CONSTERING
CONSERVATION CONSIDERERS CONSOCIATIONAL CONSPICUITIES CONSTERNATE
CONSERVATIONAL CONSIDERING CONSOCIATIONS CONSPICUITY CONSTERNATED
CONSERVATIONIST CONSIDERINGLY CONSOLABLE CONSPICUOUS CONSTERNATES
CONSERVATIONS CONSIGLIERE CONSOLATED CONSPICUOUSLY CONSTERNATING
CONSERVATISE CONSIGLIERES CONSOLATES CONSPICUOUSNESS CONSTERNATION

CONSTERNATIONS	CONSTRINGENCE	CONSUETUDES	CONSUMPTION	CONTAMINANTS
CONSTIPATE	CONSTRINGENCES	CONSUETUDINARY	CONSUMPTIONS	CONTAMINATE
CONSTIPATED	CONSTRINGENCIES	CONSULAGES	CONSUMPTIVE	CONTAMINATED
CONSTIPATES	CONSTRINGENCY	CONSULATES	CONSUMPTIVELY	CONTAMINATES
CONSTIPATING	CONSTRINGENT	CONSULSHIP	CONSUMPTIVENESS	CONTAMINATING
CONSTIPATION	CONSTRINGES	CONSULSHIPS	CONSUMPTIVES	CONTAMINATION
CONSTIPATIONS	CONSTRINGING	CONSULTABLE	CONSUMPTIVITIES	CONTAMINATIONS
CONSTITUENCIES	CONSTRUABILITY	CONSULTANCIES	CONSUMPTIVITY	CONTAMINATIVE
CONSTITUENCY	CONSTRUABLE	CONSULTANCY	CONTABESCENCE	CONTAMINATOR
CONSTITUENT	CONSTRUALS	CONSULTANT	CONTABESCENCES	CONTAMINATORS
CONSTITUENTLY	CONSTRUCTABLE	CONSULTANTS	CONTABESCENT	CONTANGOED
CONSTITUENTS	CONSTRUCTED	CONSULTANTSHIP	CONTACTABLE	CONTANGOES
CONSTITUTE	CONSTRUCTER	CONSULTANTSHIPS	CONTACTEES	CONTANGOING
CONSTITUTED	CONSTRUCTERS	CONSULTATION	CONTACTING	CONTEMNERS
CONSTITUTER	CONSTRUCTIBLE	CONSULTATIONS	CONTACTLESS	CONTEMNIBLE
CONSTITUTERS	CONSTRUCTING	CONSULTATIVE	CONTACTORS	CONTEMNIBLY
CONSTITUTES	CONSTRUCTION	CONSULTATIVELY	CONTACTUAL	CONTEMNING
CONSTITUTING	CONSTRUCTIONAL	CONSULTATORY	CONTACTUALLY	CONTEMNORS
CONSTITUTION	CONSTRUCTIONISM	CONSULTEES	CONTADINAS	CONTEMPERATION
CONSTITUTIONAL	CONSTRUCTIONIST	CONSULTERS	CONTAGIONIST	CONTEMPERATIONS
CONSTITUTIONALS	CONSTRUCTIONS	CONSULTING	CONTAGIONISTS	CONTEMPERATURE
CONSTITUTIONIST	CONSTRUCTIVE	CONSULTIVE	CONTAGIONS	CONTEMPERATURES
CONSTITUTIONS	CONSTRUCTIVELY	CONSULTORS	CONTAGIOUS	CONTEMPERED
CONSTITUTIVE	CONSTRUCTIVISM	CONSULTORY	CONTAGIOUSLY	CONTEMPERING
CONSTITUTIVELY	CONSTRUCTIVISMS	CONSUMABLE	CONTAGIOUSNESS	CONTEMPERS
CONSTITUTOR	CONSTRUCTIVIST	CONSUMABLES	CONTAINABLE	CONTEMPLABLE
CONSTITUTORS	CONSTRUCTIVISTS	CONSUMEDLY	CONTAINERBOARD	CONTEMPLANT
CONSTRAINABLE	CONSTRUCTOR	CONSUMERISM	CONTAINERBOARDS	CONTEMPLANTS
CONSTRAINED	CONSTRUCTORS	CONSUMERISMS	CONTAINERISE	CONTEMPLATE
CONSTRAINEDLY	CONSTRUCTS	CONSUMERIST	CONTAINERISED	CONTEMPLATED
CONSTRAINER	CONSTRUCTURE	CONSUMERISTIC	CONTAINERISES	CONTEMPLATES
CONSTRAINERS	CONSTRUCTURES	CONSUMERISTS	CONTAINERISING	CONTEMPLATING
CONSTRAINING	CONSTRUERS	CONSUMERSHIP	CONTAINERIZE	CONTEMPLATION
CONSTRAINS	CONSTRUING	CONSUMERSHIPS	CONTAINERIZED	CONTEMPLATIONS
CONSTRAINT	CONSTUPRATE	CONSUMINGLY	CONTAINERIZES	CONTEMPLATIST
CONSTRAINTS	CONSTUPRATED	CONSUMINGS	CONTAINERIZING	CONTEMPLATISTS
CONSTRICTED	CONSTUPRATES	CONSUMMATE	CONTAINERLESS	CONTEMPLATIVE
CONSTRICTING	CONSTUPRATING	CONSUMMATED	CONTAINERPORT	CONTEMPLATIVELY
CONSTRICTION	CONSTUPRATION	CONSUMMATELY	CONTAINERPORTS	CONTEMPLATIVES
CONSTRICTIONS	CONSTUPRATIONS	CONSUMMATES	CONTAINERS	CONTEMPLATOR
CONSTRICTIVE	CONSUBSIST	CONSUMMATING	CONTAINERSHIP	CONTEMPLATORS
CONSTRICTIVELY	CONSUBSISTED	CONSUMMATION	CONTAINERSHIPS	CONTEMPORANEAN
CONSTRICTOR	CONSUBSISTING	CONSUMMATIONS	CONTAINING	CONTEMPORANEANS
CONSTRICTORS	CONSUBSISTS	CONSUMMATIVE	CONTAINMENT	CONTEMPORANEITY
CONSTRICTS	CONSUBSTANTIAL	CONSUMMATOR	CONTAINMENTS	CONTEMPORANEOUS
CONSTRINGE	CONSUBSTANTIATE	CONSUMMATORS	CONTAMINABLE	CONTEMPORARIES
CONSTRINGED	CONSUETUDE	CONSUMMATORY	CONTAMINANT	CONTEMPORARILY

CONTEMPORARY	CONTESTABLY	CONTINGENTLY	CONTORTIONS	CONTRACTUAL
CONTEMPORISE	CONTESTANT	CONTINGENTS	CONTORTIVE	CONTRACTUALLY
CONTEMPORISED	CONTESTANTS	CONTINUABLE	CONTOURING	CONTRACTURAL
CONTEMPORISES	CONTESTATION	CONTINUALITIES	CONTRABAND	CONTRACTURE
CONTEMPORISING	CONTESTATIONS	CONTINUALITY	CONTRABANDISM	CONTRACTURES
CONTEMPORIZE	CONTESTERS	CONTINUALLY	CONTRABANDISMS	CONTRACYCLICAL
CONTEMPORIZED	CONTESTING	CONTINUALNESS	CONTRABANDIST	CONTRADANCE
CONTEMPORIZES	CONTESTINGLY	CONTINUALNESSES	CONTRABANDISTS	CONTRADANCES
CONTEMPORIZING	CONTEXTLESS	CONTINUANCE	CONTRABANDS	CONTRADICT
CONTEMPTIBILITY	CONTEXTUAL	CONTINUANCES	CONTRABASS	CONTRADICTABLE
CONTEMPTIBLE	CONTEXTUALISE	CONTINUANT	CONTRABASSES	CONTRADICTED
CONTEMPTIBLY	CONTEXTUALISED	CONTINUANTS	CONTRABASSI	CONTRADICTER
CONTEMPTUOUS	CONTEXTUALISES	CONTINUATE	CONTRABASSIST	CONTRADICTERS
CONTEMPTUOUSLY	CONTEXTUALISING	CONTINUATION	CONTRABASSISTS	CONTRADICTING
CONTENDENT	CONTEXTUALIZE	CONTINUATIONS	CONTRABASSO	CONTRADICTION
CONTENDENTS	CONTEXTUALIZED	CONTINUATIVE	CONTRABASSOON	CONTRADICTIONS
CONTENDERS	CONTEXTUALIZES	CONTINUATIVELY	CONTRABASSOONS	CONTRADICTIOUS
CONTENDING	CONTEXTUALIZING	CONTINUATIVES	CONTRABASSOS	CONTRADICTIVE
CONTENDINGLY	CONTEXTUALLY	CONTINUATOR	CONTRABBASSI	CONTRADICTIVELY
CONTENDINGS	CONTEXTURAL	CONTINUATORS	CONTRABBASSO	CONTRADICTOR
CONTENEMENT	CONTEXTURE	CONTINUEDLY	CONTRABBASSOS	CONTRADICTORIES
CONTENEMENTS	CONTEXTURES	CONTINUEDNESS	CONTRACEPTION	CONTRADICTORILY
CONTENTATION	CONTIGNATION	CONTINUEDNESSES	CONTRACEPTIONS	CONTRADICTORS
CONTENTATIONS	CONTIGNATIONS	CONTINUERS	CONTRACEPTIVE	CONTRADICTORY
CONTENTEDLY	CONTIGUITIES	CONTINUING	CONTRACEPTIVES	CONTRADICTS
CONTENTEDNESS	CONTIGUITY	CONTINUINGLY	CONTRACLOCKWISE	CONTRAFAGOTTO
CONTENTEDNESSES	CONTIGUOUS	CONTINUITIES	CONTRACTABILITY	CONTRAFAGOTTOS
CONTENTING	CONTIGUOUSLY	CONTINUITY	CONTRACTABLE	CONTRAFLOW
CONTENTION	CONTIGUOUSNESS	CONTINUOUS	CONTRACTED	CONTRAFLOWS
CONTENTIONS	CONTINENCE	CONTINUOUSLY	CONTRACTEDLY	CONTRAGESTION
CONTENTIOUS	CONTINENCES	CONTINUOUSNESS	CONTRACTEDNESS	CONTRAGESTIONS
CONTENTIOUSLY	CONTINENCIES	CONTINUUMS	CONTRACTIBILITY	CONTRAGESTIVE
CONTENTIOUSNESS	CONTINENCY	CONTORNIATE	CONTRACTIBLE	CONTRAGESTIVES
CONTENTLESS	CONTINENTAL	CONTORNIATES	CONTRACTIBLY	CONTRAHENT
CONTENTMENT	CONTINENTALISM	CONTORTEDLY	CONTRACTILE	CONTRAHENTS
CONTENTMENTS	CONTINENTALISMS	CONTORTEDNESS	CONTRACTILITIES	CONTRAINDICANT
CONTERMINAL	CONTINENTALIST	CONTORTEDNESSES	CONTRACTILITY	CONTRAINDICANTS
CONTERMINALLY	CONTINENTALISTS	CONTORTING	CONTRACTING	CONTRAINDICATE
CONTERMINANT	CONTINENTALLY	CONTORTION	CONTRACTION	CONTRAINDICATED
CONTERMINATE	CONTINENTALS	CONTORTIONAL	CONTRACTIONAL	CONTRAINDICATES
CONTERMINOUS	CONTINENTLY	CONTORTIONATE	CONTRACTIONARY	CONTRALATERAL
CONTERMINOUSLY	CONTINENTS	CONTORTIONED	CONTRACTIONS	CONTRALTOS
CONTESSERATION	CONTINGENCE	CONTORTIONISM	CONTRACTIVE	CONTRANATANT
CONTESSERATIONS	CONTINGENCES	CONTORTIONISMS	CONTRACTIVELY	CONTRAOCTAVE
CONTESTABILITY	CONTINGENCIES	CONTORTIONIST	CONTRACTIVENESS	CONTRAOCTAVES
CONTESTABLE	CONTINGENCY	CONTORTIONISTIC	CONTRACTOR	CONTRAPLEX
CONTESTABLENESS	CONTINGENT	CONTORTIONISTS	CONTRACTORS	CONTRAPOSITION

CONVERTING

CONTRAPOSITIONS	CONTRAYERVA	CONTROLLED	CONVALESCENCY	CONVENTIONISTS
CONTRAPOSITIVE	CONTRAYERVAS	CONTROLLER	CONVALESCENT	CONVENTIONS
CONTRAPOSITIVES	CONTRECOUP	CONTROLLERS	CONVALESCENTLY	CONVENTUAL
CONTRAPPOSTO	CONTRECOUPS	CONTROLLERSHIP	CONVALESCENTS	CONVENTUALLY
CONTRAPPOSTOS	CONTREDANCE	CONTROLLERSHIPS	CONVALESCES	CONVENTUALS
CONTRAPROP	CONTREDANCES	CONTROLLING	CONVALESCING	CONVERGENCE
CONTRAPROPELLER	CONTREDANSE	CONTROLMENT	CONVECTING	CONVERGENCES
CONTRAPROPS	CONTREDANSES	CONTROLMENTS	CONVECTION	CONVERGENCIES
CONTRAPTION	CONTRETEMPS	CONTROULED	CONVECTIONAL	CONVERGENCY
CONTRAPTIONS	CONTRIBUTABLE	CONTROULING	CONVECTIONS	CONVERGENT
CONTRAPUNTAL	CONTRIBUTARIES	CONTROVERSE	CONVECTIVE	CONVERGING
CONTRAPUNTALIST	CONTRIBUTARY	CONTROVERSES	CONVECTORS	CONVERSABLE
CONTRAPUNTALLY	CONTRIBUTE	CONTROVERSIAL	CONVENABLE	CONVERSABLENESS
CONTRAPUNTIST	CONTRIBUTED	CONTROVERSIALLY	CONVENANCE	CONVERSABLY
CONTRAPUNTISTS	CONTRIBUTES	CONTROVERSIES	CONVENANCES	CONVERSANCE
CONTRARIAN	CONTRIBUTING	CONTROVERSY	CONVENERSHIP	CONVERSANCES
CONTRARIANS	CONTRIBUTION	CONTROVERT	CONVENERSHIPS	CONVERSANCIES
CONTRARIED	CONTRIBUTIONS	CONTROVERTED	CONVENIENCE	CONVERSANCY
CONTRARIES	CONTRIBUTIVE	CONTROVERTER	CONVENIENCES	CONVERSANT
CONTRARIETIES	CONTRIBUTIVELY	CONTROVERTERS	CONVENIENCIES	CONVERSANTLY
CONTRARIETY	CONTRIBUTOR	CONTROVERTIBLE	CONVENIENCY	CONVERSATION
CONTRARILY	CONTRIBUTORIES	CONTROVERTIBLY	CONVENIENT	CONVERSATIONAL
CONTRARINESS	CONTRIBUTORS	CONTROVERTING	CONVENIENTLY	CONVERSATIONISM
CONTRARINESSES	CONTRIBUTORY	CONTROVERTIST	CONVENORSHIP	CONVERSATIONIST
CONTRARIOUS	CONTRISTATION	CONTROVERTISTS	CONVENORSHIPS	CONVERSATIONS
CONTRARIOUSLY	CONTRISTATIONS	CONTROVERTS	CONVENTICLE	CONVERSATIVE
CONTRARIOUSNESS	CONTRISTED	CONTUBERNAL	CONVENTICLED	CONVERSAZIONE
CONTRARIWISE	CONTRISTING	CONTUBERNYAL	CONVENTICLER	CONVERSAZIONES
CONTRARYING	CONTRITELY	CONTUMACIES	CONVENTICLERS	CONVERSAZIONI
CONTRASEXUAL	CONTRITENESS	CONTUMACIOUS	CONVENTICLES	CONVERSELY
CONTRASEXUALS	CONTRITENESSES	CONTUMACIOUSLY	CONVENTICLING	CONVERSERS
CONTRASTABLE	CONTRITION	CONTUMACITIES	CONVENTING	CONVERSING
CONTRASTABLY	CONTRITIONS	CONTUMACITY	CONVENTION	CONVERSION
CONTRASTED	CONTRITURATE	CONTUMELIES	CONVENTIONAL	CONVERSIONAL
CONTRASTING	CONTRITURATED	CONTUMELIOUS	CONVENTIONALISE	CONVERSIONARY
CONTRASTIVE	CONTRITURATES	CONTUMELIOUSLY	CONVENTIONALISM	CONVERSIONS
CONTRASTIVELY	CONTRITURATING	CONTUNDING	CONVENTIONALIST	CONVERTAPLANE
CONTRATERRENE	CONTRIVABLE	CONTUSIONED	CONVENTIONALITY	CONVERTAPLANES
CONTRAVALLATION	CONTRIVANCE	CONTUSIONS	CONVENTIONALIZE	CONVERTEND
CONTRAVENE	CONTRIVANCES	CONUNDRUMS	CONVENTIONALLY	CONVERTENDS
CONTRAVENED	CONTRIVEMENT	CONURBATION	CONVENTIONALS	CONVERTERS
CONTRAVENER	CONTRIVEMENTS	CONURBATIONS	CONVENTIONARY	CONVERTIBILITY
CONTRAVENERS	CONTRIVERS	CONVALESCE	CONVENTIONEER	CONVERTIBLE
CONTRAVENES	CONTRIVING	CONVALESCED	CONVENTIONEERS	CONVERTIBLENESS
CONTRAVENING	CONTROLLABILITY	CONVALESCENCE	CONVENTIONER	CONVERTIBLES
CONTRAVENTION	CONTROLLABLE	CONVALESCENCES	CONVENTIONERS	CONVERTIBLY
CONTRAVENTIONS	CONTROLLABLY	CONVALESCENCIES	CONVENTIONIST	CONVERTING

CONVERTIPLANE	CONVINCINGNESS	COOKSHACKS	COPARCENERY	COPRESENCES
CONVERTIPLANES	CONVIVIALIST	COOKSTOVES	COPARCENIES	COPRESENTED
CONVERTITE	CONVIVIALISTS	COOLHEADED	COPARENTED	COPRESENTING
CONVERTITES	CONVIVIALITIES	COOLHOUSES	COPARENTING	COPRESENTS
CONVERTIVE	CONVIVIALITY	COOLINGNESS	COPARTNERED	COPRESIDENT
CONVERTOPLANE	CONVIVIALLY	COOLINGNESSES	COPARTNERIES	COPRESIDENTS
CONVERTOPLANES	CONVOCATED	COOLNESSES	COPARTNERING	COPRINCIPAL
CONVERTORS	CONVOCATES	COOMCEILED	COPARTNERS	COPRINCIPALS
CONVEXEDLY	CONVOCATING	COONHOUNDS	COPARTNERSHIP	COPRISONER
CONVEXITIES	CONVOCATION	COOPERAGES	COPARTNERSHIPS	COPRISONERS
CONVEXNESS	CONVOCATIONAL	COOPERATED	COPARTNERY	COPROCESSING
CONVEXNESSES	CONVOCATIONIST	COOPERATES	COPATRIOTS	COPROCESSOR
CONVEYABLE	CONVOCATIONISTS	COOPERATING	COPAYMENTS	COPROCESSORS
CONVEYANCE	CONVOCATIONS	COOPERATION	COPESTONES	COPRODUCED
CONVEYANCER	CONVOCATIVE	COOPERATIONIST	COPINGSTONE	COPRODUCER
CONVEYANCERS	CONVOCATOR	COOPERATIONISTS	COPINGSTONES	COPRODUCERS
CONVEYANCES	CONVOCATORS	COOPERATIONS	COPIOUSNESS	COPRODUCES
CONVEYANCING	CONVOLUTED	COOPERATIVE	COPIOUSNESSES	COPRODUCING
CONVEYANCINGS	CONVOLUTEDLY	COOPERATIVELY	COPLANARITIES	COPRODUCTION
CONVEYORISATION	CONVOLUTEDNESS	COOPERATIVENESS	COPLANARITY	COPRODUCTIONS
CONVEYORISE	CONVOLUTELY	COOPERATIVES	COPLOTTING	COPRODUCTS
CONVEYORISED	CONVOLUTES	COOPERATIVITIES	COPOLYMERIC	COPROLALIA
CONVEYORISES	CONVOLUTING	COOPERATIVITY	COPOLYMERISE	COPROLALIAC
CONVEYORISING	CONVOLUTION	COOPERATOR	COPOLYMERISED	COPROLALIAS
CONVEYORIZATION	CONVOLUTIONAL	COOPERATORS	COPOLYMERISES	COPROLITES
CONVEYORIZE	CONVOLUTIONARY	COOPERINGS	COPOLYMERISING	COPROLITHS
CONVEYORIZED	CONVOLUTIONS	COOPTATION	COPOLYMERIZE	COPROLITIC
CONVEYORIZES	CONVOLVING	COOPTATIONS	COPOLYMERIZED	COPROLOGIES
CONVEYORIZING	CONVOLVULACEOUS	COOPTATIVE	COPOLYMERIZES	COPROMOTER
CONVICINITIES	CONVOLVULI	COORDINANCE	COPOLYMERIZING	COPROMOTERS
CONVICINITY	CONVOLVULUS	COORDINANCES	COPOLYMERS	COPROPHAGAN
CONVICTABLE	CONVOLVULUSES	COORDINATE	COPPERASES	COPROPHAGANS
CONVICTIBLE	CONVULSANT	COORDINATED	COPPERHEAD	COPROPHAGIC
CONVICTING	CONVULSANTS	COORDINATELY	COPPERHEADS	COPROPHAGIES
CONVICTION	CONVULSIBLE	COORDINATENESS	COPPERINGS	COPROPHAGIST
CONVICTIONAL	CONVULSING	COORDINATES	COPPERPLATE	COPROPHAGISTS
CONVICTIONS	CONVULSION	COORDINATING	COPPERPLATES	COPROPHAGOUS
CONVICTISM	CONVULSIONAL	COORDINATION	COPPERSKIN	COPROPHAGY
CONVICTISMS	CONVULSIONARIES	COORDINATIONS	COPPERSKINS	COPROPHILIA
CONVICTIVE	CONVULSIONARY	COORDINATIVE	COPPERSMITH	COPROPHILIAC
CONVICTIVELY	CONVULSIONIST	COORDINATOR	COPPERSMITHS	COPROPHILIACS
CONVINCEMENT	CONVULSIONISTS	COORDINATORS	COPPERWORK	COPROPHILIAS
CONVINCEMENTS	CONVULSIONS	COPARCENARIES	COPPERWORKS	COPROPHILIC
CONVINCERS	CONVULSIVE	COPARCENARY	COPPERWORM	COPROPHILOUS
CONVINCIBLE	CONVULSIVELY	COPARCENER	COPPERWORMS	COPROPRIETOR
CONVINCING	CONVULSIVENESS	COPARCENERIES	COPPICINGS	COPROPRIETORS
CONVINCINGLY	COOKHOUSES	COPARCENERS	COPRESENCE	COPROSPERITIES

C

COPROSPERITY	COQUETTING	CORDLESSES	CORINTHIANIZING	CORNFLOWERS
COPROSTEROL	COQUETTISH	CORDOCENTESES	CORIVALLED	CORNHUSKER
COPROSTEROLS	COQUETTISHLY	CORDOCENTESIS	CORIVALLING	CORNHUSKERS
COPSEWOODS	COQUETTISHNESS	CORDONNETS	CORIVALRIES	CORNHUSKING
COPUBLISHED	COQUIMBITE	CORDOTOMIES	CORIVALSHIP	CORNHUSKINGS
COPUBLISHER	COQUIMBITES	CORDUROYED	CORIVALSHIPS	CORNICHONS
COPUBLISHERS	CORACIIFORM	CORDUROYING	CORKBOARDS	CORNICULATE
COPUBLISHES	CORADICATE	CORDWAINER	CORKBORERS	CORNICULUM
COPUBLISHING	CORALBELLS	CORDWAINERIES	CORKINESSES	CORNICULUMS
COPULATING	CORALBERRIES	CORDWAINERS	CORKSCREWED	CORNIFEROUS
COPULATION	CORALBERRY	CORDWAINERY	CORKSCREWING	CORNIFICATION
COPULATIONS	CORALLACEOUS	CORDYLINES	CORKSCREWS	CORNIFICATIONS
COPULATIVE	CORALLIFEROUS	CORECIPIENT	CORMOPHYTE	CORNIFYING
COPULATIVELY	CORALLIFORM	CORECIPIENTS	CORMOPHYTES	CORNIGEROUS
COPULATIVES	CORALLIGENOUS	COREDEEMED	CORMOPHYTIC	CORNINESSES
COPULATORY	CORALLINES	COREDEEMING	CORMORANTS	CORNOPEANS
COPURIFIED	CORALLITES	COREFERENTIAL	CORNACEOUS	CORNROWING
COPURIFIES	CORALLOIDAL	COREGONINE	CORNBORERS	CORNSTALKS
COPURIFYING	CORALROOTS	CORELATING	CORNBRAIDED	CORNSTARCH
COPYCATTED	CORALWORTS	CORELATION	CORNBRAIDING	CORNSTARCHES
COPYCATTING	CORBEILLES	CORELATIONS	CORNBRAIDS	CORNSTONES
COPYEDITED	CORBELINGS	CORELATIVE	CORNBRANDIES	CORNUCOPIA
COPYEDITING	CORBELLING	CORELATIVES	CORNBRANDY	CORNUCOPIAN
COPYFIGHTS	CORBELLINGS	CORELIGIONIST	CORNBRASHES	CORNUCOPIAS
COPYGRAPHS	CORBICULAE	CORELIGIONISTS	CORNBREADS	COROLLACEOUS
COPYHOLDER	CORBICULATE	COREOPSISES	CORNCOCKLE	COROLLARIES
COPYHOLDERS	CORDECTOMIES	COREPRESSOR	CORNCOCKLES	COROLLIFLORAL
COPYLEFTED	CORDECTOMY	COREPRESSORS	CORNCRAKES	COROLLIFLOROUS
COPYLEFTING	CORDELLING	COREQUISITE	CORNEITISES	COROLLIFORM
COPYREADER	CORDGRASSES	COREQUISITES	CORNELIANS	COROMANDEL
COPYREADERS	CORDIALISE	CORESEARCHER	CORNEMUSES	COROMANDELS
COPYREADING	CORDIALISED	CORESEARCHERS	CORNERBACK	CORONAGRAPH
COPYREADINGS	CORDIALISES	CORESIDENT	CORNERBACKS	CORONAGRAPHS
COPYRIGHTABLE	CORDIALISING	CORESIDENTIAL	CORNERSTONE	CORONARIES
COPYRIGHTED	CORDIALITIES	CORESIDENTS	CORNERSTONES	CORONATING
COPYRIGHTER	CORDIALITY	CORESPONDENT	CORNERWAYS	CORONATION
COPYRIGHTERS	CORDIALIZE	CORESPONDENTS	CORNERWISE	CORONATIONS
COPYRIGHTING	CORDIALIZED	CORFHOUSES	CORNETCIES	CORONAVIRUS
COPYRIGHTS	CORDIALIZES	CORIACEOUS	CORNETISTS	CORONAVIRUSES
COPYTAKERS	CORDIALIZING	CORIANDERS	CORNETTINI	CORONERSHIP
COPYWRITER	CORDIALNESS	CORINTHIANISE	CORNETTINO	CORONERSHIPS
COPYWRITERS	CORDIALNESSES	CORINTHIANISED	CORNETTIST	CORONOGRAPH
COPYWRITING	CORDIERITE	CORINTHIANISES	CORNETTISTS	CORONOGRAPHS
COPYWRITINGS	CORDIERITES	CORINTHIANISING	CORNFIELDS	COROTATING
COQUELICOT ·	CORDILLERA	CORINTHIANIZE	CORNFLAKES	COROTATION
COQUELICOTS	CORDILLERAN	CORINTHIANIZED	CORNFLOURS	COROTATIONS
COQUETRIES	CORDILLERAS	CORINTHIANIZES	CORNFLOWER	CORPORALES

CORPORALITIES	CORPOREITY	CORRELATIVE	CORROBORATIVES	CORSETIERES
CORPORALITY	CORPORIFICATION	CORRELATIVELY	CORROBORATOR	CORSETIERS
CORPORALLY	CORPORIFIED	CORRELATIVENESS	CORROBORATORS	CORSETRIES
CORPORALSHIP	CORPORIFIES	CORRELATIVES	CORROBORATORY	CORTICALLY
CORPORALSHIPS	CORPORIFYING	CORRELATIVITIES	CORROBOREE	CORTICATED
CORPORASES	CORPOSANTS	CORRELATIVITY	CORROBOREED	CORTICATION
CORPORATELY	CORPULENCE	CORRELATOR	CORROBOREEING	CORTICATIONS
CORPORATENESS	CORPULENCES	CORRELATORS	CORROBOREES	CORTICOIDS
CORPORATENESSES	CORPULENCIES	CORRELIGIONIST	CORRODANTS	CORTICOLOUS
CORPORATES	CORPULENCY	CORRELIGIONISTS	CORRODENTS	CORTICOSTEROID
CORPORATION	CORPULENTLY	CORREPTION	CORRODIBILITIES	CORTICOSTEROIDS
CORPORATIONS	CORPUSCLES	CORREPTIONS	CORRODIBILITY	CORTICOSTERONE
CORPORATISE	CORPUSCULAR	CORRESPOND	CORRODIBLE	CORTICOSTERONES
CORPORATISED	CORPUSCULARIAN	CORRESPONDED	CORROSIBILITIES	CORTICOTROPHIC
CORPORATISES	CORPUSCULARIANS	CORRESPONDENCE	CORROSIBILITY	CORTICOTROPHIN
CORPORATISING	CORPUSCULARITY	CORRESPONDENCES	CORROSIBLE	CORTICOTROPHINS
CORPORATISM	CORPUSCULE	CORRESPONDENCY	CORROSIONS	CORTICOTROPIC
CORPORATISMS	CORPUSCULES	CORRESPONDENT	CORROSIVELY	CORTICOTROPIN
CORPORATIST	CORRALLING	CORRESPONDENTLY	CORROSIVENESS	CORTICOTROPINS
CORPORATISTS	CORRASIONS	CORRESPONDENTS	CORROSIVENESSES	CORTISONES
CORPORATIVE	CORRECTABLE	CORRESPONDING	CORROSIVES	CORUSCATED
CORPORATIVISM	CORRECTEST	CORRESPONDINGLY	CORRUGATED	CORUSCATES
CORPORATIVISMS	CORRECTIBLE	CORRESPONDS	CORRUGATES	CORUSCATING
CORPORATIZE	CORRECTING	CORRESPONSIVE	CORRUGATING	CORUSCATION
CORPORATIZED	CORRECTION	CORRIGENDA	CORRUGATION	CORUSCATIONS
CORPORATIZES	CORRECTIONAL	CORRIGENDUM	CORRUGATIONS	CORVETTING
CORPORATIZING	CORRECTIONER	CORRIGENTS	CORRUGATOR	CORYBANTES
CORPORATOR	CORRECTIONERS	CORRIGIBILITIES	CORRUGATORS	CORYBANTIC
CORPORATORS	CORRECTIONS	CORRIGIBILITY	CORRUPTERS	CORYBANTISM
CORPOREALISE	CORRECTITUDE	CORRIGIBLE	CORRUPTEST	CORYBANTISMS
CORPOREALISED	CORRECTITUDES	CORRIGIBLY	CORRUPTIBILITY	CORYDALINE
CORPOREALISES	CORRECTIVE	CORRIVALLED	CORRUPTIBLE	CORYDALINES
CORPOREALISING	CORRECTIVELY	CORRIVALLING	CORRUPTIBLENESS	CORYDALISES
CORPOREALISM	CORRECTIVES	CORRIVALRIES	CORRUPTIBLY	CORYLOPSES
CORPOREALISMS	CORRECTNESS	CORRIVALRY	CORRUPTING	CORYLOPSIS
CORPOREALIST	CORRECTNESSES	CORRIVALSHIP	CORRUPTION	CORYMBOSELY
CORPOREALISTS	CORRECTORS	CORRIVALSHIPS	CORRUPTIONIST	CORYNEBACTERIA
CORPOREALITIES	CORRECTORY	CORROBORABLE	CORRUPTIONISTS	CORYNEBACTERIAL
CORPOREALITY	CORREGIDOR	CORROBORANT	CORRUPTIONS	CORYNEBACTERIUM
CORPOREALIZE	CORREGIDORS	CORROBORATE	CORRUPTIVE	CORYNEFORM
CORPOREALIZED	CORRELATABLE	CORROBORATED	CORRUPTIVELY	CORYPHAEUS
CORPOREALIZES	CORRELATED	CORROBORATES	CORRUPTNESS	CORYPHENES
CORPOREALIZING	CORRELATES	CORROBORATING	CORRUPTNESSES	COSCINOMANCIES
CORPOREALLY	CORRELATING	CORROBORATION	CORRUPTORS	COSCINOMANCY
CORPOREALNESS	CORRELATION	CORROBORATIONS	CORSELETTE	COSCRIPTED
CORPOREALNESSES	CORRELATIONAL	CORROBORATIVE	CORSELETTES	COSCRIPTING
CORPOREITIES	CORRELATIONS	CORROBORATIVELY	CORSETIERE	COSEISMALS

COSEISMICS	COSMOGRAPHERS	COSTALGIAS	COTTIERISMS	COUNCILORSHIP
COSENTIENT	COSMOGRAPHIC	COSTARDMONGER	COTTONADES	COUNCILORSHIPS
COSHERINGS	COSMOGRAPHICAL	COSTARDMONGERS	COTTONMOUTH	COUNCILWOMAN
COSIGNATORIES	COSMOGRAPHIES	COSTARRING	COTTONMOUTHS	COUNCILWOMEN
COSIGNATORY	COSMOGRAPHIST	COSTEANING	COTTONOCRACIES	COUNSELABLE
COSIGNIFICATIVE	COSMOGRAPHISTS	COSTEANINGS	COTTONOCRACY	COUNSELEES
COSINESSES	COSMOGRAPHY	COSTERMONGER	COTTONSEED	COUNSELING
COSMECEUTICAL	COSMOLATRIES	COSTERMONGERS	COTTONSEEDS	COUNSELINGS
COSMECEUTICALS	COSMOLATRY	COSTIVENESS	COTTONTAIL	COUNSELLABLE
COSMETICAL	COSMOLINED	COSTIVENESSES	COTTONTAILS	COUNSELLED
COSMETICALLY	COSMOLINES	COSTLESSLY	COTTONWEED	COUNSELLING
COSMETICIAN	COSMOLINING	COSTLINESS	COTTONWEEDS	COUNSELLINGS
COSMETICIANS	COSMOLOGIC	COSTLINESSES	COTTONWOOD	COUNSELLOR
COSMETICISE	COSMOLOGICAL	COSTMARIES	COTTONWOODS	COUNSELLORS
COSMETICISED	COSMOLOGICALLY	COSTOTOMIES	COTURNIXES	COUNSELLORSHIP
COSMETICISES	COSMOLOGIES	COSTUMERIES	COTYLEDONAL	COUNSELLORSHIPS
COSMETICISING	COSMOLOGIST	COSTUMIERS	COTYLEDONARY	COUNSELORS
COSMETICISM	COSMOLOGISTS	COSURFACTANT	COTYLEDONOID	COUNSELORSHIP
COSMETICISMS	COSMONAUTICS	COSURFACTANTS	COTYLEDONOUS	COUNSELORSHIPS
COSMETICIZE	COSMONAUTS	COTANGENTIAL	COTYLEDONS	COUNTABILITIES
COSMETICIZED	COSMOPLASTIC	COTANGENTS	COTYLIFORM	COUNTABILITY
COSMETICIZES	COSMOPOLIS	COTELETTES	COTYLOIDAL	COUNTBACKS
COSMETICIZING	COSMOPOLISES	COTEMPORANEOUS	COTYLOIDALS	COUNTDOWNS
COSMETICOLOGIES	COSMOPOLITAN	COTEMPORARY	COTYLOSAUR	COUNTENANCE
COSMETICOLOGY	COSMOPOLITANISM	COTENANCIES	COTYLOSAURS	COUNTENANCED
COSMETOLOGIES	COSMOPOLITANS	COTERMINOUS	COUCHETTES	COUNTENANCER
COSMETOLOGIST	COSMOPOLITE	COTERMINOUSLY	COULIBIACA	COUNTENANCERS
COSMETOLOGISTS	COSMOPOLITES	COTILLIONS	COULIBIACAS	COUNTENANCES
COSMETOLOGY	COSMOPOLITIC	COTONEASTER	COULIBIACS	COUNTENANCING
COSMICALLY	COSMOPOLITICAL	COTONEASTERS	COULOMBMETER	COUNTERACT
COSMOCHEMICAL	COSMOPOLITICS	COTRANSDUCE	COULOMBMETERS	COUNTERACTED
COSMOCHEMIST	COSMOPOLITISM	COTRANSDUCED	COULOMETER	COUNTERACTING
COSMOCHEMISTRY	COSMOPOLITISMS	COTRANSDUCES	COULOMETERS	COUNTERACTION
COSMOCHEMISTS	COSMORAMAS	COTRANSDUCING	COULOMETRIC	COUNTERACTIONS
COSMOCRATIC	COSMORAMIC	COTRANSDUCTION	COULOMETRICALLY	COUNTERACTIVE
COSMOCRATS	COSMOSPHERE	COTRANSDUCTIONS	COULOMETRIES	COUNTERACTIVELY
COSMODROME	COSMOSPHERES	COTRANSFER	COULOMETRY	COUNTERACTS
COSMODROMES	COSMOTHEISM	COTRANSFERS	COUMARILIC	COUNTERAGENT
COSMOGENIC	COSMOTHEISMS	COTRANSPORT	COUMARONES	COUNTERAGENTS
COSMOGENIES	COSMOTHETIC	COTRANSPORTED	COUNCILLOR	COUNTERARGUE
COSMOGONAL	COSMOTHETICAL	COTRANSPORTING	COUNCILLORS	COUNTERARGUED
COSMOGONIC	COSMOTRONS	COTRANSPORTS	COUNCILLORSHIP	COUNTERARGUES
COSMOGONICAL	COSPONSORED	COTRUSTEES	COUNCILLORSHIPS	COUNTERARGUING
COSMOGONIES	COSPONSORING	COTTABUSES	COUNCILMAN	COUNTERARGUMENT
COSMOGONIST	COSPONSORS	COTTAGINGS	COUNCILMANIC	COUNTERASSAULT
COSMOGONISTS	COSPONSORSHIP	COTTERLESS	COUNCILMEN	COUNTERASSAULTS
COSMOGRAPHER	COSPONSORSHIPS	COTTIERISM	COUNCILORS	COUNTERATTACK

COUNTERATTACKED	COUNTERCHECKED	COUNTERFOILS	COUNTERMURE	COUNTERPOINT
COUNTERATTACKER	COUNTERCHECKING	COUNTERFORCE	COUNTERMURED	COUNTERPOINTED
COUNTERATTACKS	COUNTERCHECKS	COUNTERFORCES	COUNTERMURES	COUNTERPOINTING
COUNTERBALANCE	COUNTERCLAIM	COUNTERFORT	COUNTERMURING	COUNTERPOINTS
COUNTERBALANCED	COUNTERCLAIMANT	COUNTERFORTS	COUNTERMYTH	COUNTERPOISE
COUNTERBALANCES	COUNTERCLAIMED	COUNTERGLOW	COUNTERMYTHS	COUNTERPOISED
COUNTERBASE	COUNTERCLAIMING	COUNTERGLOWS	COUNTEROFFER	COUNTERPOISES
COUNTERBASES	COUNTERCLAIMS	COUNTERGUERILLA	COUNTEROFFERS	COUNTERPOISING
COUNTERBID	COUNTERCOUP	COUNTERIMAGE	COUNTERORDER	COUNTERPOSE
COUNTERBIDDER	COUNTERCOUPS	COUNTERIMAGES	COUNTERORDERED	COUNTERPOSED
COUNTERBIDDERS	COUNTERCRIES	COUNTERING	COUNTERORDERING	COUNTERPOSES
COUNTERBIDS	COUNTERCRY	COUNTERINSTANCE	COUNTERORDERS	COUNTERPOSING
COUNTERBLAST	COUNTERCULTURAL	COUNTERION	COUNTERPACE	COUNTERPOWER
COUNTERBLASTS	COUNTERCULTURE	COUNTERIONS	COUNTERPACES	COUNTERPOWERS
COUNTERBLOCKADE	COUNTERCULTURES	COUNTERIRRITANT	COUNTERPANE	COUNTERPRESSURE
COUNTERBLOW	COUNTERCURRENT	COUNTERLIGHT	COUNTERPANES	COUNTERPROJECT
COUNTERBLOWS	COUNTERCURRENTS	COUNTERLIGHTS	COUNTERPART	COUNTERPROJECTS
COUNTERBLUFF	COUNTERCYCLICAL	COUNTERMAN	COUNTERPARTIES	COUNTERPROOF
COUNTERBLUFFS	COUNTERDEMAND	COUNTERMAND	COUNTERPARTS	COUNTERPROOFS
COUNTERBOND	COUNTERDEMANDS	COUNTERMANDABLE	COUNTERPARTY	COUNTERPROPOSAL
COUNTERBONDS	COUNTERDRAW	COUNTERMANDED	COUNTERPEISE	COUNTERPROTEST
COUNTERBORE	COUNTERDRAWING	COUNTERMANDING	COUNTERPEISED	COUNTERPROTESTS
COUNTERBORED	COUNTERDRAWN	COUNTERMANDS	COUNTERPEISES	COUNTERPUNCH
COUNTERBORES	COUNTERDRAWS	COUNTERMARCH	COUNTERPEISING	COUNTERPUNCHED
COUNTERBORING	COUNTERDREW	COUNTERMARCHED	COUNTERPETITION	COUNTERPUNCHER
COUNTERBRACE	COUNTEREFFORT	COUNTERMARCHES	COUNTERPICKET	COUNTERPUNCHERS
COUNTERBRACED	COUNTEREFFORTS	COUNTERMARCHING	COUNTERPICKETED	COUNTERPUNCHES
COUNTERBRACES	COUNTEREVIDENCE	COUNTERMARK	COUNTERPICKETS	COUNTERPUNCHING
COUNTERBRACING	COUNTEREXAMPLE	COUNTERMARKS	COUNTERPLAN	COUNTERQUESTION
COUNTERBUFF	COUNTEREXAMPLES	COUNTERMEASURE	COUNTERPLANS	COUNTERRAID
COUNTERBUFFED	COUNTERFACTUAL	COUNTERMEASURES	COUNTERPLAY	COUNTERRAIDS
COUNTERBUFFING	COUNTERFACTUALS	COUNTERMELODIES	COUNTERPLAYER	COUNTERRALLIED
COUNTERBUFFS	COUNTERFECT	COUNTERMELODY	COUNTERPLAYERS	COUNTERRALLIES
COUNTERCAMPAIGN	COUNTERFEISANCE	COUNTERMEMO	COUNTERPLAYS	COUNTERRALLY
COUNTERCHANGE	COUNTERFEIT	COUNTERMEMOS	COUNTERPLEA	COUNTERRALLYING
COUNTERCHANGED	COUNTERFEITED	COUNTERMEN	COUNTERPLEAD	COUNTERREACTION
COUNTERCHANGES	COUNTERFEITER	COUNTERMINE	COUNTERPLEADED	COUNTERREFORM
COUNTERCHANGING	COUNTERFEITERS	COUNTERMINED	COUNTERPLEADING	COUNTERREFORMER
COUNTERCHARGE	COUNTERFEITING	COUNTERMINES	COUNTERPLEADS	COUNTERREFORMS
COUNTERCHARGED	COUNTERFEITLY	COUNTERMINING	COUNTERPLEAS	COUNTERRESPONSE
COUNTERCHARGES	COUNTERFEITS	COUNTERMOTION	COUNTERPLED	COUNTERSANK
COUNTERCHARGING	COUNTERFESAUNCE	COUNTERMOTIONS	COUNTERPLOT	COUNTERSCARP
COUNTERCHARM	COUNTERFIRE	COUNTERMOVE	COUNTERPLOTS	COUNTERSCARPS
COUNTERCHARMED	COUNTERFIRES	COUNTERMOVED	COUNTERPLOTTED	COUNTERSEAL
COUNTERCHARMING	COUNTERFLOW	COUNTERMOVEMENT	COUNTERPLOTTING	COUNTERSEALED
COUNTERCHARMS	COUNTERFLOWS	COUNTERMOVES	COUNTERPLOY	COUNTERSEALING
COUNTERCHECK	COUNTERFOIL	COUNTERMOVING	COUNTERPLOYS	COUNTERSEALS

C

COUNTERSHADING	COUNTERSUES	COUNTERWORKING	COURTEOUSNESSES	COVENANTEES
COUNTERSHADINGS	COUNTERSUING	COUNTERWORKS	COURTESANS	COVENANTER
COUNTERSHAFT	COUNTERSUIT	COUNTERWORLD	COURTESIED	COVENANTERS
COUNTERSHAFTS	COUNTERSUITS	COUNTERWORLDS	COURTESIES	COVENANTING
COUNTERSHOT	COUNTERSUNK	COUNTESSES	COURTESYING	COVENANTOR
COUNTERSHOTS	COUNTERTACTIC	COUNTINGHOUSE	COURTEZANS	COVENANTORS
COUNTERSIGN	COUNTERTACTICS	COUNTINGHOUSES	COURTHOUSE	COVERALLED
COUNTERSIGNED	COUNTERTENDENCY	COUNTLESSLY	COURTHOUSES	COVERMOUNT
COUNTERSIGNING	COUNTERTENOR	COUNTLINES	COURTIERISM	COVERMOUNTED
COUNTERSIGNS	COUNTERTENORS	COUNTRIFIED	COURTIERISMS	COVERMOUNTING
COUNTERSINK	COUNTERTERROR	COUNTROLLED	COURTIERLIKE	COVERMOUNTS
COUNTERSINKING	COUNTERTERRORS	COUNTROLLING	COURTIERLY	COVERSINES
COUNTERSINKS	COUNTERTHREAT	COUNTRYFIED	COURTLIEST	COVERSLIPS
COUNTERSNIPER	COUNTERTHREATS	COUNTRYISH	COURTLINESS	COVERTNESS
COUNTERSNIPERS	COUNTERTHRUST	COUNTRYMAN	COURTLINESSES	COVERTNESSES
COUNTERSPELL	COUNTERTHRUSTS	COUNTRYMEN	COURTLINGS	COVERTURES
COUNTERSPELLS	COUNTERTOP	COUNTRYSEAT	COURTROOMS	COVETINGLY
COUNTERSPIES	COUNTERTOPS	COUNTRYSEATS	COURTSHIPS	COVETIVENESS
COUNTERSPY	COUNTERTRADE	COUNTRYSIDE	COURTSIDES	COVETIVENESSES
COUNTERSPYING	COUNTERTRADED	COUNTRYSIDES	COURTYARDS	COVETOUSLY
COUNTERSPYINGS	COUNTERTRADES	COUNTRYWIDE	COUSCOUSES	COVETOUSNESS
COUNTERSTAIN	COUNTERTRADING	COUNTRYWOMAN	COUSCOUSOU	COVETOUSNESSES
COUNTERSTAINED	COUNTERTREND	COUNTRYWOMEN	COUSCOUSOUS	COWARDICES
COUNTERSTAINING	COUNTERTRENDS	COUNTSHIPS	COUSINAGES	COWARDLINESS
COUNTERSTAINS	COUNTERTYPE	COUPLEDOMS	COUSINHOOD	COWARDLINESSES
COUNTERSTATE	COUNTERTYPES	COUPLEMENT	COUSINHOODS	COWARDRIES
COUNTERSTATED	COUNTERVAIL	COUPLEMENTS	COUSINRIES	COWARDSHIP
COUNTERSTATES	COUNTERVAILABLE	COUPONINGS	COUSINSHIP	COWARDSHIPS
COUNTERSTATING	COUNTERVAILED	COURAGEFUL	COUSINSHIPS	COWBERRIES
COUNTERSTEP	COUNTERVAILING	COURAGEOUS	COUTURIERE	COWCATCHER
COUNTERSTEPS	COUNTERVAILS	COURAGEOUSLY	COUTURIERES	COWCATCHERS
COUNTERSTRATEGY	COUNTERVIEW	COURAGEOUSNESS	COUTURIERS	COWERINGLY
COUNTERSTREAM	COUNTERVIEWS	COURANTOES	COVALENCES	COWFEEDERS
COUNTERSTREAMS	COUNTERVIOLENCE	COURBARILS	COVALENCIES	COWFETERIA
COUNTERSTRICKEN	COUNTERWEIGH	COURBETTES	COVALENTLY	COWFETERIAS
COUNTERSTRIKE	COUNTERWEIGHED	COURGETTES	COVARIANCE	COWGRASSES
COUNTERSTRIKES	COUNTERWEIGHING	COURIERING	COVARIANCES	COWLSTAFFS
COUNTERSTRIKING	COUNTERWEIGHS	COURSEBOOK	COVARIANTS	COWLSTAVES
COUNTERSTROKE	COUNTERWEIGHT	COURSEBOOKS	COVARIATES	COWPUNCHER
COUNTERSTROKES	COUNTERWEIGHTED	COURSEWARE	COVARIATION	COWPUNCHERS
COUNTERSTRUCK	COUNTERWEIGHTS	COURSEWARES	COVARIATIONS	COXCOMBICAL
COUNTERSTYLE	COUNTERWORD	COURSEWORK	COVELLINES	COXCOMBICALITY
COUNTERSTYLES	COUNTERWORDS	COURSEWORKS	COVELLITES	COXCOMBICALLY
COUNTERSUBJECT	COUNTERWORK	COURTCRAFT	COVENANTAL	COXCOMBRIES
COUNTERSUBJECTS	COUNTERWORKED	COURTCRAFTS	COVENANTALLY	COXCOMICAL
COUNTERSUE	COUNTERWORKER	COURTEOUSLY	COVENANTED	COXINESSES
COUNTERSUED	COUNTERWORKERS	COURTEOUSNESS	COVENANTEE	COXSWAINED

COXSWAINING
COYISHNESS
COYISHNESSES
COYOTILLOS
COZINESSES
CRABAPPLES
CRABBEDNESS
CRABBEDNESSES
CRABBINESS
CRABBINESSES
CRABEATERS
CRABGRASSES
CRABSTICKS
CRACKAJACK
CRACKAJACKS
CRACKBACKS
CRACKBERRIES
CRACKBERRY
CRACKBRAIN
CRACKBRAINED
CRACKBRAINS
CRACKDOWNS
CRACKERJACK
CRACKERJACKS
CRACKHEADS
CRACKLEWARE
CRACKLEWARES
CRACKLIEST
CRACKLINGS
CRACOVIENNE
CRACOVIENNES
CRADLESONG
CRADLESONGS
CRADLEWALK
CRADLEWALKS
CRAFTINESS
CRAFTINESSES
CRAFTMANSHIP
CRAFTMANSHIPS
CRAFTSMANLIKE
CRAFTSMANLY
CRAFTSMANSHIP
CRAFTSMANSHIPS
CRAFTSPEOPLE
CRAFTSPERSON
CRAFTSPERSONS
CRAFTSWOMAN

CRAFTSWOMEN
CRAFTWORKS
CRAGGEDNESS
CRAGGEDNESSES
CRAGGINESS
CRAGGINESSES
CRAIGFLUKE
CRAIGFLUKES
CRAKEBERRIES
CRAKEBERRY
CRAMBOCLINK
CRAMBOCLINKS
CRAMOISIES
CRAMPBARKS
CRAMPFISHES
CRAMPONING
CRANACHANS
CRANBERRIES
CRANEFLIES
CRANESBILL
CRANESBILLS
CRANIECTOMIES
CRANIECTOMY
CRANIOCEREBRAL
CRANIOFACIAL
CRANIOGNOMIES
CRANIOGNOMY
CRANIOLOGICAL
CRANIOLOGICALLY
CRANIOLOGIES
CRANIOLOGIST
CRANIOLOGISTS
CRANIOLOGY
CRANIOMETER
CRANIOMETERS
CRANIOMETRIC
CRANIOMETRICAL
CRANIOMETRIES
CRANIOMETRIST
CRANIOMETRISTS
CRANIOMETRY
CRANIOPAGI
CRANIOPAGUS
CRANIOSACRAL
CRANIOSCOPIES
CRANIOSCOPIST
CRANIOSCOPISTS

CRANIOSCOPY
CRANIOTOMIES
CRANIOTOMY
CRANKCASES
CRANKHANDLE
CRANKHANDLES
CRANKINESS
CRANKINESSES
CRANKNESSES
CRANKSHAFT
CRANKSHAFTS
CRANREUCHS
CRAPEHANGER
CRAPEHANGERS
CRAPEHANGING
CRAPEHANGINGS
CRAPSHOOTER
CRAPSHOOTERS
CRAPSHOOTS
CRAPULENCE
CRAPULENCES
CRAPULENTLY
CRAPULOSITIES
CRAPULOSITY
CRAPULOUSLY
CRAPULOUSNESS
CRAPULOUSNESSES
CRAQUELURE
CRAQUELURES
CRASHINGLY
CRASHWORTHINESS
CRASHWORTHY
CRASSAMENTA
CRASSAMENTUM
CRASSITUDE
CRASSITUDES
CRASSNESSES
CRASSULACEAN
CRASSULACEOUS
CRATERIFORM
CRATERINGS
CRATERLESS
CRATERLETS
CRATERLIKE
CRAUNCHABLE
CRAUNCHIER
CRAUNCHIEST

CRAUNCHINESS
CRAUNCHINESSES
CRAUNCHING
CRAVATTING
CRAVENNESS
CRAVENNESSES
CRAWDADDIES
CRAWFISHED
CRAWFISHES
CRAWFISHING
CRAWLINGLY
CRAYFISHES
CRAYONISTS
CRAZINESSES
CRAZYWEEDS
CREAKINESS
CREAKINESSES
CREAKINGLY
CREAMERIES
CREAMINESS
CREAMINESSES
CREAMPUFFS
CREAMWARES
CREASELESS
CREASOTING
CREATININE
CREATININES
CREATIONAL
CREATIONISM
CREATIONISMS
CREATIONIST
CREATIONISTIC
CREATIONISTS
CREATIVELY
CREATIVENESS
CREATIVENESSES
CREATIVITIES
CREATIVITY
CREATORSHIP
CREATORSHIPS
CREATRESSES
CREATRIXES
CREATUREHOOD
CREATUREHOODS
CREATURELINESS
CREATURELY
CREATURESHIP

CREATURESHIPS
CREDENTIAL
CREDENTIALED
CREDENTIALING
CREDENTIALISM
CREDENTIALISMS
CREDENTIALLED
CREDENTIALLING
CREDENTIALS
CREDIBILITIES
CREDIBILITY
CREDIBLENESS
CREDIBLENESSES
CREDITABILITIES
CREDITABILITY
CREDITABLE
CREDITABLENESS
CREDITABLY
CREDITLESS
CREDITWORTHY
CREDULITIES
CREDULOUSLY
CREDULOUSNESS
CREDULOUSNESSES
CREEPINESS
CREEPINESSES
CREEPINGLY
CREEPMOUSE
CREESHIEST
CREMAILLERE
CREMAILLERES
CREMASTERS
CREMATIONISM
CREMATIONISMS
CREMATIONIST
CREMATIONISTS
CREMATIONS
CREMATORIA
CREMATORIAL
CREMATORIES
CREMATORIUM
CREMATORIUMS
CREMOCARPS
CRENATIONS
CRENATURES
CRENELATED
CRENELATES

C

CRENELATING	CRESCENTIC	CRIMINALIZES	CRISPATURE	CROCHETING
CRENELATION	CRESCIVELY	CRIMINALIZING	CRISPATURES	CROCHETINGS
CRENELATIONS	CRESCOGRAPH	CRIMINALLY	CRISPBREAD	CROCIDOLITE
CRENELLATE	CRESCOGRAPHS	CRIMINATED	CRISPBREADS	CROCIDOLITES
CRENELLATED	CRESTFALLEN	CRIMINATES	CRISPENING	CROCKERIES
CRENELLATES	CRESTFALLENLY	CRIMINATING	CRISPHEADS	CROCODILES
CRENELLATING	CRESTFALLENNESS	CRIMINATION	CRISPINESS	CROCODILIAN
CRENELLATION	CRETACEOUS	CRIMINATIONS	CRISPINESSES	CROCODILIANS
CRENELLATIONS	CRETACEOUSES	CRIMINATIVE	CRISPNESSES	CROCOISITE
CRENELLING	CRETACEOUSLY	CRIMINATOR	CRISSCROSS	CROCOISITES
CRENULATED	CRETINISED	CRIMINATORS	CRISSCROSSED	CROCOSMIAS
CRENULATION	CRETINISES	CRIMINATORY	CRISSCROSSES	CROISSANTS
CRENULATIONS	CRETINISING	CRIMINOGENIC	CRISSCROSSING	CROKINOLES
CREOLISATION	CRETINISMS	CRIMINOLOGIC	CRISTIFORM	CROOKBACKED
CREOLISATIONS	CRETINIZED	CRIMINOLOGICAL	CRISTOBALITE	CROOKBACKS
CREOLISING	CRETINIZES	CRIMINOLOGIES	CRISTOBALITES	CROOKEDEST
CREOLIZATION	CRETINIZING	CRIMINOLOGIST	CRITERIONS	CROOKEDNESS
CREOLIZATIONS	CRETINOIDS	CRIMINOLOGISTS	CRITERIUMS	CROOKEDNESSES
CREOLIZING	CREVASSING	CRIMINOLOGY	CRITHIDIAL	CROOKERIES
CREOPHAGIES	CREWELISTS	CRIMINOUSNESS	CRITHOMANCIES	CROOKNECKS
CREOPHAGOUS	CREWELLERIES	CRIMINOUSNESSES	CRITHOMANCY	CROPDUSTER
CREOSOTING	CREWELLERY	CRIMSONING	CRITICALITIES	CROPDUSTERS
CREPEHANGER	CREWELLING	CRIMSONNESS	CRITICALITY	CROQUANTES
CREPEHANGERS	CREWELWORK	CRIMSONNESSES	CRITICALLY	CROQUETING
CREPEHANGING	CREWELWORKS	CRINGELING	CRITICALNESS	CROQUETTES
CREPEHANGINGS	CRIBRATION	CRINGELINGS	CRITICALNESSES	CROQUIGNOLE
CREPINESSES	CRIBRATIONS	CRINGEWORTHY	CRITICASTER	CROQUIGNOLES
CREPITATED	CRIBRIFORM	CRINGINGLY	CRITICASTERS	CROREPATIS
CREPITATES	CRICKETERS	CRINICULTURAL	CRITICISABLE	CROSSABILITIES
CREPITATING	CRICKETING	CRINIGEROUS	CRITICISED	CROSSABILITY
CREPITATION	CRICKETINGS	CRINKLEROOT	CRITICISER	CROSSANDRA
CREPITATIONS	CRIMEWAVES	CRINKLEROOTS	CRITICISERS	CROSSANDRAS
CREPITATIVE	CRIMINALESE	CRINKLIEST	CRITICISES	CROSSBANDED
CREPITUSES	CRIMINALESES	CRINOIDEAN	CRITICISING	CROSSBANDING
CREPOLINES	CRIMINALISATION	CRINOIDEANS	CRITICISINGLY	CROSSBANDINGS
CREPUSCLES	CRIMINALISE	CRINOLETTE	CRITICISMS	CROSSBANDS
CREPUSCULAR	CRIMINALISED	CRINOLETTES	CRITICIZABLE	CROSSBARRED
CREPUSCULE	CRIMINALISES	CRINOLINED	CRITICIZED	CROSSBARRING
CREPUSCULES	CRIMINALISING	CRINOLINES	CRITICIZER	CROSSBEAMS
CREPUSCULOUS	CRIMINALIST	CRIPPLEDOM	CRITICIZERS	CROSSBEARER
CRESCENDOED	CRIMINALISTICS	CRIPPLEDOMS	CRITICIZES	CROSSBEARERS
CRESCENDOES	CRIMINALISTS	CRIPPLEWARE	CRITICIZING	CROSSBENCH
CRESCENDOING	CRIMINALITIES	CRIPPLEWARES	CRITICIZINGLY	CROSSBENCHER
CRESCENDOS	CRIMINALITY	CRIPPLINGLY	CRITIQUING	CROSSBENCHERS
CRESCENTADE	CRIMINALIZATION	CRIPPLINGS	CROAKINESS	CROSSBENCHES
CRESCENTADES	CRIMINALIZE	CRISPATION	CROAKINESSES	CROSSBILLS
CRESCENTED	CRIMINALIZED	CRISPATIONS	CROCHETERS	CROSSBIRTH

CROSSBIRTHS	CROSSPIECE	CRUCIFIXION	CRYOBIOLOGIES	CRYPTANALYSES
CROSSBITES	CROSSPIECES	CRUCIFIXIONS	CRYOBIOLOGIST	CRYPTANALYSIS
CROSSBITING	CROSSROADS	CRUCIFORMLY	CRYOBIOLOGISTS	CRYPTANALYST
CROSSBITTEN	CROSSRUFFED	CRUCIFORMS	CRYOBIOLOGY	CRYPTANALYSTS
CROSSBONES	CROSSRUFFING	CRUCIFYING	CRYOCABLES	CRYPTANALYTIC
CROSSBOWER	CROSSRUFFS	CRUCIVERBAL	CRYOCONITE	CRYPTANALYTICAL
CROSSBOWERS	CROSSTALKS	CRUCIVERBALISM	CRYOCONITES	CRYPTARITHM
CROSSBOWMAN	CROSSTREES	CRUCIVERBALISMS	CRYOGENICALLY	CRYPTARITHMS
CROSSBOWMEN	CROSSWALKS	CRUCIVERBALIST	CRYOGENICS	CRYPTESTHESIA
CROSSBREDS	CROSSWINDS	CRUCIVERBALISTS	CRYOGENIES	CRYPTESTHESIAS
CROSSBREED	CROSSWORDS	CRUDENESSES	CRYOGLOBULIN	CRYPTICALLY
CROSSBREEDING	CROSSWORTS	CRUELNESSES	CRYOGLOBULINS	CRYPTOBIONT
CROSSBREEDINGS	CROTALARIA	CRUISERWEIGHT	CRYOHYDRATE	CRYPTOBIONTS
CROSSBREEDS	CROTALARIAS	CRUISERWEIGHTS	CRYOHYDRATES	CRYPTOBIOSES
CROSSBUCKS	CROTALISMS	CRUISEWAYS	CRYOMETERS	CRYPTOBIOSIS
CROSSCHECK	CROTCHETED	CRUISEWEAR	CRYOMETRIC	CRYPTOCLASTIC
CROSSCHECKED	CROTCHETEER	CRUISEWEARS	CRYOMETRIES	CRYPTOCOCCAL
CROSSCHECKING	CROTCHETEERS	CRUMBCLOTH	CRYOPHILIC	CRYPTOCOCCI
CROSSCHECKS	CROTCHETIER	CRUMBCLOTHS	CRYOPHORUS	CRYPTOCOCCOSES
CROSSCLAIM	CROTCHETIEST	CRUMBLIEST	CRYOPHORUSES	CRYPTOCOCCOSIS
CROSSCLAIMS	CROTCHETINESS	CRUMBLINESS	CRYOPHYSICS	CRYPTOCOCCUS
CROSSCOURT	CROTCHETINESSES	CRUMBLINESSES	CRYOPHYTES	CRYPTOGAMIAN
CROSSCURRENT	CROTONBUGS	CRUMBLINGS	CRYOPLANKTON	CRYPTOGAMIC
CROSSCURRENTS	CROUPINESS	CRUMMINESS	CRYOPLANKTONS	CRYPTOGAMIES
CROSSCUTTING	CROUPINESSES	CRUMMINESSES	CRYOPRECIPITATE	CRYPTOGAMIST
CROSSCUTTINGS	CROUSTADES	CRUMPLIEST	CRYOPRESERVE	CRYPTOGAMISTS
CROSSETTES	CROWBARRED	CRUMPLINGS	CRYOPRESERVED	CRYPTOGAMOUS
CROSSFALLS	CROWBARRING	CRUNCHABLE	CRYOPRESERVES	CRYPTOGAMS
CROSSFIELD	CROWBERRIES	CRUNCHIEST	CRYOPRESERVING	CRYPTOGAMY
CROSSFIRES	CROWDEDNESS	CRUNCHINESS	CRYOPROBES	CRYPTOGENIC
CROSSFISHES	CROWDEDNESSES	CRUNCHINESSES	CRYOPROTECTANT	CRYPTOGRAM
CROSSHAIRS	CROWDSOURCE	CRUNCHINGS	CRYOPROTECTANTS	CRYPTOGRAMS
CROSSHATCH	CROWDSOURCED	CRUSHABILITIES	CRYOPROTECTIVE	CRYPTOGRAPH
CROSSHATCHED	CROWDSOURCES	CRUSHABILITY	CRYOSCOPES	CRYPTOGRAPHER
CROSSHATCHES	CROWDSOURCING	CRUSHINGLY	CRYOSCOPIC	CRYPTOGRAPHERS
CROSSHATCHING	CROWDSOURCINGS	CRUSHPROOF	CRYOSCOPIES	CRYPTOGRAPHIC
CROSSHATCHINGS	CROWKEEPER	CRUSTACEAN	CRYOSTATIC	CRYPTOGRAPHICAL
CROSSHEADS	CROWKEEPERS	CRUSTACEANS	CRYOSURGEON	CRYPTOGRAPHIES
CROSSJACKS	CROWNLANDS	CRUSTACEOUS	CRYOSURGEONS	CRYPTOGRAPHIST
CROSSLIGHT	CROWNPIECE	CRUSTATION	CRYOSURGERIES	CRYPTOGRAPHISTS
CROSSLIGHTS	CROWNPIECES	CRUSTATIONS	CRYOSURGERY	CRYPTOGRAPHS
CROSSLINGUISTIC	CROWNWORKS	CRUSTINESS	CRYOSURGICAL	CRYPTOGRAPHY
CROSSNESSES	CROWSTEPPED	CRUSTINESSES	CRYOTHERAPIES	CRYPTOLOGIC
CROSSOPTERYGIAN	CRUCIATELY	CRUTCHINGS	CRYOTHERAPY	CRYPTOLOGICAL
CROSSOVERS	CRUCIFEROUS	CRYMOTHERAPIES	CRYPTAESTHESIA	CRYPTOLOGIES
CROSSPATCH	CRUCIFIERS	CRYMOTHERAPY	CRYPTAESTHESIAS	CRYPTOLOGIST
CROSSPATCHES	CRUCIFIXES	CRYOBIOLOGICAL	CRYPTAESTHETIC	CRYPTOLOGISTS

CRYPTOLOGY
CRYPTOMERIA
CRYPTOMERIAS
CRYPTOMETER
CRYPTOMETERS
CRYPTOMNESIA
CRYPTOMNESIAS
CRYPTOMNESIC
CRYPTONYMOUS
CRYPTONYMS
CRYPTOPHYTE
CRYPTOPHYTES
CRYPTOPHYTIC
CRYPTORCHID
CRYPTORCHIDISM
CRYPTORCHIDISMS
CRYPTORCHIDS
CRYPTORCHISM
CRYPTORCHISMS
CRYPTOSPORIDIA
CRYPTOSPORIDIUM
CRYPTOZOIC
CRYPTOZOITE
CRYPTOZOITES
CRYPTOZOOLOGIES
CRYPTOZOOLOGIST
CRYPTOZOOLOGY
CRYSTALISABLE
CRYSTALISATION
CRYSTALISATIONS
CRYSTALISE
CRYSTALISED
CRYSTALISER
CRYSTALISERS
CRYSTALISES
CRYSTALISING
CRYSTALIZABLE
CRYSTALIZATION
CRYSTALIZATIONS
CRYSTALIZE
CRYSTALIZED
CRYSTALIZER
CRYSTALIZERS
CRYSTALIZES
CRYSTALIZING
CRYSTALLINE
CRYSTALLINES

CRYSTALLINITIES
CRYSTALLINITY
CRYSTALLISABLE
CRYSTALLISATION
CRYSTALLISE
CRYSTALLISED
CRYSTALLISER
CRYSTALLISERS
CRYSTALLISES
CRYSTALLISING
CRYSTALLITE
CRYSTALLITES
CRYSTALLITIC
CRYSTALLITIS
CRYSTALLITISES
CRYSTALLIZABLE
CRYSTALLIZATION
CRYSTALLIZE
CRYSTALLIZED
CRYSTALLIZER
CRYSTALLIZERS
CRYSTALLIZES
CRYSTALLIZING
CRYSTALLOGRAPHY
CRYSTALLOID
CRYSTALLOIDAL
CRYSTALLOIDS
CRYSTALLOMANCY
CTENOPHORAN
CTENOPHORANS
CTENOPHORE
CTENOPHORES
CUADRILLAS
CUBANELLES
CUBBYHOLES
CUBICALNESS
CUBICALNESSES
CUBICITIES
CUBISTICALLY
CUCKOLDING
CUCKOLDISE
CUCKOLDISED
CUCKOLDISES
CUCKOLDISING
CUCKOLDIZE
CUCKOLDIZED
CUCKOLDIZES

CUCKOLDIZING
CUCKOLDOMS
CUCKOLDRIES
CUCKOOFLOWER
CUCKOOFLOWERS
CUCKOOPINT
CUCKOOPINTS
CUCULIFORM
CUCULLATED
CUCULLATELY
CUCUMIFORM
CUCURBITACEOUS
CUCURBITAL
CUDDLESOME
CUDGELLERS
CUDGELLING
CUDGELLINGS
CUFFUFFLES
CUIRASSIER
CUIRASSIERS
CUIRASSING
CUISINARTS
CUISINIERS
CULICIFORM
CULINARIAN
CULINARIANS
CULINARILY
CULLENDERS
CULMIFEROUS
CULMINATED
CULMINATES
CULMINATING
CULMINATION
CULMINATIONS
CULPABILITIES
CULPABILITY
CULPABLENESS
CULPABLENESSES
CULTISHNESS
CULTISHNESSES
CULTIVABILITIES
CULTIVABILITY
CULTIVABLE
CULTIVATABLE
CULTIVATED
CULTIVATES
CULTIVATING

CULTIVATION
CULTIVATIONS
CULTIVATOR
CULTIVATORS
CULTRIFORM
CULTURABLE
CULTURALLY
CULTURELESS
CULTURISTS
CULVERINEER
CULVERINEERS
CULVERTAGE
CULVERTAGES
CULVERTAILED
CUMBERBUND
CUMBERBUNDS
CUMBERLESS
CUMBERMENT
CUMBERMENTS
CUMBERSOME
CUMBERSOMELY
CUMBERSOMENESS
CUMBRANCES
CUMBROUSLY
CUMBROUSNESS
CUMBROUSNESSES
CUMMERBUND
CUMMERBUNDS
CUMMINGTONITE
CUMMINGTONITES
CUMULATELY
CUMULATING
CUMULATION
CUMULATIONS
CUMULATIVE
CUMULATIVELY
CUMULATIVENESS
CUMULIFORM
CUMULOCIRRI
CUMULOCIRRUS
CUMULONIMBI
CUMULONIMBUS
CUMULONIMBUSES
CUMULOSTRATI
CUMULOSTRATUS
CUNCTATION
CUNCTATIONS

CUNCTATIOUS
CUNCTATIVE
CUNCTATORS
CUNCTATORY
CUNEIFORMS
CUNNILINCTUS
CUNNILINCTUSES
CUNNILINGUS
CUNNILINGUSES
CUNNINGEST
CUNNINGNESS
CUNNINGNESSES
CUPBEARERS
CUPBOARDED
CUPBOARDING
CUPELLATION
CUPELLATIONS
CUPFERRONS
CUPIDINOUS
CUPIDITIES
CUPRAMMONIUM
CUPRAMMONIUMS
CUPRESSUSES
CUPRIFEROUS
CUPRONICKEL
CUPRONICKELS
CUPULIFEROUS
CURABILITIES
CURABILITY
CURABLENESS
CURABLENESSES
CURANDERAS
CURANDEROS
CURARISATION
CURARISATIONS
CURARISING
CURARIZATION
CURARIZATIONS
CURARIZING
CURATESHIP
CURATESHIPS
CURATIVELY
CURATIVENESS
CURATIVENESSES
CURATORIAL
CURATORSHIP
CURATORSHIPS

CURATRIXES
CURBSTONES
CURCUMINES
CURDINESSES
CURETTAGES
CURETTEMENT
CURETTEMENTS
CURFUFFLED
CURFUFFLES
CURFUFFLING
CURIALISMS
CURIALISTIC
CURIALISTS
CURIETHERAPIES
CURIETHERAPY
CURIOSITIES
CURIOUSEST
CURIOUSNESS
CURIOUSNESSES
CURLICUING
CURLIEWURLIE
CURLIEWURLIES
CURLINESSES
CURLPAPERS
CURMUDGEON
CURMUDGEONLY
CURMUDGEONS
CURMURRING
CURMURRINGS
CURNAPTIOUS
CURRAJONGS
CURRANTIER
CURRANTIEST
CURRAWONGS
CURREJONGS
CURRENCIES
CURRENTNESS
CURRENTNESSES
CURRICULAR
CURRICULUM
CURRICULUMS
CURRIERIES
CURRIJONGS
CURRISHNESS
CURRISHNESSES
CURRYCOMBED
CURRYCOMBING
CURRYCOMBS
CURSEDNESS

CURSEDNESSES
CURSELARIE
CURSIVENESS
CURSIVENESSES
CURSORINESS
CURSORINESSES
CURSTNESSES
CURTAILERS
CURTAILING
CURTAILMENT
CURTAILMENTS
CURTAINING
CURTAINLESS
CURTALAXES
CURTATIONS
CURTILAGES
CURTNESSES
CURTSEYING
CURVACEOUS
CURVACEOUSLY
CURVACIOUS
CURVATIONS
CURVATURES
CURVEBALLED
CURVEBALLING
CURVEBALLS
CURVEDNESS
CURVEDNESSES
CURVETTING
CURVICAUDATE
CURVICOSTATE
CURVIFOLIATE
CURVILINEAL
CURVILINEALLY
CURVILINEAR
CURVILINEARITY
CURVILINEARLY
CURVINESSES
CURVIROSTRAL
CUSHINESSES
CUSHIONETS
CUSHIONING
CUSHIONLESS
CUSPIDATED
CUSPIDATION
CUSPIDATIONS
CUSPIDORES
CUSSEDNESS
CUSSEDNESSES

CUSTODIANS
CUSTODIANSHIP
CUSTODIANSHIPS
CUSTODIERS
CUSTOMABLE
CUSTOMARIES
CUSTOMARILY
CUSTOMARINESS
CUSTOMARINESSES
CUSTOMHOUSE
CUSTOMHOUSES
CUSTOMISATION
CUSTOMISATIONS
CUSTOMISED
CUSTOMISER
CUSTOMISERS
CUSTOMISES
CUSTOMISING
CUSTOMIZATION
CUSTOMIZATIONS
CUSTOMIZED
CUSTOMIZER
CUSTOMIZERS
CUSTOMIZES
CUSTOMIZING
CUSTOMSHOUSE
CUSTOMSHOUSES
CUSTUMARIES
CUTABILITIES
CUTABILITY
CUTANEOUSLY
CUTCHERIES
CUTCHERRIES
CUTENESSES
CUTGRASSES
CUTINISATION
CUTINISATIONS
CUTINISING
CUTINIZATION
CUTINIZATIONS
CUTINIZING
CUTTHROATS
CUTTLEBONE
CUTTLEBONES
CUTTLEFISH
CUTTLEFISHES
CYANAMIDES
CYANIDATION
CYANIDATIONS

CYANIDINGS
CYANOACETYLENE
CYANOACETYLENES
CYANOACRYLATE
CYANOACRYLATES
CYANOBACTERIA
CYANOBACTERIUM
CYANOCOBALAMIN
CYANOCOBALAMINE
CYANOCOBALAMINS
CYANOETHYLATE
CYANOETHYLATED
CYANOETHYLATES
CYANOETHYLATING
CYANOETHYLATION
CYANOGENAMIDE
CYANOGENAMIDES
CYANOGENESES
CYANOGENESIS
CYANOGENETIC
CYANOGENIC
CYANOHYDRIN
CYANOHYDRINS
CYANOMETER
CYANOMETERS
CYANOPHYTE
CYANOPHYTES
CYANOTYPES
CYANURATES
CYATHIFORM
CYBERATHLETE
CYBERATHLETES
CYBERATHLETICS
CYBERCAFES
CYBERCASTS
CYBERCHONDRIA
CYBERCHONDRIAC
CYBERCHONDRIACS
CYBERCHONDRIAS
CYBERCRIME
CYBERCRIMES
CYBERCRIMINAL
CYBERCRIMINALS
CYBERNATED
CYBERNATES
CYBERNATING
CYBERNATION
CYBERNATIONS
CYBERNAUTS

CYBERNETIC
CYBERNETICAL
CYBERNETICALLY
CYBERNETICIAN
CYBERNETICIANS
CYBERNETICIST
CYBERNETICISTS
CYBERNETICS
CYBERPHOBIA
CYBERPHOBIAS
CYBERPHOBIC
CYBERPORNS
CYBERPUNKS
CYBERSECURITIES
CYBERSECURITY
CYBERSEXES
CYBERSPACE
CYBERSPACES
CYBERSQUATTER
CYBERSQUATTERS
CYBERSQUATTING
CYBERSQUATTINGS
CYBERTERRORISM
CYBERTERRORISMS
CYBERTERRORIST
CYBERTERRORISTS
CYBRARIANS
CYCADACEOUS
CYCADEOIDS
CYCADOPHYTE
CYCADOPHYTES
CYCLAMATES
CYCLANDELATE
CYCLANDELATES
CYCLANTHACEOUS
CYCLAZOCINE
CYCLAZOCINES
CYCLEPATHS
CYCLICALITIES
CYCLICALITY
CYCLICALLY
CYCLICISMS
CYCLICITIES
CYCLISATION
CYCLISATIONS
CYCLIZATION
CYCLIZATIONS
CYCLIZINES
CYCLOADDITION

C

CYCLOADDITIONS
CYCLOALIPHATIC
CYCLOALKANE
CYCLOALKANES
CYCLOBARBITONE
CYCLOBARBITONES
CYCLODEXTRIN
CYCLODEXTRINS
CYCLODIALYSES
CYCLODIALYSIS
CYCLODIENE
CYCLODIENES
CYCLOGENESES
CYCLOGENESIS
CYCLOGIROS
CYCLOGRAPH
CYCLOGRAPHIC
CYCLOGRAPHS
CYCLOHEXANE
CYCLOHEXANES
CYCLOHEXANONE
CYCLOHEXANONES
CYCLOHEXIMIDE
CYCLOHEXIMIDES
CYCLOHEXYLAMINE
CYCLOIDALLY
CYCLOIDIAN
CYCLOIDIANS
CYCLOLITHS
CYCLOMETER
CYCLOMETERS
CYCLOMETRIES
CYCLOMETRY
CYCLONICAL
CYCLONICALLY
CYCLONITES
CYCLOOLEFIN
CYCLOOLEFINIC
CYCLOOLEFINS
CYCLOPAEDIA
CYCLOPAEDIAS
CYCLOPAEDIC
CYCLOPAEDIST
CYCLOPAEDISTS
CYCLOPARAFFIN
CYCLOPARAFFINS
CYCLOPEDIA
CYCLOPEDIAS

CYCLOPEDIC
CYCLOPEDIST
CYCLOPEDISTS
CYCLOPENTADIENE
CYCLOPENTANE
CYCLOPENTANES
CYCLOPENTOLATE
CYCLOPENTOLATES
CYCLOPLEGIA
CYCLOPLEGIAS
CYCLOPLEGIC
CYCLOPROPANE
CYCLOPROPANES
CYCLORAMAS
CYCLORAMIC
CYCLOSERINE
CYCLOSERINES
CYCLOSPERMOUS
CYCLOSPORIN
CYCLOSPORINE
CYCLOSPORINES
CYCLOSPORINS
CYCLOSTOMATE
CYCLOSTOMATOUS
CYCLOSTOME
CYCLOSTOMES
CYCLOSTOMOUS
CYCLOSTYLE
CYCLOSTYLED
CYCLOSTYLES
CYCLOSTYLING
CYCLOTHYME
CYCLOTHYMES
CYCLOTHYMIA
CYCLOTHYMIAC
CYCLOTHYMIACS
CYCLOTHYMIAS
CYCLOTHYMIC
CYCLOTHYMICS
CYCLOTOMIC
CYCLOTRONS
CYLINDERED
CYLINDERING
CYLINDRACEOUS
CYLINDRICAL
CYLINDRICALITY
CYLINDRICALLY
CYLINDRICALNESS

CYLINDRICITIES
CYLINDRICITY
CYLINDRIFORM
CYLINDRITE
CYLINDRITES
CYLINDROID
CYLINDROIDS
CYMAGRAPHS
CYMBALEERS
CYMBALISTS
CYMBIDIUMS
CYMIFEROUS
CYMOGRAPHIC
CYMOGRAPHS
CYMOPHANES
CYMOPHANOUS
CYMOTRICHIES
CYMOTRICHOUS
CYMOTRICHY
CYNGHANEDD
CYNGHANEDDS
CYNICALNESS
CYNICALNESSES
CYNOMOLGUS
CYNOPHILIA
CYNOPHILIAS
CYNOPHILIST
CYNOPHILISTS
CYNOPHOBIA
CYNOPHOBIAS
CYNOPODOUS
CYPERACEOUS
CYPRINODONT
CYPRINODONTS
CYPRINOIDS
CYPRIPEDIA
CYPRIPEDIUM
CYPRIPEDIUMS
CYPROHEPTADINE
CYPROHEPTADINES
CYPROTERONE
CYPROTERONES
CYSTEAMINE
CYSTEAMINES
CYSTECTOMIES
CYSTECTOMY
CYSTICERCI
CYSTICERCOID

CYSTICERCOIDS
CYSTICERCOSES
CYSTICERCOSIS
CYSTICERCUS
CYSTIDEANS
CYSTINOSES
CYSTINOSIS
CYSTINURIA
CYSTINURIAS
CYSTITIDES
CYSTITISES
CYSTOCARPIC
CYSTOCARPS
CYSTOCELES
CYSTOGENOUS
CYSTOGRAPHIES
CYSTOGRAPHY
CYSTOLITHIASES
CYSTOLITHIASIS
CYSTOLITHS
CYSTOSCOPE
CYSTOSCOPES
CYSTOSCOPIC
CYSTOSCOPIES
CYSTOSCOPY
CYSTOSTOMIES
CYSTOSTOMY
CYSTOTOMIES
CYTOCHALASIN
CYTOCHALASINS
CYTOCHEMICAL
CYTOCHEMISTRIES
CYTOCHEMISTRY
CYTOCHROME
CYTOCHROMES
CYTODIAGNOSES
CYTODIAGNOSIS
CYTOGENESES
CYTOGENESIS
CYTOGENETIC
CYTOGENETICAL
CYTOGENETICALLY
CYTOGENETICIST
CYTOGENETICISTS
CYTOGENETICS
CYTOGENIES
CYTOKINESES
CYTOKINESIS

CYTOKINETIC
CYTOKININS
CYTOLOGICAL
CYTOLOGICALLY
CYTOLOGIES
CYTOLOGIST
CYTOLOGISTS
CYTOLYSINS
CYTOMEGALIC
CYTOMEGALOVIRUS
CYTOMEMBRANE
CYTOMEMBRANES
CYTOMETERS
CYTOMETRIC
CYTOMETRIES
CYTOPATHIC
CYTOPATHOGENIC
CYTOPATHOLOGIES
CYTOPATHOLOGY
CYTOPENIAS
CYTOPHILIC
CYTOPHOTOMETRIC
CYTOPHOTOMETRY
CYTOPLASMIC
CYTOPLASMICALLY
CYTOPLASMS
CYTOPLASTIC
CYTOPLASTS
CYTOSKELETAL
CYTOSKELETON
CYTOSKELETONS
CYTOSTATIC
CYTOSTATICALLY
CYTOSTATICS
CYTOTAXONOMIC
CYTOTAXONOMIES
CYTOTAXONOMIST
CYTOTAXONOMISTS
CYTOTAXONOMY
CYTOTECHNOLOGY
CYTOTOXICITIES
CYTOTOXICITY
CYTOTOXINS
CZAREVICHES
CZAREVITCH
CZAREVITCHES

D

DABBLINGLY	DAILINESSES	DAMPISHNESS	DARRAYNING	DAYDREAMER
DACHSHUNDS	DAILYNESSES	DAMPISHNESSES	DARTBOARDS	DAYDREAMERS
DACOITAGES	DAINTINESS	DAMPNESSES	DARTITISES	DAYDREAMING
DACQUOISES	DAINTINESSES	DAMSELFISH	DASHBOARDS	DAYDREAMLIKE
DACTYLICALLY	DAIRYMAIDS	DAMSELFISHES	DASTARDIES	DAYFLOWERS
DACTYLIOGRAPHY	DAISYWHEEL	DAMSELFLIES	DASTARDLINESS	DAYLIGHTED
DACTYLIOLOGIES	DAISYWHEELS	DANCEHALLS	DASTARDLINESSES	DAYLIGHTING
DACTYLIOLOGY	DALLIANCES	DANDELIONS	DASTARDNESS	DAYLIGHTINGS
DACTYLIOMANCIES	DALMATIANS	DANDIFICATION	DASTARDNESSES	DAYSAILERS
DACTYLIOMANCY	DALTONISMS	DANDIFICATIONS	DASYMETERS	DAYSAILORS
DACTYLISTS	DAMAGEABILITIES	DANDIFYING	DASYPAEDAL	DAYSPRINGS
DACTYLOGRAM	DAMAGEABILITY	DANDIPRATS	DASYPHYLLOUS	DAYWORKERS
DACTYLOGRAMS	DAMAGEABLE	DANDYFUNKS	DATABASING	DAZEDNESSES
DACTYLOGRAPHER	DAMAGINGLY	DANDYISHLY	DATABUSSES	DAZZLEMENT
DACTYLOGRAPHERS	DAMASCEENE	DANDYPRATS	DATAGLOVES	DAZZLEMENTS
DACTYLOGRAPHIC	DAMASCEENED	DANGERLESS	DATAMATION	DAZZLINGLY
DACTYLOGRAPHIES	DAMASCEENES	DANGEROUSLY	DATAMATIONS	DEACIDIFICATION
DACTYLOGRAPHY	DAMASCEENING	DANGEROUSNESS	DATAVEILLANCE	DEACIDIFIED
DACTYLOLOGIES	DAMASCENED	DANGEROUSNESSES	DATAVEILLANCES	DEACIDIFIES
DACTYLOLOGY	DAMASCENES	DANGLINGLY	DATEDNESSES	DEACIDIFYING
DACTYLOSCOPIES	DAMASCENING	DANKNESSES	DATELINING	DEACONESSES
DACTYLOSCOPY	DAMASCENINGS	DANNEBROGS	DAUGHTERHOOD	DEACONHOOD
DAFFADOWNDILLY	DAMASKEENED	DANTHONIAS	DAUGHTERHOODS	DEACONHOODS
DAFFINESSES	DAMASKEENING	DAPPERLING	DAUGHTERLESS	DEACONRIES
DAFFODILLIES	DAMASKEENS	DAPPERLINGS	DAUGHTERLINESS	DEACONSHIP
DAFFODILLY	DAMASKINED	DAPPERNESS	DAUGHTERLING	DEACONSHIPS
DAFTNESSES	DAMASKINING	DAPPERNESSES	DAUGHTERLINGS	DEACTIVATE
DAGGERBOARD	DAMASQUINED	DAREDEVILRIES	DAUGHTERLY	DEACTIVATED
DAGGERBOARDS	DAMASQUINING	DAREDEVILRY	DAUNDERING	DEACTIVATES
DAGGERLIKE	DAMASQUINS	DAREDEVILS	DAUNOMYCIN	DEACTIVATING
DAGUERREAN	DAMINOZIDE	DAREDEVILTRIES	DAUNOMYCINS	DEACTIVATION
DAGUERREOTYPE	DAMINOZIDES	DAREDEVILTRY	DAUNORUBICIN	DEACTIVATIONS
DAGUERREOTYPED	DAMNABILITIES	DARINGNESS	DAUNORUBICINS	DEACTIVATOR
DAGUERREOTYPER	DAMNABILITY	DARINGNESSES	DAUNTINGLY	DEACTIVATORS
DAGUERREOTYPERS	DAMNABLENESS	DARKNESSES	DAUNTLESSLY	DEADENINGLY
DAGUERREOTYPES	DAMNABLENESSES	DARLINGNESS	DAUNTLESSNESS	DEADENINGS
DAGUERREOTYPIES	DAMNATIONS	DARLINGNESSES	DAUNTLESSNESSES	DEADHEADED
DAGUERREOTYPING	DAMNEDESTS	DARNATIONS	DAUNTONING	DEADHEADING
DAGUERREOTYPIST	DAMNIFICATION	DARNEDESTS	DAUPHINESS	DEADHOUSES
DAGUERREOTYPY	DAMNIFICATIONS	DARRAIGNED	DAUPHINESSES	DEADLIFTED
DAHABEEAHS	DAMNIFYING	DARRAIGNES	DAVENPORTS	DEADLIFTING
DAHABEEYAH	DAMOISELLE	DARRAIGNING	DAWDLINGLY	DEADLIGHTS
DAHABEEYAHS	DAMOISELLES	DARRAIGNMENT	DAWSONITES	DEADLINESS
DAHABIYAHS	DAMPCOURSE	DARRAIGNMENTS	DAYCENTRES	DEADLINESSES
DAHABIYEHS	DAMPCOURSES	DARRAINING	DAYDREAMED	DEADLINING

DEADLOCKED	DEARTICULATING	DEBAUCHING	DECALCIFIED	DECAPITATOR
DEADLOCKING	DEASPIRATE	DEBAUCHMENT	DECALCIFIER	DECAPITATORS
DEADNESSES	DEASPIRATED	DEBAUCHMENTS	DECALCIFIERS	DECAPODANS
DEADPANNED	DEASPIRATES	DEBEARDING	DECALCIFIES	DECAPODOUS
DEADPANNER	DEASPIRATING	DEBENTURED	DECALCIFYING	DECAPSULATE
DEADPANNERS	DEASPIRATION	DEBENTURES	DECALCOMANIA	DECAPSULATED
DEADPANNING	DEASPIRATIONS	DEBILITATE	DECALCOMANIAS	DECAPSULATES
DEADSTOCKS	DEATHBLOWS	DEBILITATED	DECALESCENCE	DECAPSULATING
DEADSTROKE	DEATHLESSLY	DEBILITATES	DECALESCENCES	DECAPSULATION
DEADWEIGHT	DEATHLESSNESS	DEBILITATING	DECALESCENT	DECAPSULATIONS
DEADWEIGHTS	DEATHLESSNESSES	DEBILITATION	DECALITERS	DECARBONATE
DEAERATING	DEATHLIEST	DEBILITATIONS	DECALITRES	DECARBONATED
DEAERATION	DEATHLINESS	DEBILITATIVE	DECALOGIST	DECARBONATES
DEAERATIONS	DEATHLINESSES	DEBILITIES	DECALOGISTS	DECARBONATING
DEAERATORS	DEATHTRAPS	DEBONAIRLY	DECALOGUES	DECARBONATION
DEAFENINGLY	DEATHWARDS	DEBONAIRNESS	DECAMERONIC	DECARBONATIONS
DEAFENINGS	DEATHWATCH	DEBONAIRNESSES	DECAMEROUS	DECARBONATOR
DEAFNESSES	DEATHWATCHES	DEBONNAIRE	DECAMETERS	DECARBONATORS
DEALATIONS	DEATTRIBUTE	DEBOUCHING	DECAMETHONIUM	DECARBONISATION
DEALBATION	DEATTRIBUTED	DEBOUCHMENT	DECAMETHONIUMS	DECARBONISE
DEALBATIONS	DEATTRIBUTES	DEBOUCHMENTS	DECAMETRES	DECARBONISED
DEALERSHIP	DEATTRIBUTING	DEBOUCHURE	DECAMETRIC	DECARBONISER
DEALERSHIPS	DEBAGGINGS	DEBOUCHURES	DECAMPMENT	DECARBONISERS
DEALFISHES	DEBARCATION	DEBRIDEMENT	DECAMPMENTS	DECARBONISES
DEAMBULATORIES	DEBARCATIONS	DEBRIDEMENTS	DECANDRIAN	DECARBONISING
DEAMBULATORY	DEBARKATION	DEBRIEFERS	DECANDROUS	DECARBONIZATION
DEAMINASES	DEBARKATIONS	DEBRIEFING	DECANEDIOIC	DECARBONIZE
DEAMINATED	DEBARMENTS	DEBRIEFINGS	DECANICALLY	DECARBONIZED
DEAMINATES	DEBARRASSED	DEBRUISING	DECANTATED	DECARBONIZER
DEAMINATING	DEBARRASSES	DEBUTANTES	DECANTATES	DECARBONIZERS
DEAMINATION	DEBARRASSING	DECACHORDS	DECANTATING	DECARBONIZES
DEAMINATIONS	DEBASEDNESS	DECADENCES	DECANTATION	DECARBONIZING
DEAMINISATION	DEBASEDNESSES	DECADENCIES	DECANTATIONS	DECARBOXYLASE
DEAMINISATIONS	DEBASEMENT	DECADENTLY	DECAPITALISE	DECARBOXYLASES
DEAMINISED	DEBASEMENTS	DECAFFEINATE	DECAPITALISED	DECARBOXYLATE
DEAMINISES	DEBASINGLY	DECAFFEINATED	DECAPITALISES	DECARBOXYLATED
DEAMINISING	DEBATEABLE	DECAFFEINATES	DECAPITALISING	DECARBOXYLATES
DEAMINIZATION	DEBATEMENT	DECAFFEINATING	DECAPITALIZE	DECARBOXYLATING
DEAMINIZATIONS	DEBATEMENTS	DECAGONALLY	DECAPITALIZED	DECARBOXYLATION
DEAMINIZED	DEBATINGLY	DECAGRAMME	DECAPITALIZES	DECARBURATION
DEAMINIZES	DEBAUCHEDLY	DECAGRAMMES	DECAPITALIZING	DECARBURATIONS
DEAMINIZING	DEBAUCHEDNESS	DECAGYNIAN	DECAPITATE	DECARBURISATION
DEARBOUGHT	DEBAUCHEDNESSES	DECAGYNOUS	DECAPITATED	DECARBURISE
DEARNESSES	DEBAUCHEES	DECAHEDRAL	DECAPITATES	DECARBURISED
DEARTICULATE	DEBAUCHERIES	DECAHEDRON	DECAPITATING	DECARBURISES
DEARTICULATED	DEBAUCHERS	DECAHEDRONS	DECAPITATION	DECARBURISING
DEARTICULATES	DEBAUCHERY	DECALCIFICATION	DECAPITATIONS	DECARBURIZATION

DECARBURIZE	DECENNIUMS	DECHLORINATED	DECIMETRIC	DECLARATIONS
DECARBURIZED	DECENNOVAL	DECHLORINATES	DECINORMAL	DECLARATIVE
DECARBURIZES	DECENTERED	DECHLORINATING	DECIPHERABILITY	DECLARATIVELY
DECARBURIZING	DECENTERING	DECHLORINATION	DECIPHERABLE	DECLARATOR
DECASTERES	DECENTNESS	DECHLORINATIONS	DECIPHERED	DECLARATORILY
DECASTICHS	DECENTNESSES	DECHRISTIANISE	DECIPHERER	DECLARATORS
DECASTYLES	DECENTRALISE	DECHRISTIANISED	DECIPHERERS	DECLARATORY
DECASUALISATION	DECENTRALISED	DECHRISTIANISES	DECIPHERING	DECLAREDLY
DECASUALIZATION	DECENTRALISES	DECHRISTIANIZE	DECIPHERMENT	DECLASSIFIABLE
DECASYLLABIC	DECENTRALISING	DECHRISTIANIZED	DECIPHERMENTS	DECLASSIFIED
DECASYLLABICS	DECENTRALIST	DECHRISTIANIZES	DECISIONAL	DECLASSIFIES
DECASYLLABLE	DECENTRALISTS	DECIDABILITIES	DECISIONED	DECLASSIFY
DECASYLLABLES	DECENTRALIZE	DECIDABILITY	DECISIONING	DECLASSIFYING
DECATHLETE	DECENTRALIZED	DECIDEDNESS	DECISIVELY	DECLASSING
DECATHLETES	DECENTRALIZES	DECIDEDNESSES	DECISIVENESS	DECLENSION
DECATHLONS	DECENTRALIZING	DECIDUOUSLY	DECISIVENESSES	DECLENSIONAL
DECAUDATED	DECENTRING	DECIDUOUSNESS	DECISTERES	DECLENSIONALLY
DECAUDATES	DECEPTIBILITIES	DECIDUOUSNESSES	DECITIZENISE	DECLENSIONS
DECAUDATING	DECEPTIBILITY	DECIGRAMME	DECITIZENISED	DECLINABLE
DECEITFULLY	DECEPTIBLE	DECIGRAMMES	DECITIZENISES	DECLINATION
DECEITFULNESS	DECEPTIONAL	DECILITERS	DECITIZENISING	DECLINATIONAL
DECEITFULNESSES	DECEPTIONS	DECILITRES	DECITIZENIZE	DECLINATIONS
DECEIVABILITIES	DECEPTIOUS	DECILLIONS	DECITIZENIZED	DECLINATOR
DECEIVABILITY	DECEPTIVELY	DECILLIONTH	DECITIZENIZES	DECLINATORS
DECEIVABLE	DECEPTIVENESS	DECILLIONTHS	DECITIZENIZING	DECLINATORY
DECEIVABLENESS	DECEPTIVENESSES	DECIMALISATION	DECIVILISE	DECLINATURE
DECEIVABLY	DECEREBRATE	DECIMALISATIONS	DECIVILISED	DECLINATURES
DECEIVINGLY	DECEREBRATED	DECIMALISE	DECIVILISES	DECLINISTS
DECEIVINGS	DECEREBRATES	DECIMALISED	DECIVILISING	DECLINOMETER
DECELERATE	DECEREBRATING	DECIMALISES	DECIVILIZE	DECLINOMETERS
DECELERATED	DECEREBRATION	DECIMALISING	DECIVILIZED	DECLIVITIES
DECELERATES	DECEREBRATIONS	DECIMALISM	DECIVILIZES	DECLIVITOUS
DECELERATING	DECEREBRISE	DECIMALISMS	DECIVILIZING	DECLUTCHED
DECELERATION	DECEREBRISED	DECIMALIST	DECKCHAIRS	DECLUTCHES
DECELERATIONS	DECEREBRISES	DECIMALISTS	DECKHOUSES	DECLUTCHING
DECELERATOR	DECEREBRISING	DECIMALIZATION	DECLAIMANT	DECLUTTERED
DECELERATORS	DECEREBRIZE	DECIMALIZATIONS	DECLAIMANTS	DECLUTTERING
DECELEROMETER	DECEREBRIZED	DECIMALIZE	DECLAIMERS	DECLUTTERS
DECELEROMETERS	DECEREBRIZES	DECIMALIZED	DECLAIMING	DECOCTIBLE
DECELERONS	DECEREBRIZING	DECIMALIZES	DECLAIMINGS	DECOCTIONS
DECEMVIRAL	DECERTIFICATION	DECIMALIZING	DECLAMATION	DECOCTURES
DECEMVIRATE	DECERTIFIED	DECIMATING	DECLAMATIONS	DECOHERENCE
DECEMVIRATES	DECERTIFIES	DECIMATION	DECLAMATORILY	DECOHERENCES
DECENARIES	DECERTIFYING	DECIMATIONS	DECLAMATORY	DECOHERERS
DECENNARIES	DECESSIONS	DECIMATORS	DECLARABLE	DECOLLATED
DECENNIALLY	DECHEANCES	DECIMETERS	DECLARANTS	DECOLLATES
DECENNIALS	DECHLORINATE	DECIMETRES	DECLARATION	DECOLLATING

DECOLLATION	DECOLOURISE	DECONCENTRATE	DECORATIONS	DECRESCENDO
DECOLLATIONS	DECOLOURISED	DECONCENTRATED	DECORATIVE	DECRESCENDOS
DECOLLATOR	DECOLOURISES	DECONCENTRATES	DECORATIVELY	DECRESCENT
DECOLLATORS	DECOLOURISING	DECONCENTRATING	DECORATIVENESS	DECRETALIST
DECOLLETAGE	DECOLOURIZATION	DECONCENTRATION	DECORATORS	DECRETALISTS
DECOLLETAGES	DECOLOURIZE	DECONDITION	DECOROUSLY	DECRETISTS
DECOLLETES	DECOLOURIZED	DECONDITIONED	DECOROUSNESS	DECRIMINALISE
DECOLONISATION	DECOLOURIZES	DECONDITIONING	DECOROUSNESSES	DECRIMINALISED
DECOLONISATIONS	DECOLOURIZING	DECONDITIONS	DECORTICATE	DECRIMINALISES
DECOLONISE	DECOMMISSION	DECONGESTANT	DECORTICATED	DECRIMINALISING
DECOLONISED	DECOMMISSIONED	DECONGESTANTS	DECORTICATES	DECRIMINALIZE
DECOLONISES	DECOMMISSIONER	DECONGESTED	DECORTICATING	DECRIMINALIZED
DECOLONISING	DECOMMISSIONERS	DECONGESTING	DECORTICATION	DECRIMINALIZES
DECOLONIZATION	DECOMMISSIONING	DECONGESTION	DECORTICATIONS	DECRIMINALIZING
DECOLONIZATIONS	DECOMMISSIONS	DECONGESTIONS	DECORTICATOR	DECROWNING
DECOLONIZE	DECOMMITTED	DECONGESTIVE	DECORTICATORS	DECRUSTATION
DECOLONIZED	DECOMMITTING	DECONGESTS	DECOUPAGED	DECRUSTATIONS
DECOLONIZES	DECOMPENSATE	DECONSECRATE	DECOUPAGES	DECRYPTING
DECOLONIZING	DECOMPENSATED	DECONSECRATED	DECOUPAGING	DECRYPTION
DECOLORANT	DECOMPENSATES	DECONSECRATES	DECOUPLERS	DECRYPTIONS
DECOLORANTS	DECOMPENSATING	DECONSECRATING	DECOUPLING	DECUMBENCE
DECOLORATE	DECOMPENSATION	DECONSECRATION	DECOUPLINGS	DECUMBENCES
DECOLORATED	DECOMPENSATIONS	DECONSECRATIONS	DECRASSIFIED	DECUMBENCIES
DECOLORATES	DECOMPOSABILITY	DECONSTRUCT	DECRASSIFIES	DECUMBENCY
DECOLORATING	DECOMPOSABLE	DECONSTRUCTED	DECRASSIFY	DECUMBENTLY
DECOLORATION	DECOMPOSED	DECONSTRUCTING	DECRASSIFYING	DECUMBITURE
DECOLORATIONS	DECOMPOSER	DECONSTRUCTION	DECREASING	DECUMBITURES
DECOLORING	DECOMPOSERS	DECONSTRUCTIONS	DECREASINGLY	DECURIONATE
DECOLORISATION	DECOMPOSES	DECONSTRUCTIVE	DECREASINGS	DECURIONATES
DECOLORISATIONS	DECOMPOSING	DECONSTRUCTOR	DECREEABLE	DECURRENCIES
DECOLORISE	DECOMPOSITE	DECONSTRUCTORS	DECREMENTAL	DECURRENCY
DECOLORISED	DECOMPOSITION	DECONSTRUCTS	DECREMENTED	DECURRENTLY
DECOLORISER	DECOMPOSITIONS	DECONTAMINANT	DECREMENTING	DECURSIONS
DECOLORISERS	DECOMPOUND	DECONTAMINANTS	DECREMENTS	DECURSIVELY
DECOLORISES	DECOMPOUNDABLE	DECONTAMINATE	DECREPITATE	DECURVATION
DECOLORISING	DECOMPOUNDED	DECONTAMINATED	DECREPITATED	DECURVATIONS
DECOLORIZATION	DECOMPOUNDING	DECONTAMINATES	DECREPITATES	DECUSSATED
DECOLORIZATIONS	DECOMPOUNDS	DECONTAMINATING	DECREPITATING	DECUSSATELY
DECOLORIZE	DECOMPRESS	DECONTAMINATION	DECREPITATION	DECUSSATES
DECOLORIZED	DECOMPRESSED	DECONTAMINATIVE	DECREPITATIONS	DECUSSATING
DECOLORIZER	DECOMPRESSES	DECONTAMINATOR	DECREPITLY	DECUSSATION
DECOLORIZERS	DECOMPRESSING	DECONTAMINATORS	DECREPITNESS	DECUSSATIONS
DECOLORIZES	DECOMPRESSION	DECONTROLLED	DECREPITNESSES	DEDICATEDLY
DECOLORIZING	DECOMPRESSIONS	DECONTROLLING	DECREPITUDE	DEDICATEES
DECOLOURED	DECOMPRESSIVE	DECONTROLS	DECREPITUDES	DEDICATING
DECOLOURING	DECOMPRESSOR	DECORATING	DECRESCENCE	DEDICATION
DECOLOURISATION	DECOMPRESSORS	DECORATION	DECRESCENCES	DEDICATIONAL

DEDICATIONS	DEERSTALKINGS	DEFECTIVELY	DEFERENTIALLY	DEFICIENTS
DEDICATIVE	DEFACEABLE	DEFECTIVENESS	DEFERMENTS	DEFILADING
DEDICATORIAL	DEFACEMENT	DEFECTIVENESSES	DEFERRABLE	DEFILEMENT
DEDICATORS	DEFACEMENTS	DEFECTIVES	DEFERRABLES	DEFILEMENTS
DEDICATORY	DEFACINGLY	DEFEMINISATION	DEFERVESCENCE	DEFILIATION
DEDIFFERENTIATE	DEFAECATED	DEFEMINISATIONS	DEFERVESCENCES	DEFILIATIONS
DEDRAMATISE	DEFAECATES	DEFEMINISE	DEFERVESCENCIES	DEFINABILITIES
DEDRAMATISED	DEFAECATING	DEFEMINISED	DEFERVESCENCY	DEFINABILITY
DEDRAMATISES	DEFAECATION	DEFEMINISES	DEFEUDALISE	DEFINEMENT
DEDRAMATISING	DEFAECATIONS	DEFEMINISING	DEFEUDALISED	DEFINEMENTS
DEDRAMATIZE	DEFAECATOR	DEFEMINIZATION	DEFEUDALISES	DEFINIENDA
DEDRAMATIZED	DEFAECATORS	DEFEMINIZATIONS	DEFEUDALISING	DEFINIENDUM
DEDRAMATIZES	DEFALCATED	DEFEMINIZE	DEFEUDALIZE	DEFINIENTIA
DEDRAMATIZING	DEFALCATES	DEFEMINIZED	DEFEUDALIZED	DEFINITELY
DEDUCEMENT	DEFALCATING	DEFEMINIZES	DEFEUDALIZES	DEFINITENESS
DEDUCEMENTS	DEFALCATION	DEFEMINIZING	DEFEUDALIZING	DEFINITENESSES
DEDUCIBILITIES	DEFALCATIONS	DEFENCELESS	DEFIANTNESS	DEFINITION
DEDUCIBILITY	DEFALCATOR	DEFENCELESSLY	DEFIANTNESSES	DEFINITIONAL
DEDUCIBLENESS	DEFALCATORS	DEFENCELESSNESS	DEFIBRILLATE	DEFINITIONS
DEDUCIBLENESSES	DEFAMATION	DEFENCEMAN	DEFIBRILLATED	DEFINITISE
DEDUCTIBILITIES	DEFAMATIONS	DEFENCEMEN	DEFIBRILLATES	DEFINITISED
DEDUCTIBILITY	DEFAMATORILY	DEFENDABLE	DEFIBRILLATING	DEFINITISES
DEDUCTIBLE	DEFAMATORY	DEFENDANTS	DEFIBRILLATION	DEFINITISING
DEDUCTIBLES	DEFAULTERS	DEFENESTRATE	DEFIBRILLATIONS	DEFINITIVE
DEDUCTIONS	DEFAULTING	DEFENESTRATED	DEFIBRILLATOR	DEFINITIVELY
DEDUCTIVELY	DEFEASANCE	DEFENESTRATES	DEFIBRILLATORS	DEFINITIVENESS
DEDUPLICATE	DEFEASANCED	DEFENESTRATING	DEFIBRINATE	DEFINITIVES
DEDUPLICATED	DEFEASANCES	DEFENESTRATION	DEFIBRINATED	DEFINITIZE
DEDUPLICATES	DEFEASIBILITIES	DEFENESTRATIONS	DEFIBRINATES	DEFINITIZED
DEDUPLICATING	DEFEASIBILITY	DEFENSATIVE	DEFIBRINATING	DEFINITIZES
DEDUPLICATION	DEFEASIBLE	DEFENSATIVES	DEFIBRINATION	DEFINITIZING
DEDUPLICATIONS	DEFEASIBLENESS	DEFENSELESS	DEFIBRINATIONS	DEFINITUDE
DEEMSTERSHIP	DEFEATISMS	DEFENSELESSLY	DEFIBRINISE	DEFINITUDES
DEEMSTERSHIPS	DEFEATISTS	DEFENSELESSNESS	DEFIBRINISED	DEFLAGRABILITY
DEEPFREEZE	DEFEATURED	DEFENSEMAN	DEFIBRINISES	DEFLAGRABLE
DEEPFREEZES	DEFEATURES	DEFENSEMEN	DEFIBRINISING	DEFLAGRATE
DEEPFREEZING	DEFEATURING	DEFENSIBILITIES	DEFIBRINIZE	DEFLAGRATED
DEEPFROZEN	DEFECATING	DEFENSIBILITY	DEFIBRINIZED	DEFLAGRATES
DEEPNESSES	DEFECATION	DEFENSIBLE	DEFIBRINIZES	DEFLAGRATING
DEEPWATERMAN	DEFECATIONS	DEFENSIBLENESS	DEFIBRINIZING	DEFLAGRATION
DEEPWATERMEN	DEFECATORS	DEFENSIBLY	DEFICIENCE	DEFLAGRATIONS
DEERBERRIES	DEFECTIBILITIES	DEFENSIVELY	DEFICIENCES	DEFLAGRATOR
DEERGRASSES	DEFECTIBILITY	DEFENSIVENESS	DEFICIENCIES	DEFLAGRATORS
DEERHOUNDS	DEFECTIBLE	DEFENSIVENESSES	DEFICIENCY	DEFLATIONARY
DEERSTALKER	DEFECTIONIST	DEFENSIVES	DEFICIENTLY	DEFLATIONIST
DEERSTALKERS	DEFECTIONISTS	DEFERENCES	DEFICIENTNESS	DEFLATIONISTS
DEERSTALKING	DEFECTIONS	DEFERENTIAL	DEFICIENTNESSES	DEFLATIONS

DEFLECTABLE	DEFORESTATIONS	DEFUNCTIONS	DEGLUTITORY	DEHUMANISING
DEFLECTING	DEFORESTED	DEFUNCTIVE	DEGRADABILITIES	DEHUMANIZATION
DEFLECTION	DEFORESTER	DEFUNCTNESS	DEGRADABILITY	DEHUMANIZATIONS
DEFLECTIONAL	DEFORESTERS	DEFUNCTNESSES	DEGRADABLE	DEHUMANIZE
DEFLECTIONS	DEFORESTING	DEGARNISHED	DEGRADATION	DEHUMANIZED
DEFLECTIVE	DEFORMABILITIES	DEGARNISHES	DEGRADATIONS	DEHUMANIZES
DEFLECTORS	DEFORMABILITY	DEGARNISHING	DEGRADATIVE	DEHUMANIZING
DEFLEXIONAL	DEFORMABLE	DEGAUSSERS	DEGRADEDLY	DEHUMIDIFIED
DEFLEXIONS	DEFORMALISE	DEGAUSSING	DEGRADINGLY	DEHUMIDIFIER
DEFLEXURES	DEFORMALISED	DEGEARINGS	DEGRADINGNESS	DEHUMIDIFIERS
DEFLOCCULANT	DEFORMALISES	DEGENDERED	DEGRADINGNESSES	DEHUMIDIFIES
DEFLOCCULANTS	DEFORMALISING	DEGENDERING	DEGRANULATION	DEHUMIDIFY
DEFLOCCULATE	DEFORMALIZE	DEGENERACIES	DEGRANULATIONS	DEHUMIDIFYING
DEFLOCCULATED	DEFORMALIZED	DEGENERACY	DEGREASANT	DEHYDRATED
DEFLOCCULATES	DEFORMALIZES	DEGENERATE	DEGREASANTS	DEHYDRATER
DEFLOCCULATING	DEFORMALIZING	DEGENERATED	DEGREASERS	DEHYDRATERS
DEFLOCCULATION	DEFORMATION	DEGENERATELY	DEGREASING	DEHYDRATES
DEFLOCCULATIONS	DEFORMATIONAL	DEGENERATENESS	DEGREELESS	DEHYDRATING
DEFLORATED	DEFORMATIONS	DEGENERATES	DEGRESSION	DEHYDRATION
DEFLORATES	DEFORMATIVE	DEGENERATING	DEGRESSIONS	DEHYDRATIONS
DEFLORATING	DEFORMEDLY	DEGENERATION	DEGRESSIVE	DEHYDRATOR
DEFLORATION	DEFORMEDNESS	DEGENERATIONIST	DEGRESSIVELY	DEHYDRATORS
DEFLORATIONS	DEFORMEDNESSES	DEGENERATIONS	DEGRINGOLADE	DEHYDROGENASE
DEFLOWERED	DEFORMITIES	DEGENERATIVE	DEGRINGOLADED	DEHYDROGENASES
DEFLOWERER	DEFRAGGERS	DEGENEROUS	DEGRINGOLADES	DEHYDROGENATE
DEFLOWERERS	DEFRAGGING	DEGLACIATED	DEGRINGOLADING	DEHYDROGENATED
DEFLOWERING	DEFRAGGINGS	DEGLACIATION	DEGRINGOLER	DEHYDROGENATES
DEFLUXIONS	DEFRAGMENT	DEGLACIATIONS	DEGRINGOLERED	DEHYDROGENATING
DEFOCUSING	DEFRAGMENTED	DEGLAMORISATION	DEGRINGOLERING	DEHYDROGENATION
DEFOCUSSED	DEFRAGMENTING	DEGLAMORISE	DEGRINGOLERS	DEHYDROGENISE
DEFOCUSSES	DEFRAGMENTS	DEGLAMORISED	DEGUSTATED	DEHYDROGENISED
DEFOCUSSING	DEFRAUDATION	DEGLAMORISES	DEGUSTATES	DEHYDROGENISES
DEFOLIANTS	DEFRAUDATIONS	DEGLAMORISING	DEGUSTATING	DEHYDROGENISING
DEFOLIATED	DEFRAUDERS	DEGLAMORIZATION	DEGUSTATION	DEHYDROGENIZE
DEFOLIATES	DEFRAUDING	DEGLAMORIZE	DEGUSTATIONS	DEHYDROGENIZED
DEFOLIATING	DEFRAUDMENT	DEGLAMORIZED	DEGUSTATORY	DEHYDROGENIZES
DEFOLIATION	DEFRAUDMENTS	DEGLAMORIZES	DEHISCENCE	DEHYDROGENIZING
DEFOLIATIONS	DEFRAYABLE	DEGLAMORIZING	DEHISCENCES	DEHYDRORETINOL
DEFOLIATOR	DEFRAYMENT	DEGLUTINATE	DEHORTATION	DEHYDRORETINOLS
DEFOLIATORS	DEFRAYMENTS	DEGLUTINATED	DEHORTATIONS	DEHYPNOTISATION
DEFORCEMENT	DEFREEZING	DEGLUTINATES	DEHORTATIVE	DEHYPNOTISE
DEFORCEMENTS	DEFROCKING	DEGLUTINATING	DEHORTATORY	DEHYPNOTISED
DEFORCIANT	DEFROSTERS	DEGLUTINATION	DEHUMANISATION	DEHYPNOTISES
DEFORCIANTS	DEFROSTING	DEGLUTINATIONS	DEHUMANISATIONS	DEHYPNOTISING
DEFORCIATION	DEFTNESSES	DEGLUTITION	DEHUMANISE	DEHYPNOTIZATION
DEFORCIATIONS	DEFUELLING	DEGLUTITIONS	DEHUMANISED	DEHYPNOTIZE
DEFORESTATION	DEFUNCTION	DEGLUTITIVE	DEHUMANISES	DEHYPNOTIZED

DEHYPNOTIZES	DELAYERINGS	DELIBERATIONS	DELINQUENT	DELTIOLOGIST
DEHYPNOTIZING	DELAYINGLY	DELIBERATIVE	DELINQUENTLY	DELTIOLOGISTS
DEICTICALLY	DELECTABILITIES	DELIBERATIVELY	DELINQUENTS	DELTIOLOGY
DEIFICATION	DELECTABILITY	DELIBERATOR	DELIQUESCE	DELTOIDEUS
DEIFICATIONS	DELECTABLE	DELIBERATORS	DELIQUESCED	DELUDINGLY
DEINDEXING	DELECTABLENESS	DELICACIES	DELIQUESCENCE	DELUNDUNGS
DEINDIVIDUATION	DELECTABLES	DELICATELY	DELIQUESCENCES	DELUSIONAL
DEINDUSTRIALISE	DELECTABLY	DELICATENESS	DELIQUESCENT	DELUSIONARY
DEINDUSTRIALIZE	DELECTATED	DELICATENESSES	DELIQUESCES	DELUSIONIST
DEINONYCHUS	DELECTATES	DELICATESSEN	DELIQUESCING	DELUSIONISTS
DEINONYCHUSES	DELECTATING	DELICATESSENS	DELIQUIUMS	DELUSIVELY
DEINOSAURS	DELECTATION	DELICIOUSLY	DELIRATION	DELUSIVENESS
DEINOTHERE	DELECTATIONS	DELICIOUSNESS	DELIRATIONS	DELUSIVENESSES
DEINOTHERES	DELEGACIES	DELICIOUSNESSES	DELIRIFACIENT	DELUSTERED
DEINOTHERIUM	DELEGATEES	DELIGATION	DELIRIFACIENTS	DELUSTERING
DEINOTHERIUMS	DELEGATING	DELIGATIONS	DELIRIOUSLY	DELUSTRANT
DEIONISATION	DELEGATION	DELIGHTEDLY	DELIRIOUSNESS	DELUSTRANTS
DEIONISATIONS	DELEGATIONS	DELIGHTEDNESS	DELIRIOUSNESSES	DEMAGNETISATION
DEIONISERS	DELEGATORS	DELIGHTEDNESSES	DELITESCENCE	DEMAGNETISE
DEIONISING	DELEGITIMATION	DELIGHTERS	DELITESCENCES	DEMAGNETISED
DEIONIZATION	DELEGITIMATIONS	DELIGHTFUL	DELITESCENT	DEMAGNETISER
DEIONIZATIONS	DELEGITIMISE	DELIGHTFULLY	DELIVERABILITY	DEMAGNETISERS
DEIONIZERS	DELEGITIMISED	DELIGHTFULNESS	DELIVERABLE	DEMAGNETISES
DEIONIZING	DELEGITIMISES	DELIGHTING	DELIVERANCE	DEMAGNETISING
DEIPNOSOPHIST	DELEGITIMISING	DELIGHTLESS	DELIVERANCES	DEMAGNETIZATION
DEIPNOSOPHISTS	DELEGITIMIZE	DELIGHTSOME	DELIVERERS	DEMAGNETIZE
DEISTICALLY	DELEGITIMIZED	DELIMITATE	DELIVERIES	DEMAGNETIZED
DEJECTEDLY	DELEGITIMIZES	DELIMITATED	DELIVERING	DEMAGNETIZER
DEJECTEDNESS	DELEGITIMIZING	DELIMITATES	DELIVERYMAN	DEMAGNETIZERS
DEJECTEDNESSES	DELETERIOUS	DELIMITATING	DELIVERYMEN	DEMAGNETIZES
DEJECTIONS	DELETERIOUSLY	DELIMITATION	DELOCALISATION	DEMAGNETIZING
DEKALITERS	DELETERIOUSNESS	DELIMITATIONS	DELOCALISATIONS	DEMAGOGICAL
DEKALITRES	DELEVERAGE	DELIMITATIVE	DELOCALISE	DEMAGOGICALLY
DEKALOGIES	DELEVERAGED	DELIMITERS	DELOCALISED	DEMAGOGIES
DEKAMETERS	DELEVERAGES	DELIMITING	DELOCALISES	DEMAGOGING
DEKAMETRES	DELEVERAGING	DELINEABLE	DELOCALISING	DEMAGOGISM
DEKAMETRIC	DELFTWARES	DELINEATED	DELOCALIZATION	DEMAGOGISMS
DELAMINATE	DELIBATING	DELINEATES	DELOCALIZATIONS	DEMAGOGUED
DELAMINATED	DELIBATION	DELINEATING	DELOCALIZE	DEMAGOGUERIES
DELAMINATES	DELIBATIONS	DELINEATION	DELOCALIZED	DEMAGOGUERY
DELAMINATING	DELIBERATE	DELINEATIONS	DELOCALIZES	DEMAGOGUES
DELAMINATION	DELIBERATED	DELINEATIVE	DELOCALIZING	DEMAGOGUING
DELAMINATIONS	DELIBERATELY	DELINEATOR	DELPHICALLY	DEMAGOGUISM
DELAPSIONS	DELIBERATENESS	DELINEATORS	DELPHINIUM	DEMAGOGUISMS
DELASSEMENT	DELIBERATES	DELINEAVIT	DELPHINIUMS	DEMANDABLE
DELASSEMENTS	DELIBERATING	DELINQUENCIES	DELPHINOID	DEMANDANTS
DELAYERING	DELIBERATION	DELINQUENCY	DELTIOLOGIES	DEMANDINGLY

DEMANDINGNESS	DEMILITARISED	DEMOBILIZATIONS	DEMOLISHED	DEMONOCRACY
DEMANDINGNESSES	DEMILITARISES	DEMOBILIZE	DEMOLISHER	DEMONOLATER
DEMANNINGS	DEMILITARISING	DEMOBILIZED	DEMOLISHERS	DEMONOLATERS
DEMANTOIDS	DEMILITARIZE	DEMOBILIZES	DEMOLISHES	DEMONOLATRIES
DEMARCATED	DEMILITARIZED	DEMOBILIZING	DEMOLISHING	DEMONOLATRY
DEMARCATES	DEMILITARIZES	DEMOCRACIES	DEMOLISHMENT	DEMONOLOGIC
DEMARCATING	DEMILITARIZING	DEMOCRATIC	DEMOLISHMENTS	DEMONOLOGICAL
DEMARCATION	DEMIMONDAINE	DEMOCRATICAL	DEMOLITION	DEMONOLOGIES
DEMARCATIONS	DEMIMONDAINES	DEMOCRATICALLY	DEMOLITIONIST	DEMONOLOGIST
DEMARCATOR	DEMIMONDES	DEMOCRATIES	DEMOLITIONISTS	DEMONOLOGISTS
DEMARCATORS	DEMINERALISE	DEMOCRATIFIABLE	DEMOLITIONS	DEMONOLOGY
DEMARKATION	DEMINERALISED	DEMOCRATISATION	DEMOLOGIES	DEMONOMANIA
DEMARKATIONS	DEMINERALISER	DEMOCRATISE	DEMONESSES	DEMONOMANIAS
DEMARKETED	DEMINERALISERS	DEMOCRATISED	DEMONETARISE	DEMONSTRABILITY
DEMARKETING	DEMINERALISES	DEMOCRATISER	DEMONETARISED	DEMONSTRABLE
DEMATERIALISE	DEMINERALISING	DEMOCRATISERS	DEMONETARISES	DEMONSTRABLY
DEMATERIALISED	DEMINERALIZE	DEMOCRATISES	DEMONETARISING	DEMONSTRATE
DEMATERIALISES	DEMINERALIZED	DEMOCRATISING	DEMONETARIZE	DEMONSTRATED
DEMATERIALISING	DEMINERALIZER	DEMOCRATIST	DEMONETARIZED	DEMONSTRATES
DEMATERIALIZE	DEMINERALIZERS	DEMOCRATISTS	DEMONETARIZES	DEMONSTRATING
DEMATERIALIZED	DEMINERALIZES	DEMOCRATIZATION	DEMONETARIZING	DEMONSTRATION
DEMATERIALIZES	DEMINERALIZING	DEMOCRATIZE	DEMONETISATION	DEMONSTRATIONAL
DEMATERIALIZING	DEMIPIQUES	DEMOCRATIZED	DEMONETISATIONS	DEMONSTRATIONS
DEMEANOURS	DEMIRELIEF	DEMOCRATIZER	DEMONETISE	DEMONSTRATIVE
DEMEASNURE	DEMIRELIEFS	DEMOCRATIZERS	DEMONETISED	DEMONSTRATIVELY
DEMEASNURES	DEMIREPDOM	DEMOCRATIZES	DEMONETISES	DEMONSTRATIVES
DEMENTATED	DEMIREPDOMS	DEMOCRATIZING	DEMONETISING	DEMONSTRATOR
DEMENTATES	DEMISEMIQUAVER	DEMODULATE	DEMONETIZATION	DEMONSTRATORS
DEMENTATING	DEMISEMIQUAVERS	DEMODULATED	DEMONETIZATIONS	DEMONSTRATORY
DEMENTEDLY	DEMISSIONS	DEMODULATES	DEMONETIZE	DEMORALISATION
DEMENTEDNESS	DEMITASSES	DEMODULATING	DEMONETIZED	DEMORALISATIONS
DEMENTEDNESSES	DEMIURGEOUS	DEMODULATION	DEMONETIZES	DEMORALISE
DEMERGERED	DEMIURGICAL	DEMODULATIONS	DEMONETIZING	DEMORALISED
DEMERGERING	DEMIURGICALLY	DEMODULATOR	DEMONIACAL	DEMORALISER
DEMERITING	DEMIURGUSES	DEMODULATORS	DEMONIACALLY	DEMORALISERS
DEMERITORIOUS	DEMIVEGGES	DEMOGRAPHER	DEMONIACISM	DEMORALISES
DEMERITORIOUSLY	DEMIVIERGE	DEMOGRAPHERS	DEMONIACISMS	DEMORALISING
DEMERSIONS	DEMIVIERGES	DEMOGRAPHIC	DEMONIANISM	DEMORALISINGLY
DEMIBASTION	DEMIVOLTES	DEMOGRAPHICAL	DEMONIANISMS	DEMORALIZATION
DEMIBASTIONS	DEMIWORLDS	DEMOGRAPHICALLY	DEMONICALLY	DEMORALIZATIONS
DEMICANTON	DEMOBILISATION	DEMOGRAPHICS	DEMONISATION	DEMORALIZE
DEMICANTONS	DEMOBILISATIONS	DEMOGRAPHIES	DEMONISATIONS	DEMORALIZED
DEMIGODDESS	DEMOBILISE	DEMOGRAPHIST	DEMONISING	DEMORALIZER
DEMIGODDESSES	DEMOBILISED	DEMOGRAPHISTS	DEMONIZATION	DEMORALIZERS
DEMIGRATION	DEMOBILISES	DEMOGRAPHY	DEMONIZATIONS	DEMORALIZES
DEMIGRATIONS	DEMOBILISING	DEMOISELLE	DEMONIZING	DEMORALIZING
DEMILITARISE	DEMOBILIZATION	DEMOISELLES	DEMONOCRACIES	DEMORALIZINGLY

DEMOSCENES

DEMOSCENES
DEMOTICIST
DEMOTICISTS
DEMOTIVATE
DEMOTIVATED
DEMOTIVATES
DEMOTIVATING
DEMOUNTABLE
DEMOUNTING
DEMULCENTS
DEMULSIFICATION
DEMULSIFIED
DEMULSIFIER
DEMULSIFIERS
DEMULSIFIES
DEMULSIFYING
DEMULTIPLEXER
DEMULTIPLEXERS
DEMURENESS
DEMURENESSES
DEMURRABLE
DEMURRAGES
DEMUTUALISATION
DEMUTUALISE
DEMUTUALISED
DEMUTUALISES
DEMUTUALISING
DEMUTUALIZATION
DEMUTUALIZE
DEMUTUALIZED
DEMUTUALIZES
DEMUTUALIZING
DEMYELINATE
DEMYELINATED
DEMYELINATES
DEMYELINATING
DEMYELINATION
DEMYELINATIONS
DEMYSTIFICATION
DEMYSTIFIED
DEMYSTIFIES
DEMYSTIFYING
DEMYTHOLOGISE
DEMYTHOLOGISED
DEMYTHOLOGISER
DEMYTHOLOGISERS
DEMYTHOLOGISES

DEMYTHOLOGISING
DEMYTHOLOGIZE
DEMYTHOLOGIZED
DEMYTHOLOGIZER
DEMYTHOLOGIZERS
DEMYTHOLOGIZES
DEMYTHOLOGIZING
DENATIONALISE
DENATIONALISED
DENATIONALISES
DENATIONALISING
DENATIONALIZE
DENATIONALIZED
DENATIONALIZES
DENATIONALIZING
DENATURALISE
DENATURALISED
DENATURALISES
DENATURALISING
DENATURALIZE
DENATURALIZED
DENATURALIZES
DENATURALIZING
DENATURANT
DENATURANTS
DENATURATION
DENATURATIONS
DENATURING
DENATURISE
DENATURISED
DENATURISES
DENATURISING
DENATURIZE
DENATURIZED
DENATURIZES
DENATURIZING
DENAZIFICATION
DENAZIFICATIONS
DENAZIFIED
DENAZIFIES
DENAZIFYING
DENDRACHATE
DENDRACHATES
DENDRIFORM
DENDRIMERS
DENDRITICAL
DENDRITICALLY

DENDROBIUM
DENDROBIUMS
DENDROGLYPH
DENDROGLYPHS
DENDROGRAM
DENDROGRAMS
DENDROIDAL
DENDROLATRIES
DENDROLATRY
DENDROLOGIC
DENDROLOGICAL
DENDROLOGIES
DENDROLOGIST
DENDROLOGISTS
DENDROLOGOUS
DENDROLOGY
DENDROMETER
DENDROMETERS
DENDROPHIS
DENDROPHISES
DENEGATION
DENEGATIONS
DENERVATED
DENERVATES
DENERVATING
DENERVATION
DENERVATIONS
DENIABILITIES
DENIABILITY
DENIGRATED
DENIGRATES
DENIGRATING
DENIGRATION
DENIGRATIONS
DENIGRATIVE
DENIGRATOR
DENIGRATORS
DENIGRATORY
DENISATION
DENISATIONS
DENITRATED
DENITRATES
DENITRATING
DENITRATION
DENITRATIONS
DENITRIFICATION
DENITRIFICATOR

DENITRIFICATORS
DENITRIFIED
DENITRIFIER
DENITRIFIERS
DENITRIFIES
DENITRIFYING
DENIZATION
DENIZATIONS
DENIZENING
DENIZENSHIP
DENIZENSHIPS
DENOMINABLE
DENOMINATE
DENOMINATED
DENOMINATES
DENOMINATING
DENOMINATION
DENOMINATIONAL
DENOMINATIONS
DENOMINATIVE
DENOMINATIVELY
DENOMINATIVES
DENOMINATOR
DENOMINATORS
DENOTATING
DENOTATION
DENOTATIONS
DENOTATIVE
DENOTATIVELY
DENOTEMENT
DENOTEMENTS
DENOUEMENT
DENOUEMENTS
DENOUNCEMENT
DENOUNCEMENTS
DENOUNCERS
DENOUNCING
DENSENESSES
DENSIFICATION
DENSIFICATIONS
DENSIFIERS
DENSIFYING
DENSIMETER
DENSIMETERS
DENSIMETRIC
DENSIMETRIES
DENSIMETRY

DENSITOMETER
DENSITOMETERS
DENSITOMETRIC
DENSITOMETRIES
DENSITOMETRY
DENTALITIES
DENTALIUMS
DENTATIONS
DENTICULATE
DENTICULATED
DENTICULATELY
DENTICULATION
DENTICULATIONS
DENTIFRICE
DENTIFRICES
DENTIGEROUS
DENTILABIAL
DENTILINGUAL
DENTILINGUALS
DENTIROSTRAL
DENTISTRIES
DENTITIONS
DENTURISTS
DENUCLEARISE
DENUCLEARISED
DENUCLEARISES
DENUCLEARISING
DENUCLEARIZE
DENUCLEARIZED
DENUCLEARIZES
DENUCLEARIZING
DENUDATING
DENUDATION
DENUDATIONS
DENUDEMENT
DENUDEMENTS
DENUMERABILITY
DENUMERABLE
DENUMERABLY
DENUNCIATE
DENUNCIATED
DENUNCIATES
DENUNCIATING
DENUNCIATION
DENUNCIATIONS
DENUNCIATIVE
DENUNCIATOR

DENUNCIATORS	DEOXIDIZER	DEPAUPERIZED	DEPIGMENTED	DEPOLITICIZE
DENUNCIATORY	DEOXIDIZERS	DEPAUPERIZES	DEPIGMENTING	DEPOLITICIZED
DEOBSTRUENT	DEOXIDIZES	DEPAUPERIZING	DEPIGMENTS	DEPOLITICIZES
DEOBSTRUENTS	DEOXIDIZING	DEPEINCTED	DEPILATING	DEPOLITICIZING
DEODORANTS	DEOXYCORTONE	DEPEINCTING	DEPILATION	DEPOLYMERISE
DEODORISATION	DEOXYCORTONES	DEPENDABILITIES	DEPILATIONS	DEPOLYMERISES
DEODORISATIONS	DEOXYGENATE	DEPENDABILITY	DEPILATORIES	DEPOLYMERISING
DEODORISED	DEOXYGENATED	DEPENDABLE	DEPILATORS	DEPOLYMERIZE
DEODORISER	DEOXYGENATES	DEPENDABLENESS	DEPILATORY	DEPOLYMERIZED
DEODORISERS	DEOXYGENATING	DEPENDABLY	DEPLETABLE	DEPOLYMERIZES
DEODORISES	DEOXYGENATION	DEPENDANCE	DEPLETIONS	DEPOLYMERIZING
DEODORISING	DEOXYGENATIONS	DEPENDANCES	DEPLORABILITIES	DEPOPULATE
DEODORIZATION	DEOXYGENISE	DEPENDANCIES	DEPLORABILITY	DEPOPULATED
DEODORIZATIONS	DEOXYGENISED	DEPENDANCY	DEPLORABLE	DEPOPULATES
DEODORIZED	DEOXYGENISES	DEPENDANTS	DEPLORABLENESS	DEPOPULATING
DEODORIZER	DEOXYGENISING	DEPENDENCE	DEPLORABLY	DEPOPULATION
DEODORIZERS	DEOXYGENIZE	DEPENDENCES	DEPLORATION	DEPOPULATIONS
DEODORIZES	DEOXYGENIZED	DEPENDENCIES	DEPLORATIONS	DEPOPULATOR
DEODORIZING	DEOXYGENIZES	DEPENDENCY	DEPLORINGLY	DEPOPULATORS
DEONTOLOGICAL	DEOXYGENIZING	DEPENDENTLY	DEPLOYABLE	DEPORTABLE
DEONTOLOGIES	DEOXYRIBOSE	DEPENDENTS	DEPLOYMENT	DEPORTATION
DEONTOLOGIST	DEOXYRIBOSES	DEPENDINGLY	DEPLOYMENTS	DEPORTATIONS
DEONTOLOGISTS	DEPAINTING	DEPEOPLING	DEPLUMATION	DEPORTMENT
DEONTOLOGY	DEPANNEURS	DEPERSONALISE	DEPLUMATIONS	DEPORTMENTS
DEOPPILATE	DEPARTEMENT	DEPERSONALISED	DEPOLARISATION	DEPOSITARIES
DEOPPILATED	DEPARTEMENTS	DEPERSONALISES	DEPOLARISATIONS	DEPOSITARY
DEOPPILATES	DEPARTINGS	DEPERSONALISING	DEPOLARISE	DEPOSITATION
DEOPPILATING	DEPARTMENT	DEPERSONALIZE	DEPOLARISED	DEPOSITATIONS
DEOPPILATION	DEPARTMENTAL	DEPERSONALIZED	DEPOLARISER	DEPOSITING
DEOPPILATIONS	DEPARTMENTALISE	DEPERSONALIZES	DEPOLARISERS	DEPOSITION
DEOPPILATIVE	DEPARTMENTALISM	DEPERSONALIZING	DEPOLARISES	DEPOSITIONAL
DEORBITING	DEPARTMENTALIZE	DEPHLEGMATE	DEPOLARISING	DEPOSITIONS
DEOXIDATED	DEPARTMENTALLY	DEPHLEGMATED	DEPOLARIZATION	DEPOSITIVE
DEOXIDATES	DEPARTMENTS	DEPHLEGMATES	DEPOLARIZATIONS	DEPOSITORIES
DEOXIDATING	DEPARTURES	DEPHLEGMATING	DEPOLARIZE	DEPOSITORS
DEOXIDATION	DEPASTURED	DEPHLEGMATION	DEPOLARIZED	DEPOSITORY
DEOXIDATIONS	DEPASTURES	DEPHLEGMATIONS	DEPOLARIZER	DEPRAVATION
DEOXIDISATION	DEPASTURING	DEPHLEGMATOR	DEPOLARIZERS	DEPRAVATIONS
DEOXIDISATIONS	DEPAUPERATE	DEPHLEGMATORS	DEPOLARIZES	DEPRAVEDLY
DEOXIDISED	DEPAUPERATED	DEPHLOGISTICATE	DEPOLARIZING	DEPRAVEDNESS
DEOXIDISER	DEPAUPERATES	DEPHOSPHORYLATE	DEPOLISHED	DEPRAVEDNESSES
DEOXIDISERS	DEPAUPERATING	DEPICTIONS	DEPOLISHES	DEPRAVEMENT
DEOXIDISES	DEPAUPERISE	DEPICTURED	DEPOLISHING	DEPRAVEMENTS
DEOXIDISING	DEPAUPERISED	DEPICTURES	DEPOLITICISE	DEPRAVINGLY
DEOXIDIZATION	DEPAUPERISES	DEPICTURING	DEPOLITICISED	DEPRAVITIES
DEOXIDIZATIONS	DEPAUPERISING	DEPIGMENTATION	DEPOLITICISES	DEPRECABLE
DEOXIDIZED	DEPAUPERIZE	DEPIGMENTATIONS	DEPOLITICISING	

D

DEPRECATED	DEPRESSOMOTORS	DERACIALIZES	DEREGULATORY	DERIVATIZED
DEPRECATES	DEPRESSORS	DERACIALIZING	DERELICTION	DERIVATIZES
DEPRECATING	DEPRESSURISE	DERACINATE	DERELICTIONS	DERIVATIZING
DEPRECATINGLY	DEPRESSURISED	DERACINATED	DERELIGIONISE	DERMABRASION
DEPRECATION	DEPRESSURISES	DERACINATES	DERELIGIONISED	DERMABRASIONS
DEPRECATIONS	DEPRESSURISING	DERACINATING	DERELIGIONISES	DERMAPTERAN
DEPRECATIVE	DEPRESSURIZE	DERACINATION	DERELIGIONISING	DERMAPTERANS
DEPRECATIVELY	DEPRESSURIZED	DERACINATIONS	DERELIGIONIZE	DERMATITIS
DEPRECATOR	DEPRESSURIZES	DERAIGNING	DERELIGIONIZED	DERMATITISES
DEPRECATORILY	DEPRESSURIZING	DERAIGNMENT	DERELIGIONIZES	DERMATOGEN
DEPRECATORS	DEPRIVABLE	DERAIGNMENTS	DERELIGIONIZING	DERMATOGENS
DEPRECATORY	DEPRIVATION	DERAILLEUR	DEREPRESSED	DERMATOGLYPHIC
DEPRECIABLE	DEPRIVATIONS	DERAILLEURS	DEREPRESSES	DERMATOGLYPHICS
DEPRECIATE	DEPRIVATIVE	DERAILMENT	DEREPRESSING	DERMATOGRAPHIA
DEPRECIATED	DEPRIVEMENT	DERAILMENTS	DEREPRESSION	DERMATOGRAPHIAS
DEPRECIATES	DEPRIVEMENTS	DERANGEMENT	DEREPRESSIONS	DERMATOGRAPHIC
DEPRECIATING	DEPROGRAMED	DERANGEMENTS	DEREQUISITION	DERMATOGRAPHIES
DEPRECIATINGLY	DEPROGRAMING	DERATIONED	DEREQUISITIONED	DERMATOGRAPHY
DEPRECIATION	DEPROGRAMME	DERATIONING	DEREQUISITIONS	DERMATOLOGIC
DEPRECIATIONS	DEPROGRAMMED	DEREALISATION	DERESTRICT	DERMATOLOGICAL
DEPRECIATIVE	DEPROGRAMMER	DEREALISATIONS	DERESTRICTED	DERMATOLOGIES
DEPRECIATOR	DEPROGRAMMERS	DEREALIZATION	DERESTRICTING	DERMATOLOGIST
DEPRECIATORS	DEPROGRAMMES	DEREALIZATIONS	DERESTRICTION	DERMATOLOGISTS
DEPRECIATORY	DEPROGRAMMING	DERECOGNISE	DERESTRICTIONS	DERMATOLOGY
DEPREDATED	DEPROGRAMS	DERECOGNISED	DERESTRICTS	DERMATOMAL
DEPREDATES	DEPURATING	DERECOGNISES	DERIDINGLY	DERMATOMES
DEPREDATING	DEPURATION	DERECOGNISING	DERISIVELY	DERMATOMIC
DEPREDATION	DEPURATIONS	DERECOGNITION	DERISIVENESS	DERMATOMYOSITIS
DEPREDATIONS	DEPURATIVE	DERECOGNITIONS	DERISIVENESSES	DERMATOPHYTE
DEPREDATOR	DEPURATIVES	DERECOGNIZE	DERIVATION	DERMATOPHYTES
DEPREDATORS	DEPURATORS	DERECOGNIZED	DERIVATIONAL	DERMATOPHYTIC
DEPREDATORY	DEPURATORY	DERECOGNIZES	DERIVATIONIST	DERMATOPHYTOSES
DEPREHENDED	DEPUTATION	DERECOGNIZING	DERIVATIONISTS	DERMATOPHYTOSIS
DEPREHENDING	DEPUTATIONS	DEREGISTER	DERIVATIONS	DERMATOPLASTIC
DEPREHENDS	DEPUTISATION	DEREGISTERED	DERIVATISATION	DERMATOPLASTIES
DEPRESSANT	DEPUTISATIONS	DEREGISTERING	DERIVATISATIONS	DERMATOPLASTY
DEPRESSANTS	DEPUTISING	DEREGISTERS	DERIVATISE	DERMATOSES
DEPRESSIBLE	DEPUTIZATION	DEREGISTRATION	DERIVATISED	DERMATOSIS
DEPRESSING	DEPUTIZATIONS	DEREGISTRATIONS	DERIVATISES	DERMESTIDS
DEPRESSINGLY	DEPUTIZING	DEREGULATE	DERIVATISING	DERMOGRAPHIES
DEPRESSION	DEQUEUEING	DEREGULATED	DERIVATIVE	DERMOGRAPHY
DEPRESSIONS	DERACIALISE	DEREGULATES	DERIVATIVELY	DEROGATELY
DEPRESSIVE	DERACIALISED	DEREGULATING	DERIVATIVENESS	DEROGATING
DEPRESSIVELY	DERACIALISES	DEREGULATION	DERIVATIVES	DEROGATION
DEPRESSIVENESS	DERACIALISING	DEREGULATIONS	DERIVATIZATION	DEROGATIONS
DEPRESSIVES	DERACIALIZE	DEREGULATOR	DERIVATIZATIONS	DEROGATIVE
DEPRESSOMOTOR	DERACIALIZED	DEREGULATORS	DERIVATIZE	DEROGATIVELY

DEROGATORILY | DESCENDERS | DESEGREGATION | DESEXUALIZES | DESILVERISES
DEROGATORINESS | DESCENDEUR | DESEGREGATIONS | DESEXUALIZING | DESILVERISING
DEROGATORY | DESCENDEURS | DESELECTED | DESHABILLE | DESILVERIZATION
DERRICKING | DESCENDIBLE | DESELECTING | DESHABILLES | DESILVERIZE
DERRINGERS | DESCENDING | DESELECTION | DESICCANTS | DESILVERIZED
DESACRALISATION | DESCENDINGS | DESELECTIONS | DESICCATED | DESILVERIZES
DESACRALISE | DESCENSION | DESENSITISATION | DESICCATES | DESILVERIZING
DESACRALISED | DESCENSIONAL | DESENSITISE | DESICCATING | DESINENCES
DESACRALISES | DESCENSIONS | DESENSITISED | DESICCATION | DESINENTIAL
DESACRALISING | DESCHOOLED | DESENSITISER | DESICCATIONS | DESIPIENCE
DESACRALIZATION | DESCHOOLER | DESENSITISERS | DESICCATIVE | DESIPIENCES
DESACRALIZE | DESCHOOLERS | DESENSITISES | DESICCATIVES | DESIPRAMINE
DESACRALIZED | DESCHOOLING | DESENSITISING | DESICCATOR | DESIPRAMINES
DESACRALIZES | DESCHOOLINGS | DESENSITIZATION | DESICCATORS | DESIRABILITIES
DESACRALIZING | DESCRAMBLE | DESENSITIZE | DESIDERATA | DESIRABILITY
DESAGREMENT | DESCRAMBLED | DESENSITIZED | DESIDERATE | DESIRABLENESS
DESAGREMENTS | DESCRAMBLER | DESENSITIZER | DESIDERATED | DESIRABLENESSES
DESALINATE | DESCRAMBLERS | DESENSITIZERS | DESIDERATES | DESIRABLES
DESALINATED | DESCRAMBLES | DESENSITIZES | DESIDERATING | DESIRELESS
DESALINATES | DESCRAMBLING | DESENSITIZING | DESIDERATION | DESIROUSLY
DESALINATING | DESCRIBABLE | DESERPIDINE | DESIDERATIONS | DESIROUSNESS
DESALINATION | DESCRIBERS | DESERPIDINES | DESIDERATIVE | DESIROUSNESSES
DESALINATIONS | DESCRIBING | DESERTIFICATION | DESIDERATIVES | DESISTANCE
DESALINATOR | DESCRIPTION | DESERTIFIED | DESIDERATUM | DESISTANCES
DESALINATORS | DESCRIPTIONS | DESERTIFIES | DESIDERIUM | DESISTENCE
DESALINISATION | DESCRIPTIVE | DESERTIFYING | DESIDERIUMS | DESISTENCES
DESALINISATIONS | DESCRIPTIVELY | DESERTIONS | DESIGNABLE | DESKILLING
DESALINISE | DESCRIPTIVENESS | DESERTISATION | DESIGNATED | DESKILLINGS
DESALINISED | DESCRIPTIVISM | DESERTISATIONS | DESIGNATES | DESMODIUMS
DESALINISES | DESCRIPTIVISMS | DESERTIZATION | DESIGNATING | DESMODROMIC
DESALINISING | DESCRIPTIVIST | DESERTIZATIONS | DESIGNATION | DESMOSOMAL
DESALINIZATION | DESCRIPTOR | DESERTLESS | DESIGNATIONS | DESMOSOMES
DESALINIZATIONS | DESCRIPTORS | DESERVEDLY | DESIGNATIVE | DESNOODING
DESALINIZE | DESCRIVING | DESERVEDNESS | DESIGNATOR | DESOBLIGEANTE
DESALINIZED | DESECRATED | DESERVEDNESSES | DESIGNATORS | DESOBLIGEANTES
DESALINIZES | DESECRATER | DESERVINGLY | DESIGNATORY | DESOLATELY
DESALINIZING | DESECRATERS | DESERVINGNESS | DESIGNEDLY | DESOLATENESS
DESALTINGS | DESECRATES | DESERVINGNESSES | DESIGNINGLY | DESOLATENESSES
DESATURATION | DESECRATING | DESERVINGS | DESIGNINGS | DESOLATERS
DESATURATIONS | DESECRATION | DESEXUALISATION | DESIGNLESS | DESOLATING
DESCANTERS | DESECRATIONS | DESEXUALISE | DESIGNMENT | DESOLATINGLY
DESCANTING | DESECRATOR | DESEXUALISED | DESIGNMENTS | DESOLATION
DESCENDABLE | DESECRATORS | DESEXUALISES | DESILVERED | DESOLATIONS
DESCENDANT | DESEGREGATE | DESEXUALISING | DESILVERING | DESOLATORS
DESCENDANTS | DESEGREGATED | DESEXUALIZATION | DESILVERISATION | DESOLATORY
DESCENDENT | DESEGREGATES | DESEXUALIZE | DESILVERISE | DESORIENTE
DESCENDENTS | DESEGREGATING | DESEXUALIZED | DESILVERISED | DESORPTION

DESORPTIONS	DESPONDENCES	DESTABILIZER	DESULFURING	DETAILINGS
DESOXYRIBOSE	DESPONDENCIES	DESTABILIZERS	DESULFURISATION	DETAINABLE
DESOXYRIBOSES	DESPONDENCY	DESTABILIZES	DESULFURISE	DETAINMENT
DESPAIRERS	DESPONDENT	DESTABILIZING	DESULFURISED	DETAINMENTS
DESPAIRFUL	DESPONDENTLY	DESTAINING	DESULFURISES	DETANGLERS
DESPAIRING	DESPONDING	DESTEMPERED	DESULFURISING	DETANGLING
DESPAIRINGLY	DESPONDINGLY	DESTEMPERING	DESULFURIZATION	DETASSELED
DESPATCHED	DESPONDINGS	DESTEMPERS	DESULFURIZE	DETASSELING
DESPATCHER	DESPOTATES	DESTINATED	DESULFURIZED	DETASSELLED
DESPATCHERS	DESPOTICAL	DESTINATES	DESULFURIZES	DETASSELLING
DESPATCHES	DESPOTICALLY	DESTINATING	DESULFURIZING	DETECTABILITIES
DESPATCHING	DESPOTICALNESS	DESTINATION	DESULPHURATE	DETECTABILITY
DESPERADOES	DESPOTISMS	DESTINATIONS	DESULPHURATED	DETECTABLE
DESPERADOS	DESPOTOCRACIES	DESTITUTED	DESULPHURATES	DETECTIBLE
DESPERATELY	DESPOTOCRACY	DESTITUTENESS	DESULPHURATING	DETECTIONS
DESPERATENESS	DESPUMATED	DESTITUTENESSES	DESULPHURATION	DETECTIVELIKE
DESPERATENESSES	DESPUMATES	DESTITUTES	DESULPHURATIONS	DETECTIVES
DESPERATION	DESPUMATING	DESTITUTING	DESULPHURED	DETECTIVIST
DESPERATIONS	DESPUMATION	DESTITUTION	DESULPHURING	DETECTIVISTS
DESPICABILITIES	DESPUMATIONS	DESTITUTIONS	DESULPHURISE	DETECTOPHONE
DESPICABILITY	DESQUAMATE	DESTOCKING	DESULPHURISED	DETECTOPHONES
DESPICABLE	DESQUAMATED	DESTROYABLE	DESULPHURISER	DETECTORIST
DESPICABLENESS	DESQUAMATES	DESTROYERS	DESULPHURISERS	DETECTORISTS
DESPICABLY	DESQUAMATING	DESTROYING	DESULPHURISES	DETENTIONS
DESPIRITUALISE	DESQUAMATION	DESTRUCTED	DESULPHURISING	DETENTISTS
DESPIRITUALISED	DESQUAMATIONS	DESTRUCTIBILITY	DESULPHURIZE	DETERGENCE
DESPIRITUALISES	DESQUAMATIVE	DESTRUCTIBLE	DESULPHURIZED	DETERGENCES
DESPIRITUALIZE	DESQUAMATORY	DESTRUCTING	DESULPHURIZER	DETERGENCIES
DESPIRITUALIZED	DESSERTSPOON	DESTRUCTION	DESULPHURIZERS	DETERGENCY
DESPIRITUALIZES	DESSERTSPOONFUL	DESTRUCTIONAL	DESULPHURIZES	DETERGENTS
DESPISABLE	DESSERTSPOONS	DESTRUCTIONIST	DESULPHURIZING	DETERIORATE
DESPISEDNESS	DESSIATINE	DESTRUCTIONISTS	DESULPHURS	DETERIORATED
DESPISEDNESSES	DESSIATINES	DESTRUCTIONS	DESULTORILY	DETERIORATES
DESPISEMENT	DESSIGNMENT	DESTRUCTIVE	DESULTORINESS	DETERIORATING
DESPISEMENTS	DESSIGNMENTS	DESTRUCTIVELY	DESULTORINESSES	DETERIORATION
DESPITEFUL	DESSYATINE	DESTRUCTIVENESS	DETACHABILITIES	DETERIORATIONS
DESPITEFULLY	DESSYATINES	DESTRUCTIVES	DETACHABILITY	DETERIORATIVE
DESPITEFULNESS	DESTABILISATION	DESTRUCTIVIST	DETACHABLE	DETERIORISM
DESPITEOUS	DESTABILISE	DESTRUCTIVISTS	DETACHABLY	DETERIORISMS
DESPITEOUSLY	DESTABILISED	DESTRUCTIVITIES	DETACHEDLY	DETERIORITIES
DESPOILERS	DESTABILISER	DESTRUCTIVITY	DETACHEDNESS	DETERIORITY
DESPOILING	DESTABILISERS	DESTRUCTOR	DETACHEDNESSES	DETERMENTS
DESPOILMENT	DESTABILISES	DESTRUCTORS	DETACHMENT	DETERMINABILITY
DESPOILMENTS	DESTABILISING	DESTRUCTOS	DETACHMENTS	DETERMINABLE
DESPOLIATION	DESTABILIZATION	DESUETUDES	DETAILEDLY	DETERMINABLY
DESPOLIATIONS	DESTABILIZE	DESUGARING	DETAILEDNESS	DETERMINACIES
DESPONDENCE	DESTABILIZED	DESULFURED	DETAILEDNESSES	DETERMINACY

DETERMINANT	DETHRONEMENT	DETRIBALISING	DEUTEROSCOPIES	DEVELOPPES
DETERMINANTAL	DETHRONEMENTS	DETRIBALIZATION	DEUTEROSCOPY	DEVERBATIVE
DETERMINANTS	DETHRONERS	DETRIBALIZE	DEUTEROSTOME	DEVERBATIVES
DETERMINATE	DETHRONING	DETRIBALIZED	DEUTEROSTOMES	DEVIANCIES
DETERMINATED	DETHRONINGS	DETRIBALIZES	DEUTEROTOKIES	DEVIATIONISM
DETERMINATELY	DETONABILITIES	DETRIBALIZING	DEUTEROTOKY	DEVIATIONISMS
DETERMINATENESS	DETONABILITY	DETRIMENTAL	DEUTOPLASM	DEVIATIONIST
DETERMINATES	DETONATABLE	DETRIMENTALLY	DEUTOPLASMIC	DEVIATIONISTS
DETERMINATING	DETONATING	DETRIMENTALS	DEUTOPLASMS	DEVIATIONS
DETERMINATION	DETONATION	DETRIMENTS	DEUTOPLASTIC	DEVILESSES
DETERMINATIONS	DETONATIONS	DETRITIONS	DEVALORISATION	DEVILFISHES
DETERMINATIVE	DETONATIVE	DETRITOVORE	DEVALORISATIONS	DEVILISHLY
DETERMINATIVELY	DETONATORS	DETRITOVORES	DEVALORISE	DEVILISHNESS
DETERMINATIVES	DETORSIONS	DETRUNCATE	DEVALORISED	DEVILISHNESSES
DETERMINATOR	DETORTIONS	DETRUNCATED	DEVALORISES	DEVILMENTS
DETERMINATORS	DETOXICANT	DETRUNCATES	DEVALORISING	DEVILSHIPS
DETERMINED	DETOXICANTS	DETRUNCATING	DEVALORIZATION	DEVILTRIES
DETERMINEDLY	DETOXICATE	DETRUNCATION	DEVALORIZATIONS	DEVILWOODS
DETERMINEDNESS	DETOXICATED	DETRUNCATIONS	DEVALORIZE	DEVIOUSNESS
DETERMINER	DETOXICATES	DETRUSIONS	DEVALORIZED	DEVIOUSNESSES
DETERMINERS	DETOXICATING	DETUMESCENCE	DEVALORIZES	DEVITALISATION
DETERMINES	DETOXICATION	DETUMESCENCES	DEVALORIZING	DEVITALISATIONS
DETERMINING	DETOXICATIONS	DETUMESCENT	DEVALUATED	DEVITALISE
DETERMINISM	DETOXIFICATION	DEUTERAGONIST	DEVALUATES	DEVITALISED
DETERMINISMS	DETOXIFICATIONS	DEUTERAGONISTS	DEVALUATING	DEVITALISES
DETERMINIST	DETOXIFIED	DEUTERANOMALIES	DEVALUATION	DEVITALISING
DETERMINISTIC	DETOXIFIES	DEUTERANOMALOUS	DEVALUATIONS	DEVITALIZATION
DETERMINISTS	DETOXIFYING	DEUTERANOMALY	DEVANAGARI	DEVITALIZATIONS
DETERRABILITIES	DETRACTING	DEUTERANOPE	DEVANAGARIS	DEVITALIZE
DETERRABILITY	DETRACTINGLY	DEUTERANOPES	DEVASTATED	DEVITALIZED
DETERRABLE	DETRACTINGS	DEUTERANOPIA	DEVASTATES	DEVITALIZES
DETERRENCE	DETRACTION	DEUTERANOPIAS	DEVASTATING	DEVITALIZING
DETERRENCES	DETRACTIONS	DEUTERANOPIC	DEVASTATINGLY	DEVITRIFICATION
DETERRENTLY	DETRACTIVE	DEUTERATED	DEVASTATION	DEVITRIFIED
DETERRENTS	DETRACTIVELY	DEUTERATES	DEVASTATIONS	DEVITRIFIES
DETERSIONS	DETRACTORS	DEUTERATING	DEVASTATIVE	DEVITRIFYING
DETERSIVES	DETRACTORY	DEUTERATION	DEVASTATOR	DEVOCALISE
DETESTABILITIES	DETRACTRESS	DEUTERATIONS	DEVASTATORS	DEVOCALISED
DETESTABILITY	DETRACTRESSES	DEUTERIDES	DEVASTAVIT	DEVOCALISES
DETESTABLE	DETRAINING	DEUTERIUMS	DEVASTAVITS	DEVOCALISING
DETESTABLENESS	DETRAINMENT	DEUTEROGAMIES	DEVELOPABLE	DEVOCALIZE
DETESTABLY	DETRAINMENTS	DEUTEROGAMIST	DEVELOPERS	DEVOCALIZED
DETESTATION	DETRAQUEES	DEUTEROGAMISTS	DEVELOPING	DEVOCALIZES
DETESTATIONS	DETRIBALISATION	DEUTEROGAMY	DEVELOPMENT	DEVOCALIZING
DETHATCHED	DETRIBALISE	DEUTEROPLASM	DEVELOPMENTAL	DEVOLUTION
DETHATCHES	DETRIBALISED	DEUTEROPLASMS	DEVELOPMENTALLY	DEVOLUTIONARY
DETHATCHING	DETRIBALISES	DEUTEROSCOPIC	DEVELOPMENTS	DEVOLUTIONIST

DEVOLUTIONISTS	DEXTROCARDIAS	DIACHRONOUS	DIAGONALIZES	DIALYSATES
DEVOLUTIONS	DEXTROGLUCOSE	DIACHYLONS	DIAGONALIZING	DIALYSATION
DEVOLVEMENT	DEXTROGLUCOSES	DIACHYLUMS	DIAGONALLY	DIALYSATIONS
DEVOLVEMENTS	DEXTROGYRATE	DIACODIONS	DIAGRAMING	DIALYTICALLY
DEVONPORTS	DEXTROGYRE	DIACODIUMS	DIAGRAMMABLE	DIALYZABILITIES
DEVOTEDNESS	DEXTROROTARY	DIACONATES	DIAGRAMMATIC	DIALYZABILITY
DEVOTEDNESSES	DEXTROROTATION	DIACONICON	DIAGRAMMATICAL	DIALYZABLE
DEVOTEMENT	DEXTROROTATIONS	DIACONICONS	DIAGRAMMED	DIALYZATES
DEVOTEMENTS	DEXTROROTATORY	DIACOUSTIC	DIAGRAMMING	DIALYZATION
DEVOTIONAL	DEXTRORSAL	DIACOUSTICS	DIAGRAPHIC	DIALYZATIONS
DEVOTIONALIST	DEXTRORSELY	DIACRITICAL	DIAHELIOTROPIC	DIAMAGNETIC
DEVOTIONALISTS	DEXTROUSLY	DIACRITICALLY	DIAHELIOTROPISM	DIAMAGNETICALLY
DEVOTIONALITIES	DEXTROUSNESS	DIACRITICS	DIAKINESES	DIAMAGNETISM
DEVOTIONALITY	DEXTROUSNESSES	DIACTINISM	DIAKINESIS	DIAMAGNETISMS
DEVOTIONALLY	DEZINCKING	DIACTINISMS	DIALECTALLY	DIAMAGNETS
DEVOTIONALNESS	DHARMSALAS	DIADELPHOUS	DIALECTICAL	DIAMANTIFEROUS
DEVOTIONALS	DHARMSHALA	DIADOCHIES	DIALECTICALLY	DIAMANTINE
DEVOTIONIST	DHARMSHALAS	DIADROMOUS	DIALECTICIAN	DIAMETRALLY
DEVOTIONISTS	DIABETICAL	DIAGENESES	DIALECTICIANS	DIAMETRICAL
DEVOURINGLY	DIABETOGENIC	DIAGENESIS	DIALECTICISM	DIAMETRICALLY
DEVOURMENT	DIABETOLOGIST	DIAGENETIC	DIALECTICISMS	DIAMONDBACK
DEVOURMENTS	DIABETOLOGISTS	DIAGENETICALLY	DIALECTICS	DIAMONDBACKS
DEVOUTNESS	DIABLERIES	DIAGEOTROPIC	DIALECTOLOGICAL	DIAMONDIFEROUS
DEVOUTNESSES	DIABOLICAL	DIAGEOTROPISM	DIALECTOLOGIES	DIAMONDING
DEVVELLING	DIABOLICALLY	DIAGEOTROPISMS	DIALECTOLOGIST	DIAMORPHINE
DEWATERERS	DIABOLICALNESS	DIAGNOSABILITY	DIALECTOLOGISTS	DIAMORPHINES
DEWATERING	DIABOLISED	DIAGNOSABLE	DIALECTOLOGY	DIANTHUSES
DEWATERINGS	DIABOLISES	DIAGNOSEABLE	DIALLAGOID	DIAPASONAL
DEWBERRIES	DIABOLISING	DIAGNOSING	DIALOGICAL	DIAPASONIC
DEWINESSES	DIABOLISMS	DIAGNOSTIC	DIALOGICALLY	DIAPAUSING
DEXAMETHASONE	DIABOLISTS	DIAGNOSTICAL	DIALOGISED	DIAPEDESES
DEXAMETHASONES	DIABOLIZED	DIAGNOSTICALLY	DIALOGISES	DIAPEDESIS
DEXAMPHETAMINE	DIABOLIZES	DIAGNOSTICIAN	DIALOGISING	DIAPEDETIC
DEXAMPHETAMINES	DIABOLIZING	DIAGNOSTICIANS	DIALOGISMS	DIAPERINGS
DEXIOTROPIC	DIABOLOGIES	DIAGNOSTICS	DIALOGISTIC	DIAPHANEITIES
DEXTERITIES	DIABOLOLOGIES	DIAGOMETER	DIALOGISTICAL	DIAPHANEITY
DEXTEROUSLY	DIABOLOLOGY	DIAGOMETERS	DIALOGISTS	DIAPHANOMETER
DEXTEROUSNESS	DIACATHOLICON	DIAGONALISABLE	DIALOGITES	DIAPHANOMETERS
DEXTEROUSNESSES	DIACATHOLICONS	DIAGONALISATION	DIALOGIZED	DIAPHANOUS
DEXTERWISE	DIACAUSTIC	DIAGONALISE	DIALOGIZES	DIAPHANOUSLY
DEXTRALITIES	DIACAUSTICS	DIAGONALISED	DIALOGIZING	DIAPHANOUSNESS
DEXTRALITY	DIACHRONIC	DIAGONALISES	DIALOGUERS	DIAPHONIES
DEXTRANASE	DIACHRONICALLY	DIAGONALISING	DIALOGUING	DIAPHORASE
DEXTRANASES	DIACHRONIES	DIAGONALIZABLE	DIALYPETALOUS	DIAPHORASES
DEXTROCARDIA	DIACHRONISM	DIAGONALIZATION	DIALYSABILITIES	DIAPHORESES
DEXTROCARDIAC	DIACHRONISMS	DIAGONALIZE	DIALYSABILITY	DIAPHORESIS
DEXTROCARDIACS	DIACHRONISTIC	DIAGONALIZED	DIALYSABLE	DIAPHORETIC

D

DIAPHORETICS
DIAPHOTOTROPIC
DIAPHOTOTROPIES
DIAPHOTOTROPISM
DIAPHOTOTROPY
DIAPHRAGMAL
DIAPHRAGMATIC
DIAPHRAGMATITIS
DIAPHRAGMED
DIAPHRAGMING
DIAPHRAGMS
DIAPHYSEAL
DIAPHYSIAL
DIAPIRISMS
DIAPOPHYSES
DIAPOPHYSIAL
DIAPOPHYSIS
DIAPOSITIVE
DIAPOSITIVES
DIAPYETICS
DIARCHICAL
DIARRHETIC
DIARRHOEAL
DIARRHOEAS
DIARRHOEIC
DIARTHRODIAL
DIARTHROSES
DIARTHROSIS
DIASCORDIUM
DIASCORDIUMS
DIASKEUAST
DIASKEUASTS
DIASTALSES
DIASTALSIS
DIASTALTIC
DIASTEMATA
DIASTEMATIC
DIASTEREOISOMER
DIASTEREOMER
DIASTEREOMERIC
DIASTEREOMERS
DIASTROPHIC
DIASTROPHICALLY
DIASTROPHISM
DIASTROPHISMS
DIATESSARON
DIATESSARONS

DIATHERMACIES
DIATHERMACY
DIATHERMAL
DIATHERMANCIES
DIATHERMANCY
DIATHERMANEITY
DIATHERMANOUS
DIATHERMIA
DIATHERMIAS
DIATHERMIC
DIATHERMIES
DIATHERMOUS
DIATOMACEOUS
DIATOMICITIES
DIATOMICITY
DIATOMISTS
DIATOMITES
DIATONICALLY
DIATONICISM
DIATONICISMS
DIATRETUMS
DIATRIBIST
DIATRIBISTS
DIATROPISM
DIATROPISMS
DIAZEUCTIC
DIAZOMETHANE
DIAZOMETHANES
DIAZONIUMS
DIAZOTISATION
DIAZOTISATIONS
DIAZOTISED
DIAZOTISES
DIAZOTISING
DIAZOTIZATION
DIAZOTIZATIONS
DIAZOTIZED
DIAZOTIZES
DIAZOTIZING
DIBASICITIES
DIBASICITY
DIBENZOFURAN
DIBENZOFURANS
DIBRANCHIATE
DIBRANCHIATES
DIBROMIDES
DICACITIES

DICACODYLS
DICARBOXYLIC
DICARPELLARY
DICASTERIES
DICENTRICS
DICEPHALISM
DICEPHALISMS
DICEPHALOUS
DICHASIALLY
DICHLAMYDEOUS
DICHLORACETIC
DICHLORIDE
DICHLORIDES
DICHLOROBENZENE
DICHLOROETHANE
DICHLOROETHANES
DICHLOROMETHANE
DICHLORVOS
DICHLORVOSES
DICHOGAMIC
DICHOGAMIES
DICHOGAMOUS
DICHONDRAS
DICHOTICALLY
DICHOTOMIC
DICHOTOMIES
DICHOTOMISATION
DICHOTOMISE
DICHOTOMISED
DICHOTOMISES
DICHOTOMISING
DICHOTOMIST
DICHOTOMISTS
DICHOTOMIZATION
DICHOTOMIZE
DICHOTOMIZED
DICHOTOMIZES
DICHOTOMIZING
DICHOTOMOUS
DICHOTOMOUSLY
DICHOTOMOUSNESS
DICHROISCOPE
DICHROISCOPES
DICHROISCOPIC
DICHROISMS
DICHROITES
DICHROITIC

DICHROMATE
DICHROMATES
DICHROMATIC
DICHROMATICISM
DICHROMATICISMS
DICHROMATICS
DICHROMATISM
DICHROMATISMS
DICHROMATS
DICHROMISM
DICHROMISMS
DICHROOSCOPE
DICHROOSCOPES
DICHROOSCOPIC
DICHROSCOPE
DICHROSCOPES
DICHROSCOPIC
DICKCISSEL
DICKCISSELS
DICKEYBIRD
DICKEYBIRDS
DICKYBIRDS
DICLINISMS
DICOTYLEDON
DICOTYLEDONOUS
DICOTYLEDONS
DICOUMARIN
DICOUMARINS
DICOUMAROL
DICOUMAROLS
DICROTISMS
DICTATIONAL
DICTATIONS
DICTATORIAL
DICTATORIALLY
DICTATORIALNESS
DICTATORSHIP
DICTATORSHIPS
DICTATRESS
DICTATRESSES
DICTATRICES
DICTATRIXES
DICTATURES
DICTIONALLY
DICTIONARIES
DICTIONARY
DICTYOGENS

DICTYOPTERAN
DICTYOPTERANS
DICTYOSOME
DICTYOSOMES
DICTYOSTELE
DICTYOSTELES
DICUMAROLS
DICYNODONT
DICYNODONTS
DIDACTICAL
DIDACTICALLY
DIDACTICISM
DIDACTICISMS
DIDACTYLISM
DIDACTYLISMS
DIDACTYLOUS
DIDASCALIC
DIDELPHIAN
DIDELPHIDS
DIDELPHINE
DIDELPHOUS
DIDGERIDOO
DIDGERIDOOS
DIDJERIDOO
DIDJERIDOOS
DIDJERIDUS
DIDRACHMAS
DIDYNAMIAN
DIDYNAMIES
DIDYNAMOUS
DIECIOUSLY
DIECIOUSNESS
DIECIOUSNESSES
DIEFFENBACHIA
DIEFFENBACHIAS
DIELECTRIC
DIELECTRICALLY
DIELECTRICS
DIENCEPHALA
DIENCEPHALIC
DIENCEPHALON
DIENCEPHALONS
DIESELINGS
DIESELISATION
DIESELISATIONS
DIESELISED
DIESELISES

DIESELISING DIFFICULTY DIGESTIBLENESS DIGLADIATOR DILAPIDATIONS
DIESELIZATION DIFFIDENCE DIGESTIBLY DIGLADIATORS DILAPIDATOR
DIESELIZATIONS DIFFIDENCES DIGESTIONAL DIGLOSSIAS DILAPIDATORS
DIESELIZED DIFFIDENTLY DIGESTIONS DIGLYCERIDE DILATABILITIES
DIESELIZES DIFFORMITIES DIGESTIVELY DIGLYCERIDES DILATABILITY
DIESELIZING DIFFORMITY DIGESTIVES DIGNIFICATION DILATABLENESS
DIESINKERS DIFFRACTED DIGITALINS DIGNIFICATIONS DILATABLENESSES
DIESTRUSES DIFFRACTING DIGITALISATION DIGNIFIEDLY DILATANCIES
DIETARIANS DIFFRACTION DIGITALISATIONS DIGNIFIEDNESS DILATATION
DIETETICAL DIFFRACTIONS DIGITALISE DIGNIFIEDNESSES DILATATIONAL
DIETETICALLY DIFFRACTIVE DIGITALISED DIGNIFYING DILATATIONS
DIETHYLAMIDE DIFFRACTIVELY DIGITALISES DIGNITARIES DILATATORS
DIETHYLAMIDES DIFFRACTIVENESS DIGITALISING DIGONEUTIC DILATOMETER
DIETHYLAMINE DIFFRACTOMETER DIGITALISM DIGONEUTISM DILATOMETERS
DIETHYLAMINES DIFFRACTOMETERS DIGITALISMS DIGONEUTISMS DILATOMETRIC
DIETHYLENE DIFFRACTOMETRIC DIGITALIZATION DIGRAPHICALLY DILATOMETRIES
DIETHYLENES DIFFRACTOMETRY DIGITALIZATIONS DIGRESSERS DILATOMETRY
DIETICIANS DIFFRANGIBILITY DIGITALIZE DIGRESSING DILATORILY
DIETITIANS DIFFRANGIBLE DIGITALIZED DIGRESSION DILATORINESS
DIFFARREATION DIFFUSEDLY DIGITALIZES DIGRESSIONAL DILATORINESSES
DIFFARREATIONS DIFFUSEDNESS DIGITALIZING DIGRESSIONARY DILEMMATIC
DIFFERENCE DIFFUSEDNESSES DIGITATELY DIGRESSIONS DILETTANTE
DIFFERENCED DIFFUSENESS DIGITATION DIGRESSIVE DILETTANTEISH
DIFFERENCES DIFFUSENESSES DIGITATIONS DIGRESSIVELY DILETTANTEISM
DIFFERENCIED DIFFUSIBILITIES DIGITIFORM DIGRESSIVENESS DILETTANTEISMS
DIFFERENCIES DIFFUSIBILITY DIGITIGRADE DIHYBRIDISM DILETTANTES
DIFFERENCING DIFFUSIBLE DIGITIGRADES DIHYBRIDISMS DILETTANTI
DIFFERENCY DIFFUSIBLENESS DIGITISATION DIHYDROCODEINE DILETTANTISH
DIFFERENCYING DIFFUSIONAL DIGITISATIONS DIHYDROCODEINES DILETTANTISM
DIFFERENTIA DIFFUSIONISM DIGITISERS DIHYDROGEN DILETTANTISMS
DIFFERENTIABLE DIFFUSIONISMS DIGITISING DIJUDICATE DILIGENCES
DIFFERENTIAE DIFFUSIONIST DIGITIZATION DIJUDICATED DILIGENTLY
DIFFERENTIAL DIFFUSIONISTS DIGITIZATIONS DIJUDICATES DILLYDALLIED
DIFFERENTIALLY DIFFUSIONS DIGITIZERS DIJUDICATING DILLYDALLIES
DIFFERENTIALS DIFFUSIVELY DIGITIZING DIJUDICATION DILLYDALLY
DIFFERENTIATE DIFFUSIVENESS DIGITONINS DIJUDICATIONS DILLYDALLYING
DIFFERENTIATED DIFFUSIVENESSES DIGITORIUM DILACERATE DILTIAZEMS
DIFFERENTIATES DIFFUSIVITIES DIGITORIUMS DILACERATED DILUCIDATE
DIFFERENTIATING DIFFUSIVITY DIGITOXIGENIN DILACERATES DILUCIDATED
DIFFERENTIATION DIFUNCTIONAL DIGITOXIGENINS DILACERATING DILUCIDATES
DIFFERENTIATOR DIFUNCTIONALS DIGITOXINS DILACERATION DILUCIDATING
DIFFERENTIATORS DIGASTRICS DIGLADIATE DILACERATIONS DILUCIDATION
DIFFERENTLY DIGESTANTS DIGLADIATED DILAPIDATE DILUCIDATIONS
DIFFERENTNESS DIGESTEDLY DIGLADIATES DILAPIDATED DILUTABLES
DIFFERENTNESSES DIGESTIBILITIES DIGLADIATING DILAPIDATES DILUTENESS
DIFFICULTIES DIGESTIBILITY DIGLADIATION DILAPIDATING DILUTENESSES
DIFFICULTLY DIGESTIBLE DIGLADIATIONS DILAPIDATION DILUTIONARY

DILUVIALISM	DIMINUTIVENESS	DIOPTOMETER	DIPHTHONGED	DIPLOMATISE
DILUVIALISMS	DIMINUTIVES	DIOPTOMETERS	DIPHTHONGIC	DIPLOMATISED
DILUVIALIST	DIMORPHISM	DIOPTOMETRIES	DIPHTHONGING	DIPLOMATISES
DILUVIALISTS	DIMORPHISMS	DIOPTOMETRY	DIPHTHONGISE	DIPLOMATISING
DIMENHYDRINATE	DIMORPHOUS	DIOPTRICAL	DIPHTHONGISED	DIPLOMATIST
DIMENHYDRINATES	DIMPLEMENT	DIOPTRICALLY	DIPHTHONGISES	DIPLOMATISTS
DIMENSIONAL	DIMPLEMENTS	DIORISTICAL	DIPHTHONGISING	DIPLOMATIZE
DIMENSIONALITY	DINANDERIE	DIORISTICALLY	DIPHTHONGIZE	DIPLOMATIZED
DIMENSIONALLY	DINANDERIES	DIORTHOSES	DIPHTHONGIZED	DIPLOMATIZES
DIMENSIONED	DINARCHIES	DIORTHOSIS	DIPHTHONGIZES	DIPLOMATIZING
DIMENSIONING	DINGDONGED	DIORTHOTIC	DIPHTHONGIZING	DIPLOMATOLOGIES
DIMENSIONLESS	DINGDONGING	DIOSCOREACEOUS	DIPHTHONGS	DIPLOMATOLOGY
DIMENSIONS	DINGINESSES	DIOSGENINS	DIPHYCERCAL	DIPLONEMAS
DIMERCAPROL	DINGLEBERRIES	DIOTHELETE	DIPHYLETIC	DIPLOPHASE
DIMERCAPROLS	DINGLEBERRY	DIOTHELETES	DIPHYLLOUS	DIPLOPHASES
DIMERISATION	DINITROBENZENE	DIOTHELETIC	DIPHYODONT	DIPLOSTEMONOUS
DIMERISATIONS	DINITROBENZENES	DIOTHELETICAL	DIPHYODONTS	DIPLOTENES
DIMERISING	DINITROGEN	DIOTHELISM	DIPHYSITES	DIPNETTING
DIMERIZATION	DINITROPHENOL	DIOTHELISMS	DIPHYSITISM	DIPPERFULS
DIMERIZATIONS	DINITROPHENOLS	DIOTHELITE	DIPHYSITISMS	DIPPINESSES
DIMERIZING	DINNERLESS	DIOTHELITES	DIPLEIDOSCOPE	DIPRIONIDIAN
DIMETHOATE	DINNERTIME	DIOXONITRIC	DIPLEIDOSCOPES	DIPROPELLANT
DIMETHOATES	DINNERTIMES	DIPEPTIDASE	DIPLOBIONT	DIPROPELLANTS
DIMETHYLAMINE	DINNERWARE	DIPEPTIDASES	DIPLOBIONTIC	DIPROTODON
DIMETHYLAMINES	DINNERWARES	DIPEPTIDES	DIPLOBIONTS	DIPROTODONS
DIMETHYLANILINE	DINOCERASES	DIPETALOUS	DIPLOBLASTIC	DIPROTODONT
DIMIDIATED	DINOFLAGELLATE	DIPHENHYDRAMINE	DIPLOCARDIAC	DIPROTODONTID
DIMIDIATES	DINOFLAGELLATES	DIPHENYLAMINE	DIPLOCOCCAL	DIPROTODONTIDS
DIMIDIATING	DINOMANIAS	DIPHENYLAMINES	DIPLOCOCCI	DIPROTODONTS
DIMIDIATION	DINOSAURIAN	DIPHENYLENIMINE	DIPLOCOCCIC	DIPSOMANIA
DIMIDIATIONS	DINOSAURIC	DIPHENYLKETONE	DIPLOCOCCUS	DIPSOMANIAC
DIMINISHABLE	DINOTHERES	DIPHENYLKETONES	DIPLODOCUS	DIPSOMANIACAL
DIMINISHED	DINOTHERIUM	DIPHOSGENE	DIPLODOCUSES	DIPSOMANIACS
DIMINISHES	DINOTHERIUMS	DIPHOSGENES	DIPLOGENESES	DIPSOMANIAS
DIMINISHING	DINOTURBATION	DIPHOSPHATE	DIPLOGENESIS	DIPSWITCHES
DIMINISHINGLY	DINOTURBATIONS	DIPHOSPHATES	DIPLOIDIES	DIPTERISTS
DIMINISHINGS	DINUCLEOTIDE	DIPHTHERIA	DIPLOMACIES	DIPTEROCARP
DIMINISHMENT	DINUCLEOTIDES	DIPHTHERIAL	DIPLOMAING	DIPTEROCARPOUS
DIMINISHMENTS	DIOECIOUSLY	DIPHTHERIAS	DIPLOMATED	DIPTEROCARPS
DIMINUENDO	DIOECIOUSNESS	DIPHTHERIC	DIPLOMATES	DIPTEROSES
DIMINUENDOES	DIOECIOUSNESSES	DIPHTHERITIC	DIPLOMATESE	DIRECTEDNESS
DIMINUENDOS	DIOESTRUSES	DIPHTHERITIS	DIPLOMATESES	DIRECTEDNESSES
DIMINUTION	DIOICOUSLY	DIPHTHERITISES	DIPLOMATIC	DIRECTIONAL
DIMINUTIONS	DIOICOUSNESS	DIPHTHEROID	DIPLOMATICAL	DIRECTIONALITY
DIMINUTIVAL	DIOICOUSNESSES	DIPHTHEROIDS	DIPLOMATICALLY	DIRECTIONLESS
DIMINUTIVE	DIOPHYSITE	DIPHTHONGAL	DIPLOMATICS	DIRECTIONS
DIMINUTIVELY	DIOPHYSITES	DIPHTHONGALLY	DIPLOMATING	DIRECTIVES

DIRECTIVITIES	DISACCORDS	DISAFFOREST	DISANNULLER	DISARMAMENT
DIRECTIVITY	DISACCREDIT	DISAFFORESTED	DISANNULLERS	DISARMAMENTS
DIRECTNESS	DISACCREDITED	DISAFFORESTING	DISANNULLING	DISARMINGLY
DIRECTNESSES	DISACCREDITING	DISAFFORESTMENT	DISANNULLINGS	DISARRANGE
DIRECTORATE	DISACCREDITS	DISAFFORESTS	DISANNULMENT	DISARRANGED
DIRECTORATES	DISACCUSTOM	DISAGGREGATE	DISANNULMENTS	DISARRANGEMENT
DIRECTORIAL	DISACCUSTOMED	DISAGGREGATED	DISANOINTED	DISARRANGEMENTS
DIRECTORIALLY	DISACCUSTOMING	DISAGGREGATES	DISANOINTING	DISARRANGES
DIRECTORIES	DISACCUSTOMS	DISAGGREGATING	DISANOINTS	DISARRANGING
DIRECTORSHIP	DISACKNOWLEDGE	DISAGGREGATION	DISAPPAREL	DISARRAYED
DIRECTORSHIPS	DISACKNOWLEDGED	DISAGGREGATIONS	DISAPPARELLED	DISARRAYING
DIRECTRESS	DISACKNOWLEDGES	DISAGGREGATIVE	DISAPPARELLING	DISARTICULATE
DIRECTRESSES	DISADORNED	DISAGREEABILITY	DISAPPARELS	DISARTICULATED
DIRECTRICE	DISADORNING	DISAGREEABLE	DISAPPEARANCE	DISARTICULATES
DIRECTRICES	DISADVANCE	DISAGREEABLES	DISAPPEARANCES	DISARTICULATING
DIRECTRIXES	DISADVANCED	DISAGREEABLY	DISAPPEARED	DISARTICULATION
DIREFULNESS	DISADVANCES	DISAGREEING	DISAPPEARING	DISARTICULATOR
DIREFULNESSES	DISADVANCING	DISAGREEMENT	DISAPPEARS	DISARTICULATORS
DIREMPTING	DISADVANTAGE	DISAGREEMENTS	DISAPPLICATION	DISASSEMBLE
DIREMPTION	DISADVANTAGED	DISALLOWABLE	DISAPPLICATIONS	DISASSEMBLED
DIREMPTIONS	DISADVANTAGEOUS	DISALLOWANCE	DISAPPLIED	DISASSEMBLER
DIRENESSES	DISADVANTAGES	DISALLOWANCES	DISAPPLIES	DISASSEMBLERS
DIRIGIBILITIES	DISADVANTAGING	DISALLOWED	DISAPPLYING	DISASSEMBLES
DIRIGIBILITY	DISADVENTURE	DISALLOWING	DISAPPOINT	DISASSEMBLIES
DIRIGIBLES	DISADVENTURES	DISALLYING	DISAPPOINTED	DISASSEMBLING
DIRIGISMES	DISADVENTUROUS	DISAMBIGUATE	DISAPPOINTEDLY	DISASSEMBLY
DIRTINESSES	DISAFFECTED	DISAMBIGUATED	DISAPPOINTING	DISASSIMILATE
DISABILITIES	DISAFFECTEDLY	DISAMBIGUATES	DISAPPOINTINGLY	DISASSIMILATED
DISABILITY	DISAFFECTEDNESS	DISAMBIGUATING	DISAPPOINTMENT	DISASSIMILATES
DISABLEMENT	DISAFFECTING	DISAMBIGUATION	DISAPPOINTMENTS	DISASSIMILATING
DISABLEMENTS	DISAFFECTION	DISAMBIGUATIONS	DISAPPOINTS	DISASSIMILATION
DISABLISMS	DISAFFECTIONATE	DISAMENITIES	DISAPPROBATION	DISASSIMILATIVE
DISABLISTS	DISAFFECTIONS	DISAMENITY	DISAPPROBATIONS	DISASSOCIATE
DISABUSALS	DISAFFECTS	DISANALOGIES	DISAPPROBATIVE	DISASSOCIATED
DISABUSING	DISAFFILIATE	DISANALOGOUS	DISAPPROBATORY	DISASSOCIATES
DISACCHARID	DISAFFILIATED	DISANALOGY	DISAPPROPRIATE	DISASSOCIATING
DISACCHARIDASE	DISAFFILIATES	DISANCHORED	DISAPPROPRIATED	DISASSOCIATION
DISACCHARIDASES	DISAFFILIATING	DISANCHORING	DISAPPROPRIATES	DISASSOCIATIONS
DISACCHARIDE	DISAFFILIATION	DISANCHORS	DISAPPROVAL	DISASTROUS
DISACCHARIDES	DISAFFILIATIONS	DISANIMATE	DISAPPROVALS	DISASTROUSLY
DISACCHARIDS	DISAFFIRMANCE	DISANIMATED	DISAPPROVE	DISATTIRED
DISACCOMMODATE	DISAFFIRMANCES	DISANIMATES	DISAPPROVED	DISATTIRES
DISACCOMMODATED	DISAFFIRMATION	DISANIMATING	DISAPPROVER	DISATTIRING
DISACCOMMODATES	DISAFFIRMATIONS	DISANNEXED	DISAPPROVERS	DISATTRIBUTION
DISACCORDANT	DISAFFIRMED	DISANNEXES	DISAPPROVES	DISATTRIBUTIONS
DISACCORDED	DISAFFIRMING	DISANNEXING	DISAPPROVING	DISATTUNED
DISACCORDING	DISAFFIRMS	DISANNULLED	DISAPPROVINGLY	DISATTUNES

DISATTUNING	DISBOWELING	DISCEPTATORS	DISCIPLINES	DISCOMBOBULATES
DISAUTHORISE	DISBOWELLED	DISCEPTING	DISCIPLING	DISCOMEDUSAN
DISAUTHORISED	DISBOWELLING	DISCERNABLE	DISCIPLINING	DISCOMEDUSANS
DISAUTHORISES	DISBRANCHED	DISCERNABLY	DISCIPULAR	DISCOMFIT
DISAUTHORISING	DISBRANCHES	DISCERNERS	DISCISSION	DISCOMFITER
DISAUTHORIZE	DISBRANCHING	DISCERNIBLE	DISCISSIONS	DISCOMFITERS
DISAUTHORIZED	DISBUDDING	DISCERNIBLY	DISCLAIMED	DISCOMFITING
DISAUTHORIZES	DISBURDENED	DISCERNING	DISCLAIMER	DISCOMFITS
DISAUTHORIZING	DISBURDENING	DISCERNINGLY	DISCLAIMERS	DISCOMFITURE
DISAVAUNCE	DISBURDENMENT	DISCERNMENT	DISCLAIMING	DISCOMFITURES
DISAVAUNCED	DISBURDENMENTS	DISCERNMENTS	DISCLAMATION	DISCOMFORT
DISAVAUNCES	DISBURDENS	DISCERPIBILITY	DISCLAMATIONS	DISCOMFORTABLE
DISAVAUNCING	DISBURSABLE	DISCERPIBLE	DISCLIMAXES	DISCOMFORTED
DISAVENTROUS	DISBURSALS	DISCERPING	DISCLOSERS	DISCOMFORTING
DISAVENTURE	DISBURSEMENT	DISCERPTIBLE	DISCLOSING	DISCOMFORTS
DISAVENTURES	DISBURSEMENTS	DISCERPTION	DISCLOSURE	DISCOMMEND
DISAVOUCHED	DISBURSERS	DISCERPTIONS	DISCLOSURES	DISCOMMENDABLE
DISAVOUCHES	DISBURSING	DISCERPTIVE	DISCOBOLOS	DISCOMMENDATION
DISAVOUCHING	DISBURTHEN	DISCHARGEABLE	DISCOBOLUS	DISCOMMENDED
DISAVOWABLE	DISBURTHENED	DISCHARGED	DISCOBOLUSES	DISCOMMENDING
DISAVOWALS	DISBURTHENING	DISCHARGEE	DISCOGRAPHER	DISCOMMENDS
DISAVOWEDLY	DISBURTHENS	DISCHARGEES	DISCOGRAPHERS	DISCOMMISSION
DISAVOWERS	DISCALCEATE	DISCHARGER	DISCOGRAPHIC	DISCOMMISSIONED
DISAVOWING	DISCALCEATES	DISCHARGERS	DISCOGRAPHICAL	DISCOMMISSIONS
DISBANDING	DISCANDERING	DISCHARGES	DISCOGRAPHIES	DISCOMMODE
DISBANDMENT	DISCANDERINGS	DISCHARGING	DISCOGRAPHY	DISCOMMODED
DISBANDMENTS	DISCANDIED	DISCHUFFED	DISCOLOGIES	DISCOMMODES
DISBARKING	DISCANDIES	DISCHURCHED	DISCOLOGIST	DISCOMMODING
DISBARMENT	DISCANDYING	DISCHURCHES	DISCOLOGISTS	DISCOMMODIOUS
DISBARMENTS	DISCANDYINGS	DISCHURCHING	DISCOLORATION	DISCOMMODIOUSLY
DISBARRING	DISCANTERS	DISCIPLESHIP	DISCOLORATIONS	DISCOMMODITIES
DISBELIEFS	DISCANTING	DISCIPLESHIPS	DISCOLORED	DISCOMMODITY
DISBELIEVE	DISCAPACITATE	DISCIPLINABLE	DISCOLORING	DISCOMMONED
DISBELIEVED	DISCAPACITATED	DISCIPLINAL	DISCOLORMENT	DISCOMMONING
DISBELIEVER	DISCAPACITATES	DISCIPLINANT	DISCOLORMENTS	DISCOMMONS
DISBELIEVERS	DISCAPACITATING	DISCIPLINANTS	DISCOLOURATION	DISCOMMUNITIES
DISBELIEVES	DISCARDABLE	DISCIPLINARIAN	DISCOLOURATIONS	DISCOMMUNITY
DISBELIEVING	DISCARDERS	DISCIPLINARIANS	DISCOLOURED	DISCOMPOSE
DISBELIEVINGLY	DISCARDING	DISCIPLINARILY	DISCOLOURING	DISCOMPOSED
DISBENCHED	DISCARDMENT	DISCIPLINARITY	DISCOLOURMENT	DISCOMPOSEDLY
DISBENCHES	DISCARDMENTS	DISCIPLINARIUM	DISCOLOURMENTS	DISCOMPOSES
DISBENCHING	DISCARNATE	DISCIPLINARIUMS	DISCOLOURS	DISCOMPOSING
DISBENEFIT	DISCEPTATION	DISCIPLINARY	DISCOMBOBERATE	DISCOMPOSINGLY
DISBENEFITS	DISCEPTATIONS	DISCIPLINE	DISCOMBOBERATED	DISCOMPOSURE
DISBOSOMED	DISCEPTATIOUS	DISCIPLINED	DISCOMBOBERATES	DISCOMPOSURES
DISBOSOMING	DISCEPTATOR	DISCIPLINER	DISCOMBOBULATE	DISCOMYCETE
DISBOWELED	DISCEPTATORIAL	DISCIPLINERS	DISCOMBOBULATED	DISCOMYCETES

DISCOMYCETOUS	DISCONTIGUITIES	DISCOURAGEMENT	DISCRETEST	DISCUSSING
DISCONCERT	DISCONTIGUITY	DISCOURAGEMENTS	DISCRETION	DISCUSSION
DISCONCERTED	DISCONTIGUOUS	DISCOURAGER	DISCRETIONAL	DISCUSSIONAL
DISCONCERTEDLY	DISCONTINUANCE	DISCOURAGERS	DISCRETIONALLY	DISCUSSIONS
DISCONCERTING	DISCONTINUANCES	DISCOURAGES	DISCRETIONARILY	DISCUSSIVE
DISCONCERTINGLY	DISCONTINUATION	DISCOURAGING	DISCRETIONARY	DISCUTIENT
DISCONCERTION	DISCONTINUE	DISCOURAGINGLY	DISCRETIONS	DISCUTIENTS
DISCONCERTIONS	DISCONTINUED	DISCOURING	DISCRETIVE	DISDAINFUL
DISCONCERTMENT	DISCONTINUER	DISCOURSAL	DISCRETIVELY	DISDAINFULLY
DISCONCERTMENTS	DISCONTINUERS	DISCOURSED	DISCRIMINABLE	DISDAINFULNESS
DISCONCERTS	DISCONTINUES	DISCOURSER	DISCRIMINABLY	DISDAINING
DISCONFIRM	DISCONTINUING	DISCOURSERS	DISCRIMINANT	DISEASEDNESS
DISCONFIRMATION	DISCONTINUITIES	DISCOURSES	DISCRIMINANTS	DISEASEDNESSES
DISCONFIRMED	DISCONTINUITY	DISCOURSING	DISCRIMINATE	DISEASEFUL
DISCONFIRMING	DISCONTINUOUS	DISCOURSIVE	DISCRIMINATED	DISECONOMIES
DISCONFIRMS	DISCONTINUOUSLY	DISCOURTEISE	DISCRIMINATELY	DISECONOMY
DISCONFORMABLE	DISCOPHILE	DISCOURTEOUS	DISCRIMINATES	DISEMBARKATION
DISCONFORMITIES	DISCOPHILES	DISCOURTEOUSLY	DISCRIMINATING	DISEMBARKATIONS
DISCONFORMITY	DISCOPHORAN	DISCOURTESIES	DISCRIMINATION	DISEMBARKED
DISCONNECT	DISCOPHORANS	DISCOURTESY	DISCRIMINATIONS	DISEMBARKING
DISCONNECTED	DISCOPHOROUS	DISCOVERABLE	DISCRIMINATIVE	DISEMBARKMENT
DISCONNECTEDLY	DISCORDANCE	DISCOVERED	DISCRIMINATOR	DISEMBARKMENTS
DISCONNECTER	DISCORDANCES	DISCOVERER	DISCRIMINATORS	DISEMBARKS
DISCONNECTERS	DISCORDANCIES	DISCOVERERS	DISCRIMINATORY	DISEMBARRASS
DISCONNECTING	DISCORDANCY	DISCOVERIES	DISCROWNED	DISEMBARRASSED
DISCONNECTION	DISCORDANT	DISCOVERING	DISCROWNING	DISEMBARRASSES
DISCONNECTIONS	DISCORDANTLY	DISCOVERTURE	DISCULPATE	DISEMBARRASSING
DISCONNECTIVE	DISCORDFUL	DISCOVERTURES	DISCULPATED	DISEMBELLISH
DISCONNECTS	DISCORDING	DISCREDITABLE	DISCULPATES	DISEMBELLISHED
DISCONNEXION	DISCORPORATE	DISCREDITABLY	DISCULPATING	DISEMBELLISHES
DISCONNEXIONS	DISCOTHEQUE	DISCREDITED	DISCUMBERED	DISEMBELLISHING
DISCONSENT	DISCOTHEQUES	DISCREDITING	DISCUMBERING	DISEMBITTER
DISCONSENTED	DISCOUNSEL	DISCREDITS	DISCUMBERS	DISEMBITTERED
DISCONSENTING	DISCOUNSELLED	DISCREETER	DISCURSION	DISEMBITTERING
DISCONSENTS	DISCOUNSELLING	DISCREETEST	DISCURSIONS	DISEMBITTERS
DISCONSOLATE	DISCOUNSELS	DISCREETLY	DISCURSIST	DISEMBODIED
DISCONSOLATELY	DISCOUNTABLE	DISCREETNESS	DISCURSISTS	DISEMBODIES
DISCONSOLATION	DISCOUNTED	DISCREETNESSES	DISCURSIVE	DISEMBODIMENT
DISCONSOLATIONS	DISCOUNTENANCE	DISCREPANCE	DISCURSIVELY	DISEMBODIMENTS
DISCONTENT	DISCOUNTENANCED	DISCREPANCES	DISCURSIVENESS	DISEMBODYING
DISCONTENTED	DISCOUNTENANCES	DISCREPANCIES	DISCURSORY	DISEMBOGUE
DISCONTENTEDLY	DISCOUNTER	DISCREPANCY	DISCURSUSES	DISEMBOGUED
DISCONTENTFUL	DISCOUNTERS	DISCREPANT	DISCUSSABLE	DISEMBOGUEMENT
DISCONTENTING	DISCOUNTING	DISCREPANTLY	DISCUSSANT	DISEMBOGUEMENTS
DISCONTENTMENT	DISCOURAGE	DISCRETELY	DISCUSSANTS	DISEMBOGUES
DISCONTENTMENTS	DISCOURAGEABLE	DISCRETENESS	DISCUSSERS	DISEMBOGUING
DISCONTENTS	DISCOURAGED	DISCRETENESSES	DISCUSSIBLE	DISEMBOSOM

DISEMBOSOMED	DISENCHANT	DISENSLAVED	DISENTRANCING	DISFEATUREMENTS
DISEMBOSOMING	DISENCHANTED	DISENSLAVES	DISENTRAYLE	DISFEATURES
DISEMBOSOMS	DISENCHANTER	DISENSLAVING	DISENTRAYLED	DISFEATURING
DISEMBOWEL	DISENCHANTERS	DISENTAILED	DISENTRAYLES	DISFELLOWSHIP
DISEMBOWELED	DISENCHANTING	DISENTAILING	DISENTRAYLING	DISFELLOWSHIPED
DISEMBOWELING	DISENCHANTINGLY	DISENTAILMENT	DISENTWINE	DISFELLOWSHIPS
DISEMBOWELLED	DISENCHANTMENT	DISENTAILMENTS	DISENTWINED	DISFIGURATION
DISEMBOWELLING	DISENCHANTMENTS	DISENTAILS	DISENTWINES	DISFIGURATIONS
DISEMBOWELMENT	DISENCHANTRESS	DISENTANGLE	DISENTWINING	DISFIGURED
DISEMBOWELMENTS	DISENCHANTS	DISENTANGLED	DISENVELOP	DISFIGUREMENT
DISEMBOWELS	DISENCLOSE	DISENTANGLEMENT	DISENVELOPED	DISFIGUREMENTS
DISEMBRANGLE	DISENCLOSED	DISENTANGLES	DISENVELOPING	DISFIGURER
DISEMBRANGLED	DISENCLOSES	DISENTANGLING	DISENVELOPS	DISFIGURERS
DISEMBRANGLES	DISENCLOSING	DISENTHRAL	DISENVIRON	DISFIGURES
DISEMBRANGLING	DISENCUMBER	DISENTHRALL	DISENVIRONED	DISFIGURING
DISEMBROIL	DISENCUMBERED	DISENTHRALLED	DISENVIRONING	DISFLESHED
DISEMBROILED	DISENCUMBERING	DISENTHRALLING	DISENVIRONS	DISFLESHES
DISEMBROILING	DISENCUMBERMENT	DISENTHRALLMENT	DISEPALOUS	DISFLESHING
DISEMBROILS	DISENCUMBERS	DISENTHRALLS	DISEQUILIBRATE	DISFLUENCIES
DISEMBURDEN	DISENCUMBRANCE	DISENTHRALMENT	DISEQUILIBRATED	DISFLUENCY
DISEMBURDENED	DISENCUMBRANCES	DISENTHRALMENTS	DISEQUILIBRATES	DISFORESTATION
DISEMBURDENING	DISENDOWED	DISENTHRALS	DISEQUILIBRIA	DISFORESTATIONS
DISEMBURDENS	DISENDOWER	DISENTHRONE	DISEQUILIBRIUM	DISFORESTED
DISEMPLOYED	DISENDOWERS	DISENTHRONED	DISEQUILIBRIUMS	DISFORESTING
DISEMPLOYING	DISENDOWING	DISENTHRONES	DISESPOUSE	DISFORESTS
DISEMPLOYMENT	DISENDOWMENT	DISENTHRONING	DISESPOUSED	DISFORMING
DISEMPLOYMENTS	DISENDOWMENTS	DISENTITLE	DISESPOUSES	DISFRANCHISE
DISEMPLOYS	DISENFRANCHISE	DISENTITLED	DISESPOUSING	DISFRANCHISED
DISEMPOWER	DISENFRANCHISED	DISENTITLES	DISESTABLISH	DISFRANCHISES
DISEMPOWERED	DISENFRANCHISES	DISENTITLING	DISESTABLISHED	DISFRANCHISING
DISEMPOWERING	DISENGAGED	DISENTOMBED	DISESTABLISHES	DISFROCKED
DISEMPOWERMENT	DISENGAGEDNESS	DISENTOMBING	DISESTABLISHING	DISFROCKING
DISEMPOWERMENTS	DISENGAGEMENT	DISENTOMBS	DISESTEEMED	DISFUNCTION
DISEMPOWERS	DISENGAGEMENTS	DISENTRAIL	DISESTEEMING	DISFUNCTIONS
DISEMVOWEL	DISENGAGES	DISENTRAILED	DISESTEEMS	DISFURNISH
DISEMVOWELLED	DISENGAGING	DISENTRAILING	DISESTIMATION	DISFURNISHED
DISEMVOWELLING	DISENNOBLE	DISENTRAILS	DISESTIMATIONS	DISFURNISHES
DISEMVOWELS	DISENNOBLED	DISENTRAIN	DISFAVORED	DISFURNISHING
DISENABLED	DISENNOBLES	DISENTRAINED	DISFAVORING	DISFURNISHMENT
DISENABLEMENT	DISENNOBLING	DISENTRAINING	DISFAVOURED	DISFURNISHMENTS
DISENABLEMENTS	DISENROLLED	DISENTRAINMENT	DISFAVOURER	DISGARNISH
DISENABLES	DISENROLLING	DISENTRAINMENTS	DISFAVOURERS	DISGARNISHED
DISENABLING	DISENSHROUD	DISENTRAINS	DISFAVOURING	DISGARNISHES
DISENCHAIN	DISENSHROUDED	DISENTRANCE	DISFAVOURS	DISGARNISHING
DISENCHAINED	DISENSHROUDING	DISENTRANCED	DISFEATURE	DISGARRISON
DISENCHAINING	DISENSHROUDS	DISENTRANCEMENT	DISFEATURED	DISGARRISONED
DISENCHAINS	DISENSLAVE	DISENTRANCES	DISFEATUREMENT	DISGARRISONING

DISGARRISONS	DISGUSTFULLY	DISHERITOR	DISILLUSIONISED	DISINFECTION
DISGAVELLED	DISGUSTFULNESS	DISHERITORS	DISILLUSIONISES	DISINFECTIONS
DISGAVELLING	DISGUSTING	DISHEVELED	DISILLUSIONIZE	DISINFECTOR
DISGESTING	DISGUSTINGLY	DISHEVELING	DISILLUSIONIZED	DISINFECTORS
DISGESTION	DISGUSTINGNESS	DISHEVELLED	DISILLUSIONIZES	DISINFECTS
DISGESTIONS	DISHABILITATE	DISHEVELLING	DISILLUSIONMENT	DISINFESTANT
DISGLORIFIED	DISHABILITATED	DISHEVELMENT	DISILLUSIONS	DISINFESTANTS
DISGLORIFIES	DISHABILITATES	DISHEVELMENTS	DISILLUSIVE	DISINFESTATION
DISGLORIFY	DISHABILITATING	DISHONESTIES	DISIMAGINE	DISINFESTATIONS
DISGLORIFYING	DISHABILITATION	DISHONESTLY	DISIMAGINED	DISINFESTED
DISGORGEMENT	DISHABILLE	DISHONESTY	DISIMAGINES	DISINFESTING
DISGORGEMENTS	DISHABILLES	DISHONORABLE	DISIMAGINING	DISINFESTS
DISGORGERS	DISHABITED	DISHONORABLY	DISIMMURED	DISINFLATION
DISGORGING	DISHABITING	DISHONORARY	DISIMMURES	DISINFLATIONARY
DISGOSPELLING	DISHABLING	DISHONORED	DISIMMURING	DISINFLATIONS
DISGOWNING	DISHALLOWED	DISHONORER	DISIMPASSIONED	DISINFORMATION
DISGRACEFUL	DISHALLOWING	DISHONORERS	DISIMPRISON	DISINFORMATIONS
DISGRACEFULLY	DISHALLOWS	DISHONORING	DISIMPRISONED	DISINFORMED
DISGRACEFULNESS	DISHARMONIC	DISHONOURABLE	DISIMPRISONING	DISINFORMING
DISGRACERS	DISHARMONIES	DISHONOURABLY	DISIMPRISONMENT	DISINFORMS
DISGRACING	DISHARMONIOUS	DISHONOURED	DISIMPRISONS	DISINGENUITIES
DISGRACIOUS	DISHARMONIOUSLY	DISHONOURER	DISIMPROVE	DISINGENUITY
DISGRADATION	DISHARMONISE	DISHONOURERS	DISIMPROVED	DISINGENUOUS
DISGRADATIONS	DISHARMONISED	DISHONOURING	DISIMPROVES	DISINGENUOUSLY
DISGRADING	DISHARMONISES	DISHONOURS	DISIMPROVING	DISINHERISON
DISGREGATION	DISHARMONISING	DISHORNING	DISINCARCERATE	DISINHERISONS
DISGREGATIONS	DISHARMONIZE	DISHORSING	DISINCARCERATED	DISINHERIT
DISGRUNTLE	DISHARMONIZED	DISHOUSING	DISINCARCERATES	DISINHERITANCE
DISGRUNTLED	DISHARMONIZES	DISHTOWELS	DISINCENTIVE	DISINHERITANCES
DISGRUNTLEMENT	DISHARMONIZING	DISHUMOURED	DISINCENTIVES	DISINHERITED
DISGRUNTLEMENTS	DISHARMONY	DISHUMOURING	DISINCLINATION	DISINHERITING
DISGRUNTLES	DISHCLOTHS	DISHUMOURS	DISINCLINATIONS	DISINHERITS
DISGRUNTLING	DISHCLOUTS	DISHWASHER	DISINCLINE	DISINHIBIT
DISGUISABLE	DISHDASHAS	DISHWASHERS	DISINCLINED	DISINHIBITED
DISGUISEDLY	DISHDASHES	DISHWATERS	DISINCLINES	DISINHIBITING
DISGUISEDNESS	DISHEARTEN	DISILLUDED	DISINCLINING	DISINHIBITION
DISGUISEDNESSES	DISHEARTENED	DISILLUDES	DISINCLOSE	DISINHIBITIONS
DISGUISELESS	DISHEARTENING	DISILLUDING	DISINCLOSED	DISINHIBITORY
DISGUISEMENT	DISHEARTENINGLY	DISILLUMINATE	DISINCLOSES	DISINHIBITS
DISGUISEMENTS	DISHEARTENMENT	DISILLUMINATED	DISINCLOSING	DISINHUMED
DISGUISERS	DISHEARTENMENTS	DISILLUMINATES	DISINCORPORATE	DISINHUMES
DISGUISING	DISHEARTENS	DISILLUMINATING	DISINCORPORATED	DISINHUMING
DISGUISINGS	DISHELMING	DISILLUSION	DISINCORPORATES	DISINTEGRABLE
DISGUSTEDLY	DISHERISON	DISILLUSIONARY	DISINFECTANT	DISINTEGRATE
DISGUSTEDNESS	DISHERISONS	DISILLUSIONED	DISINFECTANTS	DISINTEGRATED
DISGUSTEDNESSES	DISHERITED	DISILLUSIONING	DISINFECTED	DISINTEGRATES
DISGUSTFUL	DISHERITING	DISILLUSIONISE	DISINFECTING	DISINTEGRATING

DISINTEGRATION	DISINVOLVES	DISLOYALTIES	DISNATURALISED	DISORGANIZER
DISINTEGRATIONS	DISINVOLVING	DISLOYALTY	DISNATURALISES	DISORGANIZERS
DISINTEGRATIVE	DISJECTING	DISLUSTRED	DISNATURALISING	DISORGANIZES
DISINTEGRATOR	DISJECTION	DISLUSTRES	DISNATURALIZE	DISORGANIZING
DISINTEGRATORS	DISJECTIONS	DISLUSTRING	DISNATURALIZED	DISORIENTATE
DISINTEREST	DISJOINABLE	DISMALITIES	DISNATURALIZES	DISORIENTATED
DISINTERESTED	DISJOINING	DISMALLEST	DISNATURALIZING	DISORIENTATES
DISINTERESTEDLY	DISJOINTED	DISMALNESS	DISNATURED	DISORIENTATING
DISINTERESTING	DISJOINTEDLY	DISMALNESSES	DISNESTING	DISORIENTATION
DISINTERESTS	DISJOINTEDNESS	DISMANNING	DISOBEDIENCE	DISORIENTATIONS
DISINTERMENT	DISJOINTING	DISMANTLED	DISOBEDIENCES	DISORIENTED
DISINTERMENTS	DISJUNCTION	DISMANTLEMENT	DISOBEDIENT	DISORIENTING
DISINTERRED	DISJUNCTIONS	DISMANTLEMENTS	DISOBEDIENTLY	DISORIENTS
DISINTERRING	DISJUNCTIVE	DISMANTLER	DISOBEYERS	DISOWNMENT
DISINTHRAL	DISJUNCTIVELY	DISMANTLERS	DISOBEYING	DISOWNMENTS
DISINTHRALLED	DISJUNCTIVES	DISMANTLES	DISOBLIGATION	DISPARAGED
DISINTHRALLING	DISJUNCTOR	DISMANTLING	DISOBLIGATIONS	DISPARAGEMENT
DISINTHRALS	DISJUNCTORS	DISMASKING	DISOBLIGATORY	DISPARAGEMENTS
DISINTOXICATE	DISJUNCTURE	DISMASTING	DISOBLIGED	DISPARAGER
DISINTOXICATED	DISJUNCTURES	DISMASTMENT	DISOBLIGEMENT	DISPARAGERS
DISINTOXICATES	DISLEAFING	DISMASTMENTS	DISOBLIGEMENTS	DISPARAGES
DISINTOXICATING	DISLEAVING	DISMAYEDNESS	DISOBLIGES	DISPARAGING
DISINTOXICATION	DISLIKABLE	DISMAYEDNESSES	DISOBLIGING	DISPARAGINGLY
DISINTRICATE	DISLIKEABLE	DISMAYFULLY	DISOBLIGINGLY	DISPARATELY
DISINTRICATED	DISLIKEFUL	DISMAYINGLY	DISOBLIGINGNESS	DISPARATENESS
DISINTRICATES	DISLIKENED	DISMAYLING	DISOPERATION	DISPARATENESSES
DISINTRICATING	DISLIKENESS	DISMEMBERED	DISOPERATIONS	DISPARATES
DISINURING	DISLIKENESSES	DISMEMBERER	DISORDERED	DISPARITIES
DISINVENTED	DISLIKENING	DISMEMBERERS	DISORDEREDLY	DISPARKING
DISINVENTING	DISLIMBING	DISMEMBERING	DISORDEREDNESS	DISPARTING
DISINVENTS	DISLIMNING	DISMEMBERMENT	DISORDERING	DISPASSION
DISINVESTED	DISLINKING	DISMEMBERMENTS	DISORDERLIES	DISPASSIONATE
DISINVESTING	DISLOADING	DISMEMBERS	DISORDERLINESS	DISPASSIONATELY
DISINVESTITURE	DISLOCATED	DISMISSALS	DISORDERLY	DISPASSIONS
DISINVESTITURES	DISLOCATEDLY	DISMISSIBLE	DISORDINATE	DISPATCHED
DISINVESTMENT	DISLOCATES	DISMISSING	DISORDINATELY	DISPATCHER
DISINVESTMENTS	DISLOCATING	DISMISSION	DISORGANIC	DISPATCHERS
DISINVESTS	DISLOCATION	DISMISSIONS	DISORGANISATION	DISPATCHES
DISINVIGORATE	DISLOCATIONS	DISMISSIVE	DISORGANISE	DISPATCHFUL
DISINVIGORATED	DISLODGEMENT	DISMISSIVELY	DISORGANISED	DISPATCHING
DISINVIGORATES	DISLODGEMENTS	DISMISSORY	DISORGANISER	DISPATHIES
DISINVIGORATING	DISLODGING	DISMOUNTABLE	DISORGANISERS	DISPAUPERED
DISINVITED	DISLODGMENT	DISMOUNTED	DISORGANISES	DISPAUPERING
DISINVITES	DISLODGMENTS	DISMOUNTING	DISORGANISING	DISPAUPERISE
DISINVITING	DISLOIGNED	DISMUTATION	DISORGANIZATION	DISPAUPERISED
DISINVOLVE	DISLOIGNING	DISMUTATIONS	DISORGANIZE	DISPAUPERISES
DISINVOLVED	DISLOYALLY	DISNATURALISE	DISORGANIZED	DISPAUPERISING

DISPAUPERIZE	DISPIRITED	DISPONDEES	DISPRIVILEGED	DISPUTATIOUS
DISPAUPERIZED	DISPIRITEDLY	DISPONGING	DISPRIVILEGES	DISPUTATIOUSLY
DISPAUPERIZES	DISPIRITEDNESS	DISPORTING	DISPRIVILEGING	DISPUTATIVE
DISPAUPERIZING	DISPIRITING	DISPORTMENT	DISPRIZING	DISPUTATIVELY
DISPAUPERS	DISPIRITINGLY	DISPORTMENTS	DISPROFESS	DISPUTATIVENESS
DISPELLERS	DISPIRITMENT	DISPOSABILITIES	DISPROFESSED	DISQUALIFIABLE
DISPELLING	DISPIRITMENTS	DISPOSABILITY	DISPROFESSES	DISQUALIFIED
DISPENCING	DISPITEOUS	DISPOSABLE	DISPROFESSING	DISQUALIFIER
DISPENDING	DISPITEOUSLY	DISPOSABLENESS	DISPROFITS	DISQUALIFIERS
DISPENSABILITY	DISPITEOUSNESS	DISPOSABLES	DISPROOVED	DISQUALIFIES
DISPENSABLE	DISPLACEABLE	DISPOSEDLY	DISPROOVES	DISQUALIFY
DISPENSABLENESS	DISPLACEMENT	DISPOSINGLY	DISPROOVING	DISQUALIFYING
DISPENSABLY	DISPLACEMENTS	DISPOSINGS	DISPROPERTIED	DISQUANTITIED
DISPENSARIES	DISPLACERS	DISPOSITION	DISPROPERTIES	DISQUANTITIES
DISPENSARY	DISPLACING	DISPOSITIONAL	DISPROPERTY	DISQUANTITY
DISPENSATION	DISPLANTATION	DISPOSITIONED	DISPROPERTYING	DISQUANTITYING
DISPENSATIONAL	DISPLANTATIONS	DISPOSITIONS	DISPROPORTION	DISQUIETED
DISPENSATIONS	DISPLANTED	DISPOSITIVE	DISPROPORTIONAL	DISQUIETEDLY
DISPENSATIVE	DISPLANTING	DISPOSITIVELY	DISPROPORTIONED	DISQUIETEDNESS
DISPENSATIVELY	DISPLAYABLE	DISPOSITOR	DISPROPORTIONS	DISQUIETEN
DISPENSATOR	DISPLAYERS	DISPOSITORS	DISPROPRIATE	DISQUIETENED
DISPENSATORIES	DISPLAYING	DISPOSSESS	DISPROPRIATED	DISQUIETENING
DISPENSATORILY	DISPLEASANCE	DISPOSSESSED	DISPROPRIATES	DISQUIETENS
DISPENSATORS	DISPLEASANCES	DISPOSSESSES	DISPROPRIATING	DISQUIETFUL
DISPENSATORY	DISPLEASANT	DISPOSSESSING	DISPROVABLE	DISQUIETING
DISPENSERS	DISPLEASED	DISPOSSESSION	DISPROVALS	DISQUIETINGLY
DISPENSING	DISPLEASEDLY	DISPOSSESSIONS	DISPROVERS	DISQUIETIVE
DISPEOPLED	DISPLEASEDNESS	DISPOSSESSOR	DISPROVIDE	DISQUIETLY
DISPEOPLES	DISPLEASES	DISPOSSESSORS	DISPROVIDED	DISQUIETNESS
DISPEOPLING	DISPLEASING	DISPOSSESSORY	DISPROVIDES	DISQUIETNESSES
DISPERMOUS	DISPLEASINGLY	DISPOSTING	DISPROVIDING	DISQUIETOUS
DISPERSALS	DISPLEASINGNESS	DISPOSURES	DISPROVING	DISQUIETUDE
DISPERSANT	DISPLEASURE	DISPRAISED	DISPUNGING	DISQUIETUDES
DISPERSANTS	DISPLEASURED	DISPRAISER	DISPURSING	DISQUISITION
DISPERSEDLY	DISPLEASURES	DISPRAISERS	DISPURVEYANCE	DISQUISITIONAL
DISPERSEDNESS	DISPLEASURING	DISPRAISES	DISPURVEYANCES	DISQUISITIONARY
DISPERSEDNESSES	DISPLENISH	DISPRAISING	DISPURVEYED	DISQUISITIONS
DISPERSERS	DISPLENISHED	DISPRAISINGLY	DISPURVEYING	DISQUISITIVE
DISPERSIBLE	DISPLENISHES	DISPREADING	DISPURVEYS	DISQUISITORY
DISPERSING	DISPLENISHING	DISPREDDEN	DISPUTABILITIES	DISRANKING
DISPERSION	DISPLENISHMENT	DISPREDDING	DISPUTABILITY	DISREGARDED
DISPERSIONS	DISPLENISHMENTS	DISPRINCED	DISPUTABLE	DISREGARDER
DISPERSIVE	DISPLODING	DISPRISONED	DISPUTABLENESS	DISREGARDERS
DISPERSIVELY	DISPLOSION	DISPRISONING	DISPUTABLY	DISREGARDFUL
DISPERSIVENESS	DISPLOSIONS	DISPRISONS	DISPUTANTS	DISREGARDFULLY
DISPERSOID	DISPLUMING	DISPRIVACIED	DISPUTATION	DISREGARDING
DISPERSOIDS	DISPONDAIC	DISPRIVILEGE	DISPUTATIONS	DISREGARDS

DISRELATED	DISSECTION	DISSENTIENTLY	DISSILIENT	DISSOCIALITIES
DISRELATION	DISSECTIONS	DISSENTIENTS	DISSIMILAR	DISSOCIALITY
DISRELATIONS	DISSECTIVE	DISSENTING	DISSIMILARITIES	DISSOCIALIZE
DISRELISHED	DISSECTORS	DISSENTINGLY	DISSIMILARITY	DISSOCIALIZED
DISRELISHES	DISSEISEES	DISSENTION	DISSIMILARLY	DISSOCIALIZES
DISRELISHING	DISSEISING	DISSENTIONS	DISSIMILARS	DISSOCIALIZING
DISREMEMBER	DISSEISINS	DISSENTIOUS	DISSIMILATE	DISSOCIATE
DISREMEMBERED	DISSEISORS	DISSEPIMENT	DISSIMILATED	DISSOCIATED
DISREMEMBERING	DISSEIZEES	DISSEPIMENTAL	DISSIMILATES	DISSOCIATES
DISREMEMBERS	DISSEIZING	DISSEPIMENTS	DISSIMILATING	DISSOCIATING
DISREPAIRS	DISSEIZINS	DISSERTATE	DISSIMILATION	DISSOCIATION
DISREPUTABILITY	DISSEIZORS	DISSERTATED	DISSIMILATIONS	DISSOCIATIONS
DISREPUTABLE	DISSELBOOM	DISSERTATES	DISSIMILATIVE	DISSOCIATIVE
DISREPUTABLY	DISSELBOOMS	DISSERTATING	DISSIMILATORY	DISSOLUBILITIES
DISREPUTATION	DISSEMBLANCE	DISSERTATION	DISSIMILES	DISSOLUBILITY
DISREPUTATIONS	DISSEMBLANCES	DISSERTATIONAL	DISSIMILITUDE	DISSOLUBLE
DISREPUTES	DISSEMBLED	DISSERTATIONIST	DISSIMILITUDES	DISSOLUBLENESS
DISRESPECT	DISSEMBLER	DISSERTATIONS	DISSIMULATE	DISSOLUTELY
DISRESPECTABLE	DISSEMBLERS	DISSERTATIVE	DISSIMULATED	DISSOLUTENESS
DISRESPECTED	DISSEMBLES	DISSERTATOR	DISSIMULATES	DISSOLUTENESSES
DISRESPECTFUL	DISSEMBLIES	DISSERTATORS	DISSIMULATING	DISSOLUTES
DISRESPECTFULLY	DISSEMBLING	DISSERTING	DISSIMULATION	DISSOLUTION
DISRESPECTING	DISSEMBLINGLY	DISSERVICE	DISSIMULATIONS	DISSOLUTIONISM
DISRESPECTS	DISSEMBLINGS	DISSERVICEABLE	DISSIMULATIVE	DISSOLUTIONISMS
DISROBEMENT	DISSEMINATE	DISSERVICES	DISSIMULATOR	DISSOLUTIONIST
DISROBEMENTS	DISSEMINATED	DISSERVING	DISSIMULATORS	DISSOLUTIONISTS
DISROOTING	DISSEMINATES	DISSEVERANCE	DISSIPABLE	DISSOLUTIONS
DISRUPTERS	DISSEMINATING	DISSEVERANCES	DISSIPATED	DISSOLUTIVE
DISRUPTING	DISSEMINATION	DISSEVERATION	DISSIPATEDLY	DISSOLVABILITY
DISRUPTION	DISSEMINATIONS	DISSEVERATIONS	DISSIPATEDNESS	DISSOLVABLE
DISRUPTIONS	DISSEMINATIVE	DISSEVERED	DISSIPATER	DISSOLVABLENESS
DISRUPTIVE	DISSEMINATOR	DISSEVERING	DISSIPATERS	DISSOLVENT
DISRUPTIVELY	DISSEMINATORS	DISSEVERMENT	DISSIPATES	DISSOLVENTS
DISRUPTIVENESS	DISSEMINULE	DISSEVERMENTS	DISSIPATING	DISSOLVERS
DISRUPTORS	DISSEMINULES	DISSHEATHE	DISSIPATION	DISSOLVING
DISSATISFACTION	DISSENSION	DISSHEATHED	DISSIPATIONS	DISSOLVINGS
DISSATISFACTORY	DISSENSIONS	DISSHEATHES	DISSIPATIVE	DISSONANCE
DISSATISFIED	DISSENSUSES	DISSHEATHING	DISSIPATOR	DISSONANCES
DISSATISFIEDLY	DISSENTERISH	DISSHIVERED	DISSIPATORS	DISSONANCIES
DISSATISFIES	DISSENTERISM	DISSHIVERING	DISSOCIABILITY	DISSONANCY
DISSATISFY	DISSENTERISMS	DISSHIVERS	DISSOCIABLE	DISSONANTLY
DISSATISFYING	DISSENTERS	DISSIDENCE	DISSOCIABLENESS	DISSUADABLE
DISSAVINGS	DISSENTIENCE	DISSIDENCES	DISSOCIABLY	DISSUADERS
DISSEATING	DISSENTIENCES	DISSIDENTLY	DISSOCIALISE	DISSUADING
DISSECTIBLE	DISSENTIENCIES	DISSIDENTS	DISSOCIALISED	DISSUASION
DISSECTING	DISSENTIENCY	DISSILIENCE	DISSOCIALISES	DISSUASIONS
DISSECTINGS	DISSENTIENT	DISSILIENCES	DISSOCIALISING	DISSUASIVE

DISSUASIVELY

DISSUASIVELY	DISTHRONISES	DISTORTEDNESS	DISTRIBUENDS	DISULFIDES
DISSUASIVENESS	DISTHRONISING	DISTORTEDNESSES	DISTRIBUTABLE	DISULFIRAM
DISSUASIVES	DISTHRONIZE	DISTORTERS	DISTRIBUTARIES	DISULFIRAMS
DISSUASORIES	DISTHRONIZED	DISTORTING	DISTRIBUTARY	DISULFOTON
DISSUASORY	DISTHRONIZES	DISTORTION	DISTRIBUTE	DISULFOTONS
DISSUNDERED	DISTHRONIZING	DISTORTIONAL	DISTRIBUTED	DISULPHATE
DISSUNDERING	DISTICHOUS	DISTORTIONS	DISTRIBUTEE	DISULPHATES
DISSUNDERS	DISTICHOUSLY	DISTORTIVE	DISTRIBUTEES	DISULPHIDE
DISSYLLABIC	DISTILLABLE	DISTRACTABLE	DISTRIBUTER	DISULPHIDES
DISSYLLABLE	DISTILLAND	DISTRACTED	DISTRIBUTERS	DISULPHURET
DISSYLLABLES	DISTILLANDS	DISTRACTEDLY	DISTRIBUTES	DISULPHURETS
DISSYMMETRIC	DISTILLATE	DISTRACTEDNESS	DISTRIBUTING	DISULPHURIC
DISSYMMETRICAL	DISTILLATES	DISTRACTER	DISTRIBUTION	DISUNIONIST
DISSYMMETRIES	DISTILLATION	DISTRACTERS	DISTRIBUTIONAL	DISUNIONISTS
DISSYMMETRY	DISTILLATIONS	DISTRACTIBILITY	DISTRIBUTIONS	DISUNITERS
DISTAINING	DISTILLATORY	DISTRACTIBLE	DISTRIBUTIVE	DISUNITIES
DISTANCELESS	DISTILLERIES	DISTRACTING	DISTRIBUTIVELY	DISUNITING
DISTANCING	DISTILLERS	DISTRACTINGLY	DISTRIBUTIVES	DISUTILITIES
DISTANTNESS	DISTILLERY	DISTRACTION	DISTRIBUTIVITY	DISUTILITY
DISTANTNESSES	DISTILLING	DISTRACTIONS	DISTRIBUTOR	DISVALUING
DISTASTEFUL	DISTILLINGS	DISTRACTIVE	DISTRIBUTORS	DISVOUCHED
DISTASTEFULLY	DISTILMENT	DISTRACTIVELY	DISTRICTED	DISVOUCHES
DISTASTEFULNESS	DISTILMENTS	DISTRAINABLE	DISTRICTING	DISVOUCHING
DISTASTING	DISTINCTER	DISTRAINED	DISTRINGAS	DISWORSHIP
DISTELFINK	DISTINCTEST	DISTRAINEE	DISTRINGASES	DISWORSHIPS
DISTELFINKS	DISTINCTION	DISTRAINEES	DISTROUBLE	DISYLLABIC
DISTEMPERATE	DISTINCTIONS	DISTRAINER	DISTROUBLED	DISYLLABIFIED
DISTEMPERATURE	DISTINCTIVE	DISTRAINERS	DISTROUBLES	DISYLLABIFIES
DISTEMPERATURES	DISTINCTIVELY	DISTRAINING	DISTROUBLING	DISYLLABIFY
DISTEMPERED	DISTINCTIVENESS	DISTRAINMENT	DISTRUSTED	DISYLLABIFYING
DISTEMPERING	DISTINCTIVES	DISTRAINMENTS	DISTRUSTER	DISYLLABISM
DISTEMPERS	DISTINCTLY	DISTRAINOR	DISTRUSTERS	DISYLLABISMS
DISTENDERS	DISTINCTNESS	DISTRAINORS	DISTRUSTFUL	DISYLLABLE
DISTENDING	DISTINCTNESSES	DISTRAINTS	DISTRUSTFULLY	DISYLLABLES
DISTENSIBILITY	DISTINCTURE	DISTRAUGHT	DISTRUSTFULNESS	DITCHDIGGER
DISTENSIBLE	DISTINCTURES	DISTRAUGHTLY	DISTRUSTING	DITCHDIGGERS
DISTENSILE	DISTINGUEE	DISTRESSED	DISTRUSTLESS	DITCHWATER
DISTENSION	DISTINGUISH	DISTRESSER	DISTURBANCE	DITCHWATERS
DISTENSIONS	DISTINGUISHABLE	DISTRESSERS	DISTURBANCES	DITHEISTIC
DISTENSIVE	DISTINGUISHABLY	DISTRESSES	DISTURBANT	DITHEISTICAL
DISTENTION	DISTINGUISHED	DISTRESSFUL	DISTURBANTS	DITHELETES
DISTENTIONS	DISTINGUISHER	DISTRESSFULLY	DISTURBATIVE	DITHELETIC
DISTHRONED	DISTINGUISHERS	DISTRESSFULNESS	DISTURBERS	DITHELETICAL
DISTHRONES	DISTINGUISHES	DISTRESSING	DISTURBING	DITHELETISM
DISTHRONING	DISTINGUISHING	DISTRESSINGLY	DISTURBINGLY	DITHELETISMS
DISTHRONISE	DISTINGUISHMENT	DISTRESSINGS	DISUBSTITUTED	DITHELISMS
DISTHRONISED	DISTORTEDLY	DISTRIBUEND	DISULFATES	DITHELITISM

DITHELITISMS	DIVARICATORS	DIVERTISEMENTS	DIVORCEMENTS	DOCTORLESS
DITHERIEST	DIVEBOMBED	DIVERTISSEMENT	DIVULGATED	DOCTORSHIP
DITHIOCARBAMATE	DIVEBOMBING	DIVERTISSEMENTS	DIVULGATER	DOCTORSHIPS
DITHIONATE	DIVELLICATE	DIVESTIBLE	DIVULGATERS	DOCTRESSES
DITHIONATES	DIVELLICATED	DIVESTITURE	DIVULGATES	DOCTRINAIRE
DITHIONITE	DIVELLICATES	DIVESTITURES	DIVULGATING	DOCTRINAIRES
DITHIONITES	DIVELLICATING	DIVESTMENT	DIVULGATION	DOCTRINAIRISM
DITHIONOUS	DIVERGEMENT	DIVESTMENTS	DIVULGATIONS	DOCTRINAIRISMS
DITHYRAMBIC	DIVERGEMENTS	DIVESTURES	DIVULGATOR	DOCTRINALITIES
DITHYRAMBICALLY	DIVERGENCE	DIVIDEDNESS	DIVULGATORS	DOCTRINALITY
DITHYRAMBIST	DIVERGENCES	DIVIDEDNESSES	DIVULGEMENT	DOCTRINALLY
DITHYRAMBISTS	DIVERGENCIES	DIVIDENDLESS	DIVULGEMENTS	DOCTRINARIAN
DITHYRAMBS	DIVERGENCY	DIVINATION	DIVULGENCE	DOCTRINARIANISM
DITRANSITIVE	DIVERGENTLY	DIVINATIONS	DIVULGENCES	DOCTRINARIANS
DITRANSITIVES	DIVERGINGLY	DIVINATORIAL	DIVULSIONS	DOCTRINARISM
DITRIGLYPH	DIVERSENESS	DIVINATORS	DIZENMENTS	DOCTRINARISMS
DITRIGLYPHIC	DIVERSENESSES	DIVINATORY	DIZZINESSES	DOCTRINISM
DITRIGLYPHS	DIVERSIFIABLE	DIVINENESS	DIZZYINGLY	DOCTRINISMS
DITROCHEAN	DIVERSIFICATION	DIVINENESSES	DJELLABAHS	DOCTRINIST
DITROCHEES	DIVERSIFIED	DIVINERESS	DOBSONFLIES	DOCTRINISTS
DITSINESSES	DIVERSIFIER	DIVINERESSES	DOCENTSHIP	DOCUDRAMAS
DITTANDERS	DIVERSIFIERS	DIVINIFIED	DOCENTSHIPS	DOCUMENTABLE
DITTOGRAPHIC	DIVERSIFIES	DIVINIFIES	DOCHMIACAL	DOCUMENTAL
DITTOGRAPHIES	DIVERSIFORM	DIVINIFYING	DOCHMIUSES	DOCUMENTALIST
DITTOGRAPHY	DIVERSIFYING	DIVINISATION	DOCIBILITIES	DOCUMENTALISTS
DITTOLOGIES	DIVERSIONAL	DIVINISATIONS	DOCIBILITY	DOCUMENTARIAN
DITZINESSES	DIVERSIONARY	DIVINISING	DOCIBLENESS	DOCUMENTARIANS
DIURETICALLY	DIVERSIONIST	DIVINITIES	DOCIBLENESSES	DOCUMENTARIES
DIURETICALNESS	DIVERSIONISTS	DIVINIZATION	DOCILITIES	DOCUMENTARILY
DIURNALIST	DIVERSIONS	DIVINIZATIONS	DOCIMASIES	DOCUMENTARISE
DIURNALISTS	DIVERSITIES	DIVINIZING	DOCIMASTIC	DOCUMENTARISED
DIUTURNITIES	DIVERTIBILITIES	DIVISIBILITIES	DOCIMOLOGIES	DOCUMENTARISES
DIUTURNITY	DIVERTIBILITY	DIVISIBILITY	DOCIMOLOGY	DOCUMENTARISING
DIVAGATING	DIVERTIBLE	DIVISIBLENESS	DOCKISATION	DOCUMENTARIST
DIVAGATION	DIVERTICULA	DIVISIBLENESSES	DOCKISATIONS	DOCUMENTARISTS
DIVAGATIONS	DIVERTICULAR	DIVISIONAL	DOCKIZATION	DOCUMENTARIZE
DIVALENCES	DIVERTICULATE	DIVISIONALLY	DOCKIZATIONS	DOCUMENTARIZED
DIVALENCIES	DIVERTICULATED	DIVISIONARY	DOCKMASTER	DOCUMENTARIZES
DIVARICATE	DIVERTICULITIS	DIVISIONISM	DOCKMASTERS	DOCUMENTARIZING
DIVARICATED	DIVERTICULOSES	DIVISIONISMS	DOCKWORKER	DOCUMENTARY
DIVARICATELY	DIVERTICULOSIS	DIVISIONIST	DOCKWORKERS	DOCUMENTATION
DIVARICATES	DIVERTICULUM	DIVISIONISTS	DOCQUETING	DOCUMENTATIONAL
DIVARICATING	DIVERTIMENTI	DIVISIVELY	DOCTORANDS	DOCUMENTATIONS
DIVARICATINGLY	DIVERTIMENTO	DIVISIVENESS	DOCTORATED	DOCUMENTED
DIVARICATION	DIVERTIMENTOS	DIVISIVENESSES	DOCTORATES	DOCUMENTER
DIVARICATIONS	DIVERTINGLY	DIVORCEABLE	DOCTORATING	DOCUMENTERS
DIVARICATOR	DIVERTISEMENT	DIVORCEMENT	DOCTORESSES	DOCUMENTING

DODDERIEST
DODDIPOLLS
DODDYPOLLS
DODECAGONAL
DODECAGONS
DODECAGYNIAN
DODECAGYNOUS
DODECAHEDRA
DODECAHEDRAL
DODECAHEDRON
DODECAHEDRONS
DODECANDROUS
DODECANOIC
DODECAPHONIC
DODECAPHONIES
DODECAPHONISM
DODECAPHONISMS
DODECAPHONIST
DODECAPHONISTS
DODECAPHONY
DODECASTYLE
DODECASTYLES
DODECASYLLABIC
DODECASYLLABLE
DODECASYLLABLES
DODGEBALLS
DODGINESSES
DOGARESSAS
DOGBERRIES
DOGBERRYISM
DOGBERRYISMS
DOGCATCHER
DOGCATCHERS
DOGFIGHTING
DOGFIGHTINGS
DOGGEDNESS
DOGGEDNESSES
DOGGINESSES
DOGGISHNESS
DOGGISHNESSES
DOGGONEDER
DOGGONEDEST
DOGLEGGING
DOGMATICAL
DOGMATICALLY
DOGMATICALNESS
DOGMATISATION

DOGMATISATIONS
DOGMATISED
DOGMATISER
DOGMATISERS
DOGMATISES
DOGMATISING
DOGMATISMS
DOGMATISTS
DOGMATIZATION
DOGMATIZATIONS
DOGMATIZED
DOGMATIZER
DOGMATIZERS
DOGMATIZES
DOGMATIZING
DOGMATOLOGIES
DOGMATOLOGY
DOGNAPINGS
DOGNAPPERS
DOGNAPPING
DOGNAPPINGS
DOGROBBERS
DOGSBODIED
DOGSBODIES
DOGSBODYING
DOGSLEDDED
DOGSLEDDER
DOGSLEDDERS
DOGSLEDDING
DOGTROTTED
DOGTROTTING
DOGWATCHES
DOLABRIFORM
DOLCELATTE
DOLCELATTES
DOLCEMENTE
DOLEFULLER
DOLEFULLEST
DOLEFULNESS
DOLEFULNESSES
DOLESOMELY
DOLICHOCEPHAL
DOLICHOCEPHALIC
DOLICHOCEPHALS
DOLICHOCEPHALY
DOLICHOSAURUS
DOLICHOSAURUSES

DOLICHOSES
DOLICHURUS
DOLICHURUSES
DOLLARBIRD
DOLLARBIRDS
DOLLARFISH
DOLLARFISHES
DOLLARISATION
DOLLARISATIONS
DOLLARISED
DOLLARISES
DOLLARISING
DOLLARIZATION
DOLLARIZATIONS
DOLLARIZED
DOLLARIZES
DOLLARIZING
DOLLARLESS
DOLLAROCRACIES
DOLLAROCRACY
DOLLARSHIP
DOLLARSHIPS
DOLLHOUSES
DOLLINESSES
DOLLISHNESS
DOLLISHNESSES
DOLLYBIRDS
DOLOMITISATION
DOLOMITISATIONS
DOLOMITISE
DOLOMITISED
DOLOMITISES
DOLOMITISING
DOLOMITIZATION
DOLOMITIZATIONS
DOLOMITIZE
DOLOMITIZED
DOLOMITIZES
DOLOMITIZING
DOLORIFEROUS
DOLORIMETRIES
DOLORIMETRY
DOLOROUSLY
DOLOROUSNESS
DOLOROUSNESSES
DOLOSTONES
DOLPHINARIA

DOLPHINARIUM
DOLPHINARIUMS
DOLPHINETS
DOLPHINFISH
DOLPHINFISHES
DOLTISHNESS
DOLTISHNESSES
DOMESTICABLE
DOMESTICAL
DOMESTICALLY
DOMESTICATE
DOMESTICATED
DOMESTICATES
DOMESTICATING
DOMESTICATION
DOMESTICATIONS
DOMESTICATIVE
DOMESTICATOR
DOMESTICATORS
DOMESTICISE
DOMESTICISED
DOMESTICISES
DOMESTICISING
DOMESTICITIES
DOMESTICITY
DOMESTICIZE
DOMESTICIZED
DOMESTICIZES
DOMESTICIZING
DOMICILIARY
DOMICILIATE
DOMICILIATED
DOMICILIATES
DOMICILIATING
DOMICILIATION
DOMICILIATIONS
DOMICILING
DOMINANCES
DOMINANCIES
DOMINANTLY
DOMINATING
DOMINATINGLY
DOMINATION
DOMINATIONS
DOMINATIVE
DOMINATORS
DOMINATRICES

DOMINATRIX
DOMINATRIXES
DOMINEERED
DOMINEERING
DOMINEERINGLY
DOMINEERINGNESS
DOMINICKER
DOMINICKERS
DOMINIQUES
DONATARIES
DONATISTIC
DONATISTICAL
DONATORIES
DONENESSES
DONEPEZILS
DONKEYWORK
DONKEYWORKS
DONNICKERS
DONNISHNESS
DONNISHNESSES
DONNYBROOK
DONNYBROOKS
DONORSHIPS
DOODLEBUGS
DOOHICKEYS
DOOHICKIES
DOOMSAYERS
DOOMSAYING
DOOMSAYINGS
DOOMSDAYER
DOOMSDAYERS
DOOMWATCHED
DOOMWATCHER
DOOMWATCHERS
DOOMWATCHES
DOOMWATCHING
DOOMWATCHINGS
DOORFRAMES
DOORKEEPER
DOORKEEPERS
DOORKNOCKED
DOORKNOCKER
DOORKNOCKERS
DOORKNOCKING
DOORKNOCKS
DOORNBOOMS
DOORPLATES

DOORSTEPPED	DOTCOMMERS	DOVETAILINGS	DOWNSHIFTINGS	DRACONIANISM
DOORSTEPPER	DOTTINESSES	DOVISHNESS	DOWNSHIFTS	DRACONIANISMS
DOORSTEPPERS	DOUBLEHEADER	DOVISHNESSES	DOWNSIZERS	DRACONICALLY
DOORSTEPPING	DOUBLEHEADERS	DOWDINESSES	DOWNSIZING	DRACONISMS
DOORSTEPPINGS	DOUBLENESS	DOWELLINGS	DOWNSIZINGS	DRACONITES
DOORSTONES	DOUBLENESSES	DOWFNESSES	DOWNSLIDES	DRACONTIASES
DOPAMINERGIC	DOUBLESPEAK	DOWITCHERS	DOWNSPOUTS	DRACONTIASIS
DOPESHEETS	DOUBLESPEAKER	DOWNBURSTS	DOWNSTAGES	DRACUNCULUS
DOPEYNESSES	DOUBLESPEAKERS	DOWNCOMERS	DOWNSTAIRS	DRACUNCULUSES
DOPINESSES	DOUBLESPEAKS	DOWNDRAFTS	DOWNSTAIRSES	DRAFTINESS
DOPPELGANGER	DOUBLETHINK	DOWNDRAUGHT	DOWNSTATER	DRAFTINESSES
DOPPELGANGERS	DOUBLETHINKS	DOWNDRAUGHTS	DOWNSTATERS	DRAFTSMANSHIP
DOPPLERITE	DOUBLETONS	DOWNFALLEN	DOWNSTATES	DRAFTSMANSHIPS
DOPPLERITES	DOUBLETREE	DOWNFORCES	DOWNSTREAM	DRAFTSPERSON
DORBEETLES	DOUBLETREES	DOWNGRADED	DOWNSTROKE	DRAFTSPERSONS
DORKINESSES	DOUBTFULLY	DOWNGRADES	DOWNSTROKES	DRAGGINGLY
DORMANCIES	DOUBTFULNESS	DOWNGRADING	DOWNSWINGS	DRAGGLETAILED
DORMITIONS	DOUBTFULNESSES	DOWNHEARTED	DOWNTHROWS	DRAGHOUNDS
DORMITIVES	DOUBTINGLY	DOWNHEARTEDLY	DOWNTOWNER	DRAGONESSES
DORMITORIES	DOUBTLESSLY	DOWNHEARTEDNESS	DOWNTOWNERS	DRAGONFLIES
DORONICUMS	DOUBTLESSNESS	DOWNHILLER	DOWNTRENDED	DRAGONHEAD
DORSIBRANCHIATE	DOUBTLESSNESSES	DOWNHILLERS	DOWNTRENDING	DRAGONHEADS
DORSIFEROUS	DOUCENESSES	DOWNINESSES	DOWNTRENDS	DRAGONISED
DORSIFIXED	DOUCEPERES	DOWNLIGHTER	DOWNTRODDEN	DRAGONISES
DORSIFLEXION	DOUCHEBAGS	DOWNLIGHTERS	DOWNTURNED	DRAGONISING
DORSIFLEXIONS	DOUGHBALLS	DOWNLIGHTS	DOWNWARDLY	DRAGONISMS
DORSIGRADE	DOUGHFACED	DOWNLINKED	DOWNWARDNESS	DRAGONIZED
DORSIVENTRAL	DOUGHFACES	DOWNLINKING	DOWNWARDNESSES	DRAGONIZES
DORSIVENTRALITY	DOUGHINESS	DOWNLOADABLE	DOWNWASHES	DRAGONIZING
DORSIVENTRALLY	DOUGHINESSES	DOWNLOADED	DOWNZONING	DRAGONLIKE
DORSOLATERAL	DOUGHNUTLIKE	DOWNLOADING	DOXOGRAPHER	DRAGONNADE
DORSOLUMBAR	DOUGHNUTTED	DOWNLOOKED	DOXOGRAPHERS	DRAGONNADED
DORSOVENTRAL	DOUGHNUTTING	DOWNPLAYED	DOXOGRAPHIC	DRAGONNADES
DORSOVENTRALITY	DOUGHNUTTINGS	DOWNPLAYING	DOXOGRAPHIES	DRAGONNADING
DORSOVENTRALLY	DOUGHTIEST	DOWNREGULATION	DOXOGRAPHY	DRAGONROOT
DORTINESSES	DOUGHTINESS	DOWNREGULATIONS	DOXOLOGICAL	DRAGONROOTS
DOSEMETERS	DOUGHTINESSES	DOWNRIGHTLY	DOXOLOGICALLY	DRAGOONAGE
DOSIMETERS	DOULOCRACIES	DOWNRIGHTNESS	DOXOLOGIES	DRAGOONAGES
DOSIMETRIC	DOULOCRACY	DOWNRIGHTNESSES	DOXORUBICIN	DRAGOONING
DOSIMETRICIAN	DOUPPIONIS	DOWNRUSHES	DOXORUBICINS	DRAGSTRIPS
DOSIMETRICIANS	DOURNESSES	DOWNSCALED	DOXYCYCLINE	DRAINLAYER
DOSIMETRIES	DOUROUCOULI	DOWNSCALES	DOXYCYCLINES	DRAINLAYERS
DOSIMETRIST	DOUROUCOULIS	DOWNSCALING	DOZINESSES	DRAINPIPES
DOSIMETRISTS	DOVEISHNESS	DOWNSHIFTED	DRABBINESS	DRAKESTONE
DOSIOLOGIES	DOVEISHNESSES	DOWNSHIFTER	DRABBINESSES	DRAKESTONES
DOSOLOGIES	DOVETAILED	DOWNSHIFTERS	DRABBLINGS	DRAMATICAL
DOSSHOUSES	DOVETAILING	DOWNSHIFTING	DRABNESSES	DRAMATICALLY

DRAMATICISM
DRAMATICISMS
DRAMATISABLE
DRAMATISATION
DRAMATISATIONS
DRAMATISED
DRAMATISER
DRAMATISERS
DRAMATISES
DRAMATISING
DRAMATISTS
DRAMATIZABLE
DRAMATIZATION
DRAMATIZATIONS
DRAMATIZED
DRAMATIZER
DRAMATIZERS
DRAMATIZES
DRAMATIZING
DRAMATURGE
DRAMATURGES
DRAMATURGIC
DRAMATURGICAL
DRAMATURGICALLY
DRAMATURGIES
DRAMATURGIST
DRAMATURGISTS
DRAMATURGS
DRAMATURGY
DRAPABILITIES
DRAPABILITY
DRAPEABILITIES
DRAPEABILITY
DRAPERYING
DRASTICALLY
DRATCHELLS
DRAUGHTBOARD
DRAUGHTBOARDS
DRAUGHTERS
DRAUGHTIER
DRAUGHTIEST
DRAUGHTILY
DRAUGHTINESS
DRAUGHTINESSES
DRAUGHTING
DRAUGHTMAN
DRAUGHTMEN

DRAUGHTSMAN
DRAUGHTSMANSHIP
DRAUGHTSMEN
DRAUGHTSWOMAN
DRAUGHTSWOMEN
DRAWBRIDGE
DRAWBRIDGES
DRAWERFULS
DRAWKNIVES
DRAWLINGLY
DRAWLINGNESS
DRAWLINGNESSES
DRAWNWORKS
DRAWPLATES
DRAWSHAVES
DRAWSTRING
DRAWSTRINGS
DRAYHORSES
DREADFULLY
DREADFULNESS
DREADFULNESSES
DREADLESSLY
DREADLESSNESS
DREADLESSNESSES
DREADLOCKED
DREADLOCKS
DREADNAUGHT
DREADNAUGHTS
DREADNOUGHT
DREADNOUGHTS
DREAMBOATS
DREAMERIES
DREAMFULLY
DREAMFULNESS
DREAMFULNESSES
DREAMHOLES
DREAMINESS
DREAMINESSES
DREAMINGLY
DREAMLANDS
DREAMLESSLY
DREAMLESSNESS
DREAMLESSNESSES
DREAMTIMES
DREAMWHILE
DREAMWHILES
DREAMWORLD

DREAMWORLDS
DREARIHEAD
DREARIHEADS
DREARIHOOD
DREARIHOODS
DREARIMENT
DREARIMENTS
DREARINESS
DREARINESSES
DREARISOME
DRECKSILLS
DREGGINESS
DREGGINESSES
DREIKANTER
DREIKANTERS
DRENCHINGS
DREPANIUMS
DRERIHEADS
DRESSGUARD
DRESSGUARDS
DRESSINESS
DRESSINESSES
DRESSMAKER
DRESSMAKERS
DRESSMAKES
DRESSMAKING
DRESSMAKINGS
DRIBBLIEST
DRICKSIEST
DRIFTINGLY
DRIFTWOODS
DRILLABILITIES
DRILLABILITY
DRILLHOLES
DRILLMASTER
DRILLMASTERS
DRILLSHIPS
DRILLSTOCK
DRILLSTOCKS
DRINKABILITIES
DRINKABILITY
DRINKABLENESS
DRINKABLENESSES
DRINKABLES
DRIPSTONES
DRIVABILITIES
DRIVABILITY

DRIVEABILITIES
DRIVEABILITY
DRIVELINES
DRIVELLERS
DRIVELLING
DRIVENNESS
DRIVENNESSES
DRIVERLESS
DRIVESHAFT
DRIVESHAFTS
DRIVETHROUGH
DRIVETHROUGHS
DRIVETRAIN
DRIVETRAINS
DRIZZLIEST
DRIZZLINGLY
DROICHIEST
DROLLERIES
DROLLNESSES
DROMEDARES
DROMEDARIES
DROMOPHOBIA
DROMOPHOBIAS
DRONISHNESS
DRONISHNESSES
DRONKVERDRIET
DROOPINESS
DROOPINESSES
DROOPINGLY
DROPCLOTHS
DROPFORGED
DROPFORGES
DROPFORGING
DROPKICKER
DROPKICKERS
DROPLIGHTS
DROPPERFUL
DROPPERFULS
DROPPERSFUL
DROPSICALLY
DROPSONDES
DROPSTONES
DROSERACEOUS
DROSOMETER
DROSOMETERS
DROSOPHILA
DROSOPHILAE

DROSOPHILAS
DROSSINESS
DROSSINESSES
DROUGHTIER
DROUGHTIEST
DROUGHTINESS
DROUGHTINESSES
DROUTHIEST
DROUTHINESS
DROUTHINESSES
DROWSIHEAD
DROWSIHEADS
DROWSIHEDS
DROWSINESS
DROWSINESSES
DRUCKENNESS
DRUCKENNESSES
DRUDGERIES
DRUDGINGLY
DRUGMAKERS
DRUGSTORES
DRUIDESSES
DRUMBEATER
DRUMBEATERS
DRUMBEATING
DRUMBEATINGS
DRUMBLEDOR
DRUMBLEDORS
DRUMBLEDRANE
DRUMBLEDRANES
DRUMFISHES
DRUMSTICKS
DRUNKATHON
DRUNKATHONS
DRUNKENNESS
DRUNKENNESSES
DRUPACEOUS
DRYASDUSTS
DRYBEATING
DRYOPITHECINE
DRYOPITHECINES
DRYSALTERIES
DRYSALTERS
DRYSALTERY
DRYWALLING
DUALISTICALLY
DUBIOSITIES

DUBIOUSNESS	DUMBFOUNDING	DUODECIMALLY	DUSTCOVERS	DYNAMOTORS
DUBIOUSNESSES	DUMBFOUNDS	DUODECIMALS	DUSTINESSES	DYNASTICAL
DUBITANCIES	DUMBLEDORE	DUODECIMOS	DUSTSHEETS	DYNASTICALLY
DUBITATING	DUMBLEDORES	DUODENECTOMIES	DUSTSTORMS	DYNORPHINS
DUBITATION	DUMBNESSES	DUODENECTOMY	DUTEOUSNESS	DYOPHYSITE
DUBITATIONS	DUMBSTRICKEN	DUODENITIS	DUTEOUSNESSES	DYOPHYSITES
DUBITATIVE	DUMBSTRUCK	DUODENITISES	DUTIABILITIES	DYOTHELETE
DUBITATIVELY	DUMBWAITER	DUOPOLISTIC	DUTIABILITY	DYOTHELETES
DUCHESSING	DUMBWAITERS	DUOPSONIES	DUTIFULNESS	DYOTHELETIC
DUCKBOARDS	DUMFOUNDED	DUPABILITIES	DUTIFULNESSES	DYOTHELETICAL
DUCKSHOVED	DUMFOUNDER	DUPABILITY	DUUMVIRATE	DYOTHELETISM
DUCKSHOVER	DUMFOUNDERED	DUPLEXITIES	DUUMVIRATES	DYOTHELETISMS
DUCKSHOVERS	DUMFOUNDERING	DUPLICABILITIES	DWARFISHLY	DYOTHELISM
DUCKSHOVES	DUMFOUNDERS	DUPLICABILITY	DWARFISHNESS	DYOTHELISMS
DUCKSHOVING	DUMFOUNDING	DUPLICABLE	DWARFISHNESSES	DYOTHELITE
DUCKWALKED	DUMMELHEAD	DUPLICANDS	DWARFNESSES	DYOTHELITES
DUCKWALKING	DUMMELHEADS	DUPLICATED	DWINDLEMENT	DYOTHELITIC
DUCTILENESS	DUMMINESSES	DUPLICATELY	DWINDLEMENTS	DYOTHELITICAL
DUCTILENESSES	DUMORTIERITE	DUPLICATES	DYADICALLY	DYSAESTHESIA
DUCTILITIES	DUMORTIERITES	DUPLICATING	DYARCHICAL	DYSAESTHESIAS
DUENNASHIP	DUMOSITIES	DUPLICATION	DYEABILITIES	DYSAESTHETIC
DUENNASHIPS	DUMPINESSES	DUPLICATIONS	DYEABILITY	DYSARTHRIA
DUFFERDOMS	DUMPISHNESS	DUPLICATIVE	DYINGNESSES	DYSARTHRIAS
DUFFERISMS	DUMPISHNESSES	DUPLICATOR	DYNAMETERS	DYSBINDINS
DUIKERBOKS	DUMPTRUCKS	DUPLICATORS	DYNAMICALLY	DYSCALCULIA
DUKKERIPEN	DUNDERFUNK	DUPLICATURE	DYNAMICIST	DYSCALCULIAS
DUKKERIPENS	DUNDERFUNKS	DUPLICATURES	DYNAMICISTS	DYSCHROIAS
DULCAMARAS	DUNDERHEAD	DUPLICIDENT	DYNAMISING	DYSCRASIAS
DULCETNESS	DUNDERHEADED	DUPLICITIES	DYNAMISTIC	DYSCRASITE
DULCETNESSES	DUNDERHEADISM	DUPLICITOUS	DYNAMITARD	DYSCRASITES
DULCIFICATION	DUNDERHEADISMS	DUPLICITOUSLY	DYNAMITARDS	DYSENTERIC
DULCIFICATIONS	DUNDERHEADS	DURABILITIES	DYNAMITERS	DYSENTERIES
DULCIFLUOUS	DUNDERPATE	DURABILITY	DYNAMITING	DYSFUNCTION
DULCIFYING	DUNDERPATES	DURABLENESS	DYNAMIZING	DYSFUNCTIONAL
DULCILOQUIES	DUNDREARIES	DURABLENESSES	DYNAMOELECTRIC	DYSFUNCTIONS
DULCILOQUY	DUNGEONERS	DURALUMINIUM	DYNAMOGENESES	DYSGENESES
DULCIMORES	DUNGEONING	DURALUMINIUMS	DYNAMOGENESIS	DYSGENESIS
DULCITUDES	DUNIEWASSAL	DURALUMINS	DYNAMOGENIES	DYSGRAPHIA
DULLNESSES	DUNIEWASSALS	DURATIONAL	DYNAMOGENY	DYSGRAPHIAS
DULLSVILLE	DUNIWASSAL	DURCHKOMPONIERT	DYNAMOGRAPH	DYSGRAPHIC
DULLSVILLES	DUNIWASSALS	DURCHKOMPONIRT	DYNAMOGRAPHS	DYSHARMONIC
DULOCRACIES	DUNNIEWASSAL	DURICRUSTS	DYNAMOMETER	DYSKINESIA
DUMBFOUNDED	DUNNIEWASSALS	DUROMETERS	DYNAMOMETERS	DYSKINESIAS
DUMBFOUNDER	DUODECENNIAL	DUSKINESSES	DYNAMOMETRIC	DYSKINETIC
DUMBFOUNDERED	DUODECILLION	DUSKISHNESS	DYNAMOMETRICAL	DYSLECTICS
DUMBFOUNDERING	DUODECILLIONS	DUSKISHNESSES	DYNAMOMETRIES	DYSLOGISTIC
DUMBFOUNDERS	DUODECIMAL	DUSKNESSES	DYNAMOMETRY	DYSLOGISTICALLY

DYSMENORRHEA

DYSMENORRHEA	DYSPATHETIC	DYSPHEMISMS	DYSSYNERGIA	DYSTOPIANS
DYSMENORRHEAL	DYSPATHIES	DYSPHEMISTIC	DYSSYNERGIAS	DYSTROPHIA
DYSMENORRHEAS	DYSPEPSIAS	DYSPHONIAS	DYSTELEOLOGICAL	DYSTROPHIAS
DYSMENORRHEIC	DYSPEPSIES	DYSPHORIAS	DYSTELEOLOGIES	DYSTROPHIC
DYSMENORRHOEA	DYSPEPTICAL	DYSPLASIAS	DYSTELEOLOGIST	DYSTROPHIES
DYSMENORRHOEAL	DYSPEPTICALLY	DYSPLASTIC	DYSTELEOLOGISTS	DYSTROPHIN
DYSMENORRHOEAS	DYSPEPTICS	DYSPRAXIAS	DYSTELEOLOGY	DYSTROPHINS
DYSMENORRHOEIC	DYSPHAGIAS	DYSPROSIUM	DYSTHESIAS	DZIGGETAIS
DYSMORPHIC	DYSPHAGIES	DYSPROSIUMS	DYSTHYMIAC	
DYSMORPHOPHOBIA	DYSPHASIAS	DYSRHYTHMIA	DYSTHYMIACS	
DYSPAREUNIA	DYSPHASICS	DYSRHYTHMIAS	DYSTHYMIAS	
DYSPAREUNIAS	DYSPHEMISM	DYSRHYTHMIC	DYSTHYMICS	

E

EAGERNESSES	EARTHSHAKERS	EBOULEMENT	ECCLESIASTICAL	ECHOPRAXIS
EAGLEHAWKS	EARTHSHAKING	EBOULEMENTS	ECCLESIASTICISM	ECHOVIRUSES
EAGLESTONE	EARTHSHAKINGLY	EBRACTEATE	ECCLESIASTICS	ECLAIRCISSEMENT
EAGLESTONES	EARTHSHATTERING	EBRACTEOLATE	ECCLESIASTS	ECLAMPSIAS
EAGLEWOODS	EARTHSHINE	EBRILLADES	ECCLESIOLATER	ECLAMPSIES
EARBASHERS	EARTHSHINES	EBRIOSITIES	ECCLESIOLATERS	ECLECTICALLY
EARBASHING	EARTHSTARS	EBULLIENCE	ECCLESIOLATRIES	ECLECTICISM
EARBASHINGS	EARTHWARDS	EBULLIENCES	ECCLESIOLATRY	ECLECTICISMS
EARLIERISE	EARTHWAXES	EBULLIENCIES	ECCLESIOLOGICAL	ECLIPSISES
EARLIERISED	EARTHWOLVES	EBULLIENCY	ECCLESIOLOGIES	ECLIPTICALLY
EARLIERISES	EARTHWOMAN	EBULLIENTLY	ECCLESIOLOGIST	ECOCATASTROPHE
EARLIERISING	EARTHWOMEN	EBULLIOMETER	ECCLESIOLOGISTS	ECOCATASTROPHES
EARLIERIZE	EARTHWORKS	EBULLIOMETERS	ECCLESIOLOGY	ECOCENTRIC
EARLIERIZED	EARTHWORMS	EBULLIOMETRIES	ECCOPROTIC	ECOCLIMATE
EARLIERIZES	EARWIGGING	EBULLIOMETRY	ECCOPROTICS	ECOCLIMATES
EARLIERIZING	EARWIGGINGS	EBULLIOSCOPE	ECCREMOCARPUS	ECOFEMINISM
EARLINESSES	EARWITNESS	EBULLIOSCOPES	ECCREMOCARPUSES	ECOFEMINISMS
EARLYWOODS	EARWITNESSES	EBULLIOSCOPIC	ECCRINOLOGIES	ECOFEMINIST
EARMARKING	EASEFULNESS	EBULLIOSCOPICAL	ECCRINOLOGY	ECOFEMINISTS
EARNESTNESS	EASEFULNESSES	EBULLIOSCOPIES	ECDYSIASTS	ECOFRIENDLY
EARNESTNESSES	EASINESSES	EBULLIOSCOPY	ECHELONING	ECOLOGICAL
EARSPLITTING	EASSELGATE	EBULLITION	ECHEVERIAS	ECOLOGICALLY
EARTHBOUND	EASSELWARD	EBULLITIONS	ECHIDNINES	ECOLOGISTS
EARTHENWARE	EASTERLIES	EBURNATION	ECHINACEAS	ECOMMERCES
EARTHENWARES	EASTERLING	EBURNATIONS	ECHINOCOCCI	ECONOBOXES
EARTHFALLS	EASTERLINGS	EBURNIFICATION	ECHINOCOCCOSES	ECONOMETRIC
EARTHFLAXES	EASTERMOST	EBURNIFICATIONS	ECHINOCOCCOSIS	ECONOMETRICAL
EARTHINESS	EASTERNERS	ECARDINATE	ECHINOCOCCUS	ECONOMETRICALLY
EARTHINESSES	EASTERNMOST	ECBLASTESES	ECHINODERM	ECONOMETRICIAN
EARTHLIEST	EASTWARDLY	ECBLASTESIS	ECHINODERMAL	ECONOMETRICIANS
EARTHLIGHT	EASYGOINGNESS	ECCALEOBION	ECHINODERMATOUS	ECONOMETRICS
EARTHLIGHTS	EASYGOINGNESSES	ECCALEOBIONS	ECHINODERMS	ECONOMETRIST
EARTHLINESS	EAVESDRIPS	ECCENTRICAL	ECHIUROIDS	ECONOMETRISTS
EARTHLINESSES	EAVESDROPPED	ECCENTRICALLY	ECHOCARDIOGRAM	ECONOMICAL
EARTHLINGS	EAVESDROPPER	ECCENTRICITIES	ECHOCARDIOGRAMS	ECONOMICALLY
EARTHMOVER	EAVESDROPPERS	ECCENTRICITY	ECHOGRAPHIES	ECONOMISATION
EARTHMOVERS	EAVESDROPPING	ECCENTRICS	ECHOGRAPHS	ECONOMISATIONS
EARTHMOVING	EAVESDROPPINGS	ECCHYMOSED	ECHOGRAPHY	ECONOMISED
EARTHMOVINGS	EAVESDROPS	ECCHYMOSES	ECHOICALLY	ECONOMISER
EARTHQUAKE	EAVESTROUGH	ECCHYMOSIS	ECHOLALIAS	ECONOMISERS
EARTHQUAKED	EAVESTROUGHS	ECCHYMOTIC	ECHOLOCATION	ECONOMISES
EARTHQUAKES	EBIONISING	ECCLESIARCH	ECHOLOCATIONS	ECONOMISING
EARTHQUAKING	EBIONITISM	ECCLESIARCHS	ECHOPRAXES	ECONOMISMS
EARTHRISES	EBIONITISMS	ECCLESIAST	ECHOPRAXIA	ECONOMISTIC
EARTHSHAKER	EBIONIZING	ECCLESIASTIC	ECHOPRAXIAS	ECONOMISTS

ECONOMIZATION	ECTOBLASTS	ECUMENISMS	EDUCATABLE	EFFECTUATION
ECONOMIZATIONS	ECTOCRINES	ECUMENISTS	EDUCATEDNESS	EFFECTUATIONS
ECONOMIZED	ECTODERMAL	ECZEMATOUS	EDUCATEDNESSES	EFFEMINACIES
ECONOMIZER	ECTODERMIC	EDACIOUSLY	EDUCATIONAL	EFFEMINACY
ECONOMIZERS	ECTOENZYME	EDACIOUSNESS	EDUCATIONALIST	EFFEMINATE
ECONOMIZES	ECTOENZYMES	EDACIOUSNESSES	EDUCATIONALISTS	EFFEMINATED
ECONOMIZING	ECTOGENESES	EDAPHICALLY	EDUCATIONALLY	EFFEMINATELY
ECOPHOBIAS	ECTOGENESIS	EDAPHOLOGIES	EDUCATIONESE	EFFEMINATENESS
ECOPHYSIOLOGIES	ECTOGENETIC	EDAPHOLOGY	EDUCATIONESES	EFFEMINATES
ECOPHYSIOLOGY	ECTOGENICALLY	EDELWEISSES	EDUCATIONIST	EFFEMINATING
ECOREGIONS	ECTOGENIES	EDENTULATE	EDUCATIONISTS	EFFEMINISE
ECOSPECIES	ECTOGENOUS	EDENTULOUS	EDUCATIONS	EFFEMINISED
ECOSPECIFIC	ECTOMORPHIC	EDGINESSES	EDUCEMENTS	EFFEMINISES
ECOSPHERES	ECTOMORPHIES	EDIBILITIES	EDULCORANT	EFFEMINISING
ECOSSAISES	ECTOMORPHS	EDIBLENESS	EDULCORATE	EFFEMINIZE
ECOSYSTEMS	ECTOMORPHY	EDIBLENESSES	EDULCORATED	EFFEMINIZED
ECOTARIANS	ECTOMYCORRHIZA	EDIFICATION	EDULCORATES	EFFEMINIZES
ECOTECTURE	ECTOMYCORRHIZAE	EDIFICATIONS	EDULCORATING	EFFEMINIZING
ECOTECTURES	ECTOMYCORRHIZAS	EDIFICATORY	EDULCORATION	EFFERENCES
ECOTERRORISM	ECTOPARASITE	EDIFYINGLY	EDULCORATIONS	EFFERENTLY
ECOTERRORISMS	ECTOPARASITES	EDITIONING	EDULCORATIVE	EFFERVESCE
ECOTERRORIST	ECTOPARASITIC	EDITORIALISE	EDULCORATOR	EFFERVESCED
ECOTERRORISTS	ECTOPHYTES	EDITORIALISED	EDULCORATORS	EFFERVESCENCE
ECOTOURISM	ECTOPHYTIC	EDITORIALISER	EDUTAINMENT	EFFERVESCENCES
ECOTOURISMS	ECTOPICALLY	EDITORIALISERS	EDUTAINMENTS	EFFERVESCENCIES
ECOTOURIST	ECTOPLASMIC	EDITORIALISES	EELGRASSES	EFFERVESCENCY
ECOTOURISTS	ECTOPLASMS	EDITORIALISING	EERINESSES	EFFERVESCENT
ECOTOXICOLOGIES	ECTOPLASTIC	EDITORIALIST	EFFACEABLE	EFFERVESCENTLY
ECOTOXICOLOGIST	ECTOPROCTS	EDITORIALISTS	EFFACEMENT	EFFERVESCES
ECOTOXICOLOGY	ECTOSARCOUS	EDITORIALIZE	EFFACEMENTS	EFFERVESCIBLE
ECOTYPICALLY	ECTOTHERMIC	EDITORIALIZED	EFFECTIBLE	EFFERVESCING
ECPHONESES	ECTOTHERMS	EDITORIALIZER	EFFECTIVELY	EFFERVESCINGLY
ECPHONESIS	ECTOTROPHIC	EDITORIALIZERS	EFFECTIVENESS	EFFETENESS
ECPHRACTIC	ECTROPIONS	EDITORIALIZES	EFFECTIVENESSES	EFFETENESSES
ECPHRACTICS	ECTROPIUMS	EDITORIALIZING	EFFECTIVES	EFFICACIES
ECRITOIRES	ECTYPOGRAPHIES	EDITORIALLY	EFFECTIVITIES	EFFICACIOUS
ECSTASISED	ECTYPOGRAPHY	EDITORIALS	EFFECTIVITY	EFFICACIOUSLY
ECSTASISES	ECUMENICAL	EDITORSHIP	EFFECTLESS	EFFICACIOUSNESS
ECSTASISING	ECUMENICALISM	EDITORSHIPS	EFFECTUALITIES	EFFICACITIES
ECSTASIZED	ECUMENICALISMS	EDITRESSES	EFFECTUALITY	EFFICACITY
ECSTASIZES	ECUMENICALLY	EDRIOPHTHALMIAN	EFFECTUALLY	EFFICIENCE
ECSTASIZING	ECUMENICISM	EDRIOPHTHALMIC	EFFECTUALNESS	EFFICIENCES
ECSTASYING	ECUMENICISMS	EDRIOPHTHALMOUS	EFFECTUALNESSES	EFFICIENCIES
ECSTATICALLY	ECUMENICIST	EDUCABILITIES	EFFECTUATE	EFFICIENCY
ECTHLIPSES	ECUMENICISTS	EDUCABILITY	EFFECTUATED	EFFICIENTLY
ECTHLIPSIS	ECUMENICITIES	EDUCATABILITIES	EFFECTUATES	EFFICIENTS
ECTOBLASTIC	ECUMENICITY	EDUCATABILITY	EFFECTUATING	EFFIERCING

E

EFFIGURATE	EGOCENTRICITY	EIGHTSCORES	ELASTICATE	ELECTORALLY
EFFIGURATION	EGOCENTRICS	EIGHTSOMES	ELASTICATED	ELECTORATE
EFFIGURATIONS	EGOCENTRISM	EINSTEINIUM	ELASTICATES	ELECTORATES
EFFLEURAGE	EGOCENTRISMS	EINSTEINIUMS	ELASTICATING	ELECTORESS
EFFLEURAGED	EGOISTICAL	EIRENICALLY	ELASTICATION	ELECTORESSES
EFFLEURAGES	EGOISTICALLY	EIRENICONS	ELASTICATIONS	ELECTORIAL
EFFLEURAGING	EGOMANIACAL	EISTEDDFOD	ELASTICISE	ELECTORIALLY
EFFLORESCE	EGOMANIACALLY	EISTEDDFODAU	ELASTICISED	ELECTORSHIP
EFFLORESCED	EGOMANIACS	EISTEDDFODIC	ELASTICISES	ELECTORSHIPS
EFFLORESCENCE	EGOTHEISMS	EISTEDDFODS	ELASTICISING	ELECTRESSES
EFFLORESCENCES	EGOTISTICAL	EJACULATED	ELASTICITIES	ELECTRICAL
EFFLORESCENT	EGOTISTICALLY	EJACULATES	ELASTICITY	ELECTRICALLY
EFFLORESCES	EGREGIOUSLY	EJACULATING	ELASTICIZE	ELECTRICALS
EFFLORESCING	EGREGIOUSNESS	EJACULATION	ELASTICIZED	ELECTRICIAN
EFFLUENCES	EGREGIOUSNESSES	EJACULATIONS	ELASTICIZES	ELECTRICIANS
EFFLUVIUMS	EGRESSIONS	EJACULATIVE	ELASTICIZING	ELECTRICITIES
EFFLUXIONS	EGRESSIVES	EJACULATOR	ELASTICNESS	ELECTRICITY
EFFORTFULLY	EGURGITATE	EJACULATORS	ELASTICNESSES	ELECTRIFIABLE
EFFORTFULNESS	EGURGITATED	EJACULATORY	ELASTOMERIC	ELECTRIFICATION
EFFORTFULNESSES	EGURGITATES	EJECTAMENTA	ELASTOMERS	ELECTRIFIED
EFFORTLESS	EGURGITATING	EJECTIVELY	ELATEDNESS	ELECTRIFIER
EFFORTLESSLY	EICOSANOID	EJECTMENTS	ELATEDNESSES	ELECTRIFIERS
EFFORTLESSNESS	EICOSANOIDS	EKISTICIAN	ELATERITES	ELECTRIFIES
EFFRONTERIES	EIDERDOWNS	EKISTICIANS	ELATERIUMS	ELECTRIFYING
EFFRONTERY	EIDETICALLY	ELABORATED	ELBOWROOMS	ELECTRIFYINGLY
EFFULGENCE	EIDOGRAPHS	ELABORATELY	ELDERBERRIES	ELECTRISATION
EFFULGENCES	EIGENFREQUENCY	ELABORATENESS	ELDERBERRY	ELECTRISATIONS
EFFULGENTLY	EIGENFUNCTION	ELABORATENESSES	ELDERCARES	ELECTRISED
EFFUSIOMETER	EIGENFUNCTIONS	ELABORATES	ELDERLINESS	ELECTRISES
EFFUSIOMETERS	EIGENMODES	ELABORATING	ELDERLINESSES	ELECTRISING
EFFUSIVELY	EIGENTONES	ELABORATION	ELDERSHIPS	ELECTRIZATION
EFFUSIVENESS	EIGENVALUE	ELABORATIONS	ELECAMPANE	ELECTRIZATIONS
EFFUSIVENESSES	EIGENVALUES	ELABORATIVE	ELECAMPANES	ELECTRIZED
EGALITARIAN	EIGENVECTOR	ELABORATOR	ELECTABILITIES	ELECTRIZES
EGALITARIANISM	EIGENVECTORS	ELABORATORIES	ELECTABILITY	ELECTRIZING
EGALITARIANISMS	EIGHTBALLS	ELABORATORS	ELECTIONEER	ELECTROACOUSTIC
EGALITARIANS	EIGHTEENMO	ELABORATORY	ELECTIONEERED	ELECTROACTIVE
EGAREMENTS	EIGHTEENMOS	ELAEOLITES	ELECTIONEERER	ELECTROACTIVITY
EGGBEATERS	EIGHTEENTH	ELAEOPTENE	ELECTIONEERERS	ELECTROANALYSES
EGGHEADEDNESS	EIGHTEENTHLY	ELAEOPTENES	ELECTIONEERING	ELECTROANALYSIS
EGGHEADEDNESSES	EIGHTEENTHS	ELAIOSOMES	ELECTIONEERINGS	ELECTROANALYTIC
EGLANDULAR	EIGHTFOILS	ELASMOBRANCH	ELECTIONEERS	ELECTROBIOLOGY
EGLANDULOSE	EIGHTIETHS	ELASMOBRANCHS	ELECTIVELY	ELECTROCAUTERY
EGLANTINES	EIGHTPENCE	ELASMOSAUR	ELECTIVENESS	ELECTROCEMENT
EGOCENTRIC	EIGHTPENCES	ELASMOSAURS	ELECTIVENESSES	ELECTROCEMENTS
EGOCENTRICALLY	EIGHTPENNY	ELASTANCES	ELECTIVITIES	ELECTROCHEMIC
EGOCENTRICITIES	EIGHTSCORE	ELASTICALLY	ELECTIVITY	ELECTROCHEMICAL

E

ELECTROCHEMIST	ELECTROJET	ELECTROMOTOR	ELECTROSONDES	ELEMENTARY
ELECTROCHEMISTS	ELECTROJETS	ELECTROMOTORS	ELECTROSTATIC	ELEOPTENES
ELECTROCLASH	ELECTROKINETIC	ELECTROMYOGRAM	ELECTROSTATICS	ELEPHANTIASES
ELECTROCLASHES	ELECTROKINETICS	ELECTROMYOGRAMS	ELECTROSURGERY	ELEPHANTIASIC
ELECTROCULTURE	ELECTROLESS	ELECTROMYOGRAPH	ELECTROSURGICAL	ELEPHANTIASIS
ELECTROCULTURES	ELECTROLIER	ELECTRONEGATIVE	ELECTROTECHNICS	ELEPHANTINE
ELECTROCUTE	ELECTROLIERS	ELECTRONIC	ELECTROTHERAPY	ELEPHANTOID
ELECTROCUTED	ELECTROLOGIES	ELECTRONICA	ELECTROTHERMAL	ELEUTHERARCH
ELECTROCUTES	ELECTROLOGIST	ELECTRONICALLY	ELECTROTHERMIC	ELEUTHERARCHS
ELECTROCUTING	ELECTROLOGISTS	ELECTRONICAS	ELECTROTHERMICS	ELEUTHERIAN
ELECTROCUTION	ELECTROLOGY	ELECTRONICS	ELECTROTHERMIES	ELEUTHEROCOCCI
ELECTROCUTIONS	ELECTROLYSATION	ELECTRONVOLT	ELECTROTHERMY	ELEUTHEROCOCCUS
ELECTROCYTE	ELECTROLYSE	ELECTRONVOLTS	ELECTROTINT	ELEUTHERODACTYL
ELECTROCYTES	ELECTROLYSED	ELECTROOSMOSES	ELECTROTINTS	ELEUTHEROMANIA
ELECTRODEPOSIT	ELECTROLYSER	ELECTROOSMOSIS	ELECTROTONIC	ELEUTHEROMANIAS
ELECTRODEPOSITS	ELECTROLYSERS	ELECTROOSMOTIC	ELECTROTONUS	ELEUTHEROPHOBIA
ELECTRODERMAL	ELECTROLYSES	ELECTROPHILE	ELECTROTONUSES	ELEUTHEROPHOBIC
ELECTRODES	ELECTROLYSING	ELECTROPHILES	ELECTROTYPE	ELEVATIONAL
ELECTRODIALYSES	ELECTROLYSIS	ELECTROPHILIC	ELECTROTYPED	ELEVATIONS
ELECTRODIALYSIS	ELECTROLYTE	ELECTROPHONE	ELECTROTYPER	ELEVENTHLY
ELECTRODIALYTIC	ELECTROLYTES	ELECTROPHONES	ELECTROTYPERS	ELFISHNESS
ELECTRODYNAMIC	ELECTROLYTIC	ELECTROPHONIC	ELECTROTYPES	ELFISHNESSES
ELECTRODYNAMICS	ELECTROLYTICS	ELECTROPHORESE	ELECTROTYPIC	ELICITABLE
ELECTROFISHING	ELECTROLYZATION	ELECTROPHORESED	ELECTROTYPIES	ELICITATION
ELECTROFISHINGS	ELECTROLYZE	ELECTROPHORESES	ELECTROTYPING	ELICITATIONS
ELECTROFLUOR	ELECTROLYZED	ELECTROPHORESIS	ELECTROTYPIST	ELIGIBILITIES
ELECTROFLUORS	ELECTROLYZER	ELECTROPHORETIC	ELECTROTYPISTS	ELIGIBILITY
ELECTROFORM	ELECTROLYZERS	ELECTROPHORI	ELECTROTYPY	ELIMINABILITIES
ELECTROFORMED	ELECTROLYZES	ELECTROPHORUS	ELECTROVALENCE	ELIMINABILITY
ELECTROFORMING	ELECTROLYZING	ELECTROPHORUSES	ELECTROVALENCES	ELIMINABLE
ELECTROFORMINGS	ELECTROMAGNET	ELECTROPLATE	ELECTROVALENCY	ELIMINANTS
ELECTROFORMS	ELECTROMAGNETIC	ELECTROPLATED	ELECTROVALENT	ELIMINATED
ELECTROGEN	ELECTROMAGNETS	ELECTROPLATER	ELECTROVALENTLY	ELIMINATES
ELECTROGENESES	ELECTROMER	ELECTROPLATERS	ELECTROWEAK	ELIMINATING
ELECTROGENESIS	ELECTROMERIC	ELECTROPLATES	ELECTROWINNING	ELIMINATION
ELECTROGENIC	ELECTROMERISM	ELECTROPLATING	ELECTROWINNINGS	ELIMINATIONS
ELECTROGENS	ELECTROMERISMS	ELECTROPLATINGS	ELECTUARIES	ELIMINATIVE
ELECTROGILDING	ELECTROMERS	ELECTROPOLAR	ELEDOISINS	ELIMINATOR
ELECTROGILDINGS	ELECTROMETER	ELECTROPOSITIVE	ELEEMOSYNARY	ELIMINATORS
ELECTROGRAM	ELECTROMETERS	ELECTRORECEPTOR	ELEGANCIES	ELIMINATORY
ELECTROGRAMS	ELECTROMETRIC	ELECTRORHEOLOGY	ELEGIACALLY	ELLIPSOGRAPH
ELECTROGRAPH	ELECTROMETRICAL	ELECTROSCOPE	ELEMENTALISM	ELLIPSOGRAPHS
ELECTROGRAPHIC	ELECTROMETRIES	ELECTROSCOPES	ELEMENTALISMS	ELLIPSOIDAL
ELECTROGRAPHIES	ELECTROMETRY	ELECTROSCOPIC	ELEMENTALLY	ELLIPSOIDS
ELECTROGRAPHS	ELECTROMOTANCE	ELECTROSHOCK	ELEMENTALS	ELLIPTICAL
ELECTROGRAPHY	ELECTROMOTANCES	ELECTROSHOCKS	ELEMENTARILY	ELLIPTICALLY
ELECTROING	ELECTROMOTIVE	ELECTROSONDE	ELEMENTARINESS	ELLIPTICALNESS

ELLIPTICALS	ELVISHNESSES	EMBARCADEROS	EMBITTERINGS	EMBOLISING
ELLIPTICITIES	ELYTRIFORM	EMBARCATION	EMBITTERMENT	EMBOLISMAL
ELLIPTICITY	ELYTRIGEROUS	EMBARCATIONS	EMBITTERMENTS	EMBOLISMIC
ELOCUTIONARY	EMACIATING	EMBARGOING	EMBLAZONED	EMBOLIZATION
ELOCUTIONIST	EMACIATION	EMBARKATION	EMBLAZONER	EMBOLIZATIONS
ELOCUTIONISTS	EMACIATIONS	EMBARKATIONS	EMBLAZONERS	EMBOLIZING
ELOCUTIONS	EMALANGENI	EMBARKMENT	EMBLAZONING	EMBONPOINT
ELOIGNMENT	EMANATIONAL	EMBARKMENTS	EMBLAZONMENT	EMBONPOINTS
ELOIGNMENTS	EMANATIONS	EMBARQUEMENT	EMBLAZONMENTS	EMBORDERED
ELOINMENTS	EMANATISTS	EMBARQUEMENTS	EMBLAZONRIES	EMBORDERING
ELONGATING	EMANCIPATE	EMBARRASSABLE	EMBLAZONRY	EMBOSCATAS
ELONGATION	EMANCIPATED	EMBARRASSED	EMBLEMATIC	EMBOSOMING
ELONGATIONS	EMANCIPATES	EMBARRASSEDLY	EMBLEMATICAL	EMBOSSABLE
ELOPEMENTS	EMANCIPATING	EMBARRASSES	EMBLEMATICALLY	EMBOSSMENT
ELOQUENCES	EMANCIPATION	EMBARRASSING	EMBLEMATISE	EMBOSSMENTS
ELOQUENTLY	EMANCIPATIONIST	EMBARRASSINGLY	EMBLEMATISED	EMBOTHRIUM
ELSEWHITHER	EMANCIPATIONS	EMBARRASSMENT	EMBLEMATISES	EMBOTHRIUMS
ELUCIDATED	EMANCIPATIVE	EMBARRASSMENTS	EMBLEMATISING	EMBOUCHURE
ELUCIDATES	EMANCIPATOR	EMBARRINGS	EMBLEMATIST	EMBOUCHURES
ELUCIDATING	EMANCIPATORS	EMBASEMENT	EMBLEMATISTS	EMBOUNDING
ELUCIDATION	EMANCIPATORY	EMBASEMENTS	EMBLEMATIZE	EMBOURGEOISE
ELUCIDATIONS	EMANCIPIST	EMBASSADES	EMBLEMATIZED	EMBOURGEOISED
ELUCIDATIVE	EMANCIPISTS	EMBASSADOR	EMBLEMATIZES	EMBOURGEOISES
ELUCIDATOR	EMARGINATE	EMBASSADORS	EMBLEMATIZING	EMBOURGEOISING
ELUCIDATORS	EMARGINATED	EMBASSAGES	EMBLEMENTS	EMBOWELING
ELUCIDATORY	EMARGINATELY	EMBATTLEMENT	EMBLEMISED	EMBOWELLED
ELUCUBRATE	EMARGINATES	EMBATTLEMENTS	EMBLEMISES	EMBOWELLING
ELUCUBRATED	EMARGINATING	EMBATTLING	EMBLEMISING	EMBOWELMENT
ELUCUBRATES	EMARGINATION	EMBAYMENTS	EMBLEMIZED	EMBOWELMENTS
ELUCUBRATING	EMARGINATIONS	EMBEDDINGS	EMBLEMIZES	EMBOWERING
ELUCUBRATION	EMASCULATE	EMBEDMENTS	EMBLEMIZING	EMBOWERMENT
ELUCUBRATIONS	EMASCULATED	EMBELLISHED	EMBLOOMING	EMBOWERMENTS
ELUSIVENESS	EMASCULATES	EMBELLISHER	EMBLOSSOMED	EMBOWMENTS
ELUSIVENESSES	EMASCULATING	EMBELLISHERS	EMBLOSSOMING	EMBRACEABLE
ELUSORINESS	EMASCULATION	EMBELLISHES	EMBLOSSOMS	EMBRACEMENT
ELUSORINESSES	EMASCULATIONS	EMBELLISHING	EMBODIMENT	EMBRACEMENTS
ELUTRIATED	EMASCULATIVE	EMBELLISHINGLY	EMBODIMENTS	EMBRACEORS
ELUTRIATES	EMASCULATOR	EMBELLISHMENT	EMBOITEMENT	EMBRACERIES
ELUTRIATING	EMASCULATORS	EMBELLISHMENTS	EMBOITEMENTS	EMBRACINGLY
ELUTRIATION	EMASCULATORY	EMBEZZLEMENT	EMBOLDENED	EMBRACINGNESS
ELUTRIATIONS	EMBALLINGS	EMBEZZLEMENTS	EMBOLDENER	EMBRACINGNESSES
ELUTRIATOR	EMBALMINGS	EMBEZZLERS	EMBOLDENERS	EMBRAIDING
ELUTRIATORS	EMBALMMENT	EMBEZZLING	EMBOLDENING	EMBRANCHMENT
ELUVIATING	EMBALMMENTS	EMBITTERED	EMBOLECTOMIES	EMBRANCHMENTS
ELUVIATION	EMBANKMENT	EMBITTERER	EMBOLECTOMY	EMBRANGLED
ELUVIATIONS	EMBANKMENTS	EMBITTERERS	EMBOLISATION	EMBRANGLEMENT
ELVISHNESS	EMBARCADERO	EMBITTERING	EMBOLISATIONS	EMBRANGLEMENTS

EMBRANGLES	EMBRYOLOGISTS	EMOLLESCENCE	EMPANOPLIES	EMPHYTEUSES
EMBRANGLING	EMBRYOLOGY	EMOLLESCENCES	EMPANOPLYING	EMPHYTEUSIS
EMBRASURED	EMBRYONATE	EMOLLIATED	EMPARADISE	EMPHYTEUTIC
EMBRASURES	EMBRYONATED	EMOLLIATES	EMPARADISED	EMPIECEMENT
EMBRAZURES	EMBRYONICALLY	EMOLLIATING	EMPARADISES	EMPIECEMENTS
EMBREADING	EMBRYOPHYTE	EMOLLIENCE	EMPARADISING	EMPIERCING
EMBREATHED	EMBRYOPHYTES	EMOLLIENCES	EMPARLAUNCE	EMPIRICALLY
EMBREATHES	EMBRYOTICALLY	EMOLLIENTS	EMPARLAUNCES	EMPIRICALNESS
EMBREATHING	EMBRYOTOMIES	EMOLLITION	EMPASSIONATE	EMPIRICALNESSES
EMBRITTLED	EMBRYOTOMY	EMOLLITIONS	EMPASSIONED	EMPIRICALS
EMBRITTLEMENT	EMBRYULCIA	EMOLUMENTAL	EMPATHETIC	EMPIRICISM
EMBRITTLEMENTS	EMBRYULCIAS	EMOLUMENTARY	EMPATHETICALLY	EMPIRICISMS
EMBRITTLES	EMENDATING	EMOLUMENTS	EMPATHICALLY	EMPIRICIST
EMBRITTLING	EMENDATION	EMOTIONABLE	EMPATHISED	EMPIRICISTS
EMBROCATED	EMENDATIONS	EMOTIONALISE	EMPATHISES	EMPIRICUTIC
EMBROCATES	EMENDATORS	EMOTIONALISED	EMPATHISING	EMPLACEMENT
EMBROCATING	EMENDATORY	EMOTIONALISES	EMPATHISTS	EMPLACEMENTS
EMBROCATION	EMERGENCES	EMOTIONALISING	EMPATHIZED	EMPLASTERED
EMBROCATIONS	EMERGENCIES	EMOTIONALISM	EMPATHIZES	EMPLASTERING
EMBROGLIOS	EMERGENTLY	EMOTIONALISMS	EMPATHIZING	EMPLASTERS
EMBROIDERED	EMETICALLY	EMOTIONALIST	EMPATRONED	EMPLASTICS
EMBROIDERER	EMETOPHOBIA	EMOTIONALISTIC	EMPATRONING	EMPLASTRON
EMBROIDERERS	EMETOPHOBIAS	EMOTIONALISTS	EMPEACHING	EMPLASTRONS
EMBROIDERIES	EMICATIONS	EMOTIONALITIES	EMPENNAGES	EMPLASTRUM
EMBROIDERING	EMIGRATING	EMOTIONALITY	EMPEOPLING	EMPLASTRUMS
EMBROIDERS	EMIGRATION	EMOTIONALIZE	EMPERISHED	EMPLEACHED
EMBROIDERY	EMIGRATIONAL	EMOTIONALIZED	EMPERISHES	EMPLEACHES
EMBROILERS	EMIGRATIONIST	EMOTIONALIZES	EMPERISHING	EMPLEACHING
EMBROILING	EMIGRATIONISTS	EMOTIONALIZING	EMPERISING	EMPLECTONS
EMBROILMENT	EMIGRATIONS	EMOTIONALLY	EMPERIZING	EMPLECTUMS
EMBROILMENTS	EMIGRATORY	EMOTIONLESS	EMPERORSHIP	EMPLONGING
EMBROWNING	EMINENCIES	EMOTIONLESSLY	EMPERORSHIPS	EMPLOYABILITIES
EMBRUEMENT	EMINENTIAL	EMOTIONLESSNESS	EMPHASISED	EMPLOYABILITY
EMBRUEMENTS	EMISSARIES	EMOTIVENESS	EMPHASISES	EMPLOYABLE
EMBRYECTOMIES	EMISSIVITIES	EMOTIVENESSES	EMPHASISING	EMPLOYABLES
EMBRYECTOMY	EMISSIVITY	EMOTIVISMS	EMPHASIZED	EMPLOYMENT
EMBRYOGENESES	EMITTANCES	EMOTIVITIES	EMPHASIZES	EMPLOYMENTS
EMBRYOGENESIS	EMMARBLING	EMPACKETED	EMPHASIZING	EMPOISONED
EMBRYOGENETIC	EMMENAGOGIC	EMPACKETING	EMPHATICAL	EMPOISONING
EMBRYOGENIC	EMMENAGOGUE	EMPALEMENT	EMPHATICALLY	EMPOISONMENT
EMBRYOGENIES	EMMENAGOGUES	EMPALEMENTS	EMPHATICALNESS	EMPOISONMENTS
EMBRYOGENY	EMMENOLOGIES	EMPANELING	EMPHRACTIC	EMPOLDERED
EMBRYOLOGIC	EMMENOLOGY	EMPANELLED	EMPHRACTICS	EMPOLDERING
EMBRYOLOGICAL	EMMETROPES	EMPANELLING	EMPHYSEMAS	EMPOVERISH
EMBRYOLOGICALLY	EMMETROPIA	EMPANELMENT	EMPHYSEMATOUS	EMPOVERISHED
EMBRYOLOGIES	EMMETROPIAS	EMPANELMENTS	EMPHYSEMIC	EMPOVERISHER
EMBRYOLOGIST	EMMETROPIC	EMPANOPLIED	EMPHYSEMICS	EMPOVERISHERS

EMPOVERISHES	EMUNCTORIES	ENCAMPMENTS	ENCEPHALOID	ENCIRCLING
EMPOVERISHING	ENABLEMENT	ENCANTHISES	ENCEPHALOMA	ENCLASPING
EMPOVERISHMENT	ENABLEMENTS	ENCAPSULATE	ENCEPHALOMAS	ENCLITICALLY
EMPOVERISHMENTS	ENACTMENTS	ENCAPSULATED	ENCEPHALOMATA	ENCLOISTER
EMPOWERING	ENALAPRILS	ENCAPSULATES	ENCEPHALON	ENCLOISTERED
EMPOWERMENT	ENAMELISTS	ENCAPSULATING	ENCEPHALONS	ENCLOISTERING
EMPOWERMENTS	ENAMELLERS	ENCAPSULATION	ENCEPHALOPATHIC	ENCLOISTERS
EMPRESSEMENT	ENAMELLING	ENCAPSULATIONS	ENCEPHALOPATHY	ENCLOSABLE
EMPRESSEMENTS	ENAMELLINGS	ENCAPSULED	ENCEPHALOTOMIES	ENCLOSURES
EMPTINESSES	ENAMELLIST	ENCAPSULES	ENCEPHALOTOMY	ENCLOTHING
EMPURPLING	ENAMELLISTS	ENCAPSULING	ENCEPHALOUS	ENCLOUDING
EMPYREUMATA	ENAMELWARE	ENCARNALISE	ENCHAINING	ENCODEMENT
EMPYREUMATIC	ENAMELWARES	ENCARNALISED	ENCHAINMENT	ENCODEMENTS
EMPYREUMATICAL	ENAMELWORK	ENCARNALISES	ENCHAINMENTS	ENCOIGNURE
EMPYREUMATISE	ENAMELWORKS	ENCARNALISING	ENCHANTERS	ENCOIGNURES
EMPYREUMATISED	ENAMORADOS	ENCARNALIZE	ENCHANTING	ENCOLOURED
EMPYREUMATISES	ENAMOURING	ENCARNALIZED	ENCHANTINGLY	ENCOLOURING
EMPYREUMATISING	ENANTHEMAS	ENCARNALIZES	ENCHANTMENT	ENCOLPIONS
EMPYREUMATIZE	ENANTIODROMIA	ENCARNALIZING	ENCHANTMENTS	ENCOLPIUMS
EMPYREUMATIZED	ENANTIODROMIAS	ENCARPUSES	ENCHANTRESS	ENCOMENDERO
EMPYREUMATIZES	ENANTIODROMIC	ENCASEMENT	ENCHANTRESSES	ENCOMENDEROS
EMPYREUMATIZING	ENANTIOMER	ENCASEMENTS	ENCHARGING	ENCOMIASTIC
EMULATIONS	ENANTIOMERIC	ENCASHABLE	ENCHARMING	ENCOMIASTICAL
EMULATIVELY	ENANTIOMERS	ENCASHMENT	ENCHEASONS	ENCOMIASTICALLY
EMULATRESS	ENANTIOMORPH	ENCASHMENTS	ENCHEERING	ENCOMIASTS
EMULATRESSES	ENANTIOMORPHIC	ENCAUSTICALLY	ENCHEIRIDION	ENCOMIENDA
EMULGENCES	ENANTIOMORPHIES	ENCAUSTICS	ENCHEIRIDIONS	ENCOMIENDAS
EMULOUSNESS	ENANTIOMORPHISM	ENCEPHALALGIA	ENCHILADAS	ENCOMPASSED
EMULOUSNESSES	ENANTIOMORPHOUS	ENCEPHALALGIAS	ENCHIRIDIA	ENCOMPASSES
EMULSIFIABLE	ENANTIOMORPHS	ENCEPHALIC	ENCHIRIDION	ENCOMPASSING
EMULSIFICATION	ENANTIOMORPHY	ENCEPHALIN	ENCHIRIDIONS	ENCOMPASSMENT
EMULSIFICATIONS	ENANTIOPATHIES	ENCEPHALINE	ENCHONDROMA	ENCOMPASSMENTS
EMULSIFIED	ENANTIOPATHY	ENCEPHALINES	ENCHONDROMAS	ENCOPRESES
EMULSIFIER	ENANTIOSES	ENCEPHALINS	ENCHONDROMATA	ENCOPRESIS
EMULSIFIERS	ENANTIOSIS	ENCEPHALITIC	ENCHONDROMATOUS	ENCOPRETIC
EMULSIFIES	ENANTIOSTYLIES	ENCEPHALITIDES	ENCINCTURE	ENCOUNTERED
EMULSIFYING	ENANTIOSTYLOUS	ENCEPHALITIS	ENCINCTURED	ENCOUNTERER
EMULSIONISE	ENANTIOSTYLY	ENCEPHALITISES	ENCINCTURES	ENCOUNTERERS
EMULSIONISED	ENANTIOTROPIC	ENCEPHALITOGEN	ENCINCTURING	ENCOUNTERING
EMULSIONISES	ENANTIOTROPIES	ENCEPHALITOGENS	ENCIPHERED	ENCOUNTERS
EMULSIONISING	ENANTIOTROPY	ENCEPHALOCELE	ENCIPHERER	ENCOURAGED
EMULSIONIZE	ENARRATION	ENCEPHALOCELES	ENCIPHERERS	ENCOURAGEMENT
EMULSIONIZED	ENARRATIONS	ENCEPHALOGRAM	ENCIPHERING	ENCOURAGEMENTS
EMULSIONIZES	ENARTHRODIAL	ENCEPHALOGRAMS	ENCIPHERMENT	ENCOURAGER
EMULSIONIZING	ENARTHROSES	ENCEPHALOGRAPH	ENCIPHERMENTS	ENCOURAGERS
EMULSOIDAL	ENARTHROSIS	ENCEPHALOGRAPHS	ENCIRCLEMENT	ENCOURAGES
EMUNCTIONS	ENCAMPMENT	ENCEPHALOGRAPHY	ENCIRCLEMENTS	ENCOURAGING

E

ENCOURAGINGLY	ENCYCLOPAEDIA	ENDEAVOURMENTS	ENDOCUTICLES	ENDOPARASITE
ENCOURAGINGS	ENCYCLOPAEDIAS	ENDEAVOURS	ENDOCYTOSES	ENDOPARASITES
ENCRADLING	ENCYCLOPAEDIC	ENDECAGONS	ENDOCYTOSIS	ENDOPARASITIC
ENCREASING	ENCYCLOPAEDISM	ENDEIXISES	ENDOCYTOTIC	ENDOPARASITISM
ENCRIMSONED	ENCYCLOPAEDISMS	ENDEMICALLY	ENDODERMAL	ENDOPARASITISMS
ENCRIMSONING	ENCYCLOPAEDIST	ENDEMICITIES	ENDODERMIC	ENDOPEPTIDASE
ENCRIMSONS	ENCYCLOPAEDISTS	ENDEMICITY	ENDODERMIS	ENDOPEPTIDASES
ENCRINITAL	ENCYCLOPEDIA	ENDEMIOLOGIES	ENDODERMISES	ENDOPEROXIDE
ENCRINITES	ENCYCLOPEDIAN	ENDEMIOLOGY	ENDODONTAL	ENDOPEROXIDES
ENCRINITIC	ENCYCLOPEDIAS	ENDENIZENED	ENDODONTIC	ENDOPHAGIES
ENCROACHED	ENCYCLOPEDIC	ENDENIZENING	ENDODONTICALLY	ENDOPHAGOUS
ENCROACHER	ENCYCLOPEDICAL	ENDENIZENS	ENDODONTICS	ENDOPHYLLOUS
ENCROACHERS	ENCYCLOPEDISM	ENDERGONIC	ENDODONTIST	ENDOPHYTES
ENCROACHES	ENCYCLOPEDISMS	ENDERMATIC	ENDODONTISTS	ENDOPHYTIC
ENCROACHING	ENCYCLOPEDIST	ENDERMICAL	ENDOENZYME	ENDOPHYTICALLY
ENCROACHINGLY	ENCYCLOPEDISTS	ENDLESSNESS	ENDOENZYMES	ENDOPLASMIC
ENCROACHMENT	ENCYSTATION	ENDLESSNESSES	ENDOGAMIES	ENDOPLASMS
ENCROACHMENTS	ENCYSTATIONS	ENDOBIOTIC	ENDOGAMOUS	ENDOPLASTIC
ENCRUSTATION	ENCYSTMENT	ENDOBLASTIC	ENDOGENIES	ENDOPLEURA
ENCRUSTATIONS	ENCYSTMENTS	ENDOBLASTS	ENDOGENOUS	ENDOPLEURAS
ENCRUSTING	ENDAMAGEMENT	ENDOCARDIA	ENDOGENOUSLY	ENDOPODITE
ENCRUSTMENT	ENDAMAGEMENTS	ENDOCARDIAC	ENDOLITHIC	ENDOPODITES
ENCRUSTMENTS	ENDAMAGING	ENDOCARDIAL	ENDOLYMPHATIC	ENDOPOLYPLOID
ENCRYPTING	ENDAMOEBAE	ENDOCARDITIC	ENDOLYMPHS	ENDOPOLYPLOIDY
ENCRYPTION	ENDAMOEBAS	ENDOCARDITIS	ENDOMETRIA	ENDOPROCTS
ENCRYPTIONS	ENDANGERED	ENDOCARDITISES	ENDOMETRIAL	ENDORADIOSONDE
ENCULTURATE	ENDANGERER	ENDOCARDIUM	ENDOMETRIOSES	ENDORADIOSONDES
ENCULTURATED	ENDANGERERS	ENDOCARPAL	ENDOMETRIOSIS	ENDORHIZAL
ENCULTURATES	ENDANGERING	ENDOCARPIC	ENDOMETRITIS	ENDORPHINS
ENCULTURATING	ENDANGERMENT	ENDOCENTRIC	ENDOMETRITISES	ENDORSABLE
ENCULTURATION	ENDANGERMENTS	ENDOCHONDRAL	ENDOMETRIUM	ENDORSATION
ENCULTURATIONS	ENDARCHIES	ENDOCHYLOUS	ENDOMITOSES	ENDORSATIONS
ENCULTURATIVE	ENDARTERECTOMY	ENDOCRANIA	ENDOMITOSIS	ENDORSEMENT
ENCUMBERED	ENDEARINGLY	ENDOCRANIAL	ENDOMITOTIC	ENDORSEMENTS
ENCUMBERING	ENDEARINGNESS	ENDOCRANIUM	ENDOMIXISES	ENDOSCOPES
ENCUMBERINGLY	ENDEARINGNESSES	ENDOCRINAL	ENDOMORPHIC	ENDOSCOPIC
ENCUMBERMENT	ENDEARMENT	ENDOCRINES	ENDOMORPHIES	ENDOSCOPICALLY
ENCUMBERMENTS	ENDEARMENTS	ENDOCRINIC	ENDOMORPHISM	ENDOSCOPIES
ENCUMBRANCE	ENDEAVORED	ENDOCRINOLOGIC	ENDOMORPHISMS	ENDOSCOPIST
ENCUMBRANCER	ENDEAVORER	ENDOCRINOLOGIES	ENDOMORPHS	ENDOSCOPISTS
ENCUMBRANCERS	ENDEAVORERS	ENDOCRINOLOGIST	ENDOMORPHY	ENDOSKELETAL
ENCUMBRANCES	ENDEAVORING	ENDOCRINOLOGY	ENDOMYCORRHIZA	ENDOSKELETON
ENCURTAINED	ENDEAVOURED	ENDOCRINOPATHIC	ENDONEURIA	ENDOSKELETONS
ENCURTAINING	ENDEAVOURER	ENDOCRINOPATHY	ENDONEURIUM	ENDOSMOMETER
ENCURTAINS	ENDEAVOURERS	ENDOCRINOUS	ENDONUCLEASE	ENDOSMOMETERS
ENCYCLICAL	ENDEAVOURING	ENDOCRITIC	ENDONUCLEASES	ENDOSMOMETRIC
ENCYCLICALS	ENDEAVOURMENT	ENDOCUTICLE	ENDONUCLEOLYTIC	ENDOSMOSES

ENDOSMOSIS	ENDURABLENESSES	ENFORCEDLY	ENGLOOMING	ENHEARTENS
ENDOSMOTIC	ENDURANCES	ENFORCEMENT	ENGLUTTING	ENHUNGERED
ENDOSMOTICALLY	ENDURINGLY	ENFORCEMENTS	ENGORGEMENT	ENHUNGERING
ENDOSPERMIC	ENDURINGNESS	ENFORESTED	ENGORGEMENTS	ENHYDRITES
ENDOSPERMS	ENDURINGNESSES	ENFORESTING	ENGOUEMENT	ENHYDRITIC
ENDOSPORES	ENERGETICAL	ENFOULDERED	ENGOUEMENTS	ENHYDROSES
ENDOSPOROUS	ENERGETICALLY	ENFRAMEMENT	ENGOUMENTS	ENHYPOSTASIA
ENDOSTEALLY	ENERGETICS	ENFRAMEMENTS	ENGRAFFING	ENHYPOSTASIAS
ENDOSTOSES	ENERGISATION	ENFRANCHISE	ENGRAFTATION	ENHYPOSTATIC
ENDOSTOSIS	ENERGISATIONS	ENFRANCHISED	ENGRAFTATIONS	ENHYPOSTATISE
ENDOSTYLES	ENERGISERS	ENFRANCHISEMENT	ENGRAFTING	ENHYPOSTATISED
ENDOSULFAN	ENERGISING	ENFRANCHISER	ENGRAFTMENT	ENHYPOSTATISES
ENDOSULFANS	ENERGIZATION	ENFRANCHISERS	ENGRAFTMENTS	ENHYPOSTATISING
ENDOSYMBIONT	ENERGIZATIONS	ENFRANCHISES	ENGRAILING	ENHYPOSTATIZE
ENDOSYMBIONTS	ENERGIZERS	ENFRANCHISING	ENGRAILMENT	ENHYPOSTATIZED
ENDOSYMBIOSES	ENERGIZING	ENFREEDOMED	ENGRAILMENTS	ENHYPOSTATIZES
ENDOSYMBIOSIS	ENERGUMENS	ENFREEDOMING	ENGRAINEDLY	ENHYPOSTATIZING
ENDOSYMBIOTIC	ENERVATING	ENFREEDOMS	ENGRAINEDNESS	ENIGMATICAL
ENDOTHECIA	ENERVATION	ENFREEZING	ENGRAINEDNESSES	ENIGMATICALLY
ENDOTHECIAL	ENERVATIONS	ENGAGEMENT	ENGRAINERS	ENIGMATISE
ENDOTHECIUM	ENERVATIVE	ENGAGEMENTS	ENGRAINING	ENIGMATISED
ENDOTHELIA	ENERVATORS	ENGAGINGLY	ENGRAMMATIC	ENIGMATISES
ENDOTHELIAL	ENFACEMENT	ENGAGINGNESS	ENGRASPING	ENIGMATISING
ENDOTHELIOID	ENFACEMENTS	ENGAGINGNESSES	ENGRAVERIES	ENIGMATIST
ENDOTHELIOMA	ENFEEBLEMENT	ENGARLANDED	ENGRAVINGS	ENIGMATISTS
ENDOTHELIOMAS	ENFEEBLEMENTS	ENGARLANDING	ENGRENAGES	ENIGMATIZE
ENDOTHELIOMATA	ENFEEBLERS	ENGARLANDS	ENGRIEVING	ENIGMATIZED
ENDOTHELIUM	ENFEEBLING	ENGARRISON	ENGROOVING	ENIGMATIZES
ENDOTHERMAL	ENFELONING	ENGARRISONED	ENGROSSEDLY	ENIGMATIZING
ENDOTHERMIC	ENFEOFFING	ENGARRISONING	ENGROSSERS	ENIGMATOGRAPHY
ENDOTHERMICALLY	ENFEOFFMENT	ENGARRISONS	ENGROSSING	ENJAMBEMENT
ENDOTHERMIES	ENFEOFFMENTS	ENGENDERED	ENGROSSINGLY	ENJAMBEMENTS
ENDOTHERMISM	ENFESTERED	ENGENDERER	ENGROSSMENT	ENJAMBMENT
ENDOTHERMISMS	ENFETTERED	ENGENDERERS	ENGROSSMENTS	ENJAMBMENTS
ENDOTHERMS	ENFETTERING	ENGENDERING	ENGUARDING	ENJOINDERS
ENDOTHERMY	ENFEVERING	ENGENDERMENT	ENGULFMENT	ENJOINMENT
ENDOTOXINS	ENFIERCING	ENGENDERMENTS	ENGULFMENTS	ENJOINMENTS
ENDOTRACHEAL	ENFILADING	ENGENDRURE	ENGULPHING	ENJOYABLENESS
ENDOTROPHIC	ENFLESHING	ENGENDRURES	ENGYSCOPES	ENJOYABLENESSES
ENDOWMENTS	ENFLEURAGE	ENGENDURES	ENHANCEMENT	ENJOYMENTS
ENDPLAYING	ENFLEURAGES	ENGINEERED	ENHANCEMENTS	ENKEPHALIN
ENDUNGEONED	ENFLOWERED	ENGINEERING	ENHARMONIC	ENKEPHALINE
ENDUNGEONING	ENFLOWERING	ENGINEERINGS	ENHARMONICAL	ENKEPHALINES
ENDUNGEONS	ENFOLDMENT	ENGINERIES	ENHARMONICALLY	ENKEPHALINS
ENDURABILITIES	ENFOLDMENTS	ENGIRDLING	ENHEARSING	ENKERNELLED
ENDURABILITY	ENFORCEABILITY	ENGLACIALLY	ENHEARTENED	ENKERNELLING
ENDURABLENESS	ENFORCEABLE	ENGLISHING	ENHEARTENING	ENKINDLERS

ENKINDLING	ENORMOUSNESS	ENSCROLLED	ENSTEEPING	ENTEROCOELE
ENLACEMENT	ENORMOUSNESSES	ENSCROLLING	ENSTRUCTURED	ENTEROCOELES
ENLACEMENTS	ENOUNCEMENT	ENSEPULCHRE	ENSWATHEMENT	ENTEROCOELIC
ENLARGEABLE	ENOUNCEMENTS	ENSEPULCHRED	ENSWATHEMENTS	ENTEROCOELOUS
ENLARGEDLY	ENPHYTOTIC	ENSEPULCHRES	ENSWATHING	ENTEROCOELS
ENLARGEDNESS	ENQUEUEING	ENSEPULCHRING	ENSWEEPING	ENTEROCOLITIS
ENLARGEDNESSES	ENQUIRATION	ENSERFMENT	ENTABLATURE	ENTEROCOLITISES
ENLARGEMENT	ENQUIRATIONS	ENSERFMENTS	ENTABLATURES	ENTEROGASTRONE
ENLARGEMENTS	ENRAGEMENT	ENSHEATHED	ENTABLEMENT	ENTEROGASTRONES
ENLARGENED	ENRAGEMENTS	ENSHEATHES	ENTABLEMENTS	ENTEROHEPATITIS
ENLARGENING	ENRANCKLED	ENSHEATHING	ENTAILMENT	ENTEROKINASE
ENLEVEMENT	ENRANCKLES	ENSHELLING	ENTAILMENTS	ENTEROKINASES
ENLEVEMENTS	ENRANCKLING	ENSHELTERED	ENTAMOEBAE	ENTEROLITH
ENLIGHTENED	ENRAPTURED	ENSHELTERING	ENTAMOEBAS	ENTEROLITHS
ENLIGHTENER	ENRAPTURES	ENSHELTERS	ENTANGLEMENT	ENTEROPATHIES
ENLIGHTENERS	ENRAPTURING	ENSHIELDED	ENTANGLEMENTS	ENTEROPATHY
ENLIGHTENING	ENRAUNGING	ENSHIELDING	ENTANGLERS	ENTEROPNEUST
ENLIGHTENMENT	ENRAVISHED	ENSHRINEES	ENTANGLING	ENTEROPNEUSTAL
ENLIGHTENMENTS	ENRAVISHES	ENSHRINEMENT	ENTELECHIES	ENTEROPNEUSTS
ENLIGHTENS	ENRAVISHING	ENSHRINEMENTS	ENTELLUSES	ENTEROPTOSES
ENLIGHTING	ENREGIMENT	ENSHRINING	ENTENDERED	ENTEROPTOSIS
ENLISTMENT	ENREGIMENTED	ENSHROUDED	ENTENDERING	ENTEROSTOMAL
ENLISTMENTS	ENREGIMENTING	ENSHROUDING	ENTERCHAUNGE	ENTEROSTOMIES
ENLIVENERS	ENREGIMENTS	ENSIGNCIES	ENTERCHAUNGED	ENTEROSTOMY
ENLIVENING	ENREGISTER	ENSIGNSHIP	ENTERCHAUNGES	ENTEROTOMIES
ENLIVENMENT	ENREGISTERED	ENSIGNSHIPS	ENTERCHAUNGING	ENTEROTOMY
ENLIVENMENTS	ENREGISTERING	ENSILABILITIES	ENTERDEALE	ENTEROTOXIN
ENLUMINING	ENREGISTERS	ENSILABILITY	ENTERDEALED	ENTEROTOXINS
ENMESHMENT	ENRHEUMING	ENSILAGEING	ENTERDEALES	ENTEROVIRAL
ENMESHMENTS	ENRICHMENT	ENSILAGING	ENTERDEALING	ENTEROVIRUS
ENNEAGONAL	ENRICHMENTS	ENSLAVEMENT	ENTERECTOMIES	ENTEROVIRUSES
ENNEAGRAMS	ENROLLMENT	ENSLAVEMENTS	ENTERECTOMY	ENTERPRISE
ENNEAHEDRA	ENROLLMENTS	ENSNAREMENT	ENTERITIDES	ENTERPRISED
ENNEAHEDRAL	ENROLMENTS	ENSNAREMENTS	ENTERITISES	ENTERPRISER
ENNEAHEDRON	ENROUGHING	ENSNARLING	ENTEROBACTERIA	ENTERPRISERS
ENNEAHEDRONS	ENROUNDING	ENSORCELED	ENTEROBACTERIAL	ENTERPRISES
ENNEANDRIAN	ENSAMPLING	ENSORCELING	ENTEROBACTERIUM	ENTERPRISING
ENNEANDROUS	ENSANGUINATED	ENSORCELLED	ENTEROBIASES	ENTERPRISINGLY
ENNEASTYLE	ENSANGUINE	ENSORCELLING	ENTEROBIASIS	ENTERTAINED
ENNOBLEMENT	ENSANGUINED	ENSORCELLMENT	ENTEROCELE	ENTERTAINER
ENNOBLEMENTS	ENSANGUINES	ENSORCELLMENTS	ENTEROCELES	ENTERTAINERS
ENOKIDAKES	ENSANGUINING	ENSORCELLS	ENTEROCENTESES	ENTERTAINING
ENOKITAKES	ENSCHEDULE	ENSOULMENT	ENTEROCENTESIS	ENTERTAININGLY
ENOLOGICAL	ENSCHEDULED	ENSOULMENTS	ENTEROCOCCAL	ENTERTAININGS
ENOLOGISTS	ENSCHEDULES	ENSPHERING	ENTEROCOCCI	ENTERTAINMENT
ENORMITIES	ENSCHEDULING	ENSTAMPING	ENTEROCOCCUS	ENTERTAINMENTS
ENORMOUSLY	ENSCONCING	ENSTATITES	ENTEROCOEL	ENTERTAINS

ENTERTAKEN	ENTIRETIES	ENTOURAGES	ENTREPRENEUSES	ENVELOPMENT
ENTERTAKES	ENTITATIVE	ENTRAILING	ENTROPICALLY	ENVELOPMENTS
ENTERTAKING	ENTITLEMENT	ENTRAINEMENT	ENTROPIONS	ENVENOMING
ENTERTISSUED	ENTITLEMENTS	ENTRAINEMENTS	ENTROPIUMS	ENVENOMISATION
ENTHALPIES	ENTOBLASTIC	ENTRAINERS	ENTRUSTING	ENVENOMISATIONS
ENTHRALDOM	ENTOBLASTS	ENTRAINING	ENTRUSTMENT	ENVENOMIZATION
ENTHRALDOMS	ENTODERMAL	ENTRAINMENT	ENTRUSTMENTS	ENVENOMIZATIONS
ENTHRALLED	ENTODERMIC	ENTRAINMENTS	ENTWINEMENT	ENVERMEILED
ENTHRALLER	ENTOILMENT	ENTRAMMELLED	ENTWINEMENTS	ENVERMEILING
ENTHRALLERS	ENTOILMENTS	ENTRAMMELLING	ENTWISTING	ENVERMEILS
ENTHRALLING	ENTOMBMENT	ENTRAMMELS	ENUCLEATED	ENVIABLENESS
ENTHRALLMENT	ENTOMBMENTS	ENTRANCEMENT	ENUCLEATES	ENVIABLENESSES
ENTHRALLMENTS	ENTOMOFAUNA	ENTRANCEMENTS	ENUCLEATING	ENVIOUSNESS
ENTHRALMENT	ENTOMOFAUNAE	ENTRANCEWAY	ENUCLEATION	ENVIOUSNESSES
ENTHRALMENTS	ENTOMOFAUNAS	ENTRANCEWAYS	ENUCLEATIONS	ENVIRONICS
ENTHRONEMENT	ENTOMOLOGIC	ENTRANCING	ENUMERABILITIES	ENVIRONING
ENTHRONEMENTS	ENTOMOLOGICAL	ENTRANCINGLY	ENUMERABILITY	ENVIRONMENT
ENTHRONING	ENTOMOLOGICALLY	ENTRAPMENT	ENUMERABLE	ENVIRONMENTAL
ENTHRONISATION	ENTOMOLOGIES	ENTRAPMENTS	ENUMERATED	ENVIRONMENTALLY
ENTHRONISATIONS	ENTOMOLOGISE	ENTRAPPERS	ENUMERATES	ENVIRONMENTS
ENTHRONISE	ENTOMOLOGISED	ENTRAPPING	ENUMERATING	ENVISAGEMENT
ENTHRONISED	ENTOMOLOGISES	ENTREASURE	ENUMERATION	ENVISAGEMENTS
ENTHRONISES	ENTOMOLOGISING	ENTREASURED	ENUMERATIONS	ENVISAGING
ENTHRONISING	ENTOMOLOGIST	ENTREASURES	ENUMERATIVE	ENVISIONED
ENTHRONIZATION	ENTOMOLOGISTS	ENTREASURING	ENUMERATOR	ENVISIONING
ENTHRONIZATIONS	ENTOMOLOGIZE	ENTREATABLE	ENUMERATORS	ENVOYSHIPS
ENTHRONIZE	ENTOMOLOGIZED	ENTREATIES	ENUNCIABLE	ENWALLOWED
ENTHRONIZED	ENTOMOLOGIZES	ENTREATING	ENUNCIATED	ENWALLOWING
ENTHRONIZES	ENTOMOLOGIZING	ENTREATINGLY	ENUNCIATES	ENWHEELING
ENTHRONIZING	ENTOMOLOGY	ENTREATIVE	ENUNCIATING	ENWRAPMENT
ENTHUSIASM	ENTOMOPHAGIES	ENTREATMENT	ENUNCIATION	ENWRAPMENTS
ENTHUSIASMS	ENTOMOPHAGOUS	ENTREATMENTS	ENUNCIATIONS	ENWRAPPING
ENTHUSIAST	ENTOMOPHAGY	ENTRECHATS	ENUNCIATIVE	ENWRAPPINGS
ENTHUSIASTIC	ENTOMOPHILIES	ENTRECOTES	ENUNCIATIVELY	ENWREATHED
ENTHUSIASTICAL	ENTOMOPHILOUS	ENTREMESSE	ENUNCIATOR	ENWREATHES
ENTHUSIASTS	ENTOMOPHILY	ENTREMESSES	ENUNCIATORS	ENWREATHING
ENTHYMEMATIC	ENTOMOSTRACAN	ENTRENCHED	ENUNCIATORY	ENZOOTICALLY
ENTHYMEMATICAL	ENTOMOSTRACANS	ENTRENCHER	ENUREDNESS	ENZYMATICALLY
ENTHYMEMES	ENTOMOSTRACOUS	ENTRENCHERS	ENUREDNESSES	ENZYMICALLY
ENTICEABLE	ENTOPHYTAL	ENTRENCHES	ENUREMENTS	ENZYMOLOGICAL
ENTICEMENT	ENTOPHYTES	ENTRENCHING	ENURESISES	ENZYMOLOGIES
ENTICEMENTS	ENTOPHYTIC	ENTRENCHMENT	ENVASSALLED	ENZYMOLOGIST
ENTICINGLY	ENTOPHYTOUS	ENTRENCHMENTS	ENVASSALLING	ENZYMOLOGISTS
ENTICINGNESS	ENTOPLASTRA	ENTREPRENEUR	ENVAULTING	ENZYMOLOGY
ENTICINGNESSES	ENTOPLASTRAL	ENTREPRENEURIAL	ENVEIGLING	ENZYMOLYSES
ENTIRENESS	ENTOPLASTRON	ENTREPRENEURS	ENVELOPERS	ENZYMOLYSIS
ENTIRENESSES	ENTOPROCTS	ENTREPRENEUSE	ENVELOPING	ENZYMOLYTIC

EOHIPPUSES	EPHEBOPHILIA	EPICURISMS	EPIGASTRIA	EPIGRAPHIST
EOSINOPHIL	EPHEBOPHILIAS	EPICURIZED	EPIGASTRIAL	EPIGRAPHISTS
EOSINOPHILE	EPHEDRINES	EPICURIZES	EPIGASTRIC	EPILATIONS
EOSINOPHILES	EPHEMERALITIES	EPICURIZING	EPIGASTRIUM	EPILEPSIES
EOSINOPHILIA	EPHEMERALITY	EPICUTICLE	EPIGENESES	EPILEPTICAL
EOSINOPHILIAS	EPHEMERALLY	EPICUTICLES	EPIGENESIS	EPILEPTICALLY
EOSINOPHILIC	EPHEMERALNESS	EPICUTICULAR	EPIGENESIST	EPILEPTICS
EOSINOPHILOUS	EPHEMERALNESSES	EPICYCLICAL	EPIGENESISTS	EPILEPTIFORM
EOSINOPHILS	EPHEMERALS	EPICYCLOID	EPIGENETIC	EPILEPTOGENIC
EPAGOMENAL	EPHEMERIDES	EPICYCLOIDAL	EPIGENETICALLY	EPILEPTOID
EPANADIPLOSES	EPHEMERIDIAN	EPICYCLOIDS	EPIGENETICIST	EPILIMNION
EPANADIPLOSIS	EPHEMERIDS	EPIDEICTIC	EPIGENETICISTS	EPILIMNIONS
EPANALEPSES	EPHEMERIST	EPIDEICTICAL	EPIGENETICS	EPILOBIUMS
EPANALEPSIS	EPHEMERISTS	EPIDEMICAL	EPIGENISTS	EPILOGISED
EPANALEPTIC	EPHEMERONS	EPIDEMICALLY	EPIGLOTTAL	EPILOGISES
EPANAPHORA	EPHEMEROPTERAN	EPIDEMICITIES	EPIGLOTTIC	EPILOGISING
EPANAPHORAL	EPHEMEROPTERANS	EPIDEMICITY	EPIGLOTTIDES	EPILOGISTIC
EPANAPHORAS	EPHEMEROUS	EPIDEMIOLOGIC	EPIGLOTTIS	EPILOGISTS
EPANODOSES	EPHORALTIES	EPIDEMIOLOGICAL	EPIGLOTTISES	EPILOGIZED
EPANORTHOSES	EPIBLASTIC	EPIDEMIOLOGIES	EPIGNATHOUS	EPILOGIZES
EPANORTHOSIS	EPICALYCES	EPIDEMIOLOGIST	EPIGONISMS	EPILOGIZING
EPANORTHOTIC	EPICALYXES	EPIDEMIOLOGISTS	EPIGRAMMATIC	EPILOGUING
EPARCHATES	EPICANTHIC	EPIDEMIOLOGY	EPIGRAMMATICAL	EPILOGUISE
EPAULEMENT	EPICANTHUS	EPIDENDRONE	EPIGRAMMATISE	EPILOGUISED
EPAULEMENTS	EPICARDIAC	EPIDENDRONES	EPIGRAMMATISED	EPILOGUISES
EPAULETTED	EPICARDIAL	EPIDENDRUM	EPIGRAMMATISER	EPILOGUISING
EPAULETTES	EPICARDIUM	EPIDENDRUMS	EPIGRAMMATISERS	EPILOGUIZE
EPEIROGENESES	EPICENISMS	EPIDERMISES	EPIGRAMMATISES	EPILOGUIZED
EPEIROGENESIS	EPICENTERS	EPIDERMOID	EPIGRAMMATISING	EPILOGUIZES
EPEIROGENETIC	EPICENTRAL	EPIDERMOLYSES	EPIGRAMMATISM	EPILOGUIZING
EPEIROGENIC	EPICENTRES	EPIDERMOLYSIS	EPIGRAMMATISMS	EPIMELETIC
EPEIROGENICALLY	EPICENTRUM	EPIDIASCOPE	EPIGRAMMATIST	EPIMERASES
EPEIROGENIES	EPICHEIREMA	EPIDIASCOPES	EPIGRAMMATISTS	EPIMERISED
EPEIROGENY	EPICHEIREMAS	EPIDIDYMAL	EPIGRAMMATIZE	EPIMERISES
EPENCEPHALA	EPICHLOROHYDRIN	EPIDIDYMIDES	EPIGRAMMATIZED	EPIMERISING
EPENCEPHALIC	EPICONDYLE	EPIDIDYMIS	EPIGRAMMATIZER	EPIMERISMS
EPENCEPHALON	EPICONDYLES	EPIDIDYMITIS	EPIGRAMMATIZERS	EPIMERIZED
EPENCEPHALONS	EPICONDYLITIS	EPIDIDYMITISES	EPIGRAMMATIZES	EPIMERIZES
EPENTHESES	EPICONDYLITISES	EPIDIORITE	EPIGRAMMATIZING	EPIMERIZING
EPENTHESIS	EPICONTINENTAL	EPIDIORITES	EPIGRAMMATISM	EPIMORPHIC
EPENTHETIC	EPICRANIUM	EPIDOSITES	EPIGRAPHED	EPIMORPHOSES
EPEOLATRIES	EPICUREANISM	EPIDOTISATION	EPIGRAPHER	EPIMORPHOSIS
EPEXEGESES	EPICUREANISMS	EPIDOTISATIONS	EPIGRAPHERS	EPINASTICALLY
EPEXEGESIS	EPICUREANS	EPIDOTISED	EPIGRAPHIC	EPINASTIES
EPEXEGETIC	EPICURISED	EPIDOTIZATION	EPIGRAPHICAL	EPINEPHRIN
EPEXEGETICAL	EPICURISES	EPIDOTIZATIONS	EPIGRAPHICALLY	EPINEPHRINE
EPEXEGETICALLY	EPICURISING	EPIDOTIZED	EPIGRAPHIES	EPINEPHRINES

EPINEPHRINS	EPISCOPATE	EPISTOLISING	EPITHELIZED	EPOXIDIZING
EPINEURIAL	EPISCOPATED	EPISTOLIST	EPITHELIZES	EPROUVETTE
EPINEURIUM	EPISCOPATES	EPISTOLISTS	EPITHELIZING	EPROUVETTES
EPINEURIUMS	EPISCOPATING	EPISTOLIZE	EPITHEMATA	EPULATIONS
EPINICIONS	EPISCOPIES	EPISTOLIZED	EPITHERMAL	EPURATIONS
EPINIKIONS	EPISCOPISE	EPISTOLIZES	EPITHETICAL	EQUABILITIES
EPIPELAGIC	EPISCOPISED	EPISTOLIZING	EPITHETICALLY	EQUABILITY
EPIPETALOUS	EPISCOPISES	EPISTOLOGRAPHY	EPITHETING	EQUABLENESS
EPIPHANIES	EPISCOPISING	EPISTROPHE	EPITHETONS	EQUABLENESSES
EPIPHANOUS	EPISCOPIZE	EPISTROPHES	EPITHYMETIC	EQUALISATION
EPIPHENOMENA	EPISCOPIZED	EPITAPHERS	EPITOMICAL	EQUALISATIONS
EPIPHENOMENAL	EPISCOPIZES	EPITAPHIAL	EPITOMISATION	EQUALISERS
EPIPHENOMENALLY	EPISCOPIZING	EPITAPHIAN	EPITOMISATIONS	EQUALISING
EPIPHENOMENON	EPISEMATIC	EPITAPHING	EPITOMISED	EQUALITARIAN
EPIPHONEMA	EPISEPALOUS	EPITAPHIST	EPITOMISER	EQUALITARIANISM
EPIPHONEMAS	EPISIOTOMIES	EPITAPHISTS	EPITOMISERS	EQUALITARIANS
EPIPHRAGMS	EPISIOTOMY	EPITAXIALLY	EPITOMISES	EQUALITIES
EPIPHYLLOUS	EPISODICAL	EPITHALAMIA	EPITOMISING	EQUALIZATION
EPIPHYSEAL	EPISODICALLY	EPITHALAMIC	EPITOMISTS	EQUALIZATIONS
EPIPHYSIAL	EPISOMALLY	EPITHALAMION	EPITOMIZATION	EQUALIZERS
EPIPHYTICAL	EPISPASTIC	EPITHALAMIUM	EPITOMIZATIONS	EQUALIZING
EPIPHYTICALLY	EPISPASTICS	EPITHALAMIUMS	EPITOMIZED	EQUALNESSES
EPIPHYTISM	EPISTASIES	EPITHELIAL	EPITOMIZER	EQUANIMITIES
EPIPHYTISMS	EPISTAXISES	EPITHELIALISE	EPITOMIZERS	EQUANIMITY
EPIPHYTOLOGIES	EPISTEMICALLY	EPITHELIALISED	EPITOMIZES	EQUANIMOUS
EPIPHYTOLOGY	EPISTEMICS	EPITHELIALISES	EPITOMIZING	EQUANIMOUSLY
EPIPHYTOTIC	EPISTEMOLOGICAL	EPITHELIALISING	EPITRACHELION	EQUATABILITIES
EPIPHYTOTICS	EPISTEMOLOGIES	EPITHELIALIZE	EPITRACHELIONS	EQUATABILITY
EPIPLASTRA	EPISTEMOLOGIST	EPITHELIALIZED	EPITROCHOID	EQUATIONAL
EPIPLASTRAL	EPISTEMOLOGISTS	EPITHELIALIZES	EPITROCHOIDS	EQUATIONALLY
EPIPLASTRON	EPISTEMOLOGY	EPITHELIALIZING	EPIZEUXISES	EQUATORIAL
EPIPOLISMS	EPISTERNAL	EPITHELIOID	EPIZOOTICALLY	EQUATORIALLY
EPIROGENETIC	EPISTERNUM	EPITHELIOMA	EPIZOOTICS	EQUATORIALS
EPIROGENIC	EPISTERNUMS	EPITHELIOMAS	EPIZOOTIES	EQUATORWARD
EPIROGENIES	EPISTILBITE	EPITHELIOMATA	EPIZOOTIOLOGIC	EQUESTRIAN
EPIRRHEMAS	EPISTILBITES	EPITHELIOMATOUS	EPIZOOTIOLOGIES	EQUESTRIANISM
EPIRRHEMATIC	EPISTOLARIAN	EPITHELISATION	EPIZOOTIOLOGY	EQUESTRIANISMS
EPISCOPACIES	EPISTOLARIANS	EPITHELISATIONS	EPONYCHIUM	EQUESTRIANS
EPISCOPACY	EPISTOLARIES	EPITHELISE	EPONYCHIUMS	EQUESTRIENNE
EPISCOPALIAN	EPISTOLARY	EPITHELISED	EPONYMOUSLY	EQUESTRIENNES
EPISCOPALIANISM	EPISTOLATORY	EPITHELISES	EPOXIDATION	EQUIANGULAR
EPISCOPALIANS	EPISTOLERS	EPITHELISING	EPOXIDATIONS	EQUIANGULARITY
EPISCOPALISM	EPISTOLETS	EPITHELIUM	EPOXIDISED	EQUIBALANCE
EPISCOPALISMS	EPISTOLICAL	EPITHELIUMS	EPOXIDISES	EQUIBALANCED
EPISCOPALLY	EPISTOLISE	EPITHELIZATION	EPOXIDISING	EQUIBALANCES
EPISCOPANT	EPISTOLISED	EPITHELIZATIONS	EPOXIDIZED	EQUIBALANCING
EPISCOPANTS	EPISTOLISES	EPITHELIZE	EPOXIDIZES	EQUICALORIC

EQUIDIFFERENT	EQUIPOISES	EQUIVOCATINGLY	ERGATOMORPHS	EROTICISING
EQUIDISTANCE	EQUIPOISING	EQUIVOCATION	ERGODICITIES	EROTICISMS
EQUIDISTANCES	EQUIPOLLENCE	EQUIVOCATIONS	ERGODICITY	EROTICISTS
EQUIDISTANT	EQUIPOLLENCES	EQUIVOCATOR	ERGOGRAPHS	EROTICIZATION
EQUIDISTANTLY	EQUIPOLLENCIES	EQUIVOCATORS	ERGOMANIAC	EROTICIZATIONS
EQUIFINALLY	EQUIPOLLENCY	EQUIVOCATORY	ERGOMANIACS	EROTICIZED
EQUILATERAL	EQUIPOLLENT	EQUIVOQUES	ERGOMANIAS	EROTICIZES
EQUILATERALLY	EQUIPOLLENTLY	ERADIATING	ERGOMETERS	EROTICIZING
EQUILATERALS	EQUIPOLLENTS	ERADIATION	ERGOMETRIC	EROTISATION
EQUILIBRANT	EQUIPONDERANCE	ERADIATIONS	ERGOMETRIES	EROTISATIONS
EQUILIBRANTS	EQUIPONDERANCES	ERADICABLE	ERGONOMICALLY	EROTIZATION
EQUILIBRATE	EQUIPONDERANCY	ERADICABLY	ERGONOMICS	EROTIZATIONS
EQUILIBRATED	EQUIPONDERANT	ERADICANTS	ERGONOMIST	EROTOGENIC
EQUILIBRATES	EQUIPONDERATE	ERADICATED	ERGONOMISTS	EROTOGENOUS
EQUILIBRATING	EQUIPONDERATED	ERADICATES	ERGONOVINE	EROTOLOGICAL
EQUILIBRATION	EQUIPONDERATES	ERADICATING	ERGONOVINES	EROTOLOGIES
EQUILIBRATIONS	EQUIPONDERATING	ERADICATION	ERGOPHOBIA	EROTOLOGIST
EQUILIBRATOR	EQUIPOTENT	ERADICATIONS	ERGOPHOBIAS	EROTOLOGISTS
EQUILIBRATORS	EQUIPOTENTIAL	ERADICATIVE	ERGOSTEROL	EROTOMANIA
EQUILIBRATORY	EQUIPOTENTIALS	ERADICATOR	ERGOSTEROLS	EROTOMANIAC
EQUILIBRIA	EQUIPROBABILITY	ERADICATORS	ERGOTAMINE	EROTOMANIACS
EQUILIBRIST	EQUIPROBABLE	ERASABILITIES	ERGOTAMINES	EROTOMANIAS
EQUILIBRISTIC	EQUISETACEOUS	ERASABILITY	ERGOTISING	EROTOPHOBIA
EQUILIBRISTS	EQUISETIFORM	ERASEMENTS	ERGOTIZING	EROTOPHOBIAS
EQUILIBRITIES	EQUISETUMS	ERECTILITIES	ERICACEOUS	ERRANTRIES
EQUILIBRITY	EQUITABILITIES	ERECTILITY	ERINACEOUS	ERRATICALLY
EQUILIBRIUM	EQUITABILITY	ERECTNESSES	ERIOMETERS	ERRATICISM
EQUILIBRIUMS	EQUITABLENESS	EREMACAUSES	ERIOPHOROUS	ERRATICISMS
EQUIMOLECULAR	EQUITABLENESSES	EREMACAUSIS	ERIOPHORUM	ERRONEOUSLY
EQUIMULTIPLE	EQUITATION	EREMITICAL	ERIOPHORUMS	ERRONEOUSNESS
EQUIMULTIPLES	EQUITATIONS	EREMITISMS	ERIOPHYIDS	ERRONEOUSNESSES
EQUINITIES	EQUIVALENCE	EREMURUSES	ERIOSTEMON	ERUBESCENCE
EQUINOCTIAL	EQUIVALENCES	ERETHISMIC	ERIOSTEMONS	ERUBESCENCES
EQUINOCTIALLY	EQUIVALENCIES	ERETHISTIC	ERISTICALLY	ERUBESCENCIES
EQUINOCTIALS	EQUIVALENCY	ERGASTOPLASM	ERODIBILITIES	ERUBESCENCY
EQUINUMEROUS	EQUIVALENT	ERGASTOPLASMIC	ERODIBILITY	ERUBESCENT
EQUIPAGING	EQUIVALENTLY	ERGASTOPLASMS	EROGENEITIES	ERUBESCITE
EQUIPARATE	EQUIVALENTS	ERGATANDROMORPH	EROGENEITY	ERUBESCITES
EQUIPARATED	EQUIVOCALITIES	ERGATANERS	EROSIONALLY	ERUCTATING
EQUIPARATES	EQUIVOCALITY	ERGATIVITIES	EROSIVENESS	ERUCTATION
EQUIPARATING	EQUIVOCALLY	ERGATIVITY	EROSIVENESSES	ERUCTATIONS
EQUIPARATION	EQUIVOCALNESS	ERGATOCRACIES	EROSIVITIES	ERUCTATIVE
EQUIPARATIONS	EQUIVOCALNESSES	ERGATOCRACY	EROTICALLY	ERUDITENESS
EQUIPARTITION	EQUIVOCATE	ERGATOGYNE	EROTICISATION	ERUDITENESSES
EQUIPARTITIONS	EQUIVOCATED	ERGATOGYNES	EROTICISATIONS	ERUDITIONS
EQUIPMENTS	EQUIVOCATES	ERGATOMORPH	EROTICISED	ERUPTIONAL
EQUIPOISED	EQUIVOCATING	ERGATOMORPHIC	EROTICISES	ERUPTIVELY

ERUPTIVENESS
ERUPTIVENESSES
ERUPTIVITIES
ERUPTIVITY
ERVALENTAS
ERYSIPELAS
ERYSIPELASES
ERYSIPELATOUS
ERYSIPELOID
ERYSIPELOIDS
ERYTHEMATIC
ERYTHEMATOUS
ERYTHORBATE
ERYTHORBATES
ERYTHRAEMIA
ERYTHRAEMIAS
ERYTHREMIA
ERYTHREMIAS
ERYTHRINAS
ERYTHRISMAL
ERYTHRISMS
ERYTHRISTIC
ERYTHRITES
ERYTHRITIC
ERYTHRITOL
ERYTHRITOLS
ERYTHROBLAST
ERYTHROBLASTIC
ERYTHROBLASTS
ERYTHROCYTE
ERYTHROCYTES
ERYTHROCYTIC
ERYTHROMELALGIA
ERYTHROMYCIN
ERYTHROMYCINS
ERYTHRONIUM
ERYTHRONIUMS
ERYTHROPENIA
ERYTHROPENIAS
ERYTHROPHOBIA
ERYTHROPHOBIAS
ERYTHROPOIESES
ERYTHROPOIESIS
ERYTHROPOIETIC
ERYTHROPOIETIN
ERYTHROPOIETINS
ERYTHROPSIA

ERYTHROPSIAS
ERYTHROSIN
ERYTHROSINE
ERYTHROSINES
ERYTHROSINS
ESCABECHES
ESCADRILLE
ESCADRILLES
ESCALADERS
ESCALADING
ESCALADOES
ESCALATING
ESCALATION
ESCALATIONS
ESCALATORS
ESCALATORY
ESCALLONIA
ESCALLONIAS
ESCALLOPED
ESCALLOPING
ESCALOPING
ESCAMOTAGE
ESCAMOTAGES
ESCAPADOES
ESCAPELESS
ESCAPEMENT
ESCAPEMENTS
ESCAPOLOGIES
ESCAPOLOGIST
ESCAPOLOGISTS
ESCAPOLOGY
ESCARMOUCHE
ESCARMOUCHES
ESCARPMENT
ESCARPMENTS
ESCHAROTIC
ESCHAROTICS
ESCHATOLOGIC
ESCHATOLOGICAL
ESCHATOLOGIES
ESCHATOLOGIST
ESCHATOLOGISTS
ESCHATOLOGY
ESCHEATABLE
ESCHEATAGE
ESCHEATAGES
ESCHEATING

ESCHEATMENT
ESCHEATMENTS
ESCHEATORS
ESCHSCHOLTZIA
ESCHSCHOLTZIAS
ESCHSCHOLZIA
ESCHSCHOLZIAS
ESCLANDRES
ESCOPETTES
ESCORTAGES
ESCRIBANOS
ESCRITOIRE
ESCRITOIRES
ESCRITORIAL
ESCUTCHEON
ESCUTCHEONED
ESCUTCHEONS
ESEMPLASIES
ESEMPLASTIC
ESEMPLASTICALLY
ESOPHAGEAL
ESOPHAGOSCOPE
ESOPHAGOSCOPES
ESOPHAGUSES
ESOTERICALLY
ESOTERICISM
ESOTERICISMS
ESOTERICIST
ESOTERICISTS
ESOTERISMS
ESOTROPIAS
ESPADRILLE
ESPADRILLES
ESPAGNOLES
ESPAGNOLETTE
ESPAGNOLETTES
ESPALIERED
ESPALIERING
ESPECIALLY
ESPERANCES
ESPIEGLERIE
ESPIEGLERIES
ESPIONAGES
ESPLANADES
ESPRESSIVO
ESQUIRESSES
ESSAYETTES

ESSAYISTIC
ESSENTIALISE
ESSENTIALISED
ESSENTIALISES
ESSENTIALISING
ESSENTIALISM
ESSENTIALISMS
ESSENTIALIST
ESSENTIALISTS
ESSENTIALITIES
ESSENTIALITY
ESSENTIALIZE
ESSENTIALIZED
ESSENTIALIZES
ESSENTIALIZING
ESSENTIALLY
ESSENTIALNESS
ESSENTIALNESSES
ESSENTIALS
ESTABLISHABLE
ESTABLISHED
ESTABLISHER
ESTABLISHERS
ESTABLISHES
ESTABLISHING
ESTABLISHMENT
ESTABLISHMENTS
ESTAFETTES
ESTAMINETS
ESTANCIERO
ESTANCIEROS
ESTATESMAN
ESTATESMEN
ESTERIFICATION
ESTERIFICATIONS
ESTERIFIED
ESTERIFIES
ESTERIFYING
ESTHESIOGEN
ESTHESIOGENS
ESTHESISES
ESTHETICAL
ESTHETICALLY
ESTHETICIAN
ESTHETICIANS
ESTHETICISM
ESTHETICISMS

ESTIMABLENESS
ESTIMABLENESSES
ESTIMATING
ESTIMATION
ESTIMATIONS
ESTIMATIVE
ESTIMATORS
ESTIPULATE
ESTIVATING
ESTIVATION
ESTIVATIONS
ESTIVATORS
ESTOPPAGES
ESTRADIOLS
ESTRAMAZONE
ESTRAMAZONES
ESTRANGEDNESS
ESTRANGEDNESSES
ESTRANGELO
ESTRANGELOS
ESTRANGEMENT
ESTRANGEMENTS
ESTRANGERS
ESTRANGHELO
ESTRANGHELOS
ESTRANGING
ESTRAPADES
ESTREATING
ESTREPEMENT
ESTREPEMENTS
ESTRILDIDS
ESTROGENIC
ESTROGENICALLY
ESURIENCES
ESURIENCIES
ESURIENTLY
ETEPIMELETIC
ETERNALISATION
ETERNALISATIONS
ETERNALISE
ETERNALISED
ETERNALISES
ETERNALISING
ETERNALIST
ETERNALISTS
ETERNALITIES
ETERNALITY

ETERNALIZATION	ETHERISING	ETHNOHISTORIC	ETYMOLOGICAL	EUDAEMONISTS
ETERNALIZATIONS	ETHERIZATION	ETHNOHISTORICAL	ETYMOLOGICALLY	EUDAIMONISM
ETERNALIZE	ETHERIZATIONS	ETHNOHISTORIES	ETYMOLOGICON	EUDAIMONISMS
ETERNALIZED	ETHERIZERS	ETHNOHISTORY	ETYMOLOGICUM	EUDEMONIAS
ETERNALIZES	ETHERIZING	ETHNOLINGUIST	ETYMOLOGIES	EUDEMONICS
ETERNALIZING	ETHEROMANIA	ETHNOLINGUISTIC	ETYMOLOGISE	EUDEMONISM
ETERNALNESS	ETHEROMANIAC	ETHNOLINGUISTS	ETYMOLOGISED	EUDEMONISMS
ETERNALNESSES	ETHEROMANIACS	ETHNOLOGIC	ETYMOLOGISES	EUDEMONIST
ETERNISATION	ETHEROMANIAS	ETHNOLOGICAL	ETYMOLOGISING	EUDEMONISTIC
ETERNISATIONS	ETHICALITIES	ETHNOLOGICALLY	ETYMOLOGIST	EUDEMONISTICAL
ETERNISING	ETHICALITY	ETHNOLOGIES	ETYMOLOGISTS	EUDEMONISTS
ETERNITIES	ETHICALNESS	ETHNOLOGIST	ETYMOLOGIZE	EUDIALYTES
ETERNIZATION	ETHICALNESSES	ETHNOLOGISTS	ETYMOLOGIZED	EUDICOTYLEDON
ETERNIZATIONS	ETHICISING	ETHNOMEDICINE	ETYMOLOGIZES	EUDICOTYLEDONS
ETERNIZING	ETHICIZING	ETHNOMEDICINES	ETYMOLOGIZING	EUDIOMETER
ETHAMBUTOL	ETHIONAMIDE	ETHNOMUSICOLOGY	EUBACTERIA	EUDIOMETERS
ETHAMBUTOLS	ETHIONAMIDES	ETHNOSCIENCE	EUBACTERIUM	EUDIOMETRIC
ETHANEDIOIC	ETHIONINES	ETHNOSCIENCES	EUCALYPTOL	EUDIOMETRICAL
ETHANEDIOL	ETHNARCHIES	ETHOLOGICAL	EUCALYPTOLE	EUDIOMETRICALLY
ETHANEDIOLS	ETHNICALLY	ETHOLOGICALLY	EUCALYPTOLES	EUDIOMETRIES
ETHANOATES	ETHNICISMS	ETHOLOGIES	EUCALYPTOLS	EUDIOMETRY
ETHANOLAMINE	ETHNICITIES	ETHOLOGIST	EUCALYPTUS	EUGENECIST
ETHANOLAMINES	ETHNOBIOLOGIES	ETHOLOGISTS	EUCALYPTUSES	EUGENECISTS
ETHEOSTOMINE	ETHNOBIOLOGY	ETHOXYETHANE	EUCARYOTES	EUGENICALLY
ETHEREALISATION	ETHNOBOTANICAL	ETHOXYETHANES	EUCARYOTIC	EUGENICIST
ETHEREALISE	ETHNOBOTANIES	ETHYLAMINE	EUCHARISES	EUGENICISTS
ETHEREALISED	ETHNOBOTANIST	ETHYLAMINES	EUCHARISTIC	EUGEOSYNCLINAL
ETHEREALISES	ETHNOBOTANISTS	ETHYLATING	EUCHLORINE	EUGEOSYNCLINE
ETHEREALISING	ETHNOBOTANY	ETHYLATION	EUCHLORINES	EUGEOSYNCLINES
ETHEREALITIES	ETHNOCENTRIC	ETHYLATIONS	EUCHLORINS	EUGLENOIDS
ETHEREALITY	ETHNOCENTRICITY	ETHYLBENZENE	EUCHOLOGIA	EUGLOBULIN
ETHEREALIZATION	ETHNOCENTRISM	ETHYLBENZENES	EUCHOLOGIES	EUGLOBULINS
ETHEREALIZE	ETHNOCENTRISMS	ETIOLATING	EUCHOLOGION	EUHARMONIC
ETHEREALIZED	ETHNOCIDES	ETIOLATION	EUCHROMATIC	EUHEMERISE
ETHEREALIZES	ETHNOGENIC	ETIOLATIONS	EUCHROMATIN	EUHEMERISED
ETHEREALIZING	ETHNOGENIES	ETIOLOGICAL	EUCHROMATINS	EUHEMERISES
ETHEREALLY	ETHNOGENIST	ETIOLOGICALLY	EUCRYPHIAS	EUHEMERISING
ETHEREALNESS	ETHNOGENISTS	ETIOLOGIES	EUDAEMONIA	EUHEMERISM
ETHEREALNESSES	ETHNOGRAPHER	ETIOLOGIST	EUDAEMONIAS	EUHEMERISMS
ETHERIFICATION	ETHNOGRAPHERS	ETIOLOGISTS	EUDAEMONIC	EUHEMERIST
ETHERIFICATIONS	ETHNOGRAPHIC	ETIQUETTES	EUDAEMONICS	EUHEMERISTIC
ETHERIFIED	ETHNOGRAPHICA	ETONOGESTREL	EUDAEMONIES	EUHEMERISTS
ETHERIFIES	ETHNOGRAPHICAL	ETONOGESTRELS	EUDAEMONISM	EUHEMERIZE
ETHERIFYING	ETHNOGRAPHIES	ETOURDERIE	EUDAEMONISMS	EUHEMERIZED
ETHERISATION	ETHNOGRAPHY	ETOURDERIES	EUDAEMONIST	EUHEMERIZES
ETHERISATIONS	ETHNOHISTORIAN	ETRANGERES	EUDAEMONISTIC	EUHEMERIZING
ETHERISERS	ETHNOHISTORIANS	ETYMOLOGICA	EUDAEMONISTICAL	EUKARYOTES

EUKARYOTIC	EUPHONIOUSLY	EUROPHOBIAS	EUTHERIANS	EVANGELISATION
EULOGISERS	EUPHONIOUSNESS	EUROPHOBIC	EUTHYROIDS	EVANGELISATIONS
EULOGISING	EUPHONISED	EUROTERMINAL	EUTRAPELIA	EVANGELISE
EULOGISTIC	EUPHONISES	EUROTERMINALS	EUTRAPELIAS	EVANGELISED
EULOGISTICAL	EUPHONISING	EURYBATHIC	EUTRAPELIES	EVANGELISER
EULOGISTICALLY	EUPHONISMS	EURYHALINE	EUTROPHICATION	EVANGELISERS
EULOGIZERS	EUPHONIUMS	EURYPTERID	EUTROPHICATIONS	EVANGELISES
EULOGIZING	EUPHONIZED	EURYPTERIDS	EUTROPHIES	EVANGELISING
EUMELANINS	EUPHONIZES	EURYPTEROID	EVACUATING	EVANGELISM
EUNUCHISED	EUPHONIZING	EURYPTEROIDS	EVACUATION	EVANGELISMS
EUNUCHISES	EUPHORBIACEOUS	EURYTHERMAL	EVACUATIONS	EVANGELIST
EUNUCHISING	EUPHORBIAS	EURYTHERMIC	EVACUATIVE	EVANGELISTARIES
EUNUCHISMS	EUPHORBIUM	EURYTHERMOUS	EVACUATIVES	EVANGELISTARION
EUNUCHIZED	EUPHORBIUMS	EURYTHERMS	EVACUATORS	EVANGELISTARY
EUNUCHIZES	EUPHORIANT	EURYTHMICAL	EVAGATIONS	EVANGELISTIC
EUNUCHIZING	EUPHORIANTS	EURYTHMICS	EVAGINATED	EVANGELISTS
EUNUCHOIDISM	EUPHORICALLY	EURYTHMIES	EVAGINATES	EVANGELIZATION
EUNUCHOIDISMS	EUPHRASIAS	EUSPORANGIATE	EVAGINATING	EVANGELIZATIONS
EUNUCHOIDS	EUPHRASIES	EUSTATICALLY	EVAGINATION	EVANGELIZE
EUONYMUSES	EUPHUISING	EUTECTOIDS	EVAGINATIONS	EVANGELIZED
EUPATORIUM	EUPHUISTIC	EUTHANASED	EVALUATING	EVANGELIZER
EUPATORIUMS	EUPHUISTICAL	EUTHANASES	EVALUATION	EVANGELIZERS
EUPATRIDAE	EUPHUISTICALLY	EUTHANASIA	EVALUATIONS	EVANGELIZES
EUPEPTICITIES	EUPHUIZING	EUTHANASIAS	EVALUATIVE	EVANGELIZING
EUPEPTICITY	EUPLASTICS	EUTHANASIAST	EVALUATORS	EVANISHING
EUPHAUSIACEAN	EUPLOIDIES	EUTHANASIASTS	EVANESCENCE	EVANISHMENT
EUPHAUSIACEANS	EURHYTHMIC	EUTHANASIC	EVANESCENCES	EVANISHMENTS
EUPHAUSIDS	EURHYTHMICAL	EUTHANASIES	EVANESCENT	EVANITIONS
EUPHAUSIID	EURHYTHMICS	EUTHANASING	EVANESCENTLY	EVAPORABILITIES
EUPHAUSIIDS	EURHYTHMIES	EUTHANATISE	EVANESCING	EVAPORABILITY
EUPHEMISED	EURHYTHMIST	EUTHANATISED	EVANGELIAR	EVAPORABLE
EUPHEMISER	EURHYTHMISTS	EUTHANATISES	EVANGELIARIES	EVAPORATED
EUPHEMISERS	EUROCHEQUE	EUTHANATISING	EVANGELIARION	EVAPORATES
EUPHEMISES	EUROCHEQUES	EUTHANATIZE	EVANGELIARIONS	EVAPORATING
EUPHEMISING	EUROCREEPS	EUTHANATIZED	EVANGELIARIUM	EVAPORATION
EUPHEMISMS	EUROCURRENCIES	EUTHANATIZES	EVANGELIARIUMS	EVAPORATIONS
EUPHEMISTIC	EUROCURRENCY	EUTHANATIZING	EVANGELIARS	EVAPORATIVE
EUPHEMISTICALLY	EURODEPOSIT	EUTHANAZED	EVANGELIARY	EVAPORATOR
EUPHEMISTS	EURODEPOSITS	EUTHANAZES	EVANGELICAL	EVAPORATORS
EUPHEMIZED	EURODOLLAR	EUTHANAZING	EVANGELICALISM	EVAPORIMETER
EUPHEMIZER	EURODOLLARS	EUTHANISED	EVANGELICALISMS	EVAPORIMETERS
EUPHEMIZERS	EUROMARKET	EUTHANISES	EVANGELICALLY	EVAPORITES
EUPHEMIZES	EUROMARKETS	EUTHANISING	EVANGELICALNESS	EVAPORITIC
EUPHEMIZING	EUROPHILES	EUTHANIZED	EVANGELICALS	EVAPOROGRAPH
EUPHONICAL	EUROPHILIA	EUTHANIZES	EVANGELICISM	EVAPOROGRAPHS
EUPHONICALLY	EUROPHILIAS	EUTHANIZING	EVANGELICISMS	EVAPOROMETER
EUPHONIOUS	EUROPHOBIA	EUTHENISTS	EVANGELIES	EVAPOROMETERS

E

EVASIVENESS	EVERYWOMAN	EXACTINGLY	EXARCHISTS	EXCEPTLESS
EVASIVENESSES	EVERYWOMEN	EXACTINGNESS	EXASPERATE	EXCERPTERS
EVECTIONAL	EVIDENCING	EXACTINGNESSES	EXASPERATED	EXCERPTIBLE
EVENEMENTS	EVIDENTIAL	EXACTITUDE	EXASPERATEDLY	EXCERPTING
EVENHANDED	EVIDENTIALLY	EXACTITUDES	EXASPERATER	EXCERPTINGS
EVENHANDEDLY	EVIDENTIARY	EXACTMENTS	EXASPERATERS	EXCERPTION
EVENHANDEDNESS	EVILDOINGS	EXACTNESSES	EXASPERATES	EXCERPTIONS
EVENNESSES	EVILNESSES	EXACTRESSES	EXASPERATING	EXCERPTORS
EVENTFULLY	EVINCEMENT	EXAGGERATE	EXASPERATINGLY	EXCESSIVELY
EVENTFULNESS	EVINCEMENTS	EXAGGERATED	EXASPERATION	EXCESSIVENESS
EVENTFULNESSES	EVISCERATE	EXAGGERATEDLY	EXASPERATIONS	EXCESSIVENESSES
EVENTRATED	EVISCERATED	EXAGGERATEDNESS	EXASPERATIVE	EXCHANGEABILITY
EVENTRATES	EVISCERATES	EXAGGERATES	EXASPERATOR	EXCHANGEABLE
EVENTRATING	EVISCERATING	EXAGGERATING	EXASPERATORS	EXCHANGEABLY
EVENTRATION	EVISCERATION	EXAGGERATINGLY	EXCAMBIONS	EXCHANGERS
EVENTRATIONS	EVISCERATIONS	EXAGGERATION	EXCAMBIUMS	EXCHANGING
EVENTUALISE	EVISCERATOR	EXAGGERATIONS	EXCARNATED	EXCHEQUERED
EVENTUALISED	EVISCERATORS	EXAGGERATIVE	EXCARNATES	EXCHEQUERING
EVENTUALISES	EVITATIONS	EXAGGERATOR	EXCARNATING	EXCHEQUERS
EVENTUALISING	EVITERNALLY	EXAGGERATORS	EXCARNATION	EXCIPIENTS
EVENTUALITIES	EVITERNITIES	EXAGGERATORY	EXCARNATIONS	EXCISIONAL
EVENTUALITY	EVITERNITY	EXAHERTZES	EXCAVATING	EXCITABILITIES
EVENTUALIZE	EVOCATIONS	EXALBUMINOUS	EXCAVATION	EXCITABILITY
EVENTUALIZED	EVOCATIVELY	EXALTATION	EXCAVATIONAL	EXCITABLENESS
EVENTUALIZES	EVOCATIVENESS	EXALTATIONS	EXCAVATIONS	EXCITABLENESSES
EVENTUALIZING	EVOCATIVENESSES	EXALTEDNESS	EXCAVATORS	EXCITANCIES
EVENTUALLY	EVOLUTIONAL	EXALTEDNESSES	EXCEEDABLE	EXCITATION
EVENTUATED	EVOLUTIONARILY	EXAMINABILITIES	EXCEEDINGLY	EXCITATIONS
EVENTUATES	EVOLUTIONARY	EXAMINABILITY	EXCELLENCE	EXCITATIVE
EVENTUATING	EVOLUTIONISM	EXAMINABLE	EXCELLENCES	EXCITATORY
EVENTUATION	EVOLUTIONISMS	EXAMINANTS	EXCELLENCIES	EXCITEDNESS
EVENTUATIONS	EVOLUTIONIST	EXAMINATES	EXCELLENCY	EXCITEDNESSES
EVERBLOOMING	EVOLUTIONISTIC	EXAMINATION	EXCELLENTLY	EXCITEMENT
EVERDURING	EVOLUTIONISTS	EXAMINATIONAL	EXCELSIORS	EXCITEMENTS
EVERGLADES	EVOLUTIONS	EXAMINATIONS	EXCENTRICS	EXCITINGLY
EVERGREENS	EVOLVEMENT	EXAMINATOR	EXCEPTANTS	EXCLAIMERS
EVERLASTING	EVOLVEMENTS	EXAMINATORS	EXCEPTIONABLE	EXCLAIMING
EVERLASTINGLY	EVONYMUSES	EXAMINERSHIP	EXCEPTIONABLY	EXCLAMATION
EVERLASTINGNESS	EVULGATING	EXAMINERSHIPS	EXCEPTIONAL	EXCLAMATIONAL
EVERLASTINGS	EXACERBATE	EXANIMATION	EXCEPTIONALISM	EXCLAMATIONS
EVERYDAYNESS	EXACERBATED	EXANIMATIONS	EXCEPTIONALISMS	EXCLAMATIVE
EVERYDAYNESSES	EXACERBATES	EXANTHEMAS	EXCEPTIONALITY	EXCLAMATORILY
EVERYPLACE	EXACERBATING	EXANTHEMATA	EXCEPTIONALLY	EXCLAMATORY
EVERYTHING	EXACERBATION	EXANTHEMATIC	EXCEPTIONALNESS	EXCLAUSTRATION
EVERYWHENCE	EXACERBATIONS	EXANTHEMATOUS	EXCEPTIONALS	EXCLAUSTRATIONS
EVERYWHERE	EXACERBESCENCE	EXARATIONS	EXCEPTIONS	EXCLOSURES
EVERYWHITHER	EXACERBESCENCES	EXARCHATES	EXCEPTIOUS	EXCLUDABILITIES

E

EXCLUDABILITY	EXCORTICATED	EXCURSIVELY	EXEMPLIFIER	EXHAUSTLESSLY
EXCLUDABLE	EXCORTICATES	EXCURSIVENESS	EXEMPLIFIERS	EXHAUSTLESSNESS
EXCLUDIBLE	EXCORTICATING	EXCURSIVENESSES	EXEMPLIFIES	EXHEREDATE
EXCLUSIONARY	EXCORTICATION	EXCURSUSES	EXEMPLIFYING	EXHEREDATED
EXCLUSIONISM	EXCORTICATIONS	EXCUSABLENESS	EXEMPTIONS	EXHEREDATES
EXCLUSIONISMS	EXCREMENTA	EXCUSABLENESSES	EXENTERATE	EXHEREDATING
EXCLUSIONIST	EXCREMENTAL	EXCUSATORY	EXENTERATED	EXHEREDATION
EXCLUSIONISTS	EXCREMENTITIAL	EXECRABLENESS	EXENTERATES	EXHEREDATIONS
EXCLUSIONS	EXCREMENTITIOUS	EXECRABLENESSES	EXENTERATING	EXHIBITERS
EXCLUSIVELY	EXCREMENTS	EXECRATING	EXENTERATION	EXHIBITING
EXCLUSIVENESS	EXCREMENTUM	EXECRATION	EXENTERATIONS	EXHIBITION
EXCLUSIVENESSES	EXCRESCENCE	EXECRATIONS	EXEQUATURS	EXHIBITIONER
EXCLUSIVES	EXCRESCENCES	EXECRATIVE	EXERCISABLE	EXHIBITIONERS
EXCLUSIVISM	EXCRESCENCIES	EXECRATIVELY	EXERCISERS	EXHIBITIONISM
EXCLUSIVISMS	EXCRESCENCY	EXECRATORS	EXERCISING	EXHIBITIONISMS
EXCLUSIVIST	EXCRESCENT	EXECRATORY	EXERCITATION	EXHIBITIONIST
EXCLUSIVISTS	EXCRESCENTIAL	EXECUTABLE	EXERCITATIONS	EXHIBITIONISTIC
EXCLUSIVITIES	EXCRESCENTLY	EXECUTABLES	EXERCYCLES	EXHIBITIONISTS
EXCLUSIVITY	EXCRETIONS	EXECUTANCIES	EXERGAMING	EXHIBITIONS
EXCOGITABLE	EXCRETORIES	EXECUTANCY	EXERGAMINGS	EXHIBITIVE
EXCOGITATE	EXCRUCIATE	EXECUTANTS	EXERTAINMENT	EXHIBITIVELY
EXCOGITATED	EXCRUCIATED	EXECUTARIES	EXERTAINMENTS	EXHIBITORS
EXCOGITATES	EXCRUCIATES	EXECUTIONER	EXFOLIANTS	EXHIBITORY
EXCOGITATING	EXCRUCIATING	EXECUTIONERS	EXFOLIATED	EXHILARANT
EXCOGITATION	EXCRUCIATINGLY	EXECUTIONS	EXFOLIATES	EXHILARANTS
EXCOGITATIONS	EXCRUCIATION	EXECUTIVELY	EXFOLIATING	EXHILARATE
EXCOGITATIVE	EXCRUCIATIONS	EXECUTIVES	EXFOLIATION	EXHILARATED
EXCOGITATOR	EXCULPABLE	EXECUTORIAL	EXFOLIATIONS	EXHILARATES
EXCOGITATORS	EXCULPATED	EXECUTORSHIP	EXFOLIATIVE	EXHILARATING
EXCOMMUNICABLE	EXCULPATES	EXECUTORSHIPS	EXFOLIATOR	EXHILARATINGLY
EXCOMMUNICATE	EXCULPATING	EXECUTRESS	EXFOLIATORS	EXHILARATION
EXCOMMUNICATED	EXCULPATION	EXECUTRESSES	EXHALATION	EXHILARATIONS
EXCOMMUNICATES	EXCULPATIONS	EXECUTRICES	EXHALATIONS	EXHILARATIVE
EXCOMMUNICATING	EXCULPATORY	EXECUTRIES	EXHAUSTEDLY	EXHILARATOR
EXCOMMUNICATION	EXCURSIONED	EXECUTRIXES	EXHAUSTERS	EXHILARATORS
EXCOMMUNICATIVE	EXCURSIONING	EXEGETICAL	EXHAUSTIBILITY	EXHILARATORY
EXCOMMUNICATOR	EXCURSIONISE	EXEGETICALLY	EXHAUSTIBLE	EXHORTATION
EXCOMMUNICATORS	EXCURSIONISED	EXEGETISTS	EXHAUSTING	EXHORTATIONS
EXCOMMUNICATORY	EXCURSIONISES	EXEMPLARILY	EXHAUSTINGLY	EXHORTATIVE
EXCOMMUNION	EXCURSIONISING	EXEMPLARINESS	EXHAUSTION	EXHORTATORY
EXCOMMUNIONS	EXCURSIONIST	EXEMPLARINESSES	EXHAUSTIONS	EXHUMATING
EXCORIATED	EXCURSIONISTS	EXEMPLARITIES	EXHAUSTIVE	EXHUMATION
EXCORIATES	EXCURSIONIZE	EXEMPLARITY	EXHAUSTIVELY	EXHUMATIONS
EXCORIATING	EXCURSIONIZED	EXEMPLIFIABLE	EXHAUSTIVENESS	EXIGENCIES
EXCORIATION	EXCURSIONIZES	EXEMPLIFICATION	EXHAUSTIVITIES	EXIGUITIES
EXCORIATIONS	EXCURSIONIZING	EXEMPLIFICATIVE	EXHAUSTIVITY	EXIGUOUSLY
EXCORTICATE	EXCURSIONS	EXEMPLIFIED	EXHAUSTLESS	EXIGUOUSNESS

EXIGUOUSNESSES

EXIGUOUSNESSES
EXILEMENTS
EXIMIOUSLY
EXISTENCES
EXISTENTIAL
EXISTENTIALISM
EXISTENTIALISMS
EXISTENTIALIST
EXISTENTIALISTS
EXISTENTIALLY
EXISTENTIALS
EXOBIOLOGICAL
EXOBIOLOGIES
EXOBIOLOGIST
EXOBIOLOGISTS
EXOBIOLOGY
EXOCENTRIC
EXOCUTICLE
EXOCUTICLES
EXOCYTOSED
EXOCYTOSES
EXOCYTOSING
EXOCYTOSIS
EXOCYTOTIC
EXODERMISES
EXODONTIAS
EXODONTICS
EXODONTIST
EXODONTISTS
EXOENZYMES
EXOERYTHROCYTIC
EXOGENETIC
EXOGENISMS
EXOGENOUSLY
EXONERATED
EXONERATES
EXONERATING
EXONERATION
EXONERATIONS
EXONERATIVE
EXONERATOR
EXONERATORS
EXONUCLEASE
EXONUCLEASES
EXONUMISTS
EXOPARASITE
EXOPARASITES

EXOPARASITIC
EXOPEPTIDASE
EXOPEPTIDASES
EXOPHAGIES
EXOPHAGOUS
EXOPHTHALMIA
EXOPHTHALMIAS
EXOPHTHALMIC
EXOPHTHALMOS
EXOPHTHALMOSES
EXOPHTHALMUS
EXOPHTHALMUSES
EXOPLANETS
EXOPODITES
EXOPODITIC
EXORABILITIES
EXORABILITY
EXORATIONS
EXORBITANCE
EXORBITANCES
EXORBITANCIES
EXORBITANCY
EXORBITANT
EXORBITANTLY
EXORBITATE
EXORBITATED
EXORBITATES
EXORBITATING
EXORCISERS
EXORCISING
EXORCISTIC
EXORCISTICAL
EXORCIZERS
EXORCIZING
EXOSKELETAL
EXOSKELETON
EXOSKELETONS
EXOSPHERES
EXOSPHERIC
EXOSPHERICAL
EXOSPORIUM
EXOSPOROUS
EXOTERICAL
EXOTERICALLY
EXOTERICISM
EXOTERICISMS
EXOTHERMAL

EXOTHERMALLY
EXOTHERMIC
EXOTHERMICALLY
EXOTHERMICITIES
EXOTHERMICITY
EXOTICALLY
EXOTICISMS
EXOTICISTS
EXOTICNESS
EXOTICNESSES
EXOTROPIAS
EXPANDABILITIES
EXPANDABILITY
EXPANDABLE
EXPANSIBILITIES
EXPANSIBILITY
EXPANSIBLE
EXPANSIBLY
EXPANSIONAL
EXPANSIONARY
EXPANSIONISM
EXPANSIONISMS
EXPANSIONIST
EXPANSIONISTIC
EXPANSIONISTS
EXPANSIONS
EXPANSIVELY
EXPANSIVENESS
EXPANSIVENESSES
EXPANSIVITIES
EXPANSIVITY
EXPATIATED
EXPATIATES
EXPATIATING
EXPATIATION
EXPATIATIONS
EXPATIATIVE
EXPATIATOR
EXPATIATORS
EXPATIATORY
EXPATRIATE
EXPATRIATED
EXPATRIATES
EXPATRIATING
EXPATRIATION
EXPATRIATIONS
EXPATRIATISM

EXPATRIATISMS
EXPECTABLE
EXPECTABLY
EXPECTANCE
EXPECTANCES
EXPECTANCIES
EXPECTANCY
EXPECTANTLY
EXPECTANTS
EXPECTATION
EXPECTATIONAL
EXPECTATIONS
EXPECTATIVE
EXPECTATIVES
EXPECTEDLY
EXPECTEDNESS
EXPECTEDNESSES
EXPECTINGLY
EXPECTINGS
EXPECTORANT
EXPECTORANTS
EXPECTORATE
EXPECTORATED
EXPECTORATES
EXPECTORATING
EXPECTORATION
EXPECTORATIONS
EXPECTORATIVE
EXPECTORATOR
EXPECTORATORS
EXPEDIENCE
EXPEDIENCES
EXPEDIENCIES
EXPEDIENCY
EXPEDIENTIAL
EXPEDIENTIALLY
EXPEDIENTLY
EXPEDIENTS
EXPEDITATE
EXPEDITATED
EXPEDITATES
EXPEDITATING
EXPEDITATION
EXPEDITATIONS
EXPEDITELY
EXPEDITERS
EXPEDITING

EXPEDITION
EXPEDITIONARY
EXPEDITIONS
EXPEDITIOUS
EXPEDITIOUSLY
EXPEDITIOUSNESS
EXPEDITIVE
EXPEDITORS
EXPELLABLE
EXPELLANTS
EXPELLENTS
EXPENDABILITIES
EXPENDABILITY
EXPENDABLE
EXPENDABLES
EXPENDABLY
EXPENDITURE
EXPENDITURES
EXPENSIVELY
EXPENSIVENESS
EXPENSIVENESSES
EXPERIENCE
EXPERIENCEABLE
EXPERIENCED
EXPERIENCELESS
EXPERIENCER
EXPERIENCERS
EXPERIENCES
EXPERIENCING
EXPERIENTIAL
EXPERIENTIALISM
EXPERIENTIALIST
EXPERIENTIALLY
EXPERIMENT
EXPERIMENTAL
EXPERIMENTALISE
EXPERIMENTALISM
EXPERIMENTALIST
EXPERIMENTALIZE
EXPERIMENTALLY
EXPERIMENTATION
EXPERIMENTATIVE
EXPERIMENTED
EXPERIMENTER
EXPERIMENTERS
EXPERIMENTING
EXPERIMENTIST

EXPERIMENTISTS	EXPLICITLY	EXPOSITORY	EXPROBRATING	EXSANGUINITIES
EXPERIMENTS	EXPLICITNESS	EXPOSITRESS	EXPROBRATION	EXSANGUINITY
EXPERTISED	EXPLICITNESSES	EXPOSITRESSES	EXPROBRATIONS	EXSANGUINOUS
EXPERTISES	EXPLOITABLE	EXPOSTULATE	EXPROBRATIVE	EXSCINDING
EXPERTISING	EXPLOITAGE	EXPOSTULATED	EXPROBRATORY	EXSECTIONS
EXPERTISMS	EXPLOITAGES	EXPOSTULATES	EXPROMISSION	EXSERTIONS
EXPERTIZED	EXPLOITATION	EXPOSTULATING	EXPROMISSIONS	EXSICCATED
EXPERTIZES	EXPLOITATIONS	EXPOSTULATINGLY	EXPROMISSOR	EXSICCATES
EXPERTIZING	EXPLOITATIVE	EXPOSTULATION	EXPROMISSORS	EXSICCATING
EXPERTNESS	EXPLOITATIVELY	EXPOSTULATIONS	EXPROPRIABLE	EXSICCATION
EXPERTNESSES	EXPLOITERS	EXPOSTULATIVE	EXPROPRIATE	EXSICCATIONS
EXPIATIONS	EXPLOITING	EXPOSTULATOR	EXPROPRIATED	EXSICCATIVE
EXPIRATION	EXPLOITIVE	EXPOSTULATORS	EXPROPRIATES	EXSICCATOR
EXPIRATIONS	EXPLORATION	EXPOSTULATORY	EXPROPRIATING	EXSICCATORS
EXPIRATORY	EXPLORATIONAL	EXPOSTURES	EXPROPRIATION	EXSOLUTION
EXPISCATED	EXPLORATIONIST	EXPOUNDERS	EXPROPRIATIONS	EXSOLUTIONS
EXPISCATES	EXPLORATIONISTS	EXPOUNDING	EXPROPRIATOR	EXSTIPULATE
EXPISCATING	EXPLORATIONS	EXPRESSAGE	EXPROPRIATORS	EXSTROPHIES
EXPISCATION	EXPLORATIVE	EXPRESSAGES	EXPUGNABLE	EXSUFFLATE
EXPISCATIONS	EXPLORATIVELY	EXPRESSERS	EXPUGNATION	EXSUFFLATED
EXPISCATORY	EXPLORATORY	EXPRESSIBLE	EXPUGNATIONS	EXSUFFLATES
EXPLAINABLE	EXPLOSIBLE	EXPRESSING	EXPULSIONS	EXSUFFLATING
EXPLAINERS	EXPLOSIONS	EXPRESSION	EXPUNCTING	EXSUFFLATION
EXPLAINING	EXPLOSIVELY	EXPRESSIONAL	EXPUNCTION	EXSUFFLATIONS
EXPLANATION	EXPLOSIVENESS	EXPRESSIONISM	EXPUNCTIONS	EXSUFFLICATE
EXPLANATIONS	EXPLOSIVENESSES	EXPRESSIONISMS	EXPURGATED	EXTEMPORAL
EXPLANATIVE	EXPLOSIVES	EXPRESSIONIST	EXPURGATES	EXTEMPORALLY
EXPLANATIVELY	EXPONENTIAL	EXPRESSIONISTIC	EXPURGATING	EXTEMPORANEITY
EXPLANATORILY	EXPONENTIALLY	EXPRESSIONISTS	EXPURGATION	EXTEMPORANEOUS
EXPLANATORY	EXPONENTIALS	EXPRESSIONLESS	EXPURGATIONS	EXTEMPORARILY
EXPLANTATION	EXPONENTIATION	EXPRESSIONS	EXPURGATOR	EXTEMPORARINESS
EXPLANTATIONS	EXPONENTIATIONS	EXPRESSIVE	EXPURGATORIAL	EXTEMPORARY
EXPLANTING	EXPORTABILITIES	EXPRESSIVELY	EXPURGATORS	EXTEMPORES
EXPLETIVELY	EXPORTABILITY	EXPRESSIVENESS	EXPURGATORY	EXTEMPORISATION
EXPLETIVES	EXPORTABLE	EXPRESSIVITIES	EXQUISITELY	EXTEMPORISE
EXPLICABLE	EXPORTATION	EXPRESSIVITY	EXQUISITENESS	EXTEMPORISED
EXPLICABLY	EXPORTATIONS	EXPRESSMAN	EXQUISITENESSES	EXTEMPORISER
EXPLICATED	EXPOSEDNESS	EXPRESSMEN	EXQUISITES	EXTEMPORISERS
EXPLICATES	EXPOSEDNESSES	EXPRESSNESS	EXSANGUINATE	EXTEMPORISES
EXPLICATING	EXPOSITING	EXPRESSNESSES	EXSANGUINATED	EXTEMPORISING
EXPLICATION	EXPOSITION	EXPRESSURE	EXSANGUINATES	EXTEMPORIZATION
EXPLICATIONS	EXPOSITIONAL	EXPRESSURES	EXSANGUINATING	EXTEMPORIZE
EXPLICATIVE	EXPOSITIONS	EXPRESSWAY	EXSANGUINATION	EXTEMPORIZED
EXPLICATIVELY	EXPOSITIVE	EXPRESSWAYS	EXSANGUINATIONS	EXTEMPORIZER
EXPLICATOR	EXPOSITIVELY	EXPROBRATE	EXSANGUINE	EXTEMPORIZERS
EXPLICATORS	EXPOSITORILY	EXPROBRATED	EXSANGUINED	EXTEMPORIZES
EXPLICATORY	EXPOSITORS	EXPROBRATES	EXSANGUINEOUS	EXTEMPORIZING

E

EXTENDABILITIES	EXTERIORISING	EXTINCTING	EXTRACTANTS	EXTRANUCLEAR
EXTENDABILITY	EXTERIORITIES	EXTINCTION	EXTRACTIBLE	EXTRAORDINAIRE
EXTENDABLE	EXTERIORITY	EXTINCTIONS	EXTRACTING	EXTRAORDINARIES
EXTENDEDLY	EXTERIORIZATION	EXTINCTIVE	EXTRACTION	EXTRAORDINARILY
EXTENDEDNESS	EXTERIORIZE	EXTINCTURE	EXTRACTIONS	EXTRAORDINARY
EXTENDEDNESSES	EXTERIORIZED	EXTINCTURES	EXTRACTIVE	EXTRAPOLATE
EXTENDIBILITIES	EXTERIORIZES	EXTINGUISH	EXTRACTIVELY	EXTRAPOLATED
EXTENDIBILITY	EXTERIORIZING	EXTINGUISHABLE	EXTRACTIVES	EXTRAPOLATES
EXTENDIBLE	EXTERIORLY	EXTINGUISHANT	EXTRACTORS	EXTRAPOLATING
EXTENSIBILITIES	EXTERMINABLE	EXTINGUISHANTS	EXTRACURRICULAR	EXTRAPOLATION
EXTENSIBILITY	EXTERMINATE	EXTINGUISHED	EXTRADITABLE	EXTRAPOLATIONS
EXTENSIBLE	EXTERMINATED	EXTINGUISHER	EXTRADITED	EXTRAPOLATIVE
EXTENSIBLENESS	EXTERMINATES	EXTINGUISHERS	EXTRADITES	EXTRAPOLATOR
EXTENSIFICATION	EXTERMINATING	EXTINGUISHES	EXTRADITING	EXTRAPOLATORS
EXTENSIMETER	EXTERMINATION	EXTINGUISHING	EXTRADITION	EXTRAPOLATORY
EXTENSIMETERS	EXTERMINATIONS	EXTINGUISHMENT	EXTRADITIONS	EXTRAPOSED
EXTENSIONAL	EXTERMINATIVE	EXTINGUISHMENTS	EXTRADOSES	EXTRAPOSES
EXTENSIONALISM	EXTERMINATOR	EXTIRPABLE	EXTRADOTAL	EXTRAPOSING
EXTENSIONALISMS	EXTERMINATORS	EXTIRPATED	EXTRADURAL	EXTRAPOSITION
EXTENSIONALITY	EXTERMINATORY	EXTIRPATES	EXTRADURALS	EXTRAPOSITIONS
EXTENSIONALLY	EXTERMINED	EXTIRPATING	EXTRAEMBRYONIC	EXTRAPYRAMIDAL
EXTENSIONIST	EXTERMINES	EXTIRPATION	EXTRAFLORAL	EXTRASENSORY
EXTENSIONISTS	EXTERMINING	EXTIRPATIONS	EXTRAFORANEOUS	EXTRASOLAR
EXTENSIONS	EXTERNALISATION	EXTIRPATIVE	EXTRAGALACTIC	EXTRASYSTOLE
EXTENSITIES	EXTERNALISE	EXTIRPATOR	EXTRAHEPATIC	EXTRASYSTOLES
EXTENSIVELY	EXTERNALISED	EXTIRPATORS	EXTRAJUDICIAL	EXTRATEXTUAL
EXTENSIVENESS	EXTERNALISES	EXTIRPATORY	EXTRAJUDICIALLY	EXTRATROPICAL
EXTENSIVENESSES	EXTERNALISING	EXTOLLINGLY	EXTRALEGAL	EXTRAUTERINE
EXTENSIVISATION	EXTERNALISM	EXTOLMENTS	EXTRALEGALLY	EXTRAVAGANCE
EXTENSIVIZATION	EXTERNALISMS	EXTORSIVELY	EXTRALIMITAL	EXTRAVAGANCES
EXTENSOMETER	EXTERNALIST	EXTORTIONARY	EXTRALIMITARY	EXTRAVAGANCIES
EXTENSOMETERS	EXTERNALISTS	EXTORTIONATE	EXTRALINGUISTIC	EXTRAVAGANCY
EXTENUATED	EXTERNALITIES	EXTORTIONATELY	EXTRALITERARY	EXTRAVAGANT
EXTENUATES	EXTERNALITY	EXTORTIONER	EXTRALITIES	EXTRAVAGANTLY
EXTENUATING	EXTERNALIZATION	EXTORTIONERS	EXTRALOGICAL	EXTRAVAGANZA
EXTENUATINGLY	EXTERNALIZE	EXTORTIONIST	EXTRAMARITAL	EXTRAVAGANZAS
EXTENUATINGS	EXTERNALIZED	EXTORTIONISTS	EXTRAMARITALLY	EXTRAVAGATE
EXTENUATION	EXTERNALIZES	EXTORTIONS	EXTRAMETRICAL	EXTRAVAGATED
EXTENUATIONS	EXTERNALIZING	EXTRABOLDS	EXTRAMUNDANE	EXTRAVAGATES
EXTENUATIVE	EXTERNALLY	EXTRACANONICAL	EXTRAMURAL	EXTRAVAGATING
EXTENUATOR	EXTERNSHIP	EXTRACELLULAR	EXTRAMURALLY	EXTRAVAGATION
EXTENUATORS	EXTERNSHIPS	EXTRACELLULARLY	EXTRAMUSICAL	EXTRAVAGATIONS
EXTENUATORY	EXTEROCEPTIVE	EXTRACORPOREAL	EXTRANEITIES	EXTRAVASATE
EXTERIORISATION	EXTEROCEPTOR	EXTRACRANIAL	EXTRANEITY	EXTRAVASATED
EXTERIORISE	EXTEROCEPTORS	EXTRACTABILITY	EXTRANEOUS	EXTRAVASATES
EXTERIORISED	EXTERRITORIAL	EXTRACTABLE	EXTRANEOUSLY	EXTRAVASATING
EXTERIORISES	EXTERRITORIALLY	EXTRACTANT	EXTRANEOUSNESS	EXTRAVASATION

EXTRAVASATIONS	EXTRICABLE	EXTRUDABILITY	EXULCERATING	EYEBROWLESS
EXTRAVASCULAR	EXTRICATED	EXTRUDABLE	EXULCERATION	EYEDNESSES
EXTRAVEHICULAR	EXTRICATES	EXTRUSIBLE	EXULCERATIONS	EYEDROPPER
EXTRAVERSION	EXTRICATING	EXTRUSIONS	EXULTANCES	EYEDROPPERS
EXTRAVERSIONS	EXTRICATION	EXTUBATING	EXULTANCIES	EYEGLASSES
EXTRAVERSIVE	EXTRICATIONS	EXUBERANCE	EXULTANTLY	EYELETEERS
EXTRAVERSIVELY	EXTRINSICAL	EXUBERANCES	EXULTATION	EYELETTING
EXTRAVERTED	EXTRINSICALITY	EXUBERANCIES	EXULTATIONS	EYEOPENERS
EXTRAVERTING	EXTRINSICALLY	EXUBERANCY	EXULTINGLY	EYEPOPPERS
EXTRAVERTS	EXTROVERSION	EXUBERANTLY	EXURBANITE	EYESHADOWS
EXTREMENESS	EXTROVERSIONS	EXUBERATED	EXURBANITES	EYESTRAINS
EXTREMENESSES	EXTROVERSIVE	EXUBERATES	EXUVIATING	EYESTRINGS
EXTREMISMS	EXTROVERSIVELY	EXUBERATING	EXUVIATION	EYEWITNESS
EXTREMISTS	EXTROVERTED	EXUDATIONS	EXUVIATIONS	EYEWITNESSES
EXTREMITIES	EXTROVERTING	EXULCERATE	EYEBALLING	
EXTREMOPHILE	EXTROVERTS	EXULCERATED	EYEBRIGHTS	
EXTREMOPHILES	EXTRUDABILITIES	EXULCERATES	EYEBROWING	

E

F

FABRICANTS	FACILITATORS	FACTORSHIP	FAIRNYTICKLE	FALSENESSES
FABRICATED	FACILITATORY	FACTORSHIPS	FAIRNYTICKLES	FALSEWORKS
FABRICATES	FACILITIES	FACTORYLIKE	FAIRNYTICLE	FALSIDICAL
FABRICATING	FACINERIOUS	FACTSHEETS	FAIRNYTICLES	FALSIFIABILITY
FABRICATION	FACINOROUS	FACTUALISM	FAIRYFLOSS	FALSIFIABLE
FABRICATIONS	FACINOROUSNESS	FACTUALISMS	FAIRYFLOSSES	FALSIFICATION
FABRICATIVE	FACSIMILED	FACTUALIST	FAIRYHOODS	FALSIFICATIONS
FABRICATOR	FACSIMILEING	FACTUALISTIC	FAIRYLANDS	FALSIFIERS
FABRICATORS	FACSIMILES	FACTUALISTS	FAITHFULLY	FALSIFYING
FABRICKING	FACSIMILIST	FACTUALITIES	FAITHFULNESS	FALTERINGLY
FABULATING	FACSIMILISTS	FACTUALITY	FAITHFULNESSES	FALTERINGS
FABULATORS	FACTICITIES	FACTUALNESS	FAITHLESSLY	FAMILIARISATION
FABULISING	FACTIONALISM	FACTUALNESSES	FAITHLESSNESS	FAMILIARISE
FABULISTIC	FACTIONALISMS	FACULTATIVE	FAITHLESSNESSES	FAMILIARISED
FABULIZING	FACTIONALIST	FACULTATIVELY	FAITHWORTHINESS	FAMILIARISER
FABULOSITIES	FACTIONALISTS	FACUNDITIES	FAITHWORTHY	FAMILIARISERS
FABULOSITY	FACTIONALLY	FADDINESSES	FALANGISMS	FAMILIARISES
FABULOUSLY	FACTIONARIES	FADDISHNESS	FALANGISTS	FAMILIARISING
FABULOUSNESS	FACTIONARY	FADDISHNESSES	FALCATIONS	FAMILIARITIES
FABULOUSNESSES	FACTIONIST	FADEDNESSES	FALCONIFORM	FAMILIARITY
FACEBOOKED	FACTIONISTS	FADELESSLY	FALCONRIES	FAMILIARIZATION
FACEBOOKING	FACTIOUSLY	FADOMETERS	FALDERALED	FAMILIARIZE
FACECLOTHS	FACTIOUSNESS	FAGGOTINGS	FALDERALING	FAMILIARIZED
FACELESSNESS	FACTIOUSNESSES	FAGGOTRIES	FALDISTORIES	FAMILIARIZER
FACELESSNESSES	FACTITIOUS	FAGOTTISTS	FALDISTORY	FAMILIARIZERS
FACELIFTED	FACTITIOUSLY	FAINEANCES	FALDSTOOLS	FAMILIARIZES
FACELIFTING	FACTITIOUSNESS	FAINEANCIES	FALLACIOUS	FAMILIARIZING
FACEPLATES	FACTITIVELY	FAINEANTISE	FALLACIOUSLY	FAMILIARLY
FACEPRINTS	FACTORABILITIES	FAINEANTISES	FALLACIOUSNESS	FAMILIARNESS
FACETIOUSLY	FACTORABILITY	FAINNESSES	FALLALERIES	FAMILIARNESSES
FACETIOUSNESS	FACTORABLE	FAINTHEARTED	FALLALISHLY	FAMILISTIC
FACETIOUSNESSES	FACTORAGES	FAINTHEARTEDLY	FALLBOARDS	FAMISHMENT
FACEWORKER	FACTORIALLY	FAINTINGLY	FALLFISHES	FAMISHMENTS
FACEWORKERS	FACTORIALS	FAINTISHNESS	FALLIBILISM	FAMOUSNESS
FACIALISTS	FACTORINGS	FAINTISHNESSES	FALLIBILISMS	FAMOUSNESSES
FACILENESS	FACTORISATION	FAINTNESSES	FALLIBILIST	FANATICALLY
FACILENESSES	FACTORISATIONS	FAIRGROUND	FALLIBILISTS	FANATICALNESS
FACILITATE	FACTORISED	FAIRGROUNDS	FALLIBILITIES	FANATICALNESSES
FACILITATED	FACTORISES	FAIRLEADER	FALLIBILITY	FANATICISE
FACILITATES	FACTORISING	FAIRLEADERS	FALLIBLENESS	FANATICISED
FACILITATING	FACTORIZATION	FAIRNESSES	FALLIBLENESSES	FANATICISES
FACILITATION	FACTORIZATIONS	FAIRNITICKLE	FALLOWNESS	FANATICISING
FACILITATIONS	FACTORIZED	FAIRNITICKLES	FALLOWNESSES	FANATICISM
FACILITATIVE	FACTORIZES	FAIRNITICLE	FALSEFACES	FANATICISMS
FACILITATOR	FACTORIZING	FAIRNITICLES	FALSEHOODS	FANATICIZE

FANATICIZED	FANTASTICS	FARRANDINES	FASHIONING	FATHOMLESSNESS
FANATICIZES	FANTASTRIES	FARRIERIES	FASHIONIST	FATIDICALLY
FANATICIZING	FANTASYING	FARSIGHTED	FASHIONISTA	FATIGABILITIES
FANCIFULLY	FANTASYLAND	FARSIGHTEDLY	FASHIONISTAS	FATIGABILITY
FANCIFULNESS	FANTASYLANDS	FARSIGHTEDNESS	FASHIONISTS	FATIGABLENESS
FANCIFULNESSES	FANTOCCINI	FARTHERMORE	FASHIONMONGER	FATIGABLENESSES
FANCIFYING	FARADISATION	FARTHERMOST	FASHIONMONGERS	FATIGATING
FANCINESSES	FARADISATIONS	FARTHINGALE	FASHIONMONGING	FATIGUABLE
FANCYWORKS	FARADISERS	FARTHINGALES	FASHIOUSNESS	FATIGUABLENESS
FANDANGLES	FARADISING	FARTHINGLAND	FASHIOUSNESSES	FATIGUELESS
FANDANGOES	FARADIZATION	FARTHINGLANDS	FASTBALLER	FATIGUINGLY
FANFARADES	FARADIZATIONS	FARTHINGLESS	FASTBALLERS	FATISCENCE
FANFARONADE	FARADIZERS	FARTHINGSWORTH	FASTENINGS	FATISCENCES
FANFARONADED	FARADIZING	FARTHINGSWORTHS	FASTIDIOUS	FATSHEDERA
FANFARONADES	FARANDINES	FASCIATELY	FASTIDIOUSLY	FATSHEDERAS
FANFARONADING	FARANDOLES	FASCIATION	FASTIDIOUSNESS	FATTENABLE
FANFARONAS	FARAWAYNESS	FASCIATIONS	FASTIGIATE	FATTENINGS
FANFOLDING	FARAWAYNESSES	FASCICULAR	FASTIGIATED	FATTINESSES
FANTABULOUS	FARBOROUGH	FASCICULARLY	FASTIGIUMS	FATUOUSNESS
FANTASISED	FARBOROUGHS	FASCICULATE	FASTNESSES	FATUOUSNESSES
FANTASISER	FARCEMEATS	FASCICULATED	FATALISTIC	FAULCHIONS
FANTASISERS	FARCICALITIES	FASCICULATELY	FATALISTICALLY	FAULTFINDER
FANTASISES	FARCICALITY	FASCICULATION	FATALITIES	FAULTFINDERS
FANTASISING	FARCICALLY	FASCICULATIONS	FATALNESSES	FAULTFINDING
FANTASISTS	FARCICALNESS	FASCICULES	FATBRAINED	FAULTFINDINGS
FANTASIZED	FARCICALNESSES	FASCICULUS	FATEFULNESS	FAULTINESS
FANTASIZER	FARCIFYING	FASCIITISES	FATEFULNESSES	FAULTINESSES
FANTASIZERS	FAREWELLED	FASCINATED	FATHEADEDLY	FAULTLESSLY
FANTASIZES	FAREWELLING	FASCINATEDLY	FATHEADEDNESS	FAULTLESSNESS
FANTASIZING	FARFETCHEDNESS	FASCINATES	FATHEADEDNESSES	FAULTLESSNESSES
FANTASMALLY	FARINACEOUS	FASCINATING	FATHERHOOD	FAULTLINES
FANTASMICALLY	FARINOSELY	FASCINATINGLY	FATHERHOODS	FAUNISTICALLY
FANTASQUES	FARKLEBERRIES	FASCINATION	FATHERINGS	FAUXBOURDON
FANTASTICAL	FARKLEBERRY	FASCINATIONS	FATHERLAND	FAUXBOURDONS
FANTASTICALITY	FARMERESSES	FASCINATIVE	FATHERLANDS	FAVORABLENESS
FANTASTICALLY	FARMERETTE	FASCINATOR	FATHERLESS	FAVORABLENESSES
FANTASTICALNESS	FARMERETTES	FASCINATORS	FATHERLESSNESS	FAVOREDNESS
FANTASTICATE	FARMHOUSES	FASCIOLIASES	FATHERLIKE	FAVOREDNESSES
FANTASTICATED	FARMSTEADS	FASCIOLIASIS	FATHERLINESS	FAVORINGLY
FANTASTICATES	FARMWORKER	FASCISTICALLY	FATHERLINESSES	FAVORITISM
FANTASTICATING	FARMWORKERS	FASCITISES	FATHERSHIP	FAVORITISMS
FANTASTICATION	FARNARKELED	FASHIONABILITY	FATHERSHIPS	FAVOURABLE
FANTASTICATIONS	FARNARKELING	FASHIONABLE	FATHOMABLE	FAVOURABLENESS
FANTASTICISM	FARNARKELINGS	FASHIONABLENESS	FATHOMETER	FAVOURABLY
FANTASTICISMS	FARNARKELS	FASHIONABLES	FATHOMETERS	FAVOUREDNESS
FANTASTICO	FARRAGINOUS	FASHIONABLY	FATHOMLESS	FAVOUREDNESSES
FANTASTICOES	FARRANDINE	FASHIONERS	FATHOMLESSLY	FAVOURINGLY

FAVOURITES	FEATHERINGS	FEDERALISMS	FELICITATING	FEMININENESS
FAVOURITISM	FEATHERLESS	FEDERALIST	FELICITATION	FEMININENESSES
FAVOURITISMS	FEATHERLIGHT	FEDERALISTIC	FELICITATIONS	FEMININISM
FAVOURLESS	FEATHERSTITCH	FEDERALISTS	FELICITATOR	FEMININISMS
FAWNINGNESS	FEATHERSTITCHED	FEDERALIZATION	FELICITATORS	FEMININITIES
FAWNINGNESSES	FEATHERSTITCHES	FEDERALIZATIONS	FELICITIES	FEMININITY
FAZENDEIRO	FEATHERWEIGHT	FEDERALIZE	FELICITOUS	FEMINISATION
FAZENDEIROS	FEATHERWEIGHTS	FEDERALIZED	FELICITOUSLY	FEMINISATIONS
FEARFULLER	FEATLINESS	FEDERALIZES	FELICITOUSNESS	FEMINISING
FEARFULLEST	FEATLINESSES	FEDERALIZING	FELINENESS	FEMINISTIC
FEARFULNESS	FEATURELESS	FEDERARIES	FELINENESSES	FEMINITIES
FEARFULNESSES	FEATURELESSNESS	FEDERATING	FELINITIES	FEMINIZATION
FEARLESSLY	FEATURETTE	FEDERATION	FELLATIONS	FEMINIZATIONS
FEARLESSNESS	FEATURETTES	FEDERATIONS	FELLATRICES	FEMINIZING
FEARLESSNESSES	FEBRICITIES	FEDERATIVE	FELLATRIXES	FEMTOSECOND
FEARNAUGHT	FEBRICULAS	FEDERATIVELY	FELLMONGER	FEMTOSECONDS
FEARNAUGHTS	FEBRICULES	FEDERATORS	FELLMONGERED	FENCELESSNESS
FEARNOUGHT	FEBRIFACIENT	FEEBLEMINDED	FELLMONGERIES	FENCELESSNESSES
FEARNOUGHTS	FEBRIFACIENTS	FEEBLEMINDEDLY	FELLMONGERING	FENDERLESS
FEARSOMELY	FEBRIFEROUS	FEEBLENESS	FELLMONGERINGS	FENESTELLA
FEARSOMENESS	FEBRIFUGAL	FEEBLENESSES	FELLMONGERS	FENESTELLAE
FEARSOMENESSES	FEBRIFUGES	FEEDGRAINS	FELLMONGERY	FENESTELLAS
FEASIBILITIES	FEBRILITIES	FEEDINGSTUFF	FELLNESSES	FENESTRALS
FEASIBILITY	FECKLESSLY	FEEDINGSTUFFS	FELLOWSHIP	FENESTRATE
FEASIBLENESS	FECKLESSNESS	FEEDSTOCKS	FELLOWSHIPED	FENESTRATED
FEASIBLENESSES	FECKLESSNESSES	FEEDSTUFFS	FELLOWSHIPING	FENESTRATION
FEATEOUSLY	FECULENCES	FEEDTHROUGH	FELLOWSHIPPED	FENESTRATIONS
FEATHERBED	FECULENCIES	FEEDTHROUGHS	FELLOWSHIPPING	FENNELFLOWER
FEATHERBEDDED	FECUNDATED	FEEDWATERS	FELLOWSHIPS	FENNELFLOWERS
FEATHERBEDDING	FECUNDATES	FEELINGLESS	FELONIOUSLY	FENUGREEKS
FEATHERBEDDINGS	FECUNDATING	FEELINGNESS	FELONIOUSNESS	FEOFFMENTS
FEATHERBEDS	FECUNDATION	FEELINGNESSES	FELONIOUSNESSES	FERACITIES
FEATHERBRAIN	FECUNDATIONS	FEIGNEDNESS	FELSPATHIC	FERETORIES
FEATHERBRAINED	FECUNDATOR	FEIGNEDNESSES	FELSPATHOID	FERMENTABILITY
FEATHERBRAINS	FECUNDATORS	FEIGNINGLY	FELSPATHOIDS	FERMENTABLE
FEATHEREDGE	FECUNDATORY	FEISTINESS	FELSPATHOSE	FERMENTATION
FEATHEREDGED	FECUNDITIES	FEISTINESSES	FEMALENESS	FERMENTATIONS
FEATHEREDGES	FEDERACIES	FELDSCHARS	FEMALENESSES	FERMENTATIVE
FEATHEREDGING	FEDERALESE	FELDSCHERS	FEMALITIES	FERMENTATIVELY
FEATHERHEAD	FEDERALESES	FELDSPATHIC	FEMETARIES	FERMENTERS
FEATHERHEADED	FEDERALISATION	FELDSPATHOID	FEMINACIES	FERMENTESCIBLE
FEATHERHEADS	FEDERALISATIONS	FELDSPATHOIDS	FEMINALITIES	FERMENTING
FEATHERIER	FEDERALISE	FELDSPATHOSE	FEMINALITY	FERMENTITIOUS
FEATHERIEST	FEDERALISED	FELDSPATHS	FEMINEITIES	FERMENTIVE
FEATHERINESS	FEDERALISES	FELICITATE	FEMINILITIES	FERMENTORS
FEATHERINESSES	FEDERALISING	FELICITATED	FEMINILITY	FERNALLIES
FEATHERING	FEDERALISM	FELICITATES	FEMININELY	FERNITICKLE

FERNITICKLES	FERROGRAMS	FERTILIZATIONS	FETIPAROUS	FEUILLETONISM
FERNITICLE	FERROGRAPHIES	FERTILIZED	FETISHISATION	FEUILLETONISMS
FERNITICLES	FERROGRAPHY	FERTILIZER	FETISHISATIONS	FEUILLETONIST
FERNTICKLE	FERROMAGNESIAN	FERTILIZERS	FETISHISED	FEUILLETONISTIC
FERNTICKLED	FERROMAGNET	FERTILIZES	FETISHISES	FEUILLETONISTS
FERNTICKLES	FERROMAGNETIC	FERTILIZING	FETISHISING	FEUILLETONS
FERNTICLED	FERROMAGNETISM	FERULACEOUS	FETISHISMS	FEVERISHLY
FERNTICLES	FERROMAGNETISMS	FERVENCIES	FETISHISTIC	FEVERISHNESS
FERNYTICKLE	FERROMAGNETS	FERVENTEST	FETISHISTICALLY	FEVERISHNESSES
FERNYTICKLES	FERROMANGANESE	FERVENTNESS	FETISHISTS	FEVEROUSLY
FERNYTICLE	FERROMANGANESES	FERVENTNESSES	FETISHIZATION	FEVERROOTS
FERNYTICLES	FERROMOLYBDENUM	FERVESCENT	FETISHIZATIONS	FEVERWEEDS
FEROCIOUSLY	FERRONICKEL	FERVIDITIES	FETISHIZED	FEVERWORTS
FEROCIOUSNESS	FERRONICKELS	FERVIDNESS	FETISHIZES	FIANCAILLES
FEROCIOUSNESSES	FERRONIERE	FERVIDNESSES	FETISHIZING	FIANCHETTI
FEROCITIES	FERRONIERES	FESCENNINE	FETOLOGIES	FIANCHETTO
FERRANDINE	FERRONNIERE	FESTILOGIES	FETOLOGIST	FIANCHETTOED
FERRANDINES	FERRONNIERES	FESTINATED	FETOLOGISTS	FIANCHETTOES
FERREDOXIN	FERROPRUSSIATE	FESTINATELY	FETOPROTEIN	FIANCHETTOING
FERREDOXINS	FERROPRUSSIATES	FESTINATES	FETOPROTEINS	FIANCHETTOS
FERRELLING	FERROSILICON	FESTINATING	FETOSCOPES	FIBERBOARD
FERRETINGS	FERROSILICONS	FESTINATION	FETOSCOPIES	FIBERBOARDS
FERRICYANIC	FERROSOFERRIC	FESTINATIONS	FETTERLESS	FIBERFILLS
FERRICYANIDE	FERROTYPED	FESTIVALGOER	FETTERLOCK	FIBERGLASS
FERRICYANIDES	FERROTYPES	FESTIVALGOERS	FETTERLOCKS	FIBERGLASSED
FERRICYANOGEN	FERROTYPING	FESTIVENESS	FETTUCCINE	FIBERGLASSES
FERRICYANOGENS	FERRUGINEOUS	FESTIVENESSES	FETTUCCINES	FIBERGLASSING
FERRIFEROUS	FERRUGINOUS	FESTIVITIES	FETTUCCINI	FIBERISATION
FERRIMAGNET	FERRYBOATS	FESTOLOGIES	FETTUCINES	FIBERISATIONS
FERRIMAGNETIC	FERTIGATED	FESTOONERIES	FETTUCINIS	FIBERISING
FERRIMAGNETISM	FERTIGATES	FESTOONERY	FEUDALISATION	FIBERIZATION
FERRIMAGNETISMS	FERTIGATING	FESTOONING	FEUDALISATIONS	FIBERIZATIONS
FERRIMAGNETS	FERTIGATION	FESTSCHRIFT	FEUDALISED	FIBERIZING
FERROCENES	FERTIGATIONS	FESTSCHRIFTEN	FEUDALISES	FIBERSCOPE
FERROCHROME	FERTILENESS	FESTSCHRIFTS	FEUDALISING	FIBERSCOPES
FERROCHROMES	FERTILENESSES	FETCHINGLY	FEUDALISMS	FIBREBOARD
FERROCHROMIUM	FERTILISABLE	FETICHISED	FEUDALISTIC	FIBREBOARDS
FERROCHROMIUMS	FERTILISATION	FETICHISES	FEUDALISTS	FIBREFILLS
FERROCONCRETE	FERTILISATIONS	FETICHISING	FEUDALITIES	FIBREGLASS
FERROCONCRETES	FERTILISED	FETICHISMS	FEUDALIZATION	FIBREGLASSES
FERROCYANIC	FERTILISER	FETICHISTIC	FEUDALIZATIONS	FIBREOPTIC
FERROCYANIDE	FERTILISERS	FETICHISTS	FEUDALIZED	FIBRESCOPE
FERROCYANIDES	FERTILISES	FETICHIZED	FEUDALIZES	FIBRESCOPES
FERROCYANOGEN	FERTILISING	FETICHIZES	FEUDALIZING	FIBRILLARY
FERROCYANOGENS	FERTILITIES	FETICHIZING	FEUDATORIES	FIBRILLATE
FERROELECTRIC	FERTILIZABLE	FETIDITIES	FEUILLETES	FIBRILLATED
FERROELECTRICS	FERTILIZATION	FETIDNESSES	FEUILLETON	FIBRILLATES

FIBRILLATING	FICTIONALISES	FIDEICOMMISSA	FIGURATIVE	FILMOGRAPHIES
FIBRILLATION	FICTIONALISING	FIDEICOMMISSARY	FIGURATIVELY	FILMOGRAPHY
FIBRILLATIONS	FICTIONALITIES	FIDEICOMMISSUM	FIGURATIVENESS	FILMSETTER
FIBRILLIFORM	FICTIONALITY	FIDELISMOS	FIGUREHEAD	FILMSETTERS
FIBRILLINS	FICTIONALIZE	FIDELISTAS	FIGUREHEADS	FILMSETTING
FIBRILLOSE	FICTIONALIZED	FIDELITIES	FIGURELESS	FILMSETTINGS
FIBRILLOUS	FICTIONALIZES	FIDGETIEST	FIGUREWORK	FILMSTRIPS
FIBRINOGEN	FICTIONALIZING	FIDGETINESS	FIGUREWORKS	FILOPLUMES
FIBRINOGENIC	FICTIONALLY	FIDGETINESSES	FILAGGRINS	FILOPODIUM
FIBRINOGENOUS	FICTIONEER	FIDGETINGLY	FILAGREEING	FILOSELLES
FIBRINOGENS	FICTIONEERING	FIDUCIALLY	FILAMENTARY	FILOVIRUSES
FIBRINOIDS	FICTIONEERINGS	FIDUCIARIES	FILAMENTOUS	FILTERABILITIES
FIBRINOLYSES	FICTIONEERS	FIDUCIARILY	FILARIASES	FILTERABILITY
FIBRINOLYSIN	FICTIONISATION	FIELDBOOTS	FILARIASIS	FILTERABLE
FIBRINOLYSINS	FICTIONISATIONS	FIELDCRAFT	FILATORIES	FILTERABLENESS
FIBRINOLYSIS	FICTIONISE	FIELDCRAFTS	FILCHINGLY	FILTHINESS
FIBRINOLYTIC	FICTIONISED	FIELDFARES	FILEFISHES	FILTHINESSES
FIBRINOPEPTIDE	FICTIONISES	FIELDMOUSE	FILIALNESS	FILTRABILITIES
FIBRINOPEPTIDES	FICTIONISING	FIELDPIECE	FILIALNESSES	FILTRABILITY
FIBROBLAST	FICTIONIST	FIELDPIECES	FILIATIONS	FILTRATABLE
FIBROBLASTIC	FICTIONISTS	FIELDSTONE	FILIBUSTER	FILTRATING
FIBROBLASTS	FICTIONIZATION	FIELDSTONES	FILIBUSTERED	FILTRATION
FIBROCARTILAGE	FICTIONIZATIONS	FIELDSTRIP	FILIBUSTERER	FILTRATIONS
FIBROCARTILAGES	FICTIONIZE	FIELDSTRIPPED	FILIBUSTERERS	FIMBRIATED
FIBROCEMENT	FICTIONIZED	FIELDSTRIPPING	FILIBUSTERING	FIMBRIATES
FIBROCEMENTS	FICTIONIZES	FIELDSTRIPS	FILIBUSTERINGS	FIMBRIATING
FIBROCYSTIC	FICTIONIZING	FIELDVOLES	FILIBUSTERISM	FIMBRIATION
FIBROCYTES	FICTITIOUS	FIELDWARDS	FILIBUSTERISMS	FIMBRIATIONS
FIBROLINES	FICTITIOUSLY	FIELDWORKER	FILIBUSTEROUS	FIMBRILLATE
FIBROLITES	FICTITIOUSNESS	FIELDWORKERS	FILIBUSTERS	FIMICOLOUS
FIBROMATOUS	FICTIVENESS	FIELDWORKS	FILICINEAN	FINABLENESS
FIBROMYALGIA	FICTIVENESSES	FIENDISHLY	FILIGRAINS	FINABLENESSES
FIBROMYALGIAS	FIDDIOUSED	FIENDISHNESS	FILIGRANES	FINALISATION
FIBRONECTIN	FIDDIOUSES	FIENDISHNESSES	FILIGREEING	FINALISATIONS
FIBRONECTINS	FIDDIOUSING	FIERCENESS	FILIOPIETISTIC	FINALISERS
FIBROSARCOMA	FIDDLEBACK	FIERCENESSES	FILIPENDULOUS	FINALISING
FIBROSARCOMAS	FIDDLEBACKS	FIERINESSES	FILLAGREED	FINALISTIC
FIBROSARCOMATA	FIDDLEDEDEE	FIFTEENERS	FILLAGREEING	FINALITIES
FIBROSITIS	FIDDLEDEEDEE	FIFTEENTHLY	FILLAGREES	FINALIZATION
FIBROSITISES	FIDDLEHEAD	FIFTEENTHS	FILLESTERS	FINALIZATIONS
FIBROUSNESS	FIDDLEHEADS	FIGHTBACKS	FILLIPEENS	FINALIZERS
FIBROUSNESSES	FIDDLENECK	FIGURABILITIES	FILLISTERS	FINALIZING
FIBROVASCULAR	FIDDLENECKS	FIGURABILITY	FILMICALLY	FINANCIALIST
FICKLENESS	FIDDLESTICK	FIGURANTES	FILMINESSES	FINANCIALISTS
FICKLENESSES	FIDDLESTICKS	FIGURATELY	FILMMAKERS	FINANCIALLY
FICTIONALISE	FIDDLEWOOD	FIGURATION	FILMMAKING	FINANCIERED
FICTIONALISED	FIDDLEWOODS	FIGURATIONS	FILMMAKINGS	FINANCIERING

FINANCIERS	FINICALITY	FIRELIGHTER	FISSICOSTATE	FLACCIDNESSES
FINANCINGS	FINICALNESS	FIRELIGHTERS	FISSILINGUAL	FLACKERIES
FINEABLENESS	FINICALNESSES	FIRELIGHTS	FISSILITIES	FLACKERING
FINEABLENESSES	FINICKETIER	FIREPLACED	FISSIONABILITY	FLAFFERING
FINENESSES	FINICKETIEST	FIREPLACES	FISSIONABLE	FLAGELLANT
FINESSINGS	FINICKIEST	FIREPOWERS	FISSIONABLES	FLAGELLANTISM
FINGERBOARD	FINICKINESS	FIREPROOFED	FISSIONING	FLAGELLANTISMS
FINGERBOARDS	FINICKINESSES	FIREPROOFING	FISSIPALMATE	FLAGELLANTS
FINGERBOWL	FINICKINGS	FIREPROOFINGS	FISSIPARISM	FLAGELLATE
FINGERBOWLS	FINISHINGS	FIREPROOFS	FISSIPARISMS	FLAGELLATED
FINGERBREADTH	FINITENESS	FIRESCREEN	FISSIPARITIES	FLAGELLATES
FINGERBREADTHS	FINITENESSES	FIRESCREENS	FISSIPARITY	FLAGELLATING
FINGERGLASS	FINNICKIER	FIRESTONES	FISSIPAROUS	FLAGELLATION
FINGERGLASSES	FINNICKIEST	FIRESTORMS	FISSIPAROUSLY	FLAGELLATIONS
FINGERGUARD	FINNOCHIOS	FIRETHORNS	FISSIPAROUSNESS	FLAGELLATOR
FINGERGUARDS	FINOCCHIOS	FIRETRUCKS	FISSIPEDAL	FLAGELLATORS
FINGERHOLD	FIORATURAE	FIREWALLED	FISSIPEDES	FLAGELLATORY
FINGERHOLDS	FIREBALLER	FIREWALLING	FISSIROSTRAL	FLAGELLIFEROUS
FINGERHOLE	FIREBALLERS	FIREWARDEN	FISTFIGHTS	FLAGELLIFORM
FINGERHOLES	FIREBALLING	FIREWARDENS	FISTICUFFS	FLAGELLINS
FINGERINGS	FIREBOARDS	FIREWATERS	FITFULNESS	FLAGELLOMANIA
FINGERLESS	FIREBOMBED	FIRMAMENTAL	FITFULNESSES	FLAGELLOMANIAC
FINGERLIKE	FIREBOMBER	FIRMAMENTS	FITTINGNESS	FLAGELLOMANIACS
FINGERLING	FIREBOMBERS	FIRMNESSES	FITTINGNESSES	FLAGELLOMANIAS
FINGERLINGS	FIREBOMBING	FIRSTBORNS	FIVEFINGER	FLAGELLUMS
FINGERMARK	FIREBOMBINGS	FIRSTFRUITS	FIVEFINGERS	FLAGEOLETS
FINGERMARKS	FIREBRANDS	FIRSTLINGS	FIVEPENCES	FLAGGINESS
FINGERNAIL	FIREBREAKS	FIRSTNESSES	FIXEDNESSES	FLAGGINESSES
FINGERNAILS	FIREBRICKS	FISCALISTS	FIXTURELESS	FLAGGINGLY
FINGERPICK	FIREBUSHES	FISHABILITIES	FIZGIGGING	FLAGITATED
FINGERPICKED	FIRECRACKER	FISHABILITY	FIZZENLESS	FLAGITATES
FINGERPICKING	FIRECRACKERS	FISHBURGER	FIZZINESSES	FLAGITATING
FINGERPICKINGS	FIRECRESTS	FISHBURGERS	FLABBERGAST	FLAGITATION
FINGERPICKS	FIREDRAGON	FISHERFOLK	FLABBERGASTED	FLAGITATIONS
FINGERPLATE	FIREDRAGONS	FISHERWOMAN	FLABBERGASTING	FLAGITIOUS
FINGERPLATES	FIREDRAKES	FISHERWOMEN	FLABBERGASTS	FLAGITIOUSLY
FINGERPOST	FIREFANGED	FISHFINGER	FLABBINESS	FLAGITIOUSNESS
FINGERPOSTS	FIREFANGING	FISHFINGERS	FLABBINESSES	FLAGRANCES
FINGERPRINT	FIREFIGHTER	FISHIFYING	FLABELLATE	FLAGRANCIES
FINGERPRINTED	FIREFIGHTERS	FISHINESSES	FLABELLATION	FLAGRANTLY
FINGERPRINTING	FIREFIGHTING	FISHMONGER	FLABELLATIONS	FLAGRANTNESS
FINGERPRINTINGS	FIREFIGHTINGS	FISHMONGERS	FLABELLIFORM	FLAGRANTNESSES
FINGERPRINTS	FIREFIGHTS	FISHPLATES	FLABELLUMS	FLAGSTAFFS
FINGERSTALL	FIREFLOATS	FISHTAILED	FLACCIDEST	FLAGSTAVES
FINGERSTALLS	FIREFLOODS	FISHTAILING	FLACCIDITIES	FLAGSTICKS
FINGERTIPS	FIREGUARDS	FISHWIFELY	FLACCIDITY	FLAGSTONES
FINICALITIES	FIREHOUSES	FISHYBACKS	FLACCIDNESS	FLAKINESSES

FLAMBEEING	FLAPPERISH	FLATULENTLY	FLEECHINGS	FLICHTERING
FLAMBOYANCE	FLAPTRACKS	FLATWASHES	FLEECHMENT	FLICKERING
FLAMBOYANCES	FLAREBACKS	FLAUGHTERED	FLEECHMENTS	FLICKERINGLY
FLAMBOYANCIES	FLASHBACKED	FLAUGHTERING	FLEECINESS	FLICKERTAIL
FLAMBOYANCY	FLASHBACKING	FLAUGHTERS	FLEECINESSES	FLICKERTAILS
FLAMBOYANT	FLASHBACKS	FLAUGHTING	FLEERINGLY	FLIGHTIEST
FLAMBOYANTE	FLASHBOARD	FLAUNCHING	FLEETINGLY	FLIGHTINESS
FLAMBOYANTES	FLASHBOARDS	FLAUNCHINGS	FLEETINGNESS	FLIGHTINESSES
FLAMBOYANTLY	FLASHBULBS	FLAUNTIEST	FLEETINGNESSES	FLIGHTLESS
FLAMBOYANTS	FLASHCARDS	FLAUNTINESS	FLEETNESSES	FLIMFLAMMED
FLAMEPROOF	FLASHCUBES	FLAUNTINESSES	FLEHMENING	FLIMFLAMMER
FLAMEPROOFED	FLASHINESS	FLAUNTINGLY	FLEMISHING	FLIMFLAMMERIES
FLAMEPROOFER	FLASHINESSES	FLAVANONES	FLESHHOODS	FLIMFLAMMERS
FLAMEPROOFERS	FLASHLAMPS	FLAVESCENT	FLESHINESS	FLIMFLAMMERY
FLAMEPROOFING	FLASHLIGHT	FLAVIVIRUS	FLESHINESSES	FLIMFLAMMING
FLAMEPROOFS	FLASHLIGHTS	FLAVIVIRUSES	FLESHLIEST	FLIMSINESS
FLAMETHROWER	FLASHMOBBING	FLAVONOIDS	FLESHLINESS	FLIMSINESSES
FLAMETHROWERS	FLASHMOBBINGS	FLAVOPROTEIN	FLESHLINESSES	FLINCHINGLY
FLAMINGOES	FLASHOVERS	FLAVOPROTEINS	FLESHLINGS	FLINCHINGS
FLAMINICAL	FLASHPACKER	FLAVOPURPURIN	FLESHMENTS	FLINDERSIA
FLAMMABILITIES	FLASHPACKERS	FLAVOPURPURINS	FLESHMONGER	FLINDERSIAS
FLAMMABILITY	FLASHTUBES	FLAVORFULLY	FLESHMONGERS	FLINTHEADS
FLAMMABLES	FLATBREADS	FLAVORINGS	FLESHWORMS	FLINTIFIED
FLAMMIFEROUS	FLATFISHES	FLAVORISTS	FLETCHINGS	FLINTIFIES
FLAMMULATED	FLATFOOTED	FLAVORLESS	FLEURETTES	FLINTIFYING
FLAMMULATION	FLATFOOTING	FLAVORSOME	FLEXECUTIVE	FLINTINESS
FLAMMULATIONS	FLATLANDER	FLAVOURDYNAMICS	FLEXECUTIVES	FLINTINESSES
FLANCHINGS	FLATLANDERS	FLAVOURERS	FLEXIBILITIES	FLINTLOCKS
FLANCONADE	FLATLINERS	FLAVOURFUL	FLEXIBILITY	FLIPFLOPPED
FLANCONADES	FLATLINING	FLAVOURFULLY	FLEXIBLENESS	FLIPFLOPPING
FLANGELESS	FLATNESSES	FLAVOURING	FLEXIBLENESSES	FLIPPANCIES
FLANKERING	FLATSCREEN	FLAVOURINGS	FLEXICURITIES	FLIPPANTLY
FLANNELBOARD	FLATSCREENS	FLAVOURLESS	FLEXICURITY	FLIPPANTNESS
FLANNELBOARDS	FLATSHARES	FLAVOURSOME	FLEXIHOURS	FLIPPANTNESSES
FLANNELETS	FLATTENERS	FLAWLESSLY	FLEXIONLESS	FLIRTATION
FLANNELETTE	FLATTENING	FLAWLESSNESS	FLEXITARIAN	FLIRTATIONS
FLANNELETTES	FLATTERABLE	FLAWLESSNESSES	FLEXITARIANISM	FLIRTATIOUS
FLANNELGRAPH	FLATTERERS	FLEAHOPPER	FLEXITARIANISMS	FLIRTATIOUSLY
FLANNELGRAPHS	FLATTERIES	FLEAHOPPERS	FLEXITARIANS	FLIRTATIOUSNESS
FLANNELING	FLATTERING	FLECHETTES	FLEXITIMES	FLIRTINGLY
FLANNELLED	FLATTERINGLY	FLECKERING	FLEXOGRAPHIC	FLITTERING
FLANNELLING	FLATTEROUS	FLECTIONAL	FLEXOGRAPHIES	FLITTERMICE
FLANNELMOUTHED	FLATTEROUSLY	FLECTIONLESS	FLEXOGRAPHY	FLITTERMOUSE
FLAPDOODLE	FLATULENCE	FLEDGELING	FLEXTIMERS	FLOATABILITIES
FLAPDOODLES	FLATULENCES	FLEDGELINGS	FLEXUOUSLY	FLOATABILITY
FLAPPERHOOD	FLATULENCIES	FLEDGLINGS	FLIBBERTIGIBBET	FLOATATION
FLAPPERHOODS	FLATULENCY	FLEECELESS	FLICHTERED	FLOATATIONS

F

FLOATINGLY	FLORESCENCE	FLOWERETTES	FLUNITRAZEPAMS	FLUOROACETATE
FLOATPLANE	FLORESCENCES	FLOWERIEST	FLUNKEYDOM	FLUOROACETATES
FLOATPLANES	FLORESCENT	FLOWERINESS	FLUNKEYDOMS	FLUOROCARBON
FLOCCILLATION	FLORIATION	FLOWERINESSES	FLUNKEYISH	FLUOROCARBONS
FLOCCILLATIONS	FLORIATIONS	FLOWERINGS	FLUNKEYISM	FLUOROCHROME
FLOCCULANT	FLORIBUNDA	FLOWERLESS	FLUNKEYISMS	FLUOROCHROMES
FLOCCULANTS	FLORIBUNDAS	FLOWERLIKE	FLUNKYISMS	FLUOROGRAPHIC
FLOCCULATE	FLORICANES	FLOWERPOTS	FLUORAPATITE	FLUOROGRAPHIES
FLOCCULATED	FLORICULTURAL	FLOWINGNESS	FLUORAPATITES	FLUOROGRAPHY
FLOCCULATES	FLORICULTURE	FLOWINGNESSES	FLUORESCED	FLUOROMETER
FLOCCULATING	FLORICULTURES	FLOWMETERS	FLUORESCEIN	FLUOROMETERS
FLOCCULATION	FLORICULTURIST	FLOWSTONES	FLUORESCEINE	FLUOROMETRIC
FLOCCULATIONS	FLORICULTURISTS	FLUCTUATED	FLUORESCEINES	FLUOROMETRIES
FLOCCULATOR	FLORIDEANS	FLUCTUATES	FLUORESCEINS	FLUOROMETRY
FLOCCULATORS	FLORIDEOUS	FLUCTUATING	FLUORESCENCE	FLUOROPHORE
FLOCCULENCE	FLORIDITIES	FLUCTUATION	FLUORESCENCES	FLUOROPHORES
FLOCCULENCES	FLORIDNESS	FLUCTUATIONAL	FLUORESCENT	FLUOROSCOPE
FLOCCULENCIES	FLORIDNESSES	FLUCTUATIONS	FLUORESCENTS	FLUOROSCOPED
FLOCCULENCY	FLORIFEROUS	FLUEGELHORN	FLUORESCER	FLUOROSCOPES
FLOCCULENT	FLORIFEROUSNESS	FLUEGELHORNS	FLUORESCERS	FLUOROSCOPIC
FLOCCULENTLY	FLORIGENIC	FLUENTNESS	FLUORESCES	FLUOROSCOPIES
FLOODGATES	FLORILEGIA	FLUENTNESSES	FLUORESCING	FLUOROSCOPING
FLOODLIGHT	FLORILEGIUM	FLUFFINESS	FLUORIDATE	FLUOROSCOPIST
FLOODLIGHTED	FLORISTICALLY	FLUFFINESSES	FLUORIDATED	FLUOROSCOPISTS
FLOODLIGHTING	FLORISTICS	FLUGELHORN	FLUORIDATES	FLUOROSCOPY
FLOODLIGHTINGS	FLORISTRIES	FLUGELHORNIST	FLUORIDATING	FLUOROTYPE
FLOODLIGHTS	FLOSCULOUS	FLUGELHORNISTS	FLUORIDATION	FLUOROTYPES
FLOODMARKS	FLOTATIONS	FLUGELHORNS	FLUORIDATIONS	FLUOROURACIL
FLOODPLAIN	FLOUNCIEST	FLUIDEXTRACT	FLUORIDISE	FLUOROURACILS
FLOODPLAINS	FLOUNCINGS	FLUIDEXTRACTS	FLUORIDISED	FLUORSPARS
FLOODTIDES	FLOUNDERED	FLUIDIFIED	FLUORIDISES	FLUOXETINE
FLOODWALLS	FLOUNDERING	FLUIDIFIES	FLUORIDISING	FLUOXETINES
FLOODWATER	FLOURISHED	FLUIDIFYING	FLUORIDIZE	FLUPHENAZINE
FLOODWATERS	FLOURISHER	FLUIDISATION	FLUORIDIZED	FLUPHENAZINES
FLOORBOARD	FLOURISHERS	FLUIDISATIONS	FLUORIDIZES	FLUSHNESSES
FLOORBOARDS	FLOURISHES	FLUIDISERS	FLUORIDIZING	FLUSHWORKS
FLOORCLOTH	FLOURISHING	FLUIDISING	FLUORIMETER	FLUSTEREDLY
FLOORCLOTHS	FLOURISHINGLY	FLUIDITIES	FLUORIMETERS	FLUSTERING
FLOORHEADS	FLOUTINGLY	FLUIDIZATION	FLUORIMETRIC	FLUSTERMENT
FLOORSHOWS	FLOUTINGSTOCK	FLUIDIZATIONS	FLUORIMETRIES	FLUSTERMENTS
FLOORWALKER	FLOUTINGSTOCKS	FLUIDIZERS	FLUORIMETRY	FLUSTRATED
FLOORWALKERS	FLOWCHARTING	FLUIDIZING	FLUORINATE	FLUSTRATES
FLOPHOUSES	FLOWCHARTINGS	FLUIDNESSES	FLUORINATED	FLUSTRATING
FLOPPINESS	FLOWCHARTS	FLUKINESSES	FLUORINATES	FLUSTRATION
FLOPPINESSES	FLOWERAGES	FLUMMERIES	FLUORINATING	FLUSTRATIONS
FLORENTINE	FLOWERBEDS	FLUMMOXING	FLUORINATION	FLUTEMOUTH
FLORENTINES	FLOWERETTE	FLUNITRAZEPAM	FLUORINATIONS	FLUTEMOUTHS

FLUTTERBOARD	FOETATIONS	FOMENTATIONS	FOOTLAMBERT	FORBIDDANCES
FLUTTERBOARDS	FOETICIDAL	FONCTIONNAIRE	FOOTLAMBERTS	FORBIDDENLY
FLUTTERERS	FOETICIDES	FONCTIONNAIRES	FOOTLESSLY	FORBIDDERS
FLUTTERING	FOETIDNESS	FONDLINGLY	FOOTLESSNESS	FORBIDDING
FLUTTERINGLY	FOETIDNESSES	FONDNESSES	FOOTLESSNESSES	FORBIDDINGLY
FLUVIALIST	FOETIPAROUS	FONTANELLE	FOOTLIGHTS	FORBIDDINGNESS
FLUVIALISTS	FOETOSCOPIES	FONTANELLES	FOOTLOCKER	FORBIDDINGS
FLUVIATILE	FOETOSCOPY	FONTICULUS	FOOTLOCKERS	FORCEDNESS
FLUVIOMARINE	FOGGINESSES	FONTINALIS	FOOTNOTING	FORCEDNESSES
FLUVOXAMINE	FOGRAMITES	FONTINALISES	FOOTPLATEMAN	FORCEFULLY
FLUVOXAMINES	FOGRAMITIES	FOODLESSNESS	FOOTPLATEMEN	FORCEFULNESS
FLUXIONALLY	FOISONLESS	FOODLESSNESSES	FOOTPLATES	FORCEFULNESSES
FLUXIONARY	FOLIACEOUS	FOODSTUFFS	FOOTPLATEWOMAN	FORCEMEATS
FLUXIONIST	FOLIATIONS	FOOLBEGGED	FOOTPLATEWOMEN	FORCEPSLIKE
FLUXIONISTS	FOLIATURES	FOOLFISHES	FOOTPRINTS	FORCIBILITIES
FLUXMETERS	FOLKISHNESS	FOOLHARDIER	FOOTSLOGGED	FORCIBILITY
FLYBLOWING	FOLKISHNESSES	FOOLHARDIEST	FOOTSLOGGER	FORCIBLENESS
FLYBRIDGES	FOLKLORISH	FOOLHARDILY	FOOTSLOGGERS	FORCIBLENESSES
FLYCATCHER	FOLKLORIST	FOOLHARDINESS	FOOTSLOGGING	FORCIPATED
FLYCATCHERS	FOLKLORISTIC	FOOLHARDINESSES	FOOTSLOGGINGS	FORCIPATION
FLYPITCHER	FOLKLORISTS	FOOLHARDISE	FOOTSORENESS	FORCIPATIONS
FLYPITCHERS	FOLKSINESS	FOOLHARDISES	FOOTSORENESSES	FOREARMING
FLYPITCHES	FOLKSINESSES	FOOLHARDIZE	FOOTSTALKS	FOREBITTER
FLYPOSTERS	FOLKSINGER	FOOLHARDIZES	FOOTSTALLS	FOREBITTERS
FLYPOSTING	FOLKSINGERS	FOOLISHEST	FOOTSTOCKS	FOREBODEMENT
FLYPOSTINGS	FOLKSINGING	FOOLISHNESS	FOOTSTONES	FOREBODEMENTS
FLYRODDERS	FOLKSINGINGS	FOOLISHNESSES	FOOTSTOOLED	FOREBODERS
FLYSCREENS	FOLKSONOMIES	FOOTBALLENE	FOOTSTOOLS	FOREBODIES
FLYSPECKED	FOLKSONOMY	FOOTBALLENES	FOPPISHNESS	FOREBODING
FLYSPECKING	FOLKTRONICA	FOOTBALLER	FOPPISHNESSES	FOREBODINGLY
FLYSTRIKES	FOLKTRONICAS	FOOTBALLERS	FORAMINATED	FOREBODINGNESS
FLYSWATTER	FOLLICULAR	FOOTBALLING	FORAMINIFER	FOREBODINGS
FLYSWATTERS	FOLLICULATE	FOOTBALLIST	FORAMINIFERA	FOREBRAINS
FLYWEIGHTS	FOLLICULATED	FOOTBALLISTS	FORAMINIFERAL	FORECABINS
FOAMFLOWER	FOLLICULIN	FOOTBOARDS	FORAMINIFERAN	FORECADDIE
FOAMFLOWERS	FOLLICULINS	FOOTBRAKES	FORAMINIFERANS	FORECADDIES
FOAMINESSES	FOLLICULITIS	FOOTBREADTH	FORAMINIFEROUS	FORECARRIAGE
FOCALISATION	FOLLICULITISES	FOOTBREADTHS	FORAMINIFERS	FORECARRIAGES
FOCALISATIONS	FOLLICULOSE	FOOTBRIDGE	FORAMINOUS	FORECASTABLE
FOCALISING	FOLLICULOUS	FOOTBRIDGES	FORBEARANCE	FORECASTED
FOCALIZATION	FOLLOWABLE	FOOTCLOTHS	FORBEARANCES	FORECASTER
FOCALIZATIONS	FOLLOWERSHIP	FOOTDRAGGER	FORBEARANT	FORECASTERS
FOCALIZING	FOLLOWERSHIPS	FOOTDRAGGERS	FORBEARERS	FORECASTING
FOCIMETERS	FOLLOWINGS	FOOTFAULTED	FORBEARING	FORECASTINGS
FOCOMETERS	FOLLOWSHIP	FOOTFAULTING	FORBEARINGLY	FORECASTLE
FODDERINGS	FOLLOWSHIPS	FOOTFAULTS	FORBIDDALS	FORECASTLES
FOEDERATUS	FOMENTATION	FOOTGUARDS	FORBIDDANCE	FORECHECKED

FORECHECKER	FOREIGNERS	FOREPLANNED	FORESIGNIFIES	FORETHINKING
FORECHECKERS	FOREIGNISM	FOREPLANNING	FORESIGNIFY	FORETHINKS
FORECHECKING	FOREIGNISMS	FOREPOINTED	FORESIGNIFYING	FORETHOUGHT
FORECHECKS	FOREIGNNESS	FOREPOINTING	FORESKIRTS	FORETHOUGHTFUL
FORECHOSEN	FOREIGNNESSES	FOREPOINTS	FORESLACKED	FORETHOUGHTS
FORECLOSABLE	FOREJUDGED	FOREQUARTER	FORESLACKING	FORETOKENED
FORECLOSED	FOREJUDGEMENT	FOREQUARTERS	FORESLACKS	FORETOKENING
FORECLOSES	FOREJUDGEMENTS	FOREREACHED	FORESLOWED	FORETOKENINGS
FORECLOSING	FOREJUDGES	FOREREACHES	FORESLOWING	FORETOKENS
FORECLOSURE	FOREJUDGING	FOREREACHING	FORESPEAKING	FORETOPMAN
FORECLOSURES	FOREJUDGMENT	FOREREADING	FORESPEAKS	FORETOPMAST
FORECLOTHS	FOREJUDGMENTS	FOREREADINGS	FORESPENDING	FORETOPMASTS
FORECOURSE	FOREKNOWABLE	FORERUNNER	FORESPENDS	FORETOPMEN
FORECOURSES	FOREKNOWING	FORERUNNERS	FORESPOKEN	FORETRIANGLE
FORECOURTS	FOREKNOWINGLY	FORERUNNING	FORESTAGES	FORETRIANGLES
FOREDAMNED	FOREKNOWLEDGE	FORESAYING	FORESTAIRS	FOREVERMORE
FOREDATING	FOREKNOWLEDGES	FORESEEABILITY	FORESTALLED	FOREVERNESS
FOREDOOMED	FORELADIES	FORESEEABLE	FORESTALLER	FOREVERNESSES
FOREDOOMING	FORELAYING	FORESEEING	FORESTALLERS	FOREVOUCHED
FOREFATHER	FORELENDING	FORESEEINGLY	FORESTALLING	FOREWARNED
FOREFATHERLY	FORELIFTED	FORESHADOW	FORESTALLINGS	FOREWARNER
FOREFATHERS	FORELIFTING	FORESHADOWED	FORESTALLMENT	FOREWARNERS
FOREFEELING	FORELOCKED	FORESHADOWER	FORESTALLMENTS	FOREWARNING
FOREFEELINGLY	FORELOCKING	FORESHADOWERS	FORESTALLS	FOREWARNINGLY
FOREFENDED	FOREMANSHIP	FORESHADOWING	FORESTALMENT	FOREWARNINGS
FOREFENDING	FOREMANSHIPS	FORESHADOWINGS	FORESTALMENTS	FOREWEIGHED
FOREFINGER	FOREMASTMAN	FORESHADOWS	FORESTATION	FOREWEIGHING
FOREFINGERS	FOREMASTMEN	FORESHANKS	FORESTATIONS	FOREWEIGHS
FOREFRONTS	FOREMEANING	FORESHEETS	FORESTAYSAIL	FORFAIRING
FOREGATHER	FOREMENTIONED	FORESHEWED	FORESTAYSAILS	FORFAITERS
FOREGATHERED	FOREMOTHER	FORESHEWING	FORESTLAND	FORFAITING
FOREGATHERING	FOREMOTHERS	FORESHOCKS	FORESTLANDS	FORFAITINGS
FOREGATHERS	FORENIGHTS	FORESHORES	FORESTLESS	FORFEITABLE
FOREGLEAMS	FORENSICALITIES	FORESHORTEN	FORESTRIES	FORFEITERS
FOREGOINGS	FORENSICALITY	FORESHORTENED	FORESWEARING	FORFEITING
FOREGONENESS	FORENSICALLY	FORESHORTENING	FORESWEARS	FORFEITURE
FOREGONENESSES	FOREORDAIN	FORESHORTENINGS	FORETASTED	FORFEITURES
FOREGROUND	FOREORDAINED	FORESHORTENS	FORETASTES	FORFENDING
FOREGROUNDED	FOREORDAINING	FORESHOWED	FORETASTING	FORFEUCHEN
FOREGROUNDING	FOREORDAINMENT	FORESHOWING	FORETAUGHT	FORFICULATE
FOREGROUNDS	FOREORDAINMENTS	FORESIGHTED	FORETEACHES	FORFOUGHEN
FOREHANDED	FOREORDAINS	FORESIGHTEDLY	FORETEACHING	FORFOUGHTEN
FOREHANDEDLY	FOREORDINATION	FORESIGHTEDNESS	FORETELLER	FORGATHERED
FOREHANDEDNESS	FOREORDINATIONS	FORESIGHTFUL	FORETELLERS	FORGATHERING
FOREHANDING	FOREPASSED	FORESIGHTLESS	FORETELLING	FORGATHERS
FOREHENTING	FOREPAYMENT	FORESIGHTS	FORETHINKER	FORGEABILITIES
FOREHOOVES	FOREPAYMENTS	FORESIGNIFIED	FORETHINKERS	FORGEABILITY

FORGETFULLY
FORGETFULNESS
FORGETFULNESSES
FORGETTABLE
FORGETTERIES
FORGETTERS
FORGETTERY
FORGETTING
FORGETTINGLY
FORGETTINGS
FORGIVABLE
FORGIVABLY
FORGIVENESS
FORGIVENESSES
FORGIVINGLY
FORGIVINGNESS
FORGIVINGNESSES
FORGOTTENNESS
FORGOTTENNESSES
FORHAILING
FORHENTING
FORHOOIEING
FORINSECAL
FORISFAMILIATE
FORISFAMILIATED
FORISFAMILIATES
FORJUDGING
FORJUDGMENT
FORJUDGMENTS
FORKEDNESS
FORKEDNESSES
FORKINESSES
FORKLIFTED
FORKLIFTING
FORLENDING
FORLORNEST
FORLORNNESS
FORLORNNESSES
FORMABILITIES
FORMABILITY
FORMALDEHYDE
FORMALDEHYDES
FORMALISABLE
FORMALISATION
FORMALISATIONS
FORMALISED
FORMALISER

FORMALISERS
FORMALISES
FORMALISING
FORMALISMS
FORMALISTIC
FORMALISTICALLY
FORMALISTS
FORMALITER
FORMALITIES
FORMALIZABLE
FORMALIZATION
FORMALIZATIONS
FORMALIZED
FORMALIZER
FORMALIZERS
FORMALIZES
FORMALIZING
FORMALNESS
FORMALNESSES
FORMAMIDES
FORMATIONAL
FORMATIONS
FORMATIVELY
FORMATIVENESS
FORMATIVENESSES
FORMATIVES
FORMATTERS
FORMATTING
FORMFITTING
FORMICARIA
FORMICARIES
FORMICARIUM
FORMICATED
FORMICATES
FORMICATING
FORMICATION
FORMICATIONS
FORMIDABILITIES
FORMIDABILITY
FORMIDABLE
FORMIDABLENESS
FORMIDABLY
FORMLESSLY
FORMLESSNESS
FORMLESSNESSES
FORMULAICALLY
FORMULARIES

FORMULARISATION
FORMULARISE
FORMULARISED
FORMULARISER
FORMULARISERS
FORMULARISES
FORMULARISING
FORMULARISTIC
FORMULARIZATION
FORMULARIZE
FORMULARIZED
FORMULARIZER
FORMULARIZERS
FORMULARIZES
FORMULARIZING
FORMULATED
FORMULATES
FORMULATING
FORMULATION
FORMULATIONS
FORMULATOR
FORMULATORS
FORMULISED
FORMULISES
FORMULISING
FORMULISMS
FORMULISTIC
FORMULISTS
FORMULIZED
FORMULIZES
FORMULIZING
FORNICATED
FORNICATES
FORNICATING
FORNICATION
FORNICATIONS
FORNICATOR
FORNICATORS
FORNICATRESS
FORNICATRESSES
FORSAKENLY
FORSAKENNESS
FORSAKENNESSES
FORSAKINGS
FORSLACKED
FORSLACKING
FORSLOEING

FORSLOWING
FORSPEAKING
FORSPENDING
FORSTERITE
FORSTERITES
FORSWEARER
FORSWEARERS
FORSWEARING
FORSWINKED
FORSWINKING
FORSWORNNESS
FORSWORNNESSES
FORSYTHIAS
FORTALICES
FORTEPIANIST
FORTEPIANISTS
FORTEPIANO
FORTEPIANOS
FORTHCOMES
FORTHCOMING
FORTHCOMINGNESS
FORTHGOING
FORTHGOINGS
FORTHINKING
FORTHOUGHT
FORTHRIGHT
FORTHRIGHTLY
FORTHRIGHTNESS
FORTHRIGHTS
FORTIFIABLE
FORTIFICATION
FORTIFICATIONS
FORTIFIERS
FORTIFYING
FORTIFYINGLY
FORTILAGES
FORTISSIMI
FORTISSIMO
FORTISSIMOS
FORTISSISSIMO
FORTITUDES
FORTITUDINOUS
FORTNIGHTLIES
FORTNIGHTLY
FORTNIGHTS
FORTRESSED
FORTRESSES

FORTRESSING
FORTRESSLIKE
FORTUITIES
FORTUITISM
FORTUITISMS
FORTUITIST
FORTUITISTS
FORTUITOUS
FORTUITOUSLY
FORTUITOUSNESS
FORTUNATELY
FORTUNATENESS
FORTUNATENESSES
FORTUNATES
FORTUNELESS
FORTUNIZED
FORTUNIZES
FORTUNIZING
FORWANDERED
FORWANDERING
FORWANDERS
FORWARDERS
FORWARDEST
FORWARDING
FORWARDINGS
FORWARDNESS
FORWARDNESSES
FORWARNING
FORWASTING
FORWEARIED
FORWEARIES
FORWEARYING
FOSCARNETS
FOSSICKERS
FOSSICKING
FOSSICKINGS
FOSSILIFEROUS
FOSSILISABLE
FOSSILISATION
FOSSILISATIONS
FOSSILISED
FOSSILISES
FOSSILISING
FOSSILIZABLE
FOSSILIZATION
FOSSILIZATIONS
FOSSILIZED

F

FOSSILIZES	FOURTEENER	FRACTIONIZATION	FRAGRANTLY	FRANGIPANES
FOSSILIZING	FOURTEENERS	FRACTIONIZE	FRAGRANTNESS	FRANGIPANI
FOSTERAGES	FOURTEENTH	FRACTIONIZED	FRAGRANTNESSES	FRANGIPANIS
FOSTERINGS	FOURTEENTHLY	FRACTIONIZES	FRAICHEURS	FRANGIPANNI
FOSTERLING	FOURTEENTHS	FRACTIONIZING	FRAILNESSES	FRANKALMOIGN
FOSTERLINGS	FOVEOLATED	FRACTIONLET	FRAMBESIAS	FRANKALMOIGNS
FOSTRESSES	FOXBERRIES	FRACTIONLETS	FRAMBOESIA	FRANKFORTS
FOTHERGILLA	FOXHUNTERS	FRACTIOUSLY	FRAMBOESIAS	FRANKFURTER
FOTHERGILLAS	FOXHUNTING	FRACTIOUSNESS	FRAMBOISES	FRANKFURTERS
FOUDROYANT	FOXHUNTINGS	FRACTIOUSNESSES	FRAMESHIFT	FRANKFURTS
FOUGHTIEST	FOXINESSES	FRACTOCUMULI	FRAMESHIFTS	FRANKINCENSE
FOULBROODS	FOXTROTTED	FRACTOCUMULUS	FRAMEWORKS	FRANKINCENSES
FOULDERING	FOXTROTTING	FRACTOGRAPHIES	FRANCHISED	FRANKLINITE
FOULMOUTHED	FOZINESSES	FRACTOGRAPHY	FRANCHISEE	FRANKLINITES
FOULNESSES	FRABJOUSLY	FRACTOSTRATI	FRANCHISEES	FRANKNESSES
FOUNDATION	FRACTALITIES	FRACTOSTRATUS	FRANCHISEMENT	FRANKPLEDGE
FOUNDATIONAL	FRACTALITY	FRACTURABLE	FRANCHISEMENTS	FRANKPLEDGES
FOUNDATIONALLY	FRACTIONAL	FRACTURERS	FRANCHISER	FRANSERIAS
FOUNDATIONARY	FRACTIONALISE	FRACTURING	FRANCHISERS	FRANTICALLY
FOUNDATIONER	FRACTIONALISED	FRAGILENESS	FRANCHISES	FRANTICNESS
FOUNDATIONERS	FRACTIONALISES	FRAGILENESSES	FRANCHISING	FRANTICNESSES
FOUNDATIONLESS	FRACTIONALISING	FRAGILITIES	FRANCHISOR	FRATCHIEST
FOUNDATIONS	FRACTIONALISM	FRAGMENTAL	FRANCHISORS	FRATERNALISM
FOUNDERING	FRACTIONALISMS	FRAGMENTALLY	FRANCISATION	FRATERNALISMS
FOUNDEROUS	FRACTIONALIST	FRAGMENTARILY	FRANCISATIONS	FRATERNALLY
FOUNDLINGS	FRACTIONALISTS	FRAGMENTARINESS	FRANCISING	FRATERNISATION
FOUNDRESSES	FRACTIONALIZE	FRAGMENTARY	FRANCIZATION	FRATERNISATIONS
FOUNTAINED	FRACTIONALIZED	FRAGMENTATE	FRANCIZATIONS	FRATERNISE
FOUNTAINHEAD	FRACTIONALIZES	FRAGMENTATED	FRANCIZING	FRATERNISED
FOUNTAINHEADS	FRACTIONALIZING	FRAGMENTATES	FRANCOLINS	FRATERNISER
FOUNTAINING	FRACTIONALLY	FRAGMENTATING	FRANCOMANIA	FRATERNISERS
FOUNTAINLESS	FRACTIONARY	FRAGMENTATION	FRANCOMANIAS	FRATERNISES
FOURCHETTE	FRACTIONATE	FRAGMENTATIONS	FRANCOPHIL	FRATERNISING
FOURCHETTES	FRACTIONATED	FRAGMENTED	FRANCOPHILE	FRATERNITIES
FOURDRINIER	FRACTIONATES	FRAGMENTING	FRANCOPHILES	FRATERNITY
FOURDRINIERS	FRACTIONATING	FRAGMENTISE	FRANCOPHILS	FRATERNIZATION
FOURFOLDNESS	FRACTIONATION	FRAGMENTISED	FRANCOPHOBE	FRATERNIZATIONS
FOURFOLDNESSES	FRACTIONATIONS	FRAGMENTISES	FRANCOPHOBES	FRATERNIZE
FOURPENCES	FRACTIONATOR	FRAGMENTISING	FRANCOPHOBIA	FRATERNIZED
FOURPENNIES	FRACTIONATORS	FRAGMENTIZE	FRANCOPHOBIAS	FRATERNIZER
FOURPLEXES	FRACTIONED	FRAGMENTIZED	FRANCOPHONE	FRATERNIZERS
FOURRAGERE	FRACTIONING	FRAGMENTIZES	FRANCOPHONES	FRATERNIZES
FOURRAGERES	FRACTIONISATION	FRAGMENTIZING	FRANGIBILITIES	FRATERNIZING
FOURSCORTH	FRACTIONISE	FRAGRANCED	FRANGIBILITY	FRATRICIDAL
FOURSQUARE	FRACTIONISED	FRAGRANCES	FRANGIBLENESS	FRATRICIDE
FOURSQUARELY	FRACTIONISES	FRAGRANCIES	FRANGIBLENESSES	FRATRICIDES
FOURSQUARENESS	FRACTIONISING	FRAGRANCING	FRANGIPANE	FRAUDFULLY

F

FRAUDSTERS	FREEHANDEDNESS	FREEZINGLY	FRETBOARDS	FRIGIDNESSES
FRAUDULENCE	FREEHEARTED	FREIGHTAGE	FRETFULNESS	FRIGORIFIC
FRAUDULENCES	FREEHEARTEDLY	FREIGHTAGES	FRETFULNESSES	FRIGORIFICO
FRAUDULENCIES	FREEHOLDER	FREIGHTERS	FRIABILITIES	FRIGORIFICOS
FRAUDULENCY	FREEHOLDERS	FREIGHTING	FRIABILITY	FRIKKADELS
FRAUDULENT	FREELANCED	FREIGHTLESS	FRIABLENESS	FRILLINESS
FRAUDULENTLY	FREELANCER	FREMESCENCE	FRIABLENESSES	FRILLINESSES
FRAUDULENTNESS	FREELANCERS	FREMESCENCES	FRIARBIRDS	FRINGELESS
FRAUGHTAGE	FREELANCES	FREMESCENT	FRICANDEAU	FRINGILLACEOUS
FRAUGHTAGES	FREELANCING	FREMITUSES	FRICANDEAUS	FRINGILLID
FRAUGHTEST	FREELOADED	FRENCHIFICATION	FRICANDEAUX	FRINGILLIFORM
FRAUGHTING	FREELOADER	FRENCHIFIED	FRICANDOES	FRINGILLINE
FRAXINELLA	FREELOADERS	FRENCHIFIES	FRICASSEED	FRIPONNERIE
FRAXINELLAS	FREELOADING	FRENCHIFYING	FRICASSEEING	FRIPONNERIES
FREAKERIES	FREELOADINGS	FRENETICAL	FRICASSEES	FRIPPERERS
FREAKINESS	FREEMARTIN	FRENETICALLY	FRICATIVES	FRIPPERIES
FREAKINESSES	FREEMARTINS	FRENETICISM	FRICTIONAL	FRISKINESS
FREAKISHLY	FREEMASONIC	FRENETICISMS	FRICTIONALLY	FRISKINESSES
FREAKISHNESS	FREEMASONRIES	FRENETICNESS	FRICTIONLESS	FRISKINGLY
FREAKISHNESSES	FREEMASONRY	FRENETICNESSES	FRICTIONLESSLY	FRITHBORHS
FRECKLIEST	FREEMASONS	FRENZIEDLY	FRIEDCAKES	FRITHSOKEN
FRECKLINGS	FREENESSES	FREQUENCES	FRIENDINGS	FRITHSOKENS
FREEBASERS	FREEPHONES	FREQUENCIES	FRIENDLESS	FRITHSTOOL
FREEBASING	FREESHEETS	FREQUENTABLE	FRIENDLESSNESS	FRITHSTOOLS
FREEBOARDS	FREESTANDING	FREQUENTATION	FRIENDLIER	FRITILLARIA
FREEBOOTED	FREESTONES	FREQUENTATIONS	FRIENDLIES	FRITILLARIAS
FREEBOOTER	FREESTYLED	FREQUENTATIVE	FRIENDLIEST	FRITILLARIES
FREEBOOTERIES	FREESTYLER	FREQUENTATIVES	FRIENDLILY	FRITILLARY
FREEBOOTERS	FREESTYLERS	FREQUENTED	FRIENDLINESS	FRITTERERS
FREEBOOTERY	FREESTYLES	FREQUENTER	FRIENDLINESSES	FRITTERING
FREEBOOTIES	FREESTYLING	FREQUENTERS	FRIENDSHIP	FRIVOLITIES
FREEBOOTING	FREESTYLINGS	FREQUENTEST	FRIENDSHIPS	FRIVOLLERS
FREEBOOTINGS	FREETHINKER	FREQUENTING	FRIEZELIKE	FRIVOLLING
FREECOOLING	FREETHINKERS	FREQUENTLY	FRIGATOONS	FRIVOLOUSLY
FREECOOLINGS	FREETHINKING	FREQUENTNESS	FRIGHTENED	FRIVOLOUSNESS
FREECYCLED	FREETHINKINGS	FREQUENTNESSES	FRIGHTENER	FRIVOLOUSNESSES
FREECYCLES	FREEWHEELED	FRESCOINGS	FRIGHTENERS	FRIZZINESS
FREECYCLING	FREEWHEELER	FRESCOISTS	FRIGHTENING	FRIZZINESSES
FREEDIVERS	FREEWHEELERS	FRESHENERS	FRIGHTENINGLY	FRIZZLIEST
FREEDIVING	FREEWHEELING	FRESHENING	FRIGHTFULLY	FRIZZLINESS
FREEDIVINGS	FREEWHEELINGLY	FRESHERDOM	FRIGHTFULNESS	FRIZZLINESSES
FREEDWOMAN	FREEWHEELINGS	FRESHERDOMS	FRIGHTFULNESSES	FROGFISHES
FREEDWOMEN	FREEWHEELS	FRESHMANSHIP	FRIGHTSOME	FROGGERIES
FREEGANISM	FREEWRITES	FRESHMANSHIPS	FRIGIDARIA	FROGHOPPER
FREEGANISMS	FREEWRITING	FRESHNESSES	FRIGIDARIUM	FROGHOPPERS
FREEHANDED	FREEWRITINGS	FRESHWATER	FRIGIDITIES	FROGMARCHED
FREEHANDEDLY	FREEWRITTEN	FRESHWATERS	FRIGIDNESS	FROGMARCHES

FROGMARCHING	FROSTBITES	FRUGALISTS	FRUTESCENCES	FULMINATION
FROGMOUTHS	FROSTBITING	FRUGALITIES	FRUTESCENT	FULMINATIONS
FROGSPAWNS	FROSTBITINGS	FRUGALNESS	FRUTIFYING	FULMINATOR
FROLICKERS	FROSTBITTEN	FRUGALNESSES	FUCIVOROUS	FULMINATORS
FROLICKING	FROSTBOUND	FRUGIFEROUS	FUCOXANTHIN	FULMINATORY
FROLICSOME	FROSTFISHES	FRUGIVORES	FUCOXANTHINS	FULMINEOUS
FROLICSOMELY	FROSTINESS	FRUGIVOROUS	FUGACIOUSLY	FULSOMENESS
FROLICSOMENESS	FROSTINESSES	FRUITARIAN	FUGACIOUSNESS	FULSOMENESSES
FROMENTIES	FROSTLINES	FRUITARIANISM	FUGACIOUSNESSES	FUMATORIES
FRONDESCENCE	FROSTWORKS	FRUITARIANISMS	FUGACITIES	FUMATORIUM
FRONDESCENCES	FROTHERIES	FRUITARIANS	FUGGINESSES	FUMATORIUMS
FRONDESCENT	FROTHINESS	FRUITCAKES	FUGITATION	FUMBLINGLY
FRONDIFEROUS	FROTHINESSES	FRUITERERS	FUGITATIONS	FUMBLINGNESS
FRONTAGERS	FROUGHIEST	FRUITERESS	FUGITIVELY	FUMBLINGNESSES
FRONTALITIES	FROUZINESS	FRUITERESSES	FUGITIVENESS	FUMIGATING
FRONTALITY	FROUZINESSES	FRUITERIES	FUGITIVENESSES	FUMIGATION
FRONTBENCHER	FROWARDNESS	FRUITFULLER	FUGITOMETER	FUMIGATIONS
FRONTBENCHERS	FROWARDNESSES	FRUITFULLEST	FUGITOMETERS	FUMIGATORS
FRONTCOURT	FROWNINGLY	FRUITFULLY	FULFILLERS	FUMIGATORY
FRONTCOURTS	FROWSINESS	FRUITFULNESS	FULFILLING	FUMITORIES
FRONTENISES	FROWSINESSES	FRUITFULNESSES	FULFILLINGS	FUMOSITIES
FRONTIERED	FROWSTIEST	FRUITINESS	FULFILLMENT	FUNAMBULATE
FRONTIERING	FROWSTINESS	FRUITINESSES	FULFILLMENTS	FUNAMBULATED
FRONTIERSMAN	FROWSTINESSES	FRUITLESSLY	FULFILMENT	FUNAMBULATES
FRONTIERSMEN	FROWZINESS	FRUITLESSNESS	FULFILMENTS	FUNAMBULATING
FRONTIERSWOMAN	FROWZINESSES	FRUITLESSNESSES	FULGENCIES	FUNAMBULATION
FRONTIERSWOMEN	FROZENNESS	FRUITWOODS	FULGURATED	FUNAMBULATIONS
FRONTISPIECE	FROZENNESSES	FRUMENTACEOUS	FULGURATES	FUNAMBULATOR
FRONTISPIECED	FRUCTIFEROUS	FRUMENTARIOUS	FULGURATING	FUNAMBULATORS
FRONTISPIECES	FRUCTIFEROUSLY	FRUMENTATION	FULGURATION	FUNAMBULATORY
FRONTISPIECING	FRUCTIFICATION	FRUMENTATIONS	FULGURATIONS	FUNAMBULISM
FRONTLESSLY	FRUCTIFICATIONS	FRUMENTIES	FULGURITES	FUNAMBULISMS
FRONTLINES	FRUCTIFIED	FRUMPINESS	FULIGINOSITIES	FUNAMBULIST
FRONTLISTS	FRUCTIFIER	FRUMPINESSES	FULIGINOSITY	FUNAMBULISTS
FRONTOGENESES	FRUCTIFIERS	FRUMPISHLY	FULIGINOUS	FUNCTIONAL
FRONTOGENESIS	FRUCTIFIES	FRUMPISHNESS	FULIGINOUSLY	FUNCTIONALISM
FRONTOGENETIC	FRUCTIFYING	FRUMPISHNESSES	FULIGINOUSNESS	FUNCTIONALISMS
FRONTOLYSES	FRUCTIVOROUS	FRUSEMIDES	FULLBLOODS	FUNCTIONALIST
FRONTOLYSIS	FRUCTUARIES	FRUSTRATED	FULLERENES	FUNCTIONALISTIC
FRONTPAGED	FRUCTUATED	FRUSTRATER	FULLERIDES	FUNCTIONALISTS
FRONTPAGES	FRUCTUATES	FRUSTRATERS	FULLERITES	FUNCTIONALITIES
FRONTPAGING	FRUCTUATING	FRUSTRATES	FULLMOUTHED	FUNCTIONALITY
FRONTRUNNER	FRUCTUATION	FRUSTRATING	FULLNESSES	FUNCTIONALLY
FRONTRUNNERS	FRUCTUATIONS	FRUSTRATINGLY	FULMINANTS	FUNCTIONALS
FRONTRUNNING	FRUCTUOUSLY	FRUSTRATION	FULMINATED	FUNCTIONARIES
FRONTRUNNINGS	FRUCTUOUSNESS	FRUSTRATIONS	FULMINATES	FUNCTIONARY
FRONTWARDS	FRUCTUOUSNESSES	FRUTESCENCE	FULMINATING	FUNCTIONATE

FUNCTIONATED
FUNCTIONATES
FUNCTIONATING
FUNCTIONED
FUNCTIONING
FUNCTIONLESS
FUNDAMENTAL
FUNDAMENTALISM
FUNDAMENTALISMS
FUNDAMENTALIST
FUNDAMENTALISTS
FUNDAMENTALITY
FUNDAMENTALLY
FUNDAMENTALNESS
FUNDAMENTALS
FUNDAMENTS
FUNDHOLDER
FUNDHOLDERS
FUNDHOLDING
FUNDHOLDINGS
FUNDRAISED
FUNDRAISER
FUNDRAISERS
FUNDRAISES
FUNDRAISING
FUNDRAISINGS
FUNEREALLY
FUNGIBILITIES
FUNGIBILITY
FUNGICIDAL
FUNGICIDALLY
FUNGICIDES

FUNGISTATIC
FUNGISTATICALLY
FUNGISTATS
FUNGOSITIES
FUNICULARS
FUNICULATE
FUNKINESSES
FUNNELFORM
FUNNELLING
FUNNINESSES
FURACIOUSNESS
FURACIOUSNESSES
FURACITIES
FURALDEHYDE
FURALDEHYDES
FURANOSIDE
FURANOSIDES
FURAZOLIDONE
FURAZOLIDONES
FURBEARERS
FURBELOWED
FURBELOWING
FURBISHERS
FURBISHING
FURCATIONS
FURCIFEROUS
FURFURACEOUS
FURFURACEOUSLY
FURFURALDEHYDE
FURFURALDEHYDES
FURFUROLES
FURIOSITIES

FURIOUSNESS
FURIOUSNESSES
FURLOUGHED
FURLOUGHING
FURMENTIES
FURNIMENTS
FURNISHERS
FURNISHING
FURNISHINGS
FURNISHMENT
FURNISHMENTS
FURNITURES
FUROSEMIDE
FUROSEMIDES
FURRIERIES
FURRINESSES
FURROWLESS
FURSHLUGGINER
FURTHCOMING
FURTHCOMINGS
FURTHERANCE
FURTHERANCES
FURTHERERS
FURTHERING
FURTHERMORE
FURTHERMOST
FURTHERSOME
FURTIVENESS
FURTIVENESSES
FURUNCULAR
FURUNCULOSES
FURUNCULOSIS

FURUNCULOUS
FUSHIONLESS
FUSIBILITIES
FUSIBILITY
FUSIBLENESS
FUSIBLENESSES
FUSILLADED
FUSILLADES
FUSILLADING
FUSILLATION
FUSILLATIONS
FUSIONISMS
FUSIONISTS
FUSIONLESS
FUSSBUDGET
FUSSBUDGETS
FUSSBUDGETY
FUSSINESSES
FUSTANELLA
FUSTANELLAS
FUSTANELLE
FUSTANELLES
FUSTIANIST
FUSTIANISTS
FUSTIANIZE
FUSTIANIZED
FUSTIANIZES
FUSTIANIZING
FUSTIGATED
FUSTIGATES
FUSTIGATING
FUSTIGATION

FUSTIGATIONS
FUSTIGATOR
FUSTIGATORS
FUSTIGATORY
FUSTILARIAN
FUSTILARIANS
FUSTILIRIAN
FUSTILIRIANS
FUSTILLIRIAN
FUSTILLIRIANS
FUSTINESSES
FUSULINIDS
FUTILENESS
FUTILENESSES
FUTILITARIAN
FUTILITARIANISM
FUTILITARIANS
FUTILITIES
FUTURELESS
FUTURELESSNESS
FUTURISTIC
FUTURISTICALLY
FUTURISTICS
FUTURITIES
FUTURITION
FUTURITIONS
FUTUROLOGICAL
FUTUROLOGIES
FUTUROLOGIST
FUTUROLOGISTS
FUTUROLOGY
FUZZINESSES

G

GABAPENTIN
GABAPENTINS
GABARDINES
GABBINESSES
GABBLEMENT
GABBLEMENTS
GABBROITIC
GABERDINES
GABERLUNZIE
GABERLUNZIES
GABIONADES
GABIONAGES
GABIONNADE
GABIONNADES
GADGETEERS
GADGETRIES
GADOLINITE
GADOLINITES
GADOLINIUM
GADOLINIUMS
GADROONING
GADROONINGS
GADZOOKERIES
GADZOOKERY
GAELICISED
GAELICISES
GAELICISING
GAELICISMS
GAELICIZED
GAELICIZES
GAELICIZING
GAILLARDIA
GAILLARDIAS
GAINFULNESS
GAINFULNESSES
GAINGIVING
GAINGIVINGS
GAINLESSNESS
GAINLESSNESSES
GAINLINESS
GAINLINESSES
GAINSAYERS
GAINSAYING
GAINSAYINGS
GAINSTRIVE

GAINSTRIVED
GAINSTRIVEN
GAINSTRIVES
GAINSTRIVING
GAINSTROVE
GAITERLESS
GALABIYAHS
GALACTAGOGUE
GALACTAGOGUES
GALACTOMETER
GALACTOMETERS
GALACTOMETRIES
GALACTOMETRY
GALACTOPHOROUS
GALACTOPOIESES
GALACTOPOIESIS
GALACTOPOIETIC
GALACTOPOIETICS
GALACTORRHEA
GALACTORRHEAS
GALACTORRHOEA
GALACTORRHOEAS
GALACTOSAEMIA
GALACTOSAEMIAS
GALACTOSAMINE
GALACTOSAMINES
GALACTOSEMIA
GALACTOSEMIAS
GALACTOSEMIC
GALACTOSES
GALACTOSIDASE
GALACTOSIDASES
GALACTOSIDE
GALACTOSIDES
GALACTOSYL
GALACTOSYLS
GALANTAMINE
GALANTAMINES
GALANTINES
GALAVANTED
GALAVANTING
GALDRAGONS
GALENGALES
GALENICALS
GALEOPITHECINE

GALEOPITHECOID
GALIMATIAS
GALIMATIASES
GALINGALES
GALIONGEES
GALIVANTED
GALIVANTING
GALLABEAHS
GALLABIAHS
GALLABIEHS
GALLABIYAH
GALLABIYAHS
GALLABIYAS
GALLABIYEH
GALLABIYEHS
GALLAMINES
GALLANTEST
GALLANTING
GALLANTNESS
GALLANTNESSES
GALLANTRIES
GALLBLADDER
GALLBLADDERS
GALLEASSES
GALLERISTS
GALLERYGOER
GALLERYGOERS
GALLERYING
GALLERYITE
GALLERYITES
GALLIAMBIC
GALLIAMBICS
GALLIARDISE
GALLIARDISES
GALLIASSES
GALLICISATION
GALLICISATIONS
GALLICISED
GALLICISES
GALLICISING
GALLICISMS
GALLICIZATION
GALLICIZATIONS
GALLICIZED
GALLICIZES

GALLICIZING
GALLIGASKINS
GALLIMAUFRIES
GALLIMAUFRY
GALLINACEAN
GALLINACEANS
GALLINACEOUS
GALLINAZOS
GALLINIPPER
GALLINIPPERS
GALLINULES
GALLISISED
GALLISISES
GALLISISING
GALLISIZED
GALLISIZES
GALLISIZING
GALLIVANTED
GALLIVANTING
GALLIVANTS
GALLIWASPS
GALLOGLASS
GALLOGLASSES
GALLONAGES
GALLOPADED
GALLOPADES
GALLOPADING
GALLOWGLASS
GALLOWGLASSES
GALLOWSNESS
GALLOWSNESSES
GALLSICKNESS
GALLSICKNESSES
GALLSTONES
GALLUMPHED
GALLUMPHING
GALLYGASKINS
GALRAVAGED
GALRAVAGES
GALRAVAGING
GALRAVITCH
GALRAVITCHED
GALRAVITCHES
GALRAVITCHING
GALUMPHERS

GALUMPHING
GALVANICAL
GALVANICALLY
GALVANISATION
GALVANISATIONS
GALVANISED
GALVANISER
GALVANISERS
GALVANISES
GALVANISING
GALVANISMS
GALVANISTS
GALVANIZATION
GALVANIZATIONS
GALVANIZED
GALVANIZER
GALVANIZERS
GALVANIZES
GALVANIZING
GALVANOMETER
GALVANOMETERS
GALVANOMETRIC
GALVANOMETRICAL
GALVANOMETRIES
GALVANOMETRY
GALVANOPLASTIC
GALVANOPLASTIES
GALVANOPLASTY
GALVANOSCOPE
GALVANOSCOPES
GALVANOSCOPIC
GALVANOSCOPIES
GALVANOSCOPY
GALVANOTROPIC
GALVANOTROPISM
GALVANOTROPISMS
GAMAHUCHED
GAMAHUCHES
GAMAHUCHING
GAMARUCHED
GAMARUCHES
GAMARUCHING
GAMBADOING
GAMBOLLING
GAMEBREAKER

G

GAMEBREAKERS	GAMOTROPISMS	GARGANTUAS	GARRULITIES	GASTROENTERITIC
GAMEKEEPER	GAMYNESSES	GARGARISED	GARRULOUSLY	GASTROENTERITIS
GAMEKEEPERS	GANDERISMS	GARGARISES	GARRULOUSNESS	GASTROLITH
GAMEKEEPING	GANGBANGED	GARGARISING	GARRULOUSNESSES	GASTROLITHS
GAMEKEEPINGS	GANGBANGER	GARGARISMS	GARRYOWENS	GASTROLOGER
GAMENESSES	GANGBANGERS	GARGARIZED	GASBAGGING	GASTROLOGERS
GAMESMANSHIP	GANGBANGING	GARGARIZES	GASCONADED	GASTROLOGICAL
GAMESMANSHIPS	GANGBOARDS	GARGARIZING	GASCONADER	GASTROLOGIES
GAMESOMELY	GANGBUSTER	GARGOYLISM	GASCONADERS	GASTROLOGIST
GAMESOMENESS	GANGBUSTERS	GARGOYLISMS	GASCONADES	GASTROLOGISTS
GAMESOMENESSES	GANGBUSTING	GARIBALDIS	GASCONADING	GASTROLOGY
GAMETANGIA	GANGBUSTINGS	GARISHNESS	GASCONISMS	GASTROMANCIES
GAMETANGIAL	GANGLIATED	GARISHNESSES	GASEOUSNESS	GASTROMANCY
GAMETANGIUM	GANGLIFORM	GARLANDAGE	GASEOUSNESSES	GASTRONOME
GAMETICALLY	GANGLIONATED	GARLANDAGES	GASHLINESS	GASTRONOMER
GAMETOCYTE	GANGLIONIC	GARLANDING	GASHLINESSES	GASTRONOMERS
GAMETOCYTES	GANGLIOSIDE	GARLANDLESS	GASHOLDERS	GASTRONOMES
GAMETOGENESES	GANGLIOSIDES	GARLANDRIES	GASIFIABLE	GASTRONOMIC
GAMETOGENESIS	GANGPLANKS	GARLICKIER	GASIFICATION	GASTRONOMICAL
GAMETOGENIC	GANGRENING	GARLICKIEST	GASIFICATIONS	GASTRONOMICALLY
GAMETOGENIES	GANGRENOUS	GARLICKING	GASOMETERS	GASTRONOMICS
GAMETOGENOUS	GANGSHAGGED	GARMENTING	GASOMETRIC	GASTRONOMIES
GAMETOGENY	GANGSHAGGING	GARMENTLESS	GASOMETRICAL	GASTRONOMIST
GAMETOPHORE	GANGSTERDOM	GARMENTURE	GASOMETRIES	GASTRONOMISTS
GAMETOPHORES	GANGSTERDOMS	GARMENTURES	GASPEREAUS	GASTRONOMY
GAMETOPHORIC	GANGSTERISH	GARNETIFEROUS	GASPEREAUX	GASTROPODAN
GAMETOPHYTE	GANGSTERISM	GARNIERITE	GASPINESSES	GASTROPODANS
GAMETOPHYTES	GANGSTERISMS	GARNIERITES	GASSINESSES	GASTROPODOUS
GAMETOPHYTIC	GANGSTERLAND	GARNISHEED	GASTEROPOD	GASTROPODS
GAMEYNESSES	GANGSTERLANDS	GARNISHEEING	GASTEROPODOUS	GASTROPUBS
GAMINERIES	GANNETRIES	GARNISHEEMENT	GASTEROPODS	GASTROSCOPE
GAMINESQUE	GANNISTERS	GARNISHEEMENTS	GASTIGHTNESS	GASTROSCOPES
GAMINESSES	GANTELOPES	GARNISHEES	GASTIGHTNESSES	GASTROSCOPIC
GAMMERSTANG	GANTLETING	GARNISHERS	GASTNESSES	GASTROSCOPIES
GAMMERSTANGS	GAOLBREAKS	GARNISHING	GASTRAEUMS	GASTROSCOPIST
GAMMOCKING	GAOLERESSES	GARNISHINGS	GASTRALGIA	GASTROSCOPISTS
GAMMONINGS	GARAGISTES	GARNISHMENT	GASTRALGIAS	GASTROSCOPY
GAMOGENESES	GARBAGEMAN	GARNISHMENTS	GASTRALGIC	GASTROSOPH
GAMOGENESIS	GARBAGEMEN	GARNISHRIES	GASTRECTOMIES	GASTROSOPHER
GAMOGENETIC	GARBOLOGIES	GARNITURES	GASTRECTOMY	GASTROSOPHERS
GAMOGENETICAL	GARBOLOGIST	GAROTTINGS	GASTRITIDES	GASTROSOPHIES
GAMOGENETICALLY	GARBOLOGISTS	GARRETEERS	GASTRITISES	GASTROSOPHS
GAMOPETALOUS	GARDENFULS	GARRISONED	GASTROCNEMII	GASTROSOPHY
GAMOPHYLLOUS	GARDENINGS	GARRISONING	GASTROCNEMIUS	GASTROSTOMIES
GAMOSEPALOUS	GARDENLESS	GARROTTERS	GASTROCOLIC	GASTROSTOMY
GAMOTROPIC	GARDEROBES	GARROTTING	GASTRODUODENAL	GASTROTOMIES
GAMOTROPISM	GARGANTUAN	GARROTTINGS	GASTROENTERIC	GASTROTOMY

GASTROTRICH	GAZILLIONAIRES	GELATINOID	GENDERIZED	GENERALLED
GASTROTRICHS	GAZILLIONS	GELATINOIDS	GENDERIZES	GENERALLING
GASTROVASCULAR	GAZUNDERED	GELATINOUS	GENDERIZING	GENERALNESS
GASTRULATE	GAZUNDERER	GELATINOUSLY	GENDERLESS	GENERALNESSES
GASTRULATED	GAZUNDERERS	GELATINOUSNESS	GENEALOGIC	GENERALSHIP
GASTRULATES	GAZUNDERING	GELIDITIES	GENEALOGICAL	GENERALSHIPS
GASTRULATING	GEALOUSIES	GELIDNESSES	GENEALOGICALLY	GENERATING
GASTRULATION	GEANTICLINAL	GELIGNITES	GENEALOGIES	GENERATION
GASTRULATIONS	GEANTICLINE	GELLIFLOWRE	GENEALOGISE	GENERATIONAL
GATECRASHED	GEANTICLINES	GELLIFLOWRES	GENEALOGISED	GENERATIONALLY
GATECRASHER	GEARCHANGE	GELSEMINES	GENEALOGISES	GENERATIONISM
GATECRASHERS	GEARCHANGES	GELSEMININE	GENEALOGISING	GENERATIONISMS
GATECRASHES	GEARSHIFTS	GELSEMININES	GENEALOGIST	GENERATIONS
GATECRASHING	GEARWHEELS	GELSEMIUMS	GENEALOGISTS	GENERATIVE
GATEHOUSES	GEEKINESSES	GEMEINSCHAFT	GENEALOGIZE	GENERATORS
GATEKEEPER	GEEKSPEAKS	GEMEINSCHAFTEN	GENEALOGIZED	GENERATRICES
GATEKEEPERS	GEFUFFLING	GEMEINSCHAFTS	GENEALOGIZES	GENERATRIX
GATEKEEPING	GEGENSCHEIN	GEMFIBROZIL	GENEALOGIZING	GENERICALLY
GATHERABLE	GEGENSCHEINS	GEMFIBROZILS	GENECOLOGIES	GENERICNESS
GATHERINGS	GEHLENITES	GEMINATELY	GENECOLOGY	GENERICNESSES
GAUCHENESS	GEITONOGAMIES	GEMINATING	GENERALATE	GENEROSITIES
GAUCHENESSES	GEITONOGAMOUS	GEMINATION	GENERALATES	GENEROSITY
GAUCHERIES	GEITONOGAMY	GEMINATIONS	GENERALCIES	GENEROUSLY
GAUDEAMUSES	GELANDESPRUNG	GEMMACEOUS	GENERALISABLE	GENEROUSNESS
GAUDINESSES	GELANDESPRUNGS	GEMMATIONS	GENERALISATION	GENEROUSNESSES
GAUFFERING	GELATINATE	GEMMIFEROUS	GENERALISATIONS	GENETHLIAC
GAUFFERINGS	GELATINATED	GEMMINESSES	GENERALISE	GENETHLIACAL
GAULEITERS	GELATINATES	GEMMIPAROUS	GENERALISED	GENETHLIACALLY
GAULTHERIA	GELATINATING	GEMMIPAROUSLY	GENERALISER	GENETHLIACON
GAULTHERIAS	GELATINATION	GEMMOLOGICAL	GENERALISERS	GENETHLIACONS
GAUNTLETED	GELATINATIONS	GEMMOLOGIES	GENERALISES	GENETHLIACS
GAUNTLETING	GELATINISATION	GEMMOLOGIST	GENERALISING	GENETHLIALOGIC
GAUNTNESSES	GELATINISATIONS	GEMMOLOGISTS	GENERALISSIMO	GENETHLIALOGIES
GAUSSMETER	GELATINISE	GEMMULATION	GENERALISSIMOS	GENETHLIALOGY
GAUSSMETERS	GELATINISED	GEMMULATIONS	GENERALIST	GENETICALLY
GAUZINESSES	GELATINISER	GEMOLOGICAL	GENERALISTS	GENETICIST
GAVELKINDS	GELATINISERS	GEMOLOGIES	GENERALITIES	GENETICISTS
GAWKIHOODS	GELATINISES	GEMOLOGIST	GENERALITY	GENETOTROPHIC
GAWKINESSES	GELATINISING	GEMOLOGISTS	GENERALIZABLE	GENETRICES
GAWKISHNESS	GELATINIZATION	GEMUTLICHKEIT	GENERALIZATION	GENETRIXES
GAWKISHNESSES	GELATINIZATIONS	GEMUTLICHKEITS	GENERALIZATIONS	GENEVRETTE
GAZEHOUNDS	GELATINIZE	GENDARMERIE	GENERALIZE	GENEVRETTES
GAZETTEERED	GELATINIZED	GENDARMERIES	GENERALIZED	GENIALISED
GAZETTEERING	GELATINIZER	GENDARMERY	GENERALIZER	GENIALISES
GAZETTEERISH	GELATINIZERS	GENDERISED	GENERALIZERS	GENIALISING
GAZETTEERS	GELATINIZES	GENDERISES	GENERALIZES	GENIALITIES
GAZILLIONAIRE	GELATINIZING	GENDERISING	GENERALIZING	GENIALIZED

G

G

GENIALIZES	GENTIANELLAS	GENUFLECTORS	GEOGRAPHIC	GEOMETRISTS
GENIALIZING	GENTILESSE	GENUFLECTS	GEOGRAPHICAL	GEOMETRIZATION
GENIALNESS	GENTILESSES	GENUFLEXION	GEOGRAPHICALLY	GEOMETRIZATIONS
GENIALNESSES	GENTILHOMME	GENUFLEXIONS	GEOGRAPHIES	GEOMETRIZE
GENICULATE	GENTILISED	GENUINENESS	GEOHYDROLOGIC	GEOMETRIZED
GENICULATED	GENTILISES	GENUINENESSES	GEOHYDROLOGIES	GEOMETRIZES
GENICULATELY	GENTILISING	GEOBOTANIC	GEOHYDROLOGIST	GEOMETRIZING
GENICULATES	GENTILISMS	GEOBOTANICAL	GEOHYDROLOGISTS	GEOMORPHIC
GENICULATING	GENTILITIAL	GEOBOTANIES	GEOHYDROLOGY	GEOMORPHOGENIC
GENICULATION	GENTILITIAN	GEOBOTANIST	GEOLATRIES	GEOMORPHOGENIES
GENICULATIONS	GENTILITIES	GEOBOTANISTS	GEOLINGUISTICS	GEOMORPHOGENIST
GENISTEINS	GENTILITIOUS	GEOCACHING	GEOLOGIANS	GEOMORPHOGENY
GENITALIAL	GENTILIZED	GEOCACHINGS	GEOLOGICAL	GEOMORPHOLOGIC
GENITIVALLY	GENTILIZES	GEOCARPIES	GEOLOGICALLY	GEOMORPHOLOGIES
GENITIVELY	GENTILIZING	GEOCENTRIC	GEOLOGISED	GEOMORPHOLOGIST
GENITOURINARY	GENTILSHOMMES	GEOCENTRICAL	GEOLOGISES	GEOMORPHOLOGY
GENITRICES	GENTLEFOLK	GEOCENTRICALLY	GEOLOGISING	GEOPHAGIAS
GENITRIXES	GENTLEFOLKS	GEOCENTRICISM	GEOLOGISTS	GEOPHAGIES
GENOCIDAIRE	GENTLEHOOD	GEOCENTRICISMS	GEOLOGIZED	GEOPHAGISM
GENOCIDAIRES	GENTLEHOODS	GEOCHEMICAL	GEOLOGIZES	GEOPHAGISMS
GENOPHOBIA	GENTLEMANHOOD	GEOCHEMICALLY	GEOLOGIZING	GEOPHAGIST
GENOPHOBIAS	GENTLEMANHOODS	GEOCHEMIST	GEOMAGNETIC	GEOPHAGISTS
GENOTYPICAL	GENTLEMANLIKE	GEOCHEMISTRIES	GEOMAGNETICALLY	GEOPHAGOUS
GENOTYPICALLY	GENTLEMANLINESS	GEOCHEMISTRY	GEOMAGNETISM	GEOPHILOUS
GENOTYPICITIES	GENTLEMANLY	GEOCHEMISTS	GEOMAGNETISMS	GEOPHYSICAL
GENOTYPICITY	GENTLEMANSHIP	GEOCHRONOLOGIC	GEOMAGNETIST	GEOPHYSICALLY
GENOUILLERE	GENTLEMANSHIPS	GEOCHRONOLOGIES	GEOMAGNETISTS	GEOPHYSICIST
GENOUILLERES	GENTLENESS	GEOCHRONOLOGIST	GEOMANCERS	GEOPHYSICISTS
GENSDARMES	GENTLENESSE	GEOCHRONOLOGY	GEOMANCIES	GEOPHYSICS
GENTAMICIN	GENTLENESSES	GEOCORONAE	GEOMECHANICS	GEOPOLITICAL
GENTAMICINS	GENTLEPERSON	GEOCORONAS	GEOMEDICAL	GEOPOLITICALLY
GENTEELEST	GENTLEPERSONS	GEODEMOGRAPHICS	GEOMEDICINE	GEOPOLITICIAN
GENTEELISE	GENTLEWOMAN	GEODESICAL	GEOMEDICINES	GEOPOLITICIANS
GENTEELISED	GENTLEWOMANLY	GEODESISTS	GEOMETRICAL	GEOPOLITICS
GENTEELISES	GENTLEWOMEN	GEODETICAL	GEOMETRICALLY	GEOPONICAL
GENTEELISH	GENTRIFICATION	GEODETICALLY	GEOMETRICIAN	GEOPRESSURED
GENTEELISING	GENTRIFICATIONS	GEODYNAMIC	GEOMETRICIANS	GEORGETTES
GENTEELISM	GENTRIFIED	GEODYNAMICAL	GEOMETRICS	GEOSCIENCE
GENTEELISMS	GENTRIFIER	GEODYNAMICIST	GEOMETRIDS	GEOSCIENCES
GENTEELIZE	GENTRIFIERS	GEODYNAMICISTS	GEOMETRIES	GEOSCIENTIFIC
GENTEELIZED	GENTRIFIES	GEODYNAMICS	GEOMETRISATION	GEOSCIENTIST
GENTEELIZES	GENTRIFYING	GEOGNOSIES	GEOMETRISATIONS	GEOSCIENTISTS
GENTEELIZING	GENUFLECTED	GEOGNOSTIC	GEOMETRISE	GEOSPATIAL
GENTEELNESS	GENUFLECTING	GEOGNOSTICAL	GEOMETRISED	GEOSPHERES
GENTEELNESSES	GENUFLECTION	GEOGNOSTICALLY	GEOMETRISES	GEOSTATICS
GENTIANACEOUS	GENUFLECTIONS	GEOGRAPHER	GEOMETRISING	GEOSTATIONARY
GENTIANELLA	GENUFLECTOR	GEOGRAPHERS	GEOMETRIST	GEOSTRATEGIC

G

GEOSTRATEGICAL	GERMANISATIONS	GERONTOPHOBIA	GHETTOISATIONS	GIGANTICNESS
GEOSTRATEGIES	GERMANISED	GERONTOPHOBIAS	GHETTOISED	GIGANTICNESSES
GEOSTRATEGIST	GERMANISES	GERRYMANDER	GHETTOISES	GIGANTISMS
GEOSTRATEGISTS	GERMANISING	GERRYMANDERED	GHETTOISING	GIGANTOLOGIES
GEOSTRATEGY	GERMANITES	GERRYMANDERER	GHETTOIZATION	GIGANTOLOGY
GEOSTROPHIC	GERMANIUMS	GERRYMANDERERS	GHETTOIZATIONS	GIGANTOMACHIA
GEOSTROPHICALLY	GERMANIZATION	GERRYMANDERING	GHETTOIZED	GIGANTOMACHIAS
GEOSYNCHRONOUS	GERMANIZATIONS	GERRYMANDERINGS	GHETTOIZES	GIGANTOMACHIES
GEOSYNCLINAL	GERMANIZED	GERRYMANDERS	GHETTOIZING	GIGANTOMACHY
GEOSYNCLINE	GERMANIZES	GERUNDIVAL	GHOSTLIEST	GIGGLESOME
GEOSYNCLINES	GERMANIZING	GERUNDIVELY	GHOSTLINESS	GIGGLINGLY
GEOTACTICAL	GERMICIDAL	GERUNDIVES	GHOSTLINESSES	GIGMANITIES
GEOTACTICALLY	GERMICIDES	GESELLSCHAFT	GHOSTWRITE	GILDSWOMAN
GEOTECHNIC	GERMINABILITIES	GESELLSCHAFTEN	GHOSTWRITER	GILDSWOMEN
GEOTECHNICAL	GERMINABILITY	GESELLSCHAFTS	GHOSTWRITERS	GILLFLIRTS
GEOTECHNICS	GERMINABLE	GESNERIADS	GHOSTWRITES	GILLIFLOWER
GEOTECHNOLOGIES	GERMINALLY	GESSAMINES	GHOSTWRITING	GILLIFLOWERS
GEOTECHNOLOGY	GERMINATED	GESTALTISM	GHOSTWRITTEN	GILLNETTED
GEOTECTONIC	GERMINATES	GESTALTISMS	GHOSTWROTE	GILLNETTER
GEOTECTONICALLY	GERMINATING	GESTALTIST	GHOULISHLY	GILLNETTERS
GEOTECTONICS	GERMINATION	GESTALTISTS	GHOULISHNESS	GILLNETTING
GEOTEXTILE	GERMINATIONS	GESTATIONAL	GHOULISHNESSES	GILLRAVAGE
GEOTEXTILES	GERMINATIVE	GESTATIONS	GIANTESSES	GILLRAVAGED
GEOTHERMAL	GERMINATOR	GESTATORIAL	GIANTHOODS	GILLRAVAGES
GEOTHERMALLY	GERMINATORS	GESTICULANT	GIANTLIEST	GILLRAVAGING
GEOTHERMIC	GERMINESSES	GESTICULATE	GIANTSHIPS	GILLRAVITCH
GEOTHERMOMETER	GERMPLASMS	GESTICULATED	GIARDIASES	GILLRAVITCHED
GEOTHERMOMETERS	GERONTOCRACIES	GESTICULATES	GIARDIASIS	GILLRAVITCHES
GEOTROPICALLY	GERONTOCRACY	GESTICULATING	GIBBERELLIC	GILLRAVITCHING
GEOTROPISM	GERONTOCRAT	GESTICULATION	GIBBERELLIN	GILLYFLOWER
GEOTROPISMS	GERONTOCRATIC	GESTICULATIONS	GIBBERELLINS	GILLYFLOWERS
GERANIACEOUS	GERONTOCRATS	GESTICULATIVE	GIBBERISHES	GILRAVAGED
GERATOLOGICAL	GERONTOLOGIC	GESTICULATOR	GIBBETTING	GILRAVAGER
GERATOLOGIES	GERONTOLOGICAL	GESTICULATORS	GIBBOSITIES	GILRAVAGERS
GERATOLOGIST	GERONTOLOGIES	GESTICULATORY	GIBBOUSNESS	GILRAVAGES
GERATOLOGISTS	GERONTOLOGIST	GESTURALLY	GIBBOUSNESSES	GILRAVAGING
GERATOLOGY	GERONTOLOGISTS	GESUNDHEIT	GIDDINESSES	GILRAVITCH
GERFALCONS	GERONTOLOGY	GETTERINGS	GIFTEDNESS	GILRAVITCHED
GERIATRICIAN	GERONTOMORPHIC	GEWURZTRAMINER	GIFTEDNESSES	GILRAVITCHES
GERIATRICIANS	GERONTOPHIL	GEWURZTRAMINERS	GIFTWRAPPED	GILRAVITCHING
GERIATRICS	GERONTOPHILE	GEYSERITES	GIFTWRAPPING	GILSONITES
GERIATRIST	GERONTOPHILES	GHASTFULLY	GIGACYCLES	GIMBALLING
GERIATRISTS	GERONTOPHILIA	GHASTLIEST	GIGAHERTZES	GIMCRACKERIES
GERMANDERS'	GERONTOPHILIAS	GHASTLINESS	GIGANTESQUE	GIMCRACKERY
GERMANENESS	GERONTOPHILS	GHASTLINESSES	GIGANTICALLY	GIMMICKIER
GERMANENESSES	GERONTOPHOBE	GHASTNESSES	GIGANTICIDE	GIMMICKIEST
GERMANISATION	GERONTOPHOBES	GHETTOISATION	GIGANTICIDES	GIMMICKING

G

GIMMICKRIES	GLACIOLOGICAL	GLAMOURING	GLASSWARES	GLISSANDOS
GINGELLIES	GLACIOLOGIES	GLAMOURISE	GLASSWORKER	GLISTENING
GINGERADES	GLACIOLOGIST	GLAMOURISED	GLASSWORKERS	GLISTENINGLY
GINGERBREAD	GLACIOLOGISTS	GLAMOURISES	GLASSWORKS	GLISTERING
GINGERBREADED	GLACIOLOGY	GLAMOURISING	GLASSWORMS	GLISTERINGLY
GINGERBREADS	GLADDENERS	GLAMOURIZE	GLASSWORTS	GLITCHIEST
GINGERBREADY	GLADDENING	GLAMOURIZED	GLASSYHEADED	GLITTERAND
GINGERLINESS	GLADFULNESS	GLAMOURIZES	GLAUBERITE	GLITTERATI
GINGERLINESSES	GLADFULNESSES	GLAMOURIZING	GLAUBERITES	GLITTERIER
GINGERROOT	GLADIATORIAL	GLAMOURLESS	GLAUCESCENCE	GLITTERIEST
GINGERROOTS	GLADIATORIAN	GLAMOUROUS	GLAUCESCENCES	GLITTERING
GINGERSNAP	GLADIATORS	GLAMOUROUSLY	GLAUCESCENT	GLITTERINGLY
GINGERSNAPS	GLADIATORSHIP	GLAMOUROUSNESS	GLAUCOMATOUS	GLITTERINGS
GINGIVECTOMIES	GLADIATORSHIPS	GLAMOURPUSS	GLAUCONITE	GLITZINESS
GINGIVECTOMY	GLADIATORY	GLAMOURPUSSES	GLAUCONITES	GLITZINESSES
GINGIVITIS	GLADIOLUSES	GLANCINGLY	GLAUCONITIC	GLOATINGLY
GINGIVITISES	GLADNESSES	GLANDEROUS	GLAUCOUSLY	GLOBALISATION
GINGLIMOID	GLADSOMELY	GLANDIFEROUS	GLAUCOUSNESS	GLOBALISATIONS
GIPSYHOODS	GLADSOMENESS	GLANDIFORM	GLAUCOUSNESSES	GLOBALISED
GIPSYWORTS	GLADSOMENESSES	GLANDULARLY	GLAZIERIES	GLOBALISES
GIRANDOLAS	GLADSOMEST	GLANDULIFEROUS	GLAZINESSES	GLOBALISING
GIRANDOLES	GLADSTONES	GLANDULOUS	GLEAMINGLY	GLOBALISMS
GIRDLECAKE	GLADWRAPPED	GLANDULOUSLY	GLEEFULNESS	GLOBALISTS
GIRDLECAKES	GLADWRAPPING	GLARINESSES	GLEEFULNESSES	GLOBALIZATION
GIRDLESCONE	GLAIKETNESS	GLARINGNESS	GLEEMAIDEN	GLOBALIZATIONS
GIRDLESCONES	GLAIKETNESSES	GLARINGNESSES	GLEEMAIDENS	GLOBALIZED
GIRDLESTEAD	GLAIKITNESS	GLASNOSTIAN	GLEGNESSES	GLOBALIZES
GIRDLESTEADS	GLAIKITNESSES	GLASNOSTIC	GLEISATION	GLOBALIZING
GIRLFRIEND	GLAIRINESS	GLASSBLOWER	GLEISATIONS	GLOBEFISHES
GIRLFRIENDS	GLAIRINESSES	GLASSBLOWERS	GLEIZATION	GLOBEFLOWER
GIRLISHNESS	GLAMORISATION	GLASSBLOWING	GLEIZATIONS	GLOBEFLOWERS
GIRLISHNESSES	GLAMORISATIONS	GLASSBLOWINGS	GLENDOVEER	GLOBESITIES
GIRTHLINES	GLAMORISED	GLASSHOUSE	GLENDOVEERS	GLOBETROTS
GISMOLOGIES	GLAMORISER	GLASSHOUSES	GLENGARRIES	GLOBETROTTED
GITTARONES	GLAMORISERS	GLASSIFIED	GLIBNESSES	GLOBETROTTER
GITTERNING	GLAMORISES	GLASSIFIES	GLIDEPATHS	GLOBETROTTERS
GIVENNESSES	GLAMORISING	GLASSIFYING	GLIMMERING	GLOBETROTTING
GIZMOLOGIES	GLAMORIZATION	GLASSINESS	GLIMMERINGLY	GLOBETROTTINGS
GLABRESCENT	GLAMORIZATIONS	GLASSINESSES	GLIMMERINGS	GLOBIGERINA
GLABROUSNESS	GLAMORIZED	GLASSMAKER	GLIOBLASTOMA	GLOBIGERINAE
GLABROUSNESSES	GLAMORIZER	GLASSMAKERS	GLIOBLASTOMAS	GLOBIGERINAS
GLACIALIST	GLAMORIZERS	GLASSMAKING	GLIOBLASTOMATA	GLOBOSENESS
GLACIALISTS	GLAMORIZES	GLASSMAKINGS	GLIOMATOSES	GLOBOSENESSES
GLACIATING	GLAMORIZING	GLASSPAPER	GLIOMATOSIS	GLOBOSITIES
GLACIATION	GLAMOROUSLY	GLASSPAPERED	GLIOMATOUS	GLOBULARITIES
GLACIATIONS	GLAMOROUSNESS	GLASSPAPERING	GLISSADERS	GLOBULARITY
GLACIOLOGIC	GLAMOROUSNESSES	GLASSPAPERS	GLISSADING	GLOBULARLY

GLOBULARNESS
GLOBULARNESSES
GLOBULIFEROUS
GLOBULITES
GLOCHIDIATE
GLOCHIDIUM
GLOCKENSPIEL
GLOCKENSPIELS
GLOMERATED
GLOMERATES
GLOMERATING
GLOMERATION
GLOMERATIONS
GLOMERULAR
GLOMERULATE
GLOMERULES
GLOMERULUS
GLOOMFULLY
GLOOMINESS
GLOOMINESSES
GLORIFIABLE
GLORIFICATION
GLORIFICATIONS
GLORIFIERS
GLORIFYING
GLORIOUSLY
GLORIOUSNESS
GLORIOUSNESSES
GLOSSARIAL
GLOSSARIALLY
GLOSSARIES
GLOSSARIST
GLOSSARISTS
GLOSSATORS
GLOSSECTOMIES
GLOSSECTOMY
GLOSSINESS
GLOSSINESSES
GLOSSINGLY
GLOSSITISES
GLOSSODYNIA
GLOSSODYNIAS
GLOSSOGRAPHER
GLOSSOGRAPHERS
GLOSSOGRAPHICAL
GLOSSOGRAPHIES
GLOSSOGRAPHY

GLOSSOLALIA
GLOSSOLALIAS
GLOSSOLALIST
GLOSSOLALISTS
GLOSSOLOGICAL
GLOSSOLOGIES
GLOSSOLOGIST
GLOSSOLOGISTS
GLOSSOLOGY
GLOTTIDEAN
GLOTTOGONIC
GLOTTOLOGIES
GLOTTOLOGY
GLOWERINGLY
GLOWSTICKS
GLUCINIUMS
GLUCOCORTICOID
GLUCOCORTICOIDS
GLUCOKINASE
GLUCOKINASES
GLUCONATES
GLUCONEOGENESES
GLUCONEOGENESIS
GLUCONEOGENIC
GLUCOPHORE
GLUCOPHORES
GLUCOPROTEIN
GLUCOPROTEINS
GLUCOSAMINE
GLUCOSAMINES
GLUCOSIDAL
GLUCOSIDASE
GLUCOSIDASES
GLUCOSIDES
GLUCOSIDIC
GLUCOSURIA
GLUCOSURIAS
GLUCOSURIC
GLUCURONIDASE
GLUCURONIDASES
GLUCURONIDE
GLUCURONIDES
GLUEYNESSES
GLUINESSES
GLUMACEOUS
GLUMIFEROUS
GLUMNESSES

GLUTAMATES
GLUTAMINASE
GLUTAMINASES
GLUTAMINES
GLUTAMINIC
GLUTARALDEHYDE
GLUTARALDEHYDES
GLUTATHIONE
GLUTATHIONES
GLUTETHIMIDE
GLUTETHIMIDES
GLUTINOSITIES
GLUTINOSITY
GLUTINOUSLY
GLUTINOUSNESS
GLUTINOUSNESSES
GLUTTINGLY
GLUTTONIES
GLUTTONISE
GLUTTONISED
GLUTTONISES
GLUTTONISH
GLUTTONISING
GLUTTONIZE
GLUTTONIZED
GLUTTONIZES
GLUTTONIZING
GLUTTONOUS
GLUTTONOUSLY
GLUTTONOUSNESS
GLYCAEMIAS
GLYCATIONS
GLYCERALDEHYDE
GLYCERALDEHYDES
GLYCERIDES
GLYCERIDIC
GLYCERINATE
GLYCERINATED
GLYCERINATES
GLYCERINATING
GLYCERINES
GLYCOCOLLS
GLYCOGENESES
GLYCOGENESIS
GLYCOGENETIC
GLYCOGENIC
GLYCOGENOLYSES

GLYCOGENOLYSIS
GLYCOGENOLYTIC
GLYCOLIPID
GLYCOLIPIDS
GLYCOLYSES
GLYCOLYSIS
GLYCOLYTIC
GLYCONEOGENESES
GLYCONEOGENESIS
GLYCOPEPTIDE
GLYCOPEPTIDES
GLYCOPHYTE
GLYCOPHYTES
GLYCOPHYTIC
GLYCOPROTEIN
GLYCOPROTEINS
GLYCOSIDASE
GLYCOSIDASES
GLYCOSIDES
GLYCOSIDIC
GLYCOSIDICALLY
GLYCOSURIA
GLYCOSURIAS
GLYCOSURIC
GLYCOSYLATE
GLYCOSYLATED
GLYCOSYLATES
GLYCOSYLATING
GLYCOSYLATION
GLYCOSYLATIONS
GLYOXALINE
GLYOXALINES
GLYPHOGRAPH
GLYPHOGRAPHER
GLYPHOGRAPHERS
GLYPHOGRAPHIC
GLYPHOGRAPHICAL
GLYPHOGRAPHIES
GLYPHOGRAPHS
GLYPHOGRAPHY
GLYPTODONT
GLYPTODONTS
GLYPTOGRAPHER
GLYPTOGRAPHERS
GLYPTOGRAPHIC
GLYPTOGRAPHICAL
GLYPTOGRAPHIES

GLYPTOGRAPHY
GLYPTOTHECA
GLYPTOTHECAE
GMELINITES
GNAPHALIUM
GNAPHALIUMS
GNASHINGLY
GNATCATCHER
GNATCATCHERS
GNATHONICAL
GNATHONICALLY
GNATHOSTOMATOUS
GNATHOSTOME
GNATHOSTOMES
GNEISSITIC
GNETOPHYTE
GNETOPHYTES
GNOMICALLY
GNOMONICAL
GNOMONICALLY
GNOMONOLOGIES
GNOMONOLOGY
GNOSEOLOGIES
GNOSEOLOGY
GNOSIOLOGIES
GNOSIOLOGY
GNOSTICALLY
GNOSTICISM
GNOSTICISMS
GNOTOBIOLOGICAL
GNOTOBIOLOGIES
GNOTOBIOLOGY
GNOTOBIOSES
GNOTOBIOSIS
GNOTOBIOTE
GNOTOBIOTES
GNOTOBIOTIC
GNOTOBIOTICALLY
GNOTOBIOTICS
GOALKEEPER
GOALKEEPERS
GOALKEEPING
GOALKEEPINGS
GOALKICKER
GOALKICKERS
GOALKICKING
GOALKICKINGS

G

GOALMOUTHS	GOITROGENICITY	GOLOPTIOUS	GOODFELLAS	GORGONEION
GOALTENDER	GOITROGENS	GOLUPTIOUS	GOODFELLOW	GORGONIANS
GOALTENDERS	GOLDBEATER	GOMBEENISM	GOODFELLOWS	GORGONISED
GOALTENDING	GOLDBEATERS	GOMBEENISMS	GOODFELLOWSHIP	GORGONISES
GOALTENDINGS	GOLDBRICKED	GONADECTOMIES	GOODFELLOWSHIPS	GORGONISING
GOATFISHES	GOLDBRICKING	GONADECTOMISED	GOODINESSES	GORGONIZED
GOATISHNESS	GOLDBRICKS	GONADECTOMIZED	GOODLIHEAD	GORGONIZES
GOATISHNESSES	GOLDCRESTS	GONADECTOMY	GOODLIHEADS	GORGONIZING
GOATSBEARD	GOLDENBERRIES	GONADOTROPHIC	GOODLINESS	GORILLAGRAM
GOATSBEARDS	GOLDENBERRY	GONADOTROPHIN	GOODLINESSES	GORILLAGRAMS
GOATSUCKER	GOLDENEYES	GONADOTROPHINS	GOODLYHEAD	GORINESSES
GOATSUCKERS	GOLDENNESS	GONADOTROPIC	GOODLYHEADS	GORMANDISE
GOBBELINES	GOLDENNESSES	GONADOTROPIN	GOODNESSES	GORMANDISED
GOBBLEDEGOOK	GOLDENRODS	GONADOTROPINS	GOODNIGHTS	GORMANDISER
GOBBLEDEGOOKS	GOLDENSEAL	GONDOLIERS	GOODWILLED	GORMANDISERS
GOBBLEDYGOOK	GOLDENSEALS	GONENESSES	GOOEYNESSES	GORMANDISES
GOBBLEDYGOOKS	GOLDFIELDS	GONFALONIER	GOOFINESSES	GORMANDISING
GOBSMACKED	GOLDFINCHES	GONFALONIERS	GOOGLEWHACK	GORMANDISINGS
GOBSTOPPER	GOLDFINNIES	GONGORISTIC	GOOGLEWHACKS	GORMANDISM
GOBSTOPPERS	GOLDFISHES	GONIATITES	GOOGOLPLEX	GORMANDISMS
GODCHILDREN	GOLDILOCKS	GONIATITOID	GOOGOLPLEXES	GORMANDIZE
GODDAMMING	GOLDILOCKSES	GONIATITOIDS	GOOINESSES	GORMANDIZED
GODDAMNDEST	GOLDMINERS	GONIMOBLAST	GOONEYBIRD	GORMANDIZER
GODDAMNEDEST	GOLDSINNIES	GONIMOBLASTS	GOONEYBIRDS	GORMANDIZERS
GODDAMNING	GOLDSMITHERIES	GONIOMETER	GOOPINESSES	GORMANDIZES
GODDAUGHTER	GOLDSMITHERY	GONIOMETERS	GOOSANDERS	GORMANDIZING
GODDAUGHTERS	GOLDSMITHRIES	GONIOMETRIC	GOOSEBERRIES	GORMANDIZINGS
GODDESSHOOD	GOLDSMITHRY	GONIOMETRICAL	GOOSEBERRY	GOSLARITES
GODDESSHOODS	GOLDSMITHS	GONIOMETRICALLY	GOOSEFISHES	GOSPELISED
GODFATHERED	GOLDSPINKS	GONIOMETRIES	GOOSEFLESH	GOSPELISES
GODFATHERING	GOLDSTICKS	GONIOMETRY	GOOSEFLESHES	GOSPELISING
GODFATHERS	GOLDSTONES	GONIOSCOPE	GOOSEFOOTS	GOSPELIZED
GODFORSAKEN	GOLDTHREAD	GONIOSCOPES	GOOSEGRASS	GOSPELIZES
GODLESSNESS	GOLDTHREADS	GONOCOCCAL	GOOSEGRASSES	GOSPELIZING
GODLESSNESSES	GOLIARDERIES	GONOCOCCIC	GOOSEHERDS	GOSPELLERS
GODLIKENESS	GOLIARDERY	GONOCOCCOID	GOOSENECKED	GOSPELLING
GODLIKENESSES	GOLIARDIES	GONOCOCCUS	GOOSENECKS	GOSPELLINGS
GODLINESSES	GOLIATHISE	GONOPHORES	GOOSINESSES	GOSPELLISE
GODMOTHERED	GOLIATHISED	GONOPHORIC	GOPHERWOOD	GOSPELLISED
GODMOTHERING	GOLIATHISES	GONOPHOROUS	GOPHERWOODS	GOSPELLISES
GODMOTHERS	GOLIATHISING	GONORRHEAS	GORBELLIES	GOSPELLISING
GODPARENTS	GOLIATHIZE	GONORRHEAS	GORBLIMEYS	GOSPELLIZE
GODROONING	GOLIATHIZED	GONORRHEIC	GORBLIMIES	GOSPELLIZED
GODROONINGS	GOLIATHIZES	GONORRHOEA	GOREHOUNDS	GOSPELLIZES
GOFFERINGS	GOLIATHIZING	GONORRHOEAL	GORGEOUSLY	GOSPELLIZING
GOGGLEBOXES	GOLLIWOGGS	GONORRHOEAS	GORGEOUSNESS	GOSSIPINGLY
GOITROGENIC	GOLOMYNKAS	GONORRHOEIC	GORGEOUSNESSES	GOSSIPINGS

GOSSIPMONGER	GOVERNMENTALLY	GRADUALNESS	GRAMMATICISMS	GRANDIOSITIES
GOSSIPMONGERS	GOVERNMENTESE	GRADUALNESSES	GRAMMATICIZE	GRANDIOSITY
GOSSIPPERS	GOVERNMENTESES	GRADUATESHIP	GRAMMATICIZED	GRANDMAMAS
GOSSIPPING	GOVERNMENTS	GRADUATESHIPS	GRAMMATICIZES	GRANDMAMMA
GOSSIPRIES	GOVERNORATE	GRADUATING	GRAMMATICIZING	GRANDMAMMAS
GOTHICALLY	GOVERNORATES	GRADUATION	GRAMMATIST	GRANDMASTER
GOTHICISED	GOVERNORSHIP	GRADUATIONS	GRAMMATISTS	GRANDMASTERS
GOTHICISES	GOVERNORSHIPS	GRADUATORS	GRAMMATOLOGIES	GRANDMOTHER
GOTHICISING	GOWDSPINKS	GRAECISING	GRAMMATOLOGIST	GRANDMOTHERLY
GOTHICISMS	GOWPENFULS	GRAECIZING	GRAMMATOLOGISTS	GRANDMOTHERS
GOTHICIZED	GRACEFULLER	GRAFFITIED	GRAMMATOLOGY	GRANDNEPHEW
GOTHICIZES	GRACEFULLEST	GRAFFITIING	GRAMOPHONE	GRANDNEPHEWS
GOTHICIZING	GRACEFULLY	GRAFFITING	GRAMOPHONES	GRANDNESSES
GOURDINESS	GRACEFULNESS	GRAFFITIST	GRAMOPHONIC	GRANDNIECE
GOURDINESSES	GRACEFULNESSES	GRAFFITISTS	GRAMOPHONICALLY	GRANDNIECES
GOURMANDISE	GRACELESSLY	GRAINFIELD	GRAMOPHONIES	GRANDPAPAS
GOURMANDISED	GRACELESSNESS	GRAINFIELDS	GRAMOPHONIST	GRANDPARENT
GOURMANDISES	GRACELESSNESSES	GRAININESS	GRAMOPHONISTS	GRANDPARENTAL
GOURMANDISING	GRACILENESS	GRAININESSES	GRAMOPHONY	GRANDPARENTHOOD
GOURMANDISM	GRACILENESSES	GRALLATORIAL	GRANADILLA	GRANDPARENTS
GOURMANDISMS	GRACILITIES	GRALLOCHED	GRANADILLAS	GRANDSIRES
GOURMANDIZE	GRACIOSITIES	GRALLOCHING	GRANDADDIES	GRANDSTAND
GOURMANDIZED	GRACIOSITY	GRAMERCIES	GRANDAUNTS	GRANDSTANDED
GOURMANDIZES	GRACIOUSLY	GRAMICIDIN	GRANDBABIES	GRANDSTANDER
GOURMANDIZING	GRACIOUSNESS	GRAMICIDINS	GRANDCHILD	GRANDSTANDERS
GOUTINESSES	GRACIOUSNESSES	GRAMINACEOUS	GRANDCHILDREN	GRANDSTANDING
GOUVERNANTE	GRADABILITIES	GRAMINEOUS	GRANDDADDIES	GRANDSTANDS
GOUVERNANTES	GRADABILITY	GRAMINICOLOUS	GRANDDADDY	GRANDSTOOD
GOVERNABILITIES	GRADABLENESS	GRAMINIVOROUS	GRANDDAUGHTER	GRANDUNCLE
GOVERNABILITY	GRADABLENESSES	GRAMINOLOGIES	GRANDDAUGHTERS	GRANDUNCLES
GOVERNABLE	GRADATIONAL	GRAMINOLOGY	GRANDEESHIP	GRANGERISATION
GOVERNABLENESS	GRADATIONALLY	GRAMMALOGUE	GRANDEESHIPS	GRANGERISATIONS
GOVERNALLS	GRADATIONED	GRAMMALOGUES	GRANDFATHER	GRANGERISE
GOVERNANCE	GRADATIONS	GRAMMARIAN	GRANDFATHERED	GRANGERISED
GOVERNANCES	GRADDANING	GRAMMARIANS	GRANDFATHERING	GRANGERISER
GOVERNANTE	GRADELIEST	GRAMMARLESS	GRANDFATHERLY	GRANGERISERS
GOVERNANTES	GRADIENTER	GRAMMATICAL	GRANDFATHERS	GRANGERISES
GOVERNESSED	GRADIENTERS	GRAMMATICALITY	GRANDIFLORA	GRANGERISING
GOVERNESSES	GRADIOMETER	GRAMMATICALLY	GRANDIFLORAS	GRANGERISM
GOVERNESSING	GRADIOMETERS	GRAMMATICALNESS	GRANDILOQUENCE	GRANGERISMS
GOVERNESSY	GRADUALISM	GRAMMATICASTER	GRANDILOQUENCES	GRANGERIZATION
GOVERNMENT	GRADUALISMS	GRAMMATICASTERS	GRANDILOQUENT	GRANGERIZATIONS
GOVERNMENTAL	GRADUALIST	GRAMMATICISE	GRANDILOQUENTLY	GRANGERIZE
GOVERNMENTALISE	GRADUALISTIC	GRAMMATICISED	GRANDILOQUOUS	GRANGERIZED
GOVERNMENTALISM	GRADUALISTS	GRAMMATICISES	GRANDIOSELY	GRANGERIZER
GOVERNMENTALIST	GRADUALITIES	GRAMMATICISING	GRANDIOSENESS	GRANGERIZERS
GOVERNMENTALIZE	GRADUALITY	GRAMMATICISM	GRANDIOSENESSES	GRANGERIZES

G

G

GRANGERIZING	GRANULITIC	GRAPHOLOGICAL	GRATILLITIES	GRAVITATIONALLY
GRANITELIKE	GRANULITISATION	GRAPHOLOGIES	GRATILLITY	GRAVITATIONS
GRANITEWARE	GRANULITIZATION	GRAPHOLOGIST	GRATINATED	GRAVITATIVE
GRANITEWARES	GRANULOCYTE	GRAPHOLOGISTS	GRATINATES	GRAVITINOS
GRANITIFICATION	GRANULOCYTES	GRAPHOLOGY	GRATINATING	GRAVITOMETER
GRANITIFORM	GRANULOCYTIC	GRAPHOMANIA	GRATINEEING	GRAVITOMETERS
GRANITISATION	GRANULOMAS	GRAPHOMANIAS	GRATITUDES	GRAYBEARDED
GRANITISATIONS	GRANULOMATA	GRAPHOMOTOR	GRATUITIES	GRAYBEARDS
GRANITISED	GRANULOMATOUS	GRAPHOPHOBIA	GRATUITOUS	GRAYFISHES
GRANITISES	GRANULOSES	GRAPHOPHOBIAS	GRATUITOUSLY	GRAYHOUNDS
GRANITISING	GRANULOSIS	GRAPINESSES	GRATUITOUSNESS	GRAYNESSES
GRANITITES	GRAPEFRUIT	GRAPLEMENT	GRATULATED	GRAYWACKES
GRANITIZATION	GRAPEFRUITS	GRAPLEMENTS	GRATULATES	GRAYWATERS
GRANITIZATIONS	GRAPELOUSE	GRAPPLINGS	GRATULATING	GREASEBALL
GRANITIZED	GRAPESEEDS	GRAPTOLITE	GRATULATION	GREASEBALLS
GRANITIZES	GRAPESHOTS	GRAPTOLITES	GRATULATIONS	GREASEBAND
GRANITIZING	GRAPESTONE	GRAPTOLITIC	GRATULATORY	GREASEBANDS
GRANIVORES	GRAPESTONES	GRASPINGLY	GRAUNCHERS	GREASEBUSH
GRANIVOROUS	GRAPETREES	GRASPINGNESS	GRAUNCHING	GREASEBUSHES
GRANNIEING	GRAPEVINES	GRASPINGNESSES	GRAVADLAXES	GREASELESS
GRANODIORITE	GRAPHEMICALLY	GRASSBIRDS	GRAVELLING	GREASEPAINT
GRANODIORITES	GRAPHEMICS	GRASSFINCH	GRAVENESSES	GREASEPAINTS
GRANODIORITIC	GRAPHICACIES	GRASSFINCHES	GRAVEOLENT	GREASEPROOF
GRANOLITHIC	GRAPHICACY	GRASSHOOKS	GRAVESIDES	GREASEPROOFS
GRANOLITHICS	GRAPHICALLY	GRASSHOPPER	GRAVESITES	GREASEWOOD
GRANOLITHS	GRAPHICALNESS	GRASSHOPPERS	GRAVESTONE	GREASEWOODS
GRANOPHYRE	GRAPHICALNESSES	GRASSINESS	GRAVESTONES	GREASINESS
GRANOPHYRES	GRAPHICNESS	GRASSINESSES	GRAVEYARDS	GREASINESSES
GRANOPHYRIC	GRAPHICNESSES	GRASSLANDS	GRAVIDITIES	GREATCOATED
GRANTSMANSHIP	GRAPHITISABLE	GRASSPLOTS	GRAVIDNESS	GREATCOATS
GRANTSMANSHIPS	GRAPHITISATION	GRASSQUITS	GRAVIDNESSES	GREATENING
GRANULARITIES	GRAPHITISATIONS	GRASSROOTS	GRAVIMETER	GREATHEARTED
GRANULARITY	GRAPHITISE	GRASSWRACK	GRAVIMETERS	GREATHEARTEDLY
GRANULARLY	GRAPHITISED	GRASSWRACKS	GRAVIMETRIC	GREATNESSES
GRANULATED	GRAPHITISES	GRATEFULLER	GRAVIMETRICAL	GRECIANISE
GRANULATER	GRAPHITISING	GRATEFULLEST	GRAVIMETRICALLY	GRECIANISED
GRANULATERS	GRAPHITIZABLE	GRATEFULLY	GRAVIMETRIES	GRECIANISES
GRANULATES	GRAPHITIZATION	GRATEFULNESS	GRAVIMETRY	GRECIANISING
GRANULATING	GRAPHITIZATIONS	GRATEFULNESSES	GRAVIPERCEPTION	GRECIANIZE
GRANULATION	GRAPHITIZE	GRATICULATION	GRAVITASES	GRECIANIZED
GRANULATIONS	GRAPHITIZED	GRATICULATIONS	GRAVITATED	GRECIANIZES
GRANULATIVE	GRAPHITIZES	GRATICULES	GRAVITATER	GRECIANIZING
GRANULATOR	GRAPHITIZING	GRATIFICATION	GRAVITATERS	GREEDINESS
GRANULATORS	GRAPHITOID	GRATIFICATIONS	GRAVITATES	GREEDINESSES
GRANULIFEROUS	GRAPHOLECT	GRATIFIERS	GRAVITATING	GREENBACKER
GRANULIFORM	GRAPHOLECTS	GRATIFYING	GRAVITATION	GREENBACKERS
GRANULITES	GRAPHOLOGIC	GRATIFYINGLY	GRAVITATIONAL	GREENBACKISM

GREENBACKISMS
GREENBACKS
GREENBELTS
GREENBONES
GREENBOTTLE
GREENBOTTLES
GREENBRIER
GREENBRIERS
GREENCLOTH
GREENCLOTHS
GREENERIES
GREENFIELD
GREENFIELDS
GREENFINCH
GREENFINCHES
GREENFLIES
GREENGAGES
GREENGROCER
GREENGROCERIES
GREENGROCERS
GREENGROCERY
GREENHANDS
GREENHEADS
GREENHEART
GREENHEARTS
GREENHORNS
GREENHOUSE
GREENHOUSES
GREENISHNESS
GREENISHNESSES
GREENKEEPER
GREENKEEPERS
GREENLIGHT
GREENLIGHTED
GREENLIGHTING
GREENLIGHTS
GREENLINGS
GREENMAILED
GREENMAILER
GREENMAILERS
GREENMAILING
GREENMAILS
GREENNESSES
GREENOCKITE
GREENOCKITES
GREENROOMS
GREENSANDS

GREENSHANK
GREENSHANKS
GREENSICKNESS
GREENSICKNESSES
GREENSKEEPER
GREENSKEEPERS
GREENSOMES
GREENSPEAK
GREENSPEAKS
GREENSTICK
GREENSTONE
GREENSTONES
GREENSTUFF
GREENSTUFFS
GREENSWARD
GREENSWARDS
GREENWASHED
GREENWASHES
GREENWASHING
GREENWEEDS
GREENWINGS
GREENWOODS
GREGARIANISM
GREGARIANISMS
GREGARINES
GREGARINIAN
GREGARIOUS
GREGARIOUSLY
GREGARIOUSNESS
GREISENISATION
GREISENISATIONS
GREISENISE
GREISENISED
GREISENISES
GREISENISING
GREISENIZATION
GREISENIZATIONS
GREISENIZE
GREISENIZED
GREISENIZES
GREISENIZING
GREMOLATAS
GRENADIERS
GRENADILLA
GRENADILLAS
GRENADINES
GRESSORIAL

GRESSORIOUS
GREVILLEAS
GREWHOUNDS
GREWSOMEST
GREYBEARDED
GREYBEARDS
GREYHOUNDS
GREYLISTED
GREYLISTING
GREYNESSES
GREYSCALES
GREYSTONES
GREYWACKES
GREYWETHER
GREYWETHERS
GRIDDLEBREAD
GRIDDLEBREADS
GRIDDLECAKE
GRIDDLECAKES
GRIDIRONED
GRIDIRONING
GRIDLOCKED
GRIDLOCKING
GRIEVANCES
GRIEVINGLY
GRIEVOUSLY
GRIEVOUSNESS
GRIEVOUSNESSES
GRIFFINISH
GRIFFINISM
GRIFFINISMS
GRILLERIES
GRILLROOMS
GRILLSTEAK
GRILLSTEAKS
GRILLWORKS
GRIMACINGLY
GRIMALKINS
GRIMINESSES
GRIMLOOKED
GRIMNESSES
GRINDELIAS
GRINDERIES
GRINDHOUSE
GRINDHOUSES
GRINDINGLY
GRINDSTONE

GRINDSTONES
GRINNINGLY
GRIPPINGLY
GRISAILLES
GRISEOFULVIN
GRISEOFULVINS
GRISLINESS
GRISLINESSES
GRISTLIEST
GRISTLINESS
GRISTLINESSES
GRISTMILLS
GRITSTONES
GRITTINESS
GRITTINESSES
GRIVATIONS
GRIZZLIEST
GROANINGLY
GROATSWORTH
GROATSWORTHS
GROCETERIA
GROCETERIAS
GROGGERIES
GROGGINESS
GROGGINESSES
GROMMETING
GROOVELESS
GROOVELIKE
GROOVINESS
GROOVINESSES
GROSGRAINS
GROSSIERETE
GROSSIERETES
GROSSNESSES
GROSSULARITE
GROSSULARITES
GROSSULARS
GROTESQUELY
GROTESQUENESS
GROTESQUENESSES
GROTESQUER
GROTESQUERIE
GROTESQUERIES
GROTESQUERY
GROTESQUES
GROTESQUEST
GROTTINESS

GROTTINESSES
GROUCHIEST
GROUCHINESS
GROUCHINESSES
GROUNDAGES
GROUNDBAIT
GROUNDBAITED
GROUNDBAITING
GROUNDBAITS
GROUNDBREAKER
GROUNDBREAKERS
GROUNDBREAKING
GROUNDBREAKINGS
GROUNDBURST
GROUNDBURSTS
GROUNDEDLY
GROUNDFISH
GROUNDFISHES
GROUNDHOGS
GROUNDINGS
GROUNDLESS
GROUNDLESSLY
GROUNDLESSNESS
GROUNDLING
GROUNDLINGS
GROUNDMASS
GROUNDMASSES
GROUNDNUTS
GROUNDOUTS
GROUNDPLOT
GROUNDPLOTS
GROUNDPROX
GROUNDPROXES
GROUNDSELL
GROUNDSELLS
GROUNDSELS
GROUNDSHARE
GROUNDSHARED
GROUNDSHARES
GROUNDSHARING
GROUNDSHEET
GROUNDSHEETS
GROUNDSILL
GROUNDSILLS
GROUNDSKEEPER
GROUNDSKEEPERS
GROUNDSMAN

G

G

GROUNDSMEN	GRUFFNESSES	GUBERNATORIAL	GUILLOCHING	GURGITATIONS
GROUNDSPEED	GRUMBLIEST	GUBERNATORS	GUILLOTINE	GUSHINESSES
GROUNDSPEEDS	GRUMBLINGLY	GUBERNIYAS	GUILLOTINED	GUSSETINGS
GROUNDSWELL	GRUMBLINGS	GUDGEONING	GUILLOTINER	GUSTATIONS
GROUNDSWELLS	GRUMMETING	GUERDONERS	GUILLOTINERS	GUSTATORILY
GROUNDWATER	GRUMNESSES	GUERDONING	GUILLOTINES	GUSTINESSES
GROUNDWATERS	GRUMPINESS	GUERILLAISM	GUILLOTINING	GUTBUCKETS
GROUNDWOOD	GRUMPINESSES	GUERILLAISMS	GUILTINESS	GUTLESSNESS
GROUNDWOODS	GRUMPISHLY	GUERRILLAISM	GUILTINESSES	GUTLESSNESSES
GROUNDWORK	GRUMPISHNESS	GUERRILLAISMS	GUILTLESSLY	GUTSINESSES
GROUNDWORKS	GRUMPISHNESSES	GUERRILLAS	GUILTLESSNESS	GUTTATIONS
GROUPTHINK	GRUNTINGLY	GUERRILLERO	GUILTLESSNESSES	GUTTERBLOOD
GROUPTHINKS	GUACAMOLES	GUERRILLEROS	GUITARFISH	GUTTERBLOODS
GROUPUSCULE	GUACHAMOLE	GUESSINGLY	GUITARFISHES	GUTTERINGS
GROUPUSCULES	GUACHAMOLES	GUESSTIMATE	GUITARISTS	GUTTERSNIPE
GROUPWARES	GUACHAROES	GUESSTIMATED	GULLIBILITIES	GUTTERSNIPES
GROUPWORKS	GUANABANAS	GUESSTIMATES	GULLIBILITY	GUTTERSNIPISH
GROUSELIKE	GUANAZOLOS	GUESSTIMATING	GULOSITIES	GUTTIFEROUS
GROVELINGLY	GUANETHIDINE	GUESSWORKS	GUMMIFEROUS	GUTTURALISATION
GROVELLERS	GUANETHIDINES	GUESTBOOKS	GUMMINESSES	GUTTURALISE
GROVELLING	GUANIDINES	GUESTENING	GUMMOSITIES	GUTTURALISED
GROVELLINGLY	GUANIFEROUS	GUESTHOUSE	GUMSHIELDS	GUTTURALISES
GROVELLINGS	GUANOSINES	GUESTHOUSES	GUMSHOEING	GUTTURALISING
GROWLERIES	GUARANTEED	GUESTIMATE	GUMSUCKERS	GUTTURALISM
GROWLINESS	GUARANTEEING	GUESTIMATED	GUNCOTTONS	GUTTURALISMS
GROWLINESSES	GUARANTEES	GUESTIMATES	GUNFIGHTER	GUTTURALITIES
GROWLINGLY	GUARANTIED	GUESTIMATING	GUNFIGHTERS	GUTTURALITY
GROWTHIEST	GUARANTIES	GUIDEBOOKS	GUNFIGHTING	GUTTURALIZATION
GROWTHINESS	GUARANTORS	GUIDELINES	GUNFIGHTINGS	GUTTURALIZE
GROWTHINESSES	GUARANTYING	GUIDEPOSTS	GUNKHOLING	GUTTURALIZED
GROWTHISTS	GUARDEDNESS	GUIDESHIPS	GUNMANSHIP	GUTTURALIZES
GRUBBINESS	GUARDEDNESSES	GUIDEWORDS	GUNMANSHIPS	GUTTURALIZING
GRUBBINESSES	GUARDHOUSE	GUIDWILLIE	GUNNERSHIP	GUTTURALLY
GRUBSTAKED	GUARDHOUSES	GUILDHALLS	GUNNERSHIPS	GUTTURALNESS
GRUBSTAKER	GUARDIANSHIP	GUILDSHIPS	GUNNYSACKS	GUTTURALNESSES
GRUBSTAKERS	GUARDIANSHIPS	GUILDSWOMAN	GUNPOWDERS	GYMNASIARCH
GRUBSTAKES	GUARDRAILS	GUILDSWOMEN	GUNPOWDERY	GYMNASIARCHS
GRUBSTAKING	GUARDROOMS	GUILEFULLY	GUNRUNNERS	GYMNASIAST
GRUDGELESS	GUARDSHIPS	GUILEFULNESS	GUNRUNNING	GYMNASIASTS
GRUDGINGLY	GUARISHING	GUILEFULNESSES	GUNRUNNINGS	GYMNASIUMS
GRUELINGLY	GUAYABERAS	GUILELESSLY	GUNSLINGER	GYMNASTICAL
GRUELLINGLY	GUBERNACULA	GUILELESSNESS	GUNSLINGERS	GYMNASTICALLY
GRUELLINGS	GUBERNACULAR	GUILELESSNESSES	GUNSLINGING	GYMNASTICS
GRUESOMELY	GUBERNACULUM	GUILLEMETS	GUNSLINGINGS	GYMNORHINAL
GRUESOMENESS	GUBERNATION	GUILLEMOTS	GUNSMITHING	GYMNOSOPHIES
GRUESOMENESSES	GUBERNATIONS	GUILLOCHED	GUNSMITHINGS	GYMNOSOPHIST
GRUESOMEST	GUBERNATOR	GUILLOCHES	GURGITATION	GYMNOSOPHISTS

GYMNOSOPHS
GYMNOSOPHY
GYMNOSPERM
GYMNOSPERMIES
GYMNOSPERMOUS
GYMNOSPERMS
GYMNOSPERMY
GYNAECEUMS
GYNAECOCRACIES
GYNAECOCRACY
GYNAECOCRATIC
GYNAECOLOGIC
GYNAECOLOGICAL
GYNAECOLOGIES
GYNAECOLOGIST
GYNAECOLOGISTS
GYNAECOLOGY
GYNAECOMAST
GYNAECOMASTIA
GYNAECOMASTIAS

GYNAECOMASTIES
GYNAECOMASTS
GYNAECOMASTY
GYNANDRIES
GYNANDRISM
GYNANDRISMS
GYNANDROMORPH
GYNANDROMORPHIC
GYNANDROMORPHS
GYNANDROMORPHY
GYNANDROUS
GYNARCHIES
GYNECOCRACIES
GYNECOCRACY
GYNECOCRATIC
GYNECOLOGIC
GYNECOLOGICAL
GYNECOLOGIES
GYNECOLOGIST
GYNECOLOGISTS

GYNECOLOGY
GYNECOMASTIA
GYNECOMASTIAS
GYNIATRICS
GYNIATRIES
GYNIOLATRIES
GYNIOLATRY
GYNOCRACIES
GYNOCRATIC
GYNODIOECIOUS
GYNODIOECISM
GYNODIOECISMS
GYNOGENESES
GYNOGENESIS
GYNOGENETIC
GYNOMONOECIOUS
GYNOMONOECISM
GYNOMONOECISMS
GYNOPHOBES
GYNOPHOBIA

GYNOPHOBIAS
GYNOPHOBIC
GYNOPHOBICS
GYNOPHORES
GYNOPHORIC
GYNOSTEMIA
GYNOSTEMIUM
GYPSIFEROUS
GYPSOPHILA
GYPSOPHILAS
GYPSYHOODS
GYPSYWORTS
GYRATIONAL
GYRFALCONS
GYROCOMPASS
GYROCOMPASSES
GYROCOPTER
GYROCOPTERS
GYROFREQUENCIES
GYROFREQUENCY

GYROMAGNETIC
GYROMAGNETISM
GYROMAGNETISMS
GYROMANCIES
GYROPILOTS
GYROPLANES
GYROSCOPES
GYROSCOPIC
GYROSCOPICALLY
GYROSCOPICS
GYROSTABILISER
GYROSTABILISERS
GYROSTABILIZER
GYROSTABILIZERS
GYROSTATIC
GYROSTATICALLY
GYROSTATICS
GYROVAGUES

G

H

HAANEPOOTS	HACKMATACK	HAEMATOLOGIC	HAEMOGLOBINS	HAGIARCHIES
HABERDASHER	HACKMATACKS	HAEMATOLOGICAL	HAEMOGLOBINURIA	HAGIOCRACIES
HABERDASHERIES	HACKNEYING	HAEMATOLOGIES	HAEMOLYSES	HAGIOCRACY
HABERDASHERS	HACKNEYISM	HAEMATOLOGIST	HAEMOLYSIN	HAGIOGRAPHER
HABERDASHERY	HACKNEYISMS	HAEMATOLOGISTS	HAEMOLYSINS	HAGIOGRAPHERS
HABERDINES	HACKNEYMAN	HAEMATOLOGY	HAEMOLYSIS	HAGIOGRAPHIC
HABERGEONS	HACKNEYMEN	HAEMATOLYSES	HAEMOLYTIC	HAGIOGRAPHICAL
HABILATORY	HACKSAWING	HAEMATOLYSIS	HAEMOPHILE	HAGIOGRAPHIES
HABILIMENT	HACQUETONS	HAEMATOMAS	HAEMOPHILES	HAGIOGRAPHIST
HABILIMENTS	HADROSAURS	HAEMATOMATA	HAEMOPHILIA	HAGIOGRAPHISTS
HABILITATE	HADROSAURUS	HAEMATOPHAGOUS	HAEMOPHILIAC	HAGIOGRAPHY
HABILITATED	HADROSAURUSES	HAEMATOPOIESES	HAEMOPHILIACS	HAGIOLATER
HABILITATES	HAECCEITIES	HAEMATOPOIESIS	HAEMOPHILIAS	HAGIOLATERS
HABILITATING	HAEMACHROME	HAEMATOPOIETIC	HAEMOPHILIC	HAGIOLATRIES
HABILITATION	HAEMACHROMES	HAEMATOSES	HAEMOPHILIOID	HAGIOLATROUS
HABILITATIONS	HAEMACYTOMETER	HAEMATOSIS	HAEMOPOIESES	HAGIOLATRY
HABILITATOR	HAEMACYTOMETERS	HAEMATOTHERMAL	HAEMOPOIESIS	HAGIOLOGIC
HABILITATORS	HAEMAGGLUTINATE	HAEMATOXYLIC	HAEMOPOIETIC	HAGIOLOGICAL
HABITABILITIES	HAEMAGGLUTININ	HAEMATOXYLIN	HAEMOPTYSES	HAGIOLOGIES
HABITABILITY	HAEMAGGLUTININS	HAEMATOXYLINS	HAEMOPTYSIS	HAGIOLOGIST
HABITABLENESS	HAEMAGOGUE	HAEMATOXYLON	HAEMORRHAGE	HAGIOLOGISTS
HABITABLENESSES	HAEMAGOGUES	HAEMATOXYLONS	HAEMORRHAGED	HAGIOSCOPE
HABITATION	HAEMANGIOMA	HAEMATOZOA	HAEMORRHAGES	HAGIOSCOPES
HABITATIONAL	HAEMANGIOMAS	HAEMATOZOON	HAEMORRHAGIC	HAGIOSCOPIC
HABITATIONS	HAEMANGIOMATA	HAEMATURIA	HAEMORRHAGING	HAILSTONES
HABITAUNCE	HAEMATEINS	HAEMATURIAS	HAEMORRHOID	HAILSTORMS
HABITAUNCES	HAEMATEMESES	HAEMATURIC	HAEMORRHOIDAL	HAIRBRAINED
HABITUALLY	HAEMATEMESIS	HAEMOCHROME	HAEMORRHOIDS	HAIRBREADTH
HABITUALNESS	HAEMATINIC	HAEMOCHROMES	HAEMOSTASES	HAIRBREADTHS
HABITUALNESSES	HAEMATINICS	HAEMOCOELS	HAEMOSTASIA	HAIRBRUSHES
HABITUATED	HAEMATITES	HAEMOCONIA	HAEMOSTASIAS	HAIRCLOTHS
HABITUATES	HAEMATITIC	HAEMOCONIAS	HAEMOSTASIS	HAIRCUTTER
HABITUATING	HAEMATOBLAST	HAEMOCYANIN	HAEMOSTATIC	HAIRCUTTERS
HABITUATION	HAEMATOBLASTIC	HAEMOCYANINS	HAEMOSTATICS	HAIRCUTTING
HABITUATIONS	HAEMATOBLASTS	HAEMOCYTES	HAEMOSTATS	HAIRCUTTINGS
HABITUDINAL	HAEMATOCELE	HAEMOCYTOMETER	HAGBERRIES	HAIRDRESSER
HACENDADOS	HAEMATOCELES	HAEMOCYTOMETERS	HAGBUTEERS	HAIRDRESSERS
HACIENDADO	HAEMATOCRIT	HAEMODIALYSER	HAGBUTTERS	HAIRDRESSING
HACIENDADOS	HAEMATOCRITS	HAEMODIALYSERS	HAGGADICAL	HAIRDRESSINGS
HACKAMORES	HAEMATOCRYAL	HAEMODIALYSES	HAGGADISTIC	HAIRDRIERS
HACKBERRIES	HAEMATOGENESES	HAEMODIALYSIS	HAGGADISTS	HAIRDRYERS
HACKBUTEER	HAEMATOGENESIS	HAEMODIALYZER	HAGGARDNESS	HAIRINESSES
HACKBUTEERS	HAEMATOGENETIC	HAEMODIALYZERS	HAGGARDNESSES	HAIRLESSES
HACKBUTTER	HAEMATOGENIC	HAEMOFLAGELLATE	HAGGISHNESS	HAIRLESSNESS
HACKBUTTERS	HAEMATOGENOUS	HAEMOGLOBIN	HAGGISHNESSES	HAIRLESSNESSES

HAIRPIECES	HALLELUJAH	HALOPHILOUS	HAMPEREDNESS	HANDICUFFS
HAIRSBREADTH	HALLELUJAHS	HALOPHOBES	HAMPEREDNESSES	HANDINESSES
HAIRSBREADTHS	HALLMARKED	HALOPHYTES	HAMSHACKLE	HANDIWORKS
HAIRSPLITTER	HALLMARKING	HALOPHYTIC	HAMSHACKLED	HANDKERCHER
HAIRSPLITTERS	HALLOWEDNESS	HALOPHYTISM	HAMSHACKLES	HANDKERCHERS
HAIRSPLITTING	HALLOWEDNESSES	HALOPHYTISMS	HAMSHACKLING	HANDKERCHIEF
HAIRSPLITTINGS	HALLOYSITE	HALOTHANES	HAMSTRINGED	HANDKERCHIEFS
HAIRSPRAYS	HALLOYSITES	HALTERBREAK	HAMSTRINGING	HANDKERCHIEVES
HAIRSPRING	HALLSTANDS	HALTERBREAKING	HAMSTRINGS	HANDLANGER
HAIRSPRINGS	HALLUCINATE	HALTERBREAKS	HANDBAGGED	HANDLANGERS
HAIRSTREAK	HALLUCINATED	HALTERBROKE	HANDBAGGING	HANDLEABLE
HAIRSTREAKS	HALLUCINATES	HALTERBROKEN	HANDBAGGINGS	HANDLEBARS
HAIRSTYLES	HALLUCINATING	HALTERNECK	HANDBALLED	HANDLELESS
HAIRSTYLING	HALLUCINATION	HALTERNECKS	HANDBALLER	HANDMAIDEN
HAIRSTYLINGS	HALLUCINATIONAL	HALTINGNESS	HANDBALLERS	HANDMAIDENS
HAIRSTYLIST	HALLUCINATIONS	HALTINGNESSES	HANDBALLING	HANDPASSED
HAIRSTYLISTS	HALLUCINATIVE	HAMADRYADES	HANDBARROW	HANDPASSES
HAIRWEAVING	HALLUCINATOR	HAMADRYADS	HANDBARROWS	HANDPASSING
HAIRWEAVINGS	HALLUCINATORS	HAMADRYASES	HANDBASKET	HANDPHONES
HAIRYBACKS	HALLUCINATORY	HAMAMELIDACEOUS	HANDBASKETS	HANDPICKED
HALACHISTS	HALLUCINOGEN	HAMAMELISES	HANDBRAKES	HANDPICKING
HALAKHISTS	HALLUCINOGENIC	HAMANTASCH	HANDBREADTH	HANDPRESSES
HALBERDIER	HALLUCINOGENICS	HAMANTASCHEN	HANDBREADTHS	HANDPRINTS
HALBERDIERS	HALLUCINOGENS	HAMARTHRITIS	HANDCLASPS	HANDSBREADTH
HALCYONIAN	HALLUCINOSES	HAMARTHRITISES	HANDCRAFTED	HANDSBREADTHS
HALENESSES	HALLUCINOSIS	HAMARTIOLOGIES	HANDCRAFTING	HANDSELING
HALFENDEALE	HALOBIONTIC	HAMARTIOLOGY	HANDCRAFTS	HANDSELLED
HALFHEARTED	HALOBIONTS	HAMBURGERS	HANDCRAFTSMAN	HANDSELLING
HALFHEARTEDLY	HALOBIOTIC	HAMESUCKEN	HANDCRAFTSMEN	HANDSHAKES
HALFHEARTEDNESS	HALOCARBON	HAMESUCKENS	HANDCUFFED	HANDSHAKING
HALFNESSES	HALOCARBONS	HAMFATTERED	HANDCUFFING	HANDSHAKINGS
HALFPENNIES	HALOCLINES	HAMFATTERING	HANDEDNESS	HANDSOMELY
HALFPENNYWORTH	HALOGENATE	HAMFATTERS	HANDEDNESSES	HANDSOMENESS
HALFPENNYWORTHS	HALOGENATED	HAMMERCLOTH	HANDFASTED	HANDSOMENESSES
HALFSERIOUSLY	HALOGENATES	HAMMERCLOTHS	HANDFASTING	HANDSOMEST
HALFTRACKS	HALOGENATING	HAMMERHEAD	HANDFASTINGS	HANDSPIKES
HALFWITTED	HALOGENATION	HAMMERHEADED	HANDFEEDING	HANDSPRING
HALFWITTEDLY	HALOGENATIONS	HAMMERHEADS	HANDICAPPED	HANDSPRINGS
HALFWITTEDNESS	HALOGENOID	HAMMERINGS	HANDICAPPER	HANDSTAFFS
HALIEUTICS	HALOGENOUS	HAMMERKOPS	HANDICAPPERS	HANDSTAMPED
HALIPLANKTON	HALOGETONS	HAMMERLESS	HANDICAPPING	HANDSTAMPING
HALIPLANKTONS	HALOMORPHIC	HAMMERLOCK	HANDICRAFT	HANDSTAMPS
HALLALLING	HALOPERIDOL	HAMMERLOCKS	HANDICRAFTER	HANDSTANDS
HALLEFLINTA	HALOPERIDOLS	HAMMERSTONE	HANDICRAFTERS	HANDSTAVES
HALLEFLINTAS	HALOPHILES	HAMMERSTONES	HANDICRAFTS	HANDSTROKE
HALLELUIAH	HALOPHILIC	HAMMERTOES	HANDICRAFTSMAN	HANDSTROKES
HALLELUIAHS	HALOPHILIES	HAMMINESSES	HANDICRAFTSMEN	HANDSTURNS

H

HANDTOWELS	HAPLOLOGIC	HARDHEADED	HARMONICAL	HARNESSING
HANDWHEELS	HAPLOLOGIES	HARDHEADEDLY	HARMONICALLY	HARNESSLESS
HANDWORKED	HAPLOSTEMONOUS	HARDHEADEDNESS	HARMONICAS	HARPOONEER
HANDWORKER	HAPLOTYPES	HARDHEARTED	HARMONICHORD	HARPOONEERS
HANDWORKERS	HAPPENCHANCE	HARDHEARTEDLY	HARMONICHORDS	HARPOONERS
HANDWRINGER	HAPPENCHANCES	HARDHEARTEDNESS	HARMONICIST	HARPOONING
HANDWRINGERS	HAPPENINGS	HARDIHEADS	HARMONICISTS	HARPSICHORD
HANDWRITES	HAPPENSTANCE	HARDIHOODS	HARMONICON	HARPSICHORDIST
HANDWRITING	HAPPENSTANCES	HARDIMENTS	HARMONICONS	HARPSICHORDISTS
HANDWRITINGS	HAPPINESSES	HARDINESSES	HARMONIOUS	HARPSICHORDS
HANDWRITTEN	HAPTOGLOBIN	HARDINGGRASS	HARMONIOUSLY	HARQUEBUSE
HANDWROUGHT	HAPTOGLOBINS	HARDINGGRASSES	HARMONIOUSNESS	HARQUEBUSES
HANDYPERSON	HAPTOTROPIC	HARDLINERS	HARMONIPHON	HARQUEBUSIER
HANDYPERSONS	HAPTOTROPISM	HARDMOUTHED	HARMONIPHONE	HARQUEBUSIERS
HANDYWORKS	HAPTOTROPISMS	HARDNESSES	HARMONIPHONES	HARQUEBUSS
HANGABILITIES	HARAMZADAS	HARDSCRABBLE	HARMONIPHONS	HARQUEBUSSES
HANGABILITY	HARAMZADIS	HARDSTANDING	HARMONISABLE	HARROWINGLY
HANKERINGS	HARANGUERS	HARDSTANDINGS	HARMONISATION	HARROWINGS
HANSARDISE	HARANGUING	HARDSTANDS	HARMONISATIONS	HARROWMENT
HANSARDISED	HARASSEDLY	HARDWAREMAN	HARMONISED	HARROWMENTS
HANSARDISES	HARASSINGLY	HARDWAREMEN	HARMONISER	HARRUMPHED
HANSARDISING	HARASSINGS	HARDWIRING	HARMONISERS	HARRUMPHING
HANSARDIZE	HARASSMENT	HARDWORKING	HARMONISES	HARSHENING
HANSARDIZED	HARASSMENTS	HAREBRAINED	HARMONISING	HARSHNESSES
HANSARDIZES	HARBINGERED	HARELIPPED	HARMONISTIC	HARTBEESES
HANSARDIZING	HARBINGERING	HARESTAILS	HARMONISTICALLY	HARTBEESTS
HANSELLING	HARBINGERS	HARIOLATED	HARMONISTS	HARTEBEEST
HANTAVIRUS	HARBORAGES	HARIOLATES	HARMONIUMIST	HARTEBEESTS
HANTAVIRUSES	HARBORFULS	HARIOLATING	HARMONIUMISTS	HARTSHORNS
HAPAXANTHIC	HARBORLESS	HARIOLATION	HARMONIUMS	HARUMPHING
HAPAXANTHOUS	HARBORMASTER	HARIOLATIONS	HARMONIZABLE	HARUSPICAL
HAPHAZARDLY	HARBORMASTERS	HARLEQUINADE	HARMONIZATION	HARUSPICATE
HAPHAZARDNESS	HARBORSIDE	HARLEQUINADES	HARMONIZATIONS	HARUSPICATED
HAPHAZARDNESSES	HARBOURAGE	HARLEQUINED	HARMONIZED	HARUSPICATES
HAPHAZARDRIES	HARBOURAGES	HARLEQUINING	HARMONIZER	HARUSPICATING
HAPHAZARDRY	HARBOURERS	HARLEQUINS	HARMONIZERS	HARUSPICATION
HAPHAZARDS	HARBOURING	HARLOTRIES	HARMONIZES	HARUSPICATIONS
HAPHTARAHS	HARBOURLESS	HARMALINES	HARMONIZING	HARUSPICES
HAPHTAROTH	HARDBACKED	HARMATTANS	HARMONOGRAM	HARUSPICIES
HAPLESSNESS	HARDBOARDS	HARMDOINGS	HARMONOGRAMS	HARVESTABLE
HAPLESSNESSES	HARDBOUNDS	HARMFULNESS	HARMONOGRAPH	HARVESTERS
HAPLOBIONT	HARDCOVERS	HARMFULNESSES	HARMONOGRAPHS	HARVESTING
HAPLOBIONTIC	HARDENINGS	HARMLESSLY	HARMONOMETER	HARVESTINGS
HAPLOBIONTS	HARDFISTED	HARMLESSNESS	HARMONOMETERS	HARVESTLESS
HAPLOGRAPHIES	HARDGRASSES	HARMLESSNESSES	HARMOSTIES	HARVESTMAN
HAPLOGRAPHY	HARDHANDED	HARMOLODIC	HARMOTOMES	HARVESTMEN
HAPLOIDIES	HARDHANDEDNESS	HARMOLODICS	HARNESSERS	HARVESTTIME

HARVESTTIMES	HAVERSINES	HEADMASTER	HEALTHFULNESSES	HEARTSINKS
HASENPFEFFER	HAWFINCHES	HEADMASTERLY	HEALTHIEST	HEARTSOMELY
HASENPFEFFERS	HAWKISHNESS	HEADMASTERS	HEALTHINESS	HEARTSOMENESS
HASHEESHES	HAWKISHNESSES	HEADMASTERSHIP	HEALTHINESSES	HEARTSOMENESSES
HASTEFULLY	HAWKSBEARD	HEADMASTERSHIPS	HEALTHISMS	HEARTSTRING
HASTINESSES	HAWKSBEARDS	HEADMISTRESS	HEALTHLESS	HEARTSTRINGS
HATBRUSHES	HAWKSBILLS	HEADMISTRESSES	HEALTHLESSNESS	HEARTTHROB
HATCHABILITIES	HAWSEHOLES	HEADMISTRESSY	HEALTHSOME	HEARTTHROBS
HATCHABILITY	HAWSEPIPES	HEADPEACES	HEAPSTEADS	HEARTWARMING
HATCHBACKS	HAYMAKINGS	HEADPHONES	HEARKENERS	HEARTWATER
HATCHELING	HAZARDABLE	HEADPIECES	HEARKENING	HEARTWATERS
HATCHELLED	HAZARDIZES	HEADQUARTER	HEARTACHES	HEARTWOODS
HATCHELLER	HAZARDOUSLY	HEADQUARTERED	HEARTBEATS	HEARTWORMS
HATCHELLERS	HAZARDOUSNESS	HEADQUARTERING	HEARTBREAK	HEATEDNESS
HATCHELLING	HAZARDOUSNESSES	HEADQUARTERS	HEARTBREAKER	HEATEDNESSES
HATCHERIES	HAZARDRIES	HEADREACHED	HEARTBREAKERS	HEATHBERRIES
HATCHETTITE	HAZINESSES	HEADREACHES	HEARTBREAKING	HEATHBERRY
HATCHETTITES	HEADACHIER	HEADREACHING	HEARTBREAKINGLY	HEATHBIRDS
HATCHLINGS	HEADACHIEST	HEADSCARVES	HEARTBREAKS	HEATHCOCKS
HATCHMENTS	HEADBANGED	HEADSHAKES	HEARTBROKE	HEATHENDOM
HATEFULNESS	HEADBANGING	HEADSHEETS	HEARTBROKEN	HEATHENDOMS
HATEFULNESSES	HEADBANGINGS	HEADSHRINKER	HEARTBROKENLY	HEATHENESSE
HATELESSNESS	HEADBOARDS	HEADSHRINKERS	HEARTBROKENNESS	HEATHENESSES
HATELESSNESSES	HEADBOROUGH	HEADSPACES	HEARTBURNING	HEATHENISE
HATEWORTHY	HEADBOROUGHS	HEADSPRING	HEARTBURNINGS	HEATHENISED
HATLESSNESS	HEADCHAIRS	HEADSPRINGS	HEARTBURNS	HEATHENISES
HATLESSNESSES	HEADCHEESE	HEADSQUARE	HEARTENERS	HEATHENISH
HAUBERGEON	HEADCHEESES	HEADSQUARES	HEARTENING	HEATHENISHLY
HAUBERGEONS	HEADCLOTHS	HEADSTALLS	HEARTENINGLY	HEATHENISHNESS
HAUGHTIEST	HEADCOUNTS	HEADSTANDS	HEARTHRUGS	HEATHENISING
HAUGHTINESS	HEADDRESSES	HEADSTICKS	HEARTHSTONE	HEATHENISM
HAUGHTINESSES	HEADFISHES	HEADSTOCKS	HEARTHSTONES	HEATHENISMS
HAUNTINGLY	HEADFOREMOST	HEADSTONES	HEARTIKINS	HEATHENIZE
HAUSFRAUEN	HEADFRAMES	HEADSTREAM	HEARTINESS	HEATHENIZED
HAUSSMANNISE	HEADGUARDS	HEADSTREAMS	HEARTINESSES	HEATHENIZES
HAUSSMANNISED	HEADHUNTED	HEADSTRONG	HEARTLANDS	HEATHENIZING
HAUSSMANNISES	HEADHUNTER	HEADSTRONGLY	HEARTLESSLY	HEATHENNESS
HAUSSMANNISING	HEADHUNTERS	HEADSTRONGNESS	HEARTLESSNESS	HEATHENNESSES
HAUSSMANNIZE	HEADHUNTING	HEADWAITER	HEARTLESSNESSES	HEATHENRIES
HAUSSMANNIZED	HEADHUNTINGS	HEADWAITERS	HEARTLINGS	HEATHENRIER
HAUSSMANNIZES	HEADINESSES	HEADWATERS	HEARTRENDING	HEATHERIEST
HAUSSMANNIZING	HEADLEASES	HEADWORKER	HEARTRENDINGLY	HEATHFOWLS
HAUSTELLATE	HEADLESSNESS	HEADWORKERS	HEARTSEASE	HEATHLANDS
HAUSTELLUM	HEADLESSNESSES	HEALTHCARE	HEARTSEASES	HEATSTROKE
HAUSTORIAL	HEADLIGHTS	HEALTHCARES	HEARTSEEDS	HEATSTROKES
HAUSTORIUM	HEADLINERS	HEALTHFULLY	HEARTSICKNESS	HEAVENLIER
HAVERSACKS	HEADLINING	HEALTHFULNESS	HEARTSICKNESSES	HEAVENLIEST

HEAVENLINESS	HECTOGRAPHIES	HEIGHTENED	HELIOGRAPHERS	HELIOTROPICALLY
HEAVENLINESSES	HECTOGRAPHING	HEIGHTENER	HELIOGRAPHIC	HELIOTROPIES
HEAVENWARD	HECTOGRAPHS	HEIGHTENERS	HELIOGRAPHICAL	HELIOTROPIN
HEAVENWARDS	HECTOGRAPHY	HEIGHTENING	HELIOGRAPHIES	HELIOTROPINS
HEAVINESSES	HECTOLITER	HEIGHTISMS	HELIOGRAPHING	HELIOTROPISM
HEAVYHEARTED	HECTOLITERS	HEINOUSNESS	HELIOGRAPHS	HELIOTROPISMS
HEAVYHEARTEDLY	HECTOLITRE	HEINOUSNESSES	HELIOGRAPHY	HELIOTROPY
HEAVYWEIGHT	HECTOLITRES	HEKTOGRAMS	HELIOGRAVURE	HELIOTYPED
HEAVYWEIGHTS	HECTOMETER	HELDENTENOR	HELIOGRAVURES	HELIOTYPES
HEBDOMADAL	HECTOMETERS	HELDENTENORS	HELIOLATER	HELIOTYPIC
HEBDOMADALLY	HECTOMETRE	HELIACALLY	HELIOLATERS	HELIOTYPIES
HEBDOMADAR	HECTOMETRES	HELIANTHEMUM	HELIOLATRIES	HELIOTYPING
HEBDOMADARIES	HECTORINGLY	HELIANTHEMUMS	HELIOLATROUS	HELIOZOANS
HEBDOMADARS	HECTORINGS	HELIANTHUS	HELIOLATRY	HELIPILOTS
HEBDOMADARY	HECTORISMS	HELIANTHUSES	HELIOLITHIC	HELISPHERIC
HEBDOMADER	HECTORSHIP	HELIBUSSES	HELIOLOGIES	HELISPHERICAL
HEBDOMADERS	HECTORSHIPS	HELICHRYSUM	HELIOMETER	HELLACIOUS
HEBEPHRENIA	HECTOSTERE	HELICHRYSUMS	HELIOMETERS	HELLACIOUSLY
HEBEPHRENIAC	HECTOSTERES	HELICITIES	HELIOMETRIC	HELLBENDER
HEBEPHRENIACS	HEDGEBILLS	HELICLINES	HELIOMETRICAL	HELLBENDERS
HEBEPHRENIAS	HEDGEHOPPED	HELICOGRAPH	HELIOMETRICALLY	HELLBROTHS
HEBEPHRENIC	HEDGEHOPPER	HELICOGRAPHS	HELIOMETRIES	HELLDIVERS
HEBEPHRENICS	HEDGEHOPPERS	HELICOIDAL	HELIOMETRY	HELLEBORES
HEBETATING	HEDGEHOPPING	HELICOIDALLY	HELIOPAUSE	HELLEBORINE
HEBETATION	HEDGEHOPPINGS	HELICONIAS	HELIOPAUSES	HELLEBORINES
HEBETATIONS	HEDONICALLY	HELICOPTED	HELIOPHILOUS	HELLENISATION
HEBETATIVE	HEDONISTIC	HELICOPTER	HELIOPHOBIC	HELLENISATIONS
HEBETUDINOSITY	HEDONISTICALLY	HELICOPTERED	HELIOPHYTE	HELLENISED
HEBETUDINOUS	HEDYPHANES	HELICOPTERING	HELIOPHYTES	HELLENISES
HEBRAISATION	HEEDFULNESS	HELICOPTERS	HELIOSCIOPHYTE	HELLENISING
HEBRAISATIONS	HEEDFULNESSES	HELICOPTING	HELIOSCIOPHYTES	HELLENIZATION
HEBRAISING	HEEDINESSES	HELICTITES	HELIOSCOPE	HELLENIZATIONS
HEBRAIZATION	HEEDLESSLY	HELIDROMES	HELIOSCOPES	HELLENIZED
HEBRAIZATIONS	HEEDLESSNESS	HELILIFTED	HELIOSCOPIC	HELLENIZES
HEBRAIZING	HEEDLESSNESSES	HELILIFTING	HELIOSPHERE	HELLENIZING
HECKELPHONE	HEELPIECES	HELIOCENTRIC	HELIOSPHERES	HELLGRAMITE
HECKELPHONES	HEELPLATES	HELIOCENTRICISM	HELIOSTATIC	HELLGRAMITES
HEÇOGENINS	HEFTINESSES	HELIOCENTRICITY	HELIOSTATS	HELLGRAMMITE
HECTICALLY	HEGEMONIAL	HELIOCHROME	HELIOTACTIC	HELLGRAMMITES
HECTOCOTYLI	HEGEMONICAL	HELIOCHROMES	HELIOTAXES	HELLHOUNDS
HECTOCOTYLUS	HEGEMONIES	HELIOCHROMIC	HELIOTAXIS	HELLISHNESS
HECTOGRAMME	HEGEMONISM	HELIOCHROMIES	HELIOTHERAPIES	HELLISHNESSES
HECTOGRAMMES	HEGEMONISMS	HELIOCHROMY	HELIOTHERAPY	HELMETLIKE
HECTOGRAMS	HEGEMONIST	HELIOGRAMS	HELIOTROPE	HELMINTHIASES
HECTOGRAPH	HEGEMONISTS	HELIOGRAPH	HELIOTROPES	HELMINTHIASIS
HECTOGRAPHED	HEGUMENIES	HELIOGRAPHED	HELIOTROPIC	HELMINTHIC
HECTOGRAPHIC	HEGUMENOSES	HELIOGRAPHER	HELIOTROPICAL	HELMINTHICS

HELMINTHOID	HEMATOLOGIST	HEMIHEDRAL	HEMITROPIES	HEMORRHAGED
HELMINTHOLOGIC	HEMATOLOGISTS	HEMIHEDRIES	HEMITROPISM	HEMORRHAGES
HELMINTHOLOGIES	HEMATOLOGY	HEMIHEDRISM	HEMITROPISMS	HEMORRHAGIC
HELMINTHOLOGIST	HEMATOLYSES	HEMIHEDRISMS	HEMITROPOUS	HEMORRHAGING
HELMINTHOLOGY	HEMATOLYSIS	HEMIHEDRON	HEMIZYGOUS	HEMORRHOID
HELMINTHOUS	HEMATOMATA	HEMIHEDRONS	HEMOCHROMATOSES	HEMORRHOIDAL
HELMSMANSHIP	HEMATOPHAGOUS	HEMIHYDRATE	HEMOCHROMATOSIS	HEMORRHOIDALS
HELMSMANSHIPS	HEMATOPOIESES	HEMIHYDRATED	HEMOCHROME	HEMORRHOIDS
HELOPHYTES	HEMATOPOIESIS	HEMIHYDRATES	HEMOCHROMES	HEMOSIDERIN
HELPFULNESS	HEMATOPOIETIC	HEMIMETABOLOUS	HEMOCYANIN	HEMOSIDERINS
HELPFULNESSES	HEMATOPORPHYRIN	HEMIMORPHIC	HEMOCYANINS	HEMOSTASES
HELPLESSLY	HEMATOTHERMAL	HEMIMORPHIES	HEMOCYTOMETER	HEMOSTASIA
HELPLESSNESS	HEMATOXYLIN	HEMIMORPHISM	HEMOCYTOMETERS	HEMOSTASIAS
HELPLESSNESSES	HEMATOXYLINS	HEMIMORPHISMS	HEMODIALYSES	HEMOSTASIS
HELVETIUMS	HEMATOZOON	HEMIMORPHITE	HEMODIALYSIS	HEMOSTATIC
HEMACHROME	HEMATURIAS	HEMIMORPHITES	HEMODILUTION	HEMOSTATICS
HEMACHROMES	HEMELYTRAL	HEMIMORPHY	HEMODILUTIONS	HEMOTOXINS
HEMACYTOMETER	HEMELYTRON	HEMIONUSES	HEMODYNAMIC	HEMSTITCHED
HEMACYTOMETERS	HEMELYTRUM	HEMIOPSIAS	HEMODYNAMICALLY	HEMSTITCHER
HEMAGGLUTINATE	HEMERALOPIA	HEMIPARASITE	HEMODYNAMICS	HEMSTITCHERS
HEMAGGLUTINATED	HEMERALOPIAS	HEMIPARASITES	HEMOFLAGELLATE	HEMSTITCHES
HEMAGGLUTINATES	HEMERALOPIC	HEMIPARASITIC	HEMOFLAGELLATES	HEMSTITCHING
HEMAGGLUTININ	HEMEROCALLIS	HEMIPLEGIA	HEMOGLOBIN	HENCEFORTH
HEMAGGLUTININS	HEMEROCALLISES	HEMIPLEGIAS	HEMOGLOBINS	HENCEFORWARD
HEMAGOGUES	HEMERYTHRIN	HEMIPLEGIC	HEMOGLOBINURIA	HENCEFORWARDS
HEMANGIOMA	HEMERYTHRINS	HEMIPLEGICS	HEMOGLOBINURIAS	HENCHPERSON
HEMANGIOMAS	HEMIACETAL	HEMIPTERAL	HEMOGLOBINURIC	HENCHPERSONS
HEMANGIOMATA	HEMIACETALS	HEMIPTERAN	HEMOLYMPHS	HENCHWOMAN
HEMATEMESES	HEMIALGIAS	HEMIPTERANS	HEMOLYSING	HENCHWOMEN
HEMATEMESIS	HEMIANOPIA	HEMIPTERON	HEMOLYSINS	HENDECAGON
HEMATINICS	HEMIANOPIAS	HEMIPTERONS	HEMOLYZING	HENDECAGONAL
HEMATOBLAST	HEMIANOPSIA	HEMIPTEROUS	HEMOPHILES	HENDECAGONS
HEMATOBLASTIC	HEMIANOPSIAS	HEMISPACES	HEMOPHILIA	HENDECAHEDRA
HEMATOBLASTS	HEMIANOPTIC	HEMISPHERE	HEMOPHILIAC	HENDECAHEDRON
HEMATOCELE	HEMICELLULOSE	HEMISPHERES	HEMOPHILIACS	HENDECAHEDRONS
HEMATOCELES	HEMICELLULOSES	HEMISPHERIC	HEMOPHILIAS	HENDECASYLLABIC
HEMATOCRIT	HEMICHORDATE	HEMISPHERICAL	HEMOPHILIC	HENDECASYLLABLE
HEMATOCRITS	HEMICHORDATES	HEMISPHEROID	HEMOPHILICS	HENDIADYSES
HEMATOCRYAL	HEMICRANIA	HEMISPHEROIDAL	HEMOPHILIOID	HENOTHEISM
HEMATOGENESES	HEMICRANIAS	HEMISPHEROIDS	HEMOPOIESES	HENOTHEISMS
HEMATOGENESIS	HEMICRYPTOPHYTE	HEMISTICHAL	HEMOPOIESIS	HENOTHEIST
HEMATOGENETIC	HEMICRYSTALLINE	HEMISTICHS	HEMOPOIETIC	HENOTHEISTIC
HEMATOGENIC	HEMICYCLES	HEMITERPENE	HEMOPROTEIN	HENOTHEISTS
HEMATOGENOUS	HEMICYCLIC	HEMITERPENES	HEMOPROTEINS	HENPECKERIES
HEMATOLOGIC	HEMIELYTRA	HEMITROPAL	HEMOPTYSES	HENPECKERY
HEMATOLOGICAL	HEMIELYTRAL	HEMITROPES	HEMOPTYSIS	HENPECKING
HEMATOLOGIES	HEMIELYTRON-	HEMITROPIC	HEMORRHAGE	HEORTOLOGICAL

H

HEORTOLOGIES	HEPTADECANOIC	HERBIVOROUSNESS	HERESIOLOGISTS	HERMITISMS
HEORTOLOGIST	HEPTAGONAL	HERBOLOGIES	HERESIOLOGY	HERMITRIES
HEORTOLOGISTS	HEPTAGYNOUS	HERBORISATION	HERESTHETIC	HERNIATING
HEORTOLOGY	HEPTAHEDRA	HERBORISATIONS	HERESTHETICAL	HERNIATION
HEPARINISED	HEPTAHEDRAL	HERBORISED	HERESTHETICIAN	HERNIATIONS
HEPARINIZED	HEPTAHEDRON	HERBORISES	HERESTHETICIANS	HERNIORRHAPHIES
HEPARINOID	HEPTAHEDRONS	HERBORISING	HERESTHETICS	HERNIORRHAPHY
HEPATECTOMIES	HEPTAMEROUS	HERBORISTS	HERETICALLY	HERNIOTOMIES
HEPATECTOMISED	HEPTAMETER	HERBORIZATION	HERETICATE	HERNIOTOMY
HEPATECTOMIZED	HEPTAMETERS	HERBORIZATIONS	HERETICATED	HEROICALLY
HEPATECTOMY	HEPTAMETRICAL	HERBORIZED	HERETICATES	HEROICALNESS
HEPATICOLOGICAL	HEPTANDROUS	HERBORIZES	HERETICATING	HEROICALNESSES
HEPATICOLOGIES	HEPTANGULAR	HERBORIZING	HERETOFORE	HEROICISED
HEPATICOLOGIST	HEPTAPODIC	HERCOGAMIES	HERETOFORES	HEROICISES
HEPATICOLOGISTS	HEPTAPODIES	HERCOGAMOUS	HERETRICES	HEROICISING
HEPATICOLOGY	HEPTARCHAL	HERCULESES	HERETRIXES	HEROICIZED
HEPATISATION	HEPTARCHIC	HERCYNITES	HERIOTABLE	HEROICIZES
HEPATISATIONS	HEPTARCHIES	HEREABOUTS	HERITABILITIES	HEROICIZING
HEPATISING	HEPTARCHIST	HEREAFTERS	HERITABILITY	HEROICNESS
HEPATITIDES	HEPTARCHISTS	HEREDITABILITY	HERITRESSES	HEROICNESSES
HEPATITISES	HEPTASTICH	HEREDITABLE	HERITRICES	HEROICOMIC
HEPATIZATION	HEPTASTICHS	HEREDITABLY	HERITRIXES	HEROICOMICAL
HEPATIZATIONS	HEPTASYLLABIC	HEREDITAMENT	HERKOGAMIES	HEROINISMS
HEPATIZING	HEPTATHLETE	HEREDITAMENTS	HERMANDADS	HERONSHAWS
HEPATOCELLULAR	HEPTATHLETES	HEREDITARIAN	HERMAPHRODITE	HERPESVIRUS
HEPATOCYTE	HEPTATHLON	HEREDITARIANISM	HERMAPHRODITES	HERPESVIRUSES
HEPATOCYTES	HEPTATHLONS	HEREDITARIANIST	HERMAPHRODITIC	HERPETOFAUNA
HEPATOGENOUS	HEPTATONIC	HEREDITARIANS	HERMAPHRODITISM	HERPETOFAUNAE
HEPATOLOGIES	HEPTAVALENT	HEREDITARILY	HERMATYPIC	HERPETOFAUNAS
HEPATOLOGIST	HERALDICALLY	HEREDITARINESS	HERMENEUTIC	HERPETOLOGIC
HEPATOLOGISTS	HERALDISTS	HEREDITARY	HERMENEUTICAL	HERPETOLOGICAL
HEPATOLOGY	HERALDRIES	HEREDITIES	HERMENEUTICALLY	HERPETOLOGIES
HEPATOMATA	HERALDSHIP	HEREDITIST	HERMENEUTICS	HERPETOLOGIST
HEPATOMEGALIES	HERALDSHIPS	HEREDITISTS	HERMENEUTIST	HERPETOLOGISTS
HEPATOMEGALY	HERBACEOUS	HEREINABOVE	HERMENEUTISTS	HERPETOLOGY
HEPATOPANCREAS	HERBACEOUSLY	HEREINAFTER	HERMETICAL	HERRENVOLK
HEPATOSCOPIES	HERBALISMS	HEREINBEFORE	HERMETICALLY	HERRENVOLKS
HEPATOSCOPY	HERBALISTS	HEREINBELOW	HERMETICISM	HERRIMENTS
HEPATOTOXIC	HERBARIANS	HERENESSES	HERMETICISMS	HERRINGBONE
HEPATOTOXICITY	HERBARIUMS	HERESIARCH	HERMETICITIES	HERRINGBONED
HEPHTHEMIMER	HERBICIDAL	HERESIARCHS	HERMETICITY	HERRINGBONES
HEPHTHEMIMERAL	HERBICIDALLY	HERESIOGRAPHER	HERMETISMS	HERRINGBONING
HEPHTHEMIMERS	HERBICIDES	HERESIOGRAPHERS	HERMETISTS	HERRINGERS
HEPTACHLOR	HERBIVORES	HERESIOGRAPHIES	HERMITAGES	HERRYMENTS
HEPTACHLORS	HERBIVORIES	HERESIOGRAPHY	HERMITESSES	HERSTORIES
HEPTACHORD	HERBIVOROUS	HERESIOLOGIES	HERMITICAL	HESITANCES
HEPTACHORDS	HERBIVOROUSLY	HERESIOLOGIST	HERMITICALLY	HESITANCIES

HESITANTLY	HETEROCHRONY	HETEROGENIES	HETEROPHIL	HETEROSTYLOUS
HESITATERS	HETEROCLITE	HETEROGENOUS	HETEROPHILE	HETEROSTYLY
HESITATING	HETÉROCLITES	HETEROGENY	HETEROPHONIES	HETEROTACTIC
HESITATINGLY	HETEROCLITIC	HETEROGONIC	HETEROPHONY	HETEROTACTOUS
HESITATION	HETEROCLITOUS	HETEROGONIES	HETEROPHYLLIES	HETEROTAXES
HESITATIONS	HETEROCONT	HETEROGONOUS	HETEROPHYLLOUS	HETEROTAXIA
HESITATIVE	HETEROCONTS	HETEROGONOUSLY	HETEROPHYLLY	HETEROTAXIAS
HESITATORS	HETEROCYCLE	HETEROGONY	HETEROPLASIA	HETEROTAXIC
HESITATORY	HETEROCYCLES	HETEROGRAFT	HETEROPLASIAS	HETEROTAXIES
HESPERIDIA	HETEROCYCLIC	HETEROGRAFTS	HETEROPLASTIC	HETEROTAXIS
HESPERIDIN	HETEROCYCLICS	HETEROGRAPHIC	HETEROPLASTIES	HETEROTAXY
HESPERIDINS	HETEROCYST	HETEROGRAPHICAL	HETEROPLASTY	HETEROTHALLIC
HESPERIDIUM	HETEROCYSTOUS	HETEROGRAPHIES	HETEROPLOID	HETEROTHALLIES
HESPERIDIUMS	HETEROCYSTS	HETEROGRAPHY	HETEROPLOIDIES	HETEROTHALLISM
HESSONITES	HETERODACTYL	HETEROGYNOUS	HETEROPLOIDS	HETEROTHALLISMS
HETAERISMIC	HETERODACTYLOUS	HETEROKARYON	HETEROPLOIDY	HETEROTHALLY
HETAERISMS	HETERODACTYLS	HETEROKARYONS	HETEROPODS	HETEROTHERMAL
HETAERISTIC	HETERODONT	HETEROKARYOSES	HETEROPOLAR	HETEROTOPIA
HETAERISTS	HETERODOXIES	HETEROKARYOSIS	HETEROPOLARITY	HETEROTOPIAS
HETAIRISMIC	HETERODOXY	HETEROKARYOTIC	HETEROPTERAN	HETEROTOPIC
HETAIRISMS	HETERODUPLEX	HETEROKONT	HETEROPTERANS	HETEROTOPIES
HETAIRISTIC	HETERODUPLEXES	HETEROKONTAN	HETEROPTEROUS	HETEROTOPOUS
HETAIRISTS	HETERODYNE	HETEROKONTS	HETEROSCEDASTIC	HETEROTOPY
HETERARCHIES	HETERODYNED	HETEROLECITHAL	HETEROSCIAN	HETEROTROPH
HETERARCHY	HETERODYNES	HETEROLOGIES	HETEROSCIANS	HETEROTROPHIC
HETERAUXESES	HETERODYNING	HETEROLOGOUS	HETEROSEXISM	HETEROTROPHIES
HETERAUXESIS	HETEROECIOUS	HETEROLOGOUSLY	HETEROSEXISMS	HETEROTROPHS
HETEROATOM	HETEROECISM	HETEROLOGY	HETEROSEXIST	HETEROTROPHY
HETEROATOMS	HETEROECISMS	HETEROLYSES	HETEROSEXISTS	HETEROTYPIC
HETEROAUXIN	HETEROFLEXIBLE	HETEROLYSIS	HETEROSEXUAL	HETEROTYPICAL
HETEROAUXINS	HETEROFLEXIBLES	HETEROLYTIC	HETEROSEXUALITY	HETEROUSIAN
HETEROBLASTIC	HETEROGAMETE	HETEROMEROUS	HETEROSEXUALLY	HETEROUSIANS
HETEROBLASTIES	HETEROGAMETES	HETEROMORPHIC	HETEROSEXUALS	HETEROZYGOSES
HETEROBLASTY	HETEROGAMETIC	HETEROMORPHIES	HETEROSOCIAL	HETEROZYGOSIS
HETEROCARPOUS	HETEROGAMETIES	HETEROMORPHISM	HETEROSOCIALITY	HETEROZYGOSITY
HETEROCERCAL	HETEROGAMETY	HETEROMORPHISMS	HETEROSOMATOUS	HETEROZYGOTE
HETEROCERCALITY	HETEROGAMIES	HETEROMORPHOUS	HETEROSPECIFIC	HETEROZYGOTES
HETEROCERCIES	HETEROGAMOUS	HETEROMORPHY	HETEROSPORIES	HETEROZYGOUS
HETEROCERCY	HETEROGAMY	HETERONOMIES	HETEROSPOROUS	HETHERWARD
HETEROCHROMATIC	HETEROGENEITIES	HETERONOMOUS	HETEROSPORY	HETMANATES
HETEROCHROMATIN	HETEROGENEITY	HETERONOMOUSLY	HETEROSTROPHIC	HETMANSHIP
HETEROCHROMOUS	HETEROGENEOUS	HETERONOMY	HETEROSTROPHIES	HETMANSHIPS
HETEROCHRONIC	HETEROGENEOUSLY	HETERONYMOUS	HETEROSTROPHY	HEULANDITE
HETEROCHRONIES	HETEROGENESES	HETERONYMOUSLY	HETEROSTYLED	HEULANDITES
HETEROCHRONISM	HETEROGENESIS	HETERONYMS	HETEROSTYLIES	HEURISTICALLY
HETEROCHRONISMS	HETEROGENETIC	HETEROOUSIAN	HETEROSTYLISM	HEURISTICS
HETEROCHRONOUS	HETEROGENIC	HETEROOUSIANS	HETEROSTYLISMS	HEXACHLORETHANE

H

HEXACHLORIDE	HEXAMETRISING	HIBERNICISING	HIERARCHIZING	HIEROPHOBIA
HEXACHLORIDES	HEXAMETRIST	HIBERNICIZE	HIERATICAL	HIEROPHOBIAS
HEXACHLOROPHANE	HEXAMETRISTS	HIBERNICIZED	HIERATICALLY	HIEROPHOBIC
HEXACHLOROPHENE	HEXAMETRIZE	HIBERNICIZES	HIERATICAS	HIEROSCOPIES
HEXACHORDS	HEXAMETRIZED	HIBERNICIZING	HIEROCRACIES	HIEROSCOPY
HEXACOSANOIC	HEXAMETRIZES	HIBERNISATION	HIEROCRACY	HIERURGICAL
HEXACTINAL	HEXAMETRIZING	HIBERNISATIONS	HIEROCRATIC	HIERURGIES
HEXACTINELLID	HEXANDRIAN	HIBERNISED	HIEROCRATICAL	HIGHBALLED
HEXACTINELLIDS	HEXANDROUS	HIBERNISES	HIEROCRATS	HIGHBALLING
HEXADACTYLIC	HEXANGULAR	HIBERNISING	HIERODULES	HIGHBINDER
HEXADACTYLOUS	HEXAPLARIAN	HIBERNIZATION	HIERODULIC	HIGHBINDERS
HEXADECANE	HEXAPLARIC	HIBERNIZATIONS	HIEROGLYPH	HIGHBLOODED
HEXADECANES	HEXAPLOIDIES	HIBERNIZED	HIEROGLYPHED	HIGHBROWED
HEXADECANOIC	HEXAPLOIDS	HIBERNIZES	HIEROGLYPHIC	HIGHBROWISM
HEXADECIMAL	HEXAPLOIDY	HIBERNIZING	HIEROGLYPHICAL	HIGHBROWISMS
HEXADECIMALS	HEXAPODIES	HIBISCUSES	HIEROGLYPHICS	HIGHCHAIRS
HEXAEMERIC	HEXARCHIES	HICCOUGHED	HIEROGLYPHING	HIGHERMOST
HEXAEMERON	HEXASTICHAL	HICCOUGHING	HIEROGLYPHIST	HIGHFALUTIN
HEXAEMERONS	HEXASTICHIC	HICCUPPING	HIEROGLYPHISTS	HIGHFALUTING
HEXAFLUORIDE	HEXASTICHON	HIDALGOISH	HIEROGLYPHS	HIGHFALUTINGS
HEXAFLUORIDES	HEXASTICHONS	HIDALGOISM	HIEROGRAMMAT	HIGHFALUTINS
HEXAGONALLY	HEXASTICHS	HIDALGOISMS	HIEROGRAMMATE	HIGHFLIERS
HEXAGRAMMOID	HEXASTYLES	HIDDENITES	HIEROGRAMMATES	HIGHFLYERS
HEXAGRAMMOIDS	HEXATEUCHAL	HIDDENMOST	HIEROGRAMMATIC	HIGHJACKED
HEXAGYNIAN	HEXAVALENT	HIDDENNESS	HIEROGRAMMATIST	HIGHJACKER
HEXAGYNOUS	HEXOBARBITAL	HIDDENNESSES	HIEROGRAMMATS	HIGHJACKERS
HEXAHEDRAL	HEXOBARBITALS	HIDEOSITIES	HIEROGRAMS	HIGHJACKING
HEXAHEDRON	HEXOKINASE	HIDEOUSNESS	HIEROGRAPH	HIGHJACKINGS
HEXAHEDRONS	HEXOKINASES	HIDEOUSNESSES	HIEROGRAPHER	HIGHLANDER
HEXAHEMERIC	HEXOSAMINIDASE	HIERACIUMS	HIEROGRAPHERS	HIGHLANDERS
HEXAHEMERON	HEXOSAMINIDASES	HIERACOSPHINGES	HIEROGRAPHIC	HIGHLIGHTED
HEXAHEMERONS	HEXYLRESORCINOL	HIERACOSPHINX	HIEROGRAPHICAL	HIGHLIGHTER
HEXAHYDRATE	HIBAKUSHAS	HIERACOSPHINXES	HIEROGRAPHIES	HIGHLIGHTERS
HEXAHYDRATED	HIBERNACLE	HIERARCHAL	HIEROGRAPHS	HIGHLIGHTING
HEXAHYDRATES	HIBERNACLES	HIERARCHIC	HIEROGRAPHY	HIGHLIGHTS
HEXAMERISM	HIBERNACULA	HIERARCHICAL	HIEROLATRIES	HIGHNESSES
HEXAMERISMS	HIBERNACULUM	HIERARCHICALLY	HIEROLATRY	HIGHTAILED
HEXAMEROUS	HIBERNATED	HIERARCHIES	HIEROLOGIC	HIGHTAILING
HEXAMETERS	HIBERNATES	HIERARCHISE	HIEROLOGICAL	HIGHWAYMAN
HEXAMETHONIUM	HIBERNATING	HIERARCHISED	HIEROLOGIES	HIGHWAYMEN
HEXAMETHONIUMS	HIBERNATION	HIERARCHISES	HIEROLOGIST	HIGHWROUGHT
HEXAMETRAL	HIBERNATIONS	HIERARCHISING	HIEROLOGISTS	HIJACKINGS
HEXAMETRIC	HIBERNATOR	HIERARCHISM	HIEROMANCIES	HILARIOUSLY
HEXAMETRICAL	HIBERNATORS	HIERARCHISMS	HIEROMANCY	HILARIOUSNESS
HEXAMETRISE	HIBERNICISE	HIERARCHIZE	HIEROPHANT	HILARIOUSNESSES
HEXAMETRISED	HIBERNICISED	HIERARCHIZED	HIEROPHANTIC	HILARITIES
HEXAMETRISES	HIBERNICISES	HIERARCHIZES	HIEROPHANTS	HILLBILLIES

HILLCRESTS	HIPPODAMES	HISPANICISING	HISTOLOGICAL	HISTRIONICALLY
HILLINESSES	HIPPODAMIST	HISPANICISM	HISTOLOGICALLY	HISTRIONICISM
HILLSLOPES	HIPPODAMISTS	HISPANICISMS	HISTOLOGIES	HISTRIONICISMS
HILLWALKER	HIPPODAMOUS	HISPANICIZE	HISTOLOGIST	HISTRIONICS
HILLWALKERS	HIPPODROME	HISPANICIZED	HISTOLOGISTS	HISTRIONISM
HILLWALKING	HIPPODROMES	HISPANICIZES	HISTOLYSES	HISTRIONISMS
HILLWALKINGS	HIPPODROMIC	HISPANICIZING	HISTOLYSIS	HITCHHIKED
HINDBERRIES	HIPPOGRIFF	HISPANIDAD	HISTOLYTIC	HITCHHIKER
HINDBRAINS	HIPPOGRIFFS	HISPANIDADS	HISTOLYTICALLY	HITCHHIKERS
HINDCASTED	HIPPOGRYPH	HISPANIOLISE	HISTOPATHOLOGIC	HITCHHIKES
HINDCASTING	HIPPOGRYPHS	HISPANIOLISED	HISTOPATHOLOGY	HITCHHIKING
HINDERANCE	HIPPOLOGIES	HISPANIOLISES	HISTOPHYSIOLOGY	HITHERMOST
HINDERANCES	HIPPOLOGIST	HISPANIOLISING	HISTOPLASMOSES	HITHERSIDE
HINDERINGLY	HIPPOLOGISTS	HISPANIOLIZE	HISTOPLASMOSIS	HITHERSIDES
HINDERINGS	HIPPOMANES	HISPANIOLIZED	HISTORIANS	HITHERWARD
HINDERLAND	HIPPOPHAGIES	HISPANIOLIZES	HISTORIATED	HITHERWARDS
HINDERLANDS	HIPPOPHAGIST	HISPANIOLIZING	HISTORICAL	HOACTZINES
HINDERLANS	HIPPOPHAGISTS	HISPANISMS	HISTORICALLY	HOARFROSTS
HINDERLINGS	HIPPOPHAGOUS	HISPIDITIES	HISTORICALNESS	HOARHOUNDS
HINDERLINS	HIPPOPHAGY	HISTAMINASE	HISTORICISE	HOARINESSES
HINDERMOST	HIPPOPHILE	HISTAMINASES	HISTORICISED	HOARSENESS
HINDFOREMOST	HIPPOPHILES	HISTAMINERGIC	HISTORICISES	HOARSENESSES
HINDQUARTER	HIPPOPHOBE	HISTAMINES	HISTORICISING	HOARSENING
HINDQUARTERS	HIPPOPHOBES	HISTAMINIC	HISTORICISM	HOBBITRIES
HINDRANCES	HIPPOPOTAMI	HISTIDINES	HISTORICISMS	HOBBLEBUSH
HINDSHANKS	HIPPOPOTAMIAN	HISTIOCYTE	HISTORICIST	HOBBLEBUSHES
HINDSIGHTS	HIPPOPOTAMIC	HISTIOCYTES	HISTORICISTS	HOBBLEDEHOY
HINTERLAND	HIPPOPOTAMUS	HISTIOCYTIC	HISTORICITIES	HOBBLEDEHOYDOM
HINTERLANDS	HIPPOPOTAMUSES	HISTIOLOGIES	HISTORICITY	HOBBLEDEHOYDOMS
HIPPEASTRUM	HIPPURITES	HISTIOLOGY	HISTORICIZE	HOBBLEDEHOYHOOD
HIPPEASTRUMS	HIPPURITIC	HISTIOPHOROID	HISTORICIZED	HOBBLEDEHOYISH
HIPPIATRIC	HIPSTERISM	HISTOBLAST	HISTORICIZES	HOBBLEDEHOYISM
HIPPIATRICS	HIPSTERISMS	HISTOBLASTS	HISTORICIZING	HOBBLEDEHOYISMS
HIPPIATRIES	HIRCOCERVUS	HISTOCHEMICAL	HISTORIETTE	HOBBLEDEHOYS
HIPPIATRIST	HIRCOCERVUSES	HISTOCHEMICALLY	HISTORIETTES	HOBBLINGLY
HIPPIATRISTS	HIRCOSITIES	HISTOCHEMIST	HISTORIFIED	HOBBYHORSE
HIPPIEDOMS	HIRSELLING	HISTOCHEMISTRY	HISTORIFIES	HOBBYHORSED
HIPPIENESS	HIRSUTENESS	HISTOCHEMISTS	HISTORIFYING	HOBBYHORSES
HIPPIENESSES	HIRSUTENESSES	HISTOCOMPATIBLE	HISTORIOGRAPHER	HOBBYHORSING
HIPPINESSES	HIRSUTISMS	HISTOGENESES	HISTORIOGRAPHIC	HOBGOBLINISM
HIPPOCAMPAL	HIRUDINEAN	HISTOGENESIS	HISTORIOGRAPHY	HOBGOBLINISMS
HIPPOCAMPI	HIRUDINEANS	HISTOGENETIC	HISTORIOLOGIES	HOBGOBLINRIES
HIPPOCAMPUS	HIRUDINOID	HISTOGENIC	HISTORIOLOGY	HOBGOBLINRY
HIPPOCENTAUR	HIRUDINOUS	HISTOGENICALLY	HISTORISMS	HOBGOBLINS
HIPPOCENTAURS	HISPANICISE	HISTOGENIES	HISTORYING	HOBJOBBERS
HIPPOCRASES	HISPANICISED	HISTOGRAMS	HISTRIONIC	HOBJOBBING
HIPPOCREPIAN	HISPANICISES	HISTOLOGIC	HISTRIONICAL	HOBJOBBINGS

H

HOBNAILING	HOLOCAUSTAL	HOMALOGRAPHIC	HOMEOTYPIC	HOMINIZING
HOBNOBBERS	HOLOCAUSTIC	HOMALOIDAL	HOMEOTYPICAL	HOMOBLASTIC
HOBNOBBING	HOLOCAUSTS	HOMEBIRTHS	HOMEOWNERS	HOMOBLASTIES
HOCHMAGANDIES	HOLOCRYSTALLINE	HOMEBODIES	HOMEOWNERSHIP	HOMOBLASTY
HOCHMAGANDY	HOLODISCUS	HOMEBUYERS	HOMEOWNERSHIPS	HOMOCENTRIC
HODGEPODGE	HOLODISCUSES	HOMECOMERS	HOMEPLACES	HOMOCENTRICALLY
HODGEPODGES	HOLOENZYME	HOMECOMING	HOMEPORTED	HOMOCERCAL
HODMANDODS	HOLOENZYMES	HOMECOMINGS	HOMEPORTING	HOMOCERCIES
HODOGRAPHIC	HOLOGAMIES	HOMECRAFTS	HOMESCHOOL	HOMOCHLAMYDEOUS
HODOGRAPHS	HOLOGRAPHED	HOMELESSNESS	HOMESCHOOLED	HOMOCHROMATIC
HODOMETERS	HOLOGRAPHER	HOMELESSNESSES	HOMESCHOOLER	HOMOCHROMATISM
HODOMETRIES	HOLOGRAPHERS	HOMELINESS	HOMESCHOOLERS	HOMOCHROMATISMS
HODOSCOPES	HOLOGRAPHIC	HOMELINESSES	HOMESCHOOLING	HOMOCHROMIES
HOGGISHNESS	HOLOGRAPHICALLY	HOMEMAKERS	HOMESCHOOLS	HOMOCHROMOUS
HOGGISHNESSES	HOLOGRAPHIES	HOMEMAKING	HOMESCREETCH	HOMOCHROMY
HOIDENISHNESS	HOLOGRAPHING	HOMEMAKINGS	HOMESCREETCHES	HOMOCYCLIC
HOIDENISHNESSES	HOLOGRAPHS	HOMEOBOXES	HOMESHORING	HOMOCYSTEINE
HOJATOLESLAM	HOLOGRAPHY	HOMEOMERIC	HOMESHORINGS	HOMOCYSTEINES
HOJATOLESLAMS	HOLOGYNIES	HOMEOMERIES	HOMESICKNESS	HOMOEOMERIC
HOJATOLISLAM	HOLOHEDRAL	HOMEOMEROUS	HOMESICKNESSES	HOMOEOMERIES
HOJATOLISLAMS	HOLOHEDRISM	HOMEOMORPH	HOMESOURCING	HOMOEOMEROUS
HOKEYNESSES	HOLOHEDRISMS	HOMEOMORPHIC	HOMESOURCINGS	HOMOEOMERY
HOKEYPOKEY	HOLOHEDRON	HOMEOMORPHIES	HOMESTALLS	HOMOEOMORPH
HOKEYPOKEYS	HOLOHEDRONS	HOMEOMORPHISM	HOMESTANDS	HOMOEOMORPHIC
HOKINESSES	HOLOMETABOLIC	HOMEOMORPHISMS	HOMESTEADED	HOMOEOMORPHIES
HOKYPOKIES	HOLOMETABOLISM	HOMEOMORPHOUS	HOMESTEADER	HOMOEOMORPHISM
HOLARCHIES	HOLOMETABOLISMS	HOMEOMORPHS	HOMESTEADERS	HOMOEOMORPHISMS
HOLDERBATS	HOLOMETABOLOUS	HOMEOMORPHY	HOMESTEADING	HOMOEOMORPHOUS
HOLDERSHIP	HOLOMORPHIC	HOMEOPATHIC	HOMESTEADINGS	HOMOEOMORPHS
HOLDERSHIPS	HOLOPHOTAL	HOMEOPATHICALLY	HOMESTEADS	HOMOEOMORPHY
HOLIDAYERS	HOLOPHOTES	HOMEOPATHIES	HOMESTRETCH	HOMOEOPATH
HOLIDAYING	HOLOPHRASE	HOMEOPATHIST	HOMESTRETCHES	HOMOEOPATHIC
HOLIDAYMAKER	HOLOPHRASES	HOMEOPATHISTS	HOMEWORKER	HOMOEOPATHIES
HOLIDAYMAKERS	HOLOPHRASTIC	HOMEOPATHS	HOMEWORKERS	HOMOEOPATHIST
HOLINESSES	HOLOPHYTES	HOMEOPATHY	HOMEWORKING	HOMOEOPATHISTS
HOLISTICALLY	HOLOPHYTIC	HOMEOSTASES	HOMEWORKINGS	HOMOEOPATHS
HOLLANDAISE	HOLOPHYTISM	HOMEOSTASIS	HOMEYNESSES	HOMOEOPATHY
HOLLANDAISES	HOLOPHYTISMS	HOMEOSTATIC	HOMICIDALLY	HOMOEOSTASES
HOLLOWARES	HOLOPLANKTON	HOMEOTELEUTON	HOMILETICAL	HOMOEOSTASIS
HOLLOWNESS	HOLOPLANKTONS	HOMEOTELEUTONS	HOMILETICALLY	HOMOEOSTATIC
HOLLOWNESSES	HOLOSTERIC	HOMEOTHERM	HOMILETICS	HOMOEOTELEUTON
HOLLOWWARE	HOLOTHURIAN	HOMEOTHERMAL	HOMINESSES	HOMOEOTELEUTONS
HOLLOWWARES	HOLOTHURIANS	HOMEOTHERMIC	HOMINISATION	HOMOEOTHERMAL
HOLLYHOCKS	HOLSTERING	HOMEOTHERMIES	HOMINISATIONS	HOMOEOTHERMIC
HOLOBENTHIC	HOLYSTONED	HOMEOTHERMOUS	HOMINISING	HOMOEOTHERMOUS
HOLOBLASTIC	HOLYSTONES	HOMEOTHERMS	HOMINIZATION	HOMOEOTYPIC
HOLOBLASTICALLY	HOLYSTONING	HOMEOTHERMY	HOMINIZATIONS	HOMOEOTYPICAL

HOMOEROTIC	HOMOIOTHERMIES	HOMOOUSIAN	HOMOTAXIALLY	HONEYMONTHS
HOMOEROTICISM	HOMOIOTHERMS	HOMOOUSIANS	HOMOTHALLIC	HONEYMOONED
HOMOEROTICISMS	HOMOIOTHERMY	HOMOPHILES	HOMOTHALLIES	HONEYMOONER
HOMOEROTISM	HOMOIOUSIAN	HOMOPHOBES	HOMOTHALLISM	HONEYMOONERS
HOMOEROTISMS	HOMOIOUSIANS	HOMOPHOBIA	HOMOTHALLISMS	HONEYMOONING
HOMOGAMETIC	HOMOLOGATE	HOMOPHOBIAS	HOMOTHALLY	HONEYMOONS
HOMOGAMIES	HOMOLOGATED	HOMOPHOBIC	HOMOTHERMAL	HONEYSUCKER
HOMOGAMOUS	HOMOLOGATES	HOMOPHONES	HOMOTHERMIC	HONEYSUCKERS
HOMOGENATE	HOMOLOGATING	HOMOPHONIC	HOMOTHERMIES	HONEYSUCKLE
HOMOGENATES	HOMOLOGATION	HOMOPHONICALLY	HOMOTHERMOUS	HONEYSUCKLED
HOMOGENEITIES	HOMOLOGATIONS	HOMOPHONIES	HOMOTHERMY	HONEYSUCKLES
HOMOGENEITY	HOMOLOGICAL	HOMOPHONOUS	HOMOTONIES	HONEYTRAPS
HOMOGENEOUS	HOMOLOGICALLY	HOMOPHYLIES	HOMOTONOUS	HONORABILITIES
HOMOGENEOUSLY	HOMOLOGIES	HOMOPHYLLIC	HOMOTRANSPLANT	HONORABILITY
HOMOGENEOUSNESS	HOMOLOGISE	HOMOPLASIES	HOMOTRANSPLANTS	HONORABLENESS
HOMOGENESES	HOMOLOGISED	HOMOPLASMIES	HOMOTYPIES	HONORABLENESSES
HOMOGENESIS	HOMOLOGISER	HOMOPLASMY	HOMOUSIANS	HONORARIES
HOMOGENETIC	HOMOLOGISERS	HOMOPLASTIC	HOMOZYGOSES	HONORARILY
HOMOGENETICAL	HOMOLOGISES	HOMOPLASTICALLY	HOMOZYGOSIS	HONORARIUM
HOMOGENIES	HOMOLOGISING	HOMOPLASTIES	HOMOZYGOSITIES	HONORARIUMS
HOMOGENISATION	HOMOLOGIZE	HOMOPLASTY	HOMOZYGOSITY	HONORIFICAL
HOMOGENISATIONS	HOMOLOGIZED	HOMOPOLARITIES	HOMOZYGOTE	HONORIFICALLY
HOMOGENISE	HOMOLOGIZER	HOMOPOLARITY	HOMOZYGOTES	HONORIFICS
HOMOGENISED	HOMOLOGIZERS	HOMOPOLYMER	HOMOZYGOTIC	HONOURABLE
HOMOGENISER	HOMOLOGIZES	HOMOPOLYMERIC	HOMOZYGOUS	HONOURABLENESS
HOMOGENISERS	HOMOLOGIZING	HOMOPOLYMERS	HOMOZYGOUSLY	HONOURABLY
HOMOGENISES	HOMOLOGOUMENA	HOMOPTERAN	HOMUNCULAR	HONOURLESS
HOMOGENISING	HOMOLOGOUS	HOMOPTERANS	HOMUNCULES	HOODEDNESS
HOMOGENIZATION	HOMOLOGRAPHIC	HOMOPTEROUS	HOMUNCULUS	HOODEDNESSES
HOMOGENIZATIONS	HOMOLOGUES	HOMORGANIC	HONESTNESS	HOODLUMISH
HOMOGENIZE	HOMOLOGUMENA	HOMOSCEDASTIC	HONESTNESSES	HOODLUMISM
HOMOGENIZED	HOMOLOSINE	HOMOSEXUAL	HONEYBUNCH	HOODLUMISMS
HOMOGENIZER	HOMOMORPHIC	HOMOSEXUALISM	HONEYBUNCHES	HOODOOISMS
HOMOGENIZERS	HOMOMORPHIES	HOMOSEXUALISMS	HONEYCOMBED	HOODWINKED
HOMOGENIZES	HOMOMORPHISM	HOMOSEXUALIST	HONEYCOMBING	HOODWINKER
HOMOGENIZING	HOMOMORPHISMS	HOMOSEXUALISTS	HONEYCOMBINGS	HOODWINKERS
HOMOGENOUS	HOMOMORPHOSES	HOMOSEXUALITIES	HONEYCOMBS	HOODWINKING
HOMOGONIES	HOMOMORPHOSIS	HOMOSEXUALITY	HONEYCREEPER	HOOFPRINTS
HOMOGONOUS	HOMOMORPHOUS	HOMOSEXUALLY	HONEYCREEPERS	HOOKCHECKS
HOMOGONOUSLY	HOMOMORPHS	HOMOSEXUALS	HONEYDEWED	HOOKEDNESS
HOMOGRAFTS	HOMOMORPHY	HOMOSOCIAL	HONEYEATER	HOOKEDNESSES
HOMOGRAPHIC	HOMONUCLEAR	HOMOSOCIALITIES	HONEYEATERS	HOOLACHANS
HOMOGRAPHS	HOMONYMIES	HOMOSOCIALITY	HONEYGUIDE	HOOLIGANISM
HOMOIOMEROUS	HOMONYMITIES	HOMOSPORIES	HONEYGUIDES	HOOLIGANISMS
HOMOIOTHERM	HOMONYMITY	HOMOSPOROUS	HONEYMONTH	HOOPSKIRTS
HOMOIOTHERMAL	HOMONYMOUS	HOMOSTYLIES	HONEYMONTHED	HOOTANANNIE
HOMOIOTHERMIC	HOMONYMOUSLY	HOMOTAXIAL	HONEYMONTHING	HOOTANANNIES

H

HOOTANANNY
HOOTENANNIE
HOOTENANNIES
HOOTENANNY
HOOTNANNIE
HOOTNANNIES
HOPEFULNESS
HOPEFULNESSES
HOPELESSLY
HOPELESSNESS
HOPELESSNESSES
HOPLOLOGIES
HOPLOLOGIST
HOPLOLOGISTS
HOPPERCARS
HOPSACKING
HOPSACKINGS
HOPSCOTCHED
HOPSCOTCHES
HOPSCOTCHING
HOREHOUNDS
HORIATIKIS
HORIZONLESS
HORIZONTAL
HORIZONTALITIES
HORIZONTALITY
HORIZONTALLY
HORIZONTALNESS
HORIZONTALS
HORMOGONIA
HORMOGONIUM
HORMONALLY
HORMONELIKE
HORNBLENDE
HORNBLENDES
HORNBLENDIC
HORNEDNESS
HORNEDNESSES
HORNINESSES
HORNLESSNESS
HORNLESSNESSES
HORNSTONES
HORNSWOGGLE
HORNSWOGGLED
HORNSWOGGLES
HORNSWOGGLING
HORNWRACKS

HORNYHEADS
HORNYWINKS
HOROGRAPHER
HOROGRAPHERS
HOROGRAPHIES
HOROGRAPHY
HOROLOGERS
HOROLOGICAL
HOROLOGIES
HOROLOGION
HOROLOGIONS
HOROLOGIST
HOROLOGISTS
HOROLOGIUM
HOROLOGIUMS
HOROMETRICAL
HOROMETRIES
HOROSCOPES
HOROSCOPIC
HOROSCOPIES
HOROSCOPIST
HOROSCOPISTS
HORRENDOUS
HORRENDOUSLY
HORRENDOUSNESS
HORRIBLENESS
HORRIBLENESSES
HORRIDNESS
HORRIDNESSES
HORRIFICALLY
HORRIFICATION
HORRIFICATIONS
HORRIFYING
HORRIFYINGLY
HORRIPILANT
HORRIPILATE
HORRIPILATED
HORRIPILATES
HORRIPILATING
HORRIPILATION
HORRIPILATIONS
HORRISONANT
HORRISONOUS
HORSEBACKS
HORSEBEANS
HORSEBOXES
HORSEFEATHERS

HORSEFLESH
HORSEFLESHES
HORSEFLIES
HORSEHAIRS
HORSEHIDES
HORSELAUGH
HORSELAUGHS
HORSELEECH
HORSELEECHES
HORSEMANSHIP
HORSEMANSHIPS
HORSEMEATS
HORSEMINTS
HORSEPLAYER
HORSEPLAYERS
HORSEPLAYS
HORSEPONDS
HORSEPOWER
HORSEPOWERS
HORSEPOXES
HORSERACES
HORSERADISH
HORSERADISHES
HORSESHITS
HORSESHOED
HORSESHOEING
HORSESHOEINGS
HORSESHOER
HORSESHOERS
HORSESHOES
HORSETAILS
HORSEWEEDS
HORSEWHIPPED
HORSEWHIPPER
HORSEWHIPPERS
HORSEWHIPPING
HORSEWHIPS
HORSEWOMAN
HORSEWOMEN
HORSINESSES
HORTATIONS
HORTATIVELY
HORTATORILY
HORTICULTURAL
HORTICULTURALLY
HORTICULTURE
HORTICULTURES

HORTICULTURIST
HORTICULTURISTS
HOSANNAING
HOSPITABLE
HOSPITABLENESS
HOSPITABLY
HOSPITAGES
HOSPITALER
HOSPITALERS
HOSPITALES
HOSPITALISATION
HOSPITALISE
HOSPITALISED
HOSPITALISES
HOSPITALISING
HOSPITALIST
HOSPITALISTS
HOSPITALITIES
HOSPITALITY
HOSPITALIZATION
HOSPITALIZE
HOSPITALIZED
HOSPITALIZES
HOSPITALIZING
HOSPITALLER
HOSPITALLERS
HOSTELINGS
HOSTELLERS
HOSTELLING
HOSTELLINGS
HOSTELRIES
HOSTESSING
HOSTILITIES
HOTCHPOTCH
HOTCHPOTCHES
HOTDOGGERS
HOTDOGGING
HOTELLINGS
HOTFOOTING
HOTHEADEDLY
HOTHEADEDNESS
HOTHEADEDNESSES
HOTHOUSING
HOTHOUSINGS
HOTPRESSED
HOTPRESSES
HOTPRESSING

HOTTENTOTS
HOUGHMAGANDIE
HOUGHMAGANDIES
HOUNDFISHES
HOURGLASSES
HOURPLATES
HOUSEBOATER
HOUSEBOATERS
HOUSEBOATS
HOUSEBOUND
HOUSEBREAK
HOUSEBREAKER
HOUSEBREAKERS
HOUSEBREAKING
HOUSEBREAKINGS
HOUSEBREAKS
HOUSEBROKE
HOUSEBROKEN
HOUSECARLS
HOUSECLEAN
HOUSECLEANED
HOUSECLEANING
HOUSECLEANINGS
HOUSECLEANS
HOUSECOATS
HOUSECRAFT
HOUSECRAFTS
HOUSEDRESS
HOUSEDRESSES
HOUSEFATHER
HOUSEFATHERS
HOUSEFLIES
HOUSEFRONT
HOUSEFRONTS
HOUSEGUEST
HOUSEGUESTS
HOUSEHOLDER
HOUSEHOLDERS
HOUSEHOLDERSHIP
HOUSEHOLDS
HOUSEHUSBAND
HOUSEHUSBANDS
HOUSEKEEPER
HOUSEKEEPERS
HOUSEKEEPING
HOUSEKEEPINGS
HOUSEKEEPS

HOUSELEEKS	HOVERTRAIN	HUMANISTICALLY	HUMIDISTAT	HUNDREDTHS
HOUSELESSNESS	HOVERTRAINS	HUMANITARIAN	HUMIDISTATS	HUNDREDWEIGHT
HOUSELESSNESSES	HOWLROUNDS	HUMANITARIANISM	HUMIDITIES	HUNDREDWEIGHTS
HOUSELIGHTS	HOWTOWDIES	HUMANITARIANIST	HUMIDNESSES	HUNGERINGLY
HOUSELINES	HOYDENHOOD	HUMANITARIANS	HUMIFICATION	HUNGRINESS
HOUSELLING	HOYDENHOODS	HUMANITIES	HUMIFICATIONS	HUNGRINESSES
HOUSELLINGS	HOYDENISHNESS	HUMANIZATION	HUMILIATED	HUNTIEGOWK
HOUSEMAIDS	HOYDENISHNESSES	HUMANIZATIONS	HUMILIATES	HUNTIEGOWKS
HOUSEMASTER	HOYDENISMS	HUMANIZERS	HUMILIATING	HUNTRESSES
HOUSEMASTERS	HUBRISTICALLY	HUMANIZING	HUMILIATINGLY	HUNTSMANSHIP
HOUSEMATES	HUCKABACKS	HUMANKINDS	HUMILIATION	HUNTSMANSHIPS
HOUSEMISTRESS	HUCKLEBERRIES	HUMANNESSES	HUMILIATIONS	HUPAITHRIC
HOUSEMISTRESSES	HUCKLEBERRY	HUMBLEBEES	HUMILIATIVE	HURLBARROW
HOUSEMOTHER	HUCKLEBERRYING	HUMBLENESS	HUMILIATOR	HURLBARROWS
HOUSEMOTHERS	HUCKLEBERRYINGS	HUMBLENESSES	HUMILIATORS	HURRICANES
HOUSEPAINTER	HUCKLEBONE	HUMBLESSES	HUMILIATORY	HURRICANOES
HOUSEPAINTERS	HUCKLEBONES	HUMBLINGLY	HUMILITIES	HURRIEDNESS
HOUSEPARENT	HUCKSTERAGE	HUMBUCKERS	HUMMELLERS	HURRIEDNESSES
HOUSEPARENTS	HUCKSTERAGES	HUMBUGGABLE	HUMMELLING	HURRYINGLY
HOUSEPERSON	HUCKSTERED	HUMBUGGERIES	HUMMINGBIRD	HURTFULNESS
HOUSEPERSONS	HUCKSTERESS	HUMBUGGERS	HUMMINGBIRDS	HURTFULNESSES
HOUSEPLANT	HUCKSTERESSES	HUMBUGGERY	HUMMOCKING	HURTLEBERRIES
HOUSEPLANTS	HUCKSTERIES	HUMBUGGING	HUMORALISM	HURTLEBERRY
HOUSEROOMS	HUCKSTERING	HUMDINGERS	HUMORALISMS	HURTLESSLY
HOUSESITTING	HUCKSTERISM	HUMDRUMNESS	HUMORALIST	HURTLESSNESS
HOUSEWARES	HUCKSTERISMS	HUMDRUMNESSES	HUMORALISTS	HURTLESSNESSES
HOUSEWARMING	HUCKSTRESS	HUMDUDGEON	HUMORESQUE	HUSBANDAGE
HOUSEWARMINGS	HUCKSTRESSES	HUMDUDGEONS	HUMORESQUES	HUSBANDAGES
HOUSEWIFELINESS	HUDIBRASTIC	HUMECTANTS	HUMORISTIC	HUSBANDERS
HOUSEWIFELY	HUFFINESSES	HUMECTATED	HUMORLESSLY	HUSBANDING
HOUSEWIFERIES	HUFFISHNESS	HUMECTATES	HUMORLESSNESS	HUSBANDLAND
HOUSEWIFERY	HUFFISHNESSES	HUMECTATING	HUMORLESSNESSES	HUSBANDLANDS
HOUSEWIFESHIP	HUGENESSES	HUMECTATION	HUMOROUSLY	HUSBANDLESS
HOUSEWIFESHIPS	HUGEOUSNESS	HUMECTATIONS	HUMOROUSNESS	HUSBANDLIKE
HOUSEWIFESKEP	HUGEOUSNESSES	HUMECTIVES	HUMOROUSNESSES	HUSBANDMAN
HOUSEWIFESKEPS	HULLABALLOO	HUMGRUFFIAN	HUMOURLESS	HUSBANDMEN
HOUSEWIFEY	HULLABALLOOS	HUMGRUFFIANS	HUMOURLESSNESS	HUSBANDRIES
HOUSEWIVES	HULLABALOO	HUMGRUFFIN	HUMOURSOME	HUSHABYING
HOUSEWORKER	HULLABALOOS	HUMGRUFFINS	HUMOURSOMENESS	HUSHPUPPIES
HOUSEWORKERS	HUMANENESS	HUMICOLOUS	HUMPBACKED	HUSKINESSES
HOUSEWORKS	HUMANENESSES	HUMIDIFICATION	HUMPINESSES	HYACINTHINE
HOUSTONIAS	HUMANHOODS	HUMIDIFICATIONS	HUNCHBACKED	HYALINISATION
HOVERCRAFT	HUMANISATION	HUMIDIFIED	HUNCHBACKS	HYALINISATIONS
HOVERCRAFTS	HUMANISATIONS	HUMIDIFIER	HUNDREDERS	HYALINISED
HOVERFLIES	HUMANISERS	HUMIDIFIERS	HUNDREDFOLD	HYALINISES
HOVERINGLY	HUMANISING	HUMIDIFIES	HUNDREDFOLDS	HYALINISING
HOVERPORTS	HUMANISTIC	HUMIDIFYING	HUNDREDORS	HYALINIZATION

H

HYALINIZATIONS

HYALINIZATIONS	HYDRALAZINES	HYDROCHLORIDE	HYDROGENISE	HYDROLYTIC
HYALINIZED	HYDRANGEAS	HYDROCHLORIDES	HYDROGENISED	HYDROLYTICALLY
HYALINIZES	HYDRARGYRAL	HYDROCHORE	HYDROGENISES	HYDROLYZABLE
HYALINIZING	HYDRARGYRIA	HYDROCHORES	HYDROGENISING	HYDROLYZATE
HYALOMELAN	HYDRARGYRIAS	HYDROCHORIC	HYDROGENIZATION	HYDROLYZATES
HYALOMELANE	HYDRARGYRIC	HYDROCODONE	HYDROGENIZE	HYDROLYZATION
HYALOMELANES	HYDRARGYRISM	HYDROCODONES	HYDROGENIZED	HYDROLYZATIONS
HYALOMELANS	HYDRARGYRISMS	HYDROCOLLOID	HYDROGENIZES	HYDROLYZED
HYALONEMAS	HYDRARGYRUM	HYDROCOLLOIDAL	HYDROGENIZING	HYDROLYZER
HYALOPHANE	HYDRARGYRUMS	HYDROCOLLOIDS	HYDROGENOLYSES	HYDROLYZERS
HYALOPHANES	HYDRARTHROSES	HYDROCORAL	HYDROGENOLYSIS	HYDROLYZES
HYALOPLASM	HYDRARTHROSIS	HYDROCORALLINE	HYDROGENOUS	HYDROLYZING
HYALOPLASMIC	HYDRASTINE	HYDROCORALLINES	HYDROGEOLOGICAL	HYDROMAGNETIC
HYALOPLASMS	HYDRASTINES	HYDROCORALS	HYDROGEOLOGIES	HYDROMAGNETICS
HYALURONIC	HYDRASTININE	HYDROCORTISONE	HYDROGEOLOGIST	HYDROMANCER
HYALURONIDASE	HYDRASTININES	HYDROCORTISONES	HYDROGEOLOGISTS	HYDROMANCERS
HYALURONIDASES	HYDRASTISES	HYDROCRACK	HYDROGEOLOGY	HYDROMANCIES
HYBRIDISABLE	HYDRATIONS	HYDROCRACKED	HYDROGRAPH	HYDROMANCY
HYBRIDISATION	HYDRAULICALLY	HYDROCRACKER	HYDROGRAPHER	HYDROMANIA
HYBRIDISATIONS	HYDRAULICKED	HYDROCRACKERS	HYDROGRAPHERS	HYDROMANIAS
HYBRIDISED	HYDRAULICKING	HYDROCRACKING	HYDROGRAPHIC	HYDROMANTIC
HYBRIDISER	HYDRAULICS	HYDROCRACKINGS	HYDROGRAPHICAL	HYDROMECHANICAL
HYBRIDISERS	HYDRAZIDES	HYDROCRACKS	HYDROGRAPHIES	HYDROMECHANICS
HYBRIDISES	HYDRAZINES	HYDROCYANIC	HYDROGRAPHS	HYDROMEDUSA
HYBRIDISING	HYDRICALLY	HYDRODYNAMIC	HYDROGRAPHY	HYDROMEDUSAE
HYBRIDISMS	HYDROACOUSTICS	HYDRODYNAMICAL	HYDROKINETIC	HYDROMEDUSAN
HYBRIDISTS	HYDROBIOLOGICAL	HYDRODYNAMICIST	HYDROKINETICAL	HYDROMEDUSANS
HYBRIDITIES	HYDROBIOLOGIES	HYDRODYNAMICS	HYDROKINETICS	HYDROMEDUSAS
HYBRIDIZABLE	HYDROBIOLOGIST	HYDROELASTIC	HYDROLASES	HYDROMEDUSOID
HYBRIDIZATION	HYDROBIOLOGISTS	HYDROELECTRIC	HYDROLOGIC	HYDROMEDUSOIDS
HYBRIDIZATIONS	HYDROBIOLOGY	HYDROEXTRACTOR	HYDROLOGICAL	HYDROMETALLURGY
HYBRIDIZED	HYDROBROMIC	HYDROEXTRACTORS	HYDROLOGICALLY	HYDROMETEOR
HYBRIDIZER	HYDROCARBON	HYDROFLUORIC	HYDROLOGIES	HYDROMETEORS
HYBRIDIZERS	HYDROCARBONS	HYDROFOILS	HYDROLOGIST	HYDROMETER
HYBRIDIZES	HYDROCASTS	HYDROFORMING	HYDROLOGISTS	HYDROMETERS
HYBRIDIZING	HYDROCELES	HYDROFORMINGS	HYDROLYSABLE	HYDROMETRIC
HYBRIDOMAS	HYDROCELLULOSE	HYDROGENASE	HYDROLYSATE	HYDROMETRICAL
HYDANTOINS	HYDROCELLULOSES	HYDROGENASES	HYDROLYSATES	HYDROMETRICALLY
HYDATHODES	HYDROCEPHALIC	HYDROGENATE	HYDROLYSATION	HYDROMETRIES
HYDATIDIFORM	HYDROCEPHALICS	HYDROGENATED	HYDROLYSATIONS	HYDROMETRY
HYDNOCARPATE	HYDROCEPHALIES	HYDROGENATES	HYDROLYSED	HYDROMORPHIC
HYDNOCARPATES	HYDROCEPHALOID	HYDROGENATING	HYDROLYSER	HYDRONAUTS
HYDNOCARPIC	HYDROCEPHALOUS	HYDROGENATION	HYDROLYSERS	HYDRONEPHROSES
HYDRAEMIAS	HYDROCEPHALUS	HYDROGENATIONS	HYDROLYSES	HYDRONEPHROSIS
HYDRAGOGUE	HYDROCEPHALUSES	HYDROGENATOR	HYDROLYSING	HYDRONEPHROTIC
HYDRAGOGUES	HYDROCEPHALY	HYDROGENATORS	HYDROLYSIS	HYDRONICALLY
HYDRALAZINE	HYDROCHLORIC	HYDROGENISATION	HYDROLYTES	HYDRONIUMS

HYDROPATHIC	HYDROPOWERS	HYDROTHORACES	HYGIENISTS	HYLOTOMOUS
HYDROPATHICAL	HYDROPSIES	HYDROTHORACIC	HYGRISTORS	HYLOZOICAL
HYDROPATHICALLY	HYDROPULTS	HYDROTHORAX	HYGROCHASIES	HYLOZOISMS
HYDROPATHICS	HYDROQUINOL	HYDROTHORAXES	HYGROCHASTIC	HYLOZOISTIC
HYDROPATHIES	HYDROQUINOLS	HYDROTROPIC	HYGROCHASY	HYLOZOISTICALLY
HYDROPATHIST	HYDROQUINONE	HYDROTROPICALLY	HYGRODEIKS	HYLOZOISTS
HYDROPATHISTS	HYDROQUINONES	HYDROTROPISM	HYGROGRAPH	HYMENEALLY
HYDROPATHS	HYDROSCOPE	HYDROTROPISMS	HYGROGRAPHIC	HYMENOPHORE
HYDROPATHY	HYDROSCOPES	HYDROVANES	HYGROGRAPHICAL	HYMENOPHORES
HYDROPEROXIDE	HYDROSCOPIC	HYDROXIDES	HYGROGRAPHS	HYMENOPLASTIES
HYDROPEROXIDES	HYDROSCOPICAL	HYDROXONIUM	HYGROLOGIES	HYMENOPLASTY
HYDROPHANE	HYDROSERES	HYDROXONIUMS	HYGROMETER	HYMENOPTERA
HYDROPHANES	HYDROSOLIC	HYDROXYAPATITE	HYGROMETERS	HYMENOPTERAN
HYDROPHANOUS	HYDROSOMAL	HYDROXYAPATITES	HYGROMETRIC	HYMENOPTERANS
HYDROPHILE	HYDROSOMATA	HYDROXYBUTYRATE	HYGROMETRICAL	HYMENOPTERON
HYDROPHILES	HYDROSOMATOUS	HYDROXYLAMINE	HYGROMETRICALLY	HYMENOPTERONS
HYDROPHILIC	HYDROSOMES	HYDROXYLAMINES	HYGROMETRIES	HYMENOPTEROUS
HYDROPHILICITY	HYDROSPACE	HYDROXYLAPATITE	HYGROMETRY	HYMNODICAL
HYDROPHILIES	HYDROSPACES	HYDROXYLASE	HYGROPHILE	HYMNODISTS
HYDROPHILITE	HYDROSPHERE	HYDROXYLASES	HYGROPHILES	HYMNOGRAPHER
HYDROPHILITES	HYDROSPHERES	HYDROXYLATE	HYGROPHILOUS	HYMNOGRAPHERS
HYDROPHILOUS	HYDROSPHERIC	HYDROXYLATED	HYGROPHOBE	HYMNOGRAPHIES
HYDROPHILY	HYDROSTATIC	HYDROXYLATES	HYGROPHYTE	HYMNOGRAPHY
HYDROPHOBIA	HYDROSTATICAL	HYDROXYLATING	HYGROPHYTES	HYMNOLOGIC
HYDROPHOBIAS	HYDROSTATICALLY	HYDROXYLATION	HYGROPHYTIC	HYMNOLOGICAL
HYDROPHOBIC	HYDROSTATICS	HYDROXYLATIONS	HYGROSCOPE	HYMNOLOGIES
HYDROPHOBICITY	HYDROSTATS	HYDROXYLIC	HYGROSCOPES	HYMNOLOGIST
HYDROPHOBOUS	HYDROSULPHATE	HYDROXYPROLINE	HYGROSCOPIC	HYMNOLOGISTS
HYDROPHONE	HYDROSULPHATES	HYDROXYPROLINES	HYGROSCOPICAL	HYOPLASTRA
HYDROPHONES	HYDROSULPHIDE	HYDROXYUREA	HYGROSCOPICALLY	HYOPLASTRAL
HYDROPHYTE	HYDROSULPHIDES	HYDROXYUREAS	HYGROSCOPICITY	HYOPLASTRON
HYDROPHYTES	HYDROSULPHITE	HYDROXYZINE	HYGROSTATS	HYOSCYAMINE
HYDROPHYTIC	HYDROSULPHITES	HYDROXYZINES	HYLOGENESES	HYOSCYAMINES
HYDROPHYTON	HYDROSULPHURIC	HYDROZINCITE	HYLOGENESIS	HYOSCYAMUS
HYDROPHYTONS	HYDROSULPHUROUS	HYDROZINCITES	HYLOMORPHIC	HYOSCYAMUSES
HYDROPHYTOUS	HYDROTACTIC	HYDROZOANS	HYLOMORPHISM	HYPABYSSAL
HYDROPLANE	HYDROTAXES	HYETOGRAPH	HYLOMORPHISMS	HYPABYSSALLY
HYDROPLANED	HYDROTAXIS	HYETOGRAPHIC	HYLOPATHISM	HYPAESTHESIA
HYDROPLANES	HYDROTHECA	HYETOGRAPHICAL	HYLOPATHISMS	HYPAESTHESIAS
HYDROPLANING	HYDROTHECAE	HYETOGRAPHIES	HYLOPATHIST	HYPAESTHESIC
HYDROPNEUMATIC	HYDROTHERAPIC	HYETOGRAPHS	HYLOPATHISTS	HYPAETHRAL
HYDROPOLYP	HYDROTHERAPIES	HYETOGRAPHY	HYLOPHAGOUS	HYPAETHRON
HYDROPOLYPS	HYDROTHERAPIST	HYETOLOGIES	HYLOPHYTES	HYPAETHRONS
HYDROPONIC	HYDROTHERAPISTS	HYETOMETER	HYLOTHEISM	HYPALGESIA
HYDROPONICALLY	HYDROTHERAPY	HYETOMETERS	HYLOTHEISMS	HYPALGESIAS
HYDROPONICS	HYDROTHERMAL	HYETOMETROGRAPH	HYLOTHEIST	HYPALGESIC
HYDROPOWER	HYDROTHERMALLY	HYGIENICALLY	HYLOTHEISTS	HYPALLACTIC

H

HYPALLAGES	HYPERBOLISED	HYPERCRITICALLY	HYPERFUNCTIONS	HYPERLINKS
HYPANTHIAL	HYPERBOLISES	HYPERCRITICISE	HYPERGAMIES	HYPERLIPEMIA
HYPANTHIUM	HYPERBOLISING	HYPERCRITICISED	HYPERGAMOUS	HYPERLIPEMIAS
HYPERACIDITIES	HYPERBOLISM	HYPERCRITICISES	HYPERGEOMETRIC	HYPERLIPEMIC
HYPERACIDITY	HYPERBOLISMS	HYPERCRITICISM	HYPERGLYCAEMIA	HYPERLIPIDAEMIA
HYPERACTION	HYPERBOLIST	HYPERCRITICISMS	HYPERGLYCAEMIAS	HYPERLIPIDEMIA
HYPERACTIONS	HYPERBOLISTS	HYPERCRITICIZE	HYPERGLYCAEMIC	HYPERLIPIDEMIAS
HYPERACTIVE	HYPERBOLIZE	HYPERCRITICIZED	HYPERGLYCEMIA	HYPERLYDIAN
HYPERACTIVES	HYPERBOLIZED	HYPERCRITICIZES	HYPERGLYCEMIAS	HYPERMANIA
HYPERACTIVITIES	HYPERBOLIZES	HYPERCRITICS	HYPERGLYCEMIC	HYPERMANIAS
HYPERACTIVITY	HYPERBOLIZING	HYPERCUBES	HYPERGOLIC	HYPERMANIC
HYPERACUITIES	HYPERBOLOID	HYPERDACTYL	HYPERGOLICALLY	HYPERMARKET
HYPERACUITY	HYPERBOLOIDAL	HYPERDACTYLIES	HYPERHIDROSES	HYPERMARKETS
HYPERACUSES	HYPERBOLOIDS	HYPERDACTYLY	HYPERHIDROSIS	HYPERMARTS
HYPERACUSIS	HYPERBOREAN	HYPERDORIAN	HYPERICINS	HYPERMASCULINE
HYPERACUTE	HYPERBOREANS	HYPERDULIA	HYPERICUMS	HYPERMEDIA
HYPERACUTENESS	HYPERCALCAEMIA	HYPERDULIAS	HYPERIDROSES	HYPERMEDIAS
HYPERADRENALISM	HYPERCALCAEMIAS	HYPERDULIC	HYPERIDROSIS	HYPERMETABOLIC
HYPERAEMIA	HYPERCALCEMIA	HYPERDULICAL	HYPERIMMUNE	HYPERMETABOLISM
HYPERAEMIAS	HYPERCALCEMIAS	HYPEREFFICIENT	HYPERIMMUNISE	HYPERMETER
HYPERAEMIC	HYPERCALCEMIC	HYPEREMESES	HYPERIMMUNISED	HYPERMETERS
HYPERAESTHESIA	HYPERCAPNIA	HYPEREMESIS	HYPERIMMUNISES	HYPERMETRIC
HYPERAESTHESIAS	HYPERCAPNIAS	HYPEREMETIC	HYPERIMMUNISING	HYPERMETRICAL
HYPERAESTHESIC	HYPERCAPNIC	HYPEREMIAS	HYPERIMMUNIZE	HYPERMETROPIA
HYPERAESTHETIC	HYPERCARBIA	HYPEREMOTIONAL	HYPERIMMUNIZED	HYPERMETROPIAS
HYPERAGGRESSIVE	HYPERCARBIAS	HYPERENDEMIC	HYPERIMMUNIZES	HYPERMETROPIC
HYPERALERT	HYPERCATABOLISM	HYPERENERGETIC	HYPERIMMUNIZING	HYPERMETROPICAL
HYPERALGESIA	HYPERCATALECTIC	HYPERESTHESIA	HYPERINFLATED	HYPERMETROPIES
HYPERALGESIAS	HYPERCATALEXES	HYPERESTHESIAS	HYPERINFLATION	HYPERMETROPY
HYPERALGESIC	HYPERCATALEXIS	HYPERESTHETIC	HYPERINFLATIONS	HYPERMILING
HYPERAROUSAL	HYPERCAUTIOUS	HYPEREUTECTIC	HYPERINOSES	HYPERMILINGS
HYPERAROUSALS	HYPERCHARGE	HYPEREUTECTOID	HYPERINOSIS	HYPERMNESIA
HYPERAWARE	HYPERCHARGED	HYPEREXCITABLE	HYPERINOTIC	HYPERMNESIAS
HYPERAWARENESS	HYPERCHARGES	HYPEREXCITED	HYPERINSULINISM	HYPERMNESIC
HYPERBARIC	HYPERCHARGING	HYPEREXCITEMENT	HYPERINTENSE	HYPERMOBILITIES
HYPERBARICALLY	HYPERCIVILISED	HYPEREXCRETION	HYPERINVOLUTION	HYPERMOBILITY
HYPERBATIC	HYPERCIVILIZED	HYPEREXCRETIONS	HYPERIRRITABLE	HYPERMODERN
HYPERBATICALLY	HYPERCOAGULABLE	HYPEREXTEND	HYPERKERATOSES	HYPERMODERNIST
HYPERBATON	HYPERCOLOUR	HYPEREXTENDED	HYPERKERATOSIS	HYPERMODERNISTS
HYPERBATONS	HYPERCOLOURS	HYPEREXTENDING	HYPERKERATOTIC	HYPERMUTABILITY
HYPERBOLAE	HYPERCOMPLEX	HYPEREXTENDS	HYPERKINESES	HYPERMUTABLE
HYPERBOLAS	HYPERCONSCIOUS	HYPEREXTENSION	HYPERKINESIA	HYPERNATRAEMIA
HYPERBOLES	HYPERCORRECT	HYPEREXTENSIONS	HYPERKINESIAS	HYPERNATRAEMIAS
HYPERBOLIC	HYPERCORRECTION	HYPERFASTIDIOUS	HYPERKINESIS	HYPERNOVAE
HYPERBOLICAL	HYPERCORRECTLY	HYPERFOCAL	HYPERKINETIC	HYPERNOVAS
HYPERBOLICALLY	HYPERCRITIC	HYPERFUNCTION	HYPERLINKED	HYPERNYMIES
HYPERBOLISE	HYPERCRITICAL	HYPERFUNCTIONAL	HYPERLINKING	HYPEROPIAS

H

HYPEROREXIA	HYPERPYRETIC	HYPERSPACE	HYPERTYPICAL	HYPNOGOGIC
HYPEROREXIAS	HYPERPYREXIA	HYPERSPACES	HYPERURBANISM	HYPNOIDISE
HYPEROSMIA	HYPERPYREXIAL	HYPERSPATIAL	HYPERURBANISMS	HYPNOIDISED
HYPEROSMIAS	HYPERPYREXIAS	HYPERSTATIC	HYPERURICEMIA	HYPNOIDISES
HYPEROSTOSES	HYPERRATIONAL	HYPERSTHENE	HYPERURICEMIAS	HYPNOIDISING
HYPEROSTOSIS	HYPERREACTIVE	HYPERSTHENES	HYPERVELOCITIES	HYPNOIDIZE
HYPEROSTOTIC	HYPERREACTIVITY	HYPERSTHENIA	HYPERVELOCITY	HYPNOIDIZED
HYPERPARASITE	HYPERREACTOR	HYPERSTHENIAS	HYPERVENTILATE	HYPNOIDIZES
HYPERPARASITES	HYPERREACTORS	HYPERSTHENIC	HYPERVENTILATED	HYPNOIDIZING
HYPERPARASITIC	HYPERREALISM	HYPERSTHENITE	HYPERVENTILATES	HYPNOLOGIC
HYPERPARASITISM	HYPERREALISMS	HYPERSTHENITES	HYPERVIGILANCE	HYPNOLOGICAL
HYPERPHAGIA	HYPERREALIST	HYPERSTIMULATE	HYPERVIGILANCES	HYPNOLOGIES
HYPERPHAGIAS	HYPERREALISTIC	HYPERSTIMULATED	HYPERVIGILANT	HYPNOLOGIST
HYPERPHAGIC	HYPERREALISTS	HYPERSTIMULATES	HYPERVIRULENT	HYPNOLOGISTS
HYPERPHRYGIAN	HYPERREALITIES	HYPERSTRESS	HYPERVISCOSITY	HYPNOPAEDIA
HYPERPHYSICAL	HYPERREALITY	HYPERSTRESSES	HYPESTHESIA	HYPNOPAEDIAS
HYPERPHYSICALLY	HYPERREALS	HYPERSURFACE	HYPESTHESIAS	HYPNOPOMPIC
HYPERPIGMENTED	HYPERRESPONSIVE	HYPERSURFACES	HYPESTHESIC	HYPNOTHERAPIES
HYPERPITUITARY	HYPERROMANTIC	HYPERTENSE	HYPHENATED	HYPNOTHERAPIST
HYPERPLANE	HYPERROMANTICS	HYPERTENSION	HYPHENATES	HYPNOTHERAPISTS
HYPERPLANES	HYPERSALINE	HYPERTENSIONS	HYPHENATING	HYPNOTHERAPY
HYPERPLASIA	HYPERSALINITIES	HYPERTENSIVE	HYPHENATION	HYPNOTICALLY
HYPERPLASIAS	HYPERSALINITY	HYPERTENSIVES	HYPHENATIONS	HYPNOTISABILITY
HYPERPLASTIC	HYPERSALIVATION	HYPERTEXTS	HYPHENISATION	HYPNOTISABLE
HYPERPLOID	HYPERSARCOMA	HYPERTHERMAL	HYPHENISATIONS	HYPNOTISATION
HYPERPLOIDIES	HYPERSARCOMAS	HYPERTHERMIA	HYPHENISED	HYPNOTISATIONS
HYPERPLOIDS	HYPERSARCOMATA	HYPERTHERMIAS	HYPHENISES	HYPNOTISED
HYPERPLOIDY	HYPERSARCOSES	HYPERTHERMIC	HYPHENISING	HYPNOTISER
HYPERPNEAS	HYPERSARCOSIS	HYPERTHERMIES	HYPHENISMS	HYPNOTISERS
HYPERPNEIC	HYPERSECRETION	HYPERTHERMY	HYPHENIZATION	HYPNOTISES
HYPERPNOEA	HYPERSECRETIONS	HYPERTHYMIA	HYPHENIZATIONS	HYPNOTISING
HYPERPNOEAS	HYPERSENSITISE	HYPERTHYMIAS	HYPHENIZED	HYPNOTISMS
HYPERPOLARISE	HYPERSENSITISED	HYPERTHYROID	HYPHENIZES	HYPNOTISTIC
HYPERPOLARISED	HYPERSENSITISES	HYPERTHYROIDISM	HYPHENIZING	HYPNOTISTS
HYPERPOLARISES	HYPERSENSITIVE	HYPERTHYROIDS	HYPHENLESS	HYPNOTIZABILITY
HYPERPOLARISING	HYPERSENSITIZE	HYPERTONIA	HYPNAGOGIC	HYPNOTIZABLE
HYPERPOLARIZE	HYPERSENSITIZED	HYPERTONIAS	HYPNOANALYSES	HYPNOTIZATION
HYPERPOLARIZED	HYPERSENSITIZES	HYPERTONIC	HYPNOANALYSIS	HYPNOTIZATIONS
HYPERPOLARIZES	HYPERSENSUAL	HYPERTONICITIES	HYPNOANALYTIC	HYPNOTIZED
HYPERPOLARIZING	HYPERSEXUAL	HYPERTONICITY	HYPNOBIRTHING	HYPNOTIZER
HYPERPOWER	HYPERSEXUALITY	HYPERTROPHIC	HYPNOBIRTHINGS	HYPNOTIZERS
HYPERPOWERS	HYPERSOMNIA	HYPERTROPHICAL	HYPNOGENESES	HYPNOTIZES
HYPERPRODUCER	HYPERSOMNIAS	HYPERTROPHIED	HYPNOGENESIS	HYPNOTIZING
HYPERPRODUCERS	HYPERSOMNOLENCE	HYPERTROPHIES	HYPNOGENETIC	HYPOACIDITIES
HYPERPRODUCTION	HYPERSONIC	HYPERTROPHOUS	HYPNOGENIC	HYPOACIDITY
HYPERPROSEXIA	HYPERSONICALLY	HYPERTROPHY	HYPNOGENIES	HYPOAEOLIAN
HYPERPROSEXIAS	HYPERSONICS	HYPERTROPHYING	HYPNOGENOUS	HYPOALLERGENIC

H

HYPOBLASTIC	HYPODERMICS	HYPONASTIC	HYPOSPADIASES	HYPOTENUSES
HYPOBLASTS	HYPODERMIS	HYPONASTICALLY	HYPOSTASES	HYPOTHALAMI
HYPOCALCEMIA	HYPODERMISES	HYPONASTIES	HYPOSTASIS	HYPOTHALAMIC
HYPOCALCEMIAS	HYPODIPLOID	HYPONATRAEMIA	HYPOSTASISATION	HYPOTHALAMUS
HYPOCALCEMIC	HYPODIPLOIDIES	HYPONATRAEMIAS	HYPOSTASISE	HYPOTHECAE
HYPOCAUSTS	HYPODIPLOIDY	HYPONITRITE	HYPOSTASISED	HYPOTHECARY
HYPOCENTER	HYPODORIAN	HYPONITRITES	HYPOSTASISES	HYPOTHECATE
HYPOCENTERS	HYPOEUTECTIC	HYPONITROUS	HYPOSTASISING	HYPOTHECATED
HYPOCENTRAL	HYPOEUTECTOID	HYPONYMIES	HYPOSTASIZATION	HYPOTHECATES
HYPOCENTRE	HYPOGAEOUS	HYPOPHARYNGES	HYPOSTASIZE	HYPOTHECATING
HYPOCENTRES	HYPOGASTRIA	HYPOPHARYNX	HYPOSTASIZED	HYPOTHECATION
HYPOCHLORITE	HYPOGASTRIC	HYPOPHARYNXES	HYPOSTASIZES	HYPOTHECATIONS
HYPOCHLORITES	HYPOGASTRIUM	HYPOPHOSPHATE	HYPOSTASIZING	HYPOTHECATOR
HYPOCHLOROUS	HYPOGENOUS	HYPOPHOSPHATES	HYPOSTATIC	HYPOTHECATORS
HYPOCHONDRIA	HYPOGLOSSAL	HYPOPHOSPHITE	HYPOSTATICAL	HYPOTHENUSE
HYPOCHONDRIAC	HYPOGLOSSALS	HYPOPHOSPHITES	HYPOSTATICALLY	HYPOTHENUSES
HYPOCHONDRIACAL	HYPOGLYCAEMIA	HYPOPHOSPHORIC	HYPOSTATISATION	HYPOTHERMAL
HYPOCHONDRIACS	HYPOGLYCAEMIAS	HYPOPHOSPHOROUS	HYPOSTATISE	HYPOTHERMIA
HYPOCHONDRIAS	HYPOGLYCAEMIC	HYPOPHRYGIAN	HYPOSTATISED	HYPOTHERMIAS
HYPOCHONDRIASES	HYPOGLYCEMIA	HYPOPHYGES	HYPOSTATISES	HYPOTHERMIC
HYPOCHONDRIASIS	HYPOGLYCEMIAS	HYPOPHYSEAL	HYPOSTATISING	HYPOTHESES
HYPOCHONDRIASM	HYPOGLYCEMIC	HYPOPHYSECTOMY	HYPOSTATIZATION	HYPOTHESIS
HYPOCHONDRIASMS	HYPOGLYCEMICS	HYPOPHYSES	HYPOSTATIZE	HYPOTHESISE
HYPOCHONDRIAST	HYPOGNATHISM	HYPOPHYSIAL	HYPOSTATIZED	HYPOTHESISED
HYPOCHONDRIASTS	HYPOGNATHISMS	HYPOPHYSIS	HYPOSTATIZES	HYPOTHESISER
HYPOCHONDRIUM	HYPOGNATHOUS	HYPOPITUITARISM	HYPOSTATIZING	HYPOTHESISERS
HYPOCORISM	HYPOGYNIES	HYPOPITUITARY	HYPOSTHENIA	HYPOTHESISES
HYPOCORISMA	HYPOGYNOUS	HYPOPLASIA	HYPOSTHENIAS	HYPOTHESISING
HYPOCORISMAS	HYPOKALEMIA	HYPOPLASIAS	HYPOSTHENIC	HYPOTHESIST
HYPOCORISMS	HYPOKALEMIAS	HYPOPLASTIC	HYPOSTOMES	HYPOTHESISTS
HYPOCORISTIC	HYPOKALEMIC	HYPOPLASTIES	HYPOSTRESS	HYPOTHESIZE
HYPOCORISTICAL	HYPOLIMNIA	HYPOPLASTRA	HYPOSTRESSES	HYPOTHESIZED
HYPOCOTYLOUS	HYPOLIMNION	HYPOPLASTRON	HYPOSTROPHE	HYPOTHESIZER
HYPOCOTYLS	HYPOLIMNIONS	HYPOPLASTY	HYPOSTROPHES	HYPOTHESIZERS
HYPOCRISIES	HYPOLYDIAN	HYPOPLOIDIES	HYPOSTYLES	HYPOTHESIZES
HYPOCRITES	HYPOMAGNESAEMIA	HYPOPLOIDS	HYPOSULPHATE	HYPOTHESIZING
HYPOCRITIC	HYPOMAGNESEMIA	HYPOPLOIDY	HYPOSULPHATES	HYPOTHETIC
HYPOCRITICAL	HYPOMAGNESEMIAS	HYPOPNOEAS	HYPOSULPHITE	HYPOTHETICAL
HYPOCRITICALLY	HYPOMANIAS	HYPOSENSITISE	HYPOSULPHITES	HYPOTHETICALLY
HYPOCRYSTALLINE	HYPOMANICS	HYPOSENSITISED	HYPOSULPHURIC	HYPOTHETISE
HYPOCYCLOID	HYPOMENORRHEA	HYPOSENSITISES	HYPOSULPHUROUS	HYPOTHETISED
HYPOCYCLOIDAL	HYPOMENORRHEAS	HYPOSENSITISING	HYPOTACTIC	HYPOTHETISES
HYPOCYCLOIDS	HYPOMENORRHOEA	HYPOSENSITIZE	HYPOTENSION	HYPOTHETISING
HYPODERMAL	HYPOMENORRHOEAS	HYPOSENSITIZED	HYPOTENSIONS	HYPOTHETIZE
HYPODERMAS	HYPOMIXOLYDIAN	HYPOSENSITIZES	HYPOTENSIVE	HYPOTHETIZED
HYPODERMIC	HYPOMORPHIC	HYPOSENSITIZING	HYPOTENSIVES	HYPOTHETIZES
HYPODERMICALLY	HYPOMORPHS	HYPOSPADIAS	HYPOTENUSE	HYPOTHETIZING

HYPOTHYMIA	HYPOXAEMIAS	HYPSOMETRICAL	HYSTERANTHOUS	HYSTERICALLY
HYPOTHYMIAS	HYPOXAEMIC	HYPSOMETRICALLY	HYSTERECTOMIES	HYSTERICKY
HYPOTHYROID	HYPOXANTHINE	HYPSOMETRIES	HYSTERECTOMISE	HYSTERITIS
HYPOTHYROIDISM	HYPOXANTHINES	HYPSOMETRIST	HYSTERECTOMISED	HYSTERITISES
HYPOTHYROIDISMS	HYPOXEMIAS	HYPSOMETRISTS	HYSTERECTOMISES	HYSTEROGENIC
HYPOTHYROIDS	HYPSOCHROME	HYPSOMETRY	HYSTERECTOMIZE	HYSTEROGENIES
HYPOTONIAS	HYPSOCHROMES	HYPSOPHOBE	HYSTERECTOMIZED	HYSTEROGENY
HYPOTONICITIES	HYPSOCHROMIC	HYPSOPHOBES	HYSTERECTOMIZES	HYSTEROIDAL
HYPOTONICITY	HYPSOGRAPHIC	HYPSOPHOBIA	HYSTERECTOMY	HYSTEROMANIA
HYPOTROCHOID	HYPSOGRAPHICAL	HYPSOPHOBIAS	HYSTERESES	HYSTEROMANIAS
HYPOTROCHOIDS	HYPSOGRAPHIES	HYPSOPHYLL	HYSTERESIAL	HYSTEROTOMIES
HYPOTYPOSES	HYPSOGRAPHY	HYPSOPHYLLARY	HYSTERESIS	HYSTEROTOMY
HYPOTYPOSIS	HYPSOMETER	HYPSOPHYLLS	HYSTERETIC	HYSTRICOMORPH
HYPOVENTILATION	HYPSOMETERS	HYRACOIDEAN	HYSTERETICALLY	HYSTRICOMORPHIC
HYPOXAEMIA	HYPSOMETRIC	HYRACOIDEANS	HYSTERICAL	HYSTRICOMORPHS

H

IAMBICALLY	ICHTHYOLITIC	ICONOLATERS	IDEALIZATIONS	IDEOLOGIZE
IAMBOGRAPHER	ICHTHYOLOGIC	ICONOLATRIES	IDEALIZERS	IDEOLOGIZED
IAMBOGRAPHERS	ICHTHYOLOGICAL	ICONOLATROUS	IDEALIZING	IDEOLOGIZES
IATROCHEMICAL	ICHTHYOLOGIES	ICONOLATRY	IDEALNESSES	IDEOLOGIZING
IATROCHEMIST	ICHTHYOLOGIST	ICONOLOGICAL	IDEALOGIES	IDEOLOGUES
IATROCHEMISTRY	ICHTHYOLOGISTS	ICONOLOGIES	IDEALOGUES	IDEOPHONES
IATROCHEMISTS	ICHTHYOLOGY	ICONOLOGIST	IDEATIONAL	IDEOPOLISES
IATROGENIC	ICHTHYOPHAGIES	ICONOLOGISTS	IDEATIONALLY	IDEOPRAXIST
IATROGENICALLY	ICHTHYOPHAGIST	ICONOMACHIES	IDEMPOTENCIES	IDEOPRAXISTS
IATROGENICITIES	ICHTHYOPHAGISTS	ICONOMACHIST	IDEMPOTENCY	IDIOBLASTIC
IATROGENICITY	ICHTHYOPHAGOUS	ICONOMACHISTS	IDEMPOTENT	IDIOBLASTS
IATROGENIES	ICHTHYOPHAGY	ICONOMACHY	IDEMPOTENTS	IDIOGLOSSIA
IBUPROFENS	ICHTHYOPSID	ICONOMATIC	IDENTICALLY	IDIOGLOSSIAS
ICEBOATERS	ICHTHYOPSIDAN	ICONOMATICISM	IDENTICALNESS	IDIOGRAPHIC
ICEBOATING	ICHTHYOPSIDANS	ICONOMATICISMS	IDENTICALNESSES	IDIOGRAPHS
ICEBOATINGS	ICHTHYOPSIDS	ICONOMETER	IDENTIFIABLE	IDIOLECTAL
ICEBREAKER	ICHTHYORNIS	ICONOMETERS	IDENTIFIABLY	IDIOLECTIC
ICEBREAKERS	ICHTHYORNISES	ICONOMETRIES	IDENTIFICATION	IDIOMATICAL
ICEBREAKING	ICHTHYOSAUR	ICONOMETRY	IDENTIFICATIONS	IDIOMATICALLY
ICHNEUMONS	ICHTHYOSAURI	ICONOPHILISM	IDENTIFIED	IDIOMATICALNESS
ICHNOFOSSIL	ICHTHYOSAURIAN	ICONOPHILISMS	IDENTIFIER	IDIOMATICNESS
ICHNOFOSSILS	ICHTHYOSAURIANS	ICONOPHILIST	IDENTIFIERS	IDIOMATICNESSES
ICHNOGRAPHIC	ICHTHYOSAURS	ICONOPHILISTS	IDENTIFIES	IDIOMORPHIC
ICHNOGRAPHICAL	ICHTHYOSAURUS	ICONOSCOPE	IDENTIFYING	IDIOMORPHICALLY
ICHNOGRAPHIES	ICHTHYOSAURUSES	ICONOSCOPES	IDENTIKITS	IDIOMORPHISM
ICHNOGRAPHY	ICHTHYOSES	ICONOSTASES	IDENTITIES	IDIOMORPHISMS
ICHNOLITES	ICHTHYOSIS	ICONOSTASIS	IDEOGRAMIC	IDIOPATHIC
ICHNOLOGICAL	ICHTHYOTIC	ICOSAHEDRA	IDEOGRAMMATIC	IDIOPATHICALLY
ICHNOLOGIES	ICKINESSES	ICOSAHEDRAL	IDEOGRAMMIC	IDIOPATHIES
ICHTHYOCOLLA	ICONICALLY	ICOSAHEDRON	IDEOGRAPHIC	IDIOPHONES
ICHTHYOCOLLAS	ICONICITIES	ICOSAHEDRONS	IDEOGRAPHICAL	IDIOPHONIC
ICHTHYODORULITE	ICONIFYING	ICOSANDRIAN	IDEOGRAPHICALLY	IDIOPLASMATIC
ICHTHYODORYLITE	ICONOCLASM	ICOSANDROUS	IDEOGRAPHIES	IDIOPLASMIC
ICHTHYOFAUNA	ICONOCLASMS	ICOSITETRAHEDRA	IDEOGRAPHS	IDIOPLASMS
ICHTHYOFAUNAE	ICONOCLAST	ICTERICALS	IDEOGRAPHY	IDIORHYTHMIC
ICHTHYOFAUNAL	ICONOCLASTIC	ICTERITIOUS	IDEOLOGICAL	IDIORRHYTHMIC
ICHTHYOFAUNAS	ICONOCLASTS	IDEALISATION	IDEOLOGICALLY	IDIOSYNCRASIES
ICHTHYOIDAL	ICONOGRAPHER	IDEALISATIONS	IDEOLOGIES	IDIOSYNCRASY
ICHTHYOIDS	ICONOGRAPHERS	IDEALISERS	IDEOLOGISE	IDIOSYNCRATIC
ICHTHYOLATRIES	ICONOGRAPHIC	IDEALISING	IDEOLOGISED	IDIOSYNCRATICAL
ICHTHYOLATROUS	ICONOGRAPHICAL	IDEALISTIC	IDEOLOGISES	IDIOTHERMOUS
ICHTHYOLATRY	ICONOGRAPHIES	IDEALISTICALLY	IDEOLOGISING	IDIOTICALLY
ICHTHYOLITE	ICONOGRAPHY	IDEALITIES	IDEOLOGIST	IDIOTICALNESS
ICHTHYOLITES	ICONOLATER	IDEALIZATION	IDEOLOGISTS	IDIOTICALNESSES

IDIOTICONS	IGNORAMUSES	ILLIBERALISE	ILLUMINATED	ILLUSTRIOUSLY
IDLENESSES	IGNORANCES	ILLIBERALISED	ILLUMINATES	ILLUSTRIOUSNESS
IDOLATRESS	IGNORANTLY	ILLIBERALISES	ILLUMINATI	ILLUSTRISSIMO
IDOLATRESSES	IGNORANTNESS	ILLIBERALISING	ILLUMINATING	ILLUVIATED
IDOLATRIES	IGNORANTNESSES	ILLIBERALISM	ILLUMINATINGLY	ILLUVIATES
IDOLATRISE	IGNORATION	ILLIBERALISMS	ILLUMINATION	ILLUVIATING
IDOLATRISED	IGNORATIONS	ILLIBERALITIES	ILLUMINATIONAL	ILLUVIATION
IDOLATRISER	IGUANODONS	ILLIBERALITY	ILLUMINATIONS	ILLUVIATIONS
IDOLATRISERS	ILEOSTOMIES	ILLIBERALIZE	ILLUMINATIVE	IMAGINABLE
IDOLATRISES	ILLAQUEABLE	ILLIBERALIZED	ILLUMINATO	IMAGINABLENESS
IDOLATRISING	ILLAQUEATE	ILLIBERALIZES	ILLUMINATOR	IMAGINABLY
IDOLATRIZE	ILLAQUEATED	ILLIBERALIZING	ILLUMINATORS	IMAGINARIES
IDOLATRIZED	ILLAQUEATES	ILLIBERALLY	ILLUMINERS	IMAGINARILY
IDOLATRIZER	ILLAQUEATING	ILLIBERALNESS	ILLUMINING	IMAGINARINESS
IDOLATRIZERS	ILLAQUEATION	ILLIBERALNESSES	ILLUMINISM	IMAGINARINESSES
IDOLATRIZES	ILLAQUEATIONS	ILLICITNESS	ILLUMINISMS	IMAGINATION
IDOLATRIZING	ILLATIVELY	ILLICITNESSES	ILLUMINIST	IMAGINATIONAL
IDOLATROUS	ILLAUDABLE	ILLIMITABILITY	ILLUMINISTS	IMAGINATIONS
IDOLATROUSLY	ILLAUDABLY	ILLIMITABLE	ILLUSIONAL	IMAGINATIVE
IDOLATROUSNESS	ILLAWARRAS	ILLIMITABLENESS	ILLUSIONARY	IMAGINATIVELY
IDOLISATION	ILLEGALISATION	ILLIMITABLY	ILLUSIONED	IMAGINATIVENESS
IDOLISATIONS	ILLEGALISATIONS	ILLIMITATION	ILLUSIONISM	IMAGINEERED
IDOLIZATION	ILLEGALISE	ILLIMITATIONS	ILLUSIONISMS	IMAGINEERING
IDOLIZATIONS	ILLEGALISED	ILLIQUATION	ILLUSIONIST	IMAGINEERS
IDOLOCLAST	ILLEGALISES	ILLIQUATIONS	ILLUSIONISTIC	IMAGININGS
IDOLOCLASTS	ILLEGALISING	ILLIQUIDITIES	ILLUSIONISTS	IMAGINISTS
IDONEITIES	ILLEGALITIES	ILLIQUIDITY	ILLUSIVELY	IMAGISTICALLY
IDOXURIDINE	ILLEGALITY	ILLITERACIES	ILLUSIVENESS	IMBALANCED
IDOXURIDINES	ILLEGALIZATION	ILLITERACY	ILLUSIVENESSES	IMBALANCES
IDYLLICALLY	ILLEGALIZATIONS	ILLITERATE	ILLUSORILY	IMBECILELY
IFFINESSES	ILLEGALIZE	ILLITERATELY	ILLUSORINESS	IMBECILICALLY
IGNESCENTS	ILLEGALIZED	ILLITERATENESS	ILLUSORINESSES	IMBECILITIES
IGNIMBRITE	ILLEGALIZES	ILLITERATES	ILLUSTRATABLE	IMBECILITY
IGNIMBRITES	ILLEGALIZING	ILLOCUTION	ILLUSTRATE	IMBIBITION
IGNIPOTENT	ILLEGIBILITIES	ILLOCUTIONARY	ILLUSTRATED	IMBIBITIONAL
IGNITABILITIES	ILLEGIBILITY	ILLOCUTIONS	ILLUSTRATEDS	IMBIBITIONS
IGNITABILITY	ILLEGIBLENESS	ILLOGICALITIES	ILLUSTRATES	IMBITTERED
IGNITIBILITIES	ILLEGIBLENESSES	ILLOGICALITY	ILLUSTRATING	IMBITTERING
IGNITIBILITY	ILLEGITIMACIES	ILLOGICALLY	ILLUSTRATION	IMBOLDENED
IGNOBILITIES	ILLEGITIMACY	ILLOGICALNESS	ILLUSTRATIONAL	IMBOLDENING
IGNOBILITY	ILLEGITIMATE	ILLOGICALNESSES	ILLUSTRATIONS	IMBORDERED
IGNOBLENESS	ILLEGITIMATED	ILLUMINABLE	ILLUSTRATIVE	IMBORDERING
IGNOBLENESSES	ILLEGITIMATELY	ILLUMINANCE	ILLUSTRATIVELY	IMBOSOMING
IGNOMINIES	ILLEGITIMATES	ILLUMINANCES	ILLUSTRATOR	IMBOWERING
IGNOMINIOUS	ILLEGITIMATING	ILLUMINANT	ILLUSTRATORS	IMBRANGLED
IGNOMINIOUSLY	ILLEGITIMATION	ILLUMINANTS	ILLUSTRATORY	IMBRANGLES
IGNOMINIOUSNESS	ILLEGITIMATIONS	ILLUMINATE	ILLUSTRIOUS	IMBRANGLING

IMBRICATED	IMMANITIES	IMMERGENCES	IMMITIGABILITY	IMMORTALISE
IMBRICATELY	IMMANTLING	IMMERITOUS	IMMITIGABLE	IMMORTALISED
IMBRICATES	IMMARCESCIBLE	IMMERSIBLE	IMMITIGABLY	IMMORTALISER
IMBRICATING	IMMARGINATE	IMMERSIONISM	IMMITTANCE	IMMORTALISERS
IMBRICATION	IMMATERIAL	IMMERSIONISMS	IMMITTANCES	IMMORTALISES
IMBRICATIONS	IMMATERIALISE	IMMERSIONIST	IMMIXTURES	IMMORTALISING
IMBROCCATA	IMMATERIALISED	IMMERSIONISTS	IMMOBILISATION	IMMORTALITIES
IMBROCCATAS	IMMATERIALISES	IMMERSIONS	IMMOBILISATIONS	IMMORTALITY
IMBROGLIOS	IMMATERIALISING	IMMETHODICAL	IMMOBILISE	IMMORTALIZATION
IMBROWNING	IMMATERIALISM	IMMETHODICALLY	IMMOBILISED	IMMORTALIZE
IMBRUEMENT	IMMATERIALISMS	IMMIGRANTS	IMMOBILISER	IMMORTALIZED
IMBRUEMENTS	IMMATERIALIST	IMMIGRATED	IMMOBILISERS	IMMORTALIZER
IMBUEMENTS	IMMATERIALISTS	IMMIGRATES	IMMOBILISES	IMMORTALIZERS
IMIDAZOLES	IMMATERIALITIES	IMMIGRATING	IMMOBILISING	IMMORTALIZES
IMINAZOLES	IMMATERIALITY	IMMIGRATION	IMMOBILISM	IMMORTALIZING
IMINOUREAS	IMMATERIALIZE	IMMIGRATIONAL	IMMOBILISMS	IMMORTALLY
IMIPRAMINE	IMMATERIALIZED	IMMIGRATIONS	IMMOBILITIES	IMMORTELLE
IMIPRAMINES	IMMATERIALIZES	IMMIGRATOR	IMMOBILITY	IMMORTELLES
IMITABILITIES	IMMATERIALIZING	IMMIGRATORS	IMMOBILIZATION	IMMOTILITIES
IMITABILITY	IMMATERIALLY	IMMIGRATORY	IMMOBILIZATIONS	IMMOTILITY
IMITABLENESS	IMMATERIALNESS	IMMINENCES	IMMOBILIZE	IMMOVABILITIES
IMITABLENESSES	IMMATURELY	IMMINENCIES	IMMOBILIZED	IMMOVABILITY
IMITANCIES	IMMATURENESS	IMMINENTLY	IMMOBILIZER	IMMOVABLENESS
IMITATIONAL	IMMATURENESSES	IMMINENTNESS	IMMOBILIZERS	IMMOVABLENESSES
IMITATIONS	IMMATURITIES	IMMINENTNESSES	IMMOBILIZES	IMMOVABLES
IMITATIVELY	IMMATURITY	IMMINGLING	IMMOBILIZING	IMMOVEABILITIES
IMITATIVENESS	IMMEASURABILITY	IMMINUTION	IMMODERACIES	IMMOVEABILITY
IMITATIVENESSES	IMMEASURABLE	IMMINUTIONS	IMMODERACY	IMMOVEABLE
IMMACULACIES	IMMEASURABLY	IMMISCIBILITIES	IMMODERATE	IMMOVEABLENESS
IMMACULACY	IMMEASURED	IMMISCIBILITY	IMMODERATELY	IMMOVEABLES
IMMACULATE	IMMEDIACIES	IMMISCIBLE	IMMODERATENESS	IMMOVEABLY
IMMACULATELY	IMMEDIATELY	IMMISCIBLY	IMMODERATION	IMMUNIFACIENT
IMMACULATENESS	IMMEDIATENESS	IMMISERATION	IMMODERATIONS	IMMUNISATION
IMMANACLED	IMMEDIATENESSES	IMMISERATIONS	IMMODESTIES	IMMUNISATIONS
IMMANACLES	IMMEDIATISM	IMMISERISATION	IMMODESTLY	IMMUNISERS
IMMANACLING	IMMEDIATISMS	IMMISERISATIONS	IMMOLATING	IMMUNISING
IMMANATION	IMMEDICABLE	IMMISERISE	IMMOLATION	IMMUNITIES
IMMANATIONS	IMMEDICABLENESS	IMMISERISED	IMMOLATIONS	IMMUNIZATION
IMMANENCES	IMMEDICABLY	IMMISERISES	IMMOLATORS	IMMUNIZATIONS
IMMANENCIES	IMMEMORIAL	IMMISERISING	IMMOMENTOUS	IMMUNIZERS
IMMANENTAL	IMMEMORIALLY	IMMISERIZATION	IMMORALISM	IMMUNIZING
IMMANENTISM	IMMENSENESS	IMMISERIZATIONS	IMMORALISMS	IMMUNOASSAY
IMMANENTISMS	IMMENSENESSES	IMMISERIZE	IMMORALIST	IMMUNOASSAYABLE
IMMANENTIST	IMMENSITIES	IMMISERIZED	IMMORALISTS	IMMUNOASSAYIST
IMMANENTISTIC	IMMENSURABILITY	IMMISERIZES	IMMORALITIES	IMMUNOASSAYISTS
IMMANENTISTS	IMMENSURABLE	IMMISERIZING	IMMORALITY	IMMUNOASSAYS
IMMANENTLY	IMMERGENCE	IMMISSIONS	IMMORTALISATION	IMMUNOBLOT

IMMUNOBLOTS	IMMUREMENT	IMPARTIALLY	IMPECCANCY	IMPERCEIVABLE
IMMUNOBLOTTING	IMMUREMENTS	IMPARTIALNESS	IMPECUNIOSITIES	IMPERCEPTIBLE
IMMUNOBLOTTINGS	IMMUTABILITIES	IMPARTIALNESSES	IMPECUNIOSITY	IMPERCEPTIBLY
IMMUNOCHEMICAL	IMMUTABILITY	IMPARTIBILITIES	IMPECUNIOUS	IMPERCEPTION
IMMUNOCHEMIST	IMMUTABLENESS	IMPARTIBILITY	IMPECUNIOUSLY	IMPERCEPTIONS
IMMUNOCHEMISTRY	IMMUTABLENESSES	IMPARTIBLE	IMPECUNIOUSNESS	IMPERCEPTIVE
IMMUNOCHEMISTS	IMPACTIONS	IMPARTIBLY	IMPEDANCES	IMPERCEPTIVELY
IMMUNOCOMPETENT	IMPACTITES	IMPARTMENT	IMPEDIMENT	IMPERCEPTIVITY
IMMUNOCOMPLEX	IMPAINTING	IMPARTMENTS	IMPEDIMENTA	IMPERCIPIENCE
IMMUNOCOMPLEXES	IMPAIRABLE	IMPASSABILITIES	IMPEDIMENTAL	IMPERCIPIENCES
IMMUNODEFICIENT	IMPAIRINGS	IMPASSABILITY	IMPEDIMENTARY	IMPERCIPIENT
IMMUNODIAGNOSES	IMPAIRMENT	IMPASSABLE	IMPEDIMENTS	IMPERCIPIENTLY
IMMUNODIAGNOSIS	IMPAIRMENTS	IMPASSABLENESS	IMPEDINGLY	IMPERFECTIBLE
IMMUNODIFFUSION	IMPALEMENT	IMPASSABLY	IMPEDITIVE	IMPERFECTION
IMMUNOGENESES	IMPALEMENTS	IMPASSIBILITIES	IMPELLENTS	IMPERFECTIONS
IMMUNOGENESIS	IMPALPABILITIES	IMPASSIBILITY	IMPENDENCE	IMPERFECTIVE
IMMUNOGENETIC	IMPALPABILITY	IMPASSIBLE	IMPENDENCES	IMPERFECTIVELY
IMMUNOGENETICAL	IMPALPABLE	IMPASSIBLENESS	IMPENDENCIES	IMPERFECTIVES
IMMUNOGENETICS	IMPALPABLY	IMPASSIBLY	IMPENDENCY	IMPERFECTLY
IMMUNOGENIC	IMPALUDISM	IMPASSIONATE	IMPENETRABILITY	IMPERFECTNESS
IMMUNOGENICALLY	IMPALUDISMS	IMPASSIONED	IMPENETRABLE	IMPERFECTNESSES
IMMUNOGENICITY	IMPANATION	IMPASSIONEDLY	IMPENETRABLY	IMPERFECTS
IMMUNOGENS	IMPANATIONS	IMPASSIONEDNESS	IMPENETRATE	IMPERFORABLE
IMMUNOGLOBULIN	IMPANELING	IMPASSIONING	IMPENETRATED	IMPERFORATE
IMMUNOGLOBULINS	IMPANELLED	IMPASSIONS	IMPENETRATES	IMPERFORATED
IMMUNOLOGIC	IMPANELLING	IMPASSIVELY	IMPENETRATING	IMPERFORATION
IMMUNOLOGICAL	IMPANELMENT	IMPASSIVENESS	IMPENETRATION	IMPERFORATIONS
IMMUNOLOGICALLY	IMPANELMENTS	IMPASSIVENESSES	IMPENETRATIONS	IMPERIALISE
IMMUNOLOGIES	IMPANNELLED	IMPASSIVITIES	IMPENITENCE	IMPERIALISED
IMMUNOLOGIST	IMPANNELLING	IMPASSIVITY	IMPENITENCES	IMPERIALISES
IMMUNOLOGISTS	IMPARADISE	IMPASTATION	IMPENITENCIES	IMPERIALISING
IMMUNOLOGY	IMPARADISED	IMPASTATIONS	IMPENITENCY	IMPERIALISM
IMMUNOMODULATOR	IMPARADISES	IMPATIENCE	IMPENITENT	IMPERIALISMS
IMMUNOPATHOLOGY	IMPARADISING	IMPATIENCES	IMPENITENTLY	IMPERIALIST
IMMUNOPHORESES	IMPARIDIGITATE	IMPATIENTLY	IMPENITENTNESS	IMPERIALISTIC
IMMUNOPHORESIS	IMPARIPINNATE	IMPEACHABILITY	IMPENITENTS	IMPERIALISTS
IMMUNOREACTION	IMPARISYLLABIC	IMPEACHABLE	IMPERATIVAL	IMPERIALITIES
IMMUNOREACTIONS	IMPARITIES	IMPEACHERS	IMPERATIVE	IMPERIALITY
IMMUNOREACTIVE	IMPARKATION	IMPEACHING	IMPERATIVELY	IMPERIALIZE
IMMUNOSORBENT	IMPARKATIONS	IMPEACHMENT	IMPERATIVENESS	IMPERIALIZED
IMMUNOSORBENTS	IMPARLANCE	IMPEACHMENTS	IMPERATIVES	IMPERIALIZES
IMMUNOSUPPRESS	IMPARLANCES	IMPEARLING	IMPERATORIAL	IMPERIALIZING
IMMUNOTHERAPIES	IMPARTABLE	IMPECCABILITIES	IMPERATORIALLY	IMPERIALLY
IMMUNOTHERAPY	IMPARTATION	IMPECCABILITY	IMPERATORS	IMPERIALNESS
IMMUNOTOXIC	IMPARTATIONS	IMPECCABLE	IMPERATORSHIP	IMPERIALNESSES
IMMUNOTOXIN	IMPARTIALITIES	IMPECCABLY	IMPERATORSHIPS	IMPERILING
IMMUNOTOXINS	IMPARTIALITY	IMPECCANCIES	IMPERCEABLE	IMPERILLED

IMPERILLING	IMPERTINENCIES	IMPLACABILITIES	IMPLICITLY	IMPORTUNATE
IMPERILMENT	IMPERTINENCY	IMPLACABILITY	IMPLICITNESS	IMPORTUNATELY
IMPERILMENTS	IMPERTINENT	IMPLACABLE	IMPLICITNESSES	IMPORTUNATENESS
IMPERIOUSLY	IMPERTINENTLY	IMPLACABLENESS	IMPLODENTS	IMPORTUNED
IMPERIOUSNESS	IMPERTURBABLE	IMPLACABLY	IMPLORATION	IMPORTUNELY
IMPERIOUSNESSES	IMPERTURBABLY	IMPLACENTAL	IMPLORATIONS	IMPORTUNER
IMPERISHABILITY	IMPERTURBATION	IMPLANTABLE	IMPLORATOR	IMPORTUNERS
IMPERISHABLE	IMPERTURBATIONS	IMPLANTATION	IMPLORATORS	IMPORTUNES
IMPERISHABLES	IMPERVIABILITY	IMPLANTATIONS	IMPLORATORY	IMPORTUNING
IMPERISHABLY	IMPERVIABLE	IMPLANTERS	IMPLORINGLY	IMPORTUNINGS
IMPERMANENCE	IMPERVIABLENESS	IMPLANTING	IMPLOSIONS	IMPORTUNITIES
IMPERMANENCES	IMPERVIOUS	IMPLAUSIBILITY	IMPLOSIVELY	IMPORTUNITY
IMPERMANENCIES	IMPERVIOUSLY	IMPLAUSIBLE	IMPLOSIVES	IMPOSINGLY
IMPERMANENCY	IMPERVIOUSNESS	IMPLAUSIBLENESS	IMPLUNGING	IMPOSINGNESS
IMPERMANENT	IMPETICOSSED	IMPLAUSIBLY	IMPOCKETED	IMPOSINGNESSES
IMPERMANENTLY	IMPETICOSSES	IMPLEACHED	IMPOCKETING	IMPOSITION
IMPERMEABILITY	IMPETICOSSING	IMPLEACHES	IMPOLDERED	IMPOSITIONS
IMPERMEABLE	IMPETIGINES	IMPLEACHING	IMPOLDERING	IMPOSSIBILISM
IMPERMEABLENESS	IMPETIGINOUS	IMPLEADABLE	IMPOLICIES	IMPOSSIBILISMS
IMPERMEABLY	IMPETRATED	IMPLEADERS	IMPOLITELY	IMPOSSIBILIST
IMPERMISSIBLE	IMPETRATES	IMPLEADING	IMPOLITENESS	IMPOSSIBILISTS
IMPERMISSIBLY	IMPETRATING	IMPLEDGING	IMPOLITENESSES	IMPOSSIBILITIES
IMPERSCRIPTIBLE	IMPETRATION	IMPLEMENTAL	IMPOLITEST	IMPOSSIBILITY
IMPERSEVERANT	IMPETRATIONS	IMPLEMENTATION	IMPOLITICAL	IMPOSSIBLE
IMPERSISTENT	IMPETRATIVE	IMPLEMENTATIONS	IMPOLITICALLY	IMPOSSIBLENESS
IMPERSONAL	IMPETRATOR	IMPLEMENTED	IMPOLITICLY	IMPOSSIBLES
IMPERSONALISE	IMPETRATORS	IMPLEMENTER	IMPOLITICNESS	IMPOSSIBLY
IMPERSONALISED	IMPETRATORY	IMPLEMENTERS	IMPOLITICNESSES	IMPOSTHUMATE
IMPERSONALISES	IMPETUOSITIES	IMPLEMENTING	IMPONDERABILIA	IMPOSTHUMATED
IMPERSONALISING	IMPETUOSITY	IMPLEMENTOR	IMPONDERABILITY	IMPOSTHUMATES
IMPERSONALITIES	IMPETUOUSLY	IMPLEMENTORS	IMPONDERABLE	IMPOSTHUMATING
IMPERSONALITY	IMPETUOUSNESS	IMPLEMENTS	IMPONDERABLES	IMPOSTHUMATION
IMPERSONALIZE	IMPETUOUSNESSES	IMPLETIONS	IMPONDERABLY	IMPOSTHUMATIONS
IMPERSONALIZED	IMPICTURED	IMPLEXIONS	IMPONDEROUS	IMPOSTHUME
IMPERSONALIZES	IMPIERCEABLE	IMPLEXUOUS	IMPORTABILITIES	IMPOSTHUMED
IMPERSONALIZING	IMPIGNORATE	IMPLICATED	IMPORTABILITY	IMPOSTHUMES
IMPERSONALLY	IMPIGNORATED	IMPLICATES	IMPORTABLE	IMPOSTOROUS
IMPERSONATE	IMPIGNORATES	IMPLICATING	IMPORTANCE	IMPOSTROUS
IMPERSONATED	IMPIGNORATING	IMPLICATION	IMPORTANCES	IMPOSTUMATE
IMPERSONATES	IMPIGNORATION	IMPLICATIONAL	IMPORTANCIES	IMPOSTUMATED
IMPERSONATING	IMPIGNORATIONS	IMPLICATIONS	IMPORTANCY	IMPOSTUMATES
IMPERSONATION	IMPINGEMENT	IMPLICATIVE	IMPORTANTLY	IMPOSTUMATING
IMPERSONATIONS	IMPINGEMENTS	IMPLICATIVELY	IMPORTATION	IMPOSTUMATION
IMPERSONATOR	IMPIOUSNESS	IMPLICATIVENESS	IMPORTATIONS	IMPOSTUMATIONS
IMPERSONATORS	IMPIOUSNESSES	IMPLICATURE	IMPORTINGS	IMPOSTUMED
IMPERTINENCE	IMPISHNESS	IMPLICATURES	IMPORTUNACIES	IMPOSTUMES
IMPERTINENCES	IMPISHNESSES	IMPLICITIES	IMPORTUNACY	IMPOSTURES

IMPOSTUROUS	IMPREGNATE	IMPROBABILITY	IMPROVISATRICES	IMPUTABLENESSES
IMPOTENCES	IMPREGNATED	IMPROBABLE	IMPROVISATRIX	IMPUTATION
IMPOTENCIES	IMPREGNATES	IMPROBABLENESS	IMPROVISATRIXES	IMPUTATIONS
IMPOTENTLY	IMPREGNATING	IMPROBABLY	IMPROVISED	IMPUTATIVE
IMPOTENTNESS	IMPREGNATION	IMPROBATION	IMPROVISER	IMPUTATIVELY
IMPOTENTNESSES	IMPREGNATIONS	IMPROBATIONS	IMPROVISERS	INABILITIES
IMPOUNDABLE	IMPREGNATOR	IMPROBITIES	IMPROVISES	INABSTINENCE
IMPOUNDAGE	IMPREGNATORS	IMPROMPTUS	IMPROVISING	INABSTINENCES
IMPOUNDAGES	IMPREGNING	IMPROPERLY	IMPROVISOR	INACCESSIBILITY
IMPOUNDERS	IMPRESARIO	IMPROPERNESS	IMPROVISORS	INACCESSIBLE
IMPOUNDING	IMPRESARIOS	IMPROPERNESSES	IMPROVVISATORE	INACCESSIBLY
IMPOUNDMENT	IMPRESCRIPTIBLE	IMPROPRIATE	IMPROVVISATORES	INACCURACIES
IMPOUNDMENTS	IMPRESCRIPTIBLY	IMPROPRIATED	IMPROVVISATRICE	INACCURACY
IMPOVERISH	IMPRESSERS	IMPROPRIATES	IMPRUDENCE	INACCURATE
IMPOVERISHED	IMPRESSIBILITY	IMPROPRIATING	IMPRUDENCES	INACCURATELY
IMPOVERISHER	IMPRESSIBLE	IMPROPRIATION	IMPRUDENTLY	INACCURATENESS
IMPOVERISHERS	IMPRESSING	IMPROPRIATIONS	IMPSONITES	INACTIVATE
IMPOVERISHES	IMPRESSION	IMPROPRIATOR	IMPUDENCES	INACTIVATED
IMPOVERISHING	IMPRESSIONABLE	IMPROPRIATORS	IMPUDENCIES	INACTIVATES
IMPOVERISHMENT	IMPRESSIONAL	IMPROPRIETIES	IMPUDENTLY	INACTIVATING
IMPOVERISHMENTS	IMPRESSIONALLY	IMPROPRIETY	IMPUDENTNESS	INACTIVATION
IMPOWERING	IMPRESSIONISM	IMPROVABILITIES	IMPUDENTNESSES	INACTIVATIONS
IMPRACTICABLE	IMPRESSIONISMS	IMPROVABILITY	IMPUDICITIES	INACTIVELY
IMPRACTICABLY	IMPRESSIONIST	IMPROVABLE	IMPUDICITY	INACTIVENESS
IMPRACTICAL	IMPRESSIONISTIC	IMPROVABLENESS	IMPUGNABLE	INACTIVENESSES
IMPRACTICALITY	IMPRESSIONISTS	IMPROVABLY	IMPUGNATION	INACTIVITIES
IMPRACTICALLY	IMPRESSIONS	IMPROVEMENT	IMPUGNATIONS	INACTIVITY
IMPRACTICALNESS	IMPRESSIVE	IMPROVEMENTS	IMPUGNMENT	INADAPTABLE
IMPRECATED	IMPRESSIVELY	IMPROVIDENCE	IMPUGNMENTS	INADAPTATION
IMPRECATES	IMPRESSIVENESS	IMPROVIDENCES	IMPUISSANCE	INADAPTATIONS
IMPRECATING	IMPRESSMENT	IMPROVIDENT	IMPUISSANCES	INADAPTIVE
IMPRECATION	IMPRESSMENTS	IMPROVIDENTLY	IMPUISSANT	INADEQUACIES
IMPRECATIONS	IMPRESSURE	IMPROVINGLY	IMPULSIONS	INADEQUACY
IMPRECATORY	IMPRESSURES	IMPROVISATE	IMPULSIVELY	INADEQUATE
IMPRECISELY	IMPRIMATUR	IMPROVISATED	IMPULSIVENESS	INADEQUATELY
IMPRECISENESS	IMPRIMATURS	IMPROVISATES	IMPULSIVENESSES	INADEQUATENESS
IMPRECISENESSES	IMPRINTERS	IMPROVISATING	IMPULSIVITIES	INADEQUATES
IMPRECISION	IMPRINTING	IMPROVISATION	IMPULSIVITY	INADMISSIBILITY
IMPRECISIONS	IMPRINTINGS	IMPROVISATIONAL	IMPUNDULUS	INADMISSIBLE
IMPREDICATIVE	IMPRISONABLE	IMPROVISATIONS	IMPUNITIES	INADMISSIBLY
IMPREGNABILITY	IMPRISONED	IMPROVISATOR	IMPURENESS	INADVERTENCE
IMPREGNABLE	IMPRISONER	IMPROVISATORE	IMPURENESSES	INADVERTENCES
IMPREGNABLENESS	IMPRISONERS	IMPROVISATORES	IMPURITIES	INADVERTENCIES
IMPREGNABLY	IMPRISONING	IMPROVISATORI	IMPURPLING	INADVERTENCY
IMPREGNANT	IMPRISONMENT	IMPROVISATORIAL	IMPUTABILITIES	INADVERTENT
IMPREGNANTS	IMPRISONMENTS	IMPROVISATORS	IMPUTABILITY	INADVERTENTLY
IMPREGNATABLE	IMPROBABILITIES	IMPROVISATORY	IMPUTABLENESS	INADVISABILITY

INADVISABLE	INAPPROPRIATELY	INBRINGING	INCAPSULATIONS	INCENTIVES
INADVISABLENESS	INAPTITUDE	INBRINGINGS	INCARCERATE	INCENTIVISATION
INADVISABLY	INAPTITUDES	INCALCULABILITY	INCARCERATED	INCENTIVISE
INALIENABILITY	INAPTNESSES	INCALCULABLE	INCARCERATES	INCENTIVISED
INALIENABLE	INARGUABLE	INCALCULABLY	INCARCERATING	INCENTIVISES
INALIENABLENESS	INARGUABLY	INCALESCENCE	INCARCERATION	INCENTIVISING
INALIENABLY	INARTICULACIES	INCALESCENCES	INCARCERATIONS	INCENTIVIZATION
INALTERABILITY	INARTICULACY	INCALESCENT	INCARCERATOR	INCENTIVIZE
INALTERABLE	INARTICULATE	INCANDESCE	INCARCERATORS	INCENTIVIZED
INALTERABLENESS	INARTICULATELY	INCANDESCED	INCARDINATE	INCENTIVIZES
INALTERABLY	INARTICULATES	INCANDESCENCE	INCARDINATED	INCENTIVIZING
INAMORATAS	INARTICULATION	INCANDESCENCES	INCARDINATES	INCEPTIONS
INAMORATOS	INARTICULATIONS	INCANDESCENCIES	INCARDINATING	INCEPTIVELY
INANENESSES	INARTIFICIAL	INCANDESCENCY	INCARDINATION	INCEPTIVES
INANIMATELY	INARTIFICIALLY	INCANDESCENT	INCARDINATIONS	INCERTAINTIES
INANIMATENESS	INARTISTIC	INCANDESCENTLY	INCARNADINE	INCERTAINTY
INANIMATENESSES	INARTISTICALLY	INCANDESCENTS	INCARNADINED	INCERTITUDE
INANIMATION	INATTENTION	INCANDESCES	INCARNADINING	INCERTITUDES
INANIMATIONS	INATTENTIONS	INCANDESCING	INCARNATED	INCESSANCIES
INANITIONS	INATTENTIVE	INCANTATION	INCARNATES	INCESSANCY
INAPPARENT	INATTENTIVELY	INCANTATIONAL	INCARNATING	INCESSANTLY
INAPPARENTLY	INATTENTIVENESS	INCANTATIONS	INCARNATION	INCESSANTNESS
INAPPEASABLE	INAUDIBILITIES	INCANTATOR	INCARNATIONS	INCESSANTNESSES
INAPPELLABLE	INAUDIBILITY	INCANTATORS	INCARVILLEA	INCESTUOUS
INAPPETENCE	INAUDIBLENESS	INCANTATORY	INCARVILLEAS	INCESTUOUSLY
INAPPETENCES	INAUDIBLENESSES	INCAPABILITIES	INCASEMENT	INCESTUOUSNESS
INAPPETENCIES	INAUGURALS	INCAPABILITY	INCASEMENTS	INCHARITABLE
INAPPETENCY	INAUGURATE	INCAPABLENESS	INCATENATION	INCHOATELY
INAPPETENT	INAUGURATED	INCAPABLENESSES	INCATENATIONS	INCHOATENESS
INAPPLICABILITY	INAUGURATES	INCAPABLES	INCAUTIONS	INCHOATENESSES
INAPPLICABLE	INAUGURATING	INCAPACIOUS	INCAUTIOUS	INCHOATING
INAPPLICABLY	INAUGURATION	INCAPACIOUSNESS	INCAUTIOUSLY	INCHOATION
INAPPOSITE	INAUGURATIONS	INCAPACITANT	INCAUTIOUSNESS	INCHOATIONS
INAPPOSITELY	INAUGURATOR	INCAPACITANTS	INCEDINGLY	INCHOATIVE
INAPPOSITENESS	INAUGURATORS	INCAPACITATE	INCENDIARIES	INCHOATIVELY
INAPPRECIABLE	INAUGURATORY	INCAPACITATED	INCENDIARISM	INCHOATIVES
INAPPRECIABLY	INAUSPICIOUS	INCAPACITATES	INCENDIARISMS	INCIDENCES
INAPPRECIATION	INAUSPICIOUSLY	INCAPACITATING	INCENDIARY	INCIDENTAL
INAPPRECIATIONS	INAUTHENTIC	INCAPACITATION	INCENDIVITIES	INCIDENTALLY
INAPPRECIATIVE	INAUTHENTICITY	INCAPACITATIONS	INCENDIVITY	INCIDENTALNESS
INAPPREHENSIBLE	INBOUNDING	INCAPACITIES	INCENSATION	INCIDENTALS
INAPPREHENSION	INBREATHED	INCAPACITY	INCENSATIONS	INCINERATE
INAPPREHENSIONS	INBREATHES	INCAPSULATE	INCENSEMENT	INCINERATED
INAPPREHENSIVE	INBREATHING	INCAPSULATED	INCENSEMENTS	INCINERATES
INAPPROACHABLE	INBREEDERS	INCAPSULATES	INCENSORIES	INCINERATING
INAPPROACHABLY	INBREEDING	INCAPSULATING	INCENSORIES	INCINERATION
INAPPROPRIATE	INBREEDINGS	INCAPSULATION	INCENTIVELY	INCINERATIONS

INCINERATOR	INCLUSIVENESS	INCOMMUTABILITY	INCONCLUSIONS	INCONSPICUOUSLY
INCINERATORS	INCLUSIVENESSES	INCOMMUTABLE	INCONCLUSIVE	INCONSTANCIES
INCIPIENCE	INCLUSIVITIES	INCOMMUTABLY	INCONCLUSIVELY	INCONSTANCY
INCIPIENCES	INCLUSIVITY	INCOMPARABILITY	INCONDENSABLE	INCONSTANT
INCIPIENCIES	INCOAGULABLE	INCOMPARABLE	INCONDENSIBLE	INCONSTANTLY
INCIPIENCY	INCOERCIBLE	INCOMPARABLY	INCONDITELY	INCONSTRUABLE
INCIPIENTLY	INCOGITABILITY	INCOMPARED	INCONFORMITIES	INCONSUMABLE
INCISIFORM	INCOGITABLE	INCOMPATIBILITY	INCONFORMITY	INCONSUMABLY
INCISIVELY	INCOGITANCIES	INCOMPATIBLE	INCONGRUENCE	INCONTESTABLE
INCISIVENESS	INCOGITANCY	INCOMPATIBLES	INCONGRUENCES	INCONTESTABLY
INCISIVENESSES	INCOGITANT	INCOMPATIBLY	INCONGRUENT	INCONTIGUOUS
INCISORIAL	INCOGITATIVE	INCOMPETENCE	INCONGRUENTLY	INCONTIGUOUSLY
INCITATION	INCOGNISABLE	INCOMPETENCES	INCONGRUITIES	INCONTINENCE
INCITATIONS	INCOGNISANCE	INCOMPETENCIES	INCONGRUITY	INCONTINENCES
INCITATIVE	INCOGNISANCES	INCOMPETENCY	INCONGRUOUS	INCONTINENCIES
INCITATIVES	INCOGNISANT	INCOMPETENT	INCONGRUOUSLY	INCONTINENCY
INCITEMENT	INCOGNITAS	INCOMPETENTLY	INCONGRUOUSNESS	INCONTINENT
INCITEMENTS	INCOGNITOS	INCOMPETENTS	INCONSCIENT	INCONTINENTLY
INCITINGLY	INCOGNIZABLE	INCOMPLETE	INCONSCIENTLY	INCONTROLLABLE
INCIVILITIES	INCOGNIZANCE	INCOMPLETELY	INCONSCIONABLE	INCONTROLLABLY
INCIVILITY	INCOGNIZANCES	INCOMPLETENESS	INCONSCIOUS	INCONVENIENCE
INCLASPING	INCOGNIZANT	INCOMPLETION	INCONSECUTIVE	INCONVENIENCED
INCLEMENCIES	INCOHERENCE	INCOMPLETIONS	INCONSECUTIVELY	INCONVENIENCES
INCLEMENCY	INCOHERENCES	INCOMPLIANCE	INCONSEQUENCE	INCONVENIENCIES
INCLEMENTLY	INCOHERENCIES	INCOMPLIANCES	INCONSEQUENCES	INCONVENIENCING
INCLEMENTNESS	INCOHERENCY	INCOMPLIANCIES	INCONSEQUENT	INCONVENIENCY
INCLEMENTNESSES	INCOHERENT	INCOMPLIANCY	INCONSEQUENTIAL	INCONVENIENT
INCLINABLE	INCOHERENTLY	INCOMPLIANT	INCONSEQUENTLY	INCONVENIENTLY
INCLINABLENESS	INCOHERENTNESS	INCOMPLIANTLY	INCONSIDERABLE	INCONVERSABLE
INCLINATION	INCOMBUSTIBLE	INCOMPOSED	INCONSIDERABLY	INCONVERSANT
INCLINATIONAL	INCOMBUSTIBLES	INCOMPOSITE	INCONSIDERATE	INCONVERTIBLE
INCLINATIONS	INCOMBUSTIBLY	INCOMPOSSIBLE	INCONSIDERATELY	INCONVERTIBLY
INCLINATORIA	INCOMMENSURABLE	INCOMPREHENSION	INCONSIDERATION	INCONVINCIBLE
INCLINATORIUM	INCOMMENSURABLY	INCOMPREHENSIVE	INCONSISTENCE	INCONVINCIBLY
INCLINATORY	INCOMMENSURATE	INCOMPRESSIBLE	INCONSISTENCES	INCOORDINATE
INCLININGS	INCOMMISCIBLE	INCOMPRESSIBLY	INCONSISTENCIES	INCOORDINATION
INCLINOMETER	INCOMMODED	INCOMPUTABILITY	INCONSISTENCY	INCOORDINATIONS
INCLINOMETERS	INCOMMODES	INCOMPUTABLE	INCONSISTENT	INCORONATE
INCLIPPING	INCOMMODING	INCOMPUTABLY	INCONSISTENTLY	INCORONATED
INCLOSABLE	INCOMMODIOUS	INCOMUNICADO	INCONSOLABILITY	INCORONATION
INCLOSURES	INCOMMODIOUSLY	INCONCEIVABLE	INCONSOLABLE	INCORONATIONS
INCLUDABLE	INCOMMODITIES	INCONCEIVABLES	INCONSOLABLY	INCORPORABLE
INCLUDEDNESS	INCOMMODITY	INCONCEIVABLY	INCONSONANCE	INCORPORAL
INCLUDEDNESSES	INCOMMUNICABLE	INCONCINNITIES	INCONSONANCES	INCORPORALL
INCLUDIBLE	INCOMMUNICABLY	INCONCINNITY	INCONSONANT	INCORPORATE
INCLUSIONS	INCOMMUNICADO	INCONCINNOUS	INCONSONANTLY	INCORPORATED
INCLUSIVELY	INCOMMUNICATIVE	INCONCLUSION	INCONSPICUOUS	INCORPORATES

INCORPORATING

INCORPORATING	INCREDIBILITY	INCUBATING	INCURABLES	INDECORUMS
INCORPORATION	INCREDIBLE	INCUBATION	INCURIOSITIES	INDEFATIGABLE
INCORPORATIONS	INCREDIBLENESS	INCUBATIONAL	INCURIOSITY	INDEFATIGABLY
INCORPORATIVE	INCREDIBLY	INCUBATIONS	INCURIOUSLY	INDEFEASIBILITY
INCORPORATOR	INCREDULITIES	INCUBATIVE	INCURIOUSNESS	INDEFEASIBLE
INCORPORATORS	INCREDULITY	INCUBATORS	INCURIOUSNESSES	INDEFEASIBLY
INCORPOREAL	INCREDULOUS	INCUBATORY	INCURRABLE	INDEFECTIBILITY
INCORPOREALITY	INCREDULOUSLY	INCULCATED	INCURRENCE	INDEFECTIBLE
INCORPOREALLY	INCREDULOUSNESS	INCULCATES	INCURRENCES	INDEFECTIBLY
INCORPOREITIES	INCREMATED	INCULCATING	INCURSIONS	INDEFENSIBILITY
INCORPOREITY	INCREMATES	INCULCATION	INCURVATED	INDEFENSIBLE
INCORPSING	INCREMATING	INCULCATIONS	INCURVATES	INDEFENSIBLY
INCORRECTLY	INCREMATION	INCULCATIVE	INCURVATING	INDEFINABILITY
INCORRECTNESS	INCREMATIONS	INCULCATOR	INCURVATION	INDEFINABLE
INCORRECTNESSES	INCREMENTAL	INCULCATORS	INCURVATIONS	INDEFINABLENESS
INCORRIGIBILITY	INCREMENTALISM	INCULCATORY	INCURVATURE	INDEFINABLES
INCORRIGIBLE	INCREMENTALISMS	INCULPABILITIES	INCURVATURES	INDEFINABLY
INCORRIGIBLES	INCREMENTALIST	INCULPABILITY	INCURVITIES	INDEFINITE
INCORRIGIBLY	INCREMENTALISTS	INCULPABLE	INDAGATING	INDEFINITELY
INCORRODIBLE	INCREMENTALLY	INCULPABLENESS	INDAGATION	INDEFINITENESS
INCORROSIBLE	INCREMENTALS	INCULPABLY	INDAGATIONS	INDEFINITES
INCORRUPTED	INCREMENTED	INCULPATED	INDAGATIVE	INDEHISCENCE
INCORRUPTIBLE	INCREMENTING	INCULPATES	INDAGATORS	INDEHISCENCES
INCORRUPTIBLES	INCREMENTS	INCULPATING	INDAGATORY	INDEHISCENT
INCORRUPTIBLY	INCRESCENT	INCULPATION	INDAPAMIDE	INDELIBILITIES
INCORRUPTION	INCRETIONARY	INCULPATIONS	INDAPAMIDES	INDELIBILITY
INCORRUPTIONS	INCRETIONS	INCULPATIVE	INDEBTEDNESS	INDELIBLENESS
INCORRUPTIVE	INCRIMINATE	INCULPATORY	INDEBTEDNESSES	INDELIBLENESSES
INCORRUPTLY	INCRIMINATED	INCUMBENCIES	INDECENCIES	INDELICACIES
INCORRUPTNESS	INCRIMINATES	INCUMBENCY	INDECENTER	INDELICACY
INCORRUPTNESSES	INCRIMINATING	INCUMBENTLY	INDECENTEST	INDELICATE
INCRASSATE	INCRIMINATION	INCUMBENTS	INDECENTLY	INDELICATELY
INCRASSATED	INCRIMINATIONS	INCUMBERED	INDECIDUATE	INDELICATENESS
INCRASSATES	INCRIMINATOR	INCUMBERING	INDECIDUOUS	INDEMNIFICATION
INCRASSATING	INCRIMINATORS	INCUMBERINGLY	INDECIPHERABLE	INDEMNIFIED
INCRASSATION	INCRIMINATORY	INCUMBRANCE	INDECIPHERABLY	INDEMNIFIER
INCRASSATIONS	INCROSSBRED	INCUMBRANCES	INDECISION	INDEMNIFIERS
INCRASSATIVE	INCROSSBREDS	INCUNABLES	INDECISIONS	INDEMNIFIES
INCREASABLE	INCROSSBREED	INCUNABULA	INDECISIVE	INDEMNIFYING
INCREASEDLY	INCROSSBREEDING	INCUNABULAR	INDECISIVELY	INDEMNITIES
INCREASEFUL	INCROSSBREEDS	INCUNABULIST	INDECISIVENESS	INDEMONSTRABLE
INCREASERS	INCROSSING	INCUNABULISTS	INDECLINABLE	INDEMONSTRABLY
INCREASING	INCRUSTANT	INCUNABULUM	INDECLINABLY	INDENTATION
INCREASINGLY	INCRUSTANTS	INCURABILITIES	INDECOMPOSABLE	INDENTATIONS
INCREASINGS	INCRUSTATION	INCURABILITY	INDECOROUS	INDENTIONS
INCREATELY	INCRUSTATIONS	INCURABLENESS	INDECOROUSLY	INDENTURED
INCREDIBILITIES	INCRUSTING	INCURABLENESSES	INDECOROUSNESS	INDENTURES

INDENTURESHIP	INDICOLITES	INDIGNANCES	INDISPUTABLY	INDIVIDUATING
INDENTURESHIPS	INDICTABLE	INDIGNANTLY	INDISSOCIABLE	INDIVIDUATION
INDENTURING	INDICTABLY	INDIGNATION	INDISSOCIABLY	INDIVIDUATIONS
INDEPENDENCE	INDICTIONAL	INDIGNATIONS	INDISSOLUBILITY	INDIVIDUATOR
INDEPENDENCES	INDICTIONS	INDIGNIFIED	INDISSOLUBLE	INDIVIDUATORS
INDEPENDENCIES	INDICTMENT	INDIGNIFIES	INDISSOLUBLY	INDIVIDUUM
INDEPENDENCY	INDICTMENTS	INDIGNIFYING	INDISSOLVABLE	INDIVISIBILITY
INDEPENDENT	INDIFFERENCE	INDIGNITIES	INDISSUADABLE	INDIVISIBLE
INDEPENDENTLY	INDIFFERENCES	INDIGOLITE	INDISSUADABLY	INDIVISIBLENESS
INDEPENDENTS	INDIFFERENCIES	INDIGOLITES	INDISTINCT	INDIVISIBLES
INDESCRIBABLE	INDIFFERENCY	INDIGOTINS	INDISTINCTION	INDIVISIBLY
INDESCRIBABLES	INDIFFERENT	INDINAVIRS	INDISTINCTIONS	INDOCILITIES
INDESCRIBABLY	INDIFFERENTISM	INDIRECTION	INDISTINCTIVE	INDOCILITY
INDESIGNATE	INDIFFERENTISMS	INDIRECTIONS	INDISTINCTIVELY	INDOCTRINATE
INDESTRUCTIBLE	INDIFFERENTIST	INDIRECTLY	INDISTINCTLY	INDOCTRINATED
INDESTRUCTIBLY	INDIFFERENTISTS	INDIRECTNESS	INDISTINCTNESS	INDOCTRINATES
INDETECTABLE	INDIFFERENTLY	INDIRECTNESSES	INDISTRIBUTABLE	INDOCTRINATING
INDETECTIBLE	INDIFFERENTS	INDIRUBINS	INDITEMENT	INDOCTRINATION
INDETERMINABLE	INDIGENCES	INDISCERNIBLE	INDITEMENTS	INDOCTRINATIONS
INDETERMINABLY	INDIGENCIES	INDISCERNIBLY	INDIVERTIBLE	INDOCTRINATOR
INDETERMINACIES	INDIGENISATION	INDISCERPTIBLE	INDIVERTIBLY	INDOCTRINATORS
INDETERMINACY	INDIGENISATIONS	INDISCIPLINABLE	INDIVIDABLE	INDOLEACETIC
INDETERMINATE	INDIGENISE	INDISCIPLINE	INDIVIDUAL	INDOLEBUTYRIC
INDETERMINATELY	INDIGENISED	INDISCIPLINED	INDIVIDUALISE	INDOLENCES
INDETERMINATION	INDIGENISES	INDISCIPLINES	INDIVIDUALISED	INDOLENCIES
INDETERMINED	INDIGENISING	INDISCOVERABLE	INDIVIDUALISER	INDOLENTLY
INDETERMINISM	INDIGENITIES	INDISCREET	INDIVIDUALISERS	INDOMETHACIN
INDETERMINISMS	INDIGENITY	INDISCREETLY	INDIVIDUALISES	INDOMETHACINS
INDETERMINIST	INDIGENIZATION	INDISCREETNESS	INDIVIDUALISING	INDOMITABILITY
INDETERMINISTIC	INDIGENIZATIONS	INDISCRETE	INDIVIDUALISM	INDOMITABLE
INDETERMINISTS	INDIGENIZE	INDISCRETELY	INDIVIDUALISMS	INDOMITABLENESS
INDEXATION	INDIGENIZED	INDISCRETENESS	INDIVIDUALIST	INDOMITABLY
INDEXATIONS	INDIGENIZES	INDISCRETION	INDIVIDUALISTIC	INDOPHENOL
INDEXICALS	INDIGENIZING	INDISCRETIONARY	INDIVIDUALISTS	INDOPHENOLS
INDEXTERITIES	INDIGENOUS	INDISCRETIONS	INDIVIDUALITIES	INDORSABLE
INDEXTERITY	INDIGENOUSLY	INDISCRIMINATE	INDIVIDUALITY	INDORSEMENT
INDICATABLE	INDIGENOUSNESS	INDISPENSABLE	INDIVIDUALIZE	INDORSEMENTS
INDICATING	INDIGENTLY	INDISPENSABLES	INDIVIDUALIZED	INDRAUGHTS
INDICATION	INDIGESTED	INDISPENSABLY	INDIVIDUALIZER	INDRENCHED
INDICATIONAL	INDIGESTIBILITY	INDISPOSED	INDIVIDUALIZERS	INDRENCHES
INDICATIONS	INDIGESTIBLE	INDISPOSEDNESS	INDIVIDUALIZES	INDRENCHING
INDICATIVE	INDIGESTIBLES	INDISPOSES	INDIVIDUALIZING	INDUBITABILITY
INDICATIVELY	INDIGESTIBLY	INDISPOSING	INDIVIDUALLY	INDUBITABLE
INDICATIVES	INDIGESTION	INDISPOSITION	INDIVIDUALS	INDUBITABLENESS
INDICATORS	INDIGESTIONS	INDISPOSITIONS	INDIVIDUATE	INDUBITABLY
INDICATORY	INDIGESTIVE	INDISPUTABILITY	INDIVIDUATED	INDUCEMENT
INDICOLITE	INDIGNANCE	INDISPUTABLE	INDIVIDUATES	INDUCEMENTS

INDUCIBILITIES

INDUCIBILITIES	INDUSTRIOUS	INELABORATELY	INERASIBLY	INEXISTENCY
INDUCIBILITY	INDUSTRIOUSLY	INELASTICALLY	INERRABILITIES	INEXISTENT
INDUCTANCE	INDUSTRIOUSNESS	INELASTICITIES	INERRABILITY	INEXORABILITIES
INDUCTANCES	INDUSTRYWIDE	INELASTICITY	INERRABLENESS	INEXORABILITY
INDUCTILITIES	INDWELLERS	INELEGANCE	INERRABLENESSES	INEXORABLE
INDUCTILITY	INDWELLING	INELEGANCES	INERRANCIES	INEXORABLENESS
INDUCTIONAL	INDWELLINGS	INELEGANCIES	INERTIALLY	INEXORABLY
INDUCTIONS	INEARTHING	INELEGANCY	INERTNESSES	INEXPANSIBLE
INDUCTIVELY	INEBRIANTS	INELEGANTLY	INESCAPABLE	INEXPECTANCIES
INDUCTIVENESS	INEBRIATED	INELIGIBILITIES	INESCAPABLY	INEXPECTANCY
INDUCTIVENESSES	INEBRIATES	INELIGIBILITY	INESCULENT	INEXPECTANT
INDUCTIVITIES	INEBRIATING	INELIGIBLE	INESCUTCHEON	INEXPECTATION
INDUCTIVITY	INEBRIATION	INELIGIBLENESS	INESCUTCHEONS	INEXPECTATIONS
INDULGENCE	INEBRIATIONS	INELIGIBLES	INESSENTIAL	INEXPEDIENCE
INDULGENCED	INEBRIETIES	INELIGIBLY	INESSENTIALITY	INEXPEDIENCES
INDULGENCES	INEDIBILITIES	INELOQUENCE	INESSENTIALS	INEXPEDIENCIES
INDULGENCIES	INEDIBILITY	INELOQUENCES	INESTIMABILITY	INEXPEDIENCY
INDULGENCING	INEDUCABILITIES	INELOQUENT	INESTIMABLE	INEXPEDIENT
INDULGENCY	INEDUCABILITY	INELOQUENTLY	INESTIMABLENESS	INEXPEDIENTLY
INDULGENTLY	INEDUCABLE	INELUCTABILITY	INESTIMABLY	INEXPENSIVE
INDULGINGLY	INEFFABILITIES	INELUCTABLE	INEVITABILITIES	INEXPENSIVELY
INDUMENTUM	INEFFABILITY	INELUCTABLY	INEVITABILITY	INEXPENSIVENESS
INDUMENTUMS	INEFFABLENESS	INELUDIBILITIES	INEVITABLE	INEXPERIENCE
INDUPLICATE	INEFFABLENESSES	INELUDIBILITY	INEVITABLENESS	INEXPERIENCED
INDUPLICATED	INEFFACEABILITY	INELUDIBLE	INEVITABLES	INEXPERIENCES
INDUPLICATION	INEFFACEABLE	INELUDIBLY	INEVITABLY	INEXPERTLY
INDUPLICATIONS	INEFFACEABLY	INENARRABLE	INEXACTITUDE	INEXPERTNESS
INDURATING	INEFFECTIVE	INEPTITUDE	INEXACTITUDES	INEXPERTNESSES
INDURATION	INEFFECTIVELY	INEPTITUDES	INEXACTNESS	INEXPIABLE
INDURATIONS	INEFFECTIVENESS	INEPTNESSES	INEXACTNESSES	INEXPIABLENESS
INDURATIVE	INEFFECTUAL	INEQUALITIES	INEXCITABLE	INEXPIABLY
INDUSTRIAL	INEFFECTUALITY	INEQUALITY	INEXCUSABILITY	INEXPLAINABLE
INDUSTRIALISE	INEFFECTUALLY	INEQUATION	INEXCUSABLE	INEXPLAINABLY
INDUSTRIALISED	INEFFECTUALNESS	INEQUATIONS	INEXCUSABLENESS	INEXPLICABILITY
INDUSTRIALISES	INEFFICACIES	INEQUIPOTENT	INEXCUSABLY	INEXPLICABLE
INDUSTRIALISING	INEFFICACIOUS	INEQUITABLE	INEXECRABLE	INEXPLICABLY
INDUSTRIALISM	INEFFICACIOUSLY	INEQUITABLENESS	INEXECUTABLE	INEXPLICIT
INDUSTRIALISMS	INEFFICACITIES	INEQUITABLY	INEXECUTION	INEXPLICITLY
INDUSTRIALIST	INEFFICACITY	INEQUITIES	INEXECUTIONS	INEXPLICITNESS
INDUSTRIALISTS	INEFFICACY	INEQUIVALVE	INEXHAUSTED	INEXPRESSIBLE
INDUSTRIALIZE	INEFFICIENCIES	INEQUIVALVED	INEXHAUSTIBLE	INEXPRESSIBLES
INDUSTRIALIZED	INEFFICIENCY	INERADICABILITY	INEXHAUSTIBLY	INEXPRESSIBLY
INDUSTRIALIZES	INEFFICIENT	INERADICABLE	INEXHAUSTIVE	INEXPRESSIVE
INDUSTRIALIZING	INEFFICIENTLY	INERADICABLY	INEXISTANT	INEXPRESSIVELY
INDUSTRIALLY	INEFFICIENTS	INERASABLE	INEXISTENCE	INEXPUGNABILITY
INDUSTRIALS	INEGALITARIAN	INERASABLY	INEXISTENCES	INEXPUGNABLE
INDUSTRIES	INELABORATE	INERASIBLE	INEXISTENCIES	INEXPUGNABLY

INEXPUNGIBLE	INFANTILITIES	INFERIORLY	INFINITESIMAL	INFLECTEDNESSES
INEXTENDED	INFANTILITY	INFERNALITIES	INFINITESIMALLY	INFLECTING
INEXTENSIBILITY	INFANTILIZATION	INFERNALITY	INFINITESIMALS	INFLECTION
INEXTENSIBLE	INFANTILIZE	INFERNALLY	INFINITIES	INFLECTIONAL
INEXTENSION	INFANTILIZED	INFERRABLE	INFINITIVAL	INFLECTIONALLY
INEXTENSIONS	INFANTILIZES	INFERRIBLE	INFINITIVALLY	INFLECTIONLESS
INEXTIRPABLE	INFANTILIZING	INFERTILELY	INFINITIVE	INFLECTIONS
INEXTRICABILITY	INFANTRIES	INFERTILITIES	INFINITIVELY	INFLECTIVE
INEXTRICABLE	INFANTRYMAN	INFERTILITY	INFINITIVES	INFLECTORS
INEXTRICABLY	INFANTRYMEN	INFESTANTS	INFINITUDE	INFLEXIBILITIES
INFALLIBILISM	INFARCTION	INFESTATION	INFINITUDES	INFLEXIBILITY
INFALLIBILISMS	INFARCTIONS	INFESTATIONS	INFIRMARER	INFLEXIBLE
INFALLIBILIST	INFATUATED	INFEUDATION	INFIRMARERS	INFLEXIBLENESS
INFALLIBILISTS	INFATUATEDLY	INFEUDATIONS	INFIRMARIAN	INFLEXIBLY
INFALLIBILITIES	INFATUATES	INFIBULATE	INFIRMARIANS	INFLEXIONAL
INFALLIBILITY	INFATUATING	INFIBULATED	INFIRMARIES	INFLEXIONALLY
INFALLIBLE	INFATUATION	INFIBULATES	INFIRMITIES	INFLEXIONLESS
INFALLIBLENESS	INFATUATIONS	INFIBULATING	INFIRMNESS	INFLEXIONS
INFALLIBLES	INFEASIBILITIES	INFIBULATION	INFIRMNESSES	INFLEXURES
INFALLIBLY	INFEASIBILITY	INFIBULATIONS	INFIXATION	INFLICTABLE
INFAMISING	INFEASIBLE	INFIDELITIES	INFIXATIONS	INFLICTERS
INFAMIZING	INFEASIBLENESS	INFIDELITY	INFLAMABLE	INFLICTING
INFAMONISE	INFECTIONS	INFIELDERS	INFLAMINGLY	INFLICTION
INFAMONISED	INFECTIOUS	INFIELDSMAN	INFLAMMABILITY	INFLICTIONS
INFAMONISES	INFECTIOUSLY	INFIELDSMEN	INFLAMMABLE	INFLICTIVE
INFAMONISING	INFECTIOUSNESS	INFIGHTERS	INFLAMMABLENESS	INFLICTORS
INFAMONIZE	INFECTIVELY	INFIGHTING	INFLAMMABLES	INFLORESCENCE
INFAMONIZED	INFECTIVENESS	INFIGHTINGS	INFLAMMABLY	INFLORESCENCES
INFAMONIZES	INFECTIVENESSES	INFILLINGS	INFLAMMATION	INFLORESCENT
INFAMONIZING	INFECTIVITIES	INFILTRATE	INFLAMMATIONS	INFLOWINGS
INFAMOUSLY	INFECTIVITY	INFILTRATED	INFLAMMATORILY	INFLUENCEABLE
INFAMOUSNESS	INFECUNDITIES	INFILTRATES	INFLAMMATORY	INFLUENCED
INFAMOUSNESSES	INFECUNDITY	INFILTRATING	INFLATABLE	INFLUENCER
INFANGTHIEF	INFEFTMENT	INFILTRATION	INFLATABLES	INFLUENCERS
INFANGTHIEFS	INFEFTMENTS	INFILTRATIONS	INFLATEDLY	INFLUENCES
INFANTHOOD	INFELICITIES	INFILTRATIVE	INFLATEDNESS	INFLUENCING
INFANTHOODS	INFELICITOUS	INFILTRATOR	INFLATEDNESSES	INFLUENTIAL
INFANTICIDAL	INFELICITOUSLY	INFILTRATORS	INFLATINGLY	INFLUENTIALLY
INFANTICIDE	INFELICITY	INFINITANT	INFLATIONARY	INFLUENTIALS
INFANTICIDES	INFEOFFING	INFINITARY	INFLATIONISM	INFLUENZAL
INFANTILISATION	INFERENCES	INFINITATE	INFLATIONISMS	INFLUENZAS
INFANTILISE	INFERENCING	INFINITATED	INFLATIONIST	INFLUXIONS
INFANTILISED	INFERENCINGS	INFINITATES	INFLATIONISTS	INFOLDINGS
INFANTILISES	INFERENTIAL	INFINITATING	INFLATIONS	INFOLDMENT
INFANTILISING	INFERENTIALLY	INFINITELY	INFLATUSES	INFOLDMENTS
INFANTILISM	INFERIORITIES	INFINITENESS	INFLECTABLE	INFOMANIAS
INFANTILISMS	INFERIORITY	INFINITENESSES	INFLECTEDNESS	INFOMERCIAL

INFOMERCIALS	INFRASOUND	INGEMINATE	INGRAVESCENCE	INHARMONICITIES
INFOPRENEURIAL	INFRASOUNDS	INGEMINATED	INGRAVESCENCES	INHARMONICITY
INFORMABLE	INFRASPECIFIC	INGEMINATES	INGRAVESCENT	INHARMONIES
INFORMALITIES	INFRASTRUCTURAL	INGEMINATING	INGREDIENT	INHARMONIOUS
INFORMALITY	INFRASTRUCTURE	INGEMINATION	INGREDIENTS	INHARMONIOUSLY
INFORMALLY	INFRASTRUCTURES	INGEMINATIONS	INGRESSION	INHAUSTING
INFORMANTS	INFREQUENCE	INGENERATE	INGRESSIONS	INHEARSING
INFORMATICIAN	INFREQUENCES	INGENERATED	INGRESSIVE	INHERENCES
INFORMATICIANS	INFREQUENCIES	INGENERATES	INGRESSIVENESS	INHERENCIES
INFORMATICS	INFREQUENCY	INGENERATING	INGRESSIVES	INHERENTLY
INFORMATION	INFREQUENT	INGENERATION	INGROOVING	INHERITABILITY
INFORMATIONAL	INFREQUENTLY	INGENERATIONS	INGROSSING	INHERITABLE
INFORMATIONALLY	INFRINGEMENT	INGENIOUSLY	INGROWNNESS	INHERITABLENESS
INFORMATIONS	INFRINGEMENTS	INGENIOUSNESS	INGROWNNESSES	INHERITABLY
INFORMATIVE	INFRINGERS	INGENIOUSNESSES	INGULFMENT	INHERITANCE
INFORMATIVELY	INFRINGING	INGENUITIES	INGULFMENTS	INHERITANCES
INFORMATIVENESS	INFRUCTUOUS	INGENUOUSLY	INGULPHING	INHERITING
INFORMATORILY	INFRUCTUOUSLY	INGENUOUSNESS	INGURGITATE	INHERITORS
INFORMATORY	INFUNDIBULA	INGENUOUSNESSES	INGURGITATED	INHERITRESS
INFORMEDLY	INFUNDIBULAR	INGESTIBLE	INGURGITATES	INHERITRESSES
INFORMIDABLE	INFUNDIBULATE	INGESTIONS	INGURGITATING	INHERITRICES
INFORMINGLY	INFUNDIBULIFORM	INGLENEUKS	INGURGITATION	INHERITRIX
INFORTUNES	INFUNDIBULUM	INGLENOOKS	INGURGITATIONS	INHERITRIXES
INFOSPHERE	INFURIATED	INGLORIOUS	INHABITABILITY	INHIBITABLE
INFOSPHERES	INFURIATELY	INGLORIOUSLY	INHABITABLE	INHIBITEDLY
INFOTAINMENT	INFURIATES	INGLORIOUSNESS	INHABITANCE	INHIBITERS
INFOTAINMENTS	INFURIATING	INGRAFTATION	INHABITANCES	INHIBITING
INFRACOSTAL	INFURIATINGLY	INGRAFTATIONS	INHABITANCIES	INHIBITION
INFRACTING	INFURIATION	INGRAFTING	INHABITANCY	INHIBITIONS
INFRACTION	INFURIATIONS	INGRAFTMENT	INHABITANT	INHIBITIVE
INFRACTIONS	INFUSCATED	INGRAFTMENTS	INHABITANTS	INHIBITORS
INFRACTORS	INFUSIBILITIES	INGRAINEDLY	INHABITATION	INHIBITORY
INFRAGRANT	INFUSIBILITY	INGRAINEDNESS	INHABITATIONS	INHOLDINGS
INFRAHUMAN	INFUSIBLENESS	INGRAINEDNESSES	INHABITERS	INHOMOGENEITIES
INFRAHUMANS	INFUSIBLENESSES	INGRAINERS	INHABITING	INHOMOGENEITY
INFRALAPSARIAN	INFUSIONISM	INGRAINING	INHABITIVENESS	INHOMOGENEOUS
INFRALAPSARIANS	INFUSIONISMS	INGRATEFUL	INHABITORS	INHOSPITABLE
INFRAMAXILLARY	INFUSIONIST	INGRATIATE	INHABITRESS	INHOSPITABLY
INFRANGIBILITY	INFUSIONISTS	INGRATIATED	INHABITRESSES	INHOSPITALITIES
INFRANGIBLE	INFUSORIAL	INGRATIATES	INHALATION	INHOSPITALITY
INFRANGIBLENESS	INFUSORIAN	INGRATIATING	INHALATIONAL	INHUMANELY
INFRANGIBLY	INFUSORIANS	INGRATIATINGLY	INHALATIONS	INHUMANITIES
INFRAORBITAL	INGATHERED	INGRATIATION	INHALATORIUM	INHUMANITY
INFRAPOSED	INGATHERER	INGRATIATIONS	INHALATORIUMS	INHUMANNESS
INFRAPOSITION	INGATHERERS	INGRATIATORY	INHALATORS	INHUMANNESSES
INFRAPOSITIONS	INGATHERING	INGRATITUDE	INHARMONIC	INHUMATING
INFRASONIC	INGATHERINGS	INGRATITUDES	INHARMONICAL	INHUMATION

INHUMATIONS	INITIATRESS	INNOCENCIES	INOBSERVANCES	INORDINACY
INIMICALITIES	INITIATRESSES	INNOCENTER	INOBSERVANT	INORDINATE
INIMICALITY	INITIATRICES	INNOCENTEST	INOBSERVANTLY	INORDINATELY
INIMICALLY	INITIATRIX	INNOCENTLY	INOBSERVATION	INORDINATENESS
INIMICALNESS	INITIATRIXES	INNOCUITIES	INOBSERVATIONS	INORDINATION
INIMICALNESSES	INJECTABLE	INNOCUOUSLY	INOBTRUSIVE	INORDINATIONS
INIMICITIOUS	INJECTABLES	INNOCUOUSNESS	INOBTRUSIVELY	INORGANICALLY
INIMITABILITIES	INJECTANTS	INNOCUOUSNESSES	INOBTRUSIVENESS	INORGANISATION
INIMITABILITY	INJECTIONS	INNOMINABLE	INOCCUPATION	INORGANISATIONS
INIMITABLE	INJELLYING	INNOMINABLES	INOCCUPATIONS	INORGANISED
INIMITABLENESS	INJOINTING	INNOMINATE	INOCULABILITIES	INORGANIZATION
INIMITABLY	INJUDICIAL	INNOVATING	INOCULABILITY	INORGANIZATIONS
INIQUITIES	INJUDICIALLY	INNOVATION	INOCULABLE	INORGANIZED
INIQUITOUS	INJUDICIOUS	INNOVATIONAL	INOCULANTS	INOSCULATE
INIQUITOUSLY	INJUDICIOUSLY	INNOVATIONIST	INOCULATED	INOSCULATED
INIQUITOUSNESS	INJUDICIOUSNESS	INNOVATIONISTS	INOCULATES	INOSCULATES
INITIALERS	INJUNCTING	INNOVATIONS	INOCULATING	INOSCULATING
INITIALING	INJUNCTION	INNOVATIVE	INOCULATION	INOSCULATION
INITIALISATION	INJUNCTIONS	INNOVATIVELY	INOCULATIONS	INOSCULATIONS
INITIALISATIONS	INJUNCTIVE	INNOVATIVENESS	INOCULATIVE	INPATIENTS
INITIALISE	INJUNCTIVELY	INNOVATORS	INOCULATOR	INPAYMENTS
INITIALISED	INJURIOUSLY	INNOVATORY	INOCULATORS	INPOURINGS
INITIALISES	INJURIOUSNESS	INNOXIOUSLY	INOCULATORY	INQUIETING
INITIALISING	INJURIOUSNESSES	INNOXIOUSNESS	INODOROUSLY	INQUIETUDE
INITIALISM	INJUSTICES	INNOXIOUSNESSES	INODOROUSNESS	INQUIETUDES
INITIALISMS	INKBERRIES	INNUENDOED	INODOROUSNESSES	INQUILINES
INITIALIZATION	INKHOLDERS	INNUENDOES	INOFFENSIVE	INQUILINIC
INITIALIZATIONS	INKINESSES	INNUENDOING	INOFFENSIVELY	INQUILINICS
INITIALIZE	INMARRIAGE	INNUMERABILITY	INOFFENSIVENESS	INQUILINISM
INITIALIZED	INMARRIAGES	INNUMERABLE	INOFFICIOUS	INQUILINISMS
INITIALIZES	INMIGRANTS	INNUMERABLENESS	INOFFICIOUSLY	INQUILINITIES
INITIALIZING	INNATENESS	INNUMERABLY	INOFFICIOUSNESS	INQUILINITY
INITIALLED	INNATENESSES	INNUMERACIES	INOPERABILITIES	INQUILINOUS
INITIALLER	INNAVIGABLE	INNUMERACY	INOPERABILITY	INQUINATED
INITIALLERS	INNAVIGABLY	INNUMERATE	INOPERABLE	INQUINATES
INITIALLING	INNERMOSTS	INNUMERATES	INOPERABLENESS	INQUINATING
INITIALNESS	INNERNESSES	INNUMEROUS	INOPERABLY	INQUINATION
INITIALNESSES	INNERSOLES	INNUTRIENT	INOPERATIVE	INQUINATIONS
INITIATING	INNERSPRING	INNUTRITION	INOPERATIVENESS	INQUIRATION
INITIATION	INNERVATED	INNUTRITIONS	INOPERCULATE	INQUIRATIONS
INITIATIONS	INNERVATES	INNUTRITIOUS	INOPERCULATES	INQUIRENDO
INITIATIVE	INNERVATING	INOBEDIENCE	INOPPORTUNE	INQUIRENDOS
INITIATIVELY	INNERVATION	INOBEDIENCES	INOPPORTUNELY	INQUIRINGLY
INITIATIVES	INNERVATIONS	INOBEDIENT	INOPPORTUNENESS	INQUISITION
INITIATORIES	INNERWEARS	INOBEDIENTLY	INOPPORTUNITIES	INQUISITIONAL
INITIATORS	INNKEEPERS	INOBSERVABLE	INOPPORTUNITY	INQUISITIONIST
INITIATORY	INNOCENCES	INOBSERVANCE	INORDINACIES	INQUISITIONISTS

INQUISITIONS	INSCRIPTIONS	INSENSATELY	INSIGNIFICANT	INSOLUBILISES
INQUISITIVE	INSCRIPTIVE	INSENSATENESS	INSIGNIFICANTLY	INSOLUBILISING
INQUISITIVELY	INSCRIPTIVELY	INSENSATENESSES	INSIGNIFICATIVE	INSOLUBILITIES
INQUISITIVENESS	INSCROLLED	INSENSIBILITIES	INSINCERELY	INSOLUBILITY
INQUISITOR	INSCROLLING	INSENSIBILITY	INSINCERITIES	INSOLUBILIZE
INQUISITORIAL	INSCRUTABILITY	INSENSIBLE	INSINCERITY	INSOLUBILIZED
INQUISITORIALLY	INSCRUTABLE	INSENSIBLENESS	INSINEWING	INSOLUBILIZES
INQUISITORS	INSCRUTABLENESS	INSENSIBLY	INSINUATED	INSOLUBILIZING
INQUISITRESS	INSCRUTABLY	INSENSITIVE	INSINUATES	INSOLUBLENESS
INQUISITRESSES	INSCULPING	INSENSITIVELY	INSINUATING	INSOLUBLENESSES
INQUISITURIENT	INSCULPTURE	INSENSITIVENESS	INSINUATINGLY	INSOLUBLES
INRUSHINGS	INSCULPTURED	INSENSITIVITIES	INSINUATION	INSOLVABILITIES
INSALIVATE	INSCULPTURES	INSENSITIVITY	INSINUATIONS	INSOLVABILITY
INSALIVATED	INSCULPTURING	INSENSUOUS	INSINUATIVE	INSOLVABLE
INSALIVATES	INSECTARIES	INSENTIENCE	INSINUATOR	INSOLVABLY
INSALIVATING	INSECTARIUM	INSENTIENCES	INSINUATORS	INSOLVENCIES
INSALIVATION	INSECTARIUMS	INSENTIENCIES	INSINUATORY	INSOLVENCY
INSALIVATIONS	INSECTICIDAL	INSENTIENCY	INSIPIDITIES	INSOLVENTS
INSALUBRIOUS	INSECTICIDALLY	INSENTIENT	INSIPIDITY	INSOMNIACS
INSALUBRIOUSLY	INSECTICIDE	INSEPARABILITY	INSIPIDNESS	INSOMNIOUS
INSALUBRITIES	INSECTICIDES	INSEPARABLE	INSIPIDNESSES	INSOMNOLENCE
INSALUBRITY	INSECTIFORM	INSEPARABLENESS	INSIPIENCE	INSOMNOLENCES
INSALUTARY	INSECTIFUGE	INSEPARABLES	INSIPIENCES	INSOUCIANCE
INSANENESS	INSECTIFUGES	INSEPARABLY	INSIPIENTLY	INSOUCIANCES
INSANENESSES	INSECTIONS	INSEPARATE	INSISTENCE	INSOUCIANT
INSANITARINESS	INSECTIVORE	INSERTABLE	INSISTENCES	INSOUCIANTLY
INSANITARY	INSECTIVORES	INSERTIONAL	INSISTENCIES	INSOULMENT
INSANITATION	INSECTIVOROUS	INSERTIONS	INSISTENCY	INSOULMENTS
INSANITATIONS	INSECTOLOGIES	INSESSORIAL	INSISTENTLY	INSOURCING
INSANITIES	INSECTOLOGIST	INSEVERABLE	INSISTINGLY	INSOURCINGS
INSATIABILITIES	INSECTOLOGISTS	INSHEATHED	INSNAREMENT	INSPANNING
INSATIABILITY	INSECTOLOGY	INSHEATHES	INSNAREMENTS	INSPECTABLE
INSATIABLE	INSECURELY	INSHEATHING	INSOBRIETIES	INSPECTING
INSATIABLENESS	INSECURENESS	INSHELLING	INSOBRIETY	INSPECTINGLY
INSATIABLY	INSECURENESSES	INSHELTERED	INSOCIABILITIES	INSPECTION
INSATIATELY	INSECURITIES	INSHELTERING	INSOCIABILITY	INSPECTIONAL
INSATIATENESS	INSECURITY	INSHELTERS	INSOCIABLE	INSPECTIONS
INSATIATENESSES	INSELBERGE	INSHIPPING	INSOCIABLY	INSPECTIVE
INSATIETIES	INSELBERGS	INSHRINING	INSOLATING	INSPECTORAL
INSCIENCES	INSEMINATE	INSIDIOUSLY	INSOLATION	INSPECTORATE
INSCONCING	INSEMINATED	INSIDIOUSNESS	INSOLATIONS	INSPECTORATES
INSCRIBABLE	INSEMINATES	INSIDIOUSNESSES	INSOLENCES	INSPECTORIAL
INSCRIBABLENESS	INSEMINATING	INSIGHTFUL	INSOLENTLY	INSPECTORS
INSCRIBERS	INSEMINATION	INSIGHTFULLY	INSOLIDITIES	INSPECTORSHIP
INSCRIBING	INSEMINATIONS	INSIGNIFICANCE	INSOLIDITY	INSPECTORSHIPS
INSCRIPTION	INSEMINATOR	INSIGNIFICANCES	INSOLUBILISE	INSPHERING
INSCRIPTIONAL	INSEMINATORS	INSIGNIFICANCY	INSOLUBILISED	INSPIRABLE

INSPIRATION	INSTANTIATE	INSTITUTIONARY	INSUFFERABLE	INSURGENCY
INSPIRATIONAL	INSTANTIATED	INSTITUTIONS	INSUFFERABLY	INSURGENTLY
INSPIRATIONALLY	INSTANTIATES	INSTITUTIST	INSUFFICIENCE	INSURGENTS
INSPIRATIONISM	INSTANTIATING	INSTITUTISTS	INSUFFICIENCES	INSURMOUNTABLE
INSPIRATIONISMS	INSTANTIATION	INSTITUTIVE	INSUFFICIENCIES	INSURMOUNTABLY
INSPIRATIONIST	INSTANTIATIONS	INSTITUTIVELY	INSUFFICIENCY	INSURRECTION
INSPIRATIONISTS	INSTANTNESS	INSTITUTOR	INSUFFICIENT	INSURRECTIONAL
INSPIRATIONS	INSTANTNESSES	INSTITUTORS	INSUFFICIENTLY	INSURRECTIONARY
INSPIRATIVE	INSTARRING	INSTREAMING	INSUFFLATE	INSURRECTIONISM
INSPIRATOR	INSTATEMENT	INSTREAMINGS	INSUFFLATED	INSURRECTIONIST
INSPIRATORS	INSTATEMENTS	INSTRESSED	INSUFFLATES	INSURRECTIONS
INSPIRATORY	INSTAURATION	INSTRESSES	INSUFFLATING	INSUSCEPTIBLE
INSPIRINGLY	INSTAURATIONS	INSTRESSING	INSUFFLATION	INSUSCEPTIBLY
INSPIRITED	INSTAURATOR	INSTRUCTED	INSUFFLATIONS	INSUSCEPTIVE
INSPIRITER	INSTAURATORS	INSTRUCTIBLE	INSUFFLATOR	INSUSCEPTIVELY
INSPIRITERS	INSTIGATED	INSTRUCTING	INSUFFLATORS	INSWATHING
INSPIRITING	INSTIGATES	INSTRUCTION	INSULARISM	INSWINGERS
INSPIRITINGLY	INSTIGATING	INSTRUCTIONAL	INSULARISMS	INTACTNESS
INSPIRITMENT	INSTIGATINGLY	INSTRUCTIONS	INSULARITIES	INTACTNESSES
INSPIRITMENTS	INSTIGATION	INSTRUCTIVE	INSULARITY	INTAGLIATED
INSPISSATE	INSTIGATIONS	INSTRUCTIVELY	INSULATING	INTAGLIOED
INSPISSATED	INSTIGATIVE	INSTRUCTIVENESS	INSULATION	INTAGLIOING
INSPISSATES	INSTIGATOR	INSTRUCTOR	INSULATIONS	INTANGIBILITIES
INSPISSATING	INSTIGATORS	INSTRUCTORS	INSULATORS	INTANGIBILITY
INSPISSATION	INSTILLATION	INSTRUCTORSHIP	INSULINASE	INTANGIBLE
INSPISSATIONS	INSTILLATIONS	INSTRUCTORSHIPS	INSULINASES	INTANGIBLENESS
INSPISSATOR	INSTILLERS	INSTRUCTRESS	INSULSITIES	INTANGIBLES
INSPISSATORS	INSTILLING	INSTRUCTRESSES	INSULTABLE	INTANGIBLY
INSTABILITIES	INSTILLMENT	INSTRUMENT	INSULTINGLY	INTEGRABILITIES
INSTABILITY	INSTILLMENTS	INSTRUMENTAL	INSULTMENT	INTEGRABILITY
INSTALLANT	INSTILMENT	INSTRUMENTALISM	INSULTMENTS	INTEGRABLE
INSTALLANTS	INSTILMENTS	INSTRUMENTALIST	INSUPERABILITY	INTEGRALITIES
INSTALLATION	INSTINCTIVE	INSTRUMENTALITY	INSUPERABLE	INTEGRALITY
INSTALLATIONS	INSTINCTIVELY	INSTRUMENTALLY	INSUPERABLENESS	INTEGRALLY
INSTALLERS	INSTINCTIVITIES	INSTRUMENTALS	INSUPERABLY	INTEGRANDS
INSTALLING	INSTINCTIVITY	INSTRUMENTATION	INSUPPORTABLE	INTEGRANTS
INSTALLMENT	INSTINCTUAL	INSTRUMENTED	INSUPPORTABLY	INTEGRATED
INSTALLMENTS	INSTINCTUALLY	INSTRUMENTING	INSUPPRESSIBLE	INTEGRATES
INSTALMENT	INSTITORIAL	INSTRUMENTS	INSUPPRESSIBLY	INTEGRATING
INSTALMENTS	INSTITUTED	INSUBJECTION	INSURABILITIES	INTEGRATION
INSTANCIES	INSTITUTER	INSUBJECTIONS	INSURABILITY	INTEGRATIONIST
INSTANCING	INSTITUTERS	INSUBORDINATE	INSURANCER	INTEGRATIONISTS
INSTANTANEITIES	INSTITUTES	INSUBORDINATELY	INSURANCERS	INTEGRATIONS
INSTANTANEITY	INSTITUTING	INSUBORDINATES	INSURANCES	INTEGRATIVE
INSTANTANEOUS	INSTITUTION	INSUBORDINATION	INSURGENCE	INTEGRATOR
INSTANTANEOUSLY	INSTITUTIONAL	INSUBSTANTIAL	INSURGENCES	INTEGRATORS
INSTANTIAL	INSTITUTIONALLY	INSUBSTANTIALLY	INSURGENCIES	INTEGRITIES

INTEGUMENT	INTENDANCIES	INTERACTANT	INTERCALATE	INTERCHANNEL
INTEGUMENTAL	INTENDANCY	INTERACTANTS	INTERCALATED	INTERCHAPTER
INTEGUMENTARY	INTENDANTS	INTERACTED	INTERCALATES	INTERCHAPTERS
INTEGUMENTS	INTENDEDLY	INTERACTING	INTERCALATING	INTERCHURCH
INTELLECTED	INTENDERED	INTERACTION	INTERCALATION	INTERCIPIENT
INTELLECTION	INTENDERING	INTERACTIONAL	INTERCALATIONS	INTERCIPIENTS
INTELLECTIONS	INTENDMENT	INTERACTIONISM	INTERCALATIVE	INTERCLASS
INTELLECTIVE	INTENDMENTS	INTERACTIONISMS	INTERCAMPUS	INTERCLAVICLE
INTELLECTIVELY	INTENERATE	INTERACTIONIST	INTERCASTE	INTERCLAVICLES
INTELLECTS	INTENERATED	INTERACTIONISTS	INTERCEDED	INTERCLAVICULAR
INTELLECTUAL	INTENERATES	INTERACTIONS	INTERCEDENT	INTERCLUDE
INTELLECTUALISE	INTENERATING	INTERACTIVE	INTERCEDER	INTERCLUDED
INTELLECTUALISM	INTENERATION	INTERACTIVELY	INTERCEDERS	INTERCLUDES
INTELLECTUALIST	INTENERATIONS	INTERACTIVITIES	INTERCEDES	INTERCLUDING
INTELLECTUALITY	INTENSATED	INTERACTIVITY	INTERCEDING	INTERCLUSION
INTELLECTUALIZE	INTENSATES	INTERAGENCY	INTERCELLULAR	INTERCLUSIONS
INTELLECTUALLY	INTENSATING	INTERALLELIC	INTERCENSAL	INTERCLUSTER
INTELLECTUALS	INTENSATIVE	INTERALLIED	INTERCEPTED	INTERCOASTAL
INTELLIGENCE	INTENSATIVES	INTERAMBULACRA	INTERCEPTER	INTERCOLLEGIATE
INTELLIGENCER	INTENSENESS	INTERAMBULACRAL	INTERCEPTERS	INTERCOLLINE
INTELLIGENCERS	INTENSENESSES	INTERAMBULACRUM	INTERCEPTING	INTERCOLONIAL
INTELLIGENCES	INTENSIFICATION	INTERANIMATION	INTERCEPTION	INTERCOLONIALLY
INTELLIGENT	INTENSIFIED	INTERANIMATIONS	INTERCEPTIONS	INTERCOLUMNAR
INTELLIGENTIAL	INTENSIFIER	INTERANNUAL	INTERCEPTIVE	INTERCOMMUNAL
INTELLIGENTLY	INTENSIFIERS	INTERARCHED	INTERCEPTOR	INTERCOMMUNE
INTELLIGENTSIA	INTENSIFIES	INTERARCHES	INTERCEPTORS	INTERCOMMUNED
INTELLIGENTSIAS	INTENSIFYING	INTERARCHING	INTERCEPTS	INTERCOMMUNES
INTELLIGENTZIA	INTENSIONAL	INTERATOMIC	INTERCESSION	INTERCOMMUNING
INTELLIGENTZIAS	INTENSIONALITY	INTERBASIN	INTERCESSIONAL	INTERCOMMUNION
INTELLIGIBILITY	INTENSIONALLY	INTERBEDDED	INTERCESSIONS	INTERCOMMUNIONS
INTELLIGIBLE	INTENSIONS	INTERBEDDING	INTERCESSOR	INTERCOMMUNITY
INTELLIGIBLY	INTENSITIES	INTERBEDDINGS	INTERCESSORIAL	INTERCOMPANY
INTEMERATE	INTENSITIVE	INTERBEHAVIOR	INTERCESSORS	INTERCOMPARE
INTEMERATELY	INTENSITIVES	INTERBEHAVIORAL	INTERCESSORY	INTERCOMPARED
INTEMERATENESS	INTENSIVELY	INTERBEHAVIORS	INTERCHAIN	INTERCOMPARES
INTEMPERANCE	INTENSIVENESS	INTERBOROUGH	INTERCHAINED	INTERCOMPARING
INTEMPERANCES	INTENSIVENESSES	INTERBRAIN	INTERCHAINING	INTERCOMPARISON
INTEMPERANT	INTENSIVES	INTERBRAINS	INTERCHAINS	INTERCONNECT
INTEMPERANTS	INTENTIONAL	INTERBRANCH	INTERCHANGE	INTERCONNECTED
INTEMPERATE	INTENTIONALITY	INTERBREED	INTERCHANGEABLE	INTERCONNECTING
INTEMPERATELY	INTENTIONALLY	INTERBREEDING	INTERCHANGEABLY	INTERCONNECTION
INTEMPERATENESS	INTENTIONED	INTERBREEDINGS	INTERCHANGED	INTERCONNECTOR
INTEMPESTIVE	INTENTIONS	INTERBREEDS	INTERCHANGEMENT	INTERCONNECTORS
INTEMPESTIVELY	INTENTNESS	INTERBROKER	INTERCHANGER	INTERCONNECTS
INTEMPESTIVITY	INTENTNESSES	INTERCALAR	INTERCHANGERS	INTERCONNEXION
INTENDANCE	INTERABANG	INTERCALARILY	INTERCHANGES	INTERCONNEXIONS
INTENDANCES	INTERABANGS	INTERCALARY	INTERCHANGING	INTERCONVERSION

INTERCONVERT	INTERDEPEND	INTERESTINGLY	INTERFLUVIAL	INTERIONIC
INTERCONVERTED	INTERDEPENDED	INTERESTINGNESS	INTERFOLDED	INTERIORISATION
INTERCONVERTING	INTERDEPENDENCE	INTERETHNIC	INTERFOLDING	INTERIORISE
INTERCONVERTS	INTERDEPENDENCY	INTERFACED	INTERFOLDS	INTERIORISED
INTERCOOLED	INTERDEPENDENT	INTERFACES	INTERFOLIATE	INTERIORISES
INTERCOOLER	INTERDEPENDING	INTERFACIAL	INTERFOLIATED	INTERIORISING
INTERCOOLERS	INTERDEPENDS	INTERFACIALLY	INTERFOLIATES	INTERIORITIES
INTERCORPORATE	INTERDIALECTAL	INTERFACING	INTERFOLIATING	INTERIORITY
INTERCORRELATE	INTERDICTED	INTERFACINGS	INTERFRATERNITY	INTERIORIZATION
INTERCORRELATED	INTERDICTING	INTERFACULTY	INTERFRETTED	INTERIORIZE
INTERCORRELATES	INTERDICTION	INTERFAITH	INTERFRONTAL	INTERIORIZED
INTERCORTICAL	INTERDICTIONS	INTERFAMILIAL	INTERFUSED	INTERIORIZES
INTERCOSTAL	INTERDICTIVE	INTERFAMILY	INTERFUSES	INTERIORIZING
INTERCOSTALLY	INTERDICTIVELY	INTERFASCICULAR	INTERFUSING	INTERIORLY
INTERCOSTALS	INTERDICTOR	INTERFEMORAL	INTERFUSION	INTERISLAND
INTERCOUNTRY	INTERDICTORS	INTERFERED	INTERFUSIONS	INTERJACENCIES
INTERCOUNTY	INTERDICTORY	INTERFERENCE	INTERGALACTIC	INTERJACENCY
INTERCOUPLE	INTERDICTS	INTERFERENCES	INTERGENERATION	INTERJACENT
INTERCOURSE	INTERDIFFUSE	INTERFERENTIAL	INTERGENERIC	INTERJACULATE
INTERCOURSES	INTERDIFFUSED	INTERFERER	INTERGLACIAL	INTERJACULATED
INTERCRATER	INTERDIFFUSES	INTERFERERS	INTERGLACIALS	INTERJACULATES
INTERCROPPED	INTERDIFFUSING	INTERFERES	INTERGRADATION	INTERJACULATING
INTERCROPPING	INTERDIFFUSION	INTERFERING	INTERGRADATIONS	INTERJACULATORY
INTERCROPS	INTERDIFFUSIONS	INTERFERINGLY	INTERGRADE	INTERJECTED
INTERCROSS	INTERDIGITAL	INTERFEROGRAM	INTERGRADED	INTERJECTING
INTERCROSSED	INTERDIGITATE	INTERFEROGRAMS	INTERGRADES	INTERJECTION
INTERCROSSES	INTERDIGITATED	INTERFEROMETER	INTERGRADIENT	INTERJECTIONAL
INTERCROSSING	INTERDIGITATES	INTERFEROMETERS	INTERGRADING	INTERJECTIONARY
INTERCRURAL	INTERDIGITATING	INTERFEROMETRIC	INTERGRAFT	INTERJECTIONS
INTERCULTURAL	INTERDIGITATION	INTERFEROMETRY	INTERGRAFTED	INTERJECTOR
INTERCULTURALLY	INTERDINED	INTERFERON	INTERGRAFTING	INTERJECTORS
INTERCULTURE	INTERDINES	INTERFERONS	INTERGRAFTS	INTERJECTORY
INTERCURRENCE	INTERDINING	INTERFERTILE	INTERGRANULAR	INTERJECTS
INTERCURRENCES	INTERDISTRICT	INTERFERTILITY	INTERGROUP	INTERJECTURAL
INTERCURRENT	INTERDIVISIONAL	INTERFIBER	INTERGROWING	INTERJOINED
INTERCURRENTLY	INTERDOMINION	INTERFILED	INTERGROWN	INTERJOINING
INTERCUTTING	INTERELECTRODE	INTERFILES	INTERGROWS	INTERJOINS
INTERDASHED	INTERELECTRON	INTERFILING	INTERGROWTH	INTERKINESES
INTERDASHES	INTERELECTRONIC	INTERFLOWED	INTERGROWTHS	INTERKINESIS
INTERDASHING	INTEREPIDEMIC	INTERFLOWING	INTERINDIVIDUAL	INTERKNITS
INTERDEALER	INTERESSED	INTERFLOWS	INTERINDUSTRY	INTERKNITTED
INTERDEALERS	INTERESSES	INTERFLUENCE	INTERINFLUENCE	INTERKNITTING
INTERDEALING	INTERESSING	INTERFLUENCES	INTERINFLUENCES	INTERKNOTS
INTERDEALS	INTERESTED	INTERFLUENT	INTERINVOLVE	INTERKNOTTED
INTERDEALT	INTERESTEDLY	INTERFLUOUS	INTERINVOLVED	INTERKNOTTING
INTERDENTAL	INTERESTEDNESS	INTERFLUVE	INTERINVOLVES	INTERLACED
INTERDENTALLY	INTERESTING	INTERFLUVES	INTERINVOLVING	INTERLACEDLY

INTERLACEMENT	INTERLINGUALLY	INTERMARRIED	INTERMINABILITY	INTERNALIZED
INTERLACEMENTS	INTERLINGUAS	INTERMARRIES	INTERMINABLE	INTERNALIZES
INTERLACES	INTERLINING	INTERMARRY	INTERMINABLY	INTERNALIZING
INTERLACING	INTERLININGS	INTERMARRYING	INTERMINGLE	INTERNALLY
INTERLACUSTRINE	INTERLINKED	INTERMATTED	INTERMINGLED	INTERNALNESS
INTERLAMINAR	INTERLINKING	INTERMATTING	INTERMINGLES	INTERNALNESSES
INTERLAMINATE	INTERLINKS	INTERMAXILLA	INTERMINGLING	INTERNATIONAL
INTERLAMINATED	INTERLOANS	INTERMAXILLAE	INTERMISSION	INTERNATIONALLY
INTERLAMINATES	INTERLOBULAR	INTERMAXILLARY	INTERMISSIONS	INTERNATIONALS
INTERLAMINATING	INTERLOCAL	INTERMEDDLE	INTERMISSIVE	INTERNECINE
INTERLAMINATION	INTERLOCATION	INTERMEDDLED	INTERMITOTIC	INTERNECIVE
INTERLAPPED	INTERLOCATIONS	INTERMEDDLER	INTERMITTED	INTERNEURAL
INTERLAPPING	INTERLOCKED	INTERMEDDLERS	INTERMITTENCE	INTERNEURON
INTERLARDED	INTERLOCKER	INTERMEDDLES	INTERMITTENCES	INTERNEURONAL
INTERLARDING	INTERLOCKERS	INTERMEDDLING	INTERMITTENCIES	INTERNEURONS
INTERLARDS	INTERLOCKING	INTERMEDIA	INTERMITTENCY	INTERNISTS
INTERLAYER	INTERLOCKS	INTERMEDIACIES	INTERMITTENT	INTERNMENT
INTERLAYERED	INTERLOCUTION	INTERMEDIACY	INTERMITTENTLY	INTERNMENTS
INTERLAYERING	INTERLOCUTIONS	INTERMEDIAL	INTERMITTER	INTERNODAL
INTERLAYERS	INTERLOCUTOR	INTERMEDIARIES	INTERMITTERS	INTERNODES
INTERLAYING	INTERLOCUTORILY	INTERMEDIARY	INTERMITTING	INTERNODIAL
INTERLEAVE	INTERLOCUTORS	INTERMEDIATE	INTERMITTINGLY	INTERNSHIP
INTERLEAVED	INTERLOCUTORY	INTERMEDIATED	INTERMITTOR	INTERNSHIPS
INTERLEAVES	INTERLOCUTRESS	INTERMEDIATELY	INTERMITTORS	INTERNUCLEAR
INTERLEAVING	INTERLOCUTRICE	INTERMEDIATES	INTERMIXED	INTERNUCLEON
INTERLENDING	INTERLOCUTRICES	INTERMEDIATING	INTERMIXES	INTERNUCLEONIC
INTERLENDS	INTERLOCUTRIX	INTERMEDIATION	INTERMIXING	INTERNUCLEOTIDE
INTERLEUKIN	INTERLOCUTRIXES	INTERMEDIATIONS	INTERMIXTURE	INTERNUNCIAL
INTERLEUKINS	INTERLOOPED	INTERMEDIATOR	INTERMIXTURES	INTERNUNCIO
INTERLIBRARY	INTERLOOPING	INTERMEDIATORS	INTERMODAL	INTERNUNCIOS
INTERLINEAL	INTERLOOPS	INTERMEDIATORY	INTERMODULATION	INTEROBSERVER
INTERLINEALLY	INTERLOPED	INTERMEDIN	INTERMOLECULAR	INTEROCEAN
INTERLINEAR	INTERLOPER	INTERMEDINS	INTERMONTANE	INTEROCEANIC
INTERLINEARLY	INTERLOPERS	INTERMEDIUM	INTERMOUNTAIN	INTEROCEPTIVE
INTERLINEARS	INTERLOPES	INTERMEMBRANE	INTERMUNDANE	INTEROCEPTOR
INTERLINEATE	INTERLOPING	INTERMENSTRUAL	INTERMURED	INTEROCEPTORS
INTERLINEATED	INTERLUDED	INTERMENTS	INTERMURES	INTEROCULAR
INTERLINEATES	INTERLUDES	INTERMESHED	INTERMURING	INTEROFFICE
INTERLINEATING	INTERLUDIAL	INTERMESHES	INTERNALISATION	INTEROPERABLE
INTERLINEATION	INTERLUDING	INTERMESHING	INTERNALISE	INTEROPERATIVE
INTERLINEATIONS	INTERLUNAR	INTERMETALLIC	INTERNALISED	INTERORBITAL
INTERLINED	INTERLUNARY	INTERMETALLICS	INTERNALISES	INTERORGAN
INTERLINER	INTERLUNATION	INTERMEZZI	INTERNALISING	INTEROSCULANT
INTERLINERS	INTERLUNATIONS	INTERMEZZO	INTERNALITIES	INTEROSCULATE
INTERLINES	INTERMARGINAL	INTERMEZZOS	INTERNALITY	INTEROSCULATED
INTERLINGUA	INTERMARRIAGE	INTERMIGRATION	INTERNALIZATION	INTEROSCULATES
INTERLINGUAL	INTERMARRIAGES	INTERMIGRATIONS	INTERNALIZE	INTEROSCULATING

INTEROSCULATION	INTERPLANTS	INTERPRETATIONS	INTERRELATES	INTERSCRIBE
INTEROSSEAL	INTERPLAYED	INTERPRETATIVE	INTERRELATING	INTERSCRIBED
INTEROSSEOUS	INTERPLAYING	INTERPRETED	INTERRELATION	INTERSCRIBES
INTERPAGED	INTERPLAYS	INTERPRETER	INTERRELATIONS	INTERSCRIBING
INTERPAGES	INTERPLEAD	INTERPRETERS	INTERRELIGIOUS	INTERSECTED
INTERPAGING	INTERPLEADED	INTERPRETERSHIP	INTERRENAL	INTERSECTING
INTERPANDEMIC	INTERPLEADER	INTERPRETESS	INTERROBANG	INTERSECTION
INTERPARIETAL	INTERPLEADERS	INTERPRETESSES	INTERROBANGS	INTERSECTIONAL
INTERPARISH	INTERPLEADING	INTERPRETING	INTERROGABLE	INTERSECTIONS
INTERPAROCHIAL	INTERPLEADS	INTERPRETIVE	INTERROGANT	INTERSECTS
INTERPAROXYSMAL	INTERPLEURAL	INTERPRETIVELY	INTERROGANTS	INTERSEGMENT
INTERPARTICLE	INTERPLUVIAL	INTERPRETRESS	INTERROGATE	INTERSEGMENTAL
INTERPARTY	INTERPOINT	INTERPRETRESSES	INTERROGATED	INTERSENSORY
INTERPELLANT	INTERPOLABLE	INTERPRETS	INTERROGATEE	INTERSEPTAL
INTERPELLANTS	INTERPOLAR	INTERPROVINCIAL	INTERROGATEES	INTERSERTAL
INTERPELLATE	INTERPOLATE	INTERPROXIMAL	INTERROGATES	INTERSERTED
INTERPELLATED	INTERPOLATED	INTERPSYCHIC	INTERROGATING	INTERSERTING
INTERPELLATES	INTERPOLATER	INTERPUNCTION	INTERROGATINGLY	INTERSERTS
INTERPELLATING	INTERPOLATERS	INTERPUNCTIONS	INTERROGATION	INTERSERVICE
INTERPELLATION	INTERPOLATES	INTERPUNCTUATE	INTERROGATIONAL	INTERSESSION
INTERPELLATIONS	INTERPOLATING	INTERPUNCTUATED	INTERROGATIONS	INTERSESSIONS
INTERPELLATOR	INTERPOLATION	INTERPUNCTUATES	INTERROGATIVE	INTERSEXES
INTERPELLATORS	INTERPOLATIONS	INTERPUPILLARY	INTERROGATIVELY	INTERSEXUAL
INTERPENETRABLE	INTERPOLATIVE	INTERQUARTILE	INTERROGATIVES	INTERSEXUALISM
INTERPENETRANT	INTERPOLATOR	INTERRACIAL	INTERROGATOR	INTERSEXUALISMS
INTERPENETRATE	INTERPOLATORS	INTERRACIALLY	INTERROGATORIES	INTERSEXUALITY
INTERPENETRATED	INTERPONED	INTERRADIAL	INTERROGATORILY	INTERSEXUALLY
INTERPENETRATES	INTERPONES	INTERRADIALLY	INTERROGATORS	INTERSIDEREAL
INTERPERCEPTUAL	INTERPONING	INTERRADII	INTERROGATORY	INTERSOCIETAL
INTERPERMEATE	INTERPOPULATION	INTERRADIUS	INTERROGEE	INTERSOCIETY
INTERPERMEATED	INTERPOSABLE	INTERRADIUSES	INTERROGEES	INTERSPACE
INTERPERMEATES	INTERPOSAL	INTERRAILED	INTERRUPTED	INTERSPACED
INTERPERMEATING	INTERPOSALS	INTERRAILER	INTERRUPTEDLY	INTERSPACES
INTERPERSONAL	INTERPOSED	INTERRAILERS	INTERRUPTER	INTERSPACING
INTERPERSONALLY	INTERPOSER	INTERRAILING	INTERRUPTERS	INTERSPATIAL
INTERPETIOLAR	INTERPOSERS	INTERRAILS	INTERRUPTIBLE	INTERSPATIALLY
INTERPHALANGEAL	INTERPOSES	INTERRAMAL	INTERRUPTING	INTERSPECIES
INTERPHASE	INTERPOSING	INTERREGAL	INTERRUPTION	INTERSPECIFIC
INTERPHASES	INTERPOSITION	INTERREGES	INTERRUPTIONS	INTERSPERSAL
INTERPHONE	INTERPOSITIONS	INTERREGIONAL	INTERRUPTIVE	INTERSPERSALS
INTERPHONES	INTERPRETABLE	INTERREGNA	INTERRUPTIVELY	INTERSPERSE
INTERPILASTER	INTERPRETABLY	INTERREGNAL	INTERRUPTOR	INTERSPERSED
INTERPILASTERS	INTERPRETATE	INTERREGNUM	INTERRUPTORS	INTERSPERSEDLY
INTERPLANETARY	INTERPRETATED	INTERREGNUMS	INTERRUPTS	INTERSPERSES
INTERPLANT	INTERPRETATES	INTERRELATE	INTERSCAPULAR	INTERSPERSING
INTERPLANTED	INTERPRETATING	INTERRELATED	INTERSCHOLASTIC	INTERSPERSION
INTERPLANTING	INTERPRETATION	INTERRELATEDLY	INTERSCHOOL	INTERSPERSIONS

INTERSPINAL	INTERTRAFFIC	INTERVENTIONIST	INTESTINAL	INTONATORS
INTERSPINOUS	INTERTRAFFICS	INTERVENTIONS	INTESTINALLY	INTONINGLY
INTERSTADIAL	INTERTRIAL	INTERVENTOR	INTESTINES	INTORSIONS
INTERSTADIALS	INTERTRIBAL	INTERVENTORS	INTHRALLED	INTORTIONS
INTERSTAGE	INTERTRIGO	INTERVERTEBRAL	INTHRALLING	INTOXICABLE
INTERSTATE	INTERTRIGOS	INTERVIEWED	INTHRONING	INTOXICANT
INTERSTATES	INTERTROOP	INTERVIEWEE	INTIFADAHS	INTOXICANTS
INTERSTATION	INTERTROPICAL	INTERVIEWEES	INTIFADEHS	INTOXICATE
INTERSTELLAR	INTERTWINE	INTERVIEWER	INTIMACIES	INTOXICATED
INTERSTELLARY	INTERTWINED	INTERVIEWERS	INTIMATELY	INTOXICATEDLY
INTERSTERILE	INTERTWINEMENT	INTERVIEWING	INTIMATENESS	INTOXICATES
INTERSTERILITY	INTERTWINEMENTS	INTERVIEWS	INTIMATENESSES	INTOXICATING
INTERSTICE	INTERTWINES	INTERVILLAGE	INTIMATERS	INTOXICATINGLY
INTERSTICES	INTERTWINING	INTERVISIBILITY	INTIMATING	INTOXICATION
INTERSTIMULUS	INTERTWININGLY	INTERVISIBLE	INTIMATION	INTOXICATIONS
INTERSTITIAL	INTERTWININGS	INTERVISITATION	INTIMATIONS	INTOXICATIVE
INTERSTITIALLY	INTERTWIST	INTERVITAL	INTIMIDATE	INTOXICATOR
INTERSTITIALS	INTERTWISTED	INTERVOCALIC	INTIMIDATED	INTOXICATORS
INTERSTRAIN	INTERTWISTING	INTERVOLVE	INTIMIDATES	INTOXIMETER
INTERSTRAND	INTERTWISTINGLY	INTERVOLVED	INTIMIDATING	INTOXIMETERS
INTERSTRATIFIED	INTERTWISTS	INTERVOLVES	INTIMIDATINGLY	INTRACAPSULAR
INTERSTRATIFIES	INTERUNION	INTERVOLVING	INTIMIDATION	INTRACARDIAC
INTERSTRATIFY	INTERUNIONS	INTERWEAVE	INTIMIDATIONS	INTRACARDIAL
INTERSUBJECTIVE	INTERUNIVERSITY	INTERWEAVED	INTIMIDATOR	INTRACARDIALLY
INTERSYSTEM	INTERURBAN	INTERWEAVEMENT	INTIMIDATORS	INTRACAVITARY
INTERTANGLE	INTERVALES	INTERWEAVEMENTS	INTIMIDATORY	INTRACELLULAR
INTERTANGLED	INTERVALLEY	INTERWEAVER	INTIMISTES	INTRACELLULARLY
INTERTANGLEMENT	INTERVALLIC	INTERWEAVERS	INTIMITIES	INTRACEREBRAL
INTERTANGLES	INTERVALLUM	INTERWEAVES	INTINCTION	INTRACEREBRALLY
INTERTANGLING	INTERVALLUMS	INTERWEAVING	INTINCTIONS	INTRACOMPANY
INTERTARSAL	INTERVALOMETER	INTERWINDING	INTITULING	INTRACRANIAL
INTERTENTACULAR	INTERVALOMETERS	INTERWINDS	INTOLERABILITY	INTRACRANIALLY
INTERTERMINAL	INTERVARSITY	INTERWORKED	INTOLERABLE	INTRACTABILITY
INTERTEXTS	INTERVEINED	INTERWORKING	INTOLERABLENESS	INTRACTABLE
INTERTEXTUAL	INTERVEINING	INTERWORKINGS	INTOLERABLY	INTRACTABLENESS
INTERTEXTUALITY	INTERVEINS	INTERWORKS	INTOLERANCE	INTRACTABLY
INTERTEXTUALLY	INTERVENED	INTERWOUND	INTOLERANCES	INTRACUTANEOUS
INTERTEXTURE	INTERVENER	INTERWOVEN	INTOLERANT	INTRADERMAL
INTERTEXTURES	INTERVENERS	INTERWREATHE	INTOLERANTLY	INTRADERMALLY
INTERTIDAL	INTERVENES	INTERWREATHED	INTOLERANTNESS	INTRADERMIC
INTERTIDALLY	INTERVENIENT	INTERWREATHES	INTOLERANTS	INTRADERMICALLY
INTERTILLAGE	INTERVENING	INTERWREATHING	INTOLERATION	INTRADOSES
INTERTILLAGES	INTERVENOR	INTERWROUGHT	INTOLERATIONS	INTRAFALLOPIAN
INTERTILLED	INTERVENORS	INTERZONAL	INTONATING	INTRAFASCICULAR
INTERTILLING	INTERVENTION	INTERZONES	INTONATION	INTRAGALACTIC
INTERTILLS	INTERVENTIONAL	INTESTACIES	INTONATIONAL	INTRAGENIC
INTERTISSUED	INTERVENTIONISM	INTESTATES	INTONATIONS	INTRAMEDULLARY

INTRAMERCURIAL	INTRATELLURIC	INTRINSICAL	INTROSPECTS	INTUMESCENCY
INTRAMOLECULAR	INTRATHECAL	INTRINSICALITY	INTROSUSCEPTION	INTUMESCENT
INTRAMUNDANE	INTRATHECALLY	INTRINSICALLY	INTROVERSIBLE	INTUMESCES
INTRAMURAL	INTRATHORACIC	INTRINSICALNESS	INTROVERSION	INTUMESCING
INTRAMURALLY	INTRAUTERINE	INTRINSICATE	INTROVERSIONS	INTURBIDATE
INTRAMUSCULAR	INTRAVASATION	INTRODUCED	INTROVERSIVE	INTURBIDATED
INTRAMUSCULARLY	INTRAVASATIONS	INTRODUCER	INTROVERSIVELY	INTURBIDATES
INTRANASAL	INTRAVASCULAR	INTRODUCERS	INTROVERTED	INTURBIDATING
INTRANASALLY	INTRAVASCULARLY	INTRODUCES	INTROVERTING	INTUSSUSCEPT
INTRANATIONAL	INTRAVENOUS	INTRODUCIBLE	INTROVERTIVE	INTUSSUSCEPTED
INTRANSIGEANCE	INTRAVENOUSLY	INTRODUCING	INTROVERTS	INTUSSUSCEPTING
INTRANSIGEANCES	INTRAVITAL	INTRODUCTION	INTRUDINGLY	INTUSSUSCEPTION
INTRANSIGEANT	INTRAVITALLY	INTRODUCTIONS	INTRUSIONAL	INTUSSUSCEPTIVE
INTRANSIGEANTLY	INTRAVITAM	INTRODUCTIVE	INTRUSIONIST	INTUSSUSCEPTS
INTRANSIGEANTS	INTRAZONAL	INTRODUCTORILY	INTRUSIONISTS	INTWINEMENT
INTRANSIGENCE	INTREATFULL	INTRODUCTORY	INTRUSIONS	INTWINEMENTS
INTRANSIGENCES	INTREATING	INTROFYING	INTRUSIVELY	INTWISTING
INTRANSIGENCIES	INTREATINGLY	INTROGRESSANT	INTRUSIVENESS	INUMBRATED
INTRANSIGENCY	INTREATMENT	INTROGRESSANTS	INTRUSIVENESSES	INUMBRATES
INTRANSIGENT	INTREATMENTS	INTROGRESSION	INTRUSIVES	INUMBRATING
INTRANSIGENTISM	INTRENCHANT	INTROGRESSIONS	INTRUSTING	INUNCTIONS
INTRANSIGENTIST	INTRENCHED	INTROGRESSIVE	INTRUSTMENT	INUNDATING
INTRANSIGENTLY	INTRENCHER	INTROITUSES	INTRUSTMENTS	INUNDATION
INTRANSIGENTS	INTRENCHERS	INTROJECTED	INTUBATING	INUNDATIONS
INTRANSITIVE	INTRENCHES	INTROJECTING	INTUBATION	INUNDATORS
INTRANSITIVELY	INTRENCHING	INTROJECTION	INTUBATIONS	INUNDATORY
INTRANSITIVITY	INTRENCHMENT	INTROJECTIONS	INTUITABLE	INURBANELY
INTRANSMISSIBLE	INTRENCHMENTS	INTROJECTIVE	INTUITIONAL	INURBANITIES
INTRANSMUTABLE	INTREPIDITIES	INTROJECTS	INTUITIONALISM	INURBANITY
INTRANUCLEAR	INTREPIDITY	INTROMISSIBLE	INTUITIONALISMS	INUREDNESS
INTRAOCULAR	INTREPIDLY	INTROMISSION	INTUITIONALIST	INUREDNESSES
INTRAOCULARLY	INTREPIDNESS	INTROMISSIONS	INTUITIONALISTS	INUREMENTS
INTRAPARIETAL	INTREPIDNESSES	INTROMISSIVE	INTUITIONALLY	INURNMENTS
INTRAPARTUM	INTRICACIES	INTROMITTED	INTUITIONISM	INUSITATION
INTRAPERITONEAL	INTRICATELY	INTROMITTENT	INTUITIONISMS	INUSITATIONS
INTRAPERSONAL	INTRICATENESS	INTROMITTER	INTUITIONIST	INUTILITIES
INTRAPETIOLAR	INTRICATENESSES	INTROMITTERS	INTUITIONISTS	INUTTERABLE
INTRAPLATE	INTRIGANTE	INTROMITTING	INTUITIONS	INVAGINABLE
INTRAPOPULATION	INTRIGANTES	INTRORSELY	INTUITIVELY	INVAGINATE
INTRAPRENEUR	INTRIGANTS	INTROSPECT	INTUITIVENESS	INVAGINATED
INTRAPRENEURIAL	INTRIGUANT	INTROSPECTED	INTUITIVENESSES	INVAGINATES
INTRAPRENEURS	INTRIGUANTE	INTROSPECTING	INTUITIVISM	INVAGINATING
INTRAPSYCHIC	INTRIGUANTES	INTROSPECTION	INTUITIVISMS	INVAGINATION
INTRASEXUAL	INTRIGUANTS	INTROSPECTIONAL	INTUMESCED	INVAGINATIONS
INTRASPECIES	INTRIGUERS	INTROSPECTIONS	INTUMESCENCE	INVALIDATE
INTRASPECIFIC	INTRIGUING	INTROSPECTIVE	INTUMESCENCES	INVALIDATED
INTRASTATE	INTRIGUINGLY	INTROSPECTIVELY	INTUMESCENCIES	INVALIDATES

INVALIDATING	INVENTIONAL	INVETERACY	INVISIBILITIES	INVULTUATION
INVALIDATION	INVENTIONLESS	INVETERATE	INVISIBILITY	INVULTUATIONS
INVALIDATIONS	INVENTIONS	INVETERATELY	INVISIBLENESS	INWARDNESS
INVALIDATOR	INVENTIVELY	INVETERATENESS	INVISIBLENESSES	INWARDNESSES
INVALIDATORS	INVENTIVENESS	INVIABILITIES	INVISIBLES	INWORKINGS
INVALIDHOOD	INVENTIVENESSES	INVIABILITY	INVITATION	INWRAPPING
INVALIDHOODS	INVENTORIABLE	INVIABLENESS	INVITATIONAL	INWREATHED
INVALIDING	INVENTORIAL	INVIABLENESSES	INVITATIONALS	INWREATHES
INVALIDINGS	INVENTORIALLY	INVIDIOUSLY	INVITATIONS	INWREATHING
INVALIDISM	INVENTORIED	INVIDIOUSNESS	INVITATORIES	IODINATING
INVALIDISMS	INVENTORIES	INVIDIOUSNESSES	INVITATORY	IODINATION
INVALIDITIES	INVENTORYING	INVIGILATE	INVITEMENT	IODINATIONS
INVALIDITY	INVENTRESS	INVIGILATED	INVITEMENTS	IODISATION
INVALIDNESS	INVENTRESSES	INVIGILATES	INVITINGLY	IODISATIONS
INVALIDNESSES	INVERACITIES	INVIGILATING	INVITINGNESS	IODIZATION
INVALUABLE	INVERACITY	INVIGILATION	INVITINGNESSES	IODIZATIONS
INVALUABLENESS	INVERITIES	INVIGILATIONS	INVOCATING	IODOMETRIC
INVALUABLY	INVERNESSES	INVIGILATOR	INVOCATION	IODOMETRICAL
INVARIABILITIES	INVERSIONS	INVIGILATORS	INVOCATIONAL	IODOMETRICALLY
INVARIABILITY	INVERTASES	INVIGORANT	INVOCATIONS	IODOMETRIES
INVARIABLE	INVERTEBRAL	INVIGORANTS	INVOCATIVE	IONICITIES
INVARIABLENESS	INVERTEBRATE	INVIGORATE	INVOCATORS	IONISATION
INVARIABLES	INVERTEBRATES	INVIGORATED	INVOCATORY	IONISATIONS
INVARIABLY	INVERTEDLY	INVIGORATES	INVOLUCELLA	IONIZATION
INVARIANCE	INVERTIBILITIES	INVIGORATING	INVOLUCELLATE	IONIZATIONS
INVARIANCES	INVERTIBILITY	INVIGORATINGLY	INVOLUCELLATED	IONOPAUSES
INVARIANCIES	INVERTIBLE	INVIGORATION	INVOLUCELLUM	IONOPHORES
INVARIANCY	INVESTABLE	INVIGORATIONS	INVOLUCELS	IONOPHORESES
INVARIANTS	INVESTIBLE	INVIGORATIVE	INVOLUCRAL	IONOPHORESIS
INVASIVENESS	INVESTIGABLE	INVIGORATIVELY	INVOLUCRATE	IONOSONDES
INVASIVENESSES	INVESTIGATE	INVIGORATOR	INVOLUCRES	IONOSPHERE
INVEAGLING	INVESTIGATED	INVIGORATORS	INVOLUCRUM	IONOSPHERES
INVECTIVELY	INVESTIGATES	INVINCIBILITIES	INVOLUNTARILY	IONOSPHERIC
INVECTIVENESS	INVESTIGATING	INVINCIBILITY	INVOLUNTARINESS	IONOSPHERICALLY
INVECTIVENESSES	INVESTIGATION	INVINCIBLE	INVOLUNTARY	IONOTROPIC
INVECTIVES	INVESTIGATIONAL	INVINCIBLENESS	INVOLUTEDLY	IONOTROPIES
INVEIGHERS	INVESTIGATIONS	INVINCIBLY	INVOLUTELY	IONTOPHORESES
INVEIGHING	INVESTIGATIVE	INVIOLABILITIES	INVOLUTING	IONTOPHORESIS
INVEIGLEMENT	INVESTIGATOR	INVIOLABILITY	INVOLUTION	IONTOPHORETIC
INVEIGLEMENTS	INVESTIGATORS	INVIOLABLE	INVOLUTIONAL	IPECACUANHA
INVEIGLERS	INVESTIGATORY	INVIOLABLENESS	INVOLUTIONS	IPECACUANHAS
INVEIGLING	INVESTITIVE	INVIOLABLY	INVOLVEDLY	IPRATROPIUM
INVENDIBILITIES	INVESTITURE	INVIOLACIES	INVOLVEMENT	IPRATROPIUMS
INVENDIBILITY	INVESTITURES	INVIOLATED	INVOLVEMENTS	IPRINDOLES
INVENDIBLE	INVESTMENT	INVIOLATELY	INVULNERABILITY	IPRONIAZID
INVENTABLE	INVESTMENTS	INVIOLATENESS	INVULNERABLE	IPRONIAZIDS
INVENTIBLE	INVETERACIES	INVIOLATENESSES	INVULNERABLY	IPSELATERAL

IPSILATERAL	IRONMONGERIES	IRREALIZABLE	IRREFRAGABLE	IRREPAIRABLE
IPSILATERALLY	IRONMONGERS	IRREBUTTABLE	IRREFRAGABLY	IRREPARABILITY
IRACUNDITIES	IRONMONGERY	IRRECEPTIVE	IRREFRANGIBLE	IRREPARABLE
IRACUNDITY	IRONNESSES	IRRECIPROCAL	IRREFRANGIBLY	IRREPARABLENESS
IRACUNDULOUS	IRONSMITHS	IRRECIPROCITIES	IRREFUTABILITY	IRREPARABLY
IRASCIBILITIES	IRONSTONES	IRRECIPROCITY	IRREFUTABLE	IRREPEALABILITY
IRASCIBILITY	IRONWORKER	IRRECLAIMABLE	IRREFUTABLENESS	IRREPEALABLE
IRASCIBLENESS	IRONWORKERS	IRRECLAIMABLY	IRREFUTABLY	IRREPEALABLY
IRASCIBLENESSES	IRRADIANCE	IRRECOGNISABLE	IRREGARDLESS	IRREPLACEABLE
IRATENESSES	IRRADIANCES	IRRECOGNITION	IRREGULARITIES	IRREPLACEABLY
IREFULNESS	IRRADIANCIES	IRRECOGNITIONS	IRREGULARITY	IRREPLEVIABLE
IREFULNESSES	IRRADIANCY	IRRECOGNIZABLE	IRREGULARLY	IRREPLEVISABLE
IRENICALLY	IRRADIATED	IRRECONCILABLE	IRREGULARS	IRREPREHENSIBLE
IRENICISMS	IRRADIATES	IRRECONCILABLES	IRRELATION	IRREPREHENSIBLY
IRENOLOGIES	IRRADIATING	IRRECONCILABLY	IRRELATIONS	IRREPRESSIBLE
IRIDACEOUS	IRRADIATION	IRRECONCILED	IRRELATIVE	IRREPRESSIBLY
IRIDECTOMIES	IRRADIATIONS	IRRECONCILEMENT	IRRELATIVELY	IRREPROACHABLE
IRIDECTOMY	IRRADIATIVE	IRRECOVERABLE	IRRELATIVENESS	IRREPROACHABLY
IRIDESCENCE	IRRADIATOR	IRRECOVERABLY	IRRELEVANCE	IRREPRODUCIBLE
IRIDESCENCES	IRRADIATORS	IRRECUSABLE	IRRELEVANCES	IRREPROVABLE
IRIDESCENT	IRRADICABLE	IRRECUSABLY	IRRELEVANCIES	IRREPROVABLY
IRIDESCENTLY	IRRADICABLY	IRREDEEMABILITY	IRRELEVANCY	IRRESISTANCE
IRIDISATION	IRRADICATE	IRREDEEMABLE	IRRELEVANT	IRRESISTANCES
IRIDISATIONS	IRRADICATED	IRREDEEMABLES	IRRELEVANTLY	IRRESISTIBILITY
IRIDIZATION	IRRADICATES	IRREDEEMABLY	IRRELIEVABLE	IRRESISTIBLE
IRIDIZATIONS	IRRADICATING	IRREDENTAS	IRRELIGION	IRRESISTIBLY
IRIDOCYTES	IRRATIONAL	IRREDENTISM	IRRELIGIONIST	IRRESOLUBILITY
IRIDOLOGIES	IRRATIONALISE	IRREDENTISMS	IRRELIGIONISTS	IRRESOLUBLE
IRIDOLOGIST	IRRATIONALISED	IRREDENTIST	IRRELIGIONS	IRRESOLUBLY
IRIDOLOGISTS	IRRATIONALISES	IRREDENTISTS	IRRELIGIOUS	IRRESOLUTE
IRIDOSMINE	IRRATIONALISING	IRREDUCIBILITY	IRRELIGIOUSLY	IRRESOLUTELY
IRIDOSMINES	IRRATIONALISM	IRREDUCIBLE	IRRELIGIOUSNESS	IRRESOLUTENESS
IRIDOSMIUM	IRRATIONALISMS	IRREDUCIBLENESS	IRREMEABLE	IRRESOLUTION
IRIDOSMIUMS	IRRATIONALIST	IRREDUCIBLY	IRREMEABLY	IRRESOLUTIONS
IRIDOTOMIES	IRRATIONALISTIC	IRREDUCTIBILITY	IRREMEDIABLE	IRRESOLVABILITY
IRISATIONS	IRRATIONALISTS	IRREDUCTION	IRREMEDIABLY	IRRESOLVABLE
IRKSOMENESS	IRRATIONALITIES	IRREDUCTIONS	IRREMISSIBILITY	IRRESOLVABLY
IRKSOMENESSES	IRRATIONALITY	IRREFLECTION	IRREMISSIBLE	IRRESPECTIVE
IRONFISTED	IRRATIONALIZE	IRREFLECTIONS	IRREMISSIBLY	IRRESPECTIVELY
IRONHANDED	IRRATIONALIZED	IRREFLECTIVE	IRREMISSION	IRRESPIRABLE
IRONHEARTED	IRRATIONALIZES	IRREFLEXION	IRREMISSIONS	IRRESPONSIBLE
IRONICALLY	IRRATIONALIZING	IRREFLEXIONS	IRREMISSIVE	IRRESPONSIBLES
IRONICALNESS	IRRATIONALLY	IRREFLEXIVE	IRREMOVABILITY	IRRESPONSIBLY
IRONICALNESSES	IRRATIONALNESS	IRREFORMABILITY	IRREMOVABLE	IRRESPONSIVE
IRONMASTER	IRRATIONALS	IRREFORMABLE	IRREMOVABLENESS	IRRESPONSIVELY
IRONMASTERS	IRREALISABLE	IRREFORMABLY	IRREMOVABLY	IRRESTRAINABLE
IRONMONGER	IRREALITIES	IRREFRAGABILITY	IRRENOWNED	IRRESUSCITABLE

IRRESUSCITABLY	ISCHAEMIAS	ISOCHRONISING	ISOGLOSSIC	ISONIAZIDES
IRRETENTION	ISCHURETIC	ISOCHRONISM	ISOGLOTTAL	ISONIAZIDS
IRRETENTIONS	ISCHURETICS	ISOCHRONISMS	ISOGLOTTIC	ISONITRILE
IRRETENTIVE	ISEIKONIAS	ISOCHRONIZE	ISOGRAFTED	ISONITRILES
IRRETENTIVENESS	ISENTROPIC	ISOCHRONIZED	ISOGRAFTING	ISOOCTANES
IRRETRIEVABLE	ISENTROPICALLY	ISOCHRONIZES	ISOHYETALS	ISOPACHYTE
IRRETRIEVABLY	ISINGLASSES	ISOCHRONIZING	ISOIMMUNISATION	ISOPACHYTES
IRREVERENCE	ISLOMANIAS	ISOCHRONOUS	ISOIMMUNIZATION	ISOPERIMETER
IRREVERENCES	ISMATICALNESS	ISOCHRONOUSLY	ISOKINETIC	ISOPERIMETERS
IRREVERENT	ISMATICALNESSES	ISOCHROOUS	ISOKONTANS	ISOPERIMETRICAL
IRREVERENTIAL	ISOAGGLUTININ	ISOCLINALS	ISOLABILITIES	ISOPERIMETRIES
IRREVERENTLY	ISOAGGLUTININS	ISOCLINICS	ISOLABILITY	ISOPERIMETRY
IRREVERSIBILITY	ISOALLOXAZINE	ISOCRACIES	ISOLATABLE	ISOPIESTIC
IRREVERSIBLE	ISOALLOXAZINES	ISOCRYMALS	ISOLATIONISM	ISOPIESTICALLY
IRREVERSIBLY	ISOAMINILE	ISOCYANATE	ISOLATIONISMS	ISOPLETHIC
IRREVOCABILITY	ISOAMINILES	ISOCYANATES	ISOLATIONIST	ISOPOLITIES
IRREVOCABLE	ISOANTIBODIES	ISOCYANIDE	ISOLATIONISTS	ISOPRENALINE
IRREVOCABLENESS	ISOANTIBODY	ISOCYANIDES	ISOLATIONS	ISOPRENALINES
IRREVOCABLY	ISOANTIGEN	ISODIAMETRIC	ISOLECITHAL	ISOPRENOID
IRRIDENTAS	ISOANTIGENIC	ISODIAMETRICAL	ISOLEUCINE	ISOPROPYLS
IRRIGATING	ISOANTIGENS	ISODIAPHERE	ISOLEUCINES	ISOPROTERENOL
IRRIGATION	ISOBARISMS	ISODIAPHERES	ISOMAGNETIC	ISOPROTERENOLS
IRRIGATIONAL	ISOBAROMETRIC	ISODIMORPHIC	ISOMAGNETICS	ISOPTERANS
IRRIGATIONS	ISOBILATERAL	ISODIMORPHISM	ISOMERASES	ISOPTEROUS
IRRIGATIVE	ISOBUTANES	ISODIMORPHISMS	ISOMERISATION	ISOPYCNALS
IRRIGATORS	ISOBUTENES	ISODIMORPHOUS	ISOMERISATIONS	ISOPYCNICS
IRRITABILITIES	ISOBUTYLENE	ISODONTALS	ISOMERISED	ISORHYTHMIC
IRRITABILITY	ISOBUTYLENES	ISODYNAMIC	ISOMERISES	ISOSEISMAL
IRRITABLENESS	ISOCALORIC	ISODYNAMICS	ISOMERISING	ISOSEISMALS
IRRITABLENESSES	ISOCARBOXAZID	ISOELECTRIC	ISOMERISMS	ISOSEISMIC
IRRITANCIES	ISOCARBOXAZIDS	ISOELECTRONIC	ISOMERIZATION	ISOSEISMICS
IRRITATEDLY	ISOCHASMIC	ISOENZYMATIC	ISOMERIZATIONS	ISOSMOTICALLY
IRRITATING	ISOCHEIMAL	ISOENZYMES	ISOMERIZED	ISOSPONDYLOUS
IRRITATINGLY	ISOCHEIMALS	ISOENZYMIC	ISOMERIZES	ISOSPORIES
IRRITATION	ISOCHEIMENAL	ISOFLAVONE	ISOMERIZING	ISOSPOROUS
IRRITATIONS	ISOCHEIMENALS	ISOFLAVONES	ISOMETRICAL	ISOSTACIES
IRRITATIVE	ISOCHEIMIC	ISOGAMETES	ISOMETRICALLY	ISOSTASIES
IRRITATORS	ISOCHIMALS	ISOGAMETIC	ISOMETRICS	ISOSTATICALLY
IRROTATIONAL	ISOCHROMATIC	ISOGENETIC	ISOMETRIES	ISOSTEMONOUS
IRRUPTIONS	ISOCHROMOSOME	ISOGEOTHERM	ISOMETROPIA	ISOSTHENURIA
IRRUPTIVELY	ISOCHROMOSOMES	ISOGEOTHERMAL	ISOMETROPIAS	ISOSTHENURIAS
IRUKANDJIS	ISOCHRONAL	ISOGEOTHERMALS	ISOMORPHIC	ISOTENISCOPE
ISABELLINE	ISOCHRONALLY	ISOGEOTHERMIC	ISOMORPHICALLY	ISOTENISCOPES
ISABELLINES	ISOCHRONES	ISOGEOTHERMICS	ISOMORPHISM	ISOTHERALS
ISALLOBARIC	ISOCHRONISE	ISOGEOTHERMS	ISOMORPHISMS	ISOTHERMAL
ISALLOBARS	ISOCHRONISED	ISOGLOSSAL	ISOMORPHOUS	ISOTHERMALLY
ISAPOSTOLIC	ISOCHRONISES	ISOGLOSSES	ISONIAZIDE	ISOTHERMALS

ISOTONICALLY	ITACOLUMITES	ITALICISED	ITERATIVENESS	ITINERARIES
ISOTONICITIES	ITALIANATE	ITALICISES	ITERATIVENESSES	ITINERATED
ISOTONICITY	ITALIANATED	ITALICISING	ITEROPARITIES	ITINERATES
ISOTOPICALLY	ITALIANATES	ITALICIZATION	ITEROPARITY	ITINERATING
ISOTRETINOIN	ITALIANATING	ITALICIZATIONS	ITEROPAROUS	ITINERATION
ISOTRETINOINS	ITALIANISE	ITALICIZED	ITHYPHALLI	ITINERATIONS
ISOTROPICALLY	ITALIANISED	ITALICIZES	ITHYPHALLIC	IVERMECTIN
ISOTROPIES	ITALIANISES	ITALICIZING	ITHYPHALLICS	IVERMECTINS
ISOTROPISM	ITALIANISING	ITCHINESSES	ITHYPHALLUS	IVORYBILLS
ISOTROPISMS	ITALIANIZE	ITEMISATION	ITHYPHALLUSES	IVORYWOODS
ISOTROPOUS	ITALIANIZED	ITEMISATIONS	ITINERACIES	IZVESTIYAS
ISOXSUPRINE	ITALIANIZES	ITEMIZATION	ITINERANCIES	
ISOXSUPRINES	ITALIANIZING	ITEMIZATIONS	ITINERANCY	
ISPAGHULAS	ITALICISATION	ITERATIONS	ITINERANTLY	
ITACOLUMITE	ITALICISATIONS	ITERATIVELY	ITINERANTS	

I

J

JABBERINGLY	JACKSTONES	JARGONELLE	JEALOUSHOODS	JERKWATERS
JABBERINGS	JACKSTRAWS	JARGONELLES	JEALOUSIES	JERRYMANDER
JABBERWOCK	JACQUERIES	JARGONISATION	JEALOUSING	JERRYMANDERED
JABBERWOCKIES	JACTATIONS	JARGONISATIONS	JEALOUSNESS	JERRYMANDERING
JABBERWOCKS	JACTITATION	JARGONISED	JEALOUSNESSES	JERRYMANDERS
JABBERWOCKY	JACTITATIONS	JARGONISES	JEISTIECOR	JESSAMINES
JABORANDIS	JACULATING	JARGONISING	JEISTIECORS	JESSERANTS
JABOTICABA	JACULATION	JARGONISTIC	JEJUNENESS	JESUITICAL
JABOTICABAS	JACULATIONS	JARGONISTS	JEJUNENESSES	JESUITICALLY
JACARANDAS	JACULATORS	JARGONIZATION	JEJUNITIES	JESUITISMS
JACKALLING	JACULATORY	JARGONIZATIONS	JEJUNOSTOMIES	JESUITRIES
JACKANAPES	JADEDNESSES	JARGONIZED	JEJUNOSTOMY	JETSTREAMS
JACKANAPESES	JAGGEDNESS	JARGONIZES	JELLIFICATION	JETTATURAS
JACKAROOED	JAGGEDNESSES	JARGONIZING	JELLIFICATIONS	JETTINESSES
JACKAROOING	JAGGHERIES	JARLSBERGS	JELLIFYING	JETTISONABLE
JACKASSERIES	JAGHIRDARS	JAROVISING	JELLYBEANS	JETTISONED
JACKASSERY	JAGUARONDI	JAROVIZING	JELLYFISHES	JETTISONING
JACKBOOTED	JAGUARONDIS	JASMONATES	JELLYGRAPH	JEWELFISHES
JACKBOOTING	JAGUARUNDI	JASPERISED	JELLYGRAPHED	JEWELLERIES
JACKEROOED	JAGUARUNDIS	JASPERISES	JELLYGRAPHING	JEWELWEEDS
JACKEROOING	JAILBREAKS	JASPERISING	JELLYGRAPHS	JICKAJOGGED
JACKETLESS	JAILERESSES	JASPERIZED	JELLYROLLS	JICKAJOGGING
JACKFISHES	JAILHOUSES	JASPERIZES	JEMMINESSES	JIGAJIGGED
JACKFRUITS	JAILORESSES	JASPERIZING	JENNETINGS	JIGAJIGGING
JACKHAMMER	JAMAHIRIYA	JASPERWARE	JEOPARDERS	JIGAJOGGED
JACKHAMMERED	JAMAHIRIYAS	JASPERWARES	JEOPARDIED	JIGAJOGGING
JACKHAMMERING	JAMBALAYAS	JASPIDEOUS	JEOPARDIES	JIGAMAREES
JACKHAMMERS	JAMBOKKING	JASPILITES	JEOPARDING	JIGGERMAST
JACKKNIFED	JAMBOLANAS	JAUNDICING	JEOPARDISE	JIGGERMASTS
JACKKNIFES	JANISARIES	JAUNTINESS	JEOPARDISED	JIGGUMBOBS
JACKKNIFING	JANISSARIES	JAUNTINESSES	JEOPARDISES	JIGJIGGING
JACKKNIVES	JANITORIAL	JAUNTINGLY	JEOPARDISING	JILLFLIRTS
JACKLIGHTED	JANITORSHIP	JAVELINING	JEOPARDIZE	JIMPNESSES
JACKLIGHTING	JANITORSHIPS	JAWBATIONS	JEOPARDIZED	JIMSONWEED
JACKLIGHTS	JANITRESSES	JAWBONINGS	JEOPARDIZES	JIMSONWEEDS
JACKPLANES	JANITRIXES	JAWBREAKER	JEOPARDIZING	JINGOISTIC
JACKRABBIT	JANIZARIAN	JAWBREAKERS	JEOPARDOUS	JINGOISTICALLY
JACKRABBITS	JANIZARIES	JAWCRUSHER	JEOPARDOUSLY	JINRICKSHA
JACKROLLED	JAPANISING	JAWCRUSHERS	JEOPARDYING	JINRICKSHAS
JACKROLLING	JAPANIZING	JAYHAWKERS	JEQUERITIES	JINRICKSHAW
JACKSCREWS	JAPONAISERIE	JAYWALKERS	JEQUIRITIES	JINRICKSHAWS
JACKSHAFTS	JAPONAISERIES	JAYWALKING	JERFALCONS	JINRIKISHA
JACKSMELTS	JARDINIERE	JAYWALKINGS	JERKINESSES	JINRIKISHAS
JACKSMITHS	JARDINIERES	JAZZINESSES	JERKINHEAD	JINRIKSHAS
JACKSNIPES	JARGONEERS	JEALOUSHOOD	JERKINHEADS	JITTERBUGGED

JITTERBUGGING	JOLLIFICATION	JOURNEYWORK	JUDICATURES	JURISPRUDENCE
JITTERBUGS	JOLLIFICATIONS	JOURNEYWORKS	JUDICIALLY	JURISPRUDENCES
JITTERIEST	JOLLIFYING	JOUYSAUNCE	JUDICIARIES	JURISPRUDENT
JITTERINESS	JOLLIMENTS	JOUYSAUNCES	JUDICIARILY	JURISPRUDENTIAL
JITTERINESSES	JOLLINESSES	JOVIALITIES	JUDICIOUSLY	JURISPRUDENTS
JOBCENTRES	JOLLYBOATS	JOVIALNESS	JUDICIOUSNESS	JURISTICAL
JOBERNOWLS	JOLLYHEADS	JOVIALNESSES	JUDICIOUSNESSES	JURISTICALLY
JOBHOLDERS	JOLTERHEAD	JOVIALTIES	JUGGERNAUT	JUSTICESHIP
JOBLESSNESS	JOLTERHEADS	JOVYSAUNCE	JUGGERNAUTS	JUSTICESHIPS
JOBLESSNESSES	JONNYCAKES	JOVYSAUNCES	JUGGLERIES	JUSTICIABILITY
JOBSEEKERS	JOSEPHINITE	JOWLINESSES	JUGGLINGLY	JUSTICIABLE
JOBSWORTHS	JOSEPHINITES	JOYFULLEST	JUGLANDACEOUS	JUSTICIALISM
JOCKEYISMS	JOSTLEMENT	JOYFULNESS	JUGULATING	JUSTICIALISMS
JOCKEYSHIP	JOSTLEMENTS	JOYFULNESSES	JUGULATION	JUSTICIARIES
JOCKEYSHIPS	JOUISANCES	JOYLESSNESS	JUGULATIONS	JUSTICIARS
JOCKSTRAPS	JOURNALESE	JOYLESSNESSES	JUICEHEADS	JUSTICIARSHIP
JOCKTELEGS	JOURNALESES	JOYOUSNESS	JUICINESSES	JUSTICIARSHIPS
JOCOSENESS	JOURNALING	JOYOUSNESSES	JULIENNING	JUSTICIARY
JOCOSENESSES	JOURNALISATION	JOYPOPPERS	JUMBLINGLY	JUSTIFIABILITY
JOCOSERIOUS	JOURNALISATIONS	JOYPOPPING	JUMBOISING	JUSTIFIABLE
JOCOSITIES	JOURNALISE	JOYRIDINGS	JUMBOIZING	JUSTIFIABLENESS
JOCULARITIES	JOURNALISED	JUBILANCES	JUMHOURIYA	JUSTIFIABLY
JOCULARITY	JOURNALISER	JUBILANCIES	JUMHOURIYAS	JUSTIFICATION
JOCULATORS	JOURNALISERS	JUBILANTLY	JUMPINESSES	JUSTIFICATIONS
JOCUNDITIES	JOURNALISES	JUBILARIAN	JUNCACEOUS	JUSTIFICATIVE
JOCUNDNESS	JOURNALISING	JUBILARIANS	JUNCTIONAL	JUSTIFICATOR
JOCUNDNESSES	JOURNALISM	JUBILATING	JUNEATINGS	JUSTIFICATORS
JOHANNESES	JOURNALISMS	JUBILATION	JUNGLEGYMS	JUSTIFICATORY
JOHNNYCAKE	JOURNALIST	JUBILATIONS	JUNGLELIKE	JUSTIFIERS
JOHNNYCAKES	JOURNALISTIC	JUDGEMENTAL	JUNIORATES	JUSTIFYING
JOHNSONGRASS	JOURNALISTS	JUDGEMENTALLY	JUNIORITIES	JUSTNESSES
JOHNSONGRASSES	JOURNALIZATION	JUDGEMENTS	JUNKETEERED	JUVENESCENCE
JOINTEDNESS	JOURNALIZATIONS	JUDGESHIPS	JUNKETEERING	JUVENESCENCES
JOINTEDNESSES	JOURNALIZE	JUDGMATICAL	JUNKETEERS	JUVENESCENT
JOINTNESSES	JOURNALIZED	JUDGMATICALLY	JUNKETINGS	JUVENILELY
JOINTRESSES	JOURNALIZER	JUDGMENTAL	JUNKETTERS	JUVENILENESS
JOINTURESS	JOURNALIZERS	JUDGMENTALLY	JUNKETTING	JUVENILENESSES
JOINTURESSES	JOURNALIZES	JUDICATION	JUNKINESSES	JUVENILITIES
JOINTURING	JOURNALIZING	JUDICATIONS	JURIDICALLY	JUVENILITY
JOINTWEEDS	JOURNALLED	JUDICATIVE	JURISCONSULT	JUXTAPOSED
JOINTWORMS	JOURNALLING	JUDICATORIAL	JURISCONSULTS	JUXTAPOSES
JOKESMITHS	JOURNEYERS	JUDICATORIES	JURISDICTION	JUXTAPOSING
JOKINESSES	JOURNEYING	JUDICATORS	JURISDICTIONAL	JUXTAPOSITION
JOLIOTIUMS	JOURNEYMAN	JUDICATORY	JURISDICTIONS	JUXTAPOSITIONAL
JOLLEYINGS	JOURNEYMEN	JUDICATURE	JURISDICTIVE	JUXTAPOSITIONS

J

K

KABALISTIC	KAMELAUKION	KARYOLYSIS	KEFUFFLING	KERAUNOGRAPHS
KABARAGOYA	KAMELAUKIONS	KARYOLYTIC	KEKERENGUS	KERBSTONES
KABARAGOYAS	KAMERADING	KARYOMAPPING	KELYPHITIC	KERCHIEFED
KABBALISMS	KANAMYCINS	KARYOMAPPINGS	KENNELLING	KERCHIEFING
KABBALISTIC	KANGAROOED	KARYOPLASM	KENNETTING	KERCHIEVES
KABBALISTS	KANGAROOING	KARYOPLASMIC	KENOGENESES	KERFUFFLED
KABELJOUWS	KANTIKOYED	KARYOPLASMS	KENOGENESIS	KERFUFFLES
KADAITCHAS	KANTIKOYING	KARYOSOMES	KENOGENETIC	KERFUFFLING
KAFFEEKLATSCH	KAOLINISED	KARYOTYPED	KENOGENETICALLY	KERMESITES
KAFFEEKLATSCHES	KAOLINISES	KARYOTYPES	KENOPHOBIA	KERNELLING
KAFFIRBOOM	KAOLINISING	KARYOTYPIC	KENOPHOBIAS	KERNICTERUS
KAFFIRBOOMS	KAOLINITES	KARYOTYPICAL	KENOTICIST	KERNICTERUSES
KAHIKATEAS	KAOLINITIC	KARYOTYPICALLY	KENOTICISTS	KERNMANTEL
KAHIKATOAS	KAOLINIZED	KARYOTYPING	KENSPECKLE	KERPLUNKED
KAIKAWAKAS	KAOLINIZES	KATABOLICALLY	KENTLEDGES	KERPLUNKING
KAIKOMAKOS	KAOLINIZING	KATABOLISM	KERATECTOMIES	KERSANTITE
KAILYAIRDS	KAOLINOSES	KATABOLISMS	KERATECTOMY	KERSANTITES
KAINOGENESES	KAOLINOSIS	KATABOTHRON	KERATINISATION	KERSEYMERE
KAINOGENESIS	KAPELLMEISTER	KATABOTHRONS	KERATINISATIONS	KERSEYMERES
KAINOGENETIC	KAPELLMEISTERS	KATADROMOUS	KERATINISE	KERYGMATIC
KAIROMONES	KARABINERS	KATATHERMOMETER	KERATINISED	KETOGENESES
KAISERDOMS	KARANGAING	KATAVOTHRON	KERATINISES	KETOGENESIS
KAISERISMS	KARATEISTS	KATAVOTHRONS	KERATINISING	KETONAEMIA
KAISERSHIP	KARMICALLY	KATHAKALIS	KERATINIZATION	KETONAEMIAS
KAISERSHIPS	KARSTIFICATION	KATHAREVOUSA	KERATINIZATIONS	KETONEMIAS
KAKISTOCRACIES	KARSTIFICATIONS	KATHAREVOUSAS	KERATINIZE	KETONURIAS
KAKISTOCRACY	KARSTIFIED	KATHAROMETER	KERATINIZED	KETOSTEROID
KALAMKARIS	KARSTIFIES	KATHAROMETERS	KERATINIZES	KETOSTEROIDS
KALANCHOES	KARSTIFYING	KATZENJAMMER	KERATINIZING	KETTLEDRUM
KALASHNIKOV	KARUHIRUHI	KATZENJAMMERS	KERATINOPHILIC	KETTLEDRUMMER
KALASHNIKOVS	KARUHIRUHIS	KAWANATANGA	KERATINOUS	KETTLEDRUMMERS
KALEIDOPHONE	KARYOGAMIC	KAWANATANGAS	KERATITIDES	KETTLEDRUMS
KALEIDOPHONES	KARYOGAMIES	KAZATSKIES	KERATITISES	KETTLEFULS
KALEIDOSCOPE	KARYOGRAMS	KAZILLIONS	KERATOGENOUS	KETTLESTITCH
KALEIDOSCOPES	KARYOKINESES	KEELHALING	KERATOMATA	KETTLESTITCHES
KALEIDOSCOPIC	KARYOKINESIS	KEELHAULED	KERATOMETER	KEYBOARDED
KALENDARED	KARYOKINETIC	KEELHAULING	KERATOMETERS	KEYBOARDER
KALENDARING	KARYOLOGIC	KEELHAULINGS	KERATOPHYRE	KEYBOARDERS
KALIPHATES	KARYOLOGICAL	KEELIVINES	KERATOPHYRES	KEYBOARDING
KALLIKREIN	KARYOLOGIES	KEELYVINES	KERATOPLASTIC	KEYBOARDINGS
KALLIKREINS	KARYOLOGIST	KEENNESSES	KERATOPLASTIES	KEYBOARDIST
KALLITYPES	KARYOLOGISTS	KEEPERLESS	KERATOPLASTY	KEYBOARDISTS
KALSOMINED	KARYOLYMPH	KEEPERSHIP	KERATOTOMIES	KEYBUTTONS
KALSOMINES	KARYOLYMPHS	KEEPERSHIPS	KERATOTOMY	KEYLOGGERS
KALSOMINING	KARYOLYSES	KEESHONDEN	KERAUNOGRAPH	KEYLOGGING

KEYLOGGINGS	KIDDISHNESSES	KINDERGARTENER	KINESTHESIS	KISSPEPTINS
KEYPUNCHED	KIDDYWINKS	KINDERGARTENERS	KINESTHETIC	KITCHENALIA
KEYPUNCHER	KIDNAPINGS	KINDERGARTENS	KINESTHETICALLY	KITCHENALIAS
KEYPUNCHERS	KIDNAPPEES	KINDERGARTNER	KINETHEODOLITE	KITCHENDOM
KEYPUNCHES	KIDNAPPERS	KINDERGARTNERS	KINETHEODOLITES	KITCHENDOMS
KEYPUNCHING	KIDNAPPING	KINDERSPIEL	KINETICALLY	KITCHENERS
KEYSTONING	KIDNAPPINGS	KINDERSPIELS	KINETICIST	KITCHENETS
KEYSTROKED	KIDNEYLIKE	KINDHEARTED	KINETICISTS	KITCHENETTE
KEYSTROKES	KIDOLOGIES	KINDHEARTEDLY	KINETOCHORE	KITCHENETTES
KEYSTROKING	KIDOLOGIST	KINDHEARTEDNESS	KINETOCHORES	KITCHENING
KEYSTROKINGS	KIDOLOGISTS	KINDLESSLY	KINETOGRAPH	KITCHENWARE
KEYWORKERS	KIESELGUHR	KINDLINESS	KINETOGRAPHS	KITCHENWARES
KHALIFATES	KIESELGUHRS	KINDLINESSES	KINETONUCLEI	KITEBOARDS
KHANSAMAHS	KIESELGURS	KINDNESSES	KINETONUCLEUS	KITESURFING
KHEDIVATES	KIESERITES	KINDREDNESS	KINETONUCLEUSES	KITESURFINGS
KHEDIVIATE	KILDERKINS	KINDREDNESSES	KINETOPLAST	KITSCHIEST
KHEDIVIATES	KILLIFISHES	KINDREDSHIP	KINETOPLASTS	KITSCHIFIED
KHIDMUTGAR	KILLIKINICK	KINDREDSHIPS	KINETOSCOPE	KITSCHIFIES
KHIDMUTGARS	KILLIKINICKS	KINEMATICAL	KINETOSCOPES	KITSCHIFYING
KHITMUTGAR	KILOCALORIE	KINEMATICALLY	KINETOSOME	KITSCHNESS
KHITMUTGARS	KILOCALORIES	KINEMATICS	KINETOSOMES	KITSCHNESSES
KHUSKHUSES	KILOCURIES	KINEMATOGRAPH	KINGCRAFTS	KITTENISHLY
KIBBITZERS	KILOCYCLES	KINEMATOGRAPHER	KINGDOMLESS	KITTENISHNESS
KIBBITZING	KILOGAUSSES	KINEMATOGRAPHIC	KINGFISHER	KITTENISHNESSES
KIBBUTZNIK	KILOGRAMME	KINEMATOGRAPHS	KINGFISHERS	KITTIWAKES
KIBBUTZNIKS	KILOGRAMMES	KINEMATOGRAPHY	KINGFISHES	KIWIFRUITS
KICKABOUTS	KILOHERTZES	KINESCOPED	KINGLIHOOD	KIWISPORTS
KICKAROUND	KILOJOULES	KINESCOPES	KINGLIHOODS	KLANGFARBE
KICKAROUNDS	KILOLITERS	KINESCOPING	KINGLINESS	KLANGFARBES
KICKBOARDS	KILOLITRES	KINESIATRIC	KINGLINESSES	KLEBSIELLA
KICKBOXERS	KILOMETERS	KINESIATRICS	KINGMAKERS	KLEBSIELLAS
KICKBOXING	KILOMETRES	KINESIOLOGIES	KINGSNAKES	KLEINHUISIE
KICKBOXINGS	KILOMETRIC	KINESIOLOGIST	KINKINESSES	KLEINHUISIES
KICKFLIPPED	KILOMETRICAL	KINESIOLOGISTS	KINNIKINIC	KLENDUSITIES
KICKFLIPPING	KILOPARSEC	KINESIOLOGY	KINNIKINICK	KLENDUSITY
KICKSHAWSES	KILOPARSECS	KINESIPATH	KINNIKINICKS	KLEPHTISMS
KICKSORTER	KILOPASCAL	KINESIPATHIC	KINNIKINICS	KLEPTOCRACIES
KICKSORTERS	KILOPASCALS	KINESIPATHIES	KINNIKINNICK	KLEPTOCRACY
KICKSTANDS	KILOTONNES	KINESIPATHIST	KINNIKINNICKS	KLEPTOCRATIC
KICKSTARTED	KIMBERLITE	KINESIPATHISTS	KINTLEDGES	KLEPTOMANIA
KICKSTARTING	KIMBERLITES	KINESIPATHS	KIRBIGRIPS	KLEPTOMANIAC
KICKSTARTS	KINAESTHESES	KINESIPATHY	KIRKYAIRDS	KLEPTOMANIACS
KIDDIEWINK	KINAESTHESIA	KINESITHERAPIES	KIRSCHWASSER	KLEPTOMANIAS
KIDDIEWINKIE	KINAESTHESIAS	KINESITHERAPY	KIRSCHWASSERS	KLETTERSCHUH
KIDDIEWINKIES	KINAESTHESIS	KINESTHESES	KISSAGRAMS	KLETTERSCHUHE
KIDDIEWINKS	KINAESTHETIC	KINESTHESIA	KISSOGRAMS	KLINOSTATS
KIDDISHNESS	KINDERGARTEN	KINESTHESIAS	KISSPEPTIN	KLIPSPRINGER

K

KLIPSPRINGERS

KLIPSPRINGERS
KLONDIKERS
KLONDIKING
KLONDYKERS
KLONDYKING
KLOOCHMANS
KLOOTCHMAN
KLOOTCHMANS
KLOOTCHMEN
KLUTZINESS
KLUTZINESSES
KNACKERIES
KNACKERING
KNACKINESS
KNACKINESSES
KNACKWURST
KNACKWURSTS
KNAGGINESS
KNAGGINESSES
KNAPSACKED
KNAVESHIPS
KNAVISHNESS
KNAVISHNESSES
KNEECAPPED
KNEECAPPING
KNEECAPPINGS
KNEEPIECES
KNEVELLING
KNICKERBOCKER
KNICKERBOCKERS
KNICKKNACK
KNICKKNACKS
KNICKPOINT

KNICKPOINTS
KNIFEPOINT
KNIFEPOINTS
KNIFERESTS
KNIGHTAGES
KNIGHTHEAD
KNIGHTHEADS
KNIGHTHOOD
KNIGHTHOODS
KNIGHTLESS
KNIGHTLIER
KNIGHTLIEST
KNIGHTLINESS
KNIGHTLINESSES
KNIPHOFIAS
KNOBBINESS
KNOBBINESSES
KNOBBLIEST
KNOBKERRIE
KNOBKERRIES
KNOBSTICKS
KNOCKABOUT
KNOCKABOUTS
KNOCKDOWNS
KNOCKWURST
KNOCKWURSTS
KNOTGRASSES
KNOTTINESS
KNOTTINESSES
KNOWABLENESS
KNOWABLENESSES
KNOWINGEST
KNOWINGNESS

KNOWINGNESSES
KNOWLEDGABILITY
KNOWLEDGABLE
KNOWLEDGABLY
KNOWLEDGEABLE
KNOWLEDGEABLY
KNOWLEDGED
KNOWLEDGES
KNOWLEDGING
KNUBBLIEST
KNUCKLEBALL
KNUCKLEBALLER
KNUCKLEBALLERS
KNUCKLEBALLS
KNUCKLEBONE
KNUCKLEBONES
KNUCKLEDUSTER
KNUCKLEDUSTERS
KNUCKLEHEAD
KNUCKLEHEADED
KNUCKLEHEADS
KNUCKLIEST
KOEKSISTER
KOEKSISTERS
KOHLRABIES
KOHUTUHUTU
KOHUTUHUTUS
KOLINSKIES
KOLKHOZNIK
KOLKHOZNIKI
KOLKHOZNIKS
KOMONDOROCK
KOMONDOROK

KONIMETERS
KONIOLOGIES
KONISCOPES
KOOKABURRA
KOOKABURRAS
KOOKINESSES
KOTAHITANGA
KOTAHITANGAS
KOTTABOSES
KOTUKUTUKU
KOTUKUTUKUS
KOULIBIACA
KOULIBIACAS
KOURBASHED
KOURBASHES
KOURBASHING
KOUSKOUSES
KOWHAIWHAI
KOWHAIWHAIS
KRAKOWIAKS
KREASOTING
KREMLINOLOGIES
KREMLINOLOGIST
KREMLINOLOGISTS
KREMLINOLOGY
KREOSOTING
KRIEGSPIEL
KRIEGSPIELS
KRIEGSSPIEL
KRIEGSSPIELS
KROMESKIES
KRUGERRAND
KRUGERRANDS

KRUMMHORNS
KRYOMETERS
KUMARAHOUS
KUMMERBUND
KUMMERBUNDS
KUNDALINIS
KURBASHING
KURCHATOVIUM
KURCHATOVIUMS
KURDAITCHA
KURDAITCHAS
KURFUFFLED
KURFUFFLES
KURFUFFLING
KURRAJONGS
KURTOSISES
KVETCHIEST
KVETCHINESS
KVETCHINESSES
KWASHIORKOR
KWASHIORKORS
KYANISATION
KYANISATIONS
KYANIZATION
KYANIZATIONS
KYMOGRAPHIC
KYMOGRAPHIES
KYMOGRAPHS
KYMOGRAPHY

L

LABANOTATION	LABRADOODLE	LACINIATIONS	LACTOFLAVINS	LAICISATION
LABANOTATIONS	LABRADOODLES	LACKADAISICAL	LACTOGENIC	LAICISATIONS
LABDACISMS	LABRADORESCENT	LACKADAISICALLY	LACTOGLOBULIN	LAICIZATION
LABEFACTATION	LABRADORITE	LACKADAISY	LACTOGLOBULINS	LAICIZATIONS
LABEFACTATIONS	LABRADORITES	LACKLUSTER	LACTOMETER	LAIRDSHIPS
LABEFACTION	LABYRINTHAL	LACKLUSTERS	LACTOMETERS	LAKEFRONTS
LABEFACTIONS	LABYRINTHIAN	LACKLUSTRE	LACTOPROTEIN	LAKESHORES
LABELLINGS	LABYRINTHIC	LACKLUSTRES	LACTOPROTEINS	LALAPALOOZA
LABELLISTS	LABYRINTHICAL	LACONICALLY	LACTOSCOPE	LALAPALOOZAS
LABELMATES	LABYRINTHICALLY	LACONICISM	LACTOSCOPES	LALLAPALOOZA
LABIALISATION	LABYRINTHINE	LACONICISMS	LACTOSURIA	LALLAPALOOZAS
LABIALISATIONS	LABYRINTHITIS	LACQUERERS	LACTOSURIAS	LALLATIONS
LABIALISED	LABYRINTHITISES	LACQUERING	LACTOVEGETARIAN	LALLYGAGGED
LABIALISES	LABYRINTHODONT	LACQUERINGS	LACUNOSITIES	LALLYGAGGING
LABIALISING	LABYRINTHODONTS	LACQUERWARE	LACUNOSITY	LAMASERAIS
LABIALISMS	LABYRINTHS	LACQUERWARES	LACUSTRINE	LAMASERIES
LABIALITIES	LACCOLITES	LACQUERWORK	LADDERLIKE	LAMBASTING
LABIALIZATION	LACCOLITHIC	LACQUERWORKS	LADDISHNESS	LAMBDACISM
LABIALIZATIONS	LACCOLITHS	LACQUEYING	LADDISHNESSES	LAMBDACISMS
LABIALIZED	LACCOLITIC	LACRIMARIES	LADIESWEAR	LAMBDOIDAL
LABIALIZES	LACERABILITIES	LACRIMATION	LADIESWEARS	LAMBENCIES
LABIALIZING	LACERABILITY	LACRIMATIONS	LADYFINGER	LAMBITIVES
LABILITIES	LACERATING	LACRIMATOR	LADYFINGERS	LAMBREQUIN
LABIODENTAL	LACERATION	LACRIMATORS	LADYFISHES	LAMBREQUINS
LABIODENTALS	LACERATIONS	LACRIMATORY	LADYLIKENESS	LAMBRUSCOS
LABIONASAL	LACERATIVE	LACRYMATOR	LADYLIKENESSES	LAMEBRAINED
LABIONASALS	LACERTIANS	LACRYMATORS	LAEOTROPIC	LAMEBRAINS
LABIOVELAR	LACERTILIAN	LACRYMATORY	LAEVIGATED	LAMELLARLY
LABIOVELARS	LACERTILIANS	LACTALBUMIN	LAEVIGATES	LAMELLATED
LABORATORIES	LACHRYMALS	LACTALBUMINS	LAEVIGATING	LAMELLATELY
LABORATORY	LACHRYMARIES	LACTARIANS	LAEVOGYRATE	LAMELLATION
LABOREDNESS	LACHRYMARY	LACTATIONAL	LAEVOROTARY	LAMELLATIONS
LABOREDNESSES	LACHRYMATION	LACTATIONALLY	LAEVOROTATION	LAMELLIBRANCH
LABORINGLY	LACHRYMATIONS	LACTATIONS	LAEVOROTATIONS	LAMELLIBRANCHS
LABORIOUSLY	LACHRYMATOR	LACTESCENCE	LAEVOROTATORY	LAMELLICORN
LABORIOUSNESS	LACHRYMATORIES	LACTESCENCES	LAEVULOSES	LAMELLICORNS
LABORIOUSNESSES	LACHRYMATORS	LACTESCENT	LAGENIFORM	LAMELLIFORM
LABORSAVING	LACHRYMATORY	LACTIFEROUS	LAGERPHONE	LAMELLIROSTRAL
LABOUREDLY	LACHRYMOSE	LACTIFEROUSNESS	LAGERPHONES	LAMELLIROSTRATE
LABOUREDNESS	LACHRYMOSELY	LACTIFLUOUS	LAGGARDNESS	LAMELLOSITIES
LABOUREDNESSES	LACHRYMOSITIES	LACTIVISMS	LAGGARDNESSES	LAMELLOSITY
LABOURINGLY	LACHRYMOSITY	LACTIVISTS	LAGNIAPPES	LAMENESSES
LABOURISMS	LACINESSES	LACTOBACILLI	LAGOMORPHIC	LAMENTABLE
LABOURISTS	LACINIATED	LACTOBACILLUS	LAGOMORPHOUS	LAMENTABLENESS
LABOURSOME	LACINIATION	LACTOFLAVIN	LAGOMORPHS	LAMENTABLY

LAMENTATION
LAMENTATIONS
LAMENTEDLY
LAMENTINGLY
LAMENTINGS
LAMESTREAM
LAMESTREAMS
LAMINARIAN
LAMINARIANS
LAMINARIAS
LAMINARINS
LAMINARISE
LAMINARISED
LAMINARISES
LAMINARISING
LAMINARIZE
LAMINARIZED
LAMINARIZES
LAMINARIZING
LAMINATING
LAMINATION
LAMINATIONS
LAMINATORS
LAMINECTOMIES
LAMINECTOMY
LAMINGTONS
LAMINITISES
LAMMERGEIER
LAMMERGEIERS
LAMMERGEYER
LAMMERGEYERS
LAMPADARIES
LAMPADEDROMIES
LAMPADEDROMY
LAMPADEPHORIA
LAMPADEPHORIAS
LAMPADISTS
LAMPADOMANCIES
LAMPADOMANCY
LAMPBLACKS
LAMPHOLDER
LAMPHOLDERS
LAMPLIGHTER
LAMPLIGHTERS
LAMPLIGHTS
LAMPOONERIES
LAMPOONERS

LAMPOONERY
LAMPOONING
LAMPOONIST
LAMPOONISTS
LAMPROPHYRE
LAMPROPHYRES
LAMPROPHYRIC
LAMPSHADES
LAMPSHELLS
LANCEJACKS
LANCEOLATE
LANCEOLATED
LANCEOLATELY
LANCEWOODS
LANCINATED
LANCINATES
LANCINATING
LANCINATION
LANCINATIONS
LANDAMMANN
LANDAMMANNS
LANDAMMANS
LANDAULETS
LANDAULETTE
LANDAULETTES
LANDBOARDING
LANDBOARDINGS
LANDBOARDS
LANDDAMNED
LANDDAMNES
LANDDAMNING
LANDDROSES
LANDDROSTS
LANDFILLED
LANDFILLING
LANDFILLINGS
LANDFORCES
LANDGRAVATE
LANDGRAVATES
LANDGRAVES
LANDGRAVIATE
LANDGRAVIATES
LANDGRAVINE
LANDGRAVINES
LANDHOLDER
LANDHOLDERS
LANDHOLDING

LANDHOLDINGS
LANDLADIES
LANDLESSNESS
LANDLESSNESSES
LANDLOCKED
LANDLOPERS
LANDLORDISM
LANDLORDISMS
LANDLUBBER
LANDLUBBERLY
LANDLUBBERS
LANDLUBBING
LANDMARKED
LANDMARKING
LANDMASSES
LANDMINING
LANDMININGS
LANDOWNERS
LANDOWNERSHIP
LANDOWNERSHIPS
LANDOWNING
LANDOWNINGS
LANDSCAPED
LANDSCAPER
LANDSCAPERS
LANDSCAPES
LANDSCAPING
LANDSCAPINGS
LANDSCAPIST
LANDSCAPISTS
LANDSHARKS
LANDSKIPPED
LANDSKIPPING
LANDSKNECHT
LANDSKNECHTS
LANDSLIDDEN
LANDSLIDES
LANDSLIDING
LANDWAITER
LANDWAITERS
LANGBEINITE
LANGBEINITES
LANGLAUFER
LANGLAUFERS
LANGOSTINO
LANGOSTINOS
LANGOUSTES

LANGOUSTINE
LANGOUSTINES
LANGRIDGES
LANGSPIELS
LANGUAGELESS
LANGUAGING
LANGUESCENT
LANGUETTES
LANGUIDNESS
LANGUIDNESSES
LANGUISHED
LANGUISHER
LANGUISHERS
LANGUISHES
LANGUISHING
LANGUISHINGLY
LANGUISHINGS
LANGUISHMENT
LANGUISHMENTS
LANGUOROUS
LANGUOROUSLY
LANGUOROUSNESS
LANIFEROUS
LANIGEROUS
LANKINESSES
LANKNESSES
LANOSITIES
LANSQUENET
LANSQUENETS
LANTERLOOS
LANTERNING
LANTERNIST
LANTERNISTS
LANTHANIDE
LANTHANIDES
LANTHANONS
LANTHANUMS
LANUGINOSE
LANUGINOUS
LANUGINOUSNESS
LANZKNECHT
LANZKNECHTS
LAODICEANS
LAPAROSCOPE
LAPAROSCOPES
LAPAROSCOPIC
LAPAROSCOPIES

LAPAROSCOPIST
LAPAROSCOPISTS
LAPAROSCOPY
LAPAROTOMIES
LAPAROTOMY
LAPIDARIAN
LAPIDARIES
LAPIDARIST
LAPIDARISTS
LAPIDATING
LAPIDATION
LAPIDATIONS
LAPIDESCENCE
LAPIDESCENCES
LAPIDESCENT
LAPIDICOLOUS
LAPIDIFICATION
LAPIDIFICATIONS
LAPIDIFIED
LAPIDIFIES
LAPIDIFYING
LAPILLIFORM
LAPSTRAKES
LAPSTREAKS
LARCENISTS
LARCENOUSLY
LARDACEOUS
LARDALITES
LARGEHEARTED
LARGEMOUTH
LARGEMOUTHS
LARGENESSES
LARGHETTOS
LARGITIONS
LARKINESSES
LARKISHNESS
LARKISHNESSES
LARRIKINISM
LARRIKINISMS
LARVICIDAL
LARVICIDES
LARVIKITES
LARVIPAROUS
LARYNGEALLY
LARYNGEALS
LARYNGECTOMEE
LARYNGECTOMEES

L

LARYNGECTOMIES	LATERALISED	LATISEPTATE	LAUNDRYWOMEN	LAWYERINGS
LARYNGECTOMISED	LATERALISES	LATITANCIES	LAURACEOUS	LAWYERLIKE
LARYNGECTOMIZED	LATERALISING	LATITATION	LAURDALITE	LAXATIVENESS
LARYNGECTOMY	LATERALITIES	LATITATIONS	LAURDALITES	LAXATIVENESSES
LARYNGISMUS	LATERALITY	LATITUDINAL	LAUREATESHIP	LAYBACKING
LARYNGISMUSES	LATERALIZATION	LATITUDINALLY	LAUREATESHIPS	LAYPERSONS
LARYNGITIC	LATERALIZATIONS	LATITUDINARIAN	LAUREATING	LAZARETTES
LARYNGITIS	LATERALIZE	LATITUDINARIANS	LAUREATION	LAZARETTOS
LARYNGITISES	LATERALIZED	LATITUDINOUS	LAUREATIONS	LAZINESSES
LARYNGOLOGIC	LATERALIZES	LATRATIONS	LAURELLING	LEACHABILITIES
LARYNGOLOGICAL	LATERALIZING	LATROCINIA	LAURUSTINE	LEACHABILITY
LARYNGOLOGIES	LATERALLED	LATROCINIES	LAURUSTINES	LEADENNESS
LARYNGOLOGIST	LATERALLING	LATROCINIUM	LAURUSTINUS	LEADENNESSES
LARYNGOLOGISTS	LATERBORNS	LATTERMATH	LAURUSTINUSES	LEADERBOARD
LARYNGOLOGY	LATERIGRADE	LATTERMATHS	LAURVIKITE	LEADERBOARDS
LARYNGOPHONIES	LATERISATION	LATTERMOST	LAURVIKITES	LEADERENES
LARYNGOPHONY	LATERISATIONS	LATTICEWORK	LAVALIERES	LEADERETTE
LARYNGOSCOPE	LATERISING	LATTICEWORKS	LAVALLIERE	LEADERETTES
LARYNGOSCOPES	LATERITIOUS	LATTICINGS	LAVALLIERES	LEADERLESS
LARYNGOSCOPIC	LATERIZATION	LATTICINIO	LAVATIONAL	LEADERSHIP
LARYNGOSCOPIES	LATERIZATIONS	LAUDABILITIES	LAVATORIAL	LEADERSHIPS
LARYNGOSCOPIST	LATERIZING	LAUDABILITY	LAVATORIES	LEADPLANTS
LARYNGOSCOPISTS	LATEROVERSION	LAUDABLENESS	LAVENDERED	LEADSCREWS
LARYNGOSCOPY	LATEROVERSIONS	LAUDABLENESSES	LAVENDERING	LEAFCUTTER
LARYNGOSPASM	LATESCENCE	LAUDATIONS	LAVERBREAD	LEAFHOPPER
LARYNGOSPASMS	LATESCENCES	LAUDATIVES	LAVERBREADS	LEAFHOPPERS
LARYNGOTOMIES	LATHERIEST	LAUDATORIES	LAVEROCKED	LEAFINESSES
LARYNGOTOMY	LATHYRISMS	LAUGHABLENESS	LAVEROCKING	LEAFLESSNESS
LASCIVIOUS	LATHYRITIC	LAUGHABLENESSES	LAVISHMENT	LEAFLESSNESSES
LASCIVIOUSLY	LATHYRUSES	LAUGHINGLY	LAVISHMENTS	LEAFLETEER
LASCIVIOUSNESS	LATICIFEROUS	LAUGHINGSTOCK	LAVISHNESS	LEAFLETEERS
LASERDISCS	LATICIFERS	LAUGHINGSTOCKS	LAVISHNESSES	LEAFLETERS
LASERDISKS	LATICLAVES	LAUGHLINES	LAVOLTAING	LEAFLETING
LASERWORTS	LATIFUNDIA	LAUGHWORTHY	LAWBREAKER	LEAFLETTED
LASSITUDES	LATIFUNDIO	LAUNCEGAYE	LAWBREAKERS	LEAFLETTING
LASTINGNESS	LATIFUNDIOS	LAUNCEGAYES	LAWBREAKING	LEAFSTALKS
LASTINGNESSES	LATIFUNDIUM	LAUNCHPADS	LAWBREAKINGS	LEAGUERING
LATCHSTRING	LATIMERIAS	LAUNDERERS	LAWFULNESS	LEAKINESSES
LATCHSTRINGS	LATINISATION	LAUNDERETTE	LAWFULNESSES	LEANNESSES
LATECOMERS	LATINISATIONS	LAUNDERETTES	LAWGIVINGS	LEAPFROGGED
LATEENRIGGED	LATINISING	LAUNDERING	LAWLESSNESS	LEAPFROGGING
LATENESSES	LATINITIES	LAUNDRESSES	LAWLESSNESSES	LEARINESSES
LATENSIFICATION	LATINIZATION	LAUNDRETTE	LAWMAKINGS	LEARNABILITIES
LATERALING	LATINIZATIONS	LAUNDRETTES	LAWMONGERS	LEARNABILITY
LATERALISATION	LATINIZING	LAUNDRYMAN	LAWNMOWERS	LEARNEDNESS
LATERALISATIONS	LATIROSTRAL	LAUNDRYMEN	LAWRENCIUM	LEARNEDNESSES
LATERALISE	LATIROSTRATE	LAUNDRYWOMAN	LAWRENCIUMS	LEASEBACKS

L

LEASEHOLDER	LEECHCRAFT	LEGIONNAIRES	LEGITIMISMS	LEMNISCATE
LEASEHOLDERS	LEECHCRAFTS	LEGISLATED	LEGITIMIST	LEMNISCATES
LEASEHOLDS	LEERINESSES	LEGISLATES	LEGITIMISTIC	LEMONFISHES
LEASTAWAYS	LEETSPEAKS	LEGISLATING	LEGITIMISTS	LEMONGRASS
LEATHERBACK	LEFTWARDLY	LEGISLATION	LEGITIMIZATION	LEMONGRASSES
LEATHERBACKS	LEGALISATION	LEGISLATIONS	LEGITIMIZATIONS	LEMONWOODS
LEATHERETTE	LEGALISATIONS	LEGISLATIVE	LEGITIMIZE	LENGTHENED
LEATHERETTES	LEGALISERS	LEGISLATIVELY	LEGITIMIZED	LENGTHENER
LEATHERGOODS	LEGALISING	LEGISLATIVES	LEGITIMIZER	LENGTHENERS
LEATHERHEAD	LEGALISTIC	LEGISLATOR	LEGITIMIZERS	LENGTHENING
LEATHERHEADS	LEGALISTICALLY	LEGISLATORIAL	LEGITIMIZES	LENGTHIEST
LEATHERIER	LEGALITIES	LEGISLATORS	LEGITIMIZING	LENGTHINESS
LEATHERIEST	LEGALIZATION	LEGISLATORSHIP	LEGLESSNESS	LENGTHINESSES
LEATHERINESS	LEGALIZATIONS	LEGISLATORSHIPS	LEGLESSNESSES	LENGTHSMAN
LEATHERINESSES	LEGALIZERS	LEGISLATRESS	LEGUMINOUS	LENGTHSMEN
LEATHERING	LEGALIZING	LEGISLATRESSES	LEGWARMERS	LENGTHWAYS
LEATHERINGS	LEGATARIES	LEGISLATURE	LEIOMYOMAS	LENGTHWISE
LEATHERJACKET	LEGATESHIP	LEGISLATURES	LEIOMYOMATA	LENIENCIES
LEATHERJACKETS	LEGATESHIPS	LEGITIMACIES	LEIOTRICHIES	LENITIVELY
LEATHERLEAF	LEGATIONARY	LEGITIMACY	LEIOTRICHOUS	LENOCINIUM
LEATHERLEAVES	LEGATISSIMO	LEGITIMATE	LEIOTRICHY	LENOCINIUMS
LEATHERLIKE	LEGATORIAL	LEGITIMATED	LEISHMANIA	LENTAMENTE
LEATHERNECK	LEGENDARIES	LEGITIMATELY	LEISHMANIAE	LENTICELLATE
LEATHERNECKS	LEGENDARILY	LEGITIMATENESS	LEISHMANIAL	LENTICULAR
LEATHERWOOD	LEGENDISED	LEGITIMATES	LEISHMANIAS	LENTICULARLY
LEATHERWOODS	LEGENDISES	LEGITIMATING	LEISHMANIASES	LENTICULARS
LEAVENINGS	LEGENDISING	LEGITIMATION	LEISHMANIASIS	LENTICULES
LEBENSRAUM	LEGENDISTS	LEGITIMATIONS	LEISHMANIOSES	LENTIGINES
LEBENSRAUMS	LEGENDIZED	LEGITIMATISE	LEISHMANIOSIS	LENTIGINOSE
LECHEROUSLY	LEGENDIZES	LEGITIMATISED	LEISTERING	LENTIGINOUS
LECHEROUSNESS	LEGENDIZING	LEGITIMATISES	LEISURABLE	LENTISSIMO
LECHEROUSNESSES	LEGENDRIES	LEGITIMATISING	LEISURABLY	LENTIVIRUS
LECITHINASE	LEGERDEMAIN	LEGITIMATIZE	LEISURELINESS	LENTIVIRUSES
LECITHINASES	LEGERDEMAINIST	LEGITIMATIZED	LEISURELINESSES	LEONTIASES
LECTIONARIES	LEGERDEMAINISTS	LEGITIMATIZES	LEITMOTIFS	LEONTIASIS
LECTIONARY	LEGERDEMAINS	LEGITIMATIZING	LEITMOTIVS	LEONTOPODIUM
LECTISTERNIA	LEGERITIES	LEGITIMATOR	LEMMATISATION	LEONTOPODIUMS
LECTISTERNIUM	LEGGINESSES	LEGITIMATORS	LEMMATISATIONS	LEOPARDESS
LECTORATES	LEGIBILITIES	LEGITIMISATION	LEMMATISED	LEOPARDESSES
LECTORSHIP	LEGIBILITY	LEGITIMISATIONS	LEMMATISES	LEPIDODENDROID
LECTORSHIPS	LEGIBLENESS	LEGITIMISE	LEMMATISING	LEPIDODENDROIDS
LECTOTYPES	LEGIBLENESSES	LEGITIMISED	LEMMATIZATION	LEPIDOLITE
LECTRESSES	LEGIONARIES	LEGITIMISER	LEMMATIZATIONS	LEPIDOLITES
LECTURESHIP	LEGIONELLA	LEGITIMISERS	LEMMATIZED	LEPIDOMELANE
LECTURESHIPS	LEGIONELLAE	LEGITIMISES	LEMMATIZES	LEPIDOMELANES
LECYTHIDACEOUS	LEGIONELLAS	LEGITIMISING	LEMMATIZING	LEPIDOPTERA
LEDERHOSEN	LEGIONNAIRE	LEGITIMISM	LEMMINGLIKE	LEPIDOPTERAN

LEPIDOPTERANS
LEPIDOPTERIST
LEPIDOPTERISTS
LEPIDOPTEROLOGY
LEPIDOPTERON
LEPIDOPTERONS
LEPIDOPTEROUS
LEPIDOSIREN
LEPIDOSIRENS
LEPRECHAUN
LEPRECHAUNISH
LEPRECHAUNS
LEPRECHAWN
LEPRECHAWNS
LEPROMATOUS
LEPROSARIA
LEPROSARIUM
LEPROSARIUMS
LEPROSERIE
LEPROSERIES
LEPROSITIES
LEPROUSNESS
LEPROUSNESSES
LEPTOCEPHALI
LEPTOCEPHALIC
LEPTOCEPHALOUS
LEPTOCEPHALUS
LEPTOCERCAL
LEPTODACTYL
LEPTODACTYLOUS
LEPTODACTYLS
LEPTOKURTIC
LEPTOPHOSES
LEPTOPHYLLOUS
LEPTORRHINE
LEPTOSOMATIC
LEPTOSOMES
LEPTOSOMIC
LEPTOSPIRAL
LEPTOSPIRE
LEPTOSPIRES
LEPTOSPIROSES
LEPTOSPIROSIS
LEPTOTENES
LESBIANISM
LESBIANISMS
LESPEDEZAS

LESSEESHIP
LESSEESHIPS
LESSONINGS
LETHALITIES
LETHARGICAL
LETHARGICALLY
LETHARGIED
LETHARGIES
LETHARGISE
LETHARGISED
LETHARGISES
LETHARGISING
LETHARGIZE
LETHARGIZED
LETHARGIZES
LETHARGIZING
LETHIFEROUS
LETTERBOXED
LETTERBOXES
LETTERBOXING
LETTERBOXINGS
LETTERFORM
LETTERFORMS
LETTERHEAD
LETTERHEADS
LETTERINGS
LETTERLESS
LETTERPRESS
LETTERPRESSES
LETTERSETS
LETTERSPACING
LETTERSPACINGS
LEUCAEMIAS
LEUCAEMOGEN
LEUCAEMOGENIC
LEUCAEMOGENS
LEUCHAEMIA
LEUCHAEMIAS
LEUCITOHEDRA
LEUCITOHEDRON
LEUCITOHEDRONS
LEUCOBLAST
LEUCOBLASTS
LEUCOCIDIN
LEUCOCIDINS
LEUCOCRATIC
LEUCOCYTES

LEUCOCYTHAEMIA
LEUCOCYTHAEMIAS
LEUCOCYTIC
LEUCOCYTOLYSES
LEUCOCYTOLYSIS
LEUCOCYTOPENIA
LEUCOCYTOPENIAS
LEUCOCYTOSES
LEUCOCYTOSIS
LEUCOCYTOTIC
LEUCODEPLETED
LEUCODERMA
LEUCODERMAL
LEUCODERMAS
LEUCODERMIA
LEUCODERMIAS
LEUCODERMIC
LEUCOMAINE
LEUCOMAINES
LEUCOPENIA
LEUCOPENIAS
LEUCOPENIC
LEUCOPLAKIA
LEUCOPLAKIAS
LEUCOPLAST
LEUCOPLASTID
LEUCOPLASTIDS
LEUCOPLASTS
LEUCOPOIESES
LEUCOPOIESIS
LEUCOPOIETIC
LEUCORRHOEA
LEUCORRHOEAL
LEUCORRHOEAS
LEUCOTOMES
LEUCOTOMIES
LEUKAEMIAS
LEUKAEMOGENESES
LEUKAEMOGENESIS
LEUKEMOGENESES
LEUKEMOGENESIS
LEUKEMOGENIC
LEUKOBLAST
LEUKOBLASTS
LEUKOCYTES
LEUKOCYTIC
LEUKOCYTOSES

LEUKOCYTOSIS
LEUKOCYTOTIC
LEUKODERMA
LEUKODERMAL
LEUKODERMAS
LEUKODERMIC
LEUKODYSTROPHY
LEUKOPENIA
LEUKOPENIAS
LEUKOPENIC
LEUKOPLAKIA
LEUKOPLAKIAS
LEUKOPLAKIC
LEUKOPOIESES
LEUKOPOIESIS
LEUKOPOIETIC
LEUKORRHEA
LEUKORRHEAL
LEUKORRHEAS
LEUKOTOMIES
LEUKOTRIENE
LEUKOTRIENES
LEVANTINES
LEVELHEADED
LEVELHEADEDNESS
LEVELLINGS
LEVELNESSES
LEVERAGING
LEVIATHANS
LEVIGATING
LEVIGATION
LEVIGATIONS
LEVIGATORS
LEVIRATICAL
LEVIRATION
LEVIRATIONS
LEVITATING
LEVITATION
LEVITATIONAL
LEVITATIONS
LEVITATORS
LEVITICALLY
LEVOROTARY
LEVOROTATORY
LEWDNESSES
LEXICALISATION
LEXICALISATIONS

LEXICALISE
LEXICALISED
LEXICALISES
LEXICALISING
LEXICALITIES
LEXICALITY
LEXICALIZATION
LEXICALIZATIONS
LEXICALIZE
LEXICALIZED
LEXICALIZES
LEXICALIZING
LEXICOGRAPHER
LEXICOGRAPHERS
LEXICOGRAPHIC
LEXICOGRAPHICAL
LEXICOGRAPHIES
LEXICOGRAPHIST
LEXICOGRAPHISTS
LEXICOGRAPHY
LEXICOLOGICAL
LEXICOLOGICALLY
LEXICOLOGIES
LEXICOLOGIST
LEXICOLOGISTS
LEXICOLOGY
LEXIGRAPHIC
LEXIGRAPHICAL
LEXIGRAPHIES
LEXIGRAPHY
LEYLANDIIS
LHERZOLITE
LHERZOLITES
LIABILITIES
LIABLENESS
LIABLENESSES
LIBATIONAL
LIBATIONARY
LIBECCHIOS
LIBELLANTS
LIBELLINGS
LIBELLOUSLY
LIBERALISATION
LIBERALISATIONS
LIBERALISE
LIBERALISED
LIBERALISER

L

LIBERALISERS	LIBIDINOUSLY	LIEUTENANTSHIP	LIGHTPLANE	LIMACOLOGY
LIBERALISES	LIBIDINOUSNESS	LIEUTENANTSHIPS	LIGHTPLANES	LIMBERNESS
LIBERALISING	LIBRAIRIES	LIFEBLOODS	LIGHTPROOF	LIMBERNESSES
LIBERALISM	LIBRARIANS	LIFEGUARDED	LIGHTSHIPS	LIMBURGITE
LIBERALISMS	LIBRARIANSHIP	LIFEGUARDING	LIGHTSOMELY	LIMBURGITES
LIBERALIST	LIBRARIANSHIPS	LIFEGUARDS	LIGHTSOMENESS	LIMELIGHTED
LIBERALISTIC	LIBRATIONAL	LIFELESSLY	LIGHTSOMENESSES	LIMELIGHTER
LIBERALISTS	LIBRATIONS	LIFELESSNESS	LIGHTTIGHT	LIMELIGHTERS
LIBERALITIES	LIBRETTIST	LIFELESSNESSES	LIGHTWEIGHT	LIMELIGHTING
LIBERALITY	LIBRETTISTS	LIFELIKENESS	LIGHTWEIGHTS	LIMELIGHTS
LIBERALIZATION	LICENSABLE	LIFELIKENESSES	LIGHTWOODS	LIMESCALES
LIBERALIZATIONS	LICENSURES	LIFEMANSHIP	LIGNICOLOUS	LIMESTONES
LIBERALIZE	LICENTIATE	LIFEMANSHIPS	LIGNIFICATION	LIMEWASHES
LIBERALIZED	LICENTIATES	LIFESAVERS	LIGNIFICATIONS	LIMEWATERS
LIBERALIZER	LICENTIATESHIP	LIFESAVING	LIGNIFYING	LIMICOLINE
LIBERALIZERS	LICENTIATESHIPS	LIFESAVINGS	LIGNIPERDOUS	LIMICOLOUS
LIBERALIZES	LICENTIATION	LIFESTYLER	LIGNIVOROUS	LIMINESSES
LIBERALIZING	LICENTIATIONS	LIFESTYLERS	LIGNOCAINE	LIMITABLENESS
LIBERALNESS	LICENTIOUS	LIFESTYLES	LIGNOCAINES	LIMITABLENESSES
LIBERALNESSES	LICENTIOUSLY	LIFEWORLDS	LIGNOCELLULOSE	LIMITARIAN
LIBERATING	LICENTIOUSNESS	LIGAMENTAL	LIGNOCELLULOSES	LIMITARIANS
LIBERATION	LICHANOSES	LIGAMENTARY	LIGNOCELLULOSIC	LIMITATION
LIBERATIONISM	LICHENISMS	LIGAMENTOUS	LIGNOSULFONATE	LIMITATIONAL
LIBERATIONISMS	LICHENISTS	LIGATURING	LIGNOSULFONATES	LIMITATIONS
LIBERATIONIST	LICHENOLOGICAL	LIGHTBULBS	LIGULIFLORAL	LIMITATIVE
LIBERATIONISTS	LICHENOLOGIES	LIGHTENERS	LIKABILITIES	LIMITEDNESS
LIBERATIONS	LICHENOLOGIST	LIGHTENING	LIKABILITY	LIMITEDNESSES
LIBERATORS	LICHENOLOGISTS	LIGHTENINGS	LIKABLENESS	LIMITINGLY
LIBERATORY	LICHENOLOGY	LIGHTERAGE	LIKABLENESSES	LIMITLESSLY
LIBERTARIAN	LICHTLYING	LIGHTERAGES	LIKEABILITIES	LIMITLESSNESS
LIBERTARIANISM	LICITNESSES	LIGHTERING	LIKEABILITY	LIMITLESSNESSES
LIBERTARIANISMS	LICKERISHLY	LIGHTERMAN	LIKEABLENESS	LIMITROPHE
LIBERTARIANS	LICKERISHNESS	LIGHTERMEN	LIKEABLENESSES	LIMIVOROUS
LIBERTICIDAL	LICKERISHNESSES	LIGHTFACED	LIKELIHOOD	LIMNOLOGIC
LIBERTICIDE	LICKPENNIES	LIGHTFACES	LIKELIHOODS	LIMNOLOGICAL
LIBERTICIDES	LICKSPITTLE	LIGHTFASTNESS	LIKELINESS	LIMNOLOGICALLY
LIBERTINAGE	LICKSPITTLES	LIGHTFASTNESSES	LIKELINESSES	LIMNOLOGIES
LIBERTINAGES	LIDOCAINES	LIGHTHEARTED	LIKENESSES	LIMNOLOGIST
LIBERTINES	LIEBFRAUMILCH	LIGHTHEARTEDLY	LILIACEOUS	LIMNOLOGISTS
LIBERTINISM	LIEBFRAUMILCHS	LIGHTHOUSE	LILLIPUTIAN	LIMNOPHILOUS
LIBERTINISMS	LIENTERIES	LIGHTHOUSEMAN	LILLIPUTIANS	LIMOUSINES
LIBIDINALLY	LIEUTENANCIES	LIGHTHOUSEMEN	LILTINGNESS	LIMPIDITIES
LIBIDINIST	LIEUTENANCY	LIGHTHOUSES	LILTINGNESSES	LIMPIDNESS
LIBIDINISTS	LIEUTENANT	LIGHTLYING	LIMACIFORM	LIMPIDNESSES
LIBIDINOSITIES	LIEUTENANTRIES	LIGHTNESSES	LIMACOLOGIES	LIMPNESSES
LIBIDINOSITY	LIEUTENANTRY	LIGHTNINGED	LIMACOLOGIST	LINCOMYCIN
LIBIDINOUS	LIEUTENANTS	LIGHTNINGS	LIMACOLOGISTS	LINCOMYCINS

L

LINCRUSTAS	LINKSLANDS	LIPPINESSES	LIQUORICES	LITERALIZES
LINEALITIES	LINOLEATES	LIPPITUDES	LIQUORISHLY	LITERALIZING
LINEAMENTAL	LINOTYPERS	LIPREADERS	LIQUORISHNESS	LITERALNESS
LINEAMENTS	LINOTYPING	LIPREADING	LIQUORISHNESSES	LITERALNESSES
LINEARISATION	LINTSTOCKS	LIPREADINGS	LIRIODENDRA	LITERARILY
LINEARISATIONS	LINTWHITES	LIPSTICKED	LIRIODENDRON	LITERARINESS
LINEARISED	LIONCELLES	LIPSTICKING	LIRIODENDRONS	LITERARINESSES
LINEARISES	LIONFISHES	LIQUATIONS	LISSENCEPHALOUS	LITERARYISM
LINEARISING	LIONHEARTED	LIQUEFACIENT	LISSOMENESS	LITERARYISMS
LINEARITIES	LIONHEARTEDNESS	LIQUEFACIENTS	LISSOMENESSES	LITERATELY
LINEARIZATION	LIONISATION	LIQUEFACTION	LISSOMNESS	LITERATENESS
LINEARIZATIONS	LIONISATIONS	LIQUEFACTIONS	LISSOMNESSES	LITERATENESSES
LINEARIZED	LIONIZATION	LIQUEFACTIVE	LISSOTRICHOUS	LITERATION
LINEARIZES	LIONIZATIONS	LIQUEFIABLE	LISTENABILITIES	LITERATIONS
LINEARIZING	LIPECTOMIES	LIQUEFIERS	LISTENABILITY	LITERATORS
LINEATIONS	LIPIDOPLAST	LIQUEFYING	LISTENABLE	LITERATURE
LINEBACKER	LIPIDOPLASTS	LIQUESCENCE	LISTENERSHIP	LITERATURED
LINEBACKERS	LIPOCHROME	LIQUESCENCES	LISTENERSHIPS	LITERATURES
LINEBACKING	LIPOCHROMES	LIQUESCENCIES	LISTENINGS	LITEROSITIES
LINEBACKINGS	LIPODYSTROPHIES	LIQUESCENCY	LISTERIOSES	LITEROSITY
LINEBREEDING	LIPODYSTROPHY	LIQUESCENT	LISTERIOSIS	LITHENESSES
LINEBREEDINGS	LIPOGENESES	LIQUESCING	LISTLESSLY	LITHESOMENESS
LINECASTER	LIPOGENESIS	LIQUEURING	LISTLESSNESS	LITHESOMENESSES
LINECASTERS	LIPOGRAMMATIC	LIQUIDAMBAR	LISTLESSNESSES	LITHIFICATION
LINECASTING	LIPOGRAMMATISM	LIQUIDAMBARS	LITENESSES	LITHIFICATIONS
LINECASTINGS	LIPOGRAMMATISMS	LIQUIDATED	LITERACIES	LITHIFYING
LINEOLATED	LIPOGRAMMATIST	LIQUIDATES	LITERALISATION	LITHISTIDS
LINERBOARD	LIPOGRAMMATISTS	LIQUIDATING	LITERALISATIONS	LITHOCHROMATIC
LINERBOARDS	LIPOGRAPHIES	LIQUIDATION	LITERALISE	LITHOCHROMATICS
LINGBERRIES	LIPOGRAPHY	LIQUIDATIONS	LITERALISED	LITHOCHROMIES
LINGERINGLY	LIPOMATOSES	LIQUIDATOR	LITERALISER	LITHOCHROMY
LINGERINGS	LIPOMATOSIS	LIQUIDATORS	LITERALISERS	LITHOCLAST
LINGONBERRIES	LIPOMATOUS	LIQUIDISED	LITERALISES	LITHOCLASTS
LINGONBERRY	LIPOPHILIC	LIQUIDISER	LITERALISING	LITHOCYSTS
LINGUIFORM	LIPOPLASTS	LIQUIDISERS	LITERALISM	LITHODOMOUS
LINGUISTER	LIPOPROTEIN	LIQUIDISES	LITERALISMS	LITHOGENOUS
LINGUISTERS	LIPOPROTEINS	LIQUIDISING	LITERALIST	LITHOGLYPH
LINGUISTIC	LIPOSCULPTURE	LIQUIDITIES	LITERALISTIC	LITHOGLYPHS
LINGUISTICAL	LIPOSCULPTURES	LIQUIDIZED	LITERALISTS	LITHOGRAPH
LINGUISTICALLY	LIPOSUCKED	LIQUIDIZER	LITERALITIES	LITHOGRAPHED
LINGUISTICIAN	LIPOSUCKING	LIQUIDIZERS	LITERALITY	LITHOGRAPHER
LINGUISTICIANS	LIPOSUCTION	LIQUIDIZES	LITERALIZATION	LITHOGRAPHERS
LINGUISTICS	LIPOSUCTIONS	LIQUIDIZING	LITERALIZATIONS	LITHOGRAPHIC
LINGUISTRIES	LIPOTROPIC	LIQUIDNESS	LITERALIZE	LITHOGRAPHICAL
LINGUISTRY	LIPOTROPIES	LIQUIDNESSES	LITERALIZED	LITHOGRAPHIES
LINGULATED	LIPOTROPIN	LIQUIDUSES	LITERALIZER	LITHOGRAPHING
LINISHINGS	LIPOTROPINS	LIQUIFYING	LITERALIZERS	LITHOGRAPHS

L

LITHOGRAPHY	LITHOTOMIC	LITTLENECK	LIXIVIATION	LOCALISING
LITHOLAPAXIES	LITHOTOMICAL	LITTLENECKS	LIXIVIATIONS	LOCALISTIC
LITHOLAPAXY	LITHOTOMIES	LITTLENESS	LOADMASTER	LOCALITIES
LITHOLATRIES	LITHOTOMIST	LITTLENESSES	LOADMASTERS	LOCALIZABILITY
LITHOLATROUS	LITHOTOMISTS	LITTLEWORTH	LOADSAMONEY	LOCALIZABLE
LITHOLATRY	LITHOTOMOUS	LITURGICAL	LOADSAMONEYS	LOCALIZATION
LITHOLOGIC	LITHOTRIPSIES	LITURGICALLY	LOADSAMONIES	LOCALIZATIONS
LITHOLOGICAL	LITHOTRIPSY	LITURGIOLOGIES	LOADSPACES	LOCALIZERS
LITHOLOGICALLY	LITHOTRIPTER	LITURGIOLOGIST	LOADSTONES	LOCALIZING
LITHOLOGIES	LITHOTRIPTERS	LITURGIOLOGISTS	LOAMINESSES	LOCALNESSES
LITHOLOGIST	LITHOTRIPTIC	LITURGIOLOGY	LOANSHIFTS	LOCATEABLE
LITHOLOGISTS	LITHOTRIPTICS	LITURGISMS	LOATHEDNESS	LOCATIONAL
LITHOMANCIES	LITHOTRIPTIST	LITURGISTIC	LOATHEDNESSES	LOCATIONALLY
LITHOMANCY	LITHOTRIPTISTS	LITURGISTS	LOATHFULNESS	LOCKHOUSES
LITHOMARGE	LITHOTRIPTOR	LIVABILITIES	LOATHFULNESSES	LOCKKEEPER
LITHOMARGES	LITHOTRIPTORS	LIVABILITY	LOATHINGLY	LOCKKEEPERS
LITHOMETEOR	LITHOTRITE	LIVABLENESS	LOATHLINESS	LOCKMAKERS
LITHOMETEORS	LITHOTRITES	LIVABLENESSES	LOATHLINESSES	LOCKSMITHERIES
LITHONTHRYPTIC	LITHOTRITIC	LIVEABILITIES	LOATHNESSES	LOCKSMITHERY
LITHONTHRYPTICS	LITHOTRITICS	LIVEABILITY	LOATHSOMELY	LOCKSMITHING
LITHONTRIPTIC	LITHOTRITIES	LIVEABLENESS	LOATHSOMENESS	LOCKSMITHINGS
LITHONTRIPTICS	LITHOTRITISE	LIVEABLENESSES	LOATHSOMENESSES	LOCKSMITHS
LITHONTRIPTIST	LITHOTRITISED	LIVELIHEAD	LOBECTOMIES	LOCKSTITCH
LITHONTRIPTISTS	LITHOTRITISES	LIVELIHEADS	LOBLOLLIES	LOCKSTITCHED
LITHONTRIPTOR	LITHOTRITISING	LIVELIHOOD	LOBOTOMIES	LOCKSTITCHES
LITHONTRIPTORS	LITHOTRITIST	LIVELIHOODS	LOBOTOMISE	LOCKSTITCHING
LITHOPHAGOUS	LITHOTRITISTS	LIVELINESS	LOBOTOMISED	LOCOMOBILE
LITHOPHANE	LITHOTRITIZE	LIVELINESSES	LOBOTOMISES	LOCOMOBILES
LITHOPHANES	LITHOTRITIZED	LIVENESSES	LOBOTOMISING	LOCOMOBILITIES
LITHOPHILOUS	LITHOTRITIZES	LIVERISHLY	LOBOTOMIZE	LOCOMOBILITY
LITHOPHYSA	LITHOTRITIZING	LIVERISHNESS	LOBOTOMIZED	LOCOMOTING
LITHOPHYSAE	LITHOTRITOR	LIVERISHNESSES	LOBOTOMIZES	LOCOMOTION
LITHOPHYSE	LITHOTRITORS	LIVERLEAVES	LOBOTOMIZING	LOCOMOTIONS
LITHOPHYSES	LITHOTRITY	LIVERWORTS	LOBSCOUSES	LOCOMOTIVE
LITHOPHYTE	LITIGATING	LIVERWURST	LOBSTERERS	LOCOMOTIVELY
LITHOPHYTES	LITIGATION	LIVERWURSTS	LOBSTERING	LOCOMOTIVENESS
LITHOPHYTIC	LITIGATIONS	LIVESTOCKS	LOBSTERINGS	LOCOMOTIVES
LITHOPONES	LITIGATORS	LIVETRAPPED	LOBSTERLIKE	LOCOMOTIVITIES
LITHOPRINT	LITIGIOUSLY	LIVETRAPPING	LOBSTERMAN	LOCOMOTIVITY
LITHOPRINTS	LITIGIOUSNESS	LIVIDITIES	LOBSTERMEN	LOCOMOTORS
LITHOSPERMUM	LITIGIOUSNESSES	LIVIDNESSES	LOBULATION	LOCOMOTORY
LITHOSPERMUMS	LITTERATEUR	LIVINGNESS	LOBULATIONS	LOCOPLANTS
LITHOSPHERE	LITTERATEURS	LIVINGNESSES	LOCALISABILITY	LOCORESTIVE
LITHOSPHERES	LITTERBAGS	LIVRAISONS	LOCALISABLE	LOCULAMENT
LITHOSPHERIC	LITTERBUGS	LIXIVIATED	LOCALISATION	LOCULAMENTS
LITHOSTATIC	LITTERMATE	LIXIVIATES	LOCALISATIONS	LOCULATION
LITHOTOMES	LITTERMATES	LIXIVIATING	LOCALISERS	LOCULATIONS

LOCULICIDAL
LOCUTIONARY
LOCUTORIES
LODESTONES
LODGEMENTS
LODGEPOLES
LOFTINESSES
LOGAGRAPHIA
LOGAGRAPHIAS
LOGANBERRIES
LOGANBERRY
LOGANIACEOUS
LOGAOEDICS
LOGARITHMIC
LOGARITHMICAL
LOGARITHMICALLY
LOGARITHMS
LOGGERHEAD
LOGGERHEADED
LOGGERHEADS
LOGICALITIES
LOGICALITY
LOGICALNESS
LOGICALNESSES
LOGICISING
LOGICIZING
LOGINESSES
LOGISTICAL
LOGISTICALLY
LOGISTICIAN
LOGISTICIANS
LOGJAMMING
LOGNORMALITIES
LOGNORMALITY
LOGNORMALLY
LOGODAEDALIC
LOGODAEDALIES
LOGODAEDALUS
LOGODAEDALUSES
LOGODAEDALY
LOGOGRAMMATIC
LOGOGRAPHER
LOGOGRAPHERS
LOGOGRAPHIC
LOGOGRAPHICAL
LOGOGRAPHICALLY
LOGOGRAPHIES

LOGOGRAPHS
LOGOGRAPHY
LOGOGRIPHIC
LOGOGRIPHS
LOGOMACHIES
LOGOMACHIST
LOGOMACHISTS
LOGOPAEDIC
LOGOPAEDICS
LOGOPEDICS
LOGOPHILES
LOGORRHEAS
LOGORRHEIC
LOGORRHOEA
LOGORRHOEAS
LOGOTHETES
LOGOTYPIES
LOGROLLERS
LOGROLLING
LOGROLLINGS
LOINCLOTHS
LOITERINGLY
LOITERINGS
LOLLAPALOOZA
LOLLAPALOOZAS
LOLLYGAGGED
LOLLYGAGGING
LOMENTACEOUS
LONELINESS
LONELINESSES
LONENESSES
LONESOMELY
LONESOMENESS
LONESOMENESSES
LONGAEVOUS
LONGANIMITIES
LONGANIMITY
LONGANIMOUS
LONGBOARDS
LONGBOWMAN
LONGBOWMEN
LONGCLOTHS
LONGEVITIES
LONGHAIRED
LONGHEADED
LONGHEADEDNESS
LONGHOUSES

LONGICAUDATE
LONGICORNS
LONGINQUITIES
LONGINQUITY
LONGIPENNATE
LONGIROSTRAL
LONGITUDES
LONGITUDINAL
LONGITUDINALLY
LONGJUMPED
LONGJUMPING
LONGLEAVES
LONGLISTED
LONGLISTING
LONGNESSES
LONGPRIMER
LONGPRIMERS
LONGSHOREMAN
LONGSHOREMEN
LONGSHORING
LONGSHORINGS
LONGSIGHTED
LONGSIGHTEDNESS
LONGSOMELY
LONGSOMENESS
LONGSOMENESSES
LONGWEARING
LOOKALIKES
LOONINESSES
LOOPHOLING
LOOPINESSES
LOOSEBOXES
LOOSENESSES
LOOSESTRIFE
LOOSESTRIFES
LOOYENWORK
LOOYENWORKS
LOPGRASSES
LOPHOBRANCH
LOPHOBRANCHIATE
LOPHOBRANCHS
LOPHOPHORATE
LOPHOPHORE
LOPHOPHORES
LOPSIDEDLY
LOPSIDEDNESS
LOPSIDEDNESSES

LOQUACIOUS
LOQUACIOUSLY
LOQUACIOUSNESS
LOQUACITIES
LORAZEPAMS
LORDLINESS
LORDLINESSES
LORDOLATRIES
LORDOLATRY
LORGNETTES
LORICATING
LORICATION
LORICATIONS
LORNNESSES
LOSABLENESS
LOSABLENESSES
LOSSMAKERS
LOSSMAKING
LOSTNESSES
LOTHNESSES
LOTUSLANDS
LOUDHAILER
LOUDHAILERS
LOUDMOUTHED
LOUDMOUTHS
LOUDNESSES
LOUDSPEAKER
LOUDSPEAKERS
LOUNDERING
LOUNDERINGS
LOUNGEWEAR
LOUNGEWEARS
LOUNGINGLY
LOUSEWORTS
LOUSINESSES
LOUTISHNESS
LOUTISHNESSES
LOVABILITIES
LOVABILITY
LOVABLENESS
LOVABLENESSES
LOVASTATIN
LOVASTATINS
LOVEABILITIES
LOVEABILITY
LOVEABLENESS
LOVEABLENESSES

LOVELESSLY
LOVELESSNESS
LOVELESSNESSES
LOVELIGHTS
LOVELIHEAD
LOVELIHEADS
LOVELINESS
LOVELINESSES
LOVELORNNESS
LOVELORNNESSES
LOVEMAKERS
LOVEMAKING
LOVEMAKINGS
LOVESICKNESS
LOVESICKNESSES
LOVESTRUCK
LOVEWORTHY
LOVINGNESS
LOVINGNESSES
LOWBALLING
LOWBALLINGS
LOWBROWISM
LOWBROWISMS
LOWERCASED
LOWERCASES
LOWERCASING
LOWERCLASSMAN
LOWERCLASSMEN
LOWERINGLY
LOWLANDERS
LOWLIGHTED
LOWLIGHTING
LOWLIHEADS
LOWLINESSES
LOWSENINGS
LOXODROMES
LOXODROMIC
LOXODROMICAL
LOXODROMICALLY
LOXODROMICS
LOXODROMIES
LOYALNESSES
LUBBERLINESS
LUBBERLINESSES
LUBRICANTS
LUBRICATED
LUBRICATES

L

LUBRICATING

LUBRICATING
LUBRICATION
LUBRICATIONAL
LUBRICATIONS
LUBRICATIVE
LUBRICATOR
LUBRICATORS
LUBRICIOUS
LUBRICIOUSLY
LUBRICITIES
LUBRICOUSLY
LUBRITORIA
LUBRITORIUM
LUBRITORIUMS
LUCIDITIES
LUCIDNESSES
LUCIFERASE
LUCIFERASES
LUCIFERINS
LUCIFEROUS
LUCIFUGOUS
LUCKENBOOTH
LUCKENBOOTHS
LUCKENGOWAN
LUCKENGOWANS
LUCKINESSES
LUCKLESSLY
LUCKLESSNESS
LUCKLESSNESSES
LUCKPENNIES
LUCRATIVELY
LUCRATIVENESS
LUCRATIVENESSES
LUCTATIONS
LUCUBRATED
LUCUBRATES
LUCUBRATING
LUCUBRATION
LUCUBRATIONS
LUCUBRATOR
LUCUBRATORS
LUCULENTLY
LUDICROUSLY
LUDICROUSNESS
LUDICROUSNESSES
LUETICALLY
LUFTMENSCH

LUFTMENSCHEN
LUGUBRIOUS
LUGUBRIOUSLY
LUGUBRIOUSNESS
LUKEWARMISH
LUKEWARMLY
LUKEWARMNESS
LUKEWARMNESSES
LUKEWARMTH
LUKEWARMTHS
LULLABYING
LUMBAGINOUS
LUMBERINGLY
LUMBERINGNESS
LUMBERINGNESSES
LUMBERINGS
LUMBERJACK
LUMBERJACKET
LUMBERJACKETS
LUMBERJACKS
LUMBERSOME
LUMBERSOMENESS
LUMBERYARD
LUMBERYARDS
LUMBOSACRAL
LUMBRICALES
LUMBRICALIS
LUMBRICALISES
LUMBRICALS
LUMBRICIFORM
LUMBRICOID
LUMBRICUSES
LUMINAIRES
LUMINANCES
LUMINARIAS
LUMINARIES
LUMINARISM
LUMINARISMS
LUMINARIST
LUMINARISTS
LUMINATION
LUMINATIONS
LUMINESCED
LUMINESCENCE
LUMINESCENCES
LUMINESCENT
LUMINESCES

LUMINESCING
LUMINIFEROUS
LUMINOSITIES
LUMINOSITY
LUMINOUSLY
LUMINOUSNESS
LUMINOUSNESSES
LUMISTEROL
LUMISTEROLS
LUMPECTOMIES
LUMPECTOMY
LUMPFISHES
LUMPINESSES
LUMPISHNESS
LUMPISHNESSES
LUMPSUCKER
LUMPSUCKERS
LUNARNAUTS
LUNATICALLY
LUNCHBOXES
LUNCHEONED
LUNCHEONETTE
LUNCHEONETTES
LUNCHEONING
LUNCHMEATS
LUNCHROOMS
LUNCHTIMES
LUNGFISHES
LUNINESSES
LUNKHEADED
LURIDNESSES
LUSCIOUSLY
LUSCIOUSNESS
LUSCIOUSNESSES
LUSHNESSES
LUSKISHNESS
LUSKISHNESSES
LUSTERLESS
LUSTERWARE
LUSTERWARES
LUSTFULNESS
LUSTFULNESSES
LUSTIHEADS
LUSTIHOODS
LUSTINESSES
LUSTRATING
LUSTRATION

LUSTRATIONS
LUSTRATIVE
LUSTRELESS
LUSTREWARE
LUSTREWARES
LUSTROUSLY
LUSTROUSNESS
LUSTROUSNESSES
LUTEINISATION
LUTEINISATIONS
LUTEINISED
LUTEINISES
LUTEINISING
LUTEINIZATION
LUTEINIZATIONS
LUTEINIZED
LUTEINIZES
LUTEINIZING
LUTEOTROPHIC
LUTEOTROPHIN
LUTEOTROPHINS
LUTEOTROPIC
LUTEOTROPIN
LUTEOTROPINS
LUTESTRING
LUTESTRINGS
LUVVIEDOMS
LUXULIANITE
LUXULIANITES
LUXULLIANITE
LUXULLIANITES
LUXULYANITE
LUXULYANITES
LUXURIANCE
LUXURIANCES
LUXURIANCIES
LUXURIANCY
LUXURIANTLY
LUXURIATED
LUXURIATES
LUXURIATING
LUXURIATION
LUXURIATIONS
LUXURIOUSLY
LUXURIOUSNESS
LUXURIOUSNESSES
LYCANTHROPE

LYCANTHROPES
LYCANTHROPIC
LYCANTHROPIES
LYCANTHROPIST
LYCANTHROPISTS
LYCANTHROPY
LYCHNOSCOPE
LYCHNOSCOPES
LYCOPODIUM
LYCOPODIUMS
LYMPHADENITIS
LYMPHADENITISES
LYMPHADENOPATHY
LYMPHANGIAL
LYMPHANGIOGRAM
LYMPHANGIOGRAMS
LYMPHANGITIC
LYMPHANGITIDES
LYMPHANGITIS
LYMPHANGITISES
LYMPHATICALLY
LYMPHATICS
LYMPHOADENOMA
LYMPHOADENOMAS
LYMPHOADENOMATA
LYMPHOBLAST
LYMPHOBLASTIC
LYMPHOBLASTS
LYMPHOCYTE
LYMPHOCYTES
LYMPHOCYTIC
LYMPHOCYTOPENIA
LYMPHOCYTOSES
LYMPHOCYTOSIS
LYMPHOCYTOTIC
LYMPHOGRAM
LYMPHOGRAMS
LYMPHOGRANULOMA
LYMPHOGRAPHIC
LYMPHOGRAPHIES
LYMPHOGRAPHY
LYMPHOKINE
LYMPHOKINES
LYMPHOMATA
LYMPHOMATOID
LYMPHOMATOSES
LYMPHOMATOSIS

L

LYMPHOMATOUS	LYOPHILISATIONS	LYOPHILIZER	LYSIGENETIC	LYSOGENISES
LYMPHOPENIA	LYOPHILISE	LYOPHILIZERS	LYSIGENOUS	LYSOGENISING
LYMPHOPENIAS	LYOPHILISED	LYOPHILIZES	LYSIMETERS	LYSOGENIZATION
LYMPHOPOIESES	LYOPHILISER	LYOPHILIZING	LYSIMETRIC	LYSOGENIZATIONS
LYMPHOPOIESIS	LYOPHILISERS	LYOSORPTION	LYSOGENICITIES	LYSOGENIZE
LYMPHOPOIETIC	LYOPHILISES	LYOSORPTIONS	LYSOGENICITY	LYSOGENIZED
LYMPHOSARCOMA	LYOPHILISING	LYRICALNESS	LYSOGENIES	LYSOGENIZES
LYMPHOSARCOMAS	LYOPHILIZATION	LYRICALNESSES	LYSOGENISATION	LYSOGENIZING
LYMPHOSARCOMATA	LYOPHILIZATIONS	LYRICISING	LYSOGENISATIONS	LYSOLECITHIN
LYMPHOTROPHIC	LYOPHILIZE	LYRICIZING	LYSOGENISE	LYSOLECITHINS
LYOPHILISATION	LYOPHILIZED	LYSERGIDES	LYSOGENISED	LYTHRACEOUS

L

M

MACABERESQUE
MACADAMIAS
MACADAMISATION
MACADAMISATIONS
MACADAMISE
MACADAMISED
MACADAMISER
MACADAMISERS
MACADAMISES
MACADAMISING
MACADAMIZATION
MACADAMIZATIONS
MACADAMIZE
MACADAMIZED
MACADAMIZER
MACADAMIZERS
MACADAMIZES
MACADAMIZING
MACARISING
MACARIZING
MACARONICALLY
MACARONICS
MACARONIES
MACCARONIES
MACCARONIS
MACCHERONCINI
MACCHERONCINIS
MACCHIATOS
MACEBEARER
MACEBEARERS
MACEDOINES
MACERANDUBA
MACERANDUBAS
MACERATERS
MACERATING
MACERATION
MACERATIONS
MACERATIVE
MACERATORS
MACHAIRODONT
MACHAIRODONTS
MACHIAVELIAN
MACHIAVELIANS
MACHIAVELLIAN
MACHIAVELLIANS

MACHICOLATE
MACHICOLATED
MACHICOLATES
MACHICOLATING
MACHICOLATION
MACHICOLATIONS
MACHINABILITIES
MACHINABILITY
MACHINABLE
MACHINATED
MACHINATES
MACHINATING
MACHINATION
MACHINATIONS
MACHINATOR
MACHINATORS
MACHINEABILITY
MACHINEABLE
MACHINEGUN
MACHINEGUNNED
MACHINEGUNNING
MACHINEGUNS
MACHINELESS
MACHINELIKE
MACHINEMAN
MACHINEMEN
MACHINERIES
MACHINIMAS
MACHININGS
MACHINISTS
MACHMETERS
MACHTPOLITIK
MACHTPOLITIKS
MACINTOSHES
MACKINTOSH
MACKINTOSHES
MACONOCHIE
MACONOCHIES
MACRENCEPHALIA
MACRENCEPHALIAS
MACRENCEPHALIES
MACRENCEPHALY
MACROAGGREGATE
MACROAGGREGATED
MACROAGGREGATES

MACROBIOTA
MACROBIOTE
MACROBIOTES
MACROBIOTIC
MACROBIOTICS
MACROCARPA
MACROCARPAS
MACROCEPHALIA
MACROCEPHALIAS
MACROCEPHALIC
MACROCEPHALIES
MACROCEPHALOUS
MACROCEPHALY
MACROCLIMATE
MACROCLIMATES
MACROCLIMATIC
MACROCODES
MACROCOPIES
MACROCOSMIC
MACROCOSMICALLY
MACROCOSMS
MACROCYCLE
MACROCYCLES
MACROCYCLIC
MACROCYSTS
MACROCYTES
MACROCYTIC
MACROCYTOSES
MACROCYTOSIS
MACRODACTYL
MACRODACTYLIC
MACRODACTYLIES
MACRODACTYLOUS
MACRODACTYLY
MACRODIAGONAL
MACRODIAGONALS
MACRODOMES
MACROECONOMIC
MACROECONOMICS
MACROEVOLUTION
MACROEVOLUTIONS
MACROFAUNA
MACROFAUNAE
MACROFAUNAS
MACROFLORA

MACROFLORAE
MACROFLORAS
MACROFOSSIL
MACROFOSSILS
MACROGAMETE
MACROGAMETES
MACROGLIAS
MACROGLOBULIN
MACROGLOBULINS
MACROGRAPH
MACROGRAPHIC
MACROGRAPHS
MACROLIDES
MACROLOGIES
MACROMERES
MACROMOLECULAR
MACROMOLECULE
MACROMOLECULES
MACROMOLES
MACRONUCLEAR
MACRONUCLEI
MACRONUCLEUS
MACRONUTRIENT
MACRONUTRIENTS
MACROPHAGE
MACROPHAGES
MACROPHAGIC
MACROPHAGOUS
MACROPHOTOGRAPH
MACROPHYLA
MACROPHYLUM
MACROPHYSICS
MACROPHYTE
MACROPHYTES
MACROPHYTIC
MACROPINAKOID
MACROPINAKOIDS
MACROPRISM
MACROPRISMS
MACROPSIAS
MACROPTEROUS
MACROSCALE
MACROSCALES
MACROSCOPIC
MACROSCOPICALLY

MACROSOCIOLOGY
MACROSPORANGIA
MACROSPORANGIUM
MACROSPORE
MACROSPORES
MACROSTRUCTURAL
MACROSTRUCTURE
MACROSTRUCTURES
MACROZAMIA
MACROZAMIAS
MACTATIONS
MACULATING
MACULATION
MACULATIONS
MACULATURE
MACULATURES
MADBRAINED
MADDENINGLY
MADDENINGNESS
MADDENINGNESSES
MADEFACTION
MADEFACTIONS
MADELEINES
MADEMOISELLE
MADEMOISELLES
MADERISATION
MADERISATIONS
MADERISING
MADERIZATION
MADERIZATIONS
MADERIZING
MADONNAISH
MADONNAWISE
MADRASSAHS
MADREPORAL
MADREPORES
MADREPORIAN
MADREPORIANS
MADREPORIC
MADREPORITE
MADREPORITES
MADREPORITIC
MADRIGALESQUE
MADRIGALIAN
MADRIGALIST

MADRIGALISTS	MAGNATESHIPS	MAGNIFIABLE	MAILABILITIES	MAISONETTE
MADRILENES	MAGNESITES	MAGNIFICAL	MAILABILITY	MAISONETTES
MAELSTROMS	MAGNESIUMS	MAGNIFICALLY	MAILCOACHES	MAISONNETTE
MAENADICALLY	MAGNESSTONE	MAGNIFICAT	MAILGRAMMED	MAISONNETTES
MAENADISMS	MAGNESSTONES	MAGNIFICATION	MAILGRAMMING	MAISTERDOME
MAFFICKERS	MAGNETICAL	MAGNIFICATIONS	MAILMERGED	MAISTERDOMES
MAFFICKING	MAGNETICALLY	MAGNIFICATS	MAILMERGES	MAISTERING
MAFFICKINGS	MAGNETICIAN	MAGNIFICENCE	MAILMERGING	MAISTRINGS
MAGALOGUES	MAGNETICIANS	MAGNIFICENCES	MAILPOUCHES	MAJESTICAL
MAGAZINIST	MAGNETISABLE	MAGNIFICENT	MAILSHOTTED	MAJESTICALLY
MAGAZINISTS	MAGNETISATION	MAGNIFICENTLY	MAILSHOTTING	MAJESTICALNESS
MAGDALENES	MAGNETISATIONS	MAGNIFICENTNESS	MAIMEDNESS	MAJESTICNESS
MAGGOTIEST	MAGNETISED	MAGNIFICOES	MAIMEDNESSES	MAJESTICNESSES
MAGGOTORIA	MAGNETISER	MAGNIFICOS	MAINBRACES	MAJOLICAWARE
MAGGOTORIUM	MAGNETISERS	MAGNIFIERS	MAINFRAMES	MAJOLICAWARES
MAGIANISMS	MAGNETISES	MAGNIFYING	MAINLANDER	MAJORDOMOS
MAGISTERIAL	MAGNETISING	MAGNILOQUENCE	MAINLANDERS	MAJORETTES
MAGISTERIALLY	MAGNETISMS	MAGNILOQUENCES	MAINLINERS	MAJORETTING
MAGISTERIALNESS	MAGNETISTS	MAGNILOQUENT	MAINLINING	MAJORETTINGS
MAGISTERIES	MAGNETITES	MAGNILOQUENTLY	MAINLININGS	MAJORITAIRE
MAGISTERIUM	MAGNETITIC	MAGNITUDES	MAINPERNOR	MAJORITAIRES
MAGISTERIUMS	MAGNETIZABLE	MAGNITUDINOUS	MAINPERNORS	MAJORITARIAN
MAGISTRACIES	MAGNETIZATION	MAGNOLIACEOUS	MAINPRISES	MAJORITARIANISM
MAGISTRACY	MAGNETIZATIONS	MAHARAJAHS	MAINSHEETS	MAJORITARIANS
MAGISTRALITIES	MAGNETIZED	MAHARANEES	MAINSPRING	MAJORITIES
MAGISTRALITY	MAGNETIZER	MAHARISHIS	MAINSPRINGS	MAJORSHIPS
MAGISTRALLY	MAGNETIZERS	MAHATMAISM	MAINSTREAM	MAJUSCULAR
MAGISTRALS	MAGNETIZES	MAHATMAISMS	MAINSTREAMED	MAJUSCULES
MAGISTRAND	MAGNETIZING	MAHLSTICKS	MAINSTREAMING	MAKEREADIES
MAGISTRANDS	MAGNETOCHEMICAL	MAHOGANIES	MAINSTREAMINGS	MAKESHIFTS
MAGISTRATE	MAGNETOELECTRIC	MAIASAURAS	MAINSTREAMS	MAKEWEIGHT
MAGISTRATES	MAGNETOGRAPH	MAIDENHAIR	MAINSTREETING	MAKEWEIGHTS
MAGISTRATESHIP	MAGNETOGRAPHS	MAIDENHAIRS	MAINSTREETINGS	MAKUNOUCHI
MAGISTRATESHIPS	MAGNETOMETER	MAIDENHEAD	MAINTAINABILITY	MAKUNOUCHIS
MAGISTRATIC	MAGNETOMETERS	MAIDENHEADS	MAINTAINABLE	MALABSORPTION
MAGISTRATICAL	MAGNETOMETRIC	MAIDENHOOD	MAINTAINED	MALABSORPTIONS
MAGISTRATICALLY	MAGNETOMETRIES	MAIDENHOODS	MAINTAINER	MALACHITES
MAGISTRATURE	MAGNETOMETRY	MAIDENLIKE	MAINTAINERS	MALACOLOGICAL
MAGISTRATURES	MAGNETOMOTIVE	MAIDENLINESS	MAINTAINING	MALACOLOGIES
MAGMATISMS	MAGNETOPAUSE	MAIDENLINESSES	MAINTENANCE	MALACOLOGIST
MAGNALIUMS	MAGNETOPAUSES	MAIDENWEED	MAINTENANCED	MALACOLOGISTS
MAGNANIMITIES	MAGNETOSPHERE	MAIDENWEEDS	MAINTENANCES	MALACOLOGY
MAGNANIMITY	MAGNETOSPHERES	MAIDISHNESS	MAINTENANCING	MALACOPHILIES
MAGNANIMOUS	MAGNETOSPHERIC	MAIDISHNESSES	MAINTOPMAST	MALACOPHILOUS
MAGNANIMOUSLY	MAGNETOSTATIC	MAIDSERVANT	MAINTOPMASTS	MALACOPHILY
MAGNANIMOUSNESS	MAGNETOSTATICS	MAIDSERVANTS	MAINTOPSAIL	MALACOPHYLLOUS
MAGNATESHIP	MAGNETRONS	MAIEUTICAL	MAINTOPSAILS	MALACOPTERYGIAN

M

M

MALACOSTRACAN	MALAXATIONS	MALFUNCTIONINGS	MALODOROUSLY	MAMMITIDES
MALACOSTRACANS	MALAXATORS	MALFUNCTIONS	MALODOROUSNESS	MAMMOCKING
MALACOSTRACOUS	MALCONFORMATION	MALICIOUSLY	MALOLACTIC	MAMMOGENIC
MALADAPTATION	MALCONTENT	MALICIOUSNESS	MALONYLUREA	MAMMOGRAMS
MALADAPTATIONS	MALCONTENTED	MALICIOUSNESSES	MALONYLUREAS	MAMMOGRAPH
MALADAPTED	MALCONTENTEDLY	MALIGNANCE	MALPIGHIACEOUS	MAMMOGRAPHIC
MALADAPTIVE	MALCONTENTS	MALIGNANCES	MALPOSITION	MAMMOGRAPHIES
MALADAPTIVELY	MALDEPLOYMENT	MALIGNANCIES	MALPOSITIONS	MAMMOGRAPHS
MALADDRESS	MALDEPLOYMENTS	MALIGNANCY	MALPRACTICE	MAMMOGRAPHY
MALADDRESSES	MALDISTRIBUTION	MALIGNANTLY	MALPRACTICES	MAMMONISMS
MALADJUSTED	MALEDICENT	MALIGNANTS	MALPRACTITIONER	MAMMONISTIC
MALADJUSTIVE	MALEDICTED	MALIGNITIES	MALPRESENTATION	MAMMONISTS
MALADJUSTMENT	MALEDICTING	MALIGNMENT	MALTALENTS	MAMMONITES
MALADJUSTMENTS	MALEDICTION	MALIGNMENTS	MALTINESSES	MAMMOPLASTIES
MALADMINISTER	MALEDICTIONS	MALIMPRINTED	MALTREATED	MAMMOPLASTY
MALADMINISTERED	MALEDICTIVE	MALIMPRINTING	MALTREATER	MANAGEABILITIES
MALADMINISTERS	MALEDICTORY	MALIMPRINTINGS	MALTREATERS	MANAGEABILITY
MALADROITLY	MALEFACTION	MALINGERED	MALTREATING	MANAGEABLE
MALADROITNESS	MALEFACTIONS	MALINGERER	MALTREATMENT	MANAGEABLENESS
MALADROITNESSES	MALEFACTOR	MALINGERERS	MALTREATMENTS	MANAGEABLY
MALADROITS	MALEFACTORS	MALINGERIES	MALVACEOUS	MANAGEMENT
MALAGUENAS	MALEFACTORY	MALINGERING	MALVERSATION	MANAGEMENTAL
MALAGUETTA	MALEFACTRESS	MALLANDERS	MALVERSATIONS	MANAGEMENTS
MALAGUETTAS	MALEFACTRESSES	MALLEABILITIES	MALVOISIES	MANAGERESS
MALAKATOONE	MALEFFECTS	MALLEABILITY	MAMAGUYING	MANAGERESSES
MALAKATOONES	MALEFICALLY	MALLEABLENESS	MAMILLATED	MANAGERIAL
MALAPERTLY	MALEFICENCE	MALLEABLENESSES	MAMILLATION	MANAGERIALISM
MALAPERTNESS	MALEFICENCES	MALLEATING	MAMILLATIONS	MANAGERIALISMS
MALAPERTNESSES	MALEFICENT	MALLEATION	MAMILLIFORM	MANAGERIALIST
MALAPPORTIONED	MALEFICIAL	MALLEATIONS	MAMMALIANS	MANAGERIALISTS
MALAPPROPRIATE	MALENESSES	MALLEIFORM	MAMMALIFEROUS	MANAGERIALLY
MALAPPROPRIATED	MALENGINES	MALLEMAROKING	MAMMALITIES	MANAGERSHIP
MALAPPROPRIATES	MALENTENDU	MALLEMAROKINGS	MAMMALOGICAL	MANAGERSHIPS
MALAPROPIAN	MALENTENDUS	MALLEMUCKS	MAMMALOGIES	MANCHESTER
MALAPROPISM	MALEVOLENCE	MALLENDERS	MAMMALOGIST	MANCHESTERS
MALAPROPISMS	MALEVOLENCES	MALLEOLUSES	MAMMALOGISTS	MANCHINEEL
MALAPROPIST	MALEVOLENT	MALLOPHAGOUS	MAMMAPLASTIES	MANCHINEELS
MALAPROPISTS	MALEVOLENTLY	MALLOWPUFF	MAMMAPLASTY	MANCIPATED
MALAPROPOS	MALFEASANCE	MALLOWPUFFS	MAMMECTOMIES	MANCIPATES
MALARIOLOGIES	MALFEASANCES	MALMSTONES	MAMMECTOMY	MANCIPATING
MALARIOLOGIST	MALFEASANT	MALNOURISHED	MAMMETRIES	MANCIPATION
MALARIOLOGISTS	MALFEASANTS	MALNUTRITION	MAMMIFEROUS	MANCIPATIONS
MALARIOLOGY	MALFORMATION	MALNUTRITIONS	MAMMILLARIA	MANCIPATORY
MALASSIMILATION	MALFORMATIONS	MALOCCLUDED	MAMMILLARIAS	MANDAMUSED
MALATHIONS	MALFUNCTION	MALOCCLUSION	MAMMILLARY	MANDAMUSES
MALAXATING	MALFUNCTIONED	MALOCCLUSIONS	MAMMILLATE	MANDAMUSING
MALAXATION	MALFUNCTIONING	MALODOROUS	MAMMILLATED	MANDARINATE

MANDARINATES	MANGEMANGE	MANIFOLDNESS	MANRIKIGUSARI	MANZANITAS
MANDARINES	MANGEMANGES	MANIFOLDNESSES	MANRIKIGUSARIS	MAPMAKINGS
MANDARINIC	MANGETOUTS	MANIPULABILITY	MANSERVANT	MAPPEMONDS
MANDARINISM	MANGINESSES	MANIPULABLE	MANSIONARIES	MAQUILADORA
MANDARINISMS	MANGOLDWURZEL	MANIPULARS	MANSIONARY	MAQUILADORAS
MANDATARIES	MANGOLDWURZELS	MANIPULATABLE	MANSLAUGHTER	MAQUILLAGE
MANDATORIES	MANGOSTANS	MANIPULATE	MANSLAUGHTERS	MAQUILLAGES
MANDATORILY	MANGOSTEEN	MANIPULATED	MANSLAYERS	MAQUISARDS
MANDIBULAR	MANGOSTEENS	MANIPULATES	MANSONRIES	MARABUNTAS
MANDIBULATE	MANGOUSTES	MANIPULATING	MANSUETUDE	MARANATHAS
MANDIBULATED	MANGULATED	MANIPULATION	MANSUETUDES	MARASCHINO
MANDIBULATES	MANGULATES	MANIPULATIONS	MANTELLETTA	MARASCHINOS
MANDILIONS	MANGULATING	MANIPULATIVE	MANTELLETTAS	MARASMUSES
MANDIOCCAS	MANHANDLED	MANIPULATIVELY	MANTELPIECE	MARATHONER
MANDOLINES	MANHANDLES	MANIPULATOR	MANTELPIECES	MARATHONERS
MANDOLINIST	MANHANDLING	MANIPULATORS	MANTELSHELF	MARATHONING
MANDOLINISTS	MANHATTANS	MANIPULATORY	MANTELSHELVES	MARATHONINGS
MANDRAGORA	MANHUNTERS	MANLINESSES	MANTELTREE	MARAUDINGS
MANDRAGORAS	MANIACALLY	MANNEQUINS	MANTELTREES	MARBELISED
MANDUCABLE	MANICOTTIS	MANNERISMS	MANTICALLY	MARBELISES
MANDUCATED	MANICURING	MANNERISTIC	MANTICORAS	MARBELISING
MANDUCATES	MANICURIST	MANNERISTICAL	MANTICORES	MARBELIZED
MANDUCATING	MANICURISTS	MANNERISTICALLY	MANTLETREE	MARBELIZES
MANDUCATION	MANIFESTABLE	MANNERISTS	MANTLETREES	MARBELIZING
MANDUCATIONS	MANIFESTANT	MANNERLESS	MANUBRIUMS	MARBLEISED
MANDUCATORY	MANIFESTANTS	MANNERLESSNESS	MANUFACTORIES	MARBLEISES
MANDYLIONS	MANIFESTATION	MANNERLINESS	MANUFACTORY	MARBLEISING
MANEUVERABILITY	MANIFESTATIONAL	MANNERLINESSES	MANUFACTURABLE	MARBLEIZED
MANEUVERABLE	MANIFESTATIONS	MANNIFEROUS	MANUFACTURAL	MARBLEIZES
MANEUVERED	MANIFESTATIVE	MANNISHNESS	MANUFACTURE	MARBLEIZING
MANEUVERER	MANIFESTED	MANNISHNESSES	MANUFACTURED	MARBLEWOOD
MANEUVERERS	MANIFESTER	MANOEUVRABILITY	MANUFACTURER	MARBLEWOODS
MANEUVERING	MANIFESTERS	MANOEUVRABLE	MANUFACTURERS	MARCANTANT
MANEUVERINGS	MANIFESTIBLE	MANOEUVRED	MANUFACTURES	MARCANTANTS
MANFULNESS	MANIFESTING	MANOEUVRER	MANUFACTURING	MARCASITES
MANFULNESSES	MANIFESTLY	MANOEUVRERS	MANUFACTURINGS	MARCASITICAL
MANGABEIRA	MANIFESTNESS	MANOEUVRES	MANUMISSION	MARCATISSIMO
MANGABEIRAS	MANIFESTNESSES	MANOEUVRING	MANUMISSIONS	MARCELLERS
MANGALSUTRA	MANIFESTOED	MANOEUVRINGS	MANUMITTED	MARCELLING
MANGALSUTRAS	MANIFESTOES	MANOMETERS	MANUMITTER	MARCESCENCE
MANGANATES	MANIFESTOING	MANOMETRIC	MANUMITTERS	MARCESCENCES
MANGANESES	MANIFESTOS	MANOMETRICAL	MANUMITTING	MARCESCENT
MANGANESIAN	MANIFOLDED	MANOMETRICALLY	MANURANCES	MARCESCIBLE
MANGANIFEROUS	MANIFOLDER	MANOMETRIES	MANUSCRIPT	MARCHANTIA
MANGANITES	MANIFOLDERS	MANORIALISM	MANUSCRIPTS	MARCHANTIAS
MANGELWURZEL	MANIFOLDING	MANORIALISMS	MANZANILLA	MARCHIONESS
MANGELWURZELS	MANIFOLDLY	MANOSCOPIES	MANZANILLAS	MARCHIONESSES

MARCHLANDS	MARGUERITES	MARKSMANSHIPS	MARQUISETTES	MARTENSITIC
MARCHPANES	MARIALITES	MARKSWOMAN	MARRIAGEABILITY	MARTENSITICALLY
MARCONIGRAM	MARICULTURE	MARKSWOMEN	MARRIAGEABLE	MARTIALISM
MARCONIGRAMS	MARICULTURES	MARLACIOUS	MARROWBONE	MARTIALISMS
MARCONIGRAPH	MARICULTURIST	MARLINESPIKE	MARROWBONES	MARTIALIST
MARCONIGRAPHED	MARICULTURISTS	MARLINESPIKES	MARROWFATS	MARTIALISTS
MARCONIGRAPHING	MARIGRAPHS	MARLINGSPIKE	MARROWLESS	MARTIALNESS
MARCONIGRAPHS	MARIHUANAS	MARLINGSPIKES	MARROWSKIED	MARTIALNESSES
MARCONIING	MARIJUANAS	MARLINSPIKE	MARROWSKIES	MARTINETISH
MARESCHALS	MARIMBAPHONE	MARLINSPIKES	MARROWSKYING	MARTINETISM
MARGARINES	MARIMBAPHONES	MARLSTONES	MARSEILLES	MARTINETISMS
MARGARITAS	MARIMBISTS	MARMALADES	MARSHALCIES	MARTINGALE
MARGARITES	MARINADING	MARMALISED	MARSHALERS	MARTINGALES
MARGARITIC	MARINATING	MARMALISES	MARSHALING	MARTINGALS
MARGARITIFEROUS	MARINATION	MARMALISING	MARSHALLED	MARTYRDOMS
MARGENTING	MARINATIONS	MARMALIZED	MARSHALLER	MARTYRISATION
MARGINALIA	MARIONBERRIES	MARMALIZES	MARSHALLERS	MARTYRISATIONS
MARGINALISATION	MARIONBERRY	MARMALIZING	MARSHALLING	MARTYRISED
MARGINALISE	MARIONETTE	MARMARISED	MARSHALLINGS	MARTYRISES
MARGINALISED	MARIONETTES	MARMARISING	MARSHALSHIP	MARTYRISING
MARGINALISES	MARISCHALLED	MARMARIZED	MARSHALSHIPS	MARTYRIZATION
MARGINALISING	MARISCHALLING	MARMARIZES	MARSHBUCKS	MARTYRIZATIONS
MARGINALISM	MARISCHALS	MARMARIZING	MARSHINESS	MARTYRIZED
MARGINALISMS	MARIVAUDAGE	MARMAROSES	MARSHINESSES	MARTYRIZES
MARGINALIST	MARIVAUDAGES	MARMAROSIS	MARSHLANDER	MARTYRIZING
MARGINALISTS	MARKEDNESS	MARMELISED	MARSHLANDERS	MARTYROLOGIC
MARGINALITIES	MARKEDNESSES	MARMELISES	MARSHLANDS	MARTYROLOGICAL
MARGINALITY	MARKETABILITIES	MARMELISING	MARSHLOCKS	MARTYROLOGIES
MARGINALIZATION	MARKETABILITY	MARMELIZED	MARSHLOCKSES	MARTYROLOGIST
MARGINALIZE	MARKETABLE	MARMELIZES	MARSHMALLOW	MARTYROLOGISTS
MARGINALIZED	MARKETABLENESS	MARMELIZING	MARSHMALLOWS	MARTYROLOGY
MARGINALIZES	MARKETABLY	MARMOREALLY	MARSHMALLOWY	MARVELLING
MARGINALIZING	MARKETEERS	MAROONINGS	MARSHWORTS	MARVELLOUS
MARGINALLY	MARKETINGS	MARPRELATE	MARSIPOBRANCH	MARVELLOUSLY
MARGINATED	MARKETISATION	MARPRELATED	MARSIPOBRANCHS	MARVELLOUSNESS
MARGINATES	MARKETISATIONS	MARPRELATES	MARSQUAKES	MARVELOUSLY
MARGINATING	MARKETISED	MARPRELATING	MARSUPIALIAN	MARVELOUSNESS
MARGINATION	MARKETISES	MARQUESSATE	MARSUPIALIANS	MARVELOUSNESSES
MARGINATIONS	MARKETISING	MARQUESSATES	MARSUPIALS	MASCARAING
MARGRAVATE	MARKETIZATION	MARQUESSES	MARSUPIANS	MASCARPONE
MARGRAVATES	MARKETIZATIONS	MARQUETERIE	MARSUPIUMS	MASCARPONES
MARGRAVIAL	MARKETIZED	MARQUETERIES	MARTELLANDO	MASCULINELY
MARGRAVIATE	MARKETIZES	MARQUETRIES	MARTELLANDOS	MASCULINENESS
MARGRAVIATES	MARKETIZING	MARQUISATE	MARTELLATO	MASCULINENESSES
MARGRAVINE	MARKETPLACE	MARQUISATES	MARTELLING	MASCULINES
MARGRAVINES	MARKETPLACES	MARQUISETTE	MARTENSITE	MASCULINISATION
MARGUERITE	MARKSMANSHIP	MARQUISETTE	MARTENSITES	MASCULINISE

MASCULINISED	MASSINESSES	MASTICATING	MATCHMAKERS	MATEYNESSES
MASCULINISES	MASSIVENESS	MASTICATION	MATCHMAKES	MATFELLONS
MASCULINISING	MASSIVENESSES	MASTICATIONS	MATCHMAKING	MATGRASSES
MASCULINIST	MASSOTHERAPIES	MASTICATOR	MATCHMAKINGS	MATHEMATIC
MASCULINISTS	MASSOTHERAPIST	MASTICATORIES	MATCHMARKED	MATHEMATICAL
MASCULINITIES	MASSOTHERAPISTS	MASTICATORS	MATCHMARKING	MATHEMATICALLY
MASCULINITY	MASSOTHERAPY	MASTICATORY	MATCHMARKS	MATHEMATICIAN
MASCULINIZATION	MASSPRIEST	MASTIGOPHORAN	MATCHPLAYS	MATHEMATICIANS
MASCULINIZE	MASSPRIESTS	MASTIGOPHORANS	MATCHSTICK	MATHEMATICISE
MASCULINIZED	MASSYMORES	MASTIGOPHORE	MATCHSTICKS	MATHEMATICISED
MASCULINIZES	MASTECTOMIES	MASTIGOPHORES	MATCHWOODS	MATHEMATICISES
MASCULINIZING	MASTECTOMY	MASTIGOPHORIC	MATELASSES	MATHEMATICISING
MASCULISTS	MASTERATES	MASTIGOPHOROUS	MATELLASSE	MATHEMATICISM
MASHGICHIM	MASTERCLASS	MASTITIDES	MATELLASSES	MATHEMATICISMS
MASKALLONGE	MASTERCLASSES	MASTITISES	MATELOTTES	MATHEMATICIZE
MASKALLONGES	MASTERDOMS	MASTODONIC	MATERFAMILIAS	MATHEMATICIZED
MASKALONGE	MASTERFULLY	MASTODONTIC	MATERFAMILIASES	MATHEMATICIZES
MASKALONGES	MASTERFULNESS	MASTODONTS	MATERIALISATION	MATHEMATICIZING
MASKANONGE	MASTERFULNESSES	MASTODYNIA	MATERIALISE	MATHEMATICS
MASKANONGES	MASTERHOOD	MASTODYNIAS	MATERIALISED	MATHEMATISATION
MASKINONGE	MASTERHOODS	MASTOIDECTOMIES	MATERIALISER	MATHEMATISE
MASKINONGES	MASTERINGS	MASTOIDECTOMY	MATERIALISERS	MATHEMATISED
MASKIROVKA	MASTERLESS	MASTOIDITIS	MATERIALISES	MATHEMATISES
MASKIROVKAS	MASTERLINESS	MASTOIDITISES	MATERIALISING	MATHEMATISING
MASOCHISMS	MASTERLINESSES	MASTOPEXIES	MATERIALISM	MATHEMATIZATION
MASOCHISTIC	MASTERMIND	MASTURBATE	MATERIALISMS	MATHEMATIZE
MASOCHISTICALLY	MASTERMINDED	MASTURBATED	MATERIALIST	MATHEMATIZED
MASOCHISTS	MASTERMINDING	MASTURBATES	MATERIALISTIC	MATHEMATIZES
MASONICALLY	MASTERMINDS	MASTURBATING	MATERIALISTICAL	MATHEMATIZING
MASQUERADE	MASTERPIECE	MASTURBATION	MATERIALISTS	MATINESSES
MASQUERADED	MASTERPIECES	MASTURBATIONS	MATERIALITIES	MATRESFAMILIAS
MASQUERADER	MASTERSHIP	MASTURBATOR	MATERIALITY	MATRIARCHAL
MASQUERADERS	MASTERSHIPS	MASTURBATORS	MATERIALIZATION	MATRIARCHALISM
MASQUERADES	MASTERSINGER	MASTURBATORY	MATERIALIZE	MATRIARCHALISMS
MASQUERADING	MASTERSINGERS	MATACHINAS	MATERIALIZED	MATRIARCHATE
MASSACRERS	MASTERSTROKE	MATAGOURIS	MATERIALIZER	MATRIARCHATES
MASSACRING	MASTERSTROKES	MATCHBOARD	MATERIALIZERS	MATRIARCHIC
MASSAGISTS	MASTERWORK	MATCHBOARDING	MATERIALIZES	MATRIARCHIES
MASSARANDUBA	MASTERWORKS	MATCHBOARDINGS	MATERIALIZING	MATRIARCHS
MASSARANDUBAS	MASTERWORT	MATCHBOARDS	MATERIALLY	MATRIARCHY
MASSASAUGA	MASTERWORTS	MATCHBOOKS	MATERIALNESS	MATRICIDAL
MASSASAUGAS	MASTHEADED	MATCHBOXES	MATERIALNESSES	MATRICIDES
MASSERANDUBA	MASTHEADING	MATCHLESSLY	MATERNALISM	MATRICLINIC
MASSERANDUBAS	MASTHOUSES	MATCHLESSNESS	MATERNALISMS	MATRICLINOUS
MASSETERIC	MASTICABLE	MATCHLESSNESSES	MATERNALISTIC	MATRICULANT
MASSIFICATION	MASTICATED	MATCHLOCKS	MATERNALLY	MATRICULANTS
MASSIFICATIONS	MASTICATES	MATCHMAKER	MATERNITIES	MATRICULAR

MATRICULAS	MATROYSHKAS	MAXIMAPHILY	MEASLINESSES	MECHANIZED
MATRICULATE	MATRYOSHKA	MAXIMATION	MEASURABILITIES	MECHANIZER
MATRICULATED	MATRYOSHKI	MAXIMATIONS	MEASURABILITY	MECHANIZERS
MATRICULATES	MATSUTAKES	MAXIMISATION	MEASURABLE	MECHANIZES
MATRICULATING	MATTAMORES	MAXIMISATIONS	MEASURABLENESS	MECHANIZING
MATRICULATION	MATTERLESS	MAXIMISERS	MEASURABLY	MECHANOCHEMICAL
MATRICULATIONS	MATTIFYING	MAXIMISING	MEASUREDLY	MECHANOMORPHISM
MATRICULATOR	MATTRASSES	MAXIMIZATION	MEASUREDNESS	MECHANORECEPTOR
MATRICULATORS	MATTRESSES	MAXIMIZATIONS	MEASUREDNESSES	MECHANOTHERAPY
MATRICULATORY	MATURATING	MAXIMIZERS	MEASURELESS	MECHATRONIC
MATRIFOCAL	MATURATION	MAXIMIZING	MEASURELESSLY	MECHATRONICS
MATRIFOCALITIES	MATURATIONAL	MAYFLOWERS	MEASURELESSNESS	MECLIZINES
MATRIFOCALITY	MATURATIONS	MAYONNAISE	MEASUREMENT	MECONOPSES
MATRILINEAL	MATURATIVE	MAYONNAISES	MEASUREMENTS	MECONOPSIS
MATRILINEALLY	MATURENESS	MAYORALTIES	MEASURINGS	MEDAILLONS
MATRILINEAR	MATURENESSES	MAYORESSES	MEATINESSES	MEDALLIONED
MATRILINIES	MATURITIES	MAYORSHIPS	MEATLOAVES	MEDALLIONING
MATRILOCAL	MATUTINALLY	MAYSTERDOME	MEATPACKING	MEDALLIONS
MATRILOCALITIES	MAUDLINISM	MAYSTERDOMES	MEATPACKINGS	MEDALLISTS
MATRILOCALITY	MAUDLINISMS	MAZARINADE	MEATSCREEN	MEDALPLAYS
MATRILOCALLY	MAUDLINNESS	MAZARINADES	MEATSCREENS	MEDDLESOME
MATRIMONIAL	MAUDLINNESSES	MAZEDNESSES	MEATSPACES	MEDDLESOMELY
MATRIMONIALLY	MAULSTICKS	MAZINESSES	MECAMYLAMINE	MEDDLESOMENESS
MATRIMONIES	MAUMETRIES	MEADOWLAND	MECAMYLAMINES	MEDDLINGLY
MATRIOSHKA	MAUNDERERS	MEADOWLANDS	MECHANICAL	MEDEVACING
MATRIOSHKI	MAUNDERING	MEADOWLARK	MECHANICALISM	MEDEVACKED
MATROCLINAL	MAUNDERINGS	MEADOWLARKS	MECHANICALISMS	MEDEVACKING
MATROCLINIC	MAUSOLEUMS	MEADOWSWEET	MECHANICALLY	MEDIAEVALISM
MATROCLINIES	MAVERICKED	MEADOWSWEETS	MECHANICALNESS	MEDIAEVALISMS
MATROCLINOUS	MAVERICKING	MEAGERNESS	MECHANICALS	MEDIAEVALIST
MATROCLINY	MAVOURNEEN	MEAGERNESSES	MECHANICIAN	MEDIAEVALISTIC
MATRONAGES	MAVOURNEENS	MEAGRENESS	MECHANICIANS	MEDIAEVALISTS
MATRONHOOD	MAVOURNINS	MEAGRENESSES	MECHANISABLE	MEDIAEVALLY
MATRONHOODS	MAWKISHNESS	MEALINESSES	MECHANISATION	MEDIAEVALS
MATRONISED	MAWKISHNESSES	MEALYMOUTHED	MECHANISATIONS	MEDIAGENIC
MATRONISES	MAWMETRIES	MEANDERERS	MECHANISED	MEDIASTINA
MATRONISING	MAXILLARIES	MEANDERING	MECHANISER	MEDIASTINAL
MATRONIZED	MAXILLIPED	MEANDERINGLY	MECHANISERS	MEDIASTINUM
MATRONIZES	MAXILLIPEDARY	MEANINGFUL	MECHANISES	MEDIATENESS
MATRONIZING	MAXILLIPEDE	MEANINGFULLY	MECHANISING	MEDIATENESSES
MATRONLINESS	MAXILLIPEDES	MEANINGFULNESS	MECHANISMS	MEDIATIONAL
MATRONLINESSES	MAXILLIPEDS	MEANINGLESS	MECHANISTIC	MEDIATIONS
MATRONSHIP	MAXILLOFACIAL	MEANINGLESSLY	MECHANISTICALLY	MEDIATISATION
MATRONSHIPS	MAXILLULAE	MEANINGLESSNESS	MECHANISTS	MEDIATISATIONS
MATRONYMIC	MAXIMALIST	MEANNESSES	MECHANIZABLE	MEDIATISED
MATRONYMICS	MAXIMALISTS	MEANWHILES	MECHANIZATION	MEDIATISES
MATROYSHKA	MAXIMAPHILIES	MEASLINESS	MECHANIZATIONS	MEDIATISING

MEDIATIZATION	MEDIEVALIST	MEGAFAUNAL	MEGAPHONED	MELANCHOLIACS
MEDIATIZATIONS	MEDIEVALISTIC	MEGAFAUNAS	MEGAPHONES	MELANCHOLIAE
MEDIATIZED	MEDIEVALISTS	MEGAFLORAE	MEGAPHONIC	MELANCHOLIAS
MEDIATIZES	MEDIEVALLY	MEGAFLORAS	MEGAPHONICALLY	MELANCHOLIC
MEDIATIZING	MEDIOCRACIES	MEGAGAMETE	MEGAPHONING	MELANCHOLICALLY
MEDIATORIAL	MEDIOCRACY	MEGAGAMETES	MEGAPHYLLS	MELANCHOLICS
MEDIATORIALLY	MEDIOCRITIES	MEGAGAMETOPHYTE	MEGAPIXELS	MELANCHOLIES
MEDIATORSHIP	MEDIOCRITY	MEGAGAUSSES	MEGAPLEXES	MELANCHOLILY
MEDIATORSHIPS	MEDITATING	MEGAHERBIVORE	MEGAPROJECT	MELANCHOLINESS
MEDIATRESS	MEDITATION	MEGAHERBIVORES	MEGAPROJECTS	MELANCHOLIOUS
MEDIATRESSES	MEDITATIONS	MEGAHERTZES	MEGASCOPES	MELANCHOLY
MEDIATRICES	MEDITATIVE	MEGAJOULES	MEGASCOPIC	MELANISATION
MEDIATRIXES	MEDITATIVELY	MEGAKARYOCYTE	MEGASCOPICALLY	MELANISATIONS
MEDICALISATION	MEDITATIVENESS	MEGAKARYOCYTES	MEGASPORANGIA	MELANISING
MEDICALISATIONS	MEDITATORS	MEGAKARYOCYTIC	MEGASPORANGIUM	MELANISTIC
MEDICALISE	MEDITERRANEAN	MEGALITHIC	MEGASPORES	MELANIZATION
MEDICALISED	MEDIUMISTIC	MEGALITRES	MEGASPORIC	MELANIZATIONS
MEDICALISES	MEDIUMSHIP	MEGALOBLAST	MEGASPOROPHYLL	MELANIZING
MEDICALISING	MEDIUMSHIPS	MEGALOBLASTIC	MEGASPOROPHYLLS	MELANOBLAST
MEDICALIZATION	MEDIVACING	MEGALOBLASTS	MEGASTORES	MELANOBLASTS
MEDICALIZATIONS	MEDIVACKED	MEGALOCARDIA	MEGASTRUCTURE	MELANOCHROI
MEDICALIZE	MEDIVACKING	MEGALOCARDIAS	MEGASTRUCTURES	MELANOCHROIC
MEDICALIZED	MEDRESSEHS	MEGALOCEPHALIC	MEGATECHNOLOGY	MELANOCHROOUS
MEDICALIZES	MEDULLATED	MEGALOCEPHALIES	MEGATHERES	MELANOCYTE
MEDICALIZING	MEDULLOBLASTOMA	MEGALOCEPHALOUS	MEGATHERIAN	MELANOCYTES
MEDICAMENT	MEDUSIFORM	MEGALOCEPHALY	MEGATONNAGE	MELANOGENESES
MEDICAMENTAL	MEEKNESSES	MEGALOMANIA	MEGATONNAGES	MELANOGENESIS
MEDICAMENTALLY	MEERSCHAUM	MEGALOMANIAC	MEGAVERTEBRATE	MELANOMATA
MEDICAMENTARY	MEERSCHAUMS	MEGALOMANIACAL	MEGAVERTEBRATES	MELANOPHORE
MEDICAMENTED	MEETINGHOUSE	MEGALOMANIACS	MEGAVITAMIN	MELANOPHORES
MEDICAMENTING	MEETINGHOUSES	MEGALOMANIAS	MEGAVITAMINS	MELANOSITIES
MEDICAMENTOUS	MEETNESSES	MEGALOMANIC	MEIOFAUNAE	MELANOSITY
MEDICAMENTS	MEFLOQUINE	MEGALOPOLIS	MEIOFAUNAL	MELANOSOME
MEDICASTER	MEFLOQUINES	MEGALOPOLISES	MEIOFAUNAS	MELANOSOMES
MEDICASTERS	MEGACEPHALIC	MEGALOPOLITAN	MEIOSPORES	MELANOTROPIN
MEDICATING	MEGACEPHALIES	MEGALOPOLITANS	MEIOTICALLY	MELANOTROPINS
MEDICATION	MEGACEPHALOUS	MEGALOPSES	MEITNERIUM	MELANTERITE
MEDICATIONS	MEGACEPHALY	MEGALOSAUR	MEITNERIUMS	MELANTERITES
MEDICATIVE	MEGACHURCH	MEGALOSAURI	MEKOMETERS	MELANURIAS
MEDICINABLE	MEGACHURCHES	MEGALOSAURIAN	MELACONITE	MELAPHYRES
MEDICINALLY	MEGACITIES	MEGALOSAURIANS	MELACONITES	MELASTOMACEOUS
MEDICINALS	MEGACORPORATION	MEGALOSAURS	MELALEUCAS	MELATONINS
MEDICINERS	MEGACURIES	MEGALOSAURUS	MELAMPODES	MELIACEOUS
MEDICINING	MEGACYCLES	MEGANEWTON	MELANAEMIA	MELICOTTON
MEDICOLEGAL	MEGADEATHS	MEGANEWTONS	MELANAEMIAS	MELICOTTONS
MEDIEVALISM	MEGAFARADS	MEGAPARSEC	MELANCHOLIA	MELIORABLE
MEDIEVALISMS	MEGAFAUNAE	MEGAPARSECS	MELANCHOLIAC	MELIORATED

MELIORATES

MELIORATES	MELODRAMATISE	MEMORIALISING	MENINGOCOCCAL	MENTHOLATED
MELIORATING	MELODRAMATISED	MEMORIALIST	MENINGOCOCCI	MENTICIDES
MELIORATION	MELODRAMATISES	MEMORIALISTS	MENINGOCOCCIC	MENTIONABLE
MELIORATIONS	MELODRAMATISING	MEMORIALIZATION	MENINGOCOCCUS	MENTIONERS
MELIORATIVE	MELODRAMATIST	MEMORIALIZE	MENISCECTOMIES	MENTIONING
MELIORATIVES	MELODRAMATISTS	MEMORIALIZED	MENISCECTOMY	MENTONNIERE
MELIORATOR	MELODRAMATIZE	MEMORIALIZER	MENISCUSES	MENTONNIERES
MELIORATORS	MELODRAMATIZED	MEMORIALIZERS	MENISPERMACEOUS	MENTORINGS
MELIORISMS	MELODRAMATIZES	MEMORIALIZES	MENISPERMUM	MENTORSHIP
MELIORISTIC	MELODRAMATIZING	MEMORIALIZING	MENISPERMUMS	MENTORSHIPS
MELIORISTS	MELODRAMES	MEMORIALLY	MENOLOGIES	MENUISIERS
MELIORITIES	MELOMANIAC	MEMORISABLE	MENOMINEES	MEPACRINES
MELIPHAGOUS	MELOMANIACS	MEMORISATION	MENOPAUSAL	MEPERIDINE
MELISMATIC	MELOMANIAS	MEMORISATIONS	MENOPAUSES	MEPERIDINES
MELLIFEROUS	MELONGENES	MEMORISERS	MENOPAUSIC	MEPHITICAL
MELLIFICATION	MELOXICAMS	MEMORISING	MENOPOLISES	MEPHITICALLY
MELLIFICATIONS	MELPHALANS	MEMORIZABLE	MENORRHAGIA	MEPHITISES
MELLIFLUENCE	MELTABILITIES	MEMORIZATION	MENORRHAGIAS	MEPHITISMS
MELLIFLUENCES	MELTABILITY	MEMORIZATIONS	MENORRHAGIC	MEPROBAMATE
MELLIFLUENT	MELTINGNESS	MEMORIZERS	MENORRHEAS	MEPROBAMATES
MELLIFLUENTLY	MELTINGNESSES	MEMORIZING	MENORRHOEA	MERBROMINS
MELLIFLUOUS	MELTWATERS	MENACINGLY	MENORRHOEAS	MERCANTILE
MELLIFLUOUSLY	MELUNGEONS	MENADIONES	MENSERVANTS	MERCANTILISM
MELLIFLUOUSNESS	MEMBERLESS	MENAGERIES	MENSTRUALLY	MERCANTILISMS
MELLIPHAGOUS	MEMBERSHIP	MENAQUINONE	MENSTRUATE	MERCANTILIST
MELLIVOROUS	MEMBERSHIPS	MENAQUINONES	MENSTRUATED	MERCANTILISTIC
MELLOPHONE	MEMBRANACEOUS	MENARCHEAL	MENSTRUATES	MERCANTILISTS
MELLOPHONES	MEMBRANEOUS	MENARCHIAL	MENSTRUATING	MERCAPTANS
MELLOTRONS	MEMBRANOUS	MENDACIOUS	MENSTRUATION	MERCAPTIDE
MELLOWNESS	MEMBRANOUSLY	MENDACIOUSLY	MENSTRUATIONS	MERCAPTIDES
MELLOWNESSES	MEMOIRISMS	MENDACIOUSNESS	MENSTRUOUS	MERCAPTOPURINE
MELLOWSPEAK	MEMOIRISTS	MENDACITIES	MENSTRUUMS	MERCAPTOPURINES
MELLOWSPEAKS	MEMORABILE	MENDELEVIUM	MENSURABILITIES	MERCENARIES
MELOCOTONS	MEMORABILIA	MENDELEVIUMS	MENSURABILITY	MERCENARILY
MELOCOTOON	MEMORABILITIES	MENDICANCIES	MENSURABLE	MERCENARINESS
MELOCOTOONS	MEMORABILITY	MENDICANCY	MENSURATION	MERCENARINESSES
MELODICALLY	MEMORABLENESS	MENDICANTS	MENSURATIONAL	MERCENARISM
MELODIOUSLY	MEMORABLENESSES	MENDICITIES	MENSURATIONS	MERCENARISMS
MELODIOUSNESS	MEMORANDUM	MENINGIOMA	MENSURATIVE	MERCERISATION
MELODIOUSNESSES	MEMORANDUMS	MENINGIOMAS	MENTALESES	MERCERISATIONS
MELODISERS	MEMORATIVE	MENINGIOMATA	MENTALISMS	MERCERISED
MELODISING	MEMORIALISATION	MENINGITIC	MENTALISTIC	MERCERISER
MELODIZERS	MEMORIALISE	MENINGITIDES	MENTALISTICALLY	MERCERISERS
MELODIZING	MEMORIALISED	MENINGITIS	MENTALISTS	MERCERISES
MELODRAMAS	MEMORIALISER	MENINGITISES	MENTALITIES	MERCERISING
MELODRAMATIC	MEMORIALISERS	MENINGOCELE	MENTATIONS	MERCERIZATION
MELODRAMATICS	MEMORIALISES	MENINGOCELES	MENTHACEOUS	MERCERIZATIONS

MERCERIZED	MERCURIALISMS	MEROGONIES	MESHUGASEN	MESOGASTRIC
MERCERIZER	MERCURIALIST	MEROMORPHIC	MESHUGGENAH	MESOGASTRIUM
MERCERIZERS	MERCURIALISTS	MEROMYOSIN	MESHUGGENAHS	MESOGLOEAS
MERCERIZES	MERCURIALITIES	MEROMYOSINS	MESHUGGENEH	MESOGNATHIES
MERCERIZING	MERCURIALITY	MERONYMIES	MESHUGGENEHS	MESOGNATHISM
MERCHANDISE	MERCURIALIZE	MEROPIDANS	MESHUGGENER	MESOGNATHISMS
MERCHANDISED	MERCURIALIZED	MEROPLANKTON	MESHUGGENERS	MESOGNATHOUS
MERCHANDISER	MERCURIALIZES	MEROPLANKTONS	MESITYLENE	MESOGNATHY
MERCHANDISERS	MERCURIALIZING	MEROZOITES	MESITYLENES	MESOHIPPUS
MERCHANDISES	MERCURIALLY	MERPEOPLES	MESMERICAL	MESOHIPPUSES
MERCHANDISING	MERCURIALNESS	MERRIMENTS	MESMERICALLY	MESOKURTIC
MERCHANDISINGS	MERCURIALNESSES	MERRINESSES	MESMERISATION	MESOMERISM
MERCHANDIZE	MERCURIALS	MERRYMAKER	MESMERISATIONS	MESOMERISMS
MERCHANDIZED	MERCURISED	MERRYMAKERS	MESMERISED	MESOMORPHIC
MERCHANDIZER	MERCURISES	MERRYMAKING	MESMERISER	MESOMORPHIES
MERCHANDIZERS	MERCURISING	MERRYMAKINGS	MESMERISERS	MESOMORPHISM
MERCHANDIZES	MERCURIZED	MERRYTHOUGHT	MESMERISES	MESOMORPHISMS
MERCHANDIZING	MERCURIZES	MERRYTHOUGHTS	MESMERISING	MESOMORPHOUS
MERCHANDIZINGS	MERCURIZING	MERVEILLEUSE	MESMERISMS	MESOMORPHS
MERCHANTABILITY	MERDIVOROUS	MERVEILLEUSES	MESMERISTS	MESOMORPHY
MERCHANTABLE	MEREOLOGICAL	MERVEILLEUX	MESMERIZATION	MESONEPHRIC
MERCHANTED	MEREOLOGIES	MERVEILLEUXES	MESMERIZATIONS	MESONEPHROI
MERCHANTING	MERESTONES	MESALLIANCE	MESMERIZED	MESONEPHROS
MERCHANTINGS	MERETRICIOUS	MESALLIANCES	MESMERIZER	MESONEPHROSES
MERCHANTLIKE	MERETRICIOUSLY	MESATICEPHALIC	MESMERIZERS	MESOPAUSES
MERCHANTMAN	MERGANSERS	MESATICEPHALIES	MESMERIZES	MESOPELAGIC
MERCHANTMEN	MERIDIONAL	MESATICEPHALOUS	MESMERIZING	MESOPHILES
MERCHANTRIES	MERIDIONALITIES	MESATICEPHALY	MESNALTIES	MESOPHILIC
MERCHANTRY	MERIDIONALITY	MESCALINES	MESOAMERICAN	MESOPHYLLIC
MERCHILDREN	MERIDIONALLY	MESCALISMS	MESOBENTHOS	MESOPHYLLOUS
MERCIFULLY	MERIDIONALS	MESDEMOISELLES	MESOBENTHOSES	MESOPHYLLS
MERCIFULNESS	MERISTEMATIC	MESENCEPHALA	MESOBLASTIC	MESOPHYTES
MERCIFULNESSES	MERISTICALLY	MESENCEPHALIC	MESOBLASTS	MESOPHYTIC
MERCIFYING	MERITOCRACIES	MESENCEPHALON	MESOCEPHALIC	MESOSCAPHE
MERCILESSLY	MERITOCRACY	MESENCEPHALONS	MESOCEPHALICS	MESOSCAPHES
MERCILESSNESS	MERITOCRAT	MESENCHYMAL	MESOCEPHALIES	MESOSPHERE
MERCILESSNESSES	MERITOCRATIC	MESENCHYMATOUS	MESOCEPHALISM	MESOSPHERES
MERCURATED	MERITOCRATS	MESENCHYME	MESOCEPHALISMS	MESOSPHERIC
MERCURATES	MERITORIOUS	MESENCHYMES	MESOCEPHALOUS	MESOTHELIA
MERCURATING	MERITORIOUSLY	MESENTERIAL	MESOCEPHALY	MESOTHELIAL
MERCURATION	MERITORIOUSNESS	MESENTERIC	MESOCRANIES	MESOTHELIOMA
MERCURATIONS	MERMAIDENS	MESENTERIES	MESOCRATIC	MESOTHELIOMAS
MERCURIALISE	MEROBLASTIC	MESENTERITIS	MESOCYCLONE	MESOTHELIOMATA
MERCURIALISED	MEROBLASTICALLY	MESENTERITISES	MESOCYCLONES	MESOTHELIUM
MERCURIALISES	MEROGENESES	MESENTERON	MESODERMAL	MESOTHELIUMS
MERCURIALISING	MEROGENESIS	MESENTERONIC	MESODERMIC	MESOTHERAPIES
MERCURIALISM	MEROGENETIC	MESHUGAASEN	MESOGASTRIA	MESOTHERAPY

MESOTHORACES	METACENTRE	METAGRABOLIZING	METALLOGRAPHERS	METANEPHRIC
MESOTHORACIC	METACENTRES	METAGROBOLISE	METALLOGRAPHIC	METANEPHROI
MESOTHORAX	METACENTRIC	METAGROBOLISED	METALLOGRAPHIES	METANEPHROS
MESOTHORAXES	METACENTRICS	METAGROBOLISES	METALLOGRAPHIST	METAPERIODIC
MESOTHORIUM	METACERCARIA	METAGROBOLISING	METALLOGRAPHY	METAPHASES
MESOTHORIUMS	METACERCARIAE	METAGROBOLIZE	METALLOIDAL	METAPHORIC
MESOTROPHIC	METACERCARIAL	METAGROBOLIZED	METALLOIDS	METAPHORICAL
MESQUINERIE	METACHROMATIC	METAGROBOLIZES	METALLOPHONE	METAPHORICALLY
MESQUINERIES	METACHROMATISM	METAGROBOLIZING	METALLOPHONES	METAPHORIST
MESSAGINGS	METACHROMATISMS	METALANGUAGE	METALLURGIC	METAPHORISTS
MESSALINES	METACHRONISM	METALANGUAGES	METALLURGICAL	METAPHOSPHATE
MESSEIGNEURS	METACHRONISMS	METALDEHYDE	METALLURGICALLY	METAPHOSPHATES
MESSENGERED	METACHROSES	METALDEHYDES	METALLURGIES	METAPHOSPHORIC
MESSENGERING	METACHROSIS	METALEPSES	METALLURGIST	METAPHRASE
MESSENGERS	METACINNABARITE	METALEPSIS	METALLURGISTS	METAPHRASED
MESSIAHSHIP	METACOGNITION	METALEPTIC	METALLURGY	METAPHRASES
MESSIAHSHIPS	METACOGNITIONS	METALEPTICAL	METALMARKS	METAPHRASING
MESSIANICALLY	METACOMPUTER	METALHEADS	METALSMITH	METAPHRASIS
MESSIANISM	METACOMPUTERS	METALINGUISTIC	METALSMITHS	METAPHRAST
MESSIANISMS	METACOMPUTING	METALINGUISTICS	METALWARES	METAPHRASTIC
MESSINESSES	METACOMPUTINGS	METALISING	METALWORKER	METAPHRASTICAL
MESTRANOLS	METAETHICAL	METALIZATION	METALWORKERS	METAPHRASTS
METABOLICALLY	METAETHICS	METALIZATIONS	METALWORKING	METAPHYSIC
METABOLIES	METAFEMALE	METALIZING	METALWORKINGS	METAPHYSICAL
METABOLISABLE	METAFEMALES	METALLICALLY	METALWORKS	METAPHYSICALLY
METABOLISE	METAFICTION	METALLIDING	METAMATHEMATICS	METAPHYSICIAN
METABOLISED	METAFICTIONAL	METALLIDINGS	METAMERICALLY	METAPHYSICIANS
METABOLISES	METAFICTIONIST	METALLIFEROUS	METAMERISM	METAPHYSICISE
METABOLISING	METAFICTIONISTS	METALLINGS	METAMERISMS	METAPHYSICISED
METABOLISM	METAFICTIONS	METALLISATION	METAMICTISATION	METAPHYSICISES
METABOLISMS	METAGALACTIC	METALLISATIONS	METAMICTIZATION	METAPHYSICISING
METABOLITE	METAGALAXIES	METALLISED	METAMORPHIC	METAPHYSICIST
METABOLITES	METAGALAXY	METALLISES	METAMORPHICALLY	METAPHYSICISTS
METABOLIZABLE	METAGENESES	METALLISING	METAMORPHISM	METAPHYSICIZE
METABOLIZE	METAGENESIS	METALLISTS	METAMORPHISMS	METAPHYSICIZED
METABOLIZED	METAGENETIC	METALLIZATION	METAMORPHIST	METAPHYSICIZES
METABOLIZES	METAGENETICALLY	METALLIZATIONS	METAMORPHISTS	METAPHYSICIZING
METABOLIZING	METAGNATHISM	METALLIZED	METAMORPHOSE	METAPHYSICS
METABOLOME	METAGNATHISMS	METALLIZES	METAMORPHOSED	METAPLASES
METABOLOMES	METAGNATHOUS	METALLIZING	METAMORPHOSES	METAPLASIA
METABOLOMICS	METAGRABOLISE	METALLOCENE	METAMORPHOSING	METAPLASIAS
METABOTROPIC	METAGRABOLISED	METALLOCENES	METAMORPHOSIS	METAPLASIS
METACARPAL	METAGRABOLISES	METALLOGENETIC	METAMORPHOUS	METAPLASMIC
METACARPALS	METAGRABOLISING	METALLOGENIC	METANALYSES	METAPLASMS
METACARPUS	METAGRABOLIZE	METALLOGENIES	METANALYSIS	METAPLASTIC
METACENTER	METAGRABOLIZED	METALLOGENY	METANARRATIVE	METAPOLITICAL
METACENTERS	METAGRABOLIZES	METALLOGRAPHER	METANARRATIVES	METAPOLITICS

METAPSYCHIC	METATHESIZE	METEOROIDAL	METHODISER	METHYLPHENOL
METAPSYCHICAL	METATHESIZED	METEOROIDS	METHODISERS	METHYLPHENOLS
METAPSYCHICS	METATHESIZES	METEOROLITE	METHODISES	METHYLTHIONINE
METAPSYCHOLOGY	METATHESIZING	METEOROLITES	METHODISING	METHYLTHIONINES
METARCHONS	METATHETIC	METEOROLOGIC	METHODISMS	METHYLXANTHINE
METASEQUOIA	METATHETICAL	METEOROLOGICAL	METHODISTIC	METHYLXANTHINES
METASEQUOIAS	METATHETICALLY	METEOROLOGIES	METHODISTS	METHYSERGIDE
METASILICATE	METATHORACES	METEOROLOGIST	METHODIZATION	METHYSERGIDES
METASILICATES	METATHORACIC	METEOROLOGISTS	METHODIZATIONS	METICULOSITIES
METASILICIC	METATHORAX	METEOROLOGY	METHODIZED	METICULOSITY
METASOMATA	METATHORAXES	METERSTICK	METHODIZER	METICULOUS
METASOMATIC	METATUNGSTIC	METERSTICKS	METHODIZERS	METICULOUSLY
METASOMATISM	METAVANADIC	METESTICKS	METHODIZES	METICULOUSNESS
METASOMATISMS	METAVERSES	METESTROUS	METHODIZING	METOESTROUS
METASOMATOSES	METAXYLEMS	METESTRUSES	METHODOLOGICAL	METOESTRUS
METASOMATOSIS	METECDYSES	METFORMINS	METHODOLOGIES	METOESTRUSES
METASTABILITIES	METECDYSIS	METHACRYLATE	METHODOLOGIST	METONYMICAL
METASTABILITY	METEMPIRIC	METHACRYLATES	METHODOLOGISTS	METONYMICALLY
METASTABLE	METEMPIRICAL	METHACRYLIC	METHODOLOGY	METONYMIES
METASTABLES	METEMPIRICALLY	METHADONES	METHOMANIA	METOPOSCOPIC
METASTABLY	METEMPIRICISM	METHAEMOGLOBIN	METHOMANIAS	METOPOSCOPICAL
METASTASES	METEMPIRICISMS	METHAEMOGLOBINS	METHOTREXATE	METOPOSCOPIES
METASTASIS	METEMPIRICIST	METHAMPHETAMINE	METHOTREXATES	METOPOSCOPIST
METASTASISE	METEMPIRICISTS	METHANATION	METHOXIDES	METOPOSCOPISTS
METASTASISED	METEMPIRICS	METHANATIONS	METHOXYBENZENE	METOPOSCOPY
METASTASISES	METEMPSYCHOSES	METHANOMETER	METHOXYBENZENES	METRALGIAS
METASTASISING	METEMPSYCHOSIS	METHANOMETERS	METHOXYCHLOR	METRICALLY
METASTASIZE	METEMPSYCHOSIST	METHAQUALONE	METHOXYCHLORS	METRICATED
METASTASIZED	METENCEPHALA	METHAQUALONES	METHOXYFLURANE	METRICATES
METASTASIZES	METENCEPHALIC	METHEDRINE	METHOXYFLURANES	METRICATING
METASTASIZING	METENCEPHALON	METHEDRINES	METHYLAMINE	METRICATION
METASTATIC	METENCEPHALONS	METHEGLINS	METHYLAMINES	METRICATIONS
METASTATICALLY	METEORICALLY	METHEMOGLOBIN	METHYLASES	METRICIANS
METATARSAL	METEORISMS	METHEMOGLOBINS	METHYLATED	METRICISED
METATARSALS	METEORISTS	METHENAMINE	METHYLATES	METRICISES
METATARSUS	METEORITAL	METHENAMINES	METHYLATING	METRICISING
METATHEORETICAL	METEORITES	METHICILLIN	METHYLATION	METRICISMS
METATHEORIES	METEORITIC	METHICILLINS	METHYLATIONS	METRICISTS
METATHEORY	METEORITICAL	METHINKETH	METHYLATOR	METRICIZED
METATHERIAN	METEORITICIST	METHIONINE	METHYLATORS	METRICIZES
METATHERIANS	METEORITICISTS	METHIONINES	METHYLCELLULOSE	METRICIZING
METATHESES	METEORITICS	METHODICAL	METHYLDOPA	METRIFICATION
METATHESIS	METEOROGRAM	METHODICALLY	METHYLDOPAS	METRIFICATIONS
METATHESISE	METEOROGRAMS	METHODICALNESS	METHYLENES	METRIFIERS
METATHESISED	METEOROGRAPH	METHODISATION	METHYLMERCURIES	METRIFYING
METATHESISES	METEOROGRAPHIC	METHODISATIONS	METHYLMERCURY	METRITISES
METATHESISING	METEOROGRAPHS	METHODISED	METHYLPHENIDATE	METROLOGIC

M

METROLOGICAL	MICRIFYING	MICROCAPSULES	MICROCRACKING	MICROFILAMENTS
METROLOGICALLY	MICROAEROPHILE	MICROCARDS	MICROCRACKINGS	MICROFILARIA
METROLOGIES	MICROAEROPHILES	MICROCASSETTE	MICROCRACKS	MICROFILARIAE
METROLOGIST	MICROAEROPHILIC	MICROCASSETTES	MICROCRYSTAL	MICROFILARIAL
METROLOGISTS	MICROAMPERE	MICROCELEBRITY	MICROCRYSTALS	MICROFILING
METROMANIA	MICROAMPERES	MICROCEPHAL	MICROCULTURAL	MICROFILINGS
METROMANIAS	MICROANALYSES	MICROCEPHALIC	MICROCULTURE	MICROFILMABLE
METRONIDAZOLE	MICROANALYSIS	MICROCEPHALICS	MICROCULTURES	MICROFILMED
METRONIDAZOLES	MICROANALYST	MICROCEPHALIES	MICROCURIE	MICROFILMER
METRONOMES	MICROANALYSTS	MICROCEPHALOUS	MICROCURIES	MICROFILMERS
METRONOMIC	MICROANALYTIC	MICROCEPHALS	MICROCYTES	MICROFILMING
METRONOMICAL	MICROANALYTICAL	MICROCEPHALY	MICROCYTIC	MICROFILMS
METRONOMICALLY	MICROANATOMICAL	MICROCHEMICAL	MICRODETECTION	MICROFILTER
METRONYMIC	MICROANATOMIES	MICROCHEMISTRY	MICRODETECTIONS	MICROFILTERS
METRONYMICS	MICROANATOMY	MICROCHIPPED	MICRODETECTOR	MICROFLOPPIES
METROPLEXES	MICROARRAY	MICROCHIPPING	MICRODETECTORS	MICROFLOPPY
METROPOLIS	MICROARRAYS	MICROCHIPS	MICRODISSECTION	MICROFLORA
METROPOLISES	MICROBALANCE	MICROCIRCUIT	MICRODONTOUS	MICROFLORAE
METROPOLITAN	MICROBALANCES	MICROCIRCUITRY	MICRODRIVE	MICROFLORAL
METROPOLITANATE	MICROBAROGRAPH	MICROCIRCUITS	MICRODRIVES	MICROFLORAS
METROPOLITANISE	MICROBAROGRAPHS	MICROCLIMATE	MICROEARTHQUAKE	MICROFORMS
METROPOLITANISM	MICROBEAMS	MICROCLIMATES	MICROECONOMIC	MICROFOSSIL
METROPOLITANIZE	MICROBIOLOGIC	MICROCLIMATIC	MICROECONOMICS	MICROFOSSILS
METROPOLITANS	MICROBIOLOGICAL	MICROCLINE	MICROELECTRODE	MICROFUNGI
METROPOLITICAL	MICROBIOLOGIES	MICROCLINES	MICROELECTRODES	MICROFUNGUS
METRORRHAGIA	MICROBIOLOGIST	MICROCOCCAL	MICROELECTRONIC	MICROGAMETE
METRORRHAGIAS	MICROBIOLOGISTS	MICROCOCCI	MICROELEMENT	MICROGAMETES
METROSEXUAL	MICROBIOLOGY	MICROCOCCUS	MICROELEMENTS	MICROGAMETOCYTE
METROSEXUALS	MICROBIOTA	MICROCODES	MICROEVOLUTION	MICROGENERATION
METROSTYLE	MICROBLOGGER	MICROCOMPONENT	MICROEVOLUTIONS	MICROGLIAS
METROSTYLES	MICROBLOGGERS	MICROCOMPONENTS	MICROFARAD	MICROGRAMS
METTLESOME	MICROBLOGGING	MICROCOMPUTER	MICROFARADS	MICROGRANITE
METTLESOMENESS	MICROBLOGGINGS	MICROCOMPUTERS	MICROFAUNA	MICROGRANITES
MEZCALINES	MICROBLOGS	MICROCOMPUTING	MICROFAUNAE	MICROGRANITIC
MEZZALUNAS	MICROBREWER	MICROCOMPUTINGS	MICROFAUNAL	MICROGRAPH
MEZZANINES	MICROBREWERIES	MICROCOPIED	MICROFAUNAS	MICROGRAPHED
MEZZOTINTED	MICROBREWERS	MICROCOPIES	MICROFELSITIC	MICROGRAPHER
MEZZOTINTER	MICROBREWERY	MICROCOPYING	MICROFIBER	MICROGRAPHERS
MEZZOTINTERS	MICROBREWING	MICROCOPYINGS	MICROFIBERS	MICROGRAPHIC
MEZZOTINTING	MICROBREWINGS	MICROCOSMIC	MICROFIBRE	MICROGRAPHICS
MEZZOTINTO	MICROBREWS	MICROCOSMICAL	MICROFIBRES	MICROGRAPHIES
MEZZOTINTOS	MICROBUBBLES	MICROCOSMICALLY	MICROFIBRIL	MICROGRAPHING
MEZZOTINTS	MICROBURST	MICROCOSMOS	MICROFIBRILLAR	MICROGRAPHS
MIAROLITIC	MICROBURSTS	MICROCOSMOSES	MICROFIBRILS	MICROGRAPHY
MIASMATICAL	MICROBUSES	MICROCOSMS	MICROFICHE	MICROGRAVITIES
MIASMATOUS	MICROBUSSES	MICROCRACK	MICROFICHES	MICROGRAVITY
MIASMICALLY	MICROCAPSULE	MICROCRACKED	MICROFILAMENT	MICROGREENS

MICROGROOVE	MICROMETEOROIDS	MICROPEGMATITE	MICROPROCESSORS	MICROSKIRTS
MICROGROOVES	MICROMETER	MICROPEGMATITES	MICROPROGRAM	MICROSLEEP
MICROHABITAT	MICROMETERS	MICROPEGMATITIC	MICROPROGRAMS	MICROSLEEPS
MICROHABITATS	MICROMETHOD	MICROPHAGE	MICROPROJECTION	MICROSMATIC
MICROIMAGE	MICROMETHODS	MICROPHAGES	MICROPROJECTOR	MICROSOMAL
MICROIMAGES	MICROMETRE	MICROPHAGOUS	MICROPROJECTORS	MICROSOMES
MICROINCHES	MICROMETRES	MICROPHONE	MICROPSIAS	MICROSPECIES
MICROINJECT	MICROMETRIC	MICROPHONES	MICROPTEROUS	MICROSPHERE
MICROINJECTED	MICROMETRICAL	MICROPHONIC	MICROPUBLISHER	MICROSPHERES
MICROINJECTING	MICROMETRIES	MICROPHONICS	MICROPUBLISHERS	MICROSPHERICAL
MICROINJECTION	MICROMETRY	MICROPHOTOGRAPH	MICROPUBLISHING	MICROSPORANGIA
MICROINJECTIONS	MICROMICROCURIE	MICROPHOTOMETER	MICROPULSATION	MICROSPORANGIUM
MICROINJECTS	MICROMICROFARAD	MICROPHOTOMETRY	MICROPULSATIONS	MICROSPORE
MICROLIGHT	MICROMILLIMETRE	MICROPHYLL	MICROPUMPS	MICROSPORES
MICROLIGHTING	MICROMINIATURE	MICROPHYLLOUS	MICROPUNCTURE	MICROSPORIC
MICROLIGHTINGS	MICROMINIS	MICROPHYLLS	MICROPUNCTURES	MICROSPOROCYTE
MICROLIGHTS	MICROMOLAR	MICROPHYSICAL	MICROPYLAR	MICROSPOROCYTES
MICROLITER	MICROMOLES	MICROPHYSICALLY	MICROPYLES	MICROSPOROPHYLL
MICROLITERS	MICROMORPHOLOGY	MICROPHYSICS	MICROPYROMETER	MICROSPOROUS
MICROLITES	MICRONATION	MICROPHYTE	MICROPYROMETERS	MICROSTATE
MICROLITHIC	MICRONATIONS	MICROPHYTES	MICROQUAKE	MICROSTATES
MICROLITHS	MICRONEEDLE	MICROPHYTIC	MICROQUAKES	MICROSTOMATOUS
MICROLITIC	MICRONEEDLES	MICROPIPET	MICRORADIOGRAPH	MICROSTOMOUS
MICROLOANS	MICRONISATION	MICROPIPETS	MICROREADER	MICROSTRUCTURAL
MICROLOGIC	MICRONISATIONS	MICROPIPETTE	MICROREADERS	MICROSTRUCTURE
MICROLOGICAL	MICRONISED	MICROPIPETTES	MICROSATELLITE	MICROSTRUCTURES
MICROLOGICALLY	MICRONISES	MICROPLANKTON	MICROSATELLITES	MICROSURGEON
MICROLOGIES	MICRONISING	MICROPLANKTONS	MICROSCALE	MICROSURGEONS
MICROLOGIST	MICRONIZATION	MICROPOLIS	MICROSCALES	MICROSURGERIES
MICROLOGISTS	MICRONIZATIONS	MICROPOLISES	MICROSCOPE	MICROSURGERY
MICROLUCES	MICRONIZED	MICROPORES	MICROSCOPES	MICROSURGICAL
MICROLUXES	MICRONIZES	MICROPOROSITIES	MICROSCOPIC	MICROSWITCH
MICROMANAGE	MICRONIZING	MICROPOROSITY	MICROSCOPICAL	MICROSWITCHES
MICROMANAGED	MICRONUCLEI	MICROPOROUS	MICROSCOPICALLY	MICROTECHNIC
MICROMANAGEMENT	MICRONUCLEUS	MICROPOWER	MICROSCOPIES	MICROTECHNICS
MICROMANAGER	MICRONUCLEUSES	MICROPOWERS	MICROSCOPIST	MICROTECHNIQUE
MICROMANAGERS	MICRONUTRIENT	MICROPRINT	MICROSCOPISTS	MICROTECHNIQUES
MICROMANAGES	MICRONUTRIENTS	MICROPRINTED	MICROSCOPY	MICROTECHNOLOGY
MICROMANAGING	MICROORGANISM	MICROPRINTING	MICROSECOND	MICROTOMES
MICROMARKETING	MICROORGANISMS	MICROPRINTINGS	MICROSECONDS	MICROTOMIC
MICROMARKETINGS	MICROPARASITE	MICROPRINTS	MICROSEISM	MICROTOMICAL
MICROMERES	MICROPARASITES	MICROPRISM	MICROSEISMIC	MICROTOMIES
MICROMESHES	MICROPARASITIC	MICROPRISMS	MICROSEISMICAL	MICROTOMIST
MICROMETEORITE	MICROPARTICLE	MICROPROBE	MICROSEISMICITY	MICROTOMISTS
MICROMETEORITES	MICROPARTICLES	MICROPROBES	MICROSEISMS	MICROTONAL
MICROMETEORITIC	MICROPAYMENT	MICROPROCESSING	MICROSITES	MICROTONALITIES
MICROMETEOROID	MICROPAYMENTS	MICROPROCESSOR	MICROSKIRT	MICROTONALITY

M

MICROTONALLY	MIDDLEWEIGHTS	MILITANTLY	MILLENARISMS	MILLIMOLAR
MICROTONES	MIDDLINGLY	MILITANTNESS	MILLENNIAL	MILLIMOLES
MICROTUBULAR	MIDFIELDER	MILITANTNESSES	MILLENNIALISM	MILLINERIES
MICROTUBULE	MIDFIELDERS	MILITARIES	MILLENNIALISMS	MILLIONAIRE
MICROTUBULES	MIDINETTES	MILITARILY	MILLENNIALIST	MILLIONAIRES
MICROTUNNELLING	MIDISKIRTS	MILITARISATION	MILLENNIALISTS	MILLIONAIRESS
MICROVASCULAR	MIDLANDERS	MILITARISATIONS	MILLENNIALLY	MILLIONAIRESSES
MICROVILLAR	MIDLATITUDE	MILITARISE	MILLENNIANISM	MILLIONARY
MICROVILLI	MIDLATITUDES	MILITARISED	MILLENNIANISMS	MILLIONFOLD
MICROVILLOUS	MIDLITTORAL	MILITARISES	MILLENNIARISM	MILLIONNAIRE
MICROVILLUS	MIDLITTORALS	MILITARISING	MILLENNIARISMS	MILLIONNAIRES
MICROVOLTS	MIDNIGHTLY	MILITARISM	MILLENNIUM	MILLIONNAIRESS
MICROWATTS	MIDRASHOTH	MILITARISMS	MILLENNIUMS	MILLIONTHS
MICROWAVABLE	MIDSAGITTAL	MILITARIST	MILLEPEDES	MILLIOSMOL
MICROWAVEABLE	MIDSECTION	MILITARISTIC	MILLEPORES	MILLIOSMOLS
MICROWAVED	MIDSECTIONS	MILITARISTS	MILLERITES	MILLIPEDES
MICROWAVES	MIDSHIPMAN	MILITARIZATION	MILLESIMAL	MILLIPROBE
MICROWAVING	MIDSHIPMATE	MILITARIZATIONS	MILLESIMALLY	MILLIPROBES
MICROWIRES	MIDSHIPMATES	MILITARIZE	MILLESIMALS	MILLIRADIAN
MICROWORLD	MIDSHIPMEN	MILITARIZED	MILLHOUSES	MILLIRADIANS
MICROWORLDS	MIDSTORIES	MILITARIZES	MILLIAMPERE	MILLIROENTGEN
MICROWRITER	MIDSTREAMS	MILITARIZING	MILLIAMPERES	MILLIROENTGENS
MICROWRITERS	MIDSUMMERS	MILITATING	MILLIARIES	MILLISECOND
MICRURGIES	MIDWATCHES	MILITATION	MILLICURIE	MILLISECONDS
MICTURATED	MIDWIFERIES	MILITATIONS	MILLICURIES	MILLISIEVERT
MICTURATES	MIDWINTERS	MILITIAMAN	MILLIDEGREE	MILLISIEVERTS
MICTURATING	MIFEPRISTONE	MILITIAMEN	MILLIDEGREES	MILLIVOLTS
MICTURITION	MIFEPRISTONES	MILKFISHES	MILLIGRAMME	MILLIWATTS
MICTURITIONS	MIFFINESSES	MILKINESSES	MILLIGRAMMES	MILLOCRACIES
MIDDELMANNETJIE	MIGHTINESS	MILKSHAKES	MILLIGRAMS	MILLOCRACY
MIDDELSKOT	MIGHTINESSES	MILKSOPISM	MILLIHENRIES	MILLOCRATS
MIDDELSKOTS	MIGMATITES	MILKSOPISMS	MILLIHENRY	MILLSCALES
MIDDENSTEAD	MIGNONETTE	MILKSOPPING	MILLIHENRYS	MILLSTONES
MIDDENSTEADS	MIGNONETTES	MILKTOASTS	MILLILAMBERT	MILLSTREAM
MIDDLEBREAKER	MIGRAINEUR	MILLBOARDS	MILLILAMBERTS	MILLSTREAMS
MIDDLEBREAKERS	MIGRAINEURS	MILLEFEUILLE	MILLILITER	MILLWHEELS
MIDDLEBROW	MIGRAINOUS	MILLEFEUILLES	MILLILITERS	MILLWRIGHT
MIDDLEBROWED	MIGRATIONAL	MILLEFIORI	MILLILITRE	MILLWRIGHTS
MIDDLEBROWISM	MIGRATIONIST	MILLEFIORIS	MILLILITRES	MILOMETERS
MIDDLEBROWISMS	MIGRATIONISTS	MILLEFLEUR	MILLILUCES	MILQUETOAST
MIDDLEBROWS	MIGRATIONS	MILLEFLEURS	MILLILUXES	MILQUETOASTS
MIDDLEBUSTER	MILDNESSES	MILLENARIAN	MILLIMETER	MIMEOGRAPH
MIDDLEBUSTERS	MILEOMETER	MILLENARIANISM	MILLIMETERS	MIMEOGRAPHED
MIDDLEMOST	MILEOMETERS	MILLENARIANISMS	MILLIMETRE	MIMEOGRAPHING
MIDDLEWARE	MILESTONES	MILLENARIANS	MILLIMETRES	MIMEOGRAPHS
MIDDLEWARES	MILITANCES	MILLENARIES	MILLIMICRON	MIMETICALLY
MIDDLEWEIGHT	MILITANCIES	MILLENARISM	MILLIMICRONS	MIMIVIRUSES

MIMMICKING	MINERALIZERS	MINIATURIZES	MINISTERIUM	MIRKINESSES
MIMOGRAPHER	MINERALIZES	MINIATURIZING	MINISTERSHIP	MIRRORLIKE
MIMOGRAPHERS	MINERALIZING	MINIBIKERS	MINISTERSHIPS	MIRRORWISE
MIMOGRAPHIES	MINERALOGIC	MINIBREAKS	MINISTRANT	MIRTHFULLY
MIMOGRAPHY	MINERALOGICAL	MINIBUDGET	MINISTRANTS	MIRTHFULNESS
MIMOSACEOUS	MINERALOGICALLY	MINIBUDGETS	MINISTRATION	MIRTHFULNESSES
MINACIOUSLY	MINERALOGIES	MINIBUSSES	MINISTRATIONS	MIRTHLESSLY
MINACITIES	MINERALOGISE	MINICABBING	MINISTRATIVE	MIRTHLESSNESS
MINATORIAL	MINERALOGISED	MINICABBINGS	MINISTRESS	MIRTHLESSNESSES
MINATORIALLY	MINERALOGISES	MINICOMPUTER	MINISTRESSES	MISACCEPTATION
MINATORILY	MINERALOGISING	MINICOMPUTERS	MINISTRIES	MISACCEPTATIONS
MINAUDERIE	MINERALOGIST	MINICOURSE	MINISTROKE	MISADAPTED
MINAUDERIES	MINERALOGISTS	MINICOURSES	MINISTROKES	MISADAPTING
MINAUDIERE	MINERALOGIZE	MINIDISHES	MINITOWERS	MISADDRESS
MINAUDIERES	MINERALOGIZED	MINIDRESSES	MINITRACKS	MISADDRESSED
MINCEMEATS	MINERALOGIZES	MINIFICATION	MINIVOLLEY	MISADDRESSES
MINDBLOWER	MINERALOGIZING	MINIFICATIONS	MINIVOLLEYS	MISADDRESSING
MINDBLOWERS	MINERALOGY	MINIFLOPPIES	MINNESINGER	MISADJUSTED
MINDEDNESS	MINESHAFTS	MINIFLOPPY	MINNESINGERS	MISADJUSTING
MINDEDNESSES	MINESTONES	MINIMALISM	MINNICKING	MISADJUSTS
MINDFULNESS	MINESTRONE	MINIMALISMS	MINNOCKING	MISADVENTURE
MINDFULNESSES	MINESTRONES	MINIMALIST	MINORITAIRE	MISADVENTURED
MINDLESSLY	MINESWEEPER	MINIMALISTS	MINORITAIRES	MISADVENTURER
MINDLESSNESS	MINESWEEPERS	MINIMAXING	MINORITIES	MISADVENTURERS
MINDLESSNESSES	MINESWEEPING	MINIMISATION	MINORSHIPS	MISADVENTURES
MINDSHARES	MINESWEEPINGS	MINIMISATIONS	MINOXIDILS	MISADVENTUROUS
MINEFIELDS	MINGIMINGI	MINIMISERS	MINSTRELSIES	MISADVERTENCE
MINEHUNTER	MINGIMINGIS	MINIMISING	MINSTRELSY	MISADVERTENCES
MINEHUNTERS	MINGINESSES	MINIMIZATION	MINUSCULAR	MISADVICES
MINELAYERS	MINGLEMENT	MINIMIZATIONS	MINUSCULES	MISADVISED
MINERALISABLE	MINGLEMENTS	MINIMIZERS	MINUTENESS	MISADVISEDLY
MINERALISATION	MINGLINGLY	MINIMIZING	MINUTENESSES	MISADVISEDNESS
MINERALISATIONS	MINIATIONS	MINIRUGBIES	MIRABELLES	MISADVISES
MINERALISE	MINIATURED	MINISCHOOL	MIRABILISES	MISADVISING
MINERALISED	MINIATURES	MINISCHOOLS	MIRACIDIAL	MISALIGNED
MINERALISER	MINIATURING	MINISCULES	MIRACIDIUM	MISALIGNING
MINERALISERS	MINIATURISATION	MINISERIES	MIRACULOUS	MISALIGNMENT
MINERALISES	MINIATURISE	MINISKIRTED	MIRACULOUSLY	MISALIGNMENTS
MINERALISING	MINIATURISED	MINISKIRTS	MIRACULOUSNESS	MISALLEGED
MINERALIST	MINIATURISES	MINISTATES	MIRANDISED	MISALLEGES
MINERALISTS	MINIATURISING	MINISTERED	MIRANDISES	MISALLEGING
MINERALIZABLE	MINIATURIST	MINISTERIA	MIRANDISING	MISALLIANCE
MINERALIZATION	MINIATURISTIC	MINISTERIAL	MIRANDIZED	MISALLIANCES
MINERALIZATIONS	MINIATURISTS	MINISTERIALIST	MIRANDIZES	MISALLOCATE
MINERALIZE	MINIATURIZATION	MINISTERIALISTS	MIRANDIZING	MISALLOCATED
MINERALIZED	MINIATURIZE	MINISTERIALLY	MIRIFICALLY	MISALLOCATES
MINERALIZER	MINIATURIZED	MINISTERING	MIRINESSES	MISALLOCATING

M

MISALLOCATION	MISARRANGE	MISBEHAVIOR	MISCARRIAGE	MISCHARACTERISE
MISALLOCATIONS	MISARRANGED	MISBEHAVIORS	MISCARRIAGES	MISCHARACTERIZE
MISALLOTMENT	MISARRANGEMENT	MISBEHAVIOUR	MISCARRIED	MISCHARGED
MISALLOTMENTS	MISARRANGEMENTS	MISBEHAVIOURS	MISCARRIES	MISCHARGES
MISALLOTTED	MISARRANGES	MISBELIEFS	MISCARRYING	MISCHARGING
MISALLOTTING	MISARRANGING	MISBELIEVE	MISCASTING	MISCHIEFED
MISALLYING	MISARTICULATE	MISBELIEVED	MISCATALOG	MISCHIEFING
MISALTERED	MISARTICULATED	MISBELIEVER	MISCATALOGED	MISCHIEVOUS
MISALTERING	MISARTICULATES	MISBELIEVERS	MISCATALOGING	MISCHIEVOUSLY
MISANALYSES	MISARTICULATING	MISBELIEVES	MISCATALOGS	MISCHIEVOUSNESS
MISANALYSIS	MISASSAYED	MISBELIEVING	MISCEGENATE	MISCHMETAL
MISANDRIES	MISASSAYING	MISBESEEMED	MISCEGENATED	MISCHMETALS
MISANDRIST	MISASSEMBLE	MISBESEEMING	MISCEGENATES	MISCHOICES
MISANDRISTS	MISASSEMBLED	MISBESEEMS	MISCEGENATING	MISCHOOSES
MISANDROUS	MISASSEMBLES	MISBESTOWAL	MISCEGENATION	MISCHOOSING
MISANTHROPE	MISASSEMBLING	MISBESTOWALS	MISCEGENATIONAL	MISCIBILITIES
MISANTHROPES	MISASSIGNED	MISBESTOWED	MISCEGENATIONS	MISCIBILITY
MISANTHROPIC	MISASSIGNING	MISBESTOWING	MISCEGENATOR	MISCITATION
MISANTHROPICAL	MISASSIGNS	MISBESTOWS	MISCEGENATORS	MISCITATIONS
MISANTHROPIES	MISASSUMPTION	MISBIASING	MISCEGENES	MISCLAIMED
MISANTHROPIST	MISASSUMPTIONS	MISBIASSED	MISCEGENETIC	MISCLAIMING
MISANTHROPISTS	MISATONING	MISBIASSES	MISCEGENIST	MISCLASSED
MISANTHROPOS	MISATTRIBUTE	MISBIASSING	MISCEGENISTS	MISCLASSES
MISANTHROPOSES	MISATTRIBUTED	MISBILLING	MISCEGINES	MISCLASSIFIED
MISANTHROPY	MISATTRIBUTES	MISBINDING	MISCELLANARIAN	MISCLASSIFIES
MISAPPLICATION	MISATTRIBUTING	MISBRANDED	MISCELLANARIANS	MISCLASSIFY
MISAPPLICATIONS	MISATTRIBUTION	MISBRANDING	MISCELLANEA	MISCLASSIFYING
MISAPPLIED	MISATTRIBUTIONS	MISBUILDING	MISCELLANEOUS	MISCLASSING
MISAPPLIES	MISAUNTERS	MISBUTTONED	MISCELLANEOUSLY	MISCOINING
MISAPPLYING	MISAVERRED	MISBUTTONING	MISCELLANIES	MISCOLORED
MISAPPRAISAL	MISAVERRING	MISBUTTONS	MISCELLANIST	MISCOLORING
MISAPPRAISALS	MISAWARDED	MISCALCULATE	MISCELLANISTS	MISCOLOURED
MISAPPRECIATE	MISAWARDING	MISCALCULATED	MISCELLANY	MISCOLOURING
MISAPPRECIATED	MISBALANCE	MISCALCULATES	MISCHALLENGE	MISCOLOURS
MISAPPRECIATES	MISBALANCED	MISCALCULATING	MISCHALLENGES	MISCOMPREHEND
MISAPPRECIATING	MISBALANCES	MISCALCULATION	MISCHANCED	MISCOMPREHENDED
MISAPPRECIATION	MISBALANCING	MISCALCULATIONS	MISCHANCEFUL	MISCOMPREHENDS
MISAPPRECIATIVE	MISBECOMES	MISCALCULATOR	MISCHANCES	MISCOMPUTATION
MISAPPREHEND	MISBECOMING	MISCALCULATORS	MISCHANCING	MISCOMPUTATIONS
MISAPPREHENDED	MISBECOMINGNESS	MISCALLERS	MISCHANNEL	MISCOMPUTE
MISAPPREHENDING	MISBEGINNING	MISCALLING	MISCHANNELED	MISCOMPUTED
MISAPPREHENDS	MISBEGOTTEN	MISCANTHUS	MISCHANNELING	MISCOMPUTES
MISAPPREHENSION	MISBEHAVED	MISCANTHUSES	MISCHANNELLED	MISCOMPUTING
MISAPPREHENSIVE	MISBEHAVER	MISCAPTION	MISCHANNELLING	MISCONCEIT
MISAPPROPRIATE	MISBEHAVERS	MISCAPTIONED	MISCHANNELS	MISCONCEITED
MISAPPROPRIATED	MISBEHAVES	MISCAPTIONING	MISCHANTER	MISCONCEITING
MISAPPROPRIATES	MISBEHAVING	MISCAPTIONS	MISCHANTERS	MISCONCEITS

MISCONCEIVE	MISCORRECTIONS	MISDESCRIBED	MISEMPHASISED	MISESTIMATION
MISCONCEIVED	MISCORRECTS	MISDESCRIBES	MISEMPHASISES	MISESTIMATIONS
MISCONCEIVER	MISCORRELATION	MISDESCRIBING	MISEMPHASISING	MISEVALUATE
MISCONCEIVERS	MISCORRELATIONS	MISDESCRIPTION	MISEMPHASIZE	MISEVALUATED
MISCONCEIVES	MISCOUNSEL	MISDESCRIPTIONS	MISEMPHASIZED	MISEVALUATES
MISCONCEIVING	MISCOUNSELLED	MISDESERTS	MISEMPHASIZES	MISEVALUATING
MISCONCEPTION	MISCOUNSELLING	MISDEVELOP	MISEMPHASIZING	MISEVALUATION
MISCONCEPTIONS	MISCOUNSELS	MISDEVELOPED	MISEMPLOYED	MISEVALUATIONS
MISCONDUCT	MISCOUNTED	MISDEVELOPING	MISEMPLOYING	MISFALLING
MISCONDUCTED	MISCOUNTING	MISDEVELOPS	MISEMPLOYMENT	MISFARINGS
MISCONDUCTING	MISCREANCE	MISDEVOTION	MISEMPLOYMENTS	MISFEASANCE
MISCONDUCTS	MISCREANCES	MISDEVOTIONS	MISEMPLOYS	MISFEASANCES
MISCONJECTURE	MISCREANCIES	MISDIAGNOSE	MISENROLLED	MISFEASORS
MISCONJECTURED	MISCREANCY	MISDIAGNOSED	MISENROLLING	MISFEATURE
MISCONJECTURES	MISCREANTS	MISDIAGNOSES	MISENROLLS	MISFEATURED
MISCONJECTURING	MISCREATED	MISDIAGNOSING	MISENTERED	MISFEATURES
MISCONNECT	MISCREATES	MISDIAGNOSIS	MISENTERING	MISFEATURING
MISCONNECTED	MISCREATING	MISDIALING	MISENTREAT	MISFEEDING
MISCONNECTING	MISCREATION	MISDIALLED	MISENTREATED	MISFEIGNED
MISCONNECTION	MISCREATIONS	MISDIALLING	MISENTREATING	MISFEIGNING
MISCONNECTIONS	MISCREATIVE	MISDIRECTED	MISENTREATS	MISFIELDED
MISCONNECTS	MISCREATOR	MISDIRECTING	MISENTRIES	MISFIELDING
MISCONSTER	MISCREATORS	MISDIRECTION	MISERABILISM	MISFITTING
MISCONSTERED	MISCREAUNCE	MISDIRECTIONS	MISERABILISMS	MISFOCUSED
MISCONSTERING	MISCREAUNCES	MISDIRECTS	MISERABILIST	MISFOCUSES
MISCONSTERS	MISCREDITED	MISDISTRIBUTION	MISERABILISTS	MISFOCUSING
MISCONSTRUCT	MISCREDITING	MISDIVIDED	MISERABLENESS	MISFOCUSSED
MISCONSTRUCTED	MISCREDITS	MISDIVIDES	MISERABLENESSES	MISFOCUSSES
MISCONSTRUCTING	MISCUTTING	MISDIVIDING	MISERABLES	MISFOCUSSING
MISCONSTRUCTION	MISDEALERS	MISDIVISION	MISERABLISM	MISFORMATION
MISCONSTRUCTS	MISDEALING	MISDIVISIONS	MISERABLISMS	MISFORMATIONS
MISCONSTRUE	MISDEEMFUL	MISDOUBTED	MISERABLIST	MISFORMING
MISCONSTRUED	MISDEEMING	MISDOUBTFUL	MISERABLISTS	MISFORTUNE
MISCONSTRUES	MISDEEMINGS	MISDOUBTING	MISERICORD	MISFORTUNED
MISCONSTRUING	MISDEFINED	MISDRAWING	MISERICORDE	MISFORTUNES
MISCONTENT	MISDEFINES	MISDRAWINGS	MISERICORDES	MISFRAMING
MISCONTENTED	MISDEFINING	MISDRIVING	MISERICORDS	MISFUNCTION
MISCONTENTING	MISDEMEANANT	MISEDITING	MISERLIEST	MISFUNCTIONED
MISCONTENTMENT	MISDEMEANANTS	MISEDUCATE	MISERLINESS	MISFUNCTIONING
MISCONTENTMENTS	MISDEMEANED	MISEDUCATED	MISERLINESSES	MISFUNCTIONS
MISCONTENTS	MISDEMEANING	MISEDUCATES	MISESTEEMED	MISGAUGING
MISCOOKING	MISDEMEANOR	MISEDUCATING	MISESTEEMING	MISGIVINGS
MISCOPYING	MISDEMEANORS	MISEDUCATION	MISESTEEMS	MISGOVERNAUNCE
MISCORRECT	MISDEMEANOUR	MISEDUCATIONS	MISESTIMATE	MISGOVERNAUNCES
MISCORRECTED	MISDEMEANOURS	MISEMPHASES	MISESTIMATED	MISGOVERNED
MISCORRECTING	MISDEMEANS	MISEMPHASIS	MISESTIMATES	MISGOVERNING
MISCORRECTION	MISDESCRIBE	MISEMPHASISE	MISESTIMATING	MISGOVERNMENT

MISGOVERNMENTS

MISGOVERNMENTS	MISIMPROVED	MISKNOWLEDGE	MISMEASURED	MISPARSING
MISGOVERNOR	MISIMPROVEMENT	MISKNOWLEDGES	MISMEASUREMENT	MISPARTING
MISGOVERNORS	MISIMPROVEMENTS	MISLABELED	MISMEASUREMENTS	MISPATCHED
MISGOVERNS	MISIMPROVES	MISLABELING	MISMEASURES	MISPATCHES
MISGRADING	MISIMPROVING	MISLABELLED	MISMEASURING	MISPATCHING
MISGRAFTED	MISINFERRED	MISLABELLING	MISMEETING	MISPENNING
MISGRAFTING	MISINFERRING	MISLABORED	MISMETRING	MISPERCEIVE
MISGROWING	MISINFORMANT	MISLABORING	MISNOMERED	MISPERCEIVED
MISGROWTHS	MISINFORMANTS	MISLEADERS	MISNOMERING	MISPERCEIVES
MISGUESSED	MISINFORMATION	MISLEADING	MISNUMBERED	MISPERCEIVING
MISGUESSES	MISINFORMATIONS	MISLEADINGLY	MISNUMBERING	MISPERCEPTION
MISGUESSING	MISINFORMED	MISLEARNED	MISNUMBERS	MISPERCEPTIONS
MISGUGGLED	MISINFORMER	MISLEARNING	MISOBSERVANCE	MISPERSUADE
MISGUGGLES	MISINFORMERS	MISLEEKING	MISOBSERVANCES	MISPERSUADED
MISGUGGLING	MISINFORMING	MISLIGHTED	MISOBSERVE	MISPERSUADES
MISGUIDANCE	MISINFORMS	MISLIGHTING	MISOBSERVED	MISPERSUADING
MISGUIDANCES	MISINSTRUCT	MISLIKINGS	MISOBSERVES	MISPERSUASION
MISGUIDEDLY	MISINSTRUCTED	MISLIPPENED	MISOBSERVING	MISPERSUASIONS
MISGUIDEDNESS	MISINSTRUCTING	MISLIPPENING	MISOCAPNIC	MISPHRASED
MISGUIDEDNESSES	MISINSTRUCTION	MISLIPPENS	MISOGAMIES	MISPHRASES
MISGUIDERS	MISINSTRUCTIONS	MISLOCATED	MISOGAMIST	MISPHRASING
MISGUIDING	MISINSTRUCTS	MISLOCATES	MISOGAMISTS	MISPICKELS
MISHALLOWED	MISINTELLIGENCE	MISLOCATING	MISOGYNIES	MISPLACEMENT
MISHANDLED	MISINTENDED	MISLOCATION	MISOGYNIST	MISPLACEMENTS
MISHANDLES	MISINTENDING	MISLOCATIONS	MISOGYNISTIC	MISPLACING
MISHANDLING	MISINTENDS	MISLODGING	MISOGYNISTICAL	MISPLANNED
MISHANTERS	MISINTERPRET	MISLUCKING	MISOGYNISTS	MISPLANNING
MISHAPPENED	MISINTERPRETED	MISMANAGED	MISOGYNOUS	MISPLANTED
MISHAPPENING	MISINTERPRETER	MISMANAGEMENT	MISOLOGIES	MISPLANTING
MISHAPPENS	MISINTERPRETERS	MISMANAGEMENTS	MISOLOGIST	MISPLAYING
MISHAPPING	MISINTERPRETING	MISMANAGER	MISOLOGISTS	MISPLEADED
MISHEARING	MISINTERPRETS	MISMANAGERS	MISONEISMS	MISPLEADING
MISHEGAASEN	MISINTERRED	MISMANAGES	MISONEISTIC	MISPLEADINGS
MISHGUGGLE	MISINTERRING	MISMANAGING	MISONEISTS	MISPLEASED
MISHGUGGLED	MISJOINDER	MISMANNERS	MISORDERED	MISPLEASES
MISHGUGGLES	MISJOINDERS	MISMARKING	MISORDERING	MISPLEASING
MISHGUGGLING	MISJOINING	MISMARRIAGE	MISORIENTATION	MISPOINTED
MISHITTING	MISJUDGEMENT	MISMARRIAGES	MISORIENTATIONS	MISPOINTING
MISHMASHES	MISJUDGEMENTS	MISMARRIED	MISORIENTED	MISPOISING
MISHMOSHES	MISJUDGERS	MISMARRIES	MISORIENTING	MISPOSITION
MISIDENTIFIED	MISJUDGING	MISMARRYING	MISORIENTS	MISPOSITIONED
MISIDENTIFIES	MISJUDGMENT	MISMATCHED	MISPACKAGE	MISPOSITIONING
MISIDENTIFY	MISJUDGMENTS	MISMATCHES	MISPACKAGED	MISPOSITIONS
MISIDENTIFYING	MISKEEPING	MISMATCHING	MISPACKAGES	MISPRAISED
MISIMPRESSION	MISKENNING	MISMATCHMENT	MISPACKAGING	MISPRAISES
MISIMPRESSIONS	MISKICKING	MISMATCHMENTS	MISPAINTED	MISPRAISING
MISIMPROVE	MISKNOWING	MISMEASURE	MISPAINTING	MISPRICING

M

MISPRINTED	MISREGISTERED	MISSILERIES	MISSTARTED	MISTRAINING
MISPRINTING	MISREGISTERING	MISSILRIES	MISSTARTING	MISTRANSCRIBE
MISPRISING	MISREGISTERS	MISSIOLOGIES	MISSTATEMENT	MISTRANSCRIBED
MISPRISION	MISREGISTRATION	MISSIOLOGY	MISSTATEMENTS	MISTRANSCRIBES
MISPRISIONS	MISRELATED	MISSIONARIES	MISSTATING	MISTRANSCRIBING
MISPRIZERS	MISRELATES	MISSIONARISE	MISSTEERED	MISTRANSLATE
MISPRIZING	MISRELATING	MISSIONARISED	MISSTEERING	MISTRANSLATED
MISPROGRAM	MISRELATION	MISSIONARISES	MISSTEPPED	MISTRANSLATES
MISPROGRAMED	MISRELATIONS	MISSIONARISING	MISSTEPPING	MISTRANSLATING
MISPROGRAMING	MISRELYING	MISSIONARIZE	MISSTOPPED	MISTRANSLATION
MISPROGRAMMED	MISREMEMBER	MISSIONARIZED	MISSTOPPING	MISTRANSLATIONS
MISPROGRAMMING	MISREMEMBERED	MISSIONARIZES	MISSTRICKEN	MISTRAYNED
MISPROGRAMS	MISREMEMBERING	MISSIONARIZING	MISSTRIKES	MISTREADING
MISPRONOUNCE	MISREMEMBERS	MISSIONARY	MISSTRIKING	MISTREADINGS
MISPRONOUNCED	MISRENDERED	MISSIONERS	MISSTYLING	MISTREATED
MISPRONOUNCES	MISRENDERING	MISSIONING	MISSUITING	MISTREATING
MISPRONOUNCING	MISRENDERS	MISSIONISATION	MISSUMMATION	MISTREATMENT
MISPROPORTION	MISREPORTED	MISSIONISATIONS	MISSUMMATIONS	MISTREATMENTS
MISPROPORTIONED	MISREPORTER	MISSIONISE	MISTAKABLE	MISTRESSED
MISPROPORTIONS	MISREPORTERS	MISSIONISED	MISTAKABLY	MISTRESSES
MISPUNCTUATE	MISREPORTING	MISSIONISER	MISTAKEABLE	MISTRESSING
MISPUNCTUATED	MISREPORTS	MISSIONISERS	MISTAKEABLY	MISTRESSLESS
MISPUNCTUATES	MISREPRESENT	MISSIONISES	MISTAKENLY	MISTRESSLY
MISPUNCTUATING	MISREPRESENTED	MISSIONISING	MISTAKENNESS	MISTRUSTED
MISPUNCTUATION	MISREPRESENTER	MISSIONIZATION	MISTAKENNESSES	MISTRUSTER
MISPUNCTUATIONS	MISREPRESENTERS	MISSIONIZATIONS	MISTAKINGS	MISTRUSTERS
MISQUOTATION	MISREPRESENTING	MISSIONIZE	MISTEACHES	MISTRUSTFUL
MISQUOTATIONS	MISREPRESENTS	MISSIONIZED	MISTEACHING	MISTRUSTFULLY
MISQUOTERS	MISROUTEING	MISSIONIZER	MISTELLING	MISTRUSTFULNESS
MISQUOTING	MISROUTING	MISSIONIZERS	MISTEMPERED	MISTRUSTING
MISRAISING	MISSAYINGS	MISSIONIZES	MISTEMPERING	MISTRUSTINGLY
MISREADING	MISSEATING	MISSIONIZING	MISTEMPERS	MISTRUSTLESS
MISREADINGS	MISSEEMING	MISSISHNESS	MISTENDING	MISTRYSTED
MISRECKONED	MISSEEMINGS	MISSISHNESSES	MISTERMING	MISTRYSTING
MISRECKONING	MISSELLING	MISSORTING	MISTHINKING	MISTUTORED
MISRECKONINGS	MISSELLINGS	MISSOUNDED	MISTHOUGHT	MISTUTORING
MISRECKONS	MISSENDING	MISSOUNDING	MISTHOUGHTS	MISUNDERSTAND
MISRECOLLECTION	MISSETTING	MISSPACING	MISTHROWING	MISUNDERSTANDS
MISRECORDED	MISSHAPENLY	MISSPEAKING	MISTIGRISES	MISUNDERSTOOD
MISRECORDING	MISSHAPENNESS	MISSPELLED	MISTINESSES	MISUTILISATION
MISRECORDS	MISSHAPENNESSES	MISSPELLING	MISTITLING	MISUTILISATIONS
MISREFERENCE	MISSHAPERS	MISSPELLINGS	MISTLETOES	MISUTILIZATION
MISREFERENCES	MISSHAPING	MISSPENDER	MISTOUCHED	MISUTILIZATIONS
MISREFERRED	MISSHEATHED	MISSPENDERS	MISTOUCHES	MISVALUING
MISREFERRING	MISSILEERS	MISSPENDING	MISTOUCHING	MISVENTURE
MISREGARDS	MISSILEMAN	MISSTAMPED	MISTRACING	MISVENTURES
MISREGISTER	MISSILEMEN	MISSTAMPING	MISTRAINED	MISVENTUROUS

MISVOCALISATION	MITRAILLEUSES	MODAFINILS	MODILLIONS	MOLECULARLY
MISVOCALIZATION	MITREWORTS	MODALISTIC	MODISHNESS	MOLENDINAR
MISWANDRED	MITTIMUSES	MODALITIES	MODISHNESSES	MOLENDINARIES
MISWEENING	MIXABILITIES	MODELLINGS	MODULABILITIES	MOLENDINARS
MISWENDING	MIXABILITY	MODERATELY	MODULABILITY	MOLENDINARY
MISWORDING	MIXEDNESSES	MODERATENESS	MODULARISED	MOLESTATION
MISWORDINGS	MIXMASTERS	MODERATENESSES	MODULARITIES	MOLESTATIONS
MISWORSHIP	MIXOBARBARIC	MODERATING	MODULARITY	MOLIMINOUS
MISWORSHIPPED	MIXOLOGIES	MODERATION	MODULARIZED	MOLLIFIABLE
MISWORSHIPPING	MIXOLOGIST	MODERATIONS	MODULATING	MOLLIFICATION
MISWORSHIPS	MIXOLOGISTS	MODERATISM	MODULATION	MOLLIFICATIONS
MISWRITING	MIXOLYDIAN	MODERATISMS	MODULATIONS	MOLLIFIERS
MISWRITTEN	MIXOTROPHIC	MODERATORS	MODULATIVE	MOLLIFYING
MITERWORTS	MIZENMASTS	MODERATORSHIP	MODULATORS	MOLLITIOUS
MITHRADATIC	MIZZENMAST	MODERATORSHIPS	MODULATORY	MOLLUSCANS
MITHRIDATE	MIZZENMASTS	MODERATRICES	MOISTENERS	MOLLUSCICIDAL
MITHRIDATES	MIZZONITES	MODERATRIX	MOISTENING	MOLLUSCICIDE
MITHRIDATIC	MNEMONICAL	MODERATRIXES	MOISTIFIED	MOLLUSCICIDES
MITHRIDATISE	MNEMONICALLY	MODERNISATION	MOISTIFIES	MOLLUSCOID
MITHRIDATISED	MNEMONISTS	MODERNISATIONS	MOISTIFYING	MOLLUSCOIDAL
MITHRIDATISES	MNEMOTECHNIC	MODERNISED	MOISTNESSES	MOLLUSCOIDS
MITHRIDATISING	MNEMOTECHNICS	MODERNISER	MOISTURELESS	MOLLUSCOUS
MITHRIDATISM	MNEMOTECHNIST	MODERNISERS	MOISTURISE	MOLLUSKANS
MITHRIDATISMS	MNEMOTECHNISTS	MODERNISES	MOISTURISED	MOLLYCODDLE
MITHRIDATIZE	MOBCASTING	MODERNISING	MOISTURISER	MOLLYCODDLED
MITHRIDATIZED	MOBCASTINGS	MODERNISMS	MOISTURISERS	MOLLYCODDLER
MITHRIDATIZES	MOBILISABLE	MODERNISTIC	MOISTURISES	MOLLYCODDLERS
MITHRIDATIZING	MOBILISATION	MODERNISTICALLY	MOISTURISING	MOLLYCODDLES
MITIGATING	MOBILISATIONS	MODERNISTS	MOISTURIZE	MOLLYCODDLING
MITIGATION	MOBILISERS	MODERNITIES	MOISTURIZED	MOLLYHAWKS
MITIGATIONS	MOBILISING	MODERNIZATION	MOISTURIZER	MOLLYMAWKS
MITIGATIVE	MOBILITIES	MODERNIZATIONS	MOISTURIZERS	MOLOCHISED
MITIGATIVES	MOBILIZABLE	MODERNIZED	MOISTURIZES	MOLOCHISES
MITIGATORS	MOBILIZATION	MODERNIZER	MOISTURIZING	MOLOCHISING
MITIGATORY	MOBILIZATIONS	MODERNIZERS	MOITHERING	MOLOCHIZED
MITOCHONDRIA	MOBILIZERS	MODERNIZES	MOLALITIES	MOLOCHIZES
MITOCHONDRIAL	MOBILIZING	MODERNIZING	MOLARITIES	MOLOCHIZING
MITOCHONDRION	MOBLOGGERS	MODERNNESS	MOLASSESES	MOLYBDATES
MITOGENETIC	MOBOCRACIES	MODERNNESSES	MOLDABILITIES	MOLYBDENITE
MITOGENICITIES	MOBOCRATIC	MODIFIABILITIES	MOLDABILITY	MOLYBDENITES
MITOGENICITY	MOBOCRATICAL	MODIFIABILITY	MOLDAVITES	MOLYBDENOSES
MITOMYCINS	MOCHINESSES	MODIFIABLE	MOLDBOARDS	MOLYBDENOSIS
MITOTICALLY	MOCKERNUTS	MODIFIABLENESS	MOLDINESSES	MOLYBDENOUS
MITRAILLES	MOCKINGBIRD	MODIFICATION	MOLECATCHER	MOLYBDENUM
MITRAILLEUR	MOCKINGBIRDS	MODIFICATIONS	MOLECATCHERS	MOLYBDENUMS
MITRAILLEURS	MOCKUMENTARIES	MODIFICATIVE	MOLECULARITIES	MOLYBDOSES
MITRAILLEUSE	MOCKUMENTARY	MODIFICATORY	MOLECULARITY	MOLYBDOSIS

MOMENTANEOUS	MONDEGREEN	MONGRELIZER	MONOCHROIC	MONOCYCLES
MOMENTARILY	MONDEGREENS	MONGRELIZERS	MONOCHROICS	MONOCYCLIC
MOMENTARINESS	MONECIOUSLY	MONGRELIZES	MONOCHROMASIES	MONOCYTOID
MOMENTARINESSES	MONERGISMS	MONGRELIZING	MONOCHROMASY	MONODACTYLOUS
MOMENTOUSLY	MONESTROUS	MONILIASES	MONOCHROMAT	MONODELPHIAN
MOMENTOUSNESS	MONETARILY	MONILIASIS	MONOCHROMATE	MONODELPHIC
MOMENTOUSNESSES	MONETARISM	MONILIFORM	MONOCHROMATES	MONODELPHOUS
MONACHISMS	MONETARISMS	MONISTICAL	MONOCHROMATIC	MONODICALLY
MONACHISTS	MONETARIST	MONISTICALLY	MONOCHROMATICS	MONODISPERSE
MONACTINAL	MONETARISTS	MONITORIAL	MONOCHROMATISM	MONODRAMAS
MONADELPHOUS	MONETISATION	MONITORIALLY	MONOCHROMATISMS	MONODRAMATIC
MONADICALLY	MONETISATIONS	MONITORIES	MONOCHROMATOR	MONOECIOUS
MONADIFORM	MONETISING	MONITORING	MONOCHROMATORS	MONOECIOUSLY
MONADISTIC	MONETIZATION	MONITORINGS	MONOCHROMATS	MONOECISMS
MONADNOCKS	MONETIZATIONS	MONITORSHIP	MONOCHROME	MONOESTERS
MONADOLOGIES	MONETIZING	MONITORSHIPS	MONOCHROMES	MONOFILAMENT
MONADOLOGY	MONEYCHANGER	MONITRESSES	MONOCHROMIC	MONOFILAMENTS
MONANDRIES	MONEYCHANGERS	MONKEYGLAND	MONOCHROMICAL	MONOGAMIES
MONANDROUS	MONEYGRUBBING	MONKEYISMS	MONOCHROMIES	MONOGAMIST
MONANTHOUS	MONEYGRUBBINGS	MONKEYPODS	MONOCHROMIST	MONOGAMISTIC
MONARCHALLY	MONEYLENDER	MONKEYPOTS	MONOCHROMISTS	MONOGAMISTS
MONARCHIAL	MONEYLENDERS	MONKEYSHINE	MONOCHROMY	MONOGAMOUS
MONARCHICAL	MONEYLENDING	MONKEYSHINES	MONOCLINAL	MONOGAMOUSLY
MONARCHICALLY	MONEYLENDINGS	MONKFISHES	MONOCLINALLY	MONOGAMOUSNESS
MONARCHIES	MONEYMAKER	MONKISHNESS	MONOCLINALS	MONOGASTRIC
MONARCHISE	MONEYMAKERS	MONKISHNESSES	MONOCLINES	MONOGENEAN
MONARCHISED	MONEYMAKING	MONKSHOODS	MONOCLINIC	MONOGENEANS
MONARCHISES	MONEYMAKINGS	MONOACIDIC	MONOCLINISM	MONOGENESES
MONARCHISING	MONEYSPINNING	MONOAMINERGIC	MONOCLINISMS	MONOGENESIS
MONARCHISM	MONEYWORTS	MONOAMINES	MONOCLINOUS	MONOGENETIC
MONARCHISMS	MONGERINGS	MONOATOMIC	MONOCLONAL	MONOGENICALLY
MONARCHIST	MONGOLISMS	MONOBLEPSES	MONOCLONALS	MONOGENIES
MONARCHISTIC	MONGOLOIDS	MONOBLEPSIS	MONOCOQUES	MONOGENISM
MONARCHISTS	MONGRELISATION	MONOCARBOXYLIC	MONOCOTYLEDON	MONOGENISMS
MONARCHIZE	MONGRELISATIONS	MONOCARDIAN	MONOCOTYLEDONS	MONOGENIST
MONARCHIZED	MONGRELISE	MONOCARPELLARY	MONOCOTYLS	MONOGENISTIC
MONARCHIZES	MONGRELISED	MONOCARPIC	MONOCRACIES	MONOGENISTS
MONARCHIZING	MONGRELISER	MONOCARPOUS	MONOCRATIC	MONOGENOUS
MONASTERIAL	MONGRELISERS	MONOCEROSES	MONOCRYSTAL	MONOGLYCERIDE
MONASTERIES	MONGRELISES	MONOCEROUS	MONOCRYSTALLINE	MONOGLYCERIDES
MONASTICAL	MONGRELISING	MONOCHASIA	MONOCRYSTALS	MONOGONIES
MONASTICALLY	MONGRELISM	MONOCHASIAL	MONOCULARLY	MONOGRAMED
MONASTICISM	MONGRELISMS	MONOCHASIUM	MONOCULARS	MONOGRAMING
MONASTICISMS	MONGRELIZATION	MONOCHLAMYDEOUS	MONOCULOUS	MONOGRAMMATIC
MONAURALLY	MONGRELIZATIONS	MONOCHLORIDE	MONOCULTURAL	MONOGRAMMED
MONCHIQUITE	MONGRELIZE	MONOCHLORIDES	MONOCULTURE	MONOGRAMMER
MONCHIQUITES	MONGRELIZED	MONOCHORDS	MONOCULTURES	MONOGRAMMERS

M

M

MONOGRAMMING	MONOLOGISES	MONONUCLEARS	MONOPODIES	MONOSACCHARIDES
MONOGRAPHED	MONOLOGISING	MONONUCLEATE	MONOPODIUM	MONOSATURATED
MONOGRAPHER	MONOLOGIST	MONONUCLEATED	MONOPOLIES	MONOSEMIES
MONOGRAPHERS	MONOLOGISTS	MONONUCLEOSES	MONOPOLISATION	MONOSEPALOUS
MONOGRAPHIC	MONOLOGIZE	MONONUCLEOSIS	MONOPOLISATIONS	MONOSKIERS
MONOGRAPHICAL	MONOLOGIZED	MONONUCLEOTIDE	MONOPOLISE	MONOSKIING
MONOGRAPHICALLY	MONOLOGIZES	MONONUCLEOTIDES	MONOPOLISED	MONOSKIINGS
MONOGRAPHIES	MONOLOGIZING	MONOPETALOUS	MONOPOLISER	MONOSODIUM
MONOGRAPHING	MONOLOGUED	MONOPHAGIES	MONOPOLISERS	MONOSOMICS
MONOGRAPHIST	MONOLOGUES	MONOPHAGOUS	MONOPOLISES	MONOSOMIES
MONOGRAPHISTS	MONOLOGUING	MONOPHASIC	MONOPOLISING	MONOSPACED
MONOGRAPHS	MONOLOGUISE	MONOPHOBIA	MONOPOLISM	MONOSPECIFIC
MONOGRAPHY	MONOLOGUISED	MONOPHOBIAS	MONOPOLISMS	MONOSPECIFICITY
MONOGYNIAN	MONOLOGUISES	MONOPHOBIC	MONOPOLIST	MONOSPERMAL
MONOGYNIES	MONOLOGUISING	MONOPHOBICS	MONOPOLISTIC	MONOSPERMOUS
MONOGYNIST	MONOLOGUIST	MONOPHONIC	MONOPOLISTS	MONOSTABLE
MONOGYNISTS	MONOLOGUISTS	MONOPHONICALLY	MONOPOLIZATION	MONOSTELES
MONOGYNOUS	MONOLOGUIZE	MONOPHONIES	MONOPOLIZATIONS	MONOSTELIC
MONOHYBRID	MONOLOGUIZED	MONOPHOSPHATE	MONOPOLIZE	MONOSTELIES
MONOHYBRIDS	MONOLOGUIZES	MONOPHOSPHATES	MONOPOLIZED	MONOSTICHIC
MONOHYDRATE	MONOLOGUIZING	MONOPHTHONG	MONOPOLIZER	MONOSTICHOUS
MONOHYDRATED	MONOMACHIA	MONOPHTHONGAL	MONOPOLIZERS	MONOSTICHS
MONOHYDRATES	MONOMACHIAS	MONOPHTHONGISE	MONOPOLIZES	MONOSTOMOUS
MONOHYDRIC	MONOMACHIES	MONOPHTHONGISED	MONOPOLIZING	MONOSTROPHE
MONOHYDROGEN	MONOMANIAC	MONOPHTHONGISES	MONOPRIONIDIAN	MONOSTROPHES
MONOHYDROXY	MONOMANIACAL	MONOPHTHONGIZE	MONOPROPELLANT	MONOSTROPHIC
MONOICOUSLY	MONOMANIACALLY	MONOPHTHONGIZED	MONOPROPELLANTS	MONOSTROPHICS
MONOLATERS	MONOMANIACS	MONOPHTHONGIZES	MONOPSONIES	MONOSTYLAR
MONOLATRIES	MONOMANIAS	MONOPHTHONGS	MONOPSONIST	MONOSTYLOUS
MONOLATRIST	MONOMEROUS	MONOPHYLETIC	MONOPSONISTIC	MONOSYLLABIC
MONOLATRISTS	MONOMETALLIC	MONOPHYLIES	MONOPSONISTS	MONOSYLLABICITY
MONOLATROUS	MONOMETALLISM	MONOPHYLLOUS	MONOPTERAL	MONOSYLLABISM
MONOLAYERS	MONOMETALLISMS	MONOPHYODONT	MONOPTEROI	MONOSYLLABISMS
MONOLINGUAL	MONOMETALLIST	MONOPHYODONTS	MONOPTERON	MONOSYLLABLE
MONOLINGUALISM	MONOMETALLISTS	MONOPHYSITE	MONOPTEROS	MONOSYLLABLES
MONOLINGUALISMS	MONOMETERS	MONOPHYSITES	MONOPTEROSES	MONOSYMMETRIC
MONOLINGUALS	MONOMETRIC	MONOPHYSITIC	MONOPTOTES	MONOSYMMETRICAL
MONOLINGUIST	MONOMETRICAL	MONOPHYSITISM	MONOPULSES	MONOSYMMETRIES
MONOLINGUISTS	MONOMOLECULAR	MONOPHYSITISMS	MONORCHIDISM	MONOSYMMETRY
MONOLITHIC	MONOMOLECULARLY	MONOPLANES	MONORCHIDISMS	MONOSYNAPTIC
MONOLITHICALLY	MONOMORPHEMIC	MONOPLEGIA	MONORCHIDS	MONOTASKED
MONOLOGGED	MONOMORPHIC	MONOPLEGIAS	MONORCHISM	MONOTASKING
MONOLOGGING	MONOMORPHISM	MONOPLEGIC	MONORCHISMS	MONOTASKINGS
MONOLOGICAL	MONOMORPHISMS	MONOPLEGICS	MONORHINAL	MONOTELEPHONE
MONOLOGIES	MONOMORPHOUS	MONOPLOIDS	MONORHYMED	MONOTELEPHONES
MONOLOGISE	MONOMYARIAN	MONOPODIAL	MONORHYMES	MONOTERPENE
MONOLOGISED	MONONUCLEAR	MONOPODIALLY	MONOSACCHARIDE	MONOTERPENES

MONOTHALAMIC	MONOUNSATURATED	MONUMENTALISE	MOONWALKING	MORIBUNDITY
MONOTHALAMOUS	MONOUNSATURATES	MONUMENTALISED	MOORBUZZARD	MORIBUNDLY
MONOTHECAL	MONOVALENCE	MONUMENTALISES	MOORBUZZARDS	MORIGERATE
MONOTHECOUS	MONOVALENCES	MONUMENTALISING	MOOSEBIRDS	MORIGERATION
MONOTHEISM	MONOVALENCIES	MONUMENTALITIES	MOOSEWOODS	MORIGERATIONS
MONOTHEISMS	MONOVALENCY	MONUMENTALITY	MOOSEYARDS	MORIGEROUS
MONOTHEIST	MONOVALENT	MONUMENTALIZE	MOOTNESSES	MORONICALLY
MONOTHEISTIC	MONOXYLONS	MONUMENTALIZED	MOPINESSES	MORONITIES
MONOTHEISTICAL	MONOXYLOUS	MONUMENTALIZES	MOPISHNESS	MOROSENESS
MONOTHEISTS	MONOZYGOTIC	MONUMENTALIZING	MOPISHNESSES	MOROSENESSES
MONOTHELETE	MONOZYGOUS	MONUMENTALLY	MORALISATION	MOROSITIES
MONOTHELETES	MONSEIGNEUR	MONUMENTED	MORALISATIONS	MORPHACTIN
MONOTHELETIC	MONSIGNORI	MONUMENTING	MORALISERS	MORPHACTINS
MONOTHELETICAL	MONSIGNORIAL	MONZONITES	MORALISING	MORPHALLAXES
MONOTHELETISM	MONSIGNORS	MONZONITIC	MORALISTIC	MORPHALLAXIS
MONOTHELETISMS	MONSTERING	MOODINESSES	MORALISTICALLY	MORPHEMICALLY
MONOTHELISM	MONSTERINGS	MOONCALVES	MORALITIES	MORPHEMICS
MONOTHELISMS	MONSTRANCE	MOONCHILDREN	MORALIZATION	MORPHINISM
MONOTHELITE	MONSTRANCES	MOONFISHES	MORALIZATIONS	MORPHINISMS
MONOTHELITES	MONSTROSITIES	MOONFLOWER	MORALIZERS	MORPHINOMANIA
MONOTHELITISM	MONSTROSITY	MOONFLOWERS	MORALIZING	MORPHINOMANIAC
MONOTHELITISMS	MONSTROUSLY	MOONINESSES	MORATORIUM	MORPHINOMANIACS
MONOTHERAPIES	MONSTROUSNESS	MOONLIGHTED	MORATORIUMS	MORPHINOMANIAS
MONOTHERAPY	MONSTROUSNESSES	MOONLIGHTER	MORBIDEZZA	MORPHOGENESES
MONOTOCOUS	MONSTRUOSITIES	MOONLIGHTERS	MORBIDEZZAS	MORPHOGENESIS
MONOTONICALLY	MONSTRUOSITY	MOONLIGHTING	MORBIDITIES	MORPHOGENETIC
MONOTONICITIES	MONSTRUOUS	MOONLIGHTINGS	MORBIDNESS	MORPHOGENIC
MONOTONICITY	MONTADALES	MOONLIGHTS	MORBIDNESSES	MORPHOGENIES
MONOTONIES	MONTAGNARD	MOONPHASES	MORBIFEROUS	MORPHOGENS
MONOTONING	MONTAGNARDS	MOONQUAKES	MORBIFICALLY	MORPHOGENY
MONOTONISE	MONTBRETIA	MOONRAKERS	MORBILLIFORM	MORPHOGRAPHER
MONOTONISED	MONTBRETIAS	MOONRAKING	MORBILLIVIRUS	MORPHOGRAPHERS
MONOTONISES	MONTELIMAR	MOONRAKINGS	MORBILLIVIRUSES	MORPHOGRAPHIES
MONOTONISING	MONTELIMARS	MOONSCAPES	MORBILLOUS	MORPHOGRAPHY
MONOTONIZE	MONTGOLFIER	MOONSHINED	MORDACIOUS	MORPHOLINO
MONOTONIZED	MONTGOLFIERS	MOONSHINER	MORDACIOUSLY	MORPHOLINOS
MONOTONIZES	MONTHLINGS	MOONSHINERS	MORDACIOUSNESS	MORPHOLOGIC
MONOTONIZING	MONTICELLITE	MOONSHINES	MORDACITIES	MORPHOLOGICAL
MONOTONOUS	MONTICELLITES	MOONSHINING	MORDANCIES	MORPHOLOGICALLY
MONOTONOUSLY	MONTICOLOUS	MOONSTONES	MORDANTING	MORPHOLOGIES
MONOTONOUSNESS	MONTICULATE	MOONSTRICKEN	MORENESSES	MORPHOLOGIST
MONOTREMATOUS	MONTICULES	MOONSTRIKE	MORGANATIC	MORPHOLOGISTS
MONOTREMES	MONTICULOUS	MOONSTRIKES	MORGANATICALLY	MORPHOLOGY
MONOTRICHIC	MONTICULUS	MOONSTRUCK	MORGANITES	MORPHOMETRIC
MONOTRICHOUS	MONTICULUSES	MOONWALKED	MORGENSTERN	MORPHOMETRICS
MONOTROCHS	MONTMORILLONITE	MOONWALKER	MORGENSTERNS	MORPHOMETRIES
MONOUNSATURATE	MONUMENTAL	MOONWALKERS	MORIBUNDITIES	MORPHOMETRY

M

MORPHOPHONEME	MOSCHATELS	MOTIONLESSNESS	MOTORIZATIONS	MOUNTEBANKINGS
MORPHOPHONEMES	MOSCHIFEROUS	MOTIVATING	MOTORIZING	MOUNTEBANKISM
MORPHOPHONEMIC	MOSKONFYTS	MOTIVATION	MOTORMOUTH	MOUNTEBANKISMS
MORPHOPHONEMICS	MOSQUITOES	MOTIVATIONAL	MOTORMOUTHS	MOUNTEBANKS
MORPHOTROPIC	MOSQUITOEY	MOTIVATIONALLY	MOTORSHIPS	MOUNTENANCE
MORPHOTROPIES	MOSSBACKED	MOTIVATIONS	MOTORTRUCK	MOUNTENANCES
MORPHOTROPY	MOSSBLUITER	MOTIVATIVE	MOTORTRUCKS	MOUNTENAUNCE
MORSELLING	MOSSBLUITERS	MOTIVATORS	MOUCHARABIES	MOUNTENAUNCES
MORTADELLA	MOSSBUNKER	MOTIVELESS	MOUCHARABY	MOURNFULLER
MORTADELLAS	MOSSBUNKERS	MOTIVELESSLY	MOUDIEWART	MOURNFULLEST
MORTADELLE	MOSSINESSES	MOTIVELESSNESS	MOUDIEWARTS	MOURNFULLY
MORTALISED	MOSSPLANTS	MOTIVITIES	MOUDIEWORT	MOURNFULNESS
MORTALISES	MOSSTROOPER	MOTOCROSSES	MOUDIEWORTS	MOURNFULNESSES
MORTALISING	MOSSTROOPERS	MOTONEURON	MOUDIWARTS	MOURNINGLY
MORTALITIES	MOTETTISTS	MOTONEURONAL	MOUDIWORTS	MOURNIVALS
MORTALIZED	MOTHBALLED	MOTONEURONS	MOULDABILITIES	MOUSEBIRDS
MORTALIZES	MOTHBALLING	MOTORBICYCLE	MOULDABILITY	MOUSEOVERS
MORTALIZING	MOTHERBOARD	MOTORBICYCLES	MOULDBOARD	MOUSEPIECE
MORTARBOARD	MOTHERBOARDS	MOTORBIKED	MOULDBOARDS	MOUSEPIECES
MORTARBOARDS	MOTHERCRAFT	MOTORBIKES	MOULDERING	MOUSETAILS
MORTARLESS	MOTHERCRAFTS	MOTORBIKING	MOULDINESS	MOUSETRAPPED
MORTCLOTHS	MOTHERESES	MOTORBOATED	MOULDINESSES	MOUSETRAPPING
MORTGAGEABLE	MOTHERFUCKER	MOTORBOATER	MOULDWARPS	MOUSETRAPS
MORTGAGEES	MOTHERFUCKERS	MOTORBOATERS	MOULDYWARP	MOUSINESSES
MORTGAGERS	MOTHERFUCKING	MOTORBOATING	MOULDYWARPS	MOUSQUETAIRE
MORTGAGING	MOTHERHOOD	MOTORBOATINGS	MOUNDBIRDS	MOUSQUETAIRES
MORTGAGORS	MOTHERHOODS	MOTORBOATS	MOUNTAINBOARD	MOUSSELINE
MORTICIANS	MOTHERHOUSE	MOTORBUSES	MOUNTAINBOARDER	MOUSSELINES
MORTIFEROUS	MOTHERHOUSES	MOTORBUSSES	MOUNTAINBOARDS	MOUSTACHED
MORTIFEROUSNESS	MOTHERINGS	MOTORCADED	MOUNTAINED	MOUSTACHES
MORTIFICATION	MOTHERLAND	MOTORCADES	MOUNTAINEER	MOUSTACHIAL
MORTIFICATIONS	MOTHERLANDS	MOTORCADING	MOUNTAINEERED	MOUSTACHIO
MORTIFIERS	MOTHERLESS	MOTORCOACH	MOUNTAINEERING	MOUSTACHIOS
MORTIFYING	MOTHERLESSNESS	MOTORCOACHES	MOUNTAINEERINGS	MOUTHBREATHER
MORTIFYINGLY	MOTHERLINESS	MOTORCYCLE	MOUNTAINEERS	MOUTHBREATHERS
MORTIFYINGS	MOTHERLINESSES	MOTORCYCLED	MOUNTAINOUS	MOUTHBREEDER
MORTUARIES	MOTHERWORT	MOTORCYCLES	MOUNTAINOUSLY	MOUTHBREEDERS
MORULATION	MOTHERWORTS	MOTORCYCLING	MOUNTAINOUSNESS	MOUTHBROODER
MORULATIONS	MOTHPROOFED	MOTORCYCLINGS	MOUNTAINSIDE	MOUTHBROODERS
MOSAICALLY	MOTHPROOFER	MOTORCYCLIST	MOUNTAINSIDES	MOUTHFEELS
MOSAICISMS	MOTHPROOFERS	MOTORCYCLISTS	MOUNTAINTOP	MOUTHPARTS
MOSAICISTS	MOTHPROOFING	MOTORHOMES	MOUNTAINTOPS	MOUTHPIECE
MOSAICKING	MOTHPROOFS	MOTORICALLY	MOUNTEBANK	MOUTHPIECES
MOSAICLIKE	MOTILITIES	MOTORISATION	MOUNTEBANKED	MOUTHWASHES
MOSASAURUS	MOTIONISTS	MOTORISATIONS	MOUNTEBANKERIES	MOUTHWATERING
MOSBOLLETJIE	MOTIONLESS	MOTORISING	MOUNTEBANKERY	MOUTHWATERINGLY
MOSBOLLETJIES	MOTIONLESSLY	MOTORIZATION	MOUNTEBANKING	MOUVEMENTE

MOVABILITIES	MUCKSPREADER	MUGWUMPISH	MULTICENTRIC	MULTIFACED
MOVABILITY	MUCKSPREADERS	MUGWUMPISM	MULTICHAIN	MULTIFACETED
MOVABLENESS	MUCKSPREADING	MUGWUMPISMS	MULTICHAMBERED	MULTIFACTOR
MOVABLENESSES	MUCKSPREADS	MUJAHEDEEN	MULTICHANNEL	MULTIFACTORIAL
MOVEABILITIES	MUCKSWEATS	MUJAHIDEEN	MULTICHARACTER	MULTIFAMILY
MOVEABILITY	MUCKYMUCKS	MULATTRESS	MULTICIDES	MULTIFARIOUS
MOVEABLENESS	MUCOCUTANEOUS	MULATTRESSES	MULTICIPITAL	MULTIFARIOUSLY
MOVEABLENESSES	MUCOMEMBRANOUS	MULBERRIES	MULTICLIENT	MULTIFIDLY
MOVELESSLY	MUCOPEPTIDE	MULIEBRITIES	MULTICOATED	MULTIFIDOUS
MOVELESSNESS	MUCOPEPTIDES	MULIEBRITY	MULTICOLOR	MULTIFILAMENT
MOVELESSNESSES	MUCOPROTEIN	MULISHNESS	MULTICOLORED	MULTIFILAMENTS
MOVIEGOERS	MUCOPROTEINS	MULISHNESSES	MULTICOLORS	MULTIFLASH
MOVIEGOING	MUCOPURULENT	MULLAHISMS	MULTICOLOUR	MULTIFLORA
MOVIEGOINGS	MUCOSANGUINEOUS	MULLARKIES	MULTICOLOURED	MULTIFLORAS
MOVIELANDS	MUCOSITIES	MULLIGATAWNIES	MULTICOLOURS	MULTIFLOROUS
MOVIEMAKER	MUCOVISCIDOSES	MULLIGATAWNY	MULTICOLUMN	MULTIFOCAL
MOVIEMAKERS	MUCOVISCIDOSIS	MULLIGRUBS	MULTICOMPONENT	MULTIFOILS
MOVIEMAKING	MUCRONATED	MULLIONING	MULTICONDUCTOR	MULTIFOLIATE
MOVIEMAKINGS	MUCRONATION	MULTANGULAR	MULTICOSTATE	MULTIFOLIOLATE
MOWBURNING	MUCRONATIONS	MULTANIMOUS	MULTICOUNTY	MULTIFORMITIES
MOWDIEWART	MUDCAPPING	MULTARTICULATE	MULTICOURSE	MULTIFORMITY
MOWDIEWARTS	MUDDINESSES	MULTEITIES	MULTICULTI	MULTIFORMS
MOWDIEWORT	MUDDLEDNESS	MULTIACCESS	MULTICULTIS	MULTIFREQUENCY
MOWDIEWORTS	MUDDLEDNESSES	MULTIACCESSES	MULTICULTURAL	MULTIFUNCTION
MOXIBUSTION	MUDDLEHEADED	MULTIAGENCY	MULTICULTURALLY	MULTIFUNCTIONAL
MOXIBUSTIONS	MUDDLEHEADEDLY	MULTIANGULAR	MULTICURIE	MULTIGENIC
MOZZARELLA	MUDDLEMENT	MULTIARMED	MULTICURRENCIES	MULTIGRADE
MOZZARELLAS	MUDDLEMENTS	MULTIARTICULATE	MULTICURRENCY	MULTIGRAIN
MRIDAMGAMS	MUDDLINGLY	MULTIAUTHOR	MULTICUSPID	MULTIGRAVIDA
MRIDANGAMS	MUDHOPPERS	MULTIAXIAL	MULTICUSPIDATE	MULTIGRAVIDAE
MUCEDINOUS	MUDLARKING	MULTIBARREL	MULTICUSPIDS	MULTIGRAVIDAS
MUCHNESSES	MUDLOGGERS	MULTIBARRELED	MULTICYCLE	MULTIGROUP
MUCIDITIES	MUDLOGGING	MULTIBILLION	MULTICYCLES	MULTIHEADED
MUCIDNESSES	MUDLOGGINGS	MULTIBLADED	MULTIDENTATE	MULTIHOSPITAL
MUCIFEROUS	MUDPUPPIES	MULTIBRANCHED	MULTIDIALECTAL	MULTIHULLS
MUCILAGINOUS	MUDSKIPPER	MULTIBUILDING	MULTIDIGITATE	MULTIJUGATE
MUCILAGINOUSLY	MUDSKIPPERS	MULTICAMERATE	MULTIDISCIPLINE	MULTIJUGOUS
MUCINOGENS	MUDSLINGER	MULTICAMPUS	MULTIDIVISIONAL	MULTILANES
MUCKAMUCKED	MUDSLINGERS	MULTICAPITATE	MULTIDOMAIN	MULTILATERAL
MUCKAMUCKING	MUDSLINGING	MULTICARBON	MULTIELECTRODE	MULTILATERALISM
MUCKAMUCKS	MUDSLINGINGS	MULTICASTS	MULTIELEMENT	MULTILATERALIST
MUCKENDERS	MUFFETTEES	MULTICAULINE	MULTIEMPLOYER	MULTILATERALLY
MUCKINESSES	MUFFINEERS	MULTICAUSAL	MULTIEMPLOYERS	MULTILAYER
MUCKRAKERS	MUGEARITES	MULTICELLED	MULTIENGINE	MULTILAYERED
MUCKRAKING	MUGGINESSES	MULTICELLULAR	MULTIENZYME	MULTILEVEL
MUCKRAKINGS	MUGWUMPERIES	MULTICENTER	MULTIETHNIC	MULTILEVELED
MUCKSPREAD	MUGWUMPERY	MULTICENTRAL	MULTIETHNICS	MULTILINEAL

M

M

MULTILINEAR	MULTIPARAE	MULTIPLIES	MULTISPIRAL	MULTIVERSITY
MULTILINGUAL	MULTIPARAMETER	MULTIPLYING	MULTISPORT	MULTIVIBRATOR
MULTILINGUALISM	MULTIPARAS	MULTIPOLAR	MULTISTAGE	MULTIVIBRATORS
MULTILINGUALLY	MULTIPARITIES	MULTIPOLARITIES	MULTISTATE	MULTIVIOUS
MULTILINGUIST	MULTIPARITY	MULTIPOLARITY	MULTISTEMMED	MULTIVITAMIN
MULTILINGUISTS	MULTIPAROUS	MULTIPOLES	MULTISTOREY	MULTIVITAMINS
MULTILOBATE	MULTIPARTICLE	MULTIPOTENT	MULTISTOREYS	MULTIVOCAL
MULTILOBED	MULTIPARTITE	MULTIPOTENTIAL	MULTISTORIED	MULTIVOCALS
MULTILOBES	MULTIPARTY	MULTIPOWER	MULTISTORIES	MULTIVOLTINE
MULTILOBULAR	MULTIPARTYISM	MULTIPRESENCE	MULTISTORY	MULTIVOLUME
MULTILOBULATE	MULTIPARTYISMS	MULTIPRESENCES	MULTISTRANDED	MULTIWARHEAD
MULTILOCATIONAL	MULTIPEDES	MULTIPRESENT	MULTISTRIKE	MULTIWAVELENGTH
MULTILOCULAR	MULTIPHASE	MULTIPROBLEM	MULTISTRIKES	MULTIWINDOW
MULTILOCULATE	MULTIPHASIC	MULTIPROCESSING	MULTISULCATE	MULTIWINDOWS
MULTILOQUENCE	MULTIPHOTON	MULTIPROCESSOR	MULTISYLLABIC	MULTOCULAR
MULTILOQUENCES	MULTIPICTURE	MULTIPROCESSORS	MULTISYSTEM	MULTUNGULATE
MULTILOQUENT	MULTIPIECE	MULTIPRODUCT	MULTITALENTED	MULTUNGULATES
MULTILOQUIES	MULTIPISTON	MULTIPRONGED	MULTITASKED	MUMBLEMENT
MULTILOQUOUS	MULTIPLANE	MULTIPURPOSE	MULTITASKING	MUMBLEMENTS
MULTILOQUY	MULTIPLANES	MULTIRACIAL	MULTITASKINGS	MUMBLETYPEG
MULTIMANNED	MULTIPLANT	MULTIRACIALISM	MULTITASKS	MUMBLETYPEGS
MULTIMEDIA	MULTIPLAYER	MULTIRACIALISMS	MULTITERMINAL	MUMBLINGLY
MULTIMEDIAS	MULTIPLAYERS	MULTIRACIALLY	MULTITHREADING	MUMCHANCES
MULTIMEGATON	MULTIPLETS	MULTIRAMIFIED	MULTITHREADINGS	MUMMICHOGS
MULTIMEGAWATT	MULTIPLEXED	MULTIRANGE	MULTITIERED	MUMMIFICATION
MULTIMEGAWATTS	MULTIPLEXER	MULTIREGIONAL	MULTITONES	MUMMIFICATIONS
MULTIMEMBER	MULTIPLEXERS	MULTIRELIGIOUS	MULTITOOLS	MUMMIFYING
MULTIMETALLIC	MULTIPLEXES	MULTISCIENCE	MULTITOWERED	MUMPISHNESS
MULTIMETER	MULTIPLEXING	MULTISCIENCES	MULTITRACK	MUMPISHNESSES
MULTIMETERS	MULTIPLEXOR	MULTISCREEN	MULTITRILLION	MUMPSIMUSES
MULTIMILLENNIAL	MULTIPLEXORS	MULTISENSE	MULTITUDES	MUNCHABLES
MULTIMILLION	MULTIPLIABLE	MULTISENSORY	MULTITUDINARY	MUNDANENESS
MULTIMODAL	MULTIPLICABLE	MULTISEPTATE	MULTITUDINOUS	MUNDANENESSES
MULTIMOLECULAR	MULTIPLICAND	MULTISERIAL	MULTITUDINOUSLY	MUNDANITIES
MULTINATION	MULTIPLICANDS	MULTISERIATE	MULTIUNION	MUNDIFICATION
MULTINATIONAL	MULTIPLICATE	MULTISERVICE	MULTIVALENCE	MUNDIFICATIONS
MULTINATIONALS	MULTIPLICATES	MULTISIDED	MULTIVALENCES	MUNDIFICATIVE
MULTINOMIAL	MULTIPLICATION	MULTISKILL	MULTIVALENCIES	MUNDIFYING
MULTINOMIALS	MULTIPLICATIONS	MULTISKILLED	MULTIVALENCY	MUNDUNGUSES
MULTINOMINAL	MULTIPLICATIVE	MULTISKILLING	MULTIVALENT	MUNICIPALISE
MULTINUCLEAR	MULTIPLICATOR	MULTISKILLINGS	MULTIVALENTS	MUNICIPALISED
MULTINUCLEATE	MULTIPLICATORS	MULTISKILLS	MULTIVARIABLE	MUNICIPALISES
MULTINUCLEATED	MULTIPLICITIES	MULTISONANT	MULTIVARIATE	MUNICIPALISING
MULTINUCLEOLATE	MULTIPLICITY	MULTISOURCE	MULTIVARIOUS	MUNICIPALISM
MULTIORGASMIC	MULTIPLIED	MULTISPECIES	MULTIVERSE	MUNICIPALISMS
MULTIPACKS	MULTIPLIER	MULTISPECTRAL	MULTIVERSES	MUNICIPALIST
MULTIPANED	MULTIPLIERS	MULTISPEED	MULTIVERSITIES	MUNICIPALISTS

MUNICIPALITIES	MUSCAVADOS	MUSICOLOGISTS	MUTENESSES	MYASTHENIA
MUNICIPALITY	MUSCOLOGIES	MUSICOLOGY	MUTESSARIF	MYASTHENIAS
MUNICIPALIZE	MUSCOVADOS	MUSICOTHERAPIES	MUTESSARIFAT	MYASTHENIC
MUNICIPALIZED	MUSCOVITES	MUSICOTHERAPY	MUTESSARIFATS	MYASTHENICS
MUNICIPALIZES	MUSCULARITIES	MUSKELLUNGE	MUTESSARIFS	MYCETOLOGIES
MUNICIPALIZING	MUSCULARITY	MUSKELLUNGES	MUTILATING	MYCETOLOGY
MUNICIPALLY	MUSCULARLY	MUSKETEERS	MUTILATION	MYCETOMATA
MUNICIPALS	MUSCULATION	MUSKETOONS	MUTILATIONS	MYCETOMATOUS
MUNIFICENCE	MUSCULATIONS	MUSKETRIES	MUTILATIVE	MYCETOPHAGOUS
MUNIFICENCES	MUSCULATURE	MUSKINESSES	MUTILATORS	MYCETOZOAN
MUNIFICENT	MUSCULATURES	MUSKMELONS	MUTINEERED	MYCETOZOANS
MUNIFICENTLY	MUSCULOSKELETAL	MUSQUASHES	MUTINEERING	MYCOBACTERIA
MUNIFICENTNESS	MUSEOLOGICAL	MUSQUETOON	MUTINOUSLY	MYCOBACTERIAL
MUNIFIENCE	MUSEOLOGIES	MUSQUETOONS	MUTINOUSNESS	MYCOBACTERIUM
MUNIFIENCES	MUSEOLOGIST	MUSSELCRACKER	MUTINOUSNESSES	MYCOBIONTS
MUNITIONED	MUSEOLOGISTS	MUSSELCRACKERS	MUTOSCOPES	MYCODOMATIA
MUNITIONEER	MUSHINESSES	MUSSINESSES	MUTTERATION	MYCODOMATIUM
MUNITIONEERS	MUSHMOUTHS	MUSSITATED	MUTTERATIONS	MYCOFLORAE
MUNITIONER	MUSHROOMED	MUSSITATES	MUTTERINGLY	MYCOFLORAS
MUNITIONERS	MUSHROOMER	MUSSITATING	MUTTERINGS	MYCOLOGICAL
MUNITIONETTE	MUSHROOMERS	MUSSITATION	MUTTONBIRD	MYCOLOGICALLY
MUNITIONETTES	MUSHROOMING	MUSSITATIONS	MUTTONBIRDER	MYCOLOGIES
MUNITIONING	MUSICALISATION	MUSTACHIOED	MUTTONBIRDERS	MYCOLOGIST
MURDERBALL	MUSICALISATIONS	MUSTACHIOS	MUTTONBIRDS	MYCOLOGISTS
MURDERBALLS	MUSICALISE	MUSTELINES	MUTTONCHOPS	MYCOPHAGIES
MURDERESSES	MUSICALISED	MUSTINESSES	MUTTONFISH	MYCOPHAGIST
MURDEROUSLY	MUSICALISES	MUTABILITIES	MUTTONFISHES	MYCOPHAGISTS
MURDEROUSNESS	MUSICALISING	MUTABILITY	MUTTONHEAD	MYCOPHAGOUS
MURDEROUSNESSES	MUSICALITIES	MUTABLENESS	MUTTONHEADED	MYCOPHILES
MURGEONING	MUSICALITY	MUTABLENESSES	MUTTONHEADS	MYCOPLASMA
MURKINESSES	MUSICALIZATION	MUTAGENESES	MUTUALISATION	MYCOPLASMAL
MURMURATION	MUSICALIZATIONS	MUTAGENESIS	MUTUALISATIONS	MYCOPLASMAS
MURMURATIONS	MUSICALIZE	MUTAGENICALLY	MUTUALISED	MYCOPLASMATA
MURMURINGLY	MUSICALIZED	MUTAGENICITIES	MUTUALISES	MYCOPLASMOSES
MURMURINGS	MUSICALIZES	MUTAGENICITY	MUTUALISING	MYCOPLASMOSIS
MURMUROUSLY	MUSICALIZING	MUTAGENISE	MUTUALISMS	MYCORHIZAE
MURTHERERS	MUSICALNESS	MUTAGENISED	MUTUALISTIC	MYCORHIZAL
MURTHERING	MUSICALNESSES	MUTAGENISES	MUTUALISTS	MYCORHIZAS
MUSCADELLE	MUSICIANER	MUTAGENISING	MUTUALITIES	MYCORRHIZA
MUSCADELLES	MUSICIANERS	MUTAGENIZE	MUTUALIZATION	MYCORRHIZAE
MUSCADINES	MUSICIANLY	MUTAGENIZED	MUTUALIZATIONS	MYCORRHIZAL
MUSCARDINE	MUSICIANSHIP	MUTAGENIZES	MUTUALIZED	MYCORRHIZAS
MUSCARDINES	MUSICIANSHIPS	MUTAGENIZING	MUTUALIZES	MYCOTOXICOSES
MUSCARINES	MUSICOLOGICAL	MUTATIONAL	MUTUALIZING	MYCOTOXICOSIS
MUSCARINIC	MUSICOLOGICALLY	MUTATIONALLY	MUTUALNESS	MYCOTOXINS
MUSCATORIA	MUSICOLOGIES	MUTATIONIST	MUTUALNESSES	MYCOTOXOLOGIES
MUSCATORIUM	MUSICOLOGIST	MUTATIONISTS	MUZZINESSES	MYCOTOXOLOGY

M

MYCOTROPHIC	MYOCARDIAL	MYRINGOTOMIES	MYSTIFICATIONS	MYTHOLOGISES
MYCOVIRUSES	MYOCARDIOGRAPH	MYRINGOTOMY	MYSTIFIERS	MYTHOLOGISING
MYDRIATICS	MYOCARDIOGRAPHS	MYRIORAMAS	MYSTIFYING	MYTHOLOGIST
MYELENCEPHALA	MYOCARDIOPATHY	MYRIOSCOPE	MYSTIFYINGLY	MYTHOLOGISTS
MYELENCEPHALIC	MYOCARDITIS	MYRIOSCOPES	MYTHICALLY	MYTHOLOGIZATION
MYELENCEPHALON	MYOCARDITISES	MYRISTICIVOROUS	MYTHICISATION	MYTHOLOGIZE
MYELENCEPHALONS	MYOCARDIUM	MYRMECOCHORIES	MYTHICISATIONS	MYTHOLOGIZED
MYELINATED	MYOCLONUSES	MYRMECOCHORY	MYTHICISED	MYTHOLOGIZER
MYELITIDES	MYOELECTRIC	MYRMECOLOGIC	MYTHICISER	MYTHOLOGIZERS
MYELITISES	MYOELECTRICAL	MYRMECOLOGICAL	MYTHICISERS	MYTHOLOGIZES
MYELOBLAST	MYOFIBRILLAR	MYRMECOLOGIES	MYTHICISES	MYTHOLOGIZING
MYELOBLASTIC	MYOFIBRILS	MYRMECOLOGIST	MYTHICISING	MYTHOMANES
MYELOBLASTS	MYOFILAMENT	MYRMECOLOGISTS	MYTHICISMS	MYTHOMANIA
MYELOCYTES	MYOFILAMENTS	MYRMECOLOGY	MYTHICISTS	MYTHOMANIAC
MYELOCYTIC	MYOGLOBINS	MYRMECOPHAGOUS	MYTHICIZATION	MYTHOMANIACS
MYELOFIBROSES	MYOGRAPHIC	MYRMECOPHILE	MYTHICIZATIONS	MYTHOMANIAS
MYELOFIBROSIS	MYOGRAPHICAL	MYRMECOPHILES	MYTHICIZED	MYTHOPOEIA
MYELOFIBROTIC	MYOGRAPHICALLY	MYRMECOPHILIES	MYTHICIZER	MYTHOPOEIAS
MYELOGENOUS	MYOGRAPHIES	MYRMECOPHILOUS	MYTHICIZERS	MYTHOPOEIC
MYELOGRAMS	MYOGRAPHIST	MYRMECOPHILY	MYTHICIZES	MYTHOPOEISM
MYELOGRAPHIES	MYOGRAPHISTS	MYRMIDONES	MYTHICIZING	MYTHOPOEISMS
MYELOGRAPHY	MYOINOSITOL	MYRMIDONIAN	MYTHMAKERS	MYTHOPOEIST
MYELOMATOID	MYOINOSITOLS	MYROBALANS	MYTHMAKING	MYTHOPOEISTS
MYELOMATOUS	MYOLOGICAL	MYRTACEOUS	MYTHMAKINGS	MYTHOPOESES
MYELOPATHIC	MYOLOGISTS	MYSOPHOBIA	MYTHOGENESES	MYTHOPOESIS
MYELOPATHIES	MYOMANCIES	MYSOPHOBIAS	MYTHOGENESIS	MYTHOPOETIC
MYELOPATHY	MYOMECTOMIES	MYSTAGOGIC	MYTHOGRAPHER	MYTHOPOETICAL
MYIOPHILIES	MYOMECTOMY	MYSTAGOGICAL	MYTHOGRAPHERS	MYTHOPOETS
MYIOPHILOUS	MYOPATHIES	MYSTAGOGICALLY	MYTHOGRAPHIES	MYTILIFORM
MYLOHYOIDS	MYOPHILIES	MYSTAGOGIES	MYTHOGRAPHY	MYXAMOEBAE
MYLONITISATION	MYOPHILOUS	MYSTAGOGUE	MYTHOLOGER	MYXAMOEBAS
MYLONITISATIONS	MYOPICALLY	MYSTAGOGUES	MYTHOLOGERS	MYXEDEMATOUS
MYLONITISE	MYOSITISES	MYSTAGOGUS	MYTHOLOGIAN	MYXOEDEMAS
MYLONITISED	MYOSOTISES	MYSTAGOGUSES	MYTHOLOGIANS	MYXOEDEMATOUS
MYLONITISES	MYOSTATINS	MYSTERIOUS	MYTHOLOGIC	MYXOEDEMIC
MYLONITISING	MYRIADFOLD	MYSTERIOUSLY	MYTHOLOGICAL	MYXOMATOSES
MYLONITIZATION	MYRIADFOLDS	MYSTERIOUSNESS	MYTHOLOGICALLY	MYXOMATOSIS
MYLONITIZATIONS	MYRIAPODAN	MYSTICALLY	MYTHOLOGIES	MYXOMATOUS
MYLONITIZE	MYRIAPODOUS	MYSTICALNESS	MYTHOLOGISATION	MYXOMYCETE
MYLONITIZED	MYRINGITIS	MYSTICALNESSES	MYTHOLOGISE	MYXOMYCETES
MYLONITIZES	MYRINGITISES	MYSTICETES	MYTHOLOGISED	MYXOMYCETOUS
MYLONITIZING	MYRINGOSCOPE	MYSTICISMS	MYTHOLOGISER	MYXOVIRUSES
MYOBLASTIC	MYRINGOSCOPES	MYSTIFICATION	MYTHOLOGISERS	

M

N

NABOBERIES	NANOPUBLISHINGS	NARCOLEPTICS	NASALISATIONS	NATIONALIZING
NABOBESSES	NANOSECOND	NARCOSYNTHESES	NASALISING	NATIONALLY
NACHTMAALS	NANOSECONDS	NARCOSYNTHESIS	NASALITIES	NATIONHOOD
NAFFNESSES	NANOTECHNOLOGY	NARCOTERRORISM	NASALIZATION	NATIONHOODS
NAIFNESSES	NANOTESLAS	NARCOTERRORISMS	NASALIZATIONS	NATIONLESS
NAILBITERS	NANOWORLDS	NARCOTERRORIST	NASALIZING	NATIONWIDE
NAILBRUSHES	NAPHTHALENE	NARCOTERRORISTS	NASCENCIES	NATIVENESS
NAISSANCES	NAPHTHALENES	NARCOTICALLY	NASEBERRIES	NATIVENESSES
NAIVENESSES	NAPHTHALIC	NARCOTINES	NASOFRONTAL	NATIVISTIC
NAKEDNESSES	NAPHTHALIN	NARCOTISATION	NASOGASTRIC	NATIVITIES
NALBUPHINE	NAPHTHALINE	NARCOTISATIONS	NASOLACRYMAL	NATRIURESES
NALBUPHINES	NAPHTHALINES	NARCOTISED	NASOPHARYNGEAL	NATRIURESIS
NALORPHINE	NAPHTHALINS	NARCOTISES	NASOPHARYNGES	NATRIURETIC
NALORPHINES	NAPHTHALISE	NARCOTISING	NASOPHARYNX	NATRIURETICS
NALTREXONE	NAPHTHALISED	NARCOTISMS	NASOPHARYNXES	NATROLITES
NALTREXONES	NAPHTHALISES	NARCOTISTS	NASTINESSES	NATTERJACK
NAMAYCUSHES	NAPHTHALISING	NARCOTIZATION	NASTURTIUM	NATTERJACKS
NAMECHECKED	NAPHTHALIZE	NARCOTIZATIONS	NASTURTIUMS	NATTINESSES
NAMECHECKING	NAPHTHALIZED	NARCOTIZED	NATALITIAL	NATURALISATION
NAMECHECKS	NAPHTHALIZES	NARCOTIZES	NATALITIES	NATURALISATIONS
NAMELESSLY	NAPHTHALIZING	NARCOTIZING	NATATIONAL	NATURALISE
NAMELESSNESS	NAPHTHENES	NARGHILIES	NATATORIAL	NATURALISED
NAMELESSNESSES	NAPHTHENIC	NARGHILLIES	NATATORIUM	NATURALISES
NAMEPLATES	NAPHTHYLAMINE	NARGUILEHS	NATATORIUMS	NATURALISING
NAMEWORTHY	NAPHTHYLAMINES	NARRATABLE	NATHELESSE	NATURALISM
NANDROLONE	NAPOLEONITE	NARRATIONAL	NATIONALISATION	NATURALISMS
NANDROLONES	NAPOLEONITES	NARRATIONS	NATIONALISE	NATURALIST
NANISATION	NAPPINESSES	NARRATIVELY	NATIONALISED	NATURALISTIC
NANISATIONS	NAPRAPATHIES	NARRATIVES	NATIONALISER	NATURALISTS
NANIZATION	NAPRAPATHY	NARRATOLOGICAL	NATIONALISERS	NATURALIZATION
NANIZATIONS	NARCISSISM	NARRATOLOGIES	NATIONALISES	NATURALIZATIONS
NANNOPLANKTON	NARCISSISMS	NARRATOLOGIST	NATIONALISING	NATURALIZE
NANNOPLANKTONS	NARCISSIST	NARRATOLOGISTS	NATIONALISM	NATURALIZED
NANOGRAMME	NARCISSISTIC	NARRATOLOGY	NATIONALISMS	NATURALIZES
NANOGRAMMES	NARCISSISTS	NARROWBAND	NATIONALIST	NATURALIZING
NANOMATERIAL	NARCISSUSES	NARROWBANDS	NATIONALISTIC	NATURALNESS
NANOMATERIALS	NARCOANALYSES	NARROWCAST	NATIONALISTS	NATURALNESSES
NANOMETERS	NARCOANALYSIS	NARROWCASTED	NATIONALITIES	NATURISTIC
NANOMETRES	NARCOCATHARSES	NARROWCASTING	NATIONALITY	NATUROPATH
NANOPARTICLE	NARCOCATHARSIS	NARROWCASTINGS	NATIONALIZATION	NATUROPATHIC
NANOPARTICLES	NARCOHYPNOSES	NARROWCASTS	NATIONALIZE	NATUROPATHIES
NANOPHYSICS	NARCOHYPNOSIS	NARROWINGS	NATIONALIZED	NATUROPATHS
NANOPLANKTON	NARCOLEPSIES	NARROWNESS	NATIONALIZER	NATUROPATHY
NANOPLANKTONS	NARCOLEPSY	NARROWNESSES	NATIONALIZERS	NAUGAHYDES
NANOPUBLISHING	NARCOLEPTIC	NASALISATION	NATIONALIZES	NAUGHTIEST

NAUGHTINESS	NEARSIGHTED	NECKCLOTHS	NECROPHOBE	NEEDLEPOINT
NAUGHTINESSES	NEARSIGHTEDLY	NECKERCHIEF	NECROPHOBES	NEEDLEPOINTS
NAUMACHIAE	NEARSIGHTEDNESS	NECKERCHIEFS	NECROPHOBIA	NEEDLESSLY
NAUMACHIAS	NEARTHROSES	NECKERCHIEVES	NECROPHOBIAS	NEEDLESSNESS
NAUMACHIES	NEARTHROSIS	NECKLACING	NECROPHOBIC	NEEDLESSNESSES
NAUPLIIFORM	NEATNESSES	NECKLACINGS	NECROPHOROUS	NEEDLESTICK
NAUSEATING	NEBBISHERS	NECKPIECES	NECROPOLEIS	NEEDLEWOMAN
NAUSEATINGLY	NEBENKERNS	NECKVERSES	NECROPOLES	NEEDLEWOMEN
NAUSEATION	NEBUCHADNEZZAR	NECROBIOSES	NECROPOLIS	NEEDLEWORK
NAUSEATIONS	NEBUCHADNEZZARS	NECROBIOSIS	NECROPOLISES	NEEDLEWORKER
NAUSEATIVE	NEBULISATION	NECROBIOTIC	NECROPSIED	NEEDLEWORKERS
NAUSEOUSLY	NEBULISATIONS	NECROGRAPHER	NECROPSIES	NEEDLEWORKS
NAUSEOUSNESS	NEBULISERS	NECROGRAPHERS	NECROPSYING	NEESBERRIES
NAUSEOUSNESSES	NEBULISING	NECROLATER	NECROSCOPIC	NEFARIOUSLY
NAUTICALLY	NEBULIZATION	NECROLATERS	NECROSCOPICAL	NEFARIOUSNESS
NAUTILOIDS	NEBULIZATIONS	NECROLATRIES	NECROSCOPIES	NEFARIOUSNESSES
NAUTILUSES	NEBULIZERS	NECROLATRY	NECROSCOPY	NEGATIONAL
NAVARCHIES	NEBULIZING	NECROLOGIC	NECROTISED	NEGATIONIST
NAVELWORTS	NEBULOSITIES	NECROLOGICAL	NECROTISES	NEGATIONISTS
NAVICULARE	NEBULOSITY	NECROLOGIES	NECROTISING	NEGATIVELY
NAVICULARES	NEBULOUSLY	NECROLOGIST	NECROTIZED	NEGATIVENESS
NAVICULARS	NEBULOUSNESS	NECROLOGISTS	NECROTIZES	NEGATIVENESSES
NAVIGABILITIES	NEBULOUSNESSES	NECROMANCER	NECROTIZING	NEGATIVING
NAVIGABILITY	NECESSAIRE	NECROMANCERS	NECROTOMIES	NEGATIVISM
NAVIGABLENESS	NECESSAIRES	NECROMANCIES	NECROTROPH	NEGATIVISMS
NAVIGABLENESSES	NECESSARIAN	NECROMANCY	NECROTROPHIC	NEGATIVIST
NAVIGATING	NECESSARIANISM	NECROMANIA	NECROTROPHS	NEGATIVISTIC
NAVIGATION	NECESSARIANISMS	NECROMANIAC	NECTAREOUS	NEGATIVISTS
NAVIGATIONAL	NECESSARIANS	NECROMANIACS	NECTAREOUSNESS	NEGATIVITIES
NAVIGATIONALLY	NECESSARIES	NECROMANIAS	NECTARIFEROUS	NEGATIVITY
NAVIGATIONS	NECESSARILY	NECROMANTIC	NECTARINES	NEGLECTABLE
NAVIGATORS	NECESSARINESS	NECROMANTICAL	NECTARIVOROUS	NEGLECTEDNESS
NAYSAYINGS	NECESSARINESSES	NECROMANTICALLY	NECTOCALYCES	NEGLECTEDNESSES
NAZIFICATION	NECESSITARIAN	NECROPHAGOUS	NECTOCALYX	NEGLECTERS
NAZIFICATIONS	NECESSITARIANS	NECROPHILE	NEEDCESSITIES	NEGLECTFUL
NEANDERTAL	NECESSITATE	NECROPHILES	NEEDCESSITY	NEGLECTFULLY
NEANDERTALER	NECESSITATED	NECROPHILIA	NEEDFULNESS	NEGLECTFULNESS
NEANDERTALERS	NECESSITATES	NECROPHILIAC	NEEDFULNESSES	NEGLECTING
NEANDERTALS	NECESSITATING	NECROPHILIACS	NEEDINESSES	NEGLECTINGLY
NEANDERTHAL	NECESSITATION	NECROPHILIAS	NEEDLECORD	NEGLECTION
NEANDERTHALER	NECESSITATIONS	NECROPHILIC	NEEDLECORDS	NEGLECTIONS
NEANDERTHALERS	NECESSITATIVE	NECROPHILIES	NEEDLECRAFT	NEGLECTIVE
NEANDERTHALOID	NECESSITIED	NECROPHILISM	NEEDLECRAFTS	NEGLECTORS
NEANDERTHALS	NECESSITIES	NECROPHILISMS	NEEDLEFISH	NEGLIGEABLE
NEAPOLITAN	NECESSITOUS	NECROPHILOUS	NEEDLEFISHES	NEGLIGENCE
NEAPOLITANS	NECESSITOUSLY	NECROPHILS	NEEDLEFULS	NEGLIGENCES
NEARNESSES	NECESSITOUSNESS	NECROPHILY	NEEDLELIKE	NEGLIGENTLY

NEGLIGIBILITIES	NEIGHBOURLESS	NEOCONSERVATISM	NEOPAGANISM	NEPHELINITE
NEGLIGIBILITY	NEIGHBOURLINESS	NEOCONSERVATIVE	NEOPAGANISMS	NEPHELINITES
NEGLIGIBLE	NEIGHBOURLY	NEOCORTEXES	NEOPAGANIZE	NEPHELINITIC
NEGLIGIBLENESS	NEIGHBOURS	NEOCORTICAL	NEOPAGANIZED	NEPHELITES
NEGLIGIBLY	NELUMBIUMS	NEOCORTICES	NEOPAGANIZES	NEPHELOMETER
NEGOCIANTS	NEMATHELMINTH	NEODYMIUMS	NEOPAGANIZING	NEPHELOMETERS
NEGOTIABILITIES	NEMATHELMINTHIC	NEOGENESES	NEOPHILIAC	NEPHELOMETRIC
NEGOTIABILITY	NEMATHELMINTHS	NEOGENESIS	NEOPHILIACS	NEPHELOMETRIES
NEGOTIABLE	NEMATICIDAL	NEOGENETIC	NEOPHILIAS	NEPHELOMETRY
NEGOTIANTS	NEMATICIDE	NEOGOTHICS	NEOPHOBIAS	NEPHOGRAMS
NEGOTIATED	NEMATICIDES	NEOGRAMMARIAN	NEOPILINAS	NEPHOGRAPH
NEGOTIATES	NEMATOBLAST	NEOGRAMMARIANS	NEOPLASIAS	NEPHOGRAPHS
NEGOTIATING	NEMATOBLASTS	NEOLIBERAL	NEOPLASTIC	NEPHOLOGIC
NEGOTIATION	NEMATOCIDAL	NEOLIBERALISM	NEOPLASTICISM	NEPHOLOGICAL
NEGOTIATIONS	NEMATOCIDE	NEOLIBERALISMS	NEOPLASTICISMS	NEPHOLOGIES
NEGOTIATOR	NEMATOCIDES	NEOLIBERALS	NEOPLASTICIST	NEPHOLOGIST
NEGOTIATORS	NEMATOCYST	NEOLOGIANS	NEOPLASTICISTS	NEPHOLOGISTS
NEGOTIATORY	NEMATOCYSTIC	NEOLOGICAL	NEOPLASTIES	NEPHOSCOPE
NEGOTIATRESS	NEMATOCYSTS	NEOLOGICALLY	NEOREALISM	NEPHOSCOPES
NEGOTIATRESSES	NEMATODIRIASES	NEOLOGISED	NEOREALISMS	NEPHRALGIA
NEGOTIATRICES	NEMATODIRIASIS	NEOLOGISES	NEOREALIST	NEPHRALGIAS
NEGOTIATRIX	NEMATODIRUS	NEOLOGISING	NEOREALISTIC	NEPHRALGIC
NEGOTIATRIXES	NEMATODIRUSES	NEOLOGISMS	NEOREALISTS	NEPHRALGIES
NEGRITUDES	NEMATOLOGICAL	NEOLOGISTIC	NEOSTIGMINE	NEPHRECTOMIES
NEGROHEADS	NEMATOLOGIES	NEOLOGISTICAL	NEOSTIGMINES	NEPHRECTOMISE
NEGROPHILE	NEMATOLOGIST	NEOLOGISTICALLY	NEOTEINIAS	NEPHRECTOMISED
NEGROPHILES	NEMATOLOGISTS	NEOLOGISTS	NEOTERICAL	NEPHRECTOMISES
NEGROPHILISM	NEMATOLOGY	NEOLOGIZED	NEOTERICALLY	NEPHRECTOMISING
NEGROPHILISMS	NEMATOPHORE	NEOLOGIZES	NEOTERICALS	NEPHRECTOMIZE
NEGROPHILIST	NEMATOPHORES	NEOLOGIZING	NEOTERISED	NEPHRECTOMIZED
NEGROPHILISTS	NEMERTEANS	NEONATALLY	NEOTERISES	NEPHRECTOMIZES
NEGROPHILS	NEMERTIANS	NEONATICIDE	NEOTERISING	NEPHRECTOMIZING
NEGROPHOBE	NEMERTINES	NEONATICIDES	NEOTERISMS	NEPHRECTOMY
NEGROPHOBES	NEMOPHILAS	NEONATOLOGIES	NEOTERISTS	NEPHRIDIAL
NEGROPHOBIA	NEOANTHROPIC	NEONATOLOGIST	NEOTERIZED	NEPHRIDIUM
NEGROPHOBIAS	NEOARSPHENAMINE	NEONATOLOGISTS	NEOTERIZES	NEPHRITICAL
NEIGHBORED	NEOCLASSIC	NEONATOLOGY	NEOTERIZING	NEPHRITICS
NEIGHBORHOOD	NEOCLASSICAL	NEONOMIANISM	NEOTROPICS	NEPHRITIDES
NEIGHBORHOODS	NEOCLASSICISM	NEONOMIANISMS	NEOVITALISM	NEPHRITISES
NEIGHBORING	NEOCLASSICISMS	NEONOMIANS	NEOVITALISMS	NEPHROBLASTOMA
NEIGHBORLESS	NEOCLASSICIST	NEOORTHODOX	NEOVITALIST	NEPHROBLASTOMAS
NEIGHBORLINESS	NEOCLASSICISTS	NEOORTHODOXIES	NEOVITALISTS	NEPHROLEPIS
NEIGHBORLY	NEOCOLONIAL	NEOORTHODOXY	NEPENTHEAN	NEPHROLEPISES
NEIGHBOURED	NEOCOLONIALISM	NEOPAGANISE	NEPHALISMS	NEPHROLOGICAL
NEIGHBOURHOOD	NEOCOLONIALISMS	NEOPAGANISED	NEPHALISTS	NEPHROLOGIES
NEIGHBOURHOODS	NEOCOLONIALIST	NEOPAGANISES	NEPHELINES	NEPHROLOGIST
NEIGHBOURING	NEOCOLONIALISTS	NEOPAGANISING	NEPHELINIC	NEPHROLOGISTS

N

NEPHROLOGY	NETIQUETTE	NEUROCHEMISTS	NEUROLOGIC	NEUROSPORA
NEPHROPATHIC	NETIQUETTES	NEUROCHIPS	NEUROLOGICAL	NEUROSPORAS
NEPHROPATHIES	NETMINDERS	NEUROCOELE	NEUROLOGICALLY	NEUROSURGEON
NEPHROPATHY	NETTLELIKE	NEUROCOELES	NEUROLOGIES	NEUROSURGEONS
NEPHROPEXIES	NETTLESOME	NEUROCOELS	NEUROLOGIST	NEUROSURGERIES
NEPHROPEXY	NETWORKERS	NEUROCOGNITIVE	NEUROLOGISTS	NEUROSURGERY
NEPHROPTOSES	NETWORKING	NEUROCOMPUTER	NEUROLYSES	NEUROSURGICAL
NEPHROPTOSIS	NETWORKINGS	NEUROCOMPUTERS	NEUROLYSIS	NEUROSURGICALLY
NEPHROSCOPE	NEURALGIAS	NEUROCOMPUTING	NEUROMARKETING	NEUROSYPHILIS
NEPHROSCOPES	NEURAMINIDASE	NEUROCOMPUTINGS	NEUROMARKETINGS	NEUROSYPHILISES
NEPHROSCOPIES	NEURAMINIDASES	NEUROECTODERMAL	NEUROMASTS	NEUROTICALLY
NEPHROSCOPY	NEURASTHENIA	NEUROENDOCRINE	NEUROMATOUS	NEUROTICISM
NEPHROSTOME	NEURASTHENIAC	NEUROETHOLOGIES	NEUROMUSCULAR	NEUROTICISMS
NEPHROSTOMES	NEURASTHENIACS	NEUROETHOLOGY	NEUROPATHIC	NEUROTOMIES
NEPHROTICS	NEURASTHENIAS	NEUROFEEDBACK	NEUROPATHICAL	NEUROTOMIST
NEPHROTOMIES	NEURASTHENIC	NEUROFEEDBACKS	NEUROPATHICALLY	NEUROTOMISTS
NEPHROTOMY	NEURASTHENICS	NEUROFIBRIL	NEUROPATHIES	NEUROTOXIC
NEPHROTOXIC	NEURATIONS	NEUROFIBRILAR	NEUROPATHIST	NEUROTOXICITIES
NEPHROTOXICITY	NEURECTOMIES	NEUROFIBRILLAR	NEUROPATHISTS	NEUROTOXICITY
NEPOTISTIC	NEURECTOMY	NEUROFIBRILLARY	NEUROPATHOLOGIC	NEUROTOXIN
NEPTUNIUMS	NEURILEMMA	NEUROFIBRILS	NEUROPATHOLOGY	NEUROTOXINS
NERDINESSES	NEURILEMMAL	NEUROFIBROMA	NEUROPATHS	NEUROTROPHIC
NERVATIONS	NEURILEMMAS	NEUROFIBROMAS	NEUROPATHY	NEUROTROPHIES
NERVATURES	NEURILITIES	NEUROFIBROMATA	NEUROPEPTIDE	NEUROTROPHY
NERVELESSLY	NEURITIDES	NEUROGENESES	NEUROPEPTIDES	NEUROTROPIC
NERVELESSNESS	NEURITISES	NEUROGENESIS	NEUROPHYSIOLOGY	NEUROVASCULAR
NERVELESSNESSES	NEUROACTIVE	NEUROGENIC	NEUROPLASM	NEURULATION
NERVINESSES	NEUROANATOMIC	NEUROGENICALLY	NEUROPLASMS	NEURULATIONS
NERVOSITIES	NEUROANATOMICAL	NEUROGLIAL	NEUROPSYCHIATRY	NEURYPNOLOGIES
NERVOUSNESS	NEUROANATOMIES	NEUROGLIAS	NEUROPSYCHOLOGY	NEURYPNOLOGY
NERVOUSNESSES	NEUROANATOMIST	NEUROGRAMS	NEUROPTERA	NEUTRALISATION
NERVURATION	NEUROANATOMISTS	NEUROHORMONAL	NEUROPTERAN	NEUTRALISATIONS
NERVURATIONS	NEUROANATOMY	NEUROHORMONE	NEUROPTERANS	NEUTRALISE
NESCIENCES	NEUROBIOLOGICAL	NEUROHORMONES	NEUROPTERIST	NEUTRALISED
NESHNESSES	NEUROBIOLOGIES	NEUROHUMOR	NEUROPTERISTS	NEUTRALISER
NESSELRODE	NEUROBIOLOGIST	NEUROHUMORAL	NEUROPTERON	NEUTRALISERS
NESSELRODES	NEUROBIOLOGISTS	NEUROHUMORS	NEUROPTEROUS	NEUTRALISES
NETBALLERS	NEUROBIOLOGY	NEUROHYPNOLOGY	NEURORADIOLOGY	NEUTRALISING
NETHERLINGS	NEUROBLAST	NEUROHYPOPHYSES	NEUROSCIENCE	NEUTRALISM
NETHERMORE	NEUROBLASTOMA	NEUROHYPOPHYSIS	NEUROSCIENCES	NEUTRALISMS
NETHERMOST	NEUROBLASTOMAS	NEUROLEMMA	NEUROSCIENTIFIC	NEUTRALIST
NETHERSTOCK	NEUROBLASTOMATA	NEUROLEMMAS	NEUROSCIENTIST	NEUTRALISTIC
NETHERSTOCKS	NEUROBLASTS	NEUROLEPTIC	NEUROSCIENTISTS	NEUTRALISTS
NETHERWARD	NEUROCHEMICAL	NEUROLEPTICS	NEUROSECRETION	NEUTRALITIES
NETHERWARDS	NEUROCHEMICALS	NEUROLINGUIST	NEUROSECRETIONS	NEUTRALITY
NETHERWORLD	NEUROCHEMIST	NEUROLINGUISTIC	NEUROSECRETORY	NEUTRALIZATION
NETHERWORLDS	NEUROCHEMISTRY	NEUROLINGUISTS	NEUROSENSORY	NEUTRALIZATIONS

NEUTRALIZE	NEWSMONGER	NICKNAMING	NIGGERDOMS	NIGHTSHIRTS
NEUTRALIZED	NEWSMONGERS	NICKPOINTS	NIGGERHEAD	NIGHTSIDES
NEUTRALIZER	NEWSPAPERDOM	NICKSTICKS	NIGGERHEADS	NIGHTSPOTS
NEUTRALIZERS	NEWSPAPERDOMS	NICKUMPOOP	NIGGERISMS	NIGHTSTAND
NEUTRALIZES	NEWSPAPERED	NICKUMPOOPS	NIGGERLING	NIGHTSTANDS
NEUTRALIZING	NEWSPAPERING	NICOMPOOPS	NIGGERLINGS	NIGHTSTICK
NEUTRALNESS	NEWSPAPERISM	NICOTIANAS	NIGGLINGLY	NIGHTSTICKS
NEUTRALNESSES	NEWSPAPERISMS	NICOTINAMIDE	NIGHNESSES	NIGHTTIDES
NEUTRETTOS	NEWSPAPERMAN	NICOTINAMIDES	NIGHTBIRDS	NIGHTTIMES
NEUTRINOLESS	NEWSPAPERMEN	NICOTINISM	NIGHTBLIND	NIGHTWALKER
NEUTROPENIA	NEWSPAPERS	NICOTINISMS	NIGHTCLASS	NIGHTWALKERS
NEUTROPENIAS	NEWSPAPERWOMAN	NICROSILAL	NIGHTCLASSES	NIGHTWEARS
NEUTROPHIL	NEWSPAPERWOMEN	NICROSILALS	NIGHTCLOTHES	NIGRESCENCE
NEUTROPHILE	NEWSPEOPLE	NICTATIONS	NIGHTCLUBBED	NIGRESCENCES
NEUTROPHILES	NEWSPERSON	NICTITATED	NIGHTCLUBBER	NIGRESCENT
NEUTROPHILIC	NEWSPERSONS	NICTITATES	NIGHTCLUBBERS	NIGRIFYING
NEUTROPHILS	NEWSPRINTS	NICTITATING	NIGHTCLUBBING	NIGRITUDES
NEVERMINDS	NEWSREADER	NICTITATION	NIGHTCLUBBINGS	NIGROMANCIES
NEVERTHELESS	NEWSREADERS	NICTITATIONS	NIGHTCLUBS	NIGROMANCY
NEVERTHEMORE	NEWSSTANDS	NIDAMENTAL	NIGHTDRESS	NIGROSINES
NEWFANGLED	NEWSTRADES	NIDAMENTUM	NIGHTDRESSES	NIHILISTIC
NEWFANGLEDLY	NEWSWEEKLIES	NIDDERINGS	NIGHTFALLS	NIHILITIES
NEWFANGLEDNESS	NEWSWEEKLY	NIDDERLING	NIGHTFARING	NIKETHAMIDE
NEWFANGLENESS	NEWSWORTHINESS	NIDDERLINGS	NIGHTFIRES	NIKETHAMIDES
NEWFANGLENESSES	NEWSWORTHY	NIDERLINGS	NIGHTGEARS	NILPOTENTS
NEWISHNESS	NEWSWRITING	NIDICOLOUS	NIGHTGLOWS	NIMBLENESS
NEWISHNESSES	NEWSWRITINGS	NIDIFICATE	NIGHTGOWNS	NIMBLENESSES
NEWMARKETS	NEXTNESSES	NIDIFICATED	NIGHTHAWKS	NIMBLESSES
NEWSAGENCIES	NIACINAMIDE	NIDIFICATES	NIGHTINGALE	NIMBLEWITS
NEWSAGENCY	NIACINAMIDES	NIDIFICATING	NIGHTINGALES	NIMBLEWITTED
NEWSAGENTS	NIAISERIES	NIDIFICATION	NIGHTLIFES	NIMBOSTRATI
NEWSBREAKS	NIALAMIDES	NIDIFICATIONS	NIGHTLIVES	NIMBOSTRATUS
NEWSCASTER	NIBBLINGLY	NIDIFUGOUS	NIGHTMARES	NIMBYNESSES
NEWSCASTERS	NICCOLITES	NIDULATION	NIGHTMARISH	NINCOMPOOP
NEWSCASTING	NICENESSES	NIDULATIONS	NIGHTMARISHLY	NINCOMPOOPERIES
NEWSCASTINGS	NICKELIFEROUS	NIFEDIPINE	NIGHTMARISHNESS	NINCOMPOOPERY
NEWSDEALER	NICKELINES	NIFEDIPINES	NIGHTPIECE	NINCOMPOOPS
NEWSDEALERS	NICKELISED	NIFFNAFFED	NIGHTPIECES	NINEPENCES
NEWSFLASHES	NICKELISES	NIFFNAFFING	NIGHTRIDER	NINEPENNIES
NEWSGROUPS	NICKELISING	NIFTINESSES	NIGHTRIDERS	NINESCORES
NEWSHOUNDS	NICKELIZED	NIGGARDING	NIGHTRIDING	NINETEENTH
NEWSINESSES	NICKELIZES	NIGGARDISE	NIGHTRIDINGS	NINETEENTHLY
NEWSLETTER	NICKELIZING	NIGGARDISES	NIGHTSCOPE	NINETEENTHS
NEWSLETTERS	NICKELLING	NIGGARDIZE	NIGHTSCOPES	NINETIETHS
NEWSMAGAZINE	NICKELODEON	NIGGARDIZES	NIGHTSHADE	NINHYDRINS
NEWSMAGAZINES	NICKELODEONS	NIGGARDLINESS	NIGHTSHADES	NINNYHAMMER
NEWSMAKERS	NICKNAMERS	NIGGARDLINESSES	NIGHTSHIRT	NINNYHAMMERS

N

NIPCHEESES	NITROGLYCERIN	NOCTILUCAS	NOMENCLATURE	NOMOTHETIC
NIPPERKINS	NITROGLYCERINE	NOCTILUCENCE	NOMENCLATURES	NOMOTHETICAL
NIPPINESSES	NITROGLYCERINES	NOCTILUCENCES	NOMENKLATURA	NONABRASIVE
NIPPLEWORT	NITROGLYCERINS	NOCTILUCENT	NOMENKLATURAS	NONABSORBABLE
NIPPLEWORTS	NITROMETER	NOCTILUCOUS	NOMINALISATION	NONABSORBENT
NISBERRIES	NITROMETERS	NOCTIVAGANT	NOMINALISATIONS	NONABSORPTIVE
NITPICKERS	NITROMETHANE	NOCTIVAGATION	NOMINALISE	NONABSTRACT
NITPICKIER	NITROMETHANES	NOCTIVAGATIONS	NOMINALISED	NONACADEMIC
NITPICKIEST	NITROMETRIC	NOCTIVAGOUS	NOMINALISES	NONACADEMICS
NITPICKING	NITROPARAFFIN	NOCTUARIES	NOMINALISING	NONACCEPTANCE
NITRAMINES	NITROPARAFFINS	NOCTURNALITIES	NOMINALISM	NONACCEPTANCES
NITRANILINE	NITROPHILOUS	NOCTURNALITY	NOMINALISMS	NONACCIDENTAL
NITRANILINES	NITROSAMINE	NOCTURNALLY	NOMINALIST	NONACCOUNTABLE
NITRATINES	NITROSAMINES	NOCTURNALS	NOMINALISTIC	NONACCREDITED
NITRATIONS	NITROSATION	NOCUOUSNESS	NOMINALISTS	NONACCRUAL
NITRAZEPAM	NITROSATIONS	NOCUOUSNESSES	NOMINALIZATION	NONACHIEVEMENT
NITRAZEPAMS	NITROTOLUENE	NODALISING	NOMINALIZATIONS	NONACHIEVEMENTS
NITRIDINGS	NITROTOLUENES	NODALITIES	NOMINALIZE	NONACQUISITIVE
NITRIFIABLE	NITWITTEDNESS	NODALIZING	NOMINALIZED	NONACTIONS
NITRIFICATION	NITWITTEDNESSES	NODOSITIES	NOMINALIZES	NONACTIVATED
NITRIFICATIONS	NITWITTERIES	NODULATION	NOMINALIZING	NONADAPTIVE
NITRIFIERS	NITWITTERY	NODULATIONS	NOMINATELY	NONADDICTIVE
NITRIFYING	NOBBINESSES	NOEMATICAL	NOMINATING	NONADDICTS
NITROBACTERIA	NOBILESSES	NOEMATICALLY	NOMINATION	NONADDITIVE
NITROBACTERIUM	NOBILITATE	NOISELESSLY	NOMINATIONS	NONADDITIVITIES
NITROBENZENE	NOBILITATED	NOISELESSNESS	NOMINATIVAL	NONADDITIVITY
NITROBENZENES	NOBILITATES	NOISELESSNESSES	NOMINATIVALLY	NONADHESIVE
NITROCELLULOSE	NOBILITATING	NOISEMAKER	NOMINATIVE	NONADIABATIC
NITROCELLULOSES	NOBILITATION	NOISEMAKERS	NOMINATIVELY	NONADJACENT
NITROCHLOROFORM	NOBILITATIONS	NOISEMAKING	NOMINATIVES	NONADMIRER
NITROCOTTON	NOBILITIES	NOISEMAKINGS	NOMINATORS	NONADMIRERS
NITROCOTTONS	NOBLENESSES	NOISINESSES	NOMOCRACIES	NONADMISSION
NITROFURAN	NOBLEWOMAN	NOISOMENESS	NOMOGENIES	NONADMISSIONS
NITROFURANS	NOBLEWOMEN	NOISOMENESSES	NOMOGRAPHER	NONAESTHETIC
NITROGENASE	NOCHELLING	NOMADICALLY	NOMOGRAPHERS	NONAFFILIATED
NITROGENASES	NOCICEPTIVE	NOMADISATION	NOMOGRAPHIC	NONAFFLUENT
NITROGENISATION	NOCICEPTOR	NOMADISATIONS	NOMOGRAPHICAL	NONAGENARIAN
NITROGENISE	NOCICEPTORS	NOMADISING	NOMOGRAPHICALLY	NONAGENARIANS
NITROGENISED	NOCIRECEPTOR	NOMADIZATION	NOMOGRAPHIES	NONAGESIMAL
NITROGENISES	NOCIRECEPTORS	NOMADIZATIONS	NOMOGRAPHS	NONAGESIMALS
NITROGENISING	NOCTAMBULATION	NOMADIZING	NOMOGRAPHY	NONAGGRESSION
NITROGENIZATION	NOCTAMBULATIONS	NOMARCHIES	NOMOLOGICAL	NONAGGRESSIONS
NITROGENIZE	NOCTAMBULISM	NOMENCLATIVE	NOMOLOGICALLY	NONAGGRESSIVE
NITROGENIZED	NOCTAMBULISMS	NOMENCLATOR	NOMOLOGIES	NONAGRICULTURAL
NITROGENIZES	NOCTAMBULIST	NOMENCLATORIAL	NOMOLOGIST	NONALCOHOLIC
NITROGENIZING	NOCTAMBULISTS	NOMENCLATORS	NOMOLOGISTS	NONALIGNED
NITROGENOUS	NOCTILUCAE	NOMENCLATURAL	NOMOTHETES	NONALIGNMENT

NONALIGNMENTS	NONAUTOMATIC	NONCARCINOGEN	NONCOINCIDENCES	NONCONCURRENCE
NONALLELIC	NONAUTOMOTIVE	NONCARCINOGENIC	NONCOLLECTOR	NONCONCURRENCES
NONALLERGENIC	NONAUTONOMOUS	NONCARCINOGENS	NONCOLLECTORS	NONCONCURRENT
NONALLERGIC	NONAVAILABILITY	NONCARDIAC	NONCOLLEGE	NONCONCURRING
NONALPHABETIC	NONBACTERIAL	NONCARRIER	NONCOLLEGIATE	NONCONCURS
NONALUMINUM	NONBANKING	NONCARRIERS	NONCOLLINEAR	NONCONDENSABLE
NONAMBIGUOUS	NONBARBITURATE	NONCELEBRATION	NONCOLORED	NONCONDITIONED
NONANALYTIC	NONBARBITURATES	NONCELEBRATIONS	NONCOLORFAST	NONCONDUCTING
NONANATOMIC	NONBEARING	NONCELEBRITIES	NONCOMBATANT	NONCONDUCTION
NONANSWERS	NONBEHAVIORAL	NONCELEBRITY	NONCOMBATANTS	NONCONDUCTIVE
NONANTAGONISTIC	NONBELIEFS	NONCELLULAR	NONCOMBATIVE	NONCONDUCTOR
NONANTIBIOTIC	NONBELIEVER	NONCELLULOSIC	NONCOMBUSTIBLE	NONCONDUCTORS
NONANTIBIOTICS	NONBELIEVERS	NONCENTRAL	NONCOMMERCIAL	NONCONFERENCE
NONANTIGENIC	NONBELLIGERENCY	NONCERTIFICATED	NONCOMMISSIONED	NONCONFIDENCE
NONAPPEARANCE	NONBELLIGERENT	NONCERTIFIED	NONCOMMITMENT	NONCONFIDENCES
NONAPPEARANCES	NONBELLIGERENTS	NONCHALANCE	NONCOMMITMENTS	NONCONFIDENTIAL
NONAQUATIC	NONBETTING	NONCHALANCES	NONCOMMITTAL	NONCONFLICTING
NONAQUEOUS	NONBINDING	NONCHALANT	NONCOMMITTALLY	NONCONFORM
NONARBITRARY	NONBIOGRAPHICAL	NONCHALANTLY	NONCOMMITTED	NONCONFORMANCE
NONARCHITECT	NONBIOLOGICAL	NONCHARACTER	NONCOMMUNIST	NONCONFORMANCES
NONARCHITECTS	NONBIOLOGICALLY	NONCHARACTERS	NONCOMMUNISTS	NONCONFORMED
NONARCHITECTURE	NONBIOLOGIST	NONCHARISMATIC	NONCOMMUNITY	NONCONFORMER
NONARGUMENT	NONBIOLOGISTS	NONCHARISMATICS	NONCOMMUTATIVE	NONCONFORMERS
NONARGUMENTS	NONBONDING	NONCHAUVINIST	NONCOMPARABLE	NONCONFORMING
NONARISTOCRATIC	NONBOTANIST	NONCHEMICAL	NONCOMPATIBLE	NONCONFORMISM
NONAROMATIC	NONBOTANISTS	NONCHEMICALS	NONCOMPETITION	NONCONFORMISMS
NONAROMATICS	NONBREAKABLE	NONCHROMOSOMAL	NONCOMPETITIVE	NONCONFORMIST
NONARTISTIC	NONBREATHING	NONCHURCHGOER	NONCOMPETITOR	NONCONFORMISTS
NONARTISTS	NONBREEDER	NONCHURCHGOERS	NONCOMPETITORS	NONCONFORMITIES
NONASCETIC	NONBREEDERS	NONCIRCULAR	NONCOMPLEX	NONCONFORMITY
NONASPIRIN	NONBREEDING	NONCIRCULATING	NONCOMPLIANCE	NONCONFORMS
NONASSERTIVE	NONBROADCAST	NONCITIZEN	NONCOMPLIANCES	NONCONGRUENT
NONASSOCIATED	NONBUILDING	NONCITIZENS	NONCOMPLICATED	NONCONJUGATED
NONASTRONOMICAL	NONBURNABLE	NONCLANDESTINE	NONCOMPLYING	NONCONNECTION
NONATHLETE	NONBUSINESS	NONCLASSES	NONCOMPOSER	NONCONNECTIONS
NONATHLETES	NONCABINET	NONCLASSICAL	NONCOMPOSERS	NONCONSCIOUS
NONATHLETIC	NONCALLABLE	NONCLASSIFIED	NONCOMPOUND	NONCONSECUTIVE
NONATTACHED	NONCALORIC	NONCLASSROOM	NONCOMPRESSIBLE	NONCONSENSUAL
NONATTACHMENT	NONCANCELABLE	NONCLERICAL	NONCOMPUTER	NONCONSERVATION
NONATTACHMENTS	NONCANCEROUS	NONCLINICAL	NONCOMPUTERISED	NONCONSERVATIVE
NONATTENDANCE	NONCANDIDACIES	NONCLOGGING	NONCOMPUTERIZED	NONCONSOLIDATED
NONATTENDANCES	NONCANDIDACY	NONCOERCIVE	NONCONCEPTUAL	NONCONSTANT
NONATTENDER	NONCANDIDATE	NONCOGNITIVE	NONCONCERN	NONCONSTRUCTION
NONATTENDERS	NONCANDIDATES	NONCOGNITIVISM	NONCONCERNS	NONCONSTRUCTIVE
NONAUDITORY	NONCAPITAL	NONCOGNITIVISMS	NONCONCLUSION	NONCONSUMER
NONAUTHORS	NONCAPITALIST	NONCOHERENT	NONCONCLUSIONS	NONCONSUMERS
NONAUTOMATED	NONCAPITALISTS	NONCOINCIDENCE	NONCONCURRED	NONCONSUMING

N

NONCONSUMPTION NONCUMULATIVE NONDIABETIC NONELASTIC NONEXCLUSIVE
NONCONSUMPTIONS NONCURRENT NONDIABETICS NONELECTED NONEXECUTIVE
NONCONSUMPTIVE NONCUSTODIAL NONDIALYSABLE NONELECTION NONEXECUTIVES
NONCONTACT NONCUSTOMER NONDIALYZABLE NONELECTIONS NONEXEMPTS
NONCONTAGIOUS NONCUSTOMERS NONDIAPAUSING NONELECTIVE NONEXISTENCE
NONCONTEMPORARY NONCYCLICAL NONDIDACTIC NONELECTRIC NONEXISTENCES
NONCONTIGUOUS NONDANCERS NONDIFFUSIBLE NONELECTRICAL NONEXISTENT
NONCONTINGENT NONDECEPTIVE NONDIMENSIONAL NONELECTROLYTE NONEXISTENTIAL
NONCONTINUOUS NONDECISION NONDIPLOMATIC NONELECTROLYTES NONEXPENDABLE
NONCONTRACT NONDECISIONS NONDIRECTED NONELECTRONIC NONEXPERIMENTAL
NONCONTRACTUAL NONDECREASING NONDIRECTIONAL NONELEMENTARY NONEXPERTS
NONCONTRIBUTORY NONDEDUCTIBLE NONDIRECTIVE NONEMERGENCIES NONEXPLANATORY
NONCONTROLLABLE NONDEDUCTIVE NONDISABLED NONEMERGENCY NONEXPLOITATION
NONCONTROLLED NONDEFENSE NONDISCLOSURE NONEMOTIONAL NONEXPLOITATIVE
NONCONTROLLING NONDEFERRABLE NONDISCLOSURES NONEMPHATIC NONEXPLOITIVE
NONCONVENTIONAL NONDEFORMING NONDISCOUNT NONEMPIRICAL NONEXPLOSIVE
NONCONVERTIBLE NONDEGENERATE NONDISCURSIVE NONEMPLOYEE NONEXPOSED
NONCOOPERATION NONDEGRADABLE NONDISJUNCTION NONEMPLOYEES NONFACTORS
NONCOOPERATIONS NONDELEGATE NONDISJUNCTIONS NONEMPLOYMENT NONFACTUAL
NONCOOPERATIVE NONDELEGATES NONDISPERSIVE NONEMPLOYMENTS NONFACULTY
NONCOOPERATOR NONDELIBERATE NONDISRUPTIVE NONENCAPSULATED NONFAMILIAL
NONCOOPERATORS NONDELINQUENT NONDISTINCTIVE NONENFORCEMENT NONFAMILIES
NONCOPLANAR NONDELINQUENTS NONDIVERSIFIED NONENFORCEMENTS NONFARMERS
NONCORPORATE NONDELIVERIES NONDIVIDING NONENGAGEMENT NONFATTENING
NONCORRELATION NONDELIVERY NONDOCTORS NONENGAGEMENTS NONFEASANCE
NONCORRELATIONS NONDEMANDING NONDOCTRINAIRE NONENGINEERING NONFEASANCES
NONCORRODIBLE NONDEMANDS NONDOCUMENTARY NONENTITIES NONFEDERAL
NONCORRODING NONDEMOCRATIC NONDOGMATIC NONENTRIES NONFEDERATED
NONCORROSIVE NONDEPARTMENTAL NONDOMESTIC NONENZYMATIC NONFEMINIST
NONCOUNTRY NONDEPENDENT NONDOMICILED NONENZYMIC NONFEMINISTS
NONCOVERAGE NONDEPENDENTS NONDOMINANT NONEQUILIBRIA NONFERROUS
NONCOVERAGES NONDEPLETABLE NONDORMANT NONEQUILIBRIUM NONFICTION
NONCREATIVE NONDEPLETING NONDRAMATIC NONEQUILIBRIUMS NONFICTIONAL
NONCREATIVITIES NONDEPOSITION NONDRINKER NONEQUIVALENCE NONFICTIONALLY
NONCREATIVITY NONDEPOSITIONS NONDRINKERS NONEQUIVALENCES NONFICTIONS
NONCREDENTIALED NONDEPRESSED NONDRINKING NONEQUIVALENT NONFIGURATIVE
NONCRIMINAL NONDERIVATIVE NONDRIVERS NONESSENTIAL NONFILAMENTOUS
NONCRIMINALS NONDESCRIPT NONDURABLE NONESSENTIALS NONFILTERABLE
NONCRITICAL NONDESCRIPTIVE NONEARNING NONESTABLISHED NONFINANCIAL
NONCROSSOVER NONDESCRIPTLY NONECONOMIC NONESTERIFIED NONFISSIONABLE
NONCRUSHABLE NONDESCRIPTNESS NONECONOMIST NONESUCHES NONFLAMMABILITY
NONCRYSTALLINE NONDESCRIPTS NONECONOMISTS NONETHELESS NONFLAMMABLE
NONCULINARY NONDESTRUCTIVE NONEDIBLES NONETHICAL NONFLOWERING
NONCULTIVATED NONDETACHABLE NONEDITORIAL NONETHNICS NONFLUENCIES
NONCULTIVATION NONDEVELOPMENT NONEDUCATION NONEVALUATIVE NONFLUENCY
NONCULTIVATIONS NONDEVELOPMENTS NONEDUCATIONAL NONEVIDENCE NONFLUORESCENT
NONCULTURAL NONDEVIANT NONEFFECTIVE NONEVIDENCES NONFORFEITABLE

NONFORFEITURE	NONHYSTERICAL	NONINSURANCE	NONLIBRARY	NONMINORITY
NONFORFEITURES	NONIDENTICAL	NONINSURED	NONLINEARITIES	NONMODERNS
NONFREEZING	NONIDENTITIES	NONINTEGRAL	NONLINEARITY	NONMOLECULAR
NONFRIVOLOUS	NONIDENTITY	NONINTEGRATED	NONLINGUISTIC	NONMONETARIST
NONFULFILLMENT	NONIDEOLOGICAL	NONINTELLECTUAL	NONLIQUIDS	NONMONETARISTS
NONFULFILLMENTS	NONILLIONS	NONINTERACTING	NONLITERAL	NONMONETARY
NONFUNCTIONAL	NONILLIONTH	NONINTERACTIVE	NONLITERARY	NONMONOGAMOUS
NONFUNCTIONING	NONILLIONTHS	NONINTERCOURSE	NONLITERATE	NONMORTALS
NONGASEOUS	NONIMITATIVE	NONINTERCOURSES	NONLITERATES	NONMOTILITIES
NONGENETIC	NONIMMIGRANT	NONINTEREST	NONLIVINGS	NONMOTILITY
NONGENITAL	NONIMMIGRANTS	NONINTERFERENCE	NONLOGICAL	NONMOTORISED
NONGEOMETRICAL	NONIMPLICATION	NONINTERSECTING	NONLUMINOUS	NONMOTORIZED
NONGLAMOROUS	NONIMPLICATIONS	NONINTERVENTION	NONMAGNETIC	NONMUNICIPAL
NONGOLFERS	NONIMPORTATION	NONINTIMIDATING	NONMAINSTREAM	NONMUSICAL
NONGONOCOCCAL	NONIMPORTATIONS	NONINTOXICANT	NONMALIGNANT	NONMUSICALS
NONGOVERNMENT	NONINCLUSION	NONINTOXICANTS	NONMALLEABLE	NONMUSICIAN
NONGOVERNMENTAL	NONINCLUSIONS	NONINTOXICATING	NONMANAGEMENT	NONMUSICIANS
NONGRADUATE	NONINCREASING	NONINTRUSIVE	NONMANAGERIAL	NONMUTANTS
NONGRADUATES	NONINCUMBENT	NONINTUITIVE	NONMARITAL	NONMYELINATED
NONGRAMMATICAL	NONINCUMBENTS	NONINVASIVE	NONMARKETS	NONMYSTICAL
NONGRANULAR	NONINDEPENDENCE	NONINVOLVED	NONMATERIAL	NONNARRATIVE
NONGREGARIOUS	NONINDIGENOUS	NONINVOLVEMENT	NONMATHEMATICAL	NONNATIONAL
NONGROWING	NONINDIVIDUAL	NONINVOLVEMENTS	NONMATRICULATED	NONNATIONALS
NONHALOGENATED	NONINDUCTIVE	NONIONIZING	NONMEANINGFUL	NONNATIVES
NONHANDICAPPED	NONINDUSTRIAL	NONIRRADIATED	NONMEASURABLE	NONNATURAL
NONHAPPENING	NONINDUSTRY	NONIRRIGATED	NONMECHANICAL	NONNECESSITIES
NONHAPPENINGS	NONINFECTED	NONIRRITANT	NONMECHANISTIC	NONNECESSITY
NONHARMONIC	NONINFECTIOUS	NONIRRITANTS	NONMEDICAL	NONNEGATIVE
NONHAZARDOUS	NONINFECTIVE	NONIRRITATING	NONMEETING	NONNEGLIGENT
NONHEMOLYTIC	NONINFESTED	NONJOINDER	NONMEETINGS	NONNEGOTIABLE
NONHEREDITARY	NONINFLAMMABLE	NONJOINDERS	NONMEMBERS	NONNEGOTIABLES
NONHIERARCHICAL	NONINFLAMMATORY	NONJOINERS	NONMEMBERSHIP	NONNETWORK
NONHISTONE	NONINFLATIONARY	NONJUDGEMENTAL	NONMEMBERSHIPS	NONNITROGENOUS
NONHISTORICAL	NONINFLECTIONAL	NONJUDGMENTAL	NONMERCURIAL	NONNORMATIVE
NONHOMOGENEOUS	NONINFLUENCE	NONJUDICIAL	NONMETALLIC	NONNUCLEAR
NONHOMOLOGOUS	NONINFLUENCES	NONJUSTICIABLE	NONMETAMERIC	NONNUCLEATED
NONHOMOSEXUAL	NONINFORMATION	NONKOSHERS	NONMETAPHORICAL	NONNUMERICAL
NONHOMOSEXUALS	NONINFORMATIONS	NONLANDOWNER	NONMETRICAL	NONNUTRITIOUS
NONHORMONAL	NONINFRINGEMENT	NONLANDOWNERS	NONMETROPOLITAN	NONNUTRITIVE
NONHOSPITAL	NONINITIAL	NONLANGUAGE	NONMICROBIAL	NONOBJECTIVE
NONHOSPITALISED	NONINITIATE	NONLANGUAGES	NONMIGRANT	NONOBJECTIVISM
NONHOSPITALIZED	NONINITIATES	NONLAWYERS	NONMIGRATORY	NONOBJECTIVISMS
NONHOSTILE	NONINSECTICIDAL	NONLEGUMES	NONMILITANT	NONOBJECTIVIST
NONHOUSING	NONINSECTS	NONLEGUMINOUS	NONMILITANTS	NONOBJECTIVISTS
NONHUNTERS	NONINSTALLMENT	NONLEXICAL	NONMILITARY	NONOBJECTIVITY
NONHUNTING	NONINSTALLMENTS	NONLIBRARIAN	NONMIMETIC	NONOBSCENE
NONHYGROSCOPIC	NONINSTRUMENTAL	NONLIBRARIANS	NONMINORITIES	NONOBSERVANCE

N

NONOBSERVANCES

NONOBSERVANCES
NONOBSERVANT
NONOBVIOUS
NONOCCUPATIONAL
NONOCCURRENCE
NONOCCURRENCES
NONOFFICIAL
NONOFFICIALS
NONOPERATIC
NONOPERATING
NONOPERATIONAL
NONOPERATIVE
NONOPTIMAL
NONORGANIC
NONORGASMIC
NONORTHODOX
NONOVERLAPPING
NONOXIDISING
NONOXIDIZING
NONPAPISTS
NONPARALLEL
NONPARAMETRIC
NONPARASITIC
NONPAREILS
NONPARENTS
NONPARITIES
NONPARTICIPANT
NONPARTICIPANTS
NONPARTIES
NONPARTISAN
NONPARTISANSHIP
NONPARTIZAN
NONPARTIZANSHIP
NONPASSERINE
NONPASSIVE
NONPATHOGENIC
NONPAYMENT
NONPAYMENTS
NONPERFORMANCE
NONPERFORMANCES
NONPERFORMER
NONPERFORMERS
NONPERFORMING
NONPERISHABLE
NONPERISHABLES
NONPERMANENT
NONPERMISSIVE

NONPERSISTENT
NONPERSONAL
NONPERSONS
NONPETROLEUM
NONPHILOSOPHER
NONPHILOSOPHERS
NONPHONEMIC
NONPHONETIC
NONPHOSPHATE
NONPHOTOGRAPHIC
NONPHYSICAL
NONPHYSICIAN
NONPHYSICIANS
NONPLASTIC
NONPLASTICS
NONPLAYERS
NONPLAYING
NONPLUSING
NONPLUSSED
NONPLUSSES
NONPLUSSING
NONPOISONOUS
NONPOLARISABLE
NONPOLARIZABLE
NONPOLITICAL
NONPOLITICALLY
NONPOLITICIAN
NONPOLITICIANS
NONPOLLUTING
NONPOSSESSION
NONPOSSESSIONS
NONPRACTICAL
NONPRACTICING
NONPRACTISING
NONPREGNANT
NONPRESCRIPTION
NONPROBLEM
NONPROBLEMS
NONPRODUCING
NONPRODUCTIVE
NONPRODUCTIVITY
NONPROFESSIONAL
NONPROFESSORIAL
NONPROFITS
NONPROGRAM
NONPROGRAMMER
NONPROGRAMMERS

NONPROGRESSIVE
NONPROPRIETARY
NONPROSSED
NONPROSSES
NONPROSSING
NONPROTEIN
NONPSYCHIATRIC
NONPSYCHIATRIST
NONPSYCHOTIC
NONPUNITIVE
NONPURPOSIVE
NONQUANTIFIABLE
NONQUANTITATIVE
NONRACIALLY
NONRADIOACTIVE
NONRAILROAD
NONRANDOMNESS
NONRANDOMNESSES
NONRATIONAL
NONREACTIVE
NONREACTOR
NONREACTORS
NONREADERS
NONREADING
NONREALISTIC
NONRECEIPT
NONRECEIPTS
NONRECIPROCAL
NONRECOGNITION
NONRECOGNITIONS
NONRECOMBINANT
NONRECOMBINANTS
NONRECOURSE
NONRECURRENT
NONRECURRING
NONRECYCLABLE
NONRECYCLABLES
NONREDUCING
NONREDUNDANT
NONREFILLABLE
NONREFLECTING
NONREFLEXIVE
NONREFUNDABLE
NONREGULATED
NONREGULATION
NONRELATIVE
NONRELATIVES

NONRELATIVISTIC
NONRELEVANT
NONRELIGIOUS
NONRENEWABLE
NONRENEWAL
NONREPAYABLE
NONREPRODUCTIVE
NONRESIDENCE
NONRESIDENCES
NONRESIDENCIES
NONRESIDENCY
NONRESIDENT
NONRESIDENTIAL
NONRESIDENTS
NONRESISTANCE
NONRESISTANCES
NONRESISTANT
NONRESISTANTS
NONRESONANT
NONRESPONDENT
NONRESPONDENTS
NONRESPONDER
NONRESPONDERS
NONRESPONSE
NONRESPONSES
NONRESPONSIVE
NONRESTRICTED
NONRESTRICTIVE
NONRETRACTILE
NONRETROACTIVE
NONRETURNABLE
NONRETURNABLES
NONREUSABLE
NONREVERSIBLE
NONRHOTICITIES
NONRHOTICITY
NONRIOTERS
NONRIOTING
NONROTATING
NONROUTINE
NONRUMINANT
NONRUMINANTS
NONSALABLE
NONSAPONIFIABLE
NONSCHEDULED
NONSCIENCE
NONSCIENCES

NONSCIENTIFIC
NONSCIENTIST
NONSCIENTISTS
NONSEASONAL
NONSECRETOR
NONSECRETORS
NONSECRETORY
NONSECRETS
NONSECTARIAN
NONSEDIMENTABLE
NONSEGREGATED
NONSEGREGATION
NONSEGREGATIONS
NONSELECTED
NONSELECTIVE
NONSENSATIONAL
NONSENSICAL
NONSENSICALITY
NONSENSICALLY
NONSENSICALNESS
NONSENSITIVE
NONSENSUOUS
NONSENTENCE
NONSENTENCES
NONSEPTATE
NONSEQUENTIAL
NONSERIALS
NONSERIOUS
NONSHRINKABLE
NONSIGNERS
NONSIGNIFICANT
NONSIMULTANEOUS
NONSINKABLE
NONSKATERS
NONSKELETAL
NONSMOKERS
NONSMOKING
NONSOCIALIST
NONSOCIALISTS
NONSOLUTION
NONSOLUTIONS
NONSPATIAL
NONSPEAKER
NONSPEAKERS
NONSPEAKING
NONSPECIALIST
NONSPECIALISTS

N

NONSPECIFIC	NONTALKERS	NONVALIDITIES	NORMALISATION	NORTHERNISED
NONSPECIFICALLY	NONTAXABLE	NONVALIDITY	NORMALISATIONS	NORTHERNISES
NONSPECTACULAR	NONTEACHING	NONVANISHING	NORMALISED	NORTHERNISING
NONSPECULAR	NONTECHNICAL	NONVASCULAR	NORMALISER	NORTHERNISM
NONSPECULATIVE	NONTEMPORAL	NONVECTORS	NORMALISERS	NORTHERNISMS
NONSPHERICAL	NONTENURED	NONVEGETARIAN	NORMALISES	NORTHERNIZE
NONSPORTING	NONTERMINAL	NONVEGETARIANS	NORMALISING	NORTHERNIZED
NONSTANDARD	NONTERMINALS	NONVENOMOUS	NORMALITIES	NORTHERNIZES
NONSTAPLES	NONTERMINATING	NONVERBALLY	NORMALIZABLE	NORTHERNIZING
NONSTARTER	NONTHEATRICAL	NONVETERAN	NORMALIZATION	NORTHERNMOST
NONSTARTERS	NONTHEISTIC	NONVETERANS	NORMALIZATIONS	NORTHLANDS
NONSTATIONARY	NONTHEISTS	NONVIEWERS	NORMALIZED	NORTHWARDLY
NONSTATISTICAL	NONTHEOLOGICAL	NONVINTAGE	NORMALIZER	NORTHWARDS
NONSTATIVE	NONTHEORETICAL	NONVIOLENCE	NORMALIZERS	NORTHWESTER
NONSTATIVES	NONTHERAPEUTIC	NONVIOLENCES	NORMALIZES	NORTHWESTERLIES
NONSTEROID	NONTHERMAL	NONVIOLENT	NORMALIZING	NORTHWESTERLY
NONSTEROIDAL	NONTHINKING	NONVIOLENTLY	NORMATIVELY	NORTHWESTERN
NONSTEROIDS	NONTHREATENING	NONVIRGINS	NORMATIVENESS	NORTHWESTERS
NONSTORIES	NONTOBACCO	NONVISCOUS	NORMATIVENESSES	NORTHWESTS
NONSTRATEGIC	NONTOTALITARIAN	NONVOCATIONAL	NORMOTENSIVE	NORTHWESTWARD
NONSTRIATED	NONTRADITIONAL	NONVOLATILE	NORMOTENSIVES	NORTHWESTWARDLY
NONSTRUCTURAL	NONTRANSFERABLE	NONVOLCANIC	NORMOTHERMIA	NORTHWESTWARDS
NONSTRUCTURED	NONTRANSITIVE	NONVOLUNTARY	NORMOTHERMIAS	NORTRIPTYLINE
NONSTUDENT	NONTREATMENT	NONWINNING	NORMOTHERMIC	NORTRIPTYLINES
NONSTUDENTS	NONTREATMENTS	NONWORKERS	NOROVIRUSES	NOSEBANDED
NONSUBJECT	NONTRIVIAL	NONWORKING	NORSELLERS	NOSEBLEEDING
NONSUBJECTIVE	NONTROPICAL	NONWRITERS	NORSELLING	NOSEBLEEDINGS
NONSUBJECTS	NONTURBULENT	NONYELLOWING	NORTHBOUND	NOSEBLEEDS
NONSUBSIDISED	NONTYPICAL	NOODLEDOMS	NORTHCOUNTRYMAN	NOSEDIVING
NONSUBSIDIZED	NONUNANIMOUS	NOOGENESES	NORTHCOUNTRYMEN	NOSEGUARDS
NONSUCCESS	NONUNIFORM	NOOGENESIS	NORTHEASTER	NOSEPIECES
NONSUCCESSES	NONUNIFORMITIES	NOOMETRIES	NORTHEASTERLIES	NOSEWHEELS
NONSUITING	NONUNIFORMITY	NOOSPHERES	NORTHEASTERLY	NOSINESSES
NONSUPERVISORY	NONUNIONISED	NOOTROPICS	NORTHEASTERN	NOSOCOMIAL
NONSUPPORT	NONUNIONISM	NORADRENALIN	NORTHEASTERS	NOSOGRAPHER
NONSUPPORTS	NONUNIONISMS	NORADRENALINE	NORTHEASTS	NOSOGRAPHERS
NONSURGICAL	NONUNIONIST	NORADRENALINES	NORTHEASTWARD	NOSOGRAPHIC
NONSWIMMER	NONUNIONISTS	NORADRENALINS	NORTHEASTWARDLY	NOSOGRAPHIES
NONSWIMMERS	NONUNIONIZED	NORADRENERGIC	NORTHEASTWARDS	NOSOGRAPHY
NONSYLLABIC	NONUNIQUENESS	NOREPINEPHRINE	NORTHERING	NOSOLOGICAL
NONSYMBOLIC	NONUNIQUENESSES	NOREPINEPHRINES	NORTHERLIES	NOSOLOGICALLY
NONSYMMETRIC	NONUNIVERSAL	NORETHINDRONE	NORTHERLINESS	NOSOLOGIES
NONSYMMETRICAL	NONUNIVERSITY	NORETHINDRONES	NORTHERLINESSES	NOSOLOGIST
NONSYNCHRONOUS	NONUTILITARIAN	NORETHISTERONE	NORTHERMOST	NOSOLOGISTS
NONSYSTEMATIC	NONUTILITIES	NORETHISTERONES	NORTHERNER	NOSOPHOBIA
NONSYSTEMIC	NONUTILITY	NORMALCIES	NORTHERNERS	NOSOPHOBIAS
NONSYSTEMS	NONUTOPIAN	NORMALISABLE	NORTHERNISE	NOSTALGIAS

N

NOSTALGICALLY	NOTHINGNESSES	NOURRITURES	NUCLEARISES	NUGATORINESS
NOSTALGICS	NOTICEABILITIES	NOUSELLING	NUCLEARISING	NUGATORINESSES
NOSTALGIST	NOTICEABILITY	NOVACULITE	NUCLEARIZATION	NUGGETTING
NOSTALGISTS	NOTICEABLE	NOVACULITES	NUCLEARIZATIONS	NUISANCERS
NOSTOLOGIC	NOTICEABLY	NOVELETTES	NUCLEARIZE	NULLIFICATION
NOSTOLOGICAL	NOTIFIABLE	NOVELETTISH	NUCLEARIZED	NULLIFICATIONS
NOSTOLOGIES	NOTIFICATION	NOVELETTIST	NUCLEARIZES	NULLIFIDIAN
NOSTOMANIA	NOTIFICATIONS	NOVELETTISTS	NUCLEARIZING	NULLIFIDIANS
NOSTOMANIAS	NOTIONALIST	NOVELISATION	NUCLEATING	NULLIFIERS
NOSTOPATHIES	NOTIONALISTS	NOVELISATIONS	NUCLEATION	NULLIFYING
NOSTOPATHY	NOTIONALITIES	NOVELISERS	NUCLEATIONS	NULLIPARAE
NOSTRADAMIC	NOTIONALITY	NOVELISING	NUCLEATORS	NULLIPARAS
NOTABILITIES	NOTIONALLY	NOVELISTIC	NUCLEOCAPSID	NULLIPARITIES
NOTABILITY	NOTIONISTS	NOVELISTICALLY	NUCLEOCAPSIDS	NULLIPARITY
NOTABLENESS	NOTOCHORDAL	NOVELIZATION	NUCLEOLATE	NULLIPAROUS
NOTABLENESSES	NOTOCHORDS	NOVELIZATIONS	NUCLEOLATED	NULLIPORES
NOTAPHILIC	NOTODONTID	NOVELIZERS	NUCLEONICALLY	NULLNESSES
NOTAPHILIES	NOTODONTIDS	NOVELIZING	NUCLEONICS	NUMBERABLE
NOTAPHILISM	NOTONECTAL	NOVEMDECILLION	NUCLEOPHILE	NUMBERINGS
NOTAPHILISMS	NOTORIETIES	NOVEMDECILLIONS	NUCLEOPHILES	NUMBERLESS
NOTAPHILIST	NOTORIOUSLY	NOVENARIES	NUCLEOPHILIC	NUMBERLESSLY
NOTAPHILISTS	NOTORIOUSNESS	NOVENARIES	NUCLEOPHILICITY	NUMBERLESSNESS
NOTARIALLY	NOTORIOUSNESSES	NOVICEHOOD	NUCLEOPLASM	NUMBERPLATE
NOTARISATION	NOTORNISES	NOVICEHOODS	NUCLEOPLASMATIC	NUMBERPLATES
NOTARISATIONS	NOTOTHERIUM	NOVICESHIP	NUCLEOPLASMIC	NUMBFISHES
NOTARISING	NOTOTHERIUMS	NOVICESHIPS	NUCLEOPLASMS	NUMBNESSES
NOTARIZATION	NOTOUNGULATE	NOVICIATES	NUCLEOPROTEIN	NUMBSKULLS
NOTARIZATIONS	NOTOUNGULATES	NOVITIATES	NUCLEOPROTEINS	NUMERABILITIES
NOTARIZING	NOTUNGULATE	NOVOBIOCIN	NUCLEOSIDE	NUMERABILITY
NOTARYSHIP	NOTUNGULATES	NOVOBIOCINS	NUCLEOSIDES	NUMERACIES
NOTARYSHIPS	NOTWITHSTANDING	NOVOCAINES	NUCLEOSOMAL	NUMERAIRES
NOTATIONAL	NOUGATINES	NOVOCENTENARIES	NUCLEOSOME	NUMERATING
NOTCHBACKS	NOUMENALISM	NOVOCENTENARY	NUCLEOSOMES	NUMERATION
NOTCHELING	NOUMENALISMS	NOVODAMUSES	NUCLEOSYNTHESES	NUMERATIONS
NOTCHELLED	NOUMENALIST	NOWCASTING	NUCLEOSYNTHESIS	NUMERATIVE
NOTCHELLING	NOUMENALISTS	NOWCASTINGS	NUCLEOSYNTHETIC	NUMERATORS
NOTEDNESSES	NOUMENALITIES	NOXIOUSNESS	NUCLEOTIDASE	NUMERICALLY
NOTEPAPERS	NOUMENALITY	NOXIOUSNESSES	NUCLEOTIDASES	NUMEROLOGICAL
NOTEWORTHILY	NOUMENALLY	NUBBINESSES	NUCLEOTIDE	NUMEROLOGIES
NOTEWORTHINESS	NOURISHABLE	NUBIFEROUS	NUCLEOTIDES	NUMEROLOGIST
NOTEWORTHY	NOURISHERS	NUBIGENOUS	NUDENESSES	NUMEROLOGISTS
NOTHINGARIAN	NOURISHING	NUBILITIES	NUDIBRANCH	NUMEROLOGY
NOTHINGARIANISM	NOURISHINGLY	NUCIFEROUS	NUDIBRANCHIATE	NUMEROSITIES
NOTHINGARIANS	NOURISHMENT	NUCIVOROUS	NUDIBRANCHIATES	NUMEROSITY
NOTHINGISM	NOURISHMENTS	NUCLEARISATION	NUDIBRANCHS	NUMEROUSLY
NOTHINGISMS	NOURITURES	NUCLEARISATIONS	NUDICAUDATE	NUMEROUSNESS
NOTHINGNESS	NOURRITURE	NUCLEARISE	NUDICAULOUS	NUMEROUSNESSES
		NUCLEARISED		

N

NUMINOUSES
NUMINOUSNESS
NUMINOUSNESSES
NUMISMATIC
NUMISMATICALLY
NUMISMATICS
NUMISMATIST
NUMISMATISTS
NUMISMATOLOGIES
NUMISMATOLOGIST
NUMISMATOLOGY
NUMMULATED
NUMMULATION
NUMMULATIONS
NUMMULITES
NUMMULITIC
NUMSKULLED
NUNCIATURE
NUNCIATURES
NUNCUPATED
NUNCUPATES

NUNCUPATING
NUNCUPATION
NUNCUPATIONS
NUNCUPATIVE
NUNCUPATORY
NUNNATIONS
NUNNISHNESS
NUNNISHNESSES
NUPTIALITIES
NUPTIALITY
NURSEHOUND
NURSEHOUNDS
NURSELINGS
NURSEMAIDED
NURSEMAIDING
NURSEMAIDS
NURSERYMAID
NURSERYMAIDS
NURSERYMAN
NURSERYMEN
NURTURABLE

NURTURANCE
NURTURANCES
NUTATIONAL
NUTBUTTERS
NUTCRACKER
NUTCRACKERS
NUTGRASSES
NUTHATCHES
NUTJOBBERS
NUTMEGGING
NUTPECKERS
NUTRACEUTICAL
NUTRACEUTICALS
NUTRIGENETICS
NUTRIMENTAL
NUTRIMENTS
NUTRITIONAL
NUTRITIONALLY
NUTRITIONARY
NUTRITIONIST
NUTRITIONISTS

NUTRITIONS
NUTRITIOUS
NUTRITIOUSLY
NUTRITIOUSNESS
NUTRITIVELY
NUTRITIVES
NUTTINESSES
NYCHTHEMERAL
NYCHTHEMERON
NYCHTHEMERONS
NYCTAGINACEOUS
NYCTALOPES
NYCTALOPIA
NYCTALOPIAS
NYCTALOPIC
NYCTANTHOUS
NYCTINASTIC
NYCTINASTIES
NYCTINASTY
NYCTITROPIC
NYCTITROPISM

NYCTITROPISMS
NYCTOPHOBIA
NYCTOPHOBIAS
NYCTOPHOBIC
NYMPHAEACEOUS
NYMPHAEUMS
NYMPHALIDS
NYMPHETTES
NYMPHOLEPSIES
NYMPHOLEPSY
NYMPHOLEPT
NYMPHOLEPTIC
NYMPHOLEPTS
NYMPHOMANIA
NYMPHOMANIAC
NYMPHOMANIACAL
NYMPHOMANIACS
NYMPHOMANIAS
NYSTAGMOID
NYSTAGMUSES

N

O

OAFISHNESS	OBJECTIVATES	OBLIGATIVE	OBSCENENESSES	OBSESSIONAL
OAFISHNESSES	OBJECTIVATING	OBLIGATORILY	OBSCENITIES	OBSESSIONALLY
OAKENSHAWS	OBJECTIVATION	OBLIGATORINESS	OBSCURANTIC	OBSESSIONIST
OARSMANSHIP	OBJECTIVATIONS	OBLIGATORS	OBSCURANTISM	OBSESSIONISTS
OARSMANSHIPS	OBJECTIVELY	OBLIGATORY	OBSCURANTISMS	OBSESSIONS
OASTHOUSES	OBJECTIVENESS	OBLIGEMENT	OBSCURANTIST	OBSESSIVELY
OBBLIGATOS	OBJECTIVENESSES	OBLIGEMENTS	OBSCURANTISTS	OBSESSIVENESS
OBCOMPRESSED	OBJECTIVES	OBLIGINGLY	OBSCURANTS	OBSESSIVENESSES
OBDURACIES	OBJECTIVISE	OBLIGINGNESS	OBSCURATION	OBSESSIVES
OBDURATELY	OBJECTIVISED	OBLIGINGNESSES	OBSCURATIONS	OBSIDIONAL
OBDURATENESS	OBJECTIVISES	OBLIQUATION	OBSCUREMENT	OBSIDIONARY
OBDURATENESSES-	OBJECTIVISING	OBLIQUATIONS	OBSCUREMENTS	OBSIGNATED
OBDURATING	OBJECTIVISM	OBLIQUENESS	OBSCURENESS	OBSIGNATES
OBDURATION	OBJECTIVISMS	OBLIQUENESSES	OBSCURENESSES	OBSIGNATING
OBDURATIONS	OBJECTIVIST	OBLIQUITIES	OBSCURITIES	OBSIGNATION
OBEDIENCES	OBJECTIVISTIC	OBLIQUITOUS	OBSECRATED	OBSIGNATIONS
OBEDIENTIAL	OBJECTIVISTS	OBLITERATE	OBSECRATES	OBSIGNATORY
OBEDIENTIARIES	OBJECTIVITIES	OBLITERATED	OBSECRATING	OBSOLESCED
OBEDIENTIARY	OBJECTIVITY	OBLITERATES	OBSECRATION	OBSOLESCENCE
OBEDIENTLY	OBJECTIVIZE	OBLITERATING	OBSECRATIONS	OBSOLESCENCES
OBEISANCES	OBJECTIVIZED	OBLITERATION	OBSEQUIOUS	OBSOLESCENT
OBEISANTLY	OBJECTIVIZES	OBLITERATIONS	OBSEQUIOUSLY	OBSOLESCENTLY
OBELISCOID	OBJECTIVIZING	OBLITERATIVE	OBSEQUIOUSNESS	OBSOLESCES
OBELISKOID	OBJECTLESS	OBLITERATOR	OBSERVABILITIES	OBSOLESCING
OBESENESSES	OBJECTLESSNESS	OBLITERATORS	OBSERVABILITY	OBSOLETELY
OBESOGENIC	OBJURATION	OBLIVIOUSLY	OBSERVABLE	OBSOLETENESS
OBFUSCATED	OBJURATIONS	OBLIVIOUSNESS	OBSERVABLENESS	OBSOLETENESSES
OBFUSCATES	OBJURGATED	OBLIVIOUSNESSES	OBSERVABLES	OBSOLETING
OBFUSCATING	OBJURGATES	OBLIVISCENCE	OBSERVABLY	OBSOLETION
OBFUSCATION	OBJURGATING	OBLIVISCENCES	OBSERVANCE	OBSOLETIONS
OBFUSCATIONS	OBJURGATION	OBMUTESCENCE	OBSERVANCES	OBSOLETISM
OBFUSCATORY	OBJURGATIONS	OBMUTESCENCES	OBSERVANCIES	OBSOLETISMS
OBITUARIES	OBJURGATIVE	OBMUTESCENT	OBSERVANCY	OBSTETRICAL
OBITUARIST	OBJURGATOR	OBNOXIOUSLY	OBSERVANTLY	OBSTETRICALLY
OBITUARISTS	OBJURGATORS	OBNOXIOUSNESS	OBSERVANTS	OBSTETRICIAN
OBJECTIFICATION	OBJURGATORY	OBNOXIOUSNESSES	OBSERVATION	OBSTETRICIANS
OBJECTIFIED	OBLANCEOLATE	OBNUBILATE	OBSERVATIONAL	OBSTETRICS
OBJECTIFIES	OBLATENESS	OBNUBILATED	OBSERVATIONALLY	OBSTINACIES
OBJECTIFYING	OBLATENESSES	OBNUBILATES	OBSERVATIONS	OBSTINATELY
OBJECTIONABLE	OBLATIONAL	OBNUBILATING	OBSERVATIVE	OBSTINATENESS
OBJECTIONABLY	OBLIGATELY	OBNUBILATION	OBSERVATOR	OBSTINATENESSES
OBJECTIONS	OBLIGATING	OBNUBILATIONS	OBSERVATORIES	OBSTIPATION
OBJECTIVAL	OBLIGATION	OBREPTIONS	OBSERVATORS	OBSTIPATIONS
OBJECTIVATE	OBLIGATIONAL	OBREPTITIOUS	OBSERVATORY	OBSTREPERATE
OBJECTIVATED	OBLIGATIONS	OBSCENENESS	OBSERVINGLY	OBSTREPERATED

OBSTREPERATES	OBTRUSIVELY	OCCIDENTALIZED	OCHLOCRACIES	OCTINGENARY
OBSTREPERATING	OBTRUSIVENESS	OCCIDENTALIZES	OCHLOCRACY	OCTINGENTENARY
OBSTREPEROUS	OBTRUSIVENESSES	OCCIDENTALIZING	OCHLOCRATIC	OCTOCENTENARIES
OBSTREPEROUSLY	OBTUNDENTS	OCCIDENTALLY	OCHLOCRATICAL	OCTOCENTENARY
OBSTRICTION	OBTUNDITIES	OCCIDENTALS	OCHLOCRATICALLY	OCTODECILLION
OBSTRICTIONS	OBTURATING	OCCIPITALLY	OCHLOCRATS	OCTODECILLIONS
OBSTROPALOUS	OBTURATION	OCCIPITALS	OCHLOPHOBIA	OCTODECIMO
OBSTROPULOUS	OBTURATIONS	OCCLUDENTS	OCHLOPHOBIAC	OCTODECIMOS
OBSTRUCTED	OBTURATORS	OCCLUSIONS	OCHLOPHOBIACS	OCTOGENARIAN
OBSTRUCTER	OBTUSENESS	OCCLUSIVENESS	OCHLOPHOBIAS	OCTOGENARIANS
OBSTRUCTERS	OBTUSENESSES	OCCLUSIVENESSES	OCHLOPHOBIC	OCTOGENARIES
OBSTRUCTING	OBTUSITIES	OCCLUSIVES	OCHRACEOUS	OCTOGENARY
OBSTRUCTION	OBUMBRATED	OCCULTATION	OCHROLEUCOUS	OCTOGYNOUS
OBSTRUCTIONAL	OBUMBRATES	OCCULTATIONS	OCTACHORDAL	OCTOHEDRON
OBSTRUCTIONALLY	OBUMBRATING	OCCULTISMS	OCTACHORDS	OCTOHEDRONS
OBSTRUCTIONISM	OBUMBRATION	OCCULTISTS	OCTAGONALLY	OCTONARIAN
OBSTRUCTIONISMS	OBUMBRATIONS	OCCULTNESS	OCTAHEDRAL	OCTONARIANS
OBSTRUCTIONIST	OBVENTIONS	OCCULTNESSES	OCTAHEDRALLY	OCTONARIES
OBSTRUCTIONISTS	OBVERSIONS	OCCUPANCES	OCTAHEDRITE	OCTONARIUS
OBSTRUCTIONS	OBVIATIONS	OCCUPANCIES	OCTAHEDRITES	OCTONOCULAR
OBSTRUCTIVE	OBVIOUSNESS	OCCUPATING	OCTAHEDRON	OCTOPETALOUS
OBSTRUCTIVELY	OBVIOUSNESSES	OCCUPATION	OCTAHEDRONS	OCTOPLOIDS
OBSTRUCTIVENESS	OBVOLUTION	OCCUPATIONAL	OCTAMEROUS	OCTOPODANS
OBSTRUCTIVES	OBVOLUTIONS	OCCUPATIONALLY	OCTAMETERS	OCTOPODOUS
OBSTRUCTOR	OBVOLUTIVE	OCCUPATIONS	OCTANDRIAN	OCTOPUSHER
OBSTRUCTORS	OCCASIONAL	OCCUPATIVE	OCTANDROUS	OCTOPUSHERS
OBSTRUENTS	OCCASIONALISM	OCCURRENCE	OCTANEDIOIC	OCTOPUSHES
OBTAINABILITIES	OCCASIONALISMS	OCCURRENCES	OCTANGULAR	OCTOSEPALOUS
OBTAINABILITY	OCCASIONALIST	OCCURRENTS	OCTAPEPTIDE	OCTOSTICHOUS
OBTAINABLE	OCCASIONALISTS	OCEANARIUM	OCTAPEPTIDES	OCTOSTYLES
OBTAINMENT	OCCASIONALITIES	OCEANARIUMS	OCTAPLOIDIES	OCTOSYLLABIC
OBTAINMENTS	OCCASIONALITY	OCEANFRONT	OCTAPLOIDS	OCTOSYLLABICS
OBTEMPERATE	OCCASIONALLY	OCEANFRONTS	OCTAPLOIDY	OCTOSYLLABLE
OBTEMPERATED	OCCASIONED	OCEANGOING	OCTAPODIES	OCTOSYLLABLES
OBTEMPERATES	OCCASIONER	OCEANOGRAPHER	OCTARCHIES	OCTOTHORPS
OBTEMPERATING	OCCASIONERS	OCEANOGRAPHERS	OCTASTICHON	OCTUPLICATE
OBTEMPERED	OCCASIONING	OCEANOGRAPHIC	OCTASTICHONS	OCTUPLICATES
OBTEMPERING	OCCIDENTAL	OCEANOGRAPHICAL	OCTASTICHOUS	OCULARISTS
OBTENTIONS	OCCIDENTALISE	OCEANOGRAPHIES	OCTASTICHS	OCULOMOTOR
OBTESTATION	OCCIDENTALISED	OCEANOGRAPHY	OCTASTROPHIC	ODALISQUES
OBTESTATIONS	OCCIDENTALISES	OCEANOLOGICAL	OCTASTYLES	ODDSMAKERS
OBTRUDINGS	OCCIDENTALISING	OCEANOLOGIES	OCTAVALENT	ODIOUSNESS
OBTRUNCATE	OCCIDENTALISM	OCEANOLOGIST	OCTENNIALLY	ODIOUSNESSES
OBTRUNCATED	OCCIDENTALISMS	OCEANOLOGISTS	OCTILLIONS	ODOMETRIES
OBTRUNCATES	OCCIDENTALIST	OCEANOLOGY	OCTILLIONTH	ODONATISTS
OBTRUNCATING	OCCIDENTALISTS	OCELLATION	OCTILLIONTHS	ODONATOLOGIES
OBTRUSIONS	OCCIDENTALIZE	OCELLATIONS	OCTINGENARIES	ODONATOLOGIST

O

ODONATOLOGISTS

ODONATOLOGISTS	ODOROUSNESS	OFFHANDEDLY	OFTENNESSES	OLIGOCLASES
ODONATOLOGY	ODOROUSNESSES	OFFHANDEDNESS	OFTENTIMES	OLIGOCYTHAEMIA
ODONTALGIA	OECOLOGICAL	OFFHANDEDNESSES	OILINESSES	OLIGOCYTHAEMIAS
ODONTALGIAS	OECOLOGICALLY	OFFICEHOLDER	OINOLOGIES	OLIGODENDROCYTE
ODONTALGIC	OECOLOGIES	OFFICEHOLDERS	OLDFANGLED	OLIGODENDROGLIA
ODONTALGIES	OECOLOGIST	OFFICERING	OLEAGINOUS	OLIGOGENES
ODONTOBLAST	OECOLOGISTS	OFFICIALDOM	OLEAGINOUSLY	OLIGOMERIC
ODONTOBLASTIC	OECUMENICAL	OFFICIALDOMS	OLEAGINOUSNESS	OLIGOMERISATION
ODONTOBLASTS	OECUMENICALLY	OFFICIALESE	OLEANDOMYCIN	OLIGOMERIZATION
ODONTOCETE	OEDEMATOSE	OFFICIALESES	OLEANDOMYCINS	OLIGOMEROUS
ODONTOCETES	OEDEMATOUS	OFFICIALISM	OLECRANONS	OLIGONUCLEOTIDE
ODONTOGENIC	OEDOMETERS	OFFICIALISMS	OLEIFEROUS	OLIGOPEPTIDE
ODONTOGENIES	OENOLOGICAL	OFFICIALITIES	OLEOGRAPHIC	OLIGOPEPTIDES
ODONTOGENY	OENOLOGIES	OFFICIALITY	OLEOGRAPHIES	OLIGOPHAGIES
ODONTOGLOSSUM	OENOLOGIST	OFFICIALLY	OLEOGRAPHS	OLIGOPHAGOUS
ODONTOGLOSSUMS	OENOLOGISTS	OFFICIALTIES	OLEOGRAPHY	OLIGOPHAGY
ODONTOGRAPH	OENOMANCIES	OFFICIALTY	OLEOMARGARIN	OLIGOPOLIES
ODONTOGRAPHIES	OENOMANIAS	OFFICIANTS	OLEOMARGARINE	OLIGOPOLISTIC
ODONTOGRAPHS	OENOMETERS	OFFICIARIES	OLEOMARGARINES	OLIGOPSONIES
ODONTOGRAPHY	OENOPHILES	OFFICIATED	OLEOMARGARINS	OLIGOPSONISTIC
ODONTOLITE	OENOPHILIES	OFFICIATES	OLEOPHILIC	OLIGOPSONY
ODONTOLITES	OENOPHILIST	OFFICIATING	OLEORESINOUS	OLIGOSACCHARIDE
ODONTOLOGIC	OENOPHILISTS	OFFICIATION	OLEORESINS	OLIGOSPERMIA
ODONTOLOGICAL	OENOTHERAS	OFFICIATIONS	OLERACEOUS	OLIGOSPERMIAS
ODONTOLOGIES	OESOPHAGEAL	OFFICIATOR	OLFACTIBLE	OLIGOTROPHIC
ODONTOLOGIST	OESOPHAGITIS	OFFICIATORS	OLFACTIONS	OLIGOTROPHIES
ODONTOLOGISTS	OESOPHAGITISES	OFFICINALLY	OLFACTOLOGIES	OLIGOTROPHY
ODONTOLOGY	OESOPHAGOSCOPE	OFFICINALS	OLFACTOLOGIST	OLIGURESES
ODONTOMATA	OESOPHAGOSCOPES	OFFICIOUSLY	OLFACTOLOGISTS	OLIGURESIS
ODONTOMATOUS	OESOPHAGOSCOPY	OFFICIOUSNESS	OLFACTOLOGY	OLIGURETIC
ODONTOPHOBIA	OESOPHAGUS	OFFICIOUSNESSES	OLFACTOMETER	OLIVACEOUS
ODONTOPHOBIAS	OESTRADIOL	OFFISHNESS	OLFACTOMETERS	OLIVENITES
ODONTOPHORAL	OESTRADIOLS	OFFISHNESSES	OLFACTOMETRIES	OLIVINITIC
ODONTOPHORAN	OESTROGENIC	OFFLOADING	OLFACTOMETRY	OLOGOANING
ODONTOPHORE	OESTROGENICALLY	OFFPRINTED	OLFACTORIES	OLOLIUQUIS
ODONTOPHORES	OESTROGENS	OFFPRINTING	OLFACTRONICS	OMBROGENOUS
ODONTOPHOROUS	OFFENCEFUL	OFFSADDLED	OLIGAEMIAS	OMBROMETER
ODONTORHYNCHOUS	OFFENCELESS	OFFSADDLES	OLIGARCHAL	OMBROMETERS
ODONTORNITHES	OFFENDEDLY	OFFSADDLING	OLIGARCHIC	OMBROPHILE
ODONTOSTOMATOUS	OFFENDRESS	OFFSCOURING	OLIGARCHICAL	OMBROPHILES
ODORIFEROUS	OFFENDRESSES	OFFSCOURINGS	OLIGARCHICALLY	OMBROPHILOUS
ODORIFEROUSLY	OFFENSELESS	OFFSEASONS	OLIGARCHIES	OMBROPHILS
ODORIFEROUSNESS	OFFENSIVELY	OFFSETABLE	OLIGOCHAETE	OMBROPHOBE
ODORIMETRIES	OFFENSIVENESS	OFFSETTING	OLIGOCHAETES	OMBROPHOBES
ODORIMETRY	OFFENSIVENESSES	OFFSHORING	OLIGOCHROME	OMBROPHOBOUS
ODORIPHORE	OFFENSIVES	OFFSHORINGS	OLIGOCHROMES	OMBUDSMANSHIP
ODORIPHORES	OFFERTORIES	OFFSPRINGS	OLIGOCLASE	OMBUDSMANSHIPS

O

OMINOUSNESS	OMNIVOROUS	ONEIROMANCY	ONYCHOCRYPTOSES	OPERABILITY
OMINOUSNESSES	OMNIVOROUSLY	ONEIROSCOPIES	ONYCHOCRYPTOSIS	OPERAGOERS
OMISSIVENESS	OMNIVOROUSNESS	ONEIROSCOPIST	ONYCHOMANCIES	OPERAGOING
OMISSIVENESSES	OMOPHAGIAS	ONEIROSCOPISTS	ONYCHOMANCY	OPERAGOINGS
OMITTANCES	OMOPHAGIES	ONEIROSCOPY	ONYCHOPHAGIES	OPERATICALLY
OMMATIDIAL	OMOPHAGOUS	ONEROUSNESS	ONYCHOPHAGIST	OPERATIONAL
OMMATIDIUM	OMOPHORION	ONEROUSNESSES	ONYCHOPHAGISTS	OPERATIONALISM
OMMATOPHORE	OMOPLATOSCOPIES	ONGOINGNESS	ONYCHOPHAGY	OPERATIONALISMS
OMMATOPHORES	OMOPLATOSCOPY	ONGOINGNESSES	ONYCHOPHORAN	OPERATIONALIST
OMMATOPHOROUS	OMPHACITES	ONIONSKINS	ONYCHOPHORANS	OPERATIONALISTS
OMNIBENEVOLENCE	OMPHALOMANCIES	ONOCENTAUR	OOGAMOUSLY	OPERATIONALLY
OMNIBENEVOLENT	OMPHALOMANCY	ONOCENTAURS	OOPHORECTOMIES	OPERATIONISM
OMNIBUSSES	OMPHALOSKEPSES	ONOMASIOLOGIES	OOPHORECTOMISE	OPERATIONISMS
OMNICOMPETENCE	OMPHALOSKEPSIS	ONOMASIOLOGY	OOPHORECTOMISED	OPERATIONIST
OMNICOMPETENCES	ONAGRACEOUS	ONOMASTICALLY	OOPHORECTOMISES	OPERATIONISTS
OMNICOMPETENT	ONCHOCERCIASES	ONOMASTICIAN	OOPHORECTOMIZE	OPERATIONS
OMNIDIRECTIONAL	ONCHOCERCIASIS	ONOMASTICIANS	OOPHORECTOMIZED	OPERATISED
OMNIFARIOUS	ONCOGENESES	ONOMASTICON	OOPHORECTOMIZES	OPERATISES
OMNIFARIOUSLY	ONCOGENESIS	ONOMASTICONS	OOPHORECTOMY	OPERATISING
OMNIFARIOUSNESS	ONCOGENETICIST	ONOMASTICS	OOPHORITIC	OPERATIVELY
OMNIFEROUS	ONCOGENETICISTS	ONOMATOLOGIES	OOPHORITIS	OPERATIVENESS
OMNIFICENCE	ONCOGENICITIES	ONOMATOLOGIST	OOPHORITISES	OPERATIVENESSES
OMNIFICENCES	ONCOGENICITY	ONOMATOLOGISTS	OOZINESSES	OPERATIVES
OMNIFICENT	ONCOGENOUS	ONOMATOLOGY	OPACIFIERS	OPERATIVITIES
OMNIFORMITIES	ONCOLOGICAL	ONOMATOPOEIA	OPACIFYING	OPERATIVITY
OMNIFORMITY	ONCOLOGIES	ONOMATOPOEIAS	OPALESCENCE	OPERATIZED
OMNIGENOUS	ONCOLOGIST	ONOMATOPOEIC	OPALESCENCES	OPERATIZES
OMNIPARITIES	ONCOLOGISTS	ONOMATOPOESES	OPALESCENT	OPERATIZING
OMNIPARITY	ONCOLYTICS	ONOMATOPOESIS	OPALESCENTLY	OPERATORLESS
OMNIPAROUS	ONCOMETERS	ONOMATOPOETIC	OPALESCING	OPERCULARS
OMNIPATIENT	ONCORNAVIRUS	ONOMATOPOIESES	OPAQUENESS	OPERCULATE
OMNIPOTENCE	ONCORNAVIRUSES	.ONOMATOPOIESIS	OPAQUENESSES	OPERCULATED
OMNIPOTENCES	ONCOTOMIES	ONSETTINGS	OPEIDOSCOPE	OPERCULUMS
OMNIPOTENCIES	ONCOVIRUSES	ONSHORINGS	OPEIDOSCOPES	OPERETTIST
OMNIPOTENCY	ONDOGRAPHS	ONSLAUGHTS	OPENABILITIES	OPERETTISTS
OMNIPOTENT	ONEIRICALLY	ONTOGENESES	OPENABILITY	OPEROSENESS
OMNIPOTENTLY	ONEIROCRITIC	ONTOGENESIS	OPENHANDED	OPEROSENESSES
OMNIPOTENTS	ONEIROCRITICAL	ONTOGENETIC	OPENHANDEDLY	OPEROSITIES
OMNIPRESENCE	ONEIROCRITICISM	ONTOGENETICALLY	OPENHANDEDNESS	OPHICALCITE
OMNIPRESENCES	ONEIROCRITICS	ONTOGENICALLY	OPENHEARTED	OPHICALCITES
OMNIPRESENT	ONEIRODYNIA	ONTOGENIES	OPENHEARTEDLY	OPHICLEIDE
OMNIRANGES	ONEIRODYNIAS	ONTOLOGICAL	OPENHEARTEDNESS	OPHICLEIDES
OMNISCIENCE	ONEIROLOGIES	ONTOLOGICALLY	OPENMOUTHED	OPHIDIARIA
OMNISCIENCES	ONEIROLOGY	ONTOLOGIES	OPENMOUTHEDLY	OPHIDIARIUM
OMNISCIENT	ONEIROMANCER	ONTOLOGIST	OPENMOUTHEDNESS	OPHIDIARIUMS
OMNISCIENTLY	ONEIROMANCERS	ONTOLOGISTS	OPENNESSES	OPHIOLATER
OMNIVORIES	ONEIROMANCIES	ONYCHITISES	OPERABILITIES	OPHIOLATERS

O

OPHIOLATRIES	OPINIONIST	OPPORTUNISMS	OPSONIFYING	OPTOMETRIST
OPHIOLATROUS	OPINIONISTS	OPPORTUNIST	OPSONISATION	OPTOMETRISTS
OPHIOLATRY	OPISOMETER	OPPORTUNISTIC	OPSONISATIONS	OPTOPHONES
OPHIOLITES	OPISOMETERS	OPPORTUNISTS	OPSONISING	OPULENCIES
OPHIOLITIC	OPISTHOBRANCH	OPPORTUNITIES	OPSONIZATION	ORACULARITIES
OPHIOLOGIC	OPISTHOBRANCHS	OPPORTUNITY	OPSONIZATIONS	ORACULARITY
OPHIOLOGICAL	OPISTHOCOELIAN	OPPOSABILITIES	OPSONIZING	ORACULARLY
OPHIOLOGIES	OPISTHOCOELOUS	OPPOSABILITY	OPTATIVELY	ORACULARNESS
OPHIOLOGIST	OPISTHODOMOI	OPPOSELESS	OPTIMALISATION	ORACULARNESSES
OPHIOLOGISTS	OPISTHODOMOS	OPPOSINGLY	OPTIMALISATIONS	ORACULOUSLY
OPHIOMORPH	OPISTHOGLOSSAL	OPPOSITELY	OPTIMALISE	ORACULOUSNESS
OPHIOMORPHIC	OPISTHOGNATHISM	OPPOSITENESS	OPTIMALISED	ORACULOUSNESSES
OPHIOMORPHOUS	OPISTHOGNATHOUS	OPPOSITENESSES	OPTIMALISES	ORANGEADES
OPHIOMORPHS	OPISTHOGRAPH	OPPOSITION	OPTIMALISING	ORANGERIES
OPHIOPHAGOUS	OPISTHOGRAPHIC	OPPOSITIONAL	OPTIMALITIES	ORANGEWOOD
OPHIOPHILIST	OPISTHOGRAPHIES	OPPOSITIONIST	OPTIMALITY	ORANGEWOODS
OPHIOPHILISTS	OPISTHOGRAPHS	OPPOSITIONISTS	OPTIMALIZATION	ORANGUTANS
OPHIUROIDS	OPISTHOGRAPHY	OPPOSITIONLESS	OPTIMALIZATIONS	ORATORIANS
OPHTHALMIA	OPISTHOSOMA	OPPOSITIONS	OPTIMALIZE	ORATORICAL
OPHTHALMIAS	OPISTHOSOMATA	OPPOSITIVE	OPTIMALIZED	ORATORICALLY
OPHTHALMIC	OPISTHOTONIC	OPPRESSING	OPTIMALIZES	ORATRESSES
OPHTHALMIST	OPISTHOTONOS	OPPRESSINGLY	OPTIMALIZING	ORBICULARES
OPHTHALMISTS	OPISTHOTONOSES	OPPRESSION	OPTIMISATION	ORBICULARIS
OPHTHALMITIS	OPOBALSAMS	OPPRESSIONS	OPTIMISATIONS	ORBICULARITIES
OPHTHALMITISES	OPODELDOCS	OPPRESSIVE	OPTIMISERS	ORBICULARITY
OPHTHALMOLOGIC	OPOPANAXES	OPPRESSIVELY	OPTIMISING	ORBICULARLY
OPHTHALMOLOGIES	OPOTHERAPIES	OPPRESSIVENESS	OPTIMISTIC	ORBICULATE
OPHTHALMOLOGIST	OPOTHERAPY	OPPRESSORS	OPTIMISTICAL	ORBICULATED
OPHTHALMOLOGY	OPPIGNERATE	OPPROBRIOUS	OPTIMISTICALLY	ORCHARDING
OPHTHALMOMETER	OPPIGNERATED	OPPROBRIOUSLY	OPTIMIZATION	ORCHARDINGS
OPHTHALMOMETERS	OPPIGNERATES	OPPROBRIOUSNESS	OPTIMIZATIONS	ORCHARDIST
OPHTHALMOMETRY	OPPIGNERATING	OPPROBRIUM	.OPTIMIZERS	ORCHARDISTS
OPHTHALMOPHOBIA	OPPIGNORATE	OPPROBRIUMS	OPTIMIZING	ORCHARDMAN
OPHTHALMOPLEGIA	OPPIGNORATED	OPPUGNANCIES	OPTIONALITIES	ORCHARDMEN
OPHTHALMOSCOPE	OPPIGNORATES	OPPUGNANCY	OPTIONALITY	ORCHESOGRAPHIES
OPHTHALMOSCOPES	OPPIGNORATING	OPPUGNANTLY	OPTIONALLY	ORCHESOGRAPHY
OPHTHALMOSCOPIC	OPPIGNORATION	OPPUGNANTS	OPTOACOUSTIC	ORCHESTICS
OPHTHALMOSCOPY	OPPIGNORATIONS	OPSIMATHIES	OPTOELECTRONIC	ORCHESTRAL
OPINICUSES	OPPILATING	OPSIOMETER	OPTOELECTRONICS	ORCHESTRALIST
OPINIONATED	OPPILATION	OPSIOMETERS	OPTOKINETIC	ORCHESTRALISTS
OPINIONATEDLY	OPPILATIONS	OPSOMANIAC	OPTOLOGIES	ORCHESTRALLY
OPINIONATEDNESS	OPPILATIVE	OPSOMANIACS	OPTOLOGIST	ORCHESTRAS
OPINIONATELY	OPPONENCIES	OPSOMANIAS	OPTOLOGISTS	ORCHESTRATE
OPINIONATIVE	OPPORTUNELY	OPSONIFICATION	OPTOMETERS	ORCHESTRATED
OPINIONATIVELY	OPPORTUNENESS	OPSONIFICATIONS	OPTOMETRIC	ORCHESTRATER
OPINIONATOR	OPPORTUNENESSES	OPSONIFIED	OPTOMETRICAL	ORCHESTRATERS
OPINIONATORS	OPPORTUNISM	OPSONIFIES	OPTOMETRIES	ORCHESTRATES

O

ORCHESTRATING
ORCHESTRATION
ORCHESTRATIONAL
ORCHESTRATIONS
ORCHESTRATOR
ORCHESTRATORS
ORCHESTRIC
ORCHESTRINA
ORCHESTRINAS
ORCHESTRION
ORCHESTRIONS
ORCHIDACEOUS
ORCHIDECTOMIES
ORCHIDECTOMY
ORCHIDEOUS
ORCHIDISTS
ORCHIDLIKE
ORCHIDOLOGIES
ORCHIDOLOGIST
ORCHIDOLOGISTS
ORCHIDOLOGY
ORCHIDOMANIA
ORCHIDOMANIAC
ORCHIDOMANIACS
ORCHIDOMANIAS
ORCHIECTOMIES
ORCHIECTOMY
ORCHITISES
ORDAINABLE
ORDAINMENT
ORDAINMENTS
ORDERLINESS
ORDERLINESSES
ORDINAIRES
ORDINANCES
ORDINARIER
ORDINARIES
ORDINARIEST
ORDINARILY
ORDINARINESS
ORDINARINESSES
ORDINATELY
ORDINATING
ORDINATION
ORDINATIONS
ORDONNANCE
ORDONNANCES

ORECCHIETTE
ORECCHIETTES
ORECCHIETTI
OREOGRAPHIC
OREOGRAPHICAL
OREOGRAPHICALLY
OREOGRAPHIES
OREOGRAPHY
OREOLOGICAL
OREOLOGIES
OREOLOGIST
OREOLOGISTS
OREPEARCHED
OREPEARCHES
OREPEARCHING
ORGANELLES
ORGANICALLY
ORGANICISM
ORGANICISMS
ORGANICIST
ORGANICISTIC
ORGANICISTS
ORGANICITIES
ORGANICITY
ORGANISABILITY
ORGANISABLE
ORGANISATION
ORGANISATIONAL
ORGANISATIONS
ORGANISERS
ORGANISING
ORGANISMAL
ORGANISMALLY
ORGANISMIC
ORGANISMICALLY
ORGANISTRUM
ORGANISTRUMS
ORGANITIES
ORGANIZABILITY
ORGANIZABLE
ORGANIZATION
ORGANIZATIONAL
ORGANIZATIONS
ORGANIZERS
ORGANIZING
ORGANOCHLORINE
ORGANOCHLORINES

ORGANOGENESES
ORGANOGENESIS
ORGANOGENETIC
ORGANOGENIES
ORGANOGENY
ORGANOGRAM
ORGANOGRAMS
ORGANOGRAPHIC
ORGANOGRAPHICAL
ORGANOGRAPHIES
ORGANOGRAPHIST
ORGANOGRAPHISTS
ORGANOGRAPHY
ORGANOLEPTIC
ORGANOLOGICAL
ORGANOLOGIES
ORGANOLOGIST
ORGANOLOGISTS
ORGANOLOGY
ORGANOMERCURIAL
ORGANOMETALLIC
ORGANOMETALLICS
ORGANOPHOSPHATE
ORGANOSOLS
ORGANOTHERAPIES
ORGANOTHERAPY
ORGANZINES
ORGASMICALLY
ORGASTICALLY
ORGIASTICALLY
ORICALCHES
ORICHALCEOUS
ORIENTALISE
ORIENTALISED
ORIENTALISES
ORIENTALISING
ORIENTALISM
ORIENTALISMS
ORIENTALIST
ORIENTALISTS
ORIENTALITIES
ORIENTALITY
ORIENTALIZE
ORIENTALIZED
ORIENTALIZES
ORIENTALIZING
ORIENTALLY

ORIENTATED
ORIENTATES
ORIENTATING
ORIENTATION
ORIENTATIONAL
ORIENTATIONALLY
ORIENTATIONS
ORIENTATOR
ORIENTATORS
ORIENTEERED
ORIENTEERING
ORIENTEERINGS
ORIENTEERS
ORIFLAMMES
ORIGINALITIES
ORIGINALITY
ORIGINALLY
ORIGINATED
ORIGINATES
ORIGINATING
ORIGINATION
ORIGINATIONS
ORIGINATIVE
ORIGINATIVELY
ORIGINATOR
ORIGINATORS
ORINASALLY
ORISMOLOGICAL
ORISMOLOGIES
ORISMOLOGY
ORNAMENTAL
ORNAMENTALLY
ORNAMENTALS
ORNAMENTATION
ORNAMENTATIONS
ORNAMENTED
ORNAMENTER
ORNAMENTERS
ORNAMENTING
ORNAMENTIST
ORNAMENTISTS
ORNATENESS
ORNATENESSES
ORNERINESS
ORNERINESSES
ORNITHICHNITE
ORNITHICHNITES

ORNITHINES
ORNITHISCHIAN
ORNITHISCHIANS
ORNITHODELPHIAN
ORNITHODELPHIC
ORNITHODELPHOUS
ORNITHOGALUM
ORNITHOGALUMS
ORNITHOLOGIC
ORNITHOLOGICAL
ORNITHOLOGIES
ORNITHOLOGIST
ORNITHOLOGISTS
ORNITHOLOGY
ORNITHOMANCIES
ORNITHOMANCY
ORNITHOMANTIC
ORNITHOMORPH
ORNITHOMORPHIC
ORNITHOMORPHS
ORNITHOPHILIES
ORNITHOPHILOUS
ORNITHOPHILY
ORNITHOPHOBIA
ORNITHOPHOBIAS
ORNITHOPOD
ORNITHOPODS
ORNITHOPTER
ORNITHOPTERS
ORNITHORHYNCHUS
ORNITHOSAUR
ORNITHOSAURS
ORNITHOSCOPIES
ORNITHOSCOPY
ORNITHOSES
ORNITHOSIS
OROBANCHACEOUS
OROGENESES
OROGENESIS
OROGENETIC
OROGENETICALLY
OROGENICALLY
OROGRAPHER
OROGRAPHERS
OROGRAPHIC
OROGRAPHICAL
OROGRAPHICALLY

O

OROGRAPHIES	ORTHODONTISTS	ORTHOGRAPHY	ORTHOPTEROLOGY	OSCILLOGRAM
OROLOGICAL	ORTHODOXES	ORTHOHYDROGEN	ORTHOPTERON	OSCILLOGRAMS
OROLOGICALLY	ORTHODOXIES	ORTHOHYDROGENS	ORTHOPTEROUS	OSCILLOGRAPH
OROLOGISTS	ORTHODOXLY	ORTHOMOLECULAR	ORTHOPTERS	OSCILLOGRAPHIC
OROPHARYNGEAL	ORTHODROMIC	ORTHOMORPHIC	ORTHOPTICS	OSCILLOGRAPHIES
OROPHARYNGES	ORTHODROMICS	ORTHONORMAL	ORTHOPTIST	OSCILLOGRAPHS
OROPHARYNX	ORTHODROMIES	ORTHOPAEDIC	ORTHOPTISTS	OSCILLOGRAPHY
OROPHARYNXES	ORTHODROMY	ORTHOPAEDICAL	ORTHOPYROXENE	OSCILLOSCOPE
OROROTUNDITIES	ORTHOEPICAL	ORTHOPAEDICALLY	ORTHOPYROXENES	OSCILLOSCOPES
OROROTUNDITY	ORTHOEPICALLY	ORTHOPAEDICS	ORTHOREXIA	OSCILLOSCOPIC
OROTUNDITIES	ORTHOEPIES	ORTHOPAEDIES	ORTHOREXIAS	OSCITANCES
OROTUNDITY	ORTHOEPIST	ORTHOPAEDIST	ORTHORHOMBIC	OSCITANCIES
ORPHANAGES	ORTHOEPISTS	ORTHOPAEDISTS	ORTHOSCOPE	OSCITANTLY
ORPHANHOOD	ORTHOGENESES	ORTHOPAEDY	ORTHOSCOPES	OSCITATING
ORPHANHOODS	ORTHOGENESIS	ORTHOPEDIA	ORTHOSCOPIC	OSCITATION
ORPHANISMS	ORTHOGENETIC	ORTHOPEDIAS	ORTHOSILICATE	OSCITATIONS
ORPHARIONS	ORTHOGENIC	ORTHOPEDIC	ORTHOSILICATES	OSCULATING
ORPHEOREON	ORTHOGENICALLY	ORTHOPEDICAL	ORTHOSTATIC	OSCULATION
ORPHEOREONS	ORTHOGENICS	ORTHOPEDICALLY	ORTHOSTICHIES	OSCULATIONS
ORPHICALLY	ORTHOGNATHIC	ORTHOPEDICS	ORTHOSTICHOUS	OSCULATORIES
ORRISROOTS	ORTHOGNATHIES	ORTHOPEDIES	ORTHOSTICHY	OSCULATORY
ORTANIQUES	ORTHOGNATHISM	ORTHOPEDIST	ORTHOTISTS	OSMETERIUM
ORTHOBORATE	ORTHOGNATHISMS	ORTHOPEDISTS	ORTHOTONES	OSMIDROSES
ORTHOBORATES	ORTHOGNATHOUS	ORTHOPHOSPHATE	ORTHOTONESES	OSMIDROSIS
ORTHOBORIC	ORTHOGNATHY	ORTHOPHOSPHATES	ORTHOTONESIS	OSMIRIDIUM
ORTHOCAINE	ORTHOGONAL	ORTHOPHOSPHORIC	ORTHOTONIC	OSMIRIDIUMS
ORTHOCAINES	ORTHOGONALISE	ORTHOPHYRE	ORTHOTOPIC	OSMOLALITIES
ORTHOCENTER	ORTHOGONALISED	ORTHOPHYRES	ORTHOTROPIC	OSMOLALITY
ORTHOCENTERS	ORTHOGONALISES	ORTHOPHYRIC	ORTHOTROPIES	OSMOLARITIES
ORTHOCENTRE	ORTHOGONALISING	ORTHOPINAKOID	ORTHOTROPISM	OSMOLARITY
ORTHOCENTRES	ORTHOGONALITIES	ORTHOPINAKOIDS	ORTHOTROPISMS	OSMOMETERS
ORTHOCEPHALIC	ORTHOGONALITY	ORTHOPNOEA	ORTHOTROPOUS	OSMOMETRIC
ORTHOCEPHALIES	ORTHOGONALIZE	ORTHOPNOEAS	ORTHOTROPY	OSMOMETRICALLY
ORTHOCEPHALOUS	ORTHOGONALIZED	ORTHOPRAXES	ORTHOTUNGSTIC	OSMOMETRIES
ORTHOCEPHALY	ORTHOGONALIZES	ORTHOPRAXIES	ORTHOVANADIC	OSMOREGULATION
ORTHOCHROMATIC	ORTHOGONALIZING	ORTHOPRAXIS	ORYCTOLOGIES	OSMOREGULATIONS
ORTHOCHROMATISM	ORTHOGONALLY	ORTHOPRAXY	ORYCTOLOGY	OSMOREGULATORY
ORTHOCLASE	ORTHOGRADE	ORTHOPRISM	OSCILLATED	OSMOTICALLY
ORTHOCLASES	ORTHOGRAPH	ORTHOPRISMS	OSCILLATES	OSMUNDINES
ORTHODIAGONAL	ORTHOGRAPHER	ORTHOPSYCHIATRY	OSCILLATING	OSSIFEROUS
ORTHODIAGONALS	ORTHOGRAPHERS	ORTHOPTERA	OSCILLATION	OSSIFICATION
ORTHODONTIA	ORTHOGRAPHIC	ORTHOPTERAN	OSCILLATIONAL	OSSIFICATIONS
ORTHODONTIAS	ORTHOGRAPHICAL	ORTHOPTERANS	OSCILLATIONS	OSSIFRAGAS
ORTHODONTIC	ORTHOGRAPHIES	ORTHOPTERIST	OSCILLATIVE	OSSIFRAGES
ORTHODONTICALLY	ORTHOGRAPHIST	ORTHOPTERISTS	OSCILLATOR	OSSIVOROUS
ORTHODONTICS	ORTHOGRAPHISTS	ORTHOPTEROID	OSCILLATORS	OSTEICHTHYAN
ORTHODONTIST	ORTHOGRAPHS	ORTHOPTEROIDS	OSCILLATORY	OSTEICHTHYANS

O

OSTEITIDES OSTEOLOGIES OSTRACIZING OUROBOROSES OUTBRAGGING
OSTEITISES OSTEOLOGIST OSTRACODAN OUROLOGIES OUTBRAVING
OSTENSIBILITIES OSTEOLOGISTS OSTRACODERM OUROSCOPIES OUTBRAWLED
OSTENSIBILITY OSTEOMALACIA OSTRACODERMS OUTACHIEVE OUTBRAWLING
OSTENSIBLE OSTEOMALACIAL OSTRACODES OUTACHIEVED OUTBRAZENED
OSTENSIBLY OSTEOMALACIAS OSTRACODOUS OUTACHIEVES OUTBRAZENING
OSTENSIVELY OSTEOMALACIC OSTREACEOUS OUTACHIEVING OUTBRAZENS
OSTENSORIA OSTEOMYELITIS OSTREICULTURE OUTARGUING OUTBREAKING
OSTENSORIES OSTEOMYELITISES OSTREICULTURES OUTBACKERS OUTBREATHE
OSTENSORIUM OSTEOPATHIC OSTREICULTURIST OUTBALANCE OUTBREATHED
OSTENTATION OSTEOPATHICALLY OSTREOPHAGE OUTBALANCED OUTBREATHES
OSTENTATIONS OSTEOPATHIES OSTREOPHAGES OUTBALANCES OUTBREATHING
OSTENTATIOUS OSTEOPATHIST OSTREOPHAGIES OUTBALANCING OUTBREEDING
OSTENTATIOUSLY OSTEOPATHISTS OSTREOPHAGOUS OUTBARGAIN OUTBREEDINGS
OSTEOARTHRITIC OSTEOPATHS OSTREOPHAGY OUTBARGAINED OUTBRIBING
OSTEOARTHRITICS OSTEOPATHY OSTRICHISM OUTBARGAINING OUTBUILDING
OSTEOARTHRITIS OSTEOPETROSES OSTRICHISMS OUTBARGAINS OUTBUILDINGS
OSTEOARTHROSES OSTEOPETROSIS OSTRICHLIKE OUTBARKING OUTBULGING
OSTEOARTHROSIS OSTEOPHYTE OTHERGATES OUTBARRING OUTBULKING
OSTEOBLAST OSTEOPHYTES OTHERGUESS OUTBAWLING OUTBULLIED
OSTEOBLASTIC OSTEOPHYTIC OTHERNESSES OUTBEAMING OUTBULLIES
OSTEOBLASTS OSTEOPLASTIC OTHERWHERE OUTBEGGING OUTBULLYING
OSTEOCLASES OSTEOPLASTIES OTHERWHILE OUTBIDDERS OUTBURNING
OSTEOCLASIS OSTEOPLASTY OTHERWHILES OUTBIDDING OUTBURSTING
OSTEOCLAST OSTEOPOROSES OTHERWORLD OUTBITCHED OUTCAPERED
OSTEOCLASTIC OSTEOPOROSIS OTHERWORLDISH OUTBITCHES OUTCAPERING
OSTEOCLASTS OSTEOPOROTIC OTHERWORLDLY OUTBITCHING OUTCASTING
OSTEOCOLLA OSTEOSARCOMA OTHERWORLDS OUTBLAZING OUTCATCHES
OSTEOCOLLAS OSTEOSARCOMAS OTIOSENESS OUTBLEATED OUTCATCHING
OSTEOCYTES OSTEOSARCOMATA OTIOSENESSES OUTBLEATING OUTCAVILED
OSTEODERMAL OSTEOSISES OTIOSITIES OUTBLESSED OUTCAVILING
OSTEODERMATOUS OSTEOTOMES OTOLARYNGOLOGY OUTBLESSES OUTCAVILLED
OSTEODERMIC OSTEOTOMIES OTOLOGICAL OUTBLESSING OUTCAVILLING
OSTEODERMOUS OSTLERESSES OTOLOGISTS OUTBLOOMED OUTCHARGED
OSTEODERMS OSTRACEOUS OTOPLASTIES OUTBLOOMING OUTCHARGES
OSTEOFIBROSES OSTRACISABLE OTORRHOEAS OUTBLUFFED OUTCHARGING
OSTEOFIBROSIS OSTRACISED OTOSCLEROSES OUTBLUFFING OUTCHARMED
OSTEOGENESES OSTRACISER OTOSCLEROSIS OUTBLUSHED OUTCHARMING
OSTEOGENESIS OSTRACISERS OTOSCOPIES OUTBLUSHES OUTCHEATED
OSTEOGENETIC OSTRACISES OTOTOXICITIES OUTBLUSHING OUTCHEATING
OSTEOGENIC OSTRACISING OTOTOXICITY OUTBLUSTER OUTCHIDDEN
OSTEOGENIES OSTRACISMS OTTRELITES OUTBLUSTERED OUTCHIDING
OSTEOGENOUS OSTRACIZABLE OUANANICHE OUTBLUSTERING OUTCLASSED
OSTEOGRAPHIES OSTRACIZED OUANANICHES OUTBLUSTERS OUTCLASSES
OSTEOGRAPHY OSTRACIZER OUBLIETTES OUTBOASTED OUTCLASSING
OSTEOLOGICAL OSTRACIZERS OUGHTLINGS OUTBOASTING OUTCLIMBED
OSTEOLOGICALLY OSTRACIZES OUGHTNESSES OUTBRAGGED OUTCLIMBING

OUTCOACHED	OUTDISTANCING	OUTFITTING	OUTGOINGNESSES	OUTKICKING
OUTCOACHES	OUTDODGING	OUTFITTINGS	OUTGRINNED	OUTKILLING
OUTCOACHING	OUTDOORSMAN	OUTFLANKED	OUTGRINNING	OUTKISSING
OUTCOMPETE	OUTDOORSMANSHIP	OUTFLANKING	OUTGROSSED	OUTLANDERS
OUTCOMPETED	OUTDOORSMEN	OUTFLASHED	OUTGROSSES	OUTLANDISH
OUTCOMPETES	OUTDRAGGED	OUTFLASHES	OUTGROSSING	OUTLANDISHLY
OUTCOMPETING	OUTDRAGGING	OUTFLASHING	OUTGROWING	OUTLANDISHNESS
OUTCOOKING	OUTDRAWING	OUTFLOATED	OUTGROWTHS	OUTLASTING
OUTCOUNTED	OUTDREAMED	OUTFLOATING	OUTGUESSED	OUTLAUGHED
OUTCOUNTING	OUTDREAMING	OUTFLOWING	OUTGUESSES	OUTLAUGHING
OUTCRAFTIED	OUTDRESSED	OUTFLOWINGS	OUTGUESSING	OUTLAUNCED
OUTCRAFTIES	OUTDRESSES	OUTFLUSHED	OUTGUIDING	OUTLAUNCES
OUTCRAFTYING	OUTDRESSING	OUTFLUSHES	OUTGUNNING	OUTLAUNCHED
OUTCRAWLED	OUTDRINKING	OUTFLUSHING	OUTGUSHING	OUTLAUNCHES
OUTCRAWLING	OUTDRIVING	OUTFOOLING	OUTHANDLED	OUTLAUNCHING
OUTCROPPED	OUTDROPPED	OUTFOOTING	OUTHANDLES	OUTLAUNCING
OUTCROPPING	OUTDROPPING	OUTFROWNED	OUTHANDLING	OUTLAWRIES
OUTCROPPINGS	OUTDUELING	OUTFROWNING	OUTHAULERS	OUTLEADING
OUTCROSSED	OUTDUELLED	OUTFUMBLED	OUTHEARING	OUTLEAPING
OUTCROSSES	OUTDUELLING	OUTFUMBLES	OUTHITTING	OUTLEARNED
OUTCROSSING	OUTDWELLED	OUTFUMBLING	OUTHOMERED	OUTLEARNING
OUTCROSSINGS	OUTDWELLING	OUTGAINING	OUTHOMERING	OUTLODGING
OUTCROWDED	OUTEARNING	OUTGALLOPED	OUTHOWLING	OUTLODGINGS
OUTCROWDING	OUTECHOING	OUTGALLOPING	OUTHUMORED	OUTLOOKING
OUTCROWING	OUTERCOATS	OUTGALLOPS	OUTHUMORING	OUTLUSTRED
OUTCURSING	OUTERCOURSE	OUTGAMBLED	OUTHUNTING	OUTLUSTRES
OUTDACIOUS	OUTERCOURSES	OUTGAMBLES	OUTHUSTLED	OUTLUSTRING
OUTDANCING	OUTERWEARS	OUTGAMBLING	OUTHUSTLES	OUTMANEUVER
OUTDATEDLY	OUTFABLING	OUTGASSING	OUTHUSTLING	OUTMANEUVERED
OUTDATEDNESS	OUTFANGTHIEF	OUTGASSINGS	OUTINTRIGUE	OUTMANEUVERING
OUTDATEDNESSES	OUTFANGTHIEVES	OUTGENERAL	OUTINTRIGUED	OUTMANEUVERS
OUTDAZZLED	OUTFASTING	OUTGENERALED	OUTINTRIGUES	OUTMANIPULATE
OUTDAZZLES	OUTFAWNING	OUTGENERALING	OUTINTRIGUING	OUTMANIPULATED
OUTDAZZLING	OUTFEASTED	OUTGENERALLED	OUTJESTING	OUTMANIPULATES
OUTDEBATED	OUTFEASTING	OUTGENERALLING	OUTJETTING	OUTMANIPULATING
OUTDEBATES	OUTFEELING	OUTGENERALS	OUTJETTINGS	OUTMANNING
OUTDEBATING	OUTFENCING	OUTGIVINGS	OUTJINXING	OUTMANOEUVRE
OUTDELIVER	OUTFIELDER	OUTGLARING	OUTJOCKEYED	OUTMANOEUVRED
OUTDELIVERED	OUTFIELDERS	OUTGLEAMED	OUTJOCKEYING	OUTMANOEUVRES
OUTDELIVERING	OUTFIGHTING	OUTGLEAMING	OUTJOCKEYS	OUTMANOEUVRING
OUTDELIVERS	OUTFIGHTINGS	OUTGLITTER	OUTJUGGLED	OUTMANTLED
OUTDESIGNED	OUTFIGURED	OUTGLITTERED	OUTJUGGLES	OUTMANTLES
OUTDESIGNING	OUTFIGURES	OUTGLITTERING	OUTJUGGLING	OUTMANTLING
OUTDESIGNS	OUTFIGURING	OUTGLITTERS	OUTJUMPING	OUTMARCHED
OUTDISTANCE	OUTFINDING	OUTGLOWING	OUTJUTTING	OUTMARCHES
OUTDISTANCED	OUTFISHING	OUTGNAWING	OUTJUTTINGS	OUTMARCHING
OUTDISTANCES	OUTFITTERS	OUTGOINGNESS	OUTKEEPING	OUTMARRIAGE

OUTMARRIAGES	OUTPERFORMING	OUTPRODUCES	OUTREPRODUCED	OUTSIDERNESSES
OUTMASTERED	OUTPERFORMS	OUTPRODUCING	OUTREPRODUCES	OUTSINGING
OUTMASTERING	OUTPITCHED	OUTPROMISE	OUTREPRODUCING	OUTSINNING
OUTMASTERS	OUTPITCHES	OUTPROMISED	OUTRIGGERS	OUTSITTING
OUTMATCHED	OUTPITCHING	OUTPROMISES	OUTRIGGING	OUTSKATING
OUTMATCHES	OUTPITYING	OUTPROMISING	OUTRIGHTLY	OUTSLEEPING
OUTMATCHING	OUTPLACEMENT	OUTPULLING	OUTRINGING	OUTSLICKED
OUTMEASURE	OUTPLACEMENTS	OUTPUNCHED	OUTRIVALED	OUTSLICKING
OUTMEASURED	OUTPLACERS	OUTPUNCHES	OUTRIVALING	OUTSMARTED
OUTMEASURES	OUTPLACING	OUTPUNCHING	OUTRIVALLED	OUTSMARTING
OUTMEASURING	OUTPLANNED	OUTPURSUED	OUTRIVALLING	OUTSMELLED
OUTMODEDLY	OUTPLANNING	OUTPURSUES	OUTROARING	OUTSMELLING
OUTMODEDNESS	OUTPLAYING	OUTPURSUING	OUTROCKING	OUTSMILING
OUTMODEDNESSES	OUTPLODDED	OUTPUSHING	OUTROLLING	OUTSMOKING
OUTMUSCLED	OUTPLODDING	OUTPUTTING	OUTROOPERS	OUTSNORING
OUTMUSCLES	OUTPLOTTED	OUTQUARTERS	OUTROOTING	OUTSOARING
OUTMUSCLING	OUTPLOTTING	OUTQUOTING	OUTRUNNERS	OUTSOURCED
OUTNIGHTED	OUTPOINTED	OUTRAGEOUS	OUTRUNNING	OUTSOURCES
OUTNIGHTING	OUTPOINTING	OUTRAGEOUSLY	OUTRUSHING	OUTSOURCING
OUTNUMBERED	OUTPOLITICK	OUTRAGEOUSNESS	OUTSAILING	OUTSOURCINGS
OUTNUMBERING	OUTPOLITICKED	OUTRAISING	OUTSAVORED	OUTSPANNED
OUTNUMBERS	OUTPOLITICKING	OUTRANGING	OUTSAVORING	OUTSPANNING
OUTOFFICES	OUTPOLITICKS	OUTRANKING	OUTSCHEMED	OUTSPARKLE
OUTORGANISE	OUTPOLLING	OUTREACHED	OUTSCHEMES	OUTSPARKLED
OUTORGANISED	OUTPOPULATE	OUTREACHES	OUTSCHEMING	OUTSPARKLES
OUTORGANISES	OUTPOPULATED	OUTREACHING	OUTSCOLDED	OUTSPARKLING
OUTORGANISING	OUTPOPULATES	OUTREADING	OUTSCOLDING	OUTSPEAKING
OUTORGANIZE	OUTPOPULATING	OUTREASONED	OUTSCOOPED	OUTSPECKLE
OUTORGANIZED	OUTPORTERS	OUTREASONING	OUTSCOOPING	OUTSPECKLES
OUTORGANIZES	OUTPOURERS	OUTREASONS	OUTSCORING	OUTSPEEDED
OUTORGANIZING	OUTPOURING	OUTREBOUND	OUTSCORNED	OUTSPEEDING
OUTPAINTED	OUTPOURINGS	OUTREBOUNDED	OUTSCORNING	OUTSPELLED
OUTPAINTING	OUTPOWERED	OUTREBOUNDING	OUTSCREAMED	OUTSPELLING
OUTPASSING	OUTPOWERING	OUTREBOUNDS	OUTSCREAMING	OUTSPENDING
OUTPASSION	OUTPRAYING	OUTRECKONED	OUTSCREAMS	OUTSPOKENLY
OUTPASSIONED	OUTPREACHED	OUTRECKONING	OUTSELLING	OUTSPOKENNESS
OUTPASSIONING	OUTPREACHES	OUTRECKONS	OUTSERVING	OUTSPOKENNESSES
OUTPASSIONS	OUTPREACHING	OUTRECUIDANCE	OUTSETTING	OUTSPORTED
OUTPATIENT	OUTPREENED	OUTRECUIDANCES	OUTSETTINGS	OUTSPORTING
OUTPATIENTS	OUTPREENING	OUTREDDENED	OUTSETTLEMENT	OUTSPREADING
OUTPEEPING	OUTPRESSED	OUTREDDENING	OUTSETTLEMENTS	OUTSPREADS
OUTPEERING	OUTPRESSES	OUTREDDENS	OUTSHAMING	OUTSPRINGING
OUTPEOPLED	OUTPRESSING	OUTREDDING	OUTSHINING	OUTSPRINGS
OUTPEOPLES	OUTPRICING	OUTREIGNED	OUTSHOOTING	OUTSPRINTED
OUTPEOPLING	OUTPRIZING	OUTREIGNING	OUTSHOUTED	OUTSPRINTING
OUTPERFORM	OUTPRODUCE	OUTRELIEFS	OUTSHOUTING	OUTSPRINTS
OUTPERFORMED	OUTPRODUCED	OUTREPRODUCE	OUTSIDERNESS	OUTSTANDING

O

OUTSTANDINGLY
OUTSTARING
OUTSTARTED
OUTSTARTING
OUTSTATING
OUTSTATION
OUTSTATIONS
OUTSTAYING
OUTSTEERED
OUTSTEERING
OUTSTEPPED
OUTSTEPPING
OUTSTRAINED
OUTSTRAINING
OUTSTRAINS
OUTSTRETCH
OUTSTRETCHED
OUTSTRETCHES
OUTSTRETCHING
OUTSTRIDDEN
OUTSTRIDES
OUTSTRIDING
OUTSTRIKES
OUTSTRIKING
OUTSTRIPPED
OUTSTRIPPING
OUTSTRIVEN
OUTSTRIVES
OUTSTRIVING
OUTSTROKES
OUTSTUDIED
OUTSTUDIES
OUTSTUDYING
OUTSTUNTED
OUTSTUNTING
OUTSULKING
OUTSUMMING
OUTSWEARING
OUTSWEEPING
OUTSWEETEN
OUTSWEETENED
OUTSWEETENING
OUTSWEETENS
OUTSWELLED
OUTSWELLING
OUTSWIMMING
OUTSWINGER

OUTSWINGERS
OUTSWINGING
OUTSWOLLEN
OUTTALKING
OUTTASKING
OUTTELLING
OUTTHANKED
OUTTHANKING
OUTTHIEVED
OUTTHIEVES
OUTTHIEVING
OUTTHINKING
OUTTHOUGHT
OUTTHROBBED
OUTTHROBBING
OUTTHROWING
OUTTHRUSTED
OUTTHRUSTING
OUTTHRUSTS
OUTTONGUED
OUTTONGUES
OUTTONGUING
OUTTOPPING
OUTTOWERED
OUTTOWERING
OUTTRADING
OUTTRAVELED
OUTTRAVELING
OUTTRAVELLED
OUTTRAVELLING
OUTTRAVELS
OUTTRICKED
OUTTRICKING
OUTTROTTED
OUTTROTTING
OUTTRUMPED
OUTTRUMPING
OUTVALUING
OUTVAUNTED
OUTVAUNTING
OUTVENOMED
OUTVENOMING
OUTVILLAIN
OUTVILLAINED
OUTVILLAINING
OUTVILLAINS
OUTVOICING

OUTWAITING
OUTWALKING
OUTWARDNESS
OUTWARDNESSES
OUTWARRING
OUTWASTING
OUTWATCHED
OUTWATCHES
OUTWATCHING
OUTWEARIED
OUTWEARIES
OUTWEARING
OUTWEARYING
OUTWEEDING
OUTWEEPING
OUTWEIGHED
OUTWEIGHING
OUTWELLING
OUTWHIRLED
OUTWHIRLING
OUTWICKING
OUTWILLING
OUTWINDING
OUTWINGING
OUTWINNING
OUTWISHING
OUTWITTING
OUTWORKERS
OUTWORKING
OUTWORTHED
OUTWORTHING
OUTWRESTED
OUTWRESTING
OUTWRESTLE
OUTWRESTLED
OUTWRESTLES
OUTWRESTLING
OUTWRITING
OUTWRITTEN
OUTWROUGHT
OUTYELLING
OUTYELPING
OUTYIELDED
OUTYIELDING
OUVIRANDRA
OUVIRANDRAS
OVALBUMINS

OVALNESSES
OVARIECTOMIES
OVARIECTOMISED
OVARIECTOMIZED
OVARIECTOMY
OVARIOTOMIES
OVARIOTOMIST
OVARIOTOMISTS
OVARIOTOMY
OVARITIDES
OVARITISES
OVERABOUND
OVERABOUNDED
OVERABOUNDING
OVERABOUNDS
OVERABSTRACT
OVERABUNDANCE
OVERABUNDANCES
OVERABUNDANT
OVERACCENTUATE
OVERACCENTUATED
OVERACCENTUATES
OVERACHIEVE
OVERACHIEVED
OVERACHIEVEMENT
OVERACHIEVER
OVERACHIEVERS
OVERACHIEVES
OVERACHIEVING
OVERACTING
OVERACTION
OVERACTIONS
OVERACTIVE
OVERACTIVITIES
OVERACTIVITY
OVERADJUSTMENT
OVERADJUSTMENTS
OVERADVERTISE
OVERADVERTISED
OVERADVERTISES
OVERADVERTISING
OVERADVERTIZE
OVERADVERTIZED
OVERADVERTIZES
OVERADVERTIZING
OVERAGGRESSIVE
OVERAMBITIOUS

OVERAMPLIFIED
OVERANALYSE
OVERANALYSED
OVERANALYSES
OVERANALYSING
OVERANALYSIS
OVERANALYTICAL
OVERANALYZE
OVERANALYZED
OVERANALYZES
OVERANALYZING
OVERANXIETIES
OVERANXIETY
OVERANXIOUS
OVERAPPLICATION
OVERARCHED
OVERARCHES
OVERARCHING
OVERARMING
OVERAROUSAL
OVERAROUSALS
OVERARRANGE
OVERARRANGED
OVERARRANGES
OVERARRANGING
OVERARTICULATE
OVERARTICULATED
OVERARTICULATES
OVERASSERT
OVERASSERTED
OVERASSERTING
OVERASSERTION
OVERASSERTIONS
OVERASSERTIVE
OVERASSERTS
OVERASSESSMENT
OVERASSESSMENTS
OVERATTENTION
OVERATTENTIONS
OVERATTENTIVE
OVERBAKING
OVERBALANCE
OVERBALANCED
OVERBALANCES
OVERBALANCING
OVERBEARING
OVERBEARINGLY

O

OVERBEARINGNESS	OVERBRIEFING	OVERCARRIES	OVERCLOUDED	OVERCONFIDENT
OVERBEATEN	OVERBRIEFS	OVERCARRYING	OVERCLOUDING	OVERCONFIDENTLY
OVERBEATING	OVERBRIGHT	OVERCASTED	OVERCLOUDS	OVERCONSCIOUS
OVERBEJEWELED	OVERBRIMMED	OVERCASTING	OVERCLOYED	OVERCONSTRUCT
OVERBETTED	OVERBRIMMING	OVERCASTINGS	OVERCLOYING	OVERCONSTRUCTED
OVERBETTING	OVERBROWED	OVERCATCHES	OVERCLUBBED	OVERCONSTRUCTS
OVERBIDDEN	OVERBROWING	OVERCATCHING	OVERCLUBBING	OVERCONSUME
OVERBIDDER	OVERBROWSE	OVERCAUGHT	OVERCOACHED	OVERCONSUMED
OVERBIDDERS	OVERBROWSED	OVERCAUTION	OVERCOACHES	OVERCONSUMES
OVERBIDDING	OVERBROWSES	OVERCAUTIONS	OVERCOACHING	OVERCONSUMING
OVERBIDDINGS	OVERBROWSING	OVERCAUTIOUS	OVERCOATING	OVERCONSUMPTION
OVERBILLED	OVERBRUTAL	OVERCENTRALISE	OVERCOATINGS	OVERCONTROL
OVERBILLING	OVERBUILDING	OVERCENTRALISED	OVERCOLORED	OVERCONTROLLED
OVERBLANKET	OVERBUILDS	OVERCENTRALISES	OVERCOLORING	OVERCONTROLLING
OVERBLANKETS	OVERBULKED	OVERCENTRALIZE	OVERCOLORS	OVERCONTROLS
OVERBLEACH	OVERBULKING	OVERCENTRALIZED	OVERCOLOUR	OVERCOOKED
OVERBLEACHED	OVERBURDEN	OVERCENTRALIZES	OVERCOLOURED	OVERCOOKING
OVERBLEACHES	OVERBURDENED	OVERCHARGE	OVERCOLOURING	OVERCOOLED
OVERBLEACHING	OVERBURDENING	OVERCHARGED	OVERCOLOURS	OVERCOOLING
OVERBLOUSE	OVERBURDENS	OVERCHARGES	OVERCOMERS	OVERCORRECT
OVERBLOUSES	OVERBURDENSOME	OVERCHARGING	OVERCOMING	OVERCORRECTED
OVERBLOWING	OVERBURNED	OVERCHECKS	OVERCOMMIT	OVERCORRECTING
OVERBOILED	OVERBURNING	OVERCHILLED	OVERCOMMITMENT	OVERCORRECTION
OVERBOILING	OVERBURTHEN	OVERCHILLING	OVERCOMMITMENTS	OVERCORRECTIONS
OVERBOLDLY	OVERBURTHENED	OVERCHILLS	OVERCOMMITS	OVERCORRECTS
OVERBOOKED	OVERBURTHENING	OVERCIVILISED	OVERCOMMITTED	OVERCOUNTED
OVERBOOKING	OVERBURTHENS	OVERCIVILIZED	OVERCOMMITTING	OVERCOUNTING
OVERBORROW	OVERBUSIED	OVERCLAIMED	OVERCOMMUNICATE	OVERCOUNTS
OVERBORROWED	OVERBUSIES	OVERCLAIMING	OVERCOMPENSATE	OVERCOVERED
OVERBORROWING	OVERBUSYING	OVERCLAIMS	OVERCOMPENSATED	OVERCOVERING
OVERBORROWS	OVERBUYING	OVERCLASSES	OVERCOMPENSATES	OVERCOVERS
OVERBOUGHT	OVERCALLED	OVERCLASSIFIED	OVERCOMPLEX	OVERCRAMMED
OVERBOUNDED	OVERCALLING	OVERCLASSIFIES	OVERCOMPLIANCE	OVERCRAMMING
OVERBOUNDING	OVERCANOPIED	OVERCLASSIFY	OVERCOMPLIANCES	OVERCRAWED
OVERBOUNDS	OVERCANOPIES	OVERCLASSIFYING	OVERCOMPLICATE	OVERCRAWING
OVERBRAKED	OVERCANOPY	OVERCLEANED	OVERCOMPLICATED	OVERCREDULITIES
OVERBRAKES	OVERCANOPYING	OVERCLEANING	OVERCOMPLICATES	OVERCREDULITY
OVERBRAKING	OVERCAPACITIES	OVERCLEANS	OVERCOMPRESS	OVERCREDULOUS
OVERBREATHING	OVERCAPACITY	OVERCLEARED	OVERCOMPRESSED	OVERCRITICAL
OVERBREATHINGS	OVERCAPITALISED	OVERCLEARING	OVERCOMPRESSES	OVERCROPPED
OVERBREEDING	OVERCAPITALISES	OVERCLEARS	OVERCOMPRESSING	OVERCROPPING
OVERBREEDS	OVERCAPITALISE	OVERCLOCKED	OVERCONCERN	OVERCROWDED
OVERBRIDGE	OVERCAPITALIZE	OVERCLOCKER	OVERCONCERNED	OVERCROWDING
OVERBRIDGED	OVERCAPITALIZED	OVERCLOCKERS	OVERCONCERNING	OVERCROWDINGS
OVERBRIDGES	OVERCAPITALIZES	OVERCLOCKING	OVERCONCERNS	OVERCROWDS
OVERBRIDGING	OVERCAREFUL	OVERCLOCKINGS	OVERCONFIDENCE	OVERCROWED
OVERBRIEFED	OVERCARRIED	OVERCLOCKS	OVERCONFIDENCES	OVERCROWING

O

OVERCULTIVATION	OVERDOSAGE	OVERELABORATING	OVEREXCITE	OVERFALLEN
OVERCURING	OVERDOSAGES	OVERELABORATION	OVEREXCITED	OVERFALLING
OVERCUTTING	OVERDOSING	OVEREMBELLISH	OVEREXCITES	OVERFAMILIAR
OVERDARING	OVERDRAFTS	OVEREMBELLISHED	OVEREXCITING	OVERFAMILIARITY
OVERDECKED	OVERDRAMATIC	OVEREMBELLISHES	OVEREXERCISE	OVERFASTIDIOUS
OVERDECKING	OVERDRAMATISE	OVEREMOTED	OVEREXERCISED	OVERFATIGUE
OVERDECORATE	OVERDRAMATISED	OVEREMOTES	OVEREXERCISES	OVERFATIGUED
OVERDECORATED	OVERDRAMATISES	OVEREMOTING	OVEREXERCISING	OVERFATIGUES
OVERDECORATES	OVERDRAMATISING	OVEREMOTIONAL	OVEREXERTED	OVERFAVORED
OVERDECORATING	OVERDRAMATIZE	OVEREMPHASES	OVEREXERTING	OVERFAVORING
OVERDECORATION	OVERDRAMATIZED	OVEREMPHASIS	OVEREXERTION	OVERFAVORS
OVERDECORATIONS	OVERDRAMATIZES	OVEREMPHASISE	OVEREXERTIONS	OVERFEARED
OVERDEMANDING	OVERDRAMATIZING	OVEREMPHASISED	OVEREXERTS	OVERFEARING
OVERDEPENDENCE	OVERDRAUGHT	OVEREMPHASISES	OVEREXPAND	OVERFEEDING
OVERDEPENDENCES	OVERDRAUGHTS	OVEREMPHASISING	OVEREXPANDED	OVERFERTILISE
OVERDEPENDENT	OVERDRAWING	OVEREMPHASIZE	OVEREXPANDING	OVERFERTILISED
OVERDESIGN	OVERDRESSED	OVEREMPHASIZED	OVEREXPANDS	OVERFERTILISES
OVERDESIGNED	OVERDRESSES	OVEREMPHASIZES	OVEREXPANSION	OVERFERTILISING
OVERDESIGNING	OVERDRESSING	OVEREMPHASIZING	OVEREXPANSIONS	OVERFERTILIZE
OVERDESIGNS	OVERDRINKING	OVEREMPHATIC	OVEREXPECTATION	OVERFERTILIZED
OVERDETERMINED	OVERDRINKS	OVERENAMORED	OVEREXPLAIN	OVERFERTILIZES
OVERDEVELOP	OVERDRIVEN	OVERENCOURAGE	OVEREXPLAINED	OVERFERTILIZING
OVERDEVELOPED	OVERDRIVES	OVERENCOURAGED	OVEREXPLAINING	OVERFILLED
OVERDEVELOPING	OVERDRIVING	OVERENCOURAGES	OVEREXPLAINS	OVERFILLING
OVERDEVELOPMENT	OVERDRYING	OVERENCOURAGING	OVEREXPLICIT	OVERFINENESS
OVERDEVELOPS	OVERDUBBED	OVERENERGETIC	OVEREXPLOIT	OVERFINENESSES
OVERDEVIATE	OVERDUBBING	OVERENGINEER	OVEREXPLOITED	OVERFINISHED
OVERDEVIATED	OVERDUSTED	OVERENGINEERED	OVEREXPLOITING	OVERFISHED
OVERDEVIATES	OVERDUSTING	OVERENGINEERING	OVEREXPLOITS	OVERFISHES
OVERDEVIATING	OVERDYEING	OVERENGINEERS	OVEREXPOSE	OVERFISHING
OVERDIRECT	OVEREAGERNESS	OVERENROLLED	OVEREXPOSED	OVERFLIGHT
OVERDIRECTED	OVEREAGERNESSES	OVERENTERTAINED	OVEREXPOSES	OVERFLIGHTS
OVERDIRECTING	OVEREARNEST	OVERENTHUSIASM	OVEREXPOSING	OVERFLOODED
OVERDIRECTS	OVEREATERS	OVERENTHUSIASMS	OVEREXPOSURE	OVERFLOODING
OVERDISCOUNT	OVEREATING	OVEREQUIPPED	OVEREXPOSURES	OVERFLOODS
OVERDISCOUNTED	OVEREDITED	OVERESTIMATE	OVEREXTEND	OVERFLOURISH
OVERDISCOUNTING	OVEREDITING	OVERESTIMATED	OVEREXTENDED	OVERFLOURISHED
OVERDISCOUNTS	OVEREDUCATE	OVERESTIMATES	OVEREXTENDING	OVERFLOURISHES
OVERDIVERSITIES	OVEREDUCATED	OVERESTIMATING	OVEREXTENDS	OVERFLOURISHING
OVERDIVERSITY	OVEREDUCATES	OVERESTIMATION	OVEREXTENSION	OVERFLOWED
OVERDOCUMENT	OVEREDUCATING	OVERESTIMATIONS	OVEREXTENSIONS	OVERFLOWING
OVERDOCUMENTED	OVEREDUCATION	OVEREVALUATION	OVEREXTRACTION	OVERFLOWINGLY
OVERDOCUMENTING	OVEREDUCATIONS	OVEREVALUATIONS	OVEREXTRACTIONS	OVERFLOWINGS
OVERDOCUMENTS	OVEREGGING	OVEREXAGGERATE	OVEREXTRAVAGANT	OVERFLUSHES
OVERDOMINANCE	OVERELABORATE	OVEREXAGGERATED	OVEREXUBERANT	OVERFLYING
OVERDOMINANCES	OVERELABORATED	OVEREXAGGERATES	OVEREYEING	OVERFOCUSED
OVERDOMINANT	OVERELABORATES	OVEREXCITABLE	OVERFACILE	OVERFOCUSES

O

OVERFOCUSING	OVERGILDING	OVERGREEDY	OVERHONORS	OVERINSURE
OVERFOCUSSED	OVERGIRDED	OVERGREENED	OVERHOPING	OVERINSURED
OVERFOCUSSES	OVERGIRDING	OVERGREENING	OVERHUNTED	OVERINSURES
OVERFOCUSSING	OVERGIVING	OVERGREENS	OVERHUNTING	OVERINSURING
OVERFOLDED	OVERGLAMORISE	OVERGROUND	OVERHUNTINGS	OVERINTENSE
OVERFOLDING	OVERGLAMORISED	OVERGROWING	OVERHYPING	OVERINTENSITIES
OVERFONDLY	OVERGLAMORISES	OVERGROWTH	OVERIDEALISE	OVERINTENSITY
OVERFONDNESS	OVERGLAMORISING	OVERGROWTHS	OVERIDEALISED	OVERINVESTMENT
OVERFONDNESSES	OVERGLAMORIZE	OVERHAILED	OVERIDEALISES	OVERINVESTMENTS
OVERFORWARD	OVERGLAMORIZED	OVERHAILES	OVERIDEALISING	OVERISSUANCE
OVERFORWARDNESS	OVERGLAMORIZES	OVERHAILING	OVERIDEALIZE	OVERISSUANCES
OVERFRAUGHT	OVERGLAMORIZING	OVERHALING	OVERIDEALIZED	OVERISSUED
OVERFREEDOM	OVERGLANCE	OVERHANDED	OVERIDEALIZES	OVERISSUES
OVERFREEDOMS	OVERGLANCED	OVERHANDING	OVERIDEALIZING	OVERISSUING
OVERFREELY	OVERGLANCES	OVERHANDLE	OVERIDENTIFIED	OVERJOYING
OVERFREIGHT	OVERGLANCING	OVERHANDLED	OVERIDENTIFIES	OVERJUMPED
OVERFREIGHTING	OVERGLAZED	OVERHANDLES	OVERIDENTIFY	OVERJUMPING
OVERFREIGHTS	OVERGLAZES	OVERHANDLING	OVERIDENTIFYING	OVERKEEPING
OVERFULFILL	OVERGLAZING	OVERHANGING	OVERIMAGINATIVE	OVERKILLED
OVERFULFILLED	OVERGLOOMED	OVERHARVEST	OVERIMPRESS	OVERKILLING
OVERFULFILLING	OVERGLOOMING	OVERHARVESTED	OVERIMPRESSED	OVERKINDNESS
OVERFULFILLS	OVERGLOOMS	OVERHARVESTING	OVERIMPRESSES	OVERKINDNESSES
OVERFULLNESS	OVERGOADED	OVERHARVESTS	OVERIMPRESSING	OVERLABORED
OVERFULLNESSES	OVERGOADING	OVERHASTES	OVERINCLINED	OVERLABORING
OVERFULNESS	OVERGOINGS	OVERHASTILY	OVERINDULGE	OVERLABORS
OVERFULNESSES	OVERGORGED	OVERHASTINESS	OVERINDULGED	OVERLABOUR
OVERFUNDED	OVERGORGES	OVERHASTINESSES	OVERINDULGENCE	OVERLABOURED
OVERFUNDING	OVERGORGING	OVERHATING	OVERINDULGENCES	OVERLABOURING
OVERFUNDINGS	OVERGOVERN	OVERHAULED	OVERINDULGENT	OVERLABOURS
OVERGALLED	OVERGOVERNED	OVERHAULING	OVERINDULGES	OVERLADING
OVERGALLING	OVERGOVERNING	OVERHEAPED	OVERINDULGING	OVERLANDED
OVERGANGING	OVERGOVERNS	OVERHEAPING	OVERINFLATE	OVERLANDER
OVERGARMENT	OVERGRADED	OVERHEARING	OVERINFLATED	OVERLANDERS
OVERGARMENTS	OVERGRADES	OVERHEATED	OVERINFLATES	OVERLANDING
OVERGEARED	OVERGRADING	OVERHEATING	OVERINFLATING	OVERLAPPED
OVERGEARING	OVERGRAINED	OVERHEATINGS	OVERINFLATION	OVERLAPPING
OVERGENERALISE	OVERGRAINER	OVERHENTING	OVERINFLATIONS	OVERLARDED
OVERGENERALISED	OVERGRAINERS	OVERHITTING	OVERINFORM	OVERLARDING
OVERGENERALISES	OVERGRAINING	OVERHOLDING	OVERINFORMED	OVERLAUNCH
OVERGENERALIZE	OVERGRAINS	OVERHOMOGENISE	OVERINFORMING	OVERLAUNCHED
OVERGENERALIZED	OVERGRASSED	OVERHOMOGENISED	OVERINFORMS	OVERLAUNCHES
OVERGENERALIZES	OVERGRASSES	OVERHOMOGENISES	OVERINGENIOUS	OVERLAUNCHING
OVERGENEROSITY	OVERGRASSING	OVERHOMOGENIZE	OVERINGENUITIES	OVERLAVISH
OVERGENEROUS	OVERGRAZED	OVERHOMOGENIZED	OVERINGENUITY	OVERLAYING
OVERGENEROUSLY	OVERGRAZES	OVERHOMOGENIZES	OVERINSISTENT	OVERLAYINGS
OVERGETTING	OVERGRAZING	OVERHONORED	OVERINSURANCE	OVERLEAPED
OVERGILDED	OVERGRAZINGS	OVERHONORING	OVERINSURANCES	OVERLEAPING

O

OVERLEARNED
OVERLEARNING
OVERLEARNS
OVERLEARNT
OVERLEATHER
OVERLEATHERS
OVERLEAVEN
OVERLEAVENED
OVERLEAVENING
OVERLEAVENS
OVERLENDING
OVERLENGTH
OVERLENGTHEN
OVERLENGTHENED
OVERLENGTHENING
OVERLENGTHENS
OVERLENGTHS
OVERLETTING
OVERLIGHTED
OVERLIGHTING
OVERLIGHTS
OVERLITERAL
OVERLITERARY
OVERLIVING
OVERLOADED
OVERLOADING
OVERLOCKED
OVERLOCKER
OVERLOCKERS
OVERLOCKING
OVERLOCKINGS
OVERLOOKED
OVERLOOKER
OVERLOOKERS
OVERLOOKING
OVERLORDED
OVERLORDING
OVERLORDSHIP
OVERLORDSHIPS
OVERLOVING
OVERMANAGE
OVERMANAGED
OVERMANAGES
OVERMANAGING
OVERMANNED
OVERMANNERED
OVERMANNING

OVERMANTEL
OVERMANTELS
OVERMASTED
OVERMASTER
OVERMASTERED
OVERMASTERING
OVERMASTERS
OVERMASTING
OVERMATCHED
OVERMATCHES
OVERMATCHING
OVERMATTER
OVERMATTERS
OVERMATURE
OVERMATURITIES
OVERMATURITY
OVERMEASURE
OVERMEASURED
OVERMEASURES
OVERMEASURING
OVERMEDICATE
OVERMEDICATED
OVERMEDICATES
OVERMEDICATING
OVERMEDICATION
OVERMEDICATIONS
OVERMELTED
OVERMELTING
OVERMIGHTY
OVERMILKED
OVERMILKING
OVERMINING
OVERMIXING
OVERMODEST
OVERMODESTLY
OVERMOUNTED
OVERMOUNTING
OVERMOUNTS
OVERMUCHES
OVERMULTIPLIED
OVERMULTIPLIES
OVERMULTIPLY
OVERMULTIPLYING
OVERMULTITUDE
OVERMULTITUDED
OVERMULTITUDES
OVERMULTITUDING

OVERMUSCLED
OVERNAMING
OVERNETTED
OVERNETTING
OVERNICELY
OVERNICENESS
OVERNICENESSES
OVERNIGHTED
OVERNIGHTER
OVERNIGHTERS
OVERNIGHTING
OVERNIGHTS
OVERNOURISH
OVERNOURISHED
OVERNOURISHES
OVERNOURISHING
OVERNUTRITION
OVERNUTRITIONS
OVEROBVIOUS
OVEROFFICE
OVEROFFICED
OVEROFFICES
OVEROFFICING
OVEROPERATE
OVEROPERATED
OVEROPERATES
OVEROPERATING
OVEROPINIONATED
OVEROPTIMISM
OVEROPTIMISMS
OVEROPTIMIST
OVEROPTIMISTIC
OVEROPTIMISTS
OVERORCHESTRATE
OVERORGANISE
OVERORGANISED
OVERORGANISES
OVERORGANISING
OVERORGANIZE
OVERORGANIZED
OVERORGANIZES
OVERORGANIZING
OVERORNAMENT
OVERORNAMENTED
OVERORNAMENTING
OVERORNAMENTS
OVERPACKAGE

OVERPACKAGED
OVERPACKAGES
OVERPACKAGING
OVERPACKED
OVERPACKING
OVERPAINTED
OVERPAINTING
OVERPAINTS
OVERPARTED
OVERPARTICULAR
OVERPARTING
OVERPASSED
OVERPASSES
OVERPASSING
OVERPAYING
OVERPAYMENT
OVERPAYMENTS
OVERPEDALED
OVERPEDALING
OVERPEDALLED
OVERPEDALLING
OVERPEDALS
OVERPEERED
OVERPEERING
OVERPEOPLE
OVERPEOPLED
OVERPEOPLES
OVERPEOPLING
OVERPERCHED
OVERPERCHES
OVERPERCHING
OVERPERSUADE
OVERPERSUADED
OVERPERSUADES
OVERPERSUADING
OVERPERSUASION
OVERPERSUASIONS
OVERPICTURE
OVERPICTURED
OVERPICTURES
OVERPICTURING
OVERPITCHED
OVERPITCHES
OVERPITCHING
OVERPLACED
OVERPLAIDED
OVERPLAIDS

OVERPLANNED
OVERPLANNING
OVERPLANTED
OVERPLANTING
OVERPLANTS
OVERPLAYED
OVERPLAYING
OVERPLOTTED
OVERPLOTTING
OVERPLUSES
OVERPLUSSES
OVERPLYING
OVERPOISED
OVERPOISES
OVERPOISING
OVERPOPULATE
OVERPOPULATED
OVERPOPULATES
OVERPOPULATING
OVERPOPULATION
OVERPOPULATIONS
OVERPOSTED
OVERPOSTING
OVERPOTENT
OVERPOWERED
OVERPOWERING
OVERPOWERINGLY
OVERPOWERS
OVERPRAISE
OVERPRAISED
OVERPRAISES
OVERPRAISING
OVERPRECISE
OVERPREPARATION
OVERPREPARE
OVERPREPARED
OVERPREPARES
OVERPREPARING
OVERPRESCRIBE
OVERPRESCRIBED
OVERPRESCRIBES
OVERPRESCRIBING
OVERPRESSED
OVERPRESSES
OVERPRESSING
OVERPRESSURE
OVERPRESSURES

OVERPRICED	OVERRACKING	OVERRESPONDS	OVERSELLING	OVERSLIPPED
OVERPRICES	OVERRAKING	OVERRIDDEN	OVERSENSITIVE	OVERSLIPPING
OVERPRICING	OVERRASHLY	OVERRIDERS	OVERSENSITIVITY	OVERSMOKED
OVERPRINTED	OVERRASHNESS	OVERRIDING	OVERSERIOUS	OVERSMOKES
OVERPRINTING	OVERRASHNESSES	OVERRIPENED	OVERSERIOUSLY	OVERSMOKING
OVERPRINTS	OVERRATING	OVERRIPENESS	OVERSERVICE	OVERSOAKED
OVERPRIVILEGED	OVERRAUGHT	OVERRIPENESSES	OVERSERVICED	OVERSOAKING
OVERPRIZED	OVERREACHED	OVERRIPENING	OVERSERVICES	OVERSOLICITOUS
OVERPRIZES	OVERREACHER	OVERRIPENS	OVERSERVICING	OVERSOWING
OVERPRIZING	OVERREACHERS	OVERROASTED	OVERSETTING	OVERSPECIALISE
OVERPROCESS	OVERREACHES	OVERROASTING	OVERSEWING	OVERSPECIALISED
OVERPROCESSED	OVERREACHING	OVERROASTS	OVERSHADED	OVERSPECIALISES
OVERPROCESSES	OVERREACTED	OVERRUFFED	OVERSHADES	OVERSPECIALIZE
OVERPROCESSING	OVERREACTING	OVERRUFFING	OVERSHADING	OVERSPECIALIZED
OVERPRODUCE	OVERREACTION	OVERRULERS	OVERSHADOW	OVERSPECIALIZES
OVERPRODUCED	OVERREACTIONS	OVERRULING	OVERSHADOWED	OVERSPECULATE
OVERPRODUCES	OVERREACTS	OVERRULINGS	OVERSHADOWING	OVERSPECULATED
OVERPRODUCING	OVERREADING	OVERRUNNER	OVERSHADOWS	OVERSPECULATES
OVERPRODUCTION	OVERRECKON	OVERRUNNERS	OVERSHINES	OVERSPECULATING
OVERPRODUCTIONS	OVERRECKONED	OVERRUNNING	OVERSHINING	OVERSPECULATION
OVERPROGRAM	OVERRECKONING	OVERSAILED	OVERSHIRTS	OVERSPENDER
OVERPROGRAMED	OVERRECKONS	OVERSAILING	OVERSHOOTING	OVERSPENDERS
OVERPROGRAMING	OVERREDDED	OVERSALTED	OVERSHOOTS	OVERSPENDING
OVERPROGRAMMED	OVERREDDING	OVERSALTING	OVERSHOWER	OVERSPENDS
OVERPROGRAMMING	OVERREFINE	OVERSANGUINE	OVERSHOWERED	OVERSPICED
OVERPROGRAMS	OVERREFINED	OVERSATURATE	OVERSHOWERING	OVERSPICES
OVERPROMISE	OVERREFINEMENT	OVERSATURATED	OVERSHOWERS	OVERSPICING
OVERPROMISED	OVERREFINEMENTS	OVERSATURATES	OVERSIGHTS	OVERSPILLED
OVERPROMISES	OVERREFINES	OVERSATURATING	OVERSIMPLE	OVERSPILLING
OVERPROMISING	OVERREFINING	OVERSATURATION	OVERSIMPLIFIED	OVERSPILLS
OVERPROMOTE	OVERREGULATE	OVERSATURATIONS	OVERSIMPLIFIES	OVERSPREAD
OVERPROMOTED	OVERREGULATED	OVERSAUCED	OVERSIMPLIFY	OVERSPREADING
OVERPROMOTES	OVERREGULATES	OVERSAUCES	OVERSIMPLIFYING	OVERSPREADS
OVERPROMOTING	OVERREGULATING	OVERSAUCING	OVERSIMPLISTIC	OVERSTABILITIES
OVERPROPORTION	OVERREGULATION	OVERSAVING	OVERSIMPLY	OVERSTABILITY
OVERPROPORTIONS	OVERREGULATIONS	OVERSCALED	OVERSIZING	OVERSTAFFED
OVERPROTECT	OVERRELIANCE	OVERSCHUTCHT	OVERSKIPPED	OVERSTAFFING
OVERPROTECTED	OVERRELIANCES	OVERSCORED	OVERSKIPPING	OVERSTAFFS
OVERPROTECTING	OVERRENNING	OVERSCORES	OVERSKIRTS	OVERSTAINED
OVERPROTECTION	OVERREPORT	OVERSCORING	OVERSLAUGH	OVERSTAINING
OVERPROTECTIONS	OVERREPORTED	OVERSCRUPULOUS	OVERSLAUGHED	OVERSTAINS
OVERPROTECTIVE	OVERREPORTING	OVERSCUTCHED	OVERSLAUGHING	OVERSTANDING
OVERPROTECTS	OVERREPORTS	OVERSECRETION	OVERSLAUGHS	OVERSTANDS
OVERPUMPED	OVERREPRESENTED	OVERSECRETIONS	OVERSLEEPING	OVERSTARED
OVERPUMPING	OVERRESPOND	OVERSEEDED	OVERSLEEPS	OVERSTARES
OVERQUALIFIED	OVERRESPONDED	OVERSEEDING	OVERSLEEVE	OVERSTARING
OVERRACKED	OVERRESPONDING	OVERSEEING	OVERSLEEVES	OVERSTATED

O

OVERSTATEMENT
OVERSTATEMENTS
OVERSTATES
OVERSTATING
OVERSTAYED
OVERSTAYER
OVERSTAYERS
OVERSTAYING
OVERSTEERED
OVERSTEERING
OVERSTEERS
OVERSTEPPED
OVERSTEPPING
OVERSTIMULATE
OVERSTIMULATED
OVERSTIMULATES
OVERSTIMULATING
OVERSTIMULATION
OVERSTINKING
OVERSTINKS
OVERSTIRRED
OVERSTIRRING
OVERSTOCKED
OVERSTOCKING
OVERSTOCKS
OVERSTORIES
OVERSTRAIN
OVERSTRAINED
OVERSTRAINING
OVERSTRAINS
OVERSTRESS
OVERSTRESSED
OVERSTRESSES
OVERSTRESSING
OVERSTRETCH
OVERSTRETCHED
OVERSTRETCHES
OVERSTRETCHING
OVERSTREWED
OVERSTREWING
OVERSTREWN
OVERSTREWS
OVERSTRIDDEN
OVERSTRIDE
OVERSTRIDES
OVERSTRIDING
OVERSTRIKE

OVERSTRIKES
OVERSTRIKING
OVERSTRODE
OVERSTRONG
OVERSTROOKE
OVERSTRUCK
OVERSTRUCTURED
OVERSTRUNG
OVERSTUDIED
OVERSTUDIES
OVERSTUDYING
OVERSTUFFED
OVERSTUFFING
OVERSTUFFS
OVERSUBSCRIBE
OVERSUBSCRIBED
OVERSUBSCRIBES
OVERSUBSCRIBING
OVERSUBTLE
OVERSUBTLETIES
OVERSUBTLETY
OVERSUDSED
OVERSUDSES
OVERSUDSING
OVERSUPPED
OVERSUPPING
OVERSUPPLIED
OVERSUPPLIES
OVERSUPPLY
OVERSUPPLYING
OVERSUSPICIOUS
OVERSWAYED
OVERSWAYING
OVERSWEARING
OVERSWEARS
OVERSWEETEN
OVERSWEETENED
OVERSWEETENING
OVERSWEETENS
OVERSWEETNESS
OVERSWEETNESSES
OVERSWELLED
OVERSWELLING
OVERSWELLS
OVERSWIMMING
OVERSWINGING
OVERSWINGS

OVERSWOLLEN
OVERTAKING
OVERTALKATIVE
OVERTALKED
OVERTALKING
OVERTASKED
OVERTASKING
OVERTAUGHT
OVERTAXATION
OVERTAXATIONS
OVERTAXING
OVERTEACHES
OVERTEACHING
OVERTEDIOUS
OVERTEEMED
OVERTEEMING
OVERTHINKING
OVERTHINKS
OVERTHOUGHT
OVERTHROWER
OVERTHROWERS
OVERTHROWING
OVERTHROWN
OVERTHROWS
OVERTHRUST
OVERTHRUSTS
OVERTHWART
OVERTHWARTED
OVERTHWARTING
OVERTHWARTS
OVERTIGHTEN
OVERTIGHTENED
OVERTIGHTENING
OVERTIGHTENS
OVERTIMELY
OVERTIMERS
OVERTIMING
OVERTIPPED
OVERTIPPING
OVERTIRING
OVERTNESSES
OVERTOILED
OVERTOILING
OVERTOPPED
OVERTOPPING
OVERTOPPINGS
OVERTOWERED

OVERTOWERING
OVERTOWERS
OVERTRADED
OVERTRADES
OVERTRADING
OVERTRADINGS
OVERTRAINED
OVERTRAINING
OVERTRAINS
OVERTREATED
OVERTREATING
OVERTREATMENT
OVERTREATMENTS
OVERTREATS
OVERTRICKS
OVERTRIMMED
OVERTRIMMING
OVERTRIPPED
OVERTRIPPING
OVERTRUMPED
OVERTRUMPING
OVERTRUMPS
OVERTRUSTED
OVERTRUSTING
OVERTRUSTS
OVERTURING
OVERTURNED
OVERTURNER
OVERTURNERS
OVERTURNING
OVERTYPING
OVERURGING
OVERUTILISATION
OVERUTILISE
OVERUTILISED
OVERUTILISES
OVERUTILISING
OVERUTILIZATION
OVERUTILIZE
OVERUTILIZED
OVERUTILIZES
OVERUTILIZING
OVERVALUATION
OVERVALUATIONS
OVERVALUED
OVERVALUES
OVERVALUING

OVERVEILED
OVERVEILING
OVERVIOLENT
OVERVOLTAGE
OVERVOLTAGES
OVERVOTING
OVERWARMED
OVERWARMING
OVERWASHES
OVERWATCHED
OVERWATCHES
OVERWATCHING
OVERWATERED
OVERWATERING
OVERWATERS
OVERWEARIED
OVERWEARIES
OVERWEARING
OVERWEARYING
OVERWEATHER
OVERWEATHERED
OVERWEATHERING
OVERWEATHERS
OVERWEENED
OVERWEENING
OVERWEENINGLY
OVERWEENINGNESS
OVERWEENINGS
OVERWEIGHED
OVERWEIGHING
OVERWEIGHS
OVERWEIGHT
OVERWEIGHTED
OVERWEIGHTING
OVERWEIGHTS
OVERWETTED
OVERWETTING
OVERWHELMED
OVERWHELMING
OVERWHELMINGLY
OVERWHELMINGS
OVERWHELMS
OVERWINDING
OVERWINGED
OVERWINGING
OVERWINTER
OVERWINTERED

OVERWINTERING	OVERZEALOUSNESS	OXALACETATES	OXYGENASES	OXYMORONICALLY
OVERWINTERS	OVIPARITIES	OXALOACETATE	OXYGENATED	OXYPHENBUTAZONE
OVERWISELY	OVIPAROUSLY	OXALOACETATES	OXYGENATES	OXYRHYNCHUS
OVERWITHHELD	OVIPOSITED	OXIDATIONAL	OXYGENATING	OXYRHYNCHUSES
OVERWITHHOLD	OVIPOSITING	OXIDATIONS	OXYGENATION	OXYSULPHIDE
OVERWITHHOLDING	OVIPOSITION	OXIDATIVELY	OXYGENATIONS	OXYSULPHIDES
OVERWITHHOLDS	OVIPOSITIONAL	OXIDIMETRIC	OXYGENATOR	OXYTETRACYCLINE
OVERWORKED	OVIPOSITIONS	OXIDIMETRIES	OXYGENATORS	OXYURIASES
OVERWORKING	OVIPOSITOR	OXIDIMETRY	OXYGENISED	OXYURIASIS
OVERWRAPPED	OVIPOSITORS	OXIDISABLE	OXYGENISER	OYSTERCATCHER
OVERWRAPPING	OVIRAPTORS	OXIDISATION	OXYGENISERS	OYSTERCATCHERS
OVERWRESTED	OVOVIVIPARITIES	OXIDISATIONS	OXYGENISES	OYSTERINGS
OVERWRESTING	OVOVIVIPARITY	OXIDIZABLE	OXYGENISING	OZOCERITES
OVERWRESTLE	OVOVIVIPAROUS	OXIDIZATION	OXYGENIZED	OZOKERITES
OVERWRESTLED	OVOVIVIPAROUSLY	OXIDIZATIONS	OXYGENIZER	OZONATIONS
OVERWRESTLES	OVULATIONS	OXIDOREDUCTASE	OXYGENIZERS	OZONIFEROUS
OVERWRESTLING	OVULIFEROUS	OXIDOREDUCTASES	OXYGENIZES	OZONISATION
OVERWRESTS	OWERLOUPEN	OXIMETRIES	OXYGENIZING	OZONISATIONS
OVERWRITES	OWERLOUPING	OXYACETYLENE	OXYGENLESS	OZONIZATION
OVERWRITING	OWERLOUPIT	OXYACETYLENES	OXYHAEMOGLOBIN	OZONIZATIONS
OVERWRITTEN	OWLISHNESS	OXYCEPHALIC	OXYHAEMOGLOBINS	OZONOLYSES
OVERWROUGHT	OWLISHNESSES	OXYCEPHALIES	OXYHEMOGLOBIN	OZONOLYSIS
OVERYEARED	OWNERSHIPS	OXYCEPHALOUS	OXYHEMOGLOBINS	OZONOSPHERE
OVERYEARING	OXACILLINS	OXYCEPHALY	OXYHYDROGEN	OZONOSPHERES
OVERZEALOUS	OXALACETATE	OXYCODONES	OXYMORONIC	

O

P

PACEMAKERS
PACEMAKING
PACEMAKINGS
PACESETTER
PACESETTERS
PACESETTING
PACHYCARPOUS
PACHYDACTYL
PACHYDACTYLOUS
PACHYDERMAL
PACHYDERMATOUS
PACHYDERMIA
PACHYDERMIAS
PACHYDERMIC
PACHYDERMOUS
PACHYDERMS
PACHYMENINGITIS
PACHYMETER
PACHYMETERS
PACHYSANDRA
PACHYSANDRAS
PACHYTENES
PACIFIABLE
PACIFICALLY
PACIFICATE
PACIFICATED
PACIFICATES
PACIFICATING
PACIFICATION
PACIFICATIONS
PACIFICATOR
PACIFICATORS
PACIFICATORY
PACIFICISM
PACIFICISMS
PACIFICIST
PACIFICISTS
PACIFISTIC
PACIFISTICALLY
PACKABILITIES
PACKABILITY
PACKAGINGS
PACKBOARDS
PACKCLOTHS
PACKFRAMES

PACKHORSES
PACKINGHOUSE
PACKINGHOUSES
PACKNESSES
PACKSADDLE
PACKSADDLES
PACKSHEETS
PACKSTAFFS
PACKTHREAD
PACKTHREADS
PACLITAXEL
PACLITAXELS
PACTIONING
PADDLEBALL
PADDLEBALLS
PADDLEBOARD
PADDLEBOARDS
PADDLEBOAT
PADDLEBOATS
PADDLEFISH
PADDLEFISHES
PADDOCKING
PADDYMELON
PADDYMELONS
PADDYWACKED
PADDYWACKING
PADDYWACKS
PADDYWHACK
PADDYWHACKS
PADEMELONS
PADEREROES
PADLOCKING
PADRONISMS
PADYMELONS
PAEDAGOGIC
PAEDAGOGUE
PAEDAGOGUES
PAEDERASTIC
PAEDERASTIES
PAEDERASTS
PAEDERASTY
PAEDEUTICS
PAEDIATRIC
PAEDIATRICIAN
PAEDIATRICIANS

PAEDIATRICS
PAEDIATRIES
PAEDIATRIST
PAEDIATRISTS
PAEDOBAPTISM
PAEDOBAPTISMS
PAEDOBAPTIST
PAEDOBAPTISTS
PAEDODONTIC
PAEDODONTICS
PAEDOGENESES
PAEDOGENESIS
PAEDOGENETIC
PAEDOGENIC
PAEDOLOGICAL
PAEDOLOGIES
PAEDOLOGIST
PAEDOLOGISTS
PAEDOMORPHIC
PAEDOMORPHISM
PAEDOMORPHISMS
PAEDOMORPHOSES
PAEDOMORPHOSIS
PAEDOPHILE
PAEDOPHILES
PAEDOPHILIA
PAEDOPHILIAC
PAEDOPHILIACS
PAEDOPHILIAS
PAEDOPHILIC
PAEDOPHILICS
PAEDOTRIBE
PAEDOTRIBES
PAEDOTROPHIES
PAEDOTROPHY
PAGANISATION
PAGANISATIONS
PAGANISERS
PAGANISING
PAGANISTIC
PAGANISTICALLY
PAGANIZATION
PAGANIZATIONS
PAGANIZERS
PAGANIZING

PAGEANTRIES
PAGINATING
PAGINATION
PAGINATIONS
PAIDEUTICS
PAILLASSES
PAILLETTES
PAINFULLER
PAINFULLEST
PAINFULNESS
PAINFULNESSES
PAINKILLER
PAINKILLERS
PAINKILLING
PAINLESSLY
PAINLESSNESS
PAINLESSNESSES
PAINSTAKER
PAINSTAKERS
PAINSTAKING
PAINSTAKINGLY
PAINSTAKINGNESS
PAINSTAKINGS
PAINTBALLS
PAINTBOXES
PAINTBRUSH
PAINTBRUSHES
PAINTERLINESS
PAINTERLINESSES
PAINTINESS
PAINTINESSES
PAINTRESSES
PAINTWORKS
PAKIRIKIRI
PAKIRIKIRIS
PALAEANTHROPIC
PALAEBIOLOGIES
PALAEBIOLOGIST
PALAEBIOLOGISTS
PALAEBIOLOGY
PALAEETHNOLOGY
PALAEOANTHROPIC
PALAEOBIOLOGIC
PALAEOBIOLOGIES
PALAEOBIOLOGIST

PALAEOBIOLOGY
PALAEOBOTANIC
PALAEOBOTANICAL
PALAEOBOTANIES
PALAEOBOTANIST
PALAEOBOTANISTS
PALAEOBOTANY
PALAEOCLIMATE
PALAEOCLIMATES
PALAEOCLIMATIC
PALAEOCRYSTIC
PALAEOCURRENT
PALAEOCURRENTS
PALAEOECOLOGIC
PALAEOECOLOGIES
PALAEOECOLOGIST
PALAEOECOLOGY
PALAEOETHNOLOGY
PALAEOGAEA
PALAEOGAEAS
PALAEOGEOGRAPHY
PALAEOGRAPHER
PALAEOGRAPHERS
PALAEOGRAPHIC
PALAEOGRAPHICAL
PALAEOGRAPHIES
PALAEOGRAPHIST
PALAEOGRAPHISTS
PALAEOGRAPHY
PALAEOLIMNOLOGY
PALAEOLITH
PALAEOLITHIC
PALAEOLITHS
PALAEOMAGNETIC
PALAEOMAGNETISM
PALAEONTOGRAPHY
PALAEONTOLOGIES
PALAEONTOLOGIST
PALAEONTOLOGY
PALAEOPATHOLOGY
PALAEOPEDOLOGY
PALAEOPHYTOLOGY
PALAEOTYPE
PALAEOTYPES
PALAEOTYPIC

PALAEOZOOLOGIES	PALEOBOTANICAL	PALINDROME	PALLIAMENT	PALSGRAVINE
PALAEOZOOLOGIST	PALEOBOTANIES	PALINDROMES	PALLIAMENTS	PALSGRAVINES
PALAEOZOOLOGY	PALEOBOTANIST	PALINDROMIC	PALLIASSES	PALTRINESS
PALAESTRAE	PALEOBOTANISTS	PALINDROMICAL	PALLIATING	PALTRINESSES
PALAESTRAL	PALEOBOTANY	PALINDROMIST	PALLIATION	PALUDAMENT
PALAESTRAS	PALEOECOLOGIC	PALINDROMISTS	PALLIATIONS	PALUDAMENTA
PALAESTRIC	PALEOECOLOGICAL	PALINGENESES	PALLIATIVE	PALUDAMENTS
PALAESTRICAL	PALEOECOLOGIES	PALINGENESIA	PALLIATIVELY	PALUDAMENTUM
PALAFITTES	PALEOECOLOGIST	PALINGENESIAS	PALLIATIVES	PALUDAMENTUMS
PALAGONITE	PALEOECOLOGISTS	PALINGENESIES	PALLIATORS	PALUDICOLOUS
PALAGONITES	PALEOECOLOGY	PALINGENESIS	PALLIATORY	PALUDINOUS
PALAMPORES	PALEOGEOGRAPHIC	PALINGENESIST	PALLIDITIES	PALUSTRIAN
PALANKEENS	PALEOGEOGRAPHY	PALINGENESISTS	PALLIDNESS	PALUSTRINE
PALANQUINS	PALEOGRAPHER	PALINGENESY	PALLIDNESSES	PALYNOLOGIC
PALATABILITIES	PALEOGRAPHERS	PALINGENETIC	PALMACEOUS	PALYNOLOGICAL
PALATABILITY	PALEOGRAPHIC	PALINGENETICAL	PALMATIFID	PALYNOLOGICALLY
PALATABLENESS	PALEOGRAPHICAL	PALINODIES	PALMATIONS	PALYNOLOGIES
PALATABLENESSES	PALEOGRAPHIES	PALINOPIAS	PALMATIPARTITE	PALYNOLOGIST
PALATALISATION	PALEOGRAPHY	PALINOPSIA	PALMATISECT	PALYNOLOGISTS
PALATALISATIONS	PALEOLITHS	PALINOPSIAS	PALMCORDER	PALYNOLOGY
PALATALISE	PALEOLOGIES	PALISADING	PALMCORDERS	PAMPELMOOSE
PALATALISED	PALEOMAGNETIC	PALISADOED	PALMERWORM	PAMPELMOOSES
PALATALISES	PALEOMAGNETISM	PALISADOES	PALMERWORMS	PAMPELMOUSE
PALATALISING	PALEOMAGNETISMS	PALISADOING	PALMETTOES	PAMPELMOUSES
PALATALIZATION	PALEOMAGNETIST	PALISANDER	PALMHOUSES	PAMPEREDNESS
PALATALIZATIONS	PALEOMAGNETISTS	PALISANDERS	PALMIFICATION	PAMPEREDNESSES
PALATALIZE	PALEONTOLOGIC	PALLADIOUS	PALMIFICATIONS	PAMPHLETEER
PALATALIZED	PALEONTOLOGICAL	PALLADIUMS	PALMIPEDES	PAMPHLETEERED
PALATALIZES	PALEONTOLOGIES	PALLBEARER	PALMISTERS	PAMPHLETEERING
PALATALIZING	PALEONTOLOGIST	PALLBEARERS	PALMISTRIES	PAMPHLETEERINGS
PALATIALLY	PALEONTOLOGISTS	PALLESCENCE	PALMITATES	PAMPHLETEERS
PALATIALNESS	PALEONTOLOGY	PALLESCENCES	PALOVERDES	PAMPOOTIES
PALATIALNESSES	PALEOPATHOLOGY	PALLESCENT	PALPABILITIES	PANACHAEAS
PALATINATE	PALEOZOOLOGICAL	PALLETISATION	PALPABILITY	PANAESTHESIA
PALATINATES	PALEOZOOLOGIES	PALLETISATIONS	PALPABLENESS	PANAESTHESIAS
PALAVERERS	PALEOZOOLOGIST	PALLETISED	PALPABLENESSES	PANAESTHETISM
PALAVERING	PALEOZOOLOGISTS	PALLETISER	PALPATIONS	PANAESTHETISMS
PALEACEOUS	PALEOZOOLOGY	PALLETISERS	PALPEBRATE	PANARITIUM
PALEMPORES	PALFRENIER	PALLETISES	PALPEBRATED	PANARITIUMS
PALENESSES	PALFRENIERS	PALLETISING	PALPEBRATES	PANARTHRITIS
PALEOBIOLOGIC	PALIFICATION	PALLETIZATION	PALPEBRATING	PANARTHRITISES
PALEOBIOLOGICAL	PALIFICATIONS	PALLETIZATIONS	PALPITATED	PANATELLAS
PALEOBIOLOGIES	PALILALIAS	PALLETIZED	PALPITATES	PANBROILED
PALEOBIOLOGIST	PALILLOGIES	PALLETIZER	PALPITATING	PANBROILING
PALEOBIOLOGISTS	PALIMONIES	PALLETIZERS	PALPITATION	PANCHAYATS
PALEOBIOLOGY	PALIMPSEST	PALLETIZES	PALPITATIONS	PANCHROMATIC
PALEOBOTANIC	PALIMPSESTS	PALLETIZING	PALSGRAVES	PANCHROMATISM

P

PANCHROMATISMS	PANEGYRICALLY	PANICULATELY	PANSOPHISM	PANTISOCRACY
PANCOSMISM	PANEGYRICON	PANIDIOMORPHIC	PANSOPHISMS	PANTISOCRAT
PANCOSMISMS	PANEGYRICS	PANIFICATION	PANSOPHIST	PANTISOCRATIC
PANCRATIAN	PANEGYRIES	PANIFICATIONS	PANSOPHISTS	PANTISOCRATICAL
PANCRATIAST	PANEGYRISE	PANJANDARUM	PANSPERMATIC	PANTISOCRATIST
PANCRATIASTS	PANEGYRISED	PANJANDARUMS	PANSPERMATISM	PANTISOCRATISTS
PANCRATIST	PANEGYRISES	PANJANDRUM	PANSPERMATISMS	PANTISOCRATS
PANCRATISTS	PANEGYRISING	PANJANDRUMS	PANSPERMATIST	PANTOFFLES
PANCRATIUM	PANEGYRIST	PANLEUCOPENIA	PANSPERMATISTS	PANTOGRAPH
PANCRATIUMS	PANEGYRISTS	PANLEUCOPENIAS	PANSPERMIA	PANTOGRAPHER
PANCREASES	PANEGYRIZE	PANLEUKOPENIA	PANSPERMIAS	PANTOGRAPHERS
PANCREATECTOMY	PANEGYRIZED	PANLEUKOPENIAS	PANSPERMIC	PANTOGRAPHIC
PANCREATIC	PANEGYRIZES	PANLOGISMS	PANSPERMIES	PANTOGRAPHICAL
PANCREATIN	PANEGYRIZING	PANMIXISES	PANSPERMISM	PANTOGRAPHIES
PANCREATINS	PANELLINGS	PANNICULUS	PANSPERMISMS	PANTOGRAPHS
PANCREATITIDES	PANELLISTS	PANNICULUSES	PANSPERMIST	PANTOGRAPHY
PANCREATITIS	PANENTHEISM	PANNIKELLS	PANSPERMISTS	PANTOMIMED
PANCREATITISES	PANENTHEISMS	PANOMPHAEAN	PANTAGAMIES	PANTOMIMES
PANCREOZYMIN	PANENTHEIST	PANOPHOBIA	PANTAGRAPH	PANTOMIMIC
PANCREOZYMINS	PANENTHEISTS	PANOPHOBIAS	PANTAGRAPHS	PANTOMIMICAL
PANCYTOPENIA	PANESTHESIA	PANOPHTHALMIA	PANTALEONS	PANTOMIMICALLY
PANCYTOPENIAS	PANESTHESIAS	PANOPHTHALMIAS	PANTALETTED	PANTOMIMING
PANDAEMONIUM	PANETELLAS	PANOPHTHALMITIS	PANTALETTES	PANTOMIMIST
PANDAEMONIUMS	PANETTONES	PANOPTICAL	PANTALONES	PANTOMIMISTS
PANDANACEOUS	PANGENESES	PANOPTICALLY	PANTALOONED	PANTOPHAGIES
PANDANUSES	PANGENESIS	PANOPTICON	PANTALOONERIES	PANTOPHAGIST
PANDATIONS	PANGENETIC	PANOPTICONS	PANTALOONERY	PANTOPHAGISTS
PANDECTIST	PANGENETICALLY	PANORAMICALLY	PANTALOONS	PANTOPHAGOUS
PANDECTISTS	PANGRAMMATIST	PANPHARMACON	PANTDRESSES	PANTOPHAGY
PANDEMONIAC	PANGRAMMATISTS	PANPHARMACONS	PANTECHNICON	PANTOPHOBIA
PANDEMONIACAL	PANHANDLED	PANPSYCHISM	PANTECHNICONS	PANTOPHOBIAS
PANDEMONIAN	PANHANDLER	PANPSYCHISMS	PANTHEISMS	PANTOPRAGMATIC
PANDEMONIC	PANHANDLERS	PANPSYCHIST	PANTHEISTIC	PANTOPRAGMATICS
PANDEMONIUM	PANHANDLES	PANPSYCHISTIC	PANTHEISTICAL	PANTOSCOPE
PANDEMONIUMS	PANHANDLING	PANPSYCHISTS	PANTHEISTICALLY	PANTOSCOPES
PANDERESSES	PANHARMONICON	PANRADIOMETER	PANTHEISTS	PANTOSCOPIC
PANDERISMS	PANHARMONICONS	PANRADIOMETERS	PANTHENOLS	PANTOTHENATE
PANDERMITE	PANHELLENIC	PANSEXUALISM	PANTHEOLOGIES	PANTOTHENATES
PANDERMITES	PANHELLENION	PANSEXUALISMS	PANTHEOLOGIST	PANTOTHENIC
PANDICULATION	PANHELLENIONS	PANSEXUALIST	PANTHEOLOGISTS	PANTOUFLES
PANDICULATIONS	PANHELLENIUM	PANSEXUALISTS	PANTHEOLOGY	PANTROPICAL
PANDOWDIES	PANHELLENIUMS	PANSEXUALITIES	PANTHERESS	PANTRYMAID
PANDURATED	PANICKIEST	PANSEXUALITY	PANTHERESSES	PANTRYMAIDS
PANDURIFORM	PANICMONGER	PANSEXUALS	PANTHERINE	PANTSUITED
PANEGOISMS	PANICMONGERS	PANSOPHICAL	PANTHERISH	PANTYWAIST
PANEGYRICA	PANICULATE	PANSOPHICALLY	PANTILINGS	PANTYWAISTS
PANEGYRICAL	PANICULATED	PANSOPHIES	PANTISOCRACIES	PANZEROTTO

P

PANZEROTTOS	PAPILLOMATOSES	PARABOLISING	PARADOCTORS	PARAGNATHOUS
PANZOOTICS	PAPILLOMATOSIS	PARABOLIST	PARADOXERS	PARAGNOSES
PAPALISING	PAPILLOMATOUS	PARABOLISTS	PARADOXICAL	PARAGNOSIS
PAPALIZING	PAPILLOMAVIRUS	PARABOLIZATION	PARADOXICALITY	PARAGOGICAL
PAPAPRELATIST	PAPILLOTES	PARABOLIZATIONS	PARADOXICALLY	PARAGOGICALLY
PAPAPRELATISTS	PAPILLULATE	PARABOLIZE	PARADOXICALNESS	PARAGOGUES
PAPAVERACEOUS	PAPILLULES	PARABOLIZED	PARADOXIDIAN	PARAGONING
PAPAVERINE	PAPISTICAL	PARABOLIZES	PARADOXIES	PARAGONITE
PAPAVERINES	PAPISTICALLY	PARABOLIZING	PARADOXIST	PARAGONITES
PAPAVEROUS	PAPISTRIES	PARABOLOID	PARADOXISTS	PARAGRAMMATIST
PAPERBACKED	PAPOVAVIRUS	PARABOLOIDAL	PARADOXOLOGIES	PARAGRAMMATISTS
PAPERBACKER	PAPOVAVIRUSES	PARABOLOIDS	PARADOXOLOGY	PARAGRAPHED
PAPERBACKERS	PAPPARDELLE	PARABRAKES	PARADOXURE	PARAGRAPHER
PAPERBACKING	PAPPARDELLES	PARACASEIN	PARADOXURES	PARAGRAPHERS
PAPERBACKS	PAPULATION	PARACASEINS	PARADOXURINE	PARAGRAPHIA
PAPERBARKS	PAPULATIONS	PARACENTESES	PARADROPPED	PARAGRAPHIAS
PAPERBOARD	PAPULIFEROUS	PARACENTESIS	PARADROPPING	PARAGRAPHIC
PAPERBOARDS	PAPYRACEOUS	PARACETAMOL	PARAENESES	PARAGRAPHICAL
PAPERBOUND	PAPYROLOGICAL	PARACETAMOLS	PARAENESIS	PARAGRAPHICALLY
PAPERBOUNDS	PAPYROLOGIES	PARACHRONISM	PARAENETIC	PARAGRAPHING
PAPERCLIPS	PAPYROLOGIST	PARACHRONISMS	PARAENETICAL	PARAGRAPHIST
PAPERGIRLS	PAPYROLOGISTS	PARACHUTED	PARAESTHESIA	PARAGRAPHISTS
PAPERHANGER	PAPYROLOGY	PARACHUTES	PARAESTHESIAS	PARAGRAPHS
PAPERHANGERS	PARABAPTISM	PARACHUTIC	PARAESTHETIC	PARAHELIOTROPIC
PAPERHANGING	PARABAPTISMS	PARACHUTING	PARAFFINED	PARAHYDROGEN
PAPERHANGINGS	PARABEMATA	PARACHUTIST	PARAFFINES	PARAHYDROGENS
PAPERINESS	PARABEMATIC	PARACHUTISTS	PARAFFINIC	PARAINFLUENZA
PAPERINESSES	PARABIOSES	PARACLETES	PARAFFINING	PARAINFLUENZAS
PAPERKNIFE	PARABIOSIS	PARACROSTIC	PARAFFINOID	PARAJOURNALISM
PAPERKNIVES	PARABIOTIC	PARACROSTICS	PARAGENESES	PARAJOURNALISMS
PAPERMAKER	PARABIOTICALLY	PARACYANOGEN	PARAGENESIA	PARAKEELYA
PAPERMAKERS	PARABLASTIC	PARACYANOGENS	PARAGENESIAS	PARAKEELYAS
PAPERMAKING	PARABLASTS	PARADIDDLE	PARAGENESIS	PARAKELIAS
PAPERMAKINGS	PARABLEPSES	PARADIDDLES	PARAGENETIC	PARAKITING
PAPERWARES	PARABLEPSIES	PARADIGMATIC	PARAGENETICALLY	PARAKITINGS
PAPERWEIGHT	PARABLEPSIS	PARADIGMATICAL	PARAGLIDED	PARALALIAS
PAPERWEIGHTS	PARABLEPSY	PARADISAIC	PARAGLIDER	PARALANGUAGE
PAPERWORKS	PARABLEPTIC	PARADISAICAL	PARAGLIDERS	PARALANGUAGES
PAPETERIES	PARABOLANUS	PARADISAICALLY	PARAGLIDES	PARALDEHYDE
PAPILIONACEOUS	PARABOLANUSES	PARADISEAN	PARAGLIDING	PARALDEHYDES
PAPILLATED	PARABOLICAL	PARADISIAC	PARAGLIDINGS	PARALEGALS
PAPILLIFEROUS	PARABOLICALLY	PARADISIACAL	PARAGLOSSA	PARALEIPOMENA
PAPILLIFORM	PARABOLISATION	PARADISIACALLY	PARAGLOSSAE	PARALEIPOMENON
PAPILLITIS	PARABOLISATIONS	PARADISIAL	PARAGLOSSAL	PARALEIPSES
PAPILLITISES	PARABOLISE	PARADISIAN	PARAGLOSSATE	PARALEIPSIS
PAPILLOMAS	PARABOLISED	PARADISICAL	PARAGNATHISM	PARALEXIAS
PAPILLOMATA	PARABOLISES	PARADOCTOR	PARAGNATHISMS	PARALIMNION

P

PARALIMNIONS	PARALOGIST	PARAMETERIZING	PARANORMALS	PARAPLANNER
PARALINGUISTIC	PARALOGISTIC	PARAMETERS	PARANTHELIA	PARAPLANNERS
PARALINGUISTICS	PARALOGISTS	PARAMETRAL	PARANTHELION	PARAPLEGIA
PARALIPOMENA	PARALOGIZE	PARAMETRIC	PARANTHROPUS	PARAPLEGIAS
PARALIPOMENON	PARALOGIZED	PARAMETRICAL	PARANTHROPUSES	PARAPLEGIC
PARALIPSES	PARALOGIZES	PARAMETRICALLY	PARANYMPHS	PARAPLEGICS
PARALIPSIS	PARALOGIZING	PARAMETRISATION	PARAPARESES	PARAPODIAL
PARALLACTIC	PARALOGUES	PARAMETRISE	PARAPARESIS	PARAPODIUM
PARALLACTICAL	PARALYMPIC	PARAMETRISED	PARAPARETIC	PARAPOPHYSES
PARALLACTICALLY	PARALYMPICS	PARAMETRISES	PARAPENTES	PARAPOPHYSIAL
PARALLAXES	PARALYSATION	PARAMETRISING	PARAPENTING	PARAPOPHYSIS
PARALLELED	PARALYSATIONS	PARAMETRIZATION	PARAPENTINGS	PARAPRAXES
PARALLELEPIPED	PARALYSERS	PARAMETRIZE	PARAPERIODIC	PARAPRAXIS
PARALLELEPIPEDA	PARALYSING	PARAMETRIZED	PARAPHASIA	PARAPSYCHIC
PARALLELEPIPEDS	PARALYSINGLY	PARAMETRIZES	PARAPHASIAS	PARAPSYCHICAL
PARALLELING	PARALYTICALLY	PARAMETRIZING	PARAPHASIC	PARAPSYCHISM
PARALLELINGS	PARALYTICS	PARAMILITARIES	PARAPHERNALIA	PARAPSYCHISMS
PARALLELISE	PARALYZATION	PARAMILITARY	PARAPHILIA	PARAPSYCHOLOGY
PARALLELISED	PARALYZATIONS	PARAMNESIA	PARAPHILIAC	PARAPSYCHOSES
PARALLELISES	PARALYZERS	PARAMNESIAS	PARAPHILIACS	PARAPSYCHOSIS
PARALLELISING	PARALYZING	PARAMORPHIC	PARAPHILIAS	PARAQUADRATE
PARALLELISM	PARALYZINGLY	PARAMORPHINE	PARAPHIMOSES	PARAQUADRATES
PARALLELISMS	PARAMAGNET	PARAMORPHINES	PARAPHIMOSIS	PARAQUITOS
PARALLELIST	PARAMAGNETIC	PARAMORPHISM	PARAPHONIA	PARARHYMES
PARALLELISTIC	PARAMAGNETISM	PARAMORPHISMS	PARAPHONIAS	PARAROSANILINE
PARALLELISTS	PARAMAGNETISMS	PARAMORPHOUS	PARAPHONIC	PARAROSANILINES
PARALLELIZE	PARAMAGNETS	PARAMORPHS	PARAPHRASABLE	PARARTHRIA
PARALLELIZED	PARAMASTOID	PARAMOUNCIES	PARAPHRASE	PARARTHRIAS
PARALLELIZES	PARAMASTOIDS	PARAMOUNCY	PARAPHRASED	PARASAILED
PARALLELIZING	PARAMATTAS	PARAMOUNTCIES	PARAPHRASER	PARASAILING
PARALLELLED	PARAMECIUM	PARAMOUNTCY	PARAPHRASERS	PARASAILINGS
PARALLELLING	PARAMECIUMS	PARAMOUNTLY	PARAPHRASES	PARASCENDING
PARALLELLY	PARAMEDICAL	PARAMOUNTS	PARAPHRASING	PARASCENDINGS
PARALLELOGRAM	PARAMEDICALS	PARAMYLUMS	PARAPHRAST	PARASCENIA
PARALLELOGRAMS	PARAMEDICO	PARAMYXOVIRUS	PARAPHRASTIC	PARASCENIUM
PARALLELOPIPED	PARAMEDICOS	PARAMYXOVIRUSES	PARAPHRASTICAL	PARASCEVES
PARALLELOPIPEDA	PARAMEDICS	PARANEPHRIC	PARAPHRASTS	PARASCIENCE
PARALLELOPIPEDS	PARAMENSTRUA	PARANEPHROS	PARAPHRAXES	PARASCIENCES
PARALLELWISE	PARAMENSTRUUM	PARANEPHROSES	PARAPHRAXIA	PARASELENAE
PARALOGIAS	PARAMENSTRUUMS	PARANOEICS	PARAPHRAXIAS	PARASELENE
PARALOGIES	PARAMETERISE	PARANOIACS	PARAPHRAXIS	PARASELENIC
PARALOGISE	PARAMETERISED	PARANOICALLY	PARAPHRENIA	PARASEXUAL
PARALOGISED	PARAMETERISES	PARANOIDAL	PARAPHRENIAS	PARASEXUALITIES
PARALOGISES	PARAMETERISING	PARANORMAL	PARAPHYSATE	PARASEXUALITY
PARALOGISING	PARAMETERIZE	PARANORMALITIES	PARAPHYSES	PARASHIOTH
PARALOGISM	PARAMETERIZED	PARANORMALITY	PARAPHYSIS	PARASITAEMIA
PARALOGISMS	PARAMETERIZES	PARANORMALLY	PARAPINEAL	PARASITAEMIAS

PARASITICAL	PARASYNAPSES	PARCHMENTIZING	PARFOCALISE	PAROCCIPITAL
PARASITICALLY	PARASYNAPSIS	PARCHMENTS	PARFOCALISED	PAROCHIALISE
PARASITICALNESS	PARASYNAPTIC	PARCHMENTY	PARFOCALISES	PAROCHIALISED
PARASITICIDAL	PARASYNTHESES	PARCIMONIES	PARFOCALISING	PAROCHIALISES
PARASITICIDE	PARASYNTHESIS	PARDALISES	PARFOCALITIES	PAROCHIALISING
PARASITICIDES	PARASYNTHETA	PARDALOTES	PARFOCALITY	PAROCHIALISM
PARASITISATION	PARASYNTHETIC	PARDONABLE	PARFOCALIZE	PAROCHIALISMS
PARASITISATIONS	PARASYNTHETON	PARDONABLENESS	PARFOCALIZED	PAROCHIALITIES
PARASITISE	PARATACTIC	PARDONABLY	PARFOCALIZES	PAROCHIALITY
PARASITISED	PARATACTICAL	PARDONINGS	PARFOCALIZING	PAROCHIALIZE
PARASITISES	PARATACTICALLY	PARDONLESS	PARGASITES	PAROCHIALIZED
PARASITISING	PARATANIWHA	PAREGORICS	PARGETINGS	PAROCHIALIZES
PARASITISM	PARATANIWHAS	PAREIDOLIA	PARGETTERS	PAROCHIALIZING
PARASITISMS	PARATHESES	PAREIDOLIAS	PARGETTING	PAROCHIALLY
PARASITIZATION	PARATHESIS	PARENCEPHALA	PARGETTINGS	PAROCHINES
PARASITIZATIONS	PARATHIONS	PARENCEPHALON	PARGYLINES	PARODISTIC
PARASITIZE	PARATHORMONE	PARENCHYMA	PARHELIACAL	PAROECIOUS
PARASITIZED	PARATHORMONES	PARENCHYMAL	PARHYPATES	PAROEMIACS
PARASITIZES	PARATHYROID	PARENCHYMAS	PARIPINNATE	PAROEMIOGRAPHER
PARASITIZING	PARATHYROIDS	PARENCHYMATA	PARISCHANE	PAROEMIOGRAPHY
PARASITOID	PARATROOPER	PARENCHYMATOUS	PARISCHANES	PAROEMIOLOGIES
PARASITOIDS	PARATROOPERS	PARENTAGES	PARISCHANS	PAROEMIOLOGY
PARASITOLOGIC	PARATROOPS	PARENTALLY	PARISHIONER	PARONOMASIA
PARASITOLOGICAL	PARATUNGSTIC	PARENTERAL	PARISHIONERS	PARONOMASIAS
PARASITOLOGIES	PARATYPHOID	PARENTERALLY	PARISYLLABIC	PARONOMASIES
PARASITOLOGIST	PARATYPHOIDS	PARENTHESES	PARKINSONIAN	PARONOMASTIC
PARASITOLOGISTS	PARAWALKER	PARENTHESIS	PARKINSONISM	PARONOMASTICAL
PARASITOLOGY	PARAWALKERS	PARENTHESISE	PARKINSONISMS	PARONOMASY
PARASITOSES	PARBOILING	PARENTHESISED	PARKLEAVES	PARONYCHIA
PARASITOSIS	PARBREAKED	PARENTHESISES	PARLEMENTS	PARONYCHIAL
PARASKIING	PARBREAKING	PARENTHESISING	PARLEYVOOED	PARONYCHIAS
PARASKIINGS	PARBUCKLED	PARENTHESIZE	PARLEYVOOING	PARONYMIES
PARASPHENOID	PARBUCKLES	PARENTHESIZED	PARLEYVOOS	PARONYMOUS
PARASPHENOIDS	PARBUCKLING	PARENTHESIZES	PARLIAMENT	PARONYMOUSLY
PARASTATAL	PARCELLING	PARENTHESIZING	PARLIAMENTARIAN	PAROTIDITIC
PARASTATALS	PARCELWISE	PARENTHETIC	PARLIAMENTARILY	PAROTIDITIS
PARASTICHIES	PARCENARIES	PARENTHETICAL	PARLIAMENTARISM	PAROTIDITISES
PARASTICHOUS	PARCHEDNESS	PARENTHETICALLY	PARLIAMENTARY	PAROTITISES
PARASTICHY	PARCHEDNESSES	PARENTHOOD	PARLIAMENTING	PAROXETINE
PARASUICIDE	PARCHEESIS	PARENTHOODS	PARLIAMENTINGS	PAROXETINES
PARASUICIDES	PARCHMENTISE	PARENTINGS	PARLIAMENTS	PAROXYSMAL
PARASYMBIONT	PARCHMENTISED	PARENTLESS	PARLOUSNESS	PAROXYSMALLY
PARASYMBIONTS	PARCHMENTISES	PARESTHESIA	PARLOUSNESSES	PAROXYSMIC
PARASYMBIOSES	PARCHMENTISING	PARESTHESIAS	PARMACITIE	PAROXYTONE
PARASYMBIOSIS	PARCHMENTIZE	PARESTHETIC	PARMACITIES	PAROXYTONES
PARASYMBIOTIC	PARCHMENTIZED	PARFLECHES	PARMIGIANA	PAROXYTONIC
PARASYMPATHETIC	PARCHMENTIZES	PARFLESHES	PARMIGIANO	PARQUETING

P

PARQUETRIES	PARTIALNESSES	PARTICULARS	PASQUILANT	PASSIONATE
PARQUETTED	PARTIBILITIES	PARTICULATE	PASQUILANTS	PASSIONATED
PARQUETTING	PARTIBILITY	PARTICULATES	PASQUILERS	PASSIONATELY
PARRAKEETS	PARTICIPABLE	PARTISANLY	PASQUILLED	PASSIONATENESS
PARRAMATTA	PARTICIPANT	PARTISANSHIP	PASQUILLING	PASSIONATES
PARRAMATTAS	PARTICIPANTLY	PARTISANSHIPS	PASQUINADE	PASSIONATING
PARRHESIAS	PARTICIPANTS	PARTITIONED	PASQUINADED	PASSIONFLOWER
PARRICIDAL	PARTICIPATE	PARTITIONER	PASQUINADER	PASSIONFLOWERS
PARRICIDES	PARTICIPATED	PARTITIONERS	PASQUINADERS	PASSIONING
PARRITCHES	PARTICIPATES	PARTITIONING	PASQUINADES	PASSIONLESS
PARROCKING	PARTICIPATING	PARTITIONIST	PASQUINADING	PASSIONLESSLY
PARROQUETS	PARTICIPATION	PARTITIONISTS	PASSABLENESS	PASSIONLESSNESS
PARROTFISH	PARTICIPATIONAL	PARTITIONMENT	PASSABLENESSES	PASSIVATED
PARROTFISHES	PARTICIPATIONS	PARTITIONMENTS	PASSACAGLIA	PASSIVATES
PARROTRIES	PARTICIPATIVE	PARTITIONS	PASSACAGLIAS	PASSIVATING
PARSIMONIES	PARTICIPATOR	PARTITIVELY	PASSAGEWAY	PASSIVATION
PARSIMONIOUS	PARTICIPATORS	PARTITIVES	PASSAGEWAYS	PASSIVATIONS
PARSIMONIOUSLY	PARTICIPATORY	PARTITURAS	PASSAGEWORK	PASSIVENESS
PARSONAGES	PARTICIPIAL	PARTIZANSHIP	PASSAGEWORKS	PASSIVENESSES
PARSONICAL	PARTICIPIALLY	PARTIZANSHIPS	PASSALONGS	PASSIVISMS
PARTAKINGS	PARTICIPIALS	PARTNERING	PASSAMENTED	PASSIVISTS
PARTHENOCARPIC	PARTICIPLE	PARTNERLESS	PASSAMENTING	PASSIVITIES
PARTHENOCARPIES	PARTICIPLES	PARTNERSHIP	PASSAMENTS	PASSMENTED
PARTHENOCARPOUS	PARTICLEBOARD	PARTNERSHIPS	PASSAMEZZO	PASSMENTING
PARTHENOCARPY	PARTICLEBOARDS	PARTRIDGEBERRY	PASSAMEZZOS	PASTEBOARD
PARTHENOGENESES	PARTICULAR	PARTRIDGES	PASSEMEASURE	PASTEBOARDS
PARTHENOGENESIS	PARTICULARISE	PARTURIENCIES	PASSEMEASURES	PASTEDOWNS
PARTHENOGENETIC	PARTICULARISED	PARTURIENCY	PASSEMENTED	PASTELISTS
PARTHENOSPORE	PARTICULARISER	PARTURIENT	PASSEMENTERIE	PASTELLIST
PARTHENOSPORES	PARTICULARISERS	PARTURIENTS	PASSEMENTERIES	PASTELLISTS
PARTIALISE	PARTICULARISES	PARTURIFACIENT	PASSEMENTING	PASTEURELLA
PARTIALISED	PARTICULARISING	PARTURITION	PASSEMENTS	PASTEURELLAE
PARTIALISES	PARTICULARISM	PARTURITIONS	PASSENGERS	PASTEURELLAS
PARTIALISING	PARTICULARISMS	PARTYGOERS	PASSEPIEDS	PASTEURISATION
PARTIALISM	PARTICULARIST	PARVANIMITIES	PASSERINES	PASTEURISATIONS
PARTIALISMS	PARTICULARISTIC	PARVANIMITY	PASSIBILITIES	PASTEURISE
PARTIALIST	PARTICULARISTS	PARVIFOLIATE	PASSIBILITY	PASTEURISED
PARTIALISTS	PARTICULARITIES	PARVOLINES	PASSIBLENESS	PASTEURISER
PARTIALITIES	PARTICULARITY	PARVOVIRUS	PASSIBLENESSES	PASTEURISERS
PARTIALITY	PARTICULARIZE	PARVOVIRUSES	PASSIFLORA	PASTEURISES
PARTIALIZE	PARTICULARIZED	PASIGRAPHIC	PASSIFLORACEOUS	PASTEURISING
PARTIALIZED	PARTICULARIZER	PASIGRAPHICAL	PASSIFLORAS	PASTEURISM
PARTIALIZES	PARTICULARIZERS	PASIGRAPHIES	PASSIMETER	PASTEURISMS
PARTIALIZING	PARTICULARIZES	PASIGRAPHY	PASSIMETERS	PASTEURIZATION
PARTIALLED	PARTICULARIZING	PASODOBLES	PASSIONALS	PASTEURIZATIONS
PARTIALLING	PARTICULARLY	PASQUEFLOWER	PASSIONARIES	PASTEURIZE
PARTIALNESS	PARTICULARNESS	PASQUEFLOWERS	PASSIONARY	PASTEURIZED

P

PASTEURIZER	PATELLIFORM	PATHOLOGISED	PATRIARCHISM	PATROLOGIST
PASTEURIZERS	PATENTABILITIES	PATHOLOGISES	PATRIARCHISMS	PATROLOGISTS
PASTEURIZES	PATENTABILITY	PATHOLOGISING	PATRIARCHS	PATROLWOMAN
PASTEURIZING	PATENTABLE	PATHOLOGIST	PATRIARCHY	PATROLWOMEN
PASTICCIOS	PATERCOVES	PATHOLOGISTS	PATRIATING	PATRONAGED
PASTICHEUR	PATEREROES	PATHOLOGIZE	PATRIATION	PATRONAGES
PASTICHEURS	PATERFAMILIAS	PATHOLOGIZED	PATRIATIONS	PATRONAGING
PASTINESSES	PATERFAMILIASES	PATHOLOGIZES	PATRICIANLY	PATRONESSES
PASTITSIOS	PATERNALISM	PATHOLOGIZING	PATRICIANS	PATRONISATION
PASTNESSES	PATERNALISMS	PATHOPHOBIA	PATRICIATE	PATRONISATIONS
PASTORALES	PATERNALIST	PATHOPHOBIAS	PATRICIATES	PATRONISED
PASTORALISM	PATERNALISTIC	PATHOPHYSIOLOGY	PATRICIDAL	PATRONISER
PASTORALISMS	PATERNALISTS	PATIBULARY	PATRICIDES	PATRONISERS
PASTORALIST	PATERNALLY	PATIENTEST	PATRICLINIC	PATRONISES
PASTORALISTS	PATERNITIES	PATIENTING	PATRICLINOUS	PATRONISING
PASTORALLY	PATERNOSTER	PATINATING	PATRIFOCAL	PATRONISINGLY
PASTORALNESS	PATERNOSTERS	PATINATION	PATRIFOCALITIES	PATRONIZATION
PASTORALNESSES	PATHBREAKING	PATINATIONS	PATRIFOCALITY	PATRONIZATIONS
PASTORATES	PATHETICAL	PATINISING	PATRILINEAGE	PATRONIZED
PASTORIUMS	PATHETICALLY	PATINIZING	PATRILINEAGES	PATRONIZER
PASTORSHIP	PATHFINDER	PATISSERIE	PATRILINEAL	PATRONIZERS
PASTORSHIPS	PATHFINDERS	PATISSERIES	PATRILINEALLY	PATRONIZES
PASTOURELLE	PATHFINDING	PATISSIERS	PATRILINEAR	PATRONIZING
PASTOURELLES	PATHFINDINGS	PATRESFAMILIAS	PATRILINEARLY	PATRONIZINGLY
PASTRYCOOK	PATHLESSNESS	PATRIALISATION	PATRILINIES	PATRONLESS
PASTRYCOOKS	PATHLESSNESSES	PATRIALISATIONS	PATRILOCAL	PATRONYMIC
PASTURABLE	PATHOBIOLOGIES	PATRIALISE	PATRILOCALLY	PATRONYMICS
PASTURAGES	PATHOBIOLOGY	PATRIALISED	PATRIMONIAL	PATROONSHIP
PASTURELAND	PATHOGENES	PATRIALISES	PATRIMONIALLY	PATROONSHIPS
PASTURELANDS	PATHOGENESES	PATRIALISING	PATRIMONIES	PATTERNING
PASTURELESS	PATHOGENESIS	PATRIALISM	PATRIOTICALLY	PATTERNINGS
PATAPHYSICS	PATHOGENETIC	PATRIALISMS	PATRIOTISM	PATTERNLESS
PATCHBOARD	PATHOGENIC	PATRIALITIES	PATRIOTISMS	PATTRESSES
PATCHBOARDS	PATHOGENICITIES	PATRIALITY	PATRISTICAL	PATULOUSLY
PATCHCOCKE	PATHOGENICITY	PATRIALIZATION	PATRISTICALLY	PATULOUSNESS
PATCHCOCKES	PATHOGENIES	PATRIALIZATIONS	PATRISTICISM	PATULOUSNESSES
PATCHERIES	PATHOGENOUS	PATRIALIZE	PATRISTICISMS	PAUCILOQUENT
PATCHINESS	PATHOGNOMIES	PATRIALIZED	PATRISTICS	PAUGHTIEST
PATCHINESSES	PATHOGNOMONIC	PATRIALIZES	PATROCLINAL	PAULOWNIAS
PATCHOCKES	PATHOGNOMY	PATRIALIZING	PATROCLINIC	PAUNCHIEST
PATCHOULIES	PATHOGRAPHIES	PATRIARCHAL	PATROCLINIES	PAUNCHINESS
PATCHOULIS	PATHOGRAPHY	PATRIARCHALISM	PATROCLINOUS	PAUNCHINESSES
PATCHWORKED	PATHOLOGIC	PATRIARCHALISMS	PATROCLINY	PAUPERESSES
PATCHWORKING	PATHOLOGICAL	PATRIARCHALLY	PATROLLERS	PAUPERISATION
PATCHWORKS	PATHOLOGICALLY	PATRIARCHATE	PATROLLING	PAUPERISATIONS
PATELLECTOMIES	PATHOLOGIES	PATRIARCHATES	PATROLOGICAL	PAUPERISED
PATELLECTOMY	PATHOLOGISE	PATRIARCHIES	PATROLOGIES	PAUPERISES

P

PAUPERISING	PEACHINESS	PECTISATIONS	PEDANTICISMS	PEDICULATE
PAUPERISMS	PEACHINESSES	PECTIZABLE	PEDANTICIZE	PEDICULATED
PAUPERIZATION	PEACOCKERIES	PECTIZATION	PEDANTICIZED	PEDICULATES
PAUPERIZATIONS	PEACOCKERY	PECTIZATIONS	PEDANTICIZES	PEDICULATION
PAUPERIZED	PEACOCKIER	PECTOLITES	PEDANTICIZING	PEDICULATIONS
PAUPERIZES	PEACOCKIEST	PECTORALLY	PEDANTISED	PEDICULOSES
PAUPERIZING	PEACOCKING	PECTORILOQUIES	PEDANTISES	PEDICULOSIS
PAUPIETTES	PEACOCKISH	PECTORILOQUY	PEDANTISING	PEDICULOUS
PAUSEFULLY	PEAKEDNESS	PECULATING	PEDANTISMS	PEDICURING
PAUSELESSLY	PEAKEDNESSES	PECULATION	PEDANTIZED	PEDICURIST
PAVEMENTED	PEARLASHES	PECULATIONS	PEDANTIZES	PEDICURISTS
PAVEMENTING	PEARLESCENCE	PECULATORS	PEDANTIZING	PEDIMENTAL
PAVILIONED	PEARLESCENCES	PECULIARISE	PEDANTOCRACIES	PEDIMENTED
PAVILIONING	PEARLESCENT	PECULIARISED	PEDANTOCRACY	PEDIPALPUS
PAVONAZZOS	PEARLINESS	PECULIARISES	PEDANTOCRAT	PEDOGENESES
PAWKINESSES	PEARLINESSES	PECULIARISING	PEDANTOCRATIC	PEDOGENESIS
PAWNBROKER	PEARLWORTS	PECULIARITIES	PEDANTOCRATS	PEDOGENETIC
PAWNBROKERS	PEARMONGER	PECULIARITY	PEDANTRIES	PEDOLOGICAL
PAWNBROKING	PEARMONGERS	PECULIARIZE	PEDDLERIES	PEDOLOGIES
PAWNBROKINGS	PEARTNESSES	PECULIARIZED	PEDERASTIC	PEDOLOGIST
PAWNTICKET	PEASANTRIES	PECULIARIZES	PEDERASTIES	PEDOLOGISTS
PAWNTICKETS	PEASHOOTER	PECULIARIZING	PEDEREROES	PEDOMETERS
PAYMASTERS	PEASHOOTERS	PECULIARLY	PEDESTALED	PEDOPHILES
PAYNIMRIES	PEASOUPERS	PECUNIARILY	PEDESTALING	PEDOPHILIA
PAYSAGISTS	PEBBLEDASH	PEDAGOGICAL	PEDESTALLED	PEDOPHILIAC
PEABERRIES	PEBBLEDASHED	PEDAGOGICALLY	PEDESTALLING	PEDOPHILIACS
PEACEABLENESS	PEBBLEDASHES	PEDAGOGICS	PEDESTRIAN	PEDOPHILIAS
PEACEABLENESSES	PEBBLEDASHING	PEDAGOGIES	PEDESTRIANISE	PEDOPHILIC
PEACEFULLER	PECCABILITIES	PEDAGOGISM	PEDESTRIANISED	PEDUNCULAR
PEACEFULLEST	PECCABILITY	PEDAGOGISMS	PEDESTRIANISES	PEDUNCULATE
PEACEFULLY	PECCADILLO	PEDAGOGUED	PEDESTRIANISING	PEDUNCULATED
PEACEFULNESS	PECCADILLOES	PEDAGOGUERIES	PEDESTRIANISM	PEDUNCULATION
PEACEFULNESSES	PECCADILLOS	PEDAGOGUERY	PEDESTRIANISMS	PEDUNCULATIONS
PEACEKEEPER	PECCANCIES	PEDAGOGUES	PEDESTRIANIZE	PEELGARLIC
PEACEKEEPERS	PECKERWOOD	PEDAGOGUING	PEDESTRIANIZED	PEELGARLICS
PEACEKEEPING	PECKERWOODS	PEDAGOGUISH	PEDESTRIANIZES	PEERLESSLY
PEACEKEEPINGS	PECKISHNESS	PEDAGOGUISHNESS	PEDESTRIANIZING	PEERLESSNESS
PEACELESSNESS	PECKISHNESSES	PEDAGOGUISM	PEDESTRIANS	PEERLESSNESSES
PEACELESSNESSES	PECTINACEOUS	PEDAGOGUISMS	PEDETENTOUS	PEEVISHNESS
PEACEMAKER	PECTINATED	PEDALLINGS	PEDIATRICIAN	PEEVISHNESSES
PEACEMAKERS	PECTINATELY	PEDANTICAL	PEDIATRICIANS	PEGMATITES
PEACEMAKING	PECTINATION	PEDANTICALLY	PEDIATRICS	PEGMATITIC
PEACEMAKINGS	PECTINATIONS	PEDANTICISE	PEDIATRIST	PEIRASTICALLY
PEACETIMES	PECTINESTERASE	PEDANTICISED	PEDIATRISTS	PEJORATING
PEACHBLOWS	PECTINESTERASES	PEDANTICISES	PEDICELLARIA	PEJORATION
PEACHERINO	PECTISABLE	PEDANTICISING	PEDICELLARIAE	PEJORATIONS
PEACHERINOS	PECTISATION	PEDANTICISM	PEDICELLATE	PEJORATIVE

PEJORATIVELY	PEMPHIGUSES	PENETRANCE	PENITENTIAL	PENSILENESSES
PEJORATIVES	PENALISATION	PENETRANCES	PENITENTIALLY	PENSILITIES
PELARGONIC	PENALISATIONS	PENETRANCIES	PENITENTIALS	PENSIONABLE
PELARGONIUM	PENALISING	PENETRANCY	PENITENTIARIES	PENSIONARIES
PELARGONIUMS	PENALITIES	PENETRANTS	PENITENTIARY	PENSIONARY
PELECYPODS	PENALIZATION	PENETRATED	PENITENTLY	PENSIONEER
PELLAGRINS	PENALIZATIONS	PENETRATES	PENMANSHIP	PENSIONERS
PELLAGROUS	PENALIZING	PENETRATING	PENMANSHIPS	PENSIONING
PELLETIFIED	PENANNULAR	PENETRATINGLY	PENNACEOUS	PENSIONLESS
PELLETIFIES	PENCILINGS	PENETRATION	PENNALISMS	PENSIONNAT
PELLETIFYING	PENCILLERS	PENETRATIONS	PENNATULACEOUS	PENSIONNATS
PELLETISATION	PENCILLING	PENETRATIVE	PENNATULAE	PENSIVENESS
PELLETISATIONS	PENCILLINGS	PENETRATIVELY	PENNATULAS	PENSIVENESSES
PELLETISED	PENDENCIES	PENETRATIVENESS	PENNILESSLY	PENSTEMONS
PELLETISER	PENDENTIVE	PENETRATOR	PENNILESSNESS	PENTABARBITAL
PELLETISERS	PENDENTIVES	PENETRATORS	PENNILESSNESSES	PENTABARBITALS
PELLETISES	PENDICLERS	PENETROMETER	PENNILLION	PENTACHORD
PELLETISING	PENDRAGONS	PENETROMETERS	PENNINITES	PENTACHORDS
PELLETIZATION	PENDRAGONSHIP	PENGUINERIES	PENNONCELLE	PENTACRINOID
PELLETIZATIONS	PENDRAGONSHIPS	PENGUINERY	PENNONCELLES	PENTACRINOIDS
PELLETIZED	PENDULATED	PENGUINRIES	PENNONCELS	PENTACTINAL
PELLETIZER	PENDULATES	PENHOLDERS	PENNYCRESS	PENTACYCLIC
PELLETIZERS	PENDULATING	PENICILLAMINE	PENNYCRESSES	PENTADACTYL
PELLETIZES	PENDULOSITIES	PENICILLAMINES	PENNYLANDS	PENTADACTYLE
PELLETIZING	PENDULOSITY	PENICILLATE	PENNYROYAL	PENTADACTYLES
PELLICULAR	PENDULOUSLY	PENICILLATELY	PENNYROYALS	PENTADACTYLIC
PELLITORIES	PENDULOUSNESS	PENICILLATION	PENNYWEIGHT	PENTADACTYLIES
PELLUCIDITIES	PENDULOUSNESSES	PENICILLATIONS	PENNYWEIGHTS	PENTADACTYLISM
PELLUCIDITY	PENELOPISE	PENICILLIA	PENNYWHISTLE	PENTADACTYLISMS
PELLUCIDLY	PENELOPISED	PENICILLIFORM	PENNYWHISTLES	PENTADACTYLOUS
PELLUCIDNESS	PENELOPISES	PENICILLIN	PENNYWINKLE	PENTADACTYLS
PELLUCIDNESSES	PENELOPISING	PENICILLINASE	PENNYWINKLES	PENTADACTYLY
PELMANISMS	PENELOPIZE	PENICILLINASES	PENNYWORTH	PENTADELPHOUS
PELOLOGIES	PENELOPIZED	PENICILLINS	PENNYWORTHS	PENTAGONAL
PELOTHERAPIES	PENELOPIZES	PENICILLIUM	PENNYWORTS	PENTAGONALLY
PELOTHERAPY	PENELOPIZING	PENICILLIUMS	PENOLOGICAL	PENTAGONALS
PELTATIONS	PENEPLAINS	PENINSULAR	PENOLOGICALLY	PENTAGRAMS
PELTMONGER	PENEPLANATION	PENINSULARITIES	PENOLOGIES	PENTAGRAPH
PELTMONGERS	PENEPLANATIONS	PENINSULARITY	PENOLOGIST	PENTAGRAPHS
PELVIMETER	PENEPLANES	PENINSULAS	PENOLOGISTS	PENTAGYNIAN
PELVIMETERS	PENETRABILITIES	PENINSULATE	PENONCELLE	PENTAGYNOUS
PELVIMETRIES	PENETRABILITY	PENINSULATED	PENONCELLES	PENTAHEDRA
PELVIMETRY	PENETRABLE	PENINSULATES	PENPUSHERS	PENTAHEDRAL
PELYCOSAUR	PENETRABLENESS	PENINSULATING	PENPUSHING	PENTAHEDRON
PELYCOSAURS	PENETRABLY	PENISTONES	PENPUSHINGS	PENTAHEDRONS
PEMPHIGOID	PENETRALIA	PENITENCES	PENSIEROSO	PENTALOGIES
PEMPHIGOUS	PENETRALIAN	PENITENCIES	PENSILENESS	PENTALPHAS

P

PENTAMERIES

PENTAMERIES	PENTECONTER	PEPPERMILL	PERAMBULATED	PERCIPIENTS
PENTAMERISM	PENTECONTERS	PEPPERMILLS	PERAMBULATES	PERCOIDEAN
PENTAMERISMS	PENTETERIC	PEPPERMINT	PERAMBULATING	PERCOIDEANS
PENTAMEROUS	PENTHEMIMER	PEPPERMINTS	PERAMBULATION	PERCOLABLE
PENTAMETER	PENTHEMIMERAL	PEPPERMINTY	PERAMBULATIONS	PERCOLATED
PENTAMETERS	PENTHEMIMERS	PEPPERONIS	PERAMBULATOR	PERCOLATES
PENTAMIDINE	PENTHOUSED	PEPPERTREE	PERAMBULATORS	PERCOLATING
PENTAMIDINES	PENTHOUSES	PEPPERTREES	PERAMBULATORY	PERCOLATION
PENTANDRIAN	PENTHOUSING	PEPPERWORT	PERBORATES	PERCOLATIONS
PENTANDROUS	PENTIMENTI	PEPPERWORTS	PERCALINES	PERCOLATIVE
PENTANGLES	PENTIMENTO	PEPPINESSES	PERCEIVABILITY	PERCOLATOR
PENTANGULAR	PENTLANDITE	PEPSINATED	PERCEIVABLE	PERCOLATORS
PENTAPEPTIDE	PENTLANDITES	PEPSINATES	PERCEIVABLY	PERCURRENT
PENTAPEPTIDES	PENTOBARBITAL	PEPSINATING	PERCEIVERS	PERCURSORY
PENTAPLOID	PENTOBARBITALS	PEPSINOGEN	PERCEIVING	PERCUSSANT
PENTAPLOIDIES	PENTOBARBITONE	PEPSINOGENS	PERCEIVINGS	PERCUSSING
PENTAPLOIDS	PENTOBARBITONES	PEPTALKING	PERCENTAGE	PERCUSSION
PENTAPLOIDY	PENTOSANES	PEPTICITIES	PERCENTAGES	PERCUSSIONAL
PENTAPODIC	PENTOSIDES	PEPTIDASES	PERCENTILE	PERCUSSIONIST
PENTAPODIES	PENTOXIDES	PEPTIDOGLYCAN	PERCENTILES	PERCUSSIONISTS
PENTAPOLIS	PENTSTEMON	PEPTIDOGLYCANS	PERCEPTIBILITY	PERCUSSIONS
PENTAPOLISES	PENTSTEMONS	PEPTISABLE	PERCEPTIBLE	PERCUSSIVE
PENTAPOLITAN	PENTYLENES	PEPTISATION	PERCEPTIBLY	PERCUSSIVELY
PENTAPRISM	PENULTIMAS	PEPTISATIONS	PERCEPTION	PERCUSSIVENESS
PENTAPRISMS	PENULTIMATE	PEPTIZABLE	PERCEPTIONAL	PERCUSSORS
PENTAQUARK	PENULTIMATELY	PEPTIZATION	PERCEPTIONS	PERCUTANEOUS
PENTAQUARKS	PENULTIMATES	PEPTIZATIONS	PERCEPTIVE	PERCUTANEOUSLY
PENTARCHICAL	PENUMBROUS	PEPTONISATION	PERCEPTIVELY	PERCUTIENT
PENTARCHIES	PENURIOUSLY	PEPTONISATIONS	PERCEPTIVENESS	PERCUTIENTS
PENTASTICH	PENURIOUSNESS	PEPTONISED	PERCEPTIVITIES	PERDENDOSI
PENTASTICHOUS	PENURIOUSNESSES	PEPTONISER	PERCEPTIVITY	PERDITIONABLE
PENTASTICHS	PEOPLEHOOD	PEPTONISERS	PERCEPTUAL	PERDITIONS
PENTASTYLE	PEOPLEHOODS	PEPTONISES	PERCEPTUALLY	PERDUELLION
PENTASTYLES	PEOPLELESS	PEPTONISING	PERCHERIES	PERDUELLIONS
PENTASYLLABIC	PEPEROMIAS	PEPTONIZATION	PERCHERONS	PERDURABILITIES
PENTATEUCHAL	PEPPERBOXES	PEPTONIZATIONS	PERCHLORATE	PERDURABILITY
PENTATHLETE	PEPPERCORN	PEPTONIZED	PERCHLORATES	PERDURABLE
PENTATHLETES	PEPPERCORNS	PEPTONIZER	PERCHLORIC	PERDURABLY
PENTATHLON	PEPPERCORNY	PEPTONIZERS	PERCHLORIDE	PERDURANCE
PENTATHLONS	PEPPERGRASS	PEPTONIZES	PERCHLORIDES	PERDURANCES
PENTATHLUM	PEPPERGRASSES	PEPTONIZING	PERCHLOROETHENE	PERDURATION
PENTATHLUMS	PEPPERIDGE	PERACIDITIES	PERCIPIENCE	PERDURATIONS
PENTATOMIC	PEPPERIDGES	PERACIDITY	PERCIPIENCES	PEREGRINATE
PENTATONIC	PEPPERIEST	PERADVENTURE	PERCIPIENCIES	PEREGRINATED
PENTAVALENT	PEPPERINESS	PERADVENTURES	PERCIPIENCY	PEREGRINATES
PENTAZOCINE	PEPPERINESSES	PERAEOPODS	PERCIPIENT	PEREGRINATING
PENTAZOCINES	PEPPERINGS	PERAMBULATE	PERCIPIENTLY	PEREGRINATION

PEREGRINATIONS	PERFECTIONISTS	PERFORMATORY	PERICLASES	PERIKARYAL
PEREGRINATOR	PERFECTIONS	PERFORMERS	PERICLASTIC	PERIKARYON
PEREGRINATORS	PERFECTIVE	PERFORMING	PERICLINAL	PERILOUSLY
PEREGRINATORY	PERFECTIVELY	PERFORMINGS	PERICLINES	PERILOUSNESS
PEREGRINES	PERFECTIVENESS	PERFUMELESS	PERICLITATE	PERILOUSNESSES
PEREGRINITIES	PERFECTIVES	PERFUMERIES	PERICLITATED	PERILYMPHS
PEREGRINITY	PERFECTIVITIES	PERFUMIERS	PERICLITATES	PERIMENOPAUSAL
PEREIOPODS	PERFECTIVITY	PERFUNCTORILY	PERICLITATING	PERIMENOPAUSE
PEREMPTORILY	PERFECTNESS	PERFUNCTORINESS	PERICRANIA	PERIMENOPAUSES
PEREMPTORINESS	PERFECTNESSES	PERFUNCTORY	PERICRANIAL	PERIMETERS
PEREMPTORY	PERFECTORS	PERFUSATES	PERICRANIUM	PERIMETRAL
PERENNATED	PERFERVIDITIES	PERFUSIONIST	PERICRANIUMS	PERIMETRIC
PERENNATES	PERFERVIDITY	PERFUSIONISTS	PERICULOUS	PERIMETRICAL
PERENNATING	PERFERVIDLY	PERFUSIONS	PERICYCLES	PERIMETRICALLY
PERENNATION	PERFERVIDNESS	PERGAMENEOUS	PERICYCLIC	PERIMETRIES
PERENNATIONS	PERFERVIDNESSES	PERGAMENTACEOUS	PERICYNTHIA	PERIMORPHIC
PERENNIALITIES	PERFERVORS	PERGUNNAHS	PERICYNTHION	PERIMORPHISM
PERENNIALITY	PERFERVOUR	PERIASTRON	PERICYNTHIONS	PERIMORPHISMS
PERENNIALLY	PERFERVOURS	PERIASTRONS	PERIDERMAL	PERIMORPHOUS
PERENNIALS	PERFICIENT	PERIBLASTS	PERIDERMIC	PERIMORPHS
PERENNIBRANCH	PERFIDIOUS	PERICARDIA	PERIDESMIA	PERIMYSIUM
PERENNIBRANCHS	PERFIDIOUSLY	PERICARDIAC	PERIDESMIUM	PERIMYSIUMS
PERENNITIES	PERFIDIOUSNESS	PERICARDIAL	PERIDINIAN	PERINAEUMS
PERESTROIKA	PERFLUOROCARBON	PERICARDIAN	PERIDINIANS	PERINATALLY
PERESTROIKAS	PERFOLIATE	PERICARDITIC	PERIDINIUM	PERINEPHRIA
PERFECTATION	PERFOLIATION	PERICARDITIS	PERIDINIUMS	PERINEPHRIC
PERFECTATIONS	PERFOLIATIONS	PERICARDITISES	PERIDOTITE	PERINEPHRITIS
PERFECTERS	PERFORABLE	PERICARDIUM	PERIDOTITES	PERINEPHRITISES
PERFECTEST	PERFORANSES	PERICARDIUMS	PERIDOTITIC	PERINEPHRIUM
PERFECTIBILIAN	PERFORATED	PERICARPIAL	PERIDROMES	PERINEURAL
PERFECTIBILIANS	PERFORATES	PERICARPIC	PERIEGESES	PERINEURIA
PERFECTIBILISM	PERFORATING	PERICENTER	PERIEGESIS	PERINEURIAL
PERFECTIBILISMS	PERFORATION	PERICENTERS	PERIGASTRIC	PERINEURITIC
PERFECTIBILIST	PERFORATIONS	PERICENTRAL	PERIGASTRITIS	PERINEURITIS
PERFECTIBILISTS	PERFORATIVE	PERICENTRE	PERIGASTRITISES	PERINEURITISES
PERFECTIBILITY	PERFORATOR	PERICENTRES	PERIGENESES	PERINEURIUM
PERFECTIBLE	PERFORATORS	PERICENTRIC	PERIGENESIS	PERIODATES
PERFECTING	PERFORATORY	PERICHAETIA	PERIGLACIAL	PERIODICAL
PERFECTION	PERFORATUS	PERICHAETIAL	PERIGONIAL	PERIODICALIST
PERFECTIONATE	PERFORATUSES	PERICHAETIUM	PERIGONIUM	PERIODICALISTS
PERFECTIONATED	PERFORMABILITY	PERICHONDRAL	PERIGYNIES	PERIODICALLY
PERFECTIONATES	PERFORMABLE	PERICHONDRIA	PERIGYNOUS	PERIODICALS
PERFECTIONATING	PERFORMANCE	PERICHONDRIAL	PERIHELIAL	PERIODICITIES
PERFECTIONISM	PERFORMANCES	PERICHONDRIUM	PERIHELION	PERIODICITY
PERFECTIONISMS	PERFORMATIVE	PERICHORESES	PERIHEPATIC	PERIODIDES
PERFECTIONIST	PERFORMATIVELY	PERICHORESIS	PERIHEPATITIS	PERIODISATION
PERFECTIONISTIC	PERFORMATIVES	PERICHYLOUS	PERIHEPATITISES	PERIODISATIONS

P

PERIODISED	PERIPHERIC	PERISSOSYLLABIC	PERJINKITY	PERMISSIBILITY
PERIODISES	PERIPHERICAL	PERISTALITH	PERJURIOUS	PERMISSIBLE
PERIODISING	PERIPHERIES	PERISTALITHS	PERJURIOUSLY	PERMISSIBLENESS
PERIODIZATION	PERIPHONIC	PERISTALSES	PERKINESSES	PERMISSIBLY
PERIODIZATIONS	PERIPHRASE	PERISTALSIS	PERLEMOENS	PERMISSION
PERIODIZED	PERIPHRASED	PERISTALTIC	PERLOCUTION	PERMISSIONS
PERIODIZES	PERIPHRASES	PERISTALTICALLY	PERLOCUTIONARY	PERMISSIVE
PERIODIZING	PERIPHRASING	PERISTERITE	PERLOCUTIONS	PERMISSIVELY
PERIODONTAL	PERIPHRASIS	PERISTERITES	PERLUSTRATE	PERMISSIVENESS
PERIODONTALLY	PERIPHRASTIC	PERISTERONIC	PERLUSTRATED	PERMITTANCE
PERIODONTIA	PERIPHRASTICAL	PERISTOMAL	PERLUSTRATES	PERMITTANCES
PERIODONTIAS	PERIPHYTIC	PERISTOMATIC	PERLUSTRATING	PERMITTEES
PERIODONTIC	PERIPHYTON	PERISTOMES	PERLUSTRATION	PERMITTERS
PERIODONTICALLY	PERIPHYTONS	PERISTOMIAL	PERLUSTRATIONS	PERMITTING
PERIODONTICS	PERIPLASMS	PERISTREPHIC	PERMACULTURE	PERMITTIVITIES
PERIODONTIST	PERIPLASTS	PERISTYLAR	PERMACULTURES	PERMITTIVITY
PERIODONTISTS	PERIPLUSES	PERISTYLES	PERMAFROST	PERMUTABILITIES
PERIODONTITIS	PERIPROCTS	PERITECTIC	PERMAFROSTS	PERMUTABILITY
PERIODONTITISES	PERIPTERAL	PERITHECIA	PERMALINKS	PERMUTABLE
PERIODONTOLOGY	PERIPTERIES	PERITHECIAL	PERMALLOYS	PERMUTABLENESS
PERIONYCHIA	PERISARCAL	PERITHECIUM	PERMANENCE	PERMUTABLY
PERIONYCHIUM	PERISARCOUS	PERITONAEA	PERMANENCES	PERMUTATED
PERIOSTEAL	PERISCIANS	PERITONAEAL	PERMANENCIES	PERMUTATES
PERIOSTEUM	PERISCOPES	PERITONAEUM	PERMANENCY	PERMUTATING
PERIOSTITIC	PERISCOPIC	PERITONAEUMS	PERMANENTLY	PERMUTATION
PERIOSTITIS	PERISCOPICALLY	PERITONEAL	PERMANENTNESS	PERMUTATIONAL
PERIOSTITISES	PERISELENIA	PERITONEALLY	PERMANENTNESSES	PERMUTATIONS
PERIOSTRACUM	PERISELENIUM	PERITONEOSCOPY	PERMANENTS	PERNANCIES
PERIOSTRACUMS	PERISHABILITIES	PERITONEUM	PERMANGANATE	PERNICIOUS
PERIPATETIC	PERISHABILITY	PERITONEUMS	PERMANGANATES	PERNICIOUSLY
PERIPATETICAL	PERISHABLE	PERITONITIC	PERMANGANIC	PERNICIOUSNESS
PERIPATETICALLY	PERISHABLENESS	PERITONITIS	PERMEABILITIES	PERNICKETINESS
PERIPATETICISM	PERISHABLES	PERITONITISES	PERMEABILITY	PERNICKETY
PERIPATETICISMS	PERISHABLY	PERITRACKS	PERMEABLENESS	PERNOCTATE
PERIPATETICS	PERISHINGLY	PERITRICHA	PERMEABLENESSES	PERNOCTATED
PERIPATUSES	PERISPERMAL	PERITRICHOUS	PERMEAMETER	PERNOCTATES
PERIPETEIA	PERISPERMIC	PERITRICHOUSLY	PERMEAMETERS	PERNOCTATING
PERIPETEIAN	PERISPERMS	PERITRICHS	PERMEANCES	PERNOCTATION
PERIPETEIAS	PERISPOMENON	PERITYPHLITIS	PERMEATING	PERNOCTATIONS
PERIPETIAN	PERISPOMENONS	PERITYPHLITISES	PERMEATION	PERONEUSES
PERIPETIAS	PERISSODACTYL	PERIVITELLINE	PERMEATIONS	PERORATING
PERIPETIES	PERISSODACTYLE	PERIWIGGED	PERMEATIVE	PERORATION
PERIPHERAL	PERISSODACTYLES	PERIWIGGING	PERMEATORS	PERORATIONAL
PERIPHERALITIES	PERISSODACTYLIC	PERIWINKLE	PERMETHRIN	PERORATIONS
PERIPHERALITY	PERISSODACTYLS	PERIWINKLES	PERMETHRINS	PERORATORS
PERIPHERALLY	PERISSOLOGIES	PERJINKETY	PERMILLAGE	PEROVSKIAS
PERIPHERALS	PERISSOLOGY	PERJINKITIES	PERMILLAGES	PEROVSKITE

PEROVSKITES	PERPETUATIONS	PERSEVERATIVE	PERSONALIZED	PERSPICUOUS
PEROXIDASE	PERPETUATOR	PERSEVERATOR	PERSONALIZES	PERSPICUOUSLY
PEROXIDASES	PERPETUATORS	PERSEVERATORS	PERSONALIZING	PERSPICUOUSNESS
PEROXIDATION	PERPETUITIES	PERSEVERED	PERSONALLY	PERSPIRABLE
PEROXIDATIONS	PERPETUITY	PERSEVERES	PERSONALTIES	PERSPIRATE
PEROXIDING	PERPHENAZINE	PERSEVERING	PERSONALTY	PERSPIRATED
PEROXIDISE	PERPHENAZINES	PERSEVERINGLY	PERSONATED	PERSPIRATES
PEROXIDISED	PERPLEXEDLY	PERSICARIA	PERSONATES	PERSPIRATING
PEROXIDISES	PERPLEXEDNESS	PERSICARIAS	PERSONATING	PERSPIRATION
PEROXIDISING	PERPLEXEDNESSES	PERSIENNES	PERSONATINGS	PERSPIRATIONS
PEROXIDIZE	PERPLEXERS	PERSIFLAGE	PERSONATION	PERSPIRATORY
PEROXIDIZED	PERPLEXING	PERSIFLAGES	PERSONATIONS	PERSPIRING
PEROXIDIZES	PERPLEXINGLY	PERSIFLEUR	PERSONATIVE	PERSPIRINGLY
PEROXIDIZING	PERPLEXITIES	PERSIFLEURS	PERSONATOR	PERSTRINGE
PEROXISOMAL	PERPLEXITY	PERSIMMONS	PERSONATORS	PERSTRINGED
PEROXISOME	PERQUISITE	PERSISTENCE	PERSONHOOD	PERSTRINGES
PEROXISOMES	PERQUISITES	PERSISTENCES	PERSONHOODS	PERSTRINGING
PEROXYSULPHURIC	PERQUISITION	PERSISTENCIES	PERSONIFIABLE	PERSUADABILITY
PERPENDICULAR	PERQUISITIONS	PERSISTENCY	PERSONIFICATION	PERSUADABLE
PERPENDICULARLY	PERQUISITOR	PERSISTENT	PERSONIFIED	PERSUADERS
PERPENDICULARS	PERQUISITORS	PERSISTENTLY	PERSONIFIER	PERSUADING
PERPENDING	PERRUQUIER	PERSISTENTS	PERSONIFIERS	PERSUASIBILITY
PERPETRABLE	PERRUQUIERS	PERSISTERS	PERSONIFIES	PERSUASIBLE
PERPETRATE	PERSCRUTATION	PERSISTING	PERSONIFYING	PERSUASION
PERPETRATED	PERSCRUTATIONS	PERSISTINGLY	PERSONISED	PERSUASIONS
PERPETRATES	PERSECUTED	PERSISTIVE	PERSONISES	PERSUASIVE
PERPETRATING	PERSECUTEE	PERSNICKETINESS	PERSONISING	PERSUASIVELY
PERPETRATION	PERSECUTEES	PERSNICKETY	PERSONIZED	PERSUASIVENESS
PERPETRATIONS	PERSECUTES	PERSONABLE	PERSONIZES	PERSUASIVES
PERPETRATOR	PERSECUTING	PERSONABLENESS	PERSONIZING	PERSUASORY
PERPETRATORS	PERSECUTION	PERSONABLY	PERSONNELS	PERSULFURIC
PERPETUABLE	PERSECUTIONS	PERSONAGES	PERSONPOWER	PERSULPHATE
PERPETUALISM	PERSECUTIVE	PERSONALIA	PERSONPOWERS	PERSULPHATES
PERPETUALISMS	PERSECUTOR	PERSONALISATION	PERSPECTIVAL	PERSULPHURIC
PERPETUALIST	PERSECUTORS	PERSONALISE	PERSPECTIVE	PERSWADING
PERPETUALISTS	PERSECUTORY	PERSONALISED	PERSPECTIVELY	PERTAINING
PERPETUALITIES	PERSEITIES	PERSONALISES	PERSPECTIVES	PERTINACIOUS
PERPETUALITY	PERSELINES	PERSONALISING	PERSPECTIVISM	PERTINACIOUSLY
PERPETUALLY	PERSEVERANCE	PERSONALISM	PERSPECTIVISMS	PERTINACITIES
PERPETUALS	PERSEVERANCES	PERSONALISMS	PERSPECTIVIST	PERTINACITY
PERPETUANCE	PERSEVERANT	PERSONALIST	PERSPECTIVISTS	PERTINENCE
PERPETUANCES	PERSEVERATE	PERSONALISTIC	PERSPICACIOUS	PERTINENCES
PERPETUATE	PERSEVERATED	PERSONALISTS	PERSPICACIOUSLY	PERTINENCIES
PERPETUATED	PERSEVERATES	PERSONALITIES	PERSPICACITIES	PERTINENCY
PERPETUATES	PERSEVERATING	PERSONALITY	PERSPICACITY	PERTINENTLY
PERPETUATING	PERSEVERATION	PERSONALIZATION	PERSPICUITIES	PERTINENTS
PERPETUATION	PERSEVERATIONS	PERSONALIZE	PERSPICUITY	PERTNESSES

P

PERTURBABLE	PERVICACITY	PETITIONIST	PETROLEUSES	PHAENOGAMIC
PERTURBABLY	PERVIOUSLY	PETITIONISTS	PETROLHEAD	PHAENOGAMOUS
PERTURBANCE	PERVIOUSNESS	PETNAPINGS	PETROLHEADS	PHAENOGAMS
PERTURBANCES	PERVIOUSNESSES	PETNAPPERS	PETROLIFEROUS	PHAENOLOGIES
PERTURBANT	PESKINESSES	PETNAPPING	PETROLLING	PHAENOLOGY
PERTURBANTS	PESSIMISMS	PETRIFACTION	PETROLOGIC	PHAENOMENA
PERTURBATE	PESSIMISTIC	PETRIFACTIONS	PETROLOGICAL	PHAENOMENON
PERTURBATED	PESSIMISTICAL	PETRIFACTIVE	PETROLOGICALLY	PHAENOTYPE
PERTURBATES	PESSIMISTICALLY	PETRIFICATION	PETROLOGIES	PHAENOTYPED
PERTURBATING	PESSIMISTS	PETRIFICATIONS	PETROLOGIST	PHAENOTYPES
PERTURBATION	PESTERINGLY	PETRIFIERS	PETROLOGISTS	PHAENOTYPING
PERTURBATIONAL	PESTERMENT	PETRIFYING	PETROMONEY	PHAEOMELANIN
PERTURBATIONS	PESTERMENTS	PETRISSAGE	PETROMONEYS	PHAEOMELANINS
PERTURBATIVE	PESTHOUSES	PETRISSAGES	PETROMONIES	PHAGEDAENA
PERTURBATOR	PESTICIDAL	PETROCHEMICAL	PETRONELLA	PHAGEDAENAS
PERTURBATORIES	PESTICIDES	PETROCHEMICALLY	PETRONELLAS	PHAGEDAENIC
PERTURBATORS	PESTIFEROUS	PETROCHEMICALS	PETROPHYSICAL	PHAGEDENAS
PERTURBATORY	PESTIFEROUSLY	PETROCHEMISTRY	PETROPHYSICIST	PHAGEDENIC
PERTURBEDLY	PESTIFEROUSNESS	PETROCURRENCIES	PETROPHYSICISTS	PHAGOCYTES
PERTURBERS	PESTILENCE	PETROCURRENCY	PETROPHYSICS	PHAGOCYTIC
PERTURBING	PESTILENCES	PETRODOLLAR	PETROPOUNDS	PHAGOCYTICAL
PERTURBINGLY	PESTILENTIAL	PETRODOLLARS	PETROSTATE	PHAGOCYTISE
PERTUSIONS	PESTILENTIALLY	PETRODROME	PETROSTATES	PHAGOCYTISED
PERTUSSISES	PESTILENTLY	PETRODROMES	PETTEDNESS	PHAGOCYTISES
PERVASIONS	PESTOLOGICAL	PETROGENESES	PETTEDNESSES	PHAGOCYTISING
PERVASIVELY	PESTOLOGIES	PETROGENESIS	PETTICHAPS	PHAGOCYTISM
PERVASIVENESS	PESTOLOGIST	PETROGENETIC	PETTICHAPSES	PHAGOCYTISMS
PERVASIVENESSES	PESTOLOGISTS	PETROGENIES	PETTICOATED	PHAGOCYTIZE
PERVERSELY	PETAHERTZES	PETROGLYPH	PETTICOATS	PHAGOCYTIZED
PERVERSENESS	PETALIFEROUS	PETROGLYPHIC	PETTIFOGGED	PHAGOCYTIZES
PERVERSENESSES	PETALODIES	PETROGLYPHIES	PETTIFOGGER	PHAGOCYTIZING
PERVERSEST	PETALOMANIA	PETROGLYPHS	PETTIFOGGERIES	PHAGOCYTOSE
PERVERSION	PETALOMANIAS	PETROGLYPHY	PETTIFOGGERS	PHAGOCYTOSED
PERVERSIONS	PETAURISTS	PETROGRAMS	PETTIFOGGERY	PHAGOCYTOSES
PERVERSITIES	PETCHARIES	PETROGRAPHER	PETTIFOGGING	PHAGOCYTOSING
PERVERSITY	PETERSHAMS	PETROGRAPHERS	PETTIFOGGINGS	PHAGOCYTOSIS
PERVERSIVE	PETHIDINES	PETROGRAPHIC	PETTINESSES	PHAGOCYTOTIC
PERVERTEDLY	PETIOLATED	PETROGRAPHICAL	PETTISHNESS	PHAGOMANIA
PERVERTEDNESS	PETIOLULES	PETROGRAPHIES	PETTISHNESSES	PHAGOMANIAC
PERVERTEDNESSES	PETITENESS	PETROGRAPHY	PETULANCES	PHAGOMANIACS
PERVERTERS	PETITENESSES	PETROLAGES	PETULANCIES	PHAGOMANIAS
PERVERTIBLE	PETITIONARY	PETROLATUM	PETULANTLY	PHAGOPHOBIA
PERVERTING	PETITIONED	PETROLATUMS	PEWHOLDERS	PHAGOPHOBIAS
PERVIATING	PETITIONER	PETROLEOUS	PHACOLITES	PHAGOSOMES
PERVICACIES	PETITIONERS	PETROLEUMS	PHACOLITHS	PHALANGEAL
PERVICACIOUS	PETITIONING	PETROLEURS	PHAELONION	PHALANGERS
PERVICACITIES	PETITIONINGS	PETROLEUSE	PHAELONIONS	PHALANGIDS

PHALANGIST	PHANTASMALLY	PHARMACOPOEIAL	PHENACITES	PHENOMENALISTIC
PHALANGISTS	PHANTASMATA	PHARMACOPOEIAN	PHENAKISMS	PHENOMENALISTS
PHALANSTERIAN	PHANTASMIC	PHARMACOPOEIAS	PHENAKISTOSCOPE	PHENOMENALITIES
PHALANSTERIES	PHANTASMICAL	PHARMACOPOEIC	PHENAKITES	PHENOMENALITY
PHALANSTERISM	PHANTASMICALLY	PHARMACOPOEIST	PHENANTHRENE	PHENOMENALIZE
PHALANSTERISMS	PHANTASTIC	PHARMACOPOEISTS	PHENANTHRENES	PHENOMENALIZED
PHALANSTERIST	PHANTASTICS	PHARMACOPOLIST	PHENARSAZINE	PHENOMENALIZES
PHALANSTERISTS	PHANTASTRIES	PHARMACOPOLISTS	PHENARSAZINES	PHENOMENALIZING
PHALANSTERY	PHANTASTRY	PHARMACOTHERAPY	PHENAZINES	PHENOMENALLY
PHALAROPES	PHANTASYING	PHARYNGALS	PHENCYCLIDINE	PHENOMENAS
PHALLICALLY	PHANTOMATIC	PHARYNGEAL	PHENCYCLIDINES	PHENOMENISE
PHALLICISM	PHANTOMISH	PHARYNGITIC	PHENETICIST	PHENOMENISED
PHALLICISMS	PHANTOMLIKE	PHARYNGITIDES	PHENETICISTS	PHENOMENISES
PHALLICIST	PHANTOSMES	PHARYNGITIS	PHENETIDINE	PHENOMENISING
PHALLICISTS	PHARISAICAL	PHARYNGITISES	PHENETIDINES	PHENOMENISM
PHALLOCENTRIC	PHARISAICALLY	PHARYNGOLOGICAL	PHENETOLES	PHENOMENISMS
PHALLOCENTRISM	PHARISAICALNESS	PHARYNGOLOGIES	PHENFORMIN	PHENOMENIST
PHALLOCENTRISMS	PHARISAISM	PHARYNGOLOGIST	PHENFORMINS	PHENOMENISTS
PHALLOCRAT	PHARISAISMS	PHARYNGOLOGISTS	PHENGOPHOBIA	PHENOMENIZE
PHALLOCRATIC	PHARISEEISM	PHARYNGOLOGY	PHENGOPHOBIAS	PHENOMENIZED
PHALLOCRATS	PHARISEEISMS	PHARYNGOSCOPE	PHENMETRAZINE	PHENOMENIZES
PHALLOIDIN	PHARMACEUTIC	PHARYNGOSCOPES	PHENMETRAZINES	PHENOMENIZING
PHALLOIDINS	PHARMACEUTICAL	PHARYNGOSCOPIC	PHENOBARBITAL	PHENOMENOLOGIES
PHANEROGAM	PHARMACEUTICALS	PHARYNGOSCOPIES	PHENOBARBITALS	PHENOMENOLOGIST
PHANEROGAMIC	PHARMACEUTICS	PHARYNGOSCOPY	PHENOBARBITONE	PHENOMENOLOGY
PHANEROGAMOUS	PHARMACEUTIST	PHARYNGOTOMIES	PHENOBARBITONES	PHENOMENON
PHANEROGAMS	PHARMACEUTISTS	PHARYNGOTOMY	PHENOCOPIES	PHENOMENONS
PHANEROPHYTE	PHARMACIES	PHASCOGALE	PHENOCRYST	PHENOTHIAZINE
PHANEROPHYTES	PHARMACIST	PHASCOGALES	PHENOCRYSTIC	PHENOTHIAZINES
PHANSIGARS	PHARMACISTS	PHASEDOWNS	PHENOCRYSTS	PHENOTYPED
PHANTASIAST	PHARMACODYNAMIC	PHASEOLINS	PHENOLATED	PHENOTYPES
PHANTASIASTS	PHARMACOGENOMIC	PHATICALLY	PHENOLATES	PHENOTYPIC
PHANTASIED	PHARMACOGNOSIES	PHEASANTRIES	PHENOLATING	PHENOTYPICAL
PHANTASIES	PHARMACOGNOSIST	PHEASANTRY	PHENOLOGICAL	PHENOTYPICALLY
PHANTASIME	PHARMACOGNOSTIC	PHELLODERM	PHENOLOGICALLY	PHENOTYPING
PHANTASIMES	PHARMACOGNOSY	PHELLODERMAL	PHENOLOGIES	PHENOXIDES
PHANTASIMS	PHARMACOKINETIC	PHELLODERMS	PHENOLOGIST	PHENTOLAMINE
PHANTASMAGORIA	PHARMACOLOGIC	PHELLOGENETIC	PHENOLOGISTS	PHENTOLAMINES
PHANTASMAGORIAL	PHARMACOLOGICAL	PHELLOGENIC	PHENOLPHTHALEIN	PHENYLALANIN
PHANTASMAGORIAS	PHARMACOLOGIES	PHELLOGENS	PHENOMENAL	PHENYLALANINE
PHANTASMAGORIC	PHARMACOLOGIST	PHELLOPLASTIC	PHENOMENALISE	PHENYLALANINES
PHANTASMAGORIES	PHARMACOLOGISTS	PHELLOPLASTICS	PHENOMENALISED	PHENYLALANINS
PHANTASMAGORY	PHARMACOLOGY	PHELONIONS	PHENOMENALISES	PHENYLAMINE
PHANTASMAL	PHARMACOPEIA	PHENACAINE	PHENOMENALISING	PHENYLAMINES
PHANTASMALIAN	PHARMACOPEIAL	PHENACAINES	PHENOMENALISM	PHENYLBUTAZONE
PHANTASMALITIES	PHARMACOPEIAS	PHENACETIN	PHENOMENALISMS	PHENYLBUTAZONES
PHANTASMALITY	PHARMACOPOEIA	PHENACETINS	PHENOMENALIST	PHENYLENES

P

PHENYLEPHRINE	PHILIPPINAS	PHILOSOPHER	PHLEBOTOMIC	PHOLIDOSES
PHENYLEPHRINES	PHILIPPINE	PHILOSOPHERESS	PHLEBOTOMICAL	PHOLIDOSIS
PHENYLKETONURIA	PHILIPPINES	PHILOSOPHERS	PHLEBOTOMIES	PHONASTHENIA
PHENYLKETONURIC	PHILISTIAS	PHILOSOPHES	PHLEBOTOMISE	PHONASTHENIAS
PHENYLMETHYL	PHILISTINE	PHILOSOPHESS	PHLEBOTOMISED	PHONATHONS
PHENYLMETHYLS	PHILISTINES	PHILOSOPHESSES	PHLEBOTOMISES	PHONATIONS
PHENYLTHIOUREA	PHILISTINISM	PHILOSOPHIC	PHLEBOTOMISING	PHONAUTOGRAPH
PHENYLTHIOUREAS	PHILISTINISMS	PHILOSOPHICAL	PHLEBOTOMIST	PHONAUTOGRAPHIC
PHENYTOINS	PHILLABEGS	PHILOSOPHICALLY	PHLEBOTOMISTS	PHONAUTOGRAPHS
PHEROMONAL	PHILLIBEGS	PHILOSOPHIES	PHLEBOTOMIZE	PHONECARDS
PHEROMONES	PHILLIPSITE	PHILOSOPHISE	PHLEBOTOMIZED	PHONEMATIC
PHIALIFORM	PHILLIPSITES	PHILOSOPHISED	PHLEBOTOMIZES	PHONEMATICALLY
PHILADELPHUS	PHILLUMENIES	PHILOSOPHISER	PHLEBOTOMIZING	PHONEMICALLY
PHILADELPHUSES	PHILLUMENIST	PHILOSOPHISERS	PHLEBOTOMY	PHONEMICISATION
PHILANDERED	PHILLUMENISTS	PHILOSOPHISES	PHLEGMAGOGIC	PHONEMICISE
PHILANDERER	PHILLUMENY	PHILOSOPHISING	PHLEGMAGOGUE	PHONEMICISED
PHILANDERERS	PHILODENDRA	PHILOSOPHISM	PHLEGMAGOGUES	PHONEMICISES
PHILANDERING	PHILODENDRON	PHILOSOPHISMS	PHLEGMASIA	PHONEMICISING
PHILANDERINGS	PHILODENDRONS	PHILOSOPHIST	PHLEGMASIAS	PHONEMICIST
PHILANDERS	PHILOGYNIES	PHILOSOPHISTIC	PHLEGMATIC	PHONEMICISTS
PHILANTHROPE	PHILOGYNIST	PHILOSOPHISTS	PHLEGMATICAL	PHONEMICIZATION
PHILANTHROPES	PHILOGYNISTS	PHILOSOPHIZE	PHLEGMATICALLY	PHONEMICIZE
PHILANTHROPIC	PHILOGYNOUS	PHILOSOPHIZED	PHLEGMATICNESS	PHONEMICIZED
PHILANTHROPICAL	PHILOLOGER	PHILOSOPHIZER	PHLEGMIEST	PHONEMICIZES
PHILANTHROPIES	PHILOLOGERS	PHILOSOPHIZERS	PHLEGMONIC	PHONEMICIZING
PHILANTHROPIST	PHILOLOGIAN	PHILOSOPHIZES	PHLEGMONOID	PHONENDOSCOPE
PHILANTHROPISTS	PHILOLOGIANS	PHILOSOPHIZING	PHLEGMONOUS	PHONENDOSCOPES
PHILANTHROPOID	PHILOLOGIC	PHILOSOPHY	PHLOGISTIC	PHONETICAL
PHILANTHROPOIDS	PHILOLOGICAL	PHILOXENIA	PHLOGISTICATE	PHONETICALLY
PHILANTHROPY	PHILOLOGICALLY	PHILOXENIAS	PHLOGISTICATED	PHONETICIAN
PHILATELIC	PHILOLOGIES	PHILTERING	PHLOGISTICATES	PHONETICIANS
PHILATELICALLY	PHILOLOGIST	PHISNOMIES	PHLOGISTICATING	PHONETICISATION
PHILATELIES	PHILOLOGISTS	PHLEBECTOMIES	PHLOGISTON	PHONETICISE
PHILATELIST	PHILOLOGUE	PHLEBECTOMY	PHLOGISTONS	PHONETICISED
PHILATELISTS	PHILOLOGUES	PHLEBITIDES	PHLOGOPITE	PHONETICISES
PHILHARMONIC	PHILOMATHIC	PHLEBITISES	PHLOGOPITES	PHONETICISING
PHILHARMONICS	PHILOMATHICAL	PHLEBOGRAM	PHLORIZINS	PHONETICISM
PHILHELLENE	PHILOMATHIES	PHLEBOGRAMS	PHLYCTAENA	PHONETICISMS
PHILHELLENES	PHILOMATHS	PHLEBOGRAPHIC	PHLYCTAENAE	PHONETICIST
PHILHELLENIC	PHILOMATHY	PHLEBOGRAPHIES	PHLYCTENAE	PHONETICISTS
PHILHELLENISM	PHILOMELAS	PHLEBOGRAPHY	PHOCOMELIA	PHONETICIZATION
PHILHELLENISMS	PHILOPENAS	PHLEBOLITE	PHOCOMELIAS	PHONETICIZE
PHILHELLENIST	PHILOPOENA	PHLEBOLITES	PHOCOMELIC	PHONETICIZED
PHILHELLENISTS	PHILOPOENAS	PHLEBOLOGIES	PHOCOMELIES	PHONETICIZES
PHILHORSES	PHILOSOPHASTER	PHLEBOLOGY	PHOENIXISM	PHONETICIZING
PHILIPPICS	PHILOSOPHASTERS	PHLEBOSCLEROSES	PHOENIXISMS	PHONETISATION
PHILIPPINA	PHILOSOPHE	PHLEBOSCLEROSIS	PHOENIXLIKE	PHONETISATIONS

P

PHONETISED
PHONETISES
PHONETISING
PHONETISMS
PHONETISTS
PHONETIZATION
PHONETIZATIONS
PHONETIZED
PHONETIZES
PHONETIZING
PHONEYNESS
PHONEYNESSES
PHONICALLY
PHONINESSES
PHONMETERS
PHONOCAMPTIC
PHONOCAMPTICS
PHONOCARDIOGRAM
PHONOCHEMISTRY
PHONOFIDDLE
PHONOFIDDLES
PHONOGRAMIC
PHONOGRAMICALLY
PHONOGRAMMIC
PHONOGRAMS
PHONOGRAPH
PHONOGRAPHER
PHONOGRAPHERS
PHONOGRAPHIC
PHONOGRAPHIES
PHONOGRAPHIST
PHONOGRAPHISTS
PHONOGRAPHS
PHONOGRAPHY
PHONOLITES
PHONOLITIC
PHONOLOGIC
PHONOLOGICAL
PHONOLOGICALLY
PHONOLOGIES
PHONOLOGIST
PHONOLOGISTS
PHONOMETER
PHONOMETERS
PHONOMETRIC
PHONOMETRICAL
PHONOPHOBIA

PHONOPHOBIAS
PHONOPHORE
PHONOPHORES
PHONOPORES
PHONOSCOPE
PHONOSCOPES
PHONOTACTIC
PHONOTACTICS
PHONOTYPED
PHONOTYPER
PHONOTYPERS
PHONOTYPES
PHONOTYPIC
PHONOTYPICAL
PHONOTYPIES
PHONOTYPING
PHONOTYPIST
PHONOTYPISTS
PHORMINGES
PHOSGENITE
PHOSGENITES
PHOSPHATASE
PHOSPHATASES
PHOSPHATED
PHOSPHATES
PHOSPHATIC
PHOSPHATIDE
PHOSPHATIDES
PHOSPHATIDIC
PHOSPHATIDYL
PHOSPHATIDYLS
PHOSPHATING
PHOSPHATISATION
PHOSPHATISE
PHOSPHATISED
PHOSPHATISES
PHOSPHATISING
PHOSPHATIZATION
PHOSPHATIZE
PHOSPHATIZED
PHOSPHATIZES
PHOSPHATIZING
PHOSPHATURIA
PHOSPHATURIAS
PHOSPHATURIC
PHOSPHENES
PHOSPHIDES

PHOSPHINES
PHOSPHITES
PHOSPHOCREATIN
PHOSPHOCREATINE
PHOSPHOCREATINS
PHOSPHOKINASE
PHOSPHOKINASES
PHOSPHOLIPASE
PHOSPHOLIPASES
PHOSPHOLIPID
PHOSPHOLIPIDS
PHOSPHONIC
PHOSPHONIUM
PHOSPHONIUMS
PHOSPHOPROTEIN
PHOSPHOPROTEINS
PHOSPHORATE
PHOSPHORATED
PHOSPHORATES
PHOSPHORATING
PHOSPHORESCE
PHOSPHORESCED
PHOSPHORESCENCE
PHOSPHORESCENT
PHOSPHORESCES
PHOSPHORESCING
PHOSPHORET
PHOSPHORETS
PHOSPHORETTED
PHOSPHORIC
PHOSPHORISE
PHOSPHORISED
PHOSPHORISES
PHOSPHORISING
PHOSPHORISM
PHOSPHORISMS
PHOSPHORITE
PHOSPHORITES
PHOSPHORITIC
PHOSPHORIZE
PHOSPHORIZED
PHOSPHORIZES
PHOSPHORIZING
PHOSPHOROLYSES
PHOSPHOROLYSIS
PHOSPHOROLYTIC

PHOSPHOROSCOPE
PHOSPHOROSCOPES
PHOSPHOROUS
PHOSPHORUS
PHOSPHORUSES
PHOSPHORYL
PHOSPHORYLASE
PHOSPHORYLASES
PHOSPHORYLATE
PHOSPHORYLATED
PHOSPHORYLATES
PHOSPHORYLATING
PHOSPHORYLATION
PHOSPHORYLATIVE
PHOSPHORYLS
PHOSPHURET
PHOSPHURETS
PHOSPHURETTED
PHOTICALLY
PHOTOACTINIC
PHOTOACTIVE
PHOTOAUTOTROPH
PHOTOAUTOTROPHS
PHOTOBATHIC
PHOTOBIOLOGIC
PHOTOBIOLOGICAL
PHOTOBIOLOGIES
PHOTOBIOLOGIST
PHOTOBIOLOGISTS
PHOTOBIOLOGY
PHOTOCARDS
PHOTOCATALYSES
PHOTOCATALYSIS
PHOTOCATALYTIC
PHOTOCATHODE
PHOTOCATHODES
PHOTOCELLS
PHOTOCHEMICAL
PHOTOCHEMICALLY
PHOTOCHEMIST
PHOTOCHEMISTRY
PHOTOCHEMISTS
PHOTOCHROMIC
PHOTOCHROMICS
PHOTOCHROMIES
PHOTOCHROMISM
PHOTOCHROMISMS

PHOTOCHROMY
PHOTOCOMPOSE
PHOTOCOMPOSED
PHOTOCOMPOSER
PHOTOCOMPOSERS
PHOTOCOMPOSES
PHOTOCOMPOSING
PHOTOCONDUCTING
PHOTOCONDUCTION
PHOTOCONDUCTIVE
PHOTOCONDUCTOR
PHOTOCONDUCTORS
PHOTOCOPIABLE
PHOTOCOPIED
PHOTOCOPIER
PHOTOCOPIERS
PHOTOCOPIES
PHOTOCOPYING
PHOTOCOPYINGS
PHOTOCURRENT
PHOTOCURRENTS
PHOTODEGRADABLE
PHOTODETECTOR
PHOTODETECTORS
PHOTODIODE
PHOTODIODES
PHOTODISSOCIATE
PHOTODUPLICATE
PHOTODUPLICATED
PHOTODUPLICATES
PHOTODYNAMIC
PHOTODYNAMICS
PHOTOELASTIC
PHOTOELASTICITY
PHOTOELECTRIC
PHOTOELECTRICAL
PHOTOELECTRODE
PHOTOELECTRODES
PHOTOELECTRON
PHOTOELECTRONIC
PHOTOELECTRONS
PHOTOEMISSION
PHOTOEMISSIONS
PHOTOEMISSIVE
PHOTOENGRAVE
PHOTOENGRAVED
PHOTOENGRAVER

P

PHOTOENGRAVERS

PHOTOENGRAVERS	PHOTOGRAPHY	PHOTOMETRICALLY	PHOTOPHOBIA	PHOTOSENSITISER
PHOTOENGRAVES	PHOTOGRAVURE	PHOTOMETRIES	PHOTOPHOBIAS	PHOTOSENSITISES
PHOTOENGRAVING	PHOTOGRAVURES	PHOTOMETRIST	PHOTOPHOBIC	PHOTOSENSITIVE
PHOTOENGRAVINGS	PHOTOINDUCED	PHOTOMETRISTS	PHOTOPHONE	PHOTOSENSITIZE
PHOTOEXCITATION	PHOTOINDUCTION	PHOTOMETRY	PHOTOPHONES	PHOTOSENSITIZED
PHOTOEXCITED	PHOTOINDUCTIONS	PHOTOMICROGRAPH	PHOTOPHONIC	PHOTOSENSITIZER
PHOTOFINISHER	PHOTOINDUCTIVE	PHOTOMONTAGE	PHOTOPHONIES	PHOTOSENSITIZES
PHOTOFINISHERS	PHOTOIONISATION	PHOTOMONTAGES	PHOTOPHONY	PHOTOSETTER
PHOTOFINISHING	PHOTOIONISE	PHOTOMOSAIC	PHOTOPHORE	PHOTOSETTERS
PHOTOFINISHINGS	PHOTOIONISED	PHOTOMOSAICS	PHOTOPHORES	PHOTOSETTING
PHOTOFISSION	PHOTOIONISES	PHOTOMULTIPLIER	PHOTOPHORESES	PHOTOSETTINGS
PHOTOFISSIONS	PHOTOIONISING	PHOTOMURAL	PHOTOPHORESIS	PHOTOSHOOT
PHOTOFLASH	PHOTOIONIZATION	PHOTOMURALS	PHOTOPLAYS	PHOTOSHOOTS
PHOTOFLASHES	PHOTOIONIZE	PHOTONASTIC	PHOTOPOLYMER	PHOTOSHOPPED
PHOTOFLOOD	PHOTOIONIZED	PHOTONASTIES	PHOTOPOLYMERS	PHOTOSHOPPING
PHOTOFLOODS	PHOTOIONIZES	PHOTONASTY	PHOTOPOSITIVE	PHOTOSHOPS
PHOTOFLUOROGRAM	PHOTOIONIZING	PHOTONEGATIVE	PHOTOPRODUCT	PHOTOSPHERE
PHOTOGELATINE	PHOTOJOURNALISM	PHOTONEUTRON	PHOTOPRODUCTION	PHOTOSPHERES
PHOTOGENES	PHOTOJOURNALIST	PHOTONEUTRONS	PHOTOPRODUCTS	PHOTOSPHERIC
PHOTOGENIC	PHOTOKINESES	PHOTONOVEL	PHOTOPSIAS	PHOTOSTATED
PHOTOGENICALLY	PHOTOKINESIS	PHOTONOVELS	PHOTOPSIES	PHOTOSTATIC
PHOTOGENIES	PHOTOKINETIC	PHOTONUCLEAR	PHOTOREACTION	PHOTOSTATING
PHOTOGEOLOGIC	PHOTOLITHO	PHOTOOXIDATION	PHOTOREACTIONS	PHOTOSTATS
PHOTOGEOLOGICAL	PHOTOLITHOGRAPH	PHOTOOXIDATIONS	PHOTOREALISM	PHOTOSTATTED
PHOTOGEOLOGIES	PHOTOLITHOS	PHOTOOXIDATIVE	PHOTOREALISMS	PHOTOSTATTING
PHOTOGEOLOGIST	PHOTOLUMINESCE	PHOTOOXIDISE	PHOTOREALIST	PHOTOSYNTHATE
PHOTOGEOLOGISTS	PHOTOLUMINESCED	PHOTOOXIDISED	PHOTOREALISTIC	PHOTOSYNTHATES
PHOTOGEOLOGY	PHOTOLUMINESCES	PHOTOOXIDISES	PHOTOREALISTS	PHOTOSYNTHESES
PHOTOGLYPH	PHOTOLYSABLE	PHOTOOXIDISING	PHOTORECEPTION	PHOTOSYNTHESIS
PHOTOGLYPHIC	PHOTOLYSED	PHOTOOXIDIZE	PHOTORECEPTIONS	PHOTOSYNTHESISE
PHOTOGLYPHIES	PHOTOLYSES	PHOTOOXIDIZED	PHOTORECEPTIVE	PHOTOSYNTHESIZE
PHOTOGLYPHS	PHOTOLYSING	PHOTOOXIDIZES	PHOTORECEPTOR	PHOTOSYNTHETIC
PHOTOGLYPHY	PHOTOLYSIS	PHOTOOXIDIZING	PHOTORECEPTORS	PHOTOSYSTEM
PHOTOGRAMMETRIC	PHOTOLYTIC	PHOTOPERIOD	PHOTOREDUCE	PHOTOSYSTEMS
PHOTOGRAMMETRY	PHOTOLYTICALLY	PHOTOPERIODIC	PHOTOREDUCED	PHOTOTACTIC
PHOTOGRAMS	PHOTOLYZABLE	PHOTOPERIODISM	PHOTOREDUCES	PHOTOTACTICALLY
PHOTOGRAPH	PHOTOLYZED	PHOTOPERIODISMS	PHOTOREDUCING	PHOTOTAXES
PHOTOGRAPHED	PHOTOLYZES	PHOTOPERIODS	PHOTOREDUCTION	PHOTOTAXIES
PHOTOGRAPHER	PHOTOLYZING	PHOTOPHASE	PHOTOREDUCTIONS	PHOTOTAXIS
PHOTOGRAPHERS	PHOTOMACROGRAPH	PHOTOPHASES	PHOTOREFRACTIVE	PHOTOTELEGRAPH
PHOTOGRAPHIC	PHOTOMAPPED	PHOTOPHILIC	PHOTORESIST	PHOTOTELEGRAPHS
PHOTOGRAPHICAL	PHOTOMAPPING	PHOTOPHILIES	PHOTORESISTS	PHOTOTELEGRAPHY
PHOTOGRAPHIES	PHOTOMASKS	PHOTOPHILOUS	PHOTOSCANNED	PHOTOTHERAPIES
PHOTOGRAPHING	PHOTOMECHANICAL	PHOTOPHILS	PHOTOSCANNING	PHOTOTHERAPY
PHOTOGRAPHIST	PHOTOMETER	PHOTOPHILY	PHOTOSCANS	PHOTOTHERMAL
PHOTOGRAPHISTS	PHOTOMETERS	PHOTOPHOBE	PHOTOSENSITISE	PHOTOTHERMALLY
PHOTOGRAPHS	PHOTOMETRIC	PHOTOPHOBES	PHOTOSENSITISED	PHOTOTHERMIC

PHOTOTONIC	PHRASEOGRAPHIC	PHTHIRIASES	PHYLLOQUINONES	PHYSICKING
PHOTOTONUS	PHRASEOGRAPHIES	PHTHIRIASIS	PHYLLOSILICATE	PHYSICOCHEMICAL
PHOTOTONUSES	PHRASEOGRAPHS	PHTHISICAL	PHYLLOSILICATES	PHYSIOCRACIES
PHOTOTOPOGRAPHY	PHRASEOGRAPHY	PHTHISICKY	PHYLLOSPHERE	PHYSIOCRACY
PHOTOTOXIC	PHRASEOLOGIC	PHYCOBILIN	PHYLLOSPHERES	PHYSIOCRAT
PHOTOTOXICITIES	PHRASEOLOGICAL	PHYCOBILINS	PHYLLOTACTIC	PHYSIOCRATIC
PHOTOTOXICITY	PHRASEOLOGIES	PHYCOBIONT	PHYLLOTACTICAL	PHYSIOCRATS
PHOTOTRANSISTOR	PHRASEOLOGIST	PHYCOBIONTS	PHYLLOTAXES	PHYSIOGNOMIC
PHOTOTROPE	PHRASEOLOGISTS	PHYCOCYANIN	PHYLLOTAXIES	PHYSIOGNOMICAL
PHOTOTROPES	PHRASEOLOGY	PHYCOCYANINS	PHYLLOTAXIS	PHYSIOGNOMIES
PHOTOTROPH	PHREAKINGS	PHYCOCYANS	PHYLLOTAXY	PHYSIOGNOMIST
PHOTOTROPHIC	PHREATOPHYTE	PHYCOERYTHRIN	PHYLLOXERA	PHYSIOGNOMISTS
PHOTOTROPHS	PHREATOPHYTES	PHYCOERYTHRINS	PHYLLOXERAE	PHYSIOGNOMY
PHOTOTROPIC	PHREATOPHYTIC	PHYCOLOGICAL	PHYLLOXERAS	PHYSIOGRAPHER
PHOTOTROPICALLY	PHRENESIAC	PHYCOLOGIES	PHYLOGENESES	PHYSIOGRAPHERS
PHOTOTROPIES	PHRENETICAL	PHYCOLOGIST	PHYLOGENESIS	PHYSIOGRAPHIC
PHOTOTROPISM	PHRENETICALLY	PHYCOLOGISTS	PHYLOGENETIC	PHYSIOGRAPHICAL
PHOTOTROPISMS	PHRENETICNESS	PHYCOMYCETE	PHYLOGENIC	PHYSIOGRAPHIES
PHOTOTROPY	PHRENETICNESSES	PHYCOMYCETES	PHYLOGENIES	PHYSIOGRAPHY
PHOTOTUBES	PHRENETICS	PHYCOMYCETOUS	PHYSALISES	PHYSIOLATER
PHOTOTYPED	PHRENITIDES	PHYCOPHAEIN	PHYSHARMONICA	PHYSIOLATERS
PHOTOTYPES	PHRENITISES	PHYCOPHAEINS	PHYSHARMONICAS	PHYSIOLATRIES
PHOTOTYPESET	PHRENOLOGIC	PHYCOXANTHIN	PHYSIATRIC	PHYSIOLATRY
PHOTOTYPESETS	PHRENOLOGICAL	PHYCOXANTHINS	PHYSIATRICAL	PHYSIOLOGIC
PHOTOTYPESETTER	PHRENOLOGICALLY	PHYLACTERIC	PHYSIATRICS	PHYSIOLOGICAL
PHOTOTYPIC	PHRENOLOGIES	PHYLACTERICAL	PHYSIATRIES	PHYSIOLOGICALLY
PHOTOTYPICALLY	PHRENOLOGISE	PHYLACTERIES	PHYSIATRIST	PHYSIOLOGIES
PHOTOTYPIES	PHRENOLOGISED	PHYLACTERY	PHYSIATRISTS	PHYSIOLOGIST
PHOTOTYPING	PHRENOLOGISES	PHYLARCHIES	PHYSICALISM	PHYSIOLOGISTS
PHOTOTYPOGRAPHY	PHRENOLOGISING	PHYLAXISES	PHYSICALISMS	PHYSIOLOGUS
PHOTOVOLTAIC	PHRENOLOGIST	PHYLESISES	PHYSICALIST	PHYSIOLOGUSES
PHOTOVOLTAICS	PHRENOLOGISTS	PHYLETICALLY	PHYSICALISTIC	PHYSIOLOGY
PHOTOXYLOGRAPHY	PHRENOLOGIZE	PHYLLARIES	PHYSICALISTS	PHYSIOPATHOLOGY
PHOTOZINCOGRAPH	PHRENOLOGIZED	PHYLLOCLAD	PHYSICALITIES	PHYSIOTHERAPIES
PHRAGMOPLAST	PHRENOLOGIZES	PHYLLOCLADE	PHYSICALITY	PHYSIOTHERAPIST
PHRAGMOPLASTS	PHRENOLOGIZING	PHYLLOCLADES	PHYSICALLY	PHYSIOTHERAPY
PHRASELESS	PHRENOLOGY	PHYLLOCLADS	PHYSICALNESS	PHYSITHEISM
PHRASEMAKER	PHRENSICAL	PHYLLODIAL	PHYSICALNESSES	PHYSITHEISMS
PHRASEMAKERS	PHRENSYING	PHYLLODIES	PHYSICIANCIES	PHYSITHEISTIC
PHRASEMAKING	PHRONTISTERIES	PHYLLODIUM	PHYSICIANCY	PHYSOCLISTOUS
PHRASEMAKINGS	PHRONTISTERY	PHYLLOMANIA	PHYSICIANER	PHYSOSTIGMIN
PHRASEMONGER	PHTHALATES	PHYLLOMANIAS	PHYSICIANERS	PHYSOSTIGMINE
PHRASEMONGERING	PHTHALEINS	PHYLLOPHAGOUS	PHYSICIANS	PHYSOSTIGMINES
PHRASEMONGERS	PHTHALOCYANIN	PHYLLOPLANE	PHYSICIANSHIP	PHYSOSTIGMINS
PHRASEOGRAM	PHTHALOCYANINE	PHYLLOPLANES	PHYSICIANSHIPS	PHYSOSTOMOUS
PHRASEOGRAMS	PHTHALOCYANINES	PHYLLOPODS	PHYSICISMS	PHYTOALEXIN
PHRASEOGRAPH	PHTHALOCYANINS	PHYLLOQUINONE	PHYSICISTS	PHYTOALEXINS

P

PHYTOBENTHOS	PHYTOPLANKTON	PICCOLOISTS	PICROCARMINE	PIDGINISATION
PHYTOBENTHOSES	PHYTOPLANKTONIC	PICHICIEGO	PICROCARMINES	PIDGINISATIONS
PHYTOCHEMICAL	PHYTOPLANKTONS	PICHICIEGOS	PICROTOXIN	PIDGINISED
PHYTOCHEMICALLY	PHYTOSANITARY	PICHOLINES	PICROTOXINS	PIDGINISES
PHYTOCHEMICALS	PHYTOSOCIOLOGY	PICKABACKED	PICTARNIES	PIDGINISING
PHYTOCHEMIST	PHYTOSTEROL	PICKABACKING	PICTOGRAMS	PIDGINIZATION
PHYTOCHEMISTRY	PHYTOSTEROLS	PICKABACKS	PICTOGRAPH	PIDGINIZATIONS
PHYTOCHEMISTS	PHYTOTHERAPIES	PICKADILLIES	PICTOGRAPHIC	PIDGINIZED
PHYTOCHROME	PHYTOTHERAPY	PICKADILLO	PICTOGRAPHIES	PIDGINIZES
PHYTOCHROMES	PHYTOTOMIES	PICKADILLOES	PICTOGRAPHS	PIDGINIZING
PHYTOESTROGEN	PHYTOTOMIST	PICKADILLS	PICTOGRAPHY	PIECEMEALED
PHYTOESTROGENS	PHYTOTOMISTS	PICKADILLY	PICTORIALISE	PIECEMEALING
PHYTOFLAGELLATE	PHYTOTOXIC	PICKANINNIES	PICTORIALISED	PIECEMEALS
PHYTOGENESES	PHYTOTOXICITIES	PICKANINNY	PICTORIALISES	PIECEWORKER
PHYTOGENESIS	PHYTOTOXICITY	PICKAPACKED	PICTORIALISING	PIECEWORKERS
PHYTOGENETIC	PHYTOTOXIN	PICKAPACKING	PICTORIALISM	PIECEWORKS
PHYTOGENETICAL	PHYTOTOXINS	PICKAPACKS	PICTORIALISMS	PIEDMONTITE
PHYTOGENIC	PHYTOTRONS	PICKAROONS	PICTORIALIST	PIEDMONTITES
PHYTOGENIES	PIACULARITIES	PICKBACKED	PICTORIALISTS	PIEDNESSES
PHYTOGEOGRAPHER	PIACULARITY	PICKBACKING	PICTORIALIZE	PIEMONTITE
PHYTOGEOGRAPHIC	PIANISSIMI	PICKEDNESS	PICTORIALIZED	PIEMONTITES
PHYTOGEOGRAPHY	PIANISSIMO	PICKEDNESSES	PICTORIALIZES	PIEPOWDERS
PHYTOGRAPHER	PIANISSIMOS	PICKEERERS	PICTORIALIZING	PIERCEABLE
PHYTOGRAPHERS	PIANISSISSIMO	PICKEERING	PICTORIALLY	PIERCINGLY
PHYTOGRAPHIC	PIANISTICALLY	PICKELHAUBE	PICTORIALNESS	PIERCINGNESS
PHYTOGRAPHIES	PIANOFORTE	PICKELHAUBES	PICTORIALNESSES	PIERCINGNESSES
PHYTOGRAPHY	PIANOFORTES	PICKERELWEED	PICTORIALS	PIERRETTES
PHYTOHORMONE	PIANOLISTS	PICKERELWEEDS	PICTORICAL	PIETISTICAL
PHYTOHORMONES	PICADILLOS	PICKETBOAT	PICTORICALLY	PIETISTICALLY
PHYTOLITHS	PICANINNIES	PICKETBOATS	PICTUREGOER	PIEZOCHEMISTRY
PHYTOLOGICAL	PICARESQUE	PICKETINGS	PICTUREGOERS	PIEZOELECTRIC
PHYTOLOGICALLY	PICARESQUES	PICKINESSES	PICTUREPHONE	PIEZOMAGNETIC
PHYTOLOGIES	PICAROONED	PICKPOCKET	PICTUREPHONES	PIEZOMAGNETISM
PHYTOLOGIST	PICAROONING	PICKPOCKETS	PICTURESQUE	PIEZOMAGNETISMS
PHYTOLOGISTS	PICAYUNISH	PICKTHANKS	PICTURESQUELY	PIEZOMETER
PHYTONADIONE	PICAYUNISHLY	PICNICKERS	PICTURESQUENESS	PIEZOMETERS
PHYTONADIONES	PICAYUNISHNESS	PICNICKING	PICTURISATION	PIEZOMETRIC
PHYTOPATHOGEN	PICCADILLIES	PICOCURIES	PICTURISATIONS	PIEZOMETRICALLY
PHYTOPATHOGENIC	PICCADILLO	PICOFARADS	PICTURISED	PIEZOMETRIES
PHYTOPATHOGENS	PICCADILLOES	PICOMETERS	PICTURISES	PIEZOMETRY
PHYTOPATHOLOGY	PICCADILLS	PICOMETRES	PICTURISING	PIGEONHOLE
PHYTOPHAGIC	PICCADILLY	PICORNAVIRUS	PICTURIZATION	PIGEONHOLED
PHYTOPHAGIES	PICCALILLI	PICORNAVIRUSES	PICTURIZATIONS	PIGEONHOLER
PHYTOPHAGOUS	PICCALILLIS	PICOSECOND	PICTURIZED	PIGEONHOLERS
PHYTOPHAGY	PICCANINNIES	PICOSECONDS	PICTURIZES	PIGEONHOLES
PHYTOPLANKTER	PICCANINNY	PICOWAVING	PICTURIZING	PIGEONHOLING
PHYTOPLANKTERS	PICCOLOIST	PICQUETING	PIDDLINGLY	PIGEONITES

P

PIGEONRIES	PILGRIMAGE	PIMPMOBILES	PINKISHNESSES	PIPERAZINES
PIGEONWING	PILGRIMAGED	PINACOIDAL	PINKNESSES	PIPERIDINE
PIGEONWINGS	PILGRIMAGER	PINACOTHECA	PINNACLING	PIPERIDINES
PIGGINESSES	PILGRIMAGERS	PINACOTHECAE	PINNATIFID	PIPERONALS
PIGGISHNESS	PILGRIMAGES	PINAKOIDAL	PINNATIFIDLY	PIPESTONES
PIGGISHNESSES	PILGRIMAGING	PINAKOTHEK	PINNATIONS	PIPINESSES
PIGGYBACKED	PILGRIMERS	PINAKOTHEKS	PINNATIPARTITE	PIPISTRELLE
PIGGYBACKING	PILGRIMISE	PINBALLING	PINNATIPED	PIPISTRELLES
PIGGYBACKS	PILGRIMISED	PINCERLIKE	PINNATISECT	PIPISTRELS
PIGHEADEDLY	PILGRIMISES	PINCHBECKS	PINNIEWINKLE	PIPIWHARAUROA
PIGHEADEDNESS	PILGRIMISING	PINCHCOCKS	PINNIEWINKLES	PIPIWHARAUROAS
PIGHEADEDNESSES	PILGRIMIZE	PINCHCOMMONS	PINNIPEDES	PIPSISSEWA
PIGMENTARY	PILGRIMIZED	PINCHCOMMONSES	PINNIPEDIAN	PIPSISSEWAS
PIGMENTATION	PILGRIMIZES	PINCHFISTS	PINNIPEDIANS	PIPSQUEAKS
PIGMENTATIONS	PILGRIMIZING	PINCHINGLY	PINNULATED	PIQUANCIES
PIGMENTING	PILIFEROUS	PINCHPENNIES	PINNYWINKLE	PIQUANTNESS
PIGMENTOSA	PILLARISTS	PINCHPENNY	PINNYWINKLES	PIQUANTNESSES
PIGMENTOSAS	PILLARLESS	PINCHPOINT	PINOCYTOSES	PIRACETAMS
PIGNERATED	PILLICOCKS	PINCHPOINTS	PINOCYTOSIS	PIRATICALLY
PIGNERATES	PILLIONING	PINCUSHION	PINOCYTOTIC	PIRLICUING
PIGNERATING	PILLIONIST	PINCUSHIONS	PINOCYTOTICALLY	PIROPLASMA
PIGNORATED	PILLIONISTS	PINEALECTOMIES	PINPOINTED	PIROPLASMATA
PIGNORATES	PILLIWINKS	PINEALECTOMISE	PINPOINTING	PIROPLASMS
PIGNORATING	PILLORISED	PINEALECTOMISED	PINPRICKED	PIROUETTED
PIGNORATION	PILLORISES	PINEALECTOMISES	PINPRICKING	PIROUETTER
PIGNORATIONS	PILLORISING	PINEALECTOMIZE	PINSETTERS	PIROUETTERS
PIGSCONCES	PILLORIZED	PINEALECTOMIZED	PINSPOTTER	PIROUETTES
PIGSTICKED	PILLORIZES	PINEALECTOMIZES	PINSPOTTERS	PIROUETTING
PIGSTICKER	PILLORIZING	PINEALECTOMY	PINSTRIPED	PISCATORIAL
PIGSTICKERS	PILLORYING	PINEAPPLES	PINSTRIPES	PISCATORIALLY
PIGSTICKING	PILLOWCASE	PINFEATHER	PINTADERAS	PISCATRIXES
PIGSTICKINGS	PILLOWCASES	PINFEATHERS	PINWHEELED	PISCICOLOUS
PIKEPERCHES	PILLOWSLIP	PINFOLDING	PINWHEELING	PISCICULTURAL
PIKESTAFFS	PILLOWSLIPS	PINGRASSES	PINWRENCHES	PISCICULTURALLY
PIKESTAVES	PILNIEWINKS	PINGUEFIED	PIONEERING	PISCICULTURE
PILASTERED	PILOCARPIN	PINGUEFIES	PIOUSNESSES	PISCICULTURES
PILEORHIZA	PILOCARPINE	PINGUEFYING	PIPECLAYED	PISCICULTURIST
PILEORHIZAS	PILOCARPINES	PINGUIDITIES	PIPECLAYING	PISCICULTURISTS
PILFERABLE	PILOCARPINS	PINGUIDITY	PIPEFISHES	PISCIFAUNA
PILFERAGES	PILOSITIES	PINGUITUDE	PIPEFITTER	PISCIFAUNAE
PILFERINGLY	PILOTFISHES	PINGUITUDES	PIPEFITTERS	PISCIFAUNAS
PILFERINGS	PILOTHOUSE	PINHEADEDNESS	PIPEFITTING	PISCIVORES
PILFERPROOF	PILOTHOUSES	PINHEADEDNESSES	PIPEFITTINGS	PISCIVOROUS
PILGARLICK	PIMPERNELS	PINHOOKERS	PIPELINING	PISSASPHALT
PILGARLICKS	PIMPLINESS	PINKERTONS	PIPELININGS	PISSASPHALTS
PILGARLICKY	PIMPLINESSES	PINKINESSES	PIPERACEOUS	PISTACHIOS
PILGARLICS	PIMPMOBILE	PINKISHNESS	PIPERAZINE	PISTAREENS

PISTILLARY	PITILESSNESSES	PLACODERMS	PLAINTIFFS	PLANISPHERIC
PISTILLATE	PITTOSPORUM	PLAGIARIES	PLAINTIVELY	PLANKTONIC
PISTILLODE	PITTOSPORUMS	PLAGIARISE	PLAINTIVENESS	PLANLESSLY
PISTILLODES	PITUITARIES	PLAGIARISED	PLAINTIVENESSES	PLANLESSNESS
PISTOLEERS	PITUITRINS	PLAGIARISER	PLAINTLESS	PLANLESSNESSES
PISTOLEROS	PITYRIASES	PLAGIARISERS	PLAINWORKS	PLANOBLAST
PISTOLIERS	PITYRIASIS	PLAGIARISES	PLAISTERED	PLANOBLASTS
PISTOLLING	PITYROSPORUM	PLAGIARISING	PLAISTERING	PLANOGAMETE
PITAPATTED	PITYROSPORUMS	PLAGIARISM	PLANARIANS	PLANOGAMETES
PITAPATTING	PIWAKAWAKA	PLAGIARISMS	PLANARITIES	PLANOGRAPHIC
PITCHBENDS	PIWAKAWAKAS	PLAGIARIST	PLANATIONS	PLANOGRAPHIES
PITCHBLENDE	PIXELATION	PLAGIARISTIC	PLANCHETTE	PLANOGRAPHY
PITCHBLENDES	PIXELATIONS	PLAGIARISTS	PLANCHETTES	PLANOMETER
PITCHERFUL	PIXELLATED	PLAGIARIZE	PLANELOADS	PLANOMETERS
PITCHERFULS	PIXILATION	PLAGIARIZED	PLANENESSES	PLANOMETRIC
PITCHERSFUL	PIXILATIONS	PLAGIARIZER	PLANESIDES	PLANOMETRICALLY
PITCHFORKED	PIXILLATED	PLAGIARIZERS	PLANETARIA	PLANOMETRIES
PITCHFORKING	PIXILLATION	PLAGIARIZES	PLANETARIES	PLANOMETRY
PITCHFORKS	PIXILLATIONS	PLAGIARIZING	PLANETARIUM	PLANTAGINACEOUS
PITCHINESS	PIXINESSES	PLAGIOCEPHALIES	PLANETARIUMS	PLANTATION
PITCHINESSES	PIZZICATOS	PLAGIOCEPHALY	PLANETESIMAL	PLANTATIONS
PITCHOMETER	PLACABILITIES	PLAGIOCLASE	PLANETESIMALS	PLANTIGRADE
PITCHOMETERS	PLACABILITY	PLAGIOCLASES	PLANETICAL	PLANTIGRADES
PITCHPERSON	PLACABLENESS	PLAGIOCLASTIC	PLANETLIKE	PLANTLINGS
PITCHPERSONS	PLACABLENESSES	PLAGIOCLIMAX	PLANETOIDAL	PLANTOCRACIES
PITCHPINES	PLACARDING	PLAGIOCLIMAXES	PLANETOIDS	PLANTOCRACY
PITCHPIPES	PLACATINGLY	PLAGIOSTOMATOUS	PLANETOLOGICAL	PLANTSWOMAN
PITCHPOLED	PLACATIONS	PLAGIOSTOME	PLANETOLOGIES	PLANTSWOMEN
PITCHPOLES	PLACEHOLDER	PLAGIOSTOMES	PLANETOLOGIST	PLANULIFORM
PITCHPOLING	PLACEHOLDERS	PLAGIOSTOMOUS	PLANETOLOGISTS	PLAQUETTES
PITCHSTONE	PLACEKICKED	PLAGIOTROPIC	PLANETOLOGY	PLASMAGELS
PITCHSTONES	PLACEKICKER	PLAGIOTROPISM	PLANETWIDE	PLASMAGENE
PITCHWOMAN	PLACEKICKERS	PLAGIOTROPISMS	PLANGENCIES	PLASMAGENES
PITCHWOMEN	PLACEKICKING	PLAGIOTROPOUS	PLANGENTLY	PLASMAGENIC
PITEOUSNESS	PLACEKICKS	PLAGUESOME	PLANIGRAPH	PLASMALEMMA
PITEOUSNESSES	PLACELESSLY	PLAINCHANT	PLANIGRAPHS	PLASMALEMMAS
PITHECANTHROPI	PLACEMENTS	PLAINCHANTS	PLANIMETER	PLASMAPHERESES
PITHECANTHROPUS	PLACENTALS	PLAINCLOTHES	PLANIMETERS	PLASMAPHERESIS
PITHINESSES	PLACENTATE	PLAINCLOTHESMAN	PLANIMETRIC	PLASMASOLS
PITIABLENESS	PLACENTATION	PLAINCLOTHESMEN	PLANIMETRICAL	PLASMATICAL
PITIABLENESSES	PLACENTATIONS	PLAINNESSES	PLANIMETRICALLY	PLASMINOGEN
PITIFULLER	PLACENTIFORM	PLAINSONGS	PLANIMETRIES	PLASMINOGENS
PITIFULLEST	PLACENTOLOGIES	PLAINSPOKEN	PLANIMETRY	PLASMODESM
PITIFULNESS	PLACENTOLOGY	PLAINSPOKENNESS	PLANISHERS	PLASMODESMA
PITIFULNESSES	PLACIDITIES	PLAINSTANES	PLANISHING	PLASMODESMAS
PITILESSLY	PLACIDNESS	PLAINSTONES	PLANISPHERE	PLASMODESMATA
PITILESSNESS	PLACIDNESSES	PLAINTEXTS	PLANISPHERES	PLASMODESMS

P

PLASMODIAL	PLASTICIZE	PLATINISING	PLATYRRHINIAN	PLEASANTRY
PLASMODIUM	PLASTICIZED	PLATINIZATION	PLATYRRHINIANS	PLEASINGLY
PLASMOGAMIES	PLASTICIZER	PLATINIZATIONS	PLAUDITORY	PLEASINGNESS
PLASMOGAMY	PLASTICIZERS	PLATINIZED	PLAUSIBILITIES	PLEASINGNESSES
PLASMOLYSE	PLASTICIZES	PLATINIZES	PLAUSIBILITY	PLEASURABILITY
PLASMOLYSED	PLASTICIZING	PLATINIZING	PLAUSIBLENESS	PLEASURABLE
PLASMOLYSES	PLASTIDIAL	PLATINOCYANIC	PLAUSIBLENESSES	PLEASURABLENESS
PLASMOLYSING	PLASTIDULE	PLATINOCYANIDE	PLAYABILITIES	PLEASURABLY
PLASMOLYSIS	PLASTIDULES	PLATINOCYANIDES	PLAYABILITY	PLEASUREFUL
PLASMOLYTIC	PLASTILINA	PLATINOIDS	PLAYACTING	PLEASURELESS
PLASMOLYTICALLY	PLASTILINAS	PLATINOTYPE	PLAYACTINGS	PLEASURERS
PLASMOLYZE	PLASTIQUES	PLATINOTYPES	PLAYACTORS	PLEASURING
PLASMOLYZED	PLASTISOLS	PLATITUDES	PLAYDOUGHS	PLEBEIANISE
PLASMOLYZES	PLASTOCYANIN	PLATITUDINAL	PLAYFELLOW	PLEBEIANISED
PLASMOLYZING	PLASTOCYANINS	PLATITUDINARIAN	PLAYFELLOWS	PLEBEIANISES
PLASMOSOMA	PLASTOGAMIES	PLATITUDINISE	PLAYFIELDS	PLEBEIANISING
PLASMOSOMATA	PLASTOGAMY	PLATITUDINISED	PLAYFULNESS	PLEBEIANISM
PLASMOSOME	PLASTOMETER	PLATITUDINISER	PLAYFULNESSES	PLEBEIANISMS
PLASMOSOMES	PLASTOMETERS	PLATITUDINISERS	PLAYGOINGS	PLEBEIANIZE
PLASTERBOARD	PLASTOMETRIC	PLATITUDINISES	PLAYGROUND	PLEBEIANIZED
PLASTERBOARDS	PLASTOMETRIES	PLATITUDINISING	PLAYGROUNDS	PLEBEIANIZES
PLASTERERS	PLASTOMETRY	PLATITUDINIZE	PLAYGROUPS	PLEBEIANIZING
PLASTERINESS	PLASTOQUINONE	PLATITUDINIZED	PLAYHOUSES	PLEBEIANLY
PLASTERINESSES	PLASTOQUINONES	PLATITUDINIZER	PLAYLEADER	PLEBIFICATION
PLASTERING	PLATANACEOUS	PLATITUDINIZERS	PLAYLEADERS	PLEBIFICATIONS
PLASTERINGS	PLATEAUING	PLATITUDINIZES	PLAYLISTED	PLEBIFYING
PLASTERSTONE	PLATEGLASS	PLATITUDINIZING	PLAYLISTING	PLEBISCITARY
PLASTERSTONES	PLATELAYER	PLATITUDINOUS	PLAYMAKERS	PLEBISCITE
PLASTERWORK	PLATELAYERS	PLATITUDINOUSLY	PLAYMAKING	PLEBISCITES
PLASTERWORKS	PLATEMAKER	PLATONICALLY	PLAYMAKINGS	PLECOPTERAN
PLASTICALLY	PLATEMAKERS	PLATONISMS	PLAYSCHOOL	PLECOPTERANS
PLASTICENE	PLATEMAKING	PLATOONING	PLAYSCHOOLS	PLECOPTEROUS
PLASTICENES	PLATEMAKINGS	PLATTELAND	PLAYTHINGS	PLECTOGNATH
PLASTICINE	PLATEMARKED	PLATTELANDS	PLAYWRIGHT	PLECTOGNATHIC
PLASTICINES	PLATEMARKING	PLATTERFUL	PLAYWRIGHTING	PLECTOGNATHOUS
PLASTICISATION	PLATEMARKS	PLATTERFULS	PLAYWRIGHTINGS	PLECTOGNATHS
PLASTICISATIONS	PLATERESQUE	PLATTERSFUL	PLAYWRIGHTS	PLECTOPTEROUS
PLASTICISE	PLATFORMED	PLATYCEPHALIC	PLAYWRITING	PLEDGEABLE
PLASTICISED	PLATFORMING	PLATYCEPHALOUS	PLAYWRITINGS	PLEINAIRISM
PLASTICISER	PLATFORMINGS	PLATYFISHES	PLEADINGLY	PLEINAIRISMS
PLASTICISERS	PLATINIFEROUS	PLATYHELMINTH	PLEASANCES	PLEINAIRIST
PLASTICISES	PLATINIRIDIUM	PLATYHELMINTHIC	PLEASANTER	PLEINAIRISTS
PLASTICISING	PLATINIRIDIUMS	PLATYHELMINTHS	PLEASANTEST	PLEIOCHASIA
PLASTICITIES	PLATINISATION	PLATYKURTIC	PLEASANTLY	PLEIOCHASIUM
PLASTICITY	PLATINISATIONS	PLATYPUSES	PLEASANTNESS	PLEIOMERIES
PLASTICIZATION	PLATINISED	PLATYRRHINE	PLEASANTNESSES	PLEIOMEROUS
PLASTICIZATIONS	PLATINISES	PLATYRRHINES	PLEASANTRIES	PLEIOTAXIES

P

PLEIOTROPIC	PLEROMATIC	PLIABLENESS	PLUMBERIES	PLURIPOTENT
PLEIOTROPIES	PLEROPHORIA	PLIABLENESSES	PLUMBIFEROUS	PLURIPRESENCE
PLEIOTROPISM	PLEROPHORIAS	PLIANTNESS	PLUMBISOLVENCY	PLURIPRESENCES
PLEIOTROPISMS	PLEROPHORIES	PLIANTNESSES	PLUMBISOLVENT	PLURISERIAL
PLEIOTROPY	PLEROPHORY	PLICATENESS	PLUMBNESSES	PLURISERIATE
PLENARTIES	PLESIOSAUR	PLICATENESSES	PLUMBOSOLVENCY	PLUSHINESS
PLENILUNAR	PLESIOSAURIAN	PLICATIONS	PLUMBOSOLVENT	PLUSHINESSES
PLENILUNES	PLESIOSAURS	PLICATURES	PLUMDAMASES	PLUSHNESSES
PLENIPOTENCE	PLESSIMETER	PLODDINGLY	PLUMIGEROUS	PLUTOCRACIES
PLENIPOTENCES	PLESSIMETERS	PLODDINGNESS	PLUMMETING	PLUTOCRACY
PLENIPOTENCIES	PLESSIMETRIC	PLODDINGNESSES	PLUMOSITIES	PLUTOCRATIC
PLENIPOTENCY	PLESSIMETRIES	PLOTLESSNESS	PLUMPENING	PLUTOCRATICAL
PLENIPOTENT	PLESSIMETRY	PLOTLESSNESSES	PLUMPNESSES	PLUTOCRATICALLY
PLENIPOTENTIAL	PLETHORICAL	PLOTTERING	PLUMULACEOUS	PLUTOCRATS
PLENIPOTENTIARY	PLETHORICALLY	PLOTTINGLY	PLUMULARIAN	PLUTOLATRIES
PLENISHERS	PLETHYSMOGRAM	PLOUGHABLE	PLUMULARIANS	PLUTOLATRY
PLENISHING	PLETHYSMOGRAMS	PLOUGHBOYS	PLUNDERABLE	PLUTOLOGIES
PLENISHINGS	PLETHYSMOGRAPH	PLOUGHGATE	PLUNDERAGE	PLUTOLOGIST
PLENISHMENT	PLETHYSMOGRAPHS	PLOUGHGATES	PLUNDERAGES	PLUTOLOGISTS
PLENISHMENTS	PLETHYSMOGRAPHY	PLOUGHINGS	PLUNDERERS	PLUTONISMS
PLENITUDES	PLEURAPOPHYSES	PLOUGHLAND	PLUNDERING	PLUTONIUMS
PLENITUDINOUS	PLEURAPOPHYSIS	PLOUGHLANDS	PLUNDEROUS	PLUTONOMIES
PLENTEOUSLY	PLEURISIES	PLOUGHMANSHIP	PLUPERFECT	PLUTONOMIST
PLENTEOUSNESS	PLEURITICAL	PLOUGHMANSHIPS	PLUPERFECTS	PLUTONOMISTS
PLENTEOUSNESSES	PLEURITICS	PLOUGHSHARE	PLURALISATION	PLUVIOMETER
PLENTIFULLY	PLEURITISES	PLOUGHSHARES	PLURALISATIONS	PLUVIOMETERS
PLENTIFULNESS	PLEUROCARPOUS	PLOUGHSTAFF	PLURALISED	PLUVIOMETRIC
PLENTIFULNESSES	PLEUROCENTESES	PLOUGHSTAFFS	PLURALISER	PLUVIOMETRICAL
PLENTITUDE	PLEUROCENTESIS	PLOUGHTAIL	PLURALISERS	PLUVIOMETRIES
PLENTITUDES	PLEURODONT	PLOUGHTAILS	PLURALISES	PLUVIOMETRY
PLEOCHROIC	PLEURODONTS	PLOUGHWISE	PLURALISING	PLYOMETRIC
PLEOCHROISM	PLEURODYNIA	PLOUGHWRIGHT	PLURALISMS	PLYOMETRICS
PLEOCHROISMS	PLEURODYNIAS	PLOUGHWRIGHTS	PLURALISTIC	PNEUMATHODE
PLEOMORPHIC	PLEURONIAS	PLOUTERING	PLURALISTICALLY	PNEUMATHODES
PLEOMORPHIES	PLEUROPNEUMONIA	PLOWMANSHIP	PLURALISTS	PNEUMATICAL
PLEOMORPHISM	PLEUROTOMIES	PLOWMANSHIPS	PLURALITIES	PNEUMATICALLY
PLEOMORPHISMS	PLEUROTOMY	PLOWSHARES	PLURALIZATION	PNEUMATICITIES
PLEOMORPHOUS	PLEUSTONIC	PLOWSTAFFS	PLURALIZATIONS	PNEUMATICITY
PLEOMORPHY	PLEXIGLASS	PLOWTERING	PLURALIZED	PNEUMATICS
PLEONASTES	PLEXIGLASSES	PLUCKINESS	PLURALIZER	PNEUMATOLOGICAL
PLEONASTIC	PLEXIMETER	PLUCKINESSES	PLURALIZERS	PNEUMATOLOGIES
PLEONASTICAL	PLEXIMETERS	PLUGBOARDS	PLURALIZES	PNEUMATOLOGIST
PLEONASTICALLY	PLEXIMETRIC	PLUGUGLIES	PLURALIZING	PNEUMATOLOGISTS
PLEONECTIC	PLEXIMETRIES	PLUMASSIER	PLURILITERAL	PNEUMATOLOGY
PLEONEXIAS	PLEXIMETRY	PLUMASSIERS	PLURILOCULAR	PNEUMATOLYSES
PLEROCERCOID	PLIABILITIES	PLUMBAGINACEOUS	PLURIPARAE	PNEUMATOLYSIS
PLEROCERCOIDS	PLIABILITY	PLUMBAGINOUS	PLURIPARAS	PNEUMATOLYTIC

P

PNEUMATOMETER	POCKETLESS	PODSOLIZATIONS	POIKILOTHERM	POLARISCOPIC
PNEUMATOMETERS	POCKETSFUL	PODSOLIZED	POIKILOTHERMAL	POLARISERS
PNEUMATOMETRIES	POCKMANKIES	PODSOLIZES	POIKILOTHERMIC	POLARISING
PNEUMATOMETRY	POCKMANTIE	PODSOLIZING	POIKILOTHERMIES	POLARITIES
PNEUMATOPHORE	POCKMANTIES	PODZOLISATION	POIKILOTHERMISM	POLARIZABILITY
PNEUMATOPHORES	POCKMARKED	PODZOLISATIONS	POIKILOTHERMS	POLARIZABLE
PNEUMECTOMIES	POCKMARKING	PODZOLISED	POIKILOTHERMY	POLARIZATION
PNEUMECTOMY	POCKPITTED	PODZOLISES	POINCIANAS	POLARIZATIONS
PNEUMOBACILLI	POCOCURANTE	PODZOLISING	POINSETTIA	POLARIZERS
PNEUMOBACILLUS	POCOCURANTEISM	PODZOLIZATION	POINSETTIAS	POLARIZING
PNEUMOCOCCAL	POCOCURANTEISMS	PODZOLIZATIONS	POINTEDNESS	POLAROGRAM
PNEUMOCOCCI	POCOCURANTES	PODZOLIZED	POINTEDNESSES	POLAROGRAMS
PNEUMOCOCCUS	POCOCURANTISM	PODZOLIZES	POINTELLES	POLAROGRAPH
PNEUMOCONIOSES	POCOCURANTISMS	PODZOLIZING	POINTILLISM	POLAROGRAPHIC
PNEUMOCONIOSIS	POCOCURANTIST	POENOLOGIES	POINTILLISME	POLAROGRAPHIES
PNEUMOCONIOTIC	POCOCURANTISTS	POETASTERIES	POINTILLISMES	POLAROGRAPHS
PNEUMOCONIOTICS	POCULIFORM	POETASTERING	POINTILLISMS	POLAROGRAPHY
PNEUMOCYSTIS	PODAGRICAL	POETASTERINGS	POINTILLIST	POLEMARCHS
PNEUMOCYSTISES	PODARGUSES	POETASTERS	POINTILLISTE	POLEMICALLY
PNEUMODYNAMICS	PODCASTERS	POETASTERY	POINTILLISTES	POLEMICISE
PNEUMOGASTRIC	PODCASTING	POETASTRIES	POINTILLISTIC	POLEMICISED
PNEUMOGASTRICS	PODCASTINGS	POETICALLY	POINTILLISTS	POLEMICISES
PNEUMOGRAM	PODGINESSES	POETICALNESS	POINTLESSLY	POLEMICISING
PNEUMOGRAMS	PODIATRIES	POETICALNESSES	POINTLESSNESS	POLEMICIST
PNEUMOGRAPH	PODIATRIST	POETICISED	POINTLESSNESSES	POLEMICISTS
PNEUMOGRAPHS	PODIATRISTS	POETICISES	POISONABLE	POLEMICIZE
PNEUMOKONIOSES	PODOCONIOSES	POETICISING	POISONINGS	POLEMICIZED
PNEUMOKONIOSIS	PODOCONIOSIS	POETICISMS	POISONOUSLY	POLEMICIZES
PNEUMONECTOMIES	PODOLOGIES	POETICIZED	POISONOUSNESS	POLEMICIZING
PNEUMONECTOMY	PODOLOGIST	POETICIZES	POISONOUSNESSES	POLEMISING
PNEUMONIAS	PODOLOGISTS	POETICIZING	POISONWOOD	POLEMIZING
PNEUMONICS	PODOPHTHALMOUS	POETICULES	POISONWOODS	POLEMONIACEOUS
PNEUMONITIS	PODOPHYLIN	POETRESSES	POKEBERRIES	POLEMONIUM
PNEUMONITISES	PODOPHYLINS	POGONOPHORAN	POKELOGANS	POLEMONIUMS
PNEUMOTHORACES	PODOPHYLLI	POGONOPHORANS	POKERISHLY	POLIANITES
PNEUMOTHORAX	PODOPHYLLIN	POGONOTOMIES	POKERWORKS	POLICEWOMAN
PNEUMOTHORAXES	PODOPHYLLINS	POGONOTOMY	POKINESSES	POLICEWOMEN
POACHINESS	PODOPHYLLUM	POGROMISTS	POLARIMETER	POLICYHOLDER
POACHINESSES	PODOPHYLLUMS	POHUTUKAWA	POLARIMETERS	POLICYHOLDERS
POCKETABLE	PODOSPHERE	POHUTUKAWAS	POLARIMETRIC	POLIOMYELITIDES
POCKETBIKE	PODOSPHERES	POIGNADOES	POLARIMETRIES	POLIOMYELITIS
POCKETBIKES	PODSOLISATION	POIGNANCES	POLARIMETRY	POLIOMYELITISES
POCKETBOOK	PODSOLISATIONS	POIGNANCIES	POLARISABLE	POLIORCETIC
POCKETBOOKS	PODSOLISED	POIGNANTLY	POLARISATION	POLIORCETICS
POCKETFULS	PODSOLISES	POIKILITIC	POLARISATIONS	POLIOVIRUS
POCKETKNIFE	PODSOLISING	POIKILOCYTE	POLARISCOPE	POLIOVIRUSES
POCKETKNIVES	PODSOLIZATION	POIKILOCYTES	POLARISCOPES	POLISHABLE

P

POLISHINGS	POLLENIZERS	POLYACRYLAMIDES	POLYCHROISM	POLYDEMONISMS
POLISHMENT	POLLENOSES	POLYACTINAL	POLYCHROISMS	POLYDIPSIA
POLISHMENTS	POLLENOSIS	POLYACTINE	POLYCHROMATIC	POLYDIPSIAS
POLITBUROS	POLLICITATION	POLYADELPHOUS	POLYCHROMATISM	POLYDIPSIC
POLITENESS	POLLICITATIONS	POLYALCOHOL	POLYCHROMATISMS	POLYDISPERSE
POLITENESSES	POLLINATED	POLYALCOHOLS	POLYCHROME	POLYDISPERSITY
POLITESSES	POLLINATES	POLYAMIDES	POLYCHROMED	POLYELECTROLYTE
POLITICALISE	POLLINATING	POLYAMINES	POLYCHROMES	POLYEMBRYONATE
POLITICALISED	POLLINATION	POLYAMORIES	POLYCHROMIC	POLYEMBRYONIC
POLITICALISES	POLLINATIONS	POLYANDRIES	POLYCHROMIES	POLYEMBRYONIES
POLITICALISING	POLLINATOR	POLYANDROUS	POLYCHROMING	POLYEMBRYONY
POLITICALIZE	POLLINATORS	POLYANTHAS	POLYCHROMOUS	POLYESTERS
POLITICALIZED	POLLINIFEROUS	POLYANTHUS	POLYCHROMY	POLYESTROUS
POLITICALIZES	POLLINISED	POLYANTHUSES	POLYCISTRONIC	POLYETHENE
POLITICALIZING	POLLINISER	POLYARCHIES	POLYCLINIC	POLYETHENES
POLITICALLY	POLLINISERS	POLYATOMIC	POLYCLINICS	POLYETHYLENE
POLITICASTER	POLLINISES	POLYAXIALS	POLYCLONAL	POLYETHYLENES
POLITICASTERS	POLLINISING	POLYAXONIC	POLYCOTTON	POLYGALACEOUS
POLITICIAN	POLLINIZED	POLYBASITE	POLYCOTTONS	POLYGAMIES
POLITICIANS	POLLINIZER	POLYBASITES	POLYCOTYLEDON	POLYGAMISE
POLITICISATION	POLLINIZERS	POLYBUTADIENE	POLYCOTYLEDONS	POLYGAMISED
POLITICISATIONS	POLLINIZES	POLYBUTADIENES	POLYCROTIC	POLYGAMISES
POLITICISE	POLLINIZING	POLYCARBONATE	POLYCROTISM	POLYGAMISING
POLITICISED	POLLINOSES	POLYCARBONATES	POLYCROTISMS	POLYGAMIST
POLITICISES	POLLINOSIS	POLYCARBOXYLATE	POLYCRYSTAL	POLYGAMISTS
POLITICISING	POLLTAKERS	POLYCARBOXYLIC	POLYCRYSTALLINE	POLYGAMIZE
POLITICIZATION	POLLUCITES	POLYCARPELLARY	POLYCRYSTALS	POLYGAMIZED
POLITICIZATIONS	POLLUSIONS	POLYCARPIC	POLYCULTURE	POLYGAMIZES
POLITICIZE	POLLUTANTS	POLYCARPIES	POLYCULTURES	POLYGAMIZING
POLITICIZED	POLLUTEDLY	POLYCARPOUS	POLYCYCLIC	POLYGAMOUS
POLITICIZES	POLLUTEDNESS	POLYCENTRIC	POLYCYCLICS	POLYGAMOUSLY
POLITICIZING	POLLUTEDNESSES	POLYCENTRISM	POLYCYSTIC	POLYGENESES
POLITICKED	POLLUTIONS	POLYCENTRISMS	POLYCYTHAEMIA	POLYGENESIS
POLITICKER	POLLYANNAISH	POLYCHAETE	POLYCYTHAEMIAS	POLYGENETIC
POLITICKERS	POLLYANNAISM	POLYCHAETES	POLYCYTHEMIA	POLYGENETICALLY
POLITICKING	POLLYANNAISMS	POLYCHAETOUS	POLYCYTHEMIAS	POLYGENIES
POLITICKINGS	POLLYANNAS	POLYCHASIA	POLYCYTHEMIC	POLYGENISM
POLITICOES	POLLYANNISH	POLYCHASIUM	POLYDACTYL	POLYGENISMS
POLITIQUES	POLONAISES	POLYCHETES	POLYDACTYLIES	POLYGENIST
POLLARDING	POLONISING	POLYCHLORINATED	POLYDACTYLISM	POLYGENISTS
POLLENATED	POLONIZING	POLYCHLOROPRENE	POLYDACTYLISMS	POLYGENOUS
POLLENATES	POLTERGEIST	POLYCHOTOMIES	POLYDACTYLOUS	POLYGLOTISM
POLLENATING	POLTERGEISTS	POLYCHOTOMOUS	POLYDACTYLS	POLYGLOTISMS
POLLENIFEROUS	POLTROONERIES	POLYCHOTOMY	POLYDACTYLY	POLYGLOTTAL
POLLENISER	POLTROONERY	POLYCHREST	POLYDAEMONISM	POLYGLOTTIC
POLLENISERS	POLVERINES	POLYCHRESTS	POLYDAEMONISMS	POLYGLOTTISM
POLLENIZER	POLYACRYLAMIDE	POLYCHROIC	POLYDEMONISM	POLYGLOTTISMS

POLYGLOTTOUS	POLYLYSINE	POLYNUCLEATE	POLYPROPENE	POLYSYNDETONS
POLYGLOTTS	POLYLYSINES	POLYNUCLEOTIDE	POLYPROPENES	POLYSYNTHESES
POLYGONACEOUS	POLYMASTIA	POLYNUCLEOTIDES	POLYPROPYLENE	POLYSYNTHESIS
POLYGONALLY	POLYMASTIAS	POLYOLEFIN	POLYPROPYLENES	POLYSYNTHESISM
POLYGONATUM	POLYMASTIC	POLYOLEFINS	POLYPROTODONT	POLYSYNTHESISMS
POLYGONATUMS	POLYMASTIES	POLYOMINOS	POLYPROTODONTS	POLYSYNTHETIC
POLYGONIES	POLYMASTISM	POLYONYMIC	POLYPTYCHS	POLYSYNTHETICAL
POLYGONUMS	POLYMASTISMS	POLYONYMIES	POLYRHYTHM	POLYSYNTHETISM
POLYGRAPHED	POLYMATHIC	POLYONYMOUS	POLYRHYTHMIC	POLYSYNTHETISMS
POLYGRAPHER	POLYMATHIES	POLYPARIES	POLYRHYTHMS	POLYTECHNIC
POLYGRAPHERS	POLYMERASE	POLYPARIUM	POLYRIBOSOMAL	POLYTECHNICAL
POLYGRAPHIC	POLYMERASES	POLYPEPTIDE	POLYRIBOSOME	POLYTECHNICS
POLYGRAPHICALLY	POLYMERIDE	POLYPEPTIDES	POLYRIBOSOMES	POLYTENIES
POLYGRAPHIES	POLYMERIDES	POLYPEPTIDIC	POLYSACCHARIDE	POLYTHALAMOUS
POLYGRAPHING	POLYMERIES	POLYPETALOUS	POLYSACCHARIDES	POLYTHEISM
POLYGRAPHIST	POLYMERISATION	POLYPHAGIA	POLYSACCHAROSE	POLYTHEISMS
POLYGRAPHISTS	POLYMERISATIONS	POLYPHAGIAS	POLYSACCHAROSES	POLYTHEIST
POLYGRAPHS	POLYMERISE	POLYPHAGIES	POLYSEMANT	POLYTHEISTIC
POLYGRAPHY	POLYMERISED	POLYPHAGOUS	POLYSEMANTS	POLYTHEISTICAL
POLYGYNIAN	POLYMERISES	POLYPHARMACIES	POLYSEMIES	POLYTHEISTS
POLYGYNIES	POLYMERISING	POLYPHARMACY	POLYSEMOUS	POLYTHENES
POLYGYNIST	POLYMERISM	POLYPHASIC	POLYSEPALOUS	POLYTOCOUS
POLYGYNISTS	POLYMERISMS	POLYPHENOL	POLYSILOXANE	POLYTONALISM
POLYGYNOUS	POLYMERIZATION	POLYPHENOLIC	POLYSILOXANES	POLYTONALISMS
POLYHALITE	POLYMERIZATIONS	POLYPHENOLS	POLYSOMICS	POLYTONALIST
POLYHALITES	POLYMERIZE	POLYPHLOESBOEAN	POLYSOMIES	POLYTONALISTS
POLYHEDRAL	POLYMERIZED	POLYPHLOISBIC	POLYSORBATE	POLYTONALITIES
POLYHEDRIC	POLYMERIZES	POLYPHONES	POLYSORBATES	POLYTONALITY
POLYHEDRON	POLYMERIZING	POLYPHONIC	POLYSTICHOUS	POLYTONALLY
POLYHEDRONS	POLYMEROUS	POLYPHONICALLY	POLYSTYLAR	POLYTROPHIC
POLYHEDROSES	POLYMORPHIC	POLYPHONIES	POLYSTYRENE	POLYTUNNEL
POLYHEDROSIS	POLYMORPHICALLY	POLYPHONIST	POLYSTYRENES	POLYTUNNELS
POLYHISTOR	POLYMORPHISM	POLYPHONISTS	POLYSULFIDE	POLYTYPICAL
POLYHISTORIAN	POLYMORPHISMS	POLYPHONOUS	POLYSULFIDES	POLYUNSATURATED
POLYHISTORIANS	POLYMORPHOUS	POLYPHONOUSLY	POLYSULPHIDE	POLYURETHAN
POLYHISTORIC	POLYMORPHOUSLY	POLYPHOSPHORIC	POLYSULPHIDES	POLYURETHANE
POLYHISTORIES	POLYMORPHS	POLYPHYLETIC	POLYSYLLABIC	POLYURETHANES
POLYHISTORS	POLYMYOSITIS	POLYPHYLLOUS	POLYSYLLABICAL	POLYURETHANS
POLYHISTORY	POLYMYOSITISES	POLYPHYODONT	POLYSYLLABICISM	POLYVALENCE
POLYHYBRID	POLYMYXINS	POLYPIDOMS	POLYSYLLABISM	POLYVALENCES
POLYHYBRIDS	POLYNEURITIS	POLYPLOIDAL	POLYSYLLABISMS	POLYVALENCIES
POLYHYDRIC	POLYNEURITISES	POLYPLOIDIC	POLYSYLLABLE	POLYVALENCY
POLYHYDROXY	POLYNOMIAL	POLYPLOIDIES	POLYSYLLABLES	POLYVALENT
POLYIMIDES	POLYNOMIALISM	POLYPLOIDS	POLYSYLLOGISM	POLYVINYLIDENE
POLYISOPRENE	POLYNOMIALISMS	POLYPLOIDY	POLYSYLLOGISMS	POLYVINYLIDENES
POLYISOPRENES	POLYNOMIALS	POLYPODIES	POLYSYNAPTIC	POLYVINYLS
POLYLEMMAS	POLYNUCLEAR	POLYPODOUS	POLYSYNDETON	POLYWATERS

P

POLYZOARIA	PONDEROSAS	POPPYCOCKS	PORCELLANITE	PORPHYROGENITE
POLYZOARIAL	PONDEROSITIES	POPPYHEADS	PORCELLANITES	PORPHYROGENITES
POLYZOARIES	PONDEROSITY	POPULARISATION	PORCELLANIZE	PORPHYROID
POLYZOARIUM	PONDEROUSLY	POPULARISATIONS	PORCELLANIZED	PORPHYROIDS
POMEGRANATE	PONDEROUSNESS	POPULARISE	PORCELLANIZES	PORPHYROPSIN
POMEGRANATES	PONDEROUSNESSES	POPULARISED	PORCELLANIZING	PORPHYROPSINS
POMICULTURE	PONDOKKIES	POPULARISER	PORCELLANOUS	PORPHYROUS
POMICULTURES	PONEROLOGIES	POPULARISERS	PORCHETTAS	PORPOISING
POMIFEROUS	PONEROLOGY	POPULARISES	PORCUPINES	PORRACEOUS
POMMELLING	PONIARDING	POPULARISING	PORCUPINISH	PORRECTING
POMOERIUMS	PONTIANACS	POPULARITIES	PORIFERANS	PORRECTION
POMOLOGICAL	PONTIANAKS	POPULARITY	PORIFEROUS	PORRECTIONS
POMOLOGICALLY	PONTICELLO	POPULARIZATION	PORINESSES	PORRENGERS
POMOLOGIES	PONTICELLOS	POPULARIZATIONS	PORISMATIC	PORRIGINOUS
POMOLOGIST	PONTIFICAL	POPULARIZE	PORISMATICAL	PORRINGERS
POMOLOGISTS	PONTIFICALITIES	POPULARIZED	PORISTICAL	PORTABELLA
POMOSEXUAL	PONTIFICALITY	POPULARIZER	PORKINESSES	PORTABELLAS
POMOSEXUALS	PONTIFICALLY	POPULARIZERS	PORLOCKING	PORTABELLO
POMPADOURED	PONTIFICALS	POPULARIZES	PORNIFICATION	PORTABELLOS
POMPADOURS	PONTIFICATE	POPULARIZING	PORNIFICATIONS	PORTABILITIES
POMPELMOOSE	PONTIFICATED	POPULATING	PORNOCRACIES	PORTABILITY
POMPELMOOSES	PONTIFICATES	POPULATION	PORNOCRACY	PORTAMENTI
POMPELMOUS	PONTIFICATING	POPULATIONAL	PORNOGRAPHER	PORTAMENTO
POMPELMOUSE	PONTIFICATION	POPULATIONS	PORNOGRAPHERS	PORTAPACKS
POMPELMOUSES	PONTIFICATIONS	POPULISTIC	PORNOGRAPHIC	PORTATIVES
POMPHOLYGOUS	PONTIFICATOR	POPULOUSLY	PORNOGRAPHIES	PORTCULLIS
POMPHOLYXES	PONTIFICATORS	POPULOUSNESS	PORNOGRAPHY	PORTCULLISED
POMPOSITIES	PONTIFICES	POPULOUSNESSES	PORNOTOPIA	PORTCULLISES
POMPOUSNESS	PONTIFYING	PORBEAGLES	PORNOTOPIAN	PORTCULLISING
POMPOUSNESSES	PONTLEVISES	PORCELAINEOUS	PORNOTOPIAS	PORTENDING
PONDERABILITIES	PONTONEERS	PORCELAINISE	POROGAMIES	PORTENTOUS
PONDERABILITY	PONTONIERS	PORCELAINISED	POROMERICS	PORTENTOUSLY
PONDERABLE	PONTONNIER	PORCELAINISES	POROSCOPES	PORTENTOUSNESS
PONDERABLES	PONTONNIERS	PORCELAINISING	POROSCOPIC	PORTEOUSES
PONDERABLY	PONTOONERS	PORCELAINIZE	POROSCOPIES	PORTERAGES
PONDERANCE	PONTOONING	PORCELAINIZED	POROSITIES	PORTERESSES
PONDERANCES	PONYTAILED	PORCELAINIZES	POROUSNESS	PORTERHOUSE
PONDERANCIES	POORHOUSES	PORCELAINIZING	POROUSNESSES	PORTERHOUSES
PONDERANCY	POORMOUTHED	PORCELAINLIKE	PORPENTINE	PORTFOLIOS
PONDERATED	POORMOUTHING	PORCELAINOUS	PORPENTINES	PORTHORSES
PONDERATES	POORMOUTHS	PORCELAINS	PORPHYRIAS	PORTHOUSES
PONDERATING	POORNESSES	PORCELANEOUS	PORPHYRIES	PORTIONERS
PONDERATION	POPLINETTE	PORCELLANEOUS	PORPHYRINS	PORTIONING
PONDERATIONS	POPLINETTES	PORCELLANISE	PORPHYRIOS	PORTIONIST
PONDERINGLY	POPMOBILITIES	PORCELLANISED	PORPHYRITE	PORTIONISTS
PONDERMENT	POPMOBILITY	PORCELLANISES	PORPHYRITES	PORTIONLESS
PONDERMENTS	POPPERINGS	PORCELLANISING	PORPHYRITIC	PORTLINESS

PORTLINESSES
PORTMANTEAU
PORTMANTEAUS
PORTMANTEAUX
PORTMANTLE
PORTMANTLES
PORTMANTUA
PORTMANTUAS
PORTOBELLO
PORTOBELLOS
PORTOLANOS
PORTRAITED
PORTRAITING
PORTRAITIST
PORTRAITISTS
PORTRAITURE
PORTRAITURES
PORTRAYABLE
PORTRAYALS
PORTRAYERS
PORTRAYING
PORTREEVES
PORTRESSES
PORTULACACEOUS
PORTULACAS
PORWIGGLES
POSHNESSES
POSITIONAL
POSITIONALLY
POSITIONED
POSITIONING
POSITIONINGS
POSITIVELY
POSITIVENESS
POSITIVENESSES
POSITIVEST
POSITIVISM
POSITIVISMS
POSITIVIST
POSITIVISTIC
POSITIVISTS
POSITIVITIES
POSITIVITY
POSITRONIUM
POSITRONIUMS
POSOLOGICAL
POSOLOGIES

POSSESSABLE
POSSESSEDLY
POSSESSEDNESS
POSSESSEDNESSES
POSSESSING
POSSESSION
POSSESSIONAL
POSSESSIONARY
POSSESSIONATE
POSSESSIONATES
POSSESSIONED
POSSESSIONLESS
POSSESSIONS
POSSESSIVE
POSSESSIVELY
POSSESSIVENESS
POSSESSIVES
POSSESSORS
POSSESSORSHIP
POSSESSORSHIPS
POSSESSORY
POSSIBILISM
POSSIBILISMS
POSSIBILIST
POSSIBILISTS
POSSIBILITIES
POSSIBILITY
POSSIBLEST
POSTABORTION
POSTACCIDENT
POSTADOLESCENT
POSTAMPUTATION
POSTAPOCALYPTIC
POSTARREST
POSTATOMIC
POSTATTACK
POSTBELLUM
POSTBIBLICAL
POSTBOURGEOIS
POSTBUSSES
POSTCAPITALIST
POSTCARDED
POSTCARDING
POSTCARDLIKE
POSTCLASSIC
POSTCLASSICAL
POSTCODING

POSTCOITAL
POSTCOLLEGE
POSTCOLLEGIATE
POSTCOLONIAL
POSTCONCEPTION
POSTCONCERT
POSTCONQUEST
POSTCONSONANTAL
POSTCONVENTION
POSTCOPULATORY
POSTCORONARY
POSTCRANIAL
POSTCRANIALLY
POSTCRISIS
POSTDATING
POSTDEADLINE
POSTDEBATE
POSTDEBUTANTE
POSTDELIVERY
POSTDEPRESSION
POSTDEVALUATION
POSTDILUVIAL
POSTDILUVIAN
POSTDILUVIANS
POSTDIVESTITURE
POSTDIVORCE
POSTDOCTORAL
POSTDOCTORATE
POSTEDITING
POSTELECTION
POSTEMBRYONAL
POSTEMBRYONIC
POSTEMERGENCE
POSTEMERGENCY
POSTEPILEPTIC
POSTERIORITIES
POSTERIORITY
POSTERIORLY
POSTERIORS
POSTERISATION
POSTERISATIONS
POSTERITIES
POSTERIZATION
POSTERIZATIONS
POSTEROLATERAL
POSTERUPTIVE
POSTEXERCISE

POSTEXILIAN
POSTEXILIC
POSTEXPERIENCE
POSTEXPOSURE
POSTFEMINISM
POSTFEMINISMS
POSTFEMINIST
POSTFEMINISTS
POSTFIXING
POSTFLIGHT
POSTFORMED
POSTFORMING
POSTFRACTURE
POSTFREEZE
POSTGANGLIONIC
POSTGLACIAL
POSTGRADUATE
POSTGRADUATES
POSTGRADUATION
POSTHARVEST
POSTHASTES
POSTHEMORRHAGIC
POSTHOLDER
POSTHOLDERS
POSTHOLIDAY
POSTHOLOCAUST
POSTHORSES
POSTHOSPITAL
POSTHOUSES
POSTHUMOUS
POSTHUMOUSLY
POSTHUMOUSNESS
POSTHYPNOTIC
POSTILIONS
POSTILLATE
POSTILLATED
POSTILLATES
POSTILLATING
POSTILLATION
POSTILLATIONS
POSTILLATOR
POSTILLATORS
POSTILLERS
POSTILLING
POSTILLION
POSTILLIONS
POSTIMPACT

POSTIMPERIAL
POSTINAUGURAL
POSTINDUSTRIAL
POSTINFECTION
POSTINJECTION
POSTINOCULATION
POSTIRRADIATION
POSTISCHEMIC
POSTISOLATION
POSTLANDING
POSTLAPSARIAN
POSTLAUNCH
POSTLIBERATION
POSTLIMINARY
POSTLIMINIA
POSTLIMINIARY
POSTLIMINIES
POSTLIMINIOUS
POSTLIMINIUM
POSTLIMINOUS
POSTLIMINY
POSTLITERATE
POSTMARITAL
POSTMARKED
POSTMARKING
POSTMASTECTOMY
POSTMASTER
POSTMASTERS
POSTMASTERSHIP
POSTMASTERSHIPS
POSTMATING
POSTMEDIEVAL
POSTMENOPAUSAL
POSTMENSTRUAL
POSTMERIDIAN
POSTMIDNIGHT
POSTMILLENARIAN
POSTMILLENNIAL
POSTMISTRESS
POSTMISTRESSES
POSTMODERN
POSTMODERNISM
POSTMODERNISMS
POSTMODERNIST
POSTMODERNISTS
POSTMORTEM
POSTMORTEMS

P

POSTNATALLY	POSTSTRIKE	POTAMOGETONS	POTHUNTING	POWELLITES
POSTNEONATAL	POSTSURGICAL	POTAMOLOGICAL	POTHUNTINGS	POWELLIZED
POSTNUPTIAL	POSTSYNAPTIC	POTAMOLOGIES	POTICARIES	POWELLIZES
POSTOCULAR	POSTSYNCED	POTAMOLOGIST	POTICHOMANIA	POWELLIZING
POSTOPERATIVE	POSTSYNCING	POTAMOLOGISTS	POTICHOMANIAS	POWERBOATING
POSTOPERATIVELY	POSTTENSION	POTAMOLOGY	POTLATCHED	POWERBOATINGS
POSTORBITAL	POSTTENSIONED	POTASSIUMS	POTLATCHES	POWERBOATS
POSTORGASMIC	POSTTENSIONING	POTATOBUGS	POTLATCHING	POWERFULLY
POSTPARTUM	POSTTENSIONS	POTBELLIED	POTOMETERS	POWERFULNESS
POSTPERSON	POSTTRANSFUSION	POTBELLIES	POTPOURRIS	POWERFULNESSES
POSTPERSONS	POSTTRAUMATIC	POTBOILERS	POTSHOTTING	POWERHOUSE
POSTPOLLINATION	POSTTREATMENT	POTBOILING	POTTERINGLY	POWERHOUSES
POSTPONABLE	POSTULANCIES	POTBOILINGS	POTTERINGS	POWERLESSLY
POSTPONEMENT	POSTULANCY	POTENTATES	POTTINESSES	POWERLESSNESS
POSTPONEMENTS	POSTULANTS	POTENTIALITIES	POTTINGARS	POWERLESSNESSES
POSTPONENCE	POSTULANTSHIP	POTENTIALITY	POTTINGERS	POWERLIFTER
POSTPONENCES	POSTULANTSHIPS	POTENTIALLY	POTTYMOUTH	POWERLIFTERS
POSTPONERS	POSTULATED	POTENTIALS	POTTYMOUTHS	POWERLIFTING
POSTPONING	POSTULATES	POTENTIARIES	POTWALLERS	POWERLIFTINGS
POSTPOSING	POSTULATING	POTENTIARY	POULTERERS	POWERPLAYS
POSTPOSITION	POSTULATION	POTENTIATE	POULTICING	POWERTRAIN
POSTPOSITIONAL	POSTULATIONAL	POTENTIATED	POULTROONE	POWERTRAINS
POSTPOSITIONS	POSTULATIONALLY	POTENTIATES	POULTROONES	POWSOWDIES
POSTPOSITIVE	POSTULATIONS	POTENTIATING	POULTRYMAN	POXVIRUSES
POSTPOSITIVELY	POSTULATOR	POTENTIATION	POULTRYMEN	POZZOLANAS
POSTPOSITIVES	POSTULATORS	POTENTIATIONS	POUNDCAKES	POZZOLANIC
POSTPRANDIAL	POSTULATORY	POTENTIATOR	POURBOIRES	POZZUOLANA
POSTPRIMARY	POSTULATUM	POTENTIATORS	POURPARLER	POZZUOLANAS
POSTPRISON	POSTURISED	POTENTILLA	POURPARLERS	PRACHARAKS
POSTPRODUCTION	POSTURISES	POTENTILLAS	POURPOINTS	PRACTICABILITY
POSTPRODUCTIONS	POSTURISING	POTENTIOMETER	POURSEWING	PRACTICABLE
POSTPUBERTY	POSTURISTS	POTENTIOMETERS	POURTRAHED	PRACTICABLENESS
POSTPUBESCENT	POSTURIZED	POTENTIOMETRIC	POURTRAICT	PRACTICABLY
POSTRECESSION	POSTURIZES	POTENTIOMETRIES	POURTRAICTS	PRACTICALISM
POSTRETIREMENT	POSTURIZING	POTENTIOMETRY	POURTRAYED	PRACTICALISMS
POSTRIDERS	POSTVACCINAL	POTENTISED	POURTRAYING	PRACTICALIST
POSTROMANTIC	POSTVACCINATION	POTENTISES	POUSOWDIES	PRACTICALISTS
POSTSCENIUM	POSTVAGOTOMY	POTENTISING	POUSSETTED	PRACTICALITIES
POSTSCENIUMS	POSTVASECTOMY	POTENTIZED	POUSSETTES	PRACTICALITY
POSTSCRIPT	POSTVOCALIC	POTENTIZES	POUSSETTING	PRACTICALLY
POSTSCRIPTS	POSTWEANING	POTENTIZING	POUTHERING	PRACTICALNESS
POSTSEASON	POSTWORKSHOP	POTENTNESS	POWDERIEST	PRACTICALNESSES
POSTSEASONS	POTABILITIES	POTENTNESSES	POWDERLESS	PRACTICALS
POSTSECONDARY	POTABILITY	POTHECARIES	POWDERLIKE	PRACTICERS
POSTSTIMULATION	POTABLENESS	POTHOLDERS	POWELLISED	PRACTICIAN
POSTSTIMULATORY	POTABLENESSES	POTHOLINGS	POWELLISES	PRACTICIANS
POSTSTIMULUS	POTAMOGETON	POTHUNTERS	POWELLISING	PRACTICING

PRACTICUMS	PRAGMATISED	PRAXINOSCOPE	PREADMITTING	PREARRANGES
PRACTIQUES	PRAGMATISER	PRAXINOSCOPES	PREADMONISH	PREARRANGING
PRACTISANT	PRAGMATISERS	PRAYERFULLY	PREADMONISHED	PREASSEMBLED
PRACTISANTS	PRAGMATISES	PRAYERFULNESS	PREADMONISHES	PREASSIGNED
PRACTISERS	PRAGMATISING	PRAYERFULNESSES	PREADMONISHING	PREASSIGNING
PRACTISING	PRAGMATISM	PRAYERLESS	PREADMONITION	PREASSIGNS
PRACTITIONER	PRAGMATISMS	PRAYERLESSLY	PREADMONITIONS	PREASSURANCE
PRACTITIONERS	PRAGMATIST	PRAYERLESSNESS	PREADOLESCENCE	PREASSURANCES
PRACTOLOLS	PRAGMATISTIC	PREABSORBED	PREADOLESCENCES	PREASSURED
PRAEAMBLES	PRAGMATISTS	PREABSORBING	PREADOLESCENT	PREASSURES
PRAECOCIAL	PRAGMATIZATION	PREABSORBS	PREADOLESCENTS	PREASSURING
PRAECORDIAL	PRAGMATIZATIONS	PREACCUSED	PREADOPTED	PREATTUNED
PRAEDIALITIES	PRAGMATIZE	PREACCUSES	PREADOPTING	PREATTUNES
PRAEDIALITY	PRAGMATIZED	PREACCUSING	PREAGRICULTURAL	PREATTUNING
PRAEFECTORIAL	PRAGMATIZER	PREACHABLE	PREALLOTTED	PREAUDIENCE
PRAELECTED	PRAGMATIZERS	PREACHERSHIP	PREALLOTTING	PREAUDIENCES
PRAELECTING	PRAGMATIZES	PREACHERSHIPS	PREALTERED	PREAVERRED
PRAELUDIUM	PRAGMATIZING	PREACHIEST	PREALTERING	PREAVERRING
PRAEMUNIRE	PRAISEACHS	PREACHIFIED	PREAMBLING	PREAXIALLY
PRAEMUNIRES	PRAISELESS	PREACHIFIES	PREAMBULARY	PREBENDARIES
PRAENOMENS	PRAISEWORTHILY	PREACHIFYING	PREAMBULATE	PREBENDARY
PRAENOMINA	PRAISEWORTHY	PREACHIFYINGS	PREAMBULATED	PREBIBLICAL
PRAENOMINAL	PRAISINGLY	PREACHINESS	PREAMBULATES	PREBIDDING
PRAENOMINALLY	PRALLTRILLER	PREACHINESSES	PREAMBULATING	PREBILLING
PRAEPOSTOR	PRALLTRILLERS	PREACHINGLY	PREAMBULATORY	PREBINDING
PRAEPOSTORS	PRANAYAMAS	PREACHINGS	PREAMPLIFIER	PREBIOLOGIC
PRAESIDIUM	PRANCINGLY	PREACHMENT	PREAMPLIFIERS	PREBIOLOGICAL
PRAESIDIUMS	PRANDIALLY	PREACHMENTS	PREANESTHETIC	PREBIOTICS
PRAETORIAL	PRANKINGLY	PREACQUAINT	PREANNOUNCE	PREBLESSED
PRAETORIAN	PRANKISHLY	PREACQUAINTANCE	PREANNOUNCED	PREBLESSES
PRAETORIANS	PRANKISHNESS	PREACQUAINTED	PREANNOUNCES	PREBLESSING
PRAETORIUM	PRANKISHNESSES	PREACQUAINTING	PREANNOUNCING	PREBOARDED
PRAETORIUMS	PRANKSTERS	PREACQUAINTS	PREAPPLIED	PREBOARDING
PRAETORSHIP	PRASEODYMIUM	PREACQUISITION	PREAPPLIES	PREBOILING
PRAETORSHIPS	PRASEODYMIUMS	PREADAMITE	PREAPPLYING	PREBOOKING
PRAGMATICAL	PRATFALLEN	PREADAMITES	PREAPPOINT	PREBREAKFAST
PRAGMATICALITY	PRATFALLING	PREADAPTATION	PREAPPOINTED	PREBUDGETS
PRAGMATICALLY	PRATINCOLE	PREADAPTATIONS	PREAPPOINTING	PREBUILDING
PRAGMATICALNESS	PRATINCOLES	PREADAPTED	PREAPPOINTS	PREBUTTALS
PRAGMATICISM	PRATTLEBOX	PREADAPTING	PREAPPROVE	PRECALCULI
PRAGMATICISMS	PRATTLEBOXES	PREADAPTIVE	PREAPPROVED	PRECALCULUS
PRAGMATICIST	PRATTLEMENT	PREADJUSTED	PREAPPROVES	PRECALCULUSES
PRAGMATICISTS	PRATTLEMENTS	PREADJUSTING	PREAPPROVING	PRECANCELED
PRAGMATICS	PRATTLINGLY	PREADJUSTS	PREARRANGE	PRECANCELING
PRAGMATISATION	PRAXEOLOGICAL	PREADMISSION	PREARRANGED	PRECANCELLATION
PRAGMATISATIONS	PRAXEOLOGIES	PREADMISSIONS	PREARRANGEMENT	PRECANCELLED
PRAGMATISE	PRAXEOLOGY	PREADMITTED	PREARRANGEMENTS	PRECANCELLING

P

PRECANCELS

PRECANCELS
PRECANCEROUS
PRECANCERS
PRECAPITALIST
PRECARIOUS
PRECARIOUSLY
PRECARIOUSNESS
PRECASTING
PRECAUTION
PRECAUTIONAL
PRECAUTIONARY
PRECAUTIONED
PRECAUTIONING
PRECAUTIONS
PRECAUTIOUS
PRECEDENCE
PRECEDENCES
PRECEDENCIES
PRECEDENCY
PRECEDENTED
PRECEDENTIAL
PRECEDENTIALLY
PRECEDENTLY
PRECEDENTS
PRECENSORED
PRECENSORING
PRECENSORS
PRECENTING
PRECENTORIAL
PRECENTORS
PRECENTORSHIP
PRECENTORSHIPS
PRECENTRESS
PRECENTRESSES
PRECENTRICES
PRECENTRIX
PRECENTRIXES
PRECEPTIAL
PRECEPTIVE
PRECEPTIVELY
PRECEPTORAL
PRECEPTORATE
PRECEPTORATES
PRECEPTORIAL
PRECEPTORIALS
PRECEPTORIES
PRECEPTORS

PRECEPTORSHIP
PRECEPTORSHIPS
PRECEPTORY
PRECEPTRESS
PRECEPTRESSES
PRECESSING
PRECESSION
PRECESSIONAL
PRECESSIONALLY
PRECESSIONS
PRECHARGED
PRECHARGES
PRECHARGING
PRECHECKED
PRECHECKING
PRECHILLED
PRECHILLING
PRECHOOSES
PRECHOOSING
PRECHRISTIAN
PRECIEUSES
PRECIOSITIES
PRECIOSITY
PRECIOUSES
PRECIOUSLY
PRECIOUSNESS
PRECIOUSNESSES
PRECIPICED
PRECIPICES
PRECIPITABILITY
PRECIPITABLE
PRECIPITANCE
PRECIPITANCES
PRECIPITANCIES
PRECIPITANCY
PRECIPITANT
PRECIPITANTLY
PRECIPITANTNESS
PRECIPITANTS
PRECIPITATE
PRECIPITATED
PRECIPITATELY
PRECIPITATENESS
PRECIPITATES
PRECIPITATING
PRECIPITATION
PRECIPITATIONS

PRECIPITATIVE
PRECIPITATOR
PRECIPITATORS
PRECIPITIN
PRECIPITINOGEN
PRECIPITINOGENS
PRECIPITINS
PRECIPITOUS
PRECIPITOUSLY
PRECIPITOUSNESS
PRECISENESS
PRECISENESSES
PRECISIANISM
PRECISIANISMS
PRECISIANIST
PRECISIANISTS
PRECISIANS
PRECISIONISM
PRECISIONISMS
PRECISIONIST
PRECISIONISTS
PRECISIONS
PRECLASSICAL
PRECLEANED
PRECLEANING
PRECLEARANCE
PRECLEARANCES
PRECLEARED
PRECLEARING
PRECLINICAL
PRECLINICALLY
PRECLUDABLE
PRECLUDING
PRECLUSION
PRECLUSIONS
PRECLUSIVE
PRECLUSIVELY
PRECOCIALS
PRECOCIOUS
PRECOCIOUSLY
PRECOCIOUSNESS
PRECOCITIES
PRECOGNISANT
PRECOGNISE
PRECOGNISED
PRECOGNISES
PRECOGNISING

PRECOGNITION
PRECOGNITIONS
PRECOGNITIVE
PRECOGNIZANT
PRECOGNIZE
PRECOGNIZED
PRECOGNIZES
PRECOGNIZING
PRECOGNOSCE
PRECOGNOSCED
PRECOGNOSCES
PRECOGNOSCING
PRECOLLEGE
PRECOLLEGIATE
PRECOLONIAL
PRECOMBUSTION
PRECOMBUSTIONS
PRECOMMITMENT
PRECOMMITMENTS
PRECOMPETITIVE
PRECOMPOSE
PRECOMPOSED
PRECOMPOSES
PRECOMPOSING
PRECOMPUTE
PRECOMPUTED
PRECOMPUTER
PRECOMPUTES
PRECOMPUTING
PRECONCEIT
PRECONCEITS
PRECONCEIVE
PRECONCEIVED
PRECONCEIVES
PRECONCEIVING
PRECONCEPTION
PRECONCEPTIONS
PRECONCERT
PRECONCERTED
PRECONCERTEDLY
PRECONCERTING
PRECONCERTS
PRECONCILIAR
PRECONDEMN
PRECONDEMNED
PRECONDEMNING
PRECONDEMNS

PRECONDITION
PRECONDITIONED
PRECONDITIONING
PRECONDITIONS
PRECONISATION
PRECONISATIONS
PRECONISED
PRECONISES
PRECONISING
PRECONIZATION
PRECONIZATIONS
PRECONIZED
PRECONIZES
PRECONIZING
PRECONQUEST
PRECONSCIOUS
PRECONSCIOUSES
PRECONSCIOUSLY
PRECONSONANTAL
PRECONSTRUCT
PRECONSTRUCTED
PRECONSTRUCTING
PRECONSTRUCTION
PRECONSTRUCTS
PRECONSUME
PRECONSUMED
PRECONSUMES
PRECONSUMING
PRECONTACT
PRECONTRACT
PRECONTRACTED
PRECONTRACTING
PRECONTRACTS
PRECONVENTION
PRECONVICTION
PRECONVICTIONS
PRECOOKERS
PRECOOKING
PRECOOLING
PRECOPULATORY
PRECORDIAL
PRECREASED
PRECREASES
PRECREASING
PRECRITICAL
PRECURRERS
PRECURSIVE

PRECURSORS	PREDESTINATE	PREDICATED	PREDOMINANCE	PREESTABLISHED
PRECURSORY	PREDESTINATED	PREDICATES	PREDOMINANCES	PREESTABLISHES
PRECUTTING	PREDESTINATES	PREDICATING	PREDOMINANCIES	PREESTABLISHING
PREDACEOUS	PREDESTINATING	PREDICATION	PREDOMINANCY	PREETHICAL
PREDACEOUSNESS	PREDESTINATION	PREDICATIONS	PREDOMINANT	PREEXCITED
PREDACIOUS	PREDESTINATIONS	PREDICATIVE	PREDOMINANTLY	PREEXCITES
PREDACIOUSNESS	PREDESTINATIVE	PREDICATIVELY	PREDOMINATE	PREEXCITING
PREDACITIES	PREDESTINATOR	PREDICATOR	PREDOMINATED	PREEXEMPTED
PREDATIONS	PREDESTINATORS	PREDICATORS	PREDOMINATELY	PREEXEMPTING
PREDATISMS	PREDESTINE	PREDICATORY	PREDOMINATES	PREEXEMPTS
PREDATORILY	PREDESTINED	PREDICTABILITY	PREDOMINATING	PREEXISTED
PREDATORINESS	PREDESTINES	PREDICTABLE	PREDOMINATION	PREEXISTENCE
PREDATORINESSES	PREDESTINIES	PREDICTABLENESS	PREDOMINATIONS	PREEXISTENCES
PREDECEASE	PREDESTINING	PREDICTABLY	PREDOMINATOR	PREEXISTENT
PREDECEASED	PREDESTINY	PREDICTERS	PREDOMINATORS	PREEXISTING
PREDECEASES	PREDETERMINABLE	PREDICTING	PREDOOMING	PREEXPERIMENT
PREDECEASING	PREDETERMINATE	PREDICTION	PREDRILLED	PREEXPOSED
PREDECESSOR	PREDETERMINE	PREDICTIONS	PREDRILLING	PREEXPOSES
PREDECESSORS	PREDETERMINED	PREDICTIVE	PREDYNASTIC	PREEXPOSING
PREDEDUCTED	PREDETERMINER	PREDICTIVELY	PREECLAMPSIA	PREFABBING
PREDEDUCTING	PREDETERMINERS	PREDICTORS	PREECLAMPSIAS	PREFABRICATE
PREDEDUCTS	PREDETERMINES	PREDIGESTED	PREECLAMPTIC	PREFABRICATED
PREDEFINED	PREDETERMINING	PREDIGESTING	PREEDITING	PREFABRICATES
PREDEFINES	PREDETERMINISM	PREDIGESTION	PREELECTED	PREFABRICATING
PREDEFINING	PREDETERMINISMS	PREDIGESTIONS	PREELECTING	PREFABRICATION
PREDEFINITION	PREDEVALUATION	PREDIGESTS	PREELECTION	PREFABRICATIONS
PREDEFINITIONS	PREDEVELOP	PREDIKANTS	PREELECTRIC	PREFABRICATOR
PREDELIVERY	PREDEVELOPED	PREDILECTED	PREEMBARGO	PREFABRICATORS
PREDENTATE	PREDEVELOPING	PREDILECTION	PREEMERGENCE	PREFASCIST
PREDEPARTURE	PREDEVELOPMENT	PREDILECTIONS	PREEMERGENT	PREFATORIAL
PREDEPOSIT	PREDEVELOPMENTS	PREDINNERS	PREEMINENCE	PREFATORIALLY
PREDEPOSITED	PREDEVELOPS	PREDISCHARGE	PREEMINENCES	PREFATORILY
PREDEPOSITING	PREDIABETES	PREDISCOVERIES	PREEMINENT	PREFECTORIAL
PREDEPOSITS	PREDIABETESES	PREDISCOVERY	PREEMINENTLY	PREFECTSHIP
PREDESIGNATE	PREDIABETIC	PREDISPOSAL	PREEMPLOYMENT	PREFECTSHIPS
PREDESIGNATED	PREDIABETICS	PREDISPOSALS	PREEMPTING	PREFECTURAL
PREDESIGNATES	PREDIALITIES	PREDISPOSE	PREEMPTION	PREFECTURE
PREDESIGNATING	PREDIALITY	PREDISPOSED	PREEMPTIONS	PREFECTURES
PREDESIGNATION	PREDICABILITIES	PREDISPOSES	PREEMPTIVE	PREFERABILITIES
PREDESIGNATIONS	PREDICABILITY	PREDISPOSING	PREEMPTIVELY	PREFERABILITY
PREDESIGNATORY	PREDICABLE	PREDISPOSITION	PREEMPTORS	PREFERABLE
PREDESIGNED	PREDICABLENESS	PREDISPOSITIONS	PREENACTED	PREFERABLENESS
PREDESIGNING	PREDICABLES	PREDNISOLONE	PREENACTING	PREFERABLY
PREDESIGNS	PREDICAMENT	PREDNISOLONES	PREENROLLMENT	PREFERENCE
PREDESTINABLE	PREDICAMENTAL	PREDNISONE	PREERECTED	PREFERENCES
PREDESTINARIAN	PREDICAMENTS	PREDNISONES	PREERECTING	PREFERENTIAL
PREDESTINARIANS	PREDICANTS	PREDOCTORAL	PREESTABLISH	PREFERENTIALISM

PREFERENTIALIST	PREFORMATS	PREHENSILITIES	PREJUDICANT	PRELINGUAL
PREFERENTIALITY	PREFORMATTED	PREHENSILITY	PREJUDICATE	PRELINGUALLY
PREFERENTIALLY	PREFORMATTING	PREHENSION	PREJUDICATED	PRELITERACIES
PREFERMENT	PREFORMING	PREHENSIONS	PREJUDICATES	PRELITERACY
PREFERMENTS	PREFORMULATE	PREHENSIVE	PREJUDICATING	PRELITERARY
PREFERRABLE	PREFORMULATED	PREHENSORIAL	PREJUDICATION	PRELITERATE
PREFERRERS	PREFORMULATES	PREHENSORS	PREJUDICATIONS	PRELITERATES
PREFERRING	PREFORMULATING	PREHENSORY	PREJUDICATIVE	PRELOADING
PREFIGURATE	PREFRANKED	PREHISTORIAN	PREJUDICED	PRELOCATED
PREFIGURATED	PREFRANKING	PREHISTORIANS	PREJUDICES	PRELOCATES
PREFIGURATES	PREFREEZES	PREHISTORIC	PREJUDICIAL	PRELOCATING
PREFIGURATING	PREFREEZING	PREHISTORICAL	PREJUDICIALLY	PRELOGICAL
PREFIGURATION	PREFRESHMAN	PREHISTORICALLY	PREJUDICIALNESS	PRELUDIOUS
PREFIGURATIONS	PREFRONTAL	PREHISTORIES	PREJUDICING	PRELUNCHEON
PREFIGURATIVE	PREFRONTALS	PREHISTORY	PREJUDIZES	PRELUSIONS
PREFIGURATIVELY	PREFULGENT	PREHOLIDAY	PREKINDERGARTEN	PRELUSIVELY
PREFIGURED	PREFUNDING	PREHOMINID	PRELAPSARIAN	PRELUSORILY
PREFIGUREMENT	PREGANGLIONIC	PREHOMINIDS	PRELATESHIP	PREMALIGNANT
PREFIGUREMENTS	PREGENITAL	PREIGNITION	PRELATESHIPS	PREMANDIBULAR
PREFIGURES	PREGLACIAL	PREIGNITIONS	PRELATESSES	PREMANDIBULARS
PREFIGURING	PREGNABILITIES	PREIMPLANTATION	PRELATICAL	PREMANUFACTURE
PREFINANCE	PREGNABILITY	PREIMPOSED	PRELATICALLY	PREMANUFACTURED
PREFINANCED	PREGNANCES	PREIMPOSES	PRELATIONS	PREMANUFACTURES
PREFINANCES	PREGNANCIES	PREIMPOSING	PRELATISED	PREMARITAL
PREFINANCING	PREGNANTLY	PREINAUGURAL	PRELATISES	PREMARITALLY
PREFIXALLY	PREGNENOLONE	PREINDUCTION	PRELATISING	PREMARKETED
PREFIXIONS	PREGNENOLONES	PREINDUSTRIAL	PRELATISMS	PREMARKETING
PREFIXTURE	PREGROWTHS	PREINFORMED	PRELATISTS	PREMARKETS
PREFIXTURES	PREGUIDING	PREINFORMING	PRELATIZED	PREMARRIAGE
PREFLIGHTED	PREGUSTATION	PREINFORMS	PRELATIZES	PREMATURELY
PREFLIGHTING	PREGUSTATIONS	PREINSERTED	PRELATIZING	PREMATURENESS
PREFLIGHTS	PREHALLUCES	PREINSERTING	PRELATURES	PREMATURENESSES
PREFLORATION	PREHANDLED	PREINSERTS	PRELAUNCHED	PREMATURES
PREFLORATIONS	PREHANDLES	PREINTERVIEW	PRELAUNCHES	PREMATURITIES
PREFOCUSED	PREHANDLING	PREINTERVIEWED	PRELAUNCHING	PREMATURITY
PREFOCUSES	PREHARDENED	PREINTERVIEWING	PRELECTING	PREMAXILLA
PREFOCUSING	PREHARDENING	PREINTERVIEWS	PRELECTION	PREMAXILLAE
PREFOCUSSED	PREHARDENS	PREINVASION	PRELECTIONS	PREMAXILLARIES
PREFOCUSSES	PREHARVEST	PREINVITED	PRELECTORS	PREMAXILLARY
PREFOCUSSING	PREHEADACHE	PREINVITES	PRELEXICAL	PREMAXILLAS
PREFOLIATION	PREHEATERS	PREINVITING	PRELIBATION	PREMEASURE
PREFOLIATIONS	PREHEATING	PREJUDGEMENT	PRELIBATIONS	PREMEASURED
PREFORMATION	PREHEMINENCE	PREJUDGEMENTS	PRELIMINARIES	PREMEASURES
PREFORMATIONISM	PREHEMINENCES	PREJUDGERS	PRELIMINARILY	PREMEASURING
PREFORMATIONIST	PREHENDING	PREJUDGING	PRELIMINARY	PREMEDICAL
PREFORMATIONS	PREHENSIBLE	PREJUDGMENT	PRELIMITED	PREMEDICALLY
PREFORMATIVE	PREHENSILE	PREJUDGMENTS	PRELIMITING	PREMEDICATE

PREMEDICATED	PREMONITORILY	PREOCCUPATIONS	PREPLACING	PREPOTENCES
PREMEDICATES	PREMONITORS	PREOCCUPIED	PREPLANNED	PREPOTENCIES
PREMEDICATING	PREMONITORY	PREOCCUPIES	PREPLANNING	PREPOTENCY
PREMEDICATION	PREMOTIONS	PREOCCUPYING	PREPLANTING	PREPOTENTLY
PREMEDICATIONS	PREMOVEMENT	PREOPENING	PREPOLLENCE	PREPPINESS
PREMEDIEVAL	PREMOVEMENTS	PREOPERATIONAL	PREPOLLENCES	PREPPINESSES
PREMEDITATE	PREMUNITION	PREOPERATIVE	PREPOLLENCIES	PREPRANDIAL
PREMEDITATED	PREMUNITIONS	PREOPERATIVELY	PREPOLLENCY	PREPREPARED
PREMEDITATEDLY	PREMYCOTIC	PREOPTIONS	PREPOLLENT	PREPRESIDENTIAL
PREMEDITATES	PRENATALLY	PREORDAINED	PREPOLLICES	PREPRESSES
PREMEDITATING	PRENEGOTIATE	PREORDAINING	PREPONDERANCE	PREPRICING
PREMEDITATION	PRENEGOTIATED	PREORDAINMENT	PREPONDERANCES	PREPRIMARIES
PREMEDITATIONS	PRENEGOTIATES	PREORDAINMENTS	PREPONDERANCIES	PREPRIMARY
PREMEDITATIVE	PRENEGOTIATING	PREORDAINS	PREPONDERANCY	PREPRINTED
PREMEDITATOR	PRENEGOTIATION	PREORDERED	PREPONDERANT	PREPRINTING
PREMEDITATORS	PRENEGOTIATIONS	PREORDERING	PREPONDERANTLY	PREPROCESS
PREMEIOTIC	PRENOMINAL	PREORDINANCE	PREPONDERATE	PREPROCESSED
PREMENOPAUSAL	PRENOMINATE	PREORDINANCES	PREPONDERATED	PREPROCESSES
PREMENSTRUAL	PRENOMINATED	PREORDINATION	PREPONDERATELY	PREPROCESSING
PREMENSTRUALLY	PRENOMINATES	PREORDINATIONS	PREPONDERATES	PREPROCESSOR
PREMIERING	PRENOMINATING	PREOVULATORY	PREPONDERATING	PREPROCESSORS
PREMIERSHIP	PRENOMINATION	PREPACKAGE	PREPONDERATION	PREPRODUCTION
PREMIERSHIPS	PRENOMINATIONS	PREPACKAGED	PREPONDERATIONS	PREPRODUCTIONS
PREMIGRATION	PRENOTIFICATION	PREPACKAGES	PREPORTION	PREPROFESSIONAL
PREMILLENARIAN	PRENOTIFIED	PREPACKAGING	PREPORTIONED	PREPROGRAM
PREMILLENARIANS	PRENOTIFIES	PREPACKING	PREPORTIONING	PREPROGRAMED
PREMILLENNIAL	PRENOTIFYING	PREPARATION	PREPORTIONS	PREPROGRAMING
PREMILLENNIALLY	PRENOTIONS	PREPARATIONS	PREPOSITION	PREPROGRAMMED
PREMISSING	PRENTICESHIP	PREPARATIVE	PREPOSITIONAL	PREPROGRAMMING
PREMODIFICATION	PRENTICESHIPS	PREPARATIVELY	PREPOSITIONALLY	PREPROGRAMS
PREMODIFIED	PRENTICING	PREPARATIVES	PREPOSITIONS	PREPSYCHEDELIC
PREMODIFIES	PRENUMBERED	PREPARATOR	PREPOSITIVE	PREPUBERAL
PREMODIFYING	PRENUMBERING	PREPARATORILY	PREPOSITIVELY	PREPUBERTAL
PREMOISTEN	PRENUMBERS	PREPARATORS	PREPOSITIVES	PREPUBERTIES
PREMOISTENED	PRENUPTIAL	PREPARATORY	PREPOSITOR	PREPUBERTY
PREMOISTENING	PREOBTAINED	PREPAREDLY	PREPOSITORS	PREPUBESCENCE
PREMOISTENS	PREOBTAINING	PREPAREDNESS	PREPOSSESS	PREPUBESCENCES
PREMOLDING	PREOBTAINS	PREPAREDNESSES	PREPOSSESSED	PREPUBESCENT
PREMONISHED	PREOCCUPANCIES	PREPASTING	PREPOSSESSES	PREPUBESCENTS
PREMONISHES	PREOCCUPANCY	PREPATELLAR	PREPOSSESSING	PREPUBLICATION
PREMONISHING	PREOCCUPANT	PREPAYABLE	PREPOSSESSINGLY	PREPUBLICATIONS
PREMONISHMENT	PREOCCUPANTS	PREPAYMENT	PREPOSSESSION	PREPUNCHED
PREMONISHMENTS	PREOCCUPATE	PREPAYMENTS	PREPOSSESSIONS	PREPUNCHES
PREMONITION	PREOCCUPATED	PREPENSELY	PREPOSTEROUS	PREPUNCHING
PREMONITIONS	PREOCCUPATES	PREPENSING	PREPOSTEROUSLY	PREPUNCTUAL
PREMONITIVE	PREOCCUPATING	PREPENSIVE	PREPOSTORS	PREPURCHASE
PREMONITOR	PREOCCUPATION	PREPERFORMANCE	PREPOTENCE	PREPURCHASED

P

PREPURCHASES

PREPURCHASES	PRESBYACUSIS	PRESCREENING	PRESENTIAL	PRESIDENTIAL
PREPURCHASING	PRESBYCOUSES	PRESCREENS	PRESENTIALITIES	PRESIDENTIALLY
PREQUALIFIED	PRESBYCOUSIS	PRESCRIBED	PRESENTIALITY	PRESIDENTS
PREQUALIFIES	PRESBYCUSES	PRESCRIBER	PRESENTIALLY	PRESIDENTSHIP
PREQUALIFY	PRESBYCUSIS	PRESCRIBERS	PRESENTIENT	PRESIDENTSHIPS
PREQUALIFYING	PRESBYOPES	PRESCRIBES	PRESENTIMENT	PRESIDIARY
PREREADING	PRESBYOPIA	PRESCRIBING	PRESENTIMENTAL	PRESIDIUMS
PRERECESSION	PRESBYOPIAS	PRESCRIBINGS	PRESENTIMENTS	PRESIFTING
PRERECORDED	PRESBYOPIC	PRESCRIPTIBLE	PRESENTING	PRESIGNALED
PRERECORDING	PRESBYOPICS	PRESCRIPTION	PRESENTISM	PRESIGNALING
PRERECORDS	PRESBYOPIES	PRESCRIPTIONS	PRESENTISMS	PRESIGNALLED
PREREGISTER	PRESBYTERAL	PRESCRIPTIVE	PRESENTIST	PRESIGNALLING
PREREGISTERED	PRESBYTERATE	PRESCRIPTIVELY	PRESENTIVE	PRESIGNALS
PREREGISTERING	PRESBYTERATES	PRESCRIPTIVISM	PRESENTIVENESS	PRESIGNIFIED
PREREGISTERS	PRESBYTERIAL	PRESCRIPTIVISMS	PRESENTMENT	PRESIGNIFIES
PREREGISTRATION	PRESBYTERIALLY	PRESCRIPTIVIST	PRESENTMENTS	PRESIGNIFY
PREREHEARSAL	PRESBYTERIALS	PRESCRIPTIVISTS	PRESENTNESS	PRESIGNIFYING
PRERELEASE	PRESBYTERIAN	PRESCRIPTS	PRESENTNESSES	PRESLAUGHTER
PRERELEASED	PRESBYTERIANISE	PRESEASONS	PRESERVABILITY	PRESLICING
PRERELEASES	PRESBYTERIANISM	PRESELECTED	PRESERVABLE	PRESOAKING
PRERELEASING	PRESBYTERIANIZE	PRESELECTING	PRESERVABLY	PRESOLVING
PREREQUIRE	PRESBYTERIANS	PRESELECTION	PRESERVATION	PRESORTING
PREREQUIRED	PRESBYTERIES	PRESELECTIONS	PRESERVATIONIST	PRESPECIFIED
PREREQUIRES	PRESBYTERS	PRESELECTOR	PRESERVATIONS	PRESPECIFIES
PREREQUIRING	PRESBYTERSHIP	PRESELECTORS	PRESERVATIVE	PRESPECIFY
PREREQUISITE	PRESBYTERSHIPS	PRESELECTS	PRESERVATIVES	PRESPECIFYING
PREREQUISITES	PRESBYTERY	PRESELLING	PRESERVATORIES	PRESSBOARD
PRERETIREMENT	PRESBYTISM	PRESENSION	PRESERVATORY	PRESSBOARDS
PREREVISIONIST	PRESBYTISMS	PRESENSIONS	PRESERVERS	PRESSGANGS
PREREVOLUTION	PRESCHEDULE	PRESENTABILITY	PRESERVICE	PRESSINGLY
PRERINSING	PRESCHEDULED	PRESENTABLE	PRESERVING	PRESSINGNESS
PREROGATIVE	PRESCHEDULES	PRESENTABLENESS	PRESETTING	PRESSINGNESSES
PREROGATIVED	PRESCHEDULING	PRESENTABLY	PRESETTLED	PRESSMARKS
PREROGATIVELY	PRESCHOOLER	PRESENTATION	PRESETTLEMENT	PRESSROOMS
PREROGATIVES	PRESCHOOLERS	PRESENTATIONAL	PRESETTLES	PRESSURELESS
PREROMANTIC	PRESCHOOLS	PRESENTATIONISM	PRESETTLING	PRESSURING
PRESAGEFUL	PRESCIENCE	PRESENTATIONIST	PRESHAPING	PRESSURISATION
PRESAGEFULLY	PRESCIENCES	PRESENTATIONS	PRESHIPPED	PRESSURISATIONS
PRESAGEMENT	PRESCIENTIFIC	PRESENTATIVE	PRESHIPPING	PRESSURISE
PRESAGEMENTS	PRESCIENTLY	PRESENTEEISM	PRESHOWING	PRESSURISED
PRESANCTIFIED	PRESCINDED	PRESENTEEISMS	PRESHRINKING	PRESSURISER
PRESANCTIFIES	PRESCINDENT	PRESENTEES	PRESHRINKS	PRESSURISERS
PRESANCTIFY	PRESCINDING	PRESENTENCE	PRESHRUNKEN	PRESSURISES
PRESANCTIFYING	PRESCISSION	PRESENTENCED	PRESIDENCIES	PRESSURISING
PRESBYACOUSES	PRESCISSIONS	PRESENTENCES	PRESIDENCY	PRESSURIZATION
PRESBYACOUSIS	PRESCORING	PRESENTENCING	PRESIDENTESS	PRESSURIZATIONS
PRESBYACUSES	PRESCREENED	PRESENTERS	PRESIDENTESSES	PRESSURIZE

PRESSURIZED	PRESUMPTION	PRETENTIOUSLY	PRETTINESS	PREVENTIVELY
PRESSURIZER	PRESUMPTIONS	PRETENTIOUSNESS	PRETTINESSES	PREVENTIVENESS
PRESSURIZERS	PRESUMPTIVE	PRETERHUMAN	PRETTYISMS	PREVENTIVES
PRESSURIZES	PRESUMPTIVELY	PRETERISTS	PREUNIFICATION	PREVIEWERS
PRESSURIZING	PRESUMPTIVENESS	PRETERITENESS	PREUNITING	PREVIEWING
PRESSWOMAN	PRESUMPTUOUS	PRETERITENESSES	PREUNIVERSITY	PREVIOUSLY
PRESSWOMEN	PRESUMPTUOUSLY	PRETERITES	PREVAILERS	PREVIOUSNESS
PRESSWORKS	PRESUPPOSE	PRETERITION	PREVAILING	PREVIOUSNESSES
PRESTAMPED	PRESUPPOSED	PRETERITIONS	PREVAILINGLY	PREVISIONAL
PRESTAMPING	PRESUPPOSES	PRETERITIVE	PREVAILMENT	PREVISIONARY
PRESTATION	PRESUPPOSING	PRETERMINAL	PREVAILMENTS	PREVISIONED
PRESTATIONS	PRESUPPOSITION	PRETERMINATION	PREVALENCE	PREVISIONING
PRESTERILISE	PRESUPPOSITIONS	PRETERMINATIONS	PREVALENCES	PREVISIONS
PRESTERILISED	PRESURGERY	PRETERMISSION	PREVALENCIES	PREVISITED
PRESTERILISES	PRESURMISE	PRETERMISSIONS	PREVALENCY	PREVISITING
PRESTERILISING	PRESURMISES	PRETERMITS	PREVALENTLY	PREVOCALIC
PRESTERILIZE	PRESURVEYED	PRETERMITTED	PREVALENTNESS	PREVOCALICALLY
PRESTERILIZED	PRESURVEYING	PRETERMITTER	PREVALENTNESSES	PREVOCATIONAL
PRESTERILIZES	PRESURVEYS	PRETERMITTERS	PREVALENTS	PREWARMING
PRESTERILIZING	PRESWEETEN	PRETERMITTING	PREVALUING	PREWARNING
PRESTERNUM	PRESWEETENED	PRETERNATURAL	PREVARICATE	PREWASHING
PRESTERNUMS	PRESWEETENING	PRETERNATURALLY	PREVARICATED	PREWEANING
PRESTIDIGITATOR	PRESWEETENS	PRETERPERFECT	PREVARICATES	PREWEIGHED
PRESTIGEFUL	PRESYMPTOMATIC	PRETERPERFECTS	PREVARICATING	PREWEIGHING
PRESTIGIATOR	PRESYNAPTIC	PRETESTING	PREVARICATION	PREWORKING
PRESTIGIATORS	PRESYNAPTICALLY	PRETEXTING	PREVARICATIONS	PREWRAPPED
PRESTIGIOUS	PRETASTING	PRETEXTINGS	PREVARICATOR	PREWRAPPING
PRESTIGIOUSLY	PRETELEVISION	PRETHEATER	PREVARICATORS	PREWRITING
PRESTIGIOUSNESS	PRETELLING	PRETORIANS	PREVENANCIES	PREWRITINGS
PRESTISSIMO	PRETENCELESS	PRETORSHIP	PREVENANCY	PRICELESSLY
PRESTISSIMOS	PRETENDANT	PRETORSHIPS	PREVENIENCE	PRICELESSNESS
PRESTORAGE	PRETENDANTS	PRETOURNAMENT	PREVENIENCES	PRICELESSNESSES
PRESTORING	PRETENDEDLY	PRETRAINED	PREVENIENT	PRICINESSES
PRESTRESSED	PRETENDENT	PRETRAINING	PREVENIENTLY	PRICKLIEST
PRESTRESSES	PRETENDENTS	PRETREATED	PREVENTABILITY	PRICKLINESS
PRESTRESSING	PRETENDERS	PRETREATING	PREVENTABLE	PRICKLINESSES
PRESTRICTION	PRETENDERSHIP	PRETREATMENT	PREVENTABLY	PRICKLINGS
PRESTRICTIONS	PRETENDERSHIPS	PRETREATMENTS	PREVENTATIVE	PRICKWOODS
PRESTRUCTURE	PRETENDING	PRETRIMMED	PREVENTATIVES	PRIDEFULLY
PRESTRUCTURED	PRETENDINGLY	PRETRIMMING	PREVENTERS	PRIDEFULNESS
PRESTRUCTURES	PRETENSION	PRETTIFICATION	PREVENTIBILITY	PRIDEFULNESSES
PRESTRUCTURING	PRETENSIONED	PRETTIFICATIONS	PREVENTIBLE	PRIESTCRAFT
PRESUMABLE	PRETENSIONING	PRETTIFIED	PREVENTIBLY	PRIESTCRAFTS
PRESUMABLY	PRETENSIONLESS	PRETTIFIER	PREVENTING	PRIESTESSES
PRESUMEDLY	PRETENSIONS	PRETTIFIERS	PREVENTION	PRIESTHOOD
PRESUMINGLY	PRETENSIVE	PRETTIFIES	PREVENTIONS	PRIESTHOODS
PRESUMMITS	PRETENTIOUS	PRETTIFYING	PREVENTIVE	PRIESTLIER

P

PRIESTLIEST	PRIMITIVISTS	PRINCIPALITY	PRISMOIDAL	PRIZEWINNERS
PRIESTLIKE	PRIMITIVITIES	PRINCIPALLY	PRISONMENT	PRIZEWINNING
PRIESTLINESS	PRIMITIVITY	PRINCIPALNESS	PRISONMENTS	PRIZEWOMAN
PRIESTLINESSES	PRIMNESSES	PRINCIPALNESSES	PRISSINESS	PRIZEWOMEN
PRIESTLING	PRIMOGENIAL	PRINCIPALS	PRISSINESSES	PROABORTION
PRIESTLINGS	PRIMOGENIT	PRINCIPALSHIP	PRISTINELY	PROACTIONS
PRIESTSHIP	PRIMOGENITAL	PRINCIPALSHIPS	PRIVATDOCENT	PROAIRESES
PRIESTSHIPS	PRIMOGENITARY	PRINCIPATE	PRIVATDOCENTS	PROAIRESIS
PRIGGERIES	PRIMOGENITIVE	PRINCIPATES	PRIVATDOZENT	PROBABILIORISM
PRIGGISHLY	PRIMOGENITIVES	PRINCIPIAL	PRIVATDOZENTS	PROBABILIORISMS
PRIGGISHNESS	PRIMOGENITOR	PRINCIPIUM	PRIVATEERED	PROBABILIORIST
PRIGGISHNESSES	PRIMOGENITORS	PRINCIPLED	PRIVATEERING	PROBABILIORISTS
PRIMAEVALLY	PRIMOGENITRICES	PRINCIPLES	PRIVATEERINGS	PROBABILISM
PRIMALITIES	PRIMOGENITRIX	PRINCIPLING	PRIVATEERS	PROBABILISMS
PRIMAQUINE	PRIMOGENITRIXES	PRINTABILITIES	PRIVATEERSMAN	PROBABILIST
PRIMAQUINES	PRIMOGENITS	PRINTABILITY	PRIVATEERSMEN	PROBABILISTIC
PRIMARINESS	PRIMOGENITURE	PRINTABLENESS	PRIVATENESS	PROBABILISTS
PRIMARINESSES	PRIMOGENITURES	PRINTABLENESSES	PRIVATENESSES	PROBABILITIES
PRIMATESHIP	PRIMORDIAL	PRINTERIES	PRIVATIONS	PROBABILITY
PRIMATESHIPS	PRIMORDIALISM	PRINTHEADS	PRIVATISATION	PROBATIONAL
PRIMATIALS	PRIMORDIALISMS	PRINTMAKER	PRIVATISATIONS	PROBATIONALLY
PRIMATICAL	PRIMORDIALITIES	PRINTMAKERS	PRIVATISED	PROBATIONARIES
PRIMATOLOGICAL	PRIMORDIALITY	PRINTMAKING	PRIVATISER	PROBATIONARY
PRIMATOLOGIES	PRIMORDIALLY	PRINTMAKINGS	PRIVATISERS	PROBATIONER
PRIMATOLOGIST	PRIMORDIALS	PRINTWHEEL	PRIVATISES	PROBATIONERS
PRIMATOLOGISTS	PRIMORDIUM	PRINTWHEELS	PRIVATISING	PROBATIONERSHIP
PRIMATOLOGY	PRIMROSING	PRINTWORKS	PRIVATISMS	PROBATIONS
PRIMAVERAS	PRIMULACEOUS	PRIORESSES	PRIVATISTS	PROBATIVELY
PRIMENESSES	PRIMULINES	PRIORITIES	PRIVATIVELY	PROBENECID
PRIMEVALLY	PRINCEDOMS	PRIORITISATION	PRIVATIVES	PROBENECIDS
PRIMIGENIAL	PRINCEHOOD	PRIORITISATIONS	PRIVATIZATION	PROBIOTICS
PRIMIGRAVIDA	PRINCEHOODS	PRIORITISE	PRIVATIZATIONS	PROBLEMATIC
PRIMIGRAVIDAE	PRINCEKINS	PRIORITISED	PRIVATIZED	PROBLEMATICAL
PRIMIGRAVIDAS	PRINCELETS	PRIORITISES	PRIVATIZER	PROBLEMATICALLY
PRIMIPARAE	PRINCELIER	PRIORITISING	PRIVATIZERS	PROBLEMATICS
PRIMIPARAS	PRINCELIEST	PRIORITIZATION	PRIVATIZES	PROBLEMIST
PRIMIPARITIES	PRINCELIKE	PRIORITIZATIONS	PRIVATIZING	PROBLEMISTS
PRIMIPARITY	PRINCELINESS	PRIORITIZE	PRIVILEGED	PROBOSCIDEAN
PRIMIPAROUS	PRINCELINESSES	PRIORITIZED	PRIVILEGES	PROBOSCIDEANS
PRIMITIVELY	PRINCELING	PRIORITIZES	PRIVILEGING	PROBOSCIDES
PRIMITIVENESS	PRINCELINGS	PRIORITIZING	PRIZEFIGHT	PROBOSCIDIAN
PRIMITIVENESSES	PRINCESHIP	PRIORSHIPS	PRIZEFIGHTER	PROBOSCIDIANS
PRIMITIVES	PRINCESHIPS	PRISMATICAL	PRIZEFIGHTERS	PROBOSCISES
PRIMITIVISM	PRINCESSES	PRISMATICALLY	PRIZEFIGHTING	PROBOULEUTIC
PRIMITIVISMS	PRINCESSLY	PRISMATOID	PRIZEFIGHTINGS	PROBUSINESS
PRIMITIVIST	PRINCIFIED	PRISMATOIDAL	PRIZEFIGHTS	PROCACIOUS
PRIMITIVISTIC	PRINCIPALITIES	PRISMATOIDS	PRIZEWINNER	PROCACITIES

PROCAMBIAL	PROCESSIONINGS	PROCRUSTEAN	PROCURATIONS	PRODUCTIVITY
PROCAMBIUM	PROCESSIONS	PROCRYPSES	PROCURATOR	PROEMBRYOS
PROCAMBIUMS	PROCESSORS	PROCRYPSIS	PROCURATORIAL	PROENZYMES
PROCAPITALIST	PROCESSUAL	PROCRYPTIC	PROCURATORIES	PROESTRUSES
PROCARBAZINE	PROCHRONISM	PROCRYPTICALLY	PROCURATORS	PROFANATION
PROCARBAZINES	PROCHRONISMS	PROCTALGIA	PROCURATORSHIP	PROFANATIONS
PROCARYONS	PROCIDENCE	PROCTALGIAS	PROCURATORSHIPS	PROFANATORY
PROCARYOTE	PROCIDENCES	PROCTITIDES	PROCURATORY	PROFANENESS
PROCARYOTES	PROCLAIMANT	PROCTITISES	PROCUREMENT	PROFANENESSES
PROCARYOTIC	PROCLAIMANTS	PROCTODAEA	PROCUREMENTS	PROFANITIES
PROCATHEDRAL	PROCLAIMED	PROCTODAEAL	PROCURESSES	PROFASCIST
PROCATHEDRALS	PROCLAIMER	PROCTODAEUM	PROCUREURS	PROFECTITIOUS
PROCEDURAL	PROCLAIMERS	PROCTODAEUMS	PROCURINGS	PROFEMINIST
PROCEDURALLY	PROCLAIMING	PROCTODEUM	PROCYONIDS	PROFESSEDLY
PROCEDURALS	PROCLAMATION	PROCTODEUMS	PRODIGALISE	PROFESSING
PROCEDURES	PROCLAMATIONS	PROCTOLOGIC	PRODIGALISED	PROFESSION
PROCEEDERS	PROCLAMATORY	PROCTOLOGICAL	PRODIGALISES	PROFESSIONAL
PROCEEDING	PROCLITICS	PROCTOLOGIES	PRODIGALISING	PROFESSIONALISE
PROCEEDINGS	PROCLIVITIES	PROCTOLOGIST	PRODIGALITIES	PROFESSIONALISM
PROCELEUSMATIC	PROCLIVITY	PROCTOLOGISTS	PRODIGALITY	PROFESSIONALIST
PROCELEUSMATICS	PROCOELOUS	PROCTOLOGY	PRODIGALIZE	PROFESSIONALIZE
PROCELLARIAN	PROCONSULAR	PROCTORAGE	PRODIGALIZED	PROFESSIONALLY
PROCEPHALIC	PROCONSULATE	PROCTORAGES	PRODIGALIZES	PROFESSIONALS
PROCERCOID	PROCONSULATES	PROCTORIAL	PRODIGALIZING	PROFESSIONS
PROCERCOIDS	PROCONSULS	PROCTORIALLY	PRODIGALLY	PROFESSORATE
PROCEREBRA	PROCONSULSHIP	PROCTORING	PRODIGIOSITIES	PROFESSORATES
PROCEREBRAL	PROCONSULSHIPS	PROCTORISE	PRODIGIOSITY	PROFESSORESS
PROCEREBRUM	PROCRASTINATE	PROCTORISED	PRODIGIOUS	PROFESSORESSES
PROCEREBRUMS	PROCRASTINATED	PROCTORISES	PRODIGIOUSLY	PROFESSORIAL
PROCERITIES	PROCRASTINATES	PROCTORISING	PRODIGIOUSNESS	PROFESSORIALLY
PROCESSABILITY	PROCRASTINATING	PROCTORIZE	PRODITORIOUS	PROFESSORIAT
PROCESSABLE	PROCRASTINATION	PROCTORIZED	PRODNOSING	PROFESSORIATE
PROCESSERS	PROCRASTINATIVE	PROCTORIZES	PRODROMATA	PROFESSORIATES
PROCESSIBILITY	PROCRASTINATOR	PROCTORIZING	PRODUCEMENT	PROFESSORIATS
PROCESSIBLE	PROCRASTINATORS	PROCTORSHIP	PRODUCEMENTS	PROFESSORS
PROCESSING	PROCRASTINATORY	PROCTORSHIPS	PRODUCIBILITIES	PROFESSORSHIP
PROCESSINGS	PROCREANTS	PROCTOSCOPE	PRODUCIBILITY	PROFESSORSHIPS
PROCESSION	PROCREATED	PROCTOSCOPES	PRODUCIBLE	PROFFERERS
PROCESSIONAL	PROCREATES	PROCTOSCOPIC	PRODUCTIBILITY	PROFFERING
PROCESSIONALIST	PROCREATING	PROCTOSCOPIES	PRODUCTILE	PROFICIENCE
PROCESSIONALLY	PROCREATION	PROCTOSCOPY	PRODUCTION	PROFICIENCES
PROCESSIONALS	PROCREATIONAL	PROCUMBENT	PRODUCTIONAL	PROFICIENCIES
PROCESSIONARY	PROCREATIONS	PROCURABLE	PRODUCTIONS	PROFICIENCY
PROCESSIONED	PROCREATIVE	PROCURACIES	PRODUCTIVE	PROFICIENT
PROCESSIONER	PROCREATIVENESS	PROCURANCE	PRODUCTIVELY	PROFICIENTLY
PROCESSIONERS	PROCREATOR	PROCURANCES	PRODUCTIVENESS	PROFICIENTS
PROCESSIONING	PROCREATORS	PROCURATION	PRODUCTIVITIES	PROFILINGS

P

PROFILISTS	PROGENITURES	PROGRESSED	PROINSULIN	PROLETARIANISES
PROFITABILITIES	PROGESTATIONAL	PROGRESSES	PROINSULINS	PROLETARIANISM
PROFITABILITY	PROGESTERONE	PROGRESSING	PROJECTABLE	PROLETARIANISMS
PROFITABLE	PROGESTERONES	PROGRESSION	PROJECTILE	PROLETARIANIZE
PROFITABLENESS	PROGESTINS	PROGRESSIONAL	PROJECTILES	PROLETARIANIZED
PROFITABLY	PROGESTOGEN	PROGRESSIONALLY	PROJECTING	PROLETARIANIZES
PROFITEERED	PROGESTOGENIC	PROGRESSIONARY	PROJECTINGS	PROLETARIANNESS
PROFITEERING	PROGESTOGENS	PROGRESSIONISM	PROJECTION	PROLETARIANS
PROFITEERINGS	PROGGINSES	PROGRESSIONISMS	PROJECTIONAL	PROLETARIAT
PROFITEERS	PROGLOTTIC	PROGRESSIONIST	PROJECTIONIST	PROLETARIATE
PROFITEROLE	PROGLOTTID	PROGRESSIONISTS	PROJECTIONISTS	PROLETARIATES
PROFITEROLES	PROGLOTTIDEAN	PROGRESSIONS	PROJECTIONS	PROLETARIATS
PROFITINGS	PROGLOTTIDES	PROGRESSISM	PROJECTISATION	PROLETARIES
PROFITLESS	PROGLOTTIDS	PROGRESSISMS	PROJECTISATIONS	PROLICIDAL
PROFITLESSLY	PROGLOTTIS	PROGRESSIST	PROJECTIVE	PROLICIDES
PROFITWISE	PROGNATHIC	PROGRESSISTS	PROJECTIVELY	PROLIFERATE
PROFLIGACIES	PROGNATHISM	PROGRESSIVE	PROJECTIVITIES	PROLIFERATED
PROFLIGACY	PROGNATHISMS	PROGRESSIVELY	PROJECTIVITY	PROLIFERATES
PROFLIGATE	PROGNATHOUS	PROGRESSIVENESS	PROJECTIZATION	PROLIFERATING
PROFLIGATELY	PROGNOSING	PROGRESSIVES	PROJECTIZATIONS	PROLIFERATION
PROFLIGATES	PROGNOSTIC	PROGRESSIVISM	PROJECTMENT	PROLIFERATIONS
PROFLUENCE	PROGNOSTICATE	PROGRESSIVISMS	PROJECTMENTS	PROLIFERATIVE
PROFLUENCES	PROGNOSTICATED	PROGRESSIVIST	PROJECTORS	PROLIFEROUS
PROFOUNDER	PROGNOSTICATES	PROGRESSIVISTIC	PROJECTURE	PROLIFEROUSLY
PROFOUNDEST	PROGNOSTICATING	PROGRESSIVISTS	PROJECTURES	PROLIFICACIES
PROFOUNDLY	PROGNOSTICATION	PROGRESSIVITIES	PROKARYONS	PROLIFICACY
PROFOUNDNESS	PROGNOSTICATIVE	PROGRESSIVITY	PROKARYOTE	PROLIFICAL
PROFOUNDNESSES	PROGNOSTICATOR	PROGYMNASIA	PROKARYOTES	PROLIFICALLY
PROFULGENT	PROGNOSTICATORS	PROGYMNASIUM	PROKARYOTIC	PROLIFICATION
PROFUNDITIES	PROGNOSTICS	PROGYMNASIUMS	PROKARYOTS	PROLIFICATIONS
PROFUNDITY	PROGRADATION	PROHIBITED	PROLACTINS	PROLIFICITIES
PROFUSENESS	PROGRADATIONS	PROHIBITER	PROLAMINES	PROLIFICITY
PROFUSENESSES	PROGRADING	PROHIBITERS	PROLAPSING	PROLIFICNESS
PROFUSIONS	PROGRAMABLE	PROHIBITING	PROLAPSUSES	PROLIFICNESSES
PROGENITIVE	PROGRAMERS	PROHIBITION	PROLATENESS	PROLIXIOUS
PROGENITIVENESS	PROGRAMING	PROHIBITIONARY	PROLATENESSES	PROLIXITIES
PROGENITOR	PROGRAMINGS	PROHIBITIONISM	PROLATIONS	PROLIXNESS
PROGENITORIAL	PROGRAMMABILITY	PROHIBITIONISMS	PROLEGOMENA	PROLIXNESSES
PROGENITORS	PROGRAMMABLE	PROHIBITIONIST	PROLEGOMENAL	PROLOCUTION
PROGENITORSHIP	PROGRAMMABLES	PROHIBITIONISTS	PROLEGOMENARY	PROLOCUTIONS
PROGENITORSHIPS	PROGRAMMATIC	PROHIBITIONS	PROLEGOMENON	PROLOCUTOR
PROGENITRESS	PROGRAMMED	PROHIBITIVE	PROLEGOMENOUS	PROLOCUTORS
PROGENITRESSES	PROGRAMMER	PROHIBITIVELY	PROLEPTICAL	PROLOCUTORSHIP
PROGENITRICES	PROGRAMMERS	PROHIBITIVENESS	PROLEPTICALLY	PROLOCUTORSHIPS
PROGENITRIX	PROGRAMMES	PROHIBITOR	PROLETARIAN	PROLOCUTRICES
PROGENITRIXES	PROGRAMMING	PROHIBITORS	PROLETARIANISE	PROLOCUTRIX
PROGENITURE	PROGRAMMINGS	PROHIBITORY	PROLETARIANISED	PROLOCUTRIXES

PROLOGISED	PROMINENTNESSES	PRONATIONS	PROOFROOMS	PROPELLING
PROLOGISES	PROMISCUITIES	PRONATORES	PROPAEDEUTIC	PROPELLORS
PROLOGISING	PROMISCUITY	PRONENESSES	PROPAEDEUTICAL	PROPELMENT
PROLOGISTS	PROMISCUOUS	PRONEPHRIC	PROPAEDEUTICS	PROPELMENTS
PROLOGIZED	PROMISCUOUSLY	PRONEPHROI	PROPAGABILITIES	PROPENDENT
PROLOGIZES	PROMISCUOUSNESS	PRONEPHROS	PROPAGABILITY	PROPENDING
PROLOGIZING	PROMISEFUL	PRONEPHROSES	PROPAGABLE	PROPENSELY
PROLOGUING	PROMISELESS	PRONGBUCKS	PROPAGABLENESS	PROPENSENESS
PROLOGUISE	PROMISINGLY	PRONGHORNS	PROPAGANDA	PROPENSENESSES
PROLOGUISED	PROMISSIVE	PRONOMINAL	PROPAGANDAS	PROPENSION
PROLOGUISES	PROMISSORILY	PRONOMINALISE	PROPAGANDISE	PROPENSIONS
PROLOGUISING	PROMISSORS	PRONOMINALISED	PROPAGANDISED	PROPENSITIES
PROLOGUIZE	PROMISSORY	PRONOMINALISES	PROPAGANDISER	PROPENSITY
PROLOGUIZED	PROMONARCHIST	PRONOMINALISING	PROPAGANDISERS	PROPENSIVE
PROLOGUIZES	PROMONTORIES	PRONOMINALIZE	PROPAGANDISES	PROPERDINS
PROLOGUIZING	PROMONTORY	PRONOMINALIZED	PROPAGANDISING	PROPERISPOMENA
PROLONGABLE	PROMOTABILITIES	PRONOMINALIZES	PROPAGANDISM	PROPERISPOMENON
PROLONGATE	PROMOTABILITY	PRONOMINALIZING	PROPAGANDISMS	PROPERNESS
PROLONGATED	PROMOTABLE	PRONOMINALLY	PROPAGANDIST	PROPERNESSES
PROLONGATES	PROMOTIONAL	PRONOUNCEABLE	PROPAGANDISTIC	PROPERTIED
PROLONGATING	PROMOTIONS	PRONOUNCED	PROPAGANDISTS	PROPERTIES
PROLONGATION	PROMOTIVENESS	PRONOUNCEDLY	PROPAGANDIZE	PROPERTYING
PROLONGATIONS	PROMOTIVENESSES	PRONOUNCEMENT	PROPAGANDIZED	PROPERTYLESS
PROLONGERS	PROMPTBOOK	PRONOUNCEMENTS	PROPAGANDIZER	PROPHECIES
PROLONGING	PROMPTBOOKS	PRONOUNCER	PROPAGANDIZERS	PROPHESIABLE
PROLONGMENT	PROMPTINGS	PRONOUNCERS	PROPAGANDIZES	PROPHESIED
PROLONGMENTS	PROMPTITUDE	PRONOUNCES	PROPAGANDIZING	PROPHESIER
PROLUSIONS	PROMPTITUDES	PRONOUNCING	PROPAGATED	PROPHESIERS
PROMACHOSES	PROMPTNESS	PRONOUNCINGS	PROPAGATES	PROPHESIES
PROMENADED	PROMPTNESSES	PRONUCLEAR	PROPAGATING	PROPHESYING
PROMENADER	PROMPTUARIES	PRONUCLEARIST	PROPAGATION	PROPHESYINGS
PROMENADERS	PROMPTUARY	PRONUCLEARISTS	PROPAGATIONAL	PROPHETESS
PROMENADES	PROMPTURES	PRONUCLEUS	PROPAGATIONS	PROPHETESSES
PROMENADING	PROMULGATE	PRONUCLEUSES	PROPAGATIVE	PROPHETHOOD
PROMETHAZINE	PROMULGATED	PRONUNCIAMENTO	PROPAGATOR	PROPHETHOODS
PROMETHAZINES	PROMULGATES	PRONUNCIAMENTOS	PROPAGATORS	PROPHETICAL
PROMETHEUM	PROMULGATING	PRONUNCIATION	PROPAGULES	PROPHETICALLY
PROMETHEUMS	PROMULGATION	PRONUNCIATIONAL	PROPAGULUM	PROPHETICISM
PROMETHIUM	PROMULGATIONS	PRONUNCIATIONS	PROPANEDIOIC	PROPHETICISMS
PROMETHIUMS	PROMULGATOR	PRONUNCIOS	PROPANONES	PROPHETISM
PROMILITARY	PROMULGATORS	PROOEMIONS	PROPAROXYTONE	PROPHETISMS
PROMINENCE	PROMULGING	PROOEMIUMS	PROPAROXYTONES	PROPHETSHIP
PROMINENCES	PROMUSCIDATE	PROOFREADER	PROPELLANT	PROPHETSHIPS
PROMINENCIES	PROMUSCIDES	PROOFREADERS	PROPELLANTS	PROPHYLACTIC
PROMINENCY	PROMYCELIA	PROOFREADING	PROPELLENT	PROPHYLACTICS
PROMINENTLY	PROMYCELIAL	PROOFREADINGS	PROPELLENTS	PROPHYLAXES
PROMINENTNESS	PROMYCELIUM	PROOFREADS	PROPELLERS	PROPHYLAXIS

P

PROPINQUITIES	PROPOSITAE	PROPULSIVE	PROSCRIPTION	PROSENCHYMA
PROPINQUITY	PROPOSITION	PROPULSORS	PROSCRIPTIONS	PROSENCHYMAS
PROPIONATE	PROPOSITIONAL	PROPULSORY	PROSCRIPTIVE	PROSENCHYMATA
PROPIONATES	PROPOSITIONALLY	PROPYLAEUM	PROSCRIPTIVELY	PROSENCHYMATOUS
PROPITIABLE	PROPOSITIONED	PROPYLAMINE	PROSCRIPTS	PROSEUCHAE
PROPITIATE	PROPOSITIONING	PROPYLAMINES	PROSECTING	PROSIFYING
PROPITIATED	PROPOSITIONS	PROPYLENES	PROSECTORIAL	PROSILIENCIES
PROPITIATES	PROPOSITUS	PROPYLITES	PROSECTORS	PROSILIENCY
PROPITIATING	PROPOUNDED	PROPYLITISATION	PROSECTORSHIP	PROSILIENT
PROPITIATION	PROPOUNDER	PROPYLITISE	PROSECTORSHIPS	PROSIMIANS
PROPITIATIONS	PROPOUNDERS	PROPYLITISED	PROSECUTABLE	PROSINESSES
PROPITIATIOUS	PROPOUNDING	PROPYLITISES	PROSECUTED	PROSLAMBANOMENE
PROPITIATIVE	PROPOXYPHENE	PROPYLITISING	PROSECUTES	PROSLAVERY
PROPITIATOR	PROPOXYPHENES	PROPYLITIZATION	PROSECUTING	PROSOBRANCH
PROPITIATORIES	PROPRAETOR	PROPYLITIZE	PROSECUTION	PROSOBRANCHS
PROPITIATORILY	PROPRAETORIAL	PROPYLITIZED	PROSECUTIONS	PROSODIANS
PROPITIATORS	PROPRAETORIAN	PROPYLITIZES	PROSECUTOR	PROSODICAL
PROPITIATORY	PROPRAETORS	PROPYLITIZING	PROSECUTORIAL	PROSODICALLY
PROPITIOUS	PROPRANOLOL	PRORATABLE	PROSECUTORS	PROSODISTS
PROPITIOUSLY	PROPRANOLOLS	PRORATIONS	PROSECUTRICES	PROSOPAGNOSIA
PROPITIOUSNESS	PROPRETORS	PRORECTORS	PROSECUTRIX	PROSOPAGNOSIAS
PROPLASTID	PROPRIETARIES	PROROGATED	PROSECUTRIXES	PROSOPOGRAPHER
PROPLASTIDS	PROPRIETARILY	PROROGATES	PROSELYTED	PROSOPOGRAPHERS
PROPODEONS	PROPRIETARY	PROROGATING	PROSELYTES	PROSOPOGRAPHIES
PROPODEUMS	PROPRIETIES	PROROGATION	PROSELYTIC	PROSOPOGRAPHY
PROPOLISES	PROPRIETOR	PROROGATIONS	PROSELYTING	PROSOPOPEIA
PROPONENTS	PROPRIETORIAL	PROROGUING	PROSELYTISATION	PROSOPOPEIAL
PROPORTION	PROPRIETORIALLY	PROSAICALLY	PROSELYTISE	PROSOPOPEIAS
PROPORTIONABLE	PROPRIETORS	PROSAICALNESS	PROSELYTISED	PROSOPOPOEIA
PROPORTIONABLY	PROPRIETORSHIP	PROSAICALNESSES	PROSELYTISER	PROSOPOPOEIAL
PROPORTIONAL	PROPRIETORSHIPS	PROSAICISM	PROSELYTISERS	PROSOPOPOEIAS
PROPORTIONALITY	PROPRIETRESS	PROSAICISMS	PROSELYTISES	PROSPECTED
PROPORTIONALLY	PROPRIETRESSES	PROSAICNESS	PROSELYTISING	PROSPECTING
PROPORTIONALS	PROPRIETRICES	PROSAICNESSES	PROSELYTISM	PROSPECTINGS
PROPORTIONATE	PROPRIETRIX	PROSATEURS	PROSELYTISMS	PROSPECTION
PROPORTIONATED	PROPRIETRIXES	PROSAUROPOD	PROSELYTIZATION	PROSPECTIONS
PROPORTIONATELY	PROPRIOCEPTION	PROSAUROPODS	PROSELYTIZE	PROSPECTIVE
PROPORTIONATES	PROPRIOCEPTIONS	PROSCENIUM	PROSELYTIZED	PROSPECTIVELY
PROPORTIONATING	PROPRIOCEPTIVE	PROSCENIUMS	PROSELYTIZER	PROSPECTIVENESS
PROPORTIONED	PROPRIOCEPTOR	PROSCIUTTI	PROSELYTIZERS	PROSPECTIVES
PROPORTIONING	PROPRIOCEPTORS	PROSCIUTTO	PROSELYTIZES	PROSPECTLESS
PROPORTIONINGS	PROPROCTOR	PROSCIUTTOS	PROSELYTIZING	PROSPECTOR
PROPORTIONLESS	PROPROCTORS	PROSCRIBED	PROSEMINAR	PROSPECTORS
PROPORTIONMENT	PROPUGNATION	PROSCRIBER	PROSEMINARS	PROSPECTUS
PROPORTIONMENTS	PROPUGNATIONS	PROSCRIBERS	PROSENCEPHALA	PROSPECTUSES
PROPORTIONS	PROPULSION	PROSCRIBES	PROSENCEPHALIC	PROSPERING
PROPOSABLE	PROPULSIONS	PROSCRIBING	PROSENCEPHALON	PROSPERITIES

PROSPERITY	PROSYLLOGISMS	PROTECTRIXES	PROTHALLIC	PROTOGENIC
PROSPEROUS	PROTACTINIUM	PROTEIFORM	PROTHALLIUM	PROTOGINES
PROSPEROUSLY	PROTACTINIUMS	PROTEINACEOUS	PROTHALLOID	PROTOGYNIES
PROSPEROUSNESS	PROTAGONISM	PROTEINASE	PROTHALLUS	PROTOGYNOUS
PROSTACYCLIN	PROTAGONISMS	PROTEINASES	PROTHALLUSES	PROTOHISTORIAN
PROSTACYCLINS	PROTAGONIST	PROTEINOUS	PROTHETICALLY	PROTOHISTORIANS
PROSTAGLANDIN	PROTAGONISTS	PROTEINURIA	PROTHONOTARIAL	PROTOHISTORIC
PROSTAGLANDINS	PROTAMINES	PROTEINURIAS	PROTHONOTARIAT	PROTOHISTORIES
PROSTANTHERA	PROTANDRIES	PROTENDING	PROTHONOTARIATS	PROTOHISTORY
PROSTANTHERAS	PROTANDROUS	PROTENSION	PROTHONOTARIES	PROTOHUMAN
PROSTATECTOMIES	PROTANOMALIES	PROTENSIONS	PROTHONOTARY	PROTOHUMANS
PROSTATECTOMY	PROTANOMALOUS	PROTENSITIES	PROTHORACES	PROTOLANGUAGE
PROSTATISM	PROTANOMALY	PROTENSITY	PROTHORACIC	PROTOLANGUAGES
PROSTATISMS	PROTANOPES	PROTENSIVE	PROTHORAXES	PROTOLITHIC
PROSTATITIS	PROTANOPIA	PROTENSIVELY	PROTHROMBIN	PROTOMARTYR
PROSTATITISES	PROTANOPIAS	PROTEOCLASTIC	PROTHROMBINS	PROTOMARTYRS
PROSTERNUM	PROTANOPIC	PROTEOGLYCAN	PROTISTANS	PROTOMORPHIC
PROSTERNUMS	PROTEACEOUS	PROTEOGLYCANS	PROTISTOLOGIES	PROTONATED
PROSTHESES	PROTECTANT	PROTEOLYSE	PROTISTOLOGIST	PROTONATES
PROSTHESIS	PROTECTANTS	PROTEOLYSED	PROTISTOLOGISTS	PROTONATING
PROSTHETIC	PROTECTERS	PROTEOLYSES	PROTISTOLOGY	PROTONATION
PROSTHETICALLY	PROTECTING	PROTEOLYSING	PROTOACTINIUM	PROTONATIONS
PROSTHETICS	PROTECTINGLY	PROTEOLYSIS	PROTOACTINIUMS	PROTONEMAL
PROSTHETIST	PROTECTION	PROTEOLYTIC	PROTOAVISES	PROTONEMATA
PROSTHETISTS	PROTECTIONISM	PROTEOLYTICALLY	PROTOCHORDATE	PROTONEMATAL
PROSTHODONTIA	PROTECTIONISMS	PROTEOMICS	PROTOCHORDATES	PROTONOTARIAL
PROSTHODONTIAS	PROTECTIONIST	PROTERANDRIES	PROTOCOCCAL	PROTONOTARIAT
PROSTHODONTICS	PROTECTIONISTS	PROTERANDROUS	PROTOCOLED	PROTONOTARIATS
PROSTHODONTIST	PROTECTIONS	PROTERANDRY	PROTOCOLIC	PROTONOTARIES
PROSTHODONTISTS	PROTECTIVE	PROTEROGYNIES	PROTOCOLING	PROTONOTARY
PROSTITUTE	PROTECTIVELY	PROTEROGYNOUS	PROTOCOLISE	PROTOPATHIC
PROSTITUTED	PROTECTIVENESS	PROTEROGYNY	PROTOCOLISED	PROTOPATHIES
PROSTITUTES	PROTECTIVES	PROTERVITIES	PROTOCOLISES	PROTOPATHY
PROSTITUTING	PROTECTORAL	PROTERVITY	PROTOCOLISING	PROTOPHILIC
PROSTITUTION	PROTECTORATE	PROTESTANT	PROTOCOLIST	PROTOPHLOEM
PROSTITUTIONS	PROTECTORATES	PROTESTANTS	PROTOCOLISTS	PROTOPHLOEMS
PROSTITUTOR	PROTECTORIAL	PROTESTATION	PROTOCOLIZE	PROTOPHYTE
PROSTITUTORS	PROTECTORIES	PROTESTATIONS	PROTOCOLIZED	PROTOPHYTES
PROSTOMIAL	PROTECTORLESS	PROTESTERS	PROTOCOLIZES	PROTOPHYTIC
PROSTOMIUM	PROTECTORS	PROTESTING	PROTOCOLIZING	PROTOPLANET
PROSTOMIUMS	PROTECTORSHIP	PROTESTINGLY	PROTOCOLLED	PROTOPLANETARY
PROSTRATED	PROTECTORSHIPS	PROTESTORS	PROTOCOLLING	PROTOPLANETS
PROSTRATES	PROTECTORY	PROTHALAMIA	PROTOCTIST	PROTOPLASM
PROSTRATING	PROTECTRESS	PROTHALAMION	PROTOCTISTS	PROTOPLASMAL
PROSTRATION	PROTECTRESSES	PROTHALAMIUM	PROTODERMS	PROTOPLASMATIC
PROSTRATIONS	PROTECTRICES	PROTHALLIA	PROTOGALAXIES	PROTOPLASMIC
PROSYLLOGISM	PROTECTRIX	PROTHALLIAL	PROTOGALAXY	PROTOPLASMS

P

PROTOPLAST	PROTRACTIONS	PROVENDERING	PROVISIONAL	PRUDENTIALISTS
PROTOPLASTIC	PROTRACTIVE	PROVENDERS	PROVISIONALLY	PRUDENTIALITIES
PROTOPLASTS	PROTRACTOR	PROVENIENCE	PROVISIONALS	PRUDENTIALITY
PROTOPORPHYRIN	PROTRACTORS	PROVENIENCES	PROVISIONARIES	PRUDENTIALLY
PROTOPORPHYRINS	PROTREPTIC	PROVENTRICULAR	PROVISIONARY	PRUDENTIALS
PROTOSPATAIRE	PROTREPTICAL	PROVENTRICULI	PROVISIONED	PRUDISHNESS
PROTOSPATAIRES	PROTREPTICS	PROVENTRICULUS	PROVISIONER	PRUDISHNESSES
PROTOSPATHAIRE	PROTRUDABLE	PROVERBIAL	PROVISIONERS	PRURIENCES
PROTOSPATHAIRES	PROTRUDENT	PROVERBIALISE	PROVISIONING.	PRURIENCIES
PROTOSPATHARIUS	PROTRUDING	PROVERBIALISED	PROVISIONS	PRURIENTLY
PROTOSTARS	PROTRUSIBLE	PROVERBIALISES	PROVISORILY	PRURIGINOUS
PROTOSTELE	PROTRUSILE	PROVERBIALISING	PROVITAMIN	PRURITUSES
PROTOSTELES	PROTRUSION	PROVERBIALISM	PROVITAMINS	PRUSSIANISATION
PROTOSTELIC	PROTRUSIONS	PROVERBIALISMS	PROVOCABLE	PRUSSIANISE
PROTOSTOME	PROTRUSIVE	PROVERBIALIST	PROVOCANTS	PRUSSIANISED
PROTOSTOMES	PROTRUSIVELY	PROVERBIALISTS	PROVOCATEUR	PRUSSIANISES
PROTOTHERIAN	PROTRUSIVENESS	PROVERBIALIZE	PROVOCATEURS	PRUSSIANISING
PROTOTHERIANS	PROTUBERANCE	PROVERBIALIZED	PROVOCATION	PRUSSIANIZATION
PROTOTROPH	PROTUBERANCES	PROVERBIALIZES	PROVOCATIONS	PRUSSIANIZE
PROTOTROPHIC	PROTUBERANCIES	PROVERBIALIZING	PROVOCATIVE	PRUSSIANIZED
PROTOTROPHIES	PROTUBERANCY	PROVERBIALLY	PROVOCATIVELY	PRUSSIANIZES
PROTOTROPHS	PROTUBERANT	PROVERBING	PROVOCATIVENESS	PRUSSIANIZING
PROTOTROPHY	PROTUBERANTLY	PROVIDABLE	PROVOCATIVES	PRUSSIATES
PROTOTYPAL	PROTUBERATE	PROVIDENCE	PROVOCATOR	PSALIGRAPHIES
PROTOTYPED	PROTUBERATED	PROVIDENCES	PROVOCATORS	PSALIGRAPHY
PROTOTYPES	PROTUBERATES	PROVIDENTIAL	PROVOCATORY	PSALMBOOKS
PROTOTYPIC	PROTUBERATING	PROVIDENTIALLY	PROVOKABLE	PSALMODICAL
PROTOTYPICAL	PROTUBERATION	PROVIDENTLY	PROVOKEMENT	PSALMODIES
PROTOTYPICALLY	PROTUBERATIONS	PROVINCEWIDE	PROVOKEMENTS	PSALMODISE
PROTOTYPING	PROUDHEARTED	PROVINCIAL	PROVOKINGLY	PSALMODISED
PROTOXIDES	PROUDNESSES	PROVINCIALISE	PROVOLONES	PSALMODISES
PROTOXYLEM	PROUSTITES	PROVINCIALISED	PROVOSTRIES	PSALMODISING
PROTOXYLEMS	PROVABILITIES	PROVINCIALISES	PROVOSTSHIP	PSALMODIST
PROTOZOANS	PROVABILITY	PROVINCIALISING	PROVOSTSHIPS	PSALMODISTS
PROTOZOOLOGICAL	PROVABLENESS	PROVINCIALISM	PROWLINGLY	PSALMODIZE
PROTOZOOLOGIES	PROVABLENESSES	PROVINCIALISMS	PROXIMALLY	PSALMODIZED
PROTOZOOLOGIST	PROVASCULAR	PROVINCIALIST	PROXIMATELY	PSALMODIZES
PROTOZOOLOGISTS	PROVECTION	PROVINCIALISTS	PROXIMATENESS	PSALMODIZING
PROTOZOOLOGY	PROVECTIONS	PROVINCIALITIES	PROXIMATENESSES	PSALTERIAN
PROTOZOONS	PROVEDITOR	PROVINCIALITY	PROXIMATION	PSALTERIES
PROTRACTED	PROVEDITORE	PROVINCIALIZE	PROXIMATIONS	PSALTERIUM
PROTRACTEDLY	PROVEDITORES	PROVINCIALIZED	PROXIMITIES	PSALTRESSES
PROTRACTEDNESS	PROVEDITORS	PROVINCIALIZES	PROZYMITES	PSAMMOPHIL
PROTRACTIBLE	PROVEDORES	PROVINCIALIZING	PRUDENTIAL	PSAMMOPHILE
PROTRACTILE	PROVENANCE	PROVINCIALLY	PRUDENTIALISM	PSAMMOPHILES
PROTRACTING	PROVENANCES	PROVINCIALS	PRUDENTIALISMS	PSAMMOPHILOUS
PROTRACTION	PROVENDERED	PROVIRUSES	PRUDENTIALIST	PSAMMOPHILS

PSAMMOPHYTE	PSEUDOEPHEDRINE	PSEUDOSCORPIONS	PSYCHICISM	PSYCHOGASES
PSAMMOPHYTES	PSEUDOGRAPH	PSEUDOSOLUTION	PSYCHICISMS	PSYCHOGENESES
PSAMMOPHYTIC	PSEUDOGRAPHIES	PSEUDOSOLUTIONS	PSYCHICIST	PSYCHOGENESIS
PSELLISMUS	PSEUDOGRAPHS	PSEUDOSYMMETRY	PSYCHICISTS	PSYCHOGENETIC
PSELLISMUSES	PSEUDOGRAPHY	PSEUDOVECTOR	PSYCHOACOUSTIC	PSYCHOGENETICAL
PSEPHOANALYSES	PSEUDOLOGIA	PSEUDOVECTORS	PSYCHOACOUSTICS	PSYCHOGENETICS
PSEPHOANALYSIS	PSEUDOLOGIAS	PSILANTHROPIC	PSYCHOACTIVE	PSYCHOGENIC
PSEPHOLOGICAL	PSEUDOLOGIES	PSILANTHROPIES	PSYCHOANALYSE	PSYCHOGENICALLY
PSEPHOLOGICALLY	PSEUDOLOGUE	PSILANTHROPISM	PSYCHOANALYSED	PSYCHOGERIATRIC
PSEPHOLOGIES	PSEUDOLOGUES	PSILANTHROPISMS	PSYCHOANALYSER	PSYCHOGNOSES
PSEPHOLOGIST	PSEUDOLOGY	PSILANTHROPIST	PSYCHOANALYSERS	PSYCHOGNOSIS
PSEPHOLOGISTS	PSEUDOMARTYR	PSILANTHROPISTS	PSYCHOANALYSES	PSYCHOGNOSTIC
PSEPHOLOGY	PSEUDOMARTYRS	PSILANTHROPY	PSYCHOANALYSING	PSYCHOGONIES
PSEUDAESTHESIA	PSEUDOMEMBRANE	PSILOCYBIN	PSYCHOANALYSIS	PSYCHOGONY
PSEUDAESTHESIAS	PSEUDOMEMBRANES	PSILOCYBINS	PSYCHOANALYST	PSYCHOGRAM
PSEUDARTHROSES	PSEUDOMONAD	PSILOMELANE	PSYCHOANALYSTS	PSYCHOGRAMS
PSEUDARTHROSIS	PSEUDOMONADES	PSILOMELANES	PSYCHOANALYTIC	PSYCHOGRAPH
PSEUDEPIGRAPH	PSEUDOMONADS	PSILOPHYTE	PSYCHOANALYZE	PSYCHOGRAPHIC
PSEUDEPIGRAPHA	PSEUDOMONAS	PSILOPHYTES	PSYCHOANALYZED	PSYCHOGRAPHICAL
PSEUDEPIGRAPHIC	PSEUDOMORPH	PSILOPHYTIC	PSYCHOANALYZER	PSYCHOGRAPHICS
PSEUDEPIGRAPHON	PSEUDOMORPHIC	PSITTACINE	PSYCHOANALYZERS	PSYCHOGRAPHIES
PSEUDEPIGRAPHS	PSEUDOMORPHISM	PSITTACINES	PSYCHOANALYZES	PSYCHOGRAPHS
PSEUDEPIGRAPHY	PSEUDOMORPHISMS	PSITTACOSES	PSYCHOANALYZING	PSYCHOGRAPHY
PSEUDERIES	PSEUDOMORPHOUS	PSITTACOSIS	PSYCHOBABBLE	PSYCHOHISTORIAN
PSEUDIMAGINES	PSEUDOMORPHS	PSITTACOTIC	PSYCHOBABBLER	PSYCHOHISTORIES
PSEUDIMAGO	PSEUDOMUTUALITY	PSORIATICS	PSYCHOBABBLERS	PSYCHOHISTORY
PSEUDIMAGOS	PSEUDONYMITIES	PSYCHAGOGUE	PSYCHOBABBLES	PSYCHOKINESES
PSEUDOACID	PSEUDONYMITY	PSYCHAGOGUES	PSYCHOBILLIES	PSYCHOKINESIS
PSEUDOACIDS	PSEUDONYMOUS	PSYCHASTHENIA	PSYCHOBILLY	PSYCHOKINETIC
PSEUDOALLELE	PSEUDONYMOUSLY	PSYCHASTHENIAS	PSYCHOBIOGRAPHY	PSYCHOLINGUIST
PSEUDOALLELES	PSEUDONYMS	PSYCHASTHENIC	PSYCHOBIOLOGIC	PSYCHOLINGUISTS
PSEUDOARTHROSES	PSEUDOPODAL	PSYCHASTHENICS	PSYCHOBIOLOGIES	PSYCHOLOGIC
PSEUDOARTHROSIS	PSEUDOPODIA	PSYCHEDELIA	PSYCHOBIOLOGIST	PSYCHOLOGICAL
PSEUDOBULB	PSEUDOPODIAL	PSYCHEDELIAS	PSYCHOBIOLOGY	PSYCHOLOGICALLY
PSEUDOBULBS	PSEUDOPODIUM	PSYCHEDELIC	PSYCHOCHEMICAL	PSYCHOLOGIES
PSEUDOCARP	PSEUDOPODS	PSYCHEDELICALLY	PSYCHOCHEMICALS	PSYCHOLOGISE
PSEUDOCARPOUS	PSEUDOPREGNANCY	PSYCHEDELICS	PSYCHOCHEMISTRY	PSYCHOLOGISED
PSEUDOCARPS	PSEUDOPREGNANT	PSYCHIATER	PSYCHODELIA	PSYCHOLOGISES
PSEUDOCLASSIC	PSEUDORANDOM	PSYCHIATERS	PSYCHODELIAS	PSYCHOLOGISING
PSEUDOCLASSICS	PSEUDOSCALAR	PSYCHIATRIC	PSYCHODELIC	PSYCHOLOGISM
PSEUDOCODE	PSEUDOSCALARS	PSYCHIATRICAL	PSYCHODELICALLY	PSYCHOLOGISMS
PSEUDOCODES	PSEUDOSCIENCE	PSYCHIATRICALLY	PSYCHODRAMA	PSYCHOLOGIST
PSEUDOCOEL	PSEUDOSCIENCES	PSYCHIATRIES	PSYCHODRAMAS	PSYCHOLOGISTIC
PSEUDOCOELOMATE	PSEUDOSCIENTIST	PSYCHIATRIST	PSYCHODRAMATIC	PSYCHOLOGISTS
PSEUDOCOELS	PSEUDOSCOPE	PSYCHIATRISTS	PSYCHODYNAMIC	PSYCHOLOGIZE
PSEUDOCYESES	PSEUDOSCOPES	PSYCHIATRY	PSYCHODYNAMICS	PSYCHOLOGIZED
PSEUDOCYESIS	PSEUDOSCORPION	PSYCHICALLY	PSYCHOGALVANIC	PSYCHOLOGIZES

P

PSYCHOLOGIZING	PSYCHOSURGEON	PTERODACTYLES	PUCKEROOED	PULSATANCE
PSYCHOLOGY	PSYCHOSURGEONS	PTERODACTYLS	PUCKISHNESS	PULSATANCES
PSYCHOMACHIA	PSYCHOSURGERIES	PTEROSAURIAN	PUCKISHNESSES	PULSATILITIES
PSYCHOMACHIAS	PSYCHOSURGERY	PTEROSAURIANS	PUDDENINGS	PULSATILITY
PSYCHOMACHIES	PSYCHOSURGICAL	PTEROSAURS	PUDGINESSES	PULSATILLA
PSYCHOMACHY	PSYCHOSYNTHESES	PTERYGIALS	PUDIBUNDITIES	PULSATILLAS
PSYCHOMETER	PSYCHOSYNTHESIS	PTERYGIUMS	PUDIBUNDITY	PULSATIONS
PSYCHOMETERS	PSYCHOTECHNICS	PTERYGOIDS	PUDICITIES	PULSATIVELY
PSYCHOMETRIC	PSYCHOTHERAPIES	PTERYLOGRAPHIC	PUERILISMS	PULSELESSNESS
PSYCHOMETRICAL	PSYCHOTHERAPIST	PTERYLOGRAPHIES	PUERILITIES	PULSELESSNESSES
PSYCHOMETRICIAN	PSYCHOTHERAPY	PTERYLOGRAPHY	PUERPERALLY	PULSIMETER
PSYCHOMETRICS	PSYCHOTICALLY	PTERYLOSES	PUERPERIUM	PULSIMETERS
PSYCHOMETRIES	PSYCHOTICISM	PTERYLOSIS	PUERPERIUMS	PULSOMETER
PSYCHOMETRIST	PSYCHOTICISMS	PTOCHOCRACIES	PUFFINESSES	PULSOMETERS
PSYCHOMETRISTS	PSYCHOTICS	PTOCHOCRACY	PUFFTALOONAS	PULTACEOUS
PSYCHOMETRY	PSYCHOTOMIMETIC	PTYALAGOGIC	PUFTALOONIES	PULTRUSION
PSYCHOMOTOR	PSYCHOTOXIC	PTYALAGOGUE	PUFTALOONS	PULTRUSIONS
PSYCHONEUROSES	PSYCHOTROPIC	PTYALAGOGUES	PUGGINESSES	PULVERABLE
PSYCHONEUROSIS	PSYCHOTROPICS	PTYALISING	PUGILISTIC	PULVERATION
PSYCHONEUROTIC	PSYCHROMETER	PTYALIZING	PUGILISTICAL	PULVERATIONS
PSYCHONEUROTICS	PSYCHROMETERS	PUBCRAWLER	PUGILISTICALLY	PULVERINES
PSYCHONOMIC	PSYCHROMETRIC	PUBCRAWLERS	PUGNACIOUS	PULVERISABLE
PSYCHONOMICS	PSYCHROMETRICAL	PUBERULENT	PUGNACIOUSLY	PULVERISATION
PSYCHOPATH	PSYCHROMETRIES	PUBERULOUS	PUGNACIOUSNESS	PULVERISATIONS
PSYCHOPATHIC	PSYCHROMETRY	PUBESCENCE	PUGNACITIES	PULVERISED
PSYCHOPATHICS	PSYCHROPHILIC	PUBESCENCES	PUISSANCES	PULVERISER
PSYCHOPATHIES	PTARMIGANS	PUBLICALLY	PUISSANTLY	PULVERISERS
PSYCHOPATHIST	PTERANODON	PUBLICATION	PUISSAUNCE	PULVERISES
PSYCHOPATHISTS	PTERANODONS	PUBLICATIONS	PUISSAUNCES	PULVERISING
PSYCHOPATHOLOGY	PTERIDINES	PUBLICISED	PULCHRITUDE	PULVERIZABLE
PSYCHOPATHS	PTERIDOLOGICAL	PUBLICISES	PULCHRITUDES	PULVERIZATION
PSYCHOPATHY	PTERIDOLOGIES	PUBLICISING	PULCHRITUDINOUS	PULVERIZATIONS
PSYCHOPHILIES	PTERIDOLOGIST	PUBLICISTS	PULLULATED	PULVERIZED
PSYCHOPHILY	PTERIDOLOGISTS	PUBLICITIES	PULLULATES	PULVERIZER
PSYCHOPHYSICAL	PTERIDOLOGY	PUBLICIZED	PULLULATING	PULVERIZERS
PSYCHOPHYSICIST	PTERIDOMANIA	PUBLICIZES	PULLULATION	PULVERIZES
PSYCHOPHYSICS	PTERIDOMANIAS	PUBLICIZING	PULLULATIONS	PULVERIZING
PSYCHOPOMP	PTERIDOPHILIST	PUBLICNESS	PULMOBRANCH	PULVERULENCE
PSYCHOPOMPS	PTERIDOPHILISTS	PUBLICNESSES	PULMOBRANCHIATE	PULVERULENCES
PSYCHOSEXUAL	PTERIDOPHYTE	PUBLISHABLE	PULMOBRANCHS	PULVERULENT
PSYCHOSEXUALITY	PTERIDOPHYTES	PUBLISHERS	PULMONATES	PULVILISED
PSYCHOSEXUALLY	PTERIDOPHYTIC	PUBLISHING	PULPBOARDS	PULVILIZED
PSYCHOSOCIAL	PTERIDOPHYTOUS	PUBLISHINGS	PULPIFYING	PULVILLIFORM
PSYCHOSOCIALLY	PTERIDOSPERM	PUBLISHMENT	PULPINESSES	PULVILLING
PSYCHOSOMATIC	PTERIDOSPERMS	PUBLISHMENTS	PULPITEERS	PULVILLIOS
PSYCHOSOMATICS	PTERODACTYL	PUCCINIACEOUS	PULPITRIES	PULVINATED
PSYCHOSOMIMETIC	PTERODACTYLE	PUCKERIEST	PULPSTONES	PULVINULES

P

PUMICATING	PUNDIGRION	PURGATORIAL	PURSERSHIP	PUTREFIERS
PUMMELLING	PUNDIGRIONS	PURGATORIALLY	PURSERSHIPS	PUTREFYING
PUMPERNICKEL	PUNDITRIES	PURGATORIAN	PURSINESSES	PUTRESCENCE
PUMPERNICKELS	PUNDONORES	PURGATORIES	PURSUANCES	PUTRESCENCES
PUMPKINSEED	PUNGENCIES	PURIFICATION	PURSUANTLY	PUTRESCENT
PUMPKINSEEDS	PUNICACEOUS	PURIFICATIONS	PURSUINGLY	PUTRESCIBILITY
PUNCHBALLS	PUNINESSES	PURIFICATIVE	PURSUIVANT	PUTRESCIBLE
PUNCHBOARD	PUNISHABILITIES	PURIFICATOR	PURSUIVANTS	PUTRESCIBLES
PUNCHBOARDS	PUNISHABILITY	PURIFICATORS	PURTENANCE	PUTRESCINE
PUNCHBOWLS	PUNISHABLE	PURIFICATORY	PURTENANCES	PUTRESCINES
PUNCHINELLO	PUNISHINGLY	PURISTICAL	PURULENCES	PUTRIDITIES
PUNCHINELLOES	PUNISHMENT	PURISTICALLY	PURULENCIES	PUTRIDNESS
PUNCHINELLOS	PUNISHMENTS	PURITANICAL	PURULENTLY	PUTRIDNESSES
PUNCHINESS	PUNITIVELY	PURITANICALLY	PURVEYANCE	PUTSCHISTS
PUNCHINESSES	PUNITIVENESS	PURITANICALNESS	PURVEYANCES	PUTTYROOTS
PUNCHLINES	PUNITIVENESSES	PURITANISE	PUSCHKINIA	PUZZLEDOMS
PUNCTATION	PUNKINESSES	PURITANISED	PUSCHKINIAS	PUZZLEHEADED
PUNCTATIONS	PUPIGEROUS	PURITANISES	PUSHCHAIRS	PUZZLEMENT
PUNCTATORS	PUPILABILITIES	PURITANISING	PUSHFULNESS	PUZZLEMENTS
PUNCTILIOS	PUPILABILITY	PURITANISM	PUSHFULNESSES	PUZZLINGLY
PUNCTILIOUS	PUPILARITIES	PURITANISMS	PUSHINESSES	PUZZOLANAS
PUNCTILIOUSLY	PUPILARITY	PURITANIZE	PUSHINGNESS	PYCNIDIOSPORE
PUNCTILIOUSNESS	PUPILLAGES	PURITANIZED	PUSHINGNESSES	PYCNIDIOSPORES
PUNCTUALIST	PUPILLARITIES	PURITANIZES	PUSILLANIMITIES	PYCNOCONIDIA
PUNCTUALISTS	PUPILLARITY	PURITANIZING	PUSILLANIMITY	PYCNOCONIDIUM
PUNCTUALITIES	PUPILSHIPS	PURLICUING	PUSILLANIMOUS	PYCNODYSOSTOSES
PUNCTUALITY	PUPIPAROUS	PURLOINERS	PUSILLANIMOUSLY	PYCNODYSOSTOSIS
PUNCTUALLY	PUPPETEERED	PURLOINING	PUSSYFOOTED	PYCNOGONID
PUNCTUATED	PUPPETEERING	PUROMYCINS	PUSSYFOOTER	PYCNOGONIDS
PUNCTUATES	PUPPETEERS	PURPLEHEART	PUSSYFOOTERS	PYCNOGONOID
PUNCTUATING	PUPPETLIKE	PURPLEHEARTS	PUSSYFOOTING	PYCNOMETER
PUNCTUATION	PUPPETRIES	PURPLENESS	PUSSYFOOTS	PYCNOMETERS
PUNCTUATIONIST	PUPPYHOODS	PURPLENESSES	PUSTULANTS	PYCNOMETRIC
PUNCTUATIONISTS	PURBLINDLY	PURPORTEDLY	PUSTULATED	PYCNOSPORE
PUNCTUATIONS	PURBLINDNESS	PURPORTING	PUSTULATES	PYCNOSPORES
PUNCTUATIVE	PURBLINDNESSES	PURPORTLESS	PUSTULATING	PYCNOSTYLE
PUNCTUATOR	PURCHASABILITY	PURPOSEFUL	PUSTULATION	PYCNOSTYLES
PUNCTUATORS	PURCHASABLE	PURPOSEFULLY	PUSTULATIONS	PYELITISES
PUNCTULATE	PURCHASERS	PURPOSEFULNESS	PUTANGITANGI	PYELOGRAMS
PUNCTULATED	PURCHASING	PURPOSELESS	PUTANGITANGIS	PYELOGRAPHIC
PUNCTULATION	PURCHASINGS	PURPOSELESSLY	PUTATIVELY	PYELOGRAPHIES
PUNCTULATIONS	PURDONIUMS	PURPOSELESSNESS	PUTONGHUAS	PYELOGRAPHY
PUNCTURABLE	PUREBLOODS	PURPOSIVELY	PUTREFACIENT	PYELONEPHRITIC
PUNCTURATION	PURENESSES	PURPOSIVENESS	PUTREFACTION	PYELONEPHRITIS
PUNCTURATIONS	PURGATIONS	PURPOSIVENESSES	PUTREFACTIONS	PYGOSTYLES
PUNCTURERS	PURGATIVELY	PURPRESTURE	PUTREFACTIVE	PYKNODYSOSTOSES
PUNCTURING	PURGATIVES	PURPRESTURES	PUTREFIABLE	PYKNODYSOSTOSIS

P

PYKNOMETER	PYRETOLOGIES	PYROELECTRICS	PYROMAGNETIC	PYROSTATIC
PYKNOMETERS	PYRETOLOGY	PYROGALLATE	PYROMANCER	PYROSULPHATE
PYKNOSOMES	PYRETOTHERAPIES	PYROGALLATES	PYROMANCERS	PYROSULPHATES
PYLORECTOMIES	PYRETOTHERAPY	PYROGALLIC	PYROMANCIES	PYROSULPHURIC
PYLORECTOMY	PYRGEOMETER	PYROGALLOL	PYROMANIAC	PYROTARTRATE
PYOGENESES	PYRGEOMETERS	PYROGALLOLS	PYROMANIACAL	PYROTARTRATES
PYOGENESIS	PYRHELIOMETER	PYROGENETIC	PYROMANIACS	PYROTECHNIC
PYORRHOEAL	PYRHELIOMETERS	PYROGENICITIES	PYROMANIAS	PYROTECHNICAL
PYORRHOEAS	PYRHELIOMETRIC	PYROGENICITY	PYROMANTIC	PYROTECHNICALLY
PYORRHOEIC	PYRIDOXALS	PYROGENOUS	PYROMERIDE	PYROTECHNICIAN
PYRACANTHA	PYRIDOXAMINE	PYROGNOSTIC	PYROMERIDES	PYROTECHNICIANS
PYRACANTHAS	PYRIDOXAMINES	PYROGNOSTICS	PYROMETALLURGY	PYROTECHNICS
PYRACANTHS	PYRIDOXINE	PYROGRAPHER	PYROMETERS	PYROTECHNIES
PYRALIDIDS	PYRIDOXINES	PYROGRAPHERS	PYROMETRIC	PYROTECHNIST
PYRAMIDALLY	PYRIDOXINS	PYROGRAPHIC	PYROMETRICAL	PYROTECHNISTS
PYRAMIDICAL	PYRIMETHAMINE	PYROGRAPHIES	PYROMETRICALLY	PYROTECHNY
PYRAMIDICALLY	PYRIMETHAMINES	PYROGRAPHY	PYROMETRIES	PYROVANADIC
PYRAMIDING	PYRIMIDINE	PYROGRAVURE	PYROMORPHITE	PYROXENITE
PYRAMIDION	PYRIMIDINES	PYROGRAVURES	PYROMORPHITES	PYROXENITES
PYRAMIDIONS	PYRITHIAMINE	PYROKINESES	PYRONINOPHILIC	PYROXENITIC
PYRAMIDIST	PYRITHIAMINES	PYROKINESIS	PYROPHOBIA	PYROXENOID
PYRAMIDISTS	PYRITIFEROUS	PYROLATERS	PYROPHOBIAS	PYROXENOIDS
PYRAMIDOLOGIES	PYRITISING	PYROLATRIES	PYROPHOBIC	PYROXYLINE
PYRAMIDOLOGIST	PYRITIZING	PYROLIGNEOUS	PYROPHOBICS	PYROXYLINES
PYRAMIDOLOGISTS	PYRITOHEDRA	PYROLIGNIC	PYROPHONES	PYROXYLINS
PYRAMIDOLOGY	PYRITOHEDRAL	PYROLISING	PYROPHORIC	PYRRHICIST
PYRAMIDONS	PYRITOHEDRON	PYROLIZING	PYROPHOROUS	PYRRHICISTS
PYRANOMETER	PYROBALLOGIES	PYROLOGIES	PYROPHORUS	PYRRHOTINE
PYRANOMETERS	PYROBALLOGY	PYROLUSITE	PYROPHORUSES	PYRRHOTINES
PYRANOSIDE	PYROCATECHIN	PYROLUSITES	PYROPHOSPHATE	PYRRHOTITE
PYRANOSIDES	PYROCATECHINS	PYROLYSABLE	PYROPHOSPHATES	PYRRHOTITES
PYRARGYRITE	PYROCATECHOL	PYROLYSATE	PYROPHOSPHORIC	PYRRHULOXIA
PYRARGYRITES	PYROCATECHOLS	PYROLYSATES	PYROPHOTOGRAPH	PYRRHULOXIAS
PYRENEITES	PYROCERAMS	PYROLYSERS	PYROPHOTOGRAPHS	PYRROLIDINE
PYRENOCARP	PYROCHEMICAL	PYROLYSING	PYROPHOTOGRAPHY	PYRROLIDINES
PYRENOCARPS	PYROCHEMICALLY	PYROLYTICALLY	PYROPHOTOMETER	PYTHOGENIC
PYRENOMYCETOUS	PYROCLASTIC	PYROLYZABLE	PYROPHOTOMETERS	PYTHONESSES
PYRETHRINS	PYROCLASTICS	PYROLYZATE	PYROPHOTOMETRY	PYTHONOMORPH
PYRETHROID	PYROCLASTS	PYROLYZATES	PYROPHYLLITE	PYTHONOMORPHS
PYRETHROIDS	PYROELECTRIC	PYROLYZERS	PYROPHYLLITES	
PYRETHRUMS	PYROELECTRICITY	PYROLYZING	PYROSCOPES	

P

Q

QABALISTIC	QUADRICONES	QUADRISECTIONS	QUADRUPOLE	QUANTIFYING
QINGHAOSUS	QUADRIENNIA	QUADRISECTS	QUADRUPOLES	QUANTISATION
QUACKERIES	QUADRIENNIAL	QUADRISYLLABIC	QUAESITUMS	QUANTISATIONS
QUACKSALVER	QUADRIENNIUM	QUADRISYLLABLE	QUAESTIONARIES	QUANTISERS
QUACKSALVERS	QUADRIFARIOUS	QUADRISYLLABLES	QUAESTIONARY	QUANTISING
QUACKSALVING	QUADRIFOLIATE	QUADRIVALENCE	QUAESTORIAL	QUANTITATE
QUADPLEXES	QUADRIFORM	QUADRIVALENCES	QUAESTORSHIP	QUANTITATED
QUADRAGENARIAN	QUADRIGEMINAL	QUADRIVALENCIES	QUAESTORSHIPS	QUANTITATES
QUADRAGENARIANS	QUADRIGEMINATE	QUADRIVALENCY	QUAESTUARIES	QUANTITATING
QUADRAGESIMAL	QUADRIGEMINOUS	QUADRIVALENT	QUAESTUARY	QUANTITATION
QUADRANGLE	QUADRILATERAL	QUADRIVALENTS	QUAGGINESS	QUANTITATIONS
QUADRANGLES	QUADRILATERALS	QUADRIVIAL	QUAGGINESSES	QUANTITATIVE
QUADRANGULAR	QUADRILINGUAL	QUADRIVIUM	QUAGMIRIER	QUANTITATIVELY
QUADRANGULARLY	QUADRILITERAL	QUADRIVIUMS	QUAGMIRIEST	QUANTITIES
QUADRANTAL	QUADRILITERALS	QUADROPHONIC	QUAGMIRING	QUANTITIVE
QUADRANTES	QUADRILLED	QUADROPHONICS	QUAINTNESS	QUANTITIVELY
QUADRAPHONIC	QUADRILLER	QUADROPHONIES	QUAINTNESSES	QUANTIVALENCE
QUADRAPHONICS	QUADRILLERS	QUADROPHONY	QUAKINESSES	QUANTIVALENCES
QUADRAPHONIES	QUADRILLES	QUADRUMANE	QUALIFIABLE	QUANTIVALENT
QUADRAPHONY	QUADRILLING	QUADRUMANES	QUALIFICATION	QUANTIZATION
QUADRAPLEGIA	QUADRILLION	QUADRUMANOUS	QUALIFICATIONS	QUANTIZATIONS
QUADRAPLEGIAS	QUADRILLIONS	QUADRUMANS	QUALIFICATIVE	QUANTIZERS
QUADRAPLEGIC	QUADRILLIONTH	QUADRUMVIR	QUALIFICATIVES	QUANTIZING
QUADRAPLEGICS	QUADRILLIONTHS	QUADRUMVIRATE	QUALIFICATOR	QUANTOMETER
QUADRATICAL	QUADRILOCULAR	QUADRUMVIRATES	QUALIFICATORS	QUANTOMETERS
QUADRATICALLY	QUADRINGENARIES	QUADRUMVIRS	QUALIFICATORY	QUAQUAVERSAL
QUADRATICS	QUADRINGENARY	QUADRUPEDAL	QUALIFIEDLY	QUAQUAVERSALLY
QUADRATING	QUADRINOMIAL	QUADRUPEDS	QUALIFIERS	QUARANTINE
QUADRATRIX	QUADRINOMIALS	QUADRUPLED	QUALIFYING	QUARANTINED
QUADRATRIXES	QUADRIPARTITE	QUADRUPLES	QUALIFYINGS	QUARANTINES
QUADRATURA	QUADRIPARTITION	QUADRUPLET	QUALITATIVE	QUARANTINING
QUADRATURE	QUADRIPHONIC	QUADRUPLETS	QUALITATIVELY	QUARENDENS
QUADRATURES	QUADRIPHONICS	QUADRUPLEX	QUALMISHLY	QUARENDERS
QUADRATUSES	QUADRIPLEGIA	QUADRUPLEXED	QUALMISHNESS	QUARRELERS
QUADRELLAS	QUADRIPLEGIAS	QUADRUPLEXES	QUALMISHNESSES	QUARRELING
QUADRENNIA	QUADRIPLEGIC	QUADRUPLEXING	QUANDARIES	QUARRELLED
QUADRENNIAL	QUADRIPLEGICS	QUADRUPLICATE	QUANGOCRACIES	QUARRELLER
QUADRENNIALLY	QUADRIPOLE	QUADRUPLICATED	QUANGOCRACY	QUARRELLERS
QUADRENNIALS	QUADRIPOLES	QUADRUPLICATES	QUANTIFIABLE	QUARRELLING
QUADRENNIUM	QUADRIREME	QUADRUPLICATING	QUANTIFICATION	QUARRELLINGS
QUADRENNIUMS	QUADRIREMES	QUADRUPLICATION	QUANTIFICATIONS	QUARRELLOUS
QUADRICEPS	QUADRISECT	QUADRUPLICITIES	QUANTIFIED	QUARRELSOME
QUADRICEPSES	QUADRISECTED	QUADRUPLICITY	QUANTIFIER	QUARRELSOMELY
QUADRICIPITAL	QUADRISECTING	QUADRUPLIES	QUANTIFIERS	QUARRELSOMENESS
QUADRICONE	QUADRISECTION	QUADRUPLING	QUANTIFIES	QUARRENDER

QUARRENDERS	QUARTZIFEROUS	QUEENSIDES	QUESTORIAL	QUINCENTENARY
QUARRIABLE	QUARTZITES	QUEERITIES	QUESTORSHIP	QUINCENTENNIAL
QUARRINGTON	QUARTZITIC	QUEERNESSES	QUESTORSHIPS	QUINCENTENNIALS
QUARRINGTONS	QUASICRYSTAL	QUELQUECHOSE	QUESTRISTS	QUINCUNCIAL
QUARRYINGS	QUASICRYSTALS	QUELQUECHOSES	QUIBBLINGLY	QUINCUNCIALLY
QUARRYMASTER	QUASIPARTICLE	QUENCHABLE	QUIBBLINGS	QUINCUNXES
QUARRYMASTERS	QUASIPARTICLES	QUENCHINGS	QUICKBEAMS	QUINCUNXIAL
QUARTATION	QUASIPERIODIC	QUENCHLESS	QUICKENERS	QUINDECAGON
QUARTATIONS	QUATERCENTENARY	QUENCHLESSLY	QUICKENING	QUINDECAGONS
QUARTERAGE	QUATERNARIES	QUERCETINS	QUICKENINGS	QUINDECAPLET
QUARTERAGES	QUATERNARY	QUERCETUMS	QUICKLIMES	QUINDECAPLETS
QUARTERBACK	QUATERNATE	QUERCITINS	QUICKNESSES	QUINDECENNIAL
QUARTERBACKED	QUATERNION	QUERCITRON	QUICKSANDS	QUINDECENNIALS
QUARTERBACKING	QUATERNIONIST	QUERCITRONS	QUICKSILVER	QUINDECILLION
QUARTERBACKINGS	QUATERNIONISTS	QUERIMONIES	QUICKSILVERED	QUINDECILLIONS
QUARTERBACKS	QUATERNIONS	QUERIMONIOUS	QUICKSILVERING	QUINGENTENARIES
QUARTERDECK	QUATERNITIES	QUERIMONIOUSLY	QUICKSILVERINGS	QUINGENTENARY
QUARTERDECKER	QUATERNITY	QUERNSTONE	QUICKSILVERISH	QUINIDINES
QUARTERDECKERS	QUATORZAIN	QUERNSTONES	QUICKSILVERS	QUINOLINES
QUARTERDECKS	QUATORZAINS	QUERSPRUNG	QUICKSILVERY	QUINOLONES
QUARTERERS	QUATREFEUILLE	QUERSPRUNGS	QUICKSTEPPED	QUINQUAGENARIAN
QUARTERFINAL	QUATREFEUILLES	QUERULOUSLY	QUICKSTEPPING	QUINQUAGESIMAL
QUARTERFINALIST	QUATREFOIL	QUERULOUSNESS	QUICKSTEPS	QUINQUECOSTATE
QUARTERFINALS	QUATREFOILS	QUERULOUSNESSES	QUICKTHORN	QUINQUEFARIOUS
QUARTERING	QUATTROCENTISM	QUERYINGLY	QUICKTHORNS	QUINQUEFOLIATE
QUARTERINGS	QUATTROCENTISMS	QUESADILLA	QUIDDANIES	QUINQUENNIA
QUARTERLIES	QUATTROCENTIST	QUESADILLAS	QUIDDITATIVE	QUINQUENNIAD
QUARTERLIFE	QUATTROCENTISTS	QUESTINGLY	QUIDDITCHES	QUINQUENNIADS
QUARTERLIGHT	QUATTROCENTO	QUESTIONABILITY	QUIDDITIES	QUINQUENNIAL
QUARTERLIGHTS	QUATTROCENTOS	QUESTIONABLE	QUIESCENCE	QUINQUENNIALLY
QUARTERMASTER	QUAVERIEST	QUESTIONABLY	QUIESCENCES	QUINQUENNIALS
QUARTERMASTERS	QUAVERINGLY	QUESTIONARIES	QUIESCENCIES	QUINQUENNIUM
QUARTERMISTRESS	QUAVERINGS	QUESTIONARY	QUIESCENCY	QUINQUENNIUMS
QUARTEROON	QUEACHIEST	QUESTIONED	QUIESCENTLY	QUINQUEPARTITE
QUARTEROONS	QUEASINESS	QUESTIONEE	QUIETENERS	QUINQUEREME
QUARTERSAW	QUEASINESSES	QUESTIONEES	QUIETENING	QUINQUEREMES
QUARTERSAWED	QUEBRACHOS	QUESTIONER	QUIETENINGS	QUINQUEVALENCE
QUARTERSAWING	QUEECHIEST	QUESTIONERS	QUIETISTIC	QUINQUEVALENCES
QUARTERSAWN	QUEENCAKES	QUESTIONING	QUIETNESSES	QUINQUEVALENCY
QUARTERSAWS	QUEENCRAFT	QUESTIONINGLY	QUILLBACKS	QUINQUEVALENT
QUARTERSTAFF	QUEENCRAFTS	QUESTIONINGS	QUILLWORKS	QUINQUINAS
QUARTERSTAFFS	QUEENFISHES	QUESTIONIST	QUILLWORTS	QUINQUIVALENT
QUARTERSTAVES	QUEENHOODS	QUESTIONISTS	QUINACRINE	QUINTESSENCE
QUARTETTES	QUEENLIEST	QUESTIONLESS	QUINACRINES	QUINTESSENCES
QUARTODECIMAN	QUEENLINESS	QUESTIONLESSLY	QUINAQUINA	QUINTESSENTIAL
QUARTODECIMANS	QUEENLINESSES	QUESTIONNAIRE	QUINAQUINAS	QUINTETTES
QUARTZIEST	QUEENSHIPS	QUESTIONNAIRES	QUINCENTENARIES	QUINTILLION

QUINTILLIONS	QUINTUPLING	QUIVERIEST	QUIZZIFICATION	QUOTABILITIES
QUINTILLIONTH	QUIRISTERS	QUIVERINGLY	QUIZZIFICATIONS	QUOTABILITY
QUINTILLIONTHS	QUIRKINESS	QUIVERINGS	QUIZZIFIED	QUOTABLENESS
QUINTROONS	QUIRKINESSES	QUIXOTICAL	QUIZZIFIES	QUOTABLENESSES
QUINTUPLED	QUISLINGISM	QUIXOTICALLY	QUIZZIFYING	QUOTATIONS
QUINTUPLES	QUISLINGISMS	QUIXOTISMS	QUIZZINESS	QUOTATIOUS
QUINTUPLET	QUITCLAIMED	QUIXOTRIES	QUIZZINESSES	QUOTEWORTHY
QUINTUPLETS	QUITCLAIMING	QUIZMASTER	QUODLIBETARIAN	QUOTIDIANS
QUINTUPLICATE	QUITCLAIMS	QUIZMASTERS	QUODLIBETARIANS	QUOTITIONS
QUINTUPLICATED	QUITTANCED	QUIZZERIES	QUODLIBETIC	
QUINTUPLICATES	QUITTANCES	QUIZZICALITIES	QUODLIBETICAL	
QUINTUPLICATING	QUITTANCING	QUIZZICALITY	QUODLIBETICALLY	
QUINTUPLICATION	QUIVERFULS	QUIZZICALLY	QUODLIBETS	

Q

R

RABATMENTS	RACHIOTOMY	RADIATIONAL	RADIOAUTOGRAPH	RADIOLARIANS
RABATTEMENT	RACHISCHISES	RADIATIONLESS	RADIOAUTOGRAPHS	RADIOLOCATION
RABATTEMENTS	RACHISCHISIS	RADIATIONS	RADIOAUTOGRAPHY	RADIOLOCATIONAL
RABATTINGS	RACHITIDES	RADICALISATION	RADIOBIOLOGIC	RADIOLOCATIONS
RABBINATES	RACHITISES	RADICALISATIONS	RADIOBIOLOGICAL	RADIOLOGIC
RABBINICAL	RACIALISED	RADICALISE	RADIOBIOLOGIES	RADIOLOGICAL
RABBINICALLY	RACIALISES	RADICALISED	RADIOBIOLOGIST	RADIOLOGICALLY
RABBINISMS	RACIALISING	RADICALISES	RADIOBIOLOGISTS	RADIOLOGIES
RABBINISTIC	RACIALISMS	RADICALISING	RADIOBIOLOGY	RADIOLOGIST
RABBINISTS	RACIALISTIC	RADICALISM	RADIOCARBON	RADIOLOGISTS
RABBINITES	RACIALISTS	RADICALISMS	RADIOCARBONS	RADIOLUCENCIES
RABBITBRUSH	RACIALIZED	RADICALISTIC	RADIOCHEMICAL	RADIOLUCENCY
RABBITBRUSHES	RACIALIZES	RADICALITIES	RADIOCHEMICALLY	RADIOLUCENT
RABBITFISH	RACIALIZING	RADICALITY	RADIOCHEMIST	RADIOLYSES
RABBITFISHES	RACIATIONS	RADICALIZATION	RADIOCHEMISTRY	RADIOLYSIS
RABBITINGS	RACINESSES	RADICALIZATIONS	RADIOCHEMISTS	RADIOLYTIC
RABBITRIES	RACKABONES	RADICALIZE	RADIOECOLOGIES	RADIOMETER
RABBLEMENT	RACKETEERED	RADICALIZED	RADIOECOLOGY	RADIOMETERS
RABBLEMENTS	RACKETEERING	RADICALIZES	RADIOELEMENT	RADIOMETRIC
RABIDITIES	RACKETEERINGS	RADICALIZING	RADIOELEMENTS	RADIOMETRICALLY
RABIDNESSES	RACKETEERS	RADICALNESS	RADIOGENIC	RADIOMETRIES
RACCAHOUTS	RACKETIEST	RADICALNESSES	RADIOGOLDS	RADIOMETRY
RACECOURSE	RACKETRIES	RADICATING	RADIOGONIOMETER	RADIOMICROMETER
RACECOURSES	RACONTEURING	RADICATION	RADIOGRAMS	RADIOMIMETIC
RACEGOINGS	RACONTEURINGS	RADICATIONS	RADIOGRAPH	RADIONUCLIDE
RACEHORSES	RACONTEURS	RADICCHIOS	RADIOGRAPHED	RADIONUCLIDES
RACEMATION	RACONTEUSE	RADICELLOSE	RADIOGRAPHER	RADIOPACITIES
RACEMATIONS	RACONTEUSES	RADICICOLOUS	RADIOGRAPHERS	RADIOPACITY
RACEMISATION	RACQUETBALL	RADICIFORM	RADIOGRAPHIC	RADIOPAGER
RACEMISATIONS	RACQUETBALLS	RADICIVOROUS	RADIOGRAPHIES	RADIOPAGERS
RACEMISING	RACQUETING	RADICULOSE	RADIOGRAPHING	RADIOPAGING
RACEMIZATION	RADARSCOPE	RADIESTHESIA	RADIOGRAPHS	RADIOPAGINGS
RACEMIZATIONS	RADARSCOPES	RADIESTHESIAS	RADIOGRAPHY	RADIOPAQUE
RACEMIZING	RADIALISATION	RADIESTHESIST	RADIOIODINE	RADIOPHONE
RACEMOSELY	RADIALISATIONS	RADIESTHESISTS	RADIOIODINES	RADIOPHONES
RACEMOUSLY	RADIALISED	RADIESTHETIC	RADIOISOTOPE	RADIOPHONIC
RACETRACKER	RADIALISES	RADIOACTIVATE	RADIOISOTOPES	RADIOPHONICALLY
RACETRACKERS	RADIALISING	RADIOACTIVATED	RADIOISOTOPIC	RADIOPHONICS
RACETRACKS	RADIALITIES	RADIOACTIVATES	RADIOLABEL	RADIOPHONIES
RACEWALKED	RADIALIZATION	RADIOACTIVATING	RADIOLABELED	RADIOPHONIST
RACEWALKER	RADIALIZATIONS	RADIOACTIVATION	RADIOLABELING	RADIOPHONISTS
RACEWALKERS	RADIALIZED	RADIOACTIVE	RADIOLABELLED	RADIOPHONY
RACEWALKING	RADIALIZES	RADIOACTIVELY	RADIOLABELLING	RADIOPHOSPHORUS
RACEWALKINGS	RADIALIZING	RADIOACTIVITIES	RADIOLABELS	RADIOPHOTO
RACHIOTOMIES	RADIANCIES	RADIOACTIVITY	RADIOLARIAN	RADIOPHOTOS

RADIOPROTECTION	RADULIFORM	RAIYATWARIS	RANDINESSES	RANTIPOLES
RADIOPROTECTIVE	RAFFINATES	RAJAHSHIPS	RANDOMISATION	RANTIPOLING
RADIORESISTANT	RAFFINOSES	RAJPRAMUKH	RANDOMISATIONS	RANUNCULACEOUS
RADIOSCOPE	RAFFISHNESS	RAJPRAMUKHS	RANDOMISED	RANUNCULUS
RADIOSCOPES	RAFFISHNESSES	RAKESHAMES	RANDOMISER	RANUNCULUSES
RADIOSCOPIC	RAFFLESIAS	RAKISHNESS	RANDOMISERS	RAPACIOUSLY
RADIOSCOPICALLY	RAFTERINGS	RAKISHNESSES	RANDOMISES	RAPACIOUSNESS
RADIOSCOPIES	RAGAMUFFIN	RALLENTANDI	RANDOMISING	RAPACIOUSNESSES
RADIOSCOPY	RAGAMUFFINS	RALLENTANDO	RANDOMIZATION	RAPACITIES
RADIOSENSITISE	RAGGAMUFFIN	RALLENTANDOS	RANDOMIZATIONS	RAPIDITIES
RADIOSENSITISED	RAGGAMUFFINS	RALLYCROSS	RANDOMIZED	RAPIDNESSES
RADIOSENSITISES	RAGGEDIEST	RALLYCROSSES	RANDOMIZER	RAPIERLIKE
RADIOSENSITIVE	RAGGEDNESS	RALLYINGLY	RANDOMIZERS	RAPPELLING
RADIOSENSITIZE	RAGGEDNESSES	RAMAPITHECINE	RANDOMIZES	RAPPELLINGS
RADIOSENSITIZED	RAGMATICAL	RAMAPITHECINES	RANDOMIZING	RAPPORTAGE
RADIOSENSITIZES	RAGPICKERS	RAMBLINGLY	RANDOMNESS	RAPPORTAGES
RADIOSONDE	RAILBUSSES	RAMBOUILLET	RANDOMNESSES	RAPPORTEUR
RADIOSONDES	RAILLERIES	RAMBOUILLETS	RANDOMWISE	RAPPORTEURS
RADIOSTRONTIUM	RAILROADED	RAMBUNCTIOUS	RANGATIRAS	RAPPROCHEMENT
RADIOSTRONTIUMS	RAILROADER	RAMBUNCTIOUSLY	RANGATIRATANGA	RAPPROCHEMENTS
RADIOTELEGRAM	RAILROADERS	RAMENTACEOUS	RANGATIRATANGAS	RAPSCALLION
RADIOTELEGRAMS	RAILROADING	RAMGUNSHOCH	RANGEFINDER	RAPSCALLIONS
RADIOTELEGRAPH	RAILROADINGS	RAMIFICATION	RANGEFINDERS	RAPTATORIAL
RADIOTELEGRAPHS	RAILWAYMAN	RAMIFICATIONS	RANGEFINDING	RAPTNESSES
RADIOTELEGRAPHY	RAILWAYMEN	RAMMISHNESS	RANGEFINDINGS	RAPTURELESS
RADIOTELEMETER	RAINBOWLIKE	RAMMISHNESSES	RANGELANDS	RAPTURISED
RADIOTELEMETERS	RAINCHECKS	RAMOSITIES	RANGERSHIP	RAPTURISES
RADIOTELEMETRIC	RAINFOREST	RAMPACIOUS	RANGERSHIPS	RAPTURISING
RADIOTELEMETRY	RAINFORESTS	RAMPAGEOUS	RANGINESSES	RAPTURISTS
RADIOTELEPHONE	RAININESSES	RAMPAGEOUSLY	RANIVOROUS	RAPTURIZED
RADIOTELEPHONES	RAINMAKERS	RAMPAGEOUSNESS	RANKNESSES	RAPTURIZES
RADIOTELEPHONIC	RAINMAKING	RAMPAGINGS	RANKSHIFTED	RAPTURIZING
RADIOTELEPHONY	RAINMAKINGS	RAMPALLIAN	RANKSHIFTING	RAPTUROUSLY
RADIOTELETYPE	RAINPROOFED	RAMPALLIANS	RANKSHIFTS	RAPTUROUSNESS
RADIOTELETYPES	RAINPROOFING	RAMPANCIES	RANSACKERS	RAPTUROUSNESSES
RADIOTHERAPIES	RAINPROOFS	RAMPARTING	RANSACKING	RAREFACTION
RADIOTHERAPIST	RAINSPOUTS	RAMPAUGING	RANSHACKLE	RAREFACTIONAL
RADIOTHERAPISTS	RAINSQUALL	RAMRODDING	RANSHACKLED	RAREFACTIONS
RADIOTHERAPY	RAINSQUALLS	RAMSHACKLE	RANSHACKLES	RAREFACTIVE
RADIOTHERMIES	RAINSTORMS	RANCHERIAS	RANSHACKLING	RAREFIABLE
RADIOTHERMY	RAINWASHED	RANCHERIES	RANSHAKLED	RAREFICATION
RADIOTHONS	RAINWASHES	RANCIDITIES	RANSHAKLES	RAREFICATIONAL
RADIOTHORIUM	RAINWASHING	RANCIDNESS	RANSHAKLING	RAREFICATIONS
RADIOTHORIUMS	RAINWATERS	RANCIDNESSES	RANSOMABLE	RARENESSES
RADIOTOXIC	RAISONNEUR	RANCOROUSLY	RANSOMLESS	RASCAILLES
RADIOTRACER	RAISONNEURS	RANCOROUSNESS	RANTERISMS	RASCALDOMS
RADIOTRACERS	RAIYATWARI	RANCOROUSNESSES	RANTIPOLED	RASCALISMS

R

RASCALITIES	RATIOCINATORS	RAUWOLFIAS	REACCLIMATISE	REACTIVATION
RASCALLIEST	RATIOCINATORY	RAVAGEMENT	REACCLIMATISED	REACTIVATIONS
RASCALLION	RATIONALES	RAVAGEMENTS	REACCLIMATISES	REACTIVELY
RASCALLIONS	RATIONALISABLE	RAVELLINGS	REACCLIMATISING	REACTIVENESS
RASHNESSES	RATIONALISATION	RAVELMENTS	REACCLIMATIZE	REACTIVENESSES
RASPATORIES	RATIONALISE	RAVENINGLY	REACCLIMATIZED	REACTIVITIES
RASPBERRIES	RATIONALISED	RAVENOUSLY	REACCLIMATIZES	REACTIVITY
RASPINESSES	RATIONALISER	RAVENOUSNESS	REACCLIMATIZING	REACTUATED
RASTAFARIAN	RATIONALISERS	RAVENOUSNESSES	REACCREDIT	REACTUATES
RASTAFARIANS	RATIONALISES	RAVIGOTTES	REACCREDITATION	REACTUATING
RASTERISED	RATIONALISING	RAVISHINGLY	REACCREDITED	READABILITIES
RASTERISES	RATIONALISM	RAVISHMENT	REACCREDITING	READABILITY
RASTERISING	RATIONALISMS	RAVISHMENTS	REACCREDITS	READABLENESS
RASTERIZED	RATIONALIST	RAWINSONDE	REACCUSING	READABLENESSES
RASTERIZES	RATIONALISTIC	RAWINSONDES	REACCUSTOM	READAPTATION
RASTERIZING	RATIONALISTS	RAWMAISHES	REACCUSTOMED	READAPTATIONS
RATABILITIES	RATIONALITIES	RAYGRASSES	REACCUSTOMING	READAPTING
RATABILITY	RATIONALITY	RAYLESSNESS	REACCUSTOMS	READDICTED
RATABLENESS	RATIONALIZABLE	RAYLESSNESSES	REACQUAINT	READDICTING
RATABLENESSES	RATIONALIZATION	RAZMATAZES	REACQUAINTANCE	READDRESSED
RATAPLANNED	RATIONALIZE	RAZORBACKS	REACQUAINTANCES	READDRESSES
RATAPLANNING	RATIONALIZED	RAZORBILLS	REACQUAINTED	READDRESSING
RATATOUILLE	RATIONALIZER	RAZORCLAMS	REACQUAINTING	READERSHIP
RATATOUILLES	RATIONALIZERS	RAZORFISHES	REACQUAINTS	READERSHIPS
RATBAGGERIES	RATIONALIZES	RAZZAMATAZZ	REACQUIRED	READINESSES
RATBAGGERY	RATIONALIZING	RAZZAMATAZZES	REACQUIRES	READJUSTABLE
RATCHETING	RATIONALLY	RAZZBERRIES	REACQUIRING	READJUSTED
RATEABILITIES	RATIONALNESS	RAZZMATAZZ	REACQUISITION	READJUSTER
RATEABILITY	RATIONALNESSES	RAZZMATAZZES	REACQUISITIONS	READJUSTERS
RATEABLENESS	RATTENINGS	REABSORBED	REACTANCES	READJUSTING
RATEABLENESSES	RATTINESSES	REABSORBING	REACTIONAL	READJUSTMENT
RATEMETERS	RATTLEBAGS	REABSORPTION	REACTIONARIES	READJUSTMENTS
RATEPAYERS	RATTLEBOXES	REABSORPTIONS	REACTIONARISM	READMISSION
RATHERIPES	RATTLEBRAIN	REACCEDING	REACTIONARISMS	READMISSIONS
RATHSKELLER	RATTLEBRAINED	REACCELERATE	REACTIONARIST	READMITTANCE
RATHSKELLERS	RATTLEBRAINS	REACCELERATED	REACTIONARISTS	READMITTANCES
RATIFIABLE	RATTLESNAKE	REACCELERATES	REACTIONARY	READMITTED
RATIFICATION	RATTLESNAKES	REACCELERATING	REACTIONARYISM	READMITTING
RATIFICATIONS	RATTLETRAP	REACCENTED	REACTIONARYISMS	READOPTING
RATIOCINATE	RATTLETRAPS	REACCENTING	REACTIONISM	READOPTION
RATIOCINATED	RATTLINGLY	REACCEPTED	REACTIONISMS	READOPTIONS
RATIOCINATES	RATTOONING	REACCEPTING	REACTIONIST	READORNING
RATIOCINATING	RAUCOUSNESS	REACCESSION	REACTIONISTS	READVANCED
RATIOCINATION	RAUCOUSNESSES	REACCESSIONS	REACTIVATE	READVANCES
RATIOCINATIONS	RAUNCHIEST	REACCLAIMED	REACTIVATED	READVANCING
RATIOCINATIVE	RAUNCHINESS	REACCLAIMING	REACTIVATES	READVERTISE
RATIOCINATOR	RAUNCHINESSES	REACCLAIMS	REACTIVATING	READVERTISED

READVERTISEMENT	REALIZATIONS	REAPPLICATIONS	REARTICULATED	REASSURANCES
READVERTISES	REALLOCATE	REAPPLYING	REARTICULATES	REASSURERS
READVERTISING	REALLOCATED	REAPPOINTED	REARTICULATING	REASSURING
READVERTIZE	REALLOCATES	REAPPOINTING	REASCENDED	REASSURINGLY
READVERTIZED	REALLOCATING	REAPPOINTMENT	REASCENDING	REASTINESS
READVERTIZEMENT	REALLOCATION	REAPPOINTMENTS	REASCENSION	REASTINESSES
READVERTIZES	REALLOCATIONS	REAPPOINTS	REASCENSIONS	REATTACHED
READVERTIZING	REALLOTMENT	REAPPORTION	REASONABILITIES	REATTACHES
READVISING	REALLOTMENTS	REAPPORTIONED	REASONABILITY	REATTACHING
READYMADES	REALLOTTED	REAPPORTIONING	REASONABLE	REATTACHMENT
REAEDIFIED	REALLOTTING	REAPPORTIONMENT	REASONABLENESS	REATTACHMENTS
REAEDIFIES	REALNESSES	REAPPORTIONS	REASONABLY	REATTACKED
REAEDIFYED	REALPOLITIK	REAPPRAISAL	REASONEDLY	REATTACKING
REAEDIFYES	REALPOLITIKER	REAPPRAISALS	REASONINGS	REATTAINED
REAEDIFYING	REALPOLITIKERS	REAPPRAISE	REASONLESS	REATTAINING
REAFFIRMATION	REALPOLITIKS	REAPPRAISED	REASONLESSLY	REATTEMPTED
REAFFIRMATIONS	REALTERING	REAPPRAISEMENT	REASSAILED	REATTEMPTING
REAFFIRMED	REAMENDING	REAPPRAISEMENTS	REASSAILING	REATTEMPTS
REAFFIRMING	REAMENDMENT	REAPPRAISER	REASSEMBLAGE	REATTRIBUTE
REAFFIXING	REAMENDMENTS	REAPPRAISERS	REASSEMBLAGES	REATTRIBUTED
REAFFOREST	REANALYSED	REAPPRAISES	REASSEMBLE	REATTRIBUTES
REAFFORESTATION	REANALYSES	REAPPRAISING	REASSEMBLED	REATTRIBUTING
REAFFORESTED	REANALYSING	REAPPROPRIATE	REASSEMBLES	REATTRIBUTION
REAFFORESTING	REANALYSIS	REAPPROPRIATED	REASSEMBLIES	REATTRIBUTIONS
REAFFORESTS	REANALYZED	REAPPROPRIATES	REASSEMBLING	REAUTHORISATION
REAGENCIES	REANALYZES	REAPPROPRIATING	REASSEMBLY	REAUTHORISE
REAGGREGATE	REANALYZING	REAPPROVED	REASSERTED	REAUTHORISED
REAGGREGATED	REANIMATED	REAPPROVES	REASSERTING	REAUTHORISES
REAGGREGATES	REANIMATES	REAPPROVING	REASSERTION	REAUTHORISING
REAGGREGATING	REANIMATING	REARGUARDS	REASSERTIONS	REAUTHORIZATION
REAGGREGATION	REANIMATION	REARGUMENT	REASSESSED	REAUTHORIZE
REAGGREGATIONS	REANIMATIONS	REARGUMENTS	REASSESSES	REAUTHORIZED
REALIGNING	REANNEXATION	REARHORSES	REASSESSING	REAUTHORIZES
REALIGNMENT	REANNEXATIONS	REARMAMENT	REASSESSMENT	REAUTHORIZING
REALIGNMENTS	REANNEXING	REARMAMENTS	REASSESSMENTS	REAVAILING
REALISABILITIES	REANOINTED	REAROUSALS	REASSIGNED	REAWAKENED
REALISABILITY	REANOINTING	REAROUSING	REASSIGNING	REAWAKENING
REALISABLE	REANSWERED	REARRANGED	REASSIGNMENT	REAWAKENINGS
REALISABLY	REANSWERING	REARRANGEMENT	REASSIGNMENTS	REBALANCED
REALISATION	REAPPARELLED	REARRANGEMENTS	REASSORTED	REBALANCES
REALISATIONS	REAPPARELLING	REARRANGER	REASSORTING	REBALANCING
REALISTICALLY	REAPPARELS	REARRANGERS	REASSORTMENT	REBAPTISED
REALIZABILITIES	REAPPEARANCE	REARRANGES	REASSORTMENTS	REBAPTISES
REALIZABILITY	REAPPEARANCES	REARRANGING	REASSUMING	REBAPTISING
REALIZABLE	REAPPEARED	REARRESTED	REASSUMPTION	REBAPTISMS
REALIZABLY	REAPPEARING	REARRESTING	REASSUMPTIONS	REBAPTIZED
REALIZATION	REAPPLICATION	REARTICULATE	REASSURANCE	REBAPTIZES

R

REBAPTIZING	RECALCITRANCES	RECANTATION	RECENSIONS	RECHANNELLED
REBARBATIVE	RECALCITRANCIES	RECANTATIONS	RECENSORED	RECHANNELLING
REBARBATIVELY	RECALCITRANCY	RECAPITALISE	RECENSORING	RECHANNELS
REBATEABLE	RECALCITRANT	RECAPITALISED	RECENTNESS	RECHARGEABLE
REBATEMENT	RECALCITRANTS	RECAPITALISES	RECENTNESSES	RECHARGERS
REBATEMENTS	RECALCITRATE	RECAPITALISING	RECENTRIFUGE	RECHARGING
REBBETZINS	RECALCITRATED	RECAPITALIZE	RECENTRIFUGED	RECHARTERED
REBEGINNING	RECALCITRATES	RECAPITALIZED	RECENTRIFUGES	RECHARTERING
REBELLIONS	RECALCITRATING	RECAPITALIZES	RECENTRIFUGING	RECHARTERS
REBELLIOUS	RECALCITRATION	RECAPITALIZING	RECENTRING	RECHARTING
REBELLIOUSLY	RECALCITRATIONS	RECAPITULATE	RECEPTACLE	RECHAUFFES
REBELLIOUSNESS	RECALCULATE	RECAPITULATED	RECEPTACLES	RECHEATING
REBELLOWED	RECALCULATED	RECAPITULATES	RECEPTACULA	RECHECKING
REBELLOWING	RECALCULATES	RECAPITULATING	RECEPTACULAR	RECHIPPING
REBIRTHERS	RECALCULATING	RECAPITULATION	RECEPTACULUM	RECHIPPINGS
REBIRTHING	RECALCULATION	RECAPITULATIONS	RECEPTIBILITIES	RECHOOSING
REBIRTHINGS	RECALCULATIONS	RECAPITULATIVE	RECEPTIBILITY	RECHOREOGRAPH
REBLENDING	RECALESCED	RECAPITULATORY	RECEPTIBLE	RECHOREOGRAPHED
REBLOCHONS	RECALESCENCE	RECAPPABLE	RECEPTIONIST	RECHOREOGRAPHS
REBLOOMING	RECALESCENCES	RECAPTIONS	RECEPTIONISTS	RECHRISTEN
REBLOSSOMED	RECALESCENT	RECAPTURED	RECEPTIONS	RECHRISTENED
REBLOSSOMING	RECALESCES	RECAPTURER	RECEPTIVELY	RECHRISTENING
REBLOSSOMS	RECALESCING	RECAPTURERS	RECEPTIVENESS	RECHRISTENS
REBOARDING	RECALIBRATE	RECAPTURES	RECEPTIVENESSES	RECHROMATOGRAPH
REBOATIONS	RECALIBRATED	RECAPTURING	RECEPTIVITIES	RECIDIVISM
REBORROWED	RECALIBRATES	RECARPETED	RECEPTIVITY	RECIDIVISMS
REBORROWING	RECALIBRATING	RECARPETING	RECERTIFICATION	RECIDIVIST
REBOTTLING	RECALIBRATION	RECARRYING	RECERTIFIED	RECIDIVISTIC
REBOUNDERS	RECALIBRATIONS	RECATALOGED	RECERTIFIES	RECIDIVISTS
REBOUNDING	RECALLABILITIES	RECATALOGING	RECERTIFYING	RECIDIVOUS
REBRANCHED	RECALLABILITY	RECATALOGS	RECESSIONAL	RECIPIENCE
REBRANCHES	RECALLABLE	RECATCHING	RECESSIONALS	RECIPIENCES
REBRANCHING	RECALLMENT	RECAUTIONED	RECESSIONARY	RECIPIENCIES
REBRANDING	RECALLMENTS	RECAUTIONING	RECESSIONISTA	RECIPIENCY
REBREEDING	RECALMENTS	RECAUTIONS	RECESSIONISTAS	RECIPIENTS
REBROADCAST	RECANALISATION	RECEIPTING	RECESSIONS	RECIPROCAL
REBROADCASTED	RECANALISATIONS	RECEIPTORS	RECESSIVELY	RECIPROCALITIES
REBROADCASTING	RECANALISE	RECEIVABILITIES	RECESSIVENESS	RECIPROCALITY
REBROADCASTS	RECANALISED	RECEIVABILITY	RECESSIVENESSES	RECIPROCALLY
REBUILDING	RECANALISES	RECEIVABLE	RECESSIVES	RECIPROCALS
REBUKEFULLY	RECANALISING	RECEIVABLENESS	RECHALLENGE	RECIPROCANT
REBUKINGLY	RECANALIZATION	RECEIVABLES	RECHALLENGED	RECIPROCANTS
REBUTMENTS	RECANALIZATIONS	RECEIVERSHIP	RECHALLENGES	RECIPROCATE
REBUTTABLE	RECANALIZE	RECEIVERSHIPS	RECHALLENGING	RECIPROCATED
REBUTTONED	RECANALIZED	RECEIVINGS	RECHANGING	RECIPROCATES
REBUTTONING	RECANALIZES	RECEMENTED	RECHANNELED	RECIPROCATING
RECALCITRANCE	RECANALIZING	RECEMENTING	RECHANNELING	RECIPROCATION

RECIPROCATIONS	RECLINATIONS	RECOGNIZOR	RECOMMENDABLY	RECOMPUTATION
RECIPROCATIVE	RECLOSABLE	RECOGNIZORS	RECOMMENDATION	RECOMPUTATIONS
RECIPROCATOR	RECLOTHING	RECOILLESS	RECOMMENDATIONS	RECOMPUTED
RECIPROCATORS	RECLUSENESS	RECOINAGES	RECOMMENDATORY	RECOMPUTES
RECIPROCATORY	RECLUSENESSES	RECOLLECTED	RECOMMENDED	RECOMPUTING
RECIPROCITIES	RECLUSIONS	RECOLLECTEDLY	RECOMMENDER	RECONCEIVE
RECIPROCITY	RECLUSIVELY	RECOLLECTEDNESS	RECOMMENDERS	RECONCEIVED
RECIRCLING	RECLUSIVENESS	RECOLLECTING	RECOMMENDING	RECONCEIVES
RECIRCULATE	RECLUSIVENESSES	RECOLLECTION	RECOMMENDS	RECONCEIVING
RECIRCULATED	RECLUSORIES	RECOLLECTIONS	RECOMMISSION	RECONCENTRATE
RECIRCULATES	RECODIFICATION	RECOLLECTIVE	RECOMMISSIONED	RECONCENTRATED
RECIRCULATING	RECODIFICATIONS	RECOLLECTIVELY	RECOMMISSIONING	RECONCENTRATES
RECIRCULATION	RECODIFIED	RECOLLECTS	RECOMMISSIONS	RECONCENTRATING
RECIRCULATIONS	RECODIFIES	RECOLONISATION	RECOMMITMENT	RECONCENTRATION
RECITALIST	RECODIFYING	RECOLONISATIONS	RECOMMITMENTS	RECONCEPTION
RECITALISTS	RECOGNISABILITY	RECOLONISE	RECOMMITTAL	RECONCEPTIONS
RECITATION	RECOGNISABLE	RECOLONISED	RECOMMITTALS	RECONCEPTUALISE
RECITATIONIST	RECOGNISABLY	RECOLONISES	RECOMMITTED	RECONCEPTUALIZE
RECITATIONISTS	RECOGNISANCE	RECOLONISING	RECOMMITTING	RECONCILABILITY
RECITATIONS	RECOGNISANCES	RECOLONIZATION	RECOMPACTED	RECONCILABLE
RECITATIVE	RECOGNISANT	RECOLONIZATIONS	RECOMPACTING	RECONCILABLY
RECITATIVES	RECOGNISED	RECOLONIZE	RECOMPACTS	RECONCILED
RECITATIVI	RECOGNISEE	RECOLONIZED	RECOMPENCE	RECONCILEMENT
RECITATIVO	RECOGNISEES	RECOLONIZES	RECOMPENCES	RECONCILEMENTS
RECITATIVOS	RECOGNISER	RECOLONIZING	RECOMPENSABLE	RECONCILER
RECKLESSLY	RECOGNISERS	RECOLORING	RECOMPENSE	RECONCILERS
RECKLESSNESS	RECOGNISES	RECOMBINANT	RECOMPENSED	RECONCILES
RECKLESSNESSES	RECOGNISING	RECOMBINANTS	RECOMPENSER	RECONCILIATION
RECKONINGS	RECOGNISOR	RECOMBINATION	RECOMPENSERS	RECONCILIATIONS
RECLADDING	RECOGNISORS	RECOMBINATIONAL	RECOMPENSES	RECONCILIATORY
RECLAIMABLE	RECOGNITION	RECOMBINATIONS	RECOMPENSING	RECONCILING
RECLAIMABLY	RECOGNITIONS	RECOMBINED	RECOMPILATION	RECONDENSATION
RECLAIMANT	RECOGNITIVE	RECOMBINES	RECOMPILATIONS	RECONDENSATIONS
RECLAIMANTS	RECOGNITORY	RECOMBINING	RECOMPILED	RECONDENSE
RECLAIMERS	RECOGNIZABILITY	RECOMFORTED	RECOMPILES	RECONDENSED
RECLAIMING	RECOGNIZABLE	RECOMFORTING	RECOMPILING	RECONDENSES
RECLAMATION	RECOGNIZABLY	RECOMFORTLESS	RECOMPOSED	RECONDENSING
RECLAMATIONS	RECOGNIZANCE	RECOMFORTS	RECOMPOSES	RECONDITELY
RECLASPING	RECOGNIZANCES	RECOMFORTURE	RECOMPOSING	RECONDITENESS
RECLASSIFIED	RECOGNIZANT	RECOMFORTURES	RECOMPOSITION	RECONDITENESSES
RECLASSIFIES	RECOGNIZED	RECOMMENCE	RECOMPOSITIONS	RECONDITION
RECLASSIFY	RECOGNIZEE	RECOMMENCED	RECOMPRESS	RECONDITIONED
RECLASSIFYING	RECOGNIZEES	RECOMMENCEMENT	RECOMPRESSED	RECONDITIONING
RECLEANING	RECOGNIZER	RECOMMENCEMENTS	RECOMPRESSES	RECONDITIONS
RECLIMBING	RECOGNIZERS	RECOMMENCES	RECOMPRESSING	RECONDUCTED
RECLINABLE	RECOGNIZES	RECOMMENCING	RECOMPRESSION	RECONDUCTING
RECLINATION	RECOGNIZING	RECOMMENDABLE	RECOMPRESSIONS	RECONDUCTS

R

RECONFERRED

RECONFERRED	RECONSIDER	RECONTEXTUALIZE	RECOVERABILITY	RECRUITALS
RECONFERRING	RECONSIDERATION	RECONTINUE	RECOVERABLE	RECRUITERS
RECONFIGURATION	RECONSIDERED	RECONTINUED	RECOVERABLENESS	RECRUITING
RECONFIGURE	RECONSIDERING	RECONTINUES	RECOVEREES	RECRUITMENT
RECONFIGURED	RECONSIDERS	RECONTINUING	RECOVERERS	RECRUITMENTS
RECONFIGURES	RECONSIGNED	RECONTOURED	RECOVERIES	RECRYSTALLISE
RECONFIGURING	RECONSIGNING	RECONTOURING	RECOVERING	RECRYSTALLISED
RECONFINED	RECONSIGNS	RECONTOURS	RECOVERORS	RECRYSTALLISES
RECONFINES	RECONSOLED	RECONVALESCENCE	RECOWERING	RECRYSTALLISING
RECONFINING	RECONSOLES	RECONVENED	RECREANCES	RECRYSTALLIZE
RECONFIRMATION	RECONSOLIDATE	RECONVENES	RECREANCIES	RECRYSTALLIZED
RECONFIRMATIONS	RECONSOLIDATED	RECONVENING	RECREANTLY	RECRYSTALLIZES
RECONFIRMED	RECONSOLIDATES	RECONVERSION	RECREATING	RECRYSTALLIZING
RECONFIRMING	RECONSOLIDATING	RECONVERSIONS	RECREATION	RECTANGLED
RECONFIRMS	RECONSOLIDATION	RECONVERTED	RECREATIONAL	RECTANGLES
RECONNAISSANCE	RECONSOLING	RECONVERTING	RECREATIONIST	RECTANGULAR
RECONNAISSANCES	RECONSTITUENT	RECONVERTS	RECREATIONISTS	RECTANGULARITY
RECONNECTED	RECONSTITUENTS	RECONVEYANCE	RECREATIONS	RECTANGULARLY
RECONNECTING	RECONSTITUTABLE	RECONVEYANCES	RECREATIVE	RECTIFIABILITY
RECONNECTION	RECONSTITUTE	RECONVEYED	RECREATIVELY	RECTIFIABLE
RECONNECTIONS	RECONSTITUTED	RECONVEYING	RECREATORS	RECTIFICATION
RECONNECTS	RECONSTITUTES	RECONVICTED	RECREMENTAL	RECTIFICATIONS
RECONNOISSANCE	RECONSTITUTING	RECONVICTING	RECREMENTITIAL	RECTIFIERS
RECONNOISSANCES	RECONSTITUTION	RECONVICTION	RECREMENTITIOUS	RECTIFYING
RECONNOITER	RECONSTITUTIONS	RECONVICTIONS	RECREMENTS	RECTILINEAL
RECONNOITERED	RECONSTRUCT	RECONVICTS	RECRIMINATE	RECTILINEALLY
RECONNOITERER	RECONSTRUCTED	RECONVINCE	RECRIMINATED	RECTILINEAR
RECONNOITERERS	RECONSTRUCTIBLE	RECONVINCED	RECRIMINATES	RECTILINEARITY
RECONNOITERING	RECONSTRUCTING	RECONVINCES	RECRIMINATING	RECTILINEARLY
RECONNOITERS	RECONSTRUCTION	RECONVINCING	RECRIMINATION	RECTIPETALIES
RECONNOITRE	RECONSTRUCTIONS	RECORDABLE	RECRIMINATIONS	RECTIPETALITIES
RECONNOITRED	RECONSTRUCTIVE	RECORDATION	RECRIMINATIVE	RECTIPETALITY
RECONNOITRER	RECONSTRUCTOR	RECORDATIONS	RECRIMINATOR	RECTIPETALY
RECONNOITRERS	RECONSTRUCTORS	RECORDERSHIP	RECRIMINATORS	RECTIROSTRAL
RECONNOITRES	RECONSTRUCTS	RECORDERSHIPS	RECRIMINATORY	RECTISERIAL
RECONNOITRING	RECONSULTED	RECORDINGS	RECROSSING	RECTITISES
RECONQUERED	RECONSULTING	RECORDISTS	RECROWNING	RECTITUDES
RECONQUERING	RECONSULTS	RECOUNTALS	RECRUDESCE	RECTITUDINOUS
RECONQUERS	RECONTACTED	RECOUNTERS	RECRUDESCED	RECTOCELES
RECONQUEST	RECONTACTING	RECOUNTING	RECRUDESCENCE	RECTORATES
RECONQUESTS	RECONTACTS	RECOUNTMENT	RECRUDESCENCES	RECTORESSES
RECONSECRATE	RECONTAMINATE	RECOUNTMENTS	RECRUDESCENCIES	RECTORIALS
RECONSECRATED	RECONTAMINATED	RECOUPABLE	RECRUDESCENCY	RECTORSHIP
RECONSECRATES	RECONTAMINATES	RECOUPLING	RECRUDESCENT	RECTORSHIPS
RECONSECRATING	RECONTAMINATING	RECOUPMENT	RECRUDESCES	RECTRESSES
RECONSECRATION	RECONTAMINATION	RECOUPMENTS	RECRUDESCING	RECTRICIAL
RECONSECRATIONS	RECONTEXTUALISE	RECOURSING	RECRUITABLE	RECULTIVATE

RECULTIVATED	REDBAITING	REDEMPTIBLE	REDIGRESSED	REDISSOLVES
RECULTIVATES	REDBELLIES	REDEMPTION	REDIGRESSES	REDISSOLVING
RECULTIVATING	REDBREASTS	REDEMPTIONAL	REDIGRESSING	REDISTILLATION
RECUMBENCE	REDCURRANT	REDEMPTIONER	REDINGOTES	REDISTILLATIONS
RECUMBENCES	REDCURRANTS	REDEMPTIONERS	REDINTEGRATE	REDISTILLED
RECUMBENCIES	REDDISHNESS	REDEMPTIONS	REDINTEGRATED	REDISTILLING
RECUMBENCY	REDDISHNESSES	REDEMPTIVE	REDINTEGRATES	REDISTILLS
RECUMBENTLY	REDECIDING	REDEMPTIVELY	REDINTEGRATING	REDISTRIBUTE
RECUPERABLE	REDECORATE	REDEMPTORY	REDINTEGRATION	REDISTRIBUTED
RECUPERATE	REDECORATED	REDEPLOYED	REDINTEGRATIONS	REDISTRIBUTES
RECUPERATED	REDECORATES	REDEPLOYING	REDINTEGRATIVE	REDISTRIBUTING
RECUPERATES	REDECORATING	REDEPLOYMENT	REDIRECTED	REDISTRIBUTION
RECUPERATING	REDECORATION	REDEPLOYMENTS	REDIRECTING	REDISTRIBUTIONS
RECUPERATION	REDECORATIONS	REDEPOSITED	REDIRECTION	REDISTRIBUTIVE
RECUPERATIONS	REDECORATOR	REDEPOSITING	REDIRECTIONS	REDISTRICT
RECUPERATIVE	REDECORATORS	REDEPOSITS	REDISBURSE	REDISTRICTED
RECUPERATOR	REDECRAFTS	REDESCENDED	REDISBURSED	REDISTRICTING
RECUPERATORS	REDEDICATE	REDESCENDING	REDISBURSES	REDISTRICTS
RECUPERATORY	REDEDICATED	REDESCENDS	REDISBURSING	REDIVIDING
RECURELESS	REDEDICATES	REDESCRIBE	REDISCOUNT	REDIVISION
RECURRENCE	REDEDICATING	REDESCRIBED	REDISCOUNTABLE	REDIVISIONS
RECURRENCES	REDEDICATION	REDESCRIBES	REDISCOUNTED	REDIVORCED
RECURRENCIES	REDEDICATIONS	REDESCRIBING	REDISCOUNTING	REDIVORCES
RECURRENCY	REDEEMABILITIES	REDESCRIPTION	REDISCOUNTS	REDIVORCING
RECURRENTLY	REDEEMABILITY	REDESCRIPTIONS	REDISCOVER	REDLININGS
RECURRINGLY	REDEEMABLE	REDESIGNED	REDISCOVERED	REDOLENCES
RECURSIONS	REDEEMABLENESS	REDESIGNING	REDISCOVERER	REDOLENCIES
RECURSIVELY	REDEEMABLY	REDETERMINATION	REDISCOVERERS	REDOLENTLY
RECURSIVENESS	REDEEMLESS	REDETERMINE	REDISCOVERIES	REDOUBLEMENT
RECURSIVENESSES	REDEFEATED	REDETERMINED	REDISCOVERING	REDOUBLEMENTS
RECURVIROSTRAL	REDEFEATING	REDETERMINES	REDISCOVERS	REDOUBLERS
RECUSANCES	REDEFECTED	REDETERMINING	REDISCOVERY	REDOUBLING
RECUSANCIES	REDEFECTING	REDEVELOPED	REDISCUSSED	REDOUBTABLE
RECUSATION	REDEFINING	REDEVELOPER	REDISCUSSES	REDOUBTABLENESS
RECUSATIONS	REDEFINITION	REDEVELOPERS	REDISCUSSING	REDOUBTABLY
RECYCLABLE	REDEFINITIONS	REDEVELOPING	REDISPLAYED	REDOUBTING
RECYCLABLES	REDELIVERANCE	REDEVELOPMENT	REDISPLAYING	REDOUNDING
RECYCLATES	REDELIVERANCES	REDEVELOPMENTS	REDISPLAYS	REDOUNDINGS
RECYCLEABLE	REDELIVERED	REDEVELOPS	REDISPOSED	REDRAFTING
RECYCLEABLES	REDELIVERER	REDIALLING	REDISPOSES	REDREAMING
RECYCLISTS	REDELIVERERS	REDICTATED	REDISPOSING	REDRESSABLE
REDACTIONAL	REDELIVERIES	REDICTATES	REDISPOSITION	REDRESSALS
REDACTIONS	REDELIVERING	REDICTATING	REDISPOSITIONS	REDRESSERS
REDACTORIAL	REDELIVERS	REDIGESTED	REDISSOLUTION	REDRESSIBLE
REDAMAGING	REDELIVERY	REDIGESTING	REDISSOLUTIONS	REDRESSING
REDARGUING	REDEMANDED	REDIGESTION	REDISSOLVE	REDRESSIVE
REDBAITERS	REDEMANDING	REDIGESTIONS	REDISSOLVED	REDRESSORS

R

REDRILLING	REELECTION	REENCOUNTERS	REEQUIPPING	REEXPORTATIONS
REDRUTHITE	REELECTIONS	REENDOWING	REERECTING	REEXPORTED
REDRUTHITES	REELEVATED	REENERGISE	REESCALATE	REEXPORTING
REDSHIFTED	REELEVATES	REENERGISED	REESCALATED	REEXPOSING
REDSHIRTED	REELEVATING	REENERGISES	REESCALATES	REEXPOSURE
REDSHIRTING	REELIGIBILITIES	REENERGISING	REESCALATING	REEXPOSURES
REDSTREAKS	REELIGIBILITY	REENERGIZE	REESCALATION	REEXPRESSED
REDUCIBILITIES	REELIGIBLE	REENERGIZED	REESCALATIONS	REEXPRESSES
REDUCIBILITY	REEMBARKED	REENERGIZES	REESTABLISH	REEXPRESSING
REDUCIBLENESS	REEMBARKING	REENERGIZING	REESTABLISHED	REFASHIONED
REDUCIBLENESSES	REEMBODIED	REENFORCED	REESTABLISHES	REFASHIONING
REDUCTANTS	REEMBODIES	REENFORCES	REESTABLISHING	REFASHIONMENT
REDUCTASES	REEMBODYING	REENFORCING	REESTABLISHMENT	REFASHIONMENTS
REDUCTIONAL	REEMBRACED	REENGAGEMENT	REESTIMATE	REFASHIONS
REDUCTIONISM	REEMBRACES	REENGAGEMENTS	REESTIMATED	REFASTENED
REDUCTIONISMS	REEMBRACING	REENGAGING	REESTIMATES	REFASTENING
REDUCTIONIST	REEMBROIDER	REENGINEER	REESTIMATING	REFECTIONER
REDUCTIONISTIC	REEMBROIDERED	REENGINEERED	REEVALUATE	REFECTIONERS
REDUCTIONISTS	REEMBROIDERING	REENGINEERING	REEVALUATED	REFECTIONS
REDUCTIONS	REEMBROIDERS	REENGINEERS	REEVALUATES	REFECTORIAN
REDUCTIVELY	REEMERGENCE	REENGRAVED	REEVALUATING	REFECTORIANS
REDUCTIVENESS	REEMERGENCES	REENGRAVES	REEVALUATION	REFECTORIES
REDUCTIVENESSES	REEMERGING	REENGRAVING	REEVALUATIONS	REFEREEING
REDUNDANCE	REEMISSION	REENJOYING	REEXAMINATION	REFERENCED
REDUNDANCES	REEMISSIONS	REENLARGED	REEXAMINATIONS	REFERENCER
REDUNDANCIES	REEMITTING	REENLARGES	REEXAMINED	REFERENCERS
REDUNDANCY	REEMPHASES	REENLARGING	REEXAMINES	REFERENCES
REDUNDANTLY	REEMPHASIS	REENLISTED	REEXAMINING	REFERENCING
REDUPLICATE	REEMPHASISE	REENLISTING	REEXECUTED	REFERENCINGS
REDUPLICATED	REEMPHASISED	REENLISTMENT	REEXECUTES	REFERENDARIES
REDUPLICATES	REEMPHASISES	REENLISTMENTS	REEXECUTING	REFERENDARY
REDUPLICATING	REEMPHASISING	REENROLLED	REEXHIBITED	REFERENDUM
REDUPLICATION	REEMPHASIZE	REENROLLING	REEXHIBITING	REFERENDUMS
REDUPLICATIONS	REEMPHASIZED	REENSLAVED	REEXHIBITS	REFERENTIAL
REDUPLICATIVE	REEMPHASIZES	REENSLAVES	REEXPELLED	REFERENTIALITY
REDUPLICATIVELY	REEMPHASIZING	REENSLAVING	REEXPELLING	REFERENTIALLY
REEDIFYING	REEMPLOYED	REENTERING	REEXPERIENCE	REFERRABLE
REEDINESSES	REEMPLOYING	REENTHRONE	REEXPERIENCED	REFERRIBLE
REEDITIONS	REEMPLOYMENT	REENTHRONED	REEXPERIENCES	REFIGHTING
REEDUCATED	REEMPLOYMENTS	REENTHRONES	REEXPERIENCING	REFIGURING
REEDUCATES	REENACTING	REENTHRONING	REEXPLAINED	REFILLABLE
REEDUCATING	REENACTMENT	REENTRANCE	REEXPLAINING	REFILTERED
REEDUCATION	REENACTMENTS	REENTRANCES	REEXPLAINS	REFILTERING
REEDUCATIONS	REENACTORS	REENTRANTS	REEXPLORED	REFINANCED
REEDUCATIVE	REENCOUNTER	REEQUIPMENT	REEXPLORES	REFINANCES
REEJECTING	REENCOUNTERED	REEQUIPMENTS	REEXPLORING	REFINANCING
REELECTING	REENCOUNTERING	REEQUIPPED	REEXPORTATION	REFINANCINGS

REFINEDNESS	REFLEXIBILITIES	REFORMATIONISTS	REFRACTURED	REFUGEEISMS
REFINEDNESSES	REFLEXIBILITY	REFORMATIONS	REFRACTURES	REFULGENCE
REFINEMENT	REFLEXIBLE	REFORMATIVE	REFRACTURING	REFULGENCES
REFINEMENTS	REFLEXIONAL	REFORMATORIES	REFRAINERS	REFULGENCIES
REFINERIES	REFLEXIONS	REFORMATORY	REFRAINING	REFULGENCY
REFINISHED	REFLEXIVELY	REFORMATTED	REFRAINMENT	REFULGENTLY
REFINISHER	REFLEXIVENESS	REFORMATTING	REFRAINMENTS	REFUNDABILITIES
REFINISHERS	REFLEXIVENESSES	REFORMINGS	REFRANGIBILITY	REFUNDABILITY
REFINISHES	REFLEXIVES	REFORMISMS	REFRANGIBLE	REFUNDABLE
REFINISHING	REFLEXIVITIES	REFORMISTS	REFRANGIBLENESS	REFUNDMENT
REFITMENTS	REFLEXIVITY	REFORMULATE	REFREEZING	REFUNDMENTS
REFITTINGS	REFLEXOLOGICAL	REFORMULATED	REFRESHENED	REFURBISHED
REFLAGGING	REFLEXOLOGIES	REFORMULATES	REFRESHENER	REFURBISHER
REFLATIONARY	REFLEXOLOGIST	REFORMULATING	REFRESHENERS	REFURBISHERS
REFLATIONS	REFLEXOLOGISTS	REFORMULATION	REFRESHENING	REFURBISHES
REFLECTANCE	REFLEXOLOGY	REFORMULATIONS	REFRESHENS	REFURBISHING
REFLECTANCES	REFLOATING	REFORTIFICATION	REFRESHERS	REFURBISHINGS
REFLECTERS	REFLOODING	REFORTIFIED	REFRESHFUL	REFURBISHMENT
REFLECTING	REFLOWERED	REFORTIFIES	REFRESHFULLY	REFURBISHMENTS
REFLECTINGLY	REFLOWERING	REFORTIFYING	REFRESHING	REFURNISHED
REFLECTION	REFLOWERINGS	REFOUNDATION	REFRESHINGLY	REFURNISHES
REFLECTIONAL	REFLOWINGS	REFOUNDATIONS	REFRESHMENT	REFURNISHING
REFLECTIONLESS	REFLUENCES	REFOUNDERS	REFRESHMENTS	REFUSENIKS
REFLECTIONS	REFOCILLATE	REFOUNDING	REFRIGERANT	REFUTABILITIES
REFLECTIVE	REFOCILLATED	REFRACTABLE	REFRIGERANTS	REFUTABILITY
REFLECTIVELY	REFOCILLATES	REFRACTARIES	REFRIGERATE	REFUTATION
REFLECTIVENESS	REFOCILLATING	REFRACTARY	REFRIGERATED	REFUTATIONS
REFLECTIVITIES	REFOCILLATION	REFRACTILE	REFRIGERATES	REGAINABLE
REFLECTIVITY	REFOCILLATIONS	REFRACTING	REFRIGERATING	REGAINMENT
REFLECTOGRAM	REFOCUSING	REFRACTION	REFRIGERATION	REGAINMENTS
REFLECTOGRAMS	REFOCUSSED	REFRACTIONS	REFRIGERATIONS	REGALEMENT
REFLECTOGRAPH	REFOCUSSES	REFRACTIVE	REFRIGERATIVE	REGALEMENTS
REFLECTOGRAPHS	REFOCUSSING	REFRACTIVELY	REFRIGERATOR	REGALITIES
REFLECTOGRAPHY	REFORESTATION	REFRACTIVENESS	REFRIGERATORIES	REGALNESSES
REFLECTOMETER	REFORESTATIONS	REFRACTIVITIES	REFRIGERATORS	REGARDABLE
REFLECTOMETERS	REFORESTED	REFRACTIVITY	REFRIGERATORY	REGARDFULLY
REFLECTOMETRIES	REFORESTING	REFRACTOMETER	REFRINGENCE	REGARDFULNESS
REFLECTOMETRY	REFORMABILITIES	REFRACTOMETERS	REFRINGENCES	REGARDFULNESSES
REFLECTORISE	REFORMABILITY	REFRACTOMETRIC	REFRINGENCIES	REGARDLESS
REFLECTORISED	REFORMABLE	REFRACTOMETRIES	REFRINGENCY	REGARDLESSLY
REFLECTORISES	REFORMADES	REFRACTOMETRY	REFRINGENT	REGARDLESSNESS
REFLECTORISING	REFORMADOES	REFRACTORIES	REFRINGING	REGATHERED
REFLECTORIZE	REFORMADOS	REFRACTORILY	REFRONTING	REGATHERING
REFLECTORIZED	REFORMATES	REFRACTORINESS	REFUELABLE	REGELATING
REFLECTORIZES	REFORMATION	REFRACTORS	REFUELLABLE	REGELATION
REFLECTORIZING	REFORMATIONAL	REFRACTORY	REFUELLING	REGELATIONS
REFLECTORS	REFORMATIONIST	REFRACTURE	REFUGEEISM	REGENERABLE

R

REGENERACIES	REGISTRABLE	REGULARISATION	REHARDENING	REIGNITING
REGENERACY	REGISTRANT	REGULARISATIONS	REHEARINGS	REIGNITION
REGENERATE	REGISTRANTS	REGULARISE	REHEARSALS	REIGNITIONS
REGENERATED	REGISTRARIES	REGULARISED	REHEARSERS	REILLUMINE
REGENERATELY	REGISTRARS	REGULARISES	REHEARSING	REILLUMINED
REGENERATENESS	REGISTRARSHIP	REGULARISING	REHEARSINGS	REILLUMINES
REGENERATES	REGISTRARSHIPS	REGULARITIES	REHEATINGS	REILLUMING
REGENERATING	REGISTRARY	REGULARITY	REHOSPITALISE	REILLUMINING
REGENERATION	REGISTRATION	REGULARIZATION	REHOSPITALISED	REIMAGINED
REGENERATIONS	REGISTRATIONAL	REGULARIZATIONS	REHOSPITALISES	REIMAGINES
REGENERATIVE	REGISTRATIONS	REGULARIZE	REHOSPITALISING	REIMAGINING
REGENERATIVELY	REGISTRIES	REGULARIZED	REHOSPITALIZE	REIMBURSABLE
REGENERATOR	REGLORIFIED	REGULARIZES	REHOSPITALIZED	REIMBURSED
REGENERATORS	REGLORIFIES	REGULARIZING	REHOSPITALIZES	REIMBURSEMENT
REGENERATORY	REGLORIFYING	REGULATING	REHOSPITALIZING	REIMBURSEMENTS
REGENTSHIP	REGLOSSING	REGULATION	REHOUSINGS	REIMBURSER
REGENTSHIPS	REGNANCIES	REGULATIONS	REHUMANISE	REIMBURSERS
REGGAETONS	REGRAFTING	REGULATIVE	REHUMANISED	REIMBURSES
REGIMENTAL	REGRANTING	REGULATIVELY	REHUMANISES	REIMBURSING
REGIMENTALLY	REGRATINGS	REGULATORS	REHUMANISING	REIMMERSED
REGIMENTALS	REGREDIENCE	REGULATORY	REHUMANIZE	REIMMERSES
REGIMENTATION	REGREDIENCES	REGULISING	REHUMANIZED	REIMMERSING
REGIMENTATIONS	REGREENING	REGULIZING	REHUMANIZES	REIMPLANTATION
REGIMENTED	REGREETING	REGURGITANT	REHUMANIZING	REIMPLANTATIONS
REGIMENTING	REGRESSING	REGURGITANTS	REHYDRATABLE	REIMPLANTED
REGIONALISATION	REGRESSION	REGURGITATE	REHYDRATED	REIMPLANTING
REGIONALISE	REGRESSIONS	REGURGITATED	REHYDRATES	REIMPLANTS
REGIONALISED	REGRESSIVE	REGURGITATES	REHYDRATING	REIMPORTATION
REGIONALISES	REGRESSIVELY	REGURGITATING	REHYDRATION	REIMPORTATIONS
REGIONALISING	REGRESSIVENESS	REGURGITATION	REHYDRATIONS	REIMPORTED
REGIONALISM	REGRESSIVITIES	REGURGITATIONS	REHYPNOTISE	REIMPORTER
REGIONALISMS	REGRESSIVITY	REHABILITANT	REHYPNOTISED	REIMPORTERS
REGIONALIST	REGRESSORS	REHABILITANTS	REHYPNOTISES	REIMPORTING
REGIONALISTIC	REGRETFULLY	REHABILITATE	REHYPNOTISING	REIMPOSING
REGIONALISTS	REGRETFULNESS	REHABILITATED	REHYPNOTIZE	REIMPOSITION
REGIONALIZATION	REGRETFULNESSES	REHABILITATES	REHYPNOTIZED	REIMPOSITIONS
REGIONALIZE	REGRETTABLE	REHABILITATING	REHYPNOTIZES	REIMPRESSION
REGIONALIZED	REGRETTABLY	REHABILITATION	REHYPNOTIZING	REIMPRESSIONS
REGIONALIZES	REGRETTERS	REHABILITATIONS	REICHSMARK	REINCARNATE
REGIONALIZING	REGRETTING	REHABILITATIVE	REICHSMARKS	REINCARNATED
REGIONALLY	REGRINDING	REHABILITATOR	REIDENTIFIED	REINCARNATES
REGISSEURS	REGROOMING	REHABILITATORS	REIDENTIFIES	REINCARNATING
REGISTERABLE	REGROOVING	REHAMMERED	REIDENTIFY	REINCARNATION
REGISTERED	REGROUPING	REHAMMERING	REIDENTIFYING	REINCARNATIONS
REGISTERER	REGUERDONED	REHANDLING	REIFICATION	REINCITING
REGISTERERS	REGUERDONING	REHANDLINGS	REIFICATIONS	REINCORPORATE
REGISTERING	REGUERDONS	REHARDENED	REIFICATORY	REINCORPORATED

R

REINCORPORATES	REINHABITING	REINSTATED	REINVADING	REJECTAMENTA
REINCORPORATING	REINHABITS	REINSTATEMENT	REINVASION	REJECTIBLE
REINCORPORATION	REINITIATE	REINSTATEMENTS	REINVASIONS	REJECTINGLY
REINCREASE	REINITIATED	REINSTATES	REINVENTED	REJECTIONIST
REINCREASED	REINITIATES	REINSTATING	REINVENTING	REJECTIONISTS
REINCREASES	REINITIATING	REINSTATION	REINVENTION	REJECTIONS
REINCREASING	REINJECTED	REINSTATIONS	REINVENTIONS	REJIGGERED
REINCURRED	REINJECTING	REINSTATOR	REINVESTED	REJIGGERING
REINCURRING	REINJECTION	REINSTATORS	REINVESTIGATE	REJOICEFUL
REINDEXING	REINJECTIONS	REINSTITUTE	REINVESTIGATED	REJOICEMENT
REINDICTED	REINJURIES	REINSTITUTED	REINVESTIGATES	REJOICEMENTS
REINDICTING	REINJURING	REINSTITUTES	REINVESTIGATING	REJOICINGLY
REINDICTMENT	REINNERVATE	REINSTITUTING	REINVESTIGATION	REJOICINGS
REINDICTMENTS	REINNERVATED	REINSURANCE	REINVESTING	REJOINDERS
REINDUCING	REINNERVATES	REINSURANCES	REINVESTMENT	REJOINDURE
REINDUCTED	REINNERVATING	REINSURERS	REINVESTMENTS	REJOINDURES
REINDUCTING	REINNERVATION	REINSURING	REINVIGORATE	REJONEADOR
REINDUSTRIALISE	REINNERVATIONS	REINTEGRATE	REINVIGORATED	REJONEADORA
REINDUSTRIALIZE	REINOCULATE	REINTEGRATED	REINVIGORATES	REJONEADORAS
REINFECTED	REINOCULATED	REINTEGRATES	REINVIGORATING	REJONEADORES
REINFECTING	REINOCULATES	REINTEGRATING	REINVIGORATION	REJOURNING
REINFECTION	REINOCULATING	REINTEGRATION	REINVIGORATIONS	REJUGGLING
REINFECTIONS	REINOCULATION	REINTEGRATIONS	REINVIGORATOR	REJUSTIFIED
REINFESTATION	REINOCULATIONS	REINTEGRATIVE	REINVIGORATORS	REJUSTIFIES
REINFESTATIONS	REINSERTED	REINTERMENT	REINVITING	REJUSTIFYING
REINFLAMED	REINSERTING	REINTERMENTS	REINVOKING	REJUVENATE
REINFLAMES	REINSERTION	REINTERPRET	REINVOLVED	REJUVENATED
REINFLAMING	REINSERTIONS	REINTERPRETED	REINVOLVES	REJUVENATES
REINFLATED	REINSPECTED	REINTERPRETING	REINVOLVING	REJUVENATING
REINFLATES	REINSPECTING	REINTERPRETS	REIOYNDURE	REJUVENATION
REINFLATING	REINSPECTION	REINTERRED	REIOYNDURES	REJUVENATIONS
REINFLATION	REINSPECTIONS	REINTERRING	REISSUABLE	REJUVENATOR
REINFLATIONS	REINSPECTS	REINTERROGATE	REISTAFELS	REJUVENATORS
REINFORCEABLE	REINSPIRED	REINTERROGATED	REITERANCE	REJUVENESCE
REINFORCED	REINSPIRES	REINTERROGATES	REITERANCES	REJUVENESCED
REINFORCEMENT	REINSPIRING	REINTERROGATING	REITERATED	REJUVENESCENCE
REINFORCEMENTS	REINSPIRIT	REINTERROGATION	REITERATEDLY	REJUVENESCENCES
REINFORCER	REINSPIRITED	REINTERVIEW	REITERATES	REJUVENESCENT
REINFORCERS	REINSPIRITING	REINTERVIEWED	REITERATING	REJUVENESCES
REINFORCES	REINSPIRITS	REINTERVIEWING	REITERATION	REJUVENESCING
REINFORCING	REINSTALLATION	REINTERVIEWS	REITERATIONS	REJUVENISE
REINFORMED	REINSTALLATIONS	REINTRODUCE	REITERATIVE	REJUVENISED
REINFORMING	REINSTALLED	REINTRODUCED	REITERATIVELY	REJUVENISES
REINFUNDED	REINSTALLING	REINTRODUCES	REITERATIVES	REJUVENISING
REINFUNDING	REINSTALLS	REINTRODUCING	REJACKETED	REJUVENIZE
REINFUSING	REINSTALMENT	REINTRODUCTION	REJACKETING	REJUVENIZED
REINHABITED	REINSTALMENTS	REINTRODUCTIONS	REJECTABLE	REJUVENIZES

R

REJUVENIZING	RELATIVIZATION	RELIEVABLE	RELOCATEES	REMARRIAGE
REKEYBOARD	RELATIVIZATIONS	RELIEVEDLY	RELOCATING	REMARRIAGES
REKEYBOARDED	RELATIVIZE	RELIGHTING	RELOCATION	REMARRYING
REKEYBOARDING	RELATIVIZED	RELIGIEUSE	RELOCATIONS	REMASTERED
REKEYBOARDS	RELATIVIZES	RELIGIEUSES	RELOCATORS	REMASTERING
REKINDLING	RELATIVIZING	RELIGIONARIES	RELUBRICATE	REMATCHING
REKNITTING	RELAUNCHED	RELIGIONARY	RELUBRICATED	REMATERIALISE
REKNOTTING	RELAUNCHES	RELIGIONER	RELUBRICATES	REMATERIALISED
RELABELING	RELAUNCHING	RELIGIONERS	RELUBRICATING	REMATERIALISES
RELABELLED	RELAUNDERED	RELIGIONISE	RELUBRICATION	REMATERIALISING
RELABELLING	RELAUNDERING	RELIGIONISED	RELUBRICATIONS	REMATERIALIZE
RELACQUERED	RELAUNDERS	RELIGIONISES	RELUCTANCE	REMATERIALIZED
RELACQUERING	RELAXATION	RELIGIONISING	RELUCTANCES	REMATERIALIZES
RELACQUERS	RELAXATIONS	RELIGIONISM	RELUCTANCIES	REMATERIALIZING
RELANDSCAPE	RELAXATIVE	RELIGIONISMS	RELUCTANCY	REMEASURED
RELANDSCAPED	RELAXEDNESS	RELIGIONIST	RELUCTANTLY	REMEASUREMENT
RELANDSCAPES	RELAXEDNESSES	RELIGIONISTS	RELUCTATED	REMEASUREMENTS
RELANDSCAPING	RELEARNING	RELIGIONIZE	RELUCTATES	REMEASURES
RELATEDNESS	RELEASABLE	RELIGIONIZED	RELUCTATING	REMEASURING
RELATEDNESSES	RELEASEMENT	RELIGIONIZES	RELUCTATION	REMEDIABILITIES
RELATIONAL	RELEASEMENTS	RELIGIONIZING	RELUCTATIONS	REMEDIABILITY
RELATIONALLY	RELEGATABLE	RELIGIONLESS	RELUCTIVITIES	REMEDIABLE
RELATIONISM	RELEGATING	RELIGIOSELY	RELUCTIVITY	REMEDIABLY
RELATIONISMS	RELEGATION	RELIGIOSITIES	RELUMINING	REMEDIALLY
RELATIONIST	RELEGATIONS	RELIGIOSITY	REMAINDERED	REMEDIATED
RELATIONISTS	RELENTINGS	RELIGIOUSES	REMAINDERING	REMEDIATES
RELATIONLESS	RELENTLESS	RELIGIOUSLY	REMAINDERMAN	REMEDIATING
RELATIONSHIP	RELENTLESSLY	RELIGIOUSNESS	REMAINDERMEN	REMEDIATION
RELATIONSHIPS	RELENTLESSNESS	RELIGIOUSNESSES	REMAINDERS	REMEDIATIONS
RELATIVELY	RELENTMENT	RELINQUISH	REMANDMENT	REMEDILESS
RELATIVENESS	RELENTMENTS	RELINQUISHED	REMANDMENTS	REMEDILESSLY
RELATIVENESSES	RELETTERED	RELINQUISHER	REMANENCES	REMEDILESSNESS
RELATIVISATION	RELETTERING	RELINQUISHERS	REMANENCIES	REMEMBERABILITY
RELATIVISATIONS	RELEVANCES	RELINQUISHES	REMANUFACTURE	REMEMBERABLE
RELATIVISE	RELEVANCIES	RELINQUISHING	REMANUFACTURED	REMEMBERABLY
RELATIVISED	RELEVANTLY	RELINQUISHMENT	REMANUFACTURER	REMEMBERED
RELATIVISES	RELIABILITIES	RELINQUISHMENTS	REMANUFACTURERS	REMEMBERER
RELATIVISING	RELIABILITY	RELIQUAIRE	REMANUFACTURES	REMEMBERERS
RELATIVISM	RELIABLENESS	RELIQUAIRES	REMANUFACTURING	REMEMBERING
RELATIVISMS	RELIABLENESSES	RELIQUARIES	REMARKABILITIES	REMEMBRANCE
RELATIVIST	RELICENSED	RELIQUEFIED	REMARKABILITY	REMEMBRANCER
RELATIVISTIC	RELICENSES	RELIQUEFIES	REMARKABLE	REMEMBRANCERS
RELATIVISTS	RELICENSING	RELIQUEFYING	REMARKABLENESS	REMEMBRANCES
RELATIVITIES	RELICENSURE	RELISHABLE	REMARKABLES	REMERCYING
RELATIVITIST	RELICENSURES	RELIVERING	REMARKABLY	REMIGATING
RELATIVITISTS	RELICTIONS	RELLISHING	REMARKETED	REMIGATION
RELATIVITY	RELIEFLESS	RELOCATABLE	REMARKETING	REMIGATIONS

R

REMIGRATED	REMITTENCIES	REMONSTRATINGLY	REMOVABLENESS	RENCOUNTERED
REMIGRATES	REMITTENCY	REMONSTRATION	REMOVABLENESSES	RENCOUNTERING
REMIGRATING	REMITTENTLY	REMONSTRATIONS	REMOVALIST	RENCOUNTERS
REMIGRATION	REMIXTURES	REMONSTRATIVE	REMOVALISTS	RENDERABLE
REMIGRATIONS	REMOBILISATION	REMONSTRATIVELY	REMOVEABLE	RENDERINGS
REMILITARISE	REMOBILISATIONS	REMONSTRATOR	REMOVEDNESS	RENDEZVOUS
REMILITARISED	REMOBILISE	REMONSTRATORS	REMOVEDNESSES	RENDEZVOUSED
REMILITARISES	REMOBILISED	REMONSTRATORY	REMUNERABILITY	RENDEZVOUSES
REMILITARISING	REMOBILISES	REMONTANTS	REMUNERABLE	RENDEZVOUSING
REMILITARIZE	REMOBILISING	REMONTOIRE	REMUNERATE	RENDITIONED
REMILITARIZED	REMOBILIZATION	REMONTOIRES	REMUNERATED	RENDITIONING
REMILITARIZES	REMOBILIZATIONS	REMONTOIRS	REMUNERATES	RENDITIONS
REMILITARIZING	REMOBILIZE	REMORALISATION	REMUNERATING	RENEGADING
REMINERALISE	REMOBILIZED	REMORALISATIONS	REMUNERATION	RENEGADOES
REMINERALISED	REMOBILIZES	REMORALISE	REMUNERATIONS	RENEGATION
REMINERALISES	REMOBILIZING	REMORALISED	REMUNERATIVE	RENEGATIONS
REMINERALISING	REMODELERS	REMORALISES	REMUNERATIVELY	RENEGOTIABLE
REMINERALIZE	REMODELING	REMORALISING	REMUNERATOR	RENEGOTIATE
REMINERALIZED	REMODELLED	REMORALIZATION	REMUNERATORS	RENEGOTIATED
REMINERALIZES	REMODELLING	REMORALIZATIONS	REMUNERATORY	RENEGOTIATES
REMINERALIZING	REMODIFIED	REMORALIZE	REMURMURED	RENEGOTIATING
REMINISCED	REMODIFIES	REMORALIZED	REMURMURING	RENEGOTIATION
REMINISCENCE	REMODIFYING	REMORALIZES	REMYTHOLOGISE	RENEGOTIATIONS
REMINISCENCES	REMOISTENED	REMORALIZING	REMYTHOLOGISED	RENEWABILITIES
REMINISCENT	REMOISTENING	REMORSEFUL	REMYTHOLOGISES	RENEWABILITY
REMINISCENTIAL	REMOISTENS	REMORSEFULLY	REMYTHOLOGISING	RENEWABLES
REMINISCENTLY	REMONETISATION	REMORSEFULNESS	REMYTHOLOGIZE	RENEWEDNESS
REMINISCENTS	REMONETISATIONS	REMORSELESS	REMYTHOLOGIZED	RENEWEDNESSES
REMINISCER	REMONETISE	REMORSELESSLY	REMYTHOLOGIZES	RENFORCING
REMINISCERS	REMONETISED	REMORSELESSNESS	REMYTHOLOGIZING	RENITENCES
REMINISCES	REMONETISES	REMORTGAGE	RENAISSANCE	RENITENCIES
REMINISCING	REMONETISING	REMORTGAGED	RENAISSANCES	RENOGRAPHIC
REMISSIBILITIES	REMONETIZATION	REMORTGAGES	RENASCENCE	RENOGRAPHIES
REMISSIBILITY	REMONETIZATIONS	REMORTGAGING	RENASCENCES	RENOGRAPHY
REMISSIBLE	REMONETIZE	REMOTENESS	RENATIONALISE	RENOMINATE
REMISSIBLENESS	REMONETIZED	REMOTENESSES	RENATIONALISED	RENOMINATED
REMISSIBLY	REMONETIZES	REMOTIVATE	RENATIONALISES	RENOMINATES
REMISSIONS	REMONETIZING	REMOTIVATED	RENATIONALISING	RENOMINATING
REMISSIVELY	REMONSTRANCE	REMOTIVATES	RENATIONALIZE	RENOMINATION
REMISSNESS	REMONSTRANCES	REMOTIVATING	RENATIONALIZED	RENOMINATIONS
REMISSNESSES	REMONSTRANT	REMOTIVATION	RENATIONALIZES	RENORMALISATION
REMITMENTS	REMONSTRANTLY	REMOTIVATIONS	RENATIONALIZING	RENORMALISE
REMITTABLE	REMONSTRANTS	REMOULADES	RENATURATION	RENORMALISED
REMITTANCE	REMONSTRATE	REMOULDING	RENATURATIONS	RENORMALISES
REMITTANCES	REMONSTRATED	REMOUNTING	RENATURING	RENORMALISING
REMITTENCE	REMONSTRATES	REMOVABILITIES	RENCONTRES	RENORMALIZATION
REMITTENCES	REMONSTRATING	REMOVABILITY	RENCOUNTER	RENORMALIZE

R

RENORMALIZED	REOCCURRED	REORIENTED	REPASSAGES	REPERTOIRE
RENORMALIZES	REOCCURRENCE	REORIENTING	REPASTURES	REPERTOIRES
RENORMALIZING	REOCCURRENCES	REOUTFITTED	REPATCHING	REPERTORIAL
RENOSTERVELD	REOCCURRING	REOUTFITTING	REPATRIATE	REPERTORIES
RENOSTERVELDS	REOFFENDED	REOVIRUSES	REPATRIATED	REPERUSALS
RENOTIFIED	REOFFENDER	REOXIDATION	REPATRIATES	REPERUSING
RENOTIFIES	REOFFENDERS	REOXIDATIONS	REPATRIATING	REPETITEUR
RENOTIFYING	REOFFENDING	REOXIDISED	REPATRIATION	REPETITEURS
RENOUNCEABLE	REOFFERING	REOXIDISES	REPATRIATIONS	REPETITEUSE
RENOUNCEMENT	REOPERATED	REOXIDISING	REPATRIATOR	REPETITEUSES
RENOUNCEMENTS	REOPERATES	REOXIDIZED	REPATRIATORS	REPETITION
RENOUNCERS	REOPERATING	REOXIDIZES	REPATTERNED	REPETITIONAL
RENOUNCING	REOPERATION	REOXIDIZING	REPATTERNING	REPETITIONARY
RENOVASCULAR	REOPERATIONS	REPACIFIED	REPATTERNS	REPETITIONS
RENOVATING	REOPPOSING	REPACIFIES	REPAYMENTS	REPETITIOUS
RENOVATION	REORCHESTRATE	REPACIFYING	REPEALABLE	REPETITIOUSLY
RENOVATIONS	REORCHESTRATED	REPACKAGED	REPEATABILITIES	REPETITIOUSNESS
RENOVATIVE	REORCHESTRATES	REPACKAGER	REPEATABILITY	REPETITIVE
RENOVATORS	REORCHESTRATING	REPACKAGERS	REPEATABLE	REPETITIVELY
RENSSELAERITE	REORCHESTRATION	REPACKAGES	REPEATEDLY	REPETITIVENESS
RENSSELAERITES	REORDAINED	REPACKAGING	REPEATINGS	REPHOTOGRAPH
RENTABILITIES	REORDAINING	REPAGINATE	REPECHAGES	REPHOTOGRAPHED
RENTABILITY	REORDERING	REPAGINATED	REPELLANCE	REPHOTOGRAPHING
RENTALLERS	REORDINATION	REPAGINATES	REPELLANCES	REPHOTOGRAPHS
RENUMBERED	REORDINATIONS	REPAGINATING	REPELLANCIES	REPHRASING
RENUMBERING	REORGANISATION	REPAGINATION	REPELLANCY	REPIGMENTED
RENUNCIATE	REORGANISATIONS	REPAGINATIONS	REPELLANTLY	REPIGMENTING
RENUNCIATES	REORGANISE	REPAINTING	REPELLANTS	REPIGMENTS
RENUNCIATION	REORGANISED	REPAINTINGS	REPELLENCE	REPINEMENT
RENUNCIATIONS	REORGANISER	REPAIRABILITIES	REPELLENCES	REPINEMENTS
RENUNCIATIVE	REORGANISERS	REPAIRABILITY	REPELLENCIES	REPININGLY
RENUNCIATORY	REORGANISES	REPAIRABLE	REPELLENCY	REPLACEABILITY
RENVERSEMENT	REORGANISING	REPANELING	REPELLENTLY	REPLACEABLE
RENVERSEMENTS	REORGANIZATION	REPANELLED	REPELLENTS	REPLACEMENT
RENVERSING	REORGANIZATIONS	REPANELLING	REPELLINGLY	REPLACEMENTS
REOBJECTED	REORGANIZE	REPAPERING	REPENTANCE	REPLANNING
REOBJECTING	REORGANIZED	REPARABILITIES	REPENTANCES	REPLANTATION
REOBSERVED	REORGANIZER	REPARABILITY	REPENTANTLY	REPLANTATIONS
REOBSERVES	REORGANIZERS	REPARATION	REPENTANTS	REPLANTING
REOBSERVING	REORGANIZES	REPARATIONS	REPENTINGLY	REPLASTERED
REOBTAINED	REORGANIZING	REPARATIVE	REPEOPLING	REPLASTERING
REOBTAINING	REORIENTATE	REPARATORY	REPERCUSSED	REPLASTERS
REOCCUPATION	REORIENTATED	REPARTEEING	REPERCUSSES	REPLEADERS
REOCCUPATIONS	REORIENTATES	REPARTITION	REPERCUSSING	REPLEADING
REOCCUPIED	REORIENTATING	REPARTITIONED	REPERCUSSION	REPLEDGING
REOCCUPIES	REORIENTATION	REPARTITIONING	REPERCUSSIONS	REPLENISHABLE
REOCCUPYING	REORIENTATIONS	REPARTITIONS	REPERCUSSIVE	REPLENISHED

REPLENISHER
REPLENISHERS
REPLENISHES
REPLENISHING
REPLENISHMENT
REPLENISHMENTS
REPLETENESS
REPLETENESSES
REPLETIONS
REPLEVIABLE
REPLEVINED
REPLEVINING
REPLEVISABLE
REPLEVYING
REPLICABILITIES
REPLICABILITY
REPLICABLE
REPLICANTS
REPLICASES
REPLICATED
REPLICATES
REPLICATING
REPLICATION
REPLICATIONS
REPLICATIVE
REPLICATOR
REPLICATORS
REPLOTTING
REPLUMBING
REPLUNGING
REPOINTING
REPOLARISATION
REPOLARISATIONS
REPOLARISE
REPOLARISED
REPOLARISES
REPOLARISING
REPOLARIZATION
REPOLARIZATIONS
REPOLARIZE
REPOLARIZED
REPOLARIZES
REPOLARIZING
REPOLISHED
REPOLISHES
REPOLISHING
REPOPULARISE

REPOPULARISED
REPOPULARISES
REPOPULARISING
REPOPULARIZE
REPOPULARIZED
REPOPULARIZES
REPOPULARIZING
REPOPULATE
REPOPULATED
REPOPULATES
REPOPULATING
REPOPULATION
REPOPULATIONS
REPORTABLE
REPORTAGES
REPORTEDLY
REPORTINGLY
REPORTINGS
REPORTORIAL
REPORTORIALLY
REPOSEDNESS
REPOSEDNESSES
REPOSEFULLY
REPOSEFULNESS
REPOSEFULNESSES
REPOSITING
REPOSITION
REPOSITIONED
REPOSITIONING
REPOSITIONS
REPOSITORIES
REPOSITORS
REPOSITORY
REPOSSESSED
REPOSSESSES
REPOSSESSING
REPOSSESSION
REPOSSESSIONS
REPOSSESSOR
REPOSSESSORS
REPOTTINGS
REPOUSSAGE
REPOUSSAGES
REPOUSSOIR
REPOUSSOIRS
REPOWERING
REPREEVING

REPREHENDABLE
REPREHENDED
REPREHENDER
REPREHENDERS
REPREHENDING
REPREHENDS
REPREHENSIBLE
REPREHENSIBLY
REPREHENSION
REPREHENSIONS
REPREHENSIVE
REPREHENSIVELY
REPREHENSORY
REPRESENTABLE
REPRESENTAMEN
REPRESENTAMENS
REPRESENTANT
REPRESENTANTS
REPRESENTATION
REPRESENTATIONS
REPRESENTATIVE
REPRESENTATIVES
REPRESENTED
REPRESENTEE
REPRESENTEES
REPRESENTER
REPRESENTERS
REPRESENTING
REPRESENTMENT
REPRESENTMENTS
REPRESENTOR
REPRESENTORS
REPRESENTS
REPRESSERS
REPRESSIBILITY
REPRESSIBLE
REPRESSIBLY
REPRESSING
REPRESSION
REPRESSIONIST
REPRESSIONS
REPRESSIVE
REPRESSIVELY
REPRESSIVENESS
REPRESSORS
REPRESSURISE
REPRESSURISED

REPRESSURISES
REPRESSURISING
REPRESSURIZE
REPRESSURIZED
REPRESSURIZES
REPRESSURIZING
REPRIEVABLE
REPRIEVALS
REPRIEVERS
REPRIEVING
REPRIMANDED
REPRIMANDING
REPRIMANDS
REPRINTERS
REPRINTING
REPRISTINATE
REPRISTINATED
REPRISTINATES
REPRISTINATING
REPRISTINATION
REPRISTINATIONS
REPRIVATISATION
REPRIVATISE
REPRIVATISED
REPRIVATISES
REPRIVATISING
REPRIVATIZATION
REPRIVATIZE
REPRIVATIZED
REPRIVATIZES
REPRIVATIZING
REPROACHABLE
REPROACHABLY
REPROACHED
REPROACHER
REPROACHERS
REPROACHES
REPROACHFUL
REPROACHFULLY
REPROACHFULNESS
REPROACHING
REPROACHINGLY
REPROACHLESS
REPROBACIES
REPROBANCE
REPROBANCES
REPROBATED

REPROBATER
REPROBATERS
REPROBATES
REPROBATING
REPROBATION
REPROBATIONARY
REPROBATIONS
REPROBATIVE
REPROBATIVELY
REPROBATOR
REPROBATORS
REPROBATORY
REPROCESSED
REPROCESSES
REPROCESSING
REPROCESSINGS
REPRODUCED
REPRODUCER
REPRODUCERS
REPRODUCES
REPRODUCIBILITY
REPRODUCIBLE
REPRODUCIBLES
REPRODUCIBLY
REPRODUCING
REPRODUCTION
REPRODUCTIONS
REPRODUCTIVE
REPRODUCTIVELY
REPRODUCTIVES
REPRODUCTIVITY
REPROGRAMED
REPROGRAMING
REPROGRAMMABLE
REPROGRAMME
REPROGRAMMED
REPROGRAMMES
REPROGRAMMING
REPROGRAMS
REPROGRAPHER
REPROGRAPHERS
REPROGRAPHIC
REPROGRAPHICS
REPROGRAPHIES
REPROGRAPHY
REPROOFING
REPROVABLE

R

REPROVINGLY	REPULSIVENESS	REQUISITIONED	REREVIEWED	RESECURING
REPROVISION	REPULSIVENESSES	REQUISITIONING	REREVIEWING	RESEGREGATE
REPROVISIONED	REPUNCTUATION	REQUISITIONIST	REREVISING	RESEGREGATED
REPROVISIONING	REPUNCTUATIONS	REQUISITIONISTS	REROUTEING	RESEGREGATES
REPROVISIONS	REPURCHASE	REQUISITIONS	RESADDLING	RESEGREGATING
REPTATIONS	REPURCHASED	REQUISITOR	RESALEABLE	RESEGREGATION
REPTILIANLY	REPURCHASES	REQUISITORS	RESALUTING	RESEGREGATIONS
REPTILIANS	REPURCHASING	REQUISITORY	RESAMPLING	RESEIZURES
REPTILIFEROUS	REPURIFIED	REQUITABLE	RESCHEDULE	RESELECTED
REPTILIOUS	REPURIFIES	REQUITEFUL	RESCHEDULED	RESELECTING
REPUBLICAN	REPURIFYING	REQUITELESS	RESCHEDULES	RESELECTION
REPUBLICANISE	REPURPOSED	REQUITEMENT	RESCHEDULING	RESELECTIONS
REPUBLICANISED	REPURPOSES	REQUITEMENTS	RESCHEDULINGS	RESEMBLANCE
REPUBLICANISES	REPURPOSING	REQUITTING	RESCHOOLED	RESEMBLANCES
REPUBLICANISING	REPURSUING	REQUOYLING	RESCHOOLING	RESEMBLANT
REPUBLICANISM	REPUTABILITIES	RERADIATED	RESCINDABLE	RESEMBLERS
REPUBLICANISMS	REPUTABILITY	RERADIATES	RESCINDERS	RESEMBLING
REPUBLICANIZE	REPUTATION	RERADIATING	RESCINDING	RESENSITISE
REPUBLICANIZED	REPUTATIONAL	RERADIATION	RESCINDMENT	RESENSITISED
REPUBLICANIZES	REPUTATIONLESS	RERADIATIONS	RESCINDMENTS	RESENSITISES
REPUBLICANIZING	REPUTATIONS	RERAILINGS	RESCISSIBLE	RESENSITISING
REPUBLICANS	REPUTATIVE	REREADINGS	RESCISSION	RESENSITIZE
REPUBLICATION	REPUTATIVELY	REREBRACES	RESCISSIONS	RESENSITIZED
REPUBLICATIONS	REPUTELESS	RERECORDED	RESCISSORY	RESENSITIZES
REPUBLISHED	REQUALIFIED	RERECORDING	RESCREENED	RESENSITIZING
REPUBLISHER	REQUALIFIES	REREDORTER	RESCREENING	RESENTENCE
REPUBLISHERS	REQUALIFYING	REREDORTERS	RESCRIPTED	RESENTENCED
REPUBLISHES	REQUESTERS	REREDOSSES	RESCRIPTING	RESENTENCES
REPUBLISHING	REQUESTING	REREGISTER	RESCULPTED	RESENTENCING
REPUDIABLE	REQUESTORS	REREGISTERED	RESCULPTING	RESENTFULLY
REPUDIATED	REQUICKENED	REREGISTERING	RESEALABLE	RESENTFULNESS
REPUDIATES	REQUICKENING	REREGISTERS	RESEARCHABLE	RESENTFULNESSES
REPUDIATING	REQUICKENS	REREGISTRATION	RESEARCHED	RESENTINGLY
REPUDIATION	REQUIESCAT	REREGISTRATIONS	RESEARCHER	RESENTMENT
REPUDIATIONIST	REQUIESCATS	REREGULATE	RESEARCHERS	RESENTMENTS
REPUDIATIONISTS	REQUIGHTED	REREGULATED	RESEARCHES	RESERPINES
REPUDIATIONS	REQUIGHTING	REREGULATES	RESEARCHFUL	RESERVABLE
REPUDIATÍVE	REQUIRABLE	REREGULATING	RESEARCHING	RESERVATION
REPUDIATOR	REQUIREMENT	REREGULATION	RESEARCHIST	RESERVATIONIST
REPUDIATORS	REQUIREMENTS	REREGULATIONS	RESEARCHISTS	RESERVATIONISTS
REPUGNANCE	REQUIRINGS	RERELEASED	RESEASONED	RESERVATIONS
REPUGNANCES	REQUISITELY	RERELEASES	RESEASONING	RESERVATORIES
REPUGNANCIES	REQUISITENESS	RERELEASING	RESECTABILITIES	RESERVATORY
REPUGNANCY	REQUISITENESSES	REREMINDED	RESECTABILITY	RESERVEDLY
REPUGNANTLY	REQUISITES	REREMINDING	RESECTABLE	RESERVEDNESS
REPULSIONS	REQUISITION	REREPEATED	RESECTIONAL	RESERVEDNESSES
REPULSIVELY	REQUISITIONARY	REREPEATING	RESECTIONS	RESERVICED

RESERVICES	RESILIENCE	RESKETCHING	RESOLVENTS	RESPELLING
RESERVICING	RESILIENCES	RESKILLING	RESONANCES	RESPELLINGS
RESERVISTS	RESILIENCIES	RESKILLINGS	RESONANTLY	RESPIRABILITIES
RESERVOIRED	RESILIENCY	RESMELTING	RESONATING	RESPIRABILITY
RESERVOIRING	RESILIENTLY	RESMOOTHED	RESONATION	RESPIRABLE
RESERVOIRS	RESILVERED	RESMOOTHING	RESONATIONS	RESPIRATION
RESETTABLE	RESILVERING	RESNATRONS	RESONATORS	RESPIRATIONAL
RESETTLEMENT	RESINATING	RESOCIALISATION	RESORBENCE	RESPIRATIONS
RESETTLEMENTS	RESINIFEROUS	RESOCIALISE	RESORBENCES	RESPIRATOR
RESETTLING	RESINIFICATION	RESOCIALISED	RESORCINAL	RESPIRATORS
RESHARPENED	RESINIFICATIONS	RESOCIALISES	RESORCINOL	RESPIRATORY
RESHARPENING	RESINIFIED	RESOCIALISING	RESORCINOLS	RESPIRITUALISE
RESHARPENS	RESINIFIES	RESOCIALIZATION	RESORPTION	RESPIRITUALISED
RESHINGLED	RESINIFYING	RESOCIALIZE	RESORPTIONS	RESPIRITUALISES
RESHINGLES	RESINISING	RESOCIALIZED	RESORPTIVE	RESPIRITUALIZE
RESHINGLING	RESINIZING	RESOCIALIZES	RESOUNDING	RESPIRITUALIZED
RESHIPMENT	RESINOUSLY	RESOCIALIZING	RESOUNDINGLY	RESPIRITUALIZES
RESHIPMENTS	RESINOUSNESS	RESOFTENED	RESOURCEFUL	RESPIROMETER
RESHIPPERS	RESINOUSNESSES	RESOFTENING	RESOURCEFULLY	RESPIROMETERS
RESHIPPING	RESIPISCENCE	RESOLDERED	RESOURCEFULNESS	RESPIROMETRIC
RESHOOTING	RESIPISCENCES	RESOLDERING	RESOURCELESS	RESPIROMETRIES
RESHOWERED	RESIPISCENCIES	RESOLIDIFIED	RESOURCING	RESPIROMETRY
RESHOWERING	RESIPISCENCY	RESOLIDIFIES	RESPEAKING	RESPITELESS
RESHUFFLED	RESIPISCENT	RESOLIDIFY	RESPECIFIED	RESPLENDED
RESHUFFLES	RESISTANCE	RESOLIDIFYING	RESPECIFIES	RESPLENDENCE
RESHUFFLING	RESISTANCES	RESOLUBILITIES	RESPECIFYING	RESPLENDENCES
RESIDENCES	RESISTANTS	RESOLUBILITY	RESPECTABILISE	RESPLENDENCIES
RESIDENCIES	RESISTENTS	RESOLUBLENESS	RESPECTABILISED	RESPLENDENCY
RESIDENTER	RESISTIBILITIES	RESOLUBLENESSES	RESPECTABILISES	RESPLENDENT
RESIDENTERS	RESISTIBILITY	RESOLUTELY	RESPECTABILITY	RESPLENDENTLY
RESIDENTIAL	RESISTIBLE	RESOLUTENESS	RESPECTABILIZE	RESPLENDING
RESIDENTIALLY	RESISTIBLY	RESOLUTENESSES	RESPECTABILIZED	RESPLICING
RESIDENTIARIES	RESISTINGLY	RESOLUTEST	RESPECTABILIZES	RESPLITTING
RESIDENTIARY	RESISTIVELY	RESOLUTION	RESPECTABLE	RESPONDENCE
RESIDENTSHIP	RESISTIVENESS	RESOLUTIONER	RESPECTABLENESS	RESPONDENCES
RESIDENTSHIPS	RESISTIVENESSES	RESOLUTIONERS	RESPECTABLES	RESPONDENCIES
RESIDUALLY	RESISTIVITIES	RESOLUTIONIST	RESPECTABLY	RESPONDENCY
RESIGHTING	RESISTIVITY	RESOLUTIONISTS	RESPECTANT	RESPONDENT
RESIGNATION	RESISTLESS	RESOLUTIONS	RESPECTERS	RESPONDENTIA
RESIGNATIONS	RESISTLESSLY	RESOLUTIVE	RESPECTFUL	RESPONDENTIAS
RESIGNEDLY	RESISTLESSNESS	RESOLVABILITIES	RESPECTFULLY	RESPONDENTS
RESIGNEDNESS	RESITTINGS	RESOLVABILITY	RESPECTFULNESS	RESPONDERS
RESIGNEDNESSES	RESITUATED	RESOLVABLE	RESPECTING	RESPONDING
RESIGNMENT	RESITUATES	RESOLVABLENESS	RESPECTIVE	RESPONSELESS
RESIGNMENTS	RESITUATING	RESOLVEDLY	RESPECTIVELY	RESPONSERS
RESILEMENT	RESKETCHED	RESOLVEDNESS	RESPECTIVENESS	RESPONSIBILITY
RESILEMENTS	RESKETCHES	RESOLVEDNESSES	RESPECTLESS	RESPONSIBLE

R

RESPONSIBLENESS	RESTAURATEURS	RESTORATIVELY	RESTRUCTURING	RESURRECTOR
RESPONSIBLY	RESTAURATION	RESTORATIVES	RESTRUCTURINGS	RESURRECTORS
RESPONSIONS	RESTAURATIONS	RESTRAINABLE	RESTUDYING	RESURRECTS
RESPONSIVE	RESTEMMING	RESTRAINED	RESTUFFING	RESURVEYED
RESPONSIVELY	RESTFULLER	RESTRAINEDLY	RESTUMPING	RESURVEYING
RESPONSIVENESS	RESTFULLEST	RESTRAINEDNESS	RESUBJECTED	RESUSCITABLE
RESPONSORIAL	RESTFULNESS	RESTRAINER	RESUBJECTING	RESUSCITANT
RESPONSORIALS	RESTFULNESSES	RESTRAINERS	RESUBJECTS	RESUSCITANTS
RESPONSORIES	RESTHARROW	RESTRAINING	RESUBMISSION	RESUSCITATE
RESPONSORS	RESTHARROWS	RESTRAININGS	RESUBMISSIONS	RESUSCITATED
RESPONSORY	RESTIMULATE	RESTRAINTS	RESUBMITTED	RESUSCITATES
RESPONSUMS	RESTIMULATED	RESTRENGTHEN	RESUBMITTING	RESUSCITATING
RESPOOLING	RESTIMULATES	RESTRENGTHENED	RESULTANTLY	RESUSCITATION
RESPOTTING	RESTIMULATING	RESTRENGTHENING	RESULTANTS	RESUSCITATIONS
RESPRAYING	RESTIMULATION	RESTRENGTHENS	RESULTATIVE	RESUSCITATIVE
RESPREADING	RESTIMULATIONS	RESTRESSED	RESULTLESS	RESUSCITATOR
RESPRINGING	RESTITCHED	RESTRESSES	RESULTLESSNESS	RESUSCITATORS
RESPROUTED	RESTITCHES	RESTRESSING	RESUMMONED	RESUSPENDED
RESPROUTING	RESTITCHING	RESTRETCHED	RESUMMONING	RESUSPENDING
RESSALDARS	RESTITUTED	RESTRETCHES	RESUMPTION	RESUSPENDS
RESSENTIMENT	RESTITUTES	RESTRETCHING	RESUMPTIONS	RESVERATROL
RESSENTIMENTS	RESTITUTING	RESTRICKEN	RESUMPTIVE	RESVERATROLS
RESTABILISE	RESTITUTION	RESTRICTED	RESUMPTIVELY	RESWALLOWED
RESTABILISED	RESTITUTIONISM	RESTRICTEDLY	RESUPINATE	RESWALLOWING
RESTABILISES	RESTITUTIONISMS	RESTRICTEDNESS	RESUPINATION	RESWALLOWS
RESTABILISING	RESTITUTIONIST	RESTRICTING	RESUPINATIONS	RESYNCHRONISE
RESTABILIZE	RESTITUTIONISTS	RESTRICTION	RESUPPLIED	RESYNCHRONISED
RESTABILIZED	RESTITUTIONS	RESTRICTIONISM	RESUPPLIES	RESYNCHRONISES
RESTABILIZES	RESTITUTIVE	RESTRICTIONISMS	RESUPPLYING	RESYNCHRONISING
RESTABILIZING	RESTITUTOR	RESTRICTIONIST	RESURFACED	RESYNCHRONIZE
RESTABLING	RESTITUTORS	RESTRICTIONISTS	RESURFACER	RESYNCHRONIZED
RESTACKING	RESTITUTORY	RESTRICTIONS	RESURFACERS	RESYNCHRONIZES
RESTAFFING	RESTIVENESS	RESTRICTIVE	RESURFACES	RESYNCHRONIZING
RESTAMPING	RESTIVENESSES	RESTRICTIVELY	RESURFACING	RESYNTHESES
RESTARTABLE	RESTLESSLY	RESTRICTIVENESS	RESURGENCE	RESYNTHESIS
RESTARTERS	RESTLESSNESS	RESTRICTIVES	RESURGENCES	RESYNTHESISE
RESTARTING	RESTLESSNESSES	RESTRIKING	RESURRECTED	RESYNTHESISED
RESTATEMENT	RESTOCKING	RESTRINGED	RESURRECTING	RESYNTHESISES
RESTATEMENTS	RESTORABLE	RESTRINGEING	RESURRECTION	RESYNTHESISING
RESTATIONED	RESTORABLENESS	RESTRINGENT	RESURRECTIONAL	RESYNTHESIZE
RESTATIONING	RESTORATION	RESTRINGENTS	RESURRECTIONARY	RESYNTHESIZED
RESTATIONS	RESTORATIONISM	RESTRINGES	RESURRECTIONISE	RESYNTHESIZES
RESTAURANT	RESTORATIONISMS	RESTRINGING	RESURRECTIONISM	RESYNTHESIZING
RESTAURANTEUR	RESTORATIONIST	RESTRIVING	RESURRECTIONIST	RESYSTEMATISE
RESTAURANTEURS	RESTORATIONISTS	RESTRUCTURE	RESURRECTIONIZE	RESYSTEMATISED
RESTAURANTS	RESTORATIONS	RESTRUCTURED	RESURRECTIONS	RESYSTEMATISES
RESTAURATEUR	RESTORATIVE	RESTRUCTURES	RESURRECTIVE	RESYSTEMATISING

RESYSTEMATIZE	RETENTIVES	RETINOSCOPIC	RETRANSFERRED	RETRIEVERS
RESYSTEMATIZED	RETENTIVITIES	RETINOSCOPIES	RETRANSFERRING	RETRIEVING
RESYSTEMATIZES	RETENTIVITY	RETINOSCOPIST	RETRANSFERS	RETRIEVINGS
RESYSTEMATIZING	RETESTIFIED	RETINOSCOPISTS	RETRANSFORM	RETRIMMING
RETACKLING	RETESTIFIES	RETINOSCOPY	RETRANSFORMED	RETROACTED
RETAILINGS	RETESTIFYING	RETINOSPORA	RETRANSFORMING	RETROACTING
RETAILMENT	RETEXTURED	RETINOSPORAS	RETRANSFORMS	RETROACTION
RETAILMENTS	RETEXTURES	RETINOTECTAL	RETRANSLATE	RETROACTIONS
RETAILORED	RETEXTURING	RETIRACIES	RETRANSLATED	RETROACTIVE
RETAILORING	RETHINKERS	RETIREDNESS	RETRANSLATES	RETROACTIVELY
RETAINABLE	RETHINKING	RETIREDNESSES	RETRANSLATING	RETROACTIVENESS
RETAINERSHIP	RETHREADED	RETIREMENT	RETRANSLATION	RETROACTIVITIES
RETAINERSHIPS	RETHREADING	RETIREMENTS	RETRANSLATIONS	RETROACTIVITY
RETAINMENT	RETICELLAS	RETIRINGLY	RETRANSMISSION	RETROBULBAR
RETAINMENTS	RETICENCES	RETIRINGNESS	RETRANSMISSIONS	RETROCEDED
RETALIATED	RETICENCIES	RETIRINGNESSES	RETRANSMIT	RETROCEDENCE
RETALIATES	RETICENTLY	RETORSIONS	RETRANSMITS	RETROCEDENCES
RETALIATING	RETICULARLY	RETORTIONS	RETRANSMITTED	RETROCEDENT
RETALIATION	RETICULARY	RETOTALING	RETRANSMITTING	RETROCEDES
RETALIATIONIST	RETICULATE	RETOTALLED	RETREADING	RETROCEDING
RETALIATIONISTS	RETICULATED	RETOTALLING	RETREATANT	RETROCESSION
RETALIATIONS	RETICULATELY	RETOUCHABLE	RETREATANTS	RETROCESSIONS
RETALIATIVE	RETICULATES	RETOUCHERS	RETREATERS	RETROCESSIVE
RETALIATOR	RETICULATING	RETOUCHING	RETREATING	RETROCHOIR
RETALIATORS	RETICULATION	RETRACEABLE	RETRENCHABLE	RETROCHOIRS
RETALIATORY	RETICULATIONS	RETRACEMENT	RETRENCHED	RETROCOGNITION
RETALLYING	RETICULOCYTE	RETRACEMENTS	RETRENCHES	RETROCOGNITIONS
RETARDANTS	RETICULOCYTES	RETRACKING	RETRENCHING	RETRODICTED
RETARDATES	RETICULUMS	RETRACTABILITY	RETRENCHMENT	RETRODICTING
RETARDATION	RETIGHTENED	RETRACTABLE	RETRENCHMENTS	RETRODICTION
RETARDATIONS	RETIGHTENING	RETRACTATION	RETRIBUTED	RETRODICTIONS
RETARDATIVE	RETIGHTENS	RETRACTATIONS	RETRIBUTES	RETRODICTIVE
RETARDATORY	RETINACULA	RETRACTIBILITY	RETRIBUTING	RETRODICTS
RETARDMENT	RETINACULAR	RETRACTIBLE	RETRIBUTION	RETROFIRED
RETARDMENTS	RETINACULUM	RETRACTILE	RETRIBUTIONS	RETROFIRES
RETARGETED	RETINALITE	RETRACTILITIES	RETRIBUTIVE	RETROFIRING
RETARGETING	RETINALITES	RETRACTILITY	RETRIBUTIVELY	RETROFITTED
RETEACHING	RETINISPORA	RETRACTING	RETRIBUTOR	RETROFITTING
RETELLINGS	RETINISPORAS	RETRACTION	RETRIBUTORS	RETROFITTINGS
RETEMPERED	RETINITIDES	RETRACTIONS	RETRIBUTORY	RETROFLECTED
RETEMPERING	RETINITISES	RETRACTIVE	RETRIEVABILITY	RETROFLECTION
RETENTIONIST	RETINOBLASTOMA	RETRACTIVELY	RETRIEVABLE	RETROFLECTIONS
RETENTIONISTS	RETINOBLASTOMAS	RETRACTORS	RETRIEVABLENESS	RETROFLEXED
RETENTIONS	RETINOPATHIES	RETRAINABLE	RETRIEVABLY	RETROFLEXES
RETENTIVELY	RETINOPATHY	RETRAINEES	RETRIEVALS	RETROFLEXING
RETENTIVENESS	RETINOSCOPE	RETRAINING	RETRIEVEMENT	RETROFLEXION
RETENTIVENESSES	RETINOSCOPES	RETRANSFER	RETRIEVEMENTS	RETROFLEXIONS

R

RETROGRADATION

RETROGRADATION
RETROGRADATIONS
RETROGRADE
RETROGRADED
RETROGRADELY
RETROGRADES
RETROGRADING
RETROGRESS
RETROGRESSED
RETROGRESSES
RETROGRESSING
RETROGRESSION
RETROGRESSIONAL
RETROGRESSIONS
RETROGRESSIVE
RETROGRESSIVELY
RETROJECTED
RETROJECTING
RETROJECTION
RETROJECTIONS
RETROJECTS
RETROLENTAL
RETROMINGENCIES
RETROMINGENCY
RETROMINGENT
RETROMINGENTS
RETROPACKS
RETROPERITONEAL
RETROPHILIA
RETROPHILIAC
RETROPHILIACS
RETROPHILIAS
RETROPULSION
RETROPULSIONS
RETROPULSIVE
RETROREFLECTION
RETROREFLECTIVE
RETROREFLECTOR
RETROREFLECTORS
RETROROCKET
RETROROCKETS
RETRORSELY
RETROSEXUAL
RETROSEXUALS
RETROSPECT
RETROSPECTED
RETROSPECTING

RETROSPECTION
RETROSPECTIONS
RETROSPECTIVE
RETROSPECTIVELY
RETROSPECTIVES
RETROSPECTS
RETROUSSAGE
RETROUSSAGES
RETROVERSE
RETROVERSION
RETROVERSIONS
RETROVERTED
RETROVERTING
RETROVERTS
RETROVIRAL
RETROVIRUS
RETROVIRUSES
RETURNABILITIES
RETURNABILITY
RETURNABLE
RETURNABLES
RETURNLESS
RETWISTING
REUNIFICATION
REUNIFICATIONS
REUNIFYING
REUNIONISM
REUNIONISMS
REUNIONIST
REUNIONISTIC
REUNIONISTS
REUNITABLE
REUPHOLSTER
REUPHOLSTERED
REUPHOLSTERING
REUPHOLSTERS
REUSABILITIES
REUSABILITY
REUTILISATION
REUTILISATIONS
REUTILISED
REUTILISES
REUTILISING
REUTILIZATION
REUTILIZATIONS
REUTILIZED
REUTILIZES

REUTILIZING
REUTTERING
REVACCINATE
REVACCINATED
REVACCINATES
REVACCINATING
REVACCINATION
REVACCINATIONS
REVALENTAS
REVALIDATE
REVALIDATED
REVALIDATES
REVALIDATING
REVALIDATION
REVALIDATIONS
REVALORISATION
REVALORISATIONS
REVALORISE
REVALORISED
REVALORISES
REVALORISING
REVALORIZATION
REVALORIZATIONS
REVALORIZE
REVALORIZED
REVALORIZES
REVALORIZING
REVALUATED
REVALUATES
REVALUATING
REVALUATION
REVALUATIONS
REVAMPINGS
REVANCHISM
REVANCHISMS
REVANCHIST
REVANCHISTS
REVARNISHED
REVARNISHES
REVARNISHING
REVEALABILITIES
REVEALABILITY
REVEALABLE
REVEALINGLY
REVEALINGNESS
REVEALINGNESSES
REVEALINGS

REVEALMENT
REVEALMENTS
REVEGETATE
REVEGETATED
REVEGETATES
REVEGETATING
REVEGETATION
REVEGETATIONS
REVELATION
REVELATIONAL
REVELATIONIST
REVELATIONISTS
REVELATIONS
REVELATIVE
REVELATORS
REVELATORY
REVELLINGS
REVELMENTS
REVENDICATE
REVENDICATED
REVENDICATES
REVENDICATING
REVENDICATION
REVENDICATIONS
REVENGEFUL
REVENGEFULLY
REVENGEFULNESS
REVENGELESS
REVENGEMENT
REVENGEMENTS
REVENGINGLY
REVENGINGS
REVERBERANT
REVERBERANTLY
REVERBERATE
REVERBERATED
REVERBERATES
REVERBERATING
REVERBERATION
REVERBERATIONS
REVERBERATIVE
REVERBERATOR
REVERBERATORIES
REVERBERATORS
REVERBERATORY
REVERENCED
REVERENCER

REVERENCERS
REVERENCES
REVERENCING
REVERENTIAL
REVERENTIALLY
REVERENTLY
REVERENTNESS
REVERENTNESSES
REVERIFIED
REVERIFIES
REVERIFYING
REVERSEDLY
REVERSELESS
REVERSIBILITIES
REVERSIBILITY
REVERSIBLE
REVERSIBLES
REVERSIBLY
REVERSINGS
REVERSIONAL
REVERSIONALLY
REVERSIONARIES
REVERSIONARY
REVERSIONER
REVERSIONERS
REVERSIONS
REVERSISES
REVERTANTS
REVERTIBLE
REVESTIARIES
REVESTIARY
REVESTRIES
REVETMENTS
REVIBRATED
REVIBRATES
REVIBRATING
REVICTUALED
REVICTUALING
REVICTUALLED
REVICTUALLING
REVICTUALS
REVIEWABLE
REVILEMENT
REVILEMENTS
REVILINGLY
REVINDICATE
REVINDICATED

R

REVINDICATES	REVIVIFICATIONS	REVOLVABLY	RHAMPHOTHECAE	RHETORIZING
REVINDICATING	REVIVIFIED	REVOLVENCIES	RHAPONTICS	RHEUMATEESE
REVINDICATION	REVIVIFIES	REVOLVENCY	RHAPSODICAL	RHEUMATEESES
REVINDICATIONS	REVIVIFYING	REVOLVINGLY	RHAPSODICALLY	RHEUMATICAL
REVIOLATED	REVIVINGLY	REVOLVINGS	RHAPSODIES	RHEUMATICALLY
REVIOLATES	REVIVISCENCE	REVULSIONARY	RHAPSODISE	RHEUMATICKY
REVIOLATING	REVIVISCENCES	REVULSIONS	RHAPSODISED	RHEUMATICS
REVISIONAL	REVIVISCENCIES	REVULSIVELY	RHAPSODISES	RHEUMATISE
REVISIONARY	REVIVISCENCY	REVULSIVES	RHAPSODISING	RHEUMATISES
REVISIONISM	REVIVISCENT	REWAKENING	RHAPSODIST	RHEUMATISM
REVISIONISMS	REVOCABILITIES	REWARDABLE	RHAPSODISTIC	RHEUMATISMAL
REVISIONIST	REVOCABILITY	REWARDABLENESS	RHAPSODISTS	RHEUMATISMS
REVISIONISTS	REVOCABLENESS	REWARDINGLY	RHAPSODIZE	RHEUMATIZE
REVISITANT	REVOCABLENESSES	REWARDLESS	RHAPSODIZED	RHEUMATIZES
REVISITANTS	REVOCATION	REWATERING	RHAPSODIZES	RHEUMATOID
REVISITATION	REVOCATIONS	REWEIGHING	RHAPSODIZING	RHEUMATOIDALLY
REVISITATIONS	REVOCATORY	REWIDENING	RHEOCHORDS	RHEUMATOLOGICAL
REVISITING	REVOKABILITIES	REWILDINGS	RHEOLOGICAL	RHEUMATOLOGIES
REVISUALISATION	REVOKABILITY	REWORDINGS	RHEOLOGICALLY	RHEUMATOLOGIST
REVISUALIZATION	REVOKEMENT	REWORKINGS	RHEOLOGIES	RHEUMATOLOGISTS
REVITALISATION	REVOKEMENTS	REWRAPPING	RHEOLOGIST	RHEUMATOLOGY
REVITALISATIONS	REVOLTINGLY	RHABDOCOELE	RHEOLOGISTS	RHIGOLENES
REVITALISE	REVOLUTION	RHABDOCOELES	RHEOMETERS	RHINENCEPHALA
REVITALISED	REVOLUTIONAL	RHABDOLITH	RHEOMETRIC	RHINENCEPHALIC
REVITALISES	REVOLUTIONARIES	RHABDOLITHS	RHEOMETRICAL	RHINENCEPHALON
REVITALISING	REVOLUTIONARILY	RHABDOMANCER	RHEOMETRIES	RHINENCEPHALONS
REVITALIZATION	REVOLUTIONARY	RHABDOMANCERS	RHEOMORPHIC	RHINESTONE
REVITALIZATIONS	REVOLUTIONER	RHABDOMANCIES	RHEOMORPHISM	RHINESTONED
REVITALIZE	REVOLUTIONERS	RHABDOMANCY	RHEOMORPHISMS	RHINESTONES
REVITALIZED	REVOLUTIONISE	RHABDOMANTIST	RHEOPHILES	RHINITIDES
REVITALIZES	REVOLUTIONISED	RHABDOMANTISTS	RHEORECEPTOR	RHINITISES
REVITALIZING	REVOLUTIONISER	RHABDOMERE	RHEORECEPTORS	RHINOCERICAL
REVIVABILITIES	REVOLUTIONISERS	RHABDOMERES	RHEOSTATIC	RHINOCEROS
REVIVABILITY	REVOLUTIONISES	RHABDOMYOMA	RHEOTACTIC	RHINOCEROSES
REVIVALISM	REVOLUTIONISING	RHABDOMYOMAS	RHEOTROPES	RHINOCEROT
REVIVALISMS	REVOLUTIONISM	RHABDOMYOMATA	RHEOTROPIC	RHINOCEROTE
REVIVALIST	REVOLUTIONISMS	RHABDOSPHERE	RHEOTROPISM	RHINOCEROTES
REVIVALISTIC	REVOLUTIONIST	RHABDOSPHERES	RHEOTROPISMS	RHINOCEROTIC
REVIVALISTS	REVOLUTIONISTS	RHABDOVIRUS	RHETORICAL	RHINOLALIA
REVIVEMENT	REVOLUTIONIZE	RHABDOVIRUSES	RHETORICALLY	RHINOLALIAS
REVIVEMENTS	REVOLUTIONIZED	RHACHIDIAL	RHETORICIAN	RHINOLITHS
REVIVESCENCE	REVOLUTIONIZER	RHACHILLAS	RHETORICIANS	RHINOLOGICAL
REVIVESCENCES	REVOLUTIONIZERS	RHACHITISES	RHETORISED	RHINOLOGIES
REVIVESCENCIES	REVOLUTIONIZES	RHADAMANTHINE	RHETORISES	RHINOLOGIST
REVIVESCENCY	REVOLUTIONIZING	RHAGADIFORM	RHETORISING	RHINOLOGISTS
REVIVESCENT	REVOLUTIONS	RHAMNACEOUS	RHETORIZED	RHINOPHYMA
REVIVIFICATION	REVOLVABLE	RHAMPHOTHECA	RHETORIZES	RHINOPHYMAS

R

RHINOPLASTIC

RHINOPLASTIC	RHIZOPODOUS	RHOPALISMS	RHYTHMOPOEIA	RIDABILITIES
RHINOPLASTIES	RHIZOPUSES	RHOPALOCERAL	RHYTHMOPOEIAS	RIDABILITY
RHINOPLASTY	RHIZOSPHERE	RHOPALOCEROUS	RHYTHMUSES	RIDDLINGLY
RHINORRHAGIA	RHIZOSPHERES	RHOTACISED	RHYTIDECTOMIES	RIDERSHIPS
RHINORRHAGIAS	RHIZOTOMIES	RHOTACISES	RHYTIDECTOMY	RIDGEBACKS
RHINORRHOEA	RHODAMINES	RHOTACISING	RHYTIDOMES	RIDGELINES
RHINORRHOEAL	RHODANATES	RHOTACISMS	RIBALDRIES	RIDGELINGS
RHINORRHOEAS	RHODANISED	RHOTACISTIC	RIBATTUTAS	RIDGEPOLES
RHINOSCLEROMA	RHODANISES	RHOTACISTS	RIBAUDRIES	RIDGETREES
RHINOSCLEROMAS	RHODANISING	RHOTACIZED	RIBAVIRINS	RIDICULERS
RHINOSCLEROMATA	RHODANIZED	RHOTACIZES	RIBBONFISH	RIDICULING
RHINOSCOPE	RHODANIZES	RHOTACIZING	RIBBONFISHES	RIDICULOUS
RHINOSCOPES	RHODANIZING	RHOTICITIES	RIBBONLIKE	RIDICULOUSLY
RHINOSCOPIC	RHODOCHROSITE	RHUBARBING	RIBBONRIES	RIDICULOUSNESS
RHINOSCOPIES	RHODOCHROSITES	RHUBARBINGS	RIBBONWOOD	RIEBECKITE
RHINOSCOPY	RHODODAPHNE	RHUMBATRON	RIBBONWOODS	RIEBECKITES
RHINOTHECA	RHODODAPHNES	RHUMBATRONS	RIBGRASSES	RIFACIMENTI
RHINOTHECAE	RHODODENDRA	RHYMESTERS	RIBOFLAVIN	RIFACIMENTO
RHINOVIRUS	RHODODENDRON	RHYNCHOCOEL	RIBOFLAVINE	RIFAMPICIN
RHINOVIRUSES	RHODODENDRONS	RHYNCHOCOELS	RIBOFLAVINES	RIFAMPICINS
RHIPIDIONS	RHODOLITES	RHYNCHODONT	RIBOFLAVINS	RIFAMYCINS
RHIPIDIUMS	RHODOMONTADE	RHYNCHOPHORE	RIBONUCLEASE	RIFENESSES
RHIZANTHOUS	RHODOMONTADED	RHYNCHOPHORES	RIBONUCLEASES	RIFLEBIRDS
RHIZOCARPIC	RHODOMONTADES	RHYNCHOPHOROUS	RIBONUCLEIC	RIGAMAROLE
RHIZOCARPOUS	RHODOMONTADING	RHYPAROGRAPHER	RIBONUCLEOSIDE	RIGAMAROLES
RHIZOCARPS	RHODONITES	RHYPAROGRAPHERS	RIBONUCLEOSIDES	RIGHTABLENESS
RHIZOCAULS	RHODOPHANE	RHYPAROGRAPHIC	RIBONUCLEOTIDE	RIGHTABLENESSES
RHIZOCEPHALAN	RHODOPHANES	RHYPAROGRAPHIES	RIBONUCLEOTIDES	RIGHTENING
RHIZOCEPHALANS	RHODOPSINS	RHYPAROGRAPHY	RICERCARES	RIGHTEOUSLY
RHIZOCEPHALOUS	RHOEADINES	RHYTHMICAL	RICERCATAS	RIGHTEOUSNESS
RHIZOCTONIA	RHOICISSUS	RHYTHMICALLY	RICHNESSES	RIGHTEOUSNESSES
RHIZOCTONIAS	RHOICISSUSES	RHYTHMICITIES	RICINOLEIC	RIGHTFULLY
RHIZOGENETIC	RHOMBENCEPHALA	RHYTHMICITY	RICKETIEST	RIGHTFULNESS
RHIZOGENIC	RHOMBENCEPHALON	RHYTHMISATION	RICKETINESS	RIGHTFULNESSES
RHIZOGENOUS	RHOMBENPORPHYR	RHYTHMISATIONS	RICKETINESSES	RIGHTNESSES
RHIZOMATOUS	RHOMBENPORPHYRS	RHYTHMISED	RICKETTIER	RIGHTSIZED
RHIZOMORPH	RHOMBENPORPHYRY	RHYTHMISES	RICKETTIEST	RIGHTSIZES
RHIZOMORPHOUS	RHOMBOHEDRA	RHYTHMISING	RICKETTSIA	RIGHTSIZING
RHIZOMORPHS	RHOMBOHEDRAL	RHYTHMISTS	RICKETTSIAE	RIGHTWARDLY
RHIZOPHAGOUS	RHOMBOHEDRON	RHYTHMIZATION	RICKETTSIAL	RIGHTWARDS
RHIZOPHILOUS	RHOMBOHEDRONS	RHYTHMIZATIONS	RICKETTSIAS	RIGIDIFICATION
RHIZOPHORE	RHOMBOIDAL	RHYTHMIZED	RICKSTANDS	RIGIDIFICATIONS
RHIZOPHORES	RHOMBOIDEI	RHYTHMIZES	RICKSTICKS	RIGIDIFIED
RHIZOPLANE	RHOMBOIDES	RHYTHMIZING	RICOCHETED	RIGIDIFIES
RHIZOPLANES	RHOMBOIDEUS	RHYTHMLESS	RICOCHETING	RIGIDIFYING
RHIZOPODAN	RHOMBPORPHYRIES	RHYTHMOMETER	RICOCHETTED	RIGIDISING
RHIZOPODANS	RHOMBPORPHYRY	RHYTHMOMETERS	RICOCHETTING	RIGIDITIES

R

RIGIDIZING	RIPSNORTERS	RIVERSCAPE	ROCKETEERS	ROENTGENOSCOPES
RIGIDNESSES	RIPSNORTING	RIVERSCAPES	ROCKETRIES	ROENTGENOSCOPIC
RIGMAROLES	RIPSNORTINGLY	RIVERSIDES	ROCKFISHES	ROENTGENOSCOPY
RIGORISTIC	RISIBILITIES	RIVERWARDS	ROCKHOPPER	ROGUESHIPS
RIGOROUSLY	RISIBILITY	RIVERWEEDS	ROCKHOPPERS	ROGUISHNESS
RIGOROUSNESS	RISKINESSES	RIVERWORTHINESS	ROCKHOUNDING	ROGUISHNESSES
RIGOROUSNESSES	RISORGIMENTO	RIVERWORTHY	ROCKHOUNDINGS	ROISTERERS
RIGSDALERS	RISORGIMENTOS	RIVETINGLY	ROCKHOUNDS	ROISTERING
RIGWIDDIES	RITARDANDO	ROADABILITIES	ROCKINESSES	ROISTERINGS
RIGWOODIES	RITARDANDOS	ROADABILITY	ROCKSHAFTS	ROISTEROUS
RIJKSDAALER	RITONAVIRS	ROADBLOCKED	ROCKSLIDES	ROISTEROUSLY
RIJKSDAALERS	RITORNELLE	ROADBLOCKING	ROCKSTEADIES	ROLLCOLLAR
RIJSTAFELS	RITORNELLES	ROADBLOCKS	ROCKSTEADY	ROLLCOLLARS
RIJSTTAFEL	RITORNELLI	ROADCRAFTS	ROCKWATERS	ROLLERBALL
RIJSTTAFELS	RITORNELLO	ROADHEADER	RODENTICIDE	ROLLERBALLS
RIMINESSES	RITORNELLOS	ROADHEADERS	RODENTICIDES	ROLLERBLADE
RIMOSITIES	RITORNELLS	ROADHOLDING	RODFISHERS	ROLLERBLADED
RINDERPEST	RITOURNELLE	ROADHOLDINGS	RODFISHING	ROLLERBLADER
RINDERPESTS	RITOURNELLES	ROADHOUSES	RODFISHINGS	ROLLERBLADERS
RINFORZANDO	RITUALISATION	ROADROLLER	RODGERSIAS	ROLLERBLADES
RINGBARKED	RITUALISATIONS	ROADROLLERS	RODOMONTADE	ROLLERBLADING
RINGBARKING	RITUALISED	ROADRUNNER	RODOMONTADED	ROLLERBLADINGS
RINGHALSES	RITUALISES	ROADRUNNERS	RODOMONTADER	ROLLERCOASTER
RINGLEADER	RITUALISING	ROADSTEADS	RODOMONTADERS	ROLLERCOASTERED
RINGLEADERS	RITUALISMS	ROADWORTHIES	RODOMONTADES	ROLLERCOASTERS
RINGMASTER	RITUALISTIC	ROADWORTHINESS	RODOMONTADING	ROLLICKING
RINGMASTERS	RITUALISTICALLY	ROADWORTHY	ROENTGENISATION	ROLLICKINGS
RINGSIDERS	RITUALISTS	ROBERDSMAN	ROENTGENISE	ROLLOCKING
RINGSTANDS	RITUALIZATION	ROBERDSMEN	ROENTGENISED	ROLLOCKINGS
RINGSTRAKED	RITUALIZATIONS	ROBERTSMAN	ROENTGENISES	ROMANCICAL
RINGTOSSES	RITUALIZED	ROBERTSMEN	ROENTGENISING	ROMANCINGS
RINKHALSES	RITUALIZES	ROBORATING	ROENTGENIZATION	ROMANESCOS
RINSABILITIES	RITUALIZING	ROBOTICALLY	ROENTGENIZE	ROMANICITE
RINSABILITY	RITUXIMABS	ROBOTISATION	ROENTGENIZED	ROMANICITES
RINSIBILITIES	RITZINESSES	ROBOTISATIONS	ROENTGENIZES	ROMANISATION
RINSIBILITY	RIVALESSES	ROBOTISING	ROENTGENIZING	ROMANISATIONS
RINTHEREOUT	RIVALISING	ROBOTIZATION	ROENTGENOGRAM	ROMANISING
RINTHEREOUTS	RIVALITIES	ROBOTIZATIONS	ROENTGENOGRAMS	ROMANIZATION
RIOTOUSNESS	RIVALIZING	ROBOTIZING	ROENTGENOGRAPH	ROMANIZATIONS
RIOTOUSNESSES	RIVALSHIPS	ROBUSTIOUS	ROENTGENOGRAPHS	ROMANIZING
RIPENESSES	RIVERBANKS	ROBUSTIOUSLY	ROENTGENOGRAPHY	ROMANTICAL
RIPIDOLITE	RIVERBOATS	ROBUSTIOUSNESS	ROENTGENOLOGIC	ROMANTICALITIES
RIPIDOLITES	RIVERCRAFT	ROBUSTNESS	ROENTGENOLOGIES	ROMANTICALITY
RIPIENISTS	RIVERCRAFTS	ROBUSTNESSES	ROENTGENOLOGIST	ROMANTICALLY
RIPPLINGLY	RIVERFRONT	ROCAMBOLES	ROENTGENOLOGY	ROMANTICISATION
RIPRAPPING	RIVERFRONTS	ROCKABILLIES	ROENTGENOPAQUE	ROMANTICISE
RIPSNORTER	RIVERHEADS	ROCKABILLY	ROENTGENOSCOPE	ROMANTICISED

R

ROMANTICISES	ROOFSCAPES	ROTAVATORS	ROUGHHOUSED	ROUTEMARCH
ROMANTICISING	ROOMINESSES	ROTAVIRUSES	ROUGHHOUSES	ROUTEMARCHED
ROMANTICISM	ROOTEDNESS	ROTGRASSES	ROUGHHOUSING	ROUTEMARCHES
ROMANTICISMS	ROOTEDNESSES	ROTIFERANS	ROUGHNECKED	ROUTEMARCHING
ROMANTICIST	ROOTINESSES	ROTIFEROUS	ROUGHNECKING	ROUTINEERS
ROMANTICISTS	ROOTLESSNESS	ROTISSERIE	ROUGHNECKS	ROUTINISATION
ROMANTICIZATION	ROOTLESSNESSES	ROTISSERIES	ROUGHNESSES	ROUTINISATIONS
ROMANTICIZE	ROOTSERVER	ROTOGRAPHED	ROUGHRIDER	ROUTINISED
ROMANTICIZED	ROOTSERVERS	ROTOGRAPHING	ROUGHRIDERS	ROUTINISES
ROMANTICIZES	ROOTSINESS	ROTOGRAPHS	ROULETTING	ROUTINISING
ROMANTICIZING	ROOTSINESSES	ROTOGRAVURE	ROUNCEVALS	ROUTINISMS
ROMELDALES	ROOTSTALKS	ROTOGRAVURES	ROUNDABOUT	ROUTINISTS
ROMPISHNESS	ROOTSTOCKS	ROTORCRAFT	ROUNDABOUTATION	ROUTINIZATION
ROMPISHNESSES	ROPEDANCER	ROTORCRAFTS	ROUNDABOUTED	ROUTINIZATIONS
RONDOLETTO	ROPEDANCERS	ROTOSCOPED	ROUNDABOUTEDLY	ROUTINIZED
RONDOLETTOS	ROPEDANCING	ROTOSCOPES	ROUNDABOUTILITY	ROUTINIZES
RONTGENISATION	ROPEDANCINGS	ROTOSCOPING	ROUNDABOUTING	ROUTINIZING
RONTGENISATIONS	ROPEWALKER	ROTOTILLED	ROUNDABOUTLY	ROWANBERRIES
RONTGENISE	ROPEWALKERS	ROTOTILLER	ROUNDABOUTNESS	ROWANBERRY
RONTGENISED	ROPINESSES	ROTOTILLERS	ROUNDABOUTS	ROWDINESSES
RONTGENISES	ROQUELAURE	ROTOTILLING	ROUNDARCHED	ROYALISING
RONTGENISING	ROQUELAURES	ROTOVATING	ROUNDBALLS	ROYALISTIC
RONTGENIZATION	ROSANILINE	ROTOVATORS	ROUNDEDNESS	ROYALIZING
RONTGENIZATIONS	ROSANILINES	ROTTENNESS	ROUNDEDNESSES	ROYALMASTS
RONTGENIZE	ROSANILINS	ROTTENNESSES	ROUNDELAYS	ROYSTERERS
RONTGENIZED	ROSEBUSHES	ROTTENSTONE	ROUNDHANDS	ROYSTERING
RONTGENIZES	ROSEFINCHES	ROTTENSTONED	ROUNDHEADED	ROYSTEROUS
RONTGENIZING	ROSEFISHES	ROTTENSTONES	ROUNDHEADEDNESS	RUBBERIEST
RONTGENOGRAM	ROSEMALING	ROTTENSTONING	ROUNDHEELS	RUBBERISED
RONTGENOGRAMS	ROSEMALINGS	ROTTWEILER	ROUNDHOUSE	RUBBERISES
RONTGENOGRAPH	ROSEMARIES	ROTTWEILERS	ROUNDHOUSES	RUBBERISING
RONTGENOGRAPHS	ROSETTINGS	ROTUNDITIES	ROUNDNESSES	RUBBERIZED
RONTGENOGRAPHY	ROSEWATERS	ROTUNDNESS	ROUNDTABLE	RUBBERIZES
RONTGENOLOGICAL	ROSINESSES	ROTUNDNESSES	ROUNDTABLES	RUBBERIZING
RONTGENOLOGIES	ROSINWEEDS	ROUGHBACKS	ROUNDTRIPPING	RUBBERLIKE
RONTGENOLOGIST	ROSMARINES	ROUGHCASTED	ROUNDTRIPPINGS	RUBBERNECK
RONTGENOLOGISTS	ROSTELLATE	ROUGHCASTER	ROUNDTRIPS	RUBBERNECKED
RONTGENOLOGY	ROSTELLUMS	ROUGHCASTERS	ROUNDWOODS	RUBBERNECKER
RONTGENOPAQUE	ROSTERINGS	ROUGHCASTING	ROUNDWORMS	RUBBERNECKERS
RONTGENOSCOPE	ROSTROCARINATE	ROUGHCASTS	ROUSEABOUT	RUBBERNECKING
RONTGENOSCOPES	ROSTROCARINATES	ROUGHDRIED	ROUSEABOUTS	RUBBERNECKS
RONTGENOSCOPIC	ROTACHUTES	ROUGHDRIES	ROUSEDNESS	RUBBERWEAR
RONTGENOSCOPIES	ROTAMETERS	ROUGHDRYING	ROUSEDNESSES	RUBBERWEARS
RONTGENOSCOPY	ROTAPLANES	ROUGHENING	ROUSEMENTS	RUBBISHING
RONTGENOTHERAPY	ROTATIONAL	ROUGHHEWED	ROUSSETTES	RUBBLEWORK
ROOFLESSNESS	ROTATIVELY	ROUGHHEWING	ROUSTABOUT	RUBBLEWORKS
ROOFLESSNESSES	ROTAVATING	ROUGHHOUSE	ROUSTABOUTS	RUBEFACIENT

R

RUBEFACIENTS
RUBEFACTION
RUBEFACTIONS
RUBELLITES
RUBESCENCE
RUBESCENCES
RUBIACEOUS
RUBICELLES
RUBICONING
RUBICUNDITIES
RUBICUNDITY
RUBIGINOSE
RUBIGINOUS
RUBRICALLY
RUBRICATED
RUBRICATES
RUBRICATING
RUBRICATION
RUBRICATIONS
RUBRICATOR
RUBRICATORS
RUBRICIANS
RUBYTHROAT
RUBYTHROATS
RUCTATIONS
RUDBECKIAS
RUDDERHEAD
RUDDERHEADS
RUDDERLESS
RUDDERPOST
RUDDERPOSTS
RUDDERSTOCK
RUDDERSTOCKS
RUDDINESSES

RUDENESSES
RUDIMENTAL
RUDIMENTALLY
RUDIMENTARILY
RUDIMENTARINESS
RUDIMENTARY
RUEFULNESS
RUEFULNESSES
RUFESCENCE
RUFESCENCES
RUFFIANING
RUFFIANISH
RUFFIANISM
RUFFIANISMS
RUGGEDISATION
RUGGEDISATIONS
RUGGEDISED
RUGGEDISES
RUGGEDISING
RUGGEDIZATION
RUGGEDIZATIONS
RUGGEDIZED
RUGGEDIZES
RUGGEDIZING
RUGGEDNESS
RUGGEDNESSES
RUGOSITIES
RUINATIONS
RUINOUSNESS
RUINOUSNESSES
RULERSHIPS
RUMBLEDETHUMP
RUMBLEDETHUMPS
RUMBLEGUMPTION

RUMBLEGUMPTIONS
RUMBLINGLY
RUMBULLION
RUMBULLIONS
RUMBUSTICAL
RUMBUSTIOUS
RUMBUSTIOUSLY
RUMBUSTIOUSNESS
RUMELGUMPTION
RUMELGUMPTIONS
RUMFUSTIAN
RUMFUSTIANS
RUMGUMPTION
RUMGUMPTIONS
RUMINANTLY
RUMINATING
RUMINATINGLY
RUMINATION
RUMINATIONS
RUMINATIVE
RUMINATIVELY
RUMINATORS
RUMLEGUMPTION
RUMLEGUMPTIONS
RUMMELGUMPTION
RUMMELGUMPTIONS
RUMMINESSES
RUMMLEGUMPTION
RUMMLEGUMPTIONS
RUMORMONGER
RUMORMONGERING
RUMORMONGERINGS
RUMORMONGERS
RUMRUNNERS

RUNAROUNDS
RUNECRAFTS
RUNNINESSES
RUNTINESSES
RUPESTRIAN
RUPICOLINE
RUPICOLOUS
RUPTURABLE
RUPTUREWORT
RUPTUREWORTS
RURALISATION
RURALISATIONS
RURALISING
RURALITIES
RURALIZATION
RURALIZATIONS
RURALIZING
RURALNESSES
RURIDECANAL
RUSHINESSES
RUSHLIGHTS
RUSSETINGS
RUSSETTING
RUSSETTINGS
RUSSIFYING
RUSTBUCKET
RUSTICALLY
RUSTICATED
RUSTICATES
RUSTICATING
RUSTICATINGS
RUSTICATION
RUSTICATIONS
RUSTICATOR

RUSTICATORS
RUSTICISED
RUSTICISES
RUSTICISING
RUSTICISMS
RUSTICITIES
RUSTICIZED
RUSTICIZES
RUSTICIZING
RUSTICWORK
RUSTICWORKS
RUSTINESSES
RUSTLINGLY
RUSTPROOFED
RUSTPROOFING
RUSTPROOFINGS
RUSTPROOFS
RUTHENIOUS
RUTHENIUMS
RUTHERFORD
RUTHERFORDIUM
RUTHERFORDIUMS
RUTHERFORDS
RUTHFULNESS
RUTHFULNESSES
RUTHLESSLY
RUTHLESSNESS
RUTHLESSNESSES
RUTTINESSES
RUTTISHNESS
RUTTISHNESSES
RYBAUDRYES
RYEGRASSES

R

S

SABADILLAS	SACCHARINELY	SACHEMDOMS	SACRILEGIOUSLY	SAFEGUARDS
SABBATARIAN	SACCHARINES	SACHEMSHIP	SACRILEGIST	SAFEKEEPING
SABBATICAL	SACCHARINITIES	SACHEMSHIPS	SACRILEGISTS	SAFEKEEPINGS
SABBATICALS	SACCHARINITY	SACKCLOTHS	SACRISTANS	SAFELIGHTS
SABBATISED	SACCHARINS	SACRALGIAS	SACRISTIES	SAFENESSES
SABBATISES	SACCHARISATION	SACRALISATION	SACROCOCCYGEAL	SAFFLOWERS
SABBATISING	SACCHARISATIONS	SACRALISATIONS	SACROCOSTAL	SAFRANINES
SABBATISMS	SACCHARISE	SACRALISED	SACROCOSTALS	SAGACIOUSLY
SABBATIZED	SACCHARISED	SACRALISES	SACROILIAC	SAGACIOUSNESS
SABBATIZES	SACCHARISES	SACRALISING	SACROILIACS	SAGACIOUSNESSES
SABBATIZING	SACCHARISING	SACRALITIES	SACROILIITIS	SAGACITIES
SABERMETRICIAN	SACCHARIZATION	SACRALIZATION	SACROILIITISES	SAGANASHES
SABERMETRICIANS	SACCHARIZATIONS	SACRALIZATIONS	SACROSANCT	SAGAPENUMS
SABERMETRICS	SACCHARIZE	SACRALIZED	SACROSANCTITIES	SAGEBRUSHES
SABLEFISHES	SACCHARIZED	SACRALIZES	SACROSANCTITY	SAGENESSES
SABOTAGING	SACCHARIZES	SACRALIZING	SACROSANCTNESS	SAGINATING
SABRETACHE	SACCHARIZING	SACRAMENTAL	SADDLEBACK	SAGINATION
SABRETACHES	SACCHAROID	SACRAMENTALISM	SADDLEBACKED	SAGINATIONS
SABREWINGS	SACCHAROIDAL	SACRAMENTALISMS	SADDLEBACKS	SAGITTALLY
SABULOSITIES	SACCHAROIDS	SACRAMENTALIST	SADDLEBAGS	SAGITTARIES
SABULOSITY	SACCHAROMETER	SACRAMENTALISTS	SADDLEBILL	SAGITTIFORM
SABURRATION	SACCHAROMETERS	SACRAMENTALITY	SADDLEBILLS	SAILBOARDED
SABURRATIONS	SACCHAROMYCES	SACRAMENTALLY	SADDLEBOWS	SAILBOARDER
SACAHUISTA	SACCHAROMYCETES	SACRAMENTALNESS	SADDLEBRED	SAILBOARDERS
SACAHUISTAS	SACCHAROSE	SACRAMENTS	SADDLEBREDS	SAILBOARDING
SACAHUISTE	SACCHAROSES	SACRAMENTARIAN	SADDLECLOTH	SAILBOARDINGS
SACAHUISTES	SACCHARUMS	SACRAMENTARIANS	SADDLECLOTHS	SAILBOARDS
SACCADICALLY	SACCULATED	SACRAMENTARIES	SADDLELESS	SAILBOATER
SACCHARASE	SACCULATION	SACRAMENTARY	SADDLERIES	SAILBOATERS
SACCHARASES	SACCULATIONS	SACRAMENTED	SADDLEROOM	SAILBOATING
SACCHARATE	SACCULIFORM	SACRAMENTING	SADDLEROOMS	SAILBOATINGS
SACCHARATED	SACERDOTAL	SACRAMENTS	SADDLETREE	SAILCLOTHS
SACCHARATES	SACERDOTALISE	SACREDNESS	SADDLETREES	SAILFISHES
SACCHARIDE	SACERDOTALISED	SACREDNESSES	SADISTICALLY	SAILMAKERS
SACCHARIDES	SACERDOTALISES	SACRIFICEABLE	SADOMASOCHISM	SAILMAKING
SACCHARIFEROUS	SACERDOTALISING	SACRIFICED	SADOMASOCHISMS	SAILMAKINGS
SACCHARIFIED	SACERDOTALISM	SACRIFICER	SADOMASOCHIST	SAILORINGS
SACCHARIFIES	SACERDOTALISMS	SACRIFICERS	SADOMASOCHISTIC	SAILORLESS
SACCHARIFY	SACERDOTALIST	SACRIFICES	SADOMASOCHISTS	SAILORLIKE
SACCHARIFYING	SACERDOTALISTS	SACRIFICIAL	SAFECRACKER	SAILPLANED
SACCHARIMETER	SACERDOTALIZE	SACRIFICIALLY	SAFECRACKERS	SAILPLANER
SACCHARIMETERS	SACERDOTALIZED	SACRIFICING	SAFECRACKING	SAILPLANERS
SACCHARIMETRIES	SACERDOTALIZES	SACRIFYING	SAFECRACKINGS	SAILPLANES
SACCHARIMETRY	SACERDOTALIZING	SACRILEGES	SAFEGUARDED	SAILPLANING
SACCHARINE	SACERDOTALLY	SACRILEGIOUS	SAFEGUARDING	SAINTESSES

SAINTFOINS
SAINTHOODS
SAINTLIEST
SAINTLINESS
SAINTLINESSES
SAINTLINGS
SAINTPAULIA
SAINTPAULIAS
SAINTSHIPS
SALABILITIES
SALABILITY
SALABLENESS
SALABLENESSES
SALACIOUSLY
SALACIOUSNESS
SALACIOUSNESSES
SALACITIES
SALAMANDER
SALAMANDERS
SALAMANDRIAN
SALAMANDRINE
SALAMANDROID
SALAMANDROIDS
SALANGANES
SALBUTAMOL
SALBUTAMOLS
SALEABILITIES
SALEABILITY
SALEABLENESS
SALEABLENESSES
SALERATUSES
SALESCLERK
SALESCLERKS
SALESGIRLS
SALESLADIES
SALESMANSHIP
SALESMANSHIPS
SALESPEOPLE
SALESPERSON
SALESPERSONS
SALESROOMS
SALESWOMAN
SALESWOMEN
SALIAUNCES
SALICACEOUS
SALICETUMS
SALICIONAL

SALICIONALS
SALICORNIA
SALICORNIAS
SALICYLAMIDE
SALICYLAMIDES
SALICYLATE
SALICYLATED
SALICYLATES
SALICYLATING
SALICYLISM
SALICYLISMS
SALIENCIES
SALIENTIAN
SALIENTIANS
SALIFEROUS
SALIFIABLE
SALIFICATION
SALIFICATIONS
SALIMETERS
SALIMETRIC
SALIMETRIES
SALINISATION
SALINISATIONS
SALINISING
SALINITIES
SALINIZATION
SALINIZATIONS
SALINIZING
SALINOMETER
SALINOMETERS
SALINOMETRIC
SALINOMETRIES
SALINOMETRY
SALIVATING
SALIVATION
SALIVATIONS
SALIVATORS
SALLENDERS
SALLOWNESS
SALLOWNESSES
SALLYPORTS
SALMAGUNDI
SALMAGUNDIES
SALMAGUNDIS
SALMAGUNDY
SALMANASER
SALMANASERS

SALMANAZAR
SALMANAZARS
SALMONBERRIES
SALMONBERRY
SALMONELLA
SALMONELLAE
SALMONELLAS
SALMONELLOSES
SALMONELLOSIS
SALMONOIDS
SALOMETERS
SALOPETTES
SALPIGLOSSES
SALPIGLOSSIS
SALPIGLOSSISES
SALPINGECTOMIES
SALPINGECTOMY
SALPINGIAN
SALPINGITIC
SALPINGITIS
SALPINGITISES
SALSOLACEOUS
SALSUGINOUS
SALTARELLI
SALTARELLO
SALTARELLOS
SALTATIONISM
SALTATIONISMS
SALTATIONIST
SALTATIONISTS
SALTATIONS
SALTATORIAL
SALTATORIOUS
SALTBUSHES
SALTCELLAR
SALTCELLARS
SALTCHUCKER
SALTCHUCKERS
SALTCHUCKS
SALTFISHES
SALTIGRADE
SALTIGRADES
SALTIMBANCO
SALTIMBANCOS
SALTIMBOCCA
SALTIMBOCCAS
SALTINESSES

SALTIREWISE
SALTISHNESS
SALTISHNESSES
SALTNESSES
SALTPETERS
SALTPETREMAN
SALTPETREMEN
SALTPETRES
SALTSHAKER
SALTSHAKERS
SALUBRIOUS
SALUBRIOUSLY
SALUBRIOUSNESS
SALUBRITIES
SALURETICS
SALUTARILY
SALUTARINESS
SALUTARINESSES
SALUTATION
SALUTATIONAL
SALUTATIONS
SALUTATORIAN
SALUTATORIANS
SALUTATORIES
SALUTATORILY
SALUTATORY
SALUTIFEROUS
SALVABILITIES
SALVABILITY
SALVABLENESS
SALVABLENESSES
SALVAGEABILITY
SALVAGEABLE
SALVARSANS
SALVATIONAL
SALVATIONISM
SALVATIONISMS
SALVATIONIST
SALVATIONISTS
SALVATIONS
SALVATORIES
SALVERFORM
SALVIFICAL
SALVIFICALLY
SALVINIACEOUS
SAMARIFORM
SAMARITANS

SAMARSKITE
SAMARSKITES
SAMENESSES
SAMEYNESSES
SAMNITISES
SAMPLERIES
SANATORIUM
SANATORIUMS
SANBENITOS
SANCTIFIABLE
SANCTIFICATION
SANCTIFICATIONS
SANCTIFIED
SANCTIFIEDLY
SANCTIFIER
SANCTIFIERS
SANCTIFIES
SANCTIFYING
SANCTIFYINGLY
SANCTIFYINGS
SANCTIMONIES
SANCTIMONIOUS
SANCTIMONIOUSLY
SANCTIMONY
SANCTIONABLE
SANCTIONED
SANCTIONEER
SANCTIONEERS
SANCTIONER
SANCTIONERS
SANCTIONING
SANCTIONLESS
SANCTITIES
SANCTITUDE
SANCTITUDES
SANCTUARIES
SANCTUARISE
SANCTUARISED
SANCTUARISES
SANCTUARISING
SANCTUARIZE
SANCTUARIZED
SANCTUARIZES
SANCTUARIZING
SANDALLING
SANDALWOOD
SANDALWOODS

S

SANDARACHS	SANGUIFIED	SANITORIUMS	SAPRAEMIAS	SARCOMATOUS
SANDBAGGED	SANGUIFIES	SANNYASINS	SAPROBIONT	SARCOMERES
SANDBAGGER	SANGUIFYING	SANSCULOTTE	SAPROBIONTS	SARCOPHAGAL
SANDBAGGERS	SANGUINARIA	SANSCULOTTERIE	SAPROBIOTIC	SARCOPHAGI
SANDBAGGING	SANGUINARIAS	SANSCULOTTERIES	SAPROGENIC	SARCOPHAGOUS
SANDBLASTED	SANGUINARILY	SANSCULOTTES	SAPROGENICITIES	SARCOPHAGUS
SANDBLASTER	SANGUINARINESS	SANSCULOTTIC	SAPROGENICITY	SARCOPHAGUSES
SANDBLASTERS	SANGUINARY	SANSCULOTTIDES	SAPROGENOUS	SARCOPLASM
SANDBLASTING	SANGUINELY	SANSCULOTTISH	SAPROLEGNIA	SARCOPLASMIC
SANDBLASTINGS	SANGUINENESS	SANSCULOTTISM	SAPROLEGNIAS	SARCOPLASMS
SANDBLASTS	SANGUINENESSES	SANSCULOTTISMS	SAPROLITES	SARCOSOMAL
SANDCASTLE	SANGUINEOUS	SANSCULOTTIST	SAPROLITIC	SARCOSOMES
SANDCASTLES	SANGUINEOUSNESS	SANSCULOTTISTS	SAPROPELIC	SARDONICAL
SANDCRACKS	SANGUINING	SANSEVIERIA	SAPROPELITE	SARDONICALLY
SANDERLING	SANGUINITIES	SANSEVIERIAS	SAPROPELITES	SARDONICISM
SANDERLINGS	SANGUINITY	SANTALACEOUS	SAPROPHAGOUS	SARDONICISMS
SANDERSWOOD	SANGUINIVOROUS	SANTOLINAS	SAPROPHYTE	SARDONYXES
SANDERSWOODS	SANGUINOLENCIES	SANTONICAS	SAPROPHYTES	SARGASSUMS
SANDFISHES	SANGUINOLENCY	SAPANWOODS	SAPROPHYTIC	SARKINESSES
SANDGLASSES	SANGUINOLENT	SAPIDITIES	SAPROPHYTICALLY	SARMENTACEOUS
SANDGROPER	SANGUIVOROUS	SAPIDNESSES	SAPROPHYTISM	SARMENTOSE
SANDGROPERS	SANITARIAN	SAPIENCIES	SAPROPHYTISMS	SARMENTOUS
SANDGROUSE	SANITARIANISM	SAPIENTIAL	SAPROTROPH	SARPANCHES
SANDGROUSES	SANITARIANISMS	SAPIENTIALLY	SAPROTROPHIC	SARRACENIA
SANDINESSES	SANITARIANS	SAPINDACEOUS	SAPROTROPHS	SARRACENIACEOUS
SANDLOTTER	SANITARIES	SAPLESSNESS	SAPSUCKERS	SARRACENIAS
SANDLOTTERS	SANITARILY	SAPLESSNESSES	SARABANDES	SARRUSOPHONE
SANDPAINTING	SANITARINESS	SAPODILLAS	SARBACANES	SARRUSOPHONES
SANDPAINTINGS	SANITARINESSES	SAPOGENINS	SARCASTICALLY	SARSAPARILLA
SANDPAPERED	SANITARIST	SAPONACEOUS	SARCENCHYMATOUS	SARSAPARILLAS
SANDPAPERING	SANITARISTS	SAPONACEOUSNESS	SARCENCHYME	SARTORIALLY
SANDPAPERS	SANITARIUM	SAPONARIAS	SARCENCHYMES	SARTORIUSES
SANDPAPERY	SANITARIUMS	SAPONIFIABLE	SARCOCARPS	SASKATOONS
SANDPIPERS	SANITATING	SAPONIFICATION	SARCOCOLLA	SASQUATCHES
SANDSPOUTS	SANITATION	SAPONIFICATIONS	SARCOCOLLAS	SASSAFRASES
SANDSTONES	SANITATIONIST	SAPONIFIED	SARCOCYSTIS	SASSARARAS
SANDSTORMS	SANITATIONISTS	SAPONIFIER	SARCOCYSTISES	SASSINESSES
SANDSUCKER	SANITATIONS	SAPONIFIERS	SARCOIDOSES	SASSOLITES
SANDSUCKERS	SANITISATION	SAPONIFIES	SARCOIDOSIS	SASSYWOODS
SANDWICHED	SANITISATIONS	SAPONIFYING	SARCOLEMMA	SATANICALLY
SANDWICHES	SANITISERS	SAPOTACEOUS	SARCOLEMMAL	SATANICALNESS
SANDWICHING	SANITISING	SAPPANWOOD	SARCOLEMMAS	SATANICALNESSES
SANENESSES	SANITIZATION	SAPPANWOODS	SARCOLEMMATA	SATANITIES
SANGFROIDS	SANITIZATIONS	SAPPERMENT	SARCOLOGIES	SATANOLOGIES
SANGUIFEROUS	SANITIZERS	SAPPHIRINE	SARCOMATOID	SATANOLOGY
SANGUIFICATION	SANITIZING	SAPPHIRINES	SARCOMATOSES	SATANOPHANIES
SANGUIFICATIONS	SANITORIUM	SAPPINESSES	SARCOMATOSIS	SATANOPHANY

S

SATANOPHOBIA	SATISFICED	SAUNTERINGLY	SCABBARDLESS	SCALLOPINI
SATANOPHOBIAS	SATISFICER	SAUNTERINGS	SCABBEDNESS	SCALLOPINIS
SATCHELFUL	SATISFICERS	SAURISCHIAN	SCABBEDNESSES	SCALLYWAGS
SATCHELFULS	SATISFICES	SAURISCHIANS	SCABBINESS	SCALOGRAMS
SATCHELLED	SATISFICING	SAUROGNATHOUS	SCABBINESSES	SCALOPPINE
SATCHELSFUL	SATISFICINGS	SAUROPODOUS	SCABERULOUS	SCALOPPINES
SATEDNESSES	SATISFIERS	SAUROPSIDAN	SCABIOUSES	SCALOPPINI
SATELLITED	SATISFYING	SAUROPSIDANS	SCABRIDITIES	SCALPELLIC
SATELLITES	SATISFYINGLY	SAUROPTERYGIAN	SCABRIDITY	SCALPELLIFORM
SATELLITIC	SATURABILITIES	SAUSSURITE	SCABROUSLY	SCALPRIFORM
SATELLITING	SATURABILITY	SAUSSURITES	SCABROUSNESS	SCAMBAITING
SATELLITISE	SATURATERS	SAUSSURITIC	SCABROUSNESSES	SCAMBAITINGS
SATELLITISED	SATURATING	SAVABLENESS	SCAFFOLAGE	SCAMBLINGLY
SATELLITISES	SATURATION	SAVABLENESSES	SCAFFOLAGES	SCAMBLINGS
SATELLITISING	SATURATIONS	SAVAGEDOMS	SCAFFOLDAGE	SCAMMONIATE
SATELLITIUM	SATURATORS	SAVAGENESS	SCAFFOLDAGES	SCAMMONIES
SATELLITIUMS	SATURNALIA	SAVAGENESSES	SCAFFOLDED	SCAMPERERS
SATELLITIZE	SATURNALIAN	SAVAGERIES	SCAFFOLDER	SCAMPERING
SATELLITIZED	SATURNALIANLY	SAVEABLENESS	SCAFFOLDERS	SCAMPISHLY
SATELLITIZES	SATURNALIAS	SAVEABLENESSES	SCAFFOLDING	SCAMPISHNESS
SATELLITIZING	SATURNIIDS	SAVEGARDED	SCAFFOLDINGS	SCAMPISHNESSES
SATIABILITIES	SATURNINELY	SAVEGARDING	SCAGLIOLAS	SCANDALING
SATIABILITY	SATURNINITIES	SAVINGNESS	SCAITHLESS	SCANDALISATION
SATIATIONS	SATURNINITY	SAVINGNESSES	SCALABILITIES	SCANDALISATIONS
SATINETTAS	SATURNISMS	SAVORINESS	SCALABILITY	SCANDALISE
SATINETTES	SATURNISTS	SAVORINESSES	SCALABLENESS	SCANDALISED
SATINFLOWER	SATYAGRAHA	SAVOURIEST	SCALABLENESSES	SCANDALISER
SATINFLOWERS	SATYAGRAHAS	SAVOURINESS	SCALARIFORM	SCANDALISERS
SATINWOODS	SATYAGRAHI	SAVOURINESSES	SCALARIFORMLY	SCANDALISES
SATIRICALLY	SATYAGRAHIS	SAVOURLESS	SCALATIONS	SCANDALISING
SATIRICALNESS	SATYRESQUE	SAVVINESSES	SCALDBERRIES	SCANDALIZATION
SATIRICALNESSES	SATYRESSES	SAWBONESES	SCALDBERRY	SCANDALIZATIONS
SATIRISABLE	SATYRIASES	SAWDUSTING	SCALDFISHES	SCANDALIZE
SATIRISATION	SATYRIASIS	SAWGRASSES	SCALDHEADS	SCANDALIZED
SATIRISATIONS	SAUCEBOATS	SAWTIMBERS	SCALDSHIPS	SCANDALIZER
SATIRISERS	SAUCEBOXES	SAXICAVOUS	SCALEBOARD	SCANDALIZERS
SATIRISING	SAUCERFULS	SAXICOLINE	SCALEBOARDS	SCANDALIZES
SATIRIZABLE	SAUCERLESS	SAXICOLOUS	SCALENOHEDRA	SCANDALIZING
SATIRIZATION	SAUCERLIKE	SAXIFRAGACEOUS	SCALENOHEDRON	SCANDALLED
SATIRIZATIONS	SAUCINESSES	SAXIFRAGES	SCALENOHEDRONS	SCANDALLING
SATIRIZERS	SAUCISSONS	SAXITOXINS	SCALETAILS	SCANDALMONGER
SATIRIZING	SAUERBRATEN	SAXOPHONES	SCALEWORKS	SCANDALMONGERS
SATISFACTION	SAUERBRATENS	SAXOPHONIC	SCALINESSES	SCANDALOUS
SATISFACTIONS	SAUERKRAUT	SAXOPHONIST	SCALLAWAGS	SCANDALOUSLY
SATISFACTORILY	SAUERKRAUTS	SAXOPHONISTS	SCALLOPERS	SCANDALOUSNESS
SATISFACTORY	SAUNTERERS	SCABBARDED	SCALLOPING	SCANSORIAL
SATISFIABLE	SAUNTERING	SCABBARDING	SCALLOPINGS	SCANTINESS

S

SCANTINESSES

SCANTINESSES	SCARAMOUCH	SCATTEREDLY	SCENOGRAPHERS	SCHEMATIZATIONS
SCANTITIES	SCARAMOUCHE	SCATTERERS	SCENOGRAPHIC	SCHEMATIZE
SCANTLINGS	SCARAMOUCHES	SCATTERGOOD	SCENOGRAPHICAL	SCHEMATIZED
SCANTNESSES	SCARCEMENT	SCATTERGOODS	SCENOGRAPHIES	SCHEMATIZES
SCAPEGALLOWS	SCARCEMENTS	SCATTERGRAM	SCENOGRAPHY	SCHEMATIZING
SCAPEGALLOWSES	SCARCENESS	SCATTERGRAMS	SCENTLESSNESS	SCHEMINGLY
SCAPEGOATED	SCARCENESSES	SCATTERGUN	SCENTLESSNESSES	SCHEMOZZLE
SCAPEGOATING	SCARCITIES	SCATTERGUNS	SCEPTERING	SCHEMOZZLED
SCAPEGOATINGS	SCARECROWS	SCATTERING	SCEPTERLESS	SCHEMOZZLES
SCAPEGOATISM	SCAREHEADS	SCATTERINGLY	SCEPTICALLY	SCHEMOZZLING
SCAPEGOATISMS	SCAREMONGER	SCATTERINGS	SCEPTICISM	SCHERZANDI
SCAPEGOATS	SCAREMONGERING	SCATTERLING	SCEPTICISMS	SCHERZANDO
SCAPEGRACE	SCAREMONGERINGS	SCATTERLINGS	SCEPTRELESS	SCHERZANDOS
SCAPEGRACES	SCAREMONGERS	SCATTERMOUCH	SCEUOPHYLACIA	SCHIAVONES
SCAPEMENTS	SCARFISHES	SCATTERMOUCHES	SCEUOPHYLACIUM	SCHILLERISATION
SCAPEWHEEL	SCARFSKINS	SCATTEROMETER	SCEUOPHYLAX	SCHILLERISE
SCAPEWHEELS	SCARIFICATION	SCATTEROMETERS	SCEUOPHYLAXES	SCHILLERISED
SCAPHOCEPHALI	SCARIFICATIONS	SCATTERSHOT	SCHADENFREUDE	SCHILLERISES
SCAPHOCEPHALIC	SCARIFICATOR	SCATTINESS	SCHADENFREUDES	SCHILLERISING
SCAPHOCEPHALICS	SCARIFICATORS	SCATTINESSES	SCHALSTEIN	SCHILLERIZATION
SCAPHOCEPHALISM	SCARIFIERS	SCATURIENT	SCHALSTEINS	SCHILLERIZE
SCAPHOCEPHALISM	SCARIFYING	SCAVENGERED	SCHAPPEING	SCHILLERIZED
SCAPHOCEPHALOUS	SCARIFYINGLY	SCAVENGERIES	SCHATCHENS	SCHILLERIZES
SCAPHOCEPHALUS	SCARINESSES	SCAVENGERING	SCHECHITAH	SCHILLERIZING
SCAPHOCEPHALY	SCARLATINA	SCAVENGERINGS	SCHECHITAHS	SCHILLINGS
SCAPHOPODS	SCARLATINAL	SCAVENGERS	SCHECHITAS	SCHINDYLESES
SCAPIGEROUS	SCARLATINAS	SCAVENGERY	SCHECKLATON	SCHINDYLESIS
SCAPOLITES	SCARLETING	SCAVENGING	SCHECKLATONS	SCHINDYLETIC
SCAPULARIES	SCARPERING	SCAVENGINGS	SCHEDULERS	SCHIPPERKE
SCAPULATED	SCATHEFULNESS	SCAZONTICS	SCHEDULING	SCHIPPERKES
SCAPULIMANCIES	SCATHEFULNESSES	SCELERATES	SCHEELITES	SCHISMATIC
SCAPULIMANCY	SCATHELESS	SCENARISATION	SCHEFFLERA	SCHISMATICAL
SCAPULIMANTIC	SCATHINGLY	SCENARISATIONS	SCHEFFLERAS	SCHISMATICALLY
SCAPULOMANCIES	SCATOLOGIC	SCENARISED	SCHEMATICAL	SCHISMATICALS
SCAPULOMANCY	SCATOLOGICAL	SCENARISES	SCHEMATICALLY	SCHISMATICS
SCAPULOMANTIC	SCATOLOGIES	SCENARISING	SCHEMATICS	SCHISMATISE
SCARABAEAN	SCATOLOGIST	SCENARISTS	SCHEMATISATION	SCHISMATISED
SCARABAEANS	SCATOLOGISTS	SCENARIZATION	SCHEMATISATIONS	SCHISMATISES
SCARABAEID	SCATOPHAGIES	SCENARIZATIONS	SCHEMATISE	SCHISMATISING
SCARABAEIDS	SCATOPHAGOUS	SCENARIZED	SCHEMATISED	SCHISMATIZE
SCARABAEIST	SCATOPHAGY	SCENARIZES	SCHEMATISES	SCHISMATIZED
SCARABAEISTS	SCATTERABLE	SCENARIZING	SCHEMATISING	SCHISMATIZES
SCARABAEOID	SCATTERATION	SCENESHIFTER	SCHEMATISM	SCHISMATIZING
SCARABAEOIDS	SCATTERATIONS	SCENESHIFTERS	SCHEMATISMS	SCHISTOSITIES
SCARABAEUS	SCATTERBRAIN	SCENESTERS	SCHEMATIST	SCHISTOSITY
SCARABAEUSES	SCATTERBRAINED	SCENICALLY	SCHEMATISTS	SCHISTOSOMAL
SCARABOIDS	SCATTERBRAINS	SCENOGRAPHER	SCHEMATIZATION	SCHISTOSOME

SCHISTOSOMES	SCHLEPPING	SCHOLASTICATE	SCHOOLTEACHERS	SCINTIGRAMS
SCHISTOSOMIASES	SCHLIMAZEL	SCHOLASTICATES	SCHOOLTEACHING	SCINTIGRAPHIC
SCHISTOSOMIASIS	SCHLIMAZELS	SCHOLASTICISM	SCHOOLTEACHINGS	SCINTIGRAPHIES
SCHIZAEACEOUS	SCHLOCKERS	SCHOLASTICISMS	SCHOOLTIDE	SCINTIGRAPHY
SCHIZANTHUS	SCHLOCKIER	SCHOLASTICS	SCHOOLTIDES	SCINTILLAE
SCHIZANTHUSES	SCHLOCKIEST	SCHOLIASTIC	SCHOOLTIME	SCINTILLANT
SCHIZOCARP	SCHLUMBERGERA	SCHOLIASTS	SCHOOLTIMES	SCINTILLANTLY
SCHIZOCARPIC	SCHLUMBERGERAS	SCHOOLBAGS	SCHOOLWARD	SCINTILLAS
SCHIZOCARPOUS	SCHLUMPIER	SCHOOLBOOK	SCHOOLWARDS	SCINTILLASCOPE
SCHIZOCARPS	SCHLUMPIEST	SCHOOLBOOKS	SCHOOLWORK	SCINTILLASCOPES
SCHIZOGENESES	SCHLUMPING	SCHOOLBOYISH	SCHOOLWORKS	SCINTILLATE
SCHIZOGENESIS	SCHMALTZES	SCHOOLBOYS	SCHORLACEOUS	SCINTILLATED
SCHIZOGENETIC	SCHMALTZIER	SCHOOLCHILD	SCHORLOMITE	SCINTILLATES
SCHIZOGENIC	SCHMALTZIEST	SCHOOLCHILDREN	SCHORLOMITES	SCINTILLATING
SCHIZOGNATHOUS	SCHMALZIER	SCHOOLCRAFT	SCHOTTISCHE	SCINTILLATINGLY
SCHIZOGONIC	SCHMALZIEST	SCHOOLCRAFTS	SCHOTTISCHES	SCINTILLATION
SCHIZOGONIES	SCHMEARING	SCHOOLDAYS	SCHRECKLICH	SCINTILLATIONS
SCHIZOGONOUS	SCHMEERING	SCHOOLERIES	SCHUSSBOOMER	SCINTILLATOR
SCHIZOGONY	SCHMICKEST	SCHOOLFELLOW	SCHUSSBOOMERS	SCINTILLATORS
SCHIZOIDAL	SCHMOOSING	SCHOOLFELLOWS	SCHVARTZES	SCINTILLISCAN
SCHIZOMYCETE	SCHMOOZERS	SCHOOLGIRL	SCHWARMEREI	SCINTILLISCANS
SCHIZOMYCETES	SCHMOOZIER	SCHOOLGIRLISH	SCHWARMEREIS	SCINTILLOMETER
SCHIZOMYCETIC	SCHMOOZIEST	SCHOOLGIRLS	SCHWARMERISCH	SCINTILLOMETERS
SCHIZOMYCETOUS	SCHMOOZING	SCHOOLGOING	SCHWARTZES	SCINTILLON
SCHIZOPHRENE	SCHMUTTERS	SCHOOLGOINGS	SCHWARZLOT	SCINTILLONS
SCHIZOPHRENES	SCHNAPPERS	SCHOOLHOUSE	SCHWARZLOTS	SCINTILLOSCOPE
SCHIZOPHRENETIC	SCHNAPPSES	SCHOOLHOUSES	SCIAENOIDS	SCINTILLOSCOPES
SCHIZOPHRENIA	SCHNAUZERS	SCHOOLINGS	SCIAMACHIES	SCINTISCAN
SCHIZOPHRENIAS	SCHNITZELS	SCHOOLKIDS	SCIENTIFIC	SCINTISCANNER
SCHIZOPHRENIC	SCHNORKELED	SCHOOLMAID	SCIENTIFICAL	SCINTISCANNERS
SCHIZOPHRENICS	SCHNORKELING	SCHOOLMAIDS	SCIENTIFICALLY	SCINTISCANS
SCHIZOPHYCEOUS	SCHNORKELLED	SCHOOLMARM	SCIENTIFICITIES	SCIOLISTIC
SCHIZOPHYTE	SCHNORKELLING	SCHOOLMARMISH	SCIENTIFICITY	SCIOMACHIES
SCHIZOPHYTES	SCHNORKELS	SCHOOLMARMS	SCIENTISED	SCIOMANCER
SCHIZOPHYTIC	SCHNORRERS	SCHOOLMASTER	SCIENTISES	SCIOMANCERS
SCHIZOPODAL	SCHNORRING	SCHOOLMASTERED	SCIENTISING	SCIOMANCIES
SCHIZOPODOUS	SCHNOZZLES	SCHOOLMASTERING	SCIENTISMS	SCIOMANTIC
SCHIZOPODS	SCHOLARCHS	SCHOOLMASTERISH	SCIENTISTIC	SCIOPHYTES
SCHIZOTHYMIA	SCHOLARLIER	SCHOOLMASTERLY	SCIENTISTS	SCIOPHYTIC
SCHIZOTHYMIAS	SCHOLARLIEST	SCHOOLMASTERS	SCIENTIZED	SCIOSOPHIES
SCHIZOTHYMIC	SCHOLARLINESS	SCHOOLMATE	SCIENTIZES	SCIRRHOSITIES
SCHIZZIEST	SCHOLARLINESSES	SCHOOLMATES	SCIENTIZING	SCIRRHOSITY
SCHLEMIELS	SCHOLARSHIP	SCHOOLMISTRESS	SCINCOIDIAN	SCIRRHUSES
SCHLEMIHLS	SCHOLARSHIPS	SCHOOLMISTRESSY	SCINCOIDIANS	SCISSIPARITIES
SCHLEPPERS	SCHOLASTIC	SCHOOLROOM	SCINDAPSUS	SCISSIPARITY
SCHLEPPIER	SCHOLASTICAL	SCHOOLROOMS	SCINDAPSUSES	SCISSORERS
SCHLEPPIEST	SCHOLASTICALLY	SCHOOLTEACHER	SCINTIGRAM	SCISSORING

S

SCISSORTAIL	SCLEROTISATIONS	SCOPOPHILIC	SCOUTCRAFTS	SCRAPYARDS
SCISSORTAILS	SCLEROTISE	SCOPOPHOBIA	SCOUTHERED	SCRATCHBACK
SCISSORWISE	SCLEROTISED	SCOPOPHOBIAS	SCOUTHERING	SCRATCHBACKS
SCITAMINEOUS	SCLEROTISES	SCOPTOPHILIA	SCOUTHERINGS	SCRATCHBOARD
SCLAUNDERS	SCLEROTISING	SCOPTOPHILIAS	SCOUTMASTER	SCRATCHBOARDS
SCLEREIDES	SCLEROTITIS	SCOPTOPHOBIA	SCOUTMASTERS	SCRATCHBUILD
SCLERENCHYMA	SCLEROTITISES	SCOPTOPHOBIAS	SCOWDERING	SCRATCHBUILDER
SCLERENCHYMAS	SCLEROTIUM	SCORBUTICALLY	SCOWDERINGS	SCRATCHBUILDERS
SCLERENCHYMATA	SCLEROTIZATION	SCORCHINGLY	SCOWLINGLY	SCRATCHBUILDING
SCLERIASES	SCLEROTIZATIONS	SCORCHINGNESS	SCOWTHERED	SCRATCHBUILDS
SCLERIASIS	SCLEROTIZE	SCORCHINGNESSES	SCOWTHERING	SCRATCHBUILT
SCLERITISES	SCLEROTIZED	SCORCHINGS	SCRABBLERS	SCRATCHCARD
SCLEROCAULIES	SCLEROTIZES	SCORDATURA	SCRABBLIER	SCRATCHCARDS
SCLEROCAULOUS	SCLEROTIZING	SCORDATURAS	SCRABBLIEST	SCRATCHERS
SCLEROCAULY	SCLEROTOMIES	SCOREBOARD	SCRABBLING	SCRATCHIER
SCLERODERM	SCLEROTOMY	SCOREBOARDS	SCRAGGEDNESS	SCRATCHIES
SCLERODERMA	SCOFFINGLY	SCORECARDS	SCRAGGEDNESSES	SCRATCHIEST
SCLERODERMAS	SCOLDINGLY	SCOREKEEPER	SCRAGGIEST	SCRATCHILY
SCLERODERMATA	SCOLECIFORM	SCOREKEEPERS	SCRAGGINESS	SCRATCHINESS
SCLERODERMATOUS	SCOLECITES	SCORELINES	SCRAGGINESSES	SCRATCHINESSES
SCLERODERMIA	SCOLLOPING	SCORESHEET	SCRAGGLIER	SCRATCHING
SCLERODERMIAS	SCOLOPACEOUS	SCORESHEETS	SCRAGGLIEST	SCRATCHINGLY
SCLERODERMIC	SCOLOPENDRA	SCORIACEOUS	SCRAGGLING	SCRATCHINGS
SCLERODERMITE	SCOLOPENDRAS	SCORIFICATION	SCRAICHING	SCRATCHLESS
SCLERODERMITES	SCOLOPENDRID	SCORIFICATIONS	SCRAIGHING	SCRATCHPLATE
SCLERODERMOUS	SCOLOPENDRIDS	SCORIFIERS	SCRAMBLERS	SCRATCHPLATES
SCLERODERMS	SCOLOPENDRIFORM	SCORIFYING	SCRAMBLING	SCRATTLING
SCLEROMALACIA	SCOLOPENDRINE	SCORNFULLY	SCRAMBLINGLY	SCRAUCHING
SCLEROMALACIAS	SCOLOPENDRIUM	SCORNFULNESS	SCRAMBLINGS	SCRAUGHING
SCLEROMATA	SCOLOPENDRIUMS	SCORNFULNESSES	SCRANCHING	SCRAWLIEST
SCLEROMETER	SCOLYTOIDS	SCORODITES	SCRANNIEST	SCRAWLINGLY
SCLEROMETERS	SCOMBROIDS	SCORPAENID	SCRAPBOOKED	SCRAWLINGS
SCLEROMETRIC	SCOMFISHED	SCORPAENIDS	SCRAPBOOKING	SCRAWNIEST
SCLEROPHYLL	SCOMFISHES	SCORPAENOID	SCRAPBOOKINGS	SCRAWNINESS
SCLEROPHYLLIES	SCOMFISHING	SCORPAENOIDS	SCRAPBOOKS	SCRAWNINESSES
SCLEROPHYLLOUS	SCONCHEONS	SCORPIOIDS	SCRAPEGOOD	SCREAKIEST
SCLEROPHYLLS	SCOOTCHING	SCORPIONIC	SCRAPEGOODS	SCREAMINGLY
SCLEROPHYLLY	SCOOTERIST	SCORZONERA	SCRAPEGUTS	SCREECHERS
SCLEROPROTEIN	SCOOTERISTS	SCORZONERAS	SCRAPEPENNIES	SCREECHIER
SCLEROPROTEINS	SCOPELOIDS	SCOTODINIA	SCRAPEPENNY	SCREECHIEST
SCLEROSING	SCOPOLAMINE	SCOTODINIAS	SCRAPERBOARD	SCREECHING
SCLEROTALS	SCOPOLAMINES	SCOTOMATOUS	SCRAPERBOARDS	SCREEDINGS
SCLEROTIAL	SCOPOLINES	SCOTOMETER	SCRAPHEAPS	SCREENABLE
SCLEROTICS	SCOPOPHILIA	SCOTOMETERS	SCRAPPAGES	SCREENAGER
SCLEROTINS	SCOPOPHILIAC	SCOUNDRELLY	SCRAPPIEST	SCREENAGERS
SCLEROTIOID	SCOPOPHILIACS	SCOUNDRELS	SCRAPPINESS	SCREENCRAFT
SCLEROTISATION	SCOPOPHILIAS	SCOUTCRAFT	SCRAPPINESSES	SCREENCRAFTS

S

SCREENFULS	SCRIMPNESS	SCRIVEBOARDS	SCRUMMAGERS	SCUDDALERS
SCREENINGS	SCRIMPNESSES	SCRIVENERS	SCRUMMAGES	SCULDUDDERIES
SCREENLAND	SCRIMSHANDER	SCRIVENERSHIP	SCRUMMAGING	SCULDUDDERY
SCREENLANDS	SCRIMSHANDERED	SCRIVENERSHIPS	SCRUMMIEST	SCULDUDDRIES
SCREENLIKE	SCRIMSHANDERING	SCRIVENING	SCRUMPLING	SCULDUDDRY
SCREENPLAY	SCRIMSHANDERS	SCRIVENINGS	SCRUMPOXES	SCULDUGGERIES
SCREENPLAYS	SCRIMSHANDIED	SCROBBLING	SCRUMPTIOUS	SCULDUGGERY
SCREENSAVER	SCRIMSHANDIES	SCROBICULAR	SCRUMPTIOUSLY	SCULLERIES
SCREENSAVERS	SCRIMSHANDY	SCROBICULATE	SCRUMPTIOUSNESS	SCULPTRESS
SCREENSHOT	SCRIMSHANDYING	SCROBICULATED	SCRUNCHEON	SCULPTRESSES
SCREENSHOTS	SCRIMSHANK	SCROBICULE	SCRUNCHEONS	SCULPTURAL
SCREENWRITER	SCRIMSHANKED	SCROBICULES	SCRUNCHIER	SCULPTURALLY
SCREENWRITERS	SCRIMSHANKING	SCROFULOUS	SCRUNCHIES	SCULPTURED
SCREEVINGS	SCRIMSHANKS	SCROFULOUSLY	SCRUNCHIEST	SCULPTURES
SCREICHING	SCRIMSHAWED	SCROFULOUSNESS	SCRUNCHING	SCULPTURESQUE
SCREIGHING	SCRIMSHAWING	SCROGGIEST	SCRUNCHION	SCULPTURESQUELY
SCREWBALLS	SCRIMSHAWS	SCROLLABLE	SCRUNCHIONS	SCULPTURING
SCREWBEANS	SCRIMSHONER	SCROLLINGS	SCRUNTIEST	SCULPTURINGS
SCREWDRIVER	SCRIMSHONERS	SCROLLWISE	SCRUPLELESS	SCUMBERING
SCREWDRIVERS	SCRIPOPHILE	SCROLLWORK	SCRUPULOSITIES	SCUMBLINGS
SCREWINESS	SCRIPOPHILES	SCROLLWORKS	SCRUPULOSITY	SCUMFISHED
SCREWINESSES	SCRIPOPHILIES	SCROOCHING	SCRUPULOUS	SCUMFISHES
SCREWWORMS	SCRIPOPHILIST	SCROOTCHED	SCRUPULOUSLY	SCUMFISHING
SCRIBACIOUS	SCRIPOPHILISTS	SCROOTCHES	SCRUPULOUSNESS	SCUNCHEONS
SCRIBACIOUSNESS	SCRIPOPHILY	SCROOTCHING	SCRUTABILITIES	SCUNGILLIS
SCRIBBLEMENT	SCRIPPAGES	SCROPHULARIA	SCRUTABILITY	SCUNNERING
SCRIBBLEMENTS	SCRIPTORIA	SCROPHULARIAS	SCRUTATORS	SCUPPERING
SCRIBBLERS	SCRIPTORIAL	SCROUNGERS	SCRUTINEER	SCUPPERNONG
SCRIBBLIER	SCRIPTORIUM	SCROUNGIER	SCRUTINEERS	SCUPPERNONGS
SCRIBBLIEST	SCRIPTORIUMS	SCROUNGIEST	SCRUTINIES	SCURFINESS
SCRIBBLING	SCRIPTURAL	SCROUNGING	SCRUTINISE	SCURFINESSES
SCRIBBLINGLY	SCRIPTURALISM	SCROUNGINGS	SCRUTINISED	SCURRILITIES
SCRIBBLINGS	SCRIPTURALISMS	SCROWDGING	SCRUTINISER	SCURRILITY
SCRIECHING	SCRIPTURALIST	SCRUBBABLE	SCRUTINISERS	SCURRILOUS
SCRIEVEBOARD	SCRIPTURALISTS	SCRUBBIEST	SCRUTINISES	SCURRILOUSLY
SCRIEVEBOARDS	SCRIPTURALLY	SCRUBBINESS	SCRUTINISING	SCURRILOUSNESS
SCRIGGLIER	SCRIPTURES	SCRUBBINESSES	SCRUTINISINGLY	SCURRIOURS
SCRIGGLIEST	SCRIPTURISM	SCRUBBINGS	SCRUTINIZE	SCURVINESS
SCRIGGLING	SCRIPTURISMS	SCRUBLANDS	SCRUTINIZED	SCURVINESSES
SCRIMMAGED	SCRIPTURIST	SCRUBWOMAN	SCRUTINIZER	SCUTATIONS
SCRIMMAGER	SCRIPTURISTS	SCRUBWOMEN	SCRUTINIZERS	SCUTCHEONLESS
SCRIMMAGERS	SCRIPTWRITER	SCRUFFIEST	SCRUTINIZES	SCUTCHEONS
SCRIMMAGES	SCRIPTWRITERS	SCRUFFINESS	SCRUTINIZING	SCUTCHINGS
SCRIMMAGING	SCRIPTWRITING	SCRUFFINESSES	SCRUTINIZINGLY	SCUTELLATE
SCRIMPIEST	SCRIPTWRITINGS	SCRUMDOWNS	SCRUTINOUS	SCUTELLATED
SCRIMPINESS	SCRITCHING	SCRUMMAGED	SCRUTINOUSLY	SCUTELLATION
SCRIMPINESSES	SCRIVEBOARD	SCRUMMAGER	SCRUTOIRES	SCUTELLATIONS

S

SCUTTERING

SCUTTERING
SCUTTLEBUTT
SCUTTLEBUTTS
SCUTTLEFUL
SCUTTLEFULS
SCUZZBALLS
SCYPHIFORM
SCYPHISTOMA
SCYPHISTOMAE
SCYPHISTOMAS
SCYPHOZOAN
SCYPHOZOANS
SCYTHELIKE
SDEIGNFULL
SDEIGNFULLY
SDRUCCIOLA
SEABEACHES
SEABORGIUM
SEABORGIUMS
SEABOTTLES
SEACUNNIES
SEAFARINGS
SEALIFTING
SEALPOINTS
SEAMANLIKE
SEAMANSHIP
SEAMANSHIPS
SEAMINESSES
SEAMLESSLY
SEAMLESSNESS
SEAMLESSNESSES
SEAMSTRESS
SEAMSTRESSES
SEAMSTRESSIES
SEAMSTRESSY
SEANNACHIE
SEANNACHIES
SEAQUARIUM
SEAQUARIUMS
SEARCHABLE
SEARCHINGLY
SEARCHINGNESS
SEARCHINGNESSES
SEARCHLESS
SEARCHLIGHT
SEARCHLIGHTS
SEAREDNESS

SEAREDNESSES
SEARNESSES
SEASICKEST
SEASICKNESS
SEASICKNESSES
SEASONABILITIES
SEASONABILITY
SEASONABLE
SEASONABLENESS
SEASONABLY
SEASONALITIES
SEASONALITY
SEASONALLY
SEASONALNESS
SEASONALNESSES
SEASONINGS
SEASONLESS
SEASTRANDS
SEAWORTHIER
SEAWORTHIEST
SEAWORTHINESS
SEAWORTHINESSES
SEBIFEROUS
SEBORRHEAL
SEBORRHEAS
SEBORRHEIC
SEBORRHOEA
SEBORRHOEAL
SEBORRHOEAS
SEBORRHOEIC
SECERNENTS
SECERNMENT
SECERNMENTS
SECESSIONAL
SECESSIONISM
SECESSIONISMS
SECESSIONIST
SECESSIONISTS
SECESSIONS
SECLUDEDLY
SECLUDEDNESS
SECLUDEDNESSES
SECLUSIONIST
SECLUSIONISTS
SECLUSIONS
SECLUSIVELY
SECLUSIVENESS

SECLUSIVENESSES
SECOBARBITAL
SECOBARBITALS
SECONDARIES
SECONDARILY
SECONDARINESS
SECONDARINESSES
SECONDHAND
SECONDMENT
SECONDMENTS
SECRETAGES
SECRETAGOGIC
SECRETAGOGUE
SECRETAGOGUES
SECRETAIRE
SECRETAIRES
SECRETARIAL
SECRETARIAT
SECRETARIATE
SECRETARIATES
SECRETARIATS
SECRETARIES
SECRETARYSHIP
SECRETARYSHIPS
SECRETIONAL
SECRETIONARY
SECRETIONS
SECRETIVELY
SECRETIVENESS
SECRETIVENESSES
SECRETNESS
SECRETNESSES
SECRETORIES
SECTARIANISE
SECTARIANISED
SECTARIANISES
SECTARIANISING
SECTARIANISM
SECTARIANISMS
SECTARIANIZE
SECTARIANIZED
SECTARIANIZES
SECTARIANIZING
SECTARIANS
SECTILITIES
SECTIONALISE
SECTIONALISED

SECTIONALISES
SECTIONALISING
SECTIONALISM
SECTIONALISMS
SECTIONALIST
SECTIONALISTS
SECTIONALIZE
SECTIONALIZED
SECTIONALIZES
SECTIONALIZING
SECTIONALLY
SECTIONALS
SECTIONING
SECTIONISATION
SECTIONISATIONS
SECTIONISE
SECTIONISED
SECTIONISES
SECTIONISING
SECTIONIZATION
SECTIONIZATIONS
SECTIONIZE
SECTIONIZED
SECTIONIZES
SECTIONIZING
SECTORIALS
SECTORISATION
SECTORISATIONS
SECTORISED
SECTORISES
SECTORISING
SECTORIZATION
SECTORIZATIONS
SECTORIZED
SECTORIZES
SECTORIZING
SECULARISATION
SECULARISATIONS
SECULARISE
SECULARISED
SECULARISER
SECULARISERS
SECULARISES
SECULARISING
SECULARISM
SECULARISMS
SECULARIST

SECULARISTIC
SECULARISTS
SECULARITIES
SECULARITY
SECULARIZATION
SECULARIZATIONS
SECULARIZE
SECULARIZED
SECULARIZER
SECULARIZERS
SECULARIZES
SECULARIZING
SECUNDINES
SECUNDOGENITURE
SECURANCES
SECUREMENT
SECUREMENTS
SECURENESS
SECURENESSES
SECURIFORM
SECURITANS
SECURITIES
SECURITISATION
SECURITISATIONS
SECURITISE
SECURITISED
SECURITISES
SECURITISING
SECURITIZATION
SECURITIZATIONS
SECURITIZE
SECURITIZED
SECURITIZES
SECURITIZING
SECUROCRAT
SECUROCRATS
SEDATENESS
SEDATENESSES
SEDENTARILY
SEDENTARINESS
SEDENTARINESSES
SEDGELANDS
SEDIGITATED
SEDIMENTABLE
SEDIMENTARILY
SEDIMENTARY
SEDIMENTATION

S

SEDIMENTATIONS	SEGMENTATE	SEISMOLOGIC	SELENOGRAPHIC	SEMBLANCES
SEDIMENTED	SEGMENTATION	SEISMOLOGICAL	SELENOGRAPHICAL	SEMBLATIVE
SEDIMENTING	SEGMENTATIONS	SEISMOLOGICALLY	SELENOGRAPHIES	SEMEIOLOGIC
SEDIMENTOLOGIC	SEGMENTING	SEISMOLOGIES	SELENOGRAPHIST	SEMEIOLOGICAL
SEDIMENTOLOGIES	SEGREGABLE	SEISMOLOGIST	SELENOGRAPHISTS	SEMEIOLOGIES
SEDIMENTOLOGIST	SEGREGANTS	SEISMOLOGISTS	SELENOGRAPHS	SEMEIOLOGIST
SEDIMENTOLOGY	SEGREGATED	SEISMOLOGY	SELENOGRAPHY	SEMEIOLOGISTS
SEDIMENTOUS	SEGREGATES	SEISMOMETER	SELENOLOGICAL	SEMEIOLOGY
SEDITIONARIES	SEGREGATING	SEISMOMETERS	SELENOLOGIES	SEMEIOTICALLY
SEDITIONARY	SEGREGATION	SEISMOMETRIC	SELENOLOGIST	SEMEIOTICIAN
SEDITIOUSLY	SEGREGATIONAL	SEISMOMETRICAL	SELENOLOGISTS	SEMEIOTICIANS
SEDITIOUSNESS	SEGREGATIONIST	SEISMOMETRIES	SELENOLOGY	SEMEIOTICS
SEDITIOUSNESSES	SEGREGATIONISTS	SEISMOMETRY	SELFISHNESS	SEMELPARITIES
SEDUCEABLE	SEGREGATIONS	SEISMONASTIC	SELFISHNESSES	SEMELPARITY
SEDUCEMENT	SEGREGATIVE	SEISMONASTIES	SELFLESSLY	SEMELPAROUS
SEDUCEMENTS	SEGREGATOR	SEISMONASTY	SELFLESSNESS	SEMESTRIAL
SEDUCINGLY	SEGREGATORS	SEISMOSCOPE	SELFLESSNESSES	SEMIABSTRACT
SEDUCTIONS	SEGUIDILLA	SEISMOSCOPES	SELFNESSES	SEMIABSTRACTION
SEDUCTIVELY	SEGUIDILLAS	SEISMOSCOPIC	SELFSAMENESS	SEMIANGLES
SEDUCTIVENESS	SEIGNEURIAL	SELACHIANS	SELFSAMENESSES	SEMIANNUAL
SEDUCTIVENESSES	SEIGNEURIE	SELAGINELLA	SELLOTAPED	SEMIANNUALLY
SEDUCTRESS	SEIGNEURIES	SELAGINELLAS	SELLOTAPES	SEMIAQUATIC
SEDUCTRESSES	SEIGNIORAGE	SELDOMNESS	SELLOTAPING	SEMIARBOREAL
SEDULITIES	SEIGNIORAGES	SELDOMNESSES	SELTZOGENE	SEMIARIDITIES
SEDULOUSLY	SEIGNIORALTIES	SELECTABLE	SELTZOGENES	SEMIARIDITY
SEDULOUSNESS	SEIGNIORALTY	SELECTIONIST	SELVEDGING	SEMIAUTOMATIC
SEDULOUSNESSES	SEIGNIORIAL	SELECTIONISTS	SEMAINIERS	SEMIAUTOMATICS
SEECATCHIE	SEIGNIORIES	SELECTIONS	SEMANTEMES	SEMIAUTONOMOUS
SEEDEATERS	SEIGNIORSHIP	SELECTIVELY	SEMANTICAL	SEMIBREVES
SEEDINESSES	SEIGNIORSHIPS	SELECTIVENESS	SEMANTICALLY	SEMICARBAZIDE
SEEDNESSES	SEIGNORAGE	SELECTIVENESSES	SEMANTICIST	SEMICARBAZIDES
SEEDSTOCKS	SEIGNORAGES	SELECTIVITIES	SEMANTICISTS	SEMICARBAZONE
SEEMELESSE	SEIGNORIAL	SELECTIVITY	SEMANTIDES	SEMICARBAZONES
SEEMINGNESS	SEIGNORIES	SELECTNESS	SEMAPHORED	SEMICENTENNIAL
SEEMINGNESSES	SEISMICALLY	SELECTNESSES	SEMAPHORES	SEMICENTENNIALS
SEEMLIHEAD	SEISMICITIES	SELECTORATE	SEMAPHORIC	SEMICHORUS
SEEMLIHEADS	SEISMICITY	SELECTORATES	SEMAPHORICAL	SEMICHORUSES
SEEMLIHEDS	SEISMOGRAM	SELECTORIAL	SEMAPHORICALLY	SEMICIRCLE
SEEMLINESS	SEISMOGRAMS	SELEGILINE	SEMAPHORING	SEMICIRCLED
SEEMLINESSES	SEISMOGRAPH	SELEGILINES	SEMASIOLOGICAL	SEMICIRCLES
SEEMLYHEDS	SEISMOGRAPHER	SELENIFEROUS	SEMASIOLOGIES	SEMICIRCULAR
SEERSUCKER	SEISMOGRAPHERS	SELENOCENTRIC	SEMASIOLOGIST	SEMICIRCULARLY
SEERSUCKERS	SEISMOGRAPHIC	SELENODONT	SEMASIOLOGISTS	SEMICIRQUE
SEETHINGLY	SEISMOGRAPHICAL	SELENODONTS	SEMASIOLOGY	SEMICIRQUES
SEGHOLATES	SEISMOGRAPHIES	SELENOGRAPH	SEMATOLOGIES	SEMICIVILISED
SEGMENTALLY	SEISMOGRAPHS	SELENOGRAPHER	SEMATOLOGY	SEMICIVILIZED
SEGMENTARY	SEISMOGRAPHY	SELENOGRAPHERS	SEMBLABLES	SEMICLASSIC

S

SEMICLASSICAL	SEMIFINISHED	SEMINOMADIC	SEMIQUAVER	SEMPSTRESSINGS
SEMICLASSICS	SEMIFITTED	SEMINOMADS	SEMIQUAVERS	SENARMONTITE
SEMICOLONIAL	SEMIFLEXIBLE	SEMINOMATA	SEMIRELIGIOUS	SENARMONTITES
SEMICOLONIALISM	SEMIFLUIDIC	SEMINUDITIES	SEMIRETIRED	SENATORIAL
SEMICOLONIES	SEMIFLUIDITIES	SEMINUDITY	SEMIRETIREMENT	SENATORIALLY
SEMICOLONS	SEMIFLUIDITY	SEMIOCHEMICAL	SEMIRETIREMENTS	SENATORIAN
SEMICOLONY	SEMIFLUIDS	SEMIOCHEMICALS	SEMIROUNDS	SENATORSHIP
SEMICOMATOSE	SEMIFORMAL	SEMIOFFICIAL	SEMISACRED	SENATORSHIPS
SEMICOMMERCIAL	SEMIFREDDI	SEMIOFFICIALLY	SEMISECRET	SENECTITUDE
SEMICONDUCTING	SEMIFREDDO	SEMIOLOGIC	SEMISEDENTARY	SENECTITUDES
SEMICONDUCTION	SEMIFREDDOS	SEMIOLOGICAL	SEMISHRUBBY	SENESCENCE
SEMICONDUCTIONS	SEMIGLOBULAR	SEMIOLOGICALLY	SEMISKILLED	SENESCENCES
SEMICONDUCTOR	SEMIGLOSSES	SEMIOLOGIES	SEMISOLIDS	SENESCHALS
SEMICONDUCTORS	SEMIGROUPS	SEMIOLOGIST	SEMISOLUSES	SENESCHALSHIP
SEMICONSCIOUS	SEMIHOBOES	SEMIOLOGISTS	SEMISUBMERSIBLE	SENESCHALSHIPS
SEMICONSCIOUSLY	SEMILEGENDARY	SEMIOPAQUE	SEMISYNTHETIC	SENHORITAS
SEMICRYSTALLIC	SEMILETHAL	SEMIOTICALLY	SEMITERETE	SENILITIES
SEMICRYSTALLINE	SEMILETHALS	SEMIOTICIAN	SEMITERRESTRIAL	SENIORITIES
SEMICYLINDER	SEMILIQUID	SEMIOTICIANS	SEMITONALLY	SENNACHIES
SEMICYLINDERS	SEMILIQUIDS	SEMIOTICIST	SEMITONICALLY	SENSATIONAL
SEMICYLINDRICAL	SEMILITERATE	SEMIOTICISTS	SEMITRAILER	SENSATIONALISE
SEMIDARKNESS	SEMILITERATES	SEMIOVIPAROUS	SEMITRAILERS	SENSATIONALISED
SEMIDARKNESSES	SEMILOGARITHMIC	SEMIPALMATE	SEMITRANSLUCENT	SENSATIONALISES
SEMIDEIFIED	SEMILUCENT	SEMIPALMATED	SEMITRANSPARENT	SENSATIONALISM
SEMIDEIFIES	SEMILUNATE	SEMIPALMATION	SEMITROPIC	SENSATIONALISMS
SEMIDEIFYING	SEMILUSTROUS	SEMIPALMATIONS	SEMITROPICAL	SENSATIONALIST
SEMIDEPONENT	SEMIMANUFACTURE	SEMIPARASITE	SEMITROPICS	SENSATIONALISTS
SEMIDEPONENTS	SEMIMENSTRUAL	SEMIPARASITES	SEMITRUCKS	SENSATIONALIZE
SEMIDESERT	SEMIMETALLIC	SEMIPARASITIC	SEMIVITREOUS	SENSATIONALIZED
SEMIDESERTS	SEMIMETALS	SEMIPARASITISM	SEMIVOCALIC	SENSATIONALIZES
SEMIDETACHED	SEMIMONASTIC	SEMIPARASITISMS	SEMIVOWELS	SENSATIONALLY
SEMIDIAMETER	SEMIMONTHLIES	SEMIPELLUCID	SEMIWEEKLIES	SENSATIONISM
SEMIDIAMETERS	SEMIMONTHLY	SEMIPERIMETER	SEMIWEEKLY	SENSATIONISMS
SEMIDIURNAL	SEMIMYSTICAL	SEMIPERIMETERS	SEMIYEARLY	SENSATIONIST
SEMIDIVINE	SEMINALITIES	SEMIPERMANENT	SEMPERVIVUM	SENSATIONISTS
SEMIDOCUMENTARY	SEMINALITY	SEMIPERMEABLE	SEMPERVIVUMS	SENSATIONLESS
SEMIDOMINANT	SEMINARIAL	SEMIPLUMES	SEMPITERNAL	SENSATIONS
SEMIDRYING	SEMINARIAN	SEMIPOLITICAL	SEMPITERNALLY	SENSELESSLY
SEMIDWARFS	SEMINARIANS	SEMIPOPULAR	SEMPITERNITIES	SENSELESSNESS
SEMIDWARVES	SEMINARIES	SEMIPORCELAIN	SEMPITERNITY	SENSELESSNESSES
SEMIELLIPTICAL	SEMINARIST	SEMIPORCELAINS	SEMPITERNUM	SENSIBILIA
SEMIEMPIRICAL	SEMINARISTS	SEMIPORNOGRAPHY	SEMPITERNUMS	SENSIBILITIES
SEMIEVERGREEN	SEMINATING	SEMIPOSTAL	SEMPSTERING	SENSIBILITY
SEMIFEUDAL	SEMINATION	SEMIPOSTALS	SEMPSTERINGS	SENSIBLENESS
SEMIFINALIST	SEMINATIONS	SEMIPRECIOUS	SEMPSTRESS	SENSIBLENESSES
SEMIFINALISTS	SEMINATURAL	SEMIPRIVATE	SEMPSTRESSES	SENSIBLEST
SEMIFINALS	SEMINIFEROUS	SEMIPUBLIC	SEMPSTRESSING	SENSITISATION

S

SENSITISATIONS	SENSUALIZING	SEPARATIONISM	SEPTICALLY	SEQUENCERS
SENSITISED	SENSUALNESS	SEPARATIONISMS	SEPTICEMIA	SEQUENCIES
SENSITISER	SENSUALNESSES	SEPARATIONIST	SEPTICEMIAS	SEQUENCING
SENSITISERS	SENSUOSITIES	SEPARATIONISTS	SEPTICEMIC	SEQUENCINGS
SENSITISES	SENSUOSITY	SEPARATIONS	SEPTICIDAL	SEQUENTIAL
SENSITISING	SENSUOUSLY	SEPARATISM	SEPTICIDALLY	SEQUENTIALITIES
SENSITIVELY	SENSUOUSNESS	SEPARATISMS	SEPTICITIES	SEQUENTIALITY
SENSITIVENESS	SENSUOUSNESSES	SEPARATIST	SEPTIFEROUS	SEQUENTIALLY
SENSITIVENESSES	SENTENCERS	SEPARATISTIC	SEPTIFRAGAL	SEQUESTERED
SENSITIVES	SENTENCING	SEPARATISTS	SEPTILATERAL	SEQUESTERING
SENSITIVITIES	SENTENTIAE	SEPARATIVE	SEPTILLION	SEQUESTERS
SENSITIVITY	SENTENTIAL	SEPARATIVELY	SEPTILLIONS	SEQUESTRABLE
SENSITIZATION	SENTENTIALLY	SEPARATIVENESS	SEPTILLIONTH	SEQUESTRAL
SENSITIZATIONS	SENTENTIOUS	SEPARATORIES	SEPTILLIONTHS	SEQUESTRANT
SENSITIZED	SENTENTIOUSLY	SEPARATORS	SEPTIMOLES	SEQUESTRANTS
SENSITIZER	SENTENTIOUSNESS	SEPARATORY	SEPTIVALENT	SEQUESTRATE
SENSITIZERS	SENTIENCES	SEPARATRICES	SEPTUAGENARIAN	SEQUESTRATED
SENSITIZES	SENTIENCIES	SEPARATRIX	SEPTUAGENARIANS	SEQUESTRATES
SENSITIZING	SENTIENTLY	SEPARATUMS	SEPTUAGENARIES	SEQUESTRATING
SENSITOMETER	SENTIMENTAL	SEPIOLITES	SEPTUAGENARY	SEQUESTRATION
SENSITOMETERS	SENTIMENTALISE	SEPIOSTAIRE	SEPTUPLETS	SEQUESTRATIONS
SENSITOMETRIC	SENTIMENTALISED	SEPIOSTAIRES	SEPTUPLICATE	SEQUESTRATOR
SENSITOMETRIES	SENTIMENTALISES	SEPTATIONS	SEPTUPLICATES	SEQUESTRATORS
SENSITOMETRY	SENTIMENTALISM	SEPTAVALENT	SEPTUPLING	SEQUESTRUM
SENSOMOTOR	SENTIMENTALISMS	SEPTEMVIRATE	SEPULCHERED	SEQUESTRUMS
SENSORIALLY	SENTIMENTALIST	SEPTEMVIRATES	SEPULCHERING	SERAPHICAL
SENSORIMOTOR	SENTIMENTALISTS	SEPTEMVIRI	SEPULCHERS	SERAPHICALLY
SENSORINEURAL	SENTIMENTALITY	SEPTEMVIRS	SEPULCHRAL	SERAPHINES
SENSORIUMS	SENTIMENTALIZE	SEPTENARIES	SEPULCHRALLY	SERASKIERATE
SENSUALISATION	SENTIMENTALIZED	SEPTENARII	SEPULCHRED	SERASKIERATES
SENSUALISATIONS	SENTIMENTALIZES	SEPTENARIUS	SEPULCHRES	SERASKIERS
SENSUALISE	SENTIMENTALLY	SEPTENDECILLION	SEPULCHRING	SERENADERS
SENSUALISED	SENTIMENTS	SEPTENNATE	SEPULCHROUS	SERENADING
SENSUALISES	SENTINELED	SEPTENNATES	SEPULTURAL	SERENDIPITIES
SENSUALISING	SENTINELING	SEPTENNIAL	SEPULTURED	SERENDIPITIST
SENSUALISM	SENTINELLED	SEPTENNIALLY	SEPULTURES	SERENDIPITISTS
SENSUALISMS	SENTINELLING	SEPTENNIUM	SEPULTURING	SERENDIPITOUS
SENSUALIST	SEPALODIES	SEPTENNIUMS	SEQUACIOUS	SERENDIPITOUSLY
SENSUALISTIC	SEPARABILITIES	SEPTENTRIAL	SEQUACIOUSLY	SERENDIPITY
SENSUALISTS	SEPARABILITY	SEPTENTRION	SEQUACIOUSNESS	SERENENESS
SENSUALITIES	SEPARABLENESS	SEPTENTRIONAL	SEQUACITIES	SERENENESSES
SENSUALITY	SEPARABLENESSES	SEPTENTRIONALLY	SEQUELISED	SERENITIES
SENSUALIZATION	SEPARATELY	SEPTENTRIONES	SEQUELISES	SERGEANCIES
SENSUALIZATIONS	SEPARATENESS	SEPTENTRIONS	SEQUELISING	SERGEANTIES
SENSUALIZE	SEPARATENESSES	SEPTICAEMIA	SEQUELIZED	SERGEANTSHIP
SENSUALIZED	SEPARATING	SEPTICAEMIAS	SEQUELIZES	SERGEANTSHIPS
SENSUALIZES	SEPARATION	SEPTICAEMIC	SEQUELIZING	SERIALISATION

S

SERIALISATIONS

SERIALISATIONS	SERMONETTES	SERPENTIFORM	SERRIEDNESS	SESQUICENTENARY
SERIALISED	SERMONICAL	SERPENTINE	SERRIEDNESSES	SESQUIOXIDE
SERIALISES	SERMONINGS	SERPENTINED	SERRULATED	SESQUIOXIDES
SERIALISING	SERMONISED	SERPENTINELY	SERRULATION	SESQUIPEDAL
SERIALISMS	SERMONISER	SERPENTINES	SERRULATIONS	SESQUIPEDALIAN
SERIALISTS	SERMONISERS	SERPENTINIC	SERTULARIAN	SESQUIPEDALITY
SERIALITIES	SERMONISES	SERPENTINING	SERTULARIANS	SESQUIPLICATE
SERIALIZATION	SERMONISING	SERPENTININGLY	SERVANTHOOD	SESQUISULPHIDE
SERIALIZATIONS	SERMONIZED	SERPENTININGS	SERVANTHOODS	SESQUISULPHIDES
SERIALIZED	SERMONIZER	SERPENTINISE	SERVANTING	SESQUITERPENE
SERIALIZES	SERMONIZERS	SERPENTINISED	SERVANTLESS	SESQUITERPENES
SERIALIZING	SERMONIZES	SERPENTINISES	SERVANTRIES	SESQUITERTIA
SERIATIONS	SERMONIZING	SERPENTINISING	SERVANTSHIP	SESQUITERTIAS
SERICICULTURE	SEROCONVERSION	SERPENTINITE	SERVANTSHIPS	SESSILITIES
SERICICULTURES	SEROCONVERSIONS	SERPENTINITES	SERVICEABILITY	SESSIONALLY
SERICICULTURIST	SEROCONVERT	SERPENTINIZE	SERVICEABLE	SESTERTIUM
SERICITISATION	SEROCONVERTED	SERPENTINIZED	SERVICEABLENESS	SESTERTIUS
SERICITISATIONS	SEROCONVERTING	SERPENTINIZES	SERVICEABLY	SETACEOUSLY
SERICITIZATION	SEROCONVERTS	SERPENTINIZING	SERVICEBERRIES	SETIFEROUS
SERICITIZATIONS	SERODIAGNOSES	SERPENTINOUS	SERVICEBERRY	SETIGEROUS
SERICTERIA	SERODIAGNOSIS	SERPENTISE	SERVICELESS	SETTERWORT
SERICTERIUM	SERODIAGNOSTIC	SERPENTISED	SERVICEMAN	SETTERWORTS
SERICULTURAL	SEROGROUPS	SERPENTISES	SERVICEMEN	SETTLEABLE
SERICULTURE	SEROLOGICAL	SERPENTISING	SERVICEWOMAN	SETTLEDNESS
SERICULTURES	SEROLOGICALLY	SERPENTIZE	SERVICEWOMEN	SETTLEDNESSES
SERICULTURIST	SEROLOGIES	SERPENTIZED	SERVIETTES	SETTLEMENT
SERICULTURISTS	SEROLOGIST	SERPENTIZES	SERVILENESS	SETTLEMENTS
SERIGRAPHER	SEROLOGISTS	SERPENTIZING	SERVILENESSES	SEVENPENCE
SERIGRAPHERS	SERONEGATIVE	SERPENTLIKE	SERVILISMS	SEVENPENCES
SERIGRAPHIC	SERONEGATIVITY	SERPENTRIES	SERVILITIES	SEVENPENNIES
SERIGRAPHIES	SEROPOSITIVE	SERPIGINES	SERVITORIAL	SEVENPENNY
SERIGRAPHS	SEROPOSITIVITY	SERPIGINOUS	SERVITORSHIP	SEVENTEENS
SERIGRAPHY	SEROPURULENT	SERPIGINOUSLY	SERVITORSHIPS	SEVENTEENTH
SERINETTES	SEROSITIES	SERPULITES	SERVITRESS	SEVENTEENTHLY
SERIOCOMIC	SEROTAXONOMIES	SERRADELLA	SERVITRESSES	SEVENTEENTHS
SERIOCOMICAL	SEROTAXONOMY	SERRADELLAS	SERVITUDES	SEVENTIETH
SERIOCOMICALLY	SEROTHERAPIES	SERRADILLA	SERVOCONTROL	SEVENTIETHS
SERIOUSNESS	SEROTHERAPY	SERRADILLAS	SERVOCONTROLS	SEVERABILITIES
SERIOUSNESSES	SEROTINIES	SERRANOIDS	SERVOMECHANICAL	SEVERABILITY
SERJEANCIES	SEROTINOUS	SERRASALMO	SERVOMECHANISM	SEVERALFOLD
SERJEANTIES	SEROTONERGIC	SERRASALMOS	SERVOMECHANISMS	SEVERALTIES
SERJEANTRIES	SEROTONINERGIC	SERRATIONS	SERVOMOTOR	SEVERANCES
SERJEANTRY	SEROTONINS	SERRATIROSTRAL	SERVOMOTORS	SEVERENESS
SERJEANTSHIP	SEROTYPING	SERRATULATE	SESQUIALTER	SEVERENESSES
SERJEANTSHIPS	SEROTYPINGS	SERRATURES	SESQUIALTERA	SEVERITIES
SERMONEERS	SEROUSNESS	SERRATUSES	SESQUIALTERAS	SEWABILITIES
SERMONETTE	SEROUSNESSES	SERREFILES	SESQUICARBONATE	SEWABILITY

S

SEXAGENARIAN	SEXUALISED	SHAGTASTIC	SHANKPIECE	SHATTERPROOF
SEXAGENARIANS	SEXUALISES	SHAHTOOSHES	SHANKPIECES	SHAUCHLIER
SEXAGENARIES	SEXUALISING	SHAKEDOWNS	SHANTYTOWN	SHAUCHLIEST
SEXAGENARY	SEXUALISMS	SHAKINESSES	SHANTYTOWNS	SHAUCHLING
SEXAGESIMAL	SEXUALISTS	SHAKUHACHI	SHAPELESSLY	SHAVELINGS
SEXAGESIMALLY	SEXUALITIES	SHAKUHACHIS	SHAPELESSNESS	SHAVETAILS
SEXAGESIMALS	SEXUALIZATION	SHALLOWEST	SHAPELESSNESSES	SHEARLINGS
SEXAHOLICS	SEXUALIZATIONS	SHALLOWING	SHAPELIEST	SHEARWATER
SEXANGULAR	SEXUALIZED	SHALLOWINGS	SHAPELINESS	SHEARWATERS
SEXANGULARLY	SEXUALIZES	SHALLOWNESS	SHAPELINESSES	SHEATFISHES
SEXAVALENT	SEXUALIZING	SHALLOWNESSES	SHARAWADGI	SHEATHBILL
SEXCENTENARIES	SFORZANDOS	SHAMANISMS	SHARAWADGIS	SHEATHBILLS
SEXCENTENARY	SHABBINESS	SHAMANISTIC	SHARAWAGGI	SHEATHFISH
SEXDECILLION	SHABBINESSES	SHAMANISTS	SHARAWAGGIS	SHEATHFISHES
SEXDECILLIONS	SHABRACQUE	SHAMATEURISM	SHAREABILITIES	SHEATHIEST
SEXENNIALLY	SHABRACQUES	SHAMATEURISMS	SHAREABILITY	SHEATHINGS
SEXENNIALS	SHACKLEBONE	SHAMATEURS	SHARECROPPED	SHEATHLESS
SEXERCISES	SHACKLEBONES	SHAMBLIEST	SHARECROPPER	SHEBEENERS
SEXINESSES	SHADBERRIES	SHAMBLINGS	SHARECROPPERS	SHEBEENING
SEXIVALENT	SHADBUSHES	SHAMEFACED	SHARECROPPING	SHEBEENINGS
SEXLESSNESS	SHADCHANIM	SHAMEFACEDLY	SHARECROPS	SHECHITAHS
SEXLESSNESSES	SHADINESSES	SHAMEFACEDNESS	SHAREFARMER	SHECKLATON
SEXLOCULAR	SHADKHANIM	SHAMEFASTNESS	SHAREFARMERS	SHECKLATONS
SEXOLOGICAL	SHADOWBOXED	SHAMEFASTNESSES	SHAREHOLDER	SHEEPBERRIES
SEXOLOGIES	SHADOWBOXES	SHAMEFULLY	SHAREHOLDERS	SHEEPBERRY
SEXOLOGIST	SHADOWBOXING	SHAMEFULNESS	SHAREHOLDING	SHEEPCOTES
SEXOLOGISTS	SHADOWCAST	SHAMEFULNESSES	SHAREHOLDINGS	SHEEPFOLDS
SEXPARTITE	SHADOWCASTING	SHAMELESSLY	SHAREMILKER	SHEEPHEADS
SEXPLOITATION	SHADOWCASTINGS	SHAMELESSNESS	SHAREMILKERS	SHEEPHERDER
SEXPLOITATIONS	SHADOWCASTS	SHAMELESSNESSES	SHAREWARES	SHEEPHERDERS
SEXTILLION	SHADOWGRAPH	SHAMEWORTHY	SHARKSKINS	SHEEPHERDING
SEXTILLIONS	SHADOWGRAPHIES	SHAMIANAHS	SHARKSUCKER	SHEEPHERDINGS
SEXTILLIONTH	SHADOWGRAPHS	SHAMIYANAH	SHARKSUCKERS	SHEEPISHLY
SEXTILLIONTHS	SHADOWGRAPHY	SHAMIYANAHS	SHARPBENDER	SHEEPISHNESS
SEXTODECIMO	SHADOWIEST	SHAMMASHIM	SHARPBENDERS	SHEEPISHNESSES
SEXTODECIMOS	SHADOWINESS	SHAMPOOERS	SHARPENERS	SHEEPSHANK
SEXTONESSES	SHADOWINESSES	SHAMPOOING	SHARPENING	SHEEPSHANKS
SEXTONSHIP	SHADOWINGS	SHANACHIES	SHARPNESSES	SHEEPSHEAD
SEXTONSHIPS	SHADOWLESS	SHANDRYDAN	SHARPSHOOTER	SHEEPSHEADS
SEXTUPLETS	SHADOWLIKE	SHANDRYDANS	SHARPSHOOTERS	SHEEPSHEARER
SEXTUPLICATE	SHAGGEDNESS	SHANDYGAFF	SHARPSHOOTING	SHEEPSHEARERS
SEXTUPLICATED	SHAGGEDNESSES	SHANDYGAFFS	SHARPSHOOTINGS	SHEEPSHEARING
SEXTUPLICATES	SHAGGINESS	SHANGHAIED	SHASHLICKS	SHEEPSHEARINGS
SEXTUPLICATING	SHAGGINESSES	SHANGHAIER	SHATOOSHES	SHEEPSKINS
SEXTUPLING	SHAGGYMANE	SHANGHAIERS	SHATTERERS	SHEEPTRACK
SEXUALISATION	SHAGGYMANES	SHANGHAIING	SHATTERING	SHEEPTRACKS
SEXUALISATIONS	SHAGREENED	SHANKBONES	SHATTERINGLY	SHEEPWALKS

S

SHEERNESSES
SHEETROCKED
SHEETROCKING
SHEETROCKS
SHEIKHDOMS
SHELDDUCKS
SHELDRAKES
SHELFROOMS
SHELFTALKER
SHELFTALKERS
SHELLACKED
SHELLACKER
SHELLACKERS
SHELLACKING
SHELLACKINGS
SHELLBACKS
SHELLBARKS
SHELLBOUND
SHELLCRACKER
SHELLCRACKERS
SHELLDRAKE
SHELLDRAKES
SHELLDUCKS
SHELLFIRES
SHELLFISHERIES
SHELLFISHERY
SHELLFISHES
SHELLINESS
SHELLINESSES
SHELLPROOF
SHELLSHOCK
SHELLSHOCKED
SHELLSHOCKS
SHELLWORKS
SHELLYCOAT
SHELLYCOATS
SHELTERBELT
SHELTERBELTS
SHELTERERS
SHELTERING
SHELTERINGS
SHELTERLESS
SHEMOZZLED
SHEMOZZLES
SHEMOZZLING
SHENANIGAN
SHENANIGANS

SHEPHERDED
SHEPHERDESS
SHEPHERDESSES
SHEPHERDING
SHEPHERDLESS
SHEPHERDLING
SHEPHERDLINGS
SHERARDISATION
SHERARDISATIONS
SHERARDISE
SHERARDISED
SHERARDISES
SHERARDISING
SHERARDIZATION
SHERARDIZATIONS
SHERARDIZE
SHERARDIZED
SHERARDIZES
SHERARDIZING
SHEREEFIAN
SHERGOTTITE
SHERGOTTITES
SHERIFFALTIES
SHERIFFALTY
SHERIFFDOM
SHERIFFDOMS
SHERIFFSHIP
SHERIFFSHIPS
SHEWBREADS
SHIBBOLETH
SHIBBOLETHS
SHIBUICHIS
SHIDDUCHIM
SHIELDINGS
SHIELDLESS
SHIELDLIKE
SHIELDLING
SHIELDLINGS
SHIELDRAKE
SHIELDRAKES
SHIELDWALL
SHIELDWALLS
SHIFTINESS
SHIFTINESSES
SHIFTLESSLY
SHIFTLESSNESS
SHIFTLESSNESSES

SHIFTWORKS
SHIGELLOSES
SHIGELLOSIS
SHIKARRING
SHILLABERS
SHILLALAHS
SHILLELAGH
SHILLELAGHS
SHILLELAHS
SHILLINGLESS
SHILLINGSWORTH
SHILLINGSWORTHS
SHILLYSHALLIED
SHILLYSHALLIER
SHILLYSHALLIERS
SHILLYSHALLIES
SHILLYSHALLY
SHILLYSHALLYING
SHIMMERIER
SHIMMERIEST
SHIMMERING
SHIMMERINGLY
SHIMMERINGS
SHIMOZZLES
SHINGLIEST
SHINGLINGS
SHINGUARDS
SHININESSES
SHININGNESS
SHININGNESSES
SHINLEAVES
SHINNERIES
SHINNEYING
SHINPLASTER
SHINPLASTERS
SHINSPLINTS
SHIPBOARDS
SHIPBROKER
SHIPBROKERS
SHIPBUILDER
SHIPBUILDERS
SHIPBUILDING
SHIPBUILDINGS
SHIPFITTER
SHIPFITTERS
SHIPLAPPED
SHIPLAPPING

SHIPMASTER
SHIPMASTERS
SHIPOWNERS
SHIPPOUNDS
SHIPWRECKED
SHIPWRECKING
SHIPWRECKS
SHIPWRIGHT
SHIPWRIGHTS
SHIRRALEES
SHIRTBANDS
SHIRTDRESS
SHIRTDRESSES
SHIRTFRONT
SHIRTFRONTS
SHIRTINESS
SHIRTINESSES
SHIRTLIFTER
SHIRTLIFTERS
SHIRTMAKER
SHIRTMAKERS
SHIRTSLEEVE
SHIRTSLEEVED
SHIRTSLEEVES
SHIRTTAILED
SHIRTTAILING
SHIRTTAILS
SHIRTWAIST
SHIRTWAISTER
SHIRTWAISTERS
SHIRTWAISTS
SHITHOUSES
SHITTIMWOOD
SHITTIMWOODS
SHITTINESS
SHITTINESSES
SHIVAREEING
SHIVERIEST
SHIVERINGLY
SHIVERINGS
SHLEMIEHLS
SHLEMOZZLE
SHLEMOZZLED
SHLEMOZZLES
SHLEMOZZLING
SHLIMAZELS
SHLOCKIEST

SHMALTZIER
SHMALTZIEST
SHMOOZIEST
SHOALINESS
SHOALINESSES
SHOALNESSES
SHOCKABILITIES
SHOCKABILITY
SHOCKHEADED
SHOCKINGLY
SHOCKINGNESS
SHOCKINGNESSES
SHOCKPROOF
SHOCKSTALL
SHOCKSTALLS
SHOCKUMENTARIES
SHOCKUMENTARY
SHODDINESS
SHODDINESSES
SHOEBLACKS
SHOEHORNED
SHOEHORNING
SHOEMAKERS
SHOEMAKING
SHOEMAKINGS
SHOESHINES
SHOESTRING
SHOESTRINGS
SHOGGLIEST
SHOGUNATES
SHONGOLOLO
SHONGOLOLOS
SHOOGIEING
SHOOGLIEST
SHOOTAROUND
SHOOTAROUNDS
SHOOTDOWNS
SHOPAHOLIC
SHOPAHOLICS
SHOPAHOLISM
SHOPAHOLISMS
SHOPBOARDS
SHOPBREAKER
SHOPBREAKERS
SHOPBREAKING
SHOPBREAKINGS
SHOPFITTER

S

SHOPFITTERS	SHORTHANDS	SHOWERHEAD	SHRIMPLIKE	SHUTTLEWISE
SHOPFRONTS	SHORTHEADS	SHOWERHEADS	SHRINELIKE	SHYLOCKING
SHOPKEEPER	SHORTHORNS	SHOWERIEST	SHRINKABLE	SIALAGOGIC
SHOPKEEPERS	SHORTLISTED	SHOWERINESS	SHRINKAGES	SIALAGOGUE
SHOPKEEPING	SHORTLISTING	SHOWERINESSES	SHRINKINGLY	SIALAGOGUES
SHOPKEEPINGS	SHORTLISTS	SHOWERINGS	SHRINKPACK	SIALOGOGIC
SHOPLIFTED	SHORTNESSES	SHOWERLESS	SHRINKPACKS	SIALOGOGUE
SHOPLIFTER	SHORTSIGHTED	SHOWERPROOF	SHRITCHING	SIALOGOGUES
SHOPLIFTERS	SHORTSIGHTEDLY	SHOWERPROOFED	SHRIVELING	SIALOGRAMS
SHOPLIFTING	SHORTSTOPS	SHOWERPROOFING	SHRIVELLED	SIALOGRAPHIES
SHOPLIFTINGS	SHORTSWORD	SHOWERPROOFINGS	SHRIVELLING	SIALOGRAPHY
SHOPSOILED	SHORTSWORDS	SHOWERPROOFS	SHROFFAGES	SIALOLITHS
SHOPWALKER	SHORTWAVED	SHOWGROUND	SHROUDIEST	SIALORRHOEA
SHOPWALKERS	SHORTWAVES	SHOWGROUNDS	SHROUDINGS	SIALORRHOEAS
SHOPWINDOW	SHORTWAVING	SHOWINESSES	SHROUDLESS	SIBILANCES
SHOPWINDOWS	SHOTFIRERS	SHOWJUMPED	SHRUBBERIED	SIBILANCIES
SHOREBIRDS	SHOTGUNNED	SHOWJUMPER	SHRUBBERIES	SIBILANTLY
SHOREFRONT	SHOTGUNNER	SHOWJUMPERS	SHRUBBIEST	SIBILATING
SHOREFRONTS	SHOTGUNNERS	SHOWJUMPING	SHRUBBINESS	SIBILATION
SHORELINES	SHOTGUNNING	SHOWJUMPINGS	SHRUBBINESSES	SIBILATIONS
SHORESIDES	SHOTMAKERS	SHOWMANSHIP	SHRUBLANDS	SIBILATORS
SHOREWARDS	SHOTMAKING	SHOWMANSHIPS	SHTETELACH	SIBILATORY
SHOREWEEDS	SHOTMAKINGS	SHOWPIECES	SHTICKIEST	SICCATIVES
SHORTARSES	SHOULDERED	SHOWPLACES	SHUBUNKINS	SICILIANOS
SHORTBOARD	SHOULDERING	SHOWSTOPPER	SHUDDERING	SICILIENNE
SHORTBOARDS	SHOULDERINGS	SHOWSTOPPERS	SHUDDERINGLY	SICILIENNES
SHORTBREAD	SHOUTHERED	SHOWSTOPPING	SHUDDERINGS	SICKENINGLY
SHORTBREADS	SHOUTHERING	SHREDDIEST	SHUDDERSOME	SICKENINGS
SHORTCAKES	SHOUTINGLY	SHREDDINGS	SHUFFLEBOARD	SICKERNESS
SHORTCHANGE	SHOUTLINES	SHREWDNESS	SHUFFLEBOARDS	SICKERNESSES
SHORTCHANGED	SHOVELBOARD	SHREWDNESSES	SHUFFLINGLY	SICKISHNESS
SHORTCHANGER	SHOVELBOARDS	SHREWISHLY	SHUFFLINGS	SICKISHNESSES
SHORTCHANGERS	SHOVELFULS	SHREWISHNESS	SHUNAMITISM	SICKLEBILL
SHORTCHANGES	SHOVELHEAD	SHREWISHNESSES	SHUNAMITISMS	SICKLEBILLS
SHORTCHANGING	SHOVELHEADS	SHREWMOUSE	SHUNPIKERS	SICKLEMIAS
SHORTCOMING	SHOVELLERS	SHRIECHING	SHUNPIKING	SICKLINESS
SHORTCOMINGS	SHOVELLING	SHRIEKIEST	SHUNPIKINGS	SICKLINESSES
SHORTCRUST	SHOVELNOSE	SHRIEKINGLY	SHUTTERBUG	SICKNESSES
SHORTCUTTING	SHOVELNOSES	SHRIEKINGS	SHUTTERBUGS	SICKNURSES
SHORTENERS	SHOVELSFUL	SHRIEVALTIES	SHUTTERING	SICKNURSING
SHORTENING	SHOWBIZZES	SHRIEVALTY	SHUTTERINGS	SICKNURSINGS
SHORTENINGS	SHOWBOATED	SHRILLIEST	SHUTTERLESS	SIDDHUISMS
SHORTFALLS	SHOWBOATER	SHRILLINGS	SHUTTLECOCK	SIDEBOARDS
SHORTGOWNS	SHOWBOATERS	SHRILLNESS	SHUTTLECOCKED	SIDEBURNED
SHORTHAIRED	SHOWBOATING	SHRILLNESSES	SHUTTLECOCKING	SIDECHECKS
SHORTHAIRS	SHOWBREADS	SHRIMPIEST	SHUTTLECOCKS	SIDEDNESSES
SHORTHANDED	SHOWCASING	SHRIMPINGS	SHUTTLELESS	SIDEDRESSES

S

SIDELEVERS	SIDEWINDERS	SIGNALLING	SILICIFICATION	SILVERPOINTS
SIDELIGHTS	SIEGECRAFT	SIGNALLINGS	SILICIFICATIONS	SILVERSIDE
SIDELINERS	SIEGECRAFTS	SIGNALMENT	SILICIFIED	SILVERSIDES
SIDELINING	SIEGEWORKS	SIGNALMENTS	SILICIFIES	SILVERSIDESES
SIDEPIECES	SIFFLEUSES	SIGNATORIES	SILICIFYING	SILVERSKIN
SIDERATING	SIGHTLESSLY	SIGNATURES	SILICONISED	SILVERSKINS
SIDERATION	SIGHTLESSNESS	SIGNBOARDS	SILICONIZED	SILVERSMITH
SIDERATIONS	SIGHTLESSNESSES	SIGNEURIES	SILICOTICS	SILVERSMITHING
SIDEREALLY	SIGHTLIEST	SIGNIFIABLE	SILICULOSE	SILVERSMITHINGS
SIDEROLITE	SIGHTLINES	SIGNIFICANCE	SILIQUACEOUS	SILVERSMITHS
SIDEROLITES	SIGHTLINESS	SIGNIFICANCES	SILKALENES	SILVERTAIL
SIDEROPENIA	SIGHTLINESSES	SIGNIFICANCIES	SILKALINES	SILVERTAILS
SIDEROPENIAS	SIGHTSCREEN	SIGNIFICANCY	SILKGROWER	SILVERWARE
SIDEROPHILE	SIGHTSCREENS	SIGNIFICANT	SILKGROWERS	SILVERWARES
SIDEROPHILES	SIGHTSEEING	SIGNIFICANTLY	SILKINESSES	SILVERWEED
SIDEROPHILIC	SIGHTSEEINGS	SIGNIFICANTS	SILKOLINES	SILVERWEEDS
SIDEROPHILIN	SIGHTSEERS	SIGNIFICATE	SILKSCREEN	SILVESTRIAN
SIDEROPHILINS	SIGHTWORTHY	SIGNIFICATES	SILKSCREENS	SILVICULTURAL
SIDEROSTAT	SIGILLARIAN	SIGNIFICATION	SILLIMANITE	SILVICULTURALLY
SIDEROSTATIC	SIGILLARIANS	SIGNIFICATIONS	SILLIMANITES	SILVICULTURE
SIDEROSTATS	SIGILLARID	SIGNIFICATIVE	SILLINESSES	SILVICULTURES
SIDESADDLE	SIGILLARIDS	SIGNIFICATIVELY	SILTATIONS	SILVICULTURIST
SIDESADDLES	SIGILLATION	SIGNIFICATOR	SILTSTONES	SILVICULTURISTS
SIDESHOOTS	SIGILLATIONS	SIGNIFICATORS	SILVERBACK	SILYMARINS
SIDESLIPPED	SIGMATIONS	SIGNIFICATORY	SILVERBACKS	SIMAROUBACEOUS
SIDESLIPPING	SIGMATISMS	SIGNIFIEDS	SILVERBERRIES	SIMAROUBAS
SIDESPLITTING	SIGMATRONS	SIGNIFIERS	SILVERBERRY	SIMARUBACEOUS
SIDESPLITTINGLY	SIGMOIDALLY	SIGNIFYING	SILVERBILL	SIMILARITIES
SIDESTEPPED	SIGMOIDECTOMIES	SIGNIFYINGS	SILVERBILLS	SIMILARITY
SIDESTEPPER	SIGMOIDECTOMY	SIGNIORIES	SILVEREYES	SIMILATIVE
SIDESTEPPERS	SIGMOIDOSCOPE	SIGNORINAS	SILVERFISH	SIMILISING
SIDESTEPPING	SIGMOIDOSCOPES	SIGNPOSTED	SILVERFISHES	SIMILITUDE
SIDESTREAM	SIGMOIDOSCOPIC	SIGNPOSTING	SILVERHORN	SIMILITUDES
SIDESTROKE	SIGMOIDOSCOPIES	SIKORSKIES	SILVERHORNS	SIMILIZING
SIDESTROKES	SIGMOIDOSCOPY	SILENTIARIES	SILVERIEST	SIMILLIMUM
SIDESWIPED	SIGNALINGS	SILENTIARY	SILVERINESS	SIMILLIMUMS
SIDESWIPER	SIGNALISATION	SILENTNESS	SILVERINESSES	SIMONIACAL
SIDESWIPERS	SIGNALISATIONS	SILENTNESSES	SILVERINGS	SIMONIACALLY
SIDESWIPES	SIGNALISED	SILHOUETTE	SILVERISED	SIMONISING
SIDESWIPING	SIGNALISES	SILHOUETTED	SILVERISES	SIMONIZING
SIDETRACKED	SIGNALISING	SILHOUETTES	SILVERISING	SIMPERINGLY
SIDETRACKING	SIGNALIZATION	SILHOUETTING	SILVERIZED	SIMPERINGS
SIDETRACKS	SIGNALIZATIONS	SILHOUETTIST	SILVERIZES	SIMPLEMINDED
SIDEWHEELER	SIGNALIZED	SILHOUETTISTS	SILVERIZING	SIMPLEMINDEDLY
SIDEWHEELERS	SIGNALIZES	SILICATING	SILVERLING	SIMPLENESS
SIDEWHEELS	SIGNALIZING	SILICICOLOUS	SILVERLINGS	SIMPLENESSES
SIDEWINDER	SIGNALLERS	SILICIFEROUS	SILVERPOINT	SIMPLESSES

SIMPLETONS	SINCERENESS	SINGULARITIES	SINUOUSNESSES	SITUATIONISMS
SIMPLICIAL	SINCERENESSES	SINGULARITY	SINUPALLIAL	SITUATIONS
SIMPLICIALLY	SINCERITIES	SINGULARIZATION	SINUPALLIATE	SITUTUNGAS
SIMPLICIDENTATE	SINCIPITAL	SINGULARIZE	SINUSITISES	SITZKRIEGS
SIMPLICITER	SINDONOLOGIES	SINGULARIZED	SINUSOIDAL	SIXPENNIES
SIMPLICITIES	SINDONOLOGIST	SINGULARIZES	SINUSOIDALLY	SIXTEENERS
SIMPLICITY	SINDONOLOGISTS	SINGULARIZING	SIPHONAGES	SIXTEENMOS
SIMPLIFICATION	SINDONOLOGY	SINGULARLY	SIPHONOGAM	SIXTEENTHLY
SIMPLIFICATIONS	SINDONOPHANIES	SINGULARNESS	SIPHONOGAMIES	SIXTEENTHS
SIMPLIFICATIVE	SINDONOPHANY	SINGULARNESSES	SIPHONOGAMS	SIZABLENESS
SIMPLIFICATOR	SINECURISM	SINGULTUSES	SIPHONOGAMY	SIZABLENESSES
SIMPLIFICATORS	SINECURISMS	SINICISING	SIPHONOPHORE	SIZARSHIPS
SIMPLIFIED	SINECURIST	SINICIZING	SIPHONOPHORES	SIZEABLENESS
SIMPLIFIER	SINECURISTS	SINISTERITIES	SIPHONOPHOROUS	SIZEABLENESSES
SIMPLIFIERS	SINEWINESS	SINISTERITY	SIPHONOSTELE	SIZINESSES
SIMPLIFIES	SINEWINESSES	SINISTERLY	SIPHONOSTELES	SIZZLINGLY
SIMPLIFYING	SINFONIETTA	SINISTERNESS	SIPHONOSTELIC	SJAMBOKING
SIMPLISTIC	SINFONIETTAS	SINISTERNESSES	SIPHUNCLES	SJAMBOKKED
SIMPLISTICALLY	SINFULNESS	SINISTERWISE	SIPUNCULID	SJAMBOKKING
SIMULACRES	SINFULNESSES	SINISTRALITIES	SIPUNCULIDS	SKAITHLESS
SIMULACRUM	SINGABLENESS	SINISTRALITY	SIPUNCULOID	SKALDSHIPS
SIMULACRUMS	SINGABLENESSES	SINISTRALLY	SIPUNCULOIDS	SKANKINESS
SIMULATING	SINGALONGS	SINISTRALS	SIRENISING	SKANKINESSES
SIMULATION	SINGLEDOMS	SINISTRODEXTRAL	SIRENIZING	SKATEBOARD
SIMULATIONS	SINGLEHOOD	SINISTRORSAL	SIRONISING	SKATEBOARDED
SIMULATIVE	SINGLEHOODS	SINISTRORSALLY	SIRONIZING	SKATEBOARDER
SIMULATIVELY	SINGLENESS	SINISTRORSE	SISERARIES	SKATEBOARDERS
SIMULATORS	SINGLENESSES	SINISTRORSELY	SISSINESSES	SKATEBOARDING
SIMULATORY	SINGLESTICK	SINISTROUS	SISSYNESSES	SKATEBOARDINGS
SIMULCASTED	SINGLESTICKS	SINISTROUSLY	SISTERHOOD	SKATEBOARDS
SIMULCASTING	SINGLETONS	SINLESSNESS	SISTERHOODS	SKATEPARKS
SIMULCASTS	SINGLETRACK	SINLESSNESSES	SISTERLESS	SKEDADDLED
SIMULTANEITIES	SINGLETRACKS	SINNINGIAS	SISTERLIKE	SKEDADDLER
SIMULTANEITY	SINGLETREE	SINOATRIAL	SISTERLINESS	SKEDADDLERS
SIMULTANEOUS	SINGLETREES	SINOLOGICAL	SISTERLINESSES	SKEDADDLES
SIMULTANEOUSES	SINGSONGED	SINOLOGIES	SITATUNGAS	SKEDADDLING
SIMULTANEOUSLY	SINGSONGING	SINOLOGIST	SITIOLOGIES	SKELDERING
SINANTHROPUS	SINGSPIELS	SINOLOGISTS	SITIOPHOBIA	SKELETALLY
SINANTHROPUSES	SINGULARISATION	SINOLOGUES	SITIOPHOBIAS	SKELETOGENOUS
SINARCHISM	SINGULARISE	SINSEMILLA	SITOLOGIES	SKELETONIC
SINARCHISMS	SINGULARISED	SINSEMILLAS	SITOPHOBIA	SKELETONISE
SINARCHIST	SINGULARISES	SINTERABILITIES	SITOPHOBIAS	SKELETONISED
SINARCHISTS	SINGULARISING	SINTERABILITY	SITOSTEROL	SKELETONISER
SINARQUISM	SINGULARISM	SINUATIONS	SITOSTEROLS	SKELETONISERS
SINARQUISMS	SINGULARISMS	SINUITISES	SITUATIONAL	SKELETONISES
SINARQUIST	SINGULARIST	SINUOSITIES	SITUATIONALLY	SKELETONISING
SINARQUISTS	SINGULARISTS	SINUOUSNESS	SITUATIONISM	SKELETONIZE

S

SKELETONIZED	SKILLFULNESS	SKRIMMAGING	SLACKENERS	SLATTERNLY
SKELETONIZER	SKILLFULNESSES	SKRIMSHANK	SLACKENING	SLAUGHTERABLE
SKELETONIZERS	SKILLIGALEE	SKRIMSHANKED	SLACKENINGS	SLAUGHTERED
SKELETONIZES	SKILLIGALEES	SKRIMSHANKER	SLACKNESSES	SLAUGHTERER
SKELETONIZING	SKILLIGOLEE	SKRIMSHANKERS	SLACKTIVISM	SLAUGHTERERS
SKELLOCHED	SKILLIGOLEES	SKRIMSHANKING	SLACKTIVISMS	SLAUGHTERHOUSE
SKELLOCHING	SKIMBOARDED	SKRIMSHANKS	SLACKTIVIST	SLAUGHTERHOUSES
SKELTERING	SKIMBOARDER	SKULDUDDERIES	SLACKTIVISTS	SLAUGHTERIES
SKEPTICALLY	SKIMBOARDERS	SKULDUDDERY	SLACTIVISM	SLAUGHTERING
SKEPTICALNESS	SKIMBOARDING	SKULDUGGERIES	SLACTIVISMS	SLAUGHTERMAN
SKEPTICALNESSES	SKIMBOARDS	SKULDUGGERY	SLACTIVIST	SLAUGHTERMEN
SKEPTICISM	SKIMMINGLY	SKULKINGLY	SLACTIVISTS	SLAUGHTEROUS
SKEPTICISMS	SKIMMINGTON	SKULLDUGGERIES	SLAISTERED	SLAUGHTEROUSLY
SKETCHABILITIES	SKIMMINGTONS	SKULLDUGGERY	SLAISTERIES	SLAUGHTERS
SKETCHABILITY	SKIMOBILED	SKUMMERING	SLAISTERING	SLAUGHTERY
SKETCHABLE	SKIMOBILES	SKUNKBIRDS	SLALOMISTS	SLAVEHOLDER
SKETCHBOOK	SKIMOBILING	SKUNKWEEDS	SLAMDANCED	SLAVEHOLDERS
SKETCHBOOKS	SKIMPINESS	SKUTTERUDITE	SLAMDANCES	SLAVEHOLDING
SKETCHIEST	SKIMPINESSES	SKUTTERUDITES	SLAMDANCING	SLAVEHOLDINGS
SKETCHINESS	SKIMPINGLY	SKYBRIDGES	SLAMMAKINS	SLAVERINGLY
SKETCHINESSES	SKINFLICKS	SKYDIVINGS	SLAMMERKIN	SLAVERINGS
SKETCHPADS	SKINFLINTS	SKYJACKERS	SLAMMERKINS	SLAVISHNESS
SKEUOMORPH	SKINFLINTY	SKYJACKING	SLANDERERS	SLAVISHNESSES
SKEUOMORPHIC	SKINNINESS	SKYJACKINGS	SLANDERING	SLAVOCRACIES
SKEUOMORPHISM	SKINNINESSES	SKYLARKERS	SLANDEROUS	SLAVOCRACY
SKEUOMORPHISMS	SKINTIGHTS	SKYLARKING	SLANDEROUSLY	SLAVOCRATS
SKEUOMORPHS	SKIPPERING	SKYLARKINGS	SLANDEROUSNESS	SLAVOPHILE
SKEWBACKED	SKIPPERINGS	SKYLIGHTED	SLANGINESS	SLAVOPHILES
SKEWNESSES	SKIPPINGLY	SKYROCKETED	SLANGINESSES	SLAVOPHILS
SKIAGRAPHS	SKIRMISHED	SKYROCKETING	SLANGINGLY	SLEAZEBAGS
SKIAMACHIES	SKIRMISHER	SKYROCKETS	SLANGUAGES	SLEAZEBALL
SKIASCOPES	SKIRMISHERS	SKYSCRAPER	SLANTENDICULAR	SLEAZEBALLS
SKIASCOPIES	SKIRMISHES	SKYSCRAPERS	SLANTINDICULAR	SLEAZINESS
SKIBOBBERS	SKIRMISHING	SKYSURFERS	SLANTINGLY	SLEAZINESSES
SKIBOBBING	SKIRMISHINGS	SKYSURFING	SLANTINGWAYS	SLEDGEHAMMER
SKIBOBBINGS	SKITTERIER	SKYSURFINGS	SLAPDASHED	SLEDGEHAMMERED
SKIDDOOING	SKITTERIEST	SKYWRITERS	SLAPDASHES	SLEDGEHAMMERING
SKIJORINGS	SKITTERING	SKYWRITING	SLAPDASHING	SLEDGEHAMMERS
SKIKJORING	SKITTISHLY	SKYWRITINGS	SLAPHAPPIER	SLEECHIEST
SKIKJORINGS	SKITTISHNESS	SKYWRITTEN	SLAPHAPPIEST	SLEEKENING
SKILFULNESS	SKITTISHNESSES	SLABBERERS	SLAPSTICKS	SLEEKNESSES
SKILFULNESSES	SKREEGHING	SLABBERIER	SLASHFESTS	SLEEKSTONE
SKILLCENTRE	SKREIGHING	SLABBERIEST	SLASHINGLY	SLEEKSTONES
SKILLCENTRES	SKRIECHING	SLABBERING	SLATHERING	SLEEPINESS
SKILLESSNESS	SKRIEGHING	SLABBINESS	SLATINESSES	SLEEPINESSES
SKILLESSNESSES	SKRIMMAGED	SLABBINESSES	SLATTERING	SLEEPLESSLY
SKILLFULLY	SKRIMMAGES	SLABSTONES	SLATTERNLINESS	SLEEPLESSNESS

S

SLEEPLESSNESSES	SLIMEBALLS	SLIVOWITZES	SLOVENLINESS	SLUMPFLATIONARY
SLEEPOVERS	SLIMINESSES	SLOBBERERS	SLOVENLINESSES	SLUMPFLATIONS
SLEEPSUITS	SLIMNASTICS	SLOBBERIER	SLOVENRIES	SLUNGSHOTS
SLEEPWALKED	SLIMNESSES	SLOBBERIEST	SLOWCOACHES	SLUSHINESS
SLEEPWALKER	SLIMPSIEST	SLOBBERING	SLOWNESSES	SLUSHINESSES
SLEEPWALKERS	SLINGBACKS	SLOBBISHNESS	SLUBBERING	SLUTCHIEST
SLEEPWALKING	SLINGSHOTS	SLOBBISHNESSES	SLUBBERINGLY	SLUTTERIES
SLEEPWALKINGS	SLINGSTONE	SLOCKDOLAGER	SLUBBERINGS	SLUTTINESS
SLEEPWALKS	SLINGSTONES	SLOCKDOLAGERS	SLUGGABEDS	SLUTTINESSES
SLEEPYHEAD	SLINKINESS	SLOCKDOLIGER	SLUGGARDISE	SLUTTISHLY
SLEEPYHEADED	SLINKINESSES	SLOCKDOLIGERS	SLUGGARDISED	SLUTTISHNESS
SLEEPYHEADS	SLINKSKINS	SLOCKDOLOGER	SLUGGARDISES	SLUTTISHNESSES
SLEETINESS	SLINKWEEDS	SLOCKDOLOGERS	SLUGGARDISING	SMACKDOWNS
SLEETINESSES	SLIPCOVERED	SLOCKENING	SLUGGARDIZE	SMACKHEADS
SLEEVEHAND	SLIPCOVERING	SLOEBUSHES	SLUGGARDIZED	SMALLCLOTHES
SLEEVEHANDS	SLIPCOVERS	SLOETHORNS	SLUGGARDIZES	SMALLHOLDER
SLEEVELESS	SLIPDRESSES	SLOGANEERED	SLUGGARDIZING	SMALLHOLDERS
SLEEVELETS	SLIPFORMED	SLOGANEERING	SLUGGARDLINESS	SMALLHOLDING
SLEEVELIKE	SLIPFORMING	SLOGANEERINGS	SLUGGARDLY	SMALLHOLDINGS
SLEIGHINGS	SLIPNOOSES	SLOGANEERS	SLUGGARDNESS	SMALLMOUTH
SLENDEREST	SLIPPERIER	SLOGANISED	SLUGGARDNESSES	SMALLMOUTHS
SLENDERISE	SLIPPERIEST	SLOGANISES	SLUGGISHLY	SMALLNESSES
SLENDERISED	SLIPPERILY	SLOGANISING	SLUGGISHNESS	SMALLPOXES
SLENDERISES	SLIPPERINESS	SLOGANISINGS	SLUGGISHNESSES	SMALLSWORD
SLENDERISING	SLIPPERINESSES	SLOGANIZED	SLUGHORNES	SMALLSWORDS
SLENDERIZE	SLIPPERING	SLOGANIZES	SLUICEGATE	SMALMINESS
SLENDERIZED	SLIPPERWORT	SLOGANIZING	SLUICEGATES	SMALMINESSES
SLENDERIZES	SLIPPERWORTS	SLOGANIZINGS	SLUICELIKE	SMARAGDINE
SLENDERIZING	SLIPPINESS	SLOMMOCKED	SLUICEWAYS	SMARAGDITE
SLENDERNESS	SLIPPINESSES	SLOMMOCKING	SLUMBERERS	SMARAGDITES
SLENDERNESSES	SLIPSHEETED	SLOPINGNESS	SLUMBERFUL	SMARMINESS
SLEUTHHOUND	SLIPSHEETING	SLOPINGNESSES	SLUMBERING	SMARMINESSES
SLEUTHHOUNDS	SLIPSHEETS	SLOPPINESS	SLUMBERINGLY	SMARTARSED
SLICKENERS	SLIPSHODDINESS	SLOPPINESSES	SLUMBERINGS	SMARTARSES
SLICKENING	SLIPSHODNESS	SLOPWORKER	SLUMBERLAND	SMARTASSES
SLICKENSIDE	SLIPSHODNESSES	SLOPWORKERS	SLUMBERLANDS	SMARTENING
SLICKENSIDED	SLIPSLOPPY	SLOTHFULLY	SLUMBERLESS	SMARTINGLY
SLICKENSIDES	SLIPSTREAM	SLOTHFULNESS	SLUMBEROUS	SMARTMOUTH
SLICKNESSES	SLIPSTREAMED	SLOTHFULNESSES	SLUMBEROUSLY	SMARTMOUTHS
SLICKROCKS	SLIPSTREAMING	SLOUCHIEST	SLUMBEROUSNESS	SMARTNESSES
SLICKSTERS	SLIPSTREAMS	SLOUCHINESS	SLUMBERSOME	SMARTPHONE
SLICKSTONE	SLITHERIER	SLOUCHINESSES	SLUMBROUSLY	SMARTPHONES
SLICKSTONES	SLITHERIEST	SLOUCHINGLY	SLUMGULLION	SMARTWEEDS
SLIDDERING	SLITHERING	SLOUGHIEST	SLUMGULLIONS	SMARTYPANTS
SLIGHTINGLY	SLIVOVICAS	SLOVENLIER	SLUMMOCKED	SMASHEROOS
SLIGHTNESS	SLIVOVICES	SLOVENLIEST	SLUMMOCKING	SMASHINGLY
SLIGHTNESSES	SLIVOVITZES	SLOVENLIKE	SLUMPFLATION	SMATTERERS

S

SMATTERING	SMOOCHIEST	SNAKEMOUTHS	SNEEZELESS	SNOBBOCRACY
SMATTERINGLY	SMOOTHABLE	SNAKEROOTS	SNEEZEWEED	SNOBOCRACIES
SMATTERINGS	SMOOTHBORE	SNAKESKINS	SNEEZEWEEDS	SNOBOCRACY
SMEARCASES	SMOOTHBORED	SNAKESTONE	SNEEZEWOOD	SNOBOGRAPHER
SMEARINESS	SMOOTHBORES	SNAKESTONES	SNEEZEWOODS	SNOBOGRAPHERS
SMEARINESSES	SMOOTHENED	SNAKEWEEDS	SNEEZEWORT	SNOBOGRAPHIES
SMELLINESS	SMOOTHENING	SNAKEWOODS	SNEEZEWORTS	SNOBOGRAPHY
SMELLINESSES	SMOOTHINGS	SNAKINESSES	SNICKERERS	SNOLLYGOSTER
SMELTERIES	SMOOTHNESS	SNAKISHNESS	SNICKERING	SNOLLYGOSTERS
SMICKERING	SMOOTHNESSES	SNAKISHNESSES	SNICKERSNEE	SNOOKERING
SMICKERINGS	SMOOTHPATE	SNAPDRAGON	SNICKERSNEED	SNOOPERSCOPE
SMIERCASES	SMOOTHPATES	SNAPDRAGONS	SNICKERSNEEING	SNOOPERSCOPES
SMIFLIGATE	SMORGASBORD	SNAPHANCES	SNICKERSNEES	SNOOTINESS
SMIFLIGATED	SMORGASBORDS	SNAPHAUNCE	SNIDENESSES	SNOOTINESSES
SMIFLIGATES	SMORREBROD	SNAPHAUNCES	SNIFFINESS	SNORKELERS
SMIFLIGATING	SMORREBRODS	SNAPHAUNCH	SNIFFINESSES	SNORKELING
SMILACEOUS	SMOTHERERS	SNAPHAUNCHES	SNIFFINGLY	SNORKELLED
SMILINGNESS	SMOTHERINESS	SNAPPERING	SNIFFISHLY	SNORKELLING
SMILINGNESSES	SMOTHERINESSES	SNAPPINESS	SNIFFISHNESS	SNORKELLINGS
SMIRKINGLY	SMOTHERING	SNAPPINESSES	SNIFFISHNESSES	SNORTINGLY
SMITHCRAFT	SMOTHERINGLY	SNAPPINGLY	SNIFFLIEST	SNOTTERIES
SMITHCRAFTS	SMOTHERINGS	SNAPPISHLY	SNIFTERING	SNOTTERING
SMITHEREEN	SMOULDERED	SNAPPISHNESS	SNIGGERERS	SNOTTINESS
SMITHEREENED	SMOULDERING	SNAPPISHNESSES	SNIGGERING	SNOTTINESSES
SMITHEREENING	SMOULDERINGLY	SNAPSHOOTER	SNIGGERINGLY	SNOWBALLED
SMITHEREENS	SMOULDERINGS	SNAPSHOOTERS	SNIGGERINGS	SNOWBALLING
SMITHERIES	SMUDGELESS	SNAPSHOOTING	SNIGGLINGS	SNOWBERRIES
SMITHSONITE	SMUDGINESS	SNAPSHOOTINGS	SNIPEFISHES	SNOWBLADER
SMITHSONITES	SMUDGINESSES	SNAPSHOTTED	SNIPERSCOPE	SNOWBLADERS
SMOKEBOARD	SMUGGERIES	SNAPSHOTTING	SNIPERSCOPES	SNOWBLADES
SMOKEBOARDS	SMUGGLINGS	SNARLINGLY	SNIPPERSNAPPER	SNOWBLADING
SMOKEBOXES	SMUGNESSES	SNATCHIEST	SNIPPERSNAPPERS	SNOWBLADINGS
SMOKEHOODS	SMUTCHIEST	SNATCHINGLY	SNIPPETIER	SNOWBLINKS
SMOKEHOUSE	SMUTTINESS	SNATCHINGS	SNIPPETIEST	SNOWBLOWER
SMOKEHOUSES	SMUTTINESSES	SNAZZINESS	SNIPPETINESS	SNOWBLOWERS
SMOKEJACKS	SNACKETTES	SNAZZINESSES	SNIPPETINESSES	SNOWBOARDED
SMOKELESSLY	SNAGGLETEETH	SNEAKINESS	SNIPPINESS	SNOWBOARDER
SMOKELESSNESS	SNAGGLETOOTH	SNEAKINESSES	SNIPPINESSES	SNOWBOARDERS
SMOKELESSNESSES	SNAGGLETOOTHED	SNEAKINGLY	SNITCHIEST	SNOWBOARDING
SMOKEPROOF	SNAILERIES	SNEAKINGNESS	SNIVELLERS	SNOWBOARDINGS
SMOKESCREEN	SNAILFISHES	SNEAKINGNESSES	SNIVELLING	SNOWBOARDS
SMOKESCREENS	SNAKEBIRDS	SNEAKISHLY	SNIVELLINGS	SNOWBRUSHES
SMOKESTACK	SNAKEBITES	SNEAKISHNESS	SNOBBERIES	SNOWBUSHES
SMOKESTACKS	SNAKEBITTEN	SNEAKISHNESSES	SNOBBISHLY	SNOWCAPPED
SMOKETIGHT	SNAKEFISHES	SNEAKSBIES	SNOBBISHNESS	SNOWCLONES
SMOKINESSES	SNAKEHEADS	SNEERINGLY	SNOBBISHNESSES	SNOWDRIFTS
SMOLDERING	SNAKEMOUTH	SNEESHINGS	SNOBBOCRACIES	SNOWFIELDS

SOLICITANT

SNOWFLAKES	SOBERINGLY	SOCIOBIOLOGIES	SODOMISING	SOLDIERIES
SNOWFLECKS	SOBERISING	SOCIOBIOLOGIST	SODOMITICAL	SOLDIERING
SNOWFLICKS	SOBERIZING	SOCIOBIOLOGISTS	SODOMITICALLY	SOLDIERINGS
SNOWGLOBES	SOBERNESSES	SOCIOBIOLOGY	SODOMIZING	SOLDIERLIKE
SNOWINESSES	SOBERSIDED	SOCIOCULTURAL	SOFTBALLER	SOLDIERLINESS
SNOWMAKERS	SOBERSIDEDNESS	SOCIOCULTURALLY	SOFTBALLERS	SOLDIERLINESSES
SNOWMAKING	SOBERSIDES	SOCIOECONOMIC	SOFTBOUNDS	SOLDIERSHIP
SNOWMOBILE	SOBOLIFEROUS	SOCIOGRAMS	SOFTCOVERS	SOLDIERSHIPS
SNOWMOBILER	SOBRIETIES	SOCIOHISTORICAL	SOFTENINGS	SOLECISING
SNOWMOBILERS	SOBRIQUETS	SOCIOLECTS	SOFTHEADED	SOLECISTIC
SNOWMOBILES	SOCDOLAGER	SOCIOLINGUIST	SOFTHEADEDLY	SOLECISTICAL
SNOWMOBILING	SOCDOLAGERS	SOCIOLINGUISTIC	SOFTHEADEDNESS	SOLECISTICALLY
SNOWMOBILINGS	SOCDOLIGER	SOCIOLINGUISTS	SOFTHEARTED	SOLECIZING
SNOWMOBILIST	SOCDOLIGERS	SOCIOLOGESE	SOFTHEARTEDLY	SOLEMNESSES
SNOWMOBILISTS	SOCDOLOGER	SOCIOLOGESES	SOFTHEARTEDNESS	SOLEMNIFICATION
SNOWPLOUGH	SOCDOLOGERS	SOCIOLOGIC	SOFTNESSES	SOLEMNIFIED
SNOWPLOUGHED	SOCIABILITIES	SOCIOLOGICAL	SOFTSHELLS	SOLEMNIFIES
SNOWPLOUGHING	SOCIABILITY	SOCIOLOGICALLY	SOGDOLAGER	SOLEMNIFYING
SNOWPLOUGHS	SOCIABLENESS	SOCIOLOGIES	SOGDOLAGERS	SOLEMNISATION
SNOWPLOWED	SOCIABLENESSES	SOCIOLOGISM	SOGDOLIGER	SOLEMNISATIONS
SNOWPLOWING	SOCIALISABLE	SOCIOLOGISMS	SOGDOLIGERS	SOLEMNISED
SNOWSCAPES	SOCIALISATION	SOCIOLOGIST	SOGDOLOGER	SOLEMNISER
SNOWSHOEING	SOCIALISATIONS	SOCIOLOGISTIC	SOGDOLOGERS	SOLEMNISERS
SNOWSHOERS	SOCIALISED	SOCIOLOGISTS	SOGGINESSES	SOLEMNISES
SNOWSLIDES	SOCIALISER	SOCIOMETRIC	SOILINESSES	SOLEMNISING
SNOWSTORMS	SOCIALISERS	SOCIOMETRIES	SOJOURNERS	SOLEMNITIES
SNOWSURFING	SOCIALISES	SOCIOMETRIST	SOJOURNING	SOLEMNIZATION
SNOWSURFINGS	SOCIALISING	SOCIOMETRISTS	SOJOURNINGS	SOLEMNIZATIONS
SNOWTUBING	SOCIALISMS	SOCIOMETRY	SOJOURNMENT	SOLEMNIZED
SNOWTUBINGS	SOCIALISTIC	SOCIOPATHIC	SOJOURNMENTS	SOLEMNIZER
SNUBBINESS	SOCIALISTICALLY	SOCIOPATHIES	SOKEMANRIES	SOLEMNIZERS
SNUBBINESSES	SOCIALISTS	SOCIOPATHS	SOLACEMENT	SOLEMNIZES
SNUBBINGLY	SOCIALITES	SOCIOPATHY	SOLACEMENTS	SOLEMNIZING
SNUBNESSES	SOCIALITIES	SOCIOPOLITICAL	SOLANACEOUS	SOLEMNNESS
SNUFFBOXES	SOCIALIZABLE	SOCIORELIGIOUS	SOLARIMETER	SOLEMNNESSES
SNUFFINESS	SOCIALIZATION	SOCIOSEXUAL	SOLARIMETERS	SOLENESSES
SNUFFINESSES	SOCIALIZATIONS	SOCKDOLAGER	SOLARISATION	SOLENETTES
SNUFFLIEST	SOCIALIZED	SOCKDOLAGERS	SOLARISATIONS	SOLENODONS
SNUFFLINGS	SOCIALIZER	SOCKDOLIGER	SOLARISING	SOLENOIDAL
SNUGGERIES	SOCIALIZERS	SOCKDOLIGERS	SOLARIZATION	SOLENOIDALLY
SNUGNESSES	SOCIALIZES	SOCKDOLOGER	SOLARIZATIONS	SOLEPLATES
SOAPBERRIES	SOCIALIZING	SOCKDOLOGERS	SOLARIZING	SOLEPRINTS
SOAPBOXING	SOCIALNESS	SODALITIES	SOLDATESQUE	SOLFATARAS
SOAPINESSES	SOCIALNESSES	SODBUSTERS	SOLDERABILITIES	SOLFATARIC
SOAPOLALLIE	SOCIATIONS	SODDENNESS	SOLDERABILITY	SOLFEGGIOS
SOAPOLALLIES	SOCIETALLY	SODDENNESSES	SOLDERABLE	SOLFERINOS
SOAPSTONES	SOCIOBIOLOGICAL	SODICITIES	SOLDERINGS	SOLICITANT

S

SOLICITANTS	SOLILOQUISES	SOLUBILISING	SOMATOPLEURE	SOMNAMBULANCE
SOLICITATION	SOLILOQUISING	SOLUBILITIES	SOMATOPLEURES	SOMNAMBULANCES
SOLICITATIONS	SOLILOQUIST	SOLUBILITY	SOMATOPLEURIC	SOMNAMBULANT
SOLICITIES	SOLILOQUISTS	SOLUBILIZATION	SOMATOSENSORY	SOMNAMBULANTS
SOLICITING	SOLILOQUIZE	SOLUBILIZATIONS	SOMATOSTATIN	SOMNAMBULAR
SOLICITINGS	SOLILOQUIZED	SOLUBILIZE	SOMATOSTATINS	SOMNAMBULARY
SOLICITORS	SOLILOQUIZER	SOLUBILIZED	SOMATOTENSIC	SOMNAMBULATE
SOLICITORSHIP	SOLILOQUIZERS	SOLUBILIZES	SOMATOTONIA	SOMNAMBULATED
SOLICITORSHIPS	SOLILOQUIZES	SOLUBILIZING	SOMATOTONIAS	SOMNAMBULATES
SOLICITOUS	SOLILOQUIZING	SOLUBLENESS	SOMATOTONIC	SOMNAMBULATING
SOLICITOUSLY	SOLIPEDOUS	SOLUBLENESSES	SOMATOTROPHIC	SOMNAMBULATION
SOLICITOUSNESS	SOLIPSISMS	SOLUTIONAL	SOMATOTROPHIN	SOMNAMBULATIONS
SOLICITUDE	SOLIPSISTIC	SOLUTIONED	SOMATOTROPHINS	SOMNAMBULATOR
SOLICITUDES	SOLIPSISTICALLY	SOLUTIONING	SOMATOTROPIC	SOMNAMBULATORS
SOLIDARISM	SOLIPSISTS	SOLUTIONIST	SOMATOTROPIN	SOMNAMBULE
SOLIDARISMS	SOLITAIRES	SOLUTIONISTS	SOMATOTROPINS	SOMNAMBULES
SOLIDARIST	SOLITARIAN	SOLVABILITIES	SOMATOTYPE	SOMNAMBULIC
SOLIDARISTIC	SOLITARIANS	SOLVABILITY	SOMATOTYPED	SOMNAMBULISM
SOLIDARISTS	SOLITARIES	SOLVABLENESS	SOMATOTYPES	SOMNAMBULISMS
SOLIDARITIES	SOLITARILY	SOLVABLENESSES	SOMATOTYPING	SOMNAMBULIST
SOLIDARITY	SOLITARINESS	SOLVATIONS	SOMBERNESS	SOMNAMBULISTIC
SOLIDATING	SOLITARINESSES	SOLVENCIES	SOMBERNESSES	SOMNAMBULISTS
SOLIDIFIABLE	SOLITUDINARIAN	SOLVENTLESS	SOMBRENESS	SOMNIATING
SOLIDIFICATION	SOLITUDINARIANS	SOLVOLYSES	SOMBRENESSES	SOMNIATIVE
SOLIDIFICATIONS	SOLITUDINOUS	SOLVOLYSIS	SOMBRERITE	SOMNIATORY
SOLIDIFIED	SOLIVAGANT	SOLVOLYTIC	SOMBRERITES	SOMNIFACIENT
SOLIDIFIER	SOLIVAGANTS	SOMAESTHESIA	SOMEBODIES	SOMNIFACIENTS
SOLIDIFIERS	SOLLICKERS	SOMAESTHESIAS	SOMEPLACES	SOMNIFEROUS
SOLIDIFIES	SOLMISATION	SOMAESTHESIS	SOMERSAULT	SOMNIFEROUSLY
SOLIDIFYING	SOLMISATIONS	SOMAESTHESISES	SOMERSAULTED	SOMNILOQUENCE
SOLIDITIES	SOLMIZATION	SOMAESTHETIC	SOMERSAULTING	SOMNILOQUENCES
SOLIDNESSES	SOLMIZATIONS	SOMASCOPES	SOMERSAULTS	SOMNILOQUIES
SOLIDUNGULATE	SOLONCHAKS	SOMATICALLY	SOMERSETED	SOMNILOQUISE
SOLIDUNGULOUS	SOLONETSES	SOMATOGENIC	SOMERSETING	SOMNILOQUISED
SOLIFIDIAN	SOLONETZES	SOMATOLOGIC	SOMERSETTED	SOMNILOQUISES
SOLIFIDIANISM	SOLONETZIC	SOMATOLOGICAL	SOMERSETTING	SOMNILOQUISING
SOLIFIDIANISMS	SOLONISATION	SOMATOLOGICALLY	SOMESTHESIA	SOMNILOQUISM
SOLIFIDIANS	SOLONISATIONS	SOMATOLOGIES	SOMESTHESIAS	SOMNILOQUISMS
SOLIFLUCTION	SOLONIZATION	SOMATOLOGIST	SOMESTHESIS	SOMNILOQUIST
SOLIFLUCTIONS	SOLONIZATIONS	SOMATOLOGISTS	SOMESTHESISES	SOMNILOQUISTS
SOLIFLUXION	SOLSTITIAL	SOMATOLOGY	SOMESTHETIC	SOMNILOQUIZE
SOLIFLUXIONS	SOLSTITIALLY	SOMATOMEDIN	SOMETHINGS	SOMNILOQUIZED
SOLILOQUIES	SOLUBILISATION	SOMATOMEDINS	SOMEWHENCE	SOMNILOQUIZES
SOLILOQUISE	SOLUBILISATIONS	SOMATOPLASM	SOMEWHERES	SOMNILOQUIZING
SOLILOQUISED	SOLUBILISE	SOMATOPLASMS	SOMEWHILES	SOMNILOQUOUS
SOLILOQUISER	SOLUBILISED	SOMATOPLASTIC	SOMEWHITHER	SOMNILOQUY
SOLILOQUISERS	SOLUBILISES	SOMATOPLEURAL	SOMMELIERS	SOMNOLENCE

S

SOMNOLENCES	SOOTHFASTNESS	SORBITIZED	SOULLESSLY	SOUTHEASTERLIES
SOMNOLENCIES	SOOTHFASTNESSES	SORBITIZES	SOULLESSNESS	SOUTHEASTERLY
SOMNOLENCY	SOOTHINGLY	SORBITIZING	SOULLESSNESSES	SOUTHEASTERN
SOMNOLENTLY	SOOTHINGNESS	SORCERESSES	SOUNDALIKE	SOUTHEASTERS
SOMNOLESCENT	SOOTHINGNESSES	SORDAMENTE	SOUNDALIKES	SOUTHEASTS
SONGCRAFTS	SOOTHSAYER	SORDIDNESS	SOUNDBITES	SOUTHEASTWARD
SONGFULNESS	SOOTHSAYERS	SORDIDNESSES	SOUNDBOARD	SOUTHEASTWARDS
SONGFULNESSES	SOOTHSAYING	SOREHEADED	SOUNDBOARDS	SOUTHERING
SONGLESSLY	SOOTHSAYINGS	SOREHEADEDLY	SOUNDBOXES	SOUTHERLIES
SONGOLOLOS	SOOTINESSES	SOREHEADEDNESS	SOUNDCARDS	SOUTHERLINESS
SONGSMITHS	SOPAIPILLA	SORENESSES	SOUNDINGLY	SOUTHERLINESSES
SONGSTRESS	SOPAIPILLAS	SORICIDENT	SOUNDLESSLY	SOUTHERMOST
SONGSTRESSES	SOPAPILLAS	SORORIALLY	SOUNDLESSNESS	SOUTHERNER
SONGWRITER	SOPHISTERS	SORORICIDAL	SOUNDLESSNESSES	SOUTHERNERS
SONGWRITERS	SOPHISTICAL	SORORICIDE	SOUNDNESSES	SOUTHERNISE
SONGWRITING	SOPHISTICALLY	SORORICIDES	SOUNDPOSTS	SOUTHERNISED
SONGWRITINGS	SOPHISTICATE	SORORISING	SOUNDPROOF	SOUTHERNISES
SONICATING	SOPHISTICATED	SORORITIES	SOUNDPROOFED	SOUTHERNISING
SONICATION	SOPHISTICATEDLY	SORORIZING	SOUNDPROOFING	SOUTHERNISM
SONICATIONS	SOPHISTICATES	SORRINESSES	SOUNDPROOFINGS	SOUTHERNISMS
SONICATORS	SOPHISTICATING	SORROWFULLY	SOUNDPROOFS	SOUTHERNIZE
SONIFEROUS	SOPHISTICATION	SORROWFULNESS	SOUNDSCAPE	SOUTHERNIZED
SONNETEERING	SOPHISTICATIONS	SORROWFULNESSES	SOUNDSCAPES	SOUTHERNIZES
SONNETEERINGS	SOPHISTICATOR	SORROWINGS	SOUNDSTAGE	SOUTHERNIZING
SONNETEERS	SOPHISTICATORS	SORROWLESS	SOUNDSTAGES	SOUTHERNLY
SONNETISED	SOPHISTRIES	SORTATIONS	SOUNDTRACK	SOUTHERNMOST
SONNETISES	SOPHOMORES	SORTILEGER	SOUNDTRACKED	SOUTHERNNESS
SONNETISING	SOPHOMORIC	SORTILEGERS	SOUNDTRACKING	SOUTHERNNESSES
SONNETIZED	SOPHOMORICAL	SORTILEGES	SOUNDTRACKS	SOUTHERNWOOD
SONNETIZES	SOPORIFEROUS	SORTILEGIES	SOUPSPOONS	SOUTHERNWOODS
SONNETIZING	SOPORIFEROUSLY	SORTITIONS	SOURCEBOOK	SOUTHLANDER
SONNETTING	SOPORIFICALLY	SOSTENUTOS	SOURCEBOOKS	SOUTHLANDERS
SONOFABITCH	SOPORIFICS	SOTERIOLOGIC	SOURCELESS	SOUTHLANDS
SONOGRAPHER	SOPPINESSES	SOTERIOLOGICAL	SOURDELINE	SOUTHSAYING
SONOGRAPHERS	SOPRANINOS	SOTERIOLOGIES	SOURDELINES	SOUTHWARDLY
SONOGRAPHIES	SOPRANISTS	SOTERIOLOGY	SOURDOUGHS	SOUTHWARDS
SONOGRAPHS	SORBABILITIES	SOTTISHNESS	SOURNESSES	SOUTHWESTER
SONOGRAPHY	SORBABILITY	SOTTISHNESSES	SOURPUSSES	SOUTHWESTERLIES
SONOMETERS	SORBEFACIENT	SOTTISIERS	SOUSAPHONE	SOUTHWESTERLY
SONORITIES	SORBEFACIENTS	SOUBRETTES	SOUSAPHONES	SOUTHWESTERN
SONOROUSLY	SORBITISATION	SOUBRETTISH	SOUSAPHONIST	SOUTHWESTERS
SONOROUSNESS	SORBITISATIONS	SOUBRIQUET	SOUSAPHONISTS	SOUTHWESTS
SONOROUSNESSES	SORBITISED	SOUBRIQUETS	SOUTENEURS	SOUTHWESTWARD
SOOTERKINS	SORBITISES	SOULDIERED	SOUTERRAIN	SOUTHWESTWARDLY
SOOTFLAKES	SORBITISING	SOULDIERING	SOUTERRAINS	SOUTHWESTWARDS
SOOTHERING	SORBITIZATION	SOULFULNESS	SOUTHBOUND	SOUVENIRED
SOOTHFASTLY	SORBITIZATIONS	SOULFULNESSES	SOUTHEASTER	SOUVENIRING

S

SOUVLAKIAS	SPACIOUSLY	SPARAGRASSES	SPATHULATE	SPECIALIZER
SOVENANCES	SPACIOUSNESS	SPARAXISES	SPATIALITIES	SPECIALIZERS
SOVEREIGNLY	SPACIOUSNESSES	SPARENESSES	SPATIALITY	SPECIALIZES
SOVEREIGNS	SPADASSINS	SPARGANIUM	SPATIOTEMPORAL	SPECIALIZING
SOVEREIGNTIES	SPADEFISHES	SPARGANIUMS	SPATTERDASH	SPECIALLED
SOVEREIGNTIST	SPADEWORKS	SPARINGNESS	SPATTERDASHES	SPECIALLING
SOVEREIGNTISTS	SPADICEOUS	SPARINGNESSES	SPATTERDOCK	SPECIALNESS
SOVEREIGNTY	SPADICIFLORAL	SPARKISHLY	SPATTERDOCKS	SPECIALNESSES
SOVIETISATION	SPADILLIOS	SPARKLESSLY	SPATTERING	SPECIALOGUE
SOVIETISATIONS	SPAGHETTILIKE	SPARKLIEST	SPATTERWORK	SPECIALOGUES
SOVIETISED	SPAGHETTINI	SPARKLINGLY	SPATTERWORKS	SPECIALTIES
SOVIETISES	SPAGHETTINIS	SPARKLINGS	SPEAKEASIES	SPECIATING
SOVIETISING	SPAGHETTIS	SPARKPLUGGED	SPEAKERINE	SPECIATION
SOVIETISMS	SPAGYRICAL	SPARKPLUGGING	SPEAKERINES	SPECIATIONAL
SOVIETISTIC	SPAGYRICALLY	SPARKPLUGS	SPEAKERPHONE	SPECIATIONS
SOVIETISTS	SPAGYRISTS	SPARROWFART	SPEAKERPHONES	SPECIESISM
SOVIETIZATION	SPALLATION	SPARROWFARTS	SPEAKERSHIP	SPECIESISMS
SOVIETIZATIONS	SPALLATIONS	SPARROWGRASS	SPEAKERSHIPS	SPECIESIST
SOVIETIZED	SPANAEMIAS	SPARROWGRASSES	SPEAKINGLY	SPECIESISTS
SOVIETIZES	SPANAKOPITA	SPARROWHAWK	SPEARFISHED	SPECIFIABLE
SOVIETIZING	SPANAKOPITAS	SPARROWHAWKS	SPEARFISHES	SPECIFICAL
SOVIETOLOGICAL	SPANCELING	SPARROWLIKE	SPEARFISHING	SPECIFICALLY
SOVIETOLOGIST	SPANCELLED	SPARSENESS	SPEARHEADED	SPECIFICATE
SOVIETOLOGISTS	SPANCELLING	SPARSENESSES	SPEARHEADING	SPECIFICATED
SOVRANTIES	SPANGHEWED	SPARSITIES	SPEARHEADS	SPECIFICATES
SOWBELLIES	SPANGHEWING	SPARTEINES	SPEARMINTS	SPECIFICATING
SPACEBANDS	SPANGLIEST	SPARTERIES	SPEARWORTS	SPECIFICATION
SPACEBORNE	SPANGLINGS	SPARTICLES	SPECIALEST	SPECIFICATIONS
SPACECRAFT	SPANIELLED	SPASMATICAL	SPECIALISATION	SPECIFICATIVE
SPACECRAFTS	SPANIELLING	SPASMODICAL	SPECIALISATIONS	SPECIFICITIES
SPACEFARING	SPANIOLATE	SPASMODICALLY	SPECIALISE	SPECIFICITY
SPACEFARINGS	SPANIOLATED	SPASMODIST	SPECIALISED	SPECIFIERS
SPACEFLIGHT	SPANIOLATES	SPASMODISTS	SPECIALISER	SPECIFYING
SPACEFLIGHTS	SPANIOLATING	SPASMOLYTIC	SPECIALISERS	SPECIOCIDE
SPACEPLANE	SPANIOLISE	SPASMOLYTICS	SPECIALISES	SPECIOCIDES
SPACEPLANES	SPANIOLISED	SPASTICALLY	SPECIALISING	SPECIOSITIES
SPACEPORTS	SPANIOLISES	SPASTICITIES	SPECIALISM	SPECIOSITY
SPACESHIPS	SPANIOLISING	SPASTICITY	SPECIALISMS	SPECIOUSLY
SPACESUITS	SPANIOLIZE	SPATANGOID	SPECIALIST	SPECIOUSNESS
SPACEWALKED	SPANIOLIZED	SPATANGOIDS	SPECIALISTIC	SPECIOUSNESSES
SPACEWALKER	SPANIOLIZES	SPATCHCOCK	SPECIALISTS	SPECKLEDNESS
SPACEWALKERS	SPANIOLIZING	SPATCHCOCKED	SPECIALITIES	SPECKLEDNESSES
SPACEWALKING	SPANKINGLY	SPATCHCOCKING	SPECIALITY	SPECKSIONEER
SPACEWALKS	SPANOKOPITA	SPATCHCOCKS	SPECIALIZATION	SPECKSIONEERS
SPACEWOMAN	SPANOKOPITAS	SPATHACEOUS	SPECIALIZATIONS	SPECKTIONEER
SPACEWOMEN	SPARAGMATIC	SPATHIPHYLLUM	SPECIALIZE	SPECKTIONEERS
SPACINESSES	SPARAGRASS	SPATHIPHYLLUMS	SPECIALIZED	SPECTACLED

S

SPECTACLES
SPECTACULAR
SPECTACULARITY
SPECTACULARLY
SPECTACULARS
SPECTATING
SPECTATORIAL
SPECTATORS
SPECTATORSHIP
SPECTATORSHIPS
SPECTATRESS
SPECTATRESSES
SPECTATRICES
SPECTATRIX
SPECTATRIXES
SPECTINOMYCIN
SPECTINOMYCINS
SPECTRALITIES
SPECTRALITY
SPECTRALLY
SPECTRALNESS
SPECTRALNESSES
SPECTROGRAM
SPECTROGRAMS
SPECTROGRAPH
SPECTROGRAPHIC
SPECTROGRAPHIES
SPECTROGRAPHS
SPECTROGRAPHY
SPECTROLOGICAL
SPECTROLOGIES
SPECTROLOGY
SPECTROMETER
SPECTROMETERS
SPECTROMETRIC
SPECTROMETRIES
SPECTROMETRY
SPECTROSCOPE
SPECTROSCOPES
SPECTROSCOPIC
SPECTROSCOPICAL
SPECTROSCOPIES
SPECTROSCOPIST
SPECTROSCOPISTS
SPECTROSCOPY
SPECULARITIES
SPECULARITY

SPECULARLY
SPECULATED
SPECULATES
SPECULATING
SPECULATION
SPECULATIONS
SPECULATIST
SPECULATISTS
SPECULATIVE
SPECULATIVELY
SPECULATIVENESS
SPECULATOR
SPECULATORS
SPECULATORY
SPECULATRICES
SPECULATRIX
SPECULATRIXES
SPEECHCRAFT
SPEECHCRAFTS
SPEECHFULNESS
SPEECHFULNESSES
SPEECHIFICATION
SPEECHIFIED
SPEECHIFIER
SPEECHIFIERS
SPEECHIFIES
SPEECHIFYING
SPEECHLESS
SPEECHLESSLY
SPEECHLESSNESS
SPEECHMAKER
SPEECHMAKERS
SPEECHMAKING
SPEECHMAKINGS
SPEECHWRITER
SPEECHWRITERS
SPEEDBALLED
SPEEDBALLING
SPEEDBALLINGS
SPEEDBALLS
SPEEDBOATING
SPEEDBOATINGS
SPEEDBOATS
SPEEDFREAK
SPEEDFREAKS
SPEEDFULLY
SPEEDINESS

SPEEDINESSES
SPEEDOMETER
SPEEDOMETERS
SPEEDREADING
SPEEDREADS
SPEEDSKATING
SPEEDSKATINGS
SPEEDSTERS
SPEEDWELLS
SPELAEOLOGICAL
SPELAEOLOGIES
SPELAEOLOGIST
SPELAEOLOGISTS
SPELAEOLOGY
SPELAEOTHEM
SPELAEOTHEMS
SPELDERING
SPELDRINGS
SPELEOLOGICAL
SPELEOLOGIES
SPELEOLOGIST
SPELEOLOGISTS
SPELEOLOGY
SPELEOTHEM
SPELEOTHEMS
SPELEOTHERAPIES
SPELEOTHERAPY
SPELLBINDER
SPELLBINDERS
SPELLBINDING
SPELLBINDINGLY
SPELLBINDS
SPELLBOUND
SPELLCHECK
SPELLCHECKER
SPELLCHECKERS
SPELLCHECKS
SPELLDOWNS
SPELLICANS
SPELLINGLY
SPELLSTOPT
SPELUNKERS
SPELUNKING
SPELUNKINGS
SPENDTHRIFT
SPENDTHRIFTS
SPERMACETI

SPERMACETIS
SPERMADUCT
SPERMADUCTS
SPERMAGONIA
SPERMAGONIUM
SPERMAPHYTE
SPERMAPHYTES
SPERMAPHYTIC
SPERMARIES
SPERMARIUM
SPERMATHECA
SPERMATHECAE
SPERMATHECAL
SPERMATIAL
SPERMATICAL
SPERMATICALLY
SPERMATICS
SPERMATIDS
SPERMATIUM
SPERMATOBLAST
SPERMATOBLASTIC
SPERMATOBLASTS
SPERMATOCELE
SPERMATOCELES
SPERMATOCIDAL
SPERMATOCIDE
SPERMATOCIDES
SPERMATOCYTE
SPERMATOCYTES
SPERMATOGENESES
SPERMATOGENESIS
SPERMATOGENETIC
SPERMATOGENIC
SPERMATOGENIES
SPERMATOGENOUS
SPERMATOGENY
SPERMATOGONIA
SPERMATOGONIAL
SPERMATOGONIUM
SPERMATOPHORAL
SPERMATOPHORE
SPERMATOPHORES
SPERMATOPHYTE
SPERMATOPHYTES
SPERMATOPHYTIC
SPERMATORRHEA
SPERMATORRHEAS

SPERMATORRHOEA
SPERMATORRHOEAS
SPERMATOTHECA
SPERMATOTHECAE
SPERMATOZOA
SPERMATOZOAL
SPERMATOZOAN
SPERMATOZOANS
SPERMATOZOIC
SPERMATOZOID
SPERMATOZOIDS
SPERMATOZOON
SPERMICIDAL
SPERMICIDE
SPERMICIDES
SPERMIDUCT
SPERMIDUCTS
SPERMIOGENESES
SPERMIOGENESIS
SPERMIOGENETIC
SPERMOGONE
SPERMOGONES
SPERMOGONIA
SPERMOGONIUM
SPERMOPHILE
SPERMOPHILES
SPERMOPHYTE
SPERMOPHYTES
SPERMOPHYTIC
SPERRYLITE
SPERRYLITES
SPESSARTINE
SPESSARTINES
SPESSARTITE
SPESSARTITES
SPETSNAZES
SPETZNAZES
SPEWINESSES
SPHACELATE
SPHACELATED
SPHACELATES
SPHACELATING
SPHACELATION
SPHACELATIONS
SPHACELUSES
SPHAERIDIA
SPHAERIDIUM

S

SPHAERITES	SPHEROIDIZE	SPIDERWEBS	SPININESSES	SPIRITLESS
SPHAEROCRYSTAL	SPHEROIDIZED	SPIDERWOOD	SPINMEISTER	SPIRITLESSLY
SPHAEROCRYSTALS	SPHEROIDIZES	SPIDERWOODS	SPINMEISTERS	SPIRITLESSNESS
SPHAEROSIDERITE	SPHEROIDIZING	SPIDERWORK	SPINNAKERS	SPIRITOUSNESS
SPHAGNICOLOUS	SPHEROMETER	SPIDERWORKS	SPINNERETS	SPIRITOUSNESSES
SPHAGNOLOGIES	SPHEROMETERS	SPIDERWORT	SPINNERETTE	SPIRITUALISE
SPHAGNOLOGIST	SPHEROPLAST	SPIDERWORTS	SPINNERETTES	SPIRITUALISED
SPHAGNOLOGISTS	SPHEROPLASTS	SPIEGELEISEN	SPINNERIES	SPIRITUALISER
SPHAGNOLOGY	SPHERULITE	SPIEGELEISENS	SPINNERULE	SPIRITUALISERS
SPHAIRISTIKE	SPHERULITES	SPIFFINESS	SPINNERULES	SPIRITUALISES
SPHAIRISTIKES	SPHERULITIC	SPIFFINESSES	SPINOSITIES	SPIRITUALISING
SPHALERITE	SPHINCTERAL	SPIFFLICATE	SPINSTERDOM	SPIRITUALISM
SPHALERITES	SPHINCTERIAL	SPIFFLICATED	SPINSTERDOMS	SPIRITUALISMS
SPHENDONES	SPHINCTERIC	SPIFFLICATES	SPINSTERHOOD	SPIRITUALIST
SPHENODONS	SPHINCTERS	SPIFFLICATING	SPINSTERHOODS	SPIRITUALISTIC
SPHENODONT	SPHINGOMYELIN	SPIFFLICATION	SPINSTERIAL	SPIRITUALISTS
SPHENOGRAM	SPHINGOMYELINS	SPIFFLICATIONS	SPINSTERIAN	SPIRITUALITIES
SPHENOGRAMS	SPHINGOSINE	SPIFLICATE	SPINSTERISH	SPIRITUALITY
SPHENOIDAL	SPHINGOSINES	SPIFLICATED	SPINSTERLY	SPIRITUALIZE
SPHENOPSID	SPHINXLIKE	SPIFLICATES	SPINSTERSHIP	SPIRITUALIZED
SPHENOPSIDS	SPHRAGISTIC	SPIFLICATING	SPINSTERSHIPS	SPIRITUALIZER
SPHERELESS	SPHRAGISTICS	SPIFLICATION	SPINSTRESS	SPIRITUALIZERS
SPHERELIKE	SPHYGMOGRAM	SPIFLICATIONS	SPINSTRESSES	SPIRITUALIZES
SPHERICALITIES	SPHYGMOGRAMS	SPIKEFISHES	SPINTHARISCOPE	SPIRITUALIZING
SPHERICALITY	SPHYGMOGRAPH	SPIKENARDS	SPINTHARISCOPES	SPIRITUALLY
SPHERICALLY	SPHYGMOGRAPHIC	SPIKINESSES	SPINULESCENT	SPIRITUALNESS
SPHERICALNESS	SPHYGMOGRAPHIES	SPILLIKINS	SPINULIFEROUS	SPIRITUALNESSES
SPHERICALNESSES	SPHYGMOGRAPHS	SPILLOVERS	SPIRACULAR	SPIRITUALS
SPHERICITIES	SPHYGMOGRAPHY	SPILOSITES	SPIRACULATE	SPIRITUALTIES
SPHERICITY	SPHYGMOLOGIES	SPINACENES	SPIRACULUM	SPIRITUALTY
SPHERISTERION	SPHYGMOLOGY	SPINACEOUS	SPIRALIFORM	SPIRITUELLE
SPHERISTERIONS	SPHYGMOMETER	SPINACHLIKE	SPIRALISMS	SPIRITUOSITIES
SPHEROCYTE	SPHYGMOMETERS	SPINDLELEGS	SPIRALISTS	SPIRITUOSITY
SPHEROCYTES	SPHYGMOPHONE	SPINDLESHANKS	SPIRALITIES	SPIRITUOUS
SPHEROCYTOSES	SPHYGMOPHONES	SPINDLIEST	SPIRALLING	SPIRITUOUSNESS
SPHEROCYTOSIS	SPHYGMOSCOPE	SPINDLINGS	SPIRASTERS	SPIRITUSES
SPHEROIDAL	SPHYGMOSCOPES	SPINDRIFTS	SPIRATIONS	SPIRKETTING
SPHEROIDALLY	SPHYGMUSES	SPINELESSLY	SPIRIFEROUS	SPIRKETTINGS
SPHEROIDICALLY	SPICEBERRIES	SPINELESSNESS	SPIRILLOSES	SPIROCHAETAEMIA
SPHEROIDICITIES	SPICEBERRY	SPINELESSNESSES	SPIRILLOSIS	SPIROCHAETE
SPHEROIDICITY	SPICEBUSHES	SPINESCENCE	SPIRITEDLY	SPIROCHAETES
SPHEROIDISATION	SPICILEGES	SPINESCENCES	SPIRITEDNESS	SPIROCHAETOSES
SPHEROIDISE	SPICINESSES	SPINESCENT	SPIRITEDNESSES	SPIROCHAETOSIS
SPHEROIDISED	SPICULATION	SPINIFEROUS	SPIRITINGS	SPIROCHETAL
SPHEROIDISES	SPICULATIONS	SPINIFEXES	SPIRITISMS	SPIROCHETE
SPHEROIDISING	SPIDERIEST	SPINIGEROUS	SPIRITISTIC	SPIROCHETES
SPHEROIDIZATION	SPIDERLIKE	SPINIGRADE	SPIRITISTS	SPIROCHETOSES

SPIROCHETOSIS	SPLASHINESS	SPLENITISES	SPOKESPERSON	SPONTANEITY
SPIROGRAMS	SPLASHINESSES	SPLENIUSES	SPOKESPERSONS	SPONTANEOUS
SPIROGRAPH	SPLASHINGS	SPLENIZATION	SPOKESWOMAN	SPONTANEOUSLY
SPIROGRAPHIC	SPLASHPROOF	SPLENIZATIONS	SPOKESWOMEN	SPONTANEOUSNESS
SPIROGRAPHIES	SPLATCHING	SPLENOMEGALIES	SPOLIATING	SPOOFERIES
SPIROGRAPHS	SPLATTERED	SPLENOMEGALY	SPOLIATION	SPOOKERIES
SPIROGRAPHY	SPLATTERING	SPLEUCHANS	SPOLIATIONS	SPOOKINESS
SPIROGYRAS	SPLATTERPUNK	SPLINTERED	SPOLIATIVE	SPOOKINESSES
SPIROMETER	SPLATTERPUNKS	SPLINTERIER	SPOLIATORS	SPOONBAITS
SPIROMETERS	SPLATTINGS	SPLINTERIEST	SPOLIATORY	SPOONBILLS
SPIROMETRIC	SPLAYFOOTED	SPLINTERING	SPONDAICAL	SPOONDRIFT
SPIROMETRIES	SPLAYFOOTEDLY	SPLINTLIKE	SPONDOOLICKS	SPOONDRIFTS
SPIROMETRY	SPLEENFULLY	SPLINTWOOD	SPONDULICKS	SPOONERISM
SPIRONOLACTONE	SPLEENIEST	SPLINTWOODS	SPONDYLITIC	SPOONERISMS
SPIRONOLACTONES	SPLEENLESS	SPLITTINGS	SPONDYLITICS	SPOONHOOKS
SPIROPHORE	SPLEENSTONE	SPLITTISMS	SPONDYLITIS	SPOONWORMS
SPIROPHORES	SPLEENSTONES	SPLITTISTS	SPONDYLITISES	SPORADICAL
SPIRULINAE	SPLEENWORT	SPLODGIEST	SPONDYLOLYSES	SPORADICALLY
SPIRULINAS	SPLEENWORTS	SPLODGINESS	SPONDYLOLYSIS	SPORADICALNESS
SPISSITUDE	SPLENATIVE	SPLODGINESSES	SPONDYLOSES	SPORANGIAL
SPISSITUDES	SPLENDIDER	SPLOOSHING	SPONDYLOSIS	SPORANGIOLA
SPITCHCOCK	SPLENDIDEST	SPLOTCHIER	SPONDYLOSISES	SPORANGIOLE
SPITCHCOCKED	SPLENDIDIOUS	SPLOTCHIEST	SPONDYLOUS	SPORANGIOLES
SPITCHCOCKING	SPLENDIDLY	SPLOTCHILY	SPONGEABLE	SPORANGIOLUM
SPITCHCOCKS	SPLENDIDNESS	SPLOTCHINESS	SPONGEBAGS	SPORANGIOPHORE
SPITEFULLER	SPLENDIDNESSES	SPLOTCHINESSES	SPONGELIKE	SPORANGIOPHORES
SPITEFULLEST	SPLENDIDOUS	SPLOTCHING	SPONGEWARE	SPORANGIOSPORE
SPITEFULLY	SPLENDIFEROUS	SPLURGIEST	SPONGEWARES	SPORANGIOSPORES
SPITEFULNESS	SPLENDIFEROUSLY	SPLUTTERED	SPONGEWOOD	SPORANGIUM
SPITEFULNESSES	SPLENDOROUS	SPLUTTERER	SPONGEWOODS	SPORICIDAL
SPITSTICKER	SPLENDOURS	SPLUTTERERS	SPONGICOLOUS	SPORICIDES
SPITSTICKERS	SPLENDROUS	SPLUTTERING	SPONGIFORM	SPORIDESMS
SPITTLEBUG	SPLENECTOMIES	SPLUTTERINGLY	SPONGINESS	SPOROCARPS
SPITTLEBUGS	SPLENECTOMISE	SPLUTTERINGS	SPONGINESSES	SPOROCYSTIC
SPIVVERIES	SPLENECTOMISED	SPODOGRAMS	SPONGIOBLAST	SPOROCYSTS
SPLANCHNIC	SPLENECTOMISES	SPODOMANCIES	SPONGIOBLASTIC	SPOROCYTES
SPLANCHNOCELE	SPLENECTOMISING	SPODOMANCY	SPONGIOBLASTS	SPOROGENESES
SPLANCHNOCELES	SPLENECTOMIZE	SPODOMANTIC	SPONGOLOGIES	SPOROGENESIS
SPLANCHNOLOGIES	SPLENECTOMIZED	SPODUMENES	SPONGOLOGIST	SPOROGENIC
SPLANCHNOLOGY	SPLENECTOMIZES	SPOILFIVES	SPONGOLOGISTS	SPOROGENIES
SPLASHBACK	SPLENECTOMIZING	SPOILSPORT	SPONGOLOGY	SPOROGENOUS
SPLASHBACKS	SPLENECTOMY	SPOILSPORTS	SPONSIONAL	SPOROGONIA
SPLASHBOARD	SPLENETICAL	SPOKESHAVE	SPONSORIAL	SPOROGONIAL
SPLASHBOARDS	SPLENETICALLY	SPOKESHAVES	SPONSORING	SPOROGONIC
SPLASHDOWN	SPLENETICS	SPOKESMANSHIP	SPONSORSHIP	SPOROGONIES
SPLASHDOWNS	SPLENISATION	SPOKESMANSHIPS	SPONSORSHIPS	SPOROGONIUM
SPLASHIEST	SPLENISATIONS	SPOKESPEOPLE	SPONTANEITIES	SPOROPHORE

S

SPOROPHORES	SPORTSWOMAN	SPRECHGESANG	SPRINGWATER	SQUABASHING
SPOROPHORIC	SPORTSWOMEN	SPRECHGESANGS	SPRINGWATERS	SQUABBIEST
SPOROPHOROUS	SPORTSWRITER	SPRECHSTIMME	SPRINGWOOD	SQUABBLERS
SPOROPHYLL	SPORTSWRITERS	SPRECHSTIMMES	SPRINGWOODS	SQUABBLING
SPOROPHYLLS	SPORTSWRITING	SPREETHING	SPRINGWORT	SQUADRONAL
SPOROPHYLS	SPORTSWRITINGS	SPREKELIAS	SPRINGWORTS	SQUADRONED
SPOROPHYTE	SPORULATED	SPRIGGIEST	SPRINKLERED	SQUADRONES
SPOROPHYTES	SPORULATES	SPRIGHTFUL	SPRINKLERING	SQUADRONING
SPOROPHYTIC	SPORULATING	SPRIGHTFULLY	SPRINKLERS	SQUAILINGS
SPOROPOLLENIN	SPORULATION	SPRIGHTFULNESS	SPRINKLING	SQUALIDEST
SPOROPOLLENINS	SPORULATIONS	SPRIGHTING	SPRINKLINGS	SQUALIDITIES
SPOROTRICHOSES	SPORULATIVE	SPRIGHTLESS	SPRINTINGS	SQUALIDITY
SPOROTRICHOSIS	SPOTLESSLY	SPRIGHTLIER	SPRITELIER	SQUALIDNESS
SPOROZOANS	SPOTLESSNESS	SPRIGHTLIEST	SPRITELIEST	SQUALIDNESSES
SPOROZOITE	SPOTLESSNESSES	SPRIGHTLINESS	SPRITSAILS	SQUALLIEST
SPOROZOITES	SPOTLIGHTED	SPRIGHTLINESSES	SPROUTINGS	SQUALLINGS
SPORTABILITIES	SPOTLIGHTING	SPRIGTAILS	SPRUCENESS	SQUAMATION
SPORTABILITY	SPOTLIGHTS	SPRINGALDS	SPRUCENESSES	SQUAMATIONS
SPORTANCES	SPOTTEDNESS	SPRINGBOARD	SPRYNESSES	SQUAMELLAS
SPORTCASTER	SPOTTEDNESSES	SPRINGBOARDS	SPUILZIEING	SQUAMIFORM
SPORTCASTERS	SPOTTINESS	SPRINGBOKS	SPULEBLADE	SQUAMOSALS
SPORTFISHERMAN	SPOTTINESSES	SPRINGBUCK	SPULEBLADES	SQUAMOSELY
SPORTFISHERMEN	SPOUSELESS	SPRINGBUCKS	SPULYIEING	SQUAMOSENESS
SPORTFISHING	SPOYLEFULL	SPRINGEING	SPULZIEING	SQUAMOSENESSES
SPORTFISHINGS	SPRACHGEFUHL	SPRINGHAAS	SPUMESCENCE	SQUAMOSITIES
SPORTFULLY	SPRACHGEFUHLS	SPRINGHALT	SPUMESCENCES	SQUAMOSITY
SPORTFULNESS	SPRACKLING	SPRINGHALTS	SPUMESCENT	SQUAMOUSLY
SPORTFULNESSES	SPRADDLING	SPRINGHASE	SPUNBONDED	SQUAMOUSNESS
SPORTINESS	SPRANGLING	SPRINGHEAD	SPUNKINESS	SQUAMOUSNESSES
SPORTINESSES	SPRATTLING	SPRINGHEADS	SPUNKINESSES	SQUAMULOSE
SPORTINGLY	SPRAUCHLED	SPRINGHOUSE	SPURGALLED	SQUANDERED
SPORTIVELY	SPRAUCHLES	SPRINGHOUSES	SPURGALLING	SQUANDERER
SPORTIVENESS	SPRAUCHLING	SPRINGIEST	SPURIOSITIES	SQUANDERERS
SPORTIVENESSES	SPRAUNCIER	SPRINGINESS	SPURIOSITY	SQUANDERING
SPORTSCAST	SPRAUNCIEST	SPRINGINESSES	SPURIOUSLY	SQUANDERINGLY
SPORTSCASTER	SPRAWLIEST	SPRINGINGS	SPURIOUSNESS	SQUANDERINGS
SPORTSCASTERS	SPREADABILITIES	SPRINGKEEPER	SPURIOUSNESSES	SQUANDERMANIA
SPORTSCASTS	SPREADABILITY	SPRINGKEEPERS	SPUTTERERS	SQUANDERMANIAS
SPORTSMANLIKE	SPREADABLE	SPRINGLESS	SPUTTERING	SQUAREHEAD
SPORTSMANLY	SPREADINGLY	SPRINGLETS	SPUTTERINGLY	SQUAREHEADS
SPORTSMANSHIP	SPREADINGS	SPRINGLIKE	SPUTTERINGS	SQUARENESS
SPORTSMANSHIPS	SPREADSHEET	SPRINGTAIL	SPYGLASSES	SQUARENESSES
SPORTSPEOPLE	SPREADSHEETS	SPRINGTAILS	SPYMASTERS	SQUAREWISE
SPORTSPERSON	SPREAGHERIES	SPRINGTIDE	SQUABASHED	SQUARISHLY
SPORTSPERSONS	SPREAGHERY	SPRINGTIDES	SQUABASHER	SQUARISHNESS
SPORTSWEAR	SPREATHING	SPRINGTIME	SQUABASHERS	SQUARISHNESSES
SPORTSWEARS	SPRECHERIES	SPRINGTIMES	SQUABASHES	SQUARSONAGE

SQUARSONAGES	SQUIGGLIER	SQUISHINESS	STADHOLDERS	STAINPROOF
SQUASHABLE	SQUIGGLIEST	SQUISHINESSES	STADHOLDERSHIP	STAIRCASED
SQUASHIEST	SQUIGGLING	SQUOOSHIER	STADHOLDERSHIPS	STAIRCASES
SQUASHINESS	SQUILGEEING	SQUOOSHIEST	STADIOMETER	STAIRCASING
SQUASHINESSES	SQUILLIONS	SQUOOSHING	STADIOMETERS	STAIRCASINGS
SQUATNESSES	SQUINANCIES	STABBINGLY	STADTHOLDER	STAIRFOOTS
SQUATTERED	SQUINCHING	STABILATES	STADTHOLDERATE	STAIRHEADS
SQUATTERING	SQUINNIEST	STABILISATION	STADTHOLDERATES	STAIRLIFTS
SQUATTIEST	SQUINNYING	STABILISATIONS	STADTHOLDERS	STAIRSTEPPED
SQUATTINESS	SQUINTIEST	STABILISATOR	STADTHOLDERSHIP	STAIRSTEPPING
SQUATTINESSES	SQUINTINGLY	STABILISATORS	STAFFRIDER	STAIRSTEPS
SQUATTLING	SQUINTINGS	STABILISED	STAFFRIDERS	STAIRWELLS
SQUATTOCRACIES	SQUIRALITIES	STABILISER	STAFFROOMS	STAIRWORKS
SQUATTOCRACY	SQUIRALITY	STABILISERS	STAGECOACH	STAKEHOLDER
SQUAWBUSHES	SQUIRALTIES	STABILISES	STAGECOACHES	STAKEHOLDERS
SQUAWFISHES	SQUIRARCHAL	STABILISING	STAGECOACHING	STAKHANOVISM
SQUAWKIEST	SQUIRARCHICAL	STABILITIES	STAGECOACHINGS	STAKHANOVISMS
SQUAWKINGS	SQUIRARCHIES	STABILIZATION	STAGECOACHMAN	STAKHANOVITE
SQUAWROOTS	SQUIRARCHS	STABILIZATIONS	STAGECOACHMEN	STAKHANOVITES
SQUEAKERIES	SQUIRARCHY	STABILIZATOR	STAGECRAFT	STAKTOMETER
SQUEAKIEST	SQUIREAGES	STABILIZATORS	STAGECRAFTS	STAKTOMETERS
SQUEAKINESS	SQUIREARCH	STABILIZED	STAGEHANDS	STALACTICAL
SQUEAKINESSES	SQUIREARCHAL	STABILIZER	STAGESTRUCK	STALACTIFORM
SQUEAKINGLY	SQUIREARCHICAL	STABILIZERS	STAGFLATION	STALACTITAL
SQUEAKINGS	SQUIREARCHIES	STABILIZES	STAGFLATIONARY	STALACTITE
SQUEALINGS	SQUIREARCHS	STABILIZING	STAGFLATIONS	STALACTITED
SQUEAMISHLY	SQUIREARCHY	STABLEBOYS	STAGGERBUSH	STALACTITES
SQUEAMISHNESS	SQUIREDOMS	STABLEMATE	STAGGERBUSHES	STALACTITIC
SQUEAMISHNESSES	SQUIREHOOD	STABLEMATES	STAGGERERS	STALACTITICAL
SQUEEGEEING	SQUIREHOODS	STABLENESS	STAGGERING	STALACTITICALLY
SQUEEZABILITIES	SQUIRELIKE	STABLENESSES	STAGGERINGLY	STALACTITIFORM
SQUEEZABILITY	SQUIRELING	STABLISHED	STAGGERINGS	STALACTITIOUS
SQUEEZABLE	SQUIRELINGS	STABLISHES	STAGHOUNDS	STALAGMITE
SQUEEZIEST	SQUIRESHIP	STABLISHING	STAGINESSES	STALAGMITES
SQUEEZINGS	SQUIRESHIPS	STABLISHMENT	STAGNANCES	STALAGMITIC
SQUEGGINGS	SQUIRESSES	STABLISHMENTS	STAGNANCIES	STALAGMITICAL
SQUELCHERS	SQUIRMIEST	STACATIONS	STAGNANTLY	STALAGMITICALLY
SQUELCHIER	SQUIRMINGLY	STACCATISSIMO	STAGNATING	STALAGMOMETER
SQUELCHIEST	SQUIRRELED	STACKROOMS	STAGNATION	STALAGMOMETERS
SQUELCHING	SQUIRRELFISH	STACKYARDS	STAGNATIONS	STALAGMOMETRIES
SQUELCHINGS	SQUIRRELFISHES	STACTOMETER	STAIDNESSES	STALAGMOMETRY
SQUETEAGUE	SQUIRRELING	STACTOMETERS	STAINABILITIES	STALEMATED
SQUETEAGUES	SQUIRRELLED	STADDLESTONE	STAINABILITY	STALEMATES
SQUIBBINGS	SQUIRRELLING	STADDLESTONES	STAINLESSES	STALEMATING
SQUIDGIEST	SQUIRRELLY	STADHOLDER	STAINLESSLY	STALENESSES
SQUIFFIEST	SQUIRTINGS	STADHOLDERATE	STAINLESSNESS	STALKINESS
SQUIGGLERS	SQUISHIEST	STADHOLDERATES	STAINLESSNESSES	STALKINESSES

S

STALLENGER	STANDARDIZATION	STAPHYLOMATA	STARVELING	STATOLATRIES
STALLENGERS	STANDARDIZE	STAPHYLOPLASTIC	STARVELINGS	STATOLATRY
STALLHOLDER	STANDARDIZED	STAPHYLOPLASTY	STASIDIONS	STATOLITHIC
STALLHOLDERS	STANDARDIZER	STAPHYLORRHAPHY	STASIMORPHIES	STATOLITHS
STALLINGER	STANDARDIZERS	STARBOARDED	STASIMORPHY	STATOSCOPE
STALLINGERS	STANDARDIZES	STARBOARDING	STATECRAFT	STATOSCOPES
STALLMASTER	STANDARDIZING	STARBOARDS	STATECRAFTS	STATUARIES
STALLMASTERS	STANDARDLESS	STARBURSTS	STATEHOODS	STATUESQUE
STALWARTLY	STANDARDLY	STARCHEDLY	STATEHOUSE	STATUESQUELY
STALWARTNESS	STANDDOWNS	STARCHEDNESS	STATEHOUSES	STATUESQUENESS
STALWARTNESSES	STANDFASTS	STARCHEDNESSES	STATELESSNESS	STATUETTES
STALWORTHS	STANDFIRST	STARCHIEST	STATELESSNESSES	STATUTABLE
STAMINEOUS	STANDFIRSTS	STARCHINESS	STATELIEST	STATUTABLY
STAMINIFEROUS	STANDGALES	STARCHINESSES	STATELINESS	STATUTORILY
STAMINODES	STANDISHES	STARCHLIKE	STATELINESSES	STAUNCHABLE
STAMINODIA	STANDOFFISH	STARDRIFTS	STATEMENTED	STAUNCHERS
STAMINODIES	STANDOFFISHLY	STARFISHED	STATEMENTING	STAUNCHEST
STAMINODIUM	STANDOFFISHNESS	STARFISHES	STATEMENTINGS	STAUNCHING
STAMMERERS	STANDOVERS	STARFLOWER	STATEMENTS	STAUNCHINGS
STAMMERING	STANDPATTER	STARFLOWERS	STATEROOMS	STAUNCHLESS
STAMMERINGLY	STANDPATTERS	STARFRUITS	STATESMANLIKE	STAUNCHNESS
STAMMERINGS	STANDPATTISM	STARFUCKER	STATESMANLY	STAUNCHNESSES
STAMPEDERS	STANDPATTISMS	STARFUCKERS	STATESMANSHIP	STAUROLITE
STAMPEDING	STANDPIPES	STARFUCKING	STATESMANSHIPS	STAUROLITES
STAMPEDOED	STANDPOINT	STARFUCKINGS	STATESPERSON	STAUROLITIC
STAMPEDOING	STANDPOINTS	STARGAZERS	STATESPERSONS	STAUROSCOPE
STANCHABLE	STANDSTILL	STARGAZING	STATESWOMAN	STAUROSCOPES
STANCHELLED	STANDSTILLS	STARGAZINGS	STATESWOMEN	STAUROSCOPIC
STANCHELLING	STANNARIES	STARKENING	STATICALLY	STAVESACRE
STANCHERED	STANNATORS	STARKNESSES	STATIONARIES	STAVESACRES
STANCHERING	STANNIFEROUS	STARLIGHTED	STATIONARILY	STAVUDINES
STANCHINGS	STANNOTYPE	STARLIGHTS	STATIONARINESS	STAYCATION
STANCHIONED	STANNOTYPES	STARMONGER	STATIONARY	STAYCATIONS
STANCHIONING	STAPEDECTOMIES	STARMONGERS	STATIONERIES	STAYMAKERS
STANCHIONS	STAPEDECTOMY	STAROSTIES	STATIONERS	STEADFASTLY
STANCHLESS	STAPEDIUSES	STARRINESS	STATIONERY	STEADFASTNESS
STANCHNESS	STAPHYLINE	STARRINESSES	STATIONING	STEADFASTNESSES
STANCHNESSES	STAPHYLINID	STARSHINES	STATIONMASTER	STEADINESS
STANDARDBRED	STAPHYLINIDS	STARSTONES	STATIONMASTERS	STEADINESSES
STANDARDBREDS	STAPHYLITIS	STARSTRUCK	STATISTICAL	STEAKHOUSE
STANDARDISATION	STAPHYLITISES	STARTINGLY	STATISTICALLY	STEAKHOUSES
STANDARDISE	STAPHYLOCOCCAL	STARTLEMENT	STATISTICIAN	STEALINGLY
STANDARDISED	STAPHYLOCOCCI	STARTLEMENTS	STATISTICIANS	STEALTHFUL
STANDARDISER	STAPHYLOCOCCIC	STARTLINGLY	STATISTICS	STEALTHIER
STANDARDISERS	STAPHYLOCOCCUS	STARTLINGS	STATOBLAST	STEALTHIEST
STANDARDISES	STAPHYLOMA	STARVATION	STATOBLASTS	STEALTHILY
STANDARDISING	STAPHYLOMAS	STARVATIONS	STATOCYSTS	STEALTHINESS

S

STEALTHINESSES STEELMAKINGS STEGOCEPHALIAN STENOCHROMIES STEPFAMILY
STEALTHING STEELWARES STEGOCEPHALIANS STENOCHROMY STEPFATHER
STEALTHINGS STEELWORKER STEGOCEPHALOUS STENOGRAPH STEPFATHERS
STEAMBOATS STEELWORKERS STEGODONTS STENOGRAPHED STEPHANITE
STEAMERING STEELWORKING STEGOMYIAS STENOGRAPHER STEPHANITES
STEAMFITTER STEELWORKINGS STEGOPHILIST STENOGRAPHERS STEPHANOTIS
STEAMFITTERS STEELWORKS STEGOPHILISTS STENOGRAPHIC STEPHANOTISES
STEAMINESS STEELYARDS STEGOSAURIAN STENOGRAPHICAL STEPLADDER
STEAMINESSES STEENBRASES STEGOSAURS STENOGRAPHIES STEPLADDERS
STEAMROLLED STEENBUCKS STEGOSAURUS STENOGRAPHING STEPMOTHER
STEAMROLLER STEENKIRKS STEGOSAURUSES STENOGRAPHIST STEPMOTHERLY
STEAMROLLERED STEEPDOWNE STEINBOCKS STENOGRAPHISTS STEPMOTHERS
STEAMROLLERING STEEPEDOWNE STEINKIRKS STENOGRAPHS STEPPARENT
STEAMROLLERS STEEPENING STELLARATOR STENOGRAPHY STEPPARENTING
STEAMROLLING STEEPINESS STELLARATORS STENOHALINE STEPPARENTINGS
STEAMROLLS STEEPINESSES STELLATELY STENOPAEIC STEPPARENTS
STEAMSHIPS STEEPLEBUSH STELLERIDAN STENOPETALOUS STEPSISTER
STEAMTIGHT STEEPLEBUSHES STELLERIDANS STENOPHAGOUS STEPSISTERS
STEAMTIGHTNESS STEEPLECHASE STELLERIDS STENOPHYLLOUS STEPSTOOLS
STEAROPTENE STEEPLECHASED STELLIFEROUS STENOTHERM STERADIANS
STEAROPTENES STEEPLECHASER STELLIFIED STENOTHERMAL STERCORACEOUS
STEARSMATE STEEPLECHASERS STELLIFIES STENOTHERMS STERCORANISM
STEARSMATES STEEPLECHASES STELLIFORM STENOTOPIC STERCORANISMS
STEATOCELE STEEPLECHASING STELLIFYING STENOTROPIC STERCORANIST
STEATOCELES STEEPLECHASINGS STELLIFYINGS STENOTYPED STERCORANISTS
STEATOLYSES STEEPLEJACK STELLIONATE STENOTYPER STERCORARIOUS
STEATOLYSIS STEEPLEJACKS STELLIONATES STENOTYPERS STERCORARY
STEATOMATOUS STEEPNESSES STELLULARLY STENOTYPES STERCORATE
STEATOPYGA STEERAGEWAY STELLULATE STENOTYPIC STERCORATED
STEATOPYGAS STEERAGEWAYS STEMMATOUS STENOTYPIES STERCORATES
STEATOPYGIA STEERLINGS STEMMERIES STENOTYPING STERCORATING
STEATOPYGIAS STEERSMATE STEMWINDER STENOTYPIST STERCORICOLOUS
STEATOPYGIC STEERSMATES STEMWINDERS STENOTYPISTS STERCULIACEOUS
STEATOPYGOUS STEGANOGRAM STENCHIEST STENTMASTER STERCULIAS
STEATORRHEA STEGANOGRAMS STENCILERS STENTMASTERS STEREOACUITIES
STEATORRHEAS STEGANOGRAPH STENCILING STENTORIAN STEREOACUITY
STEATORRHOEA STEGANOGRAPHER STENCILLED STEPBAIRNS STEREOBATE
STEATORRHOEAS STEGANOGRAPHERS STENCILLER STEPBROTHER STEREOBATES
STEDFASTLY STEGANOGRAPHIC STENCILLERS STEPBROTHERS STEREOBATIC
STEDFASTNESS STEGANOGRAPHIES STENCILLING STEPCHILDREN STEREOBLIND
STEDFASTNESSES STEGANOGRAPHIST STENCILLINGS STEPDANCER STEREOCARD
STEELHEADS STEGANOGRAPHS STENOBATHIC STEPDANCERS STEREOCARDS
STEELINESS STEGANOGRAPHY STENOBATHS STEPDANCING STEREOCHEMICAL
STEELINESSES STEGANOPOD STENOCARDIA STEPDANCINGS STEREOCHEMISTRY
STEELMAKER STEGANOPODOUS STENOCARDIAS STEPDAUGHTER STEREOCHROME
STEELMAKERS STEGANOPODS STENOCHROME STEPDAUGHTERS STEREOCHROMED
STEELMAKING STEGOCARPOUS STENOCHROMES STEPFAMILIES STEREOCHROMES

S

STEREOCHROMIES	STEREOSONIC	STERILIZER	STEVEDORING	STICKLEBACKS
STEREOCHROMING	STEREOSPECIFIC	STERILIZERS	STEVENGRAPH	STICKSEEDS
STEREOCHROMY	STEREOTACTIC	STERILIZES	STEVENGRAPHS	STICKTIGHT
STEREOGNOSES	STEREOTACTICAL	STERILIZING	STEWARDESS	STICKTIGHTS
STEREOGNOSIS	STEREOTAXES	STERLINGLY	STEWARDESSES	STICKWEEDS
STEREOGRAM	STEREOTAXIA	STERLINGNESS	STEWARDING	STICKWORKS
STEREOGRAMS	STEREOTAXIAS	STERLINGNESSES	STEWARDRIES	STICKYBEAK
STEREOGRAPH	STEREOTAXIC	STERNALGIA	STEWARDSHIP	STICKYBEAKED
STEREOGRAPHED	STEREOTAXICALLY	STERNALGIAS	STEWARDSHIPS	STICKYBEAKING
STEREOGRAPHIC	STEREOTAXIS	STERNALGIC	STEWARTRIES	STICKYBEAKS
STEREOGRAPHICAL	STEREOTOMIES	STERNBOARD	STIACCIATO	STIDDIEING
STEREOGRAPHIES	STEREOTOMY	STERNBOARDS	STIACCIATOS	STIFFENERS
STEREOGRAPHING	STEREOTROPIC	STERNEBRAE	STIBIALISM	STIFFENING
STEREOGRAPHS	STEREOTROPISM	STERNFASTS	STIBIALISMS	STIFFENINGS
STEREOGRAPHY	STEREOTROPISMS	STERNFOREMOST	STICCADOES	STIFFNESSES
STEREOISOMER	STEREOTYPE	STERNNESSES	STICCATOES	STIFFWARES
STEREOISOMERIC	STEREOTYPED	STERNOCOSTAL	STICHARION	STIFLINGLY
STEREOISOMERISM	STEREOTYPER	STERNOTRIBE	STICHARIONS	STIGMARIAN
STEREOISOMERS	STEREOTYPERS	STERNPORTS	STICHICALLY	STIGMARIANS
STEREOISOMETRIC	STEREOTYPES	STERNPOSTS	STICHIDIUM	STIGMASTEROL
STEREOLOGICAL	STEREOTYPIC	STERNSHEET	STICHOLOGIES	STIGMASTEROLS
STEREOLOGICALLY	STEREOTYPICAL	STERNSHEETS	STICHOLOGY	STIGMATICAL
STEREOLOGIES	STEREOTYPICALLY	STERNUTATION	STICHOMETRIC	STIGMATICALLY
STEREOLOGY	STEREOTYPIES	STERNUTATIONS	STICHOMETRICAL	STIGMATICS
STEREOMETER	STEREOTYPING	STERNUTATIVE	STICHOMETRIES	STIGMATIFEROUS
STEREOMETERS	STEREOTYPINGS	STERNUTATIVES	STICHOMETRY	STIGMATISATION
STEREOMETRIC	STEREOTYPIST	STERNUTATOR	STICHOMYTHIA	STIGMATISATIONS
STEREOMETRICAL	STEREOTYPISTS	STERNUTATORIES	STICHOMYTHIAS	STIGMATISE
STEREOMETRIES	STEREOTYPY	STERNUTATORS	STICHOMYTHIC	STIGMATISED
STEREOMETRY	STEREOVISION	STERNUTATORY	STICHOMYTHIES	STIGMATISER
STEREOPHONIC	STEREOVISIONS	STERNWARDS	STICHOMYTHY	STIGMATISERS
STEREOPHONIES	STERICALLY	STERNWORKS	STICKABILITIES	STIGMATISES
STEREOPHONY	STERIGMATA	STEROIDOGENESES	STICKABILITY	STIGMATISING
STEREOPSES	STERILANTS	STEROIDOGENESIS	STICKBALLS	STIGMATISM
STEREOPSIS	STERILISABLE	STEROIDOGENIC	STICKERING	STIGMATISMS
STEREOPTICON	STERILISATION	STERTOROUS	STICKHANDLE	STIGMATIST
STEREOPTICONS	STERILISATIONS	STERTOROUSLY	STICKHANDLED	STIGMATISTS
STEREOPTICS	STERILISED	STERTOROUSNESS	STICKHANDLER	STIGMATIZATION
STEREOREGULAR	STERILISER	STETHOSCOPE	STICKHANDLERS	STIGMATIZATIONS
STEREOSCOPE	STERILISERS	STETHOSCOPES	STICKHANDLES	STIGMATIZE
STEREOSCOPES	STERILISES	STETHOSCOPIC	STICKHANDLING	STIGMATIZED
STEREOSCOPIC	STERILISING	STETHOSCOPIES	STICKHANDLINGS	STIGMATIZER
STEREOSCOPICAL	STERILITIES	STETHOSCOPIST	STICKINESS	STIGMATIZERS
STEREOSCOPIES	STERILIZABLE	STETHOSCOPISTS	STICKINESSES	STIGMATIZES
STEREOSCOPIST	STERILIZATION	STETHOSCOPY	STICKLEADER	STIGMATIZING
STEREOSCOPISTS	STERILIZATIONS	STEVEDORED	STICKLEADERS	STIGMATOPHILIA
STEREOSCOPY	STERILIZED	STEVEDORES	STICKLEBACK	STIGMATOPHILIAS

S

STIGMATOPHILIST	STINGBULLS	STITCHWORK	STOCKPILER	STOMACHFULNESS
STIGMATOSE	STINGFISHES	STITCHWORKS	STOCKPILERS	STOMACHFULS
STILBESTROL	STINGINESS	STITCHWORT	STOCKPILES	STOMACHICAL
STILBESTROLS	STINGINESSES	STITCHWORTS	STOCKPILING	STOMACHICS
STILBOESTROL	STINGINGLY	STOCHASTIC	STOCKPILINGS	STOMACHING
STILBOESTROLS	STINGINGNESS	STOCHASTICALLY	STOCKPUNISHT	STOMACHLESS
STILETTOED	STINGINGNESSES	STOCKADING	STOCKROOMS	STOMACHOUS
STILETTOES	STINKBIRDS	STOCKBREEDER	STOCKROUTE	STOMATITIC
STILETTOING	STINKEROOS	STOCKBREEDERS	STOCKROUTES	STOMATITIDES
STILLATORIES	STINKHORNS	STOCKBREEDING	STOCKTAKEN	STOMATITIS
STILLATORY	STINKINGLY	STOCKBREEDINGS	STOCKTAKES	STOMATITISES
STILLBIRTH	STINKINGNESS	STOCKBROKER	STOCKTAKING	STOMATODAEA
STILLBIRTHS	STINKINGNESSES	STOCKBROKERAGE	STOCKTAKINGS	STOMATODAEUM
STILLBORNS	STINKSTONE	STOCKBROKERAGES	STOCKWORKS	STOMATOGASTRIC
STILLHOUSE	STINKSTONES	STOCKBROKERS	STOCKYARDS	STOMATOLOGICAL
STILLHOUSES	STINKWEEDS	STOCKBROKING	STODGINESS	STOMATOLOGIES
STILLICIDE	STINKWOODS	STOCKBROKINGS	STODGINESSES	STOMATOLOGY
STILLICIDES	STINTEDNESS	STOCKFISHES	STOECHIOLOGICAL	STOMATOPLASTIES
STILLIFORM	STINTEDNESSES	STOCKHOLDER	STOECHIOLOGIES	STOMATOPLASTY
STILLNESSES	STINTINGLY	STOCKHOLDERS	STOECHIOLOGY	STOMATOPOD
STILLROOMS	STIPELLATE	STOCKHOLDING	STOECHIOMETRIC	STOMATOPODS
STILPNOSIDERITE	STIPENDIARIES	STOCKHOLDINGS	STOECHIOMETRIES	STOMODAEAL
STILTBIRDS	STIPENDIARY	STOCKHORSE	STOECHIOMETRY	STOMODAEUM
STILTEDNESS	STIPENDIATE	STOCKHORSES	STOICALNESS	STOMODAEUMS
STILTEDNESSES	STIPENDIATED	STOCKINESS	STOICALNESSES	STOMODEUMS
STILTINESS	STIPENDIATES	STOCKINESSES	STOICHEIOLOGIES	STONEBOATS
STILTINESSES	STIPENDIATING	STOCKINETS	STOICHEIOLOGY	STONEBORER
STIMPMETER	STIPITIFORM	STOCKINETTE	STOICHEIOMETRIC	STONEBORERS
STIMPMETERS	STIPPLINGS	STOCKINETTES	STOICHEIOMETRY	STONEBRASH
STIMULABLE	STIPULABLE	STOCKINGED	STOICHIOLOGICAL	STONEBRASHES
STIMULANCIES	STIPULACEOUS	STOCKINGER	STOICHIOLOGIES	STONEBREAK
STIMULANCY	STIPULATED	STOCKINGERS	STOICHIOLOGY	STONEBREAKS
STIMULANTS	STIPULATES	STOCKINGLESS	STOICHIOMETRIC	STONECASTS
STIMULATED	STIPULATING	STOCKISHLY	STOICHIOMETRIES	STONECHATS
STIMULATER	STIPULATION	STOCKISHNESS	STOICHIOMETRY	STONECROPS
STIMULATERS	STIPULATIONS	STOCKISHNESSES	STOITERING	STONECUTTER
STIMULATES	STIPULATOR	STOCKJOBBER	STOKEHOLDS	STONECUTTERS
STIMULATING	STIPULATORS	STOCKJOBBERIES	STOKEHOLES	STONECUTTING
STIMULATINGLY	STIPULATORY	STOCKJOBBERS	STOLENWISE	STONECUTTINGS
STIMULATION	STIRABOUTS	STOCKJOBBERY	STOLIDITIES	STONEFISHES
STIMULATIONS	STIRPICULTURE	STOCKJOBBING	STOLIDNESS	STONEFLIES
STIMULATIVE	STIRPICULTURES	STOCKJOBBINGS	STOLIDNESSES	STONEGROUND
STIMULATIVES	STIRRINGLY	STOCKKEEPER	STOLONIFEROUS	STONEHANDS
STIMULATOR	STITCHCRAFT	STOCKKEEPERS	STOMACHACHE	STONEHORSE
STIMULATORS	STITCHCRAFTS	STOCKLISTS	STOMACHACHES	STONEHORSES
STIMULATORY	STITCHERIES	STOCKLOCKS	STOMACHERS	STONELESSNESS
STINGAREES	STITCHINGS	STOCKPILED	STOMACHFUL	STONELESSNESSES

S

STONEMASON
STONEMASONRIES
STONEMASONRY
STONEMASONS
STONESHOTS
STONEWALLED
STONEWALLER
STONEWALLERS
STONEWALLING
STONEWALLINGS
STONEWALLS
STONEWARES
STONEWASHED
STONEWASHES
STONEWASHING
STONEWORKER
STONEWORKERS
STONEWORKS
STONEWORTS
STONINESSES
STONISHING
STONKERING
STONYHEARTED
STOOLBALLS
STOOPBALLS
STOOPINGLY
STOPLIGHTS
STOPPERING
STOPWATCHES
STOREFRONT
STOREFRONTS
STOREHOUSE
STOREHOUSES
STOREKEEPER
STOREKEEPERS
STOREKEEPING
STOREKEEPINGS
STOREROOMS
STORESHIPS
STORIETTES
STORIOLOGIES
STORIOLOGIST
STORIOLOGISTS
STORIOLOGY
STORKSBILL
STORKSBILLS
STORMBIRDS

STORMBOUND
STORMCOCKS
STORMFULLY
STORMFULNESS
STORMFULNESSES
STORMINESS
STORMINESSES
STORMPROOF
STORMSTAYED
STORYBOARD
STORYBOARDED
STORYBOARDING
STORYBOARDS
STORYBOOKS
STORYETTES
STORYLINES
STORYTELLER
STORYTELLERS
STORYTELLING
STORYTELLINGS
STOTTERING
STOUTENING
STOUTHEARTED
STOUTHEARTEDLY
STOUTHERIE
STOUTHERIES
STOUTHRIEF
STOUTHRIEFS
STOUTNESSES
STOVEPIPES
STRABISMAL
STRABISMIC
STRABISMICAL
STRABISMOMETER
STRABISMOMETERS
STRABISMUS
STRABISMUSES
STRABOMETER
STRABOMETERS
STRABOTOMIES
STRABOTOMY
STRACCHINI
STRACCHINO
STRADDLEBACK
STRADDLERS
STRADDLING
STRAGGLERS

STRAGGLIER
STRAGGLIEST
STRAGGLING
STRAGGLINGLY
STRAGGLINGS
STRAICHTER
STRAICHTEST
STRAIGHTAWAY
STRAIGHTAWAYS
STRAIGHTBRED
STRAIGHTBREDS
STRAIGHTED
STRAIGHTEDGE
STRAIGHTEDGED
STRAIGHTEDGES
STRAIGHTEN
STRAIGHTENED
STRAIGHTENER
STRAIGHTENERS
STRAIGHTENING
STRAIGHTENS
STRAIGHTER
STRAIGHTEST
STRAIGHTFORTH
STRAIGHTFORWARD
STRAIGHTING
STRAIGHTISH
STRAIGHTJACKET
STRAIGHTJACKETS
STRAIGHTLACED
STRAIGHTLY
STRAIGHTNESS
STRAIGHTNESSES
STRAIGHTWAY
STRAIGHTWAYS
STRAINEDLY
STRAININGS
STRAITENED
STRAITENING
STRAITJACKET
STRAITJACKETED
STRAITJACKETING
STRAITJACKETS
STRAITLACED
STRAITLACEDLY
STRAITLACEDNESS
STRAITNESS

STRAITNESSES
STRAITWAISTCOAT
STRAMACONS
STRAMASHED
STRAMASHES
STRAMASHING
STRAMAZONS
STRAMINEOUS
STRAMONIES
STRAMONIUM
STRAMONIUMS
STRANDEDNESS
STRANDEDNESSES
STRANDFLAT
STRANDFLATS
STRANDLINE
STRANDLINES
STRANDWOLF
STRANDWOLVES
STRANGENESS
STRANGENESSES
STRANGERED
STRANGERING
STRANGLEHOLD
STRANGLEHOLDS
STRANGLEMENT
STRANGLEMENTS
STRANGLERS
STRANGLING
STRANGULATE
STRANGULATED
STRANGULATES
STRANGULATING
STRANGULATION
STRANGULATIONS
STRANGURIES
STRAPHANGED
STRAPHANGER
STRAPHANGERS
STRAPHANGING
STRAPHANGINGS
STRAPHANGS
STRAPLESSES
STRAPLINES
STRAPONTIN
STRAPONTINS
STRAPPADOED

STRAPPADOES
STRAPPADOING
STRAPPADOS
STRAPPIEST
STRAPPINGS
STRAPWORTS
STRATAGEMS
STRATEGETIC
STRATEGETICAL
STRATEGICAL
STRATEGICALLY
STRATEGICS
STRATEGIES
STRATEGISE
STRATEGISED
STRATEGISES
STRATEGISING
STRATEGIST
STRATEGISTS
STRATEGIZE
STRATEGIZED
STRATEGIZES
STRATEGIZING
STRATHSPEY
STRATHSPEYS
STRATICULATE
STRATICULATION
STRATICULATIONS
STRATIFICATION
STRATIFICATIONS
STRATIFIED
STRATIFIES
STRATIFORM
STRATIFYING
STRATIGRAPHER
STRATIGRAPHERS
STRATIGRAPHIC
STRATIGRAPHICAL
STRATIGRAPHIES
STRATIGRAPHIST
STRATIGRAPHISTS
STRATIGRAPHY
STRATOCRACIES
STRATOCRACY
STRATOCRAT
STRATOCRATIC
STRATOCRATS

S

STRATOCUMULI	STREAMINGS	STRENGTHENING	STRESSLESSNESS	STRIFELESS
STRATOCUMULUS	STREAMLESS	STRENGTHENINGS	STRETCHABILITY	STRIGIFORM
STRATOPAUSE	STREAMLETS	STRENGTHENS	STRETCHABLE	STRIKEBOUND
STRATOPAUSES	STREAMLIKE	STRENGTHFUL	STRETCHERED	STRIKEBREAKER
STRATOSPHERE	STREAMLINE	STRENGTHLESS	STRETCHERING	STRIKEBREAKERS
STRATOSPHERES	STREAMLINED	STRENUITIES	STRETCHERS	STRIKEBREAKING
STRATOSPHERIC	STREAMLINER	STRENUOSITIES	STRETCHIER	STRIKEBREAKINGS
STRATOSPHERICAL	STREAMLINERS	STRENUOSITY	STRETCHIEST	STRIKELESS
STRATOTANKER	STREAMLINES	STRENUOUSLY	STRETCHINESS	STRIKEOUTS
STRATOTANKERS	STREAMLING	STRENUOUSNESS	STRETCHINESSES	STRIKEOVER
STRATOVOLCANO	STREAMLINGS	STRENUOUSNESSES	STRETCHING	STRIKEOVERS
STRATOVOLCANOES	STREAMLINING	STREPEROUS	STRETCHINGS	STRIKINGLY
STRATOVOLCANOS	STREAMSIDE	STREPHOSYMBOLIA	STRETCHLESS	STRIKINGNESS
STRAUCHTED	STREAMSIDES	STREPITANT	STRETCHMARKS	STRIKINGNESSES
STRAUCHTER	STREETAGES	STREPITATION	STREWMENTS	STRINGBOARD
STRAUCHTEST	STREETBOYS	STREPITATIONS	STRIATIONS	STRINGBOARDS
STRAUCHTING	STREETCARS	STREPITOSO	STRIATURES	STRINGCOURSE
STRAUGHTED	STREETFULS	STREPITOUS	STRICKENLY	STRINGCOURSES
STRAUGHTER	STREETIEST	STREPSIPTEROUS	STRICKLING	STRINGENCIES
STRAUGHTEST	STREETKEEPER	STREPTOBACILLI	STRICTIONS	STRINGENCY
STRAUGHTING	STREETKEEPERS	STREPTOBACILLUS	STRICTNESS	STRINGENDO
STRAVAGING	STREETLAMP	STREPTOCARPUS	STRICTNESSES	STRINGENTLY
STRAVAIGED	STREETLAMPS	STREPTOCARPUSES	STRICTURED	STRINGENTNESS
STRAVAIGER	STREETLIGHT	STREPTOCOCCAL	STRICTURES	STRINGENTNESSES
STRAVAIGERS	STREETLIGHTS	STREPTOCOCCI	STRIDDLING	STRINGHALT
STRAVAIGING	STREETROOM	STREPTOCOCCIC	STRIDELEGGED	STRINGHALTED
STRAWBERRIES	STREETROOMS	STREPTOCOCCUS	STRIDELEGS	STRINGHALTS
STRAWBERRY	STREETSCAPE	STREPTOKINASE	STRIDENCES	STRINGIEST
STRAWBOARD	STREETSCAPES	STREPTOKINASES	STRIDENCIES	STRINGINESS
STRAWBOARDS	STREETSMART	STREPTOLYSIN	STRIDENTLY	STRINGINESSES
STRAWFLOWER	STREETWALKER	STREPTOLYSINS	STRIDEWAYS	STRINGINGS
STRAWFLOWERS	STREETWALKERS	STREPTOMYCES	STRIDULANCE	STRINGLESS
STRAWWEIGHT	STREETWALKING	STREPTOMYCETE	STRIDULANCES	STRINGLIKE
STRAWWEIGHTS	STREETWALKINGS	STREPTOMYCETES	STRIDULANT	STRINGPIECE
STRAWWORMS	STREETWARD	STREPTOMYCIN	STRIDULANTLY	STRINGPIECES
STRAYLINGS	STREETWARDS	STREPTOMYCINS	STRIDULATE	STRINGYBARK
STREAKIEST	STREETWEAR	STREPTOSOLEN	STRIDULATED	STRINGYBARKS
STREAKINESS	STREETWEARS	STREPTOSOLENS	STRIDULATES	STRINKLING
STREAKINESSES	STREETWISE	STREPTOTHRICIN	STRIDULATING	STRINKLINGS
STREAKINGS	STREIGNING	STREPTOTHRICINS	STRIDULATION	STRIPELESS
STREAKLIKE	STRELITZES	STRESSBUSTER	STRIDULATIONS	STRIPINESS
STREAMBEDS	STRELITZIA	STRESSBUSTERS	STRIDULATOR	STRIPINESSES
STREAMERED	STRELITZIAS	STRESSBUSTING	STRIDULATORS	STRIPLINGS
STREAMIEST	STRENGTHEN	STRESSFULLY	STRIDULATORY	STRIPOGRAM
STREAMINESS	STRENGTHENED	STRESSFULNESS	STRIDULOUS	STRIPOGRAMS
STREAMINESSES	STRENGTHENER	STRESSFULNESSES	STRIDULOUSLY	STRIPPABLE
STREAMINGLY	STRENGTHENERS	STRESSLESS	STRIDULOUSNESS	STRIPPERGRAM

S

STRIPPERGRAMS

STRIPPERGRAMS
STRIPPINGS
STRIPTEASE
STRIPTEASER
STRIPTEASERS
STRIPTEASES
STRIVINGLY
STROBILACEOUS
STROBILATE
STROBILATED
STROBILATES
STROBILATING
STROBILATION
STROBILATIONS
STROBILIFORM
STROBILINE
STROBILISATION
STROBILISATIONS
STROBILIZATION
STROBILIZATIONS
STROBILOID
STROBILUSES
STROBOSCOPE
STROBOSCOPES
STROBOSCOPIC
STROBOSCOPICAL
STROBOTRON
STROBOTRONS
STRODDLING
STROGANOFF
STROGANOFFS
STROKEPLAY
STROLLINGS
STROMATOLITE
STROMATOLITES
STROMATOLITIC
STROMATOUS
STROMBULIFEROUS
STROMBULIFORM
STROMBUSES
STRONGARMED
STRONGARMING
STRONGARMS
STRONGBOXES
STRONGHOLD
STRONGHOLDS
STRONGNESS

STRONGNESSES
STRONGPOINT
STRONGPOINTS
STRONGROOM
STRONGROOMS
STRONGYLES
STRONGYLOID
STRONGYLOIDOSES
STRONGYLOIDOSIS
STRONGYLOIDS
STRONGYLOSES
STRONGYLOSIS
STRONTIANITE
STRONTIANITES
STRONTIANS
STRONTIUMS
STROPHANTHIN
STROPHANTHINS
STROPHANTHUS
STROPHANTHUSES
STROPHICAL
STROPHIOLATE
STROPHIOLATED
STROPHIOLE
STROPHIOLES
STROPHOIDS
STROPHULUS
STROPPIEST
STROPPINESS
STROPPINESSES
STROUDINGS
STROUPACHS
STRUCTURAL
STRUCTURALISE
STRUCTURALISED
STRUCTURALISES
STRUCTURALISING
STRUCTURALISM
STRUCTURALISMS
STRUCTURALIST
STRUCTURALISTS
STRUCTURALIZE
STRUCTURALIZED
STRUCTURALIZES
STRUCTURALIZING
STRUCTURALLY
STRUCTURATION

STRUCTURATIONS
STRUCTURED
STRUCTURELESS
STRUCTURES
STRUCTURING
STRUGGLERS
STRUGGLING
STRUGGLINGLY
STRUGGLINGS
STRUMITISES
STRUMPETED
STRUMPETING
STRUTHIOID
STRUTHIOIDS
STRUTHIOUS
STRUTTINGLY
STRUTTINGS
STRYCHNIAS
STRYCHNINE
STRYCHNINED
STRYCHNINES
STRYCHNINING
STRYCHNINISM
STRYCHNINISMS
STRYCHNISM
STRYCHNISMS
STUBBINESS
STUBBINESSES
STUBBLIEST
STUBBORNED
STUBBORNER
STUBBORNEST
STUBBORNING
STUBBORNLY
STUBBORNNESS
STUBBORNNESSES
STUCCOWORK
STUCCOWORKS
STUDDINGSAIL
STUDDINGSAILS
STUDENTRIES
STUDENTSHIP
STUDENTSHIPS
STUDFISHES
STUDHORSES
STUDIEDNESS
STUDIEDNESSES

STUDIOUSLY
STUDIOUSNESS
STUDIOUSNESSES
STUFFINESS
STUFFINESSES
STULTIFICATION
STULTIFICATIONS
STULTIFIED
STULTIFIER
STULTIFIERS
STULTIFIES
STULTIFYING
STUMBLEBUM
STUMBLEBUMS
STUMBLIEST
STUMBLINGLY
STUMPINESS
STUMPINESSES
STUMPWORKS
STUNNINGLY
STUNTEDNESS
STUNTEDNESSES
STUNTWOMAN
STUNTWOMEN
STUPEFACIENT
STUPEFACIENTS
STUPEFACTION
STUPEFACTIONS
STUPEFACTIVE
STUPEFIERS
STUPEFYING
STUPEFYINGLY
STUPENDIOUS
STUPENDOUS
STUPENDOUSLY
STUPENDOUSNESS
STUPIDITIES
STUPIDNESS
STUPIDNESSES
STUPRATING
STUPRATION
STUPRATIONS
STURDINESS
STURDINESSES
STUTTERERS
STUTTERING
STUTTERINGLY

STUTTERINGS
STYLEBOOKS
STYLELESSNESS
STYLELESSNESSES
STYLIFEROUS
STYLISATION
STYLISATIONS
STYLISHNESS
STYLISHNESSES
STYLISTICALLY
STYLISTICS
STYLITISMS
STYLIZATION
STYLIZATIONS
STYLOBATES
STYLOGRAPH
STYLOGRAPHIC
STYLOGRAPHICAL
STYLOGRAPHIES
STYLOGRAPHS
STYLOGRAPHY
STYLOLITES
STYLOLITIC
STYLOMETRIES
STYLOMETRY
STYLOPHONE
STYLOPHONES
STYLOPISED
STYLOPISES
STYLOPISING
STYLOPIZED
STYLOPIZES
STYLOPIZING
STYLOPODIA
STYLOPODIUM
STYLOSTIXES
STYLOSTIXIS
STYPTICITIES
STYPTICITY
STYRACEOUS
STYROFOAMS
SUABILITIES
SUASIVENESS
SUASIVENESSES
SUAVENESSES
SUAVEOLENT
SUBABDOMINAL

S

SUBACETATE	SUBARRATION	SUBCATEGORY	SUBCLUSTERS	SUBCRITICAL
SUBACETATES	SUBARRATIONS	SUBCAVITIES	SUBCOLLECTION	SUBCRUSTAL
SUBACIDITIES	SUBARRHATION	SUBCEILING	SUBCOLLECTIONS	SUBCULTURAL
SUBACIDITY	SUBARRHATIONS	SUBCEILINGS	SUBCOLLEGE	SUBCULTURALLY
SUBACIDNESS	SUBARTICLE	SUBCELESTIAL	SUBCOLLEGIATE	SUBCULTURE
SUBACIDNESSES	SUBARTICLES	SUBCELESTIALS	SUBCOLONIES	SUBCULTURED
SUBACTIONS	SUBASSEMBLE	SUBCELLARS	SUBCOMMISSION	SUBCULTURES
SUBACUTELY	SUBASSEMBLED	SUBCELLULAR	SUBCOMMISSIONED	SUBCULTURING
SUBADOLESCENT	SUBASSEMBLES	SUBCENTERS	SUBCOMMISSIONER	SUBCURATIVE
SUBADOLESCENTS	SUBASSEMBLIES	SUBCENTRAL	SUBCOMMISSIONS	SUBCUTANEOUS
SUBAERIALLY	SUBASSEMBLING	SUBCENTRALLY	SUBCOMMITTEE	SUBCUTANEOUSLY
SUBAFFLUENT	SUBASSEMBLY	SUBCEPTION	SUBCOMMITTEES	SUBCUTISES
SUBAGENCIES	SUBASSOCIATION	SUBCEPTIONS	SUBCOMMUNITIES	SUBDEACONATE
SUBAGGREGATE	SUBASSOCIATIONS	SUBCHANTER	SUBCOMMUNITY	SUBDEACONATES
SUBAGGREGATES	SUBATMOSPHERIC	SUBCHANTERS	SUBCOMPACT	SUBDEACONRIES
SUBAGGREGATION	SUBATOMICS	SUBCHAPTER	SUBCOMPACTS	SUBDEACONRY
SUBAGGREGATIONS	SUBAUDIBLE	SUBCHAPTERS	SUBCOMPONENT	SUBDEACONS
SUBAHDARIES	SUBAUDITION	SUBCHARTER	SUBCOMPONENTS	SUBDEACONSHIP
SUBAHSHIPS	SUBAUDITIONS	SUBCHARTERS	SUBCONSCIOUS	SUBDEACONSHIPS
SUBALLIANCE	SUBAURICULAR	SUBCHASERS	SUBCONSCIOUSES	SUBDEALERS
SUBALLIANCES	SUBAVERAGE	SUBCHELATE	SUBCONSCIOUSLY	SUBDEANERIES
SUBALLOCATION	SUBAXILLARY	SUBCHLORIDE	SUBCONSULS	SUBDEANERY
SUBALLOCATIONS	SUBBASEMENT	SUBCHLORIDES	SUBCONTIGUOUS	SUBDEBUTANTE
SUBALTERNANT	SUBBASEMENTS	SUBCIRCUIT	SUBCONTINENT	SUBDEBUTANTES
SUBALTERNANTS	SUBBITUMINOUS	SUBCIRCUITS	SUBCONTINENTAL	SUBDECANAL
SUBALTERNATE	SUBBRANCHES	SUBCIVILISATION	SUBCONTINENTS	SUBDECISION
SUBALTERNATES	SUBBUREAUS	SUBCIVILISED	SUBCONTINUOUS	SUBDECISIONS
SUBALTERNATION	SUBBUREAUX	SUBCIVILIZATION	SUBCONTRACT	SUBDELIRIA
SUBALTERNATIONS	SUBCABINET	SUBCIVILIZED	SUBCONTRACTED	SUBDELIRIOUS
SUBALTERNITIES	SUBCABINETS	SUBCLASSED	SUBCONTRACTING	SUBDELIRIUM
SUBALTERNITY	SUBCALIBER	SUBCLASSES	SUBCONTRACTINGS	SUBDELIRIUMS
SUBALTERNS	SUBCALIBRE	SUBCLASSIFIED	SUBCONTRACTOR	SUBDEPARTMENT
SUBANGULAR	SUBCANTORS	SUBCLASSIFIES	SUBCONTRACTORS	SUBDEPARTMENTS
SUBANTARCTIC	SUBCAPSULAR	SUBCLASSIFY	SUBCONTRACTS	SUBDEPUTIES
SUBAPOSTOLIC	SUBCARDINAL	SUBCLASSIFYING	SUBCONTRAOCTAVE	SUBDERMALLY
SUBAPPEARANCE	SUBCARDINALS	SUBCLASSING	SUBCONTRARIES	SUBDEVELOPMENT
SUBAPPEARANCES	SUBCARRIER	SUBCLAUSES	SUBCONTRARIETY	SUBDEVELOPMENTS
SUBAQUATIC	SUBCARRIERS	SUBCLAVIAN	SUBCONTRARY	SUBDIACONAL
SUBAQUEOUS	SUBCATEGORIES	SUBCLAVIANS	SUBCOOLING	SUBDIACONATE
SUBARACHNOID	SUBCATEGORISE	SUBCLAVICULAR	SUBCORDATE	SUBDIACONATES
SUBARACHNOIDAL	SUBCATEGORISED	SUBCLIMACTIC	SUBCORIACEOUS	SUBDIALECT
SUBARBOREAL	SUBCATEGORISES	SUBCLIMAXES	SUBCORTEXES	SUBDIALECTS
SUBARBORESCENT	SUBCATEGORISING	SUBCLINICAL	SUBCORTICAL	SUBDIRECTOR
SUBARCTICS	SUBCATEGORIZE	SUBCLINICALLY	SUBCORTICES	SUBDIRECTORS
SUBARCUATE	SUBCATEGORIZED	SUBCLUSTER	SUBCOSTALS	SUBDISCIPLINE
SUBARCUATION	SUBCATEGORIZES	SUBCLUSTERED	SUBCOUNTIES	SUBDISCIPLINES
SUBARCUATIONS	SUBCATEGORIZING	SUBCLUSTERING	SUBCRANIAL	SUBDISTRICT

S

ten to fifteen letter words | 1109

SUBDISTRICTS	SUBFERTILITY	SUBINFEUDATES	SUBJECTIVELY	SUBLESSEES
SUBDIVIDABLE	SUBFEUDATION	SUBINFEUDATING	SUBJECTIVENESS	SUBLESSORS
SUBDIVIDED	SUBFEUDATIONS	SUBINFEUDATION	SUBJECTIVES	SUBLETHALLY
SUBDIVIDER	SUBFEUDATORY	SUBINFEUDATIONS	SUBJECTIVISE	SUBLETTERS
SUBDIVIDERS	SUBFOSSILS	SUBINFEUDATORY	SUBJECTIVISED	SUBLETTING
SUBDIVIDES	SUBFREEZING	SUBINFEUDED	SUBJECTIVISES	SUBLETTINGS
SUBDIVIDING	SUBFUSCOUS	SUBINFEUDING	SUBJECTIVISING	SUBLIBRARIAN
SUBDIVISIBLE	SUBGENERATION	SUBINFEUDS	SUBJECTIVISM	SUBLIBRARIANS
SUBDIVISION	SUBGENERATIONS	SUBINHIBITORY	SUBJECTIVISMS	SUBLICENSE
SUBDIVISIONAL	SUBGENERIC	SUBINSINUATION	SUBJECTIVIST	SUBLICENSED
SUBDIVISIONS	SUBGENERICALLY	SUBINSINUATIONS	SUBJECTIVISTIC	SUBLICENSES
SUBDIVISIVE	SUBGENUSES	SUBINSPECTOR	SUBJECTIVISTS	SUBLICENSING
SUBDOMINANT	SUBGLACIAL	SUBINSPECTORS	SUBJECTIVITIES	SUBLIEUTENANCY
SUBDOMINANTS	SUBGLACIALLY	SUBINTELLECTION	SUBJECTIVITY	SUBLIEUTENANT
SUBDUCTING	SUBGLOBOSE	SUBINTELLIGENCE	SUBJECTIVIZE	SUBLIEUTENANTS
SUBDUCTION	SUBGLOBULAR	SUBINTELLIGITUR	SUBJECTIVIZED	SUBLIMABLE
SUBDUCTIONS	SUBGOVERNMENT	SUBINTERVAL	SUBJECTIVIZES	SUBLIMATED
SUBDUEDNESS	SUBGOVERNMENTS	SUBINTERVALS	SUBJECTIVIZING	SUBLIMATES
SUBDUEDNESSES	SUBGROUPED	SUBINTRANT	SUBJECTLESS	SUBLIMATING
SUBDUEMENT	SUBGROUPING	SUBINTRODUCE	SUBJECTSHIP	SUBLIMATION
SUBDUEMENTS	SUBHARMONIC	SUBINTRODUCED	SUBJECTSHIPS	SUBLIMATIONS
SUBDUPLICATE	SUBHARMONICS	SUBINTRODUCES	SUBJOINDER	SUBLIMENESS
SUBECONOMIC	SUBHASTATION	SUBINTRODUCING	SUBJOINDERS	SUBLIMENESSES
SUBECONOMIES	SUBHASTATIONS	SUBINVOLUTION	SUBJOINING	SUBLIMINAL
SUBECONOMY	SUBHEADING	SUBINVOLUTIONS	SUBJUGABLE	SUBLIMINALLY
SUBEDITING	SUBHEADINGS	SUBIRRIGATE	SUBJUGATED	SUBLIMINALS
SUBEDITORIAL	SUBIMAGINAL	SUBIRRIGATED	SUBJUGATES	SUBLIMINGS
SUBEDITORS	SUBIMAGINES	SUBIRRIGATES	SUBJUGATING	SUBLIMISED
SUBEDITORSHIP	SUBIMAGOES	SUBIRRIGATING	SUBJUGATION	SUBLIMISES
SUBEDITORSHIPS	SUBINCISED	SUBIRRIGATION	SUBJUGATIONS	SUBLIMISING
SUBEMPLOYED	SUBINCISES	SUBIRRIGATIONS	SUBJUGATOR	SUBLIMITIES
SUBEMPLOYMENT	SUBINCISING	SUBITANEOUS	SUBJUGATORS	SUBLIMIZED
SUBEMPLOYMENTS	SUBINCISION	SUBITISING	SUBJUNCTION	SUBLIMIZES
SUBENTRIES	SUBINCISIONS	SUBITIZING	SUBJUNCTIONS	SUBLIMIZING
SUBEPIDERMAL	SUBINDEXES	SUBJACENCIES	SUBJUNCTIVE	SUBLINEATION
SUBEQUATORIAL	SUBINDICATE	SUBJACENCY	SUBJUNCTIVELY	SUBLINEATIONS
SUBERISATION	SUBINDICATED	SUBJACENTLY	SUBJUNCTIVES	SUBLINGUAL
SUBERISATIONS	SUBINDICATES	SUBJECTABILITY	SUBKINGDOM	SUBLITERACIES
SUBERISING	SUBINDICATING	SUBJECTABLE	SUBKINGDOMS	SUBLITERACY
SUBERIZATION	SUBINDICATION	SUBJECTIFIED	SUBLANCEOLATE	SUBLITERARY
SUBERIZATIONS	SUBINDICATIONS	SUBJECTIFIES	SUBLANGUAGE	SUBLITERATE
SUBERIZING	SUBINDICATIVE	SUBJECTIFY	SUBLANGUAGES	SUBLITERATES
SUBFACTORIAL	SUBINDICES	SUBJECTIFYING	SUBLAPSARIAN	SUBLITERATURE
SUBFACTORIALS	SUBINDUSTRIES	SUBJECTING	SUBLAPSARIANISM	SUBLITERATURES
SUBFAMILIES	SUBINDUSTRY	SUBJECTION	SUBLAPSARIANS	SUBLITTORAL
SUBFERTILE	SUBINFEUDATE	SUBJECTIONS	SUBLATIONS	SUBLITTORALS
SUBFERTILITIES	SUBINFEUDATED	SUBJECTIVE	SUBLEASING	SUBLUXATED

S

SUBLUXATES	SUBMINIATURISES	SUBOCTAVES	SUBPENAING	SUBROUTINE
SUBLUXATING	SUBMINIATURIZE	SUBOCTUPLE	SUBPERIODS	SUBROUTINES
SUBLUXATION	SUBMINIATURIZED	SUBOFFICER	SUBPHRENIC	SUBSAMPLED
SUBLUXATIONS	SUBMINIATURIZES	SUBOFFICERS	SUBPOENAED	SUBSAMPLES
SUBMANAGER	SUBMINIMAL	SUBOFFICES	SUBPOENAING	SUBSAMPLING
SUBMANAGERS	SUBMINISTER	SUBOPERCULA	SUBPOPULATION	SUBSATELLITE
SUBMANDIBULAR	SUBMINISTERS	SUBOPERCULAR	SUBPOPULATIONS	SUBSATELLITES
SUBMANDIBULARS	SUBMISSIBLE	SUBOPERCULUM	SUBPOTENCIES	SUBSATURATED
SUBMARGINAL	SUBMISSION	SUBOPTIMAL	SUBPOTENCY	SUBSATURATION
SUBMARGINALLY	SUBMISSIONS	SUBOPTIMISATION	SUBPREFECT	SUBSATURATIONS
SUBMARINED	SUBMISSIVE	SUBOPTIMISE	SUBPREFECTS	SUBSCAPULAR
SUBMARINER	SUBMISSIVELY	SUBOPTIMISED	SUBPREFECTURE	SUBSCAPULARS
SUBMARINERS	SUBMISSIVENESS	SUBOPTIMISES	SUBPREFECTURES	SUBSCHEMATA
SUBMARINES	SUBMISSNESS	SUBOPTIMISING	SUBPRIMATE	SUBSCIENCE
SUBMARINING	SUBMISSNESSES	SUBOPTIMIZATION	SUBPRIMATES	SUBSCIENCES
SUBMARKETS	SUBMITTABLE	SUBOPTIMIZE	SUBPRINCIPAL	SUBSCRIBABLE
SUBMATRICES	SUBMITTALS	SUBOPTIMIZED	SUBPRINCIPALS	SUBSCRIBED
SUBMATRIXES	SUBMITTERS	SUBOPTIMIZES	SUBPRIORESS	SUBSCRIBER
SUBMAXILLARIES	SUBMITTING	SUBOPTIMIZING	SUBPRIORESSES	SUBSCRIBERS
SUBMAXILLARY	SUBMITTINGS	SUBOPTIMUM	SUBPROBLEM	SUBSCRIBES
SUBMAXIMAL	SUBMOLECULE	SUBORBICULAR	SUBPROBLEMS	SUBSCRIBING
SUBMEDIANT	SUBMOLECULES	SUBORBITAL	SUBPROCESS	SUBSCRIBINGS
SUBMEDIANTS	SUBMONTANE	SUBORDINAL	SUBPROCESSES	SUBSCRIPTION
SUBMERGEMENT	SUBMONTANELY	SUBORDINARIES	SUBPRODUCT	SUBSCRIPTIONS
SUBMERGEMENTS	SUBMUCOSAE	SUBORDINARY	SUBPRODUCTS	SUBSCRIPTIVE
SUBMERGENCE	SUBMUCOSAL	SUBORDINATE	SUBPROFESSIONAL	SUBSCRIPTS
SUBMERGENCES	SUBMUCOSAS	SUBORDINATED	SUBPROGRAM	SUBSECRETARIES
SUBMERGIBILITY	SUBMULTIPLE	SUBORDINATELY	SUBPROGRAMS	SUBSECRETARY
SUBMERGIBLE	SUBMULTIPLES	SUBORDINATENESS	SUBPROJECT	SUBSECTION
SUBMERGIBLES	SUBMUNITION	SUBORDINATES	SUBPROJECTS	SUBSECTIONS
SUBMERGING	SUBMUNITIONS	SUBORDINATING	SUBPROLETARIAT	SUBSECTORS
SUBMERSIBILITY	SUBNASCENT	SUBORDINATION	SUBPROLETARIATS	SUBSEGMENT
SUBMERSIBLE	SUBNATIONAL	SUBORDINATIONS	SUBRATIONAL	SUBSEGMENTS
SUBMERSIBLES	SUBNATURAL	SUBORDINATIVE	SUBREFERENCE	SUBSEIZURE
SUBMERSING	SUBNETWORK	SUBORDINATOR	SUBREFERENCES	SUBSEIZURES
SUBMERSION	SUBNETWORKED	SUBORDINATORS	SUBREGIONAL	SUBSELLIUM
SUBMERSIONS	SUBNETWORKING	SUBORGANISATION	SUBREGIONS	SUBSENSIBLE
SUBMETACENTRIC	SUBNETWORKS	SUBORGANIZATION	SUBREPTION	SUBSENTENCE
SUBMETACENTRICS	SUBNORMALITIES	SUBORNATION	SUBREPTIONS	SUBSENTENCES
SUBMICROGRAM	SUBNORMALITY	SUBORNATIONS	SUBREPTITIOUS	SUBSEQUENCE
SUBMICRONS	SUBNORMALLY	SUBORNATIVE	SUBREPTITIOUSLY	SUBSEQUENCES
SUBMICROSCOPIC	SUBNORMALS	SUBOSCINES	SUBREPTIVE	SUBSEQUENT
SUBMILLIMETER	SUBNUCLEAR	SUBPANATION	SUBROGATED	SUBSEQUENTIAL
SUBMINIATURE	SUBNUCLEUS	SUBPANATIONS	SUBROGATES	SUBSEQUENTLY
SUBMINIATURES	SUBNUCLEUSES	SUBPARAGRAPH	SUBROGATING	SUBSEQUENTNESS
SUBMINIATURISE	SUBOCCIPITAL	SUBPARAGRAPHS	SUBROGATION	SUBSEQUENTS
SUBMINIATURISED	SUBOCEANIC	SUBPARALLEL	SUBROGATIONS	SUBSERVIENCE

S

SUBSERVIENCES

SUBSERVIENCES	SUBSONICALLY	SUBSTANTIVAL	SUBSTRUCTED	SUBTHERAPEUTIC
SUBSERVIENCIES	SUBSPECIALISE	SUBSTANTIVALLY	SUBSTRUCTING	SUBTHRESHOLD
SUBSERVIENCY	SUBSPECIALISED	SUBSTANTIVE	SUBSTRUCTION	SUBTILENESS
SUBSERVIENT	SUBSPECIALISES	SUBSTANTIVELY	SUBSTRUCTIONS	SUBTILENESSES
SUBSERVIENTLY	SUBSPECIALISING	SUBSTANTIVENESS	SUBSTRUCTS	SUBTILISATION
SUBSERVIENTS	SUBSPECIALIST	SUBSTANTIVES	SUBSTRUCTURAL	SUBTILISATIONS
SUBSERVING	SUBSPECIALISTS	SUBSTANTIVISE	SUBSTRUCTURE	SUBTILISED
SUBSESSILE	SUBSPECIALITIES	SUBSTANTIVISED	SUBSTRUCTURES	SUBTILISER
SUBSHRUBBY	SUBSPECIALITY	SUBSTANTIVISES	SUBSULTIVE	SUBTILISERS
SUBSIDENCE	SUBSPECIALIZE	SUBSTANTIVISING	SUBSULTORILY	SUBTILISES
SUBSIDENCES	SUBSPECIALIZED	SUBSTANTIVITIES	SUBSULTORY	SUBTILISIN
SUBSIDENCIES	SUBSPECIALIZES	SUBSTANTIVITY	SUBSULTUSES	SUBTILISING
SUBSIDENCY	SUBSPECIALIZING	SUBSTANTIVIZE	SUBSUMABLE	SUBTILISINS
SUBSIDIARIES	SUBSPECIALTIES	SUBSTANTIVIZED	SUBSUMPTION	SUBTILITIES
SUBSIDIARILY	SUBSPECIALTY	SUBSTANTIVIZES	SUBSUMPTIONS	SUBTILIZATION
SUBSIDIARINESS	SUBSPECIES	SUBSTANTIVIZING	SUBSUMPTIVE	SUBTILIZATIONS
SUBSIDIARITIES	SUBSPECIFIC	SUBSTATION	SUBSURFACE	SUBTILIZED
SUBSIDIARITY	SUBSPECIFICALLY	SUBSTATIONS	SUBSURFACES	SUBTILIZER
SUBSIDIARY	SUBSPINOUS	SUBSTELLAR	SUBSYSTEMS	SUBTILIZERS
SUBSIDISABLE	SUBSPONTANEOUS	SUBSTERNAL	SUBTACKSMAN	SUBTILIZES
SUBSIDISATION	SUBSTANCELESS	SUBSTITUENT	SUBTACKSMEN	SUBTILIZING
SUBSIDISATIONS	SUBSTANCES	SUBSTITUENTS	SUBTANGENT	SUBTILTIES
SUBSIDISED	SUBSTANDARD	SUBSTITUTABLE	SUBTANGENTS	SUBTITLING
SUBSIDISER	SUBSTANTIAL	SUBSTITUTE	SUBTEMPERATE	SUBTITULAR
SUBSIDISERS	SUBSTANTIALISE	SUBSTITUTED	SUBTENANCIES	SUBTLENESS
SUBSIDISES	SUBSTANTIALISED	SUBSTITUTES	SUBTENANCY	SUBTLENESSES
SUBSIDISING	SUBSTANTIALISES	SUBSTITUTING	SUBTENANTS	SUBTLETIES
SUBSIDIZABLE	SUBSTANTIALISM	SUBSTITUTION	SUBTENDING	SUBTOTALED
SUBSIDIZATION	SUBSTANTIALISMS	SUBSTITUTIONAL	SUBTENURES	SUBTOTALING
SUBSIDIZATIONS	SUBSTANTIALIST	SUBSTITUTIONARY	SUBTERFUGE	SUBTOTALLED
SUBSIDIZED	SUBSTANTIALISTS	SUBSTITUTIONS	SUBTERFUGES	SUBTOTALLING
SUBSIDIZER	SUBSTANTIALITY	SUBSTITUTIVE	SUBTERMINAL	SUBTOTALLY
SUBSIDIZERS	SUBSTANTIALIZE	SUBSTITUTIVELY	SUBTERNATURAL	SUBTRACTED
SUBSIDIZES	SUBSTANTIALIZED	SUBSTITUTIVITY	SUBTERRAIN	SUBTRACTER
SUBSIDIZING	SUBSTANTIALIZES	SUBSTRACTED	SUBTERRAINS	SUBTRACTERS
SUBSISTENCE	SUBSTANTIALLY	SUBSTRACTING	SUBTERRANE	SUBTRACTING
SUBSISTENCES	SUBSTANTIALNESS	SUBSTRACTION	SUBTERRANEAN	SUBTRACTION
SUBSISTENT	SUBSTANTIALS	SUBSTRACTIONS	SUBTERRANEANLY	SUBTRACTIONS
SUBSISTENTIAL	SUBSTANTIATE	SUBSTRACTOR	SUBTERRANEANS	SUBTRACTIVE
SUBSISTERS	SUBSTANTIATED	SUBSTRACTORS	SUBTERRANEOUS	SUBTRACTOR
SUBSISTING	SUBSTANTIATES	SUBSTRACTS	SUBTERRANEOUSLY	SUBTRACTORS
SUBSOCIALLY	SUBSTANTIATING	SUBSTRATAL	SUBTERRANES	SUBTRAHEND
SUBSOCIETIES	SUBSTANTIATION	SUBSTRATES	SUBTERRENE	SUBTRAHENDS
SUBSOCIETY	SUBSTANTIATIONS	SUBSTRATIVE	SUBTERRENES	SUBTREASURER
SUBSOILERS	SUBSTANTIATIVE	SUBSTRATOSPHERE	SUBTERRESTRIAL	SUBTREASURERS
SUBSOILING	SUBSTANTIATOR	SUBSTRATUM	SUBTERRESTRIALS	SUBTREASURIES
SUBSOILINGS	SUBSTANTIATORS	SUBSTRATUMS	SUBTEXTUAL	SUBTREASURY

S

SUBTRIANGULAR	SUBVERTICAL	SUCCESSORAL	SUCRALOSES	SUFFOCATIVE
SUBTRIPLICATE	SUBVERTING	SUCCESSORS	SUCTIONING	SUFFRAGANS
SUBTROPICAL	SUBVIRUSES	SUCCESSORSHIP	SUCTORIANS	SUFFRAGANSHIP
SUBTROPICALLY	SUBVISIBLE	SUCCESSORSHIPS	SUDATORIES	SUFFRAGANSHIPS
SUBTROPICS	SUBVITREOUS	SUCCINATES	SUDATORIUM	SUFFRAGETTE
SUBTRUDING	SUBVOCALISATION	SUCCINCTER	SUDATORIUMS	SUFFRAGETTES
SUBTYPICAL	SUBVOCALISE	SUCCINCTEST	SUDDENNESS	SUFFRAGETTISM
SUBUMBRELLA	SUBVOCALISED	SUCCINCTLY	SUDDENNESSES	SUFFRAGETTISMS
SUBUMBRELLAR	SUBVOCALISES	SUCCINCTNESS	SUDDENTIES	SUFFRAGISM
SUBUMBRELLAS	SUBVOCALISING	SUCCINCTNESSES	SUDORIFEROUS	SUFFRAGISMS
SUBUNGULATE	SUBVOCALIZATION	SUCCINCTORIA	SUDORIFICS	SUFFRAGIST
SUBUNGULATES	SUBVOCALIZE	SUCCINCTORIES	SUDORIPAROUS	SUFFRAGISTS
SUBURBANISATION	SUBVOCALIZED	SUCCINCTORIUM	SUEABILITIES	SUFFRUTESCENT
SUBURBANISE	SUBVOCALIZES	SUCCINCTORY	SUEABILITY	SUFFRUTICOSE
SUBURBANISED	SUBVOCALIZING	SUCCINITES	SUFFERABLE	SUFFUMIGATE
SUBURBANISES	SUBVOCALLY	SUCCINYLCHOLINE	SUFFERABLENESS	SUFFUMIGATED
SUBURBANISING	SUBWARDENS	SUCCORABLE	SUFFERABLY	SUFFUMIGATES
SUBURBANISM	SUBWOOFERS	SUCCORLESS	SUFFERANCE	SUFFUMIGATING
SUBURBANISMS	SUBWRITERS	SUCCOTASHES	SUFFERANCES	SUFFUMIGATION
SUBURBANITE	SUCCEDANEA	SUCCOURABLE	SUFFERINGLY	SUFFUMIGATIONS
SUBURBANITES	SUCCEDANEOUS	SUCCOURERS	SUFFERINGS	SUFFUSIONS
SUBURBANITIES	SUCCEDANEUM	SUCCOURING	SUFFICIENCE	SUGARALLIE
SUBURBANITY	SUCCEDANEUMS	SUCCOURLESS	SUFFICIENCES	SUGARALLIES
SUBURBANIZATION	SUCCEEDABLE	SUCCUBUSES	SUFFICIENCIES	SUGARBERRIES
SUBURBANIZE	SUCCEEDERS	SUCCULENCE	SUFFICIENCY	SUGARBERRY
SUBURBANIZED	SUCCEEDING	SUCCULENCES	SUFFICIENT	SUGARBUSHES
SUBURBANIZES	SUCCEEDINGLY	SUCCULENCIES	SUFFICIENTLY	SUGARCANES
SUBURBANIZING	SUCCENTORS	SUCCULENCY	SUFFICIENTS	SUGARCOATED
SUBURBICARIAN	SUCCENTORSHIP	SUCCULENTLY	SUFFICINGNESS	SUGARCOATING
SUBVARIETIES	SUCCENTORSHIPS	SUCCULENTS	SUFFICINGNESSES	SUGARCOATS
SUBVARIETY	SUCCESSANTLY	SUCCUMBERS	SUFFIGANCE	SUGARHOUSE
SUBVASSALS	SUCCESSFUL	SUCCUMBING	SUFFIGANCES	SUGARHOUSES
SUBVENTION	SUCCESSFULLY	SUCCURSALE	SUFFISANCE	SUGARINESS
SUBVENTIONARY	SUCCESSFULNESS	SUCCURSALES	SUFFISANCES	SUGARINESSES
SUBVENTIONS	SUCCESSION	SUCCURSALS	SUFFIXATION	SUGARLOAVES
SUBVERSALS	SUCCESSIONAL	SUCCUSSATION	SUFFIXATIONS	SUGARPLUMS
SUBVERSING	SUCCESSIONALLY	SUCCUSSATIONS	SUFFIXIONS	SUGGESTERS
SUBVERSION	SUCCESSIONIST	SUCCUSSING	SUFFLATING	SUGGESTIBILITY
SUBVERSIONARIES	SUCCESSIONISTS	SUCCUSSION	SUFFLATION	SUGGESTIBLE
SUBVERSIONARY	SUCCESSIONLESS	SUCCUSSIONS	SUFFLATIONS	SUGGESTIBLENESS
SUBVERSIONS	SUCCESSIONS	SUCCUSSIVE	SUFFOCATED	SUGGESTIBLY
SUBVERSIVE	SUCCESSIVE	SUCHNESSES	SUFFOCATES	SUGGESTING
SUBVERSIVELY	SUCCESSIVELY	SUCKERFISH	SUFFOCATING	SUGGESTION
SUBVERSIVENESS	SUCCESSIVENESS	SUCKERFISHES	SUFFOCATINGLY	SUGGESTIONISE
SUBVERSIVES	SUCCESSLESS	SUCKFISHES	SUFFOCATINGS	SUGGESTIONISED
SUBVERTEBRAL	SUCCESSLESSLY	SUCRALFATE	SUFFOCATION	SUGGESTIONISES
SUBVERTERS	SUCCESSLESSNESS	SUCRALFATES	SUFFOCATIONS	SUGGESTIONISING

S

SUGGESTIONISM	SULFONAMIDE	SULPHONAMIDE	SULPHURYLS	SUMMERTIMES
SUGGESTIONISMS	SULFONAMIDES	SULPHONAMIDES	SULTANATES	SUMMERWEIGHT
SUGGESTIONIST	SULFONATED	SULPHONATE	SULTANESSES	SUMMERWOOD
SUGGESTIONISTS	SULFONATES	SULPHONATED	SULTANSHIP	SUMMERWOODS
SUGGESTIONIZE	SULFONATING	SULPHONATES	SULTANSHIPS	SUMMITEERS
SUGGESTIONIZED	SULFONATION	SULPHONATING	SULTRINESS	SUMMITLESS
SUGGESTIONIZES	SULFONATIONS	SULPHONATION	SULTRINESSES	SUMMITRIES
SUGGESTIONIZING	SULFONIUMS	SULPHONATIONS	SUMMABILITIES	SUMMONABLE
SUGGESTIONS	SULFONYLUREA	SULPHONIUM	SUMMABILITY	SUMMONSING
SUGGESTIVE	SULFONYLUREAS	SULPHONIUMS	SUMMARINESS	SUMPHISHNESS
SUGGESTIVELY	SULFOXIDES	SULPHONMETHANE	SUMMARINESSES	SUMPHISHNESSES
SUGGESTIVENESS	SULFURATED	SULPHONMETHANES	SUMMARISABLE	SUMPSIMUSES
SUICIDALLY	SULFURATES	SULPHONYLS	SUMMARISATION	SUMPTUOSITIES
SUICIDOLOGIES	SULFURATING	SULPHONYLUREA	SUMMARISATIONS	SUMPTUOSITY
SUICIDOLOGIST	SULFURETED	SULPHONYLUREAS	SUMMARISED	SUMPTUOUSLY
SUICIDOLOGISTS	SULFURETING	SULPHURATE	SUMMARISER	SUMPTUOUSNESS
SUICIDOLOGY	SULFURETTED	SULPHURATED	SUMMARISERS	SUMPTUOUSNESSES
SUITABILITIES	SULFURETTING	SULPHURATES	SUMMARISES	SUNBATHERS
SUITABILITY	SULFURISATION	SULPHURATING	SUMMARISING	SUNBATHING
SUITABLENESS	SULFURISATIONS	SULPHURATION	SUMMARISTS	SUNBATHINGS
SUITABLENESSES	SULFURISED	SULPHURATIONS	SUMMARIZABLE	SUNBERRIES
SUITRESSES	SULFURISES	SULPHURATOR	SUMMARIZATION	SUNBONNETED
SULCALISED	SULFURISING	SULPHURATORS	SUMMARIZATIONS	SUNBONNETS
SULCALISES	SULFURIZED	SULPHUREOUS	SUMMARIZED	SUNBURNING
SULCALISING	SULFURIZES	SULPHUREOUSLY	SUMMARIZER	SUNDERABLE
SULCALIZED	SULFURIZING	SULPHUREOUSNESS	SUMMARIZERS	SUNDERANCE
SULCALIZES	SULFUROUSLY	SULPHURETED	SUMMARIZES	SUNDERANCES
SULCALIZING	SULFUROUSNESS	SULPHURETING	SUMMARIZING	SUNDERINGS
SULCATIONS	SULFUROUSNESSES	SULPHURETS	SUMMATIONAL	SUNDERMENT
SULFACETAMIDE	SULKINESSES	SULPHURETTED	SUMMATIONS	SUNDERMENTS
SULFACETAMIDES	SULLENNESS	SULPHURETTING	SUMMERHOUSE	SUNDOWNERS
SULFADIAZINE	SULLENNESSES	SULPHURING	SUMMERHOUSES	SUNDOWNING
SULFADIAZINES	SULPHACETAMIDE	SULPHURISATION	SUMMERIEST	SUNDRENCHED
SULFADIMIDINE	SULPHACETAMIDES	SULPHURISATIONS	SUMMERINESS	SUNDRESSES
SULFADIMIDINES	SULPHADIAZINE	SULPHURISE	SUMMERINESSES	SUNFLOWERS
SULFADOXINE	SULPHADIAZINES	SULPHURISED	SUMMERINGS	SUNGAZINGS
SULFADOXINES	SULPHANILAMIDE	SULPHURISES	SUMMERLESS	SUNGLASSES
SULFAMETHAZINE	SULPHANILAMIDES	SULPHURISING	SUMMERLIKE	SUNLESSNESS
SULFAMETHAZINES	SULPHATASE	SULPHURIZATION	SUMMERLONG	SUNLESSNESSES
SULFANILAMIDE	SULPHATASES	SULPHURIZATIONS	SUMMERSAULT	SUNLOUNGER
SULFANILAMIDES	SULPHATHIAZOLE	SULPHURIZE	SUMMERSAULTED	SUNLOUNGERS
SULFATASES	SULPHATHIAZOLES	SULPHURIZED	SUMMERSAULTING	SUNNINESSES
SULFATHIAZOLE	SULPHATING	SULPHURIZES	SUMMERSAULTS	SUNPORCHES
SULFATHIAZOLES	SULPHATION	SULPHURIZING	SUMMERSETS	SUNRISINGS
SULFATIONS	SULPHATIONS	SULPHUROUS	SUMMERSETTED	SUNSCREENING
SULFHYDRYL	SULPHHYDRYL	SULPHUROUSLY	SUMMERSETTING	SUNSCREENS
SULFHYDRYLS	SULPHHYDRYLS	SULPHUROUSNESS	SUMMERTIDE	SUNSEEKERS
SULFINPYRAZONE	SULPHINPYRAZONE	SULPHURWORT	SUMMERTIDES	SUNSETTING
SULFINPYRAZONES	SULPHINYLS	SULPHURWORTS	SUMMERTIME	SUNSETTINGS

S

SUNSPOTTED	SUPERATHLETE	SUPERCHARGED	SUPERCRIMINAL	SUPEREXALTS
SUNSTROKES	SUPERATHLETES	SUPERCHARGER	SUPERCRIMINALS	SUPEREXCELLENCE
SUNTANNING	SUPERATING	SUPERCHARGERS	SUPERCRITICAL	SUPEREXCELLENT
SUNWORSHIPPER	SUPERATION	SUPERCHARGES	SUPERCURRENT	SUPEREXPENSIVE
SUNWORSHIPPERS	SUPERATIONS	SUPERCHARGING	SUPERCURRENTS	SUPEREXPRESS
SUOVETAURILIA	SUPERATOMS	SUPERCHERIE	SUPERDAINTY	SUPEREXPRESSES
SUPERABILITIES	SUPERBANKS	SUPERCHERIES	SUPERDELEGATE	SUPERFAMILIES
SUPERABILITY	SUPERBAZAAR	SUPERCHURCH	SUPERDELEGATES	SUPERFAMILY
SUPERABLENESS	SUPERBAZAARS	SUPERCHURCHES	SUPERDELUXE	SUPERFARMS
SUPERABLENESSES	SUPERBAZAR	SUPERCILIARIES	SUPERDENSE	SUPERFATTED
SUPERABOUND	SUPERBAZARS	SUPERCILIARY	SUPERDIPLOMAT	SUPERFECTA
SUPERABOUNDED	SUPERBIKES	SUPERCILIOUS	SUPERDIPLOMATS	SUPERFECTAS
SUPERABOUNDING	SUPERBITCH	SUPERCILIOUSLY	SUPERDOMINANT	SUPERFEMALE
SUPERABOUNDS	SUPERBITCHES	SUPERCITIES	SUPERDOMINANTS	SUPERFEMALES
SUPERABSORBENT	SUPERBITIES	SUPERCIVILISED	SUPEREFFECTIVE	SUPERFETATE
SUPERABSORBENTS	SUPERBLOCK	SUPERCIVILIZED	SUPEREFFICIENCY	SUPERFETATED
SUPERABUNDANCE	SUPERBLOCKS	SUPERCLASS	SUPEREFFICIENT	SUPERFETATES
SUPERABUNDANCES	SUPERBNESS	SUPERCLASSES	SUPEREGOIST	SUPERFETATING
SUPERABUNDANT	SUPERBNESSES	SUPERCLEAN	SUPEREGOISTS	SUPERFETATION
SUPERABUNDANTLY	SUPERBOARD	SUPERCLUBS	SUPERELASTIC	SUPERFETATIONS
SUPERACHIEVER	SUPERBOARDS	SUPERCLUSTER	SUPERELEVATE	SUPERFICIAL
SUPERACHIEVERS	SUPERBOMBER	SUPERCLUSTERS	SUPERELEVATED	SUPERFICIALISE
SUPERACTIVE	SUPERBOMBERS	SUPERCOILED	SUPERELEVATES	SUPERFICIALISED
SUPERACTIVITIES	SUPERBOMBS	SUPERCOILING	SUPERELEVATING	SUPERFICIALISES
SUPERACTIVITY	SUPERBRAIN	SUPERCOILS	SUPERELEVATION	SUPERFICIALITY
SUPERACUTE	SUPERBRAINS	SUPERCOLLIDER	SUPERELEVATIONS	SUPERFICIALIZE
SUPERADDED	SUPERBRATS	SUPERCOLLIDERS	SUPERELITE	SUPERFICIALIZED
SUPERADDING	SUPERBRIGHT	SUPERCOLOSSAL	SUPEREMINENCE	SUPERFICIALIZES
SUPERADDITION	SUPERBUREAUCRAT	SUPERCOLUMNAR	SUPEREMINENCES	SUPERFICIALLY
SUPERADDITIONAL	SUPERCABINET	SUPERCOMPUTER	SUPEREMINENT	SUPERFICIALNESS
SUPERADDITIONS	SUPERCABINETS	SUPERCOMPUTERS	SUPEREMINENTLY	SUPERFICIALS
SUPERAGENCIES	SUPERCALENDER	SUPERCOMPUTING	SUPEREROGANT	SUPERFICIES
SUPERAGENCY	SUPERCALENDERED	SUPERCOMPUTINGS	SUPEREROGATE	SUPERFINENESS
SUPERAGENT	SUPERCALENDERS	SUPERCONDUCT	SUPEREROGATED	SUPERFINENESSES
SUPERAGENTS	SUPERCARGO	SUPERCONDUCTED	SUPEREROGATES	SUPERFIRMS
SUPERALLOY	SUPERCARGOES	SUPERCONDUCTING	SUPEREROGATING	SUPERFIXES
SUPERALLOYS	SUPERCARGOS	SUPERCONDUCTION	SUPEREROGATION	SUPERFLACK
SUPERALTAR	SUPERCARGOSHIP	SUPERCONDUCTIVE	SUPEREROGATIONS	SUPERFLACKS
SUPERALTARS	SUPERCARGOSHIPS	SUPERCONDUCTOR	SUPEREROGATIVE	SUPERFLUID
SUPERALTERN	SUPERCARRIER	SUPERCONDUCTORS	SUPEREROGATOR	SUPERFLUIDITIES
SUPERALTERNS	SUPERCARRIERS	SUPERCONDUCTS	SUPEREROGATORS	SUPERFLUIDITY
SUPERAMBITIOUS	SUPERCAUTIOUS	SUPERCONFIDENCE	SUPEREROGATORY	SUPERFLUIDS
SUPERANNUABLE	SUPERCEDED	SUPERCONFIDENT	SUPERESSENTIAL	SUPERFLUITIES
SUPERANNUATE	SUPERCEDES	SUPERCONTINENT	SUPERETTES	SUPERFLUITY
SUPERANNUATED	SUPERCEDING	SUPERCONTINENTS	SUPEREVIDENT	SUPERFLUOUS
SUPERANNUATES	SUPERCELESTIAL	SUPERCONVENIENT	SUPEREXALT	SUPERFLUOUSLY
SUPERANNUATING	SUPERCENTER	SUPERCOOLED	SUPEREXALTATION	SUPERFLUOUSNESS
SUPERANNUATION	SUPERCENTERS	SUPERCOOLING	SUPEREXALTED	SUPERFLUXES
SUPERANNUATIONS	SUPERCHARGE	SUPERCOOLS	SUPEREXALTING	SUPERFOETATION

S

SUPERFOETATIONS

SUPERFOETATIONS	SUPERHUMAN	SUPERINTENDING	SUPERMICRO	SUPERNUTRITIONS
SUPERFOODS	SUPERHUMANISE	SUPERINTENDS	SUPERMICROS	SUPEROCTAVE
SUPERFRONTAL	SUPERHUMANISED	SUPERINTENSITY	SUPERMILITANT	SUPEROCTAVES
SUPERFRONTALS	SUPERHUMANISES	SUPERIORESS	SUPERMILITANTS	SUPERORDER
SUPERFUNDS	SUPERHUMANISING	SUPERIORESSES	SUPERMINDS	SUPERORDERS
SUPERFUSED	SUPERHUMANITIES	SUPERIORITIES	SUPERMINIS	SUPERORDINAL
SUPERFUSES	SUPERHUMANITY	SUPERIORITY	SUPERMINISTER	SUPERORDINARY
SUPERFUSING	SUPERHUMANIZE	SUPERIORLY	SUPERMINISTERS	SUPERORDINATE
SUPERFUSION	SUPERHUMANIZED	SUPERIORSHIP	SUPERMODEL	SUPERORDINATED
SUPERFUSIONS	SUPERHUMANIZES	SUPERIORSHIPS	SUPERMODELS	SUPERORDINATES
SUPERGENES	SUPERHUMANIZING	SUPERJACENT	SUPERMODERN	SUPERORDINATING
SUPERGIANT	SUPERHUMANLY	SUPERJOCKS	SUPERMOTOS	SUPERORDINATION
SUPERGIANTS	SUPERHUMANNESS	SUPERJUMBO	SUPERMUNDANE	SUPERORGANIC
SUPERGLACIAL	SUPERHUMERAL	SUPERJUMBOS	SUPERNACULA	SUPERORGANICISM
SUPERGLUED	SUPERHUMERALS	SUPERKINGDOM	SUPERNACULAR	SUPERORGANICIST
SUPERGLUES	SUPERHYPED	SUPERKINGDOMS	SUPERNACULUM	SUPERORGANISM
SUPERGLUING	SUPERHYPES	SUPERLARGE	SUPERNALLY	SUPERORGANISMS
SUPERGOVERNMENT	SUPERHYPING	SUPERLATIVE	SUPERNANNIES	SUPERORGASM
SUPERGRAPHICS	SUPERIMPORTANT	SUPERLATIVELY	SUPERNANNY	SUPERORGASMS
SUPERGRASS	SUPERIMPOSABLE	SUPERLATIVENESS	SUPERNATANT	SUPEROVULATE
SUPERGRASSES	SUPERIMPOSE	SUPERLATIVES	SUPERNATANTS	SUPEROVULATED
SUPERGRAVITIES	SUPERIMPOSED	SUPERLAWYER	SUPERNATATION	SUPEROVULATES
SUPERGRAVITY	SUPERIMPOSES	SUPERLAWYERS	SUPERNATATIONS	SUPEROVULATING
SUPERGROUP	SUPERIMPOSING	SUPERLIGHT	SUPERNATES	SUPEROVULATION
SUPERGROUPS	SUPERIMPOSITION	SUPERLINER	SUPERNATION	SUPEROVULATIONS
SUPERGROWTH	SUPERINCUMBENCE	SUPERLINERS	SUPERNATIONAL	SUPEROXIDE
SUPERGROWTHS	SUPERINCUMBENCY	SUPERLOADS	SUPERNATIONALLY	SUPEROXIDES
SUPERHARDEN	SUPERINCUMBENT	SUPERLOBBYIST	SUPERNATIONS	SUPERPARASITISM
SUPERHARDENED	SUPERINDIVIDUAL	SUPERLOBBYISTS	SUPERNATURAL	SUPERPARTICLE
SUPERHARDENING	SUPERINDUCE	SUPERLOYALIST	SUPERNATURALISE	SUPERPARTICLES
SUPERHARDENS	SUPERINDUCED	SUPERLOYALISTS	SUPERNATURALISM	SUPERPATRIOT
SUPERHEATED	SUPERINDUCEMENT	SUPERLUMINAL	SUPERNATURALIST	SUPERPATRIOTIC
SUPERHEATER	SUPERINDUCES	SUPERLUNAR	SUPERNATURALIZE	SUPERPATRIOTISM
SUPERHEATERS	SUPERINDUCING	SUPERLUNARY	SUPERNATURALLY	SUPERPATRIOTS
SUPERHEATING	SUPERINDUCTION	SUPERLUXURIOUS	SUPERNATURALS	SUPERPERSON
SUPERHEATS	SUPERINDUCTIONS	SUPERLUXURY	SUPERNATURE	SUPERPERSONAL
SUPERHEAVIES	SUPERINFECT	SUPERLYING	SUPERNATURES	SUPERPERSONS
SUPERHEAVY	SUPERINFECTED	SUPERMACHO	SUPERNORMAL	SUPERPHENOMENA
SUPERHELICAL	SUPERINFECTING	SUPERMAJORITIES	SUPERNORMALITY	SUPERPHENOMENON
SUPERHELICES	SUPERINFECTION	SUPERMAJORITY	SUPERNORMALLY	SUPERPHOSPHATE
SUPERHELIX	SUPERINFECTIONS	SUPERMALES	SUPERNOVAE	SUPERPHOSPHATES
SUPERHELIXES	SUPERINFECTS	SUPERMARKET	SUPERNOVAS	SUPERPHYLA
SUPERHEROES	SUPERINSULATED	SUPERMARKETS	SUPERNUMERARIES	SUPERPHYLUM
SUPERHEROINE	SUPERINTEND	SUPERMARTS	SUPERNUMERARY	SUPERPHYSICAL
SUPERHEROINES	SUPERINTENDED	SUPERMASCULINE	SUPERNURSE	SUPERPIMPS
SUPERHETERODYNE	SUPERINTENDENCE	SUPERMASSIVE	SUPERNURSES	SUPERPLANE
SUPERHIGHWAY	SUPERINTENDENCY	SUPERMAXES	SUPERNUTRIENT	SUPERPLANES
SUPERHIGHWAYS	SUPERINTENDENT	SUPERMEMBRANE	SUPERNUTRIENTS	SUPERPLASTIC
SUPERHIVES	SUPERINTENDENTS	SUPERMEMBRANES	SUPERNUTRITION	SUPERPLASTICITY

S

SUPERPLASTICS	SUPERSATURATING	SUPERSEXES	SUPERSTRENGTH	SUPERTWISTS
SUPERPLAYER	SUPERSATURATION	SUPERSEXUALITY	SUPERSTRENGTHS	SUPERVENED
SUPERPLAYERS	SUPERSAURS	SUPERSHARP	SUPERSTRIKE	SUPERVENES
SUPERPLUSES	SUPERSAVER	SUPERSHOWS	SUPERSTRIKES	SUPERVENIENCE
SUPERPOLITE	SUPERSAVERS	SUPERSINGER	SUPERSTRING	SUPERVENIENCES
SUPERPOLYMER	SUPERSCALAR	SUPERSINGERS	SUPERSTRINGS	SUPERVENIENT
SUPERPOLYMERS	SUPERSCALE	SUPERSIZED	SUPERSTRONG	SUPERVENING
SUPERPORTS	SUPERSCHOOL	SUPERSIZES	SUPERSTRUCT	SUPERVENTION
SUPERPOSABLE	SUPERSCHOOLS	SUPERSIZING	SUPERSTRUCTED	SUPERVENTIONS
SUPERPOSED	SUPERSCOUT	SUPERSLEUTH	SUPERSTRUCTING	SUPERVIRILE
SUPERPOSES	SUPERSCOUTS	SUPERSLEUTHS	SUPERSTRUCTION	SUPERVIRTUOSI
SUPERPOSING	SUPERSCREEN	SUPERSLICK	SUPERSTRUCTIONS	SUPERVIRTUOSO
SUPERPOSITION	SUPERSCREENS	SUPERSMART	SUPERSTRUCTIVE	SUPERVIRTUOSOS
SUPERPOSITIONS	SUPERSCRIBE	SUPERSMOOTH	SUPERSTRUCTS	SUPERVIRULENT
SUPERPOWER	SUPERSCRIBED	SUPERSONIC	SUPERSTRUCTURAL	SUPERVISAL
SUPERPOWERED	SUPERSCRIBES	SUPERSONICALLY	SUPERSTRUCTURE	SUPERVISALS
SUPERPOWERFUL	SUPERSCRIBING	SUPERSONICS	SUPERSTRUCTURES	SUPERVISED
SUPERPOWERS	SUPERSCRIPT	SUPERSOUND	SUPERSTUDS	SUPERVISEE
SUPERPRAISE	SUPERSCRIPTION	SUPERSOUNDS	SUPERSUBTILE	SUPERVISEES
SUPERPRAISED	SUPERSCRIPTIONS	SUPERSPECIAL	SUPERSUBTLE	SUPERVISES
SUPERPRAISES	SUPERSCRIPTS	SUPERSPECIALIST	SUPERSUBTLETIES	SUPERVISING
SUPERPRAISING	SUPERSECRECIES	SUPERSPECIALS	SUPERSUBTLETY	SUPERVISION
SUPERPREMIUM	SUPERSECRECY	SUPERSPECIES	SUPERSURGEON	SUPERVISIONS
SUPERPREMIUMS	SUPERSECRET	SUPERSPECTACLE	SUPERSURGEONS	SUPERVISOR
SUPERPROFIT	SUPERSEDABLE	SUPERSPECTACLES	SUPERSWEET	SUPERVISORS
SUPERPROFITS	SUPERSEDEAS	SUPERSPEED	SUPERSYMMETRIC	SUPERVISORSHIP
SUPERQUALITY	SUPERSEDEASES	SUPERSPEEDS	SUPERSYMMETRIES	SUPERVISORSHIPS
SUPERRACES	SUPERSEDED	SUPERSPIES	SUPERSYMMETRY	SUPERVISORY
SUPERREALISM	SUPERSEDENCE	SUPERSTARDOM	SUPERSYSTEM	SUPERVOLUTE
SUPERREALISMS	SUPERSEDENCES	SUPERSTARDOMS	SUPERSYSTEMS	SUPERWAIFS
SUPERREALIST	SUPERSEDER	SUPERSTARS	SUPERTANKER	SUPERWAVES
SUPERREALISTS	SUPERSEDERE	SUPERSTATE	SUPERTANKERS	SUPERWEAPON
SUPERREFINE	SUPERSEDERES	SUPERSTATES	SUPERTAXES	SUPERWEAPONS
SUPERREFINED	SUPERSEDERS	SUPERSTATION	SUPERTEACHER	SUPERWEEDS
SUPERREFINES	SUPERSEDES	SUPERSTATIONS	SUPERTEACHERS	SUPERWIDES
SUPERREFINING	SUPERSEDING	SUPERSTIMULATE	SUPERTERRANEAN	SUPERWIVES
SUPERREGIONAL	SUPERSEDURE	SUPERSTIMULATED	SUPERTERRIFIC	SUPERWOMAN
SUPERREGIONALS	SUPERSEDURES	SUPERSTIMULATES	SUPERTHICK	SUPERWOMEN
SUPERROADS	SUPERSELLER	SUPERSTITION	SUPERTHRILLER	SUPINATING
SUPERROMANTIC	SUPERSELLERS	SUPERSTITIONS	SUPERTHRILLERS	SUPINATION
SUPERSAFETIES	SUPERSELLING	SUPERSTITIOUS	SUPERTIGHT	SUPINATIONS
SUPERSAFETY	SUPERSELLS	SUPERSTITIOUSLY	SUPERTITLE	SUPINATORS
SUPERSALES	SUPERSENSIBLE	SUPERSTOCK	SUPERTITLES	SUPINENESS
SUPERSALESMAN	SUPERSENSIBLY	SUPERSTOCKS	SUPERTONIC	SUPINENESSES
SUPERSALESMEN	SUPERSENSITIVE	SUPERSTORE	SUPERTONICS	SUPPEAGOES
SUPERSALTS	SUPERSENSORY	SUPERSTORES	SUPERTRAMS	SUPPEDANEA
SUPERSATURATE	SUPERSENSUAL	SUPERSTRATA	SUPERTRUCK	SUPPEDANEUM
SUPERSATURATED	SUPERSESSION	SUPERSTRATUM	SUPERTRUCKS	SUPPERLESS
SUPERSATURATES	SUPERSESSIONS	SUPERSTRATUMS	SUPERTWIST	SUPPERTIME

S

SUPPERTIMES	SUPPLYMENTS	SUPPRESSIONS	SUPREMENESS	SURGEONFISH
SUPPLANTATION	SUPPORTABILITY	SUPPRESSIVE	SUPREMENESSES	SURGEONFISHES
SUPPLANTATIONS	SUPPORTABLE	SUPPRESSIVENESS	SUPREMITIES	SURGEONSHIP
SUPPLANTED	SUPPORTABLENESS	SUPPRESSOR	SURADDITION	SURGEONSHIPS
SUPPLANTER	SUPPORTABLY	SUPPRESSORS	SURADDITIONS	SURGICALLY
SUPPLANTERS	SUPPORTANCE	SUPPURATED	SURBASEMENT	SURJECTION
SUPPLANTING	SUPPORTANCES	SUPPURATES	SURBASEMENTS	SURJECTIONS
SUPPLEJACK	SUPPORTERS	SUPPURATING	SURBEDDING	SURJECTIVE
SUPPLEJACKS	SUPPORTING	SUPPURATION	SURCEASING	SURLINESSES
SUPPLEMENT	SUPPORTINGS	SUPPURATIONS	SURCHARGED	SURMASTERS
SUPPLEMENTAL	SUPPORTIVE	SUPPURATIVE	SURCHARGEMENT	SURMISABLE
SUPPLEMENTALLY	SUPPORTIVELY	SUPPURATIVES	SURCHARGEMENTS	SURMISINGS
SUPPLEMENTALS	SUPPORTIVENESS	SUPRACHIASMIC	SURCHARGER	SURMISTRESS
SUPPLEMENTARIES	SUPPORTLESS	SUPRACILIARY	SURCHARGERS	SURMISTRESSES
SUPPLEMENTARILY	SUPPORTMENT	SUPRACOSTAL	SURCHARGES	SURMOUNTABLE
SUPPLEMENTARY	SUPPORTMENTS	SUPRACRUSTAL	SURCHARGING	SURMOUNTED
SUPPLEMENTATION	SUPPORTRESS	SUPRAGLOTTAL	SURCINGLED	SURMOUNTER
SUPPLEMENTED	SUPPORTRESSES	SUPRALAPSARIAN	SURCINGLES	SURMOUNTERS
SUPPLEMENTER	SUPPORTURE	SUPRALAPSARIANS	SURCINGLING	SURMOUNTING
SUPPLEMENTERS	SUPPORTURES	SUPRALIMINAL	SURCULUSES	SURMOUNTINGS
SUPPLEMENTING	SUPPOSABLE	SUPRALIMINALLY	SUREFOOTED	SURMULLETS
SUPPLEMENTS	SUPPOSABLY	SUPRALUNAR	SUREFOOTEDLY	SURNOMINAL
SUPPLENESS	SUPPOSEDLY	SUPRAMAXILLARY	SUREFOOTEDNESS	SURPASSABLE
SUPPLENESSES	SUPPOSINGS	SUPRAMOLECULAR	SURENESSES	SURPASSERS
SUPPLETION	SUPPOSITION	SUPRAMOLECULE	SURETYSHIP	SURPASSING
SUPPLETIONS	SUPPOSITIONAL	SUPRAMOLECULES	SURETYSHIPS	SURPASSINGLY
SUPPLETIVE	SUPPOSITIONALLY	SUPRAMUNDANE	SURFACELESS	SURPASSINGNESS
SUPPLETIVES	SUPPOSITIONARY	SUPRANATIONAL	SURFACEMAN	SURPLUSAGE
SUPPLETORILY	SUPPOSITIONLESS	SUPRANATIONALLY	SURFACEMEN	SURPLUSAGES
SUPPLETORY	SUPPOSITIONS	SUPRAOPTIC	SURFACINGS	SURPLUSING
SUPPLIABLE	SUPPOSITIOUS	SUPRAORBITAL	SURFACTANT	SURPLUSSED
SUPPLIANCE	SUPPOSITIOUSLY	SUPRAPUBIC	SURFACTANTS	SURPLUSSES
SUPPLIANCES	SUPPOSITITIOUS	SUPRARATIONAL	SURFBOARDED	SURPLUSSING
SUPPLIANTLY	SUPPOSITIVE	SUPRARENAL	SURFBOARDER	SURPRINTED
SUPPLIANTS	SUPPOSITIVELY	SUPRARENALS	SURFBOARDERS	SURPRINTING
SUPPLICANT	SUPPOSITIVES	SUPRASEGMENTAL	SURFBOARDING	SURPRISALS
SUPPLICANTS	SUPPOSITORIES	SUPRASENSIBLE	SURFBOARDINGS	SURPRISEDLY
SUPPLICATE	SUPPOSITORY	SUPRATEMPORAL	SURFBOARDS	SURPRISERS
SUPPLICATED	SUPPRESSANT	SUPRAVITAL	SURFCASTER	SURPRISING
SUPPLICATES	SUPPRESSANTS	SUPRAVITALLY	SURFCASTERS	SURPRISINGLY
SUPPLICATING	SUPPRESSED	SUPREMACIES	SURFCASTING	SURPRISINGNESS
SUPPLICATINGLY	SUPPRESSEDLY	SUPREMACISM	SURFCASTINGS	SURPRISINGS
SUPPLICATION	SUPPRESSER	SUPREMACISMS	SURFEITERS	SURPRIZING
SUPPLICATIONS	SUPPRESSERS	SUPREMACIST	SURFEITING	SURQUEDIES
SUPPLICATORY	SUPPRESSES	SUPREMACISTS	SURFEITINGS	SURQUEDRIES
SUPPLICATS	SUPPRESSIBILITY	SUPREMATISM	SURFFISHES	SURREALISM
SUPPLICAVIT	SUPPRESSIBLE	SUPREMATISMS	SURFPERCHES	SURREALISMS
SUPPLICAVITS	SUPPRESSING	SUPREMATIST	SURFRIDERS	SURREALIST
SUPPLYMENT	SUPPRESSION	SUPREMATISTS	SURGEONCIES	SURREALISTIC

S

SURREALISTS	SURVEYABLE	SUSPENSEFUL	SUSTENTATE	SWANSDOWNS
SURREBUTTAL	SURVEYANCE	SUSPENSEFULLY	SUSTENTATED	SWARAJISMS
SURREBUTTALS	SURVEYANCES	SUSPENSEFULNESS	SUSTENTATES	SWARAJISTS
SURREBUTTED	SURVEYINGS	SUSPENSELESS	SUSTENTATING	SWARTHIEST
SURREBUTTER	SURVEYORSHIP	SUSPENSERS	SUSTENTATION	SWARTHINESS
SURREBUTTERS	SURVEYORSHIPS	SUSPENSIBILITY	SUSTENTATIONS	SWARTHINESSES
SURREBUTTING	SURVIEWING	SUSPENSIBLE	SUSTENTATIVE	SWARTHNESS
SURREJOINDER	SURVIVABILITIES	SUSPENSION	SUSTENTATOR	SWARTHNESSES
SURREJOINDERS	SURVIVABILITY	SUSPENSIONS	SUSTENTATORS	SWARTNESSES
SURREJOINED	SURVIVABLE	SUSPENSIVE	SUSTENTION	SWASHBUCKLE
SURREJOINING	SURVIVALISM	SUSPENSIVELY	SUSTENTIONS	SWASHBUCKLED
SURREJOINS	SURVIVALISMS	SUSPENSIVENESS	SUSTENTIVE	SWASHBUCKLER
SURRENDERED	SURVIVALIST	SUSPENSOID	SUSURRATED	SWASHBUCKLERS
SURRENDEREE	SURVIVALISTS	SUSPENSOIDS	SUSURRATES	SWASHBUCKLES
SURRENDEREES	SURVIVANCE	SUSPENSORIA	SUSURRATING	SWASHBUCKLING
SURRENDERER	SURVIVANCES	SUSPENSORIAL	SUSURRATION	SWASHWORKS
SURRENDERERS	SURVIVORSHIP	SUSPENSORIES	SUSURRATIONS	SWATCHBOOK
SURRENDERING	SURVIVORSHIPS	SUSPENSORIUM	SUSURRUSES	SWATCHBOOKS
SURRENDEROR	SUSCEPTANCE	SUSPENSORS	SUTLERSHIP	SWATHEABLE
SURRENDERORS	SUSCEPTANCES	SUSPENSORY	SUTLERSHIPS	SWATTERING
SURRENDERS	SUSCEPTIBILITY	SUSPERCOLLATE	SUTTEEISMS	SWAYBACKED
SURRENDRIES	SUSCEPTIBLE	SUSPERCOLLATED	SUTTLETIES	SWEARWORDS
SURREPTITIOUS	SUSCEPTIBLENESS	SUSPERCOLLATES	SUTURATION	SWEATBANDS
SURREPTITIOUSLY	SUSCEPTIBLY	SUSPERCOLLATING	SUTURATIONS	SWEATBOXES
SURROGACIES	SUSCEPTIVE	SUSPICIONAL	SUZERAINTIES	SWEATERDRESS
SURROGATED	SUSCEPTIVENESS	SUSPICIONED	SUZERAINTY	SWEATERDRESSES
SURROGATES	SUSCEPTIVITIES	SUSPICIONING	SVARABHAKTI	SWEATINESS
SURROGATESHIP	SUSCEPTIVITY	SUSPICIONLESS	SVARABHAKTIS	SWEATINESSES
SURROGATESHIPS	SUSCEPTORS	SUSPICIONS	SVELTENESS	SWEATPANTS
SURROGATING	SUSCIPIENT	SUSPICIOUS	SVELTENESSES	SWEATSHIRT
SURROGATION	SUSCIPIENTS	SUSPICIOUSLY	SWAGGERERS	SWEATSHIRTS
SURROGATIONS	SUSCITATED	SUSPICIOUSNESS	SWAGGERING	SWEATSHOPS
SURROGATUM	SUSCITATES	SUSPIRATION	SWAGGERINGLY	SWEATSUITS
SURROGATUMS	SUSCITATING	SUSPIRATIONS	SWAGGERINGS	SWEEPBACKS
SURROUNDED	SUSCITATION	SUSPIRIOUS	SWAINISHNESS	SWEEPINGLY
SURROUNDING	SUSCITATIONS	SUSTAINABILITY	SWAINISHNESSES	SWEEPINGNESS
SURROUNDINGS	SUSPECTABLE	SUSTAINABLE	SWALLOWABLE	SWEEPINGNESSES
SURTARBRAND	SUSPECTEDLY	SUSTAINEDLY	SWALLOWERS	SWEEPSTAKE
SURTARBRANDS	SUSPECTEDNESS	SUSTAINERS	SWALLOWING	SWEEPSTAKES
SURTURBRAND	SUSPECTEDNESSES	SUSTAINING	SWALLOWTAIL	SWEETBREAD
SURTURBRANDS	SUSPECTERS	SUSTAININGLY	SWALLOWTAILS	SWEETBREADS
SURVEILING	SUSPECTFUL	SUSTAININGS	SWALLOWWORT	SWEETBRIAR
SURVEILLANCE	SUSPECTING	SUSTAINMENT	SWALLOWWORTS	SWEETBRIARS
SURVEILLANCES	SUSPECTLESS	SUSTAINMENTS	SWAMPINESS	SWEETBRIER
SURVEILLANT	SUSPENDERED	SUSTENANCE	SWAMPINESSES	SWEETBRIERS
SURVEILLANTS	SUSPENDERS	SUSTENANCES	SWAMPLANDS	SWEETCORNS
SURVEILLED	SUSPENDIBILITY	SUSTENTACULA	SWANKINESS	SWEETENERS
SURVEILLES	SUSPENDIBLE	SUSTENTACULAR	SWANKINESSES	SWEETENING
SURVEILLING	SUSPENDING	SUSTENTACULUM	SWANNERIES	SWEETENINGS

S

SWEETFISHES

SWEETFISHES	SWINGLINGS	SWORDPROOF	SYLLABISED	SYMBOLICALNESS
SWEETHEART	SWINGOMETER	SWORDSMANSHIP	SYLLABISES	SYMBOLISATION
SWEETHEARTED	SWINGOMETERS	SWORDSMANSHIPS	SYLLABISING	SYMBOLISATIONS
SWEETHEARTING	SWINGTREES	SWORDSTICK	SYLLABISMS	SYMBOLISED
SWEETHEARTS	SWINISHNESS	SWORDSTICKS	SYLLABIZED	SYMBOLISER
SWEETIEWIFE	SWINISHNESSES	SWORDTAILS	SYLLABIZES	SYMBOLISERS
SWEETIEWIVES	SWIRLINGLY	SYBARITICAL	SYLLABIZING	SYMBOLISES
SWEETISHLY	SWISHINGLY	SYBARITICALLY	SYLLABLING	SYMBOLISING
SWEETISHNESS	SWITCHABLE	SYBARITISH	SYLLABOGRAM	SYMBOLISMS
SWEETISHNESSES	SWITCHBACK	SYBARITISM	SYLLABOGRAMS	SYMBOLISTIC
SWEETMEATS	SWITCHBACKED	SYBARITISMS	SYLLABOGRAPHIES	SYMBOLISTICAL
SWEETNESSES	SWITCHBACKING	SYCOPHANCIES	SYLLABOGRAPHY	SYMBOLISTICALLY
SWEETSHOPS	SWITCHBACKS	SYCOPHANCY	SYLLABUSES	SYMBOLISTS
SWEETVELDS	SWITCHBLADE	SYCOPHANTIC	SYLLEPTICAL	SYMBOLIZATION
SWEETWATER	SWITCHBLADES	SYCOPHANTICAL	SYLLEPTICALLY	SYMBOLIZATIONS
SWEETWATERS	SWITCHBOARD	SYCOPHANTICALLY	SYLLOGISATION	SYMBOLIZED
SWEETWOODS	SWITCHBOARDS	SYCOPHANTISE	SYLLOGISATIONS	SYMBOLIZER
SWEIRNESSES	SWITCHEROO	SYCOPHANTISED	SYLLOGISED	SYMBOLIZERS
SWELLFISHES	SWITCHEROOS	SYCOPHANTISES	SYLLOGISER	SYMBOLIZES
SWELLHEADED	SWITCHGEAR	SYCOPHANTISH	SYLLOGISERS	SYMBOLIZING
SWELLHEADEDNESS	SWITCHGEARS	SYCOPHANTISHLY	SYLLOGISES	SYMBOLLING
SWELLHEADS	SWITCHGIRL	SYCOPHANTISING	SYLLOGISING	SYMBOLOGICAL
SWELLINGLY	SWITCHGIRLS	SYCOPHANTISM	SYLLOGISMS	SYMBOLOGIES
SWELTERING	SWITCHGRASS	SYCOPHANTISMS	SYLLOGISTIC	SYMBOLOGIST
SWELTERINGLY	SWITCHGRASSES	SYCOPHANTIZE	SYLLOGISTICAL	SYMBOLOGISTS
SWELTERINGS	SWITCHIEST	SYCOPHANTIZED	SYLLOGISTICALLY	SYMBOLOGRAPHIES
SWELTRIEST	SWITCHINGS	SYCOPHANTIZES	SYLLOGISTICS	SYMBOLOGRAPHY
SWEPTWINGS	SWITCHLIKE	SYCOPHANTIZING	SYLLOGISTS	SYMBOLOLATRIES
SWERVELESS	SWITCHOVER	SYCOPHANTLY	SYLLOGIZATION	SYMBOLOLATRY
SWIFTNESSES	SWITCHOVERS	SYCOPHANTRIES	SYLLOGIZATIONS	SYMBOLOLOGIES
SWIMFEEDER	SWITCHYARD	SYCOPHANTRY	SYLLOGIZED	SYMBOLOLOGY
SWIMFEEDERS	SWITCHYARDS	SYCOPHANTS	SYLLOGIZER	SYMMETALISM
SWIMMERETS	SWITHERING	SYLLABARIA	SYLLOGIZERS	SYMMETALISMS
SWIMMINGLY	SWIVELBLOCK	SYLLABARIES	SYLLOGIZES	SYMMETALLIC
SWIMMINGNESS	SWIVELBLOCKS	SYLLABARIUM	SYLLOGIZING	SYMMETALLISM
SWIMMINGNESSES	SWIVELLING	SYLLABICAL	SYLPHIDINE	SYMMETALLISMS
SWINDLINGS	SWOLLENNESS	SYLLABICALLY	SYLVANITES	SYMMETRIAN
SWINEHERDS	SWOLLENNESSES	SYLLABICATE	SYLVESTRAL	SYMMETRIANS
SWINEHOODS	SWOONINGLY	SYLLABICATED	SYLVESTRIAN	SYMMETRICAL
SWINEPOXES	SWOOPSTAKE	SYLLABICATES	SYLVICULTURAL	SYMMETRICALLY
SWINESTONE	SWORDBEARER	SYLLABICATING	SYLVICULTURE	SYMMETRICALNESS
SWINESTONES	SWORDBEARERS	SYLLABICATION	SYLVICULTURES	SYMMETRIES
SWINGBEATS	SWORDBILLS	SYLLABICATIONS	SYLVINITES	SYMMETRISATION
SWINGBOATS	SWORDCRAFT	SYLLABICITIES	SYMBIONTIC	SYMMETRISATIONS
SWINGEINGLY	SWORDCRAFTS	SYLLABICITY	SYMBIONTICALLY	SYMMETRISE
SWINGINGEST	SWORDFISHES	SYLLABIFICATION	SYMBIOTICAL	SYMMETRISED
SWINGINGLY	SWORDPLAYER	SYLLABIFIED	SYMBIOTICALLY	SYMMETRISES
SWINGLETREE	SWORDPLAYERS	SYLLABIFIES	SYMBOLICAL	SYMMETRISING
SWINGLETREES	SWORDPLAYS	SYLLABIFYING	SYMBOLICALLY	SYMMETRIZATION

S

SYMMETRIZATIONS	SYMPHYSEOTOMIES	SYNANDROUS	SYNCHRONISING	SYNCRETIZED
SYMMETRIZE	SYMPHYSEOTOMY	SYNANTHEROUS	SYNCHRONISM	SYNCRETIZES
SYMMETRIZED	SYMPHYSIAL	SYNANTHESES	SYNCHRONISMS	SYNCRETIZING
SYMMETRIZES	SYMPHYSIOTOMIES	SYNANTHESIS	SYNCHRONISTIC	SYNDACTYLIES
SYMMETRIZING	SYMPHYSIOTOMY	SYNANTHETIC	SYNCHRONISTICAL	SYNDACTYLISM
SYMMETROPHOBIA	SYMPHYSTIC	SYNANTHIES	SYNCHRONIZATION	SYNDACTYLISMS
SYMMETROPHOBIAS	SYMPIESOMETER	SYNANTHOUS	SYNCHRONIZE	SYNDACTYLOUS
SYMPATHECTOMIES	SYMPIESOMETERS	SYNAPHEIAS	SYNCHRONIZED	SYNDACTYLS
SYMPATHECTOMY	SYMPLASTIC	SYNAPOSEMATIC	SYNCHRONIZER	SYNDACTYLY
SYMPATHETIC	SYMPODIALLY	SYNAPOSEMATISM	SYNCHRONIZERS	SYNDERESES
SYMPATHETICAL	SYMPOSIACS	SYNAPOSEMATISMS	SYNCHRONIZES	SYNDERESIS
SYMPATHETICALLY	SYMPOSIARCH	SYNAPTASES	SYNCHRONIZING	SYNDESISES
SYMPATHETICS	SYMPOSIARCHS	SYNAPTICAL	SYNCHRONOLOGIES	SYNDESMOSES
SYMPATHIES	SYMPOSIAST	SYNAPTICALLY	SYNCHRONOLOGY	SYNDESMOSIS
SYMPATHINS	SYMPOSIASTS	SYNAPTOSOMAL	SYNCHRONOSCOPE	SYNDESMOTIC
SYMPATHIQUE	SYMPOSIUMS	SYNAPTOSOME	SYNCHRONOSCOPES	SYNDETICAL
SYMPATHISE	SYMPTOMATIC	SYNAPTOSOMES	SYNCHRONOUS	SYNDETICALLY
SYMPATHISED	SYMPTOMATICAL	SYNARCHIES	SYNCHRONOUSLY	SYNDICALISM
SYMPATHISER	SYMPTOMATICALLY	SYNARTHRODIAL	SYNCHRONOUSNESS	SYNDICALISMS
SYMPATHISERS	SYMPTOMATISE	SYNARTHRODIALLY	SYNCHROSCOPE	SYNDICALIST
SYMPATHISES	SYMPTOMATISED	SYNARTHROSES	SYNCHROSCOPES	SYNDICALISTIC
SYMPATHISING	SYMPTOMATISES	SYNARTHROSIS	SYNCHROTRON	SYNDICALISTS
SYMPATHIZE	SYMPTOMATISING	SYNASTRIES	SYNCHROTRONS	SYNDICATED
SYMPATHIZED	SYMPTOMATIZE	SYNAXARION	SYNCLASTIC	SYNDICATES
SYMPATHIZER	SYMPTOMATIZED	SYNCARPIES	SYNCLINALS	SYNDICATING
SYMPATHIZERS	SYMPTOMATIZES	SYNCARPOUS	SYNCLINORIA	SYNDICATION
SYMPATHIZES	SYMPTOMATIZING	SYNCHONDROSES	SYNCLINORIUM	SYNDICATIONS
SYMPATHIZING	SYMPTOMATOLOGIC	SYNCHONDROSIS	SYNCOPATED	SYNDICATOR
SYMPATHOLYTIC	SYMPTOMATOLOGY	SYNCHORESES	SYNCOPATES	SYNDICATORS
SYMPATHOLYTICS	SYMPTOMLESS	SYNCHORESIS	SYNCOPATING	SYNDICSHIP
SYMPATHOMIMETIC	SYMPTOMOLOGICAL	SYNCHROFLASH	SYNCOPATION	SYNDICSHIPS
SYMPATRICALLY	SYMPTOMOLOGIES	SYNCHROFLASHES	SYNCOPATIONS	SYNDIOTACTIC
SYMPATRIES	SYMPTOMOLOGY	SYNCHROMESH	SYNCOPATIVE	SYNDYASMIAN
SYMPETALIES	SYNADELPHITE	SYNCHROMESHES	SYNCOPATOR	SYNECDOCHE
SYMPETALOUS	SYNADELPHITES	SYNCHRONAL	SYNCOPATORS	SYNECDOCHES
SYMPHILIES	SYNAERESES	SYNCHRONEITIES	SYNCRETISATION	SYNECDOCHIC
SYMPHILISM	SYNAERESIS	SYNCHRONEITY	SYNCRETISATIONS	SYNECDOCHICAL
SYMPHILISMS	SYNAESTHESES	SYNCHRONIC	SYNCRETISE	SYNECDOCHICALLY
SYMPHILOUS	SYNAESTHESIA	SYNCHRONICAL	SYNCRETISED	SYNECDOCHISM
SYMPHONICALLY	SYNAESTHESIAS	SYNCHRONICALLY	SYNCRETISES	SYNECDOCHISMS
SYMPHONIES	SYNAESTHESIS	SYNCHRONICITIES	SYNCRETISING	SYNECOLOGIC
SYMPHONION	SYNAESTHETIC	SYNCHRONICITY	SYNCRETISM	SYNECOLOGICAL
SYMPHONIONS	SYNAGOGICAL	SYNCHRONIES	SYNCRETISMS	SYNECOLOGICALLY
SYMPHONIOUS	SYNAGOGUES	SYNCHRONISATION	SYNCRETIST	SYNECOLOGIES
SYMPHONIOUSLY	SYNALEPHAS	SYNCHRONISE	SYNCRETISTIC	SYNECOLOGIST
SYMPHONIST	SYNALLAGMATIC	SYNCHRONISED	SYNCRETISTS	SYNECOLOGISTS
SYMPHONISTS	SYNALOEPHA	SYNCHRONISER	SYNCRETIZATION	SYNECOLOGY
SYMPHYLOUS	SYNALOEPHAS	SYNCHRONISERS	SYNCRETIZATIONS	SYNECPHONESES
SYMPHYSEAL	SYNANDRIUM	SYNCHRONISES	SYNCRETIZE	SYNECPHONESIS

S

SYNECTICALLY	SYNONYMICONS	SYNTEXISES	SYNTHETIZER	SYSTEMATIC
SYNEIDESES	SYNONYMIES	SYNTHESISATION	SYNTHETIZERS	SYSTEMATICAL
SYNEIDESIS	SYNONYMISE	SYNTHESISATIONS	SYNTHETIZES	SYSTEMATICALLY
SYNERGETIC	SYNONYMISED	SYNTHESISE	SYNTHETIZING	SYSTEMATICIAN
SYNERGETICALLY	SYNONYMISES	SYNTHESISED	SYNTHRONUS	SYSTEMATICIANS
SYNERGICALLY	SYNONYMISING	SYNTHESISER	SYNTONICALLY	SYSTEMATICNESS
SYNERGISED	SYNONYMIST	SYNTHESISERS	SYNTONISED	SYSTEMATICS
SYNERGISES	SYNONYMISTS	SYNTHESISES	SYNTONISES	SYSTEMATISATION
SYNERGISING	SYNONYMITIES	SYNTHESISING	SYNTONISING	SYSTEMATISE
SYNERGISMS	SYNONYMITY	SYNTHESIST	SYNTONIZED	SYSTEMATISED
SYNERGISTIC	SYNONYMIZE	SYNTHESISTS	SYNTONIZES	SYSTEMATISER
SYNERGISTICALLY	SYNONYMIZED	SYNTHESIZATION	SYNTONIZING	SYSTEMATISERS
SYNERGISTS	SYNONYMIZES	SYNTHESIZATIONS	SYPHERINGS	SYSTEMATISES
SYNERGIZED	SYNONYMIZING	SYNTHESIZE	SYPHILISATION	SYSTEMATISING
SYNERGIZES	SYNONYMOUS	SYNTHESIZED	SYPHILISATIONS	SYSTEMATISM
SYNERGIZING	SYNONYMOUSLY	SYNTHESIZER	SYPHILISED	SYSTEMATISMS
SYNESTHESIA	SYNONYMOUSNESS	SYNTHESIZERS	SYPHILISES	SYSTEMATIST
SYNESTHESIAS	SYNOPSISED	SYNTHESIZES	SYPHILISING	SYSTEMATISTS
SYNESTHETIC	SYNOPSISES	SYNTHESIZING	SYPHILITIC	SYSTEMATIZATION
SYNGENESES	SYNOPSISING	SYNTHESPIAN	SYPHILITICALLY	SYSTEMATIZE
SYNGENESIOUS	SYNOPSIZED	SYNTHESPIANS	SYPHILITICS	SYSTEMATIZED
SYNGENESIS	SYNOPSIZES	SYNTHETASE	SYPHILIZATION	SYSTEMATIZER
SYNGENETIC	SYNOPSIZING	SYNTHETASES	SYPHILIZATIONS	SYSTEMATIZERS
SYNGNATHOUS	SYNOPTICAL	SYNTHETICAL	SYPHILIZED	SYSTEMATIZES
SYNKARYONIC	SYNOPTICALLY	SYNTHETICALLY	SYPHILIZES	SYSTEMATIZING
SYNKARYONS	SYNOPTISTIC	SYNTHETICISM	SYPHILIZING	SYSTEMATOLOGIES
SYNODICALLY	SYNOPTISTS	SYNTHETICISMS	SYPHILOLOGIES	SYSTEMATOLOGY
SYNOECETES	SYNOSTOSES	SYNTHETICS	SYPHILOLOGIST	SYSTEMICALLY
SYNOECIOSES	SYNOSTOSIS	SYNTHETISATION	SYPHILOLOGISTS	SYSTEMISATION
SYNOECIOSIS	SYNOVIALLY	SYNTHETISATIONS	SYPHILOLOGY	SYSTEMISATIONS
SYNOECIOUS	SYNOVITISES	SYNTHETISE	SYPHILOMAS	SYSTEMISED
SYNOECISED	SYNSEPALOUS	SYNTHETISED	SYPHILOMATA	SYSTEMISER
SYNOECISES	SYNTACTICAL	SYNTHETISER	SYPHILOPHOBIA	SYSTEMISERS
SYNOECISING	SYNTACTICALLY	SYNTHETISERS	SYPHILOPHOBIAS	SYSTEMISES
SYNOECISMS	SYNTACTICS	SYNTHETISES	SYRINGITIS	SYSTEMISING
SYNOECIZED	SYNTAGMATA	SYNTHETISING	SYRINGITISES	SYSTEMIZATION
SYNOECIZES	SYNTAGMATIC	SYNTHETISM	SYRINGOMYELIA	SYSTEMIZATIONS
SYNOECIZING	SYNTAGMATITE	SYNTHETISMS	SYRINGOMYELIAS	SYSTEMIZED
SYNOECOLOGIES	SYNTAGMATITES	SYNTHETIST	SYRINGOMYELIC	SYSTEMIZER
SYNOECOLOGY	SYNTECTICAL	SYNTHETISTS	SYRINGOTOMIES	SYSTEMIZERS
SYNOEKETES	SYNTENOSES	SYNTHETIZATION	SYRINGOTOMY	SYSTEMIZES
SYNONYMATIC	SYNTENOSIS	SYNTHETIZATIONS	SYSSARCOSES	SYSTEMIZING
SYNONYMICAL	SYNTERESES	SYNTHETIZE	SYSSARCOSIS	SYSTEMLESS
SYNONYMICON	SYNTERESIS	SYNTHETIZED	SYSSARCOTIC	SYZYGETICALLY

S

T

TABASHEERS	TABULATIONS	TACHYMETRICALLY	TAIKONAUTS	TALKATIVENESSES
TABBOULEHS	TABULATORS	TACHYMETRIES	TAILBOARDS	TALKINESSES
TABBYHOODS	TABULATORY	TACHYMETRY	TAILCOATED	TALLGRASSES
TABEFACTION	TACAMAHACS	TACHYPHASIA	TAILENDERS	TALLIATING
TABEFACTIONS	TACHEOMETER	TACHYPHASIAS	TAILGATERS	TALLNESSES
TABELLIONS	TACHEOMETERS	TACHYPHRASIA	TAILGATING	TALLYHOING
TABERNACLE	TACHEOMETRIC	TACHYPHRASIAS	TAILLESSLY	TALLYSHOPS
TABERNACLED	TACHEOMETRICAL	TACHYPHYLAXES	TAILLESSNESS	TALLYWOMAN
TABERNACLES	TACHEOMETRIES	TACHYPHYLAXIS	TAILLESSNESSES	TALLYWOMEN
TABERNACLING	TACHEOMETRY	TACHYPNEAS	TAILLIGHTS	TALMUDISMS
TABERNACULAR	TACHISTOSCOPE	TACHYPNOEA	TAILORBIRD	TAMABILITIES
TABESCENCE	TACHISTOSCOPES	TACHYPNOEAS	TAILORBIRDS	TAMABILITY
TABESCENCES	TACHISTOSCOPIC	TACITNESSES	TAILORESSES	TAMABLENESS
TABLANETTE	TACHOGRAMS	TACITURNITIES	TAILORINGS	TAMABLENESSES
TABLANETTES	TACHOGRAPH	TACITURNITY	TAILORMADE	TAMARILLOS
TABLATURES	TACHOGRAPHS	TACITURNLY	TAILORMAKE	TAMBOURERS
TABLECLOTH	TACHOMETER	TACKBOARDS	TAILORMAKES	TAMBOURINE
TABLECLOTHS	TACHOMETERS	TACKIFIERS	TAILORMAKING	TAMBOURINES
TABLELANDS	TACHOMETRIC	TACKIFYING	TAILPIECES	TAMBOURING
TABLEMATES	TACHOMETRICAL	TACKINESSES	TAILPIPING	TAMBOURINIST
TABLESPOON	TACHOMETRICALLY	TACMAHACKS	TAILPLANES	TAMBOURINISTS
TABLESPOONFUL	TACHOMETRIES	TACTFULNESS	TAILSLIDES	TAMBOURINS
TABLESPOONFULS	TACHOMETRY	TACTFULNESSES	TAILSPINNED	TAMEABILITIES
TABLESPOONS	TACHYARRHYTHMIA	TACTICALLY	TAILSPINNING	TAMEABILITY
TABLESPOONSFUL	TACHYCARDIA	TACTICIANS	TAILSTOCKS	TAMEABLENESS
TABLETTING	TACHYCARDIAC	TACTICITIES	TAILWATERS	TAMEABLENESSES
TABLEWARES	TACHYCARDIAS	TACTILISTS	TAILWHEELS	TAMELESSNESS
TABOGGANED	TACHYGRAPH	TACTILITIES	TAINTLESSLY	TAMELESSNESSES
TABOGGANING	TACHYGRAPHER	TACTLESSLY	TAKINGNESS	TAMENESSES
TABOPARESES	TACHYGRAPHERS	TACTLESSNESS	TAKINGNESSES	TAMOXIFENS
TABOPARESIS	TACHYGRAPHIC	TACTLESSNESSES	TALBOTYPES	TAMPERINGS
TABULARISATION	TACHYGRAPHICAL	TACTUALITIES	TALEBEARER	TAMPERPROOF
TABULARISATIONS	TACHYGRAPHIES	TACTUALITY	TALEBEARERS	TAMPONADES
TABULARISE	TACHYGRAPHIST	TAEKWONDOS	TALEBEARING	TAMPONAGES
TABULARISED	TACHYGRAPHISTS	TAENIACIDE	TALEBEARINGS	TANDEMWISE
TABULARISES	TACHYGRAPHS	TAENIACIDES	TALEGALLAS	TANGENCIES
TABULARISING	TACHYGRAPHY	TAENIAFUGE	TALENTLESS	TANGENTALLY
TABULARIZATION	TACHYLITES	TAENIAFUGES	TALISMANIC	TANGENTIAL
TABULARIZATIONS	TACHYLITIC	TAFFETASES	TALISMANICAL	TANGENTIALITIES
TABULARIZE	TACHYLYTES	TAFFETIZED	TALISMANICALLY	TANGENTIALITY
TABULARIZED	TACHYLYTIC	TAGLIARINI	TALKABILITIES	TANGENTIALLY
TABULARIZES	TACHYMETER	TAGLIARINIS	TALKABILITY	TANGERINES
TABULARIZING	TACHYMETERS	TAGLIATELLE	TALKATHONS	TANGHININS
TABULATING	TACHYMETRIC	TAGLIATELLES	TALKATIVELY	TANGIBILITIES
TABULATION	TACHYMETRICAL	TAHSILDARS	TALKATIVENESS	TANGIBILITY

TANGIBLENESS	TAPESCRIPTS	TARBOUCHES	TARTRAZINE	TAUTOCHRONISM
TANGIBLENESSES	TAPESTRIED	TARBOUSHES	TARTRAZINES	TAUTOCHRONISMS
TANGINESSES	TAPESTRIES	TARDIGRADE	TASEOMETER	TAUTOCHRONOUS
TANGLEFOOT	TAPESTRYING	TARDIGRADES	TASEOMETERS	TAUTOLOGIC
TANGLEFOOTS	TAPHEPHOBIA	TARDINESSES	TASIMETERS	TAUTOLOGICAL
TANGLEMENT	TAPHEPHOBIAS	TARGETABLE	TASIMETRIC	TAUTOLOGICALLY
TANGLEMENTS	TAPHEPHOBIC	TARGETEERS	TASIMETRIES	TAUTOLOGIES
TANGLESOME	TAPHONOMIC	TARGETITIS	TASKMASTER	TAUTOLOGISE
TANGLEWEED	TAPHONOMICAL	TARGETITISES	TASKMASTERS	TAUTOLOGISED
TANGLEWEEDS	TAPHONOMIES	TARGETLESS	TASKMISTRESS	TAUTOLOGISES
TANGLINGLY	TAPHONOMIST	TARIFFICATION	TASKMISTRESSES	TAUTOLOGISING
TANISTRIES	TAPHONOMISTS	TARIFFICATIONS	TASSELLING	TAUTOLOGISM
TANKBUSTER	TAPHOPHOBIA	TARIFFLESS	TASSELLINGS	TAUTOLOGISMS
TANKBUSTERS	TAPHOPHOBIAS	TARMACADAM	TASTEFULLY	TAUTOLOGIST
TANKBUSTING	TAPHROGENESES	TARMACADAMS	TASTEFULNESS	TAUTOLOGISTS
TANKBUSTINGS	TAPHROGENESIS	TARMACKING	TASTEFULNESSES	TAUTOLOGIZE
TANOREXICS	TAPOTEMENT	TARNATIONS	TASTELESSLY	TAUTOLOGIZED
TANTALATES	TAPOTEMENTS	TARNISHABLE	TASTELESSNESS	TAUTOLOGIZES
TANTALISATION	TAPSALTEERIE	TARNISHERS	TASTELESSNESSES	TAUTOLOGIZING
TANTALISATIONS	TAPSALTEERIES	TARNISHING	TASTEMAKER	TAUTOLOGOUS
TANTALISED	TAPSIETEERIE	TARPAULING	TASTEMAKERS	TAUTOLOGOUSLY
TANTALISER	TAPSIETEERIES	TARPAULINGS	TASTINESSES	TAUTOMERIC
TANTALISERS	TAPSTRESSES	TARPAULINS	TATAHASHES	TAUTOMERISM
TANTALISES	TARADIDDLE	TARRADIDDLE	TATPURUSHA	TAUTOMERISMS
TANTALISING	TARADIDDLES	TARRADIDDLES	TATPURUSHAS	TAUTOMETRIC
TANTALISINGLY	TARAMASALATA	TARRIANCES	TATTERDEMALION	TAUTOMETRICAL
TANTALISINGS	TARAMASALATAS	TARRINESSES	TATTERDEMALIONS	TAUTONYMIC
TANTALISMS	TARANTARAED	TARSALGIAS	TATTERDEMALLION	TAUTONYMIES
TANTALITES	TARANTARAING	TARSOMETATARSAL	TATTERSALL	TAUTONYMOUS
TANTALIZATION	TARANTARAS	TARSOMETATARSI	TATTERSALLS	TAUTOPHONIC
TANTALIZATIONS	TARANTASES	TARSOMETATARSUS	TATTINESSES	TAUTOPHONICAL
TANTALIZED	TARANTASSES	TARTANALIA	TATTLETALE	TAUTOPHONIES
TANTALIZER	TARANTELLA	TARTANALIAS	TATTLETALED	TAUTOPHONY
TANTALIZERS	TARANTELLAS	TARTANRIES	TATTLETALES	TAWDRINESS
TANTALIZES	TARANTISMS	TARTAREOUS	TATTLETALING	TAWDRINESSES
TANTALIZING	TARANTISTS	TARTARISATION	TATTLINGLY	TAWHEOWHEO
TANTALIZINGLY	TARANTULAE	TARTARISATIONS	TATTOOISTS	TAWHEOWHEOS
TANTALIZINGS	TARANTULAS	TARTARISED	TAUNTINGLY	TAWNINESSES
TANTALUSES	TARATANTARA	TARTARISES	TAUROBOLIA	TAXABILITIES
TANTAMOUNT	TARATANTARAED	TARTARISING	TAUROBOLIUM	TAXABILITY
TANTARARAS	TARATANTARAING	TARTARIZATION	TAUROMACHIAN	TAXABLENESS
TANZANITES	TARATANTARAS	TARTARIZATIONS	TAUROMACHIES	TAXABLENESSES
TAPERINGLY	TARAXACUMS	TARTARIZED	TAUROMACHY	TAXAMETERS
TAPERNESSES	TARBOGGINED	TARTARIZES	TAUROMORPHOUS	TAXATIONAL
TAPERSTICK	TARBOGGINING	TARTARIZING	TAUTNESSES	TAXIDERMAL
TAPERSTICKS	TARBOGGINS	TARTINESSES	TAUTOCHRONE	TAXIDERMIC
TAPESCRIPT	TARBOOSHES	TARTNESSES	TAUTOCHRONES	TAXIDERMIES

TAXIDERMISE	TEASELINGS	TECHNOCRACIES	TECHNOSPEAK	TELAESTHESIAS
TAXIDERMISED	TEASELLERS	TECHNOCRACY	TECHNOSPEAKS	TELAESTHETIC
TAXIDERMISES	TEASELLING	TECHNOCRAT	TECHNOSTRESS	TELANGIECTASES
TAXIDERMISING	TEASELLINGS	TECHNOCRATIC	TECHNOSTRESSES	TELANGIECTASIA
TAXIDERMIST	TEASPOONFUL	TECHNOCRATS	TECHNOSTRUCTURE	TELANGIECTASIAS
TAXIDERMISTS	TEASPOONFULS	TECHNOFEAR	TECTIBRANCH	TELANGIECTASIS
TAXIDERMIZE	TEASPOONSFUL	TECHNOFEARS	TECTIBRANCHIATE	TELANGIECTATIC
TAXIDERMIZED	TEATASTERS	TECHNOGRAPHIES	TECTIBRANCHS	TELAUTOGRAPHIC
TAXIDERMIZES	TEAZELLING	TECHNOGRAPHY	TECTONICALLY	TELAUTOGRAPHIES
TAXIDERMIZING	TECHINESSES	TECHNOJUNKIE	TECTONISMS	TELAUTOGRAPHY
TAXIMETERS	TECHNETIUM	TECHNOJUNKIES	TECTRICIAL	TELEARCHICS
TAXIPLANES	TECHNETIUMS	TECHNOLOGIC	TEDIOSITIES	TELEBANKING
TAXONOMERS	TECHNETRONIC	TECHNOLOGICAL	TEDIOUSNESS	TELEBANKINGS
TAXONOMICAL	TECHNICALISE	TECHNOLOGICALLY	TEDIOUSNESSES	TELEBRIDGE
TAXONOMICALLY	TECHNICALISED	TECHNOLOGIES	TEDIOUSOME	TELEBRIDGES
TAXONOMIES	TECHNICALISES	TECHNOLOGISE	TEEMINGNESS	TELECAMERA
TAXONOMIST	TECHNICALISING	TECHNOLOGISED	TEEMINGNESSES	TELECAMERAS
TAXONOMISTS	TECHNICALITIES	TECHNOLOGISES	TEENTSIEST	TELECASTED
TAXPAYINGS	TECHNICALITY	TECHNOLOGISING	TEENYBOPPER	TELECASTER
TAYASSUIDS	TECHNICALIZE	TECHNOLOGIST	TEENYBOPPERS	TELECASTERS
TAYBERRIES	TECHNICALIZED	TECHNOLOGISTS	TEETERBOARD	TELECASTING
TCHOTCHKES	TECHNICALIZES	TECHNOLOGIZE	TEETERBOARDS	TELECHIRIC
TCHOUKBALL	TECHNICALIZING	TECHNOLOGIZED	TEETHRIDGE	TELECOMMAND
TCHOUKBALLS	TECHNICALLY	TECHNOLOGIZES	TEETHRIDGES	TELECOMMANDS
TEABERRIES	TECHNICALNESS	TECHNOLOGIZING	TEETOTALED	TELECOMMUTE
TEACHABILITIES	TECHNICALNESSES	TECHNOLOGY	TEETOTALER	TELECOMMUTED
TEACHABILITY	TECHNICALS	TECHNOMANIA	TEETOTALERS	TELECOMMUTER
TEACHABLENESS	TECHNICIAN	TECHNOMANIAC	TEETOTALING	TELECOMMUTERS
TEACHABLENESSES	TECHNICIANS	TECHNOMANIACS	TEETOTALISM	TELECOMMUTES
TEACHERLESS	TECHNICISE	TECHNOMANIAS	TEETOTALISMS	TELECOMMUTING
TEACHERSHIP	TECHNICISED	TECHNOMUSIC	TEETOTALIST	TELECOMMUTINGS
TEACHERSHIPS	TECHNICISES	TECHNOMUSICS	TEETOTALISTS	TELECONFERENCE
TEACUPFULS	TECHNICISING	TECHNOPHILE	TEETOTALLED	TELECONFERENCES
TEACUPSFUL	TECHNICISM	TECHNOPHILES	TEETOTALLER	TELECONNECTION
TEAKETTLES	TECHNICISMS	TECHNOPHOBE	TEETOTALLERS	TELECONNECTIONS
TEARFULNESS	TECHNICIST	TECHNOPHOBES	TEETOTALLING	TELECONTROL
TEARFULNESSES	TECHNICISTS	TECHNOPHOBIA	TEETOTALLY	TELECONTROLS
TEARGASSED	TECHNICIZE	TECHNOPHOBIAS	TEGUMENTAL	TELECONVERTER
TEARGASSES	TECHNICIZED	TECHNOPHOBIC	TEGUMENTARY	TELECONVERTERS
TEARGASSING	TECHNICIZES	TECHNOPHOBICS	TEHSILDARS	TELECOTTAGE
TEARINESSES	TECHNICIZING	TECHNOPOLE	TEICHOPSIA	TELECOTTAGES
TEARJERKER	TECHNICOLOUR	TECHNOPOLES	TEICHOPSIAS	TELECOTTAGING
TEARJERKERS	TECHNICOLOURED	TECHNOPOLIS	TEINOSCOPE	TELECOTTAGINGS
TEARSHEETS	TECHNIKONS	TECHNOPOLISES	TEINOSCOPES	TELECOURSE
TEARSTAINED	TECHNIQUES	TECHNOPOLITAN	TEKNONYMIES	TELECOURSES
TEARSTAINS	TECHNOBABBLE	TECHNOPOLITANS	TEKNONYMOUS	TELEDILDONICS
TEARSTRIPS	TECHNOBABBLES	TECHNOPOPS	TELAESTHESIA	TELEFACSIMILE

T

TELEFACSIMILES

TELEFACSIMILES TELEMETERING TELEPHONER TELESHOPPED TELEWORKING
TELEFAXING TELEMETERS TELEPHONERS TELESHOPPING TELEWORKINGS
TELEFERIQUE TELEMETRIC TELEPHONES TELESHOPPINGS TELEWRITER
TELEFERIQUES TELEMETRICAL TELEPHONIC TELESMATIC TELEWRITERS
TELEGENICALLY TELEMETRICALLY TELEPHONICALLY TELESMATICAL TELFERAGES
TELEGNOSES TELEMETRIES TELEPHONIES TELESMATICALLY TELIOSPORE
TELEGNOSIS TELENCEPHALA TELEPHONING TELESOFTWARE TELIOSPORES
TELEGNOSTIC TELENCEPHALIC TELEPHONIST TELESOFTWARES TELLERSHIP
TELEGONIES TELENCEPHALON TELEPHONISTS TELESTEREOSCOPE TELLERSHIPS
TELEGONOUS TELENCEPHALONS TELEPHOTOGRAPH TELESTHESIA TELLURATES
TELEGRAMMATIC TELEOLOGIC TELEPHOTOGRAPHS TELESTHESIAS TELLURETTED
TELEGRAMMED TELEOLOGICAL TELEPHOTOGRAPHY TELESTHETIC TELLURIANS
TELEGRAMMIC TELEOLOGICALLY TELEPHOTOS TELESTICHS TELLURIDES
TELEGRAMMING TELEOLOGIES TELEPOINTS TELESURGERIES TELLURIONS
TELEGRAPHED TELEOLOGISM TELEPORTATION TELESURGERY TELLURISED
TELEGRAPHER TELEOLOGISMS TELEPORTATIONS TELETYPESETTING TELLURISES
TELEGRAPHERS TELEOLOGIST TELEPORTED TELETYPEWRITER TELLURISING
TELEGRAPHESE TELEOLOGISTS TELEPORTING TELETYPEWRITERS TELLURITES
TELEGRAPHESES TELEONOMIC TELEPRESENCE TELETYPING TELLURIUMS
TELEGRAPHIC TELEONOMIES TELEPRESENCES TELEUTOSPORE TELLURIZED
TELEGRAPHICALLY TELEOSAURIAN TELEPRINTER TELEUTOSPORES TELLURIZES
TELEGRAPHIES TELEOSAURIANS TELEPRINTERS TELEUTOSPORIC TELLURIZING
TELEGRAPHING TELEOSAURS TELEPROCESSING TELEVANGELICAL TELLUROMETER
TELEGRAPHIST TELEOSTEAN TELEPROCESSINGS TELEVANGELISM TELLUROMETERS
TELEGRAPHISTS TELEOSTEANS TELERECORD TELEVANGELISMS TELNETTING
TELEGRAPHS TELEOSTOME TELERECORDED TELEVANGELIST TELOCENTRIC
TELEGRAPHY TELEOSTOMES TELERECORDING TELEVANGELISTS TELOCENTRICS
TELEHEALTH TELEOSTOMOUS TELERECORDINGS TELEVERITE TELOMERASE
TELEHEALTHS TELEPATHED TELERECORDS TELEVERITES TELOMERASES
TELEJOURNALISM TELEPATHIC TELERGICALLY TELEVIEWED TELOMERISATION
TELEJOURNALISMS TELEPATHICALLY TELESCIENCE TELEVIEWER TELOMERISATIONS
TELEJOURNALIST TELEPATHIES TELESCIENCES TELEVIEWERS TELOMERIZATION
TELEJOURNALISTS TELEPATHING TELESCOPED TELEVIEWING TELOMERIZATIONS
TELEKINESES TELEPATHISE TELESCOPES TELEVIEWINGS TELOPHASES
TELEKINESIS TELEPATHISED TELESCOPIC TELEVISERS TELOPHASIC
TELEKINETIC TELEPATHISES TELESCOPICAL TELEVISING TELPHERAGE
TELEKINETICALLY TELEPATHISING TELESCOPICALLY TELEVISION TELPHERAGES
TELEMARKED TELEPATHIST TELESCOPIES TELEVISIONAL TELPHERING
TELEMARKETER TELEPATHISTS TELESCOPIFORM TELEVISIONALLY TELPHERLINE
TELEMARKETERS TELEPATHIZE TELESCOPING TELEVISIONARY TELPHERLINES
TELEMARKETING TELEPATHIZED TELESCOPIST TELEVISIONS TELPHERMAN
TELEMARKETINGS TELEPATHIZES TELESCOPISTS TELEVISORS TELPHERMEN
TELEMARKING TELEPATHIZING TELESCREEN TELEVISUAL TELPHERWAY
TELEMATICS TELEPHEMES TELESCREENS TELEVISUALLY TELPHERWAYS
TELEMEDICINE TELEPHERIQUE TELESELLING TELEWORKED TEMAZEPAMS
TELEMEDICINES TELEPHERIQUES TELESELLINGS TELEWORKER TEMERARIOUS
TELEMETERED TELEPHONED TELESERVICES TELEWORKERS TEMERARIOUSLY

TEMERARIOUSNESS	TEMPORARIES	TENANTLESS	TENDOVAGINITIS	TENSIOMETER
TEMERITIES	TEMPORARILY	TENANTRIES	TENDRESSES	TENSIOMETERS
TEMEROUSLY	TEMPORARINESS	TENANTSHIP	TENDRILLAR	TENSIOMETRIC
TEMPERABILITIES	TEMPORARINESSES	TENANTSHIPS	TENDRILLED	TENSIOMETRIES
TEMPERABILITY	TEMPORISATION	TENDENCIALLY	TENDRILLOUS	TENSIOMETRY
TEMPERABLE	TEMPORISATIONS	TENDENCIES	TENDRILOUS	TENSIONALLY
TEMPERALITIE	TEMPORISED	TENDENCIOUS	TENEBRIFIC	TENSIONERS
TEMPERALITIES	TEMPORISER	TENDENCIOUSLY	TENEBRIONID	TENSIONING
TEMPERAMENT	TEMPORISERS	TENDENCIOUSNESS	TENEBRIONIDS	TENSIONLESS
TEMPERAMENTAL	TEMPORISES	TENDENTIAL	TENEBRIOUS	TENTACULAR
TEMPERAMENTALLY	TEMPORISING	TENDENTIALLY	TENEBRIOUSNESS	TENTACULATE
TEMPERAMENTFUL	TEMPORISINGLY	TENDENTIOUS	TENEBRISMS	TENTACULIFEROUS
TEMPERAMENTS	TEMPORISINGS	TENDENTIOUSLY	TENEBRISTS	TENTACULITE
TEMPERANCE	TEMPORIZATION	TENDENTIOUSNESS	TENEBRITIES	TENTACULITES
TEMPERANCES	TEMPORIZATIONS	TENDERABLE	TENEBROSITIES	TENTACULOID
TEMPERATED	TEMPORIZED	TENDERFEET	TENEBROSITY	TENTACULUM
TEMPERATELY	TEMPORIZER	TENDERFOOT	TENEBROUSNESS	TENTATIONS
TEMPERATENESS	TEMPORIZERS	TENDERFOOTS	TENEBROUSNESSES	TENTATIVELY
TEMPERATENESSES	TEMPORIZES	TENDERHEARTED	TENEMENTAL	TENTATIVENESS
TEMPERATES	TEMPORIZING	TENDERHEARTEDLY	TENEMENTARY	TENTATIVENESSES
TEMPERATING	TEMPORIZINGLY	TENDERINGS	TENEMENTED	TENTATIVES
TEMPERATIVE	TEMPORIZINGS	TENDERISATION	TENESMUSES	TENTERHOOK
TEMPERATURE	TEMPTABILITIES	TENDERISATIONS	TENIACIDES	TENTERHOOKS
TEMPERATURES	TEMPTABILITY	TENDERISED	TENIAFUGES	TENTIGINOUS
TEMPERINGS	TEMPTABLENESS	TENDERISER	TENNANTITE	TENTMAKERS
TEMPESTING	TEMPTABLENESSES	TENDERISERS	TENNANTITES	TENTORIUMS
TEMPESTIVE	TEMPTATION	TENDERISES	TENORRHAPHIES	TENUIROSTRAL
TEMPESTUOUS	TEMPTATIONS	TENDERISING	TENORRHAPHY	TENUOUSNESS
TEMPESTUOUSLY	TEMPTATIOUS	TENDERIZATION	TENOSYNOVITIS	TENUOUSNESSES
TEMPESTUOUSNESS	TEMPTINGLY	TENDERIZATIONS	TENOSYNOVITISES	TENURIALLY
TEMPOLABILE	TEMPTINGNESS	TENDERIZED	TENOTOMIES	TEPEFACTION
TEMPORALISE	TEMPTINGNESSES	TENDERIZER	TENOTOMIST	TEPEFACTIONS
TEMPORALISED	TEMPTRESSES	TENDERIZERS	TENOTOMISTS	TEPHIGRAMS
TEMPORALISES	TEMULENCES	TENDERIZES	TENOVAGINITIS	TEPHROITES
TEMPORALISING	TEMULENCIES	TENDERIZING	TENOVAGINITISES	TEPHROMANCIES
TEMPORALITIES	TEMULENTLY	TENDERLING	TENPOUNDER	TEPHROMANCY
TEMPORALITY	TENABILITIES	TENDERLINGS	TENPOUNDERS	TEPIDARIUM
TEMPORALIZE	TENABILITY	TENDERLOIN	TENSENESSES	TEPIDITIES
TEMPORALIZED	TENABLENESS	TENDERLOINS	TENSIBILITIES	TEPIDNESSES
TEMPORALIZES	TENABLENESSES	TENDERNESS	TENSIBILITY	TERAHERTZES
TEMPORALIZING	TENACIOUSLY	TENDERNESSES	TENSIBLENESS	TERATOCARCINOMA
TEMPORALLY	TENACIOUSNESS	TENDEROMETER	TENSIBLENESSES	TERATOGENESES
TEMPORALNESS	TENACIOUSNESSES	TENDEROMETERS	TENSILENESS	TERATOGENESIS
TEMPORALNESSES	TENACITIES	TENDINITIS	TENSILENESSES	TERATOGENIC
TEMPORALTIES	TENACULUMS	TENDINITISES	TENSILITIES	TERATOGENICIST
TEMPORALTY	TENAILLONS	TENDONITIS	TENSIMETER	TERATOGENICISTS
TEMPORANEOUS	TENANTABLE	TENDONITISES	TENSIMETERS	TERATOGENICITY

T

TERATOGENIES	TERMINABILITY	TERRAFORMS	TERRORISTS	TESTICULATED
TERATOGENS	TERMINABLE	TERRAMARES	TERRORIZATION	TESTIFICATE
TERATOGENY	TERMINABLENESS	TERRAQUEOUS	TERRORIZATIONS	TESTIFICATES
TERATOLOGIC	TERMINABLY	TERRARIUMS	TERRORIZED	TESTIFICATION
TERATOLOGICAL	TERMINALLY	TERREMOTIVE	TERRORIZER	TESTIFICATIONS
TERATOLOGIES	TERMINATED	TERREPLEIN	TERRORIZERS	TESTIFICATOR
TERATOLOGIST	TERMINATES	TERREPLEINS	TERRORIZES	TESTIFICATORS
TERATOLOGISTS	TERMINATING	TERRESTRIAL	TERRORIZING	TESTIFICATORY
TERATOLOGY	TERMINATION	TERRESTRIALLY	TERRORLESS	TESTIFIERS
TERATOMATA	TERMINATIONAL	TERRESTRIALNESS	TERSANCTUS	TESTIFYING
TERATOMATOUS	TERMINATIONS	TERRESTRIALS	TERSANCTUSES	TESTIMONIAL
TERATOPHOBIA	TERMINATIVE	TERRIBILITIES	TERSENESSES	TESTIMONIALISE
TERATOPHOBIAS	TERMINATIVELY	TERRIBILITY	TERTIARIES	TESTIMONIALISED
TERCENTENARIES	TERMINATOR	TERRIBLENESS	TERVALENCIES	TESTIMONIALISES
TERCENTENARY	TERMINATORS	TERRIBLENESSES	TERVALENCY	TESTIMONIALIZE
TERCENTENNIAL	TERMINATORY	TERRICOLES	TESCHENITE	TESTIMONIALIZED
TERCENTENNIALS	TERMINISMS	TERRICOLOUS	TESCHENITES	TESTIMONIALIZES
TEREBINTHINE	TERMINISTS	TERRIFICALLY	TESSARAGLOT	TESTIMONIALS
TEREBINTHS	TERMINOLOGICAL	TERRIFIERS	TESSELATED	TESTIMONIED
TEREBRANTS	TERMINOLOGIES	TERRIFYING	TESSELATES	TESTIMONIES
TEREBRATED	TERMINOLOGIST	TERRIFYINGLY	TESSELATING	TESTIMONYING
TEREBRATES	TERMINOLOGISTS	TERRIGENOUS	TESSELLATE	TESTINESSES
TEREBRATING	TERMINOLOGY	TERRITORIAL	TESSELLATED	TESTOSTERONE
TEREBRATION	TERMINUSES	TERRITORIALISE	TESSELLATES	TESTOSTERONES
TEREBRATIONS	TERMITARIA	TERRITORIALISED	TESSELLATING	TESTUDINAL
TEREBRATULA	TERMITARIES	TERRITORIALISES	TESSELLATION	TESTUDINARY
TEREBRATULAE	TERMITARIUM	TERRITORIALISM	TESSELLATIONS	TESTUDINEOUS
TEREBRATULAS	TERMITARIUMS	TERRITORIALISMS	TESSERACTS	TESTUDINES
TEREPHTHALATE	TERNEPLATE	TERRITORIALIST	TESSITURAS	TETANICALLY
TEREPHTHALATES	TERNEPLATES	TERRITORIALISTS	TESTABILITIES	TETANISATION
TEREPHTHALIC	TEROTECHNOLOGY	TERRITORIALITY	TESTABILITY	TETANISATIONS
TERGIVERSANT	TERPENELESS	TERRITORIALIZE	TESTACEANS	TETANISING
TERGIVERSANTS	TERPENOIDS	TERRITORIALIZED	TESTACEOUS	TETANIZATION
TERGIVERSATE	TERPINEOLS	TERRITORIALIZES	TESTAMENTAL	TETANIZATIONS
TERGIVERSATED	TERPOLYMER	TERRITORIALLY	TESTAMENTAR	TETANIZING
TERGIVERSATES	TERPOLYMERS	TERRITORIALS	TESTAMENTARILY	TETARTOHEDRAL
TERGIVERSATING	TERPSICHOREAL	TERRITORIED	TESTAMENTARY	TETARTOHEDRALLY
TERGIVERSATION	TERPSICHOREAN	TERRITORIES	TESTAMENTS	TETARTOHEDRISM
TERGIVERSATIONS	TERRACELESS	TERRORISATION	TESTATIONS	TETARTOHEDRISMS
TERGIVERSATOR	TERRACETTE	TERRORISATIONS	TESTATRICES	TETCHINESS
TERGIVERSATORS	TERRACETTES	TERRORISED	TESTATRIXES	TETCHINESSES
TERGIVERSATORY	TERRACINGS	TERRORISER	TESTCROSSED	TETHERBALL
TERMAGANCIES	TERRACOTTA	TERRORISERS	TESTCROSSES	TETHERBALLS
TERMAGANCY	TERRACOTTAS	TERRORISES	TESTCROSSING	TETRABASIC
TERMAGANTLY	TERRAFORMED	TERRORISING	TESTERNING	TETRABASICITIES
TERMAGANTS	TERRAFORMING	TERRORISMS	TESTICULAR	TETRABASICITY
TERMINABILITIES	TERRAFORMINGS	TERRORISTIC	TESTICULATE	TETRABRACH

TETRABRACHS	TETRAHEDRONS	TETRASTICH	TEXTURIZES	THANATOSIS
TETRABRANCHIATE	TETRAHYDROFURAN	TETRASTICHAL	TEXTURIZING	THANEHOODS
TETRACAINE	TETRAHYMENA	TETRASTICHIC	THALAMENCEPHALA	THANESHIPS
TETRACAINES	TETRAHYMENAS	TETRASTICHOUS	THALAMICALLY	THANKFULLER
TETRACHLORIDE	TETRALOGIES	TETRASTICHS	THALAMIFLORAL	THANKFULLEST
TETRACHLORIDES	TETRAMERAL	TETRASTYLE	THALASSAEMIA	THANKFULLY
TETRACHORD	TETRAMERIC	TETRASTYLES	THALASSAEMIAS	THANKFULNESS
TETRACHORDAL	TETRAMERISM	TETRASYLLABIC	THALASSAEMIC	THANKFULNESSES
TETRACHORDS	TETRAMERISMS	TETRASYLLABICAL	THALASSEMIA	THANKLESSLY
TETRACHOTOMIES	TETRAMEROUS	TETRASYLLABLE	THALASSEMIAS	THANKLESSNESS
TETRACHOTOMOUS	TETRAMETER	TETRASYLLABLES	THALASSEMIC	THANKLESSNESSES
TETRACHOTOMY	TETRAMETERS	TETRATHEISM	THALASSEMICS	THANKSGIVER
TETRACTINAL	TETRAMETHYLLEAD	TETRATHEISMS	THALASSIAN	THANKSGIVERS
TETRACTINE	TETRAMORPHIC	TETRATHLON	THALASSIANS	THANKSGIVING
TETRACYCLIC	TETRANDRIAN	TETRATHLONS	THALASSOCRACIES	THANKSGIVINGS
TETRACYCLINE	TETRANDROUS	TETRATOMIC	THALASSOCRACY	THANKWORTHILY
TETRACYCLINES	TETRAPLEGIA	TETRAVALENCIES	THALASSOCRAT	THANKWORTHINESS
TETRADACTYL	TETRAPLEGIAS	TETRAVALENCY	THALASSOCRATS	THANKWORTHY
TETRADACTYLIES	TETRAPLEGIC	TETRAVALENT	THALASSOGRAPHER	THARBOROUGH
TETRADACTYLOUS	TETRAPLOID	TETRAVALENTS	THALASSOGRAPHIC	THARBOROUGHS
TETRADACTYLS	TETRAPLOIDIES	TETRAZOLIUM	THALASSOGRAPHY	THATCHIEST
TETRADACTYLY	TETRAPLOIDS	TETRAZOLIUMS	THALASSOTHERAPY	THATCHINGS
TETRADITES	TETRAPLOIDY	TETRAZZINI	THALATTOCRACIES	THATCHLESS
TETRADRACHM	TETRAPODIC	TETRODOTOXIN	THALATTOCRACY	THATNESSES
TETRADRACHMS	TETRAPODIES	TETRODOTOXINS	THALICTRUM	THAUMASITE
TETRADYMITE	TETRAPODOUS	TETROTOXIN	THALICTRUMS	THAUMASITES
TETRADYMITES	TETRAPOLIS	TETROTOXINS	THALIDOMIDE	THAUMATINS
TETRADYNAMOUS	TETRAPOLISES	TETROXIDES	THALIDOMIDES	THAUMATOGENIES
TETRAETHYL	TETRAPOLITAN	TEUTONISED	THALLIFORM	THAUMATOGENY
TETRAETHYLS	TETRAPTERAN	TEUTONISES	THALLOPHYTE	THAUMATOGRAPHY
TETRAFLUORIDE	TETRAPTEROUS	TEUTONISING	THALLOPHYTES	THAUMATOLATRIES
TETRAFLUORIDES	TETRAPTOTE	TEUTONIZED	THALLOPHYTIC	THAUMATOLATRY
TETRAGONAL	TETRAPTOTES	TEUTONIZES	THANATISMS	THAUMATOLOGIES
TETRAGONALLY	TETRAPYRROLE	TEUTONIZING	THANATISTS	THAUMATOLOGY
TETRAGONALNESS	TETRAPYRROLES	TEXTBOOKISH	THANATOGNOMONIC	THAUMATROPE
TETRAGONOUS	TETRARCHATE	TEXTPHONES	THANATOGRAPHIES	THAUMATROPES
TETRAGRAMMATON	TETRARCHATES	TEXTUALISM	THANATOGRAPHY	THAUMATROPICAL
TETRAGRAMMATONS	TETRARCHIC	TEXTUALISMS	THANATOLOGICAL	THAUMATURGE
TETRAGRAMS	TETRARCHICAL	TEXTUALIST	THANATOLOGIES	THAUMATURGES
TETRAGYNIAN	TETRARCHIES	TEXTUALISTS	THANATOLOGIST	THAUMATURGIC
TETRAGYNOUS	TETRASEMIC	TEXTUARIES	THANATOLOGISTS	THAUMATURGICAL
TETRAHEDRA	TETRASPORANGIA	TEXTURALLY	THANATOLOGY	THAUMATURGICS
TETRAHEDRAL	TETRASPORANGIUM	TEXTURELESS	THANATOPHOBIA	THAUMATURGIES
TETRAHEDRALLY	TETRASPORE	TEXTURISED	THANATOPHOBIAS	THAUMATURGISM
TETRAHEDRITE	TETRASPORES	TEXTURISES	THANATOPSES	THAUMATURGISMS
TETRAHEDRITES	TETRASPORIC	TEXTURISING	THANATOPSIS	THAUMATURGIST
TETRAHEDRON	TETRASPOROUS	TEXTURIZED	THANATOSES	THAUMATURGISTS

T

THAUMATURGUS	THEIRSELVES	THEOLOGIAN	THEOPHOBIA	THEOSOPHISTS
THAUMATURGUSES	THEISTICAL	THEOLOGIANS	THEOPHOBIAC	THEOSOPHIZE
THAUMATURGY	THEISTICALLY	THEOLOGICAL	THEOPHOBIACS	THEOSOPHIZED
THEANTHROPIC	THELEMENTS	THEOLOGICALLY	THEOPHOBIAS	THEOSOPHIZES
THEANTHROPIES	THELITISES	THEOLOGIES	THEOPHOBIST	THEOSOPHIZING
THEANTHROPISM	THELYTOKIES	THEOLOGISATION	THEOPHOBISTS	THEOTECHNIC
THEANTHROPISMS	THELYTOKOUS	THEOLOGISATIONS	THEOPHORIC	THEOTECHNIES
THEANTHROPIST	THEMATICALLY	THEOLOGISE	THEOPHYLLINE	THEOTECHNY
THEANTHROPISTS	THEMATISATION	THEOLOGISED	THEOPHYLLINES	THERALITES
THEANTHROPY	THEMATISATIONS	THEOLOGISER	THEOPNEUST	THERAPEUSES
THEARCHIES	THEMATIZATION	THEOLOGISERS	THEOPNEUSTIC	THERAPEUSIS
THEATERGOER	THEMATIZATIONS	THEOLOGISES	THEOPNEUSTIES	THERAPEUTIC
THEATERGOERS	THEMSELVES	THEOLOGISING	THEOPNEUSTY	THERAPEUTICALLY
THEATERGOING	THENABOUTS	THEOLOGIST	THEORBISTS	THERAPEUTICS
THEATERGOINGS	THENARDITE	THEOLOGISTS	THEOREMATIC	THERAPEUTIST
THEATRICAL	THENARDITES	THEOLOGIZATION	THEOREMATICAL	THERAPEUTISTS
THEATRICALISE	THENCEFORTH	THEOLOGIZATIONS	THEOREMATICALLY	THERAPISTS
THEATRICALISED	THENCEFORWARD	THEOLOGIZE	THEOREMATIST	THERAPSIDS
THEATRICALISES	THENCEFORWARDS	THEOLOGIZED	THEOREMATISTS	THEREABOUT
THEATRICALISING	THEOBROMINE	THEOLOGIZER	THEORETICAL	THEREABOUTS
THEATRICALISM	THEOBROMINES	THEOLOGIZERS	THEORETICALLY	THEREAFTER
THEATRICALISMS	THEOCENTRIC	THEOLOGIZES	THEORETICIAN	THEREAGAINST
THEATRICALITIES	THEOCENTRICISM	THEOLOGIZING	THEORETICIANS	THEREAMONG
THEATRICALITY	THEOCENTRICISMS	THEOLOGOUMENA	THEORETICS	THEREANENT
THEATRICALIZE	THEOCENTRICITY	THEOLOGOUMENON	THEORIQUES	THEREBESIDE
THEATRICALIZED	THEOCENTRISM	THEOLOGUES	THEORISATION	THEREINAFTER
THEATRICALIZES	THEOCENTRISMS	THEOMACHIES	THEORISATIONS	THEREINBEFORE
THEATRICALIZING	THEOCRACIES	THEOMACHIST	THEORISERS	THERENESSES
THEATRICALLY	THEOCRASIES	THEOMACHISTS	THEORISING	THERETHROUGH
THEATRICALNESS	THEOCRATIC	THEOMANCIES	THEORIZATION	THERETOFORE
THEATRICALS	THEOCRATICAL	THEOMANIAC	THEORIZATIONS	THEREUNDER
THEATRICISE	THEOCRATICALLY	THEOMANIACS	THEORIZERS	THEREWITHAL
THEATRICISED	THEODICEAN	THEOMANIAS	THEORIZING	THEREWITHIN
THEATRICISES	THEODICEANS	THEOMANTIC	THEOSOPHER	THERIANTHROPIC
THEATRICISING	THEODICIES	THEOMORPHIC	THEOSOPHERS	THERIANTHROPISM
THEATRICISM	THEODOLITE	THEOMORPHISM	THEOSOPHIC	THERIOLATRIES
THEATRICISMS	THEODOLITES	THEOMORPHISMS	THEOSOPHICAL	THERIOLATRY
THEATRICIZE	THEODOLITIC	THEONOMIES	THEOSOPHICALLY	THERIOMORPH
THEATRICIZED	THEOGONICAL	THEONOMOUS	THEOSOPHIES	THERIOMORPHIC
THEATRICIZES	THEOGONIES	THEOPATHETIC	THEOSOPHISE	THERIOMORPHISM
THEATRICIZING	THEOGONIST	THEOPATHIC	THEOSOPHISED	THERIOMORPHISMS
THEATROMANIA	THEOGONISTS	THEOPATHIES	THEOSOPHISES	THERIOMORPHOSES
THEATROMANIAS	THEOLOGASTER	THEOPHAGIES	THEOSOPHISING	THERIOMORPHOSIS
THEATROPHONE	THEOLOGASTERS	THEOPHAGOUS	THEOSOPHISM	THERIOMORPHOUS
THEATROPHONES	THEOLOGATE	THEOPHANIC	THEOSOPHISMS	THERIOMORPHS
THECODONTS	THEOLOGATES	THEOPHANIES	THEOSOPHIST	THERMAESTHESIA
THEFTUOUSLY	THEOLOGERS	THEOPHANOUS	THEOSOPHISTICAL	THERMAESTHESIAS

T

THERMALISATION	THERMOFORMABLE	THERMOPHILS	THERMOTROPISM	THIMBLERIGGING
THERMALISATIONS	THERMOFORMED	THERMOPHYLLOUS	THERMOTROPISMS	THIMBLERIGGINGS
THERMALISE	THERMOFORMING	THERMOPILE	THEROLOGIES	THIMBLERIGS
THERMALISED	THERMOFORMS	THERMOPILES	THEROPHYTE	THIMBLESFUL
THERMALISES	THERMOGENESES	THERMOPLASTIC	THEROPHYTES	THIMBLEWEED
THERMALISING	THERMOGENESIS	THERMOPLASTICS	THEROPODAN	THIMBLEWEEDS
THERMALIZATION	THERMOGENETIC	THERMORECEPTOR	THEROPODANS	THIMBLEWIT
THERMALIZATIONS	THERMOGENIC	THERMORECEPTORS	THERSITICAL	THIMBLEWITS
THERMALIZE	THERMOGENOUS	THERMOREGULATE	THESAURUSES	THIMBLEWITTED
THERMALIZED	THERMOGRAM	THERMOREGULATED	THESMOTHETE	THIMEROSAL
THERMALIZES	THERMOGRAMS	THERMOREGULATES	THESMOTHETES	THIMEROSALS
THERMALIZING	THERMOGRAPH	THERMOREGULATOR	THETICALLY	THINGAMABOB
THERMESTHESIA	THERMOGRAPHER	THERMOREMANENCE	THEURGICAL	THINGAMABOBS
THERMESTHESIAS	THERMOGRAPHERS	THERMOREMANENT	THEURGICALLY	THINGAMAJIG
THERMETTES	THERMOGRAPHIC	THERMOSCOPE	THEURGISTS	THINGAMAJIGS
THERMICALLY	THERMOGRAPHIES	THERMOSCOPES	THIABENDAZOLE	THINGAMIES
THERMIDORS	THERMOGRAPHS	THERMOSCOPIC	THIABENDAZOLES	THINGAMYBOB
THERMIONIC	THERMOGRAPHY	THERMOSCOPICAL	THIAMINASE	THINGAMYBOBS
THERMIONICS	THERMOHALINE	THERMOSETS	THIAMINASES	THINGAMYJIG
THERMISTOR	THERMOJUNCTION	THERMOSETTING	THICKENERS	THINGAMYJIGS
THERMISTORS	THERMOJUNCTIONS	THERMOSIPHON	THICKENING	THINGHOODS
THERMOBARIC	THERMOLABILE	THERMOSIPHONS	THICKENINGS	THINGINESS
THERMOBAROGRAPH	THERMOLABILITY	THERMOSPHERE	THICKHEADED	THINGINESSES
THERMOBAROMETER	THERMOLOGIES	THERMOSPHERES	THICKHEADEDNESS	THINGLINESS
THERMOCHEMICAL	THERMOLOGY	THERMOSPHERIC	THICKHEADS	THINGLINESSES
THERMOCHEMIST	THERMOLYSES	THERMOSTABILITY	THICKLEAVES	THINGNESSES
THERMOCHEMISTRY	THERMOLYSIS	THERMOSTABLE	THICKNESSES	THINGUMABOB
THERMOCHEMISTS	THERMOLYTIC	THERMOSTAT	THICKSKINS	THINGUMABOBS
THERMOCHROMIC	THERMOMAGNETIC	THERMOSTATED	THIEVERIES	THINGUMAJIG
THERMOCHROMIES	THERMOMETER	THERMOSTATIC	THIEVISHLY	THINGUMAJIGS
THERMOCHROMISM	THERMOMETERS	THERMOSTATICS	THIEVISHNESS	THINGUMBOB
THERMOCHROMISMS	THERMOMETRIC	THERMOSTATING	THIEVISHNESSES	THINGUMBOBS
THERMOCHROMY	THERMOMETRICAL	THERMOSTATS	THIGHBONES	THINGUMMIES
THERMOCLINE	THERMOMETRIES	THERMOSTATTED	THIGMOTACTIC	THINGUMMYBOB
THERMOCLINES	THERMOMETRY	THERMOSTATTING	THIGMOTAXES	THINGUMMYBOBS
THERMOCOUPLE	THERMOMOTOR	THERMOTACTIC	THIGMOTAXIS	THINGUMMYJIG
THERMOCOUPLES	THERMOMOTORS	THERMOTAXES	THIGMOTROPIC	THINGUMMYJIGS
THERMODURIC	THERMONASTIES	THERMOTAXIC	THIGMOTROPISM	THINKABLENESS
THERMODYNAMIC	THERMONASTY	THERMOTAXIS	THIGMOTROPISMS	THINKABLENESSES
THERMODYNAMICAL	THERMONUCLEAR	THERMOTENSILE	THIMBLEBERRIES	THINKINGLY
THERMODYNAMICS	THERMOPERIODIC	THERMOTHERAPIES	THIMBLEBERRY	THINKINGNESS
THERMOELECTRIC	THERMOPERIODISM	THERMOTHERAPY	THIMBLEFUL	THINKINGNESSES
THERMOELECTRON	THERMOPHIL	THERMOTICAL	THIMBLEFULS	THINKPIECE
THERMOELECTRONS	THERMOPHILE	THERMOTICS	THIMBLERIG	THINKPIECES
THERMOELEMENT	THERMOPHILES	THERMOTOLERANT	THIMBLERIGGED	THINNESSES
THERMOELEMENTS	THERMOPHILIC	THERMOTROPIC	THIMBLERIGGER	THIOALCOHOL
THERMOFORM	THERMOPHILOUS	THERMOTROPICS	THIMBLERIGGERS	THIOALCOHOLS

T

THIOBACILLI	THIXOTROPE	THOROUGHLY	THREATENINGS	THROATWORT
THIOBACILLUS	THIXOTROPES	THOROUGHNESS	THREEFOLDNESS	THROATWORTS
THIOBARBITURATE	THIXOTROPIC	THOROUGHNESSES	THREEFOLDNESSES	THROBBINGLY
THIOCARBAMIDE	THIXOTROPIES	THOROUGHPACED	THREENESSES	THROBBINGS
THIOCARBAMIDES	THIXOTROPY	THOROUGHPIN	THREEPEATED	THROMBOCYTE
THIOCYANATE	THOLEIITES	THOROUGHPINS	THREEPEATING	THROMBOCYTES
THIOCYANATES	THOLEIITIC	THOROUGHWAX	THREEPEATS	THROMBOCYTIC
THIOCYANIC	THOLOBATES	THOROUGHWAXES	THREEPENCE	THROMBOEMBOLIC
THIODIGLYCOL	THORACENTESES	THOROUGHWORT	THREEPENCES	THROMBOEMBOLISM
THIODIGLYCOLS	THORACENTESIS	THOROUGHWORTS	THREEPENCEWORTH	THROMBOGEN
THIOFURANS	THORACICALLY	THOUGHTCAST	THREEPENNIES	THROMBOGENS
THIOPENTAL	THORACOCENTESES	THOUGHTCASTS	THREEPENNY	THROMBOKINASE
THIOPENTALS	THORACOCENTESIS	THOUGHTFUL	THREEPENNYWORTH	THROMBOKINASES
THIOPENTONE	THORACOPLASTIES	THOUGHTFULLY	THREESCORE	THROMBOLYSES
THIOPENTONES	THORACOPLASTY	THOUGHTFULNESS	THREESCORES	THROMBOLYSIS
THIOPHENES	THORACOSCOPE	THOUGHTLESS	THREESOMES	THROMBOLYTIC
THIORIDAZINE	THORACOSCOPES	THOUGHTLESSLY	THREMMATOLOGIES	THROMBOLYTICS
THIORIDAZINES	THORACOSTOMIES	THOUGHTLESSNESS	THREMMATOLOGY	THROMBOPHILIA
THIOSINAMINE	THORACOSTOMY	THOUGHTWAY	THRENETICAL	THROMBOPHILIAS
THIOSINAMINES	THORACOTOMIES	THOUGHTWAYS	THRENODIAL	THROMBOPLASTIC
THIOSULFATE	THORACOTOMY	THOUSANDFOLD	THRENODIES	THROMBOPLASTIN
THIOSULFATES	THORIANITE	THOUSANDFOLDS	THRENODIST	THROMBOPLASTINS
THIOSULPHATE	THORIANITES	THOUSANDTH	THRENODISTS	THROMBOSED
THIOSULPHATES	THORNBACKS	THOUSANDTHS	THREONINES	THROMBOSES
THIOSULPHURIC	THORNBILLS	THRAIPINGS	THRESHINGS	THROMBOSING
THIOURACIL	THORNBIRDS	THRALLDOMS	THRESHOLDS	THROMBOSIS
THIOURACILS	THORNBUSHES	THRAPPLING	THRIFTIEST	THROMBOTIC
THIRDBOROUGH	THORNHEDGE	THRASHINGS	THRIFTINESS	THROMBOXANE
THIRDBOROUGHS	THORNHEDGES	THRASONICAL	THRIFTINESSES	THROMBOXANES
THIRDSTREAM	THORNINESS	THRASONICALLY	THRIFTLESS	THRONELESS
THIRDSTREAMS	THORNINESSES	THREADBARE	THRIFTLESSLY	THRONGINGS
THIRSTIEST	THORNPROOF	THREADBARENESS	THRIFTLESSNESS	THROPPLING
THIRSTINESS	THORNPROOFS	THREADFINS	THRILLIEST	THROTTLEABLE
THIRSTINESSES	THORNTREES	THREADIEST	THRILLINGLY	THROTTLEHOLD
THIRSTLESS	THOROUGHBASS	THREADINESS	THRILLINGNESS	THROTTLEHOLDS
THIRTEENTH	THOROUGHBASSES	THREADINESSES	THRILLINGNESSES	THROTTLERS
THIRTEENTHLY	THOROUGHBRACE	THREADLESS	THRIVELESS	THROTTLING
THIRTEENTHS	THOROUGHBRACED	THREADLIKE	THRIVINGLY	THROTTLINGS
THIRTIETHS	THOROUGHBRACES	THREADMAKER	THRIVINGNESS	THROUGHFARE
THIRTYFOLD	THOROUGHBRED	THREADMAKERS	THRIVINGNESSES	THROUGHFARES
THIRTYSOMETHING	THOROUGHBREDS	THREADWORM	THROATIEST	THROUGHGAUN
THISNESSES	THOROUGHER	THREADWORMS	THROATINESS	THROUGHGAUNS
THISTLEDOWN	THOROUGHEST	THREATENED	THROATINESSES	THROUGHITHER
THISTLEDOWNS	THOROUGHFARE	THREATENER	THROATLASH	THROUGHOTHER
THISTLIEST	THOROUGHFARES	THREATENERS	THROATLASHES	THROUGHOUT
THITHERWARD	THOROUGHGOING	THREATENING	THROATLATCH	THROUGHPUT
THITHERWARDS	THOROUGHGOINGLY	THREATENINGLY	THROATLATCHES	THROUGHPUTS

THROUGHWAY	THUNDERERS	THYMECTOMIZE	TICKTACKING	TILLANDSIAS
THROUGHWAYS	THUNDERFLASH	THYMECTOMIZED	TICKTACKTOE	TILLERLESS
THROWAWAYS	THUNDERFLASHES	THYMECTOMIZES	TICKTACKTOES	TILTMETERS
THROWBACKS	THUNDERHEAD	THYMECTOMIZING	TICKTOCKED	TILTROTORS
THROWDOWNS	THUNDERHEADS	THYMECTOMY	TICKTOCKING	TIMBERDOODLE
THROWSTERS	THUNDERIER	THYMELAEACEOUS	TICTACKING	TIMBERDOODLES
THRUMMIEST	THUNDERIEST	THYMIDINES	TICTOCKING	TIMBERHEAD
THRUMMINGLY	THUNDERING	THYMIDYLIC	TIDDLEDYWINK	TIMBERHEADS
THRUMMINGS	THUNDERINGLY	THYMOCYTES	TIDDLEDYWINKS	TIMBERINGS
THRUPPENCE	THUNDERINGS	THYRATRONS	TIDDLYWINK	TIMBERLAND
THRUPPENCES	THUNDERLESS	THYRISTORS	TIDDLYWINKS	TIMBERLANDS
THRUPPENNIES	THUNDEROUS	THYROCALCITONIN	TIDEWAITER	TIMBERLINE
THRUPPENNY	THUNDEROUSLY	THYROGLOBULIN	TIDEWAITERS	TIMBERLINES
THRUSTINGS	THUNDEROUSNESS	THYROGLOBULINS	TIDEWATERS	TIMBERWORK
THRUTCHING	THUNDERSHOWER	THYROIDECTOMIES	TIDINESSES	TIMBERWORKS
THUDDINGLY	THUNDERSHOWERS	THYROIDECTOMY	TIDIVATING	TIMBERYARD
THUGGERIES	THUNDERSTONE	THYROIDITIS	TIDIVATION	TIMBERYARDS
THUMBHOLES	THUNDERSTONES	THYROIDITISES	TIDIVATIONS	TIMBRELLED
THUMBIKINS	THUNDERSTORM	THYROTOXICOSES	TIEBREAKER	TIMBROLOGIES
THUMBLINGS	THUNDERSTORMS	THYROTOXICOSIS	TIEBREAKERS	TIMBROLOGIST
THUMBNAILS	THUNDERSTRICKEN	THYROTROPHIC	TIEMANNITE	TIMBROLOGISTS
THUMBPIECE	THUNDERSTRIKE	THYROTROPHIN	TIEMANNITES	TIMBROLOGY
THUMBPIECES	THUNDERSTRIKES	THYROTROPHINS	TIERCELETS	TIMBROMANIA
THUMBPRINT	THUNDERSTRIKING	THYROTROPIC	TIERCERONS	TIMBROMANIAC
THUMBPRINTS	THUNDERSTROKE	THYROTROPIN	TIGERISHLY	TIMBROMANIACS
THUMBSCREW	THUNDERSTROKES	THYROTROPINS	TIGERISHNESS	TIMBROMANIAS
THUMBSCREWS	THUNDERSTRUCK	THYROXINES	TIGERISHNESSES	TIMBROPHILIES
THUMBSTALL	THURIFEROUS	THYRSOIDAL	TIGERWOODS	TIMBROPHILIST
THUMBSTALLS	THURIFICATION	THYSANOPTEROUS	TIGGYWINKLE	TIMBROPHILISTS
THUMBTACKED	THURIFICATIONS	THYSANURAN	TIGGYWINKLES	TIMBROPHILY
THUMBTACKING	THURIFYING	THYSANURANS	TIGHTASSED	TIMEFRAMES
THUMBTACKS	THUSNESSES	THYSANUROUS	TIGHTASSES	TIMEKEEPER
THUMBWHEEL	THWACKINGS	TIBIOFIBULA	TIGHTENERS	TIMEKEEPERS
THUMBWHEELS	THWARTEDLY	TIBIOFIBULAE	TIGHTENING	TIMEKEEPING
THUMPINGLY	THWARTINGLY	TIBIOFIBULAS	TIGHTFISTED	TIMEKEEPINGS
THUNBERGIA	THWARTINGS	TIBIOTARSI	TIGHTFISTEDNESS	TIMELESSLY
THUNBERGIAS	THWARTSHIP	TIBIOTARSUS	TIGHTISHLY	TIMELESSNESS
THUNDERBIRD	THWARTSHIPS	TIBOUCHINA	TIGHTNESSES	TIMELESSNESSES
THUNDERBIRDS	THWARTWAYS	TIBOUCHINAS	TIGHTROPES	TIMELINESS
THUNDERBOLT	THWARTWISE	TICHORRHINE	TIGHTWIRES	TIMELINESSES
THUNDERBOLTS	THYLACINES	TICKETINGS	TIGRISHNESS	TIMENOGUYS
THUNDERBOX	THYLAKOIDS	TICKETLESS	TIGRISHNESSES	TIMEPASSED
THUNDERBOXES	THYMECTOMIES	TICKETTYBOO	TIKOLOSHES	TIMEPASSES
THUNDERCLAP	THYMECTOMISE	TICKLISHLY	TIKTAALIKS	TIMEPASSING
THUNDERCLAPS	THYMECTOMISED	TICKLISHNESS	TILEFISHES	TIMEPIECES
THUNDERCLOUD	THYMECTOMISES	TICKLISHNESSES	TILIACEOUS	TIMEPLEASER
THUNDERCLOUDS	THYMECTOMISING	TICKTACKED	TILLANDSIA	TIMEPLEASERS

T

TIMESAVERS	TINTINNABULATE	TITIVATIONS	TOBOGGANIST	TOLERATIONS
TIMESAVING	TINTINNABULATED	TITIVATORS	TOBOGGANISTS	TOLERATIVE
TIMESCALES	TINTINNABULATES	TITLEHOLDER	TOBOGGINED	TOLERATORS
TIMESERVER	TINTINNABULOUS	TITLEHOLDERS	TOBOGGINING	TOLLBOOTHS
TIMESERVERS	TINTINNABULUM	TITLEHOLDING	TOCCATELLA	TOLLBRIDGE
TIMESERVING	TINTOMETER	TITRATABLE	TOCCATELLAS	TOLLBRIDGES
TIMESERVINGS	TINTOMETERS	TITRATIONS	TOCCATINAS	TOLLDISHES
TIMESHARES	TINTOOKIES	TITRIMETRIC	TOCHERLESS	TOLLHOUSES
TIMESTAMPED	TIPPYTOEING	TITTERINGLY	TOCOLOGIES	TOLUIDIDES
TIMESTAMPING	TIPSIFYING	TITTERINGS	TOCOPHEROL	TOLUIDINES
TIMESTAMPS	TIPSINESSES	TITTIVATED	TOCOPHEROLS	TOMAHAWKED
TIMETABLED	TIPTRONICS	TITTIVATES	TODDLERHOOD	TOMAHAWKING
TIMETABLES	TIRAILLEUR	TITTIVATING	TODDLERHOODS	TOMATILLOES
TIMETABLING	TIRAILLEURS	TITTIVATION	TOENAILING	TOMATILLOS
TIMEWORKER	TIREDNESSES	TITTIVATIONS	TOERAGGERS	TOMBOYISHLY
TIMEWORKERS	TIRELESSLY	TITTIVATOR	TOFFISHNESS	TOMBOYISHNESS
TIMIDITIES	TIRELESSNESS	TITTIVATORS	TOFFISHNESSES	TOMBOYISHNESSES
TIMIDNESSES	TIRELESSNESSES	TITTLEBATS	TOGAVIRUSES	TOMBSTONES
TIMOCRACIES	TIRESOMELY	TITTUPPING	TOGETHERNESS	TOMCATTING
TIMOCRATIC	TIRESOMENESS	TITUBANCIES	TOGETHERNESSES	TOMFOOLERIES
TIMOCRATICAL	TIRESOMENESSES	TITUBATING	TOILETRIES	TOMFOOLERY
TIMOROUSLY	TIROCINIUM	TITUBATION	TOILFULNESS	TOMFOOLING
TIMOROUSNESS	TIROCINIUMS	TITUBATIONS	TOILFULNESSES	TOMFOOLISH
TIMOROUSNESSES	TITANESSES	TITULARIES	TOILINETTE	TOMFOOLISHNESS
TIMPANISTS	TITANICALLY	TITULARITIES	TOILINETTES	TOMOGRAPHIC
TINCTORIAL	TITANIFEROUS	TITULARITY	TOILSOMELY	TOMOGRAPHIES
TINCTORIALLY	TITANOSAUR	TOADEATERS	TOILSOMENESS	TOMOGRAPHS
TINCTURING	TITANOSAURS	TOADFISHES	TOILSOMENESSES	TOMOGRAPHY
TINDERBOXES	TITANOTHERE	TOADFLAXES	TOKENISTIC	TONALITIES
TINGLINGLY	TITANOTHERES	TOADGRASSES	TOKOLOGIES	TONALITIVE
TINGUAITES	TITARAKURA	TOADRUSHES	TOKOLOSHES	TONELESSLY
TININESSES	TITARAKURAS	TOADSTONES	TOKOLOSHIS	TONELESSNESS
TINKERINGS	TITHINGMAN	TOADSTOOLS	TOKTOKKIES	TONELESSNESSES
TINKERTOYS	TITHINGMEN	TOASTMASTER	TOLBUTAMIDE	TONETICALLY
TINKLINGLY	TITILLATED	TOASTMASTERS	TOLBUTAMIDES	TONGUELESS
TINNINESSES	TITILLATES	TOASTMISTRESS	TOLERABILITIES	TONGUELETS
TINNITUSES	TITILLATING	TOASTMISTRESSES	TOLERABILITY	TONGUELIKE
TINPLATING	TITILLATINGLY	TOBACCANALIAN	TOLERABLENESS	TONGUESTER
TINSELLING	TITILLATION	TOBACCANALIANS	TOLERABLENESSES	TONGUESTERS
TINSELRIES	TITILLATIONS	TOBACCOLESS	TOLERANCES	TONICITIES
TINSMITHING	TITILLATIVE	TOBACCONIST	TOLERANTLY	TONISHNESS
TINSMITHINGS	TITILLATOR	TOBACCONISTS	TOLERATING	TONISHNESSES
TINTINESSES	TITILLATORS	TOBOGGANED	TOLERATION	TONNISHNESS
TINTINNABULA	TITIPOUNAMU	TOBOGGANER	TOLERATIONISM	TONNISHNESSES
TINTINNABULANT	TITIPOUNAMUS	TOBOGGANERS	TOLERATIONISMS	TONOMETERS
TINTINNABULAR	TITIVATING	TOBOGGANING	TOLERATIONIST	TONOMETRIC
TINTINNABULARY	TITIVATION	TOBOGGANINGS	TOLERATIONISTS	TONOMETRIES

T

TONOPLASTS	TOPDRESSINGS	TOPSTITCHED	TORRIDNESSES	TOTALIZATION
TONSILITIS	TOPECTOMIES	TOPSTITCHES	TORRIFYING	TOTALIZATIONS
TONSILITISES	TOPGALLANT	TOPSTITCHING	TORSIBILITIES	TOTALIZATOR
TONSILLARY	TOPGALLANTS	TOPWORKING	TORSIBILITY	TOTALIZATORS
TONSILLECTOMIES	TOPHACEOUS	TORBANITES	TORSIOGRAPH	TOTALIZERS
TONSILLECTOMY	TOPIARISTS	TORBERNITE	TORSIOGRAPHS	TOTALIZING
TONSILLITIC	TOPICALITIES	TORBERNITES	TORSIONALLY	TOTAQUINES
TONSILLITIS	TOPICALITY	TORCHBEARER	TORTELLINI	TOTEMICALLY
TONSILLITISES	TOPKNOTTED	TORCHBEARERS	TORTELLINIS	TOTEMISTIC
TONSILLOTOMIES	TOPLESSNESS	TORCHIERES	TORTFEASOR	TOTIPALMATE
TONSILLOTOMY	TOPLESSNESSES	TORCHLIGHT	TORTFEASORS	TOTIPALMATION
TOOLHOLDER	TOPLOFTICAL	TORCHLIGHTS	TORTICOLLAR	TOTIPALMATIONS
TOOLHOLDERS	TOPLOFTIER	TORCHWOODS	TORTICOLLIS	TOTIPOTENCIES
TOOLHOUSES	TOPLOFTIEST	TORMENTEDLY	TORTICOLLISES	TOTIPOTENCY
TOOLMAKERS	TOPLOFTILY	TORMENTERS	TORTILITIES	TOTIPOTENT
TOOLMAKING	TOPLOFTINESS	TORMENTILS	TORTILLONS	TOTTERINGLY
TOOLMAKINGS	TOPLOFTINESSES	TORMENTING	TORTIOUSLY	TOTTERINGS
TOOLPUSHER	TOPMAKINGS	TORMENTINGLY	TORTOISESHELL	TOUCHABLENESS
TOOLPUSHERS	TOPMINNOWS	TORMENTINGS	TORTOISESHELLS	TOUCHABLENESSES
TOOTHACHES	TOPNOTCHER	TORMENTORS	TORTRICIDS	TOUCHBACKS
TOOTHBRUSH	TOPNOTCHERS	TORMENTUMS	TORTUOSITIES	TOUCHDOWNS
TOOTHBRUSHES	TOPOCENTRIC	TOROIDALLY	TORTUOSITY	TOUCHHOLES
TOOTHBRUSHING	TOPOCHEMISTRIES	TOROSITIES	TORTUOUSLY	TOUCHINESS
TOOTHBRUSHINGS	TOPOCHEMISTRY	TORPEDINOUS	TORTUOUSNESS	TOUCHINESSES
TOOTHCOMBS	TOPOGRAPHER	TORPEDOERS	TORTUOUSNESSES	TOUCHINGLY
TOOTHFISHES	TOPOGRAPHERS	TORPEDOING	TORTUREDLY	TOUCHINGNESS
TOOTHINESS	TOPOGRAPHIC	TORPEDOIST	TORTURESOME	TOUCHINGNESSES
TOOTHINESSES	TOPOGRAPHICAL	TORPEDOISTS	TORTURINGLY	TOUCHLINES
TOOTHPASTE	TOPOGRAPHICALLY	TORPEFYING	TORTURINGS	TOUCHMARKS
TOOTHPASTES	TOPOGRAPHIES	TORPESCENCE	TORTUROUSLY	TOUCHPAPER
TOOTHPICKS	TOPOGRAPHS	TORPESCENCES	TOSSICATED	TOUCHPAPERS
TOOTHSHELL	TOPOGRAPHY	TORPESCENT	TOSTICATED	TOUCHSTONE
TOOTHSHELLS	TOPOLOGICAL	TORPIDITIES	TOSTICATION	TOUCHSTONES
TOOTHSOMELY	TOPOLOGICALLY	TORPIDNESS	TOSTICATIONS	TOUCHTONES
TOOTHSOMENESS	TOPOLOGIES	TORPIDNESSES	TOTALISATION	TOUCHWOODS
TOOTHSOMENESSES	TOPOLOGIST	TORPITUDES	TOTALISATIONS	TOUGHENERS
TOOTHWASHES	TOPOLOGISTS	TORPORIFIC	TOTALISATOR	TOUGHENING
TOOTHWORTS	TOPONYMICAL	TORREFACTION	TOTALISATORS	TOUGHENINGS
TOPAGNOSES	TOPONYMICS	TORREFACTIONS	TOTALISERS	TOUGHNESSES
TOPAGNOSIA	TOPONYMIES	TORREFYING	TOTALISING	TOURBILLION
TOPAGNOSIAS	TOPONYMIST	TORRENTIAL	TOTALISTIC	TOURBILLIONS
TOPAGNOSIS	TOPONYMISTS	TORRENTIALITIES	TOTALITARIAN	TOURBILLON
TOPARCHIES	TOPOPHILIA	TORRENTIALITY	TOTALITARIANISE	TOURBILLONS
TOPAZOLITE	TOPOPHILIAS	TORRENTIALLY	TOTALITARIANISM	TOURISTICALLY
TOPAZOLITES	TOPSCORING	TORRENTUOUS	TOTALITARIANIZE	TOURMALINE
TOPCROSSES	TOPSOILING	TORRIDITIES	TOTALITARIANS	TOURMALINES
TOPDRESSING	TOPSOILINGS	TORRIDNESS	TOTALITIES	TOURMALINIC

T

TOURNAMENT	TOXIGENICITIES	TRACHEOPHYTES	TRADEMARKED	TRADUCINGS
TOURNAMENTS	TOXIGENICITY	TRACHEOSCOPIES	TRADEMARKING	TRADUCTION
TOURNEYERS	TOXIPHAGOUS	TRACHEOSCOPY	TRADEMARKS	TRADUCTIONS
TOURNEYING	TOXIPHOBIA	TRACHEOSTOMIES	TRADENAMES	TRADUCTIVE
TOURNIQUET	TOXIPHOBIAC	TRACHEOSTOMY	TRADERSHIP	TRAFFICABILITY
TOURNIQUETS	TOXIPHOBIACS	TRACHEOTOMIES	TRADERSHIPS	TRAFFICABLE
TOURTIERES	TOXIPHOBIAS	TRACHEOTOMY	TRADESCANTIA	TRAFFICATOR
TOVARICHES	TOXOCARIASES	TRACHINUSES	TRADESCANTIAS	TRAFFICATORS
TOVARISCHES	TOXOCARIASIS	TRACHITISES	TRADESFOLK	TRAFFICKED
TOVARISHES	TOXOPHILIES	TRACHOMATOUS	TRADESFOLKS	TRAFFICKER
TOWARDLINESS	TOXOPHILITE	TRACHYPTERUS	TRADESMANLIKE	TRAFFICKERS
TOWARDLINESSES	TOXOPHILITES	TRACHYPTERUSES	TRADESPEOPLE	TRAFFICKING
TOWARDNESS	TOXOPHILITIC	TRACHYTOID	TRADESPEOPLES	TRAFFICKINGS
TOWARDNESSES	TOXOPLASMA	TRACKBALLS	TRADESWOMAN	TRAFFICLESS
TOWELETTES	TOXOPLASMAS	TRACKERBALL	TRADESWOMEN	TRAGACANTH
TOWELHEADS	TOXOPLASMIC	TRACKERBALLS	TRADITIONAL	TRAGACANTHS
TOWELLINGS	TOXOPLASMOSES	TRACKLAYER	TRADITIONALISE	TRAGEDIANS
TOWERINGLY	TOXOPLASMOSIS	TRACKLAYERS	TRADITIONALISED	TRAGEDIENNE
TOWNHOUSES	TOYISHNESS	TRACKLAYING	TRADITIONALISES	TRAGEDIENNES
TOWNSCAPED	TOYISHNESSES	TRACKLAYINGS	TRADITIONALISM	TRAGELAPHINE
TOWNSCAPES	TRABEATION	TRACKLEMENT	TRADITIONALISMS	TRAGELAPHS
TOWNSCAPING	TRABEATIONS	TRACKLEMENTS	TRADITIONALIST	TRAGICALLY
TOWNSCAPINGS	TRABECULAE	TRACKLESSLY	TRADITIONALISTS	TRAGICALNESS
TOWNSFOLKS	TRABECULAR	TRACKLESSNESS	TRADITIONALITY	TRAGICALNESSES
TOWNSPEOPLE	TRABECULAS	TRACKLESSNESSES	TRADITIONALIZE	TRAGICOMEDIES
TOWNSPEOPLES	TRABECULATE	TRACKROADS	TRADITIONALIZED	TRAGICOMEDY
TOWNSWOMAN	TRABECULATED	TRACKSIDES	TRADITIONALIZES	TRAGICOMIC
TOWNSWOMEN	TRACASSERIE	TRACKSUITS	TRADITIONALLY	TRAGICOMICAL
TOXALBUMIN	TRACASSERIES	TRACKWALKER	TRADITIONARILY	TRAGICOMICALLY
TOXALBUMINS	TRACEABILITIES	TRACKWALKERS	TRADITIONARY	TRAILBASTON
TOXAPHENES	TRACEABILITY	TRACTABILITIES	TRADITIONER	TRAILBASTONS
TOXICATION	TRACEABLENESS	TRACTABILITY	TRADITIONERS	TRAILBLAZER
TOXICATIONS	TRACEABLENESSES	TRACTABLENESS	TRADITIONIST	TRAILBLAZERS
TOXICITIES	TRACELESSLY	TRACTABLENESSES	TRADITIONISTS	TRAILBLAZING
TOXICOGENIC	TRACHEARIAN	TRACTARIAN	TRADITIONLESS	TRAILBLAZINGS
TOXICOLOGIC	TRACHEARIANS	TRACTARIANS	TRADITIONS	TRAILBREAKER
TOXICOLOGICAL	TRACHEARIES	TRACTATORS	TRADITORES	TRAILBREAKERS
TOXICOLOGICALLY	TRACHEATED	TRACTILITIES	TRADUCEMENT	TRAILERABLE
TOXICOLOGIES	TRACHEATES	TRACTILITY	TRADUCEMENTS	TRAILERING
TOXICOLOGIST	TRACHEIDAL	TRACTIONAL	TRADUCIANISM	TRAILERINGS
TOXICOLOGISTS	TRACHEIDES	TRACTORATION	TRADUCIANISMS	TRAILERIST
TOXICOLOGY	TRACHEITIS	TRACTORATIONS	TRADUCIANIST	TRAILERISTS
TOXICOMANIA	TRACHEITISES	TRACTORFEED	TRADUCIANISTIC	TRAILERITE
TOXICOMANIAS	TRACHELATE	TRACTORFEEDS	TRADUCIANISTS	TRAILERITES
TOXICOPHAGOUS	TRACHEOLAR	TRACTRICES	TRADUCIANS	TRAILHEADS
TOXICOPHOBIA	TRACHEOLES	TRADECRAFT	TRADUCIBLE	TRAILINGLY
TOXICOPHOBIAS	TRACHEOPHYTE	TRADECRAFTS	TRADUCINGLY	TRAINABILITIES

TRAINABILITY	TRAMPOLINING	TRANSACTINIDE	TRANSCRIBING	TRANSFERALS
TRAINBANDS	TRAMPOLININGS	TRANSACTINIDES	TRANSCRIPT	TRANSFERASE
TRAINBEARER	TRAMPOLINIST	TRANSACTION	TRANSCRIPTASE	TRANSFERASES
TRAINBEARERS	TRAMPOLINISTS	TRANSACTIONAL	TRANSCRIPTASES	TRANSFEREE
TRAINEESHIP	TRAMPOLINS	TRANSACTIONALLY	TRANSCRIPTION	TRANSFEREES
TRAINEESHIPS	TRANCELIKE	TRANSACTIONS	TRANSCRIPTIONAL	TRANSFERENCE
TRAINLOADS	TRANQUILER	TRANSACTOR	TRANSCRIPTIONS	TRANSFERENCES
TRAINSPOTTERISH	TRANQUILEST	TRANSACTORS	TRANSCRIPTIVE	TRANSFERENTIAL
TRAIPSINGS	TRANQUILISATION	TRANSALPINE	TRANSCRIPTIVELY	TRANSFEROR
TRAITORESS	TRANQUILISE	TRANSALPINES	TRANSCRIPTOME	TRANSFERORS
TRAITORESSES	TRANQUILISED	TRANSAMINASE	TRANSCRIPTOMES	TRANSFERRABLE
TRAITORHOOD	TRANQUILISER	TRANSAMINASES	TRANSCRIPTS	TRANSFERRAL
TRAITORHOODS	TRANQUILISERS	TRANSAMINATION	TRANSCULTURAL	TRANSFERRALS
TRAITORISM	TRANQUILISES	TRANSAMINATIONS	TRANSCURRENT	TRANSFERRED
TRAITORISMS	TRANQUILISING	TRANSANDEAN	TRANSCUTANEOUS	TRANSFERRER
TRAITOROUS	TRANQUILISINGLY	TRANSANDINE	TRANSDERMAL	TRANSFERRERS
TRAITOROUSLY	TRANQUILITIES	TRANSATLANTIC	TRANSDUCED	TRANSFERRIBLE
TRAITOROUSNESS	TRANQUILITY	TRANSAXLES	TRANSDUCER	TRANSFERRIN
TRAITORSHIP	TRANQUILIZATION	TRANSCALENCIES	TRANSDUCERS	TRANSFERRING
TRAITORSHIPS	TRANQUILIZE	TRANSCALENCY	TRANSDUCES	TRANSFERRINS
TRAITRESSES	TRANQUILIZED	TRANSCALENT	TRANSDUCING	TRANSFIGURATION
TRAJECTILE	TRANQUILIZER	TRANSCAUCASIAN	TRANSDUCTANT	TRANSFIGURE
TRAJECTING	TRANQUILIZERS	TRANSCEIVER	TRANSDUCTANTS	TRANSFIGURED
TRAJECTION	TRANQUILIZES	TRANSCEIVERS	TRANSDUCTION	TRANSFIGUREMENT
TRAJECTIONS	TRANQUILIZING	TRANSCENDED	TRANSDUCTIONAL	TRANSFIGURES
TRAJECTORIES	TRANQUILIZINGLY	TRANSCENDENCE	TRANSDUCTIONS	TRANSFIGURING
TRAJECTORY	TRANQUILLER	TRANSCENDENCES	TRANSDUCTOR	TRANSFINITE
TRALATICIOUS	TRANQUILLEST	TRANSCENDENCIES	TRANSDUCTORS	TRANSFIXED
TRALATITIOUS	TRANQUILLISE	TRANSCENDENCY	TRANSECTED	TRANSFIXES
TRAMELLING	TRANQUILLISED	TRANSCENDENT	TRANSECTING	TRANSFIXING
TRAMMELERS	TRANQUILLISER	TRANSCENDENTAL	TRANSECTION	TRANSFIXION
TRAMMELING	TRANQUILLISERS	TRANSCENDENTALS	TRANSECTIONS	TRANSFIXIONS
TRAMMELLED	TRANQUILLISES	TRANSCENDENTLY	TRANSENNAS	TRANSFORMABLE
TRAMMELLER	TRANQUILLISING	TRANSCENDENTS	TRANSEPTAL	TRANSFORMATION
TRAMMELLERS	TRANQUILLITIES	TRANSCENDING	TRANSEPTATE	TRANSFORMATIONS
TRAMMELLING	TRANQUILLITY	TRANSCENDINGLY	TRANSEXUAL	TRANSFORMATIVE
TRAMONTANA	TRANQUILLIZE	TRANSCENDS	TRANSEXUALISM	TRANSFORMED
TRAMONTANAS	TRANQUILLIZED	TRANSCODED	TRANSEXUALISMS	TRANSFORMER
TRAMONTANE	TRANQUILLIZER	TRANSCODES	TRANSEXUALS	TRANSFORMERS
TRAMONTANES	TRANQUILLIZERS	TRANSCODING	TRANSFECTED	TRANSFORMING
TRAMPETTES	TRANQUILLIZES	TRANSCRANIAL	TRANSFECTING	TRANSFORMINGS
TRAMPLINGS	TRANQUILLIZING	TRANSCRIBABLE	TRANSFECTION	TRANSFORMISM
TRAMPOLINE	TRANQUILLY	TRANSCRIBE	TRANSFECTIONS	TRANSFORMISMS
TRAMPOLINED	TRANQUILNESS	TRANSCRIBED	TRANSFECTS	TRANSFORMIST
TRAMPOLINER	TRANQUILNESSES	TRANSCRIBER	TRANSFERABILITY	TRANSFORMISTIC
TRAMPOLINERS	TRANSACTED	TRANSCRIBERS	TRANSFERABLE	TRANSFORMISTS
TRAMPOLINES	TRANSACTING	TRANSCRIBES	TRANSFERAL	TRANSFORMS

T

TRANSFUSABLE
TRANSFUSED
TRANSFUSER
TRANSFUSERS
TRANSFUSES
TRANSFUSIBLE
TRANSFUSING
TRANSFUSION
TRANSFUSIONAL
TRANSFUSIONIST
TRANSFUSIONISTS
TRANSFUSIONS
TRANSFUSIVE
TRANSFUSIVELY
TRANSGENDER
TRANSGENDERED
TRANSGENDERS
TRANSGENES
TRANSGENESES
TRANSGENESIS
TRANSGENIC
TRANSGENICS
TRANSGRESS
TRANSGRESSED
TRANSGRESSES
TRANSGRESSING
TRANSGRESSION
TRANSGRESSIONAL
TRANSGRESSIONS
TRANSGRESSIVE
TRANSGRESSIVELY
TRANSGRESSOR
TRANSGRESSORS
TRANSHIPMENT
TRANSHIPMENTS
TRANSHIPPED
TRANSHIPPER
TRANSHIPPERS
TRANSHIPPING
TRANSHIPPINGS
TRANSHISTORICAL
TRANSHUMANCE
TRANSHUMANCES
TRANSHUMANT
TRANSHUMANTS
TRANSHUMED
TRANSHUMES

TRANSHUMING
TRANSIENCE
TRANSIENCES
TRANSIENCIES
TRANSIENCY
TRANSIENTLY
TRANSIENTNESS
TRANSIENTNESSES
TRANSIENTS
TRANSILIENCE
TRANSILIENCES
TRANSILIENCIES
TRANSILIENCY
TRANSILIENT
TRANSILLUMINATE
TRANSISTHMIAN
TRANSISTOR
TRANSISTORISE
TRANSISTORISED
TRANSISTORISES
TRANSISTORISING
TRANSISTORIZE
TRANSISTORIZED
TRANSISTORIZES
TRANSISTORIZING
TRANSISTORS
TRANSITABLE
TRANSITING
TRANSITION
TRANSITIONAL
TRANSITIONALLY
TRANSITIONALS
TRANSITIONARY
TRANSITIONS
TRANSITIVE
TRANSITIVELY
TRANSITIVENESS
TRANSITIVES
TRANSITIVITIES
TRANSITIVITY
TRANSITORILY
TRANSITORINESS
TRANSITORY
TRANSLATABILITY
TRANSLATABLE
TRANSLATED
TRANSLATES

TRANSLATING
TRANSLATION
TRANSLATIONAL
TRANSLATIONALLY
TRANSLATIONS
TRANSLATIVE
TRANSLATIVES
TRANSLATOR
TRANSLATORIAL
TRANSLATORS
TRANSLATORY
TRANSLEITHAN
TRANSLITERATE
TRANSLITERATED
TRANSLITERATES
TRANSLITERATING
TRANSLITERATION
TRANSLITERATOR
TRANSLITERATORS
TRANSLOCATE
TRANSLOCATED
TRANSLOCATES
TRANSLOCATING
TRANSLOCATION
TRANSLOCATIONS
TRANSLUCENCE
TRANSLUCENCES
TRANSLUCENCIES
TRANSLUCENCY
TRANSLUCENT
TRANSLUCENTLY
TRANSLUCID
TRANSLUCIDITIES
TRANSLUCIDITY
TRANSLUMENAL
TRANSLUMINAL
TRANSLUNAR
TRANSLUNARY
TRANSMANCHE
TRANSMARINE
TRANSMEMBRANE
TRANSMEWED
TRANSMEWING
TRANSMIGRANT
TRANSMIGRANTS
TRANSMIGRATE
TRANSMIGRATED

TRANSMIGRATES
TRANSMIGRATING
TRANSMIGRATION
TRANSMIGRATIONS
TRANSMIGRATIVE
TRANSMIGRATOR
TRANSMIGRATORS
TRANSMIGRATORY
TRANSMISSIBLE
TRANSMISSION
TRANSMISSIONAL
TRANSMISSIONS
TRANSMISSIVE
TRANSMISSIVELY
TRANSMISSIVITY
TRANSMISSOMETER
TRANSMITTABLE
TRANSMITTAL
TRANSMITTALS
TRANSMITTANCE
TRANSMITTANCES
TRANSMITTANCIES
TRANSMITTANCY
TRANSMITTED
TRANSMITTER
TRANSMITTERS
TRANSMITTIBLE
TRANSMITTING
TRANSMITTIVITY
TRANSMOGRIFIED
TRANSMOGRIFIES
TRANSMOGRIFY
TRANSMOGRIFYING
TRANSMONTANE
TRANSMONTANES
TRANSMOUNTAIN
TRANSMOVED
TRANSMOVES
TRANSMOVING
TRANSMUNDANE
TRANSMUTABILITY
TRANSMUTABLE
TRANSMUTABLY
TRANSMUTATION
TRANSMUTATIONAL
TRANSMUTATIONS
TRANSMUTATIVE

TRANSMUTED
TRANSMUTER
TRANSMUTERS
TRANSMUTES
TRANSMUTING
TRANSNATIONAL
TRANSNATURAL
TRANSOCEANIC
TRANSONICS
TRANSPACIFIC
TRANSPADANE
TRANSPARENCE
TRANSPARENCES
TRANSPARENCIES
TRANSPARENCY
TRANSPARENT
TRANSPARENTISE
TRANSPARENTISED
TRANSPARENTISES
TRANSPARENTIZE
TRANSPARENTIZED
TRANSPARENTIZES
TRANSPARENTLY
TRANSPARENTNESS
TRANSPERSONAL
TRANSPICUOUS
TRANSPICUOUSLY
TRANSPIERCE
TRANSPIERCED
TRANSPIERCES
TRANSPIERCING
TRANSPIRABLE
TRANSPIRATION
TRANSPIRATIONAL
TRANSPIRATIONS
TRANSPIRATORY
TRANSPIRED
TRANSPIRES
TRANSPIRING
TRANSPLACENTAL
TRANSPLANT
TRANSPLANTABLE
TRANSPLANTATION
TRANSPLANTED
TRANSPLANTER
TRANSPLANTERS
TRANSPLANTING

T

TRANSPLANTINGS	TRANSSEXUALS	TRANSVERSALS	TRASHTRIES	TRAYMOBILE
TRANSPLANTS	TRANSSHAPE	TRANSVERSE	TRATTORIAS	TRAYMOBILES
TRANSPOLAR	TRANSSHAPED	TRANSVERSED	TRAUCHLING	TRAZODONES
TRANSPONDER	TRANSSHAPES	TRANSVERSELY	TRAUMATICALLY	TREACHERER
TRANSPONDERS	TRANSSHAPING	TRANSVERSENESS	TRAUMATISATION	TREACHERERS
TRANSPONDOR	TRANSSHIPMENT	TRANSVERSES	TRAUMATISATIONS	TREACHERIES
TRANSPONDORS	TRANSSHIPMENTS	TRANSVERSING	TRAUMATISE	TREACHEROUS
TRANSPONTINE	TRANSSHIPPED	TRANSVERSION	TRAUMATISED	TREACHEROUSLY
TRANSPORTABLE	TRANSSHIPPER	TRANSVERSIONS	TRAUMATISES	TREACHEROUSNESS
TRANSPORTAL	TRANSSHIPPERS	TRANSVERTER	TRAUMATISING	TREACHETOUR
TRANSPORTALS	TRANSSHIPPING	TRANSVERTERS	TRAUMATISM	TREACHETOURS
TRANSPORTANCE	TRANSSHIPPINGS	TRANSVESTED	TRAUMATISMS	TREACHOURS
TRANSPORTANCES	TRANSSHIPS	TRANSVESTIC	TRAUMATIZATION	TREACLIEST
TRANSPORTATION	TRANSSONIC	TRANSVESTING	TRAUMATIZATIONS	TREACLINESS
TRANSPORTATIONS	TRANSTHORACIC	TRANSVESTISM	TRAUMATIZE	TREACLINESSES
TRANSPORTED	TRANSUBSTANTIAL	TRANSVESTISMS	TRAUMATIZED	TREADLINGS
TRANSPORTEDLY	TRANSUDATE	TRANSVESTIST	TRAUMATIZES	TREADMILLS
TRANSPORTEDNESS	TRANSUDATES	TRANSVESTISTS	TRAUMATIZING	TREADWHEEL
TRANSPORTER	TRANSUDATION	TRANSVESTITE	TRAUMATOLOGICAL	TREADWHEELS
TRANSPORTERS	TRANSUDATIONS	TRANSVESTITES	TRAUMATOLOGIES	TREASONABLE
TRANSPORTING	TRANSUDATORY	TRANSVESTITISM	TRAUMATOLOGY	TREASONABLENESS
TRANSPORTINGLY	TRANSUDING	TRANSVESTITISMS	TRAUMATONASTIES	TREASONABLY
TRANSPORTINGS	TRANSUMING	TRANSVESTS	TRAUMATONASTY	TREASONOUS
TRANSPORTIVE	TRANSUMPTION	TRAPANNERS	TRAVAILING	TREASURABLE
TRANSPORTS	TRANSUMPTIONS	TRAPANNING	TRAVELATOR	TREASURELESS
TRANSPOSABILITY	TRANSUMPTIVE	TRAPESINGS	TRAVELATORS	TREASURERS
TRANSPOSABLE	TRANSUMPTS	TRAPEZIFORM	TRAVELINGS	TREASURERSHIP
TRANSPOSAL	TRANSURANIAN	TRAPEZISTS	TRAVELLERS	TREASURERSHIPS
TRANSPOSALS	TRANSURANIC	TRAPEZIUMS	TRAVELLING	TREASURIES
TRANSPOSED	TRANSURANICS	TRAPEZIUSES	TRAVELLINGS	TREASURING
TRANSPOSER	TRANSURANIUM	TRAPEZOHEDRA	TRAVELOGUE	TREATABILITIES
TRANSPOSERS	TRANSVAGINAL	TRAPEZOHEDRAL	TRAVELOGUES	TREATABILITY
TRANSPOSES	TRANSVALUATE	TRAPEZOHEDRON	TRAVERSABLE	TREATMENTS
TRANSPOSING	TRANSVALUATED	TRAPEZOHEDRONS	TRAVERSALS	TREATYLESS
TRANSPOSINGS	TRANSVALUATES	TRAPEZOIDAL	TRAVERSERS	TREBBIANOS
TRANSPOSITION	TRANSVALUATING	TRAPEZOIDS	TRAVERSING	TREBLENESS
TRANSPOSITIONAL	TRANSVALUATION	TRAPNESTED	TRAVERSINGS	TREBLENESSES
TRANSPOSITIONS	TRANSVALUATIONS	TRAPNESTING	TRAVERTINE	TREBUCHETS
TRANSPOSITIVE	TRANSVALUE	TRAPPINESS	TRAVERTINES	TREBUCKETS
TRANSPOSON	TRANSVALUED	TRAPPINESSES	TRAVERTINS	TRECENTIST
TRANSPOSONS	TRANSVALUER	TRAPSHOOTER	TRAVESTIED	TRECENTISTS
TRANSPUTER	TRANSVALUERS	TRAPSHOOTERS	TRAVESTIES	TREDECILLION
TRANSPUTERS	TRANSVALUES	TRAPSHOOTING	TRAVESTYING	TREDECILLIONS
TRANSSEXUAL	TRANSVALUING	TRAPSHOOTINGS	TRAVOLATOR	TREDRILLES
TRANSSEXUALISM	TRANSVERSAL	TRASHERIES	TRAVOLATORS	TREEHOPPER
TRANSSEXUALISMS	TRANSVERSALITY	TRASHINESS	TRAWLERMAN	TREEHOPPERS
TRANSSEXUALITY	TRANSVERSALLY	TRASHINESSES	TRAWLERMEN	TREEHOUSES

T

TREELESSNESS	TRENDSETTER	TRIALLISTS	TRIBULATION	TRICHINOSIS
TREELESSNESSES	TRENDSETTERS	TRIALOGUES	TRIBULATIONS	TRICHINOTIC
TREENWARES	TRENDSETTING	TRIALWARES	TRIBUNATES	TRICHINOUS
TREGETOURS	TRENDSETTINGS	TRIAMCINOLONE	TRIBUNESHIP	TRICHLORACETIC
TREHALOSES	TRENDYISMS	TRIAMCINOLONES	TRIBUNESHIPS	TRICHLORFON
TREILLAGED	TREPANATION	TRIANDRIAN	TRIBUNICIAL	TRICHLORFONS
TREILLAGES	TREPANATIONS	TRIANDROUS	TRIBUNICIAN	TRICHLORIDE
TREKSCHUIT	TREPANNERS	TRIANGULAR	TRIBUNITIAL	TRICHLORIDES
TREKSCHUITS	TREPANNING	TRIANGULARITIES	TRIBUNITIAN	TRICHLOROACETIC
TRELLISING	TREPANNINGS	TRIANGULARITY	TRIBUTARIES	TRICHLOROETHANE
TRELLISWORK	TREPHINATION	TRIANGULARLY	TRIBUTARILY	TRICHLORPHON
TRELLISWORKS	TREPHINATIONS	TRIANGULATE	TRIBUTARINESS	TRICHLORPHONS
TREMATODES	TREPHINERS	TRIANGULATED	TRIBUTARINESSES	TRICHOBACTERIA
TREMATOIDS	TREPHINING	TRIANGULATELY	TRICAMERAL	TRICHOCYST
TREMBLEMENT	TREPHININGS	TRIANGULATES	TRICARBOXYLIC	TRICHOCYSTIC
TREMBLEMENTS	TREPIDATION	TRIANGULATING	TRICARPELLARY	TRICHOCYSTS
TREMBLIEST	TREPIDATIONS	TRIANGULATION	TRICENTENARIES	TRICHOGYNE
TREMBLINGLY	TREPIDATORY	TRIANGULATIONS	TRICENTENARY	TRICHOGYNES
TREMBLINGS	TREPONEMAL	TRIAPSIDAL	TRICENTENNIAL	TRICHOGYNIAL
TREMENDOUS	TREPONEMAS	TRIARCHIES	TRICENTENNIALS	TRICHOGYNIC
TREMENDOUSLY	TREPONEMATA	TRIATHLETE	TRICEPHALOUS	TRICHOLOGICAL
TREMENDOUSNESS	TREPONEMATOSES	TRIATHLETES	TRICERATOPS	TRICHOLOGIES
TREMOLANDI	TREPONEMATOSIS	TRIATHLONS	TRICERATOPSES	TRICHOLOGIST
TREMOLANDO	TREPONEMATOUS	TRIATOMICALLY	TRICERIONS	TRICHOLOGISTS
TREMOLANDOS	TREPONEMES	TRIAXIALITIES	TRICHIASES	TRICHOLOGY
TREMOLANTS	TRESPASSED	TRIAXIALITY	TRICHIASIS	TRICHOMONACIDAL
TREMOLITES	TRESPASSER	TRIBADISMS	TRICHINELLA	TRICHOMONACIDE
TREMOLITIC	TRESPASSERS	TRIBALISMS	TRICHINELLAE	TRICHOMONACIDES
TREMORLESS	TRESPASSES	TRIBALISTIC	TRICHINELLAS	TRICHOMONAD
TREMULANTS	TRESPASSING	TRIBALISTS	TRICHINIASES	TRICHOMONADAL
TREMULATED	TRESTLETREE	TRIBESPEOPLE	TRICHINIASIS	TRICHOMONADS
TREMULATES	TRESTLETREES	TRIBESWOMAN	TRICHINISATION	TRICHOMONAL
TREMULATING	TRESTLEWORK	TRIBESWOMEN	TRICHINISATIONS	TRICHOMONIASES
TREMULOUSLY	TRESTLEWORKS	TRIBOELECTRIC	TRICHINISE	TRICHOMONIASIS
TREMULOUSNESS	TRETINOINS	TRIBOLOGICAL	TRICHINISED	TRICHOPHYTON
TREMULOUSNESSES	TREVALLIES	TRIBOLOGIES	TRICHINISES	TRICHOPHYTONS
TRENCHANCIES	TRIABLENESS	TRIBOLOGIST	TRICHINISING	TRICHOPHYTOSES
TRENCHANCY	TRIABLENESSES	TRIBOLOGISTS	TRICHINIZATION	TRICHOPHYTOSIS
TRENCHANTLY	TRIACETATE	TRIBOMETER	TRICHINIZATIONS	TRICHOPTERAN
TRENCHARDS	TRIACETATES	TRIBOMETERS	TRICHINIZE	TRICHOPTERANS
TRENCHERMAN	TRIACONTER	TRIBRACHIAL	TRICHINIZED	TRICHOPTERIST
TRENCHERMEN	TRIACONTERS	TRIBRACHIC	TRICHINIZES	TRICHOPTERISTS
TRENDIFIED	TRIACTINAL	TRIBROMOETHANOL	TRICHINIZING	TRICHOPTEROUS
TRENDIFIES	TRIADELPHOUS	TRIBROMOMETHANE	TRICHINOSE	TRICHOTHECENE
TRENDIFYING	TRIADICALLY	TRIBULATED	TRICHINOSED	TRICHOTHECENES
TRENDINESS	TRIALITIES	TRIBULATES	TRICHINOSES	TRICHOTOMIC
TRENDINESSES	TRIALLINGS	TRIBULATING	TRICHINOSING	TRICHOTOMIES

T

TRICHOTOMISE	TRICONSONANTAL	TRIFOLIOLATE	TRILATERALIST	TRINACRIAN
TRICHOTOMISED	TRICONSONANTIC	TRIFOLIUMS	TRILATERALISTS	TRINACRIFORM
TRICHOTOMISES	TRICORNERED	TRIFURCATE	TRILATERALLY	TRINISCOPE
TRICHOTOMISING	TRICORPORATE	TRIFURCATED	TRILATERALS	TRINISCOPES
TRICHOTOMIZE	TRICORPORATED	TRIFURCATES	TRILATERATION	TRINITARIAN
TRICHOTOMIZED	TRICOSTATE	TRIFURCATING	TRILATERATIONS	TRINITRATE
TRICHOTOMIZES	TRICOTEUSE	TRIFURCATION	TRILINEATE	TRINITRATES
TRICHOTOMIZING	TRICOTEUSES	TRIFURCATIONS	TRILINGUAL	TRINITRINS
TRICHOTOMOUS	TRICOTINES	TRIGAMISTS	TRILINGUALISM	TRINITROBENZENE
TRICHOTOMOUSLY	TRICROTISM	TRIGEMINAL	TRILINGUALISMS	TRINITROCRESOL
TRICHOTOMY	TRICROTISMS	TRIGEMINALS	TRILINGUALLY	TRINITROCRESOLS
TRICHROISM	TRICROTOUS	TRIGEMINUS	TRILITERAL	TRINITROPHENOL
TRICHROISMS	TRICUSPIDAL	TRIGGERFISH	TRILITERALISM	TRINITROPHENOLS
TRICHROMAT	TRICUSPIDATE	TRIGGERFISHES	TRILITERALISMS	TRINITROTOLUENE
TRICHROMATIC	TRICUSPIDS	TRIGGERING	TRILITERALS	TRINITROTOLUOL
TRICHROMATISM	TRICYCLERS	TRIGGERLESS	TRILITHONS	TRINITROTOLUOLS
TRICHROMATISMS	TRICYCLICS	TRIGGERMAN	TRILLIONAIRE	TRINKETERS
TRICHROMATS	TRICYCLING	TRIGGERMEN	TRILLIONAIRES	TRINKETING
TRICHROMIC	TRICYCLINGS	TRIGLYCERIDE	TRILLIONTH	TRINKETINGS
TRICHROMICS	TRICYCLIST	TRIGLYCERIDES	TRILLIONTHS	TRINKETRIES
TRICHRONOUS	TRICYCLISTS	TRIGLYPHIC	TRILOBATED	TRINOCULAR
TRICHURIASES	TRIDACTYLOUS	TRIGLYPHICAL	TRILOBITES	TRINOMIALISM
TRICHURIASIS	TRIDENTATE	TRIGNESSES	TRILOBITIC	TRINOMIALISMS
TRICKERIES	TRIDIMENSIONAL	TRIGONALLY	TRILOCULAR	TRINOMIALIST
TRICKINESS	TRIDOMINIA	TRIGONOMETER	TRIMERISMS	TRINOMIALISTS
TRICKINESSES	TRIDOMINIUM	TRIGONOMETERS	TRIMESTERS	TRINOMIALLY
TRICKISHLY	TRIDYMITES	TRIGONOMETRIC	TRIMESTRAL	TRINOMIALS
TRICKISHNESS	TRIENNIALLY	TRIGONOMETRICAL	TRIMESTRIAL	TRINUCLEOTIDE
TRICKISHNESSES	TRIENNIALS	TRIGONOMETRIES	TRIMETHADIONE	TRINUCLEOTIDES
TRICKLIEST	TRIENNIUMS	TRIGONOMETRY	TRIMETHADIONES	TRIOECIOUS
TRICKLINGLY	TRIERARCHAL	TRIGRAMMATIC	TRIMETHOPRIM	TRIOXOBORIC
TRICKLINGS	TRIERARCHIES	TRIGRAMMIC	TRIMETHOPRIMS	TRIOXYGENS
TRICKSIEST	TRIERARCHS	TRIGRAPHIC	TRIMETHYLAMINE	TRIPALMITIN
TRICKSINESS	TRIERARCHY	TRIHALOMETHANE	TRIMETHYLAMINES	TRIPALMITINS
TRICKSINESSES	TRIETHYLAMINE	TRIHALOMETHANES	TRIMETHYLENE	TRIPARTISM
TRICKSTERING	TRIETHYLAMINES	TRIHEDRALS	TRIMETHYLENES	TRIPARTISMS
TRICKSTERINGS	TRIFACIALS	TRIHEDRONS	TRIMETRICAL	TRIPARTITE
TRICKSTERS	TRIFARIOUS	TRIHYBRIDS	TRIMETROGON	TRIPARTITELY
TRICKTRACK	TRIFFIDIAN	TRIHYDRATE	TRIMETROGONS	TRIPARTITION
TRICKTRACKS	TRIFLINGLY	TRIHYDRATED	TRIMMINGLY	TRIPARTITIONS
TRICLINIUM	TRIFLINGNESS	TRIHYDRATES	TRIMNESSES	TRIPEHOUND
TRICLOSANS	TRIFLINGNESSES	TRIHYDROXY	TRIMOLECULAR	TRIPEHOUNDS
TRICOLETTE	TRIFLUOPERAZINE	TRIIODOMETHANE	TRIMONTHLY	TRIPERSONAL
TRICOLETTES	TRIFLURALIN	TRIIODOMETHANES	TRIMORPHIC	TRIPERSONALISM
TRICOLORED	TRIFLURALINS	TRILATERAL	TRIMORPHISM	TRIPERSONALISMS
TRICOLOURED	TRIFOLIATE	TRILATERALISM	TRIMORPHISMS	TRIPERSONALIST
TRICOLOURS	TRIFOLIATED	TRILATERALISMS	TRIMORPHOUS	TRIPERSONALISTS

T

TRIPERSONALITY	TRIQUETROUSLY	TRITHEISMS	TRIVALENCE	TROCHOTRON
TRIPETALOUS	TRIQUETRUM	TRITHEISTIC	TRIVALENCES	TROCHOTRONS
TRIPHAMMER	TRIRADIATE	TRITHEISTICAL	TRIVALENCIES	TROCTOLITE
TRIPHAMMERS	TRIRADIATELY	TRITHEISTS	TRIVALENCY	TROCTOLITES
TRIPHENYLAMINE	TRISACCHARIDE	TRITHIONATE	TRIVALVULAR	TROGLODYTE
TRIPHENYLAMINES	TRISACCHARIDES	TRITHIONATES	TRIVIALISATION	TROGLODYTES
TRIPHIBIOUS	TRISAGIONS	TRITHIONIC	TRIVIALISATIONS	TROGLODYTIC
TRIPHOSPHATE	TRISECTING	TRITIATING	TRIVIALISE	TROGLODYTICAL
TRIPHOSPHATES	TRISECTION	TRITIATION	TRIVIALISED	TROGLODYTISM
TRIPHTHONG	TRISECTIONS	TRITIATIONS	TRIVIALISES	TROGLODYTISMS
TRIPHTHONGAL	TRISECTORS	TRITICALES	TRIVIALISING	TROLLEYBUS
TRIPHTHONGS	TRISECTRICES	TRITICALLY	TRIVIALISM	TROLLEYBUSES
TRIPHYLITE	TRISECTRIX	TRITICALNESS	TRIVIALISMS	TROLLEYBUSSES
TRIPHYLITES	TRISKELION	TRITICALNESSES	TRIVIALIST	TROLLEYING
TRIPHYLLOUS	TRISKELIONS	TRITICEOUS	TRIVIALISTS	TROLLIUSES
TRIPINNATE	TRISOCTAHEDRA	TRITICISMS	TRIVIALITIES	TROLLOPEES
TRIPINNATELY	TRISOCTAHEDRAL	TRITUBERCULAR	TRIVIALITY	TROLLOPING
TRIPITAKAS	TRISOCTAHEDRON	TRITUBERCULATE	TRIVIALIZATION	TROLLOPISH
TRIPLENESS	TRISOCTAHEDRONS	TRITUBERCULIES	TRIVIALIZATIONS	TROMBICULID
TRIPLENESSES	TRISTEARIN	TRITUBERCULISM	TRIVIALIZE	TROMBICULIDS
TRIPLETAIL	TRISTEARINS	TRITUBERCULISMS	TRIVIALIZED	TROMBIDIASES
TRIPLETAILS	TRISTESSES	TRITUBERCULY	TRIVIALIZES	TROMBIDIASIS
TRIPLICATE	TRISTFULLY	TRITURABLE	TRIVIALIZING	TROMBONIST
TRIPLICATED	TRISTFULNESS	TRITURATED	TRIVIALNESS	TROMBONISTS
TRIPLICATES	TRISTFULNESSES	TRITURATES	TRIVIALNESSES	TROMOMETER
TRIPLICATING	TRISTICHIC	TRITURATING	TRIWEEKLIES	TROMOMETERS
TRIPLICATION	TRISTICHOUS	TRITURATION	TROCHAICALLY	TROMOMETRIC
TRIPLICATIONS	TRISTIMULUS	TRITURATIONS	TROCHANTER	TROOPSHIPS
TRIPLICITIES	TRISUBSTITUTED	TRITURATOR	TROCHANTERAL	TROOSTITES
TRIPLICITY	TRISULCATE	TRITURATORS	TROCHANTERIC	TROPAEOLIN
TRIPLOBLASTIC	TRISULFIDE	TRIUMPHALISM	TROCHANTERS	TROPAEOLINS
TRIPLOIDIES	TRISULFIDES	TRIUMPHALISMS	TROCHEAMETER	TROPAEOLUM
TRIPPERISH	TRISULPHIDE	TRIUMPHALIST	TROCHEAMETERS	TROPAEOLUMS
TRIPPINGLY	TRISULPHIDES	TRIUMPHALISTS	TROCHELMINTH	TROPEOLINS
TRIPTEROUS	TRISYLLABIC	TRIUMPHALS	TROCHELMINTHS	TROPHALLACTIC
TRIPTYQUES	TRISYLLABICAL	TRIUMPHANT	TROCHILUSES	TROPHALLAXES
TRIPUDIARY	TRISYLLABICALLY	TRIUMPHANTLY	TROCHISCUS	TROPHALLAXIS
TRIPUDIATE	TRISYLLABLE	TRIUMPHERIES	TROCHISCUSES	TROPHESIAL
TRIPUDIATED	TRISYLLABLES	TRIUMPHERS	TROCHLEARS	TROPHESIES
TRIPUDIATES	TRITAGONIST	TRIUMPHERY	TROCHOIDAL	TROPHICALLY
TRIPUDIATING	TRITAGONISTS	TRIUMPHING	TROCHOIDALLY	TROPHOBIOSES
TRIPUDIATION	TRITANOPES	TRIUMPHINGS	TROCHOMETER	TROPHOBIOSIS
TRIPUDIATIONS	TRITANOPIA	TRIUMVIRAL	TROCHOMETERS	TROPHOBIOTIC
TRIPUDIUMS	TRITANOPIAS	TRIUMVIRATE	TROCHOPHORE	TROPHOBLAST
TRIQUETRAE	TRITANOPIC	TRIUMVIRATES	TROCHOPHORES	TROPHOBLASTIC
TRIQUETRAL	TRITENESSES	TRIUMVIRIES	TROCHOSPHERE	TROPHOBLASTS
TRIQUETROUS	TRITERNATE	TRIUNITIES	TROCHOSPHERES	TROPHOLOGIES

TROPHOLOGY	TROPOSPHERIC	TRUCKLOADS	TRUSTFULNESS	TSCHERNOSEMS
TROPHONEUROSES	TROPOTAXES	TRUCKMASTER	TRUSTFULNESSES	TSESAREVICH
TROPHONEUROSIS	TROPOTAXIS	TRUCKMASTERS	TRUSTINESS	TSESAREVICHES
TROPHOPLASM	TROTHPLIGHT	TRUCKSTOPS	TRUSTINESSES	TSESAREVITCH
TROPHOPLASMS	TROTHPLIGHTED	TRUCULENCE	TRUSTINGLY	TSESAREVITCHES
TROPHOTACTIC	TROTHPLIGHTING	TRUCULENCES	TRUSTINGNESS	TSESAREVNA
TROPHOTAXES	TROTHPLIGHTS	TRUCULENCIES	TRUSTINGNESSES	TSESAREVNAS
TROPHOTAXIS	TROUBADOUR	TRUCULENCY	TRUSTLESSLY	TSESAREWICH
TROPHOTROPIC	TROUBADOURS	TRUCULENTLY	TRUSTLESSNESS	TSESAREWICHES
TROPHOTROPISM	TROUBLEDLY	TRUEHEARTED	TRUSTLESSNESSES	TSESAREWITCH
TROPHOTROPISMS	TROUBLEFREE	TRUEHEARTEDNESS	TRUSTWORTHILY	TSESAREWITCHES
TROPHOZOITE	TROUBLEMAKER	TRUENESSES	TRUSTWORTHINESS	TSOTSITAAL
TROPHOZOITES	TROUBLEMAKERS	TRUEPENNIES	TRUSTWORTHY	TSOTSITAALS
TROPICALISATION	TROUBLEMAKING	TRUFFLINGS	TRUTHFULLY	TSUTSUGAMUSHI
TROPICALISE	TROUBLEMAKINGS	TRUMPERIES	TRUTHFULNESS	TSUTSUGAMUSHIS
TROPICALISED	TROUBLESHOOT	TRUMPETERS	TRUTHFULNESSES	TUBBINESSES
TROPICALISES	TROUBLESHOOTER	TRUMPETING	TRUTHINESS	TUBECTOMIES
TROPICALISING	TROUBLESHOOTERS	TRUMPETINGS	TRUTHINESSES	TUBERACEOUS
TROPICALITIES	TROUBLESHOOTING	TRUMPETLIKE	TRUTHLESSNESS	TUBERCULAR
TROPICALITY	TROUBLESHOOTS	TRUMPETWEED	TRUTHLESSNESSES	TUBERCULARLY
TROPICALIZATION	TROUBLESHOT	TRUMPETWEEDS	TRYINGNESS	TUBERCULARS
TROPICALIZE	TROUBLESOME	TRUNCATELY	TRYINGNESSES	TUBERCULATE
TROPICALIZED	TROUBLESOMELY	TRUNCATING	TRYPAFLAVINE	TUBERCULATED
TROPICALIZES	TROUBLESOMENESS	TRUNCATION	TRYPAFLAVINES	TUBERCULATELY
TROPICALIZING	TROUBLINGS	TRUNCATIONS	TRYPANOCIDAL	TUBERCULATION
TROPICALLY	TROUBLOUSLY	TRUNCHEONED	TRYPANOCIDE	TUBERCULATIONS
TROPICBIRD	TROUBLOUSNESS	TRUNCHEONER	TRYPANOCIDES	TUBERCULES
TROPICBIRDS	TROUBLOUSNESSES	TRUNCHEONERS	TRYPANOSOMAL	TUBERCULIN
TROPISMATIC	TROUGHLIKE	TRUNCHEONING	TRYPANOSOME	TUBERCULINS
TROPOCOLLAGEN	TROUNCINGS	TRUNCHEONS	TRYPANOSOMES	TUBERCULISATION
TROPOCOLLAGENS	TROUSERING	TRUNKFISHES	TRYPANOSOMIASES	TUBERCULISE
TROPOLOGIC	TROUSERINGS	TRUNKSLEEVE	TRYPANOSOMIASIS	TUBERCULISED
TROPOLOGICAL	TROUSERLESS	TRUNKSLEEVES	TRYPANOSOMIC	TUBERCULISES
TROPOLOGICALLY	TROUSSEAUS	TRUNKWORKS	TRYPARSAMIDE	TUBERCULISING
TROPOLOGIES	TROUSSEAUX	TRUNNIONED	TRYPARSAMIDES	TUBERCULIZATION
TROPOMYOSIN	TROUTLINGS	TRUSTABILITIES	TRYPSINOGEN	TUBERCULIZE
TROPOMYOSINS	TROUTSTONE	TRUSTABILITY	TRYPSINOGENS	TUBERCULIZED
TROPOPAUSE	TROUTSTONES	TRUSTAFARIAN	TRYPTAMINE	TUBERCULIZES
TROPOPAUSES	TROUVAILLE	TRUSTAFARIANS	TRYPTAMINES	TUBERCULIZING
TROPOPHILOUS	TROUVAILLES	TRUSTBUSTER	TRYPTOPHAN	TUBERCULOID
TROPOPHYTE	TROWELLERS	TRUSTBUSTERS	TRYPTOPHANE	TUBERCULOMA
TROPOPHYTES	TROWELLING	TRUSTBUSTING	TRYPTOPHANES	TUBERCULOMAS
TROPOPHYTIC	TRUANTRIES	TRUSTBUSTINGS	TRYPTOPHANS	TUBERCULOMATA
TROPOSCATTER	TRUANTSHIP	TRUSTEEING	TSAREVICHES	TUBERCULOSE
TROPOSCATTERS	TRUANTSHIPS	TRUSTEESHIP	TSAREVITCH	TUBERCULOSED
TROPOSPHERE	TRUCKLINES	TRUSTEESHIPS	TSAREVITCHES	TUBERCULOSES
TROPOSPHERES	TRUCKLINGS	TRUSTFULLY	TSCHERNOSEM	TUBERCULOSIS

T

TUBERCULOUS	TULIPOMANIAS	TUNEFULNESS	TURBULATORS	TURRICULATE
TUBERCULOUSLY	TULIPWOODS	TUNEFULNESSES	TURBULENCE	TURRICULATED
TUBERCULUM	TUMATAKURU	TUNELESSLY	TURBULENCES	TURTLEBACK
TUBERIFEROUS	TUMATAKURUS	TUNELESSNESS	TURBULENCIES	TURTLEBACKS
TUBERIFORM	TUMBLEBUGS	TUNELESSNESSES	TURBULENCY	TURTLEDOVE
TUBEROSITIES	TUMBLEDOWN	TUNESMITHS	TURBULENTLY	TURTLEDOVES
TUBEROSITY	TUMBLEHOME	TUNGSTATES	TURCOPOLES	TURTLEHEAD
TUBICOLOUS	TUMBLEHOMES	TUNGSTITES	TURCOPOLIER	TURTLEHEADS
TUBIFICIDS	TUMBLERFUL	TUNNELINGS	TURCOPOLIERS	TURTLENECK
TUBIFLOROUS	TUMBLERFULS	TUNNELLERS	TURDUCKENS	TURTLENECKED
TUBOCURARINE	TUMBLERSFUL	TUNNELLIKE	TURFGRASSES	TURTLENECKS
TUBOCURARINES	TUMBLESETS	TUNNELLING	TURFINESSES	TUTELARIES
TUBOPLASTIES	TUMBLEWEED	TUNNELLINGS	TURFSKIING	TUTIORISMS
TUBOPLASTY	TUMBLEWEEDS	TUPPENNIES	TURFSKIINGS	TUTIORISTS
TUBULARIAN	TUMEFACIENT	TURACOVERDIN	TURGENCIES	TUTORESSES
TUBULARIANS	TUMEFACTION	TURACOVERDINS	TURGESCENCE	TUTORIALLY
TUBULARITIES	TUMEFACTIONS	TURANGAWAEWAE	TURGESCENCES	TUTORISING
TUBULARITY	TUMESCENCE	TURANGAWAEWAES	TURGESCENCIES	TUTORIZING
TUBULATING	TUMESCENCES	TURBELLARIAN	TURGESCENCY	TUTORSHIPS
TUBULATION	TUMESCENTLY	TURBELLARIANS	TURGESCENT	TUTOYERING
TUBULATIONS	TUMIDITIES	TURBIDIMETER	TURGIDITIES	TUTWORKERS
TUBULATORS	TUMIDNESSES	TURBIDIMETERS	TURGIDNESS	TUTWORKMAN
TUBULATURE	TUMORGENIC	TURBIDIMETRIC	TURGIDNESSES	TUTWORKMEN
TUBULATURES	TUMORGENICITIES	TURBIDIMETRIES	TURMOILING	TWADDLIEST
TUBULIFLORAL	TUMORGENICITY	TURBIDIMETRY	TURNABOUTS	TWADDLINGS
TUBULIFLOROUS	TUMORIGENESES	TURBIDITES	TURNAGAINS	TWALPENNIES
TUBULOUSLY	TUMORIGENESIS	TURBIDITIES	TURNAROUND	TWANGINGLY
TUCKERBAGS	TUMORIGENIC	TURBIDNESS	TURNAROUNDS	TWANGLINGLY
TUCKERBOXES	TUMORIGENICITY	TURBIDNESSES	TURNBROACH	TWANGLINGS
TUFFACEOUS	TUMULOSITIES	TURBINACIOUS	TURNBROACHES	TWATTLINGS
TUFFTAFFETA	TUMULOSITY	TURBINATED	TURNBUCKLE	TWAYBLADES
TUFFTAFFETAS	TUMULTUARY	TURBINATES	TURNBUCKLES	TWEEDINESS
TUFFTAFFETIES	TUMULTUATE	TURBINATION	TURNROUNDS	TWEEDINESSES
TUFFTAFFETY	TUMULTUATED	TURBINATIONS	TURNSTILES	TWEEDLEDEE
TUFTAFFETA	TUMULTUATES	TURBOCHARGED	TURNSTONES	TWEEDLEDEED
TUFTAFFETAS	TUMULTUATING	TURBOCHARGER	TURNTABLES	TWEEDLEDEEING
TUFTAFFETIES	TUMULTUATION	TURBOCHARGERS	TURNVEREIN	TWEEDLEDEES
TUFTAFFETY	TUMULTUATIONS	TURBOCHARGING	TURNVEREINS	TWEENAGERS
TUILLETTES	TUMULTUOUS	TURBOCHARGINGS	TUROPHILES	TWEENESSES
TUILYIEING	TUMULTUOUSLY	TURBOELECTRIC	TURPENTINE	TWELVEFOLD
TUILZIEING	TUMULTUOUSNESS	TURBOGENERATOR	TURPENTINED	TWELVEMONTH
TUITIONARY	TUNABILITIES	TURBOGENERATORS	TURPENTINES	TWELVEMONTHS
TULARAEMIA	TUNABILITY	TURBOMACHINERY	TURPENTINING	TWENTIETHS
TULARAEMIAS	TUNABLENESS	TURBOPROPS	TURPENTINY	TWENTYFOLD
TULARAEMIC	TUNABLENESSES	TURBOSHAFT	TURPITUDES	TWENTYFOLDS
TULAREMIAS	TUNBELLIED	TURBOSHAFTS	TURQUOISES	TWICHILDREN
TULIPOMANIA	TUNBELLIES	TURBULATOR	TURRIBANTS	TWIDDLIEST

T

TWIDDLINGS	TYMPANIFORM	TYPEWRITES	TYPOGRAPHIES	TYRANNIZED
TWILIGHTED	TYMPANISTS	TYPEWRITING	TYPOGRAPHING	TYRANNIZER
TWILIGHTING	TYMPANITES	TYPEWRITINGS	TYPOGRAPHIST	TYRANNIZERS
TWINBERRIES	TYMPANITESES	TYPEWRITTEN	TYPOGRAPHISTS	TYRANNIZES
TWINFLOWER	TYMPANITIC	TYPHACEOUS	TYPOGRAPHS	TYRANNIZING
TWINFLOWERS	TYMPANITIS	TYPHLITISES	TYPOGRAPHY	TYRANNOSAUR
TWINKLINGS	TYMPANITISES	TYPHLOLOGIES	TYPOLOGICAL	TYRANNOSAURS
TWISTABILITIES	TYNDALLIMETRIES	TYPHLOLOGY	TYPOLOGICALLY	TYRANNOSAURUS
TWISTABILITY	TYNDALLIMETRY	TYPHLOSOLE	TYPOLOGIES	TYRANNOSAURUSES
TWITCHIEST	TYPECASTER	TYPHLOSOLES	TYPOLOGIST	TYRANNOUSLY
TWITCHINGS	TYPECASTERS	TYPHOGENIC	TYPOLOGISTS	TYRANNOUSNESS
TWITTERERS	TYPECASTING	TYPHOIDINS	TYPOMANIAS	TYRANNOUSNESSES
TWITTERING	TYPEFOUNDER	TYPICALITIES	TYPOTHETAE	TYROCIDINE
TWITTERINGLY	TYPEFOUNDERS	TYPICALITY	TYRANNESSES	TYROCIDINES
TWITTERINGS	TYPEFOUNDING	TYPICALNESS	TYRANNICAL	TYROCIDINS
TWITTINGLY	TYPEFOUNDINGS	TYPICALNESSES	TYRANNICALLY	TYROGLYPHID
TWOFOLDNESS	TYPESCRIPT	TYPIFICATION	TYRANNICALNESS	TYROGLYPHIDS
TWOFOLDNESSES	TYPESCRIPTS	TYPIFICATIONS	TYRANNICIDAL	TYROPITTAS
TWOPENCEWORTH	TYPESETTER	TYPOGRAPHED	TYRANNICIDE	TYROSINASE
TWOPENCEWORTHS	TYPESETTERS	TYPOGRAPHER	TYRANNICIDES	TYROSINASES
TWOPENNIES	TYPESETTING	TYPOGRAPHERS	TYRANNISED	TYROTHRICIN
TWOSEATERS	TYPESETTINGS	TYPOGRAPHIA	TYRANNISER	TYROTHRICINS
TYCOONATES	TYPESTYLES	TYPOGRAPHIC	TYRANNISERS	
TYCOONERIES	TYPEWRITER	TYPOGRAPHICAL	TYRANNISES	
TYLECTOMIES	TYPEWRITERS	TYPOGRAPHICALLY	TYRANNISING	

T

U

UBERSEXUAL
UBERSEXUALS
UBIQUARIAN
UBIQUINONE
UBIQUINONES
UBIQUITARIAN
UBIQUITARIANISM
UBIQUITARIANS
UBIQUITARY
UBIQUITIES
UBIQUITINATION
UBIQUITINATIONS
UBIQUITINS
UBIQUITOUS
UBIQUITOUSLY
UBIQUITOUSNESS
UDOMETRIES
UFOLOGICAL
UFOLOGISTS
UGLIFICATION
UGLIFICATIONS
UGLINESSES
UGSOMENESS
UGSOMENESSES
UINTAHITES
UINTATHERE
UINTATHERES
UITLANDERS
ULCERATING
ULCERATION
ULCERATIONS
ULCERATIVE
ULCEROGENIC
ULCEROUSLY
ULCEROUSNESS
ULCEROUSNESSES
ULOTRICHIES
ULOTRICHOUS
ULSTERETTE
ULSTERETTES
ULTERIORLY
ULTIMACIES
ULTIMATELY
ULTIMATENESS
ULTIMATENESSES

ULTIMATING
ULTIMATUMS
ULTIMOGENITURE
ULTIMOGENITURES
ULTRABASIC
ULTRABASICS
ULTRACAREFUL
ULTRACASUAL
ULTRACAUTIOUS
ULTRACENTRIFUGE
ULTRACIVILISED
ULTRACIVILIZED
ULTRACLEAN
ULTRACOMMERCIAL
ULTRACOMPACT
ULTRACOMPETENT
ULTRACONVENIENT
ULTRACREPIDATE
ULTRACREPIDATED
ULTRACREPIDATES
ULTRACRITICAL
ULTRADEMOCRATIC
ULTRADENSE
ULTRADISTANCE
ULTRADISTANT
ULTRAEFFICIENT
ULTRAENERGETIC
ULTRAEXCLUSIVE
ULTRAFAMILIAR
ULTRAFASTIDIOUS
ULTRAFEMININE
ULTRAFICHE
ULTRAFICHES
ULTRAFILTER
ULTRAFILTERED
ULTRAFILTERING
ULTRAFILTERS
ULTRAFILTRATE
ULTRAFILTRATES
ULTRAFILTRATION
ULTRAGLAMOROUS
ULTRAHAZARDOUS
ULTRAHEATED
ULTRAHEATING
ULTRAHEATS

ULTRAHEAVY
ULTRAHUMAN
ULTRAISTIC
ULTRALARGE
ULTRALEFTISM
ULTRALEFTISMS
ULTRALEFTIST
ULTRALEFTISTS
ULTRALIBERAL
ULTRALIBERALISM
ULTRALIBERALS
ULTRALIGHT
ULTRALIGHTS
ULTRAMAFIC
ULTRAMARATHON
ULTRAMARATHONER
ULTRAMARATHONS
ULTRAMARINE
ULTRAMARINES
ULTRAMASCULINE
ULTRAMICRO
ULTRAMICROMETER
ULTRAMICROSCOPE
ULTRAMICROSCOPY
ULTRAMICROTOME
ULTRAMICROTOMES
ULTRAMICROTOMY
ULTRAMILITANT
ULTRAMILITANTS
ULTRAMINIATURE
ULTRAMODERN
ULTRAMODERNISM
ULTRAMODERNISMS
ULTRAMODERNIST
ULTRAMODERNISTS
ULTRAMONTANE
ULTRAMONTANES
ULTRAMONTANISM
ULTRAMONTANISMS
ULTRAMONTANIST
ULTRAMONTANISTS
ULTRAMUNDANE
ULTRANATIONAL
ULTRAORTHODOX
ULTRAPATRIOTIC

ULTRAPHYSICAL
ULTRAPOWERFUL
ULTRAPRACTICAL
ULTRAPRECISE
ULTRAPRECISION
ULTRAQUIET
ULTRARADICAL
ULTRARADICALS
ULTRARAPID
ULTRARAREFIED
ULTRARATIONAL
ULTRAREALISM
ULTRAREALISMS
ULTRAREALIST
ULTRAREALISTIC
ULTRAREALISTS
ULTRAREFINED
ULTRARELIABLE
ULTRARIGHT
ULTRARIGHTIST
ULTRARIGHTISTS
ULTRAROMANTIC
ULTRAROYALIST
ULTRAROYALISTS
ULTRASECRET
ULTRASENSITIVE
ULTRASENSUAL
ULTRASERIOUS
ULTRASHARP
ULTRASHORT
ULTRASIMPLE
ULTRASLICK
ULTRASMALL
ULTRASMART
ULTRASMOOTH
ULTRASONIC
ULTRASONICALLY
ULTRASONICS
ULTRASONOGRAPHY
ULTRASOUND
ULTRASOUNDS
ULTRASTRUCTURAL
ULTRASTRUCTURE
ULTRASTRUCTURES
ULTRAVACUA

ULTRAVACUUM
ULTRAVACUUMS
ULTRAVIOLENCE
ULTRAVIOLENCES
ULTRAVIOLENT
ULTRAVIOLET
ULTRAVIOLETS
ULTRAVIRILE
ULTRAVIRILITIES
ULTRAVIRILITY
ULTRAVIRUS
ULTRAVIRUSES
ULTRAWIDEBAND
ULTRAWIDEBANDS
ULTRONEOUS
ULTRONEOUSLY
ULTRONEOUSNESS
ULULATIONS
UMBELLATED
UMBELLATELY
UMBELLIFER
UMBELLIFEROUS
UMBELLIFERS
UMBELLULATE
UMBELLULES
UMBILICALLY
UMBILICALS
UMBILICATE
UMBILICATED
UMBILICATION
UMBILICATIONS
UMBILICUSES
UMBILIFORM
UMBONATION
UMBONATIONS
UMBRACULATE
UMBRACULIFORM
UMBRACULUM
UMBRAGEOUS
UMBRAGEOUSLY
UMBRAGEOUSNESS
UMBRATICAL
UMBRATILOUS
UMBRELLAED
UMBRELLAING

UMBRELLOES	UNACTORISH	UNAMBIGUOUSLY	UNAPPARELLED	UNASCENDABLE
UMBRIFEROUS	UNACTUATED	UNAMBITIOUS	UNAPPARELLING	UNASCENDED
UMPIRESHIP	UNADAPTABLE	UNAMBITIOUSLY	UNAPPARELS	UNASCENDIBLE
UMPIRESHIPS	UNADDRESSED	UNAMBIVALENT	UNAPPARENT	UNASCERTAINABLE
UMPTEENTHS	UNADJUDICATED	UNAMBIVALENTLY	UNAPPEALABLE	UNASCERTAINED
UNABASHEDLY	UNADJUSTED	UNAMENABLE	UNAPPEALABLY	UNASHAMEDLY
UNABATEDLY	UNADMIRING	UNAMENDABLE	UNAPPEALING	UNASHAMEDNESS
UNABBREVIATED	UNADMITTED	UNAMIABILITIES	UNAPPEALINGLY	UNASHAMEDNESSES
UNABOLISHED	UNADMONISHED	UNAMIABILITY	UNAPPEASABLE	UNASPIRATED
UNABRIDGED	UNADOPTABLE	UNAMIABLENESS	UNAPPEASABLY	UNASPIRING
UNABROGATED	UNADULTERATE	UNAMIABLENESSES	UNAPPEASED	UNASPIRINGLY
UNABSOLVED	UNADULTERATED	UNAMORTISED	UNAPPETISING	UNASPIRINGNESS
UNABSORBED	UNADULTERATEDLY	UNAMORTIZED	UNAPPETISINGLY	UNASSAILABILITY
UNABSORBENT	UNADVENTROUS	UNAMPLIFIED	UNAPPETIZING	UNASSAILABLE
UNACADEMIC	UNADVENTUROUS	UNAMUSABLE	UNAPPETIZINGLY	UNASSAILABLY
UNACADEMICALLY	UNADVERTISED	UNAMUSINGLY	UNAPPLAUSIVE	UNASSAILED
UNACCENTED	UNADVISABLE	UNANALYSABLE	UNAPPLICABLE	UNASSEMBLED
UNACCENTUATED	UNADVISABLENESS	UNANALYSED	UNAPPOINTED	UNASSERTIVE
UNACCEPTABILITY	UNADVISABLY	UNANALYTIC	UNAPPRECIATED	UNASSERTIVELY
UNACCEPTABLE	UNADVISEDLY	UNANALYTICAL	UNAPPRECIATION	UNASSIGNABLE
UNACCEPTABLY	UNADVISEDNESS	UNANALYZABLE	UNAPPRECIATIONS	UNASSIGNED
UNACCEPTANCE	UNADVISEDNESSES	UNANALYZED	UNAPPRECIATIVE	UNASSIMILABLE
UNACCEPTANCES	UNAESTHETIC	UNANCHORED	UNAPPREHENDED	UNASSIMILATED
UNACCEPTED	UNAFFECTED	UNANCHORING	UNAPPREHENSIBLE	UNASSISTED
UNACCLIMATED	UNAFFECTEDLY	UNANESTHETISED	UNAPPREHENSIVE	UNASSISTEDLY
UNACCLIMATISED	UNAFFECTEDNESS	UNANESTHETIZED	UNAPPRISED	UNASSISTING
UNACCLIMATIZED	UNAFFECTING	UNANIMATED	UNAPPROACHABLE	UNASSOCIATED
UNACCOMMODATED	UNAFFECTIONATE	UNANIMITIES	UNAPPROACHABLY	UNASSUAGEABLE
UNACCOMMODATING	UNAFFILIATED	UNANIMOUSLY	UNAPPROACHED	UNASSUAGED
UNACCOMPANIED	UNAFFLUENT	UNANIMOUSNESS	UNAPPROPRIATE	UNASSUMING
UNACCOMPLISHED	UNAFFORDABLE	UNANIMOUSNESSES	UNAPPROPRIATED	UNASSUMINGLY
UNACCOUNTABLE	UNAGGRESSIVE	UNANNEALED	UNAPPROVED	UNASSUMINGNESS
UNACCOUNTABLY	UNAGREEABLE	UNANNOTATED	UNAPPROVING	UNATHLETIC
UNACCOUNTED	UNALIENABLE	UNANNOUNCED	UNAPPROVINGLY	UNATONABLE
UNACCREDITED	UNALIENABLY	UNANSWERABILITY	UNAPTNESSES	UNATTACHED
UNACCULTURATED	UNALIENATED	UNANSWERABLE	UNARGUABLE	UNATTAINABLE
UNACCUSABLE	UNALLEVIATED	UNANSWERABLY	UNARGUABLY	UNATTAINABLY
UNACCUSABLY	UNALLOCATED	UNANSWERED	UNARMOURED	UNATTAINTED
UNACCUSTOMED	UNALLOTTED	UNANTICIPATED	UNARRANGED	UNATTEMPTED
UNACCUSTOMEDLY	UNALLOWABLE	UNANTICIPATEDLY	UNARROGANT	UNATTENDED
UNACHIEVABLE	UNALLURING	UNAPOLOGETIC	UNARTFULLY	UNATTENDING
UNACHIEVED	UNALTERABILITY	UNAPOLOGISING	UNARTICULATE	UNATTENTIVE
UNACKNOWLEDGED	UNALTERABLE	UNAPOLOGIZING	UNARTICULATED	UNATTENUATED
UNACQUAINT	UNALTERABLENESS	UNAPOSTOLIC	UNARTIFICIAL	UNATTESTED
UNACQUAINTANCE	UNALTERABLY	UNAPOSTOLICAL	UNARTIFICIALLY	UNATTRACTIVE
UNACQUAINTANCES	UNALTERING	UNAPOSTOLICALLY	UNARTISTIC	UNATTRACTIVELY
UNACQUAINTED	UNAMBIGUOUS	UNAPPALLED	UNARTISTLIKE	UNATTRIBUTABLE

UNATTRIBUTED	UNBATTERED	UNBESEEMED	UNBLUSHINGLY	UNBUNDLERS
UNAUGMENTED	UNBEARABLE	UNBESEEMING	UNBLUSHINGNESS	UNBUNDLING
UNAUSPICIOUS	UNBEARABLENESS	UNBESEEMINGLY	UNBOASTFUL	UNBUNDLINGS
UNAUTHENTIC	UNBEARABLY	UNBESOUGHT	UNBONNETED	UNBURDENED
UNAUTHENTICATED	UNBEATABLE	UNBESPEAKING	UNBONNETING	UNBURDENING
UNAUTHENTICITY	UNBEATABLY	UNBESPEAKS	UNBORROWED	UNBUREAUCRATIC
UNAUTHORISED	UNBEAUTIFUL	UNBESPOKEN	UNBOSOMERS	UNBURNABLE
UNAUTHORITATIVE	UNBEAUTIFULLY	UNBESTOWED	UNBOSOMING	UNBURNISHED
UNAUTHORIZED	UNBEAVERED	UNBETRAYED	UNBOTTLING	UNBURROWED
UNAUTOMATED	UNBECOMING	UNBETTERABLE	UNBOTTOMED	UNBURROWING
UNAVAILABILITY	UNBECOMINGLY	UNBETTERED	UNBOUNDEDLY	UNBURTHENED
UNAVAILABLE	UNBECOMINGNESS	UNBEWAILED	UNBOUNDEDNESS	UNBURTHENING
UNAVAILABLENESS	UNBECOMINGS	UNBIASEDLY	UNBOUNDEDNESSES	UNBURTHENS
UNAVAILABLY	UNBEDIMMED	UNBIASEDNESS	UNBOWDLERISED	UNBUSINESSLIKE
UNAVAILING	UNBEDINNED	UNBIASEDNESSES	UNBOWDLERIZED	UNBUTTERED
UNAVAILINGLY	UNBEFITTING	UNBIASSEDLY	UNBRACKETED	UNBUTTONED
UNAVAILINGNESS	UNBEFRIENDED	UNBIASSEDNESS	UNBRAIDING	UNBUTTONING
UNAVERTABLE	UNBEGETTING	UNBIASSEDNESSES	UNBRANCHED	UNCALCIFIED
UNAVERTIBLE	UNBEGINNING	UNBIASSING	UNBREACHABLE	UNCALCINED
UNAVOIDABILITY	UNBEGOTTEN	UNBIBLICAL	UNBREACHED	UNCALCULATED
UNAVOIDABLE	UNBEGUILED	UNBINDINGS	UNBREAKABLE	UNCALCULATING
UNAVOIDABLENESS	UNBEGUILES	UNBIRTHDAY	UNBREATHABLE	UNCALIBRATED
UNAVOIDABLY	UNBEGUILING	UNBIRTHDAYS	UNBREATHED	UNCALLOUSED
UNAVOWEDLY	UNBEHOLDEN	UNBISHOPED	UNBREATHING	UNCANCELED
UNAWAKENED	UNBEKNOWNST	UNBISHOPING	UNBREECHED	UNCANDIDLY
UNAWAKENING	UNBELIEVABILITY	UNBLAMABLE	UNBREECHES	UNCANDIDNESS
UNAWARENESS	UNBELIEVABLE	UNBLAMABLY	UNBREECHING	UNCANDIDNESSES
UNAWARENESSES	UNBELIEVABLY	UNBLAMEABLE	UNBRIBABLE	UNCANDOURS
UNBAILABLE	UNBELIEVED	UNBLAMEABLY	UNBRIDGEABLE	UNCANNIEST
UNBALANCED	UNBELIEVER	UNBLEACHED	UNBRIDLEDLY	UNCANNINESS
UNBALANCES	UNBELIEVERS	UNBLEMISHED	UNBRIDLEDNESS	UNCANNINESSES
UNBALANCING	UNBELIEVES	UNBLENCHED	UNBRIDLEDNESSES	UNCANONICAL
UNBALLASTED	UNBELIEVING	UNBLENCHING	UNBRIDLING	UNCANONICALNESS
UNBANDAGED	UNBELIEVINGLY	UNBLESSEDNESS	UNBRILLIANT	UNCANONISE
UNBANDAGES	UNBELIEVINGNESS	UNBLESSEDNESSES	UNBROKENLY	UNCANONISED
UNBANDAGING	UNBELLIGERENT	UNBLESSING	UNBROKENNESS	UNCANONISES
UNBAPTISED	UNBENDABLE	UNBLINDFOLD	UNBROKENNESSES	UNCANONISING
UNBAPTISES	UNBENDINGLY	UNBLINDFOLDED	UNBROTHERLIKE	UNCANONIZE
UNBAPTISING	UNBENDINGNESS	UNBLINDFOLDING	UNBROTHERLY	UNCANONIZED
UNBAPTIZED	UNBENDINGNESSES	UNBLINDFOLDS	UNBUCKLING	UNCANONIZES
UNBAPTIZES	UNBENDINGS	UNBLINDING	UNBUDGEABLE	UNCANONIZING
UNBAPTIZING	UNBENEFICED	UNBLINKING	UNBUDGEABLY	UNCAPITALISED
UNBARBERED	UNBENEFICIAL	UNBLINKINGLY	UNBUDGETED	UNCAPITALIZED
UNBARRICADE	UNBENEFITED	UNBLISSFUL	UNBUDGINGLY	UNCAPSIZABLE
UNBARRICADED	UNBENIGHTED	UNBLOCKING	UNBUFFERED	UNCAPTIONED
UNBARRICADES	UNBENIGNANT	UNBLOODIED	UNBUILDABLE	UNCAPTURABLE
UNBARRICADING	UNBENIGNLY	UNBLUSHING	UNBUILDING	UNCARPETED

U

UNCASTRATED	UNCHARNELS	UNCHURCHLY	UNCLIMBABLENESS	UNCOMFORTABLE
UNCATALOGED	UNCHARTERED	UNCILIATED	UNCLINCHED	UNCOMFORTABLY
UNCATALOGUED	UNCHASTELY	UNCINARIAS	UNCLINCHES	UNCOMFORTED
UNCATCHABLE	UNCHASTENED	UNCINARIASES	UNCLINCHING	UNCOMMENDABLE
UNCATEGORISABLE	UNCHASTENESS	UNCINARIASIS	UNCLIPPING	UNCOMMENDABLY
UNCATEGORIZABLE	UNCHASTENESSES	UNCINEMATIC	UNCLOAKING	UNCOMMENDED
UNCEASINGLY	UNCHASTEST	UNCIPHERED	UNCLOGGING	UNCOMMERCIAL
UNCEASINGNESS	UNCHASTISABLE	UNCIPHERING	UNCLOISTER	UNCOMMITTED
UNCEASINGNESSES	UNCHASTISED	UNCIRCULATED	UNCLOISTERED	UNCOMMONER
UNCELEBRATED	UNCHASTITIES	UNCIRCUMCISED	UNCLOISTERING	UNCOMMONEST
UNCENSORED	UNCHASTITY	UNCIRCUMCISION	UNCLOISTERS	UNCOMMONLY
UNCENSORIOUS	UNCHASTIZABLE	UNCIRCUMCISIONS	UNCLOTHING	UNCOMMONNESS
UNCENSURED	UNCHASTIZED	UNCIRCUMSCRIBED	UNCLOUDEDLY	UNCOMMONNESSES
UNCEREBRAL	UNCHAUVINISTIC	UNCIVILISED	UNCLOUDEDNESS	UNCOMMUNICABLE
UNCEREMONIOUS	UNCHECKABLE	UNCIVILISEDLY	UNCLOUDEDNESSES	UNCOMMUNICATED
UNCEREMONIOUSLY	UNCHECKING	UNCIVILISEDNESS	UNCLOUDING	UNCOMMUNICATIVE
UNCERTAINLY	UNCHEERFUL	UNCIVILITIES	UNCLUBABLE	UNCOMMUTED
UNCERTAINNESS	UNCHEERFULLY	UNCIVILITY	UNCLUBBABLE	UNCOMPACTED
UNCERTAINNESSES	UNCHEERFULNESS	UNCIVILIZED	UNCLUTCHED	UNCOMPANIED
UNCERTAINTIES	UNCHEWABLE	UNCIVILIZEDLY	UNCLUTCHES	UNCOMPANIONABLE
UNCERTAINTY	UNCHILDING	UNCIVILIZEDNESS	UNCLUTCHING	UNCOMPANIONED
UNCERTIFICATED	UNCHILDLIKE	UNCIVILNESS	UNCLUTTERED	UNCOMPASSIONATE
UNCERTIFIED	UNCHIVALROUS	UNCIVILNESSES	UNCLUTTERING	UNCOMPELLED
UNCHAINING	UNCHIVALROUSLY	UNCLAMPING	UNCLUTTERS	UNCOMPELLING
UNCHAIRING	UNCHLORINATED	UNCLARIFIED	UNCOALESCE	UNCOMPENSATED
UNCHALLENGEABLE	UNCHOREOGRAPHED	UNCLARITIES	UNCOALESCED	UNCOMPETITIVE
UNCHALLENGEABLY	UNCHRISTEN	UNCLASPING	UNCOALESCES	UNCOMPLACENT
UNCHALLENGED	UNCHRISTENED	UNCLASSICAL	UNCOALESCING	UNCOMPLAINING
UNCHALLENGING	UNCHRISTENING	UNCLASSIFIABLE	UNCOATINGS	UNCOMPLAININGLY
UNCHANCIER	UNCHRISTENS	UNCLASSIFIED	UNCODIFIED	UNCOMPLAISANT
UNCHANCIEST	UNCHRISTIAN	UNCLEANEST	UNCOERCIVE	UNCOMPLAISANTLY
UNCHANGEABILITY	UNCHRISTIANED	UNCLEANLIER	UNCOERCIVELY	UNCOMPLETED
UNCHANGEABLE	UNCHRISTIANING	UNCLEANLIEST	UNCOFFINED	UNCOMPLIANT
UNCHANGEABLY	UNCHRISTIANISE	UNCLEANLINESS	UNCOFFINING	UNCOMPLICATED
UNCHANGING	UNCHRISTIANISED	UNCLEANLINESSES	UNCOLLECTED	UNCOMPLIMENTARY
UNCHANGINGLY	UNCHRISTIANISES	UNCLEANNESS	UNCOLLECTIBLE	UNCOMPLYING
UNCHANGINGNESS	UNCHRISTIANIZE	UNCLEANNESSES	UNCOLLECTIBLES	UNCOMPOSABLE
UNCHANNELED	UNCHRISTIANIZED	UNCLEANSED	UNCOLOURED	UNCOMPOUNDED
UNCHAPERONED	UNCHRISTIANIZES	UNCLEAREST	UNCOMATABLE	UNCOMPREHENDED
UNCHARGING	UNCHRISTIANLIKE	UNCLEARNESS	UNCOMBATIVE	UNCOMPREHENDING
UNCHARISMATIC	UNCHRISTIANLY	UNCLEARNESSES	UNCOMBINED	UNCOMPREHENSIVE
UNCHARITABLE	UNCHRISTIANS	UNCLENCHED	UNCOMBINES	UNCOMPROMISABLE
UNCHARITABLY	UNCHRONICLED	UNCLENCHES	UNCOMBINING	UNCOMPROMISING
UNCHARITIES	UNCHRONOLOGICAL	UNCLENCHING	UNCOMEATABLE	UNCOMPUTERISED
UNCHARMING	UNCHURCHED	UNCLERICAL	UNCOMELINESS	UNCOMPUTERIZED
UNCHARNELLED	UNCHURCHES	UNCLESHIPS	UNCOMELINESSES	UNCONCEALABLE
UNCHARNELLING	UNCHURCHING	UNCLIMBABLE	UNCOMFIEST	UNCONCEALED

U

UNCONCEALING
UNCONCEIVABLE
UNCONCEIVABLY
UNCONCEIVED
UNCONCERNED
UNCONCERNEDLY
UNCONCERNEDNESS
UNCONCERNING
UNCONCERNMENT
UNCONCERNMENTS
UNCONCERNS
UNCONCERTED
UNCONCILIATORY
UNCONCLUSIVE
UNCONCOCTED
UNCONDITIONAL
UNCONDITIONALLY
UNCONDITIONED
UNCONFEDERATED
UNCONFESSED
UNCONFINABLE
UNCONFINED
UNCONFINEDLY
UNCONFINES
UNCONFINING
UNCONFIRMED
UNCONFORMABLE
UNCONFORMABLY
UNCONFORMING
UNCONFORMITIES
UNCONFORMITY
UNCONFOUNDED
UNCONFUSED
UNCONFUSEDLY
UNCONFUSES
UNCONFUSING
UNCONGEALED
UNCONGEALING
UNCONGEALS
UNCONGENIAL
UNCONGENIALITY
UNCONJECTURED
UNCONJUGAL
UNCONJUGATED
UNCONJUNCTIVE
UNCONNECTED
UNCONNECTEDLY

UNCONNECTEDNESS
UNCONNIVING
UNCONQUERABLE
UNCONQUERABLY
UNCONQUERED
UNCONSCIENTIOUS
UNCONSCIONABLE
UNCONSCIONABLY
UNCONSCIOUS
UNCONSCIOUSES
UNCONSCIOUSLY
UNCONSCIOUSNESS
UNCONSECRATE
UNCONSECRATED
UNCONSECRATES
UNCONSECRATING
UNCONSENTANEOUS
UNCONSENTING
UNCONSIDERED
UNCONSIDERING
UNCONSOLED
UNCONSOLIDATED
UNCONSTANT
UNCONSTRAINABLE
UNCONSTRAINED
UNCONSTRAINEDLY
UNCONSTRAINT
UNCONSTRAINTS
UNCONSTRICTED
UNCONSTRUCTED
UNCONSTRUCTIVE
UNCONSUMED
UNCONSUMMATED
UNCONTAINABLE
UNCONTAMINATED
UNCONTEMNED
UNCONTEMPLATED
UNCONTEMPORARY
UNCONTENTIOUS
UNCONTESTABLE
UNCONTESTED
UNCONTRACTED
UNCONTRADICTED
UNCONTRIVED
UNCONTROLLABLE
UNCONTROLLABLY
UNCONTROLLED

UNCONTROLLEDLY
UNCONTROVERSIAL
UNCONTROVERTED
UNCONVENTIONAL
UNCONVERSABLE
UNCONVERSANT
UNCONVERTED
UNCONVERTIBLE
UNCONVICTED
UNCONVINCED
UNCONVINCING
UNCONVINCINGLY
UNCONVOYED
UNCOOPERATIVE
UNCOOPERATIVELY
UNCOORDINATED
UNCOPYRIGHTABLE
UNCOQUETTISH
UNCORRECTABLE
UNCORRECTED
UNCORRELATED
UNCORROBORATED
UNCORRUPTED
UNCORSETED
UNCOUNSELLED
UNCOUNTABLE
UNCOUPLERS
UNCOUPLING
UNCOURAGEOUS
UNCOURTEOUS
UNCOURTLINESS
UNCOURTLINESSES
UNCOUTHEST
UNCOUTHNESS
UNCOUTHNESSES
UNCOVENANTED
UNCOVERING
UNCREATEDNESS
UNCREATEDNESSES
UNCREATING
UNCREATIVE
UNCREDENTIALED
UNCREDIBLE
UNCREDITABLE
UNCREDITED
UNCRIPPLED
UNCRITICAL

UNCRITICALLY
UNCROSSABLE
UNCROSSING
UNCROWNING
UNCRUMPLED
UNCRUMPLES
UNCRUMPLING
UNCRUSHABLE
UNCRYSTALLISED
UNCRYSTALLIZED
UNCTIONLESS
UNCTUOSITIES
UNCTUOSITY
UNCTUOUSLY
UNCTUOUSNESS
UNCTUOUSNESSES
UNCUCKOLDED
UNCULTIVABLE
UNCULTIVATABLE
UNCULTIVATED
UNCULTURED
UNCUMBERED
UNCURBABLE
UNCURTAILED
UNCURTAINED
UNCURTAINING
UNCURTAINS
UNCUSTOMARILY
UNCUSTOMARY
UNCUSTOMED
UNCYNICALLY
UNDANCEABLE
UNDAUNTABLE
UNDAUNTEDLY
UNDAUNTEDNESS
UNDAUNTEDNESSES
UNDAZZLING
UNDEBARRED
UNDEBATABLE
UNDEBATABLY
UNDEBAUCHED
UNDECADENT
UNDECAGONS
UNDECEIVABLE
UNDECEIVED
UNDECEIVER
UNDECEIVERS

UNDECEIVES
UNDECEIVING
UNDECIDABILITY
UNDECIDABLE
UNDECIDEDLY
UNDECIDEDNESS
UNDECIDEDNESSES
UNDECIDEDS
UNDECILLION
UNDECILLIONS
UNDECIMOLE
UNDECIMOLES
UNDECIPHERABLE
UNDECIPHERED
UNDECISIVE
UNDECLARED
UNDECLINING
UNDECOMPOSABLE
UNDECOMPOSED
UNDECORATED
UNDEDICATED
UNDEFEATED
UNDEFENDED
UNDEFINABLE
UNDEFOLIATED
UNDEFORMED
UNDEIFYING
UNDELAYING
UNDELECTABLE
UNDELEGATED
UNDELETING
UNDELIBERATE
UNDELIGHTED
UNDELIGHTFUL
UNDELIGHTS
UNDELIVERABLE
UNDELIVERED
UNDEMANDING
UNDEMOCRATIC
UNDEMONSTRABLE
UNDEMONSTRATIVE
UNDENIABLE
UNDENIABLENESS
UNDENIABLY
UNDEPENDABLE
UNDEPENDING
UNDEPLORED

U

UNDEPRAVED	UNDERBREEDING	UNDERCLOTHING	UNDERDRAINED	UNDERFISHED
UNDEPRECIATED	UNDERBREEDINGS	UNDERCLOTHINGS	UNDERDRAINING	UNDERFISHES
UNDEPRESSED	UNDERBRIDGE	UNDERCLUBBED	UNDERDRAINS	UNDERFISHING
UNDEPRIVED	UNDERBRIDGES	UNDERCLUBBING	UNDERDRAWERS	UNDERFLOOR
UNDERACHIEVE	UNDERBRIMS	UNDERCLUBS	UNDERDRAWING	UNDERFLOWS
UNDERACHIEVED	UNDERBRUSH	UNDERCOATED	UNDERDRAWINGS	UNDERFONGED
UNDERACHIEVER	UNDERBRUSHED	UNDERCOATING	UNDERDRAWN	UNDERFONGING
UNDERACHIEVERS	UNDERBRUSHES	UNDERCOATINGS	UNDERDRAWS	UNDERFONGS
UNDERACHIEVES	UNDERBRUSHING	UNDERCOATS	UNDERDRESS	UNDERFOOTED
UNDERACHIEVING	UNDERBUDDED	UNDERCOOKED	UNDERDRESSED	UNDERFOOTING
UNDERACTED	UNDERBUDDING	UNDERCOOKING	UNDERDRESSES	UNDERFOOTS
UNDERACTING	UNDERBUDGET	UNDERCOOKS	UNDERDRESSING	UNDERFULFIL
UNDERACTION	UNDERBUDGETED	UNDERCOOLED	UNDERDRIVE	UNDERFULFILLED
UNDERACTIONS	UNDERBUDGETING	UNDERCOOLING	UNDERDRIVES	UNDERFULFILLING
UNDERACTIVE	UNDERBUDGETS	UNDERCOOLS	UNDEREARTH	UNDERFULFILS
UNDERACTIVITIES	UNDERBUILD	UNDERCOUNT	UNDEREATEN	UNDERFUNDED
UNDERACTIVITY	UNDERBUILDER	UNDERCOUNTED	UNDEREATING	UNDERFUNDING
UNDERACTOR	UNDERBUILDERS	UNDERCOUNTING	UNDEREDUCATED	UNDERFUNDINGS
UNDERACTORS	UNDERBUILDING	UNDERCOUNTS	UNDEREMPHASES	UNDERFUNDS
UNDERAGENT	UNDERBUILDS	UNDERCOVER	UNDEREMPHASIS	UNDERGARMENT
UNDERAGENTS	UNDERBUILT	UNDERCOVERT	UNDEREMPHASISE	UNDERGARMENTS
UNDERBAKED	UNDERBURNT	UNDERCOVERTS	UNDEREMPHASISED	UNDERGIRDED
UNDERBAKES	UNDERBUSHED	UNDERCRACKERS	UNDEREMPHASISES	UNDERGIRDING
UNDERBAKING	UNDERBUSHES	UNDERCREST	UNDEREMPHASIZE	UNDERGIRDS
UNDERBEARER	UNDERBUSHING	UNDERCRESTED	UNDEREMPHASIZED	UNDERGLAZE
UNDERBEARERS	UNDERBUYING	UNDERCRESTING	UNDEREMPHASIZES	UNDERGLAZES
UNDERBEARING	UNDERCAPITALISE	UNDERCRESTS	UNDEREMPLOYED	UNDERGOERS
UNDERBEARINGS	UNDERCAPITALIZE	UNDERCROFT	UNDEREMPLOYMENT	UNDERGOING
UNDERBEARS	UNDERCARDS	UNDERCROFTS	UNDERESTIMATE	UNDERGOWNS
UNDERBELLIES	UNDERCARRIAGE	UNDERCURRENT	UNDERESTIMATED	UNDERGRADS
UNDERBELLY	UNDERCARRIAGES	UNDERCURRENTS	UNDERESTIMATES	UNDERGRADUATE
UNDERBIDDER	UNDERCARTS	UNDERCUTTING	UNDERESTIMATING	UNDERGRADUATES
UNDERBIDDERS	UNDERCASTS	UNDERDAMPER	UNDERESTIMATION	UNDERGRADUETTE
UNDERBIDDING	UNDERCHARGE	UNDERDAMPERS	UNDEREXPOSE	UNDERGRADUETTES
UNDERBITES	UNDERCHARGED	UNDERDECKS	UNDEREXPOSED	UNDERGROUND
UNDERBITING	UNDERCHARGES	UNDERDEVELOP	UNDEREXPOSES	UNDERGROUNDER
UNDERBITTEN	UNDERCHARGING	UNDERDEVELOPED	UNDEREXPOSING	UNDERGROUNDERS
UNDERBLANKET	UNDERCLASS	UNDERDEVELOPING	UNDEREXPOSURE	UNDERGROUNDS
UNDERBLANKETS	UNDERCLASSES	UNDERDEVELOPS	UNDEREXPOSURES	UNDERGROVE
UNDERBODIES	UNDERCLASSMAN	UNDERDOERS	UNDERFEEDING	UNDERGROVES
UNDERBORNE	UNDERCLASSMEN	UNDERDOING	UNDERFEEDS	UNDERGROWN
UNDERBOSSES	UNDERCLAYS	UNDERDOSED	UNDERFELTS	UNDERGROWTH
UNDERBOUGH	UNDERCLIFF	UNDERDOSES	UNDERFINANCED	UNDERGROWTHS
UNDERBOUGHS	UNDERCLIFFS	UNDERDOSING	UNDERFINISHED	UNDERHAIRS
UNDERBOUGHT	UNDERCLOTHE	UNDERDRAIN	UNDERFIRED	UNDERHANDED
UNDERBREATH	UNDERCLOTHED	UNDERDRAINAGE	UNDERFIRES	UNDERHANDEDLY
UNDERBREATHS	UNDERCLOTHES	UNDERDRAINAGES	UNDERFIRING	UNDERHANDEDNESS

U

UNDERHANDS	UNDERLYING	UNDERPEOPLED	UNDERQUOTED	UNDERSHOOTS
UNDERHEATED	UNDERLYINGLY	UNDERPERFORM	UNDERQUOTES	UNDERSHORTS
UNDERHEATING	UNDERMANNED	UNDERPERFORMED	UNDERQUOTING	UNDERSHRUB
UNDERHEATS	UNDERMANNING	UNDERPERFORMING	UNDERRATED	UNDERSHRUBS
UNDERHONEST	UNDERMASTED	UNDERPERFORMS	UNDERRATES	UNDERSIDES
UNDERINFLATED	UNDERMEANING	UNDERPINNED	UNDERRATING	UNDERSIGNED
UNDERINFLATION	UNDERMEANINGS	UNDERPINNING	UNDERREACT	UNDERSIGNING
UNDERINFLATIONS	UNDERMENTIONED	UNDERPINNINGS	UNDERREACTED	UNDERSIGNS
UNDERINSURED	UNDERMINDE	UNDERPITCH	UNDERREACTING	UNDERSIZED
UNDERINVESTMENT	UNDERMINDED	UNDERPLANT	UNDERREACTS	UNDERSKIES
UNDERJAWED	UNDERMINDES	UNDERPLANTED	UNDERREPORT	UNDERSKINKER
UNDERKEEPER	UNDERMINDING	UNDERPLANTING	UNDERREPORTED	UNDERSKINKERS
UNDERKEEPERS	UNDERMINED	UNDERPLANTS	UNDERREPORTING	UNDERSKIRT
UNDERKEEPING	UNDERMINER	UNDERPLAYED	UNDERREPORTS	UNDERSKIRTS
UNDERKEEPS	UNDERMINERS	UNDERPLAYING	UNDERRUNNING	UNDERSLEEVE
UNDERKILLS	UNDERMINES	UNDERPLAYS	UNDERRUNNINGS	UNDERSLEEVES
UNDERKINGDOM	UNDERMINING	UNDERPLOTS	UNDERSATURATED	UNDERSLUNG
UNDERKINGDOMS	UNDERMININGS	UNDERPOPULATED	UNDERSAYING	UNDERSOILS
UNDERKINGS	UNDERNAMED	UNDERPOWERED	UNDERSCORE	UNDERSONGS
UNDERLAPPED	UNDERNEATH	UNDERPRAISE	UNDERSCORED	UNDERSPEND
UNDERLAPPING	UNDERNEATHS	UNDERPRAISED	UNDERSCORES	UNDERSPENDING
UNDERLAYER	UNDERNICENESS	UNDERPRAISES	UNDERSCORING	UNDERSPENDS
UNDERLAYERS	UNDERNICENESSES	UNDERPRAISING	UNDERSCRUB	UNDERSPENT
UNDERLAYING	UNDERNOTED	UNDERPREPARED	UNDERSCRUBS	UNDERSPINS
UNDERLAYMENT	UNDERNOTES	UNDERPRICE	UNDERSEALED	UNDERSTAFFED
UNDERLAYMENTS	UNDERNOTING	UNDERPRICED	UNDERSEALING	UNDERSTAFFING
UNDERLEASE	UNDERNOURISH	UNDERPRICES	UNDERSEALINGS	UNDERSTAFFINGS
UNDERLEASED	UNDERNOURISHED	UNDERPRICING	UNDERSEALS	UNDERSTAND
UNDERLEASES	UNDERNOURISHES	UNDERPRISE	UNDERSECRETARY	UNDERSTANDABLE
UNDERLEASING	UNDERNOURISHING	UNDERPRISED	UNDERSELLER	UNDERSTANDABLY
UNDERLEAVES	UNDERNTIME	UNDERPRISES	UNDERSELLERS	UNDERSTANDED
UNDERLETTER	UNDERNTIMES	UNDERPRISING	UNDERSELLING	UNDERSTANDER
UNDERLETTERS	UNDERNUTRITION	UNDERPRIVILEGED	UNDERSELLS	UNDERSTANDERS
UNDERLETTING	UNDERNUTRITIONS	UNDERPRIZE	UNDERSELVES	UNDERSTANDING
UNDERLETTINGS	UNDERPAINTING	UNDERPRIZED	UNDERSENSE	UNDERSTANDINGLY
UNDERLIERS	UNDERPAINTINGS	UNDERPRIZES	UNDERSENSES	UNDERSTANDINGS
UNDERLINED	UNDERPANTS	UNDERPRIZING	UNDERSERVED	UNDERSTANDS
UNDERLINEN	UNDERPARTS	UNDERPRODUCTION	UNDERSETTING	UNDERSTATE
UNDERLINENS	UNDERPASSES	UNDERPROOF	UNDERSEXED	UNDERSTATED
UNDERLINES	UNDERPASSION	UNDERPROPPED	UNDERSHAPEN	UNDERSTATEDLY
UNDERLINGS	UNDERPASSIONS	UNDERPROPPER	UNDERSHERIFF	UNDERSTATEMENT
UNDERLINING	UNDERPAYING	UNDERPROPPERS	UNDERSHERIFFS	UNDERSTATEMENTS
UNDERLOADED	UNDERPAYMENT	UNDERPROPPING	UNDERSHIRT	UNDERSTATES
UNDERLOADING	UNDERPAYMENTS	UNDERPROPS	UNDERSHIRTED	UNDERSTATING
UNDERLOADS	UNDERPEEPED	UNDERPUBLICISED	UNDERSHIRTS	UNDERSTEER
UNDERLOOKER	UNDERPEEPING	UNDERPUBLICIZED	UNDERSHOOT	UNDERSTEERED
UNDERLOOKERS	UNDERPEEPS	UNDERQUOTE	UNDERSHOOTING	UNDERSTEERING

U

UNDERSTEERS	UNDERTIMES	UNDERWOODS	UNDESTROYED	UNDISCUSSED
UNDERSTOCK	UNDERTINTS	UNDERWOOLS	UNDETECTABLE	UNDISCUSSIBLE
UNDERSTOCKED	UNDERTONED	UNDERWORKED	UNDETECTED	UNDISGUISABLE
UNDERSTOCKING	UNDERTONES	UNDERWORKER	UNDETERMINABLE	UNDISGUISED
UNDERSTOCKS	UNDERTRICK	UNDERWORKERS	UNDETERMINATE	UNDISGUISEDLY
UNDERSTOOD	UNDERTRICKS	UNDERWORKING	UNDETERMINATION	UNDISHONOURED
UNDERSTOREY	UNDERTRUMP	UNDERWORKS	UNDETERMINED	UNDISMANTLED
UNDERSTOREYS	UNDERTRUMPED	UNDERWORLD	UNDETERRED	UNDISMAYED
UNDERSTORIES	UNDERTRUMPING	UNDERWORLDS	UNDEVELOPED	UNDISORDERED
UNDERSTORY	UNDERTRUMPS	UNDERWRITE	UNDEVIATING	UNDISPATCHED
UNDERSTRAPPER	UNDERUSING	UNDERWRITER	UNDEVIATINGLY	UNDISPENSED
UNDERSTRAPPERS	UNDERUTILISE	UNDERWRITERS	UNDIAGNOSABLE	UNDISPOSED
UNDERSTRAPPING	UNDERUTILISED	UNDERWRITES	UNDIAGNOSED	UNDISPUTABLE
UNDERSTRATA	UNDERUTILISES	UNDERWRITING	UNDIALECTICAL	UNDISPUTED
UNDERSTRATUM	UNDERUTILISING	UNDERWRITINGS	UNDIDACTIC	UNDISPUTEDLY
UNDERSTRENGTH	UNDERUTILIZE	UNDERWRITTEN	UNDIFFERENCED	UNDISSEMBLED
UNDERSTUDIED	UNDERUTILIZED	UNDERWROTE	UNDIGESTED	UNDISSOCIATED
UNDERSTUDIES	UNDERUTILIZES	UNDERWROUGHT	UNDIGESTIBLE	UNDISSOLVED
UNDERSTUDY	UNDERUTILIZING	UNDESCENDABLE	UNDIGHTING	UNDISSOLVING
UNDERSTUDYING	UNDERVALUATION	UNDESCENDED	UNDIGNIFIED	UNDISTEMPERED
UNDERSUPPLIED	UNDERVALUATIONS	UNDESCENDIBLE	UNDIGNIFIES	UNDISTILLED
UNDERSUPPLIES	UNDERVALUE	UNDESCRIBABLE	UNDIGNIFYING	UNDISTINCTIVE
UNDERSUPPLY	UNDERVALUED	UNDESCRIBED	UNDIMINISHABLE	UNDISTINGUISHED
UNDERSUPPLYING	UNDERVALUER	UNDESCRIED	UNDIMINISHED	UNDISTORTED
UNDERSURFACE	UNDERVALUERS	UNDESERVED	UNDIPLOMATIC	UNDISTRACTED
UNDERSURFACES	UNDERVALUES	UNDESERVEDLY	UNDIRECTED	UNDISTRACTEDLY
UNDERTAKABLE	UNDERVALUING	UNDESERVEDNESS	UNDISAPPOINTING	UNDISTRACTING
UNDERTAKEN	UNDERVESTS	UNDESERVER	UNDISCERNED	UNDISTRIBUTED
UNDERTAKER	UNDERVIEWER	UNDESERVERS	UNDISCERNEDLY	UNDISTURBED
UNDERTAKERS	UNDERVIEWERS	UNDESERVES	UNDISCERNIBLE	UNDISTURBEDLY
UNDERTAKES	UNDERVOICE	UNDESERVING	UNDISCERNIBLY	UNDISTURBING
UNDERTAKING	UNDERVOICES	UNDESERVINGLY	UNDISCERNING	UNDIVERSIFIED
UNDERTAKINGS	UNDERVOTES	UNDESIGNATED	UNDISCERNINGS	UNDIVERTED
UNDERTAXED	UNDERWATER	UNDESIGNED	UNDISCHARGED	UNDIVERTING
UNDERTAXES	UNDERWATERS	UNDESIGNEDLY	UNDISCIPLINABLE	UNDIVESTED
UNDERTAXING	UNDERWEARS	UNDESIGNEDNESS	UNDISCIPLINE	UNDIVESTEDLY
UNDERTENANCIES	UNDERWEIGHT	UNDESIGNING	UNDISCIPLINED	UNDIVIDABLE
UNDERTENANCY	UNDERWEIGHTS	UNDESIRABILITY	UNDISCIPLINES	UNDIVIDEDLY
UNDERTENANT	UNDERWHELM	UNDESIRABLE	UNDISCLOSED	UNDIVIDEDNESS
UNDERTENANTS	UNDERWHELMED	UNDESIRABLENESS	UNDISCOMFITED	UNDIVIDEDNESSES
UNDERTHINGS	UNDERWHELMING	UNDESIRABLES	UNDISCORDANT	UNDIVORCED
UNDERTHIRST	UNDERWHELMS	UNDESIRABLY	UNDISCORDING	UNDIVULGED
UNDERTHIRSTS	UNDERWINGS	UNDESIRING	UNDISCOURAGED	UNDOCTORED
UNDERTHRUST	UNDERWIRED	UNDESIROUS	UNDISCOVERABLE	UNDOCTRINAIRE
UNDERTHRUSTING	UNDERWIRES	UNDESPAIRING	UNDISCOVERABLY	UNDOCUMENTED
UNDERTHRUSTS	UNDERWIRING	UNDESPAIRINGLY	UNDISCOVERED	UNDOGMATIC
UNDERTIMED	UNDERWIRINGS	UNDESPOILED	UNDISCUSSABLE	UNDOGMATICALLY

U

UNDOMESTIC	UNEASINESSES	UNENFORCED	UNEXAMINED	UNFAILINGNESSES
UNDOMESTICATE	UNEATABLENESS	UNENJOYABLE	UNEXAMPLED	UNFAIRNESS
UNDOMESTICATED	UNEATABLENESSES	UNENLARGED	UNEXCAVATED	UNFAIRNESSES
UNDOMESTICATES	UNECCENTRIC	UNENLIGHTENED	UNEXCELLED	UNFAITHFUL
UNDOMESTICATING	UNECLIPSED	UNENLIGHTENING	UNEXCEPTIONABLE	UNFAITHFULLY
UNDOUBLING	UNECOLOGICAL	UNENQUIRING	UNEXCEPTIONABLY	UNFAITHFULNESS
UNDOUBTABLE	UNECONOMIC	UNENRICHED	UNEXCEPTIONAL	UNFALLIBLE
UNDOUBTEDLY	UNECONOMICAL	UNENSLAVED	UNEXCEPTIONALLY	UNFALSIFIABLE
UNDOUBTFUL	UNEDIFYING	UNENTAILED	UNEXCITABLE	UNFALTERING
UNDOUBTING	UNEDUCABLE	UNENTERPRISING	UNEXCITING	UNFALTERINGLY
UNDOUBTINGLY	UNEDUCATED	UNENTERTAINED	UNEXCLUDED	UNFAMILIAR
UNDRAINABLE	UNEFFECTED	UNENTERTAINING	UNEXCLUSIVE	UNFAMILIARITIES
UNDRAMATIC	UNELABORATE	UNENTHRALLED	UNEXCLUSIVELY	UNFAMILIARITY
UNDRAMATICALLY	UNELABORATED	UNENTHUSIASTIC	UNEXECUTED	UNFAMILIARLY
UNDRAMATISED	UNELECTABLE	UNENTITLED	UNEXEMPLIFIED	UNFASHIONABLE
UNDRAMATIZED	UNELECTRIFIED	UNENVIABLE	UNEXERCISED	UNFASHIONABLY
UNDREADING	UNEMBARRASSED	UNENVIABLY	UNEXHAUSTED	UNFASHIONED
UNDREAMING	UNEMBELLISHED	UNEQUALLED	UNEXPANDED	UNFASTENED
UNDRESSING	UNEMBITTERED	UNEQUIPPED	UNEXPECTANT	UNFASTENING
UNDRESSINGS	UNEMBODIED	UNEQUITABLE	UNEXPECTED	UNFASTIDIOUS
UNDRINKABLE	UNEMOTIONAL	UNEQUIVOCABLY	UNEXPECTEDLY	UNFATHERED
UNDRIVEABLE	UNEMOTIONALLY	UNEQUIVOCAL	UNEXPECTEDNESS	UNFATHERLY
UNDROOPING	UNEMOTIONED	UNEQUIVOCALLY	UNEXPENDED	UNFATHOMABLE
UNDULANCES	UNEMPHATIC	UNEQUIVOCALNESS	UNEXPENSIVE	UNFATHOMABLY
UNDULANCIES	UNEMPHATICALLY	UNERASABLE	UNEXPENSIVELY	UNFATHOMED
UNDULATELY	UNEMPIRICAL	UNERRINGLY	UNEXPERIENCED	UNFAVORABLE
UNDULATING	UNEMPLOYABILITY	UNERRINGNESS	UNEXPERIENT	UNFAVORABLENESS
UNDULATINGLY	UNEMPLOYABLE	UNERRINGNESSES	UNEXPIATED	UNFAVORABLY
UNDULATION	UNEMPLOYABLES	UNESCAPABLE	UNEXPLAINABLE	UNFAVORITE
UNDULATIONIST	UNEMPLOYED	UNESCORTED	UNEXPLAINED	UNFAVOURABLE
UNDULATIONISTS	UNEMPLOYEDS	UNESSENCED	UNEXPLODED	UNFAVOURABLY
UNDULATIONS	UNEMPLOYMENT	UNESSENCES	UNEXPLOITED	UNFAVOURED
UNDULATORS	UNEMPLOYMENTS	UNESSENCING	UNEXPLORED	UNFEARFULLY
UNDULATORY	UNENCHANTED	UNESSENTIAL	UNEXPRESSED	UNFEASIBLE
UNDUPLICATED	UNENCLOSED	UNESSENTIALLY	UNEXPRESSIBLE	UNFEATHERED
UNDUTIFULLY	UNENCOURAGING	UNESSENTIALS	UNEXPRESSIVE	UNFEATURED
UNDUTIFULNESS	UNENCUMBERED	UNESTABLISHED	UNEXPUGNABLE	UNFEELINGLY
UNDUTIFULNESSES	UNENDANGERED	UNEVALUATED	UNEXPURGATED	UNFEELINGNESS
UNDYINGNESS	UNENDEARED	UNEVANGELICAL	UNEXTENDED	UNFEELINGNESSES
UNDYINGNESSES	UNENDEARING	UNEVENNESS	UNEXTENUATED	UNFEIGNEDLY
UNEARMARKED	UNENDINGLY	UNEVENNESSES	UNEXTINGUISHED	UNFEIGNEDNESS
UNEARTHING	UNENDINGNESS	UNEVENTFUL	UNEXTRAORDINARY	UNFEIGNEDNESSES
UNEARTHLIER	UNENDINGNESSES	UNEVENTFULLY	UNFADINGLY	UNFEIGNING
UNEARTHLIEST	UNENDURABLE	UNEVENTFULNESS	UNFADINGNESS	UNFELLOWED
UNEARTHLINESS	UNENDURABLENESS	UNEVIDENCED	UNFADINGNESSES	UNFEMININE
UNEARTHLINESSES	UNENDURABLY	UNEXACTING	UNFAILINGLY	UNFERMENTED
UNEASINESS	UNENFORCEABLE	UNEXAGGERATED	UNFAILINGNESS	UNFERTILISED

U

UNFERTILIZED	UNFORBIDDEN	UNFRAUGHTED	UNGENEROUS	UNGUARDEDNESSES
UNFETTERED	UNFORCEDLY	UNFRAUGHTING	UNGENEROUSLY	UNGUARDING
UNFETTERING	UNFORCIBLE	UNFRAUGHTS	UNGENITURED	UNGUENTARIA
UNFEUDALISE	UNFORDABLE	UNFREEDOMS	UNGENTEELLY	UNGUENTARIES
UNFEUDALISED	UNFOREBODING	UNFREEZING	UNGENTILITIES	UNGUENTARIUM
UNFEUDALISES	UNFOREKNOWABLE	UNFREQUENT	UNGENTILITY	UNGUENTARY
UNFEUDALISING	UNFOREKNOWN	UNFREQUENTED	UNGENTLEMANLIKE	UNGUERDONED
UNFEUDALIZE	UNFORESEEABLE	UNFREQUENTLY	UNGENTLEMANLY	UNGUESSABLE
UNFEUDALIZED	UNFORESEEING	UNFRIENDED	UNGENTLENESS	UNGUICULATE
UNFEUDALIZES	UNFORESEEN	UNFRIENDEDNESS	UNGENTLENESSES	UNGUICULATED
UNFEUDALIZING	UNFORESKINNED	UNFRIENDLIER	UNGENTRIFIED	UNGUICULATES
UNFILIALLY	UNFORESTED	UNFRIENDLIEST	UNGENUINENESS	UNGULIGRADE
UNFILLABLE	UNFORETOLD	UNFRIENDLILY	UNGENUINENESSES	UNHABITABLE
UNFILLETED	UNFOREWARNED	UNFRIENDLINESS	UNGERMINATED	UNHABITUATED
UNFILTERABLE	UNFORFEITED	UNFRIENDLY	UNGETATABLE	UNHACKNEYED
UNFILTERED	UNFORGETTABLE	UNFRIENDSHIP	UNGIMMICKY	UNHALLOWED
UNFILTRABLE	UNFORGETTABLY	UNFRIENDSHIPS	UNGIRTHING	UNHALLOWING
UNFINDABLE	UNFORGIVABLE	UNFRIGHTED	UNGLAMORISED	UNHAMPERED
UNFINISHED	UNFORGIVEN	UNFRIGHTENED	UNGLAMORIZED	UNHANDIEST
UNFINISHING	UNFORGIVENESS	UNFRIVOLOUS	UNGLAMOROUS	UNHANDINESS
UNFINISHINGS	UNFORGIVENESSES	UNFROCKING	UNGODLIEST	UNHANDINESSES
UNFITNESSES	UNFORGIVING	UNFRUCTUOUS	UNGODLINESS	UNHANDSELLED
UNFITTEDNESS	UNFORGIVINGNESS	UNFRUITFUL	UNGODLINESSES	UNHANDSOME
UNFITTEDNESSES	UNFORGOTTEN	UNFRUITFULLY	UNGOVERNABLE	UNHANDSOMELY
UNFITTINGLY	UNFORMALISED	UNFRUITFULNESS	UNGOVERNABLY	UNHANDSOMENESS
UNFIXEDNESS	UNFORMALIZED	UNFULFILLABLE	UNGOVERNED	UNHAPPIEST
UNFIXEDNESSES	UNFORMATTED	UNFULFILLED	UNGRACEFUL	UNHAPPINESS
UNFIXITIES	UNFORMIDABLE	UNFUNNIEST	UNGRACEFULLY	UNHAPPINESSES
UNFLAGGING	UNFORMULATED	UNFURNISHED	UNGRACEFULNESS	UNHAPPYING
UNFLAGGINGLY	UNFORSAKEN	UNFURNISHES	UNGRACIOUS	UNHARBOURED
UNFLAMBOYANT	UNFORTHCOMING	UNFURNISHING	UNGRACIOUSLY	UNHARBOURING
UNFLAPPABILITY	UNFORTIFIED	UNFURROWED	UNGRACIOUSNESS	UNHARBOURS
UNFLAPPABLE	UNFORTUNATE	UNFUSSIEST	UNGRAMMATIC	UNHARDENED
UNFLAPPABLENESS	UNFORTUNATELY	UNGAINLIER	UNGRAMMATICAL	UNHARMFULLY
UNFLAPPABLY	UNFORTUNATENESS	UNGAINLIEST	UNGRAMMATICALLY	UNHARMONIOUS
UNFLATTERING	UNFORTUNATES	UNGAINLINESS	UNGRASPABLE	UNHARNESSED
UNFLATTERINGLY	UNFORTUNED	UNGAINLINESSES	UNGRATEFUL	UNHARNESSES
UNFLAVOURED	UNFORTUNES	UNGAINSAID	UNGRATEFULLY	UNHARNESSING
UNFLESHING	UNFOSSILIFEROUS	UNGAINSAYABLE	UNGRATEFULNESS	UNHARVESTED
UNFLINCHING	UNFOSSILISED	UNGALLANTLY	UNGRATIFIED	UNHATTINGS
UNFLINCHINGLY	UNFOSSILIZED	UNGARMENTED	UNGROUNDED	UNHAZARDED
UNFLUSHING	UNFOSTERED	UNGARNERED	UNGROUNDEDLY	UNHAZARDOUS
UNFLUSTERED	UNFOUGHTEN	UNGARNISHED	UNGROUNDEDNESS	UNHEALABLE
UNFOCUSSED	UNFOUNDEDLY	UNGARTERED	UNGRUDGING	UNHEALTHFUL
UNFOLDINGS	UNFOUNDEDNESS	UNGATHERED	UNGRUDGINGLY	UNHEALTHFULLY
UNFOLDMENT	UNFOUNDEDNESSES	UNGENEROSITIES	UNGUARDEDLY	UNHEALTHFULNESS
UNFOLDMENTS	UNFRANCHISED	UNGENEROSITY	UNGUARDEDNESS	UNHEALTHIER

U

UNHEALTHIEST	UNHURTFULNESS	UNIFORMNESS	UNIMPOSING	UNINSTRUCTED
UNHEALTHILY	UNHURTFULNESSES	UNIFORMNESSES	UNIMPREGNATED	UNINSTRUCTIVE
UNHEALTHINESS	UNHUSBANDED	UNIGENITURE	UNIMPRESSED	UNINSULATED
UNHEALTHINESSES	UNHYDROLYSED	UNIGENITURES	UNIMPRESSIBLE	UNINSURABLE
UNHEARSING	UNHYDROLYZED	UNIGNORABLE	UNIMPRESSIVE	UNINSUREDS
UNHEARTING	UNHYGIENIC	UNILABIATE	UNIMPRISONED	UNINTEGRATED
UNHEEDEDLY	UNHYPHENATED	UNILATERAL	UNIMPROVED	UNINTELLECTUAL
UNHEEDFULLY	UNHYSTERICAL	UNILATERALISM	UNIMPUGNABLE	UNINTELLIGENCE
UNHEEDINGLY	UNHYSTERICALLY	UNILATERALISMS	UNINAUGURATED	UNINTELLIGENCES
UNHELMETED	UNIAXIALLY	UNILATERALIST	UNINCHANTED	UNINTELLIGENT
UNHELPABLE	UNICAMERAL	UNILATERALISTS	UNINCLOSED	UNINTELLIGENTLY
UNHELPFULLY	UNICAMERALISM	UNILATERALITIES	UNINCORPORATED	UNINTELLIGIBLE
UNHERALDED	UNICAMERALISMS	UNILATERALITY	UNINCUMBERED	UNINTELLIGIBLY
UNHEROICAL	UNICAMERALIST	UNILATERALLY	UNINDEARED	UNINTENDED
UNHEROICALLY	UNICAMERALISTS	UNILINGUAL	UNINDICTED	UNINTENTIONAL
UNHESITATING	UNICAMERALLY	UNILINGUALISM	UNINFECTED	UNINTENTIONALLY
UNHESITATINGLY	UNICELLULAR	UNILINGUALISMS	UNINFLAMED	UNINTEREST
UNHIDEBOUND	UNICELLULARITY	UNILINGUALS	UNINFLAMMABLE	UNINTERESTED
UNHINDERED	UNICENTRAL	UNILITERAL	UNINFLATED	UNINTERESTEDLY
UNHINGEMENT	UNICOLORATE	UNILLUMINATED	UNINFLECTED	UNINTERESTING
UNHINGEMENTS	UNICOLOROUS	UNILLUMINATING	UNINFLUENCED	UNINTERESTINGLY
UNHISTORIC	UNICOLOURED	UNILLUMINED	UNINFLUENTIAL	UNINTERESTS
UNHISTORICAL	UNICOSTATE	UNILLUSIONED	UNINFORCEABLE	UNINTERMITTED
UNHITCHING	UNICYCLING	UNILLUSTRATED	UNINFORCED	UNINTERMITTEDLY
UNHOARDING	UNICYCLIST	UNILOBULAR	UNINFORMATIVE	UNINTERMITTING
UNHOLINESS	UNICYCLISTS	UNILOCULAR	UNINFORMATIVELY	UNINTERPRETABLE
UNHOLINESSES	UNIDEALISM	UNIMAGINABLE	UNINFORMED	UNINTERRUPTED
UNHOMELIKE	UNIDEALISMS	UNIMAGINABLY	UNINFORMING	UNINTERRUPTEDLY
UNHOMOGENISED	UNIDEALISTIC	UNIMAGINATIVE	UNINGRATIATING	UNINTIMIDATED
UNHOMOGENIZED	UNIDENTIFIABLE	UNIMAGINATIVELY	UNINHABITABLE	UNINTOXICATING
UNHONOURED	UNIDENTIFIED	UNIMAGINED	UNINHABITED	UNINTRODUCED
UNHOPEFULLY	UNIDEOLOGICAL	UNIMMORTAL	UNINHIBITED	UNINUCLEAR
UNHOSPITABLE	UNIDIMENSIONAL	UNIMMUNISED	UNINHIBITEDLY	UNINUCLEATE
UNHOUSELED	UNIDIOMATIC	UNIMMUNIZED	UNINHIBITEDNESS	UNINVENTIVE
UNHOUZZLED	UNIDIOMATICALLY	UNIMOLECULAR	UNINITIATE	UNINVESTED
UNHUMANISE	UNIDIRECTIONAL	UNIMPAIRED	UNINITIATED	UNINVIDIOUS
UNHUMANISED	UNIFICATION	UNIMPARTED	UNINITIATES	UNINVITING
UNHUMANISES	UNIFICATIONS	UNIMPASSIONED	UNINOCULATED	UNINVOLVED
UNHUMANISING	UNIFLOROUS	UNIMPEACHABLE	UNINQUIRING	UNIONISATION
UNHUMANIZE	UNIFOLIATE	UNIMPEACHABLY	UNINQUISITIVE	UNIONISATIONS
UNHUMANIZED	UNIFOLIOLATE	UNIMPEACHED	UNINSCRIBED	UNIONISERS
UNHUMANIZES	UNIFORMEST	UNIMPEDEDLY	UNINSPECTED	UNIONISING
UNHUMANIZING	UNIFORMING	UNIMPLORED	UNINSPIRED	UNIONISTIC
UNHUMOROUS	UNIFORMITARIAN	UNIMPORTANCE	UNINSPIRING	UNIONIZATION
UNHURRIEDLY	UNIFORMITARIANS	UNIMPORTANCES	UNINSTALLED	UNIONIZATIONS
UNHURRYING	UNIFORMITIES	UNIMPORTANT	UNINSTALLING	UNIONIZERS
UNHURTFULLY	UNIFORMITY	UNIMPORTUNED	UNINSTALLS	UNIONIZING

U

UNIPARENTAL	UNIVERSALIST	UNKNOWABILITY	UNLIKELIHOOD	UNMAINTAINED
UNIPARENTALLY	UNIVERSALISTIC	UNKNOWABLE	UNLIKELIHOODS	UNMALICIOUS
UNIPARTITE	UNIVERSALISTS	UNKNOWABLENESS	UNLIKELINESS	UNMALICIOUSLY
UNIPERSONAL	UNIVERSALITIES	UNKNOWABLES	UNLIKELINESSES	UNMALLEABILITY
UNIPERSONALITY	UNIVERSALITY	UNKNOWABLY	UNLIKENESS	UNMALLEABLE
UNIPOLARITIES	UNIVERSALIZE	UNKNOWINGLY	UNLIKENESSES	UNMANACLED
UNIPOLARITY	UNIVERSALIZED	UNKNOWINGNESS	UNLIMBERED	UNMANACLES
UNIQUENESS	UNIVERSALIZES	UNKNOWINGNESSES	UNLIMBERING	UNMANACLING
UNIQUENESSES	UNIVERSALIZING	UNKNOWINGS	UNLIMITEDLY	UNMANAGEABLE
UNIRONICALLY	UNIVERSALLY	UNKNOWLEDGEABLE	UNLIMITEDNESS	UNMANAGEABLY
UNIRRADIATED	UNIVERSALNESS	UNKNOWNNESS	UNLIMITEDNESSES	UNMANFULLY
UNIRRIGATED	UNIVERSALNESSES	UNKNOWNNESSES	UNLIQUEFIED	UNMANIPULATED
UNISEPTATE	UNIVERSALS	UNLABELLED	UNLIQUIDATED	UNMANLIEST
UNISERIALLY	UNIVERSITARIAN	UNLABORIOUS	UNLIQUORED	UNMANLINESS
UNISERIATE	UNIVERSITIES	UNLABOURED	UNLISTENABLE	UNMANLINESSES
UNISERIATELY	UNIVERSITY	UNLABOURING	UNLISTENED	UNMANNERED
UNISEXUALITIES	UNIVOCALLY	UNLADYLIKE	UNLISTENING	UNMANNEREDLY
UNISEXUALITY	UNIVOLTINE	UNLAMENTED	UNLITERARY	UNMANNERLINESS
UNISEXUALLY	UNJAUNDICED	UNLATCHING	UNLIVEABLE	UNMANNERLY
UNISONALLY	UNJOINTING	UNLAUNDERED	UNLIVELINESS	UNMANTLING
UNISONANCE	UNJUSTIFIABLE	UNLAWFULLY	UNLIVELINESSES	UNMANUFACTURED
UNISONANCES	UNJUSTIFIABLY	UNLAWFULNESS	UNLOADINGS	UNMARKETABLE
UNITARIANISM	UNJUSTIFIED	UNLAWFULNESSES	UNLOCALISED	UNMARRIABLE
UNITARIANISMS	UNJUSTNESS	UNLEARNABLE	UNLOCALIZED	UNMARRIAGEABLE
UNITARIANS	UNJUSTNESSES	UNLEARNEDLY	UNLOCKABLE	UNMARRIEDS
UNITEDNESS	UNKEMPTNESS	UNLEARNEDNESS	UNLOOSENED	UNMARRYING
UNITEDNESSES	UNKEMPTNESSES	UNLEARNEDNESSES	UNLOOSENING	UNMASCULINE
UNITHOLDER	UNKENNELED	UNLEARNING	UNLOVEABLE	UNMASKINGS
UNITHOLDERS	UNKENNELING	UNLEASHING	UNLOVELIER	UNMASTERED
UNITISATION	UNKENNELLED	UNLEAVENED	UNLOVELIEST	UNMATCHABLE
UNITISATIONS	UNKENNELLING	UNLEISURED	UNLOVELINESS	UNMATERIAL
UNITIZATION	UNKINDLIER	UNLEISURELY	UNLOVELINESSES	UNMATERIALISED
UNITIZATIONS	UNKINDLIEST	UNLESSONED	UNLOVERLIKE	UNMATERIALIZED
UNIVALENCE	UNKINDLINESS	UNLETTABLE	UNLOVINGLY	UNMATERNAL
UNIVALENCES	UNKINDLINESSES	UNLETTERED	UNLOVINGNESS	UNMATHEMATICAL
UNIVALENCIES	UNKINDNESS	UNLEVELING	UNLOVINGNESSES	UNMATRICULATED
UNIVALENCY	UNKINDNESSES	UNLEVELLED	UNLUCKIEST	UNMEANINGLY
UNIVALENTS	UNKINGLIER	UNLEVELLING	UNLUCKINESS	UNMEANINGNESS
UNIVALVULAR	UNKINGLIEST	UNLIBERATED	UNLUCKINESSES	UNMEANINGNESSES
UNIVARIANT	UNKINGLIKE	UNLIBIDINOUS	UNLUXURIANT	UNMEASURABLE
UNIVARIATE	UNKNIGHTED	UNLICENSED	UNLUXURIOUS	UNMEASURABLY
UNIVERSALISE	UNKNIGHTING	UNLIFELIKE	UNMACADAMISED	UNMEASURED
UNIVERSALISED	UNKNIGHTLINESS	UNLIGHTENED	UNMACADAMIZED	UNMEASUREDLY
UNIVERSALISES	UNKNIGHTLY	UNLIGHTSOME	UNMAGNIFIED	UNMECHANIC
UNIVERSALISING	UNKNITTING	UNLIKEABLE	UNMAIDENLY	UNMECHANICAL
UNIVERSALISM	UNKNOTTING	UNLIKELIER	UNMAILABLE	UNMECHANISE
UNIVERSALISMS	UNKNOWABILITIES	UNLIKELIEST	UNMAINTAINABLE	UNMECHANISED

U

UNMECHANISES

UNMECHANISES
UNMECHANISING
UNMECHANIZE
UNMECHANIZED
UNMECHANIZES
UNMECHANIZING
UNMEDIATED
UNMEDICATED
UNMEDICINABLE
UNMEDITATED
UNMEETNESS
UNMEETNESSES
UNMELLOWED
UNMELODIOUS
UNMELODIOUSNESS
UNMEMORABLE
UNMEMORABLY
UNMENTIONABLE
UNMENTIONABLES
UNMENTIONABLY
UNMENTIONED
UNMERCENARY
UNMERCHANTABLE
UNMERCIFUL
UNMERCIFULLY
UNMERCIFULNESS
UNMERITABLE
UNMERITEDLY
UNMERITING
UNMETABOLISED
UNMETABOLIZED
UNMETALLED
UNMETAPHORICAL
UNMETAPHYSICAL
UNMETHODICAL
UNMETHODISED
UNMETHODIZED
UNMETRICAL
UNMILITARY
UNMINDFULLY
UNMINDFULNESS
UNMINDFULNESSES
UNMINGLING
UNMINISTERIAL
UNMIRACULOUS
UNMISSABLE
UNMISTAKABLE

UNMISTAKABLY
UNMISTAKEABLE
UNMISTAKEABLY
UNMISTRUSTFUL
UNMITERING
UNMITIGABLE
UNMITIGABLY
UNMITIGATED
UNMITIGATEDLY
UNMITIGATEDNESS
UNMODERATED
UNMODERNISED
UNMODERNIZED
UNMODIFIABLE
UNMODIFIED
UNMODULATED
UNMOISTENED
UNMOLESTED
UNMONITORED
UNMORALISED
UNMORALISING
UNMORALITIES
UNMORALITY
UNMORALIZED
UNMORALIZING
UNMORTGAGED
UNMORTIFIED
UNMORTISED
UNMORTISES
UNMORTISING
UNMOTHERLY
UNMOTIVATED
UNMOULDING
UNMOUNTING
UNMOVEABLE
UNMOVEABLY
UNMUFFLING
UNMUNITIONED
UNMURMURING
UNMURMURINGLY
UNMUSICALLY
UNMUSICALNESS
UNMUSICALNESSES
UNMUTILATED
UNMUZZLING
UNMUZZLINGS
UNMYELINATED

UNNAMEABLE
UNNATURALISE
UNNATURALISED
UNNATURALISES
UNNATURALISING
UNNATURALIZE
UNNATURALIZED
UNNATURALIZES
UNNATURALIZING
UNNATURALLY
UNNATURALNESS
UNNATURALNESSES
UNNAVIGABLE
UNNAVIGATED
UNNECESSARILY
UNNECESSARINESS
UNNECESSARY
UNNEEDFULLY
UNNEGOTIABLE
UNNEIGHBOURED
UNNEIGHBOURLY
UNNERVINGLY
UNNEUROTIC
UNNEWSWORTHY
UNNILHEXIUM
UNNILHEXIUMS
UNNILPENTIUM
UNNILPENTIUMS
UNNILQUADIUM
UNNILQUADIUMS
UNNILSEPTIUM
UNNILSEPTIUMS
UNNOTICEABLE
UNNOTICEABLY
UNNOTICING
UNNOURISHED
UNNOURISHING
UNNUMBERED
UNNURTURED
UNOBEDIENT
UNOBJECTIONABLE
UNOBJECTIONABLY
UNOBNOXIOUS
UNOBSCURED
UNOBSERVABLE
UNOBSERVANCE
UNOBSERVANCES

UNOBSERVANT
UNOBSERVED
UNOBSERVEDLY
UNOBSERVING
UNOBSTRUCTED
UNOBSTRUCTIVE
UNOBTAINABLE
UNOBTAINED
UNOBTRUSIVE
UNOBTRUSIVELY
UNOBTRUSIVENESS
UNOCCUPIED
UNOFFENDED
UNOFFENDING
UNOFFENSIVE
UNOFFICERED
UNOFFICIAL
UNOFFICIALLY
UNOFFICIOUS
UNOPENABLE
UNOPERATIVE
UNOPPRESSIVE
UNORDAINED
UNORDERING
UNORDINARY
UNORGANISED
UNORGANIZED
UNORIGINAL
UNORIGINALITIES
UNORIGINALITY
UNORIGINATE
UNORIGINATED
UNORNAMENTAL
UNORNAMENTED
UNORTHODOX
UNORTHODOXIES
UNORTHODOXLY
UNORTHODOXY
UNOSSIFIED
UNOSTENTATIOUS
UNOVERCOME
UNOVERTHROWN
UNOXIDISED
UNOXIDIZED
UNOXYGENATED
UNPACIFIED
UNPACKINGS

UNPAINTABLE
UNPAINTING
UNPALATABILITY
UNPALATABLE
UNPALATABLY
UNPAMPERED
UNPANELLED
UNPANELLING
UNPANNELLED
UNPANNELLING
UNPAPERING
UNPARADISE
UNPARADISED
UNPARADISES
UNPARADISING
UNPARAGONED
UNPARALLEL
UNPARALLELED
UNPARASITISED
UNPARASITIZED
UNPARDONABLE
UNPARDONABLY
UNPARDONED
UNPARDONING
UNPARENTAL
UNPARENTED
UNPARLIAMENTARY
UNPASSABLE
UNPASSABLENESS
UNPASSIONATE
UNPASSIONED
UNPASTEURISED
UNPASTEURIZED
UNPASTORAL
UNPASTURED
UNPATENTABLE
UNPATENTED
UNPATHETIC
UNPATHWAYED
UNPATRIOTIC
UNPATRIOTICALLY
UNPATRONISED
UNPATRONIZED
UNPATTERNED
UNPAVILIONED
UNPEACEABLE
UNPEACEABLENESS

U

UNPEACEFUL	UNPICKABLE	UNPOPULARLY	UNPRESSURED	UNPROGRESSIVE
UNPEACEFULLY	UNPICTURESQUE	UNPOPULATED	UNPRESSURISED	UNPROGRESSIVELY
UNPEDANTIC	UNPILLARED	UNPOPULOUS	UNPRESSURIZED	UNPROHIBITED
UNPEDIGREED	UNPILLOWED	UNPORTIONED	UNPRESUMING	UNPROJECTED
UNPEERABLE	UNPITIFULLY	UNPOSSESSED	UNPRESUMPTUOUS	UNPROLIFIC
UNPENSIONED	UNPITIFULNESS	UNPOSSESSING	UNPRETENDING	UNPROMISED
UNPEOPLING	UNPITIFULNESSES	UNPOSSIBLE	UNPRETENDINGLY	UNPROMISING
UNPEPPERED	UNPITYINGLY	UNPOWDERED	UNPRETENTIOUS	UNPROMISINGLY
UNPERCEIVABLE	UNPLAITING	UNPRACTICABLE	UNPRETENTIOUSLY	UNPROMPTED
UNPERCEIVABLY	UNPLASTERED	UNPRACTICAL	UNPRETTINESS	UNPRONOUNCEABLE
UNPERCEIVED	UNPLAUSIBLE	UNPRACTICALITY	UNPRETTINESSES	UNPRONOUNCED
UNPERCEIVEDLY	UNPLAUSIBLY	UNPRACTICALLY	UNPREVAILING	UNPROPERLY
UNPERCEPTIVE	UNPLAUSIVE	UNPRACTICALNESS	UNPREVENTABLE	UNPROPERTIED
UNPERCHING	UNPLAYABLE	UNPRACTICED	UNPREVENTED	UNPROPHETIC
UNPERFECTED	UNPLEASANT	UNPRACTISED	UNPRIESTED	UNPROPHETICAL
UNPERFECTION	UNPLEASANTLY	UNPRACTISEDNESS	UNPRIESTING	UNPROPITIOUS
UNPERFECTIONS	UNPLEASANTNESS	UNPRAISEWORTHY	UNPRIESTLY	UNPROPITIOUSLY
UNPERFECTLY	UNPLEASANTRIES	UNPRAISING	UNPRINCELY	UNPROPORTIONATE
UNPERFECTNESS	UNPLEASANTRY	UNPREACHED	UNPRINCIPLED	UNPROPORTIONED
UNPERFECTNESSES	UNPLEASING	UNPREACHES	UNPRINTABLE	UNPROPOSED
UNPERFORATED	UNPLEASINGLY	UNPREACHING	UNPRINTABLENESS	UNPROPPING
UNPERFORMABLE	UNPLEASURABLE	UNPRECEDENTED	UNPRINTABLY	UNPROSPEROUS
UNPERFORMED	UNPLEASURABLY	UNPRECEDENTEDLY	UNPRISABLE	UNPROSPEROUSLY
UNPERFORMING	UNPLOUGHED	UNPREDICTABLE	UNPRISONED	UNPROTECTED
UNPERFUMED	UNPLUGGING	UNPREDICTABLES	UNPRISONING	UNPROTECTEDNESS
UNPERILOUS	UNPLUMBING	UNPREDICTABLY	UNPRIVILEGED	UNPROTESTANTISE
UNPERISHABLE	UNPOETICAL	UNPREDICTED	UNPRIZABLE	UNPROTESTANTIZE
UNPERISHED	UNPOETICALLY	UNPREDICTING	UNPROBLEMATIC	UNPROTESTED
UNPERISHING	UNPOETICALNESS	UNPREDICTS	UNPROCEDURAL	UNPROTESTING
UNPERJURED	UNPOISONED	UNPREFERRED	UNPROCESSED	UNPROVABLE
UNPERPETRATED	UNPOISONING	UNPREGNANT	UNPROCLAIMED	UNPROVIDED
UNPERPLEXED	UNPOLARISABLE	UNPREJUDICED	UNPROCURABLE	UNPROVIDEDLY
UNPERPLEXES	UNPOLARISED	UNPREJUDICEDLY	UNPRODUCED	UNPROVIDENT
UNPERPLEXING	UNPOLARIZABLE	UNPRELATICAL	UNPRODUCTIVE	UNPROVIDES
UNPERSECUTED	UNPOLARIZED	UNPREMEDITABLE	UNPRODUCTIVELY	UNPROVIDING
UNPERSONED	UNPOLICIED	UNPREMEDITATED	UNPRODUCTIVITY	UNPROVISIONED
UNPERSONING	UNPOLISHABLE	UNPREMEDITATION	UNPROFANED	UNPROVOCATIVE
UNPERSUADABLE	UNPOLISHED	UNPREOCCUPIED	UNPROFESSED	UNPROVOKED
UNPERSUADED	UNPOLISHES	UNPREPARED	UNPROFESSIONAL	UNPROVOKEDLY
UNPERSUASIVE	UNPOLISHING	UNPREPAREDLY	UNPROFESSIONALS	UNPROVOKES
UNPERTURBED	UNPOLITELY	UNPREPAREDNESS	UNPROFITABILITY	UNPROVOKING
UNPERVERTED	UNPOLITENESS	UNPREPARES	UNPROFITABLE	UNPUBLICISED
UNPERVERTING	UNPOLITENESSES	UNPREPARING	UNPROFITABLY	UNPUBLICIZED
UNPERVERTS	UNPOLITICAL	UNPREPOSSESSED	UNPROFITED	UNPUBLISHABLE
UNPHILOSOPHIC	UNPOLLUTED	UNPREPOSSESSING	UNPROFITING	UNPUBLISHED
UNPHILOSOPHICAL	UNPOPULARITIES	UNPRESCRIBED	UNPROGRAMMABLE	UNPUCKERED
UNPHONETIC	UNPOPULARITY	UNPRESENTABLE	UNPROGRAMMED	UNPUCKERING

U

UNPUNCTUAL
UNPUNCTUALITIES
UNPUNCTUALITY
UNPUNCTUATED
UNPUNISHABLE
UNPUNISHABLY
UNPUNISHED
UNPURCHASABLE
UNPURCHASEABLE
UNPURCHASED
UNPURIFIED
UNPURPOSED
UNPURVAIDE
UNPURVEYED
UNPUTDOWNABLE
UNPUZZLING
UNQUALIFIABLE
UNQUALIFIED
UNQUALIFIEDLY
UNQUALIFIEDNESS
UNQUALIFIES
UNQUALIFYING
UNQUALITED
UNQUALITIED
UNQUANTIFIABLE
UNQUANTIFIED
UNQUANTISED
UNQUANTIZED
UNQUARRIED
UNQUEENING
UNQUEENLIER
UNQUEENLIEST
UNQUEENLIKE
UNQUENCHABLE
UNQUENCHABLY
UNQUENCHED
UNQUESTIONABLE
UNQUESTIONABLY
UNQUESTIONED
UNQUESTIONING
UNQUESTIONINGLY
UNQUICKENED
UNQUIETEST
UNQUIETING
UNQUIETNESS
UNQUIETNESSES
UNQUOTABLE

UNRANSOMED
UNRATIFIED
UNRAVELING
UNRAVELLED
UNRAVELLER
UNRAVELLERS
UNRAVELLING
UNRAVELLINGS
UNRAVELMENT
UNRAVELMENTS
UNRAVISHED
UNREACHABLE
UNREACTIVE
UNREADABILITIES
UNREADABILITY
UNREADABLE
UNREADABLENESS
UNREADABLY
UNREADIEST
UNREADINESS
UNREADINESSES
UNREALISABLE
UNREALISED
UNREALISES
UNREALISING
UNREALISMS
UNREALISTIC
UNREALISTICALLY
UNREALITIES
UNREALIZABLE
UNREALIZED
UNREALIZES
UNREALIZING
UNREASONABLE
UNREASONABLY
UNREASONED
UNREASONING
UNREASONINGLY
UNRECALLABLE
UNRECALLED
UNRECALLING
UNRECAPTURABLE
UNRECEIPTED
UNRECEIVED
UNRECEPTIVE
UNRECIPROCATED
UNRECKONABLE

UNRECKONED
UNRECLAIMABLE
UNRECLAIMABLY
UNRECLAIMED
UNRECOGNISABLE
UNRECOGNISABLY
UNRECOGNISED
UNRECOGNISING
UNRECOGNIZABLE
UNRECOGNIZABLY
UNRECOGNIZED
UNRECOGNIZING
UNRECOLLECTED
UNRECOMMENDABLE
UNRECOMMENDED
UNRECOMPENSED
UNRECONCILABLE
UNRECONCILABLY
UNRECONCILED
UNRECONCILIABLE
UNRECONSTRUCTED
UNRECORDED
UNRECOUNTED
UNRECOVERABLE
UNRECOVERABLY
UNRECOVERED
UNRECTIFIED
UNRECURING
UNRECYCLABLE
UNREDEEMABLE
UNREDEEMED
UNREDRESSED
UNREDUCIBLE
UNREFLECTED
UNREFLECTING
UNREFLECTINGLY
UNREFLECTIVE
UNREFLECTIVELY
UNREFORMABLE
UNREFORMED
UNREFRACTED
UNREFRESHED
UNREFRESHING
UNREFRIGERATED
UNREGARDED
UNREGARDING
UNREGENERACIES

UNREGENERACY
UNREGENERATE
UNREGENERATED
UNREGENERATELY
UNREGENERATES
UNREGIMENTED
UNREGISTERED
UNREGULATED
UNREHEARSED
UNREINFORCED
UNREJOICED
UNREJOICING
UNRELATIVE
UNRELENTING
UNRELENTINGLY
UNRELENTINGNESS
UNRELENTOR
UNRELENTORS
UNRELIABILITIES
UNRELIABILITY
UNRELIABLE
UNRELIABLENESS
UNRELIEVABLE
UNRELIEVED
UNRELIEVEDLY
UNRELIGIOUS
UNRELIGIOUSLY
UNRELISHED
UNRELUCTANT
UNREMAINING
UNREMARKABLE
UNREMARKABLY
UNREMARKED
UNREMEDIED
UNREMEMBERED
UNREMEMBERING
UNREMINISCENT
UNREMITTED
UNREMITTEDLY
UNREMITTENT
UNREMITTENTLY
UNREMITTING
UNREMITTINGLY
UNREMITTINGNESS
UNREMORSEFUL
UNREMORSEFULLY
UNREMORSELESS

UNREMOVABLE
UNREMUNERATIVE
UNRENDERED
UNREPAIRABLE
UNREPAIRED
UNREPEALABLE
UNREPEALED
UNREPEATABLE
UNREPEATED
UNREPELLED
UNREPENTANCE
UNREPENTANCES
UNREPENTANT
UNREPENTANTLY
UNREPENTED
UNREPENTING
UNREPENTINGLY
UNREPINING
UNREPININGLY
UNREPLACEABLE
UNREPLENISHED
UNREPORTABLE
UNREPORTED
UNREPOSEFUL
UNREPOSING
UNREPRESENTED
UNREPRESSED
UNREPRIEVABLE
UNREPRIEVED
UNREPRIMANDED
UNREPROACHED
UNREPROACHFUL
UNREPROACHING
UNREPRODUCIBLE
UNREPROVABLE
UNREPROVED
UNREPROVING
UNREPUGNANT
UNREPULSABLE
UNREQUIRED
UNREQUISITE
UNREQUITED
UNREQUITEDLY
UNRESCINDED
UNRESENTED
UNRESENTFUL
UNRESENTING

U

UNRESERVED	UNREVERTED	UNSAINTING	UNSCAVENGERED	UNSEEMLINESS
UNRESERVEDLY	UNREVIEWABLE	UNSAINTLIER	UNSCEPTRED	UNSEEMLINESSES
UNRESERVEDNESS	UNREVIEWED	UNSAINTLIEST	UNSCHEDULED	UNSEGMENTED
UNRESERVES	UNREVOLUTIONARY	UNSAINTLINESS	UNSCHOLARLIKE	UNSEGREGATED
UNRESISTANT	UNREWARDED	UNSAINTLINESSES	UNSCHOLARLY	UNSEISABLE
UNRESISTED	UNREWARDEDLY	UNSALABILITIES	UNSCHOOLED	UNSEIZABLE
UNRESISTIBLE	UNREWARDING	UNSALABILITY	UNSCIENTIFIC	UNSELECTED
UNRESISTING	UNRHETORICAL	UNSALARIED	UNSCISSORED	UNSELECTIVE
UNRESISTINGLY	UNRHYTHMIC	UNSALEABILITIES	UNSCORCHED	UNSELECTIVELY
UNRESOLVABLE	UNRHYTHMICAL	UNSALEABILITY	UNSCOTTIFIED	UNSELFCONSCIOUS
UNRESOLVED	UNRHYTHMICALLY	UNSALEABLE	UNSCRAMBLE	UNSELFISHLY
UNRESOLVEDNESS	UNRIDDLEABLE	UNSALVAGEABLE	UNSCRAMBLED	UNSELFISHNESS
UNRESPECTABLE	UNRIDDLERS	UNSANCTIFIED	UNSCRAMBLER	UNSELFISHNESSES
UNRESPECTED	UNRIDDLING	UNSANCTIFIES	UNSCRAMBLERS	UNSELLABLE
UNRESPECTIVE	UNRIDEABLE	UNSANCTIFY	UNSCRAMBLES	UNSEMINARIED
UNRESPITED	UNRIGHTEOUS	UNSANCTIFYING	UNSCRAMBLING	UNSENSATIONAL
UNRESPONSIVE	UNRIGHTEOUSLY	UNSANCTIONED	UNSCRATCHED	UNSENSIBLE
UNRESPONSIVELY	UNRIGHTEOUSNESS	UNSANDALLED	UNSCREENED	UNSENSIBLY
UNRESTFULNESS	UNRIGHTFUL	UNSANITARY	UNSCREWING	UNSENSITISED
UNRESTFULNESSES	UNRIGHTFULLY	UNSATIABLE	UNSCRIPTED	UNSENSITIVE
UNRESTINGLY	UNRIGHTFULNESS	UNSATIATED	UNSCRIPTURAL	UNSENSITIZED
UNRESTINGNESS	UNRIPENESS	UNSATIATING	UNSCRIPTURALLY	UNSENSUALISE
UNRESTINGNESSES	UNRIPENESSES	UNSATIRICAL	UNSCRUPLED	UNSENSUALISED
UNRESTORED	UNRIPPINGS	UNSATISFACTION	UNSCRUPULOSITY	UNSENSUALISES
UNRESTRAINABLE	UNRIVALLED	UNSATISFACTIONS	UNSCRUPULOUS	UNSENSUALISING
UNRESTRAINED	UNRIVETING	UNSATISFACTORY	UNSCRUPULOUSLY	UNSENSUALIZE
UNRESTRAINEDLY	UNROMANISED	UNSATISFIABLE	UNSCRUTINISED	UNSENSUALIZED
UNRESTRAINT	UNROMANIZED	UNSATISFIED	UNSCRUTINIZED	UNSENSUALIZES
UNRESTRAINTS	UNROMANTIC	UNSATISFIEDNESS	UNSCULPTURED	UNSENSUALIZING
UNRESTRICTED	UNROMANTICAL	UNSATISFYING	UNSEALABLE	UNSENTENCED
UNRESTRICTEDLY	UNROMANTICALLY	UNSATURATE	UNSEARCHABLE	UNSENTIMENTAL
UNRETARDED	UNROMANTICISED	UNSATURATED	UNSEARCHABLY	UNSEPARABLE
UNRETENTIVE	UNROMANTICIZED	UNSATURATES	UNSEARCHED	UNSEPARATED
UNRETIRING	UNROOSTING	UNSATURATION	UNSEASONABLE	UNSEPULCHRED
UNRETOUCHED	UNROUNDING	UNSATURATIONS	UNSEASONABLY	UNSERIOUSNESS
UNRETURNABLE	UNRUFFABLE	UNSAVORILY	UNSEASONED	UNSERIOUSNESSES
UNRETURNED	UNRUFFLEDNESS	UNSAVORINESS	UNSEASONEDNESS	UNSERVICEABLE
UNRETURNING	UNRUFFLEDNESSES	UNSAVORINESSES	UNSEASONING	UNSETTLEDLY
UNRETURNINGLY	UNRUFFLING	UNSAVOURILY	UNSEAWORTHINESS	UNSETTLEDNESS
UNREVEALABLE	UNRULIMENT	UNSAVOURINESS	UNSEAWORTHY	UNSETTLEDNESSES
UNREVEALED	UNRULIMENTS	UNSAVOURINESSES	UNSECONDED	UNSETTLEMENT
UNREVEALING	UNRULINESS	UNSAYABLES	UNSECTARIAN	UNSETTLEMENTS
UNREVENGED	UNRULINESSES	UNSCABBARD	UNSECTARIANISM	UNSETTLING
UNREVENGEFUL	UNSADDLING	UNSCABBARDED	UNSECTARIANISMS	UNSETTLINGLY
UNREVEREND	UNSAFENESS	UNSCABBARDING	UNSEEMINGS	UNSETTLINGS
UNREVERENT	UNSAFENESSES	UNSCABBARDS	UNSEEMLIER	UNSHACKLED
UNREVERSED	UNSAFETIES	UNSCALABLE	UNSEEMLIEST	UNSHACKLES

U

UNSHACKLING	UNSISTERED	UNSOLICITOUS	UNSTACKING	UNSTOPPERED
UNSHADOWABLE	UNSISTERLINESS	UNSOLIDITIES	UNSTAIDNESS	UNSTOPPERING
UNSHADOWED	UNSISTERLY	UNSOLIDITY	UNSTAIDNESSES	UNSTOPPERS
UNSHADOWING	UNSIZEABLE	UNSOLVABLE	UNSTAINABLE	UNSTOPPING
UNSHAKABLE	UNSKILFULLY	UNSOPHISTICATE	UNSTANCHABLE	UNSTRAINED
UNSHAKABLENESS	UNSKILFULNESS	UNSOPHISTICATED	UNSTANCHED	UNSTRAPPED
UNSHAKABLY	UNSKILFULNESSES	UNSOUNDABLE	UNSTANDARDISED	UNSTRAPPING
UNSHAKEABLE	UNSKILLFUL	UNSOUNDEST	UNSTANDARDIZED	UNSTRATIFIED
UNSHAKEABLENESS	UNSKILLFULLY	UNSOUNDNESS	UNSTARCHED	UNSTREAMED
UNSHAKEABLY	UNSKILLFULNESS	UNSOUNDNESSES	UNSTARCHES	UNSTRENGTHENED
UNSHAKENLY	UNSLAKABLE	UNSPARINGLY	UNSTARCHING	UNSTRESSED
UNSHAPELIER	UNSLEEPING	UNSPARINGNESS	UNSTARTLING	UNSTRESSES
UNSHAPELIEST	UNSLINGING	UNSPARINGNESSES	UNSTATESMANLIKE	UNSTRIATED
UNSHARPENED	UNSLIPPING	UNSPARRING	UNSTATUTABLE	UNSTRINGED
UNSHEATHED	UNSLUICING	UNSPEAKABLE	UNSTATUTABLY	UNSTRINGING
UNSHEATHES	UNSLUMBERING	UNSPEAKABLENESS	UNSTAUNCHABLE	UNSTRIPPED
UNSHEATHING	UNSLUMBROUS	UNSPEAKABLY	UNSTAUNCHED	UNSTRIPPING
UNSHELLING	UNSMILINGLY	UNSPEAKING	UNSTEADFAST	UNSTRUCTURED
UNSHELTERED	UNSMIRCHED	UNSPECIALISED	UNSTEADFASTLY	UNSUBDUABLE
UNSHIELDED	UNSMOOTHED	UNSPECIALIZED	UNSTEADFASTNESS	UNSUBJECTED
UNSHIFTING	UNSMOOTHING	UNSPECIFIABLE	UNSTEADIED	UNSUBLIMATED
UNSHINGLED	UNSMOTHERABLE	UNSPECIFIC	UNSTEADIER	UNSUBLIMED
UNSHIPPING	UNSNAGGING	UNSPECIFIED	UNSTEADIES	UNSUBMERGED
UNSHOCKABLE	UNSNAPPING	UNSPECTACLED	UNSTEADIEST	UNSUBMISSIVE
UNSHOOTING	UNSNARLING	UNSPECTACULAR	UNSTEADILY	UNSUBMITTING
UNSHOUTING	UNSNECKING	UNSPECULATIVE	UNSTEADINESS	UNSUBSCRIBE
UNSHOWERED	UNSOCIABILITIES	UNSPELLING	UNSTEADINESSES	UNSUBSCRIBED
UNSHRINKABLE	UNSOCIABILITY	UNSPHERING	UNSTEADYING	UNSUBSCRIBES
UNSHRINKING	UNSOCIABLE	UNSPIRITED	UNSTEELING	UNSUBSCRIBING
UNSHRINKINGLY	UNSOCIABLENESS	UNSPIRITUAL	UNSTEPPING	UNSUBSIDISED
UNSHROUDED	UNSOCIABLY	UNSPIRITUALISE	UNSTERCORATED	UNSUBSIDIZED
UNSHROUDING	UNSOCIALISED	UNSPIRITUALISED	UNSTERILISED	UNSUBSTANTIAL
UNSHRUBBED	UNSOCIALISM	UNSPIRITUALISES	UNSTERILIZED	UNSUBSTANTIALLY
UNSHUNNABLE	UNSOCIALISMS	UNSPIRITUALIZE	UNSTICKING	UNSUBSTANTIATED
UNSHUTTERED	UNSOCIALITIES	UNSPIRITUALIZED	UNSTIGMATISED	UNSUCCEEDED
UNSHUTTERING	UNSOCIALITY	UNSPIRITUALIZES	UNSTIGMATIZED	UNSUCCESSES
UNSHUTTERS	UNSOCIALIZED	UNSPIRITUALLY	UNSTIMULATED	UNSUCCESSFUL
UNSHUTTING	UNSOCIALLY	UNSPLINTERABLE	UNSTINTING	UNSUCCESSFULLY
UNSIGHTEDLY	UNSOCKETED	UNSPOOLING	UNSTINTINGLY	UNSUCCESSIVE
UNSIGHTING	UNSOCKETING	UNSPORTING	UNSTITCHED	UNSUCCOURED
UNSIGHTLIER	UNSOFTENED	UNSPORTSMANLIKE	UNSTITCHES	UNSUFFERABLE
UNSIGHTLIEST	UNSOFTENING	UNSPOTTEDNESS	UNSTITCHING	UNSUFFICIENT
UNSIGHTLINESS	UNSOLDERED	UNSPOTTEDNESSES	UNSTOCKING	UNSUITABILITIES
UNSIGHTLINESSES	UNSOLDERING	UNSPRINKLED	UNSTOCKINGED	UNSUITABILITY
UNSINEWING	UNSOLDIERLIKE	UNSTABLENESS	UNSTOOPING	UNSUITABLE
UNSINKABLE	UNSOLDIERLY	UNSTABLENESSES	UNSTOPPABLE	UNSUITABLENESS
UNSINNOWED	UNSOLICITED	UNSTABLEST	UNSTOPPABLY	UNSUITABLY

U

UNSUMMERED	UNSYLLABLED	UNTENANTABLE	UNTIMELIER	UNTREASURES
UNSUMMONED	UNSYMMETRICAL	UNTENANTED	UNTIMELIEST	UNTREASURING
UNSUPERFLUOUS	UNSYMMETRICALLY	UNTENANTING	UNTIMELINESS	UNTREATABLE
UNSUPERVISED	UNSYMMETRIES	UNTENDERED	UNTIMELINESSES	UNTREMBLING
UNSUPPLENESS	UNSYMMETRISED	UNTENDERLY	UNTIMEOUSLY	UNTREMBLINGLY
UNSUPPLENESSES	UNSYMMETRIZED	UNTERMINATED	UNTINCTURED	UNTREMENDOUS
UNSUPPLIED	UNSYMMETRY	UNTERRESTRIAL	UNTIRINGLY	UNTREMULOUS
UNSUPPORTABLE	UNSYMPATHETIC	UNTERRIFIED	UNTOCHERED	UNTRENCHED
UNSUPPORTED	UNSYMPATHIES	UNTERRIFYING	UNTOGETHER	UNTRESPASSING
UNSUPPORTEDLY	UNSYMPATHISING	UNTESTABLE	UNTORMENTED	UNTRIMMING
UNSUPPOSABLE	UNSYMPATHIZING	UNTETHERED	UNTORTURED	UNTROUBLED
UNSUPPRESSED	UNSYMPATHY	UNTETHERING	UNTOUCHABILITY	UNTROUBLEDLY
UNSURFACED	UNSYNCHRONISED	UNTHANKFUL	UNTOUCHABLE	UNTRUENESS
UNSURMISED	UNSYNCHRONIZED	UNTHANKFULLY	UNTOUCHABLES	UNTRUENESSES
UNSURMOUNTABLE	UNSYSTEMATIC	UNTHANKFULNESS	UNTOWARDLINESS	UNTRUSSERS
UNSURPASSABLE	UNSYSTEMATICAL	UNTHATCHED	UNTOWARDLY	UNTRUSSING
UNSURPASSABLY	UNSYSTEMATISED	UNTHATCHES	UNTOWARDNESS	UNTRUSSINGS
UNSURPASSED	UNSYSTEMATIZED	UNTHATCHING	UNTOWARDNESSES	UNTRUSTFUL
UNSURPRISED	UNTACKLING	UNTHEOLOGICAL	UNTRACEABLE	UNTRUSTINESS
UNSURPRISING	UNTAINTEDLY	UNTHEORETICAL	UNTRACKING	UNTRUSTINESSES
UNSURPRISINGLY	UNTAINTEDNESS	UNTHICKENED	UNTRACTABLE	UNTRUSTING
UNSURVEYED	UNTAINTEDNESSES	UNTHINKABILITY	UNTRACTABLENESS	UNTRUSTWORTHILY
UNSUSCEPTIBLE	UNTAINTING	UNTHINKABLE	UNTRADITIONAL	UNTRUSTWORTHY
UNSUSPECTED	UNTALENTED	UNTHINKABLENESS	UNTRADITIONALLY	UNTRUTHFUL
UNSUSPECTEDLY	UNTAMABLENESS	UNTHINKABLY	UNTRAMMELED	UNTRUTHFULLY
UNSUSPECTEDNESS	UNTAMABLENESSES	UNTHINKING	UNTRAMMELLED	UNTRUTHFULNESS
UNSUSPECTING	UNTAMEABLE	UNTHINKINGLY	UNTRAMPLED	UNTUCKERED
UNSUSPECTINGLY	UNTAMEABLENESS	UNTHINKINGNESS	UNTRANQUIL	UNTUMULTUOUS
UNSUSPENDED	UNTAMEABLY	UNTHOROUGH	UNTRANSFERABLE	UNTUNABLENESS
UNSUSPICION	UNTAMEDNESS	UNTHOUGHTFUL	UNTRANSFERRABLE	UNTUNABLENESSES
UNSUSPICIONS	UNTAMEDNESSES	UNTHOUGHTFULLY	UNTRANSFORMED	UNTUNEABLE
UNSUSPICIOUS	UNTANGIBLE	UNTHREADED	UNTRANSLATABLE	UNTUNEFULLY
UNSUSPICIOUSLY	UNTANGLING	UNTHREADING	UNTRANSLATABLY	UNTUNEFULNESS
UNSUSTAINABLE	UNTARNISHED	UNTHREATENED	UNTRANSLATED	UNTUNEFULNESSES
UNSUSTAINED	UNTASTEFUL	UNTHREATENING	UNTRANSMIGRATED	UNTURNABLE
UNSUSTAINING	UNTEACHABLE	UNTHRIFTILY	UNTRANSMISSIBLE	UNTWISTING
UNSWADDLED	UNTEACHABLENESS	UNTHRIFTINESS	UNTRANSMITTED	UNTWISTINGS
UNSWADDLES	UNTEACHING	UNTHRIFTINESSES	UNTRANSMUTABLE	UNTYPICALLY
UNSWADDLING	UNTEARABLE	UNTHRIFTYHEAD	UNTRANSMUTED	UNTYREABLE
UNSWALLOWED	UNTECHNICAL	UNTHRIFTYHEADS	UNTRANSPARENT	UNUNUNIUMS
UNSWATHING	UNTELLABLE	UNTHRIFTYHED	UNTRAVELED	UNUPLIFTED
UNSWAYABLE	UNTEMPERED	UNTHRIFTYHEDS	UNTRAVELLED	UNUSEFULLY
UNSWEARING	UNTEMPERING	UNTHRONING	UNTRAVERSABLE	UNUSEFULNESS
UNSWEARINGS	UNTENABILITIES	UNTIDINESS	UNTRAVERSED	UNUSEFULNESSES
UNSWEETENED	UNTENABILITY	UNTIDINESSES	UNTREADING	UNUSUALNESS
UNSWERVING	UNTENABLENESS	UNTILLABLE	UNTREASURE	UNUSUALNESSES
UNSWERVINGLY	UNTENABLENESSES	UNTIMBERED	UNTREASURED	UNUTILISED

U

UNUTILIZED	UNWANDERING	UNWIELDIEST	UNWORLDLINESSES	UPGATHERING
UNUTTERABLE	UNWARENESS	UNWIELDILY	UNWORSHIPFUL	UPGRADABILITIES
UNUTTERABLENESS	UNWARENESSES	UNWIELDINESS	UNWORSHIPPED	UPGRADABILITY
UNUTTERABLES	UNWARINESS	UNWIELDINESSES	UNWORTHIER	UPGRADABLE
UNUTTERABLY	UNWARINESSES	UNWIELDLILY	UNWORTHIES	UPGRADATION
UNVACCINATED	UNWARRANTABLE	UNWIELDLINESS	UNWORTHIEST	UPGRADATIONS
UNVALUABLE	UNWARRANTABLY	UNWIELDLINESSES	UNWORTHILY	UPGRADEABILITY
UNVANQUISHABLE	UNWARRANTED	UNWIFELIER	UNWORTHINESS	UPGRADEABLE
UNVANQUISHED	UNWARRANTEDLY	UNWIFELIEST	UNWORTHINESSES	UPGROWINGS
UNVARIABLE	UNWASHEDNESS	UNWIFELIKE	UNWOUNDABLE	UPHEAPINGS
UNVARIEGATED	UNWASHEDNESSES	UNWILLINGLY	UNWRAPPING	UPHILLWARD
UNVARNISHED	UNWATCHABLE	UNWILLINGNESS	UNWREATHED	UPHOARDING
UNVEILINGS	UNWATCHFUL	UNWILLINGNESSES	UNWREATHES	UPHOISTING
UNVENDIBLE	UNWATCHFULLY	UNWINDABLE	UNWREATHING	UPHOLDINGS
UNVENERABLE	UNWATCHFULNESS	UNWINDINGS	UNWRINKLED	UPHOLSTERED
UNVENTILATED	UNWATERING	UNWINKINGLY	UNWRINKLES	UPHOLSTERER
UNVERACIOUS	UNWAVERING	UNWINNABLE	UNWRINKLING	UPHOLSTERERS
UNVERACITIES	UNWAVERINGLY	UNWINNOWED	UNYIELDING	UPHOLSTERIES
UNVERACITY	UNWEAKENED	UNWISENESS	UNYIELDINGLY	UPHOLSTERING
UNVERBALISED	UNWEAPONED	UNWISENESSES	UNYIELDINGNESS	UPHOLSTERS
UNVERBALIZED	UNWEAPONING	UNWITCHING	UPBRAIDERS	UPHOLSTERY
UNVERIFIABILITY	UNWEARABLE	UNWITHDRAWING	UPBRAIDING	UPHOLSTRESS
UNVERIFIABLE	UNWEARIABLE	UNWITHERED	UPBRAIDINGLY	UPHOLSTRESSES
UNVERIFIED	UNWEARIABLY	UNWITHERING	UPBRAIDINGS	UPHOORDING
UNVIOLATED	UNWEARIEDLY	UNWITHHELD	UPBREAKING	UPKNITTING
UNVIRTUOUS	UNWEARIEDNESS	UNWITHHOLDEN	UPBRINGING	UPLIFTINGLY
UNVIRTUOUSLY	UNWEARIEDNESSES	UNWITHHOLDING	UPBRINGINGS	UPLIFTINGS
UNVISITABLE	UNWEARYING	UNWITHSTOOD	UPBUILDERS	UPLIGHTERS
UNVISORING	UNWEARYINGLY	UNWITNESSED	UPBUILDING	UPLIGHTING
UNVITIATED	UNWEATHERED	UNWITTINGLY	UPBUILDINGS	UPLINKINGS
UNVITRIFIABLE	UNWEDGABLE	UNWITTINGNESS	UPBUOYANCE	UPMANSHIPS
UNVITRIFIED	UNWEDGEABLE	UNWITTINGNESSES	UPBUOYANCES	UPMARKETED
UNVIZARDED	UNWEETINGLY	UNWOMANING	UPBURSTING	UPMARKETING
UNVIZARDING	UNWEIGHING	UNWOMANLIER	UPCATCHING	UPPERCASED
UNVOCALISED	UNWEIGHTED	UNWOMANLIEST	UPCHEERING	UPPERCASES
UNVOCALIZED	UNWEIGHTING	UNWOMANLINESS	UPCHUCKING	UPPERCASING
UNVOICINGS	UNWELCOMED	UNWOMANLINESSES	UPCLIMBING	UPPERCLASSMAN
UNVOYAGEABLE	UNWELCOMELY	UNWONTEDLY	UPCOUNTRIES	UPPERCLASSMEN
UNVULGARISE	UNWELCOMENESS	UNWONTEDNESS	UPDATEABLE	UPPERCUTTING
UNVULGARISED	UNWELCOMENESSES	UNWONTEDNESSES	UPDRAGGING	UPPERPARTS
UNVULGARISES	UNWELLNESS	UNWORKABILITIES	UPDRAUGHTS	UPPERWORKS
UNVULGARISING	UNWELLNESSES	UNWORKABILITY	UPFILLINGS	UPPISHNESS
UNVULGARIZE	UNWHISTLEABLE	UNWORKABLE	UPFLASHING	UPPISHNESSES
UNVULGARIZED	UNWHOLESOME	UNWORKMANLIKE	UPFLINGING	UPPITINESS
UNVULGARIZES	UNWHOLESOMELY	UNWORLDLIER	UPFOLLOWED	UPPITINESSES
UNVULGARIZING	UNWHOLESOMENESS	UNWORLDLIEST	UPFOLLOWING	UPPITYNESS
UNVULNERABLE	UNWIELDIER	UNWORLDLINESS	UPGATHERED	UPPITYNESSES

UPPROPPING	UPTRAINING	URBANOLOGISTS	UROGRAPHIES	USUCAPIONS
UPREACHING	UPTURNINGS	URBANOLOGY	UROKINASES	USUCAPTIBLE
UPRIGHTEOUSLY	UPVALUATION	URCEOLUSES	UROLAGNIAS	USUCAPTING
UPRIGHTING	UPVALUATIONS	UREDINIOSPORE	UROLITHIASES	USUCAPTION
UPRIGHTNESS	UPWARDNESS	UREDINIOSPORES	UROLITHIASIS	USUCAPTIONS
UPRIGHTNESSES	UPWARDNESSES	UREDIOSPORE	UROLOGICAL	USUFRUCTED
UPROARIOUS	UPWELLINGS	UREDIOSPORES	UROLOGISTS	USUFRUCTING
UPROARIOUSLY	UPWHIRLING	UREDOSORUS	UROPOIESES	USUFRUCTUARIES
UPROARIOUSNESS	URALITISATION	UREDOSPORE	UROPOIESIS	USUFRUCTUARY
UPROOTEDNESS	URALITISATIONS	UREDOSPORES	UROPYGIUMS	USURIOUSLY
UPROOTEDNESSES	URALITISED	UREOTELISM	UROSCOPIES	USURIOUSNESS
UPROOTINGS	URALITISES	UREOTELISMS	UROSCOPIST	USURIOUSNESSES
UPSETTABLE	URALITISING	URETERITIS	UROSCOPISTS	USURPATION
UPSETTINGLY	URALITIZATION	URETERITISES	UROSTEGITE	USURPATIONS
UPSETTINGS	URALITIZATIONS	URETHRITIC	UROSTEGITES	USURPATIVE
UPSHIFTING	URALITIZED	URETHRITIS	UROSTHENIC	USURPATORY
UPSHOOTING	URALITIZES	URETHRITISES	UROSTOMIES	USURPATURE
UPSIDEOWNE	URALITIZING	URETHROSCOPE	URTICACEOUS	USURPATURES
UPSITTINGS	URANALYSES	URETHROSCOPES	URTICARIAL	USURPINGLY
UPSKILLING	URANALYSIS	URETHROSCOPIC	URTICARIAS	UTERECTOMIES
UPSPEAKING	URANINITES	URETHROSCOPIES	URTICARIOUS	UTERECTOMY
UPSPEARING	URANOGRAPHER	URETHROSCOPY	URTICATING	UTERITISES
UPSPRINGING	URANOGRAPHERS	URICOSURIC	URTICATION	UTEROGESTATION
UPSTANDING	URANOGRAPHIC	URICOTELIC	URTICATIONS	UTEROGESTATIONS
UPSTANDINGNESS	URANOGRAPHICAL	URICOTELISM	USABILITIES	UTEROTOMIES
UPSTARTING	URANOGRAPHIES	URICOTELISMS	USABLENESS	UTILISABLE
UPSTEPPING	URANOGRAPHIST	URINALYSES	USABLENESSES	UTILISATION
UPSTIRRING	URANOGRAPHISTS	URINALYSIS	USEABILITIES	UTILISATIONS
UPSTREAMED	URANOGRAPHY	URINATIONS	USEABILITY	UTILITARIAN
UPSTREAMING	URANOLOGIES	URINIFEROUS	USEABLENESS	UTILITARIANISE
UPSTRETCHED	URANOMETRIES	URINIPAROUS	USEABLENESSES	UTILITARIANISED
UPSURGENCE	URANOMETRY	URINOGENITAL	USEFULNESS	UTILITARIANISES
UPSURGENCES	URANOPLASTIES	URINOLOGIES	USEFULNESSES	UTILITARIANISM
UPSWEEPING	URANOPLASTY	URINOMETER	USELESSNESS	UTILITARIANISMS
UPSWELLING	URBANENESS	URINOMETERS	USELESSNESSES	UTILITARIANIZE
UPSWINGING	URBANENESSES	URINOSCOPIES	USHERESSES	UTILITARIANIZED
UPTALKINGS	URBANISATION	URINOSCOPY	USHERETTES	UTILITARIANIZES
UPTHROWING	URBANISATIONS	UROBILINOGEN	USHERSHIPS	UTILITARIANS
UPTHRUSTED	URBANISING	UROBILINOGENS	USQUEBAUGH	UTILIZABLE
UPTHRUSTING	URBANISTIC	UROBOROSES	USQUEBAUGHS	UTILIZATION
UPTHUNDERED	URBANISTICALLY	UROCHORDAL	USTILAGINEOUS	UTILIZATIONS
UPTHUNDERING	URBANITIES	UROCHORDATE	USTILAGINOUS	UTOPIANISE
UPTHUNDERS	URBANIZATION	UROCHORDATES	USTULATION	UTOPIANISED
UPTIGHTEST	URBANIZATIONS	UROCHROMES	USTULATIONS	UTOPIANISER
UPTIGHTNESS	URBANIZING	URODYNAMICS	USUALNESSES	UTOPIANISERS
UPTIGHTNESSES	URBANOLOGIES	UROGENITAL	USUCAPIENT	UTOPIANISES
UPTITLINGS	URBANOLOGIST	UROGRAPHIC	USUCAPIENTS	UTOPIANISING

U

UTOPIANISM

UTOPIANISM	UTOPIANIZES	UTRICULITISES	UVAROVITES	UXORIOUSNESS
UTOPIANISMS	UTOPIANIZING	UTTERABLENESS	UVULITISES	UXORIOUSNESSES
UTOPIANIZE	UTRICULARIA	UTTERABLENESSES	UXORICIDAL	
UTOPIANIZED	UTRICULARIAS	UTTERANCES	UXORICIDES	
UTOPIANIZER	UTRICULATE	UTTERMOSTS	UXORILOCAL	
UTOPIANIZERS	UTRICULITIS	UTTERNESSES	UXORIOUSLY	

U

V

VACANTNESS	VAGABONDISES	VALIANCIES	VANCOMYCINS	VAPORIMETERS
VACANTNESSES	VAGABONDISH	VALIANTNESS	VANDALISATION	VAPORISABLE
VACATIONED	VAGABONDISING	VALIANTNESSES	VANDALISATIONS	VAPORISATION
VACATIONER	VAGABONDISM	VALIDATING	VANDALISED	VAPORISATIONS
VACATIONERS	VAGABONDISMS	VALIDATION	VANDALISES	VAPORISERS
VACATIONING	VAGABONDIZE	VALIDATIONS	VANDALISING	VAPORISHNESS
VACATIONIST	VAGABONDIZED	VALIDATORY	VANDALISMS	VAPORISHNESSES
VACATIONISTS	VAGABONDIZES	VALIDITIES	VANDALISTIC	VAPORISING
VACATIONLAND	VAGABONDIZING	VALIDNESSES	VANDALIZATION	VAPORIZABLE
VACATIONLANDS	VAGARIOUSLY	VALLATIONS	VANDALIZATIONS	VAPORIZATION
VACATIONLESS	VAGILITIES	VALLECULAE	VANDALIZED	VAPORIZATIONS
VACCINATED	VAGINECTOMIES	VALLECULAR	VANDALIZES	VAPORIZERS
VACCINATES	VAGINECTOMY	VALLECULATE	VANDALIZING	VAPORIZING
VACCINATING	VAGINICOLINE	VALORISATION	VANGUARDISM	VAPOROSITIES
VACCINATION	VAGINICOLOUS	VALORISATIONS	VANGUARDISMS	VAPOROSITY
VACCINATIONS	VAGINISMUS	VALORISING	VANGUARDIST	VAPOROUSLY
VACCINATOR	VAGINISMUSES	VALORIZATION	VANGUARDISTS	VAPOROUSNESS
VACCINATORS	VAGINITISES	VALORIZATIONS	VANISHINGLY	VAPOROUSNESSES
VACCINATORY	VAGOTOMIES	VALORIZING	VANISHINGS	VAPORWARES
VACCINIUMS	VAGOTONIAS	VALOROUSLY	VANISHMENT	VAPOURABILITIES
VACILLATED	VAGOTROPIC	VALPOLICELLA	VANISHMENTS	VAPOURABILITY
VACILLATES	VAGRANCIES	VALPOLICELLAS	VANITORIES	VAPOURABLE
VACILLATING	VAGRANTNESS	VALPROATES	VANPOOLING	VAPOURINGLY
VACILLATINGLY	VAGRANTNESSES	VALUABLENESS	VANPOOLINGS	VAPOURINGS
VACILLATION	VAGUENESSES	VALUABLENESSES	VANQUISHABLE	VAPOURISHNESS
VACILLATIONS	VAINGLORIED	VALUATIONAL	VANQUISHED	VAPOURISHNESSES
VACILLATOR	VAINGLORIES	VALUATIONALLY	VANQUISHER	VAPOURLESS
VACILLATORS	VAINGLORIOUS	VALUATIONS	VANQUISHERS	VAPOURWARE
VACILLATORY	VAINGLORIOUSLY	VALUELESSNESS	VANQUISHES	VAPOURWARES
VACUATIONS	VAINGLORYING	VALUELESSNESSES	VANQUISHING	VAPULATING
VACUOLATED	VAINNESSES	VALVASSORS	VANQUISHMENT	VAPULATION
VACUOLATION	VAIVODESHIP	VALVULITIS	VANQUISHMENTS	VAPULATIONS
VACUOLATIONS	VAIVODESHIPS	VALVULITISES	VANTAGELESS	VARIABILITIES
VACUOLISATION	VALEDICTION	VAMPIRISED	VANTBRACES	VARIABILITY
VACUOLISATIONS	VALEDICTIONS	VAMPIRISES	VANTBRASSES	VARIABLENESS
VACUOLIZATION	VALEDICTORIAN	VAMPIRISING	VAPIDITIES	VARIABLENESSES
VACUOLIZATIONS	VALEDICTORIANS	VAMPIRISMS	VAPIDNESSES	VARIATIONAL
VACUOUSNESS	VALEDICTORIES	VAMPIRIZED	VAPORABILITIES	VARIATIONALLY
VACUOUSNESSES	VALEDICTORY	VAMPIRIZES	VAPORABILITY	VARIATIONIST
VAGABONDAGE	VALENTINES	VAMPIRIZING	VAPORESCENCE	VARIATIONISTS
VAGABONDAGES	VALERIANACEOUS	VANADIATES	VAPORESCENCES	VARIATIONS
VAGABONDED	VALETUDINARIAN	VANADINITE	VAPORESCENT	VARICELLAR
VAGABONDING	VALETUDINARIANS	VANADINITES	VAPORETTOS	VARICELLAS
VAGABONDISE	VALETUDINARIES	VANASPATIS	VAPORIFORM	VARICELLATE
VAGABONDISED	VALETUDINARY	VANCOMYCIN	VAPORIMETER	VARICELLOID

ten to fifteen letter words | 1167

VARICELLOUS	VARNISHINGS	VASOPRESSOR	VECTORISES	VELLICATES
VARICOCELE	VARSOVIENNE	VASOPRESSORS	VECTORISING	VELLICATING
VARICOCELES	VARSOVIENNES	VASOSPASMS	VECTORIZATION	VELLICATION
VARICOLORED	VASCULARISATION	VASOSPASTIC	VECTORIZATIONS	VELLICATIONS
VARICOLOURED	VASCULARISE	VASOTOCINS	VECTORIZED	VELLICATIVE
VARICOSITIES	VASCULARISED	VASOTOMIES	VECTORIZES	VELOCIMETER
VARICOSITY	VASCULARISES	VASSALAGES	VECTORIZING	VELOCIMETERS
VARICOTOMIES	VASCULARISING	VASSALESSES	VECTORSCOPE	VELOCIMETRIES
VARICOTOMY	VASCULARITIES	VASSALISED	VECTORSCOPES	VELOCIMETRY
VARIEDNESS	VASCULARITY	VASSALISES	VEGEBURGER	VELOCIPEDE
VARIEDNESSES	VASCULARIZATION	VASSALISING	VEGEBURGERS	VELOCIPEDEAN
VARIEGATED	VASCULARIZE	VASSALIZED	VEGETABLES	VELOCIPEDEANS
VARIEGATES	VASCULARIZED	VASSALIZES	VEGETARIAN	VELOCIPEDED
VARIEGATING	VASCULARIZES	VASSALIZING	VEGETARIANISM	VELOCIPEDER
VARIEGATION	VASCULARIZING	VASSALLING	VEGETARIANISMS	VELOCIPEDERS
VARIEGATIONS	VASCULARLY	VASSALRIES	VEGETARIANS	VELOCIPEDES
VARIEGATOR	VASCULATURE	VASTIDITIES	VEGETATING	VELOCIPEDIAN
VARIEGATORS	VASCULATURES	VASTITUDES	VEGETATINGS	VELOCIPEDIANS
VARIETALLY	VASCULIFORM	VASTNESSES	VEGETATION	VELOCIPEDING
VARIFOCALS	VASCULITIDES	VATICINATE	VEGETATIONAL	VELOCIPEDIST
VARIFORMLY	VASCULITIS	VATICINATED	VEGETATIONS	VELOCIPEDISTS
VARIOLATED	VASECTOMIES	VATICINATES	VEGETATIOUS	VELOCIRAPTOR
VARIOLATES	VASECTOMISE	VATICINATING	VEGETATIVE	VELOCIRAPTORS
VARIOLATING	VASECTOMISED	VATICINATION	VEGETATIVELY	VELOCITIES
VARIOLATION	VASECTOMISES	VATICINATIONS	VEGETATIVENESS	VELODROMES
VARIOLATIONS	VASECTOMISING	VATICINATOR	VEGGIEBURGER	VELOUTINES
VARIOLATOR	VASECTOMIZE	VATICINATORS	VEGGIEBURGERS	VELUTINOUS
VARIOLATORS	VASECTOMIZED	VATICINATORY	VEHEMENCES	VELVETEENED
VARIOLISATION	VASECTOMIZES	VAUDEVILLE	VEHEMENCIES	VELVETEENS
VARIOLISATIONS	VASECTOMIZING	VAUDEVILLEAN	VEHEMENTLY	VELVETIEST
VARIOLITES	VASOACTIVE	VAUDEVILLEANS	VEILLEUSES	VELVETINESS
VARIOLITIC	VASOACTIVITIES	VAUDEVILLES	VEINSTONES	VELVETINESSES
VARIOLIZATION	VASOACTIVITY	VAUDEVILLIAN	VEINSTUFFS	VELVETINGS
VARIOLIZATIONS	VASOCONSTRICTOR	VAUDEVILLIANS	VELARISATION	VELVETLIKE
VARIOLOIDS	VASODILATATION	VAUDEVILLIST	VELARISATIONS	VENALITIES
VARIOMETER	VASODILATATIONS	VAUDEVILLISTS	VELARISING	VENATICALLY
VARIOMETERS	VASODILATATORY	VAULTINGLY	VELARIZATION	VENATIONAL
VARIOUSNESS	VASODILATION	VAUNTERIES	VELARIZATIONS	VENATORIAL
VARIOUSNESSES	VASODILATIONS	VAUNTINGLY	VELARIZING	VENDETTIST
VARISCITES	VASODILATOR	VAVASORIES	VELDSCHOEN	VENDETTISTS
VARITYPING	VASODILATORS	VECTOGRAPH	VELDSCHOENS	VENDIBILITIES
VARITYPIST	VASODILATORY	VECTOGRAPHS	VELDSKOENS	VENDIBILITY
VARITYPISTS	VASOINHIBITOR	VECTORIALLY	VELITATION	VENDIBLENESS
VARLETESSES	VASOINHIBITORS	VECTORINGS	VELITATIONS	VENDIBLENESSES
VARLETRIES	VASOINHIBITORY	VECTORISATION	VELLEITIES	VENDITATION
VARNISHERS	VASOPRESSIN	VECTORISATIONS	VELLENAGES	VENDITATIONS
VARNISHING	VASOPRESSINS	VECTORISED	VELLICATED	VENDITIONS

VENEERINGS	VENOSCLEROSES	VENTRIPOTENT	VERBICIDES	VERKRAMPTES
VENEFICALLY	VENOSCLEROSIS	VENTROLATERAL	VERBIFICATION	VERMEILING
VENEFICIOUS	VENOSITIES	VENTROMEDIAL	VERBIFICATIONS	VERMEILLED
VENEFICIOUSLY	VENOUSNESS	VENTURESOME	VERBIFYING	VERMEILLES
VENEFICOUS	VENOUSNESSES	VENTURESOMELY	VERBIGERATE	VERMEILLING
VENEFICOUSLY	VENTIDUCTS	VENTURESOMENESS	VERBIGERATED	VERMICELLI
VENENATING	VENTIFACTS	VENTURINGLY	VERBIGERATES	VERMICELLIS
VENEPUNCTURE	VENTILABLE	VENTURINGS	VERBIGERATING	VERMICIDAL
VENEPUNCTURES	VENTILATED	VENTUROUSLY	VERBIGERATION	VERMICIDES
VENERABILITIES	VENTILATES	VENTUROUSNESS	VERBIGERATIONS	VERMICULAR
VENERABILITY	VENTILATING	VENTUROUSNESSES	VERBOSENESS	VERMICULARLY
VENERABLENESS	VENTILATION	VERACIOUSLY	VERBOSENESSES	VERMICULATE
VENERABLENESSES	VENTILATIONS	VERACIOUSNESS	VERBOSITIES	VERMICULATED
VENERABLES	VENTILATIVE	VERACIOUSNESSES	VERDANCIES	VERMICULATES
VENERATING	VENTILATOR	VERACITIES	VERDIGRISED	VERMICULATING
VENERATION	VENTILATORS	VERANDAHED	VERDIGRISES	VERMICULATION
VENERATIONAL	VENTILATORY	VERAPAMILS	VERDIGRISING	VERMICULATIONS
VENERATIONS	VENTOSITIES	VERATRIDINE	VERDURELESS	VERMICULES
VENERATIVENESS	VENTRICLES	VERATRIDINES	VERGEBOARD	VERMICULITE
VENERATORS	VENTRICOSE	VERATRINES	VERGEBOARDS	VERMICULITES
VENEREOLOGICAL	VENTRICOSITIES	VERBALISATION	VERGENCIES	VERMICULOUS
VENEREOLOGIES	VENTRICOSITY	VERBALISATIONS	VERGERSHIP	VERMICULTURE
VENEREOLOGIST	VENTRICOUS	VERBALISED	VERGERSHIPS	VERMICULTURES
VENEREOLOGISTS	VENTRICULAR	VERBALISER	VERIDICALITIES	VERMIFUGAL
VENEREOLOGY	VENTRICULE	VERBALISERS	VERIDICALITY	VERMIFUGES
VENESECTION	VENTRICULES	VERBALISES	VERIDICALLY	VERMILIONED
VENESECTIONS	VENTRICULI	VERBALISING	VERIDICOUS	VERMILIONING
VENGEANCES	VENTRICULUS	VERBALISMS	VERIFIABILITIES	VERMILIONS
VENGEFULLY	VENTRILOQUAL	VERBALISTIC	VERIFIABILITY	VERMILLING
VENGEFULNESS	VENTRILOQUIAL	VERBALISTS	VERIFIABLE	VERMILLION
VENGEFULNESSES	VENTRILOQUIALLY	VERBALITIES	VERIFIABLENESS	VERMILLIONS
VENGEMENTS	VENTRILOQUIES	VERBALIZATION	VERIFIABLY	VERMINATED
VENIALITIES	VENTRILOQUISE	VERBALIZATIONS	VERIFICATION	VERMINATES
VENIALNESS	VENTRILOQUISED	VERBALIZED	VERIFICATIONS	VERMINATING
VENIALNESSES	VENTRILOQUISES	VERBALIZER	VERIFICATIVE	VERMINATION
VENIPUNCTURE	VENTRILOQUISING	VERBALIZERS	VERIFICATORY	VERMINATIONS
VENIPUNCTURES	VENTRILOQUISM	VERBALIZES	VERISIMILAR	VERMINOUSLY
VENISECTION	VENTRILOQUISMS	VERBALIZING	VERISIMILARLY	VERMINOUSNESS
VENISECTIONS	VENTRILOQUIST	VERBALLING	VERISIMILITIES	VERMINOUSNESSES
VENOGRAPHIC	VENTRILOQUISTIC	VERBARIANS	VERISIMILITUDE	VERMIVOROUS
VENOGRAPHICAL	VENTRILOQUISTS	VERBASCUMS	VERISIMILITUDES	VERNACULAR
VENOGRAPHIES	VENTRILOQUIZE	VERBENACEOUS	VERISIMILITY	VERNACULARISE
VENOGRAPHY	VENTRILOQUIZED	VERBERATED	VERISIMILOUS	VERNACULARISED
VENOLOGIES	VENTRILOQUIZES	VERBERATES	VERITABLENESS	VERNACULARISES
VENOMOUSLY	VENTRILOQUIZING	VERBERATING	VERITABLENESSES	VERNACULARISING
VENOMOUSNESS	VENTRILOQUOUS	VERBERATION	VERJUICING	VERNACULARISM
VENOMOUSNESSES	VENTRILOQUY	VERBERATIONS	VERKRAMPTE	VERNACULARISMS

VERNACULARIST	VERSIONIST	VESICULATION	VIABILITIES	VICEROYALTY
VERNACULARISTS	VERSIONISTS	VESICULATIONS	VIBRACULAR	VICEROYSHIP
VERNACULARITIES	VERSLIBRIST	VESICULOSE	VIBRACULARIA	VICEROYSHIPS
VERNACULARITY	VERSLIBRISTE	VESPERTILIAN	VIBRACULARIUM	VICHYSSOIS
VERNACULARIZE	VERSLIBRISTES	VESPERTILIONID	VIBRACULOID	VICHYSSOISE
VERNACULARIZED	VERSLIBRISTS	VESPERTILIONIDS	VIBRACULUM	VICHYSSOISES
VERNACULARIZES	VERTEBRALLY	VESPERTILIONINE	VIBRAHARPIST	VICINITIES
VERNACULARIZING	VERTEBRATE	VESPERTINAL	VIBRAHARPISTS	VICIOSITIES
VERNACULARLY	VERTEBRATED	VESPERTINE	VIBRAHARPS	VICIOUSNESS
VERNACULARS	VERTEBRATES	VESPIARIES	VIBRANCIES	VICIOUSNESSES
VERNALISATION	VERTEBRATION	VESTIARIES	VIBRAPHONE	VICISSITUDE
VERNALISATIONS	VERTEBRATIONS	VESTIBULAR	VIBRAPHONES	VICISSITUDES
VERNALISED	VERTICALITIES	VESTIBULED	VIBRAPHONIST	VICISSITUDINARY
VERNALISES	VERTICALITY	VESTIBULES	VIBRAPHONISTS	VICISSITUDINOUS
VERNALISING	VERTICALLY	VESTIBULING	VIBRATILITIES	VICOMTESSE
VERNALITIES	VERTICALNESS	VESTIBULITIS	VIBRATILITY	VICOMTESSES
VERNALIZATION	VERTICALNESSES	VESTIBULITISES	VIBRATINGLY	VICTIMHOOD
VERNALIZATIONS	VERTICILLASTER	VESTIBULUM	VIBRATIONAL	VICTIMHOODS
VERNALIZED	VERTICILLASTERS	VESTIGIALLY	VIBRATIONLESS	VICTIMISATION
VERNALIZES	VERTICILLATE	VESTIMENTAL	VIBRATIONS	VICTIMISATIONS
VERNALIZING	VERTICILLATED	VESTIMENTARY	VIBRATIUNCLE	VICTIMISED
VERNATIONS	VERTICILLATELY	VESTIMENTS	VIBRATIUNCLES	VICTIMISER
VERNISSAGE	VERTICILLATION	VESTITURES	VIBRATOLESS	VICTIMISERS
VERNISSAGES	VERTICILLATIONS	VESTMENTAL	VIBROFLOTATION	VICTIMISES
VERRUCIFORM	VERTICILLIUM	VESTMENTED	VIBROFLOTATIONS	VICTIMISING
VERRUCOSITIES	VERTICILLIUMS	VESUVIANITE	VIBROGRAPH	VICTIMIZATION
VERRUCOSITY	VERTICITIES	VESUVIANITES	VIBROGRAPHS	VICTIMIZATIONS
VERSABILITIES	VERTIGINES	VETCHLINGS	VIBROMETER	VICTIMIZED
VERSABILITY	VERTIGINOUS	VETERINARIAN	VIBROMETERS	VICTIMIZER
VERSATILELY	VERTIGINOUSLY	VETERINARIANS	VICARESSES	VICTIMIZERS
VERSATILENESS	VERTIGINOUSNESS	VETERINARIES	VICARIANCE	VICTIMIZES
VERSATILENESSES	VERTIPORTS	VETERINARY	VICARIANCES	VICTIMIZING
VERSATILITIES	VERUMONTANA	VEXATIOUSLY	VICARIANTS	VICTIMLESS
VERSATILITY	VERUMONTANUM	VEXATIOUSNESS	VICARIATES	VICTIMOLOGIES
VERSICOLOR	VERUMONTANUMS	VEXATIOUSNESSES	VICARIOUSLY	VICTIMOLOGIST
VERSICOLOUR	VESICATING	VEXEDNESSES	VICARIOUSNESS	VICTIMOLOGISTS
VERSICOLOURED	VESICATION	VEXILLARIES	VICARIOUSNESSES	VICTIMOLOGY
VERSICULAR	VESICATIONS	VEXILLATION	VICARSHIPS	VICTORESSES
VERSIFICATION	VESICATORIES	VEXILLATIONS	VICEGERENCIES	VICTORIANA
VERSIFICATIONS	VESICATORY	VEXILLOLOGIC	VICEGERENCY	VICTORINES
VERSIFICATOR	VESICULARITIES	VEXILLOLOGICAL	VICEGERENT	VICTORIOUS
VERSIFICATORS	VESICULARITY	VEXILLOLOGIES	VICEGERENTS	VICTORIOUSLY
VERSIFIERS	VESICULARLY	VEXILLOLOGIST	VICEREGALLY	VICTORIOUSNESS
VERSIFYING	VESICULATE	VEXILLOLOGISTS	VICEREGENT	VICTORYLESS
VERSIONERS	VESICULATED	VEXILLOLOGY	VICEREGENTS	VICTRESSES
VERSIONING	VESICULATES	VEXINGNESS	VICEREINES	VICTUALAGE
VERSIONINGS	VESICULATING	VEXINGNESSES	VICEROYALTIES	VICTUALAGES

V

VICTUALERS	VIGINTILLION	VILLIAGOES	VINICULTURAL	VIRGINALLING
VICTUALING	VIGINTILLIONS	VILLICATION	VINICULTURE	VIRGINALLY
VICTUALLAGE	VIGNETTERS	VILLICATIONS	VINICULTURES	VIRGINHOOD
VICTUALLAGES	VIGNETTING	VILLOSITIES	VINICULTURIST	VIRGINHOODS
VICTUALLED	VIGNETTINGS	VINAIGRETTE	VINICULTURISTS	VIRGINITIES
VICTUALLER	VIGNETTIST	VINAIGRETTES	VINIFEROUS	VIRGINIUMS
VICTUALLERS	VIGNETTISTS	VINBLASTINE	VINIFICATION	VIRIDESCENCE
VICTUALLESS	VIGORISHES	VINBLASTINES	VINIFICATIONS	VIRIDESCENCES
VICTUALLING	VIGOROUSLY	VINCIBILITIES	VINIFICATOR	VIRIDESCENT
VIDEOCASSETTE	VIGOROUSNESS	VINCIBILITY	VINIFICATORS	VIRIDITIES
VIDEOCASSETTES	VIGOROUSNESSES	VINCIBLENESS	VINOLOGIES	VIRILESCENCE
VIDEOCONFERENCE	VIKINGISMS	VINCIBLENESSES	VINOLOGIST	VIRILESCENCES
VIDEODISCS	VILDNESSES	VINCRISTINE	VINOLOGISTS	VIRILESCENT
VIDEODISKS	VILENESSES	VINCRISTINES	VINOSITIES	VIRILISATION
VIDEOGRAMS	VILIFICATION	VINDEMIATE	VINTAGINGS	VIRILISATIONS
VIDEOGRAPHER	VILIFICATIONS	VINDEMIATED	VINYLCYANIDE	VIRILISING
VIDEOGRAPHERS	VILIPENDED	VINDEMIATES	VINYLCYANIDES	VIRILITIES
VIDEOGRAPHIES	VILIPENDER	VINDEMIATING	VINYLIDENE	VIRILIZATION
VIDEOGRAPHY	VILIPENDERS	VINDICABILITIES	VINYLIDENES	VIRILIZATIONS
VIDEOLANDS	VILIPENDING	VINDICABILITY	VIOLABILITIES	VIRILIZING
VIDEOPHILE	VILLAGERIES	VINDICABLE	VIOLABILITY	VIROLOGICAL
VIDEOPHILES	VILLAGIOES	VINDICATED	VIOLABLENESS	VIROLOGICALLY
VIDEOPHONE	VILLAGISATION	VINDICATES	VIOLABLENESSES	VIROLOGIES
VIDEOPHONES	VILLAGISATIONS	VINDICATING	VIOLACEOUS	VIROLOGIST
VIDEOPHONIC	VILLAGIZATION	VINDICATION	VIOLATIONS	VIROLOGISTS
VIDEOTAPED	VILLAGIZATIONS	VINDICATIONS	VIOLENTING	VIRTUALISE
VIDEOTAPES	VILLAGREES	VINDICATIVE	VIOLINISTIC	VIRTUALISED
VIDEOTAPING	VILLAINAGE	VINDICATIVENESS	VIOLINISTICALLY	VIRTUALISES
VIDEOTELEPHONE	VILLAINAGES	VINDICATOR	VIOLINISTS	VIRTUALISING
VIDEOTELEPHONES	VILLAINESS	VINDICATORILY	VIOLONCELLI	VIRTUALISM
VIDEOTEXES	VILLAINESSES	VINDICATORS	VIOLONCELLIST	VIRTUALISMS
VIDEOTEXTS	VILLAINIES	VINDICATORY	VIOLONCELLISTS	VIRTUALIST
VIEWERSHIP	VILLAINOUS	VINDICATRESS	VIOLONCELLO	VIRTUALISTS
VIEWERSHIPS	VILLAINOUSLY	VINDICATRESSES	VIOLONCELLOS	VIRTUALITIES
VIEWFINDER	VILLAINOUSNESS	VINDICTIVE	VIOSTEROLS	VIRTUALITY
VIEWFINDERS	VILLANAGES	VINDICTIVELY	VIPERFISHES	VIRTUALIZE
VIEWINESSES	VILLANELLA	VINDICTIVENESS	VIPERIFORM	VIRTUALIZED
VIEWLESSLY	VILLANELLAS	VINEDRESSER	VIPERISHLY	VIRTUALIZES
VIEWPHONES	VILLANELLE	VINEDRESSERS	VIPEROUSLY	VIRTUALIZING
VIEWPOINTS	VILLANELLES	VINEGARETTE	VIRAGINIAN	VIRTUELESS
VIGILANCES	VILLANOUSLY	VINEGARETTES	VIRAGINOUS	VIRTUOSITIES
VIGILANTES	VILLEGGIATURA	VINEGARING	VIREONINES	VIRTUOSITY
VIGILANTISM	VILLEGGIATURAS	VINEGARISH	VIRESCENCE	VIRTUOSOSHIP
VIGILANTISMS	VILLEINAGE	VINEGARROON	VIRESCENCES	VIRTUOSOSHIPS
VIGILANTLY	VILLEINAGES	VINEGARROONS	VIRGINALIST	VIRTUOUSLY
VIGILANTNESS	VILLENAGES	VINEYARDIST	VIRGINALISTS	VIRTUOUSNESS
VIGILANTNESSES	VILLIACOES	VINEYARDISTS	VIRGINALLED	VIRTUOUSNESSES

VIRULENCES

VIRULENCES	VISIBLENESSES	VITAMINISE	VITREOUSNESS	VITUPERATORS
VIRULENCIES	VISIOGENIC	VITAMINISED	VITREOUSNESSES	VITUPERATORY
VIRULENTLY	VISIONALLY	VITAMINISES	VITRESCENCE	VIVACIOUSLY
VIRULIFEROUS	VISIONARIES	VITAMINISING	VITRESCENCES	VIVACIOUSNESS
VISAGISTES	VISIONARINESS	VITAMINIZE	VITRESCENT	VIVACIOUSNESSES
VISCACHERA	VISIONARINESSES	VITAMINIZED	VITRESCIBILITY	VIVACISSIMO
VISCACHERAS	VISIONINGS	VITAMINIZES	VITRESCIBLE	VIVACITIES
VISCERALLY	VISIONISTS	VITAMINIZING	VITRIFACTION	VIVANDIERE
VISCERATED	VISIONLESS	VITASCOPES	VITRIFACTIONS	VIVANDIERES
VISCERATES	VISIOPHONE	VITATIVENESS	VITRIFACTURE	VIVANDIERS
VISCERATING	VISIOPHONES	VITATIVENESSES	VITRIFACTURES	VIVERRINES
VISCEROMOTOR	VISITATION	VITELLICLE	VITRIFIABILITY	VIVIANITES
VISCEROPTOSES	VISITATIONAL	VITELLICLES	VITRIFIABLE	VIVIDITIES
VISCEROPTOSIS	VISITATIONS	VITELLIGENOUS	VITRIFICATION	VIVIDNESSES
VISCEROTONIA	VISITATIVE	VITELLINES	VITRIFICATIONS	VIVIFICATION
VISCEROTONIAS	VISITATORIAL	VITELLOGENESES	VITRIFYING	VIVIFICATIONS
VISCEROTONIC	VISITATORS	VITELLOGENESIS	VITRIOLATE	VIVIPARIES
VISCIDITIES	VISITORIAL	VITELLOGENIC	VITRIOLATED	VIVIPARISM
VISCIDNESS	VISITRESSES	VITELLUSES	VITRIOLATES	VIVIPARISMS
VISCIDNESSES	VISUALISATION	VITIATIONS	VITRIOLATING	VIVIPARITIES
VISCOELASTIC	VISUALISATIONS	VITICETUMS	VITRIOLATION	VIVIPARITY
VISCOELASTICITY	VISUALISED	VITICOLOUS	VITRIOLATIONS	VIVIPAROUS
VISCOMETER	VISUALISER	VITICULTURAL	VITRIOLING	VIVIPAROUSLY
VISCOMETERS	VISUALISERS	VITICULTURALLY	VITRIOLISATION	VIVIPAROUSNESS
VISCOMETRIC	VISUALISES	VITICULTURE	VITRIOLISATIONS	VIVISECTED
VISCOMETRICAL	VISUALISING	VITICULTURER	VITRIOLISE	VIVISECTING
VISCOMETRIES	VISUALISTS	VITICULTURERS	VITRIOLISED	VIVISECTION
VISCOMETRY	VISUALITIES	VITICULTURES	VITRIOLISES	VIVISECTIONAL
VISCOSIMETER	VISUALIZATION	VITICULTURIST	VITRIOLISING	VIVISECTIONALLY
VISCOSIMETERS	VISUALIZATIONS	VITICULTURISTS	VITRIOLIZATION	VIVISECTIONIST
VISCOSIMETRIC	VISUALIZED	VITIFEROUS	VITRIOLIZATIONS	VIVISECTIONISTS
VISCOSIMETRICAL	VISUALIZER	VITILITIGATE	VITRIOLIZE	VIVISECTIONS
VISCOSIMETRIES	VISUALIZERS	VITILITIGATED	VITRIOLIZED	VIVISECTIVE
VISCOSIMETRY	VISUALIZES	VITILITIGATES	VITRIOLIZES	VIVISECTOR
VISCOSITIES	VISUALIZING	VITILITIGATING	VITRIOLIZING	VIVISECTORIUM
VISCOUNTCIES	VITALISATION	VITILITIGATION	VITRIOLLED	VIVISECTORIUMS
VISCOUNTCY	VITALISATIONS	VITILITIGATIONS	VITRIOLLING	VIVISECTORS
VISCOUNTESS	VITALISERS	VITIOSITIES	VITUPERABLE	VIVISEPULTURE
VISCOUNTESSES	VITALISING	VITRAILLED	VITUPERATE	VIVISEPULTURES
VISCOUNTIES	VITALISTIC	VITRAILLIST	VITUPERATED	VIXENISHLY
VISCOUNTSHIP	VITALISTICALLY	VITRAILLISTS	VITUPERATES	VIXENISHNESS
VISCOUNTSHIPS	VITALITIES	VITRECTOMIES	VITUPERATING	VIXENISHNESSES
VISCOUSNESS	VITALIZATION	VITRECTOMY	VITUPERATION	VIZIERATES
VISCOUSNESSES	VITALIZATIONS	VITREOSITIES	VITUPERATIONS	VIZIERSHIP
VISIBILITIES	VITALIZERS	VITREOSITY	VITUPERATIVE	VIZIERSHIPS
VISIBILITY	VITALIZING	VITREOUSES	VITUPERATIVELY	VIZIRSHIPS
VISIBLENESS	VITALNESSES	VITREOUSLY	VITUPERATOR	VOCABULARIAN

VOCABULARIANS	VOETSTOETS	VOLCANISTS	VOLUMINOUS	VOODOOISTS
VOCABULARIED	VOETSTOOTS	VOLCANIZATION	VOLUMINOUSLY	VOORKAMERS
VOCABULARIES	VOGUISHNESS	VOLCANIZATIONS	VOLUMINOUSNESS	VOORTREKKER
VOCABULARY	VOGUISHNESSES	VOLCANIZED	VOLUMISERS	VOORTREKKERS
VOCABULIST	VOICEFULNESS	VOLCANIZES	VOLUMISING	VORACIOUSLY
VOCABULISTS	VOICEFULNESSES	VOLCANIZING	VOLUMIZERS	VORACIOUSNESS
VOCALICALLY	VOICELESSLY	VOLCANOLOGIC	VOLUMIZING	VORACIOUSNESSES
VOCALISATION	VOICELESSNESS	VOLCANOLOGICAL	VOLUMOMETER	VORACITIES
VOCALISATIONS	VOICELESSNESSES	VOLCANOLOGIES	VOLUMOMETERS	VORAGINOUS
VOCALISERS	VOICEMAILS	VOLCANOLOGIST	VOLUNTARIES	VORTICALLY
VOCALISING	VOICEOVERS	VOLCANOLOGISTS	VOLUNTARILY	VORTICELLA
VOCALITIES	VOICEPRINT	VOLCANOLOGY	VOLUNTARINESS	VORTICELLAE
VOCALIZATION	VOICEPRINTS	VOLITATING	VOLUNTARINESSES	VORTICELLAS
VOCALIZATIONS	VOIDABLENESS	VOLITATION	VOLUNTARISM	VORTICISMS
VOCALIZERS	VOIDABLENESSES	VOLITATIONAL	VOLUNTARISMS	VORTICISTS
VOCALIZING	VOIDNESSES	VOLITATIONS	VOLUNTARIST	VORTICITIES
VOCALNESSES	VOISINAGES	VOLITIONAL	VOLUNTARISTIC	VORTICULAR
VOCATIONAL	VOITURIERS	VOLITIONALLY	VOLUNTARISTS	VORTIGINOUS
VOCATIONALISM	VOIVODESHIP	VOLITIONARY	VOLUNTARYISM	VOTARESSES
VOCATIONALISMS	VOIVODESHIPS	VOLITIONLESS	VOLUNTARYISMS	VOTIVENESS
VOCATIONALIST	VOLATILENESS	VOLITORIAL	VOLUNTARYIST	VOTIVENESSES
VOCATIONALISTS	VOLATILENESSES	VOLKSLIEDER	VOLUNTARYISTS	VOUCHERING
VOCATIONALLY	VOLATILISABLE	VOLKSRAADS	VOLUNTATIVE	VOUCHSAFED
VOCATIVELY	VOLATILISATION	VOLLEYBALL	VOLUNTEERED	VOUCHSAFEMENT
VOCICULTURAL	VOLATILISATIONS	VOLLEYBALLS	VOLUNTEERING	VOUCHSAFEMENTS
VOCIFERANCE	VOLATILISE	VOLPLANING	VOLUNTEERISM	VOUCHSAFES
VOCIFERANCES	VOLATILISED	VOLTAMETER	VOLUNTEERISMS	VOUCHSAFING
VOCIFERANT	VOLATILISES	VOLTAMETERS	VOLUNTEERS	VOUCHSAFINGS
VOCIFERANTS	VOLATILISING	VOLTAMETRIC	VOLUNTOURISM	VOUSSOIRED
VOCIFERATE	VOLATILITIES	VOLTAMMETER	VOLUNTOURISMS	VOUSSOIRING
VOCIFERATED	VOLATILITY	VOLTAMMETERS	VOLUPTUARIES	VOUTSAFING
VOCIFERATES	VOLATILIZABLE	VOLTIGEURS	VOLUPTUARY	VOWELISATION
VOCIFERATING	VOLATILIZATION	VOLTINISMS	VOLUPTUOSITIES	VOWELISATIONS
VOCIFERATION	VOLATILIZATIONS	VOLTMETERS	VOLUPTUOSITY	VOWELISING
VOCIFERATIONS	VOLATILIZE	VOLUBILITIES	VOLUPTUOUS	VOWELIZATION
VOCIFERATOR	VOLATILIZED	VOLUBILITY	VOLUPTUOUSLY	VOWELIZATIONS
VOCIFERATORS	VOLATILIZES	VOLUBLENESS	VOLUPTUOUSNESS	VOWELIZING
VOCIFEROSITIES	VOLATILIZING	VOLUBLENESSES	VOLUTATION	VOYAGEABLE
VOCIFEROSITY	VOLCANICALLY	VOLUMENOMETER	VOLUTATIONS	VOYEURISMS
VOCIFEROUS	VOLCANICITIES	VOLUMENOMETERS	VOLVULUSES	VOYEURISTIC
VOCIFEROUSLY	VOLCANICITY	VOLUMETERS	VOMERONASAL	VOYEURISTICALLY
VOCIFEROUSNESS	VOLCANISATION	VOLUMETRIC	VOMITORIES	VRAICKINGS
VODCASTERS	VOLCANISATIONS	VOLUMETRICAL	VOMITORIUM	VRAISEMBLANCE
VODCASTING	VOLCANISED	VOLUMETRICALLY	VOMITURITION	VRAISEMBLANCES
VODCASTINGS	VOLCANISES	VOLUMETRIES	VOMITURITIONS	VULCANICITIES
VOETGANGER	VOLCANISING	VOLUMINOSITIES	VOODOOISMS	VULCANICITY
VOETGANGERS	VOLCANISMS	VOLUMINOSITY	VOODOOISTIC	VULCANISABLE

VULCANISATE VULCANIZATE VULCANOLOGY VULGARIZED VULNERATING
VULCANISATES VULCANIZATES VULGARIANS VULGARIZER VULNERATION
VULCANISATION VULCANIZATION VULGARISATION VULGARIZERS VULNERATIONS
VULCANISATIONS VULCANIZATIONS VULGARISATIONS VULGARIZES VULPECULAR
VULCANISED VULCANIZED VULGARISED VULGARIZING VULPICIDES
VULCANISER VULCANIZER VULGARISER VULNERABILITIES VULPINISMS
VULCANISERS VULCANIZERS VULGARISERS VULNERABILITY VULPINITES
VULCANISES VULCANIZES VULGARISES VULNERABLE VULTURISMS
VULCANISING VULCANIZING VULGARISING VULNERABLENESS VULVITISES
VULCANISMS VULCANOLOGICAL VULGARISMS VULNERABLY VULVOVAGINAL
VULCANISTS VULCANOLOGIES VULGARITIES VULNERARIES VULVOVAGINITIS
VULCANITES VULCANOLOGIST VULGARIZATION VULNERATED
VULCANIZABLE VULCANOLOGISTS VULGARIZATIONS VULNERATES

V

W

WACKINESSES	WAITERINGS	WALLYBALLS	WARCHALKER	WARRANTIES
WADSETTERS	WAITLISTED	WALLYDRAGS	WARCHALKERS	WARRANTING
WADSETTING	WAITLISTING	WALLYDRAIGLE	WARCHALKING	WARRANTINGS
WAFFLESTOMPER	WAITPERSON	WALLYDRAIGLES	WARCHALKINGS	WARRANTISE
WAFFLESTOMPERS	WAITPERSONS	WALNUTWOOD	WARDENRIES	WARRANTISES
WAGELESSNESS	WAITRESSED	WALNUTWOODS	WARDENSHIP	WARRANTLESS
WAGELESSNESSES	WAITRESSES	WAMBENGERS	WARDENSHIPS	WARRANTORS
WAGENBOOMS	WAITRESSING	WAMBLINESS	WARDERSHIP	WARRANTYING
WAGEWORKER	WAITRESSINGS	WAMBLINESSES	WARDERSHIPS	WARRIORESS
WAGEWORKERS	WAITSTAFFS	WAMBLINGLY	WARDRESSES	WARRIORESSES
WAGGISHNESS	WAKEBOARDED	WAMPISHING	WARDROBERS	WASHABILITIES
WAGGISHNESSES	WAKEBOARDER	WAMPUMPEAG	WARDROBING	WASHABILITY
WAGGLINGLY	WAKEBOARDERS	WAMPUMPEAGS	WAREHOUSED	WASHATERIA
WAGGONETTE	WAKEBOARDING	WANCHANCIE	WAREHOUSEMAN	WASHATERIAS
WAGGONETTES	WAKEBOARDINGS	WANDERINGLY	WAREHOUSEMEN	WASHBASINS
WAGGONLESS	WAKEBOARDS	WANDERINGS	WAREHOUSER	WASHBOARDS
WAGGONLOAD	WAKEFULNESS	WANDERLUST	WAREHOUSERS	WASHCLOTHS
WAGGONLOADS	WAKEFULNESSES	WANDERLUSTS	WAREHOUSES	WASHERWOMAN
WAGHALTERS	WALDFLUTES	WANRESTFUL	WAREHOUSING	WASHERWOMEN
WAGONETTES	WALDGRAVES	WANTHRIVEN	WAREHOUSINGS	WASHETERIA
WAGONLOADS	WALDGRAVINE	WANTONISED	WARFARINGS	WASHETERIAS
WAGONWRIGHT	WALDGRAVINES	WANTONISES	WARIBASHIS	WASHHOUSES
WAGONWRIGHTS	WALDSTERBEN	WANTONISING	WARINESSES	WASHINESSES
WAINSCOTED	WALDSTERBENS	WANTONIZED	WARLIKENESS	WASHINGTONIA
WAINSCOTING	WALKABOUTS	WANTONIZES	WARLIKENESSES	WASHINGTONIAS
WAINSCOTINGS	WALKATHONS	WANTONIZING	WARLOCKRIES	WASHSTANDS
WAINSCOTTED	WALKINGSTICK	WANTONNESS	WARLORDISM	WASPINESSES
WAINSCOTTING	WALKINGSTICKS	WANTONNESSES	WARLORDISMS	WASPISHNESS
WAINSCOTTINGS	WALKSHORTS	WAPENSCHAW	WARMBLOODS	WASPISHNESSES
WAINWRIGHT	WALLBOARDS	WAPENSCHAWS	WARMHEARTED	WASSAILERS
WAINWRIGHTS	WALLCHARTS	WAPENSHAWS	WARMHEARTEDNESS	WASSAILING
WAISTBANDS	WALLCLIMBER	WAPENTAKES	WARMNESSES	WASSAILINGS
WAISTBELTS	WALLCLIMBERS	WAPINSCHAW	WARMONGERING	WASSAILRIES
WAISTCLOTH	WALLCOVERING	WAPINSCHAWS	WARMONGERINGS	WASTEBASKET
WAISTCLOTHS	WALLCOVERINGS	WAPINSHAWS	WARMONGERS	WASTEBASKETS
WAISTCOATED	WALLFISHES	WAPPENSCHAW	WARRANDICE	WASTEFULLY
WAISTCOATEER	WALLFLOWER	WAPPENSCHAWING	WARRANDICES	WASTEFULNESS
WAISTCOATEERS	WALLFLOWERS	WAPPENSCHAWINGS	WARRANDING	WASTEFULNESSES
WAISTCOATING	WALLOPINGS	WAPPENSCHAWS	WARRANTABILITY	WASTELANDS
WAISTCOATINGS	WALLOWINGS	WAPPENSHAW	WARRANTABLE	WASTENESSES
WAISTCOATS	WALLPAPERED	WAPPENSHAWING	WARRANTABLENESS	WASTEPAPER
WAISTLINES	WALLPAPERING	WAPPENSHAWINGS	WARRANTABLY	WASTEPAPERS
WAITERAGES	WALLPAPERS	WAPPENSHAWS	WARRANTEES	WASTERFULLY
WAITERHOOD	WALLPOSTER	WARBLINGLY	WARRANTERS	WASTERFULNESS
WAITERHOODS	WALLPOSTERS	WARBONNETS	WARRANTIED	WASTERFULNESSES

W

WASTEWATER
WASTEWATERS
WASTEWEIRS
WASTNESSES
WATCHABLES
WATCHBANDS
WATCHBOXES
WATCHCASES
WATCHCRIES
WATCHDOGGED
WATCHDOGGING
WATCHFULLY
WATCHFULNESS
WATCHFULNESSES
WATCHGLASS
WATCHGLASSES
WATCHGUARD
WATCHGUARDS
WATCHLISTS
WATCHMAKER
WATCHMAKERS
WATCHMAKING
WATCHMAKINGS
WATCHSPRING
WATCHSPRINGS
WATCHSTRAP
WATCHSTRAPS
WATCHTOWER
WATCHTOWERS
WATCHWORDS
WATERBIRDS
WATERBOARDING
WATERBOARDINGS
WATERBORNE
WATERBRAIN
WATERBRAINS
WATERBUCKS
WATERBUSES
WATERBUSSES
WATERCOLOR
WATERCOLORIST
WATERCOLORISTS
WATERCOLORS
WATERCOLOUR
WATERCOLOURIST
WATERCOLOURISTS
WATERCOLOURS

WATERCOOLER
WATERCOOLERS
WATERCOURSE
WATERCOURSES
WATERCRAFT
WATERCRAFTS
WATERCRESS
WATERCRESSES
WATERDRIVE
WATERDRIVES
WATERFALLS
WATERFINDER
WATERFINDERS
WATERFLOOD
WATERFLOODED
WATERFLOODING
WATERFLOODINGS
WATERFLOODS
WATERFOWLER
WATERFOWLERS
WATERFOWLING
WATERFOWLINGS
WATERFOWLS
WATERFRONT
WATERFRONTS
WATERGLASS
WATERGLASSES
WATERHEADS
WATERINESS
WATERINESSES
WATERISHNESS
WATERISHNESSES
WATERLEAFS
WATERLESSNESS
WATERLESSNESSES
WATERLILIES
WATERLINES
WATERLOGGED
WATERLOGGING
WATERMANSHIP
WATERMANSHIPS
WATERMARKED
WATERMARKING
WATERMARKS
WATERMELON
WATERMELONS
WATERPOWER

WATERPOWERS
WATERPOXES
WATERPROOF
WATERPROOFED
WATERPROOFER
WATERPROOFERS
WATERPROOFING
WATERPROOFINGS
WATERPROOFNESS
WATERPROOFS
WATERQUAKE
WATERQUAKES
WATERSCAPE
WATERSCAPES
WATERSHEDS
WATERSIDER
WATERSIDERS
WATERSIDES
WATERSKIING
WATERSKIINGS
WATERSMEET
WATERSMEETS
WATERSPOUT
WATERSPOUTS
WATERTHRUSH
WATERTHRUSHES
WATERTIGHT
WATERTIGHTNESS
WATERWEEDS
WATERWHEEL
WATERWHEELS
WATERWORKS
WATERZOOIS
WATTLEBARK
WATTLEBARKS
WATTLEBIRD
WATTLEBIRDS
WATTLEWORK
WATTLEWORKS
WATTMETERS
WAULKMILLS
WAVEFRONTS
WAVEGUIDES
WAVELENGTH
WAVELENGTHS
WAVELESSLY
WAVELLITES

WAVEMETERS
WAVERINGLY
WAVERINGNESS
WAVERINGNESSES
WAVESHAPES
WAVINESSES
WAXBERRIES
WAXFLOWERS
WAXINESSES
WAXWORKERS
WAYFARINGS
WAYMARKING
WAYMENTING
WAYWARDNESS
WAYWARDNESSES
WAYZGOOSES
WEAKFISHES
WEAKHEARTED
WEAKISHNESS
WEAKISHNESSES
WEAKLINESS
WEAKLINESSES
WEAKNESSES
WEALTHIEST
WEALTHINESS
WEALTHINESSES
WEALTHLESS
WEAPONEERING
WEAPONEERINGS
WEAPONEERS
WEAPONISED
WEAPONISES
WEAPONISING
WEAPONIZED
WEAPONIZES
WEAPONIZING
WEAPONLESS
WEAPONRIES
WEARABILITIES
WEARABILITY
WEARIFULLY
WEARIFULNESS
WEARIFULNESSES
WEARILESSLY
WEARINESSES
WEARISOMELY
WEARISOMENESS

WEARISOMENESSES
WEARYINGLY
WEASELLERS
WEASELLING
WEATHERABILITY
WEATHERABLE
WEATHERBOARD
WEATHERBOARDED
WEATHERBOARDING
WEATHERBOARDS
WEATHERCAST
WEATHERCASTER
WEATHERCASTERS
WEATHERCASTS
WEATHERCLOTH
WEATHERCLOTHS
WEATHERCOCK
WEATHERCOCKED
WEATHERCOCKING
WEATHERCOCKS
WEATHERERS
WEATHERGIRL
WEATHERGIRLS
WEATHERGLASS
WEATHERGLASSES
WEATHERING
WEATHERINGS
WEATHERISATION
WEATHERISATIONS
WEATHERISE
WEATHERISED
WEATHERISES
WEATHERISING
WEATHERIZATION
WEATHERIZATIONS
WEATHERIZE
WEATHERIZED
WEATHERIZES
WEATHERIZING
WEATHERLINESS
WEATHERLINESSES
WEATHERMAN
WEATHERMEN
WEATHERMOST
WEATHEROMETER
WEATHEROMETERS
WEATHERPERSON

WEATHERPERSONS	WELDABILITY	WESTERNIZATIONS	WHEELBASES	WHIGMALEERIE
WEATHERPROOF	WELFARISMS	WESTERNIZE	WHEELCHAIR	WHIGMALEERIES
WEATHERPROOFED	WELFARISTIC	WESTERNIZED	WHEELCHAIRS	WHIGMALEERY
WEATHERPROOFING	WELFARISTS	WESTERNIZES	WHEELHORSE	WHILLYWHAED
WEATHERPROOFS	WELLBEINGS	WESTERNIZING	WHEELHORSES	WHILLYWHAING
WEATHERWORN	WELLHOUSES	WESTERNMOST	WHEELHOUSE	WHILLYWHAS
WEAVERBIRD	WELLINGTON	WESTWARDLY	WHEELHOUSES	WHILLYWHAW
WEAVERBIRDS	WELLINGTONIA	WETTABILITIES	WHEELWORKS	WHILLYWHAWED
WEBCASTERS	WELLINGTONIAS	WETTABILITY	WHEELWRIGHT	WHILLYWHAWING
WEBCASTING	WELLINGTONS	WHAIKORERO	WHEELWRIGHTS	WHILLYWHAWS
WEBLOGGERS	WELLNESSES	WHAIKOREROS	WHEESHTING	WHIMBERRIES
WEBMASTERS	WELLSPRING	WHAKAPAPAS	WHEEZINESS	WHIMPERERS
WEEDICIDES	WELLSPRINGS	WHALEBACKS	WHEEZINESSES	WHIMPERING
WEEDINESSES	WELTANSCHAUUNG	WHALEBOATS	WHEEZINGLY	WHIMPERINGLY
WEEDKILLER	WELTANSCHAUUNGS	WHALEBONES	WHENCEFORTH	WHIMPERINGS
WEEDKILLERS	WELTERWEIGHT	WHAREPUNIS	WHENCESOEVER	WHIMSICALITIES
WEEKENDERS	WELTERWEIGHTS	WHARFINGER	WHENSOEVER	WHIMSICALITY
WEEKENDING	WELTSCHMERZ	WHARFINGERS	WHEREABOUT	WHIMSICALLY
WEEKENDINGS	WELTSCHMERZES	WHARFMASTER	WHEREABOUTS	WHIMSICALNESS
WEEKNIGHTS	WELWITSCHIA	WHARFMASTERS	WHEREAFTER	WHIMSICALNESSES
WEELDLESSE	WELWITSCHIAS	WHATABOUTERIES	WHEREAGAINST	WHIMSINESS
WEEPINESSES	WENSLEYDALE	WHATABOUTERY	WHEREFORES	WHIMSINESSES
WEIGHBOARD	WENSLEYDALES	WHATABOUTS	WHEREINSOEVER	WHINBERRIES
WEIGHBOARDS	WENTLETRAP	WHATCHAMACALLIT	WHERENESSES	WHINGDINGS
WEIGHBRIDGE	WENTLETRAPS	WHATNESSES	WHERESOEVER	WHINGEINGLY
WEIGHBRIDGES	WEREWOLFERIES	WHATSHERNAME	WHERETHROUGH	WHINGEINGS
WEIGHTAGES	WEREWOLFERY	WHATSHERNAMES	WHEREUNDER	WHININESSES
WEIGHTIEST	WEREWOLFISH	WHATSHISNAME	WHEREUNTIL	WHINSTONES
WEIGHTINESS	WEREWOLFISM	WHATSHISNAMES	WHEREWITHAL	WHIPLASHED
WEIGHTINESSES	WEREWOLFISMS	WHATSITSNAME	WHEREWITHALS	WHIPLASHES
WEIGHTINGS	WEREWOLVES	WHATSITSNAMES	WHEREWITHS	WHIPLASHING
WEIGHTLESS	WERNERITES	WHATSOEVER	WHERRETING	WHIPPERSNAPPER
WEIGHTLESSLY	WERWOLFISH	WHATSOMEVER	WHERRITING	WHIPPERSNAPPERS
WEIGHTLESSNESS	WESTERINGS	WHEATFIELD	WHETSTONES	WHIPPETING
WEIGHTLIFTER	WESTERLIES	WHEATFIELDS	WHEWELLITE	WHIPPETINGS
WEIGHTLIFTERS	WESTERLINESS	WHEATGRASS	WHEWELLITES	WHIPPINESS
WEIGHTLIFTING	WESTERLINESSES	WHEATGRASSES	WHEYISHNESS	WHIPPINESSES
WEIGHTLIFTINGS	WESTERNERS	WHEATLANDS	WHEYISHNESSES	WHIPPLETREE
WEIMARANER	WESTERNISATION	WHEATMEALS	WHICHSOEVER	WHIPPLETREES
WEIMARANERS	WESTERNISATIONS	WHEATWORMS	WHICKERING	WHIPPOORWILL
WEIRDNESSES	WESTERNISE	WHEEDLESOME	WHIDDERING	WHIPPOORWILLS
WEISENHEIMER	WESTERNISED	WHEEDLINGLY	WHIFFLERIES	WHIPSAWING
WEISENHEIMERS	WESTERNISES	WHEEDLINGS	WHIFFLETREE	WHIPSNAKES
WELCOMENESS	WESTERNISING	WHEELBARROW	WHIFFLETREES	WHIPSTAFFS
WELCOMENESSES	WESTERNISM	WHEELBARROWED	WHIFFLINGS	WHIPSTALLED
WELCOMINGLY	WESTERNISMS	WHEELBARROWING	WHIGGAMORE	WHIPSTALLING
WELDABILITIES	WESTERNIZATION	WHEELBARROWS	WHIGGAMORES	WHIPSTALLS

WHIPSTITCH	WHITEHEADS	WHOLEGRAIN	WIDEAWAKES	WILLIEWAUGHT
WHIPSTITCHED	WHITELISTED	WHOLEHEARTED	WIDEBODIES	WILLIEWAUGHTS
WHIPSTITCHES	WHITELISTING	WHOLEHEARTEDLY	WIDECHAPPED	WILLINGEST
WHIPSTITCHING	WHITELISTS	WHOLEMEALS	WIDEMOUTHED	WILLINGNESS
WHIPSTOCKS	WHITENESSES	WHOLENESSES	WIDENESSES	WILLINGNESSES
WHIPTAILED	WHITENINGS	WHOLESALED	WIDERSHINS	WILLOWHERB
WHIRLABOUT	WHITESMITH	WHOLESALER	WIDESCREEN	WILLOWHERBS
WHIRLABOUTS	WHITESMITHS	WHOLESALERS	WIDESPREAD	WILLOWIEST
WHIRLBLAST	WHITETAILS	WHOLESALES	WIDOWBIRDS	WILLOWLIKE
WHIRLBLASTS	WHITETHORN	WHOLESALING	WIDOWERHOOD	WILLOWWARE
WHIRLIGIGS	WHITETHORNS	WHOLESOMELY	WIDOWERHOODS	WILLOWWARES
WHIRLINGLY	WHITETHROAT	WHOLESOMENESS	WIDOWHOODS	WILLPOWERS
WHIRLPOOLS	WHITETHROATS	WHOLESOMENESSES	WIELDINESS	WIMPINESSES
WHIRLWINDS	WHITEWALLS	WHOLESOMER	WIELDINESSES	WIMPISHNESS
WHIRLYBIRD	WHITEWARES	WHOLESOMEST	WIENERWURST	WIMPISHNESSES
WHIRLYBIRDS	WHITEWASHED	WHOLESTITCH	WIENERWURSTS	WINCEYETTE
WHIRRETING	WHITEWASHER	WHOLESTITCHES	WIFELINESS	WINCEYETTES
WHISKERANDO	WHITEWASHERS	WHOLEWHEAT	WIFELINESSES	WINCHESTER
WHISKERANDOED	WHITEWASHES	WHOMSOEVER	WIGWAGGERS	WINCHESTERS
WHISKERANDOS	WHITEWASHING	WHOREHOUSE	WIGWAGGING	WINCOPIPES
WHISKERIER	WHITEWASHINGS	WHOREHOUSES	WIKITORIAL	WINDBAGGERIES
WHISKERIEST	WHITEWATER	WHOREMASTER	WIKITORIALS	WINDBAGGERY
WHISKEYFIED	WHITEWINGS	WHOREMASTERIES	WILDCATTED	WINDBLASTS
WHISKIFIED	WHITEWOODS	WHOREMASTERLY	WILDCATTER	WINDBREAKER
WHISPERERS	WHITEYWOOD	WHOREMASTERS	WILDCATTERS	WINDBREAKERS
WHISPERING	WHITEYWOODS	WHOREMASTERY	WILDCATTING	WINDBREAKS
WHISPERINGLY	WHITHERING	WHOREMISTRESS	WILDCATTINGS	WINDBURNED
WHISPERINGS	WHITHERSOEVER	WHOREMISTRESSES	WILDEBEEST	WINDBURNING
WHISPEROUSLY	WHITHERWARD	WHOREMONGER	WILDEBEESTS	WINDCHEATER
WHISTLEABLE	WHITHERWARDS	WHOREMONGERIES	WILDERMENT	WINDCHEATERS
WHISTLINGLY	WHITISHNESS	WHOREMONGERS	WILDERMENTS	WINDCHILLS
WHISTLINGS	WHITISHNESSES	WHOREMONGERY	WILDERNESS	WINDFALLEN
WHITEBAITS	WHITLEATHER	WHORISHNESS	WILDERNESSES	WINDFLOWER
WHITEBASSES	WHITLEATHERS	WHORISHNESSES	WILDFLOWER	WINDFLOWERS
WHITEBEAMS	WHITTAWERS	WHORTLEBERRIES	WILDFLOWERS	WINDGALLED
WHITEBEARD	WHITTERICK	WHORTLEBERRY	WILDFOWLER	WINDHOVERS
WHITEBEARDS	WHITTERICKS	WHOSESOEVER	WILDFOWLERS	WINDINESSES
WHITEBOARD	WHITTERING	WHUNSTANES	WILDFOWLING	WINDJAMMER
WHITEBOARDS	WHITTLINGS	WHYDUNNITS	WILDFOWLINGS	WINDJAMMERS
WHITEBOYISM	WHIZZBANGS	WICKEDNESS	WILDGRAVES	WINDJAMMING
WHITEBOYISMS	WHIZZINGLY	WICKEDNESSES	WILDNESSES	WINDJAMMINGS
WHITECOATS	WHODUNITRIES	WICKERWORK	WILFULNESS	WINDLASSED
WHITECOMBS	WHODUNITRY	WICKERWORKS	WILFULNESSES	WINDLASSES
WHITEDAMPS	WHODUNNITRIES	WICKETKEEPER	WILINESSES	WINDLASSING
WHITEFACES	WHODUNNITRY	WICKETKEEPERS	WILLEMITES	WINDLESSLY
WHITEFISHES	WHODUNNITS	WICKTHINGS	WILLFULNESS	WINDLESSNESS
WHITEFLIES	WHOLEFOODS	WIDDERSHINS	WILLFULNESSES	WINDLESSNESSES

WINDLESTRAE	WINNINGNESS	WIREDRAWINGS	WITCHGRASSES	WITWANTONED
WINDLESTRAES	WINNINGNESSES	WIREFRAMES	WITCHHOODS	WITWANTONING
WINDLESTRAW	WINNOWINGS	WIREGRASSES	WITCHINGLY	WITWANTONS
WINDLESTRAWS	WINSOMENESS	WIREHAIRED	WITCHKNOTS	WIZARDRIES
WINDMILLED	WINSOMENESSES	WIRELESSED	WITCHWEEDS	WOADWAXENS
WINDMILLING	WINTERBERRIES	WIRELESSES	WITENAGEMOT	WOBBEGONGS
WINDOWINGS	WINTERBERRY	WIRELESSING	WITENAGEMOTE	WOBBLINESS
WINDOWLESS	WINTERBOURNE	WIREPHOTOS	WITENAGEMOTES	WOBBLINESSES
WINDOWPANE	WINTERBOURNES	WIREPULLER	WITENAGEMOTS	WOEBEGONENESS
WINDOWPANES	WINTERCRESS	WIREPULLERS	WITGATBOOM	WOEBEGONENESSES
WINDOWSILL	WINTERCRESSES	WIREPULLING	WITGATBOOMS	WOEFULLEST
WINDOWSILLS	WINTERFEED	WIREPULLINGS	WITHDRAWABLE	WOEFULNESS
WINDROWERS	WINTERFEEDING	WIRETAPPED	WITHDRAWAL	WOEFULNESSES
WINDROWING	WINTERFEEDS	WIRETAPPER	WITHDRAWALS	WOFULNESSES
WINDSCREEN	WINTERGREEN	WIRETAPPERS	WITHDRAWER	WOLFBERRIES
WINDSCREENS	WINTERGREENS	WIRETAPPING	WITHDRAWERS	WOLFFISHES
WINDSHAKES	WINTERIEST	WIRETAPPINGS	WITHDRAWING	WOLFHOUNDS
WINDSHIELD	WINTERINESS	WIREWALKER	WITHDRAWMENT	WOLFISHNESS
WINDSHIELDS	WINTERINESSES	WIREWALKERS	WITHDRAWMENTS	WOLFISHNESSES
WINDSTORMS	WINTERISATION	WIREWORKER	WITHDRAWNNESS	WOLFRAMITE
WINDSUCKER	WINTERISATIONS	WIREWORKERS	WITHDRAWNNESSES	WOLFRAMITES
WINDSUCKERS	WINTERISED	WIREWORKING	WITHEREDNESS	WOLFSBANES
WINDSURFED	WINTERISES	WIREWORKINGS	WITHEREDNESSES	WOLLASTONITE
WINDSURFER	WINTERISING	WIRINESSES	WITHERINGLY	WOLLASTONITES
WINDSURFERS	WINTERIZATION	WISECRACKED	WITHERINGS	WOLVERENES
WINDSURFING	WINTERIZATIONS	WISECRACKER	WITHERITES	WOLVERINES
WINDSURFINGS	WINTERIZED	WISECRACKERS	WITHERSHINS	WOMANFULLY
WINDTHROWS	WINTERIZES	WISECRACKING	WITHHOLDEN	WOMANHOODS
WINEBERRIES	WINTERIZING	WISECRACKS	WITHHOLDER	WOMANISERS
WINEBIBBER	WINTERKILL	WISENESSES	WITHHOLDERS	WOMANISHLY
WINEBIBBERS	WINTERKILLED	WISENHEIMER	WITHHOLDING	WOMANISHNESS
WINEBIBBING	WINTERKILLING	WISENHEIMERS	WITHHOLDMENT	WOMANISHNESSES
WINEBIBBINGS	WINTERKILLINGS	WISHFULNESS	WITHHOLDMENTS	WOMANISING
WINEGLASSES	WINTERKILLS	WISHFULNESSES	WITHINDOORS	WOMANISINGS
WINEGLASSFUL	WINTERLESS	WISHTONWISH	WITHOUTDOORS	WOMANIZERS
WINEGLASSFULS	WINTERLINESS	WISHTONWISHES	WITHSTANDER	WOMANIZING
WINEGROWER	WINTERLINESSES	WISPINESSES	WITHSTANDERS	WOMANIZINGS
WINEGROWERS	WINTERTIDE	WISTFULNESS	WITHSTANDING	WOMANKINDS
WINEMAKERS	WINTERTIDES	WISTFULNESSES	WITHSTANDS	WOMANLIEST
WINEPRESSES	WINTERTIME	WITBLITSES	WITHYWINDS	WOMANLINESS
WINGCHAIRS	WINTERTIMES	WITCHBROOM	WITLESSNESS	WOMANLINESSES
WINGLESSNESS	WINTERWEIGHT	WITCHBROOMS	WITLESSNESSES	WOMANNESSES
WINGLESSNESSES	WINTRINESS	WITCHCRAFT	WITNESSABLE	WOMANPOWER
WINGSPREAD	WINTRINESSES	WITCHCRAFTS	WITNESSERS	WOMANPOWERS
WINGSPREADS	WIREDRAWER	WITCHERIES	WITNESSING	WOMENFOLKS
WINNABILITIES	WIREDRAWERS	WITCHETTIES	WITTICISMS	WOMENKINDS
WINNABILITY	WIREDRAWING	WITCHGRASS	WITTINESSES	WOMENSWEAR

WOMENSWEARS	WOODENWARES	WOOLLYBACK	WORKINGMAN	WORSHIPFUL
WONDERFULLY	WOODGRAINS	WOOLLYBACKS	WORKINGMEN	WORSHIPFULLY
WONDERFULNESS	WOODGROUSE	WOOLLYBUTT	WORKINGWOMAN	WORSHIPFULNESS
WONDERFULNESSES	WOODGROUSES	WOOLLYBUTTS	WORKINGWOMEN	WORSHIPING
WONDERINGLY	WOODHORSES	WOOLLYFOOT	WORKLESSNESS	WORSHIPLESS
WONDERINGS	WOODHOUSES	WOOLLYFOOTS	WORKLESSNESSES	WORSHIPPED
WONDERKIDS	WOODINESSES	WOOLSORTER	WORKMANLIKE	WORSHIPPER
WONDERLAND	WOODLANDER	WOOLSORTERS	WORKMANSHIP	WORSHIPPERS
WONDERLANDS	WOODLANDERS	WOOMERANGS	WORKMANSHIPS	WORSHIPPING
WONDERLESS	WOODLESSNESS	WOOZINESSES	WORKMASTER	WORTHINESS
WONDERMENT	WOODLESSNESSES	WORCESTERBERRY	WORKMASTERS	WORTHINESSES
WONDERMENTS	WOODNESSES	WORCESTERS	WORKMISTRESS	WORTHLESSLY
WONDERMONGER	WOODPECKER	WORDBREAKS	WORKMISTRESSES	WORTHLESSNESS
WONDERMONGERING	WOODPECKERS	WORDINESSES	WORKPEOPLE	WORTHLESSNESSES
WONDERMONGERS	WOODPRINTS	WORDISHNESS	WORKPIECES	WORTHWHILE
WONDERWORK	WOODREEVES	WORDISHNESSES	WORKPLACES	WORTHWHILENESS
WONDERWORKS	WOODRUSHES	WORDLESSLY	WORKPRINTS	WOUNDINGLY
WONDROUSLY	WOODSCREWS	WORDLESSNESS	WORKSHEETS	WOUNDWORTS
WONDROUSNESS	WOODSHEDDED	WORDLESSNESSES	WORKSHOPPED	WRAITHLIKE
WONDROUSNESSES	WOODSHEDDING	WORDMONGER	WORKSHOPPING	WRANGLERSHIP
WONTEDNESS	WOODSHEDDINGS	WORDMONGERS	WORKSPACES	WRANGLERSHIPS
WONTEDNESSES	WOODSHOCKS	WORDSEARCH	WORKSTATION	WRANGLESOME
WOODBLOCKS	WOODSHRIKE	WORDSEARCHES	WORKSTATIONS	WRANGLINGS
WOODBORERS	WOODSHRIKES	WORDSMITHERIES	WORKSTREAM	WRAPAROUND
WOODBURYTYPE	WOODSPITES	WORDSMITHERY	WORKSTREAMS	WRAPAROUNDS
WOODBURYTYPES	WOODSTONES	WORDSMITHS	WORKTABLES	WRAPPERING
WOODCARVER	WOODSTOVES	WORKABILITIES	WORKWATCHER	WRAPROUNDS
WOODCARVERS	WOODSWALLOW	WORKABILITY	WORKWATCHERS	WRATHFULLY
WOODCARVING	WOODSWALLOWS	WORKABLENESS	WORLDBEATS	WRATHFULNESS
WOODCARVINGS	WOODTHRUSH	WORKABLENESSES	WORLDLIEST	WRATHFULNESSES
WOODCHOPPER	WOODTHRUSHES	WORKAHOLIC	WORLDLINESS	WRATHINESS
WOODCHOPPERS	WOODWAXENS	WORKAHOLICS	WORLDLINESSES	WRATHINESSES
WOODCHUCKS	WOODWORKER	WORKAHOLISM	WORLDLINGS	WREATHIEST
WOODCRAFTS	WOODWORKERS	WORKAHOLISMS	WORLDSCALE	WREATHLESS
WOODCRAFTSMAN	WOODWORKING	WORKAROUND	WORLDSCALES	WREATHLIKE
WOODCRAFTSMEN	WOODWORKINGS	WORKAROUNDS	WORLDVIEWS	WRECKFISHES
WOODCUTTER	WOOLGATHERER	WORKBASKET	WORMINESSES	WRECKMASTER
WOODCUTTERS	WOOLGATHERERS	WORKBASKETS	WORNNESSES	WRECKMASTERS
WOODCUTTING	WOOLGATHERING	WORKBENCHES	WORRIMENTS	WRENCHINGLY
WOODCUTTINGS	WOOLGATHERINGS	WORKERISTS	WORRISOMELY	WRENCHINGS
WOODENHEAD	WOOLGROWER	WORKERLESS	WORRISOMENESS	WRESTLINGS
WOODENHEADED	WOOLGROWERS	WORKFELLOW	WORRISOMENESSES	WRETCHEDER
WOODENHEADS	WOOLGROWING	WORKFELLOWS	WORRYINGLY	WRETCHEDEST
WOODENNESS	WOOLGROWINGS	WORKFORCES	WORRYWARTS	WRETCHEDLY
WOODENNESSES	WOOLINESSES	WORKGROUPS	WORSENESSES	WRETCHEDNESS
WOODENTOPS	WOOLLINESS	WORKHORSES	WORSHIPABLE	WRETCHEDNESSES
WOODENWARE	WOOLLINESSES	WORKHOUSES	WORSHIPERS	WRIGGLIEST

W

WRIGGLINGS
WRINKLELESS
WRINKLIEST
WRISTBANDS
WRISTLOCKS
WRISTWATCH

WRISTWATCHES
WRITERESSES
WRITERSHIP
WRITERSHIPS
WRITHINGLY
WRONGDOERS

WRONGDOING
WRONGDOINGS
WRONGFULLY
WRONGFULNESS
WRONGFULNESSES
WRONGHEADED

WRONGHEADEDLY
WRONGHEADEDNESS
WRONGNESSES
WRONGOUSLY
WULFENITES
WUNDERKIND

WUNDERKINDER
WUNDERKINDS
WYANDOTTES
WYLIECOATS

XYZ

XANTHATION	XENODIAGNOSES	XENOTRANSPLANTS	XEROPHYTISM	XYLOGRAPHER
XANTHATIONS	XENODIAGNOSIS	XENOTROPIC	XEROPHYTISMS	XYLOGRAPHERS
XANTHOCHROIA	XENODIAGNOSTIC	XERANTHEMUM	XERORADIOGRAPHY	XYLOGRAPHIC
XANTHOCHROIAS	XENODOCHIUM	XERANTHEMUMS	XEROSTOMAS	XYLOGRAPHICAL
XANTHOCHROIC	XENODOCHIUMS	XERISCAPES	XEROSTOMATA	XYLOGRAPHIES
XANTHOCHROID	XENOGAMIES	XEROCHASIES	XEROSTOMIA	XYLOGRAPHING
XANTHOCHROIDS	XENOGAMOUS	XERODERMAE	XEROSTOMIAS	XYLOGRAPHS
XANTHOCHROISM	XENOGENEIC	XERODERMAS	XEROTHERMIC	XYLOGRAPHY
XANTHOCHROISMS	XENOGENESES	XERODERMATIC	XEROTRIPSES	XYLOIDINES
XANTHOCHROMIA	XENOGENESIS	XERODERMATOUS	XEROTRIPSIS	XYLOLOGIES
XANTHOCHROMIAS	XENOGENETIC	XERODERMIA	XIPHIHUMERALIS	XYLOMETERS
XANTHOCHROOUS	XENOGENIES	XERODERMIAS	XIPHIPLASTRA	XYLOPHAGAN
XANTHOMATA	XENOGENOUS	XERODERMIC	XIPHIPLASTRAL	XYLOPHAGANS
XANTHOMATOUS	XENOGLOSSIA	XEROGRAPHER	XIPHIPLASTRALS	XYLOPHAGES
XANTHOMELANOUS	XENOGLOSSIAS	XEROGRAPHERS	XIPHIPLASTRON	XYLOPHAGOUS
XANTHOPHYL	XENOGLOSSIES	XEROGRAPHIC	XIPHISTERNA	XYLOPHILOUS
XANTHOPHYLL	XENOGLOSSY	XEROGRAPHICALLY	XIPHISTERNUM	XYLOPHONES
XANTHOPHYLLOUS	XENOGRAFTS	XEROGRAPHIES	XIPHISTERNUMS	XYLOPHONIC
XANTHOPHYLLS	XENOLITHIC	XEROGRAPHY	XIPHOPAGIC	XYLOPHONIST
XANTHOPHYLS	XENOMANIAS	XEROMORPHIC	XIPHOPAGOUS	XYLOPHONISTS
XANTHOPSIA	XENOMENIAS	XEROMORPHOUS	XIPHOPAGUS	XYLOPYROGRAPHY
XANTHOPSIAS	XENOMORPHIC	XEROMORPHS	XIPHOPAGUSES	XYLORIMBAS
XANTHOPTERIN	XENOMORPHICALLY	XEROPHAGIES	XIPHOPHYLLOUS	XYLOTOMIES
XANTHOPTERINE	XENOPHILES	XEROPHILES	XIPHOSURAN	XYLOTOMIST
XANTHOPTERINES	XENOPHOBES	XEROPHILIES	XIPHOSURANS	XYLOTOMISTS
XANTHOPTERINS	XENOPHOBIA	XEROPHILOUS	XYLOBALSAMUM	XYLOTOMOUS
XANTHOXYLS	XENOPHOBIAS	XEROPHTHALMIA	XYLOBALSAMUMS	XYLOTYPOGRAPHIC
XENARTHRAL	XENOPHOBIC	XEROPHTHALMIAS	XYLOCARPOUS	XYLOTYPOGRAPHY
XENOBIOTIC	XENOPHOBICALLY	XEROPHTHALMIC	XYLOCHROME	XYRIDACEOUS
XENOBIOTICS	XENOPHOBIES	XEROPHYTES	XYLOCHROMES	
XENOBLASTS	XENOPLASTIC	XEROPHYTIC	XYLOGENOUS	
XENOCRYSTS	XENOTRANSPLANT	XEROPHYTICALLY	XYLOGRAPHED	

YACHTSMANSHIP	YEARNINGLY	YELLOWHAMMERS	YELLOWWARES	YESTEREVENS
YACHTSMANSHIPS	YEASTINESS	YELLOWHEAD	YELLOWWEED	YESTEREVES
YACHTSWOMAN	YEASTINESSES	YELLOWHEADS	YELLOWWEEDS	YESTERMORN
YACHTSWOMEN	YELLOCHING	YELLOWIEST	YELLOWWOOD	YESTERMORNING
YAFFINGALE	YELLOWBACK	YELLOWISHNESS	YELLOWWOODS	YESTERMORNINGS
YAFFINGALES	YELLOWBACKS	YELLOWISHNESSES	YELLOWWORT	YESTERMORNS
YAMMERINGS	YELLOWBARK	YELLOWLEGS	YELLOWWORTS	YESTERNIGHT
YARBOROUGH	YELLOWBARKS	YELLOWNESS	YEOMANRIES	YESTERNIGHTS
YARBOROUGHS	YELLOWBIRD	YELLOWNESSES	YERSINIOSES	YESTERYEAR
YARDMASTER	YELLOWBIRDS	YELLOWTAIL	YERSINIOSIS	YESTERYEARS
YARDMASTERS	YELLOWCAKE	YELLOWTAILS	YESTERDAYS	YIELDABLENESS
YARDSTICKS	YELLOWCAKES	YELLOWTHROAT	YESTEREVEN	YIELDABLENESSES
YATTERINGLY	YELLOWFINS	YELLOWTHROATS	YESTEREVENING	YIELDINGLY
YATTERINGS	YELLOWHAMMER	YELLOWWARE	YESTEREVENINGS	YIELDINGNESS

YIELDINGNESSES
YOCTOSECOND
YOCTOSECONDS
YOHIMBINES
YOKEFELLOW
YOKEFELLOWS
YOTTABYTES

YOUNGBERRIES
YOUNGBERRY
YOUNGLINGS
YOUNGNESSES
YOUNGSTERS
YOURSELVES
YOUTHENING

YOUTHFULLY
YOUTHFULNESS
YOUTHFULNESSES
YOUTHHEADS
YOUTHHOODS
YOUTHQUAKE
YOUTHQUAKES

YPSILIFORM
YTHUNDERED
YTTERBITES
YTTERBIUMS
YTTRIFEROUS
YUCKINESSES
YUMMINESSES

YUPPIEDOMS
YUPPIFICATION
YUPPIFICATIONS
YUPPIFYING

ZABAGLIONE
ZABAGLIONES
ZALAMBDODONT
ZALAMBDODONTS
ZAMBOORAKS
ZAMINDARIES
ZAMINDARIS
ZANAMIVIRS
ZANINESSES
ZANTEDESCHIA
ZANTEDESCHIAS
ZANTHOXYLS
ZANTHOXYLUM
ZANTHOXYLUMS
ZAPATEADOS
ZAPOTILLAS
ZEALOTISMS
ZEALOTRIES
ZEALOUSNESS
ZEALOUSNESSES
ZEBRAFISHES
ZEBRAWOODS
ZEBRINNIES
ZEITGEBERS
ZEITGEISTS
ZEITGEISTY
ZELATRICES
ZELATRIXES
ZELOPHOBIA
ZELOPHOBIAS
ZELOPHOBIC
ZELOPHOBICS
ZELOTYPIAS
ZEMINDARIES
ZEMINDARIS
ZEOLITIFORM
ZEPTOSECOND
ZEPTOSECONDS
ZESTFULNESS
ZESTFULNESSES
ZETTABYTES

ZEUGLODONT
ZEUGLODONTS
ZEUGMATICALLY
ZIBELLINES
ZIDOVUDINE
ZIDOVUDINES
ZIGZAGGEDNESS
ZIGZAGGEDNESSES
ZIGZAGGERIES
ZIGZAGGERS
ZIGZAGGERY
ZIGZAGGING
ZILLIONAIRE
ZILLIONAIRES
ZILLIONTHS
ZINCIFEROUS
ZINCIFICATION
ZINCIFICATIONS
ZINCIFYING
ZINCKENITE
ZINCKENITES
ZINCKIFICATION
ZINCKIFICATIONS
ZINCKIFIED
ZINCKIFIES
ZINCKIFYING
ZINCOGRAPH
ZINCOGRAPHER
ZINCOGRAPHERS
ZINCOGRAPHIC
ZINCOGRAPHICAL
ZINCOGRAPHIES
ZINCOGRAPHS
ZINCOGRAPHY
ZINCOLYSES
ZINCOLYSIS
ZINFANDELS
ZINGIBERACEOUS
ZINJANTHROPI
ZINJANTHROPUS
ZINJANTHROPUSES

ZINKENITES
ZINKIFEROUS
ZINKIFICATION
ZINKIFICATIONS
ZINKIFYING
ZINZIBERACEOUS
ZIPLOCKING
ZIRCALLOYS
ZIRCONIUMS
ZITHERISTS
ZIZYPHUSES
ZOANTHARIAN
ZOANTHARIANS
ZOANTHROPIC
ZOANTHROPIES
ZOANTHROPY
ZOECHROMES
ZOMBIELIKE
ZOMBIFICATION
ZOMBIFICATIONS
ZOMBIFYING
ZOOCEPHALIC
ZOOCHEMICAL
ZOOCHEMISTRIES
ZOOCHEMISTRY
ZOOCHORIES
ZOOCHOROUS
ZOOCULTURE
ZOOCULTURES
ZOODENDRIA
ZOODENDRIUM
ZOOGAMETES
ZOOGEOGRAPHER
ZOOGEOGRAPHERS
ZOOGEOGRAPHIC
ZOOGEOGRAPHICAL
ZOOGEOGRAPHIES
ZOOGEOGRAPHY
ZOOGLOEOID
ZOOGONIDIA
ZOOGONIDIUM

ZOOGRAFTING
ZOOGRAFTINGS
ZOOGRAPHER
ZOOGRAPHERS
ZOOGRAPHIC
ZOOGRAPHICAL
ZOOGRAPHIES
ZOOGRAPHIST
ZOOGRAPHISTS
ZOOKEEPERS
ZOOLATRIAS
ZOOLATRIES
ZOOLATROUS
ZOOLOGICAL
ZOOLOGICALLY
ZOOLOGISTS
ZOOMAGNETIC
ZOOMAGNETISM
ZOOMAGNETISMS
ZOOMANCIES
ZOOMETRICAL
ZOOMETRIES
ZOOMORPHIC
ZOOMORPHIES
ZOOMORPHISM
ZOOMORPHISMS
ZOONOMISTS
ZOOPATHIES
ZOOPATHOLOGIES
ZOOPATHOLOGY
ZOOPERISTS
ZOOPHAGANS
ZOOPHAGIES
ZOOPHAGOUS
ZOOPHILIAS
ZOOPHILIES
ZOOPHILISM
ZOOPHILISMS
ZOOPHILIST
ZOOPHILISTS
ZOOPHILOUS

ZOOPHOBIAS
ZOOPHOBOUS
ZOOPHYSIOLOGIES
ZOOPHYSIOLOGIST
ZOOPHYSIOLOGY
ZOOPHYTICAL
ZOOPHYTOID
ZOOPHYTOLOGICAL
ZOOPHYTOLOGIES
ZOOPHYTOLOGIST
ZOOPHYTOLOGISTS
ZOOPHYTOLOGY
ZOOPLANKTER
ZOOPLANKTERS
ZOOPLANKTON
ZOOPLANKTONIC
ZOOPLANKTONS
ZOOPLASTIC
ZOOPLASTIES
ZOOPSYCHOLOGIES
ZOOPSYCHOLOGY
ZOOSCOPIES
ZOOSPERMATIC
ZOOSPERMIA
ZOOSPERMIUM
ZOOSPORANGIA
ZOOSPORANGIAL
ZOOSPORANGIUM
ZOOSPOROUS
ZOOSTEROLS
ZOOTECHNICAL
ZOOTECHNICS
ZOOTECHNIES
ZOOTHAPSES
ZOOTHAPSIS
ZOOTHECIAL
ZOOTHECIUM
ZOOTHEISMS
ZOOTHEISTIC
ZOOTHERAPIES
ZOOTHERAPY

X
Y
Z

ZOOTOMICAL

ZOOTOMICAL	ZWISCHENZUG	ZYGOCACTUSES	ZYGOMYCETE	ZYMOLOGICAL
ZOOTOMICALLY	ZWISCHENZUGS	ZYGOCARDIAC	ZYGOMYCETES	ZYMOLOGIES
ZOOTOMISTS	ZWITTERION	ZYGODACTYL	ZYGOMYCETOUS	ZYMOLOGIST
ZOOTROPHIC	ZWITTERIONIC	ZYGODACTYLIC	ZYGOPHYLLACEOUS	ZYMOLOGISTS
ZOOTROPHIES	ZWITTERIONS	ZYGODACTYLISM	ZYGOPHYTES	ZYMOMETERS
ZOOTSUITER	ZYGANTRUMS	ZYGODACTYLISMS	ZYGOPLEURAL	ZYMOSIMETER
ZOOTSUITERS	ZYGAPOPHYSEAL	ZYGODACTYLOUS	ZYGOSITIES	ZYMOSIMETERS
ZOOXANTHELLA	ZYGAPOPHYSES	ZYGODACTYLS	ZYGOSPERMS	ZYMOTECHNIC
ZOOXANTHELLAE	ZYGAPOPHYSIAL	ZYGOMATICS	ZYGOSPHENE	ZYMOTECHNICAL
ZORBONAUTS	ZYGAPOPHYSIS	ZYGOMORPHIC	ZYGOSPHENES	ZYMOTECHNICS
ZUCCHETTOS	ZYGOBRANCH	ZYGOMORPHIES	ZYGOSPORES	ZYMOTICALLY
ZUGZWANGED	ZYGOBRANCHIATE	ZYGOMORPHISM	ZYGOSPORIC	
ZUGZWANGING	ZYGOBRANCHIATES	ZYGOMORPHISMS	ZYGOTICALLY	
ZUMBOORUKS	ZYGOBRANCHS	ZYGOMORPHOUS	ZYMOGENESES	
ZWANZIGERS	ZYGOCACTUS	ZYGOMORPHY	ZYMOGENESIS	